payback

First published in Great Britain in 2009 by Old Street Publishing Ltd
40 Bowling Green Lane, London EC1R 0NE
www.oldstreetpublishing.co.uk

ISBN 978-1-906964-16-0

10 9 8 7 6 5 4 3 2 1

A CIP catalogue record for this title is available from the British Library.

Typeset by Martin Worthington

Printed and bound in Great Britain.

payback

mike nicol

Old St PUBLISHING

CONTENTS

GOING DOWN

'… in this city of bombs and pain …'
Anonymous victim

PROLOGUE

They sat for two hours waiting. Three men in an old white Toyota looking out at the sodden street. No one to notice them. No one about in this dark suburb above the city. In some of the houses lighted rooms in the upper storeys. The houses behind high walls. Below they could see the city's tall buildings drifting through the trees.

'This's up to shit,' said the one in the back, Mikey. He had a 9mm in his hand, racked the slide, released it. Racked it again.

'Doesn't matter what you think.' Abdul Abdul turned round to grin at him. 'You got no staying power, my bru.' He tapped his fingers on the steering wheel. 'Patience, hey.'

Mikey grunted. He looked up at the mountain rising black above them. Threatening as the sky. He had his window open despite the rain gusts, the cold that numbed his feet seeped into his marrow. He had his window open because Abdul and Val smoked from cigarette to cigarette.

'It's bloody freezing,' he said, putting the gun down to blow on his hands.

'Close the window.'

'Then stop smoking.'

'Isn't gonna happen,' said Abdul.

Between cigarettes Abdul brought out a joint. Mikey toted on that.

'You smoke dagga but you don't smoke cigarettes,' Abdul said to Val. 'What a stupid. Mikey the moegoe.'

Mikey heard the car approaching, said, 'Shit, man, watch it. He'll see the glow.' The car came past them, an Alfa Spider, swerved in at the open gates thirty metres down the street.

'That's him,' said Mikey. 'Mace Bishop.'

Abdul turned down Abdullah Ibrahim's *Mannenberg* that'd been on a loop in the tape system.

'And now?' said Mikey.

'We're gonna wait,' said Abdul.

'Jus wait?'

'Jus wait.'

'Maybe he's not gonna go out again.'

'He will.'

Mikey sat back, sighed. 'For how long, hey, we havta wait?'

'Long as it takes.' Abdul wound up the song.

'Enough,' said Mikey. 'We been listening to that for two hours. Three if you take it from when we left.'

'So,' said Abdul. 'It's a good song. Cape Town's theme tune.'

Mikey took a last pull at the roach. Squashed it underfoot. He went back to playing with his gun. Rack release. Rack release.

They listened to *Mannenberg* for another forty-five minutes until Mace Bishop drove out fast in the Alfa.

'Here we go,' said Mikey, hunching forward.

'Not yet,' said Abdul.

They waited five more minutes. All quiet. Mikey sitting hunched forward all that time.

Abdul started the car. 'You get the pill down the woman's throat, Mikey. That's what you gotta do.'

'Then I can bang her.'

'Thought your thing was kiddies rather,' said Val.

'Kiddies. Grown-ups. I got a bone needs picking with her.'

'Ag sies, man.' Val opened his door, spat onto the gravel.

4

'Remember,' said Abdul, 'we're here for the girl.' He turned, cuffed Mikey lightly on the cheek. 'No shit, right. No bones. What we want's the girl.' He reversed the Toyota into the driveway.

The men pulled on balaclavas. Mikey had his pistol in his hand, Val and Abdul slid their guns into their belts. Abdul fancying American style with the barrel down the crack of his arse. They stood looking at the Victorian house. No burglar bars over the front windows. Same thing as leaving a door unlocked.

'Those windows,' said Abdul.

Mikey smashed a pane and they were in. Inside stank of wet clay and turps. Before he could say anything, Abdul put his hand over Mikey's mouth. They listened, a television playing somewhere. Val pointed up. Abdul nodded.

They came out of the room into a hallway, facing a flight of stairs. Again Val pointed up.

Abdul drew his pistol, went up the stairs first, treading close to the banister. Still some of the boards groaned. Each time he stopped dead. Listened. No movement. Just the television, bangs and sirens of a cop show. He waited on the landing for Mikey and Val.

They came up separately. Mikey the only one silent as a cat.

He grinned at Abdul and Val. Mouthed: 'Good, hey.'

Abdul grimaced, pointed with his gun at the third door along the landing. The door slightly ajar. He gestured for Mikey to go in. 'The woman,' he whispered. 'Get the pill into her.'

'Relax,' said Mikey. 'Be cool like a schul.' He shoved open the door, stepped into the room. 'Hello, darlings.'

Mother and daughter lying on the bed. The woman with her eyes closed, the girl under the duvet, watching television. The woman opened her eyes, seemed to spring from the bed at the same time. Mikey had to crack her one with his pistol. She went down and he was on her. Had a good feel of her breasts in the tumble.

The girl screamed.

Abdul had her, hauled her free of the duvet. The kid's PJ top hiked up.

'Sshh, Christa,' said Abdul, squeezing the wind out of her. 'Bru,' he said to Val, 'light us a cigarette.'

Val did. Mikey was raising up the woman, his pistol hard against her neck. Blood trickled down from where he'd opened a cut on her forehead.

'Oumou,' said Abdul, 'my friend's got a pill we want you to take.' He put the cigarette to his lips, pulled gently. Blew out the smoke from the corner of his mouth. 'If yous don't' – he pushed back the girl's pyjama sleeve to expose smooth skin – 'I'm gonna put this out right here' – brushed the hot tip of the cigarette across Christa's arm.

1

Mace Bishop, wearing sunglasses, said, 'There are people I'm happy to offer my services to, Ducky. And those I take on because I owe.' He owed Ducky Donald Hartnell for five RPGs, two dozen Chinese AKs, and an assortment of pistols, grenades, ammunition. A debt Ducky had let slide fifteen years.

Fifteen years back Ducky's son Matthew was ten years old. When Ducky called in the favour, Mace had heard tell of Matthew as a stuttering dipshit cokehead running a nightclub that daddy set up.

'I'd rather come to an arrangement,' Mace told Ducky over breakfast at Café Paradiso up Kloof, among the young suits, male and female, execs one and all.

'Sure you would,' Ducky said. 'But a payback I don't need, Mace. I need someone like you. A ruthless cold bugger. To be a babysitter.'

'That I can arrange, if you like. Just not me. Or Pylon.'

Ducky wiped egg from his chin. 'How's that black bastard these days?'

'These days,' said Mace. 'In love.'

'Never could keep his pecker in.'

Mace took his espresso in a swallow. 'In love, Ducky. It's not the same thing.'

'You mean he's not balling her?'

Mace shrugged. Ducky Donald Hartnell always had been a rude pig.

'I hear you've got a neat thing going, you'n Pylon, playing muscle for the rich and famous.'

'We're doing alright.'

'Complete Security. What sorta bloody name's that? For two gun runners!'

'Times change.'

'You're not kidding.' Ducky Donald cut into his bacon. 'Look, Mace, it's a favour, okay? The boy's got bouncers, Centurion Armed Response. He's paying protection …'

'To?'

'Americans. It's their corner of town.'

Mace watched him shovel a load of bacon, mushrooms and fried banana into his mouth, half-closing it but not enough so he couldn't talk.

'I told him, you've gotta understand how the city's divided up. You pay who you must if you want to stay in business. Revenue takes their assessment, the gangs get their turf toll, and the strollers and the homeless need an allowance. So what we're a heavily taxed society? We have sea and sun. Pay the rate, don't overpay, I told him.'

He masticated for a moment.

'That much he did, I'll admit. I was proud of him. He's gonna manage this, I thought. Next thing the fundamentals start blowing up bars, even that steak house, Planet Hollywood. I warned him, Matt, they're going to come calling. Chill dad, he tells me, they're not a scare. Attitude like that suggests to me the boy's taking too much white, Mace. Know what I mean?'

Mace nodded. Matthew Hartnell's pretentious little rave cave had a reputation as the place you could get anything. For a price. But anything.

'All due respects,' Mace said, 'your son'd be safer wandering in a minefield.'

'This much I'm aware of, china. What I'm doing here is keeping the boy's mother happy in Hampshire. Reassuring her that all is well in our new land that we struggled so hard and so long to create. The land she so generously gave back to the natives by returning to the country of her forefathers. All the same, the last thing she wants is for her darling boy to get blown up. Lose a few digits like his dear old dad.'

'Would be tragic.'

Ducky glanced up from mopping a crust of toast through the eggmush and brown sauce on his plate, but Mace kept po-faced until he went back to his trough. 'What I want you to ensure is he doesn't. Do me the favour, hey. So I can tell people Mace Bishop's good for his word.'

Mace caught the threat but let it ride. Easier said than done admittedly. He picked up the empty espresso cup, put it down. Gazed out the window at the tower blocks below and the sea beyond them, brown haze turning the view murky. Most autumn days the city disappeared in the muck, only the mountain rising behind into a stark blue.

'Your son's a drug dealer,' he said. 'Here is an obstacle.'

'Sure,' Ducky said. 'I'm working on it.'

'Also, I have some sympathy with those trying to take out druglords and gangsters.'

'Don't we all. Meantime I need the protective power of my old pal Mace Bishop.' Ducky wiped a serviette across his mouth, squinted at Mace. 'Maybe I should mention two other things could help you in this.'

'Like?'

Ducky paused for effect. 'Like Cayman accounts. Like what happened at Techipa.'

Mace kept blank, Ducky leaning into his face. 'I know, china, about both. Trust me, I wanna keep your secrets.'

Mace thinking, how in Christ's name?

Ducky Donald saying, 'So how about it? Boy's got a meeting with those wonderful types in a few hours. Woman the name of Sheemina February.' Ducky grinning. The sort of grin Mace believed a hyena might have running down a zebra foal. 'Tell me you'll be there.'

2

Matthew Hartnell had an office in a sad building on Harrington, one block up from the Castle. A quarter of town nothing much happened at any time, day or night. A lick away from a major tourist site but no frumps with cameras came wandering here even by accident. Vagrants and cardboard collectors staggered about the street, Angolans ran the parking lot. Mace's little red Alfa Spider caused them some excitement. He left the top down, a holder of CDs in the glovebox, the Becker a shining invite to anyone with a screwdriver.

A car-guard sauntered over, smiling.

'Hey, Cuito,' said Mace, 'you've moved your patch?' The last time he'd seen him the Angolan was car-guarding at a shopping mall in the leafy suburbs. Had done Mace a favour by keeping an eye on a wealthy client.

Cuito gave a wide white smile. 'Sometimes the local Xhosa do not like our hard work, Mr Mace. They make trouble. It is best to move away.'

'Sorry to hear it.'

Cuito pointed at the Spider. 'It's safe,' – taking the offered ten.

'Obrigado,' Mace told him.

The foyer of No 23 Harrington Street was cold and dark and stank of urine. The lift was boarded up, the stairs stripped of what lino might once have covered them. Mace went up to Matthew Hartnell's business quarters on the first floor at the end of a corridor where every door had a security gate. Once there were probably frosted glass panes in the doors and people had their names scripted on in attractive flourishes. Obromowitz &

Sons, Jewellers. Jackman & Jackman, Shipping Chandlers. Now you didn't want to know what went on behind the closed doors. Or why club-owner Matt regarded this as a good address. Mace knocked. Matthew opened.

'Yo, the ar-arms dealer,' Matthew greeted.

Mace pushed in past him. 'Don't give me uphill, Matt, okay, I'm doing your daddy a favour. And stay off the weed before you meet people.'

Which got Matthew pouty. 'I d-d-don't need you. I got my own g-guys. I'm looked after b-better than the president. I can ha-handle this.'

Mace thought, I, I, I, bullshit. Raking a glance down the thin youth in a beanie, baggy jeans and a bomber jacket that was vogue when Neil Young sang 'Heart of Gold'.

'Matt,' he said, 'Matt, we're talking People Against Gangsters and Drugs. You've seen the pictures. They carry serious weaponry. How many bombs are we talking? How many dead? Fifteen? Twenty? I don't know. These are the people coming to see you.'

Matthew tapped his cellphone against his front teeth. 'I ca-can sort it.'

Mace took a look out the window at the side of a building an arm's length away. Gave a cursory scan of the four plastic garden chairs, the second-hand desk and the grey-green filing cabinet that served as office furniture. Pulled a chair to the side of the desk and sat down.

'Sure you can.'

Matthew took his place behind the desk.

'How long do we have to wait?'

'That's the-them,' Matthew said, the tread of the well-heeled echoing on the concrete stairs.

They came in: a woman first, then a fat man, followed by a goon who worked out so much his neck and head were a continuum. She was well-groomed: silk trouser suit, fingernails like drops of blood on her right hand, her left in a black glove, plum lipstick, eyes an ice shade of blue, a silk scarf over her hair that Mace felt was pure statement. She carried a leather briefcase, attorney-style, in the gloved hand.

Her name was Sheemina February, a senior partner in the law firm Fortune, Dadoo & Moosa, legal representatives for the anti-drug vigilantes. As Mace understood it, she'd called Matthew to suggest the meeting would be in his best interests.

The fat man was a brand name type, labels all over him. Gold wrist watch. Gold cufflinks. Open-necked shirt under a leather jacket. A short haircut giving a black fuzz to his skull. His cheeks pitted from acne, his front teeth filed to points. Mace recognised the face: Abdul Abdul, on bail facing two murder charges. Assassinations: bullet in the back of the head style.

The goon wore de rigueur snakeskin lace-ups and a black suit. Mace watched him take up a position beside the door, the way goons did it in the movies. The oddity about him was he was white.

'Matthew?' queried the woman, frowning at Mace as if she recognised him, shifting her gaze from him to Matthew.

'Mr Matthew Hartnell to you,' Mace said.

She swung at him: 'And you are?' Some aggression in her face.

'Doesn't matter. Just accept I'm here.'

'He's my ad-visor,' said Matthew.

'A lawyer?'

'Something like that.'

She extended a hand to Matthew. After he'd shaken she held it at Mace. 'Mr Advisor.'

He ignored the sarcasm and took her outstretched hand: cold, firm. 'Who's he?' pointing at the goon.

'A friend,' said Abdul. 'Mikey. Say hello, Mikey.'

'Hi,' said Mikey, his voice flat and nasal.

Sheemina February and Abdul sat down on the two chairs other side of Matthew's desk. They placed their cellphones on the table.

Mace's cell was already there, so was Matthew's. Sheemina February put her attaché case on the floor and looked at Matthew and said, 'There's drugs being sold in your club and we don't like that.'

Matthew shook his head. 'Na-na-no way. There's no shit g-going down. Out of the qu-question.'

Sheemina February shrugged. 'Well, maybe that's what you think, but that's not what's happening.'

'I don't allow d-drugs,' said Matthew. 'Not e-even weed.'

Mace marvelled the kid could say it barefaced. Shades of daddy.

Abdul Abdul laughed. Sheemina February bent down and took out of her briefcase a plastic bank packet filled with a mix of sticks and pips, flipped it onto the desk. Very casual. Very neat.

'Ganja,' Abdul said and laughed again, harsh and ugly. 'Top dagga,' he said. 'Bloody first-class weed.'

Mace raised his eyebrows, but let the bankie lie where it lay.

'Sold to one of our people on the floor last night,' said Sheemina February.

'I-I've only got your w-word for it,' came back Matthew.

'Of course.' Sheemina February tapped the bankie. 'But we've no reason to lie.' They made eye contact: Matthew looked away first. 'You say you don't allow this stuff. Then we're on the same side, Matthew. We're both against the drugs and the gangsters.'

'Who're you paying protection to?' interjected Abdul Abdul, reeling off some names: 'Twenty-eights? Americans? Pretty Boys?'

'No wh-one,' said Matthew.

Abdul gave an imitation of a laugh. 'Americans,' he said. 'Don't give me any shit. I know.'

'It's not only the grass,' said Sheemina February. 'They're selling hard stuff too.'

'Im-im-impossible,' said Matthew.

Sheemina February took another bank packet out of her briefcase, flipped it on to the table. 'Heroin,' she said.

'Could be talcum,' said Mace. 'For all we know.'

'Try it.' Abdul pushed the bankie towards Matthew. 'Take a taste, my friend, this's your scene.'

'Believe me,' said Sheemina February, placing her hand over the packet.

'You have all this,' Mace said. 'Take it to the cops.'

Abdul Abdul snorted. Sheemina February smiled vaguely then quickly turned to Matthew.

'This is killing our children.' She held up the packet of heroin.

'You have the evidence. Call the cops,' Mace said. 'The man says he knows nothing about this stuff.'

Abdul Abdul frowned at Mace and dismissed him with a flip of his hand.

The vague smile returned to Sheemina February's purple lips. 'Mr Advisor, the cops will close down your client's business.' She held his eyes. 'Do you want that?'

'No,' Matthew broke in. 'No. The-there's a way to w-work this out.'

'Good. The simple thing here Matthew is the drugs have to stop.'

The 'or' left hanging. She dropped the packet onto the desk. 'Right. Here's how we can help you.'

'You don't g-get to,' Matthew replied. 'Th-the way we work this out is you f-f-fuck off.'

A quiet, a sudden quiet that went on so long Mace could hear the rumble of the city. He let his glance slide from face to face: Sheemina February amused, Matthew staring at his hands, Abdul with a tic working below his right eye.

Abdul Abdul broke first, reached for his cellphone and shook it at Matthew. 'We are telling you,' he shouted. 'We are telling you this must stop.'

Sheemina February put her hand on Abdul's arm. He flicked her off. Said, 'You think this is fun and games, my friend? You think this is fun and games to have all these drugs? You want Ecstasy? I can push so much Ecstasy down your throat you have a straight trip to hell. You are cheap shit. You are small shit, my friend.'

Matthew stood up. The goon moved away from the door closer to his boss, flipping his jacket to show a thirty-eight tucked into his belt.

'Wh-what're you g-going to do?' Matthew hurled back. 'Th-throw a pipe bomb in my club? K-kill a whole lot of in-in-innocent p-people like you did at those res-restaurants? B-blow off some kid's feet just to t-teach me a lesson? Wh-who's the cheap shit?'

'Be careful.' Abdul Abdul was standing now, spit catching at the corner of his mouth.

Sheemina said quietly, 'Shut up.' Said louder, but not shouting, looking at Mace throughout. 'Shut up. Both of you, shut up.' Mace held her stare, not interfering, holding her eyes until she took them off him. Wondering, had they met before? Like what was her case? Her face seemed familiar. But how? From when? From the old days when there'd been women by the night? As easy as the flow of beers.

Matthew the drug dealer and Abdul Abdul the assassin shut up.

'Sit down, Matthew,' she said, 'sit down and listen to me.' He did, so did Abdul. 'Here's the deal. You lose the security. Centurion and the Americans both. You close down for a week. You speak nicely to Abdul and then we get you back up and running. Nothing different to before, just being done by other means.'

Matthew gagged, suddenly off the boil, getting only the first part of the words out. 'Ca-ca-ca,' he went.

Sheemina February waited. 'You were saying?'

'Ca-ca-ca.'

She turned to Mace. 'Perhaps you should advise him, Mr Advisor.'

Mace uncrossed his legs, tipped back the plastic chair. The thing about Sheemina February, he reckoned, was her calm blue eyes in her olive face. Eyes from a Nordic ice land. Untroubled eyes. The sort of eyes you'd remember. Eyes that mocked. Like her smile.

The purple of her lipstick against white teeth. Easy to be suckered, to believe she was the voice of reason.

'So?'

He let the chair drop forward. 'What's your percentage?'

She exposed the tips of her teeth. 'Mr Advisor, please. Matthew pays for our services. Nothing different to what he's been doing except we're cheaper. And we keep him clean. A major advantage.' Mace got a full smile before she turned to Matthew Hartnell. 'So, Matthew, what do you say?'

Matthew said, 'Ca-ca-Christ!'

'Consider it,' said Sheemina February, standing. 'Talk about it with your advisor.' She slid a card onto the desk. 'Let me know this afternoon. Before close of business.' A smile. 'No call, I'll take it you've declined the offer. Your choice. It's a free country.'

She snapped shut her briefcase, picked up her cellphone. The goon reached over and put the dope packets in his pocket.

'Think hard about it, my friends,' said Abdul Abdul, pressing his fangs into the flesh of his lower lip. 'We are worried about you.'

'Goodbye,' said Sheemina February, and the goon squeezed past her and opened the door. He stepped into the corridor and she followed him. Abdul flicked his wrist to rattle his gold watch strap. He pointed the cellphone at Matthew, raised it to his lips, pretending to blow smoke from a barrel, then was gone without closing the door. Mace listened to the strike of Sheemina February's heels along the corridor and down the stairs. He stood, shoved back the plastic chair and headed for the door. On his way out, paused. 'My deal with Donald is to give you protection for two weeks. Let me know what you're planning.'

'Wha-what d'you think?' Matthew said. His voice back now, the tremor still in his hands, though. 'You th-think I'm just gonna close up like she wa-wants? Fuck her. Ca-Christ, man, f-fuck her.'

Mace shrugged. 'You're a drug dealer, Matthew. You run a club where it's easier to score coke than Coca-Cola. More especially, you're making my life difficult.'

'So f-fuck off too.'

'I would, except this is an obligation.'

'Not to m-me.'

Mace shook his head. 'It's an honour debt Matthew. Something you wouldn't understand.'

Matthew pulled a joint from deep in the bags of his jeans and held it to a Bic, drawing long on the smoke. After the exhale he coughed, said, 'I-I-I don't wa-want you, ch-china. I g-got pro-protection. Experienced people. El-electronic s-s-surveillance. Metal detectors. The-they're not g-gonna drop a bomb on me.'

'Dream on.' Mace's cellphone rang: Pylon's name on the screen. While he thumbed him on, he kept at Matthew. 'Another thing, if I don't hear from you, your club four-fifteen is when we meet.' With that was gone.

'Let's hear it,' said Pylon in his ear. 'We got a fabulous new client?'

'A freebie.'

Pylon groaned. 'What're you saying?'

Mace told him right down to the purple lipstick, saving the best for last: Cayman and Techipa.

A long silence from Pylon. Then: 'Save me Jesus.' Then: 'You think he knows or he's guessing?'

'Cayman, it's possible. Those bankers say they're like the gnomes but stuff gets out. If someone's looking.'

'We've given no clue. No flash living. So-so business.'

Mace said, 'He starts putting this around we're buggered. Big time.'

Pylon coming in, 'What I don't get is Techipa. Everyone was dead.'

'Someone wasn't.'

'He started this with the guns? Return of a favour?'

'Yup.'

'I'd forgotten the guns.'

'Was a long time ago in another country. Hadn't been him it would've been someone else. We'd have got them in the end.'

Except in the end it was Ducky Donald who saved them from what might have been The End with slit throats. As Mace recalled it the Arab wasn't pleased that his suppliers had hit a shortfall on the consignment. No matter who the partners contacted there was nothing in that corner of the Sahel at that time that would appease their irate buyer. Until a desperate call to Ducky Donald siphoned off the requisite from a cache stockpiled in a Jo'burg mineshaft. Where the RPGs came from Mace never asked. Suffice to say he suspected Ducky Donald was also trading for the SA army. For him business was business. For Mace and Pylon at the time business was revolution. Which came to seem a quaint perspective. Which now seemed positively idealistic, Mace thought.

'We could say no,' said Pylon. 'Call his bluff.'

Mace took the last concrete step into the piss-stink of the foyer. 'We could, except Ducky isn't. Bluffing. He'd put it out and that'd be bye bye Cape Town.'

'Nice.'

'Exactly. So much for old comrades. My thoughts: better to bite the bullet for two weeks, what happens afterwards is we come to an arrangement.'

'We can do this?'

'Egg-dancing. What we were so good at. The Pylon and Mace routine.'

Dar-es-Salaam, 1984: a house up the coast north of the city. Old colonial beach place: shuttered windows, covered veranda round three sides with French doors onto the bedrooms. A short walk off the veranda across the sand scrub onto the beach into a sea, tepid and salty.

A month they spent there, waiting, playing backgammon, waiting for the buyer to collect. No one around day after day after day. Occasionally a dhow sailing along the horizon. The light pouring down. Only fish and coconuts for food. Back in the house anti-personnel mines, assorted assault rifles, Canadian Sterlings, Mats, Madsens, a few Chinese 79s, sweating in the heat. Sufficient hardware to depose an African dictator. All of it packed neatly into rooms where once the colonials frolicked their white mischief.

Mace and Pylon were extended, their credit zippo because their middleman wanted bucks on the table. If the deal went bad they could ship the stuff elsewhere, over time. Over time was the problem. Each day increased the risk of bad guys lifting the merchandise without payment. The ordinance sweated. They sweated: at night the egg-dance. Until the deal went solid, and they carried payment away in three suitcases. He who sits it out sits it out. The first time they skimmed a commission.

Freetown, 1986. On the runway the weaponry being unpacked from a Hercules transport into three UN trucks destined for a warlord in the hills. When a better offer came in. Actually came steaming out of the cane fields in a Land Rover: three soldiers, one driving, two in the back toting Brazilian Urus, a man wearing a DJ in the passenger seat. DJ put down his offer in cash, US dollars, on the bonnet of the Land Rover. Mace counted it. Said to Pylon, 'Let him have it.' Happy to fly out on the Hercules toot sweet. Pylon unsure. They confabbed. Pylon arguing, the warlord was a source they'd supplied before. Someone who, if he stayed alive, would want guns again. Mace countered, with a call to their new arms contact Isabella they could make good in two days, three max. Both of them keeping an eye on DJ, standing apart, staring into the middle distance, patiently, while they weighed the pros and cons. Decided in the end to take the cash. DJ headed off, the trucks following. Hadn't smiled once through the whole exchange.

In the air, Mace radioed the warlord that the consignment had been hijacked, they'd get back to him with new stock in two days. In two days the warlord was dead. Mace and Pylon egg-danced, diverted the new consignment whistled up by Isabella to Sierra Leone. The Mace and Pylon routine. A large wad wired to their Cayman account.

'You guys!' Isabella had said. 'If it wasn't for me you'd be dead. Or worse.' More truth in it than Mace had ever wanted to admit, fancy footwork notwithstanding.

'Stay flexible,' he said to Pylon. 'Especially where Ducky Donald's concerned. Be cool. Don't think too much about what he's holding.'

'We could move the account.'

'We could. Best option for now is to play it his way.'

Pylon agreeing, wanting to know, 'Are you going to come in at all today?' – as Mace crossed Harrington into the car park, Cuito angling towards him, a grin breaking ear to ear.

'Got to collect Oumou to see a house. Pick up Christa from school. Maybe later this afternoon. If not, Club Catastrophe four-fifteen. Could turn out to be somewhere you can take Treasure clubbing.'

'That being high on Treasure's list of to-dos.'

'Chicks want these jives.'

'This's a mama with a daughter the same age as your's we're talking about.'

'Still a chick.'

'Treasure wasn't a chick. Ever.'

They disconnected. Cuito stood grinning as Mace jiggled the Alfa's keys from the pocket of his jacket.

'Those people you come to see are the Muslims?' he said.

Mace shifted down his sunglasses to squint at the Angolan over the frames.

'They come here yesterday. Drive around. The fat one he goes up the stairs.'

Mace juggled his keys from hand to hand. 'What makes you think I want to know that?'

Cuito laughed. 'I have my eyes.'

'You know the thin guy who's got an office up there?'

Cuito nodded.

'Tell you what, you see those people again, you call me.'

'For how much?' he said.

'It'll be worth it.' Mace took out his wallet.

'Also at the club?'

Mace laughed. 'Cuito you know things.'

'Many things, Mr Mace,' he said, his fingers closing another ten into the palm of his hand.

3

Mikey, in the passenger seat of the white Toyota, said, 'In the Yellow Pages there's a place called DAWG, that has cats. In Hout Bay.'

The coloured guy driving said, 'DAWG, has cats?'

Mikey kept his finger on the advert. 'Why not? It's a pseudonym, Val. Like PAGAD.'

'An acronym.'

'A what?'

'That's what it is. DAWG stands for something. An acronym. Pseudonym's something else. Like Madonna.'

'Madonna with the pointy tits?'

'She's not doing that anymore.'

'No? Shame, hey.' He glanced at the advert. 'Says it's got kennels. People bring their pets they don't want. Same as the SPCA.'

'Sounds okay, long as it's got cats. You heard Abdul. Cats. Has to be kittens.'

Val took the Constantia off-ramp, the signs pointing to Hout Bay over the Nek, a drive he liked taking on a Sunday afternoon with a new cherry. Drive around the peninsula: sea one side, mountain the other. A1 impressive. Romantic to any chickie. Under the oaks, up the hill all the larney mansions left and right down the narrow curvy road into Hout Bay. Only thing that spoilt it, Val reckoned, was the squatter camp, Imizamo whatnot, some tongue twister like that perched right there on the mountain at the entrance, a weeping pit of human stink, their raw shit washing down every time it rained. You could understand whiteys in the valley getting upset.

Mikey said, 'Hout Bay's buggered. They've got wild crime from the squatters. Story I heard about a black family come down from Jo'burg to cycle in the Argus, they book into this expensive guesthouse, full-on security, armed response, electric fences, anyhow the black daddy gets up to take a pee in the middle of the night there's another black daddy on the landing who's got a shopping list from the shacklands, this dude does him right there, pow, nine mil smack in the chest.'

'Gives the city a bad image.'

'No kidding, bru.'

Val picked up the signs for the kennels over the bridge, turned into side roads heading back up the valley along the river away from the sea, the plots getting bigger, the road going from tar to gravel. The sign on a gate said Domestic Animal Welfare Group. He parked the car on the verge. They walked up a path to a ranch-style house set under bluegums. Everything in shadow. The house in need of paint, a glass pane in the front door cracked. A note above the buzzer said ring for attendance.

They did. And again. Twice more before a woman appeared with a parakeet on her shoulder, small dogs yapping at her feet. Mikey noticed she wore sheepskin slippers that might've been chewed by a dog.

They both said 'Hi ma'am' – gave her full smiles.

What she saw was two clean and tidy young men, dressed in chinos and v-neck polo shirts with their sunglasses stuck in the v. She smelt a hint of aftershave.

Val said, 'We're from the Mitchell's Plain Baptist Congregation, ma'am, I'm Val and this is Mikey and we're arranging a party for orphaned children from a home that is run by our church.'

Mikey held out a letter with a printed masthead. 'This is our address and charity number, ma'am, and if you'll phone our pastor he'll confirm our mission.'

She barely glanced at it. 'Alright. So what's it you want?'

'Bless you,' said Mikey.

Val said, 'We were hoping, ma'am, that you'd have twelve kittens seeking good homes because it is our intention to give our orphan charges a pet to care for. Under our supervision at all times.'

'In the name of the Lord,' Mikey said, 'our intention is to give our young charges something to love and to provide a home for neglected animals.'

'Really?' said the woman. The parakeet on her shoulder pecked at her hair and she flicked her head to stop the bird.

'All we ask, ma'am, is that the kittens be donated as all our funds are for the running of the orphanage.'

'That so?' said the woman, looking from one to the other, stopping on Val's face. 'Alright. I've got kittens I can give you. On your word you're going to care for them?'

'So help me God,' said Mikey.

'We're Christians,' said Val.

They followed the woman through the dim house that smelt of cat pee out to the kennels at the back: rows of sad dogs, cats curled asleep in patches of sun, the kittens in a wooden Zozo hut with a high reek.

'It's two litters,' said the woman. 'I've got to feed them because their mothers won't.' She stared at the men. 'You know how to feed kittens?' They said no, and she showed them, telling them how much each kitten needed.

'No problem,' said Val. 'The kids will love doing it.'

The woman fetched two cardboard boxes and divided the kittens between them.

'In God's name we thank you,' said Mikey, taking one of the boxes.

The woman glanced at him like she couldn't believe he'd said that. She indicated a path round the house they could take to get back to their car.

They put the kittens in the boot and Val took the coast road to town under the Twelve Apostles. Cranked up some R&B on the sound system. Even so, they could hear the kittens screeching.

'I hate cats,' said Mikey. 'Dogs too.'

'How about her bird,' said Val. 'It'd shat all down her jersey. Jesus Christ, some people.'

'Weird. Fully.' Mikey's cellphone rang: Abdul Abdul.

'I've got Sheemina on the other line,' Abdul said. 'I want to tell her a nice story.'

'We're passing through Camps Bay,' said Mikey. 'Lotsa babes on the beach. Moms with their kiddies under the palms.'

'Don't give me shit,' said Abdul. 'You wanna be a tour guide, I can arrange it. Give you a special interest in paraplegics.'

Mikey made a gesture of throwing the phone out the window. Said, 'Give us half an hour we'll be done. Mikey's Decorators at your service.'

He heard Abdul sigh, say, 'You stuff-up, I phone the SPCA.'

Mikey disconnected. 'What's his case?'.

Val shrugged, wondering how nice it would be in a Clifton apartment, view of the sea, view of the mountains. A place like Sheemina February had. Among the rich larneys.

4

Oumou took one look at the house and said, 'Non.' Continued in French, What was he thinking? Had he taken complete leave of his senses? Went into English so there could be no possibility of Mace misunderstanding the message. 'This is a ruin. We cannot live in a broken house. We have a daughter.' She gestured at the wild overgrown garden. 'There will be horrible insects. A little girl cannot play in a place with horrible insects. Non, non, non. The house is not in the question. We have to build a new house.'

'Whokai. Whoa, whoa, whoa, love. Don't chew his head off.'

Oumou shifted her glare from her husband to Dave Cruikshank, the estate agent.

'Love,' he said, lighting a cigarette, 'this is wonderland. Beatrix Potter, hey?' He blew a stream of smoke out the side of his mouth. 'Call in a garden service, they'll sort it out no time at all. The kiddy'll think it's magic.'

'It is a ruin,' said Oumou.

'So knock it down, love.' Dave flicked ash into the riotous vegetation. 'What I'm showing you and Mace here is a bargain. This sort of property doesn't come on the market every day. This sort of property's scarcer than hens' teeth.' He gave a display of his teeth. 'You want to build a new house, love, then that's what you do. Get your Mace to speak to his pals in the building trade. Six months' time you open the door onto shiny travertine marble.' He grinned again: his upper dentures not quite straight, and put a hand on Oumou's arm. She drew back. 'Don't look at what you see, love. Look at the potential.' Dave put the key in the front door. 'Stand back a bit, this is not a pleasant smell.'

Before he sold property, Dave sold cars. He sold Mace the Spider, a good deal and a sound buy. After an engine overhaul, a wonderful car. As he put it, 'The 1970 Alfa's class, Mace. The least you can do is give it an overhaul.'

Mace now believed it was time to give their lifestyle an overhaul. Get out of the security complex in the suburbs and into the city. If you were going to live in Cape Town, you lived in the City Bowl. The peninsula suburbs were too House and Garden, the seaboard out of his price bracket, both sides, the Atlantic and False Bay. He wanted some of the city's life: the sirens, the lights, the wail of the muezzin's call to prayer, the cotton days of fog. And to be below the mountain, to feel its heat. What he liked about the city was the whacking great mountain in its middle. Anywhere you looked, the mountain loomed. He'd heard Dave was in property. He called him. Dave said, 'Funny you should ring now, there's this place just come on our books, Mace, come'n take a look see.'

Oumou said, 'Non. Dave is a crook. What he sells there is always a story.'

Mace said, 'Let's see what he's got.'

Oumou came back, 'I know what you are going to do. You are going to buy this house. Because it is a bargain.'

Her mind was set on concrete, glass and chrome. This desert woman, who'd lived in a mud house most of her life, wanted concrete, glass and chrome. Mace couldn't understand it.

Before he opened the door, Dave said, 'Like I say, love, you could knock it down. But why would you do that when you got walls and a floor here already. You get me?'

'We are coming to the city for the view,' said Oumou.

They turned to look at the view hidden behind a hedge so thick and wild not even a bird could nest in it.

'Trim the forestry, love,' said Dave. 'You'll get all the view you want.'

He opened the door. The house exhaled must, dust, rot, and death.

'It's not good,' said Dave, 'like I said.' He took two torches out of his jacket pocket, handed one to Oumou. 'Like I say, what we've got here, love, is about dreams. Forget the present. This is the future.'

Oumou gave the torch to Mace so she could tighten the bandanna tied over her hair. Mace watched her, saw a faint smudge of clay beside her right ear where she'd hooked back a stray strand. Her dungarees, too, were stained with clay. Her canvas shoes smudged and clotted like she'd been treading in mud.

'Today is my pottery class,' she'd said to protest the time Mace set.

Dave had said, 'Move fast, my son, I'm fighting off the pack.'

'Forty-five minutes,' Mace had said to Oumou. 'I'll fetch you.'

'What we've got here,' Dave had said, 'is your deceased estate. Owner went into a home twenty years ago. Died last week. One son in Canada. Who wants shot of the hassle. What I'm telling you is any price is good.'

'And your commission?'

'Fixed as of the asking price, my son. You get below the marker, you owe me.'

Mace could hear him sucking at his dentures. 'Deal?'

He looked over Oumou's shoulder into the stench and darkness of the house. Ripped wallpaper, old newspapers, shit everywhere, much of it human.

'Mind the planks, love,' said Dave, 'bit dicey some of them.'

They followed him in, Mace in front, Oumou behind, her hand latched onto his belt. Dave opened a door off the passage into a sitting room, streaks and spots of light filtering through holes in the corrugated-iron sheeting at the windows.

'Think sun,' he said. 'Think big couches, thick carpets, sun, sun, sun. Sun all over this room. Your kiddy lying there in front of the winter fire doing her homework.' Dave rubbed his hand over the fireplace tiles. A dull green showed through the grime. 'Genuine, my son. Old Victorian. That's what you're buying here. History. Vintage Cape Town. Gracious living. What you say, love? You getting the picture here? Seeing how things could be in the not too distant?'

Mace moved the torch beam over the walls, smoke blackened, the skirtings charred. In all the rooms the same smoke markings, filth everywhere. Bottles, broken glass, tins, faeces, lumps of food dried to a powder, spider webs snagging against their faces. Behind him Oumou sneezed, cursed in French.

Dave said, 'I was into property, I'd snatch this myself.'

'Where is the problem?' said Oumou.

Dave patted his trouser pocket. 'None of the ready, love. Dave Cruikshank's right extended.'

He shuffled them back into the entrance hall. A staircase disappeared into the dimness of the upper storey.

'Bit rickety,' he said, kicking at the lower stairs. 'Take my word for it, great views.' He bent to open a door to a cupboard beneath the staircase. 'But take a decko here. Down there's your original mud-floor cellar. History bloke we contacted at the uni said probably belonged to an earlier house. He reckoned might've been a farm-house up this part of the mountain once. How's that? You get that racked up, you can lay your Cape reds down there 'n become a connoisseur.'

'You going to show us?'

Oumou's cellphone rang, and she headed for the warmth of the sunlight to answer it.

'Right now, it's best you take my word for it.' Dave closed the cupboard door. 'Spiders mostly. The history bloke said he wasn't going in there till there'd been fumigators. Not the sort of chap to excavate the pyramids. But then me neither. You convinced?'

Mace nodded, half-listening out for Oumou.

Dave dusted off his hands. 'Your wife a born Frenchie, my son? Looks like that model. The shaven-headed bird. Iman.'

'Malian. Place called Malitia. One of those mud towns.'

'Always wondered what happens when it rains. Those towns must just wash away.'

'Mostly it doesn't. Rain.'

'That right? Not a drop?'

Oumou came towards them holding out her phone. 'This woman says she is calling for you.'

Mace took the phone and answered but the connection was gone. The call register gave no number.

Behind him Dave said to Oumou. 'What you think, love? You see yourself and the kiddy living here? Your old man mowing the lawn?'

Before she could answer, Mace, riding on an instinct this might be Sheemina February, said, 'Did the caller give you her name?'

Oumou shook her head.

'She knew your name?'

'Oui.'

'She say anything else?'

'Non. She says Mrs Bishop can I speak to your husband.'

Dave locked the front door, came to stand up close. 'Children, I'm not putting pressure, far from it, thing is, you're running ahead of the pack but the dogs are closing. Quick decision is of the essence. Next twenty-four hours this place is going to be in new hands. If those were your hands I'd be happy.'

Mace's cellphone rang: Matthew Hartnell. 'You-you-you've got to c-come here,' he said. 'To the club. N-now.'

5

In the car Mace said, pointing down Molteno Road, 'Look at that. Don't you want to live with this every day?'

Cape Town city spread below them, clear now with the brown haze lifted and the sun hard on the buildings. Across the bay a white sickle of beach gleamed up the west coast for such a distance you could almost make out the bulk of the nuclear power station.

Mace revelled, 'Oh man.'

Oumou reached out to put her hand on his arm. 'Oui, this is beautiful. But not the house. In the house there is a bad feeling.'

'Ah, come on.' Mace slowed for the traffic lights at the reservoir. 'It's an old house. Get the renovators and the painters in, like Dave says, it's what the house can be, not what it is.'

Oumou smiled, took her hand off his arm.

Mace, she knew, could be stubborn and demanding. And sometimes she resisted and sometimes she didn't. This time she would wait. In the waiting much would change. Maybe they would move to this house, but maybe they wouldn't. She kept the smile, thinking of how for a time at the beginning she had resisted him, even when she didn't want to.

'You come here for your business, to my town Malitia to sell guns, you go away again,' she had told him. 'For months you are away. You come back with that woman, Isabella, I think she is your wife.'

'Isabella is a contact. American. She can get us guns. It's business.'

'You sleep with her. This is business?'

Mace had said, 'That's over' – and reached out for her hand, drawn her towards him.

She laughed at his brazenness, pushed him away.

In Paris men had been like that. She met them, she talked to them, they thought they could lay her. She told them no. Three years she'd spent fighting them off, one way or the other. Four or five she'd pulled a knife on to make her point. The ceramicist she worked for said, 'Why make pots when rich men want to screw you?'

'Because I do not want to screw them or you,' she said.

He leered at her. Always trying to feel her bum, her breasts until she threatened his groin with a knife and said she'd set free his testicles, if he didn't stop it. The gesture got them to an understanding.

When her time was up she went back to the desert, to Malitia, to shape pots from her native clay.

The potter said, 'Stay in France, you will make more money. We can organise an exhibition.'

Oumou said, maybe one day.

The man she met on her return to Malitia was Mace Bishop. He was sitting with her brother at a café where men gathered in the afternoon, smoking hookahs, drinking coffee. Playing dominoes. He looked at her as the French men had done, but said nothing. That night he ate at their house. He and the other man, Pylon, joking with her brother.

He admired her pots. He spoke to her in poor French and she told him to speak in English.

'You know English?' he said, surprised.

'Like French, it is the language of guns,' she said. 'When I was a girl there was a man here the same as you. An Englishman. If he had nothing to do he would teach me English.'

'He couldn't have been very busy.'

She laughed. As he stood grinning at her, said, 'Why must you sell guns here?'

The grin didn't leave his face. 'For the money.'

Oumou set a lump of clay on the wheel the French ceramicist had given her. 'So that people can kill each other. Kill women and children. Little babies even.'

'They do that,' he said. 'Anyhow.'

'You are a heartless man.'

He told her then about his country and the war there and the need to finance what he called 'the struggle'. He didn't tell her about Cayman. About his nest egg.

'And this makes it right, to sell guns?' she said.

'I sell guns to those who need to fight. Like we are.'

'To children.'

'In my country they took the lead. They have a future.'

'Empty words,' she said, turned to her clay, smoothed it, rounded it, began to shape a form that was long and elegant like her neck. She started the wheel and let this man who sold guns watch her make something beautiful.

For a time she resisted him, his kind attention that would tease her, never touch her, make her laugh. And then one sunset they walked through the mud streets, across the casbah where men packed away their wares and went up the steps onto the wall that had once enclosed the town, gazing into the wadi at boys playing soccer with a ball on the sand between the palm trees. Behind them the imams in their mosques called the faithful to prayer and Mace said, 'I want to sleep with you.'

The words startled her. She stiffened, broke away from him. 'You come here for your business, to Malitia, you stay for a few weeks then you go away again. Now you want a sex toy?'

Mace stepped towards her. 'That's not what I'm saying.'

'Stop.' She put a hand against his chest. Glared at him. 'If you stop the guns.'

He laughed. 'What?'

'You must stop the guns.'

He stared at her for a long time and she didn't waver. In the wadi the boys ended their game as the dusk thickened, their voices sharp in the stillness. 'Okay.' He turned away from her. 'I'll think about it.'

Two days later Mace came in from the desert with the body of her brother. She did not cry, her grief was silent. He told her he knew about those who had raped her when she was a girl. Raped her, stabbed her in the stomach, left her for dead. That her brother had told him this in the long hours he took to die. Mace told her he could not let rest the matter of her brother's death. That night she did not resist him.

But she was insistent. You must stop the guns. You must stop the guns.

When she told him she was pregnant, he said he would stop selling guns.

'This you will make as a promise?'

'Yes,' he said.

And she believed he would.

6

Matthew and Ducky Donald were standing on the pavement when Mace and Oumou pulled up. The two of them smoking. Only Ducky Donald's slight lean to the right a clue that he might be favouring a good leg. No one else in the short side-street. At night a trendy part of town; during the day not a lot went on. Some cars got repaired at a small garage. A junk dealer took in odd pieces of the city's discard. Maybe import-export happened in upstairs offices. Nor much passing traffic. The motormac and the junk dealer were keeping to themselves. Mace stopped behind Ducky Donald's SUV.

'Won't take a minute,' he said to Oumou.

'Perhaps you can let me have the car?'

'Ten minutes. That's all, ten minutes.'

She told him in French he pushed her to the limit.

Ducky Donald leant over the open Spider, grinning at Oumou. 'Hey, darling! You the one made Mace all the money in the desert? Can see why he did business with you.' He leered at Mace. 'Shouldn't hide her, boykie.'

Mace ignored him. 'What've you got me here for?'

'Art exhibition,' said Donald. 'Appeal to your pitiless heart. Step inside.' He quashed one cigarette, lit another. 'The best of gothic. Not so, Mattie boy? Bloody wonderful example.' Matthew scowled, stepped away so his father couldn't thump him a second time on the back. 'Come on, bring the wife, Mace, nothing here she wouldn't have seen before. Considering what the Arabs get up to.' He opened the door of the club and they followed him into the darkness.

Mace's eyes took a moment to adjust. Before they did he heard a mewing, very soft. Also smelt a faint odour like old cat litter. When he could see he saw that kittens had been nailed to the walls through the fur at the nape of their necks. Most were dead, a few squirmed.

'A grand display, don't you think!' said Ducky Donald, whisping a stream of exhale over their heads. 'You want Mattie to switch the lights on? The strobe's good.'

The strobe came on: pulsing at images of skulls, tombstones, ruined churches. Bats crossing a sickle moon.

'Maybe you can tell me what happened?' Mace said to Matthew.

Matthew licked the dryness of his lips. 'About ha-ha-half an hour ago I got a ca-all.'

'Cell? Landline?'

'My cell-cellphone.' He cadged a cigarette from his father. 'No num-number. This guy sa-says they've added some decor-ations to my c-club. He ha-hangs up. My first thought it's Pa-PAGAD. Second that they've t-trashed the place. I get down here the door's o-open ...'

'You called the cops?'

Matthew gave him a pained look. 'L-like what's with you-you and the c-cops?'

'Like breaking and entry. Cruelty to animals. What about Centurion?'

Matthew got red-faced. 'Wa-wasn't act-activated. The contract's ex-pired.'

'We need protection here, Mace,' said Donald. 'These people are shitting the constitution. You gonna let what we struggled for go up in a kilo of Semtex?'

'You want my protection? Call the cops.'

'Je-Jesus,' Matthew rounded on Mace, 'don't you g-get it? This isn't st-stuff for the cops. This is Sh-Sheemina Feb-February. The cops can do sweet fa-fanny about her. You see Abdul Abdul wa-walking around. Two mur-murder charges, he's out f-free. This's tha-thank you Sheemina. So what good're c-cops? Huh! You can t-tell me?'

A shadow darkened the doorway into the street and Oumou came in. Mace heard her catch her breath, say, 'Merde!' and disappear.

'That's a stunner you picked up,' said Ducky. 'You're a cagey boy, Mace Bishop.'

'You want my advice?' Mace shifted from one kitten to the next. They were well tacked in. Some had their heads busted in the hammering. Five of the twelve were alive. 'Close down. That's the best protection I can give.'

'Not possible,' said Ducky. 'We're talking business, Mace. Mattie closes down, the income stream collapses.'

'They put a pipe bomb in here it's going to explode, not just collapse.'

'What you're engaged to prevent.'

Oumou came back with a pair of pliers from the motormac.

'You gonna yank the nails out with that you gonna need visibility,' said Ducky Donald. 'Bring the lights up, Mattie, give the girl some illumination.' He closed on her. 'You need a hand there?'

Oumou ignored him. Got at the first live kitten, put the pliers to the nail head and pulled back hard with a grunt. The nail came out and the kitten fell to the floor, screeching. Ducky Donald got a load of French for not catching it. Pity was, Mace thought, he couldn't understand a word of it.

'You gonna enlighten me?' Ducky Donald asked as Mace handed him a box that must have been the container the kittens were brought in.

'In a word, you're an arsehole.'

Matthew sniggered. Oumou pulled free another kitten, gave it to Ducky with an expression suggesting arsehole was too soft a translation. She got down the five, said, 'Give this back to your neighbour' – swapping the pliers for the box. Mace followed her out.

'Ask him what he saw,' Mace called back at father and son. 'The motormac.'

Ducky Donald shouted, 'You're not running out on us Mace?'

'Till four-thirty. Meantime think of closing down.'

7

The vet saved three. While he was snipping fur, cleaning the wounds, preparing syringes, wanted to know what happened. Mace gave him a story of how he and Oumou had found them tacked to a wall in the wrong part of Woodstock, probably some sort of gang initiation. Right, he said, he'd heard of that. Dogs being crucified. Cats skewered. Even cows with their udders cut off. Once about a dozen hens plucked alive. Made you wonder what sort of drugs they took, these gangsters.

'You want me to take these to a pet's refuge?' he said. 'Should imagine if they stay alive over the next few days someone'll give them a home.'

'We are having them,' said Oumou.

The vet glanced at her sympathetically. 'You've done enough already, you don't have to feel responsible.' He flicked his eyes at Mace for confirmation.

Oumou said, 'They are for us to look after.'

Mace didn't argue. Arguing with Oumou on matters like this got nowhere.

In the car heading up the steep streets she told him it was a good idea for Christa to have pets. This was something they should have done years before. The girl was six years old; she should have a pet to look after. 'You can see this is true, no?'

Mace swung the Spider out of Kloof Street into Union, slowing on the approach to Christa's crèche.

'They're not going to live. Not all of them anyhow. How's she going to feel when they die?'

'We face that one, maybe, when it happens.'

'It's going to.'

'Maybe.' He got flashed a look a million years old. 'But maybe not.'

The crèche was hidden behind a high wall, a notice at the security gate read: 'Parents must ensure that their children are handed into the care of accredited staff at the beginning of the day.'

Oumou slid out of the car, reached the gate in two strides and punched the intercom buzzer. He heard her speak her name. The gate clicked unlocked and she went in. The noise of kids at play came loud from behind the wall. Mace opened the boot to gentle the kittens.

Christa came hurtling through the gate. She stopped at the sight of the kittens curled into one another in the box.

She wore a red T-shirt, black tracksuit bottoms and Nikes. Her hair was wild, dark, but in the sunlight it caught fire and turned almost auburn. Her eyes could have been her mother's, he believed, mysterious pools that had gathered secrets for so long they were incapable of registering surprise. She had the same texture and skin colour as her mother, a brown as golden as the head on an espresso. When he searched for traces of his genes in her expressions, movement, the tilt of her face he could find none. Other stuff, yes: pigheadedness, temper, irritability. Then again nothing there that wasn't in her mother. To look at, most times he reckoned Oumou made her alone. She was the only child they could have, and that gave her special dues he felt.

Mace took her hand, drew her closer to the boot. There was blood on the cardboard. The kitten with the leaking wound stared up, opened its mouth to mew but made no sound. Christa reached out to touch it, poking a finger into the fur.

'Softly, ma puce,' said Oumou. 'They are sore.'

'Why?' asked Christa.

'Someone hurt them,' Mace said.

The kitten opened its mouth, red as a wound, silent.

All the drive home down the peninsula, Christa didn't say a word.

8

'I'll drop you,' Mace said as they waited for the security guard to roll the gate back manually to let them in. For three days the electronics had been faulty. The man took his time, smiling at them, waving at Christa like there was no hurry in his day. Mace gritted his teeth but kept from saying anything.

'You can't have coffee?' said Oumou.

Mace shook his head. 'A meeting.'

'With that man and his boy?'

'Uh huh.'

'This is not your work, to give them protection.'

'It's a favour. I owe him.'

Oumou didn't reply, not looking at him either as they drove through the gate. Lavender Mews: neat white duplexes, BMs, SUVs, station wagons lining the pavements, toys left out on the front lawns, flowers bright in the flower beds. A street of identical townhouses, theirs in the middle of the row. A box between boxes, Mace thought of it. Spruce and clean and sanitised. Except their house had no flowers and the grass needed mowing. The sort of detail he didn't see. The sort of home neither of them wanted.

'I do not like that house,' Oumou said, getting out. 'I have a bad feeling.'

'We'll talk later,' said Mace, popping the boot to pick up the box of kittens. 'Just think about it. About what it could be.'

'For me I do not have to think about it.'

Five minutes later Mace was thinking about it, about how the hell he was going to convince Oumou on this one. She wanted to move, he wanted to move, get out of the suburbs. This was the opportunity. Except she wasn't seeing it. She wanted to build a concrete, glass and chrome number.

He pushed the thought away. More worrying, what had eaten at him all the way home, was the call to Oumou's cellphone. He drove out of the neat streets into the Main Road heading for the Blue Route highway, the mountain chain hazy against the sky. Had to be Sheemina February. Why he couldn't say. Just a feeling this was how she operated. Had to be she'd found out his name.

The on-ramp opened into three lanes and Mace pushed the Spider over the speed limit, flashing cars that didn't move out of the fast lane. Had to be she had someone inside the cellphone service providers to get the number, not just his number but his wife's. With the right contacts, anybody's phone number was only ten minutes away. No reason Sheemina February didn't have the right contacts. If one call had given him the number behind the call to Oumou, two calls could've got her to Oumou's phone.

Up Wynberg Hill Mace thumbed through to Matthew's number. He came on sounding like he'd pulled a bunch of dead kittens off a wall.

'You been in touch with Sheemina February since our meeting?' Mace said.

'She-Sheemina?'- Matthew's voice rising through the syllables, surprised.

'All I need is yes or no.'

'N-no,' he said.

Ducky Donald shouted in the background. 'When're you pitching, Mace? You've got obligations here.'

He told Matthew to tell his father thanks for the reminder, he'd be there shortly. But the traffic was slow down Edinburgh Drive through the Claremont S-bends and Newlands Forest. During the crawl Mace dialled the cellphone number used to call Oumou, found out it belonged to a woman who'd had her phone stolen the previous week.

'Off my office desk,' she said. 'You can't turn your back for a minute. Anywhere.' She laughed. 'Insurance paid out and I got an upgrade. That's how things work these days.'

He said, 'Sounds like a win-win situation' – and they both laughed. Added a new dimension to Sheemina February though. Always assuming it was her. Which he did.

The traffic eased on Hospital Bend, Mace working the Spider across four lanes, the revs up into the sweep at the top, the city opening below and the mountain grey behind. This was the city he wanted. Forget the suburbs, the townships, the shacklands. Sheemina February, he said aloud, I'm going to get your number.

By the time Mace pulled the Spider into the curb outside the club, the motormac's shop was closed, likewise the second-hand dealer. Only sign of life was a black guy settling to a meal of fish and chips in a doorway. He watched Mace walk over.

'You work for Cuito?'

The man grinned. 'My name is Dr Roberto from Luanda at your service. I am here all night.' He wiped his hand on his trousers, holding it out. They shook.

'A medical doctor or something else?'

'General practitioner.' Dr Roberto plopped a chip into his mouth. 'Excuse me, I am very hungry.' He followed the chip with a portion of fish. When he'd swallowed, said, 'My training was in Cuba. But I am not here. I do not exist.'

'Like Cuito.'

The two men laughed. 'Like Cuito. It is very sad.'

Mace pulled out a fifty, handed it to him. 'I never visited Luanda. From the photographs I've seen it looked like a beautiful city once.'

Dr Roberto sighed. 'For me it was always broken. All my life there has been the war.' He went back to his fish and chips.

'You let me know if there's anything I should know.' Mace turned towards the club. 'Any time of the night.'

'I have your phone number Mr Mace. Cuito has informed me what you want.'

Inside Club Catastrophe, Pylon, Ducky Donald, and Matthew stood in the dance zone drinking from bottles of beer. Not a trace of the kittens but some smear marks of blood on the walls. Pylon held up his hand in greeting. Ducky Donald smirked as Mace registered the blood.

'Mattie's idea,' he said. 'In memoriam.'

'You're opening tonight then?' Mace took the beer Matthew uncapped.

'Why not? What's to stop us?'

Mace caught Pylon's eye. 'Maybe you can explain it to him. Slowly.'

Pylon stepped back to rest his elbows against the bar counter. 'I already have. Didn't change the way the world spins.'

Ducky Donald put his arm round his son's shoulders. 'Accept it guys. This's the modern age. The ravers wanna rave. You can't let them down. We're opening. Hasn't even been a bomb scare yet.'

Mace took a mouthful of beer, the taste in his mouth gave it the taste of iron. 'Okay. You're set on this, we have no option.'

'That's how it is, my brother.'

Mace shook his head. 'You're wrong, Donald. You're wrong in forcing this.' He and Pylon headed off to take a look round the premises.

'Not the sort of words would've been spoken by the gung ho Bishop I used to know,' he called after them.

Out of earshot Pylon said, 'We haven't got the guys for this. We're stretched.'

Mace didn't respond.

'Putting a blanket down's going to cost us big time.'

'You've got another suggestion?'

Pylon grimaced. 'I'd known it would be like this, I'd have told Ducky Donald where to put his AKs.'

Behind the dance floor they found a chill room and toilets with skylights onto a service lane. What passed as burglar bars weren't going to stop a pipe bomb being lobbed in. Weren't going to stop anybody getting in if they wanted to. Nor was a backdoor onto the room Matthew used to store his booze stocks. Might have a security grille but a tyre iron would've sorted that in less than thirty seconds, Mace reckoned. Also, with all the walls painted black, any packages left lying around were going to disappear into the shadows. Because shadows were everywhere. Somebody managed to sneak a four-, five-pound parcel around the pat search they could put it down in a corner, walk right out, nobody'd know anything until the boom. Above the club was empty office space, above that an attic. The floors between were wooden boards, some creaking like it wasn't a good idea to stand on them. In a broom cupboard Pylon found a trapdoor; you opened that you could see how Ducky Donald was thinning on top. Pylon slid it back into place, dusted his hands.

'Nice of Ducky. At the time, choice between this and the Arab gun runner, I'd have taken the Arab.'

Mace looked down on Dr Roberto finished with his fish and chips, warming his hands round a steaming mug. He had somewhere sorted when it came to take-aways.

Pylon joined his partner at the window, said, 'You think we should get the place swept? Maybe they stashed a bomb while nailing the kittens?'

'To be on the safe side, yes. Personally I doubt it though.'

'You know that guy?'

'Medical doctor. Doing reconnaissance for us.'

'We've employed him?'

'Him and that car-guard Cuito.'

Pylon rubbed a hand over his face so hard Mace could hear the beard rasp. 'You shouldn't have asked me first?'

'Should've,' he agreed, heading for the staircase. 'Look at them as casuals. Casuals didn't need a partner's consent in our articles of association.'

'Mace.' How Pylon said the name was meant to stop Mace in his tracks. It did. He came up. 'We don't play matters that way. Never have that I can remember. And no need to change either.' They stared at one another, twenty years of history in the contact. 'If you'd asked me I'd have said do it, now I wonder what's going on here? Now I think, hey, Mace didn't tell me where he was for those two extra days in New York. Hey, seems Mace took a flight to Jozi three weeks back that I don't know the reason for. Hey, Saturday afternoon Mace didn't answer his cell, and Oumou didn't know his whereabouts. All these things are not in my understanding of Mace. In my understanding of Mace he's clinical. Efficient. Seems to be without feelings sometimes. Most times. But he doesn't go behind my back. See where I'm going? Next thing we've got two aliens on the payroll.'

'COD basis.'

'Doesn't matter. What matters is this other thing going on here. Underneath. This thing where Oumou phones me, asks if I've noticed something odd about Mace. Like what? Well, like he's angry. More specifically he's not playing with his daughter. Not playing with his wife either I would imagine. Without being told this, you understand. Just taking an informed guess.'

He let a silence fall. Mace let it lengthen. Eventually, said, 'It's nothing.'

'I don't think so. I think it's something. You asked me to guess I'd say it was a woman.'

Mace snorted a laugh. 'You'd be way off. Dead wrong.'

'I don't think so. I'd say you saw Isabella in New York.'

'You can think what you like. I'm saying you're wrong.'

Pylon kept up the glare, a small muscle working below his lower lip, as it did when he was irritated. 'Alright. Okay, bru.' He snapped his fingers. 'Now's not the time. But we must talk. I need to know what's happening.'

Downstairs father and son were cracking their third beer. Pylon and Mace declined the offer.

'You figured out how you're gonna keep Mattie safe?' Ducky Donald put the bottle to his lips and sucked hard.

'It's not about keeping anyone safe,' said Pylon. 'It's about whether we get to spot the guy with the bomb before it blows.'

'Not good enough,' said Ducky Donald. 'You're the hot shots, and that's not hot.'

'At short notice the best we can do is have Pylon and me here,' Mace said. 'We want to thank you for this opportunity, Donald.'

Ducky Donald smiled at the jibe. 'Keeping you from better things?'

'We have a business to run.'

'Looking after old dames on surgical safaris! That is some business, Mace. That is milking the rich and famous. Where's the fear margin, huh? Where's the excitement? Good morning Mrs Vanderbilt. How's the nip'n tuck healing? Ready to go watch the rhinos yet?' He mimicked the two men picking subserviently among their face-lift clients. Admittedly, Mace acknowledged, not an awe-inspiring prospect, but good business nonetheless: chaperone them in from New York, Los Angeles, wherever, babysit the op and recovery, take them game-viewing while the bruising disappears. 'What's with you guys?' Ducky went up to Pylon, clasped a hand round his bicep and gripped. Pylon, not the smallest of men, clamped a hand over Ducky Donald's and pulled him off. Ducky staggered back a pace. 'You get a kick out of jacking off the larneys? Don't worry Sandra we'll watch your back. Keep the paparazzi away.' He turned from Pylon to Mace. 'That's not a business. That's trading on the paranoid. Hyping up the neurotic. Easy money, guys.' He took another mouthful of beer. 'What we've put on your plate is real stuff. The sorta thing you grooved on.'

Fear. Destruction. Blood. Death.

The history Mace didn't need to replay. He circled the room wondering if Matthew's bouncers were good at the pat down, said, 'You got it Ducky. Our business doesn't run to club security.'

'Does now.' There came across his face the self-satisfied smirk that used to rile Mace. Still did. 'So work out a strategy.'

Mace was about to tell him the strategy was wait-and-see, when Matthew's cellphone rang. He mouthed at them Sh-Sheemina February, put the instrument to his ear.

'I wa-wasn't gonna ph-phone you,' he said, and listened.

'I've no n-need to see-ee you.'

He listened to more of her story.

'It's a f-free country,' he said. 'L-like you told us' – pressed the disconnect. 'Sh-she's outside. Com-ing in.'

'She'd better not,' said Ducky. 'This's private property.'

Matthew didn't respond.

Sheemina February was alone, sans briefcase, sans headscarf. A striking woman with a presence, to Mace's way of thinking. Took guts to walk in there. She ignored the men, ran her gaze over the black walls and the gothic images. If she saw the blood stains she gave no sign.

Said, 'Pathetic, Matthew. Childish.'

'You some kind of connoisseur?' said Ducky Donald, bristling into the beam of a spotlight.

She didn't rise to him. Said straight to Matthew, 'What've you decided?'

He put a hand up against the wall to lean, nonchalant. 'I-I already sa-said.'

'Your final word?' When Matthew said nothing, Sheemina February turned to Mace. 'Mr Advisor, this is what you've advised him?'

'You know my name,' Mace said, 'use it.'

She kept her eyes on him. 'I know more than that.' Slowly did a circuit of the wall art, stopping when her back was to him. 'I know you. I know Christa. Adorable child, Mr Bishop. Friendly. Not afraid to talk to strangers.'

A shot of red crossed Mace's eyes. The world went dark. Pylon checked him with a hand to his forearm. 'Don't.' He whispered it, but she heard.

'Don't.' She faced them. The blue eyes giving up nothing. 'The comrades: Mace and Pylon. The ice men. Stone killers to some. The people's heroes to others. Struggle veterans, arms smugglers for the glorious guerrillas of our movement. Nowadays VIP assistance. This is not your scene. Stick with the wrinklies, guys. Best to keep the pension scheme.'

'You touch her ... You touch my wife ...' Mace shook free of Pylon's grip.

'I don't touch anybody, Mr Bishop. What I do is represent people against drug dealing. If you want to, some time I'll show you good people who saw their kids become prostitutes, gangsters, criminals. Kids that were like Christa. What did the police do to help these people? Nothing. Because somewhere there's police in the supply line. What do the politicians do? Nothing. Because the druglords are building schools. From where I stand they're building a market-place. In here, this is a market-place.'

Mace took a step towards her, she held her ground. 'How'd you get my name? How'd you get my wife's phone number?'

'I recognised you, Mr Bishop. As simple as that. There was a time we were on the same side. In the same camp, so to speak.'

'Doesn't answer my question.'

'Come, come. Use your imagination.' She glanced at her watch. 'We're in power now, we probably share contacts.' She brushed past him heading for the door. 'Gentlemen,' she said, held up her gloved hand, 'I'm sorry you've taken a hardline attitude, I'd hoped for your cooperation.'

'Hardline!' Ducky Donald almost choked on his beer. But Sheemina February was gone.

'Jesus,' said Pylon, 'I remember her. She got ten years for treason. Round about the late eighties. Almost died under torture, was the story I heard.'

'Pity she didn't.' Ducky Donald launched across the room to slam the club door shut. 'She's trouble. Major trouble.'

'You still going to open?' Mace asked.

'Nose of ten the doors swing wide,' said Ducky. 'What you say, Mattie?'

Matthew nodded, not the happiest club owner in town.

9

Outside it was dusk, but warm, a berg wind blowing.

Pylon said, 'What's with the February woman getting onto Oumou?'

Mace shrugged. 'Intimidation. Christ knows. Maybe she thinks I hold some sway with the Hartnells.' He paused. 'You said she got done?'

'The way I recall it, she and two sisters planned a car bomb, going to take out the president on his way to parliament. Something like that. Got them high profile attention in the papers. Mostly because of their pretty faces. And ten years for conspiracy. Come the political amnesty, they walked. Probably did no more than a couple of years.'

Mace rocked on the curb edge, irked by a detail he couldn't get to. 'There's more,' he said. 'Only I don't know what. She's familiar.'

'She's scary.'

'No kidding. Her personally and what's behind her. The crazies. One thing, Sheemina February's not going to be hands on. She's done that.' Mace sighed. 'Once it was so easy, hey. Us and them. Now us is them. Sometimes worse I think.'

'Ah, come on.'

'No, true as. Look at this shit Ducky Donald's pulling.'

'He said something more?'

'Doesn't have to does he?'

Pylon clucked his tongue, stared off at the end of the street before he said, 'Time to talk? About you.'

The last thing Mace wanted. 'Uh uh.' He shook his head. 'Tomorrow.'

Pylon looked dubious.

'Tomorrow, okay.'

'I'm not kidding, Mace.' He flicked the automatic lock on the Merc, one of their luxury client cars. 'And this lot?' – jerking a thumb at the club. 'They're going to blow it?'

'Probably. Probably tonight I'd guess.'

Pylon slid into the car. 'That's just so exciting.' The side window came down. 'Another thing I remember about that Sheemina February, in jail she sharpened a hairbrush, stuck it into a warder's stomach.'

'Dangerous lady.'

'We should try the police. That Captain Gonsalves, maybe he'd be interested.'

'Doubt it. Like the man said, no bomb threat. What's to be worrying about? Gonsalves'll tell me to piss off.'

'Try him.'

'You try him.'

'He's white. There's your commonality.'

They agreed to meet at ten.

Three times a week, Monday, Wednesday, Thursday Mace swam with two others in the pool at the Point Health Centre. Tyrone impressed him as a suit, probably in management; Allan favoured chinos and polo shirts. He figured him for a marketing type. They didn't talk much except to greet and maybe comment on the obvious: weather, news, sport. Their rule was swimming started at six-thirty. Five minutes grace if someone was late but they didn't wait longer than this.

Tyrone and Allan were younger than Mace, Tyrone the stronger swimmer, Allan more in the iron-man league. They had a routine. For the first half-hour Mace set the pace in deference to the ten, fifteen years he pulled on them, then Allan took over for a quartile, and Tyrone hauled them through the final sector, powering it on until Mace's arms screamed and he wasn't sure if his lungs were big enough for the air he needed. At the end he was gasping, clutching the side of the pool with almost no strength left to get out at the steps. This wasn't normal. But then, he reckoned, nothing was normal anymore.

His hours in the water were time out: a reptile locked on the blue ahead and the black line along the bottom. A crocodile. No past, no future, no thoughts. Only action, only the movement of his arms and his legs, the turn of his head to draw air. The efficiency of his body propelled smoothly through the water, noiseless, churning bubbles, intent only on motion. Mace the reliable, he thought of himself. Who got things done.

After the session the men dressed more or less in silence. Maybe some comments on if they could've done a better time, no suggestion yet that Mace was slowing them down. On the way out he stopped for a fruit juice at the health bar, Tyrone and Allan giving it a rain check.

It was dark when Mace left the centre, the Spider parked to the side of the parking ground near a hedge. No overhead lights, no perimeter lights at all. A number of cars still in the lot, but not a soul else around. He threaded his way through, thoughts of Sheemina February and the bomb she'd have her minions set off uppermost in his mind. Also that she'd recognised him. That he should've recognised her.

The kids, a pack of boys, were about him like they'd been conjured from another dimension, hissing, whispering, tugging at his sport's bag and clothing, feral, stinking of booze and meths and glue. He didn't sense them, glimpse them, hear them. They had him cold. In the Spider's boot was a forty-five, but a forty-five in the Spider's boot was about as much help as a prayer, Mace thought, taking in the situation.

They were a pack of fifteen or more, swirling among the cars, on the hunt. One jumped at his back, smaller boys either side, two bigger rat-faces blocked the gap. Crouched there, grinning.

He dropped the bag as a diversion, and the kids fell on it like jackals ripping bones from a carcass. He had house and car keys in his left hand, slid out the metal shafts to protrude from his fist. Before the kids could pinion this arm he slashed a back-hander at the nearest rat-face, opening his cheek. Turned on the boy behind, knocked him down, put a boot to his head. It was the only advantage he got before they packed him. Yet he worked in two more jabs with his fist, from the screams believing the keys had punctured skin.

The boys clawed for his eyes, trying to drag him down. He tasted blood, felt its stickiness on his hands. His blood, their blood. Their blood thick with HIV, most of them rentboys for the rough-trade punters. The thought of mixing blood gave him comeback strength to shuck those racking at his chest and the momentum to crash back against a car, those behind him going down. The other rat-face was dancing foot to foot, feinting with a knife. He came in low meaning to spill Mace's guts. Fast for a glue head, except Mace knocked his arm, the blade snagging on Mace's belt-buckle, slid upwards through his shirt, finding skin. He felt it as heat. The boy skipped away, darted back to stick him. Again Mace feinted, the blade opening a cut along his arm.

From the centre came shouts. A shot. Rat-face hesitated but the pack scattered. Then he made off.

A guy ran up. 'You alright?'

Mace looked at the blood dripping off his fingers.

'Best thing would be to give them a chopper ride out to sea,' said his saviour. 'Drop them in the deep.'

10

Mace got cleaned up at the centre. The cut on his stomach needed only ointment and a plaster patch. The forearm slash was deeper. Merited a stitch or two, thought the first-aid guy. Definitely an anti-tetanus. On the HIV score he didn't think there was too serious a risk.

'Lucky,' he said. In his experience he'd seen incidents where the corpse had his hands full keeping his guts from sliding about in the dirt while his valuables were stolen.

'Who's a corpse?' Mace said.

The first-aid guy gave him a baleful glance. 'It's how the kids think of their victims. Even before the knife's gone in.'

All the way home Mace kept thinking, corpse. Dead man walking. Goner. Cadaver. What also plagued him was how he'd walked into it. Not even noticed the kids until it was too late. In the line of business that sort of negligence was scary. Enough to get you killed in the old days. Enough to get you killed in the present days too. It happened when your mind was elsewhere.

Going up Eastern Boulevard out of the city, he pressed in Captain Gonsalves's direct line. The phone went to five rings before the captain answered: 'What?'

Mace told him what. Whenever he paused he could hear the captain chewing.

'So?' said Gonsalves when Mace had finished.

'So d'you want to get there before or afterwards?' Mace said.

Gonsalves laughed. 'This's a come down, Mr Bishop?' The chewing got louder. 'Last time I looked you were security, right? Protecting the stars. I got the catch-line there? Those facelift gals're your speciality. Not so? You and that Buso fella playing wanker boys to the stars and celebs. Hey, Mr Bishop stick with it. The club scene's fulla shit. Your scenario's right, tonight you're gonna get blown up.'

'Which doesn't concern you?'

'You're a big boy, Mace Bishop. You've been around.' Chew, chew. Gonsalves laughed again and the connection went dead.

Mace took Hospital Bend in the fast lane, down the straight and up towards the Mill, tight against the centre barrier. Gonsalves he'd bump into from time to time. In security you did. There were people who said he was a good cop, kept his nose in real crime through the dark years. Nowadays the guy was staring his pension in the face, probably not a joyful prospect. Five years down the line, Mace reckoned, he could be knocking on their door pleading for a babysit.

At the entrance to the security complex, the nightwatch rolled back the gate. A new man, did it with more speed than the day guard. Mace pulled up behind Oumou's estate. Even before he'd parked, Christa came running out. A kitten had died. She'd named them Cat1, Cat2, and Cat3. Cat1 was dead.

'Probably Cat3 is also going to be dead,' she said, nodding, her mouth purposeful.

She wasn't teary, more interested in where they were going to bury Cat1.

In the back garden, Mace suggested. Or what passed for a back garden: a block of lawn surrounded by empty flower beds where only weeds grew. Once in a while Oumou had a man in to trim the grass but the neatness never lasted more than a week. Occasionally there'd been notes from the complex's body corporate complaining about the neglect, suggesting that they plant daisy bushes.

'You can put a candle on the grave,' said Oumou.

'And flowers?'

'We can buy flowers, ma puce.'

Mace searched through the cutlery for an old spoon to use as a trowel and found one spotted with rust.

'You want to dig?' Christa nodded and they went into the backyard to dig a shallow grave. While she scooped a hole in the earth, Oumou brought out a candle and Mace fetched the dead kitten.

'I will, Papa,' Christa said, taking the body, putting it carefully into the hole.

'Now you've got to cover it.'

She shook her head, suddenly clutching at her mother. Mace made to push a handful of soil over the body but Christa stopped him. He crouched to be face to face with her.

'What's it?'

Her eyes were teary, she clutched Oumou's hand.

Oumou said, 'You want to cover the kitten first, chérie, with a blanket?' Christa nodded.

They wrapped the kitten in a kitchen cloth and put it back in the hole. This time Christa let her father push over the soil and build it into a mound. Her mother lit a candle, sticking it in the ground about where the kitten's head would be. For a while they stood, hand-in-hand, watching the flame sputter, shadows dancing on the wall behind.

At supper Christa said, 'Papa, do kittens go to heaven?'

Oumou reached out to stroke her daughter's hair, her eyes fixed on Mace.

'When kittens die, they die just like us,' he said.

Christa looked at him. 'We go to heaven.'

Mace shook his head. 'We die, sweetheart. That's it. Nothing happens afterwards.'

Puzzled she turned to her mother. 'Oui, ma puce,' said Oumou softly.

Christa's face crumpled. The tears came, big slow ones.

Mace left once Christa was asleep. At the door into the garage Oumou stopped him.

'Why are you doing this?' she said. 'They are not good men.'

'You're right. But I owe him. I told you.'

'For something from the past. This is stupid, Mace.' She took his right hand and brought him round to face her. He winced as they embraced, and she stepped back. Her arms dropped. Eventually she said, 'Why are you leaving me?'

His arm ached but he couldn't see the point in telling her now about the mugging. He took her hand. 'I'm not. You're wrong.' It was an echo of what he'd told Pylon.

'Then why are you so strange? So cold.'

'Tomorrow,' he said. 'We'll talk tomorrow.'

Her expression brought a heaviness to his chest. Such desolation. Such aloneness. He went quickly, before the hurt could stop him.

11

Sheemina February, in her right hand a glass of wine, stood barefoot before the picture window looking out at the darkness. Nothing visible. Black sky, black sea. She smiled at her reflection: the woman in the trousers and loose shirt smiling back at her.

That in a single day so much could change.

She raised the glass and sipped, leaving a plum imprint of lipstick on the rim.

To recognise but not be recognised. To be seen yet remain hidden. The thought angered her that in the life of Mace Bishop her life had barely registered.

Below, a wave broke against the shore rocks. She glanced down, saw blue phosphorescence run through the white water like lightning.

Earlier, at sundown, a yacht had been anchored there inshore, pretty people lounging on the decks, the women topless. She'd watched their playfulness. A blonde boy draping his girlfriend's breasts in seagrass.

The blonde boy hard-muscled. Broad shoulders, a swimmer's figure with strong thighs. Reminded her of Mace Bishop.

What to do about Mace Bishop?

To wait.

Waiting was the trick. Drawing out the situation, setting up the moves.

He was attractive. So much the better. Cocky. Sitting there behind the desk, cool and confident. Looking at her cleavage. Shifting for a glance of her breasts when she'd leant forward. Not caring that she'd noticed. A man pleased with himself and his world. Pleased with his wife, his daughter, his sexy red sports car.

'Enjoy them, Mr Bishop,' Sheemina February said aloud.

She turned away from the window to the file on her dining room table. How quickly a man's life could be compiled. She had it all in an afternoon: the girl's name, the girl's crèche, the wife's name, the home street address, the car registrations, land-line numbers, cellphone numbers, his latest tax return, a bank statement, the work address. A photograph of the woman. Another of the child. Two of the man himself: one coming out of the swimming pool, rising up on his arms, the water sluicing off his body; the other full frontal in a black Speedo. She studied his face: the sharp line of the jaw, the flat planes of the cheeks. The dark eyebrows. The nose flaring softly at the nostrils. A face she had not expected to see again.

Her cellphone rang and she flipped the photograph onto the pile of documents. Thumbed on Abdul Abdul. Before he could speak, said, 'I told you not to phone me. I am your lawyer. Your legal advisor, not your playmate' – and disconnected. In two paces she was across at the marble kitchen countertop, filling her glass from the bottle.

'Prost, Mr Bishop.' Raising her glass to the room: large open-plan space: white couches facing the sea view, limewashed table and chairs, white flokatis on the ash flooring. A ritual of white. White votive candles scattered about, the only other light coming from a desk lamp. Everything reflected in the picture windows.

She clicked off the lamp and smiled at the order of her lair.

Sheemina February ate at her dining table facing the dark sea. Piazzolla on the sound system. Propped against the wine bottle, the photograph of Mace Bishop in his costume. Sexy. She speared the penne onto her fork and wiped them through red pesto sauce.

Later she went out on the balcony with the last of the wine. Leant against the chrome rail, the metal cold under her arms, a dampness clinging to the ozone air. She finished her wine, dangling the long-stemmed goblet from the fingers of her left hand. The glove off. She let it drop, the glass flashing twice before it disappeared, the fall too long to hear it break.

12

Even at ten the nightclub quarter was hectic. Kids stood around their cars drinking, doors open, sound systems thumping out rap and funk. Mace found a spot for Oumou's Opel estate a few streets away, checked a round into the chamber of his Ruger, slipped it into his jacket pocket. The street was quiet, some parked cars farther along, a huddle of streetkids in a shop doorway. He sat watching them: they could have been the pack that attacked him. This group was whacked on glue, meths, who knew: curled into one another, covered by plastic and cardboard. Even the slam of his car door didn't raise a head.

Assurance Street by night was a party. Loud, throbbing, kids dancing in the road. The air sweet with grass, E-pushers doing business unconcerned. Matthew had speakers belting techno mounted on the walls either side his club's neon sign, a screen now suspended over the entrance showing a loop of nuclear tests. A bomb went off here: inside the club, outside the club, either way, the collateral would be major. First the explosion's mayhem, then the panic, then the difficulty of bringing in emergency vehicles.

Mace took a look round for Dr Roberto. The guy had seen him and was angling through the throng.

'Mr Mace,' he called, 'the people you want are here' – he gestured towards the corner. 'A white man and a coloured, sitting in a Toyota car.'

'You're sure?'

'It is according to Cuito.'

'He's around?'

'For some time but he has gone now to sleep. He says I must tell you the white man is from this morning. The other man he has not seen before.'

At the club doors Mace could see Pylon waving him over. 'Watch them, Dr Roberto,' he said, making off. 'They move anywhere, even to take a pee you let me know.'

Behind him he heard Dr Roberto say, 'Maybe I will be needed as a doctor tonight?' Mace left the question unanswered.

Pylon tapped his watch. 'Ten o'clock we said. I'm missing the soccer for this: Bushbucks and Kaiser Chiefs.'

Mace gave the French shrug, pushed past him through the doors. 'Ten-twenty's not too bad. You could tape the soccer.'

'I am,' said Pylon.

Inside two bouncers with magic wands stepped up to frisk him.

Ducky Donald in white, white shirt open to show chest hair, white chinos, white socks and shoes, a black bimbo in black fastened to his arm, intervened, 'Party time, guys, they're special guests.' The one with his wand screeching over Mace's Ruger grinned. 'Fuzz?'

'Whatever you want,' said Pylon.

'You know what?' said Ducky. 'In my water it says they won't do it. And you know why?'

Pylon rolled his eyes, shouted at Matthew, 'Give us some light on the scene?' The club was as dark as a Gothic grotto.

Matthew punched up the lights. For the first time Mace saw the djs in a box about head level, staring down on them. Both shaven heads. Skinny. Androgynous. Something softer about the one's face that made her for a woman.

'You wanna know why?'

The boy dj gave a hand sign that meant nothing to Mace. He waved a greeting. The dj held up some vinyl in return.

'We're getting started,' he said into the mic.

'Not now,' said Ducky, gesticulating at the dj, pawing at Mace's sleeve. 'Not now, buddy. Give us five, hey.'

At Ducky Donald's clutching, pain seared up Mace's arm. Through a grimace to keep in the throb he said, 'Tell me Ducky. What's your theory?'

Despite the booze he caught the edge to Mace's tone, hesitated, then leered forward. 'It's because no way that woman's gonna want the kinda death toll a bomb would set up in here. You know what I mean? One or two and a coupla amputations even she can live with. The body count goes any higher, they're gonna lose the PR spin.' Triumph smeared a smile across his face. 'She blows a bomb, she's got twenty dead right off.'

'Which is why we're going to take a look around again.' Mace steered a passage to Matthew. 'The bouncers know what they're looking for?' He nodded. 'You tell them their wands burp for a tooth filling, entry's denied.'

Matthew spluttered 'Ca-ca-ca...'

'Christ,' Mace filled in for him.

Pylon and Mace did another tour of the premises, mostly by flashlight. Everything was how they'd last seen it.

'Should of arranged for dogs,' Pylon said. 'You can't tell just looking at things.' They were at the window in the empty office space upstairs: below the street partied. 'Seems they don't even wait for the club to open.'

Mace pointed out the Toyota with Sheemina February's side-kicks. The coloured guy was on his cell inside the car; the white guy leant against the bonnet, smoking. 'Mr White I recognise from this morning. Chances are they're only monitoring. No ways she'd send them in to do the job.'

Pylon rested his forehead against the windowpane. 'We're just supposed to hang around waiting for the shit to happen? Or we're going to hassle them?'

'No point in hassling.'

'You've got a plan to do anything?'

'Be patient.'

Pylon clucked. 'How about Gonsalves? You speak to him?'

'I did.'

'And?'

'And he gave me advice, same as Sheemina February did. Stick to the safaris.'

'Wonderful. Just bloody wonderful.' Pylon straightened, clicked the knuckles of his left hand. 'Talking about Sheemina February, I found out something. She's STASI trained, explains why she stuck the warder with the sharpened hairbrush. A year before she got caught, pitched up as a legal assistant in a blue-chip firm in town. One smart cookie from what I'm told. Into contractual law.'

'Now into PAGAD.'

'Someone's got to do it. Useful common interests though.'

Mace laughed. 'In bombs?'

'I believe.'

'She wore the glove then?'

'Birth defect. So the story goes.' Pylon turned back to the window to scope the street. 'There were no cars against the curb that would be a help. These guys're so into car bombs.'

'Not this time. This time they've got to blow the club. Close it down. A car bomb wouldn't do the structural damage.'

'Would if it was big enough.'

'Big enough would be beyond their league.'

Pylon gave his partner a sceptical look. 'You've got a strategy?'

'Keep Mattie boy from catching it. Like Ducky wants.'

'Everyone else can go to hell?'

'We save him, we save everyone.'

People surged in the street towards the club doors, sound came thumping up from below. The rave was on. Pylon pointed at the PAGAD guys on the corner: both were out of the car but not intent on moving. 'We'd better go party,' he said. 'Check out the patrons.'

Pylon did the circulating. Mace took the door. The bouncers were good. Everyone got the going over. If women complained there wasn't a female for the pat search, he told them if it was a problem they didn't have to come in. If the wire in their bras got the wands buzzing, he told them get rid of the underwear. They whinged but got the notion. The truly pissed-off came through tits flashing, dangling their bras from their fingertips.

Some said Mace was a pervert. Some said he was an arsehole.

Matthew came up. 'Wh-what's th-this?' Held out a red lacy number. Behind him a raging female.

Mace told him looked like a C cup. Weedy type that he was, Matthew grabbed Mace by the jacket, pulled at him, yelling, 'Yo-yo-you ca-can't do this. Ss-top. Na-now.' Again Mace's arm burnt with pain.

'Let go.' Mace spoke it quietly. Matthew wasn't coked, wasn't boozed either. He got in Mace's face, spit-white flecking at the corners of his mouth. When he didn't do as asked, Mace kneed him in the balls, catching him as he doubled over. The bouncers made a move towards them.

'Stay with it guys,' Pylon cautioned the doormen, stepping in to cover his partner. 'Keep the clubbers coming through.'

Matthew retched and groaned.

'Listen, boykie,' Mace whispered in his ear. 'Listen good. Get off our case, okay?' No response. Mace jerked him upright. 'Okay?'

He coughed, moaning at the nerves it twitched.

'You don't like what we're doing, tough shit. Got it?' Mace shook him.

'Al-alright.' Matthew pushed him away. 'Alright f-for God's sake' – staggering off into the crowd.

'Runty little bastard,' said Pylon.

'I was him, I'd get out of Ducky Donald's territory.' The pain in Mace's arm subsided.

'Something bothering you?' said Pylon.

'Nothing,' Mace told him. 'Knocked my elbow.'

They stood taking in the scene: the floor was pumping: bodies in ecstasy. Some sort of smoke rising up around the dancers' legs, the strobes jagging an effect of disjointed slow motion, like they were looking at puppets being jerked by unseen strings. Two hundred jivers when there should have been half that, dribs and drabs still arriving. One exit a single door wide. You let off a stink bomb people would get killed in the rush for fresh air.

Pylon spoke Mace's thoughts. Shouted over the beat. 'He ever intend putting a cap on the intake?'

'Seems not.' Mace indicated the back rooms. 'Better take a look there.'

In the chill room a guy chased a coke line along the armrest of a chair. Two others on a couch watched pictures in their heads. Pylon checked the windows were screwed fast the way they should be. The coke man shook his head wildly, gave a roar.

Pylon said, 'Keep the faith, brother.'

The coker roared again.

Matthew's stockroom was tight, the security grille locked, bolts latched on the door. Skylights in the male toilets likewise good. The door to the female loo was shut. Mace knocked. A voice said, 'Give us a break.' Could have been male or female. The two men waited.

Mace said, 'Take a bet?'

'Ten bucks, a dyke.'

Couple of minutes later the door opened.

'Evening ladies,' Pylon said.

'Up yours, ballbag,' said the hen who'd wanted a break, shepherding her chick away from them. The chick looked stunned, smiling stupidly.

Pylon grinned at Mace. 'Ten bucks a dyke, that's twenty.' He stepped into the loo. One person in there with the toilet and a basin left only squeeze space. Mace heard him groan. 'Window's open.'

Meant someone needed a screwdriver to open it. Meant someone had removed two screws. Meant someone was after more than fresh air. Meant someone had got in a screwdriver.

Mace said it.

'Didn't come in tonight,' Pylon replied, stepping into the passage. 'Someone had to know about how the window was fastened. My theory, the entry'd been cased already, the screwdriver came in with the kittens, they could've left it anyplace. Even in the cisterns.'

'I checked the cisterns.'

Pylon frowned. 'Problem we've got now is how we call this. You tell the people please leave the building calmly, they'll stampede.'

'Two things,' Mace said, the pain coming back to his arm unbidden. 'Ask the bouncers if anyone's left yet.' While he'd been at the door the flow was one way: in. The time was eleven fifteen. What clubber headed home before the wee hours? 'I'll have a word outside.'

'And our clients?' Pylon loaded the description with some rancour.

'Best to keep the temperature down. Mightn't even be a bomb we're talking about.'

'Then again…'

Mace pressed Dr Roberto's number into his cellphone. 'Times like this I could handle a smoke.'

'You and me both.'

'So why'd we quit then?'

'For our health.' Pylon moved towards the dancers. 'This thing blows in the next ten minutes we don't have to worry about our health.'

Mace could hear Dr Roberto on the phone, except not loud enough to hear him. 'At the entrance,' he yelled into the phone. 'Now.'

He went out through the stockroom. Locked the door behind him but not the grille. If a bomb exploded, getting back in needed to be as easy as possible. The service lane stank of drains. To the left the distant end ran into darkness, to the right people, noise, cars. Mostly the lane was empty, except for some garbage bins, a vagrant bedded down behind them. With a nudge from the toe of his boot Mace woke him, the guy reluctant to move on.

'Jou ma se poes,' he spat, swaying off down the lane towards the darkness, blanket over his head and shoulders, monk-like.

Your mother too, Mace thought, half a building came down on you, you'd be well pleased.

Where the lane entered Assurance Street, he hung back to get the scene: the Toyota hadn't moved, both guys inside now. Ditto, the street hadn't quietened. Cars still lined the kerbs bonnet to boot, kids still danced wherever, drank coolers from the bottle, smoked weed. The speakers broadcast the djs' music, the screen showed the dancers in the club. Dr Roberto waited at the entrance.

'Let's go down a bit,' Mace said, motioning towards the motor-mac's shop. Sheemina February's goon would've spotted him in the street, he didn't need to know about the watchman. Out of their line of sight Mace said, 'Anyone leave there yet, doc?'

'Only two girls,' he said.

'White, coloured, black?'

'We would call them mulatto.'

'Some time ago?'

'Maybe it is twenty, maybe it is thirty minutes.'

'Which? Twenty or thirty?'

Dr Roberto looked at the time on his cellphone. 'Twenty, I would say most accurately.'

Mace's cellphone rang. Pylon.

'Two twenty-somethings, female,' he said. 'Recognised being here a couple of nights back. Sentries stamped them both so they could get back in. A giggly pair. Stoked on E for sure, so say the knowledgeable.'

'Confirmed,' Mace told him.

'Another thing,' Pylon said, 'Ducky Donald's done a duck.'

'Not as far as I know.'

'Not as far as Mattie knows or the sentries know either. Disappeared nonetheless.'

Mace told him to hang on, to Dr Roberto said, 'You notice a guy dressed in white with a black girlfriend leaving?'

He shook his head.

To Pylon, Mace said, 'Didn't leave through the front.'

'Which means what?'

'Probably shagging under a table.'

Pylon snorted, 'We have to call on this?'

'Your sense?'

'My plan'd be no announcement, bouncers hustle them from the front, I do the back we can get rid of half before the stampede comes. When it comes maybe it's containable. Reckon fifteen minutes the situation's averted.'

'Get Matthew out first,' Mace said, 'into the back alley.'

They disconnected. To Dr Roberto he said, 'Chances are there's a bomb in there.' He got thoughtful. 'We're planning to empty the place. Watch the guys in the Toyota. The moment they leave, tell me.'

Raised voices at the entrance to the club, people stumbling into the street, hurled out. Angry, confused, milling. Someone yelled, 'Bomb!' Someone started screaming. The djs kept up a different caterwaul. The screen showed the dancers but not what was unravelling at the edges.

Mace's thoughts were on the trigger device: timer or cellphone? To date, from what he'd read in the papers, they'd been timers. Didn't mean this would be the same. If this was a situation.

In the business of protection, Mace knew sometimes you had to show not only the gun but the intention to shoot.

Before he could move off he said to Dr Roberto, 'Forget the Toyota, I'll sort it.'

The thing with muscle boys, they did not lock their car doors. Their physical size gave them immunity, or so they thought.

Mace looped unnoticed wide of the crowd, came up behind the twosome cosy in the front seats watching the commotion. The screen now showing the efforts of Pylon and the bouncers clearing the decks. The back door popped open at his grip, he slid in jamming the nine mil against the white guy's shaven head.

'Boys,' he said, 'don't even consider that I won't. Hands on the wheel, driver. Howzit, Mikey.'

They didn't look round. The coloured guy had the driver's seat, clutched the steering wheel with meaty paws, a row of gold rings visible.

'Good fellas.' Mace shifted more comfortably onto the seat. 'Who's your friend, Mikey?'

'Get stuffed,' said Mikey.

Mace tutted. Racked the slide on the automatic.

'Val,' said the coloured guy. 'I'm Val.'

'Now, Mikey and Val, here's the question: do we have a bomb inside there?'

Mikey said, 'Wouldn't you like to know?'

Val said, 'What difference it's gonna make?'

Mace came back, 'Yes I would, and good question.' For the hell of it, whacked Mikey's head, the gun sight drawing blood. Mikey howled, tried to grab backwards. Mace caught his arm, yanked down. He yodelled. Pain shot through Mace's wound. Val was poised to make a break. 'Don't,' Mace shouted, smacked the bald head again. It bled so easily. Calm returned.

'Once more: is there a bomb?'

'Fuck you,' they said in unison.

Mace brought the gun down. Asked generally, 'Either of you ever been shot before?'

In response got, 'Go fuck yourself.'

'Piss off.'

He shot Mikey through the seat through the shoulder. The exit sprayed a red mist on the windscreen, the bullet bored into the dash. Mikey screamed. Val kept his hands fastened where Mace could see them. Outside no one heard above the howling dervish.

'You wanna know,' said Val, 'I'll tell you. There's a bomb.'

'Timer or cellphone?'

'Timer.'

'For when?'

He turned his head to give Mace his profile, to show his smirk. 'Any time now,' he said.

13

The building blew before Mace had run ten paces, before he'd got Pylon on the phone.

In the first milliseconds a shock wave popped a blackened, laminated plate glass window, taking down people standing beside it on the pavement. Similarly flattened those arguing with the bouncers at the entrance.

Then came the sound, the blast, something that put Mace's pulse rate up every time, no matter how many times he'd heard it. Followed by the fall of debris, followed by a moment's silence, followed by screaming. Followed by small fires where combustible material had caught alight. Followed by the acrid smell of the explosive chemical and the whiff of burning.

In the immediate panic Mace connected with Pylon; he saw Dr Roberto rush into the building; he heard the Toyota screech away; a woman walked towards him with her face melted, her hair on fire. Later he would remember carrying people out of the dust and smoke. He would remember leaving someone to die to help someone who wouldn't. He would remember hearing the distant sirens getting closer. There was blood, there was bone, there were body parts, raw flesh. Some faces were rigid with shock, some cried, some would not stop screaming.

Eventually there was a second explosion.

14

Afterwards, hours afterwards, in Assurance Street, Mace stood with Pylon, Matthew and Ducky Donald who'd reappeared. He and Pylon were wrecked, fire-blackened, cut, bruised, blood-splattered. Neither Hartnell had extended himself.

Firemen trained a hose on the smoking building. The ambulances were gone, the paramedics putting the last bandages on the lucky. Those who needed to thank Dr Roberto wouldn't think to look for him as a car-guard.

Either end of the street, cop cars still closed off entry, emergency lights flashing. The road was cleared of vehicles, except two near the club's entrance smashed with rubble. Club Catastrophe had no roof, was gutted. Crime tape cordoned off the scene.

The first blast left four dead: a man, three women. Five criticals. Forty, fifty needed treatment. The second brought the first floor down, set the place on fire. Just so happened the paras had got everyone out by then. Mace suspected probably a cellphone trigger on the second but he kept that quiet. Suspected, too, someone in the vicinity chose the moment.

Ducky Donald said, 'I was wrong then.'

'Seems like it,' Mace said. Noticing the prick was out of his whites into a grubby tracksuit, his dolly-bird nowhere to be seen. 'Where were you?'

'Gone home,' Ducky said. 'This is Mattie's thing. Doesn't want the old fart around.'

'You didn't say goodbye,' said Pylon.

Ducky Donald lit a cigarette from the butt of the one he was finishing. 'Didn't know you cared.'

'Should have listened to us,' Mace said. 'There wouldn't be kids dead now.'

'Protection's what I wanted,' said Ducky, 'not advice. I want advice I've got a lawyer.'

Mace and Pylon let that drift. At what had been the club entrance, Captain Gonsalves appeared with the fire chief, both in oil skins, the captain clutching a black bin-liner.

Pylon said, 'Insurers won't be happy.'

'That's their problem,' said Ducky. 'We'll start the remake soon as the cops are finished their business.'

'Taking out the blown-off bits, you mean.'

Matthew jerked round at Mace, said, 'Christ!' without a stutter; Ducky Donald let out a ring of smoke. 'Not nice, Mace. Uncalled for. Even for a mean shit like you.'

It brought Mace into his face. 'Four dead. Some others maybe soon to be. Some legless. Armless. Kids we're talking. Twenty-somethings. People who're going to wake screaming in the night reliving it. Afraid to walk in the street. Scared to drink coffee at a pavement café. Maybe lose their jobs, spend their days in pain. Because you and Mattie boy have a point to make with PAGAD. You think they care? They don't care. In their heads you're the ones flicked on the timer.'

Pylon pulled his partner away, Ducky Donald shouting, 'What about your body count, you righteous saint? Not just here. All over the bloody continent. How about a figure on that? Thousands? Tens of thousands? Hundreds of more like it. You shitheap.'

Gonsalves came up. 'Mr Bishop,' he said, 'I owe an apology.' He handed the black bag to the fire chief, spat a gob of yellow muck on the pavement. 'How about a cigarette?' he said to Matthew. Matthew knocked the bottom of his pack, extended it. 'Obliged.' Gonsalves selected one delicately, started stripping off the paper, balling the tobacco in the palm of his hand.

A squat man made squatter by the oilskins, grey moustache that needed trimming, wild, random eyebrows.

'I've given up,' he said, flicking the cigarette paper into the gutter. 'Used to smoke fifty a day. Now I just chew them.' He glanced from Matthew to Ducky Donald. 'Would these be the owners?'

Mace nodded.

'Nasty situation here,' he said, 'two bombs like that. New scene for PAGAD.' He popped a pellet of tobacco into his mouth, gave it a quick hard chew. 'Splendid.' Then greeted the Hartnells. 'Seems they don't like you much, PAGAD. Makes it easy for your claims though.'

'Sure,' said Ducky Donald.

'Structural damage's severe.'

'We're covered, captain,' said Ducky Donald.

'Didn't think you wouldn't be. Everyone is these days.'

'Sign of the times.'

Gonsalves chewed on that. 'Truly. Not among my favourite people, insurers, though.' He took a step closer to Ducky Donald. 'What I've been looking forward to is retiring. Now they tell me on my pension payout, I'm not gonna doze in a sunny spot, walk the dog, settle the evening in with a single malt. Not even a blend. They tell me prepare for nightwatch work. I've got maybe nine years left before I'm sitting in the marble foyers. Not a cheerful prospect, hearing the lifts go up and down all night.'

Ducky Donald took a step back from the captain's bad breath.

'Nother thing.' Gonsalves leant forward. 'Two months ago this broker comes to see me. He says he's got a product for a person in my situation. A product, hey. Not a policy anymore. A product. Like hair shampoo. Long story short, he wants a medical. I do a medical. The assessors say I smoke too much. I'm AA so there's been no alcohol over my lips in twenty-one years. Which they like a lot. Keep it up, captain, they say. But the smoking's too much. If you want this product, you've got to stop smoking. I stop smoking. Wonderful, captain, keep it up, captain, they say. My broker says, here's your product. What he means is here's the bill. Monthly instalments at a cost of half my take-home pay. You're joking, I say to him. How'm I supposed to manage this. I've got to eat. My wife's got to eat. I can't afford this. It's because of your age, he says, that's why it's so high. I say to him there has to be another way. Another kind of product. He says to me there's no other kind. He says my only chance of staying out of the marble foyers is to pay the instalments. So I start paying the instalments. But it's hard Mr Hartnell. I've got no thoughts that are not thoughts about that premium. You with me here?'

Ducky Donald gave no sign he was but lit up a smoke right in the captain's face.

Captain Gonsalves said, 'Let me show you something' – got the bag from the fire chief. 'Take a look what we got here.' He held it open. Matthew stirred to take a peek too.

'Ah shit.' Ducky Donald staggered back. 'Ah Jesus Christ.'

Matthew said, 'Ca-ca-ca...'

'Probably a young lady,' said Gonsalves. 'A forearm that slender. Also the watch's a clue. Man's gonna have something much chunkier. Still gotta locate her hand I reckon.' He closed the bin-liner, handed it back to the fire chief. 'Probably she didn't have life cover. Who does that young?'

Captain Gonsalves nodded at each one of them, said to Matthew, 'How about tomorrow' – checked his watch – 'how about later this morning, say, ten, you rock up 'n tell me about PAGAD?'

'We'll be there,' said Ducky Donald.

Gonsalves shifted the tobacco ball about his mouth. 'Which've you runs the club?'

Ducky Donald pointed at Matthew. 'He does.'

'Then you get to talk to the insurers, Mr Hartnell. Or sleep late. It's your life. Man I wanna see is the young gent here.'

The captain walked away; Ducky Donald kept his trap shut until the cop was well off.

'What's his case? What the hell was all that about?'

'Smoke screens,' said Pylon.

'Ca-ca-ca-Christ!' said Matthew.

15

'What was his case?' Pylon said. 'The good Captain Gonsalves?'

'Not a clue.'

Mace put two coffees on the glass-topped table, clearing space among the stacks of safari brochures and large-format photographic books of wild Africa. His pistol was also there with a box of cleaning equipment. Pylon lay stretched out on one of two leather couches: kudu skin, his fingers tracing the tears and scars of the animal's life in the thornveld.

Mace said, 'Just like the old days.'

Pylon looked over. 'I don't get off on the blood and guts anymore.'

'You think I do?'

'Don't you?'

Mace thought about it. 'Doesn't bother me.'

'That's my point. Not only the shit going down, but the rev. It scares me. And I think back to the violence we stoked, and I think that was our life and it didn't freak us.'

'So?'

'So maybe we should be seeing shrinks.'

'Nah. What for? We saw worse than tonight, it wasn't a problem.'

'No.' Pylon swung his legs onto the floor. 'Look at you Mace. Look at us. We don't feel stuff. We got something missing from us.'

'You think so?'

'I do. I look at you and I think so. I get scared sometimes you're so cool. Scared for both of us.'

Mace sat down opposite Pylon on the other couch, started taking the gun apart.

'Maybe you're right. Except you look at what's out there and how're we supposed to do it otherwise? Protect people. You get a type like Ducky Donald sets his own bombs.'

'Bullshit.'

'Think about it. The second bomb was a Ducky Donald special.'

Mace sipped his coffee, reckoned French roast never tasted so good.

Pylon leant back incredulous. 'You're telling me Ducky Donald triggered number two from a cellphone.' He stared at the dark liquid in his cup. 'The forensics will pick it up.'

'Assuming the forensics get that far. So many bombs going off those guys haven't got the capacity.'

Pylon swallowed a scalding mouthful, wiped a hand across his mouth. 'Or Ducky's in with PAGAD.'

'There've been stranger partnerships.' Mace sniffed at the gun: the sweet smell of cordite in the barrel. There was a memory there from not so many years ago. Nothing troubling. He scratched for a lint rope in the box, drew it through the barrel.

Pylon watched every move he made. 'Very domestic, isn't this?'

'Had to use it earlier,' Mace said. 'Shot one of the sidekicks in the shoulder.'

Pylon got animated. 'That's what I was talking about. Earlier. You shoot a guy it's like no big deal.'

'It wasn't.'

'Exactly why you need a shrink.'

'No ways. What for?'

'Save me Jesus.' Pylon rolled his eyes, took more coffee.

Mace said, 'I'd bet on Ducky working alone. Must've made a look-a-like. Probably got all the specs over a few beers with one of his cop mates. Only bit of different technology was the cellphone. The forensics ever examine it, they'll scheme PAGAD's getting clever.'

Outside in Dunkley Square a car engine revved, tyres squealed. Two gear changes then the shriek of brakes. Again the tyre squeal before the night went quiet. Mace and Pylon glanced at one another, raised eyebrows.

Their office was on the square, in the Victorian terrace row given to small legal practices, architectural partnerships, graphic designers, and Complete Security's discreet operation. They liked the sense of professionals going about their business. Across the way, Maria's restaurant did good Greek meals; the coffee shops good coffee. Their clients liked it. They'd take them into the Company's Gardens for the noonday gun: watch the pigeons fly up at the boom. The clients were impressed. They'd gaze at the art gallery, the synagogue, the copper dome of the observatory, the mountain behind, and sigh. 'Oh Mr Bishop this has been life transforming. What a romantic city.' They'd had fat sucked from their thighs, wrinkles ironed from their faces, their boobs elevated, both males and females. They'd lounged at swimming pools watching lions at waterholes. For what Complete Security did, Dunkley Square was the best location in the city.

Pylon stood up. 'The guy you shot would need a hospital?'

'Sure. Someone to plug the hole.'

'Who's legally required to report all gunshot wounds.'

'In a perfect world.' Mace reassembled the parts. 'Most likely if a report's filled in at all it'll be attempted hijacking. Happens all the time.'

He jacked the clip into the butt, put the gun on the table. He'd shot three people with that gun. One was fatal. It had to be.

Pylon finished his coffee, went through to fix another one. From the kitchen he called out, 'Want to tell me about Isabella?'

'Nothing to tell,' Mace said. 'I haven't seen her.'

Not since Paris 1991. The Hotel Meurice. Where the Nazis had put up for their stay in the city. Mace running a double agenda, part of it a payback few days for Isabella, wining and dining her in the gilded restaurant. The two of them rampant in the bedroom suite. Isabella saying, luxury hotels were built for sex. Testing the theory sprawled on her stomach on the sheets in the late afternoon when room service wheeled in a trolley with ice bucket, Moët, and two crystal flutes. The waiter not blinking at the sight of Isabella naked. Going about his job of opening the champagne with a flourish, pouring half-glasses that rose in bubbly heads.

'À votre santé, madame, monsieur.'

'See what I mean?' said Isabella, as the door clicked closed. 'French style. Unfazed.'

'To good times,' said Mace, the crystal ringing at their toast. An amazing few days, even if they were the last time he'd been with her.

'I haven't seen her,' Mace said again to Pylon.

Pylon looked dubious. 'So tell me anyhow.'

Mace swallowed coffee, said, 'I have prostate cancer.'

Pylon said nothing, cooked up the pot, brought it through to offer him more.

'Why didn't you say?'

'It's not a death sentence.' Mace held out his mug; Pylon filled it. 'Just didn't expect it at forty-two.'

'You're having treatment?'

'Of course.'

'And the prognosis is?'

'It was discovered early. There're no complications, no need for operations, I'll be a survivor by Christmas.'

'Bru,' he said. 'Bru, bru, bru.'

'It's okay,' Mace said, 'my head's getting round it. Funny thing is Ducky Donald's been a great help. Gave me something else to think about.'

'And the knocked elbow that bleeds more like a knife cut?'

'A mugging. Street kids in the Point car park.'

A beat, then Pylon laughed. His infectious, deep belly laugh. Mace had to join him.

Oumou was awake when Mace got home. Sitting up in bed, pensive, expectant. Four-thirty, according to the radio clock on the pedestal. He'd phoned her about the bombs, the bloody mess and the death toll. Her eyes said everything he needed.

Mace bent over to kiss her. Their lips met and hers stuck hard. He gave back the pressure, felt her tongue slipping between his teeth as her arm came around to pull him to her and he went despite the pain shooting in the stab wound. But Oumou caught his flinch, broke the kiss.

'You are hurting?'

'A scrape.' His lips found hers again. Again she pulled back.

'Let me see.'

'It's nothing,' he said, sliding against her.

'That is not nothing,' she said. 'Oh Mace.'

The concern in her voice was balm. 'Say it again,' he said, burrowing in her long beautiful neck.

'No. Stop.' And she was out of bed, bending over to examine his arm, her breasts ripe fruit. 'You need a doctor.'

He pulled her naked body down, sliding beneath her.

'Non. Non.' She swore in French. 'Let me go.' Again she was up, and heading for the bathroom. 'First we must clean that wound.'

'Tomorrow,' he said, undressing, intent on what they'd started. His arm throbbed just to undo the belt buckle. When Oumou came back, he was naked, she was swaddled in a white towel. Stunning against her ebony skin.

Gently she unwrapped the bandage, blood had leaked through and dried, the wound was weeping, the gauze embedded in the rawness.

'Merde,' she whispered. 'What is this?'

He told her. While she cleaned his arm with antiseptic solution and rebound it with bandages they'd last used in the desert, he told her how streetkids had taken him blind.

'Me!' he said. 'Of all people.'

'Oui. Now tell me about the other thing. The thing that is troubling you.'

Mace looked at her. 'What d'you mean?'

'Is it Isabella?'

He shook his head, no, and explained about his prostate tumour.

'You should have told me straight away,' she said, hurt welling in her eyes.

'I couldn't.' He caught at her hand, pulled her down beside him on the bed. 'This shouldn't have happened to me.'

16

1999

A late Easter, with the days cool, shortening, Mace stood in their bedroom gazing down at the city, the bay beyond. He put the cellphone back on its unit to charge.

Below, Christa in the garden with Cat2, putting flowers from the well-trimmed hedge on the grave of Cat3 that'd lived until they moved into the renovated house, then died suddenly when stones formed in the urinary tract. Happened sometimes in males, the vet said. So he'd heard, Mace told him.

His own water works were clear. Blood tests negative. The doctor's finger test caused him to grunt, 'That's okay, meneer, just keep coming in for checkups.'

Off the gurney Mace hitched up his jeans. 'Great job you've got.'

The doctor stripped off plastic gloves, washed his hands at a basin. 'Just another day at the orifice' – handed him an invoice to pay on the way out. Between the doc and the prostate pills Mace believed he could've financed a war of liberation in Sierra Leone.

Thing was he had his health and the Victorian gem in the City Bowl.

'My son,' Dave Cruikshank said when Mace signed the papers, 'I thought your missus had your balls in her grasp. Good on yer.'

After the renovation, he said, 'I told you didn't I. A dream you were buying, I told you. My son, you've done good. This is a marketable proposition.'

'Not for sale,' Mace said.

Mace gave the house a total make-over. Not just spruced up. Redone. Olde worlde meets stainless steel and glass. Featured, after they'd moved in, in Home and Garden. The cellar even getting a special picture and a comment from the university historian that he believed it went back to the seventeenth century.

When Mace told Oumou he'd signed and sealed she said, 'This is because of your cancer, I understand. But I am telling you I will not live there.'

When he persuaded her to at least look at the renovations, she went grudgingly at first. Inspected the changes without a word, then said, 'You think you are a smart man, no?'

He smirked.

'I shall give up,' she said. 'This will be a beautiful house. We can stay here.'

Mace showed Christa her en-suite bedroom. 'Ah cool,' she said. 'Papa can I have my own TV?'

Instead he promised her the world.

They moved in a month into the new year. Handed the keys and lease to their suburban townhouse to Pylon and Treasure.

'I don't want this,' said Pylon. 'This's smaller than we've got. This is crappy. We're giving up four en-suite bedrooms, hi-tech kitchen, entrance hall, marble tiles, for what? For a better address?'

'So what?' said Treasure, stamping township dust from her shoes. 'No shit in the streets. No dead dogs in the gutters. No all-night shebeens. No slaughtering cows in the backyard. Security. No worries my daughter's going to be kidnapped. No more township. This's fine by me.'

Her daughter Pumla's rave: 'Can I have my own TV?'

Mace's wasn't the only renovating going on in those months: Ducky Donald and Mattie-boy got their insurance payout and fixed up Club Catastrophe due to rise from the ashes, according to the invite Mace got, in ten day's time. One thing he was pleased about, Ducky Donald had no more favours to call in.

He called nonetheless. Sheemina February had set up another meeting with Matthew, could Mace be present?

Mace said, 'I see on the news some of her clients are in jail. What's to meet about?'

'Same thing again.'

'So go to the newspapers. Stir the pot. People are on your side.'

'Not so easy, china. What'm I gonna tell them? We got a PAGAD lawyer threatening us?'

'Sounds good.'

'I'd rather hear her out first.'

Mace said nothing, let the silence go until Ducky said, 'Please, okay?'

'We're square,' Mace said. 'Far as I'm concerned. No more obligations to you. And you forget about Cayman and Techipa.'

'Sure. Agreed. Forgotten already.' Ducky cleared his throat. 'This's more something involving you.'

'Not interested.'

Mace could hear him swig at a drink, Ducky loving this. 'Thing is there's something else here that I don't understand. The bitch said she wants my Mattie and his advisor. Mattie tells her he hasn't got an advisor. She says Mace Bishop. He says history. She says, you, meaning you, owe her.'

'Interesting perspective.'

'Not one I comprehend, Mace.' Ducky took another gulp. 'Further, she says Mattie doesn't have you with him, Mattie's gonna be the only paraplegic club owner in the city. I tell Mattie we've got no holds on you. Debt paid up in full. The only thing I can do is put it to you, see what you say.'

Mace had encountered Sheemina February a good couple of times since PAGAD bombed Mattie's club. Each occasion had to keep himself from getting in her face about the bombings. The victims. Once had been in the foyer of the Cape Grace, another time at an evening concert in the winelands. Then again about a month back on the forecourt of the petrol station on Orange where he usually filled up. Mace was busy signing the chit, she stopped at a pump alongside. Electric blue BMW coupé open to the early autumn. This was a small city, people moved in small circles. Bumping into people you knew was nothing out of the ordinary. Point was, if she'd wanted to have her say about the hole in her goon's shoulder she could have phoned him at any time. But no, she kept her cards. Until now.

The voice in his ear said, 'So what d'you say?'

'Don't know, I can't see the leverage here.'

'Except my boy's health.'

'There's that.'

'And my memory.'

'I wouldn't go there.'

'Joke, boykie. Take half an hour of your time. Give a bit of interest to your day.'

Mace looked down at Christa in the garden, her attention now on her toys. He should have said no. He'd said, 'Alright, for this you owe me.' Thinking, maybe he'd unload some opinions of his own.

Pylon asked Mace in the weeks after the bomb, was he going to have a word with Gonsalves about his theory regarding the Hartnells? Mace had more pressing matters on his mind: getting his prostate back to size for one, rebuilding a house for another. Also he still worried Ducky would pull the Cayman and Techipa plug.

Gonsalves was in touch though to let him know Ducky Donald Hartnell had powerful friends. He mentioned the name Mo Siq early in the conversation. Asked Mace if he knew such a man. Mace said he did.

Captain Gonsalves said, 'One night the phone rings, my wife answers, says to me a Mr Siq says he wants to have a word. I leave my warm chair next to the gas heater, go out into the passage where there's no heating and it's colder than a witch's tit. My wife says we should get a cordless phone but they cost five hundred bucks, Mr Bishop. I tell her while there are pension instalments there are no cordless phones. Except while I'm out in the freezing passage listening to Mr Siq I did consider it.

'What Mr Siq had to say,' he said, 'was that anything I could do to expedite – which is the word he used – to expedite the report on the Club Catastrophe bombing would be appreciated, seeing as how it was a simple PAGAD bombing situation. Here I hesitated. Simple bombings. I dunno about simple bombings. I gave a long aaah. He then told me Mr Hartnell had made a considerable investment in the rebuilding of the club but was feeling exposed – which is also the word he used – because the insurers were waiting for the police report before they paid out. Mr Siq said he wasn't going to offer me an inducement – again his word – because that was bribery by another name, but that he had entered my details in his little book as an aide-memoire. Either way.'

'Either way what?' Mace said.

Gonsalves chewed into the mouthpiece of his phone for a moment. 'I believe you know what that means, Mr Bishop,' he said.

Mace told him, 'Uh huh.'

'The next day,' the captain continued, 'I found out that Mr Siq is known by the first name Mo and that he buys big grey ships and fast grey jets on behalf of my employer. My ultimate employer that is. What they call in the vernacular my *makulu baas*. Otherwise known as *el presidente*. I learnt that I should not mess with Mr Mo Siq.'

'You should not,' Mace said, knowing that Mo was not the guy he once was, who drank palm wine on a Lagos beach till sunrise. Mr Mo Siq now dressed in Armani suits, Rolex watches and Bally boots. Mace had no problem with the Bally boots.

'What I'm saying,' said Captain Gonsalves, 'is that I appreciate the tip-off, even if we didn't act on it as we should have. I have Matthew Hartnell's account of his – your – meetings with a person called Sheemina February, who is known to us as a PAGAD lawyer, and Abdul Abdul who we had the pleasure of hosting until he got bail. Ms February represents Abdul Abdul but that is her only association with known suspects. On the other hand she is a lawyer. In my experience they are at home in what my wife would call sleaze.'

He coughed loudly. When the spasm petered out, told Mace he would be grateful for any further information.

Below in the garden Christa arranged in a circle Cupcake, her teddy bear, the Incredible Hulk, Belinda, a Barbie doll, and Spiderwoman. She placed a cup and saucer before each and poured a brown fluid from one of Oumou's reject pots. She stood back to admire her tea party. Mace came to a decision.

In the room directly below their bedroom Oumou had her studio, she was there now, throwing clay, at the wheel fashioning tall elegant vessels. He went down and kissed her on her neck below the silver and amber earrings she was never without. These earrings were the envy of Christa who never let up to Mace on how she couldn't wait to have her ears pierced.

'I'll be an hour,' he said. 'An unexpected meeting.'

Oumou gave him lazy hooded eyes. 'This is your holiday, no?'

'Supposed to be.'

'Do not be long,' she said.

Outside Christa wanted to know, 'Papa, can I come?'

Mace swung her round on a three-sixty carousel ride until he got giddy. 'Next time, C. This is business.'

'Please, please please please,' she said, slightly giddy herself. At his shaking head changed tack, 'Can Cupcake go with you instead?'

Cupcake went with Mace on away business trips to fetch important clients. He'd been to Madrid, Milan, Munich, Hamburg, Copenhagen, London, New York, Los Angeles, Miami, Lusaka, Chobe, Victoria Falls. Also a number of cities and safari ranches within the country. Never before had Mace had to strap him into the passenger seat of the Spider and drive him about town with the top down.

When he pulled into the Harrington Street parking lot, a surly black guy handed him a slip of paper. On it was a name he couldn't make out.

'Where's the Angolan?' Mace asked. 'Cuito?'

The car-guard shrugged, gave him a hard stare.

Mace looked about, only locals. He reckoned if Cuito wasn't dead, he was probably close to it. Wondered about Dr Roberto. Locals had a hatred of foreigners, especially those with enterprise.

He pointed at his passenger. 'The bear's called Cupcake,' he said. 'He goes home with me. So does everything else in here.'

The Xhosa didn't even register he was talking to him.

17

Matthew was waiting in his hole of an office, smoking, playing a game on his cellphone. He'd smartened up his image: leather jacket, black T-shirt, regular jeans, hi-tech footwear without socks. His hair gelled into spikes. The office was unchanged, occupied but not occupied, as the corridor had been unchanged, every room locked with a security door, occupied but not occupied.

The room reeked of cigarettes: ash and two crushed butts in the saucer on the desk. Mace opened the window. It made no difference.

Matthew kept his eyes on his game. 'Th-the ma-macho with his gun?' he said.

Mace had a short-barrelled Smith & Wesson .38 in the pocket of his chinos, a loose shirt and denim jacket meant to hide the outline. He sat down where he'd sat down before. 'Don't annoy me Mattie-boy. It's not a good idea.'

Matthew flicked a head of ash into the saucer. 'D-don't call me Ma-Mattie-boy.'

Mace considered this. 'How about you try growing up first.'

Matthew put down the cellphone, still didn't look at Mace. 'Wha-what's with you ol-old guys? It's l-like you all sucked p-piss from your ma's tits. Li-lighten up, ar-sehole.' He made to pick up the cellphone again, Mace leant forward to stop his hand.

'One thing you have to watch, Mat-thew,' he said, tightening his grip, 'is your language.' He squeezed the pressure point behind Matthew's thumb until he yowled. 'You're playing in the big world, Mat-thew. You've got bodies to your name. You need help. At the moment I am that help although I do not want to be. I want to walk out of here and leave you to Sheemina February. Except that again your daddy prevailed upon me. And now you owe me, understand?'

This time they had not heard Sheemina February coming up the stairs, walking along the corridor. This time she came alone and she came on soft-soled shoes. She was standing in the doorway.

'I am not interested in boys, Mr Advisor,' she said. 'I prefer men.' She came in, sat down across the desk from Matthew but angled towards Mace. Crossed her legs with the faint rasp of pantihose. No briefcase. A shawl about her shoulders. Throughout, Mace was the object of her gaze. Not once did her eyes acknowledge Matthew. She tapped the fingers of her gloved hand on the desk, then said to the club owner, 'Do you mind not smoking.'

Matthew crushed out what was left of his cigarette.

She smiled at him. 'Thank you.'

Her Nordic eyes came back to Mace, and he held them. The smile remained, a hint of white teeth behind her gloss plum lipstick.

'Mr Advisor I'm pleased you could make it. I'm pleased Matthew's father prevailed upon you, even if you don't want to be here. Even if you don't ever want to see me again.'

Mace snorted a laugh. 'I wish. Except our paths seem to cross from time to time.'

'It's a small town.' She ironed creases from her skirt with the palm of her right hand. 'That is why we live here, isn't it? Our sense of being Capeys?'

'What do you want, exactly, Miss February?'

She held up her gloved left hand. 'I could be wearing a wedding ring, but I'm not. A good guess, Mr Advisor. Once, though, I was married. You even know my ex-husband.'

'Really?'

'Make some enquiries. You'll no doubt be amused. You'll hear that I tried to kill him. You probably won't hear that he tried to kill me too.'

'I'm fascinated.'

'You will be.'

Matthew toyed with his cigarette packet, itching to light up, flicking his Bic. In a voice that came out a note too high, said, 'Li-like he asked, wha-what's it you w-ant?'

'Don't do that.' Sheemina February pointed a red-nailed finger at his lighter. 'Like your Mr Advisor advised, Matthew, this is the big world, you have to control your nerves. Now.' She again tapped lightly on the desk. 'You are about to open your new club. Our conditions are the same as before. If you are not a drug dealer, Matthew, you will accept them.'

'Or-or you're go-onna blow us up again?'

'I'm not going to answer that, Matthew.' She turned to Mace. 'Mr Advisor you will have to explain to him the laws of resistance.' She clasped her hands in her lap. 'That's what this meeting was really all about. The laws of physics.'

Mace said, 'You heard him, he's not going with PAGAD, what next?'

'Stalemate. Back to the laws of physics. What happens when an unstoppable force hits an immovable object?' She glanced at Matthew. 'School science isn't that far back in your life.'

Matthew had no answers.

Sheemina February sighed. 'Pressure builds up.'

They sat staring at one another: she at Mace, Mace at her, Matthew concentrating on his packet of smokes. Nothing Mace could read in her blue eyes about where this was going. What did change on her face was it relaxed, small lines at the corners of her eyes faded. He waited. Breaking such an impasse was unwise.

Matthew didn't know that. 'Wha-what's with you?' he said. 'Wha-what's it you g-guys have got in for me?'

Sheemina February didn't even look at him. Smiled at Mace. 'You're a drug dealer, Matthew. This's common knowledge.'

'It's bull-bullshit,' said Matthew. 'What a-bout other clubs?'

She turned her head towards him. 'We're working on it. From the top of the alphabet.'

Matthew did his 'Ca-ca-ca-Christ!' number. 'Yo-you're fucking thre-threatening me.'

'Advising, Matthew. Advising.'

Mace stood. 'Then we've got the picture.'

'I hope so,' said Sheemina February. Matthew took Mace's lead, got to his feet. 'Mr Bishop,' she said, staying sitting, 'don't you want to know about my client's colleague? The one you shot.'

'Nope.' He moved to hold the door open. 'Like you're not concerned about the kids you killed. The ones left with bits missing.'

Sheemina February ignored him. 'Whether or not,' she said. 'He's recovered well. Back doing his daily workout at the gym. Amazing how some people snap back. A good man, my client says. Nice guy, too, I'm told. It's surprising you haven't bumped into him.' She stood. 'At the Point, I believe is where he trains.'

'Miss February,' Mace said as she went through the door. 'What was this all about?'

'Setting the ground rules.' She winked at him, touched her hair, laid a hand briefly on his arm as she went out. 'Getting to know one another better. See you around, Mr Bishop.' In the corridor she stopped. 'Oh yes, Abdul sends his regards.'

That was supposed to mean what? Mace wondered. A wink. A touch. Like she was flirting. What for, for Chrissakes? Like she was on the prowl with her doubletalk.

Mace waited five minutes, watching Matthew get through a smoke and fire a second. 'Remember you owe me,' he said, as he headed out the door, Matthew calling after him, 'Wh-why's she got it in for me-me?'

He paused, looked back. 'Get real, Matthew. You're a bloody drug dealer no matter how you want to spin it. This she doesn't like. '

'It's n-not about me,' he said. 'It's a-about you.' He laughed. 'She's ho-hot for you. I can see.'

Mace shook his head, left Matthew sitting behind his empty desk with his empty filing cabinet and his plastic chairs. 'Pop something, Mattie-boy,' he called back to him, 'you'll feel better.'

Outside, the Xhosa stood at the Harrington Street entrance to the parking lot, laughing with two others wearing orange car-guard bibs. Mace gave him back his card as he walked past, knowing he'd follow him to the Spider expecting a tip. Cupcake sat strapped in the passenger seat, waiting.

Before he could open the car door his cellphone rang, no number listed on the screen. Normally he wouldn't answer those calls, this time he did. Sheemina February, which wasn't a surprise.

She said, 'I forgot to mention, Mr Bishop, that I'm pleased you're over the prostate problem.' She disconnected before he could say anything.

The car-guard stood up against the rear bumper of the Spider, watching him.

'Let me have some space a minute, hey!'

The man backed off three paces, no change to his expression, said, 'My name is Oupa K, chief.'

Mace acknowledged him, then phoned his doctor on his cell knowing he would take the call when he saw who was making it.

'I'm in a consultation,' he said. 'What's it?'

'How're you too?' Mace said.

He heard the doctor heave a sigh. 'Mace, get to it, please.'

'Quick one: have you been burgled recently? Your surgery?'

'No.'

'Any of your patients called Sheemina February?'

'No, again. These're strange questions, Mace.'

'Forget about them. Tell your patient my apologies.' He thumbed him off.

The Xhosa stepped nearer as Mace got into his car.

'You said your name was?'

'Oupa K,' he replied.

Mace dropped a two buck coin into the man's cupped hands. Buggered if he was giving him five rand.

18

Sheemina February opened the balcony doors to smell the ocean. And paused, breathing deeply, listening to the rasp of gulls and the smack of small waves against the rocks. How good was this place during the day? Yet she seldom saw it.

She turned into the apartment, draping her shawl over the arm of a couch on her way to the fridge for mineral water. Her cellphone rang but she let it go to voicemail.

She came back to settle on the couch that faced the horizon, kicked off her shoes, curling her legs beneath her as she sat. On the glass coffee table lay her briefcase. In it, more photographs of Mace Bishop and a recording of his voice.

She brought out the tape recorder and played through to the moment he said, 'Miss February, what was this all about?'

Remembering the frown, the intensity of his eyes challenging her. Then how her wink had made him tilt his head yet he'd not moved his arm when she briefly, lightly placed her hand on it, feeling the solidity through the denim jacket.

She took out more photographs. In all of them he was at the pool alone. Most often he wore only the Speedo. Stood wet: his muscles pumped from the exercise, his stomach six-packed.

In four sessions he'd not noticed her. Not paid attention to the figure in the gown, reading, her towel bundled beside her on the bench. Hadn't imagined she was there because of him.

Once she'd even swum with him. Watched from beneath the water the easy crawl of his arms, the steady movement of his legs hardly churning bubbles. She'd matched him stroke for stroke for half a length until the effort ached.

But that was over now. She had the photographs, his voice.

Sheemina February looked up at the horizon, long and blue. Uncurled from the couch and walked onto the balcony. On the rocks below she could make out broken glass.

19

Could only have been that Sheemina February ordered a rifling of his doctor's surgery, Mace decided. No great accomplishment. That sort of service could be ordered up from the Yellow Pages. Guy goes in, gets the necessary, slips out, nobody's the wiser. Question was: why? Why the mind games? Mace had no answers there. Nor did he and Sheemina February cross paths over the following week. At least not that he was aware of.

Meanwhile Pylon got some background on the woman. Turned out she'd been married to their buddy in the arms trade and now high-flyer, Mo Siq. This, half a dozen years back for half a dozen months.

'In the first flush of the new country,' was how Pylon put it. 'Old comrades tying the knot in celebration. Sweet sentimental touch.'

'Except it didn't last.'

'This's true. Then Mo likes dipping into new things.'

They stood beside the big Merc at the entrance to the arrivals hall, Cape Town International. On the tannoy the Airport Company said they were pleased to announce the arrival of the Atlanta flight. On it their new clients. He was going tunny fishing. She was having a boob job. They didn't want muscle but they wanted protection.

'No nasty incidents, Mr Bishop,' he said over the phone. 'We have a couple of days' holiday in your fair city, we want good memories. Going to do a little shopping, visit some tourist spots, maybe spend time on the beach, eat your best food, hit some late-night venues, some clubs. This the sort of service you offer?'

Mace told him it was. Also told him it was autumn, maybe he would want to skip the beach. He laughed.

Pylon zipped up his jacket. Anyone giving the two men half a glance would have said security. The black shoes, the black chinos, the white golf shirts, the short jackets, the shades. Which was the point. One way to put out the signal: no nasty incidents.

'Mo has nothing but bad words for her. Calls her a bitch. Bitch of the first water, to be precise.'

'How's Mo?'

'Important.'

'Friendly?'

'You know Mo. Hi Pylon, what's happening? You got three minutes, I'm waiting on the minister. I say we're having some trouble with a woman called Sheemina February. He says, she told you we were married that I tried to kill her? I said that's what we'd heard. He said, "I woke up one night that bitch was about to slit my throat. Huge kitchen knife. Afterwards, she laid an assault charge on me. She's disturbed. The sort of girl pulls wings off of flies. Some advice: you want to make the problem go away, shoot her."'

'Ever the sweet-hearted Mo.'

'Tell me about it.' Pylon beeped the automatic locking on the Merc. They headed into the knot of people waiting on the concourse. 'Another thing I found, her family's Christian. No one's ever been Muslim. No one's ever heard of Sheemina converting. She got married to Mo, they did it in a registry office.'

'So what's the attraction to PAGAD?'

'Search me. She likes pulling wings off of flies.'

So what's the attraction to me, Mace was going to add but didn't.

The first-class passengers were dribbling out. They spotted their clients: late thirties, she Max Mara, he Lacombe. Difficult to guess why she needed a boob job. Perfect looking at a glance, Mace thought.

'Also, Mo was seriously concerned for a couple of weeks she would do him. Was stalking him. He'd see her behind him. She'd pitch up where he was. Restaurants. Coffee bars. Sort of chance encounters, except too many to be chance. Weird stuff like that.'

Mace and Pylon moved into their clients' line of sight, saw the relief on their faces.

'This I got from one of the guys that watched his back. He said Mo was freaked she'd get into his house.'

'Not something you associate with Mo.'

'Not usually.'

The men greeted the clients, took their luggage. At the car the clients remarked that spring in New York was colder than fall in Cape Town. 'All I see is blue sky and sunshine,' he said. She said, 'Where's the Cape of Storms?'

Mace pointed at the peninsula chain. 'Other side those mountains, a butterfly's flapping its wings.'

They got the couple to the Mount Nelson, arranged a schedule for the next five days. That sorted, Pylon and Mace agreed to meet at the Club Catastrophe at ten for the grand reopening. Pylon took off to get some family hours, Mace headed to the Point swimming pool. As he pulled into the parking lot his cellphone cheeped: Ducky Donald. He'd taken a call from him every day since the meeting with Sheemina February.

'She's phoned,' Ducky said, 'the cow.'

Mace switched off the ignition, waited. On Signal Hill the grass flared tawny in the dying light.

'She says her clients wanna know if we're opening tonight. Her clients, for God's sake! Bombers. Killers. These are the lowlifes she calls clients.'

'Anything like a direct threat?' Mace heard ice clink, said, 'Cheers.'

'Come'n have a drink, Mace?'

'I'm about to go swimming, Ducky.' He got out of the car, lifted a tog bag from the boot.

'What's with this swimming? You didn't used to be into men's health. Anyone offered a drink you took it.'

'Still happens when I'm in the mood.'

Two women came out of the gym, glanced at Mace. He held the door, went in to sweat and doof doof musak.

'Christ,' Ducky Donald said in his ear, 'sounds like hell.'

Mace nodded at trainers and familiar faces, threading through to the change rooms. His swimming mates, Tyrone and Allan, were already costumed and waiting.

'I must go, Ducky. See you later.'

'Wait,' Ducky Donald shouted. 'Mace, Mace, I've got a lotta money invested here. Another bomb I don't need.'

'She make any threats?'

'She's a goddamned lawyer, for goddamned Chrissakes.'

'Call the cops. Talk to Gonsalves. You got high-up friends. Speak to Mo.'

Ducky Donald spluttered in his drink. 'Thank you, Mace. Thank you for that advice.'

Mace disconnected. Tyrone and Allan looked quizzical. 'Man with a problem he wants me to share.' Mace grimaced. 'What's in it for me I don't get.'

They hit the water, striking the rhythm and pace that took Mace's mind off the world and Ducky Donald. No reason to think here: just follow the black line across the tiles, roll into the turn, kick against the side, straighten for the return and as his left arm came up suck in air. At that moment he glimpsed Tyrone matching his actions stroke for stroke. On his right Allan would be similar. These guys knew nothing about his prostate problems, and if his performance dropped during the months he was popping pills, they made no comment. Now, though, he was fit, easy, even when Tyrone powered it on for the last stretch. They ended clutching the sides, heaving for breath.

'Killer,' gasped Allan. 'Have to cut back on the cakes.'

Mace could feel last night's chocolate mousse oozing from his shoulders.

They showered, changed, ordered energy drinks at the bar counter. On the TV was a replay of a Tri-Nations rugby match. One of those the Boks had thrown away. A depressing spectacle.

'Enough to send you home,' said Tyrone draining his glass.

The three men went out into a parking lot as dark as it was the night the street kids packed Mace. There'd been no incidents since, plunging any moves to get lighting to the bottom of the gym's agenda.

But Mace didn't need lighting to notice the rose stuck under the windscreen wiper, the flower still a bud. He pulled it free, shouted across to Allan, 'Someone leave a rose for you too?'

Allan slammed shut his boot. 'Not a chance.'

Mace called out the same question to Tyrone. Got another negative.

The bud's colour was deep plum. The attached courtesy card said International Flowers.

When Mace got home, Christa had her mother's box of jewellery spread over the sitting-room floor. A treasure chest in one sense. In another, an ongoing dispute between father and daughter.

The pieces were silver, fine-patterned filigree work. Bangles. Amulets. Necklaces. Earrings. Silver and coral chokers. Filigreed pendants. Ropes of glass and amber beads. Work from the Tuareg, the Maghreb, the Berbers. For Oumou the pieces had talismanic powers, they were not simply pretty. They were also her past.

Something of this past drew Christa to the jewellery. At birth she was given a customary set of beads. At two years old a cast silver bracelet. At the age of eighteen, the age she became a woman, she would receive another with a moon pattern symbolising life.

'Papa,' she said, as Mace bent to kiss her, 'can I have my ears pierced?'

A question that came up from time to time to an answer that never varied. 'No problem, when you're eighteen.'

'Please.'

She held up a pair of earrings, from each dangled four red beads attached to fine silver chains. In the centre of the earrings were stylised doves, the carriers of good news. They were beautiful. Oumou had promised them to her some time back.

'No. You're too young.'

Suddenly she was not far off tears. 'Maman wasn't too young.'

Mace glanced at Oumou. She lifted a hand to stroke her daughter's hair. To her this was no big deal. It was a cultural thing. Where she came from kids had their ears pierced before they could talk.

Mace didn't see it that way.

'Where your Maman lived that was okay.'

Christa sobbed. 'Pumla's got them.'

'It's alright for Pumla too.'

Christa looked at her father, her eyes tearing. 'Why?'

'It's okay for people like Pumla and Treasure.'

Which made no sense to her.

'Please, Papa.'

Tears spilled onto her cheeks.

'Enough.' Mace crouched before her. 'I've told you, when you're older.'

She sniffed. 'Why Papa?'

'Because that's my rule.'

Oumou said, 'She is my daughter too, no?'

Mace held up an admonishing finger. 'We've been through this. My rules. You agreed. My rules.'

'Bof! They are stupid.'

Oumou glared at him. To Christa said, 'Go to your room, ma puce.' They stood listening to their daughter run up the stairs, crying hard.

'You are stupid, Mace. Stupid. You do not know what is the right thing to do. Always you must say no to her for a small thing.

You do not think that maybe I would like to have her wear these earrings.'

'She is not going to have her ears pierced.'

Quietly Oumou said, 'This is what I am going to do for her.'

'No.' Mace grasped her arm.

'Yes. Oui, oui, oui. Yes.'

'Forget it.'

She locked her free hand onto his wrist, pushed him away.

'Non. You must forget it, Mace. This is my custom. This is what I want.' She moved around him towards the door. 'She is a little girl. When she has the nightmares you are the big daddy to protect her. When she wants to do something that makes me happy, you say no. Why is this? What is this here in Mace Bishop' – she poked at his chest – 'in the heart of Mace Bishop that cannot do this little thing for his daughter? Can you tell me? Why you must be so hard?'

Mace kept blank.

'No.' Oumou sighed. 'There is no answer, no?'

She opened the door.

'Sometimes you must think of our family. There are your ways. There are my ways. For Christa we have to give her some of both. This is not a big thing to do.'

Mace didn't waver the hard stare, held his hands rigid at his sides.

'Maybe you must have some therapy.' Oumou shook her head, went upstairs to comfort their daughter.

In the kitchen, Mace sat down to supper by himself. Ate forkfuls mechanically, chewing the food without relish or taste, the anger dry in his mouth. Oumou's questioning of what was in his heart getting to him: that he'd failed his daughter? Over earrings. That he'd failed Oumou? Over earrings. That he wasn't big enough for them both. He gave them the best, what'd he get back? Some crap that he wasn't on the nail. Not attentive enough. That he was small-minded.

'To hell with it,' he said aloud, shoving back the chair as he stood. 'I'm in this too.'

He dumped the rest of the food into the rubbish bin and slammed out of the house on his way to the opening of Club Catastrophe mark two. He knew he should have gone upstairs to say goodbye. He could imagine mother and daughter curled asleep on the bed. He shouldn't have gone out feeling pissed off. But he did because he was.

20

Mikey and Val took the pistols Abdul Abdul handed over: two nine mils, eight loads each.

'I thought he wasn't gonna be there?' said Val.

'Would be a pleasure if he was,' said Mikey.

'He won't be, Val,' said Abdul, 'but you gotta watch the woman. I've found out she's the sort can get outta hand.'

'That so?' said Mikey, grinning, tucking the gun into his belt.

'Mikey,' said Abdul, 'don't work my case. I don't want shit. No shit. Wave it around all you want to but no shit.' He gave him a bottle of tablets. 'Make her eat one of these would be a good idea.'

'Like how?' said Mikey.

Abdul Abdul tapped him on the head with the knuckles of his right hand. 'Sometimes, my friend, I think you have shit for brains.' Mikey ducked away. 'How should I know how? You open her mouth, you put it on her tongue, you close her mouth, you wait till she swallows. How about that?'

'She'll spit it out.'

'So you gotta do it again. That a problem?'

Mikey shrugged. 'She's gonna get hurt.'

'So?'

'So you said no shit.'

'I said no shit with shooting. Stand on her, I don't care. Just no shit with shooting.'

'Lay on her would be better,' said Mikey. He jiggled his crotch.

Abdul Abdul glanced at him, showed his pointy teeth. 'Don't fuck around, bru. Do the job, hey?'

'I've seen her,' said Mikey. 'You see her you wanna screw her. Dude owes me anyhow.'

Abdul flicked a flame on his lighter, set fire to a spliff. He took three totes letting the exhale out slowly, passed it on to Val. Val sucked at the zol, drawing the smoke into his lungs. He took another hit, gave it to Mikey. Mikey snagged off the head of ash into an abalone shell ashtray. Took his pulls.

'What about a button?' he said. 'To set the scene.'

Abdul took the joint. 'You shoulda been a coloured. Fucked-up whitey like you. Think of something else than poes for a moment.'

Mikey giggled. Wiggled his fingers for the spliff. 'There's something else?'

They smoked the joint to the roach and Abdul crushed it in the shell. 'Short 'n sweet,' he said. 'You go in, you put down the woman, you get the kid. You come out, we're away like a sleigh.'

They took the white Toyota: Abdul driving, Val up front, Mikey lolling across the back seat. *Mannenberg* blowing through the speakers on a tape that was only this tune recorded over and over. Abdul playing second piano on the steering wheel.

The rain fell solid over the dark streets of Athlone, everyone tucked away in their little houses watching TV. Abdul drove slowly from stop street to stop street out of the suburb. As they passed a corner café Mikey said he needed a Coke. Abdul stopped, kept the engine running while Mikey bought the cans. Some smarts in the doorway of the café, standing there smoking, eyed the two men in the car. One said to Mikey he had buttons for sale. Mikey said, yeah sure, made from rat poison.

'Nee, my bru, it's proper,' said the smart, laughing all the same.

'Bloody Pretty Boys,' said Abdul, once Mikey was in the car, 'they's next. 'Strues! All the drugs they sell.'

Mikey handed cans to Val and Abdul, felt under the seat for a half-jack of whisky he'd hidden there. Abdul smelt the liquor straight off.

'None of that shit,' he said, watching Mikey in the rear-view mirror.

Mikey ignored him, swallowed a mouthful anyhow.

'I'm telling you,' said Abdul. 'None of that shit.'

'Don't tune me,' said Mikey. 'It's not my religion.'

'You with PAGAD you don't drink.'

Mikey raised the bottle for a second time. 'Sure, don't smoke boom neither.' He screwed on the cap.

'Throw it out,' said Abdul, his voice high-pitched against the engine noise.

They'd come out of Athlone, joined the freeway at the cooling towers. Abdul ran the speed to one twenty, moving right to the fast lane, a BM swerving round them, the driver giving a long blast of hooter.

'Do it. Throw it out.' Shouting.

'Don't be bloody mad.' Mikey shouting back. 'This's a bloody highway for shitsakes.'

'Now. Get it out.' Abdul tight against the centre barrier, cars locked side back and front of them: lights and spray and rain harder against the windscreen than the wipers could manage. Over the Black River bridge into the corners, the cars in formation like this was a motorcade. Abdul pushed the pedal against the floor edging on the car in front, flicking his lights. Val sat stiff: one hand gripped on the armrest.

'Yo,' yelled Mikey, 'watch your bloody driving.'

The car in front not moving from the lane.

'Throw it out. Now, now. Do it.' Abdul with both hands fastened to the steering wheel, tailgating into Hospital Bend, knocking down the gear to send the revs screaming. 'Now, now.' The Toyota losing speed on the incline, cars hooting past in anger. Abdul swung left across four lanes to the hard shoulder, skidding the car to a halt.

He half-turned in his seat to lash at Mikey, screaming, 'I wanna hear it smash, pissface, now.'

Mikey slid down the window, hurled the half-jack into the grass. No telling if it broke or not.

Abdul Abdul popped the tab on his can of Coke and drank heavily. Wiped the back of his hand across his mouth at the finish. 'Don't cause shit with me, whitey. You gonna come to grief.'

'Okay,' said Mikey. 'Okay, let's do the job.'

They drove on along De Waal with *Mannenberg* still playing, the city lights in the bowl below sometimes curtained by the fall of the rain. No one spoke, Abdul too uptight even to drum the tune.

It took Abdul a couple of passes to locate the street in the steep suburb and they cruised up and down before finding the house. He parked thirty metres back from the driveway gate.

'And now?' said Mikey.

'We wait,' said Abdul, easing down the volume on the tape.

'No one's gonna notice us?'

'You see anybody?' said Abdul – the three looking out at the dark sodden street, the houses back behind their walls, the trees hiding lighted windows. The city buildings hardly visible below. 'Isn't anyone gonna be out in this street. Not even walking his dog.'

They smoked cigarettes, except Mikey, Abdul telling him to shut up complaining, and they smoked a joint, Mikey pleased to tote on that. For near two hours they waited in the loop of *Mannenberg*. Saw Mace Bishop drive in, saw him drive out in his Alfa Spider.

21

First thing Mace noticed it was a lot quieter in Assurance Street than the last time Club Catastrophe threw an opening party. No outside speakers. No outside video display. Fewer cars in the street. No suspicious Toyotas with musclemen. A short queue of patrons at the entrance, by invitation only. No one dancing on the pavements. No Dr Roberto either.

The back service lane clear of rubbish bins, vagrants, lurkers. The windows onto it secured prison style, bars sunk in the concrete sills. The only smell, the damp fishiness of the city. The only sound his heels on the concrete as he walked back into the light.

At the main door Ducky Donald and Matthew did the meet and greet.

'You wanna dance with a celeb, you wanna dance with a politician?' shouted Ducky, trying to put a champagne flute in Mace's hand.

'I don't want to dance,' Mace said, stepping through the magic hoop to set it flashing.

The bouncers acted discreet, one whispering to him, 'Excuse me, sir.'

'He's a cowboy,' Ducky told the doorman, 'doesn't go anywhere without packing' – pulled Mace into a clumsy hug, sloshing the bubbly. Drunk. Stoned. Both probably, Mace thought. No sign of any black bimbo.

'Your buddy's here. Power Pylon.'

Over his shoulder Mace saw Pylon watching from the shadows.

'How about this, Mace?' – Ducky Donald gestured expansively at the crowd – 'Doesn't get hipper than this anywhere in the city as we speak. Miss Calendar Month puts a bomb in here she'd have judges and high-ups jumping on her afterwards.' He slurped at his drink, holding it by the stem with the thumb and index finger of his right hand. Mace reckoned either he'd sorted something after Sheemina February's phone call or he was too gone to remember. 'Wanna meet a judge?'

'Later. We're going to enjoy ourselves, we need to take a look around.'

'Security's on it,' said Ducky. 'This is party time.'

DJ Shrapnel, the renamed duo from the club's first incarnation, started a countdown, the ravers joining, 'Ten, nine ...'

Ducky Donald bellowed into Mace's ear, 'Relax buddy.'

Before he could reply the djs yelled, 'You ready?' Got the immediate response. 'Go, go, go, go.' One hundred and forty-eight beats per minute bounced off the walls.

Mace grabbed Pylon by the arm, heading through the good-time mass for the chill room and the toilets at the back. Layout-wise the new building wasn't much different to the old. More convenient access from the bar to the stockroom, otherwise unchanged. Upstairs a different set-up. Executive offices on the first floor no doubt for Ducky and Matthew. Apart from a white leather four-seater couch in one room, a pot plant with big cut-out leaves, no other furniture. Expensive light fittings with dimmer switches on the walls. Adjoined to the bigger office a full-suite bathroom in black slate: Jacuzzi, shower behind a glass door, blue uplighters embedded in the tiles.

Very chichi.

Back in the office Mace and Pylon took seats either end of the couch, sat listening to the sound of DJ Shrapnel thumping beneath their feet.

Mace said, 'You ever think we fought with the angels for this? For kids to pop Ecstacy, jump around all night.'

'Was for a revolution.'

'Was for flash greed. Rolex. Banana Republic. Merc Mls.'

'Same thing.'

'As what?'

'A revolution. You have a revolution someone's going to make money, someone's going to spend it on the high-roller life. They did then. They're doing it still.'

'Bloody politicians.'

'Not forgetting we made bucks. Shaving it off the pile.'

'As a fee. Legitimate commission. Danger pay. Because after what we'd done who gave a flying monkeys for Pylon and Mace otherwise? No one. What'd they say, give us the guns. Give us the money. Viva the struggle, viva. Bugger that.'

'We did. Viva the Cayman viva.'

They both laughed, stretching out on the couches, the beat coming up in waves through the floor.

Mace mused. 'Only trouble's getting it out. It sits there and we can't touch it.'

'Stay patient,' said Pylon. 'Time will come, we can use it. Bring it in under the radar, no questions from the bank, no Revenue types calling round. Just need the right situation.'

'Might never happen,' said Mace.

'It'll happen.' Pylon got up to take a closer look at the pot plant, asked Mace how much he spent on plants?

Mace told him he didn't know. Not much.

Pylon said, 'Few days ago I come home Treasure's bought plants. She says, we've gotta do a garden. I tell her this is a waste of money. Plants grow. You don't buy them. She wants to know if I've heard of nurseries? Also she's got bags of compost that need to be dug in she tells me. Now I'm the garden boy. A whole war I fought not to be a garden boy. In the township she didn't care we didn't have a garden. Now we must have a garden.' Pylon rolled his shoulders in agitation. 'I told her you never had a garden.'

'Now we have. A lawn to mow too. Even use a Weedeater on the edges.'

'Which got pointed out to me.'

From below came shrieks and laughter, piercing even above the pounding beat: the party rising to the boil.

'First thing I had to do was dig up the bed near the back door. Little Pumla starts to help me, what does she uncover, the bones of a cat. Not rotted away properly, still stuck with fur and putrid.'

'Cat1.'

Pylon stopped. 'Cat1?'

'That's where we buried it. One of the kittens that were hammered to the club's walls. The other one's buried in our new garden.'

'The bourgeoisie bury cats in their gardens?'

'Probably small dogs too. It's traditional.'

'But I can't kill a sheep on my patio for the ancestors?'

'Treasure wants you do to that?'

'Treasure's got no ancestors.'

'Unlike you?'

The music changed pitch, getting more hectic. The crowd loved it.

'Up until we got duplexed, yes. Now I hear them calling.' Pylon leant forward, tapped Mace on the knee. 'Another thing, it's expensive. You consider what we had. A big house, double garage, even spent less money. And now? I burp downstairs Treasure shouts at me from upstairs to say pardon. Also I'm renting. Used to be I owned the place we lived in. Where's the advantage?'

'So buy,' said Mace. 'Get into the market.'

'Buy? For what I've got to lay down on a house in the suburbs I could get five in the township.'

Mace shook his head. 'You're tight, you know that. Take the money out the bank put it into property. Spreading your portfolio, they call it.'

'What? Buying a duplex?'

'If you have to be that cheap, sure, buy a duplex.'

'I should buy something else?'

'Spend the bucks, okay. Get somewhere decent.'

'Be Mr Flash? Move into the City Bowl?'

'Why not?'

'Because it's big bucks, Mr Bishop. Big bucks. More bucks than I've got.'

'Don't kid me. I've got it, so you've got it.'

'Not enough you don't need a bank loan.'

'That's what banks're for.'

'To take your money. Sure, I've seen that. When you finish paying you could've bought the house three times.'

Mace laughed. 'Helps you get stuff' – dug in a pocket for his vibrating cellphone. An SMS. 'Bad advice, Mr Advisor.'

He handed the phone to Pylon. 'A message from Miss February.'

Pylon read it, checked the details. 'You're sure? This is her cellphone number?'

'For the moment.'

'This mean there is a bomb?'

'It means she doesn't like it the club's up and running.'

'So why send it to you?'

The phone rang. Pylon looked at the screen.

'It's Oumou.'

Mace took the phone, connected. Could hear her breath catching as if she'd been running. Heard her gasp, 'The men have Christa.'

22

Mace felt the chill in his blood. Thought: I didn't set the alarm. Oumou and Christa were asleep. He should have set the alarm. Even if one of them had woken and triggered the system, so what? So when the armed response checked back, Oumou could have told them, sorry, a mistake. Happens all the time.

If he'd set the alarm, the passives would've caught the men the moment they broke in, the sirens would've blasted high decibels all over the house. The armed response would've put through a query call. Even supposing the men had guns to Oumou's head, they'd have made her answer the phone. She'd have said, No problem, this is Oumou Bishop, but she'd have given the wrong password. Three minutes flat armed response would've been all over the set. Worst case scenario: a hostage situation.

In a hostage situation there was a high percentage chance it could be talked out. Mace knew this. Knew too, in kidnap situations the police statistics were not promising on a favourable outcome.

This was a kidnap situation. Because he didn't arm the house.

Because he didn't arm the house.

The loop that spun his head as he crossed the city, ran lights, shot stop streets, left a trail of irate hooters.

Mace rushed into the house with Pylon hard behind him. Oumou sat at the kitchen table staring at the night outside the window. She had gone deep into herself. As they held one another he could feel the tightness of her muscles, a run of shivers when she tensed.

'Tell me,' he said.

'They came in the studio,' she said.

'When?'

She shrugged out of his hold, sat where she'd been sitting to stare into the dark. Above her eyebrow was a livid bruise, a cut at its centre that had bled, blood-runs streaking her temple. 'They were in the bedroom, three men in those hats over their faces.'

'Balaclavas?' Mace took a chair opposite her. 'How long after I'd gone?'

'It wasn't many minutes. Christa was watching television while I lay with her.'

The thing about Oumou was that she didn't accuse him. She did not say: if you had not been so stubborn. If you had not argued with Christa over the earrings. If you had listened to her, then we would not have quarrelled. You would not have stormed out of the house. She said none of these things. He did not believe she even thought these things. He did. He knew that in the normal course, the house would've been armed when he left.

Pylon squatted beside her. 'Can you describe them? Their size? Blacks? Coloureds?'

She shook her head. 'Non. The one hit me too quickly.'

He looked at Mace. 'Were waiting for you to leave. Had to be.'

'And the time lapse? That was three hours ago.'

'Oui. They made me swallow something. Or they would burn Christa with a cigarette.' Oumou bowed her head not wanting Mace to see her tears.

His cellphone rang. An SMS: 'If you want to see your child, stop the club.'

Oumou reached out for the phone. 'It is about Christa?'

Pylon asked, 'Same number as the last one?

'Same number.'

Oumou gripped Mace's arm, her eyes fastened on his. Moist, pleading. 'You must tell them to stop. Quickly.'

Mace connected to Ducky Donald. To Pylon said, 'Anyone we know can run a trace on this number?'

Pylon nodded, already dialled up to his contact.

Ducky came on. 'Mace, where are you boykie?'

Mace told him he wanted him to close the club. Told him why. Told him he owed him a favour.

Ducky Donald said, 'Shouldn't you be talking to the cops?'

'You owe me,' Mace said. 'I'm calling it in.'

'Due respects, Mace, I don't owe you this big.'

'This is my child.'

'Which I appreciate.'

'So do it.'

'Any other time, Mace boykie, I would. But I can't. I've got a private party here. By invitation only.'

'One last time, Donald,' Mace said, not shouting, keeping his voice level, 'for the sake of my daughter's safety I'm asking you to stop your party.'

Ducky Donald didn't even pause to consider. 'No can do, Mace. Not the sort of thing you can tell judges and politicians.'

Mace thumbed him off before he heard anymore. Replied to the SMS that the club would be packing up.

Oumou said, 'She is gone, no?'

'No.' The word exploded from him. 'No. We are going to get her back.' He stood gripping the sides of the kitchen sink, staring at the face reflected in the window. A face with faint lines in the cheeks that one day would be deeply etched. A face with a thin mouth, eyes that were holes in this black reflection.

In this mirror he could see Oumou at the table watching him; Pylon behind her, leaning against a counter. A silence settled. The only sound the hum and throb of the fridge. For long minutes they did not move. Until his cellphone bleated an SMS: 'Everyone is still dancing.'

Pylon said, 'Phone the number, talk to them. It'll give my guy more time.'

'No need,' Mace said, 'whoever it is, is at the club.'

Ducky Donald threw his arms out, expansive, sympathetic. 'Mace, what can I say to you and your lovely lady wife.'

Pylon said, 'Cut it Ducky.'

They stood outside the entrance door, the only place you could speak without shouting.

'What I want, Ducky,' Mace said, 'is for the djs to stop for thirty seconds. That's all I'm asking.'

Ducky was stoned, his pupils pinpricks. He stared at Mace, frowning. Mace didn't blink until he looked away. 'Thirty seconds?'

'All I'm asking.'

'The favour sorted?'

'We'd be square.'

Ducky thrust back into the club, sending a bouncer tottering. Mace followed, Oumou and Pylon behind him. Saw Ducky shouting at Matthew, Matthew looking over at them, shaking his head. The expression on Matthew's face like he'd swallowed piss. Ducky pushing him aside, skipping into the dj box, a startled DJ Shrapnel staggering back as Ducky stopped the music. Took a couple of seconds for the dancers to realise they'd been abandoned.

To a rising chorus of irritation, Ducky said, 'Friends, just thirty seconds then we're back on the beat.'

Mace had already connected to the number. Even above the buzz of annoyance could hear a cellphone ringing. Could see its keypad flashing green where it lay on the bar counter. Pylon got to it first.

'This anybody's?' he called out, holding it up, not expecting an answer.

'Play the music. Play the music,' people shouted back.

DJ Shrapnel obliged while Ducky Donald saw his guests to the door. 'Can I give you some advice, Mace?' he said without waiting for the go-ahead. 'Like I said, call the cops, that guy Gonsalves.'

Mace jabbed a finger against Ducky Donald's chest. 'Tomorrow, Ducky, I want your guest list.'

At home, Mace sat long hours in Christa's room staring at her empty bed. Cat2 warm in his lap, Cupcake lying against his daughter's pillow. Sat rigid, unmoving, nausea in his stomach, a heaviness tight across his chest. He had the word kidnapped on a loop through his mind: kidnapped, kidnapped, kidnapped. Like the slap of a big man's hand belting a child. With each strike he fought to keep Christa's face before him; fought to keep out the image of her backed into a corner, bruised, frightened. He wanted to scream. He kept the howl trapped in his lungs. He wanted to act. He kept still. Before dawn he lay down on her bed, eyes fixed on a mobile of colourful birds suspended from the ceiling. It didn't move. He didn't sleep. He cursed Ducky Donald.

23

The men stood around the mattress looking down at Christa lying there drugged with anaesthetic. Wearing only a T-shirt and broekies as she had when they'd snatched her. Her legs bare, curled half-foetal. They passed a joint between them. Each taking two hits at a time, holding in the smoke, letting it out slowly.

Mikey dropped the end on the floor, ground it out. 'So what now?'

'We wait.' Abdul Abdul took a polaroid camera from his tog bag.

'Pretty kid, hey,' said Mikey.

'You wanna put your thing in her?' said Abdul.

'Why not? Pass the time.'

Abdul focused the camera on him. Mikey held his hand to the lens. 'There's people I could get hold of would pay for her. Argentinians. They're doing it all the time. Coloured kids mostly. Like her. There's a preference, so it would seem.'

'Perverts. Alla yous.' Abdul stood over the girl aiming the camera down.

'Hell,' said Mikey, 'that's old. Didn't know you could still buy those.'

'You can't,' said Abdul. 'This is old.'

'And the film? Where d'you get that?'

'A contact.'

'Pretty as a picture,' said Mikey as Abdul clicked off the photograph, the camera whirring out the result. 'Lips like that she's gonna give good head. Surfer I know, he's into kids. Once showed me some pictures of kids doing stuff you wouldn't believe. My friend says when a kid does a blow job, doesn't matter boy or girl, it's their teeth does it for him.'

Abdul peeled the strip off the image, waved it for the emulsifier to work. 'Mikey the sick whitey. Into kiddy porn, hey. Sick, my friend. Dis-gusting. You know about this, Val? Our paedophile friend. Maybe we should cut his dick off.'

Val laid a blanket over the girl.

'Spoil his fun.' Abdul Abdul laughing, holding out the slowly forming image to Mikey. 'Something for you to wank on.'

Val found another blanket and covered the girl with that too.

Abdul thrust the photograph at Mikey. 'I mean it. Give our friends an extra charge. Take it. Come'n take it.'

Mikey did, holding up the image to the light, the little kid seeming fast asleep, peaceful, her hair mussed. He looked down at her. Cute. Really cute.

'What's gonna happen with her?' said Val.

Abdul shrugged. 'Something. Depends.' He leered at Mikey. 'Hey, Mikey.'

24

8:30 a.m. For twelve hours Christa had been in the hands of her kidnappers.

Mace and Oumou stood in the front office of Fortune, Dadoo & Moosa. Mace noting well-used furniture, some framed certificates on the walls. A carpet in need of replacing. An image of we're-not-ripping-you-off. The receptionist smiled at them. Not a nicety either returned.

Mace told her they wanted to see Sheemina February.

'Do you have an appointment?' Still the smile, a batting of eyelids brushed with pale green.

'Listen,' Mace said, leaning over her console, 'just get her out here.'

'Please,' said Oumou, 'this is very urgent for us.'

The receptionist punched a button on her consul, a male voice answered. 'There are people here for Sheemina,' she said. The voice told her he would be right out.

'Please take a seat,' she said to them, a tiny diamond stud in her left nostril glinting in the light of a desk lamp.

'It's not going to be that long,' Mace said.

Oumou sat though, the hurting for Christa taking more out of her than personal suffering ever had. They waited. Mace gave them five minutes then headed for the door he reckoned must lead to the offices.

The receptionist called out. 'Excuse me.'

He ignored her, opened the door. A man in a bowtie said, 'What do you want?'

'You heard her,' Mace said. 'To see Sheemina February.'

'And you are?'

'Jesus, guy, just get her.'

'I am Reginald Fortune,' Mr Bowtie said, 'perhaps now you will tell me your name?'

Mace did.

He nodded. Ushered them back into the reception area. 'I am afraid Ms February is out of town.'

'Where? Since when?'

'That is no business of yours.'

'Damnit, it is.' Mace thumped the wall, dry wall boarding that shook at the blow. 'Get her on the phone.'

Oumou came round to face Fortune. 'Please, can you help us talk to her.'

'I'm sorry that is impossible. As we speak Ms February is in London. If you make an appointment I'm sure you'll be able to consult with her when she's back in two days' time.'

'Non. That is too late. Non.' Oumou sat down, the tears coming.

'I'm sorry,' said Fortune. 'I can't help you any further.' He gave a slight nod and made to leave.

'Wait a minute, pal,' Mace said, grabbing his shirt sleeve. 'I met with her yesterday. She didn't say anything about going away.'

Fortune shook himself free. 'Without knowing who you are, Mr Bishop, I cannot see why she should. Her business is her business.'

'PAGAD is her business.'

Fortune put his hand on the door handle. 'She represents some of that organisation's members.'

'Twice she has threatened my clients for running a nightclub.'

'I very much doubt that.'

'You think I'm lying?'

He paused. 'Mr Bishop, Sheemina February is a lawyer, she is not an activist.'

'My child has been kidnapped,' Mace shouted. 'Abducted from our house. On the night my clients reopened their nightclub. Eight hours after Sheemina February warned them not to. In my presence. Where is my daughter? Where has she got my daughter?'

Reginald Fortune didn't respond.

Mace grabbed him, bunched both hands into the lawyer's shirt, knocking off the man's bowtie. 'Where, you bastard? Where is my daughter?' Speaking each word separately, the heat suddenly out of his voice, gone cold, deliberate. 'Tell me.' Jerking the man up on his toes. 'Where is she?'

'Mace, leave the man,' said Oumou, reaching up to restrain him with one hand, rubbing the tears from her cheeks with the other. Mace let go of the lawyer and Fortune bent to pick up his bowtie, clipped it on.

'Do you want me to call the police, Mr Fortune?' said the receptionist.

He shook his head at her. 'No, no, there is no need. Mr and Mrs Bishop are just leaving.' He opened the inter-leading door to his office. 'If your daughter has been kidnapped Mr Bishop perhaps you should be talking to the police, not accusing my colleague. I shall overlook your assault.'

'Please,' said Oumou, 'where is our daughter?'

'Mrs Bishop,' said Fortune, 'I do not know. We are a firm of attorneys, not gangsters.' With that shut the door.

Mace smashed his fist against it, tugged at the handle but it was locked.

Again Oumou calmed him. 'Come, she is not here.'

'Bastard,' said Mace. Softly, then shouting it. 'You bastard.'

'Do you want to make an appointment to see Ms February?' asked the receptionist.

Mace said, 'When your Ms February phones in, tell her to call me.' He flipped a business card onto the desk. 'Immediately.'

In the car Oumou said, 'Do you believe she is in London?'

Mace eased the Spider out of the parking space into Queen Victoria Street, a car-guard holding up advocates on their way to chambers for them.

'She could be. She could be anywhere. Only thing I know she wasn't at home last night. Pylon was round there.'

'She has got Christa?'

'My guess, no. But my guess she knows about it. Could be why she's in London.'

Oumou went quiet and still. In this silence they drove Orange, Molteno, into the quiet suburb, took Woodburn, Glen Steps to the driveway of their house, the gates open. Mace drove in, parked in front of the garage door. Oumou didn't move to get out.

'This is because of the club?'

Mace looked up at the mountain, clouds down low on it with more wet weather coming in. Already the wind picking up.

'I believe so.'

'Then they will not take Christa away? For slavery?'

He put a hand over Oumou's where they lay knotted in her lap. 'She is still in the city. We'll find her.'

Oumou turned sad brown eyes on him. Said nothing.

9:50 a.m. At the office Mace went through the guest list Ducky Donald had emailed. One hundred and fifty high-end names. Predictably the cellphone didn't belong to any of them. He could scratch off about thirty people as above suspicion but even a team of ten working the phones and shoe leather mightn't have hit a link to Sheemina February or PAGAD in two weeks among the others. All the same what else could he do but make random calls on the off-chance. He started at the top.

Had they ever sought legal advice from a Sheemina February?

No.

The five people he spoke to knew the name, though. Told him, she's PAGAD.

10:20 a.m. The New York clients phoned: how about a shopping trip down at the Waterfront? Mace explained that a colleague would be collecting them.

Mr New York was unhappy. 'Is this boutique service?'

'A temporary emergency,' Mace said.

When his wife was under the knife, the New York client said, he didn't want any temporary emergencies.

Mace assured him there wouldn't be any. Went back to the list.

12:00 p.m. Bang on the noonday gun, Pylon phoned.

'This's cute,' he said, 'Business class passenger Sheemina February on last night's London flight. Due back day after tomorrow. Convenient.'

'No bloody coincidence.'

'So now?'

'Haven't a clue.' The thought of Christa came back on Mace, heavy and painful. His daughter alone, scared. Strange men about her. A thought he couldn't bear. He groaned out loud.

'What's it?' Pylon coming in fast. 'You okay?'

'Yeah,' said Mace, thinking, no, there's this bloody great pain in my chest tearing me up.

'Go swimming,' said Pylon, 'I'll come back and chase the list.'

'Wouldn't do any good.'

Pylon about to hang up when Mace said, 'Christ! The goon. She said he trains at the Point. Mitch. Mick. Micky. Mikey. Some shit like that.'

Pylon going, 'What? What're you talking about?'

Mace going, 'Get down there. Meet me down there. Now.'

12.45 p.m. The day manager at the Point told Mace, 'I can't do that. The list's private, confidential. I can't let you see it.'

Mace and Pylon sat in his office, watching the young manager squeeze an exercise grip to pump his biceps. The guy's pecs strained against his T-shirt like he was a walking advert for health and vitality.

'Alright,' said Pylon, 'there's another way we can do this. We give you a description, we give you a first name, you say, "Oh hell yes, I know blah de blah, trains here all the time, lives out at blah." How's that sound?'

The day manager looked dubious. 'Dude, what are you okes?'

'You know,' said Mace. 'You know me. I swim here three days a week. I step out of your office, ten people'll greet me.'

'I've seen you. I mean what's it you do?'

'Protection,' said Pylon. 'Celebrities. Movie stars. Business people. High net worth individuals.'

'So what's it with this chappie you wanna contact?'

Pylon leant forward, placed his hands on the manager's desk. 'Tony,' he said, picking up the manager's name from a staff schedule pinned on a notice board, 'Tony, you don't want to know. But let me tell you this, our client, a major business figure, is about to lay a charge against this man. For stalking his daughter. Here at your gym. And elsewhere. In this sort of situation we first take a soft line, try to intervene, talk the parties out of the courts.'

'Like beating him up?'

'Talking to him, I said, Tony. Talking to him.' Pylon sat back. He and Mace watching the day manager squeezing the grip.

'Another thing you have to consider,' said Mace, 'is the publicity. Especially if it comes out it could have been stopped. This guy, Mikey, hitting on her, here where she's supposed to be safe.'

'Mikey?' said Tony. 'Mikey Rheeder? No ways.'

'Muscled fella,' said Pylon, puffing out his chest. 'Like you. Surfer-type, tanned, very short blond hair. Probably a number one cut.'

'Sure,' said the day manager. 'That's Mikey Rheeder. No ways he'd do that.'

'You know him?'

'I've trained with him a few times. I don't know him. I know him like that, from training. From seeing him around. You know.'

2:15 p.m. Mace and Pylon sat in the big Merc outside a Sea Point block of flats eating salami and olive pizzas. They'd buzzed the button beside Mikey Rheeder's name, and got no response. From a public phone on Main Road, Mace had called the cellphone number the day manager had given them and Mikey had answered, at least Mace believed it was Mikey from how he remembered his voice, nasal, too high-pitched for the size of his body. Mace hadn't said anything. Mikey had said, 'Who's this? You got a wrong number, pal. Piss off.' He'd laughed. Said, 'Cheers, arsehole. Your fingers too fat for the keys.' The connection was dropped and Mace hung up the handset, waiting to see if Mikey would ring back. When the phone rang he lifted the receiver. Mikey said, 'Who's this? Stop bugging me arsehole.' This time Mace cut the connection.

'He's got my daughter,' said Mace, toying with the pizza. Not hungry suddenly. 'That's the shit part. He's sitting there with Christa. Wherever they've got her.'

The wind came up the canyon street blustery with rain, rocking the car.

Pylon looked up at the block of flats. 'Makes you wonder how this Mikey Rheeder guy can afford this. A flat in Sea Point. Alright not ocean frontage but these're rich larneys stacked in these properties. Lawyers, gynaes, chemists. How's a common goon get in among the Jews you have to ask?'

Mace didn't. He was thinking about Christa in the hands of Mikey Rheeder but he couldn't take that thought too far before he imagined the fear on Christa's face.

6.04 p.m. Pylon was saying what he didn't understand was why there'd been no word from them, the kidnappers, no demand? Not to close down the club. Not to stop Matthew dealing drugs. Not even a ransom.

'I was wondering that,' said Mace.

'The longer they hold out, the more you sweat. That's the strategy, you reckon?'

'Exactly.'

Mace's cellphone rang and both men jumped at the shrillness. No number on the screen.

Mace said, 'Maybe this's it.' He thumbed on the connection, held the phone to his ear.

'Mr Bishop this is Sheemina February. I believe you called at my office.'

Mace got a coldness in his veins, fastened his stare on the entrance to the block of flats, said, 'Where's my daughter?' – keeping his voice even as if he were asking about nothing important.

Pylon in the driver's seat glanced at him, touched his shoulder. Mouthed Sheemina February when Mace turned, Mace nodding twice.

'What about your daughter?' said Sheemina February. 'I'm sorry I don't know what you're saying.'

'My daughter is what I'm saying,' said Mace, still no heat in his voice. No emotion. 'You don't have to kid me you don't know.'

'I'm not.'

'Bullshit.'

A pause, and for a moment Mace thought he'd lost her.

'This is an international call I'm making,' she said, 'I don't need to be sworn at.'

'Where's my daughter? Where've your thugs got her?'

'I don't have thugs, Mr Bishop. I don't know anything about your daughter.'

'Jesus!' Mace let out an explosion of air. 'I'm expected to believe that. My daughter gets kidnapped. It just so happens the night you fly to London. From where I'm standing that looks like you pulled a move.'

'Mr Bishop, you're distraught. I'm sorry about your daughter.'

'I've got a description,' Mace lied. 'Of a guy called Mikey Rheeder. A guy I met in your company. A guy you told me about. About how he recovered from a bullet wound to the shoulder. One of your thugs.'

'I know of this man.'

'Sure you do. I want my daughter.'

'Mr Bishop, I'm in London. You need the police.'

'I need you to make a call, tell Abdul Abdul and this Mikey Rheeder to bring my daughter back.'

'You think I can do that? Mr Bishop, you overestimate my position. I'm a lawyer.'

Mace had his gaze fixed on the entrance to the block of flats at an elderly couple coming out, buttoned up in raincoats against the drizzle. The woman with a scarf over her hair.

'I know what you can do,' said Mace. 'You know where my daughter is. Tell me.'

A pause. He could hear no background noise, then she said, 'Some things, Mr Bishop, are not what they seem.'

The connection closed off. Mace shouted, 'You bitch. You fucking bloody bitch.' Hit the dashboard, again and again, the elderly couple edging past the front of the Merc staring at the two men inside. The one yelling, hitting the dashboard.

7:15 p.m. Oumou phoned Mace, her voice a whisper. As Mace pieced it together a man had buzzed her from the street intercom, said he was a courier with Ajax Deliveries, had a package for Mr and Mrs Bishop. Sender one François Barber. Oumou had said, No, she wasn't expecting a parcel. Didn't know anyone called Barber. The courier said, Please lady, here's the tracking number, look up Ajax in the phone book, I can't stand here all night. Oumou did, everything was kosher. She let the guy in, he handed over the parcel.

That was when her voice disappeared.

'What, Oumou, what?' Mace shouted.

'It is Christa's hair,' Mace heard her say.

He told her he'd be there in five.

He left Pylon in the Merc, took the Spider, jumping lights into Glengariff, along High Level, after the quarry going through the Bokaap side streets, down Wale into Buitengracht to Orange and steeply up to the house on Glen Steps. Rushed in shouting Oumou's name from the front door to where he found her in the kitchen. On the table the envelope, a standard over-the-counter padded number for sending documents. Beside it, a huge pile of Christa's hair, dark and soft. Mace picked up a handful, held it to his nose. Could smell his daughter.

He didn't want to imagine where she'd been when they'd shaved her head, how they'd held her, except the flash came unbidden: a bare room, his daughter on a stool in the middle, shivering. Mikey Rheeder with a hand on her neck, another on her shoulder. Abdul Abdul holding electric clippers, the cord trailing across the floor to a wall plug. Grinning, his sharp-pointed teeth grin. Behind him a woman in a long coat. Her arms crossed. Sheemina February. Didn't matter where she was, she was there. The only sound the electric hum of the clippers.

A printed note that'd been included with the hair read: 'Get your friend to close his club.'

Mace checked with Ajax who had brought in the parcel. The clerk remembered the sender, a personable man wearing a suit had paid the fee in cash. Coloured guy. His only stipulation that the delivery was urgent. They'd got it dropped in forty-five minutes. Not bad going the clerk felt, seeing as the point of departure was their northern office, twenty clicks out of the city.

Mace reckoned that's where they'd got Christa: somewhere in the northern suburbs, in one of those ranch-style houses, double garage, behind high walls in a street where nobody was going to notice anything out of the ordinary. Knowing this didn't make anything any easier.

He stayed with Oumou, the two of them sitting either side the kitchen table with Christa's hair between them.

7:40 p.m. An SMS. Disappointed in you again Mr Bishop. What next must your daughter sacrifice?

A new cellphone number.

Mace didn't show it to Oumou, told her it was an update on a client.

8:10 p.m. Pylon phoned. 'I'm sitting here with Mikey in his flat,' he said. 'Nice place. Very comfortable. He wants to tell us where Christa is, but he'd rather give it straight to her daddy. That right, Mikey?'

Mace heard Mikey say, 'Piss off, prick.'

Then Pylon: 'I can understand why you shot him. He has this effect on people.'

'I'm there,' said Mace, pocketing his phone. He reached across the table for Oumou's hand, laced his fingers into hers. 'We have someone who might know where Christa is. With a little persuasion. I won't be long.' He squeezed her fingers, unlocked their hold.

'I must come with you,' said Oumou. 'This is our daughter.'

Mace shook his head. 'No. I need you to be here, for any phone calls. Sometime they have to talk to us. Make their demands, ask us for money, whatever it is they're after. They want to hear we're desperate. Frightened for what they're doing to Christa. They've sent her hair, they have to know how they're hurting us. If they call you've got to tell them that.'

Oumou stayed focused on his eyes.

'I know,' said Mace. 'I know what you're thinking. You want to hear him say it. Tell you where she is. You have to hear it, I know. But you've got to be here.'

'They will not phone,' she said.

'We can't be sure of that. My guess is they will, in the next hours, unless this Mikey tells us first.'

'What will you do?'

Mace shrugged. 'Can't say, really. There's a way we had, Pylon and me, in our early days at the camps. Membesh especially. When people were coming through that we didn't know if they were genuine or spies. If the word was that they were spies we'd talk to them and they'd usually tell us. Quite quickly.'

Oumou said, 'I have a way too.'

'I've seen it,' said Mace. 'But this time you have to be here.' He stood, bunched his hand again into the pile of Christa's hair. 'I'm going to take some.'

Oumou reached up to him, to his fist that held their daughter's hair. 'Hurt him,' she said.

'Oh, that's likely,' Mace said, smiling at the desert in her eyes.

'I've been asked to hurt you,' were the first words he said to Mikey Rheeder fifteen, sixteen minutes later after Pylon had buzzed him into the block and he'd taken the lift to the fifth floor and gone down the corridor to number five ten and knocked and been let in. Mikey Rheeder sat on a straight-backed oak carver, one of six around a lime-washed oak dining room table. His arms were taped to the arms of the carver. The left arm he'd fastened himself under the watchful barrel of Pylon's pistol, before Pylon had done the other.

'Nice dining table,' said Mace.

'Part of the rental,' said Pylon. 'Not a reflection of Mikey's taste.' He indicated the open-plan kitchen. 'That's nice too. Well equipped. Serious knives for the serious chef. Got everything in it for someone doing a gourmet meal. Sort of thing would make Treasure rush out to Boardmans to upgrade the cutlery.'

Mace took the fistful of Christa's hair out of his jacket pocket, put it on the table, dark against the white surface. He saw Mikey's eyes flick to it and away.

'Recognise that?' he said.

'Get stuffed,' said Mikey.

'This's not an attitude I would take,' said Pylon. 'Under the circumstances. The best would be for you to treat us politely. Know what I'm saying?'

'My sense is you would recognise it,' said Mace, sitting down across the table from him. 'I have a feeling you probably helped shave my daughter's head this afternoon and your friend, the coloured guy, delivered this to the couriers, Ajax.' He pushed the clump of hair into the centre of the table. 'Surprising how soft her hair is, like that. But you'd know this from stuffing it in the envelope. When she asks me to brush it, it seems different, almost liquid. If I smell that hair, I can smell her. Amazing that. That we can tell one another from the smell of our hair.'

Mikey said, 'Up yours.'

Mace and Pylon let it go, stared at him until Mikey said, 'Look, you've got the wrong guy. I'm not on this one. I'm just security for them. They don't let me go on jobs. I'm white can't you see. White's not a colour they trust.'

'The thing is,' said Pylon, 'this's not our understanding. We believe differently. Especially about the kidnapping of Mace's daughter.'

'I'm not lying.'

'Ah, Mikey that's easy for you to say now. How you convince us is the more difficult part.' Pylon put a hand on his shoulder. 'We need you to scoot up closer to the table so's your hands are on the surface. I'll help you, keep the chair from falling over. Don't want you to hurt yourself.'

Mikey wouldn't oblige. Mace sighed, stood up and went round the table to Mikey's chair. He and Pylon manoeuvred the man against the table and got Mikey's hands where they wanted them.

'You're a big guy, Mikey,' said Mace. 'What're we talking, eighty-five, ninety kilos? Impressive. Good muscle tone, too. Is it steroids you're using? The boys do, I'm told. The serious weightlifters.'

'Look,' said Mikey, 'I'm not the man you want.'

'Are you right-handed or left-handed?' asked Pylon. 'It's important we know otherwise you've got no way of communicating with us, and you'll most certainly want to do that.'

'Right-handed,' said Mikey. 'What d'you mean anyhow?'

'We need you to write down where we can find Christa,' said Mace. 'It's that simple. Give us a clue where the paper and pens are, you write down the address, and then we go check it out. If you're sensible we could have put this whole thing behind us in … what? An hour? Hour and a half max.'

Mikey said, 'I can't give you the address. I don't know it. I'm not involved.'

'But you know about what's happened?'

'I've heard. I won't lie.'

'That's good, Mikey,' said Mace. 'Telling the truth's a good start.'

Pylon found a pad of notepaper and ballpoints in a bureau drawer, brought them over to the table. He went across to the kitchen, returned with a chopping board and mallet for tenderising steak. One of the old-fashioned wooden ones, heavy, no staining so probably unused. Pylon smacked it into the palm of his hand, said, 'Eina. Points are still sharp.' He placed board and mallet beside Mikey's left hand, just out of reach.

'Before we ask you to give us the address,' he said, 'we're going to strap you in a bit tighter. You know, fasten your ankles to the legs of the chair. What could happen is that you'll want to move around a bit with the pain but we need to keep you upright and focused.'

He bent down with the roll of duct tape but Mikey kicked out his legs and Pylon stood up again, shaking his head. 'Mikey, Mikey, Mikey. Don't do this.'

Mace pulled the Ruger from his belt and slid a round into the chamber. 'I found this worked before,' he said over Mikey's head to Pylon. 'But he screams so maybe the gag first's a good idea.'

'No, hang on,' said Mikey. 'Just a bloody minute. No, I can't help you. Don't you understand. Listen to me. Listen. I've got nothing to do with this. You've got the wrong man here. I'm no good to you. I don't know what's what. 'Strues. Hey, hey. I can give you Val's address. If you want that I can give it to you. Speak to him. He's in there. Big time. Fully. With Abdul. You know, like in the leadership.'

'Write that, too, Mikey,' said Mace. 'Because we don't want a situation where we're disturbing the neighbours.'

He put down the Ruger and gripped Mikey's head and worked his thumbs into Mikey's cheeks until Mikey opened his mouth. Pylon balled in a sponge he'd found at the sink and got the duct tape winding round Mikey's head to secure it. At the end Mikey couldn't move his jaws at all.

It took the two of them to fasten Mikey's ankles to the chair legs, the guy doing his best to be uncooperative. When they were done, Mace stood, dusting carpet-lint from the knees of his jeans.

'Spunky, Mikey,' he said. 'Perhaps not the right time, though.' He shifted the pad of paper under Mikey's right hand and fitted the pen between his fingers. Mikey flicked it away. 'I wouldn't do that,' said Mace. 'I would realise now is the moment to be cooperative. What we need to see is that you can write. For your own sake.'

He retrieved the pen and put it back in Mikey's fingers. This time Mikey scrawled 'fuck you' on the pad.

Pylon laughed. Mace smiled sadly.

'Here's the question: where can we find my daughter, Christa?'

Mikey repeated his answer.

'Fine,' said Mace. 'We're going to do things a little differently from now on.' He took a coin from his pocket, glanced at Pylon. 'Best of three?'

Pylon shrugged. 'Your call.'

Mace called heads and won. On the second flip Pylon called heads and lost. Mikey staring at them with crazed eyes.

Mace slipped the chopping board under Mikey's left hand, but Mikey balled his hand into a fist and kept it angled upwards from the wrist.

'That's not going to help,' said Mace. He raised the mallet and brought it down hard on Mikey's knuckles. The man's fingers splayed. Mace gave Mikey's index finger three piston blows, at the second smack splinters of bone showed white through the pulp.

Mikey screamed and jiggled in the chair and rolled his head and for a moment looked like he might wrench free his hands from the strapping. Then his head flopped forward.

'That used to do it,' said Pylon.

Mace got a jug of water from the kitchen, poured it over Mikey's head, which brought the big fellow round.

'All you have to do,' said Mace, 'is give us the answer. If you're right we can drop you at a hospital afterwards. That doesn't look good, that finger.'

Mikey made a movement of his head that both Mace and Pylon took to be a negative.

'Got a lot of the hero in him,' said Pylon. He pinned Mikey's splayed fingers to the board, brought the mallet down on the pinky. The blow broke the skin, pushed the nail out at an angle. Mikey jerked about until Mace put both hands on his shoulders to quieten him. When he was still Pylon smashed the pinky four, five times. Mikey fainted about the third hit.

Mace brought him back with another jug of water and put the question to him again. 'Help yourself,' he said. 'Write it down.'

Mikey was snorting through his nose as if he couldn't get in enough air. From the noises he was making, Mace wondered if he hadn't swallowed the sponge. Also the guy was scrawling on the pad but nothing that was legible.

'We're going to cut free your gag,' said Mace, 'then you can tell us in your own words.'

Pylon kept Mikey's hand fastened to the chopping board while Mace worked a boning knife into the duct tape and slit it. Mikey was heaving for breath, sobbing with pain. But he got the words out.

'Grown older, grown wiser,' said Pylon, putting down the mallet.

'There's a man,' said Mace. 'Well done.' Then made Mikey repeat the address, bending close to his mouth to hear the panted words. Mace straightened. 'Shows how wrong you can be. I guessed the northern suburbs. Paardeneiland factory land didn't spring to mind first off.'

25

'Great choice,' said Pylon, rain gusting in spurts, the wind force rocking even the big Merc. He slowed to a crawl in Section Street, a deserted zone. Most of the factories and warehouses in darkness, some showrooms with display windows blazing.

'Keep on,' Mace told him, routing them from a street map open on his lap. At Calcutta indicated right, the buildings thinning out with vacant lots between them. At Bermuda got him to slow.

To the right the street was a cul-de-sac, ended by the Salt River Canal. Down there a one-storey building, empty land either side, the canal behind it. Had to be their destination.

Before they made the turn Pylon pulled over, killing the lights. 'What's the plan?'

'Search me. Break the door down and get Christa out.'

He switched the wipers off and the street blurred. 'There'll be a guard.'

'Sure.'

The rain drummed loudly over the car while they waited for the squall to ease. In the after-lull Pylon nodded towards the back. 'And him?'

They had Mikey trussed and gagged in the boot.

Mace pulled out his Ruger, checked the clip and racked a load into the chamber. 'Could be a complication. Probably best if he walks from here. Depending on how things go down.'

Pylon said, 'Fair enough.'

From the glove compartment Mace took two full clips, pocketed one and gave the other to Pylon.

'Shotguns would've been better,' Pylon said. 'Like a twelve gauge sawn-off.'

The door to the building was wooden, protected by a concertina security grille bolted into the concrete.

'Hardly security,' said Pylon.

He levered the grille open with a tyre iron, used much the same technique on the wooden door, except it made more noise. Behind the door was a small office, another door leading out of it.

They stopped, listened. Nothing but the rain, loud on the corrugated roof-sheeting.

Mace opened the door onto what might once have been a workshop. A ghostly light filtered through the windows from the street, enough to see racks for tools on the wall above a bench, the outlines of spanners, screwdrivers, power drills. Parked facing a roller door was a small delivery van with the decal International Flowers on the side. The floor was stained with patches of engine oil. In front of Mace a metal staircase spiralled up to the mezzanine floor.

Again they stopped. Rain noise. The rumble of wind over the roof. Mace gestured to Pylon that he was going up, disappeared into the shadows of the workshop.

He paused on every step, the metal creaking with his weight. At the top of the staircase, a door. He opened it, a light clicked on.

Abdul Abdul sat on a chair holding Christa tightly against his chest, his revolver in her mouth. Christa started at the sight of her father. Abdul tightened his grip, pushing the barrel deeper into her mouth.

'Slowly, my friend,' he said, 'you gotta be careful.'

Mace put the pistol on him. 'Let her go.'

The air smelt of cinnamon and something sweeter: dagga. The remains of a joint squashed in a saucer.

'Take the gun out her mouth. Best thing is you point it at me.'

'Best thing is you shut up,' Abdul replied.

Mace took a step into the room, sideways towards a tier of bunk beds, away from where they sat other side of a table. On the table a microwave and a kettle, dirty plates in a basin.

He shifted the sight dead centre of Abdul's forehead. 'Give her up.'

Abdul snorted. 'God is great.'

Mace took a step towards them.

'No, my friend. Get back.' He jerked at Christa and she moaned.

Mace stopped.

'Back. Now, my friend. Back, back' – his voice rising in pitch.

Mace did as he wanted.

Abdul gave a grin of pointy teeth. 'Put your gun on the top bed. Like a good boy, lie down in the corner.'

Mace didn't move.

Abdul stared at him, waiting, the grin unwavering.

'This is your daughter,' he said, cocking the hammer.

'Okay, okay.' Mace placed the pistol on the bunk. 'Let her go. You can leave. I can't stop you.'

'Of course not. But you do not tell me what to do.' He took the gun out of Christa's mouth, gestured at the corner of the room. 'Lie down. On your stomach.'

'Papa,' Christa yelled before he choked off her scream.

Mace paused. 'It's alright, C. It's alright now, baby. He's going to let you go.'

'On your fucking stomach,' shouted Abdul. 'Come on. Come on.'

Christa whimpered. Mace could see scabs on her scalp where the shaver had nicked her, fresh blood leaking from a new cut. Abdul smothered her face against his torso, the gun at her bald head.

'Lie down.'

Mace went over to the corner, knelt: the lino sticky beneath his palms. 'Call it quits, Abdul. Let her come to me.'

'Get flat,' Abdul screamed. 'Stop buggering around.'

His face was livid, a pulse working in his throat. He stood up, dragging Christa, kicked Mace in the small of the back.

'Arsehole.'

Mace went down, the pain sharp, but braced on his arms and kicked out, catching Abdul off balance. He staggered against the wall and Christa screamed.

Mace heard a shot.

Heard her cry out.

Twisted into a crouch as she fell against him.

Abdul fired again.

26

A little after sunrise the storm was over, the sky clearing a thin blue line along the tops of the mountains. Mace stood among the rain puddles in the hospital car park, his hands warming around a polystyrene cup of coffee, dreading that Christa might not make it.

The what if unthinkable.

He paced across the car park to the fence. Over the road, sacred ibis and hadeda picked through a sodden field after frogs. He watched the birds, their quick stab, the small deaths. If Christa died he would lose Oumou too. Wouldn't be able to live with her eyes, brown and sad, accusing. And why? Because he'd not considered the fanatics. Their madness. Never believed his family was in danger. Or that Abdul Abdul would have no worries about snatching a child.

He closed his eyes: saw Christa's pain pulled across her face; Oumou's tearless suffering. And remembered Techipa. Snapped on it suddenly: the faces of the MKs. Contorted, howling, bloody.

Mace opened his eyes, looked up at the Constantiaberg clear in the washed sunlight. Shook his head to clear the recall.

But the men were there, lying in the bush, in the sand, the sand in their wounds. The blood on the ground.

How they'd gone from one to the next, he and Pylon. One frightened young man to the next. The men begging for help. Three of them.

Half an hour earlier they'd sold the men guns. AKs, Russian and Chinese. Some Makarovs, some grenades. Twenty landmines. The deal was payment on delivery, Mace and Pylon rocking up in a Bedford, the MK commander paying in greenbacks. Ten men in the unit going to cause shit in the mountains. Hit and runs. Mine the tracks, take out some Boer armour. No fear in them then, only laughter.

Mace and Pylon hadn't driven off three kays when they heard the firefight. Had returned to find three men alive, gut shot and going nowhere, a short way off eight Boer soldiers dead. A hopeless situation. No medicine. A day's drive to the nearest town. They flipped a coin that fell two one to Mace.

Pylon'd said the men would be dead in hours anyway. Why have them suffer. Mace said nothing. Shot two men point blank, heard the retort of Pylon's pistol behind him.

Afterwards they collected the weaponry from both sides. Trucked it to Lusaka for resale to other cadres heading over the border.

In all these years Mace hadn't thought of the two men's faces. Kept them in deep vaults he never opened. Would never have opened, he believed, if not for Ducky Donald Hartnell. Or had his daughter not been shot.

He threw the dregs of his coffee into the undergrowth. Crumpled the polystyrene cup in his fist.

A man coughed behind him. 'Ah, Mr Bishop.'

'What?' Mace spun round. 'For Chrissakes.'

Came face to face with Captain Gonsalves. 'You alright?' The cop peering at him. 'You look like shit.'

Mace wiped a hand over his face, took a breath. 'What's it?'

The cop keeping up his stare, rubbing a plug of tobacco round the palm of his left hand. 'Bit of a storm, hey, last night!'

Mace nodded.

Gonsalves popped the plug into his mouth, chewed tentatively. 'Look, tell me if I'm outta line but a coupla answers to some questions would be useful.'

'My daughter's in ICU.'

'I enquired. I'm sorry about that.' He gave the plug a more vigorous chewing. 'We could do it later at my office if you want. But now would be better. Abdul Abdul having such a, what you might call, high profile.'

Mace tossed the crushed cup into a refuse bin. 'What about Pylon?'

The captain shrugged. 'Due process, that's all. No problem. Abdul had a bloody great forty-five in his hand. Had to be self-defence. What I hear there's legislation pending that we're gonna have to charge anyone who kills in self-defence. But we're talking a couple of years' time. Right now all we gotta do is file a statement. Know what I'm saying? For the autopsy.'

Mace sighed, looked up at the red tinge on the clouds. Sailors would get the horrors at crimson dawns.

'Ten minutes of your time.' Gonsalves spat out a stray strand of tobacco. Before Mace could respond he put his own spin to it. 'This's a follow-up on the Catastrophe bombing as I read it. Not so?'

'Yeah,' Mace said, 'it is' – and gave him a brief account of Christa's abduction, how he'd tracked down Abdul through a lucky break.

'Meaning?'

'A mutual contact.'

Gonsalves looked dubious. 'That right? Within twenty-four hours?'

'Something like that.'

'Going some.' He gave the plug a suck. 'Usually we're talking days, weeks even.'

'We got lucky.' Mace pinched the bridge of his nose. Suddenly exhausted. 'Anything else?'

The captain nodded. 'Maybe. For instance, why'n't you let us know?'

'I was told to keep the cops out of it.'

'They always say that. People think they can handle it, take their time getting to us. Only causes grief.' He snapped closed his notebook. 'This's a help for now' – offered his hand, and Mace shook it. 'If I prayed I'd pray for your daughter. If I believed I'd say trust in God.'

As Mace turned away Gonsalves said, 'That lawyer Sheemina February involved in any of this?'

Mace glanced back. 'Not so's you could pin it. Made some legal threats to the Hartnells I heard.'

Gonsalves said, 'She was Abdul's attorney.'

'Then she's got one less client.'

The captain opened the door of an old Cressida. 'I'm expecting her call. Once she gets to hear, she's gonna be all over us.' He spat the tobacco plug into his hand and flicked it under a bed of shrubs edging the parking lot. The Cressida's engine swung a couple of times before it fired.

Watching the cop drive off Mace thought, Techipa. He'd looked in the guys' faces, seen fear and hope. Moved quickly from one to the next. Jesus Christ, to remember it now.

He went back into the hospital, took the stairs to the ICU wing. On the landing his phone rang: Sheemina February.

'My flight's just landed,' she said. 'I am told your daughter has been badly wounded.'

Mace walked to a corner, away from a group of people huddled on chairs, blank-eyed and stunned. He kept his voice low, controlled: 'Then you know your friend Abdul Abdul is dead.'

'Client, Mr Bishop. I represent – represented – him.'

Mace snorted. 'Of course. The detached lawyer. Well, I don't see it that way.'

'Oh, how do you see it?'

'I see your hand in this somewhere. I don't know where. But somewhere.'

Sheemina February laughed. 'How flattering, Mr Bishop. That you should think I have power over men such as Abdul.'

'Get out of my life,' said Mace. 'Out of my life, out of my family's life.' He thumbed her off, thinking, leave it, walk away, when once he wouldn't have. Once he'd have played it differently with Sheemina February, but that was once and elsewhere. Now he had to leave it. She was too high profile. Too connected. You touched her you got burned. Mace didn't want that. He had too much to lose. Had almost lost Christa, didn't want to think of losing Oumou. He put the phone in his jacket pocket, went off to find his wife.

Oumou sat in a chair, a cup of tea long cold at her elbow. The doctors were with Christa, she whispered. Mace sat beside her, held her hand. Until there was this woman, he thought, he had not known another's pain; until there was Christa he had not known fear. The fear that a life might be lost to him. The fear of being without her.

An hour they sat there, watching blankly the trail of doctors and nurses in and out of the ward. Eventually a young doctor approached, dressed like he was heading off for a round of golf. Introduced himself as the surgeon who'd operated on Christa.

He sat opposite them, said, 'Your daughter's condition is stable. We need to keep her in ICU for a few more days. For monitoring. You see the bullet went through her intestines but that's not the problem, the problem's that it grazed her spine. Severed some nerves. At the moment, Mr Bishop, Mrs Bishop, your daughter's paralysed from the waist down.'

Mace felt Oumou stiffen.

'We'll have to perform another procedure in a few days and maybe some things can be corrected. I'm not going to tell you she will walk again. All I'm telling you is we will do our best for her.' He stood up. 'I'm sorry I had to give you such news.'

There was something weird, Mace decided, about how things worked: that when you thought you were getting your life together, you weren't.

THE DEAL

'… in this city the world comes to party and traffick …'
- Anonymous businessman

1

'Ludovico,' he said to the receptionist. 'You have a reservation for me.' Speaking English not Spanish, although his Spanish was workable. Not a question but a statement. The receptionist fingering a version of his name on the keyboard.

'You spell it L-u-d-o-v-i-c-o,' he said. 'Ludovico.'

The receptionist tapped at the keys again.

'Ah, si.' She beamed at him, as she had done when he approached her. Even teeth. Full lips. 'We have a room for you over the plaza. There is more light.'

'That would be good,' he said.

She looked at the screen: 'You are with us for two days, Mr Ludovico. I hope you will enjoy your stay.'

'Yeah,' he replied.

She wrote his name and room number on a small folder that contained a smartcard key, gave this to him.

'Have a nice day,' she said. Smiling at him again, her lipstick glistening.

'Sure,' he said, handing the card to a bellhop, smiling at her.

As he turned away, she exclaimed. 'Oh! Momento! Mr Ludovico, excuse me, there is a present for you' – and bent down to a cupboard beneath the counter, coming up with a shoe-box size package wrapped in navy blue paper, fastened with a ribbon, and a gift-wrapped cylinder that could only contain a bottle of wine.

'Thank you,' he said, reaching for the parcels.

'You're welcome.'

He noticed her eyes for the first time. Happy eyes, smiling too. Reminded him what he needed was a night at the ballet.

'Any ballet on?' he asked.

'Ballet? Si, it is possible,' she said. 'I will find out in five minutes.'

'Much obliged,' said Ludo.

Riccardo Ludovico – known to his friends and enemies as Ludo – filled the bath with a few inches of cold water, sat on the edge, unfastened his shoes, eased off his socks, swung his feet into the tub. He sighed out loud at the relief. For ten minutes sat immobile, staring at the soap holder, two rounds of soap wrapped in cream waxed paper nestled there. Smoked a cigarette, flicked the ash into the water, stubbed out on one of the soaps.

'Stay at the Carrera,' Francisco had said. 'Treat yourself. This is an important job.'

But the air ticket had been economy class. The plane full, his knees jammed against the seat in front, a woman alongside him of such girth she overflowed, forcing him sideways. Ten hours of this misery, no chance of a cigarette.

'Maybe you upgrade the ticket, I'll stay at a cheaper hotel,' he'd suggested to Francisco.

'Hey, hey, hey,' came back Francisco, 'for ten hours?'

'Twenty,' said Ludo. 'Ten there. Ten back.'

'You stay at the Carrera,' said Francisco. 'Beautiful place. Like you're in England. Floral drapes. Leather armchairs. Prints of hunting scenes. That sort of decoration. You stay there, Ludo. My treat for you.'

Ludo hadn't pushed it any further. Francisco had.

'Best location, close by to everything. Okay, so you must put up with a bit of smog, but this is right there in the middle of history. Behind the palace where they shot up that president. Whatsisname? From the air.'

'That right?' said Ludo.

'Damn sure,' said Francisco. 'They got everything there. Restaurants. Health club. Pool outside. The oldest hotel in Santiago, Ludo. Be my guest. Stay a few days. Take some time out.'

Francisco's normal style: I make the arrangements, you do the job.

'Bullshit,' said Ludo, standing in the water, talking to himself in the full-length mirror at the end of the bathroom. 'Get in. Do the job. Get out. That's how we do it. That's how we always do it.'

No need to unpack, for two nights it wasn't worth it.

The phone rang. The receptionist to tell him Swan Lake. Swan Lake, his worst but what the hell. Had her book him a ticket for that night.

The phone rang again: Francisco opening with the standard line: 'That was a safe flight?'

'Yeah,' said Ludo.

'You got the package?'

'Yeah,' said Ludo, staring at the packages where he'd put them on the bed.

'Everything okay?'

'I don't know,' said Ludo.

'What d'you mean you don't know?'

'I haven't opened it yet,' said Ludo.

'Saint's sake.' Francisco's voice going up an octave. 'Why haven't you?'

'I just got here,' said Ludo. 'I got things to do. Unpacking. Maybe take a swim. Have some lunch.' Ludo smiling at himself in the cupboard mirror, the phone lodged between his shoulder and left ear. 'Is the wine good?'

'The best. Enjoy.' The line went dead.

Ludo grimaced at himself. He needed a shave. More than that he needed a drink.

At the pool bar he took a table under an umbrella. Only a few people on the patio, nobody around showing flesh any younger than his own. He took out his silver cigarette case, opened it, tapped a Camel against the case.

'Señor?' A lighter flared in front of him. Ludo looked up at a waiter's impassive face, slight smile but nothing ingratiating.

'Gracias,' he said leaning into the flame, wondering if he should try out his Spanish, deciding against this. 'You do cocktails?' he said in English.

'Si, señor.'

'Yeah. Like what?'

'Is a local drink I may suggest?'

'Uh huh.'

'Is a pisco-sour.'

'Being?'

'Señor?'

'What's it made of?'

'Is Pisco. Like aperitif and lemon that is very cold.'

'Yeah,' said Ludo.

'In a tall glass.'

'That's good.'

'For señor?'

'I guess,' said Ludo.

The waiter nodded. Ludo blew a stream of smoke up against the umbrella. With each draw he felt better, letting the smoke rub around his lungs, waiting a beat before sending out a blue plume.

'Señor.' The waiter set down the drink. Tall as he'd said, the rim encrusted with sugar, the glass opaque with condensation. 'Salud!'

As the waiter didn't leave Ludo realised he had to try the drink. A taste he took to immediately.

'Is good?' asked the waiter.

'Yeah,' said Ludo. 'Bring me another, huh.'

Halfway through the second pisco-sour Ludo remembered he hadn't locked the wallet with his passport and the air ticket and a clip of dollars in the room safe. Nor his cellphone. Left them lying on the bedside table like a classic jerk. The package unopened on the bed. Hotel of this nature there was bound to be an attendant went in every time you left the room. He took the rest of the drink in one.

First thing he saw the room had been straightened, the counterpane smoothed out, the wine and the package placed on the writing table. The wallet on the bedside pedestal, nothing missing. Also his Nokia. His Discman and his blues CDs. Great hotel! He sighed with relief, sat down at the escritoire and opened the package, this time tearing the wrapping.

The pistol inside was a used H&K 9mm with a silencer, five rounds in the magazine. Not what he'd asked for but good enough, light, easy to shoot. Also a pair of garden secateurs. Brand new.

He locked the package and his wallet and his cellphone in the safe.

That evening, Ludo did the ballet. Cringed at the opening bars, then thought, d'you wanna hate this or what? Relax. And went with the mood, even finding grace in the swans, figuring, maybe he'd been too hard before, there was beauty here if you looked unbiased. Or he'd got the romance for the first time. What the hell! He enjoyed it, bought a programme as a souvenir. The sort of thing he could show to Isabella. Isabella always threatening to overcome her prejudice. Offering a pas de cheval, neighing at the same time, whenever he talked of ballet tickets. Swan Lake in Santiago would amaze her. Amazed him. Hyped him. Back at the Carrera he toasted three pisco-sours to Tchaikovsky.

Gone one, Ludo let himself into the artist's apartment. Had on his work outfit: hooded jacket, clean sports shirt, jeans, Nikes. A cat stench hit him, made pungent by the warm weather. He found the bedroom; with the shutters closed the room was dark, but enough light to make out Señor Ramon Moraga Salazar on the far side of the bed, on his back, snoring. The woman lying on her left side facing away from him. Their only covering a sheet. Perfect situation.

Ludo drew the H&K from a pocket inside his bomber jacket, shot Señor Salazar through the heart from a distance of ten centimetres. Nice gun, low recoil, the silencer minimising the muzzle flash. The cartridge tinkling away somewhere. The man jerked at the impact like he'd had a nightmare. The woman woke up screaming. Ludo smacked her on the side of the head with the pistol stock. End of screaming. He wasn't concerned with the cartridge, give the cops some excitement. Put the pistol back in his inside pocket, took the secateurs and a Ziploc bag from the back pocket of his jeans. Señor Salazar's right hand dangled over the bed. Ludo snipped off the index finger, a crack someway between snapping a lobster leg and pruning roses, dropped the keepsake in the Ziploc, wiped the blades of the secateur along the sheet. On his way out dumped the pistol and the pruners in the kitchen garbage bin. Some more excitement for the cops.

Six hours later Ludo checked out. Full lips, the receptionist, said, 'But you have another night booked.'

'Yeah,' said Ludo. 'I don't need it.'

Then he gave her a padded envelope and asked for it to be posted airmail.

'To New York?' she asked, glancing at the address.

'Yeah,' said Ludo.

'From here?'

'Yeah,' said Ludo, smiling.

She frowned. 'It will take some days, Mr Ludovico.'

'I guess.'

What she didn't want to ask was why he didn't post it when he was back in New York. So he helped her out.

'It's a present,' he said. 'My friend likes to get presents with foreign stamps.'

2

Mace and Oumou sat other side of Elizabeth Tlali's desk. Personal account advisor was the title under her name. Mace and Oumou dressed for this meeting with the bank: Mace in a suit with an open-necked blue shirt, Oumou in a long black dress, a string of silver and amber beads round her neck. Elizabeth Tlali told them that the bank would have to foreclose. As the situation stood there had not been a single repayment for three months. 'Mr Bishop, Mrs Bishop,' she said, 'you understand our position.'

Mace said, 'It's only been built a year. We need more time.'

Oumou said, 'What is this foreclose?'

Mace could see out the window behind the personal account advisor to the lower end of Longmarket Street, people crossing over from the Town Hall to the Grand Parade, and beyond that tourist coaches pulling up outside the Castle. He and Oumou had driven down into the city in the station-wagon, no ways was Mace going to leave the Spider on the Grand Parade even with the top on. Too many skollie-boys lurking around ready to slit the hood.

'Basically,' he heard Elizabeth Tlali saying, 'what it means is that we will have to sell your house in order to recoup the money you owe us.'

'But already,' said Mace, 'the house is worth more than the money we borrowed to build it. That means you'll be throwing away our money.'

Before they'd left home he'd stood at the pool looking back at the house: Oumou's dream: lots of glass, concrete beams, straight elegant lines. Some tall stone pines behind it and you looked up beyond that at Devil's Peak. He turned to his right there was the grand face of Table Mountain, a better aspect he had to admit than from the Victorian. Not that Oumou or Christa wanted to live there after the kidnapping.

He'd wondered about bringing in some Cayman money. That wealth sitting out there that he couldn't touch. How stupid to lose the house for the fear of laundering a few thousand K. Maybe it'd come to that. In his hand was the bank's letter, just a tone short of threatening legalese.

The hell with you, he'd thought. This is our house.

'That's not how we see it,' said Elizabeth Tlali. Elizabeth Tlali wearing a pin-stripe black suit, skirt not trousers. She wore no rings, no jewellery. Her wristwatch, Mace noticed, was expensive, the name Raymond Weil discreetly on the face.

'This house is for our daughter,' said Oumou. 'She cannot walk. Everywhere is built for her wheelchair.'

'I know,' said Elizabeth Tlali. 'I am aware of your personal situation.'

'Then,' said Mace, 'you know that your bank was happy to lend us the money, more than we asked for, so we could build the house.'

Elizabeth Tlali nodded. 'I know. We make every effort to help our clients, Mr Bishop.'

'So give us more time. Extend the bond. Make it thirty years. Thirty-five years. For God's sake your money's safe. There's the house as security. Just give us a chance to pay for it.'

'We have not even lived there for two years yet,' said Oumou. 'For all that time except for the last three months we have paid.'

Elizabeth Tlali said yes that was on the record. That was why they'd allowed three months leeway. Mouthing on about the bank and its responsibility towards its client. Mace thinking, blah, blah, blah, they could put it up for auction, sell it out from under them, and not even bother to get all the money back. Still have him for the balance owing. Even when, on the open market, he could get probably a good couple of hundred thousand more. If you believed Dave Cruickshank. Which he did. Dave also telling him, 'Hang in there, my son, the market's turning up.

We're talking twenty per cent plus returns in the coming years. Cape Town's hot. We're getting international interest.'

'What you're saying,' Mace said to Elizabeth Tlali, 'is you don't care if you put us on the street. Worse, put us in financial shit without any assets. Our daughter's a paraplegic, you heard my wife, we had this house designed to make her life easy. But okay, this doesn't matter. From your perspective you just want your money. What I've got to say is I don't see any morality in this Mrs Tlali.'

'Ms,' she said.

Mace stared at her, wondering who trained bank staff to irritate the customers.

Oumou said, 'What we would like to ask for is another three months. Please. If we could have the extra months we can then afford to pay.'

Elizabeth Tlali shuffled through the papers on her desk. 'I have here your bank statements, Mrs Bishop. What they tell me is you and Mr Bishop can't afford your house.'

'In two months,' said Oumou, 'I shall have an exhibition. All the money from that will go to the house.'

Elizabeth Tlali smiled. 'I hope you are very successful, Mrs Bishop. But we cannot rely on that.'

'You have my revised business plan,' said Mace. 'You can see the potential. That's not thumbsuck. That's modelled on conservative values. By professional consultants.'

'Of course. But it is a plan. What you have proposed may not work out quite so well.'

'It was fine when you lent us the money. Not as good a business plan but that didn't matter then. Then you said, here's the money Mr Bishop. We're on your side.'

From a drawer in her desk Elizabeth Tlali took out a block of notepaper, the bank's logo top centre. She wrote the date on it. Glanced up at Mace and Oumou, said, 'Alright, I'll tell you what

I'm prepared to do. The bank has its rules and because you haven't paid, you've broken the rules. You understand that?'

Mace thought, here we go, the my hands are tied, sorry I can't help you line of bullshit.

'But I have discretionary powers, in terms of a first contravention.'

Mace didn't like the word contravention but let it ride seeing as Elizabeth Tlali seemed to be heading in the right direction.

'My suggestion is,' she said, 'that you come up with one of the missed payments within what? … say ten days. Something to show your good intentions. Something I can show upstairs. For that I can go three months, end of that time unless the bank sees some money the people upstairs are going to force me to foreclose.' She wrote on the pad, 'Decision postponed to end January 2002', Mace reading it upside down.

'Fair enough,' he said, standing up.

Elizabeth Tlali closed the file, dropped it onto a pile in an out-basket. She stood, extended her hand to Oumou. 'Good luck with your exhibition. What's it? Paintings?'

'Pottery,' said Oumou.

The woman kept hold of her hand. 'You know Clementina van der Walt's work?'

Oumou nodded.

'Is it like that? Colourful?'

'Non,' said Oumou. 'Different without the colour. More like the colours of the desert and the shape is thinner.'

'Fascinating,' said Elizabeth Tlali. 'You must send me an invitation.'

To Mace said, shaking his hand, 'We like to help our customers, Mr Bishop. Support them too in their activities.'

'I'll bear it in mind,' he said.

On Adderley Street, Mace headed Oumou down a block towards the flower sellers, their alley of stalls cool and damp in the shadow of the tall buildings. 'We need flowers,' he said. 'In celebration.'

Oumou stopped, mock-amazed. 'Mace Bishop is going to buy flowers?'

'Come on,' he said, his arm round her shoulder. 'We got extra time. Anything can happen. The bank can lose the file. We can win the lotto.'

'Maybe we must try to save some money.'

'Like how? Stop eating Norwegian salmon? Give up chocolate? I don't think so' – Mace buoyant with relief.

The flower sellers saw them coming, yelling out prices and offers, thrusting roses at Mace. He shook his head. 'Not roses, some other flowers, not roses.' The women laughing at him, 'Ag shame, Mister Gentleman, roses is for love. You got such a beautiful woman you supposed to listen to the poets.' Two of the women insistent, holding out bouquets wrapped in newsprint. 'Over there,' said Oumou, pointing at buckets of carnations. The women rushing to their stock. 'Oui, that is what we want.' She chose two bunches of carnations and daisy mix. Mace paid. The woman smiling at him while she scratched for change in a bag: the gums where her front teeth should have been bright pink. 'Flowers for the hours,' she said.

Mace laughed, taking hold of Oumou's arm walked down the alley into Parliament Street, each carrying a bouquet, Mace saying, 'Did you notice her watch, the woman in the bank?'

'It was expensive,' said Oumou.

'Raymond Weil. I have clients wear those watches.'

They came round the post office and onto the Parade, Mace grateful to be out of the shadow and into the sun, even in November the shade cooler than he wanted.

They stopped at their car. Mace opening the back, the two of them laying down the flowers like they were sleeping children. Before he closed the door Mace said, 'We could probably get more finance. If we wanted.'

Oumou said, 'That is not the problem, Mace. The problem is the first payment.'

3

'It's fantastic. I come in here every morning, I look out the window, I think, fantastic! In all these years I didn't notice the Twin Towers, now they're gone, every time I look out there I know they're gone.'

Francisco turned into the room.

'What d'you think, Paulo?'

Paulo slurped at his coffee. 'I think it's weird.'

'Weird? This isn't weird, this is terrible. What I'm saying is who noticed the Towers until they're gone?'

'That's what you said.'

'Like you only see them when they're not there.'

'Weird.'

'Two great buildings! You don't see them. The terrorists destroy them, you say, hey, that all looks so sad. But you ask me if I ever saw the Towers, I'd say, no, never.'

Francisco shot his shirt cuffs so that they rode about two centimetres out of his jacket sleeves. The way he liked it. Smart casual. Open-necked shirt, gold chain with the small crucifix just visible there dropping into his chest hairs. Informal. Relaxed. He glanced at the guy sitting drinking his coffee. His brother-in-law. A serious punk. Why Isabella didn't divorce him, get him outta their lives was a mystery. But no. Kicked him outta the home but kept him dangling. More than a little nastiness in Isabella. Francisco shrugged, examined his fingernails. The cuticles pushed back, half-moons showing. The thing about Salazar's index was that the half-moon showed. This was what Francisco noticed straight off when he saw it in the Ziploc. Before he plopped it into the bottle with the others. Wasn't often men in their middle years had the half-moon showing. A mark of distinction to do so in Francisco's reckoning.

'Paulo!' said Francisco, getting Paulo to come to the window, wrinkling his nose at the smell of the aftershave. 'You see that?' – waving at Ground Zero. 'It's like dentistry. You get two teeth knocked out side by side you have a huge gap. You never thoughta those teeth as individuals. You thoughta them as part of your set. Brushing your teeth in the mirror you didn't even see them.'

'That right?'

'Yeah. So it's only when they're gone you know they were there.'

'Right.'

'What I'm saying is sometimes we don't appreciate things till they're not there.'

Francisco headed round his desk, sat, leaning back. Paulo standing like a kid being stared at by the teacher.

'All we need's a bit of dentistry, we can fix it.' Francisco gestured at a chair. 'Take a seat.'

Paulo sat, the two of them opposite one another.

'So?' said Francisco and stopped. Not saying a word more, letting the silence drag.

Paulo dry-swallowed. 'I need about fifty G.'

Francisco clasped his hands behind his head. 'You asked Isabella?'

'Like that's a good idea?'

'I dunno. You outta pocket, she's your man. Your wife too.'

Francisco laughed. Paulo managed a weak grin, forcing it across his face.

'What you need it for?'

'Obligations.'

'Wheel debts? White devil?'

Paulo nodded, not wanting to go near the words.

'Which?'

He grimaced, Francisco reading this as both.

'What'd I tell you, Paulo?' Francisco unlaced his fingers, put his hands down on the table. Olive hands. Hands like Isabella's. The nails well-groomed. 'I told you, you handle that stuff. You want to run a line of business, while you're parta the family you come to the family. You need to open an investment, you come to the family. Isabella. Me. It doesn't matter. Wherever you're comfortable. You run the numbers by us, if we can, we help. Where we don't help is paying wheel. That's not business. For your account only. Similarly powder. That's entertainment. For your account only.'

Paulo slumped, let his eyes down to the carpet: grey with a pattern of small lighter grey squares. Every now and then an orange one to give some lift. Standard office wall-to-wall. Francisco kept focused on his brother-in-law. The telephone buzzed, he lifted the handset, said, 'Paulo, something comes up, I'll call you.' He leant forward to shake the guy's hand, at the same time saying, 'Yeah, send them in.'

As Paulo stood, Isabella and Ludovico came swinging in, Isabella wearing one of those ethnic gypsy numbers with tassels and bells. A waft of Chanel No 5.

'How about this?' Bright and perky from Isabella. 'A family gathering. Why'n't you tell me, honeypie? We coulda cooched-up in the same cab.'

'You bend to him?' Isabella wanted to know, the instant the door closed behind Paulo.

'I'm going to do a thing like that?' Francisco retorted.

'I told him …'

'Sure you did. So give him a divorce.'

Isabella laughed. 'Against my religion.' She flopped down in the chair warmed by her husband. Estranged husband. 'This's how I want it till I'm ready.'

'Him 'n that bitch? What's her name, Victoria?'

'Vittoria.'

'Yeah her exactly.'

'It suits me.'

'Well. To each his poison.' Francisco sighed. 'You look lovely.'

'Her,' she said, inclining her head, hair shimmering at the movement. Bright eyes. 'Her poison.'

Reminded Francisco of a tiger's, those eyes. He smiled at Ludo sitting down to the right of Isabella. Decided to open with the pity of Señor Ramon Moraga Salazar's death. He tipped back in his chair until the people sashaying down a path in the picture behind his head seemed about to step into his hair.

'Señor Ramon Moraga Salazar's dead.'

Ludo flicked lint from his trousers.

'Who's he?' asked Isabella.

'Was a business associate in Santiago,' said Francisco. 'Who turned bad. Who Ludo whacked. Then what happened: we get a message per email the merchandise is dispatched.'

Ludo shrugged. 'He shoulda done it earlier.'

'No doubt.'

Francisco put his elbows on the desk, made a bridge of his forearms, rested his chin on the platform of his hands. 'What happened, Isabella,' he said, 'was we paid Señor Salazar for a big shipment, ex Colombia. Up-front transaction. We knew him so no hassles. Only this time we start picking up static as the mission proceeds. When he doesn't produce, we sympathise. We give him time to make good. Lotsa time. Still he makes excuses. We tell him, look, Señor Salazar, this is not the way we're used to doing business. He says, he's sorry. This is not the way he does business either. He says his people are giving him a hard time. We tell him that's his problem. Nothing to do with us. We tell him go away and talk to his people, sort them out. He goes away, never comes back. We phone. We email. We fax. We even use the mail. He won't talk to us. So we send Ludovico.'

Isabella turned to Ludo. 'You get to the ballet in Santiago?'

'Sure. Swan Lake. You wanna see the programme?'

'Thought you didn't like Swan Lake?'

'I didn't. Maybe still don't. This was good though.'

She shook her head, swivelled back to her brother. 'And the consignment's where?'

'Sailing to Africa.'

'Nice one.' Isabella moistened her lips. Lips the colour of iced mocha. 'Where in Africa?'

'Doesn't matter where in Africa, Bella.' Francisco back with the furrow-brow. 'Anywhere's a catastrophe. This isn't wartime goods. This is goodtime goods. Africa's not a place people have a good time.'

'So where's it going? Lagos?'

'Lagos. Saints no. It was going to Lagos we wouldn't even be talking about it.'

'So where's it going?'

'Cape Town. Right down there at the bottom.'

'You figure you can't do business there?'

'Dunno. I checked out the Rough Guide, says it's a pink city. Does a gay pride party round Christmas time.'

'Didn't know you had a problem with gays.'

Francisco flopped his wrist. 'No problem, sweetie. Except these are African homosexuals. African's the part I got trouble with. Also' – he pulled open a desk drawer, took out a Wall Street Journal folded to the exchange rate page – 'it says here you need almost ten of their rands. Worse, two days ago you only needed seven of their rands to buy the dollar. Traders say next week you could need eleven. Which tells even the saints, the rand is no currency you want to hold. Even if we sell the shipment to the African homosexuals, all they've done is feed us peanuts.'

'Umm,' said Isabella.

'Big umm,' said Francisco.

Isabella tapped the desk with her fingernails. Dark mauve varnish. The men listened to the clicking, usually a prelude to some kind of solution.

'Okay,' said Isabella. 'First problem is how much're we talking?'

'Somewhere about ten kilos,' said Francisco.

Isabella smiled. 'Paulo's good for that. We send him. Second problem, we have to take on-site delivery of the merchandise. So send Ludo too to keep things steady. Third problem where to pitch the sales. Maybe try the local clubs. How about Paulo works them. And the beaches. It's their summertime, right? We're talking international holiday destination. The world gone there to party. Afrotrash, Eurotrash, Brit lager louts all mixed up sun and sand and speed. Paulo's good for that.'

Francisco held up his hand. 'You giving Paulo a long run on this?'

'Why not?' She let another smile twitch her lips. 'He's family. Also he's good at schmooze.'

'Fine.' Francisco pulled at his ear lobe. 'Problem number four: how d'you turn the whatsits into hard currency?'

Isabella winked at him. She knew a guy in Cape Town with the emotions of a shark. Had known him pretty well, once. Said, 'Give me a moment,' sliding a laptop onto Francisco's desk. Googled the name Mace Bishop, came up with Complete Security's website and email address among a list of Anglican pastoral missions. Sent him a mail with the words 'nostalgia and money' in the subject line. Below the message, she attached a photograph.

4

Paulo was hardly out of Global Enterprises than his phone rang: Vittoria. In Milan.

The reason she was in Milan was because back in the spring he'd said, 'Ria, suges, how's your fertility?'

'You want to have babies?'

He squeezed her hand. 'I've got a better proposition.'

She had fertility tests done. The results came back positive. He wanted a copy of the actual report.

'What for?' she'd asked.

'Opening discussions,' he'd replied.

'You're into selling your lover's body?' Half-joking, half-appalled. 'You're joking.'

'Is $200 large joking?'

'Sounds like it.'

'Nine, ten months work max. Not even work, really.' Paulo triumphant, gazing at her as if he was about to score a serious deal.

Vittoria laying it on the line: 'Let me understand this clearly. You're suggesting I have some guy's baby?'

'Short and sweet of it, yeah. For $200,000.'

'Don't you think we should've talked about this first?'

'The $200 thou?'

'You know what I mean.'

'We went through that.'

'Talking about my fertility is not talking about it.'

Paulo standing up from the couch, going over to the window. Her apartment, two floors up a Brooklyn brownstone, the street below empty this time of night: gone 12 a.m.

'Jesus, Vittoria, when's somebody laid this sort of money on you? Wasn't for me passing down some bills, you wouldn't have this!' A hand gesturing round the room, an expensive room, the sort of room she couldn't afford. By herself. 'I'm saying here's good money.'

'And your cut?'

He acted hurt. 'We're an item. I don't take a cut' – wheeling towards where she sat on the other couch, leaning down on her with his hands on her shoulders, their faces close. 'What d'you say?'

She pushed him away. He straightened, his eyes holding hers.

'I'm listening. Tell me the small print.'

Paulo sat down alongside her on the couch, laid an arm on the back, almost reaching her.

'Basically,' he'd said, 'an apartment in Milan for the duration. Monte Napoleone district. Classy stuff, I'm talking. High-end fittings. Use of an Alfa exclusively. House staff. Two flights home, business class.'

'For which I must?'

'Have his child.'

'How's the issue, Paulo?'

'Basically, artificial insemination.'

'He gets to screw me?'

Paulo shifting his eyes to the carpet.

'The guy's queer, Ria. He's not gonna want to screw you.'

'He might.'

'In the unlikely event, the contract limits it to days of ovulation only. Three days max at each event.'

'Event!'

'Sure.'

'Like a ball game?'

'You know what I mean.'

Vittoria reaching for the wine on the side-table behind the couch, filling her glass.

'He can screw me three days a month?'

'He's a homo.'

'How many times?'

'What d'you mean how many times?'

'How many times a day?'

'For Chrissakes. Once.'

'It's in the print?'

'Sure.'

'I'm not a whore.'

The two of them staring at one another.

'So who's this?'

'Camillo Medardo.'

'Medardo! The fashion Medardo? He's gotta be seventy!'

'Sixty-five. Looks sixty.'

'Big deal!'

'Listen, Ria, I've wrapped this for you. The guy's had two heart attacks. He goes before the contract ends you get the full payment.'

'And the kid?'

'The kid gets raised by his partner. Guy called Dieter.'

Vittoria thought about other issues, such as Camillo Medardo's sperm count.

'What happens if I don't fall pregnant?'

Paulo shrugged. 'Always a possibility. He gets six ovulations. If he doesn't score the deal's off, you're home with $60 000.'

'$60 000! That's all?'

'The best I can do. Chances are you'll go the deal first time out.'

'Bah!' Vittoria hit her wine. '$60 000. I can't believe it.'

'One other thing, you've got to marry him if he knocks you up. For the Italian laws. Also for the life insurance to kick in.'

'And afterwards?'

'Divorce proceedings start on termination of contract. No cost to you.'

This was back in the summer. Things had moved on since then, gone wide. The main reason Vittoria was phoning Paulo.

'Hi, Ria babe,' he said, pressing the down button for the elevator.

'I want you to kill this fuck,' she said, no niceties. Corrected herself: 'These fucks.'

'Hey, is it good to talk to your lover, or what?'

'Your contract's a load of shit,' she said next. 'They just wanted a whore.'

What happened the first time was that Camillo and Dieter actually drove her to the clinic. In his Saab. Champagne, chocolates, flowers in the private ward, made her stay there three days while they hoped the miracle of conception occurred. Or rather kept her on her back so that none of the stuff could dribble out. During this she decided Paulo's idea was not a bad deal, that she could even get to like these two queers fussing over her.

Then spot on comes her next period, everyone's disappointed. Dieter goes sulky for a few hours. Camillo bites his lip. Tries to comfort her. Hello, when it's his piss-poor ratings on the sperm count. Camillo saying, 'Maybe we've got to pamper you even more this time, baby. Get the doctor to come to you.'

Which is what he organises. She tells Camillo when the bleeding stops, a week later her apartment's flooded with bouquets. She stays in bed. Camillo chats to her about the royals he's dressed. Dieter looks in with tea. They're constantly on about her temperature. They're both in attendance when the doctor comes, either side of her, each holding a hand, peering at what the doctor's doing. She doesn't feel happy about this. Especially when it happens the next day and the next. But they're sweet. Flapping about her like nannies.

Again the blood comes. Dieter throws a heavy sulk. She overhears him talking to Camillo in German, understands enough to know he's questioning the fertility tests. Suggesting that Camillo's been taken for a ride. Camillo's less prone to jump to conclusions. He doesn't talk to her about this. Tells her of his disappointment, like it's her fault. Like she's doing something to prevent the pregnancy.

Next time he says to hell with modern science. They're going to do it like daddy and mommy. He keeps to the contract's stipulation of once a day, three days only. He's disgusting.

The month after, nothing's changed. Except they're taking her to Cape Town for the Christmas holidays. 'Cos they wanna go to some queer party.

To Paulo in distant New York she said, 'I'm not going to this place Cape Town to be a sex toy. I've gotta have time off, Paulo. I've gotta see you.'

'What's happening?' he responded, that tone of you're-being-a-prima-donna in his voice. 'Where's Cape Town?'

'Fucking Africa. Any place's more boring than Milan it's Africa.'

'Slowly, suges. Go again, slowly.'

'What's happening is your queer that doesn't touch women's found that maybe it's not such a bad ride.' A hiss that could be the transatlantic connection. 'Three times a day!'

'Hey, man! For an old guy like that!'

Vittoria considered whether she needed another line to keep talking rationally to her lover.

'You're not hearing me,' she said. 'We're talking bisexual. AC DC. That wants a sex toy on holiday.'

'This happens,' said Paulo, serious now. 'What can I say? That's the deal.'

'The deal's not Ria-the-Hooker. I'm gonna kill him. Him and the boyfriend. They're perverts.'

Silence. A long silence. Vittoria let it drag, the longer it went, the more Paulo would know she was serious. She spilled more coke on the dressing table.

'Hang in there, suges,' he said. 'This'll work out.'

'I wanna see you,' she said. 'I'm dying here. I'm bored, Paulo. Bored, bored, bored.'

Another silence, which she broke. 'It's heavy. I'm not gonna last this. You don't come here 'n see me, something's gonna snap.'

Paulo said, 'Think of the bucks.'

'The bucks aren't enough, Paulo.'

'Okay, baby, okay. It's almost over.'

'Big deal. Know what?'

'What?'

'There's not going to be a kid. Medardo had sago for jism there'd be more chance. I'm gonna kill them. Dirty queens.'

'Stay cool.'

'And that Isabella. Get you outta her clutches, the way she's dangling you. Power-tripping. I'm gonna kill her too.' The thought of all the dead bodies suddenly very appealing.

5

Mace, sitting in his office on a warm November afternoon, stared at the photograph filling his screen and thought, now what? Simultaneously had to smile at the image.

The photograph showed him and Isabella buttoned in long coats, huddled into one another, standing among rags of snow. Behind them a canal, on the canal a gunboat, a man in the boat watching them through binoculars. The only colour in the photograph that wasn't grey was the black of their coats and her red boots, bright against the snow. They were both laughing.

West Berlin, January 1989, Mace recalled. After he'd returned from meeting a bunch of comrades who needed AKs and ammunition ten thousand kilometres away otherside the Limpopo River in five days' time. AKs and ammunition that Mace hadn't sourced yet. No problem, he'd said to the comrades. Walked back through Checkpoint Charlie and said to Isabella after he'd made five phone calls from the payphone in Café Adler, 'How am I going to do this? Pylon's up the Congo, everyone's out of stock. I'm on a limb over a shit pond.'

'Maybe I can oblige,' she'd said. 'Once again.'

Her chance to work the phone although it only took one call and she returned to their table in the window to say, 'You've got it.'

'What?' he said.

'Basically, whatever you want. At Francistown. How you get it over the river's your issue.'

'Bullets too.'

'Everything.'

'I won't ask,' he said.

'I wouldn't,' she said. 'Just think of the money.'

Which was why they were laughing in the photograph. Well, not the only reason Mace remembered. The other reason was the Kempinski, more particularly their suite, as Isabella indulged her flamboyance for fine hotels.

'Next time in the Meurice,' she'd said.

The Kempinski suite stacked with antique furniture, a mammoth bed, in the bathroom a double marble bath and gold taps, a shower with adjustable head. You could set it for a massage, the water pulsing out in needle jets.

She'd booked in a few hours ahead of him. Was sitting on the bed in a towelling robe painting her toenails green when he arrived, cold, dog-tired after a four-plane trip from Mogadishu. She'd looked up, the gown loosely tied and gaping, his eyes plunging from her face to her breasts half-revealed. Isabella standing and walking towards him, long-limbed, the gown framing her, the girdle looped across the curve of her stomach.

As Mace remembered, it'd been a lost two days before he met the comrades.

'Perhaps we should try the shower first,' she'd said. 'It's got this effect you have to feel.'

He had an image of her that the photograph brought back: her hands white against the black marble tiles of the shower, her hair wet in the nape of her neck, soap froth on the curve of her back, her breasts almost liquid in his hands.

'Bloody hell,' he thought, snapping to the photograph, 'what're you thinking?'

It was why they were laughing. Going back to the Kempinski for another of those showers before they flew out separately the next morning. The penultimate time they had an expensive fling like that. Couple of months later he'd waltzed into Malitia and seen the irresistible Oumou.

Hi Mace, Isabella's email read, neat website. I heard that security had become a big thing for you guys. But Complete Security? Who're you trying to kid? Anyhow this is not about that, this is about something you're good at. It'll fatten up your bank balance, too. And how's this photie for old time's sake? When next are you in New York so we can talk? There's been a lot of water. Isabella.

Dangerous, Mace thought. Dangerous Isabella. When next you're in New York... He'd be in New York in a week to baby-sit a banker flying out for a holiday at the Fairest Cape.

When he'd told her at the Meurice that they were off, that he'd committed to Oumou, she'd put a Makarov to his head and asked if there was one good reason she shouldn't pull the trigger. Very melodramatic. Very Isabella. Then she'd laughed and set down the pistol. Stripped off her shirt and capris, said, 'You're a bastard, Mace Bishop. Two days you spend screwing me to come out with this?' For the last time they'd had sex. Nothing loving in it: rough and dry and quick. Afterwards Isabella said, 'Don't think we're finished, Mace. It doesn't work like that.'

Yet in all this time, ten years, there'd not been a word out of her. For which he was thankful. So now what?

6

Across the Company Gardens from the offices of Complete Security, Sheemina February in the firm's offices got Isabella's email to Mace Bishop and his response to Isabella bundled in a message from her contact at the service provider not long after Mace sent it.

Sheemina February double clicked the attachment to bring up the photograph of happy Mace and Isabella clasped together beside the canal. How quaint, an old flame suddenly rekindled. Had to be Berlin, she reckoned. The Spree, judging by the gunboat and the wall and the dark buildings behind it. Such a beautiful couple. Could be on their honeymoon, tourists getting off on Cold War glamour. The sort of photograph Sheemina February doubted Mace Bishop had ever shown his lovely wife.

She saved it in a folder named 'Membesh' after the guerrilla camp where she'd served.

7

The call to Paulo came from Francisco himself. Made Paulo feel, wow, this was a thing. Not usual for Francisco to put through his own calls.

'Here's the situation, Paulo,' said Francisco, 'we need someone we can trust.'

Paulo heard him out, thought, incredible, a place you've never heard of scores twice in so many days. Cape Town in Africa. Thought Ria, suges, you're not gonna believe this. Dialled her on the turn.

Vittoria was sitting in the Café Cova, wondering if white powder was big in Cape Town when her cell gave the Star Wars ringtone, her personal signature for Paulo. She picked up the phone lying next to the cooling espresso, clicked on.

'Baby,' he said. 'Like how's this? I'm gonna be doing a little business in Cape Town. Right about when you're there.'

That brought a reaction from Vittoria. She licked a finger, dipped it into a sachet of powder open in her bag, sucked the candy, feeling a whole lot better even before it got to work. She had a large swallow of the espresso too. Said, 'Tell me everything' – took the rest of the espresso in a second gulp while Paulo outlined Francisco's scheme.

'She going to be there?' Vittoria wanted to know when he'd finished.

'Isabella? Most likely. Also Francisco's hitman, Ludo.'

'Francisco up on my movements?' Vittoria said.

'No ways,' Paulo came back, 'this is just a coincidence.'

'Gives us a great opportunity,' said Vittoria. 'Also, I've been thinking, I'm not going through another session. You get the kill fee before that happens.'

A pause. Paulo catching up; Vittoria waiting.

'What're you on about?'

'The money. Like the contract says. Before my next egg comes on stream.'

'Ria!'

'I'll call you when we get there,' said Vittoria. 'Give you the address. They're gonna want to start trying for baby about a few days after we get in. If my body's running to schedule.'

She thumbed off, headed for the toilet. In the cubicle she ran a short line on her compact, drew it up through a fuzzy thousand-lire note. Half the powder got stuck on the fuzz. The sooner they went to euro the better, Italy needed some clean new notes. Nonetheless the hit was enough. Made her feel a whole lot better.

8

Pylon, at the wheel of the big Merc on De Waal Drive, said, 'The reason I don't have a fancy car, is because of the crap it gets you into. Maintenance plans. Garage bills.'

'No car at all, you mean,' said Mace.

'Alright, no car at all. You want to go that route we could buy another company car, you could sell the Spider. That'd cover your house repayment.'

'Sell the Spider?'

'Why not? It's an old car, Mace. Old-fashioned. I don't get this thing with cars. Cars're cars.'

Mace stared down into the Bowl, afternoon haze distancing the city. 'Since I first saw that car,' he said, 'I wanted one. I was what?

Fourteen. Something like that. A neighbour in the flats got this bluey-green number with a white hood, a white stripe down the side. I was standing there, in the parking area looking at it and he came down and asked if I wanted a ride. What's his name?' Mace clicked his fingers. 'Sampson, Randal Sampson. Chelsea boots and tight trousers. Had chicks in and out of his flat like he ran a fashion house. Randy by name and nature I guess. I said sure. We hop in, spin to Llandudno, Hout Bay, over Chappies to Noordhoek. Noordhoek under the oaks he pulls out a zol and we tote this. My first Spider, my first grass. Heaven. The sweet smell, the sweet sound of the engine. That explain it?'

'Save me Jesus,' said Pylon, taking the inside lane past the hospital with the traffic picking up. 'That's bullshit. Sentimental pap.'

Mace grinned. 'I drive a Duetto. You horde money. Same thing really.'

'Invest. To invest isn't to horde. What we've got in the Cayman's a horde, in case you'd forgotten. But in our land of milk and honey I invest. Which is why I can get you out of the shit you're in. And keep us squeaky clean.'

'One month,' said Mace. 'That's all.'

The traffic slowed bumper to bumper.

'One month is five thousand bucks, if I heard you correctly.' Pylon glanced at his watch. 'What time's your flight?'

'Seven. It's okay. No rush.' Mace coughed. 'The other way is I take it out of the business. Increase the bond on the Dunkley Square building.'

'We don't need that,' said Pylon.

'Write it off against tax.'

'I don't think so. I think the best is I lend it to you. Trouble is what happens after that?'

'I've got three months,' said Mace. 'I told you. We make this payment and the bank extends. January, February there's extra income from Oumou's exhibition. We're out of the brown stuff.'

Pylon took a gap to the right, accelerating into the taxi lane. 'Face it,' he said. 'The house's the problem. Too larney. Door handles like you've got, Italian door handles. Who needs Italian door handles to open a door? Travertine marble. What's that about? Fancy French hob. And gas. What's wrong with electricity? People in the township cook on gas.'

'Our investment,' said Mace. 'Dave Cruikshank's philosophy: buy high. Five years down the track you're smiling.'

'If you can make it five years down the track.'

'Also it's for Christa, remember.'

'Right. Lifts for Christa. This's the point, Mace. Somewhere on the flat would've been better for Christa.'

'Comes back to an investment. The mountain's where it's at. So Dave says.'

'Dave says. Right. Second-hand car dealer. Estate agent. Dave says.'

'One month,' said Mace. 'It's all I'm asking for. No big deal. The way the business is going it's back in your pocket by the end of the year. Interest included.

'Eight per cent's the deal.'

'Loan shark.'

'Hey. You want it or you don't want it?'

Mace leant back against the headrest, turned to Pylon. 'Thanks, hey. Much appreciated. I can fly away relaxed.' He blew out a sigh of relief.

'To New York? Nobody can fly into New York with relief.' Pylon switched lanes back to the left for the airport turn-off. 'See this bridge?' he said pointing at a pedestrian footbridge arching over the highway. 'This's the one you have to watch out for.'

'I thought so,' said Mace. 'The woman died, you know, I heard it earlier on the news.'

'A bloody block of concrete, they dropped. You get a block of concrete through the windscreen at one twenty, you're lucky to live long enough to get to hospital. Even a brick's bad news. Every time I drive under here I check for pedestrians. Someone who looks like they're into a bit of gratuitous. Because most times it happens, it's from this bridge. Why they don't close it, build a subway I don't know.'

'Then people'll be mugged. Women raped.'

'This's the problem.'

At the junction to the airport, Pylon slowed, edging into the traffic flow.

'I've been meaning to tell you,' said Mace. 'I had a mail from Isabella.'

'Just like that?' Pylon frowned.

'Just like that. No kidding.'

'When?'

'About a week ago.'

'A week ago, and you keep it quiet!'

'It's business. The possibility of business.'

'Which is why you should've mentioned it earlier.'

'Not really. It was something I had to think about first. The implications.'

'And having thought about the implications you're going to meet her?'

'I am. For lunch.'

'For a friendly chat?'

'About something she thinks we could handle.'

'Yeah,' said Pylon, giving a hooter blast to get a tourist operator out of the drop zone at international departures. 'I bet.'

9

Mace took a cab to the restaurant. Told the cabby Cesca's, 164 West 75th Street.

The table was reserved in the name of Isabella Medicis, a table at the window so he could watch her get out of the cab: the black calf-length boots emerging first, her skirt ridden up slightly to show knee and thigh in black tights as she moved through that awkward moment between sliding off the car seat and standing on the sidewalk. Once it was over, she was all grace. Wardrobe and make-up perfect. Choreography professional.

Mace appreciated it. Got just long enough to take this in before the action started and she headed for the door, long-legged, confident. The way he'd seen her move in jungle and desert.

Next she was beside the table, being helped off with her coat. Ten years had gone since they'd last seen each other. The thing about Isabella he realised was that you couldn't take your eyes off her. Maybe her beauty was even more startling with the extra years. He watched a smile sneak across her lips.

'Isn't this cosy for a reunion?'

Mace shrugged. 'Very nice.'

She picked up the wine list. 'Who's the client?'

'A banker.'

She gave him a raised eyebrow. 'You fly all the way over here to babysit a banker going on holiday.'

'Part of the service.'

'Who gives a shit what happens to a banker?'

'She does. Her husband and kiddies too.'

Isabella shook her head. 'The world's paranoid. You want merlot? Or pinot noir?'

'Merlot.'

She ordered pinot noir, giving him the wide smile that had worked him up in their arms-dealing jungle days.

Mace rolled with it.

'Do you remember,' she said, 'the first words I ever said to you?' – a glint in her eyes.

'I hope you want to have sex.'

She smiled. 'Quite a memory!'

'Hardly the sort of opener you're likely to forget.'

Isabella nodded. 'That was a hopeless situation. How you walked right into it, not a care in the world. I'm watching you switch off the Jeep, start down the path towards me, wondering when's he going to realise what's going down?'

Mace shrugged. 'You could've given me a clue.'

'What? Like I hope you want to have sex isn't a clue?'

'I thought you'd been in the bush too long.'

'Oh right. I was desperate for it.'

'I even said it. Made a joke about you being bush-happy. Then you got all tight-lipped, said something about being serious and I wasn't to run ...'

'Or do anything I was going to regret.'

'Words to that effect.'

Mace thinking back to this stunning woman: hair short, ragged and self-cut against the dripping heat. A face out of some Italian renaissance painting: hooded brown eyes, smooth skin, roman nose, small lovely mouth, delicate cheek bones. This woman standing in the doorway of the hut. Unsmiling.

'Then you got the general idea.'

'I did.'

The waiter brought the wine, showing the label to Isabella.

She smiled up at him. 'Let's have it.'

The waiter cut the seal, twisted an old-fashioned corkscrew into the cork and pulled it with a grimace. Splashed an eighth into Isabella's glass. She swirled it, tasted, nodded at the man to pour.

When he was done she raised her glass to Mace, toasted, 'To getting out alive.'

They clinked glasses and drank, Mace taking a little more than a sip.

'You approve?'

'It's not Merlot,' he said.

'And you've become a wine connoisseur?'

'Hardly.'

'It doesn't get any better than this.'

Mace shrugged. 'I'll take your word for it.' Took another decent mouthful. 'Where was that?' he said. 'Where were we? Uganda?'

'Zaire, Mace. Outskirts of Kinshasa. On the edge of a rainforest. The way I remember it there was a hut on a track through fields of banana palms. A bit further off, a small village near the tree edge but not so far away you couldn't hear voices now and then. Not sure when we'd made the arrangement or even how but I'd got the hardware for you: a stack of Czech assault rifles.'

'The first time I'd sourced from you.'

'The way it began I didn't think we had a future. Walking straight into kiddie-bandits like that.'

'Before I left the hotel, the dive we were staying at, I told Pylon, it's a simple pick-up, only one of us needed to go. Told him to stay in case you called. He said, how's that supposed to happen when the phone's down? So I joked maybe there'd be a messenger with a letter in a forked stick.'

'Pity about that. That he didn't come with you.'

'No harm done.'

'Very nearly though. Remember the little boy, the frisker, patting you down, trying to undo your belt buckle and hold that Aksu at the same time?'

Mace laughed. 'I thought about making a grab for it. But his finger was on the trigger. He touched that fifteen rounds were going to go off, or the whole clip, thirty. No telling who would've died.'

'You for one.'

'Probably.'

'The thing about it I thought was how spooky they were. Like aliens. With no ideas about living and dying. Just there doing this thing. Shooting guns they could hardly lift. Killing, being killed. The leader was so cool. Giving me instructions with serious intent.'

'About us getting naked!' Mace, mimicking her accent: 'They want us to screw. I have to tell you I have my period. Menstrual blood's bad juice to them. They get their willies blooded they're in line for serious malevolence from the spirits. They'd rather see this happen to you. Jesus! You sounded like anthropology 101. I couldn't believe what I was hearing.'

'You did as you were told.'

'Anything for a screw.'

'I'm sure.'

'I had an alternative? I didn't think so.'

'Nice striptease. I enjoyed it. Until you're standing there buck naked and the main kid says you look like a snail and he's bigger than you. I could've burst out laughing at that.'

'Thanks.'

'Thing is, he was. Whipping out that great schlong. Something you have to admit, looked like a stunted leg on a kid that short.'

'Awesome,' said Mace, and Isabella spluttered.

The main kid had stood there with his hands on his hips, his crotch thrust out. Letting them get a good look at him. Then he'd zipped again, and got Isabella to lose the bra. She dropped it at her feet. The main kid whisking it up with the barrel of his rifle, pressed it to his nose, his eyes fastened on her tits. He touched the buckle of her webbing belt with his gun. Isabella unclipped the belt, the main kid studying her every move. Her eyes were on him, too. Her play slow, deliberate: the releasing of a button, opening the zip, letting the shorts fall down her legs, stepping out of them. She'd got the main kid hooked, the others standing around open-mouthed.

The main kid snagged the elastic of her underpants with the barrel of his gun. Dragged them down.

Isabella took the pants off, turned them inside out, held them for the main kid to see there was blood in the crotch. That made them step back.

Mace took a mouthful of wine. 'When you took your knickers off, showed him the crotch, I couldn't tell what he was going to do. He just kept staring at them, absorbed. The others went back a pace, he didn't move. The last thing I expected was you'd throw them in his face.'

'Didn't you?'

'Hell no. He was hypnotised. Me too.'

'Broke the spell though. Got him going. Got them all going. Screaming. Running off faster than if they'd seen the evil spirits. Still can't believe it was that easy.'

'Me neither,' said Mace. 'I kept expecting them to open fire from the forest. Even when we drove out I expected it.'

'We were lucky.' Isabella looked at him. 'What I wonder though is would you've done it?'

Mace shrugged. 'Only to stay alive.'

'Thank you.'

'Pleasure. D'you remember what you said, back in Kinshasa when I dropped you at the Consulate?'

Isabella shook her head. 'Tell me.'

'Don't think you can take up the offer anytime you want.'

'You did though.'

Mace nodded, grinned.

For lunch they made their way through the pinot noir and most of a second bottle. Not a mention of the proposition. How it'd always been with Isabella. When she had something on her mind, it was the last thing she was going to talk about. Like flying out of N'Djamena on the morning of 16 February 1986 with Isabella talking about a short break in the Seychelles maybe to celebrate the deal and not talking about the French jets flying into N'Djamena to put down the rebel offensive. Rebels Mace had just the previous day tooled up with smart weaponry. Only in the hotel that night watching a clip on television it came to Mace that Isabella had known. And not said a thing. Not in the air. Not at any time.

Simply smiled when he said she could've told him. Her current proposition equally as mysterious. Until, when the bill was paid, when they were getting their coats she said, 'I want you to see my new apartment.'

Mace inclined his head in acceptance.

In the cab she held his hand. Simply took it in hers without looking at him, put it in her lap, stared out the window.

Mace wondered about this, wondered too about her husband, Paulo, a little creep that didn't gel with her profile. 'You still married?'

'Sure.' Said without looking at him. 'Like you and the gorgeous Oumou.'

He let the barb go. When it'd come to the choice, Oumou or Isabella, there'd never been a choice.

The taxi stopped in a busy street, Upper West Side somewhere. Outside spoke of celebrity; inside spoke of money, not lavish money, comfortable money: plenty of artworks hanging wherever there was space, stacks of CDs, a row of artbooks. A number on African art. Some novels on a side table next to the telephone, half covered by a map. The name of a city caught his eye: Luanda. Strange map for her to have open, he thought, but then also not strange, if she was still in that line of business.

'You like it?' she asked.

Too many rugs everywhere, Mace reckoned. Too many African artefacts, spears, masks, pots, carved figures. Small tables covered with brass ornaments, souvenirs. Candles all over, like she'd turn the room into a grotto at night. A clutter that spoke of Isabella. Nothing here of her husband.

'Nostalgic,' he said.

'Open this,' she said, handing him a bottle of Maipo Valley cabernet, 'I've got to take a pee.'

Mace sat down on a three-seater settee while he uncorked the wine. He poured, tasted.

'You approve?'

'It's good,' he said. 'Come on, what do I know?'

'Not as heavy as a Meerlust.'

Mace shrugged. 'Wine is wine.'

They touched glasses. She sat along from him at the other end of the couch, swung her legs up, stretched until her feet pushed at his thigh. She moved her foot against him: she could be scratching an itch on the sole of her foot, she could be caressing. She'd had a thing about her toes, loved to have them massaged, he remembered. Remembered sitting out a fire-fight with her in a ruined church. The odd round thudding into the walls. Frelimo, Renamo off in the bush shooting the shit out of one another: he and Isabella on the edge of it waiting to make a break. A time he massaged her toes, and more. For two days until the shooting stopped. A craziness they'd both mainlined.

Mace took some more wine, relaxed into the cushions, ignored the pushing of her toes. The cab tasted of sun, began to lay lazily at the back of his head. They didn't say anything, made no eye contact through this, kept sipping wine, lost in the silence: one of Isabella's strategies of getting to the point.

'How's your daughter doing?' she said.

Mace laughed. 'What d'you mean?'

'She's how old now? Ten?'

'Nine going ten.' Mace wondered if he should tell her more. Decided not to.

'The family man.'

'Uh huh.' He sat up at the sarcasm in her voice.

'Relax. I got over us a long time ago.' She laughed, her ice-cold laugh that didn't show in her eyes. Their eyes met. 'Now I like the thought of Mace the former arms-dealer. Husband. Father. Muscle to the rich and famous. Jesus Christ!'

'Protection consultant.'

'What?' She kicked at his thigh. 'A goon, Macey-boy. A bloody jumped-up goon, that's what you are.'

Mace shrugged. 'You need some protection?'

'A trader,' she said, 'is what I need. Someone who knows.' She made a gesture for more wine and Mace passed the bottle. Before she filled her glass, she said, 'Real life, Mace. Not the pretend stuff.' She poured, held out the bottle to him.

He took the rest, thinking the thing about a bottle of wine was it only held four glasses.

'I need to buy a shipment.'

When Mace didn't respond she said, 'In your part of the world.'

'Luanda's not my part of the world.'

She pointed her glass at him. 'Always the observant one.'

'Go on.'

'I've got this buyer, I've got the money in your currency. All I need's the hardware.'

'Which is?'

'Full bag. Handguns, rifles, RPGs, grenades, mines, radios, boots, cam suits, medic kits.'

'Sounds like stock for USAID.'

'Very funny. So yes? So no?' She nudged her foot against his thigh. 'I need a tough guy. So yes? So no?'

Mace considered, useful to get the bank off his back, grimaced a maybe yes, maybe no. She swung her legs off the couch. 'There's someone you'll need to meet.'

'Now?'

'Now's a good time.'

The lift stopped at the seventh floor. Across a marble foyer were glass doors: Global Enterprises. This arching over an ellipse of the world, all the continents side by side. Isabella punched a code into the security lock, pushed the door open. She led him through reception to where he could hear a man talking, saying, 'You do the arithmetic, you'd want to know how many virgins there are in heaven? Those virgins having to get from here to there first. Then you'd want to know why're they virgins? Must be some sorry looking women nobody wanted to screw them in the first place.'

They entered the room. Francisco peering into a telescope, talking on his cellphone. He said to Isabella, 'You're late. I was about to call.'

Isabella ignored him, said, 'Meet my one-time lover Mace Bishop.'

Francisco said into his phone, 'I'll call you.' Disconnected. Said to Mace, 'You been to Ground Zero?' Took him by the arm. 'Come here. Get a look at Ground Zero.'

Mace put an eye to the telescope. There was not much to see of Ground Zero. Nothing moving down there at all. While he was looking Francisco explained about things that weren't noticed until they were missed. Mace pretended he was with him on this theory.

When they were seated round his desk, Francisco said, 'You hear about the suicide bomber this morning? Took out some Jews on a bus. You think these guys really reckon they're gonna get laid by seventy-eight virgins?'

'Sure,' said Isabella.

'I wanna know what Mace thinks,' Francisco said.

Mace told him probably.

'You think that's the motivation?'

'Probably.'

He glanced at Mace to see if he was taking the piss, then cut to the business at hand, said, 'Mace, you think you can pull this one off for us?'

'Probably,' said Mace. Francisco chuckled, leant on the table to let Mace know the jokes were over.

'What we've got here, Mace,' he said, 'is a delicate situation featuring a bunch of guns Isabella's wanting to acquire. Where from's where you come in. Given the logistics we're tying up the nearest market, a dive by name of Luranda.'

'Luanda,' said Isabella.

Francisco raised his eyebrows. 'Mace comes from Africa. He knows where it's positioned.' He focused on Mace again. 'What we're needing is the merchandise, someone to go there, oversee the transaction. Make things easier for you this is a no-money deal. Guys in Luranda print dollars to wipe their asses. So we told them no paper. Stones only. There's a fellow lives there, John Webster, knows about stones. Diamond John's what the Russians call him. Major merchant figure. Used to work for Debretts.'

'De Beers,' said Isabella.

'Whatever,' said Francisco. 'The payment comes in, before you release, Diamond John checks we're not being shoved a parcel of piss crystals.'

He sat back in his chair. There was a picture behind him, idyllic Italian scene, couple walking down a path about to step into his hair.

'You reckon this is a peach?'

'Probably,' Mace said.

Outside on the sidewalk Isabella said, 'You've got maybe a month, six weeks. Get back to me soonest.'

They took separate taxis. In the cab, Mace thought the thing about Isabella was their history, the lunacy of it: the jive. There'd always been that with her, a spark. On his phone he saw he had two SMSs.

The first from Christa. 'Msng u.' Made him smile, the thought of her asleep now. Probably in their bed, despite Oumou's rules. The second from Oumou. 'How you doing?'

He tapped a message back: 'Good. Off now to call on four million bucks. All love.'

To Christa: 'Hi dollface. Got you on my mind. Love Papa and Cupcake.'

Mace sat back looking at the bright streets, the dense traffic, thinking Isabella still tweaked a vibe in him, wondered how Pylon would enjoy some déjà vu.

10

Pylon didn't enjoy the prospect Mace laid out not forty-eight hours later.

'No,' he said, shaking his head. 'No, we're not into that. We're finished with those days. You told me that's what you promised Oumou. No more trading. '

'I did.'

'So what's this?'

'I need the bucks.'

'Oh save me Jesus. You want another loan?'

'No. No. I appreciate that. What you did. Like I said, that saved us. Thing is I need serious bucks. Or we'll lose the house. It's this or Cayman.'

The way they saw Cayman was keep the money hidden until Complete Security was flourishing. Sell the business, wash the stash gradually into their lifestyles so no one would know the difference. Certainly not the taxman. Be quietly rich and contented. That was the game plan.

'No.' Pylon shot out of the chair other side of Mace's desk and headed for the door. Spun round before he got there. 'No to both things. No to Cayman, no to gun deals. This's Isabella we're talking about here. Not only guns but Isabella. Miss CIA. Fun once. A good contact once. But as I seem to recall we shut that door. For the sake of family life.' He came up to Mace's desk, placed both hands on the surface, leant forward. 'We can be bad guys, I acknowledge. Except next to them we're angels. Where we're going to hesitate, they're going to kill.' He stopped to let the point sink in. 'Also, Oumou finds out you are going to be in such deep crap, losing the house will seem like fun.'

Mace said, 'This is not about Isabella.'

Pylon said nothing.

'She contacted me, out of the blue. I told you.'

'I believe it' – sounding like he didn't.

'Told me the deal, I said I'd have to discuss it.'

'Meaning I'm sold, I just got to sell it to Pylon.'

'Meaning I have to do it.'

'At the risk of your marriage?'

'I have to.'

'There's someone forcing you?'

'Yes.'

Pylon snorted. 'Sure, I know, the bank manager. Some suit.'

'Some sister with a US degree to be specific.'

Pylon said, 'No shit. It gets worse. Listen.' He sat down again. 'Listen, to me, okay. We've been out of that for what ten, eleven years? That's a different environment out there now. Big-league players. No room for the little man. Especially the little man doing a trade on the side for pocket money.'

'It isn't pocket money. It's the end of my bond. Financial relief. For you, financial gain. More investments. A holiday home up the coast. Whatever you want.'

Pylon covered his face with his hands, slowly drew them down until his eyes were showing. 'Oh yeah. Very nice. I admit it. Major problem: what do I tell Treasure?'

'About what?'

'About these new investments. The holiday home.'

'Jesus, Pylon. You make up a story. Any story. That's what investments do, they grow. You got dividends. I don't know. A company you got shares in paid out a bonus. Any story'll probably convince her. What the hell difference does it make what you tell her?'

'To Treasure it makes a difference. Treasure understands money. She wants to see the paperwork. What's it you'll tell Oumou?'

Mace rocked his chair back. 'No idea. The deal's not sorted. We haven't got the money. I'm not planning to worry about that until I have to.'

'You see, there's the difference between you and me. You don't think further than here.' Pylon held his hand up against his nose. 'Balls out for glory Mace. Another thing: we're not talking money. We're talking stones. Stones're as far from ready cash as it gets.'

'Diamonds aren't a problem,' said Mace. 'In this country never have been, never will be.'

'Oh we'll waltz into De Beers, throw a bag on the table, say, how much for these?'

'They've got people to handle this sort of stuff.'

'Of course. And you know someone who knows someone.'

'I don't know anyone.'

'No, I forgot. This's not a problem until it's a problem. Like it's not a problem that we don't even know where to get guns anymore.'

'I don't think that's a problem,' said Mace, coming forward on his chair. 'I think we probably know someone who could help us.'

'Enlighten me.'

'Mo Siq.'

'Mo Siq?'

'Mo Siq.'

Pylon stared at him. 'Are you out of your tiny mind?'

'Phone. See what he has to say. Offer him lunch, La Colombe, Uitsig, either one.'

'I thought you were off the comrades. Disillusioned by their ... What'd you call it?' Pylon snapping his fingers. 'Their politics of greed.'

'I am.'

'So this?'

'Business. Money. Why we became traders in the first place. Remember?'

'It wasn't for the struggle? I forgot.'

'The struggle for bucks.' Mace pointing at Pylon's cellphone. 'You going to phone him?'

Pylon made a call to Mo Siq's office, got as far as his PA. The PA wouldn't patch him through, the director was in a meeting, left him on hold for two, three minutes then came back that there'd been a cancellation, the director had a window in two days' time. La Colombe or Uitsig? Pylon asked. The PA said, one minute, came back inside two, said, Uitsig was the director's preference.

Pylon hung up. 'I don't even think I'm going to enjoy the lunch,' he said.

11

For starters Mace had mussels in a vinaigrette. Pylon the asparagus with a sesame dressing. Mo Siq a basket of three langoustines on a bed of couscous. Pylon chose the wine: the estate's 2000 Semillon Reserve.

From their table they looked across the vineyards towards the mountain. The afternoon sun laying a heat shimmer over the trellises.

'A good choice, Uitsig,' said Mo, rolling the wine round his mouth. He put the glass down, peeled the shell off a prawn. 'How's your girl, Mace?'

Mace swallowed a mussel, the taste of the sea strong in his mouth. 'Doing okay. She's swimming is the main thing. Getting the exercise. We're starting to notice improvements.'

'She's what now? Ten, eleven?'

'Nine.'

'Yeah, well.' Mo glanced from Mace to Pylon, his face blank. 'Not a good scene what was going on then.'

Mace chased the sea with a mouthful of wine. 'She bought my house, you know, the one where it happened.'

'Sheemina? I didn't. That a fact?'

'Ten months it'd been on the market she comes up with this offer that's short of what I want but also I need to sell. Had to sell.'

'One hard woman.'

'Cash.' Mace soaked up vinaigrette with a piece of ciabatta. 'I find out she's got a place in Clifton, on millionaire's mile. A share in a wine estate. Industrial property. The sort of portfolio that'd make brokers drool.'

'You sold to her though.'

'I didn't want to. The woman's got something about her that's disturbing. I would use the word evil.'

'So would I.' Mo forked up couscous.

'She offered a bit more. The way she did it, it came across like she was doing us a favour.'

With his serviette Mo wiped beads of couscous from the corner of his mouth. 'That clinched the deal?'

'Against my instincts.'

'What you have to ask,' said Mo, 'is why she did it? With Sheemina there's always some other reason. Something behind the obvious that it's a good place to buy at a good price. Something else.'

'I asked that question,' said Mace. 'I ask it still. Damn freaky situation.'

For the main course Mace had grilled tuna steak; Pylon ostrich medallions; Mo the lobster. Pylon ordered a Steenberg Catharina.

Said to Mo, 'You rather have a white with that?'

Mo said, 'I'm good for the red.'

While they ate Mo talked mostly, recounting this story of marlin fishing off the Seychelles with a director of Deutsche Aerospace. How two hours into one morning and twenty nautical into the sea the Kraut says, no, let's give this a miss, hop the Lear jet and have dinner at a restaurant he knows in Alexandria. Ten hours later it's nine-thirty local time, they're being shown to a table, there's a bottle of champagne waiting in ice. Mo laughed. Went a long way to persuading him that Deutsche Aerospace were serious people. Mace and Pylon chuckled with him. People at the nearby table looking over with smiles on their faces.

German tourists, Mace reckoned, maybe they'd caught the reference.

The three men skipped on the desserts, went straight to double espressos and cognacs.

'If you like we can serve them on the stoep,' said the waitress. 'There're comfortable chairs there.'

Pylon brought out three cigars. 'Can we smoke?'

'Sure.' The waitress smiled. 'No problem.'

The only other people on the stoep were two Chinese business-men and a family group of five, loud after their wine and meal. It suited Mace. Nothing they said would be overheard. He and Mo settled into cane easy-chairs, Pylon pulled up a wingback.

Mo held the cigar to his nose. Sniffed along its length. A Montecristo No 1. 'As good as anything the Krauts ever offered,' he said.

So, he believed, was the KWV brandy.

Mace and Pylon waited for him to make a move. Mo was in no hurry, talking about a short deal with a company called Industriepark Spreewald Lubben that netted twelve million on surplus ammo the cabinet steering committee had stamped for destruction.

'What they're then doing, the Krauts,' he explained, 'is selling it on to the States. Guys there can't get enough of our surplus for practicing and hunting. Mostly 5.56mm and 7.62mm. We got maybe a billion rounds supposed to be destroyed or dismantled. Which is a waste when you consider there're people willing to pay for it.' He drew on the Montecristo, blew the smoke out in a plume.

Pylon said, 'Makes you wonder what the boers were thinking, producing all those rounds. Like they were heading for a major war.'

'Silly buggers,' said Mo. 'On the other hand what we've got here is what we call unofficially The Opportunity. Not something the minister wants to hear about, but then not something he's inclined to stop either supposing he has heard about it. Which he must've. Income is income.' He flicked off a stub of ash, glanced from Pylon to Mace. 'Welcome to The Opportunity. We're happy to do business with you.'

'Again,' Mace said.

Mo chuckled. 'I suppose you could say again, in a manner of speaking. I suppose should you look at it in a certain light the cause is the same: the upliftment of the people. Fair trade. Guns 'n ammo for houses.' He pulled out the shopping list Pylon had hand-delivered earlier in the week. 'I can get these,' he said, tapping it with the damp end of his cigar, 'any time you want, as the man said.'

Mace took the last of his espresso. 'In about four, five weeks?'

Mo nodded. 'What's the deal we're talking?'

'A deposit upfront in rands. The balance on delivery. Here you've got a choice: diamonds or dollars.'

Mo grinned. 'Interesting.'

'Excepting we're not talking about delivery from you to us,' put in Pylon.

'No? There's another sort of delivery?'

'Us to them.'

Mo raised his eyebrows.

'We need a bit of slack here,' said Mace.

'No more than a few days,' said Pylon. 'Cape Town to Luanda's what? Two, two 'n a bit days' sailing. That's the sort of slack Mace's suggesting.'

To Mace, Mo didn't look happy. There was a tightening at his eyes, a thinning of his lips as if the espresso was too bitter. Mo chased it with cognac.

'You're the agents?'

'We are. Much as Pylon fears flying.'

Pylon grimaced and shrugged.

'You understand what I'm doing here?' Mo shifted his gaze between them. 'You understand I've gotta get this stuff selected from a warehouse at the depot, loaded into a truck or probably two given the quantities we're looking at, then these trucks signed onto the road for an eight hundred kilometre journey, that's twelve hours on the highway when anything can happen from a Christ-knows-how accident to maybe having to get through bloody cops doing roadblocks in the hopes they'll pick up some poor bastard shifting bales of dagga, to an inside-job hijack. You understand that's a long time in the smoke.'

'But you're government,' said Pylon.

'Quasi,' said Mo. 'Those armaments do not exist. The paper-work they're written against's going through a shredder when the trucks return to base. This is about The Opportunity. Any-one mentions The Opportunity to me, I'm going to look blankly at them. Which is why when you tell me that even on delivery to the docks I must wait five more days for a ship that probably should be scrap iron to wallow three thousand nautical miles up a coast of wild seas, I'm not happy.' He put down his snif-ter, eyed Pylon then Mace. 'Even knowing you're the receiving agents.'

'There's the deposit,' Mace said.

'It's not that,' said Mo. 'It's my experience that the crucial time is between despatch and receipt of payment. Best scenario's when the two are one and the same. Spread those two moments and you're looking at things going wrong. "Exposure" is the term a risk assessor would use.'

'Acknowledged,' said Mace. 'The two of us more so than you. Exposed that is.'

'It's how it is on this one,' said Pylon. 'Which is not to say it's how we want it.'

The men went quiet: Mo focusing on a group inspecting early season berries three or four rows back into the vineyard; Pylon contemplating the end of his cigar; Mace swirling his cognac, putting odds on Mo that he wouldn't pull out, there being too sweet a slice in the deal for his own account. He noticed the Chinese had gone, replaced by a man and a woman holding hands.

Mo said, 'Who's the party?'

Mace considered, should he, shouldn't he reveal the backers? Decided what the hell. 'New York concern. Not big players.'

Mo squinted at him. 'You've worked with them before?'

'All through the war.'

'I've met them at all?'

Mace caught Pylon's eye, a curiosity there about what he'd say. He said, 'Yeah, actually. You met in Dar es Salaam. Probably late 1986. Woman called Isabella Medicis.'

Mo shook his head. 'Means nothing.'

'Might've once been CIA,' Pylon chipped in.

'No longer,' said Mace quickly to ease the concern on Mo's face.

'Once, always,' said Mo. 'What's this about?'

'Keeping it simple,' said Mace. 'And spreading the assets. No money, no paper trail. Nothing for Revenue Services to get bitter and twisted about.'

Mo took his time with this. In fact all the time it took the happy family to usher themselves off the stoep. Into the quiet he said softly, 'Okay. I'm doing this because it's you guys. No other reason. Anybody else I'd say you were working the ends.'

'We are,' said Pylon. 'But then so's everybody else on this deal.'

'Doesn't make me rest easier.'

The waitress appeared with a bottle of cognac. 'Another, sir?' she said to Pylon. He got the nod from Mo and Mace.

'Seems like it.'

She smiled and poured them healthy shots. 'More coffee?'

'Just the bill,' said Pylon.

When she'd moved off to serve the loving couple, the three men raised their glasses in a toast.

185

Mo said, 'To The Opportunity.'

Pylon said, 'And old times.'

Mace said, 'I'll go with both of those.'

He phoned Isabella from the vineyard. Mo had left in his M5, Pylon following in their Merc, headed for an afternoon off with his family. Summer was hectic, you took the free hours whenever you could get them. Mace planned to do the same. Spend some time with Christa in the swimming pool floating over the buildings below, let Oumou get on with making stock for her pottery exhibition in the new year.

Isabella answered on the fourth ring. 'I was wondering when I'd hear from you.'

'Now's your lucky day,' said Mace. He leant against the Spider, parked in the shade of an oak tree, imagining Isabella among her masks and wooden figures. After Christmas he'd be back there, they could do a celebratory dinner.

'And so?'

'We're on,' said Mace. 'The full bag.'

Isabella laughed. 'The same old Mace. Still able to pull the moves.'

Mace grinned at the compliment, watched the hand-holding couple walk across to their car. She half-waved, he nodded. 'Payment caused a moment's concern.'

'But you smoothed it over.'

'Of course.' Mace could hear a kettle coming to the boil, the ring of cup against saucer. Isabella and Oumou, the only two women in the world wouldn't drink from mugs. 'He remembered you. And the connection.'

'I doubt that. On both counts. But thanks for the flattery.' The kettle whistled and came off the boil. 'I'll sort the logistics, no reason for you to chase around.'

'It would be,' said Mace, 'a chase around.' He opened the car door, settled into the driver's seat. 'I'll be in touch.'

'Can't wait,' she said, and Mace caught the laughter in her voice as she disconnected. The laughter that riled him. Roused him too.

12

Francisco looked at Ludo. The eyeballing returned, Ludo glancing away first, being the employee.

'Paulo, he's family,' said Francisco, pulling his right earlobe, not deflecting his gaze. 'Also a prick. Of this I've been made aware. Over the years.'

Ludo kept his opinions to himself. Lit a cigarette.

'Isabella treats him like shit. Lines him up for this opportunity. I'm missing something you think?'

Ludo sucked smoke.

Francisco stood up, walked round the desk to the telescope.

'Where he's good is clubs. Sure. He can work clubs. Ten K a night I've heard he can do. That's like two hundred sale points. That's working. Doesn't stop the punk being a prick.'

Francisco put his eye to the telescope, watched a truck coming out of Ground Zero.

'We're going to go down on this one?' said Ludo, exhaling smoke.

'I don't think so.' Francisco moved the scope to follow the truck. 'It would seem Isabella's one-time screw has come to the party. Fella called Mace Bishop. The sort of name you've gotta wonder about. Still, he's done the wonders on the one side. Question is, can he do the wonders on the front-line? Isabella's not stressing.'

'Isabella says so,' said Ludo, 'she knows the score.'

Francisco grinned, came round behind Ludo, put his hands on his shoulders, squeezed. Ludo was hard as wood.

'You got a number for her?'

Ludo's shoulders rose and fell in a shrug beneath his hands.

'It's alright, I understand. She wasn't my sister I'd have a number for her too.' He went back to his chair. 'You think Paulo can actually move that shit?'

'Sure, your Rough Guide says lotsa clubs. It's big holiday time. No reason why not.'

'You keep an eye on him. Any way to scam it, he will. I'll send you a present.'

'Sure,' said Ludo, crushing the butt in Francisco's clean ashtray.

Francisco rang the receptionist to have the dirty ashtray removed. While the receptionist was doing this, took a file from his desk, shifted it across to Ludo. Ludo yet again amazed Francisco let people smoke if he hated cigarette butts that much.

'That's the paperwork,' said Francisco. 'You go to the port, find Customs. Find a Vusi something. Give him ten thousand local, one per kilo is how they work it, he'll give you the merchandise. All you need's in the paperwork.' He tapped the file.

Ludo took it, stood up.

'Have a good flight,' said Francisco.

'Yeah,' said Ludo, thinking New York to London, five hours. Change in London wait two hours. Flight to Cape Town eleven hours. Sixteen hours flying time in economy. Also no chance of a cigarette. Some good flight.

'Ludovico,' he said to the woman who answered the door. Coloured woman about fiftyish in a blue housecoat. Steel-grey hair, glaring at him over frameless glasses. 'This is the house we're renting.' Not a question but a statement. Paulo getting out of the Grand Cherokee stretching, exclaiming, the woman staring at them, seeming bewildered.

'You speak English?' asked Ludo.

She nodded.

'Good. Like I said, my name's Ludovico. L-u-d-o-v-i-c-o.' He pulled an email out of his jacket pocket. 'It says here this is the place we rented.' He looked at the view: beach below, surfers pulling moves on the waves, sea for a hundred miles, sky forever.

The coloured woman stepped aside to let him in. He and Paulo squeezed past. Inside the place shone. The woman must have been cleaning all night.

'Spotless,' said Ludo. 'We can eat off the floor.'

'We have plates for you,' said the woman.

Paulo whistled. 'Nice one.'

Huge picture windows straight on to the exterior picture. Rim-flow off the patio. Maybe even better than California. Interior: white soft-pile carpets. Leather suite. Open-plan lounge and dining room. Ten-seater table. He went to the kitchen through a door, big black dude in there dressed all in white, even the shoes, beaming at him.

The dude said, 'I am Sibusiso. How are you?'

'Doing well,' said Paulo, stretching out a hand. They shook. 'How do you spell that?'

Sibusiso spelled it, 'S-i-b-u-s-i-s-o.'

'That Italian?'

'Zulu,' he was told. 'I am the cook.'

Paulo called out to Ludo, 'We order a cook?'

'Seems,' said Ludo. In the meantime he'd talked to the woman, found out her name was Mrs September, housekeeper. She'd told him she and the cook had premises off to the back. Hadn't smiled once during the exchange.

'Right, Mrs September,' he said, 'here's the plan. One breakfast at seven. One breakfast at eleven. You clean the rooms eleven to noon. We have lunch say three o'clock. You do any other cleaning you need to anytime you can, mostly when we're out. Five you're gone. Same with Mr Cook. We want you to do dinner we'll make advance arrangements.' He smiled at her, she didn't return it. 'How's that sound?'

'Suitable,' she said.

Ludo was wondering why she hadn't mentioned anything about a delivery of packages. Didn't want to ask, because he didn't want her to know he knew. Wanted it to seem like a surprise. Maybe best to let it unfold in its own time, he reckoned. This Mrs September was pure clam. The sort of reserve he liked. Twenty minutes later she came out with two gift-wrapped bottles of wine, gave one to each, also a box for Ludo.

How Francisco had organised this was amazing. Fedex'd over the greeting cards, got a local wine boutique to do the rest. The message to Paulo clearer than if he'd written it: I can do things everywhere.

'Nice one,' said Paulo, thinking, Jesus the guy never lets up.

Ludo fancied the rim-flow. Fancied everything about drifting round the pool looking at the ocean. Liked Sibusiso and Mrs September, especially Sibusiso bringing him coffee, Illy espresso through a Saeco wonder of wonders, the moment he sat down. All told a better deal than he could have imagined and he'd had high hopes to begin with.

La bella casa. He gazed up at it from the pool. Nice house. His room on the upper floor with the best views. Off the patio a TV lounge with a bigger flat-screen than he'd ever seen in New York. All wired up for DVD. Best of all a good sound system for his blues CDs. If there was a downside, no summer ballet season. What sort of city was this for Chrissakes? No ballet. He swam over to the side, lit a cigarette. Smoked it, supporting himself on the rim tiles, his body in the water. As he relaxed there, saw Paulo come out all smarted up, wearing wrap-around shades.

'You coming?' he wanted to know.

'Chill it,' said Ludo leaving the pool. Emerged ten minutes later jacket over his arm. Paulo looked like he was going to give him lip but didn't.

They took the Quattro. Paulo driving, well orientated to the left-hand side of the road. Both of them smoking. When they stopped at a traffic light a blue haze of smoke flowed from the windows.

'You know where we're going?' said Ludo.

'No problem,' said Paulo, 'until we get to the small stuff. That's why you've got the map.'

Ludo let this go. The only other words spoken before they got to Customs was Ludo giving directions down a street that crossed car parks, went under an elevated freeway through a gate into a fenced yard. Paulo parked.

'This's it?'

'Smells like it,' said Ludo. 'Docks smell of fish 'n oil. Everywhere in the world they smell like this.'

Turned out their man at Customs, Vusi Themba, had an office of his own, three floors up, good side of the building with a view of the docks. Other side of the building, third floor was level with a motorway.

Vusi Themba was easy-going. Big friendly face, coffee-coloured, nose looked like it'd been squashed onto his face. Gold Rolex weighing down his left wrist. He greeted them, shaking hands. Invited them in, shut the office door, sat them down, poured coffee from a filter machine, asked how they liked the city?

Paulo told him it was a great place.

Ludo asked if he minded people smoking.

Vusi brought out a pack and offered it round. Lit their cigarettes with a Zippo. Then wanted to know if they were going to visit a shebeen, spend a night in one of the township B&Bs, like an experience of a lifetime, man. Not to be missed. They wanted partying, then a township shebeen was the place for it. Okay, the city clubs were good. The type of clubs you found anywhere in the world though. You wanted something different, you hit a shebeen.

What's he saying here? Paulo thought. Paulo wanted clubs like you found anywhere in the world. On the other hand maybe this fella was dropping hints. Laying out a business plan. Opening up a new market. Maybe he wasn't so much Customs as Trade and Industry, Paulo thought.

Ludo thought, suave. Very suave. Ludo also thought, What's he saying here? Ten thousand isn't enough? Decided to give him the envelope with twelve grand. For the advice.

Vusi grinned at them both, stubbed his cigarette, scooted his chair across to a wall safe. Keyed in a code, not even trying to hide it. Ludo noted the numbers out of habit. Vusi reached in, brought out a cardboard box wrapped in brown paper tied up with string, the knots sealed with red wax. A battered cardboard box.

Jesus, thought Ludo, wasn't that the most obvious package you'd ever seen? No two ways about what was in there.

'Here's your coffee,' said Vusi, whisking it onto the desk. Ten kilos no effort in the arms of a big guy like him.

'Much obliged,' said Paulo. Judging by the state of the box they were lucky it hadn't broken.

Ludo opened his leather shoulder bag, flipped through the paperwork to one of the envelopes he'd prefilled, offered it to Vusi.

'Thanks,' said Vusi, searching round his desk for a paperknife, finding a silver one with the handle a naked woman. Very tasteful.

'Nice paperknife,' said Paulo.

'Carrol Boyes,' said Vusi. 'Local artist. Advance Christmas present from an importer. Jewish guy, brings in fashion accessories.'

Vusi counted through the notes while they watched. Stashed the envelope in the safe, closed it.

'So, gents,' he said. 'Have a good time' – taking them through the drill of a brother's handshake on the way out.

13

Paulo went in clean the first night. Smack on the witching hour.

That morning had checked out the clubs' whereabouts. Cruised in the Quattro. Found Club Catastrophe up a side street, the sort of urban terrain he recognised: at midday not much activity. Other side of the street from the club's metal door a motormac's garage, some cars on the pavement being repaired. Small-time stuff. Two doors down a junk dealer's store. Overhead premises either storage or cheap office space, he reckoned. Other doors on the street grilled up.

'Rave here, you rave among the movers and shakers, the bright young things,' Paulo read from a club guide. 'On any night there's more financial muscle getting down than you'll find in the office blocks during the day.' How about that?

'My kind of market,' he said aloud.

Midnight the traffic was chaotic. Kids everywhere. The glitzy off the beaches, more diamond belly-button studs than Paulo had seen in the jeweller's tray when he went with Vittoria to buy hers. Average age in the street probably mid-teens. Good enough trade on a slow night but not capable of the sort of turnover he needed.

Paulo parked a block away, ramping the Audi onto a traffic island. He angled back through the kids, assessed the situation, believed it was worth a G local between the car and the club door. Saw two coloured heps dealing and a black dude, large snapper, hung with gold chains, shades, cut-away T-shirt, gold-studded belt, black jeans, boots, moving leisurely, a boy-tart clutching at him. Two markers, less conspicuous, tracking them. The black making no contacts. The kids opening before him like the Red Sea. Paulo took note.

He kept the smart and his entourage in mind, picked out a couple of other sales points. Nothing major. Dope, mostly, Ecstasy for the desperate.

Getting through the bouncers was easy, cursory wave of the magic wand, not even a pat down. Paulo was all smiles, could bring in a kilo of powder no one would know. Thought, Jesus, man, kiddy city, yes. Good scene. Gothic graphics on the walls. Serious tendency towards cats. Some evil felines with luminous eyes painted everywhere, watching. You're freaking they'd be howling at you, scratching your eyes out. Paulo shook his head. Freaking cats. Had to be an acidhead you went for freaking cats. Tuned out these thoughts, zipped to the music pitched to the range of loudness he preferred, blocking all other sound. Blocked your thoughts if you let it. He got down to dancing.

By five he'd cased five clubs, decided to abandon the sixth to another night. He was hopping. He'd done two Es from the black, more particularly from the fella's markers. One straight off in the Catastrophe, another in number four, the Jean Pool. By then he and the schwarzer were on eyeball terms. Picking one another out each club they hit.

Either the guy was cool or a cop. In Paulo's estimation, the dude was a dude. The way he figured it, a potential outlet to get rid of a big pile of shit in one easy go. He had thirty days. Minus Christmas and New Year holidays and Sundays he had maybe twenty-four. The way the division came out that was four hundred singles a night. That was working. That was slave labour. So what he had to do was to move a big pile. Sweeten the dude.

He was standing next to the car still ramped up the traffic island. The city quiet. Early light. The frigging great big mountain looming up behind. The clubbers gone, the workers not awake yet. He fixed two short lines on the bonnet. Rolled a brown twenty and zoomed.

'A for away,' he said, pinching his nose, licking the grains from his fingertips. Had to give it to the big F, he sourced grade-A shit.

He drove off, his plan to sink a few beers on the patio, take in one of Sibusiso's English breakfasts, crash for the day.

Three early mornings later, about three-tenish Paulo phoned Vittoria. He was outside the Catastrophe. Flying. Her voice came on sleepy.

'Babe,' he said. 'Babe, I love you.'

'Jesus, Paulo,' was the response this got. 'It's two o'clock.' Vittoria not wanting to wake.

'You gotta be here, babe,' he said. 'You gotta see this kind of wonderful.'

The sleep thick in her head. Where the fuck was Paulo? What the fuck was he doing? Then she remembered, Cape Town. He was in Cape Town. She looked again at the radio clock. Fucking two o'clock.

This voice going in her ear: 'You gotta see this, babe. You gotta see this huge mountain. All the kiddies dancing in the street. Thanks to the sugar they buy from Uncle Paulo. Dance kiddies dance.'

'Paulo,' she said, raising her voice to break through his chatter. 'Paulo listen to me. It's two o'clock, I've gotta sleep. My tits are sore, I've got a headache. I feel like hell. Premenstrual. You heard of PMT?'

'Ah baby,' he said. 'Poor baby.'

'I'm going to disconnect you now,' she said. 'Phone me when you're going to sleep?'

'Baby,' he soothed. 'Babe, I love you.'

'Ciao, Paulo,' she said.

'Babe, I just shot the moon,' he said.

She thumbed him off. Four days she'd be there. Get rid of the fruits, get her life back.

Why Paulo was flying, why he'd just shot the moon, was because Paulo had scored big-time.

He'd gone in there the second night and dished out loss-leaders, half-gram sweeteners. Dished them out for free. Punters poked their noses once in that direction they were hooked. Wanted more. Tomorrow, guys, promised Paulo, trying to keep the scene cool. On the tomorrow he came back all set up to do business, pushed three hundred and fifty units. And did a deal. Which was why he'd come on to Vittoria all hyper at three in the a.m.

'Unreal man, unheard of,' he told Ludo back at the palace.

Ludo said he was impressed. This was after the second breakfast sitting, Paulo too wound up to sleep. He and Ludo lounging under an umbrella.

'Phone the man. Tell him,' said Paulo. 'Tell Francisco I'm going to move a kilo unit. A single deal.'

'That right?' said Ludo.

'Damn right,' said Paulo.

What had happened was he'd met up with the Xhosa of the bling. Club Catastrophe, the chill room. Paulo danced watching-not-watching, dazed. The jig came in, minus the tart. Minus the markers. They nodded. The guy put a hand on his shoulder, not rough, not gentle either, forceful, and squeezed.

Paulo said, 'You carry on doing that man, I'll put six inches of Carrol Boyes in your stomach.'

He'd really fancied the paperknife he'd seen in the Customs office so had bought one, sharpened it up. Its handle a naked nymph all tits and fanny. Fitted in his hand like the real parts. Paulo wore it sheathed to his wrist.

The Xhosa laughed.

'A Yank,' he said. 'Chief,' he said, 'you have just scored me a hundred note.'

He sat down next to Paulo.

'I told them only a Yank could come in the way you did.'

He held out his hand in greeting.

'You want to know about me, you ask anyone about Oupa K,' he said, flashing gold teeth. 'What a Yank doesn't know is Oupa stands for grandfather, K stands for kaffir. I hear a white man use that word he gets six inches of bicycle spoke poked through his lungs. Such a tiny hole it doesn't even bleed. All the air goes out whoosh.'

He grinned at Paulo, who grinned back, shook his hand, said, 'Paulo.'

'So who's Carrol, Paulo?'

Paulo slipped her from his sleeve.

Oupa K said, 'Stylish.'

Paulo slipped her back, took out one of his sweetener sachets.

'This is what we have to indaba about, chief,' said Oupa K. 'What a Yank can probably guess is indaba means par-lay. Talk the talk.'

Two guys tried to crash the chill room, without looking up Oupa K told them, Get. They did.

'Chief,' he said, stretching back, eyes closed, 'I don't want you here.'

Paulo said, 'Run this, then we'll what you call indaba.'

Oupa K opened lazy eyes that said, you're full of shit. Nonetheless wetted a finger, dipped it in the powder, sucked it off. Fine fine granules. Paulo lined the remainder with his Amex on the seat. Oupa K vroomed this in a quick snort.

They both sat back watching-not-watching the dancers on a TV screen.

Paulo said, 'What they indaba at business schools is partnerships. Win-win situations.'

Oupa K said nothing.

'The sort of partnerships I'm exploring here,' Paulo was saying, 'would extend brand reach.'

Oupa K burst out laughing. Paulo joined him.

Oupa K said, 'Lay it on me, chief.'

Paulo outlined a deal. Oupa K bought a kilo at a knockdown price for sale in the shebeens. Only in the shebeens. In addition, he, Paulo, would cut him a five per cent commission on all local sales. For the right to trade.

'Ten per cent,' said Oupa K.

'Five,' said Paulo, figuring if he doctored the stock he could recoup the five per cent, easy. Ten per cent started lessening brand edge. In a tight market not a wise strategy.

'Five,' he said.

Oupa K said, 'You could bullshit the commission.'

'I could,' said Paulo.

They watched the camera dollying along over the heads, people shuddering below in the strobe light like they were puppets.

'End of the day,' said Paulo, 'it comes down to trust.'

Oupa K gave him a quick glance. 'For a whitey you have a strange idea of business.'

As a way of detailing this strangeness, Paulo let him take the price down fifty thousand, privately calling it a discount. Unsure of how he was going to recoup, knowing it would fire up Ludo. Oupa K thinking the Yank must be holding out on something to be fixing so low for such quality.

They set the exchange for Mouille Point, in the car park next to the lighthouse, a position Paulo had cleared for major deals. Good visibility. Enough people about walking themselves, their children, their dogs. Anonymous. The Xhosa sure to send his markers, not likely to pitch himself given his image in the context. It came to it, an environment Paulo and Ludo could handle.

Oupa K stood up. They went through the brother's handshake. 'Keep the air in your lungs,' he said, heading out the chill room.

'Phone the man,' said Paulo. 'Tell him.'

Ludo crushed his cigarette, picked up his cellphone, clicked into the contacts menu, selected Francisco, thumbed on, exhaled a grey breath.

Francisco went straight into a spiel about how the playboy better get his act together because Isabella was lining up a major major deal mid-January, cash, no bullshit, so the playboy better have changed the white devil into rand bucks like tomorrow. This didn't happen there was going to be huge shit. Mega important contracts being flighted here.

'Sure,' Ludo said. 'D'you wanna hear some good news.'

But Francisco had thumbed him off.

They used the Quattro for the getaway, Ludo parked it in a bay facing the ocean, grassy side of the parking lot an hour early. He then wandered along the promenade to take a seat on a bench not far from the vehicle. Man his age sauntering around like that wouldn't scare a pigeon. Ludo was packing. Boos were boos, you didn't take chances.

Paulo parked the Cherokee in a back street, waited until ten minutes before the agreed time. The charlie was in a packet that'd held white flour an hour ago, this in a 7Eleven bag. In another bag a litre bottle of Coke. Looked like he was just coming back from the store. He headed off between the blocks of apartments along the beach road, crossed the lawns, coming onto the promenade far enough away from the lighthouse to be unnoticed, should anyone be watching out. Which he doubted. Oupa K's style, he reckoned, would be more like get there, do the trade, split. Don't anticipate, deal with what goes down. What worried him as he strolled along the seaside was that they'd take the powder and not hand over the money. How good were Ludo and his nine mil going to be then?

Ludo saw Paulo when he was crossing the lawns. He had no specific thoughts about the arrangements. He'd watched enough of them transact to know that give or take a bit of verbal, a bit of aggro posing, mostly what happened was what was supposed to happen. Paulo's fears he considered extreme.

Paulo stopped on the promenade, in front of the Quattro as agreed. Leant against the railings, put the bags at his feet, lit a cigarette. After a few draws reached down for the Coke, unscrewed the top, took a long pull. Anyone watching would see a man going home with his shopping, taking a break to admire the view.

Ludo strolled to a closer bench, sat down, fired up too. Right on the appointed time. His presence didn't disturb a single pigeon, some gulls circled though, cried at him.

Fifteen minutes they passed like this. Then another ten.

Paulo went through four cigarettes, drank most of the Coke.

After half an hour Ludo thought, no, it wasn't going to happen, or it had the makings of a cop bust. Paulo could be ID'd but the difficulty for the cops would be connecting the pieces. Worst-case scenario was the loss of a major portion of the income. Technically this happened Paulo would be dead come the end of the job. Ludo scoped the cars and the people, couldn't pick out anything that suggested a bust. In this situation the plan was, drift away, meet behind the apartment blocks. He was about to do just that.

Paulo moved a pace off the powder. Was within grabbing distance if he needed to run. Like Ludo he was thinking cops. Like Ludo he couldn't spot one. Should the passing power-walkers turn to drug squaddies he knew nothing about the 7Eleven bags. He was pissed, though. He hadn't had Oupa K for a bullshit artist. He'd had Oupa K for genuine. Fuck was the Big F going to say if they lost the candy? Have his ass. Paulo grabbed the bag, started to move off per the plan.

Ludo saw him do this. Thought he'd give him a few minutes, then drive off in the Quattro when a van grumbled in. Tinted windows. Graffitied sides top back front. Requiem music at full volume.

The panel door slid open, out stepped Oupa K. Shifted up his shades, squinted at Paulo, shouting for him to bring the stuff. Some soprano motor-mouth on the sound system giving a full Ave Maria. Not a person within fifty metres wasn't watching. Ludo included, fascinated by the style.

Paulo came up. 'What goddamned time is this?'

Oupa K said, 'African time.'

'Jesus,' said Paulo. 'I say five. I don't mean quarter to six.'

'Chief,' said Oupa K, stretching for the shopping bag, 'remember what I told you.'

Paulo held the bag away, said, 'Where's the money?'

Oupa K smiled. 'In the van. Come listen to the music.'

'Nah,' said Paulo. 'You bring it out here.'

'Chief, my Yankee chief, where's the trust, brother?'

Paulo shrugged.

They swapped packages. Paulo held the money.

'It's all here?'

Oupa K grinned at him. 'Have faith, my brother.'

A guy in the van weighed the 7Eleven bag, no attempt to hide the obvious. Oupa K tasted the contents, nodded.

Paulo thought, must be someone watching this about to call the cops.

Ludo was thinking similarly. On the other hand such in-your-face audacity froze the spectators. Nobody really believing their eyes. He heard Paulo say, 'I'm not sure.' He heard the jimbo say, 'Trust, chief, we gotta do this on trust.'

The schwarzer got into the van. The van exited. So did Paulo in the Quattro. Ludo was pleased he'd changed the car's plates.

As he got up to leave a white woman with her grandchildren said, 'What's that all about?'

'Dunno,' said Ludo. 'Drugs, I reckon' – ambling off, the granny going, 'Fucking munts.'

14

Leaving Milan was not a hardship. It couldn't happen fast enough. Early-afternoon Vittoria was packed. Sitting on the bed, agitated, plugged into Bon Jovi on her Discman. Enough devil left for two hits, one like now, the other as soon as the cabs arrived.

She did the line on the dressing table, went back to lying on the bed, Bon Jovi wound up loud.

Twenty minutes later Vittoria was coming off the monkey. Paulo better have shit waiting, she thought, after all the bragging he'd done. Worried her, being without it. By her count door-to-door would be, maybe, sixteen, seventeen hours. Two hours check in at Milan. Forty-five minute flight. Two hours wait in Rome for the connection. Ten hours onwards. Then Paulo. Pop the assholes, enjoy the holiday.

When she heard the taxis arrive she chased the last line, every bit of it, like a vacuum cleaner. Grinned to herself at the image. Left the suite without a backward glance.

On my way to a killing was the thought running round her head going down the stairs into the hall, hefting her own suit-case. A single suitcase. The entrance hall stacked with luggage like there was a fashion shoot about to happen. The effect weird in the mirrored walls. Suitcases ad infinitum. Made Vittoria laugh.

'They got no washing machines in Cape Town?' she said, one step off the ground, surveying the luggage.

Dieter snapped back. 'You shut up, bitch.'

The taxi drivers humping the suitcases into the cabs, grinned at such love and happiness.

'Temper, temper,' Vittoria chanted. Dieter was flustered with the last minute demands, Camillo barking from up the stairs: 'Have you got the air tickets? Where are our passports? I can't find the talc. Why are you not taking the white suit? This is summer we're going to. I like you in the white suit.'

These sort of questions and niggles when they'd been packing for two days, never mind that half the suitcases were now locked and in the cabs.

In English Vittoria said softly, but loudly enough for Dieter to hear, 'Dorky fags.'

Hadn't expected a fisted backhander that caught her on the cheekbone. Dieter pirouetting half ballet-dancer, half kick-boxer in the action. The blow stung, staggered her, even had the taxi drivers protesting on her behalf. Vittoria lurching against the mirrors hand to cheek, eyes darting for a weapon, seeing umbrellas, making a grab for one. Would have run Dieter through, fencer-style. Except Camillo coming down the stairs shouted in German, 'What are you doing? Stop that! Stop that!'

Vittoria checked the lunge, went at Dieter in Italian for a cock-sucking latex Nazi.

Dieter shouting that it was time Camillo sent the useless bitch back to New York. That the cunt was as fertile as house dust. This last in Italian for the benefit of the taxi drivers.

'Get in the taxi,' Camillo said, meaning both of them.

They rode out to Linate in silence, Dieter sulking, sitting in front staring out the windscreen at rain pouring down. Vittoria happy to be leaving Milan, just wishing she could spit on the pavements. Her cheek throbbing.

Camillo said, 'Aren't you pleased we are going to the sun?'

Vittoria thought, You better be good for it, Paulo. Answered, 'Delighted.'

Cape Town International, Camillo had arranged security: two dapper guys in black introduced themselves as Mace and Pylon from Complete Security. Friendly, good-looking types who gave her the once-over, Vittoria happy to preen. On the drive into the city, Mace and Pylon up front chauffeuring a minibus they'd had to hire at the last minute. Camillo asked her, 'How do you like this?'

'Wonderful.' Vittoria saying it offhand, her attention on the glowing mountain, a sky of sunshine over it like she hadn't seen in months. 'If it wasn't for the shanties.'

'The blacks are a problem,' said Dieter. 'Too many children.' When Vittoria didn't respond he said, 'Moreover they are with AIDS.'

'But our child will not be,' said Camillo. 'He will have everything. Perhaps we can start trying for baby tomorrow, don't you think?'

Vittoria thought, Like hell we can.

'What do you say?' said Dieter, turning round to snigger.

'Get stuffed,' said Vittoria, watching a black guy on the centre isle of the highway making to run across. Dieter glared at her. The black man started running. Vittoria shut her eyes, heard behind them the screech of tyres, long blasts of hooting. She checked the scene behind: the black man safely across, waving at the traffic.

The house was way up the mountain slopes above the city. The security men carried the luggage piece by piece into the mansion.

Camillo held out a tip. The one called Mace said, no it was part of the service.

'You want to go out, just call,' said the other one with the funny name. 'Any time.' Further explaining that if it was a dire situation, the armed response control panel was a better bet than a cellphone call. Or to push a panic button. 'Two minutes and the armed response'll have men with guns here,' he said.

They left, both giving Vittoria another once-over.

Vittoria headed for the swimming pool, sat on the edge with her feet in the water, soon on her cell to Paulo, desperate for freedom and charlie.

Was saying, 'That prick, Camillo, wants to start tomorrow, but it's too early. Anyway, I told you not again.'

'What's the worst case?' Paulo wanted to know. 'One lay more, that's all.'

'No,' said Vittoria. 'You come here and fix it. Now.' At the edge of her nerves, ragged for a hit.

She heard Paulo sigh. 'Not that easy, suges.'

'Hell Paulo.'

'Like the piece is Ludo's. I've got to sneak it. Without the gun the homos're not gonna be serious.'

'So sneak it. Just get here.'

'Okay. Okay. Wait. Okay, wait.'

'I'm waiting.' She gave him the street address, disconnected. It felt like she had glass in her eyes.

Vittoria got up, went back to the house. Dieter standing on the patio eyeing her all the way in.

'Nice view,' he said.

'Fabulous,' she replied.

'Enjoy it, darling. You've only got four days.'

Vittoria stopped. 'Meaning?'

Dieter waved a floppy hand at her. 'Bye, bye Vittoria. When we're finished. You're going home to mamma.'

Camillo came out, showered, changed, fresh. Like an advert for first-class air travel.

'What's this?' she said to him.

'Mmmm?' he said.

'This four days shit.'

'Better for all of us, don't you think?' said Camillo. 'We don't like you. You don't like us.'

Vittoria thought, so far so good. 'In four days I only start ovulating.'

Dieter said, 'Shit.'

Camillo considered this, said, 'Alright we have to wait a bit longer. Why not?'

'If I get pregnant?'

'If,' said Camillo. 'We do DNA testing. If it is my baby, I will honour the contract.'

Dieter popped the champagne. Camillo said to her, 'Isn't it romantic?' – took a sip of the Moët looking at her while he did.

Vittoria thought, to hell with this. Fully understanding the expression on his face, why he kept moistening his lips while he poured her a glass of champagne and handed it to her, toasting, 'To your success.'

'I'm going to rest,' Vittoria responded, leaving the two fruits sitting there in the cane chairs taking in the view.

An hour later the intercom bell rang. She got up to answer. Paulo said, 'I'm here' – and she buzzed him in.

15

They sat on a tartan blanket among the Sunday concert crowd at Kirstenbosch Gardens: Mace, Oumou, Treasure, Pylon, the girls, Christa and Pumla, reading books. The hell was it with kids, Mace wondered, that they did so much reading? He stretched out, his head against Oumou's thigh, his bare feet nudging at his daughter, irritating her. Christa smacked at his ankles, not breaking her concentration, not using any force, more as if she were brushing off an insect.

'Mace,' said Oumou, 'leave her' – also telling him in French to stop annoying the girl.

About them the crowd had thickened, not a patch of lawn visible beneath the blankets and the cotton throws. People snacking on picnics, quaffing down wine like it was an obligation in the city of the grape. Oumou and Treasure drinking sparkling from long-stem glasses, Mace and Pylon tooting beer.

'So what d'you think, Oumou?' said Treasure, 'about their taking a weekend away.'

'It's business,' said Pylon, his voice high in protest.

'You said. Like you're going to go somewhere in a plane if it's business? Mace does the flying.'

'Protecting the high 'n mighty,' said Pylon. 'That's what we do.'

'Both of you, over a weekend?

'I think it's alright,' said Oumou. She glanced down at Mace, smiling.

'There's a festival on,' said Treasure. 'They're going to party.'

'In Luanda?' said Mace. 'I don't think so. I could think of better places.'

'A festival?' said Oumou.

But Mace didn't get a chance to explain as the Blues Broers in dark suits and shades drifted onto the stage: base guitarist Big Rob in a floppy hat, the Doc with his pork-pie; Big Rob going into a harp conversation with Albert Frost's lead guitar, Agent Orange bringing up the keyboard with a riff that had Mace gazing out across the sunlit suburbs towards the cooling towers and the urban sprawl beyond, high burnished windows in the office blocks.

There were risks, he knew, about this sort of deal. There always were. But if it came off and no reason why it shouldn't, they'd be home and dry. Not bond-free perhaps, but getting there. The world beginning to look a decidedly less scary place. Mace shifted against Oumou, excited at the possibilities.

At the movement Oumou ran her palm over his short hair, put fingers onto his scalp and massaged. Mace closed his eyes, brought his attention back to the song Agent Orange sang about a guy taking a train ride, coming to the end of his journey, entering a dark railway station in a distant city. Feeling a stranger where everyone else was at home. Been a long time since he'd had those sorts of feelings, Mace realised. Which was the way he preferred it these days: the family man.

At the end of the song Oumou bent down to him and said, 'What is this festival?'

'I've no idea,' said Mace, sitting up. 'Not a clue.'

Above the applause, Treasure said, 'Any other time they could choose, they choose one with a festival.'

'Wasn't our choice,' said Pylon. 'That's when the client's got his meetings. What can we do?'

'You jealous, Treasure?' said Mace. 'The two boys out having some fun.'

Oumou smiled at the tease.

Treasure said, 'He could be at home helping me in the garden.'

Mace wasn't sure if she was serious or not. From the look on Pylon's face could tell he wasn't either.

The band went into a run of songs back to back that had the audience on its feet jiving to the music like cultists at some summer rite. Mace hoisted up his daughter and Christa slung her arms around his neck and Oumou's and they balanced her between them, her legs dangling, a rhythm in her body even so.

When the band was through Mace went off in search of Cokes for the girls. Left Oumou and Treasure stretched out on the blanket, Pylon with his eyes closed. Probably dreaming of money, Mace reckoned. He wandered down the lawns to the café, the gardens in shadow and the mountain dark behind. Everywhere people enjoying the twilight and the warm air.

On the bridge over a stream, someone touched his arm from behind and he glanced back to find the ice eyes of Sheemina February glinting at him.

'Enjoy the concert?' she said.

Mace nodded. 'What d'you want?' Keeping his voice tight, noticing the white top giving a glimpse of the rise of her breasts, her left hand buried in her jacket pocket.

'Just to tell you how much I'm enjoying your old house. Home.' She corrected. 'It has a sense of peace. Despite what happened.'

'Aren't you the lucky one,' said Mace, turning away. Then came back at her. 'One thing… One thing I can't figure out.'

She raised her eyebrows, quizzical, amused. 'That is?'

'What sort of kicks you get out of this?'

'Kicks?' She laughed. 'It's not about kicks. It's about right and wrong, justice. That's why I'm a lawyer.'

'I'd call it stalking,' said Mace. 'Perverted. I heard it's what you do.'

She stiffened, her ice eyes came on him. 'Ask yourself that question, who's the pervert? Who is guilty?' And as quickly smiled. 'Our family man Mace Bishop. The loving father. The loving husband. Don't fool yourself.'

She raised her right hand, waved with her fingers, leaving Mace watching her walk away. His eyes on her arse in the tight jeans, what was visible below the jacket.

Screw you, Mace thought. Screw you for buggering up my day.

16

Monday morning Mace and Pylon were on Dunkley Square for an early cappuccino. Relaxed in the shade of an umbrella, the heat already oppressive. Along the mountain-top, a wisp of cloud suggested a breeze over False Bay but in the city the air was unmoving, faintly petrol-fumed.

Mace said, 'So we're in the clear with the girls?'

Pylon folded his newspaper, put it aside. 'Treasure wanted more info. Like who's this guy he needs two bodyguards? I told her that's confidential. Can't give his name. Can't give the name of his company. She looks at me like who'm I trying to kid, so I go, honest believe me this is a fine arrangement. Good money for just standing around. She says the guy must be paranoid he wants both of us. I say, that's right, he's neurotic, never looks you in the eye, always glancing over his shoulder. Now he's having to visit Angola. Then she comes at me, so it's going to be dangerous? What can I say? I'm in the corner. I have to answer. Sure, I say, it's dangerous, I won't lie to you. But no more dangerous than here, if you keep your eyes open. I don't want you to go, she says. I have to babe, I tell her. It's business. For three days she doesn't speak to me. Even yesterday, when we left for the concert, she wasn't speaking to me.'

The coffees came, Pylon paid.

'Oumou didn't give you any shit?'

'Nothing. Told me to be careful, that's all.'

'Maybe you're a better liar than me.'

Mace grinned. 'First thing this deal's going to sort out for me is my bond. Get the bank off my back.'

Pylon spooned up foam. 'Sure sure. They'll love your diamonds.'

'Inter account transaction,' said Mace. 'I've lined it up.'

Pylon looked dubious. 'Already. A dealer?'

'Your investment analyst, that's what he does, isn't it?'

'Wait, wait, wait. You're going to my investment analyst?'

'Sure. You swear by him.' Mace fished for his cellphone in his chinos. It vibrated, pulsed with light, gave a ringtone like a frog. The name on the screen was Gonsalves.

'Here's a strange one,' he said, connecting to the cop. 'Long time, captain,' he said.

'Absolutely,' said Gonsalves without wasting a beat, saying, 'I've got something here you're not gonna like. Two bodies. Been dead maybe all weekend. The renting agent, guy called Dave Cruikshank, says he knows you, says you were providing protection services. Maybe you'd like to see how effective you've been?'

'We're there,' said Mace. He thumbed off the cop, gave Pylon a baleful stare.

'What's it?'

'A stuff-up,' said Mace. 'The Italian homos are dead.'

Dave Cruikshank stood at the gate outside the police tape.

'Not the sort of scene that's going to boost your enterprise, my son,' he said as Mace and Pylon flashed company ID at the duty officers. 'One bloke's sitting there minus his willy.'

'You find them, Dave?' asked Mace.

'Came round to check everything's hunky-dory, like you probably were going to do eventually, walked right in. Front gate unlatched, front door locked but you go round the side the sliding door onto the pool's open wide.'

Mace looked over at the house, Captain Gonsalves watching them, his jaws chewing the cud.

'Anyone could've walked in. Know what I'm saying. Come in off the street at any time.' Dave's lips glistened with gloating.

'Thanks for calling us first.' Mace started after Pylon down the gravel path.

'It's a cop job,' said Dave, 'you're supposed to prevent this sort of thing, my son.'

Mace gave him the finger. 'Oi,' Dave called out, 'give my best to the missus.'

As they approached, Gonsalves held up a business card with the name Complete Security embossed on it in gold, beneath that the strap line: Your safety is our concern. Then the names Mace Bishop and Pylon Buso in black, and landline and cellphone numbers. 'Found this on the coffee table, where you might have left it,' he said. 'Don't you guys check on your clients at all?' He moved a plug of tobacco from one cheek to the other.

'They got armed response for that,' said Pylon. 'We look like armed response?'

Gonsalves shrugged. 'Doesn't concern me. Still your clients. Like to tell me what you know?'

They followed him into the house, Pylon summarising: they'd picked them up from the airport, brought them here, unloaded their suitcases, told them call any time of day or night they felt concerned.

'That's the deal?' said Gonsalves. 'Any time they want you?'

'That's it,' said Pylon. 'People employ us for out and about. They're sitting in their houses, they feel safe. Got panic buttons on the walls, maybe even strapped to their wrists.'

'Makes you wonder why they come here?'

''Cos it's safe,' said Pylon.

They were stopped before the body of a man tied to a dining room chair, his mouth taped up. A bullet wound in the centre of his forehead.

'This your client?' said Gonsalves.

'The German one,' said Mace. 'Name of Dieter Dreske. Made all the bookings in the name of Camillo Medardo, his partner. We figured them for old queens. The Italian being some big deal in Milan fashion.'

They went through to the bedroom.

'Save me Jesus!' said Pylon, moving behind the corpse so he didn't have to see the bloody crotch.

'My thoughts,' said Gonsalves. He pointed at the dead man. 'You would say this is the Eyetie?'

'It is,' said Mace. 'Bit of rough trade going on here, possibly.'

'You're telling me or you're asking me?' said Gonsalves.

'Either.' Mace glanced round the room, noted the narrow-bladed boning knife on a bedside table, the cheque book, and the white smear Pylon pointed at on the dressing table's glass top. 'Coke?'

'Most probably,' said Pylon. To Gonsalves he said, 'The woman killed too?'

Gonsalves said, 'What woman?'

'We picked up three of them,' said Pylon. 'The deal was for the two gays, we took the woman for maybe a niece. A last minute addition. We had to hire a minibus. This happens more'n you'd believe. We go out with one car, except we need two 'cos the party's doubled.'

'There is no woman,' said Gonsalves.

Mace and Pylon exchanged glances. Mace thinking, oh really?

'No trace of a woman,' said Gonsalves. 'Only suitcases here've got men's things.'

Mace thought, That so? Ran through some scenarios: she did it, she was in on it, she'd been kidnapped. Whichever way, the shooting was spot-on accurate so probably not the niece. Didn't disqualify option two but his gut favoured a kidnapping.

Gonsalves said, 'How about talking to the face artist.'

Mace said, sure.

Pylon said, 'Long legs, helluva arse. Very J-Lo.'

Gonsalves stared him out, chewing vigorously until Pylon

212

turned away. The three men walked back to the patio. One empty glass, two flutes still with champagne on the table, the level of the Moët slightly under half.

'Seems to have started merrily enough,' said Mace.

Gonsalves spat the tobacco plug into his hand, tossed it into a bed of roses. 'Any idea what a penis costs nowadays?'

'About a hundred bucks,' Pylon said. 'But if this was for muti they'd have taken both. I'd reckon it's about something else.'

'Any opinions, Mr Bishop?'

Mace shook his head. 'You're the detective.'

'Bloody wonderful job, hey.' Gonsalves took out a cigarette, started stripping off the paper.

17

A week later the case was nowhere, except an international sensation. Cops had had radio time on the talk shows, identikits in the dailies, not one response. 'Maybe you should of kept your eyes off her arse and on her face,' Gonsalves told Mace when he phoned for an update. 'We could of got a better likeness then.' Mace let it go, the identikit was as good as identikits got.

What the cops did know was her name: Vittoria Corombona. A US citizen, address in New York, no one home. Immigration confirmed her entry at Cape Town International. No exit from any border post. Gonsalves also had some weird story from the polizia or carabiniere or whatever they were called that Medardo was paying the goose, Mace smiled at the word, thinking he hadn't heard it since he was at school, to have his baby. This nugget from the Milan housekeeper.

'Unbelievable,' Gonsalves said, 'an old poofter wanting a baby the traditional way. But there you were, you had money you could buy anything. So hardly likely she was going to shoot him then, was it? Those sorts of deals you had to take to full term or you didn't get paid.'

This was true, Mace agreed.

In between, Mace had to pacify Mo Siq getting ratty about was the deal on or off.

'I need lead time, my friend,' he told Mace. Mace clicked him to the speakerphone for Pylon's benefit. 'This doesn't happen overnight.'

'We're still on for three, four weeks' time.'

'That's my point,' said Mo. 'Three weeks, four weeks when? What date? What day? Know what I'm saying? It's got to be exact. There's sorting time, loading time, hours on the road, transference shore to ship. We're not playing bush games here. Real world, guys. Real time. Countdowns. Precision. Yeah. A closed loop, everybody on the information. What you've got to give me is when and where. When you've got to give me this is soonest. Like end of business today.'

'We're arranging logistics,' said Pylon.

'Well arrange faster.' A pause. 'And what's the deal with payment. You've got clarity there yet?'

'Same as we agreed.'

'That's a shit story, Mace. Where's the money, my friend? We're not talking trust and warm feelings here. We're talking money. Understand?'

'Nothing's changed,' said Mace. 'The deal's as it was.'

'Jesus,' Mo hissed. 'You guys' – and hung up.

Mace and Pylon shrugged at one another.

'Man has a point,' said Pylon. 'Dates would be nice.'

But when Mace called her, Isabella wasn't committing. 'What's the saying? Hang loose, Macey. Chill. We're getting there.'

'Getting where? Bloody hell, Bella, I've got to book cargo space. I've got a man getting jumpy.'

'See you in New York,' she said, blowing him transatlantic kisses.

Pylon wasn't impressed. 'That woman plays cat games with you,' he said. 'All these years 'n she's still got you by the balls.'

'Leave it,' said Mace.

'Are you screwing her again?'

'Short answer. No.'

Pylon snorted. 'I believe you, bru. I told the story to a thousand others, they mightn't.'

After Christmas, on the day Mace was to fly to New York to set up a surgical safari, Pylon said he had the diamond problem sorted out.

'Just like that?' said Mace. 'Didn't know you were working on it.'

'I wasn't. Not particularly. And not sorted out, exactly.'

'Make sense,' said Mace.

'Half an hour ago,' said Pylon, 'I got a call from my cousin. Big businessman, used to work for De Beers. His son was hijacked. Handed over an Audi TT at the Claremont traffic lights.'

'Eina!'

What happened, Pylon said, was the jackers put a gun in the boy's face, pulled him out of the car with some force. The boy was unhurt, jittery, though. Long and short of it was the cousin phoned a friend who phoned a friend who came back with the chopshop address of where the Audi TT was being made over in the township. Terrible mistake, apologies, no hard feelings. What the cousin wanted was for Pylon to go with the boy to collect the car. The boy had never set foot in a township, the boy was shit scared of townships.

'I said, no problem. Do a man like Stones a favour, is a pleasure.'

Mace laughed. 'Stones?'

'Previously known as. Goes by his initials these days, AC. AC Mkize.'

'You kept him quiet.'

'I'm connected,' said Pylon. 'A network where you wouldn't believe.'

They took the big Merc and a nine mil each, Pylon driving. First stop was to collect the boy from a palace in Bishop's Court. On the way Mace said, 'So who's AC?'

Pylon said, 'Like I said, a businessman.'

'Ex-De Beers, you also said.'

'Sure.'

'A black chappie in De Beers! How'd a black man get into De Beers?'

Pylon made a clucking sound which Mace knew meant he was weighing up the pros and cons of how much to tell. Eventually said, 'Once he was a trader. Before he got in with De Beers, he worked for a Chinese.'

'There's a thing,' said Mace.

'Starting out as a fahfee runner for the Chinese,' said Pylon, 'doing a couple of streets in the Joburg worker suburbs. This little kid, the aunties loved him. Gave him sweets and Cokes with their bets.'

'I've heard of fahfee,' said Mace.

'The way it works,' said Pylon, 'is you bet on your dreams. You dream about a monkey, you play two. A horse is twenty-two. Up to thirty-five. Fahfee, it's more Joburg and Durban, than Cape Town, wherever there's lots of Chinese. Probably start in Cape Town now with all the chinks moving in. Those days it was illegal 'cos it was gambling, like playing roulette.

'What AC's job was was to run down the lanes collecting all the bets, the numbers people were playing. Thing about fahfee is everyone does it on trust. The white aunties trust the black runner to take their money to the Chinese, like they trust the Chinese to pull a number and pay up on it. Then everyone trusts the black runner's going to take the winnings back to the winners. Lots of room for someone wanting to make a break. Except the Chinese is smart. He's got plenty of AC-type runners so no one's carrying big money, a couple of hundred maybe, not enough to run off with.

I mean you can but three days later you're dead. Not a wise move. The point about fahfee is that it's lots of little bets. Nobody's betting much, nobody's winning much but there's a lot of money coming in.

'AC keeps his nose clean. The Chinese likes him. Upgrades him to a bigger game where the stakes are high. Serious players. Serious money. AC handles it. Then the Chinese shows him some stones. Starts to tell him about various kinds of stones, which ones are valuable, how to look at a diamond, what makes one better than another. AC could do this. Like as a lightie he could glance at a stone, weigh it in his hand, take a closer look through the Chinese's magnifying glass and tell you how much a jeweller would tell you.

'The Chinese is a sharp man. When all the brothers are picking up our hardware to fight the good fight, the Chinese has got AC in Berkley, some place like that, studying rocks. Geology. He comes back graduated, the Chinese says to him no more IDB, get a job at De Beers. They see a black man walk in with these qualifications, this know-how, they're going to show you the fast track: big salary, share options, BMW cars, low-interest housing loans, expenses-paid holidays. Go there. AC does. Which is why we're driving to Bishop's Court.'

'And the Chinese?'

'Dead now,' said Pylon. 'He kept dealing 'n AC let him. That's when they set up a process of fencing illicit stones. Keep a handle on things.'

Pylon turned right off Edinburgh Drive at the traffic lights into Upper Bishop's Court, the mountain green in the morning light, going third right into Forest and up to Dunkeld, Mace wondering what people did in mansions. Like did they sleep in different rooms every night? You looked at these places there had to be six, seven bedrooms probably all en-suite before you got to counting sitting and dining rooms. All set in gardens that'd need full-time attention. Tennis courts, swimming pools, three garages, serious money.

They went right into Dunkeld, cruised slowly under the trees to a pair of wrought-iron gates between two columns, statues of lions at the base of each column. Mace whistled as the gates swung open on a cobbled drive curving to a mansion with a columned portico. This man was on his way to being an icon, Pylon said. Up there with the Ramaphosas, Motsepes, Sexwales, fronting the black empowerment deals. Rolling in it.

Aren't they all, thought Mace. The old soldiers.

Pylon saying, talk was he'd even become a Freemason to put a crack in the white brotherhood. On the portico stood AC and his son. The boy was about eighteen, just old enough to get his driving licence. Geared up hip-hop. His father suited.

Pylon introduced Mace, AC shaking his hand Western-style only. No one introduced the boy.

'Shouldn't be a problem,' said AC. 'The man has apologised. He gives you any trouble let me know.' AC going back into the house even before Pylon had the car in gear.

The boy said nothing on the way out. Neither did Mace and Pylon, Pylon driving the N2 without hurry, the traffic dense past the cooling towers, easing after the airport. Mace sat at an angle in the passenger seat staring at the shacklands teetering on the dunes down to the concrete fence that bordered the highway. Here and there the palisades were smashed through for herders to drive their goats and cattle onto the good grazing along the road verge. The boy was wired into a Discman, a tinny rap audible to Mace and Pylon.

Pylon took the Khayelitsha exit ramp, deciding what he'd do for the boy was give him a tour: breezeblock houses, pot-holed roads, electricity wires sandbagged across the streets, filth and dead dogs everywhere. Down to the market, trolleys of tripe, stalls of goats' heads. The boy wasn't listening to his rap anymore.

Pylon switched off the air conditioner, slid down all the windows to a heavy smell of fried onions and meat. The throughways were narrow here, more lanes than streets, people having to back up against the stalls as the Merc crawled along.

Pylon stopped at a woman braaiing chicken bits on a brazier, ordered a mixed KFC short tub of wings and feet. The boy said, no thanks, but Pylon kept the tub held over the seat until the boy took a wing. In Xhosa he said, you're going to insult her if you don't take one but the boy didn't seem to understand. To the woman Pylon said, city boys only eat from Woolworths, and the woman laughed uproariously. Pylon bit into a foot, tearing at the toughness. When the boy asked what he should do with the bone, Pylon said throw it out the window.

The house was a double storey in a street of government twenty-by-twenties: metal window frames, walls needing plaster. A bright patch of green lawn with a child's swing on it, a sprinkler going. Major gangster, said Pylon. Drugs, cars, protection, pirate videos and CDs, even a bit of small-arms trading. Major taxi owner too. Mace noticed two men standing in the yard of the house opposite. Three down the street; two others back a bit making snazzy moves with a soccer ball.

Pylon stopped behind a van with tinted windows, the word Sanctus writ large across the back. He cut the engine. In the silence Mace heard what sounded like church singing. Choirs. The music was turned down, a tall guy with a six-pack stomach, wearing only shorts, a flap of jackal skin hanging in the front, appeared in the house's doorway.

Pylon pressed the window down. 'Heita.'

'Chief,' the man said, not moving from the front door.

Pylon gave him some lip in Xhosa about buggering up big time in hijacking the boykie of such a main man brother.

The man grinned, said, You're about to fill an order, you're not too bothered about the supplier.

Pylon laughed. Turned to the boy. 'You catch any of that?'

The boy shook his head.

'Too bad.' Pylon opened his door. 'Okay, let's get this over.' He and Mace got out but the boy stayed put. Pylon ducked back in. 'Out, boetie. Showtime.' The boy looked terrified, all the same did as he was told.

'Where's the car?' Pylon asked.

The man indicated a garage across the street, said, 'Who's the mlungu, chief? Cop or what?'

'My partner,' said Pylon.

Mace caught the mlungu bit, but kept zipped. The young men with the football had edged closer, ditto the three down the street, ditto the two opposite, now lounging at the street gate.

'Hey, chief,' the man said in English, pointing at Mace. 'You guys fucked up hey!' He displayed a mouth studded with gold teeth.

Mace said, 'How's that?'

'Letting the girl take out the homosexuals.'

Mace said to Pylon, 'What's he on about?'

Pylon shrugged. 'Who's this, Oupa?'

The man switched back to Xhosa told Pylon they were stupids, moegoes, like the cops. This woman that killed the Italians was living it up in the city, swinging through the nightclubs. He'd seen her. Her and her boyfriend. Yankee doodles. He laughed. Hell, what sort of bodyguards were they. Bloody useless. Just like the cops.

'Which clubs?' asked Pylon.

The man waved his arms, told him to go hamba, fuck off and do his own work. Followed this with a stream of invective about the state of the world.

Pylon let him finish. 'Where the car keys Oupa?'

Oupa K threw them into the street.

Mace said to the boy. 'Go pick them up. Get the car out the garage. Stick behind us.'

The boy glanced at the groups of men, closer now.

Mace said, 'Come, china, let's move it.'

The boy went round the Merc into the street and picked up the keys. He stood hesitant, the ball players jogging, flicking the ball between them. One called to him, lined up a shot and kicked, the ball catching the boy hard in the stomach. He bent double, staggered, the men laughing as the ball rolled towards Mace. He trapped it under his foot.

Pylon said, 'Don't do this.'

'Come, come,' the guy who'd kicked shouted, 'kick, man.'

And Mace did, lifting the ball over their heads.

'David Beckham,' they joked, one running to retrieve it.

Pylon got into the car, fired the engine. Mace waited while the boy opened the garage doors, reversed the TT into the street. He stalled it, swung the engine again with the accelerator floored, the revs howling. The young men all stood next to the van now, none of them smiling. Pylon gave a beep on the hooter and Mace eased into the passenger seat, said, 'Let's go.'

On the highway the boy took off without a wave of thank you and Pylon let him go, clucking his disapproval. 'Bloody rich kids.'

Mace said, 'Who's the fella back there?'

'Oupa K,' said Pylon. 'Started off as a car-guard. He reckons he's seen the chick, Vittoria what's her name?'

'Sure he does.'

'No, I'd believe him,' said Pylon. 'On the club scene, Oupa K's the operator. He's the merchant. Es from Amsterdam. Coke from Columbia. Oupa K has it all.'

'Attractive man.'

'Embittered man. Thought when he came back from the bush war, the powers would set him up. They did. With a chauffeuring job. Not exactly what Oupa K had in mind.'

Pylon took the off-ramp into the airport. 'Probably what I'll do while you're away is hang out in the clubs for a while.'

'Exciting,' said Mace.

18

Two nights later Pylon hit Club Catastrophe a little after midnight. The building pumped, the street was jumping. On the corner Oupa K's van issued a low requiem. He imagined the man inside watching him pass, knowing his reason for being there, probably smiling to himself. For a moment wondered if he shouldn't knock on the tinted windows but didn't. What for? Let the guy chill to his weird music in peace.

At the club door Pylon had to shout at the bouncers, 'Ducky Donald around by any chance?'

The doorman looked over his head at the kids dancing in the street. 'Who's asking?'

Pylon told him.

The man spoke into the mic clipped to his lapel, kept his eyes on Pylon moving aside to let a couple of white boys stagger out, both wiggers, their hip-hop gear falling off their bums, their Nike laces whipping about like snakes. White kids, black kids, street cool was ridiculous.

The bouncer tapped Pylon on the shoulder, indicating with his thumb that he could go inside. 'At the bar,' he shouted. 'Wait there.'

Pylon nodded, headed into the thundering drone of the club's dark interior. Nothing seemed changed since he'd last been there, had to be almost three years back in '99: the same gothic style on the walls, the images of hanged cats.

At the bar Matthew shouted at him to go upstairs where Pylon found Ducky Donald sprawled on the not-so-white leather couch watching a movie of a bare-torsoed Ben Kingsley mouthing off at himself in a mirror.

'Grab a beer, take a pew,' said Ducky, flapping a hand towards a drinks counter that ran the length of the wall. Ducky sitting there in green tracksuit bottoms, a red T-shirt, bare feet. No sign of any female company. The room a pit of old newspapers, magazines, stacks of videos. A polystyrene box from the Hot Wok takeaway perched on a tower of discs. Ashtrays of butts on the bar and coffee table, the air heavy with cigarette smoke and not a window open on this hot night.

Pylon got a Becks from the bar fridge, uncapped it with a waiter's friend. One thing he had to give Ducky, the noise insulation was good, only a dim boom audible from below.

'Cheers,' said Ducky, patting the white leather. 'Siddown, watch this. Sexy Beast it's called. I got a pirate. Bloody best movie Kingsley ever made.'

Pylon scooped newspapers off the couch, dumped them on the coffee table and sat.

'Check this.' Ducky Donald rewound to Kingsley aka Don Logan dissing Ray Winstone aka Gal.

The two guys facing off, Logan going: 'Look at you, fuckin' suntan, like leather! Like a leather man, your skin, you could make a fuckin' suitcase out of you, holdall! Look like a crocodile, fat crocodile, fat bastard, you look like fuckin' Idi Amin, know what I mean?'

Ducky slapped at his thighs. 'Isn't that great. Bloody wonderful. Wouldn't you say?' – and spun back for a replay.

Pylon sipped his beer, thinking fat Ducky Donald with his sunbed tan was only a shade or two off Idi Amin himself.

When the scene came to an end, Ducky paused the movie, an image of the bald psychopath in a tight white shirt with a face like a demon filling the screen. He tossed the remote onto a woven grass plate, gave Pylon a toothy smile. 'So what you want, boykie?'

Pylon said, 'I'm looking for a girl looks like this' – he handed Ducky two newspaper clippings: one the cop's identikit, the other of a passport mug shot. 'She's been around the clubs, I heard.'

'Hundreds of broads look like this,' said Ducky, giving Pylon back the cuttings. He took a cigarette from a pack, fired it with a

Bic. Said, 'Let me show you something' – blowing smoke from the corner of his mouth as he picked out a remote from the four lying in the bowl, aimed it at a black box standing on the floor below the screen. Logan disappeared; the club's dance floor popped up, a packed mob swaying with their hands snaking above their heads. 'I can sit here, keep an eye on the ravers.'

Ducky zoomed in on a couple, ecstasy written over their faces. 'How about that? Truly bombed, hey!'

He switched cameras: the doormen having words with a kid waving a knife in their faces. The one bouncer took the knife away like the kid had given it to him. Ducky Donald laughed. 'Got sound too.' He powered up the volume, the kid shrieking about how they were racists, not letting blacks in. Ducky Donald sighed out a stream of smoke. 'We get that all the time.'

The bouncer sneered. 'What, you an MK? The bloody spear of the rainbow nation. Piss off arsehole.'

Ducky Donald jumped to a camera in the chill room, no one there. 'In here's where the shit happens,' he said. 'The things I've seen you wouldn't believe people'd do in public.'

'This cover the loos too?' said Pylon.

The screen filled with dancers, the speakers blasted an amplified sound. Ducky shut down the volume, zooming on and off faces. 'We're thinking of that.'

Pylon thought, Yeah, sure, like that wasn't the first place they installed the system. He watched the play of the camera, had to be on some track across the ceiling.

'Goddamned wonderful piece of hi-tech,' said Ducky, dollying slowly over the crowd.

Pylon caught an upturned face, said, 'Stop. Go back.' Ducky Donald opened the angle. 'There. That one. With the black hair.' The camera came tight on her: eyes closed, sweat glistening on her forehead, mouth slightly open to show the tips of her teeth.

It could be. An outside chance, something about the shape of her face. He leant forward. 'What d'you think?'

Ducky Donald pulled at his cigarette. 'You're gonna tell me that's her?'

'I reckon.'

Ducky squinted at the screen. 'Nah. Not a chance.'

'It is,' said Pylon. 'Except last time I saw her she was blonde.' He took a long swallow at his beer, watching the young woman dancing, not a care in the world. Seemed to be dancing all by herself. Attractive babe.

'And why's she of note?'

'Cops're after her.'

'I gathered. Question is, why are you?'

'Long story,' said Pylon. He drained the bottle of beer, stood the empty at the foot of the couch. 'Thanks for the help.'

Ducky Donald shrugged. 'Just don't cause any shit on the premises.'

'Wouldn't dream of it,' said Pylon.

Two hours later he watched the woman leave the club with a man that had a decade on her at least. The two of them walking hand-in-hand casually through the dark streets to an Audi Quattro parked a block away. He followed them across the city, up and over the Nek, along the coastal stretch to Llandudno, down into the suburb. Not another car about this time of the morning. At a fork he lost them, then saw headlights sweep into a street below. He made it down in time to see an automatic gate rolling closed. Lights came on in the house. Pylon went back to his car, tapped an SMS through to Mace in New York.

19

'Trust me. I'm a dealer.' Isabella ran a finger down Mace Bishop's cheek. Opened the door to her apartment, going in ahead of him.

'You're not the problem.'

'So what is?'

'Mo's the problem.'

'Schmooze him.'

In the lounge Mace took off his coat, draped it over the back of an armchair. 'All I want to know are two things: when, and that the deposit's secure.'

'You can't believe me?' Isabella collapsed on the couch, eased off her shoes. 'It's going to work out, Macey. I've got my little husband on the case.'

That, Mace thought, was the real problem. The little husband didn't have a great track record from what he could gather.

'I'm not going to leave you out in the blue exhaust, am I now? There's lots riding on this, Mace. A cool fortune.' She patted the seat of the couch, enticing.

He sat in the armchair. 'Exactly. So when?'

She ignored him, kept patting the couch leather. 'Come and keep me company.'

'Not a good idea,' said Mace.

'You wouldn't have said that once.'

'Once was once. Times change.'

'I forgot. The family man.'

Mace nodded. 'So when, exactly?'

'That last time in the Meurice,' she said, getting up, kneeling down beside him, 'wasn't good. Not the sort of memory I like for what we had. What d'you say?' Reached up to take his hands.

'You said you'd got over it.'

She nibbled at his fingers. 'I lied.'

'Bella,' he said, 'don't do this.'

'No? Then why're you here, Mace? Tell me? I didn't ask you. You came up. Or is this my Macey-boy the smuggler, daring all, suddenly getting cold feet?' She sat astride him, lap-dancer style, her skirt riding up, and took his face in her hands.

Mace said, 'No.'

Isabella grinned at him, her hand pressed into his crotch. 'No? I'd have thought, yes, by the feel of it.' Her lips came down to his, pushing hard against his teeth.

Mace thought, Don't. Felt his hand on her thigh. Her hand covering his, taking it higher. The touch of her on his fingers brought a rasp to his breath.

Afterwards he had to leave. Right away. Isabella lying on the couch beneath a throw, amused at his hurry. His searching for shoes under the furniture, mismatching his button holes.

'You can stay the night,' she said. 'We could do it again, in bed.'

'I don't think so.' Mace shrugged into his coat.

'Oumou on your conscience. How cute. Not like you, Mace, to have a conscience.'

'What we haven't settled,' said Mace, 'is the date.'

'Ever the Pitbull.' She sighed. 'Never lets go' – watching him flip open a small diary, scanning a calendar. 'For heaven's sake, Mace, it was just a screw. Something we used to do before you met Oumou. It's not like I'm a new lay.'

'When in January?'

'You tell me.'

'Saturday 18th?'

'That's good, if it's good for you.' Isabella put her head coquettishly at an angle. 'It was good for you, I could tell.'

She was right, Mace admitted back at his hotel, sex with Isabella smelt of guns. Always had done. A brush of linseed when her body heat came up. You could taste it if you licked her skin. That excitement that possessed you.

He stared at himself in the bathroom mirror: the lines at the corners of his eyes that hardened his gaze. The curve of his lips, tightening. A redness at the flanges of his nostrils. 'Why'd you do it?' he said aloud. 'You weak bastard.'

Oumou'd know. Sense it somehow. Just know. Truth was he felt like shit. Really bad. Sick in his gut.

'You think you can get away with it?' He searched in his eyes for a remorse that frightened him. In their marriage he hadn't betrayed her, always respected her. Until now. He spat in the basin. Rinsed his mouth and spat again, the taste of bile still on his tongue.

He went through to the bedroom and from the minibar poured a whisky. This took away the taste and the lurking edge of unease. He chased it with another, drinking without pleasure. The second down, he stripped off and showered, over the jet of water could hear his cellphone beeping. Five minutes he let the water drum against his skull, thinking, how was this going to end?

The message was from Christa: What r u dng?

A towel wrapped round his waist, he sat on the bed to respond: Why are you awake?

He knew she went through spells of waking in the night. At first she'd called out to them and they'd rushed through to her. Lay with her, held her while she sobbed with terror. But over the last year she'd moved out of that, reached some accommodation with her fate, become accepting. If she woke, she read. In a household of no books, Christa took to reading. Some mornings he'd find her asleep with the bedside light on, a book fallen on the floor, Cat2 and Cupcake entangled at the bottom of the bed. Her thing with books he couldn't understand. Stories had no fascination for him. Unless they were real.

Christa replied: Reading Harry Potter. What u do 2day?

Major shit, he thought. Thumbed back: Saw some people. Walked in Central Park. Very very cold. Had supper in a little bistro.

The message sent, he unscrewed a third miniature from the minibar, filling this with soda. Hoping as he sipped it to hear again from his daughter. The queasiness still in his stomach. The room phone rang. Isabella.

'Just to say goodbye,' she said. 'See you in Cape Town.' Her voice light with laughter.

I'll bet, thought Mace, entirely sure having Isabella in the same city as Oumou was a bad idea. 'Till the 18th,' he said, a silence opening between them. His cellphone beeped twice.

'Such a busy boy,' said Isabella. 'Keep the faith, Mace, you're still a good screw.' She hung up before he could think of a reply.

He checked his messages.

The first was from Pylon: Found her in Llandudno.

The second from Christa: Poor daddy all alone. Should have taken Cupcake.

20

When Mace got back from New York the first thing he checked on was Vittoria Corombona. Found her on a packed Llandudno beach under the noonday sun.

'No question,' he said to Pylon.

'Pleased I got it right.' Pylon handed Mace back a photograph of Isabella's husband. 'Makes this a bit messy.'

'No kidding. Gonsalves on her tail and we're supposed to do business with him.'

They watched the couple walking in the shallows hand-in-hand.

'Question is how soon's Gonsalves likely to find his way here?'

Mace slipped off his shoes, rolled up the bottom of his chinos. 'Perhaps he needs delaying.'

'Meaning?'

'Search me. Maybe something like a contribution to his pension.'

Pylon wiped a hand over his face, said, 'How about an ice-cream?'

They bought mint-chocolates on a stick from a vendor sitting on his coolbox eyeing the tanga babes.

'The problem with mint-chocolate,' said Pylon, 'is it tastes like mouthwash.'

'Only to you. My ice-cream of choice.' Mace took a bite, letting the chocolate and mint fuse in his mouth. 'The trick is catching the chocolate before it falls off.'

They ambled onto the sand towards the water, feeling over-dressed among the sun worshippers.

'You think Gonsalves might be tempted?'

'Possibility. I seem to recall retirement held some terrors for him.'

At the far end of the beach Vittoria and Paulo reached the boulders that shaped the bay and turned, heading slowly back.

'She'll recognise us,' said Pylon, watching the couple. 'Which would not be a good thing.'

Mace picked at the remains of the chocolate coating his ice-cream, freed a sizeable piece and dropped it into his mouth. Crunched it, said, 'We'd not be asking much of him. Just a postponement.'

'And the reason?'

'No reason. Why's there have to be a reason? The money's the reason he won't be interested in any other reason.'

Pylon flicked his ice-cream wrapper and stick into a dirtbin. 'If you say so.'

Top down in the Spider they drove back to town, getting into a bumper-to-bumper along the Camps Bay strip, the traffic moving slower than the bikini moms pushing prams under the palms.

Mace said, 'What I hate about the season is traffic jams. Every beach round the peninsula there's a snarl-up.' He pressed the hooter to get the driver in front concentrating on the road instead of the beautiful bodies playing volleyball.

Pylon said, 'How much were you thinking of?'

'We could start low. Say ten K. Raise it to a max of say fifteen. I wouldn't be comfortable going beyond that.'

Pylon whistled. 'Just to keep him off for a few days?'

'Actually almost three weeks.'

'Almost a thousand a day!'

'Sounds attractive, doesn't it?'

'No kidding.'

They met Gonsalves at the Long Street Café. On a stinking after-noon the day after New Year the place was empty, everybody headed for the sea. Mace and Pylon flopped onto two couches in a corner. Ordered Kahlúa Dom Pedros and tall sparkling waters. As the order arrived Gonsalves came in, carrying his jacket over his shoulder, his shirt stained with sweat at the armpits. He gave off a blast of tobacco and BO.

'I'll have two of those,' he told the waiter, pointing at the Dom Pedros. 'With whisky, not the fancy stuff. Oh 'n hey, you got an ashtray for me?'

'Sorry, sir, smoking's outside,' said the waiter.

'Who said I'm gonna smoke?' – Gonsalves collapsed into an easy chair, fished in his jacket pocket for a cigarette. 'Heat I can't take.'

'Sir…' stammered the waiter.

'It's alright,' said Pylon, 'he's not planning to smoke it. Just bring the drinks, okay.'

The waiter backed off dubiously.

Gonsalves said, 'So what you want?'

Mace cleared his throat. 'More or less to find out how things're going.'

'In a nutshell: up to shit.' Gonsalves stripped paper off the cigarette. 'I got the commissioner wanting to know every second day where's the poppie? His word. Poppie. You ever heard anyone wasn't an Afrikaner use that word? Meet my commissioner. A black man. Been in the force as long as me, now he's a commissioner, I'm a white man with a foot in the marble foyers. What the French say c'est la vie. Never mind. The commissioner's point is how come a poppie can go missing in our fair city? Because this is not good for tourism, captain, this is not the sort of incident what they call the gateway city, the mother city, wants riding on its name. We've got a brand here, captain, he tells me, this brand can't be tarnished or all the lovely Germans, English, Americans, Japanese gonna take their lovely euros, pounds, dollars, yen off to Malaysia. Find the poppie, captain. Find the killers. Get the Italians off my back. Know what I mean. This is pink city, captain, we can't have gays being butchered. Think of the brand. Get out there, captain, talk to people.' Gonsalves balled tobacco between the palms of his hands. 'This commissioner, Khumalo, talks of whistle-blowers. Somewhere there's gotta be a whistle-blower. Find the whistle-blower, captain, help him blow his whistle.'

The waiter brought the two Dom Pedros and an ashtray.

Gonsalves popped the plug of tobacco into his mouth, surveyed the mess of tobacco bits strewn over his trousers and the floor, said, 'Bit late with that' – indicating the ashtray. He reached for a Dom Pedro, sucked down half of the mix without coming up for air.

Mace wondered how he did that and kept from swallowing the tobacco.

'Another thing,' Gonsalves wiped his mouth with the back of his hand, 'you ever heard of irritable bowel syndrome?'

Mace and Pylon shook their heads.

'Well that's what the commissioner's given me. It's virulent. I wake up about two, three in the morning with this pain like someone's got their fist in my gut. I lie there breathing shallow 'cos this fist's pressing against my lungs too. Then the pain starts in my side, sharp, like a stitch except worse, slowly it slides down into my colon and I know okay it's going, soon I'm gonna be okay again. Except sometimes it goes on for six hours. Khumalo's gut-ache I call it.' He finished the Dom Pedro, sucking noisily around the ice. 'Sorry you asked, hey?'

Mace said, 'That's a pity.'

Gonsalves glanced at him. 'More'n a pity, china. Hope it's not in your destiny.' He licked ice-cream from the straw. 'So what've you got to tell me?'

Pylon said, 'Just wanted to know if there was some way we could be of help.'

'Such as?'

Mace leant forward. 'Such as, letting you in on some information.'

'Meaning you know where she is?'

'In a manner of speaking. Only problem is there's a time issue involved.'

'What sort of period are we talking?'

'Till, say, the middle of January.'

Gonsalves swirled the straw through the mixture. 'You've got a good reason for this?'

'We have.'

'Which's obviously confidential?'

'That sort of thing.'

The captain sucked at his Dom Pedro. 'What if I get to her before then? In the normal course of events.'

Mace said, 'Maybe we could talk about it. At that point.'

'Anything's possible.' Gonsalves finished the drink, ran a finger round the inside of the glass and licked it clean. 'We in the service're open to discussion as long as justice is served.'

'It will be.'

'Splendid.' Gonsalves wiped his fingers on a serviette. 'What've you got in mind?'

Pylon moved a leather briefcase across the floor until it bumped against the policeman's leg. Gonsalves looked at him, them, for a long time. 'I'll have your balls,' he said. 'Both of you.'

'It's cool,' said Pylon.

Gonsalves chewed at what was left of the tobacco wad in his mouth, staring at them both. 'Don't get me wrong, about this. I can make you think car-guarding's a good option.'

Mace said, 'We'll deliver. Tuesday 21 January. Scout's honour.'

Gonsalves ignored the humour. 'If we need to talk again, we need to talk again.'

'Of course.'

Captain Gonsalves rose, hawked the tobacco into the ashtray, dusted his trousers. 'Happy New Year.'

'Likewise,' said Mace.

Pylon nodded. 'Don't forget your briefcase.'

'No intention of doing that.' Gonsalves smiled at the two men, stooping to grip the briefcase by its handle. 'Real leather.' He patted it. 'How thoughtful.'

21

Five days into the New Year, Mace and Pylon set up a logistics meeting with Mo Siq.

'Make it my apartment,' he said. 'Come'n be jealous of my view.'

Getting to the Waterfront was a nightmare, Mace and Pylon pulled in twenty minutes late. Mo waved aside their apologies. Mo was expansive, until Mace and Pylon explained the situation. Then Mo, in shorts and a flashy Madiba shirt worn loose, was not relaxed. Paced the balcony of his apartment most agitated. Mace and Pylon standing, beers in hand, letting the man adjust to the information. Typical Mo, Mace thought, the ostentatious address. Rich Jews his only neighbours. From three floors up good view, though, across the V&A to the harbour and back to the mountain. Nothing to be jealous about, given his own aspects. When he beat the bank off.

The situation they'd outlined to Mo ran: cargo scheduled for loading Wednesday afternoon, Duncan Dock, Berth D, ship sails that night, deposit paid the next day.

Mo stopped to take a swallow of a single malt he'd splashed with water. 'Again. I'm dispatching early Wednesday morning, therefore loaded Wednesday afternoon, and your boat sails away with my goodies and only twenty-four hours later do I get to see some money.'

'As agreed,' said Pylon.

Mo stared at him. 'I took it you were joking. I thought in this day 'n age you'd do business better. Professionally.'

'It's straight,' said Mace. 'You have our word.'

'Word's not what I care for. What I care for is this' – he held up his right hand, rubbed his thumb against his fingers. 'Moolah, Mace Bishop. Moolah.'

'The arrangement's solid,' said Pylon.

'Yeah sure it is. I've got to take the say-so of security guards.'

Mace said, 'What? What'd you say?'

'Goons. Thick necks. The word of guard dogs.'

'Up yours, Mo.' Mace feeling heat rising in his face, taking a step forward.

Mo smirked. 'The boy's flushing. Macey the hammer. Good to smash fingers, the only thing he could do. You're nowhere, Mace. Nowhere 'n no one.' Mo gesturing like he was throwing corn to chickens. Turned away.

Mace angled to get past Pylon, reaching to get a grip on Mo's fancy shirt. 'Don't come the high and mighty.'

Mo squirmed out of Mace's hold, keeping Pylon as a shield. Pylon blocking Mace.

'You cheap shit-' but Mace got no further, Pylon shouting, 'Okay, okay, let's cool it.'

Mo grinned. 'Touched a nerve, hey! Bit raw there.'

'Stuff off,' said Mace.

'Guys,' said Pylon. 'Guys. Help me out here. Wind it down.'

Mace shrugged free of Pylon's hold. 'This was the deal, Mo. This was the deal in November. This is the deal now.'

'Except in November you were gonna pay me on delivery.'

'A deposit.'

'On delivery. Now you tell me one day later. Like I'm smelling a set-up. I'm thinking you're hanging me out here. I'm feeling done over.'

'It's nothing like that,' said Pylon.

'Convince me.'

Pylon set his beer bottle on a table beside the remains of Mo's breakfast. 'What more can we say?' He faced Mo, holding out his hands. 'This is the way it is, bru. We're all taking a risk. Me and Mace most of all. It's our lives on the table.'

'My career,' snapped Mo.

'Sure it is. But you wouldn't be doing it if you didn't consider this worth the pot.'

Mo grunted dismissively. 'Get me,' he said, putting a finger in Pylon's face. 'Understand me word for word. I find out something else's going down here, you'll become unhappy. You will want your life to end.'

Pylon stared him out.

Mace said, 'Oh shit.'

'Try me,' Mo said.

Going down in the lift Mace thought, we do things for people, what thanks do we get? Nothing but grief. Said, 'It's not as if he's even putting out personally. So what's with the heavy stuff?'

'Can't help it,' said Pylon. 'That's part of Mo. In the old days, in exile, Mo was paranoid all the time. Never went to London because he reckoned someone would stick him with a poisoned umbrella.'

The lift doors opened onto what would be a marina but was still a building site. 'Bloody paranoid,' said Mace, imitating Mo's accent. 'Why doesn't he bugger off back to the curry basin, I ask you?'

22

Isabella slept off her jet-lag before she called Paulo. Stood now at the hotel window looking over the trees towards the city's downtown. What she'd seen coming in from the airport a nice place for an African city, if you ignored the squatter mess either side of the highway: tin shacks, igloos of black plastic sheeting, goats, cows. You turned away from that, not a bad place to spend your last days as Paulo was doing. She thumbed in her husband's cellphone number. He came on groggy in the middle of the afternoon.

'Honeypie! Did I wake you?'

Paulo's voice coming over irritated: 'Why're you calling?'

Isabella loved it. 'Oh, hon, I'm concerned. I'm here to cheer you.'

'Here?'

'Same place you are. Think you should come to mamma quickly. Leave the little bimbo for a couple of hours, huh!'

She smiled at the silence. Paulo eventually saying, 'Ludo told you?'

'Hon, Ludo tells me everything. I told Ludo, relax, no harm done, if she's gonna make you work better then wonderful.'

What she'd also told Ludo was to make an arrangement for Paulo and Vittoria for after. Which made Ludo happy.

'So surprise, surprise, hon. Here I am. Bit earlier than expected but a wife has to support her hubby too. Come 'n talk to me.'

'Where?'

'Pink place called Mount Nelson. Say in an hour?'

'Jesus, Isabella.'

'Jesus nothing,' said Isabella. 'I'll be waiting.'

Next she hit Mace Bishop in her contacts list.

'Was wondering when I'd hear from you,' he said.

Isabella laughed. 'Such a welcome to your beautiful city. You're sounding a bit stressed Macey-boy.'

'Just a little,' said Mace. 'Mostly about a payment that's due.'

'Relax.' She turned from the window. Slipped into her shoes. 'In about an hour you're going to hear it from the horse's mouth.'

'Really. From your husband?'

'The great man himself. All the details. So how about dinner?'

'Could be arranged,' said Mace. 'Where're you? The Nellie?'

'If that's Mount Nelson.'

'I'll pick you up. About eight?'

'Oh, and Mace,' she said before he could disconnect, 'go easy on my beloved. Paulo's Paulo, that's one thing he can't help.'

Vittoria shifted onto an elbow, watching Paulo head for the shower. 'That Isabella?'

Paulo's affirmative coming over the toilet flush.

'She's in town already? Where?'

'Hotel called Mount Nelson.'

'Think we should do her now?'

Paulo came back into the bedroom. 'Too many complications. We gotta sell the snow. Get the cash to her, sort it out after. What we don't want is Francisco on our ass.'

Vittoria dipped a wet finger in her bedside supply. 'Thing is, Paulo, what if she flies away again?'

'Let me find out, okay? Get her schedule.'

Vittoria sucked her finger. 'Best thing's to kill her now, Paulo. Statistics say a tourist's gonna get killed it's gonna happen in the first forty-eight hours.'

Paulo shook his head. 'You take too much of that stuff.' He disappeared into the shower steam, still shaking his head.

'You not gonna go soft on me, baby?'

Paulo didn't answer.

Vittoria lay back wondering if Paulo had the balls or was he going to move out of this the way he'd tried with the queers.

When his cellphone rang she took it. 'Yeah!'

Isabella's voice: 'Where's Paulo?'

'Taking a shower.'

'Let me talk to him.'

Vittoria thought, Screw you. Said in mock posh English, 'Of course, ma'am' – and took the cellphone to Paulo, lobbing it over the glass panel, 'Catch, Paulo.'

Isabella heard Paulo swearing, the sound of the shower, the phone bouncing around. The noises stopped.

'Honeypie,' she said, 'bring the money with you.'

Paulo got to Isabella's room and she hit straight into the stuff he was jumpy about. Counted the money, wanted to know why he was so far off the target.

Had him wound up with her bitchy voice. 'Paulo, honeypie, this is me, your wife, on the line here. Not you, or Ludo, or Francisco, but me.' Talking down to him, really talking down to him as if he were ten years old. Paulo having to sit on the edge of the bed while she played teacher. 'So Francisco would be disappointed. Nobody likes to lose money. But Francisco loses this, he doesn't notice it. Not really. People who notice it are people like me. My agents. People who've really got their asses in the flames. They're the ones going to get burned, Paulo. Not just third degree. I'm talking full-on cinderisation. Full-on black stump and crispy. And why? Because my little honeypie didn't pull his finger out. Kept it waggling in his girlfriend's pussy when he should've been out there pitching, pitching, pitching.'

Paulo shifted uneasily.

'You stop being useful, Paulo, you're finished. Worm chow.'

She went to stand at the window so he could see nothing but this black spectre against the light. Thinking, Vittoria's right, the bitch's at the end of usefulness. Time for an accident. Time to move on. After the job.

'You want to listen now, honeypie, hear a thing or two about the loop you're working?'

Paulo nodded. What options?

'Let me hear you.'

'Yeah.' He cleared his throat. 'Tell me.'

Isabella smiled. 'What you're doing, hon, is not simply turning chemicals into money. What you're doing is setting up a stream. Cash becomes hardware. Hardware becomes diamonds. Diamonds become dollars. As I said, a lot of people're drinking from this stream. Mostly people who don't drink from your cut-glass crystal. What I'm saying is, you don't set up the stream you're the man who gets fingered first.'

She came away from the window took her cellphone off the dressing table, put in a number, and listened. 'Who I'm phoning is a guy called Mace Bishop. I'm going to tell him you're the money man for the down payment and the whole deal. You're going to tell him your landline number and address. That address is where he comes to collect the cash.'

Turned out Mace Bishop was cool about this arrangement. Isabella gave the phone to Paulo.

'Hey,' said Paulo.

'I'm listening,' came the response.

Paulo gave the Llandudno address and the house telephone number.

Mace said, 'I'll be round to collect the down-payment Saturday morning. Say about eleven. Be waiting.'

'Fuck you,' said Paulo.

'That's not the line you want to take,' said Mace. 'Be nice and friendly.'

Paulo disconnected.

'I wouldn't say things like that to him,' said Isabella. 'The guy's a hyena.'

'Like everyone,' said Paulo, handed the cellphone back to Isabella. 'What if I don't make the down-payment?'

Isabella tapped the phone against the palm of her hand. 'I don't think you won't. Four nights to go, one of those a Friday. Shouldn't be a problem.'

Paulo thought, Shit, she's hanging me out. Said, 'I can do it.'

'Course you can. Dealer like you this is no hassle at all.' She gave him a dazzler, flash of teeth, lips thinned. Dangerous as a snake Paulo had always found that smile.

'And if I don't?'

She grimaced. 'Perhaps we shouldn't go there' – held out her hand to him, 'How about a cream tea?'

Paulo dabbed the scone first with strawberry jam, then cream. The only problem with the English habit was how to get it in your mouth without hoovering cream up your nostrils. Not an issue for anyone else he'd noticed. A lounge of them going at the scones and cream.

'What you think?' Isabella said. 'Something else, you must admit.'

Paulo took the serviette to the cream smearing his upper lip. He swallowed. 'What would be a help, would be getting say ten days out of your friend. Five days is tight.'

'Nothing I can do, hon. Out of my hands. The deal's going down Saturday. Why's there a problem here?'

Paulo thought, A problem here! A problem like how to get four hundred K from three hundred K max worth of powder. In four days. Pushing it in every sense of the word. 'No problem,' he said.

Isabella leant across, holding out a serviette. Paulo pulled back. 'There's a tag of jam on the end of your nose,' she said, blotting at it. 'Better' – and sat back. 'Don't you love this place?' – gesturing round the hotel lounge, popping what was left of a scone into her mouth. 'Probably they didn't even have to theme it colonial.'

'Maybe I should drop the money with you?' Paulo watched Isabella top up his coffee, coffee that was as piss poor as instant.

'Would make sense. He's your friend. Your contact. Maybe you should close the deal with him.'

'Ordinarily, that's how it would've gone. Except this time I want you in the loop. Prove something to Francisco. I want you to handle this all the way.' She brushed crumbs from her lap.

'What about Ludovico?'

'Paulo, hon. I told you. You want in with Francisco, you do this. Ludo'll be around.' She reached across to stroke his hand. 'It's just a pick-up. You worried, get your girl on the scene. Mace goes weak at the sight of a babe.' Isabella's fingers curled over his, she stood.

Paulo looked up at her smiling down at him. 'Poor honeypie.'

Afterwards Paulo felt like shit. Walked back to his car thinking, Christ, Christ, Christ, why'd he let her dangle him like that? Freaking bitch. To hell with her.

He Zippo'd a smoke. His hands shaking. Anger, humiliation, the indignity of obeying her giving him the sweats the more he thought about it. He needed to be calm, to consider this thing through. Sat in the car staring down the avenue of palms to the fella in the pith helmet at the bottom directing a 4x4 between the pillars. An entrance like a Greek temple: columns and plinths. The 4x4 roared up in low gear, a Grand Cherokee, Ludo at the wheel.

The shit was going on? Paulo about to find out, half-opened the car door when his head cleared: Nah, to hell with them. Time to go on safari. See the Big Five. Chill in an African lodge. Yeah! Up yours Francisco. He fished in the pockets of his chinos for his cell, found Oupa K's number.

'Oupa K, it's Paulo.'

'You're saying, chief?'

'Paulo. You remember ...'

'What you want, Paulo?'

'What's happening, man? How're you doing?'

'Hanging.'

Paulo laughed. The Xhosa playing so hard he must be desperate for stocks. 'You got a moment?'

'You've had a moment. What you want, yankee?'

'Maybe we can talk again?'

'That's what we're doing already.'

'Sure.'

'So talk.'

'About our arrangement: I'm thinking half as candy, half as rocks.'

'That right, chief? You worked out a tag?'

'Sure. I'm thinking three, four hundred K.'

'Crap, yankee.'

'I'm doing the chemistry, man. You're going to put that out at double. Maybe more. You're scoring here. Way I'm looking at it you're turning a profit here close to two hundred thou. Maybe more. You hearing me, dude? You comprehensive here? Listen up again: half powder, half rocks, four hundred K. Sweet?'

Was when Paulo realised he was talking into the ether. 'Motherfucker,' he yelled, hitting the redial. The voicemail came on after ten rings, telling him to leave a message. 'Jesus, assholes,' he screamed, banging the steering wheel with both hands, almost smashing the cell. Fired up another cigarette. Halfway down the stick he crushed it. Redialled.

Oupa K came on, saying, 'Alright.'

'You hung up on me, man. Nobody hangs up on me.'

'I said, it's good.'

Paulo heard this for the first time.

'Friday morning, yankee. There at the lighthouse. Ten a.m.'

Paulo eased the Quattro down the avenue, shaking another cigarette from the pack. At the gate the pith helmet snapped him a salute as he swung into the traffic without a rightward glance. In the rear-view mirror caught an on-coming car flashing lights at him.

Heading out of the city up the Nek, over, the Atlantic wide below, down into the coke strip of Camps Bay with all the chic coffee bars along the sidewalk, Paulo was scheming: get to work on the crack, Vittoria to check out the safari operations. Only problem remained getting rid of Isabella. Wouldn't be any problem at all to walk out on Ludo. He wouldn't know they'd gone for like ten, twelve hours. Meantime he and Vittoria would be blowing the bucks. Five-star safari time.

Paulo's mood was singing when he pulled into the Llandudno drive. Ran into the house shouting, 'Ria, suges, I've worked it out, babe' – the intercom bell rang catching him in the entrance hall. He answered. On the screen was a guy in a white open-necked shirt, chewing a cigarette.

Paulo said, 'How can I help you?' On the patio he could see Vittoria, bare-boobed to the sun.

The man said, 'Ja, um.' Stared up at the camera, shifted the cigarette round his lips with his tongue. The cigarette was unlit.

'There something you want?' said Paulo.

'Mr Ludovico?' asked the man.

'He's out,' said Paulo.

'Mr Paulo Cave-dag... Cavedag-na?'

Paulo thought, cop. Thought, Be cool.

'Sure. You're?'

'Captain Gonsalves. Maybe I can come in for a moment?'

'There's a problem, captain?'

'No. No problem.'

Big problem, thought Paulo.

'You got a badge? Some ID, captain?'

The cop grinned at the camera. 'This is what I always tell people, Mr Cave-dag-na. Don't open the door till you've seen some ID. Do like the Americans do in the movies. Ask for ID.' The captain held a card up to the camera, Paulo couldn't read a thing written on it. 'You an American, Mr Cave-dag-na?'

'One moment, please,' said Paulo, turning off the intercom, calling, 'Vittoria, Vittoria.' Thinking, this is a cop. He knows my name, he knows Ludovico's. He's gotta be looking for Vittoria.

'What's it?' Vittoria said, sitting up. 'Give me a break won't you?'

'Cops,' said Paulo which got Vittoria inside and up the stairs fast.

Paulo pressed the intercom button. 'Come in, captain.'

He stalled the policeman in the driveway.

'Captain, I'm Paulo Cavedagna' – shaking the captain's hand, guiding him towards the front door, showing him inside to the living room.

'Nice place for a holiday,' said Gonsalves, looking about.

'Been a wonderful vacation,' said Paulo.

'A good thing coming to an end?'

'Yup. We'll be Stateside next week. But you got a great country, captain, we'll be back. For sure.'

The captain took out a notebook, flipped to the last page. 'There somebody called Vittoria Corombona with you and Mr Ludovico?'

Paulo shook his head. 'Was. She came for Christmas. Flew home a week ago.'

'She a friend of yours?'

'A relation. Why? You looking for her?'

'I believe she can help me,' said Gonsalves. 'In an investigation.'

23

Come the afternoon of Tuesday 14 January, when Mace took the call from Isabella, he couldn't decide if he was pleased or not. The excitement and fear he'd known in New York. Except with a cold edge: Isabella in the same city as Oumou was tricky. The woman a loose cannon on any deck. Still, he set up a dinner date. Better to keep her humoured than feeling spurned. Somewhat of an hour later he had Paulo, confirming the collection details. A whine to his voice. The guy trying some tough stuff, which amused Mace.

When Mace disconnected, Pylon stood in the doorway to his office, grinning at how the exchange had ended.

'What a prick,' said Mace.

'It happens.' Pylon couldn't stop the grin. 'Got your goat didn't he?'

'Maybe you should call Mo tell him the deal's good.'

'Maybe you should.'

'Cut me some slack, hey.'

Pylon sighed. 'Sometimes you must face your demons' – at the same time flipped open his cellphone.

Mo Siq answered right off. 'Yes or no?'

'Yes,' said Pylon.

'Midnight my trucks are rolling. What about the money?'

'Tell him Saturday morning half past eleven,' said Mace. 'His apartment.'

Pylon did.

'And the rest?'

'On the Monday.'

Mo gave his grunt, disconnecting.

Pylon stared at his phone, said, 'Have a nice day to you too Mr Siq' – and clipped the phone shut. 'It's so rewarding doing business with him.'

Mace chuckled, suggested why didn't they take a break, have a Coke float at the café in the Gardens. Surely a good idea on a long and hot day with something to celebrate? Especially as come Saturday they were headed for a place where it'd cost a month's salary in hard US for a Coke float. Or they wouldn't be able to order one at all.

Pylon said, 'Don't remind me.'

'Relax,' said Mace, 'it's a short flight.'

'I don't do any sort of flying. Remember.' Pylon slipped his phone into the pocket of his slacks. 'That was our agreement. You fly. I stay on the ground.'

'This is different.'

'Don't tell me.'

They shut the office, ambled up Barnet, down Dunkley, crossed Hatfield into Avenue behind the Gardens Commercial High, the school shuttered for the holidays, and turned right into Paddock beneath the oaks. Dappled shade but no relief from the heat. Both men breaking a sweat in their armpits. At the fish ponds they came out of the shadow into the heaviness of the sun, the light blinding even through sunglasses. In Government Avenue the tree canopy took the weight off their heads. Mace glanced up the avenue at the distant pillared entrance to the Mount Nelson, wondering what Isabella was doing with that jerk, her husband. Considered too that he, Oumou and Isabella hadn't been in the same town in twelve years, since their last days in Malitia. The thought brought out a flush behind the perspiration. Caused a nervous cough.

Pylon thumped his back. 'You alright?'

'Yeah,' said Mace. 'Nothing a swig of Coke won't wash down.'

They took a table where the shade was deepest, near the bird cages, the canaries in loud song, untroubled by the sweltering afternoon. Only other people on the terrace were a couple eating burgers and a group of backpackers in the full sun like cancer wasn't an option. Next time he looked a woman, her hair covered by a shawl, had taken a table on the far side of the terrace. She was bent over a document, a highlighter clasped in her right hand. Mace felt something about the woman seemed familiar but he wasn't troubled enough to mention it.

The Coke and ice-cream went down smoothly, Mace not saying much, Pylon getting into his stride about Treasure wanting to adopt an AIDS orphan. Didn't want to have one of their own because of these kids stacking up in the shacks and huts, being looked after by grandparents. Was alright for her to talk, she had Pumla. But what about him? He didn't have a kid of his own. His own blood. Instead she's uptight about social responsibility. The new black middle class in their rich houses and SUVs not showing any compassion. What Arch Tutu called ubuntu. Like she expected differently?

Mace listened with half an ear, his eyes drawn to the quiet woman at the far table. She looked up, smiled at him: Sheemina February.

At the same time his cellphone rang, a new number on the screen.

'I'm standing at a public phone kiosk in Llandudno,' were Captain Gonsalves's opening words. 'The one just before you go onto the beach. Just had this interesting talk with a Mr Cave-dag-no. Name mean anything to you?'

Mace told him no. Asked where did Mr Cave-dag-no stay?

Gonsalves gave the address.

Mace said, 'Maybe we could sort this out the same way as last time?'

'Depends.'

'Always does,' said Mace. He could hear the cop's slow chewing. 'Anything specific you have in mind?'

'I've got the commissioner on my back you have to understand. The man wants the poppie because the Italians are about to send people out to show us up.'

'I hear you,' said Mace.

'We agreed next Tuesday. I can't do next Tuesday anymore. This's drawing in.'

'Can you do Saturday?'

'Saturday would be easier.'

'That would suit us.'

The line went quiet, Mace could hear excited children shriek-ing, the noise blocking Gonsalves's voice. 'Normally I wouldn't be doing it this way, Mr Bishop,' he was saying. 'Normally I would go straight in there with a warrant, get the mess cleaned up.'

'Sure,' said Mace. 'I appreciate that. I appreciate your call. Listen, let's say you can go knocking there from eleven-thirty Saturday morning. How would that do?'

'I can live with that.'

'We can maybe ease the waiting too. Like by three grand.'

'I didn't hear that,' said Gonsalves.

'Next Tuesday we'll sort you out,' said Mace. 'Adios.'

'Three large,' exclaimed Pylon. 'We're not a bank.'

Mace shrugged. 'The commission we're pulling, we'll not miss it.'

'Long as it ends there.'

'He's a cop for Chrissakes. He's honourable.' The two men laughed. Mace looked over at the table on the edge of the terrace. Sheemina February had left.

'Sheemina February was behind you,' said Mace.

Pylon turned round. 'Where?'

'She's gone. Seems to me we're bumping into her a bit too often.'

'Coincidence,' said Pylon. 'Lawyers hang out here. Huguenot Chambers is full of lawyers. High Court's round the corner, it's to be expected.'

'All the same,' said Mace.

At five Mace was home to pick up his daughter for their swimming session. He called downstairs to Oumou in her studio that they were off and heard her call back, 'Oui. Enjoy the water.'

Christa, in a black Speedo under one of Mace's T-shirts, ears glittering with studs he'd bought her, closed her book, said, 'Let's go, Papa. Let's go, we're late.'

Mace scooped her up from the couch and carried her through to the garage where the Spider ticked quietly. She was still a child's weight although he sensed the strength of the muscles in her arms hugging his neck. She squeezed.

He mock-gagged. 'You're strangling me?'

'We've got to move,' she said, setting Cupcake on the dashboard as a mascot.

'What's it? There's some boys you want to impress?'

She giggled. 'Papa!'

Mace plopped her in the Spider, fitted her wheelchair into the space behind the seats. Before he could start the engine Christa slotted a Britney Spears CD into the player, saying, 'Don't even say aargh,' but Mace did and she slapped at his shoulder.

He drove fast down Molteno, the city spread below them, Christa singing Britney's words, both of them exhilarated by the speed. At the Annandale traffic lights he bought a joke sheet from a cross-dresser in a blonde wig and an orange miniskirt, the trans squealing at him 'Hello, how are you, what a sweetie,' poncing and pouting all the time it took Mace to dig out some change. He gave the photostatted sheet to Christa, said, 'Read us a joke.'

She read two, neither funny, and scrunched up the sheet in disgust.

'Bit of a waste of time,' he said.

'I know better ones,' she replied, going back to singing with Britney.

At the gym Mace wheeled her through to the pool, running a shower of greetings along the way, his daughter a hero with everyone. And she was. Maybe she couldn't walk yet but there was movement in her legs when she swam and he lived in hope that each session in the pool brought her a day closer to walking. He got her out of the chair into the water, watched her take off for the other side in her dragging crawl, her legs mostly trailing. What he admired in her was the fierce determination. Like her mother she didn't give up.

Mace changed and hit the water, getting into sync with his daughter until she tired. Then they stopped and he held her by the arms while she tried to coax a kick into her legs. A year they'd been doing this. In the beginning she hadn't the strength to hold her body out, and her legs had drooped down, useless. Now she floated easily, legs out, gently rising and falling, her little bum tight with effort. The thought of her grit choked Mace.

When she was tired he piggy-backed her to the side and set off for a couple of lengths at a pace way off what he'd managed with Tyrone and Allan. After Tyrone's death in a car crash eighteen months back, the sessions at the pool had petered to a halt. He hadn't seen Allan in a while; the guy could've left the city for all he knew.

Ten lengths later he surfaced beside his daughter. 'One more for luck?'

She shook her head.

'A smoothie?'

She nodded. Mace caught a change in her mood. 'Something's wrong?' Again she shook her head but he could see she wasn't far from tears. In the end they skipped on the smoothie and went straight out to the car.

Neither of them noticed Cupcake wasn't where they'd left him until they were almost home.

'Cupcake? Where's Cupcake, Papa?' Christa pointed at the dashboard. 'Someone's stolen him.' This time the tears came.

Mace reached a hand across to comfort her, thinking, had he or hadn't he locked the car? Sure that he had. But the bear was missing.

'Cupcake's gone. Someone stole him out of the car,' Christa told Oumou, the tears coming again as Mace carried her into the kitchen and eased her onto a stool at the centre island where Oumou stood preparing a salad, a glass of chardonnay at hand.

'Ma puce,' said Oumou, hugging her daughter, looking at Mace. 'This is terrible. Maybe he fell out.'

'No,' said Mace. 'I couldn't have locked the car.'

'And there were no car-guards watching?'

'Gone home already.'

'Oh ma puce,' said Oumou, wiping her daughter's tears. 'This is sad on a day when Maman has a celebration.'

'What celebration?' said Christa.

'Yeah, what?' said Mace, picking at the calamari strips and black mussels simmering on the gas hob, shooing off Cat2 from clawing his leg.

'You have to congratulate me.'

'For what, Maman? For what?' Cupcake's loss temporarily put aside.

'For my exhibition that is all sold out.'

'Wow!' said Christa.

'Hey!' said Mace. 'That's wonderful.'

'Today,' said Oumou. 'This afternoon quite late a tourist bought everything that was not sold. The gallery phoned to tell me a cash payment.'

'A sell-out.'

'What is best for me is the exhibition is only open a week.' She clutched their hands. 'This is wonderful. It will be something to shut up the bank woman.'

Mace hugged her, said, 'We should celebrate but I can't. That's a pity.'

'You are going out?'

'Aah Papa.'

'Dinner with clients,' he said. 'I have to be on the schmooze.' He saw it took the smile off Oumou's face but she said nothing.

Mace and Isabella had dinner at the hotel.

'I'm tired,' she said. 'I don't want to make a night of it. We can hit the town some other time.'

'The hotel's fine,' said Mace wondering when that other time would be. He wasn't sure two nights on the trot with Isabella would be a good idea.

They took a drink first in the bar with a guy called Ludovico who Mace couldn't remember meeting back when he'd agreed to the deal. Ludovico didn't have much to say, seemed distracted, Mace thought, and a bit uptight even in his bright shirt and white slacks.

'My brother's watcher,' Isabella reminded him over dinner. 'Keeping an eye on business.'

'Like the money?'

'The money's fine.'

Mace took a mouthful of grilled fish. Before he'd swallowed it, said, 'When do I get to know the details? Of who we're selling to.'

Isabella set her knife and fork neatly on her plate, the only remains of her meal a grey jacket of fish skin folded to the side.

'Not a bad fish,' she said. 'Needs the sauce though.' She sipped her wine, dabbed her lips. 'What'd you call it, a kind of cob?'

'Kabeljou,' said Mace.

'Would've risked being bland otherwise.' She sat back to let the waiter take the plate. When he was gone, said, 'It goes like this, Mace. A man called John Webster's going to be in touch. Probably at your hotel. Old-hand trader. Guns, diamonds, even ivory, at one time I heard. Art too. Masks and carved figures. Some of my best stuff in New York came through him. He's got this contact, politician, chief, warlord, I don't know what exactly, who needs to improve his standing. This consignment he reckons will do that. Shouldn't be a hassle at all.'

'And the diamonds come via Webster?'

'In him we trust.'

'Like you say, no hassle then.'

They finished the bottle of wine and ordered espressos.

Isabella said, 'Macey-boy what I'd appreciate doing while I'm here is to see where you live, maybe meet your daughter?'

Mace felt the chill of that suggestion in his veins. He shook his head. 'Not a good idea. I don't want Oumou to even suspect you're here.'

Isabella smiled. 'I bought out her exhibition. I'd say for that you owe me one small favour.'

Mace looked down at the black surface of the coffee, mottled with golden froth. Thought, Christ, didn't she ever stop. 'I should've guessed.'

'She excited about a sell-out?' Isabella couldn't keep the smirk from her voice.

Mace glanced up at her. 'Why'd you do it?'

'I liked the stuff. She does good work. Hell, Mace, why not? What was left? Some bowls, plates, vases.'

'About fifty grand's worth.'

'In dollars, peanuts.'

'That's not the point.

'No? But she's happy, I'll bet. Flying.'

'Because she thinks some stranger walked in and snapped it up.'

'That's about right. There hadn't been a flyer for the exhibition on the concierge's desk I wouldn't have known. She wouldn't have sold out, I wouldn't own some of her pieces. What's the big deal here? I'm not allowed to buy her pottery?'

'It's patronising. What you did's like taking the piss.'

Isabella laughed. 'Come on. Lighten up.' She opened the foil on the round of Belgian noir that came with the coffee, popped it on her tongue, sucked loud enough for Mace to hear. 'Not bad.' Sipped coffee over the chocolate melting in her mouth. 'So what d'you say, Mace?' – leant across the table to stroke his cheek.

24

Mace and Pylon spent Wednesday running ragged, juggling their time between two sets of clients. The one couple about to head off for their post-op safari, both of them surgically sculpted and still a little puffy and bruised about the gills. Neither much concerned about their war wounds.

'Hell,' the husband said, 'like I should give a damn.' His wife adding, 'These people on the safari we're never going to meet again.' Predictable attitude in Mace's experience, yet always amused him seeing as appearance was the nip-and-tuck brigade's major motivation. While he got them to the airport in the big Merc, Pylon logged in a gay couple for their detox at a hydro in the winelands.

On the highway back to town Mace took a call from Isabella.

'So, when're you gonna pick me up? Show me your fair city.'

'I'm not,' said Mace. 'I'm flat-out, Bella. Also we're taking over the consignment this afternoon.'

'Count me in.'

'Don't want to disappoint you again, but no.'

'Sweetie! So macho. Dinner then?'

'Okay,' said Mace, thinking what he'd do was cancel in the late afternoon. Maybe fob her off with lunch on Friday.

They agreed a time and disconnected. For sure, Isabella in his home town was big-time maintenance.

Mace and Pylon met up at the quay to watch Mo Siq's trucks unload twenty wooden crates marked engineering equipment. All the paperwork stamped, the ship's captain relaxed, happy to share a beer with them on the bridge. The wind freshening through the afternoon, the mountain under a tablecloth of cloud, and the harbour water choppy. A murky green, ominous looking. Across in Duncan Basin the wharf cranes loaded containers onto a trio of ships. Back of that the city skyline floated low in the wind haze. The sight gave Mace a charge, like this was the old times.

Going down the gangplank he said, 'Maybe we should do this more often.'

Pylon stopped. 'Did I hear you correctly?'

'Just a thought. Hitch a ride with Mo's Opportunity?'

'Forget it. We don't need the exposure.'

'Good bucks though.'

'We're doing alright last time I looked.'

They reached their cars. Mo's trucks were already gone. Some sailors huddled out of the wind behind a container playing cards, a long-haired dog beside them.

'That's it,' said Mace. 'May as well head home for an early one.'

Pylon beeped his car's remote locking. 'Give Isabella my best.'

'I'm not seeing her.'

'No?'

'No. A family evening.'

Pylon held his gaze. 'I'm pleased. I was wondering there.'

Mace laughed. 'You don't think …? Come on. No.'

'Have to admit it crossed my mind.'

'You mean you would've?'

'For the nostalgia. I might've taken a night out. That sort of thing's tempting.'

'Forget it.' Mace opened the Alfa's door, staring over the car at a white Toyota coming fast along the quay. 'This situation's worth a lot of money but it's not worth that, blowing it with Oumou.' The Toyota stopped, out jumped a nifty dresser, all smiles. Came forward, his hand extended.

'You're Mo Siq's guys,' he said. 'My name's Vusi Themba, Customs and Excise.'

'That so,' said Mace, shaking the offered hand. Pylon approached, did the brother's clasp.

'Establishing that everything went as it should.' He grinned from one to the other, giving them a lot of teeth behind thick lips. Mace thought his nose looked like it'd been beaten onto his face. A round friendly face.

'No problems,' said Pylon.

Vusi said, 'I've just passed the trucks heading out. Couldn't have taken more than forty-five minutes to unload.' He hauled up a heavy Rolex to check the time. 'Yeah, forty-five, fifty minutes.'

Neither Mace nor Pylon made a comment.

Vusi took out a pack of Marlboros, tapped the base and offered it. The two men shook their heads. 'I've gotta stop,' he said, picking out a white, firing it with a Zippo. He blew the exhale from a corner of his mouth, the wind bringing it back on Mace and Pylon. Vusi gestured at the ship. 'Argentinian?'

Mace nodded. 'That's right.'

'Heading up the coast?'

'Haven't asked their schedule. The captain's up there if you want to know.'

Vusi turned his back to the wind, the strength picking up, getting unpleasant and gritty. 'Sailing tonight I believe.'

'If that's the schedule.'

'According to the harbour log, it is.' Vusi flicked ash. 'Once I've signed off the paperwork.' He stuck the cigarette in his mouth, pulled out a sheaf of forms from his jacket pocket, said with the Marlboro bobbing on his lip, 'Wouldn't want to lose these in the breeze.' The documentation fluttered in his hand.

'What's it you want?' said Pylon switching to Xhosa, knowing the answer all too well.

The custom's officer stuck to English. 'To talk. Mo said I should speak to you.'

Pylon looked at his partner, gestured his head at the big Merc. Mace nodded, said to Vusi, 'We'd appreciate no smoking in the car.'

Vusi grinned, dropped the remains of the cigarette and crushed it.

Mace held the front passenger door open for him then slid himself in along the back seat. Pylon went behind the wheel.

'Nice car,' said Vusi, 'leather, hey, really smooth,' patting the seats, turning sideways so he faced Pylon and could see Mace behind the headrest. 'Look, guys,' he said. 'This is awkward for me. My understanding is you'd have been expecting me. Maybe even have come in to see me. In my office. We could've had coffee.

257

That would've been easier. More comfortable.' He spread his hands. 'Mo should've told you the way it works.'

'Maybe you should now,' said Pylon.

Vusi nodded vigorously. 'That's right. Okay. Okay. Take it this way. The way this works is you wouldn't be here without me. You understand what I'm saying?' He glanced from one to the other.

'Sure,' said Pylon. 'Continue.'

'What I'm saying is that I'm the link that makes the chain. Otherwise you got two bits dangling in your hands.' He laughed. Nervous, cutting the laugh short at their non-response. 'Mo should've told you that.' He sighed. 'Sometimes Mo's not good on the detail.'

'Seems like it,' said Pylon. 'So how much is the bribe?'

Vusi grimaced. 'Commission,' he said. 'Same as any professional consultant.'

'Well?'

'How about twenty grand?'

'How about it.'

'My estimation. As this's for Mo, that's a base rate.'

'So maybe you should talk to him.'

'That's right,' said Vusi. 'I should, normally. Except he said to talk to you.'

'Fifteen thousand, tops' said Mace. 'Saturday midday at Mo's flat. You know where it is?'

Vusi nodded. 'Now would be better.'

'Now we don't have it. Ask Mo. This thing's structured on trust.' Mace leant over, touched Vusi on the shoulder. 'We're grateful for your help, Mr ...'

'...Vusi. Vusi Themba ...'

'... Mr Vusi Themba. But this's how things are. Till Saturday.' He opened his hand and the custom's officer hooked his arm up awkwardly to shake it.

Mace and Pylon saw him into his car, watched him drive off.

'How come we're always the suckers paying the hired help?' said Pylon.

Mace headed for the Spider. 'This sort of thing all comes out in the wash.'

On his way across the docks Mace put through a call to Isabella.

'You're cancelling?' she said when she heard his voice. 'You're taking the chicken option.'

Mace smiled, Isabella always getting in ahead of the game. He gave her the excuse of clients needing a run around.

'Nanny work,' she said. 'When're you going to get a proper job?'

'It buys the beer.'

Isabella laughed. 'You're a bad liar, Mace. Go'n, run home to mommy.' She hung up.

He considered ringing back, then had second thoughts. Better to head for the Hot Wok and get takeout Chinese. Put him into Oumou's and Christa's good books.

25

Mace woke with Christa's screams, and found her sitting up in bed, eyes screwed shut, mouth open, hands in tight fists over her ears, shrieking. He and Oumou dropped either side of her, Oumou clutching her, Mace holding them both while Christa subsided into deep sobs.

'Shoosh, ma puce, shoosh,' said Oumou, the three of them rocking gently while the echo of the screams bounced around Mace's head. The vision rising of Abdul Abdul shooting, Christa's cry, and the gun coming back on them again. He closed his eyes, felt the trembling of his daughter and pushed away the memory. It'd been a while since she'd woken screaming, so many months back he'd hoped the nightmare was over. But no. Some things didn't end.

For a long time they held one another until Mace said, 'I'll get you a drink of milk' – and went through to the kitchen to warm a glassful, stirring in a teaspoon of honey. He brought this back with a tranquilliser popped from a blister pack.

Christa said, 'It was that man. I could smell him.'

'What smell?'

'Like cinnamon.' She finished the milk, handed the glass to Mace.

'It's okay,' he said, 'just your mind playing tricks.'

Oumou fussed with the pillows and the sheet. 'Come, ma puce, lie down' – easing her back, Christa's face softening under her mother's hands.

'I can still smell the cinnamon,' she said.

'There's no cinnamon,' said Mace.

'Don't go.' Christa reached up to both of them.

'You must sleep,' said Oumou.

'Please.'

'Okay.' Oumou and Mace stretched out either side of their daughter.

She'll get through it, Mace thought, it takes time. And what time was three years? Not much. What he couldn't fathom was what triggered the flashback. Yesterday she'd been laughing. Rough and tumbling with him in the swimming pool before supper. Ravenous for the Chinese takeout, giggling over their game of rummy. A happy young girl. Except she was paralysed. Except she'd once been shot. Because of him. The thought worked into his mind: a splinter under a fingernail.

It was gone eight when Mace got up, shifting Cat2 from where she was curled behind his knees. He'd slept badly off and on, aware of Christa's every move beside him. In the kitchen he spooned coffee into the Bialetti and set it on the hob. Stared out at the city, already bright and growling. He heard Oumou come down the passage and pause in the kitchen door.

'She alright?'

'Of course, why not?' Oumou hugged him from behind.

'When is it going to stop?' said Mace.

Oumou rubbed her chin between his shoulder blades. 'Maybe it will take a long time. Maybe it won't go away. It is not over for me. I can still see the man with the knife. What is it Pylon says? There is a way of things, no?'

Mace turned in her embrace. 'I don't go with that stuff. We make our lives.'

'I didn't make what the men did to me.'

'But look at you now.'

'And look at Christa. One day she will walk again.'

'I don't know.'

'She will.'

Mace reached behind to unlock her hands. 'I'm going to take a swim at the centre,' he said. 'Work off some of this.'

'If you wait till Christa wakes, she could go with you, no?' Oumou took the coffee pot off the hob, poured two cups. 'This will be good for her.' She handed Mace a cup, her eyes on him.

He met her gaze and smiled. 'I'll do that.'

Oumou took his hand. 'Then we can go back to bed.'

Mace stood, eyes closed under the shower, thinking, this was on the edge, this wasn't New York. The unease in his gut again. He let the water run full in his face, water restrictions or no water restrictions. The city could be drying up in the heat, he needed water. Turned to get the jet on his back, adjusted the rose until the water was hard and sharp. The cascade drummed against him. He switched off the hot tap, let the cold water bring out the gooseflesh before he tightened that tap too and stepped from the cubicle.

'Any longer and you'd have run the hotel dry,' Isabella said, leaning now against the bathroom doorway, flicking a comb through her wet hair, watching him. 'This thing with you and water. Very mother's womb.'

Mace towelled himself. 'We all have our hang-ups.'

'Some more than others.' She stood aside to let him into the bedroom. 'Still, lunch and a fuck in a strange city's always something to be appreciated.'

Mace stopped at the tone, halfway into a T-shirt, his arms in the sleeves. 'What's this about?'

Isabella looked at him. 'My requests, Mace. Two small things. A drive past your house. A chance to say hello to your daughter. Not much to ask, I'd have thought.'

'No.' He pulled on his T-shirt. 'I told you. Out of the question.'

'What you don't understand,' she said, 'is that girl, your daughter, is just a name to me. I want to meet her.'

'And then?'

'And then she's real. We have a connection, Mace. The four of us. You, me, Oumou, Christa.'

Mace snorted. 'Yeah, sure.'

'I could be a client for all she has to know.'

'Not going to happen.' Mace fastened his belt, sat down next to her to put on his shoes. 'Accept it, Bella. I'm not going there.'

Isabella launched off the bed to stand at the window with her back to him. Her shoulders rigid, her arms folded tightly across her chest.

'You need help, Mace. A full-time shrink. Give you back some feelings.'

Mace looked at her silhouette. Mistake. It'd been a mistake in New York, a lapse, a moment's weakness. Which he'd deeply regretted. This wasn't a mistake. This was foolish. Utter craziness.

'Come on, be reasonable,' he said.

She turned to face him. 'Do me a favour, Mace Bishop. Fuck off.'

Mace did, slamming out the room, thinking, up yours too Isabella.

26

Saturday morning Vittoria lay listening to Paulo's breathing. Rhythmical. Like the guy hadn't got a care in the world. Amazing thing about Paulo was he'd done a number. Cut the crap. Got focused. Got a life. Started with him getting rid of the cop, smooth-talking him back out the gate. So where'd this come from? Little Paulo the rollover suddenly become the schemer, the dealer, the action man. The lover. The. Lover. This Paulo. Twice a night in the last three nights. The stud was stoned on adrenaline. Didn't even need to chase a line.

Had done a huge deal with the schwarzer, Oupa K, selling him a portion cut seventy/thirty with baby powder. Rat poison laced into the rock. A self-concocted and made recipe. Paulo over the moon that this was better than a pure pipe. He went out alone, walked away with four hundred K in a five-minute transaction. Not good enough for Paulo the dealer. He set up a run of drops with small-timers that pulled down close to sixty grand. The dude was a hero. She wondered, where's this Paulo been all my life?

She asked him: what about Isabella? He came back, Isabella's toast. Maybe babe I just been wiped over one go too many. Like, enough man. So here's the plan: once the diamonds come in we're going on safari. Give Isabella the finger. Francisco too.

The guy was serious, he was talking giraffes, lions, crocodiles, hippopotamuses. Not only talking, he dropped a bundle of game lodge brochures in her lap, said, whichever one you want make the booking. How long? He'd shrugged. Coupla three, four days?

Vittoria dipped a wetted finger in her bedside candy bag, rubbed it over her gums. The clock radio gave 9:41.

The powder ritzing her, she stuck her tongue in Paulo's ear to wake him. He was hard, ready for a quickie before he'd opened his eyes. What the hell, she thought, it was making for that sort of day. Sat astride him. He reached up, tweaked her nipples, that silly smile on his face.

'You okay?' he said.

She angled forward to float her boobs across his chest.

He asked what the time was.

Almost 9:45 she told him.

'You ready?' he said.

'Getting there.'

He slid a finger in and that did it for her.

10:45 heading downstairs, Paulo was all joy and light. Called to Ludo on the patio, 'What's happening man?' Ludo busy on his phone held up a hand to hush Paulo.

'All good,' he said, disconnected. To Paulo: 'You got the money?'

'Right upstairs. That was who? Isabella?'

'Francisco.'

Paulo walked off two paces as the intercom buzzed.

'Has to be the collection men,' said Ludo plonking himself down in front of the television. 'All yours pal.'

27

Eleven on the nose, Pylon brought the big Merc to a stop before the gates of the Llandudno house, he and Mace on their cells.

Mace to Isabella, 'The flowers weren't a good idea.'

'What flowers? Like I'm going to send you flowers after Thursday.'

Mo to Pylon, 'You get the guy to ring me and tell me how much is in the bag. Then you get here chop chop.'

'That's our schedule,' Pylon said, then said, 'Hang on' – and buzzed the intercom, telling the person who answered they'd come to collect.

Mo said, 'Another thing, I got a call from Vusi.'

Isabella to Mace, 'I don't even know your address to send you flowers. You've got a secret admirer. Or Oumou has.' She laughed. 'Who got them, you or her?'

'She did,' said Mace.

'And she thinks they're from you?'

The gates opened. Pylon drove in pulling up close to the front door. Mace caught the movement of someone at a window, thought, no, the weasel wouldn't try it surely. Wondering whether to take the Ruger from the glove box. He and Pylon got out, leant against the car to finish their conversations, scoping the grounds and the house.

To Isabella he said, 'She does. Thinks I've given them to her because she sold out her exhibition.'

'How sweet.'

Mo said to Pylon, 'I don't like Vusi. Vusi's a slimeball. I don't want him coming here.'

'Have to go,' said Pylon, disconnecting.

Isabella said to Mace, 'No bad blood?'

'We'll survive,' he said.

'Keep in touch,' she said. 'And Mace, bon voyage.'

Mace pocketed his phone, then he and Pylon walked up to the front door, rang the bell.

Paulo buzzed them in: a big black Merc. Two guys got out: smart types in jeans and T-shirts, shades. Both on their cells, leaning against the car finishing their conversations, watching the place while they talked. Difficult to tell which was the man, the white one he supposed. Paulo waited for them to ring the doorbell. The bag with the money on the table. Ludo tuned to a sports channel. The doorbell rang, Paulo opened.

'You're Paulo?'

'That's the name I'm known by.'

'This is Pylon. I'm Mace.'

'The money's on the table,' said Paulo, letting them follow him into the dining room.

'Nice place.' Pylon, nodded at Ludo, asked what was the cricket score?

'Fifty-seven for two,' said Ludo. 'Pakistan bowling big-time.'

Mace opened the bag, took out some bundles of notes at random. 'These in thousands?' he said.

Paulo nodded.

'Can you get me a damp sponge?'

'If you want.'

'I do.'

Paulo fetched one from the kitchen, by the time he returned Mace was sitting at the table, the elastic bands off a bundle, ready to be counted. The guy Pylon chatting to Ludo, saying, he didn't know Americans were into cricket.

'Couldn't tell a stump from a six before I got here,' said Ludo, laughing.

'What they say about travel broadening the mind.'

'Sure thing,' said Ludo.

Mace counted off notes into a stack of fifteen grand, stuffed them into an envelope, slipped an elastic band over the rest of the bundle. Everything went back into the bag.

Pylon brought out his phone, connected to Mo Siq. To Paulo said, 'When the man answers, tell him how much is in the bag.'

Paulo took the phone and headed back into the kitchen, not wanting them to hear the figures. He returned shaking his head. 'Who's that guy?' – gave the phone to Pylon.

'Not someone you want to meet,' said Mace.

'Enjoy the cricket,' said Pylon to Ludo on his way out. Mace walking ahead with the bag of money, Paulo on his heels.

At the front door Mace turned to Paulo. 'You Isabella's husband?'

'What's it to you?'

'Nothing,' said Mace, with that bopped Paulo two power punches: the first on the mouth, the second on the cheekbone, both split skin, drawing blood. Paulo staggered back, hands going to his face. Mace dancing forward, arms like lightning dealing two short five-finger stabs to Paulo's ribs.

'Oof,' the breath knocked out of Paulo, doubling him up.

Ludo scooted to the door at the sound of the scuffle. 'Hey, hey, hey, guys, what's the problem!'

'No problem,' said Mace. 'Nothing that a block of ice and a Band-aid won't sort out.'

'Yeah, well let it go,' said Ludo, stepping in front of Paulo.

'Obliged,' said Mace. 'Give my regards to your wife.'

Paulo dabbed at his lips, blood smeared over his face.

'Serious people,' said Ludo, conjuring his cellphone from a trouser pocket as the Merc pulled out. Thumbed a number, said, 'Deal's done.'

'That was Isabella?' asked Paulo.

'Francisco,' said Ludo, very elegant today: white shirt, pale avocado slacks, suede slip-ons. He disappeared upstairs came back down carrying a suitcase.

'You're leaving?'

'Yeah. I were you, I would too. Given the cop's interest in your ladyfriend, you don't wanna be hanging around here anymore. Either you or her.'

Paulo waited for more explanation, none was forthcoming. 'Where're you going?'

'Best you don't know. Find a little B&B. Keep in touch.'

'I wanna see Isabella,' said Paulo. 'You tell her.'

'Tell her yourself.' Ludo headed for the Jeep. 'She's your wife.'

28

At the Mount Nelson Isabella upgraded to a luxury suite with two separate bedrooms, the second for Ludo. This her idea while they waited for the collection. 'May as well treat ourselves,' she'd said. 'Also better for security.'

The situation gave Ludo a rush yet he pretended nonchalance at the thought of getting to sleep that close to the woman of his daydreams. That she had him in the next room as muscle was not a reality he let infringe on the fantasy.

The first thing that spoiled the fantasy for Ludo was he couldn't find his gun. Here he was in this paradise room over the trees, bright swimming pool down below, four days with Isabella ahead, he couldn't find his gun. He unpacked some shirts, put underwear into a drawer, hung up jackets, he couldn't find his gun. It was there when he packed. Sure it was there when he packed. He went through jacket pockets, trouser pockets, laid out his clothes on the bed. No gun.

He shook out a smoke, lit it. The punk. The gigolo punk.

From the other room came Isabella, 'You smoking, Ludo?'

'Yeah, yeah, sorry.' He pulled twice quickly, then stubbed the Camel and went through to the suite's lounge. 'Paulo's got my gun,' he said to her bare-foot image in the mirror. She was changing, had on unfastened jeans and a cream camisole, a bead choker round her neck.

She looked at his reflection in the mirror. 'This's a problem?' Isabella came out of the room, fixing diamond clip-ons to her ears. The flies of her jeans still undone. 'Probably makes him feel macho.'

'He said he wanted you to call him.'

'Sure he does.' She closed the zip. 'He knows where I am. He wants to talk to me he'll call.' She fastened the belt, shook her head, giving Ludo a broad smile of amusement. 'Would you credit it. Paulo pulls a move. The punk I thought was a jerk.' She went over to a mirror, applied lipstick. Chuckling, mmmed her lips, padding back to her bedroom.

'He's got my gun.'

'What you think he's going to do? Shoot someone?'

Isabella strapped on sandals, slung a small bag over her shoulder, Ludo watching her in the mirror: some cool woman this.

'Let's go get a coffee.' As they were leaving the suite said, 'You think the pussy gave him the balls?'

Ludo patted his pockets for the reassurance of a Camel packet, desperate for a cigarette the moment they hit fresh air. 'Probably.' He pressed for the lift. They travelled down two floors in silence.

Halfway through their coffees, Isabella's phone rang. Ludo watched her reach for it on the table, the phone vibrating across the glass top. She flipped it open. 'There we go. The little man on cue' – and gave her husband a bright 'How'r you, hon?', smiling the while at Ludo sprawled in the cane chair opposite.

Ludo thought, not for the first time, strange game she played with the asshole, listening patiently while the jock mouthed on.

'More than talk I would think,' she said eventually, studying the nails of her right hand. 'What's that? A coffee shop. Mugg & Bean? You think that's the best place to discuss this sort of thing, hon?'

Ludo signalled to her that the hotel would be good, but she shook her head.

'How about one o'clock? You want to do it when there're lots of people, that's alright.' She lent over to spoon froth from her cappuccino, paused with the teaspoon halfway to her mouth. 'Alone? Hubby and wifey doing lunch, how sweet.'

Now Ludo shook his head, pointing at himself then at her to say no ways would she be going alone. Tell him, he mouthed, tell him I'll be with you.

Isabella put the teaspoon in her mouth and swallowed the froth, put the spoon back on the tray. Ludo made a pistol out of his right hand, held it up to catch Isabella's eye. She nodded. Tell him I want it back, he mouthed.

'Another thing, hon, 'fore you go. Bring the gun. It's what Francisco would call crucial. And crucial is best to swing with.' She disconnected before Paulo could respond, and flipped the phone closed.

'A Mugg & Bean,' she said. 'Can you take seriously a guy that wants to talk money in a Mugg & Bean?'

29

Mace and Pylon in the departure lounge ordered filter coffees at a stand-up bar. Pylon wanting to know what was it that they couldn't serve it in a china cup and saucer or even a china mug? Why'd it have to be this polystyrene nonsense? The cashier told him the price without a smile.

'What d'you call it?' he said. 'Not a mug, it's a container, even has a lid on it. Like where else will I drink this but standing here, hey sisi?'

The cashier scratched at a stain on her apron, flaking off a white powder.

Pylon turned to Mace, 'A two-plane airport like Malitia's, no more'n an airfield and a hangar, they served coffee in proper cups. Back then.' He fidgeted change from his pocket.

'When they served coffee,' said Mace taking away both containers to a counter that'd still to be wiped clean, littered with an assortment of polystyrene cups stacked into one another.

He prised off the lid, sipped at the liquid. That it was hot was about all you could say for it.

Pylon said, 'Look at all this shit. Can't they get it right to clean when the customers leave? You could put your elbow in a coffee ring if you weren't watching.'

An attendant came up, swept the empties into a black bin liner, wiped a damp cloth over the counter top.

'This's too late,' said Pylon. 'The time to've done this was before we got here.' The woman apologised. 'It's important,' he said, 'otherwise the place feels dirty. Everything's sticky where people've spilt sugar and slopped their drinks. You can feel it.' He patted his hand on the table top where she hadn't wiped. Held up his palm. 'See there, there's sugar sticking to it. See what I mean?'

Mace said, 'Pylon.'

Pylon said, 'No, this's an issue. Here's a place with a captive market but just because of that they've still got to treat people properly. What's needed here is some competition. Get everybody on their toes. Or decent management. Someone who's concerned. Gives the staff some training, keeps the customers satisfied.' He popped the lid on his coffee, tore open a sachet of sugar and poured it in. Before he'd stirred it he said, 'I have to go again. Excuse me' – and headed for the toilets at a clip.

Mace took another swallow of coffee, noted twenty minutes to boarding time. Gazed across at the Hottentots Holland mountains hazed by the heat and the strengthening wind, and thought, thirty-six hours he'd be home and dry with enough moolah to shut up the bank chick. Goddamned woman. What a moment that would be.

His cellphone rang, no caller identity on the screen. Normally he didn't take those, this time he did. The voice he recognised straight off: Sheemina February.

'How'd you like the flowers?'

'Very nice,' said Mace.

'Bit confusing, maybe,' she said and clicked her tongue. 'After the way you left Isabella maybe you thought they were from her. All these women in your life.'

Mace stayed calm. 'You're bugging hotels now?'

'I don't have to. Still, with the CIA it's not a bad idea.'

'Ex.'

'Ex? Not from what I heard, Mr Bishop. From what I heard you had a lapse for old time's sake. So maybe the lovely Isabella's not ex-CIA either.'

'What's your point?' said Mace.

'A courtesy call. To wish you well on your trip. And a cautionary: drop it with Isabella before word gets out. I mean to Oumou.'

Mace took a mouthful of coffee and swallowed. 'Then one courtesy deserves another.'

'How wonderful.'

'Don't fuck with me, okay. Or my wife.'

Sheemina February laughed. 'That's not my style.'

Mace said good, and Sheemina February said have a pleasant flight and that brought Mace back to the thing she'd first said: to wish you well on your trip.

'And what trip's this I'm supposed to be on?' he said. Could sense her shaking her head.

'Oh come now, Mr Bishop. There's no need to pretend with me. Please' – and she disconnected, leaving Mace to thumb his phone off thoughtfully.

'How much more?' said Pylon, coming up. 'Three times since we've got here, I've still got the squirts.'

'I've just had a call from Sheemina February,' said Mace. 'She knows about this trip.'

'Hey?' said Pylon, stirring his coffee with a plastic spoon, frowning at Mace. 'She's saying what?' He put the spoon on the counter, took a mouthful of coffee. 'She's saying she knows about this?'

Mace nodded.

'Bloody save me Jesus.' Pylon drank again, dabbed at his mouth with a paper serviette. 'It won't be from Mo she heard.'

'I wouldn't imagine either. But it makes you wonder where she did hear.'

'Maybe,' said Pylon, 'it's not so much where as how.'

30

Paulo stood at the French doors leading onto the deck: the rim-flow at the far end, Vittoria topless in a tanga stretched on the boards, wired for sound, a bottle of sparkling stuck in a cooler bucket close to hand. He dropped the cellphone into the pocket of his shorts, touched the swelling on his cheek and winced. Didn't hurt as badly as his ribs, but to the touch, burnt like hell. The cut on his mouth stung too. Still, nothing to how Isabella was going to hurt. Taking a glass off the bar, he joined Vittoria, filling both their glasses.

Vittoria unplugged her ears. 'You fix it with the bitch?'

'For one o'clock.' Before he could click his glass against hers, his phone rang.

'My name's Dave Cruikshank,' said the voice, 'from City Bowl Properties. I am phoning to make sure everything's to your liking.'

'Yeah, great,' said Paulo. 'Great place.'

'Well, enjoy. Any problems big or small you need attending to, you've got our number. Whatever hour of day or night.'

'Appreciate it,' said Paulo. 'You're who again?'

'Dave Cruikshank. MD City Bowl Properties.'

How about that? Paulo put down the cellphone and sipped from his glass. 'The MD himself of the rental company. Nice service touch. Here's to the best fuckpad in the city, Mr MD. What you think, huh, babe? Tell me it's not goddamned paradise.' This their new self-catering in the City Bowl, mountain rising behind, the view from the deck across the city to the bay.

Vittoria took half her wine in a swallow. 'Paulo the organiser.'

'You better believe it.'

'All we need's some white to keep the devil smiling.'

Paulo dug into his pocket, flipped a Ziploc of powder onto her stomach. 'Like that?'

'Hey!' Vittoria sat up. 'There's a babe.'

'Numero uno?'

'You got it.' She laid out a line on the deck. 'You want one?'

Paulo sipped at his wine, shook his head. 'Monday we take possession on Francisco's behalf, we can be on safari the very next day. With his stones.'

'Whatever, baby.' Vittoria snorted the coke.

'Lions under every tree.'

'What about giraffes?'

'It's got them,' he said, reaching for the brochure of the place Vittoria had chosen. 'Says here lions under every tree. The big five. Night-time we take a ride with spotlights, get up close.'

Vittoria rubbed at her nose. 'Surprising where a few hours can take you. You walk out of one life, you walk into another.' She rolled over to sun her backside, plugging Massive Attack into her ears.

'Want me to cream your back?' Paulo knelt beside her, slid his hand over the curve of her ass. The pain at his ribs cut through the movement so fast he couldn't stop the groan, sat down hard on the deck.

'Poor baby,' said Vittoria, turning her head towards him.

Paulo collapsed on his back, the pain beading perspiration over his body. The hell reason the guy had to get physical made no sense. Except if Isabella had suggested it as a cautionary. Unwise of her under the circumstances. Isabella about to get her's big time. He lay still, eyes closed letting the pain recede, Vittoria's fingers stroking his arm.

31

Ludo stared up at the mountain, cloud starting to roll across its top. What he'd learnt in five weeks, the cloud meant wind. Hard, shrieking south-east wind that scraped along your nerves. No escaping it. Even in a house wind-howl chewed at you, after five days you wanted to scream enough already, stop for Chrissakes. Going to be no hardship kissing this place goodbye.

The trouble Ludo had been mulling over was the little dipshit, Paulo, and the discomfort of being without his nine mil. Especially with Isabella insisting on the meeting alone.

'This is a marriage thing,' she'd told him two hours back. 'I know how to handle it.'

They'd gone up in the lift Ludo thinking the Paulo situation felt all wrong. Something else going down. In the suite Isabella said what she was going to do was take a taxi to the café, listen to Paulo, offer him a lifestyle.

'The guy's a prick,' she'd said. 'I tell him something he believes it.'

Ludo had watched the cricket on television till he got antsy. Two hours gone and she wasn't back. He told himself cool it, go take a drive. Drove up the mountain past the cable station to the lookout under Devil's Peak. At the lookout a bunch of coloured heps toting reefer and quarts of beer, their sound-system thumping techno. Ugly types, not one of them with front teeth. How that improved their looks a mystery to Ludo. He stopped a way off from them: they caused a hassle he'd leave. A pity the trash always spoilt the magic spots. Tourists came here for the view of mountain, city, bay. They got human detritus.

He lit a cigarette. In the distance a plane lowering to the air-port. Which was the moment Francisco called wanting to know what was happening. Ludo did the pacifying number, once they'd disconnected dialled Isabella. Got her voicemail.

The coloured scum were starting to pay him some attention now, lined up like the wild bunch, grinning toothless. Ludo fired the Cherokee, spun off the lookout point in a shower of gravel. He could hear the bastards laughing. He had the gun he'd maybe handle it differently.

At the hotel, no Isabella and her phone still on voicemail. The same with Paulo. He uncapped a beer from the minibar, pacing the room while he drank from the bottle: the question was what to do? Start at the Mugg & Bean he reckoned. If they weren't there wasn't a circumstance he wanted to contemplate. But the chances were Isabella wouldn't go wandering off somewhere quiet with the guy.

Ludo finished the beer in a swallow, leaving the empty on the counter top. By force of habit he felt along his belt for where the nine would usually be. That Paulo had it and he didn't was a major concern.

32

Paulo walked into the Mugg & Bean, took a table near the outside door. He waved to Vittoria waiting in the Merc two parking bays down. The plan was that as soon as he and Isabella stood, she would drive up and they'd be off. Isabella persuaded to the venture by the barrel of Ludo's short nine in her back, in a worst-case scenario.

Ten minutes later Isabella came in from the mall side of the café, Paulo watching her confident long-legged stride that didn't deviate for anyone, people getting out of her way like a sixth sense told them to move. That was the thing about her – arrogance. As if nobody else mattered a flyblown damn. She caught his eye as she passed the wait-here-to-be-seated notice, waving at the waitress that they could do with service. Paulo smiled in response. Why not? She was the one hadn't the merest notion of what was playing out.

'Hon,' she said, standing next to him, 'isn't this sweet. Like a married couple on holiday in foreign climes.'

He pulled back from her attempt at an air kiss. 'You could say.'

'Except I won't.'

'Ease up, Isabella,' he said. 'We got things to discuss.'

'Hey,' she said, sitting down opposite him, 'you walk into a wall?'

Paulo touched the bruises on his face.

'Does that hurt?'

'You have nice friends.'

'Mace Bishop did that? What for?'

'I thought I'd find out from you.'

'How should I know?'

'You could've asked him to, is what I suspect.'

'Hon, you're off beam. Way off.'

'Maybe,' said Paulo and ordered two Americanos from the waitress hovering beside him.

'That'll do me fine,' said Isabella when the waitress looked at her for confirmation. 'He reads my mind.' Her eyes locked on Paulo's face but he kept his gaze past her at Vittoria watching from the Merc. 'You haven't done a clever thing, hon, taking Ludo's gun. So let's hear where you're going so we can make some sense of the situation.'

Paulo said, 'Don't patronise, okay. That's a start.'

Isabella reached across to stroke his hand. He grabbed hers and squeezed hard. 'Don't.' He released her.

'Hey, hon, that's a grip you've developed. You grab her tits that hard?'

Paulo felt the pressure come up in his chest, told himself not to rise to her. What she wanted was for him to lose it, right here in public. Instead he grinned, looking her smack in the eyes. 'Yeah, something like that.' And revelled in the sharp glance she gave him.

Their coffees arrived, the waitress telling them they were bottomless cups, all they had to do was get a refill from the spigot. As the girl backed off, Isabella said, 'So what's your opening gambit, hon?' She twisted the top off a sachet of sugar, poured half into her cup. 'I'm assuming that's what we're about. Sitting here.'

'Something like that,' said Paulo.

'So what's it to be?' Isabella gave her coffee two quick stirs. 'Give me some idea of where you're heading in the figure work.'

'Sixty per cent of the arms sale.'

Isabella sat back. 'Not a bad opener, hon. Way over the top, the sort of figure would give Francisco the apoplectics. If you wanted advice I would say ten per cent would be good. A regular agent's commission. For that you get a divorce.'

'I'm not a regular agent.'

'Say fifteen per cent then?'

'Say sixty.' Paulo sipped at his coffee, intrigued by the frown furrow on her forehead that he'd never noticed before. 'Sixty's because of all the work I had to do to make this possible for you.'

'For Francisco.'

'Whatever. Sixty's the opener. Sixty's the closer.'

'Hon, that's unreasonable.'

'Sure. But also you're paying to keep me shut-up about all the stuff I've gathered over the years. Also this way Francisco gets his money back. All I'm asking is the profits.'

'Francisco'd be pissed about that, he didn't make any interest.'

Paulo shrugged. 'This isn't a bother to me.' He watched Isabella sip at her coffee, put the cup down, dab at her mouth with a paper serviette taking off her lipstick gloss in the process.

'Think what you're walking away from. The sort of position Francisco could give you.'

'Never gonna happen, I know that. This way he gets rid of me, you get rid of me, I get rid of you, everybody's happy. To Francisco this is small change we're talking.'

'You think that's the settlement between us? For a divorce.'

'I do. Maybe I'm even short-changing myself.' Paulo finished his coffee. 'New life, Isabella. For all of us. Hey, you should be thanking me.' He called over the waitress for the bill. 'Finish up, hon, we've gotta get this show on the boards.'

'Meaning?'

'We're going to a place where you can tell Francisco how the game's shaping.'

'No,' said Isabella. 'We do it here. I guarantee you fifteen per cent and the divorce.'

Paulo paid the bill and told the waitress to keep the change. He rose and circled the table as if he were to help his companion out of her chair. In Isabella's ear he said, 'Sometimes you can be stupid. This is not about fifteen or twenty or twenty-five, this is about sixty per cent. Read my lips: sixty.' He straightened and grinned at her. 'You want to stay outta trouble, you have to come and conference. One of those phone sessions with Francisco.'

'Wait.' He felt Isabella's hand clutch at his arm. 'That's it? You're walking away?'

'Uh-huh.' Paulo moved off a pace.

'I haven't finished yet.'

'Doesn't matter, I have.'

He left her without a backward glance, moving to the door and pushing out through it as a Merc slid alongside him. Paulo opened the passenger door wondering whether the hell Isabella was calling his bluff when he heard Vittoria say, 'She's coming.' All the same he didn't look round, much as he wanted to. He got in, closed his door. 'Okay?' said Vittoria.

'Sure,' said Paulo, 'we're gonna win this one.'

The rear door opened and Isabella peered in. 'Mind if I join you?'

'We're waiting,' said Vittoria, releasing the brake to let the car roll forward.

All the way back to their self-catering Isabella was on about how this was going to annoy Francisco. How she'd have to explain away Paulo's duplicity. No matter what kind of deal they settled on there would be collateral. Unquestionably. Indubitably. Francisco was a businessman only the stupid crossed. All Paulo had to do was ask Ludo what happened to the guy in Santiago, just the latest in a long list of Francisco's ex-associates. Best thing here was to go with Francisco's generosity.

Vittoria said, 'Won't you tell your wife to shut the fuck up.'

Paulo said, 'Isabella, shut the fuck up.'

Isabella said, 'You're cute. The both of you. Regular natural born Mickey and Mallory.'

At the apartment Vittoria drove into the garage and pressed the remote to bring the door down. Paulo was out first moving back to open Isabella's door, Vittoria going down the other side of the car to pop the boot.

'You're such a hon,' said Isabella manoeuvring herself off the leather seat straight into a blast of the mace can Vittoria had passed across to Paulo. As she doubled he went at her face with the spray, Isabella gasping, trying to crawl away from him across the back seat. Vittoria came in the other side with the ether on a hand towel, clamping it to Isabella's face until she stopped moving. Wasn't too much difficulty from then on to heft her into the boot, tie her wrists and ankles with duct tape, do a couple of swirls around her jaw to keep her silent.

They swapped positions, this time with Paulo driving. He headed out of town along the side of a golf course to a beach-front strip of apartment blocks that looked across the bay to the mountain. Vittoria rapped along to P-Diddy and Paulo thought amazing how easy some things could be. All they had to do now was shoot her. No big deal he'd discovered. Wasn't even really a rush, certainly not like hitting a line of coke.

At a traffic light he swung left on to the West Coast road, making for a region of sand dunes that he'd come across when the idea to top Isabella first mooted itself.

Vittoria sighted down the long road, said, 'Where're we going?'

'Another ten clicks,' said Paulo, 'quiet little place I found. Anyone gets round to stumbling on her in the short term it's gonna be an accident.'

Vittoria took the nine mil out of the glove compartment. 'You going to do this? Or me?'

'We can take turns.'

'That's a waste.' Vittoria took a coin from her pocket. 'Heads or tails?'

Paulo said tails.

Vittoria flipped the coin, caught it, smacked it onto the back of her left hand. 'Heads.' She looked at him. 'You want to make it best of three?'

Paulo said, 'Sure. Heads this time.'

He won but Vittoria took the next with another win for heads. 'Isn't that weird,' she said, 'tails didn't come up once.' She flipped for fun and it was tails.

'This is it,' said Paulo turning off onto a dirt road that led to a gate. 'The gate's not locked,' he said. 'Just a chain's holding it.'

Vittoria got out to open the gate. They drove slowly along the track into the dunes until the sand became too soft. Paulo killed the engine and they sat in the sudden quiet of the white sand. No bird noise. Only insects. The heat noticeable without the aircon. The glare intense. Among these tall dunes with the heat simmering across the sand, it could be in the middle of a desert. Yet it was only a few hundred metres from the coast road, a car passing every two or three minutes.

Isabella was wide-eyed when they opened the boot. Struggling. Making a rasping noise at the back of her throat.

They heaved her from the car and dragged her to a copse of dune grass. Vittoria cocked the nine, took out Isabella with a single shot between the eyes.

33

After takeoff Mace ordered a Windhoek from the steward pushing the drinks trolley. For Pylon, in the aisle seat, a still mineral water. He'd been up and to the loo as soon as the seatbelt lights pinged off, and looked, Mace thought, a whiter shade of brown, if that were possible.

'Have a drink?' he said. 'It'll relax you.'

Pylon said he'd stick with the water, breaking out tablets to stop the runs and any nausea.

'Suit yourself,' said Mace settling back to watch the desert, the swirls of white river beds, the shadows darkening in the mountain kloofs. Here and there the glint of a corrugated-iron roof, a homestead in the brown emptiness, smoke rising from an outside fire.

His thoughts went to Sheemina February, about what was her case exactly? Like suddenly she was right there again. In six weeks had popped up at a concert, at a café, then started the strange stuff: the flowers, the blatant telephone call. Okay, so the concert was a coincidence, the café explainable, the flowers and the call weren't subtle but they didn't mean the same without the other two incidents. Funny how it kicked in as the deal firmed. Pointing to Mo. Except what was his advantage? Or a leak in Mo's office, which was a scary notion. But more likely if she was keeping tabs on him for future gain. Leverage? Revenge? A payoff? The first two he could credit, the last was an outside runner, probably a handy by-product of her main play. Hence her portfolio of properties. Yet he couldn't see her calling for a cut on this transaction, more likely she'd stay clean, keep the moral high ground, to call large when she needed to. Mostly, though, the way he reckoned it, that was Mo's problem. His problem was something else.

Starting with Christa, the kidnapping, that'd had Sheemina February in the background somewhere. Collateral damage in Ducky Donald's estimation but Mace didn't believe so, although he had no other explanation. And then she'd bought their house. How weird was that? A detail he'd kept from Oumou. Not that Oumou had given a damn about the buyer. Just wanted to get rid of the house. Fair enough. After that Sheemina February had gone quiet until ... until there'd been a need to talk to Mo. Then hey ho, Sheemina February's back on the scene. But then surely Mo was the common denominator, an explicable line of association. More collateral damage? That was what it looked like. So why the moral angle about Isabella? Or did the woman just like causing shit?

Mace ordered another beer with his lunch. Nudged Pylon, the guy sitting upright in his seat, hands gripped to the armrests, eyes shut tight behind his sunglasses.

Pylon groaned. 'What's it?'

Mace said, 'Sheemina February, after you'd found out about her and Mo, was that where you stopped?'

Pylon took off his sunglasses, pinched the bridge of his nose. 'More or less. Like what else're you thinking about?'

'Education, maybe. To be a lawyer you need degrees.'

'Wouldn't believe it, the way they act,' said Pylon. 'Don't remember going into that.'

'I think she's in this. Working an angle somehow.'

Pylon groaned. 'Save me Jesus.'

Mace couldn't tell if it was at what he'd said or a passage of bumps the plane flew through.

'You're joking?'

'No. Not this time.'

'I'm going to be sick.' Pylon heaved, got out the barf-bag not a moment too soon.

Not an ideal way to travel, Mace thought. He pushed Sheemina February out of mind. What was the sense in obsessing about it at a time like this?

An hour out of Luanda the plane hit serious turbulence. A summer afternoon over the savannah, the towers of cumulonimbus building, the plane was going to hit turbulence. A given.

'Shit,' said Pylon, 'I can't take this. I hate this.' His body a panic of nerves, his stomach in agony, his palms sweaty. 'Why'm I doing this, oh Lord?'

Ping – the seat-belt light came on.

Mace closed his magazine. 'Sometimes there are great big holes in the air,' he said. 'I heard about a jumbo fell into one of those. Didn't go all the way down but some people got badly flung around.'

Ping. The plane dropped, bounced, the taste of mayonnaise from lunch rising in Mace's mouth.

Ping. Pylon groaned, closed his eyes, gripped the armrests.

The stewardess staggered the aisle. 'Your seat-belt, sir, seat-belt please.'

'After an event like that,' Mace said, 'a lot of people won't get into an aeroplane again. The one I heard about was somewhere over Mali. Long haul Cape Town to London. They've been going five, six hours, it's the middle of the night, people are sleeping, watching movies, not many people're strapped in. Suddenly the plane falls into the hole. Jesus, the way these people recounted it, what wasn't held down went flying: people, trolleys, bottles banging off the ceiling, things smashing, people breaking limbs, ribs, getting cut up. Like about two kilometres down the plane punches through the hole but the inside's a disaster zone. What they need is to land fast, get the injured attended to. But, hey, they're over Africa. No coms, except with other planes. No radar tracking anyone so they can't head off for the nearest airport because, hell, they might hit another flight. Besides it's night-time, there's no one there. The nearest airport they can talk to is Marseilles, three hours away. That's where they come down, people groaning and crying and shit scared for three hours. Then, those that don't need hospitalisation have to get on a flight to London. The people I heard this story from said that was bad, being so terrified that it might happen all over again. They couldn't stop shaking all the way until they touched down at Heathrow. But they're flying without too much trouble these days.'

'Wonderful,' said Pylon. 'I appreciate the story.'

'The thing is,' said Mace, 'the plane didn't crash. That's what's important to remember.'

'Sometimes they do,' said Pylon, referring to once flying into Malitia on a Dakota, an engine stopped, leaving only one prop to get them down. The pilot had to force-land in a field, stripping off some vital parts of the plane in the process. Everyone walked away with only cuts and bruises.

'Sure,' said Mace, knowing what Pylon meant, 'but propeller planes are better fliers. Easier to get down than jets, if there's trouble.'

Pylon sucked in air as the plane jolted. 'The last place I need to be is on any plane. Bloody Lear jet or a bloody turboprop like this.' He groaned.

Ping. The plane fell and Pylon grabbed at the sickbag, losing what little was left of his stomach contents.

'Where's your sense of adventure?' said Mace, staring down on the empty land. Land-mined, shot out, peopleless land. Thirty years of war didn't do anyone any favours, unless you sold the ordinance.

Luanda was a party.

On the twilight streets people singing and dancing: men in wedding dresses, women in tight minis, everyone whooping in a carnival. Mace and Pylon checked into the hotel, wanting to know what all the fun was about.

'For a festival,' said the reception clerk. 'Every year it happens. The people like it.'

Mace left it there, asked if there were any messages for them. The clerk shook her head.

'Anyone calls for us, tell them we'll be back in an hour.'

'No senhor, no. Is dangerous. Without a guard you cannot leave the hotel.'

'We'll manage,' said Pylon.

Out on the streets people laughed at them, tried to pull them into the procession.

Pylon said, 'What the hell's this about?'

A man came past with a severed cat's head dangling round his neck, the tabby's body draped over his shoulder, blood spatters on his T-shirt. Pylon tried to stop him, getting caught up in a group led by a young boy with a ginger kitten nailed to a cross. The kitten still alive. Meeuwing. Men followed wearing blue robes, blue paint daubed on their faces. Chanting solemnly: Bin La-den, Bin La-den. Behind them a knot of cross-dressers holding aloft a crucified chicken.

Pylon pulled aside the man with the severed cat's head, wanted to know in pidgin Portuguese what was with killing the cat.

Was told, 'Porque o gato é gatuno,' – getting a hard stare, the man fondling the ears of the cathead. Finally spat on Pylon's brand new square-toed lace-up Cats.

Pylon jumped forward, but the brother took off.

'What's he say?' said Mace.

'Ah shit! Can you believe this?'

'Sure,' Mace said. 'This's Africa. So what's happening here?'

'I should know,' said Pylon, wiping the phlegm from his shoes with a piece of litter.

'You didn't understand him?'

'He said something about the cat was a thief.'

'For that he hacks its head off?'

'Apparently.'

'Nice people,' said Mace, wondering what it was about cats that got them so reviled.

Pylon flicked aside the piece of paper, straightened up as a pack of children howled out of the carnival to paw at them, going, 'Camel, Benson, Peters.' Their lips were smeared with pink lipstick, they wore padded bras over skinny chests.

Pylon shouted above the melee, 'Treasure thinks this's a festival!'

'Let's duck.' Mace pointed up the street. 'Get to the hotel.'

They fought free of the kids, edging back against the crowds the way they'd come, people trying to drag them into the procession every step of the way. A woman with burning cigarettes in her ears and nose offered Mace a mouthful of the snake she was eating. Her friend in bra and miniskirt flashed Pylon a full-frontal that wasn't female at all. Pylon gawped. Thought to tap the silly bitch a back-hander but Mace pulled him away, the two of them bulldozing a passage clear.

The hotel's dining room was a clutch of flimsy tables, the Formica tops scorched with cigarette burns, the metal legs rusting, the chairs plastic. No other diners. Flies circled the ceiling fans. The fans long since stopped. A black-and-white photograph of Agustinho Neto on one wall, when he was president. The only picture on the walls. Not even one of the current president, though neither Mace nor Pylon could remember who that was.

A waiter came through the batwing doors from the kitchen when they were seated, all smiles, a tea-towel folded over his arm. 'You would like to order?' he asked.

Mace smiled back at him. 'Sure. What're you offering?'

The waiter told them the menu was steak and chips or fish and chips. Mace said, fish would be good.

'Yesterday is fish,' said the waiter. 'Today is steak.'

'Okay, steaks,' said Mace. 'And beers.'

In the silence after the waiter had gone, Pylon said, 'Before, I thought the Wodaabe were weird, pretty boys prancing about in all that makeup. Except that was at least something they'd been doing for a long time. A tradition. And they didn't kill things. But what's this about, huh?'

'A local version of Rio?'

'Bit extreme.'

The waiter brought their beers, uncapped them at the table.

Pylon asked if he was going to party with the carnival.

'Of course, senhor.' The waiter grinned. 'After I am finished in the hotel, I dance.' He did a quick jive, laughed. 'You like it?'

'Not tonight, José,' said Mace, reading the man's name off his lapel badge.

José bowed out. 'I bring your steak soon.'

Mace and Pylon clinked bottles, and drank, talking some more about the nightmare of the carnival. Fifteen minutes later José laid down huge plates of steak and chips.

'Very rare,' he said. 'You can taste the blood. Good eating.'

They were: the steaks tender, the juice welling red at the corners of their mouths as they ate.

Through a mouthful Pylon said, 'Our Mr Webster's taking his time, don't you think? I'd expected some call of welcome by now.'

Mace shrugged, cutting loose a piece of pink flesh. 'Maybe he's at the carnival.'

'Why not phone Isabella. Get her onto it.'

'She didn't have a number.'

'Shit, Mace, she's got to have made the deal with him somehow.'

Mace chewed, thinking, for a broken city the steak was melt-in-the-mouth. Could teach the Spur Ranches a thing or two.

'Just call her.'

Mace did and got her voicemail.

Pylon shook his head. 'Great handler. You got guys out in the field for you, you switch your phone to voicemail. That's what I like about Isabella. Care and concern.' He stabbed at the last of his chips. 'Down to the flowers.'

'You shouldn't listen to other people's conversations.'

'I listen to everything.'

'Anyhow, she didn't send them.'

'That's what she says.'

'She doesn't know my address.'

'That's what you say.'

They drank two more beers in the lounge, not much happening there except a group of USAID-types talking in a corner about securing people's trust. 'They don't trust us,' a big black guy was saying, 'we're going to get no cooperation. No cooperation means no more budget, bottom line. Our asses get hauled back to Washington' – the rest of the group nodding at him. 'We get hauled back to Washington, these poor folks stay starved. First thing we do tomorrow is give them candy. Sweeten them up, hey?' The group laughed. Mace and Pylon exchanged a wry glance on their way out the lounge.

In his room Mace paused, thinking he'd left his suitcase on the bed, not the rack, but maybe a maid had moved it. Then again this wasn't the sort of hotel to have maids cleaning up a room every time a guest stepped out. He checked through his suitcase. Nothing missing but it had been gone through. Neatly enough repacked but the order of things wrong.

He phoned Pylon. Pylon answered, saying, 'Yeah, someone's been through my bag, too.'

34

Saturday night Ludo went on a bender. Starting with the mini-bar. Hit back four Chivas and sodas, before taking the brandies neat. The sun dropped below Signal Hill he cried. Ludo couldn't remember the last time he'd cried. Standing at the window looking over the tree-tops, sunlight reflecting off the high-rise windows, he cried. His face crumpled. He sobbed. Deep agonising sobs. And groaned. A groan that came from his heart. Hurt in his chest like he'd taken a solid right roundhouse.

'Oh shit,' he heaved. 'Oh shit, oh shit, oh shit.' Smearing tears across his face with the back of his hand. The brandy in the other hand trembling.

He didn't want to think about Isabella. He couldn't think about anyone but Isabella. Imagine where she was lying. In a ditch. A dumpster. Among scrapped autos at some industrial site. These images haunting him. What if she wasn't dead? Was bleeding out. Alone. Dying alone. Enough to agitate him to do something. Anything.

He dialled Paulo, surprised at the connection.

'What the fuck've you done with her?' he shouted.

'Hell, I left her at Mugg & Bean,' Paulo said. 'Hours ago.'

'Tell me,' screamed Ludo but the connection was cut.

'Bastards,' he howled, sitting down, letting go. Knowing what Paulo must've done. 'Bastards.'

Slowly the shaking subsided. Ludo sat back, took deep breaths. Lit up again. The ashtray a mess of butts. There would be revenge. He would tell Francisco the punk had killed her. The least he could do. The news going to wreck Francisco, Francisco going to want to kill the messenger, knowing him. As if his pain for Isabella was all the pain there could be. Jesus, Ludo sighed, the heartache unbearable. The guilt, too. He'd gone with her this wouldn't have happened. Even without a gun.

This thought fired him again, brought down more vitriol on Paulo. Ludo knocked off the brandy, chased it with a beer. Fuck them. The best place he could think of to start was at the Llandudno house. Take it from there step by step. If they were around, really grind them over. Do what Francisco would want.

Ludo showered, dressed to kill. In Isabella's room, looked at her clothes folded on the shelves, a strappy dress hanging up. Probably what she would've worn to dinner that evening. Would have been something, the two of them dining together. Like a couple.

At Llandudno he left the Cherokee at the beach parking, walked to the house along a path at the back. Entered from the garden gate, cutting across the lawn to the swimming pool, surprised to find the patio door unlocked. He went in, called out, got no response. Upstairs he checked out Paulo's room: a goddamned mess of newspapers, magazines, brochures, maps, flyers, even ticket stubs. Their clothes gone. Among all the shit he found a portfolio of B&Bs and holiday rentals, one place circled – Molteno Road. Ludo thought, careless prick, came from thinking he'd covered all the angles.

He got out of Llandudno, driving to a cafe on the zooty beach strip. Took a table inside beneath a light, ordered a double Jack Daniel's while he located the street on a map. What he needed was a gun. Without a gun the world was too risky a place. He sipped at the sour mash. The best guy to organise a gun Ludo reckoned, short of Francisco, would be none other than Paulo's contact, Oupa K.

While he was toying with this, he was not thinking of Isabella, but the gun brought the heartache back. There'd been a gun, things could've played out differently. Instead she was probably dead. He hit the rest of the Jack to dull the grief.

He tried Isabella's number again. Voicemail. The same with Paulo's cell.

Ludo left the cafe, considering he needed to waste two, three hours before cruising for Oupa K. His preference in the interlude being a bar of drinkers, pool players, darts-types, men and women, there for the drink and the smoke and the company. Sometimes these summer nights he'd found it at the Perseverance, more usually at the Stag's Head. He made it the Stag's Head, a part of the city dim and empty this hour of a Saturday evening. Suitable to his mood. A place to grieve.

In the bar he was pulled a draught and a shot of Jack besides, taking these to a back bench behind the pool players. Set down the beer and whiskey on cork coasters, beside them laying his packet of Camels, a Zippo, his cellphone. The pool players paid no heed. Ludo sipped the beer: to Isabella. The thought of her become a dull ache in his chest. He lit a cigarette, drew smoke into his lungs, keeping it there for a ten-count, releasing it through his nose. What the hell! Put down half the Jack, chasing it with beer. He leant back, closed his eyes. The balls clicked, the players grunted approval. Ludo reckoned what was the problem here was he couldn't remember feeling so lousy. Ever. He'd felt better in worse situations. Like he didn't have the heart for this. Like what was the point? Go home, punter, go home. Catch the next flight. He got another beer and chaser.

Just after half eleven he left the Stag's Head, carrying a bottle of Jack Daniel's and headed for the Club Catastrophe that Paulo had raved of often enough. Getting there the town changing from dark and empty to a different quarter: traffic jams, cruisers, kids, the sound level booming. A block away he got a parking space, a Golf trying to squeeze him for it, Ludo pushing right on in, the Golf screeched off, hooting.

Before he left the car Ludo broke the seal on the Jack and took a pull and a second mouthful, went searching for Oupa K.

At the door of the club the bouncer said, 'You're looking for?' – meaning this is not your scene daddyo.

Ludo eyeballed him. 'Black fella name of Oupa K.'

The bouncer looked past him. 'That so? This's Africa, friend, most people're black.'

'I believe you know the man,' said Ludo, ignoring the jibe. 'I believe he hangs here.'

The man glanced at him, decided to leave it there. 'Maybe. You go inside you can find out.'

'Surely.' Ludo stepped forward and the bouncer let him pass, the bouncer smelling of the aftershave Paulo favoured, powerful cloying scent of sweat mixed with tar.

Ludo pushed into the dancers. Women in skimpy clothes everywhere, men with their shirts off, shuddering around the dance floor like zombies. They called this a club? Like hell it was. Pictures of cats crucified on the walls. Scenes from some junkhead's worst nightmare.

A tall thin guy came at him, shouting over the techno. 'M-my name's Ma-Matthew. I heard you're lo-looking for some-one?'

'Yeah,' Ludo shouted back. 'You heard right.'

'You a-aiming to score?'

The guy had attitude. Ludo grinned at this. 'Other business.'

'Sh-sh-shit doesn't go dow-down here.'

'Sure, pal.'

The Matthew guy indicated he should follow through the bodies and foam pumping from nozzles like it was a freaking bubble bath. Everybody raving on E. And the Matthew guy said shit didn't go down. The Matthew guy had his eyes closed. Probably getting some kickback.

They came to a door. Ludo heard the thin man shout at him, 'Ch-chill room.' He went inside, there was a black sucking the face of a latte boy. The black had his eyes wide open.

'You Oupa K?' said Ludo, kicking the schwarzer's boot, hand-tooled cowboy, product of the USA.

The man got back his mouth, said, 'Who the shit're you?'

'Doesn't matter, pal.' Ludo fished out his Camels, took one of the sticks from the packet with his lips. 'I'm in the market for a pistol. What're you selling?'

'Hey, hey, hey.' The black laughing, pushed away the latte rent, said to him, 'Go dance, baby.' Said to Ludo, 'You Yanks reckon you run the world.'

Ludo lit the cigarette, puffed out the smoke without drawing it down. '$250 cash. Here and now.'

Oupa K stretched his legs. 'You not notice the hulk at the door, chief? He's going to let me in with a tray of hardware.'

Ludo shrugged. '$250.'

Oupa K said nothing, staring at him. Suddenly exploded, 'Who you think I am? Who're you, Yank, you can walk in here even think I'm going to snivel, yes, boss, anything you want boss? Your problem, your white problem is you've all got this arrogance. The white man speaks the black man obeys. Hey, up yours, Yank. Screw you, man. You run the world so well, go ask one of your honky honchos. Don't put this bullshit on me.'

Ludo smoked through to the end of the cigarette, both of them staring past one another now.

'No offence, pal.' He killed the butt with the toe of his shoe. Frigging jigs, always the image problem. Oupa K wasn't his only hope, he'd walk out. Find another darkie sharper at the business end. 'Like I said, though. You can help me I'd appreciate it.'

Oupa K sprang up. 'Stuff you, mlungu.' Grabbed Ludo's open bomber jacket, pulling him towards the door. 'You want a tool? What're you want? 9mm? .38? Magnum? Huh! Huh! Tell me, Yankee. Let the niggerboy run for the white master.'

'A nine would be good,' said Ludo.

Oupa K leered at him. 'A nine would be good. Hooray for you, Yankee. Come. Come.'

Oupa K was off through the dancers, Ludo following him out the door past the grinning bouncer calling after them, 'Follow your noses, grandads,' through the throngs a block down the street, a right, and four cars away was Oupa K's van, rocking. Not only with requiems, but the human connection. Oupa K banged on the panel door. The door slid back, a guy with a straight up monkey squinted out.

'Ah shit,' said Oupa K. Then stood back for Ludo to see. 'Be amazed, Yankee. Be amazed at the darkie's big dick.'

The guy with the hard-on disappeared, Oupa K shouting, 'Where's your pistol, bro? Gimme your pistol.' Turned to Ludo. 'You want something, you're going to take whatever?'

Ludo nodded. 'If it works.'

'It works, Yankee. It works.' Oupa K reaching in for a pistol being offered grip first from the dark of the van. He raised it sighting at a streetlight, firing, missing, the slug gouging into a wall behind. 'You do any better, Doodle-dandy?'

Ludo took the gun, brought his arm up, popped the streetlight.

'$250,' said Oupa K, feigning unimpressed.

Ludo looked at the gun. A Czech CZ75. Not a corner of the world they didn't get to. Praise the Lord. Even in the midst of darkness you could be blessed. The first positive in a bad day. Ludo released the magazine: eight rounds. Jacked it back in with the palm of his hand.

'You have more ammunition?'

Oupa K tapped the roof of the van. 'What you see is what you get.' Oupa K getting jumpy at the length of this transaction. 'You want it? You don't want it?'

Ludo slipped the shooter into the pocket of his jacket, took out a roll of dollar bills. Counted off two hundreds and a fifty, handed them across, Oupa K eyeing the remainder.

'You Yanks got a strange attitude,' said Oupa K, folding the money into his pocket.

'I'm obliged,' said Ludo. He turned away, walking off fast.

'Hey, chief,' shouted Oupa K, 'go down easy, man. Say a prayer to Jesus.'

At the corner Ludo made for the crowds, his right hand in his jacket pocket, fingers curled round the grip of the Czech, his thumb working the safety catch. On, off. On, off. On. Life was better with a gun. Life would be even better with a mouthful of whiskey, the gap since the last lengthening further than it should. Still he went easy through the crowds, rolling with the bumps and pushes, stepping round the teen-scene knots, causing no aggro, everyone here for a good time after all. Stepped out of the club quarter into the quiet street where he'd parked. Here he was jumped, a knife going into his right shoulder and out, the second strike intended as a gut-rip.

Ludo felt no pain, staggering from the mugger's body-rush against a car, bringing his free hand up to save his belly. Realising this was what he'd wanted: action, something happening. He went down easy as the man had said, not praying to Jesus but slipping off the safety catch. The mugger following to stick him in the neck, his arm pulled back for the swing. Ludo shot him, the gun still in his pocket. The wonder of the CZ you didn't need a cocked hammer. The other wonder its reliability. You could lie awkward in a gutter against some Beemer's Pirelli, watch the ballet of a mugger dying. A pretty performance: pas ciseaux, pas allé, pas chasse, le grand écarté. Only at the moment of the dipshit's dropping, feel the pain.

Ludo brought his left hand to his shoulder, blood on his palm. He levered himself up, moved off in search of the Jeep, not giving the mugger a second glance. Even with his clothes on, the jig recognisable as Oupa K's stud. The trouble with jimbos their sheer greed and avarice. Their honour code non-existent.

In the car Ludo took two long hits at the Jack Daniel's. Stripped off his jacket and shirt, fingering around the puncture. From what he could tell a muscle stick wound that hurt like hell but needed no more than a wad. For the wad used a handkerchief to soak the bleeding. Carefully, grimacing, put on his shirt and jacket, keeping the wad positioned beneath the clothing.

The whiskey level was under half, Ludo wondered if he went back to the Stag's Head would the barmaid sell him another? It was worth a try. Fifteen minutes later walked into the Stag's Head, the right sleeve of his jacket bloody. The barmaid saw him coming, raised a thumb and forefinger to indicate a shot glass, at Ludo's nod poured him a Bushmills single malt.

'A nightcap,' she called it, sliding the taste of heaven towards him.

'Much obliged,' he said. She glanced at his arm. 'Just got mugged,' he said. 'Some Elastoplast would be handy. And another of those bottles.'

Poker-faced she nodded. Got the bottle from below the counter, cut a long strip of adhesive plaster off a roll kept in a drawer. 'In case of breakages,' she offered as explanation. 'You need ointment?'

Ludo pointed at the Tennessee sour mash. 'That'll do.' She nodded again.

Ludo took his time over the Bushmills, Paulo on his mind. He were Paulo he wouldn't be whooping it up, would be keeping a low profile in the apartment he'd rented. Ludo finished the malt. Couldn't help licking his lips.

'Another?' asked the barmaid without smiling.

'I'm done,' said Ludo.

She rang up, gave him the chit. The price of the bottle wasn't on it, she took that money separately, counting the change into the palm of his left hand.

'You want a room for the night, we've some above?'

'I'm fine,' he said.

She gave him a dimple-smile as he nodded goodbye. 'Take care,' she said. 'Or take more care.'

Ludo liked that, for a moment it even eased the burning in his shoulder. A nice lady, he thought. Another time, another place he might have had a different attitude.

Instead he drove to the street address on the brochure, parked some distance back from the house, settled in for a range of hard sore hours until a time Paulo would least expect him. He drank. He smoked. He played blues CDs at low volume, sometimes passing out from the pain, the whiskey, the fatigue, the ache of Isabella hurting in his chest.

Morning came to Cape Town. Ludo watched the dawn spreading over the city, the mountain, tender orange changing to the clear of day. He moved, balanced the pain with the whiskey, and went knocking. When Paulo opened the door Ludo put the Czech in his face.

'Surprise, surprise.'

Paulo stepping back, said, 'Oh, shit!'

'Right,' said Ludo, feeling himself fall into the guy's arms.

35

Ludo came back for his dying, the ringing of his cellphone fetching him up through the black. The phone in his hand.

Francisco. 'Hi, Ludo. Ludo, what's happening? You're supposed to be keeping me on the score. You and Isabella.'

'Dancing,' said Ludo. 'Dancing on the dunes.'

'What's that? You're breaking up there.'

'Boogie woogie,' said Ludo. 'Boom, boom, boom, boom.' Hooker doing a riff behind the lyrics.

'You're faint. You've gotta get back to me, Ludo.'

Ludo brought Isabella up in his arms, a harp loud in his ear: James Cotton: 'Fire Down Under the Hill'. He shuffled her about the bad terrain, her head bowed in rigor mortis, resting on his shoulder. The piano coming under the harmonica, talking, the guitar joining. The harp saying the words he couldn't.

Francisco shouted, 'You gotta get back to me, Ludo. Give me a report on the situation. How the deal's going. You tell Isabella she can answer her phone sometimes.'

Ludo boogied, staggered, Isabella falling away from him, the two of them going down among the dune grass.

'You guys gotta return,' said Francisco. 'This's a bad connection, Ludo? Hey, Ludo!'

Ludo dropped the cellphone, took hold of Isabella.

Harsh sunlight on white sand, the dying and the dead. The harp wailing. Wha-ah. Wha-ah. Wha-ah.

36

Sunday morning Pylon contracted a taxi driver outside the hotel. Guy said his name was Joao. Spoke no English, didn't look older than sixteen. Drove a 1970s model Mercedes Benz that might once have been green but was eaten out by rust, the skeleton showing in the doors and bonnet. Bald tyres, a holed exhaust. The interior: plastic chair seats tied with wire to the spring coils, the dashboard mostly missing. Mace got in the back, Pylon in the front telling the guy the harbour. A run that took ten minutes out of the city into a terrain of rusted hardware: lorries, engines, rail stock, ships, like half the world's old fishing fleet came there to die. Joao turned down an alley following rail tracks that came out of the warehouses on the seaward side of the harbour, heading along the outer breakwater past an old tanker towards a familiar boat.

'At least something's right,' said Pylon.

'Relax,' said Mace. 'Webster'll rock up soon enough.'

Pylon snorted, sceptical. 'Soon enough was yesterday.'

They got out of the taxi, Pylon telling the driver to wait, and found the captain on the bridge eating sausages.

'Can you unload for us?' said Mace.

The captain licked his fingers, told them he already had and the crates were in the container yard under the watch of one Buffalo.

'What?' said Pylon. 'Are you crazy?'

The captain told him, no, he always left stuff with Buffalo. Never had any problems before.

'So where do we find him?' said Mace.

The captain took a swig of beer, pointing down the breakwater at a wire-fenced compound.

They found Buffalo sitting in the doorway of a container, stirring a stew over a low fire. Bob Marley singing softly from a boombox. Mace could see the container was done out inside like a bed-sitting room, two collapsed armchairs in the front, a steel cabinet and a bed behind. For decor the Rasta had made mobiles of bones and shells and old china and cutlery: the collections chiming on the breeze. Leaning against the door an RPG grenade launcher; within arm's reach a Kalashnikov and two spare clips. Rasta Buffalo didn't look up from his stirring even when their shadows stopped over him.

Pylon said in his pidgin Portuguese, pointing back at the boat, 'The captain there says you're got our crates?'

The man looked up, his dreads falling about his face: blank eyes, a twitch at the corner of his mouth. He nodded at a container about fifty metres away, said, 'Two hundred US.'

Pylon shook his head. 'Too much.'

The Rasta went back to stirring his pot, brought up a spoonful of broth with a piece of white flesh in it, tasted the liquid, dropped the flesh back into the pot. 'Two hundred US.'

'What's he want?' said Mace.

Pylon told him and Mace whistled. 'Try half that.'

Pylon squatted before the Rasta to make their offer. It got no visible reaction except the man repeated his position: 'You pay two hundred' – offering Pylon a spoonful of the stew.

'Don't refuse it,' said Mace, going down on his haunches beside him.

Pylon tasted the stew and passed the spoon back to the Rasta. He dipped into the pot, held the spoon to Mace. Mace took it, smelling the pungency of the fish and mussels before he sipped at the liquid, the Rasta watching him, unsmiling. The soup was salty, the flesh in the mouthful rubbery.

The Rasta held up a key. 'Two hundred.'

Pylon brought out a hundred dollar note, said that first they wanted to inspect their crates, when they collected they'd pay the balance. Maybe today. Maybe tomorrow.

The Rasta thought about this, staring at Pylon eventually nodded okay, flipped him the key.

'He's accepting half?' said Mace.

'It gets us the key,' said Pylon, standing, the two of them moving away. 'The rest when we collect.'

'Non-negotiable,' said the Rasta in English, back at his stirring, ignoring Mace and Pylon stopped in their tracks, gazing at him.

Pylon clucked his tongue, muttered, 'Bloody pothead.'

The crates were stacked at the back of an empty container. They levered off the lids with a crowbar borrowed from the Rasta, revealing the hardware carefully packed in blankets. Enough blankets to excite a charity. Pylon took out a nine mil, said, 'Look at this. When last did you see one of these?'

'Nice gun,' said Mace, taking it from him, a Z-88, old police stock made to beat the international arms embargo. Better, he believed, than the Beretta 92 it was modelled on. As he racked it, his phone rang, the voice he connected to said, 'This's John Webster.'

'That right?' said Mace. 'We were starting to wonder about you.'

Webster ignored him. 'The consignment's ready?'

Mace said, 'I'm staring at it.'

'Where's this?'

'In a safe place.'

Webster didn't answer, let the silence drag. Eventually said, 'Someone'll collect you this afternoon. Two-thirty, three at the hotel.' He disconnected.

Mace thumbed off his phone, said, 'Ummm.' Said, 'Maybe we should take precautions.' He put the Z-88 back into a crate, took out a nine mil Taurus. Pylon already had one in his hand, loading the clip from a box in the ammunition crate.

On their way out Mace waved at the Rasta, 'Cheers, and thanks for the fish.'

37

They'd been driving around all morning. Paulo hyper, stopping twice to ritz some powder. Talking a blue streak about a condo in Miami or settling in Hawaii somewhere with a sea view. Or scrub that, some Caribbean hideaway island, pelicans circling overhead, water so clear you could snorkel without a mask. All they'd need would be an inflatable to go out fishing on the reef, maybe scooters for transport into the nearest town.

'The thing is,' Paulo said, 'to have low aspirations. I mean not want the big-ticket numbers: no flash. Choose a good lifestyle. Then the money's gonna last and nobody's gonna be stressed out having to work again at any sorta job. That's what I don't wanna do, work again. I wanna wake up each morning thinking this is it, no problems. Money in the bank gently compounding. Nothing I have to do today but swim, maybe drift over to the reef in the Zodiac, dive some lobster. Lunch time take my usual stool at the Oyster Pond, eat some seafood, drink some beers, talk to the tourists. Laze through the afternoon trying to work out where to eat, like at the Orient again, or the Rouge this time or Captain Oliver's Restaurant.'

They'd driven round the glitz strip, Sea Point, Clifton, Camps Bay, come back over the Nek, Paulo saying why return to the apartment on a day like this, taking De Waal down the peninsula through Newlands Forest, Cecelia Forest, across Constantia through the vineyards up and over the mountain till coming down into Sun Valley Vittoria said, 'I've gotta eat, Paulo. It's one o'clock. I've gotta eat' – and Paulo had swung into Longbeach Mall saying, 'A Wimpy should do,' finding a parking space right at the entrance, the car-guard giving him a slip of paper that said Amos was pleased to watch his car, have a nice day.

Taking the card, Paulo said, 'The thing I'm not gonna miss about this place is you guys.'

The Wimpy was loud with kids and grandparents but a granny leaving with two brats freed up a cubicle in the window for Paulo and Vittoria – a view of the parking lot and the mountains beyond. A waitress took their order for all-day breakfasts and fast coffees.

Vittoria stared out at the fat people wheeling trolley loads of groceries to their cars. Could be a home-mall if you blinked, everyone as badly dressed. 'I'm not sure I want that,' she said. 'The paradise island.'

'Babe. We try it, you'll like it. Trust me.'

The coffees came, he finished his before she'd had a sip, still selling her the Caribbean idyll.

'The way I look at it,' Vittoria said, 'this is a start.'

Paulo shook his head vigorously. 'That's the point. Keep off the greed. The greed's what kills people.'

The waitress put two full-house plates on the table: bacon, sausages, eggs sunny side up, French fries, fried tomato, two slices of white bread toast. Filled up their coffees. 'Anything else?'

Paulo said, 'This is good.'

They ate in silence, Vittoria relishing each mouthful, Paulo getting through an egg and a slice of toast.

'If you're not eating it, I'll have your bacon,' said Vittoria, heisting the rashers from his plate. 'So what's the plan, tomorrow?'

Paulo said, 'Shit that reminds me' – taking out Isabella's cellphone – 'I better keep her lover smiling, after all the messages he's left.'

SMSed: 'Hold tight, babe, talk to you soon.' Repeated it to Vittoria.

'That's gonna please him?'

'Sounds to me like what Isabella would say.'

'She'd call him.'

'Yeah, well, this time she hasn't.' He pressed send.

Vittoria clattered her knife and fork on the empty plate. 'Breakfast for lunch is as good as breakfast at breakfast.' She wiped her mouth. 'Still haven't told me what the plan is.'

'Simple. We meet. They give us the diamonds, we cut them their share. Adios amigos.'

'You think?'

'Sure. Where's the hitch?'

'No Isabella. No Ludo.'

'Tonight she's going to send him a message, she's at the airport on standby, got to fly home urgently, Paulo'll take care of everything. Talk tomorrow.'

'He'll buy that?'

'Can't see why not. Shit happens all the time.'

38

Two-thirty came, two-thirty went. Three came and went. Mace and Pylon were sitting on the hotel terrace under an umbrella watching two women in thong bikinis drifting about the pool on lilos, their shapely bodies some distraction in the heat. Mace had tried phoning Isabella after her SMS, got her voicemail again. Even put through a call to Francisco in New York, got his voicemail.

Pylon said, 'This is wrong.'

Mace said, 'Give it time.'

'Why's she not talking to you?'

Mace held up his hands. 'A message is fine.'

At close to half past three the waiter José brought them a slip of hotel notepaper with an address. Said the man on the phone said they must get a taxi.

'What'd I say,' said Pylon. 'Mr Webster's pulling the moves.'

'That's okay,' said Mace, patting the bulge of the nine on his hip. 'We've got our own moves.'

They found Joao playing cards with the other drivers on the street outside the hotel. Pylon waved him over, showed him the address, and Joao smiled, told him big houses, swimming pools, rich people, government people.

The house was Italianate. Double storey. Columns. Balconies. Shutters on the windows, marble porch. Stucco walls. Dark-stained woodwork. A black Mercedes Benz on the circular drive.

'Politico,' said Joao.

Mace eased out of the bucket-seat onto the gravel. Saw a couple of teenage girls playing tennis on a clay court. An umbrella and loungers at the pool, empty glasses on the table.

He said, 'You didn't know this was Luanda, you wouldn't know this was Luanda. You'd think posh Santiago, Singapore, Cape Town. You wouldn't think there was a war on. Not with so many trees.'

Pylon paid off Joao, told him if they needed collecting they'd phone the hotel. Joao protested no he had a cellphone, they could phone him direct, bringing out a blue Nokia to prove it. Pylon entered the number, then he and Mace crunched up to the wide-open front door and pressed the bell, could hear it ringing in two different places. But the buzzing brought no reaction. The only sound in the house a soccer match on television.

'They aren't about to hear above that,' said Pylon, pressing the buzzer again.

Through the hall Mace could see glass doors giving onto a lawn mown in neat stripes. Some peacocks wandering on it, dragging their tails. Pylon gave the bell another long session. Again the two men waited, Pylon reading off the seconds: thirty seconds, one minute, minute and a half, said, 'Shit, this's ridiculous.'

Above them a voice said, 'Welcome to my house, gentlemen, sorry that you are kept waiting. Tão, please to come in and up the stair.'

Standing at the top of the stairs was a moon-faced man, thick-necked, the flesh bulging over his collar. A short dumpy man in a pale blue shirt, the white collar fastened with a tie. He flashed them a smile of bright teeth. 'Bom, I am Dr Kiambu. Tão, please. Join with me.'

On the landing he shook their hands. 'You enjoy soccer, gentlemen?' A Portuguese accent tingeing his English.

Mace and Pylon nodded. 'I am afraid the match is almost full-time, but come. Manchester United against Spurs. This is what I would call a mid-period time for Gascoigne at the end of the season of 1989-90. You like soccer?'

He took them into a long dim room, the shutters up, a wall of bookcases, on the other walls paintings in ornate gold frames of Portuguese sailing ships and peasants tilling fields. Persians on the parquet flooring. What was missing, Mace thought, was a suit of armour. At the one end a desk, at the other leather armchairs facing a television screen. The only light from the television, a man's head silhouetted against it. On screen a moment of tension: Manchester taking a corner. The ball goes up, is intercepted, kicked away mid-field.

'Frigging useless,' said the man in the armchair, half-turning towards the group behind him.

'Tão please,' said Dr Kiambu, 'let me introduce you to John Webster.'

John Webster came off the chair sideways like a hunting spider. A thin-lipped thin man in jeans and a green open-necked shirt worn loose Madiba-style. Mace took one look at him and didn't like him. Didn't like freckled faces, ginger hair, in tight waves close to the scalp.

They shook hands, Webster putting more clinch into it than necessary. Mace held the grip, caught the devil in the man's eyes, mocking him.

'Everything in order?' Webster said, no niceties, his thin lips pulled into a sneer.

'No reason it shouldn't be,' said Mace, jerking free his hand.

Webster kept his smirk. 'Good, then let's see what the frig you've brought us.'

'Us?' said Pylon. 'You're the diamond checker, right?'

'Good gentlemen,' said Kiambu. 'Tão please. My friend John checks diamonds for you, and weapons for me. Is there a problem?' He laid a podgy hand on Webster's arm, glanced from Pylon to Mace.

'This isn't how we expected it,' said Mace.

Dr Kiambu beamed. 'Come please Mr Bishop. In Angola certain skills are in what we call short supply. We must fix our arrangements in the best way we can. Mr Webster is a professional. He can make these judgements without compromise. Surely? Or your Ms Medicis would not have sought him out to advise you.' He picked up a remote, switched off the television set. 'Tão, we go to business. I would be happy if Mr Buso comes with me. Mr Bishop, perhaps you will accompany with John, yes? Afterwards we can place you at your hotel, no problem.'

Mace caught Pylon's eye, saw there the same unease he felt. He frowned, but said nothing as Kiambu ushered them down the stairs.

In the driveway the black Mercedes had been joined by a second. The chauffeurs were big men, wore guns holstered on their belts.

'Where to?' said Webster.

'The harbour.' Mace slipped into the back seat, smelling new leather.

'Where the frig else.' Webster slammed Mace's door closed, got in the front. 'Let me guess, huh.' He leered round at Mace. 'You're storing in the Rasta's compound.' Webster laughed. 'Amazing.' Gave directions to the driver in Portuguese. 'I heard tell you once were major traders. That right?'

Mace didn't respond.

'I'd have thought you might have made other arrangements. Not left enough hardware to stage a frigging coup lying in the hands of a mushbrain so that every nignog with his mother's AK could pop round to liberate it.' He gave his thin-lipped sneer. 'Get my meaning?'

Mace stared at him until Webster turned away, grunting, 'Frigging arsehole.'

Mace leant forward, whispered in Webster's ear. 'I wouldn't push it any further, okay.'

'I'll push it any frigging way I want,' said Webster.

Mace sat back, smiled at the driver's eyes watching him in the rear-view mirror. Heard Webster put through a brief cellphone call in Portuguese.

* * *

The Mercs stopped at the gates to the compound, the Rasta sitting in the shade watching them get out. The drivers yelled at him to open up and he sauntered over, no servility in his manner, taking his time unlocking the chains. Mace noted the Argentinian had sailed, only the old tanker moored against the wharf. By the state of it had been moored there a long time. As he turned away he glimpsed two men come out on the upper deck and wave down at them. He raised a hand in greeting. Second to the Rasta's job, securing a rusting hulk in a wrecked harbour had to be the pits. They had his sympathy. He went through the security gates and joined Dr Kiambu while Pylon unlocked the container.

Kiambu stepped inside, mopping at the perspiration on his face with a handkerchief. 'Táo please tell me, this is everything we requested?'

The firing started before either Mace or Pylon could answer, the bullets slamming loud against the steel container. Mace spun, grabbed the door to pull it closed as Webster scooted in. Saw one driver running off, the other crouched behind the Merc. No sign of the Rasta. The volley ceased, a couple of single shots then quiet.

'How many?' said Pylon.

'Two for sure.' Mace eased the door open to widen the line of sight. The driver was where he'd been, a pistol in his hand.

Webster called to him and the guy raised his head and may have said something but the shooting came again. Webster cursed, said, 'Where's that Rasta? This's gotta be his setup.'

In the quiet Mace could hear someone whistling. 'Why's that?' he said, pushing the door open a crack to let in light.

Webster came round on him. 'What d'you think this is about, frigger? This's about guns 'n diamonds and about arseholes who waltz in here like it's a picnic.'

'The Rasta's gone,' said Pylon. 'So's the driver now.'

Webster snorted. 'Frigging likely.'

'See for yourself.' Pylon stood back from the door. 'See him run.'

Webster looked. 'Arsehole.'

'Please,' said Kiambu, 'it could also be that I am the target. Before they have tried to kidnap me for a ransom.'

Mace said, 'What makes you so precious?'

'He's a frigging cabinet minister.' Webster flicked a cigarette from a pack. 'Jesus. Who're you guys?'

'I am minister for transport,' said Kiambu. 'In our politics there is great suspicion. Everyone is watching his back.'

Pylon shook his head. 'Unlikely this is about you. How was anyone gonna know you'd be here?'

Kiambu smiled. 'In Luanda they say there are no secrets. Everywhere there are spies finding out all the business. It could be that someone has heard about these' – he pointed at the crates – 'and so they think they can make a nice killing.' He kept his smile. 'That is what you say in English, sim?' Sweat stained Kiambu's shirt, dark spots where the material pulled across his breasts and under his armpits. He dabbed at his face. 'What do you think, John? Should we call for some help? Tamoda, maybe.'

'Wouldn't the bastard just rush to help you.'

'Then Xitu.'

'Ha, Xitu. Xitu would love this.'

Kiambu sighed. 'I suppose so.'

'Face it, doctor. You've got no leverage there.' Webster stood at the half-open door, blowing exhale out the corner of his mouth. He held the cigarette cupped into his hand.

'So what do you think?'

'I think it's a mess, is what I think. Doesn't matter what it's about. We're stuck in this shit-pit.'

'Until it's dark,' said Mace. 'They don't make a move before then we'll walk away.'

'Yeah. And leave all this stuff. No chance, mate. No way in hell.'

Pylon turned to Mace. 'Take a look, they're just standing up there on the deck.' He waved, and one of the figures brought up his gun and unleashed a clip, the bullets zinging and clanging against the container. They waited for the silence. 'Stalemate.' Pylon pointed at the crates. 'Somewhere in this lot has to be a rifle we can use to slot them.'

Mace's cellphone rang. He thumbed it on. 'This is New York,' the voice said. 'Am I talking to Mace Bishop?' Saying before Mace could answer, 'This is Francisco Medicis calling to find out what's happening.'

'It's not a good time,' said Mace.

Francisco talking over him. 'I'm getting voicemail every connection I make to Isabella's phone, and Mr Ludovico was breaking up last time we spoke. Since then only his voicemail. What I need to know're the circumstances, Mr Bishop. Like where you're at geographically speaking.'

Mace said, 'Luanda. Your man John Webster's right here.'

'That right,' said Francisco, 'this deal is going down?'

'Not how we expected,' said Mace.

'Again,' said Francisco. 'I'm getting interference.'

Mace said, 'What's happening here is we have the weapons. We have the buyer. We have not seen the diamonds. We are being shot at.'

'Say again. You're dropping, Mr Bishop.'

Mace shouted, 'This is a heist situation' – the connection broke and Mace thumbed it off. 'Christ!' To Webster. 'That was the man who put this together.'

Webster came off the crates, ground the butt into the container's wooden floor. 'Like I give a damn.' He drew out a .38 from beneath the loose hang of his shirt, put it on Mace and Pylon. 'Back there. With the good doctor.'

'John!' exclaimed Kiambu. 'What is this?'

'It's what he said,' said Webster, pushing the cabinet minister against the crates until he sat down. 'The only thing our friend here's got right all afternoon. This's a heist. Come gents, come.' He levelled the gun on Mace and Pylon. 'Oblige me. Sit down here beside our little politician.' He dug in his jeans pocket for his cellphone and pressed digits, half an eye on his captives. 'Excuse me one moment.'

Mace nudged Pylon but Webster caught the movement and smiled. 'Be good. Don't try it on, yeah. You'll be a frigging dead smart-arse.' He brought up the phone, spoke in Portuguese. When he thumbed it off, said, 'Any last minute calls you guys want to make?'

'John... Who is that?'

'Some friends, doctor. People you're gonna spend some time with. Nothing to stress about.' He turned to Mace and Pylon. 'How about you, what's your name, Pylon? Hey, what's with you guys? Mace and Pylon? Like a comedy act. Pylon. What sort of frigging name's Pylon? You have pylons running past your village, that was the first thing your mother saw after you wriggled out? So cute, you darkies, calling your babies all these weird names.'

Pylon stared at him blank-eyed.

'And Mace. Macey-boy. Someone had a sense of humour here? So who's out there, boys? Gotta have some chicks somewhere. Two blokes like you two. Macho types. Gun dealers. Men of the world. What d'you say Pylon? No girlfriend, wife, mother to say goodbye to?'

Pylon held out his hand for the phone.

'Who's it to be mate? Your wife? She sitting there in the shack with all the piccanins waiting for her hubby to bring home the kill like a good Zulu.'

'Xhosa,' said Pylon.

'There's a difference?'

Pylon didn't answer.

In the distance Mace could hear a truck grinding in low gear, saw Webster focused on Pylon, heard the lorry change up to second, and closer someone calling Webster's name. Webster yelling at Pylon, 'Zulu, Xhosa, Zulu, Xhosa' getting close to Pylon, putting the gun right in his face. Webster screaming, 'You frigging golliwog.'

Mace heard the click of the misfire. Even in the fracas, loud as a gunshot. He pulled the Taurus from his belt, wracked it, gut shot Webster, saw Pylon wrench the pistol from the guy's hand, heard men shouting, running, the truck closer now. Webster bent double and Mace grabbed him about the neck, walked him step by step to the door, the gun at the diamond man's head.

'What you have to do,' he said to Webster, 'is tell your frigging chinas to go home.'

Webster spat blood, groaned something that sounded to Mace like no human words. Mace shook the guy, getting the pain of the gut wound to make Webster buckle in his grip. He pulled him up, feeling the stickiness of blood underfoot. Webster as heavy as deadweight.

Pylon pushed past to open the container door. Outside stood two men with AKs pointing at them.

'Stage's all yours,' said Mace, digging the gun into Webster's ear. 'Talk to them.' At the same time felt his phone vibrating in his pocket, the ringing lasting for seven counts until the call went to voicemail.

39

Captain Gonsalves heard the voicemail click in and cursed, left a message, 'Call me, Bishop. ASAP.' He disconnected, walked away, stripping the cigarette he'd cadged. The site busy as a shopping mall. Bloody Sunday afternoon everyone dragged away from their braais and their families, his wife not even looking up from her crochet work when he took the call-out. Just a 'See you later.' He sighed, headed up the sand dune to get some perspective. The climb winded him, the sand hot and loose and filling his shoes. Halfway up Gonsalves rested, sat down to consider the scene.

He could see over the dunes to the road, busy now at this time of the afternoon with people coming back from their West Coast getaways. The farm gate visible too, a couple of cops in a marked car sitting there to secure the area. Below, the technicians did their work, combing through the dune grass, sifting the sand. He didn't reckon they were going to find much. Or anything at all.

Gonsalves rolled the tobacco between his palms, popped the pellet into his mouth.

He watched the medics strap the bodies onto stretchers. Funny way they'd fallen: the one on top of the other. Strange scuffle markings in the sand like after the male had been shot he recovered enough to try and pick up the woman, before he collapsed again. The end of it beyond that. His cellphone dropped as he fell. Why would you bring somebody out here and let them keep their cellphone? Let them keep their wallet. Minus cash and credit cards admittedly. Only clue a photo of the dead women in the wallet holder. But no ID. And nothing on the woman. Then she'd have had everything in a handbag. Which was easy to dump. Still didn't explain the cellphone. Like it was an up-yours gesture. Deliberate. Like whoever this was telling you they weren't planning to be around long. First clue: all the numbers in the cellphone were American. Mostly New York.

Gonsalves sucked at the tobacco plug.

Yankees. Tourists. Jesus. He unlaced his shoes, emptied out the sand. Tied the laces in neat bows again.

What this shooting reminded him of was the homo killing, the one queer shot smack in the centre of the forehead. Just like the woman here: right between the eyes. A major difference: both of them brought out to be done on the spot, the doc guessing anything up to fifteen hours separating the shootings. The man taking it in the chest, a lung hit, which was why he'd come back to life temporarily. Which might mean there'd been two killers. Because why not go for the same shot again, if you were the shooter? Also, if you were the shooter and going for the heart, you'd hit the heart. Not put a stray one through the lungs.

Still, cocky bastards not even trying to hide the bodies. Believing that outta the way in the thick dune grass no one was gonna stumble on them in a month of Sundays. And probably a fair assumption. If it wasn't for quad bikers tearing up the dunes, almost ramping right over the corpses. Might have been a couple of weeks otherwise. Instead of four or five hours.

At the base of the dune, the medics loaded the bodies into the ambulance and closed the doors, the doctor waving up at Gonsalves. The captain got up slowly, his right knee cracking. He flexed his leg muscles, working the joint. What was puzzling was Mace Bishop's cellphone number in the phone. Chances were the guy wasn't one of Bishop's clients. Although the woman could've been. She was expensive. But not the man, too chain store in his clothing. Gonsalves spat out the tobacco and started down the dune, the sand cramming his shoes with each step.

40

The men with the AKs shouted in Portuguese. Pylon yelling back they should shut up or Mr Webster would take another bullet. The men highly agitated, dancing about like the ground was hot.

Behind them Mace could see the truck stopped other side of the Mercs, its engine running, the driver watching the stand-off. Mace shook Webster. 'Talk to your buddies. Let them hear you.'

Webster groaned, his head flopping forward, Mace thinking, Christ, the frigger's dead meat, and tightened his grip to keep Webster from dropping. Wasn't any way Webster would be talking to his buddies.

Shouted at Pylon, 'He's bloody dead.'

Pylon gesticulating at the two men with the nine mil in one hand, Webster's dud thirty-eight in the other, telling them they would die beyond the count of three if they didn't get their arses in the truck and vanish, catching the movement of Mace tossing Webster's body aside and behind him Dr Kiambu. The politician appearing with an R34 assault rifle in his hands like this was nothing new.

Pylon yelling at him to stay back.

Mace going, 'What the fuck?'

The attackers with the AKs hesitating at the appearance of the short man in the jacket and tie. In that hesitation losing the moment as Kiambu sprayed half a clip into them, their bodies jiggling at the impacts, spinning to fall face down.

Mace felt shells bouncing off him, his head booming with the automatic fire, thinking, with some men you just couldn't tell. They looked the talking type, the last sort you'd expect to know about guns, let alone killing. Then when it came down to the nail they pulled a stunt. You had to give it to him.

Kiambu handed the rifle to Pylon. 'A dangerous weapon, I think. Perhaps it is of more use to you.' He pointed at the truck. 'That transport would be useful, I believe.'

The driver saw this scenario too, in his haste to reverse at the sight of Pylon running towards him stalled the engine.

Pylon came up with a grin, said in pidgin, 'Don't cause any shit.' The man shook his head, climbed out of the cab and stood peeing his pants. 'Ah, save me Jesus.' Pylon rolled his eyes to the heavens. 'There's no need for that.' The driver was a short way off tears too. Pylon prodded him in the ribs with the rifle barrel, pushed him backwards. 'Go. Deixar. Piss off' – indicating the road into the warehouses. The man looked at him. 'Ciao! Goodbye,' said Pylon, 'go' – and the man took off, running, glancing back, about a hundred metres away bringing up a pistol from somewhere in his trousers. He fired twice on the run, his aim high. Pylon watched him, thinking, why bro, why're you doing that? Wondering, should he take down the brother? Decided, no, what was the point?

'In politics,' said Dr Kiambu 'there are always enemies. Some of these will want to kill you. Myself I believe in the case of dictators this is a good thing. The killing. This is what should happen in Zimbabwe, yes? Many years ago they should have shot Mugabe.'

He lined up a range of single malts on the counter top: Glenmorangie. Speyburn. Ben Nevis. Laphroaig.

Laphroaig, the only one Mace recognised.

'You would agree, about Mugabe? Such a good leader in the beginning. But he gets money, he gets power, a new young wife, what is to stop a man when he has these things?' Kiambu held up between his thumb and index finger an AK47 round. 'This. This is the friend of the ordinary citizen. You would agree? When the man becomes a monster then pow, finished, the saint kills the dragon.' He stood the bullet next to a photograph of a woman and two teenage girls. 'Who was that saint?'

'Saint George,' said Pylon.

'I should not forget.' Kiambu set a row of four glasses before Mace and four in front of Pylon. 'It is important you try each one to choose what you want to drink. Myself I drink Ben Nevis.' He poured a tot for Mace and Pylon, a triple for himself. 'For me it is the vanilla and orange. Por favor, please, taste it.'

They did. Mace thinking if there was vanilla and orange in there it was hidden. Good smooth Scotch, though. You could settle in with this for a winter's night. Not quite the drink in thirty degrees and high humidity. A beer would've been better, but the doctor was on a victory roll.

Kiambu picked up the Glenmorangie. 'This is my second choice. My colleagues will not drink anything else. But some of them are bush monkeys so this is no recommendation. Try for yourself. Also you will taste the vanilla.' He poured. 'Bom.'

Pylon said, 'That's it, doctor. That's the one.'

Kiambu smiled. 'You would have friends in our cabinet.'

Mace couldn't tell the difference. Why bother, it was hellish good anyhow.

'What I have difficulty with understanding,' said Kiambu, uncapping the Speyburn, 'is that there are people that want to kill me. Why I do not know. I mean why I have this difficulty with understanding it. All my life people have been shooting at me to kill me. This is what happens in war. But then the war stops but the people do not want to stop shooting at me.' He poured a shot into their glasses. 'This one you will notice is more sweeter. Like honey. Also very very good, but not for my palate.'

Mace could taste the sweetness, decided this suited him better than any of the others although he sipped the Laphroaig out of politeness.

'Please, gentlemen. Let me guess which one you prefer. Mr Buso I have no doubt is a Glenmorangie man. Yes?' Pylon nodded. 'Mr Bishop I would say is Speyburn.'

Mace grinned. 'How'd you guess?'

'It was simple. With the first two, there was a little tightening in your lips. Same with the Laphroaig. With the Speyburn, nothing. Am I right?'

'Spot on.'

'Then.' Kiambu gave them triples of their choice.

Mace said, 'Some ice perhaps?'

'Ah, Mr Bishop...' He shook his head. 'You are not a whisky drinker. Ice will stop the flavours from coming out.'

Mace shrugged.

'But you are a guest and this I will honour.' He took a tray of ice blocks from the bar fridge. 'Please, help yourself.'

While Mace did, Kiambu brought out Montecristos in cellophane wrappers.

'I suppose what it is difficult for me to understand after this afternoon is my friend John Webster. For ten years we have done business, I would even say he was a friend. We are both soccer fans. He has slept here in my house. He has invited me to his fine house in Scotland. Together we have visited the distilleries. We have had these lovely times, he and myself.'

While the doctor spoke, Mace broke the wrapper, slipped out the cigar and slid it back and forth beneath his nose.

'This afternoon at our lunch he asked why did I not come again this summer to catch trout in his streams? I said, yes, why not? I was pleased. I was happy about this possibility. But he was going to kill me. He could sit here and look at me and know I would be dead tonight. Pah! What sort of man is this, I ask you?'

Dr Kiambu contemplated his cigar, cut the end off, passed the snippers to Pylon.

'I find this behaviour beyond my belief.' He shook his head. 'What has he to gain? The guns. The diamonds. My ransom. What is this worth? A droplet. Over the years there would be much more. I was a good contact for him. Here in the country, but outside too. John Webster did not know everybody.'

Kiambu clicked up a flame on a heavy gold lighter, sucked until the cigar burned. He blew out a stream of smoke. Waited while Pylon and Mace went through the ritual. 'Shall we sit?'

The chairs were leather, deep, would not have been out of place in the foyer of a five-star hotel.

'Sometimes I believe we know so little of what it is that is going on. We walk into someone else's agenda and things happen that appear to be completely without meaning. For that someone it is all naturally logical, this game they are playing. For us it can be strange, it can be dangerous. It can be deadly.' He sipped at his whisky. 'Myself I would not have thought this of my friend John Webster.'

He drew on the cigar, sending the smoke up at the chandelier.

'And you two gentlemen. Strangers until this afternoon. I could say strangers even now because what do I know about how you have lived? But you have saved my life.'

A silence settled. Mace smoked, then rolled the scotch around his mouth. He considered contacting Isabella. Wondered what she'd known of John Webster?

Dr Kiambu broke into his thoughts. 'Bom. Please, gentlemen. Perhaps we should call this the end of the night?' He glanced at his watch. 'Sim, yes. It is after ten o'clock. If you do not mind I will drive you to the hotel.'

Mace took the rest of his whisky in a single swallow. Felt the weight of the diamonds against his hip. Hell, after the peri-peri crab, the French Chablis, the scotch, he could understand the man's need to sleep.

In his hotel room Mace spilled the stones from their pouch onto his bed, divided the heap in half.

Said, 'That's your lot. Just in case.'

'Just in case what?'

'Kiambu sends heavies round to get them back.'

'He won't.'

'You can be so sure?'

Pylon said, 'I think you're being paranoid,' – funnelling his share back into the pouch.

'Not a bad thing to be in this country it would seem,' said Mace. 'A nightcap?'

Pylon considered, shook his head. 'Nah, I won't. Enough excitement.'

Alone, Mace uncapped a beer from the minibar and sat on the edge of the bed, suddenly exhausted. The sort of exhaustion that wasn't tiredness but anger at John Webster. At why couldn't he have let the deal happen without the duplicity? At why the goddamned hell he had to be a greedy bastard? Always there was someone out to score. Never content to take a cut, wanting it all. And when that happened the world turned nasty. He shuddered, recalling the click of the misfire. That could've been Pylon gone.

For a heap of stones. Mace rolled the diamonds beneath his palm, thinking, he'd not thought about Pylon being killed before, or himself for that matter. A prospect that'd been a real possibility with each deal they'd floated in the old days. There were times they both could have taken a bullet. But he'd not stopped to think about it then. Not for an instant. Certainly not gone maudlin. He grabbed a handful of the stones, let them drop from his fist one by one. Pretty enough. Although in a heap of gravel you'd have to be a prospector to find them all. Blood diamonds. Three deaths written against their record in one afternoon, and how many before?

He sighed, said aloud, 'You're getting past it, Mace. These are an old man's thoughts' – and flicked the unlock on his cellphone. He thumbed to the call register.

A missed call from Francisco. At international rates not worth a call back.

A missed call from Mo Siq. Ditto. Let alone that Mo wouldn't appreciate being woken at what would be going one a.m.

A missed call from Captain Gonsalves. Nothing there, Mace reckoned that couldn't be dealt with back home. Probably to tell him they'd arrested the woman.

Nothing from Isabella which puzzled and disappointed him. Usually she'd have rung back. Especially given the urgency of his messages.

In the inbox a message from Oumou: 'Let me know you're okay.' He replied straight off: 'Everything fine. See you tomorrow afternoon.'

And one from Isabella. 'After standby for two hours now on the New York flight. Had to go urgently. Paulo will contact you. Talk to you soonest. Love you babe.'

Love you babe!

In all this time she'd never said anything like that, let alone written it. Getting soft with the years. He smiled. Sentimentality got even the hard cases. He keyed in a message: 'Webster pulled a move. His last one. Trust the diamonds are what they're supposed to be.' The moment she switched her phone on and that came through, she'd be dialling him. With a bit of luck he wouldn't be in the air.

Mace finished the beer and stretched out on the bed. He closed his eyes, fell asleep in his clothes, the light on.

His phone woke him at seven-thirty. He came up groggy, for a moment unsure where he was. Light and heat flooded the room. Mace groped for the phone vibrating across the bedside table, in the movement caught the reek of sweat from his clothes and grimaced. Saw the cluster of diamonds he'd heaped into an ashtray, the empty beer bottle. Gonsalves' name on the screen.

'Captain,' he said, his voice croaky, his mouth dry and sour. He swung his legs off the bed and sat upright. Again the sweaty release of his body odour.

'I left a message,' said Gonsalves. 'I expect you'd have got to it one day.'

'It's seven-thirty. You woke me.'

'Eight-thirty.' Gonsalves paused. 'Monday morning. Everybody's on the job, hangover or not. You got a hangover, Mr Bishop?'

Mace wiped his hand over his face, his skin bristly, sticky with perspiration. 'I'm in Luanda,' he said. 'But don't let it bother you.'

'I won't. Luanda, hey. Nice place before the war. I had family there. Even spent a Christmas with them, 1969 or '70, long before the shit started. From what I hear it's buggered now.'

'Totally.'

'Ja, well, what can you say?'

Mace said nothing.

Gonsalves said, 'The reason I phoned is we have two bodies found on the Atlantis dunes. No ID. One male. One female. Male's about two metres tall, eighty-five kilos, thin sandy hair going grey, mid-fifties probably.'

Mace thought, why're you telling me? Started to say, 'What's this got …' but Gonsalves talked him down.

'Give me a minute, okay? Just listen. Female about one eight, say weighing sixty, sixty-five kilos, hair dark, styled in what they call a bob, I would guess about ten years younger. Male's dressed okay but nothing special. Female's more classy. Expensive-looking clothes. Male shot in the chest. Female shot in the head between the eyes. Female dead about fifteen hours before the male.'

Mace said, 'Shot in the head?'

Gonsalves said, 'Ah, the man's not so babalaas. My thoughts too, Mr Bishop. Where'd I seen this type of shooting before? I asked myself.'

'You've got the chick?'

'Negative, no. She's gone. Vanished without trace. What we got at the Llandudno place was sweet fanny. Everybody done a runner.' He paused and Mace heard paper tearing. 'Why I'm ringing you specifically is because near the twosome in the dunes we found a cellphone. Only local number in it is yours. This one I'm phoning. Could be clients of yours? What I'm gonna do is phone you, see if you recognise the name.'

He disconnected. While he waited Mace thought, unlikely it was a client, even if the profile fitted maybe two couples on their books. Except on both counts the men were snazzy dressers.

His phone rang. Number restricted on the screen. He thumbed it on, told Gonsalves this wasn't going anywhere.

'How about coming round to confirm?' said the captain.

'That's all I need.' Mace stood up to stretch his back.

'When're you back?'

'Tomorrow,' he lied.

'Give me a call,' said Gonsalves.

'I'll do that,' said Mace, as he put down the cellphone and headed for the bathroom and a long shower. Supposing there was long water. Afterwards he checked on his clients. No one missing.

At breakfast he raised the idea with Pylon of giving Gonsalves the chick's whereabouts after they'd done the deal with Paulo.

'Ten to one she's with him. Right?'

Pylon nodded.

'All we do is follow him home afterwards. We phone Gonsalves, the cops call round and get her. Get him too on suspicion.'

'And turn up a parcel of diamonds meant for your Isabella.'

'There're ways round that?'

'Gonsalves?'

'A pension contribution.'

Pylon spread margarine on his toast, toast thin and dry that cracked into pieces under his knife. He looked at Mace in exasperation. 'How do they do this? Why can't they make toast that's like toast? You know, warm bread lightly browned both sides.'

Mace ignored him. 'So where does the exchange happen? Our offices? Mo's place? Somewhere neutral?' Thinking, not Mo's place if Sheemina February was on his case.

'Like hire a room?' Pylon crunched down on the toast. 'Our offices are fine.'

Mace SMS'd Paulo the address and time. Copied it to Mo Siq. 'Now all we need is your cousin AC.'

Pylon wiped crumbs from his fingers, pulled out his cellphone. 'Toast is so easy. The toaster we've got now, in six months there's not one piece I've had to scrape off the charred stuff. I hate that, when it burns. A slice burns, you get the taste goes right through the toast. I'd throw that away. Not Treasure. No. That's wasting. There're kids would die for a piece of burnt toast, so you've got to scrape it off and eat it. May as well toast cardboard.' He thumbed an SMS into his phone. Pressed send. 'So now, with the new toaster, you can't burn the toast. Even if you forget it's on, it pops up.' He smeared margarine on another piece. Bit into it and choked.

'Come,' said Mace, thumping his partner on the back, 'let's go, we've got a plane to catch.'

41

With the last rays of the afternoon at the window and the aircon up high, they sat round the table in what Mace and Pylon grandly called their boardroom, the diamonds in the centre, refracting sunlight against the dark wood. Mo Siq, AC Mkize, and Mace and Pylon waiting on Paulo.

AC was impressed with the diamonds.

'Tell me again. You walked in with these in your pockets. Through Customs?'

Mace grinned. 'Who's to guess? No one even checked the baggage.'

AC laughed. More relaxed than the last time Mace had seen him. Not suited, drinking a beer from the bottle. He and Mo reminiscing about some deal they'd done in Luanda at a dinner party to fund the war effort.

Mo saying, 'There we were in penguin suits, Stones and me, at this huge colonial house modelled on some Lisbon mansion that the minister of defence had moved into after the owners left for Portugal, and there's maybe fifty people at the do, seated at tables on the back patio and at our table this Cuban colonel's all over the wife of the minister of defence, in front of the minister of defence. Which was embarrassing,' Mo said, 'except the minister of defence's not getting fraught and his wife's touching the colonel almost as much as he's touching her.'

'Until they disappear,' said AC. 'One minute they're there, the next they're gone. At which point I look at Mo and he nods towards the minister of defence who's rising from his seat, not in much of a hurry, keeping on a conversation with his neighbour, smiling like there was no problem in the world.'

'We watched him walk out,' said Mo, 'but as we'd not seen which direction the colonel and the minister's wife had taken, who could tell what was going on? And Stones is other side of the table so I can't be too blatant.'

'Probably he wasn't gone more than five minutes,' said AC, 'when he comes back and sits down, not a problem in the world.'

'And five minutes later the colonel returns not looking quite as happy as when he went out,' Mo said.

'The next thing I noticed,' said AC, 'was that the minister's wife is sitting at another table talking to another Cuban officer. Now she's got on a different dress, different jewellery, maybe her hair was even done in a new style. The colonel can't stop looking at her but she has her attention on the colonel's colleague. Eventually the colonel at our table is so embarrassed he leaves the party. The next morning,' said AC, 'we heard the Cubans were sending in troops, vehicles, jet fighters to stop the Boer army from invading. What we never established was what part the minister of defence's wife played in the alliance.'

After the laughter AC said, 'This is a good pile' – sorting through the diamonds, picking out ones for a special examination under his eyeglass. Mace explained how the deal had to be divided and AC began shifting the diamonds into three groups, asking Mace could he tell him anything of their provenance?

'Nothing,' said Mace. 'There was a guy called John Webster involved. But that's all we know.'

'Oh yes,' said AC, glancing up. 'A big fish. Major IDB player.'

'Was,' said Pylon.

'Was?' AC shifted his gaze from Pylon to Mace, back to Pylon, slow, half-hooded eyes. 'Interesting. You want to tell me more?'

'Not really,' said Pylon.

AC laughed. 'I'm curious that's all.'

'Situations change,' said Pylon.

The doorbell rang. Mace said, 'Our man Paulo.'

He brought in Paulo, Paulo stopping abruptly at the sight of three men staring at him. 'Go in,' said Mace. 'You're among friends' – introducing Mo Siq and explaining AC Mkize's part.

'It's all divided up there on the table,' said Mace, pointing at the piles. 'The big one's how much you owe Mo. The small one's how much you owe Pylon and me, the other belongs to Francisco. According to AC that's worth a good few dollars. And that small stone is his commission. Out of your heap.'

'And I've gotta trust you?'

Mace shrugged. 'Isabella does.' He went over to the drinks' cabinet. 'What's your fancy?'

'I won't,' said Paulo. 'Thank you.'

'You should,' said Pylon. 'Considering what we did to get this for you. A toast's the least you could share with us.'

Paulo hesitated, moving to gather up the diamonds. Pylon restrained him.

'Let them lie. A toast first.'

Paulo shook him off. 'What's with you guys?'

'Part of the way we do business.'

'Like this,' said Paulo, indicating the cut on his cheek, his split lip, the three-day-old wounds still red and crusted.

'Nasty,' said Mace. 'But not like that, no. Whisky doesn't have the same effect. Nor beer.' He poured Paulo a shot of whisky without waiting to hear what he wanted. 'Here. You'll like it.'

Paulo took it, not looking happy, frowning at the amber liquid in the glass.

'These are very good diamonds,' said AC. 'You should be happy.'

'I'm happy,' said Mo.

'So're we,' said Pylon.

Mace said, 'Give us the toast then, Paulo?'

Paulo shifted from foot to foot, keeping his gaze focused on the diamonds, avoiding any eye contact with the men standing round the table. They waited. Watching him, expectant. Paulo flushed, couldn't get to something witty. Something with a double meaning. Ended up with: 'Okay, here's to having pulled it off.'

Mace clipped bottles with Pylon. 'I'll drink to that.'

Paulo smirked, holding out his glass for everyone to tap it. He took the single malt in a swallow. 'I'm outta here, guys,' he said, scooping his pile of diamonds and this time no one persuaded him otherwise.

'Treat them carefully,' said AC, 'that's serious value you're carrying.'

'Don't worry,' said Paulo, backing out, Mace and Pylon seeing him to the door. A taxi waited outside.

'Give my best to Francisco,' said Mace.

Paulo nodded from the backseat, that smirk writ large across his face.

'Makes you want to smash in his dial,' said Pylon as the taxi pulled out of Dunkley Square down Barnet Street.

'Not sure there'll be an opportunity if you don't get after them,' said Mace, although Pylon was already unlocking the white Toyota parked at the curb. As he eased away the taxi reached the bottom of Barnet, turned left into Vrede Street.

'Shouldn't be too taxing,' Mace called after him, Pylon giving him the thumbs down at the bad pun.

Mace smiled, went inside to join Mo and AC for another drink.

'And Pylon?' said Mo.

'Filling in the details,' said Mace, 'following our erstwhile associate to wherever he's going.'

Mo said, 'Problems?'

Mace brushed it aside. 'No big deal.'

They weren't finished their drinks, AC was on a story about how De Beers operators moved in what he called 'the IDB environment' when Pylon phoned that Paulo was paying off his taxi on the forecourt of the Table Bay Hotel. 'Must be flush,' he added before disconnecting.

AC picked up then on a story about how a diver in the restricted coastal zone used carrier pigeons to get out his illegals, those birds doing a round trip of near on three hundred kilometres with a halfway stop at a farm to lighten their payload. If a kid with an airgun hadn't shot down a bird before it left the zone there was no telling how long the scam would've lasted.

'Honest little bugger to report it,' said Mo.

'According to the diver, not all of it,' said AC. 'The parcel was supposed to be a six-pack, the bird was only carrying four when security got involved.'

Mace's phone rang again. Pylon said, 'I've lost him. He's not booked in. Never has been. Not in his name at least, and no one knows the description.'

Mace thought, Nice one. All Paulo had to do was walk through the hotel foyer out the other side into the Waterfront, get another taxi at one of the entrances.

'Clever,' said Mace, 'we'll have to rethink this.' To Mo and AC he said, 'Our bird's flown the coop too.' Put through a call to a contact at the airport but his birds weren't listed on international flights. Didn't mean they weren't going under different names. Mace considered the possibilities, decided that given the hotel ruse, Paulo and Vittoria probably had another plan.

What Paulo did was walk through the hotel foyer and out the other side into the Waterfront. He took the first entrance into the shopping mall towards the Mugg & Bean where he'd met Isabella, thinking, Isabella if you could see me now, and fingered the diamonds in his pocket as he stepped onto the escalator down to the underground parking. Almost at the exit, Vittoria sat in their hired Merc. He could see her watching his approach in the rear-view mirror and did a dance step to amuse her. From where it was stuck in his belt under his shirt, Paulo tugged out Ludo's pistol, wiped the grip with his shirt, dropped the gun in a wastebin. A present for some cleaner. What would he do with it? Hand it in to the cops? Sell it? Keep it? Paulo believed one of the last two options. He opened the passenger door.

'They follow you to the hotel?' said Vittoria as he got in.

'No idea,' he said. 'But if they did they're gonna be really pissed' – showing her a handful of diamonds. 'Let's go kiddo. We're on safari.'

They drove to the airport, took a late domestic flight out of the city. In the air Vittoria leant across and kissed Paulo on the mouth. 'You've got the style, babe.'

'Sure have,' he said.

They asked for two dinky bottles of sparkling wine from the stewardess and Paulo said, 'I had to make a toast this evening for the diamonds. May as well drink to the same thing again.'

'What's that?' said Vittoria.

'To having pulled it off.'

42

Mace woke with Oumou's hand on his stomach and turned towards her, reaching out to draw her closer, feeling her shift easily into his arms and come hard against him, thigh to thigh. Her lips sealed on his and his hand trailed down her back to the swell of her buttocks, resting there, his fingers pressing into the flesh. He hugged her fiercely, this woman who would look at him sometimes with sad eyes but never respond to his 'What? What is it?' except to maybe smile slightly as if she knew all about him. Everything he did. Everything he thought. Yet did not judge him. Her leg lifted over his thigh and he opened his eyes to find her watching him.

Afterwards they slept and Mace woke with the sunlight, and Oumou gently rocking him.

'Mon chéri,' she whispered in his ear, 'there is a telephone call.'

Mace glanced at the bedside clock: 6:40. Who was going to phone at 6:40?

'He said he is a policeman. Captain somebody,' said Oumou. 'Three times I ask him who but I cannot understand his name.'

'Gonsalves,' said Mace, pulling her down until she fell across him. 'You are simply the best,' he said into her hair but she pushed herself up and looked at him the way she had done earlier and said, 'Oui, that is what you always say,' laughing as she said it, holding out the cellphone.

Gonsalves said, 'Mr Bishop you were supposed to call me.'

'It was past your bedtime,' said Mace.

Gonsalves ignored him. 'How about this morning, first off?' he said. 'Another thing you might like to know: it was the same gun that killed the queers. And the man's name is Riccardo Ludovico. Ring any bells?'

'Yes,' said Mace, 'I've met him.'

'Good. The morgue. Say eight o'clock.'

'Eight-thirty,' said Mace, but he was talking to dead air.

Mace showered and half an hour later put through a call to Dave Cruikshank, on the off-chance.

'Seven-fifteen,' said Dave, 'is no time to be calling even if I haven't heard from you since your famous clients were forcibly passed on. But I'll overlook that, being as I am a man of generous nature. Well-disposed towards his fellow human beings, not inclined to disturb their early mornings without so much as a how are you? So how are you, my son? How's the lovely Oumou? And the darling Christa who I heard tell along the grapevine is to be seen in the swimming pool giving her old man something to consider? The girl's doing alright then?'

Mace said she was and reiterated his question: did he have any Americans on his books who'd signed for holiday lets in recent days?

'Could be, my son, could be. But I need more clues.'

'I'm looking for a guy called Paulo Cavedagno,' said Mace. 'Might be staying in a hotel, a self-catering flat, a B&B for all I know. Mightn't even be in the city any longer for that matter.'

'Doesn't ring a bell, my son,' said Dave. 'A name like that would ring a bell.'

* * *

Salt River wasn't Mace's favourite part of town. Not at any time, especially not in a gritty wind. Wide Durham Street with its factory shops wasn't his idea of a good address. Nor did the morgue's palisade concrete fence topped with barbed wire thrill him. Nor the whipping flag. Nor the morgue itself, brown facebrick, a barrack-like building with an incongruous gable. Nondescript if you were driving past, too obviously visiting the dead if you were not. He registered at the security post.

'No public until twelve o'clock,' said the guard.

'I'm with him.' Mace pointed at the figure of Captain Gonsalves hunched at the entrance door, his back to the wind.

The guard grunted, pressed knobs to open the electronic gate.

Mace parked in the yard, as he killed the Spider's ignition his phone rang: Dave Cruikshank.

'My son, you're in luck and as always it goes to show my finger is on the pulse. Turns out my young colleague here entered a Mr Paulo Cavedagno on our books. Even turns out I spoke to the selfsame man on Saturday afternoon. Not that the name stirred the dust when you mentioned it but then what does these days, all the names that come through my agency? Now, my colleague is a chatty sort and engaged Mr Cavedagno in some light conversation and learnt that after his stay at our fair Cape our client was headed up to a safari lodge for a few days before going home. Chap was doing a whistle-stop round the country. Only booked the house from Friday to Monday which is not our favourite rental but it happened last minute and the place was free so we did it. Money is money, my son, as you'd know.'

Mace could see Gonsalves waiting for him at the door, said, 'Was he alone?'

'A bachelor, my young colleague assumed, to use the old-fashioned term. Very personable, I'm informed. Drove a Merc. Came in himself to collect the keys. Paid with an American Express. Not our favourite card but when you're dealing with our American cousins you take what they're offering.'

'That's helpful,' said Mace. 'Any chance your colleague remembers the name of the lodge.'

He heard Dave relay the question and the answer: Hippo Pools.

'You hear that?' said Dave.

'I got it,' said Mace.

'Nice chatting, then. Got to rush, my son, morning call of nature. My best to your lovely lady wife.'

Mace thought, well, wasn't Hippo Pools in for some exciting times, deciding not to tell Gonsalves until he'd checked out the information.

The captain was shrugged into a jacket with leather patches at the elbows. 'This's not my favourite place,' he said as Mace approached.

'Not anywhere I've been before,' said Mace.

'I bring people here usually they're going to be looking at someone they love who was alive the last time they looked.' He made no move to go inside. 'This Ludovico, how'd you meet him?'

'He was at a house in Llandudno. I was there on business.'

'Business?'

'For a client.'

Gonsalves chewed on this, then gestured at the morgue. 'He's American, this Ludovico?'

'Certainly sounded it.'

'So why's he dead?'

'I wouldn't know. My business wasn't with him. My client was a Paulo Cavedagno.'

'Smooth talker,' said Gonsalves. 'I met him the day I went there looking for the bird. What was it you did for him?'

'Hey!' said Mace, 'why the questions?'

Gonsalves shrugged. 'So tell me, what? When? How?'

'The man was interested in a surgical safari, I went to explain the details.'

'And this Ludovico was there?'

'Watching the cricket on television. Pylon even talked to him about the game.'

Gonsalves nodded. 'You know what the dead smell like in here?

Before Mace could answer, he said, 'Disinfectant. Jeyes fluid. Ammonia. Dettol. Toilet cleaner. Everything you eat for the rest of the day's gonna taste like the morgue.' He pushed at the glass and aluminium entrance door and led the way into the building, down a corridor and through swing doors into a room with two gurneys, bodies on both of them, side by side. The attendant uncovered the face of the nearest one and Mace looked down at the man who'd been watching television, who'd come out to intervene after he'd slammed some punches into the arsehole Paulo. 'That's him,' he said. Dread filling his stomach, the certainty coming on him hard and cold that Isabella was the other body.

'You want to take a look at the female?' the attendant asked without waiting for an answer, pulling down the sheet.

Mace forcing himself to glance over, taking in the wound between the eyes, the pallid skin, knowing it was her before he recognised the face.

'Jesus!'

He stepped closer, reached out to touch her face, saying her name, 'Bella. Bella.' Heard Gonsalves say, 'You know this woman?' – the voice coming from a distance as Mace gripped the side of the gurney, bent over the body, his breathing loud and ragged in his ears. He looked at her: her closed eyes, the roman nose, her lips unsmiling, the angry rose in her forehead where the bullet had smashed in. He stood like that looking down at her and it might have been five minutes or half an hour, there were no thoughts but her name on a loop through his mind and behind it the realisation: She's dead. She is dead.

They gave him sugared tea in an office, he and Gonsalves alone, sitting at a table. The captain waited until Mace finished the tea before he said, 'For now what I need to know is her name, okay, and where she was staying. Some contact numbers too if you've got them.' He pushed a notepad and pencil across the desk to Mace. 'This'd be a help, okay? Statements can come later.'

Mace nodded. He picked up the pencil, a tremor in his hand and wrote down the name: Isabella Medicis. Brought out his cellphone, copied the numbers he had for her, and for Francisco. 'The last one's her brother,' he said. 'In New York.'

Gonsalves stretched over for the pad. 'Any idea where she was staying.'

Mace told him the Mount Nelson.

Gonsalves stood. 'I've gotta go. If you want some more time with her that's okay. Just ask them.'

Mace shook his head.

'Then how about you come to my office about eleven, eleven-thirty? That give you enough time?'

'Sure,' Mace said, the word grating in his throat.

He heard Gonsalves pause, then turn away and go out, closing the door quietly. For a while he sat tracing beneath his fingertip a pattern formed by the gouges and gashes in the table top, round and round. No thoughts, only the distracted circling of his finger from scar to scar until slowly he refocused, the image of two people walking hand-in-hand on Llandudno beach rising in his mind's eye. Paulo and the woman Vittoria.

He pulled out his cellphone. Directory inquiries gave him the telephone number of Hippo Pools. The receptionist at Hippo Pools confirmed that Mr and Mrs Cavedagno were expected during the morning for a short stay. Was there anything she could do for him? But Mace had disconnected and was thumbing through his contacts for the travel agent he used. He had her book him onto a noon departure to the airport nearest Hippo Pools. A three-hour flight, maybe an hour's drive from the airport to the lodge. Beyond that he wasn't planning.

Mace left the room. He found the attendant drinking tea in the corridor and arranged for five minutes with the body of the woman who'd been his lover once. Who'd tempted him again for old-time's sake.

'No problem,' said the attendant, taking him to the room they'd been in first, the gurneys as they'd left them.

'I need to be alone,' said Mace. 'Can you get him out?' – waiting until the other trolley was wheeled away before he lifted off the sheet to expose her head and shoulders, her marbled whiteness.

'Nice guy you picked for a husband,' he said, feeling her hair between his fingers, not the soft texture he'd felt mere days back but strands, coarse and sandy. 'The issue is how you'd like him to die?' He trailed his fingers down her face over the curve of her jaw and down her neck to the hollows at her collarbone, but the flesh wasn't her flesh anymore. It was meat. 'Personally I'd opt for hanging. Both of them. Side by side from a fever tree. Or maybe staking them out on an anthill for the hyenas.' He bent towards her and caught a faint hint of the Chanel, and sniffed closer to her skin but the scent was gone. He swung away. 'Jesus, Bella. This, after everything. This arsehole.'

Paulo and Vittoria's plane touched down mid-morning at a small airport only used now for tourist flights but had once been an airforce base in the border-war years, the pilot told them. Admitted he'd been stationed there, Number Two Mirage Squadron. Those were the days, folks. Enjoy your stay, folks.

They stepped out into heat and glare, white heads of cumulus building on the sky's horizon.

'Real Africa,' Paulo said as the courtesy Land Rover took them to the lodge along a dirt track through scrub mopani and bushwillow woodlands, the air dry and singing. At the sight of grazing impala, Vittoria made the driver stop and he said, 'Lady, by tonight you're not gonna want to see another one of these buck. They're everywhere.'

'But now is not tonight,' said Vittoria, snapping off a picture on the digital she'd bought courtesy of Isabella's credit card.

The lodge accommodation thrilled them: a stand-alone wooden and thatch-roofed chalet under this tree the porter said was called a jackalberry tree. Right at the edge of a waterhole. Inside bushveld chic: exposed rafters over a large bed with white linen, grass mats on the tiled floors. From the bedroom window Vittoria could see pig creatures on their knees rooting in the grass along the banks of the water. And what could have been a log but what the porter said was a crocodile at the far end of the pool.

'Sometimes at night,' he said, 'we get lions in the camp. It is best not to wander around after your dinner.'

'Exciting,' said Paulo.

They arranged for a night game-viewing drive then settled on the deck with beers from the minibar.

'Nice place,' said Vittoria. 'Maybe four days isn't going to be long enough.'

Six hours later Mace landed at the same airport. He was travelling light: from the overhead locker took down a plastic packet with a coil of thick rope and a torch, the pockets of his bush jacket carried a tape recorder and a twenty-pack of cigarettes, and at the exit the stewardess handed him his nine mil with a full clip and a Leatherman that'd been stowed in the plane's safe. Told him the car hire desk was in the terminal.

On the flight he'd spent time with a map and a layout of Hippo Pools pulled off their website. The place ran a small guest lodge and five individual chalets overlooking a waterhole, each one located for privacy which was good. The guest lodge of ten rooms, a dining room and bar fronted a river and the hippo pools that gave the reserve its name. Well to the side were staff quarters, probably hidden from the lodge by thick bush. Outside the main building a small parking lot. All this in thirty thousand hectares of rolling hills savannah. Pure paradise for Paulo and his chick. Mace saw Isabella's dead face and thought, It's going to be hell, pal.

The map showed two entrances to Hippo Pools: one a private dirt track through the bush from the airport for the shuttle Jeeps so the guests never knew they were fifteen kilometres from a small town and granite mine; the other a ten kilometre stretch of tar road off the main north/south arterial. He would have to use that and bullshit his way through the main gate.

In the town Mace bought a Big Jack steak and kidney pie, two toasted cheese sandwiches and a litre of Coke from a Kwikspar. At the junction to Hippo Pools pulled off the road to eat the pie and sort through the messages on his cellphone: a list of irate callers, including four voicemails from Gonsalves up to half an hour ago wanting to know where he was, what he was playing at, to get in touch with him ASAP; five from Pylon saying call me urgently; three from Francisco that were incoherent; two from Oumou, the least panicked of the bunch. Five SMS messages: four from Pylon, one from Oumou. He reckoned by now Pylon would have been onto Gonsalves or vice versa and would know the details but that's where the trail would stop. He wasn't going to respond to either because they'd have him located to the nearest cellphone mast in half an hour. To Oumou he sent a message telling her where he was, that he would be off-air, that he'd speak to her first thing in the morning. And not to tell anyone, not even Pylon, that she'd heard from him. That Pylon and Gonsalves had contacted her he took for granted. He switched off his phone and headed for the main gate to Hippo Pools Safari Lodge.

The guard on the gate was in his mid-thirties, a dapper sort in pressed khakis and a wide-brimmed hat. Mace stopped at the boom and got out. The guard sauntered over and Mace went into a routine that involved sharing a smoke and a chat about how they were in the same line of business, Mace whipping out his SIRA licence to make the point and mentioning that he'd been asked to look over the security arrangements at the lodge following one or two incidents in the other private game reserves where bandits had walked out of the bush and robbed expensive tourists at gunpoint. In the exchange he learnt the guard – 'I am Zwide' – was on a six-to-six daily shift, seven days on seven days off. Day five of his current shift ending in an hour. Mace said he'd better be getting on before it got too late, he'd see Zwide on his way out in the morning. Pressed on him the pack of smokes and as he'd expected the guy opened the boom, not bothering to radio reception for clearance.

Mace parked among the other guests cars with a clear line of sight across a rockery of aloes to the front doors of the lodge. He checked there was cellphone connectivity, then sat and waited for dark.

Shortly before sunset, people gathered at the entrance for the night drive, among them Paulo and Vittoria. He watched them get onto the first Land Rover, choosing the highest seat at the back, the woman clutching her man like they were on honeymoon. When the vehicles left, Mace went to find their chalet.

Number one was occupied, number two contained the neat order of Germans, number three was where he would've put his money even without checking the passports lying on the table. The open suitcases, the rumpled bed, the towels strewn about the floor, the empty bottles outside on the deck, the traces of white powder along the glass top of the dressing table: exactly how he imagined Paulo and Vittoria. He did a cursory search of the room although he couldn't see Paulo putting the diamonds anywhere but in the jewellery safe. How quickly Paulo opened that safe would depend on Paulo but Mace believed he'd be cooperative.

He went back to his car to eat a soggy sandwich, and wait.

43

From the darkness he watched the Land Rovers return. Watched Paulo and Vittoria talking to the ranger. Watched them sucking up to him, the ranger enjoying their adoration. Watched them shake his hand, head off for the dining room, the ranger fixated on her arse.

Mace walked quickly down the path to their chalet. Order had been restored: the towels replaced, the bed made, the empty bottles removed. Five-star lodge service.

He sat on the bed, shook the rope from the bag and measured out two four-metre lengths, hand to chin, cut them with the Leatherman and fashioned a hangman's noose in each.

They were the first things Paulo saw when he and Vittoria, slightly drunk, getting off on the scare of lions on the walk from the dining room to their chalet, stumbled in, fumbled for the light switch, giggling.

The nooses hung side by side from the main truss over the bed.

'What the fuck?' said Paulo.

Behind them Mace cocked the nine mil and shut the door. The couple turned to face him.

'Who the hell're you?' said Vittoria.

'Ask your boyfriend,' said Mace. 'Meantime we've got business. The sooner we do it, the sooner it's over. So let's have your head in a noose, either one, the choice is yours, and your hands behind your back.'

She didn't move. 'Paulo?'

Paulo sneered at Mace. 'Her one-time screw. Isabella's old gigolo.'

Mace whipped the pistol across Paulo's face, opening the cut that had almost healed, Paulo staggering back clutching at his mouth.

'You bastard,' screamed Vittoria, and Mace hit her too, Vittoria collapsing against the bed.

'Cooperate,' he said. 'Make it easier for all of us.'

'What d'you want?' said Paulo, the words slurred through his bleeding lips.

'I told you once,' said Mace. 'For her to put her head in a noose, either one. You don't want me to repeat it.'

'We haven't got the diamonds.'

Mace hit him again and Paulo fell, Vittoria sliding over to him crying 'Baby, baby.' Mace tapped her on the head with the gun butt.

'Into the noose.'

She spat blood at him, coming up fast to make a run for the door.

'Not a good idea,' said Mace, and caught her by the hair and slammed her hard into the wall, hearing her nose break at the impact.

'Listen to me people, okay? Before you get truly hurt.' He pushed Vittoria towards the bed. 'Humour me.'

She did and stood unsteadily beneath the noose but the noose was too high.

'Stand on the pillows,' said Mace, 'and you' – he kicked at Paulo – 'go on, help your girlfriend.'

Raised by two pillows Vittoria put her head into the noose. Mace told Paulo how to tighten it and had him tie Vittoria's hands behind her back with a length of rope.

'Now you,' he said, 'down here' – and had Paulo kneel on the floor while Mace tied his hands. Paulo saying all the time, they hadn't got the diamonds. 'That's alright,' said Mace, 'at this point we don't need the diamonds.' When he was done, helped Paulo onto the bed, brought the noose over his head and tightened the knot against the side of Paulo's face. Paulo stretched up on tiptoe to stop choking.

Mace sat down on a chair behind them and the room went quiet.

'Please,' rasped Paulo. 'Enough.'

'I hope so,' said Mace.

Vittoria screamed then which brought Mace out of the chair to sweep away the pillows from beneath her feet and Vittoria dangled, her cry choked off. Mace let her hang. Paulo in tears going, 'Please, please, she's gonna die.' Until Mace put the pillows back beneath Vittoria's jerking feet.

'Screaming wasn't a good idea,' he said, the woman gasping and heaving, almost losing her balance. Mace steadied her. 'What I want you to do is think about your situation. I want you to think about the diamonds you have stolen but more than that I want you to think about the two people you killed on the weekend, and you' – he dug the pistol's barrel into Vittoria's back, 'you must also think about the two men you killed last month. That wasn't nice. Especially cutting off the one's dick.'

While he spoke Mace searched through the suitcases, fishing out a bra that he used to gag her, Vittoria snorting and snuffling through the blood of her broken nose.

'And when you've done enough thinking then tell me and you can make your confession into this tape recorder.' He held it up for them to see. 'But what you need most now is some time to think about the dead and about your situation.' He opened the mini-bar and selected a beer and uncapped it. 'Take as long as you want, there's no hurry.'

It took Paulo half an hour before he moaned, 'Please, please, help me.'

'I'd like to,' said Mace. 'Really I would. But what I have in my head is this picture of Isabella with a hole right here between her eyes. Isabella lying on a mortuary slab. That's not how I like to think of Isabella.'

'The diamonds …'

'Forget the diamonds for a moment, Paulo. Mourn for your wife. The woman who married you to give you opportunities.' Mace paused, heard Paulo sniffing. 'Good, Paulo. Good. You should get emotional. Let the grief come out.' He paused again, seeing the shake in Paulo's shoulders. 'Let me tell you how I'm feeling. How Isabella's old gigolo's dealing with his grief. Right now Isabella's old gigolo cannot accept she's dead. He has to keep reminding himself of the corpse he saw in the morgue. That that corpse was once Isabella. The woman who was his friend and, you're right, lover once upon a time. Isabella's old gigolo's got a problem dealing with these emotions. Can you understand this, Paulo?'

'The diamonds ...'

Mace waited. Watched Vittoria jerk towards her lover, making muffled noises which could've meant anything.

'... in the safe.'

He got up and went to the safe, looking across at Paulo expectantly. The guy's face was red, streaked with tears.

Between sobs Paulo gave the combination numbers and Mace pressed them into the safe's keypad. The diamonds inside in a draw-string pouch.

'This's a start,' said Mace, spilling some of the stones into the palm of his hand. 'It goes a little way towards demonstrating remorse. Maybe even sorrow.'

He uncapped another beer, sat down again to drink it. The problem, he thought, was that at this rate Paulo would be done and dusted within an hour, while the chick wasn't anywhere near being obliging. You had to admire her, holding out even with a broken nose.

After he'd finished the beer, Mace waited in the chair, half an hour slipping past before Paulo broke down again, crying, enough, he couldn't stand it, he'd talk.

'Okay,' said Mace coming round to face him, holding up the tape recorder. 'It's got a sensitive mic, all you have to do is speak clearly. Start by giving your name, followed by the sequence of events that led to you shooting Isabella and Ludovico.'

'Then you'll go?'

Mace shrugged. 'Maybe. Depends on what you say.'

'In court,' said Paulo, sobbing still, 'I'll say I was tortured.'

'I know.' Mace adjusted the volume on the tape recorder. 'This isn't about evidence. Nor about courts of law. It's personal. It's about how Isabella died. It's about admitting the truth. That's what we do here, Paulo. That's our party trick.'

'She shot her,' said Paulo. 'She shot the gay guys too.'

'Slowly,' said Mace. 'I want you to start with your name.'

Paulo's confession had Vittoria as the shooter of both Isabella and Ludovico. When he'd finished Mace said to Vittoria, 'You want to talk now?'

But Vittoria made a muffled noise and Mace went back to his chair. 'I can wait.'

'You … you said you'd go,' said Paulo. 'Please go.'

'Not yet. Not without her story.'

Paulo said, 'Ria, please Ria.' Vittoria giving him no response.

'Like I said,' said Mace. 'I can wait.'

He sat watching them over the next few hours until the first red of dawn started low in the east. Quarter to five. Another hour until the friendly guard came on the gate. He took the sodden bra out of Vittoria's mouth and held up the tape recorder by way of asking did she want to talk? But the woman was past it. Mace clicked off the tape, glanced from one to the another, Paulo snivelling. Another time, another place he'd have done it differently, he thought. He shook his head, partly in disgust at the twosome, partly in wonder at his change of approach. From the chair picked up the pouch of diamonds and weighed it from hand to hand, the stones clicking. Slipped it into his pocket.

Mace slowed to a stop at the gate and slipped the gear into neutral. Zwide came smiling towards him.

'You are the first person out of the paradise this morning.'

'Some of us have to work.' Mace grinned at him. 'One day what I'd like to do is come back and do nothing with the rich people.'

Zwide laughed. 'Me, I want to see New York. One American said he would send me a ticket for the jumbo jet but maybe the ticket is lost in the post.' And again he laughed, lifting the boom for Mace to drive through.

'Hope you get to New York,' Mace said, holding his hand up in salute, seeing Zwide in the rear-view mirror waving goodbye like they were big buddies.

PAYBACK

'… in this city rise up the angry bones …'
Anonymous imam

1

At 6:00 p.m. the barometer measured 1000 millibars. Down two hundred over six hours. Mo Siq tapped the instrument through the day, watching it drop as the storm came in. Watching the storm come in. From the first slates of high cloud in the morning to the dense, low greyness of the sky by late afternoon. From the stillness when he'd stepped onto his balcony mid-morning to make a cellphone call, to the gusts of wind that now buffeted his windows. New flush-fitting anodised windows that shook nonetheless. At times during the afternoon he stood at these windows looking out at Signal Hill, at how the wind flurries chased patterns through the tall grass. He stared down at the little yacht basin, no longer a building site, two yachts moored against a jetty.

Once, while Mo stood there smoking a cigarette, he watched a man wearing a beanie and thick jersey hurry onto the further boat and test the ropes and the knots and the pins that secured the hatches, then dash back into the apartment block. Mo smiled. The man considered himself an old salt, would hold cocktail evenings on his yacht for people with too much jewellery. Mo had been to one, got a deal going with an Israeli to supply five hundred thousand rounds of 7.62mm they could use in their carbines. At that party the old salt promised Mo a sail into the wild ocean. Mo took a rain check, then again he'd never seen the old salt put to sea. At 6:00 p.m. Mo set the marker on the barometer at 1000 millibars.

Mo Siq, in a baggy tracksuit, was unshaven, his bed unmade. Through the day he drank five cups of coffee and the five dirty mugs were scattered about the apartment: one on the bedside table next to a paperback of Cogan's Trade, the bookmark at page one-sixty-five where Cogan runs the 30-06 Savage semi-automatic rifle out the rear window of the car he's in and puts five shots into a designated hit; another two mugs on the dining room table where Mo sat most of the day preparing a report; a fourth on the kitchen counter beside a plate with the remains, the crusts, of a cheese sandwich; the fifth on a coffee table next to a leather armchair in the lounge.

He smoked sixteen cigarettes: one stubbed out in an ashtray on the bedside table, twelve while writing the report, although he twice emptied the ashtray into the kitchen bin, three extinguished in a small soapstone dish on the coffee table beside his armchair. Alongside the dish and his coffee mug was the video case of the movie The Usual Suspects. Shortly after setting the barometer at 1000 millibars, Mo Siq sat down to watch one of his favourite films. Afterwards he ordered a marguerita pizza with anchovy, olives and capers from the St Elmo's at the Waterfront.

The report Mo spent the day working on concerned opening an avenue for the minister of defence around the restrictive memorandum No 4 of 1997 that consigned surplus ammunition smaller than, and including, 12.7mm to be destroyed. Mo Siq believed that by circumventing this memo, not only would the state earn revenue, but he could arrange commissions that would benefit The Opportunity. At the end of his report, filed on his laptop under the heading New Regulations, a paragraph concluded that an export permit could not be issued for surplus state or parastatal stock that had been designated for destruction. Which gave the minister the loophole not to designate any stock as surplus. Mo reckoned nine million rounds would be made available with the minister's signature.

Mo took the day off, a Friday, to work unhindered. He unplugged his landline, switched to silent his official cellphone, but left his private cell open. He made twelve calls on this phone: to his sister, to three women in different parts of the country, to a travel agent in India and a wine distributor in Ireland, to three hunting organisations in the United States, a Lufthansa freight manager, a former minister in the Yemen government, and finally to order the pizza. He made a single call on his official cellphone to ask his staff for clarity on some financial implications and this call he took on the balcony.

The pizza was delivered at 8:40 p.m. according to the chit, and Mo put the box on the kitchen counter and ate from it. He uncapped an Amstel and drank the beer from the bottle. While he ate, Mo stared at the lights of the Waterfront hazed by the rain beating against the windowpanes. He thought about The Usual Suspects and the nature of truth, and with this thought went over to his laptop and reread his report, marvelling at how a single word could change a situation. The gale threw a loud rattle of rain against the windows and Mo shivered, on the thermostat behind him switched up the underfloor heating two degrees. He hadn't finished the beer or the pizza, three slices remained, when his intercom phone buzzed. He groaned: to answer or to leave it? He answered.

'Mo I have to talk to you.' He could barely make out the words against the storm noise.

'Who is this?'

'Mo. Let me up.'

'Who's it?'

No response. Then: 'Mo, this is urgent.'

He recognised the voice now. 'Ah for bloody hell's sake, Sheemina!' he said, pushing the lock release.

He saved the file on his laptop, brought down the screen and clicked it closed. Waited there until his doorbell rang, wondering what this was about.

The moment he opened the door, it slammed back against him and through the pain Mo saw a man rush at him, a blow smashed his nose, cartilage broke. Mo went down on his hands and knees, blood flooding his nostrils, leaking into his throat. He took two kicks to the kidneys in that position and collapsed on a kelim given to him by the travel agent in India. He didn't lie there long: the man had him up by his tracksuit top, walked him on air into the lounge, dropped him in the armchair. The point when Mo saw the silenced nine mil in the guy's hand. A big man, blond hair, surfer's tan.

Mo probed gentle fingers at the hurt of his nose, the throb excruciating. Still managed to say, 'Where's Sheemina?'

'Doesn't matter,' said the invader, 'I'm what matters.'

Mo said, 'What'da she wan?' – the words running into one another with the pain of talking. 'Who're you?' The stream of blood out his nose not letting him pronounce properly.

'Questions, questions,' said the surfer. 'Slow down, china. Take it easy a minute, hey. Put your head back, it'll stop the blood.'

Mo did, wondering why he listened to this thug, swallowing blood now but aware it was easing. He watched the invader picking his way round the room, examining photographs, objects, the video collection.

The guy said, 'I'm Mikey Rheeder, I'm telling you that to be polite. No other reason.' Mikey Rheeder then finding the pizza box on the counter top with the three uneaten pieces. 'St Elmo's,' he said, lifting an olive from the topping, elastic bands of mozzarella coming away with it. Holding it in his left hand that was rigid like a claw. 'Personally I prefer Moma Roma. A better kinda base. St Elmo's they could make two pizzas outta one, I always think. They've got this thick crust here that gets too doughy. Especially when it's not hot anymore.' He turned to Mo. 'You mind if I help myself?' – lifting out a triangle anyhow. 'You want another piece?'

Mo said, 'Nug.'

Mikey said, 'I understand.' He put down the pistol on the counter, using both hands to hold the pizza slice to his mouth. Chewing and swallowing rapidly. 'I saw this movie once, these dudes, two black suits, talking about the best burgers they'd eaten.

Discussing the finer points. On their way to cause all kindsa shit they're talking about burgers. That's hectic, hey?'

'Wha thew wan?' said Mo, bringing his head down to test if the bleeding had stopped. It had.

Mikey lifted out another slice of pizza and took two bites. Chewing, looking over at Mo. He put the remains of the slice back in the box, wiped his hands on a dish towel. 'If it was a thin crust, I'd probably have finished it,' he said, taking the gun off the counter. 'The thing is this, Mo, Sheemina told me to tell you this isn't about you and her. I don't know what that means, she didn't tell me. But whatever that was about, it's not about that. What she told me to tell you this is about is what she called misappropriation. More than that I can't tell you.'

Mo said, 'Misapplopliation! Shi-t.'

'Something like that,' said Mikey, raising the nine to put one through Mo Siq's heart, so much nosebleed on his T-shirt that the extra seep wasn't noticeable. Most of the wound being at the exit point anyhow.

In the after-quiet, the rain against the window was like a child's tapping. The wind gusts howling along the building.

Mikey found the casing, unscrewed the silencer, putting it in the left pocket of his leather jacket, the pistol going into the right. He took a look round the apartment, hesitated over the laptop. Leave everything was a standard rule. Crap, he decided, why not? Worst case: he could sell it. Then again, depending on what was Mo Siq's line of business, Sheemina February might be interested in shelling out a couple of Ks extra as a bonus.

2

The cellar had been prepared. You came down the wooden staircase and opened the door on a room six metres long by four metres wide, the same size as the sitting room above, lit by a buzzing neon strip over the door.

The walls were hand-cut blocks of Table Mountain sandstone, cleaned of two centuries of grime and damp, freshly white-washed. The floor, an overlay of flagstones on a foundation slurry of dung and mud, tamped down to a hard surface, the flagstones set into this. The ceiling of planking supported by thick rough-hewn beams.

The only furniture was a metal bed and a foam mattress, the foam new and spongy. No pillow or blankets on the bed.

Into the far wall of the cellar, low down, about ten centimetres from the floor was a thick iron pin with an eye. A length of chain was fastened with a padlock to the iron pin and ended in a hand-cuff. The length of chain was long enough to allow whoever was manacled to lie without discomfort on the bed. The length of chain was not long enough to allow the captive to reach the door. The length was such that the captive would have to stretch to reach any bowl of food placed on the floor by the captor.

When the door was closed, someone held captive in the cellar could scream and shout and never be heard even by those upstairs. There was no one upstairs. The house was empty. City Bowl Properties had a laminated For Sale sign tied to two metal rods staked on the pavement.

3

Mace Bishop wasn't pleased to hear Ducky Donald Hartnell's voice on his cellphone but he wasn't surprised. He looked out the window at a dripping Dunkley Square, the cloud down low on Devil's Peak and no let-up in the rain visible, and thought, Why'd I expect this?

From what he'd read in the papers, he knew the bones had become a major headache for Ducky Donald. Then again he thought Ducky had been handling the matter with unusual sensitivity.

'I need protection,' Ducky Donald said. 'They wanna kill me.'

On and off in your life, Mace wanted to say, someone has always wanted to kill you. Instead said, 'We're not in that kind of business, Ducky.'

'What're you saying, boykie? Just 'cos I'm not some dazzling New Yorker wanting a face job, you're not interested. I'm not asking a favour. I'm asking for a professional service. I've come to the best place in town.'

'Very flattering.'

'Not supposed to be. I'm getting phone calls from people who wanna unravel my intestines. It's on tape. You interested to hear it?'

'Enter the cops.'

'Ah, come on. Do me a favour. Of course I've told the cops. The first thing I did, but they're not gonna protect me, are they? They're not watching my back. I need that, Mace. Protection. When I'm out there I need someone with my interests at heart because I'm paying him to do that. Someone like you.'

Mace sighed. Probably louder than he should have.

'Maybe this sounds tedious to you,' Ducky Donald said, 'but to me it sounds bloody frightening. Now, I'll say it again, I'm paying.'

'Forget it.'

'It's my life. I'm on my knees Mace, okay. What more? I'm offering to do this straight up.'

'There's another way?'

'Sure, square one: Cayman and Techipa.'

Mace groaned. 'Not that again.'

'It's always there.'

'What's there?'

'Stories for the taxman. War story for a magazine: two men's act of mercy.'

'That's bullshit.'

'No question. Except I'm shit scared, china, 'and I need you on this one so don't push me.'

Mace laughed. 'If you blab you're not going to get me anyhow. Doesn't solve your problem.'

Ducky Donald went quiet for a beat. Then, 'Mace, chommie, do it. Please. One last time. Fifty large up-front.'

'Cash.'

'If that's what it's gonna take.'

'It is,' said Mace.

They agreed to meet at Hartnell's warehouse, some place with a Paardeneiland address, in half an hour.

A gust of northwester brought the rain against the windowpane and blurred the world. It was warm in the office. Quiet and cosy. The last thing Mace wanted, the last thing he needed, was to stand in a cold warehouse while Ducky Donald Hartnell explained why persons unknown wanted to withdraw his intestines from a hole in his gut.

Mace gave Pylon the good news. Pylon lay on the couch in his office reading a travel magazine. Said, 'Is the guy shitting himself?'

'As much as Ducky Donald ever sounds like it, it sounds like it.'

'Good.' He held up the magazine. 'How about this? Lake Garda, Italy. Glorious, hey? I think maybe that's where I'll take Treasure. Get away from this miserable weather for a few weeks.'

'That's a fly-in destination?'

Pylon looked hurt. 'I can handle it.' He tossed the magazine onto his desk. 'Is this a paid job we're discussing?'

'Absolutely.'

'Our rates or his?'

'Hey. I said we'd hear him out. Maybe it's not even a job.'

Pylon laced up his boots. 'With Ducky Donald you know you're never going to score.'

Mace knew the story, at least the part that was public news. Come the end of the last summer, Club Catastrophe shut its doors. An event that got space in the papers and talk-radio time as Ducky Donald maximised the publicity. Spinning, it's the end of an era that had seen its share of tragedy, the end of a personal journey. Even some star-sign bullshit that it was time for him to initiate new ventures. Nothing about what part his son Matthew played in this, although Mace believed he might have heard that he was going on to greater things, Ib-Ib-Ibiza or somewhere.

He'd been invited to the bash on the last night but hadn't gone. Didn't want to be reminded of Christa's kidnapping. But gossip had it this was a party to rival the opening, or rather the second opening after the bombing. Much the same crowd made up the guest list. Ducky Donald might be moving on but the direction he was headed required the influence of the same movers and shakers.

Someone who hadn't been at the opening but was at the closing was the estate agent Dave Cruikshank. Just before that party, he and Ducky Donald were quoted together in a property article. Dave was on about the 'rejuvenation of the city centre' as developers converted vacant office space into apartments while Ducky Donald talked about a desire to 'contribute to the urban fabric of the city'. His words, though Mace felt he must have borrowed them. What it came down to was that Ducky and Dave had formed a partnership to develop the site.

A month after the closing of the club, the demolishers moved in, and a couple of weeks later Ducky Donald and his new mate Dave were pictured in the Saturday Argus pretending to dig the foundations. Next to this photograph was an architect's drawing of the proposed seven-storey block with loft apartments.

Two days later they were back in the press. The excavations had been brought to a halt by a pile of bones. The archaeologists moved on site. Ducky Donald's proposed contribution to the urban fabric had sunk its foundations into an old graveyard. Worse. These were not merely the bones of colonial Capeys, these were the bones of slaves.

What a find, said the archaeologists holding skulls with teeth filed to points as television cameras swept over a jumble of skeletons sticking up through the mud and sand. Like they were trying to get out.

Not a moment later but priests, imams, community leaders, politicians were clamouring for the remains of their ancestors. This was a sacred site. It should be a memorial. Part of the national heritage. It had to be protected. These people whose lives had been lived under the whip of slavery deserved to be honoured and left in peace. They were the builders of the city and yet again they were being abused. Tempers were raised. The situation got ugly. But until Ducky Donald's call, Mace had thought a truce of sorts prevailed.

They found the warehouse down a side-street in the middle of a row of buildings, each one closed against the rain and wind. The only cars in the street Ducky Donald's BM and Dave's Volvo.

'Not a lot going on,' said Pylon. 'Where're the sentries? The way everybody talks about these bones I'd expected them under twenty-four hour guard.'

Mace parked the Merc close to the entrance and they made a dash for the door, Dave standing there holding it open, a cigarette dangling from his lips.

'Hello, my son,' he said, 'never thought I'd be one of your clients, did you? Never wanted to neither. Still and all, welcome to the ossuary of Hartnell and Cruikshank. Keepers of the sacred dead.'

The warehouse was an old building, wooden floors, exposed wooden rafters, a wooden catwalk running round two sides some three metres off the floor. Ducky Donald standing on the stairs to the walkway surveying a stack of seven hundred boxes. He raised a hand in greeting, came down to meet Mace and Pylon.

'I've stored stuff in my time,' he said. 'Stuff you could do things with. Shoot it. Drive it. Eat it on one occasion. Merchandise with value. Bones're not my style. Nevertheless I hired this warehouse to store them. I'm paying the rent.'

'We, my son,' said Dave Cruikshank. 'Out of the development budget.'

'Every day,' said Ducky not taking in Dave's interjection, 'I'm losing money. Every day nothing happens I might as well have flushed hundreds of thousands of bucks down the toilet. Hear what I'm saying? I'm saying we've got schedules, contractors, contracts with penalty clauses, not to mention the loans we're financing while these ponces in their frocks, Christian and Muslim both, tell us sorry boykies this is the same as a massacre site. Bullshit! It's a bloody graveyard. That's what it is. But no, to them it's a site of atrocity. A place of mourning. On this spot the brutality of white oppression exacted – that's the word they use – exacted its inhuman toll. I'm quoting. That's the sorta shit they spit in our faces. You ask the archaeologists is this right, they tell you no these people died of old age, illnesses, the kinds of things that normal people die from normally. Okay. Alright. I understand the sentiment. In my day I was on their side. Much of what they're saying I don't even dispute. But Chrissakes we're talking eight years later. Eight years into democracy. We've gotta let go of that stuff. So nevertheless I think, fine, this is a sore spot, these people have been dished shit for centuries what can I do here to defuse the situation?'

'We, my son. We.'

Ducky Donald spun on Dave. 'What? What's it?'

'We,' said Dave. 'Our partnership.'

'Jesus,' said Ducky Donald, 'I'm telling these two, they know what I mean, okay!' He stared at Dave. 'Now I've lost it. Chrissakes, what was I saying?'

'Defusing the situation,' said Dave.

'Right.' Ducky Donald flipped open a box, picked out a bone, a long femur. 'We held a meeting. Asked them what can we do to be accommodating. No, more'n that, brought stuff to the table. Said we'd give the archaeologists three months to dig the site. Which, okay, legally we're obliged to do. But over and above we give them a financial donation, your actual cash-in-hand out of our expensive loans which no bank manager's saying, ag shame, let me chip in here for national reconciliation. Bugger me no. The banks want their interest. To hell with the touchy-feely. Leave that to the poor bastard on the ground. Anyhow, all this I do. We do. And more. Much bloody more. 'Cos now there's a problem with all these bones. Goddamned hundreds and hundreds of goddamned bones that've got to be stored. The archi blokes suggest the Castle. Lots of space. The military's gone, the place's been sanitised for the people. Why not? Get some poetic justice going here. The Castle protecting the remains of the people it brutalised. But hell no, that's the original terrain of horror. That's the place that caused all the shit in everybody's lives in the first instance. Sending them there's like dropping them in the dungeons. Donker gat here we come. Okay, okay. We hear them. We might think it's crappy logic but we hear their pain. We put our hands in our pocket, we find a warehouse that is suitable to all concerned. Everybody's happy. Let's get on with the future.'

Ducky Donald whacked the side of a box with the femur.

'The dozers move in. The hole starts going down 'cos we've gotta go down a depth for the underground parking. No problem, it's just ground down there now. Dave here and me put our feet up. There's been a blood-letting but hey we're recouping. Next thing, outta the blue, slap bang an interdict, the bones've gotta be part of the building, there's gotta be a museum on the ground floor. No more development until this is sorted. I thought about it. I thought how can we work around this. Maybe it's possible. But then reality-check. Are you gonna live in an apartment that's got a goddamned huge pile of bones in a room downstairs? Where every time you come home dog-tired at the end of the day there's a memorial telling you how shitty were the lives of the people whose skeletons are stored in the room under your million rands of luxury. This's not gonna work. Anyhow they can't ask this. They know it.

We know it. We go to court. We get the interdict chucked out. Hasn't solved the problem of what about the bones? The frocks are still on about the bones of their ancestors. About disrespect. About the denigration of human rights. Writing articles in the newspapers. Phoning us at the office, at home. Wanting meetings. Harassment it's called. I told Dave here, one day there's gonna be a death threat. And one day, tru'as bob, there was. Not one either. Plenty. Only thing they haven't done yet is nailed my pussycat to the front door.'

Ducky Donald dropped the bone into a box, wasn't the box it had come out of but that didn't bother him.

'But the day's gonna come.' He glanced from Pylon to Mace. 'What I want from you guys is personal protection. Every time I step outside my front door. The same for Dave here.'

'It's costly,' Mace said.

'We'll pay.' He kicked at a box. 'All this shit for a bunch of old bones.'

4

That afternoon Mace opened the door on a black couple, mid-thirties, smart and trim, he in leather jacket, roll neck, black pants, brogues, she in an open duffel coat, white blouse, tartan skirt, calf-length boots, both huddled under a J&B golf umbrella. The man with a wispy moustache; the woman with a face the colour of dry clay, careful eye-liner, red lipstick. They looked at him, the woman flicking her eyes behind Mace into the passage. The man said, 'Mr Bishop?'

Mace said, yes, thought, spooks.

The man didn't introduce himself or his colleague, said, 'Can we talk to you? And Mr Buso if he's in?'

'About?' said Mace, keeping them out in the rain. 'Where're you from?'

They didn't answer that. The woman, her hands buried in her coat pockets, said in an English accent, 'Can we rather do this somewhere warmer.'

Returnee back from exile, went through Mace's mind as he stood aside to let them in, the man collapsing the umbrella, leaving it to drip outside the door.

'Get stolen there,' said Mace.

'I don't think so.' Mr Brogues grinned at him, pointed at a BMW in the square, a black bulk visible in the driver's seat. 'He's watching.'

Bloody wonderful, Mace thought, not potential clients then. He closed the front door, directed them down the passage to the boardroom, calling upstairs for Pylon that there were visitors. The two went in, stood on the far side of the table, hands resting on the back of the chairs like clergy at a synod.

Mace said, 'What's this about?'

'Shall we wait for your colleague,' said the woman. 'In the meantime do you mind if we sit? This won't take long, but no reason to stand on ceremony.'

Mace gestured at the chairs. 'That's what they're for' – sitting down opposite them.

Pylon came in, said, 'Save me Jesus, the NIA.'

The man smiled slightly, barely twitching his lips beneath the wispy hairs, the woman kept blank-faced. She could be a sheriff of the court delivering a summons, Mace reckoned.

'You know them?' he said.

'No,' said Pylon, 'but you can tell can't you? From the attitude. The clothing too. Smart-casual. Blend in with the crowd. Hi guys, I'm Pylon Buso'- extending his hand.

The man shook, the brother's shake. The woman kept her hands knotted before her on the table.

Pylon shrugged, took a chair beside Mace. 'So the National Intelligent Agency's after some protection?'

'Very funny, Mr Buso, but no,' said the woman. 'We're here on another matter.'

'Perhaps you should tell us who you are,' said Mace. 'Show us some ID.'

'That's not necessary,' she said. 'Seeing as how Mr Buso knows where we're from.'

'Bit mysterious,' said Mace. 'Very secret service.'

'Think of it this way,' said the woman, 'if it's going to help you. We could give you our names and show you ID and you wouldn't know if it was real or not. So we're not going through the charade.'

'Thoughtful of you,' said Mace. 'Charades would've been good though.'

The agents exchanged a glance, the man getting straight to the point. 'We're not here on official business, not investigating anything, nothing like that. We're not cops. All we're wanting to do is put you ahead of the game.'

'Huh!' said Mace.

'We believe you know a man called Mr Mo Siq. You were comrades.'

'You asking or telling?' said Mace.

The man ignored him. 'Since the settlement have you kept in touch?'

'Are you investigating him?' said Pylon.

'As my colleague told you we are not investigating anything or anyone,' said the woman. 'Believe it or not we are here to help you.'

Simultaneously Mace and Pylon pushed back their chairs.

She said quickly, 'Let me be frank. We know you had lunch with Mr Siq at Uitsig restaurant in November last year. We know you visited him at his apartment in early January this year. We know that in the same month he came here to your offices. We have the records of landline and cellphone conversations, not the conversations, but the times and duration of these conversations between both of you and him over the same period. We know you have not been in touch with Mr Siq subsequently.' She looked from Mace to Pylon.

Mace thinking, they're onto Mo about the weapons transfers. Probably they also knew about the weekend jaunt to Luanda.

'You can see that this might be of interest, under the circumstances?'

'Under what circumstances?' said Pylon.

Again she looked from one to the other. The man also watching them. 'Under the circumstances of his death, his murder,' she said.

Pylon said, 'Jesus.'

Mace said, 'Christ.'

Pylon said, 'How?'

'I'm afraid we'll have to leave that for the newspapers,' she said. 'Mr Buso, Mr Bishop, you will understand that we interpret your dealings with Mr Siq as of a business nature. Our concern is not with the nature of that business but to ensure that this information goes no further. We believe that it is probably not in your best interests either. Consequently we have taken the liberty of amending the records of the telephone calls, unfortunately we could not do the same for Mr Siq's diaries. The police will follow up those leads. They will call on you. They will want to know why you had lunch with Mr Siq, why you visited him, why he came to your offices. They might even ask you why you have had no subsequent contact. May we suggest you get your ducks in a row. I have found that often the simplest stories are the best in such cases. You were comrades after all. Old friends.' She stood, for the first time smiled. 'I'm sorry I had to bring you such sad news.'

Afterwards they poured double scotches to toast Mo's life.

Pylon said, 'Could be any one of hundreds of people.'

'The thing is how much the cops will find out.'

'Not much,' said Pylon, 'if Ms Pasty Face and her sidekick do their job properly. What I want to know is how? And where? Mo wasn't the sort of guy to let that sort of thing happen to him.'

'Did though.'

'This's a problem. Probably says something for all of us.'

'Like what?' said Mace.

'Like I can't say. Like we all need protection from our lives.'

5

On the day the news broke about the murder of Mo Siq, Ducky Donald Hartnell was shot leaving his house, 10:24 in the morning. The shooter firing two 5.56mm rounds, probably from a revolver the cops said, as they didn't find any shells. But then you wouldn't, Mace thought, if the gun was a pistol and was fired from inside a car.

The first lead clipped the wing mirror of Ducky's car, the second hit him in the hand he had clamped on the steering wheel. Not good shooting given the range: less than four metres. And the fact it was done from a stationary vehicle. At that distance anyone half-way hot with a handgun would've scored two head hits, in Mace's opinion. Ducky Donald would've been no more. Which raised the questions for Mace: was it a botched job? Or did they just want to frighten the developer?

He decided it was a botched job. If you wanted to frighten someone what you did was pump two bullets close together into the metal work. What you're telling that person, should he or she care to think about it, was that you knew how to group your shots and that where you put them was where you meant to put them. Next time, supposing there needed to be a next time, you were going to arrange them differently.

'Lucky Ducky,' Mace told him the first opportunity he got.

'Very funny,' Ducky said, propped up in his hospital bed, private ward, one of Complete Security's heavies stationed at the door. 'I sign you up, two days later I get shot. I told you they wanna kill me. You don't believe me? You give me that quizzical look, like I'm a drama queen. So now what d'you think? That maybe I've got a point? Huh!'

Mace nodded. 'Seems so.'

'Bloody goddamned right it seems so. Right now Donald Hartnell should be on the slab. That's hectic. A radical position. That's ratcheting up the heat. Anybody takes that kind of stance is declaring war. Know what I'm saying: they've opened a range of possibilities. So guess what? I'm gonna bring them war. We're building a democracy here. You don't run around shooting people.'

Mace thrust a newspaper at him. 'You seen this about Mo Siq?'

'What?'

'Shot in the head, in his apartment. One of those larney ones in the Waterfront. People run around shooting people.'

Ducky waved his good hand dismissively. 'Mo Siq, schmo prick.'

'Helped you out once.'

'Once. 'Cos he owed me. What I'm saying, Mace, is you gotta protect me. That's all I'm asking here. I do the fighting. You keep me safe. Then I don't get to end up like Mo.'

'Easier said than done.'

He caught the critical tone.

'I was outta line. Accepted. Such a thing won't happen again.'

'Better not,' said Mace, 'or you're history' – walking out of the ward, leaving Ducky Donald lying there with a sheepish grin on his dial.

What had happened was they were waiting for Ducky. A shooter and a driver. Had actually called him out. And Ducky Donald, a hipster, a streetwise dude, a trader in a range of merchandise legal and illegal, a club owner, the father of a known drug dealer, this man of the world, fell for trick number one: if you want a guy to act stupidly pull his dick.

At 9:46 a.m. Ducky Donald Hartnell's latest black bimbo puts through a cellphone call: come rescue me Ducky the cops have got me for partying. I'm on my way, says Ducky, grabbing his cheque book to pay the fine. Never for a moment pausing to consider, hey, I've only known this chick for two weeks, is she worth the hassle? Let alone thinking, wait a minute, disturbing the peace is no major event, most times you're gonna get off with a warning. What's she done that there's an admission of guilt fine? Let me check with the cop shop. At this point smelling the proverbial rat: is someone setting me up? Seeing as a sector of the community have already told you they want to uncoil your intestines. A suggestion you've taken seriously and hired people to prevent. But no, you do not proceed cautiously. No, Mr White Knight hops into his BMW presses the remote to open the garage door, reverses down the driveway, presses the remote again to slide open the wooden gate onto the street. Slowly exits. Parked at the curb on the wrong side of the street, in other words facing the oncoming traffic and looking straight at him, are two people in a white car. Make unknown. One of these people is holding a gun. Bang, bang.

Mace's arrangement with Ducky Donald was simple: he didn't step outside the house without either Mace or Pylon holding his hand. Technically the same went for Dave Cruikshank. Though Dave wasn't being targeted. Nobody had written or phoned to let him know they wanted to spill his guts. At least not yet. But then Dave didn't have the profile. He kept out of the glare. And when Pylon showed him the splendours of Lake Garda he started talking about taking a holiday. Which was a good idea, to Mace's way of thinking. The three of them in Complete Security's offices talking over some alternatives.

'Just go,' he told Dave. 'Why not? You wouldn't want to be where your partner is now. Or worse. I've seen him, he's not a happy camper.'

'You're right, my old son,' said Dave. 'Phone a travel agent, get the missus to pack our cases, just go.' He flicked a finger against the Lake Garda brochure. 'Be good to get away from here. Out of all this nonsense.'

'Wouldn't it?' said Pylon. 'Let Ducky Donald handle the shit.'

Dave glanced at him. 'I'm not running away.'

'I didn't mean that,' said Pylon. 'Thing like this is a Hartnell situation. We have experience of it.'

'Right then, I'm away,' said Dave, launching himself off Pylon's couch. 'What you reckon, two, three weeks should wrap it?'

'Three,' said Mace. 'Treat yourself.'

'Should be fun, my son.' At the door he paused. 'Yeah, Mace, a thing I meant to tell you. Your old house, the Victorian's, on the market again. She phoned me, the woman who bought it, said she was moved out, could I sell it. No hurry, but she wants her price.'

'Sheemina February?'

'Her, yes. Very modern miss. That's quick, I say to her by way of pleasantry. It being, what, three years she was there. Too suburban, she tells me. Not her scene. Says she wants to live with a bit more life around her.' He waved the brochure. 'Ta-rar then. Best to the missus, Mace.' Calling back, 'I can see myself out.'

They heard him clomp down the stairs, the front door slam closed. The office went quiet.

Pylon said, 'Months go by you don't hear a name. Suddenly it's there in the ether again. Strange how that stuff works.'

'Isn't it?' said Mace. 'With her ex-husband suddenly dead.'

'Coincidence.'

'No such thing. Another word for the brown stuff's going to hit the fan.'

'You reckon it's her?'

'I'm not saying that. I'm saying it's a factor, the sort of thing I'd be investigating if I was the cops. Okay, Mo was into a heap of shit with that arms business. But Mo was a smart operator. No ways he'd let someone into his flat unless he knew them.' Mace took up the newspaper, ran his finger down the page three story, nice photograph mid-way in the column of Mo dancing at the party thrown to celebrate the acceptance of the constitution. 'What's it say here? "Police said there was no sign of forcible entry."'

'Could be a colleague. Could be a deal's gone bad, the people are pissed off. Doesn't have to be Sheemina February. She's not likely to do it herself.'

'She tried it once before,' Mace said. 'According to Mo. And herself, she admitted it.'

'They were married. They've been divorced for how long, years? Maybe ten years. Why's she waited this long?'

'There's two factors why I'd say it wasn't her,' said Mace. 'She's not hands-on, even considering what's said about revenge tasting sweet when it's cold.'

'Served,' said Pylon.

'Served what?'

'Served cold. That's the saying.'

'Served, tasting, it's about eating.'

'Serving's not eating,' said Pylon. 'That's the point.'

'I can't see it.' Mace stood and stretched. 'What I'm grateful for, though, is our friends from the agency. They could start a cleaning service with all the dusting they do.' He pulled his car keys from the back pocket of his jeans.

'You're ducking?'

'Actually, yes. With the arsehole in hospital, what's the need to hang around?'

'This's true.' Pylon searched under the travel brochures for his keys. 'A drink somewhere?'

Mace shook his head. 'Quality time with Oumou.'

'Racking up brownie points,' said Pylon.

'A man can't have enough, the way I see it.'

After the death of Isabella, Mace reckoned that all he had worked for, all that he valued, was in danger of breaking. Those that he loved he almost threw away. Mace didn't want to go there again.

Isabella's murder made the headlines: "Foreign tourists found shot in sand dunes." At some point he knew Oumou had to hear about it. But he didn't tell her. One night, getting into bed, she said, 'I cannot sleep with you anymore. Please go. Sleep in another room.'

Mace said, 'What? What for?'

'I have heard about Isabella,' she said. 'She was here.'

Mace looked at her, at how she hugged herself standing there in one of his T-shirts, the hem riding high on her thighs. Saw her fierce beauty in that moment. 'Isabella was murdered,' he said.

'You should have told me. I should not get this picture in my email.' From her bedside drawer she took a print-out of Isabella and Mace, dressed in long coats, clutching one another. 'In the email it says, I should be happy this woman is dead.'

'What email?' said Mace, grabbing at the print-out. 'Who sent this?'

'It does not matter,' said Oumou. 'You should have told me.'

'Told you what? What should I have told you for Chrissakes? That she was here? That she was murdered?'

'Both of them.'

'Jesus, Oumou. She's dead. She was shot between the eyes.'

'You knew that. When you came back from Luanda you knew that. That is why you disappeared for that night.'

'Yes, okay. Yes, I got back from Luanda, I found out she'd been killed. I knew who'd killed her. I had to sort it out.'

'But you could not tell me. Me, the person who is your wife, you keep this a secret from me.'

'Don't you understand,' said Mace, walking up and down the room, up and down. 'Don't you understand, she was murdered.'

'Before that,' said Oumou, 'she was here. In Cape Town. A couple of times you went to her, no? When you said you are with clients you went to her. You have secrets. Inside you keep these things hidden from me. All of my life you know about but you hide your life from me. Oumou can know that. But Oumou cannot know this. You have been sleeping with her, no?'

'No. You're wrong. You're wrong about that.' Mace afraid even of coming close to the truth.

She stared at him, a long brown stare of anger. 'I cannot believe you. For all these years. When you fly to New York you go to her. You make fun of me. You think I am cheap. A toy like your motor car?'

'No. It's not like that. Not like that at all.' He balled the print-out in his hand, hurled it across the room. 'How can I convince you?'

'Why do you lie?' she said. 'Tell me the truth. I do not want your stories.'

'You want the truth,' Mace said, 'okay this's the truth. You want to hear this?'

'Of course,' said Oumou. 'Tell me. Let me hear if it is more lies.' Going to sit in a chair, dumping his clothes on the floor.

Mace thinking fast, considering how much should he tell, fearing that if he said too much she'd leave. Take Christa and walk out. He said, 'I knew Isabella was here. Yes, I knew that. She phoned me before she came over from New York and I saw her while she was here. Yes, I did that. We had supper. Nothing more, me and her. For old-times' sake. She was on business, I didn't ask her what. With her husband and a colleague. She wanted to see you and meet Christa. I said no, I didn't think that was a good idea.'

Oumou said, 'Oui, I am listening.'

'Then I was away for that weekend in Luanda. With Pylon. We get back I find out she's been murdered. Her and her colleague. Ludo-something. But her husband's missing. Vanished. I talk to her brother in New York, he tells me it's got to be Isabella's husband, who's killed her. The man's distraught. Sobbing on the phone. Find him for me, he says. I'm asking you.'

'Why?' said Oumou. 'This is what I do not understand.'

'Why what?'

'Why you did not tell me. Why I must find out from this email.'

'I can't answer that. I'm sorry. All right, I should've told you. I'm sorry. I messed up there. I wasn't thinking straight at the time.'

'This is because you had been to bed with her.'

'You think that?'

'I do not want to,' said Oumou quietly, getting up from the chair, going to the bed. Standing and looking at him. 'In my heart I am not sure. I see in the photograph that you are laughing. You and her.'

'That was before I met you,' said Mace. 'That was in Berlin. Before the wall came down. I hadn't been to Malitia yet. I've told you all this. What's worrying me now is who sent the email.'

Oumou held up her hand. 'Don't talk.' She touched the swell of her breasts. 'Here,' she said, 'in here you can hurt me. Even now my heart is sore. I can hear what you are saying but I know this man, Mace Bishop. I know he has done bad things. Also, I know he has done good things. Long ago, I thought to myself, this man can take my heart. I can give it to him. If I did not think this there would be no Christa.'

Mace moved towards her round the bed. Again she held up her hand.

'Tonight,' she said. 'Tonight I must be alone.'

He stopped. 'Okay. Okay, I can respect that. But then it's over. Tomorrow we're on new ground.'

Except Isabella was on the new ground too. A month later Oumou learnt it was Isabella who'd bought up her exhibition. Another anonymous email.

'I do not want her money,' she screamed at Mace, the two of them in her studio late into the night.

'She liked your work,' said Mace. 'She bought it. I can't see the issue here.'

'How does she know?' said Oumou. 'How does she know about my exhibition? Because you have told her. Because maybe you took her there.'

'I didn't,' said Mace. 'I had nothing to do with it.'

'She told you about buying the pieces?'

'She could've. Maybe she did, maybe she didn't. I can't remember.'

'But this is another little secret from Oumou. Now we have Isabella's money to pay for the house. We must say thank you Isabella because the bank is happy.'

'She bought your work,' said Mace. 'She didn't dish out charity.'

'From Isabella it is blood money.'

'It is money you earned from your pottery,' said Mace. 'Full stop. Without it we'd be selling our house. We'd be on the street. That money kept us here.' He watched her waver, hesitant about her argument, the weight it carried.

'I had nothing going with Isabella,' he said. 'She liked your work and she came across it and she bought it. That's all. It's not blood money or anything like that. What's at the bottom of this is your work. The pots you made here have kept us in this house.'

He could see he'd convinced her, that she wasn't going to argue anymore. Went over to her where she sat on her stool and stood behind her, his hands on her shoulders, kneading. She leant back until her head rested against him and he felt the tension go out of her. He'd been working hard on her over the month: telling her everything that happened in his day. Every smallest detail. Almost. They'd been to the bank together, paid in the money from her exhibition that'd brought their bond payments back in line. He still noticed her looking at him sometimes, frowning. He'd come up on her then, do something unexpected: give her a kiss, hug her, maybe work her towards the bedroom. What he never told her about though were the diamonds. Or that he'd gone against the broker's advice and kept them. To Mace's way of thinking, the diamonds were a fall-back and easier to hide than an investment account, no matter where in the world you put it.

What did faze him were the emails: how someone had got the photograph; known about Isabella buying up Oumou's exhibition. He was stone-walled here.

On the afternoon Mace notched up brownie points, he took Oumou and Christa to the five o'clock showing of Lord of The Rings at the V&A. Christa's choice which was fine by him, plenty of action to stir the blood. Afterwards, Oumou said why didn't they go downstairs to the Fish Market for calamari, Christa's favourite and a restaurant easy to get the wheelchair in and out of. The Fish Market another fine choice, Mace thought, this time saying it out loud. And that all the on-screen fighting had made him thirsty for a long Windhoek.

They got inside no problem, the restaurant not too busy this early in the evening. Ordered a Coke for Christa, white wine for Oumou and the draught, the waiter then going into his spiel about the fresh fish on special that could be grilled and served with baby potatoes or pan-fried with butter, without butter, with garlic, without garlic, served with a baked potato or chips. French pommes frites-type chips. They ordered calamari and onion rings and baked potatoes with sour cream dressing all-round.

When the drinks arrived Mace said, 'What'll we toast to?'

And Christa answered, 'Frodo.'

Oumou laughed. 'Frodo, ma puce! With the hairy feet.'

'I liked him,' she said, 'for wanting to get rid of the ring. That was cool.'

'Yeah,' said Mace. 'It was an evil thing.'

'But pretty, oui?' Oumou fingering some of the amber beads in her necklace.

'Just shows how people fight over pretty things.' Mace took a long pull at the beer. It left a moustache on his upper lip that made Christa laugh and he used the back of his hand to wipe it off.

'Men,' said Oumou. 'Men fight, no.'

'This's true,' said Mace. 'But there's always a woman in it somewhere.'

'Cate Blanchett's my favourite,' said Christa.

'See,' said Mace. 'That's what I mean.'

'But if there wasn't a ring, Papa,' said Christa, 'the fighting wouldn't have happened. She didn't make them fight.'

Mace reached across and brushed her cheek with the fingers of his right hand. 'You win, C, I give up.' Looking at his daughter sitting there, her legs hanging down. Glanced too at his wife and saw the flight of hurt cross her face. Still, the swimming was bringing a little movement back into Christa's legs. He could see it. A bit of strength too. Not enough yet to stand, but enough that he could feel resistance if he held her up, her feet pressed against the floor.

'Maybe some things can be corrected,' the surgeon had said. 'I'm not going to tell you she will walk again.'

Their calamari came and Mace said that perhaps in the school holidays he should take time off and they could get away somewhere, like to a game reserve.

'The Kruger Park?' said Christa, her eyes on her father, Mace saying through a mouthful that yes, Kruger was an option.

'I will see,' said Oumou, 'where we can get bookings.'

Mace believed, watching mother and daughter making plans, that if he sold one or two of the smaller stones it should cover costs with money to spare. What a pleasure!

'But how do we have the money for this holiday?' Oumou wanted to know when they sat side by side on the couch in their lounge, a fire in the grate, Mace nursing a Johnny Walker black that he wished was blue, Dr Kiambu's whisky tasting having given him a liking for finer things.

'We can afford it,' he said. 'In the summer we've got so many clients signed we won't be sleeping, either Pylon or me. Nor's Kruger Italy where Pylon wants to go. That's expensive. He's talking airfares for the three of them that'd equal our holiday.'

Oumou reached for his whisky, took a sip.

Mace said, 'I can get you one?'

'Non.' Oumou shaking her head, pulled a face at the taste.

He took back the glass. 'Something else?'

She curled against him. 'I can think of it.'

Mace could too. Sometimes, you acted on the spur of the moment you could score all down the line. Tomorrow, on the way to fetch Ducky Donald from the hospital, he'd stop at the broker's, get the fellow to make an arrangement. Now he ran a hand under Oumou's jersey, his fingers touching the scars across her stomach, sliding towards her breasts.

'Hey,' he said, 'no bra!'

6

Ten days after the killing of Mo Siq, the city crouched, drenched and shivering under a low sky. The sort of day that was a copy of the last one Mo Siq lived.

On this morning, Sheemina February, opening the front door of the house she was selling, said to Mikey Rheeder, 'Mikey, let me tell you something about this house.'

'That you used to live here,' said Mikey Rheeder. 'You've told me.'

'Mikey' – she stepped into the hall, the heels of her boots hard on the floorboards, echoing through the empty house – 'shut up and listen.'

He came inside and closed the door. They stood in the hall, Sheemina February staring down the passage to the kitchen, Mikey looking up the stairs at the landing.

'What for?' he said. 'I can't hear anything.'

'Shh,' said Sheemina February. 'Hear how this house creaks and groans.'

'Houses do that. What's the big deal?'

'Like someone's in the house, walking about.'

Mikey Rheeder listened and said, 'Hey, that's weird. That's really weird. Who's it up there? A ghost?'

'No one. Just the house.'

He squeezed past her into the lounge, looked around at the marks on the fitted carpet where furniture had stood. 'You wouldn't catch me living in a place like this.'

'Scared are you, Mikey? Scared of strange noises?'

'There're ghosts,' he said. 'I've been on this tour this guy runs in Cape Town. You go to all the houses where there's ghosts. Some rooms in the Castle, that spook house on the bend there in Rondebosch, the one with the turrets, other places he said people were murdered. 'Strues, I got this really cold sensation in my blood. Like someone's stroking down my arm very lightly, raising my hairs. That's spooky stuff.'

'I lived here three years, I never saw a ghost.' Sheemina February opened the door beneath the staircase, switched on a light.

'Still cleared out though.'

'I move around, Mikey. Different parts of the city, depending on my mood.'

'What's down there?' He stepped back into the hall to peer down the stairwell, a short flight of wooden stairs ending at a door.

'A cellar. That's what I wanted to tell you about. Come, let me show you.'

She went down first, bending to enter the low doorway, taking the stairs carefully, one gloved hand steadying herself against the wall. Unlocked the rough plank door, switched on a neon light that hummed and popped as it lit up inside the cellar. The cold was physical, like walking into a fridge.

Mikey dug his hands into the pockets of his jacket. 'This's grim. 'And it smells.'

'I found out,' said Sheemina February, 'that this was the cellar of the first house built here, probably a one-roomed farmhouse.'

'I'm supposed to be impressed?' said Mikey.

She shrugged. 'Some people are. It's history. I found out that house was burned down in seventeen eighty-one. Set alight by a mob. Inside was the owner, an English doctor. The reason the mob burned it down was because they thought he was a paedophile. Afterwards, no one could find his corpse.'

'You better tell this to the man who runs the ghost tours.'

Sheemina February sat down on the bed, on the new foam mattress, smoothing the creases from her skirt. She picked up a chain that was fastened to an iron wall-pin at one end and to a pair of handcuffs at the other. 'I'm telling you, Mikey.'

'What's that?' said Mikey. 'Hey, what's that shit?'

'Let me finish. I said I'm telling you because underneath this floor we're standing on is earth. You lift up these flagstones, that's what's below. No concrete foundation, nothing but earth.'

'So?' Mikey cocked his head.

'So you've got some unfinished business, and I've got some unfinished business. Both with the same man.'

Mikey frowned. 'Who's this?'

Sheemina February sighed. 'How about Mace Bishop?'

'Yeah,' said Mikey, 'that's true, yeah' – taking his hands out of his pocket. His left hand buckled and bent, shaping his right into a gun, going 'Pow, pow'- grinning.

'What I'm getting to,' said Sheemina February, smiling at Mikey slowly coming up to speed, 'is that before I sell, maybe it would be better to throw a concrete floor in here.' She held out the house keys and he took them. 'The house is on the market, but the market's quiet. Also the agent's taking a holiday out of the country. Nobody's got any business here for ten days, two weeks. Neighbours see a bunch of building boys mixing cement, they're going to think I'm doing minor repairs to meet a sale. Nothing out of the ordinary.'

'Alright,' said Mikey, jangling the bunch of keys. 'I see where you're going. I can see uses for that chain.'

'Good,' said Sheemina February. 'Problems solved then.' She got up and headed for the cellar door. 'Let's get out of this freezing cold.' She paused. 'Tomorrow. Nothing dramatic, Mikey, you understand me. Keep it toned down.'

Mikey switched the light off, locked the door, following her up the stairs, his eyes on her larney boots rising into her long coat. 'Same deal as with the other one?'

'That's fine.' She waited for him on the stoep, the outside warmer than the inside of the house. Which had been one of the drawbacks to living there, that the place was an ice-chest in winter.

Mikey came out. 'You suppose the English doctor's down there?'

'Wouldn't you?'

He laughed. 'It's gonna get crowded then.'

Sheemina February, driving away from the house, thought it didn't matter how Mikey Rheeder played this one, or Mace Bishop for that matter either, the outcome was going to be satisfactory. As a gesture, though, she bought a single deep purple long-stemmed rose in a box from a florist on Kloof. Had it delivered to Mace Bishop's office.

Mikey Rheeder, standing on the driveway looking up at the house, thought he could have some fun here. Keep the guy in the cellar for a while, smash some of his fingers to show him what it's like. Mace Bishop could scream his lungs out down there, wasn't going to be anybody who'd hear him.

Then other thoughts occurred: that he'd heard about Mace Bishop doing a diamond deal, also that maybe there was a way to get Sheemina meshed in. People he knew would pay for that.

Mikey Rheeder said aloud, 'Hey, who's a clever dude?'

7

On this wild morning, either Mace or Pylon was to collect Ducky Donald Hartnell for a site visit.

To Mace, the newspaper spread across his desk, a mug of coffee at hand, the heater warming his feet, the thought of chauffeuring Ducky Donald Hartnell to a site meeting never had been a must-do and was becoming moment by moment less so. He listened to the fall of rain on the corrugated-iron roof and said, 'I'll flip you best of three.'

To Pylon on the couch, a newspaper across his lap, a mug of coffee at hand, the thought of chauffeuring Ducky Donald Hartnell to a site meeting was a non-starter. He listened to the drum of the rain and said, 'D'you think the cops are doing anything?'

'About what?' said Mace, searching for a five-rand coin in a jar of change he kept for car-guard tips.

'About Mo's killing.'

'I suppose. Why not?'

'In five days not a mention in the newspapers. Not a cop on our doorstep. This's how they investigate?'

'Must be a long list of people to see,' said Mace emptying the jar on his newspaper, spreading the coins across the print. 'Our names aren't a high priority.' He found a coin. 'Heads or tails?'

'I'm not doing that,' said Pylon. 'This's got your name on it.'

'Forget it. Not in this weather. Come on, fair's fair.'

'Also, you'd think the newspapers would be worrying at it. Writing those reports where the cops say they're at a sensitive stage. Except they aren't. Writing them I mean.'

'Probably the cops aren't at a sensitive stage either. Heads or tails?'

'How about you offering for once?'

'You mean like you do?'

'It's been known.'

'Uh uh, china, not today.'

Pylon said, 'Shit, who came up with this idea anyway?'

'The way I recall it,' said Mace, 'you did. All those years ago. Heads or tails?'

'Tails.'

Mace flipped: tails. Pylon called tails again. Mace flipped: tails.

'Want to see if you'll win the third one?' Pylon said.

Mace flipped, caught the coin in his palm, slapped it down on the back of his hand and kept it covered. Pylon called heads. Mace took away his hand: heads.

'If you flipped and I called I'd win,' said Mace.

'Sure,' said Pylon 'but I'm not going to.' He cracked a page of his newspaper. 'Look at it another way, bro, you've got a more exciting life.'

'Isn't it?' said Mace.

He took the Spider parked at the curb, intending to use Ducky's BMW for the downtown leg. If Ducky was going to get shot at again, Mace didn't want bullet holes in his car, or blood splatter on the upholstery. Also, he had to admit, the BM was faster in a tight situation.

At the bottom of Barnet he noticed a grey Camry hard on his pipe. Followed him into Vrede, right into St John's, down Plein to the traffic light. A lone driver, difficult to tell if it was a man or a woman. Not that he was concerned at this point.

The light went green, the Camry tracked him left into Spin, Adderley, Wale, up to Buitengracht, down to Strand. Another red traffic light, the Camry one car back. Mace's interest aroused, but the situation far from critical.

On the green he took Strand to the robot at Chiappini, and a sudden right down the hill, only a block or two above Ducky Donald's building site. The Camry followed. No longer a coincidence. Mace braked hard in the middle of the street, and leaped out, shouting. The Camry swerved and accelerated, jumped the red light into Somerset on squealing tyres. Hooters blared at this craziness, cars skidding about the intersection. Not a pleasant sight, but Mace got the number and phoned it through to Pylon for his contact at Traffic to do a quick scan. The rest of the way to Ducky, wondered what advantage was to be had from harassing him? Although he'd been there before.

'A site visit's not a secret,' said Ducky. 'Architect, engineer, builder, project manager, building inspector, a couple of secretaries, have to be about seven people know of the meeting excluding the two of us. Someone in there's keeping tabs on me, they're gonna know about it. Stands to reason. Also have to know that I've engaged you. So they start the nonsense to put a cracker in your jocks even before you've got here.' He laughed. 'Seems to have worked, I'd say.'

Nor did Pylon come back with helpful news. The plates on the Camry belonged to a twenty-five-year-old Datsun registered to a woman on the Flats.

'Not even worth checking out,' he said.

'Worth a phone call,' Mace said.

Pylon groaned. 'Ease up, bru. It's going nowhere.'

Still, came back three minutes later that the Datsun in question was up on bricks in the woman's backyard, had been like that for ten years and no it didn't have number plates on it anymore. 'Satisfied?'

Mace told him he was a great help.

On the drive from Ducky's house to the site, Mace was pleased not a grey Camry to be seen. Didn't seem to be any car following them.

At the site, despite the rain, about twenty, thirty people crowded the entrance, waving placards, singing songs they'd last sang at the barricades during the eighties. Some priests and imams stoking the emotions but no politicians that Mace could see. The cops had been called and kept the mob back from the gate. All the same, he reckoned, if someone in their midst pulled a gun, Ducky Donald was going to be very close to the action as he walked past.

Mace stopped the car a block away before anyone had seen them.

'Not good, Ducky.'

They sat considering: staring at the demonstration through each pass of the wipers. Didn't take a psychologist to see the people were worked up. Not even the wet and cold were going to send them home.

'Maybe someone's office would be a better idea?'

Ducky Donald drummed the armrest with the fingers of his good hand. 'No ways. This lot have gotta know I'm not shit scared.'

He looked shit scared to Mace. Licking his lips, his voice coming from a dry mouth.

'Last thing they're gonna do is hit me out here. In front of the cops. It's not their style. Their style's your drive-by. Your pipebomb hurled through the bedroom window. Out here, on the street, they want publicity. Give the reporters something to write about. Don't you think?'

Mace shrugged. 'My advice is we drive away.'

'Nah, Mace.' He opened the door. 'You're going soft. That's crap. What I've done's been patient and understanding. I'm looking after their bones for heaven's sake. My conscience's clear. What I'm not gonna do is store their bones in my new building. That's outta the question. Completely. Is that unreasonable? I ask you? Come'n tell me? All they gotta do is find somewhere to bury the bones, I'll even pay to dig the hole. I've told them. Just not in my building.' He got out of the car, leant back in. 'Switch off. Let's go. You've gotta be there to take the bullet for me.' And pulled his hyena grin.

That was exactly the problem Mace could foresee: being in the line of something meant for Ducky Donald.

They weren't halfway down the block when the horde realised the man in the long black raincoat, advancing with his hobble gait towards them, was none other than the hated developer. This gave them new vim and vigour. Unleashed some stones but nothing Mace and Ducky couldn't dodge. The cops got active; even the mob's leaders called for calm. Didn't stop the chanting though.

Gathered at the entrance to the site were the people Ducky Donald was to meet. Not a happy crew. Clustered under golf umbrellas clutching their plans and files.

Among the enemy, a priest Mace recognised from television and a man he didn't, started calling to Ducky, the police restraining them.

Ducky said, 'What's your problem reverend? We've got channels for this sorta stuff.'

'See how angry people are,' said the man in a soaked kurta. 'You have desecrated a grave.'

Ducky waved him aside. 'Yeah, yeah. We've been through this, Ahmed. We've gotta move on. Do me a favour, hey. Find somewhere new for your bones. Okay? Then we can talk.' He turned away from them, started shaking hands with the people he'd come to meet.

Mace kept facing the horde, saw the half-brick lobbed from the back but was too late in pulling Ducky aside. It caught the developer on the shoulder, staggered him into the arms of his architect. Unleashed a roar of outrage. Ducky Donald swung round on the pack even as it surged forward, his wounded hand raised, shouting,

'You bastards. What's your bloody problem, you bastards?' While Mace bunched a fist into his jacket and hauled him inside the site entrance.

'Lemme go. Jesus damnit, Mace. Lemme go.' Ducky found his feet. Straightened the clothing Mace had pulled awry. 'The bastards. The bloody bastards.'

'Alright,' Mace said restraining him again. 'Let the cops deal with it, okay. They're breaking it up.'

'They want war,' he said. 'They've got war.'

The second time Mace had heard him threaten this, but believed Ducky was probably a three-bells man.

He quietened down, the consultants grouped around shuffling nervously.

While they held their meeting on a platform suspended over the hole, Mace stood at the entrance, admiring the police efforts. No hard-line tactics, a gentle pushing and shoving, moving the people up the street. Nor were the leaders putting up any resistance. Everyone went peacefully enough, still singing. Eventually only the priest was left, a wet figure at the top of the road holding a sodden newspaper over his head. He made a cellphone call during the time Mace watched but he couldn't have said more than a dozen words before he disconnected. Nor did he move from that spot or change his stance until Ducky appeared. Then he was gone onto Somerset Road.

'Who's the priest?' Mace asked Ducky in the car. 'He looks familiar.'

'Oh,' he raised his bandaged hand dismissively. 'Holy called Thomas Carney. Got a huge chip on his shoulder. Got huge chips on both shoulders actually. Does TV stuff.'

Mace eased into Prestwich Street, drove slowly past the building site. No action any longer, even the cops were gone.

'All this bloody rain, how're you supposed to get a bloody building built?' Ducky stared at his fence of corrugated-iron sheeting surrounding the excavation. 'You take a look down there at all the water?'

'Uh huh.'

'Like a swimming pool. Seeps up from underneath. Buckets down from the heavens.'

'You wanted to be the developer.' Mace turned into Chiappini, heading towards Somerset. There on the corner was the reverend. 'Want to give your friend a lift?'

'Of course, yes, why don't we? Dump him to hell 'n gone in the Karoo. Let him walk outta the desert like a prophet.'

Mace stopped at the traffic light. The priest came quickly at them, slapped his sodden newspaper on the bonnet of the car. Shouted, 'Damn you to hell Mr Hartnell.'

Ducky lowered the side window. 'Not very charitable, reverend.' The man glared at him. 'Can we give you a lift?'

'Fuck you. Just fuck you.' And the reverend hit the car again, taking off towards the city in long strides.

'Crazy man,' said Ducky bringing up the window. 'A priest saying things like that. Jesus Christ!'

The light changed and Mace drove across to where he'd had the altercation with the grey Camry. Got stopped again at the intersection into High Level Road.

'What sort of priest?'

'Anglican. Church of England, whatever you call it. In the struggle days saw the insides of prisons more than the insides of churches. A righteous man. Starved himself when the Boers locked him up.'

'He did?'

'A hunger strike got him on the front page for ten days. I checked.'

'Always hoping for an angle.'

Ducky chuckled. 'Why not? You never know.'

Mace turned into High Level, accelerating up the hill.

'He's just a poor rev nobody can even bum money off. So when the bones come up he jumps to the frontline. Something to vent his spleen. Get him back in the news. Gives me crap all the time without let-up.'

When Mace next glanced in the rear-view mirror there was the blurred front end of a grey Camry, a lone driver.

'We're going for a little ride,' he told Ducky, shifting forward to draw the Ruger from his belt. 'Don't look back. Let's keep it calm.'

Ducky hit the dashboard, nonetheless. 'I don't bloody believe it.'

'Mightn't be anything but a little more aggro. To let you know they're watching.'

'Bugger them. This is war now Mace. Know what I'm saying? War.'

He kept rigid in the seat though, facing forward. All the way along High Level, down Fresnaye into Queen's onto Victoria, slowly along the coastal curves through Clifton, through Camps Bay, the Camry keeping steadily behind them, not too close, until the road opened under the Apostles, then narrowing the distance. Mace let him come up, figuring not too many options in his hand.

The weather was black and raw here: breaking in squalls off a high sea. Spume and debris on the road. The wind tugging the wheels. Mace let the Camry move out to overtake, changed down, put foot.

'Are you bloody mad?' yelled Ducky, as they went into the first bend, the cars sliding on the wet, side by side. For any on-coming traffic the Camry was solid in their lane. Also he had the drop-away to the sea at his elbow. Mace edged closer, but the driver didn't frighten, kept his speed until the Camry was door for door. Swept through a left curve, a right, a tight left, the Camry twinning his moves.

'Goddamned maniac,' Mace shouted.

Ducky going, 'Jesus! Fuck! The bugger's got a gun.'

Mace caught this out of the corner of his eye: the driver's grin, the pistol and damaged hand raised in profile. A face he recognised. Glanced ahead, the road wide and rising on a straight.

The BM had power to spare, would outstrip the Camry in a few hundred metres. Instead Mace braked, stood hard on the pedal, the ABS kicking in, even on the wet the car not fishtailing. It got him a couple of seconds, the Camry braking too but sliding right, loose on the road. Mace jerked the handbrake, brought the car round in a tight left. Slapped down the gears and watched the needle climb.

He remembered the face. And the hand. Mikey Rheeder.

In the rear-view saw the Camry slew to a stop across the road, saw muzzle flash as Mikey pulled off two rounds but he and Ducky were laughing, could hardly hear the retorts. Saw the Camry make a three-point and come after them again.

'Bloody hell,' said Ducky, skewed in the seat to look back. 'Would you bloody believe it? Doesn't this guy know when's enough?'

'Seems not.'

Mace ran the speed higher to Camps Bay, taking Geneva up to the Nek and back to town, losing the Camry.

'And now?' said Ducky when they drove into Dunkley Square.

'And now,' Mace said, 'we're going to organise a meeting with your priest and the imam and whoever else's got themselves frothing at the mouth. Right here. Right today.'

'Nothing more to be said with them.'

Mace parked the BM on the square. 'Bullshit. For starters, they can pull off the heavies. Maybe you can offer some concession.'

'Oh yeah. Like what?'

'Hell, Ducky. How should I know? A plaque in the entrance. For Godssake. Anything.'

They made a dash through the rain for the office. Stood shaking off like wet dogs in the hall. Pylon came downstairs holding a rose in a box, grinning at Mace.

'For you,' he said.

A deep purple, long-stemmed rosebud.

Mace took it, opened the attached envelope: no name, no message on the florist's courtesy card. 'Any clues?'

Pylon shook his head, still grinning. 'The florist delivered. Poor guy on a motorbike. On a pissing-down day like this. But, hey, it's for the irresistible Mace Bishop.'

'Seven months off Valentine's,' said Ducky.

'And Gonsalves is after you. Wants to know why you don't answer his calls.'

8

The meeting was set for 5:00 p.m., Mace and Pylon hosting. The reverend and the imam not overly keen. A quiet chat they were told, to sort out some issues.

On the phone, the Reverend Carney got up on his hind legs. 'We will not be bullied. 'You cannot intimidate us.'

'I don't imagine so,' Mace said, 'considering your tactics.'

'Protest is not intimidation.'

'Trying to kill us is.'

'People are upset. They throw stones when they're frustrated.'

'I'm not talking about stones, reverend.'

A silence. Then: 'I don't know what you mean.'

'Yes you do. And it wasn't very Christian either.'

'God's gonna get you,' Ducky Donald shouted from where he sat across the room.

'What's he say? What's he say?' said the reverend. 'We will not stand for any abuse.'

'Till five,' Mace said, disconnecting.

'They won't rock up,' said Ducky. 'I'll bet you.'

Mace didn't respond.

Pylon said, 'They will. They can't afford not to.'

They took Ducky Donald home, giving him a lecture on the way about the need for a concession.

'That's why I've got you,' he said. 'So I don't have to do that. What you want's a PR job 'n since when've you been experts in that field, huh?'

'Think about it,' said Pylon. 'It might save your life.'

Ducky Donald wasn't happy at the prospect of thinking about it but Mace wasn't happy about grey Camrys on his tail. Also if Gonsalves was agitated Mace needed to clear some space. His voicemail message: 'Get back to me asap, Mr Bishop, some serious shit's gonna hit the fan about those Americans.' Undoubtedly, Mace believed. But first things first.

The florist turned out to be a boutique high up Kloof. You went in a bell tinkled, a young man sucking his pencil behind the counter, said, 'Hi there, can I help you?'

Mace held up the rosebud in its box. 'This was delivered to me. I'd like to know from who.'

'Ooo,' he said. 'You are Mr …?'

Mace told him.

He licked his thumb, paged back in his delivery book. 'A lady bought it for you. Yesterday.' He sucked his pencil, smiling. 'A lovely lady.'

'Help me out,' Mace said, 'what's her name?'

'Ooo no, sir. I don't have her name. Cash payment. Secret admirers never use credit cards.' The pencil went back between his lips.

'How about a description?'

'Lovely, but I told you. A bit shorter than sir. In a beautiful coat with a hood. Swanky boots too.'

'The colour of her hair?'

'I would say dark.'

'You didn't see it?'

'She kept on the hood, sir. So cool. Black gloves, Ray-Bans. Even in the bad weather. I can't tell you. Very juze.' He tapped his teeth with the pencil. 'Ringing any bells for sir?'

In the car Pylon said, 'What'd that get you?'

'A female monk by the sounds of it.'

'What can I say?' He accelerated down Kloof. 'Beware of cloisters.'

Back in the office, Mace settled with a coffee and the gas heater punched up to three panels, and phoned Captain Gonsalves.

'Whyn't you answer your phone more often?' the captain said.

Mace sipped coffee, watched steam rising from his socks. 'Busy life. You know, clients to satisfy.'

Gonsalves snorted. 'Come down, we need to talk.'

Mace told him, 'Sorry, captain, no can do. I'm up against it.'

Gonsalves chewed on this. 'The busy life, huh?'

'Something like that.'

'Listen, Bishop, we've got a bad situation developing. They're gonna subpoena you tomorrow.'

'Oh yeah?' The news gave Mace's heart a kick though. 'For all the good it'll do they could subpoena the president if they wanted. It's my word against theirs that I was even there.'

'They can put you there Bishop. Airplane ticket to and from. Car hire. One cellphone SMS from the local point of presence, I believe they call it, to your wife.'

'So what? I was in the district. Doesn't mean squat. A coincidence that's all.'

'Helluva coincidence two and a half thousand kilometres from your home.'

'Happens all the time. First thing: it's a fact I was there somewhere but the court wants facts of where exactly I was. Second thing: a subpoena's not a charge, captain. I don't have to lay out an alibi.'

'Remember the guard on the gate. Guy called Zwide something or other, Ramatlhodi. He ID'd you.'

'No chance.'

'It's an affidavit. Time in, time out. Registration of the car. Colour and make. Logged up on their book in his handwriting. All that's missing is your name.'

'And he ID'd me. How?'

'From a photograph included here. Looks like you're coming out of your office door. Doesn't flatter you but it's good enough.' He chuckled. 'Sharp lawyers they've got. People've been snapping you when you're not paying attention. Scary hey?'

'Not possible that he could've made a positive ID. I had on sunglasses. A floppy hat. He's a black for Chrissakes. He didn't look me in the eyes.'

'All the same. It's here: sworn and attested.'

'But full of holes.'

'Admittedly. But what a story for the papers. Investigating officer gets a mysterious call that natural born killers are relaxing in a game lodge. The boys in blue shoot over, find our NBKs dangling from the rafters. Not literally but you know what I mean. Standing there tied up with nooses round their necks. Question is, who did this? Deduction suggests the man in the hire car. The hire car that came in at sunset 'n went out at sunrise, half an hour before the investigating officer got his anonymous call. Know what else?'

'Surprise me.'

'Zwide says this guy in the hire car told him they were in the same line of business: security. Now, was that a smart thing to say?'

'And the point is?'

'What point?'

'The point of all this? They're nailed. You've got the case tied up. What's all this supposed to get them?'

'A lighter sentence. Maybe some sympathy.'

'They killed four people.'

'Allegedly.'

'Ah for heaven's sake!'

'Exactly. Point is Bishop, this isn't gonna help me. There're other questions here the lawyers are gonna bring up. Like why we didn't find who did this to them? That's what they'll put to me. Make me look incompetent. Or worse, colluding.'

'Nasty,' said Mace.

'Bloody nasty.'

'So?'

'So what?'

'So what about fixing it.'

'Shit, Bishop. What d'you think I am?'

'A good man.'

The captain disconnected. Mace thought, cops, sometimes you had to spell it out for them.

At 5:00 p.m. the doorbell rang and there was the Reverend Carney and the Imam Ahmed Jabaar on the front stoep shaking out their umbrellas. Pylon opened for them, Carney starting immediately, 'We will not be lectured to. We have come in good faith. We have a mandate.' Mace heard Pylon pacifying, 'It's exploratory, okay. To work something out.'

Mace had collected Ducky Donald already, set up a tea-and-scones sideboard in the room with the round table. Told him, no war. Alright they've stirred the shit to start with, but enough. No more drive-bys, no more car chases, no more skop, skiet en donder. And no funny stuff.

'Me! What've I done? Except stay calm under the worst provocation.'

'Keep it that way.'

Pylon ushered in Carney and Jabaar.

Ducky held up his bandaged right, 'Hey, I'd shake hands if I wasn't shot.'

Before Carney could answer, the doorbell rang again.

'Someone else?' Mace asked the priests.

'Our lawyer,' said Jabaar

Mace went to the front door, opened it to Sheemina February.

'Mr Bishop,' she said. 'Isn't this cosy.' Stood there, wearing a coat she hadn't bought in Cape Town, leather briefcase in her right hand, rain beaded in her hair, those pale blue eyes levelled at Mace. 'Such a small city.'

'You weren't invited,' he said.

She smiled. 'Client's request.' Looked over his shoulder down the passage. 'Perhaps we should get started. I assume my clients are waiting?'

'So what?' Mace keeping the passageway blocked, the air between them saturated with her perfume. Nothing subtle about it.

She said, 'Let me through' – waving her left hand to move him aside. 'Please.' Not subservient, ironic.

Mace nodded, keeping eye contact, drawing out the moment. 'Okay.' He stepped aside. 'Oh yeah, my condolences on the death, the murder, of your ex-husband.'

She brushed past him, stopped, half turned towards him. 'No need. It couldn't have happened to a nicer man.' Again the smile. 'But perhaps I should offer you condolences for the loss of a business partner?'

'Hardly,' said Mace. 'Not our league.'

'No? I think very much your league. From what I remember. That little Luanda adventure.'

Before he could answer, Pylon, standing in the doorway of the boardroom, said, 'What's she doing here?'

'Ah, the gallant Mr Buso,' Sheemina February said. 'What a pleasure.'

Pylon stepped in front of her. Said to Mace, 'You're letting her in?'

'It's alright.'

'Be gracious,' she said, 'like Mr Bishop. I'm their legal representative.' The passage was narrow, they were close together. 'Don't carry grudges, Mr Buso, they lead to intestinal problems. Ulcers.

Irritable bowel syndrome. Now, please. My clients and I have matters to settle with Mr Hartnell. That, I believe, is why we're here.'

'No crap,' said Pylon. 'You got that?'

She flashed her smile: the white teeth, the plum lipstick. 'Or what?' She waggled the fingers of her right hand. 'Or what, Mr Buso?'

Pylon took a pace back to let her into the room. 'Don't push it.'

'Oh I know my place,' she said. 'The question is, do you?'

He caught her by the shoulder but she made no effort to shrug off his grasp. Merely waited until he let her go.

'You're muscle, Mr Buso. You look strong but in here' – she tapped his chest with her left hand, 'you're weak.' With that entered the room. Pylon caught Mace's eye, and drew a finger across his throat.

'What we want,' Sheemina February told Ducky Donald half an hour later, 'is for the bones to go back where they came from.'

He shook his head, 'No ways. No ways in hell.' Turned to Mace. 'We've been through this, boykie. A thousand times. I said no before. I'm saying no still.' Holding up his bandaged hand to her. 'I don't scare.'

Sheemina February touched the glove on her left hand as if she might take it off, said, 'Nor do I.'

'Congratulations,' said Ducky. 'Doesn't mean shit. I'm talking about the hits you ordered.'

'What we want,' Mace said, 'is for you' – pointing at her and the priests – 'to call off the hitman.'

'That has nothing to do with us,' said Carney.

'Absolutely,' said Jabaar. 'We condemn it.'

Sheemina February leant back in her chair. 'That is a radical group. We have no control over them.'

'But you know who they are.'

'We suspect we know who they are,' corrected Carney, Jabaar nodding agreement.

'I know them, yes,' said Sheemina February. 'They're radicals. They will not listen to Reverend Carney or Imam Jabaar. They have had enough talk. Since 1994 they have been preached to but nothing changes. Once a woman called us God's stepchildren. We are still that.'

'Ah, save me Jesus!' Pylon threw up his hands. 'My heart bleeds.'

'You're black,' she said. 'What do you know of our lives?'

Ducky Donald was enjoying this, grinning hugely at Pylon and Sheemina February trading insults, Carney and Jabaar supporting her. Abruptly he thumped his hand on the table. 'Children, children. I give in.'

A sudden silence, everyone looking at him.

'You can have your crypt. A small room in the basement not the foyer. A symbolic gesture. That's it. What you do with the rest of the bones is your indaba.'

Mace watched Ducky, the man's small eyes beneath the wiry eyebrows darting from Sheemina February to Carney, Jabaar, back to the lawyer. The priests not believing what they were hearing, Sheemina February poker-faced.

Pylon said, 'Hallelujah brothers.'

Mace wasn't so sure, knowing Ducky Donald Hartnell.

'What about a plaque?' said the imam.

'Sure, whatever.' Ducky held up his hands about half a metre apart. 'About this square I can live with. In brass. Tasteful, alright. No shitty wording about oppressive colonial masters. Any stuff like that it doesn't go up. And it's your baby. You're the descendants. So you pay. Bring it to me with four screws I'll put it up.'

'Prominently.' This from Sheemina February.

'How about next to the lifts?'

Mace frowned in wonder at what he was hearing. Ducky Donald at a hundred and eighty degrees and sounding like Jesus Christ.

Reverend Carney looked satisfied. 'God is great,' said Imam Jabaar.

The two priests shook hands as if they'd achieved a significant victory.

Sheemina February said, 'We'll need it in writing.'

'Write it now, I'll sign it,' said Ducky. 'You're the lawyer.'

'I'll draft it,' she said, stacking her papers. 'A proper contract.'

'Then send it to my lawyers,' said Ducky, rattling off the name of a legal firm. 'The buggers charge enough, they can argue with you about the wording.'

When the priests and Sheemina February had left, Pylon said to Ducky, 'What was that about?'

'Seeing the light, boykie,' he said, helping himself to a single malt from their cabinet. 'You get to a point where you think, what the hell? What does this mean anyway? Hey? A stack of bones in a locked room. Ten, twenty years' time someone's gonna clear them out, throw them away. Who's gonna know the difference?' He glanced from Pylon to Mace. 'A plaque in the foyer. 'People'll stop seeing it. Any friends they have come visiting are gonna say, hey, isn't this cool? Imagine that?'

'Not what you said before,' Mace reminded him.

'Like I said, what's it mean? Call it weaving in the historic heritage of our city.' He sipped his drink. 'That's good don't you think? Something for the spin doctors.'

9

Mace sat up that night after Oumou and Christa had gone to bed with two words in his head: Sheemina February. Threw rooikrans faggots on a log fire and nursed a tawny port. Thought: why'd this woman bother him? Outside a gale crashed through the stone pines: the mountain howling.

During the meeting, at every moment, he was aware that across the table sat the woman who'd okayed Christa's kidnapping. Probably okayed, wasn't in it, he was sure she had. Abdul Abdul being no more than a sidekick really. Sheemina February, the woman who gave Christa the pain. The nightmares. The flashbacks. The woman who put her in a wheelchair. If he looked up, Sheemina February would catch his eye. Sometimes smile, taunting. Always hold his glance for too long. Sitting there blatantly. Challenging. Daring him. Like she knew something he didn't.

The pale blue eyes. The delicate nose. The lipstick on her Penelope Cruz lips. The perfume. Her hair uncovered. What was he supposed to do here? What was he supposed to feel? Hate? Anger? Fear?

He felt some of that, the hate, the anger. Was disconcerted by her, he had to admit that. He could do without having her pitching up in his business.

After the meeting Pylon had said, 'How could you let her in here? Are you mad? After what happened, how could you? Save me Jesus! She kidnapped your daughter. Could've got Christa killed. She's evil. Pure bloody undiluted evil. And you let her walk in like this isn't our place to say who comes in, who we keep out. What's in your head?'

What, Mace wondered, what was in his head?

That he hadn't stood up to her? Why was that?

Something in some dark corner he couldn't remember?

Or something else? Her words at the concert: that he was guilty. Of what though? Trying to get the truth? Selling guns?

More like he'd let her in out of curiosity. To see where it would go. How matters would pan out. Once there hadn't been time for that sort of consideration. You acted. Earlier times he'd never have left the two Yanks alive, that Paulo and his bird, for the justice system to deal with. The justice system had more chance of cocking it up than of dishing out justice. Earlier times he'd have done them, saved everyone the trouble. Maybe even have done something about Sheemina February in earlier times. A weakness creeping in here. A sense that it made no difference.

He sighed, took a long swallow of the port.

Perhaps Pylon was right. He should've been decisive, kept her out.

After the meeting he'd had a swimming session with Christa. Coaxed her to put in two extra lengths, working her harder than normal. Willing strength into her legs. Mace watched her and thought, this is the triumph. The defeat of Sheemina February.

Some defeat, getting Christa to swim extra lengths.

He let the fire burn down, finished the port. Went to bed with the thought: Sheemina February's rubbing your nose in it. What the it was, he couldn't imagine.

10

Ducky Donald shouted into his phone, 'What's your problem? What's it you don't understand?'

Oupa K said, 'What?'

So Ducky told him again at full volume.

Oupa K said, 'Now?' Then, 'Chief, come again.'

At which Ducky Donald took the phone from his ear and looked at it in wonder as if the instrument wasn't working properly.

He heard the words, 'Alwyn, shit man, don't do that.' Then Oupa K talking to him again, saying, 'Shh. There's no need to shout. Talk nicely, okay?'

Ducky Donald stared at the television screen: a car chase through shopping arcades of the Via Roma. He put the phone back to his ear and said, 'What's this Alwyn doing that I'm straining to get your attention?'

'Taking all the duvet,' said Oupa K, the grunts of a tug-of-war audible to Ducky.

'Five thou, I'm offering. Why's that a problem?'

The Minis going up onto a rooftop, racing round a test track.

'It's midnight,' said Oupa K. 'That's a problem place to start with.'

'Keep off the boys, pal. That's a problem place to start with.'

He heard Oupa K sigh. 'I'm listening to you. I don't need shit.'

'Ten grand.'

'I am at home, in my bed. I was asleep.'

Ducky Donald barked a laugh. 'Sure, sure. You and Alwyn nice 'n cosy.'

The Minis now bouncing down the stairs of a church, a wedding happening in the background. Leaving the cops in the Alfas looking stupid.

'Also it is storming. And it is cold.'

'Then this's gonna warm you up,' said Ducky, aiming the remote at the TV screen, getting back to the main menu. He clicked on scene selection: started the car scene all over again.

'Tomorrow,' said Oupa K. 'When I can get some guys to do it.'

Ducky Donald watched the loot being loaded into the Minis. 'Tomorrow's good. It's what I've been talking about. You leave right now, it's tomorrow by the time you get there.'

'Uh-uh. Not my party. I got people do this for me.'

On screen, it's mayhem in the arcades. Ducky set down the remote to pick up a tumbler of brandy and Coke, his teeth clicking against the glass. He'd been to Oupa K's house once with Matthew and had peeked in the bedroom: a kingsize mattress and base set on a shaggy white rug that was almost wall to wall. The rug smelt of dog, even though Oupa K kept his dogs chained in the yard. Probably all the shit from the street that Oupa K and his bumboys tramped in embedded in the fur.

Ducky scene-hopped to the end, the bus teetering on the edge of a cliff, gold sliding down the floor.

'What else're you doing tonight that's gonna earn you ten grand? For an outlay of what? I dunno. Maybe five hundred bucks. And two hours of your time. Three hours max including travelling.'

''Cos I'm lying here. Cosy like you said. So tomorrow night.'

'Don't you understand?' Ducky raising his voice again. 'For Chrissakes, I need it done now. Come'n Oupa. Do me a favour.'

He paused for Oupa K to come in but the guy didn't. 'It's easy, okay. Nothing to it. No security, no alarms, nothing. You're back in your bed before morning.'

This time Ducky didn't fill the silence, forcing Oupa K into it.

'At seven I coulda made a plan. At ten I coulda made a plan. At nearly twelve I'm not gonna make a plan. Why didn't you tell me earlier?'

''Cos I didn't know earlier. You didn't occur to me earlier. I only thought of you now.'

'Tomorrow, chief. That's it. Duze time.'

'Fifteen.'

'Hey, hey, hey, chief. Five, ten, fifteen. In five minutes of talking. Another five minutes you're gonna be at thirty.'

The man had a point, fifteen was way beyond its worth but Ducky wanted it handled and he wanted it handled tonight. 'That's it. Take it or leave it. I know other fish in the sea.'

Oupa K laughed. 'Hey, what're you talking? I'm not asking any price, chief. You came to me. Other fish've got nothing to do with this. Maybe you should slow down the brandies.'

'Hell, Oupa! Must I go on my knees? That gonna make you happier than fifteen K?'

'That's what Alwyn's doing.'

Ducky flicked back to watch the opening shots coming down the pass.

'I don't wanna know what Alwyn's doing. I wanna know if you're going to help me out.'

Oupa K gave a long sigh of pleasure. 'Oooooo ... Alright. Alright. Say I do this, chief. How're you paying?'

Ducky paused the movie. 'The soon as you do it, the soon as you get here, it's all yours. Just bring the video of the fire as evidence so's I can see it.'

Silence from Oupa K. Then: 'You got an address for me there, chief?'

Ducky Donald gave him directions. 'Leave now, Oupa. I wanna hear it on the morning news.'

Before he thumbed off the connection he heard Oupa say, 'We're on our way, chief. Any moment now.'

11

For Mace the day started badly. He had to collect Francisco off the London flight at 7:00 a.m. 7:00 a.m. was still deep into what he considered a dark and stormy night. To make matters worse he phoned ahead and was told, the flight's on schedule. So 7:00 a.m. his wheels were rolling: fifteen minutes to Cape Town International at that time of the morning against the traffic. His thinking was: Francisco's disembarking, going through passport control, collecting his baggage, hitting the queues at Customs, it was going to be quarter to eight, eight o'clock before he'd cleared. Enough time to relax with the paper and a cappuccino, maybe also a blueberry muffin, at a concourse café.

Wrong.

On the N2 outgoing a lorry's lost its load, the traffic's at a dead stop for thirty minutes. Bang goes the coffee break.

It's gone eight by the time he gets to the airport, there's a different story on the ground. Sorry, sir, the flight's been delayed for thirty minutes because of bad weather.

Okay, he reverts to plan A: a cappuccino, a blueberry muffin and the newspaper.

Only problem: no more blueberry muffins, no more newspapers. Sorry, sir, everybody wants a newspaper, sir, because of the delays.

He gets the cappuccino which is more a latte and a second-hand Cape Times with a story torn out on page three. This means the article on page four about the court case due to open in the High Court in a few hours is mostly missing. The court case featuring Francisco's brother-in-law, the punkish Paulo and his delightful bint, the viper Vittoria. The lead paragraphs are about the murder of the American tourists and the link to the earlier killing of the Italian couturiers but that's all. Mace has to wait until he can get someone else's discarded paper to find that he's made the last paragraph:

'In a surprise development, security operator, Mr Mace Bishop, is to be subpoenaed by the accused on allegations of torture. According to the police, no charges have been laid against Mr Bishop. He is not under investigation.'

He's staring at these words thinking so much for Gonsalves sorting it when Gonsalves calls. 'Nice write up,' he says. 'A fine achievement to make the news.' He gives Mace the sound effects of tobacco chewing.

'I thought you'd organised something.'

'You know with miracles they take a little longer' – a slurp of saliva causing the captain to drag out the last word. 'The sheriff's men been on to you yet?'

Mace tells him, I'm not at home, I'm not at the office, the way the day's shaping I'm not even going to be in at the start of the trial.

'Keep on ducking and diving,' Gonsalves says, 'stay ahead of the law.'

For which advice Mace thanked him and joined the chauffeurs and the company drivers and the tour couriers holding up signs for Mr and Mrs So and So. Francisco came out ahead of the pack.

No preliminaries, no beating about the bush. 'What I wanna do first, Mace,' he said, 'is tour the sight. This's haunting me, the exact location of the final moments of her life. Maybe it doesn't make sense to you. But me, I can't get it outta my mind.'

Mace checked his watch. 'The court'll be sitting round about now.'

'We got time for the court after. This first.'

They drove out to the sand dunes, Francisco silent all the way, staring at the low grey sky and the wild sea. The mountain and the city across that stretch of water a brooding dark.

Where the road comes down into Big Bay Francisco said, 'Would that be Robben Island out there?'

Mace told him yes.

He said, 'I heard about it.'

They drove on in silence for the next ten, fifteen kilometres, Francisco sitting there tense in his Burberry and brogues, giving off a faint scent of mint. At the junction to Atlantis he said, 'This's a long way outta the city. How'd that asshole think to come here?'

'He talks about that,' Mace said. 'On the tape.'

'You gonna let me hear his squealing?'

'Up to you. I can make copies and drop them off. Except some of it's harsh, I have to say.'

Francisco didn't respond beyond a shrug.

In that gloom the dunes came up white, rolling away into a fog bank. Mace slowed, anticipating the farm gate beyond them but even so, overshot and had to U-turn, driving back along the gravel shoulder.

The gate was locked. The farm track mostly under water. Only advantage was the rain had stopped.

'It's here?' said Francisco.

Mace pointed down the track and into the dunes. 'About two hundred metres.'

Francisco conjured a camera from his raincoat pocket, took some snaps of the gate and the track and the dunes beyond.

'You've been out here a coupla times?' he said.

Mace nodded, tested the wire strands of the fence and climbed over. 'In the summer. Not since.'

They stood either side of the gate.

'You and her had this thing, right?'

'Once. We went back some years.'

'I'm assuming. She never talked about it, her feelings, just every now 'n then the name Mace Bishop would drop into her conversation.'

Mace held out his hand. 'I'll take the camera while you climb over.'

Francisco gave it to him. 'This's not interrogational Mace, I'm telling you is all.' He put his foot on the middle strand of wire and jiggled it. 'Isabella I couldn't figure. Her marrying the jerk. Her not putting the romantic clinch on you. This's mysterious to me. I reckon she had other scenes. A woman like that musta done. But she holds tight to the dickhead till he fucking does her.' He climbed onto the gate and Mace steadied him but he came down the other side badly, falling on a knee and a hand, soaking the cuff of his coat, likewise his lower trouser leg. 'Ah shit. Ah for saint's sake, man. Ah Lord Jesus look at this?' He picked himself up. 'This is what I truly need.' He flapped his arm, stared down at his brogues. 'One thing I've no partiality to is wet socks.' He shook his head. 'Okay, this's my safari. This is what I have to do. So we better do it.'

Mace gave him back the camera and he took it, gripping Mace's hand.

'What I'm asking now Mace is, she mean anything to you'- he thumped his chest – 'here in your heart?'

Mace didn't answer him. Held his eyes until Francisco, releasing his grasp, said, 'Yeah, I guessed, I suppose.'

They walked down the track without speaking, wading through vlei sponge that put water into their shoes. About a hundred metres farther, a path forked left off the track into the dunes, the going easier on the hard wet sand. The dune grass thickened and they entered the hollow where Isabella had been shot. Except the hollow was now under water.

Francisco stood beside Mace, his breathing fast. 'This's it?'

'In the summer it's dry,' Mace said. 'Though you wouldn't believe so.'

'And the spot's in there? Under the water.'

Mace nodded.

'Ah bloody saints,' Francisco said, taking a small, framed photograph of Isabella from his coat pocket. 'I wanted to lay this there.' He flipped it into the centre of the pond and they watched it sink, zigzagging out of sight. 'That about right you think?'

Mace told him it was, and for ten minutes they stood there until Francisco said, 'Are you a praying man, Mace?'

Mace told him no.

Francisco picked at a head of dune grass, threw it on the surface. 'In the sense I'm meaning, me neither. I do mass. I'd want a priest at my dying. But I don't pray. Isabella wouldn't even believe I asked you that question.'

Mace's phone started ringing.

'I reckon standing here's as good as that. All the places she'd been she could of died. Yet this is it. A sainting pond in a sand dune outside a city in saint knows where.' He clicked off some photographs. 'God's divine scheme this's supposed to be. Tell me about it, pal. Tell me where there's the hand of God, for saint's sake.'

Mace fished his cell from the inside pocket of his jacket: Ducky Donald's name on the screen. He thumbed him on, said, 'I'll call you back' – disconnecting before the other man could get a word in.

Francisco turned to face him, red-eyed. 'After your justice's gone the course, that's not the end of it for Paulo. The broad neither.'

Mace held his gaze. 'Probably justice won't go its course.'

'I was wondering about that.' He nodded, offered his hand. They shook. 'You better get onto your caller.'

As they headed back across the sand, Mace phoned Ducky.

'Chrissake,' Ducky yelled. 'You cut me off. I'm dealing with major shit here, Mace, 'n you cut me off.'

Mace grimaced at the sky, speckles of rain on the wind again. 'What's it, Ducky?'

'Big trouble. Like you wouldn't believe.'

'Why don't you tell me?'

Ducky gave his hyena laugh. 'The goddamned warehouse burnt down. How about that! In all the rain. Wooma it's gone. Dust to dust, bones to ashes.'

Mace waited at the gate while Francisco climbed over. 'That wasn't smart, Ducky.'

'Shit happens,' he said. 'I need to get there Mace. Pronto, show my disappointment and dismay at this disaster.'

The roof of the warehouse had burnt out completely, not a blackened rafter remaining. The walls stood but everything that was wood had gone up: the doors, the floor boards, the catwalk, the stairs to the walkway. Metal window frames warped in the heat, the panes of glass blown out. You didn't have to be a fireman to know this had been a fierce blaze.

By the time Mace got there the drama was well over: the street still blocked off by a fire services' car and a cop van pulled across it either end, but the fire tenders long gone. In the smouldering shell stood a knot of men, Ducky Donald and Pylon among them. With the sprung floor burnt away, the foundation cellar seemed an ancient ruin of columns and short walls, black sludge and mud. Like being in Pompeii, Mace thought, jumping down. Roofing sheets and other charred debris scattered about. The ground still hot.

Pylon walked him aside before he could join the group. 'This's him again?'

'I'd reckon.'

'But you wouldn't tell from how he's acting. In character as soon's I picked him up: "this is a tragedy, just when everything's sorted out" – words to that effect.'

'And the bones?'

'Ashes, mostly. Odd bits here and there where you can see anything under the roof sheeting. But what's wood ash 'n what's human ash who can tell?

'The priests will love this.' Mace looked over at the group of men. 'What's the fire chief say?'

'He's talking a probable electrical fault but he's dubious. Because of the intensity. Also a fault would've triggered the alarm. The alarm would've brought out the security patrol. Didn't happen.'

'What did?'

'Smoke detector next-door got the fire services here before the street went up. The timeline's something like: security logs a fire alarm at five-fifty thereabouts, the patrol checks it out, calls the fire brigade maybe six minutes later, it takes them ten minutes to get an engine here. Say six-twentyish they're on the job. Seven the fire's doused. Most of the damage done before anybody knew about it.'

'And Ducky's security system didn't trigger.'

'Probably I'd say it was switched off.'

'Bloody pyromaniac.'

'What's puzzling the fire chief is why the floor burnt first. Usually it's the roof he says.'

Mace noticed the knot of men breaking up, Ducky Donald limping towards them.

'The forensics'll get him. Or rather put it down to arson. But what's that prove? Ducky'll say it was a set-up, probably caused by the same people as are trying to kill him. Makes sense.'

'Except for the security system failing.'

'Dud technology. Why not? Happens all the time.'

Ducky Donald called out. 'Christ, do I need this?'

'Don't you?' Mace asked 'Seems to me to sort out a problem.'

'What's that?' Ducky dusted his hands.

'Nothing left to fight over.'

He squinted at Mace. 'Boykie, you're too cynical. Anybody ever told you that?'

'Also frees up the storage commitment.'

'I was good for that. You heard me tell her.'

'Tell her what?' said the voice of Sheemina February, and they looked up and she stood there in what had once been the doorway, their heads level with her boots.

At any other time Mace might have said he could see what Mo Siq had seen when he married her. This alluring woman – black coat, black gloves, black hair – the flash in her pale blue eyes and the half-smile. The tips of her teeth white against her lipstick. At any other time.

'Last night,' she said, 'we had an arrangement, Mr Hartnell. Draw up the contract, I'll sign it. you said.' She held out her briefcase. 'It's in here. I took you on good faith. Funny thing this fire should happen now.'

'Changes nothing,' said Ducky. 'I'm good for my word.'

She forced a laugh. 'Good for what? Taking a scoop of sand and ash from where you're standing and plastering it onto a wall.'

'Of course. Make the ancestors part of the building.'

'Nice try, Mr Hartnell. But we don't want our ancestors churned up in a concrete mixer.'

She stared at the men, each one in turn. Mace met her eyes, held them until she said, 'I'm calling a press conference. For tomorrow morning, in the Slave Lodge probably. Be there.' And swirled away, Ducky Donald shouting after her, 'Wait, wait.'

'Forget it,' Mace said.

'Ah, shit, man.' Ducky groaned. 'They're gonna crucify me.'

Pylon patted him on the shoulder. 'Keep spinning, bro, you'll think of something.'

Mace drove a subdued Ducky Donald home, didn't stop for the coffee and a shot he offered.

'You'll get me to the lion's den tomorrow?'

'As per our agreement.'

Ducky didn't think it was funny, slammed closed the Spider's door.

When Mace got back to the office the sheriff's man was waiting with a subpoena. A day starts badly it continues like that all the way, he thought.

12

Christa phoned Mace at 4:03 p.m. To remind him they were swimming that afternoon.

'At five,' he said, 'I'm collecting you as usual, right?'

'Just checking.'

'You want to skip this one because of the weather?'

It'd rained all day. It was cold. People were calling into the radio talk-shows to say there was snow on the lower slopes of the Hottentots Hollands, it must be thick higher up. If you could even see higher up, the clouds were so low.

Christa giggled. 'Never.'

'I'll see you at five.'

'You can come earlier.'

'No chance C, I've got this client, seriously strange man' – and he dropped his voice to describe him.

'Papa,' she said, not really listening, 'could we go to the mountains? To see the snow.'

'Hey, there's an idea,' he said. 'Why not? Talk to your mother. She's at home?'

'Downstairs.'

'Ask her to make a booking for the weekend. At a farm B&B. The farmers do it when there's snow.'

'Papa,' she said, drawing out the vowels, 'what about our holiday?'

'Your mother's working on it,' said Mace, 'talk to her.'

At 4:12 p.m. Oumou phoned Mace.

'What is it Christa is talking about?'

'There's snow on the mountains. She wants to see it.'

'Ah oui. This is what she is saying, about sleeping on a farm.'

'See if you can't make a booking somewhere. I'd do it but I haven't got the time.'

'Later you swim?'

'Five o'clock. I told Christa five. As usual, I'll pick her up. You coming with us?'

'This is possible.'

'Make her day. Mine too.'

At 5:15 p.m. Oumou phoned Mace again. Got his voicemail and left a message: 'Why are you late? We are waiting.' Called again at 5:34 p.m. And then at 5:52 p.m.

'Where's your father?' she said after the last call. 'He said he would be here at five o'clock.'

'He's always late, Maman,' said Christa. 'You know.' She put down her book, switched on the television to see the snow on the news.

'For your swimming times he is never late.'

She phoned Pylon, said, 'Is my husband with you?'

'I'm at home,' he said. 'Mace said he was going swimming.'

'We are waiting for him. Since five o'clock.'

'You've phoned him?'

'Oui. Three times already. There is just his voicemail.'

'I'll call you back,' said Pylon.

At 6:01 p.m. Pylon phoned Mace and got his voicemail. He called Oumou immediately and said Mace was going to stop at the Mount Nelson on his way home to drop off some audio tapes. With an American called Francisco. About the murder case.

'This is Isabella's brother? He told me.'

'Yes,' said Pylon. 'Maybe they're having a drink.'

'He would have phoned to tell Christa.'

'I'll talk to Francisco,' said Pylon.

He phoned the hotel, was patched through to Francisco in the bar.

'So where's your partner, amigo?' Francisco said. 'He tells me half past four, I get here half past four, the barman puts together a dry martini that it turns out he learnt how to make in New York, but I'm stood up. Undeniably. I tell the barman give me another, my man says he's coming, my man keeps his word. Like the French Louis says it, punctuality is the politeness of kings. Nothing truer my friend. To show respect. An attribution I believed of Mace Bishop. Up till an hour thirty ago. That's way over my leeside. Ten minutes, this happens at the end of the day. Bad traffic. You're running late through your schedule. This I understand. But you call. You say, give me ten, fifteen, whatever. This I would've thought of Mace. How he strikes me is what they call fastidious. Know what I mean?'

Pylon told Francisco that when Mace pitched up would he ask him to make some phone calls urgently. To his wife for starters, and to him, Pylon.

'We're talking some unusualness here?' said Francisco. 'Like maybe he's had an accident?'

'Wouldn't know. I'm checking.'

Pylon got through to his contacts on the paramedics. The guys laughed. No crashes involving red Alfa Spiders in living memory let alone the last hour. Two Golfs, one Beemer, a taxi minibus, one pedestrian dead on the highway. Nothing serious otherwise. Fender benders in the wet.

He hung up, went through to Treasure in the kitchen. 'I'm supposed to worry about Mace, d'you think?'

She asked him: worry about Mace doing what? He told her. She said, 'He's got a woman, maybe?'

Pylon thought about this. About the rosebud in the box. About Mace and women. But it didn't gel: Mace looked but wouldn't go further. Whatever the rosebud was about, a secret admirer, a client getting cute, Mace wasn't on the prowl. That he'd put money on.

'I don't think so,' he said. 'Something must've come up. Could be over the fire. Could be Gonsalves about the case.'

'He'd have let you know.'

'This's true.'

'Unless it's a woman.'

'I can't see that.'

Treasure kept stirring the risotto.

Pylon tapped his fingers on the countertop. 'The best thing here is to sit it out.'

At 6:51 p.m. Oumou phoned Mace, the call went to voicemail. Christa wasn't watching television anymore. The television was on, but she was staring at a book open on her lap not reading it either. Waiting. Oumou had to do something. Couldn't sit there, went to the kitchen to put a meal together: a pot of fish stew on the hob, a ciabatta warming in the oven like Mace was going to walk in at any moment – Hey, girls, sorry I'm late, this client, you just wouldn't believe … – stooping to give Christa a kiss, giving her a hug as he now did every evening. The loving Mace. At 6:51 p.m. she picked up the cellphone lying on the counter: names, search, Mace, thumbed on the key with the little green icon of a telephone. Listened to seven rings willing him to answer until the voicemail clicked in. She didn't leave a message. Put the cell on the countertop, took the lid off the stew to stir it, turned the heat to its lowest setting. Replaced the lid, balanced the wooden spoon against the hob. She looked up, stared at the city lights smudged by the condensation on the window. Swallowed to stop the hollowness in her stomach, and phoned Pylon.

'Something has happened,' she said. 'Please.'

Pylon forked up another mouthful of risotto, his favourite risotto with the toasted almond flakes and the croutons. Began to wonder if settling in front of the TV to watch the Bafana match mightn't be at stake here.

'It is two hours,' said Oumou. 'This is not normal for Mace. At five o'clock he was swimming with Christa. That was what he arranged. For his swimming, Mace would not be late. Please. Something has happened. Still he is not answering.'

Pylon put down the forkful of risotto. Two hours in the life of Mace Bishop was not a long time to go missing.

'Why don't we wait another hour,' he said. 'You know Mace.'

'Non,' she said. 'Not for this time. For this time he is in trouble. I can feel it.'

Pylon glanced across the table at Treasure and Pumla. Both were looking at him. Treasure reached out her hand for the phone. He gave it to her, thinking, so much for the chances of watching soccer.

'Oumou,' she said. 'What's it?'

He could hear Oumou talking, Treasure nodding as she listened. He ate the forkful of risotto, crunching almond flakes.

Treasure said, 'Alright, alright. Oumou listen. We're coming over. Give us half an hour.' She put down the phone, said to Pylon. 'She's crying. She knows something's wrong. Oumou doesn't cry for nothing.'

He scraped his fork around the plate. 'So it's not another woman suddenly?'

'No.'

'Still Mace we're talking about. For twenty-four hours he disappeared the last time. Playing the big white hunter. Didn't tell anybody where he was going. Just poof, Mace's gone.'

'He told Oumou.'

'Oumou didn't know.'

'She did. Mace told her. I know that. Also Mace wouldn't do it to Christa.'

Pylon pushed his plate aside. 'He forgot. Something came up. Could be half a dozen reasons.'

'Let's go,' said Treasure.

***

Pylon dropped Treasure and Pumla with Oumou and Christa. The women really worked up about this. He couldn't take it seriously that Mace had disappeared, but okay he'd go through the motions: check Mace's diary, see if there were any notes lying about on his desk. Put through a few calls to clients. Ducky Donald. Gonsalves. Francisco again. On a night like this it was the last thing he wanted, running through the rain from his car to the office door. The restaurants on Dunkley Square empty. No cars in the parking lot. Every sensible person indoors. What I don't do for you Mace Bishop, he thought.

Mace's diary had Francisco, Mount Nelson written at 4:30 and Christa at 5:00 p.m. No other engagements for the night. He paged back, but no strange names, no unattributed telephone numbers leapt out. Then Mace wasn't a doodler, his diary a sparse record of appointments. No notes in the waste bin either.

Pylon made his phone calls, telling each one he was trying to track down Mace.

Ducky said, 'I'm my brother's keeper? Hell, china, if nobody knows where Mace is then Mace's gotta be screwing his arse off somewhere. Randy bugger. So he should of been home three hours ago. So that's news? Mace is a grown man last time I looked.'

Gonsalves said, 'When you find him, tell him he can relax. Tear up the subpoena. The captain's waved his wand.'

Francisco said, 'I'm eating this cabulyou fish, got good texture to the flesh like I like it. No fishiness like I like it. Not bad with a sharp sauce. The waiter says to me, they've got it in fresh today, it's their specialisation, been nowhere near the inside of a freezer. Bring it on John I tell him. Mace'd played his cards right he coulda been eating this too with some chardonnay. Tell him he missed out big time. Tell him justice is a donkey's ass.'

Pylon sat back in Mace's chair, played through the sequence so it looked to Oumou like he'd done the homework.

Four o'clock Mace tells Christa he'll pick her up at five. Fifteen minutes later he tells Oumou he's going to be home at five. He's supposed to drop audio tapes at the Nellie at four-thirty. Must have been about four twenty-five, Mace shouted he was leaving. He gets into his car he drives out of Dunkley Square down Dunkley Street, left into Hatfield up to the traffic lights. Goes right into Orange, two hundred metres later swings left into the Nelson between the columns. Maximum couldn't have taken more than three minutes even allowing for a red robot. Four-thirty Francisco's waiting for him. He never pitches. In five minutes Mace Bishop disappears.

You laid it out like that, Pylon thought, it looked wrong. Unlikely that Mace suddenly thought of something he should have done. He would have made calls. He would have made the drop with Francisco, he was right there. No point in not doing it. So what happened?

Pylon locked up, drove to the Mount Nelson. Two security men at the entrance in trench coats and pith helmets came out of their warm sentry box when he beckoned.

Polite in the rain: 'Can we help you, sir?'

Pylon asked if they could recall a red Alfa Spider coming in about four-thirty. The old style. They shook their heads, water spraying off their helmets. The one said he'd have remembered that sort of car, he'd seen it before, just a few days ago in fact. Probably, said Pylon, and made a U-turn on Orange, thinking, this was not a good scenario to lay before Oumou. Not encouraging at all.

He'd been through nights like this one was shaping up to be. They were long and dark, waiting for someone to pitch up. He put through a call to the vehicle tracking company that monitored their cars, asked the controller to get a reading on Mace's Spider.

Not thirty seconds later the controller said, 'I'd say he's at home. Or in the vicinity. On that block of the grid anyway.'

'Wonderful,' said Pylon, hanging up, thinking any minute he'd get a call to say Mace had walked in. Maybe watching the soccer match was still a goer.

13

Mace opened his eyes, the only movement he made. He felt like shit. His head pounding, his throat dry, an ache in the calf muscle of his left leg. He lay trying to put together the run of events, listening, looking, smelling.

The smell was of damp, distemper. The paint job seemed recent but it couldn't hide the smell. A familiar smell as the room was familiar. Not a room, more a cellar, his eyes taking in the stonework and the beams. A cellar like there'd been in the Victorian, cold as that too. Silent as that. He couldn't hear any noise, no bumps, no footfall, nothing above the buzz of the fluorescent tube. In the cellar in the Victorian you couldn't hear anybody moving above you either. Might be a wooden ceiling but there had to be stone and mortar packed on top of the boards.

Mace eased up onto his elbows, the pain hammering through his skull. He waited blinking, letting the throb settle. Saw then the handcuff on his left ankle, the chain running off the bed to the iron pin in the wall. He knew where he was then. He groaned, collapsed back on the mattress, something stiff and furry falling against his face. Mace reached for it, held up a child's teddy bear: Cupcake, he reckoned. Had to be, the same spot on the back where the fur was worn away. The bear that'd gone missing, what, six months ago when the car was parked at the gym? So not some random theft, something deliberate.

That brought events back. Seeing himself clutching his jacket closed, running head down through the rain to the Spider, not looking around. Not paying attention. Beeping open the automatic locks from a couple of metres off. Dropping into the driver's seat, the guy getting into the passenger seat at the same time. The guy in the Camry with the gun. The guy who put the same gun in his face, saying, 'Roll outta here, brother, 'n don't tune any grief.' The guy Mikey Rheeder.

Replying to him, 'Piss off.'

Mikey Rheeder digging the barrel deep into Mace's left kidney, telling him that at that range there'd be little left of the near kidney and probably very little of the other and a great deal of chewed up intestine in between.

Mace said, 'Relax, okay.'

Mikey said, 'Put the keys in, get us the fuck outta here. I can pull a trigger as easy as you.'

Mace remembered doing what the prick wanted: starting the car, driving slowly into Dunkley to the corner with Hatfield. Not challenging him with eye contact, playing submissive. 'Don't get worked up. Tell me what you want. I'm not going to cause you any shit.'

Mikey Rheeder laughing. 'You bloody right there' – coming round with his left hand, jabbing a syringe right into Mace's neck. From there on it wasn't clear to Mace what happened next, except the car going hard against the curb and stalling.

Mace touched his neck, winced as his fingers found the stick wound.

He sat up then, swinging his legs off the bed, ignoring the pressure bouncing round his skull. His wristwatch was gone, likewise his credit card holder, his belt, his shoes. Also the pen from the inside pocket of his jacket. A thorough guy was Mikey Rheeder. Mace stood, his calf hurt to put weight on, but was only a muscle-ache like he'd pulled a tendon. He shuffled to the end of the chain's length, hardly enough slack to let him move beyond the bed. Sat down on the edge when he heard a key going into the lock. In came Mikey Rheeder.

'Hey, bro, you're up, hey.'

Mace said, 'What's your problem?'

Mikey, dangling a bottle of Black Label from his fingers, said, 'My problem?' Drank a mouthful of beer. 'My problem. Hey dude, you shoot me through the shoulder. You smash my fingers, you ask me what's my problem?' He stayed in the doorway, leaning against the architrave, pointing at Mace with the bottle of beer. 'I'll tell you what's my problem. What was my problem. You was my problem. Except now you're not my problem anymore. Now you're your problem. Your own problem.'

Mace said, 'Where's this place?'

'For someone chained to a wall you know what, you ask too many questions,' said Mikey.

'I know this house,' said Mace.

'Yeah. You're a detective.'

'It belongs to Sheemina February. Your boss, right? It's empty now. On the market.'

Mikey grinned. 'Like I said, clever dick.' He took a swig of beer. 'Know what's gonna happen here? One day she's gonna have a show house. The agent's gonna open up 'n think, Jesus, rats musta died in here. 'N 'strues bob, in the cellar they're gonna find this dead rat. 'N they're gonna call the cops and the cops're gonna say Miss February what's going on here? Especially they're gonna be interested when they find the bullet in you comes from the same gun that put a bullet in someone else just a coupla weeks ago. That's gonna make them wanna talk in detail to her.'

'I'd think twice about a plan like that Mikey. Anything involving Sheemina February I'd think twice.'

'I have,' said Mikey. 'I thought the best would be not to be around. You see what I heard was that you've got some diamonds stuck away. I'm figuring to get those first. I'm thinking to send your wife a little video presentation. My idea is to do that now, get the show on the road.'

'Had some diamonds,' said Mace. 'That is true. But I sold them.'

'Sure,' said Mikey. 'I'd also say something like that in your position.' He reached into a pocket of his cargo pants and brought out a camcorder. 'What I want you to say is, "Get the diamonds".' He raised the camera, focusing tightly on Mace. 'Nothing more. Just get the diamonds. Okay, go.'

Mace said, 'I'm being held captive at our old home.'

'Nice one, Mace,' said Mikey shutting off the camera. 'That's what I heard about you, always the macho big prick. That's okay, I got enough for what I want. Like they say, tomorrow's another day. See you around, china.' He turned to leave, stopped. 'Oh yeah, I forgot to mention. What I'm gonna do later on is smash a couple of your fingers. Till then, my apologies, no room service, no plumbing. But, there's your teddy bear and, hey, you're not dead yet.'

14

A grey dawn, cold and dripping. The city below ghosting tall buildings through the mist; the sea beyond invisible. Cloud down on Lion's Head and Devil's Peak and veiling the face of the mountain. And in the kitchens of the houses and flats, lights on for breakfast; a smell of porridge and of toast, the raised voices of children and the television news. People leaving for their offices, kissing goodbye.

'Please,' said Oumou to Pylon, 'you must find him.' He held her hands, stared at the sadness in her brown eyes. The sadness that Mace was always on about, as if her eyes had seen too much.

For a couple of hours after midnight Pylon had driven the neighbourhood streets: round Gardens, Vredehoek, even into Higgovale. Nada, nix, nothing. Which was the weird thing about this, he felt. The car was nearby. Mace was nearby. The hell was Mace up to? The hell was going on?

The rest of the night they'd watched television, the five of them in the lounge drinking coffee, Pylon putting calls through to Mace's cellphone every half hour. The girls slept, Pumla most of the time, Christa intermittently. Pylon thought he might have dozed off in the chair but never for long, and each time he jerked awake, Oumou and Treasure were staring at the television. Twice he phoned emergency services, drew negatives. The same with the cops at a range of police stations through the city and down the peninsula. Twice, too, the tracker company. 'He moves, we'll call you,' the operator said.

In the grey dawn Pylon said to Oumou, 'He's not moved by eight, half past eight then the tracking company's got a mobile scanner which'll find the car. A couple of hours that's all it'll take.'

'Oui,' she said. 'But why must we wait? They could have done this in the night.'

'They couldn't,' said Pylon. 'They've only got one mobile. That was somewhere else last night. They said to me they'll have it here by half past eight. If Mace hasn't shown up.'

Oumou looked at the kitchen clock: half past seven. 'We are wasting time,' she said. 'There is trouble for Mace.'

Pylon turned away from her and back again. 'What can I do Oumou? I don't know what else to do until they get the scanner here.'

'It is too late at half past eight,' she said.

'Phone them, tell them yourself.'

She did. They told her the other job had taken longer than they thought, it was about tennish they expected the scanner back.

'It is too late,' she said. 'You must get here sooner.'

'Lady,' the operator said, 'that's how long it takes to drive it here, all right, from where it is now. The guy's on his way. Full speed.'

Oumou looked at Pylon, no tears in her eyes but the anguish in them stung him. 'Please,' she said. 'You must find him.'

When Pylon got to the office there was a CD in the letter box. No packaging, no address, no instructions. It came up on his laptop as a video clip and there's Mace against a white background but the focus too tight to give anything away, Mace mouthing something. At the end a voice saying, 'You want him back, I'll do a swap: I get his diamonds, you get him.'

Not a long clip, enough to see Mace's lips moving but not make out the words. The voice no one's Pylon recognised. Cape Town white accent, although you got black and coloured guys with that accent too depending on the schools they got into. Which narrowed things down to about a couple of hundred thousand males.

Pylon thought probably not the sort of thing to show Oumou. At least not yet. Probably best not to tell her even. The thing being that Mace and his car might be well separated. The car dumped in a parking garage. In the tracking company's block there being about four he could think of. He called them, suggested they start with the parking garages.

'When the mobile gets here,' said the operator.

Pylon said, 'I'm not hassling. I know your problems, I'm just making a suggestion.'

He hung up, went back to the disc in his laptop. 'You want him back, I'll do a swap: I get his diamonds, you get him.' Played that over and over.

The thing here being the diamonds. Weren't too many knew about that deal. He wrote down the names on a notepad: Mo Siq, Stones Mkize, Mace's broker. Brokers being brokers could let out this sort of information. Stones wouldn't. Mo was dead. Pylon drew a circle round Mo's name, wondering if there was a link in his killing to Mace's disappearance. Remembering someone else who knew about the deal was Sheemina February. Remembering the call Mace had got from her before they flew to Angola. While they were waiting in the departure lounge. Wondering if that had something to do with this. Getting a bad sense. The sort that made him look out the window on a pissing-down Dunkley Square at a scattering of empty cars, no one staking him out. Made him think maybe he needed to get someone in, do a sweep of the office for bugs. A thought he put on hold, better now to let the cameraman play his game, no suspicions raised.

Instead Pylon called for the telephone records, his contacts wanting to know why he couldn't wait a couple of days to the end of the month when he'd get the detailed billing anyhow. A special favour, he replied, and like urgent, guys, this morning would be good.

He spoke to Francisco. 'Wanna know my sense here, pal,' Francisco said, 'my sense is the same as with Isabella. I try to get connectivity with her hour after hour. Into the second day I know she's dead. I don't sleep, I don't eat until I get the call from Mace confirming. Then I howl. Make noises like I don't believe a human can make. That's disconcerting. People don't answer their cellphones, it means they can't. They're dead or dying I'd say.'

Thanks for that, Pylon thought, hanging up, the phone ringing immediately. Gonsalves.

'He pitched up yet?' said the cop.

'Not a trace.'

'The case gets postponed 'n he still disappears!'

'This's not about the case. This's about something else.'

'So report a missing person?'

Pylon snorted. 'They'll tell me wait forty-eight hours.'

'That's bullshit,' said Gonsalves. 'Some desk jockey gives you that kinda crap, call me.'

He didn't take the advice, instead worked up another scenario: a hijacking. A long long shot: someone had an order on a red Alfa Spider vintage 1970s or whatever and some cool dudes pulled it in the rain. Stored it in a garage nearby. Stranger things had happened. Oupa K didn't think so.

'Chief, chief,' Oupa K told Pylon in English, 'listen to me chief' – switching to Xhosa. 'Nobody's gonna want that car south of Lusaka. Not to drive around. The person wants that car's gonna put it in a garage.'

'Exactly.'

'There's what,' said Oupa K back in English, 'about two red Spiders in the city? Three tops. If I'm gonna roll that type of car I'd find out the owners. Settle on the one's likely to cause the least shit.'

Pylon in vernacular said if he got any whispers to call.

'Only a mlungu,' said Oupa K. 'No big deal.'

At 9:45 Pylon heard from the tracking company that they'd have the mobile scanner on the job in an hour, hour and a half max. At 10:30 they called to say they were starting the search, doing the Gardens section of the block first.

'No,' said Pylon. 'The parking garages first. And you find it, you do nothing except call me. Nobody touches it before me.'

'Nobody's gonna want to,' said the operator.

Half an hour later Pylon collected Ducky Donald for the press conference. Ducky less concerned about Mace than how the press was going to angle the story.

'Bones, ashes, what's the difference?' he said to Pylon in the car. 'They didn't have cremation those days, or there wouldn't have been bones to start with, know what I'm saying? Pity, when you think about it. Ashes are better. Ashes are less emotional. 'Cos ashes can be anything: wood, plants, humans. When they're ashes there's no telling them apart. Not like a skeleton. That looks like us. We know it's us. These people with pointy teeth look at skulls with pointy teeth and they go, ancestor. You can't look at ashes in the same way. So there's that. I can't see her problem with how I wanna handle the ashes. Makes them part of the building. One of the ways you can look at this is that the building's their memorial. A living monument. There's a point, wouldn't you think?'

Pylon didn't respond.

'What I called in that article a contribution to the urban fabric of the city, takes on a second meaning under the circumstances.' He half-turned towards Pylon. 'You see the thing we're talking about isn't bones or ashes, it's dignity. Recognition. Acknowledgement.'

'When you're finished building you could be a PR,' said Pylon.

Ducky beamed. 'There's this possibility.'

The press conference was full, maybe ten, twelve journalists: newspapers, radio, even television. Pylon stood back at the entrance to the foyer, Ducky Donald's safety in this situation a low priority. At the table up front Sheemina February, the reverend, the imam, the public relations-types. Ducky's lawyers huddled with their client, no doubt trying to talk down the developer's gung-ho spiel.

Pylon stood listening, not listening, heard Ducky get defensive, the imam and the priest lashing him about the fire, Sheemina February alert and stern through it, coming in with the business that among those bones could have been those of her ancestors. Her slave ancestors that built the city. Pylon heard that as his phone rang: Oumou. He ducked away to take the call.

He told her the tracking company had started the search, been on it over an hour, he expected to hear from them at any time.

'I know,' she said, 'I have called the operator. Perhaps you should be with them?'

'I can't,' said Pylon, 'nor will that make them go any faster. One thing, the car's not been left in a parking garage. It has to be on private property.'

'That is not better,' said Oumou. 'Then someone has caught him.'

'I don't know,' said Pylon. 'I don't know what's going on.' He heard her gasp and disconnect. He dialled Treasure.

'She's okay,' said Treasure. 'Where're you?'

He told her the Slave Lodge and she said, 'It's the waiting, the not knowing. Can't you do something?'

'There's a call holding,' he said, 'I have to go.'

The call was from the tracking company. They'd found the house. A long-wheelbase Isuzu in the driveway, no sign of the Spider. Had to be in the garage, the technician said. Pylon took down the address, thinking, that's familiar. Thinking, Save me Jesus, Mace's old address, the Victorian, the house Sheemina February bought. Looked at her holding forth to the journalists, and walked out. Didn't seem like anyone intended hanging an arson charge on Ducky either. Guy had more luck than was good for him. Or anyone else. Pylon put an SMS through to Ducky Donald to get a lift home with his lawyer.

15

Mace, cold, dehydrated, needing badly to piss. Did so in the corner closest to the foot of the bed. A puddle forming, trickling back towards his feet, making him dance away. This was shit, he thought, this was up the creek. The options not looking good.

Mikey Rheeder couldn't be so stupid he wouldn't ditch the Spider. He did that, what hope was there?

That Sheemina February had put Mikey up to this didn't take a rocket scientist's calculations. The future, to Mace's way of thinking, looked like nothing but anguish, pain and death. Bloody wonderful.

He zipped, sat at the head of the bed rubbing his arms to bring in some warmth. Felt something hard beneath his backside, digging into the flesh of his left cheek. He stood, lifted the foam mattress: there taped to the base slats a tiny, stainless steel, double-action, North American Arms Guardian .32. He undid the tape, picked up the gun. It disappeared in his fist, the barrel no longer than his index finger.

'Jesus,' he said aloud, 'the hell I'm supposed to do with this?' The featherweight of it, the bullet going to be little more than a bee-sting to a rhinoceros. He slid out the clip, a full load of six rounds. Hollow-points. At least hollow-points would go some way to persuading Mikey Rheeder to listen. He sat down again to think things through, wondering what Sheemina February was playing at?

Had to be her who'd taped it there, without a doubt. The only obvious explanation she wanted him to blow away Mikey Rheeder. Then die of thirst and hunger himself. Always assuming Mikey Rheeder didn't get a shot in too. The two of them killing each other in a shoot-out. Had to be the way of her thinking. The intention to get rid of them both. Very curious. What Mace did appreciate was that now he had some bargaining power with Mikey Rheeder.

Sitting there waiting for Mikey Rheeder he also wondered why the guy wanted to line up Sheemina February for a fall. She was the boss, why would he want to do that? Unless he was working a financial angle somewhere. Such possibilities didn't do anything for Mace's headache.

He lay down on the bed with the gun in his hand and waited for Mikey to return. Closed his eyes against the neon light, even drifting in and out of sleep.

The slap of soft-soled trainers on the staircase and the scrape of the key in the lock brought Mace up wide awake. The door swung open, Mikey Rheeder standing there with a chopping board and mallet in his bent hand, a small cannon, Smith & Wesson L frame, in the other.

'Time for some tender moments,' Mikey said.

Mace said, 'I don't think so' – brought up the Guardian. 'Listen to me, okay?'

Mikey said, 'Hey, what the fuck!' – edged backwards.

Mace said, 'Don't do that' – shot him in the torso.

Mikey staggered, dropping both chopping board and mallet, clutched at his stomach, brought up the S&W.

It looked to Mace like hollow-point or no hollow-point, Mikey was intending to use the gun.

16

Pylon stopped behind the mobile-scanner van, checked his pistol and chambered a round before he joined the technicians in the van. The two men inside almost invisible in the cigarette smoke. The smoke sending Pylon into a coughing fit so savage he had to back out to clear his lungs.

'It's going to kill you,' he said to the techies.

'This or something else,' said the one, butt lighting another Marlboro. 'Get in outta the rain.'

'No,' said Pylon, 'this is not how I fancy dying.'

'Suit yourself,' the techie said, switching on the instrument, the signal loud, a long screech.

'We had a look over the wall,' said the second techie, 'there's a garage just the other side, 'n that's where we'd guess the car is. For a signal this strong.'

'Nobody around?'

'Nobody we've noticed. A bakkie delivery van standing in the driveway though.'

'All yours now,' said the first techie. 'Should be fun.'

Pylon waited until they'd driven away before he buzzed the gate intercom, wondering what he was going to say if someone answered? No one did. Buzzed three times, then hauled himself over the gate. Dropped down and crouched. No movement at the windows. No shouts that he'd been seen from the street. No one out in the drizzle anyway.

The driveway was cobbled now that had been a tarred strip in Mace's day. Went right up to the steps at the stoep. Otherwise not much had changed. The garden neater, the lawn trimmed. The house recently painted and in good shape for the market.

He peered in the windows of the Isuzu: the cab a mess of sweet papers, KFC takeaway boxes, polystyrene cups; in the back a surfboard, a wetsuit bundled in a plastic bucket. The canopy door unlocked, but the cab secured, a security light flashing in the dashboard.

Pylon tried the front door of the house, locked, but you had to test the obvious. Made a funnel of his hand against the glass, and listened. Could hear what might have been a radio on somewhere deep in the house.

The thing here, he thought, was where to break in?

The curtains were drawn at the sitting-room windows, the same at the front room that'd been Oumou's studio, where the men got in. Not one of the windows open even a chink. He walked round the house, through the gate that led to a paved courtyard at the back. The kitchen light on, blinds at the window slatted open enough for him to see the room was empty. A takeaway packet on the counter top. A six-pack of beer unopened and a couple of bottles next to the takeaway remains. A world-band radio.

He broke a back window to get in. Stood in the kitchen listening, the radio playing rap music. He switched it off. The only sound now the tick of a kitchen clock. He waited while the second hand did a full circle. Stepped into the hallway leading to the front door, with each step the floorboards creaking. Stopped at the foot of the staircase. Looked up. Could feel the house paused about him.

Only then noticed the door to the cellar, unlatched, slightly ajar, a bulkhead light on in the stairwell. Pylon started down the steps, calling out, 'Mace, Mace' – seeing the body lying in the doorway, a mess of blood on the flagstone floor.

Pylon, in the cellar's doorway, said, 'Save me Jesus.'

'I'd go with that,' said Mace, 'at this point.'

'What a mess.'

'I'd go with that, too,' Mace said, 'bastard tried to shoot me.'

Pylon pointed at the gun lying on the bed beside Mace. 'And that little toy?'

'Left for me, under the mattress. It works though.'

'Jesus Christ Almighty. I mean what? How?'

So Mace told Pylon how he'd been jacked by Mikey and everything that'd followed up to the point it seemed Mikey intended to use the revolver so he, Mace, had laid two more shots into Mikey's chest. And how Mikey got a strange expression like he was going to be sick, and spewed up blood and pink matter. Still on his feet though. Then how he took a step forward, unsteady, waving the gun about, falling down on his hands, coughing up more of the pink matter. Mace said he thought he might have to shoot Mikey again but the guy's arms gave way and he dropped flat, his legs splaying behind him. Lay twitching on his stomach. 'Watching him bleed out wasn't the best time of my life,' Mace said.

'Save me Jesus,' said Pylon again. 'You don't realise people have so much blood.'

'The keys,' said Mace. 'Just get me loose.'

Pylon took a step back. 'I'm supposed to go through his pockets, all that blood 'n shit? Scumbag like this'll be HIV.'

'Wash your hands afterwards,' said Mace. 'Water's got that purifying quality.'

Pylon said, 'Who're you kidding' – prodded at Mikey's pockets with the toe of his shoe until he found the bulge of the keys and eased them out, bloodying his hands nonetheless. 'Ah shit,' he said, 'this's asking for death' – and rushed upstairs to wash his hands and the bunch of keys.

Mace shouting after him, 'You could get me loose first.'

Pylon came back drying his hands on his jeans. 'I forgot to mention,' he said, bending to the handcuffs, 'that I got a kidnap video this morning, through the letter box, at the office. Nice shot of you, against the wall, I'd say. Couldn't make out what you were saying, though, 'cos there's a voice-over, probably by Mikey here, that he'll swap you for your diamonds.'

'That right?' said Mace.

Pylon found the right key, unsnapped the lock. 'I didn't tell Oumou. I thought it premature.'

'Good,' said Mace, rubbing the pain in his calf. 'How's she?'

'In a bad way. Very cut up. I was you, I'd phone her, like now' – offering Mace his cellphone.

Mace took it. 'I thought I would die here. Lie there dying, all shot up by that Mikey is what Sheemina February wanted. Him and me going out together. What the hell's her case? What's she think she's playing at?'

Pylon shrugged. 'Search me. We could go'n ask her. After you've done the ET phone home bit.' He started up the stairs, paused. 'Yeah, another thing. Gonz phoned.'

'To say what?'

'The case is adjourned.'

'For how long?'

'No idea. How long's a piece of string.'

'He's a good man, Gonz.'

Pylon came down a step. 'Only adjourned, Mace. Postponed. Stuff like that bounces back.'

Sheemina February agreed to meet them at the café in the Gardens. She didn't ask about Mikey Rheeder or even sound surprised to hear from Mace.

'A hard bitch,' Mace said to Pylon, 'that Mikey Rheeder was thinking of setting her up. For a price no doubt. Saw himself getting diamonds and a payout on her. Silly bugger. Probably she knew this. Realised Mikey was on the take, thought here's a solution.'

Sheemina February was waiting when they walked in, a filter coffee before her, untouched.

Mace and Pylon sat down, ordered the same. Mace put the gun on the table. 'Didn't work out as you wanted.'

She shrugged, barely moving her shoulders. 'You lived up to my expectations: the man who always shoots first. Who I over-estimated was Mikey.'

Pylon covered the pistol with a serviette, shoved it towards her.

'You can keep it,' she said. 'As a souvenir.'

'What shit are you playing?' said Mace.

Sheemina February took a sip of coffee, leaving the outline of her lipstick on the rim of the cup. 'I'll tell you, Mr Bishop. Although I am disappointed in you and Mr Buso that you haven't realised. But maybe it was routine for people like you? Maybe you weren't bothered. You especially, Mr Bishop. Unable to even recognise me. That's how much it all meant. Minor stuff. Waste and discard.' She smiled at them, Mace seeing no humour in her Nordic eyes.

'That sidekick of yours killed Mo, didn't he? You were setting him up. Wanted us both dead in the cellar?'

'Mr Bishop, you asked a question, I'm trying to answer it.'

'Jesus,' said Mace, 'what's with you?'

Sheemina February pushed away the cup of coffee. 'Can I talk?'

'Yeah,' said Mace. 'Talk. Amuse us.'

'Oh, it'll amuse you,' said Sheemina February, 'if you've got the imagination.'

Mace was about to come in again, Pylon put a restraining hand on his arm.

'Thank you, Mr Buso,' she said. And paused once more, looking from one to the other. 'This is about a young girl. Eighteen, just matriculated. Idealistic. An activist. Saw the inside of a prison for the first time when she was sixteen. Used to teargas. Used to throwing stones. Even used to the sound of gunfire. And deaths. She's been to the funerals of her friends, people as young as she is.

'Imagine this young girl going north, hitching rides in trucks, walking through the bush across borders until she gets to the camps. Membesh, the camp where freedom fighters train. What she wants is to learn to shoot guns, and go back to the war.

'What happens to her is nobody believes her story. Nobody believes that she has been travelling for a month. Alone. That some nights she slept in ditches, that some nights she was too scared to sleep. A young girl, alone? Impossible. All the way from Cape Town to Lusaka? Forget it. She is called a spy. She is put in a room, tied to a chair, her hands flat on the table. Two young men come in. They ask her questions, the same questions she has been asked before. She gives the same answers as always. They say they do not believe her. That she must tell them the truth. It is the truth, she says. They explain what is going to happen. They show her the mallet. She is crying, through her sobs she tells them she has told the truth. They flip a coin. Best of three, heads wins.'

She looked at Mace, the white of her teeth lightly pressing on the purple of her lips.

'You won, Mr Bishop. You called heads.'

Twenty years ago the times were paranoid, Mace thought. Shit happened. He kept her stare, didn't say a word.

'Should I tell you what happened to the young girl afterwards?' She held up her gloved hand. 'And I don't mean this, this disfigurement.' She lowered her hand. 'Or is that too shameful for the ears of heroes, what happened to your victims?' Sheemina February glanced from Mace to Pylon. 'Yes? No? Yes, let me tell you. The young girl was raped by the leaders. Not once. Not twice. Every day for months. Because you would not believe her.'

Sheemina February got up from the table. Seemed about to add something else but didn't. Might have had the edge of a smile on her lips but Mace wasn't sure. She pushed in the chair, walked away. At the door turned back to face them. 'I wasn't going to mention this, boys, but perhaps you should know that I know about the diamonds.'

They watched Sheemina February in her long black coat, black gloves, pause outside to put up an umbrella. She didn't look round, headed off through the Company Gardens, beneath the dripping trees.

When she was out of sight Pylon said, 'That's bad. About the diamonds.'

'No question.'

They stared into the grey morning, drank their weak Americanos. Pylon finished his, wiped his hand across the back of his mouth. 'You believe that story of her's?'

Mace pocketed the pistol, said, 'Probably not. Nobody did then. Why should we now?'

Mike Nicol was born in Cape Town, where is is a full-time author of fiction and non-fiction. His previous novels have been published by Bloomsbury in the United Kingdom, and by Knopf in the United States. He is currently at work on *Black Heart*, third in The Revenge Trilogy.

Chapter 9 Silicon   328

Chapter 10 Germanium, Tin and Lead   367

Chapter 11 Nitrogen   406

Chapter 15   Sulfur **645**

Chapter 16   Selenium, Tellurium and Polonium **747**

Chapter 22   Vanadium, Niobium and Tantalum   976

Chapter 23   Chromium, Molybdenum and Tungsten   1002

Chapter 24   Manganese, Technetium and Rhenium   1040

Chapter 25   Iron, Ruthenium and Osmium   1070

Chapter 26   Cobalt, Rhodium and Iridium   1113

Preface to the Second Edition

When this book first appeared in 1984 it rapidly established itself as one of the foremost textbooks and references on the subject. It was enthusiastically adopted by both students and teachers and has already been translated into several European and Asian languages. The novel features which it adopted (see Preface to the First Edition) were clearly much appreciated and we have been pressed for some time now to bring out a second edition. Accordingly we have completely revised and updated the text and have incorporated over 2000 new literature references to work which has appeared since the first edition was published. In addition, innumerable modifications and extensions incorporating recent advances have been made throughout the text and, indeed, no single page has been left unaltered. However, by judicious editing we have ensured that all the features which made the first edition so attractive to its readers have been retained.

The main plan of the book has been left unchanged except that the general section on organometallic chemistry has been removed from Chapter 8 (Carbon) and has been incorporated, together with a summary of other aspects of coordination chemistry, in a restyled Chapter 19. However, the chemistry of even the simplest elements has been considerably enriched during the past few years, sometimes by quite dramatic advances. Thus the chemistry of the alkali metals has a complexity that was undreamt of one or two decades ago and lithium, for example, is now known in at least 20 coordination geometries having coordination numbers from 1 to 12. Compounds of alkali metal *anions* and even electrides are known. Likewise, there is expanding interest in the organometallic chemistry of the heavier congeners of magnesium, particularly those with bulky ligands. Boron continues to amaze and confound, and its cluster chemistry continues to expand, as does sulfur–nitrogen chemistry, heteropolyacid chemistry, bioinorganic aspects of the chemistry of many of the elements, lower-valent lanthanide element chemistry, and so on through each of the chapters, up to the synthesis and characterization of the heaviest trans-actinide element, $Z = 112$. It is salutory to reflect that there are now 49 more elements known than the 63 known to Mendeleev when he devised the periodic table of the elements.

A further indication of the rapid advances that have occurred in the chemistry of the elements during the past 15 years can be gauged from the several completely new sections which have been added to review work in what were previously both nonexistent and unsuspected areas. These include (a) coordination compounds of dihapto-dihydrogen, (b) the fullerenes and their many derivatives, (c) the metcars, and (d) high-temperature oxide superconductors.

We hope that this new edition of *Chemistry of the Elements* will continue to stimulate and inform its readers, and that they will experience something of the excitement and fascination which we ourselves feel for this burgeoning subject. We should also like to thank our many correspondents who have kept us informed of their work and the School of Chemistry in the University of Leeds for providing us with facilities.

N. N. Greenwood
A. Earnshaw
August, 1997

Preface to the First Edition

IN this book we have tried to give a balanced, coherent and comprehensive account of the chemistry of the elements for both undergraduate and postgraduate students. This crucial central area of chemistry is full of ingenious experiments, intriguing compounds and exciting new discoveries. We have specifically avoided the term *inorganic chemistry* since this emphasizes an outmoded view of chemistry which is no longer appropriate in the closing decades of the 20th century. Accordingly, we deal not only with inorganic chemistry but also with those aspects which might be called analytical, theoretical, industrial, organometallic, bio-inorganic or any other of the numerous branches of the subject currently in vogue.

We make no apology for giving pride of place to the phenomena of chemistry and to the factual basis of the subject. Of course the chemistry of the elements is discussed within the context of an underlying theoretical framework that gives cohesion and structure to the text, but at all times it is the chemical chemistry that is emphasized. There are several reasons for this. First, theories change whereas facts do so less often — a greater permanency and value therefore attaches to a treatment based on a knowledge and understanding of the factual basis of the subject. We recognize, of course, that though the facts may not change dramatically, their significance frequently does. It is therefore important to learn how to assess observations and to analyse information reliably. Numerous examples are provided throughout the text. Moreover, it is scientifically unsound to present a theory and then describe experiments which purport to prove it. It is essential to distinguish between facts and theories and to recognize that, by their nature, theories are ephemeral and continually changing. Science advances by removing error, not by establishing truth, and no amount of experimentation can "prove" a theory, only that the theory is consistent with the facts as known *so far*. (At a more subtle level we also recognize that all facts are theory-laden.)

It is also important to realize that chemistry is not a static body of knowledge as defined by the contents of a textbook. Chemistry came from somewhere and is at present heading in various specific directions. It is a living self-stimulating discipline, and we have tried to transmit this sense of growth and excitement by reference to the historical development of the subject when appropriate. The chemistry of the elements is presented in a logical and academically consistent way but is interspersed with additional material which illuminates, exemplifies, extends or otherwise enhances the chemistry being discussed.

Chemistry is a human activity and its results have a substantial impact on our daily lives. However, we have not allowed ourselves to become obsessed by "relevance". Today's relevance is tomorrow's obsolescence. On the other hand, it would be obtuse in the modern world not to recognize that chemistry, in addition to being academically stimulating and aesthetically satisfying, is frequently also useful. This gives added point to much of the chemistry of the elements and indeed a great deal of that chemistry has been specifically developed because of society's needs. To many this is one of the most attractive aspects of the subject — its potential usefulness. We therefore wrote to over 500 chemically based firms throughout the world asking for information about the chemicals they manufactured or used, in what quantities and for what purposes. This produced an immense wealth of technical information which has proved to be an invaluable resource in discussing the chemistry of the elements. Our own experience as teachers had already alerted us to the difficulty of acquiring such topical information and we have incorporated much of this material where appropriate throughout the text. We believe it is important to know whether a given compound was made perhaps once in milligram amounts, or is produced annually in tonne quantities, and for what purpose.

In a textbook devoted to the chemistry of the elements it seemed logical to begin with such questions as: where do the elements come from, how were they made, why do they have their observed terrestrial abundances, what determines their atomic weights, and so on. Such questions, through usually ignored in textbooks and certainly difficult to answer, are ones which are currently being actively pursued, and some tentative answers and suggestions are given in the opening chapter. This followed by a brief description of chemical periodicity and the periodic table before the chemistry of the individual elements and their group relationships are discussed on a systematic basis.

We have been much encouraged by the careful assessment and comments on individual chapters by numerous colleagues not only throughout the U.K. but also in Australia, Canada, Denmark, the Federal Republic of Germany, Japan, the U.S.A and several other countries. We believe that this new approach will be widely welcomed as a basis for discussing the very diverse behaviour of the chemical elements and their compounds.

It is a pleasure to record our gratitude to the staff of the Edward Boyle Library in the University of Leeds for their unfailing help over many years during the writing of this book. We should also like to express our deep appreciation to Mrs Jean Thomas for her perseverance and outstanding skill in preparing the manuscript for the publishers. Without her generous help and the understanding of our families this work could not have been completed.

N. N. GREENWOOD
A. EARNSHAW

1

Origin of the Elements.
Isotopes and Atomic Weights

1.1 Introduction

This book presents a unified treatment of the chemistry of the elements. At present 112 elements are known, though not all occur in nature: of the 92 elements from hydrogen to uranium all except technetium and promethium are found on earth and technetium has been detected in some stars. To these elements a further 20 have been added by artificial nuclear syntheses in the laboratory. Why are there only 90 elements in nature? Why do they have their observed abundances and why do their individual isotopes occur with the particular relative abundances observed? Indeed, we must also ask to what extent these isotopic abundances commonly vary in nature, thus causing variability in atomic weights and possibly jeopardizing the classical means of determining chemical composition and structure by chemical analysis.

Theories abound, and it is important at all times to distinguish carefully between what has been experimentally established, what is a useful model for suggesting further experiments, and what is a currently acceptable theory which interprets the known facts. The tentative nature of our knowledge is perhaps nowhere more evident than in the first few sections of this chapter dealing with the origin of the chemical elements and their present isotopic composition. This is not surprising, for it is only in the last few decades that progress in this enormous enterprise has been made possible by discoveries in nuclear physics, astrophysics, relativity and quantum theory.

1.2 Origin of the Universe

At present, the most widely accepted theory for the origin and evolution of the universe to its present form is the "hot big bang".[1] It is supposed that all the matter in the universe

---

[1] J. SILK, *The Big Bang: The Creation and Evolution of the Universe*, 2nd edn., W. H. Freeman, New York, 1989, 485 pp. J. D. BARROW and J. SILK, *The Left Hand of Creation: The Origin and Evolution of the Expanding Universe*, Heinemann, London, 1984, 256 pp. E. W. KOLB and M. S. TURNER, *The Early Universe*, Addison-Wesley, Redwood City, CA, 1990, 547 pp.

was once contained in a primeval nucleus of immense density ($\sim 10^{96}$ g cm^{-3}) and temperature ($\sim 10^{32}$ K) which, for some reason, exploded and distributed radiation and matter uniformly throughout space. As the universe expanded it cooled; this allowed the four main types of force to become progressively differentiated, and permitted the formation of various types of particle to occur. Nothing scientific can be said about the conditions obtaining at times shorter than the Planck time, t_P $[(Gh/c^5)^{1/2} = 1.33 \times 10^{-43}$ s] at which moment the forces of gravity and electromagnetism, and the weak and strong nuclear forces were all undifferentiated and equally powerful. At 10^{-43} s after the big bang ($T = 10^{31}$ K) gravity separated as a distinct force, and at 10^{-35} s (10^{28} K) the strong nuclear force separated from the still combined electro-weak force. These are, of course, inconceivably short times and unimaginably high temperatures: for example, it takes as long as 10^{-24} s for a photon (travelling at the speed of light) to traverse a distance equal to the diameter of an atomic nucleus. When a time interval of 10^{-10} s had elapsed from the big bang the temperature is calculated to have fallen to 10^{15} K and this enabled the electromagnetic and weak nuclear forces to separate. By 6×10^{-6} s (1.4×10^{12} K) protons and neutrons had been formed from quarks, and this was followed by stabilization of electrons. One second after the big bang, after a period of extensive particle–antiparticle annihilation to form electromagnetic photons, the universe was populated by particles which sound familiar to chemists — protons, neutrons and electrons.

Shortly thereafter, the strong nuclear force ensured that large numbers of protons and neutrons rapidly combined to form deuterium nuclei (p + n), then helium (2p + 2n). *The process of element building had begun.* During this small niche of cosmic history, from about 10–500 s after the big bang, the entire universe is thought to have behaved as a colossal homogeneous fusion reactor converting hydrogen into helium. Previously no helium nuclei could exist — the temperature was so high that the sea

of radiation would have immediately decomposed them back to protons and neutrons. Subsequently, the continuing expansion of the universe was such that the particle density was too low for these strong (but short-range) interactions to occur. Thus, within the time slot of about eight minutes, it has been calculated that about one-quarter of the mass of the universe was converted to helium nuclei and about three-quarters remained as hydrogen. Simultaneously, a minute 10^{-3}% was converted to deuterons and about 10^{-6}% to lithium nuclei. These remarkable predictions of the big bang cosmological theory are borne out by experimental observations. Wherever one looks in the universe — the oldest stars in our own galaxy, or the "more recent" stars in remote galaxies — the universal abundance of helium is about 25%. Even more remarkably, the expected concentration of deuterium has been detected in interstellar clouds. Yet, as we shall shortly see, stars can only destroy deuterium as soon as it is formed; they cannot create any appreciable equilibrium concentration of deuterium nuclei because of the high temperature of the stellar environment. The sole source of deuterium in the universe seems to be the big bang. At present no other cosmological theory can explain this observed ratio of H:He:D.

Two other features of the universe find ready interpretation in terms of the big bang theory. First, as observed originally by E. Hubble in 1929, the light received on earth from distant galaxies is shifted increasingly towards the red end of the spectrum as the distance of the source increases. This implies that the universe is continually expanding and, on certain assumptions, extrapolation backwards in time indicates that the big bang occurred some 15 billion years ago. Estimates from several other independent lines of evidence give reassuringly similar values for the age of the universe. Secondly, the theory convincingly explains (indeed predicted) the existence of an all-pervading isotropic cosmic black-body radiation. This radiation (which corresponds to a temperature of 2.735 ± 0.06 K according to the most recent measurements) was discovered in

1965 by A. A. Penzias and R. W. Wilson[2] and is seen as the dying remnants of the big bang. No other comological theory yet proposed is able to interpret all these diverse observations.

1.3 Abundances of the Elements in the Universe

Information on the abundances of at least some of the elements in the sun, stars, gaseous nebulae and the interstellar regions has been obtained from detailed spectroscopic analysis using various regions of the electromagnetic spectrum. This data can be supplemented by direct analysis of samples from the earth, from meteorites, and increasingly from comets, the moon, and the surfaces of other planets and satellites in the solar system. The results indicate extensive differentiation in the solar system and in some stars, but the overall picture is one of astonishing uniformity of composition. Hydrogen is by far the most abundant element in the universe, accounting for some 88.6% of all atoms (or nuclei). Helium is about eightfold less abundant (11.3%), but these two elements together account for over 99.9% of the atoms and nearly 99% of the mass of the universe. Clearly nucleosynthesis of the heavier elements from hydrogen and helium has not yet proceeded very far.

Various estimates of the universal abundances of the elements have been made and, although these sometimes differ in detail for particular elements, they rarely do so by more than a factor of 3 ($10^{0.5}$) on a scale that spans more than 12 orders of magnitude. Representative values are plotted in Fig. 1.1, which shows a number of features that must be explained by any satisfactory theory of the origin of the elements. For example:

(i) Abundances decrease approximately exponentially with increase in atomic mass number A until $A \sim 100$ (i.e. $Z \sim 42$); thereafter the decrease is more gradual and is sometimes masked by local fluctuations.

(ii) There is a pronounced peak between $Z = 23-28$ including V, Cr, Mn, Fe, Co and Ni, and rising to a maximum at Fe which is $\sim 10^3$ more abundant than expected from the general trend.

(iii) Deuterium (D), Li, Be and B are rare compared with the neighbouring H, He, C and N.

(iv) Among the lighter nuclei (up to Sc, $Z = 21$), those having an atomic mass number A divisible by 4 are more abundant than their neighbours, e.g. ^{16}O, ^{20}Ne, ^{24}Mg, ^{28}Si, ^{32}S, ^{36}Ar and ^{40}Ca (rule of G. Oddo, 1914).

(v) Atoms with A even are more abundant than those with A odd. (This is seen in Fig. 1.1 as an upward displacement of the curve for Z even, the exception at beryllium being due to the non-existence of $^{8}_{4}$Be, the isotope $^{9}_{4}$Be being the stable species.)

Two further features become apparent when abundances are plotted against A rather than Z:

(vi) Atoms of heavy elements tend to be neutron rich; heavy proton-rich nuclides are rare.

(vii) Double-peaked abundance maxima occur at $A = 80$, 90; $A = 130$, 138; and $A = 196$, 208 (see Fig. 1.5 on p. 11).

It is also necessary to explain the existence of naturally occurring radioactive elements whose half-lives (or those of their precursors) are substantially less than the presumed age of the universe.

As a result of extensive studies over the past four decades it is now possible to give a detailed and convincing explanation of the experimental abundance data summarized above. The historical sequence of events which led to our present

---

[2] R. W. WILSON, The cosmic microwave background radiation, pp. 113–33 in *Les Prix Nobel 1978*, Almqvist & Wiksell International, Stockholm 1979. A. A. PENZIAS, The origin of the elements, pp. 93–106 in *Les Prix Nobel 1978* (also in *Science* **105**, 549–54 (1979)).

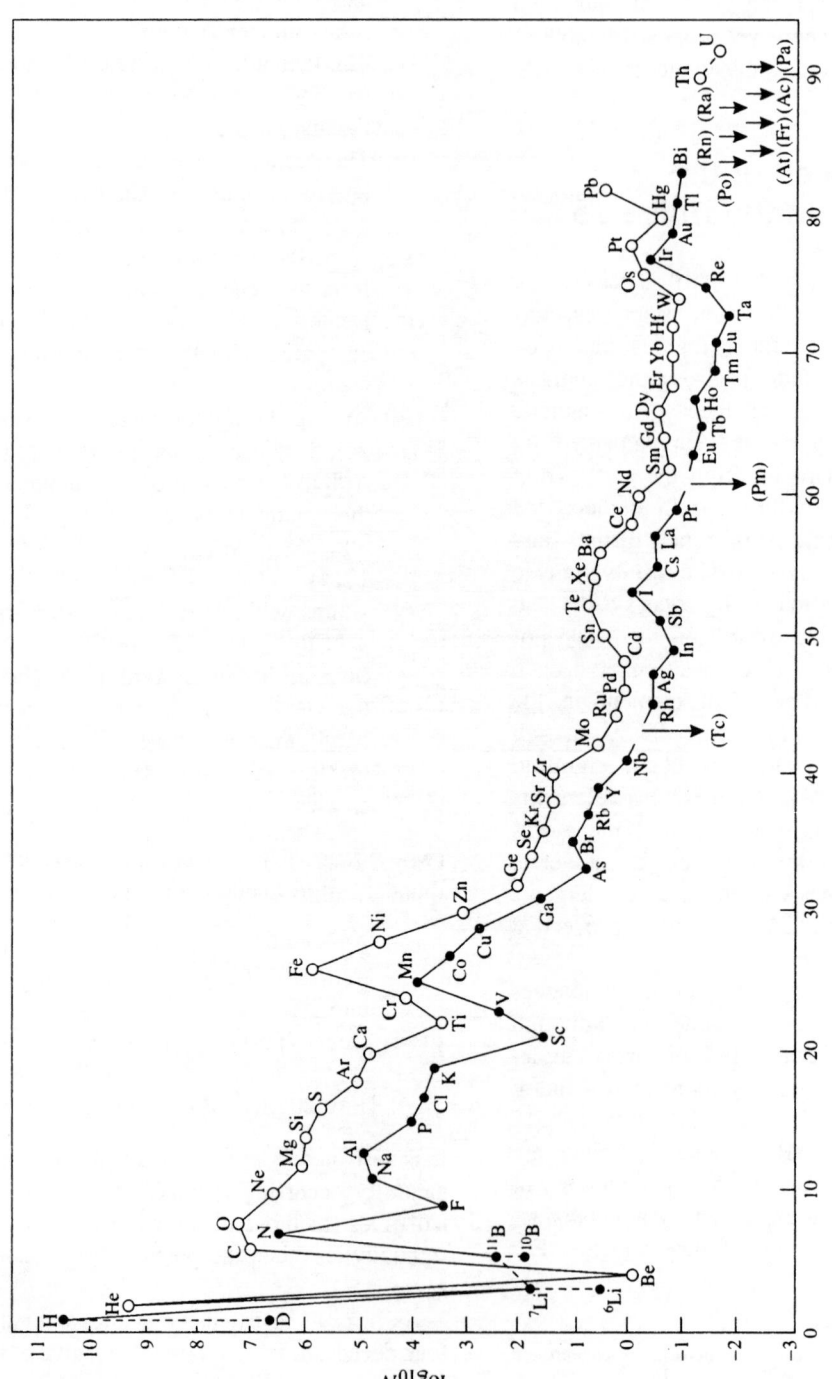

Figure 1.1   Cosmic abundances of the elements as a function of atomic number Z. Abundances are expressed as numbers of atoms per 10^6 atoms of Si and are plotted on a logarithmic scale. (From A. G. W. Cameron, *Space Sci. Rev.* **15**, 121–46 (1973), with some updating.)

understanding is briefly summarized in the Panel. As the genesis of the elements is closely linked with theories of stellar evolution, a short description of the various types of star is given in the next section and this is then followed by a fuller discussion of the various processes by which the chemical elements are synthesized.

1.4 Stellar Evolution and the Spectral Classes of Stars[3,4]

In broad outline stars are thought to evolve by the following sequence of events. First, there is self-gravitational accretion from the cooled primordial

hydrogen and helium. For a star the size and mean density of the sun (mass = 1.991×10^{30} kg = 1 M$_\odot$) this might take $\sim$20 y. This gravitational contraction releases heat energy, some of which is lost by radiation; however, the continued contraction results in a steady rise in temperature until at $\sim$10^7 K the core can sustain nuclear reactions. These reactions release enough additional energy to compensate for radiational losses and a temporary equilibrium or steady state is established.

When $\sim$10% of the hydrogen in the core has been consumed gravitational contraction again occurs until at a temperature of $\sim$2 $\times$ 10^8 K helium burning (fusion) can occur. This is followed by a similar depletion, contraction and temperature rise until nuclear reactions involving

[3] I. S. SHKLOVSKII, *Stars: Their Birth, Life and Death* (translated by R. B. Rodman), W. H. Freeman, San Francisco, 1978, 442 pp. M. HARWIT, *Astrophysical Concepts* (2nd edn) Springer Verlag, New York, 1988, 626 pp.

[4] D. H. CLARK and F. R. STEPHENSON, *The Historical Supernovae*, Pergamon Press, Oxford, 1977, 233 pp.

L. A. MARSCHALL, *The Supernova Story*, Plenum Press, New York, 1989, 276 pp. P. MURDIN, *End in Fire: The Supernova in the Large Magellanic Cloud*, Cambridge University Press, 1990, 253 pp.

Genesis of the Elements — Historical Landmarks

1890s	First systematic studies on the terrestrial abundances of the elements	F. W. Clarke; H. S. Washington and others
1905	Special relativity theory: $E = mc^2$	A. Einstein
1911	Nuclear model of the atom	E. Rutherford
1913	First observation of isotopes in a stable element (Ne)	J. J. Thompson
1919	First artificial transmutation of an element $^{14}_{7}$N$(\alpha,p)^{17}_{8}$O	E. Rutherford
1925–8	First abundance data on stars (spectroscopy)	Cecilia H. Payne; H. N. Russell
1929	First proposal of stellar nucleosynthesis by proton fusion to helium and heavier nuclides	R. D'E. Atkinson and F. G. Houtermans
1937	The "missing element" $Z = 43$ (technetium) synthesized by $^{99}_{42}$Mo$(d,n)^{99}_{43}$Tc	C. Perrier and E. G. Segré
1938	Catalytic CNO process independently proposed to assist nuclear synthesis in stars	H. A. Bethe; C. F. von Weizsäcker
1938	Uranium fission discovered experimentally	O. Hahn and F. Strassmann
1940	First transuranium element $^{239}_{93}$Np synthesized	E. M. McMillan and P. Abelson
1947	The last "missing element" $Z = 61$ (Pm) discovered among uranium fission products	J. A. Marinsky, L. E. Glendenin and C. D. Coryell
1948	Hot big-bang theory of expanding universe includes an (incorrect) theory of nucleogenesis	R. A. Alpher, H. A. Bethe and G. Gamow
1952–4	Helium burning as additional process for nucleogenesis	E. E. Salpeter; F. Hoyle
1954	Slow neutron absorption added to stellar reactions	A. G. W. Cameron
1955–7	Comprehensive theory of stellar synthesis of all elements in observed cosmic abundances	E. M. Burbidge, G. R. Burbidge, W. A. Fowler and F. Hoyle
1965	2.7 K radiation detected	A. P. Penzias and R. W. Wilson

still heavier nuclei ($Z = 8$–22) can occur at $\sim 10^9$ K. The time scale of these processes depends sensitively on the mass of the star, taking perhaps 10^{12} y for a star of mass 0.2 $M_\odot$, 10^{10} y for a star of 1 solar mass, 10^7 y for mass 10 $M_\odot$, and only 8×10^4 y for a star of 50 $M_\odot$; i.e. the more massive the star, the more rapidly it consumes its nuclear fuel. Further catastrophic changes may then occur which result in much of the stellar material being ejected into space, where it becomes incorporated together with further hydrogen and helium in the next generation of stars. It should be noted, however, that, as iron is at the maximum of the nuclear binding energy curve, only those elements up to iron ($Z = 26$) can be produced by exothermic processes of the type just considered, which occur automatically if the temperature rises sufficiently. Beyond iron, an input of energy is required to promote further element building.

The evidence on which this theory of stellar evolution is based comes not only from known nuclear reactions and the relativistic equivalence of mass and energy, but also from the spectroscopic analysis of the light reaching us from the stars. This leads to the spectral classification of stars, which is the cornerstone of modern experimental astrophysics. The spectroscopic analysis of starlight reveals much information about the chemical composition of stars — the identity of the elements present and their relative concentrations. In addition, the "red shift" or Doppler effect can be used to gauge the relative motions of the stars and their distance from the earth. More subtly, the surface temperature of stars can be determined from the spectral characteristics of their "blackbody" radiation, the higher the temperature the shorter the wavelength of maximum emission. Thus cooler stars appear red, and successively hotter stars appear progressively yellow, white, and blue. Differences in colour are also associated with differences in chemical composition as indicated in Table 1.1.

If the spectral classes (or temperatures) of stars are plotted against their absolute magnitudes (or luminosities) the resulting diagram shows several preferred regions into which most of the stars fall. Such diagrams were first made, independently, by E. Hertzsprung and H. N. Russell about 1913 and are now called HR diagrams (Fig. 1.2). More than 90% of all stars fall on a broad band called the main sequence, which covers the full range of spectral classes and magnitudes from the large, hot, massive O stars at the top to the small, dense, reddish M stars at the bottom. However, it should be emphasized that the terms "large" and "small" are purely relative since all stars within the main sequence are classified as dwarfs.

Table 1.1 Spectral classes of stars

Class[a]	Colour	Surface (T/K)	Spectral characterization	Examples
O	Blue	>25 000	Lines of ionized He and other elements; H lines weak	10 Lacertae
B	Blue-white	11 000–25 000	H and He prominent	Rigel, Spica
A	White	7500–11 000	H lines very strong	Sirius, Vega
F	Yellow-white	6000–7000	H weaker; lines of ionized metals becoming prominent	Canopus, Procyon
G	Yellow	5000–6000	Lines of ionized and neutral metals prominent (especially Ca)	Sun, Capella
K	Orange	3500–5000	Lines of neutral metals and band spectra of simple radicals (e.g. CN, OH, CH)	Arcturus, Aldebaran
M	Red	2000–3500	Band spectra of many simple compounds prominent (e.g. TiO)	Betelgeuse, Antares

[a]Further division of each class into 10 subclasses is possible, e.g. ... F8, F9, G0, G1, G2, ... The sun is G2 with a surface temperature of 5780 K. This curious alphabetical sequence of classes arose historically and can perhaps best be remembered by the mnemonic "Oh Be A Fine Girl (Guy), Kiss Me".

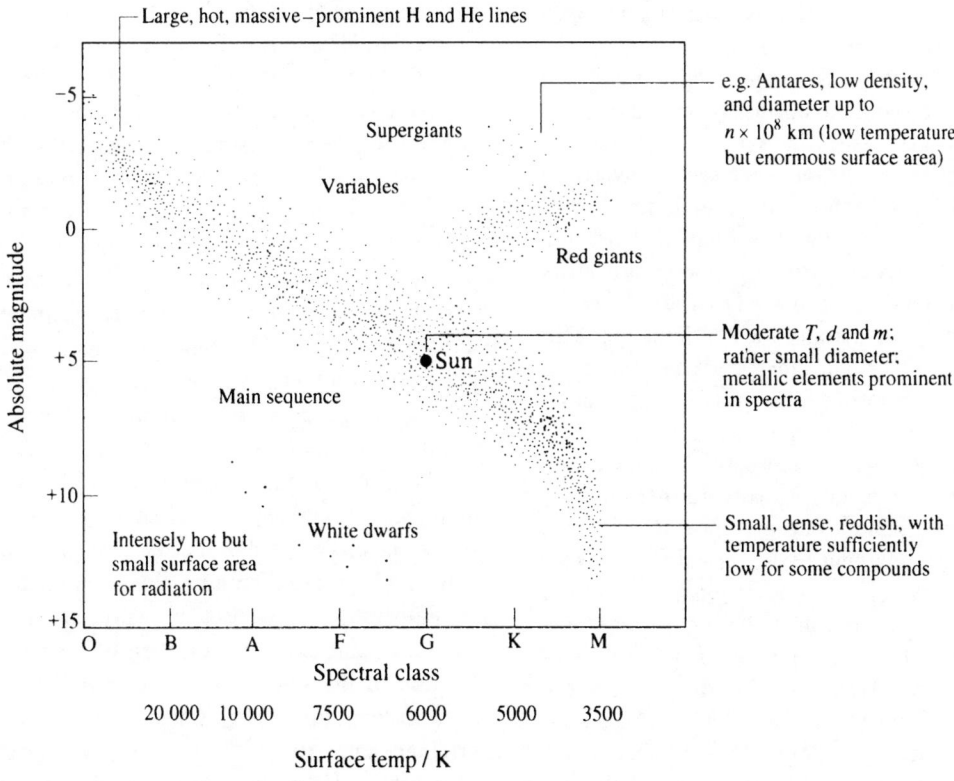

Figure 1.2   The Hertzsprung-Russell diagram for stars with known luminosities and spectra.

The next most numerous group of stars lie above and to the right of the main sequence and are called red giants. For example, Capella and the sun are both G-type stars yet Capella is 100 times more luminous than the sun; since they both have the same temperature it is concluded that Capella must have a radiating surface 100 times larger than the sun and thus has about 10 times its radius. Lying above the red giants are the supergiants such as Antares (Fig. 1.3), which has a surface temperature only half that of the sun but is 10 000 times more luminous: it is concluded that its radius is 100 times that of the sun. By contrast, the lower left-hand corner of the HR diagram is populated with relatively hot stars of low luminosity which implies that they are very small. These are the white dwarfs such as Sirius B which is only about the size of the earth though its mass is that of the sun: the implied density

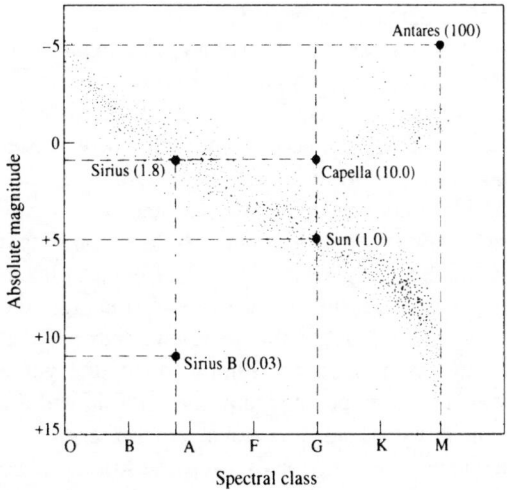

Figure 1.3   The comparison of various stars on the HR diagram. The number in parentheses indicates the approximate diameter of the star (sun = 1.0).

of $\sim5 \times 10^4$ g cm^{-3} indicates the extraordinarily compact nature of these bodies.

It is now possible to connect this description of stellar types with the discussion of the thermonuclear processes and the synthesis of the elements to be given in the next section. When a protostar begins to form by gravitational contraction from interstellar hydrogen and helium, its temperature rises until the temperature in its core can sustain proton burning (p. 9). A star of approximately the mass of the sun joins the main sequence at this point and spends perhaps 90% of its life there, losing little mass but generating colossal amounts of energy. Subsequent exhaustion of the hydrogen in the core (but not in the outer layers of the star) leads to further contraction to form a helium-burning core which forces much of the remaining hydrogen into a vast tenuous outer envelope — the star has become a red giant since its enormous radiating surface area can no longer be maintained at such a high temperature as previously despite the higher core temperature. Typical red giants have surface temperatures in the range 3500–5500 K; their luminosities are about 10^2–10^4 times that of the sun and diameters about 10–100 times that of the sun. Carbon burning (p. 10) can follow in older red giants followed by the α-process (p. 11) during its final demise to white dwarf status.

Many stars are in fact partners in a binary system of two stars revolving around each other. If, as frequently occurs, the two stars have different masses, the more massive one will evolve faster and reach the white-dwarf stage before its partner. Then, as the second star expands to become a red giant its extended atmosphere encompasses the neighbouring white dwarf and induces instabilities which result in an outburst of energy and transfer of matter to the more massive partner. During this process the luminosity of the white dwarf increases perhaps ten-thousandfold and the event is witnessed as a nova (since the preceding binary was previously invisible to the naked eye).

As we shall see in the description of the e-process and the γ-process (p. 12), even more spectacular instabilities can develop in larger main sequence stars. If the initial mass is greater than about 3.5 solar masses, current theories suggest that gravitational collapse may be so catastrophic that the system implodes beyond nuclear densities to become a black hole. For main sequence stars in the mass range 1.4–3.5 $M_{\odot}$, implosion probably halts at nuclear densities to give a rapidly rotating neutron star (density $\sim10^{14}$ g cm^{-3}) which may be observable as a pulsar emitting electromagnetic radiation over a wide range of frequencies in pulses at intervals of a fraction of a second. During this process of star implosion the sudden arrest of the collapsing core at nuclear densities yields an enormous temperature ($\sim10^{12}$ K) and high pressure which produces an outward-moving shock wave. This strikes the star's outer envelope with resulting rapid compression, a dramatic rise in temperature, the onset of many new nuclear reactions, and explosive ejection of a significant fraction of the star's mass. The overall result is a supernova up to 10^8 times as bright as the original star. At this point a single supernova is comparable in brightness to the whole of the rest of the galaxy in which it is formed, after which the brightness decays exponentially, often with a half-life of about two months. Supernovae, novae, and unstable variables from dying red giants are thus all candidates for the synthesis of heavier elements and their ejection into interstellar regions for subsequent processing in later generations of condensing main sequence stars such as the sun. It should be stressed, however, that these various theories of the origin of the chemical elements are all very recent and the detailed processes are by no means all fully understood. Since this is at present a very active area of research, some of the conclusions given in this chapter are correspondingly tentative, and will undoubtedly be modified and refined in the light of future experimental and theoretical studies. With this caveat we now turn to a more detailed description of the individual nuclear processes thought to be involved in the synthesis of the elements.

1.5 Synthesis of the Elements[5-9]

The following types of nuclear reactions have been proposed to account for the various types of stars and the observed abundances of the elements:

(i) Exothermic processes in stellar interiors: these include (successively) hydrogen burning, helium burning, carbon burning, the α-process, and the equilibrium or e-process.

(ii) Neutron capture processes: these include the s-process (slow neutron capture) and the r-process (rapid neutron capture).

(iii) Miscellaneous processes: these include the p-process (proton capture) and spallation within the stars, and the x-process which involves spallation (p. 14) by galactic cosmic rays in interstellar regions.

1.5.1 Hydrogen burning

When the temperature of a contracting mass of hydrogen and helium atoms reaches about 10^7 K, a sequence of thermonuclear reactions is possible of which the most important are as shown in Table 1.2.

The overall reaction thus converts 4 protons into 1 helium nucleus plus 2 positrons and 2 neutrinos:

$$4\,^1\text{H} \longrightarrow {}^4\text{He} + 2e^+ + 2\nu_e; \quad Q = 26.72 \text{ MeV}$$

[5] D. N. SCHRAMM and R. WAGONER, Element production in the early universe, *A. Rev. Nucl. Sci.* **27**, 37–74 (1977).

[6] E. M. BURBIDGE, G. R. BURBIDGE, W. A. FOWLER and F. HOYLE, Synthesis of the elements in stars, *Rev. Mod. Phys.* **29**, 547–650 (1957). This is the definitive review on which all later work has been based.

[7] L. H. ALLER, *The Abundance of the Elements*, Interscience, New York, 1961, 283 pp.

[7a] L. H. AHRENS (ed.), *Origin and Distribution of the Elements*, Pergamon Press, Oxford, 1979, 920 pp.

[8] R. J. TAYLOR, *The Origin of Chemical Elements*, Wykeham Publications, London, 1972, 169 pp.

[9] W. A. FOWLER, The quest for the origin of the elements (Nobel Lecture), *Angew. Chem. Int. Edn. Engl.* **23**, 645–71 (1984).

Table 1.2 Thermonucleaf consumption of protons

Reaction	Energy evolved, Q	Reaction time[a]
$^1\text{H} + {}^1\text{H} \rightarrow {}^2\text{H} + e^+ + \nu_e$	1.44 MeV	1.4×10^{10} y
$^2\text{H} + {}^1\text{H} \rightarrow {}^3\text{He} + \gamma$	5.49 MeV	0.6 s
$^3\text{He} + {}^3\text{He} \rightarrow {}^4\text{He} + 2\,^1\text{H}$	12.86 MeV	10^6 y

[a]The reaction time quoted is the time required for half the constituents involved to undergo reaction — this is sensitively dependent on both temperature and density; the figures given are appropriate for the centre of the sun, i.e. 1.3×10^7 K and 200 g cm^{-3}.
1 MeV per atom $\equiv 96.485 \times 10^6$ kJ mol^{-1}.

Making allowance for the energy carried away by the 2 neutrinos (2×0.25 MeV) this leaves a total of 26.22 MeV for radiation, i.e. 4.20 pJ per atom of helium or 2.53×10^9 kJ mol^{-1}. This vast release of energy arises mainly from the difference between the rest mass of the helium-4 nucleus and the 4 protons from which it was formed (0.028 atomic mass units). There are several other peripheral reactions between the protons, deuterons and ^{3}He nuclei, but these need not detain us. It should be noted, however, that only 0.7% of the mass is lost during this transformation, so that the star remains approximately constant in mass. For example, in the sun during each second, some 600×10^6 tonnes (600×10^9 kg) of hydrogen are processed into 595.5×10^6 tonnes of helium, the remaining 4.5×10^6 tonnes of matter being transformed into energy. This energy is released deep in the sun's interior as high-energy γ-rays which interact with stellar material and are gradually transformed into photons with longer wavelengths; these work their way to the surface taking perhaps 10^6 y to emerge.

In fact, the sun is not a first-generation main-sequence star since spectroscopic evidence shows the presence of many heavier elements thought to be formed in other types of stars and subsequently distributed throughout the galaxy for eventual accretion into later generations of main-sequence stars. In the presence of heavier elements, particularly carbon and nitrogen, a catalytic sequence of nuclear reactions aids the fusion of protons to helium (H. A. Bethe

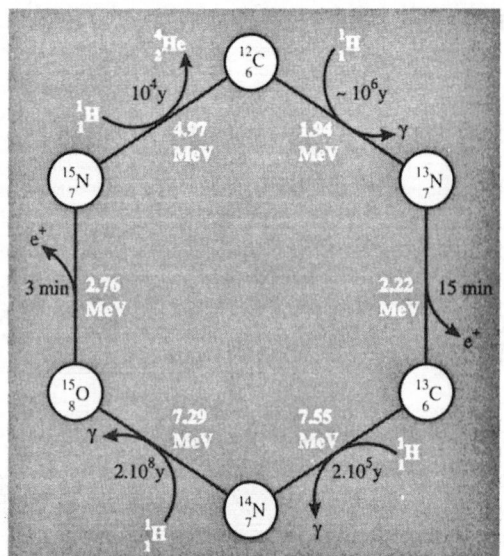

Figure 1.4 Catalytic C–N–O cycle for conversion of ^{1}H to ^{4}He. The times quoted are the calculated half-lives for the individual steps at 1.5×10^7 K.

and C. F. von Weizsäcker, 1938) (Fig. 1.4). The overall reaction is precisely as before with the evolution of 26.72 MeV, but the 2 neutrinos now carry away 0.7 and 1.0 MeV respectively, leaving 25.0 MeV (4.01 pJ) per cycle for radiation. The coulombic energy barriers in the C–N–O cycle are some 6–7 times greater than for the direct proton–proton reaction and hence the catalytic cycle does not predominate until about 1.6×10^7 K. In the sun, for example, it is estimated that about 10% of the energy comes from this process and most of the rest comes from the straightforward proton–proton reaction.

When approximately 10% of the hydrogen in a main-sequence star like the sun has been consumed in making helium, the outward thermal pressure of radiation is insufficient to counteract the gravitational attraction and a further stage of contraction ensues. During this process the helium concentrates in a dense central core ($\rho \sim 10^5$ g cm^{-3}) and the temperature rises to perhaps 2×10^8 K. This is sufficient to overcome the coulombic potential energy barriers surrounding the helium nuclei, and helium burning (fusion)

can occur. The hydrogen forms a vast tenuous envelope around this core with the result that the star evolves rapidly from the main sequence to become a red giant (p. 7). It is salutory to note that hydrogen burning in main-sequence stars has so far contributed an amount of helium to the universe which is only about 20% of that which was formed in the few minutes directly following the big bang (p. 2).

1.5.2 Helium burning and carbon burning

The main nuclear reactions occurring in helium burning are:

$$^4\text{He} + {^4\text{He}} \rightleftharpoons {^8\text{Be}}$$

and

$$^8\text{Be} + {^4\text{He}} \rightleftharpoons {^{12}\text{C}^*} \longrightarrow {^{12}\text{C}} + \gamma$$

The nucleus ^{8}Be is unstable to α-particle emission ($t_{1/2} \sim 2 \times 10^{-16}$ s) being 0.094 MeV less stable than its constituent helium nuclei; under the conditions obtaining in the core of a red giant the calculated equilibrium ratio of ^{8}Be to ^{4}He is $\sim 10^{-9}$. Though small, this enables the otherwise improbable 3-body collision to occur. It is noteworthy that, from consideration of stellar nucleogenesis, F. Hoyle predicted in 1954 that the nucleus of ^{12}C would have a radioactive excited state ^{12}C* 7.70 MeV above its ground state, some three years before this activity was observed experimentally at 7.653 MeV. Experiments also indicate that the energy difference $Q(^{12}\text{C}^* - 3\,^4\text{He})$ is 0.373 MeV, thus leading to the overall reaction energy

$$3\,^4\text{He} \longrightarrow {^{12}\text{C}} + \gamma; \quad Q = 7.281 \text{ MeV}$$

Further helium-burning reactions can now follow during which even heavier nuclei are synthesized:

$$^{12}\text{C} + {^4\text{He}} \longrightarrow {^{16}\text{O}} + \gamma; \quad Q = 7.148 \text{ MeV}$$

$$^{16}\text{O} + {^4\text{He}} \longrightarrow {^{20}\text{Ne}} + \gamma; \quad Q = 4.75 \text{ MeV}$$

$$^{20}\text{Ne} + {^4\text{He}} \longrightarrow {^{24}\text{Mg}} + \gamma; \quad Q = 9.31 \text{ MeV}$$

These reactions result in the exhaustion of helium previously produced in the hydrogen-burning process and an inner core of carbon, oxygen and neon develops which eventually undergoes gravitational contraction and heating as before. At a temperature of $\sim 5 \times 10^8$ K carbon burning becomes possible in addition to other processes which must be considered. Thus, ageing red giant stars are now thought to be capable of generating a carbon-rich nuclear reactor core at densities of the order of 10^4 g cm^{-3}. Typical initial reactions would be:

$$^{12}C + {}^{12}C \longrightarrow {}^{24}Mg + \gamma; \qquad Q = 13.85 \text{ MeV}$$

$$^{12}C + {}^{12}C \longrightarrow {}^{23}Na + {}^{1}H; \qquad Q = 2.23 \text{ MeV}$$

$$^{12}C + {}^{12}C \longrightarrow {}^{20}Ne + {}^{4}He; \qquad Q = 4.62 \text{ MeV}$$

The time scale of such reactions is calculated to be $\sim 10^5$ y at 6×10^8 K and ~ 1 y at 8.5×10^8 K. It will be noticed that hydrogen and helium nuclei are regenerated in these processes and numerous subsequent reactions become possible, generating numerous nuclides in this mass range.

1.5.3 The α-process

The evolution of a star after it leaves the red-giant phase depends to some extent on its mass. If it is not more than about 1.4 $M_\odot$ it may contract appreciably again and then enter an oscillatory phase of its life before becoming a white dwarf (p. 7). When core contraction following helium and carbon depletion raises the temperature above $\sim 10^9$ K the γ-rays in the stellar assembly become sufficiently energetic to promote the (endothermic) reaction $^{20}Ne(\gamma,\alpha)^{16}O$. The α-particle released can penetrate the coulomb barrier of other neon nuclei to form ^{24}Mg in a strongly exothermic reaction:

$$^{20}Ne + \gamma \longrightarrow {}^{16}O + {}^4He;$$
$$Q = -4.75 \text{ MeV}$$
$$^{20}Ne + {}^4He \longrightarrow {}^{24}Mg + \gamma;$$
$$Q = +9.31 \text{ MeV}$$
i.e. $\quad 2{}^{20}Ne \longrightarrow {}^{16}O + {}^{24}Mg + \gamma;$
$$Q = +4.56 \text{ MeV}$$

Some of the released α-particles can also scour out ^{12}C to give more ^{16}O and the ^{24}Mg formed can react further by $^{24}Mg(\alpha,\gamma)^{28}Si$. Likewise for ^{32}S, ^{36}Ar and ^{40}Ca. It is this process that is considered to be responsible for building up the decreasing proportion of these so-called α-particle nuclei (Figs. 1.1 and 1.5). The relevant numerical data (including for comparison those for ^{20}Ne which is produced in helium and carbon burning) are as follows:

Nuclide	(^{20}Ne)	^{24}Mg	^{28}Si	^{32}S	^{36}Ar	^{40}Ca	^{44}Ca	^{48}Ti
Q_α/MeV	(9.31)	10.00	6.94	6.66	7.04	5.28	9.40	9.32
Relative abundance (as observed)	(8.4)	0.78	1.00	0.39	0.14	0.052	0.0011	0.0019

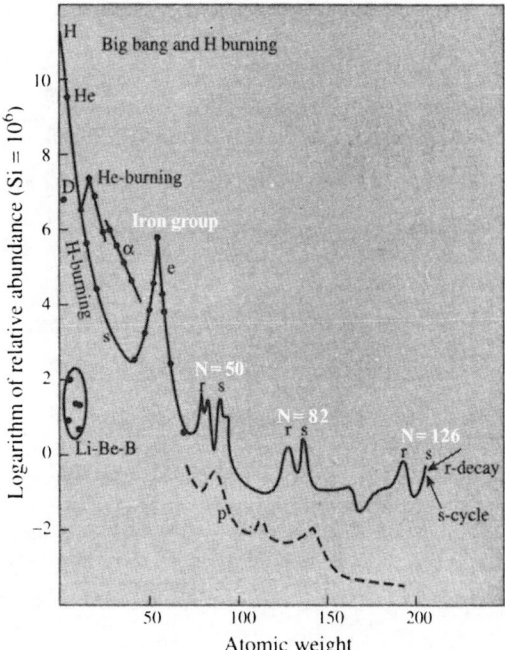

Figure 1.5   Schematic representation of the main features of the curve of cosmic abundances shown in Fig. 1.1, labelled according to the various stellar reactions considered to be responsible for the synthesis of the elements. (After E. M. Burbidge *et al.*[6].)

In a sense the α-process resembles helium burning but is distinguished from it by the quite different source of the α-particles consumed. The straightforward α-process stops at ^{40}Ca since ^{44}Ti* is unstable to electron-capture decay. Hence (and including atomic numbers Z as subscripts for clarity):

$$^{40}_{20}\text{Ca} + ^4_2\text{He} \longrightarrow ^{44}_{22}\text{Ti}^* + \gamma$$

$$^{44}_{22}\text{Ti}^* + e^- \longrightarrow ^{44}_{21}\text{Sc}^* + \nu_+;$$
$$t_{1/2} \sim 49 \text{ y}$$

$$^{44}_{21}\text{Sc}^* \longrightarrow ^{44}_{20}\text{Ca} + \beta^+ + \nu_+;$$
$$t_{1/2} \ 3.93 \text{ h}$$

Then $\ ^{44}_{20}\text{Ca} + ^4_2\text{He} \longrightarrow ^{48}_{22}\text{Ti} + \gamma$

The total time spent by a star in this α-phase may be $\sim 10^2 - 10^4$ y (Fig. 1.6).

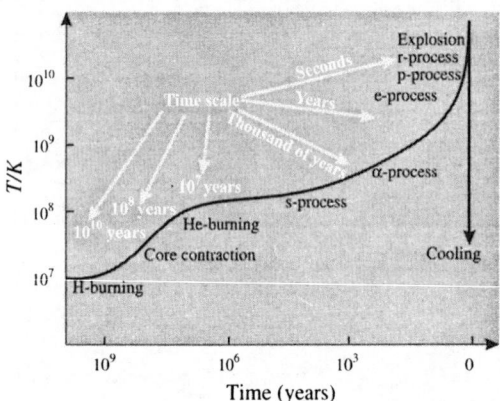

Figure 1.6   The time-scales of the various processes of element synthesis in stars. The curve gives the central temperature as a function of time for a star of about one solar mass. The curve is schematic.[6]

1.5.4 The e-process (equilibrium process)

More massive stars in the upper part of the main-sequence diagram (i.e. stars with masses in the range $1.4-3.5$ M$_\odot$) have a somewhat different history to that considered in the preceding sections. We have seen (p. 6) that such stars consume their hydrogen much more rapidly than do smaller stars and hence spend less time in the main sequence. Helium reactions begin in their interiors long before the hydrogen is exhausted, and in the middle part of their life they may expand only slightly. Eventually they become unstable and explode violently, emitting enormous amounts of material into interstellar space. Such explosions are seen on earth as supernovae, perhaps 10 000 times more luminous than ordinary novae. In the seconds (or minutes) preceding this catastrophic outburst, at temperatures above $\sim 3 \times 10^9$ K, many types of nuclear reactions can occur in great profusion, e.g. (γ,α), (γ,p), (γ,n), (α,n), (p,γ), (n,γ), (p,n), etc. (Fig. 1.6). This enables numerous interconversions to occur with the rapid establishment of a statistical equilibrium between the various nuclei and the free protons and neutrons. This is believed to explain the cosmic abundances of elements from $_{22}$Ti to $_{29}$Cu. Specifically, since $^{56}_{26}$Fe is at the peak of the nuclear binding-energy curve, this element is considerably more abundant than those further removed from the most stable state.

1.5.5 The s- and r-processes (slow and rapid neutron absorption)

Slow neutron capture with emission of γ-rays is thought to be responsible for synthesizing most of the isotopes in the mass range $A = 63-209$ and also the majority of non-α-process nuclei in the range $A = 23-46$. These processes probably occur in pulsating red giants over a time span of $\sim 10^7$ y, and production loops for individual isotopes are typically in the range $10^2 - 10^5$ y. Several stellar neutron sources have been proposed, but the most likely candidates are the exothermic reactions ^{13}C$(\alpha,n)^{16}$O (2.20 MeV) and ^{21}Ne$(\alpha,n)^{24}$Mg (2.58 MeV). In both cases the target nuclei ($A = 4n + 1$) would be produced by a (p,γ) reaction on the more stable $4n$ nucleus followed by positron emission.

Because of the long time scale involved in the s-process, unstable nuclides formed by (n,γ) reactions have time to decay subsequently by β^- decay (electron emission). The crucial factor in determining the relative abundance of elements formed by this process is thus the neutron capture cross-section of the precursor nuclide. In this way the process provides an ingenious explanation of the local peaks in abundance that occur near $A = 90$, 138 and 208, since these occur near unusually stable nuclei (neutron "magic numbers" 50, 82 and 126) which have very low capture cross-sections (Fig. 1.5). Their concentration therefore builds up by resisting further reaction. In this way the relatively high abundances of specific isotopes such as $^{89}_{39}Y$ and $^{90}_{40}Zr$, $^{138}_{56}Ba$ and $^{140}_{58}Ce$, $^{208}_{82}Pb$ and $^{209}_{83}Bi$ can be understood.

In contrast to the more leisured processes considered in preceding paragraphs, conditions can arise (e.g. at $\sim 10^9$ K in supernovae outbursts) where many neutrons are rapidly added successively to a nucleus before subsequent β-decay becomes possible. The time scale for the r-process is envisaged as $\sim 0.01 - 10$ s, so that, for example, some 200 neutrons might be added to an iron nucleus in $10 - 100$ s. Only when β^- instability of the excessively neutron-rich product nuclei becomes extreme and the cross-section for further neutron absorption diminishes near the "magic numbers", does a cascade of some $8 - 10$ β^- emissions bring the product back into the region of stable isotopes. This gives a convincing interpretation of the local abundance peaks near $A = 80$, 130 and 194, i.e. some $8 - 10$ mass units below the nuclides associated with the s-process maxima (Fig. 1.5). It has also been suggested that neutron-rich isotopes of several of the lighter elements might also be the products of an r-process, e.g. ^{36}S, ^{46}Ca, ^{48}Ca and perhaps ^{47}Ti, ^{49}Ti and ^{50}Ti. These isotopes, though not as abundant as others of these elements, nevertheless do exist as stable species and cannot be so readily synthesized by other potential routes.

The problem of the existence of the heavy elements must also be considered. The short half-lives of all isotopes of technetium and promethium adequately accounts for their absence on earth. However, no element with atomic number greater than $_{83}Bi$ has any stable isotope. Many of these (notably $_{84}Po$, $_{85}At$, $_{86}Rn$, $_{87}Fr$, $_{88}Ra$, $_{89}Ac$ and $_{91}Pa$) can be

understood on the basis of secular equilibria with radioactive precursors, and their relative concentrations are determined by the various half-lives of the isotopes in the radioactive series which produce them. The problem then devolves on explaining the cosmic presence of thorium and uranium, the longest lived of whose isotopes are ^{232}Th ($t_{1/2}$ 1.4×10^{10} y), ^{238}U ($t_{1/2}$ 4.5×10^9 y) and ^{235}U ($t_{1/2}$ 7.0×10^8 y). The half-life of thorium is commensurate with the age of the universe ($\sim 1.5 \times 10^{10}$ y) and so causes no difficulty. If all the present terrestrial uranium was produced by an r-process in a single supernova event then this occurred 6.6×10^9 y ago (p. 1257). If, as seems more probable, many supernovae contributed to this process, then such events, distributed uniformly in time, must have started $\sim 10^{10}$ y ago. In either case the uranium appears to have been formed long before the formation of the solar system $(4.6 - 5.0) \times 10^9$ y ago. More recent considerations of the formation and decay of ^{232}Th, ^{235}U and ^{238}U suggest that our own galaxy is $(1.2 - 2.0) \times 10^{10}$ y old.

1.5.6 The p-process (proton capture)

Proton capture processes by heavy nuclei have already been briefly mentioned in several of the preceding sections. The (p,γ) reaction can also be invoked to explain the presence of a number of proton-rich isotopes of lower abundance than those of nearby normal and neutron-rich isotopes (Fig. 1.5). Such isotopes would also result from expulsion of a neutron by a γ-ray, i.e. (γ,n). Such processes may again be associated with supernovae activity on a very short time scale. With the exceptions of ^{113}In and ^{115}Sn, all of the 36 isotopes thought to be produced in this way have even atomic mass numbers; the lightest is $^{74}_{34}Se$ and the heaviest $^{196}_{80}Hg$.

1.5.7 The x-process

One of the most obvious features of Figs. 1.1 and 1.5 is the very low cosmic abundance of the stable isotopes of lithium, beryllium and boron.[10] Paradoxically, the problem is not to explain why these abundances are so low but why these elements exist at all since their isotopes are bypassed by the normal chain of thermonuclear reactions described on the preceding pages. Again, deuterium and ^{3}He, though part of the hydrogen-burning process, are also virtually completely consumed by it, so that their existence in the universe, even at relatively low abundances, is very surprising. Moreover, even if these various isotopes were produced in stars, they would not survive the intense internal heat since their bonding energies imply that deuterium would be destroyed above 0.5×10^6 K, Li above 2×10^6 K, Be above 3.5×10^6 and B above 5×10^6. Deuterium and ^{3}He are absent from the spectra of almost all stars and are now generally thought to have been formed by nucleosynthesis during the last few seconds of the original big bang; their main agent of destruction is stellar processing.

It now seems likely that the 5 stable isotopes ^{6}Li, ^{7}Li, ^{9}Be, ^{10}B and ^{11}B are formed predominantly by spallation reactions (i.e. fragmentation) effected by galactic cosmic-ray bombardment (the x-process). Cosmic rays consist of a wide variety of atomic particles moving through the galaxy at relativistic velocities. Nuclei ranging from hydrogen to uranium have been detected in cosmic rays though ^{1}H and ^{4}He are by far the most abundant components [^{1}H: 500; ^{4}He: 40; all particles with atomic numbers from 3 to 9: 5; all particles with $Z \geq 10$: ~1]. However, there is a striking deviation from stellar abundances since Li, Be and B are vastly over abundant as are Sc, Ti, V and Cr (immediately preceding the abundance peak near iron). The simplest interpretation of these facts is that the (heavier) particles comprising cosmic rays, travelling as they do great distances in the galaxy, occasionally collide with atoms of the interstellar gas (predominantly ^{1}H and ^{4}He) and thereby fragment. This fragmentation, or spallation as it

is called, produces lighter nuclei from heavier ones. Conversely, high-speed ^{4}He particles may occasionally collide with interstellar iron-group elements and other heavy nuclei, thus inducing spallation and forming Li, Be and B (and possibly even some ^{2}H and ^{3}He), on the one hand, and elements in the range Sc–Cr, on the other. As we have seen, the lighter transition elements are also formed in various stellar processes, but the presence of elements in the mass range 6–12 suggest the need for a low-temperature low-density extra-stellar process. In addition to spallation, interstellar (p,α) reactions in the wake of supernova shock waves may contribute to the synthesis of boron isotopes:

$$^{13}C(p,\alpha)^{10}B \quad \text{and} \quad ^{14}N(p,\alpha)^{11}C \xrightarrow{\beta^+} {}^{11}B.$$

A further intriguing possibility has recently been mooted.[11] If the universe were not completely isotropic and uniform in density during the first few minutes after the big bang, then the high-density regions would have a greater concentration of protons than expected and the low-density regions would have more neutrons; this is because the diffusion of protons from high to low density regions would be inhibited by the presence of oppositely charged electrons whereas the electrically neutral neutrons can diffuse more readily. In the neutron-abundant lower-density regions certain neutron-rich species can then be synthesized. For example, in the homogeneous big bang, most of the ^{7}Li formed is rapidly destroyed by proton bombardment (^{7}Li + p → 2^4He) but in a neutron-rich region the radioactive isotope ^{8}Li* can be formed:

$$^7\text{Li} + \text{n} \longrightarrow {}^8\text{Li}^* \ (t_{1/2} \ 0.84\,\text{s} \longrightarrow \beta^- + 2^4\text{He})$$

If, before it decays, ^{8}Li* is struck by a prevalent ^{4}He nucleus then ^{11}B can be formed (^{8}Li* + ^{4}He → ^{11}B + n) and this will survive longer than in a proton-rich environment (^{11}B + p → 3^4He). Other neutron-rich species could also be synthesized and survive in greater numbers than would

---

[10] H. REEVES, Origin of the light elements, *A. Rev. Astron. Astrophys.* **12**, 437–69 (1974).

[11] K. CROSSWELL, *New Scientist,* 9 Nov. 1991, 42–8.

be possible with higher concentrations of protons, e.g.:

$$^7Li + {}^3H \longrightarrow {}^9Be + n$$
$$^9Be + {}^3H \longrightarrow {}^{11}B + n$$

The relative abundances of the various isotopes of the light elements Li, Be and B therefore depend to some extent on which detailed model of the big bang is adopted, and experimentally determined abundances may in time permit conclusions to be drawn as to the relative importance of these processes as compared to x-process spallation reactions.

In overall summary, using a variety of nuclear syntheses it is now possible to account for the presence of the 270 known stable isotopes of the elements up to $^{209}_{83}Bi$ and to understand, at least in broad outline, their relative concentrations in the universe. The tremendous number of hypothetically possible internuclear conversions and reactions makes detailed computation extremely difficult. Energy changes are readily calculated from the known relative atomic masses of the various nuclides, but the cross-sections (probabilities) of many of the reactions are unknown and this prevents precise calculation of reaction rates and equilibrium concentrations in the extreme conditions occurring even in stable stars. Conditions and reactions occurring during supernova outbursts are even more difficult to define precisely. However, it is clear that substantial progress has been made in the last few decades in interpreting the bewildering variety of isotopic abundances which comprise the elements used by chemists. The approximate constancy of the isotopic composition of the individual elements is a fortunate result of the quasi-steady-state conditions obtaining in the universe during the time required to form the solar system. It is tempting to speculate whether chemistry could ever have emerged as a quantitative science if the elements had had widely varying isotopic composition, since gravimetric analysis would then have been impossible and the great developments of the nineteenth century could hardly have occurred. Equally, it should no longer cause surprise that the atomic weights of the

elements are not necessarily always "constants of nature", and variations are to be expected, particularly among the lighter elements, which can have appreciable effects on physicochemical measurements and quantitative analysis.

1.6 Atomic Weights[12]

The concept of "atomic weight" or "mean relative atomic mass" is fundamental to the development of chemistry. Dalton originally supposed that all atoms of a given element had the same unalterable weight but, after the discovery of isotopes earlier this century, this property was transferred to them. Today the possibility of variable isotopic composition of an element (whether natural or artificially induced) precludes the possibility of defining *the* atomic weight of most elements, and the tendency nowadays is to define *an* atomic weight of an element as "the ratio of the average mass per atom of an element to one-twelfth of the mass of an atom of ^{12}C". It is important to stress that atomic weights (mean relative atomic masses) of the elements are dimensionless numbers (ratios) and therefore have no units.

Because of their central importance in chemistry, atomic weights have been continually refined and improved since the first tabulations by Dalton (1803–5). By 1808 Dalton had included 20 elements in his list and these results were substantially extended and improved by Berzelius during the following decades. An illustration of the dramatic and continuing improvement in accuracy and precision during the past 100 y is given in Table 1.3. In 1874 no atomic weight was quoted to better than one part in 200, but by 1903 33 elements had values quoted to one part in 10^3 and 2 of these (silver and

---

[12] N. N. Greenwood, Atomic weights, Ch. 8 in Part I, Vol. 1, Section C, of Kolthoff and Elving's *Treatise on Analytical Chemistry*, pp. 453–78, Interscience, New York, 1978. This gives a fuller account of the history and techniques of atomic weight determinations and their significance, and incorporates a full bibliographical list of Reports on Atomic Weights.

iodine) were quoted to 1 in 10^4. Today the majority of values are known to 1 in 10^4 and 26 elements have an accuracy exceeding 1 in 10^6. This improvement was first due to improved chemical methods, particularly between 1900 and 1935 when increasing use of fused silica ware and electric furnaces reduced the possibility of contamination. More recently the use of mass spectrometry has effected a further improvement in precision. Mass spectrometric data were first used in a confirmatory role in the 1935 table of atomic weights, and by 1938 mass spectrometric values were preferred to chemical determinations for hydrogen and osmium and to gas-density values for helium. In 1959 the atomic weight values of over 50 elements were still based on classical chemical methods, but by 1973 this number had dwindled to 9 (Ti, Ge, Se, Mo, Sn, Sb, Te, Hg and Tl) or to 10 if the coulometric determination for Zn is counted as chemical. The values for a further 8 elements were based on a judicious blend of chemical and mass-spectrometric data, but the values quoted for all other elements were based entirely on mass-spectrometric data.

Accurate atomic weight values do not automatically follow from precise measurements of relative atomic masses, however, since the relative abundance of the various isotopes must also be determined. That this can be a limiting factor is readily seen from Table 1.3: the value for praseodymium (which has only 1 stable naturally occurring isotope) has two more significant figures than the value for the neighbouring element cerium which has 4 such isotopes. In the twelve years since the first edition of this book was published the atomic weight values of no fewer than 55 elements have been improved, sometimes spectacularly, e.g. Ni from 58.69(1) to 58.6934(2).

1.6.1 Uncertainty in atomic weights

Numerical values for the atomic weights of the elements are now reviewed every 2 y by the Commission on Atomic Weights and Isotopic

Table 1.3 Evolution of atomic weight values for selected elements[a]; (the dates selected were chosen for the reasons given below)

Element	1873–5	1903	1925	1959	1961	1997	
H	1	1.008	1.008	1.0080	1.007 97	1.007 94(7)	gmr
C	12	12.00	12.000	12.011 15	12.011 15	12.0107(8)	g r
O	16	16.00	16.000	**16**	15.9994	15.9994(3)	g r
P	31	31.0	31.027	30.975	30.9738	30.973 761(2)	
Ti	50	48.1	48.1	47.90	47.90	47.867(1)	
Zn	65	65.4	65.38	65.38	65.37	65.39(2)	
Se	79	79.2	79.2	78.96	78.96	78.96(3)	
Ag	108	107.93	107.880	107.880	107.870	107.8682(2)	g
I	127	126.85	126.932	126.91	126.9044	126.90447(3)	
Ce	92	140.0	140.25	140.13	140.12	140.116(1)	g
Pr	—	140.5	140.92	140.92	140.907	140.907 65(2)	
Re	—	—	188.7[b]	186.22	186.22	186.207(1)	
Hg	200	200.0	200.61	200.61	200.59	200.59(2)	

[a] The annotations g, m and r appended to some values in the final column have the same meanings as those in the definitive table (facing inside front cover). The numbers in parentheses are the uncertainties in the last digit of the quoted value.
[b] The value for rhenium was first listed in 1929.
Note on dates:
    1874 Foundation of the American Chemical Society (64 elements listed).
    1903 First international table of atomic weights (78 elements listed).
    1925 Major review of table (83 elements listed).
    1959 Last table to be based on oxygen = 16 (83 elements listed).
    1961 Complete reassessment of data and revision to ^{12}C = 12 (83 elements).
    1997 Latest available IUPAC values (84 + 28 elements listed).

Abundances of IUPAC (the International Union of Pure and Applied Chemistry). Their most recent recommendations[13] are tabulated on the inside front fly sheet. From this it is clear that there is still a wide variation in the reliability of the data. The most accurately quoted value is that for fluorine which is known to better than 1 part in 38 million; the least accurate is for boron (1 part in 1500, i.e. 7 parts in 10^4). Apart from boron all values are reliable to better than 5 parts in 10^4 and the majority are reliable to better than 1 part in 10^4. For some elements (such as boron) the rather large uncertainty arises not because of experimental error, since the use of mass-spectrometric measurements has yielded results of very high precision, but because the natural variation in the relative abundance of the 2 isotopes ^{10}B and ^{11}B results in a range of values of at least ± 0.003 about the quoted value of 10.811. By contrast, there is no known variation in isotopic abundances for elements such as selenium and osmium, but calibrated mass-spectrometric data are not available, and the existence of 6 and 7 stable isotopes respectively for these elements makes high precision difficult to obtain: they are thus prime candidates for improvement.

Atomic weights are known most accurately for elements which have only 1 stable isotope; the relative atomic mass of this isotope can be determined to at least 1 ppm and there is no possibility of variability in nature. There are 20 such elements: Be, F, Na, Al, P, Sc, Mn, Co, As, Y, Nb, Rh, I, Cs, Pr, Tb, Ho, Tm, Au and Bi. (Note that all of these elements except beryllium have odd atomic numbers — why?)

Elements with 1 predominant isotope can also, potentially, permit very precise atomic weight determinations since variations in isotopic composition or errors in its determination have a correspondingly small effect on the mass-spectrometrically determined value of the atomic weight. Nine elements have 1 isotope that is more than 99% abundant (H, He, N, O, Ar, V, La, Ta

---

[13] IUPAC Inorganic Chemistry Division, Atomic Weights of the Elements 1995, *Pure Appl. Chem.* **68**, 2339–59 (1996).

and U) and carbon also approaches this category (^{13}C 1.11% abundant).

Known variations in the isotopic composition of normal terrestrial material prevent a more accurate atomic weight being given for 13 elements and these carry the footnote r in the Table of Atomic Weights. For each of these elements (H, He, Li, B, C, N, O, Si, S, Ar, Cu, Sr and Pb) the accuracy attainable in an atomic weight determination on a given sample is greater than that implied by the recommended value since this must be applicable to any sample and so must embrace all known variations in isotopic composition from commercial terrestrial sources. For example, for hydrogen the present attainable accuracy of calibrated mass-spectrometric atomic weight determinations is about ± 1 in the sixth significant figure, but the recommended value of 1.00794(± 7) is so given because of the natural terrestrial variation in the deuterium content. The most likely value relevant to laboratory chemicals (e.g. H_2O) is 1.00797, but it should be noted that hydrogen gas used in laboratories is often inadvertently depleted during its preparation by electrolysis, and for such samples the atomic weight is close to 1.00790. By contrast, intentional fractionation to yield heavy water (thousands of tonnes annually) or deuterated chemicals implies an atomic weight approaching 2.014, and great care should be taken to avoid contamination of "normal" samples when working with or disposing of such enriched materials.

Fascinating stories of natural variability could be told for each of the 13 elements having the footnote r and, indeed, determinations of such variations in isotopic composition are now an essential tool in unravelling the geochemical history of various ore bodies. For example, the atomic weight of sulfur obtained from virgin Texas sulfur is detectably different from that obtained from sulfate ores, and an overall range approaching ± 0.01 is found for terrestrial samples; this limits the value quoted to 32.066(6) though the accuracy of atomic weight determinations on individual samples is ± 0.00015. Boron is even more adversely affected, as previously noted, and the actual atomic weight can vary from 10.809 to 10.812 depending on whether the mineral source is Turkey or the USA.

Even more disconcerting are the substantial deviations in atomic weight that can occur in commercially available material because of inadvertent or undisclosed changes in isotopic composition (footnote m in the Table of Atomic Weights). This situation at present obtains for 8 elements (H, Li, B, Ne, Cl, Kr, Xe and U) and may well also soon affect others (such as C, N and O). The separated or partially enriched isotopes of Li, B and U are now extensively used in nuclear reactor technology and weaponry, and the unwanted residues, depleted in the desired isotopes, are sometimes dumped on the market and sold as "normal" material. Thus lithium salts may unsuspectingly be purchased which have been severely depleted in ^{6}Li (natural abundance 7.5%), and a major commercial supplier has marketed lithium containing as little as 3.75% of this isotope, thereby inducing an atomic weight change of 0.53%. For this reason practically all lithium compounds now obtainable in the USA are suspect and quantitative data obtained on them are potentially unreliable. Again, the practice of "milking" fission-product rare gases from reactor fuels and marketing these materials, produces samples with anomalous isotopic compositions. The effect, particularly on physicochemical computations, can be serious and, whilst not wishing to strike an alarmist note, the possibility of such deviations must continually be borne in mind for elements carrying the footnote m in the Table of Atomic Weights.

The related problem arising from radioactive elements is considered in the next section.

1.6.2 The problem of radioactive elements

Elements with radioactive nuclides amongst their naturally occurring isotopes have a built-in time variation of the relative concentration of their isotopes and hence a continually varying atomic weight. Whether this variation is chemically significant depends on the half-life of the transition and the relative abundance of the various isotopes. Similarly, the actual concentration of stable isotopes of several elements (e.g. Ar, Ca and Pb) may be influenced by association of those elements with radioactive precursors (i.e. ^{40}K, ^{238}U, etc.) which generate potentially variable amounts of the stable isotopes concerned. Again, some elements (such as technetium, promethium and the transuranium elements) are synthesized by nuclear reactions which produce a single isotope of the element. The "atomic weight" therefore depends on which particular isotope is being synthesized, and the concept of a "normal" atomic weight is irrelevant. For example, cyclotron production of technetium yields ^{97}Tc ($t_{1/2}$ 2.6 × 10^6 y) with an atomic weight of 96.9064, whereas fission product technetium is ^{99}Tc ($t_{1/2}$ 2.11 × 10^5 y), atomic weight 98.9063, and the isotope of longest half-life is ^{98}Tc ($t_{1/2}$ 4.2 × 10^6 y), atomic weight 97.9072.

At least 19 elements not usually considered to be radioactive do in fact have naturally occurring unstable isotopes. The minute traces of naturally occurring ^{3}H ($t_{1/2}$ 12.33 y) and ^{14}C ($t_{1/2}$ 5730 y) have no influence on the atomic weights of these elements though, of course, they are of crucial importance in other areas of study. The radioactivity of ^{40}K ($t_{1/2}$ 1.28 × 10^9 y) influences the atomic weights of its daughter elements argon (by electron capture) and calcium (by β^- emission) but fortunately does not significantly affect the atomic weight of potassium itself because of the low absolute abundance of this particular isotope (0.0117%). The half-lives of the radioactive isotopes of the 16 other "stable" elements are all greater than 10^{10} y and so normally have little influence on the atomic weight of these elements even when, as in the case of ^{115}In ($t_{1/2}$ 4.41 × 10^{14} y, 95.7% abundant) and ^{187}Re ($t_{1/2}$ 4.35 × 10^{10} y, 62.6% abundant), they are the most abundant isotopes. Note, however, that on a geological time scale it has been possible to build up significant concentrations of ^{187}Os in rhenium-containing ores (by β^- decay of ^{187}Re), thereby generating samples of osmium with an anomalous atomic weight nearer to 187 than to the published value of 190.23(3). Lead was the first element known to be subject to such isotopic disturbances and, indeed, the discovery and interpretation of the significance of isotopes was itself hastened by the reluctant conclusion of T. W. Richards at the turn of the century that a group of lead samples of differing geological origins were identical chemically but differed in atomic weight — the possible variation is now known to span almost the complete range from 204 to 208. Such elements, for which geological specimens are known in which the element has an anomalous isotopic composition, are given the footnote g in the Table of Atomic Weights. In addition to Ar, Ca, Os and Pb just discussed, such variability affects at least 38 other elements, including Sr (resulting from the β^- decay of ^{87}Rb), Ra, Th and U. A spectacular example, which affects virtually every element in the central third of the periodic table, has recently come to light with the discovery of prehistoric natural nuclear reactors at Oklo in Africa (see p. 1257). Fortunately this mine is a source of uranium ore only and so will not affect commercially available samples of the other elements involved.

In summary, as a consequence of the factors considered in this and the preceding section, the atomic weights of only the 20 mononuclidic elements can be regarded as "constants of nature". For all other elements variability in atomic weight is potentially possible and in several instances is known to occur to an extent which affects the reliability of quantitative results of even modest precision.

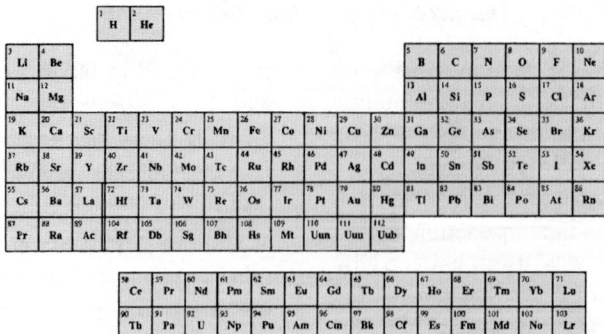

2

Chemical Periodicity and the Periodic Table

2.1 Introduction

The concept of chemical periodicity is central to the study of inorganic chemistry. No other generalization rivals the periodic table of the elements in its ability to systematize and rationalize known chemical facts or to predict new ones and suggest fruitful areas for further study. Chemical periodicity and the periodic table now find their natural interpretation in the detailed electronic structure of the atom; indeed, they played a major role at the turn of the century in elucidating the mysterious phenomena of radioactivity and the quantum effects which led ultimately to Bohr's theory of the hydrogen atom. Because of this central position it is perhaps not surprising that innumerable articles and books have been written on the subject since the seminal papers by Mendeleev in 1869, and some 700 forms of the periodic table (classified into 146 different types or subtypes) have been proposed.[1-3] A brief historical survey of these developments is summarized in the Panel opposite.

There is no single *best* form of the periodic table since the choice depends on the purpose for which the table is used. Some forms emphasize chemical relations and valence, whereas others stress the electronic configuration of the elements or the dependence of the periods on the shells and subshells of the atomic structure. The most convenient form for our purpose is the so-called "long form" with separate panels for the lanthanide and actinide elements (see inside front cover). There has been a lively debate during the past decade as to the best numbering system to be used for the individual

---

[1] F. P. VENABLE, *The Development of the Periodic Law*, Chemical Publishing Co., Easton, Pa., 1896. This is the first general review of periodic tables and has an almost complete collection of those published to that time. J. W. VAN SPRONSEN, *The Periodic System of the Chemical Elements*, Elsevier, Amsterdam, 1969, 368 pp. An excellent modern account of the historical developments leading up to Mendeleev's table.

[2] E. G. MAZURS, *Graphic Representation of the Periodic System during One Hundred Years*, University of Alabama Press, Alabama, 1974. An exhaustive topological classification of over 700 forms of the periodic table.

groups in the table; we will adopt the 1–18 numbering scheme recommended by IUPAC.[3] The following sections of this chapter summarize:

(a) the interpretation of the periodic law in terms of the electronic structure of atoms;

(b) the use of the periodic table and graphs to systematize trends in physical and chemical properties and to detect possible errors, anomalies, and inconsistencies;

(c) the use of the periodic table to predict new elements and compounds, and to suggest new areas of research.

---

[3] E. FLUCK, *Pure Appl. Chem.* **60**, 432–6 (1988); G. J. LEIGH (ed.), *Nomenclature of Inorganic Chemistry: IUPAC Recommendations 1990*, Blackwell, Oxford, 1990, 289 pp. The "Red Book".

2.2 The Electronic Structure of Atoms[4]

The ubiquitous electron was discovered by J. J. Thompson in 1897 some 25 y after the original work on chemical periodicity by D. I. Mendeleev and Lothar Meyer; however, a further 20 y were to pass before G. N. Lewis and then I. Langmuir connected the electron with valency and chemical bonding. Refinements continued via wave mechanics and molecular orbital theory, and the symbiotic relation between experiment and theory still continues

---

[4] N. N. GREENWOOD, *Principles of Atomic Orbitals*, revised SI edition, Monograph for Teachers, No. 8, Chemical Society, London, 1980, 48 pp.

Mendeleev's Periodic Table

Precursors and Successors

1772	L. B. G. de Morveau made the first table of "chemically simple" substances. A. L. Lavoisier used this in his *Traité Elémentaire de Chimie* published in 1789.
1817–29	J. W. Döbereiner discovered many triads of elements and compounds, the combining weight of the central component being the average of its partners (e.g. CaO, SrO, BaO, and NiO, CuO, ZnO).
1843	L. Gmelin included a V-shaped arrangement of 16 triads in the 4th edition of his *Handbuch der Chemie.*
1857	J. B. Dumas published a rudimentary table of 32 elements in 8 columns indicating their relationships.
1862	A. E. B. de Chancourtois first arranged the elements in order of increasing atomic weight; he located similar elements in this way and published a helical form in 1863.
1864	L. Meyer published a table of valences for 49 elements.
1864	W. Odling drew up an almost correct table with 17 vertical columns and including 57 elements.
1865	J. A. R. Newlands propounded his law of octaves after several partial classifications during the preceding 2 y; he also correctly predicted the atomic weight of the undiscovered element germanium.
1868–9	L. Meyer drew up an atomic volume curve and a periodic table, but this latter was not published until 1895.
1869	D. I. Mendeleev enunciated his periodic law that "the properties of the elements are a periodic function of their atomic weights". He published several forms of periodic table, one containing 63 elements.
1871	D. I. Mendeleev modified and improved his tables and predicted the discovery of 10 elements (now known as Sc, Ga, Ge, Tc, Re, Po, Fr, Ra, Ac and Pa). He fully described with amazing prescience the properties of 4 of these (Sc, Ga, Ge, Po). Note, however, that it was not possible to predict the existence of the noble gases or the number of lanthanide elements.
1894–8	Lord Rayleigh, W. Ramsay and M. W. Travers detected and then isolated the noble gases (He), Ne, Ar, Kr, Xe.
1913	N. Bohr explained the form of the periodic table on the basis of his theory of atomic structure and showed that there could be only 14 lanthanide elements.
1913	H. G. J. Moseley observed regularities in the characteristic X-ray spectra of the elements; he thereby discovered atomic numbers Z and provided justification for the ordinal sequence of the elements.
1940	E. McMillan and P. Abelson synthesized the first transuranium element $_{93}Np$. Others were synthesized by G. T. Seaborg and his colleagues during the next 15 y.
1944	G. T. Seaborg proposed the actinide hypothesis and predicted 14 elements (up to $Z = 103$) in this group.

today. It should always be remembered, however, that it is incorrect to "deduce" known chemical phenomena from theoretical models; the proper relationship is that the currently accepted theoretical models interpret the facts and suggest new experiments — they will be modified (or discarded and replaced) when new results demand it. Theories can never be proved by experiment — only refuted, the best that can be said of a theory is that it is consistent with a wide range of information which it interprets logically and that it is a fruitful source of predictions and new experiments.

Our present views on the electronic structure of atoms are based on a variety of experimental results and theoretical models which are fully discussed in many elementary texts. In summary, an atom comprises a central, massive, positively charged nucleus surrounded by a more tenuous envelope of negative electrons. The nucleus is composed of neutrons ($_0^1$n) and protons ($_1^1$p, i.e. $_1^1$H$^+$) of approximately equal mass tightly bound by the force field of mesons. The number of protons (Z) is called the atomic number and this, together with the number of neutrons (N), gives the atomic mass number of the nuclide ($A = N + Z$). An element consists of atoms all of which have the same number of protons (Z) and this number determines the position of the element in the periodic table (H. G. J. Moseley, 1913). Isotopes of an element all have the same value of Z but differ in the number of neutrons in their nuclei. The charge on the electron (e^-) is equal in size but opposite in sign to that of the proton and the ratio of their masses is 1/1836.1527.

The arrangement of electrons in an atom is described by means of four quantum numbers which determine the spatial distribution, energy, and other properties, see Appendix 1 (p. 1285). The principal quantum number n defines the general energy level or "shell" to which the electron belongs. Electrons with $n = 1, 2, 3, 4, \ldots$, are sometimes referred to as K, L, M, N, $\ldots$, electrons. The orbital quantum number l defines both the shape of the electron charge distribution and its orbital angular momentum. The number of possible values for l for a given electron depends on its principal quantum number n; it can have n values running from 0 to $n - 1$, and electrons with $l = 0, 1, 2, 3, \ldots$, are designated s, p, d, f, $\ldots$, electrons. Whereas n is the prime determinant of an electron's energy this also depends to some extent on l (for atoms or ions containing more than one electron). It is found that the sequence of increasing electron energy levels in an atom follows the sequence of values $n + l$; if 2 electrons have the same value of $n + l$ then the one with smaller n is the more tightly bound.

The third quantum number m is called the magnetic quantum number for it is only in an applied magnetic field that it is possible to define a direction within the atom with respect to which the orbital can be directed. In general, the magnetic quantum number can take up $2l + 1$ values (i.e. $0, \pm 1, \ldots, \pm l$); thus an s electron (which is spherically symmetrical and has zero orbital angular momentum) can have only one orientation, but a p electron can have three (frequently chosen to be the x, y, and z directions in Cartesian coordinates). Likewise there are five possibilities for d orbitals and seven for f orbitals.

The fourth quantum number m_s is called the spin angular momentum quantum number for historical reasons. In relativistic (four-dimensional) quantum mechanics this quantum number is associated with the property of symmetry of the wave function and it can take on one of two values designated as $+\frac{1}{2}$ and $-\frac{1}{2}$, or simply α and β. All electrons in atoms can be described by means of these four quantum numbers and, as first enumerated by W. Pauli in his *Exclusion Principle* (1926), each electron in an atom must have a unique set of the four quantum numbers.

It can now be seen that there is a direct and simple correspondence between this description of electronic structure and the form of the periodic table. Hydrogen, with 1 proton and 1 electron, is the first element, and, in the ground state (i.e. the state of lowest energy) it has the electronic configuration 1s^1 with zero orbital angular momentum. Helium, $Z = 2$, has the configuration 1s^2, and this completes the first period since no other unique combination of $n = 1$, $l = m = 0$, $m_s = \pm\frac{1}{2}$ exists. The second period begins with lithium ($Z = 3$), the least tightly bound electron having the configuration $2s^1$. The same situation obtains for each of the other periods in the table, the number of the period being the principal quantum number of the least tightly bound electron of the first element in the period. It will also be seen that there is a direct relation between the various blocks of elements in the periodic table and the electronic configuration of the atoms it contains; the s block is 2 elements wide, the p block 6 elements wide, the d block 10, and the f block 14, i.e. $2(2l + 1)$, the factor 2 appearing because of the spins.

In so far as the chemical (and physical) properties of an element derive from its electronic configuration, and especially the configuration of its least tightly bound electrons, it follows that chemical periodicity and the form of the periodic table can be elegantly interpreted in terms of electronic structure.

2.3 Periodic Trends in Properties[5,6]

General similarities and trends in the *chemical* properties of the elements had been noticed increasingly since the end of the eighteenth century and predated the observation of periodic variations in *physical* properties which were not noted until about 1868. However, it is more convenient to invert this order and to look at trends in atomic and physical properties first.

2.3.1 Trends in atomic and physical properties

Figure 2.1 shows a modern version of Lothar Meyer's atomic volume curve: the alkali metals

[5] R. RICH, *Periodic Correlations*, W. A. Benjamin, New York, 1965, 159 pp.

[6] R. T. SANDERSON, *Inorganic Chemistry*, Reinhold Publishing Corp., New York, 1967, 430 pp.

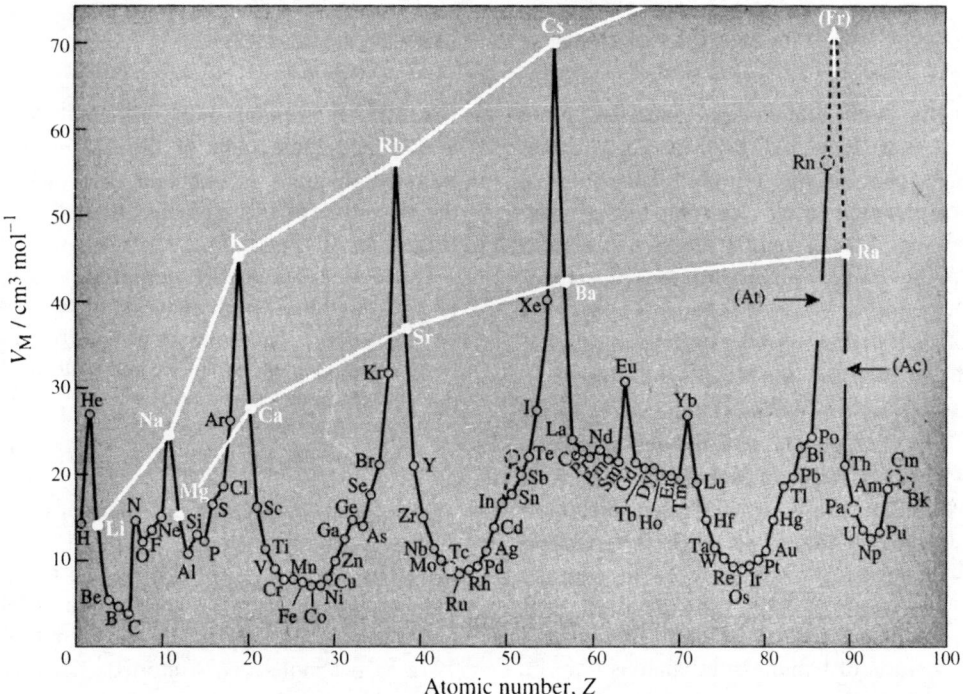

Figure 2.1 Atomic volumes (molar volumes) of the elements in the solid state.

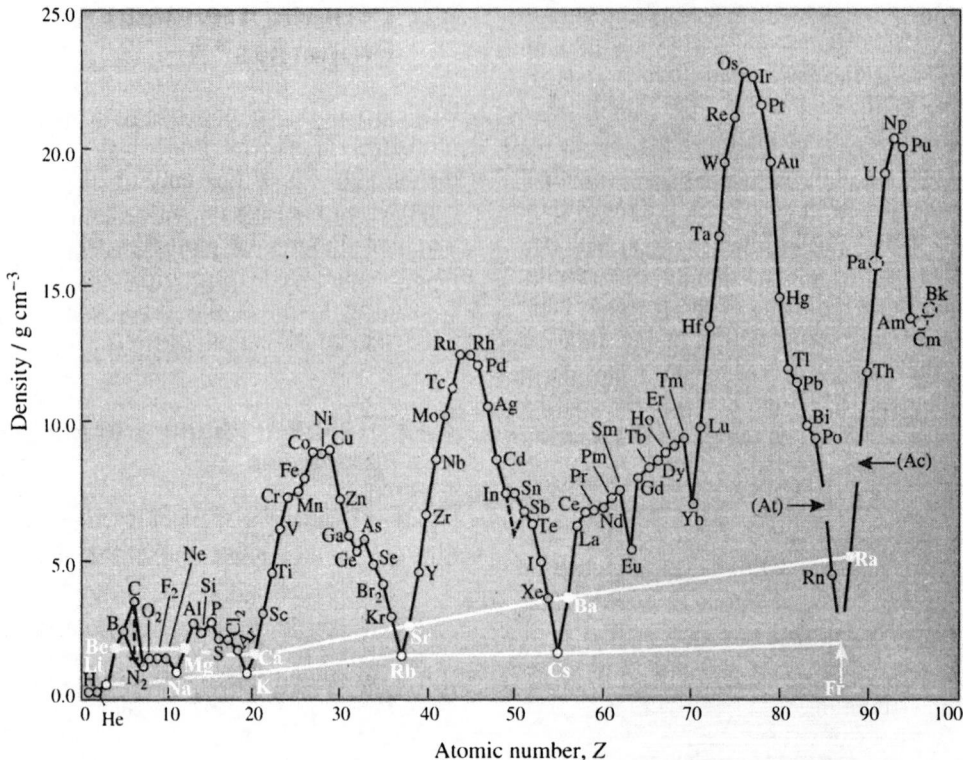

Figure 2.2 Densities of the elements in the solid state.

appear at the peaks and elements near the centre of each period (B, C; Al, Si; Mn, Fe, Co; Ru; and Os) appear in the troughs. This finds a ready interpretation on the electronic theory since the alkali metals have only 1 electron per atom to contribute to the binding of the 8 nearest-neighbour atoms, whereas elements near the centre of each period have the maximum number of electrons available for bonding. Elements in other groups fall on corresponding sections of the curve in each period, and in several groups there is a steady trend to higher volumes with the increasing atomic number. Closer inspection reveals that a much more detailed interpretation would be required to encompass all the features of the curve which includes data on solids held by very diverse types of bonding. Note also that the position of helium is anomalous (why?), and that there are local anomalies at europium and ytterbium in the lanthanide elements (see

Chapter 30). Similar plots are obtained for the atomic and ionic radii of the elements and an inverted diagram is obtained, as expected, for the densities of the elements in the solid state (Fig. 2.2).

Of more fundamental importance is the plot of first-stage ionization energies of the elements, i.e. the energy I_M required to remove the least tightly bound electron from the neutral atom in the gas phase:

$$M(g) \longrightarrow M^+(g) + e^-; \quad \Delta H^\circ = I_M$$

These are shown in Fig. 2.3 and illustrate most convincingly the various quantum shells and subshells described in the preceding section. The energy required to remove the 1 electron from an atom of hydrogen is 13.606 eV (i.e. 1312 kJ per mole of H atoms). This rises to 2372 kJ mol^{-1} for He (1s^2) since the positive charge on the helium nucleus is twice that of the

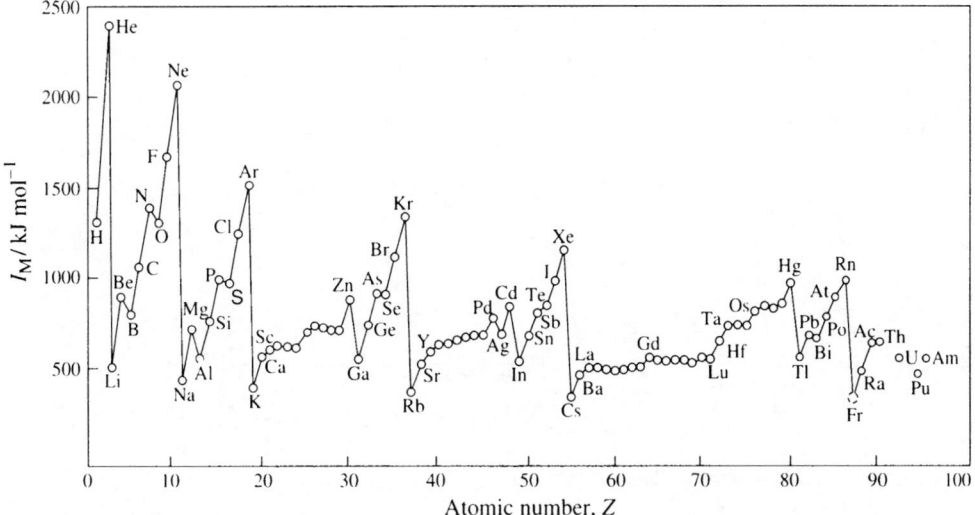

Figure 2.3　First-stage ionization energies of the elements.

proton and the additional charge is not completely shielded by the second electron. There is a large drop in ionization energy between helium and lithium ($1s^2 2s^1$) because the principal quantum number n increases from 1 to 2, after which the ionization energy rises somewhat for beryllium ($1s^2 2s^2$), though not to a value which is so high that beryllium would be expected to be an inert gas. The interpretation that is placed on the other values in Fig. 2.3 is as follows. The slight decrease at boron ($1s^2 2s^2 2p^1$) is due to the increase in orbital quantum number l from 0 to 1 and the similar decrease between nitrogen and oxygen is due to increased interelectronic coulomb repulsion as the fourth p electron is added to the 3 already occupying $2p_x$, $2p_y$, and $2p_z$. The ionization energy then continues to increase with increasing Z until the second quantum shell is filled at neon ($2s^2 sp^6$). The process is precisely repeated from sodium ($3s^1$) to argon ($3s^2 3p^6$) which again occurs at a peak in the curve, although at this point the third quantum shell is not yet completed (3d). This is because the next added electron for the next element potassium ($Z = 19$) enters the 4s shell ($n + l = 4$) rather than the 3d ($n + l = 5$). After calcium ($Z = 20$) the 3d shell fills and then the 4p ($n + l = 5$, but n higher than for 3d). The

implications of this and of the subsequent filling of later s, p, d, and f levels will be elaborated in considerable detail in later chapters. Suffice it to note for the moment that the chemical inertness of the lighter noble gases correlates with their high ionization energies whereas the extreme reactivity of the alkali metals (and their prominent flame tests) finds a ready interpretation in their much lower ionization energies.

Electronegativities also show well-developed periodic trends though the concept of electronegativity itself, as introduced by L. Pauling,[7] is rather qualitative: "Electronegativity is the power of an atom *in a molecule* to attract electrons to itself." It is to be expected that the electronegativity of an element will depend to some extent not only on the other atoms to which it is bonded but also on its coordination number and oxidation state; for example, the electronegativity of a given atom increases with increase in its oxidation state. Fortunately, however, these effects do not obscure the main trends. Various measures of electronegativity have been proposed by L. Pauling, by R. S. Mulliken, by A. L. Allred

---

[7] L. PAULING, *J. Am. Chem. Soc.* **54**, 3570 (1932); *The Nature of the Chemical Bond*, 3rd edn., pp. 88–107. Cornell University Press, Ithaca, NY, 1960.

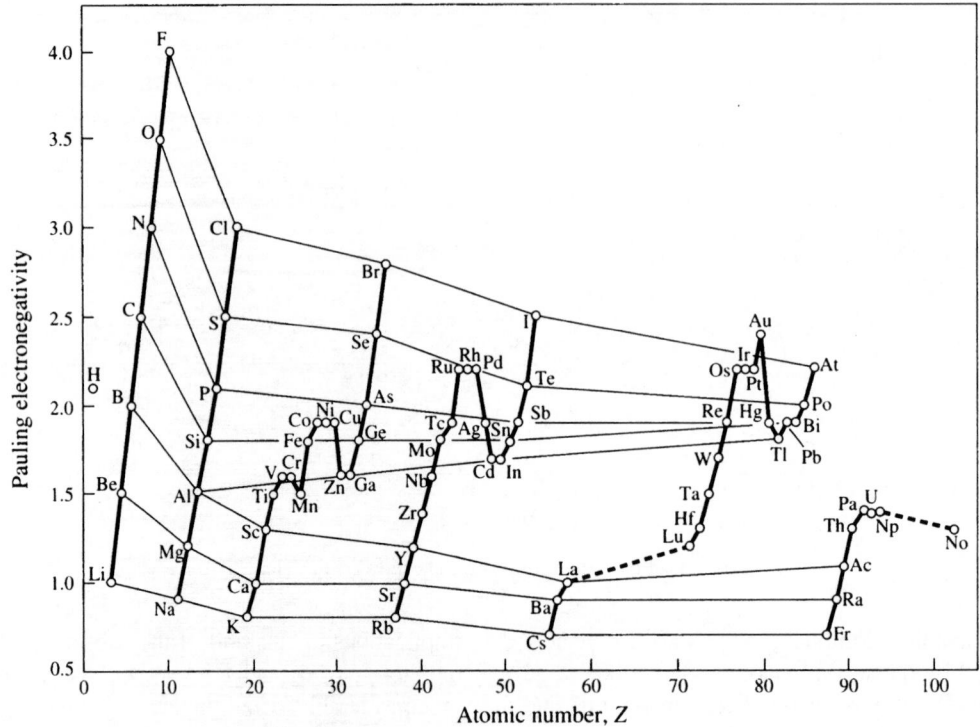

Figure 2.4   Values of electronegativity of the elements.

and E. Rochow, and by R. T. Sanderson, and all give roughly parallel scales. Figure 2.4, which incorporates Pauling's values, illustrates the trends observed; electronegativities tend to increase with increasing atomic number within a given period (e.g. Li to F, or K to Br) and to decrease with increasing atomic number within a given group (e.g. F to At, or O to Po). Numerous reviews are available.[8]

Many other properties have been found to show periodic variations and these can be displayed graphically or by circles of varying size on a periodic table, e.g. melting points of the elements, boiling points, heats of fusion, heats of vaporization, energies of atomization, etc.[6] Similarly, the properties of simple binary

compounds of the elements can be plotted, e.g. heats of formation, melting points and boiling points of hydrides, fluorides, chlorides, bromides, iodides, oxides, sulfides, etc.[6] Trends immediately become apparent, and the selection of compounds with specific values for particular properties is facilitated. Such trends also permit interpolation to give estimates of undetermined values of properties for a given compound though such a procedure can be misleading and should only be used as a first rough guide. Extrapolation has also frequently been used, and to good effect, though it too can be hazardous and unreliable particularly when new or unsuspected effects are involved. Perhaps the classic example concerns the dissociation energy of the fluorine molecule which is difficult to measure experimentally: for many years this was taken to be ~265 kJ mol^{-1} by extrapolation of the values for iodine, bromine, and chlorine (151, 193, and 243 kJ mol^{-1}), whereas the

---

[8] K. D. SEN and C. K. JØRGENSEN (eds.), *Structure and Bonding* **66** *Electronegativity*, Springer-Verlag, Berlin, 1987, 198 pp. J. Mullay, *J. Am. Chem. Soc.* **106**, 5842–7 (1984). R. T. Sanderson, *Inorg. Chem.* **25**, 1856–8 (1986). R. G. Pearson, *Inorg. Chem.* **27**, 734–40 (1988).

most recent experimental values are close to 159 kJ mol^{-1} (see Chapter 17). The detection of such anomalous data from periodic plots thus serves to identify either inaccurate experimental observations or inadequate theories (or both).

2.3.2 Trends in chemical properties

These, though more difficult to describe quantitatively than the trends in atomic and physical properties described in the preceding subsection, also become apparent when the elements are compared in each group and along each period. Such trends will be discussed in detail in later chapters and it is only necessary here to enumerate briefly the various types of behaviour that frequently recur.

The most characteristic chemical property of an element is its valence. There are numerous measures of valency each with its own area of usefulness and applicability. Simple definitions refer to the number of hydrogen atoms that can combine with an element in a binary hydride or to twice the number of oxygen atoms combining with an element in its oxide(s). It was noticed from the beginning that there was a close relation between the position of an element in the periodic table and the stoichiometry of its simple compounds. Hydrides of main group elements have the formula MH_n where n was related to the group number N by the equations $n = N$ ($N \leq 4$), and $n = 18 - N$ for $N > 14$. By contrast, oxygen elicited an increasing valence in the highest normal oxide of each element and this was directly related to the group number, i.e. M_2O, MO, M_2O_3, ..., M_2O_7. These periodic regularities find a ready explanation in terms of the electronic configuration of the elements and simple theories of chemical bonding. In more complicated chemical formulae involving more than 2 elements, it is convenient to define the "oxidation state" of an element as the formal charge remaining on the element when all other atoms have been removed as their normal ions. For example, nitrogen has an oxidation state of -3 in ammonium chloride $[NH_4Cl - (4H^+ + Cl^-) = N^{3-}]$ and manganese

has an oxidation state of $+7$ in potassium permanganate {tetraoxomanganate(1−)} [$KMnO_4 - (K^+ + 4O^{2-}) = Mn^{7+}$]. For a compound such as Fe_3O_4 iron has an average oxidation state of $+2.67$ [i.e. $(4 \times 2)/3$] which may be thought of as comprising $1Fe^{2+}$ and $2Fe^{3+}$. It should be emphasized that these charges are formal, not actual, and that the concept of oxidation state is not particularly helpful when considering predominantly covalent compounds (such as organic compounds) or highly catenated inorganic compounds such as S_7NH.

The periodicity in the oxidation state or valence shown by the elements was forcefully illustrated by Mendeleev in one of his early forms of the periodic system and this is shown in an extended form in Fig. 2.5 which incorporates more recent information. The predictive and interpolative powers of such a plot are obvious and have been a fruitful source of chemical experimentation for over a century.

Other periodic trends which occur in the chemical properties of the elements and which are discussed in more detail throughout later chapters are:

(i) The "anomalous" properties of elements in the first short period (from lithium to fluorine) — see Chapters 4, 5, 6, 8, 11, 14 and 17.

(ii) The "anomalies" in the post-transition element series (from gallium to bromine) related to the d-block contraction — see Chapters 7, 10, 13, 16 and 17.

(iii) The effects of the lanthanide contraction — see Chapters 21–30.

(iv) Diagonal relationships between lithium and magnesium, beryllium and aluminium, boron and silicon.

(v) The so-called inert pair effect (see Chapters 7, 10 and 13) and the variation of oxidation state in the main group elements in steps of 2 (e.g. IF, IF_3, IF_5, IF_7).

(vi) Variability in the oxidation state of transition elements in steps of 1.

(vii) Trends in the basicity and electropositivity of elements — both vertical trends

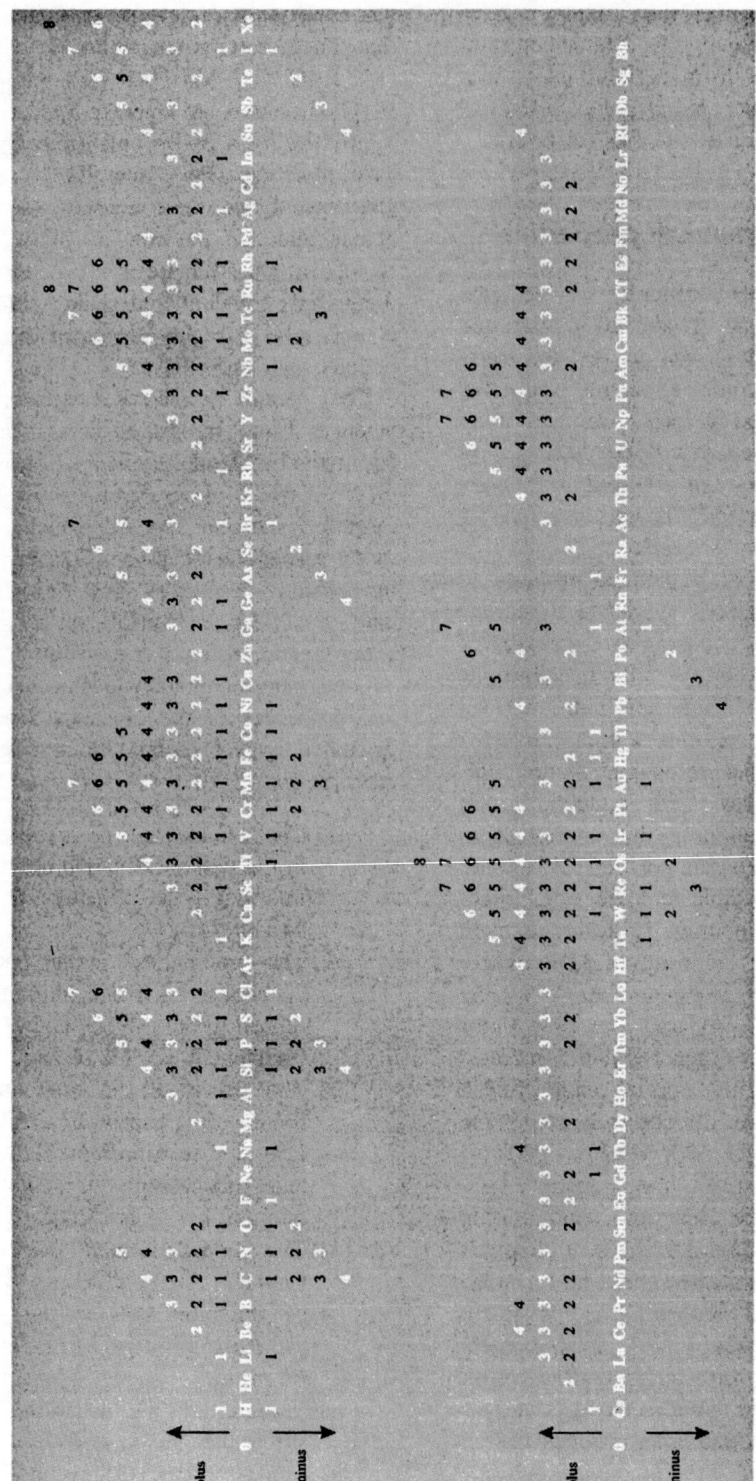

Figure 2.5   Formal oxidation states of the elements displayed in a format originally devised by Mendeleev in 1889. The more common oxidation states (including zero) are shown in white. Nonintegral values, as in B_5H_9, C_3H_8, HN_3, S_8^{2+}, etc., are not included.

within groups and horizontal trends along periods.

(viii) Trends in bond type with position of the elements in the table and with oxidation state for a given element.

(ix) Trends in stability of compounds and regularities in the methods used to extract the elements from their compounds.

(x) Trends in the stability of coordination complexes and the electron-donor power of various series of ligands.

2.4 Prediction of New Elements and Compounds

Newlands (1864) was the first to predict correctly the existence of a "missing element" when he calculated an atomic weight of 73 for an element between silicon and tin, close to the present value of 72.61 for germanium (discovered by C. A. Winkler in 1886). However, his method of detecting potential triads was unreliable and he predicted (non-existent) elements between

rhodium and iridium, and between palladium and platinum. Mendeleev's predictions 1869–71 were much more extensive and reliable, as indicated in the historical panel on p. 21. The depth of his insight and the power of his method remain impressive even today, but in the state of development of the subject in 1869 they were monumental. A comparison of the properties of eka-silicon predicted by Mendeleev and those determined experimentally for germanium is shown in Table 2.1. Similarly accurate predictions were made for eka-aluminium and gallium and for eka-boron and scandium.

Of the remaining 26 undiscovered elements between hydrogen and uranium, 11 were lanthanoids which Mendeleev's system was unable to characterize because of their great chemical similarity and the new numerological feature dictated by the filling of the 4f orbitals. Only cerium, terbium and erbium were established with certainty in 1871, and the others (except promethium, 1945) were separated and identified in the period 1879–1907. The isolation of the (unpredicted) noble gases also occurred at this time (1894–8).

Table 2.1

Mendeleev's predictions (1871) for eka-silicon, M		Observed properties (1995) of germanium (discovered 1886)	
Atomic weight	72	Atomic weight	72.61(2)
Density/g cm^{-3}	5.5	Density/g cm^{-3}	5.323
Molar volume/cm^3 mol^{-1}	13.1	Molar volume/cm^3 mol^{-1}	13.64
MP/°C	high	MP/°C	945
Specific heat/J g^{-1} K^{-1}	0.305	Specific heat/J g^{-1} K^{-1}	0.309
Valence	4	Valence	4
Colour	dark grey	Colour	greyish-white
M will be obtained from MO_2 or K_2MF_6 by reaction with Na		Ge is obtained by reaction of K_2GeF_6 with Na	
M will be slightly attacked by acids such as HCl and will resist alkalis such as NaOH		Ge is not dissolved by HCl or dilute NaOH but reacts with hot conc HNO_3	
M, on being heated, will form MO_2 with high mp, and d 4.7 g cm^{-3}		Ge reacts with oxygen to give GeO_2, mp 1086°, d 4.228 g cm^{-3}	
M will give a hydrated MO_2 soluble in acid and easily reprecipitated		"$Ge(OH)_4$" dissolves in conc acid and is reprecipitated on dilution or addition of base	
MS_2 will be insoluble in water but soluble in ammonium sulfide		GeS_2 is insoluble in water and dilute acid but readily soluble in ammonium sulfide	
MCl_4 will be a volatile liquid with bp a little under 100°C and d 1.9 g cm^{-3}		$GeCl_4$ is a volatile liquid with bp 83°C and d 1.8443 g cm^{-3}	
M will form MEt_4 bp 160°C		$GeEt_4$ bp 185°C	

The isolation and identification of 4 radioactive elements in minute amounts took place at the turn of the century, and in each case the insight provided by the periodic classification into the predicted chemical properties of these elements proved invaluable. Marie Curie identified polonium in 1898 and, later in the same year working with Pierre Curie, isolated radium. Actinium followed in 1899 (A. Debierne) and the heaviest noble gas, radon, in 1900 (F. E. Dorn). Details will be found in later chapters which also recount the discoveries made in the present century of protactinium (O. Hahn and Lise Meitner, 1917), hafnium (D. Coster and G. von Hevesey, 1923), rhenium (W. Noddack, Ida Tacke and O. Berg, 1925), technetium (C. Perrier and E. Segré, 1937), francium (Marguerite Perey, 1939) and promethium (J. A. Marinsky, L. E. Glendenin and C. D. Coryell, 1945).

A further group of elements, the transuranium elements, has been synthesized by artificial nuclear reactions in the period from 1940 onwards; their relation to the periodic table is discussed fully in Chapter 31 and need not be repeated here. Perhaps even more striking today are the predictions, as yet unverified, for the properties of the currently non-existent superheavy elements.[9] Elements up to lawrencium ($Z = 103$) are actinides (5f) and the 6d transition series starts with element 104. So far only elements 104–112 have been synthesized,[10] and, because there is as yet no agreement on trivial names for some of these elements (see pp. 1280–1), they are here referred to by their atomic numbers. A systematic naming scheme was approved by IUPAC in 1977 but is not widely used by researchers in the field. It involves the use of three-letter symbols derived directly from the atomic number by using the

following numerical roots:

0	1	2	3	4	5	6	7	8	9
nil	un	bi	tri	quad	pent	hex	sept	oct	enn

These names and symbols can be used for elements 110 and beyond until agreed trivial names have been internationally approved. Hence, 110 is un-un-nilium (Uun), 111 is un-un-unium (Uuu), and 112 is un-un-bium, (Uub). These elements are increasingly unstable with respect to α-decay or spontaneous fission with half-lives of less than 1 s. It is therefore unlikely that much chemistry will ever be carried out on them though their ionization energies, mps, bps, densities, atomic and metallic radii, etc., have all been predicted. Element 112 is expected to be eka-mercury at the end of the 6d transition series, and should be, followed by the 7p and 8s configurations $Z = 113$–120. On the basis of present theories of nuclear structure an "island of stability" is expected near element 114 with half-lives in the region of years. Much effort is being concentrated on attempts to make these elements, and oxidation states are expected to follow the main group trends (e.g. 113: eka-thallium mainly + 1). Other physical properties have been predicted by extrapolation of known periodic trends. Still heavier elements have been postulated, though it is unlikely (on present theories) that their chemistry will ever be studied because of their very short predicted half-lives. Calculated energy levels for the range $Z = 121$–154 lead to the expectation of an unprecedented 5g series of 18 elements followed by fourteen 6f elements.

In addition to the prediction of new elements and their probable properties, the periodic table has proved invaluable in suggesting fruitful lines of research in the preparation of new compounds. Indeed, this mode of thinking is now so ingrained in the minds of chemists that they rarely pause to reflect how extraordinarily difficult their task would be if periodic trends were unknown. It is the ability to anticipate the effect of changing an element or a group in a compound which enables work to be planned effectively, though the prudent chemist is always alert to the possibility of

⁹ B. Fricke, Superheavy elements, *Structure and Bonding* **21**, 89 (1975). A full account of the predicted stabilities and chemical properties of elements with atomic numbers in the range $Z = 104$–184.

¹⁰ R. C. Barber, N. N. Greenwood, A. Z. Hrynkiewicz, M. Lefort, M. Sakai, I. Ulehla, A. H. Wapstra and D. H. Wilkinson, *Progr. in Particle and Nuclear Physics*, **29**, 453–530 (1992); also published in *Pure Appl. Chem.* **65**, 1757–824 (1993). See also §31.4.

new effects or unsuspected factors which might surprisingly intervene.

Typical examples taken from the developments of the past two or three decades include:

(i) the organometallic chemistry of lithium and thallium (Chapters 4 and 7);

(ii) the use of boron hydrides as ligands (Chapter 6);

(iii) solvent systems and preparative chemistry based on the interhalogens (Chapter 17);

(iv) the development of the chemistry of xenon (Chapter 18);

(v) ferrocene — leading to ruthenocene and dibenzene chromium, etc. (Chapters 19, 25 and 23 respectively);

(vi) the development of solid-state chemistry.

Indeed, the influence of Mendeleev's fruitful generalization pervades the whole modern approach to the chemistry of the elements.

3

Hydrogen

3.1 Introduction

Hydrogen is the most abundant element in the universe and is also common on earth, being the third most abundant element (after oxygen and silicon) on the surface of the globe. Hydrogen in combined form accounts for about 15.4% of the atoms in the earth's crust and oceans and is the ninth element in order of abundance by weight (0.9%). In the crustal rocks alone it is tenth in order of abundance (0.15 wt%). The gradual recognition of hydrogen as an element during the sixteenth and seventeenth centuries forms part of the obscure and tangled web of experiments that were carried out as chemistry emerged from alchemy to become a modern science.[1] Until almost the end of the eighteenth century the element was inextricably entwined with the concept of phlogiston and H. Cavendish, who is generally regarded as having finally isolated and identified the gas in 1766, and who established conclusively that water was a compound of oxygen and hydrogen, actually communicated his findings to the Royal Society in January 1784 in the following words: "There seems to be the utmost reason to think that dephlogisticated air is only water deprived of its phlogiston" and that "water consists of dephlogisticated air united with phlogiston".

The continued importance of hydrogen in the development of experimental and theoretical chemistry is further illustrated by some of the dates listed in the Panel on the page opposite.

Hydrogen was recognized as the essential element in acids by H. Davy after his work on the hydrohalic acids, and theories of acids and bases have played an important role ever since. The electrolytic dissociation theory of S. A. Arrhenius and W. Ostwald in the 1880s, the introduction of the pH scale for hydrogen-ion concentrations by S. P. L. Sørensen in 1909, the theory of acid–base titrations and indicators, and J. N. Brønsted's fruitful concept of acids and conjugate bases as proton donors and acceptors (1923) are other land marks (see p. 48). The discovery of *ortho-* and *para-* hydrogen in 1924, closely followed by the discovery of heavy hydrogen (deuterium) and

---

[1] J. W. MELLOR, *A Comprehensive Treatise on Inorganic and Theoretical Chemistry*, Vol. 1, Chap. 3, Longmans, Green & Co., London, 1922.

tritium in the 1930s, added a further range of phenomena that could be studied by means of this element (pp. 34–43). In more recent times, the technique of nmr spectroscopy, which was first demonstrated in 1946 using the hydrogen nucleus, has revolutionized the study of structural chemistry and permitted previously unsuspected phenomena such as fluxionality to be studied. Simultaneously, the discovery of complex metal hydrides such as $LiAlH_4$ has had a major impact on synthetic chemistry and enabled new classes of compound to be readily prepared in high yield (p. 229). The most important compound of hydrogen is, of course, water,

---

Hydrogen — Some Significant Dates

1671	R. Boyle showed that dilute sulfuric acid acting on iron gave a flammable gas; several other seventeenth-century scientists made similar observations.
1766	H. Cavendish established the true properties of hydrogen by reacting several acids with iron, zinc and tin; he showed that it was much lighter than air.
1781	H. Cavendish showed quantitatively that water was formed when hydrogen was exploded with oxygen, and that water was therefore not an element as had previously been supposed.
1783	A. L. Lavoisier proposed the name "hydrogen" (Greek ὕδωρ γείνομαι, water former).
1800	W. Nicholson and A. Carlisle decomposed water electrolytically into hydrogen and oxygen which were then recombined by explosion to resynthesize water.
1810–15	Hydrogen recognized as the essential element in acids by H. Davy (contrary to Lavoisier who originally considered oxygen to be essential — hence Greek ὀξύς γείνομαι, acid former).
1866	The remarkable solubility of hydrogen in palladium discovered by T. Graham following the observation of hydrogen diffusion through red-hot platinum and iron by H. St. C. Deville and L. Troost, 1863.
1878	Hydrogen detected spectroscopically in the sun's chromosphere (J. N. Lockyer).
1895	Hydrogen first liquefied in sufficient quantity to show a meniscus (J. Dewar) following earlier observations of mists and droplets by others, 1877–85.
1909	The pH scale for hydrogen-ion concentration introduced by S. P. L. Sørensen.
1912	H_3^+ discovered mass-spectrometrically by J. J. Thompson.
1920	The concept of hydrogen bonding introduced by W. M. Latimer and W. H. Rodebush (and by M. L. Huggins, 1921).
1923	J. N. Brønsted defined an acid as a species that tended to lose a proton: $A \rightleftharpoons B + H^+$.
1924	*Ortho-* and *para*-hydrogen discovered spectroscopically by R. Mecke and interpreted quantum-mechanically by W. Heisenberg, 1927.
1929–30	Concept of quantum-mechanical tunnelling in proton-transfer reactions introduced (without experimental evidence) by several authors.
1931	First hydrido complex of a transition metal prepared by W. Hieber and F. Leutert.
1932	Deuterium discovered spectroscopically and enriched by gaseous diffusion of hydrogen and by electrolysis of water (H. C. Urey, F. G. Brickwedde and G. M. Murphy).
1932	Acidity function H_0 proposed by L. P. Hammett for assessing the strength of very strong acids.
1934	Tritium first made by deuteron bombardment of D_3PO_4 and $(ND_4)_2SO_4$ (i.e. $^2D + ^2D = ^3T + ^1H$); M. L. E. Oliphant, P. Harteck and E. Rutherford.
1939	Tritium found to be radioactive by L. W. Alvarez and R. Cornog after a prediction by T. W. Bonner in 1938.
1946	Proton nmr first detected in bulk matter by E. M. Purcell, H. C. Torrey and R. V. Pound; and by F. Bloch, W. W. Hansen and M. E. Packard.
1947	$LiAlH_4$ first prepared and subsequently shown to be a versatile reducing agent; A. E. Finholt, A. C. Bond and H. I. Schlesinger.
1950	Tritium first detected in atmospheric hydrogen (V. Faltings and P. Harteck) and later shown to be present in rain water (W. F. Libby *et al.*, 1951).
1954	Detonation of the first hydrogen bomb on Bikini Atoll.
1960s	"Superacids" (10^7–10^{19} times stronger than sulfuric acid) studied systematically by G. A. Olah's group and by R. J. Gillespie's group.
1966	The term "magic acid" coined in G. A. Olah's laboratory for the non-aqueous system HSO_3F/SbF_5.
1976–79	Encapsulated H atom detected and located in octahedral polynuclear carbonyls such as $[HRu_6(CO)_{18}]^-$ and $[HCo_6(CO)_{15}]^-$ following A. Simon's characterization of interstitial H in HNb_6I_{11}.
1984	Stable transition-metal complexes of dihapto-dihydrogen (η^2-H_2) discovered by G. Kubas.

and a detailed discussion of this compound is given on pp. 620–33 in the chapter on oxygen. In fact, hydrogen forms more chemical compounds than any other element, including carbon, and a survey of its chemistry therefore encompasses virtually the whole periodic table. However, before embarking on such a review in Sections 3.4–3.7 it is convenient to summarize the atomic and physical properties of the various forms of hydrogen (Section 3.2), to enumerate the various methods used for its preparation and industrial production, and to indicate some of its many applications and uses (Section 3.3).

3.2 Atomic and Physical Properties of Hydrogen[2]

Despite its very simple electronic configuration ($1s^1$) hydrogen can, paradoxically, exist in over 50 different forms most of which have been well characterized. This multiplicity of forms arises firstly from the existence of atomic, molecular and ionized species in the gas phase: H, H_2, H^+, H^-, H_2^+, H_3^+ ..., H_{11}^+; secondly, from the existence of three isotopes, $_1^1H$, $_1^2H(D)$ and $_1^3H(T)$, and correspondingly of D, D_2, HD, DT, etc.; and, finally, from the existence of nuclear spin isomers for the homonuclear diatomic species,

---

[2] K. M. MACKAY, The element hydrogen, *Comprehensive Inorganic Chemistry*, Vol. 1, Chap. 1. K. M. MACKAY and M. F. A. DOVE, Deuterium and tritium, *ibid.*, Vol. 1, Chap. 3, Pergamon Press, Oxford, 1973.

i.e. *ortho*- and *para*-dihydrogen, -dideuterium and -ditritium.[†]

3.2.1 Isotopes of hydrogen

Hydrogen as it occurs in nature is predominantly composed of atoms in which the nucleus is a single proton. In addition, terrestrial hydrogen contains about 0.0156% of deuterium atoms in which the nucleus also contains a neutron, and this is the reason for its variable atomic weight (p. 17). Addition of a second neutron induces instability and tritium is radioactive, emitting low-energy β^- particles with a half-life of 12.33 y. Some characteristic properties of these 3 atoms are given in Table 3.1, and their implications for stable isotope studies, radioactive tracer studies, and nmr spectroscopy are obvious.

In the molecular form, dihydrogen is a stable, colourless, odourless, tasteless gas with a very low mp and bp. Data are in Table 3.2 from which it is clear that the values for deuterium and tritium are substantially higher.

[†] The term dihydrogen (like dinitrogen, dioxygen, etc.) is used when it is necessary to refer unambiguously to the molecule H_2 (or N_2, O_2, etc.) rather than to the element as a substance or to an atom of the element. Strictly, one should use "diprotium" when referring specifically to the species H_2 and "dihydrogen" when referring to an undifferentiated isotopic mixture such as would be obtained from materials having the natural isotopic abundances of H and D; likewise "proton" only when referring specifically to H^+, but "hydron" when referring to an undifferentiated isotopic mixture.

Table 3.1   Atomic properties of hydrogen (protium), deuterium, and tritium

Property	H	D	T
Relative atomic mass	1.007 825	2.014 102	3.016 049
Nuclear spin quantum number	$\frac{1}{2}$	1	$\frac{1}{2}$
Nuclear magnetic moment/(nuclear magnetons)[a]	2.792 70	0.857 38	2.978 8
NMR frequency (at 2.35 tesla)/MHz	100.56	15.360	104.68
NMR relative sensitivity (constant field)	1.000	0.009 64	1.21
Nuclear quadrupole moment/(10^{-28} m^2)	0	2.766×10^{-3}	0
Radioactive stability	Stable	Stable	β^- $t_{\frac{1}{2}}$ 12.33 y[b]

[a] Nuclear magneton $\mu_N = e\hbar/2m_p = 5.0508 \times 10^{-27}$ J T^{-1}.

[b] E_{max} 18.6 keV; E_{mean} 5.7 keV; range in air ~6 mm; range in water ~6 μm.

Table 3.2   Physical properties of hydrogen, deuterium and tritium

Property[a]	H_2	D_2	T_2
MP/K	13.957	18.73	20.62
BP/K	20.39	23.67	25.04
Heat of fusion/kJ mol^{-1}	0.117	0.197	0.250
Heat of vaporization/kJ mol^{-1}	0.904	1.226	1.393
Critical temperature/K	33.19	38.35	40.6 (calc)
Critical pressure/atm[b]	12.98	16.43	18.1 (calc)
Heat of dissociation/kJ mol^{-1} (at 298.2 K)	435.88	443.35	446.9
Zero point energy/kJ mol^{-1}	25.9	18.5	15.1
Internuclear distance/pm	74.14	74.14	(74.14)

[a]Data refer to H_2 of normal isotopic composition (i.e. containing 0.0156 atom % of deuterium, predominantly as HD). All data refer to the mixture of *ortho*- and *para*-forms that are in equilibrium at room temperature.

[b]1 atm $= 101.325 \, kN \, m^{-2} = 101.325 \, kPa$.

For example, the mp of T_2 is above the bp of H_2. Other forms such as HD and DT tend to have properties intermediate between those of their components. Thus HD has mp 16.60 K, bp 22.13 K, ΔH_{fus} 0.159 kJ mol^{-1}, ΔH_{vap} 1.075 kJ mol^{-1}, T_c 35.91 K, P_c 14.64 atm and ΔH_{dissoc} 439.3 kJ mol^{-1}. The critical temperature T_c is the temperature above which a gas cannot be liquefied simply by application of pressure, and the critical pressure P_c is the pressure required for liquefaction at this point.

Table 3.2 also indicates that the heat of dissociation of the hydrogen molecule is extremely high, the H–H bond energy being larger than for almost all other single bonds. This contributes to the relative unreactivity of hydrogen at room temperature. Significant thermal decomposition into hydrogen atoms occurs only above 2000 K: the percentage of atomic H is 0.081 at this temperature, and this rises to 7.85% at 3000 K and 95.5% at 5000 K. Atomic hydrogen can, however, be conveniently prepared in low-pressure glow discharges, and the study of its reactions forms an important branch of chemical gas kinetics. The high heat of recombination of hydrogen atoms finds application in the atomic hydrogen torch — dihydrogen is dissociated in an arc and the atoms then recombine on the surface of a metal, generating temperatures in the region of 4000 K which can be used to weld very high melting metals such as tantalum and tungsten.

3.2.2 Ortho- *and* para-*hydrogen*

All homonuclear diatomic molecules having nuclides with non-zero spin are expected to show nuclear spin isomers. The effect was first detected in dihydrogen where it is particularly noticeable, and it has also been established for D_2, T_2, $^{14}N_2$, $^{15}N_2$, $^{17}O_2$, etc. When the two nuclear spins are parallel (*ortho*-hydrogen) the resultant nuclear spin quantum number is 1 (i.e. $\frac{1}{2} + \frac{1}{2}$) and the state is threefold degenerate (2S + 1). When the two proton spins are antiparallel, however, the resultant nuclear spin is zero and the state is non-degenerate. Conversion between the two states involves a forbidden triplet–singlet transition and is normally slow unless catalysed by interaction with solids or paramagnetic species which either break the H–H bond, weaken it, or allow magnetic perturbations. Typical catalysts are Pd, Pt, active Fe_2O_3 and NO. *Para*-hydrogen (spins antiparallel) has the lower energy and this state is favoured at low temperatures. Above 0 K (100% *para*) the equilibrium concentration of *ortho*-hydrogen gradually increases until, above room temperature, the statistically weighted proportion of 3 *ortho*:1 *para* is obtained, i.e. 25% *para*. Typical equilibrium concentrations of *para*-hydrogen are 99.8% at 20 K, 65.4% at 60 K, 38.5% at 100 K, 25.7% at 210 K, and 25.1% at 273 K (Fig. 3.1). It follows that, whereas essentially pure *para*-hydrogen can be obtained, it is never possible to obtain a sample

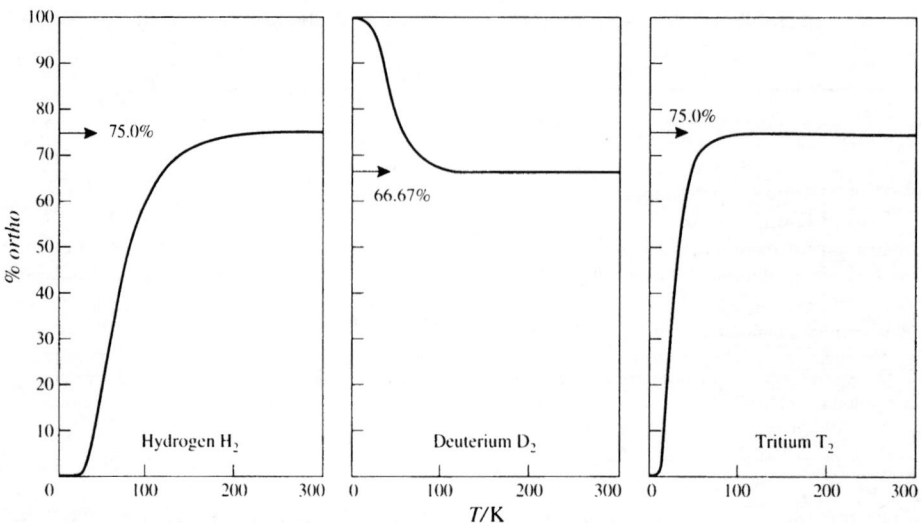

Figure 3.1   *Ortho-para* equilibria for H_2, D_2 and T_2.

containing more than 75% of *ortho*-hydrogen. Experimentally, the presence of both o-H_2 and p-H_2 is seen as an alternation in the intensities of successive rotational lines in the fine structure of the electronic band spectrum of H_2. It also explains the curious temperature dependence of the heat capacity of hydrogen gas.

Similar principles apply to *ortho*- and *para*-deuterium except that, as the nuclear spin quantum number of the deuteron is 1 rather than $\frac{1}{2}$ as for the proton, the system is described by Bose–Einstein statistics rather than the more familiar Fermi–Dirac statistics. For this reason, the stable low-temperature form is *ortho*-deuterium and at high temperatures the statistical weights are 6 *ortho*:3 *para* leading to an upper equilibrium concentration of 33.3% *para*-deuterium above about 190 K as shown in Fig. 3.1. Tritium (spin $\frac{1}{2}$) resembles H_2 rather than D_2.

Most physical properties are but little affected by nuclear-spin isomerism though the thermal conductivity of p-H_2 is more than 50% greater than that of o-H_2, and this forms a ready means of analysing mixtures. The mp of p-H_2 (containing only 0.21% o-H_2) is 0.15 K below that of "normal" hydrogen (containing 75% o-H_2), and by extrapolation the mp of (unobtainable) pure

o-H_2 is calculated to be 0.24 K above that of p-H_2. Similar differences are found for the bps which occur at the following temperatures: normal-H_2 20.39 K, o-H_2 20.45 K. For deuterium the converse relation holds, o-D_2 melting some 0.03 K below "normal"-D_2 (66.7% *ortho*) and boiling some 0.04 K below. The effects for other elements are even smaller.

3.2.3 Ionized forms of hydrogen

This section briefly considers the proton H^+, the hydride ion H^-, the hydrogen molecule ion H_2^+, the triatomic 2-electron species H_3^+ and the recently established cluster species H_n^+,[3,4].

The hydrogen atom has a high ionization energy (1312 kJ mol^{-1}) and in this it resembles the halogens rather than the alkali metals. Removal of the 1s electron leaves a bare proton which, having a radius of only about 1.5×10^{-3} pm, is not a stable chemical entity in the condensed phase. However, when bonded to other species it is well known in solution and in

[3] N. J. KIRCHNER and M. T. BOWERS, *J. Chem. Phys.* **86**, 1301–10 (1987).

[4] M. OKUMURA, L. I. YEH and Y. T. LEE, *J. Chem. Phys.* **88**, 79–91 (1988), and references cited therein.

solids, e.g. H_3O^+, NH_4^+, etc. The proton affinity of water and the enthalpy of solution of H^+ in water have been estimated by several authors and typical values that are currently accepted are:

$$H^+(g) + H_2O(g) \longrightarrow H_3O^+(g);$$
$$-\Delta H \sim 710 \, kJ \, mol^{-1}$$
$$H^+(g) \longrightarrow H_3O^+(aq);$$
$$-\Delta H \sim 1090 \, kJ \, mol^{-1}$$

It follows that the heat of solution of the oxonium ion in water is $\sim 380 \, kJ \, mol^{-1}$, intermediate between the values calculated for Na^+ ($405 \, kJ \, mol^{-1}$) and K^+ ($325 \, kJ \, mol^{-1}$). Reactions involving proton transfer will be considered in more detail in Section 3.5.

The hydrogen atom, like the alkali metals (ns^1) and halogens (ns^2np^5), has an affinity for the electron and heat is evolved in the following process:

$$H(g) + e^- \longrightarrow H^-(g); \quad -\Delta H_{calc} = 72 \, kJ \, mol^{-1}$$

This is larger than the corresponding value for Li ($57 \, kJ \, mol^{-1}$) but substantially smaller than the value for F ($333 \, kJ \, mol^{-1}$). The hydride ion H^- has the same electron configuration as helium but is much less stable because the single positive charge on the proton must now control the 2 electrons. The hydride ion is thus readily deformable and this constitutes a characteristic feature of its structural chemistry (see p. 66).

The species H_2^+ and H_3^+ are important as model systems for chemical bonding theory. The hydrogen molecule ion H_2^+ comprises 2 protons and 1 electron and is extremely unstable even in a low-pressure gas discharge system; the energy of dissociation and the internuclear distance (with the corresponding values for H_2 in parentheses) are:

$$\Delta H_{dissoc} \; 255(436) \, kJ \, mol^{-1};$$
$$r(H–H) \; 106(74.2) \, pm$$

The triatomic hydrogen molecule ion H_3^+ was first detected by J. J. Thomson in gas discharges and later fully characterized by mass spectrometry; its relative atomic mass, 3.0235, clearly distinguishes it from HD (3.0219) and from tritium

(3.0160). The "observed" equilateral triangular 3-centre, 2-electron structure is more stable than the hypothetical linear structure, and the comparative stability of the species is shown by the following gas-phase enthalpies:

$$H + H + H^+ = H_3^+; \quad -\Delta H \; 855.9 \, kJ \, mol^{-1}$$
$$H_2 + H^+ = H_3^+; \quad -\Delta H \; 423.8 \, kJ \, mol^{-1}$$
$$H + H_2^+ = H_3^+; \quad -\Delta H \; 600.2 \, kJ \, mol^{-1}$$

The H_3^+ ion is the simplest possible example of a three-centre two-electron bond (see discussion of bonding in boranes on p. 157) and is also a model for the dihapto bonding mode of the ligand η^2-H_2 (pp. 44–7):

A series of ions H_n^+ with n-odd up to 15 and n-even up to 10 have recently been observed mass-spectrometrically and characterized for the first time.[3,4] The odd-numbered species are much more stable than the even-numbered members, as shown in the subjoined table which gives the relative intensities, I, as a function of n (in H_n^+) obtained in a particular experiment with a high-pressure ion source, relative to H_3^+:[3]

n	1	2	3	4	5	6
$10^4 I$	160	50	**10 000**	4.2	4200	210

n	7	8	9	10	11
$10^4 I$	3200	7.4	2600	18	34

The structures of H_5^+, H_7^+ and H_9^+ are related to that of H_3^+ with H_2 molecules added perpendicularly at the corners, whereas those of H_4^+, H_6^+ and H_8^+ feature an added H atom at the first corner. Typical structures are shown below. The structures of higher members of the series, with $n \geq 10$ are unknown but may involve further loosely bonded H_2 molecules above and below the H_3^+ plane. Enthalpies of dissociation are ΔH°_{300} ($H_5^+ \rightleftharpoons H_3^+ + H_2$) $28 \, kJ \, mol^{-1}$ and ΔH°_{300} ($H_7^+ \rightleftharpoons H_5^+ + H_2$) $13 \, kJ \, mol^{-1}$.[4]

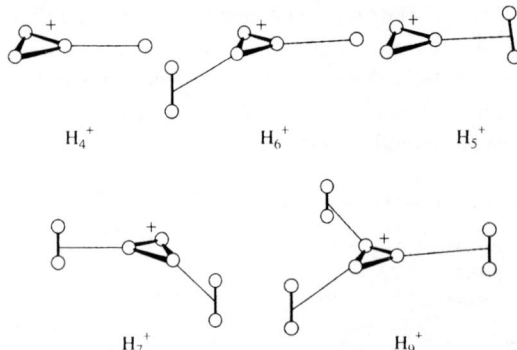

$$H_4^+ \qquad\qquad H_6^+ \qquad\qquad H_5^+$$

$$H_7^+ \qquad\qquad\qquad H_9^+$$

3.3 Preparation, Production and Uses[(5.6)]

3.3.1 Hydrogen

Hydrogen can be prepared by the reaction of water or dilute acids on electropositive metals such as the alkali metals, alkaline earth metals, the metals of Groups 3, 4 and the lanthanoids. The reaction can be explosively violent. Convenient laboratory methods employ sodium amalgam or calcium with water, or zinc with hydrochloric acid. The reaction of aluminium or ferrosilicon with aqueous sodium hydroxide has also been used. For small-scale preparations the hydrolysis of metal hydrides is convenient, and this generates twice the amount of hydrogen as contained in the hydride, e.g.:

$$CaH_2 + 2H_2O \longrightarrow Ca(OH)_2 + 2H_2$$

Electrolysis of acidified water using platinum electrodes is a convenient source of hydrogen (and oxygen) and, on a larger scale, very pure hydrogen (>99.95%) can be obtained from the electrolysis of warm aqueous solutions of barium hydroxide between nickel electrodes. The method is expensive but becomes economical

on an industrial scale when integrated with the chloralkali industry (p. 798). Other bulk processes involve the (endothermic) reaction of steam on hydrocarbons or coke:

$$CH_4 + H_2O \xrightarrow{1100°C} CO + 3H_2$$

$$C + H_2O \xrightarrow{1000°C} CO + H_2 \quad \text{(water gas)}$$

In both processes the CO can be converted to CO_2 by passing the gases and steam over an iron oxide or cobalt oxide catalyst at 400°C, thereby generating more hydrogen:

$$CO + H_2O \xrightarrow[\text{catalyst}]{400°C} CO_2 + H_2$$

This is the so-called water–gas shift reaction $(-\Delta G^{\circ}_{298} 19.9\,\text{kJ mol}^{-1})$ and it can also be effected by low-temperature homogeneous catalysts in aqueous acid solutions.[(7)] The extent of subsequent purification of the hydrogen depends on the use to which it will be put.

The industrial production of hydrogen is considered in more detail in the Panel. The largest single use of hydrogen is in ammonia synthesis (p. 421) but other major applications are in the catalytic hydrogenation of unsaturated liquid vegetable oils to solid, edible fats (margarine), and in the manufacture of bulk organic chemicals, particularly methanol (by the "oxo" or hydroformylation process):

$$CO + 2H_2 \xrightarrow[\text{catalyst}]{\text{cobalt}} MeOH$$

Direct reaction of hydrogen with chlorine is a major source of hydrogen chloride (p. 811), and a smaller, though still substantial use is in the manufacture of metal hydrides and complex metal hydrides (p. 64). Hydrogen is used in metallurgy to reduce oxides to metals (e.g. Mo, W) and to produce a reducing atmosphere. Direct reduction of iron ores in steelmaking is also now becoming technically and economically feasible.

[5] T. A. CZUPPON, S. A. KNEZ and D. S. NEWSOME, Hydrogen, in *Kirk–Othmer Encyclopedia of Chemical Technology*, 4th edn., Vol. 13, Wiley, New York, 1995, pp. 838–94.

[6] P. HÄUSSINGER R. LOHMÜLLER and A. M. WATSON, Hydrogen, in *Ullmann's Encyclopedia of Industrial Chemistry*, 5th edn., Vol. A13, VCH, Weinheim, 1989, pp. 297–442.

[7] C.-H. CHENG and R. EISENBERG, *J. Am. Chem. Soc.* **100**, 5969–70 (1978).

Industrial Production of Hydrogen

Many reactions are available for the preparation of hydrogen and the one chosen depends on the amount needed, the purity required, and the availability of raw materials. Most (~97%) of the hydrogen produced in industry is consumed in integrated plants on site (e.g. ammonia synthesis, petrochemical works, etc.). Even so, vast amounts of the gas are produced for the general market, e.g. ~6.5 × 10^{10} m^3 or 5.4 million tonnes yearly in the USA alone. Small generators may have a capacity of 100–4000 m^3 h^{-1}, medium-sized plants 4000–10 000 m^3 h^{-1}, and large plants can produce 10^4–10^5 m^3 h^{-1}. The dominant large-scale process in integrated plants is the catalytic steam–hydrocarbon reforming process using natural gas or oil-refinery feedstock. After desulfurization (to protect catalysts) the feedstock is mixed with process steam and passed over a nickel-based catalyst at 700–1000°C to convert it irreversibly to CO and H$_2$, e.g.

$$C_3H_8 + 3H_2O \xrightarrow[\text{catalyst}]{900°C} 3CO + 7H_2$$

Two reversible reactions also occur to give an equilibrium mixture of H$_2$, CO, CO$_2$ and H$_2$O:

$$CO + H_2O \rightleftharpoons CO_2 + H_2$$

$$CO + 3H_2 \rightleftharpoons CH_4 + H_2O$$

The mixture is cooled to ~350°C before entering a high-temperature shift convertor where the major portion of the CO is catalytically and exothermically converted to CO$_2$ and hydrogen by reaction with H$_2$O. The issuing gas is further cooled to 200° before entering the low-temperature shift convertor which reduces the CO content to 0.2 vol%. The product is further cooled and CO$_2$ absorbed in a liquid contacter. Further removal of residual CO and CO$_2$ can be effected by methanation at 350°C to a maximum of 10 ppm. Provided that the feedstock contains no nitrogen the product purity is about 98%. Alternatively the low-temperature shift process and methanation stage can be replaced by a single pressure-swing absorption (PSA) system in which the hydrogen is purified by molecular sieves. The sieves are regenerated by adiabatic depressurization at ambient temperature (hence the name) and the product has a purity of ≥99.9%.

At present about 77% of the industrial hydrogen produced is from petrochemicals, 18% from coal, 4% by electrolysis of aqueous solutions and at most 1% from other sources. Thus, hydrogen is produced as a byproduct of the brine electrolysis process for the manufacture of chlorine and sodium hydroxide (p. 798). The ratio of H$_2$:Cl$_2$:NaOH is, of course, fixed by stoichiometry and this is an economic determinant since bulk transport of the byproduct hydrogen is expensive. To illustrate the scale of the problem: the total world chlorine production capacity is about 38 million tonnes per year which corresponds to 105 000 tonnes of hydrogen (1.3 × 10^{10} m^3). Plants designed specifically for the electrolytic manufacture of hydrogen as the main product, use steel cells and aqueous potassium hydroxide as electrolyte. The cells may be operated at atmospheric pressure (Knowles cells) or at 30 atm (Lonza cells).

When relatively small amounts of hydrogen are required, perhaps in remote locations such as weather stations, then small transportable generators can be used which can produce 1–17 m^3 h^{-1}. During production a 1:1 molar mixture of methanol and water is vaporized and passed over a "base–metal chromite" type catalyst at 400°C where it is cracked into hydrogen and carbon monoxide; subsequently steam reacts with the carbon monoxide to produce the dioxide and more hydrogen:

$$MeOH \xrightarrow[\text{catalyst}]{400°C} CO + 2H_2$$

$$CO + H_2O \longrightarrow CO_2 + H_2$$

All the gases are then passed through a diffuser separator comprising a large number of small-diameter thin-walled tubes of palladium-silver alloy tightly packed in a stainless steel case. The solubility of hydrogen in palladium is well known (p. 1150) and the alloy with silver is used to prolong the life of the diffuser by avoiding troublesome changes in dimensions during the passage of hydrogen. The hydrogen which emerges is cool, pure, dry and ready for use via a metering device.

Another medium-scale use is in oxyhydrogen torches and atomic hydrogen torches for welding and cutting. Liquid hydrogen is used in bubble chambers for studying high-energy particles and as a rocket fuel (with oxygen) in the space programme. Hydrogen gas is potentially a large-scale fuel for use in internal combustion engines and fuel cells if the notional "hydrogen economy" (see Panel on p. 40) is ever developed.

3.3.2 Deuterium

Deuterium is invariably prepared from heavy water, D$_2$O, which is itself now manufactured

The Hydrogen Economy[6,8−11]

The growing recognition during the past decades that world reserves of coal and oil are finite and that nuclear power cannot supply all our energy requirements, particularly for small mobile units such as cars, has prompted an active search for alternatives. One solution which has many attractive features is the "hydrogen economy" whereby energy is transported and stored in the form of liquid or gaseous hydrogen. Enthusiasts point out that such a major change in the source of energy, though apparently dramatic, is not unprecedented and has in fact occurred twice during the past 100 y. In 1880 wood was overtaken by coal as the main world supplier of energy and now it accounts for only about 2% of the total. Likewise in 1960 coal was itself overtaken by oil and now accounts for only 15% of the total. (Note, however, that this does not imply a decrease in the total amount of coal used: in 1930 this was 14.5×10^6 barrels per day of oil equivalent and was 75% of the then total energy supply whereas in 1975 coal had increased in absolute terms by 11% to 16.2×10^6 b/d oe, but this was only 18% of the total energy supply which had itself increased 4.6-fold in the interim.) Another change may well be in the offing since nuclear power, which was effectively non-existent as an industrial source of energy in 1950, now accounts for 16% of the world supply of electricity; it has already overtaken coal as a source of energy and may well overtake oil during the next century. The aim of the "hydrogen economy" is to transmit this energy, not as electric power but in the form of hydrogen; this overcomes the great problem of electricity — that it cannot be stored — and also reduces the costs of power transmission.

The technology already exists for producing hydrogen electrically and storing it in bulk. For example huge quantities of liquid hydrogen are routinely stored in vacuum insulated cryogenic tanks for the US space programme, one such tank alone holding over $3400 \, m^3$ (900 000 US gallons). Liquid hydrogen can be transported by road or by rail tankers of $75.7 \, m^3$ capacity (20 000 US gallons). Underground storage of the type currently used for hydrogen — natural gas mixtures and transmission through large pipes is also feasible, and pipelines carrying hydrogen up to 80 km in the USA and South Africa and 200 km in Europe have been in operation for many years. Smaller storage units based on metal alloy systems have also been suggested, e.g. $LaNi_5$ can absorb up to 7 moles of H atoms per mole of $LaNi_5$ at room temperature and 2.5 atm, the density of contained hydrogen being twice that in the liquid element itself. Other systems include $Mg-MgH_2$, $Mg_2Ni-Mg_2NiH_4$, $Ti-TiH_2$ and $TiFe-TiFeH_{1.95}$.

The advantages claimed for hydrogen as an automobile fuel are the greater energy release per unit weight of fuel and the absence of polluting emissions such as CO, CO_2, NO_x, SO_2, hydrocarbons, aldehydes and lead compounds. The product of combustion is water with only traces of nitrogen oxides. Several conventional internal-combustion petrol engines have already been simply and effectively modified to run on hydrogen. Fuel cells for the regeneration of electric power have also been successfully operated commercially with a conversion efficiency of 70%, and test cells at higher pressures have achieved 85% efficiency.

Non-electrolytic sources of hydrogen have also been studied. The chemical problem is how to transfer the correct amount of free energy to a water molecule in order to decompose it. In the last few years about 10 000 such thermochemical water-splitting cycles have been identified, most of them with the help of computers, though it is significant that the most promising ones were discovered first by the intuition of chemists.

The stage is thus set, and further work to establish safe and economically viable sources of hydrogen for general energy usage seems destined to flourish as an active area of research for some while.

on the multitonne scale by the electrolytic enrichment of normal water.[12,13] The enrichment is expressed as a separation factor between the gaseous and liquid phases:

$$s = (H/D)_g / (H/D)_l$$

The equilibrium constant for the exchange reaction

$$H_2O + HD \rightleftharpoons HDO + H_2$$

is about 3 at room temperature and this would lead to a value of $s = 3$ if this were the only effect. However, the choice of the metal used for the electrodes can also affect the various electrode processes, and this increases the separation still further. Using alkaline solutions s values in

[8] D. P. GREGORY, The hydrogen economy, Chap. 23 in *Chemistry in the Environment*, Readings from *Scientific American*, 1973, pp. 219–27.

[9] L. B. McGOWN and J. O'M. BOCKRIS, *How to Obtain Abundant Clean Energy*, Plenum, New York, 1980, 275 pp. L. O. WILLIAMS, *Hydrogen Power*, Pergamon Press, Oxford, 1980, 158 pp.

[10] C. J. WINTER and J. NITSCH (eds.), *Hydrogen as an Energy Carrier*, Springer Verlag, Berlin, 1988, 377 pp.

[11] B. BOGDANOVIĆ, *Angew. Chem. Int. Edn. Engl.* **24**, 262–73 (1985).

[12] G. VASARU, D. URSU, A. MIHĂILĂ and P. SZENT-GYÖRGYI, *Deuterium and Heavy Water*, Elsevier, Amsterdam, 1975, 404 pp.

[13] H. K. RAE (ed.), *Separation of Hydrogen Isotopes*, ACS Symposium Series No. 68, 1978, 184 pp.

the range 5–7.6 are obtained for many metals, rising to 13.9 for platinum cathodes and even higher for gold. By operating a large number of cells in cascade, and burning the evolved H_2/D_2 mixture to replenish the electrolyte of earlier cells in the sequence, any desired degree of enrichment can ultimately be attained. Thus, starting with normal water (0.0156% of hydrogen as deuterium) and a separation factor of 5, the deuterium content rises to 10% after the original volume has been reduced by a factor of 2400. Reduction by 66 000 is required for 90% deuterium and by 130 000 for 99% deuterium. If, however, the separation factor is 10, then 99% deuterium can be obtained by a volume reduction on electrolysis of 22 000. Prior enrichment of the electrolyte to 15% deuterium can be achieved by a chemical exchange between H_2S and H_2O after which a fortyfold volume reduction produces heavy water with 99% deuterium content. Other enrichment processes are now rarely used but include fractional distillation of water (which also enriches ^{18}O), thermal diffusion of gaseous hydrogen, and diffusion of H_2/D_2 through palladium metal.

Many methods have been used to determine the deuterium content of hydrogen gas or water. For H_2/D_2 mixtures mass spectroscopy and thermal conductivity can be used together with gas chromatography (alumina activated with manganese chloride at 77 K). For heavy water the deuterium content can be determined by density measurements, refractive index change, or infrared spectroscopy.

The main uses of deuterium are in tracer studies to follow reaction paths and in kinetic studies to determine isotope effects.[14] A good discussion with appropriate references is in *Comprehensive Inorganic Chemistry*, Vol. 1, pp. 99–116. The use of deuterated solvents is widespread in proton nmr studies to avoid interference from solvent hydrogen atoms, and deuteriated compounds are also valuable in structural studies involving neutron diffraction techniques.

3.3.3 Tritium [15]

Tritium differs from the other two isotopes of hydrogen in being radioactive and this immediately indicates its potential uses and its method of detection. Tritium occurs naturally to the extent of about 1 atom per 10^{18} hydrogen atoms as a result of nuclear reactions induced by cosmic rays in the upper atmosphere:

$$^{14}_{7}N + ^{1}_{0}n = ^{3}_{1}H + ^{12}_{6}C$$

$$^{14}_{7}N + ^{1}_{1}H = ^{3}_{1}H + \text{fragments}$$

$$^{2}_{1}H + ^{2}_{1}H = ^{3}_{1}H + ^{1}_{1}H$$

The concentration of tritium increased by over a hundredfold when thermonuclear weapon testing began on Bikini Atoll in March 1954 but has now subsided as a result of the ban on atmospheric weapon testing and the natural radioactivity of the isotope ($t_{\frac{1}{2}}$ 12.33 y).

Numerous reactions are available for the artificial production of tritium and it is now made on a large scale by neutron irradiation of enriched ^6Li in a nuclear reactor:

$$^{6}_{3}Li + ^{1}_{0}n = ^{4}_{2}He + ^{3}_{1}H$$

The lithium is in the form of an alloy with magnesium or aluminium which retains much of the tritium until it is released by treatment with acid. Alternatively the tritium can be produced by neutron irradiation of enriched LiF at 450° in a vacuum and then recovered from the gaseous products by diffusion through a palladium barrier. As a result of the massive production of tritium for thermonuclear devices and research into energy production by fusion reactions, tritium is available cheaply on the megacurie scale for peaceful purposes.† The most convenient way of storing the gas is to react it with finely divided uranium

---

[14] L. MELANDER and W. H. SAUNDERS, *Reaction Rates of Isotopic Molecules*, Wiley, New York, 1980, 331 pp.

[15] E. A. EVANS, *Tritium and its Compounds*, 2nd edn., Butterworths, London, 1974, 840 pp. E. A. EVANS, D. C. WARRELL, J. A. ELVIDGE and J. R. JONES, *Handbook of Tritium NMR Spectroscopy and Applications*, Wiley, Chichester, 1985, 249 pp.

† See also p. 18 for the influence on the atomic weight of commercially available lithium in some countries.

to give UT$_3$ from which it can be released by heating above 400°C.

Besides being one of the least expensive radio-isotopes, tritium has certain unique advantages as a tracer. Like ^{14}C it is a pure low-energy β^- emitter with no associated γ-rays. The radiation is stopped by $\sim$6 mm of air or $\sim$6 μm of material of density 1 g cm^{-3} (e.g. water). As the range is inversely proportional to the density, this is reduced to only $\sim$1 μm in photographic emulsion ($\rho \sim$3.5 g cm^{-3}) thus making tritium ideal for high-resolution autoradiography. Moreover, tritium has a high specific activity. The weight of tritium equal to an activity of 1 Ci is 0.103 mg and 1 mmol T$_2$ has an activity of 58.25 Ci. [Note: 1 Ci (curie) = 3.7 × 10^{10} Bq (becquerel); 1 Bq = 1 s^{-1}.] Tritium is one of the least toxic of radio-isotopes and shielding is unnecessary; however, precautions must be taken against ingestion, and no work should be carried out without appropriate statutory authorization and adequate radiochemical facilities.

Tritium has been used extensively in hydrological studies to follow the movement of ground waters and to determine the age of various bodies of water. It has also been used to study the adsorption of hydrogen and the hydrogenation of ethylene on a nickel catalyst and to study the absorption of hydrogen in metals. Autoradiography has been used extensively to study the distribution of tritium in multiphase alloys, though care must be taken to correct for the photographic darkening caused by emanated tritium gas. Increasing use is also being made of tritium as a tracer for hydrogen in the study of reaction mechanisms and kinetics and in work on homogeneous catalysis.

The production of tritium-labelled organic compounds was enormously facilitated by K. E. Wilzbach's discovery in 1956 that tritium could be introduced merely by storing a compound under tritium gas for a few days or weeks: the β^- radiation induces exchange reactions between the hydrogen atoms in the compound and the tritium gas. The excess of gas is recovered for further use and the tritiated compound is purified chromatographically. Another widely used method of

general applicability is catalytic exchange in solution using either a tritiated solution or tritium gas. This is valuable for the routine production of tritium compounds in high radiochemical yield and at high specific activity ($>$50 mCi mmol^{-1}). For example, although ammonium ions exchange relatively slowly with D$_2$O, tritium exchange equilibria are established virtually instantaneously: tritiated ammonium salts can therefore be readily prepared by dissolving the salt in tritiated water and then removing the water by evaporation:

$$(NH_4)_2SO_4 + HTO \rightleftharpoons (NH_3T)_2SO_4 + H_2O, \text{ etc.}$$

For exchange of non-labile organic hydrogen atoms, acid–base catalysis (or some other catalytic hydrogen-transfer agent such as palladium or platinum) is required. The method routinely gives tritiated products having a specific activity almost 1000 times that obtained by the Wilzbach method; shorter times are required (2–12 h) and subsequent purification is easier.

When specifically labelled compounds are required, direct chemical synthesis may be necessary. The standard techniques of preparative chemistry are used, suitably modified for small-scale work with radioactive materials. The starting material is tritium gas which can be obtained at greater than 98% isotopic abundance. Tritiated water can be made either by catalytic oxidation over palladium or by reduction of a metal oxide:

$$2T_2 + O_2 \xrightarrow{\text{Pd}} 2T_2O$$

$$T_2 + CuO \longrightarrow T_2O + Cu$$

Note, however, that pure tritiated water is virtually never used since 1 ml would contain 2650 Ci; it is self-luminescent, irradiates itself at the rate of 6 × 10^{17} eV ml^{-1} s^{-1} ($\sim$10^9 rad day^{-1}), undergoes rapid self-radiolysis, and also causes considerable radiation damage to dissolved species. In chemical syntheses or exchange reactions tritiated water of 1% tritium abundance (580 mCi mmol^{-1}) is usually sufficient to produce compounds having a specific activity of at least 100 mCi mmol^{-1}. Other useful synthetic reagents are NaT, LiAlH$_3$T, NaBH$_3$T, NaBT$_4$, B$_2$T$_6$ and tritiated Grignard reagents. Typical preparations are as follows:

$$LiH + T_2 \xrightarrow{350°C} LiT + HT$$

$$LiBH_4 + T_2 \xrightarrow{200°C} LiBH_3T + HT$$

$$4LiT + AlBr_3 \xrightarrow{ether} LiAlT_4 + 3LiBr$$

$$B_2H_6 + T_2 \xrightarrow{55°C} B_2H_5T + HT$$

$$3NaBT_4 + 4BF_3.OEt_2 \longrightarrow 2B_2T_6 + 3NaBF_4$$

$$3T_2O(g) + P(CN)_3 \longrightarrow 3TCN + T_3PO_3$$

$$2AgCl + T_2 \xrightarrow{700°C} 2TCl + 2Ag$$

$$Br_2 + T_2 \xrightarrow{uv} 2TBr$$

$$P(red) + I_2 + HTO \longrightarrow TI + HI + \ldots$$

$$NH_3 + T_2 \longrightarrow NH_2T + TH$$

$$Mg_3N_2 + 6T_2O \xrightarrow{100°C} 2NT_3 + 3Mg(OT)_2$$

$$M + \frac{x}{2}T_2 \xrightarrow{heat} MT_x$$

The preparation and use of LiEt$_3$BT and LiAlT$_4$ at maximum specific activity (57.5 Ci mmol^{-1}) has also been described.[16]

3.4 Chemical Properties and Trends

Hydrogen is a colourless, tasteless, odourless gas which has only low solubility in liquid solvents. It is comparatively unreactive at room temperature though it combines with fluorine even in the dark and readily reduces aqueous solutions of palladium(II) chloride:

$$PdCl_2(aq) + H_2 \longrightarrow Pd(s) + 2HCl(aq)$$

---

16 H. ANDRES, H. MORIMOTO and P. G. WILLIAMS, *J. Chem. Soc., Chem. Commun.*, 627–8 (1990).

This reaction can be used as a sensitive test for the presence of hydrogen. At higher temperatures hydrogen reacts vigorously, even explosively, with many metals and non-metals to give the corresponding hydrides. Activation can also be induced photolytically, by heterogeneous catalysts (Raney nickel, Pd, Pt, etc.), or by means of homogeneous hydrogenation catalysts. Industrially important processes include the hydrogenation of many organic compounds and the use of cobalt compounds as catalysts in the hydroformylation of olefins to aldehydes and alcohols at high temperatures and pressures (p. 1140):

$$RCH{=}CH_2 + H_2 + CO \longrightarrow RCH_2CH_2CHO$$

$$RCH_2CH_2CHO + H_2 \longrightarrow RCH_2CH_2CH_2OH$$

An even more effective homogeneous hydrogenation catalyst is the complex [RhCl(PPh$_3$)$_3$] which permits rapid reduction of alkenes, alkynes and other unsaturated compounds in benzene solution at 25°C and 1 atm pressure (p. 1134). The Haber process, which uses iron metal catalysts for the direct synthesis of ammonia from nitrogen and hydrogen at high temperatures and pressures, is a further example (p. 421).

The hydrogen atom has a unique electronic configuration 1s^1: accordingly it can gain an electron to give H$^-$ with the helium configuration 1s^2 or it can lose an electron to give the proton H$^+$ (p. 36). There are thus superficial resemblances both to the halogens which can gain an electron to give an inert-gas configuration ns^2np^6, and to the alkali metals which can lose an electron to give M$^+$ (ns^2np^6). However, because hydrogen has no other electrons in its structure there are sufficient differences from each of these two groups to justify placing hydrogen outside either. For example, the proton is so small ($r \sim 1.5 \times 10^{-3}$ pm compared with normal atomic and ionic sizes of $\sim$50–220 pm) that it cannot exist in condensed systems unless associated with other atoms or molecules. The transfer of protons between chemical species constitutes the basis of acid–base phenomena (see Section 3.5). The hydrogen atom is also frequently found in close association with 2 other atoms in linear array; this particularly important type of interaction is called hydrogen bonding (see Section 3.6). Again, the ability to penetrate metals to form nonstoichiometric metallic hydrides, though not unique to hydrogen, is one of its more characteristic properties as is its ability to form nonlinear hydrogen bridge bonds in many of its compounds. These properties will be further discussed during the general classification of the hydrides of the elements in section 3.7. The most important compound of hydrogen is, of course, water and a detailed discussion of this compound is given on pp. 620–33 in the chapter on oxygen.

3.4.1 The coordination chemistry of hydrogen

Perhaps the most exciting recent development in the chemistry of hydrogen is the discovery that, in transition metal polyhydrides, the molecule H_2 can act as a dihapto ligand, η^2-H_2 (see below). Even the H atom itself can form compounds in which its coordination number (CN) is not just 1 (as expected) but also 2, 3, 4, 5 or even 6. A rich and unexpectedly varied coordination chemistry is thus emerging. We shall deal with the H atom first and then with the H_2 molecule.

By far the most common CN of hydrogen is 1, as in HCl, H_2S, PH_3, CH_4 and most other covalent hydrides and organic compounds. Bridging modes in which the H atom has a higher CN are shown schematically in the next column — in these structures M is typically a transition metal but, particularly in the μ_2-mode and to some extent in the μ_3-mode, one or more of the M can represent a main-group element such as B, Al; C, Si; N etc. Typical examples are in Table 3.3.[17–19] Fuller discussion and references, when appropriate, will be found in later chapters dealing with the individual elements concerned.

[17] D. S. MOORE and S. D. ROBINSON, *Chem. Soc. Revs.* **12**, 415–52 (1983).

[18] A. DEDIEU (ed.), *Transition Metal Hydrides*, VCH, Berlin, 1991, 416 pp.

[19] T. P. FEHLNER, *Polyhedron*, **9**, 1955–63 (1990).

Table 3.3 Stereochemistry of hydrogen

CN	Examples
1	HCl, H_2S, PH_3, NH_4^+, BH_4^-, etc.; [HMn(CO)$_5$], [H_2Fe(CO)$_4$], [H_3Ta(C_5H_5)$_2$], [H_4Cr(dmpe)$_2$], [CoH$_5$]$^{4-}$, [H_6W(PR$_3$)$_3$], [{H_7Re(PR$_3$)$_2$}$_2$Ag]$^+$, [H_8Re(PR$_3$)]$^-$, [ReH$_9$]$^{2-}$
2	B_2H_6, [Me$_2$NAlH$_2$]$_3$, [H_3BHCu(PMePh$_2$)$_3$], [*nido*-Ir(B$_5$H$_8$)(CO)(PPh$_3$)$_2$], [(CO)$_5$WHW(CO)$_5$]$^-$, [(C_5Me$_5$)Ir(μ_2-H)$_3$Ir(C_5Me$_5$)]
3	[*closo*-B_6H_6(μ_3-H)]$^-$, [(μ_3-H)Rh$_3$(C_5H_5)$_4$], [(μ_3-H)$_4$Co$_4$(C_5H_5)$_4$]
4	[(μ_4-H)Ru$_6$(CO)$_{21}$H]$^{2-}$
5	β-Mg$_2$NiH$_4$(d$_4$) (1 "covalent" Ni–D 149 pm plus 4 "ionic" Mg–D 230 pm)
6	[HNb$_6$I$_{11}$], [HRu$_6$(CO)$_{18}$]$^-$, [HCo$_6$(CO)$_{15}$]$^-$, [(μ_6-H)$_2$Ni$_{12}$(CO)$_{21}$]$^{2-}$, [(μ_6-H)Ni$_{12}$(CO)$_{21}$]$^{3-}$

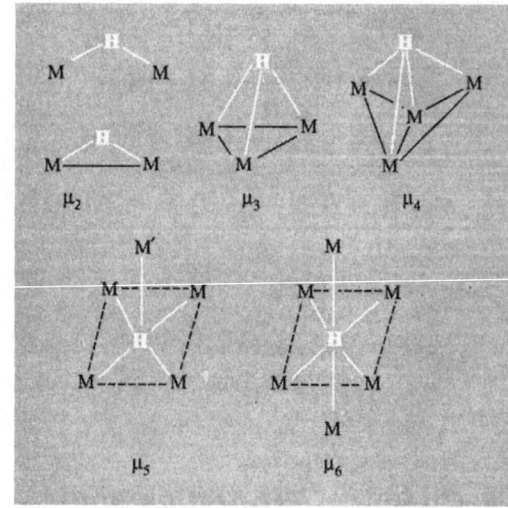

The crucial experiment suggesting that the H_2 molecule might act as a dihapto ligand to transition metals was the dramatic observation[20] that toluene solutions of the deep purple coordinatively unsaturated 16-electron complexes [Mo(CO)$_3$(PCy$_3$)$_2$] and [W(CO)$_3$-(PCy$_3$)$_2$] (where Cy = cyclohexyl) react readily and cleanly with H_2 (1 atm) at low temperatures to precipitate yellow crystals of [M(CO)$_3H_2$(PCy$_3$)$_2$] in 85–95% yield. The

[20] G. J. KUBAS, *J. Chem. Soc., Chem. Commun.*, 61–2 (1980).

H_2 could be quantitatively removed at room temperature either by partial evacuation or by sparging the solution with argon. Definitive confirmation that the complexes did indeed contain η^2-H_2 came from X-ray and neutron diffraction studies on the bis(tri i-propylphosphine) analogue at $-100°$, which revealed the side-on coordination of H_2 as shown in Fig. 3.2.[21] During the past decade many other such compounds have been prepared and studied in great detail, and the field has been well reviewed.[22-24]

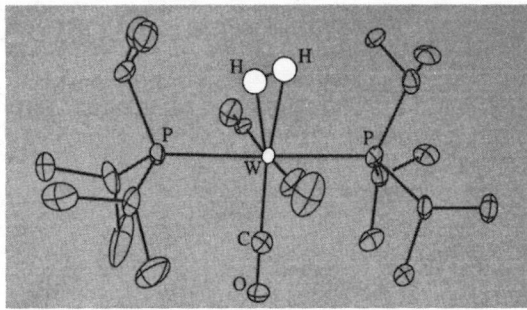

Figure 3.2 The geometry of *mer-trans*-[W(CO)₃-(η^2-H_2)(PPr$_3^i$)₂] from X-ray and neutron diffraction data: r(H–H) 84 pm (compared with 74.14 pm for free H_2), r(W–H) 175 pm. Infrared vibration spectroscopy gives ν(H–H) 2690 cm^{-1} compared with 4159 cm^{-1} (Raman) for free H_2.

There are two general routes to η^2-H_2 complexes. The first involves direct addition of molecular H_2 either to an unoccupied coordination site in a 16-electron complex (as above) or by displacement of a ligand such as CO, Cl, H_2O in the coordination sphere of an 18-electron complex; in this latter case ultraviolet irradiation may be required to assist in the

substitution reaction. Examples are:

$$[W(CO)_3(PPr_3^i)_2] + H_2 \longrightarrow$$
$$[W(CO)_3(\eta^2\text{-}H_2)(PPr_3^i)_2]$$

$$[FeClH(R_2PCH_2CH_2PR_2)_2] + H_2 + NaBPh_4$$
$$\longrightarrow [FeH(\eta^2\text{-}H_2)(R_2PCH_2CH_2PR_2)_2]^+$$
$$+ BPh_4^- + NaCl$$

$$trans\text{-}[IrH(H_2O)(PPh_3)_2(Bq)]^+ + H_2 \longrightarrow$$
$$trans\text{-}[IrH(\eta^2\text{-}H_2)(PPh_3)_2(Bq)]^+$$

$$[Cr(CO)_6] + H_2 \xrightarrow[\text{liq. Xe}]{h\nu} [Cr(CO)_5(\eta^2\text{-}H_2)] + CO$$

$$Co(CO)_3(NO) + H_2 \xrightarrow[\text{liq. Xe}]{h\nu}$$
$$[Co(CO)_2(\eta^2\text{-}H_2)(NO)] + CO$$

The second general method involves the protonation of a polyhydrido complex using a strong acid such as HBF₄.Et₂O. Typical examples involving d^2, d^4, d^6 or d^8 metal centres are:

$$(d^2) \quad [MoH_4(dppe)_2] + 2H^+ \longrightarrow$$
$$[MoH_4(\eta^2\text{-}H_2)(dppe)_2]^{2+}$$

$$d^4) \quad [IrH_5(PCy_3)_2] \underset{NEt_3}{\overset{H^+}{\rightleftharpoons}}$$
$$[IrH_2(\eta^2\text{-}H_2)_2(PCy_3)_2]^+$$

$$(d^6) \quad [RuH_2(dppe)_2] + H^+ \longrightarrow$$
$$[RuH(\eta^2\text{-}H_2)(dppe)_2]^+$$

$$(d^8) \quad [RhH\{P(CH_2CH_2PPh_2)_3\}] + H^+ \longrightarrow$$
$$[Rh(\eta^2\text{-}H_2)\{P(CH_2CH_2PPh_2)_3\}]^+$$

There is even a rare example involving a d^0 polyhydride:[25]

$$(d^0) \quad [ReH_7(PCy_3)_2] \underset{NEt_3}{\overset{H^+(-80°)}{\rightleftharpoons}}$$
$$[ReH_{8-2x}(\eta^2\text{-}H_2)_x(PCy_3)_2]^+$$

[21] G. J. KUBAS, R. R. RYAN, B. I. SWANSON, P. I. VERGAMINI and H. J. WASSERMAN, *J. Am. Chem. Soc.* **106**, 452–4 (1984).

[22] G. J. KUBAS, *Acc. Chem. Res.* **21**, 120–8 (1988).

[23] R. H. CRABTREE and D. G. HAMILTON, *Adv. Organomet. Chem.* **28**, 299–338 (1988); R. H. CRABTREE, *Acc. Chem. Res.* **23**, 95–101 (1990).

[24] A. G. GINZBURG and A. A. BAGATUR'ANTS, *Organomet. Chem. in USSR* **2**, 111–26 (1989).

[25] X. L. R. FONTAINE, E. H. FOWLES and B. L. SHAW, *J. Chem. Soc., Chem. Commun.*, 482–3 (1988).

If deuterio acids are used then η^2-HD complexes are formed; these are particularly useful in establishing the retention of substantive H–H bonding in the coordinated ligand by observation of a 1:1:1 triplet in the proton nmr spectrum (the proton signal being split by coupling to deuterium with nuclear spin $J = 1$).

The stability of η^2-H$_2$ complexes varies considerably, from those which can be observed only in low-temperature matrix-isolation experiments to those which are moderately robust even at room temperature and above. Stability depends on the electron configuration of the metal centre, the electronic and steric nature of the co-ligands, the overall charge on the complex, the state of aggregation and, of course, the temperature. Most η^2-H$_2$ complexes involve transition metals in Groups 6–8, in oxidation states having a formal d^6 electron configuration. No η^2-H$_2$ complexes are yet known for transition metals in Groups 3 or 4 of the periodic table, although examples involving Group 5 metals have recently been reported, e.g. the d^4 species [V(η^5-C$_5$H$_5$)(CO)$_3$(η^2-H$_2$)][26] and [Nb(η^5-C$_5$H$_5$)(CO)$_3$(η^2-H$_2$)].[27] Within a given Group, the first and second members more readily form η^2-H$_2$ complexes while the third member tends to form polyhydrido species, e.g. [Fe(H)$_2$(η^2-H$_2$)(PEtPh$_2$)$_3$] and [Ru(H)$_2$(η^2-H$_2$)(PPh$_3$)$_3$] but [Os(H)$_4$(P(o-tol)$_3$)$_3$].[28] Stability is also enhanced by an overall cationic charge on the complex (remember protonation as a route to η^2-H$_2$ complexes). In such cases, however, stability of the resulting compound depends on the presence of a non-coordinating anion such as BF$_4^-$, otherwise there is a risk of decomposition by displacement of the more weakly coordinating (η^2-H$_2$). Neutral complexes are also well known, but no examples of anionic η^2-H$_2$ complexes have been reported.

[26] M. T. Haward, M. W. George, S. M. Howdle and M. Poliakoff, *J. Chem. Soc., Chem. Commun.*, 913–5 (1990).

[27] M. T. Haward, M. W. George, P. Hamley and M. Poliakoff, *J. Chem. Soc., Chem. Commun.*, 1101–3 (1991).

[28] R. H. Crabtree and D. G. Hamilton, *J. Am. Chem. Soc.* **108** 3124–5 (1986).

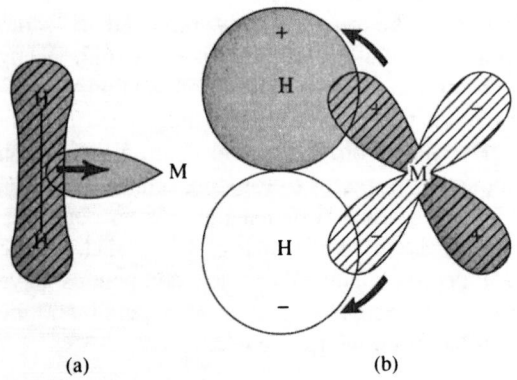

(a)   (b)

Figure 3.3 Schematic representation of the two components of the η^2-H$_2$-metal bond: (a) donation from the filled (hatched) σ-H$_2$ bonding orbital into a vacant hybrid orbital on M; (b) π-back donation from a filled d orbital (or hybrid) on M into the vacant σ^* antibonding orbital of H$_2$.

Most of the observed facts can be understood in terms of a bonding scheme which envisages donation of electron density from the σ bond of H$_2$ into a vacant hybrid orbital on the metal, plus a certain amount of synergic back donation from an occupied d orbital on the metal into the σ^* antibonding orbital of H$_2$ (see Fig. 3.3). This is reminiscent of the bonding in the well known metal–alkene complexes (to be discussed in more detail on p. 931) but with two significant differences: (a) the electron density being donated from the H$_2$ ligand is in the single-bond σ orbital whereas for alkenes such as H$_2$C=CH$_2$ it is in the π component of the double bond; and (b) the H$_2$ antibonding orbital involved in accepting back-donated electron density has σ^* symmetry rather than π^* as in alkenes. It is clear from this description that an overall positive charge on the metal centre encourages forward donation to form the 3-centre bond, but diminishes the extent of back donation. By contrast, an overall negative charge might be expected to enhance back donation into the σ^* antibonding orbital and thus promote rupture of the H$_2$ single bond, with concomitant formation of two new hydrido M–H bonds.

The bonding scheme is also consistent with the observed lengthening of the H–H distance to about 84–90 pm in the η^2-H$_2$ complexes (as compared with 74 pm in free molecular H$_2$), and with the lowering of the ν(H–H) vibration frequency from 4159 cm^{-1} in free H$_2$ to values typically in the range 2650–3250 cm^{-1} in the complexes.

There is evidently a very fine balance between the two options {M(η^2-H$_2$)} and {M(H)$_2$}; indeed, examples of an equilibrium between the two forms have recently been discovered:[27,29,30]

$$[\text{Nb}(\eta^5\text{-C}_5\text{H}_5)(\text{CO})_3(\eta^2\text{-H}_2)] \xrightleftharpoons{-78° \text{ to } +25°}$$

$$[\text{Nb}(\eta^5\text{-C}_5\text{H}_5)(\text{CO})_3(\text{H})_2]$$

$$[\text{Re}(\text{CO})(\eta^2\text{-H}_2)(\text{H})_2(\text{PMe}_2\text{Ph})_3]^+ \xrightleftharpoons{-85° \text{ to } -65°}$$

$$[\text{Re}(\text{CO})(\text{H})_4(\text{PMe}_2\text{Ph})_3]^+$$

$$[\text{Ru}(\eta^2\text{-H}_2)(\eta^2\text{-O}_2\text{CCF}_3)(\text{PCy}_3)_2] \xrightleftharpoons{\text{hexane/r.t.}}$$

$$[\text{Ru}(\text{H})_2(\eta^2\text{-O}_2\text{CCF}_3)(\text{PCy}_3)_2]$$

In the niobium system[27] the η^2-H$_2$ form is marginally the more stable, with $\Delta H = 2.0$ kJ mol^{-1}, whereas in the rhenium system,[29] it is the tetrahydrido form which is the more stable, with $-\Delta G_{208} = 2.5$ kJ mol^{-1} and $-\Delta H = 4.6$ kJ mol^{-1}.

In a sense the formation of η^2-H$_2$ complexes can be thought of as an intermediate stage in the oxidative addition of H$_2$ to form two M–H bonds and, as such, the complexes might serve as a model for this process and for catalytic hydrogenation reactions by metal hydrides.[31] Indeed, intermediate cases between η^2-H$_2$ and (σ-H)$_2$ coordination are occasionally observed, as in [ReH$_7$(P(p-tol)$_3$)$_2$], where neutron-diffraction

studies[32] have revealed one H···H contact of 137.7(7) pm whereas all other H···H distances in the complex are greater than 174 pm. (This distance of 137.7 pm is seen to be intermediate between values of *ca.* 80 pm typical of η^2-H$_2$ complexes and values greater than *ca.* 160 pm which are found in classical hydrido complexes.) Likewise, some trihydrogen complexes, such as [Ir(η^5-C$_5$H$_5$)H$_3$(PMe$_3$)],[33] have nmr behaviour which suggests the presence of a bent (or possibly triangular) η^3-H$_3$ ligand which is bonded "side-on" rather like an allylic group (pp. 933–5).

The possibility of η^1-H$_2$ "end-on" coordination has also been mooted. For example, deposition of Pd atoms onto a krypton matrix doped with H$_2$ at 12 K apparently yields both Pd(η^1-H$_2$) and Pd(η^2-H$_2$) species, whereas with a Xe/H$_2$ matrix only Pd(η^2-H$_2$) was obtained.[34] Again, the complex [ReCl(H$_2$)(PMePh$_2$)$_4$] appears to feature an asymmetrically-bonded H$_2$ ligand which may well be (η^1-H$_2$).[35]

Nearly one hundred η^2-H$_2$ complexes have so far been prepared and the crystal and molecular structure of about half a dozen have been determined by X-ray/neutron diffraction. Some are dinuclear, such as the homobimetallic [(P–N)(η^2-H$_2$)**Ru**(μ-Cl)$_2$(μ-H)**Ru**(H)(PPh$_3$)$_2$][36] and the heterobimetallic [(PPh$_3$)$_2$H**Re**(μ-H)(μ-Cl)$_2$(μ-CO)**Ru**(η^2-H$_2$)(PPh$_3$)$_2$]$^+$.[37]

The coordination chemistry of hydrogen is still being intensively studied and new developments are continually being reported.

[29] X.-L. LUO and R. H. CRABTREE, *J. Chem. Soc., Chem. Commun.*, 189–90 (1990).

[30] T. ANLIGUIE and B. CHAUDRET, *J. Chem. Soc., Chem. Commun.*, 155–7 (1989).

[31] C. BIANCHINI, C. MEALLI, A. MELI, M. PERUZZINI and F. ZANOBINI, *J. Am. Chem. Soc.* **110**, 8725–6 (1988). See also L. D. FIELD, A. V. GEORGE, E. Y. MALOUF and D. J. YOUNG, *Chem. Soc., Chem. Commun.*, 931–3 (1990).

[32] L. BRAMMER, J. A. K. HOWARD, O. JOHNSON, T. F. KOETZLE, J. L. SPENCER and A. M. STRINGER, *J. Chem. Soc., Chem. Commun.*, 241–3 (1991).

[33] D. M. HEINEKEY, N. G. PAYNE and G. K. SCHULTE, *J. Am. Chem. Soc.* **110**, 2303–5 (1988).

[34] G. A. OZIN and J. GARCIA-PRIETO, *J. Am. Chem. Soc.* **108**, 3099–100 (1986).

[35] F. A. COTTON and R. L. LUCK, *Inorg. Chem.* **30**, 767–74 (1991).

[36] C. HAMPTON, W. R. CULLEN and B. R. JAMES, *J. Am. Chem. Soc.* **110**, 6918–9 (1988). In this compound, P–N is a complex substituted ferrocene ligand. See also A. M. JOSHI and B. R. JAMES, *J. Chem. Soc., Chem. Commun.*, 1785–6 (1989).

[37] M. CAZANOUE, Z. HE, D. NEILBECKER and R. MATHIEU, *J. Chem. Soc., Chem. Commun.*, 307–9 (1991).

3.5 Protonic acids and bases[38]

Many compounds that contain hydrogen can donate protons to a solvent such as water and so behave as acids. Water itself undergoes ionic dissociation to a small extent by means of autoprotolysis; the process is usually represented formally by the equilibrium

$$H_2O + H_2O \rightleftharpoons H_3O^+ + OH^-$$

though it should be remembered that both ions are further solvated and that the time a proton spends in close association with any one water molecule is probably only about 10^{-13} s. (See also pp. 630–2 for structural studies on $[H(OH_2)_n]^+$ $n = 1$–6.) Depending on what aspect of the process is being emphasized, the species $H_3O^+(aq)$ can be called an oxonium ion, a hydrogen ion, or simply a solvated (hydrated) proton. The equilibrium constant for autoprotolysis is

$$K_1 = [H_3O^+][OH^-]/[H_2O]^2$$

and, since the concentration of water is essentially constant, the ionic product of water can be written as

$$K_w = [H_3O^+][OH^-] \, \text{mol}^2 \, l^{-2}$$

The value of K_w depends on the temperature, being $0.69 \times 10^{-14} \, \text{mol}^2 \, l^{-2}$ at 0°C, 1.00×10^{-14} at 25°C and 47.6×10^{-14} at 100°C. It follows that the hydrogen-ion concentration in pure water at 25°C is $10^{-7} \, \text{mol} \, l^{-1}$. Acids increase this concentration by means of the reaction

$$HA + H_2O \rightleftharpoons H_3O^+ + A^-;$$

$$K = \frac{[H_3O^+][A^-]}{[HA][H_2O]}$$

It is to be understood that all the species are in aqueous solution and the symbol HA implies only that the (aquated) species can act as a proton donor: it can be a neutral species (e.g. H_2S), an anion (e.g. $H_2PO_4^-$) or a cation such as

$[Fe(H_2O)_6]^{3+}$. The hydrogen-ion concentration is usually expressed as pH (see Panel). In dilute solution the concentration of water molecules is constant at 25°C ($55.345 \, \text{mol} \, l^{-1}$), and the dissociation of the acid is often rewritten as

$$HA \rightleftharpoons H^+ + A^-;$$

$$K_a = [H^+][A^-]/[HA] \, \text{mol} \, l^{-1}$$

The acid constant K_a can also be expressed by the relation

$$pK_a = -\log K_a. \quad \text{Hence, as } K_a = 55.345 \, K$$

$$pK_a = pK - 1.734$$

Further, as the free energy of dissociation is given by

$$\Delta G^\circ = -RT \ln K = -2.3026 RT \log K,$$

the standard free energy of dissociation is

$$\Delta G^\circ_{298.15} = 5.708 pK$$

$$= 5.708(pK_a + 1.734) \, \text{kJ} \, \text{mol}^{-1}$$

Textbooks of analytical chemistry should be consulted for further details concerning the ionization of weak acids and bases and the theory of indicators, buffer solutions, and acid–alkali titrations.[39-41]

Various trends have long been noted in the acid strengths of many binary hydrides and oxoacids.[38] Values for some simple hydrides are given in Table 3.4 from which it is clear that acid strength increases with atomic number both in any one horizontal period and in any

---

[38] R. P. BELL, *The Proton in Chemistry*, 2nd edn. Chapman & Hall, London, 1973, 223 pp.

[39] A. I. VOGEL, *Quantitative Chemical Analysis*, 5th edn., Sections 2.12–2.27, pp. 31–60. Longman, London, 1989.
[40] A. HULANICKI, *Reactions of Acids and Bases in Analytical Chemistry*, Ellis Horwood (Wiley), Chichester, 1987, 308 pp.
[41] D. ROSENTHAL and P. ZUMAN, Acid–base equilibria, buffers and titrations in water, Chap. 18 in I. M. KOLTHOFF and P. J. ELVING (eds.), *Treatise on Analytical Chemistry*, 2nd edn., Vol. 2, Part 1, 1979, pp. 157–236. Succeeding chapters (pp. 237–440) deal with acid–base equilibria and titrations in non-aqueous solvents.

The Concept of pH

The now universally used measure of the hydrogen-ion concentration was introduced in 1909 by the Danish biochemist S. P. L. Sørensen during his work at the Carlsberg Breweries (*Biochem. Z.* **21**, 131, 1909):

$$pH = -\log[H^+]$$

The symbol pH derives from the French *puissance d'hydrogéne*, referring to the exponent or "power of ten" used to express the concentration. Thus a hydrogen-ion concentration of $10^{-7}\,\text{mol}\,l^{-1}$ is designated pH 7, whilst acid solutions with higher hydrogen-ion concentrations have a lower pH. For example, a strong acid of concentration $1\,\text{mmol}\,l^{-1}$ has pH 3, whereas a strong alkali of the same concentration has pH 11 since $[H_3O^+] = 10^{-14}/[OH^-] = 10^{-11}$.

Unfortunately, it is far simpler to define pH than to measure it, despite the commercial availability of instruments that purport to do this. Most instruments use an electrochemical cell such as

glass electrode|test solution|3.5 M KCl(aq)|Hg_2Cl_2|Hg

Assuming that the glass electrode shows an ideal hydrogen electrode response, the emf of the cell still depends on the magnitude of the liquid junction potential E_j and the activity coefficients γ of the ionic species:

$$E = E° - \frac{RT}{F}\ln \gamma_{Cl}[Cl^-] + E_j - \frac{RT}{F}\ln \gamma_H[H^+]$$

For this reason, the pH as measured by any of the existing national standards is an operational quantity which has no simple fundamental significance. It is defined by the equation

$$pH(X) = pH(S) + \frac{(E_x - E_s)F}{RT\ln 10}$$

where pH(S) is the *assigned* pH of a standard buffer solution such as those supplied with pH meters.

Only in the case of dilute aqueous solutions ($<0.1\,\text{mol}\,l^{-1}$) which are neither strongly acid or alkaline ($2 < pH < 12$) is pH(X) such that

$$pH(X) = -\log[H^+]\gamma_\pm \pm 0.02$$

where $\gamma_\pm$, the mean ionic activity coefficient of a typical uni-univalent electrolyte, is given by

$$-\log\gamma_\pm = AI^{\frac{1}{2}}(1 + I)^{-\frac{1}{2}}$$

In this expression I is the ionic strength of the solution and A is a temperature-dependent constant ($0.511^{\frac{1}{2}}\,\text{mol}^{-\frac{1}{2}}$ at 25°C; $0.501^{\frac{1}{2}}\,\text{mol}^{-\frac{1}{2}}$ at 15°C). It is clearly unwise to associate a pH meter reading too closely with pH unless under very controlled conditions, and still less sensible to relate the reading to the actual hydrogen-ion concentration in solution. For further discussion of pH measurements, see *Pure Appl. Chem.* **57**, 531–42 (1985): Definition of pH Scales, Standard Reference Values, Measurement of pH and Related Terminology. Also *C&E News*, Oct. 20, 1997, p. 6.

Table 3.4 Approximate values of pK_a for simple hydrides

CH_4	46	NH_3	35	OH_2	16	FH	3
		PH_3	27	SH_2	7	ClH	−7
				SeH_2	4	BrH	−9
				TeH_2	3	IH	−10

vertical group. Several attempts have been made to interpret these trends, at least qualitatively, but the situation is complex. The trend to increasing acidity from left to right in the periodic table could be ascribed to the increasing electronegativity of the elements which would favour release of the proton, but this is clearly not the dominant effect within any one group since the trend there is in precisely the opposite direction. Within a group it is the diminution in bond strength with increasing atomic number that prevails, and entropies of solvation are also important. It should, perhaps, also be emphasized that thermodynamic computations do not "explain" the observed acid strengths; they merely allocate the overall values of ΔG,

ΔH and ΔS to various notional subprocesses such as bond dissociation energies, ionization energies, electron affinities, heats and entropies of hydration, etc., which themselves have empirically observed values that are difficult to compute *ab initio*.

Regularities in the observed strengths of oxoacids have been formulated in terms of two rules by L. Pauling and others:

(i) for polybasic mononuclear oxoacids, successive acid dissociation constants diminish approximately in the ratios $1:10^{-5}:10^{-10}:\ldots$;

(ii) the value of the first ionization constant for acids of formula $XO_m(OH)_n$ depends sensitively on m but is approximately independent of n and X for constant m, being $\leq 10^{-8}$ for $m = 0$, $\sim 10^{-2}$ for $m = 1$, $\sim 10^3$ for $m = 2$, and $> 10^8$ for $m = 3$.

Thus to illustrate the first rule:

$$H_3PO_4 \rightleftharpoons H^+ + H_2PO_4^-;$$

$$K_1 = \frac{[H^+][H_2PO_4^-]}{[H_3PO_4]} = 7.11 \times 10^{-3}\,mol\,l^{-1};$$

$$pK_1 = 2.15$$

$$H_2PO_4^- \rightleftharpoons H^+ + HPO_4^{2-};$$

$$K_2 = \frac{[H^+][HPO_4^{2-}]}{[H_2PO_4^-]} = 6.31 \times 10^{-8}\,mol\,l^{-1};$$

$$pK_2 = 7.20$$

$$HPO_4^{2-} \rightleftharpoons H^+ + PO_4^{3-};$$

$$K_3 = \frac{[H^+][PO_4^{3-}]}{[HPO_4^{2-}]} = 4.22 \times 10^{-13}\,mol\,l^{-1};$$

$$pK_3 = 12.37$$

Qualitatively, a reduction in pK_a for each successive stage of ionization is to be expected since the proton must separate from an anion of increasingly negative charge, though the approximately constant reduction factor of 10^5 is more difficult to rationalize quantitatively.

Acids which illustrate the second rule are summarized in Table 3.5. The qualitative explanation for this regularity is that, with increasing numbers of oxygen atoms the single negative charge on the anion can be spread more widely, thereby reducing the electrostatic energy attracting the proton and facilitating the ionization. On this basis one might expect an even more dramatic effect if the anion were monoatomic (e.g. S^{2-}, Se^{2-}, Te^{2-}) since the attraction of these dianions for protons will be very strong and the acid dissociation constant of SH^-, SeH^- and TeH^- correspondingly small; this is indeed observed and the ratio of

Table 3.5 Values of pK_a for some mononuclear oxoacids $XO_m(OH)_n$ ($pK_a \approx 8 - 5n$)

X(OH)$_n$ (very weak)		XO(OH)$_n$ (weak)		XO$_2$(OH)$_n$ (strong)		XO$_3$(OH)$_n$ (very strong)	
Cl(OH)	7.2	NO(OH)	3.3	NO$_2$(OH)	-1.4	ClO$_3$(OH)	(-10)
Br(OH)	8.7	ClO(OH)	2.0	ClO$_2$(OH)	-1	MnO$_3$(OH)	—
I(OH)	10.0	CO(OH)$_2$	3.9[a]	IO$_2$(OH)	0.8		
B(OH)$_3$	9.2	SO(OH)$_2$	1.9	SO$_2$(OH)$_2$	<0		
As(OH)$_3$	9.2	SeO(OH)$_2$	2.6	SeO$_2$(OH)$_2$	<0		
Sb(OH)$_3$	11.0	TeO(OH)$_2$	2.7				
Si(OH)$_4$	10.0	PO(OH)$_3$	2.1				
Ge(OH)$_4$	8.6	AsO(OH)$_3$	2.3				
Te(OH)$_6$	8.8	IO(OH)$_5$	1.6				
		HPO(OH)$_2$	1.8[b]				
		H$_2$PO(OH)	2.0[b]				

[a] Corrected for the fact that only 0.4% of dissolved CO_2 is in the form of H_2CO_3; the conventional value is pK_a 6.5.

[b] Note that the value of pK_a for hypophosphorous acid H_3PO_3 is consistent with its (correct) formulation as $HPO(OH)_2$ rather than as $P(OH)_3$, which would be expected to have $pK_a > 8$. Similarly for H_3PO_2, which is $H_2PO(OH)$ rather than $HP(OH)_2$.

Table 3.6 First and second ionization constants for H_2S, H_2Se and H_2Te

	pK_1	pK_2	ΔpK
H_2S	7	14	7
H_2Se	4	12	8
H_2Te	3	11	8

the first and second dissociation constants is $\sim 10^8$ rather than 10^5 (Table 3.6).

The results for dinuclear and polynuclear oxoacids are also consistent with this interpretation. Thus for phosphoric acid, $H_4P_2O_7$, the successive pK_a values are 1.5, 2.4, 6.6 and 9.2; the ~ 10-fold decrease between pK_1 and pK_2 (instead of a decrease of 10^5) is related to the fact that ionization occurs from two different PO_4 units. The third stage ionization, however, is $\sim 10^5$ less than the first stage and the difference between the mean of the first two and the last two ionization constants is $\sim 5 \times 10^5$.

Another phenomenon that is closely associated with acid–base equilibria is the so-called hydrolysis of metal cations in aqueous solution, which is probably better considered as the protolysis of hydrated cations, e.g.:

"hydrolysis":

$$Fe^{3+} + H_2O \rightleftharpoons [Fe(OH)]^{2+} + H^+$$

protolysis:

$$[Fe(H_2O)_6]^{3+} + H_2O \rightleftharpoons$$
$$[Fe(H_2O)_5(OH)]^{2+} + H_3O^+; \quad pK_a \; 3.05$$

$$[Fe(H_2O)_5(OH)]^{2+} + H_2O \rightleftharpoons$$
$$[Fe(H_2O)_4(OH)_2]^+ + H_3O^+; \quad pK_a \; 3.26$$

It is these reactions that impart the characteristic yellow to reddish-brown coloration of the hydroxoaquo species to aqueous solutions of iron(III) salts, whereas the undissociated ion $[Fe(H_2O)_6]^{3+}$ is pale mauve, as seen in crystals of iron(III) alum $\{[Fe(H_2O)_6][K(H_2O)_6](SO_4)_2\}$ and iron(III) nitrate $\{[Fe(H_2O)_6](NO_3)_3.3H_2O\}$. Such reactions may proceed to the stage where the diminished charge on the hydrated cation permits the formation of oxobridged,

or hydroxobridged polynuclear species that eventually precipitate as hydrous oxides (see discussion of the chemistry of many elements in later chapters). A useful summary is in Fig. 3.4. By contrast, extensive studies of the pK_a values of hydrated metal ions in solution has generated a wealth of numerical data but no generalizations such as those just discussed for the hydrides and oxoacids of the non-metals.[42] Typical pK_a values fall in the range 3–14 and, as expected, there is a general tendency for protolysis to be greater (pK_a values to be lower) the higher the cationic charge. For example, aqueous solutions of iron(III) salts are more acidic than solutions of the corresponding iron(II) salts. However, it is difficult to discern any regularities in pK_a for series of cations of the same ionic charge, and it is clear that specific "chemical" effects must also be considered.

Brønsted acidity is not confined to dilute aqueous solutions and the ideas developed in the preceding pages can be extended to proton donors in nonaqueous solutions.[43,44] In organic solvents and anhydrous protonic liquids the concepts of hydrogen-ion concentration and pH, if not actually meaningless, are certainly operationally inapplicable and acidity must be defined on some other scale. The one most frequently used is the Hammett acidity function H_0 which enables various acids to be compared in a given solvent and a given acid to be compared in various solvents. For the equilibrium between a base and its conjugate acid (frequently a coloured indicator)

$$B + H^+ \rightleftharpoons BH^+$$

the acidity function is defined as

$$H_0 = pK_{BH^+} - \log\{[BH^+]/[B]\}$$

In very dilute solutions

$$K_{BH^+} = [B][H^+]/[BH^+]$$

[42] L. G. SILLÉN, *Q. Rev. (London)* **13**, 146–68 (1969); *Pure Appl. Chem.* **17**, 55–78 (1968).

[43] C. H. ROCHESTER, *Acidity Functions*, Academic Press, London, 1970, 300 pp.

[44] G. A. OLAH, G. K. S. PRAKASH and J. SOMMER, *Super-acids*, Wiley, New York, 1985, 371 pp.

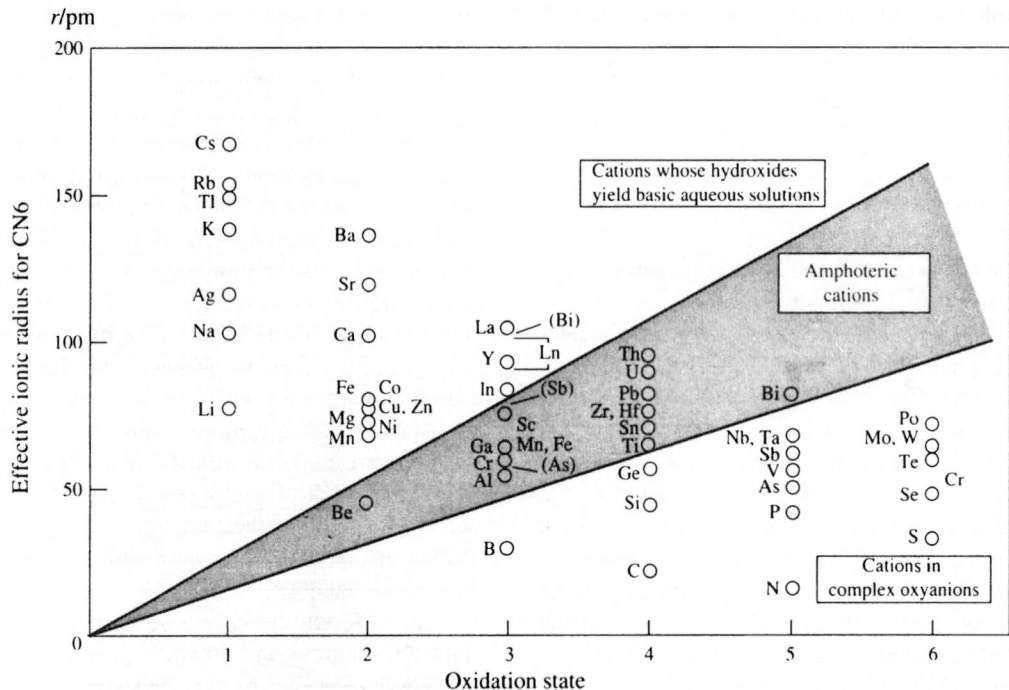

Figure 3.4   Plot of effective ionic radii *versus* oxidation state for various elements.

so that in water H_0 becomes the same as pH. Some values for typical anhydrous acids are in Table 3.7 and these are discussed in more detail in appropriate sections of later chapters.

Table 3.7   Hammett acidity functions for some anhydrous acids

Acid	$-H_0$	Acid	$-H_0$
$HSO_3F + SbF_5$	15–27	HF	~11
$HF + SbF_5$ (1M)	20.4	H_3PO_4	5.0
HSO_3F	15.0	H_2SO_4 (63% in H_2O)	4.9
H_2SO_4	12.0	HCO_2H	2.2

It will be noted that addition of SbF_5 to HF considerably enhances its acidity and the same effect can be achieved by other fluoride acceptors such as BF_3 and TaF_5:

$$2HF + MF_n \rightleftharpoons H_2F^+ + MF_{n+1}^-$$

The enhancement of the acidity of HSO_3F by the addition of SbF_5 is more complex and the equilibria involved are discussed on p. 570.

3.6 The Hydrogen Bond[45-7]

The properties of many substances suggest that, in addition to the "normal" chemical bonding between the atoms and ions, there exists some further interaction involving a hydrogen atom placed between two or more other groups of atoms. Such interaction is called hydrogen bonding and, though normally weak (10–60 kJ per mol of H-bonded H), it frequently has a decisive influence on the structure and properties of the substance. A hydrogen bond can be said to exist between 2 atoms A and B when these atoms approach more closely than would otherwise be expected in the absence of the hydrogen atom and when, as a result, the system has a lower total energy. The bond is represented

[45] G. C. PIMENTEL and A. L. McCLELLAN, *The Hydrogen Bond*, W. H. Freeman, San Francisco, 1960, 475 pp.

[46] W. C. HAMILTON and J. A. IBERS, *Hydrogen Bonding in Solids*, W. A. Benjamin, New York, 1968, 284 pp.

[47] J. EMSLEY, *Chem. Soc. Revs.* **9**, 91–124 (1980).

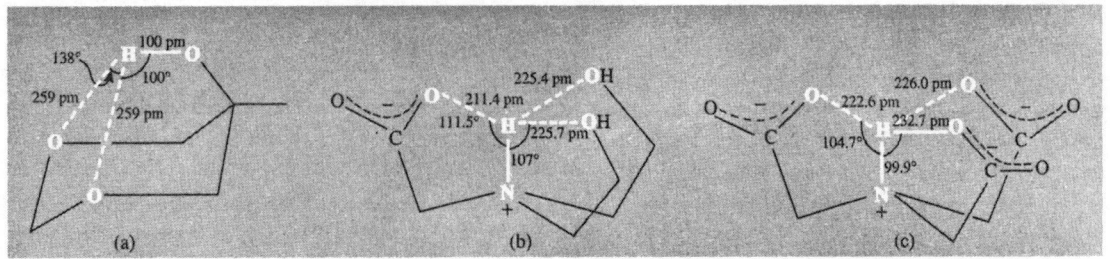

Figure 3.5 Some examples of branched H bonds: (a) the bifurcated bond in 1,3–dioxanol–5[49]; and trifurcated bonds in (b) *N,N*-bis(2–hydroxyethyl)glycine[50] and (c) the nitrilotriacetate dianion.[51]

as A–H···B and usually occurs when A is sufficiently electronegative to enhance the acidic nature of H (proton donor) and where the acceptor B has a region of high electron density (such as a lone pair of electrons) which can interact strongly with the acidic hydrogen. In fact, the H bond in A–H···B can be either linear as in schematic structure (1) or significantly non-linear as in structures (1b) and (1c). H-bonds can also join three adjacent atoms (bifurcated) as in structure (2) or even four atoms (trifurcated) as in structure (3).

$$A—H···B \qquad \begin{array}{c} H \\ A \quad B \end{array} \qquad \begin{array}{c} H \\ A \quad\quad B \\ H \end{array}$$

(1a)   (1b)   (1c)

$$A—H\begin{array}{c} B_1 \\ \\ B_2 \end{array} \qquad A—H\begin{array}{c} B_1 \\ B_2 \\ B_2 \end{array}$$

(2)   (3)

Thus, in a recent survey of 1509 N–H···O=C hydrogen bonds in organic carbonyls or carboxylates, nearly 80% (1199) were unbranched, some 20% (304) were bifurcated, but only 0.4% (6) were trifurcated.[48] Some examples are in Fig. 3.5.

It will be convenient first to indicate the range of phenomena which are influenced by H bonding and then to discuss more specifically the nature of the bond itself according to current theories. The experimental evidence suggests that strong H bonds can be formed when A is F, O or N; weaker H bonds are sometimes formed when A is C or a second row element, P, S, Cl or even Br, I. Strong H bonds are favoured when the atom B is F, O or N; the other halogens Cl, Br, I are less effective unless negatively charged and the atoms C, S and P can also sometimes act as B in weak H bonds. Recent examples of C–H···N and C–H···C bonds are in bis(phenylsulfonyl)trimethylbutylamine (4)[52] and the carbanion of [1.1]ferrocenophane (5).[53]

$$\begin{array}{c} H···NMe_2 \\ \diagup \qquad \diagdown \\ X_2CCH_2CH(Me)CH_2 \end{array} \qquad \begin{array}{c} X \text{ is the S-bonded} \\ PhSO_2 \text{ group} \end{array} \qquad \left[\begin{array}{ccc} C_5H_4 & ···CH··· & C_5H_4 \\ | & | & | \\ Fe & H & Fe \\ | & | & | \\ C_5H_4 & ···CH··· & C_5H_4 \end{array}\right]$$

(4)   (5)

3.6.1 Influence on properties

It is well known that the mps and bps of NH_3, H_2O and HF are anomalously high when compared with the mps and bps of the hydrides of other elements in Groups 15, 16 and 17, and the

[48] R. TAYLOR, O. KENNARD and W. VERICHEL, *J. Am. Chem. Soc.* **106**, 244–8 (1984).

[49] J. L. ALONSO and E. B. WILSON, *J. Am. Chem. Soc.* **102**, 1248–51 (1980).

[50] V. CODY, J. HAZEL and D. LANGS, *Acta Crystallogr.* **B33**, 905–7 (1977).

[51] S. H. WHITLOW, *Acta Crystallogr.* **B28**, 1914–9 (1972).

[52] R. L. HARLOW, C. LI and M. P. SAMMES, *J. Chem. Soc., Chem. Commun.*, 818–9 (1984).

[53] P. AHLBERG and O. DAVIDSSON, *J. Chem. Soc., Chem. Commun.*, 623–4 (1987).

same effect is noted for the heats of vaporization, as shown in Fig. 3.6. The explanation normally given is that there is some residual interaction (H bonding) between the molecules of NH_3, H_2O and HF which is absent for methane, and either absent or much weaker for heavier hydrides. This argument is probably correct in outline but is deceptively oversimplified since it depends on the assumption that only some of the H bonds in solid HF (for example) are broken during the melting process and that others are broken on vaporization, though not all, since HF is known to be substantially polymerized even in the gas phase. The mp is the temperature at which there is zero

free-energy change on passing from the solid to the liquid phase:

$$\Delta G_m = \Delta H_m - T_m \Delta S_m = 0;$$

hence $\quad T_m = \Delta H_m / \Delta S_m$

It can be seen that a high mp implies either a high enthalpy of melting, or a low entropy of melting, or both. Similar arguments apply to vaporization and the bp, and indicate the difficulties in quantifying the discussion.

Other properties that are influenced by H bonding are solubility and miscibility, heats of mixing, phase-partitioning properties, the

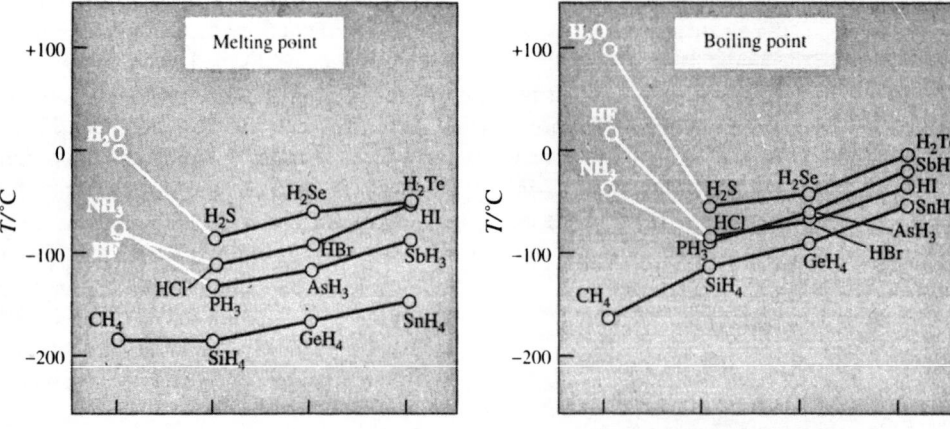

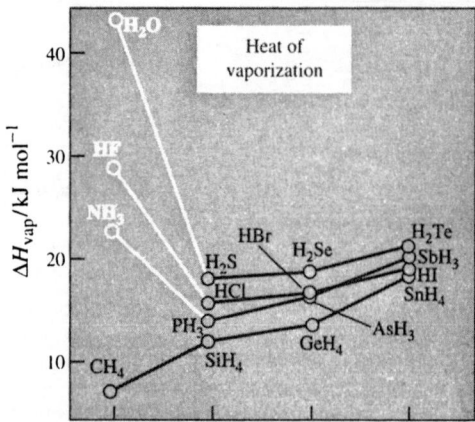

Figure 3.6 Plots showing the high values of mp, bp and heat of vaporization of NH_3, H_2O and HF when compared with other hydrides. Note also that the mp of CH_4 ($-182.5°C$) is slightly higher than that of SiH_4 ($-185°C$).

existence of azeotropes, and the sensitivity of chromatographic separation. Liquid crystals (or mesophases) which can be regarded as "partly melted" solids also frequently involve molecules that have H-bonded groups (e.g. cholesterols, polypeptides, etc.). Again, H bonding frequently results in liquids having a higher density and lower molar volume than would otherwise have been expected, and viscosity is also affected (e.g. glycerol, anhydrous H_2SO_4, H_3PO_4, etc.).

Electrical properties of liquids and solids are sometimes crucially influenced by H bonding. The ionic mobility and conductance of H_3O^+ and OH^- in aqueous solutions are substantially greater than those of other univalent ions due to a proton-switch mechanism in the H-bonded associated solvent, water. For example, at 25°C the conductance of H_3O^+ and OH^- are 350 and 192 $ohm^{-1}\,cm^2\,mol^{-1}$, whereas for other (viscosity-controlled) ions the values fall

mainly in the range 50–75 $ohm^{-1}\,cm^2\,mol^{-1}$. (To convert to mobility, $v\,cm^2\,s^{-1}\,V^{-1}$, divide by 96 485 $C\,mol^{-1}$.) It is also notable that the dielectric constant is not linearly related to molecular dipole moments for H-bonded liquids being much higher due to the orientating effect of the H bonds: large domains are able to align in an applied electric field so that the molecular dipoles reinforce one another rather than cancelling each other due to random thermal motion. Some examples are given in Fig. 3.7, which also illustrates the substantial influence of temperature on the dielectric constant of H-bonded liquids presumably due to the progressive thermal dissociation of the H bonds. Even more dramatic are the properties of ferroelectric crystals where there is a stable permanent electric polarization (see Fig. 3.8). Hydrogen bonding is one of the important ordering mechanisms

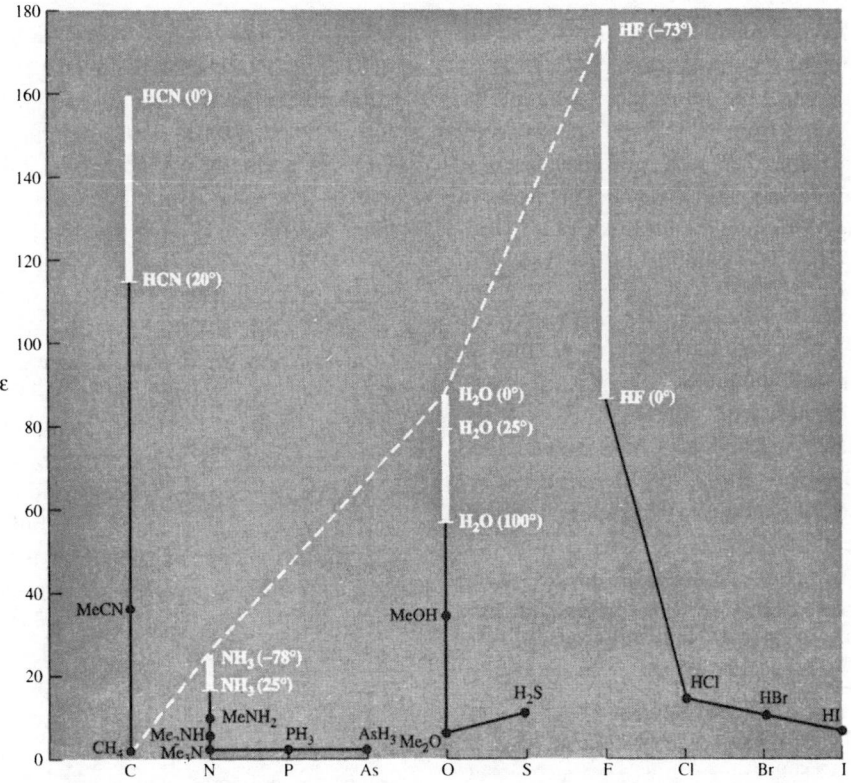

Figure 3.7 Dielectric constant of selected liquids.

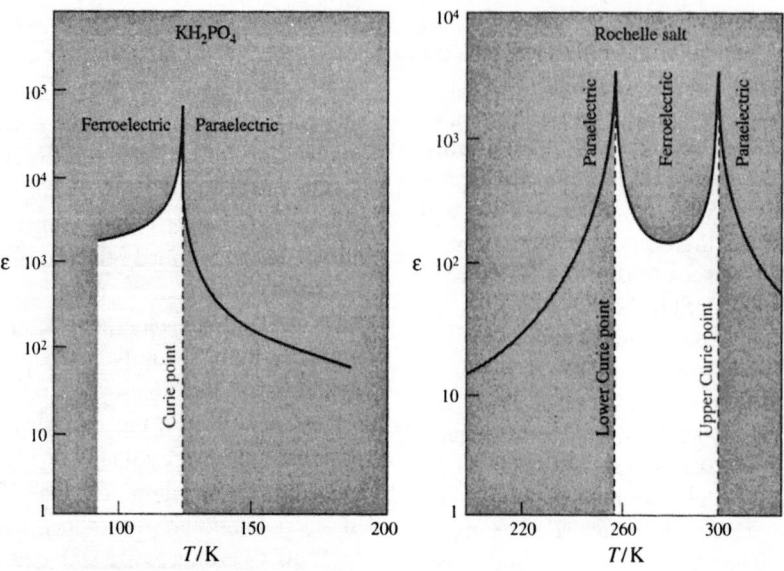

Figure 3.8   Anomalous temperature dependence of relative dielectric constant of ferroelectric crystals at the transition temperature (Curie point).

responsible for this phenomenon as discussed in more detail in the Panel opposite.[54,55]

Intimate information about the nature of the H bond has come from vibrational spectroscopy (infrared and Raman), proton nmr spectroscopy, and diffraction techniques (X-ray and neutron). In vibrational spectroscopy the presence of a hydrogen bond A–H $\cdots$ B is manifest by the following effects:

(i) the A–H stretching frequency ν shifts to lower wave numbers;

(ii) the breadth and intensity of ν(A–H) increase markedly, often more than tenfold;

(iii) the bending mode δ(A–H) shifts to higher wave numbers;

(iv) new stretching and bending modes of the H bond itself sometimes appear at very low wave numbers (20–200 cm^{-1}).

[54] C. KITTELL, *Introduction to Solid State Physics*, 5th edn., Chap. 13, pp. 399–431. Wiley, New York, 1976.

[55] H.-G. UNRUH, Ferroelectrics in *Ullmann's Encyclopedia of Industrial Chemistry*, Vol. A10, VCH, Weinheim, 1987, pp. 309–21, and references cited therein.

Most of these effects correlate roughly with the strength of the H bond and are particularly noticeable when the bond is strong. For example, for isolated non-H-bonded hydrogen groups, ν(O–H) normally occurs near 3500–3600 cm^{-1} and is less than 10 cm^{-1} broad whereas in the presence of O–H $\cdots$ O bonding $\nu_{antisym}$ drops to ~1700–2000 cm^{-1}, is several hundred cm^{-1} broad, and much more intense. A similar effect of $\Delta\nu \sim$ 1500–2000 cm^{-1} is noted on F–H $\cdots$ F formation and smaller shifts have been found for N–H $\cdots$ F ($\Delta\nu \leq$ 1000 cm^{-1}), N–H $\cdots$ O ($\Delta\nu \leq$ 400 cm^{-1}), O–H $\cdots$ N ($\Delta\nu \leq$ 100 cm^{-1}), etc. A full discussion of these effects, including the influence of solvent, concentration, temperature and pressure, is given in ref. 45. Suffice it to note that the magnitude of the effect is much greater than expected on a simple electrostatic theory of hydrogen bonding, and this implies appreciable electron delocalization (covalency) particularly for the stronger H bonds.

Proton nmr spectroscopy has also proved valuable in studying H-bonded systems. As might be expected, substantial chemical shifts are observed and information can be obtained

Ferroelectric Crystals[54,55]

A ferroelectric crystal is one that has an electric dipole moment even in the absence of an external electric field. This arises because the centre of positive charge in the crystal does not coincide with the centre of negative charge. The phenomenon was discovered in 1920 by J. Valasek in Rochelle salt, which is the H-bonded hydrated d-tartrate $NaKC_4H_4O_6.4H_2O$. In such compounds the dielectric constant can rise to enormous values of 10^3 or more due to presence of a stable permanent electric polarization. Before considering the effect further, it will be helpful to recall various definitions and SI units:

electric polarization $P = D - \varepsilon_0 E (C\,m^{-2})$

where D is the electric displacement $(C\,m^{-2})$

      E is the electric field strength $(V\,m^{-1})$

      ε_0 is the permittivity of vacuum $(F\,m^{-1} = A\,s\,V^{-1}\,m^{-1})$

dielectric constant $\varepsilon = \dfrac{\varepsilon_0 E + P}{\varepsilon_0 E} = 1 + \chi$ (dimensionless)

where $\chi = \varepsilon - 1 = P/\varepsilon_0 E$ is the dielectric susceptibility.

There are two main types of ferroelectric crystal:

(a) those in which the polarization arises from an ordering process typically by H bonding;
(b) those in which the polarization arises by a displacement of one sublattice with respect to another, as in perovskite-type structures like barium titanate (p. 963).

The ferroelectricity usually disappears above a certain transition temperature (often called a Curie temperature) above which the crystal is said to be paraelectric; this is because thermal motion has destroyed the ferroelectric order. Occasionally the crystal melts or decomposes before the paraelectric state is reached. There are thus some analogies to ferromagnetic and paramagnetic compounds though it should be noted that there is no iron in ferroelectric compounds. Some typical examples, together with their transition temperatures and spontaneous permanent electric polarization P_s, are given in the Table.

Table   Properties of some ferroelectric compounds

Compound	T_c/K	$P_s/\mu C\,cm^{-2}$ [a]	(at T/K)
KH_2PO_4	123	5.3	(96)
KD_2PO_4	213	4.5	—
KH_2AsO_4	96	3.0	(80)
KD_2AsO_4	162		
RbH_2PO_4	147	5.6	(90)
$(NH_2CH_2CO_2H)_3.H_2SO_4$ [b]	322	2.8	(293)
$(NH_2CH_2CO_2H)_3.H_2SeO_4$ [b]	295	3.2	(273)
$BaTiO_3$	393	26.0	(296)
$KNbO_3$	712	30.0	(523)
$PbTiO_3$	763	>50.0	(300)
$LiTaO_3$	890	23.0	(720)
$LiNbO_3$	1470	300.0	—

[a] To convert to the basic SI unit of $C\,m^{-2}$ divide the tabulated values of P_s by 10^2; to convert to the CGS unit of esu cm^{-2} multiply by 3×10^3. For a full compilation see E. C. Subbarao, *Ferroelectrics* **5**, 267 (1973).

[b] Triglycinesulfate and selenate.

In KH_2PO_4 and related compounds each tetrahedral $[PO_2(OH)_2]^-$ group is joined by H bonds to neighbouring $[PO_2(OH)_2]^-$ groups; below the transition temperature all the short O–H bonds are ordered on the same side of the PO_4 units, and by appropriate application of an electric field, the polarization of the H bonds can be reversed. The dramatic effect of deuterium substitution in raising the transition temperature of such compounds can be seen from the Table; this has been ascribed to a quantum-mechanical effect involving the mass dependence of the de Broglie wavelength of hydrogen. Other examples of H-bonded ferroelectrics are $(NH_4)H_2PO_4$, $(NH_4)H_2AsO_4$, $Ag_2H_3IO_6$, $(NH_4)Al(SO_4)_2.6H_2O$ and $(NH_4)_2SO_4$. Rochelle salt is unusual in having both an upper and a lower critical temperature between which the compound is ferroelectric.

Panel continues

The closely related phenomenon of antiferroelectric behaviour is also known, in which there is an ordered, self-cancelling arrangement of permanent electric dipole moments below a certain transition temperature; H bonding is again implicated in the ordering mechanism for several ammonium salts of this type, e.g. $(NH_4)H_2PO_4$ 148 K, $(NH_4)D_2PO_4$ 242 K, $(NH_4)H_2AsO_4$ 216 K, $(NH_4)D_2AsO_4$ 304 K and $(NH_4)_2H_3IO_6$ 254 K. As with ferroelectrics, antiferroelectrics can also arise by a displacive mechanism in perovskite-type structures, and typical examples, with their transition temperatures, are:

$PbZrO_3$ 506 K, $PbHfO_3$ 488 K, $NaNbO_3$ 793, 911 K, WO_3 1010 K.

Ferroelectrics have many practical applications: they can be used as miniature ceramic capacitors because of their large capacitance, and their electro-optical characteristics enable them to modulate and deflect laser beams. The temperature dependence of spontaneous polarization induces a strong pyroelectric effect which can be exploited in thermal and infrared detection. Many applications depend on the fact that all ferroelectrics are also piezoelectrics. Piezoelectricity is the property of acquiring (or altering) an electric polarization P under external mechanical stress, or conversely, the property of changing size (or shape) when subjected to an external electric field E. Thus ferroelectrics have been used as transducers to convert mechanical pulses into electrical ones and vice versa, and find extensive application in ultrasonic generators, microphones, and gramophone pickups; they can also be used as frequency controllers, electric filters, modulating devices, frequency multipliers, and as switches, counters and other bistable elements in computer circuits. A further ingeneous application is in delay lines by means of which an electric signal is transformed piezoelectrically into an acoustic signal which passes down the piezoelectric rod at the velocity of sound until, at the other end, it is reconverted into a (delayed) electric signal.

It should be noted that, whereas ferroelectrics are necessarily piezoelectrics, the converse need not apply. The necessary condition for a crystal to be piezoelectric is that it must lack a centre of inversion symmetry. Of the 32 point groups, 20 qualify for piezoelectricity on this criterion, but for ferroelectric behaviour a further criterion is required (the possession of a single non-equivalent direction) and only 10 space groups meet this additional requirement. An example of a crystal that is piezoelectric but not ferroelectric is quartz, and indeed this is a particularly important example since the use of quartz for oscillator stabilization has permitted the development of extremely accurate clocks (1 in 10^8) and has also made possible the whole of modern radio and television broadcasting including mobile radio communications with aircraft and ground vehicles.

concerning H-bond dissociation, proton exchange times, and other relaxation processes. The chemical shift always occurs to low field and some typical values are tabulated below for the shifts which occur between the gas and liquid phases or on dilution in an inert solvent:

Compound	CH_4	C_2H_6	$CHCl_3$	HCN	NH_3	PH_3
δ ppm	0	0	0.30	1.65	1.05	0.78
Compound	H_2O	H_2S	HF	HCl	HBr	HI
δ ppm	4.58	1.50	6.65	2.05	1.78	2.55

The low-field shift is generally interpreted, at least qualitatively, in terms of a decrease in diamagnetic shielding of the proton: the formation of $A-H\cdots B$ tends to draw H towards B and to repel the bonding electrons in $A-H$ towards A thus reducing the electron density about H and reducing the shielding. The strong electric field due to B also inhibits the diamagnetic circulation within the H atom and this further reduces the shielding. In addition,

there is a magnetic anisotropy effect due to B; this will be positive (upfield shift) if the principal symmetry axis of B is towards the H bond, but the effect is presumably small since the overall shift is always downfield.

Ultraviolet and visible spectra are also influenced by H bonding, but the effects are more difficult to quantify and have been rather less used than ir and nmr. It has been found that the $n \rightarrow \pi^*$ transition of the base B always moves to high frequency (blue shift) on H-bond formation, the magnitude of $\Delta\nu$ being $\sim 300-4000$ cm^{-1} for bands in the region 15 000–35 000 cm^{-1}. By contrast $\pi \rightarrow \pi^*$ transitions on the base B usually move to lower frequencies (red shift) and shifts are in the range -500 to -2300 cm^{-1} for bands in the region 30 000–47 000 cm^{-1}. Detailed interpretations of these data are somewhat complex and obscure, but it will be noted that the shifts are approximately of the same magnitude as the enthalpy of formation of many H bonds (83.59 cm^{-1} per atom $\equiv$ 1 kJ mol^{-1}).

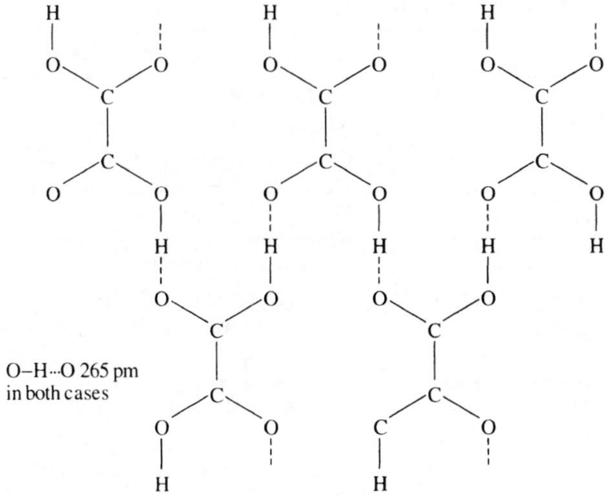

α-form : layer structure with easy cleavage (H bonds remain intact)

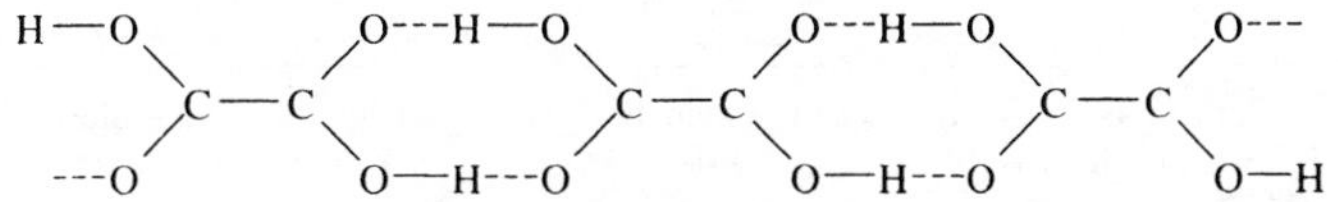

O–H···O 265 pm
in both cases

β-form : long chains giving crystals that cleave into laths parallel to the chain

Figure 3.9   Schematic representation of the two forms of oxalic acid, $(-CO_2H)_2$.

3.6.2 Influence on structure [56,57]

The crystal structure of many compounds is dominated by the effect of H bonds, and numerous examples will emerge in ensuing chapters. Ice (p. 624) is perhaps the classic example, but the layer lattice structure of $B(OH)_3$ (p. 203) and the striking difference between the α- and β-forms of oxalic and other dicarboxylic acids is notable (Fig. 3.9). The more subtle distortions that lead to ferroelectric phenomena in KH_2PO_4 and other crystals have already been noted (p. 57). Hydrogen bonds between fluorine atoms result in the formation of infinite zigzag chains in crystalline hydrogen fluoride

with F–H $\cdots$ F distance 249 pm and the angle HFH 120.1°. Likewise, the crystal structure of NH_4HF_2 is completely determined by H bonds, each nitrogen atom being surrounded by 8 fluorines, 4 in tetrahedral array at 280 pm due to the formation of N–H $\cdots$ F bonds, and 4 further away at about 310 pm; the two sets of fluorine atoms are themselves bonded pairwise at 232 pm by F–H–F interactions. Ammonium azide NH_4N_3 has the same structure as NH_4HF_2, with N–H $\cdots$ N 298 pm. Hydrogen bonding also leads NH_4F to crystallize with a structure different from that of the other ammonium (and alkali) halides: NH_4Cl, NH_4Br and NH_4I each have a low-temperature CsCl-type structure and a high-temperature NaCl-type structure, but NH_4F adopts the wurtzite (ZnS) structure in which each NH_4^+ group is surrounded tetrahedrally by 4 F to which it is bonded by 4 N–H $\cdots$ F bonds at 271 pm. This is very similar to the structure

[56] L. PAULING, *The Nature of the Chemical Bond*, 3rd edn., Chap. 12, Cornell University Press, Ithaca, 1960.
[57] A. F. WELLS, *Structural Inorganic Chemistry*, 5th edn., Clarendon Press, Oxford, 1984, 1382 pp.

Table 3.8 Length of typical H bonds[46,57]

Bond	Length/pm	Σ/pm[a]	Examples
F–H–F	227	(270)	$NaHF_2$, KHF_2
F–H$\cdots$F	245–249	(270)	KH_4F_5, HF
O–H$\cdots$F	265–287	(275)	$CuF_2.2H_2O$, $FeSiF_6.6H_2O$
O–H$\cdots$Cl	295–310	(320)	$HCl.H_2O$, $(NH_3OH)Cl$, $CuCl_2.2H_2O$
O–H$\cdots$Br	320–340	(335)	$NaBr.2H_2O$, $HBr.4H_2O$
O–H–O	240–263	(280)	Ni dimethylglyoxime, KH maleate, $HCrO_2$ $Na_3H(CO_3)_2.2H_2O$
O–H$\cdots$O	248–290	(280)	KH_2PO_4, $NH_4H_2PO_4$, KH_2AsO_4, AlOOH, α-HIO_3, numerous hydrated metal sulfates and nitrates
O–H$\cdots$S	310–340	(325)	$MgS_2O_3.6H_2O$
O–H$\cdots$N	268–279	(290)	$N_2H_4.4MeOH$, $N_2H_4.H_2O$
N–H$\cdots$F	262–296	(285)	NH_4F, $N_2H_6F_2$, $(N_2H_6)SiF_6$
N–H$\cdots$Cl	300–320	(330)	Me_3NHCl, Me_2NH_2Cl, $(NH_3OH)Cl$
N–H$\cdots$I	346	(365)	Me_3NHI
N–H$\cdots$O	281–304	(290)	HSO_3NH_2, $(NH_4)_2SO_4$, NH_4OOCH, $CO(NH_2)_2$
N–H$\cdots$S	323, 329	(335)	$N_2H_5(HS)$
N–H$\cdots$N	294–315	(300)	NH_4N_3, $NCNC(NH_2)_2$ (i.e. dicyandiamide)
P–H$\cdots$I	424	(405)	PH_4I

[a] Σ = sum of van der Waals' radii (in pm) of A and B (ignoring H which has a value of ~120 pm) and using the values F 135, Cl 180, Br 195, I 215; O 140, S 185; N 150, P 190.

of ordinary ice. Typical values of A–H$\cdots$B distances found in crystals are given in Table 3.8.

The precise position of the H atom in crystalline compounds containing H bonds has excited considerable experimental and theoretical interest. In situations where a symmetric H bond is possible in principle, it is frequently difficult to decide whether the proton is vibrating with a large amplitude about a single potential minimum or whether it is vibrating with a smaller amplitude but is also statistically disordered between two close sites, the potential energy barrier between the two sites being small.[46,47] It now seems well established that the F–H–F bond is symmetrical in $NaHF_2$ and KHF_2, and that the O–H–O bond is symmetrical in $HCrO_2$. Other examples are the intra-molecular H bonds in potassium hydrogen maleate, $K^+[cis\text{-}\overline{CH}=CHC(O)O\text{-}H\text{-}O\overline{C}(O)]^-$ and its monochloro derivative: Numerous other examples of H bonding will be found in later chapters.

In summary, we can see that H bonding influences crystal structure by linking atoms or groups into larger structural units. These may be:

> finite groups: HF_2^-; $[O_2CO\text{-}H\cdots OCO_2]^{3-}$ in $Na_3H(CO_3)_2.2H_2O$ dimers of carboxylic acids, etc.;
>
> infinite chains: HF, HCN, HCO_3^-, HSO_4^-, etc.;
>
> infinite layers: $N_2H_6F_2$, $B(OH)_3$, $B_3O_3(OH)_3$, H_2SO_4, etc.;
>
> three-dimensional nets: NH_4F, H_2O, H_2O_2, $Te(OH)_6$, $H_2PO_4^-$ in KH_2PO_4, etc.

H bonding also vitally influences the conformation and detailed structure of the polypeptide chains of protein molecules and the complementary intertwined polynucleotide chains which form the double helix in nucleic acids.[56,58] Thus, proteins are built up from polypeptide chains of the type shown at the top of the next column.

These chains are coiled in a precise way which is determined to a large extent by N–H$\cdots$O hydrogen bonds of length 279 ±

---

[58] G. A. JEFFREY and W. SAENGER, *Hydrogen Bonding in Biological Structures*, Springer Verlag, Berlin, 1991, 567 pp.

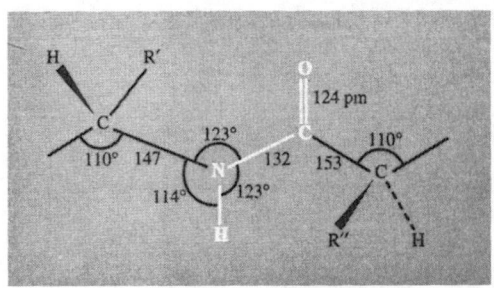

12 pm depending on the amino–acid residue involved. Each amide group is attached by such a hydrogen bond to the third amide group from it in both directions along the chain, resulting in an α-helix of pitch (total rise of helix per turn) of about 538 pm, corresponding to 3.60 amino–acid residues per turn. These helical chains can, in turn, become stretched and form hydrogen bonds with neighbouring chains to generate either parallel-chain pleated sheets (repeat distances 650 pm) or antiparallel-chain pleated sheets (700 pm).

Nucleic acids, which control the synthesis of proteins in the cells of living organisms and which transfer heredity information via genes, are also dominated by H bonding. Their structure involves two polynucleotide chains intertwined to form a double helix. The complimentariness in the structure of the two chains is ascribed to the formation of H bonds between the pyrimidine residue (thymine or cytosine) in one chain and the purine residue (adenine or guanine) in the other as illustrated in Fig. 3.10. Whilst there is still some uncertainty as to the precise configuration of the N–H $\cdots$ O and N–H $\cdots$ N hydrogen bonds in particular cases, the extraordinary fruitfulness of these basic ideas has led to a profusion

of developments of fundamental importance in biochemistry.[58]

3.6.3 Strength of hydrogen bonds and theoretical description [59]

Measurement of the properties of H-bonded systems over a range of temperatures leads to experimental values of ΔG, ΔH and ΔS for H-bond formation, and these data have been supplemented in recent years by increasingly reliable *ab initio* quantum-mechanical calculations.[60] Some typical values for the enthalpy of dissociation of H-bonded pairs in the gas phase are in Table 3.9.

The uncertainty in these values varies between ± 1 and $\pm 6\,kJ\,mol^{-1}$. In general, H bonds of energy $<25\,kJ\,mol^{-1}$ are classified as weak; those in the range 25–$40\,kJ\,mol^{-1}$ are medium; and those having $\Delta H > 40\,kJ\,mol^{-1}$ are strong. Until recently, it was thought that the strongest H bond was that in the hydrogendifluoride ion $[F-H-F]^-$; this is difficult to determine experimentally and values in the range 150–$250\,kJ\,mol^{-1}$ have been reported. A recent theoretically computed value is $169\,kJ\,mol^{-1}$ which agrees well with the value of $163 \pm 4\,kJ\,mol^{-1}$ from ion cyclotron resonance studies.[61] In fact, it now seems that the H bond between formic acid and the fluoride ion,

[59] A. C. LEGON and D. J. MILLEN, *Chem. Soc. Revs.* **21**, 71–8 (1992).

[60] P. A. KOLLMAN, Chap. 3 in H. F. SCHAEFFER (ed.), *Applications of Electronic Structure Theory*, Plenum Press, New York, 1977.

[61] J. EMSLEY, *Polyhedron* **4**, 489–90 (1985).

Table 3.9 Enthalpy of dissociation of H-bonded pairs in the gas phase, $\Delta H_{298}(A-H \cdots B)/kJ\,mol^{-1}$

Weak		Medium		Strong	
HSH$\cdots$SH$_2$	7	FH$\cdots$FH	29	HOH$\cdots$Cl$^-$	55
NCH$\cdots$NCH	16	ClH$\cdots$OMe$_2$	30	HCONH$_2$ $\cdots$OCHNH$_2$	59
H$_2$NH$\cdots$NH$_3$	17	FH$\cdots$OH$_2$	38	HCOOH$\cdots$OCHOH	59
MeOH$\cdots$OHMe	19			HOH$\cdots$F$^-$	98
HOH$\cdots$OH$_2$	22			H$_2$OH$^+\cdots$OH$_2$	151
				FH$\cdots$F$^-$	169
				HCO$_2$H$\cdots$F$^-$	~200

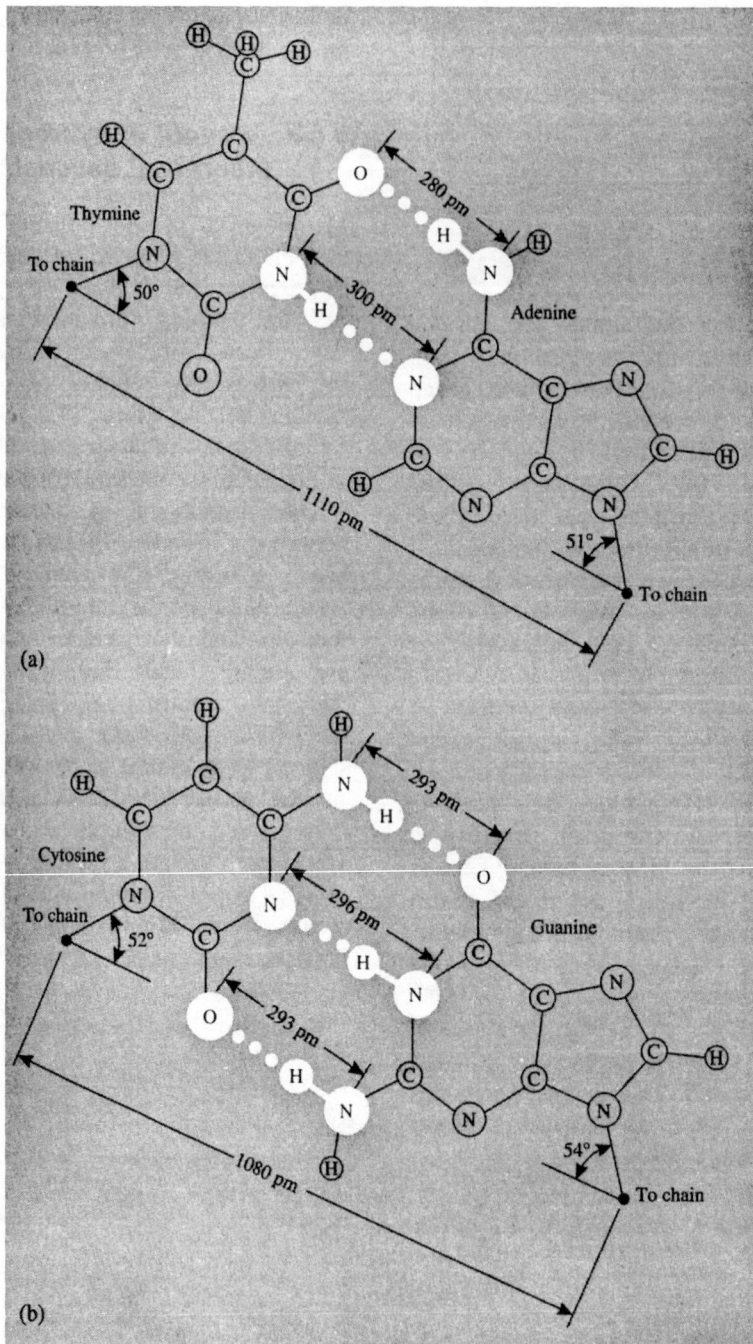

Figure 3.10 Structural details of the bridging units between pairs of bases in separate strands of the double helix of DNA: (a) the thymine–adenine pair (b) the cytosine–guanine pair.

$[HCO_2H\cdots F^-]$, is some $30\,kJ\,mol^{-1}$ stronger than that calculated on the same basis for HF_2^{-}.[62]

Early discussions on the nature of the hydrogen bond tended to adopt an electrostatic approach in order to avoid the implication of a covalency greater than one for hydrogen. Indeed, such calculations can reproduce the experimental H-bond energies and dipole moments, but this is not a particularly severe test because of the parametric freedom in positioning the charges. However, the purely electrostatic theory is unable to account for the substantial increase in intensity of the stretching vibration $\nu(A-H)$ on H bonding or for the lowered intensity of the bending mode $\delta(A-H)$. More seriously, such a theory does not account for the absence of correlation between H-bond strength and dipole moment of the base, and it leaves the frequency shifts in the electronic transitions unexplained. Nonlinear $A-H\cdots B$ bonds would also be unexpected, though numerous examples of angles in the range $150-180°$ are known.[46]

Valence-bond descriptions envisage up to five contributions to the total bond wave function,[45] but these are now considered to be merely computational devices for approximating to the true wave function. Perturbation theory has also been employed and apportions the resultant bond energy between (1) the electrostatic energy of interaction between the fixed nuclei and the electron distribution of the component molecules, (2) Pauli exchange repulsion energy between electrons of like spin, (3) polarization energy resulting from the attraction between the polarizable charge cloud of one molecule and the permanent multipoles of the other molecule, (4) quantum-mechanical charge-transfer energy, and (5) dispersion energy, resulting from second-order induced dipole-induced dipole attraction. The results suggest that electrostatic effects predominate, particularly for weak bonds, but that covalency effects increase in importance as the strength of the bond increases. It is also

possible to apportion the energy obtained from *ab initio* SCF-MO calculations in this way.[63] For example, in one particular calculation for the water dimer $HOH\cdots OH_2$, the five energy terms enumerated above were calculated to be: $E_{elec\ stat}\ -26.5$, $E_{Pauli}\ +18$, $E_{polar}\ -2$, $E_{ch\ tr}\ -7.5$, $E_{disp}\ 0\,kJ\,mol^{-1}$. There was also a coupling interaction $E_{mix}\ -0.5$, making in all a total attractive force $\Delta E_0 = E_{dimer} - E_{monomers} = -18.5\,kJ\,mol^{-1}$. To calculate the enthalpy change ΔH_{298} as listed on p. 61, it is also necessary to consider the work of expansion and the various spectroscopic degrees of freedom:

$$\Delta H_{298} = E_0 + \Delta(PV) + \Delta E_{trans} + \Delta E_{vib} + \Delta E_{rot}$$

Such calculations can also give an indication of the influence of H-bond formation on the detailed electron distribution within the interacting components. There is general agreement that in the system $X-A-H\cdots B-Y$ as compared with the isolated species XAH and BY, there is a net gain of electron density by X, A and B and a net loss of electrons by H and Y. There is also a small transfer of electronic charge ($\sim$0.05 electrons) from BY to XAH in moderately strong H bonds ($20-40\,kJ\,mol^{-1}$). In virtually all neutral dimers, the increase in the A–H bond length on H-bond formation is quite small (<5 pm), the one exception so far studied theoretically being $ClH\cdots NH_3$, where the proton position in the H bond is half-way between completely transferred to NH_3 and completely fixed on HCl.

It follows from the preceding discussion that the unbranched H bond can be regarded as a 3-centre 4-electron bond $A-H\cdots B$ in which the 2 pairs of electrons involved are the bond pair in A–H and the lone pair on B. The degree of charge separation on bond formation will depend on the nature of the proton-donor group AH and the Lewis base B. The relation between this 3-centre bond formalism and the 3-centre bond descriptions frequently used for boranes, polyhalides and compounds of xenon is particularly instructive and is elaborated in

[62] J. EMSLEY, O. P. A. HOYTE and R. E. OVERILL, *J. Chem. Soc., Chem. Commun.*, 225 (1977).

[63] H. UMEYAMA and K. MOROKUMA, *J. Am. Chem. Soc.* **99**, 1316–32 (1977).

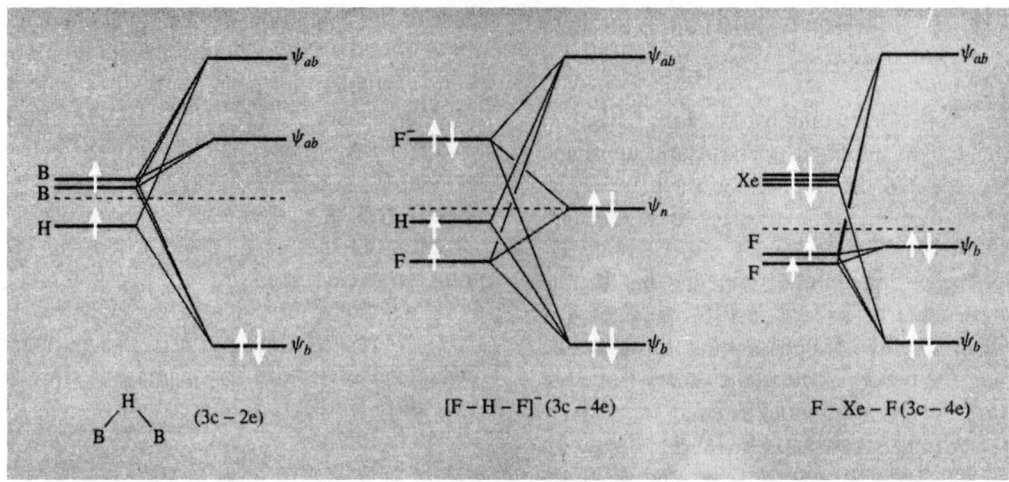

Figure 3.11 Schematic representation of the energy levels in various types of 3-centre bond. The B–H–B ("electron deficient") bond is non-linear, the ("electron excess") F–Xe–F bond is linear, and the A–H ··· B hydrogen bond can be either linear or non-linear depending on the compound.

Fig. 3.11. Numerous examples are also known in which hydrogen acts as a bridge between metallic elements in binary and more complex hydrides, and some of these will be mentioned in the following section which considers the general question of the hydrides of the elements.

3.7 Hydrides of the Elements[64-6]

Hydrogen combines with many elements to form binary hydrides MH_x (or M_mH_n). All the main-group elements except the noble gases and perhaps indium and thallium form hydrides, as do all the lanthanoids and actinoids that have been studied. Hydrides are also formed by the more electropositive transition elements, notably Sc, Y, La, Ac; Ti, Zr, Hf; and to a lesser

extent V, Nb, Ta; Cr; Cu; and Zn. Hydrides of other transition elements are either non-existent or poorly characterized, with the spectacular exception of palladium which has been more studied than any other metal hydride system.[67] The situation is summarized in Fig. 3.12; this indicates the idealized formulae of the known hydrides though many of the d-block and f-block elements form phases of variable compositions.

It has been customary to group the binary hydrides of the elements into various classes according to the presumed nature of their bonding: ionic, metallic, covalent, polymeric, and "intermediate" or "borderline". However, this is unsatisfactory because the nature of the bonding is but poorly understood in many cases and the classification obscures the important point that there is an almost continuous gradation in properties — and bond types(?) — between members of the various classes. It is also somewhat misleading in implying that the various bond types are mutually exclusive whereas it seems likely that more than one type of bonding is present in many cases. The situation is not unique to hydrides but is also well known for

[64] K. M. MACKAY, *Hydrogen Compounds of the Metallic Elements*, E. and F. N. Spon, London, 1966, 168 pp.; Hydrides, *Comprehensive Inorganic Chemistry*, Vol. 1, Chap. 2, Pergamon Press, Oxford, 1973.

[65] E. WIBERG and E. AMBERGER, *Hydrides of the Elements of Main Groups I–IV*, Elsevier, Amsterdam, 1971, 785 pp.

[66] W. M. MUELLER, J. P. BLACKLEDGE and G. G. LIBOWITZ (eds.), *Metal Hydrides*, Academic Press, New York, 1968, 791 pp.

[67] F. A. LEWIS, *The Palladium-Hydrogen System*, Academic Press, London, 1967, 178 pp.

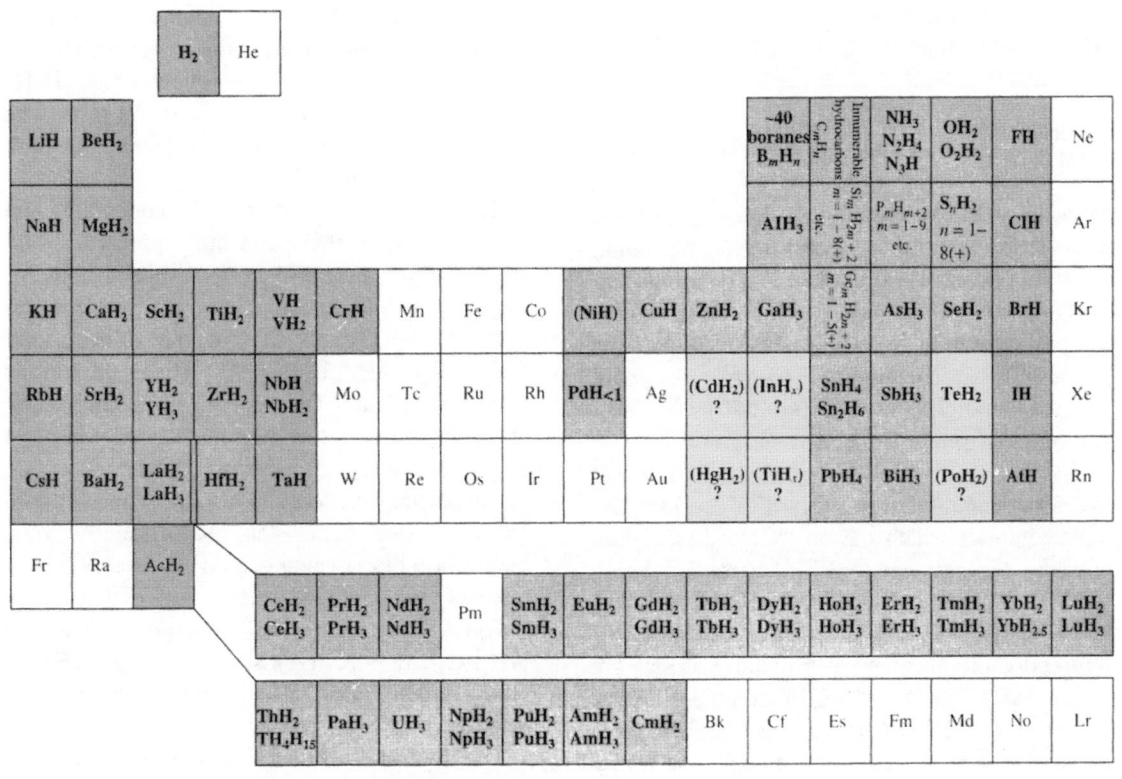

Figure 3.12 The hydrides of the elements.

binary halides, oxides, sulfides, etc.: this serves to remind us that the various bond models represent grossly oversimplified limiting cases and that in most actual systems the position is more complex. For example, oxides might be classed as ionic (MgO), metallic (TiO, ReO_3), covalent (CO_2), polymeric (SiO_2), or as intermediate between these various classes, though any adequate bonding theory would recognize the arbitrary nature of these distinctions which merely emphasize particular features of the overall assembly of molecular orbitals and electron populations.

The metals in Groups 1 and 2 of the periodic table react directly with hydrogen to form white, crystalline, stoichiometric hydrides of formula MX and MX_2 respectively. The salt-like character of these compounds was recognized by G. N. Lewis in 1916 and he suggested that they contained the hydride ion H^-. Shortly thereafter

(1920) K. Moers showed that electrolysis of molten LiH (mp 692°C) gave the appropriate amount of hydrogen at the anode; the other hydrides tended to decompose before they could be melted. As expected, the ionic-bond model is most satisfactory for the later (larger) members of each group, and the tendency towards covalency becomes more marked for the smaller elements LiH, MgH_2, and particularly BeH_2, which is best described in terms of polymeric covalent bridge bonds. X-ray and neutron diffraction studies show that the alkali metal hydrides adopt the cubic NaCl structure (p. 242) whereas MgH_2 has the tetragonal TiO_2 (rutile type) structure (p. 961) and CaH_2, SrH_2 and BaH_2 adopt the orthorhombic $PbCl_2$-type structure (p. 382). The implied radius of the hydride ion H^- ($1s^2$) varies considerably with the nature of the metal because of the ready deformability of the pair of electrons surrounding a single proton. Typical values are given below and these can be compared with $r(F^-) \sim 133$ pm and $r(Cl^-) \sim 184$ pm.

Compound	MgH$_2$	LiH	NaH	KH	RbH	CsH	Free H$^-$ (calculated)
r(H$^-$)/pm	130	137	146	152	154	152	208

The closest M−M approach in these compounds is often less than for the metal itself: this should occasion no surprise since this is a common feature of many compounds in which there is substantial separation of charge. For example, the shortest Ca−Ca interatomic distance is 393 pm in calcium metal, 360 pm in CaH$_2$, 380 pm in CaF$_2$, and only 340 pm in CaO (why?).

The thermal stability of the alkali metal hydrides decreases from lithium to caesium, the temperature at which the reversible dissociation pressure of hydrogen reaches 10 mmHg being $\sim$550°C for LiH, $\sim$210°C for NaH and KH, and $\sim$170°C for RbH and CsH. The corresponding figures for the alkaline earth metal hydrides are CaH$_2$ 885°C, SrH$_2$ 585°C and BaH$_2$ 230°C, though for MgH$_2$ it is only 85°C. Chemical reactivity depends markedly on both the purity and the state of subdivision but increases from lithium to caesium and from calcium to barium with CaH$_2$ being rather less reactive than LiH. The reaction of water with these latter two compounds forms a convenient portable source of hydrogen, but with NaH the reaction is more violent than with sodium itself. RbH and CsH actually ignite spontaneously in dry air.

Turning next to Group 3, Fig. 3.12 indicates that hydrides of limiting stoichiometry MH$_2$ are also formed by Sc, Y, La, Ac and by most of the lanthanoids and actinoids. In the special case of EuH$_2$ (Eu^{II} 4f^7) and YbH$_2$ (Yb^{II}4f^{14}) the hydrides are isostructural with CaH$_2$ and the ionic bonding model gives a reasonable description of the observed properties; however, YbH$_2$ can absorb more hydrogen up to about YbH$_{2.5}$. The other hydrides adopt the fluorite (CaF$_2$) crystal structure (p. 118) and the supernumerary valence electron is delocalized, thereby conferring considerable metallic conductivity. For example, LaH$_2$ is a dark-coloured, brittle compound with a conductivity of about 10 ohm^{-1} cm^{-1} ($\sim$1% of

that of La metal). Further uptake of hydrogen progressively diminishes this conductivity to $<10^{-1}$ ohm^{-1} cm^{-1} for the cubic phase LaH$_3$ (cf. $\sim$3 × 10^{-5} ohm^{-1} cm^{-1} for YbH$_2$). The other Group 3 elements and the lanthanoids and actinoids are similar.

There is a lively controversy concerning the interpretation of these and other properties, and cogent arguments have been advanced both for the presence of hydride ions H$^-$ and for the presence of protons H$^+$ in the d-block and f-block hydride phases.[64,66] These difficulties emphasize again the problems attending any classification based on presumed bond type, and a phenomenological approach which describes the observed properties is a sounder initial basis for discussion. Thus the predominantly ionic nature of a phase cannot safely be inferred either from crystal structure or from calculated lattice energies since many metallic alloys adopt the NaCl-type or CsCl-type structures (e.g. LaBi, β-brass) and enthalpy calculations are notoriously insensitive to bond type.

The hydrides of limiting composition MH$_3$ have complex structures and there is evidence that the third hydrogen is sometimes less strongly bound in the crystal. For the earlier (larger) lanthanoids La, Ce, Pr and Nd, hydrogen enters octahedral sites and LnH$_3$ has the cubic Li$_3$Bi structure.[57] For Y and the smaller lanthanoids Sm, Gd, Tb, Dy, Ho, Er, Tm and Lu, as well as for the actinoids Np, Pu and Am, the hexagonal HoH$_3$ structure is adopted. This is a rather complex structure based on an extended unit cell containing 6 Ho and 18 H atoms.[68] The idealized structure has hcp Ho atoms with 12 tetrahedrally coordinated H atoms and 6 octahedrally coordinated H atoms; however, to make room for the bulky Ho atoms, close pairs of tetrahedral H atoms are slightly displaced and there is a more substantial movement of the "octahedral" H atoms towards the planes of the Ho atoms so that 2 of the H atoms are actually in the Ho planes and are trigonal 3-coordinate. The

68 M. MANSMANN and W. E. WALLACE *J. de Physique* **25**, 454–9 (1964).

hydrogen atoms are thus of three types having respectively 14, 11, and 9 H neighbours for the distorted trigonal, octahedral and tetrahedral sites. Each H atom has 3 Ho neighbours at either 210 or 217 or 224–299 pm respectively, and each Ho has 11 hydrogen neighbours, 9 at 210–229 pm and 2 somewhat further away at 248 pm. The 3-coordinate hydrogen is most unusual, the only other hydride in which it occurs being the complex cubic phase Th_4H_{15}.

Uranium forms two hydrides of stoichiometric composition UH_3. The normal β-form has a complex cubic structure and is the only one formed when the preparation is carried out above 200°C. Below this temperature increasing amounts of the slightly denser cubic α-form occur and this can be transformed to the β-phase by warming to 250°C. Both phases have ferromagnetic and metallic properties. Uranium hydride is commonly used as a starting material for the preparation of uranium compounds as it is finely powdered and extremely reactive. It is also used for purifying and regenerating hydrogen (or deuterium) gas.

The hydrides of Ti, Zr and Hf are characterized by considerable variability in composition and structure. When pure, the limiting phases MH_2 form massive, metallic crystals of fluorite structure (TiH_2) or body-centred tetragonal structure (ZrH_2, HfH_2, ThH_2), but there are also several hydrogen-deficient phases of variable composition and complex structure in which several M–H distances occur.[57,64,66] These phases (and others based on Y, Ce and Nb) have been extensively investigated in recent years because of their potential applications as moderators, reflectors, or shield components for high-temperature, mobile nuclear reactors.

Other hydrides with interstitial or metallic properties are formed by V, Nb and Ta; they are, however, very much less stable than the compounds we have been considering and have extensive ranges of composition. Chromium also forms a hydride, CrH, though this must be prepared electrolytically rather than by direct reaction of the metal with hydrogen. It has the anti-NiAs structure (p. 555). Most other elements

in this area of the periodic table have little or no affinity for hydrogen and this has given rise to the phrase "hydrogen gap". The notable exception is the palladium–hydrogen system which is discussed on p. 1150.

The hydrides of the later main-group elements present few problems of classification and are best discussed during the detailed treatment of the individual elements. Many of these hydrides are covalent, molecular species, though association via H bonding sometimes occurs, as already noted (p. 53). Catenation flourishes in Group 14 and the complexities of the boron hydrides merit special attention (p. 151). The hydrides of aluminium, gallium, zinc (and beryllium) tend to be more extensively associated via M–H–M bonds, but their characterization and detailed structural elucidation has proved extremely difficult.

Two further important groups of hydride compounds should be mentioned and will receive detailed attention in later chapters. One is the group of complex metal hydrides of which notable examples are $LiBH_4$, $NaBH_4$, $LiAlH_4$, $Al(BH_4)_3$, etc.[69] The other is the growing number of compounds in which the hydrogen atom is a monodentate or bidentate (bridging) ligand to a transition element:[70-73] these date from the early 1930s when W. Hieber discovered $[Fe(CO)_4H_2]$ and $[Co(CO)_4H]$ and now cover an astonishing variety of structural types. The modest steric requirements of the H atom enable complexes such as $[ReH_9]^{2-}$ to be synthesized, and bridged complexes such as the linear $[Cr_2(CO)_{10}H]^-$ and bent $[W_2(CO)_9H(NO)]$, are known. For η^2-H_2 complexes see pp. 44–7. The role of hydrido complexes in homogeneous catalysis is also exciting considerable attention.

---

[69] A. HAJOS, *Complex Hydrides*, Elsevier, Amsterdam, 1979, 398 pp.

[70] J. C. GREEN and M. L. H. GREEN, *Comprehensive Inorganic Chemistry*, Vol. 4, Chap. 48, Pergamon Press, Oxford, 1973.

[71] H. D. KAESZ and R. B. SAILLANT, *Chem. Rev.* **72**, 231–81 (1972).

[72] A. P. HUMPHRIES and H. D. KAESZ, *Progr. Inorg. Chem.* **25**, 145–222 (1979).

[73] G. L. GEOFFROY, *Progr. Inorg. Chem.* **27**, 123–51 (1980).

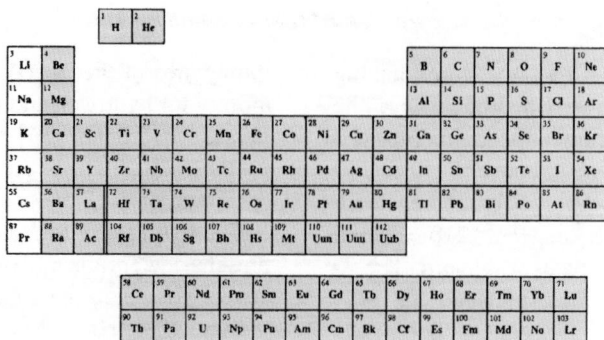

4

Lithium, Sodium, Potassium, Rubidium, Caesium and Francium

4.1 Introduction

The alkali metals form a homogeneous group of extremely reactive elements which illustrate well the similarities and trends to be expected from the periodic classification, as discussed in Chapter 2. Their physical and chemical properties are readily interpreted in terms of their simple electronic configuration, ns^1, and for this reason they have been extensively studied by the full range of experimental and theoretical techniques. Compounds of sodium and potassium have been known from ancient times and both elements are essential for animal life. They are also major items of trade, commerce and chemical industry. Lithium was first recognized as a separate element at the beginning of the nineteenth century but did not assume major industrial importance until about 40 y ago. Rubidium and caesium are of considerable academic interest but so far have few industrial applications. Francium, the elusive element 87, has only fleeting existence in nature due to its very short radioactive half-life, and this delayed its discovery until 1939.

4.2 The Elements

4.2.1 Discovery and isolation

The spectacular success (in 1807) of Humphry Davy, then aged 29 y, in isolating metallic potassium by electrolysis of molten caustic potash (KOH) is too well known to need repeating in detail.[1] Globules of molten sodium were similarly prepared by him a few days later from molten caustic soda. Earlier experiments with aqueous solutions had been unsuccessful because of the great reactivity of these new elements. The names chosen by Davy reflect the sources of the elements.

Lithium was recognized as a new alkali metal by J. A. Arfvedson in 1817 whilst he was working as a young assistant in J. J. Berzelius's laboratory. He noted that Li compounds were similar to those of Na and K but that the carbonate and hydroxide were much less soluble

[1] M. E. WEEKS, *Discovery of the Elements*, Journal of Chemical Education, Easton, 6th edn., 1956, 910 pp.

in water. Lithium was first isolated from the sheet silicate mineral petalite, $LiAlSi_4O_{10}$, and Arfvedson also showed it was present in the pyroxene silicate spodumene, $LiAlSi_2O_6$, and in the mica lepidolite, which has an approximate composition $K_2Li_3Al_4Si_7O_{21}(OH,F)_3$. He chose the name lithium (Greek $\lambda\iota\theta o\varsigma$, stone) to contrast it with the vegetable origin of Davy's sodium and potassium. Davy isolated the metal in 1818 by electrolysing molten Li_2O.

Rubidium was discovered as a minor constituent of lepidolite by R. W. Bunsen and G. R. Kirchhoff in 1861 only a few months after their discovery of caesium (1860) in mineral spa waters. These two elements were the first to be discovered by means of the spectroscope, which Bunsen and Kirchhoff had invented the previous year (1859); accordingly their names refer to the colour of the most prominent lines in their spectra (Latin *rubidus*, deepest red; *caesius*, sky blue).

Francium was first identified in 1939 by the elegant radiochemical work of Marguerite Perey who named the element in honour of her native country. It occurs in minute traces in nature as a result of the rare (1.38%) branching decay of ^{227}Ac in the ^{235}U series:

$$^{227}_{89}Ac \xrightarrow[t_{1/2}\ 21.77\ y]{\alpha\ (1.38\%)} {}^{223}_{87}Fr \xrightarrow[\textbf{21.8 min}]{\beta^-} {}^{223}_{88}Ra \xrightarrow{\alpha} {}_{11.43\ d}$$

Its terrestrial abundance has been estimated as 2×10^{-18} ppm, which corresponds to a total of only 15 g in the top 1 km of the earth's crust. Other isotopes have since been produced by nuclear reactions but all have shorter half-lives than ^{223}Fr, which decays by energetic β^- emission, $t_{1/2}$ 21.8 min. Because of this intense radioactivity it is only possible to work with tracer amounts of the element.

4.2.2 Terrestrial abundance and distribution

Despite their chemical similarity, Li, Na and K are not closely associated in their occurrence, mainly because of differences in size (see Table on p. 75). Lithium tends to occur in ferromagnesian minerals where it partly replaces magnesium; it occurs to the extent of about 18 ppm by weight in crustal rocks, and this reflects its relatively low abundance in the cosmos (Chapter 1). It is about as abundant as gallium (19 ppm) and niobium (20 ppm). The most important mineral commercially is spodumene, $LiAlSi_2O_6$, and large deposits occur in the USA, Canada, Brazil, Argentina, the former USSR, Spain, China, Zimbabwe and the Congo. An indication of the industrial uses of lithium and its compounds is given in the Panel. World production of lithium compounds in 1994 corresponded to some 5700 tonnes of contained lithium (equivalent to 30 000 tonnes of lithium carbonate) of which over 70% was in the USA.

Sodium, 22 700 ppm (2.27%) is the seventh most abundant element in crustal rocks and the fifth most abundant metal, after Al, Fe, Ca and Mg. Potassium (18 400 ppm) is the next most abundant element after sodium. Vast deposits of both Na and K salts occur in relatively pure form on all continents as a result of evaporation of ancient seas, and this process still continues today in the Great Salt Lake (Utah), the Dead Sea and elsewhere. Sodium occurs as rock-salt (NaCl) and as the carbonate (trona), nitrate (saltpetre), sulfate (mirabilite), borate (borax, kernite), etc. Potassium occurs principally as the simple chloride (sylvite), as the double chloride $KCl.MgCl_2.6H_2O$ (carnallite) and the anhydrous sulfate $K_2Mg_2(SO_4)_3$ (langbeinite). There are also unlimited supplies of NaCl in natural brines and oceanic waters (~ 30 kg m^{-3}). Thus, it has been calculated that rock-salt equivalent to the NaCl in the oceans of the world would occupy 19 million cubic km (i.e. 50% more than the total volume of the North American continent above sea-level). Alternatively stated, a one-km square prism would stretch from the earth to the moon 47 times. Note also that, although Na and K are almost equally abundant in the crustal rocks of the earth, Na is some 30 times as abundant as K in the oceans. This is partly because K salts with the larger anions tend to be less soluble than the Na salts and, likewise, K is more strongly bound to

Lithium and its Compounds[2−4]

The dramatic transformation of Li from a small-scale specialist commodity to a multikilotonne industry during the past three decades is due to the many valuable properties of its compounds. About 35 compounds of Li are currently available in bulk, and a similar number again can be obtained in developmental or research quantities. A major industrial use of Li is in the form of **lithium stearate** which is used as a thickener and gelling agent to transform oils into lubricating greases. These "all-purpose" greases combine high water resistance with good low-temperature properties (−20°C) and excellent high-temperature stability (>150°C); they are readily prepared from $LiOH.H_2O$ and tallow or other natural fats and have captured nearly half the total market for automotive greases in the USA.

Lithium carbonate is the most important industrial compound of lithium and is the starting point for the production of most other lithium compounds. It is also used as a flux in porcelain enamel formulations and in the production of special toughened glasses (by replacement of the larger Na ions): Li can either be incorporated within the glass itself or the preformed Na-glass can be dipped in a molten-salt bath containing Li ions to effect a surface cation exchange. In another application, the use of Li_2CO_3 by primary aluminium producers has risen sharply in recent years since it increases production capacity by 7–10% by lowering the mp of the cell content and permitting larger current flow; in addition, troublesome fluorine emissions are reduced by 25–50% and production costs are appreciably lowered. In 1987 the price for bulk quantities of Li_2CO_3 in the USA was $3.30 per kg.

The first commercial use of **Li metal** (in the 1920s) was as an alloying agent with lead to give toughened bearings; currently it is used to produce high-strength, low-density aluminium alloys for aircraft construction. With magnesium it forms an extremely tough low-density alloy which is used for armour plate and for aerospace components (e.g. LA 141, d 1.35 g cm^{-3}, contains 14% Li, 1% Al, 85% Mg). Other metallurgical applications employ **LiCl** as an invaluable brazing flux for Al automobile parts.

LiOH is used in the manufacture of lithium stearate greases (see above) and for CO_2 absorption in closed environments such as space capsules (light weight) and submarines. **LiH** is used to generate hydrogen in military, meteorological, and other applications, and the use of LiD in thermonuclear weaponry and research has been mentioned (p. 18). Likewise, the important applications of **LiAlH$_4$, Li/NH$_3$** and **organolithium reagents** in synthetic organic chemistry are well known, though these account for only a small percentage of the lithium produced. Other specialist uses include the growing market for ferroelectrics such as **LiTaO$_3$** to modulate laser beams (p. 57), and increasing use of thermoluminescent LiF in X-ray dosimetry.

Perhaps one of the most exciting new applications stems from the discovery in 1949 that small daily doses (1–2 g) of **Li$_2$CO$_3$** taken orally provide an effective treatment for manic-depressive psychoses. The mode of action is not well understood but there appear to be no undesirable side effects. The dosage maintains the level of Li in the blood at about 1 mmol l^{-1} and its action may be related to the influence of Li on the Na/K balance and (or) the Mg/Ca balance since Li is related chemically to both pairs of elements.

Looking to the future, Li/FeS$_x$ battery systems are emerging as a potentially viable energy storage system for off-peak electricity and as a non-polluting silent source of power for electric cars. The battery resembles the conventional lead–acid battery in having solid electrodes (Li/Si alloy, negative; FeS$_x$ positive) and a liquid electrolyte (molten LiCl/KCl at 400°C). Other battery systems which have reached the prototype stage include the Li/S and Na/S cells (see p. 678).

the complex silicates and alumino silicates in the soils (ion exchange in clays). Again, K leached from rocks is preferentially absorbed and used by plants whereas Na can proceed to the sea. Potassium is an essential element for plant life and the growth of wild plants is often limited by the supply of K available to them.

[2] *Kirk–Othmer Encyclopedia of Chemical Technology*, 4th edn., 1995, Vol 15, pp. 434–63.

[3] J. E. LLOYD in R. THOMPSON (ed.) *Speciality Inorganic Chemicals*, Royal Society of Chemistry, London, 1981, pp. 98–122.

[4] W. BÜCHNER, R. SCHLIEBS, G. WINTER and K. H. BÜCHEL, *Industrial Inorganic Chemistry*, VCH, New York, 1989, pp. 215–8.

The vital importance of NaCl in the heavy chemical industry is indicated in the Panel opposite, and information on potassium salts is given in the Panel on p. 73.

Rubidium (78 ppm, similar to Ni, Cu, Zn) and caesium (2.6 ppm, similar to Br, Hf, U) are much less abundant than Na and K and have only recently become available in quantity. No purely Rb-containing mineral is known and much of the commercially available material is obtained as a byproduct of lepidolite processing for Li. Caesium occurs as the hydrated aluminosilicate pollucite, $Cs_4Al_4Si_9O_{26}.H_2O$, but the world's only commercial source is at Bernic Lake,

Production and Uses of Salt[5−7]

More NaCl is used for inorganic chemical manufacture than is any other material. It is approached only by phosphate rock, and world consumption of each exceeds 150 million tonnes annually, the figure for NaCl in 1982 being 168.7 million tonnes. Production is dominated by Europe (39%), North America (34%) and Asia (20%), whilst South America and Oceania have only 3% each and Africa 1%. Rock-salt occurs as vast subterranean deposits often hundreds of metres thick and containing >90% NaCl. The Cheshire salt field (which is the principal UK source of NaCl) is typical, occupying an area of 60 km × 24 km and being some 400 m thick: this field alone corresponds to reserves of $>10^{11}$ tonnes. Similar deposits occur near Carlsbad New Mexico, in Saskachewan Canada and in many other places. Production methods vary with locality and with the use to be made of the salt. For example, in the UK 82% is extracted as brine for direct use in the chemical industry and 18% is mined as rock-salt, mainly for use on roads; less than 1% is obtained by solar evaporation. By contrast, in the USA only 55% comes from brine, whereas 32% is mined as rock salt, 8% is obtained by vacuum pan evaporation, 4% by solar evaporation and 1% by the open pan process.

Major sections of the inorganic heavy chemicals industry are based on salt and, indeed, this compound was the very starting point of the chemical industry. Nicolas Leblanc (1742–1806), physician to the Duke of Orleans, devised a satisfactory process for making NaOH from NaCl in 1787 (Patent 1791) and this achieved enormous technological significance in Europe during most of the nineteenth century as the first industrial chemical process to be worked on a really large scale. It was, however, never important in the USA since it was initially cheaper to import from Europe and, by the time the US chemical industry began to develop in the last quarter of the century, the Leblanc process had been superseded by the electrolytic process. Thus in 1874 world production of NaOH was 525 000 tonnes of which 495 000 were by the Leblanc process; by 1902 production had risen to 1 800 000 tonnes, but only 150 000 tonnes of this was Leblanc. Despite its long history, there is still great scope for innovation and development in the chlor-alkali and related industries. For example, in recent years there has been a steady switch from mercury electrolysis cells to diaphragm and membrane cells for environmental and economic reasons.[7] Similarly, the ammonia-soda (Solvay) process for Na_2CO_3 is being phased out because of the difficulty of disposing of embarrassing byproducts such as NH_4Cl and $CaCl_2$, coupled with the increasing cost of NH_3 and the possibility of direct mining for trona, $Na_2CO_3.NaHCO_3.2H_2O$. The closely interlocking chemical processes based on salt are set out in the flow sheet (Fig. 4.1). The detailed balance of the processes differs somewhat in the various industrial nations but data for the usage of salt in the USA are typical: of the 34.8 million tonnes consumed in 1982, 48% was used for chlor-alkali production and Na_2CO_3, 24% for the salting of roads, 6% for food and food processing, 5% for animal feeds, 5% for various industries such as paper pulp, textiles, metal manufacturing and the rubber and oil industries, 2% for all other chemical manufacturing, and the remaining 10% for a wide variety of other purposes. Further discussion on the industrial production and uses of many of these chemicals (e.g. NaOH, Na_2CO_3, Na_2SO_4) is given on p. 89.

Current industrial prices are ~$5 per tonne for salt in brine and ~$55 per tonne for solid salt, depending on quality.

Manitoba and Cs (like Rb) is mainly obtained as a byproduct of the Li industry. The intense interest in Li for thermonuclear purposes since about 1958, coupled with its extensive use in automotive greases (p. 70), has consequently made Rb and Cs compounds much more available than formerly: annual production is in the region of 5 tonnes for each.

⁵ L. F. HABER, *The Chemical Industry during the Nineteenth Century*, Oxford University Press, Oxford, 1958, 292 pp. T. K. DERRY and T. I. WILLIAMS, *A Short History of Chemical Technology*, Oxford University Press, Oxford, 1960, 782 pp.

⁶ *Kirk–Othmer Encyclopedia of Chemical Technology*, 3rd edn., 1983, Vol. 21 pp. 205–23.

⁷ W. BÜCHNER, R. SCHLIEBS, G. WINTER and K. H. BÜCHEL, *Industrial Inorganic Chemistry*, VCH, New York, 1989, 149 ff., 218 ff.

4.2.3 Production and uses of the metals

Most commercial Li ores have 1–3% Li and this is increased by flotation to 4–6%. Spodumene, $LiAlSi_2O_6$, is heated to ~1100° to convert the α-form into the less-dense, more friable β-form, which is then washed with H_2SO_4 at 250°C and water-leached to give $Li_2SO_4.H_2O$. Successive treatment with Na_2CO_3 and HCl gives Li_2CO_3 (insol) and LiCl. Alternatively, the chloride can be obtained by calcining the washed ore with limestone ($CaCO_3$) at 1000° followed by water leaching to give LiOH and then treatment with HCl. Recovery from natural brines is also extensively used in the USA (Searles Lake, California and Clayton Valley, Nevada).

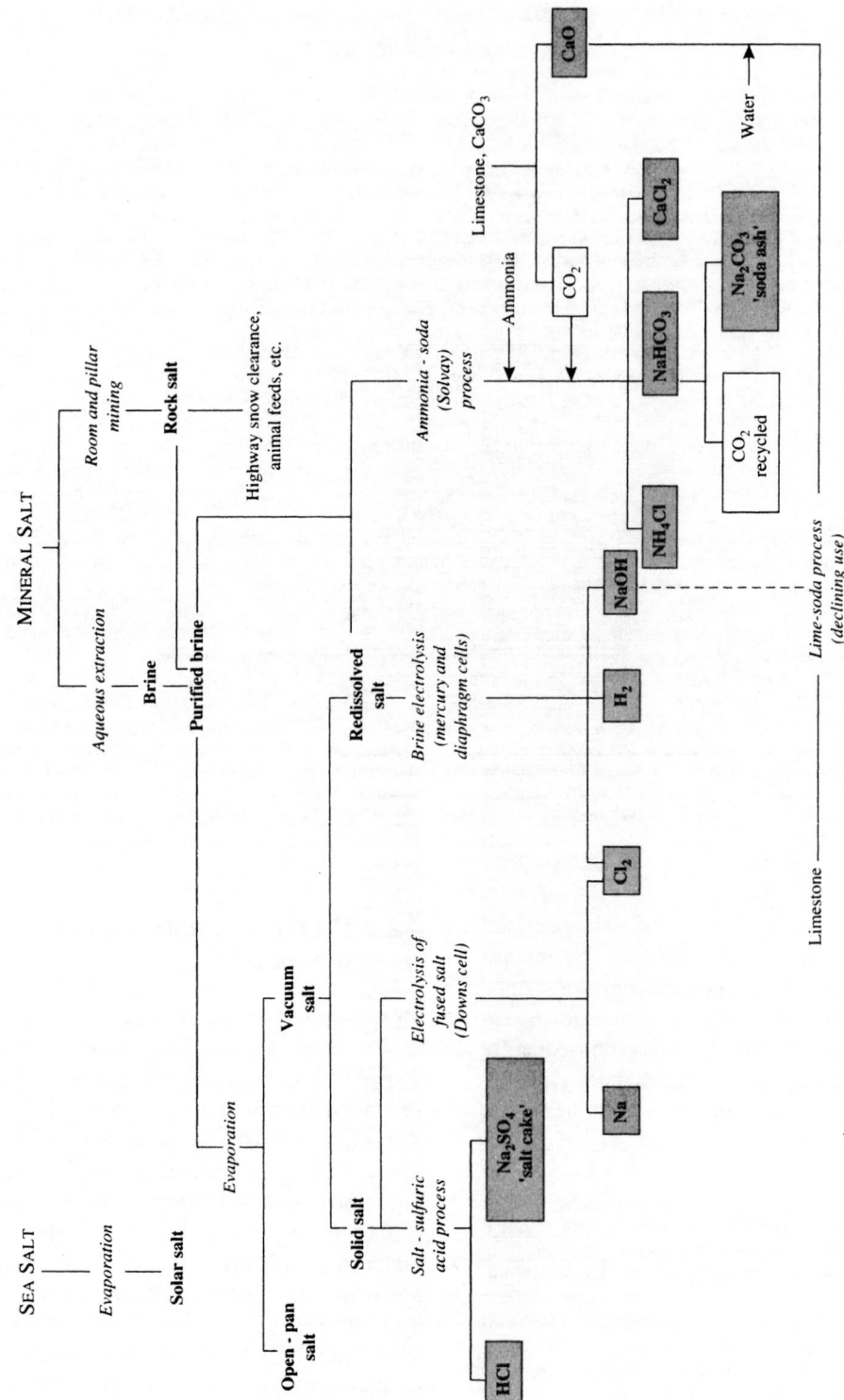

Figure 4.1   Flow sheet on chemical processes based on salt.

Production of Potassium Salts[8-10]

Sylvite (KCl) and sylvinite (mixed NaCl, KCl) are the most important K minerals for chemical industry; carnallite is also mined. Ocean waters contain only about 0.06% KCl, though this can rise to as high as 1.5% in some inland marshes and seas such as Searle's Lake, the Great Salt Lake, or the Dead Sea, thereby making recovery economically feasible. Soluble minerals of K are generally referred to (incorrectly) as potash, and production figures are always expressed as the weight of K_2O equivalent. Massive evaporite beds of soluble K salts were first discovered at Stassfurt, Germany, in 1856 and were worked there for potash and rock-salt from 1861 until 1972. World production was 28.6 million tonnes K_2O equivalent in 1986 of which 35% was produced in the USSR and 24% Canada.

In the UK workable potash deposits are confined to the Cleveland–North Yorkshire bed which is ~11 m thick and has reserves of >500 million tonnes. Massive recovery is also possible from brines; e.g. Jordan has a huge plant capable of recovering up to a million tonnes pa from the Dead Sea and the annual production by this country and by Israel now matches that of the USA and France.

Potassium is a major essential element for plant growth and potassic fertilizers account for the overwhelming proportion of production (95%). Again KCl is dominant, accounting for more than 90% of the K used in fertilizers; K_2SO_4 is also used. KNO_3, though an excellent fertilizer, is now of only minor importance because of production costs. In addition to its dominant use in fertilizers, KCl is used mainly to manufacture KOH by electrolysis using the mercury and membrane processes (about 0.7 million tonnes of KOH worldwide in 1985). This in turn is used to make a variety of other compounds and materials such as those listed below (the figures referring to the percentage usage of KOH in the USA in 1984): K_2CO_3 25%, liquid fertilizers 15%, soaps 10%, liquid detergents ($K_4P_2O_7$) 9%, synthetic rubber 5%, crop protection agents 3%, $KMnO_4$ 2%, other chemicals 26% and export 5%. The manufacture of metallic K is relatively minor, the world production in 1994 amounting only to about 500 tonnes. Prices in 1994 were $30–40 per kg for bulk K and $16–22 per kg for NaK (78% K).

The main industrial uses of potassium compounds other than KCl and KOH are:

K_2CO_3 (from KOH and CO_2), used chiefly in high-quality decorative glassware, in optical lenses, colour TV tubes and fluorescent lamps; it is also used in china ware, textile dyes and pigments.

KNO_3, a powerful oxidizing agent now used mainly in gunpowders and pyrotechnics, and in fertilizers.

$KMnO_4$, an oxidizer, decolorizer, bleacher and purification agent; its major application is in the manufacture of saccharin.

KO_2, used in breathing apparatus (p. 74).

$KClO_3$, used in small amounts in matches and explosives (pp. 509, 862).

KBr, used extensively in photography and as the usual source of bromine in organic syntheses; formerly used as a sedative.

It is interesting to note the effect of varying the alkali metal cation on the properties of various compounds and industrial materials. For example, a soap is an alkali metal salt formed by neutralizing a long-chain organic acid such as stearic acid, $CH_3(CH_2)_{16}CO_2H$, with MOH. Potassium soaps are soft and low melting, and are therefore used in liquid detergents. Sodium soaps have higher mps and are the basis for the familiar domestic "hard soaps" or bar soaps. Lithium soaps have still higher mps and are therefore used as thickening agents for high-temperature lubricating oils and greases — their job is to hold the oil in contact with the metal under conditions when the oil by itself would run off.

The metal is obtained by electrolysis of a fused mixture of 55% LiCl, 45% KCl at ~450°C, the first commercial production being by Metallgesellschaft AG, in Germany, 1923. Current world production of Li metal is about 1000 tonnes pa. Far greater tonnages of Li compounds are, of course, produced and their major commercial applications have already been noted (p. 70).

[8] *Kirk–Othmer Encyclopedia of Chemical Technology*, 4th edn., 1996, Vol. 19, pp. 1047–92.

[9] P. CROWSON, *Minerals Handbook 1988–89*, Stockton Press, New York, 1988, pp. 216–21

[10] Ref. 7 pp. 228–31.

Sodium metal is produced commercially on the kilotonne scale by the electrolysis of a fused eutectic mixture of 40% NaCl, 60% $CaCl_2$ at ~580°C in a Downs cell (introduced by du Pont, Niagara Falls, 1921). Metallic Na and Ca are liberated at the cylindrical steel cathode and rise through a cooled collecting pipe which allows the calcium to solidify and fall back into the melt. Chlorine liberated at the central graphite anode is collected in a nickel dome and subsequently purified. Potassium cannot be produced in this way because it is too soluble in the molten chloride to float on top of the cell for collection and because it vaporizes readily at the operating temperatures, creating hazardous conditions. Superoxide formation is an added difficulty since this reacts explosively with K metal. Consequently, commercial production of K relies on reduction of molten KCl with metallic Na at 850°C.[†] A similar process using Ca metal at 750°C under reduced pressure is used to produce metallic Rb and Cs.

Industrial uses of Na metal reflect its strong reducing properties. Much of the world production was used to make $PbEt_4$ (or $PbMe_4$) for gasoline antiknocks via the high-pressure reaction of alkyl chlorides with Na/Pb alloy, though this use is declining rapidly for environmental reasons. A further major use is to produce Ti, Zr and other metals by reduction of their chlorides, and a smaller amount is used to make compounds such as NaH, NaOR and Na_2O_2. Sodium dispersions are also a valuable catalyst for the production of some artificial rubbers and elastomers. A growing use is as a heat-exchange liquid in fast breeder nuclear reactors where sodium's low mp, low viscosity and low neutron absorption cross-section combine with its exceptionally high heat capacity and thermal conductivity to make it (and its alloys with K) the most-favoured material.[11] The annual production of metallic Na in the USA fell steadily from 170 000 tonnes in 1974 to 86 000 tonnes in 1985 and is still falling. Potassium metal, being more difficult and expensive to produce, is manufactured on a much smaller scale. One of its main uses is to make the superoxide KO_2 by direct combustion; this compound is used in breathing masks as an auxiliary supply of O_2 in mines, submarines and space vehicles:

$$4KO_2 + 2CO_2 \longrightarrow 2K_2CO_3 + 3O_2$$

$$4KO_2 + 4CO_2 + 2H_2O \longrightarrow 4KHCO_3 + 3O_2$$

An indication of the relative cost of the alkali metals in bulk at 1980–82 prices (USA) is:

Metal	Li	Na	K	Rb	Cs
Price/\$ kg^{-1}	36.3	1.50	34.4	827	716
Relative cost (per kg)	24	1	23	550	477
Relative cost (per mol)	7.3	1	39	2050	2760

4.2.4 Properties of the alkali metals

The Group 1 elements are soft, low-melting metals which crystallize with bcc lattices. All are silvery-white except caesium which is golden yellow;[12] in fact, caesium is one of only three metallic elements which are intensely coloured, the other two being copper and gold (see also pp. 112, 1177, 1232). Lithium is harder than sodium but softer than lead. Atomic properties are summarized in Table 4.1 and general physical properties are in Table 4.2. Further physical properties of the alkali metals, together with a review of the chemical properties and industrial applications of the metals in the molten state are in ref. 11.

Lithium has a variable atomic weight (p. 18) whereas sodium and caesium, being mononuclidic, have very precisely known and invariant atomic weights. Potassium and rubidium are both radioactive but the half-lives of their radioisotopes are so long that the atomic weight does not vary significantly from this cause. The large size and low ionization energies of the alkali metals compared with all other elements have already been noted (pp. 23–5) and this confers on the elements their characteristic properties. The group usually shows smooth trends in properties, and the weak bonding of the single valence electron leads to low mp, bp and density, and low heats of sublimation, vaporization and dissociation. Conversely, the elements have large atomic and ionic radii and extremely high thermal and electrical conductivity. Lithium is the smallest element in the group and has the highest ionization energy, mp and heat

---

[†] This reduction of KCl by Na appears to be contrary to the normal order of reactivity (K > Na). However, at 850–880° an equilibrium is set up: $Na(g) + K^+(l) \rightleftharpoons Na^+(l) + K(g)$. Since K is the more volatile (p. 75), it distils off more readily, thus displacing the equilibrium and allowing the reaction to proceed. By fractional distillation through a packed tower, K of 99.5% purity can be obtained but usually an Na/K mixture is drawn off because alloys with 15–55% Na are liquid at room temperature and therefore easier to transport.

[11] C. C. ADDISON, *The Chemistry of Liquid Alkali Metals*, Wiley, Chichester, 1984, 330 pp.

[12] R. J. MOOLENAAR, *Journal of Metals* **16**, 21–4 (1964).

Table 4.1 Atomic properties of the alkali metals

Property	Li	Na	K	Rb	Cs	Fr
Atomic number	3	11	19	37	55	87
Number of naturally occurring isotopes	2	1	$2 + 1^{(a)}$	$1 + 1^{(a)}$	1	$1^{(a)}$
Atomic weight	6.941(2)	22.989 768(6)	39.0983(1)	85.4678(3)	132.90543(5)	(223)
Electronic configuration	$[He]2s^1$	$[Ne]3s^1$	$[Ar]4s^1$	$[Kr]5s^1$	$[Xe]6s^1$	$[Rn]7s^1$
Ionization energy/kJ mol^{-1}	520.2	495.8	418.8	403.0	375.7	$\sim$375
Electron affinity/kJ mol^{-1}	59.8	52.9	46.36	46.88	45.5	(44.0)
ΔH_{dissoc}/kJ mol^{-1} (M$_2$)	106.5	73.6	57.3	45.6	44.77	—
Metal radius/pm	152	186	227	248	265	—
Ionic radius (6-coordinate)/pm	76	102	138	152	167	(180)
$E°$/V for M$^+$(aq) + e$^- \longrightarrow$ M(s)	−3.045	−2.714	−2.925	−2.925	−2.923	—

$^{(a)}$Radioactive: ^{40}K $t_{1/2}$ 1.277 × 10^9 y; ^{87}Rb $t_{1/2}$ 4.75 × 10^{10} y; ^{223}Fr $t_{1/2}$ 21.8 min.

Table 4.2 Physical properties of the alkali metals

Property	Li	Na	K	Rb	Cs
MP/°C	180.6	97.8	63.7	39.5	28.4
BP/°C	1342	883	759	688	671
Density (20°C)/g cm^{-3}	0.534	0.968	0.856	1.532	1.90
ΔH_{fus}/kJ mol^{-1}	2.93	2.64	2.39	2.20	2.09
ΔH_{vap}/kJ mol^{-1}	148	99	79	76	67
ΔH_{f} (monatomic gas)/kJ mol^{-1}	162	108	89.6	82.0	78.2
Electrical resistivity (25°C)/μohm cm	9.47	4.89	7.39	13.1	20.8

of atomization; it also has the lowest density of any solid at room temperature.

All the alkali metals have characteristic flame colorations due to the ready excitation of the outermost electron, and this is the basis of their analytical determination by flame photometry or atomic absorption spectroscopy. The colours and principal emission (or absorption) wavelengths, λ, are given below but it should be noted that these lines do not all refer to the same transition; for example, the Na D-line doublet at 589.0, 589.6 nm arises from the $3s^1 - 3p^1$ transition in Na atoms formed by reduction of Na$^+$ in the flame, whereas the red line for lithium is associated with the short-lived species LiOH.

Element	Li	Na	K	Rb	Cs
Colour	Crimson	Yellow	Violet	Red-violet	Blue
λ/nm	670.8	589.2	766.5	780.0	455.5

The reduction potential for lithium appears at first sight to be anomalous and is one of the

few properties that does not show a smooth trend with increasing atomic number in the group. This arises from the small size and very large hydration energy of the free gaseous lithium ion. The standard reduction potential $E°$ refers to the reaction Li$^+$(aq) + e$^- \longrightarrow$ Li(s) and is related to the free-energy change: $\Delta G° = -nFE°$. The ionization energy I_M, which is the enthalpy change of the gas-phase reaction Li(g) $\longrightarrow$ Li$^+$(g) + e$^-$, is only one component of this, as can be seen from the following cycle:

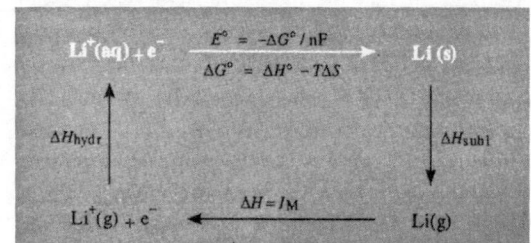

Estimates of the heat of hydration of Li$^+$(g) give values near 520 kJ mol^{-1} compared with

$405 \, \text{kJ mol}^{-1}$ for $Na^+(g)$ and only $265 \, \text{kJ mol}^{-1}$ for $Cs^+(g)$. This factor, although opposed by the much larger entropy change for the lithium electrode reaction (due to the more severe disruption of the water structure by the lithium ion), is sufficient to reverse the position of lithium and make it the most electropositive of the alkali metals (as measured by electrode potential) despite the fact that it is the most difficult element of the group to ionize in the gas phase.

4.2.5 Chemical reactivity and trends

The ease of involving the outermost ns^1 electron in bonding, coupled with the very high second-stage ionization energy of the alkali metals, immediately explains both the great chemical reactivity of these elements and the fact that their oxidation state in compounds never exceeds $+1$. The metals have a high lustre when freshly cut but tarnish rapidly in air due to reaction with O_2 and moisture. Reaction with the halogens is vigorous; even explosive in some cases. All the alkali metals react with hydrogen (p. 65) and with proton donors such as alcohols, gaseous ammonia and even alkynes. They also act as powerful reducing agents towards many oxides and halides and so can be used to prepare many metallic elements or their alloys.

The small size of lithium frequently confers special properties on its compounds and for this reason the element is sometimes termed "anomalous". For example, it is miscible with Na only above 380° and is immiscible with molten K, Rb and Cs, whereas all other pairs of alkali metals are miscible with each other in all proportions. (The ternary alloy containing 12% Na, 47% K and 41% Cs has the lowest known mp, $-78°C$, of any metallic system.) Li shows many similarities to Mg. This so-called "diagonal relationship" stems from the similarity in ionic size of the two elements: $r(Li^+)$ 76 pm, $r(Mg^{2+})$ 72 pm, compared with $r(Na^+)$ 102 pm. Thus, as first noted by Arfvedson in establishing lithium as a new element, LiOH and Li_2CO_3 are much less soluble than the corresponding

Na and K compounds and the carbonate (like $MgCO_3$) decomposes more readily on being heated. Similarly, LiF (like MgF_2) is much less soluble in water than are the other alkali metal fluorides because of the large lattice energy associated with the small size of both the cation and the anion. By contrast, lithium salts of large, non-polarizable anions such as ClO_4^- are much more soluble than those of the other alkali metals, presumably because of the high energy of solvation of Li^+. For the same reason many simple lithium salts are normally hydrated (p. 88) and the anhydrous salts are extremely hygroscopic: this great affinity for water forms the basis of the widespread use of LiCl and LiBr brines in dehumidifying and air-conditioning units. More subtly there is also a close structural relation between the hydrogen-bonded structures of $LiClO_4.3H_2O$ and $Mg(ClO_4)_2.6H_2O$ in which the face-shared octahedral groups of $[Li(H_2O)_6]^+$ are replaced alternately by half the number of discrete $[Mg(H_2O)_6]^{2+}$ groups.[13] Lithium sulfate, unlike the other alkali metal sulfates, does not form alums $[M(H_2O)_6]^+[Al(H_2O)_6]^{3+}$-$[SO_4]^{2-}_2$ because the hydrated lithium cation is too small to fill the appropriate site in the alum structure.

Lithium is unusual in reacting directly with N_2 to form the nitride Li_3N; no other alkali metal has this property, which lithium shares with magnesium (which readily forms Mg_3N_2). On the basis of size, it would be expected that Li would be tetrahedrally coordinated by N but, as pointed out by A. F. Wells,[13] this would require 12 tetrahedra to meet at a point which is a geometrical impossibility, 8 being the maximum number theoretically possible; accordingly Li_3N has a unique structure (see p. 92) in which one-third of the Li have 2 N atoms as nearest neighbours (at 194 pm) and the remainder have 3 N atoms as neighbours (at 213 pm); each N is surrounded by 2 Li at 194 pm and 6 more at 213 pm.

---

13 A. F. WELLS, *Structural Inorganic Chemistry*, 5th edn., Oxford University Press, Oxford, 1984, 1382 pp.

4.2.6 Solutions in liquid ammonia and other solvents [14]

One of the most remarkable features of the alkali metals is their ready solubility in liquid ammonia to give bright blue, metastable solutions with unusual properties. Such solutions have been extensively studied since they were first observed by T. Weyl in 1863,[†] and it is now known that similar solutions are formed by the heavier alkaline earth metals (Ca, Sr and Ba) and the divalent lanthanoids europium and ytterbium in liquid ammonia. Many amines share with ammonia this ability though to a much lesser extent. It is clear that solubility is favoured by low metal lattice energy, low ionization energies and high cation solvation energy. The most striking physical properties of the solutions are their colour, electrical conductivity and magnetic susceptibility. The solutions all have the same blue colour when dilute, suggesting the presence of a common coloured species, and they become bronze-coloured and metallic at higher concentrations. The conductivity of the dilute solutions is an order of magnitude higher than that of completely ionized salts in water; as the solutions become more concentrated the conductivity at first diminishes to a minimum value at about 0.04 M and then increases dramatically to approach values typical of liquid metals. Dilute solutions are paramagnetic with a susceptibility appropriate to the presence of 1 free electron per metal atom; this susceptibility diminishes with increase in concentration, the

solutions becoming diamagnetic in the region of the conductivity minimum and then weakly paramagnetic again at still higher concentrations.

The interpretation of these remarkable properties has excited considerable interest: whilst there is still some uncertainty as to detail, it is now generally agreed that in dilute solution the alkali metals ionize to give a cation M^+ and a quasi-free electron which is distributed over a cavity in the solvent of radius 300–340 pm formed by displacement of 2–3 NH_3 molecules. This species has a broad absorption band extending into the infrared with a maximum at ∼1500 nm and it is the short wavelength tail of this band which gives rise to the deep-blue colour of the solutions. The cavity model also interprets the fact that dissolution occurs with considerable expansion of volume so that the solutions have densities that are appreciably lower than that of liquid ammonia itself. The variation of properties with concentration can best be explained in terms of three equilibria between five solute species M, M_2, M^+, M^- and e^-:

$$M_{am} \rightleftharpoons M_{am}^+ + e_{am}^-; \quad K \sim 10^{-2} \, mol \, l^{-1}$$

$$M_{am}^- \rightleftharpoons M_{am} + e_{am}^-; \quad K \sim 10^{-3} \, mol \, l^{-1}$$

$$(M_2)_{am} \rightleftharpoons 2M_{am}; \quad\quad K \sim 2 \times 10^{-4} \, mol \, l^{-1}$$

The subscript am indicates that the species are dissolved in liquid ammonia and may be solvated. At very low concentrations the first equilibrium predominates and the high ionic conductivity stems from the high mobility of the electron which is some 280 times that of the cation. The species M_{am} can be thought of as an ion pair in which M_{am}^+ and e_{am}^- are held together by coulombic forces. As the concentration is raised the second equilibrium begins to remove mobile electrons e_{am}^- as the complex M_{am}^- and the conductivity drops. Concurrently M_{am} begins to dimerize to give $(M_2)_{am}$ in which the interaction between the 2 electrons is sufficiently strong to lead to spin-pairing and diamagnetism. At still higher concentrations the system behaves as a molten metal in which the metal cations are ammoniated. Saturated solutions are indeed extremely concentrated as indicated by the following table:

[14] W. L. JOLLY and C. J. HALLADA, Liquid ammonia, Chap. 1 in T. C. WADDINGTON (ed.), *Non-aqueous Solvent Systems*, pp. 1–45, Academic Press, London, 1965. J. C. THOMPSON, The physical properties of metal solutions in non-aqueous solvents, Chap. 6 in J. LAGOWSKI (ed.), *The Chemistry of Non-aqueous Solvents*, Vol. 2, pp. 265–317, Academic Press, New York, 1967. J. JANDER (ed.), *Chemistry in Anhydrous Liquid Ammonia*, Wiley, Interscience, New York, 1966, 561 pp.

[†] Actually, the first observation was probably made by Sir Humphry Davy some 55 years earlier: an unpublished observation in his Notebook for November 1807 reads "When 8 grains of potassium were heated in ammoniacal gas it assumed a beautiful metallic appearance and gradually became of a pure blue colour".

Solute	Li	Na	K	Rb	Cs
$T/^\circ C$	-33.2°	-33.5°	-33.2°	–	-50°
$g(M)/kg(NH_3)$	108.7	251.4	463.7	–	3335
$mol(NH_3)/$					
$mol(M)$	3.75	5.37	4.95	–	2.34

The lower solubility of Li on a wt/wt basis reflects its lower atomic weight and, when compared on a molar basis, it is nearly 50% more soluble than Na (15.66 mol/kg NH_3 compared to 10.93 mol/kg NH_3). Note that it requires only 2.34 mol NH_3 (39.8 g) to dissolve 1 mol Cs (132.9 g).

Solutions of alkali metals in liquid ammonia are valuable as powerful and selective reducing agents. The solutions are themselves unstable with respect to amide formation:

$$M + NH_3 \longrightarrow MNH_2 + \tfrac{1}{2}H_2$$

However, under anhydrous conditions and in the absence of catalytic impurities such as transition metal ions, solutions can be stored for several days with only a few per cent decomposition. Some reductions occur without bond cleavage as in the formation of alkali metal superoxides and peroxide (p. 84).

$$O_2 \xrightarrow{e_{am}^-} O_2^- \xrightarrow{e_{am}^-} O_2^{2-}$$

Transition metal complexes can be reduced to unusually low oxidation states either with or without bond cleavage, e.g.:

$$K_2[Ni(CN)_4] + 2K \xrightarrow{NH_3/-33^\circ} K_4[Ni(CN)_4];$$
$$\text{i.e. Ni(0)}$$

$$[Pt(NH_3)_4]Br_2 + 2K \xrightarrow{NH_3/-33^\circ} [Pt(NH_3)_4] + 2KBr;$$
$$\text{i.e. Pt(0)}$$

$$Mn_2(CO)_{10} + 2K \xrightarrow{NH_3/-33^\circ} 2K[Mn(CO)_5];$$
$$\text{i.e. Mn}(-1)$$

$$Fe(CO)_5 + 2Na \xrightarrow{NH_3/-33^\circ} Na_2[Fe(CO)_4] + CO;$$
$$\text{i.e. Fe}(-2)$$

Salts of several heavy main-group elements can be reduced to form polyanions such as $Na_4[Sn_9]$, $Na_3[Sb_3]$ and $Na_3[Sb_7]$ (p. 588).

Many protonic species react with liberation of hydrogen:

$$RC{\equiv}CH + e_{am}^- \longrightarrow RC{\equiv}C^- + \tfrac{1}{2}H_2$$

$$GeH_4 + e_{am}^- \longrightarrow GeH_3^{\,-} + \tfrac{1}{2}H_2$$

$$NH_4^+ + e_{am}^- \longrightarrow NH_3 + \tfrac{1}{2}H_2$$

$$AsH_3 + e_{am}^- \longrightarrow AsH_2^{\,-} + \tfrac{1}{2}H_2$$

$$EtOH + e_{am}^- \longrightarrow EtO^- + \tfrac{1}{2}H_2$$

These and similar reactions have considerable synthetic utility. Other reactions which result in bond cleavage by the addition of one electron are:

$$R_2S + e_{am}^- \longrightarrow RS^- + \tfrac{1}{2}R_2$$

$$Et_3SnBr + e_{am}^- \longrightarrow Et_3Sn^\bullet + Br^-$$

When a bond is broken by addition of 2 electrons, either 2 anions or a dianion is formed:

$$Ge_2H_6 + 2e_{am}^- \longrightarrow 2GeH_3^{\,-}$$

$$PhNHNH_2 + 2e_{am}^- \longrightarrow PhNH^- + NH_2^{\,-}$$

$$PhN{=}O + 2e_{am}^- \longrightarrow PhN^- {-} O^-$$

$$S_8 + 2e_{am}^- \longrightarrow S_8^{\,2-}$$

Subsequent ammonolysis may also occur:

$$RCH{=}CH_2 + 2e_{am}^- \longrightarrow \{RCH{-}CH_2^{\,2-}\}$$

$$\xrightarrow{2NH_3} RCH_2CH_3 + 2NH_2^{\,-}$$

$$N_2O + 2e_{am}^- \longrightarrow \{N_2 + O^{2-}\}$$

$$\xrightarrow{NH_3} N_2 + OH^- + NH_2^{\,-}$$

$$NCO^- + 2e_{am}^- \longrightarrow \{CN^- + O^{2-}\}$$

$$\xrightarrow{NH_3} CN^- + OH^- + NH_2^-$$

$$EtBr + 2e_{am}^- \longrightarrow \{Br^- + Et^-\}$$

$$\xrightarrow{NH_3} Br^- + C_2H_6 + NH_2^-$$

Solutions of alkali metals in liquid ammonia have been developed as versatile reducing agents which effect reactions with organic compounds that are otherwise difficult or impossible.[15] Aromatic systems are reduced smoothly to cyclic mono- or di-olefins and alkynes are reduced stereospecifically to *trans*-alkenes (in contrast to Pd/H_2 which gives *cis*-alkenes).

The alkali metals are also soluble in aliphatic amines and hexamethylphosphoramide, $P(NMe_2)_3$ to give coloured solutions which are strong reducing agents. These solutions appear to be similar in many respects to the dilute solutions in liquid ammonia though they are less stable with respect to decomposition into amide and H_2. Likewise, fairly stable solutions of the larger alkali metals K, Rb and Cs have been obtained in tetrahydrofuran, ethylene glycol dimethyl ether and other polyethers. These and similar solutions have been successfully used as strong reducing agents in situations where protonic solvents would have caused solvolysis. For example, naphthalene reacts with Na in tetrahydrofuran to form deep-green solutions of the paramagnetic sodium naphthenide, $NaC_{10}H_8$, which can be used directly in the presence of a bis(tertiary phosphine) ligand to reduce the anhydrous chlorides VCl_3, $CrCl_3$, $MoCl_5$ and WCl_6 to the zerovalent octahedral complexes $[M(Me_2PCH_2CH_2PMe_2)_3]$, where M = V, Cr, Mo, W. Similarly the planar complex $[Fe(Me_2PCH_2CH_2PMe_2)_2]$ was obtained from *trans*-$[Fe(Me_2PCH_2CH_2PMe_2)_2Cl_2]$, and the corresponding tetrahedral Co(0) compound from $CoCl_2$.[16]

4.3 Compounds[17]

4.3.1 Introduction: the ionic-bond model[18]

The alkali metals form a complete range of compounds with all the common anions and have long been used to illustrate group similarities and trends. It has been customary to discuss the simple binary compounds in terms of the ionic bond model and there is little doubt that there is substantial separation of charge between the cationic and anionic components of the crystal lattice. On this model the ions are considered as hard, undeformable spheres carrying charges which are integral multiples of the electronic charge $z_i e^+$. Corrections can be incorporated for zero-point energies, London dispersion energies, ligand-field stabilization energies and non-spherical ions (such as NO_3^-, etc.). The attractive simplicity of this model, and its considerable success during the past 70 y in interpreting many of the properties of simple salts, should not, however, be allowed to obscure the growing realization of its inadequacy.[18,19] In particular, as already noted, success in calculating lattice energies and hence enthalpy of formation via the Born–Haber cycle, does not establish the correctness of the model but merely indicates that it is consistent with these particular observations. For example, the ionic model is quite successful in reproducing the enthalpy of formation of BF_3, SiF_4, PF_5 and even SF_6 on the assumption that they are assemblies of point charges at the known interatomic distance, i.e. $B^{3+}(F^-)_3$, etc.,[20] but this is not a sound reason

---

[15] A. J. BIRCH, *Qt. Rev.* **4**, 69–93 (1950); A. J. BIRCH and H. SMITH, *Qt. Rev.* **12**, 17–33 (1958).

[16] J. CHATT and H. R. WATSON, Complexes of zerovalent transition metals with the ditertiary phosphine, $Me_2PCH_2CH_2PMe_2$, *J. Chem. Soc.* 2545–9 (1962).

[17] W. A. HART and O. F. BEUMEL, Lithium and its compounds, *Comprehensive Inorganic Chemistry*, Vol. 1, Chap. 7, Pergamon Press, Oxford, 1973. T. P. WHALEY, Sodium, potassium, rubidium, caesium and francium, *ibid.*, Chap. 8.

[18] N. N. GREENWOOD, *Ionic Crystals, Lattice Defects and Nonstoichiometry*, Butterworths, London, 1968, 194 pp.

[19] D. M. ADAMS, *Inorganic Solids: An Introduction to Concepts in Solid-State Structural Chemistry*, Wiley, London, 1974, 336 pp.

[20] F. J. GARRICK, *Phil. Mag.* **14**, 914–37 (1932). It is instructive to repeat some of these calculations with more recent values for the constants and properties used.

for considering these molecular compounds as ionic. Likewise, the known lattice energy of lithium metal can be reproduced quite well by assuming that the observed bcc arrangement of atoms is made up from alternating ions Li^+Li^- in the CsCl structure;[21] the discrepancy is no worse than that obtained using the same model for AgCl (which has the NaCl structure). It appears that the ionic-bond model is self compensating and that the decrease in the hypothetical binding energy which accompanies the diminution of formal charges on the atoms is accompanied by an equivalent increase in binding energy which could be described as "covalent" (BF_3) or "metallic" (Li metal).

Indeed, the inherent improbability of the ionic bond model can be appreciated when it is realized that all simple cations have a positive charge and several vacant orbitals (and are therefore potentially electron pair acceptors) whereas all simple anions have a negative charge and several lone pairs of electrons (and are therefore potentially electron pair donors). The close juxtaposition of these electron-pair donor and acceptor species is thus likely to result in the transfer of at least some charge density by coordination, thereby introducing a substantial measure of covalency into the bonding of the alkali metal halides and related compounds. A more satisfactory procedure, at least conceptually, would be to describe crystalline salts and other solid compounds in terms of molecular orbitals. Quantitative calculations are difficult to carry out but the model allows flexibility in placing "partial ionic charges" on atoms by modifying orbital coefficients and populations, and it can also incorporate metallic behaviour by modifying the extent to which partly filled individual molecular orbitals are either separated by energy gaps or overlap.

The compounds which most nearly fit the classical conception of ionic bonding are the alkali metal halides. However, even here, one must ask to what extent it is reasonable to maintain that positively charged cations M^+ with favourably

directed vacant p orbitals remain uncoordinated by the surrounding anionic ligands X^- to form extended (bridged) complexes. Such interaction would be expected to increase from Cs^+ to Li^+ and from F^- to I^- (why?) and would place some electron density between the cation and anion. Some evidence on this comes from very precise electron density plots obtained by X-ray diffraction experiments on LiF, NaCl, KCl, MgO and CaF_2.[22] Data for LiF are shown in Fig. 4.2a from which it is clear that the Li^+ ion is no longer spherical and that the electron density, while it falls to a low value between the ions, does not become zero. Even more significantly, as shown in Fig. 4.2b, the minimum does not occur at the position to be expected from the conventional ionic radii: whatever set of tabulated values is used the cation is always larger than expected and the anion smaller. This is consistent with a transfer of some electronic density from anion to cation since the smaller resultant positive charge on the cation exerts smaller coulombic attraction for the electrons and the ion expands. The opposite holds for the anion. These results also call into question the use of radius-ratio rules to calculate the coordination number of cations and leave undecided the numerical value of the ionic radii to be used (see also p. 66, hydrides). In fact, the radius-ratio rules are particularly unhelpful for the alkali halides, since they predict (incorrectly) that LiCl, LiBr and LiI should have tetrahedral coordination and that NaF, KF, KCl, RbF, RbCl, RbBr and CsF should all have the CsCl structure. It may be significant that adoption of the NaCl structure by all these compounds maximizes the p orbital overlap along the orthogonal x-, y- and z-directions, and so favours molecular orbital formation in these directions. Further information on the variation in apparent radius of the hydride, halide and other anions in compounds with the alkali metals and other cations is in ref. 23.

[21] C. S. G. PHILLIPS and R. J. P. WILLIAMS, *Inorganic Chemistry*, Vol. 1, Chap. 5, "The ionic model", pp. 142–87, Oxford University Press, Oxford, 1965.

[22] H. WITTE and E. WÖLFEL, *Z. phys. Chem.* **3**, 296–329 (1955). J. KRUG, H. WITTE and E. WÖLFEL, *ibid.* **4**, 36–64 (1955). H. WITTE and E. WÖLFEL, *Rev. Mod. Phys.* **30**, 51–5 (1958).

[23] O. JOHNSON, *Inorg. Chem.* **12**, 780–5 (1973).

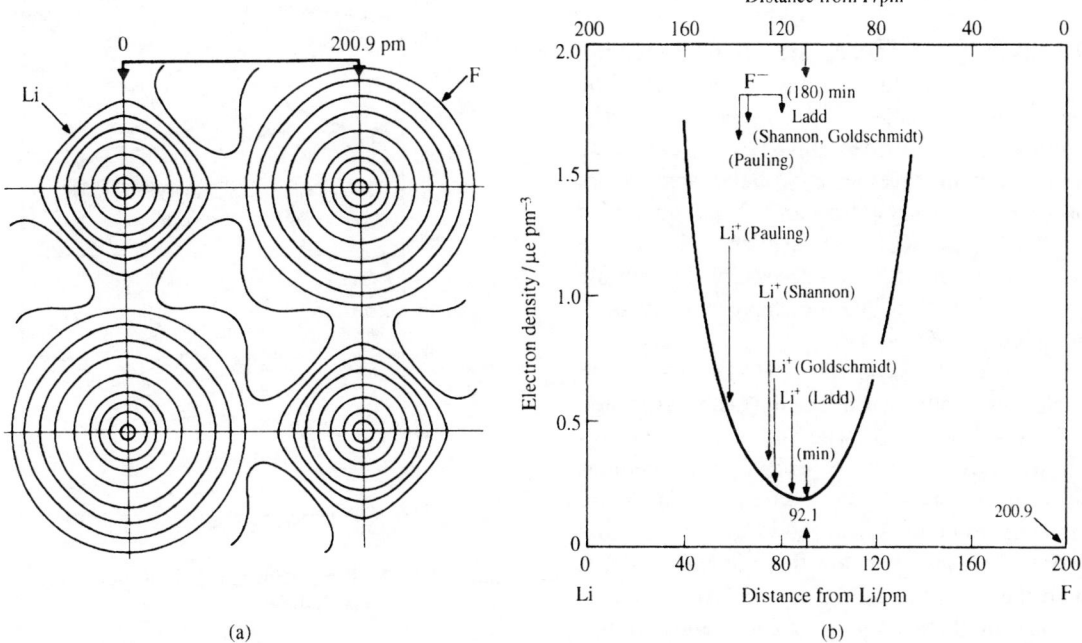

Figure 4.2   (a) Distribution of electron density ($\mu e/pm^3$) in the *xyo* plane of LiF, and (b) variation of electron density along the Li–F direction near the minimum. The electron density rises to $17.99\,\mu e\,pm^{-3}$ at Li and to $115.63\,\mu e\,pm^{-3}$ at F. (The unit $\mu e\,pm^{-3}$ is numerically identical to $e\,\text{Å}^{-3}$.)

Deviations from the simple ionic model are expected to increase with increasing formal charge on the cation or anion and with increasing size and ease of distortion of the anion. Again, deviations tend to be greater for smaller cations and for those (such as Cu^+, Ag^+, etc.) which do not have an inert-gas configuration.[18] The gradual transition from predominantly ionic to covalent is illustrated by the "isoelectronic" series:

$$NaF, MgF_2, AlF_3, SiF_4, PF_5, SF_6, IF_7, F_2$$

A similar transition towards metallic bonding is illustrated by the series:

$$NaCl, Na_2O, Na_2S, Na_3P, Na_3As, Na_3Sb, Na_3Bi, Na$$

Alkali metal alloys with gold have the CsCl structure and, whilst NaAu and KAu are essentially metallic, RbAu and CsAu have partial ionic bonding and are n-type semiconductors. These factors should constantly be borne in mind during the discussion of compounds in later chapters.

The extent to which charge is transferred back from the anion towards the cation in the alkali metal halides themselves is difficult to determine precisely. Calculations indicate that it is probably only a few percent for some salts such as NaCl, whereas for others (e.g. LiI) it may amount to more than $0.33\,e^-$ per atom. Direct experimental evidence on these matters is available for some other elements from techniques such as Mössbauer spectroscopy,[24] electron spin resonance spectroscopy,[25] and neutron scattering form factors.[26]

[24] N. N. GREENWOOD and T. C. GIBB, *Mössbauer Spectroscopy*, Chapman & Hall, London, 1971, 659 pp.

[25] P. B. AYSCOUGH, *Electron Spin Resonance in Chemistry*, pp. 300–1, Methuen, London, 1967. P. W. ATKINS and M. C. R. SYMONS, *The Structure of Inorganic Radicals*, pp. 51–73, Elsevier, Amsterdam, 1967.

[26] G. E. BACON, *Neutron Diffraction*, 3rd edn., Oxford University Press, Oxford, 1975, 636 pp.

4.3.2 Halides and hydrides

The alkali metal halides are all high-melting, colourless crystalline solids which can be conveniently prepared by reaction of the appropriate hydroxide (MOH) or carbonate (M_2CO_3) with aqueous hydrohalic acid (HX), followed by recrystallization. Vast quantities of NaCl and KCl are available in nature and can be purified if necessary by simple crystallization. The hydrides have already been discussed (p. 65).

Trends in the properties of MX have been much studied and typical examples are illustrated in Figs. 4.3 and 4.4. The mp and bp always follow the trend F > Cl > Br > I except perhaps for some of the Cs salts where the data are uncertain. Figure 4.3 also shows that the mp and bp of LiX are always below those of NaX and that (with the exception of the mp of KI) the values for NaX are the maximum for each series. Trends in enthalpy of formation ΔH_f° and lattice energy U_L are even more regular (Fig. 4.4) and can readily be interpreted in terms of the Born–Haber cycle, providing one assumes an invariant charge corresponding to loss or gain of one complete electron per ion, M^+X^-. The Born–Haber cycle considers two possible routes to the formation of MX and equates the corresponding enthalpy changes by applying Hess's law:[18]

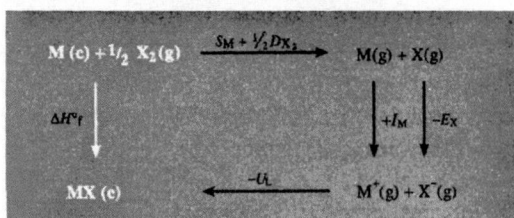

Hence

$$\Delta H_f^\circ(MX) = S_M + \tfrac{1}{2}D_{X_2} + I_M - E_X - U_L$$

where S_M is the heat of sublimation of M(c) to a monatomic gas (Table 4.2), D_{X_2} is the dissociation energy of X_2(g) (Table 4.2), I_M is the ionization energy of M(g) (Table 4.2), and E_X the electron affinity of X(g) (Table 17.3, p. 800). The

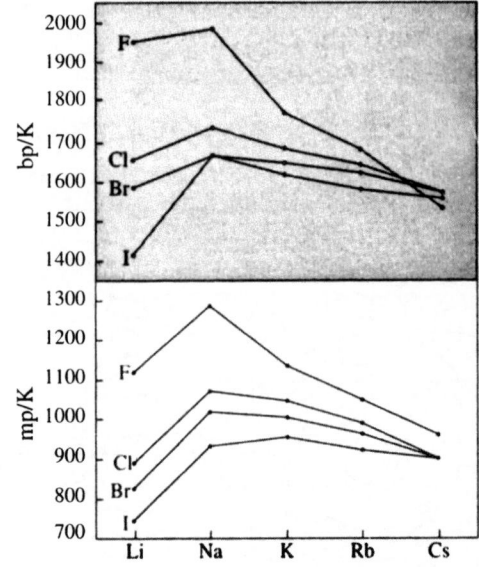

Figure 4.3   Melting point and boiling point of alkali metal halides.

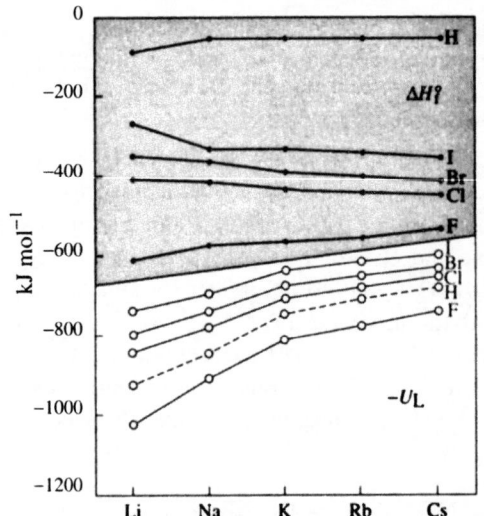

Figure 4.4   Standard enthalpies of formation (ΔH_f°) and lattice energies (plotted as $-U_L$) for alkali metal halides and hydrides.

lattice energy U_L is given approximately by the expression

$$U_L = \frac{N_0 A e^2}{4\pi\varepsilon_0 r_0}\left(1 - \frac{\rho}{r_0}\right)$$

where N_0 is the Avogadro constant, A is a geometrical factor, the Madelung constant (which has the value of 1.7627 for the CsCl structure and 1.7476 for the NaCl structure), r_0 is the shortest internuclear distance between M^+ and X^- in the crystal, and ρ is a measure of the close-range repulsion force which resists mutual interpenetration of the ions. It is clear that the sequence of lattice energies is determined primarily by r_0, so that the lattice energy is greatest for LiF and smallest for CsI, as shown in Fig. 4.4. In the Born–Haber expression for ΔH_f° this factor predominates for the fluorides and there is a trend to smaller enthalpies of formation from LiF to CsF (Fig. 4.4). The same incipient trend is noted for the hydrides MH, though here the numerical values of ΔH_f° are all much smaller than those for MX because of the much higher heat of dissociation of H_2 compared to X_2. By contrast with the fluorides, the lattice energy for the larger halides is smaller and less dominant, and the resultant trend of ΔH_f° is to larger values, thus reflecting the greater ease of subliming and ionizing the heavier alkali metals.

The Born–Haber cycle is also useful in examining the possibility of forming alkali–metal halides of stoichiometry MX_2. The dominant term will clearly be the very large second-stage ionization energy for the process $M^+(g) \longrightarrow M^{2+}(g) + e^-$; this is $7297\,kJ\,mol^{-1}$ for Li but drops to $2255\,kJ\,mol^{-1}$ for Cs. The largest possible lattice energy to compensate for this would be obtained with the smallest halogen F and (making plausible assumptions on lattice structure and ionic radius) calculations indicate that CsF_2 could indeed be formed exothermically from its elements:

$$Cs(s) + F_2(g) = CsF_2(s); \quad \Delta H_f^\circ \simeq -125\,kJ\,mol^{-1}$$

However, the compound cannot be prepared because of the much greater enthalpy of formation of CsF which makes CsF_2 unstable with respect to decomposition:

$$Cs(s) + \tfrac{1}{2}F_2(g) = CsF(s); \quad \Delta H_f^\circ = -530\,kJ\,mol^{-1}$$

whence

$$CsF_2(s) = CsF(s) + \tfrac{1}{2}F_2; \quad \Delta H_{disprop} \simeq -405\,kJ\,mol^{-1}$$

There is some evidence that Cs^{3+} can be formed by cyclic voltammetry of $Cs^+[OTeF_5]^-$ in pure MeCN at the extremely high oxidizing potential of 3 V, and that Cs^{3+} might be stabilized by 18-crown-6 and cryptand (see pp. 96 and 97 for nomenclature).[27] However, the isolation of pure compounds containing Cs^{3+} has so far not been reported.

Ternary alkali-metal halide oxides are known and have the expected structures. Thus Na_3ClO and the yellow K_3BrO have the anti-perovskite structure (p. 963) whereas Na_4Br_2O, Na_4I_2O and K_4Br_2O have the tetragonal anti-K_2NiF_4 structure.[28]

The alkali metal halides, particularly NaCl and KCl, find extensive application in industry (pp. 71 and 73). The hydrides are frequently used as reducing agents, the product being a hydride or complex metal hydride depending on the conditions used, or the free element if the hydride is unstable. Illustrative examples using NaH are:

$$2BF_3 + 6NaH \xrightarrow{200^\circ} B_2H_6 + 6NaF$$

$$BF_3 + 4NaH \xrightarrow{Et_2O/125^\circ} NaBH_4 + 3NaF$$

$$B(OMe)_3 + NaH \xrightarrow{reflux} Na[BH(OMe)_3]$$

$$B(OMe)_3 + 4NaH \xrightarrow{225-275^\circ} NaBH_4 + 3NaOMe$$

$$AlBr_3 + 4NaH \xrightarrow{Me_2O} NaAlH_4 + 3NaBr$$

$$TiCl_4 + 4NaH \xrightarrow{400^\circ} Ti + 4NaCl + 2H_2$$

Sulfur dioxide is uniquely reduced to dithionite (a process useful in bleaching paper pulp, p. 720). CO_2 gives the formate:

$$2SO_2(l) + 2NaH \longrightarrow Na_2S_2O_4 + H_2$$

$$CO_2(g) + NaH \longrightarrow HCO_2Na$$

Particularly reactive (pyrophoric) forms of LiH, NaH and KH can be prepared simply and in high yield by the direct hydrogenation of

[27] K. Moock and K. Seppelt, *Angew. Chem. Int. Edn. Engl.* **28**, 1676–8 (1989).

[28] S. Sitta, K. Hippler, P. Vogt and H. Sabrowsky, *Z. anorg. allg. Chem.* **597**, 197–200 (1991).

hexane solutions of MBu^n in the presence of tetramethylethylenediamine (tmeda) and these have proved extremely useful reagents for the metalation of organic compounds which have an active hydrogen site.[29]

4.3.3 Oxides, peroxides, superoxides and suboxides

The alkali metals form a fascinating variety of binary compounds with oxygen, the most versatile being Cs which forms 9 compounds with stoichiometries ranging from Cs_7O to CsO_3. When the metals are burned in a free supply of air the predominant product depends on the metal: Li forms the oxide Li_2O (plus some Li_2O_2), Na forms the peroxide Na_2O_2 (plus some Na_2O) whilst K, Rb and Cs form the superoxide MO_2. Under the appropriate conditions pure compounds M_2O, M_2O_2 and MO_2 can be prepared for all five metals.

The "normal" oxides M_2O (Li, Na, K, Rb) have the antifluorite structure as do many of the corresponding sulfides, selenides and tellurides. This structure is related to the CaF_2 structure (p. 118) but with the sites occupied by the cations and anions interchanged so that M replaces F and O replaces Ca in the structure. Cs_2O has the anti-$CdCl_2$ layer structure (p. 1211). There is a trend to increasing coloration with increasing atomic number, Li_2O and Na_2O being pure white, K_2O yellowish white, Rb_2O bright yellow and Cs_2O orange. The compounds are fairly stable towards heat, and thermal decomposition is not extensive below about 500°. Pure Li_2O is best prepared by thermal decomposition of Li_2O_2 (see below) at 450°C. Na_2O is obtained by reaction of Na_2O_2, NaOH or preferably $NaNO_2$ with the Na metal:

$$Na_2O_2 + 2Na \longrightarrow 2Na_2O$$

$$NaOH + Na \longrightarrow Na_2O + \tfrac{1}{2}H_2$$

$$NaNO_2 + 3Na \longrightarrow 2Na_2O + \tfrac{1}{2}N_2$$

In this last reaction Na can be replaced by the azide NaN_3 to give the same products. The normal oxides of the other alkali metals can be prepared similarly.

The peroxides M_2O_2 contain the peroxide ion O_2^{2-} which is isoelectronic with F_2. Li_2O_2 is prepared industrially by the reaction of $LiOH.H_2O$ with hydrogen peroxide, followed by dehydration of the hydroperoxide by gentle heating under reduced pressure:

$$LiOH.H_2O + H_2O_2 \longrightarrow LiOOH.H_2O + H_2O$$

$$2LiOOH.H_2O \xrightarrow{\text{heat}} Li_2O_2 + H_2O_2 + 2H_2O$$

It is a thermodynamically stable, white, crystalline solid which decomposes to Li_2O on being heated above 195°C.

Na_2O_2, is prepared as pale-yellow powder by first oxidizing Na to Na_2O in a limited supply of dry oxygen (air) and then reacting this further to give Na_2O_2:

$$2Na + \tfrac{1}{2}O_2 \xrightarrow{\text{heat}} Na_2O \xrightarrow{\tfrac{1}{2}O_2} Na_2O_2$$

Preparation of pure K_2O_2, Rb_2O_2 and Cs_2O_2 by this route is difficult because of the ease with which they oxidize further to the superoxides MO_2. Oxidation of the metals with NO has been used but the best method is the quantitative oxidation of the metals in liquid ammonia solution (p. 78). The peroxides can be regarded as salts of the dibasic acid H_2O_2. Thus reaction with acids or water quantitatively liberates H_2O_2:

$$M_2O_2 + H_2SO_4 \longrightarrow M_2SO_4 + H_2O_2;$$

$$M_2O_2 + H_2O \longrightarrow 2MOH + H_2O_2$$

Sodium peroxide finds widespread use industrially as a bleaching agent for fabrics, paper pulp, wood, etc., and as a powerful oxidant; it explodes with powdered aluminium or charcoal, reacts with sulfur with incandescence and ignites many organic liquids. Carbon monoxide forms the carbonate, and CO_2 liberates oxygen (an important application in breathing apparatus for divers, firemen, and in submarines — space capsules use the lighter Li_2O_2):

$$Na_2O_2 + CO \longrightarrow Na_2CO_3$$

[29] P. A. A. KLUSENER, L. BRANDSMA, H. D. VERKRUIJSSE, P. v. R. SCHLEYER, T. FRIEDL and R. PI, *Angew. Chem. Int. Edn. Engl.* **25**, 465 (1986).

$$Na_2O_2 + CO_2 \longrightarrow Na_2CO_3 + \tfrac{1}{2}O_2$$

In the absence of oxygen or oxidizable material, the peroxides (except Li_2O_2) are stable towards thermal decomposition up to quite high temperatures, e.g. $Na_2O_2 \sim 675°C$, $Cs_2O_2 \sim 590°C$.

The superoxides MO_2 contain the paramagnetic ion O_2^- which is stable only in the presence of large cations such as K, Rb, Cs (and Sr, Ba, etc.). LiO_2 has only been prepared by matrix isolation experiments at 15 K and positive evidence for NaO_2 was first obtained by reaction of O_2 with Na dissolved in liquid NH_3; it can be obtained pure by reacting Na with O_2 at 450°C and 150 atm pressure. By contrast, the normal products of combustion of the heavier alkali metals in air are KO_2 (orange), mp 380°C, RbO_2 (dark brown), mp 412°C and CsO_2 (orange), mp 432°C. NaO_2 is trimorphic, having the marcasite structure (p. 680) at low temperatures, the pyrite structure (p. 680) between $-77°$ and $-50°C$ and a pseudo-NaCl structure above this, due to disordering of the O_2^- ions by rotation. The heavier congeners adopt the tetragonal CaC_2 structure (p. 298) at room temperature and the pseudo-NaCl structure at high temperature.

Sesquoxides "M_2O_3" have been prepared as dark-coloured paramagnetic powders by careful thermal decomposition of MO_2 (K, Rb, Cs). They can also be obtained by oxidation of liquid ammonia solutions of the metals or by controlled oxidation of the peroxides, and are considered to be peroxide disuperoxides $[(M^+)_4(O_2^{2-})(O_2^-)_2]$. Indeed, pure Rb_4O_6, prepared by solid-state reaction between Rb_2O_2 and $2RbO_2$, has recently been shown to be $[Rb_4(O_2^{2-})(O_2^-)_2]$ by single-crystal diffractometry, although the two types of diatomic anion could not be distinguished in the cubic unit cell even at $-60°C$; the compound is thermodynamically stable and melts at $461°C$[30]

Ozonides MO_3 have been prepared for Na, K, Rb and Cs by the reaction of O_3 on powdered anhydrous MOH at low temperature and extraction of the red MO_3 by liquid NH_3:

[30] M. JANSEN and N. KORBER, *Z. anorg. allg. Chem.* **598/599**, 163–73 (1991).

$$3MOH(c) + 2O_3(g) \longrightarrow 2MO_3(c)$$
$$+ MOH.H_2O(c) + \tfrac{1}{2}O_2(g)$$

Under similar conditions Li gives $[Li(NH_3)_4]O_3$ which decomposes on attempted removal of the coordinated NH_3, again emphasizing the important role of cation size in stabilizing catenated oxygen anions. Improved techniques involving the reaction of oxygen/ozone mixtures on the preformed peroxide, followed by extraction with liquid ammonia, now permit gram amounts of the pure crystalline ozonides of K, Rb and Cs to be prepared.[31] (See also p. 98, p. 610.) The ozonides, on standing, slowly decompose to oxygen and the superoxide MO_2, but on hydrolysis they appear to go directly to the hydroxide:

$$MO_3 \longrightarrow MO_2 + \tfrac{1}{2}O_2$$
$$4MO_3 + 2H_2O \longrightarrow 4MOH + 5O_2$$

In addition to the above oxides M_2O, M_2O_2, M_4O_6, MO_2 and MO_3 in which the alkali metal has the constant oxidation state +1, rubidium and caesium also form suboxides in which the formal oxidation state of the metal is considerably lower. Some of these intriguing compounds have been known since the turn of the century but only recently have their structures been elucidated by single crystal X-ray analysis.[32] Partial oxidation of Rb at low temperatures gives Rb_6O which decomposes above $-7.3°C$ to give copper-coloured metallic crystals of Rb_9O_2:

$$2Rb_6O \xrightarrow{-7.3°} Rb_9O_2 + 3Rb$$

Rb_9O_2 inflames with H_2O and melts incongruently at $40.2°$ to give $2Rb_2O + 5Rb$. The structure of Rb_9O_2 comprises two ORb_6 octahedra sharing a common face (Fig. 4.5). It thus has the anti-$[Tl_2Cl_9]^{3-}$ structure. The Rb–Rb distance within this unit is only 352 pm (compared with 485 pm in Rb metal) and the nearest Rb–Rb distance

[31] W. SCHNICK and M. JANSEN, *Z. anorg. allg. Chem.* **532**, 37–46 (1986).

[32] A. SIMON, *Naturwiss.* **58**, 622–3 (1971); *Z. anorg. allg. Chem.* **395**, 301 (1973); *Struct. Bonding* **36**, 81–'127 (1979); *Angew. Chem. Int. Edn. Engl.* **27**, 159–83 (1988).

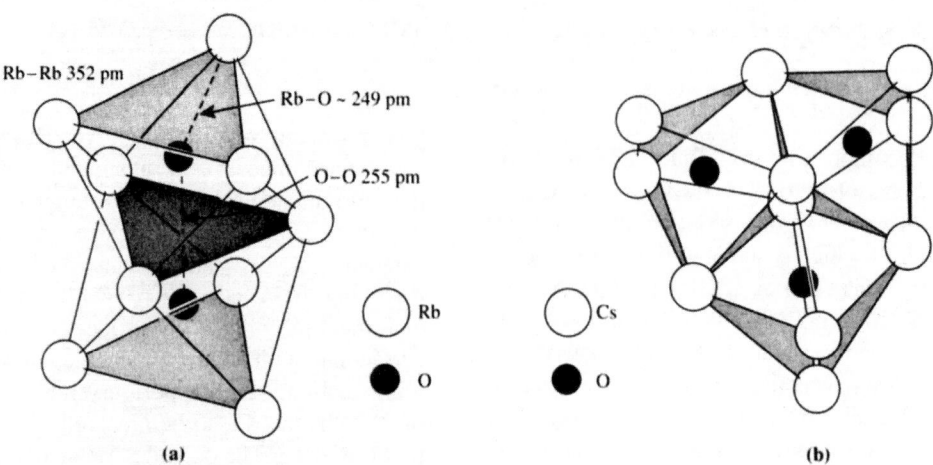

Figure 4.5 (a) The confacial bioctahedral Rb_9O_2 group in Rb_9O_2 and Rb_6O, and (b) the confacial trioctahedral $Cs_{11}O_3$ group in Cs_7O.

between groups is 511 pm. The Rb–O distance is ~249 pm, much less than the sum of the conventional ionic radii (289 pm) and the metallic character of the oxide comes from the excess of at least 5 electrons above that required for simple bookkeeping. Crystalline Rb_6O has a unit cell containing 4 formula units, i.e. $Rb_{24}O_4$, and the structure consists of alternating layers of Rb_9O_2 and close-packed metal atoms parallel to (001) to give the structural formula $[(Rb_9O_2)Rb_3]$.

Caesium forms an even more extensive series of suboxides:[32] Cs_7O, bronze-coloured, mp +4.3°C; Cs_4O, red-violet, decomposes >10.5°; $Cs_{11}O_3$, violet crystals, mp (incongruent) 52.5°C; and $Cs_{3+x}O$, a nonstoichiometric phase up to Cs_4O, which decomposes at 166°C. Cs_7O reacts vigorously with O_2 and H_2O and the unit cell is found to be $Cs_{21}O_3$, i.e. $[(Cs_{11}O_3)Cs_{10}]$. The unit $Cs_{11}O_3$ comprises 3 octahedral OCs_6 groups each sharing 2 adjacent faces to form the trigonal group shown in Fig. 4.5b. These groups form chains along (001) and are also surrounded by the other Cs atoms. The Cs–Cs distance within the $Cs_{11}O_3$ group is only 376 pm, whereas between groups it is 527 pm; this latter distance is also the shortest distance between Cs in a group and the other 10 Cs atoms, and is similar to the interatomic distance in Cs metal. The structures of the other 3 suboxides are more complex

but it is salutory to realize that Cs forms at least 9 crystalline oxides whose structures can be rationalized in terms of general bonding systematics.

4.3.4 Hydroxides

Evaporation of aqueous solutions of LiOH under normal conditions produces the monohydrate, and this can be readily dehydrated by heating in an inert atmosphere or under reduced pressure. $LiOH.H_2O$ has a crystal structure built up of double chains in which both Li and H_2O have 4 nearest neighbours (Fig. 4.6a); Li is tetrahedrally coordinated by 2OH and $2H_2O$, and each tetrahedron shares an edge (2OH) and two corners ($2H_2O$) to produce double chains which are held laterally by H bonds. Each H_2O molecule is tetrahedrally coordinated by 2Li from the same chain and 2OH from other chains. Anhydrous LiOH has a layer lattice of edge-shared $Li(OH)_4$ tetrahedra (Fig. 4.6b) in which each Li in a plane is surrounded tetrahedrally by 4OH, and each OH has 4Li neighbours all lying on one side; neutron diffraction shows that the OH bonds are normal to the layer plane and there is no H bonding between layers.

Numerous hydrates have been prepared from aqueous solutions of the heavier alkali metal

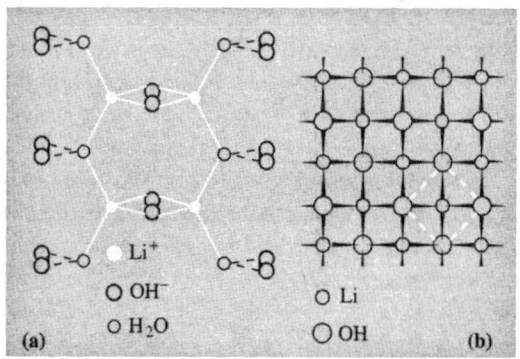

Figure 4.6 (a) The double-chain structure of LiOH.H$_2$O, and (b) the layer structure of anhydrous LiOH (see text).

hydroxides (e.g. NaOH.nH$_2$O, where n = 1, 2, 2.5, 3.5, 4, 5.25 and 7) but little detailed structural information is available.[33] The anhydrous compounds all show the influence of oriented OH groups on the structure,[13] and there is evidence of weak O—H$\cdots$O bonding for KOH and RbOH. Melting points are substantially lower than those of the halides, decreasing from 471°C for LiOH to 272° for CsOH, and the mp of the hydrates is even lower, e.g. 2.5°C (incongr.) for CsOH.2H$_2$O and −5.5°C for the trihydrate.

The alkali metal hydroxides are the most basic of all hydroxides. They react with acids to form salts and with alcohols to form alkoxides. The alkoxides are oligomeric and the degree of polymerization can vary depending on the particular metal and the state of aggregation. The *tert*-butoxides, MOBu^t, (Bu^t = OCMe$_3$) can be considered as an example. Crystalline (KOBu^t)$_4$ has a cubane-like structure and the tetramer persists in tetrahydrofuran solution and in the gas phase.[34,35] By contrast, (NaOBu^t)$_4$ is exclusively tetrameric in thf, but is a mixture of hexamers and nonamers

in the crystalline state and of hexamers and heptamers in the vapour phase. The lithium analogue is tetrameric in thf but is hexameric in benzene, toluene or cyclohexane and in the gas phase. The degree of polymerization can also be influenced by the nature of the organic residue. Thus X-ray crystallography shows that lithium 2,6-di-*tert*-butyl-4-methylphenolate is dimeric whereas the closely related phenolate {LiOC$_6$H$_2$(CH$_2$NMe$_2$)$_2$-2,6-Me-4}$_3$ provides the first example of a trimeric structure, with an essentially planar central Li$_3$O$_3$ heterocyclic ring.[36] The trimer, like the dimer, features unusually short Li–O and C$_{ipso}$–O bonds (186.5 and 130.1 pm, respectively) perhaps suggesting quasi-aromaticity of the Li$_3$O$_3$ ring, the delocalized π-electrons originating from the lone pairs on the oxygen atoms.

The alkali metal hydroxides are also readily absorb CO$_2$ and H$_2$S to form carbonates (or hydrogencarbonates) and sulfides (or hydrogensulfides), and are extensively used to remove mercaptans from petroleum products. Amphoteric oxides such as those of Al, Zn, Sn and Pb react with MOH to form aluminates, zincates, stannates and plumbates, and even SiO$_2$ (and silicate glasses) are attacked.

Production and uses of LiOH have already been discussed (p. 70). Huge tonnages of NaOH and KOH are produced by electrolysis of brine (pp. 71, 73) and the enormous industrial importance of these chemicals has already been alluded to.

4.3.5 Oxoacid salts and other compounds

Many binary and pseudo-binary compounds of the alkali metals are more conveniently treated within the context of the chemistry of the other element and for this reason discussion is deferred to later chapters, e.g. borides (p. 145),

[33] H. JACOBS and U. METZNER, *Z. anorg. allg. Chem.* **597**, 97–106 (1991). D. MOOTZ and H. RUTTER, *Z. anorg. allg. Chem*, **608**, 123–30 (1992).

[34] M. H. CHISHOLM, S. R. DRAKE, A. A. NAIINI and W. E. STREIB, *Polyhehron* **10**, 337–43 (1991).

[35] M. BRAUN, D. WALDMÜLLER and B. MAYER, *Angew. Chem. Int. Edn. Engl.* **28**, 895–6 (1989).

[36] P. A. VAN DER SCHAAF, M. P. HOGERHEIDE, D. M. GROVE, A. L. SPEK and G. VAN KOTEN, *J. Chem. Soc., Chem. Commun.*, 1703–5 (1992).

graphite intercalation compounds (p. 293), carbides, cyanides, cyanates, etc. (pp. 297, 319), silicides (p. 335), germanides (p. 393), nitrides, azides and amides (p. 417), phosphides (p. 489), arsenides (p. 554), sulfides (p. 676), selenides and tellurides (p. 765), polyhalides (p. 835), etc. Likewise, the alkali metals form stable salts with virtually all oxoacids and these are also discussed in later chapters.

Lithium salts show a great propensity to crystallize as hydrates, the trihydrates being particularly common, e.g. $LiX.3H_2O$, X = Cl, Br, I, ClO_3, ClO_4, MnO_4, NO_3, BF_4, etc. In most of these Li is coordinated by $6H_2O$ to form chains of face-sharing octahedra:

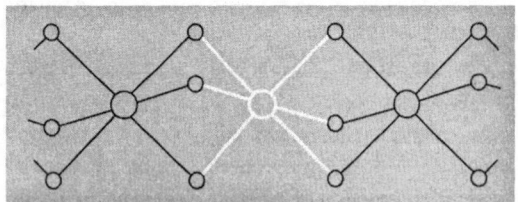

By contrast Li_2CO_3 is anhydrous and sparingly soluble (1.28 wt% at 25°C, i.e. $0.17 \, mol \, l^{-1}$). The nitrate is also anhydrous but is hygroscopic and much more soluble (45.8 wt% at 25°C, i.e. $6.64 \, mol \, l^{-1}$).

The heavier alkali metals form a wide variety of hydrated carbonates, hydrogencarbonates, sesquicarbonates and mixed-metal combinations of these, e.g. $Na_2CO_3.H_2O$, $Na_2CO_3.7H_2O$, $Na_2CO_3.10H_2O$, $Na_2CO_3.NaHCO_3.2H_2O$, $Na_2CO_3.3NaHCO_3$, $NaKCO_3.nH_2O$, $K_2CO_3.NaHCO_3.2H_2O$, etc. These systems have been studied in great detail because of their industrial and geochemical significance (see Panel). Some solubility data are in Fig. 4.7, which indicates the considerable solubility of Rb_2CO_3 and Cs_2CO_3 and the lower solubility of the hydrogencarbonates. The various stoichiometries reflect differing ways of achieving charge balance, preferred coordination polyhedra, and H bonding. Thus $Na_2CO_3.H_2O$ has two types of 6-coordinate Na, half being surrounded by $1H_2O$ plus 5 oxygen atoms from CO_3 groups and half by

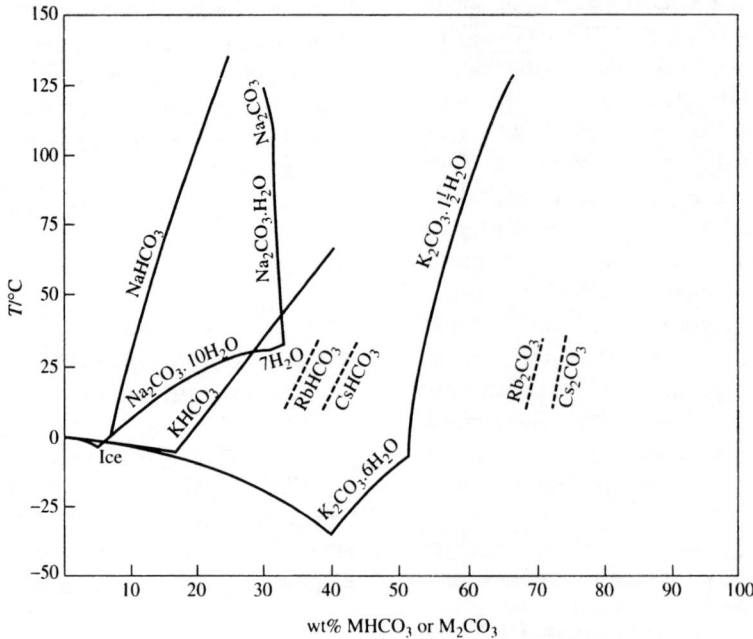

Figure 4.7 Solubilities of alkali carbonates and bicarbonates (hydrogencarbonates). (H. Stephen and T. Stephen, *Solubilities of Inorganic and Organic Compounds*, Vol. 1, Part 1, Macmillan, New York.).

Industrial Production and Uses of Sodium Carbonate, Hydroxide and Sulfate[37]

Na_2CO_3 (soda ash) is interchangeable with NaOH in many of its applications (e.g. paper pulping, soap, detergents) and this gives a valuable flexibility to the chlor-alkali industry. About half the Na_2CO_3 produced is used in the glass industry. One developing application is in the reduction of sulfur pollution resulting from stack gases of power plants and other large furnaces: powdered Na_2CO_3 is injected with the fuel and reacts with SO_2 to give solids such as Na_2SO_3 which can be removed by filtration or precipitation. World production of Na_2CO_3 was 28.7 million tonnes in 1985: the five leading countries were the USA, the USSR, China, Bulgaria and the Federal Republic of Germany, and they accounted for over 70% of production. Most of this material was synthetic (Solvay), but the increasing use of natural carbonate (trona) is notable, particularly in the USA where it is now the sole source of Na_2CO_3, the last synthetic unit having been closed in 1985: reserves in the Green River, Wyoming, deposit alone exceed 10^{10} tonnes and occur in beds up to 3 m thick over an area of 2300 km^2. About one third of the world production is now from natural deposits.

Formerly Na_2CO_3 found extensive use as "washing soda" but this market has now disappeared due to the domestic use of detergents. The related compound $NaHCO_3$ is, however, still used, particularly because of its ready decomposition in the temperature range 50-100°C:

$$2NaHCO_3 \longrightarrow Na_2CO_3 + H_2O + CO_2$$

Production in the USA is ~350 000 tonnes annually of which 30% is used in baking-powder formulations, 20% in animal feedstuffs, 15% in chemicals manufacture, 11% in pharmaceuticals, 9% in fire extinguishers and the remaining 15% in the textile, leather and paper industries and in soaps, detergents and neutralizing agents.

Caustic soda (NaOH) is industry's most important alkali. It is manufactured on a huge scale by the electrolysis of brine (p. 72) and annual production in the USA alone is over 10 million tonnes. Electrolysis is followed by concentration of the alkali in huge tandem evaporators such as those at PPG Industries' Lake Charles plant. The evaporators, which are perhaps the world's largest, are 41 m high and 12 m in diameter. About half the caustic produced is used directly in chemical production; a detailed breakdown of usage (USA, 1985) is: organic chemicals 30%, inorganic chemicals 20%, paper and pulp 20%, export 10%, soap and detergents 5%, oil industry 5%, textiles 4%, bauxite digestion 3% and miscellaneous 3%. Principal applications are in acid neutralization, the manufacture of phenol, resorcinol, β-naphthol, etc., and the production of sodium hypochlorite, phosphate, sulfide, aluminates, etc.

Salt cake (Na_2SO_4) is a byproduct of HCl manufacture using H_2SO_4 and is also the end-product of hundreds of industrial operations in which H_2SO_4 used for processing is neutralized by NaOH. For long it had few uses, but now it is the mainstay of the paper industry, being a key chemical in the kraft process for making brown wrapping paper and corrugated boxes: digestion of wood chips or saw-mill waste in very hot alkaline solutions of Na_2SO_4 dissolves the lignin (the brown resinous component of wood which cements the fibres together) and liberates the cellulose fibres as pulp which then goes to the paper-making screens. The remaining solution is evaporated until it can be burned, thereby producing steam for the plant and heat for the evaporation: the fused Na_2SO_4 and NaOH survive the flames and can be reused. Total world production of Na_2SO_4 (1985) was ~4.5 million tonnes (45% natural, 55% synthetic). Most of this (~70%) is used in the paper industry and smaller amounts are used in glass manufacture and detergents (~10% each). The hydrated form, $Na_2SO_4.10H_2O$, Glauber's salt, is now less used than formerly. Further information on the industrial production and uses of Na_2CO_3, NaOH and Na_2SO_4 are given in *Kirk-Othmer Encyclopedia of Chemical Technology*, 4th edn., Vol. 1, 1991, pp. 1025-39 and Vol. 22, 1997, pp. 354-419.

$2H_2O$ plus 4 oxygen atoms from CO_3 groups. The decahydrate has octahedral $Na(H_2O)_6$ groups associated in pairs by edge sharing to give $[Na_2(H_2O)_{10}]$. The hydrogencarbonate $NaHCO_3$ has infinite one-dimensional chains of HCO_3 formed by unsymmetrical $O-H\cdots O$ bonds (261 pm) which are held laterally by Na ions. The sesquicarbonates $Na_3H(CO_3)_2.2H_2O$ have short,

symmetrical $O-H-O$ bonds (253 pm) which link the carbonate ions in pairs, and longer $O-H\cdots O$ bonds (275 pm) which link these pairs to water molecules. Similar phases are known for the other alkali metals.

Alkali metal nitrates can be prepared by direct reaction of aqueous nitric acid on the appropriate hydroxide or carbonate. $LiNO_3$ is used for scarlet flares and pyrotechnic displays. Large deposits of $NaNO_3$ (saltpetre) are found in Chile and were probably formed by bacterial decay of small marine organisms: the NH_3 initially produced

[37] Ref. 4, pp. 149-63 and 219-25. See also *Kirk-Othmer Encyclopedia of Chemical Technology*, 4th edn., Vol. 1, 1991, Chlorine and sodium hydroxide, pp. 938-1025. Sodium carbonate, pp. 1025-39.

presumably oxidized to nitrous acid and nitric acid which would then react with dissolved NaCl. KNO_3 was formerly prepared by metathesis of $NaNO_3$ and KCl but is now obtained directly as part of the synthetic ammonia/nitric acid industry (p. 421).

Alkali metal nitrates are low-melting salts that decompose with evolution of oxygen above about 500°C, e.g.

$$2NaNO_3 \underset{\sim500°}{\rightleftharpoons} 2NaNO_2 + O_2;$$

$$2NaNO_3 \underset{\sim800°}{\rightleftharpoons} Na_2O + N_2 + \tfrac{5}{2}O_2$$

Thermal stability increases with increasing atomic weight, as expected. Nitrates have been widely used as molten salt baths and heat transfer media, e.g. the 1:1 mixture $LiNO_3$:KNO_3 melts at 125°C and the ternary mixture of 40% $NaNO_2$, 7% $NaNO_3$ and 53% KNO_3 can be used from its mp 142° up to about 600°C.

The corresponding nitrites, MNO_2, can be prepared by thermal decomposition of MNO_3 as indicated above or by reaction of NO with the hydroxide:

$$4NO + 2MOH \longrightarrow 2MNO_2 + N_2O + H_2O$$

$$6NO + 4MOH \longrightarrow 4MNO_2 + N_2 + 2H_2O$$

Chemical reduction of nitrates has also been employed:

$$KNO_3 + Pb \longrightarrow KNO_2 + PbO$$

$$2RbNO_3 + C \longrightarrow 2RbNO_2 + CO_2$$

The commercial production of $NaNO_2$ is achieved by absorbing oxides of nitrogen in aqueous Na_2CO_3 solution:

$$Na_2CO_3 + NO + NO_2 \longrightarrow 2NaNO_2 + CO_2$$

Nitrites are white, crystalline hygroscopic salts that are very soluble in water. When heated in the absence of air they disproportionate:

$$5NaNO_2 \longrightarrow 3NaNO_3 + Na_2O + N_2$$

$NaNO_2$, in addition to its use with nitrates in heat-transfer molten-salt baths, is much used in the production of azo dyes and other organo-nitrogen compounds, as a corrosion inhibitor and in curing meats.

Other oxoacid salts of the alkali metals are discussed in later chapters, e.g. borates (p. 205), silicates (p. 347), phosphites and phosphates (p. 510), sulfites, hydrogensulfates, thiosulfates, etc. (p. 706) selenites, selenates, tellurites and tellurates (p. 781), hypohalites, halites, halates and perhalates (p. 853), etc.

4.3.6 Coordination chemistry [38-42]

Exciting developments have occurred in the coordination chemistry of the alkali metals during the last few years that have completely rejuvenated what appeared to be a largely predictable and worked-out area of chemistry. Conventional beliefs had reinforced the predominant impression of very weak coordinating ability, and had rationalized this in terms of the relatively large size and low charge of the cations M^+. On this view, stability of coordination complexes should diminish in the sequence Li > Na > K > Rb > Cs, and this is frequently observed, though the reverse sequence is also known for the formation constants of, for example, the weak complexes with sulfate, peroxosulfate, thiosulfate and the hexacyanoferrates in aqueous solutions.[39] It was also known that the alkali metal cations formed numerous hydrates, or aqua-complexes, as discussed in the preceding section, and there is a definite, though smaller tendency to form ammine complexes such as $[Li(NH_3)_4]I$. Other well-defined complexes include the extremely stable adducts $LiX.5Ph_3PO$, $LiX.4Ph_3PO$ and $NaX.5Ph_3PO$, where X is a large anion such as I, NO_3, ClO_4, BPh_4, SbF_6, $AuCl_4$, etc.; these compounds melt in the range 200–315° and are stable to air and water (in which they are insoluble).

---
[38] P. N. KAPOOR and R. C. MEHROTRA, *Coord. Chem. Rev.* **14**, 1–27 (1974).

[39] D. MIDGLEY, *Chem. Soc. Revs.* **4**, 549–68 (1975).

[40] N. S. POONIA and A. V. BAJAJ, *Chem. Revs.* **79**, 389–445 (1979).

[41] W. SETZER and P. v. R. SCHLEYER, *Adv. Organomet. Chem.* **24**, 353–451 (1985).

[42] C. SCHADE and P. v. R. SCHLEYER, *Adv. Organomet. Chem.* **27**, 169–278 (1987).

They probably all contain the tetrahedral ion $[Li(OPPh_3)_4]^+$ which was established by X-ray crystallography for the compound $LiI.5Ph_3PO$; the fifth molecule of Ph_3PO is uncoordinated.

In recent years this simple picture has been completely transformed and it is now recognized that the alkali metals have a rich and extremely varied coordination chemistry which frequently transcends even that of the transition metals. The efflorescence is due to several factors such as the emerging molecular chemistry of lithium in particular, the imaginative use of bulky ligands, the burgeoning numbers of metal amides, alkoxides, enolates and organometallic compounds, and the exploitation of multidentate crown and cryptand ligands. Some of these aspects will be dealt with more fully in subsequent subsections (4.3.7 and 4.3.8).

Lithium is now known in at least 20 coordination geometries with coordination numbers ranging from 1–12. Some illustrative examples are in Table 4.3 and in the accompanying Figs. 4.8 and 4.9 which will repay close attention. The bulky ligand bis(trimethylsilyl)methyl forms a derivative in which Li is 1-coordinate in the gas phase but which polymerizes in the crystalline form to give bent 2-coordinate Li (and 5-coordinate carbon). The related ligand tris(trimethylsilyl)methyl gives an anionic complex in which Li is linear 2-coordinate, and the

Table 4.3 Stereochemistry of lithium

CN and shape	Examples	Remarks	Ref.
1	$[LiCH(SiMe_3)_2]$	Gas-phase electron diffr. Li–C 203 pm	43
2 linear	$[Li\{C(SiMe_3)_3\}_2]^-$	Li–C 216 pm, C–Li–C 180°. Cation is $[Li(thf)_4]^+$	44
	Li_3N	Li_I–N 194 pm. See Fig. 4.8a	45
bent	$\{LiCH(SiMe_3)_2\}_\infty$	Note 5-Coord C_α, Li–C 214, 222 pm; C–Li–C 147–152°, Li–C–Li 152°	43
	$[\{Li(\mu\text{-}OCBu^t_3)\}_2]$	Li–O 167.7 pm, O–Li–O 103°	46
3 planar	$[\{Li(\mu\text{-}NR_2)(OEt_2)\}_2]$	R = $SiMe_3$; Li–N 206 pm, Li–O 195 pm; N–Li–N 105°, N–Li–O 127.5°. See also Fig. 4.13 below	47
pyramidal	$[Li_5(N{=}CPh_2)_6\{O{=}P(NMe_2)_3\}]^-$	Cluster anion, see Fig. 4.8b	48
angular	$[(LiEt)_4]$	Cubane-like cluster, See Fig. 4.8c	49
	$[(LiOCMe_2Ph)_6]$; $[\{Li(c\text{-hexyl})\}_6]$	Hexagonal prism, see Fig. 4.8d	50
4 tetrahedral	$[Li(MeOH)_4]I$	See also $[Li(thf)_4]^+$ in line 3, above, and Fig. 4.8b	51
	$\{LiAl(\mu\text{-}C_2H_5)_4\}_\infty$		
5 trigonal-bipyramidal	$[LiBr(phen)_2].Pr^iOH$	Br equatorial, one N from each phen axial; N–Li–N 169°; Pr^iOH uncoordinated	52
	$[LiL][ClO_4]$	L is the aza cage shown in Fig. 4.8e	53

[43] J. L. ATWOOD, T. FJELDBERG, M. F. LAPPERT, N. T. LUONG-THI, R. SHAKIR and A. J. THORNE, *J. Chem. Soc., Chem. Commun.*, 1163–5 (1984).

[44] C. EABORN, P. B. HITCHOCK, J. D. SMITH and A. C. SULLIVAN, *J. Chem. Soc., Chem. Commun.*, 827–8 (1983).

[45] U. v. ALPEN, *J. Solid State Chem.* **29**, 379–92 (1979), and refs. therein.

[46] G. BECK, P. B. HITCHOCK, M. F. LAPPERT and I. A. MACKINNON, *J. Chem. Soc., Chem. Commun.*, 1313–4 (1989); see also ref. d.

[47] T. FJELDBERG, P. B. HITCHOCK, M. F. LAPPERT and A. J. THORNE, *J. Chem. Soc., Chem. Commun.*, 822–4 (1984).

[48] D. BARR, W. CLEGG, R. E. MULVEY and R. SNAITH, *J. Chem. Soc., Chem. Commun.*, 226–7 (1984).

[49] H. DIETRICH, *J.Organomet. Chem.* **205**, 291–9 (1981).

[50] M. H. CHISHOLM, S. R. DRAKE, A. A. NAIINI and W. E. STRIEB, *Polyhedron* **10**, 805–10 (1991).

[51] W. WEPPNER, W. WELZEL, R. KNIEP and A. RABENAU, *Angew. Chem. Int. Edn. Engl.* **25**, 1087–9 (1986).

[52] W. C. PATALINGHUG, C. R. WHITAKER and A. H. WHITE, *Aust. J. Chem.* **43**, 635–7 (1990).

[53] A. BENCINI, A. BIANCHI, A. BORSELLI, M. CIAMPOLINI, M. MICHELONI, N. NARDI, P. PAOLI, B. VALTANCOLI, S. CHIMICHI and P. DAPPORTO, *J. Chem. Soc., Chem. Commun.*, 174–5 (1990).

Table 4.3 *continued*

CN and shape	Examples	Remarks	Ref.
sq. pyramidal	[LiL'][BPh$_4$]	L' is the aza cage shown in Fig. 4.8f	54
	[{Li(thf)}$_4$(C$_4$Bu$_2^t$)$_2$]	Dimeric dilithiobutatriene complex, Fig. 4.8g	55
planar	[LiL''][PF$_6$]	L'' is the pentadentate ligand in Fig, 4.8h	56
6 octahedral	LiX	NaCl-type, X = H, F, Cl, Br, I. Also LiIO$_3$; LiNO$_3$ (calcite-type); LiAlSi$_2$O$_6$ (spodumene)	
planar	Li$_3$N	See Fig. 4.8a. Li$_{II}$ has 3 Li$_{II}$ and 3 N at 213 pm	45
pentag. pyram.	[LiL*(MeOH)][PF$_6$]	See Fig. 4.8i	57
irregular	[Li$_2$(μ-η^4,η^4-C$_6$H$_8$(tmeda)$_2$)]	See Fig. 4.9a	58
7 irregular	[Li(η^5-C$_5$H$_4$SiMe$_3$)(tmeda)]	5C at 227 pm, 2N at 215 pm. See Fig. 4.9b	59
	[Li$_2$(μ-η^5,η^5-C$_8$H$_6$)(dme)$_2$]	Pentalene-dimethoxyethane complex, Fig. 4.9c	60
8 cubic	Li metal	Body-centered cubic	
	LiHg, LiTl	CsCl-type	
irregular	[Li$_2$(μ-η^6,η^6-C$_{10}$H$_8$)(tmeda)$_2$]	Dilithionaphthalene complex, Fig. 4.9d	61
9 irregular	[Na$_2$Ph(Et$_2$O$_2$(Ph$_2$Ni)$_2$N$_2$Na-Li$_6$(OEt)$_4$(Et$_2$O)]$_2$	Fig. 4.9e. 4Li are 9-coord (1, 2, 5, 6), Li(4) is 7-coord and Li(3) is 6 coord	62
12 cuboctahedron	Li metal (cold worked, ccp)	Below 78 K Li is hcp (12 coord)	
hexag. prism.	[Li$_2$(μ-C$_{19}$H$_{12}$)$_2$]	Lithium 7bH-indenofluorenide dimer, see Fig. 4.9f	63

[54] A. Bencini, A. Bianchi, M. Ciampolini, E. Garcia-Espana, P. Dapporto, M. Micheloni, P. Paoli, J. A. Ramirez and B. Valtancoli, *J. Chem. Soc., Chem. Commun.*, 701–3 (1989).

[55] W. Neugebauer, G. A. P. Geiger, A. J. Kos, J. J. Stezowski and P. v. R. Schleyer, *Chem. Ber.* **118**, 1504–16 (1985).

[56] E. C. Constable, M. J. Doyle, J. Healy and P. R. Raithby, *J. Chem. Soc., Chem. Commun.*, 1262–4 (1988).

[57] E. C. Constable, L.-Y. Chung, J. Lewis and P. R. Raithby, *J. Chem. Soc., Chem. Commun.*, 1719–20 (1986).

[58] S. K. Arora, R. B. Bates, W. A. Beavers and R. S. Cutler, *J. Am. Chem. Soc.* **97**, 6271–2 (1975).

[59] M. F. Lappert, A. Singh, L. M. Engelhart and A. H. White, *J. Organomet Chem.* **262**, 271–8 (1984).

[60] J. J. Stezowski, H. Oier, D. Wilhelm, T. Clark and P. v. R. Schleyer, *J. Chem. Soc., Chem. Commun.*, 1263–4 (1985).

[61] J. J. Brooks, W. Rhine, G. D. Stucky *J. Am. Chem. Soc.* **94**, 7346–51 (1972).

[62] K. Jonas, D. J. Brauer, C. Krüger, P. J. Roberts and Y.-H. Tsay *J. Am. Chem. Soc.* **98**, 74–81 (1976).

[63] D. Bladauski, H. Dietrich, H.-J. Hecht and D. Rewicki, *Angew. Chem. Int. Edn. Engl.* **16**, 474–5 (1977).

same stereochemistry is observed in the unique structure of Li$_3$N (Fig. 4.8a) which also features the highly unusual planar 6-coordination mode; the structure comprises hexagonal sheets of overall composition Li$_2$N stacked alternately with planes containing the 2-coordinate Li. The coordination number of N is 8 (hexagonal bipyramidal). Three-coordinate Li is known in planar, pyramidal and angular geometries, the latter two modes being illustrated in Fig. 4.8b, c and d. Numerous examples of 4-coordinate Li have already been mentioned. Five-coordinate Li can be trigonal bipyramidal as in [LiBr(phen)$_2$]

and the aza cage cation shown in Fig. 4.8e, square pyramidal (Fig. 4.8f and g) or planar (Fig. 4.8h).

Table 4.3 indicates that octahedral coordination is a common mode for Li. Less usual is planar 6-fold coordination (Fig. 4.8a), pentagonal pyramidal coordination (Fig. 4.8i) or irregular 6-fold coordination (Fig. 4.9a). Examples of 7-fold coordination are in Fig. 4.9b and c. Lithium has cubic 8-fold coordination in the metallic form and in several of its alloys with metals of large radius. It is also 8-coordinate in the dilithionaphthalene complex shown in Fig. 4.9d; here the aromatic hydrocarbon bonds to two lithium atoms in a bis-hexahapto bridging mode and each lithium is also coordinated by a chelating diamine. A much more complicated dimeric cluster compound, whose central ($Li_6Na_2Ni_2$) core is shown schematically in Fig. 4.9e, includes 9-coordinate lithium among its many fascinating structural features.

When Li metal is cold-worked it transforms from body-centred cubic to cubic close-packed in which each atom is surrounded by 12 others in twinned cuboctahedral coordination; below 78 K the stable crystalline modification is hexagonal close-packed in which each lithium atom has 12 nearest neighbours in the form of a cuboctahedron. This very high coordination

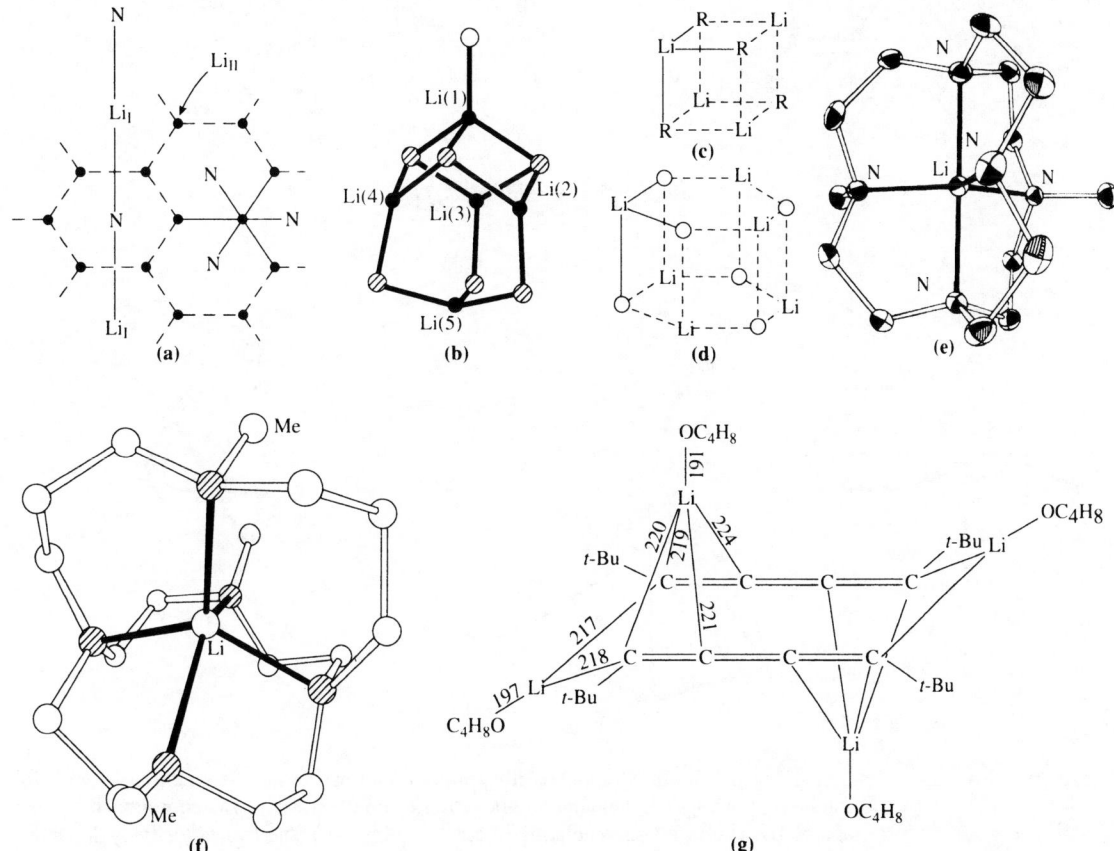

Figure 4.8 Structures of selected lithium compounds having coordination numbers ranging from 2 to 6. **(a)** The unique structure of $Li_3N^{(45)}$ **(b)** The cluster anion $[Li_5(N=CPh_2)_6\{O=P(NMe_2)_3\}]^-$ showing four pyramidal and one tetrahedral Li[48] [● = Li, ○ = $(Me_2N)_3P=O$, ⊘ = $Ph_2C=N$]. **(c)** Schematic structure of the cubane-like cluster $[(LiEt)_4]$ (rings are puckered).[49] **(d)** Schematic structure of the hexagonal prismatic cluster $[(LiOCMe)_2Ph_6]$ (rings puckered).[50] **(e)** Li^+ encapsulated trigonal-bipyramidally by the cryptand dimethylpentaaza[5.5.5]heptadecane (L).[53] **(f)** Li^+ encapsulated square-pyramidally by the cryptand trimethylpentaazabicyclo[7.5.5]nonadecane (L′).[54] **(g)** The dimeric dilithiobutatriene complex showing square-pyramidal coordination of two Li and trigonal coordination of the other two Li.[55] **(h)** Coordination of Li^+ by the planar pentadentate macrocycle dimethyltetraaza[6.0.0]pyridinophanediene (L″).[56] **(i)** Pentagonal-pyramidal coordination of Li^+ by the pentadentate macrocycle (L*) and an apical MeOH ligand,; L* = (bis-2-hydroxyethyl)-6*H*,13*H*-tripyridoheptaazapentadecine.[57]

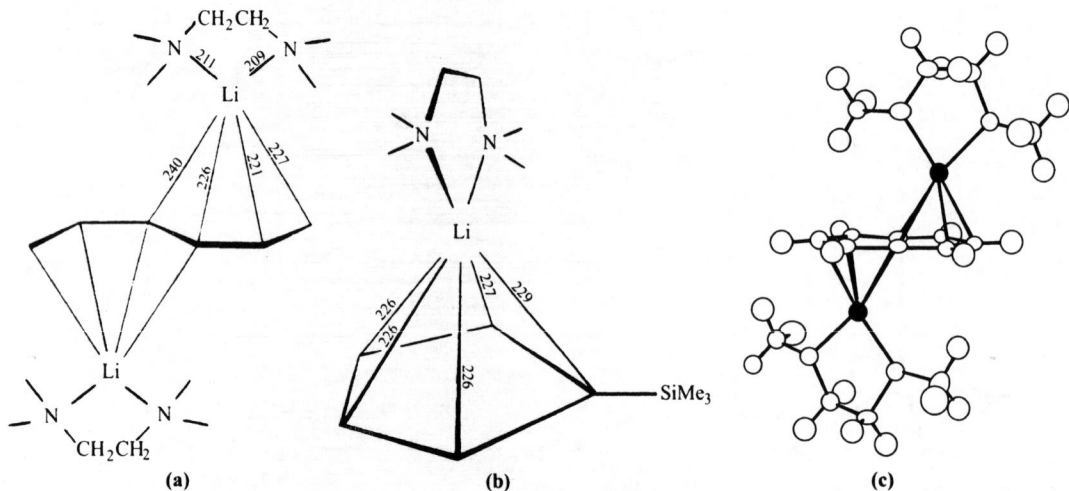

(h)   **(i)**

Figure 4.8   *continued*

(a)   **(b)**   **(c)**

Figure 4.9 Structures of selected organolithium compounds illustrating coordination numbers ranging from 6 to 12. **(a)** The dilithiobis(tetramethylethylenediamine)hexatriene complex; each Li is coordinated by the bridging bistetrahapto triene and by one chelating tmeda ligand.[58] **(b)** The trimethylsilylcyclopentadienyllithium complex with tmeda.[59] **(c)** The dilithiopentalene-dimethoxyethane complex.[60] **(d)** The dilithionaphthalene complex with tmeda.[61]   **(e)** The $Li_6Na_2Ni_2$ core in the cluster $[(Na_2Ph(Et_2O)_2(Ph_2Ni)_2N_2NaLi_6(OEt)_4(Et_2O)]_2]$ showing the four 9-coordinate Li atoms (1, 2, 5, 6), together with the 7-coordinate Li(4) and 6-coordinate Li(3) atoms.[62] **(f)** Hexagonal-prismatic 12-fold coordination of Li in its *H*–indenofluorenide dimer.[63]

number is also found in the dimeric sandwich compound that Li forms with the extended planar hydrocarbon 7b*H*-indeno[1,2,3-*jk*]fluorene; in this case, as can be seen from Fig. 4.9f, the coordination geometry about the metal atoms is hexagonal prismatic.

Similar structural diversity has been established for the heavier alkali metals also but it is unnecessary to deal with this in detail. The structural chemistry of the organometallic compounds in particular, and of related complexes, has been well reviewed.[41,42]

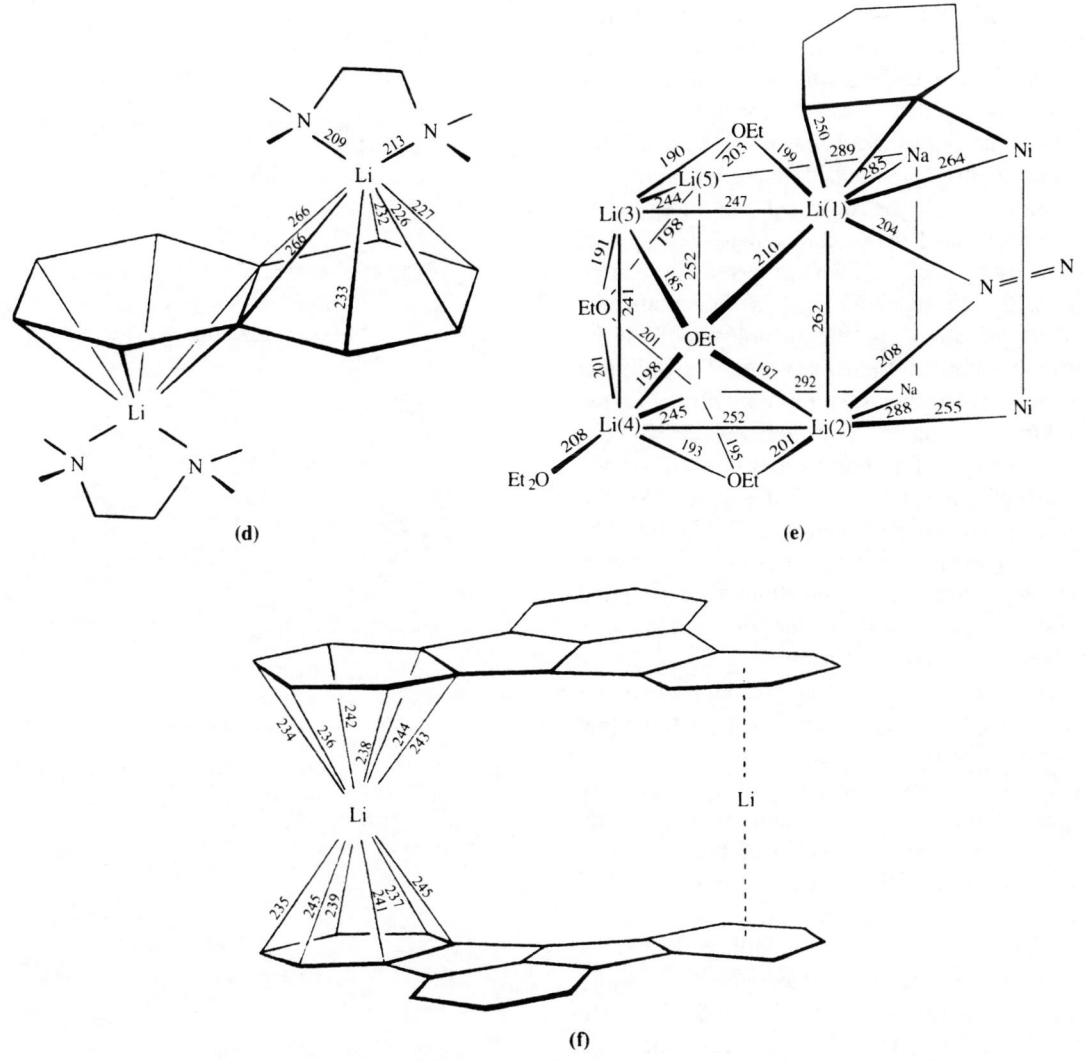

Figure 4.9 *continued*

Complexes with chelating organic reagents such as salicylaldehyde and β-diketonates were first prepared by N. V. Sidgwick and his students in 1925, and many more have since been characterized. Stability, as measured by equilibrium formation constants, is rather low and almost invariably decreases in the sequence Li > Na > K. This situation changed dramatically in 1967 when C. J. Pedersen announced the synthesis of several macrocyclic polyethers which were shown to form stable complexes with alkali metal and other cations.[64] The stability of the complexes was found to depend on the number and geometrical disposition of the ether oxygen atoms and in particular on the size and shape of potential coordination polyhedra relative to the size of the cation. For this reason stability could peak at any particular cation

[64] C. J. PEDERSEN, *J. Am. Chem. Soc.* **89**, 2495, 7017–36 (1967). See also C. J. PEDERSEN and H. K. FRENSDORF, *Angew. Chem. Int. Edn. Engl.* **11**, 16–25 (1972).

and, for M^I, this was often K and sometimes Na or Rb rather than Li. Pedersen, who was awarded a Nobel Prize for these discoveries, coined the epithet "crown" for this class of macrocyclic polyethers because, as he said "the molecular structure looked like one and, with it, cations could be crowned and uncrowned without physical damage to either".[65] Typical examples of such "crown" ethers are given in Fig. 4.10, the numerical prefix indicating the number of atoms in the heterocycle and the suffix the number of ether oxygens. The aromatic rings can be substituted, replaced by naphthalene residues, or reduced to cyclohexyl derivatives. The "hole size" for coordination depends on the number of atoms in the ring and is compared with conventional ionic diameters in Table 4.4. The best complexing agents are rings of 15–24 atoms including 5 to eight oxygen atoms. Nitrogen and sulfur can also serve as the donor atoms in analogous macroheterocycles.

The X-ray crystal structures of many of these complexes have now been determined: representative examples are shown in Fig. 4.11 from which it is clear that, at least for the larger cations, coordinative saturation and bond directionality are far less significant factors than in many transition element complexes.[66,67] Further interest in these ligands stems from their use in biochemical modelling since they sometimes mimic the behaviour of naturally occurring, neutral, macrocyclic antibiotics such as valinomycin, monactin, nonactin, nigericin

[65] C. J. PEDERSON, Nobel Lecture, *Angew. Chem. Int. Edn. Engl.* **27**, 1021–7 (1988).

[66] J.-M. LEHN, *Struct. Bonding* **16**, 1–69 (1973).

[67] M. R. TRUTER, *Struct. Bonding* **16**, 71–111 (1973).

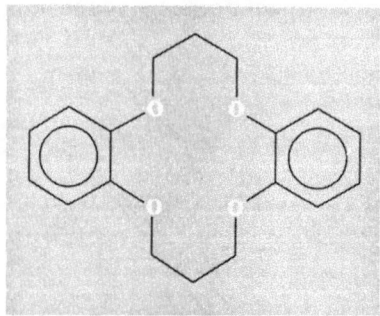

Dibenzo-14-crown-4

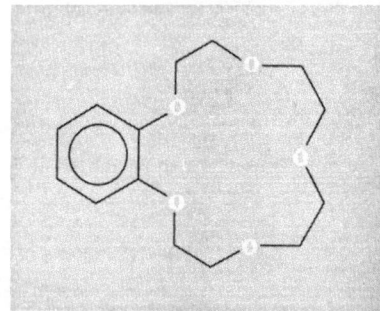

Benzo-15-crown-5

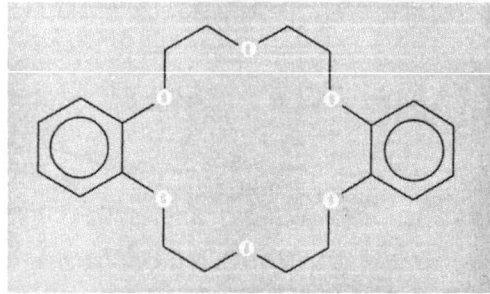

Dibenzo-18-crown-6

Figure 4.10 Schematic representation of the (non-planar) structure of some typical crown ethers.

Table 4.4 Comparison of ionic diameters and crown ether "hole sizes"

Cation	Ionic diam/pm	Cation	Ionic diam/pm	Polyether ring	"Hole size"/pm
Li^+	152	Mg^{2+}	144	14-crown-4	120–150
Na^+	204	Ca^{2+}	200	15-crown-5	170–220
K^+	276	Sr^{2+}	236	18-crown-6	260–320
Rb^+	304	Ba^{2+}	270	21-crown-7	340–430
Cs^+	334	Ra^{2+}	296	—	—

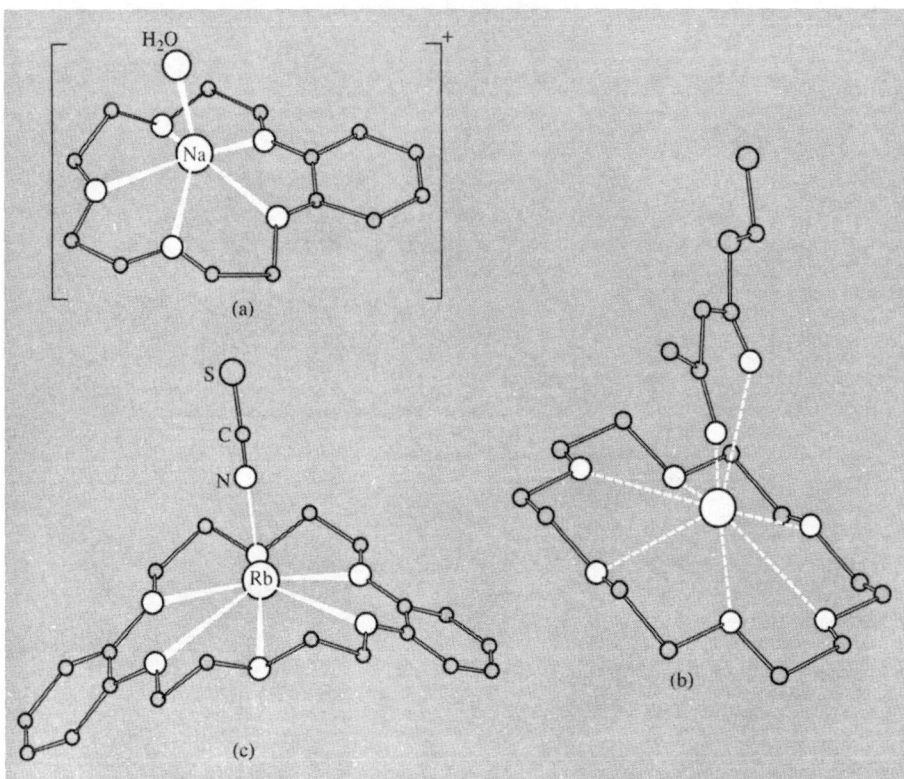

Figure 4.11 Molecular structures of typical crown-ether complexes with alkali metal cations: (a) sodium-water-benzo-15-crown-5 showing pentagonal-pyramidal coordination of Na by 6 oxygen atoms; (b) 18-crown-6-potassium-ethyl acetoacetate enolate showing unsymmetrical coordination of K by 8 oxygen atoms; and (c) the RbNCS ion pair coordinated by dibenzo-18-crown-6 to give seven-fold coordination about Rb.

and enneatin.[68,69] They may also shed some light on the perplexing and remarkably efficient selectivity between Na and K in biological systems.[68–70]

Another group of very effective ligands that have recently been employed to coordinate alkali metal cations are the macrobicyclic polydentate ligands that J.-M. Lehn has termed "cryptands",[71] e.g. N{(CH$_2$CH$_2$O)$_2$CH$_2$CH$_2$}$_3$N (Fig. 4.13a, b). This forms a complex [Rb(crypt)]CNS.H$_2$O in which the ligand encapsulates the cation with a bicapped trigonal prismatic coordination polyhedron (Fig. 4.12c, d). Such complexes are finding increasing use in solvent extraction, phase-transfer catalysis,[72] the

[68] W. SIMON, W. E. MORF and P. Ch. MEIER, *Struct. Bonding* **16**, 113–60 (1973).

[69] D. J. CRAM, Nobel Lecture, *Angew. Chem. Int. Edn. Engl.* **27**, 1009–20 (1988). See also F. VÖGTLE (ed.) *Host Guest Complex Chemistry, I, II and III*, Springer-Verlag, *Topics in Current Chemistry* **98**, 1–197 (1981); **101**, 1–203 (1982); **121**, 1–224 (1984).

[70] R. M. IZATT, D. J. EATOUGH, and J. J. CHRISTENSEN, *Struct. Bonding* **16**, 161–89 (1973).

[71] J.-M. LEHN, Nobel Lecture, *Angew. Chem. Int. Edn. Engl.* **27**, 89–112. (1988).

[72] W. P. WEBER and G. W. GOKEL, *Phase Transfer Catalysis in Organic Synthesis*, Vol. 4 of *Reactivity and Structure*, Springer-Verlag, 1977, 250 pp. C. M. STARKS and C. LIOTTA, *Phase Transfer Catalysis*, Academic Press, New York, 1978, 365 pp. F. MONTANARI, D. LANDINI and F. ROLLA, *Topics in Current Chemistry* **101**, 149–201 (1982). E. V. DEHMLOW and S. S. DEHMLOW, *Phase Transfer Catalysis* (2nd edn.), VCH Publishers, London 1983, 386 pp. T. G. SOUTHERN, *Polyhedron* **8**, 407–13 (1989).

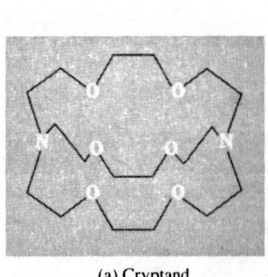

(a) Cryptand

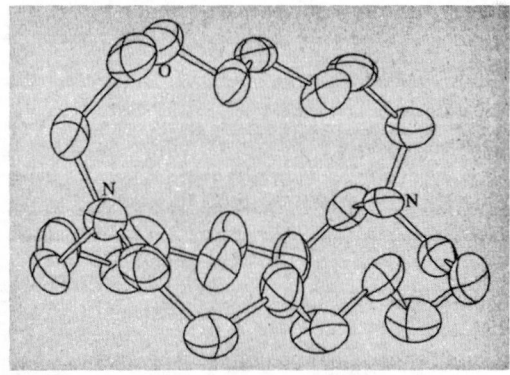

(b) Molecular structure and conformation of the free macrobicyclic cryptand ligand

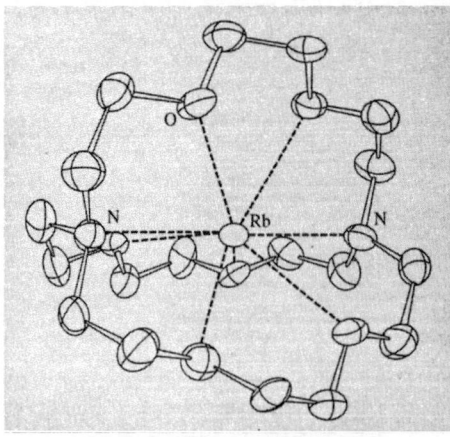

(c) Molecular structure of complex cation of RbSCN with cryptand.

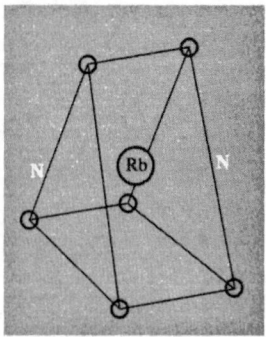

(d) Schematic representation of bicapped trigonal prismatic coordination about Rb+.

Figure 4.12 A typical cryptand and its complex.

stabilization of uncommon or reactive oxidation states and the promotion of otherwise improbable reactions. Extraordinarily pronounced selectivity in complexation can be achieved by suitably designed ligands, some of the more spectacular being $K^+/Na^+ \sim 10^5$, $Cu^{2+}/Zn^{2+} \sim 10^8$, $Cd^{2+}/Zn^{2+} \sim 10^9$.

A growing application of cryptands and other macrocyclic polydentate ligands is in protecting sensitive anions from the polarizing and destabilizing effect of cationic charges, by encapsulating or crowning the cation and so preventing its close approach to the anion. For example, ozonides of K, Rb and Cs form stable solutions in typical organic solvents (such as CH_2Cl_2, tetrahydrofuran or MeCN) when the cation is coordinated by crown ethers or cryptands, thus enabling the previously unstudied solution chemistry of O_3^- to be investigated at room temperature.[73] Slow evaporation of ammonia solutions of such complexes yields red crystalline products and an X-ray structure of $[Rb(\eta^6\text{-}18\text{-crown-6})(\eta^2\text{-}O_3)(NH_3)]$ reveals 9-coordinate Rb, the chelating ozonide ion itself having O–O distances of 129 and 130 pm and an O–O–O angle of 117°.

---

[73] N. KORBER and M. JANSEN, *J. Chem. Soc., Chem. Commun.*, 1654–5 (1990).

A particularly imaginative application of this concept has led to the isolation of compounds which contain monatomic alkali metal *anions*. For example, Na was reacted with cryptand in the presence of $EtNH_2$ to give the first example of a sodide salt of Na^-.[74]

$$2Na + N\{(C_2H_4O)_2C_2H_4\}_3N \xrightarrow{EtNH_2}$$

$$[Na(cryptand)]^+Na^-$$

The Na^- is 555 pm from the nearest N and 516 pm from the nearest O, indicating that it is a separate entity in the structure. Potassides, rubidides and caesides have similarly been prepared.[74] The same technique has been used to prepare solutions and even crystals of electrides, in which trapped electrons can play the role of anion. Typical examples are $[K(cryptand)]^+e^-$ and $[Cs(18\text{-crown-}6)]^+e^-$.[74,75]

Macrocycles, though extremely effective as polydentate ligands, are not essential for the production of stable alkali metal complexes; additional conformational flexibility without loss of coordinating power can be achieved by synthesizing benzene derivatives with 2–6 pendant mercapto-polyether groups $C_6H_{6-n}R_n$, where R is $—SC_2H_4OC_2H_4OMe$, $—S(C_2H_4O)_3Bu$, etc. Such "octopus" ligands are more effective than crowns and often equally as effective as cryptands in sequestering alkali metal cations.[76] Indeed, it is not even essential to invoke organic ligands at all since an inorganic cryptate which completely surrounds Na has been identified in the heteropolytungstate $(NH_4)_{17}Na[NaW_{21}Sb_9O_{86}].14H_2O$; the compound was also found to have pronounced antiviral activity.[77]

[74] J. L. DYE, J. M. CERASE, M. T. LOK, B. L. BARNETT and F. J. TEHAN, *J. Am. Chem. Soc.* **96**, 608–9, 7203–8 (1974). J. L. DYE, *Angew. Chem. Int. Edn. Engl.* **18**, 587–98 (1979).

[75] J. L. DYE, *Prog. Inorg. Chem.* **32**, 327–441 (1984); J. L. DYE and R.-H. HUANG, *Chem. in Britain* March, 239–44 (1990).

[76] F. VÖGTLE and E. WEBER, *Angew. Chem. Int. Edn. Engl.* **13**, 814–5 (1974).

[77] J. FISCHER, L. RICHARD and R. WEISS, *J. Am. Chem. Soc.* **98**, 3050–2 (1976).

4.3.7 Imides, amides and related compounds [78,79]

Before discussing the organometallic compounds of the alkali metals (which contain direct M–C bonds, Section 4.3.8) it is convenient to mention another important class of compounds: those which involve M–N bonds. In this way we shall resume the sequence of compounds which started with those having M–X bonds (i.e. halides, Section 4.3.2), through those with M–O bonds (oxides, hydroxides etc., Sections 4.3.3–4.3.5) to those with M–N and finally those with M–C bonds. As we shall see, several significant perceptions have emerged in this field during the past decade. For example, it is now generally agreed that in all these classes of compound the bond from the main group element to the alkali metal is predominantly ionic. Furthermore, structural studies of compounds with Li–N bonds in particular have led to the seminal concepts of *ring-stacking* and *ring-laddering* which, in turn, have permitted the rationalization of many otherwise puzzling structural features.

Lithium imides (imidolithiums) are airsensitive compounds of general formula $(RR'C{=}NLi)_n$. They can be prepared in high yield either by the addition of an organolithium compound across the triple bond of a nitrile (equation (1)) or by lithiation of a ketimine (equation (2)).

$$R'Li + RC{\equiv}N \longrightarrow RR'C{=}NLi \qquad (1)$$

$$R''Li + RR'C{=}NH \longrightarrow RR'C{=}NLi + R''H \qquad (2)$$

Lithium imides have proved to be useful reagents for the synthesis of imino derivatives of a wide variety of other elements, e.g. Be, B, Al, Si, P, Mo, W and Fe as in equation (3).

$$R''_3SiCl + RR'C{=}NLi \longrightarrow RR'C{=}NSiR''_3 + LiCl \qquad (3)$$

When R and R' are both aryl groups the resulting lithium imides are amorphous, insoluble

[78] R. E. MULVEY, *Chem. Soc. Rev.* **20**, 167–209 (1991).

[79] K. GREGORY, P. v. R. SCHLEYER and R. SNAITH. *Adv. Inorg. Chem.* **37**, 47–142 (1991).

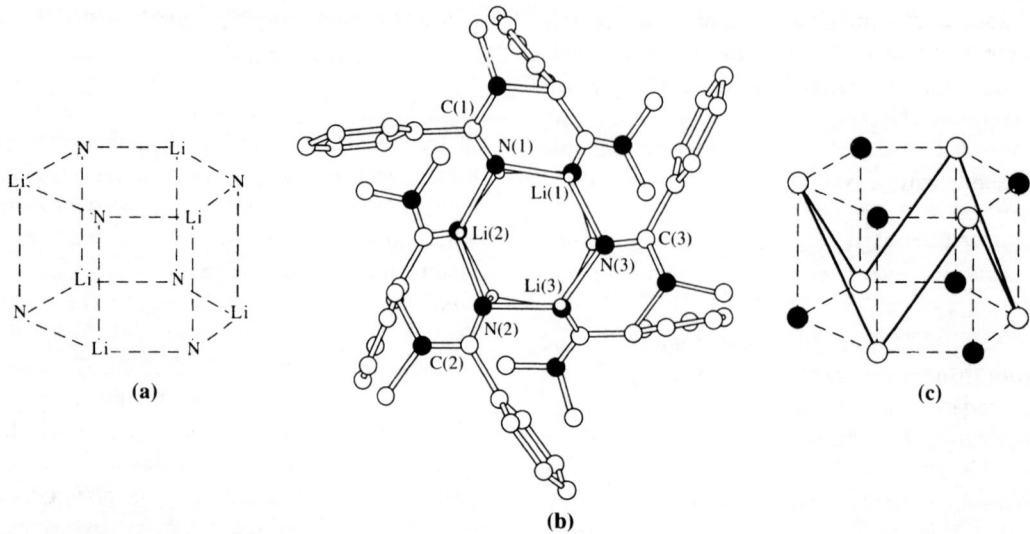

Figure 4.13   (a) Schematic representation of the Li_6N_6 core cluster in hexameric lithium imides. (b) The X-ray structure of $[Me_2N(Ph)C{=}NLi]_6$ viewed from above showing the stacking of two 6-membered Li_3N_3 rings. (c) Each Li atom has two nearest-neighbour Li atoms in the adjacent ring at 248 pm, shown here joined by full lines; the mean Li–N distances (broken lines) are 198 pm within each ring and 206 pm between rings.[80]

(presumably polymeric) solids, but if only one or neither of R, R' is an aryl group, soluble crystalline hexamers are obtained. The skeletal structure of these hexamers comprises an Li_6N_6 cluster formed by the stacking of two slightly puckered heterocyclic Li_3N_3 rings so that the Li atoms in each ring are almost directly above or below the N atoms in the adjacent ring. This is illustrated schematically in Fig. 4.13a (cf. Fig. 4.8d for the analogous hexameric alkoxide structure). An alternative view, looking down onto the open 6-membered face of the stack, is shown in Fig. 4.13b for the case of $[Me_2N(Ph)C{=}NLi]_6$. Formation of such hexamers can be viewed as a stepwise process. Initially formed ion-pairs (monomers), $Li^+[N{=}CRR']^-$, with 1-coordinate Li^+, associate at first to cyclic trimers, $(LiN{=}CRR')_3$, containing 2-coordinate Li^+ centres. Such rings are essentially planar systems [the planarity of the $(LiN)_3$ ring itself extending outwards through the imido C up to

and including the α-atoms of R and R'] and so two such rings can come together, sharing their $(LiN)_3$ faces and so raising the Li^+ coordination number to 3. Such stacking necessitates a loss in planarity of the original trimeric rings thus normally preventing more extensive stacking. A further feature of the stacked hexameric structure is the close approach of neighbouring Li atoms across the diagonals of the square faces (Fig. 4.13c), each Li atom being only 248 pm from its two nearest neighbours. This is much less that the Li–Li distance in Li metal (304 pm) or even in the necessarily covalent diatomic molecule Li_2 (274 pm), but this does not imply either metallic or covalent metal–metal bonding. Such close approaches merely reflect the small size of the Li^+ ion. For example, the Li–Li distance in LiF (which has the NaCl-type crystal structure) is 284 pm, which is 7% less than the Li–Li distance in Li metal itself.

The ring-stacking concept used in the preceding paragraph to explain the occurrence and structure of lithium imide hexamers can be applied more widely to Li–C, Li–N and Li–O rings and

[80] D. BARR, W. CLEGG, R. E. MULVEY, R. SNAITH and K. WADE, *J. Chem. Soc., Chem. Commun.*, 295–7 (1986).

clusters of various sizes.[(78,79)] but the details lie outside the scope of the present treatment.

In contrast to the planar (sp^2) nitrogen centres in lithium imides, lithium amides, $(RR'NLi)_n$, feature tetrahedral (sp^3) nitrogen. The exocyclic R groups are thus above and below the $(LiN)_n$ plane and this prevents ring stacking. Rings of varying size are known, with $n = 2$, 3 or 4 depending on the nature of the substituents (Fig. 4.14a, b and c). In the important case of $n = 2$, the 4-membered Li_2N_2 heterocycles can associate further by edge fusion (rather than by face fusion) to form laddered structures as shown schematically in Fig. 4.14d. Specific examples of amidolithium heterocycles are $[(Me_3Si)_2NLi]_2$ (gas-phase), $[(PhCH_2)_2NLi]_3$ (Fig. 4.15a) and the tetramethylpiperidinatolithium tetramer $[Me_2\overline{C(CH_2)_3CMe_2N}Li]_4$ (Fig. 4.15b). By contrast, lithiation of the cyclic amine pyrrolidine

in the presence of the chelating ligand tetramethylethylenediamine (tmeda) affords the

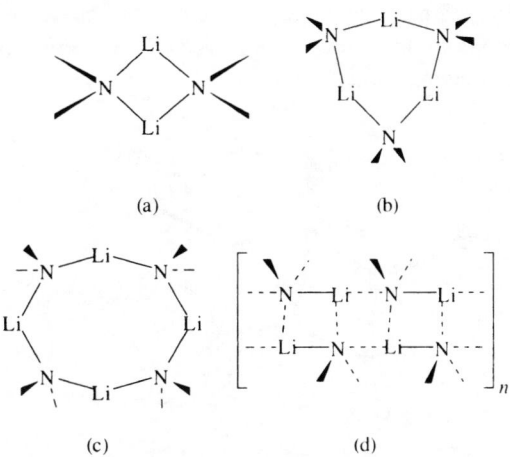

(a)   (b)

(c)   (d)

Figure 4.14 Schematic representation of (a) 4-membered, (b) 6-membered and (c) 8-membered $(LiN)_n$ heterocycles showing pendant groups on N lying both above and below the plane of the ring. (d) the laddered structure formed by lateral bonding of two Li_2N_2 units.

[81] D. R. ARMSTRONG, R. E. MULVEY, G. T. WALKER, D. BARR, R. SNAITH, W. CLEGG and D. REED, *J. Chem. Soc., Dalton Trans.*, 617–28 (1988).

[82] M. F. LAPPERT, M. J. SLADE, A. SINGH, J. L. ATWOOD, R. D. ROGERS and R. SHAKIR, *J. Am. Chem. Soc.* **105**, 302–3 (1983).

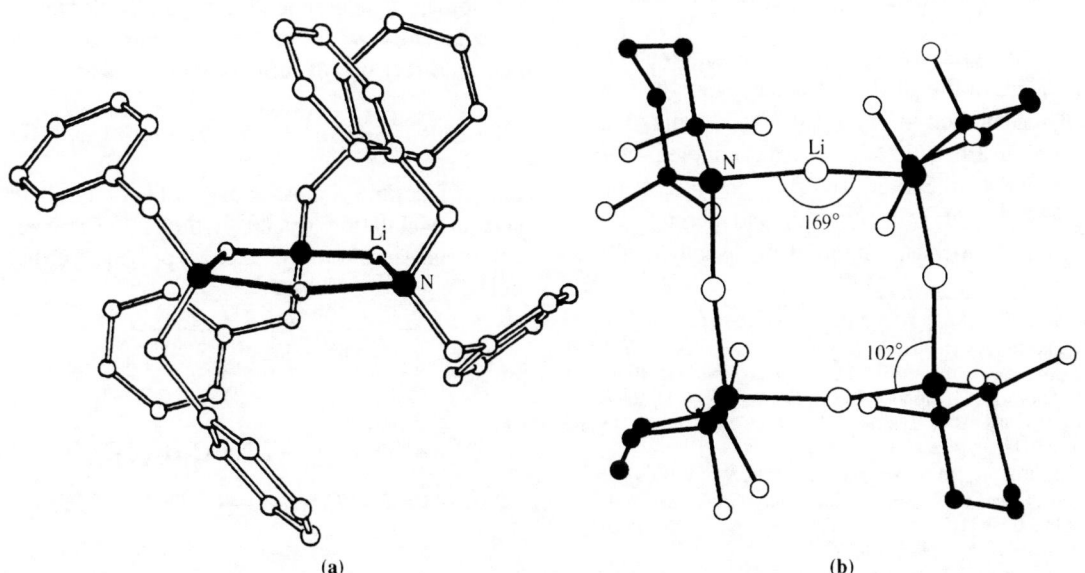

(a)   (b)

Figure 4.15 X-ray structure of (a) dibenzylamidolithium, $[(PhCH_2)_2NLi]_3$[(81)] and (b) tetramethylpiperidinato-lithium, $[Me_2\overline{C(CH_2)_3CMe_2N}Li]_4$.[(82)]

laddered complex $[(H_2\overline{C(CH_2)_3NLi})_2.tmeda]_2$ (Fig. 4.16). Detailed examination of the inter-atomic distances in this structure clearly indicate that laddering is achieved by the lateral connection of the two outer Li_2N_2 rings. The Li–N bonds in all these compounds are considered to be predominantly ionic.

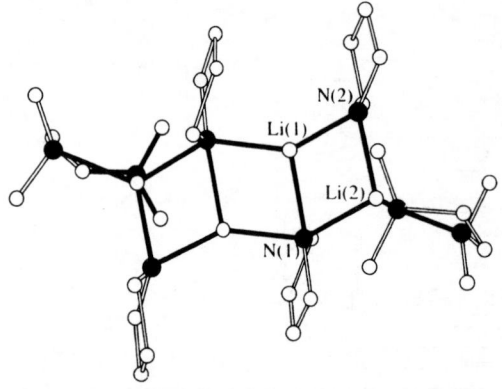

Figure 4.16   X-ray structure of the laddered complex $[H_2\overline{C(CH_2)_3NLi}]_2.tmeda]_2$ where tmeda is tetramethylethylenediamine.[83]

4.3.8 Organometallic compounds [41,42,84,85]

Some structural aspects of the organometallic compounds of the alkali metals have already been briefly mentioned in Section 4.3.6. The diagonal relation of Li with Mg (p. 76), coupled with the known synthetic utility of Grignard reagents (pp. 132–5), suggests that Li, and perhaps the other alkali metals, might afford synthetically

useful organometallic reagents. Such is found to be the case.[86]

Organolithium compounds can readily be prepared from metallic Li and this is one of the major uses of the metal. Because of the great reactivity both of the reactants and the products, air and moisture must be rigorously excluded by use of an inert atmosphere. Lithium can be reacted directly with alkyl halides in light petroleum, cyclohexane, benzene or ether, the chlorides generally being preferred:

$$2Li + RX \xrightarrow{\text{solvent}} LiR + LiX$$

Reactivity and yields are greatly enhanced by the presence of 0.5–1% Na in the Li. The reaction is also generally available for the preparation of metal alkyls of the heavier Group 1 metals. Lithium aryls are best prepared by metal–halogen exchange using $LiBu^n$ and an aryl iodide, and transmetalation is the most convenient route to vinyl, allyl and other unsaturated derivatives:

$$LiBu^n + ArI \xrightarrow{\text{ether}} LiAr + Bu^nI$$

$$4LiPh + Sn(CH{=}CH_2)_4 \xrightarrow{\text{ether}} 4LiCH{=}CH_2 + SnPh_4$$

The reaction between an excess of Li and an organomercury compound is a useful alternative when isolation of the product is required, rather than its direct use in further synthetic work:

$$2Li + HgR_2(\text{or } HgAr_2) \xrightarrow[\text{benzene}]{\text{petrol or}} 2LiR(\text{or } LiAr) + Hg$$

Similar reactions are available for the other alkali metals. Metalation (metal–hydrogen exchange) and metal addition to alkenes provide further routes, e.g.

$$2Na + 3C_5H_6 \longrightarrow 2NaC_5H_5 + C_5H_8$$

[83] D. R. Armstrong, D. Barr, W. Clegg, R. E. Mulvey, D. Reed, R. Snaith and K. Wade, *J. Chem. Soc., Chem. Commun.*, 869–70 (1986). D. R. Armstrong, D. Barr, W. Clegg, S. M. Hodgson, R. E. Mulvey, D. Reed, R. Snaith and D. S. Wright, *J. Am. Chem. Soc.*, **111**, 4719–27 (1989).

[84] G. E. Coates, M. L. H. Green and K. Wade, *Organometallic Compounds*, Vol. 1, *The Main Group Elements*, 3rd edn., Chap. 1, The alkali metals, pp. 1–70, Methuen, London, 1967.

[85] G. Wilkinson, F. G. A. Stone and E. W. Abel (eds.) *Comprehensive Organometallic Chemistry*, Pergamon Press, Oxford, 1982, Vol. 1, Chap. 2. J. L. Wardell, Alkali Metals, pp. 43–120.

[86] B. J. Wakefield, *Organolithium Methods*, Academic Press, New York, 1988, 189 pp.

$$2Cs + CH_2{=}CH_2 \longrightarrow CsCH_2CH_2Cs$$

In the presence of certain ethers such as Me_2O, $MeOCH_2CH_2OMe$ or tetrahydrofuran, Na forms deep-green highly reactive paramagnetic adducts with polynuclear aromatic hydrocarbons such as naphthalene, phenanthrene, anthracene, etc.:

These compounds are in many ways analogous to the solutions of alkali metals in liquid ammonia (p. 77).

The most ionic of the organometallic derivatives of Group 1 elements are the acetylides and dicarbides formed by the deprotonation of alkynes in liquid ammonia solutions:

$$Li + HC{\equiv}CH \xrightarrow{\text{liq NH}_3} LiC{\equiv}CH + \tfrac{1}{2}H_2$$

$$2Li + HC{\equiv}CH \xrightarrow{\text{liq NH}_3} Li_2C_2 + H_2$$

The largest industrial use of LiC_2H is in the production of vitamin A, where it effects ethynylation of methyl vinyl ketone to produce a key tertiary carbinol intermediate. The acetylides and dicarbides of the other alkali metals are prepared similarly. It is not always necessary to prepare this type of compound in liquid ammonia and, indeed, further substitution to give the bright red perlithiopropyne Li_4C_3 can be effected in hexane under reflux:[87]

$$4LiBu^n + CH_3C{\equiv}CH \xrightarrow{\text{hexane}} Li_3CC{\equiv}CLi + 4C_4H_{10}$$

[87] R. WEST, P. A. CARNEY and I. C. MINEO. *J. Am. Chem. Soc.* **87**, 3788–9 (1965).

Organolithium compounds tend to be thermally unstable and most of them decompose to LiH and an alkene on standing at room temperature or above. Among the more stable compounds are the colourless, crystalline solids LiMe (decomp above 200°C), LiBu^n and LiBu^t (which shows little decomposition over a period of days at 100°C) Common lithium alkyls have unusual tetrameric or hexameric structures (see preceding sections). The physical properties of these oligomers are similar to those often associated with covalent compounds (e.g. moderately high volatility, high solubility in organic solvents and low electrical conductivity when fused). Despite this it is now generally agreed that the central $(LiC)_n$ core is held together by predominantly ionic forces, though estimates of the precise extent of charge separation vary from about 55 to 95%.[88–91]. The resolution of this apparent paradox lies in the realization that continued polymerization of (Li^+R^-) monomers into infinite ionic arrays, such as are found in the alkali-metal halides, is hindered by the bulky nature of the R groups. Furthermore, these organic groups, which are covalently bonded within themselves, almost completely surround the ionic core and so dominate the bulk physical properties. Such ionic/covalent oligomers have been termed "supramolecules".[92]

The structure and bonding in lithium methyl have been particularly fully studied. The crystal structure consists of interconnected tetrameric units $(LiMe)_4$ as shown in Fig. 4.17: the individual Li_4C_4 clusters consist of a tetrahedron

[88] A. STREITWIESER, J. E. WILLIAMS, S. ALEXANDRATOS and J. M. McKELVEY, *J. Am. Chem. Soc.* **98**, 4778–84 (1976). A. STREITWIESER, *Acc. Chem. Res.* **17**, 353–7 (1984).

[89] E. D. JEMMIS, J. CHANDRASEKHAR and P. V. R. SCHLEYER, *J. Am. Chem. Soc.* **101**, 2848–56 (1979). P. V. R. SCHLEYER, *Pure Appl. Chem.* **55**, 355–62 (1983); **56**, 151–62 (1984).

[90] G. D. GRAHAM, D. S. MARYNICK and W. N. LIPSCOMB, *J. Am. Chem. Soc.* **102**, 4572–8 (1980).

[91] D. BARR, R. SNAITH, R. E. MULVEY and P. G. PERKINS, *Polyhedron* **7**, 2119–28 (1988).

[92] D. SEEBACH, *Angew. Chem. Int. Edn. Engl.* **27**, 1624–54 (1988).

[93] K. WADE, *Electron Deficient Compounds*, Nelson, London, 1971, 203 pp.

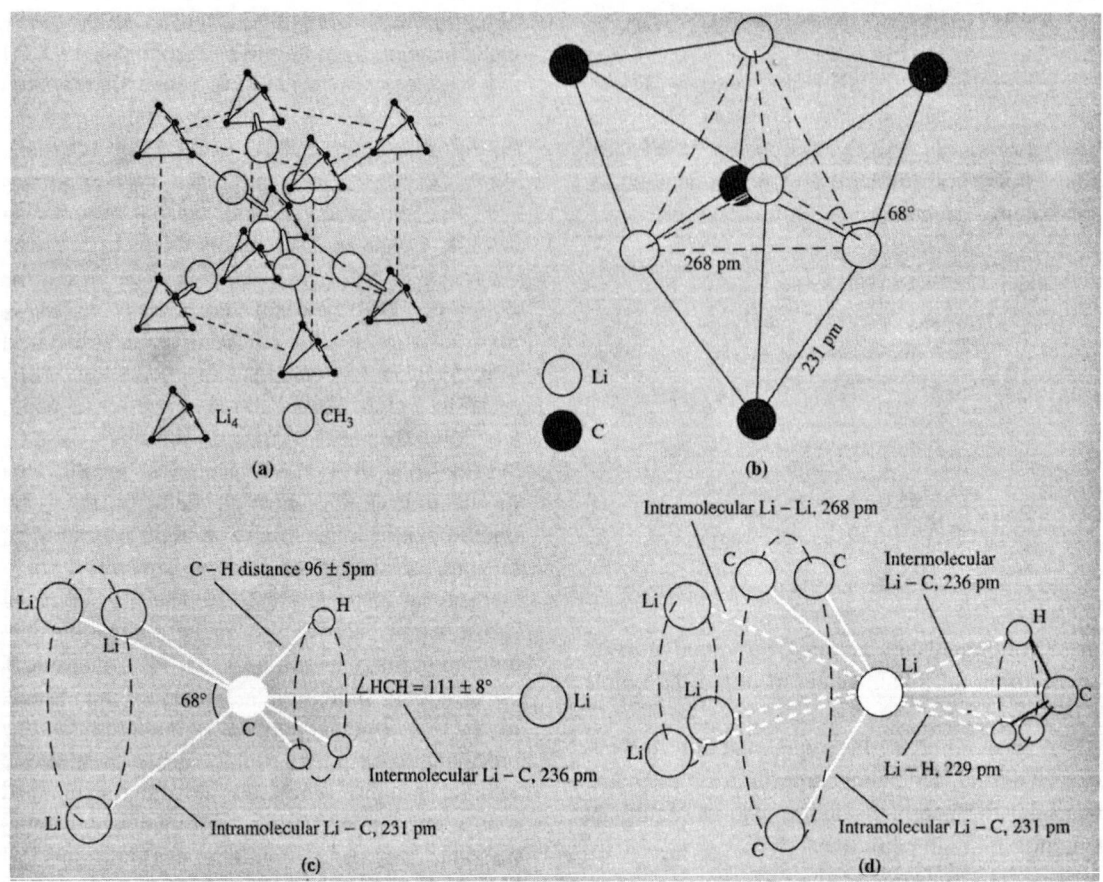

Figure 4.17 Crystal and molecular structure of (LiMe)$_4$ showing (a) the unit cell of lithium methyl, (b) the Li$_4$C$_4$ skeleton of the tetramer viewed approximately along one of the threefold axes, (c) the 7-coordinate environment of each C atom, and (d) the (4 + 3 + 3)-coordinate environment of each Li atom. After ref. 93, modified to include Li—H contacts.

of 4Li with a triply-bridging C above the centre of each face to complete a distorted cube. The clusters are interconnected along cube diagonals via the bridging CH$_3$ groups and the intercluster Li–C distance (236 pm) is very similar to the Li–C distance within each cluster (231 pm). The carbon atoms are thus essentially 7-coordinate being bonded directly to 3H and 4Li. The Li–Li distance within the cluster is 268 pm, which is virtually identical with the value of 267.3 pm for the gaseous Li$_2$ molecule and substantially smaller than the value of 304 pm in Li metal (where each Li has 8 nearest neighbours). Each Li atom is

therefore closely associated with three other Li atoms and three C atoms within its own cluster and with one C and three H atoms in an adjoining cluster. Detailed calculations show that the C–H$\cdots$Li interactions make a substantial contribution to the overall bonding.[91] Such "agostic" interactions were indeed first noted in lithium methyl long before their importance in transition metal organometallic compounds was recognized. The effect is most pronounced in (LiEt)$_4$ where the α-H on the ethyl group comes within 198 pm of its neighbouring Li atom;[79,91] cf. 204.3 pm in solid LiH, which has the NaCl structure (pp. 65, 82).

Higher alkyls of lithium adopt similar structures in which polyhedral clusters of metal atoms are bridged by alkyl groups located over the triangular faces of these clusters. For example, crystalline lithium *t*-butyl is tetrameric and the structural units $(LiBu^t)_4$ persist in solution; by contrast lithium ethyl, which is tetrameric in the solid state, dissolves in hydrocarbons as the hexamer $(LiEt)_6$ which probably consists of octahedra of Li_6 with triply bridging $-CH_2CH_3$ groups above 6 of the 8 faces. As the atomic number of the alkali metal increases there is a gradual trend away from these oligomeric structures towards structures which are more typical of polarized ionic compounds. Thus, although NaMe is tetrameric like LiMe, NaEt adopts a layer structure in which the CH_2 groups have a trigonal pyramidal array of Na neighbours, and KMe adopts a NiAs-type structure (p. 679) in which each Me is surrounded by a trigonal prismatic array of K. The extent to which this is considered to be $K^+CH_3^-$ is a matter for discussion though it will be noted that CH_3^- is isoelectronic with the molecule NH_3.

The structure of the organometallic complex lithium tetramethylborate $LiBMe_4$ is discussed on pp. 127–8 alongside that of polymeric $BeMe_2$ with which it is isoelectronic.

Organometallic compounds of the alkali metals (particularly LiMe and $LiBu^n$) are valuable synthetic reagents and have been increasingly used in industrial and laboratory-scale organic syntheses during the past 20 y.[86,94,95]. The annual production of $LiBu^n$ alone has leapt from a few kilograms to about 1000 tonnes. Large scale applications are as a polymerization catalyst, alkylating agent and precursor to metalated organic reagents. Many of the synthetic reactions parallel those of Grignard reagents over which they sometimes have distinct advantages in terms of speed of reaction, freedom from complicating side reactions or convenience of handling. Reactions are

[94] B. J. WAKEFIELD, *The Chemistry of Organolithium Compounds*, Pergamon Press, Oxford, 1976, 337 pp.

[95] K. SMITH, Lithiation and organic synthesis, *Chem.. in Br.* **18(1)**, 29–32 (1982)

those to be expected for carbanions, though free-radical mechanisms occasionally occur.

Halogens regenerate the parent alkyl (or aryl) halide and proton donors give the corresponding hydrocarbon:

$$LiR + X_2 \longrightarrow LiX + RX$$

$$LiR + H^+ \longrightarrow Li^+ + RH$$

$$LiR + R'I \longrightarrow LiI + RR'$$

C–C bonds can be formed by reaction with alkyl iodides or more usefully by reaction with metal carbonyls to give aldehydes and ketones: e.g. $Ni(CO)_4$ reacts with LiR to form an unstable acyl nickel carbonyl complex which can be attacked by electrophiles such as H^+ or $R'Br$ to give aldehydes or ketones by solvent-induced reductive elimination:

$[Fe(CO)_5]$ reacts similarly. Aldehydes and ketones can also be obtained from *N,N*-disubstituted amides, and symmetrical ketones are formed by reaction with CO:

$$LiR + HCONMe_2 \longrightarrow LiNMe_2 + RCHO$$

$$LiR + R'CONMe_2 \longrightarrow LiNMe_2 + R'COR$$

$$2LiR + 3CO \longrightarrow 2LiCO + R_2CO$$

Thermal decomposition of LiR eliminates a β-hydrogen atom to give an olefin and LiH, a process of industrial importance for long-chain terminal alkenes. Alkenes can also be produced by treatment of ethers, the organometallic reacting here as a very strong base (proton acceptor):

Lithium aryls react as typical carbanions in non-polar solvents giving carboxylic acids with CO_2

and tertiary carbinols with aryl ketones:

$$LiAr + CO_2 \longrightarrow ArCO_2Li \xrightarrow{H_2O}$$

$$LiOH + ArCO_2H$$

$$LiAr + Ar_2'CO \longrightarrow [Ar_2'C(Ar)OLi]$$

$$\xrightarrow{H_2O} LiOH + Ar_2'C(Ar)OH$$

Organolithium reagents are also valuable in the synthesis of other organometallic compounds via metal–halogen exchange:

$$3LiR + BCl_3 \longrightarrow 3LiCl + BR_3$$

$$(4-x)LiR + SnCl_4 \longrightarrow$$

$$(4-x)LiCl + SnCl_xR_{4-x} \quad (1 \leq x \leq 4)$$

$$3LiAr + P(OEt)_3 \longrightarrow 3LiOEt + PAr_3$$

Similar reactions have been used to produce organo derivatives of As, Sb, Bi; Si, Ge and many other elements.

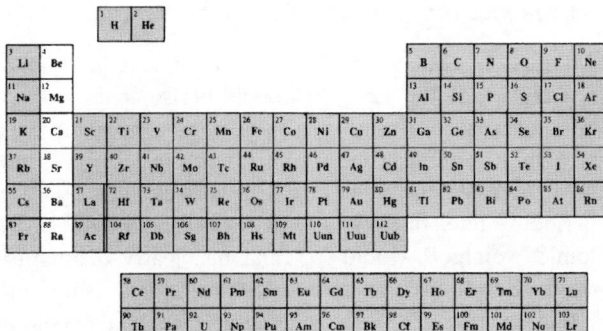

5

Beryllium, Magnesium, Calcium, Strontium, Barium and Radium

5.1 Introduction

The Group 2 or alkaline earth metals exemplify and continue the trends in properties noted for the alkali metals. No new principles are involved, but the ideas developed in the preceding chapter gain emphasis and clarity by their further application and extension. Indeed, there is an impressively close parallelism between the two groups as will become increasingly clear throughout the chapter.

The discovery of beryllium in 1798 followed an unusual train of events.[1] The mineralogist R.-J. Haüy had observed the remarkable similarity in external crystalline structure, hardness and density of a beryl from Limoges and an emerald from Peru, and suggested to L.-N. Vauquelin that he should analyse them to see if they were chemically identical.[†] As a result, Vauquelin showed that both minerals contained not only alumina and silica as had previously been known, but also a new earth, beryllia, which closely resembled alumina but gave no alums, apparently did not dissolve in an excess of KOH (perhaps because it had been fused?) and had a sweet rather than an astringent taste. *Caution*: beryllium compounds are now known to be extremely toxic, especially as dusts or smokes;[2] it seems likely that this toxicity results from the ability of Be^{II} to displace Mg^{II} from Mg-activated enzymes due to its stronger coordinating ability.

Both beryl and emerald were found to be essentially $Be_3Al_2Si_6O_{18}$, the only difference between them being that emerald also contains ~2% Cr, the source of its green colour. The combining weight of Be was ~4.7 but the similarity (diagonal relation) between Be and

[1] M. E. WEEKS, *Discovery of the Elements*, 6th edn., Journal of Chemical Education, Easton, Pa, 1956, 910 pp.

[2] J. SCHUBERT, Beryllium and berylliosis, Chap. 34 (1958), in *Chemistry in the Environment*, pp. 321–7, Readings from *Scientific American*, W. H. Freeman, San Francisco, 1973.

[†] A similar observation had been made (with less dramatic consequences) nearly 2000 y earlier by Pliny the Elder when he wrote: "Beryls, it is thought, are of the same nature as the smaragdus (emerald), or at least closely analogous" (*Historia Naturalis*, Book 37).

Al led to considerable confusion concerning the valency and atomic weight of Be $(2 \times 4.7$ or $3 \times 4.7)$; this was not resolved until Mendeleev 70 y later stated that there was no room for a tervalent element of atomic weight 14 near nitrogen in his periodic table, but that a divalent element of atomic weight 9 would fit snugly between Li and B. Beryllium metal was first prepared by F. Wöhler in 1828 (the year he carried out his celebrated synthesis of urea from NH_4CNO); he suggested the name by allusion to the mineral (Latin *beryllus* from Greek βηρυλλος). The metal was independently isolated in the same year by A.-B. Bussy using the same method — reduction of $BeCl_2$ with metallic K. The first electrolytic preparation was by P. Lebeau in 1898 and the first commercial process (electrolysis of a fused mixture of BeF_2 and BaF_2) was devised by A. Stock and H. Goldschmidt in 1932. The close parallel with the development of Li technology (pp. 68–70) is notable.

Compounds of Mg and Ca, like those of their Group 1 neighbours Na and K, have been known from ancient times though nothing was known of their chemical nature until the seventeenth century. Magnesian stone (Greek Μαγνησία λιθος) was the name given to the soft white mineral steatite (otherwise called soapstone or talc) which was found in the Magnesia district of Thessally, whereas calcium derives from the Latin *calx*, *calcis* — lime. The Romans used a mortar prepared from sand and lime (obtained by heating limestone, $CaCO_3$) because these lime mortars withstood the moist climate of Italy better than the Egyptian mortars based on partly dehydrated gypsum ($CaSO_4.2H_2O$); these had been used, for example, in the Great Pyramid of Gizeh, and all the plaster in Tutankhamun's tomb was based on gypsum. The names of the elements themselves were coined by H. Davy in 1808 when he isolated Mg and Ca, along with Sr and Ba by an electrolytic method following work by J. J. Berzelius and M. M. Pontin: the moist earth (oxide) was mixed with one-third its weight of HgO on a Pt plate which served as anode; the cathode was a Pt wire dipping into a pool of Hg and electrolysis

gave an amalgam from which the desired metal could be isolated by distilling off the Hg.

A mineral found in a lead mine near Strontian, Scotland, in 1787 was shown to be a compound of a new element by A. Crawford in 1790. This was confirmed by T. C. Hope the following year and he clearly distinguished the compounds of Ba, Sr and Ca, using amongst other things their characteristic flame colorations: Ba yellow-green, Sr bright red, Ca orange-red. Barium-containing minerals had been known since the seventeenth century but the complex process of unravelling the relation between them was not accomplished until the independent work of C. W. Scheele and J. G. Gahn between 1774 and 1779: heavy spar was found to be $BaSO_4$ and called barite or barytes (Greek βαρυς, heavy), whence Scheele's new base baryta (BaO) from which Davy isolated barium in 1808.

Radium, the last element in the group, was isolated in trace amounts as the chloride by P. and M. Curie in 1898 after their historic processing of tonnes of pitchblende. It was named by Mme Curie in allusion to its radioactivity, a word also coined by her (Latin *radius*, a ray); the element itself was isolated electrolytically via an amalgam by M. Curie and A. Debierne in 1910 and its compounds give a carmine-red flame test.

5.2 The Elements

5.2.1 Terrestrial abundance and distribution

Beryllium, like its neighbours Li and B, is relatively unabundant in the earth's crust; it occurs to the extent of about 2 ppm and is thus similar to Sn (2.1 ppm), Eu (2.1 ppm) and As (1.8 ppm). However, its occurrence as surface deposits of beryl in pegmatite rocks (which are the last portions of granite domes to crystallize) makes it readily accessible. Crystals as large as 1 m on edge and weighing up to 60 tonnes have been reported. World reserves in commercial deposits are about 4 million tonnes of contained Be and mined production in 1985–86 was USA

223, USSR 76 and Brazil 37 tonnes of contained Be, which together accounted for 98% of world production. The cost of Be metal was $690/kg in 1987. By contrast, world supplies of magnesium are virtually limitless: it occurs to the extent of 0.13% in sea water, and electrolytic extraction at the present annual rate, if continued for a million years, would only reduce this to 0.12%.

Magnesium, like its heavier congeners Ca, Sr and Ba, occurs in crustal rocks mainly as the insoluble carbonates and sulfates, and (less accessibly) as silicates. Estimates of its total abundance depend sensitively on the geochemical model used, particularly on the relative weightings given to the various igneous and sedimentary rock types, and values ranging from 20 000 to 133 000 ppm are current.[3] Perhaps the most acceptable value is 27 640 ppm (2.76%), which places Mg sixth in order of abundance by weight immediately following Ca (4.66%) and preceding Na (2.27%) and K (1.84%). Large land masses such as the Dolomites in Italy consist predominantly of the magnesian limestone mineral dolomite [$MgCa(CO_3)_2$], and there are substantial deposits of magnesite ($MgCO_3$), epsomite ($MgSO_4.7H_2O$) and other evaporites such as carnallite ($K_2MgCl_4.6H_2O$) and langbeinite [$K_2Mg_2(SO_4)_3$]. Silicates are represented by the common basaltic mineral olivine [$(Mg,Fe)_2SiO_4$] and by soapstone (talc) [$Mg_3Si_4O_{10}(OH)_2$], asbestos (chrysotile) [$Mg_3Si_2O_5(OH)_4$] and micas. Spinel ($MgAl_2O_4$) is a metamorphic mineral and gemstone. It should also be remembered that the green leaves of plants, though not a commercial source of Mg, contain chlorophylls which are the Mg-porphine complexes primarily involved in photosynthesis.

Calcium, as noted above, is the fifth most abundant element in the earth's crust and hence the third most abundant metal after Al and Fe. Vast sedimentary deposits of $CaCO_3$, which represent the fossilized remains of earlier marine life, occur over large parts of the earth's surface. The deposits are of two main types — rhombohedral calcite, which is the more common, and orthorhombic aragonite, which sometimes forms in more temperate seas. Representative minerals of the first type are limestone itself, dolomite, marble, chalk and iceland spar. Extensive beds of the aragonite form of $CaCO_3$ make up the Bahamas, the Florida Keys and the Red Sea basin. Corals, sea shells and pearls are also mainly $CaCO_3$. Other important minerals are gypsum ($CaSO_4.2H_2O$), anhydrite ($CaSO_4$), fluorite (CaF_2: also blue john and fluorspar) and apatite [$Ca_5(PO_4)_3F$].

Strontium (384 ppm) and barium (390 ppm) are respectively the fifteenth and fourteenth elements in order of abundance, being bracketed by S (340 ppm) and F (544 ppm). The most important mineral of Sr is celestite ($SrSO_4$), and strontianite ($SrCO_3$) is also mined. The largest producers are Mexico, Spain, Turkey and the UK, and the world production of these two minerals in 1985 was 10^5 tonnes. The main uses of Sr compounds, especially $SrCO_3$, are in the manufacture of special glasses for colour television and computer monitors (53%), for pyrotechnic displays (14%) and magnetic materials (11%). Strontium carbonate and sulfate are critical raw materials for the USA which is totally dependent on imports for supplies. The sulfate (barite) is also the most important mineral of Ba: it is mined commercially in over 40 countries throughout the world. Production in 1985 was 6.0 million tonnes, of which 44% was mined in the USA. The major use of $BaSO_4$ (92%) is as a heavy mud slurry in well drilling; production of Ba chemicals accounts for only 7%.

Radium occurs only in association with uranium (Chapter 31); the observed ratio $^{226}Ra/U$ is ~1 mg per 3 kg, leading to a terrestrial abundance for Ra of ~10^{-6} ppm. As uranium ores normally contain only a few hundred ppm of U, it follows that about 10 tonnes of ore must be processed for 1 mg Ra. The total amount of Ra available worldwide is of the order of a few kilograms, but its use in cancer therapy has been superseded by the use of other isotopes, and the

---

[3] K. K. Turekian, Elements, geochemical distribution of, *McGraw Hill Encyclopedia of Science and Technology*, Vol. 4, pp. 627–30, 1977.

annual production of separated Ra compounds is probably now only about 100 g. Chief suppliers are Belgium, Canada, Czechoslovakia, the UK, and the former Soviet Union. ^{226}Ra decays by α-emission with a half-life of 1600 y, although 3 in every 10^{11} decays occur by ^{14}C emission ($^{226}_{88}Ra \longrightarrow {}^{212}_{82}Pb + {}^{14}_{6}C$). This exceedingly rare form of radioactivity was discovered in 1984 in the rare naturally occurring radium isotope ^{223}Ra where about 1 in 10^9 of the atoms decays by ^{14}C rather than α-emission.[4]

5.2.2 Production and uses of the metals [5]

Beryllium is extracted from beryl by roasting the mineral with Na_2SiF_6 at 700–750°C, leaching the soluble fluoride with water and then precipitating $Be(OH)_2$ at about pH 12. The metal is usually prepared by reduction of BeF_2 (p. 116) with Mg at about 1300°C or by electrolysis of fused mixtures of $BeCl_2$ and alkali metal chlorides. It is one of the lightest metals known and has one of the highest mps of the light metals. Its modulus of elasticity is one-third greater than that of steel. The largest use of Be is in high-strength alloys of Cu and Ni (see Panel below).

Magnesium is produced on a large scale (400 000 tonnes in 1985) either by electrolysis or

silicothermal reduction. The major producers are the USA (43%), the former Soviet Union (26%), and Norway (17%). The electrolytic process uses either fused anhydrous $MgCl_2$ at 750°C or partly hydrated $MgCl_2$ from sea water at a slightly lower temperature. The silicothermal process uses calcined dolomite and ferrosilicon alloy under reduced pressure at 1150°C:

$$2(MgO.CaO) + FeSi \longrightarrow 2Mg + Ca_2SiO_4 + Fe$$

Magnesium is industry's lightest constructional metal, having a density less than two-thirds that of Al (see Panel on the next page). The price of the metal (99.8% purity) was $3.4/kg in 1994.

The other alkaline earth metals Ca, Sr and Ba are produced on a much smaller scale than Mg. Calcium is produced by electrolysis of fused $CaCl_2$ (obtained either as a byproduct of the Solvay process (p. 71) or by the action of HCl or $CaCO_3$). It is less reactive than Sr or Ba, forming a protective oxide-nitride coating in air which enables it to be machined in a lathe or handled by other standard metallurgical techniques. Calcium metal is used mainly as an alloying agent to strengthen Al bearings, to control graphitic C in cast-iron and to remove Bi from Pb. Chemically it is used as a scavenger in the steel industry (O, S and P), as a getter for oxygen and nitrogen, to remove N_2 from argon and as a reducing agent in the production of other metals such as Cr, Zr, Th and U. Calcium also reacts directly with H_2 to give CaH_2, which is a useful source of H_2. World production of

[4] H. J. ROSE and G. A. JONES, *Nature* **307**, 245–7 (1984).

[5] W. BÜCHNER, R. SCHLIEBS, G. WINTER and K. H. BÜCHEL, *Industrial Inorganic Chemistry*, VCH, New York, 1989, pp. 231–46.

Uses of Beryllium Metal and Alloys

The ability of Be to age-harden Cu was discovered by M. G. Corson in 1926 and it is now known that ~2% of Be increases the strength of Cu sixfold. In addition, the alloys (which also usually contain 0.25% Co) have good electrical conductivity, high strength, unusual wear resistance, and resistance to anelastic behaviour (hysteresis, damping, etc.): they are non-magnetic and corrosion resistant, and find numerous applications in critical moving parts of aero-engines, key components in precision instruments, control relays and electronics. They are also non-sparking and are thus of great use for hand tools in the petroleum industry. A nickel alloy containing 2% Be is used for high-temperature springs, clips, bellows and electrical connections. Another major use for Be is in nuclear reactors since it is one of the most effective neutron moderators and reflectors known. A small, but important, use of Be is as a window material in X-ray tubes: it transmits X-rays 17 times better than Al and 8 times better than Lindemann glass. A mixture of compounds of radium and beryllium has long been used as a convenient laboratory source of neutrons and, indeed, led to the discovery of the neutron by J. Chadwick in 1932: $^9Be(\alpha,n)^{12}C$.

Magnesium Metal and Alloys

The principal advantage of Mg as a structural metal is its low density ($1.7\,\mathrm{g\,cm^{-3}}$ compared with 2.70 for Al and 7.80 for steel). For equal strength, the best Mg alloy weighs only a quarter as much as steel, and the best Al alloy weighs about one-third as much as steel. In addition, Mg has excellent machinability and it can be cast or fabricated by any of the standard metallurgical methods (rolling, extruding, drawing, forging, welding, brazing or riveting). Its major use therefore is as a light-weight construction metal, not only in aircraft but also in luggage, photographic and optical equipment, etc. It is also used for cathodic protection of other metals from corrosion, as an oxygen scavenger, and as a reducing agent in the production of Be, Ti, Zr, Hf and U. World production approaches 400 000 tonnes pa.

Magnesium alloys typically contain >90% Mg together with 2–9% Al, 1–3% Zn and 0.2–1% Mn. Greatly improved retention of strength at high temperature (up to 450°C) is achieved by alloying with rare-earth metals (e.g. Pr/Nd) or Th. These alloys can be used for automobile engine casings and for aeroplane fuselages and landing wheels. Other uses are in light-weight tread-plates, dock-boards, loading platforms, gravity conveyors and shovels.

Up to 5% Mg is added to most commercial Al to improve its mechanical properties, weldability and resistance to corrosion.

For further details see *Kirk–Othmer Encyclopedia of Chemical Technology*, 4th edn., 1995, Vol. 15, pp. 622–74.

the metal is about 2500 tonnes pa of which >50% was in the USA (price \$5.00–8.00/kg in 1991).

Metallic Sr and Ba are best prepared by high-temperature reduction of their oxides with Al in an evacuated retort or by small-scale electrolysis of fused chloride baths. They have limited use as getters, and a Ni–Ba alloy is used for spark-plug wire because of its high emissivity. Annual production of Ba metal is about 20–30 tonnes worldwide and the 1991 price about \$80–140/kg depending on quality.

5.2.3 Properties of the elements

Table 5.1 lists some of the atomic properties of the Group 2 elements. Comparison with the data for Group 1 elements (p. 75) shows the substantial increase in the ionization energies; this is related to their smaller size and higher nuclear charge, and is particularly notable for Be. Indeed, the "ionic radius" of Be is purely a notional figure since no compounds are known in which uncoordinated Be has a 2+ charge. In aqueous solutions the reduction potential of

Table 5.1 Atomic properties of the alkaline earth metals

Property	Be	Mg	Ca	Sr	Ba	Ra
Atomic number	4	12	20	38	56	88
Number of naturally occurring isotopes	1	3	6	4	7	4[a]
Atomic weight	9.012 182(3)	24.3050(6)	40.078(4)	87.62(1)	137.327(7)	(226.0254)[b]
Electronic configuration	$[\mathrm{He}]2s^2$	$[\mathrm{Ne}]3s^2$	$[\mathrm{Ar}]4s^2$	$[\mathrm{Kr}]5s^2$	$[\mathrm{Xe}]6s^2$	$[\mathrm{Rn}]7s^2$
Ionization energies/ kJ mol^{-1}	899.4 1757.1	737.7 1450.7	589.8 1145.4	549.5 1064.2	502.9 965.2	509.3 979.0
Metal radius/pm	112	160	197	215	222	—
Ionic radius (6 coord)/pm	(27)[c]	72	100	118	135	148
$E°$/V for $\mathrm{M^{2+}(aq)} + 2e^- \longrightarrow \mathrm{M(s)}$	−1.97	−2.356	−2.84	−2.89	−2.92	−2.916

[a] All isotopes are radioactive: longest $t_{1/2}$ 1600 y for Ra(226).

[b] Value refers to isotope with longest half-life.

[c] Four-coordinate.

Be is much less than that of its congeners, again indicating its lower electropositivity. By contrast, Ca, Sr, Ba and Ra have reduction potentials which are almost identical with those of the heavier alkali metals; Mg occupies an intermediate position.

Be and Mg are silvery white metals whereas Ca, Sr and Ba are pale yellow (as are the divalent rare earth metals Eu and Yb) although the colour is less intense than for Cs (p. 74). All the alkaline earth metals are lustrous and relatively soft, and their physical properties (Table 5.2), when compared with those of Group 1 metals, show that they have a substantially higher mp, bp, density and enthalpies of fusion and vaporization. This can be understood in terms of the size factor mentioned in the preceding paragraph and the fact that 2 valency electrons per atom are now available for bonding. Again, Be is notable in melting more than 1100° above Li and being nearly 3.5 times as dense; its enthalpy of fusion is more than 5 times that of Li. Beryllium resembles Al in being stable in moist air due to the formation of a protective oxide layer, and highly polished specimens retain their shine indefinitely. Magnesium also resists oxidation but the heavier metals tarnish readily. Beryllium, like Mg and the high-temperature form of Ca (>450°C), crystallizes in the hcp arrangement, and this confers a marked anisotropy on its properties; Sr is fcc, Ba and Ra are bcc like the alkali metals.

5.2.4 Chemical reactivity and trends

Beryllium metal is relatively unreactive at room temperature, particularly in its massive form. It does not react with water or steam even at red heat and does not oxidize in air below 600°C, though powdered Be burns brilliantly on ignition to give BeO and Be_3N_2. The halogens (X_2) react above about 600°C to give BeX_2 but the chalcogens (S, Se, Te) require even higher temperatures to form BeS, etc. Ammonia reacts above 1200°C to give Be_3N_2 and carbon forms Be_2C at 1700°C. In contrast with the other Group 2 metals, Be does not react directly with hydrogen, and BeH_2 must be prepared indirectly (p. 115). Cold, concentrated HNO_3 passivates Be but the metal dissolves readily in dilute aqueous acids (HCl, H_2SO_4, HNO_3) with evolution of hydrogen. Beryllium is sharply distinguished from the other alkaline earth metals in reacting with aqueous alkalis (NaOH, KOH) with evolution of hydrogen. It also dissolves rapidly in aqueous NH_4HF_2 (as does $Be(OH)_2$), a reaction of some technological importance in the preparation of anhydrous BeF_2 and purified Be:

$$2NH_4HF_2(aq) + Be(s) \longrightarrow (NH_4)_2BeF_4 + H_2(g)$$

$$(NH_4)_2BeF_4(s) \xrightarrow{280°} BeF_2(s) + 2NH_4F \text{ (subl)}$$

Magnesium is more electropositive than the amphoteric Be and reacts more readily with most of the non-metals. It ignites with the halogens, particularly when they are moist, to give MgX_2, and burns with dazzling brilliance in air to give MgO and Mg_3N_2. It also reacts directly with the other elements in Groups 15 and 16 (and Group 14) when heated and even forms MgH_2 with hydrogen at 570° and 200 atm. Steam produces MgO (or $Mg(OH)_2$) plus H_2, and ammonia reacts at elevated temperature to give Mg_3N_2. Methanol reacts at 200° to give $Mg(OMe)_2$ and ethanol (when activated

Table 5.2 Physical properties of the alkaline earth metals

Property	Be	Mg	Ca	Sr	Ba	Ra
MP/°C	1289	650	842	769	729	700
BP/°C	2472	1090	1494	1382	1805	(1700)
Density (20°C)/g cm^{-3}	1.848	1.738	1.55	2.63	3.59	5.5
ΔH_{fus}/kJ mol^{-1}	15	8.9	8.6	8.2	7.8	(8.5)
ΔH_{vap}/kJ mol^{-1}	309	127.4	155	158	136	(113)
ΔH_f(monatomic gas)/kJ mol^{-1}	324	146	178	164	178	—
Electrical resistivity (25°C)/μohm cm	3.70	4.48	3.42	13.4	34.0	(100)

by a trace of iodine) reacts similarly at room temperature. Alkyl and aryl halides react with Mg to give Grignard reagents RMgX (pp. 132–5).

The heavier alkaline earth metals Ca, Sr, Ba (and Ra) react even more readily with non-metals, and again the direct formation of nitrides M_3N_2 is notable. Other products are similar though the hydrides are more stable (p. 65) and the carbides less stable than for Be and Mg. There is also a tendency, previously noted for the alkali metals (p. 84), to form peroxides MO_2 of increasing stability in addition to the normal oxides MO. Calcium, Sr and Ba dissolve in liquid NH_3 to give deep blue-black solutions from which lustrous, coppery, ammoniates $M(NH_3)_6$ can be recovered on evaporation; these ammoniates gradually decompose to the corresponding amides, especially in the presence of catalysts:

$$[M(NH_3)_6](s) \longrightarrow M(NH_2)_2(s)$$

$$+ 4NH_3(g) + H_2(g)$$

In these properties, as in many others, the heavier alkaline earth metals resemble the alkali metals rather than Mg (which has many similarities to Zn) or Be (which is analogous to Al).

5.3 Compounds

5.3.1 Introduction

The predominant divalence of the Group 2 metals can be interpreted in terms of their electronic configuration, ionization energies, and size (see Table 5.1). Further ionization to give simple salts of stoichiometry MX_3 is precluded by the magnitude of the energies involved, the third stage ionization being $14\,849\,kJ\,mol^{-1}$ for Be, $7733\,kJ\,mol^{-1}$ for Mg and $4912\,kJ\,mol^{-1}$ for Ca; even for Ra the estimated value of $3281\,kJ\,mol^{-1}$ involves far more energy than could be recovered by additional bonding even if this were predominantly covalent. Reasons for the absence of *univalent* compounds MX are less obvious. The first-stage ionization energies for Ca, Sr, Ba and Ra are similar to that of Li (p. 75) though the larger

size of the hypothetical univalent Group 2 ions, when compared to Li, would reduce the lattice energy somewhat (p. 82). By making plausible assumptions about the ionic radius and structure we can estimate the approximate enthalpy of formation of such compounds and they are predicted to be stable with respect to the constituent elements; their non-existence is related to the much higher enthalpy of formation of the conventional compounds MX_2, which leads to rapid and complete disproportionation. For example, the standard enthalpy of formation of hypothetical crystalline MgCl, assuming the NaCl structure, is $\sim\!-125\,kJ\,mol^{-1}$, which is substantially greater than for many known stable compounds and essentially the same as the experimentally observed value for AgCl: $\Delta H_f^\circ = -127\,kJ\,mol^{-1}$. However, the corresponding (experimental) value for $\Delta H_f^\circ(MgCl_2)$ is $-642\,kJ\,mol^{-1}$, whence an enthalpy of disproportionation of $-196\,kJ\,mol^{-1}$:

$$Mg(c) + Cl_2(g) = MgCl_2(c);$$

$$\Delta H_f^\circ = -642 \text{ kJ/(mol of } MgCl_2)$$

$$2Mg(c) + Cl_2(g) = 2MgCl(c);$$

$$\Delta H_f^\circ = -250 \text{ kJ/(2 mol of MgCl)}$$

$$2MgCl(c) = Mg(c) + MgCl_2(c);$$

$$\Delta H_{disprop}^\circ = -392 \text{ kJ/(2 mol of MgCl)}$$

It is clear that, if synthetic routes could be devised which would mechanistically hinder disproportionation, such compounds might be preparable. Although univalent compounds of the Group 2 metals have not yet been isolated, there is some evidence for the formation of Mg^I species during electrolysis with Mg electrodes. Thus H_2 is evolved at the anode when an aqueous solution of NaCl is electrolysed and the amount of Mg lost from the anode corresponds to an oxidation state of 1.3. Similarly, when aqueous Na_2SO_4 is electrolysed, the amount of H_2 evolved corresponds to the oxidation by water of Mg ions having an average oxidation state of 1.4:

$$Mg^{1.4+}(aq) + 0.6H_2O \longrightarrow Mg^{2+}(aq)$$

$$+ 0.6OH^-(aq) + 0.3H_2(g)$$

On the basis of the discussion on pp. 79–81 the elements in Group 2 would be expected to deviate further from simple ionic bonding than do the alkali metals. The charge on M^{2+} is higher and the radius for corresponding ions is smaller, thereby inducing more distortion of the surrounding anions. This is reflected in the decreased thermal stability of oxoacid salts such as nitrates, carbonates and sulfates. For example, the temperature at which the carbonate reaches a dissociation pressure of 1 atm CO_2 is: $BeCO_3$ 250°, $MgCO_3$ 540°, $CaCO_3$ 900°, $SrCO_3$ 1289°, $BaCO_3$ 1360°. The tendency towards covalency is greatest with Be, and this element forms no compounds in which the bonding is predominantly ionic. For similar reasons Be (and to a lesser extent Mg) forms numerous stable coordination compounds; organometallic compounds are also well characterized, and these frequently involve multicentre (electron deficient) bonding similar to that found in analogous compounds of Li and B.

Many compounds of the Group 2 elements are much less soluble in water than their Group 1 counterparts. This is particularly true for the fluorides, carbonates and sulfates of the heavier members, and is related to their higher lattice energies. These solubility relations have had a profound influence on the mineralization of these elements as noted on p. 109. The ready solubility of BeF_2 (~20 000 times that of CaF_2) is presumably related to the very high solvation enthalpy of Be to give $[Be(H_2O)_4]^{2+}$.

Beryllium, because of its small size, almost invariably has a coordination number of 4. This is important in analytical chemistry since it ensures that edta, which coordinates strongly to Mg, Ca (and Al), does not chelate Be appreciably. BeO has the wurtzite (ZnS, p. 1209) structure whilst the other Be chalcogenides adopt the zinc blende modification. BeF_2 has the cristobalite (SiO_2, p. 342) structure and has only a very low electrical conductivity when fused. Be_2C and Be_2B have extended lattices of the antifluorite type with 4-coordinate Be and 8-coordinate C or B. Be_2SiO_4 has the phenacite structure (p. 347) in which both Be and Si

are tetrahedrally coordinated, and Li_2BeF_4 has the same structure. $[Be(H_2O)_4]SO_4$ features a tetrahedral aquo-ion which is H bonded to the surrounding sulfate groups in such a way that Be–O is 161 pm and the O–H $\cdots$ O are 262

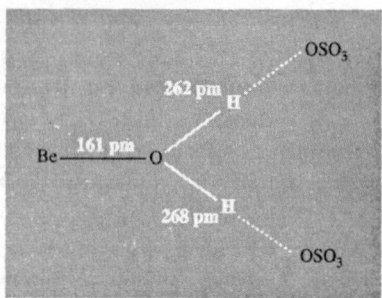

and 268 pm. Further examples of tetrahedral coordination to Be are to be found in later sections. Other configurations, involving linear (two-fold) coordination (e.g. $BeBu_2^t$) or trigonal coordination [e.g. cyclic $(MeBeNMe_2)_2$] are rare and most compounds which might appear to have such coordination (e.g. $BeMe_2$, $CsBeF_3$, etc.) achieve 4-coordination by polymerization. However K_2BeO_2,[6] Y_2BeO_4[7] and one or two more complex structures[8] do indeed contain trigonal planar $\{BeO_3\}$ units with Be–O ca. 155 pm, i.e. some 11 pm shorter than in tetrahedral $\{BeO_4\}$. Likewise, K_4BeE_2 (E = P, As, Sb) feature linear anions $[E–Be–E]^{4-}$ isoelectronic with $BeCl_2$ molecules (p. 117).[9] (See also p. 123). Six-coordination has been observed in $K_3Zr_6Cl_{15}Be$ and $Be_3Zr_6Cl_{18}Be$, in which the Be atom is encapsulated by and contributes two bonding elections to the octahedral Zr_6 cluster.[10] Trigonal-pyramidal

[6] P. KASTNER and R. HOPPE, *Naturwiss.* **61**, 79 (1974).

[7] L. A. HARRIS and H. L. YANKEL, *Acta Cryst.* **22**, 354–60 (1967).

[8] R. A. HOWIE and A. R. WEST, *Nature* **259**, 473 (1976). D. SCHULDT and R. HOPPE, *Z. anorg. allg. Chem.*, **578** 119–32 (1989), **594**, 87–94 (1991).

[9] M. SOMER, M. HARTWEG, K. PETERS, T. POPP and H.-G. VON SCHNERING, *Z. anorg. allg. Chem.* **595**, 217–23 (1991).

[10] R. P. ZIEBARTH and J. D. CORBETT, *J. Am. Chem. Soc.* **110**. 1132–9 (1988). J. ZHANG and J. D. CORBETT, *Z. anorg. allg. Chem.* **598/599**, 363–70 (1991).

6-fold coordination of Be by H is found in $Be(BH_4)_2$ (p. 116).

The stereochemistry of Mg and the heavier alkaline earth metals is more flexible than that of Be and, in addition to occasional compounds which feature low coordination numbers (2, 3 and 4), there are many examples of 6, 8 and 12 coordination, some with 7, 9 or 10 coordination, and even some with coordination numbers as high as 22 or 24, as in $SrCd_{11}$, $BaCd_{11}$ and $(Ca, Sr \text{ or } Ba)Zn_{13}$.[11] Strontium is 5-coordinate on the hemisolvate $[Sr(OC_6H_2Bu^t_3)_2(thf)_3].\frac{1}{2}thf$ which features a distorted trigonal bipyramidal structure with the two aryloxides in equatorial positions.[11a]

5.3.2 Hydrides and halides

Many features of the structure, bonding and stability of the Group 2 hydrides have already been discussed (p. 65) and it is only necessary to add some comments on BeH_2, which is the most difficult of these compounds to prepare and the least stable. BeH_2 (contaminated with variable amounts of ether) was first prepared in 1951 by reduction of $BeCl_2$ with LiH and by the reaction of $BeMe_2$ with $LiAlH_4$. A purer sample can be made by pyrolysis of $BeBu^t_2$ at 210°C and the best product is obtained by displacing BH_3 from BeB_2H_8 using PPh_3 in a sealed tube reaction at 180°:

$$BeB_2H_8 + 2PPh_3 \longrightarrow 2Ph_3PBH_3 + BeH_2$$

BeH_2 is an amorphous white solid (d 0.65 g cm^{-3}) which begins to evolve hydrogen when heated above 250°; it is moderately stable in air or water but is rapidly hydrolysed by acids, liberating H_2. A hexagonal crystalline form (d 0.78 g cm^{-3}) has been prepared by compaction fusion at 6.2 kbar and 130° in the presence of ~1% Li as catalyst.[12] In all forms BeH_2 appears to be highly polymerized by means of BeHBe

3-centre bonds and its structure is probably similar to that of crystalline $BeCl_2$ and $BeMe_2$ (see below). A related compound is the volatile mixed hydride BeB_2H_8, which is readily prepared (in the absence of solvent) by the reaction of $BeCl_2$ with $LiBH_4$ in a sealed tube:

$$BeCl_2 + 2LiBH_4 \xrightarrow{120°C} BeB_2H_8 + 2LiCl$$

BeB_2H_8 inflames in air, reacts almost explosively with water and reacts with dry HCl even at low temperatures:

$$BeB_2H_8 + 2HCl \longrightarrow BeCl_2 + B_2H_6 + 2H_2$$

The structure of this compound has proved particularly elusive and at least nine different structures have been proposed; it therefore affords an instructive example of the difficulties which attend the use of physical techniques for the structural determination of compounds in the gaseous, liquid or solution phases. In the gas phase it now seems likely that more than one species is present[13] and the compound certainly shows fluxional behaviour which makes all the hydrogen atoms equivalent on the nmr time scale.[14] A linear structure such as (a), with possible admixture of singly bridged B–H–B and triply bridged BeH$_3$B variants is now favoured, after a period in which triangular structures such as (b) had been vigorously canvassed. Even structure (c), which features planar 3-coordinate Be, had been advocated because it was thought to fit best much of the infrared and electron diffraction data and also accounted for the ready formation of adducts (d) with typical ligands such as Et$_2$O, thf, R$_3$N, R$_3$P, etc. In the solid state the structure has recently been established with some certainty by single-crystal X-ray analysis.[15] BeB_2H_8 consists of helical polymers of BH$_4$Be

[11] A. F. WELLS, *Structural Inorganic Chemistry*, 5th edn., Oxford University Press, Oxford, 1984, 1382 pp.

[11a] S. R. DRAKE, D. J. OTWAY, M. B. HURSTHOUSE and K. M. A. MALIK, *Polyhedron* **11**, 1995–2007 (1992).

[12] G. J. BRENDEL, E. M. MARLETT and L. M. NIEBYLSKI, *Inorg. Chem.* **17**, 3589–92 (1978).

[13] K. BRENDHAUGEN, A. HAARLAND and D. P. NOVAK, *Acta Chem. Scand.* **A29**, 801–2 (1975).

[14] D. F. GAINES, J. L. WALSH and D. F. HILLENBRAND, *J. Chem. Soc., Chem. Commun.*, 224–5 (1977).

[15] D. S. MARYNICK and W. N. LIPSCOMB, *Inorg. Chem.* **11**, 820–3 (1972). D. S. MARYNICK, *J. Am. Chem. Soc.* **101**, 6876–80 (1979). [See also J. F. STANTON, W. N. LIPSCOMB and R. J. BARTLETT, *J. Chem. Phys.* **88**, 5726–34 (1988) for results of high-level computations.]

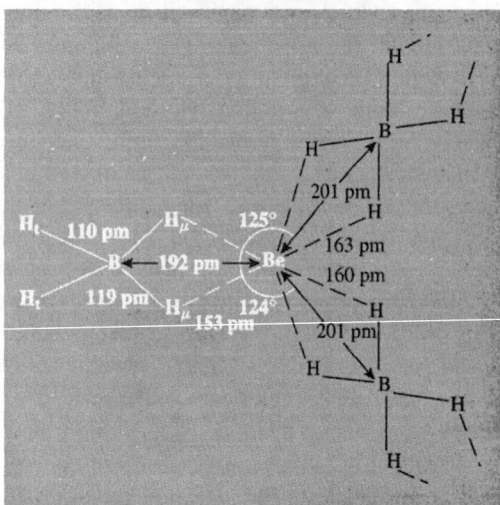

(a) Probable "linear" structure · (b) Hypothetical triangular
(fluxional)   structure

(c) Alternative triangular   (d) Proposed structure for
structure   LBeB₂H₈

Figure 5.1 Polymeric structure of crystalline Be(BH₄)₂ showing a section of the ···(H₂BH₂)Be(H₂BH₂)··· helix and one "terminal" or non-bridging group {(H$_t$)₂B(H$_μ$)₂}.

units linked by an equal number of bridging BH₄ units (Fig. 5.1). Of the 8 H atoms only 2 are not involved in bonding to Be; the Be is thus 6-coordinate (distorted trigonal prism) though the H atoms are much closer to B (~110 pm) than to Be (2 at ~153 pm and 4 at ~162 pm). The Be ··· B distance within the helical chain is 201 pm and in the branch is 192 pm. The relationship of this

structure to those of Al(BH₄)₃ and AlH₃ itself (p. 227) is noteworthy.

Anhydrous beryllium halides cannot be obtained from reactions in aqueous solutions because of the formation of hydrates such as [Be(H₂O)₄]F₂ and the subsequent hydrolysis which attends attempted dehydration. Thermal decomposition of (NH₄)₂BeF₄ is the best route for BeF₂, and BeCl₂ is conveniently made from the oxide

$$BeO + C + Cl_2 \xrightarrow{600-800°} BeCl_2 + CO$$

BeCl₂ can also be prepared by direct high-temperature chlorination of metallic Be or Be₂C, and these reactions are also used for the bromide and iodide. BeF₂ is a glassy material that is difficult to crystallize; it consists of a random network of 4-coordinate F-bridged Be atoms similar to the structure of vitreous silica, SiO₂. Above 270°, BeF₂ spontaneously crystallizes to give the quartz modification (p. 342) and, like quartz, it exists in a low-temperature α-form which transforms to the β-form at 227°; crystobalite and tridymite forms (p. 343) have also been prepared. The structural similarities between BeF₂ and SiO₂ extend to fluoroberyllates and silicates, and numerous parallels have been drawn: e.g. the phase diagram, compounds, and structures in the system NaF–BeF₂ resemble those for CaO–SiO₂; the system CaF₂–BeF₂ resembles ZrO₂–SiO₂; the compound KZnBe₃F₉ is isostructural with benitoite, BaTiSi₃O₉, etc.

BeCl₂ has an unusual chain structure (a) which can be cleaved by weak ligands such as Et₂O to give 4-coordinate molecular complexes L₂BeCl₂ (b); stronger donors such as H₂O or NH₃ lead

(a)

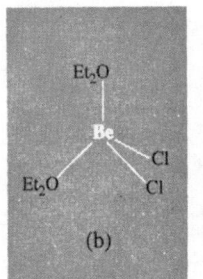

(b)

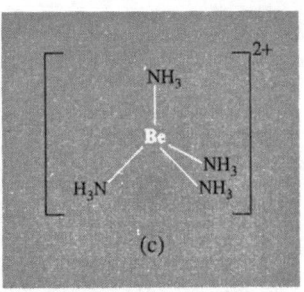

(c)

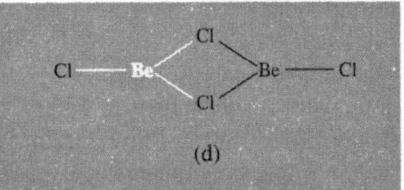

(d)

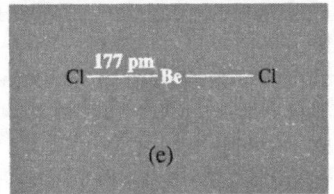

(e)

to ionic complexes $[BeL_4]^{2+}[Cl]^-{}_2$ (c). In all these forms Be can be considered to use the s, p_x, p_y and p_z orbitals for bonding; the ClBeCl angle is substantially less than the tetrahedral angle of 109° probably because this lessens the repulsive interaction between neighbouring Be atoms in the chain by keeping them further apart and also enables a wider angle than 71° to be accommodated at each Cl atom, consistent with its predominant use of two p orbitals. The detailed interatomic distances and angles therefore differ significantly from those in the analogous chain structure BeMe₂ (p. 128), which is best described in terms of 3-centred "electron-deficient" bonding as the Me groups, leading to a BeCBe angle of 66° and a much closer approach of neighbouring Be atoms (209 pm). In the vapour phase BeCl₂ tends to form a bridged sp² dimer (d) and dissociation to the linear (sp) monomer (e) is not complete below about 900°; in contrast, BeF₂ is monomeric and shows little tendency to dimerize in the gas phase.

The shapes of the monomeric molecules of the Group 2 halides (gas phase or matrix isolation) pose some interesting problems for those who are content with simple theories of bonding and molecular geometry. Thus, as expected on the basis of either sp hybridization or the VSEPR model, the dihalides of Be and Mg and the heavier halides of Ca and Sr are essentially linear. However, the other dihalides are appreciably bent, e.g. CaF₂ ~ 145°, SrF₂ ~ 120°, BaF₂ ~ 108°; SrCl₂ ~ 130°, BaCl₂ ~ 115°; BaBr₂ ~ 115°; BaI₂ ~ 105°. The uncertainties on these bond angles are often quite large (±10°) and the molecules are rather flexible, but there seems little doubt that the equilibrium geometry is substantially non-linear. This has been interpreted in terms of sd (rather than sp) hybridization[16] or by a suitable *ad hoc* modification of the VSEPR theory[17].

The *crystal* structures of the halides of the heavier Group 2 elements also show some interesting trends (Table 5.3). For the fluorides, increasing size of the metal enables its

---

[16] R.L. DeKock, M. A. Peterson, L. A. Timmer, E. J. Baerends and P. Vernooijs, *Polyhedron* **9**, 1919–34 (1990) and references cited therein. D. M. Hassett and C. J. Marsden, *J. Chem. Soc., Chem. Commun.*, 667–9 (1990).

[17] R. J. Gillespie, *Chem. Soc. Revs.* **21**, 59–69 (1992).

Table 5.3 Crystal structures of alkaline earth halides[a]

	Be	Mg	Ca	Sr	Ba
F	Quartz	Rutile(TiO₂)	Fluorite	Fluorite	Fluorite
Cl	Chain	CdCl₂	Deformed TiO₂	Deformed TiO₂	PbCl₂
Br	Chain	CdI₂	Deformed TiO₂	Deformed PbCl₂	PbCl₂
I	—	CdI₂	CdI₂	SrI₂	PbCl₂

[a]For description of these structures see: quartz (p. 342), rutile (p. 961), CdCl₂ (p. 1212), CdI₂ (p. 1212), PbCl₂ (p. 382); the fluorite, BeCl₂-chain and SrI₂ structures are described in this subsection.

coordination number to increase from 4 (Be) to 6 (Mg) and 8 (Ca, Sr, Ba). CaF_2 (fluorite) is a standard crystal structure type and its cubic unit cell is illustrated in Fig. 5.2. The other halides (Cl, Br, I) show an increasing trend away from three-dimensional structures, the Be halides forming chains (as discussed above) and the others tending towards layer-lattice structures such as $CdCl_2$, CdI_2 and PbI_2. SrI_2 is unique in this group in having sevenfold coordination (Fig. 5.3); a similar coordination polyhedron is found in EuI_2, but the way they are interconnected differs in the two compounds.[18]

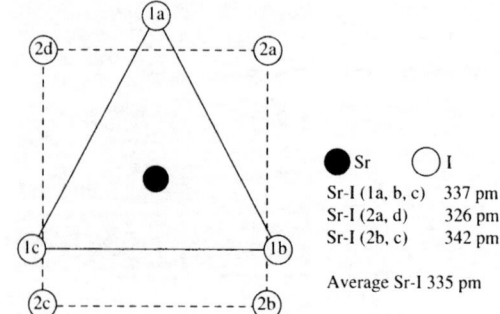

Sr-I (1a, b, c) 337 pm
Sr-I (2a, d)   326 pm
Sr-I (2b, c)   342 pm

Average Sr-I 335 pm

Figure 5.3 Structure of SrI_2 showing sevenfold coordination of Sr by I. The planes 1 and 2 are almost parallel (4.5°) and the planes 1a2a2d and 1b2b2c1c are at an angle of 12° to each other.[9]

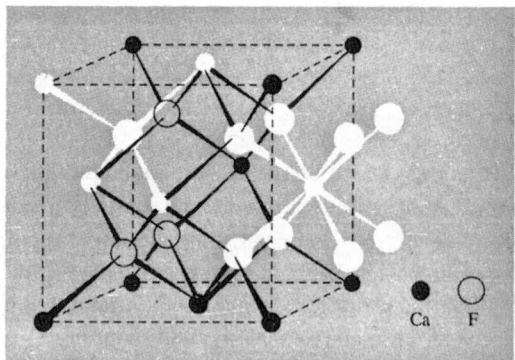

Figure 5.2 Unit cell of CaF_2 showing eightfold (cubic) coordination of Ca by 8F and fourfold (tetrahedral) coordination of F by 4Ca. The structure can be thought of as an fcc array of Ca in which all the tetrahedral interstices are occupied by F.

The most important fluoride of the alkaline earth metals is CaF_2 since this mineral (fluorspar) is the only large-scale source of fluorine (p. 795). Annual world production now exceeds 5 million tonnes the principal suppliers (in 1984) being Mexico (15%), Mongolia (15%), China (14%), USSR (13%) and South Africa (7%). The largest consumer is the USA, though 85% of its needs must be imported. CaF_2 is a white, high-melting (1418°C) solid whose low solubility in water permits quantitative analytical precipitation. The

other fluorides (except BeF_2) are also high-melting and rather insoluble. By contrast, the chlorides tend to be deliquescent and to have much lower mps (715–960°); they readily form numerous hydrates and are soluble in alcohols. $MgCl_2$ is one of the most important salts of Mg industrially (p. 110) and its concentration in sea water is exceeded only by NaCl. $CaCl_2$ is also of great importance, as noted earlier; its production in the US is in the megatonne region and its 1990 price was: bulk $182/tonne, granules $360/tonne, i.e 36 cents/kg. Its traditional uses include:

(a) brine for refrigeration plants (and for filling inflated tires of tractors and earth-moving equipment to increase traction);

(b) control of snow and ice on highways and pavements (side walks) — the $CaCl_2$–H_2O eutectic at 30 wt% $CaCl_2$ melts at −55°C (compared with NaCl–H_2O at −18°C);

(c) dust control on secondary roads, unpaved streets, and highway shoulders;

(d) freeze-proofing of coal and ores in shipping and stock piling;

(e) use in concrete mixes to give quicker initial set, higher early strength, and greater ultimate strength.

The bromides and iodides continue the trends to lower mps and higher solubilities

---

[18] E. T. RIETSCHEL and H. BÄRNIGHAUSEN, *Z. anorg. allg. Chem.* **368**, 62–72 (1969).

in water and their ready solubility in alcohols, ethers, etc., is also notable; indeed, $MgBr_2$ forms numerous crystalline solvates such as $MgBr_2.6ROH$ (R = Me, Et, Pr), $MgBr_2.6Me_2CO$, $MgBr_2.3Et_2O$, in addition to numerous ammines $MgBr_2.nNH_3$ ($n = 2-6$). The ability of Group 2 cations to form coordination complexes is clearly greater than that of Group 1 cations (p. 90).

Alkaline earth salts MHX, where M = Ca, Sr or Ba and X = Cl, Br or I can be prepared by fusing the hydride MH_2 with the appropriate halide MX_2 or by heating $M + MX_2$ in an atmosphere of H_2 at 900°. These hydride halides appear to have the PbClF layer lattice structure though the H atoms were not directly located. The analogous compounds of Mg have proved more elusive and the preceding preparative routes merely yield physical mixtures. However, MgClH and MgBrH can be prepared as solvated dimers by the reaction of specially activated MgH_2 with MgX_2 in thf:

$$MgR_2 + LiAlH_4 \xrightarrow{Et_2O} MgH_2 + LiAlH_2R_2$$

$$MgH_2 + MgX_2 \xrightarrow{thf} [HMgX(thf)]_2$$

The chloride can be crystallized but the bromide disproportionates. On the basis of mol wt and infrared spectroscopic evidence the proposed structure is:

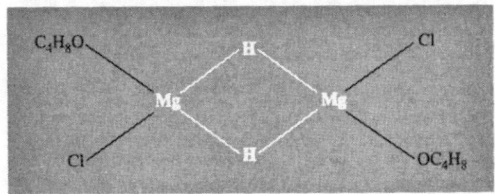

5.3.3 Oxides and hydroxides [19,20]

The oxides MO are best obtained by calcining the carbonates (pp. 114 and 122); dehydration of the hydroxides at red heat offers an alternative route. BeO (like the other Be chalcogenides)

has the wurtzite structure (p. 1210) and is an excellent refractory, combining a high mp (2507°C) with negligible vapour pressure below this temperature; it has good chemical stability and a very high thermal conductivity which is greater than that of any other non-metal and even exceeds that of some metals. The other oxides in the group all have the NaCl structure and this structure is also adopted by the chalcogenides (except MgTe which has the wurtzite structure). Lattice energies and mps are again very high: MgO mp 2832°, CaO 2627°, SrO 2665°, BaO 1913°C (all ± ca. 30°). The compounds are comparatively unreactive in bulk but their reactivity increases markedly with decrease in particle size and increase in atomic weight. Notable reactions (which reverse those used to prepare the oxides) are with CO_2 and with H_2O. MgO is extensively used as a refractory: like BeO it is unusual in being both an excellent thermal conductor and a good electrical insulator, thus finding widespread use as the insulating radiator in domestic heating ranges and similar appliances. CaO (lime) is produced on an enormous scale in many countries and, indeed, is one of the half-dozen largest tonnage industrial chemicals to be manufactured (see Panel on p. 120). Production in 1991 exceeded 16 million tonnes in the USA alone. Its major end uses (in descending tonnages) are as a flux in steel manufacture; in the production of Ca chemicals; in the treatment of municipal water supplies, industrial wastes and sewage; in mortars and cements; in the pulp and paper industries; and in non-ferrous metal production. Price for bulk quantities is ∼$45 per tonne.

In addition to the oxides MO, peroxides MO_2 are known for the heavier alkaline earth metals and there is some evidence for yellow superoxides $M(O_2)_2$ of Ca, Sr and Ba; impure ozonides $Ca(O_3)_2$ and $Ba(O_3)_2$ have also been reported.[21] As with the alkali metals, stability

[19] D. A. EVEREST, Beryllium, *Comprehensive Inorganic Chemistry* Vol. 1, pp. 531–90 Pergamon Press, Oxford (1973).

[20] R. D. GOODENOUGH and V. A. STENGER, Magnesium, calcium, strontium, barium and radium, *Comprehensive Inorganic Chemistry*, Vol. 1, pp. 591–664 (1973).

[21] N.-G. VANNERBERG, *Prog. Inorg. Chem.* **4**, 125–97 (1962).

Industrial Uses of Limestone and Lime

Limestone rock is the commonest form of calcium carbonate, which also occurs as chalk, marble, corals, calcite, aragonite, etc., and (with Mg) as dolomite. Limestone and dolomite are widely used as building materials and road aggregate and both are quarried on a vast scale worldwide. $CaCO_3$ is also a major industrial chemical and is indispensable as the precursor of quick lime (CaO) and slaked lime, $Ca(OH)_2$. These chemicals are crucial to large sections of the chemical, metallurgical and construction industries, as noted below, and are produced on a scale exceeded by very few other materials.[22] Thus, world production of lime exceeds 110 million tonnes, and even this is dwarfed by Portland cement (793 million tonnes in 1984) which is made by roasting limestone and sand with clay (p. 252).

Large quantities of lime are consumed in the steel industry where it is used as a flux to remove P, S, Si and to a lesser extent Mn. The basic oxygen steel process typically uses 75 kg lime per tonne of steel, or a rather larger quantity (100–300 kg) of dolomitic quick lime, which markedly extends the life of the refractory furnace linings. Lime is also used as a lubricant in steel wire drawing and in neutralizing waste sulfuric-acid-based pickling liquors. Another metallurgical application is in the production of Mg (p. 110): the ferro-silicon (Pidgeon) process (1) uses dolomitic lime and both of the Dow electrolytic methods (2), (3), also require lime.

$$2(CaO.MgO) + Si/Fe \longrightarrow 2Mg + Ca_2SiO_4/Fe \tag{1}$$

$$CaO.MgO + CaCl_2.MgCl_2\,(\text{brine}) + CO_2 \longrightarrow 2CaCO_3 + 2MgCl_2 \text{ (then electrolysis)} \tag{2}$$

$$\left. \begin{array}{l} Ca(OH)_2 + MgCl_2\,(\text{seawater}) \longrightarrow Mg(OH)_2 + CaCl_2 \\[2mm] Mg(OH)_2 + 2HCl \longrightarrow 2H_2O + MgCl_2 \text{ (then electrolysis)} \end{array} \right\} \tag{3}$$

Lime is the largest tonnage chemical used in the treatment of potable and industrial water supplies. In conjunction with alum or iron salts it is used to coagulate suspended solids and remove turbidity. It is also used in water softening to remove temporary (bicarbonate) hardness. Typical reactions are:

$$Ca(HCO_3)_2 + Ca(OH)_2 \longrightarrow 2CaCO_3\downarrow + 2H_2O$$

$$Mg(HCO_3)_2 + Ca(OH)_2 \longrightarrow MgCO_3\downarrow + CaCO_3\downarrow + 2H_2O$$

$$MgCO_3 + Ca(OH)_2 \longrightarrow Mg(OH)_2\downarrow + CaCO_3\downarrow \text{ etc.}$$

The neutralization of acid waters (and industrial wastes) and the maintenance of optimum pH for the biological oxidation of sewage are further applications. Another major use of lime is in scrubbers to remove SO_2/H_2S from stack gases of fossil-fuel-powered generating stations and metallurgical smelters.

The chemical industry uses lime in the manufacture of calcium carbide (for acetylene, p. 297), cyanamide (p. 323), and numerous other chemicals. Glass manufacturing is also a major consumer, most common glasses having ~12% CaO in their formulation. The insecticide calcium arsenate, obtained by neutralizing arsenic acid with lime, is much used for controlling the cotton boll weevil, codling moth, tobacco worm, and Colorado potato beetle. Lime-sulfur sprays and Bordeaux mixtures [$(CuSO_4/Ca(OH)_2)$] are important fungicides.

The paper and pulp industries consume large quantities of $Ca(OH)_2$ and precipitated (as distinct from naturally occurring) $CaCO_3$. The largest application of lime in pulp manufacture is as a causticizing agent in sulfate (kraft) plants (p. 89). Here the waste Na_2CO_3 solution is reacted with lime to regenerate the caustic soda used in the process:

$$Na_2CO_3 + CaO + H_2O \longrightarrow CaCO_3 + 2NaOH$$

About 95% of the $CaCO_3$ mud is dried and recalcined in rotary kilns to recover the CaO. Calcium hypochlorite bleaching liquor (p. 860) for paper pulp is obtained by reacting lime and Cl_2.

The manufacture of high quality paper involves the extensive use of specially precipitated $CaCO_3$. This is formed by calcining limestone and collecting the CO_2 and CaO separately; the latter is then hydrated and recarbonated to give the desired product. The type of crystals obtained, as well as their size and habit, depend on the temperature, pH, rate of mixing, concentration and presence of additives. The fine crystals ($<45\,\mu$m) are often subsequently coated with fatty acids, resins and wetting agents to improve their flow properties. US prices (1991) range from 5–45 cents per kg depending on grade and the amounts consumed are immense, e.g. 5.9 million tonnes p.a. in the USA alone. $CaCO_3$ adds brightness, opacity, ink receptivity and smoothness to paper and, in higher concentration, counteracts the high gloss produced by kaolin additives and produces a matte or dull finish which is particularly popular for textbooks. Such papers may contain 5–50% by weight of precipitated $CaCO_3$. The compound is also used as a filler in rubbers, latex, wallpaints and enamels, and in plastics (~10% by weight) to improve their heat resistance, dimensional stability, stiffness, hardness and processability.

Panel continues

---

[22] R. S. BOYNTON, *Chemistry and Technology of Lime and Limestone*, 2nd edn., Wiley, Chichester, 1980, 579 pp.

Domestic and pharmaceutical uses of precipitated $CaCO_3$ include its direct use as an antacid, a mild abrasive in toothpastes, a source of Ca enrichment in diets, a constituent of chewing gum and a filler in cosmetics.

In the dairy industry lime finds many uses. Lime water is often added to cream when separated from whole milk, in order to reduce its acidity prior to pasteurization and conversion to butter. The skimmed milk is then acidified to separate casein which is mixed with lime to produce calcium caseinate glue. Fermentation of the remaining skimmed milk (whey) followed by addition of lime yields calcium lactate which is used as a medicinal or to produce lactic acid on reacidification. Likewise the sugar industry relies heavily on lime: the crude sugar juice is reacted with lime to precipitate calcium sucrate which permits purification from phosphatic and organic impurities. Subsequent treatment with CO_2 produces insoluble $CaCO_3$ and purified soluble sucrose. The cycle is usually repeated several times; cane sugar normally requires $\sim$3–5 kg lime per tonne but beet sugar requires 100 times this amount i.e. $\sim\frac{1}{4}$ tonne lime per tonne of sugar.

increases with electropositive character and size: no peroxide of Be is known; anhydrous MgO_2 can only be made in liquid NH_3 solution, aqueous reactions leading to various peroxide hydrates; CaO_2 can be obtained by dehydrating $CaO_2.8H_2O$ but not by direct oxidation, whereas SrO_2 can be synthesized directly at high oxygen pressures and BaO_2 forms readily in air at 500°. Reactions with aqueous reagents are as expected, and the compounds can be used as oxidizing agents and bleaches:

$$CaO_2(s) + H_2SO_4(aq) \longrightarrow CaSO_4(s) + H_2O_2(aq)$$

$$Ca(O_2)_2 + H_2SO_4(aq) \longrightarrow CaSO_4(s)$$
$$+ H_2O_2(aq) + O_2(g)$$

MgO_2 has the pyrite structure (p. 680) and the Ca, Sr and Ba analogues have the CaC_2 structure (p. 298).

The hydroxides of Group 2 elements show a smooth gradation in properties, with steadily increasing basicity, solubility, and heats of formation from the corresponding oxide. $Be(OH)_2$ is amphoteric and $Mg(OH)_2$ is a mild base which, as an aqueous suspension (milk of magnesia), is widely used as a digestive antacid. Note that, though mild, $Mg(OH)_2$ will neutralize 1.37 times as much acid as NaOH, weight for weight, and 2.85 times as much as $NaHCO_3$. $Ca(OH)_2$ and $Sr(OH)_2$ are moderately strong to strong bases and $Ba(OH)_2$ approaches the alkali hydroxides in strength.

Beryllium salts rapidly hydrolyse in water to give a series of hydroxo complexes of undetermined structure; the equilibria depend sensitively on initial concentration, pH, temperature, etc., and precipitation begins when the ratio $OH^-/Be^{2+}(aq) > 1$. Addition of further alkali redissolves the precipitate and the properties of the resultant solution are consistent (at least qualitatively) with the presence of isopolyanions of the type $[(HO)_2\{Be(\mu\text{-}OH)_2\}_n Be(OH)_2]^{2-}$. Further addition of alkali progressively depolymerizes this chain anion by hydroxyl addition until ultimately the mononuclear beryllate anion $[Be(OH)_4]^{2-}$ is formed. The analogy with $Zn(OH)_2$ and $Al(OH)_3$ is clear.

The solubility of $Be(OH)_2$ in water is only $\sim 3 \times 10^{-4}\,g\,l^{-1}$ at room temperature, compared with $\sim 3 \times 10^{-2}\,g\,l^{-1}$ for $Mg(OH)_2$ and $\sim 1.3\,g\,l^{-1}$ for $Ca(OH)_2$. Strontium and barium hydroxides have even greater solubilities (8 and 38 g l^{-1} respectively at 20°).

The crystal structures of $M(OH)_2$ also follow group trends.[11] $Be(OH)_2$ crystallizes with 4-coordinate Be in the $Zn(OH)_2$ structure which can be considered as a diamond or cristobalite (SiO_2) lattice distorted by H bonding. $Mg(OH)_2$ (brucite) and $Ca(OH)_2$ have 6-coordinate cations in a CdI_2 layer lattice structure with OH bonds perpendicular to the layers and strong $O-H\cdots O$ bonding between them. Strontium is too large for the CdI_2 structure and $Sr(OH)_2$ features 7-coordinate Sr $(3 + 4)$, the structure being built up of edge-sharing monocapped trigonal prisms with no H bonds. (The monohydrate has bicapped trigonal prismatic coordination about Sr.) The structure of $Ba(OH)_2$ is complex and has not yet been fully determined.

5.3.4 Oxoacid salts and coordination complexes

The chemical trends and geochemical significance of the oxoacid salts of the alkaline earth metals have already been mentioned (p. 109) and the immense industrial importance of the carbonates and sulfates in particular can hardly be over emphasized (see Panel on limestone and lime). A speciality use can also be noted: mother-of-pearl (nacre) is a material composed of thin plates of chalk (in the form of aragonite) stuck together with a protein glue. It is irridescent and highly decorative when polished and, despite being 95% chalk, is very strong.

Calcium sulfate usually occurs as the dihydrate (gypsum) though anhydrite ($CaSO_4$) is also mined. Alabaster is a compact, massive, finegrained form of $CaSO_4.2H_2O$ resembling marble. When gypsum is calcined at 150–165°C it looses approximately three-quarters of its water of crystallization to give the hemihydrate $CaSO_4.\frac{1}{2}H_2O$, also known as plaster of Paris because it was originally obtained from gypsum quarried at Montmartre. Heating at higher temperatures yields various anhydrous forms:

$$CaSO_4.2H_2O \xrightarrow{\sim 150°} CaSO_4.\tfrac{1}{2}H_2O \xrightarrow{\sim 200°}$$

$$\gamma\text{-}CaSO_4 \xrightarrow{\sim 600°} \beta\text{-}CaSO_4 \xrightarrow{\sim 1100°} CaO + SO_3$$

Gypsum, though not mined on the same scale as limestone, is nevertheless still a major industrial mineral. World production in 1990 was 97.7 million tonnes, the major producing countries being the USA (15.2%), Canada (8.4%), Iran (8.2%), China (8.2%), Japan (6.5%), Mexico (6.1%), Thailand (5.9%), France (5.8%) and Spain (5.1%); the remaining 30.6% (30 million tonnes) was distributed between over 20 other countries including the former Soviet Union (4.8%) and the UK (4.1%). A representative price in 1990 was $5.5 per tonne. In the USA about 28% of the gypsum used is uncalcined and most of this is for Portland cement (p. 252) or agricultural purposes. Of calcined gypsum, virtually all (95%) is used for prefabricated products, mainly wall board, and the rest is for industrial and building plasters. The hemihydrate expands slightly (0.2–0.3% linear) on rehydration with water and this is crucial to its use in mouldings and plasters; the expansion can be modified in the range 0.03–1.2% by the use of additives.

Other oxoacid salts and binary compounds are more conveniently discussed under the chemistry of the appropriate non-metals in later chapters.

Beryllium is unique in forming a series of stable, volatile, molecular oxide-carboxylates of general formula $[OBe_4(RCO_2)_6]$, where R = H, Me, Et, Pr, Ph, etc. These white crystalline compounds, of which "basic beryllium acetate" (R = Me) is typical, are readily soluble in organic solvents, including alkanes, but are insoluble in water or the lower alcohols. They are best prepared simply by refluxing the hydroxide or oxide with the carboxylic acid; mixed oxide carboxylates can be prepared by reacting a given compound with another organic acid or acid chloride. The structure (Fig. 5.4) features a central O atom tetrahedrally surrounded by 4 Be. The 6 edges of the tetrahedron so formed are bridged by the 6 acetate groups in such a way that each Be is also tetrahedrally coordinated by 4 oxygens. $[OBe_4(MeCO_2)_6]$ melts at 285° and boils at 330°; it is stable to heat and oxidation except under drastic conditions, is only slowly hydrolysed by hot water, but is decomposed rapidly by mineral acids to give an aqueous solution of the corresponding beryllium salt and free carboxylic acid. The basic nitrate $[OBe_4(NO_3)_6]$ appears to have a similar structure with bridging nitrate groups. The compound is formed by first dissolving $BeCl_2$ in N_2O_4/ethyl-acetate to give the crystalline solvate $[Be(NO_3)_2.2N_2O_4]$; when heated to 50° this gives $Be(NO_3)_2$ which decomposes suddenly at 125°C into N_2O_4 and $[OBe_4(NO_3)_6]$.

In addition to the oxide carboxylates, beryllium forms numerous chelating and bridged complexes with ligands such as the oxalate ion $C_2O_4^{2-}$, alkoxides, β-diketonates and 1,3-diketonates.[20] These almost invariably feature 4-coordinate Be

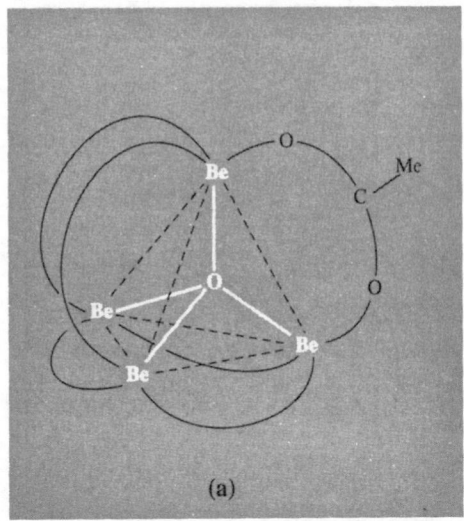
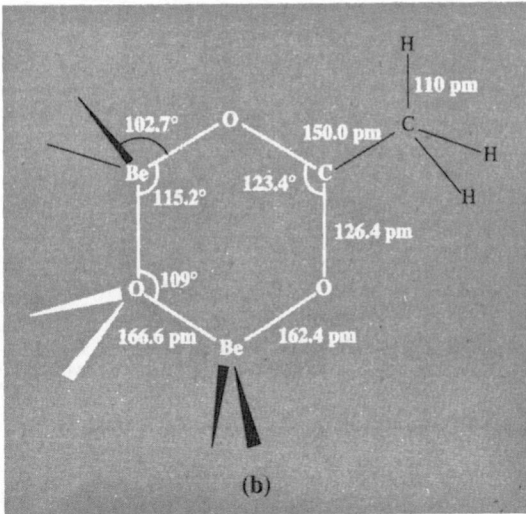

Figure 5.4   The molecular structure of "basic beryllium acetate" showing (a) the regular tetrahedral arrangement of 4 Be about the central oxygen and the octahedral arrangement of the 6 bridging acetate groups, and (b) the detailed dimensions of one of the six non-planar 6-membered heterocycles. (The Be atoms are 24 pm above and below the plane of the acetate group.) The 2 oxygen atoms in each acetate group are equivalent. The central Be–O distances (166.6 pm) are very close to that in BeO itself (165 pm).

though severe steric crowding can reduce the coordination number to 3 or even 2; for example, the very volatile dimeric perfluoroalkoxide (a) was prepared in 1975 and the unique monomeric bis(2,6-di-t-butylphenoxy)beryllium (b) has been known since 1972.

Halide complexes are also well known but complexes with nitrogen-containing ligands are rare. An exception is the blue phthalocyanine complex formed by reaction of Be metal with phthalonitrile, $1,2-C_6H_4(CN)_2$, and this affords an unusual example of planar 4-coordinate Be (Fig. 5.5). The complex readily picks up two molecules of H_2O to form an extremely stable dihydrate, perhaps by dislodging 2 adjacent Be–N bonds and forming 2 Be–O bonds at the preferred tetrahedral angle above and below the plane of the macrocycle.

Magnesium forms few halide complexes of the type MX_4^{2-}, though $[NEt_4]_2[MgCl_4]$ has been reported; examples of $MX_n^{(n-2)-}$ for the heavier alkaline earths are lacking, though hydrates and

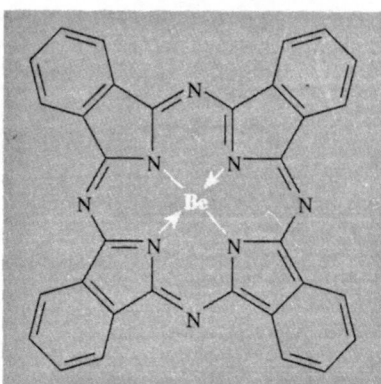

Figure 5.5   The beryllium phthalocyanine complex.

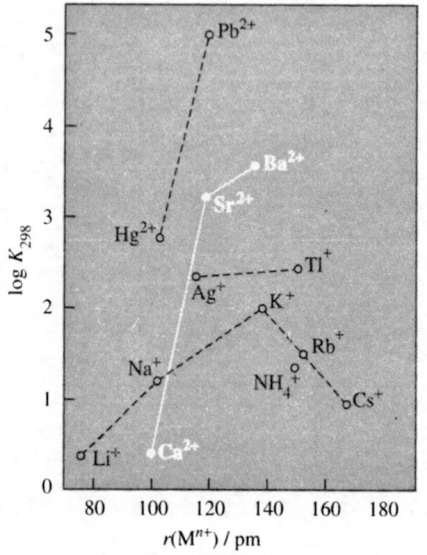

Figure 5.6   Formation constants K for complexes of dicyclohexyl-18-crown-6 ether with various cations. Note that, although the radii of Ca^{2+}, Na^+ and Hg^{2+} are very similar, the ratio of the formation constants is 1:6.3:225. Again, K^+ and Ba^{2+} have similar radii but the ratio of K is 1:35 in the reverse direction (note log scale).

other solvates are well known. The first examples of monomeric six-coordinate (octahedral) complexes of strontium salts have recently been characterized, viz. *trans*-$[SrI_2(hmpa)_4]$ and *cis*-$[Sr(NCS)_2(hmpa)_4]$ where hmpa is $(Me_2N)_3PO$; they were made as colourless crystals by refluxing a mixture of NH_4I (or NH_4SCN) with metallic Sr and hmpa in toluene for 1 hour.[23]

Oxygen chelates such as those of edta and polyphosphates are of importance in analytical chemistry and in removing Ca ions from hard water. There is no unique sequence of stabilities since these depend sensitively on a variety of factors: where geometrical considerations are not important the smaller ions tend to form the stronger complexes but in polydentate macrocycles steric factors can be crucial. Thus dicyclohexyl-18-crown-6 (p. 96) forms much stronger complexes with Sr and Ba than with Ca (or the alkali metals) as shown in Fig. 5.6.[24] Structural data are also available and an example of a solvated 8-coordinate Ca complex $[(benzo-15-crown-5)-Ca(NCS)_2.MeOH]$ is shown in Fig. 5.7. The coordination polyhedron is not regular: Ca lies above the mean plane of the 5 ether oxygens

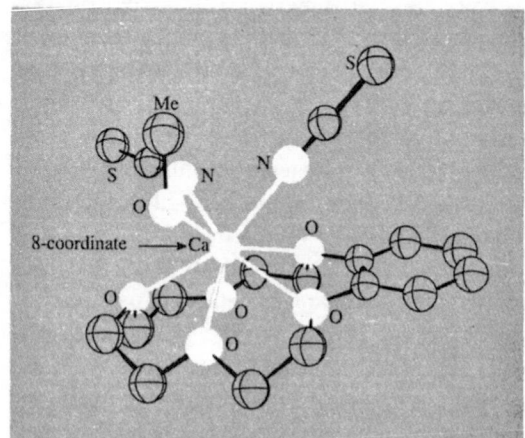

Figure 5.7   Molecular structure of benzo-15-crown-5-$Ca(NCS)_2.MeOH$.

(mean Ca–O 253 pm) and is coordinated on the other side by a methanol molecule (Ca–O 239 pm) and two non-equivalent isothiocyanate

[23] D. BARR, A. T. BROOKER, M. J. DOYLE, S. R. DRAKE, P. R. RAITHBY, R. SNAITH and D. S. WRIGHT, *J. Chem. Soc., Chem. Commun.*, 893–5 (1989).

[24] See refs. 38 and 66 of Chapter 4.

groups (Ca–N 244 pm) which make angles Ca–N–CS of 153° and 172° respectively.[25] Cryptates (pp. 97–8) are also known and usually follow the stability sequence Mg < Ca < Sr < Ba.[24] The first monomeric barium alkoxides, $[Ba\{O(CH_2CH_2O)_nMe\}_2]$ ($n = 2$, 3), which incorporate coordinating polyether functions, were isolated in 1991; the compounds, which are unusual in being liquids at room temperature and which feature 6- and 8-coordinate Ba, respectively, were made by direct reaction of Ba metal with the oligoether alcohols in thf.[26]

Preeminent in importance among the macrocyclic complexes of Group 2 elements are the chlorophylls, which are modified porphyrin complexes of Mg. These compounds are vital to the process of photosynthesis in green plants (see Panel). Magnesium and Ca are also intimately involved in biochemical processes in animals: Mg ions are required to trigger phosphate transfer enzymes, for nerve impulse transmissions and carbohydrate metabolism; Mg ions are also involved in muscle action, which is triggered by Ca ions. Ca is required for the formation of bones and teeth, maintaining heart rhythm, and in blood clotting.[27a–f]

---

[25] J. D. OWEN and J. N. WINGFIELD, *J. Chem. Soc., Chem. Commun.*, 318–9 (1976).

[26] W. S. REES and D. A. MORENO, *J. Chem. Soc., Chem. Commun.*, 1759–60 (1991).

[27a] W. E. C. WACKER, *Magnesium and Man*, Harvard University Press, London, 1980.

[27b] M. N. HUGHES, *The Inorganic Chemistry of Biological Processes*, Wiley, London, 1972, Chap. 8, pp. 256–82.

[27c] G. L. EICHHORN (ed.), *Inorganic Biochemistry*, Elsevier, Amsterdam, 1973, 2 Vols., 1263 pp.

[27d] B. S. COOPERMAN, Chap. 2 in H. SIGAL (ed.), *Metal Ions in Biological Systems*, Vol. 5, Dekker, New York, 1976, pp. 80–125.

[27e] K. S. RAJAN, R. W. COLBURN and J. M. DAVIS, Chap. 5 in H. SIGAL (ed.), *Metal Ions in Biological Systems*, Vol. 6, Dekker, New York, 1976, pp. 292–321. Also F. N. BRIGGS and R. J. SOLARO, Chap. 6, pp. 324–98 in the same volume.

[27f] H. SCHEER, *Chlorophylls*, CRC Press, Boca Raton, 1991.

[28] M. CALVIN, The path of carbon in photosynthesis, *Nobel Lectures in Chemistry 1942–62*, Elsevier, Amsterdam, 1964, 618–44.

Chlorophylls and Photosynthesis

Photosynthesis is the process by which green plants convert atmospheric CO_2 into carbohydrates such as glucose. The overall chemical change can be expressed as

$$6CO_2 + 6H_2O \xrightarrow{h\nu} C_6H_{12}O_6 + 6O_2$$

though this is a gross and somewhat misleading over-simplification. The process is initiated in the photoreceptors of the green magnesium-containing pigments which have the generic name chlorophyll (Greek: χλωρός, *chloros* green; φύλλον, *phyllon* leaf), but many of the subsequent steps can proceed in the dark. The overall process is endothermic ($\Delta H^\circ \sim 469$ kJ per mole of CO_2) and involves more than one type of chlorophyll. It also involves a manganese complex of unknown composition, various iron-containing cytochromes and ferredoxin (p. 1102), and a copper containing plastocyanin.

Photosynthesis is essentially the conversion of radiant electromagnetic energy (light) into chemical energy in the form of adenosine triphosphate (ATP) and reduced nicotinamide adenine dinucleotide phosphate (NADP). This energy eventually permits the fixation of CO_2 into carbohydrates, with the liberation of O_2. As such, the process is the basis for the nutrition of all living things and also provides mankind with fuel (wood, coal, petroleum), fibres (cellulose) and innumerable useful chemical compounds. About 90–95% of the dry weight of crops is derived from the CO_2/H_2O fixed from the air during photosynthesis — only about 5–10% comes from minerals and nitrogen taken from the soil. The detailed sequence of events is still not fully understood but tremendous advances were made from 1948 onwards by use of the then newly available radioactive $^{14}CO_2$ and paper chromatography. With these tools and classical organic chemistry M. Calvin and his group were able to probe the biosynthetic pathways and thus laid the basis for our present understanding of the complex series of reactions. Calvin was awarded the 1961 Nobel Prize in Chemistry "for his research on the carbon dioxide assimilation in plants".[28]

Panel continues

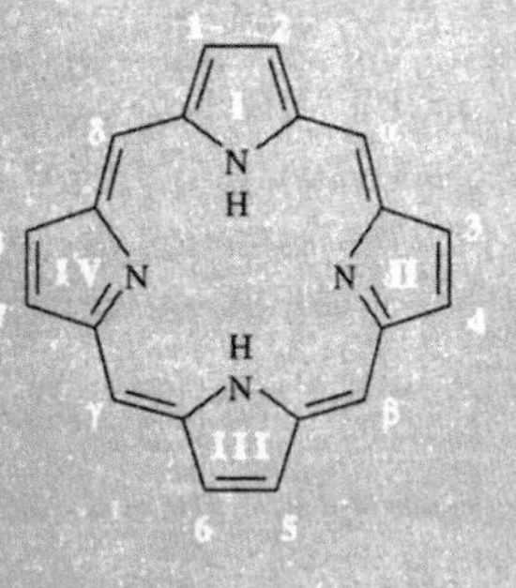

(1) Porphin

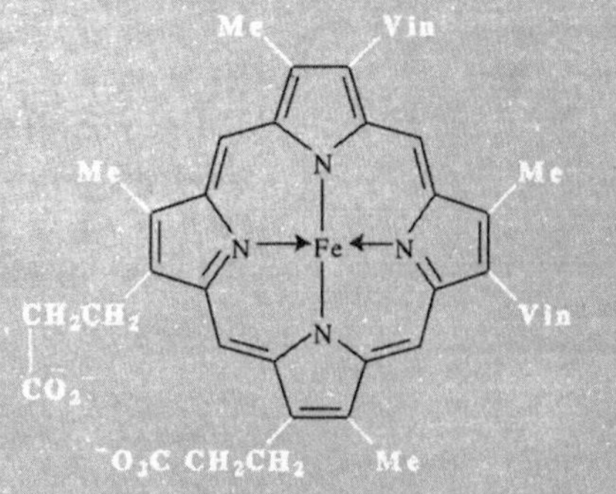

(2) Haem

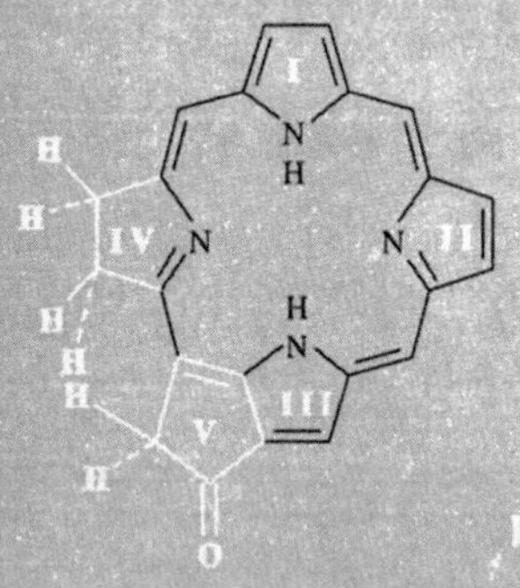

(3) Chlorin

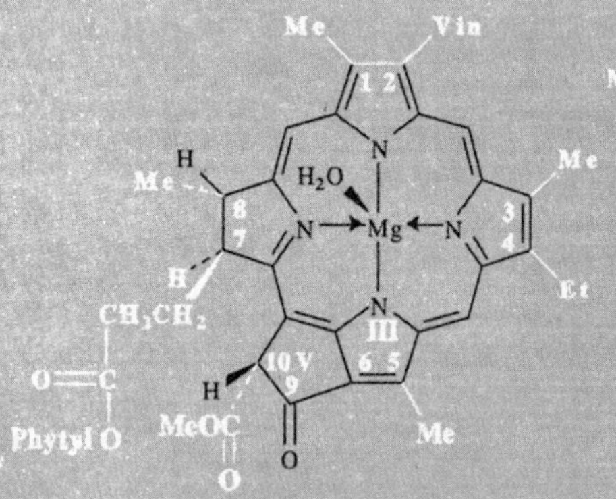

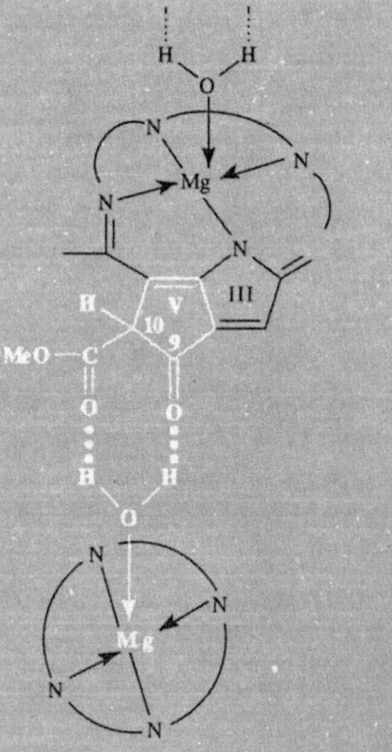

(4) Chlorophyll *a* [the phytyl isoprenoid group is ——CH_2CH=$C(CH_2)_3CH(CH_2)_3CH(CH_2)_3CHMe$]

(5)

Chlorophylls are complexes of Mg with macrocyclic ligands derived from the parent tetrapyrrole molecule porphin (structure 1). They are thus related to the porphyrin (substituted porphin) complexes which occur in haem proteins[†] such as haemoglobin, myoglobin and the cytochromes (p. 1101). [The word haem and the prefix haemo derive directly from the Greek word αἷμα, blood, whereas porphyrins derive their name from the characteristic purple-red coloration which these alkaloids give when acidified (Greek πόρφυρ-ος, *porphyros* purple).] The haem group is illustrated in structure 2. When the C=C double bond in the pyrrole-ring IV of porphin is *trans* hydrogenated and when a cyclopentanone ring is formed between ring III and the adjacent (γ) methine bridge then the chlorin macrocycle (structure 3) is produced, and this is the basis for the various chlorophylls. Chlorophyll *a* (Chl *a*) is shown in structure 4; this is the most common of the chlorophylls and is found in all O_2-evolving organisms. It was synthesized with complete chiral integrity by R. B. Woodward and his group in 1960 — an achievement of remarkable virtuosity. Variants of chlorophyll are:

Chlorophyll *b*, in which the 3-Me group is replaced by –CHO; this occurs in higher plants and green algae, the ratio CHl *b*:Chl *a* being ~1:3.
Chlorophyll *c*, in which position 7 is substituted by acrylic acid, –CH=CHCO$_2$H; it occurs in diatoms and brown algae.
Chlorophyll *d*, in which 2-vinyl is replaced by –CHO.

Panel continues

[†]The first time that these two apparently very different but actually closely related coloured materials, chlorophyll and haemoglobin, were connected was in an extraordinarily percipient poem written in 1612 by the English poet John Donne who mused: Why grass is green or why our blood is red/Are mysteries that none have reached unto.

It is important to note that the chlorin macrocycle is "ruffled" rather than completely planar and the Mg atom is ~30–50 pm above the plane of the 4 N atoms. In fact the Mg is not 4-coordinate but carries one (or sometimes two) other ligands, notably water molecules, which play a crucial role in interconnecting the basic chlorophyll units into stacks by H bonding to the cyclopentanone ring V of an adjacent chlorophyll molecule (see structure 5).

The function of the chlorophyll in the chloroplast is to absorb photons in the red part of the visible spectrum (near 680–700 nm) and to pass this energy of excitation on to other chemical intermediates in the complex reaction scheme. At least two photosystems are involved: the initiating photosystem II (P680) which absorbs at 680 nm and the subsequent photosystem I (P700). The detailed redox processes occurring, and the enzyme-catalysed synthetic pathways (dark reactions) in-so-far as they have yet been elucidated, are described in biochemical texts and fall outside our present scope. The Mg ion apparently serves several purposes: (a) it keeps the macrocycles fairly rigid so that energy is not so readily dissipated by thermal vibrations; (b) it coordinates the H_2O molecules which mediate in the H bonding between adjacent molecules in the stack; and (c) it thereby enhances the rate at which the short-lived singlet excited state formed initially by absorption of a photon by the macrocycle is transformed to the corresponding longer-lived triplet state which is involved in the redox chain (since this involves the H bonded system between several individual chlorophyll units over a distance of some 1500–2000 pm). However, it is by no means clear why, of all metals, Mg is uniquely suited for this purpose.

5.3.5 Organometallic compounds [29–31]

Compounds containing M–C bonds are well established for Be and Mg but, as with the alkali metals, reactivity within the group increases with increasing electropositivity, and relatively few organometallic compounds of Ca, Sr or Ba have been isolated.

Beryllium [30]

Beryllium dialkyls (BeR$_2$, R = Me, Et, Pr^n, Pr^i, Bu^i etc.) can be made by reacting lithium alkyls or Grignard reagents with $BeCl_2$ in ethereal solution, but the products are difficult to free from ether and, when pure compounds rather than solutions are required, a better route is by heating Be metal with the appropriate mercury dialkyl:

$$BeCl_2 + 2LiMe \xrightarrow{Et_2O} BeMe_2.nEt_2O + 2LiCl$$

$$BeCl_2 + 2MeMgCl \xrightarrow{Et_2O} BeMe_2.nEt_2O + 2MgCl_2$$

$$Be + HgMe_2 \xrightarrow{110°} BeMe_2 + Hg$$

BePh$_2$ (mp 245°) can be prepared similarly, using LiPh or HgPh$_2$; an excess of the former reagent yields Li[BePh$_3$]. Beryllium dialkyls are colourless solids or viscous liquids which are spontaneously flammable in air and explosively hydrolysed by water. BeMe$_2$ (like MgMe$_2$, p. 131) has been shown by X-ray analysis to have a chain structure analogous to that found in BeCl$_2$ (p. 116) though the bonding is probably best described in terms of 2-electron 3-centre bridge bonds involving ·CH$_3$ groups rather than that adopted by bridging Cl atoms which each form two 2-electron 2-centre bonds involving a total of 4 electrons per Be–Cl–Be bridge (Fig. 5.8). Each C atom has a coordination number of 5 (cf. bonding in boranes, carbaboranes, etc., p. 157). Higher alkyls are progressively less highly polymerized and the sterically crowded BeBu$^t_2$ is monomeric. As with polymeric BeCl$_2$, addition of strong ligands results in depolymerization and the eventual formation of monomeric adducts, e.g. [BeMe$_2$(PMe$_3$)$_2$], [BeMe$_2$(Me$_2$NCH$_2$CH$_2$NMe$_2$)], etc. Pyrolysis eliminates alkenes and leads to mixed hydrido species of variable composition (see also p. 115).

[29] G. E. COATES, M. L. H. GREEN and K. WADE, *Organometallic Compounds*, Vol. 1, *The Main Group Elements*, 3rd edn., Chap. II, Group II, pp. 71–121, Methuen, London, 1967.

[30] N. A. BELL, Chap. 3, Beryllium in G. WILKINSON, F. G. A. STONE and E. W. ABEL (eds.) *Comprehensive Organometallic Chemistry*, Pergamon Press, Oxford, 1982, pp. 121–53.

[31] W. E. LINDSELL, Chap. 4, Mg, Ca, Sr and Ba, in G. WILKINSON, F. G. A. STONE and E. W. ABEL (eds.) *Comprehensive Organometallic Chemistry*, Pergamon Press, Oxford, 1982, pp. 155–252.

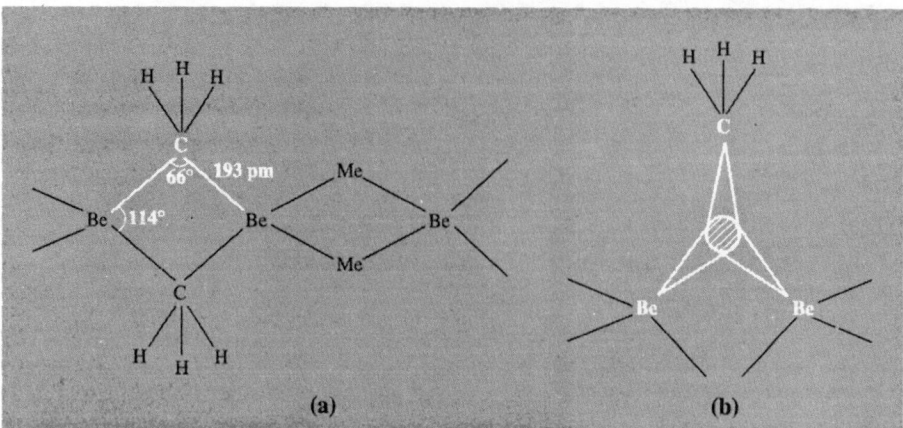

Figure 5.8   (a) Chain structure of BeMe$_2$ showing the acute angle at the bridging methyl group; the Be $\cdots$ Be distance is 209 pm and the distance between the 2 C atoms across the bridge is 315 pm. (b) Pictorial representation of the 3 approximately sp^3 orbitals used to form one 3-centre bridge bond; this description of the bonding is consistent with the acute bridging angle at C and the close approach of adjacent Be atoms noted in (a).

Alkylberyllium hydrides of more precise stoichiometry can be prepared by reducing BeBr$_2$ with LiH in the presence of BeR$_2$, e.g.:

$$\text{BeMe}_2 + \text{BeBr}_2 + 2\text{LiH} \xrightarrow{\text{Et}_2\text{O}}
\begin{array}{ccc}
\text{Me} & \text{H} & \text{OEt}_2 \\
& & \searrow \\
\text{Be} & & \text{Be} \\
\nearrow & & \diagdown \\
\text{Et}_2\text{O} & \text{H} & \text{Me}
\end{array}
+ 2\text{LiBr}$$

The coordinated ether molecules can be replaced by tertiary amines. Use of NaH in the absence of halide produces the related compound Na$_2$[Me$_2$BeH$_2$BeMe$_2$]; the corresponding ethyl derivative crystallizes with 1 mole of Et$_2$O per Na but this can readily be removed under reduced pressure. The crystal structure of the etherate is shown in Fig. 5.9[32] and is important in illustrating once more (cf. p. 103) how misleading it can be to differentiate too sharply between different kinds of bonding in solids, for example: ionic [Na(OEt$_2$)]$_2$$^+$[Et$_2BeH_2$BeEt$_2$]$^{2-}$ or polymeric [Et$_2$ONaHBeEt$_2$]$_n$. Thus in the structure shown in Fig. 5.9 each Be is surrounded tetrahedrally by 2 Et and 2 bridging H to form a subunit

$$\left[
\begin{array}{ccccc}
\text{Et} & & \text{H} & & \text{Et} \\
\diagdown & & & & \diagup \\
& \text{Be} & & \text{Be} & \\
\diagup & & & & \diagdown \\
\text{Et} & & \text{H} & & \text{Et}
\end{array}
\right]$$

In addition, each H is coordinated tetrahedrally by 2 Be and 2 Na, and each Na is directly bonded to 1 Et$_2$O. Be–C is 180 pm and Be–H is 140 pm, close to expected values; Na–H is 240 pm, equal to that in NaH. The distance Na $\cdots$ Na is 362 pm which is less than in Na metal (372 pm) but greater than in NaH (345 pm), where each Na is surrounded by 6H; Be $\cdots$ Be is 220 pm as in Be metal. It is therefore misleading to consider the structure as being built up from the isolated ions [Na(OEt$_2$)]$^+$ and [Et$_2$BeH$_2$BeEt$_2$]$^{2-}$ and it is perhaps better to regard it as a chain polymer [Et$_2$ONaHBeEt$_2$]$_n$ which in plane projection can be written as:

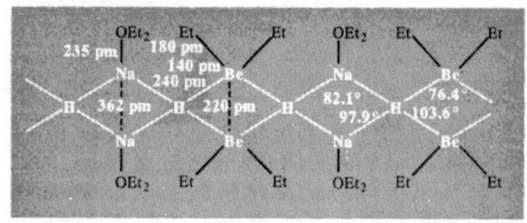

[32] G. W. ADAMSON and H. M. M. SHEARER, *J. Chem. Soc., Chem. Commun.*, 240 (1965).

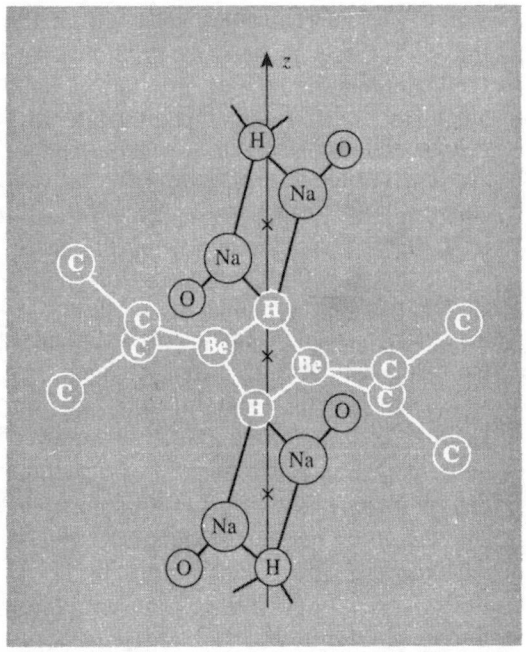
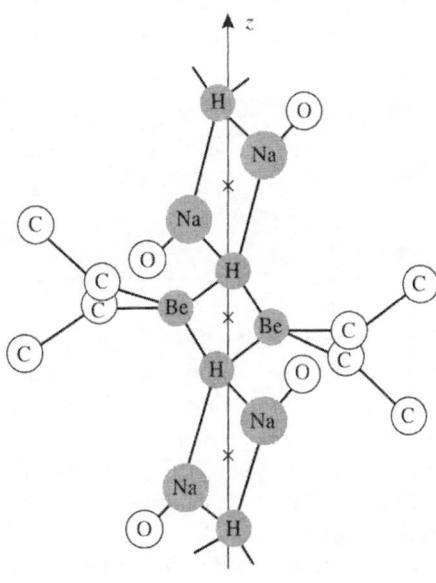

Figure 5.9 Crystal structure of the etherate of polymeric sodium hydridodiethylberyllate $(Et_2ONaHBeEt_2)_n$ emphasizing two features of the structure (see text).

Alkylberyllium alkoxides (RBeOR′) can be prepared from BeR_2 by a variety of routes such as alcoholysis with R′OH, addition to carbonyls, cleavage of peroxides R′OOR′ or redistribution with the appropriate dialkoxide $Be(OR')_2$, e.g.:

$$4BeMe_2 + 4Bu^tOH$$
$$\downarrow -4CH_4$$
$$2BeMe_2 + 2Be(OBu^t)_2 \rightleftharpoons (MeBeOBu^t)_4$$
$$4BeMe_2 + 2Bu^tOOBu^t \qquad 4BeMe_2 + 4Me_2C{=}O$$

Ring opening of ethylene oxide has also been used:

$$4BeMe_2 + 4CH_2{-}CH_2 \longrightarrow (MeBeOPr^n)_4$$
$$\underset{O}{\diagdown\diagup}$$

The compounds are frequently tetrameric and probably have the "cubane-like" structure established for the zinc analogue $(MeZnOMe)_4$. The methylberyllium alkoxides $(MeBeOR')_4$ are reactive, low-melting solids (mp for R′ = Me 25°, Et 30°, Pr^n 40°, Pr^i 136°, Bu^t 93°). Bulky substituents may reduce the degree of oligomerization, e.g. trimeric $(EtBeOCEt_3)_3$, and reaction with coordinating solvents or strong ligands can also lead to depolymerization, e.g. dimeric $(MeBeOBu^t.py)_2$ and monomeric $PhBeOMe.2Et_2O$:

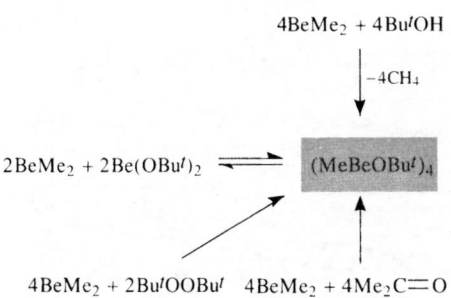

Reaction of beryllium dialkyls with an excess of alcohol yields the alkoxides $Be(OR)_2$. The methoxide and ethoxide are insoluble and probably polymeric, whereas the *t*-butoxide (mp 112°) is readily soluble as a trimer in benzene or hexane; the proposed structure:

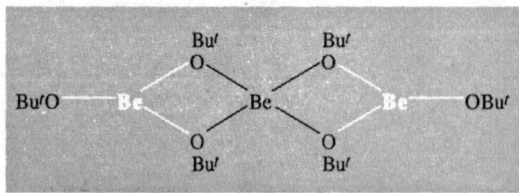

involves both 3- and 4-coordinate Be and is consistent with the observation of 2 proton nmr signals at τ 8.60 and 8.75 with intensities in the ratio 2:1. (A precisely analogous structure has been established by X-ray diffraction analysis for the "isoelectronic" linear trimer [Be(NMe$_2$)$_2$]$_3$.)[33]

Beryllium forms a series of cyclopentadienyl complexes [Be(η^5-C$_5$H$_5$Y] with Y = H, Cl, Br, Me, —C≡CH and BH$_4$, all of which show the expected C_{5v} symmetry (Fig. 5.10a). If the *pentahapto*-cyclopentadienyl group (p. 937) contributes 5 electrons to the bonding, then these are all 8-electron Be complexes consistent with the octet rule for elements of the first short

period.[34] The bis(cyclopentadienyl) compound (mp 59°C), first prepared by E. O. Fischer and H. P. Hofmann in 1959, is also known but does not adopt the ferrocene-type structure (p. 937) presumably because this would require 12 electrons in the valence shell of Be. Instead, the complex has C_s symmetry and is, in fact, [Be(η^1-C$_5$H$_5$)(η^5-C$_5$H$_5$)], as shown in Fig. 5.10b.[35] The σ-bonded Be–C distance is significantly shorter than the five other Be–C distances and there is some alternation of C–C distances in the σ-bonded cyclopentadienyl group. All H atoms are coplanar with the rings except for the one adjacent to the Be–C$_\sigma$ bond. For free molecules in the gas phase it seems unlikely that the two cyclopentadienyl rings are coplanar, and the most recent calculations[36] suggest a dihedral angle between the rings of 117° with Be–C$_\sigma$ 172 pm, Be–C$_\pi$ 187 pm, and the angle Be–C$_\sigma$–H 108°.

[33] J. L. ATWOOD and G. D. STUCKY, *Chem. Comm.* 1967, 1169–70.

[34] E. D. JEMMIS, S. ALEXANDRATOS, P. v. R. SCHLEYER, A. STREITWIESER and H. F. SCHAEFFER, *J. Am. Chem. Soc.* **100**, 5695–700 (1978).

[35] C.-H. WONG, T.-Y. LEE, K.-J. CHAO and S. LEE, *Acta Cryst.* **B28**, 1662–5 (1972); C. WONG, T. Y. LEE, T. J. LEE, T. W. CHANG and C. S. LIU, *Inorg. Nucl. Chem. Lett.* **9**, 667–73 (1973).

[36] D. S. MARYNICK, *J. Am. Chem. Soc.* **99**, 1436–41 (1977). See also J. B. COLLINS and P. v. R. SCHLEYER, *Inorg. Chem.* **16**, 152–5 (1977).

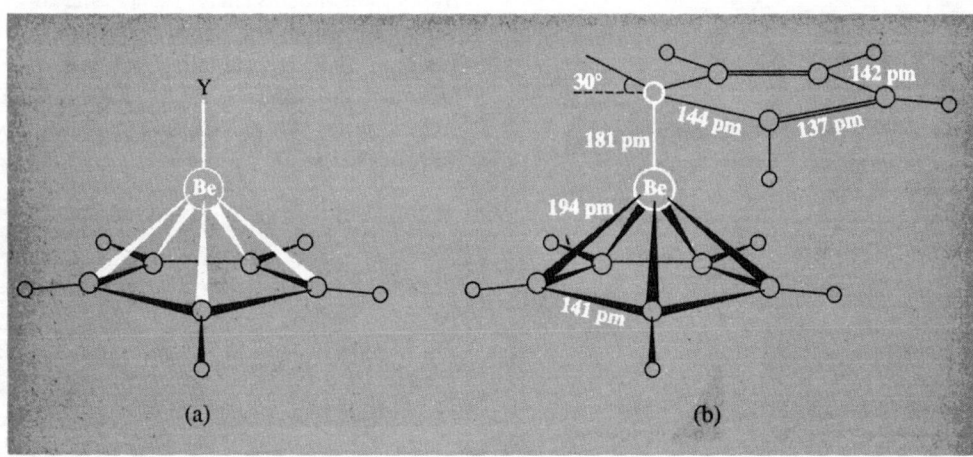

Figure 5.10 Cyclopentadienyl derivatives of beryllium showing (a) the C_{5v} structure of [Be(η^5-C$_5$H$_5$)Y] and (b) the structure of crystalline [Be(η^1-C$_5$H$_5$)(η^5-C$_5$H$_5$)] at $-120°$ (see text).

Pentamethylcyclopentadienyl derivatives are also known, e.g. [$(\eta^5\text{-}C_5Me_5)BeCl$]; this reacts with $LiPBu_2^t$ in Et_2O at $-78°$ to give colourless crystals of [$(\eta^5\text{-}C_5Me_5)BePBu_2^t$] in high yield.[37] Here the dibutylphosphido group is acting as a 1-electron ligand to Be to form a covalent bond of length 208.3 pm almost perpendicular to the C_5 plane: angle $P-Be-C_5$(centroid) 168.3° Interestingly, the $Be-C_5$(centroid) distance (148 pm) is notably shorter than that found in [$(\eta^5\text{-}C_5H_5BeMe)$] (190.7 pm), implying stronger bonding in the pentamethyl derivative. Because the Be nucleus has a spin of 3/2, the $^{31}P\{^1H\}$ nmr signal consists of a 1:1:1:1 quartet with a coupling constant $^1J_{Be-P}$ of 50.0 Hz; this is an order of magnitude greater than for Lewis-base (2-electron) tertiary phosphine adducts of Be.

Magnesium [31]

Magnesium dialkyls and diaryls, though well established, have been relatively little studied by comparison with the vast amount of work which has been published on the Grignard reagents RMgX. The dialkyls (and diaryls) can be conveniently made by the reaction of LiR (LiAr) on Grignard reagents, or by the reaction of HgR_2 ($HgAr_2$) on Mg metal (sometimes in the presence of ether). On an industrial scale, alkenes can be reacted at 100° under pressure with MgH_2 or with Mg in the presence of H_2:

$$LiR + RMgX \xrightarrow{Et_2O} MgR_2 + LiX$$

$$HgR_2 + Mg \xrightarrow{Et_2O} MgR_2 + Hg$$

$$2C_2H_4 + H_2 + Mg \xrightarrow[100°]{pressure} MgEt_2$$

A suitable laboratory method is to shift the Schlenk equilibrium in a Grignard solution (p. 132) by adding dioxan to precipitate the complex MgX_2.diox; this enables MgR_2 to be isolated by careful removal of solvent under reduced pressure:

$$2RMgX \rightleftharpoons MgR_2 + MgX_2 \xrightarrow{C_4H_8O_2} MgR_2 + MgX_2.C_4H_8O_2$$

$MgMe_2$ is a white involatile polymeric solid which is insoluble in hydrocarbons and only slightly soluble in ether. Its structure is very similar to that of $BeMe_2$ (p. 128) the corresponding dimensions for $MgMe_2$ being: $Mg-C$ 224 pm, $Mg-C-Mg$ 75°, $C-Mg-C$ 105°, $Mg\cdots Mg$ 272 pm and $C\cdots C$ (across the bridge) 357 pm. Precisely analogous bridging Me groups are found in dimeric Al_2Me_6 (p. 259) and in the monomeric compound $Mg(AlMe_4)_2$ which can be formed by direct reaction of $MgMe_2$ and Al_2Me_6:

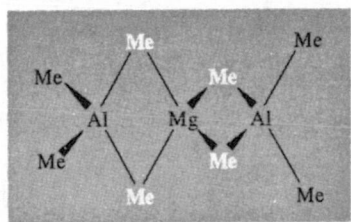

$MgEt_2$ and higher homologues are very similar to $MgMe_2$ except that they decompose at a lower temperature (175–200° instead of ~250°C) to give the corresponding alkene and MgH_2 in a reaction which reverses their preparation. $MgPh_2$ is similar: it is insoluble in benzene dissolves in ether to give the monomeric complex $MgPh_2.2Et_2O$ and pyrolyses at 280° to give Ph_2 and Mg metal. Like $BePh_2$ it reacts with an excess of LiPh to give the colourless complex $Li[MgPh_3]$.

The first organosilylmagnesium compound [$Mg(SiMe_3)_2$].($-CH_2OMe)_2$, was isolated in 1977;[38] it was obtained as colourless, spontaneously flammable crystals by reaction of bis(trimethylsilyl)mercury with Mg powder in

[37] J. L. ATWOOD, S. G. BOTT, R. A. JONES and S. U. KOSCHMIEDER, *J. Chem. Soc., Chem. Commun.,* 692–3 (1990).

[38] L. RÖSCH, *Angew. Chem. Int. Edn. Engl.* **16,** 247–8 (1977).

1,2-dimethoxyethane. More recently[39] the bulkier bis{tris(trimethylsilyl)methyl} derivative, [Mg{C(SiMe$_3$)$_3$}$_2$], was obtained as an unsolvated crystalline monomer; this was the first example of 2-coordinate (linear) Mg in the solid state, though this geometry had been established earlier by electron diffraction in the gas phase for bis(neopentyl)magnesium.[40]

Grignard reagents are the most important organometallic compounds of Mg and are probably the most extensively used of all organometallic reagents because of their easy preparation and synthetic versatility. Despite this, their constitution in solution has been a source of considerable uncertainty until recent times.[41] It now seems well established that solutions of Grignard reagents can contain a variety of chemical species interlinked by mobile equilibria whose position depends critically on at least five factors: (i) the steric and electronic nature of the alkyl (or aryl) group R, (ii) the nature of the halogen X (size, electron-donor power, etc.), (iii) the nature of the solvent (Et$_2$O, thf, benzene, etc.), (iv) the concentration

and (v) the temperature. The species present may also depend on the presence of trace impurities such as H$_2$O or O$_2$. Neglecting solvation in the first instance, the general scheme of equilibria can be set out as shown below. Thus "monomeric" (solvated) RMgX can disproportionate to MgR$_2$ and MgX$_2$ by the Schlenk equilibrium or can dimerize to RMgX$_2$MgR. Both the monomer and the dimer can ionize, and reassociation can give the alternative dimer R$_2$MgX$_2$Mg. Note that only halogen atoms X are involved in the bridging of these species.

Evidence for these species and the associated equilibria comes from a variety of techniques such as vibration spectroscopy, nmr spectroscopy, molecular-weight determinations, radioisotopic exchange using ^{28}Mg, electrical conductivity, etc. In some cases equilibria can be displaced by crystallization or by the addition of complexing agents such as dioxan (p. 131) or NEt$_3$. The crystal structures of several pertinent adducts have recently been determined (Fig. 5.11). None call for special comment except the curious solvated dimer [EtMg$_2$Cl$_3$(OC$_4$H$_8$)$_3$]$_2$ which features both 5-coordinate trigonal bipyramidal and 6-coordinate octahedral Mg groups; note also that, whilst 4 of the Cl atoms each bridge 2 Mg atoms, the remaining 2 Cl atoms are triply bridging.

[39] S. S. Al-Juaid,   C. Eaborn,   P. B. Hitchcock, C. A. McGeary and J. D. Smith, *J. Chem. Soc., Chem. Commun.*, 273–4 (1989).

[40] E. C. Ashby, L. Fernholt, A. Haaland, R. Seip and R. C. Smith, *Acta Chem. Scand., Ser. A* **34**, 213–7 (1980).

[41] E. C. Ashby, *Qt. Rev.* **21**, 259–85 (1967).

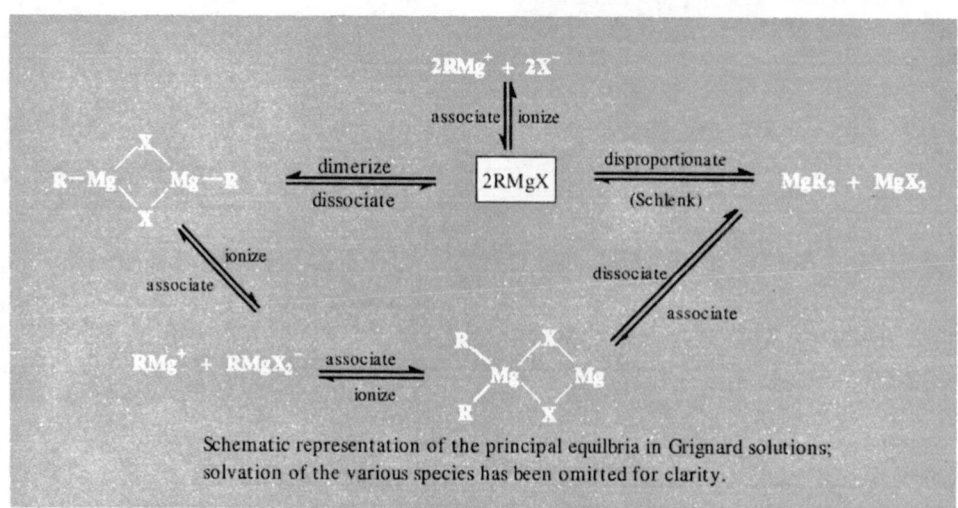

Schematic representation of the principal equilbria in Grignard solutions; solvation of the various species has been omitted for clarity.

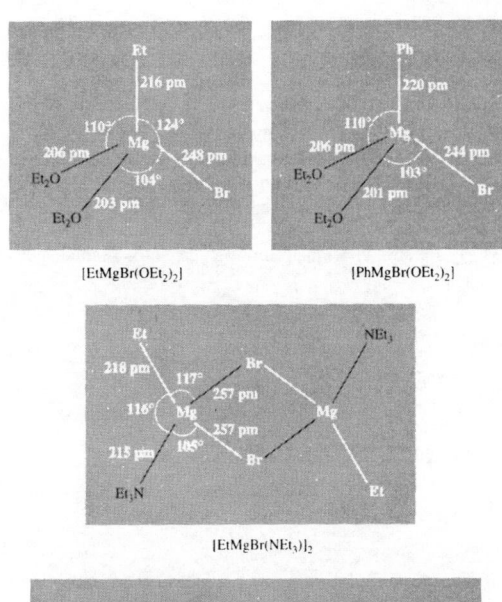

[EtMgBr(OEt$_2$)$_2$] [PhMgBr(OEt$_2$)$_2$]

[EtMgBr(NEt$_3$)]$_2$

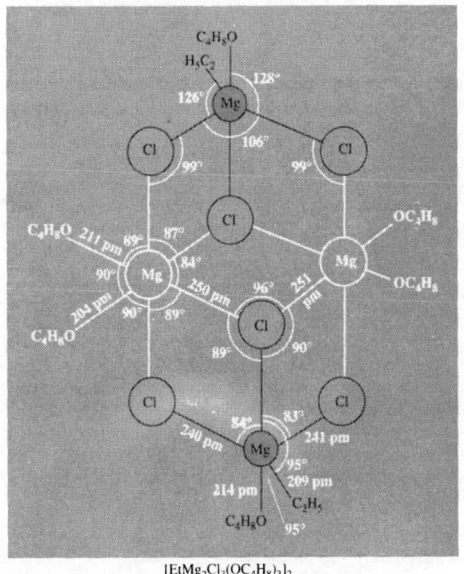

[EtMg$_2$Cl$_3$(OC$_4$H$_8$)$_3$]$_2$

Figure 5.11 Crystal structures of adducts of Grignard reagents.

Grignard reagents are normally prepared by the slow addition of the organic halide to a stirred suspension of magnesium turnings in the appropriate solvent and with rigorous exclusion of air and moisture. The reaction, which usually begins slowly after an induction period, can be initiated by addition of a small crystal of iodine; this penetrates the protective layer of oxide (hydroxide) on the surface of the metal. The order of reactivity of RX is I > Br > Cl and alkyl > aryl. The mechanism has been much studied but is not fully understood.[42] The fluorides RMgF (R = Me, Et, Bu, Ph) can be prepared by reacting MgR$_2$ with mild fluorinating agents such as BF$_3$.OEt$_2$, Bu$_3$SnF or SiF$_4$.[43] The scope of Grignard reagents in syntheses has been greatly extended by a recently developed method for preparing very reactive Mg (by reduction of MgX$_2$ with K in the presence of KI).[44] Grignard reagents have a wide range of application in the synthesis of alcohols, aldehydes, ketones, carboxylic acids, esters and amides, and are probably the most versatile reagents for constructing C–C bonds by carbanion (or occasionally[45] free-radical) mechanisms. Standard Grignard methods are also available for constructing C–N, C–O, C–S (Se, Te) and C–X bonds (see Panel on pp. 134–5).

A related class of compounds are the alkyl-magnesium alkoxides: these can be prepared by reaction of MgR$_2$ with an alcohol or ketone or by reaction of Mg metal with the appropriate alcohol and alkyl chloride in methylcyclohexane solvent, e.g.:

$$4MgEt_2 + 4Bu^iOH \longrightarrow$$
$$(EtMgOBu^i)_4 + 4C_2H_6$$

$$2MgMe_2 + 2Ph_2CO \xrightarrow{Et_2O}$$
$$(MeMgOCMePh_2.Et_2O)_2$$

$$6Mg + 6Bu^nCl + 3Pr^iOH \longrightarrow$$
$$(Bu^nMgOPr^i)_3 + 3MgCl_2 + 3C_4H_{10}$$

[42] H. R. ROGERS, C. L. HILL, Y. FUJIWARA, R. J. ROGERS, H. L. MITCHELL and G. M. WHITESIDES, *J. Am. Chem. Soc.* **102**, 217–26 (1980), and the three following papers, pp. 226–43.

[43] E. C. ASHBY and J. NACKASHI, *J. Organometall. Chem.* **72**, 203–11 (1974).

[44] R. D. RIEKE and S. E. BALES, *J. Am. Chem. Soc.* **96**, 1775–81 (1974).

[45] C. WALLING, *J. Am. Chem. Soc.* **110**, 6846–50 (1988).

Synthetic Uses of Grignard Reagents

Victor Grignard (1871–1935) showed in 1900 that Mg reacts with alkyl halides in dry ether at room temperature to give ether-soluble organomagnesium compounds; the use of these reagents to synthesize acids, alcohols, and hydrocarbons formed the substance of his doctorate thesis at the University of Lyon in 1901, and further studies on the synthetic utility of Grignard reagents won him the Nobel Prize for Chemistry in 1912. The range of applications is now enormous and some indication of the extraordinary versatility of organomagnesium compounds can be gauged from the following brief summary.

Standard procedures convert RMgX into ROH, RCH_2OH, RCH_2CH_2OH and an almost unlimited range of secondary and tertiary alcohols:

$$RMgX + O_2 \longrightarrow ROOMgX \xrightarrow{RMgX} 2ROMgX \xrightarrow{acid} 2ROH$$

$$RMgX + HCHO \longrightarrow RCH_2OMgX \xrightarrow{acid} RCH_2OH$$

$$RMgX + CH_2\underset{O}{\diagdown\diagup}CH_2 \longrightarrow RCH_2CH_2OMgX \xrightarrow{acid} RCH_2CH_2OH$$

$$RMgX + R'CHO \longrightarrow RR'CHOMgX \xrightarrow{acid} RR'CHOH$$

$$RMgX + R'COR'' \longrightarrow RR'R''COMgX \xrightarrow{acid} RR'R''COH$$

Aldehydes and carboxylic acids having 1 C atom more than R, as well as ketones, amides and esters can be prepared similarly, the reaction always proceeding in the direction predicted for potential carbanion attack on the unsaturated C atom:

$$RMgX + HC(OEt)_3 \xrightarrow{acid} RCH(OEt)_2 \xrightarrow{acid} RCHO$$

$$RMgX + CO_2 \longrightarrow RCO_2MgX \xrightarrow{acid} RCO_2H$$

$$RMgX + R'CN \longrightarrow [RR'C{=}NMgX] \xrightarrow{acid} RR'C{=}O$$

$$RMgX + R'NCO \longrightarrow [RCNR'(OMgX)] \xrightarrow{acid} RC(O)NHR'$$

$$RMgX + EtOCOCl \longrightarrow [RC(OEt)Cl(OMgX)] \xrightarrow{acid} RCO_2Et$$

Grignard reagents are rapidly hydrolysed by water or acid to give the parent hydrocarbon, RH, but this reaction is rarely of synthetic importance. Hydrocarbons can also be synthesized by nucleophilic displacement of halide ion from a reactive alkyl halide, e.g.

$$MeMgCl + {\diagup}{\diagdown}C{=}CHCH_2Cl \longrightarrow {\diagup}{\diagdown}C{=}CHCH_2Me + MgCl_2$$

However, other products may be formed simultaneously by a free-radical process, especially in the presence of catalytic amounts of $CoCl_2$ or CuCl:

$$2\ {\diagup}{\diagdown}C{=}CHCH_2Cl \xrightarrow[CoCl_2]{MeMgCl} {\diagup}{\diagdown}C{=}CHCH_2CH_2CH{=}C{\diagdown}{\diagup}$$

$$2\ {\diagup}{\diagdown}C{=}\underset{MgX}{C}{\diagdown}{\diagup} \xrightarrow{CuCl/thf} {\diagup}{\diagdown}C{=}C{\diagdown}{\diagup}\underset{C{=}C}{\diagdown}{\diagdown}{\diagup}$$

Panel continues

Similarly, aromatic Grignard reagents undergo free-radical self-coupling reactions when treated with MCl_2 (M=Cr, Mn, Fe, Co, Ni), e.g.:

$$2PhMgBr + CrCl_2 \longrightarrow 2\text{``MgBrCl''} +$$

$$Ph_2 + Cr \xleftarrow{\ heat\ }$$

Alkenes can be synthesized from aldehydes or ketones using the Grignard reagent derived from CH_2Br_2:

$$CH_2(MgBr)_2 + RR'C{=}O \longrightarrow \left[\begin{array}{c} R \quad OMgBr \\ \diagdown \diagup \\ C \\ \diagup \diagdown \\ R \quad CH_2MgBr \end{array}\right] \longrightarrow RR'C{=}CH_2 + MgO + MgBr_2$$

The formation of C–N bonds can be achieved by using chloramine or *O*-methylhydroxylamine to yield primary amines; aryl diazonium salts yield azo-compounds:

$$RMgX + ClNH_2 \longrightarrow RNH_2 + \text{``MgClX''}$$

$$RMgX + MeONH_2 \longrightarrow RNH_2 + MeOMgX$$

$$RMgX + [ArN_2]X \longrightarrow RN{=}NAr + MgX_2$$

Carbon-oxygen bonds can be made using the synthetically uninteresting conversion of RMgX into ROH (shown as the first reaction listed above); direct acid hydrolysis of the peroxo compound ROOMgX yields the hydroperoxide ROOH. Carbon-sulfur bonds can be constructed using S_8 to make thiols or thioethers, and similar reactions are known for Se and Te:

$$RMgX + S_8 \longrightarrow RS_xMgX \xrightarrow{RMgX} RSMgX$$

$$RSMgX \begin{cases} \xrightarrow{\ acid\ } RSH + MgX_2 \\ \xrightarrow{\ RMgX\ } R_2S + MgX_2 + Mg \\ \xrightarrow{\ R'I\ } RSR' + \text{``MgIX''} \end{cases}$$

Formation of C–X bonds is not normally a problem but the Grignard route can occasionally be useful when normal halogen exchange fails. Thus iodination of Me_3CCH_2Cl cannot be achieved by reaction with NaI or similar reagents but direct iodination of the corresponding Grignard effects a smooth conversion:

$$Me_3CCH_2MgCl + I_2 \longrightarrow Me_3CCH_2I + \text{``MgClI''}$$

Further examples of the ingenious use of Grignard reagents will be found in many books on synthetic organic chemistry and much recent work in this area was reviewed in a special edition of *Bull. Soc. Chim. France*, 1972, 2127–86, which commemorated the centenary of Victor Grignard's birth.

As with the Grignard reagents, the structure and degree of association of the product depend on the bulk of the organic groups, the coordinating ability of the solvent, etc. This is well illustrated by MeMgOR (R = Pr^n, Pr^i, Bu^t, $CMePh_2$) in thf, Et_2O and benzene:[46] the strongly coordinating solvent thf favours solvated dimers (A) but prevents the formation both of oligomers (B) involving the relatively weak Me bridges and of cubane structures (C) involving the relatively weak triply bonding oxygen bridges.

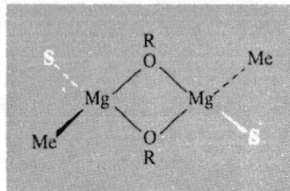

A, solvated dimer

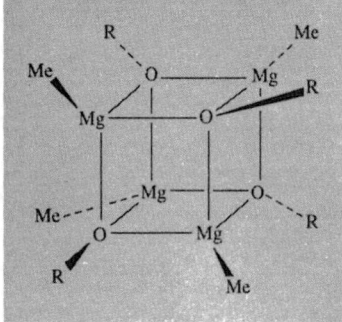

B, linear oligomer (various isomers are possible e.g. involving OR

Mg   Mg bridges, etc.)
         Me

C, cubane tetramer (unsolvated)

By contrast, in the more weakly coordinating solvent Et_2O, Me bridges and μ_3-OR bridges can form, leading to linear oligomers and cubanes, provided OR is not too bulky. Thus when R = $CMePh_2$, oligomerization and cubane formation are blocked and $MeMgOCMePh_2$ exists only as a solvated dimer even in Et_2O. In benzene, R = Bu^t and Pr^i form cubane tetramers but Pr^n can form an oligomer of 7–9 monomer units. The sensitive dependence of the structure of a compound on solvation energy, lattice energy and the relative coordinating abilities of its component atoms and groups will be a recurring theme in many subsequent chapters.

Dicyclopentadienylmagnesium [$Mg(\eta^5\text{-}C_5H_5)_2$], mp 176°, can be made in good yield by direct reaction of Mg and cyclopentadiene at 500–600°; it is very reactive towards air, moisture, CO_2 and CS_2, and reacts with transition-metal halides to give transition-element cyclopentadienyls. It has the staggered (D_{5d}) "sandwich" structure (cf. ferrocene p. 1109) with Mg–C 230 pm and C–C 139 pm;[47] the bonding is thought to be intermediate between ionic and covalent but the actual extent of the charge separation between the central atom and the rings is still being discussed.

Calcium, strontium and barium[31,48]

Organometallic compounds of Ca, Sr and Ba are far more reactive than those of Mg and have been much less studied until recently. For example, although about 50 000 papers have been published on organomagnesium compounds and reagents, less than 1% of this number have appeared for the heavier triad of elements. Many of the differences in reactivity can be traced to the larger radii of the cations (Ca^{2+} 100, Sr^{2+} 118, Ba^{2+} 135 pm) when compared to Mg^{2+} (72 pm) — i.e the lower (charge/size) ratio enhances still further the ionic character of the bonding and thus increases the kinetic lability of the ligands. Coordinative unsaturation also plays a rôle and, indeed, the organometallic behaviour of the heavier alkali metals often resembles

[46] E. C. ASHBY, J. NACKASHI and G. E. PARRIS, *J. Am. Chem. Soc.* **97**, 3162–71 (1975).

[47] W. BÜNDER and E. WEISS, [$Mg(\eta^5\text{-}C_5H_5)_2$], *J. Organometall. Chem.* **92**, 1–6 (1975).

[48] T. P. HANUSA, *Polyhedron* **9**, 1345–62 (1990)

that of the similarly-sized divalent lanthanide elements (Yb^{2+} 102, Eu^{2+} 117, Sm^{2+} 122 pm) rather than that of Mg. In these circumstances it became clear that stability would be enhanced by the use of bulky ligands. Early work showed that the reactive compounds MR$_2$ (M = Ca, Sr, Ba; R = Me, Et, allyl, Ph, PhCH$_2$, etc.) can be prepared using HgR$_2$ under appropriate conditions, often at low temperature. Compounds of the type RCaI (R = Bu, Ph, tolyl) have also been known for some time and can now be isolated as crystals.

Calcium (and Sr) dicyclopentadienyl can be made by direct reaction of the metal with either [Hg(C$_5$H$_5$)$_2$] or with cyclo-C$_5$H$_6$ itself; cyclopentadiene also reacts with CaC$_2$ in liquid NH$_3$ to form [Ca(C$_5$H$_5$)$_2$] and HC≡CH. The barium analogue [Ba(C$_5$H$_5$)$_2$] is best made (though still in small yield) by treating cyclo-C$_5$H$_6$ with BaH$_2$. The structure of [Ca(C$_5$H$_5$)$_2$] is unique.[49] Each Ca is surrounded by 4 planar cyclopentadienyl rings and the overall structure involves a complex sharing of rings which bridge the various Ca atoms. The coordination geometry about a given Ca atom is shown in Fig. 5.12:

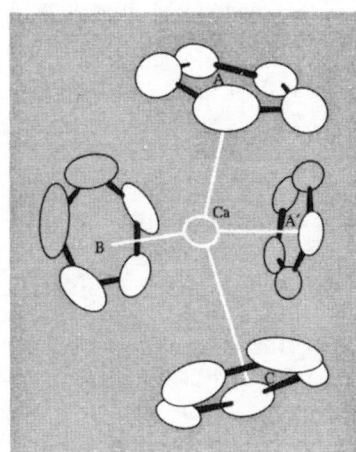

Figure 5.12 Coordination geometry about Ca in polymeric [Ca(C$_5$H$_5$)$_2$] showing 2 × η^5-, η^3- and η^1- bonding (see text).

two of the rings (A, C) are η^5, with all Ca–C distances 275 pm. A third ring (B) is η^3 with one Ca–C distance 270, two at 279, and two longer distances at 295 pm. These three polyhapto rings (A, B, C) are arranged so that their centroids are disposed approximately trigonally about the Ca atom. The fourth ring (A') is η^1, with only 1 Ca–C within bonding distance (310 pm) and this bond is approximately perpendicular to the plane formed by the centroids of the other 3 rings. The structure is the first example in which η^5-, η^3- and η^1-C$_5$H$_5$ groups are all present. Indeed, the structure is even more complex than this implies because of the ring-bridging between adjacent Ca atoms; for example ring A (and A') is simultaneously bonded η^5 to 1 Ca (248 pm from the ring centre) and η^1 to another on the opposite side of the ring, whereas ring C is equally associated in *pentahapto* mode with 2 Ca atoms each 260 pm from the plane of the ring.

Replacement of the ligand C$_5$H$_5$ by the bulkier C$_5$Me$_5$ results in improved solubility, volatility and kinetic stability of the compound, and all three complexes [M(η^5-C$_5$Me$_5$)$_2$] have been prepared in >65% yield by the reaction of NaC$_5$Me$_5$ (or KC$_5$Me$_5$) with the appropriate diiodide, MI$_2$, in diethyl ether or thf, followed by removal of the coordinated ether (or thf) by refluxing the product in toluene. [Ca(C$_5$Me$_5$)$_2$(thf)$_2$] has also been prepared in 48% yield by the reaction of C$_5$HMe$_5$ and Ca(NH$_2$)$_2$ in liquid ammonia. The greater tractability of these complexes enabled the first (gas-phase) molecular structures of organo-Sr and organo-Ba compounds to be determined,[50] and also the first organo-Ba crystal structure.[51] Group comparisons show that the angle subtended by the two C$_5$Me$_5$ ring centroids at the metal atom in the gas phase is almost the same (to within 1 esd) for the three metals (154 ± 4°) but that this drops to 131.0° for crystalline [Ba(C$_5$Me$_5$)$_2$]. A theoretical rationalization for these angles, especially in the gas phase, is not obvious.[48]

[49] R. ZERGER and G. STUCKY, *J. Organometall. Chem.* **80**, 7–17 (1974).

[50] R. A. ANDERSEN, R. BLOM, C. J. BURNS and H. V. VOLDEN, *J. Chem. Soc., Chem. Commun.*, 768–9 (1987).

[51] R. A. WILLIAMS, T. P. HANUSA and J. C. HUFFMAN, *J. Chem. Soc., Chem. Commun.*, 1045–6 (1988).

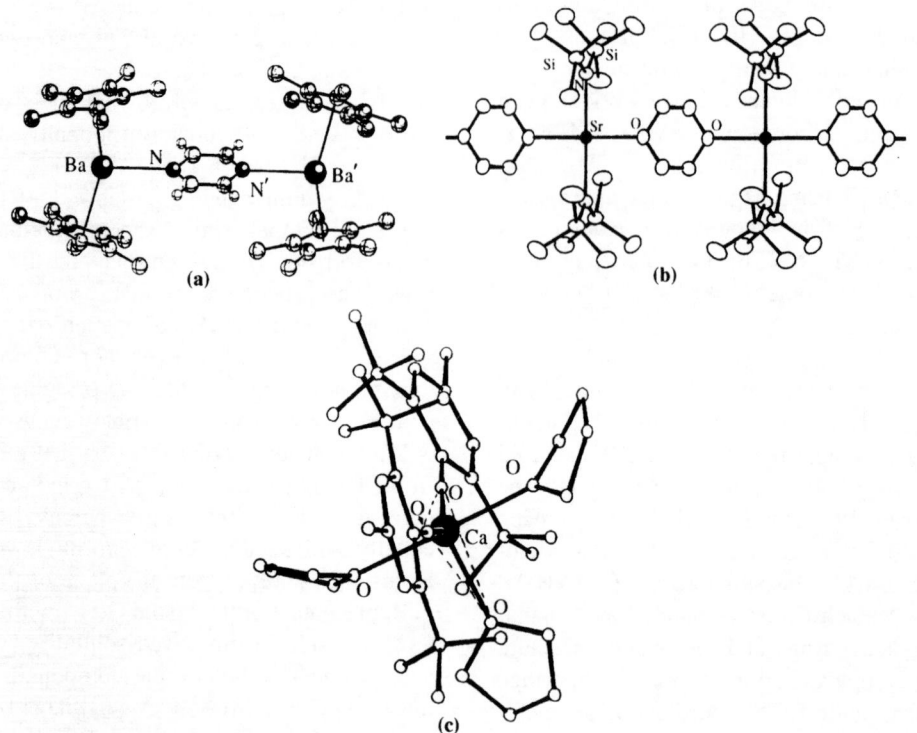

Figure 5.13 (a) Structure of [{Ba(η^5-C$_5$Me$_5$)$_2$}$_2$(μ-1,4-C$_4$H$_4$N$_2$)] in which the pyrazine ligand bridges two bent {BaCp*$_2$} units to give a centrosymmetric adduct with an essentially linear disposition of the four atoms BaNNBa. (b) The polymeric dioxane-bridged structure of [{*trans*-Sr(NR$_2$)$_2$(μ-1,4C$_4$H$_8$O$_2$)}] (R = SiMe$_3$) showing the 4-coordinate square-planar stereochemistry of the Sr atoms. (c) The 5-coordinate trigonal-bipyramidal structure of [Ca(OAr)$_2$(thf)$_3$] (Ar = C$_6$H$_2$-2,6-Bu$^t_2$-4-Me) showing one equatorial and two axial thf ligands.

Attempts to prepare the mono(cyclopentadienyl) derivatives are sometimes frustrated by a Schlenk-type equilibrium (see p. 132), but judicious choice of ligands, solvent etc. occasionally permits the isolation of such compounds, e.g. the centrosymmetric halogen-bridged dimer [{(η^5-C$_5$Me$_5$)Ca(μ-1)(thf)$_2$}$_2$] which crystallizes from toluene solution. The complex is isostructural with the dimeric organosamarium(II) analogue.[52]

Other interesting structures of organometallic and related complexes of the heavier Group 2 metals include those of the centrosymmetric pyrazine adduct [{Ba(η^5-C$_5$Me$_5$)$_2$}$_2$(μ-1,4-C$_4$H$_4$N$_2$)], (Fig. 5.13a)[48], the square-planar Sr complex [{*trans*-Sr(NR$_2$)$_2$(μ-1,4-C$_4$H$_8$O$_2$)}] (R = SiMe$_3$), Fig. 5.13b[53] and the 5-coordinate trigonal-bipyramidal Ca complex [Ca(OAr)$_2$-(thf)$_3$] (Ar = C$_6$H$_2$-2,6-Bu$^t_2$-4-Me), Fig. 5.13c.[54]

52 W. J. EVANS,   J. W. GRATE,   H. W. CHOI,   I. BLOOM, W. E. HUNTER and J. L. ATWOOD, *J. Am. Chem. Soc.* **107**, 941–6 (1985).

53 F. G. N. CLOKE,   P. B. HITCHCOCK,   M. F. LAPPERT, G. A. LAWLESS and B. ROYO, *J. Chem. Soc., Chem. Commun.*, 724–6 (1991).

54 P. B. HITCHCOCK, M. F. LAPPERT, G. A. LAWLESS and B. ROYO, *J. Chem. Soc., Chem. Commun.*, 1141–2 (1990).

1 H																	2 He
3 Li	4 Be											5 B	6 C	7 N	8 O	9 F	10 Ne
11 Na	12 Mg											13 Al	14 Si	15 P	16 S	17 Cl	18 Ar
19 K	20 Ca	21 Sc	22 Ti	23 V	24 Cr	25 Mn	26 Fe	27 Co	28 Ni	29 Cu	30 Zn	31 Ga	32 Ge	33 As	34 Se	35 Br	36 Kr
37 Rb	38 Sr	39 Y	40 Zr	41 Nb	42 Mo	43 Tc	44 Ru	45 Rh	46 Pd	47 Ag	48 Cd	49 In	50 Sn	51 Sb	52 Te	53 I	54 Xe
55 Cs	56 Ba	57 La	72 Hf	73 Ta	74 W	75 Re	76 Os	77 Ir	78 Pt	79 Au	80 Hg	81 Tl	82 Pb	83 Bi	84 Po	85 At	86 Rn
87 Fr	88 Ra	89 Ac	104 Rf	105 Db	106 Sg	107 Bh	108 Hs	109 Mt	110 Uun	111 Uuu	112 Uub						

58 Ce	59 Pr	60 Nd	61 Pm	62 Sm	63 Eu	64 Gd	65 Tb	66 Dy	67 Ho	68 Er	69 Tm	70 Yb	71 Lu
90 Th	91 Pa	92 U	93 Np	94 Pu	95 Am	96 Cm	97 Bk	98 Cf	99 Es	100 Fm	101 Md	102 No	103 Lr

6

Boron

6.1 Introduction

Boron is a unique and exciting element. Over the years it has proved a constant challenge and stimulus not only to preparative chemists and theoreticians, but also to industrial chemists and technologists. It is the only non-metal in Group 13 of the periodic table and shows many similarities to its neighbour, carbon, and its diagonal relative, silicon. Thus, like C and Si, it shows a marked propensity to form covalent, molecular compounds, but it differs sharply from them in having one less valence electron than the number of valence orbitals, a situation sometimes referred to as "electron deficiency". This has a dominant effect on its chemistry.

Borax was known in the ancient world where it was used to prepare glazes and hard (borosilicate) glasses. Sporadic investigations during the eighteenth century led ultimately to the isolation of very impure boron by H. Davy and by J. L. Gay Lussac and L. J. Thénard in 1808, but it was not until 1892 that H. Moissan obtained samples of 95–98% purity by reducing B_2O_3 with Mg. High-purity boron (>99%) is a product of this century, and the various crystalline forms have been obtained only during the last few decades mainly because of the highly refractory nature of the element and its rapid reaction at high temperatures with nitrogen, oxygen and most metals. The name *boron* was proposed by Davy to indicate the source of the element and its similarity to carbon, i.e. *bor*(ax + carb)*on*.

Boron is comparatively unabundant in the universe (p. 14); it occurs to the extent of about 9 ppm in crustal rocks and is therefore rather less abundant than lithium (18 ppm) or lead (13 ppm) but is similar to praseodymium (9.1 ppm) and thorium (8.1 ppm). It occurs almost invariably as borate minerals or as borosilicates. Commercially valuable deposits are rare, but where they do occur, as in California or Turkey, they can be vast (see Panel). Isolated deposits are also worked in the former Soviet Union, Tibet and Argentina.

The structural complexity of borate minerals (p. 205) is surpassed only by that of silicate minerals (p. 347). Even more complex are the structures of the metal borides and the various allotropic modifications of boron itself. These factors, together with the unique structural and bonding problems of the boron hydrides, dictate that boron should be treated in a separate chapter.

Borate Minerals

The world's major deposits of borate minerals occur in areas of former volcanic activity and appear to be associated with the waters from former hot springs. The primary mineral that first crystallized was normally ulexite, $NaCa[B_5O_6(OH)_6].5H_2O$, but this was frequently mixed with lesser amounts of borax, $Na_2[B_4O_5(OH)_4].8H_2O$ (p. 206). Exposure and subsequent weathering (e.g. in the Mojave Desert, California) resulted in leaching by surface waters, leaving a residue of the less-soluble mineral colemanite,$Ca[B_3O_4(OH)_3].H_2O$ (p. 206). The leached (secondary) borax sometimes reaccumulated and sometimes underwent other changes to form other secondary minerals such as the commercially important kernite, $Na_2[B_4O_5(OH)_4].2H_2O$, at Boron, California: This is the world's largest single source of borates and comprises a deposit 6.5 km long, 1.5 km wide and 25–50 m thick containing material that averages 75% of hydrated sodium tetraborates (borax and kernite). World reserves (expressed as B_2O_3 content) exceed 315 million tonnes (Turkey 45%, USA 21%, Kazakhstan 17%, China 8.6%, Argentina 7.3%). Annual world production of borates was 2.67 million tonnes in 1990. Production in Turkey has expanded dramatically in the last two decades and now exceeds that of the USA, the 1990 production figures being 1.20 and 1.09 Mt respectively. Smaller producers (10^3 t) are: "Russia" 175, Chile 132, China 27. Argentina 26 and Peru 18. The 1991 bulk price per tonne of borax in USA was $264 for technical grade and $2222 for refined granules.

The main chemical products produced from these minerals are (a) boron oxides, boric acid and borates, (b) esters of boric acid, (c) refractory boron compounds (borides, etc.), (d) boron halides, (e) boranes and carbaboranes and (f) organoboranes. The main industrial and domestic uses of boron compounds in Europe (USA in parentheses) are:

Heat resistant glasses (e.g. Pyrex), glass wool, fibre glass	26%	(60%)
Detergents, soaps, cleaners and cosmetics	37%	(7%)
Porcelain enamels	16%	(3%)
Synthetic herbicides and fertilizers	2%	(4%)
Miscellaneous (nuclear shielding. metallurgy, corrosion control. leather tanning, flame-proofing, catalysts)	19%	(26%)

The uses in the glass and ceramics industries reflect the diagonal relation between boron and silicon and the similarity of vitreous borate and silicate networks (pp. 203, 206 and 347). In the UK and continental Europe (but not in the USA or Japan) sodium perborate (p. 206) is a major constituent of washing powders since it hydrolyses to H_2O_2 and acts as a bleaching agent in very hot water ($\sim 90°C$); in the USA domestic washing machines rarely operate above 70°, at which temperature perborates are ineffective as bleaches.

Details of other uses of boron compounds are noted at appropriate places in the text.

The general group trends, and a comparison with the chemistry of the metallic elements of Group 13 (Al, Ga, In and Tl), will be deferred until the next chapter.

6.2 Boron[1]

6.2.1 Isolation and purification of the element

There are four main methods of isolating boron from its compounds:

[1] N. N. GREENWOOD, *Boron*, Pergamon Press. Oxford, 1975, 327 pp.; also as Chap. 11 in *Comprehensive Inorganic Chemistry*, Vol. 1, Pergamon Press, Oxford, 1973.

(i) Reduction by metals at high temperature, e.g. the strongly exothermic reaction

$$B_2O_3 + 3Mg \longrightarrow 2B + 3MgO$$

(Moissan boron, 95–98% pure)

Other electropositive elements have been used (e.g. Li, Na, K, Be, Ca, Al, Fe), but the product is generally amorphous and contaminated with refractory impurities such as metal borides. Massive crystalline boron (96%) has been prepared by reacting BCl_3 with zinc in a flow system at 900°C.

(ii) Electrolytic reduction of fused borates or tetrafluoroborates, e.g. KBF_4 in molten KCl/KF at 800°. The process is comparatively cheap but yields only powdered boron of 95% purity.

(iii) Reduction of volatile boron compounds by H_2, e.g. the reaction of $BBr_3 + H_2$ on a heated tantalum metal filament. This method, which was introduced in 1922 and can now be operated on the kilogram scale, is undoubtedly the most effective general preparation for high purity boron (>99.9%). Crystallinity improves with increasing temperature, amorphous products being obtained below 1000°C, α- and β-rhombohedral modifications between 1000–1200° and tetragonal crystals above this. BCl_3 can be substituted for BBr_3 but BI_3 is unsatisfactory because it is expensive and too difficult to purify sufficiently. Free energy calculations indicate that BF_3 would require impracticably high temperatures (>2000°).

(iv) Thermal decomposition of boron hydrides and halides. Boranes decompose to amorphous boron when heated at temperatures up to 900° and crystalline products can be obtained by thermal decomposition of BI_3. Indeed, the first recognized sample of α-rhombohedral B was prepared (in 1960) by decomposition of BI_3 on Ta at 800–1000°, and this is still an excellent exclusive preparation of this allotrope.

6.2.2 Structure of crystalline boron [1-3]

Boron is unique among the elements in the structural complexity of its allotropic modifications; this reflects the variety of ways in which boron seeks to solve the problem of having fewer electrons than atomic orbitals available for bonding. Elements in this situation usually adopt metallic bonding, but the small size and high ionization energies of B (p. 222) result in covalent rather than metallic bonding. The structural unit which dominates the various allotropes of B is the B_{12} icosahedron (Fig. 6.1), and this also occurs in several metal boride structures and in certain boron hydride derivatives. Because of the fivefold rotation symmetry at the individual B atoms, the B_{12} icosahedra pack rather inefficiently and there

[2] V. I. MATKOVICH (ed.), *Boron and Refractory Borides*, Springer-Verlag, Berlin, 1977, 656 pp.

[3] GMELIN, *Handbook of Inorganic Chemistry, Boron, Supplement Vol. 2: Elemental Boron. Boron Carbides*, 1981, 242 pp.

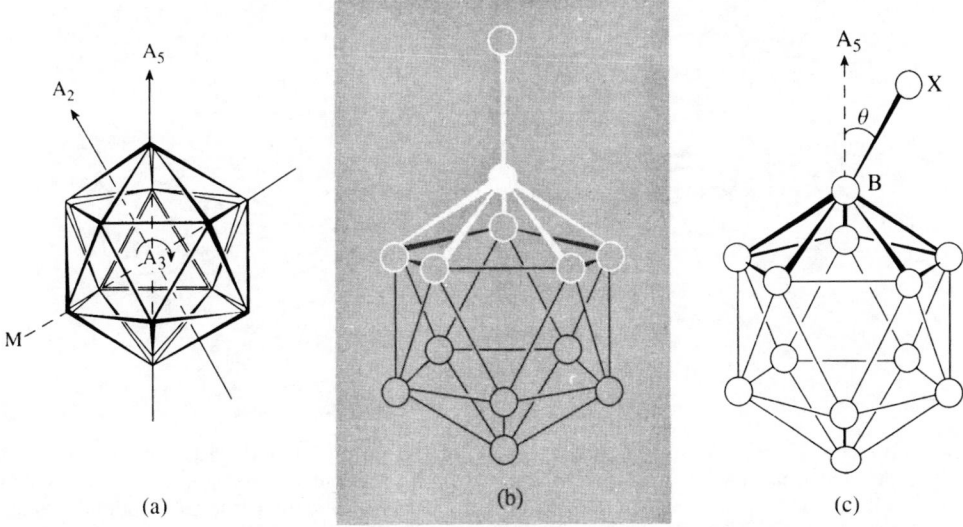

(a)   (b)   (c)

Figure 6.1   The icosahedron and some of its symmetry elements. (a) An icosahedron has 12 vertices and 20 triangular faces defined by 30 edges. (b) The preferred pentagonal pyramidal coordination polyhedron for 6-coordinate boron in icosahedral structures; as it is not possible to generate an infinite three-dimensional lattice on the basis of fivefold symmetry, various distortions, translations and voids occur in the actual crystal structures. (c) The distortion angle θ, which varies from 0° to 25°, for various boron atoms in crystalline boron and metal borides.

are regularly spaced voids which are large enough to accommodate additional boron (or metal) atoms. Even in the densest form of boron, the α-rhombohedral modification, the percentage of space occupied by atoms is only 37% (compared with 74% for closest packing of spheres).

The α-rhombohedral form of boron is the simplest allotropic modification and consists of nearly regular B_{12} icosahedra in slightly deformed cubic close packing. The rhombohedral unit cell (Fig. 6.2) has a_0 505.7 pm, α 58.06° (60° for regular ccp) and contains 12 B atoms. *It is important to remember that in Fig. 6.2, as in most other structural diagrams in this chapter, the lines merely define the geometry of the clusters of boron atoms; they do not usually represent 2-centre 2-electron bonds between pairs of atoms.* In terms of the MO theory to be discussed on p. 157, the 36 valence electrons of each B_{12} unit are distributed as follows: 26 electrons just fill the 13 available bonding MOs within the icosahedron and 6 electrons share with 6 other electrons from 6 neighbouring icosahedra in adjacent planes to

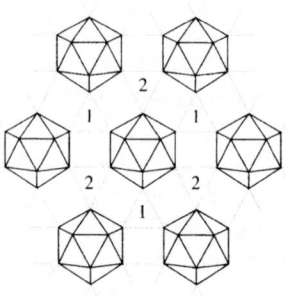

Figure 6.2 Basal plane of α-rhombohedral boron showing close-packed arrangement of B_{12} icosahedra. The B–B distances within each icosahedron vary regularly between 173–179 pm. Dotted lines show the 3-centre bonds between the 6 equatorial boron atoms in each icosahedron to 6 other icosahedra in the same sheet at 202.5 pm. The sheets are stacked so that each icosahedron is bonded by six 2-centre B–B bonds at 171 pm (directed rhombohedrally, 3 above and 3 below the icosahedron). B_{12} units in the layer above are centred over 1 and those in the layer below are centred under 2.

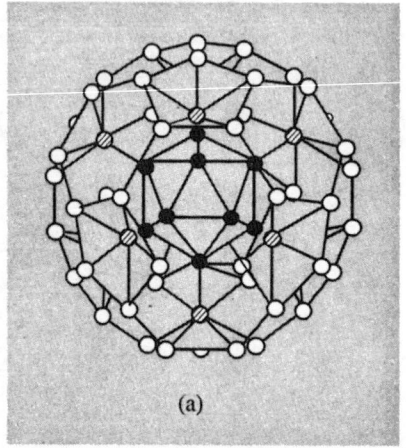

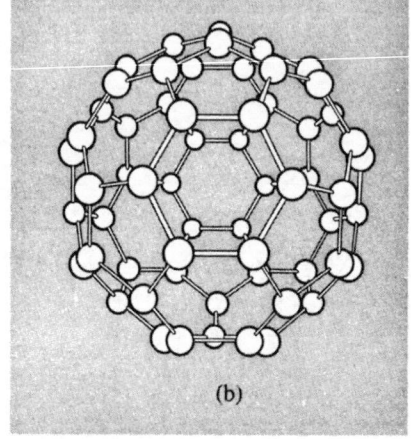

(a)   (b)

Figure 6.3 (a) The B_{84} unit in β-rhombohedral boron comprising a central B_{12} icosahedron and 12 outwardly directed pentagonal pyramids of boron atoms. The 12 outer icosahedra are completed by linking with the B_{10} subunits as described in the text. The central icosahedron (●) is almost exactly regular with B–B 176.7 pm. The shortest B–B distances (162–172 pm) are between the central icosahedron and the apices of the 12 surrounding pentagonal pyramids (⊘). The B–B distances within the $12B_6$ pentagonal pyramids (half-icosahedra) are somewhat longer (185 pm) and the longest B–B distances (188–192 pm) occur within the hexagonal rings surrounding the 3-fold symmetry axes of the B_{84} polyhedron. Note that if the 24 "internal" B atoms (● and ⊘) are removed from the B_{84} unit then a B_{60} unit (b) remains which has precisely the fullerene structure subsequently found some 25 years later for C_{60} (p. 279).

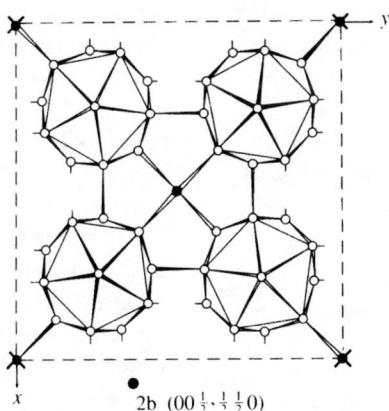

$2b \ (00\tfrac{1}{2}, \tfrac{1}{2}\tfrac{1}{2}0)$

Figure 6.4   Crystal structure of α-tetragonal boron. This was originally thought to be B_{50} ($4B_{12} + 2B$) but is now known to be either $B_{50}C_2$ or $B_{50}N_2$ in which the 2C (or 2N) occupy the 2(b) positions; the remaining 2B are distributed statistically at other "vacant" sites in the lattice. Note that this reformulation solves three problems which attended the description of the α-tetragonal phase as a crystalline modification of pure B:

1. The lattice parameters showed considerable variation from one crystal to another with average values a 875 pm, c 506 pm; this is now thought to arise from variable composition depending on the precise preparative conditions used.
2. The interatomic distances involving the single 4-coordinate atoms at 2(b) were only 160 pm; this is unusually short for B–B but reasonable for B–C or B–N distances.
3. The structure requires 160 valence electrons per unit cell computed as follows: internal bonding within the 4 icosahedra ($4 \times 26 = 104$); external bonds for the 4 icosahedra ($4 \times 12 = 48$); bonds shared by the atoms in 2(b) positions ($2 \times 4 = 8$). However, 50 B atoms have only 150 valence electrons and even with the maximum possible excess of boron in the unit cell (0.75 B) this rises to only 152 electrons. The required extra 8 or 10 electrons are now supplied by 2C or 2N though the detailed description of the bonding is more intricate than this simple numerology implies.

form the 6 rhombohedrally directed normal 2-centre 2-electron bonds; this leaves 4 electrons which is just the number required for contribution to the 6 equatorial 3-centre 2-electron bonds ($6 \times \tfrac{2}{3} = 4$).

The thermodynamically most stable polymorph of boron is the β-rhombohedral modification which has a much more complex structure with 105 B atoms in the unit cell (a_0 1014.5 pm, α 65.28°). The basic unit can be thought of as a central B_{12} icosahedron surrounded by an icosahedron of icosahedra; this can be visualized as 12 of the B_7 units in Fig. 6.1b arranged so that the apex atoms form the central B_{12} surrounded by 12 radially disposed pentagonal dishes to give the B_{84} unit shown in Fig. 6.3a. The 12 half-icosahedra are then completed by means of 2 complicated B_{10} subunits per unit cell,

each comprising a central 9-coordinate B atom surrounded by 9 B atoms in the form of 4 fused pentagonal rings. This arrangement corresponds to 104 B ($84 + 10 + 10$) and there is, finally, a 6-coordinate B atom at the centre of symmetry between 2 adjacent B_{10} condensed units, bringing the total to 105 B atoms in the unit cell.

The first crystalline polymorph of B to be prepared (1943) was termed α-tetragonal boron and was found to have 50 B atoms in the unit cell ($4B_{12} + 2B$) (Fig. 6.4). Paradoxically, however, more recent work (1974) suggests that this phase never forms in the absence of carbon or nitrogen as impurity and that it is, in reality, $B_{50}C_2$ or $B_{50}N_2$ depending on the preparative conditions; yields are increased considerably when the BBr_3/H_2 mixture is purposely doped with a few per cent of CH_4, $CHBr_3$ or N_2. The work illustrates the great difficulties attending preparative and structural studies in this area. The crystal structures of other boron polymorphs, particularly the β-tetragonal phase with 192 B atoms in the unit cell (a 1012, c 1414 pm), are even more complex and have so far defied elucidation despite extensive work by many investigators.[3]

6.2.3 Atomic and physical properties of boron

Boron has 2 stable naturally occurring isotopes and the variability of their concentration (particularly the difference between borates from California (low in ^{10}B) and Turkey (high in ^{10}B) prevents the atomic weight of boron being quoted more precisely than 10.811(7) (p. 17). Each isotope has a nuclear spin (Table 6.1) and this has proved particularly valuable in nmr spectroscopy, especially for ^{11}B.[4] The great difference in neutron absorption cross-section of the 2 isotopes is also notable, and this has led to the development of viable separation processes on an industrial scale. The commercial availability of the separated isotopes has greatly assisted the solution of structural and mechanistic problems in boron chemistry and has led to the development of boron-10 neutron capture therapy for the treatment of certain types of brain tumour (see p. 179).

[4] J. D. KENNEDY, Chap. 8 in J. MASON (ed.), *Multinuclear NMR*, Plenum, New York, pp. 221–58 (1987). T. L. VENABLE, W. C. HUTTON and R. N. GRIMES, *J. Am. Chem. Soc.* **106**, 29–37 (1984). D. REED, *Chem. Soc. Rev.* **22**, 109–16 (1993).

Boron is the fifth element in the periodic table and its ground-state electronic configuration is $[He]2s^2 2p^1$. The first 3 ionization energies are 800.6, 2427.1 and 3659.7 kJ mol^{-1}, all substantially larger than for the other elements in Group 13. (The values for this and other properties of B are compared with those for Al, Ga, In and Tl on p. 222). The electronegativity (p. 25) of B is 2.0, which is close to the values for H (2.1) Si (1.8) and Ge (1.8) but somewhat less than the value for C (2.5). The implied reversal of the polarity of B–H and C–H bonds is an important factor in discussing hydroboration (p. 166) and other reactions.

The determination of precise physical properties for elemental boron is bedevilled by the twin difficulties of complex polymorphism and contamination by irremovable impurities. Boron is an extremely hard refractory solid of high mp, low density and very low electrical conductivity. Crystalline forms are dark red in transmitted light and powdered forms are black. The most stable (β-rhombohedral) modification has mp 2092°C (exceeded only by C among the non-metals), bp ~4000°C, d 2.35 g cm^{-3} (α-rhombohedral form 2.45 g cm^{-3}), $\Delta H_{sublimation}$ 570 kJ per mol of B, electrical conductivity at room temperature 1.5 × 10^{-6} ohm^{-1} cm^{-1}.

6.2.4 Chemical properties

It has been argued[1] that the inorganic chemistry of boron is more diverse and complex than that of any other element in the periodic table. Indeed, it is only during the last three decades that the enormous range of structural types has begun to

Table 6.1 Nuclear properties of boron isotopes

Property	^{10}B	^{11}B
Relative mass ($^{12}C = 12$)	10.012 939	11.009 305
Natural abundance/(%)	19.055–20.316	80.945–79.684
Nuclear spin (parity)	3(+)	$\frac{3}{2}(-)$
Magnetic moment/(nuclear magnetons)[a]	+1.800 63	+2.688 57
Quadrupole moment/barns[b]	+0.074	+0.036
Cross-section for (n,α)/barns[b]	3835($\pm$10)	0.005

[a] 1 nuclear magneton = 5.0505×10^{-27} A m^2 in SI.
[b] 1 barn = 10^{-28} m^2 in SI; the cross-section for natural boron (~20% ^{10}B) is ~767 barns.

be elucidated and the subtle types of bonding appreciated. The chemical nature of boron is influenced primarily by its small size and high ionization energy, and these factors, coupled with the similarity in electronegativity of B, C and H, lead to an extensive and unusual type of covalent (molecular) chemistry. The electronic configuration $2s^2 2p^1$ is reflected in a predominant tervalence, and bond energies involving B are such that there is no tendency to form univalent compounds of the type which increasingly occur in the chemistry of Al, Ga, In and Tl. However, the availability of only 3 electrons to contribute to covalent bonding involving the 4 orbitals s, p_x, p_y and p_z confers a further range of properties on B leading to electron-pair acceptor behaviour (Lewis acidity) and multicentre bonding (p. 157). The high affinity for oxygen is another dominant characteristic which forms the basis of the extensive chemistry of borates and related oxo complexes (p. 203). Finally, the small size of B enables many interstitial alloy-type metal borides to be prepared, and the range of these is considerably extended by the propensity of B to form branched and unbranched chains, planar networks, and three-dimensional arrays of great intrinsic stability which act as host frameworks to house metal atoms in various stoichiometric proportions.

It is thus possible to distinguish five types of boron compound, each having its own chemical systematics which can be rationalized in terms of the type of bonding involved, and each resulting in highly individualistic structures and chemical reactions:

(i) metal borides ranging from M_5B to MB_{66} (or even $MB_{>100}$) (see below);

(ii) boron hydrides and their derivatives including carbaboranes and polyhedral borane-metal complexes (p. 151);

(iii) boron trihalides and their adducts and derivatives (p. 195);

(iv) oxo compounds including polyborates, borosilicates, peroxoborates, etc. (p. 203);

(v) organoboron compounds and B–N compounds (B–N being isoelectronic with C–C) (p. 207).

The chemical reactivity of boron itself obviously depends markedly on the purity, crystallinity, state of subdivision and temperature. Boron reacts with F_2 at room temperature and is superficially attacked by O_2 but is otherwise inert. At higher temperatures boron reacts directly with all the non-metals except H, Ge, Te and the noble gases. It also reacts readily and directly with almost all metals at elevated temperatures, the few exceptions being the heavier members of groups 11–15 (Ag, Au; Cd, Hg; Ga, In, Tl; Sn, Pb; Sb, Bi).

The general chemical inertness of boron at lower temperatures can be gauged by the fact that it resists attack by boiling concentrated aqueous NaOH or by fused NaOH up to 500°, though it is dissolved by fused $Na_2CO_3/NaNO_3$ mixtures at 900°C. A 2:1 mixture of hot concentrated H_2SO_4/HNO_3 is also effective for dissolving elemental boron for analysis but non-oxidizing acids do not react.

6.3 Borides[1-3]

6.3.1 Introduction

The borides comprise a group of over 200 binary compounds which show an amazing diversity of stoichiometries and structural types; e.g. M_5B, M_4B, M_3B, M_5B_2, M_7B_3, M_2B, M_5B_3, M_3B_2, $M_{11}B_8$, MB, $M_{10}B_{11}$, M_3B_4, M_2B_3, M_3B_5, MB_2, M_2B_5, MB_3, MB_4, MB_6, M_2B_{13}, MB_{10}, MB_{12}, MB_{15}, MB_{18} and MB_{66}. There are also numerous nonstoichiometric phases of variable composition and many ternary and more complex phases in which more than one metal combines with boron. The rapid advance in our understanding of these compounds during the past few decades has been based mainly on X-ray diffraction analysis and the work has been stimulated not only by the inherent academic challenge implied by the existence of these unusual compounds but also by the extensive industrial interest generated by their unique combination of desirable physical and chemical properties (see Panel).

Properties and Uses of Borides

Metal-rich borides are extremely hard, chemically inert, involatile, refractory materials with mps and electrical conductivities which often exceed those of the parent metals. Thus the highly conducting diborides of Zr, Hf, Nb and Ta all have mps > 3000°C and TiB_2 (mp 2980°C) has a conductivity 5 times greater than that of Ti metal. Borides are normally prepared as powders but can be fabricated into the desired form by standard techniques of powder metallurgy and ceramic technology. TiB_2, ZrB_2 and CrB_2 find application as turbine blades, combustion chamber liners, rocket nozzles and ablation shields. Ability to withstand attack by molten metals, slags and salts have commended borides or boride-coated metals as high-temperature reactor vessels, vaporizing boats, crucibles, pump impellers and thermocouple sheaths. Inertness to chemical attack' at high temperatures, coupled with excellent electrical conductivity, suggest application as electrodes in industrial processes.

Nuclear applications turn on the very high absorption cross-section of ^{10}B for thermal neutrons (p. 144) and the fact that this property is retained for high-energy neutrons (10^4–10^6 eV) more effectively than for any other nuclide. Another advantage of ^{10}B is that the products of the (n,α) reaction are the stable, non-radioactive elements Li and He. Accordingly, metal borides and boron carbide have been used extensively as neutron shields and control rods since the beginning of the nuclear power industry. More dramatically, following the disaster at Chernobyl in the early hours of 26 April 1986, some 40 tonnes of boron carbide particles were dumped from helicopters onto the stricken reactor to prevent further runaway fission occurring. (In addition there were 800 tonnes of dolomite to provide a CO_2 gas blanket, 1800 t of clay and sand to quench the fires and filter radionuclides, plus 2400 t of lead to absorb heat by melting and to provide a liquid layer that would in time solidify and seal the top of the core of the vault.)

The principal non-nuclear industrial use of boron carbide is as an abrasive grit or powder for polishing or grinding; it is also used on brake and clutch linings. In addition, there is much current interest in its use as light-weight protective armour, and tests have indicated that boron carbide and beryllium borides offer the best choice; applications are in bullet-proof protective clothing and in protective armour for aircraft. More elegantly, boron carbide can now be produced in fibre form by reacting BCl_3/H_2 with carbon yarn at 1600–1900°C:

$$4BCl_3 + 6H_2 + C(fibres) \longrightarrow B_4C(fibres) + 12HCl$$

Fibre curling can be eliminated by heat treatment under tension near the mp, and the resulting fibres have a tensile strength of 3.5×10^5 psi (1 psi = 6895 N m^{-2}) and an elastic modulus of 50×10^6 psi at a density of 2.35 g cm^{-3}; the form was 1 ply, 720 filament yarn with a filament diameter of 11–12 μm. The fibres are inert to hot acid and alkali, resistant to Cl_2 up to 700° and air up to 800°C.

Boron itself has been used for over two decades in filament form in various composites; BCl_3/H_2 is reacted at 1300° on the surface of a continuously moving tungsten fibre 12 μm in diameter. US production capacity is about 20 tonnes pa and the price in about \$800/kg. The primary use so far has been in military aircraft and space shuttles, but boron fibre composites are also being studied as reinforcement materials for commercial aircraft. At the domestic level they are finding increasing application in golf shafts, tennis rackets and bicycle frames.

6.3.2 Preparation and stoichiometry

Eight general methods are available for the synthesis of borides, the first four being appropriate for small-scale laboratory preparations and the remaining four for commercial production on a scale ranging from kilogram amounts to tonne quantities. Because high temperatures are involved and the products are involatile, borides are not easy to prepare pure and subsequent purification is often difficult; precise stoichiometry is also sometimes hard to achieve because of differential volatility or high activation energies. The methods are:

(i) Direct combination of the elements: this is probably the most widely used technique, e.g.

$$Cr + nB \xrightarrow{1150°} CrB_n$$

(ii) Reduction of metal oxide with B (rather wasteful of expensive elemental B), e.g.

$$Sc_2O_3 + 7B \xrightarrow{1800°} 2ScB_2 + 3BO$$

(iii) Co-reduction of volatile mixed halides with H_2 using a metal filament, hot tube or plasma torch, e.g.

$$2TiCl_4 + 4BCl_3 + 10H_2 \xrightarrow{1300°}$$
$$2TiB_2 + 20HCl$$

(iv) Reduction of BCl_3 (or BX_3) with a metal (sometimes assisted by H_2), e.g.

$$nBX_3 + (x + 1)M \longrightarrow$$
$$MB_n + xMX_{3n/x}$$

$$BCl_3 + W \xrightarrow{H_2/1200°} WB + Cl_2 + HCl$$

(v) Electrolytic deposition from fused salts: this is particularly effective for MB_6 (M = alkaline earth or rare earth metal) and for the borides of Mo, W, Fe, Co and Ni. The metal oxide and B_2O_3 or borax are dissolved in a suitable, molten salt bath and electrolysed at 700–1000° using a graphite anode; the boride is deposited on the cathode which can be graphite or steel.

(vi) Co-reduction of oxides with carbon at temperatures up to 2000°, e.g.

$$V_2O_5 + B_2O_3 + 8C \xrightarrow{1500°} 2VB + 8CO$$

(vii) Reduction of metal oxide (or $M + B_2O_3$) with boron carbide, e.g.

$$Eu_2O_3 + 3B_4C \xrightarrow{1600°} 2EuB_6 + 3CO$$

$$7Ti + B_2O_3 + 3B_4C \xrightarrow{2000°} 7TiB_2 + 3CO$$

Boron carbide (p. 149) is a most useful and economic source of B and will react with most metals or their oxides. It is produced in tonnage quantities by direct reduction of B_2O_3 with C at 1600°: a C resistor is embedded in a mixture of B_2O_3 and C, and a heavy electric current passed.

(viii) Co-reduction of mixed oxides with metals (Mg or Al) in a thermite-type reaction — this usually gives contaminated products including ternary borides, e.g. $Mo_7Al_6B_7$. Alternatively, alkali metals or Ca can be used as reductants, e.g.

$$TiO_2 + B_2O_3 \xrightarrow{molten Na} TiB_2$$

The various stoichiometries are not equally common, as can be seen from Fig. 6.5; the most frequently occurring are M_2B, MB, MB_2, MB_4 and MB_6, and these five classes account for 75% of the compounds. At the other extreme $Ru_{11}B_8$ is the only known example of this stoichiometry. Metal-rich borides tend to be formed by the transition elements whereas the boron-rich borides are characteristic of the more electropositive elements in Groups 1–3, the lanthanides and the actinides. Only the diborides MB_2 are common to both classes.

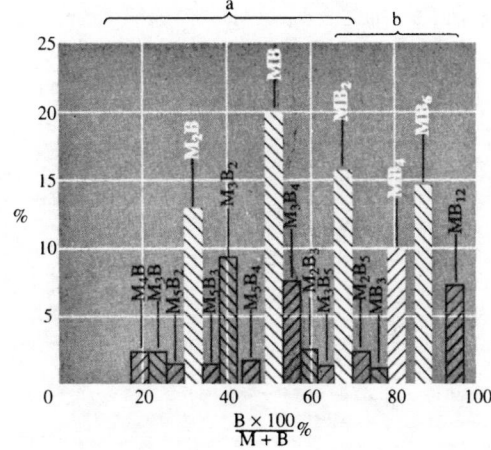

Figure 6.5 Frequency of occurrence of various stoichiometries among boride phases: (a) field of borides of d elements, and (b) field of borides of s, p and f elements.

6.3.3 Structures of borides [1-3,5]

The structures of metal-rich borides can be systematized by the schematic arrangements shown in Fig. 6.6, which illustrates the increasing tendency of B atoms to catenate as their concentration in the boride phase increases; the B atoms are often at the centres of trigonal prisms of metal atoms (Fig. 6.7) and the various stoichiometries are accommodated as follows:

---

[5] T. LUNDSTRÖM, *Pure Appl. Chem.* **57**, 1383–90 (1985).

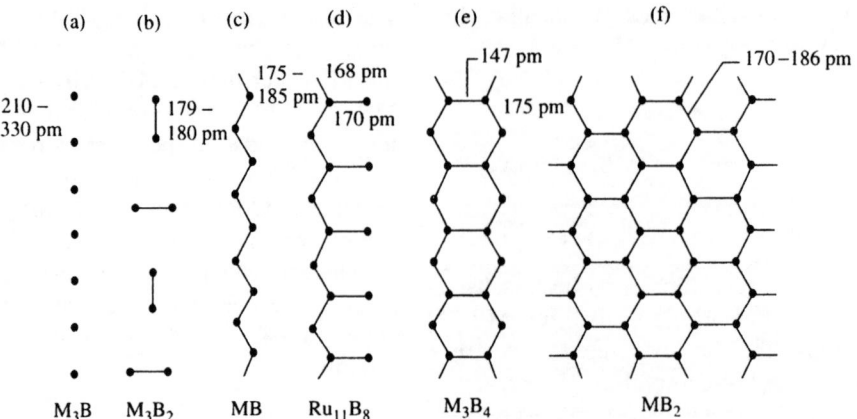

Figure 6.6 Idealized patterns of boron catenation in metal-rich borides. Examples of the structures (a)–(f) are given in the text. Boron atoms are often surrounded by trigonal prisms of M atoms as shown in Fig. 6.7.

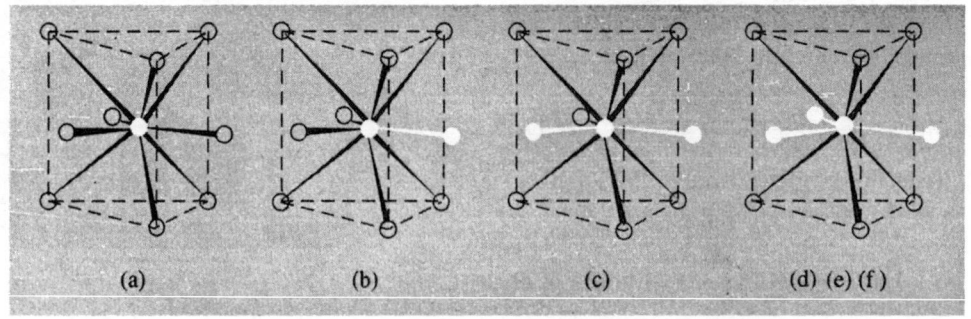

Figure 6.7 Idealized boron environment in metal-rich borides (see text): (a) isolated B atoms in M_3B and M_7B_3; (b) pairs of B atoms in Cr_5B_3 and M_3B_2; (c) zigzag chains of B atoms in Ni_3B_4 and MB; (d) branched chains in $Ru_{11}B_8$; and (e), (f) double chains and plane nets in M_3B_4, MB_2 and M_2B_5.

(a) isolated B atoms:	Mn_4B; M_3B (Tc, Re, Co, Ni, Pd); Pd_5B_2; M_7B_3 (Tc, Re, Ru, Rh); M_2B (Ta, Mo, W, Mn, Fe, Co, Ni);
(b) isolated pairs B_2:	Cr_5B_3; M_3B_2 (V, Nb, Ta);
(c) zigzag chains of B atoms:	M_3B_4 (Ti; V, Nb, Ta; Cr, Mn, Ni); MB (Ti, Hf; V, Nb, Ta; Cr, Mo, W; Mn, Fe, Co, Ni);
(d) branched chains of B atoms:	$Ru_{11}B_8$;
(e) double chains of B atoms:	M_3B_4 (V, Nb, Ta; Cr, Mn);
(f) plane (or puckered) nets:	MB_2 (Mg, Al; Sc, Y; Ti, Zr, Hf; V, Nb, Ta; Cr, Mo, W; Mn, Tc, Re; Ru, Os; U, Pu); M_2B_5 (Ti; Mo, W).

It will be noted from Fig. 6.6 that structures with isolated B atoms can have widely differing interatomic B–B distances, but all other classes involve appreciable bonding between B atoms, and the B–B distances remain almost invariant despite the extensive variation in the size of the metal atoms.

The structures of boron-rich borides (e.g. MB_4, MB_6, MB_{10}, MB_{12}, MB_{66}) are even more effectively dominated by inter-B bonding, and the structures comprise three-dimensional networks of B atoms and clusters in which the metal atoms occupy specific voids or otherwise vacant sites. The structures are often exceedingly complicated (for the reasons given in Section 6.2.2): for example, the cubic unit cell of YB_{66} has a_0 2344 pm and contains 1584 B and 24 Y atoms; the basic structural unit is the 13-icosahedron unit of 156 B atoms found in β-rhombohedral B (p. 142); there are 8 such units (1248 B) in the unit cell and the remaining 336 B atoms are statistically distributed in channels formed by the packing of the 13-icosahedron units.

Another compound which is even more closely related to β-rhombohedral boron is boron carbide, "B_4C"; this is now more correctly written as $B_{13}C_2$,[6] but the phase can vary over wide composition ranges which approach the stoichiometry $B_{12}C_3$. The structure is best thought of in terms of B_{84} polyhedra (p. 142) but these are now interconnected simply by linear C–B–C units instead of the larger B_{10}–B–B_{10} units in β-rhombohedral B. The result is a more compact packing of the 13-icosahedron units so generated and this is reflected in the unit cell dimensions (a 517.5 pm, α 65.74°). A notable feature of the structure (Fig. 6.8) is the presence of regular hexagonal planar rings B_4C_2 (shaded). Stringent tests had to be applied to distinguish confidently between B and C atoms in this structure and to establish that it was indeed B_{12} CBC and not $B_{12}C_3$ as had previously been thought. [This view has recently been challenged as a result of a ^{13}C nmr study using magic-angle spinning, which suggests that the carbon is present only as C_3 chains and that the structure is in fact still best represented as $B_{12}C_3$ (or $B_{12}^{2-}C_3^{2+}$).][7] It is salutory to recall that boron carbide, which was first made by H. Moissan in 1899 and which has been manufactured in tonne amounts for several decades, still waits definitive

structural characterization. On one view the wide variation in stoichiometry from "$B_{6.5}C$" to "B_4C" is due to progressive vacancies in the CBC chain ($B_{12}C_2 \equiv B_6C$) and/or progressive substitution of one C for B in the icosahedron [($B_{11}C$)CBC $\equiv B_4C$)]. Related phases are $B_{12}PBP$ and $B_{12}X_2$ (X = P, As, O, S). See also p. 288 for B_nC_{60-n} ($n = 1-6$).

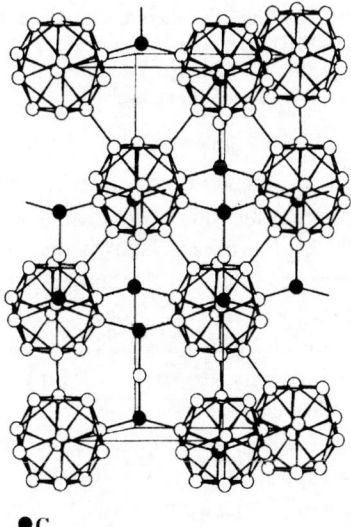

● C

Figure 6.8 Crystal structure of $B_{13}C_2$ showing the planar hexagonal rings connecting the B_{12} icosahedra. These rings are perpendicular to the C–B–C chains.

By contrast with the many complex structures formally related to β-rhombohedral boron, the structures of the large and important groups of cubic borides MB_{12} and MB_6 are comparatively simple. MB_{12} is formed by many large electropositive metals (e.g. Sc, Y, Zr, lanthanides and actinides) and has an "NaCl-type" fcc structure in which M atoms alternate with B_{12} cubo-octahedral clusters (Fig. 6.9). (Note that the B_{12} cluster is not an icosahedron.) Similarly, the cubic hexaborides MB_6 consist of a simple CsCl-type lattice in which the halogen is replaced by B_6 octahedra (Fig. 6.10); these B_6 octahedra are linked together in all 6 orthogonal directions to give a rigid but open framework which can accommodate large,

[6] G. WILL and K. H. KOSSOBUTZKI, *J. Less-Common Metals* **47**, 43–8 (1976).

[7] T. M. DUNCAN, *J. Am. Chem. Soc.* **106**, 2270–5 (1984).

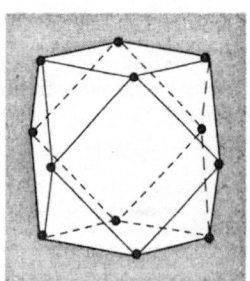

Figure 6.9 B_{12} Cubo-octahedral cluster as found in MB_{12}. This B_{12} cluster alternates with M atoms on an fcc lattice as in NaCl, the B_{12} cluster replacing Cl.

electropositive metal atoms at the corners of the interpenetrating cubic sublattice. The rigidity of the B framework is shown by the very small linear coefficient of thermal expansion of hexaborides ($6-8 \times 10^{-6}$ deg^{-1}) and by the narrow range of lattice constants of these phases which vary by only 4% (410–427 pm), whereas the diameters of the constituent metal atoms vary by 25% (355–445 pm). Bonding theory for isolated groups such as $B_6H_6^{2-}$ (p. 160) requires the transfer of 2 electrons to the borane cluster to fill all the bonding MOs; however, complete

transfer of 2e per B_6 unit is not required in a three-dimensional crystal lattice and calculations for MB_6 (Ca, Sr, Ba) indicate the transfer of only 0.9–1.0e.[8] This also explains why metal-deficit phases $M_{1-x}B_6$ remain stable and why the alkali metals (Na, K) can form hexaborides. The $M^{II}B_6$ hexaborides (Ca, Sr, Ba, Eu, Yb) are semiconductors but $M^{III}B_6$ and $M^{IV}B_6$ (M^{III} = Y, La, lanthanides; M^{IV} = Th) have a high metallic conductivity at room temperature ($10^4 - 10^5$ ohm^{-1} cm^{-1}).

The "radius" of the 24-coordinate metal site in MB_6 is too large (215–225 pm) to be comfortably occupied by the later (smaller) lanthanide elements Ho, Er, Tm and Lu, and these form MB_4 instead, where the metal site has a radius of 185–200 pm. The structure of MB_4 (also formed by Ca, Y, Mo and W) consists of a tetragonal lattice formed by chains of B_6 octahedra linked along the c-axis and joined laterally by pairs of B_2 atoms in the xy plane so as to form a 3D skeleton with tunnels along the c-axis that are filled by metal atoms (Fig. 6.11). The pairs of boron atoms are thus surrounded by trigonal prisms of

---

8 P. G. PERKINS, pp. 31–51 in ref. 2.

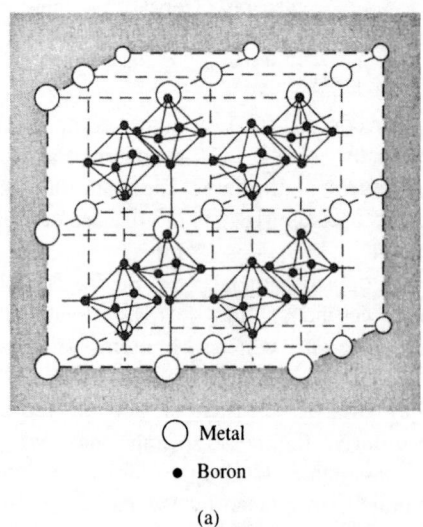

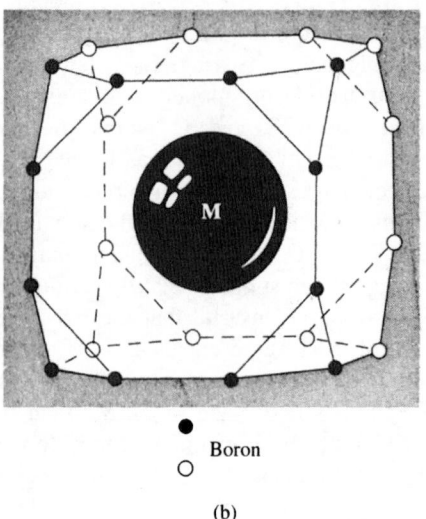

| ◯ Metal |
| • Boron |

(a)

| • Boron |
| ◯ |

(b)

Figure 6.10 Cubic MB_6 showing (a) boron octahedra (B–B in range 170–174 pm), and (b) 24-atom coordination polyhedron around each metal atom.

metal atoms and the structure represents a transition between the puckered layer structures of MB_2 and the cubic MB_6.

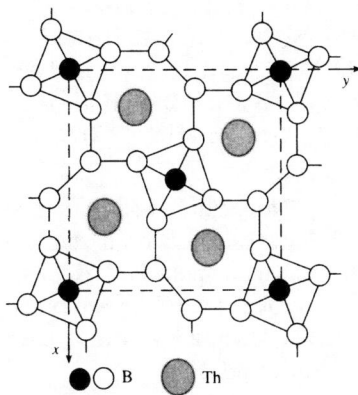

B ◯● Th ⬤

Figure 6.11 Structure of ThB_4.

The structure and properties of many borides emphasize again the inadequacy of describing bonding in inorganic compounds as either ionic, covalent or metallic. For example, in conventional terminology LaB_6 would be described as a rigid, covalently bonded network of B_6 clusters having multicentred bonding within each cluster and 2-centre covalent B–B bonds between the clusters; this requires the transfer of up to 2 electrons from the metal to the boron sublattice and so could be said also to involve ionic bonding ($La^{2+}B_6{}^{2-}$) in addition to the covalent inter-boron bonding. Finally, the third valency electron on La is delocalized in a conduction band of the crystal (mainly metal based) and the electrical conductivity of the boride is actually greater than that of La metal itself so that this aspect of the bonding could be called metallic. The resulting description of the bonding is an *ad hoc* mixture of four oversimplified limiting models and should more logically be replaced by a generalized MO approach.[8] It will also be clear from the preceding paragraphs that a classification of borides according to the periodic table does not result in the usual change in stoichiometry from one group to the next; instead, a classification

in terms of the type of boron network and the size and electropositivity of the other atoms is frequently more helpful and revealing of periodic trends.

6.4 Boranes (Boron Hydrides)[1,9]

6.4.1 Introduction

Borane chemistry began in 1912 with A. Stock's classic investigations,[10] and the numerous compounds prepared by his group during the following 20 y proved to be the forerunners of an amazingly diverse and complex new area of chemistry. During the past few decades the chemistry of boranes and the related carbaboranes (p. 181) has been one of the major growth areas in inorganic chemistry, and interest continues unabated. The importance of boranes stems from three factors: first, the completely unsuspected structural principles involved; secondly, the growing need to extend covalent MO bond theory considerably to cope with the unusual stoichiometries; and finally, the emergence of a versatile and extremely extensive reaction chemistry which parallels but is quite distinct from that of organic and organometallic chemistry. This efflorescence of activity culminated (in the centenary year of Stock's birth) in the award of the 1976 Nobel Prize for Chemistry to W. N. Lipscomb (Harvard) "for his studies of boranes which have illuminated problems of chemical bonding".

Over 50 neutral boranes, B_nH_m, and an even larger number of borane anions $B_nH_m{}^{x-}$ have been characterized;[11] these can be classified

[9] E. L. MUETTERTIES (ed.), *Boron Hydride Chemistry*, Academic Press, New York, 1975, 532 pp.

[10] A. STOCK, *Hydrides of Boron and Silicon*, Cornell University Press, Ithaca, New York, 1933, 250 pp.

[11] N. N. GREENWOOD, Boron Hydride Clusters, in H. W. ROESKY (ed.) *Rings, Clusters and Polymers of Main Group and Transition Elements*, Elsevier, Amsterdam, 1989, pp. 49–105.

according to structure and stoichiometry into 5 series though examples of neutral or unsubstituted boranes themselves are not known for all 5 classes:

closo-boranes (from Greek κλωβός, *clovos*, a cage) have complete, closed polyhedral clusters of n boron atoms;

nido-boranes (from Latin *nidus*, a nest) have non-closed structures in which the B_n cluster occupies n corners of an $(n + 1)$-cornered polyhedron;

arachno-boranes (from Greek ἀράχνη, *arachne*, a spider's web) have even more open clusters in which the B atoms occupy n contiguous corners of an $(n + 2)$-cornered polyhedron;

hypho-boranes (from Greek ὑφή, *hyphe*, a net) have the most open clusters in which the B atoms occupy n corners of an $(n + 3)$-cornered polyhedron;

conjuncto-boranes (from Latin *conjuncto*, I join together) have structures formed by linking two (or more) of the preceding types of cluster together.

Examples of these various series are listed below and illustrated in the accompanying structural diagrams. Their interrelations are further discussed in connection with carborane structures 51–81.

Closo-boranes:

$B_n H_n^{2-}$ ($n = 6$–12) see structures 1–7. The neutral boranes $B_n H_{n+2}$ are not known.

Nido-boranes:

$B_n H_{n+4}$, e.g. $B_2 H_6$ (8), $B_5 H_9$ (9), $B_6 H_{10}$ (10), $B_{10} H_{14}$ (11); $B_8 H_{12}$ also has this formula but has a rather more open structure (12) which can be visualized as being formed from $B_{10} H_{14}$ by removal of B(9) and B(10).

$B_n H_{n+3}^{-}$ formed by removal of 1 bridge proton from $B_n H_{n+4}$, e.g. $B_5 H_8^{-}$, $B_{10} H_{13}^{-}$; other anions in this series such as $B_4 H_7^{-}$ and $B_9 H_{12}^{-}$ are known though the parent boranes have proved too

fugitive to isolate; BH_4^{-} can be thought of as formed by addition of H^- to BH_3.

$B_n H_{n+2}^{2-}$, e.g. $B_{10} H_{12}^{2-}$, $B_{11} H_{13}^{2-}$.

Arachno-boranes:

$B_n H_{n+6}$, e.g. $B_4 H_{10}$ (13), $B_5 H_{11}$ (14), $B_6 H_{12}$ (15), $B_8 H_{14}$ (16), n-$B_9 H_{15}$ (17), i-$B_9 H_{15}$.

$B_n H_{n+5}^{-}$, e.g. $B_2 H_7^{-}$ (18), $B_3 H_8^{-}$ (19), $B_5 H_{10}^{-}$, $B_9 H_{14}^{-}$ (20), $B_{10} H_{15}^{-}$.

$B_n H_{n+4}^{2-}$, e.g. $B_{10} H_{14}^{2-}$ (21).

Hypho-boranes:

$B_n H_{n+8}$. No neutral borane has yet been definitely established in this series but the known compounds $B_8 H_{16}$ and $B_{10} H_{18}$ may prove to be *hypho*-boranes and several adducts are known to have *hypho*-structures (pp. 171–2).

Conjuncto-boranes:

$B_n H_m$. At least five different structure types of interconnected borane clusters have been identified; they have the following features:

(a) fusion by sharing a single common B atom, e.g. $B_{15} H_{23}$ (22);

(b) formation of a direct 2-centre B–B σ bond between 2 clusters, e.g. $B_8 H_{18}$, i.e. $(B_4 H_9)_2$ (23), $B_{10} H_{16}$, i.e. $(B_5 H_8)_2$ (3 isomers) (24), $B_{20} H_{26}$, i.e. $(B_{10} H_{13})_2$ (11 possible isomers of which most have been prepared and separated), (e.g. 25a, b, c); anions in this subgroup are represented by the 3 isomers of $B_{20} H_{18}^{4-}$, i.e. $(B_{10} H_9^{2-})_2$ (26);

(c) fusion of 2 clusters via 2 B atoms at a common edge, e.g. $B_{13} H_{19}$ (27), $B_{14} H_{18}$ (28), $B_{14} H_{20}$ (29), $B_{16} H_{20}$ (30), n-$B_{18} H_{22}$ (31), i-$B_{18} H_{22}$ (32);

(d) fusion of two clusters via 3 B atoms at a common face: no neutral borane or borane anion is yet known with this conformation but the solvated complex $(MeCN)_2 B_{20} H_{16} \cdot MeCN$ has this structure (33);

(e) more extensive fusion involving 4 B atoms in various configurations, e.g. $B_{20} H_{16}$ (34), $B_{20} H_{18}^{2-}$ (35).

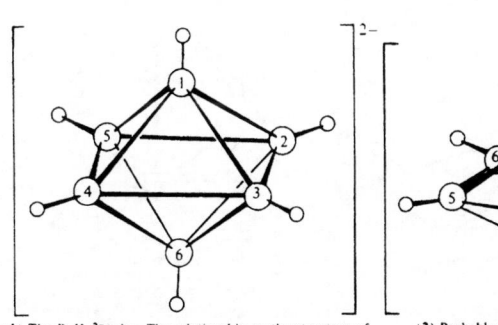

(1) The $B_6H_6^{2-}$ anion. The relationship to the structure of the B_6 network in CaB_6 and the boron cluster in B_5H_9 should be noted

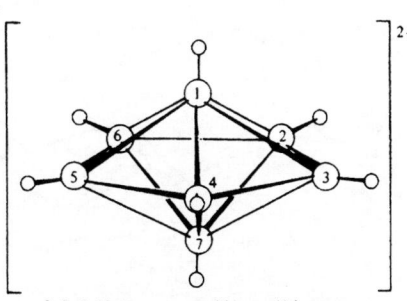

(2) Probable D_{5h} pentagonal bipyramidal structure of the anion $B_7H_7^{2-}$ in solution

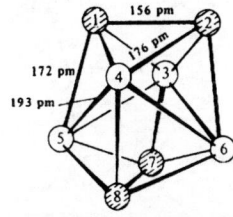

(3) The D_{2d} configuration of the boron atoms in $B_8H_8^{2-}$ showing the two structurally non-equivalent sets of 4 boron atoms

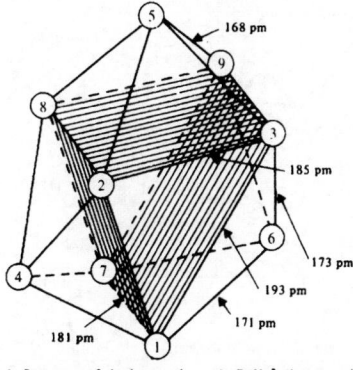

(4) Structure of the boron cluster in $B_9H_9^{2-}$ (interatomic distances ± 1.5 pm) The four unique B-H distances are 107, 110, 127 and 144 ± 15 pm

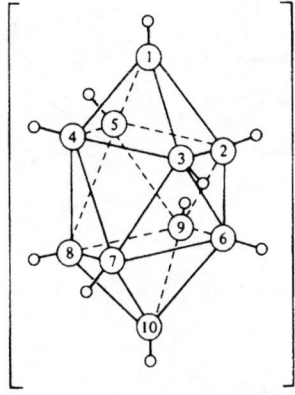

(5) $B_{10}H_{10}^{2-}$: decahydro-*closo*-decaborate (2–)

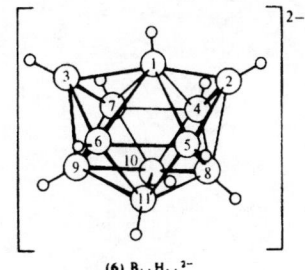

(6) $B_{11}H_{11}^{2-}$

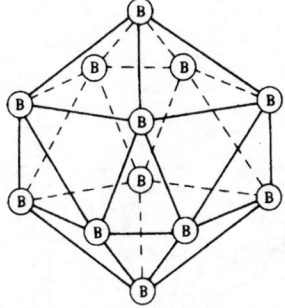

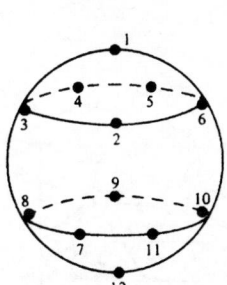

(7) Position of boron atoms and numbering system in the icosahedral borane anion $B_{12}H_{12}^{2-}$. The hydrogen atoms, which are attached radially to each boron atom, are omitted for clarity. There are six B-B distances of 175.5 pm and 24 of 178 pm

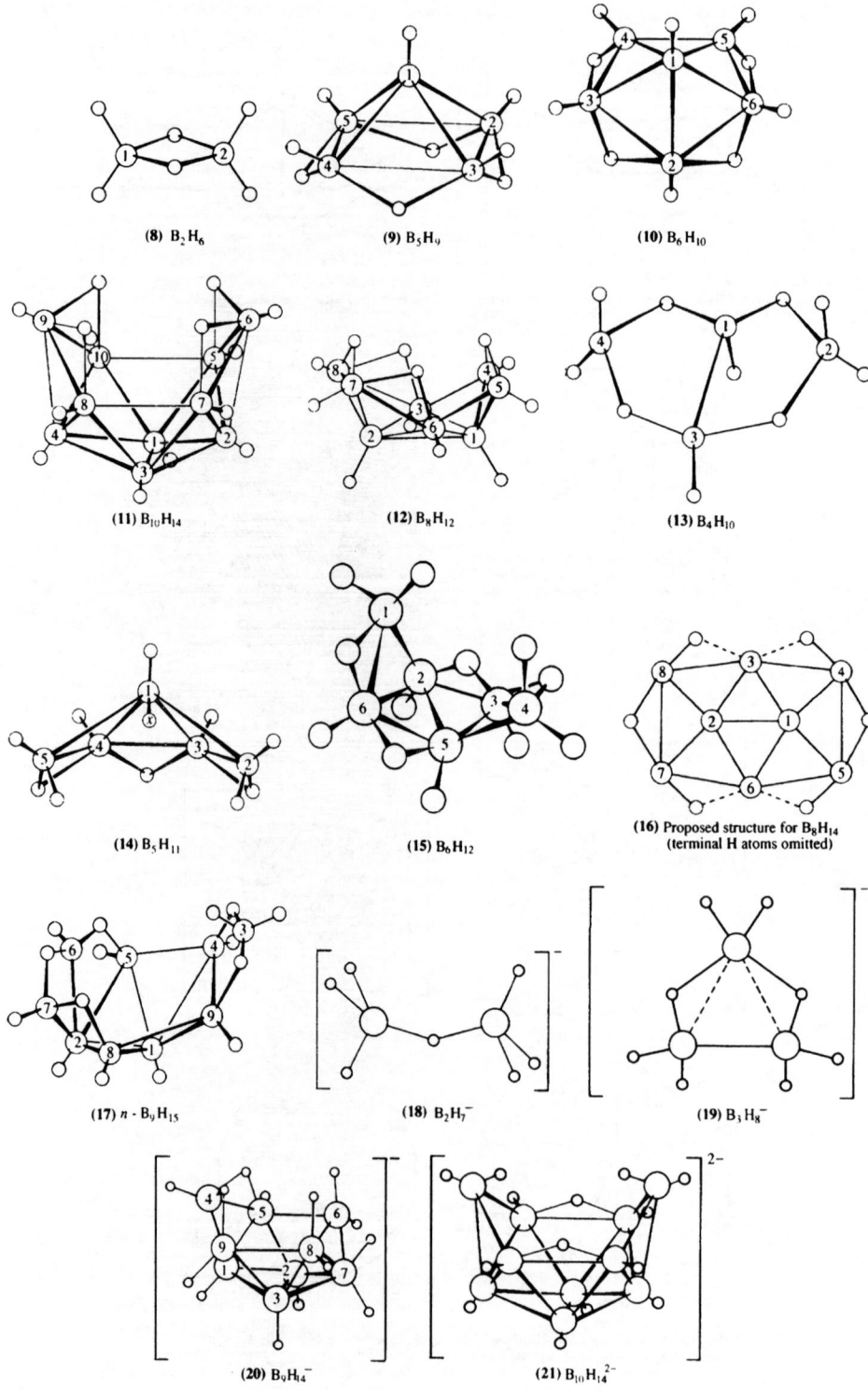

(8) B_2H_6

(9) B_5H_9

(10) B_6H_{10}

(11) $B_{10}H_{14}$

(12) B_8H_{12}

(13) B_4H_{10}

(14) B_5H_{11}

(15) B_6H_{12}

(16) Proposed structure for B_8H_{14}
(terminal H atoms omitted)

(17) n - B_9H_{15}

(18) $B_2H_7^-$

(19) $B_3H_8^-$

(20) $B_9H_{14}^-$

(21) $B_{10}H_{14}^{2-}$

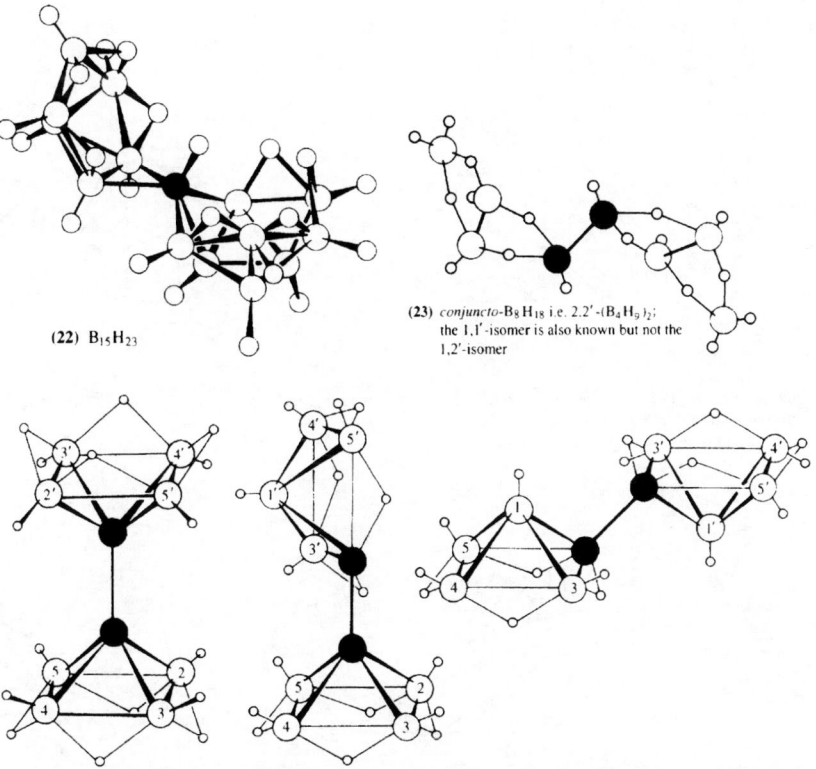

(22) $B_{15}H_{23}$

(23) *conjuncto*-B_8H_{18} i.e. 2.2'-$(B_4H_9)_2$; the 1,1'-isomer is also known but not the 1,2'-isomer

(24) Structures of the three isomers of $B_{10}H_{16}$. The 1,1' isomer comprises two pentaborane(9) groups linked in eclipsed configuration via the apex boron atoms to give overall D_{4h} symmetry; the B-B bond distances are 174 pm for the linking bond, 176 pm for the slant edge of the pyramids, and 171 pm for the basal boron atoms

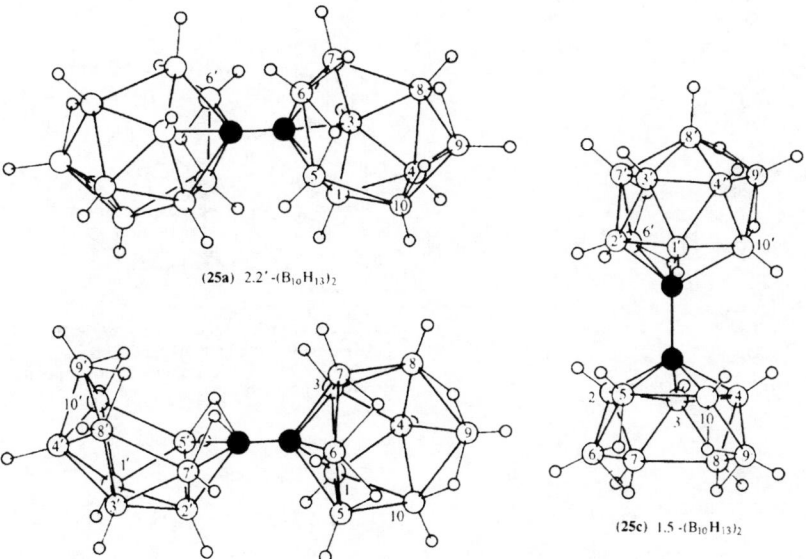

(25a) 2.2'-$(B_{10}H_{13})_2$

(25b) 2.6'-$(B_{10}H_{13})_2$

(25c) 1.5-$(B_{10}H_{13})_2$

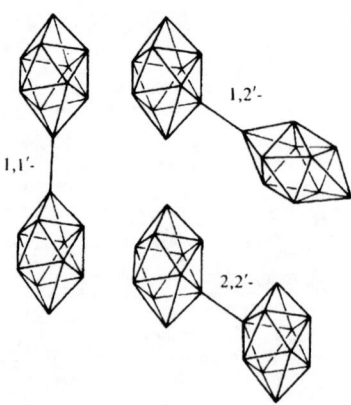

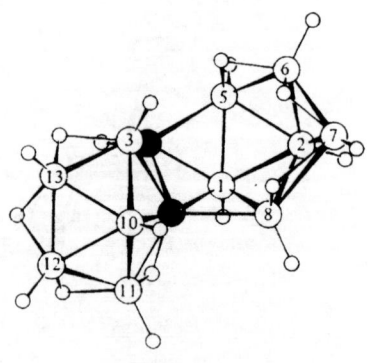

(26) Proposed structures for the three isomers of $[B_{20}H_{18}]^{4-}$; terminal hydrogen atoms omitted for clarity. (See also p. 180)

(27) $B_{13}H_{19}$

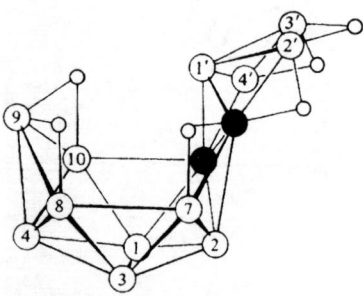

(28) Proposed structure of $B_{14}H_{18}$, omitting terminal hydrogen atoms for clarity

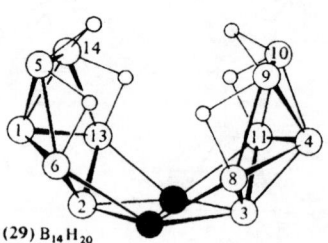

(29) $B_{14}H_{20}$ Terminal hydrogen atoms have been omitted for clarity

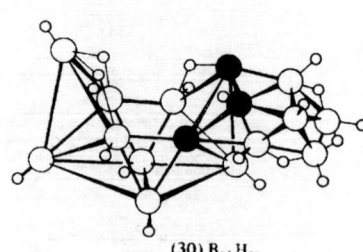

(30) $B_{16}H_{20}$

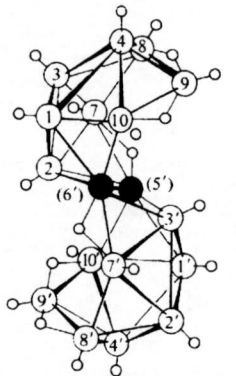

(31) $n\text{-}B_{18}H_{22}$ (centrosymmetric)

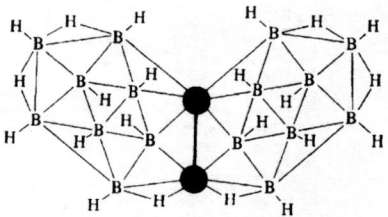

(32) Plane projection of the structure of $i\text{-}B_{18}H_{22}$. The two decaborane units are fused at the 5(7′) and 6(6′) positions to give a non-centrosymmetric structure with C_2 symmetry

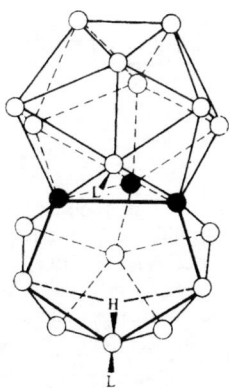 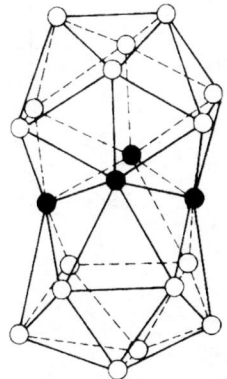 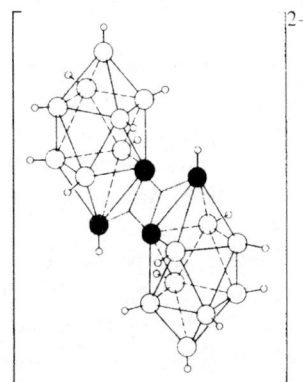

(33) Molecular structure of $(MeCN)_2 B_{20}H_{16}$ as found in crystals of the solvate $(MeCN)_2 B_{20}H_{16} \cdot MeCN$ (see text)

(34) The boron atom arrangement in *closo*-$B_{20}H_{16}$. Each boron atom except the 4 "fusion borons" carries an external hydrogen atom and there are no BHB bridges

(35) Structure of the $B_{20}H_{18}{}^{2-}$ ion. The two 3-centre BBB bonds joining the 2 $B_{10}H_9{}^{-}$ units are shown by broad shaded lines

Boranes are usually named[12] by indicating the number of B atoms with a latin prefix and the number of H atoms by an arabic number in parentheses, e.g. B_5H_9, pentaborane(9); B_5H_{11}, pentaborane(11). Names for anions end in "ate" rather than "ane" and specify both the number of H and B atoms and the charge, e.g. $B_5H_8{}^{-}$ octahydropentaborate(1−). Further information can be provided by the optional inclusion of the italicized descriptors *closo-*, *nido-*, *arachno-*, *hypho-* and *conjuncto-*, e.g.:

$B_{10}H_{10}{}^{2-}$: decahydro-*closo*-decaborate(2−) [structure (5)]

$B_{10}H_{14}$: *nido*-decaborane(14) [structure (11)]

$B_{10}H_{14}{}^{2-}$: tetradecahydro-*arachno*-decaborate(2−) [structure (21)]

$B_{10}H_{16}$: 1,1′-*conjuncto*-decaborane(16) [structure (24a)] [i.e. 1,1′-bi(*nido*-pentaboranyl)]

The detailed numbering schemes are necessarily somewhat complicated but, in all other respects, standard nomenclature practices are followed.[12]

Derivatives of the boranes include not only simple substituted compounds in which H has been replaced by halogen, OH, alkyl or aryl groups, etc., but also the much more diverse and numerous class of compounds in which one or more B atom in the cluster is replaced by another main-group element such as C, P or S, or by a wide range of metal atoms or coordinated metal groups. These will be considered in later sections.

6.4.2 Bonding and topology

The definitive structural chemistry of the boranes began in 1948 with the X-ray crystallographic determination of the structure of decaborane(14); this showed the presence of 4 bridging H atoms and an icosahedral fragment of 10 B atoms. This was rapidly followed in 1951 by the unequivocal demonstration of the H-bridged structure of diborane(6) and by the determination of the structure of pentaborane(9). Satisfactory theories of bonding in boranes date from the introduction of the concept of the 3-centre 2-electron B−H−B bond by H. C. Longuet-Higgins in 1949; he also extended the principle of 3-centre bonding and multicentre bonding to the higher boranes. These ideas have been extensively developed and

---

[12] G. J. LEIGH (ed.), *Nomenclature of Inorganic Chemistry: Recommendations 1990* (The IUPAC "Red Book"), Blackwell, Oxford, 1990, Chap. 11, pp. 207–37.

refined by W. N. Lipscomb and his group during the past four decades.[13]

In simple covalent bonding theory molecular orbitals (MOs) are formed by the linear combination of atomic orbitals (LCAO); for example, 2 AOs can combine to give 1 bonding and 1 antibonding MO and the orbital of lower energy will be occupied by a pair of electrons. This is a special case of a more general situation in which a number of AOs are combined together by the LCAO method to construct an equal number of MOs of differing energies, some of which will be bonding, some possibly nonbonding and some antibonding. In this way 2-centre, 3-centre, and multicentre orbitals can be envisaged. The three criteria that determine whether particular AOs can combine to form MOs are that the AOs must (a) be similar in energy, (b) have appreciable spatial overlap, and (c) have appropriate symmetry. In borane chemistry two types of 3-centre bond find considerable application: B–H–B bridge bonds (Fig. 6.12) and central 3-centre BBB bonds (Fig. 6.13). Open 3-centre B–B–B bonds are not now thought to occur in boranes and their anions though they are still useful in describing the bonding in carbaboranes and other heteroatom clusters (p. 194). The relation between the 3-centre bond formation for B–H–B, where the bond angle at H is ~90° and the 3-centre bond formation for approximately linear H bonds A–H···B is given on pp. 63–4.

Localized 3-centre bond formalism can readily be used to rationalize the structure and bonding in most of the non-*closo*-boranes. This is illustrated for some typical *nido*- and *arachno*-boranes in the following plane-projection diagrams which use an obvious symbolism for normal 2-centre bonds: B–B O—O, B–H$_t$ O—●, (t = terminal),

central 3-centre bonds $\bigwedge$, and B–H$_\mu$–B

bridge bonds $\bigcirc\!\!\!\!\nearrow\!\!\!\!\bullet\!\!\!\!\searrow\!\!\!\!\bigcirc$. It is particularly important

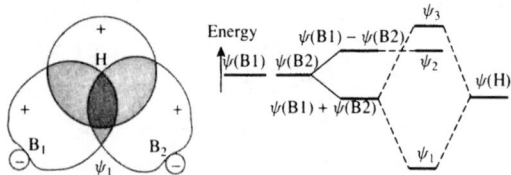

Figure 6.12 Formation of a bonding 3-centre B–H–B orbital ψ_1 from an sp^x hybrid orbital on each of B(1), B(2) and the H 1s orbital, ψ(H). The 3 AOs have similar energy and appreciable spatial overlap, but only the combination ψ(B1) + ψ(B2) has the correct symmetry to combine linearly with ψ(H).

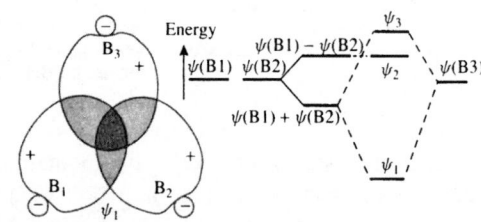

Figure 6.13 Formation of a bonding, central 3-centre bond ψ_1 and schematic representation of the relative energies of the 3 molecular orbitals ψ_1, ψ_2 and ψ_3.

to realize that the latter two symbols each represent a single (3-centre) bond involving one pair of electrons. As each B atom has 3 valence electrons, and each B–H$_t$ bond requires 1 electron from B and one from H, it follows that each B–H$_t$ group can contribute the remaining 2 electrons on B towards the bonding of the cluster (including B–H–B bonds), and likewise each BH$_2$ group can contribute 1 electron for cluster bonding. The overall bonding is sometimes codified in a 4-digit number, the so-called *styx* number, where s is the number of B–H–B bonds, t is the number of 3-centre BBB bonds, y the number of 2-centre BB bonds, and x the number of BH$_2$ groups.[13] Examples are on p. 159.

Electron counting and orbital bookkeeping can easily be checked in these diagrams: as each B has 4 valency orbitals (s + 3p) there should be 4 lines emanating from each open circle; likewise, as each B atom contributes 3 electrons in all and each H atom contributes 1 electron, the total

[13] W. N. LIPSCOMB, Chap. 2 in ref. 9, pp. 30–78. W. N. LIPSCOMB, *Boron. Hydrides*, Benjamin, New York, 1963, 275 pp. W. N. LIPSCOMB, Nobel Prize Lecture, *Science* **196**, 1047–55 (1977).

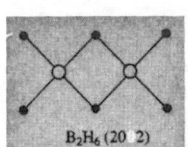

B₂H₆ (20 2)

Each terminal BH₂ group and each (bridging) H$_\mu$ contributes 1 electron to the bridging; these 4 electrons just fill the two B–H–B bonds.

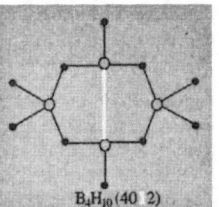

B₄H₁₀(40 2)

Each of the 4 B and 4H$_\mu$ contribute 1 electron to the B–H–B bonds, i.e. 4 pairs of electrons for the 4 (3-centre) bonds. The 2 "hinge" BH$_t$ groups each have 1 remaining electron and 1 orbital which interact to give the 2-centre B–B bond.

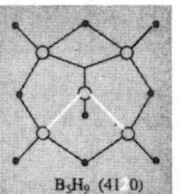

B₅H₉ (41 0)

In B₅H₉ the bonding can be thought of as involving the structure shown and 3 other equivalent structures in which successive pairs of adjacent basal B atoms are combined with the apex B in a 3-centre bond.

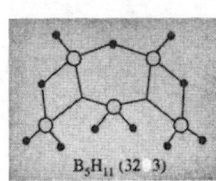

B₅H₁₁ (32 3)

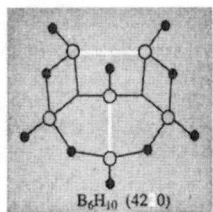

B₆H₁₀ (42 0)

number of valence electrons for a borane of formula B_nH_m is $(3n + m)$ and the number of bonds shown in the structure should be just half this. It follows, too, that the number of electron-pair bonds in the molecule is n plus the sum of the individual *styx* numbers (e.g. 13 for B_5H_{11}, 14 for B_6H_{10}) and this constitutes a further check.[†] An appropriate number of additional electrons should be added for anionic species.

For *closo*-boranes and for the larger open-cluster boranes it becomes increasingly difficult to write a simple satisfactory localized orbital structure, and a full MO treatment is required. Intermediate cases, such as B_5H_9, require several "resonance hybrids" in the localized orbital

formation and, by the time $B_{10}H_{14}$ is considered there are 24 resonance hybrids, even assuming that no open 3-centre B–B–B bonds occur. The best single compromise structure in this case is the (4620) arrangement shown at the foot of the page, but the open 3-centre B–B–B bonds can be avoided if "fractional" central 3-centre bonds replace the B–B and B–B–B bonds in pairs:

[†] Further checks, which can readily be verified from the equations of balance, are (a) the number of atoms in a neutral borane molecule $= 2(s + t + y + x)$, and (b) there are as many framework electrons as there are atoms in a neutral borane B_nH_m since each BH group supplies 2 electrons and each of the $(m - n)$ "extra" H atoms supplies 1 electron, making $n + m$ in all.

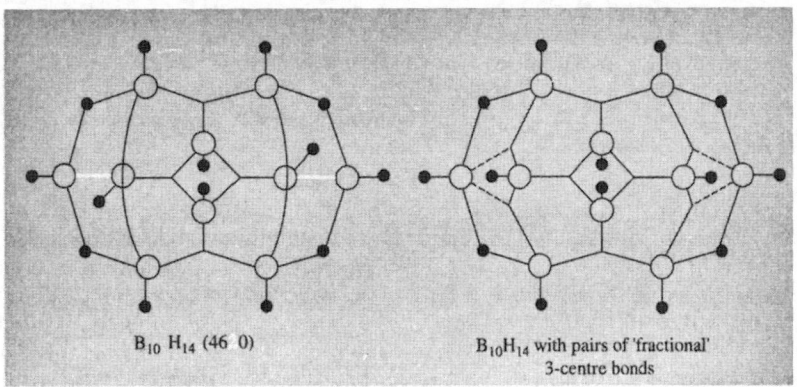

B₁₀H₁₄ (46 0)   B₁₀H₁₄ with pairs of 'fractional' 3-centre bonds

MO Description of Bonding in *closo*-$B_6H_6{}^{2-}$

Closo $B_6H_6{}^{2-}$ (structure 1) has a regular octahedral cluster of 6 B atoms surrounded by a larger octahedron of 6 radially disposed H atoms. Framework MOs for the B_6 cluster are constructed (LCAO) using the 2s, $2p_x$, $2p_y$ and $2p_z$ boron AOs. The symmetry of the octahedron suggests the use of sp hybrids directed radially outwards and inwards from each B along the cartesian axes (see figure) and 2 pure p orbitals at right angles to these (i.e. oriented tangentially to the B_6 octahedron). These sets of AOs are combined, with due regard to symmetry, to give 24 MOs as follows: the 24 AOs on the 6 B combine to give 24 MOs of which 7 (i.e. $n + 1$) are bonding framework MOs, 6 are used to form B–H_t bonds, and the remaining 11 are antibonding.

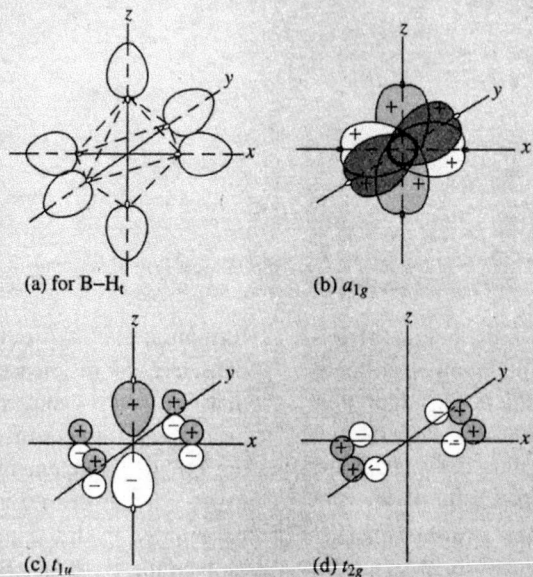

Symmetry of orbitals on the B_6 octahedron. (a) Six outward-pointing (sp) orbitals used for σ bonding to 6 H_t. (b) Six inward-pointing (sp) orbitals used to form the a_{1g} framework bonding molecular orbital. (c) Components for one of the t_{1u} framework bonding molecular orbitals — the other two molecular orbitals are in the yz and zx planes. (d) Components for one of the t_{2g} framework bonding molecular orbitals — the other two molecular orbitals are in the yz and zx planes.

The diagrams also indicate why neutral *closo*-boranes B_nH_{n+2} are unknown since the 2 anionic charges are effectively located in the low-lying inwardly directed a_{1g} orbital which has no overlap with protons outside the cluster (e.g. above the edges or faces of the B_6 octahedron). Replacement of the 6 H_t by 6 further B_6 builds up the basic three-dimensional network of hexaborides MB_6 (p. 150) just as replacement of the 4 H_t in CH_4 begins to build up the diamond lattice.

The diagrams, with minor modification, also describe the bonding in isoelectronic species such as *closo*-$CB_5H_6{}^-$, 1,2-*closo*-$C_2B_4H_6$, 1,6-*closo*-$C_2B_4H_6$, etc. (pp. 181–2). Similar though more complex diagrams can be derived for all *closo*-$B_nH_n{}^{2-}$ ($n = 6$–12); these have the common feature of a low lying a_{1g} orbital and n other framework bonding MOs; in each case, therefore $(n + 1)$ pairs of electrons are required to fill these orbitals as indicated in Wade's rules (p. 161). It is a triumph for MO theory that the existence of $B_6H_6{}^{2-}$ and $B_{12}H_{12}{}^{2-}$ were predicted by H. C. Longuet-Higgins in 1954–5,[14] a decade before $B_6H_6{}^{2-}$ was first synthesized and some 5 y before the (accidental) preparation of $B_{10}H_{10}{}^{2-}$ and $B_{12}H_{12}{}^{2-}$ were reported.[15,16]

[14] H. C. LONGUET-HIGGINS and M. DE V. ROBERTS, *Proc. R. Soc.* A, **230**, 110–19 (1955); see also idem *ibid.* A, **224**, 336–47 (1954).

[15] J. L. BOONE, *J. Am. Chem. Soc.* **86**, 5036 (1964).

[16] M. F. HAWTHORNE and A. R. PITTOCHELLI, *J. Am. Chem. Soc.* **81**, 5519 (and also 5833–4) (1959); *J. Am. Chem. Soc.* **82**, 3228–9 (1960).

A simplified MO approach to the bonding in *closo*-$B_6H_6{}^{2-}$ (structure 1, p. 153) is shown in the Panel. It is a general feature of *closo*-$B_nH_n{}^{2-}$ anions that there are no B–H–B or BH_2 groups and the $4n$ boron atomic orbitals are always distributed as follows:

n in the $n(B-H_t)$ bonding orbitals

$(n + 1)$ in framework bonding MOs

$(2n - 1)$ in nonbonding and antibonding framework MOs

As each B atom contributes 1 electron to its $B-H_t$ bond and 2 electrons to the framework MOs, the $(n + 1)$ framework bonding MOs are just filled by the $2n$ electrons from nB atoms and the 2 electrons from the anionic charge. Further, it is possible (conceptually) to remove a BH_t group and replace it by 2 electrons to compensate for the 2 electrons contributed by the BH_t group to the MOs. Electroneutrality can then be achieved by adding the appropriate number of protons; this does not alter the number of electrons in the system and hence all bonding MOs remain just filled.

$$B_6H_6{}^{2-} \xrightarrow{-BH + 2e^-} \{B_5H_5{}^{4-}\} \xrightarrow{4H^+} B_5H_9$$
(structure 1, p. 153)   (structure 9, p. 154)

$$\Bigg\downarrow \begin{array}{c} (-BH + 2e^-) \\ +2H^+ \end{array}$$

$$B_6H_6{}^{2-} \xrightarrow{-2BH + 4e^-} \{B_4H_4{}^{6-}\} \xrightarrow{6H^+} B_4H_{10}$$
(structure 13)

The structural interrelationship of all the various *closo*-, *nido*- and *arachno*-boranes thus becomes evident; a further example is shown at the foot of the page.

These relationships were codified in 1971 by K. Wade in a set of rules which have been extremely helpful not only in rationalizing known structures, but also in suggesting the probable structures of new species.[17] Wade's rules can be stated in extended form as follows:

> *closo*-borane anions have the formula $B_nH_n{}^{2-}$; the B atoms occupy all n corners of an n-cornered triangulated polyhedron, and the structures require $(n + 1)$ pairs of framework bonding electrons;
>
> *nido*-boranes have the formula B_nH_{n+4} with B atoms at n corners of an $(n + 1)$ cornered polyhedron; they require $(n + 2)$ pairs of framework-bonding electrons;
>
> *arachno*-boranes: B_nH_{n+6}, n corners of an $(n + 2)$ cornered polyhedron, requiring $(n + 3)$ pairs of framework-bonding electrons;
>
> *hypho*-boranes: B_nH_{n+8}: n corners of an $(n + 3)$ cornered polyhedron, requiring $(n + 4)$ pairs of framework-bonding electrons.

The rules can readily be extended to isoelectronic anions and carbaboranes ($BH \equiv B^- \equiv C$) and also to metalloboranes (p. 174), metallocarbaboranes (p. 194) and even to metal clusters themselves, though they become less reliable the further one moves away from boron in atomic size, ionization energy, electronegativity, etc.

―――――――――
[17] K. WADE, *Adv. Inorg. Chem. Radiochem.* **18**, 1-66 (1976).

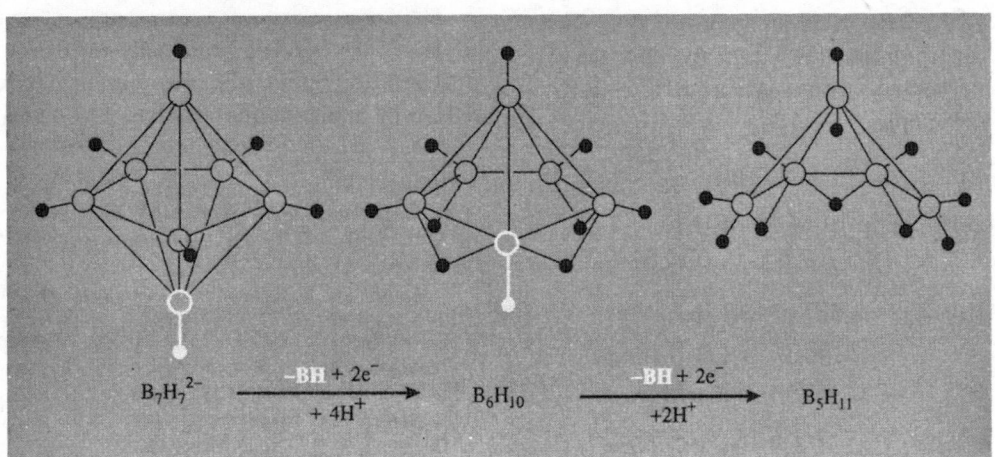

$$B_7H_7{}^{2-} \xrightarrow[+ 4H^+]{-BH + 2e^-} B_6H_{10} \xrightarrow[+2H^+]{-BH + 2e^-} B_5H_{11}$$

More sophisticated and refined calculations lead to orbital populations and electron charge distributions within the borane molecules and to predictions concerning the sites of electrophilic and nucleophilic attack. In general, the highest electron charge density (and the preferred site of electrophilic attack) occurs at apical B atoms which are furthest removed from open faces; conversely the lowest electron charge density (and the preferred site of nucleophilic attack) occurs on B atoms involved in B–H–B bonding. The consistency of this correlation implies that the electron distribution in the activated complex formed during reaction must follow a similar sequence to that in the ground state. Bridge H atoms tend to be more acidic than terminal H atoms and are the ones first lost during the formation of anions in acid-base reactions.

6.4.3 Preparation and properties of boranes

Earlier methods for preparing the boron hydrides were tedious and inefficient[10] but have now been superseded by modern high-yield routes.[11,18] The first great advance was to replace the reaction between protonic hydrogen and negative boride clusters by the reaction of hydridic species such as LiH or $LiAlH_4$ with boron halides or alkoxides which contain more positive boron centres. Subsequently, S. G. Shore and his group developed a systematic synthesis by using the Lewis acid properties of BX_3 ($X = F$, Cl, Br) to abstract H^- from the now readily available borane anions such as BH_4^-, $B_3H_8^-$ etc. For example:[19]

$$BX_3 + BH_4^- \longrightarrow HBX_3^- + (BH_3) \longrightarrow 1/2B_2H_6$$

$$BX_3 + B_3H_8^- \longrightarrow HBX_3^- + \{B_3H_7\} \longrightarrow$$
$$1/2B_4H_{10} + 1/2\text{“}B_2H_4\text{”} \text{ polymer}$$

$$BX_3 + B_4H_9^- \longrightarrow HBX_3^- + \{B_4H_8\} \longrightarrow$$
$$1/2B_5H_{11} + 1/2\text{“}B_3H_5\text{”} \text{ polymer}$$

$$BX_3 + B_9H_{14}^- \longrightarrow HBX_3^- + \{B_9H_{13}\} \longrightarrow$$
$$1/2B_{10}H_{14} + 1/2\text{“}B_8H_{10}\text{”} \text{ polymer} + 1/2H_2$$

The perception by R. Schaeffer that *nido*-B_6H_{10} (structure 10, pp. 154, 159) could act as a Lewis base towards reactive (vacant orbital) borance radicals has led to several new *conjucto*-boranes, e.g.:[20]

$$B_6H_{10} + 1/2B_2H_6 \xrightarrow{-H_2} \{B_7H_{11}\}$$

$$\xrightarrow{B_6H_{10}} B_{13}H_{19} + H_2$$

$$B_6H_{10} + B_8H_{12} \longrightarrow B_{14}H_{22}$$

$$B_6H_{10} + \textit{iso-}B_9H_{15} \longrightarrow B_{15}H_{23}(22) + H_2$$

A useful route to B–B bonded *conjuncto*-boranes involves the photolysis of parent *nido*-boranes. Thus, ultraviolet irradiation of B_5H_9 (9) yields the three isomers of *conjuncto*-$B_{10}H_{16}$ (24) and similar treatment of $B_{10}H_{14}$ (11) yields a mixture of 1,2′- and 2,2′-$(B_{10}H_{13})_2$ (25a). High-yield catalytic routes to specific B–B coupled *conjuncto*-boranes (using $PtBr_2$) have been developed by L. G. Sneddon and his group[21], e.g. B_5H_9 gave 1,2′-$(B_5H_8)_2$ (24), B_4H_{10} gave 1,1′-$(B_4H_9)_2$ (i.e. *conjuncto*-B_8H_{18}, of which the 2,2′-isomer is shown in 23), and a mixture of B_4H_{10} and B_5H_9 yielded 1,2′-$(B_4H_9)(B_5H_8)$, i.e. *conjuncto*-B_9H_{17}. When applied to a mixture of B_2H_6 and B_5H_9 in decane at room temperature, the method gave the first authenticated neutral heptaborane, B_7H_{13}, in which one of the bridging H atoms in diborane has been replaced by a basal B atom of the B_5 unit, i.e. $1,2-\mu(2-B_5H_8)B_2H_5$.

The synthesis of *closo*-borane dianions $B_nH_n^{2-}$ (1–7) relies principally on thermolysis reactions of boranes in the presence of either BH_4^- or amino-borane adducts.[9,11] The yields

[18] R. W. PARRY and M. K. WALTER, in W. L. JOLLY (ed.), *Preparative Inorganic Reactions* **5**, 45–102 (1968).

[19] M. A. TOFT, J. B. LEACH, F. L. HIMPSL and S. G. SHORE *Inorg. Chem.* **21**, 1952–7 (1982).

[20] J. RATHKE and R. SCHAEFFER, *Inorg. Chem.* **13**, 3008–11 (1974); J. RATHKE, D. C. MOODY and R. SCHAEFFER, *Inorg. Chem.* **13**, 3040–2 (1974); J. C. HUFFMAN, D. C. MOODY and R. SCHAEFFER, *Inorg. Chem.* **20**, 741–5 (1981).

[21] E. W. CORCORAN and L. G. SNEDDON, *J. Am. Chem. Soc.* **106**, 7793–7800 (1984); **107**, 7446–50 (1985); L. G. SNEDDON, *Pure Appl. Chem.* **59**, 837–46 (1987).

Table 6.2 Properties of some boranes

Nido-boranes				Arachno-boranes			
Compound	mp	bp	$\Delta H_f^\circ/\text{kJ mol}^{-1}$	Compound	mp	bp	$\Delta H_f^\circ/\text{kJ mol}^{-1}$
B_2H_6	$-164.9°$	$-92.6°$	36	B_4H_{10}	$-120°$	$18°$	58
B_5H_9	$-46.8°$	$60.0°$	54	B_5H_{11}	$-122°$	$65°$	67 (or 93)
B_6H_{10}	$-62.3°$	$108°$	71	B_6H_{12}	$-82.3°$	$\sim85°$ (extrap)	111
B_8H_{12}	Decomp	above $-35°$	—	B_8H_{14}	Decomp	above $-30°$	—
$B_{10}H_{14}$	$99.5°$	$213°$	32	n-B_9H_{15}	$2.6°$	$28°/0.8$ mmHg	—

are very sensitive to conditions (solvent, pressure and temperature) and mixtures are often obtained. A more recent variant is the thermolysis of Et_4NBH_4 at $175-190°C$ for about 12 hours, which yields a mixture of *closo*-$B_9H_9^{2-}$, $B_{10}H_{10}^{2-}$, $B_{12}H_{12}^{2-}$ and *nido*-$B_{11}H_{14}^-$. The smaller *closo*-dianions ($n = 6, 7, 8$) can then be obtained (in smaller yield) by the oxidative (air) degradation of $B_9H_9^{2-}$ salts in the presence of EtOH, thf or 1,2-dimethoxyethane.

Boranes are colourless, diamagnetic, molecular compounds of moderate to low thermal stability. The lower members are gases at room temperature but with increasing molecular weight they become volatile liquids or solids (Table 6.2); bps are approximately the same as those of hydrocarbons of similar molecular weight. The boranes are all endothermic and their free energies of formation ΔG_f° are also positive; however, their thermodynamic instability results from the exceptionally strong interatomic bonds in both elemental B and H_2 rather than any weakness of the B–H bond. In this the boranes resemble the hydrocarbons. Likewise, the remarkable chemical reactivity of the boranes and their ready thermolytic interconversion (p. 164) should not be taken to imply that the bonds holding the boranes together are inherently weak. Indeed, the opposite is the case; the B–B and B–H bonds are among the strongest 2-electron bonds known, and the great reactivity of the boranes is to be sought rather in the availability of alternative structures and vacant orbitals of similar energies. Some comparative data are in Table 6.3[22] which

shows that the bond enthalpies E for the 2-centre B–B bond in boranes and for the C–C bond in C_2H_6 are essentially identical and that the value for the 3-centre 2-electron BBB bond in boranes is very similar to that for the B–C bond in BMe_3.

Table 6.3 Some enthalpies of atomization (ΔH_f°, 298 K) and comparative bond–enthalpy contributions, E

$\Delta H_f^\circ/\text{kJ mol}^{-1}$	$E/\text{kJ mol}^{-1}$		$E/\text{kJ mol}^{-1}$	
H(g) $1/2 \times 436$	B–B (2c,2e)	332	C–C	331
B(g) 566	BBB(3c,2e)	380	B–C	372
C(g) 356	B–H (2c,2e)	381	C–H	416
	BHB(3c,2e)	441	H–H	436

Boranes are extremely reactive compounds and several are spontaneously flammable in air. *Arachno*-boranes tend to be more reactive (and less stable to thermal decomposition) than *nido*-boranes and reactivity also diminishes with increasing mol wt. *Closo*-borane anions are exceptionally stable and their general chemical behaviour has suggested the term "three-dimensional aromaticity".

Boron hydrides have proved to be extremely versatile chemical reagents but the very diversity of their reactions makes a general classification unduly cumbersome. For this reason, the range of behaviour will be illustrated by typical examples taken from the chemistry of the boranes and their anions, arranged approximately according to the size of the borane cluster being discussed. Nearly all boranes are highly toxic when inhaled or absorbed through the skin though they can be safely and conveniently handled with relatively minor precautions.

---

[22] N. N. GREENWOOD and R. GREATREX, *Pure Appl. Chem.* **59**, 857–68 (1987).

6.4.4 The chemistry of small boranes and their anions ($B_1 - B_4$)

Diborane occupies a special place because all the other boranes can be prepared from it (directly or indirectly); it is also one of the most studied and synthetically useful reagents in the whole of chemistry.[1,23] B_2H_6 gas can most conveniently be prepared in small quantities by the reaction of I_2 on $NaBH_4$ in diglyme [$(MeOCH_2CH_2)_2O$], or by the reaction of a solid tetrahydroborate with an anhydrous acid:

$$2NaBH_4 + I_2 \xrightarrow[\text{(98\% yield)}]{\text{diglyme}} B_2H_6 + 2NaI + H_2$$

$$2NaBH_4(c) + 2H_3PO_4(l) \xrightarrow{\text{(70\% yield)}}$$

$$B_2H_6(g) + 2NaH_2PO_4(c) + 2H_2(g)$$

When B_2H_6 is to be used as a reaction intermediate without the need for isolation or purification, the best procedure is to add Et_2OBF_3 to $NaBH_4$ in a polyether such as diglyme:

$$3NaBH_4 + 4Et_2OBF_3 \xrightarrow[25°]{\text{diglyme}}$$

$$2B_2H_6(g) + 3NaBF_4 + 4Et_2O$$

On an industrial scale gaseous BF_3 can be reduced directly with NaH at 180° and the product trapped out as it is formed to prevent subsequent pyrolysis:

$$2BF_3(g) + 6NaH(c) \xrightarrow{180°} B_2H_6(g) + 6NaF(c)$$

Some 200 tonnes per annum of B_2H_6 is produced commercially, worldwide. Care should be taken in all these reactions because B_2H_6 is spontaneously flammable; its heat of combustion ($-\Delta H°$) is higher per unit weight of fuel than for any other substance except

H_2, BeH_2 and $Be(BH_4)_2$: [$-\Delta H°(B_2H_6) = 2165 \text{ kJ mol}^{-1} = 78.2 \text{ kJ g}^{-1}$].

The pyrolysis of gaseous B_2H_6 in sealed vessels at temperatures above 100° is exceedingly complex and has only recently been fully elucidated.[24-27] The initiating step is the unimolecular equilibrium dissociation of B_2H_6 to give $2\{BH_3\}$, and the $\{BH_3\}$ then reacts with further B_2H_6 to give $\{B_3H_7\}$ plus H_2 in a concerted rate-controlling reaction via a $\{B_3H_9\}$ transition state. This explains the observed 1.5-order of the kinetics and also successfully interprets all other aspects of the initial reaction:

$$B_2H_6 \rightleftharpoons 2\{BH_3\}$$

$$\{BH_3\} + B_2H_6 \longrightarrow \{B_3H_7\} + H_2$$

In these and subsequent reactions, unstable intermediates that have but transitory existence are placed in curly brackets, {}.

The first stable intermediate, B_4H_{10}, is then formed followed by B_5H_{11}:

$$\{BH_3\} + \{B_3H_7\} \rightleftharpoons B_4H_{10}$$

$$B_2H_6 + \{B_3H_7\} \longrightarrow \{BH_3\} + B_4H_{10}$$

$$\rightleftharpoons B_5H_{11} + H_2$$

A complex series of further steps gives B_5H_9, B_6H_{10}, B_6H_{12}, and higher boranes, culminating in $B_{10}H_{14}$ as the most stable end product, together with polymeric materials BH_x and a trace of *conjuncto*-icosaboranes $B_{20}H_{26}$.

Careful control of temperature, pressure and reaction time enables the yield of the various intermediate boranes to be optimized. For example, B_4H_{10} is best prepared by storing B_2H_6 under pressure at 25° for 10 days; this gives a 15% yield and quantitative conversion according to the

23 L. H. Long, Chap. 22 in *Mellor's Comprehensive Treatise on Inorganic and Theoretical Chemistry*, Vol. 5, Supplement 2, Part 2, pp. 52–162, Longmans, London, 1981.

24 J. F. Stanton, W. N. Lipscomb and R. J. Bartlett, *J. Am. Chem. Soc.* **111**, 5165–73 (1989).

25 R. Greatrex, N. N. Greenwood and S. M. Lucas, *J. Am. Chem. Soc.* **111**, 8721–2 (1989).

26 N. N. Greenwood and R. Greatrex, *Pure Appl. Chem.* **59**, 857–68 (1987).

27 N. N. Greenwood, *Chem. Soc. Revs.* **21**, 49–57 (1992).

overall reaction:

$$2B_2H_6 \longrightarrow B_4H_{10} + H_2$$

B_5H_{11} can be prepared in 70% yield by the reaction of B_2H_6 and B_4H_{10} in a carefully dimensioned hot/cold reactor at $+120°/-30°$:

$$2B_4H_{10} + B_2H_6 \rightleftharpoons 2B_5H_{11} + 2H_2$$

Alternative high-yield syntheses of these various boranes via hydride-ion abstraction from borane anions by BBr_3 and other Lewis acids have recently been devised[19] (see p. 162).

From the foregoing it is clear that {BH_3} is a fugitive reaction species: it exists only at exceedingly low concentrations but can be isolated and studied using matrix isolation techniques. Thus it can be generated by thermal dissociation of loosely bound 1:1 adducts with Lewis bases, such as $PF_3.BH_3$, and its reactions studied.[28] The relative stability of the adducts $L.BH_3$ has been determined from thermochemical and spectroscopic data and leads to the following unusual sequence:

$$PF_3 < CO < Et_2O < Me_2O < C_4H_8O < C_4H_8S$$

$$< Et_2S < Me_2S < py < Me_3N < H^-$$

Note that both PF_3 and CO form isolable although weak adducts, and that organic sulfide adducts are more stable than those of ethers, thereby showing that BH_3 has some class b acceptor ("soft acid") characteristics despite the absence of low-lying d orbitals on boron (see p. 909). The ligand H^- is a special case since it gives the symmetrical tetrahedral ion BH_4^-, isoelectronic with CH_4 and NH_4^+. Many other complexes of BH_3 with N, P, As, O, S etc. donor atoms are also known and they are readily formed by symmetrical homolytic (cleavage of the bridge bonds in B_2H_6. Occasionally, however, unsymmetrical (heterolytic) cleavage products result, perhaps partly as a result of steric effects,[29] e.g. NH_3, $MeNH_2$ and Me_2NH give unsymmetrical cleavage products whereas Me_3N gives the symmetrical cleavage product, $Me_3N.BH_3$ (see scheme below).

In addition to pyrolysis and cleavage reactions, B_2H_6 undergoes a wide variety of substitution, redistribution, and solvolytic reactions of which the following are representative. Gaseous HCl yields $B_2H_5Cl_t$ whereas Cl_2 (and F_2) give BX_3 directly even at low temperatures and high dilution. Methylation with $PbMe_4$ yields B_2H_5Me, but comproportionation with BMe_3 affords $Me_nB_2H_{6-n}$ ($n = 1$–4), the two BHB bridge bonds remaining intact. Hydrolysis gives the stoichiometric amount of $B(OH)_3$. The related alcoholysis reaction was much used in earlier times as a convenient means of total analysis

[28] T. P. FEHLNER, Chap. 4 in ref. 9, pp. 175–96.

[29] S. G. SHORE, Chap. 3 in ref. 9, pp. 79–174.

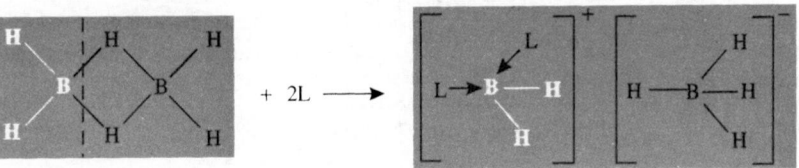

Symmetrical (homolytic)

Unsymmetrical (heterolytic)

since the volatile $B(OMe)_3$ could readily be distilled off and determined while the number of moles of H_2 evolved equalled the number of H atoms in the borane molecule:

$$B_2H_6 + 6MeOH \longrightarrow 2B(OMe)_3 + 6H_2$$

This works well for all *nido-* and *arachno-*boranes but not for the *closo-*dianions, which are much less reactive. Reactions of B_2H_6 with NH_3 are complex and, depending on the conditions, yield aminodiborane, $H_2B(\mu\text{-}H)(\mu\text{-}NH_2)BH_2$, or the diammoniate of diborane, $[BH_2(NH_3)_2]$-$[BH_4]$ (p. 165); at higher temperatures the benzene analogue borazine, $(HNBH)_3$, results (see p. 210).

The remarkably facile addition of B_2H_6 to alkenes and alkynes in ether solvents at room temperatures was discovered by H. C. Brown and B. C. Subba Rao in 1956:

$$3RCH{=}CH_2 + \tfrac{1}{2}B_2H_6 \longrightarrow B(CH_2CH_2R)_3$$

This reaction, now termed hydroboration, has opened up the quantitative preparation of organoboranes and these, in turn, have proved to be of outstanding synthetic utility.[30,31] It was for his development of this field that H. C. Brown (Purdue) was awarded the 1979 Nobel Prize in Chemistry. Hydroboration is regiospecific, the boron showing preferential attachment to the least substituted C atom (anti-Markovnikov). This finds ready interpretation in terms of electronic factors and relative bond polarities (p. 144); steric factors also work in the same direction. The addition is stereospecific *cis (syn)*. Recent extensions of the methodology have encompassed the significant development of generalized chiral syntheses.[32]

---

[30] H. C. Brown, *Organic Syntheses via Boranes*, Wiley, New York, 1975, 283 pp., *Boranes in Organic Chemistry*, Cornell University Press, Ithaca, New York, 1972, 462 pp.

[31] D. J. Pasto, Solution reactions of borane and substituted boranes, Chap. 5 in ref. 7, pp. 197–222.

[32] H. C. Brown and B. Singaram, *Pure Appl. Chem.* **59**, 879–94 (1987); H. C. Brown and P. V. Ramachandran, *Pure Appl. Chem.* **63**, 307–16 (1991) and references cited therein.

Diborane reacts slowly over a period of days with metals such as Na, K, Ca or their amalgams and more rapidly in the presence of ether:

$$2B_2H_6 + 2Na \longrightarrow NaBH_4 + NaB_3H_8$$

$B_3H_8{}^-$ prepared in this way was the first polyborane anion (1955); it is now more conveniently made by the reaction

$$B_2H_6 + NaBH_4 \xrightarrow[100°]{\text{diglyme}} NaB_3H_8 + H_2$$

Alternatively, BH_3.thf can be reduced by alkali metal amalgams (M = K, Rb, Cs) to give good yields of solvent-free products:[33]

$$2M/Hg + 4BH_3.thf \xrightarrow{\text{thf}} MBH_4 + MB_3H_8$$

Tetrahydroborates, $M(BH_4)_x$, were first identified in 1940 (M = Li, Be, Al) and since then have been widely exploited as versatile nucleophilic reducing agents which attack centres of low electron density (cf. electrophiles such as B_2H_6 and LBH_3 which attack electron-rich centres). The most stable are the alkali derivatives MBH_4: $LiBH_4$ decomposes above $\sim 380°$ but the others (Na–Cs) are stable up to $\sim 600°$. MBH_4 are readily soluble in water and many other coordinating solvents such as liquid ammonia, amines, ethers ($LiBH_4$) and polyethers ($NaBH_4$). They can be prepared by direct reaction of MH with either B_2H_6 or BX_3 at room temperature though the choice of solvent is often crucial, e.g.:

$$2LiH + B_2H_6 \xrightarrow{Et_2O} 2LiBH_4$$

$$2NaH + B_2H_6 \xrightarrow{\text{diglyme}} 2NaBH_4$$

$$4LiH + Et_2OBF_3 \longrightarrow LiBH_4 + 3LiF + Et_2O$$

$$4NaH + BCl_3 \xrightarrow{Al_2Et_6} NaBH_4 + 3NaCl$$

These laboratory-scale syntheses are clearly unsuitable for large-scale industrial production;

---

[33] T. G. Hill, R. A. Godfroid, J. P. White and S. G. Shore, *Inorg. Chem.* **30**, 2952–4 (1991).

here the preferred route, introduced in the early 1960s is the Bayer process which uses borax (or ulexite), quartz, Na and H_2 under moderate pressure at 450–500°:[34]

$$(Na_2B_4O_7 + 7SiO_2) + 16Na + 8H_2$$

$$\longrightarrow 4NaBH_4 + 7Na_2SiO_3$$

The resulting mixture is extracted under pressure with liquid NH_3 and the product obtained as a 98% pure powder (or pellets) by evaporation. An alternative route is:

$$B(OMe)_3 + 4NaH \xrightarrow{250-270°} NaBH_4 + 3NaOMe$$

The resulting mixture is hydrolysed with water and the aqueous phase extracted with Pr^iNH_2.

Worldwide production of $NaBH_4$ is now about 3000 tonnes per annum (1990) and the price for powdered $NaBH_4$ in 1991 was \$48.39/kg.

Reaction of MBH_4 with electronegative elements is also often crucially dependent on the solvent and on the temperature and stoichiometry of reagents. Thus $LiBH_4$ reacts with S at $-50°$ in the presence of Et_2O to give $Li[BH_3SH]$, whereas at room temperature the main products are Li_2S, $Li[B_3S_2H_6]$, and H_2; at 200° in the absence of solvent $LiBH_4$ reacts with S to give $LiBS_2$ and either H_2 or H_2S depending on whether S is in excess. Similarly, MBH_4 react with I_2 in cyclohexane at room temperature to give BI_3, HI and MI, whereas in diglyme B_2H_6 is formed quantitatively (p. 164).

The product of reaction of BH_4^- with element halides depends on the electropositivity of the element. Halides of the electropositive elements tend to form the corresponding $M(BH_4)_x$, e.g. M = Be, Mg, Ca, Sr, Ba; Zn, Cd; Al, Ga, Tl^I; lanthanides; Ti, Zr, Hf and U^{IV}. Halides of the less electropositive elements tend to give the hydride or a hydrido-complex since the BH_4 derivative is either unstable or non-existent: thus $SiCl_4$ gives SiH_4;

PCl_3 and PCl_5 give PH_3; Ph_2AsCl gives Ph_2AsH; $[Fe(\eta^5\text{-}C_5H_5)(CO)_2Cl]$ gives $[Fe(\eta^5\text{-}C_5H_5)(CO)_2H]$, etc.

A particularly interesting reaction (and one of considerable commercial value in the BOROL process for the *in situ* bleaching of wood pulp) is the production of dithionite, $S_2O_4{}^{2-}$, from SO_2:

$$NaBH_4 + 8NaOH + 8SO_2 \xrightarrow{90\% \text{ yield}}$$

$$4Na_2S_2O_4 + NaBO_2 + 6H_2O$$

In reactions with organic compounds, $LiBH_4$ is a stronger (less selective) reducing agent than $NaBH_4$ and can be used, for example, to reduce esters to alcohols. $NaBH_4$ reduces ketones, acid chlorides and aldehydes under mild conditions but leaves other functions (such as $-CN$, $-NO_2$, esters) untouched; it can be used as a solution in alcohols, ethers, dimethylsulfoxide, or even aqueous alkali (pH > 10). Perhaps the classic example of its selectivity is shown below where an aldehyde group is hydrogenated in high yield without any attack on the nitro group, the bromine atom, the olefinic bond, or the thiophene ring:

Industrial interest in $LiBH_4$, and particularly $NaBH_4$, stems not only from their use as versatile reducing agents for organic functional groups and their use in the bleaching of wood pulp, but also for their application in the electroless (chemical) plating of metals. Traditionally, either sodium hypophosphite, NaH_2PO_2, or formaldehyde have been used (as in the silvering of glass), but $NaBH_4$ was introduced on an industrial scale in the early 1960s, notably for the deposition of Ni on metal or non-metallic substrates; this gives corrosion-resistant, hard, protective coatings, and is also useful for metallizing plastics prior to

---

[34] R. WADE, in R. THOMPSON (ed.), *Speciality Inorganic Chemistry*, Royal Soc. Chem., London, 1981, pp. 25–58; see also *Kirk–Othmer Encyclopedia of Chemical Technology*, 4th edn., John Wiley, New York, 1992, Vol. 4, pp. 490–501.

further electroplating or for depositing contacts in electronics. Chemical plating also achieves a uniform thickness of deposit independent of the geometric shape, however complicated.

The BH_4^- ion is essentially non-coordinating in its alkali metal salts. However, despite the fact that it is isoelectronic with methane, BH_4^- has been found to act as a versatile ligand, forming many coordination compounds by means of 3-centre $B-H \rightarrow M$ bonds to somewhat less electropositive metals.[35-37] Indeed, BH_4^-

affords a rare example of a ligand that can act in at least 6 coordination modes: η^1, η^2, η^3, $\mu(\eta^2,\eta^2)$, $\mu(\eta^3)$ and $\mu(\eta^4)$. Such complexes are usually readily prepared by reacting the corresponding (or closely related) halides with BH_4^- in what are essentially ligand replacement reactions. Some examples follow:

η^1: $[Cu(\eta^1\text{-}\dot{B}H_4)(PMePh_2)_3]$ (see Fig. 6.14a); $[Cu(\eta^1\text{-}BH_4)\{MeC(CH_2PPh_2)_3\}]$; $[FeH(\eta^1\text{-}BH_4)$-

[35] B. D. JAMES and M. G. H. WALLBRIDGE, *Prog. Inorg. Chem.* **11**, 99–231 (1970).

[36] P. A. WEGNER, Chap. 12 in ref. 9, pp. 431–80.
[37] T. J. MARKS and J. R. KOLB, *Chem. Rev.* **77**, 263–93 (1977).

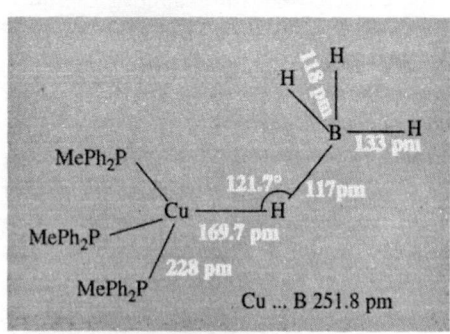

(a) $[Cu^I(\eta^1\text{-}BH_4)(PMePh_2)_3]$

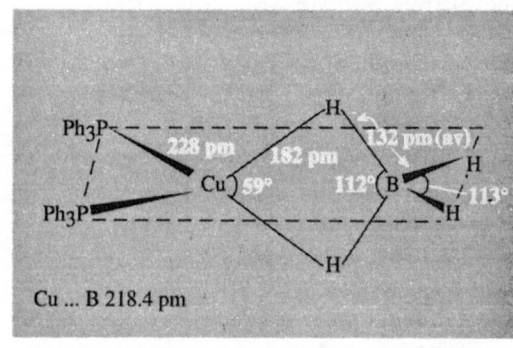

(b) $[Cu^I(\eta^2\text{-}BH_4)(PPh_3)_2]$

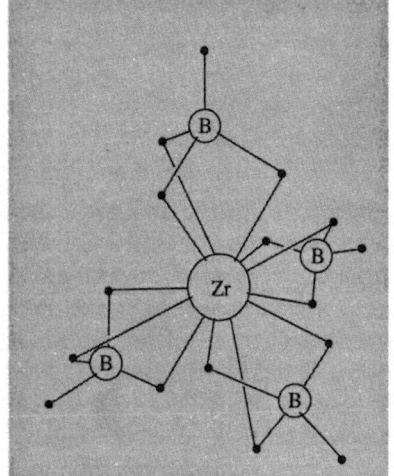

(c) $[Zr^{IV}(\eta^3\text{-}BH_4)_4]$

(d) $[\{RuH(tripod)\}_2 \, (\mu\text{:}\eta^2,\eta^2\text{-}BH_4)]^+$

Figure 6.14 Examples of the various coordination modes of BH_4^- (continued on facing page).

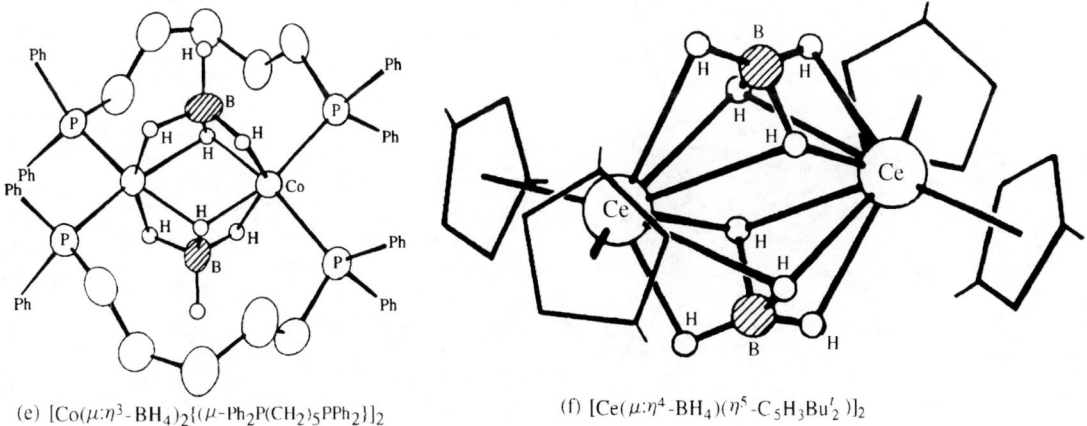

(e) $[Co(\mu{:}\eta^3{-}BH_4)_2\{(\mu{-}Ph_2P(CH_2)_5PPh_2)\}]_2$

(f) $[Ce(\mu{:}\eta^4{-}BH_4)(\eta^5{-}C_5H_3Bu^t_2)]_2$

Figure 6.14　continued

(dmpe)] (dmpe = Me₂PCH₂CH₂PMe₂); [*trans*-V(η^1-BH₄)₂ (dmpe)₂]; (also B₂H₇⁻, i.e. [BH₃(η^1-BH₄)]⁻)

η^2: [Al(η^2-BH₄)₃] (see p. 230); [Cu(η^2-BH₄)-(PPh₃)₂] (Fig. 6.14b); [Ti^III(η^2-BH₄)₃(dme)] (dme = 1,2-dimethoxyethane); [Sc(η^2-BH₄)(η^5-Cp^II)₂] (Cp^II = {C₅H₃(SiMe₃)₂}); [Y(η^2-BH₄)-(η^5-Cp^II)₂(thf)]

η^3: [M(η^3-BH₄)₄] (M = Zr, Hf, Np, Pu; see Fig. 6.14c); [Ln(η^3-BH₄)(η^5-Cp^II)₂(thf)] (Ln = La, Pr, Nd, Sm); [U^IV(η^3-BH₄)₃(η^5-C₅H₅)]

$\mu(\eta^2,\eta^2)$: [{RuH(tripod)}₂($\mu{:}\eta^2,\eta^2$-BH₄)]⁺ (Fig. 6.14d)

$\mu(\eta^3)$: [Co($\mu{:}\eta^3$-BH₄){μ-Ph₂P(CH₂)₅PPh₂}]₂ (Fig. 6.14e); [(tmeda)Li-$\mu(\eta^3$-BH₄)]₂ (tmeda = tetramethylethylenediamine)

$\mu(\eta^4)$: [Ce($\mu{:}\eta^4$-BH₄)(η^5-C₅H₃Bu'₂)]₂ (Fig. 6.14f)

Many complexes have more than one coordination mode of BH₄⁻ featured in their structure, e.g. [U^III(η^2-BH₄)(η^3-BH₄)₂(dmpe)₂]. Likewise, whereas [M(BH₄)₄] are monomeric 12-coordinate complexes for M = Zr, Hf, Np, Pu, they are polymeric for M = Th, Pa, U: the coordination number rises to 14 and each metal centre is coordinated by two η^3-BH₄⁻ and four bridging η^2-BH₄⁻ groups. It is clear that among the factors which determine the mode adopted are the size of the metal atom and the steric requirements of the co-ligands. Many of the complexes

are fluxional on an nmr timescale in solution; indeed, this property of fluxionality, which has been increasingly recognized to occur in many inorganic and organometallic systems, was first observed (1955) on the tris-bidentate complex [Al(η^2-BH₄)₃].[38]

The B₃H₈⁻ ion (p. 166) is a triangular cluster of C_s (rather than C_{2v}) symmetry (see Fig. 6.15a);[39] the bridging H$_\mu$ atoms are essentially in the B₃ plane with H$_t$ above and below. While it has been conventional to represent the cluster bonding in terms of two BHB and one B–B bond (Fig. 6.15b), recent high-level computations[40] suggest the presence of a 3-centre BBB bond, as depicted approximately in Fig. 6.15c.

The *arachno*-anion B₃H₈⁻ is the only binary triboron species that is stable at room temperature and above. It can be viewed as a ligand-stabilized {B₃H₇} group, i.e. (L.B₃H₇], in which the ligand is H⁻ (cf. BH₄⁻). However, the ion is completely fluxional in solution, all three boron atoms (and all eight protons) being equivalent on an nmr timescale. The B₃H₈⁻ anion has an

[38] R. A. OGG and J. D. RAY, *Disc. Faraday Soc.* **19**, 239–46 (1955).

[39] H. J. DEISEROTH, O. SOMMER, H. BINDER, K. WOLFER and B. FREI, *Z. anorg. allg. Chem.* **571**, 21–8 (1989).

[40] M. SIRONI, M. RAIMONDI, D. L. COOPER and J. GERRATT, *J. Phys. Chem.* **95**, 10617–23 (1991).

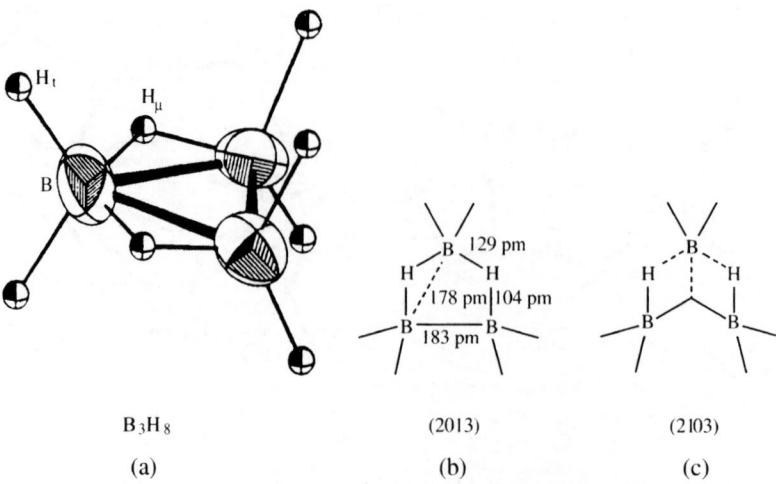

B_3H_8

(a)

(2013)

(b)

(2103)

(c)

Figure 6.15   (a) Structure of $B_3H_8^-$ showing C_s symmetry; (b) dimensions and representation of the bonding using a direct B–B bond (2013) for the longer (unbridged) B–B distance; (c) most recent (2103) description of the bonding in terms of a 3-centre BBB bond. (See p. 158 for *styx* formalism.)

extensive reaction chemistry both as a reducing agent and as a source of *arachno*-B_4H_{10} (p. 162). Conversely, unsymmetrical (heterolytic) cleavage of B_4H_{10} with ligands, L, such as NH_3 yield $[L_2BH_2]^+[B_3H_8]^-$.

The $B_3H_8^-$ ion is also a versatile ligand and forms bidentate and even tridentate complexes with many metal centres.[41] The octahedrally coordinated 18-electron manganese(I) complex $[Mn(\eta^2\text{-}B_3H_8)(CO)_4]$ is a particularly instructive example. As can be seen from Fig. 6.16a it has a cluster structure that is clearly related to that of B_4H_{10} (13). When heated to 180°C or irradiated with ultraviolet light the complex loses one of the four CO ligands and this enables a further B–H group to coordinate to give the trihapto complex *fac*-$[Mn(\eta^3\text{-}B_3H_8)(CO)_3]$ (Fig. 6.16b). Treatment of this product with an excess of CO under moderate pressure regenerates the original dihapto species by a simple ligand replacement reaction.[42]

[41] D. F. GAINES and S. J. HILDEBRANDT, Chap. 3 in R. N. GRIMES (ed.), *Metal Interactions with Boron Clusters*, Plenum Press, New York, 1982, pp. 119–43.

[42] S. J. HILDEBRANDT, D. F. GAINES and J. C. CALABRESE, *Inorg. Chem.* **17**, 790–4 (1978).

6.4.5 Intermediate-sized Boranes and their Anions (B_5–B_9)

Pentaborane(9), *nido*-B_5H_9, is by far the most studied borane in this group. It can be prepared by passing a 1:5 mixture of B_2H_6 and H_2 at subatmospheric pressure through a furnace at 250°C with a residence time of 3 s (or at 225° with a 15 s residence time); there is a 70% yield and 30% conversion. Alternatively B_2H_6 can be pyrolysed for 2.5 days in a static hot/cold reactor at 180°/–80°. B_5H_9 is a colourless, volatile liquid, bp 60.0°; it is thermally stable but chemically very reactive and spontaneously flammable in air. Its structure is essentially a square-based pyramid of B atoms each of which carries a terminal H atom and there are 4 bridging H atoms around the base (structure 9, p. 154). The slant edge of the pyramid, B(1)–B(2), is 168 pm and the basal interboron distances, B(2)–B(3) etc, are 178 pm; other key dimensions are B–H_t 122 pm, B–H_μ 135 pm and B–H_μ–B 83°. Calculations suggest that B(1) has a slightly higher electron density than the basal borons and that H_μ is slightly more positive than H_t. Apex-substituted derivatives 1-XB_5H_8 can

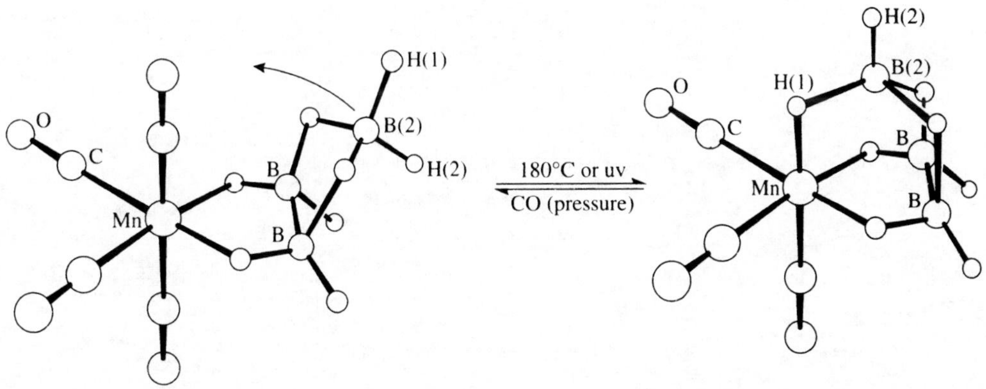

Figure 6.16 Ligand replacement reaction of $[Mn(\eta^2\text{-}B_3H_8)(CO)_4]$ (see text).

readily be prepared by electrophilic substitution (e.g. halogenation or Friedel-Crafts alkylation with RX or alkenes), whereas base-substituted derivatives $2\text{-}XB_5H_8$ result when nucleophilic reaction is induced by amines or ethers, or when $1\text{-}XB_5H_8$ is isomerized in the presence of a Lewis base such as hexamethylenetetramine or an ether:

$$B_5H_9 \xrightarrow{I_2/AlX_3} 1\text{-}IB_5H_8 \xrightarrow[(CH_2)_6N_4]{base} 2\text{-}IB_5H_8$$

$$\xrightarrow{SbF_3} 2\text{-}FB_5H_8$$

Further derivatives can be obtained by metathesis, e.g.

$$2\text{-}ClB_5H_8 + NaMn(CO)_5 \longrightarrow$$

$$2\text{-}\{(CO)_5Mn\}B_5H_8 \text{ (also Re)}$$

B_5H_9 reacts with Lewis bases (electron-pair donors) to form adducts, some of which have now been recognized as belonging to the new series of *hypho*-borane derivatives B_nH_{n+8} (p. 152). Thus PMe_3 gives the adduct $[B_5H_9(PMe_3)_2]$ which is formally analogous to $[B_5H_{11}]^{2-}$ and the (unknown) borane B_5H_{13}. $[B_5H_9(PMe_3)_2]$ has a very open structure in the form of a shallow pyramid with the ligands attached at positions 1 and 2 and with major rearrangement of the H atoms (Fig. 6.17a). Chelating phosphine ligands such as $(Ph_2P)_2CH_2$

and $(Ph_2PCH_2)_2$ have similar structures but $[B_5H_9(Me_2NCH_2CH_2NMe_2)]$ undergoes a much more severe distortion in which the ligand chelates a single boron atom, $B(2)$, which is joined to the rest of the molecule by a single bond to the apex $B(1)$ (Fig. 6.17b).[43] With NH_3 as ligand (at $-78°$) complete excision of one B atom occurs by "unsymmetrical cleavage" to give $[(NH_3)_2BH_2]^+[B_4H_7]^-$.

B_5H_9 also acts as a weak Brønsted acid and, from proton competition reactions with other boranes and borane anions, it has been established that acidity increases with increasing size of the borane cluster and that *arachno*-boranes are more acidic than *nido*-boranes:

nido : $B_5H_9 < B_6H_{10} < B_{10}H_{14} < B_{16}H_{20} < B_{18}H_{22}$

arachno : $B_4H_{10} < B_5H_{11} < B_6H_{12}$ and

$$B_4H_{10} > B_6H_{10}$$

Accordingly, B_5H_9 can be deprotonated at low temperatures by loss of H_μ to give $B_5H_8^-$ providing a sufficiently strong base such as a lithium alkyl or alkali metal hydride is used. Bridge-substituted derivatives of B_5H_9 can then be obtained by reacting MB_5H_8 with chloro compounds such as R_2PCl, Me_3SiCl, Me_3GeCl,

─────────
43 N. W. ALCOCK, H. M. COLQUHOUN, G. HARAN, J. F. SAWYER and M. G. H. WALLBRIDGE, *J. Chem. Soc., Chem. Commun.*, 368–70 (1977); *J. Chem. Soc., Dalton Trans.*, 2243–55 (1982).

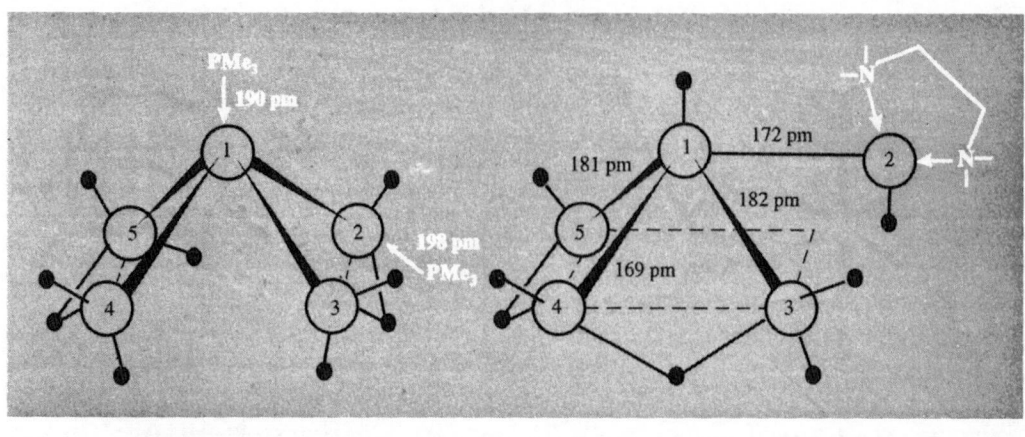

(a) [B₅H₉(PMe₃)₂]   (b) [B₅H₉(Me₂NCH₂CH₂NMe₂)]

Figure 6.17 Structure of *hypho*-borane derivatives: (a) $[B_5H_9(PMe_3)_2]$ — the distances B(1)-B(2) and B(2)-B(3) are as in B_5H_9 (p. 170) but B(3)···B(4) is 295 pm (cf. B···B 297 pm in B_5H_{11}, structure 14, p. 154), and (b) $[B_5H_9(Me_2NCH_2CH_2NMe_2)]$ — the distances B(2)···B(3) and B(2)···B(5) are 273 and 272 pm respectively.

or even Me_2BCl to give compounds in which the 3-centre $B-H_\mu-B$ bond has been replaced by a 3-centre bond between the 2 B atoms and P, Si, Ge or B respectively. Many metal-halide coordination complexes react similarly, and the products can be considered as adducts in which the $B_5H_8{}^-$ anion is acting formally as a 2-electron ligand via a 3-centre $B-M-B$ bond.[44,45] Thus $[Cu^I(B_5H_8)(PPh_3)_2]$ (Fig. 6.18a) is readily formed by the low-temperature reaction of KB_5H_8 with $[CuCl(PPh_3)_3]$ and analogous 16-electron complexes have been prepared for many of the later transition elements, e.g. $[Cd(B_5H_8)Cl(PPh_3)]$, $[Ag(B_5H_8)(PPh_3)_2]$ and $[M^{II}(B_5H_8)XL_2]$, where M^{II} = Ni, Pd, Pt; X = Cl, Br, I; L_2 = a diphosphine or related ligand. By contrast, $[Ir^I(CO)Cl(PPh_3)_2]$ reacts by oxidative insertion of Ir and consequent cluster expansion to give $[(IrB_5H_8)(CO)(PPh_3)_2]$ which, though superficially of similar formula, has the structure of an irida-*nido*-hexaborane

(Fig. 6.18b).[46] In this, the $\{Ir(CO)(PPh_3)_2\}$ moiety replaces a basal BH_tH_μ unit in B_6H_{10} (structure 10, p. 154).

Cluster-expansion and cluster-degradation reactions are a feature of many polyhedral borane species. Examples of cluster-expansion are:[11,47]

$$LiB_5H_8 + \tfrac{1}{2}B_2H_6 \xrightarrow[\text{(fast)}]{\text{Et}_2\text{O}/-78°} LiB_6H_{11}$$

$$\xrightarrow{\text{HCl}} B_6H_{12}$$

$$LiB_5H_8 + B_2H_6 \xrightarrow[\text{(slow)}]{\text{Me}_2\text{O}/-78°} \{LiB_7H_{14}\}$$

$$\longrightarrow B_6H_{10} + LiBH_4$$

$$1.8B_5H_9 + MH \xrightarrow[\text{15 h}]{\text{thf/r.t.}} MB_9H_{14} + H_2 \text{ plus}$$

minor products (M=Na, K)

[44] N. N. GREENWOOD and I. M. WARD, *Chem. Soc. Revs.* **3**, 231–71 (1974).

[45] N. N. GREENWOOD, *Pure Appl. Chem.* **49**, 791–802 (1977).

[46] N. N. GREENWOOD, J. D. KENNEDY, W. S. McDONALD, D. REED and J. STAVES, *J. Chem. Soc., Dalton Trans.*, 117–23 (1979).

[47] N. S. HOSMANE, J. R. WERMER, ZHU HONG, T. D. GETMAN and S. G. SHORE, *Inorg. Chem.* **26**, 3638–9 (1987), and references cited therein.

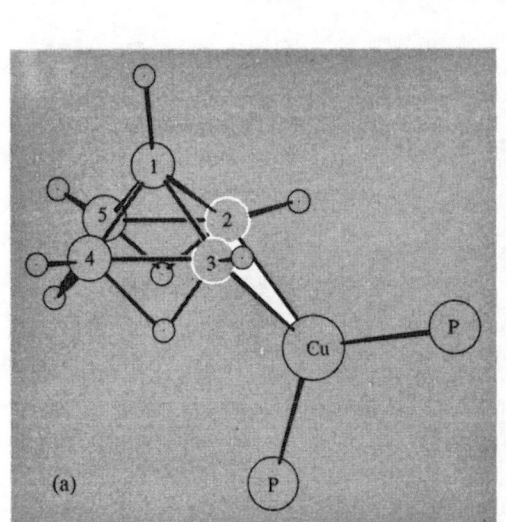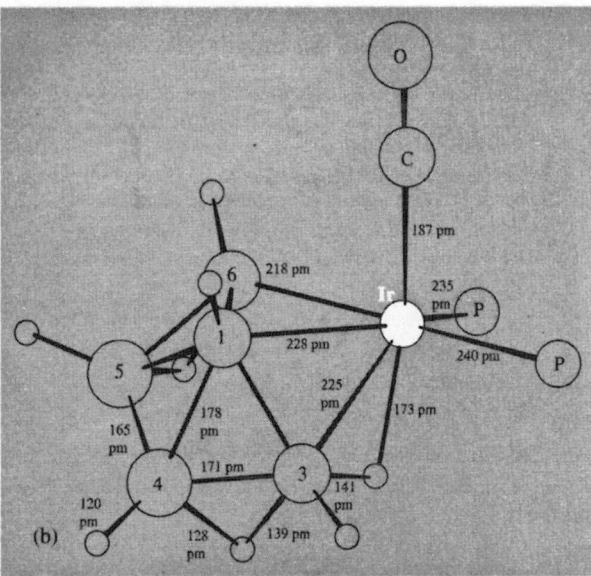

Figure 6.18 (a) Structure of [Cu(B₅H₈)(PPh₃)₂], showing η^2-bonding of B₅H₈⁻ (phenyl groups omitted for clarity); (b) Structure of [(IrB₅H₈)(CO)(PPh₃)₂] showing the structure about the iridium atom and the relationship of the metallaborane cluster to that of *nido*-B₆H₁₀.

$$KB_9H_{14} + 0.4B_5H_9 \xrightarrow[20\,h]{glyme/85°} KB_{11}H_{14} + 1.8H_2$$

Cluster degradation has already been mentioned in connection with the unsymmetrical cleavage reaction (p. 165) and other examples are:

$$[NMe_4]B_5H_8 + 6Pr^iOH \longrightarrow [NMe_4]B_3H_8$$
$$+ 2B(OPr^i)_3 + 3H_2$$

$$\text{and } B_5H_9 \xrightarrow{tmed} B_5H_9(tmed) \xrightarrow{MeOH} B_4H_8(tmed)$$
$$+ B(OMe)_3 + 2H_2$$

(where Pr^i is Me₂CH– and tmed is Me₂NCH₂-CH₂NMe₂).

Replacement of a {BH} unit in B₅H₉ by an "isoelectronic" organometallic group such as {Fe(CO)₃} or {Co(η^5-C₅H₅)} can also occur, and this illustrates the close interrelation between metalloboranes, metal–metal cluster compounds, and organometallic complexes in general (see Panel).

The structures of several other *nido-* and *arachno-* B₅–B₉ boranes are given on page 154 but a detailed discussion of their chemistry is beyond the scope of this treatment. Further information is in refs. 9, 11, 27, 51 and 52.

6.4.6 *Chemistry of* nido-*decaborane,* B₁₀H₁₄

Decaborane is the most studied of all the polyhedral boranes and at one time (mid-1950s) was manufactured on a multitonne scale in the USA as a potential high-energy fuel. It is now obtainable in research quantities by the pyrolysis of B₂H₆ at 100–200°C in the presence of catalytic amounts of Lewis bases such as Me₂O. B₁₀H₁₄ is a colourless, volatile, crystalline solid (see Table 6.2, p. 163) which

Metalloboranes, Metal Clusters and Organometallic Complexes

Copyrolysis of B_5H_9 and $[Fe(CO)_5]$ in a hot/cold reactor at $220°/20°$ for 3 days gives an orange liquid (mp $5°C$) of formula $[1-\{Fe(CO)_3\}B_4H_8]$ having the structure shown in (a).[48] The isoelectronic complex $[1-\{Co(\eta^5-C_5H_5)\}B_4H_8]$ (structure b) can be obtained as yellow crystals by pyrolysis at $200°$ of the corresponding basal derivative $[2-\{Co(\eta^5-C_5H_5)\}B_4H_8]$ (structure (c)) which is obtained as red crystals from the reaction of NaB_5H_8 and $CoCl_2$ with NaC_5H_5 in thf at $-20°$.[49] The course of these reactions is obscure and other products are also obtained.

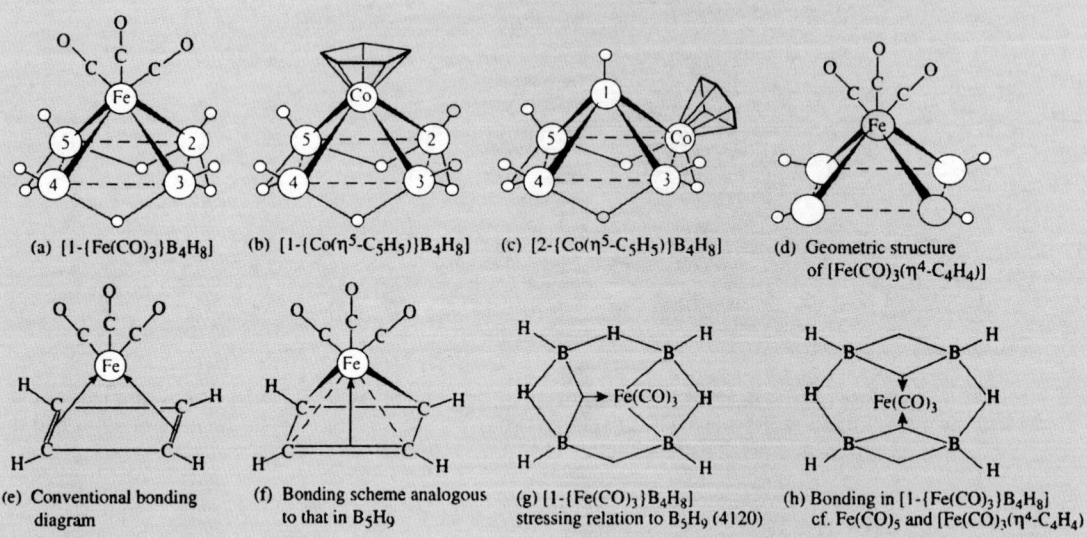

(a) $[1-\{Fe(CO)_3\}B_4H_8]$

(b) $[1-\{Co(\eta^5-C_5H_5)\}B_4H_8]$

(c) $[2-\{Co(\eta^5-C_5H_5)\}B_4H_8]$

(d) Geometric structure of $[Fe(CO)_3(\eta^4-C_4H_4)]$

(e) Conventional bonding diagram

(f) Bonding scheme analogous to that in B_5H_9

(g) $[1-\{Fe(CO)_3\}B_4H_8]$ stressing relation to B_5H_9 (4120)

(h) Bonding in $[1-\{Fe(CO)_3\}B_4H_8]$ cf. $Fe(CO)_5$ and $[Fe(CO)_3(\eta^4-C_4H_4)]$

As $\{BH_2\}$ is isoelectronic with $\{CH\}$, these metalloborane clusters are isoelectronic with the cyclobutadiene adduct $[Fe(\eta^4-C_4H_4)(CO)_3]$, see (d), (e) and (f). Likewise $\{Fe(CO)_3\}$ or $\{Co(\eta^5-C_5H_5)\}$ can replace a $\{BH\}$ group in B_5H_9 and two descriptions of the bonding are given in (g) and (h): the Fe atom supplies 2 electrons and 3 atomic orbitals to the cluster (as does BH), thereby enabling it to form 2 Fe–B σ bonds and to accept a pair of electrons from adjacent B atoms to form a 3-centre BMB bond. In this description the Fe atom is formally octahedral Fe^{II} (d^6). Alternatively, diagram (h) emphasizes the relation between $[1-\{Fe(CO)_3\}B_4H_8]$ and $[Fe(CO)_3(\eta^4-C_4H_4)]$ or $[Fe(CO)_5]$: the Fe atom accepts 2 pairs of electrons to form two 3-centre BMB bonds and is formally Fe^0 with a trigonal bipyramidal arrangement of bonds.

It is possible to replace more than one $\{BH\}$ group in B_5H_9 by a metal centre, e.g in the dimetalla species $[1,2-\{Fe(CO)_3\}_2B_3H_7]$;[50] it is also notable that the iron carbonyl cluster compound $[Fe_5(CO)_{15}C]$ (p. 1108) features the same square-pyramidal cluster in which 5 $\{Fe(CO)_3\}$ groups have replaced the five $\{BH\}$ groups in B_5H_9, and the C atom (in the centre of the base) replaces the 4 bridging H atoms by supplying the 4 electrons required to complete the bonding.

Many other equivalent groups can be envisaged and the formalism permits a unified approach to possible synthetic routes and to probable structures of a wide variety of compounds.[17,51–53]

[48] N. N. GREENWOOD, C. G. SAVORY, R. N. GRIMES, L. G. SNEDDON, A. DAVISON and S. S. WREFORD, *J. Chem. Soc., Chem. Commun.*, 718 (1974).

[49] V. R. MILLER and R. N. GRIMES, *J. Am. Chem. Soc.* **95**, 5078–80 (1973).

[50] K. J. HALLER, E. L. ANDERSEN and T. P. FEHLNER, *Inorg. Chem.* **20**, 309–13 (1981).

[51] N. N. GREENWOOD and J. D. KENNEDY, Chap. 2 in R. N. GRIMES (ed.), *Metal Interactions with Boron Clusters*, Plenum, New York, 1982, pp. 43–118.

[52] J. D. KENNEDY, *Prog. Inorg. Chem.* **32**, 519–679 (1984); **34**, 211–434 (1986).

[53] T. P. FEHLNER (ed.), *Inorganometallic Chemistry*, Plenum, New York, 1992, 401 pp.

is insoluble in H$_2$O but readily soluble in a wide range of organic solvents. Its structure (36) can be regarded as derived from the 11 B atom cluster B$_{11}$H$_{11}^{2-}$ (p. 153) by replacing the unique BH group with 2 electrons and appropriate addition of 4H$_\mu$. MO-calculations give the sequence of electron charge densities at the various B atoms as 2, 4 > 1, 3 > 5, 7, 8, 10 > 6, 9 though the total range of deviation from charge neutrality is less than ±0.1 electron per B atom. The chemistry of B$_{10}$H$_{14}$ can be conveniently discussed under the headings (a) proton abstraction, (b) electron addition, (c) adduct formation, (d) cluster rearrangements, cluster expansions, and cluster degradation reactions, and (e) metalloborane and other heteroborane compounds.

B$_{10}$H$_{14}$ can be titrated in aqueous/alcoholic media as a monobasic acid, pK_a 2.70:

$$B_{10}H_{14} + OH^- \rightleftharpoons B_{10}H_{13}^- + H_2O$$

Proton abstraction can also be effected by other strong bases such as H$^-$, OMe$^-$, NH$_2^-$, etc. The B$_{10}$H$_{13}^-$ ion is formed by loss of a bridge proton, as expected, and this results in a considerable shortening of the B(5)–B(6) distance from 179 pm in B$_{10}$H$_{14}$ to 165 pm in B$_{10}$H$_{13}^-$ (structures 36, 37). Under more forcing conditions with NaH a second H$_\mu$ can be removed to give Na$_2$B$_{10}$H$_{12}$; the probable structure of B$_{10}$H$_{12}^{2-}$ is (38) and the anion acts as a formal bidentate (tetrahapto) ligand to many metals (p. 177).

Electron addition to B$_{10}$H$_{14}$ can be achieved by direct reaction with alkali metals in ethers, benzene or liquid NH$_3$:

$$B_{10}H_{14} + 2Na \longrightarrow Na_2B_{10}H_{14}$$

A more convenient preparation of the B$_{10}$H$_{14}^{2-}$ anion uses the reaction of aqueous BH$_4^-$ in alkaline solution:

$$B_{10}H_{14} \xrightarrow{\;+BH_4^- - \{BH_3\}\;} B_{10}H_{15}^- \underset{+H^+}{\overset{-H^+}{\rightleftharpoons}} B_{10}H_{14}^{2-}$$

Structure (39) conforms to the predicted (2632) topology (p. 158) and shows that the 2 added electrons have relieved the electron deficiency to the extent that the 2 B–H$_\mu$–B groups have been

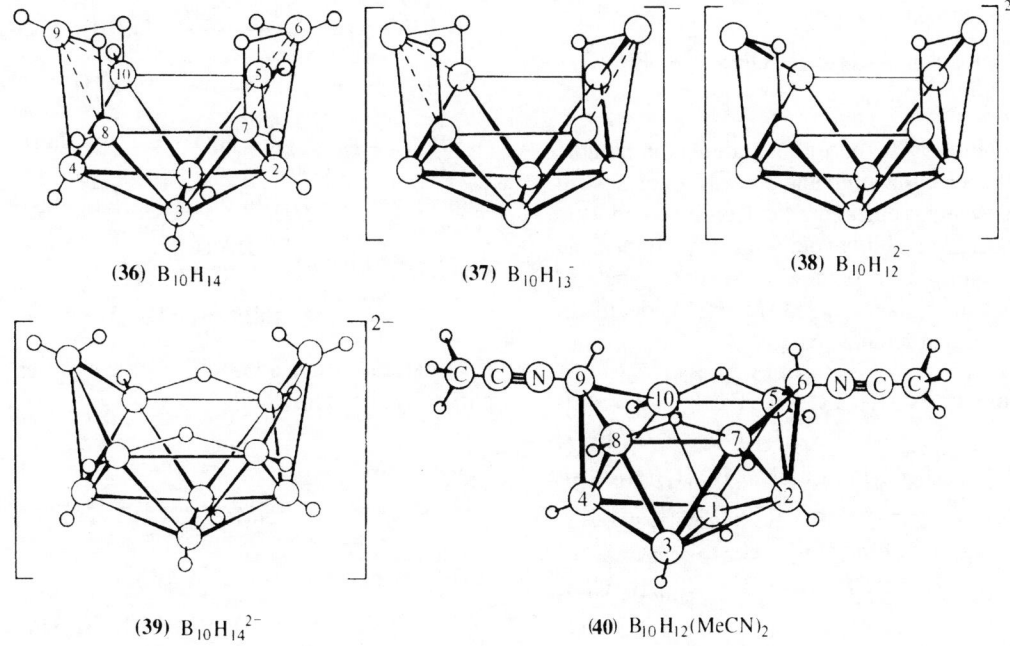

(36) B$_{10}$H$_{14}$

(37) B$_{10}$H$_{13}^-$

(38) B$_{10}$H$_{12}^{2-}$

(39) B$_{10}$H$_{14}^{2-}$

(40) B$_{10}$H$_{12}$(MeCN)$_2$

converted to $B-H_t$ with the consequent appearance of $2BH_2$ groups in the structure. Calculations show that this conversion of a *nido-* to an *arachno*-cluster reverses the sequence of electron charge density at the 2, 4 and 6, 9 positions so that for $B_{10}H_{14}{}^{2-}$ the sequence is 6, 9 > 1, 3 > 5, 7, 8, 10 > 2, 4; this is paralleled by changes in the chemistry. $B_{10}H_{14}{}^{2-}$ can formally be regarded as $B_{10}H_{12}L_2$ for the special case of $L = H^-$. Compounds of intermediate stoichiometry $B_{10}H_{13}L^-$ are formed when $B_{10}H_{14}$ is deprotonated in the presence of the ligand L:

$$B_{10}H_{14} \xrightarrow{\text{Et}_2\text{O/NaH}} B_{10}H_{13}{}^- \xrightarrow{\text{Et}_2\text{O/L}} [B_{10}H_{13}L]^-$$
$$\xrightarrow{\text{NMe}_4{}^+} [NMe_4][B_{10}H_{13}L]$$

The adducts $B_{10}H_{12}L_2$ (structure 40) can be prepared by direct reaction of $B_{10}H_{14}$ with L or by ligand replacement reactions:

$$B_{10}H_{14} + 2MeCN \longrightarrow B_{10}H_{12}(MeCN)_2 + H_2$$
$$B_{10}H_{12}L_2 + 2L' \longrightarrow B_{10}H_{12}L_2' + 2L$$

Ligands L, L' can be drawn from virtually the full range of inorganic and organic neutral and anionic ligands and, indeed, the reaction severely limits the range of donor solvents in which $B_{10}H_{14}$ can be dissolved. The approximate sequence of stability is:

$$SR_2 < RCN < AsR_3 < RCONMe_2 < P(OR)_3$$
$$< py \approx NEt_3 \approx PPh_3$$

The stability of the phosphine adducts is notable as is the fact that thioethers readily form such adducts whereas ethers do not. Bis-ligand adducts of moderate stability play an important role in activating decaborane for several types of reaction to be considered in more detail in subsequent paragraphs, e.g.:

Substitution: $B_{10}H_{12}(SR_2)_2 + HX \xrightarrow{\text{C}_6\text{H}_6/20°}$
$$6\text{-}(5\text{-})XB_{10}H_{13} \ (X = F, Cl, Br, I)$$

Cluster rearrangement: *arachno*-$B_{10}H_{12}(NEt_3)_2$
$$\longrightarrow [NEt_3H]^+{}_2[\textit{closo}\text{-}B_{10}H_{10}]^{2-}$$

Cluster addition: *arachno*-$B_{10}H_{12}(SR_2)_2 +$
$$2RC{\equiv}CR \longrightarrow \textit{closo}\text{-}B_{10}H_{10}(CR)_2$$
$$+ 2SR_2 + H_2$$

Cluster degradation: $B_{10}H_{12}L_2 + 3ROH \longrightarrow$
$$B_9H_{13}L + B(OR)_3 + L + H_2$$

In this last reaction it is the coordinated B atom at position 9 that is solvolytically cleaved from the cluster.

Electrophilic substitution of $B_{10}H_{14}$ follows the sequence of electron densities in the ground-state molecule. Thus halogenation in the presence of $AlCl_3$ leads to 1- and 2-monosubstituted derivatives and to 2,4-disubstitution. Similarly, Friedel–Crafts alkylations with $RX/AlCl_3$ (or $FeCl_3$) yield mixtures such as 2-$MeB_{10}H_{13}$, 2,4- and 1,2-$Me_2B_{10}H_{12}$, 1,2,3- and 1,2,4-$Me_3B_{10}H_{11}$, and 1,2,3,4-$Me_4B_{10}H_{10}$. By contrast, nucleophilic substitution (like the adduct formation with Lewis bases) occurs preferentially at the 6 (9) position; e.g., LiMe produces 6-$MeB_{10}H_{13}$ as the main product with smaller amounts of 5-$MeB_{10}H_{13}$, 6,5(8)-$Me_2B_{10}H_{12}$ and 6,9-$Me_2B_{10}H_{12}$.

$B_{10}H_{14}$ undergoes numerous cluster-addition reactions in which B or other atoms become incorporated in an expanded cluster. Thus in a reaction which differs from that on p. 175 $BH_4{}^-$ adds to $B_{10}H_{14}$ with elimination of H_2 to form initially the *nido*-$B_{11}H_{14}{}^-$ anion (structure 41, p. 178) and then the *closo*-$B_{12}H_{12}{}^{2-}$:

$$B_{10}H_{14} + LiBH_4 \xrightarrow{\text{monoglyme/90}°} LiB_{11}H_{14} + 2H_2$$

$$B_{10}H_{14} + 2LiBH_4 \longrightarrow Li_2B_{12}H_{12} + 5H_2$$

A more convenient high-yield synthesis of $B_{12}H_{12}{}^{2-}$ is by the direct reaction of amine-boranes with $B_{10}H_{14}$ in the absence of solvents:

$$B_{10}H_{14} + 2Et_3NBH_3 \xrightarrow{90-100°}$$
$$[NEt_3H]_2{}^+[B_{12}H_{12}]^{2-} + 3H_2$$

Heteroatom cluster addition reactions are exemplified by the following:

$$B_{10}H_{14} + Me_3NAlH_3 \xrightarrow{\text{Et}_2\text{O}}$$
$$[NMe_3H]^+[AlB_{10}H_{14}]^- + H_2$$

$$B_{10}H_{14} + 2TlMe_3 \xrightarrow{\text{Et}_2\text{O}}$$
$$[TlMe_2]^+[B_{10}H_{12}TlMe_2]^-$$

The Concept of Boranes as Ligands

Boranes are usually regarded as being electron-deficient, in the sense that they have an insufficient number of electrons to form classical 2-centre 2-electron bonds between each contiguous pair of atoms. However, in the mid-1960s several groups began to realize that, far from being deficient in electrons, many boranes and their anions could act as very effective polyhapto ligands: that is, they could form donor–acceptor complexes (coordination compounds, Chap. 19) in which the borane cluster itself was acting as the electron donor or ligand. The application of this astonishing idea has extended enormously the range of boron hydride compounds which can be made.[54] Many aspects have already been alluded to in the preceding pages and these are briefly summarized in this Panel.

Boranes can act as ligands either by forming 3-centre, 2-electron B–H–M bonds (analogous to BHB bonds) or by forming direct B_nM bonds ($n = 1$–6, analogous to B–B, BBB etc bonds). All hapticities from η^1–η^6 and occasionally beyond are known. The various coordination modes of BH_4^- and $B_3H_8^-$ were discussed on pp. 168–71; these involve the conversion of B–H_t bonds to B–H→M bonds. Likewise, the use of $B_5H_8^-$ as an η^2-ligand was described on pp. 172–3, this involves the notional donation to a metal centre of the electron pair in a B–B bond, thus forming a BMB 3-centre bond. $B_5H_8^-$ can also act as a notional η^1-donor by replacement of a terminal H atom in B_5H_9 with a metal centre; e.g. direct reaction of B_5H_8Cl or B_5H_8Br with $NaM(CO)_5$ to give $[M(\eta^1\text{-}2\text{-}B_5H_8)(CO)_5]$ (M = Mn, Re).

It is clear that some boranes are amphoteric Lewis acid/bases — that is they can act either as electron-pair donors as above or as electron-pair acceptors (e.g. in $L.BH_3$ and $L.B_3H_7$). It follows that a borane donor could conceivably ligate to a borane acceptor to form a borane–borane complex, i.e. a larger borane, e.g. $BH_4^- + \{BH_3\} \longrightarrow B_2H_7^-$ (p. 154). In this sense B_2H_6 itself could be regarded either as a coordination complex of BH_4^- with the notional cation $\{BH_2^+\}$, or as the mutual coordination of two monodentate $\{BH_3\}$ units. Replacement of these donors with stronger ligands such as NH_3 or NMe_3 would then result in either unsymmetrical or symmetrical cleavage of B_2H_6 as discussed on p. 165. Likewise, B_4H_{10} could be regarded either as a complex between $\eta^2\text{-}B_3H_8^-$ and $\{BH_2^+\}$ or as a mutual coordination between $\{B_3H_7\}$ and $\{BH_3\}$; reaction with stronger ligands, L, would then yield either $[L_2BH_2]^+[B_3H_8]^-$ or $L.B_3H_7$ and $L.BH_3$ by ligand displacement reactions (pp. 169–70).

The neutral *nido*-borane B_6H_{10} (structure 10) has a basal B–B bond (see p. 159) and this enables it to act as a ligand by displacing ethene from Zeise's salt (p. 930).

$$K[Pt(\eta^2\text{-}C_2H_4)Cl_3] + 2B_6H_{10} \longrightarrow trans\text{-}[Pt(\eta^2\text{-}B_6H_{10})_2Cl_2] + C_2H_4 + KCl$$

Similarly, reaction of B_6H_{10} with $Fe_2(CO)_9$ (p. 1104) at room temperature results in the smooth elimination of $Fe(CO)_5$ to form $[Fe(\eta^2\text{-}B_6H_{10})(CO)_4]$ as a stable, volatile yellow solid. Use of these electron-donor properties of B_6H_{10} towards reactive (vacant orbital) borane radicals resulted in the preparation of several new *conjuncto*-boranes, e.g. $B_{13}H_{19}$, $B_{14}H_{22}$ and $B_{15}H_{23}$ (p. 162).

Another important concept is the notion of stabilization by means of coordination. A classic example is the stabilization of the fugitive species cyclobutadiene, $\{C_4H_4\}$ by coordination to $\{Fe(CO)_3\}$ (p. 936). As the C atom is isoelectronic with $\{BH\}$, so $\{C_4H_4\}$ is isoelectronic with the borane fragment $\{B_4H_8\}$ which is similarly stabilized by coordination to $\{Fe(CO)_3\}$ or the isoelectronic $\{Co(\eta^5\text{-}C_5H_5)\}$ (see Panel on p. 174). Indeed it is a general feature of metallaborane chemistry that such clusters are often much more stable than are the parent boranes themselves.

As a result of the systematic application of coordination-chemistry principles, dozens of previously unsuspected structure types have been synthesized in which polyhedral boranes or their anions can be considered to act as ligands which donate electron density to metal centres, thereby forming novel metallaborane clusters.[36,44,45,51–54] Some 40 metals have been found to act as acceptors in this way (see also p. 178). The ideas have been particularly helpful in emphasizing the close interconnection between several previously separated branches of chemistry, notably boron hydride cluster chemistry, metallaborane and metallacarbaborane chemistry (pp. 189–95), organometallic chemistry and metal–metal cluster chemistry. All are now seen to be parts of a coherent whole.

It is also noteworthy that Alfred Stock, who is universally acclaimed as the discoverer of the boron hydrides (1912),[10] was also the first to propose the use of the term "ligand" (in a lecture in Berlin on 27 November 1916).[55] Both events essentially predate the formulation by G. N. Lewis of the electronic theory of valency (1916). It is therefore felicitous that, albeit some 20 years after Stock's death in 1946, two such apparently disparate aspects of his work should be connected in the emerging concept of "boranes as ligands".

[54] N. N. GREENWOOD, Chap 28 in G. B. KAUFFMAN (ed.), *Coordination Chemistry: A Century of Progress* A.C.S. Symposium Series No. 565 (1994) pp. 333–45.

[55] A. STOCK, *Berichte* **50**, 170 (1917).

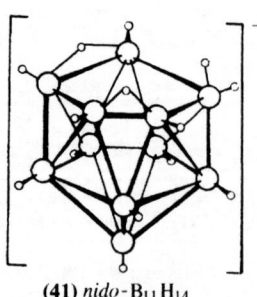

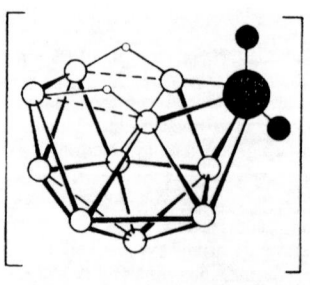

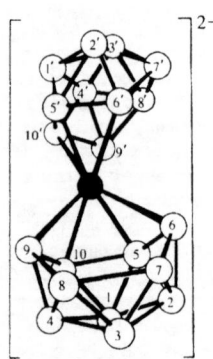

(41) *nido*-$B_{11}H_{14}$

(The open face comprises a fluxional
system involving the two H_{μ} atoms
and the *endo*-H_t atom of the BH_2
group)

(42) *nido*-$[B_{10}H_{12}TlMe_2]^-$

(43) $[Zn(B_{10}H_{12})_2]^{2-}$

$$B_{10}H_{14} + 2ZnR_2 \xrightarrow{Et_2O} [B_{10}H_{12}Zn(Et_2O)_2]$$

$$\xrightarrow{H_2O/Me_4NCl} [NMe_4]^+{}_2[Zn(B_{10}H_{12})_2]^{2-}$$

The structure of the highly reactive anion
$[AlB_{10}H_{14}]^-$ is thought to be similar to *nido*-
$B_{11}H_{14}{}^-$ with one facial B atom replaced
by Al. The metal alkyls react somewhat
differently to give extremely stable metalloborane anions which can be thought of as complexes of the bidentate ligand $B_{10}H_{12}{}^{2-}$ (structures 42, 43).[44,51,52] Many other complexes
$[M(B_{10}H_{12})_2]^{2-}$ and $[L_2M(B_{10}H_{12})]$ are known
with similar structures except that, where M =
Ni, Pd, Pt, the coordination about the metal
is essentially square-planar rather than pseudo-
tetrahedral as for Zn, Cd and Hg. Such compounds were among the first examples to be recognized of the novel and extremely fruitful perception that "electron-deficient" boranes and their
anions can, in fact, act as powerful stabilizing
electron-donor ligands (see Panel on p. 177).

6.4.7 Chemistry of closo-$B_nH_n{}^{2-(1,56,57)}$

The structures of these anions have been
indicated on p. 153. Preparative reactions are
often mechanistically obscure but thermolysis
under controlled conditions is the dominant

procedure (pp. 162–3). Many of the product
closo-boranes are not degraded even when heated
to 600°C. Salts of $B_{12}H_{12}{}^{2-}$ and $B_{10}H_{10}{}^{2-}$ are
particularly stable and their reaction chemistry
has been extensively studied. As expected
from their charge, they are extremely stable
towards nucleophiles but moderately susceptible
to electrophilic attack. For $B_{10}H_{10}{}^{2-}$ the apex
positions 1,10 are substituted preferentially to
the equatorial positions; reference to structure
(5) shows that there are 2 geometrical isomers
for monosubstituted derivatives $B_{10}H_9X_2{}^-$, 7
isomers for $B_{10}H_8X_2{}^{2-}$ and 16 for $B_{10}H_7X_3{}^{2-}$.
Many of these isomers exist, additionally,
as enantiomeric pairs. Because of its higher
symmetry $B_{12}H_{12}{}^{2-}$ has only 1 isomer for
monosubstituted species $B_{12}H_{11}X^{2-}$, 3 for
$B_{12}H_{10}X_2{}^{2-}$ (sometimes referred to as *ortho*-,
meta- and *para*-) and 5 for $B_{12}H_9X_3{}^{2-}$. A
particularly important derivative of $B_{12}H_{12}{}^{2-}$ is
the thiol $[B_{12}H_{11}(SH)]^{2-}$ which has found use in
the treatment of brain tumours by neutron capture
therapy (see Panel on next page).

Oxidation of *closo*-$B_{10}H_{10}{}^{2-}$ with aqueous
solutions of Fe^{III} or Ce^{IV} (or electrochemically)
yields *conjuncto*-$B_{20}H_{18}{}^{2-}$ (44) which can be
photoisomerized to *neo*-$B_{20}H_{18}{}^{2-}$ (45). If the
oxidation is carried out at 0° with Ce^{IV},

[56] E. L. MEUTTERTIES and W. H. KNOTH, *Polyhedral Boranes*, Marcel Dekker, New York, 1968, 197 pp.

[57] R. L. MIDDAUGH, Chap. 8 in ref. 9, pp. 273–300.

Boron-10 Neutron Capture Therapy[58,59]

Every year more than 600 000 people throughout the world contract brain tumours and about 1700 die from this cause every day. Treatment by surgical excision is usually impossible because of the site of the malignant growth and the lack of a distinct boundary (gliomas). Likewise, conventional radiotherapy (X-rays, γ-rays etc.) from outside the skull is rarely effective. An ingenious approach to this problem which has given encouraging results so far is impregnation of the tumour with a suitable boron compound, followed by irradiation with thermal neutrons which readily pass harmlessly through normal tissue but are strongly absorbed by the isotope ^{10}B. As can be seen from Table 6.1 (p. 144) ^{10}B is 767 000 times more effective than ^{11}B and, in fact, has one of the highest neutron absorption cross-sections for any nuclide. The strategy is thus to synthesize cluster compounds enriched in ^{10}B, thereby enhancing the neutron absorption cross-section of the boron nearly five-fold, and then to attach these clusters to the cells comprising the brain tumour. A single injection of, say, $Na_2[^{10}B_{12}H_{11}SH]$ usually suffices. Treatment with thermal neutrons from a nuclear reactor then releases huge amounts of energy right within the tumour tissue (and nowhere else) as a result of the nuclear reaction:

$$^{10}_{5}B + ^{1}_{0}n \longrightarrow \{^{11}_{5}B^*\} \longrightarrow ^{4}_{2}He + ^{7}_{3}Li + \gamma$$

The recoiling α-particle ($^{4}_{2}He$) and lithium nucleus ($^{7}_{3}Li$) between them carry 2.4 MeV of energy and this is shed within just a few μm, the α-particle travelling about 9 μm and the Li nucleus about 5.5 μm in the opposite direction. The radiation damage is thus confined within the cancerous tissue alone.

This is a very active area of research which involves collaboration between synthetic inorganic chemists, biochemists, neurosurgeons, nuclear physicists and reactor engineers, and there is considerable scope for advance in all of these areas.[58,60,61]

or in a two-phase system with Fe^{III} using very concentrated solutions of $B_{10}H_{10}^{2-}$, the intermediate H-bridged species $B_{20}H_{19}^{3-}$ (46) can be isolated. Reduction of *conjuncto*-$B_{20}H_{18}^{2-}$ with Na/NH_3 yields the equatorial–equatorial (ee) isomer of *conjuncto*-$B_{20}H_{18}^{4-}$ (47), and this can be successively converted by acid catalyst to the ae isomer (49) and, finally, to the aa isomer (48). Careful protonation of this aa isomer yields the elusive anion $[aa-B_{20}H_{19}]^{3-}$ in which the *conjuncto* B–B bond in structure (48) is replaced by an unsupported $B-H_{\mu}-B$ bond (angle 91(3)°, $B-H_{\mu}$ 136(5) pm, $B_a \cdots B_a$ 193.6 pm), though the two *closo* clusters still share a common axis through their B(1)-B(10) vertices.[61a] An extensive derivative chemistry of these various

species has been developed. Another important (though mechanistically obscure) reaction of *conjuncto*-$B_{20}H_{18}^{2-}$ is its degradation in high yield to n-$B_{18}H_{22}$ by passage of an enthanolic solution through an acidic ion exchange resin; i-$B_{18}H_{22}$ is also formed as a minor product. The relation of these 2 edge-fused decaborane clusters to the B_{20} species is illustrated in structures (31) and (32) (p. 156).

When salts of *closo*-$B_{10}H_{10}^{2-}$ and *closo*-$B_{12}H_{12}^{2-}$ are passed through an acid ion exchange resin, hydrates of the strong acids $H_2B_nH_n$ are obtained. For example, $[NEt_4]^+_2$-$[B_{10}H_{10}]^{2-}$ gives $H_2B_{10}H_{10}.4H_2O$ which, on careful dehydration, yields the dihydrate, $[H_3O]^+_2[B_{10}H_{10}]^{2-}$. Repeated low-pressure evaporation of benzene solutions of this acid at room temperature results in reductive cluster opening to give the *nido*-decaborane derivative $[6,6'-(B_{10}H_{13})_2O]$ in good yield, probably via *nido*-6-$B_{10}H_{13}(OH)$.[62] The structure of the readily sublimable bis(*nido*-decaboranyl) oxide,

[58] A. H. SOLOWAY, F. ALAM, R. F. BARTH, N. MAFUNE, B. BAPAT and D. M. ADAMS, in S. Heřmánek (ed.), *Boron Chemistry: Proc. 6th Internat. Meeting on Boron Chemistry*, World Scientific, Singapore, 1987, pp. 495–509.

[59] H. HATANAKA, *Boron Neutron Capture Therapy for Tumours*, Nishimura, Niigata, Japan, 1986. R. G. FAIRCHILD, V. P. BOND and A. D. WOODHEAD (eds.), *Clinical Aspects of Neutron Capture Therapy*, Plenum, New York, 1989, 370 pp.

[60] M. F. HAWTHORNE, *Pure Appl. Chem.* **63**, 327–34 (1991).

[61] B. J. ALLEN, D. E. MOORE and B. V. HARRINGTON (eds.), *Progress in Neutron Capture Therapy for Cancer* (Proc. 4th Internat. Conf.), Plenum, New York, 1992, 668 pp.

[61a] R. A. WATSON-CLARK, C. B. KNOBLER and M. F. HAWTHORNE, *Inorg. Chem.* **35**, 2963–6 (1996).

[62] B. BONNETOT, A. TANGI, M. COLOMBIER and H. MONGEOT, *Inorg. Chem. Acta* **105**, L15–L16 (1985).

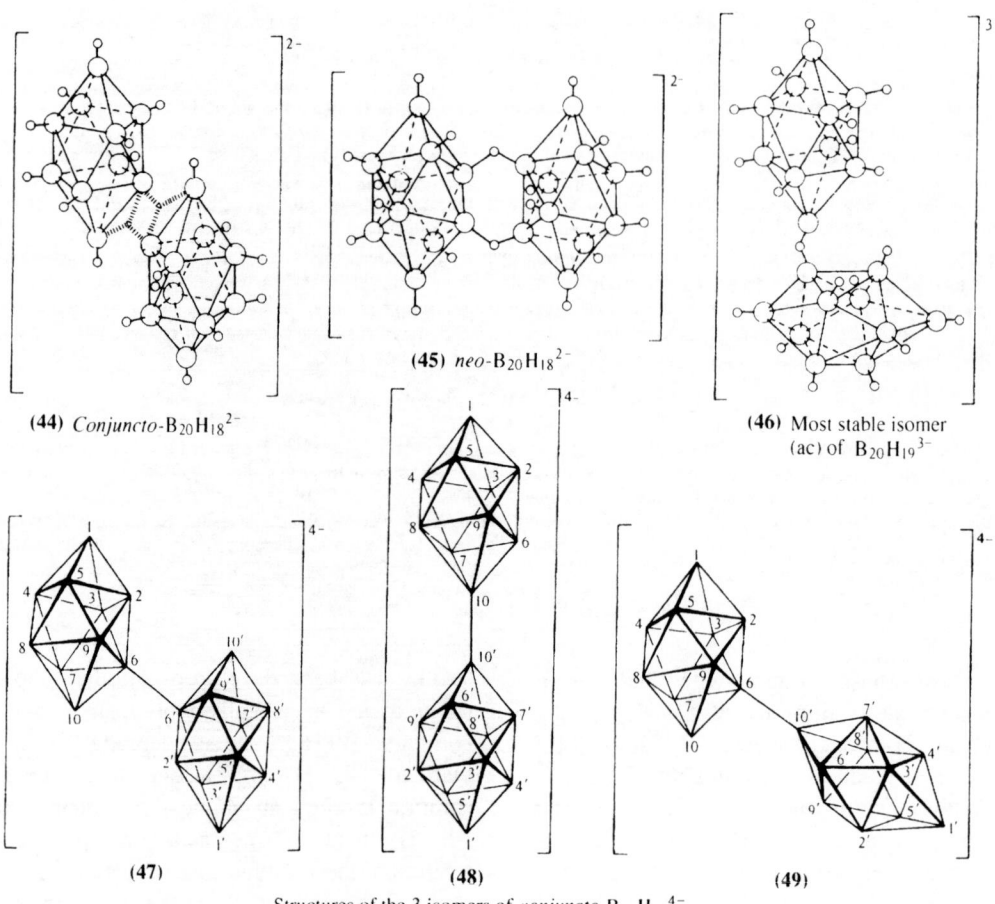

(44) *Conjuncto*-$B_{20}H_{18}^{2-}$

(45) *neo*-$B_{20}H_{18}^{2-}$

(46) Most stable isomer (ac) of $B_{20}H_{19}^{3-}$

(47)

(48)

(49)

Structures of the 3 isomers of *conjuncto*-$B_{20}H_{18}^{4-}$

$(B_{10}H_{13})_2O$, prepared by other routes, had previously been established by X-ray diffraction analysis[63] and by nmr spectroscopy.[64] Another interesting derivative is [*closo*-1,10-$B_{10}H_8(N_2)_2$] in which the apical H atoms in $B_{10}H_{10}^{2-}$ have been replaced by end-on dinitrogen ligands (see pp. 414–6): the B–N distance is 149.9 pm and the N–N distance is 109.1 pm[65] (cf 109.8 pm in gaseous N_2). The isoelectronic ligand CO fulfils the same function in [*closo*-1,10-$B_{10}H_8(CO)_2$].[66,67] The closely related stable, volatile, icosahedral molecule [*closo*-1,12-$B_{12}H_{10}(CO)_2$] can be prepared by the reaction of $H_2B_{12}H_{12}.4H_2O$ with CO at 130°C and 800–1000 atm. pressure in the presence of dicobaltoctacarbonyl as catalyst.[67] In the absence of this catalyst, approximately equal amounts of the 1,7- and 1,12-isomers are formed.

[63] N. N. GREENWOOD, W. S. MCDONALD and T. R. SPALDING, *J. Chem. Soc., Chem. Commun.*, 1251–2 (1980).

[64] J. D. KENNEDY and N. N. GREENWOOD, *Inorg. Chem. Acta* **38**, 93–6 (1980).

[65] T. WHELAN, P. BRINT, T. R. SPALDING, W. S. MCDONALD and D. R. LLOYD, *J. Chem. Soc., Dalton Trans.*, 2469–73 (1982).

[66] W. H. KNOTH, J. C. SAUER, H. C. MILLER and E. L. MUETTERTIES, *J. Amer. Chem. Soc.* **86**, 115–6 (1964).

[67] W. H. KNOTH, J. C. SAUER, J. H. BALTHIS, H. C. MILLER and E. L. MUETTERTIES, *J. Amer. Chem. Soc.* **89**, 4842–50 (1967). See also P. BRINT, B. SANGCHAKR, M. MCGRATH, T. R. SPALDING and R. J. SUFFOLK, *Inorg. Chem.* **29**, 47–52 (1990) for references to more recent work.

(50) B_6H_{10}
nido-hexaborane(10)

(51) CB_5H_9
2-carba-*nido*-
hexaborane(9)

(52) $C_2B_4H_8$
2.3-dicarba-*nido*-
hexaborane(8)

(53) $C_3B_3H_7$
2.3.4-tricarba-*nido*-
hexaborane(7)

(54) $C_4B_2H_6$
2.3.4.5-tetracarba-*nido*-
hexaborane(6)

6.5 Carboranes[1,17,68-71]

Carboranes burst onto the chemical scene in 1962–3 when classified work that had been done in the USA during the late 1950s was cleared for publication. The succeeding 30 y has seen a tremendous burgeoning of activity, as a result of which the carboranes and the related metallocarboranes (p. 189) now occupy a strategic position in the chemistry of the elements, since they overlap and give coherence to several other large areas including the chemistry of polyhedral boranes, transition-metal complexes, metal-cluster compounds and organometallic chemistry. The field has become so vast that it is only possible to give a few illustrative examples of the many thousands of known compounds, and to indicate the general structural features and reactivity. The vast majority of carboranes ($>95\%$) have two C atoms in the cluster, reflecting their ready formation from alkynes (see below). A few have one C atom and there are a growing number incorporating three or even four C atoms as cluster vertices.

Carboranes (or more correctly carbaboranes) are compounds having as the basic structural unit a number of C and B atoms arranged on

the vertices of a triangulated polyhedron. Their structures are closely related to those of the isoelectronic boranes (p. 161) [$BH \equiv B^- \equiv C$; $BH_2 \equiv BH^- \equiv B.L \equiv CH$]. For example, *nido*-$B_6H_{10}$ (structures 10, 50) provides the basic cluster structure for the 4 carboranes CB_5H_9 (51), $C_2B_4H_8$ (52), $C_3B_3H_7$ (53) and $C_4B_2H_6$ (54), each successive replacement of a basal B atom by C being compensated by the removal of one H_μ. Carboranes have the general formula $[(CH)_a(BH)_mH_b]^{c-}$ with a CH units and m BH units at the polyhedral vertices, plus b "extra" H atoms which are either bridging (H_μ) or *endo* (i.e. tangential to the surface of the polyhedron as distinct from the axial H_t atoms specified in the CH and BH groups; H_{endo} occur in BH_2 groups which are thus more precisely specified as BH_tH_{endo}). It follows that the number of electrons available for skeletal bonding is 3e from each CH unit, 2e from each BH unit, 1e from each H_μ or H_{endo}, and ce from the anionic charge. Hence:

> total number of skeletal bonding electron pairs $= \frac{1}{2}(3a + 2m + b + c) = n + \frac{1}{2}(a + b + c)$, where $n(= a + m)$ is the number of occupied vertices of the polyhedron.
> *closo*-structures have $(n + 1)$ pairs of skeletal bonding electrons (i.e. $a + b + c = 2$).
> *nido*-structures have $(n + 2)$ pairs of skeletal bonding electrons (i.e. $a + b + c = 4$).
> *arachno*-structures have $(n + 3)$ pairs of skeletal bonding electrons (i.e. $a + b + c = 6$).

If $a = 0$ the compound is a borane or borane anion rather than a carborane. If $b = 0$ there are no H_μ or H_{endo}; this is the case for all *closo*-carboranes except for the unique octahedral

[68] R. N. GRIMES, *Carboranes*, Academic Press, New York, 1970, 272 pp.

[69] H. BEALL, Chap. 9 in ref. 9, pp. 302–47. T. ONAK, Chap. 10 in ref. 9, pp. 349–82.

[70] R. E. WILLIAMS, Coordination number–pattern recognition theory of carborane structures, *Adv. Inorg. Chem. Radiochem.* **18**, 67–142 (1976). R. E. WILLIAMS, Chap. 2 in G. A. OLAH, K. WADE and R. E. WILLIAMS (eds.), *Electron Deficient Boron and Carbon Clusters*, Wiley, New York, 1991, pp. 11–93.

[71] R. N. GRIMES, *Adv. Inorg. Chem. Radiochem.* **26**, 55–117 (1983).

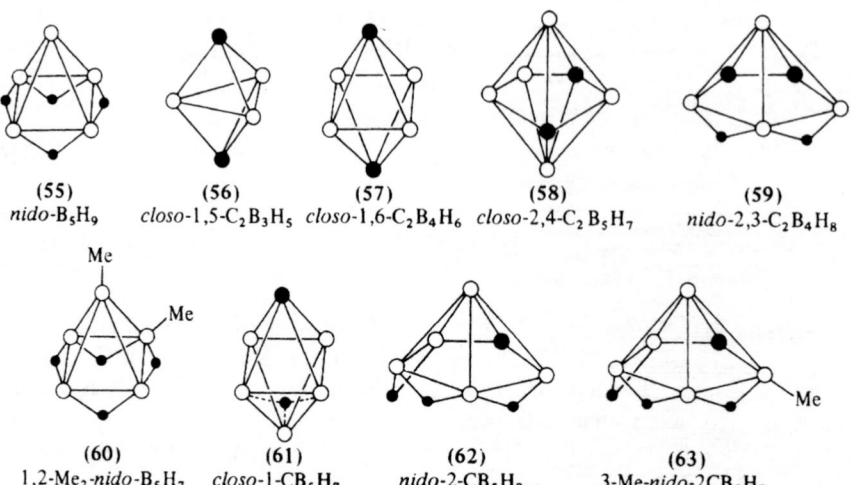

(55)   (56)   (57)   (58)   (59)
nido-B$_5$H$_9$ closo-1,5-C$_2$B$_3$H$_5$ closo-1,6-C$_2$B$_4$H$_6$ closo-2,4-C$_2$B$_5$H$_7$ nido-2,3-C$_2$B$_4$H$_8$

(60)   (61)   (62)   (63)
1,2-Me$_2$-nido-B$_5$H$_7$ closo-1-CB$_5$H$_7$ nido-2-CB$_5$H$_9$ 3-Me-nido-2CB$_5$H$_8$

monocarbaborane, 1-CB$_5$H$_7$, which has a triply bridging H$_\mu$ over one B$_3$ face of the octahedron. If $c = 0$ the compound is a neutral carborane molecule rather than an anion.

Nomenclature[12] follows the well-established oxa-aza convention of organic chemistry. Numbering begins with the apex atom of lowest coordination and successive rings or belts of polyhedral vertex atoms are numbered in a clockwise direction with C atoms being given the lowest possible numbers within these rules.[†]

Closo-carboranes are the most numerous and the most stable of the carboranes. They are colourless volatile liquids or solids (depending on mol wt.) and can be prepared from an alkyne and a borane by pyrolysis, or by reaction in a silent electric discharge. This route, which generally gives mixtures, is particularly useful for small *closo*-carboranes ($n = 5$–7) and for some intermediate *closo*-carboranes ($n = 8$–11), e.g.

$$nido\text{-}B_5H_9 \xrightarrow[500°-600°]{C_2H_2} closo\text{-}1,5\text{-}C_2B_3H_5$$
$$(55) \hspace{5cm} (56)$$
$$+ \; closo\text{-}1,6\text{-}C_2B_4H_6 + closo\text{-}2,4\text{-}C_2B_5H_7$$
$$(57) \hspace{3cm} (58)$$

[†] As frequently happens in a rapidly developing field, nomenclature and numbering for the carboranes gradually evolved to cope with increasing complexity. Consequently, many systems have been used, often by the same author in successive years, and the only safe procedure is to draw a labelled diagram and convert to the preferred numbering system.

Milder conditions provide a route to *nido*-carboranes, e.g.:

$$nido\text{-}B_5H_9 \xrightarrow[200°]{C_2H_2} nido\text{-}2,3\text{-}C_2B_4H_8 \quad (59)$$

Pyrolysis of *nido*- or *arachno*-carboranes or their reaction in a silent electric discharge also leads to *closo*-species either by loss of H$_2$ or disproportionation:

$$C_2B_nH_{n+4} \longrightarrow C_2B_nH_{n+2} + H_2$$
$$2C_2B_nH_{n+4} \longrightarrow C_2B_{n-1}H_{n+1} + C_2B_{n+1}H_{n+3} + 2H_2$$

For example, pyrolysis of the previously mentioned *nido*-2,3-C$_2$B$_4$H$_8$ gives the 3 *closo*-species shown above, whereas under the milder conditions of photolytic closure the less-stable isomer *closo*-1,2-C$_2$B$_4$H$_6$ is obtained. Pyrolysis of alkyl boranes at 500–600° is a related route which is particularly useful to monocarbaboranes though the yields are often low, e.g.:

$$1,2\text{-}Me_2\text{-}nido\text{-}B_5H_7 \longrightarrow closo\text{-}1,5\text{-}C_2B_3H_5$$
$$(60) \hspace{4cm} (56)$$
$$+ \; closo\text{-}1\text{-}CB_5H_7 + nido\text{-}2\text{-}CB_5H_9$$
$$(61) \hspace{3cm} (62)$$
$$+ \; 3\text{-}Me\text{-}nido\text{-}2\text{-}CB_5H_8$$
$$(63)$$

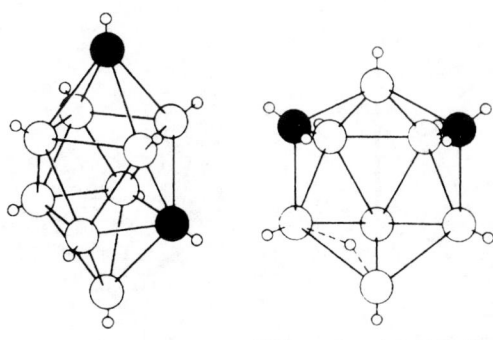

(64)   *closo*-1,6-$C_2B_8H_{10}$ **(65)** *arachno*-1,3-$C_2B_7H_{12}^-$

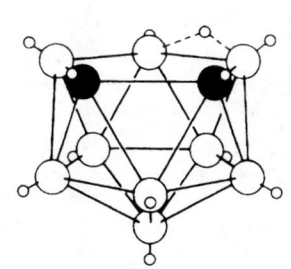

(66) *nido*-1,7-$C_2B_9H_{12}^-$

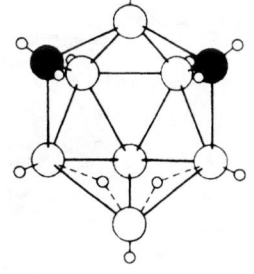

(67) *arachno*-1,3-$C_2B_7H_{13}$

Cluster expansion reactions with diborane provide an alternative route to intermediate *closo*-carboranes, e.g.:

$$closo\text{-}1,7\text{-}C_2B_6H_8 + \tfrac{1}{2}B_2H_6 \longrightarrow$$
$$closo\text{-}1,6\text{-}C_2B_7H_9 + H_2$$

$$closo\text{-}1,6\text{-}C_2B_7H_9 + \tfrac{1}{2}B_2H_6 \longrightarrow$$
$$closo\text{-}1,6\text{-}C_2B_8H_{10} + H_2$$

Conversely, cluster degradation reactions lead to more open structures, e.g.:

$$closo\text{-}1,6\text{-}C_2B_8H_{10} \xrightarrow[\text{OH}^- + 2H_2O]{\text{base hydrol}}$$
$$\text{(64)}$$

$$arachno\text{-}1,3\text{-}C_2B_7H_{12}^- + B(OH)_3$$
$$\text{(65)}$$

$$nido\text{-}1,7\text{-}C_2B_9H_{12}^- \xrightarrow[+6H_2O - 6e^-]{\text{chromic acid oxidn.}}$$
$$\text{(66)}$$

$$arachno\text{-}1,3\text{-}C_2B_7H_{13} + 2B(OH)_3 + 5H^+$$
$$\text{(67)}$$

Other convenient routes to carboranes, selected from the growing number of recently reported syntheses, are as follows. Monocarbon carboranes can be prepared in good yield by the transition-metal catalysed hydroboration of alkenes followed by thermal rearrangement of the intermediate product, e.g.[72]

$$B_5H_9 + [(MeC\equiv CMe)Co_2(CO)_6] \xrightarrow{75°}$$

$$[nido\text{-}B_5H_8\text{-}2\text{-}(CMe=CHMe)] \xrightarrow{355°}$$

$$[nido\text{-}2\text{-}CB_5H_7\text{-}2\text{-}Me\text{-}3(\text{or }4)\text{-}Et] \text{ (see structure 51).}$$

The two isomers are each obtained in about 30% yield. Again, the Me_2S-promoted reaction of *nido*-$B_{10}H_{14}$ with bis(trimethylsilyl)ethyne, $Me_3SiC\equiv CSiMe_3$, results in monocarbon insertion by internal hydroboration and $SiMe_3$ group migration to give [*nido*-7-$CB_{10}H_{11}$-7-{$(Me_3Si)_2CH$}-9-(Me_2S)] structure (68) in 28% yield.[73] New dicarbaboranes can be obtained from preformed *nido*-dicarbaboranes either by reducing them to give the corresponding *arachno* species[74] or by a capping reaction to give a *closo*-dicarbaborane,[75] e.g.

$$nido\text{-}C_2B_8H_{12} \xrightarrow[\text{EtOH/KOH}]{\text{NaBH}_4 \text{ in}} arachno\text{-}6,9\text{-}C_2B_8H_{14} \text{ (69)}$$

$$nido\text{-}2,3\text{-}Et_2C_2B_4H_6 \text{ (52)} + Et_3NBH_3 \xrightarrow{140°}$$
$$closo\text{-}2,3\text{-}Et_2C_2B_5H_5 + 2H_2 + NEt_3$$

A convenient route to three-carbon carboranes is the hydroboration of an alkyne with a preformed dicarbaborane. For example,[76] reaction of ethyne (or propyne) with *arachno*-4,5-$C_2B_7H_{13}$ (70) in hexane at 120°C gives a mixture of tri- and tetra-carbaboranes, e.g. (71), (72), (73), (74) in modest yield. Access to other

[72] R. WILCZYNSKI and L. G. SNEDDON, *J. Amer. Chem. Soc.* **102**, 2857–8 (1980).

[73] R. L. ERNEST, W. QUINTANA, R. ROSEN, P. J. CARROLL and L. G. SNEDDON, *Organometallics* **6**, 80–8 (1987).

[74] Z. JANOUŠEK, J. PLEŠEK, S. HEŘMÁNEK and B. ŠTÍBR, *Polyhedron* **4**, 1797–8 (1985).

[75] J. S. BECK, A. P. KAHN and L. G. SNEDDON, *Organometallics* **5**, 2552–3 (1986).

[76] B. ŠTÍBR, T. JELÍNEK, Z. JANOUŠEK, S. HEŘMÁNEK, E. DRDÁKOVÁ, Z. PLZÁK and J. PLEŠEK, *J. Chem. Soc., Chem. Commun.*, 1106–7 (1987). B. ŠTÍBR, T. JELÍNEK, E. DRDÁKOVÁ, S. HEŘMÁNEK and J. PLEŠEK, *Polyhedron*, **7**, 669–70 (1988).

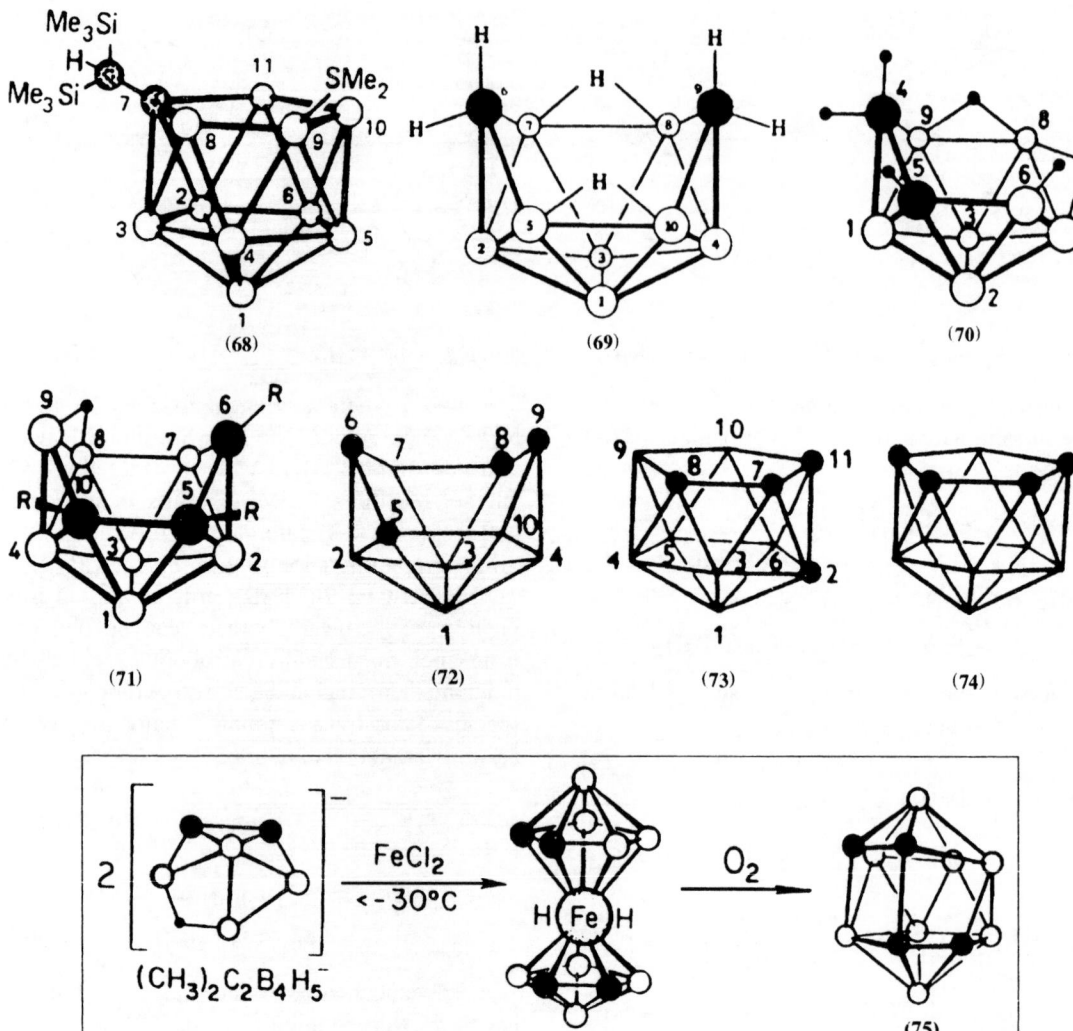

Scheme

tetracarbaboranes was greatly facilitated by the discovery of oxidative fusion reactions in 1974; these involve the construction of large clusters by metal-promoted face-to-face fusion of smaller clusters.[71] For example, bridge-deprotonation of $2,3\text{-}R_2C_2B_4H_6$ (see structure 52) with alkali metal hydride, followed by treatment with $FeCl_2$ and exposure to O_2 yields the desired product $R_4C_4B_8H_8$ (75) (see Scheme above). The starting material is available in multigram amounts via the room-temperature reaction of B_5H_9 with alkynes in the presence of NEt_3:

$$B_5H_9 + R_2C_2 + NEt_3 \longrightarrow 2,3\text{-}R_2C_2B_4H_6 \quad (52)$$
$$+ Et_3NBH_3$$

Metal-promoted alkyne-insertion reactions afford another good method (see structure 12 for cluster geometry and numbering):[77]

$$2,3\text{-}Et_2C_2B_4H_6 \ (52) + NaH + MeC\equiv CMe$$
$$+ NiCl_2 \xrightarrow{\text{thf}} 4,5,7,8\text{-}Me_2Et_2C_4B_4H_4$$

[77] M. G. L. MIRABELLI and L. G. SNEDDON, *Organometallics* **5**, 1510–11 (1986).

Some Further Generalizations Concerning Carboranes

1. Carbon tends to adopt the position of lowest coordination number on the polyhedron and to keep as far from other C atoms as possible (i.e. the most stable isomer has the greatest number of B–C connections).

2. Boron-boron distances in the cluster increase with increasing coordination number (as expected). Average B–B distances are: 5-coordinate B 170 pm, 6-coordinate B 177 pm, 7-coordinate B 186 pm.

3. Carbon is somewhat smaller than B and interatomic distances involving C are correspondingly shorter. Thus B–C and C–C distances are about 165 pm and 145 pm, respectively, for 5-coordinate C; the corresponding values for 6-coordinate C are 172 pm and 165 pm.

4. Negative electronic charge on B is computed to decrease in the sequence:

   B (not bonded to C) > B (bonded to 1C) > B (bonded to 2C).

   Within each group the B with lower coordination number has a greater negative charge than those with higher coordination.

5. CH groups tend to be more positive than BH groups with the same coordination number (despite the higher electronegativity of C). This presumably arises because each C contributes 3e for bonding within the cluster whereas each B contributes only 2e.

6. In *nido*- and *arachno*-carboranes H_μ is more acidic than H_t and is the one removed on deprotonation with NaH.

In general *nido*- (and *arachno*-) carboranes are less stable thermally than are the corresponding *closo*-compounds and they are less stable to aerial oxidation and other reactions, due to their more open structure and the presence of labile H atoms in the open face. Most *closo*-carboranes are stable to at least 400° though they may undergo rearrangement to more stable isomers in which the distance between the C atoms is increased. Some other structural and bonding generalizations are summarized in the Panel. Note, however, that kinetic control during synthesis may result in the isolation of a thermodynamically less favoured structure, with contiguous C atoms, while electronic factors in carboranes with as many as four C atoms may result in distortions or other deviations from the structures predicted on the basis of the simple application of electron counting rules.[71]

The three isomeric icosahedral carboranes (76–78) are unique both in their ease of preparation and their great stability in air, and consequently their chemistry has been the most fully studied. The 1,2-isomer in particular is available on the multikilogram scale. It is best prepared in bulk by the direct reaction of ethyne with decaborane in the presence of a Lewis base, preferably Et_2S:

$$nido\text{-}B_{10}H_{14} + 2SEt_2 \longrightarrow B_{10}H_{12}(SEt_2)_2 + H_2$$

$$B_{10}H_{12}(SEt_2)_2 + C_2H_2 \longrightarrow closo\text{-}1,2\text{-}C_2B_{10}H_{12}$$
$$+ 2SEt_2 + H_2$$

The 1,7-isomer is obtained in 90% yield by heating the 1,2-isomer in the gas phase at 470°C

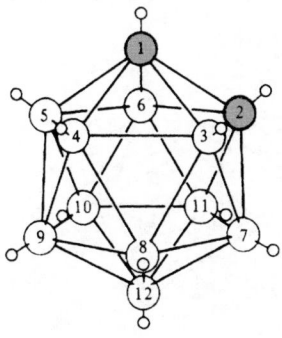

(76) *ortho*-carborane, 1,2-$C_2B_{10}H_{12}$ (mp 320°C)

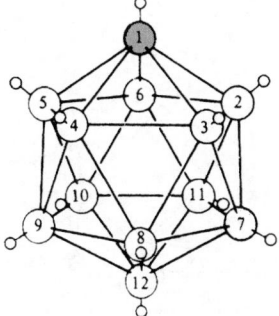

(77) *meta*-carborane, 1,7-$C_2B_{10}H_{12}$ (mp 265°C)

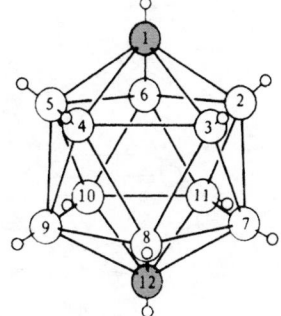

(78) *para*-carborane, 1,12-$C_2B_{10}H_{12}$ (mp 261°C)

for several hours (or in quantitative yield by flash pyrolysis at 600° for 30 s). The 1,12-isomer is most efficiently prepared (20% yield) by heating the 1,7-isomer for a few seconds at 700°C. The mechanism of these isomerizations has been the subject of considerable speculation but definitive experiments are hard to devise. The "diamond-square-diamond" mechanism has been proposed (Fig. 6.19) for the 1,2 $\rightleftharpoons$ 1,7 isomerization, but the 1,12 isomer cannot be generated by this mechanism. Moreover, the activation energy required to pass through the cubo-octahedral transition state is likely to be rather high. An alternative proposal, which could, in principle, lead to both the 1,7 and the 1,12 isomers, is the successive concerted rotation of the 3 atoms on a triangular face, and a third possible mechanism involves the concerted basal twisting of two parallel pentagonal pyramids comprising the icosahedron. Vertex extrusion to a capping position, followed by reinsertion at an adjacent site in the cluster has also been suggested. It is extremely difficult to devise experiments to test these mechanisms, but where this has been achieved (as in the case of the disubstituted derivative of (58), $closo$-5-Me-6-Cl-2,4-$C_2B_5H_6$, for example) the results rule out triangular face rotation and are consistent with a "diamond-square-diamond" mechanisms.[78] It is conceivable that for other clusters the various mechanisms operate in different temperature ranges or that two (or more) mechanisms are active simultaneously. For recent definitive work on $closo$-$C_2B_{10}H_{12}$ see refs. 79 and 80.

An entirely different form of isomerism, which is attracting increasing attention, is described in the Panel opposite.

An extensive derivative chemistry of the icosahedral carboranes has been developed, especially for 1,2-$C_2B_{10}H_{12}$. Terminal H atoms attached to B undergo facile electrophilic substitution and the sequence of reactivity follows the sequence of negative charge density on the BH_t group:[81]

$closo$-1,2-$C_2B_{10}H_{12}$:

$$(8, 10 \approx 9, 12) > 4, 5, 7, 11 > 3, 6$$

$closo$-1,7-$C_2B_{10}H_{12}$:

$$9, 10 > 4, 6, 8, 11 > 5, 12 > 2, 3$$

Similar reactions occur for other $closo$-carboranes, e.g.:

$$1,6\text{-}C_2B_7H_9 \xrightarrow{\text{Br}_2/\text{AlCl}_3} 8\text{-Br-}1,6\text{-}C_2B_7H_8 + HBr$$

$$1,10\text{-}C_2B_8H_{10} \xrightarrow{8\text{Cl}_2/\text{CCl}_4} 1,10\text{-(CH)}_2B_8Cl_8 + 8HCl$$

It is noteworthy that, despite the greater electronegativity of C, the CH group tends to be more

78 Z. J. ABDOU, G. ABDOU, T. ONAK and S. LEE, *Inorg. Chem.* **25**, 2678–83 (1986).

79 S.-H. WU and M. JONES *J. Amer. Chem. Soc.* **111**, 5373–84 (1989).

80 G. M. EDVENSON and D. F. GAINES *Inorg. Chem.* **29**, 1210–16 (1990).

81 D. A. DIXON, D. A. KLEIR, T. A. HALGREN, J. H. HALL and W. N. LIPSCOMB, *J. Am. Chem. Soc.* **99**, 6226–37 (1977).

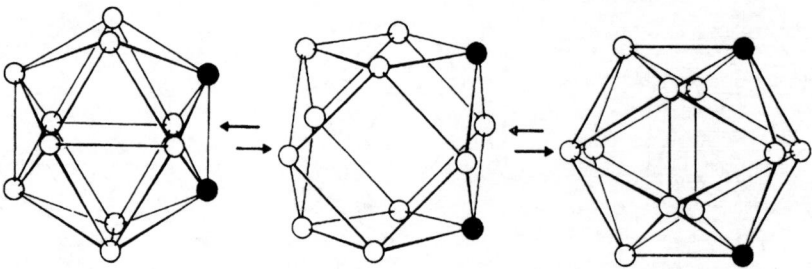

Figure 6.19   The interconversion of 1,2- and 1,7-disubstituted icosahedral species *via* a proposed cubooctahedral intermediate formed during four "diamond–square–diamond" rearrangements.

"Classical-Nonclassical" Valence Isomerism

A novel and far-reaching type of isomerism concerns the possibility of valence isomerism between "nonclassical" (electron-deficient) clusters and "classical" organoboron structures. Thus, n-vertexed *nido*-boranes, B_nH_{n+4}, have cluster structures with $4H_\mu$ — cf. (9), (10), (11) — whereas the precisely isoelectronic n-vertexed *nido*-tetracarbaboranes, $C_4B_{n-4}H_n$ have no bridging H atoms and can, in principle, adopt either a cluster borane structure or one of several classical organic structures. For example, derivatives of $C_4B_2H_6$ could adopt either the *nido*-2,3,4,5-tetracarbahexaborane structure (a) — i.e. (54) — or the 1,4-dibora-2,5-cyclohexadiene structure (b). As might be expected, the 3-coordinate B atoms in (b) are stabilized by π-donor substituents (e.g. R = F, OMe) whereas when R = alkyl, rearrangement to the *nido*-carbaborane (a) occurs.[82] The novel diborafulvene isomer (c) has also been synthesized in good yield[82,83] and two other isomers, (d) and (e), have been stabilized as ligands in Ru- and Rh-complexes.

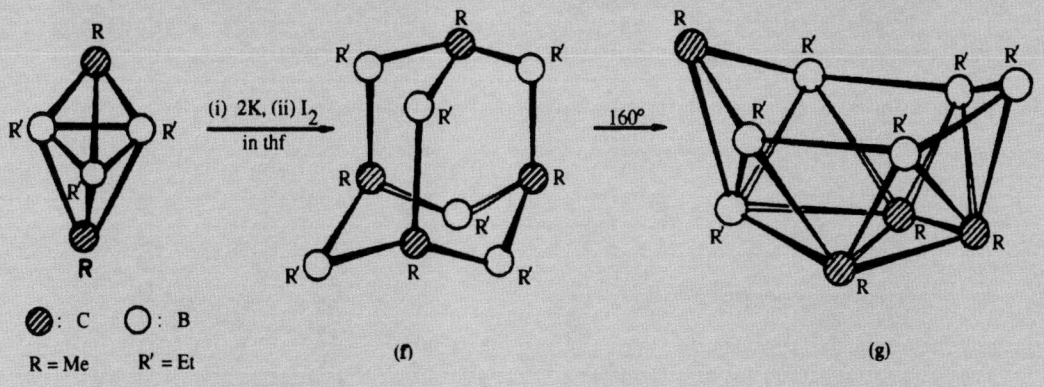

Similar possibilities arise for 10-atom clusters. Thus, dimerization of the *closo*-C_2B_3 cluster 1,5-$Me_2C_2B_3Et_3$ (56) by means of K metal then I_2 in thf yields the "classical" adamantane derivative $Me_4C_4B_6Et_6$ (f); when this is heated to 160° the *nido*-tetracarbadecaborane cluster (g) is obtained rapidly and quantitatively.[84] It will be noted that in (f) all four C atoms are 4-coordinate and all six B atoms are 3-coordinate, whereas in (g) the three C atoms in the C_3 triangular face are 5-coordinate while the boron atoms are variously 4, 5 or 6 coordinate.

[82] V. SCHÄFER, H. PRITZKOW and W. SIEBERT, *Angew. Chem. Int. Edn. Engl.* **27**, 299–300 (1988) and references cited therein. See also B. WRACKMEYER and G. KEHR, *Polyhedron* **10**, 1497–506 (1991).

[83] G. E. HERBERICH, H. OHST and H. MAYER, *Angew. Chem. Int. Edn. Engl.* **23**, 969–70 (1984).

[84] R. KÖSTER, G. SEIDEL and B. WRACKMEYER, *Angew. Chem. Int. Edn. Engl.* **24**, 326–7 (1985).

positive than the BH groups and does not normally react under these conditions.

The weakly acidic CH_t group can be deprotonated by strong nucleophiles such as LiBu or RMgX; the resulting metalated carboranes $LiCCHB_{10}H_{10}$ and $(LiC)_2B_{10}H_{10}$ can then be used to prepare a full range of C-substituted derivatives $-R$, $-X$, $-SiMe_3$, $-COOH$, $-COCl$, $-CONHR$, etc. The possibility of synthesizing extensive covalent C–C or siloxane networks with pendant carborane clusters is obvious and the excellent thermal stability of such polymers has already been exploited in several industrial applications.

Although $closo$-carboranes are stable to high temperatures and to most common reagents, M. F. Hawthorne showed (1964) that they can

be specifically degraded to $nido$-carborane anions by the reaction of strong bases in the presence of protonic solvents, e.g.:

$$1,2\text{-}C_2B_{10}H_{12} + EtO^- + 2EtOH \xrightarrow{85°C}$$

$$7,8\text{-}C_2B_9H_{12}^- + B(OEt)_3 + H_2$$

$$1,7\text{-}C_2B_{10}H_{12} + EtO^- + 2EtOH \longrightarrow$$

$$7,9\text{-}C_2B_9H_{12}^- + B(OEt)_3 + H_2$$

Figure 6.20 indicates that, in both cases, the BH vertex removed is the one adjacent to the two CH vertices: since the C atoms tend to remove electronic charge preferentially from contiguous B atoms, the reaction can be described as a nucleophilic attack by EtO^- on the most positive (most electron deficient) B atom in the

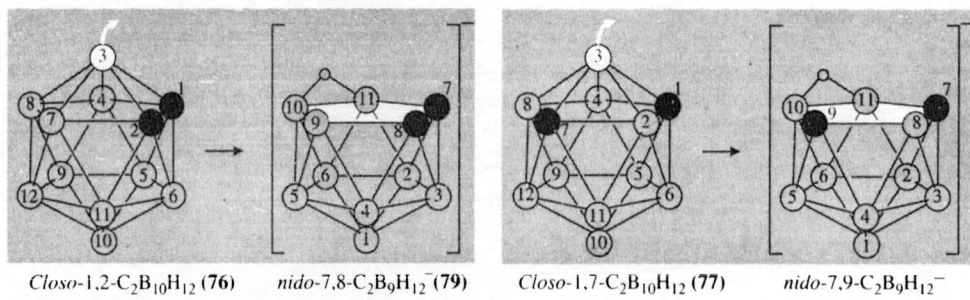

$Closo$-1,2-$C_2B_{10}H_{12}$ **(76)** $nido$-7,8-$C_2B_9H_{12}^-$ **(79)** $Closo$-1,7-$C_2B_{10}H_{12}$ **(77)** $nido$-7,9-$C_2B_9H_{12}^-$

Figure 6.20 Degradation of $closo$-carboranes to the corresponding debor-$nido$-carborane anions.

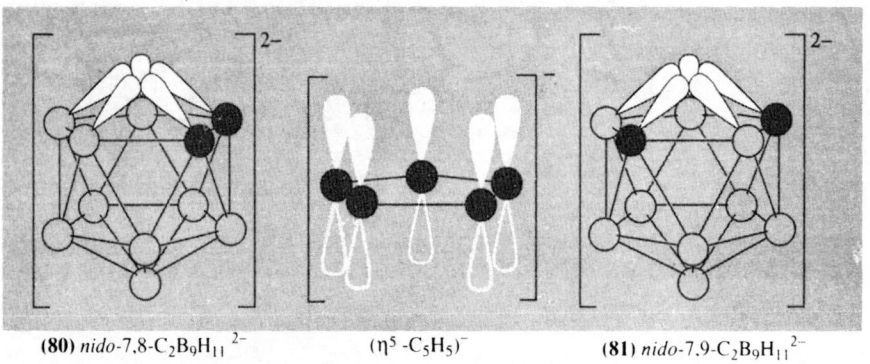

(80) $nido$-7,8-$C_2B_9H_{11}^{2-}$ $(\eta^5$-$C_5H_5)^-$ **(81)** $nido$-7,9-$C_2B_9H_{11}^{2-}$

Figure 6.21 Relation between $C_2B_9H_{11}^{2-}$ and $C_5H_5^-$. In this formalism the $closo$-carboranes $C_2B_{10}H_{12}$ are considered as a coordination complex between the pentahapto 6-electron donor $C_2B_9H_{11}^{2-}$ and the acceptor BH^{2+} (which has 3 vacant orbitals). The $closo$-structure can be regained by capping the open pentagonal face with an equivalent metal acceptor that has 3 vacant orbitals.

cluster. Deprotonation of the monoanions by NaH removes the bridge proton to give the *nido*-dianions 7,8-$C_2B_9H_{11}{}^{2-}$ (80) and 7,9-$C_2B_9H_{11}{}^{2-}$ (81). It was the perceptive recognition that the open pentagonal faces of these dianions were structurally and electronically equivalent to the pentahapto cyclopentadienide anion (η^5-C_5H_5)$^-$ (Fig. 6.21) that led to the discovery of the metallocarboranes and the development of some of the most intriguing and far-reaching reactions of the carboranes. These are considered in the next section.

6.6 Metallocarboranes$^{(1,17,85-90)}$

There are now at least a dozen synthetic routes to metallocarboranes including (i) coordination using *nido*-carborane anions as ligands, (ii) polyhedral expansion reactions, (iii) polyhedral contraction reactions, (iv) polyhedral subrogation and (v) thermal metal transfer reactions. These first five routes were all devised by M. F. Hawthorne and his group in the period 1965–74 and have since been extensively exploited and extended by several groups. Examples of each will be given before mentioning some of the more recent routes that have been developed. It is worth noting that the carborane dianions (80) and (81) are both more effective as ligands than is η^5-$C_5H_5{}^-$, perhaps because of the more favourable angles of the orbitals, the lower electronegativity of boron and the higher formal anionic charge. Thus, the carboranes form stable sandwich complexes with Cu^{II}, Al^{III} and

Si^{IV}, for example, whereas cyclopentadienyl does not.$^{(90,91)}$

(*i*) *Coordination using* nido-*carborane anions as ligands (1965)*. Reaction of $C_2B_9H_{11}{}^{2-}$ with $FeCl_2$ in tetrahydrofuran (thf) with rigorous exclusion of moisture and air gives the pink, diamagnetic bis-sandwich-type complex of Fe(II) (structure 82) which can be reversibly oxidized to the corresponding red Fe(III) complex:

$$2C_2B_9H_{11}{}^{2-} + Fe^{2+} \xrightarrow{\text{thf}} [Fe^{II}(\eta^5\text{-}C_2B_9H_{11})_2]^{2-}$$
$$(82)$$
$$\underset{+e^-}{\overset{\text{air}}{\rightleftharpoons}} [Fe^{III}(\eta^5\text{-}C_2B_9H_{11})_2]^-$$

When the reaction is carried out in the presence of NaC_5H_5 the purple mixed sandwich complex (83) is obtained:

$$C_2B_9H_{11}{}^{2-} + C_5H_5{}^- + Fe^{2+} \xrightarrow[-e^-]{\text{thf}}$$

$$[Fe^{III}(\eta^5\text{-}C_5H_5)(\eta^5\text{-}C_2B_9H_{11})] \quad (83)$$

The reaction is general and has been applied to many transition metals as well as lanthanides and actinides.$^{(92)}$ Variants use metal carbonyls and other complexes to supply the capping unit, e.g.

$$C_2B_9H_{11}{}^{2-} + Mo(CO)_6 \xrightarrow{h\nu}$$

$$[Mo(CO)_3(\eta^5\text{-}C_2B_9H_{11})]^{2-} + 3CO$$

(*ii*) *Polyhedral expansion (1970)*. This entails the 2-electron reduction of a *closo*-carborane with a strong reducing agent such as sodium naphthalide in thf followed by reaction with a transition-metal reagent:

$$2[closo\text{-}C_2B_{n-2}H_n] \xrightarrow[\text{thf}]{4Na/C_{10}H_8} 2[nido\text{-}C_2B_{n-2}H_n]^{2-}$$

$$\xrightarrow{M^{m+}} [M(C_2B_{n-2}H_n)_2]^{(m-4)+}$$

The reaction, which is quite general for *closo*-carboranes, involves the reductive opening of an *n*-vertex *closo*-cluster followed by metal

^{85} R. N. GRIMES, *Pure Appl. Chem.* **39**, 455–74 (1974).

^{86} K. P. CALLAHAN and M. F. HAWTHORNE, *Pure Appl. Chem.* **39**, 475–95 (1974).

^{87} G. B. DUNKS and M. F. HAWTHORNE, Chap. 11 in ref. 9, pp. 383–430.

^{88} K. P. CALLAHAN and M. F. HAWTHORNE, *Adv. Organometallic Chem.* **14**, 145–86 (1976).

^{89} R. N. GRIMES, Chap. 2 in E. BECHER and M. TSUTSUI (eds.), *Organometallic Reactions and Syntheses* **6**, 63–221 (1977).

^{90} D. M. SCHUBERT, M. A. BANDMAN, W. S. REES, C. B. KNOBLER, P. LU, W. NAM and M. F. HAWTHORNE, *Organometallics* **9**, 2046–61 (1990), and refs. cited therein.

^{91} D. M. SCHUBERT, W. S. REES, C. B. KNOBLER and M. F. HAWTHORNE, *Organometallics* **9**, 2938–44 (1990), and refs. cited therein.

^{92} M. J. MANNING, C. B. KNOBLER and M. F. HAWTHORNE, *J. Am. Chem. Soc.* **110**, 4458–9 (1988).

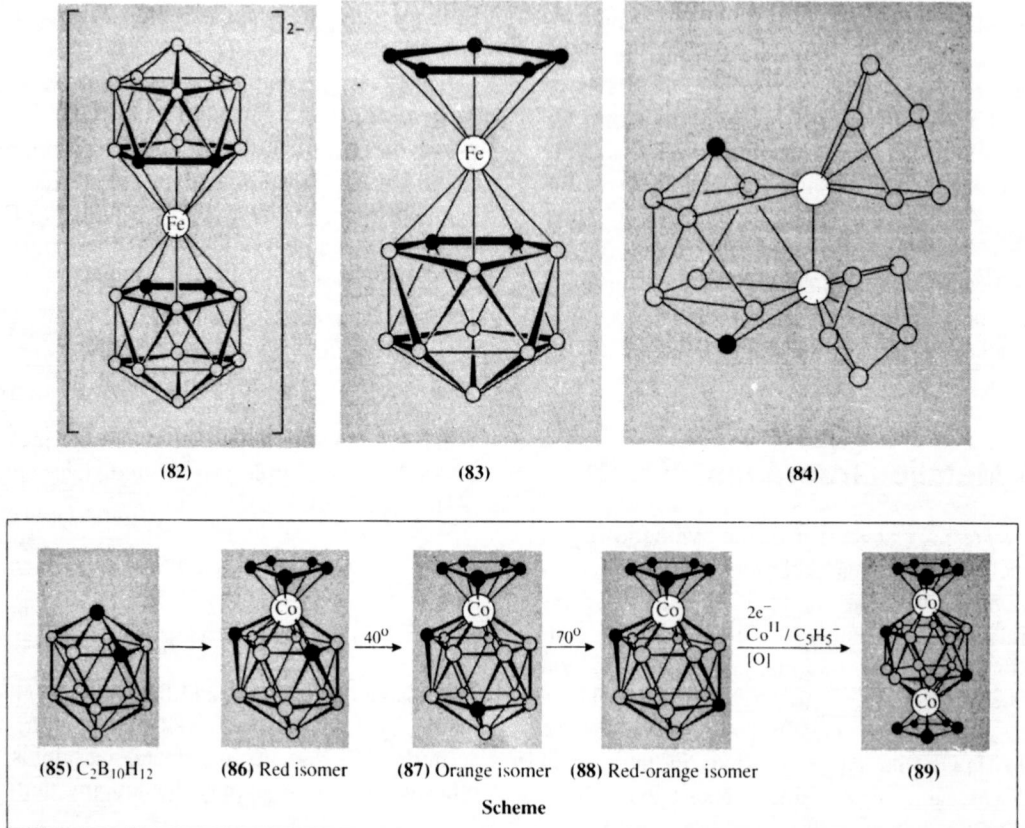

(82)   (83)   (84)

(85) $C_2B_{10}H_{12}$ (86) Red isomer   (87) Orange isomer   (88) Red-orange isomer   (89)

Scheme

insertion to give an $(n + 1)$-vertex *closo*-cluster. Numerous variants are possible including the insertion of a second metal centre into an existing metallocarborane, e.g.:

$$closo\text{-}1,7\text{-}C_2B_6H_8 \xrightarrow[\text{CoCl}_2 + \text{NaC}_5\text{H}_5]{2e^-/\text{thf}} [\text{Co}(\text{C}_5\text{H}_5)(\text{C}_2\text{B}_6\text{H}_8)]$$

$$\xrightarrow[\text{CoCl}_2 + \text{NaC}_5\text{H}_5]{2e^-/\text{thf}} [\{\text{Co}(\text{C}_5\text{H}_5)\}_2(\text{C}_2\text{B}_6\text{H}_8)] \ (84)$$

The structure of the bimetallic 10-vertex cluster was shown by X-ray diffraction to be (84). When the icosahedral carborane $1,2\text{-}C_2B_{10}H_{12}$ was used, the reaction led to the first supraicosahedral metallocarboranes with 13- and 14-vertex polyhedral structures (85)–(89). Facile isomerism of the 13-vertex monometallodicarbaboranes was observed as indicated in the scheme above (in which ● = CH and ○ = BH).

(iii) Polyhedral contraction (1972). This involves the clean removal of one BH group from a *closo*-metallocarborane by nucleophilic base degradation, followed by oxidative closure of the resulting *nido*-metallocarborane complex to a *closo*-species with one vertex less than the original, e.g.:

$$[3\text{-}\{\text{Co}(\eta^5\text{-}C_5H_5)\}(1,2\text{-}C_2B_9H_{11})](90) \xrightarrow[\text{(2) } H_2O_2]{\text{(1) } OEt^-}$$

$$[1\text{-}\{\text{Co}(\eta^5\text{-}C_5H_5)\}(2,4\text{-}C_2B_8H_{10})] \ (91)$$

Polyhedral contraction is not so general a method of preparing metallocarboranes as is polyhedral expansion since some metallocarboranes degrade completely under these conditions.

(iv) Polyhedral subrogation (1973). Replacement of a BH vertex by a metal vertex without changing the number of vertices in the cluster is termed polyhedral subrogation. It is an off-shoot of the polyhedral contraction route in that degradative removal of the BH unit is followed by reaction with a transition metal ion rather than

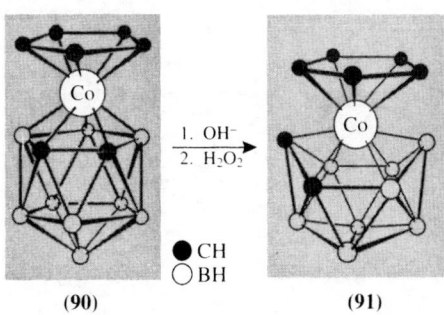

CH (filled circle)
BH (open circle)

(90)   (91)

with an oxidizing agent, e.g.:

$$[Co(\eta^5\text{-}C_5H_5)(C_2B_{10}H_{12})] \xrightarrow[\text{(2) } Co^{II}, C_5H_5^-]{\text{(1) } OH^-}$$

$$[\{Co(\eta^5\text{-}C_5H_5)\}_2(C_2B_9H_{11})]$$

The method is clearly of potential use in preparing mixed metal clusters, e.g. (Co + Ni) or (Co + Fe), and can be extended to prepare more complicated cluster arrays as depicted below, the subrogated B atom being indicated as a shaded circle in (92).

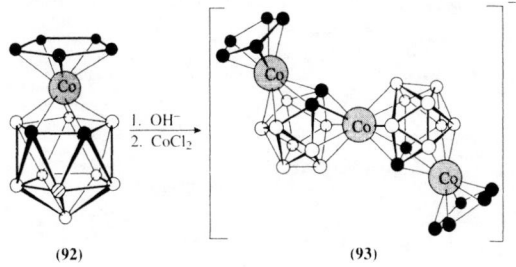

(92)   (93)

(v) *Thermal metal transfer (1974).* This method is less general and often less specific than the coordination of *nido*-anions or polyhedral expansion; it involves the pyrolysis of pre-existing metallocarboranes and consequent cluster expansion or disproportionation similar to that of the *closo*-carboranes themselves (p. 182). Mixtures of products are usually obtained, e.g.:

$$[(C_5H_5)_2Co]^+[(2,3\text{-}C_2B_8H_{10})_2Co]^-$$

$$\xrightarrow[\text{or } 270° \text{ hexadecane}]{525° \text{(hot tube)}} [(C_5H_5)_2Co_2C_2B_8H_{10}]$$

Similarly:

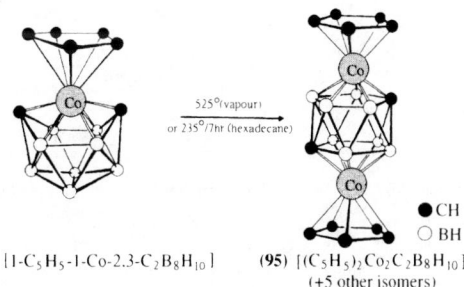

$$\xrightarrow[\text{or } 235°/7hr \text{ (hexadecane)}]{525° \text{(vapour)}}$$

CH (filled circle)
BH (open circle)

(94) [1-C₅H₅-1-Co-2.3-C₂B₈H₁₀]   (95) [(C₅H₅)₂Co₂C₂B₈H₁₀]
                                              (+5 other isomers)

A related technique (R. N. Grimes, 1973) is direct metal insertion by gas-phase reactions at elevated temperatures; typical reactions are shown in the scheme (p. 192). The reaction with $[Co(\eta^5\text{-}C_5H_5)(CO)_2]$ also gave the 7-vertex *closo*-bimetallocarborane (101) which can be considered as a rare example of a triple-decker sandwich compound; another isomer (102) can be made by base degradation of $[\{Co(\eta^5\text{-}C_5H_5)\}(C_2B_4H_6)]$ followed by deprotonation and subrogation with a second $\{Co(\eta^5\text{-}C_5H_5)\}$ unit.[85] It will be noted that the central planar formal $C_2B_3H_5^{4-}$ unit is isoelectronic with $C_5H_5^-$.

A particularly elegant route to metallacarboranes is the *direct oxidative insertion of a metal centre* into a *closo*-carborane cluster: the reaction uses zero-valent derivatives of Ni, Pd and Pt in a concerted process which involves a nett transfer of electrons from the nucleophilic metal centre to the cage:[93]

$$M^0L_{x+y} + C_2B_nH_{n+2} \longrightarrow$$

$$[M^{II}L_x(C_2B_nH_{n+2})] + yL$$

where L = PR_3, C_8H_{12}, RNC, etc. A typical reaction is

$$[Pt(PEt_3)_3] + 2,3\text{-}Me_2\text{-}2,3\text{-}C_2B_9H_9 \xrightarrow[\text{petrol}]{-30°}$$

$$[1\text{-}\{Pt(PEt_3)_2\}\text{-}2,4\text{-}(MeC)_2B_9H_9] + PEt_3$$

---

[93] F. G. A. STONE, *J. Organometallic Chem.* **100**, 257–71 (1975).

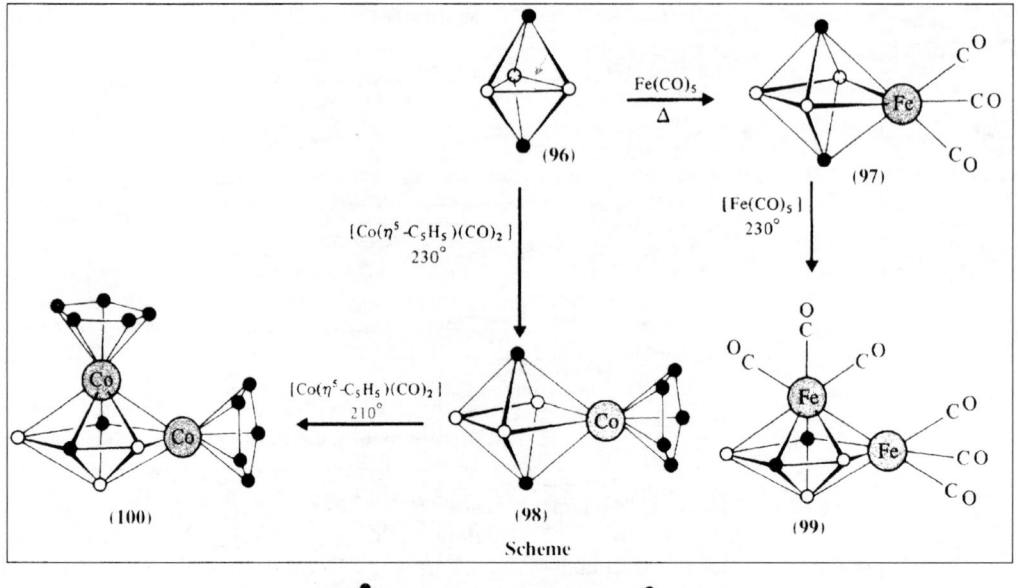

Scheme

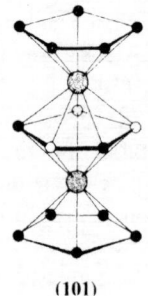

(101)

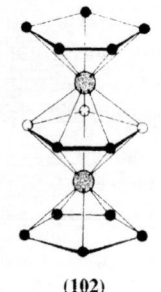

(102)

Many novel cluster compounds have now been prepared in this way, including mixed metal clusters. Further routes involve the *oxidative fusion of dicarbon metallacarborane anions* to give dimetal tetracarbon clusters such as (103) and (104);[71] the *insertion of isonitriles into metallaborane clusters* to give monocarbon metallacarboranes such as (105);[94] and the reaction of small *nido*-carboranes with alane adducts such as Et_3NAlH_3 to give the *commo* species (106):[95]

$$2[(\eta^5\text{-}C_5H_5)CoMe_2C_2B_3H_4]^- \xrightarrow[-2e^-,\ -H_2]{O_2}$$

$$[(\eta^5\text{-}C_5H_5)_2Co_2Me_4C_4B_6H_6]\ (103)$$

$$2[(Me_2C_2B_4H_4)_2FeH_2] \xrightarrow[\text{(ii) dme}]{\text{(i) thf}}$$

$$[(Me_2C_2B_4H_4)_2Fe_2(MeOCH_2CH_2OMe)]\ (104)$$

$$2EtNC + [(\eta^5\text{-}C_5Me_5)\text{-}nido\text{-}RhB_9H_{13}] \xrightarrow[-2H_2]{110°/\text{tol}}$$

$$[(\eta^5\text{-}C_5Me_5)(NHEt)(CNEt)\text{-}closo\text{-}RhCB_9H_8]\ (105)$$

$$Et_3NAlH_3 + 2[nido\text{-}Et_2C_2B_4H_6]\ (52) \xrightarrow[-3H_2]{70°/36\ h}$$

$$[commo\text{-}(Et_2C_2B_4H_4)\text{-}\mu\text{-}(AlNEt_3)(Et_2C_2B_4H_5)]\ (106)$$

[94] E. J. DITZEL, X. L. R. FONTAINE, N. N. GREENWOOD, J. D. KENNEDY, Z. SISAN, B. ŠTÍBR and M. THORNTON-PETT, *J. Chem. Soc., Chem. Commun.*, 1741–3 (1990). See also N. N. GREENWOOD and J. D. KENNEDY, *Pure Appl. Chem.* **63**, 317–26 (1991) and refs. therein.

[95] J. S. BECK and L. G. SNEDDON, *J. Am. Chem. Soc.* **110**, 3467–72 (1988).

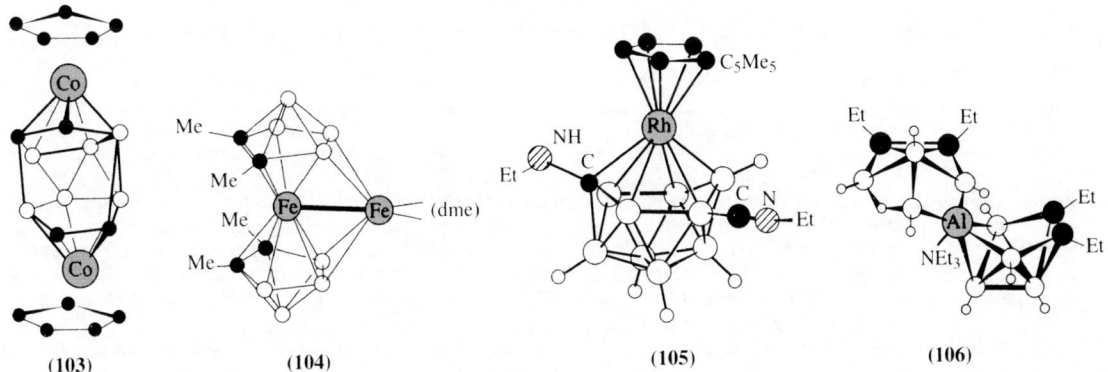

(103)   (104)   (105)   (106)

Numerous other aluminacarborane structural types have also recently been synthesized by a variety of routes[91] and, indeed, the burgeoning field of metallocarborane chemistry now encompasses the whole Periodic Table with an almost bewildering display of exotic and unprecedented structural types.

The electron-counting rules outlined for boranes (p. 161) and carboranes (p. 181) can readily be extended to the metallocarboranes (see Panel on next page). For bis-complexes of $1,2\text{-}C_2B_{10}H_{11}^{2-}$ which can be regarded as a 6-electron penta-hapto ligand, it has been found that "electron-sufficient" (18-electron) systems such as those involving d^6 metal centres (e.g. Fe^{II}, Co^{III} or Ni^{IV}) have symmetrical structures with the metal atom equidistant from the 2 C and 3 B atoms in the pentagonal face. The same is true for "electron-deficient" systems such as those involving d^2 Ti^{II} (14-electron), d^3 Cr^{III} (15-electron), etc., though here the metal-cluster bonds are somewhat longer. With "electron excess" complexes such as $[Ni^{II}(C_2B_{10}H_{11})_2]^{2-}$ and the corresponding complexes of Pd^{II}, Cu^{III} and Au^{III} (20 electrons), so-called "slipped-sandwich" structures (107) are observed in which the metal atom is significantly closer to the 3 B atoms than to the 2 C atoms. This has been thought by some to indicate π-allylic bonding to the 3 B but is more likely to arise from an occupation of orbitals that are antibonding with respect to both the metal and the cluster thereby leading to an opening of the 12-vertex

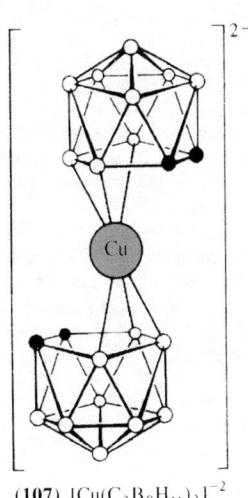

(107) $[Cu(C_2B_9H_{11})_2]^{-2}$

closo-structure to a pseudo-*nido* structure in which the 12 atoms of the cluster occupy 12 vertices of a 13-vertex polyhedron.[96] A similar type of distortion accompanies the use of metal centres with increasing numbers of electron-pairs on the metal and it seems that these electrons may also, at least in part, contribute to the framework electron count with consequent cluster opening.[97] Thus, progressive opening of the

[96] D. M. P. MINGOS, M. I. FORSYTH and A. J. WELCH, *J. Chem. Soc., Chem. Commun.*, 605–7 (1977). See also G. K. BARKER, M. GREEN, F. G. A. STONE and A. J. WELCH, *J. Chem. Soc., Dalton Trans.*, 1186–99 (1980); D. M. P. MINGOS and A. J. WELCH, *ibid.* 1674–81.

[97] H. M. COLQUHOUN, T. J. GREENHOUGH and M. G. H. WALLBRIDGE, *J. Chem. Soc., Chem. Commun.*, 737–8 (1977); see also H. M. COLQUHOUN, T. J. GREENHOUGH

Electron-counting Rules for Metallocarboranes and Other Heteroboranes

As indicated on pp. 161 and 174 each framework atom (except H) uses 3 atomic orbitals (AOs) in cluster bonding. For B, C, and other first-row elements this leaves one remaining AO to bond exopolyhedrally to $-H_t$, $-X$, $-R$, etc. In contrast, transition elements have a total of 9 valence AOs (five d, one s, three p). Hence, after contributing 3 AOs to the cluster, they have 6 remaining AOs which can be used for bonding to external ligands and for storage of nonbonding electrons. In *closo*-clusters the $(n + 1)$ MOs require $(2n + 2)$ electrons from the B, C and M vertex atoms. In its simplest form the electron counting scheme invokes only the total number of framework MOs and electrons, and requires no assumptions as to orbital hybridization or formal oxidation state. For example, the neutral moiety $\{Fe(CO)_3\}$ has 8 Fe electrons and 9 Fe AOs: since 3 AOs are involved in bonding to 3 CO and 3 AOs are used in cluster bonding, there remain 3 AOs which can accommodate 6 (nonbonding) Fe electrons, leaving 2 Fe electrons to be used in cluster bonding. Neutral $\{Fe(CO)_3\}$ is thus precisely equivalent to $\{BH\}$, as distinct from $\{CH\}$, which provides 3 electrons for the cluster. Other groups such as $\{Co(\eta^5\text{-}C_5H_5)\}$ and $\{Ni(CO)_2\}$ are clearly equivalent to $\{Fe(CO)_3\}$.

An alternative scheme that is qualitatively equivalent is to assign formal oxidation states to the metal moiety and to consider the bonding as coordination from a carborane ligand, e.g. $\{Fe(CO)_3\}^{2+}\,\eta^5$-bonded to a cyclocarborane ring as in $\{C_2B_9H_{11}\}^{2-}$. This is acceptable when the anionic ligand is well characterized as an independent entity, as in the case just cited, but for many metallocarboranes the "ligands" are not known as free species and the presumed anionic charge and metal oxidation state become somewhat arbitrary. It is therefore recommended that the metalloborane cluster be treated as a single covalently bonded structure with no artificial separation between the metal and the rest of the cluster; electron counting can then be done unambiguously on the basis of neutral atoms and attached groups.

To the structural generalizations on carboranes (p. 185) can be added the rule that, in metallocarboranes, the M atom tends to adopt a vertex with high coordination number; M occupancy of a low CN vertex is not precluded, particularly in kinetically controlled syntheses, but isomerization to more stable configurations usually results in the migration of M to high CN vertices.

Other main-group atoms besides C can occur in heteroborane clusters and the electron-counting rules can readily be extended to them.[17] Thus, whereas each $\{BH\}$ contributes 2 e and $\{CH\}$ contributes 3 e to the cluster, so $\{NH\}$ or $\{PH\}$ contributes 4 e, $\{SH\}$ contributes 5 e, $\{S\}$ contributes 4 e, etc. For example, the following 10-vertex thiaboranes (and their isoelectronic equivalents) are known: *closo*-1-SB_9H_9 ($B_{10}H_{10}^{2-}$), *nido*-6-SB_9H_{11} ($B_{10}H_{13}^{-}$) and *arachno*-6-$SB_9H_{12}^{-}$ ($B_{10}H_{14}^{2-}$). Similarly, the structures of 12-, 11- and 9-vertex thiaboranes parallel those of boranes and carbaboranes with the same skeletal electron count, the S atom in each case contributing 4 electrons to the framework plus an *exo*-polyhedral lone-pair.

cluster is noted for complexes of $1,2\text{-}C_2B_9H_{11}^{2-}$ with Re^I (d^6), Au^{III} (d^8), Hg^{II} (d^{10}) and Tl^I ($d^{10}s^2$) as shown in structures (108)–(111). Thus the Re^I (d^6) complex (108) is a symmetrically bonded 12-vertex cluster with Re–B 234 pm and Re–C 231 pm. The Au^{III} (d^8) complex (109) has the metal appreciably closer to the 3 B atoms (221 pm) than to the 2 C atoms (278 pm). With the Hg^{II} (d^{10}) complex (110) this distortion is even more pronounced and the metal is pseudo-σ-bonded to 1 B atom at 220 pm; there is

some additional though weak interaction with the other 2 B (252 pm) but the two $Hg \cdots C$ distances (290 pm) are essentially nonbonding. Finally, the Tl^I ($d^{10}s^2$) complex (111), whilst having the Tl atom more symmetrically located above the open face, has Tl–cluster distances that exceed considerably the expected covalent Tl^I–B distance of $\sim$236 pm; the shortest Tl–B distance is 266 pm and there are two other Tl–B at 274 pm and two Tl–C at 292 pm: the species can thus be regarded formally as being closer to an ion pair $[Tl^+ (C_2B_9H_{11})^{2-}]$.

In general, metallocarboranes are much less reactive (more stable) than the corresponding metallocenes and they tend to stabilize higher oxidation states of the later transition metals, e.g. $[Cu^{II}(1,2\text{-}C_2B_9H_{11})_2]^{2-}$ and $[Cu^{III}(1,2\text{-}C_2B_9H_{11})_2]^{-}$ are known whereas cuprocene

and M. G. H. WALLBRIDGE, *J. Chem. Soc., Chem. Commun.*, 1019–20 (1976); 737–8 (1977); *J. Chem. Soc., Dalton Trans.*, 619–28 (1979); *J. Chem. Soc., Chem. Commun.*, 192–4 (1980); G. K. BARKER, M. GREEN, F. G. A. STONE, A. J. WELCH and W. C. WOLSEY, *J. Chem. Soc., Chem. Commun.*, 627–9 (1980), K. NESTOR, B. ŠTÍBR, T. JELÍNEK and J. D. KENNEDY, *J. Chem. Soc., Dalton Trans.*, 1661–3 (1993).

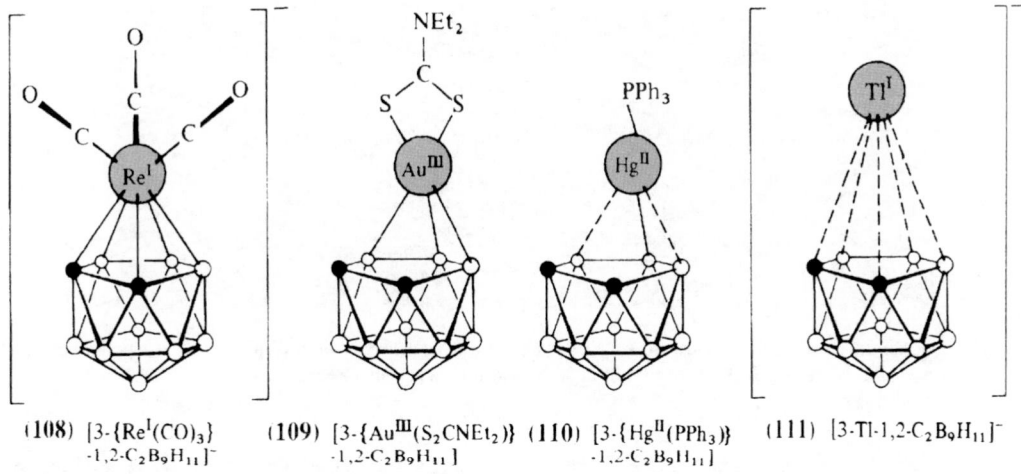

(108) $[3-\{Re^I(CO)_3\}$
$\cdot 1,2\text{-}C_2B_9H_{11}]^-$

(109) $[3-\{Au^{III}(S_2CNEt_2)\}$
$\cdot 1,2\text{-}C_2B_9H_{11}]$

(110) $[3-\{Hg^{II}(PPh_3)\}$
$\cdot 1,2\text{-}C_2B_9H_{11}]$

(111) $[3\text{-}Tl\text{-}1,2\text{-}C_2B_9H_{11}]^-$

$[Cu^{II}(\eta^5\text{-}C_5H_5)_2]$ is not. Likewise, Fe^{III} and Ni^{IV} carborane derivatives are extremely stable. Conversely, metallocarboranes tend to stabilize lower oxidation states of early transition elements and complexes are well established for Ti^{II}, Zr^{II}, Hf^{II}, V^{II}, Cr^{II} and Mn^{II}: these do not react with H_2, N_2, CO or PPh_3 as do cyclopentadienyl derivatives of these elements.

The chemistry of metallocarboranes of all cluster sizes is still rapidly developing and further unusual reactions and novel structures are continually appearing. Furthermore, as Si, Ge, Sn (and Pb) are in the same periodic group as C, heteroboranes containing these elements are to be expected (see p. 394). Likewise, as CC is isoelectronic with BN, the dicarbaboranes such as $C_2B_{10}H_{12}$ can be paralleled by $NB_{11}H_{12}$ etc. Numerous azaboranes and their metalla-derivatives are known (see p. 211) as indeed are clusters incorporating P, As, Sb (and Bi) (p. 212). The incorporation of the more electronegative element O has proved to be a greater challenge but several examples are now known. Sulfur provides an extensive thia- and polythia-borane chemistry (p. 214) and this is paralleled, although to a lesser extent, by Se and Te derivatives (p. 215). Detailed discussion of these burgeoning areas of borane cluster chemistry fall outside this present treatment but the general references cited on the above mentioned pages provide a

useful introduction into this important new area of chemistry.

6.7 Boron Halides

Boron forms numerous binary halides of which the monomeric trihalides BX_3 are the most stable and most extensively studied. They can be regarded as the first members of a homologous series B_nH_{n+2}. The second members B_2X_4 are also known for all 4 halogens but only F forms more highly catenated species containing BX_2 groups: B_3F_5, $B_4F_6.L$, B_8F_{12} (p. 201). Chlorine forms a series of neutral *closo*-polyhedral compounds B_nCl_n ($n = 4, 8-12$) and several similar compounds are known for Br ($n = 7-10$) and I (e.g. B_9I_9). There are also numerous involatile subhalides, particularly of Br and I, but these are of uncertain stoichiometry and undetermined structure.

6.7.1 Boron trihalides

The boron trihalides are volatile, highly reactive, monomeric molecular compounds which show no detectable tendency to dimerize (except perhaps in Kr matrix-isolation experiments at 20K). In

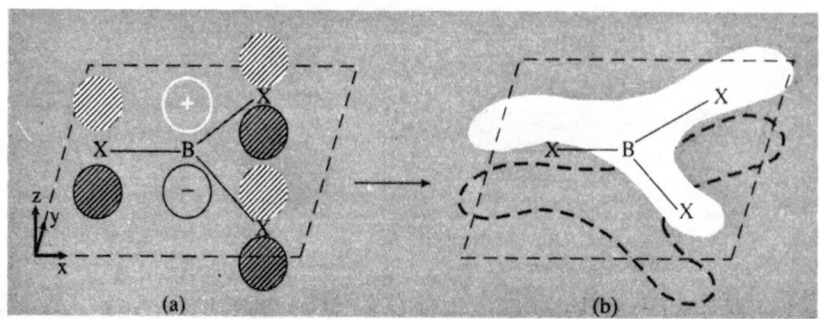

Figure 6.22 Schematic indication of the $p_\pi - p_\pi$ interaction between the "vacant" p_z orbital on B and the 3 filled p_z orbitals on the 3 X atoms leading to a bonding MO of π symmetry.

this they resemble organoboranes, BR_3, but differ sharply from diborane, B_2H_6, and the aluminium halides and alkyls, Al_2X_6, Al_2R_6 (p. 259). Some physical properties are listed in Table 6.4; mps and volatilities parallel those of the parent halogens, BF_3 and BCl_3 being gases at room temperature, BBr_3 a volatile liquid, and BI_3 a solid. All four compounds have trigonal planar molecules of D_{3h} symmetry with angle X–B–X $120°$ (Fig. 6.22a). The interatomic distances B–X are substantially less than those expected for single bonds and this has been interpreted in terms of appreciable $p_\pi - p_\pi$ interaction (Fig. 6.22b). However, there is disagreement as to whether the extent of this π bonding increases or diminishes with increasing atomic number of the halogen; this probably reflects the differing criteria used (extent of orbital overlap, percentage π-bond character, amount of π-charge transfer from X to B, π-bond energy, or reorganization energy in going from planar BX_3 to tetrahedral LBX_3, etc.).[98] For example, it is quite possible for the extent of π-charge transfer from X to B to increase in the sequence F < Cl < Br < I but for the actual magnitude of the π-bond energy to be in

the reverse sequence $BF_3 > BCl_3 > BBr_3 > BI_3$ because of the much greater bond energy of the lighter homologues. Indeed, the mean B–F bond energy in BF_3 is $646\,kJ\,mol^{-1}$, which makes it the strongest known "single" bond; if $x\%$ of this were due to π bonding, then even if $2.4x\%$ of the B–I bond energy were due to π bonding, the π-bond energy in BI_3 would be less than that in BF_3 in absolute magnitude. The point is one of some importance since the chemistry of the trihalides is dominated by interactions involving this orbital.

Table 6.4 Some physical properties of boron tri-halides

Property	BF_3	BCl_3	BBr_3	BI_3
MP/°C	−127.1	−107	−46	49.9
BP/°C	−99.9	12.5	91.3	210
r(B–X)/pm	130	175	187	210
ΔH_f° (298 K)/kJ mol^{-1} (gas)	−1123	−408	−208	+
E(B–X)/kJ mol^{-1}	646	444	368	267

BF_3 is used extensively as a catalyst in various industrial processes (p. 199) and can be prepared on a large scale by the fluorination of boric oxide or borates with fluorspar and concentrated H_2SO_4:

$$6CaF_2 + Na_2B_4O_7 + 8H_2SO_4 \longrightarrow$$
$$2NaHSO_4 + 6CaSO_4 + 7H_2O + 4BF_3$$

---

[98] Some key references will be found in D. R. ARMSTRONG and P. G. PERKINS, *J. Chem. Soc.* (A), 1967, 1218–22; and in M. F. LAPPERT, M. R. LITZOW, J. B. PEDLEY, P. N. K. RILEY and A. TWEEDALE, *J. Chem. Soc.* (A), 1968, 3105–10. Y. A. BUSLAEV, E. A. KRAVCHENKO and L. KOLDIZ, *Coord. Chem. Rev.* **82**, 9–231 (1987). V. BRANCHADELL and A. OLIVA, *J. Am. Chem. Soc.* **113**, 4132–6 (1991) and *Theochem.* **236**, 75–84 (1991).

Better yields are obtained in the more modern two-stage process:

$$Na_2B_4O_7 + 12HF \xrightarrow{-6H_2O} [Na_2O(BF_3)_4]$$

$$\xrightarrow{+2H_2SO_4} 2NaHSO_4 + H_2O + 4BF_3$$

On the laboratory scale, pure BF_3 is best made by thermal decomposition of a diazonium tetrafluoroborate (e.g. $PhN_2BF_4 \longrightarrow PhF + N_2 + BF_3$). BCl_3 and BBr_3 are prepared on an industrial scale by direct halogenation of the oxide in the presence of C, e.g.:

$$B_2O_3 + 3C + 3Cl_2 \xrightarrow{500°C} 6CO + 2BCl_3$$

Laboratory samples of the pure compounds can be made by halogen exchange between BF_3 and Al_2X_6. BI_3 is made in good yield by treating $LiBH_4$ (or $NaBH_4$) with elemental I_2 at 125° (or 200°). Both BBr_3 and BI_3 tend to decompose with liberation of free halogen when exposed to light or heat; they can be purified by treatment with Hg or Zn/Hg.

Simple BX_3 undergo rapid scrambling or redistribution reactions on being mixed and the mixed halides BX_2Y and BXY_2 have been identified by vibrational spectroscopy, mass spectrometry, or nmr spectroscopy using ^{11}B or ^{19}F. A good example of this last technique is shown in Fig. 6.23, where not only the species $BF_{3-n}X_n (n = 0, 1, 2)$ were observed but also the trihalogeno species $BFClBr$.[99] The equilibrium concentration of the various species are always approximately random (equilibrium constants between 0.5 and 2.0) but it is not possible to isolate individual mixed halides because the equilibrium is too rapidly attained from either direction (<1 s). The related systems $RBX_2/R'BY_2$ (and $ArBX_2/Ar'BY_2$) also exchange X and Y but not R (or Ar). The scrambling mechanism probably involves a 4-centre transition state. Consistent with this, complexes such as Me_2OBX_3 or Me_3NBX_3 do not scramble at room temperature, or even above, in the absence of free BX_3[100] (cf. the stability of $CFCl_3$, CF_2Cl_2, etc.) and species that are

---

99 T. D. COYLE and F. G. A. STONE, *J. Chem. Phys.* **32**, 1892–3 (1960).

100 J. S. HARTMAN and J. M. MILLER, *Adv. Inorg. Chem. Radiochem.* **21**, 147–77 (1978).

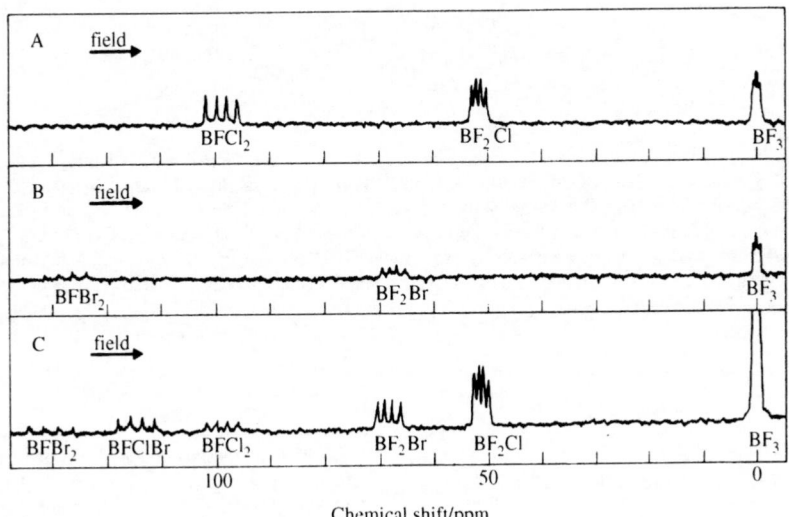

Figure 6.23 Fluorine-19 nmr spectra of mixtures of boron halides showing the presence of mixed fluorohalogenoboranes.

Factors Affecting the Stability of Donor–Acceptor Complexes[101-103]

For a given ligand, stability of the adduct LBX_3 usually increases in the sequence $BF_3 < BCl_3 < BBr_3 < BI_3$, probably because the loss of π bonding on reorganization from planar to tetrahedral geometry (p. 196) is not fully compensated for by the expected electronegativity effect. However, if the ligand has an H atom directly bonded to the donor atom, the resulting complex is susceptible to protonolysis of the B–X bond, e.g.:

$$ROH + BX_3 \longrightarrow [ROH.BX_3] \longrightarrow ROBX_2 + HX$$

In such cases the great strength of the B–F bond ensures that the BF_3 complex is more stable than the others. For example, BF_3 forms stable complexes with H_2O, MeOH, Me_2NH, etc., whereas BCl_3 reacts rapidly to give $B(OH)_3$, $B(OMe)_3$ and $B(NMe_2)_3$: with BBr_3 and BI_3 such protolytic reactions are sometimes of explosive violence. Even ethers may be cleaved by BCl_3 to give RCl and $ROBCl_2$, etc.

For a given BX_3, the stability of the complex depends on (a) the chemical nature of the donor atom, (b) the presence of polar substituents on the ligand, (c) steric effects, (d) the stoichiometric ratio of ligand to acceptor, and (e) the state of aggregation. Thus the majority of adducts have as the donor atom N, P, As; O, S; or the halide and hydride ions X^-. BX_3 (but not BH_3) can be classified as type-a acceptors, forming stronger complexes with N, O and F ligands than with P, S and Cl. However, complexes are not limited to these traditional main-group donor atoms, and, following the work of D. F. Shriver (1963), many complexes have been characterized in which the donor atom is a transition metal, e.g. $[(C_5H_5)_2H_2W^{IV} \rightarrow BF_3]$, $[(Ph_3P)_2(CO)ClRh^I \rightarrow BBr_3]$, $[(Ph_2PCH_2CH_2PPh_2)_2Rh^I(BCl_3)_2]^+$, $[(Ph_3P)_2(CO)ClIr^I(BF_3)_2]$, $[(Ph_3P)_2Pt^0(BCl_3)_2]$, etc. Displacement studies on several such complexes indicate that BF_3 is a weaker acceptor than BCl_3.

The influence of polar substituents on the ligand follows the expected sequence for electronegative groups, e.g. electron donor properties decrease in the order $NMe_3 > NMe_2Cl > NMeCl_2 \gg NCl_3$. Steric effects can also limit the electron-donor strength. For example, whereas pyridine, C_5H_5N, is a weaker base (proton acceptor) than 2-MeC_5H_4N and $2,6\text{-Me}_2C_5H_3N$, the reverse is true when BF_3 is the acceptor due to steric crowding of the α-Me groups which prevent the close approach of BF_3 to the donor atom. Steric effects also predominate in determining the decreasing stability of BF_3 etherates in the sequence $C_4H_8O(thf) > Me_2O > Et_2O > Pr^i_2O$.

The influences of stoichiometry and state of aggregation are more subtle. At first sight it is not obvious why BF_3, with 1 vacant orbital should form not only $BF_3.H_2O$ but also the more stable $BF_3.2H_2O$; similarly, the 1:2 complexes with ROH and RCOOH are always more stable than the 1:1 complexes. The second mole of ligand is held by hydrogen bonding in the solid, e.g. $BF_3.OH_2 \ldots OH_2$; however, above the mp 6.2°C the compound melts and the act of coordinate-bond formation causes sufficient change in the electron distribution within the ligand that ionization ensues and the compound is virtually completely ionized as a molten salt:[101]

The greater stability of the 1:2 complex is thus seen to be related to the formation of H_3O^+, ROH_2^+, etc., and the lower stability of the 1:1 complexes HBF_3OH, HBF_3OR, is paralleled by the instability of some other anhydrous oxo acids, e.g. H_2CO_3. The mp of the hydrate is essentially the transition temperature between an H-bonded molecular solid and an ionically dissociated liquid. A transition in the opposite sense occurs when crystalline $[PCl_4]^+[PCl_6]^-$ melts to give molecular PCl_5 (p. 498) and several other examples are known. The fact that coordination can substantially modify the type of bonding should occasion no surprise: the classic example (first observed by J. Priestley in 1774) was the reaction $NH_3(g) + HCl(g) \rightarrow NH_4Cl(c)$.

expected to form stronger π bonds than BX_3 (such as R_2NBX_2) exchange much more slowly (days or weeks).

The boron trihalides form a great many molecular addition compounds with molecules

[101] N. N. GREENWOOD and R. L. MARTIN *Qt. Revs.* **8**, 1–39 (1954).

[102] V. GUTMANN, *The Donor-Acceptor Approach to Molecular Interactions*, Plenum, New York, 1978, 279 pp.

[103] A. HAALAND, *Angew. Chem. Int. Edn. Engl.* **28**, 992–1007 (1989).

(ligands) possessing a lone-pair of electrons (Lewis base). Such adducts have assumed considerable importance since it is possible to investigate in detail the process of making and breaking one bond, and to study the effect this has on the rest of the molecule (see Panel). The tetrahalogeno borates BX_4^- are a special case in which the ligand is X^-; they are isoelectronic with BH_4^- (p. 165) and with CH_4 and CX_4. Salts of BF_4^- are readily formed by adding a suitable metal fluoride to BF_3 either in the absence of solvent or in such nonaqueous solvents as HF, BrF_3, AsF_3 or SO_2. The alkali metal salts MBF_4 are stable to hydrolysis in aqueous solutions. Some molecular fluorides such as NO_2F and RCOF react similarly. There is a significant lengthening of the B–F bond from 130 pm in BF_3 to 145 pm in BF_4^-. The other tetrahalogenoborates, BX_4^-, are less stable but may be prepared using large counter cations, e.g. Rb, Cs, pyridinium, tetraalkylammonium, tropenium, triphenylcarbonium, etc. The BF_4^- anion is a very weakly coordinating ligand, indeed one of the weakest;[104] however, unstable complexes are known in which it acts as an η^1-ligand and, in the case of [Ag(lut)$_2$(BF$_4$)] it acts as a bis(bidentate) bridging ligand [μ_4-η^2,η^2-BF$_4$]$^-$ to form a polymeric chain of 6-coordinate Ag centres[105] [lut = lutidene, i.e. 2,6-dimethylpyridine].

The importance of the trihalides as industrial chemicals stems partly from their use in preparing crystalline boron (p. 141) but mainly from their ability to catalyse a wide variety of organic reactions.[106] BF_3 is the most widely used but BCl_3 is employed in special cases. Thus, BF_3 is manufactured on the multikilotonne scale whereas the production of BCl_3 (USA, 1990) was 250 tonnes and BBr_3 was about 23 tonnes. BF_3 is shipped in steel cylinders containing 2.7 or 28 kg at a pressure of 10–12 atm, or in tube trailers

containing about 5.5 tonnes. Prices for BF_3 are in the range \$4.00–5.00/kg depending on purity and quantity; corresponding prices (USA, 1991) for BCl_3 and BBr_3 were \$8.50–16.75/kg and \$81.50/kg, respectively.

Many of the reactions of BF_3 are of the Friedel–Crafts type though they are perhaps not strictly catalytic since BF_3 is required in essentially equimolar quantities with the reactant. The mechanism is not always fully understood but it is generally agreed that in most cases ionic intermediates are produced by or promoted by the formation of a BX_3 complex; electrophilic attack of the substrate by the cation so produced completes the process. For example, in the Friedel–Crafts-type alkylation of aromatic hydrocarbons:

$$RX + BF_3 \rightleftharpoons \{R^+\}\{BF_3X^-\}$$

$$\{R^+\} + PhH \rightleftharpoons PhR + \{H^+\}$$

$$\{H^+\} + \{BF_3X^-\} \rightleftharpoons BF_3 + HX$$

Similarly, ketones are prepared via acyl carbonium ions:

$$RCOOMe + BF_3 \rightleftharpoons \{RCO^+\}\{BF_3(OMe)^-\}$$

$$\{RCO^+\} + PhH \rightleftharpoons PhCOR + \{H^+\}$$

$$\{H^+\} + \{BF_3(OMe)^-\} \rightleftharpoons MeOH.BF_3$$

Evidence for many of these ions has been extensively documented.[101]

$$ROH + BF_3 \rightleftharpoons \{H^+\} + \{BF_3(OR)^-\}$$

$$\{H^+\} + ROH \rightleftharpoons \{ROH_2{}^+\}$$

$$\xrightarrow{BF_3} \rightleftharpoons \{R^+\} + H_2OBF_3$$

$$\{R^+\} + ROH \longrightarrow R_2O + \{H^+\}$$

A similar mechanism has been proposed for the esterification of carboxylic acids:

$$\{H^+\} + RCOOH \rightleftharpoons \{RCOOH_2{}^+\}$$

$$\xrightarrow{BF_3 3} \rightleftharpoons \{RCO^+\} + H_2OBF_3$$

$$\{RCO^+\} + R'OH \longrightarrow RCOOR' + \{H^+\}$$

104 W. BECK and K. SÜNKEL, *Chem. Rev.* **88**, 1405–21 (1988).

105 E. HORM, M. R. SNOW and E. R. T. TIEKINK, *Aust. J. Chem.* **40**, 761–5 (1987).

106 G. OLAH (ed.), *Friedel–Crafts and Related Reactions*, Interscience, New York, 1963 (4 vols).

Nitration and sulfonation of aromatic compounds probably occur via the formation of the nitryl and sulfonyl cations:

$$HONO_2 + BF_3 \rightleftharpoons \{NO_2^+\} + \{BF_3(OH)^-\}$$

$$HOSO_3H + BF_3 \rightleftharpoons \{SO_3H^+\} + \{BF_3(OH)^-\}$$

Polymerization of alkenes and the isomerization of alkanes and alkenes occur in the presence of a cocatalyst such as H_2O, whereas the cracking of hydrocarbons is best performed with HF as cocatalyst. These latter reactions are of major commercial importance in the petrochemicals industry.

6.7.2 Lower halides of boron

B_2F_4 (mp $-56°$, bp $-34°C$) has a planar (D_{2h}) structure with a rather long B–B bond; in this it resembles both the oxalate ion $C_2O_4^{2-}$ and N_2O_4 with which it is precisely isoelectronic. Crystalline B_2Cl_4 (mp $-92.6°C$) has the same structure, but in the gas phase (bp $65.5°$) it adopts the staggered D_{2d} configuration (see below) with hindered rotation about the B–B bond (ΔE_r 7.7 kJ mol^{-1}). The structure of gaseous B_2Br_4 is also D_{2d} with B–B 169 pm and ΔE_r 12.8 kJ mol^{-1}. B_2I_4 is presumably similar.

B_2Cl_4 was the first compound in this series to be prepared and is the most studied; it is best made by subjecting BCl_3 vapour to an electrical discharge between mercury or copper electrodes:

$$2BCl_3 + 2Hg \longrightarrow B_2Cl_4 + Hg_2Cl_2$$

The reaction probably proceeds by formation of a {BCl} intermediate which then inserts into a B–Cl bond of BCl_3 to give the product directly.

Another route is via the more stable $B_2(NMe_2)_4$ (see reaction scheme). Thermal stabilities of these compounds parallel the expected sequence of $p_\pi-p_\pi$ bonding between the substituent and B:

$$B_2(NMe_2)_4 > B_2(OMe)_4 > B_2(OH)_4$$
$$> B_2F_4 > B_2Cl_4 > B_2Br_4$$

The halides are much less stable than the corresponding BX_3, the most stable member B_2F_4 decomposing at the rate of about 8% per day at room temperature. B_2Br_4 disproportionates so rapidly at room temperature that it is difficult to purify:

$$nB_2X_4 \longrightarrow nBX_3 + (BX)_n$$

The compounds B_2X_4 are spontaneously flammable in air and react with H_2 to give BHX_2, B_2H_6 and related hydrohalides; they form adducts with Lewis bases ($B_2Cl_4L_2$ more stable than $B_2F_4L_2$) and add across C–C multiple bonds, e.g.

Other reactions of B_2Cl_4 are shown in the scheme and many of these also occur with B_2F_4.

When BF_3 is passed over crystalline B at $1850°C$ and pressures of less than 1 mmHg, the reactive gas BF is obtained in high yield and can

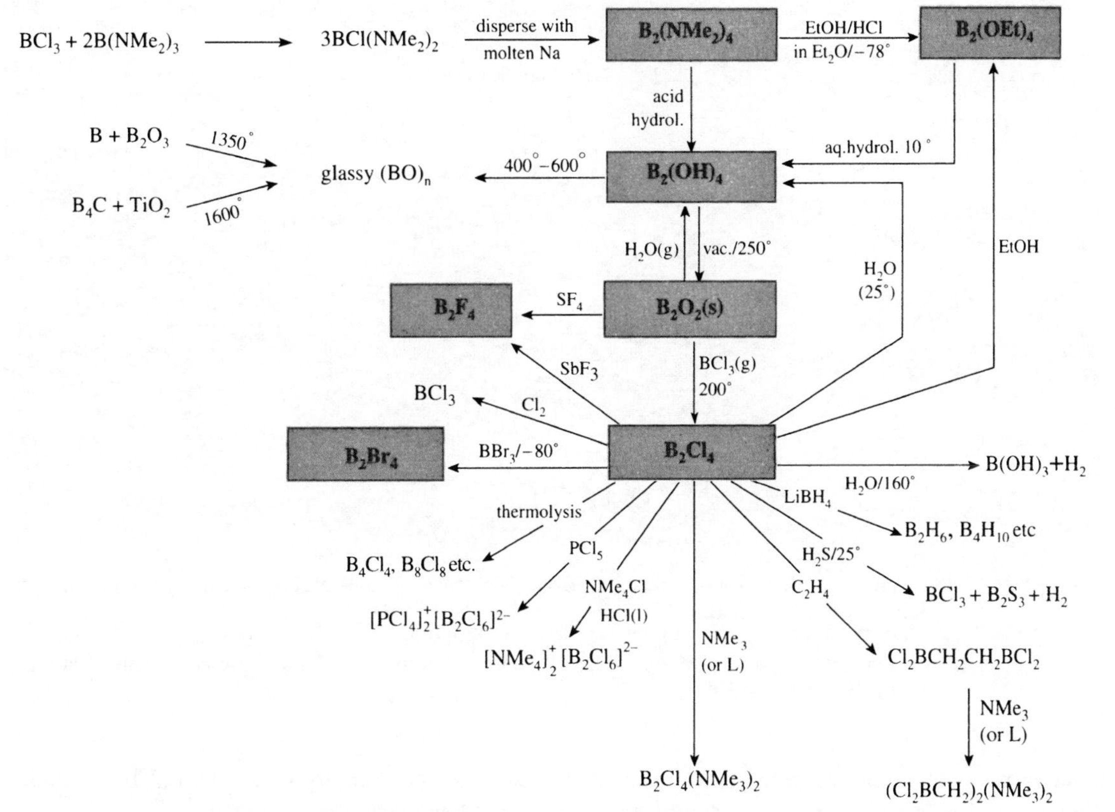

$BCl_3 + 2B(NMe_2)_3 \longrightarrow 3BCl(NMe_2)_2$ →(disperse with molten Na)→ **$B_2(NMe_2)_4$** →(EtOH/HCl in Et_2O/$-78°$)→ **$B_2(OEt)_4$**

$B + B_2O_3$ —$1350°$→

$B_4C + TiO_2$ —$1600°$→ glassy $(BO)_n$ ←$400°-600°$— **$B_2(OH)_4$**

$B_2(NMe_2)_4$ → (acid hydrol.) → $B_2(OH)_4$

$B_2(OEt)_4$ → (aq.hydrol. $10°$) → $B_2(OH)_4$

$B_2(OEt)_4$ → (EtOH) → $B_2(OH)_4$

$B_2(OH)_4$ ⇌ (H_2O(g) / vac./$250°$) ⇌ **B_2O_2(s)**

B_2F_4 ←SF_4— **B_2O_2(s)**

B_2O_2(s) →(BCl_3(g) $200°$)→ **B_2Cl_4**

B_2Cl_4 —SbF_3→ B_2F_4

B_2Cl_4 —Cl_2→ BCl_3

B_2Br_4 ←$BBr_3/-80°$— B_2Cl_4

B_2Cl_4 →(H_2O ($25°$))→ $B_2(OH)_4$

B_2Cl_4 →(H_2O/$160°$)→ $B(OH)_3 + H_2$

B_2Cl_4 →(LiBH$_4$)→ B_2H_6, B_4H_{10} etc

B_2Cl_4 →(H_2S/$25°$)→ $BCl_3 + B_2S_3 + H_2$

B_2Cl_4 →(thermolysis)→ B_4Cl_4, B_8Cl_8 etc.

B_2Cl_4 →(PCl_5)→ $[PCl_4]_2^+[B_2Cl_6]^{2-}$

B_2Cl_4 →(NMe_4Cl / HCl(l))→ $[NMe_4]_2^+[B_2Cl_6]^{2-}$

B_2Cl_4 →(NMe_3 (or L))→ $B_2Cl_4(NMe_3)_2$

B_2Cl_4 →(C_2H_4)→ $Cl_2BCH_2CH_2BCl_2$ →(NMe_3 (or L))→ $(Cl_2BCH_2)_2(NMe_3)_2$

be condensed out at $-196°$. Cocondensation with BF_3 yields B_2F_4 then B_3F_5 (i.e. $F_2B-B(F)-BF_2$). However, this latter compound is unstable and it disproportionates above $-50°$ according to

$$4(BF_2)_2BF \longrightarrow 2B_2F_4 + B_8F_{12} \quad (112)$$

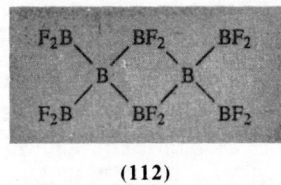

(112)

The yellow compound B_8F_{12} appears to have a diborane-like structure (112) and this readily undergoes symmetrical cleavage with a variety of ligands such as CO, PF_3, PCl_3, PH_3, AsH_3 and SMe_2 to give adducts $L.B(BF_2)_3$ which are stable at room temperature in the absence of air or moisture.

Thermolysis of B_2Cl_4[107] and B_2Br_4 at moderate temperatures gives a series of *closo*-halogenoboranes B_nX_n where $n = 4$, 8–12 for Cl, and $n = 7$–10 for Br. Other preparative routes include the high-yield halogenation of $B_9H_9^{2-}$ to $B_9X_9^{2-}$ using *N*-chlorosuccinimide, *N*-bromosuccinimide or I_2.[108] The redox sequences $B_9X_9^{2-} \rightleftharpoons B_9X_9^{\bullet -} \rightleftharpoons B_9X_9$ have also been established, the radical anions $B_9X_9^{\bullet -}$ being isolated as air-stable coloured salts.[108]

B_4Cl_4, a pale-yellow-green solid, has a regular *closo*-tetrahedral structure (Fig. 6.24a); it is hyperelectron deficient when compared with the *closo*-boranes $B_nH_n^{2-}$ (pp. 153, 160) and the

---

[107] T. DAVAN and J. A. MORRISON, *Inorg. Chem.* **25**, 2366–72 (1986).

[108] E. H. WONG and R. M. KABBANI, *Inorg. Chem.* **19**, 451–5 (1980). See also E. H. WONG, *Inorg. Chem.* **20**, 1300–2 (1981); A. J. MARKWELL, A. G. MASSEY and P. J. PORTAL, *Polyhedron* **1**, 134–5 (1982).

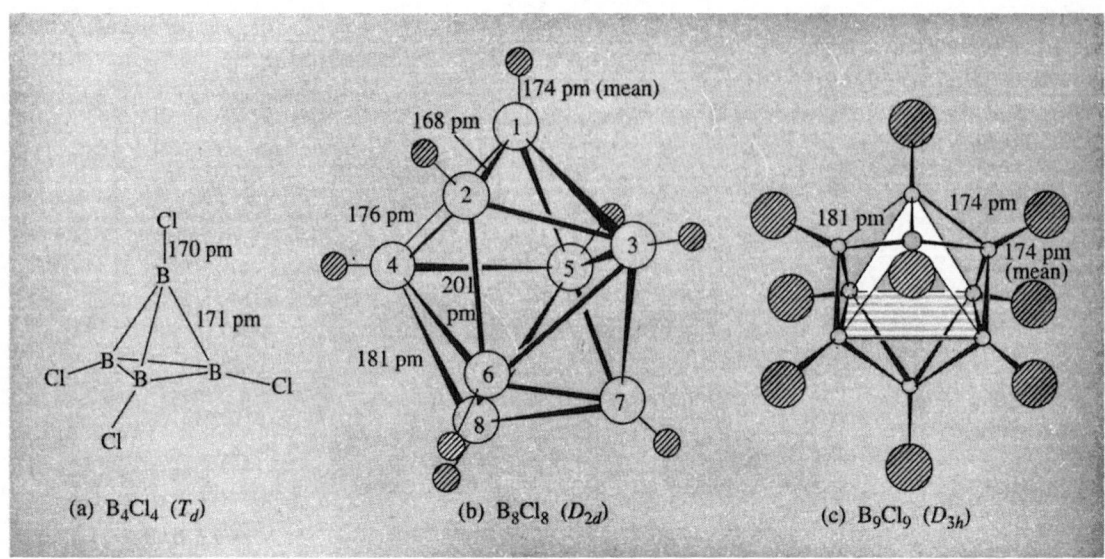

(a) B$_4$Cl$_4$ (T_d)   (b) B$_8$Cl$_8$ (D_{2d})   (c) B$_9$Cl$_9$ (D_{3h})

Figure 6.24   Molecular structures of (a) tetrahedral B$_4$Cl$_4$, (b) dodecahedral B$_8$Cl$_8$, and (c) tricapped trigonal pyramidal B$_9$Cl$_9$ and B$_9$Br$_9$. In B$_8$Cl$_8$ note that the shortest B–B distances are between two 5-coordinate B atoms, e.g. B(1)–B(2) 168 pm; the longest are between two 6-coordinate B atoms, e.g. B(4)–B(6) 201 pm and intermediate distances are between one 5- and one 6-coordinate B atom. A similar trend occurs in B$_9$Cl$_9$.

bonding has been discussed in terms of localized 3-centre bonds above the 4 tetrahedral faces supplemented by p$_\pi$ interaction with p orbitals of suitable symmetry on the 4 Cl atoms: the 8 electrons available for framework bonding from the 4 {BCl} groups fill 4 bonding MOs of class A_1 and T_2 and there are 2 additional bonding MOs of class E which have correct symmetry to mix with the Cl p$_\pi$ orbitals. B$_8$Cl$_8$ (variously described as dark red, dark purple or green-black crystals) has an irregular dodecahedral (bisphenoid) arrangement of the *closo*-B$_8$ cluster (Fig. 6.24b) with 14 B–B distances in the range 168–184 pm and 4 substantially longer B–B distances at 193–205 pm. B$_9$Br$_9$ is a particularly stable compound; it forms as dark-red crystals together with other subbromides (n = 7–10) when gaseous BBr$_3$ is subjected to a silent electric discharge in the presence of Cu wool, and can be purified by sublimation under conditions (200°C) which rapidly decompose the other products. B$_9$Br$_9$ is isostructural with B$_9$Cl$_9$ (yellow-orange) (Fig. 6.24c). The photoelectron

spectra and bonding in B$_4$Cl$_4$, B$_8$Cl$_8$ and B$_9$Cl$_9$ have been described in detail.[109]

Many mixed halides B$_n$Br$_{n-x}$Cl$_x$ (n = 9, 10, 11) have been identified by mass spectrometry and other techniques, but their separation as pure compounds has so far not been achieved. Chemical reactions of B$_n$X$_n$ resemble those of B$_2$X$_4$ except that alkenes do not cleave the B–B bonds in the *closo*-species. Thus, B$_4$Cl$_4$ reacts with LiEt to give the yellow liquids B$_4$Cl$_3$Et and B$_4$Cl$_2$Et$_2$, whereas LiBu^t afforded B$_4$Bu$^t_4$ as a glassy solid, mp 45°C.[110] By contrast, reaction with Me$_3$SnH yields *arachno*-B$_4$H$_{10}$ and LiBH$_4$ yields a mixture of *nido*-B$_5$H$_9$ and *nido*-B$_6$H$_{10}$, while B$_2$H$_6$ gave *nido*-B$_6$H$_6$Cl$_4$ and a mixture of *nido*-B$_{10}$H$_n$Cl$_{14-n}$ (n = 8–12).[111]

[109] P. R. LEBRETON, S. URANO, M. SHAHBAZ, S. L. EMERY and J. A. MORRISON, *J. Am. Chem. Soc.* **108**, 3937–46 (1986).

[110] T. DAVAN and J. A. MORRISON, *J. Chem. Soc., Chem. Commun.*, 250–1 (1981).

[111] S. L. EMERY and J. A. MORRISON, *Inorg. Chem.* **24**, 1612–13 (1985).

6.8 Boron–Oxygen Compounds[(112)]

Boron (like silicon) invariably occurs in nature as oxo compounds and is never found as the element or even directly bonded to any other element than oxygen.[†] The structural chemistry of B–O compounds is characterized by an extraordinary complexity and diversity which rivals those of the borides (p. 145) and boranes (p. 151). In addition, vast numbers of predominantly organic compounds containing B–O are known.

6.8.1 *Boron oxides and oxoacids* [(112)]

The principal oxide of boron is boric oxide, B_2O_3 (mp 450°, bp (extrap) 2250°C). It is one of the most difficult substances to crystallize and, indeed, was known only in the vitreous state until 1937. It is generally prepared by careful dehydration of boric acid $B(OH)_3$. The normal crystalline form (d 2.56 g cm^{-3}) consists of a 3D network of trigonal BO_3 groups joined through their O atoms, but there is also a dense form (d 3.11 g cm^{-3}) formed under a pressure of 35 kbar at 525°C and built up from irregular interconnected BO_4 tetrahedra. In the vitreous state ($d \simeq 1.83$ g cm^{-3}) B_2O_3 probably consists of a network of partially ordered trigonal BO_3 units in which the 6-membered $(BO)_3$ ring predominates; at higher temperatures the structure becomes increasingly disordered and above 450°C polar —B=O groups are formed. Fused B_2O_3 readily dissolves many metal oxides to give characteristically coloured borate glasses. Its major application is in the glass industry where borosilicate glasses

(e.g. Pyrex) are extensively used because of their small coefficient of thermal expansion and their easy workability. US production of B_2O_3 exceeds 25 000 tonnes pa and the price (1990) was $2780–2950 per tonne for 99% grade.

Orthoboric acid, $B(OH)_3$, is the normal end product of hydrolysis of most boron compounds and is usually made ($\simeq$160 000 tonnes pa) by acidification of aqueous solutions of borax. Price depends on quality, being $805 per tonne for technical grade and about twice that for refined material (1990). It forms flaky, white, transparent crystals in which a planar array of BO_3 units is joined by unsymmetrical H bonds as shown in Fig. 6.25. In contrast to the short O—H$\cdots$O distance of 272 pm within the plane, the distance between consecutive layers in the crystal is 318 pm, thus accounting for the pronounced basal cleavage of the waxy, plate-like crystals, and their low density (1.48 g cm^{-3}). $B(OH)_3$ is a very weak monobasic acid and acts exclusively by hydroxyl-ion acceptance rather than proton donation:

$$B(OH)_3 + 2H_2O \rightleftharpoons H_3O^+ + B(OH)_4^-;$$

$$pK = 9.25$$

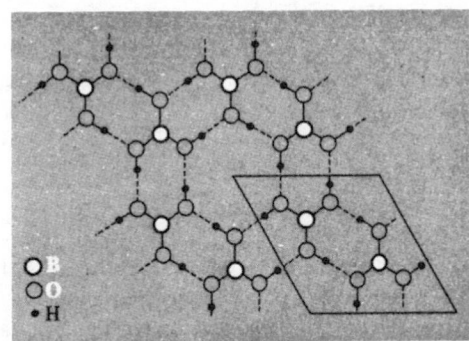

Figure 6.25   Layer structure of $B(OH)_3$. Interatomic distances are B–O 136 pm. O–H 97 pm, O—H$\cdots$O 272 pm. Angles at B are 120° and at O 126° and 114°. The H bond is almost linear.

Its acidity is considerably enhanced by chelation with polyhydric alcohols (e.g. glycerol, mannitol) and this forms the basis of its use in analytical chemistry; e.g. with mannitol pK drops to 5.15,

---

[112] *Supplement to "Mellor's Comprehensive Treatise on Inorganic and Theoretical Chemistry"*, Vol. V, Boron: Part A, *"Boron-Oxygen Compounds"*, Longman, London, 1980, 825 pp. See also J. R. BOWSER and T. P. FEHLNER, Chap. 1 in H. W. ROESKY (ed.), *Rings, Clusters and Polymers of Main Group and Transition Elements*, Elsevier, Amsterdam, 1989, pp. 1–48.

[†] Trivial exceptions to this sweeping generalization are $NaBF_4$ (ferrucite) and $(K,Cs)BF_4$ (avogadrite) which have been reported from Mt. Vesuvius, Italy.

indicating an increase in the acid equilibrium constant by a factor of more than 10^4:[113]

$$B(OH)_3 + 2 \overset{\diagdown}{\underset{\diagup}{C}}\overset{}{-}\overset{\diagdown}{\underset{\diagup}{C}} \quad \rightleftharpoons \quad H_3O^+ +$$

$$\left[\begin{array}{c} -\!\!\!-C-O \qquad O-C-\!\!\!- \\ \diagdown \quad \diagup \\ B \\ \diagup \quad \diagdown \\ -\!\!\!-C-O \qquad O-C-\!\!\!- \end{array} \right]^{-} + 2H_2O$$

$B(OH)_3$ also acts as a strong acid in anhydrous H_2SO_4:

$$B(OH)_3 + 6H_2SO_4 \longrightarrow 3H_3O^+ + 2HSO_4^-$$
$$+ [B(HSO_4)_4]^-$$

Other reactions include esterification with ROH/H_2SO_4 to give $B(OR)_3$, and coordination of this with NaH in thf to give the powerful reducing agent $Na[BH(OR)_3]$. Reaction with H_2O_2 gives peroxoboric acid solutions which probably contain the monoperoxoborate anion $[B(OH)_3OOH]^-$. A complete series of fluoroboric acids is also known in aqueous solution and several have been isolated as pure compounds:

$$H[B(OH)_4] \quad H[BF(OH)_3] \quad H[BF_2(OH)_2]$$
$$H[BF_3OH] \quad HBF_4$$

The hypohalito analogues $[B(OH)_3(OX)]^-$ (X=Cl, Br) have recently been characterized in aqueous solutions of $B(OH)_3$ containing NaOX; the stability constants $\log \beta'$ at 25°C being 2.25(1) and 1.83(4), respectively,[114] compared with 5.39(7) for $B(OH)_4^-$.

---

[113] J. M. CODDINGTON and M. J. TAYLOR, *J. Coord. Chem.* **20**, 27–38 (1989), and references cited therein, including those which describe its application to conformational analysis of carbohydrates and its use in separation and chromatographic techniques.

[114] A. BOUSHER, P. BRIMBLECOMBE and D. MIDGLEY, *J. Chem. Soc., Dalton Trans.*, 943–6 (1987).

Partial dehydration of $B(OH)_3$ above 100° yields metaboric acid HBO_2 which can exist in several crystalline modifications:

	CN of B	$d/g\ cm^{-3}$	mp/°C
Orthorhombic HBO_2	3	1.784	176°
monoclinic HBO_2	3 and 4	2.045	201°
cubic HBO_2	4	2.487	236°

$B(OH)_3 \xrightarrow{140°}$ ... rapid quench → Orthorhombic HBO_2

$B(OH)_3 \xrightarrow{175°}$ cubic HBO_2

Orthorhombic HBO_2 consists of trimeric units $B_3O_3(OH)_3$ which are linked into layers by H bonding (Fig. 6.26); all the B atoms are 3-coordinate. Monoclinic HBO_2 is built of chains of composition $[B_3O_4(OH)(H_2O)]$ in which some of the B atoms are now 4-coordinate, whereas cubic HBO_2 has a framework structure of tetrahedral BO_4 groups some of which are H bonded. The increase in CN of B is paralleled by an increase in density and mp.

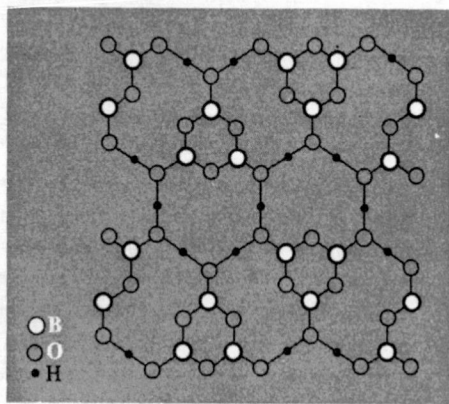

Figure 6.26   Layer structure of orthorhombic metaboric acid HBO_2(III), comprising units of formula $B_3O_3(OH)_3$ linked by $O\cdots H\cdots O$ bonds.

Boron suboxide $(BO)_n$ and subboric acid $B_2(OH)_4$ were mentioned on p. 201.

6.8.2 Borates [112,115]

The phase relations, stoichiometry and structural chemistry of the metal borates have been extensively studied because of their geochemical implications and technological importance. Borates are known in which the structural unit is mononuclear (1 B atom), bi-, tri-, tetra- or penta-nuclear, or in which there are polydimensional networks including glasses. The main structural principles underlying the bonding in crystalline metal borates are as follows:[116]

1. Boron can link either three oxygens to form a triangle or four oxygens to form a tetrahedron.
2. Polynuclear anions are formed by corner-sharing only of boron-oxygen triangles and tetrahedra in such a manner that a compact insular group results.
3. In the hydrated borates, protonatable oxygen atoms will be protonated in the following sequence: available protons are first assigned to free O^{2-} ions to convert these to free OH^- ions; additional protons are assigned to tetrahedral oxygens in the borate ion, and then to triangular oxygens in the borate ion; finally any remaining protons are assigned to free OH^- ions to form H_2O molecules.

4. The hydrated insular groups may polymerize in various ways by splitting out water; this process may be accompanied by the breaking of boron-oxygen bonds within the polyanion framework.
5. Complex borate polyanions may be modified by attachment of an individual side group, such as (but not limited to) an extra borate tetrahedron, an extra borate triangle, 2 linked triangles, an arsenate tetrahedron, and so on.
6. Isolated $B(OH)_3$ groups, or polymers of these, may exist in the presence of other anions.

Examples of minerals and compounds containing monomeric triangular, BO_3 units (structure 113) are the rare-earth orthoborates $M^{III}BO_3$ and the minerals $CaSn^{IV}(BO_3)_2$ and $Mg_3(BO_3)_2$. Binuclear trigonal planar units (114) are found in the pyroborates $Mg_2B_2O_5$, $Co^{II}_2B_2O_5$ and $Fe^{II}_2B_2O_5$. Trinuclear cyclic units (115) occur in the metaborates $NaBO_2$ and KBO_2, which should therefore be written as $M_3B_3O_6$ (cf. metaboric acid, p. 204). Polynuclear linkage of BO_3 units into infinite chains of stoichiometry BO_2 (116) occurs in $Ca(BO_2)_2$, and three-dimensional linkage of planar BO_3 units occurs in the borosilicate mineral tourmaline and in glassy B_2O_3 (p. 203).

Monomeric tetrahedral BO_4 units (117) are found in the zircon-type compound Ta^VBO_4 and in the minerals (Ta,Nb)BO_4 and $Ca_2H_4BAs^VO_8$. The related tetrahedral unit $[B(OH)_4]^-$ (118) occurs in $Na_2[B(OH)_4]Cl$ and $Cu^{II}[B(OH)_4]Cl$. Binuclear tetrahedral units (119) have been found

[115] G. HELLER, *Topics in Current Chemistry* No. 131 Springer-Verlag, Berlin, 1986, 39–98 (a survey of structural types with 568 refs.).

[116] C. L. CHRIST and J. R. CLARK, *Phys. Chem. Minerals* **2**, 59–87 (1977). See also J. B. FARMER, *Adv. Inorg. Chem. Radiochem.* **25**, 187–237 (1982).

(113) $[BO_3]^{3-}$ (114) $[B_2O_5]^{4-}$ (115) $[B_3O_6]^{3-}$ (116) $[(BO_2)^-]_n$

Units containing B in planar BO_3 coordination only

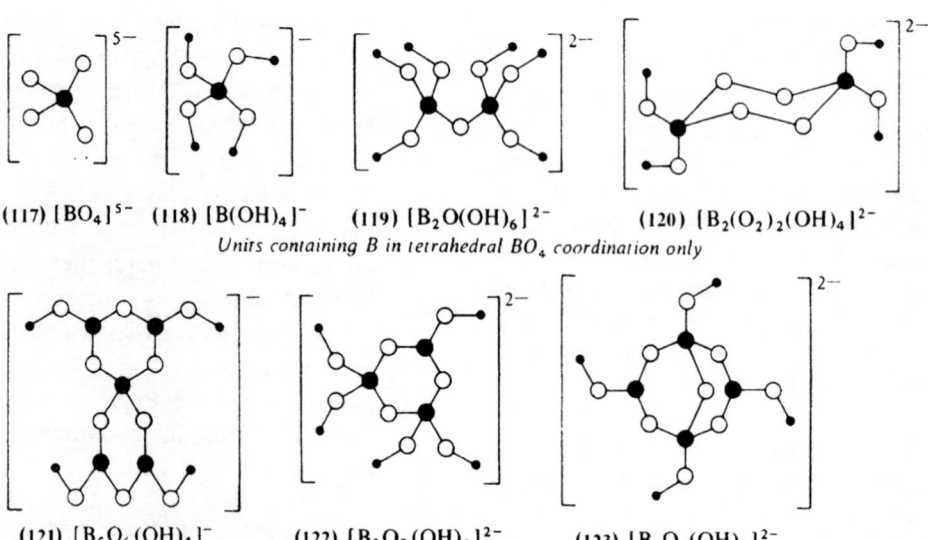

(117) $[BO_4]^{5-}$ (118) $[B(OH)_4]^-$ (119) $[B_2O(OH)_6]^{2-}$ (120) $[B_2(O_2)_2(OH)_4]^{2-}$

Units containing B in tetrahedral BO$_4$ coordination only

(121) $[B_5O_6(OH)_4]^-$ (122) $[B_3O_3(OH)_5]^{2-}$ (123) $[B_4O_5(OH)_4]^{2-}$

Units containing B in both BO$_3$ and BO$_4$ coordination

in $Mg[B_2O(OH)_6]$ and a cyclic binuclear tetrahedral structure (120) characterizes the peroxoanion $[B_2(O_2)_2(OH)_4]^{2-}$ in "sodium perborate" $NaBO_3.4H_2O$, i.e. $Na_2[B_2(O_2)_2(OH)_4].6H_2O$. A more complex polynuclear structure comprising sheets of tetrahedrally coordinated $BO_3(OH)$ units occurs in the borosilicate mineral $CaB(OH)SiO_4$ and the fully three-dimensional polynuclear structure is found in BPO_4 (cf. the isoelectronic SiO_2), $BAsO_4$ and the minerals $NaBSi_3O_8$ and $Zn_4B_6O_{13}$.

The final degree of structural complexity occurs when the polynuclear assemblages contain both planar BO_3 and tetrahedral BO_4 units joined by sharing common O atoms. The structure of monoclinic HBO_2 affords an example (p. 204). A structure in which the ring has but one BO_4 unit is the spiroanion $[B_5O_6(OH)_4]^-$ (structure 121) which occurs in hydrated potassium pentaborate $KB_5O_8.4H_2O$, i.e. $K[B_5O_6(OH)_4].2H_2O$. The anhydrous pentaborate KB_5O_8 has the same structural unit but dehydration of the OH groups link the spiroanions of structure (121) sideways into ribbon-like helical chains. The mineral $CaB_3O_3(OH)_5.H_2O$ has 2 BO_4 units in the 6-membered heterocycle (122) and related chain elements $[B_3O_4(OH)_3^{2-}]_n$ linked by a common oxygen atom are found in the

important mineral colemanite $Ca_2B_6O_{11}.5H_2O$, i.e. $[CaB_3O_4(OH)_3].H_2O$. It is clear from these examples that, without structural data, the stoichiometry of these borate minerals gives little indication of their constitution. A further illustration is afforded by borax which is normally formulated $Na_2B_4O_7.10H_2O$, but which contains tetranuclear units $[B_4O_5(OH)_4]^{2-}$ formed by fusing 2 B_3O_3 rings which each contain 2 BO_4 (shared) and 1 BO_3 unit (123); borax should therefore be written as $Na_2[B_4O_5(OH)_4].8H_2O$.

There is wide variation of B–O distances in these various structures the values increasing, as expected, with increase in coordination:

–B=O   BO$_3$ BO$_4$

|120 pm   128 pm ←————→ 143 pm ←————→ 155 pm

136.6 pm   147.5 pm

The extent to which B_3O_3 rings catenate into more complex structures or hydrolyse into smaller units such as $[B(OH)_4]^-$ clearly depends sensitively on the activity (concentration) of water in the system, on the stoichiometric ratio of metal ions to boron and on the temperature ($T\Delta S$).

Many metal borates find important industrial applications (p. 140) and annual world production exceeds 2.9 million tonnes: Turkey 1.2, USA 1.1, Argentina 0.26, the former Soviet Union 0.18, Chile 0.13 Mt. Main uses are in glass-fibre and cellular insulation, the manufacture of borosilicate glasses and enamels, and as fire retardants. Sodium perborate (for detergents) is manufactured on a 550 000 tonne pa scale.

6.8.3 Organic compounds containing boron–oxygen bonds

Only a brief classification of this very large and important class of compounds will be given; most contain trigonal planar B though many 4-coordinate complexes have also been characterized. The orthoborates $B(OR)_3$ can readily be prepared by direct reaction of BCl_3 or $B(OH)_3$ with ROH, while transesterification with $R'OH$ affords a route to unsymmetrical products $B(OR)_2(OR')$, etc. The compounds range from colourless volatile liquids to involatile white solids depending on molecular weight. R can be a primary, secondary, tertiary, substituted or unsaturated alkyl group or an aryl group, and orthoborates of polyhydric alcohols and phenols are also numerous.

Boronic acids $RB(OH)_2$ were first made over a century ago by the unlikely route of slow partial oxidation of the spontaneously flammable trialkyl boranes followed by hydrolysis of the ester so formed (E. Frankland, 1862):

$$BEt_3 + O_2 \longrightarrow EtB(OEt)_2 \xrightarrow{2H_2O} EtB(OH)_2$$

Many other routes are now available but the most used involve the reaction of Grignard reagents or lithium alkyls on orthoborates or boron trihalides:

$$B(OR)_3 + ArMgX \xrightarrow{-50°} [ArB(OR)_3]MgX$$

$$\xrightarrow{H_3O^+} ArB(OH)_2$$

Phenylboronic acid in particular has proved invaluable, since its complexes with *cis*-diols and -polyols have formed the basis of chromatographic separations, asymmetric syntheses, enzyme immobilization and the preparation of polymers capable of molecular recognition.[117]

Boronic acids readily dehydrate at moderate temperatures (or over P_4O_{10} at room temperature) to give trimeric cyclic anhydrides known as trialkyl(aryl)boroxines:

The related trialkoxyboroxines $(ROBO)_3$ can be prepared by esterifying $B(OH)_3$, B_2O_3 or metaboric acid $BO(OH)$ with the appropriate mole ratio of ROH.

Endless variations have been played on these themes and the B atom can be surrounded by innumerable combinations of groups such as acyloxy (RCOO), peroxo (ROO), halogeno (X), hydrido, etc., in either open or cyclic arrays. However, no new chemical principles emerge.

6.9 Boron–Nitrogen Compounds

Two factors have contributed to the special interest that attaches to B–N compounds. First, the B–N unit is isoelectronic with C–C and secondly, the size and electronegativity of the 3 atoms are similar, C being the mean of B and N:

	B	C	N
Number of valence electrons	3	4	5
Covalent single-bond radius/pm	88	77	70
Electronegativity	2.0	2.5	3.0

The repetition of much organic chemistry by replacing pairs of C atoms with the B–N

---

117 C. D'Silva and D. Green, *J. Chem. Soc., Chem. Commun.*, 227–9 (1991) and leading references cited therein.

grouping has led to many new classes of compound but these need not detain us.[118] By contrast, key points emerge from several other areas of B–N chemistry and, accordingly, this section deals briefly with the structure, properties and reaction chemistry of boron nitride, amine-borane adducts, aminoboranes, iminoboranes, cyclic borazines and azaborane clusters.

The synthesis of boron nitride, BN, involves considerable technical difficulty;[119] a laboratory preparation yielding relatively pure samples involves the fusion of borax with ammonium chloride, whereas technical-scale production relies on the fusion of urea with $B(OH)_3$ in an atmosphere of NH_3 at 500–950°C. Only a brave (or foolhardy) chemist would attempt to write a balanced equation for either reaction. An alternative synthesis (>99% purity) treats BCl_3 with an excess of NH_3 (see below) and pyrolyses the resulting mixture in an atmosphere of NH_3 at 750°C. The hexagonal modification of BN has a simple layer structure (Fig. 6.27) similar to graphite but with the significant difference that the layers are packed directly on top of each other so that the B atom in one layer is located over an N atom in the next layer at a distance of 333 pm. Cell dimensions and other data for BN and graphite are compared in Table 6.5. Within each layer the B–N distance is only 145 pm; this is similar to the distance of 144 pm in borazine (p. 210) but much less than the sum of single-bond covalent radii (158 pm) and this has been taken to indicate substantial additional π bonding within the layer. However, unlike graphite, BN is colourless and a good insulator; it also resists

attack by most reagents though fluorine converts it quantitatively to BF_3 and N_2 and HF gives NH_4BF_4 quantitatively. Hexagonal BN can be converted into a cubic form (zinc-blende type structure) at 1800°C and 85 000 atm pressure in the presence of an alkali or alkaline-earth metal catalyst. The lattice constant of cubic BN is 361.5 pm (cf. diamond 356.7 pm). A wurtzite-type modification (p. 1210) can be obtained at lower temperatures.

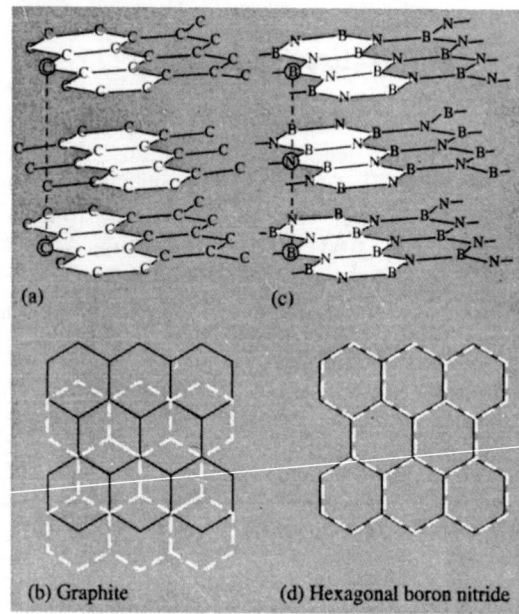

Figure 6.27 Comparison of the hexagonal layer structures of BN and graphite. In BN the atoms of one layer are located directly above the atoms of adjacent layers with B···N contacts; in graphite the C atoms in one layer are located above interstices in the adjacent layer and are directly above atoms in alternate layers only.

Amine-borane adducts have the general formula R_3NBX_3 where R = alkyl, H, etc., and

---

[118] I. ANDER, Chap. 1.21 in A. R. KATRITZKY and C. W. REES (eds.), *Comprehensive Heterocyclic Chemistry*, Pergamon, Oxford, 1984, pp. 629–63.

[119] R. T. PAINE and C. K. NARULA, *Chem. Rev.* **90**, 73–91 (1990).

Table 6.5 Comparison of hexagonal BN and graphite

	a/pm	c/pm	c/a	Inter-layer spacing/pm	Intra-layer spacing/pm	d/g cm^{-3}
BN (hexagonal)	250.4	666.1	2.66	333	144.6	2.29
Graphite	245.6	669.6	2.73	335	142	2.255

X = alkyl, H, halogen, etc. They are usually colourless, crystalline compounds with mp in the range 0–100° for X = H and 50–200° for X = halogen. Synthetic routes, and factors affecting the stability of the adducts have already been discussed (p. 165 and p. 198). In cases where diborane undergoes unsymmetrical cleavage (e.g. with NH_3) alternative routes must be devised:

$$B_2H_6 + 2NH_3 \longrightarrow [BH_2(NH_3)_2]^+ BH_4^-$$

$$NH_4Cl + LiBH_4 \longrightarrow NH_3BH_3 + LiCl + H_2$$

The nature of the bonding in amine-boranes and related adducts has been the subject of considerable theoretical discussion and has also been the source of some confusion. Conventional representations of the donor-acceptor (or coordinate) bond use symbols such as $R_3N{\rightarrow}BX_3$ or $R_3\overset{+}{N}{-}\overset{-}{B}X_3$ to indicate the origin of the bonding electrons and the direction (but not the magnitude) of charge transfer. It is important to realize that these symbols refer to the relative change in electron density with respect to the individual separate donor and acceptor molecules. Thus, $R_3\overset{+}{N}$ in the adduct has less electron density on N than has free R_3N, and $\overset{-}{B}X_3$ has more electron density on B in the adduct than has free BX_3; this does not necessarily mean that N is positive with respect to B in the adduct. Indeed, several MO calculations indicate that the change in electron density on coordination merely reduces but is insufficient to reverse the initial positive charge on the B atom. Consistent with this, experiments show that electrophilic reagents always attack N in amine-borane adducts, and nucleophilic reagents attack B.

A similar situation obtains in the aminoboranes where one or more of the substituents on B is an R_2N group (R = alkyl, aryl, H), e.g. $Me_2N{-}BMe_2$. Reference to Fig. 6.22 indicates the possibility of some p_π interaction between the lone pair on N and the "vacant" orbital on trigonal B. This is frequently indicated as

$$\text{>}N{\rightleftarrows}B\text{<} \quad \text{or} \quad \text{>}\overset{+}{N}{=}\overset{-}{B}\text{<}$$

However, as with the amine-borane adducts just considered, this does not normally indicate the actual sign of the net charges on N and B because the greater electronegativity of N causes the σ bond to be polarized in the opposite sense. Thus, N–B bond moments in aminoboranes have been found to be negligible and MO calculations again suggest that the N atom bears a larger net negative charge than does the B atom. The partial double-bond formulation of these compounds, however, is useful in implying an analogy to the isoelectronic alkenes. Coordinative saturation in aminoboranes can be achieved not only through partial double bond formation but also by association (usually dimerization) of the monomeric units to form $(B{-}N)_n$ rings. For example, in the gas phase, aminodimethylborane exists as both monomer and dimer in reversible equilibrium:

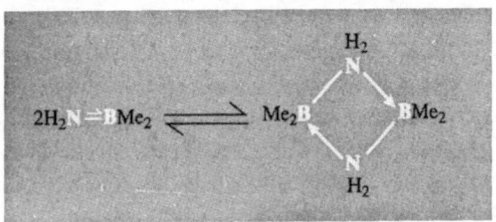

The presence of bulky groups on either B or N hinders dimer formation and favours monomers, e.g. $(Me_2NBF_2)_2$ is dimeric whereas the larger halides form monomers at least in the liquid phase. Association to form trimers (6-membered heterocycles) is less common, presumably because of even greater crowding of substituents, though triborazane $(H_2NBH_2)_3$ and its N-methyl derivatives, $(MeHNBH_2)_3$ and $(Me_2NBH_2)_3$, are known in which the B_3N_3 ring adopts the cyclohexane chair conformation.

Preparative routes to these compounds are straightforward, e.g.:

$$R_2NH_2Cl + MBH_4 \longrightarrow R_2NBH_2 + MCl + H_2$$
$$(R = H, \text{alkyl, aryl})$$

$$R_2NH + R_2'BX + NEt_3 \longrightarrow R_2NBR_2' + Et_3NHX$$
$$(R' = \text{alkyl, aryl, halide})$$

$$B(NR_2)_3 + 2BR_3 \longrightarrow 3R_2NBR_2, \text{ etc.}$$

In general monomeric products are readily hydrolysed but associated species (containing 4-coordinate B) are much more stable: e.g. $(Me_2NBH_2)_2$ does not react with H_2O at $50°$ but is rapidly hydrolysed by dilute HCl at $110°$ because at this temperature there is a significant concentration of monomer present.

Iminoboranes, $R-N{\equiv}B-R'$, are isoelectronic with alkynes and contain 2-coordinate boron; their chemistry has recently been reviewed.[120,121] Likewise for amino iminoboranes, $R_2N-B{=}NR'$.[122] In both classes of compound inductive and steric effects have an important influence on stability. Another stable 2-coordinate boron species is the linear anion $BN_2{}^{3-}$ (isoelectronic with CO_2, CNO^-, NCO^-, N_2O, $NO_2{}^+$, $N_3{}^-$ and $CN_2{}^{2-}$) which occurs in $M_3^I BN_2$ and $M_3^{II}(BN_2)_2$. For example, Na_3BN_2 can be prepared as light honey-coloured crystals by heating a 2:1 mixture of NaN_3 and BN at 4 GPa and $1000°C$; the B–N distance is 134.5 pm.[123] In neutral species, the well known decrease in interatomic distance in the sequence C–C(154 pm) > C=C(133 pm), > C≡C (118 pm) is paralleled by the analogous sequence B–N(158 pm) > B=N(140 pm) > B≡N(124 pm).

The cyclic borazine $(-BH-NH-)_3$ and its derivatives form one of the largest classes of B–N compounds. The parent compound, also known as "inorganic benzene", was first isolated as a colourless liquid from the mixture of products obtained by reacting B_2H_6 and NH_3 (A. Stock and E. Pohland, 1926):

$$3B_2H_6 + 6NH_3 \xrightarrow{180°} 2B_3N_3H_6 + 12H_2$$

It is now best prepared by reduction of the *B*-trichloro derivative:

[120] P. PAETZOLD, *Adv. Inorg. Chem.* **31**, 123–70 (1987).

[121] P. PAETZOLD, *Pure Appl. Chem.* **63**, 345–50 (1991).

[122] H. NÖTH, *Angew. Chem. Int. Edn. Engl.* **27**, 1603–22 (1988).

[123] J. EVERS, M. MÜNSTERKÖTTER, G. OEHLINGER, K. POLBORN and B. SENDLINGER, *J. Less Common Metals* **162**, L17–22 (1990). For the crystal structure of $Sr_3(BN_2)_2$, [B–N 135.8(6) pm, angle $180°$] see H. WOMELSDORF and H.-J. MEYER, *Z. anorg. allg. Chem.* **620**, 2652–5 (1994).

$$3BCl_3 + 3NH_4Cl \xrightarrow[-9HCl]{heat} (BClNH)_3$$

$$\xrightarrow{3NaBH_4} B_3N_3H_6 + 3NaCl + \tfrac{3}{2}B_2H_6$$

Borazine has a regular plane hexagonal ring structure and its physical properties closely resemble those of the isoelectronic compound benzene (Table 6.6). Although it is possible to write Kekulé-type structures with $N{\Rightarrow}B$ π bonding superimposed on the σ bonding, the weight of chemical evidence suggests that borazine has but little aromatic character. It reacts readily with H_2O, MeOH and HX to yield 1:3 adducts which eliminate $3H_2$ on being heated to $100°$, e.g.:

$$B_3N_3H_6 + 3H_2O \xrightarrow{0°} [BH(OH)NH_2]_3$$

$$\xrightarrow{100°} [B(OH)NH]_3 + 3H_2$$

Table 6.6 Comparison of borazine and benzene

Property	$B_3N_3H_6$	C_6H_6
Molecular weight	80.5	78.1
MP/°C	−57	6
BP/°C	55	80
Critical temperature	252	288
Density (l at mp)/g cm^{-3}	0.81	0.81
Density (s)/g cm^{-3}	1.00	1.01
Surface tension at mp/ dyne cm^{-1}(a)	31.1	31.0
Interatomic distances/pm	B–N 144	C–C 142
	B–H 120	C–H 108
	N–H 102	

(a) 1 dyne = 10^{-5} newton.

Numerous other reactions have been documented, most of which are initiated by nucleophilic attack on B. There is no evidence that electrophilic substitution of the borazine ring occurs and conditions required for such reactions in benzenoid systems disrupt the borazine ring by oxidation or solvolysis. However, it is known that the less-reactive hexamethyl derivative $B_3N_3Me_6$ (which can be heated to $460°$ for 3 h without significant decomposition)

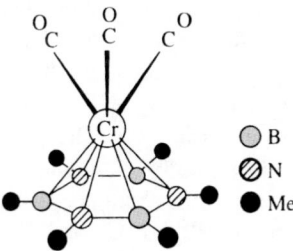

Figure 6.28　Structure of $[Cr(\eta^6\text{-}B_3N_3Me_6)(CO)_3]$.

reacts with $[Cr(CO)_3(MeCN)_3]$ to give the complex $[Cr(\eta^6\text{-}B_3N_3Me_6)(CO)_3]$ (Fig. 6.28) which closely resembles the corresponding hexamethylbenzene complex $[Cr(\eta^6\text{-}C_6Me_6)(CO)_3]$.

N-substituted and *B*-substituted borazines are readily prepared by suitable choice of amine and borane starting materials or by subsequent reaction of other borazines with Grignard reagents, etc. Thermolysis of monocyclic borazines leads to polymeric materials and to polyborazine analogues of naphthalene, biphenyl, etc.:

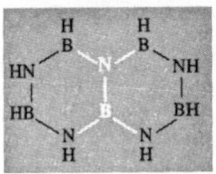
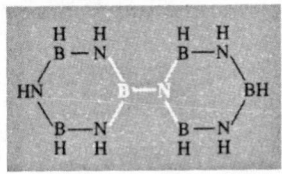

A quite different structural motif is found in the curious cyclic hexamer $[(BNMe_2)_6]$ which can be obtained as orange-red crystals by distilling the initial product formed by dehalogenation of $(Me_2N)_2BCl$ with Na/K alloy:[124]

$$2(Me_2N)_2BCl \xrightarrow{\text{Na/K}} [B_2(NMe_2)_4]$$
$$\xrightarrow{\text{thermolysis}} [(BNMe_2)_6]$$

The B_6 ring has a chair conformation (dihedral angle 57.6°) with mean B–B distances of 172 pm. All 6 B and all 6 N are trigonal planar and the 6-exocyclic NMe_2 groups are each twisted at an angle of ∼65° from the adjacent B_3 plane, with

B–N 140 pm. Structurally, this cyclohexaborane derivative resembles the radialenes, particularly the isoelectronic $[C_6(=CHMe)_6]$ in which the C_6 ring likewise adopts the chair conformation.

Finally, the conceptual isoelectronic replacement of C–C by B–N can be applied to carbaboranes, thus leading (by appropriate synthetic routes) to azaboranes in which one or more of the cluster vertices of the borane is occupied by an N atom. So far, the following species have been characterized,[125] the relevant cluster geometries and numbering schemes being given by the indicated structures on pp. 153–85: *arachno*-4-NB_8H_{13} (20), *nido*-6-NB_9H_{12} (11), *closo*-1-NB_9H_{10} (5), *arachno*-6,9-$N_2B_8H_{12}$ (21), *nido*-7-$NB_{10}H_{13}$ (41), *nido*-7-$NB_{10}H_{11}{}^{2-}$ (80), *closo*-1-$NB_{11}H_{12}$ (7, 76) and *anti*-9-$NB_{17}H_{20}$ (31).

6.10 Other Compounds of Boron

6.10.1 Compounds with bonds to P, As or Sb

Only minor echoes of the extensive themes of B–N chemistry occur in compounds containing B–P, B–As or B–Sb bonds but there are signs that the field is now beginning to expand rapidly. Few 1:1 phosphine-borane adducts are known, although the recently characterized white crystalline complex $(C_6F_5)_3B.PH_3$, which dissociates reversibly above room temperature, has been suggested as a useful storage material for the safe purification and generation of PH_3.[126] The interesting compound $Na[B(PH_2)_4]$ can readily be made by reacting BCl_3 with 4 moles of $NaPH_2$; at moderate temperatures and in the presence of thf it rearranges to the diborate analogue $Na[(PH_2)_3B\text{-}PH_2\text{-}B(PH_2)_3]$

---

[124] H. NÖTH and H. POMMERENING, *Angew. Chem. Int. Edn. Engl.* **19**, 482–3 (1980).

[125] T. JELÍNEK, J. D. KENNEDY and B. ŠTÍBR, *J. Chem. Soc., Chem. Commun.*, 677–8 (1994) and references cited therein. L. SCHNEIDER, U. ENGLERT and P. PAETZOLD, *Z. anorg. allg. Chem.* **620**, 1191–3 (1994). H.-P. HANSEN, U. E. ENGLERT and P. PAETZOLD, *Z. anorg. allg. Chem.* **621**, 719–24 (1995).

[126] D. C. BRADLEY, M. B. HURSTHOUSE, M. MOTEVALLI and Z. DAO-HONG, *J. Chem. Soc., Chem. Commun.*, 7–8 (1991).

and with $BH_3.thf$ it gives the tetrakis(borane) adduct $Na[B(PH_2.BH_3)_4]$.[127]

Phosphinoboranes, like their aminoborane analogues (p. 209), tend to oligomerize, although monomeric examples with planar B and pyramidal P atoms have recently been prepared using bulky substituents, e.g. yellow Mes_2BPPh_2,[128] orange $(Mes_2P)_2BBr$[129] and colourless $(Mes_2P)_2BOEt$, mp 163°C [130](Mes = $2,4,6-Me_3C_6H_2-$). By contrast, $B(PEt_2)_3$ is a dimer with a planar B_2P_2 ring of 4-coordinate B and P atoms (124).[130] A planar 4-membered ring of 3-coordinate planar B and pyramidal P atoms is featured in the diphosphadiboretane ${MesPB(tmp)}_2$ (125) (tmp = $2,2,6,6$-tetramethylpiperidino);[131] the corresponding diarsadiboretane is also known. A phosphorus analogue of borazine (p. 210) having a planar B_3P_3 ring is the pale yellow crystalline $(MesBPC_6H_{11})_3$ (126), synthesized by reacting $MesBBr_2$ with $C_6H_{11}PHLi$ in hexane at room temperature;[132] the B–P distances in

the boraphosphabenzene are all essentially equal, averaging 184 pm, which is considerably shorter than the known range of single-bond distances (192–196 pm). The cyclohexyl group, C_6H_{11}, can be replaced by Ph, Mes, Bu^t, etc.

Phosphaborane cluster compounds have also been synthesized. For example, thermolysis of a 1:2 mixture of $(Pr^i_2N)BCl$ and $(Pr^i_2N)B(Cl)$-$(SiMe_3)_2$ at 160°C results in the smooth elimination of Me_3SiCl to give colourless crystals of $[closo-1,5-P_2(BNPr^i_2)_3]$ (127) in high yield:[133]

$$2(Pr^i_2N)B(Cl)P(SiMe_3)_2 + (Pr^i_2N)BCl_2$$
$$\longrightarrow 4Me_3SiCl + P_2(BNPr^i_2)_3 \ (127)$$

The structural analogy with the dicarbaborane $C_2B_3H_5$ (56) is obvious. Likewise, pyrolysis of a mixture of B_2Cl_4 and PCl_3 yields $[closo-1,2-P_2B_4Cl_4]$ (128) as hygroscopic colourless crystals.[134]

(124)   (125)

(126)

(127)   (128)

Typical borane clusters incorporating As or Sb atoms are $closo-1,2-B_{10}H_{10}CHAs$ and $closo-1,2-B_{10}H_{10}CHSb$ in which the group 15 heteroatom replaces a CH vertex in the dicarbaborane (76); they are prepared in 25 and 41% yield, respectively, by direct reaction of $Na_3B_{10}H_{10}CH$ with $AsCl_3$ or SbI_3, and can be isomerized in high yield below 500°C to the 1,7-isomers. Above 500° the 1,12-isomers can be obtained but this is accompanied by substantial decomposition. The diarsa derivative $1,2-B_{10}H_{10}As_2$ is also known. Likewise, reaction of $nido-B_{10}H_{14}$ with $AsCl_3$ and NaH or $NaBH_4$ affords the 11-vertex anion $7-B_{10}H_{12}As^-$

[127] M. BAUDLER, C. BLOCK, H. BUDZIKIEWICZ and H. MÜNSTER, *Z. anorg. allg. Chem.* **569**, 7–15 (1989).

[128] Z. FENG, M. M. OLMSTEAD and P. P. POWER, *Inorg. Chem.* **25**, 4615–6 (1986).

[129] H. H. KARSCH, G. HANIKA, B. HUBER, K. MEINDL, S. KÖNIG, K. KRÜGER and G. MÜLLER, *J. Chem. Soc., Chem. Commun.*, 373–5 (1989).

[130] H. NÖTH, *Z. anorg. allg. Chem.* **555**, 79–84 (1987).

[131] A. M. ARIF, A. H. COWLEY, M. PAKULSKI and J. M. POWER, *J. Chem. Soc., Chem. Commun.*, 889–90 (1986).

[132] H. V. R. DIAS and P. P. POWER, *Angew. Chem. Int. Edn. Engl.* **26**, 1270–1 (1987); H. V. R. DIAS and P. P. POWER, *J. Am. Chem. Soc.* **111**, 144–8 (1989).

[133] G. L. WOOD, E. N. DUESLER, C. K. NARULA, R. T. PAINE and H. NÖTH, *J. Chem. Soc., Chem. Commun.*, 496–8 (1987).

[134] W. HAUBOLD, W. KELLER and G. SAWITZKI, *Angew. Chem. Int. Edn. Engl.* **27**, 925–6 (1988).

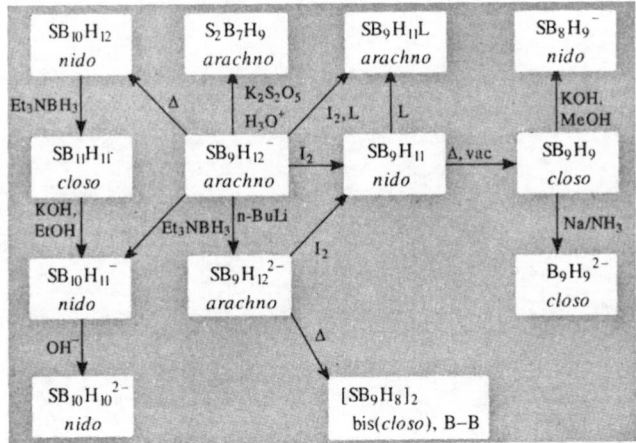

Scheme (for page 215)

and this can be capped using $Et_3N \cdot BH_3$ in diglyme at 160° to give the *closo*-icosahedral anion $B_{11}H_{11}As^-$ in 51% yield. Other examples include $B_{11}H_{11}Sb^-$, $1,2-B_{10}H_{10}Sb_2$, $1,2-B_{10}H_{10}AsSb$ and the arsenathia- and arsenaselenaboranes $B_8H_8As_2S$ and $B_8H_8As_2Se$.[135]

6.10.2 Compounds with bonds to S, Se and Te

The vast array of B–O minerals and compounds (pp. 139–40 and 203–7) finds no parallel in B–S or B–Se chemistry though thioborates of the type $B(SR)_3$, $R'B(SR)_2$ and $R'_2B(SR)$ are well documented. There are also a growing number of binary boron sulfides and boron–sulfur anions which feature chains, rings and networks. B_2S_3 itself has been known for many years as a pale-yellow solid which tends to form a glassy phase (cf. B_2O_3 and also B_2Se_3). This absence of a suitable crystalline sample prevented the structural characterization of this compound until as late as 1977. It has now been found that B_2S_3 has a fascinating layer structure which bears no resemblance to the three-dimensionally linked B_2O_3 crystal structure but is slightly reminiscent of BN. The structure (Fig. 6.29a) is made up of planar B_3S_3 6-membered rings and B_2S_2 4-membered rings linked by S bridges into almost planar two-dimensional layers.[136] All the boron atoms are trigonal planar with B–S distances averaging 181 pm and the perpendicular interlayer distance is almost twice this at 355 pm. More recently[137] a monomeric form of B_2S_3 was prepared by matrix-isolation techniques at 10 K and shown by vibrational spectroscopy to be a planar V-shaped molecule, $S=B-S-B=S$, with C_{2v} symmetry, the angle subtended at the central S atom by the linear arms being about 120°.

Another boron sulfide, of stoichiometry BS_2, can be made by heating B_2S_3 and sulfur to 300°C under very carefully defined conditions.[138] It is a colourless, moisture-sensitive material with a porphine-like molecular structure, B_8S_{16}, as shown in Fig. 6.29b. An alternative route to B_8S_{16} involves the reaction of dibromotrithiadiborolane with trithiocarbonic acid in an H_2S generator in dilute CS_2 solution:

$$4Br\overline{BSSB}(Br)S + 4(HS)_2CS \longrightarrow B_8S_{16}$$
$$+ 4CS_2 + 8HBr$$

[135] L. J. TODD, Chap. 4 in R. N. GRIMES (ed.) *Metal Interactions with Boron Clusters*, Plenum, New York, 1982, pp. 145–71.

[136] H. DIERCKS and B. KREBS, *Angew. Chem. Int. Edn. Engl.* **16**, 313 (1977).

[137] I. R. BEATTIE, P. J. JONES, D. J. WILD and T. R. GILSON, *J. Chem. Soc., Dalton Trans.*, 267–9 (1987).

[138] B. KREBS and H. U. HÜRTER, *Angew. Chem. Int. Edn. Engl.* **19**, 481–2 (1980).

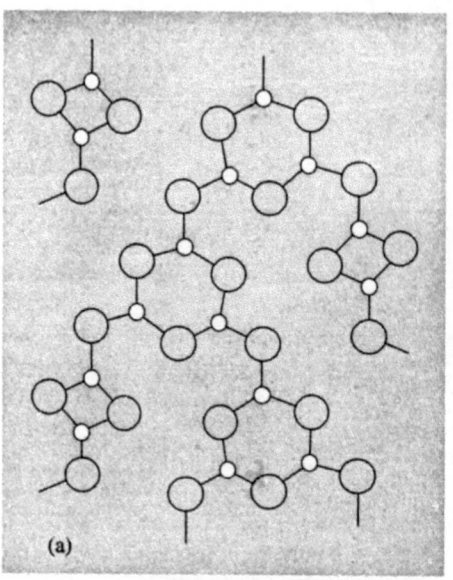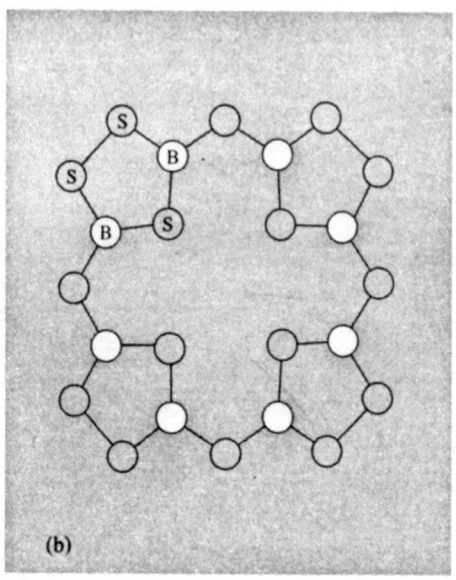

Figure 6.29 (a) Part of the layer structure of B_2S_3 perpendicular to the plane of the layer. (b) Porphine-like structure of the molecule B_8S_{16}.

The monomeric selenium compound BSe_2 has been identified mass-spectrometrically in the vapours formed by reacting solid boron with Se_2 and its thermodynamic properties evaluated.[139]

Another expanding area of B–S chemistry is the synthesis and structural characterization of anionic species. The colourless thioborate $RbBS_3$ was formed by heating the stoichiometric amounts of Rb_2S, B and S at 600°. Its structure, and that of the yellow $TlBS_3$, features polymeric anionic chains that are spirocyclically connected via tetrahedral B atoms as shown schematically below:[140]

$$\text{(chain structure with S, B atoms)}$$

The sulfur-rich analogue $Tl_3B_3S_{10}$ was likewise prepared as yellow plates from the appropriate stoichiometric mixture of $(3Tl_2S + 6B + 17S)$ at

850° and shown to have a similar polymeric anion with the extra S atoms inserted into each third pentatomic heterocycle to make it a hexatomic unit, $>B(S_2)_2B<$. With the smaller cation, Li^+, similar procedures generate $Li_5B_7S_{13}$ and $Li_9B_{19}S_{33}$ which again have novel polymeric anions. The $\{B_7S_{13}^{5-}\}_\infty$ polymer is formed by sharing B_4S_{10} and $B_{10}S_{20}$ units, i.e. $\{B_4S_6S_{4/2}^{4-}\}$ (cf. P_4O_{10}) and $\{B_{10}S_{16}S_{4/2}^{6-}\}$ both of which are built up from tetrahedral BS_4 subunits, whereas the $\{B_{19}S_{33}^{9-}\}_\infty$ polymer is formed from the conjoining of $\{B_{19}S_{30}S_{6/2}^{9-}\}$ units.[141]

The structural principles and reaction chemistry of B–S compounds have recently been reviewed.[142] This includes not only electron-precise 4-, 5- and 6-membered heterocycles of the types described above, but also electron-deficient polyhedral clusters based on *closo-*,

[139] M. BINNEWIES. *Z. anorg. allg. Chem.* **589**. 115–21 (1990).

[140] C. PÜTTMANN, F. HILTMANN, W. HAMANN, C. BRENDEL and B. KREBS. *Z. anorg. allg. Chem.* **619**, 109–16 (1993).

[141] F. HILTMANN, P. ZUM HEBEL, A. HAMMERSCHMIDT and B. KREBS. *Z. anorg. allg. Chem.* **619**, 293–302 (1993). For other novel B/S/Se anions from B. Krebs' group see *Z. anorg. allg. Chem.* **620**, 1898–1904 (1994); **621**, 424–30, 1322–9 and 1330–7 (1995).

[142] J. R. BOWSER and T. P. FEHLNER. in H. W. ROESKY (ed.), *Rings, Clusters and Polymers of Main Group and Transition Elements,* Elsevier, Amsterdam, 1989, pp. 1–48.

nido- and *arachno-*boranes. Some typical inter-conversion reactions of thiaboranes are shown in the scheme on p. 213,[142] and further examples are in references (143) and (144). Selena- and tellura-derivatives are also known[135, 145] and, like the thiaboranes, have structures that can be rationalized by the normal electron counting rules, taking the chalcogen atom as a 4-electron donor, e.g. *closo*-$B_{11}H_{11}Te$, *nido*-$B_{10}H_{12}Te$, *nido*-$B_{10}H_{11}Te^-$, *nido*-$B_9H_{11}Te$, *nido*-$B_9H_9Se_2$, *nido*-B_9H_9STe, *arachno*-$B_8H_{10}Se_2$, $[Fe(\eta^5\text{-}B_{10}H_{10}Te)_2]^{2-}$ (green) and $[Co(\eta^5\text{-}C_5H_5)(\eta^5\text{-}B_{10}H_{10}Te)]$ (yellow).

There appears to be no end to the structural ingenuity of boron and, whilst it is true that many regularities can now be discerned in its stereochemistry, much more work is still needed to unravel the reaction pathways by which the compounds are formed and to elucidate the mechanisms by which they isomerize and interconvert.

[143] T. JELINEK, J. D. KENNEDY and B. ŠTÍBR, *J. Chem. Soc., Chem. Commun.*, 1415–6 (1994).

[144] S. O. KANG and L. G. SNEDDON, Chap. 8 in G. A. OLAH, K. WADE and R. E. WILLIAMS (eds.), *Electron Deficient Boron and Carbon Clusters*, Wiley, New York, 1991, pp. 195–213.

[145] G. D. FRIESEN, T. P. HANUSA and L. J. TODD, *Inorg. Synth.* **29**, 103–7, (1992).

7

Aluminium, Gallium, Indium and Thallium

7.1 Introduction

Aluminium derives its name from alum, the double sulfate $KAl(SO_4)_2.12H_2O$, which was used medicinally as an astringent in ancient Greece and Rome (Latin *alumen*, bitter salt). Humphry Davy was unable to isolate the metal but proposed the name "alumium" and then "aluminum"; this was soon modified to aluminium and this form is used throughout the world except in North America where the ACS decided in 1925 to adopt "aluminum" in its publications. The impure metal was first isolated by the Danish scientist H. C. Oersted using the reaction of dilute potassium amalgam on $AlCl_3$. This method was improved in 1827 by H. Wöhler who used metallic potassium, but the first commercially successful process was devised by H. St.-C. Deville in 1854 using sodium. In the same year both he and R. W. Bunsen independently obtained metallic aluminium by electrolysis of fused $NaAlCl_4$. So precious was the metal at this time that it was exhibited next to the crown jewels at the Paris Exposition of 1855 and the Emperor Louis Napoleon III used Al cutlery on state occasions. The dramatic thousand-fold drop in price which occurred before the end of the century (Table 7.1) was due first to the advent of cheap electric power following the development of the dynamo by W. von Siemens in the 1870s, and secondly to the independent development in 1886 of the electrolysis of alumina dissolved in cryolite (Na_3AlF_6) by P. L. T. Héroult in France and C. M. Hall in the USA; both men were 22 years old at the time. World production rose quickly and in 1893 exceeded 1000 tonnes pa for the first time.

Gallium was predicted as eka-aluminium by D. I. Mendeleev in 1870 and was discovered by P. E. Lecoq de Boisbaudran in 1875 by means of the spectroscope; de Boisbaudran was, in fact, guided at the time by an independent theory of his own and had been searching for the missing element for some years. The first indications came with the observation of two new violet lines in the spark spectrum of a sample deposited on zinc, and within a month he had isolated 1 g of the metal starting from several hundred kilograms of crude zinc blende ore. The

Table 7.1 Price of aluminium metal ($ per kg)

1852	1854	1855	1856	1857	1858	1886	
1200	600	250	75	60	25	17	

→ |Introduction of St. C. Deville's Na/AlCl$_3$ process

1888	1890	1895	1900	1950	1965	1980	1989
11.5	5.0	1.15	0.73	0.40	0.54	1.53	1.94

→ |Introduction of Héroult-Hall   ↑
    electrolysis   minimum

Table 7.2 Comparison of predicted and observed properties of gallium

Mendeleev's predictions (1871) for eka-aluminium, M		Observed properties (1993) of gallium (discovered 1875)	
Atomic weight	~68	Atomic weight	69.723
Density/g cm^{-3}	5.9	Density/g cm^{-3}	5.904
MP	low	MP/°C	29.767
Non-volatile		Vapour pressure	10^{-3} mmHg at 1000°C
Valence	3	Valence	3
M will probably be discovered by spectroscopic analysis		Ga was discovered by means of the spectroscope	
M will have an oxide of formula M$_2$O$_3$, d 5.5 g cm^{-3}, soluble in acids to give MX$_3$		Ga has an oxide Ga$_2$O$_3$, d 5.88 g cm^{-3}, soluble in acids to give salts of the type GaX$_3$	
M should dissolve slowly in acids and alkalis and be stable in air		Ga metal dissolves slowly in acids and alkalis and is stable in air	
M(OH)$_3$ should dissolve in both acids and alkalis		Ga(OH)$_3$ dissolves in both acids and alkalis	
M salts will tend to form basic salts; the sulfate should form alums; M$_2$S$_3$ should be precipitated by H$_2$S or (NH$_4$)$_2$S; anhydrous MCl$_3$ should be more volatile than ZnCl$_2$		Ga salts readily hydrolyse and form basic salts; alums are known; Ga$_2$S$_3$ can be precipitated under special conditions by H$_2$S or (NH$_4$)$_2$S; anhydrous GaCl$_3$ is more volatile than ZnCl$_2$	

element was named in honour of France (Latin *Gallia*) and the striking similarity of its physical and chemical properties to those predicted by Mendeleev (Table 7.2) did much to establish the general acceptance of the Periodic Law (p. 20); indeed, when de Boisbaudran first stated that the density of Ga was 4.7 g cm^{-3} rather than the predicted 5.9 g cm^{-3}, Mendeleev wrote to him suggesting that he redetermine the figure (the correct value is 5.904 g cm^{-3}).

Indium and thallium were also discovered by means of the spectroscope as their names indicate. Indium was first identified in 1863 by F. Reich and H. T. Richter and named from the brilliant indigo blue line in its flame spectrum (Latin *indicum*). Thallium was discovered independently by W. Crookes and by

C. A. Lamy in the preceding year 1861/2 and named after the characteristic bright green line in its flame spectrum (Greek θαλλός, *thallos*, a budding shoot or twig).

7.2 The Elements

7.2.1 Terrestrial abundance and distribution

Aluminium is the most abundant metal in the earth's crust (8.3% by weight); it is exceeded in abundance only by O (45.5%) and Si (25.7%), and is approached only by Fe (6.2%) and Ca (4.6%). Aluminium is a major constituent of many common igneous minerals including feldspars and micas. These, in turn, weather in temperate climates to give clay minerals such as kaolinite [$Al_2(OH)_4Si_2O_5$], montmorillonite and vermiculite (p. 349). It also occurs in many well-known though rarer minerals such as cryolite (Na_3AlF_6), spinel ($MgAl_2O_4$), garnet [$Ca_3Al_2(SiO_4)_3$], beryl ($Be_3Al_2Si_6O_{18}$), and turquoise [$Al_2(OH)_3PO_4H_2O/Cu$]. Corundum (Al_2O_3) is one of the hardest substances known and is therefore used as an abrasive; many gemstones are impure forms of Al_2O_3, e.g. ruby (Cr), sapphire (Co), oriental emerald, etc. Commercially, the most important mineral is bauxite $AlO_x(OH)_{3-2x}$ ($0 < x < 1$); this occurs in a wide belt in tropical and subtropical regions as a result of the leaching out of both silica and various metals from aluminosilicates (see Panel).

Gallium, In and Tl are very much less abundant than Al and tend to occur at low concentrations in sulfide minerals rather than as oxides, though Ga is also found associated with Al in bauxite. Ga (19 ppm) is about as abundant as N, Nb, Li and Pb; it is twice as abundant as B (9 ppm) but is more difficult to extract because of the absence of major Ga-containing ores. The highest concentrations (0.1–1%) are in the rare mineral germanite (a complex sulfide of Zn, Cu, Ge and As); concentrations in sphalerite (ZnS), bauxite or coal, are a hundredfold less. Gallium always occurs in association either with Zn or Ge, its neighbours in the periodic table, or with Al in the same group. It was formerly recovered from

flue dusts emitted during sulfide roasting or coal burning (up to 1.5% Ga) but is now obtained as a byproduct of the vast Al industry. Since bauxites contain 0.003–0.01% Ga, complete recovery would yield over 1000 tonnes pa. However, present consumption, though growing rapidly, is little more than 1% of this and production is of the order of 50 tonnes pa (1986). This can be compared with the estimate of 5 tonnes for the total of Ga metal in the 90 y following its discovery (1875–1965). Its price in 1928 was $50 per g; in 1965 it was $1 per g, similar to the then price of gold ($1.1 per g), and in 1986 it was $0.45 per g, i.e. $450/kg for semiconductor grade metal (99.9999%).

Indium (0.24 ppm) is similar in abundance to Sb and Cd, whereas Tl (0.7 ppm) is close to Tm and somewhat less abundant than Mo, W and Tb (1.2 ppm). Both elements are chalcophiles (p. 648), indium tending to associate with the similarly sized Zn in its sulfide minerals whilst the larger Tl tends to replace Pb in galena, PbS. Thallium(I) has a similar radius to Rb^I and so also concentrates with this element in the late magmatic potassium minerals such as feldspars and micas.

Indium is now commercially recovered from the flue dusts emitted during the roasting of Zn/Pb sulfide ores and can also be recovered during the roasting of Fe and Cu sulfide ores. Before 1925 only 1 g of the element was available in the world but production now exceeds 80 000 000 g

Bauxite

The mixed aluminium oxide hydroxide mineral bauxite was discovered by P. Berthier in 1821 near Les Baux in Provence. In temperate countries (such as Mediterranean Europe) it occurs mainly as the "monohydrate" AlOOH (boehmite and diaspore) whereas in the tropics it is generally closer to the "trihydrate" $Al(OH)_3$ (gibbsite and hydrargillite). Since AlOOH is less soluble in aqueous NaOH than is $Al(OH)_3$, this has a major bearing on the extraction process for Al manufacture (p. 219). Typical compositions for industrially used bauxites are Al_2O_3 40–60%, combined H_2O 12–30%, SiO_2 free and combined 1–15%, Fe_2O_3 7–30%, TiO_2 3–4%. F, P_2O_5, V_2O_5, etc., 0.05–0.2%.

World production in 1989 was over 101 million tonnes and this is still increasing. Reserves are immense, being of the order of 22×10^9 tonnes in all (Guinea 5.6, Australia 4.4, Brazil 2.8, Jamaica 2.0, India 1.0, USA 0.038 Gt). Australia is currently the largest producer of alumina with 36.6%, followed by Guinea 16.6%, Brazil 8.7%, Jamaica 8.2% the former Soviet Union 4.6%, India 3.9%, etc. Bauxite is easy to mine by open-cast methods since it occurs typically in broad layers 3–10 m thick with very little topsoil or other overburden. Apart from its preponderant use (>80%) in Al extraction, bauxite is used to manufacture refractories, high-alumina cements and aluminium compounds, and smaller amounts are used as drying agents and as catalysts in the petrochemicals industry.

(i.e. 80 tonnes) each year. Prices have fluctuated widely during the past 20 years, being \$270/kg for 99.97% purity in 1987.

Thallium is likewise recovered from flue dusts emitted during sulfide roasting for H_2SO_4 manufacture, and from the smelting of Zn/Pb ores. Extraction procedures are complicated because of the need to recover Cd at the same time. There are no major commercial uses for Tl metal; world production in 1983 was estimated to be 5–15 tonnes p.a. and the price ranged from \$60 to \$80 per kg depending on purity and amount purchased.

7.2.2 Preparation and uses of the metals [1]

The huge difference in scale between the production of Al metal, on the one hand, and the other elements in the group is clear from the preceding section. The tremendous growth of the Al industry compared with all other non-ferrous metals is indicated in Table 7.3 and Al production is now exceeded only by that of iron and steel (p. 1072).

Production of Al metal involves two stages: (a) the extraction, purification and dehydration of bauxite, and (b) the electrolysis of Al_2O_3 dissolved in molten cryolite Na_3AlF_6. Bauxite is now almost universally treated by the Bayer process; this involves dissolution in aqueous NaOH, separation from insoluble impurities (red muds), partial precipitation of the trihydrate

Table 7.3   World production of some non-ferrous metals/million tonnes pa

Metal	1900	1950	1970	1980	1988
Al	0.0057	1.52	9.78	16.04	17.30
Cu	0.50	2.79	6.38	6.08	5.96
Zn	0.48	1.96	5.10	6.15	7.22
Pb	0.88	1.75	4.00	5.40	3.37

---

[1] *Kirk–Othmer Encyclopedia of Chemical Technology*, 4th edn., Vol. 2, Aluminium and aluminium alloys, pp. 184–251; Aluminium compounds, pp. 252–345. Interscience, New York, 1992.

and calcining at 1200°. Bauxites approximating to the "monohydrate" AlOOH require higher concentrations of NaOH ($200-300\,g\,l^{-1}$) and higher temperatures and pressures ($200-250°C$, 35 atm) than do bauxites approximating to $Al(OH)_3$ ($100-150\,g\,l^{-1}$ NaOH, $120-140°C$). Electrolysis is carried out at $940-980°C$ in a carbon-lined steel cell (cathode) with carbon anodes. Originally Al_2O_3 was dissolved in molten cryolite (Héroult–Hall process) but cryolite is a rather rare mineral and production from the mines in Greenland provide only about 30 000 tonnes pa, quite insufficient for world needs. Synthetic cryolite is therefore manufactured in lead-clad vessels by the reaction of HF on sodium aluminate (from the Bayer process):

$$6HF + 3NaAlO_2 \longrightarrow Na_3AlF_6 + 3H_2O + Al_2O_3$$

No further cryolite is actually needed once the smelting process is in operation because it is produced in the reduction cells by neutralizing the Na_2O brought into the cell as an impurity in the alumina using AlF_3:

$$4AlF_3 + 3Na_2O \longrightarrow 2Na_3AlF_6 + Al_2O_3$$

Thus operating cells need AlF_3 rather than cryolite, much of it being produced in a fluidized bed reactor from gaseous HF and activated alumina (made by partially calcining the alumina hydrate from the Bayer process). Typical electrolyte composition ranges are Na_3AlF_6 (80–85%), CaF_2 (5–7%), AlF_3 (5–7%), Al_2O_3 (2–8% — intermittently recharged). See also p. 70 for the beneficial use of Li_2CO_3. The detailed electrolysis mechanism is still imperfectly understood but typical operating conditions require up to 10^5 A at 4.5 V and a current density of $0.7\,A\,cm^{-2}$. One tonne Al metal requires 1.89 tonnes Al_2O_3, ~0.45 tonnes C anode material, 0.07 tonnes Na_3AlF_6 and about 15 000 kWh of electrical energy. It follows that cheap electric power is the overriding commercial consideration. World production (1988) exceeded 17 million tonnes pa, the leading producers being the USA (23%), China (21%), the former Soviet Union (14%), Canada (9%), Australia (7%),

Brazil, Norway and Czechoslovakia (5% each). In addition to this primary production, recycling of used alloys probably adds a further 3–4 million tonnes pa to the total Al metal consumed.

Some uses of Al and its alloys are noted in the Panel from which it will be seen that many of the mechanical properties of pure Al are greatly improved by alloying it with Cu, Mn, Si, Mg or Zn (Table A). The example of Cu is particularly important because of the insight which it gives into the subtle solid-state diffusion processes that occur during heat treatment. At room temperature

---

Some Uses of Aluminium Metal and Alloys

Pure aluminium is a silvery-white metal with many desirable properties: it is light, non-toxic, of pleasing appearance, and capable of taking a high polish. It has a high thermal and electrical conductivity, excellent corrosion resistance, is non-magnetic, non-sparking and stands second only to gold for malleability and sixth for ductility. Many of its alloys have high mechanical and tensile strength. Aluminium and its alloys can be cast, rolled, extruded, forged, drawn or machined, and they are readily obtained as pipes, tubes, rods, bars, wires, plates, sheets or foils.

Aluminium resists corrosion not because of its position in the electrochemical series but because of the rapid formation of a coherent, inert, oxide layer. Contact with graphite, Fe, Ni, Cu, Ag or Pb is disastrous for corrosion resistance; the effect of contact with steel, Zn and Cd depends on pH and exposure conditions. Protection is enhanced by anodizing the metal; this involves immersing it in 15–20% H_2SO_4 and connecting it to the positive terminal so that it becomes coated with alumina:

$$2Al + 3O^{2-} - 6e^- \longrightarrow Al_2O_3$$

A layer 10–20 μm thick gives excellent protection between pH 4.5–8.7 and is also adequate for external architectural use; thicker layers (50–100 μm) also impart abrasion resistance. The layer can be coloured by incorporating suitable organic or inorganic compounds in the bath and incorporation of photosensitive material enables photographic images to be developed. Decorative engraving using solutions of nitrate or NH_4HF_2 gives the metal a fine silky texture.

Table A   Some aluminium alloys

1000 Series:	Commercially pure Al (<1% of other elements); good properties except for limited mechanical strength. Used in chemical equipment, reflectors, heat exchangers, buildings and decorative trim.
2000 Series:	Cu alloys (~5%); excellent strength and machinability, limited corrosion resistance. Used for components requiring high strength/weight ratio, e.g. truck trailer panels, aircraft structure parts.
3000 Series:	Mn alloys (~1.2%); moderate strength, high workability. Used for cooking utensils, heat exchangers, storage tanks, awnings, furniture, highway signs, roofing, side panels, etc.
4000 Series:	Si alloys (≤12%); low mp and low coefficient of expansion. Used for castings and as filler material for brazing and welding; readily anodized to attractive grey colours.
5000 Series:	Mg alloys (0.3–5%); good strength and weldability coupled with excellent corrosion resistance in marine atmospheres. Used for ornamental and decorative trim, street light standards, ships, boats, cryogenic vessels, gun mounts and crane parts.
6000 Series:	Mg/Si alloys; good formability and high corrosion resistance. Used in buildings, transportation equipment, bridges, railings and welded construction.
7000 Series:	Zn alloys (3–8%) plus Mg; when heat treated and aged have very high strength. Used principally for aircraft structures, mobile equipment and equipment requiring high strength/weight ratio.

Many of the uses listed in Table A are a matter of everyday observation. In addition we may note that the electrical conductivity of pure Al is 63.5% of the conductivity of an equal *volume* of pure Cu; when the lower density of Al is considered its conductivity is 2.1 times that of Cu on a wt. for wt. basis. This, coupled with its corrosion resistance and ready workability makes it an ideal metal for power lines and, indeed, more than 90% of all overhead electrical transmission lines in the USA are Al alloy.

Aluminium is now extensively used in the construction and aerospace industries throughout the world although in the USA packaging has replaced the construction industry as the largest consumer of Al and its alloys. For example, 95% of beer and soft drinks is packaged in two-piece cans comprising an Al/Mn alloy body and Al/Mg alloy ends. There is also extensive use in food packaging, aerosol cans, collapsible tubes for toiletries and pharmaceuticals and as foil (typically 0.18 mm thick).

Al dissolves only about 0.1% Cu and this has little effect on its properties. The solubility rises to a maximum of 5.65% Cu at 548°C and this remains in metastable solid solution to give a soft workable alloy when the alloy is rapidly quenched to temperatures below 65°. Subsequent ageing of the shaped material at 100–150° for a few minutes hardens the alloy due to the formation of Guinier–Preston zones: these zones, independently discovered in 1938 by A. Guinier (France) and G. D. Preston (England), are minute discs of material higher in Cu content than the matrix — they are about 4 atoms thick and up to 100 atoms across; they mesh coherently with the host lattice in two directions, the (100) planes, but not in the third. The coherency strains which thereby develop in the lattice are the basis for the hardening of the alloy. Besides its immense technological importance, this phenomenon is particularly significant in being one of the first recognized examples of a single phase which nevertheless varies regularly in composition throughout its extent.

Gallium metal is now obtained as a byproduct of the Al industry. The Bayer process for obtaining alumina from bauxite gradually enriches the alkaline solutions from an initial weight ratio Ga/Al of about 1/5000 to about 1/300; electrolysis of these extracts with an Hg electrode gives further concentration, and the solution of sodium gallate is then electrolysed with a stainless steel cathode to give Ga metal. Ultra high-purity Ga for semiconductor uses is obtained by further chemical treatment with acids and O_2 at high temperatures followed by crystallization and zone refining. Gallium has a beautiful silvery blue appearance; it wets glass, porcelain, and most other surfaces (except quartz, graphite, and teflon) and forms a brilliant mirror when painted on to glass. Its main use is in semiconductor technology (p. 258). For example, GaAs (isoelectronic with Ge) can convert electricity directly into coherent light (laser diodes) and is employed in electroluminescent light-emitting diodes (LEDs); it is also used for doping other semiconductors and in solid-state devices such as transistors.

The compound $MgGa_2O_4$, when activated by divalent impurities such as Mn^{2+}, is used in ultraviolet-activated powders as a brilliant green phosphor. Another very important application is to improve the sensitivity of various bands used in the spectroscopic analysis of uranium. Minor uses are as high-temperature liquid seals, manometric fluids and heat-transfer media, and for low-temperature solders.

Indium, like Ga, is normally recovered by electrolysis after prior concentration in processes leading primarily to other elements (Pb/Zn). It is a soft, silvery metal with a brilliant lustre and (like Sn) it gives out a high-pitched "cry" when bent. Formerly it was much used to protect bearings against wear and corrosion but the pattern of use has been changing in recent years and now its most important applications are in low-melting alloys and in electronic devices. Thus meltable safety devices, heat regulators, and sprinklers use alloys of In with Bi, Cd, Pb and Sn (mp 50–100°C) and In-rich solders are valuable in sealing metal-nonmetal joints in high vacuum apparatus. Indium is of particular importance in the manufacture of p–n–p transistor junctions in Ge (p. 369) and to solder semiconductor leads at low temperature; the softness of the metal also minimizes stress in the Ge during subsequent cooling. So-called III–V semiconductors like InAs and InSb are used in low-temperature transistors, thermistors and optical devices (photoconductors), and InP is used for high-temperature transistors. A further minor use, which exploits the high neutron capture cross-section of In, is as a component in control rods for certain nuclear reactors.

Technical grade Tl is purified from other flue-dust elements (Ni; Zn, Cd; In; Ge, Pb; As; Se, Te) by dissolving it in warm dilute acid, then precipitating the insoluble $PbSO_4$ and adding HCl to precipitate TlCl. Further purification is effected by electrolysing Tl_2SO_4 in dilute H_2SO_4 with short Pt wire electrodes, followed by fusion of the deposited Tl metal at 350–400°C under an atmosphere of H_2. Both the element and its compounds are extremely toxic; skin-contact, ingestion and inhalation are all dangerous, and the maximum allowable concentration of soluble Tl compounds in air is $0.1 \, \text{mg m}^{-3}$. In this context the position of Tl in the periodic table will be noted — it occurs between two other poisonous heavy metals Hg and Pb. Tl_2SO_4 was formerly widely used as a rodenticide and ant killer but it is both odourless and tasteless and is now banned in many countries as being too dangerous for general use. Many suggestions have been made for the use of Tl compounds in industry but none have been substantially developed. A few specialist uses have emerged in infrared technology since TlBr and TlI are transparent to long wavelengths, and there are possibilities for photosensitive diodes and infrared detectors. The very high density of aqueous solutions of Tl formate and malonate have found application in the small-scale separation of minerals and the determination of their densities; a saturated solution containing approximately equal weights of these salts (Clerici's solution) has a density of $4.324 \, \text{g cm}^{-3}$ at $20°$ and progressively lower densities can be obtained by dilution.

7.2.3 Properties of the elements

The atomic properties of the Group 13 elements (including boron) are compared in Table 7.4. All have odd atomic numbers and correspondingly few stable isotopes. The varying precision of

atomic weights has been discussed (p. 17). The electronic configuration is ns^2np^1 in each case but the underlying core varies considerably: for B and Al it is the preceding noble gas core, for Ga and In it is noble gas plus d^{10}, and for Tl noble gas plus $4f^{14}5d^{10}$. This variation has a substantial influence on the trends in chemical properties of the group and is also reflected in the ionization energies of the elements. Thus, as shown in Fig. 7.1, the expected decrease from B to Al is not followed by a further decrease to Ga because of the "d-block contraction" in atomic size and the higher effective nuclear charge for this element which stems from the fact that the 10 added d electrons do not completely shield the extra 10 positive charges on the nucleus. Similarly, the decrease between Ga and In is reversed for Tl as a result of the further influence of the f block or lanthanide contraction. It is notable that these irregularities for the Group 13 elements do not occur for the Group 3 elements Sc, Y and La, which show a steady decrease in ionization energy from B and Al, all 5 elements having the same type of underlying core (noble gas). This has a decisive influence on the comparative chemistry of the two subgroups.

Boron is a covalently bonded, refractory, non-metallic insulator of great hardness and is thus not directly comparable in its physical properties with Al, Ga, In and Tl, which are all low-melting, rather soft metals having a very low electrical

Table 7.4　Atomic properties of Group 13 elements

Property		B	Al	Ga	In	Tl
Atomic number		5	13	31	49	81
No. of naturally occurring isotopes		2	1	2	2	2
Atomic weight		10.811(7)	26.981538(2)	69.723(1)	114.818(3)	204.3833(2)
Electronic configuration		$[He]2s^22p^1$	$[Ne]3s^23p^1$	$[Ar]3d^{10}4s^24p^1$	$[Kr]4d^{10}5s^25p^1$	$[Xe]4f^{14}5d^{10}6p^1$
Ionization energy/ kJ mol^{-1}	I	800.6	577.5	578.8	558.3	589.4
	II	2427.1	1816.7	1979.3	1820.6	1971.0
	III	3659.7	2744.8	2963	2704	2878
Metal radius/pm		(80–90)	143	135 (see text)	167	170
Ionic radius/pm (6-coord.)	III	27[a]	53.5	62.0	80.0	88.5
	I	—	—	120	140	150

[a]Nominal "ionic" radius for B^{III}.

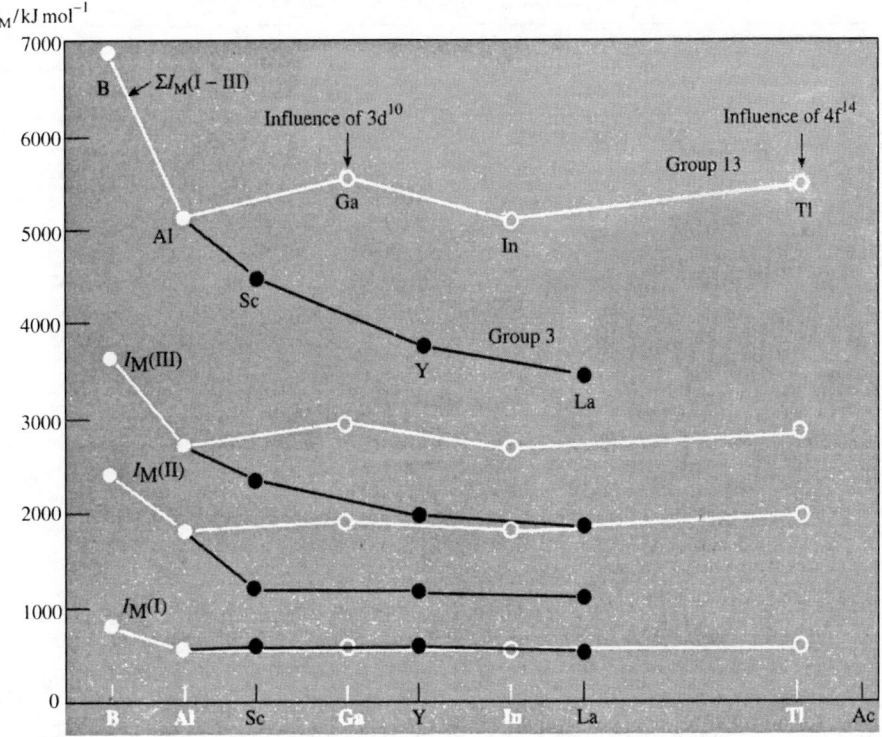

I_M/kJ mol^{-1}

Figure 7.1 Trends in successive ionization energies I_M(I), I_M(II), and I_M(III), and their sum Σ for elements in Groups 3 and 13.

resistivity (Table 7.5). The heats of fusion and vaporization of the metals are also much lower than those of boron and tend to decrease with increasing atomic number. In all these properties the metals resemble the neighbouring metals Zn, Cd, Hg; Sn, Pb, etc., and it is probable that in each case the properties are related to the rather small number of electrons available for metallic bonding. Some have seen this as a manifestation of the "inert-pair effect" (see p. 226). The interatomic distances in these elements are also somewhat longer than expected from general trends.

The crystal structure of Al is fcc, typical of many metals, each Al being surrounded by 12 nearest neighbours at 286 pm. Thallium also has a typical metallic structure (hcp) with 12 nearest neighbours at 340 pm. Indium has an unusual structure which is slightly distorted from a regular close-packed arrangement: the structure is face-centred tetragonal and each In has 4 neighbours

at 324 pm and 8 at the slightly greater distance of 336 pm Gallium has a unique orthorhombic (pseudotetragonal) structure in which each Ga has 1 very close neighbour at 244 pm and 6 further neighbours, 2 each at 270, 273 and 279 pm. The structure is very similar to that of iodine and the appearance of pseudo-molecules Ga_2 may result from partial pair-wise interaction on neighbouring atoms of the single p electron outside the $[Ar]3d^{10}4s^2$ core which immediately follows the first transition series. As such it can be compared with Hg which also has a very low mp and completes the $[Xe]4f^{14}5d^{10}6s^2$ "pseudo-noble-gas" configuration following the lanthanide elements. Note that all interatomic contacts in metallic Ga are less than those in Al, again emphasizing the presence of a "d-block contraction". Gallium is also unusual in contracting on melting, the volume of the liquid phase being 3.4% less than that of the solid; the

Table 7.5 Physical properties of Group 13 elements

Property	B	Al	Ga	In	Tl
MP/°C	2092	660.45	29.767	156.63	303.5
BP/°C	4002	2520	2205	2073	1473
Density (20°C)/g cm^{-3}	2.35	2.699	5.904	7.31	11.85
Hardness (Mohs)	11	2.75	1.5	1.2	1.2–1.3
ΔH_{fus}/kJ mol^{-1}	50.2	10.71	5.56	3.28	4.21
ΔH_{vap}/kJ mol^{-1}	480	294	254	232	166
ΔH_f (monoatomic gas)/kJ mol^{-1}	560	329.7	286.2	243	182.2
Electrical resistivity/μohm cm	6.7×10^{11}	2.655	$\sim$27$^{(a)}$	8.37	18
$E°(M^{3+} + 3e^- = M(s))$/V	$-0.890^{(b)}$	-1.676	-0.529	-0.338	$+1.26^{(c)}$
$E°(M^+ + e^- = M(s))$/V	—	0.55	-0.79(acid)	-0.18	-0.336
			-1.39(alkali)		
Electronegativity χ	2.0	1.5	1.6	1.7	1.8

$^{(a)}$The resistivity of crystalline Ga is markedly anisotropic, the values in the three orthorhombic directions being a 17.5, b 8.20, c 55.3 μohm cm. The resistivity of liquid Ga at 30° is 25.8 μohm cm.

$^{(b)}E°$ for reaction $H_3BO_3 + 3H^+ + 3e^- = B(s) + 3H_2O$.

$^{(c)}$This is the observed value for $E°(Tl^{3+}/Tl^+)$, hence the calculated value for the corresponding $E°(Tl^{3+}/Tl(s))$ is +0.73 V.

same phenomenon occurs with the next element in the periodic table Ge, and also with Sb and Bi, in addition to the well-known example of H_2O. In each case, a structural feature in the solid is broken down to permit more efficient packing of atoms in the liquid state.

The standard electrode potentials of the heavier Group 13 elements reflect the decreasing stability of the +3 oxidation state in aqueous solution and the tendency, particularly of Tl, to form compounds in the +1 oxidation state (p. 226). The trend to increasing electropositivity of the group oxidation state which was noted for Groups 1 and 2 does not occur with Group 13 but is found, as expected, in Group 3 (Fig. 7.2). Similarly, the steady decrease in electronegativity in the series B > Al > Sc > Y > La > Ac is reversed in Group 13 and there is a steady *increase* in electronegativity from Al to Tl.

7.2.4 Chemical reactivity and trends

The Group 13 metals differ sharply from the non-metallic element boron both in their greater chemical reactivity at moderate temperatures and in their well-defined cationic chemistry for aqueous solutions. The absence of a range of

volatile hydrides and other cluster compounds analogous to the boranes and carboranes is also notable. Aluminium combines with most non-metallic elements when heated to give compounds such as AlN, Al_2S_3, AlX_3, etc. It also forms intermetallic compounds with elements from all groups of the periodic table that contain metals. Because of its great affinity for oxygen it is used as a reducing agent to obtain Cr, Mn, V, etc., by means of the thermite process of J. W. Goldschmidt. Finely powdered Al metal explodes on contact with liquid O_2, but for normal samples of the metal a coherent protective oxide film prevents appreciable reaction with oxygen, water or dilute acids; amalgamation with Hg or contact with solutions of salts of certain electropositive metals destroys the film and permits further reaction. Aluminium is also readily soluble in hot concentrated hydrochloric acid and in aqueous NaOH or KOH at room temperature with liberation of H_2. This latter reaction is sometimes written as

$$Al + NaOH + H_2O \longrightarrow NaAlO_2 + \tfrac{3}{2}H_2$$

though it is likely that the species in solution is the hydrated tetrahydroxoaluminate anion $[Al(OH)_4]^-$(aq) or $[Al(H_2O)_2(OH)_4]^-$.

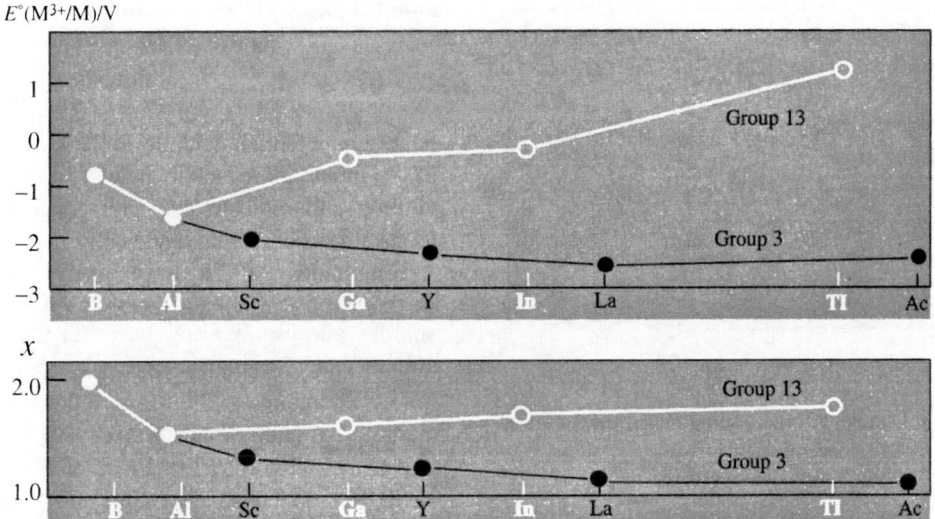

Figure 7.2   Trends in standard electrode potential $E°$ and electronegativity χ for elements in Groups 3 and 13.

$Al(OH)_3$ is amphoteric, forming both salts and aluminates (Greek άμφοτέρως, *amphoteros*, in both ways). Thus the freshly precipitated hydroxide is readily soluble in both acid and alkali:

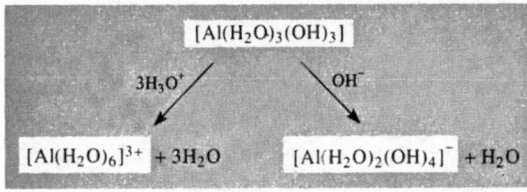

In these reactions the coordination number of Al has been assumed to be 6 throughout though direct evidence on this point is rarely available. Amphoterism is also exhibited in anhydrous reactions, e.g.:

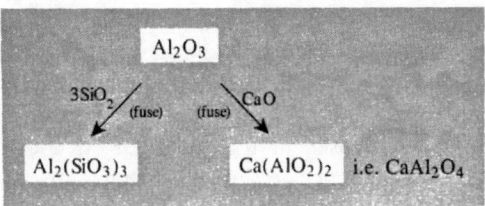

Aluminium compounds of weak acids are extensively hydrolysed to $[Al(H_2O)_3(OH)_3]$ and the corresponding hydride, e.g. $Al_2S_3 \longrightarrow$

$3H_2S$, $AlN \longrightarrow NH_3$, and $Al_4C_3 \longrightarrow 3CH_4$. Similarly, the cyanide, acetate and carbonate are unstable in aqueous solution. Hydrolysis of the halides and other salts such as the nitrate and sulfate is incomplete but aqueous solutions are acidic due to the ability of the hydrated cation $[Al(H_2O)_6]^{3+}$ to act as proton donor giving $[Al(H_2O)_5(OH)]^{2+}$, $[Al(H_2O)_4(OH)_2]^+$, etc. If the pH is gradually increased this deprotonation of the mononuclear species is accompanied by aggregation via OH bridges to give species such as

$$[(H_2O)_4Al\overset{\displaystyle OH}{\underset{\displaystyle OH}{\diamondsuit}}Al(H_2O)_4]^{4+}$$

and then to precipitation of the hydrous oxide. This is of particular use in water clarification since the precipitating hydroxide nucleates on fine suspended particles which are thereby thrown out of suspension. Still further increase in pH leads to redissolution as an aluminate (Fig. 7.3). Similar behaviour is shown by Be^{II}, Zn^{II}, Ga^{III}, Sn^{II}, Pb^{II}, etc. A detailed quantitative theory of amphoterism is difficult to construct but it is known that amphoteric behaviour occurs when (a) the cation is weakly basic, (b) its hydroxide

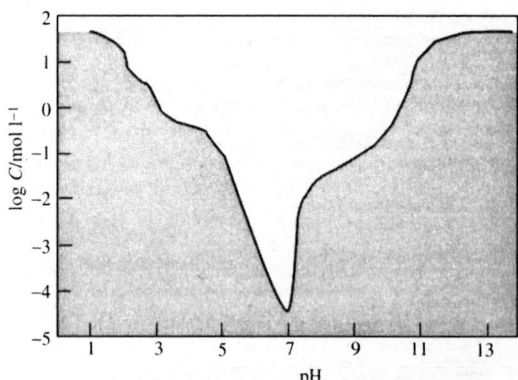

Figure 7.3 Schematic representation of the variation of concentration of an Al salt as a function of pH (see text).

is moderately insoluble, and (c) the hydrated species can also act as proton donors.[2]

Anhydrous Al salts cannot be prepared by heating the corresponding hydrate for reasons closely related to the amphoterism and hydrolysis of such compounds. For example, $AlCl_3.6H_2O$ is, in reality, $[Al(H_2O)_6]Cl_3$ and the strength of the Al–O interaction precludes the formation of Al–Cl bonds:

$$2[Al(H_2O)_6]Cl_3 \xrightarrow{\text{heat}} Al_2O_3 + 6HCl + 9H_2O$$

The amphoteric behaviour of Ga^{III} salts parallels that of Al^{III}; indeed, Ga_2O_3 is slightly *more* acidic than Al_2O_3 and solutions of gallates tend to be more stable than aluminates. Consistent with this, pK_a for the equilibrium

$$[M(H_2O)_6]^{3+} \rightleftharpoons [M(H_2O)_5OH]^{2+} + H^+$$

is 4.95 for Al and 2.60 for Ga. Indium is more basic than Ga and is only weakly amphoteric. The metal does not dissolve in aqueous alkali whereas Ga does. This alternation in the sequence of basicity can be related to the electronic and size factors mentioned on p. 222. Thallium behaves as a moderately strong base but is not strictly

[2] C. S. G. PHILLIPS and R. J. P. WILLIAMS, *Inorganic Chemistry*, Vol. 1, Chap. 14; Vol. 2, pp. 524–5, Oxford University Press, Oxford, 1966.

comparable with other members of the group because it normally exists as Tl^I in aqueous solution. Thus, Tl metal tarnishes readily and reacts with steam or moist air to give TlOH. The electrode potential data in Table 7.5 show that Tl^I is much more stable than Tl^{III} in aqueous solution and indicate that Tl^{III} compounds can act as strong oxidizing agents.

Compounds of Tl^I have many similarities to those of the alkali metals: TlOH is very soluble and is a strong base; Tl_2CO_3 is also soluble and resembles the corresponding Na and K compounds; Tl^I forms colourless, well-crystallized salts of many oxoacids, and these tend to be anhydrous like those of the similarly sized Rb and Cs; Tl^I salts of weak acids have a basic reaction in aqueous solution as a result of hydrolysis; Tl^I forms polysulfides (e.g. Tl_2S_5) and polyiodides, etc. In other respects Tl^I resembles the more highly polarizing ion Ag^+, e.g. in the colour and insolubility of its chromate, sulfide, arsenate and halides (except F), though it does not form ammine complexes in aqueous solution and its azide is not explosive.

The stability of the +1 oxidation state in Group 13 increases in the sequence Al < Ga < In < Tl, and numerous examples of M^I compounds will be found in the following sections. The occurrence of an oxidation state which is 2 less than the group valency is sometimes referred to as the "inert-pair effect" but it is important to recognize that this is a description not an explanation. The phenomenon is quite general among the heavier elements of the p block (i.e. the post-transition elements in Groups 13–16). For example, Sn and Pb commonly occur in both the +2 and +4 oxidation states; P, As, Sb and Bi in the +3 and +5; S, Se, Te and Po in the +2, +4, and +6 states. The term "inert-pair effect" is somewhat misleading since it implies that the energy required to involve the ns^2 electrons in bonding increases in the sequence Al < Ga < In < Tl. Reference to Table 7.4 shows that this is not so (the sequence is, in fact, In < Al < Tl < Ga). The explanation lies rather in the decrease in bond energy with increase in size from Al to Tl so that the energy required to involve the s electrons in bonding is not compensated by the energy released in forming the 2 additional bonds. The argument is difficult to quantify since the requisite energy terms are not known. Thus it is unrealistic to use the simple ionic bond model (p. 79) to calculate the heat of formation of MX_3 because compounds like $TlCl_3$ are not ionic, i.e. $[Tl^{3+}(Cl^-)_3]$ — the energy for the ionization of M(g) to M^{3+}(g) is greater than $5000 \, kJ \, mol^{-1}$ for each element and substantial covalent interaction between M^{3+} and X^- would also be expected. In the absence of semi-empirical bond energy data or *ab initio* MO calculations it is only possible to note that the higher oxidation state becomes progressively less stable with respect to the lower oxidation state as atomic number increases within the group. This is seen, for example, by comparing the standard electrode potentials in aqueous solution for M^{III} and M^I in Table 7.5. Similarly, from the somewhat fragmentary data available, it appears that the enthalpy of formation of the anhydrous halides remains approximately constant for MX but diminishes irregularly from Al to Tl for MX_3 (X = Cl, Br, I). The overall result depends not only on the simple Born–Haber terms (p. 82) but also on a combination of several other factors including changes in structure and bond type, covalency effects, enthalpies of hydration, entropy effects, etc., and a quantitative rationalization of all the data has not yet been achieved.

Group 13 metals furnish a good example of the general rule that an element is more electropositive in its lower than in its higher oxidation state: the lower oxide and hydroxide are more basic and the higher oxide and hydroxide more acidic. The reasons for this behaviour are similar to those already discussed when comparing Group 2 with Group 1 (p. 111) and turn on the relative magnitude of ionization energies, cationic size, hydration enthalpy and entropy, etc. Again, the higher the charge on an aquo cation $[M(H_2O_x)]^{n+}$ the more readily will it act as a proton donor (p. 51).

Other group trends will emerge in subsequent sections. However, it is worth noting here an important vestigial structural relation of these elements to the icosahedral units in elementary boron (p. 142). Thus, the structures of both β-rhombohedral boron and the cubic alloy phase Al_5CuLi_3 can be constructed from 60-vertex truncated icosahedra, although linked in very different ways in the 3-dimensional crystalline lattice. Likewise, Ga_{12} icosahedra have been found in intermetallic phases such as $RbGa_7$, $CsGa_7$, Li_2Ga_7, K_3Ga_{13} and $Na_{22}Ga_{39}$. This has led to the proposal[3] that the Group 13 elements should be given the collective epithet of 'icosagens'.

7.3 Compounds

7.3.1 Hydrides and related complexes [4–8]

The extensive covalent cluster chemistry of the boron hydrides finds no parallel with the heavier elements of Group 13. AlH_3 is a colourless, involatile solid which is extensively polymerized via Al–H–Al bonds; it is thermally unstable above 150–200°, is a strong reducing agent and reacts violently with water and other protic reagents to liberate H_2. Several crystalline and amorphous modifications have been described and the structure of α-AlH_3 has been determined by X-ray and neutron diffraction:[9] each Al is octahedrally surrounded by 6 H atoms at 172 pm and the Al–H–Al angle is 141°. The participation of each Al in 6 bridges, and the equivalence of all

[3] R. B. KING, *Inorg. Chim. Acta* **181**, 217–25 (1991).

[4] E. WIBERG and E. AMBERGER, *Hydrides of the Elements of Main Groups 1–IV*, Chaps. 5 and 6, pp. 381–461, Elsevier, Amsterdam, 1971.

[5] N. N. GREENWOOD Chap. 3 in E. A. V. EBSWORTH, A. G. MADDOCK, and A. G. SHARPE (eds.), *New Pathways in Inorganic Chemistry*, pp. 37–64, Cambridge University Press, Cambridge, 1968.

[6] A. R. BARRON and G. WILKINSON, *Polyhedron* **5**, 1897–1915 (1986).

[7] B. M. BULYCHEV, *Polyhedron* **9**, 387–408 (1990).

[8] C. JONES, G. A. KOUSATONIS and C. L. RASTON, *Polyhedron* **12**, 1829–48 (1993).

[9] J. W. TURLEY and H. W. RINN, *Inorg. Chem.* **8**, 18–22 (1969).

Al–H distances suggests that 3-centre 2-electron bonding occurs as in the boranes (p. 157). The closest Al $\cdots$ Al distance is 324 pm, which is appreciably shorter than in metallic Al (340 pm), but there is no direct metal–metal bonding and the density of AlH_3 ($1.477 \, g \, cm^{-3}$) is markedly less than that for Al ($2.699 \, g \, cm^{-3}$); this is because in Al metal all 12 nearest neighbours are at 340 pm whereas in AlH_3 there are 6 Al at 324 and 6 at 445 pm.

AlH_3 is best prepared by the reaction of ethereal solutions of $LiAlH_4$ and $AlCl_3$ under very carefully controlled conditions:[10]

$$3LiAlH_4 + AlCl_3 \xrightarrow{Et_2O} 4[AlH_3(Et_2O)_n] + 3LiCl$$

The LiCl is removed and the filtrate, if left at this stage, soon deposits an intractable etherate of variable composition. To avoid this, the solution is worked up with an excess of $LiAlH_4$ and some added $LiBH_4$ in the presence of a large excess of benzene under reflux at 76–79°C. Crystals of α-AlH_3 soon form. Slight variations in the conditions lead to other crystalline modifications of unsolvated AlH_3, 6 of which have been identified.

AlH_3 readily forms adducts with strong Lewis bases (L) but these are more conveniently prepared by reactions of the type

$$LiAlH_4 + NMe_3HCl \xrightarrow{Et_2O} [AlH_3(NMe_3)]$$
$$+ LiCl + H_2$$

$[AlH_3(NMe_3)]$ has a tetrahedral structure and can take up a further mole of ligand to give $[AlH_3(NMe_3)_2]$; this was the first compound in which Al was shown to adopt a 5-coordinate trigonal bipyramidal structure[11]. Such complexes are now of interest since their thermal decomposition can be used to prepare ultra-thin carbon-free Al films by chemical vapour deposition on GaAs semiconductor devices.[12]

$LiAlH_4$ is a white crystalline solid, stable in dry air but highly reactive towards moisture, protic solvents, and many organic functional groups. It is readily soluble in ether (~29 g per 100 g at room temperature) and is normally used in this solvent. $LiAlH_4$ has proved to be an outstandingly versatile reducing agent since its discovery some 50 y ago[13,14] (see Panel opposite). It can be prepared on the laboratory (and industrial) scale by the reaction

$$4LiH + AlCl_3 \xrightarrow{Et_2O} LiAlH_4 + 3LiCl$$

On the industrial (multitonne) scale it can also be prepared by direct high-pressure reaction of the elements or preferably via the intermediate formation of the Na analogue.

$$Na + Al + 2H_2 \xrightarrow[350 \, atm]{thf/140°/3h} NaAlH_4 \text{ (99\% yield)}$$

The Li salt can then be obtained by metathesis with LiCl in Et_2O. The X-ray crystal structure of $LiAlH_4$ shows the presence of tetrahedral AlH_4 groups (Al–H 155 pm) bridged by Li in such a way that each Li is surrounded by 4H at 188–200 pm (cf. 204 pm in LiH) and a fifth H at 216 pm. The bonding therefore deviates considerably from the simple ionic formulation $Li^+AlH_4^-$ and there appears to be substantial covalent bonding as found in other complex hydrides (p. 67).

Other complex hydrides of Al are known including Li_3AlH_6, M^IAlH_4 (M^I = Li, Na, K, Cs), $M^{II}(AlH_4)_2$ (M^{II} = Be, Mg, Ca), $Ga(AlH_4)_3$, $M^I(AlH_3R)$, $M^I(AlH_2R_2)$, $M^I[AlH(OEt)_3]$, etc. (see Panel). The important complex $Al(BH_4)_3$ has already been mentioned (p. 169); it is a colourless liquid, mp −64.5°, bp +44.5°. It is best prepared

[10] F. M. BROWER, N. E. MATZEK, P. F. REIGLER, H. W. RINN, C. B. ROBERTS, D. L. SCHMIDT, J. A. SHOVER and K. TERADA, *J. Am. Chem. Soc.* **98**, 2450–3 (1976).

[11] G. W. FRASER, N. N. GREENWOOD and B. P. STRAUGHAN, *J. Chem. Soc.* 3742–9 (1963). C. W. HEITSCH, C. E. NORDMAN, and R. W. PARRY, *Inorg. Chem.* **2**, 508–12 (1963).

[12] A. T. S. WEE, A. J. MURRELL, N. K. SINGH, D. O'HARE and J. S. FORD, *J. Chem Soc., Chem. Commun.*, 11–13 (1990).

[13] A. E. FINHOLD, A. C. BOND, and H. J. SCHLESINGER, *J. Am. Chem. Soc.* **9**, 1199–203 (1947).

[14] N. G. GAYLORD, *Reduction with Complex Metal Hydrides*, Interscience, New York, 1956, 1046 pp. J. S. PIZEY, *Lithium Aluminium Hydride*, Ellis Horwood, Ltd., Chichester, 1977, 288 pp.

Synthetic Reactions of LiAlH$_4$[4,14]

LiAlH$_4$ is a versatile reducing and hydrogenating reagent for both inorganic and organic compounds. With inorganic halides the product obtained depends on the relative stabilities of the corresponding tetrahydroaluminate, hydride and element. For example, BeCl$_2$ gives Be(AlH$_4$)$_2$. whereas BCl$_3$ gives B$_2$H$_6$ and HgI$_2$ gives Hg metal. The halides of Cu, Ag, Au, Zn, Cd and Hg give some evidence of unstable hydrido species at low temperatures but all are reduced to the metal at room temperature. The halides of main groups 14 and 15 yield the corresponding hydrides since the AlH$_4$ derivatives are unstable or non-existent. Thus SiCl$_4$, GeCl$_4$ and SnCl$_4$ yield MH$_4$ and substituted halides such as R$_n$SiX$_{4-n}$ give R$_n$SiH$_{4-n}$. Similarly, PCl$_3$ (and PCl$_5$), AsCl$_3$ and SbCl$_3$ afford MH$_3$ but BiCl$_3$ is reduced to the metal. PhAsCl$_2$ gives PhAsH$_2$ and Ph$_2$SbCl gives Ph$_2$SbH, etc. Less work has been done on oxides but COCl$_2$ yields MeOH, NO yields hyponitrous acid HON=NOH (which can be isolated as the Ag salt), and CO$_2$ gives LiAl(OMe)$_4$ or LiAl(OCH$_2$O)$_2$ depending on conditions.

The real importance of LiAlH$_4$ stems from the applications in organic syntheses. Its commercial introduction dates from 1948. By 1951 the number of functional groups that were known to react was 23 and this rose to more than 60 by the 1970s. Despite this, the heyday of LiAlH$_4$ seems to have been reached in the late 1960s and it has now been replaced in many systems by the more selective borohydrides (p. 167) or by organometallic hydrides (see below). Reaction is usually carried out in ether solution, followed by hydrolysis of the intermediate so formed when appropriate. Typical examples are listed below.

Compound	Product	Compound	Product
Reactive >C=C<	>CH—CH<	RCOSR	RCH$_2$OH
RCH=CH$_2$	[Al(CH$_2$CH$_2$R)$_4$]$^-$	RCSNH$_2$	RCH$_2$NH$_2$
C$_2$H$_2$	[AlH(CH=CH$_2$)$_3$]$^-$	RSCN	RSH
RC≡CH	RCH=CH$_2$	R$_2$SO	R$_2$S
RX	RH (not aryl)	R$_2$SO$_2$	R$_2$S
ROH	[Al(OR)$_4$]$^-$ or [AlH(OR)$_3$]$^-$	RSO$_2$X	RSH
RCHO	RCH$_2$OH	ROSO$_2$R', (ArOSO$_2$R')	RH, (ArOH)
R$_2$CO	R$_2$CHOH	RSO$_2$H	RSSR + RSH
Quinone	Hydroquinone	RNC or RNCO	RNHMe
RCO$_2$H or (RCO)$_2$O or RCOX	RCH$_2$OH	or RNCS	
		RCN	RCH$_2$NH$_2$ or RCHO
RCO$_2$R'	RCH$_2$OH + R'OH	R$_2$C=NOH	R$_2$CHNH$_2$
Lactones, i.e. $\overline{O(CH_2)_nC}$=O	Diols, i.e. HO(CH$_2$)$_{n+1}$OH	R$_3$NO	R$_3$N
RCONH$_2$	RCH$_2$NH$_2$ (also 2°, 3°)	R$_2$NNO	R$_2$NNH$_2$
Epoxides $\overline{OCR_2CHR}$	R$_2$C(OH)CH$_2$R	RNO$_2$, RNHOH or RN$_3$	RNH$_2$
$\overline{SCR_2—CR_2}$	R$_2$C(SH)CHR$_2$	ArNO$_2$	ArN=NAr
RSSR	RSH		

More recently, LiAlH$_4$ has been eclipsed as an organic reducing agent by the emergence of several cheaper organo-aluminium hydrides which are also safer and easier to handle than LiAlH$_4$. Pre-eminent among these are Bu$_2^i$AlH and Na[AlEt$_2$H$_2$] which were introduced commercially in the early 1970s and Na[Al(OCH$_2$CH$_2$OMe)$_2$H$_2$], VITRIDE®, which became available in bulk during 1979. All three reagents can be prepared directly:

$$2Me_2CH=CH_2 + Al + H_2 \longrightarrow Bu_2^iAlH$$

$$2CH_2=CH_2 + Al + 2H_2 \longrightarrow \tfrac{1}{2}(Et_2AlH)_2 \xrightarrow{NaH} Na[AlEt_2H_2]$$

$$2MeOCH_2CH_2OH + Al + Na \xrightarrow{H_2/PhMe} Na[Al(OCH_2CH_2OMe)_2H_2]$$

All three are substantially cheaper than LiAlH$_4$ and are now produced on a far larger scale as indicated in the table overleaf. Data refer to US industrial use in 1980 and even larger markets are available outside the chemical industry (e.g. in polymerization catalysis).

Compound	Production/kg	Price/$ kg^{-1}	$ per kg 'H'
LiAlH$_4$	6 000	88.00	835.00
Bu$_2^i$AlH	195 000	5.10	715.00
Na[AlEt$_2$H$_2$]	91 000	11.00	605.00
Na[Al(OCH$_2$CH$_2$OMe)$_2$H$_2$]	123 000	6.25	638.00

in the absence of solvent by the reaction

$$3NaBH_4 + AlCl_3 \longrightarrow Al(BH_4)_3 + 3NaCl$$

Al(BH$_4$)$_3$ was the first fluxional compound to be recognized as such (1955) and its thermal decomposition led to a new compound which was the first to be discovered and structurally characterized by means of nmr:

$$2Al(BH_4)_3 \xrightarrow{70°} Al_2B_4H_{18} + B_2H_6$$

This binuclear complex is also fluxional and has the structure shown in Fig. 7.4a. Al(BH$_4$)$_3$ reacts readily with NMe$_3$ to give a 1:1 adduct in which Al adopts the unusual pentagonal

bipyramidal 7-fold coordination as shown in Fig. 7.4b.[15]

At room temperature Al(BH$_4$)$_3$ reacts quantitatively in the gas phase with Al$_2$Me$_6$ (p. 259) to give [Al(η^2-BH$_4$)$_2$Me] (mp $-76°$) in which one of the BH$_4$ groups of the parent compound has been replaced by a Me group:

$$4Al(BH_4)_3 + Al_2Me_6 \xrightarrow{rt/2\,h} 6[Al(BH_4)_2Me]$$

Electron diffraction studies in the gas phase reveal an unusual structure in which the 5-coordinate Al atom has square-pyramidal

---

[15] N. A. BAILEY, P. H. BIRD and M. G. H. WALLBRIDGE, *Chem. Commun.*, 286–7 (1966); *Inorg. Chem.* **7**, 1575–81 (1968).

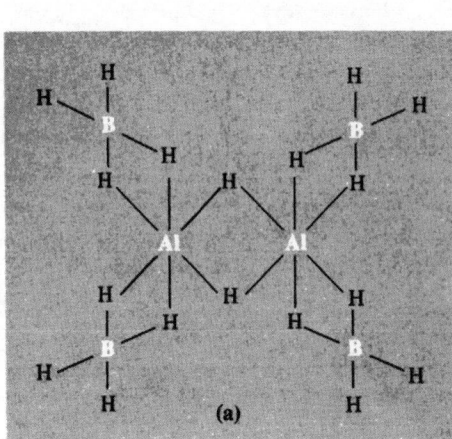

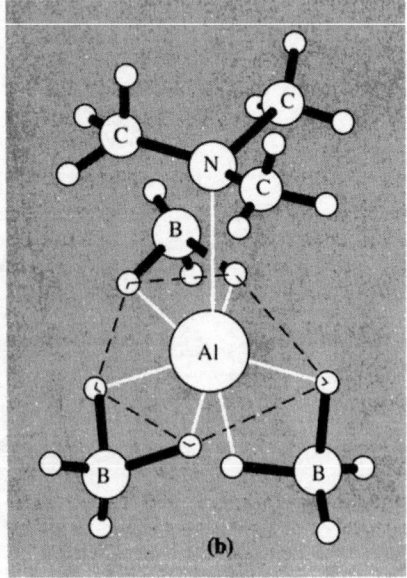

Figure 7.4   (a) Structure of Al$_2$B$_4$H$_{18}$ showing 6-coordinate Al, (b) Structure of the adduct Me$_3$N.Al(BH$_4$)$_3$ showing 7-coordinate pentagonal bipyramidal Al.

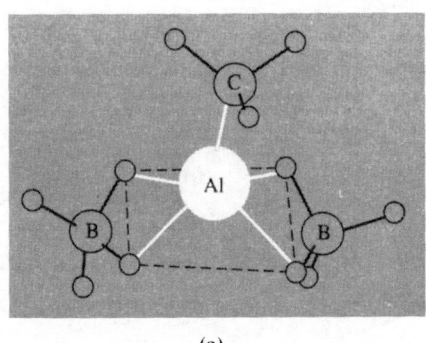
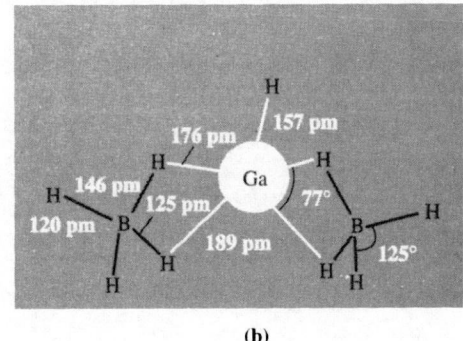

(a)   (b)

Figure 7.5   (a) Structure of $[MeAl(\eta^2\text{-}BH_4)_2]$ as revealed by electron diffraction, and (b) structure and key dimensions of $[HGa(\eta^2\text{-}BH_4)_2]$ as determined by low temperature X-ray diffractometry.

geometry (Fig. 7.5a).[16] The heavy atoms $CAlB_2$ are coplanar and the symmetry is close to C_{2v}. A similar structure (Fig. 7.5b) has been found by X-ray diffraction for $[Ga(\eta^2\text{-}BH_4)_2H]$, which was prepared by the dry reaction of $LiBH_4$ and $GaCl_3$ at $-45°C$,[17] and this geometry is emerging as a notable structural feature of many AlH_4^- complexes (see next paragraph).

Many complexes in which AlH_4^- acts as a dihapto (or bridging bis-dihapto) ligand to transition metals have recently been characterized. These are usually stabilized by coligands such as tertiary phosphines or η^5-cyclopentadienyls and are readily prepared by treating the corresponding chloro-complexes with $LiAlH_4$ in ether. Typical examples, frequently dimeric, are:[6] $[\{(C_5H_5)_2Y(AlH_4.thf)\}_2]$, $[\{(C_5Me_5)_2Ti(AlH_4)\}_2]$ (Fig. 7.6a), $[\{(C_5Me_5)_2Ta(AlH_4)\}_2]$, $[\{(PMe_3)_3\text{-}H_3W\}_2\text{-}\mu\text{-}(\eta^2,\eta^2\text{-}AlH_5)]$ (Fig. 7.6b), $[\{(dmpe)_2\text{-}Mn(AlH_4)\}_2]$ and $[\{(PPh_3)_3HRu(AlH_4)\}_2]$. A few transition metal tetrahydroaluminates $[M(AlH_4)_n]$ are also known but their structures have not yet been determined by X-ray crystallography, e.g.:[6] $[Y(AlH_3)_3]$, $[Ti(AlH_4)_4]$, $[Nb(AlH_4)_5]$ and $[Fe(AlH_4)_2]$.

The synthesis and characterization of gallane, the binary hydride of gallium, has proved even more elusive than that of alane, AlH_3. Success was finally achieved[18,19] by first preparing dimeric monochlorogallane, $\{H_2Ga(\mu\text{-}Cl)\}_2$,[20] and then reducing a freshly prepared sample of this liquid with freshly prepared $LiGaH_4$ under solvent-free conditions in an all-glass apparatus at $-30°C$:

$$2GaCl_3 + 4Me_3SiH \xrightarrow{-23°} Ga_2Cl_2H_4 + 4Me_3SiCl$$

$$Ga_2Cl_2H_4 + 2LiGaH_4 \xrightarrow{-30°} Ga_2H_6 + 2LiGaH_3Cl$$

The volatile product, obtained in about 5% yield, condensed as a white solid at $-50°$ and had a vapour pressure of about 1 mmHg at $-63°$. Gallane decomposes into its elements at ambient temperatures. In the vapour phase it has a diborane-like structure, Ga_2H_6, with $Ga\text{-}H_t$ 152 pm, $Ga\text{-}H_\mu$ 171 pm, $Ga\cdots Ga$ 258 pm and angle GaHGa 98° (electron diffraction).[19] In the solid state gallane tends to aggregate via $Ga\text{-}H\text{-}Ga$ bonds to give $(GaH_3)_n$ with n, perhaps equal to 4 but, in contrast to the structure

[16] M. T. BARLOW, C. J. DAIN, A. J. DOWNS, P. D. P. THO-MAS and D. W. H. RANKIN, *J. Chem. Soc., Dalton Trans.*, 1374–8 (1980). See also A. J. DOWNS and L. A. JONES, *Polyhedron* **13**, 2401–15 (1994) for a description of the polymeric Al analogue, $[Al(BH_4)_2H]$.

[17] M. T. BARLOW, C. J. DAIN, A. J. DOWNS, G. S. LAUREN-SON and D. W. H. RANKIN, *J. Chem. Soc., Dalton Trans.*, 597–602 (1982).

[18] A. J. DOWNS, M. J. GOODE and C. R. PULHAM, *J. Am. Chem. Soc.* **111**, 1936–7 (1989).

[19] C. R. PULHAM, A. J. DOWNS, M. J. GOODE, D. W. H. RAN-KIN and H. E. ROBERTSON, *J. Am. Chem. Soc.* **113**, 5149–62 (1991).

[20] M. J. GOODE, A. J. DOWNS, C. R. PULHAM, D. W. H. RAN-KIN and H. E. ROBERTSON, *J. Chem. Soc., Chem. Commun.*, 768–9 (1988).

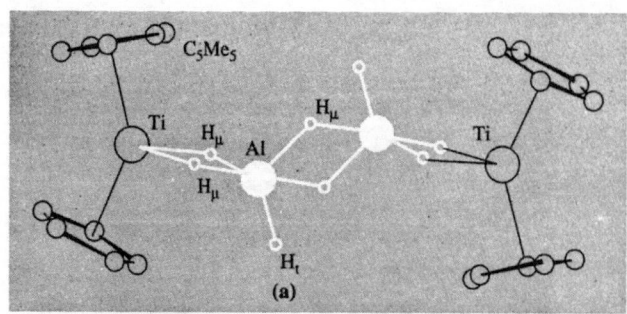
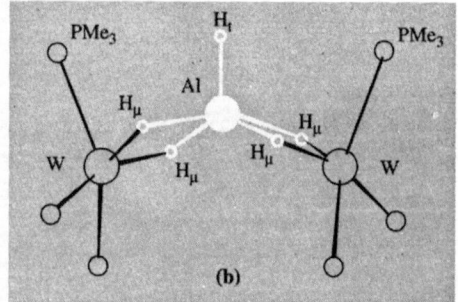

Figure 7.6 (a) The structure of $[\{(C_5Me_5)_2Ti(AlH_4)\}_2]$, i.e. $[\{(\eta^5\text{-}C_5Me_5)_2Ti(\mu\text{-}H)_2Al(H_t(\mu\text{-}H)\}_2]$; the Me groups have been omitted for clarity. (b) The structure of $[\{(PMe_3)_3H_3W\}_2\text{-}\mu\text{-}(\eta^2, \eta^2\text{-}AlH_5)]$; the Me groups have been omitted for clarity and the three H atoms on each W were not located with certainty.

of α-AlH$_3$ (p. 227), some terminal Ga–H$_t$ bonds remain.

The known reactions of gallane appear mostly to parallel those of diborane (p. 165). Thus, at $-95°$, NH$_3$ causes unsymmetrical cleavage to give $[H_2Ga(NH_3)_2]^+[GaH_4]^-$ whereas NMe$_3$ effects symmetrical cleavage to give Me$_3$N.GaH$_3$ or (Me$_3$N)$_2$GaH$_3$ according to the amount used.[19] These last two adducts were already well known. Me$_3$N.GaH$_3$ can readily be prepared as a colourless crystalline solid, mp 70.5°, by the reaction of ethereal solutions of LiGaH$_4$ and Me$_3$NHCl.[21] It is one of the most stable complexes of GaH$_3$ and, like its Al analogue, can take up a further mole of ligand to give the trigonal bipyramidal 2:1 complex.[22] Numerous other complexes have been prepared and the stabilities of the 1:1 adducts decrease in the following sequences:[5]

$$Me_2NH > Me_3N > C_5H_5N > Et_3N$$
$$> PhNMe_2 \gg Ph_3N$$
$$Me_3N \approx Me_3P > Me_2PH$$
$$Ph_3P > Ph_3N > Ph_3As$$
$$R_3N \text{ or } R_3P > R_2O \text{ or } R_2S$$

Complexes of the type $[GaH_2X(NMe_3)]$ and $[GaHX_2(NMe_3)]$ are readily prepared by reaction of HCl or HBr on the GaH$_3$ complex at low temperatures or by reactions of the type

$$2[GaH_3(NMe_3)] + [GaX_3(NMe_3)] \xrightarrow{C_6H_6}$$
$$3[GaH_2X(NMe_3)] \quad X = Cl, Br, I$$

The relative stabilities of these various complexes can be rationalized in terms of the factors discussed on p. 198. A few mixed hydrides have also been characterized, e.g. galla-diborane, $H_2Ga(\mu\text{-}H)_2BH_2$,[23] and *arachno*-2-gallatetraborane(10), $H_2GaB_3H_8$,[24] as well as derivatives such as tetramethyldigallane, $Me_2Ga(\mu\text{-}H)_2GaMe_2$.[25]

InH$_3$ and TlH$_3$ appear to be too unstable to exist in the uncoordinated state though they may have transitory existence in ethereal solutions at low temperatures. A similar decrease in thermal stability is noted for the tetrahydro complexes; e.g.the temperature at which the Li salts decompose rapidly, follows the sequence

[21] N. N. GREENWOOD, A. STORR and M. G. H. WALLBRIDGE, *Proc. Chem Soc.* 249 (1962).

[22] N. N. GREENWOOD, A. STORR and M. G. H. WALLBRIDGE, *Inorg. Chem.* **2**, 1036–9 (1963). D. F. SHRIVER and R. W. PARRY, *Inorg. Chem.* **2**, 1039–42 (1963).

[23] C. R. PULHAM, P. T. BRAIN, A. J. DOWNS, D. W. H. RANKIN and H. E. ROBERTSON, *J. Chem. Soc., Chem. Commun.*, 177–8 (1990).

[24] C. R. PULHAM, A. J. DOWNS, D. W. H. RANKIN and H. E. ROBERTSON, *J. Chem. Soc., Chem. Commun.*, 1520–1 (1990). B. J. DUKE and H. F. SCHAEFER, *J. Chem. Soc., Chem. Commun.*, 123–4 (1991).

[25] P. L. BAXTER, A. J. DOWNS, M. J. GOODE, D. W. H. RANKIN and H. E. ROBERTSON, *J. Chem. Soc., Chem. Commun.*, 805–6 (1986).

$$LiBH_4(380°) > LiAlH_4(100°) > LiGaH_4(50°)$$
$$> LiInH_4(0°) \approx LiTlH_4(0°)$$

7.3.2 Halides and halide complexes

Several important points emerge in considering the wide range of Group 13 metal halides and their complexes. Monohalides are known for all 4 metals with each halogen though for Al they occur only as short-lived diatomic species in the gas phase or as cryogenically isolated solids. This may seem paradoxical, since the bond dissociation energies for Al–X are substantially greater than for the corresponding monohalides of the other elements and fall in the range 655 kJ mol^{-1} (AlF) to 365 kJ mol^{-1} (AlI). The corresponding values for the gaseous TlX decrease from 460 to 270 kJ mol^{-1} yet it is these latter compounds that form stable crystalline solids. In fact, the instability of AlX in the condensed phase at normal temperatures is due not to the weakness of the Al–X bond but to the ready disproportionation of these compounds into the even more stable AlX$_3$:

$$AlX(s) \longrightarrow \tfrac{2}{3}Al(s) + \tfrac{1}{3}AlX_3(s);$$

$$\Delta H_{disprop} \text{ (see table below)}$$

The reverse reaction to give the gaseous species AlX(g) at high temperature accounts for the enhanced volatility of AlF$_3$ when heated in the presence of Al metal, and the ready volatilization of Al metal in the presence of AlCl$_3$. Using calculations of the type outlined on p. 82 the standard heats of formation of the crystalline monohalides AlX and their heats of disproportionation have been estimated as:

Compound (s)	AlF	AlCl	AlBr	AlI
$\Delta H_f^°$/kJ mol^{-1}	−393	−188	−126	−46
$\Delta H_{disprop}^°$/kJ mol^{-1}	−105	−46	−50	−59

The crystalline dihalides AlX$_2$ are even less stable with respect to disproportionation, value of $\Delta H_{disprop}$ falling in the range −200 to −230 kJ mol^{-1} for the reaction

$$AlX_2(s) \longrightarrow \tfrac{1}{3}Al(s) + \tfrac{2}{3}AlX_3(s)$$

Very recently the first AlI compound to be stable at room temperature, the tetrameric complex [{AlI(NEt$_3$)}$_4$], has been prepared and shown to feature a planar Al$_4$ ring with Al–Al 265 pm, Al–I 265 pm and Al–N 207 pm.[25a]

Aluminium trihalides

AlF$_3$ is made by treating Al$_2$O$_3$ with HF gas at 700° and the other trihalides are made by the direct exothermic combination of the elements. AlF$_3$ is important in the industrial production of Al metal (p. 219) and is made on a scale approaching 700 000 tonnes per annum world wide. AlCl$_3$ finds extensive use as a Friedel–Crafts catalyst (p. 236): its annual production approaches 100 000 tpa and is dominated by Western Europe, USA and Japan. The price for bulk AlCl$_3$ is about $0.35/kg.

AlF$_3$ differs from the other trihalides of Al in being involatile and insoluble, and in having a much greater heat of formation (Table 7.6). These differences probably stem from differences in coordination number (6 for AlF$_3$; change from 6 to 4 at mp for AlCl$_3$; 4 for AlBr$_3$ and AlI$_3$) and from the subtle interplay of a variety of other factors mentioned below, rather than from any discontinuous change in bond type between the fluoride and the other halides. Similar differences dictated by change in coordination number are noted for many other metal halides, e.g. SnF$_4$ and SnX$_4$ (p. 381), BiF$_3$ and BiX$_3$ (p. 559), etc., and even more dramatically for some oxides such as CO$_2$ and SiO$_2$. In AlF$_3$ each Al is surrounded by

Table 7.6   Properties of crystalline AlX$_3$

Property	AlF$_3$	AlCl$_3$	AlBr$_3$	AlI$_3$
MP/°C	1290	192.4	97.8	189.4
Sublimation pt (1 atm)/°C	1272	180	256	382
$\Delta H_f^°$/kJ mol^{-1}	1498	707	527	310

[25a] A. ECKER and H.-G. SCHNÖCKEL, *Z. anorg. allg. Chem.* **622**, 149–52 (1996).

a distorted octahedron of 6 F atoms and the 1:3 stoichiometry is achieved by the corner sharing of each F between 2 octahedra. The structure is thus related to the ReO_3 structure (p. 1047) but is somewhat distorted from ideal symmetry for reasons which are not understood. Maybe the detailed crystal structure data are wrong.[26] The relatively "open" lattice of AlF_3 provides sites for water molecules and permits the formation of a range of nonstoichiometric hydrates. In addition, well-defined hydrates $AlF_3.nH_2O$ ($n = 1, 3, 9$) are known but, curiously, no hexahydrate corresponding to the familiar $[Al(H_2O)_6]Cl_3$. In the gas phase at $1000°C$ the AlF_3 molecule has trigonal planar symmetry (D_{3h})[27] with $Al-F$ 163.0(3) pm which is considerably shorter than in the solid phase 170–190 pm (for 6-coordinate Al).

The complex fluorides of Al^{III} (and Fe^{III}) provide a good example of a family of structures with differing stoichiometries all derived by the sharing of vertices between octahedral $\{AlF_6\}$ units;[26] edge sharing and face sharing are not observed, presumably because of the destabilizing influence of the close (repulsive) approach of 2 Al atoms each of which carries a net partial positive charge. Discrete $\{AlF_6\}$ units occur in cryolite, Na_3AlF_6, and in the garnet structure $Li_3Na_3Al_2F_{12}$ (i.e. $[Al_2Na_3(LiF_4)_3]$, see p. 348) but it is misleading to think in terms of $[AlF_6]^{3-}$ ions since the Al–F bonds are not appreciably different from the other M–F bonds in the structure. Thus the Na_3AlF_6 structure is closely related to perovskite ABO_3 (p. 963) in which one-third of the Na and all the Al atoms occupy octahedral $\{MF_6\}$ sites and the remaining two-thirds of the Na occupy the 12-coordinate sites. When two opposite vertices of $\{AlF_6\}$ are shared the stoichiometry becomes $\{AlF_5\}$ as in $Tl_2^IAlF_5$ (and $Tl_2^IGaF_5$). The sharing of 4 equatorial vertices of $\{AlF_6\}$ leads to the stoichiometry $\{AlF_4\}$ in Tl^IAlF_4. The same structural motif is found in each of the "isoelectronic" 6-coordinate layer lattices of $K_2Mg^{II}F_4$, $KAl^{III}F_4$ and $Sn^{IV}F_4$, none of which contain tetrahedral $\{MF_4\}$ units.

More complex patterns of sharing give intermediate stoichiometries as in $Na_5Al_3F_{14}$ which features layers of $\{Al_3F_{14}^{5-}\}$ built up by one-third of the $\{AlF_6\}$ octahedra sharing 4 equatorial vertices and the remainder sharing 2 opposite vertices. Again, Na_2MgAlF_7 comprises linked $\{AlF_6\}$ and $\{MgF_6\}$ octahedra in which 4 vertices of $\{AlF_6\}$ and all vertices of $\{MgF_6\}$ are shared. Likewise, $Sm^{II}AlF_5$ features $\{Al_2F_{10}^{4-}\}$ bioctahedra and linear chains of *trans* corner-sharing $\{AlF_6\}$,[28] and $Ba_3Al_2F_{12}$ has a tetrameric $\{(F_4AlF_{2/2})_4^{8-}\}$ ring, i.e $[Ba_6F_4(Al_4F_{20})]$,[29] which is unique for fluorometallates, being previously encountered only in neutral molecules $(MF_5)_4$ where M is Nb, Ta (p. 990); Mo, W (p. 1020); Ru, Os (p. 1083). In all of these structures the degree of charge separation, though considerable, is unlikely to approach the formal group charges: thus AlF_3 should not be regarded as a network of alternating ions Al^{3+} and F^- nor, at the other extreme, as an alternating set of Al^{3+} and AlF_6^{3-}, and lattice energies calculated on the basis of such formal charges placed at the observed interatomic distances are bound to be of limited reliability. Equally, the structure is not well described as a covalently bonded network of Al atoms and F atoms, and detailed MO calculations would be required to assess the actual extent of charge separation, on the one hand, and of interatomic covalent bonding, on the other.

The structure of $AlCl_3$ is similarly revealing. The crystalline solid has a layer lattice with 6-coordinate Al but at the mp 192.4° the structure changes to a 4-coordinate molecular dimer Al_2Cl_6; as a result there is a dramatic increase in volume (by 85%) and an even more dramatic drop in electrical conductivity almost to zero. The mp therefore represents a substantial change in the nature of the bonding. The covalently bonded

[26] A. F. WELLS, *Structural Inorganic Chemistry*, 4th edn., Oxford University Press, Oxford, 1975, 1095 pp.

[27] M. HARGITTAI, M. KOLONITS, J. TREMMEL, J.-L. FOURQUET and G. FEREY, *Struct. Chem.* **1**, 75–8 (1989).

[28] J. KÖHLER, *Z. anorg. allg. Chem.* **619**, 181–8 (1993).

[29] R. DOMESLE and R. HOPPE, *Angew. Chem. Int. Edn. Engl.* **19**, 489–90 (1980).

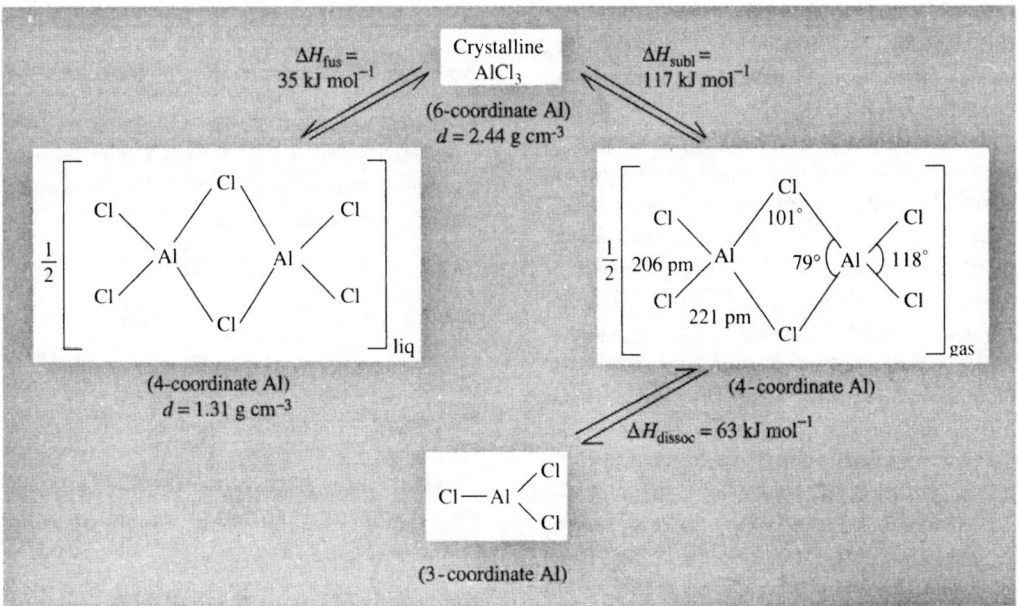

molecular dimers are also the main species in the gas phase at low temperatures ($\sim 150-200°$) but at higher temperature there is an increasing tendency to dissociate into trigonal planar $AlCl_3$ molecules isostructural with BX_3 (p. 196).

By contrast, Al_2Br_6 and Al_2I_6 form dimeric molecular units in the crystalline phase as well as in the liquid and gaseous states and fusion is not attended by such extensive changes in properties. In the gas phase $\Delta H_{dissoc} = 59\,kJ\,mol^{-1}$ for $AlBr_3$ and $50\,kJ\,mol^{-1}$ for AlI_3. In all these dimeric species, as in the analogous dimers Ga_2Cl_6, Ga_2Br_6, Ga_2I_6 and In_2I_6, the $M-X_t$ distance is $10-20\,pm$ shorter than the $M-X_\mu$ distance; the external angle X_tMX_t is in the range $110-125°$ whereas the internal angle $X_\mu MX_\mu$ is in the range $79-102°$

The trihalides of Al form a large number of addition compounds or complexes and these have been extensively studied because of their importance in understanding the nature of Friedel–Crafts catalysis.[30,31] The adducts vary enormously in stability from weak interactions to very stable complexes, and they also vary widely in their mode of bonding, structure and

properties. Aromatic hydrocarbons and olefins interact weakly though in some cases crystalline adducts can be isolated, e.g. the clathrate-like complex $Al_2Br_6.C_6H_6$, mp 37° (decomp). With mesitylene ($C_6H_3Me_3$) and the xylenes ($C_6H_4Me_2$) the interaction is slightly stronger, leading to dissociation of the dimer and the formation of weak monomeric complexes $AlBr_3L$ both in solution and in the solid state. At the other end of the stability scale NMe_3 forms two crystalline complexes: $[AlCl_3(NMe_3)]$ mp 156.9° which features molecular units with 4-coordinate tetrahedral Al, and $[AlCl_3(NMe_3)_2]$ which has 5-coordinate Al with trigonal bipyramidal geometry and *trans* axial ligands. By contrast, the adduct $AlCl_3.3NH_3$ has been shown by X-ray diffraction analysis to consist of elongated octahedra $[AlCl_2(NH_3)_4]^+$ and compressed octahedra $[AlCl_4(NH_3)_2]^-$, the

[30] N. N. GREENWOOD and K. WADE, Chap. 7 in G. A. OLAH (ed.), *Friedel–Crafts and Related Reactions*, Vol. 1, pp. 569–622, Interscience, New York, 1963.

[31] K. WADE and A. J. BANISTER, Chap. 12 in *Comprehensive Inorganic Chemistry*, Vol. 1, pp. 993–1172, Pergamon Press, Oxford, 1973.

arrangement being further stabilized by a network of N–H$\cdots$Cl hydrogen bonds.[32]

Alkyl halides interact rather weakly and vibrational spectroscopy suggests bonding of the type R–X$\cdots$AlX$_3$. However, for readily ionizable halides such as Ph$_3$CCl the degree of charge separation is much more extensive and the complex can be formulated as Ph$_3$C$^+$AlCl$_4^-$. Acyl halides RCOX may interact either through the carbonyl oxygen, PhC(Cl)=O$\rightarrow$AlCl$_3$, or through the halogen, RCOX$\cdots$AlX$_3$ or RCO$^+$AlX$_4^-$. Again, vibrational spectroscopy is a sensitive, though not always reliable, diagnostic for the mode of bonding. X-ray crystal structures of several complexes have been obtained but these do not necessarily establish the predominant species in nonaqueous solvents because of the delicate balance between the various factors which determine the structure (p. 198). Even in the crystalline state the act of coordination may lead to substantial charge separation. For example, X-ray analysis has established that AlCl$_3$ICl$_3$ comprises chains of alternating units which are best described as ICl$_2^+$ and AlCl$_4^-$ with rather weaker interactions between the ions.

Another instructive example is the ligand POCl$_3$ which forms 3 crystalline complexes AlCl$_3$POCl$_3$ mp 186.5°, AlCl$_3$(POCl$_3$)$_2$ mp 164° (d), and AlCl$_3$(POCl$_3$)$_6$ mp 41° (d). Although the crystal structures of these adducts have not been established it is known that POCl$_3$ normally coordinates through oxygen rather than chlorine and very recently a Raman spectroscopic study of the 1:1 adduct in the gas phase suggests that it is indeed Cl$_3$P=O$\rightarrow$AlCl$_3$ with C_s symmetry.[33] Also consistent with oxygen ligation is the observation that there is no exchange of radioactive ^{36}Cl when AlCl$_3$ containing ^{36}Cl is dissolved in inactive POCl$_3$. However, such solutions are good electrical conductors and spectroscopy reveals AlCl$_4^-$ as a predominant solute species. The resolution of this apparent paradox was provided by means of ^{27}Al nmr spectroscopy[34] which showed that ionization occurred according to the reaction

$$4AlCl_3 + 6POCl_3 \longrightarrow [Al(OPCl_3)_6]^{3+} + 3[AlCl_4]^-$$

It can be seen that all the Cl atoms in [AlCl$_4$]$^-$ come from the AlCl$_3$. It was further shown that the same two species predominated when Al$_2$I$_6$ was dissolved in an excess of POCl$_3$:

$$2Al_2I_6 + 12POCl_3 \rightleftharpoons 4\{AlCl_3\} + 12POCl_2I$$

$$4\{AlCl_3\} + 6POCl_3 \longrightarrow [Al(OPCl_3)_6]^{3+}$$
$$+ 3[AlCl_4]^-$$

No mixed Al species were found by ^{27}Al nmr in this case.

AlCl$_3$ is a convenient starting material for the synthesis of a wide range of other Al compounds, e.g.:

$$AlCl_3 + 3LiY \longrightarrow 3LiCl + AlY_3$$
$$(Y = R, NR_2, N=CR_2)$$

$$AlCl_3 + 4LiY \longrightarrow 3LiCl + LiAlY_4$$
$$(Y = R, NR_2, N=CR_2, H)$$

Similarly, NaOR reacts to give Al(OR)$_3$ and NaAl(OR)$_4$. AlCl$_3$ also converts non-metal fluorides into the corresponding chloride, e.g.

$$BF_3 + AlCl_3 \longrightarrow AlF_3 + BCl_3$$

This type of transhalogenation reaction, which is common amongst the halides of main group elements, always proceeds in the direction which pairs the most electropositive element with the most electronegative, since the greatest amount of energy is evolved with this combination.[35]

The major industrial use of AlCl$_3$ is in catalytic reactions of the type first observed in 1877 by C. Friedel and J. M. Crafts. AlCl$_3$ is now extensively used to effect alkylations (with RCl, ROH or RCH=CH$_2$), acylations (with RCOCl), and

---

[32] H. JACOBS and B.NÖCKER, *Z. anorg. allg. Chem.* **619**, 73–6 (1993).

[33] S. BOGHOSIAN, D. A. KARYDIS and G. A. VOYIATZIS, *Polyhedron* **12**, 771–82 (1993).

[34] R. G. KIDD and D. R. TRUAX, *J. Chem. Soc., Chem. Commun.*, 160–1 (1969).

[35] F. SEEL, *Atomic Structure and Chemical Bonding*, 4th edn. translated and revised by N. N. GREENWOOD and H. P. STADLER, Methuen, London, 1963, pp. 83–4.

various condensation, polymerization, cyclization, and isomerization reactions.[36] The reactions are examples of the more general class of electrophilic reactions that are catalysed by metal halides and other Lewis acids (electron pair acceptors). Of the 30 000 tonnes of $AlCl_3$ produced annually in the USA, about 15% is used in the synthesis of anthraquinones for the dyestuffs industry:

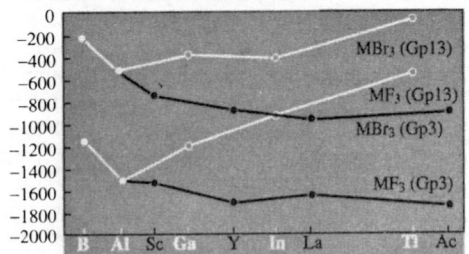

A further 15% of the $AlCl_3$ is used in the production of ethyl benzene for styrene manufacture, and 13% in making EtCl or EtBr (for $PbEt_4$):

$$CH_2{=}CH_2 + PhH \xrightarrow{AlCl_3} PhEt$$

$$CH_2{=}CH_2 + HX \xrightarrow{AlCl_3} EtX$$

The isomerization of hydrocarbons in the petroleum industry and the production of dodecyl benzene for detergents accounts for a further 10% each of the $AlCl_3$ used.

Trihalides of gallium, indium and thallium

These compounds have been mentioned several times in the preceding sections. As with AlX_3 (p. 233), the trifluorides are involatile and have much higher mps and heats of formation than the other trihalides;[31] e.g. GaF_3 melts above 1000°, sublimes at ~950° and has the 6-coordinate FeF_3-type structure, whereas $GaCl_3$ melts at 77.8°, boils at 201.2°, and has the 4-coordinate molecular structure Ga_2Cl_6. GaF_3 and

InF_3 are best prepared by thermal decomposition of $(NH_4)_3MF_6$, e.g.:

$$(NH_4)_3InF_6 \xrightarrow{120-170°} NH_4InF_4 \xrightarrow{300°} InF_3$$

Preparations using aqueous HF on $M(OH)_3$, M_2O_3, or M metal give the trihydrate. TlF_3 is best prepared by the direct fluorination of Tl_2O_3 with F_2, BrF_3 or SF_4 at 300°. Trends in the heats of formation of the Group 13 trihalides show the same divergence from BX_3, AlX_3 and the Group 3 trihalides as was found for trends in other properties such as I_M, $E°$ and χ (pp. 223–5) and for the same reasons. For example, the data for $\Delta H_f°$ for the trifluorides and tribromides are compared in Fig. 7.7 from which it is clear that the trend noted for the sequence B, Al, Sc, Y, La, Ac is not followed for the Group 13 metal trihalides which become progressively less stable from Al to Tl.

The volatile trihalides MX_3 form several ranges of addition compounds MX_3L, MX_3L_2, MX_3L_3, and these have been extensively studied because of the insight they provide on the relative influence of the underlying d^{10} electron configuration on the structure and stability of the complexes. With halide ions X^- as ligands the stoichiometry depends sensitively on crystal lattice effects or on the nature of the solvent and the relative concentration of the species in solution. Thus X-ray studies have established the tetrahedral ions $[GaX_4]^-$, $[InCl_4]^-$, etc., and these persist in ethereal

[36] G. A. OLAH (ed.), *Friedel–Crafts and Related Reactions*, Vols. 1–4, Interscience, New York, 1963. See especially Chap. 1, Historical, by G. A. OLAH and R. E. A. DEAR, and Chap. 2, Definition and scope by G. A. OLAH.

$\Delta H_f° (MF_3)$ and $\Delta H_f° (MBr_3)/kJ\,mol^{-1}$

Figure 7.7   Trends in the standard enthalpies of formation $\Delta H_f°$ for Groups 3 and 13 trihalides as illustrated by data for MF_3 and MBr_3.

solution, though in aqueous solution $[InCl_4]^-$ loses its T_d symmetry due to coordination of further molecules of H_2O. $[NEt_4]_2[InCl_5]$ is remarkable in featuring a square-pyramidal ion of C_{4v} symmetry (Fig. 7.8) and was one of the first recorded examples of this geometry in nontransition element chemistry (1969), cf SbPh$_5$ on p. 598 and the hydrido aluminate species on p. 231. The structure is apparently favoured by electrostatic packing considerations though it also persists in nonaqueous solution, possibly due to the formation of a pseudo-octahedral solvate $[InCl_5S]^{2-}$. It will be noted that $[InCl_5]^{2-}$ is not isostructural with the isoelectronic species $SnCl_5^-$ and $SbCl_5$ which have the more common D_{3h} symmetry. Substituted 5-coordinate chloroderivatives of In^{III} and Tl^{III} often have geometries intermediate between square pyramidal and trigonal bipyramidal.[37]

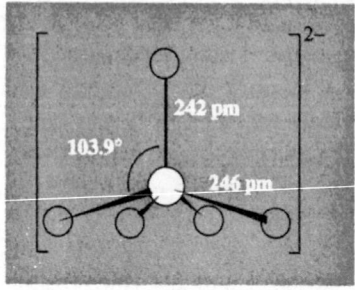

Figure 7.8 The structure of $InCl_5^{2-}$ showing square-pyramidal (C_{4v}) geometry. The In–Cl$_{apex}$ distance is significantly shorter than the In–Cl$_{base}$ distances and In is 59 pm above the basal plane; this leads to a Cl$_{apex}$–In–Cl$_{base}$ angle of 103.9° which is very close to the theoretical value required to minimize Cl$\cdots$Cl repulsions whilst still retaining C_{4v} symmetry (103.6°) calculated on the basis of a simple inverse square law for repulsion between ligands. $[NEt_4]_2[TlCl_5]$ is isomorphous with $[NEt_4]_2[InCl_5]$ and presumably has a similar structure for the anion.

With neutral ligands, L, GaX$_3$ tend to resemble AlX$_3$ in forming predominantly MX$_3$L and some MX$_3$L$_2$, whereas InX$_3$ are more varied.[38] InX$_3$L$_3$ is the commonest stoichiometry for N and O donors and these are probably predominantly 6-coordinate in the solid state, though in coordinating solvents (S) partial dissociation into ions frequently occurs:

$$InX_3L_3 + S \longrightarrow [InX_2SL_3]^+ + X^-$$

More extensive ionization occurs if, instead of the halides X$^-$, a less strongly coordinating anion Y$^-$ such as ClO$_4^-$ or NO$_3^-$ is used; in such cases the coordinating stoichiometry tends to be 1:6, e.g. $[InL_6]^{3+}(Y^-)_3$, L = Me$_2$SO, Ph$_2$SO, (Me$_2$N)$_2$CO, HCO(NMe$_2$), P(OMe)$_3$, etc. Bulky ligands such as PPh$_3$ and AsPh$_3$ tend to give 1:4 adducts $[InL_4]^{3+}(Y^-)_3$. The same effect of ionic dissociation can be achieved in 1:3 complexes of the trihalides themselves by use of bidentate chelating ligands (B) such as en, bipy, or phen, e.g. $[InB_3]^{3+}(X^-)_3$ (X = Cl, Br, I, NCO, NCS, NCSe). InX$_3$ complexes having 1:2 stoichiometry also have a variety of structures. Trigonal bipyramidal geometry with axial ligands is found for InX$_3$L$_2$, where L = MNe$_3$, PMe$_3$, PPh$_3$, Et$_2$O, etc. By contrast, the crystal structure of the 1:2 complex of InI$_3$ with Me$_2$SO shows that it is fully ionized as $[cis\text{-}InI_2(OSMe_2)_4]^+[InI_4]^-$, and fivefold coordination is avoided by a disproportionation into 6- and 4-coordinate species. Complexes having 1:1 stoichiometry are rare for InX$_3$; InCl$_3$ forms $[InCl_3(OPCl_3)]$, $[InCl_3(OCMe_2)]$ and $[InCl_3(OCPh_2)]$ and py forms a 1:1 (and a 1:3) adduct with InI$_3$. Frequently, of course, a given donor–acceptor pair combines in more than one stoichiometric ratio.

The thermochemistry of the Group 13 trihalide complexes has been extensively studied[30,31,39] and several stability sequences have been

[37] R. O. DAY and R. R. HOLMES, *Inorg. Chem.* **21**, 2379–82 (1982). H. BORGHOLTE, K. DEHNICKE, H. GOESMANN and D. FENSKE, *Z. anorg. allg. Chem.* **600**, 7–14 (1991).

[38] A. J. CARTY and D. J. TUCK, *Prog. Inorg. Chem.* **19**, 243–337 (1975).

[39] N. N. GREENWOOD *et al.*, *Pure Appl. Chem.* **2**, 55–9 (1961); *J. Chem. Soc. A*, 267–70, 270–3, 703–6 (1966); *J. Chem. Soc. A*, 753–6 (1968); 249–53, 2876–8 (1969); *Inorg. Chem.* **9**, 86–90 (1970), and references therein. R. C. GEARHART, J. D. BECK and R. H. WOOD, *Inorg. Chem.* **14**, 2413–6 (1975).

established which can be interpreted in terms of the factors listed on p. 198. In addition, Ga and In differ from B and Al in having an underlying d^{10} configuration which can, in principle, take part in $d_\pi–d_\pi$ back bonding with donors such as S (but not N or O); alternatively (or additionally), some of the trends can be interpreted in terms of the differing polarizabilities of B and Al, as compared to Ga and In, the former pair behaving as class-a or "hard" acceptors whereas Ga and In frequently behave as class-b or "soft" acceptors. Again, it should be emphasized that these categories tend to provide descriptions rather than explanations. Towards amines and ethers the acceptor strengths as measured by gas-phase enthalpies of formation decrease in the sequence $MCl_3 > MBr_3 > MI_3$ for M = Al, Ga or In. Likewise, towards phosphines the acceptor strength decreases as $GaCl_3 > GaBr_3 > GaI_3$. However, towards the "softer" sulfur donors Me_2S, Et_2S and C_4H_8S, whilst AlX_3 retains the same sequence, the order for GaX_3 and InX_3 is reversed to read $MI_3 > MBr_3 > MCl_3$. A similar reversal is noted when the acceptor strengths of individual AlX_3 are compared with those of the corresponding GaX_3: towards N and O donors the sequence is invariably $AlX_3 > GaX_3$ but for S donors the relative acceptor strength is $GaX_3 > AlX_3$. These trends emphasize the variety of factors that contribute towards the strength of chemical bonds and indicate that there are no unique series of donor or acceptor strengths when the acceptor atom is varied, e.g.:

towards $MeCO_2Et$: $BCl_3 > AlCl_3 > GaCl_3 > InCl_3$

towards py: $AlPh_3 > GaPh_3 > BPh_3 \approx InPh_3$

towards py: $AlX_3 > BX_3 > GaX_3$ (X = Cl, Br)

towards Me_2S: $GaX_3 > AlX_3 > BX_3$ (X = Cl, Br)

Regularities are more apparent when the acceptor atom remains constant and the attached groups are varied; e.g., for all ligands so far studied the acceptor strength diminishes in the sequence

$$MX_3 > MPh_3 > MMe_3 \quad (M = B, Al, Ga, In)$$

It has also been found that halide-ion donors (such as X^- in AlX_4^- and GaX_4^-) are more than twice as strong as any neutral donor such as X in M_2X_6, or N, P, O and S donors in MX_3L.[39] Finally, the complexity of factors influencing the strength of such bonds can be gauged from the curious alternation of the gas-phase enthalpies of dissociation of the dimers M_2X_6 themselves; e.g. ΔH°_{298}(dissoc) for Al_2Cl_6, Ga_2Cl_6 and In_2Cl_6 are respectively 126.8, 93.9 and 121.5 kJ mol^{-1} [40] The corresponding entropies of dissociation ΔS°_{298} are 152.3, 150.4 and 136.0 J mol^{-1}.

The trihalides of Tl are much less stable than those of the lighter Group 13 metals and are chemically quite distinct from them. TlF_3, mp 550° (decomp), is a white crystalline solid isomorphous with β-BiF_3 (p. 560); it does not form hydrates but hydrolyses rapidly to $Tl(OH)_3$ and HF. Nor does it give TlF_4^- in aqueous solution, and the compounds $LiTlF_4$ and $NaTlF_4$ have structures related to fluorite, CaF_2 (p. 118): in $NaTlF_4$ the cations have very similar 8-coordinate radii (Na 116 pm, Tl 100 pm) and are disordered on the Ca sites (Ca 112 pm); in $LiTlF_4$, the smaller size of Li ($\sim$83 pm for eightfold coordination) favours a superlattice structure in which Li and Tl are ordered on the Ca sites. Na_3TlF_6 has the cryolite structure (p. 234).

$TlCl_3$ and $TlBr_3$ are obtained from aqueous solution as the stable tetrahydrates and $TlCl_3.4H_2O$ can be dehydrated with $SOCl_2$ to give anhydrous $TlCl_3$, mp 155°; it has the YCl_3-type structure which can be described as NaCl-type with two-thirds of the cations missing in an ordered manner.

TlI_3 is an intriguing compound which is isomorphous with NH_4I_3 and CsI_3 (p. 836); it therefore contains the linear I_3^- ion[†] and is a compound of Tl^I rather than Tl^{III}. It is obtained as black crystals by evaporating an equimolar solution of TlI and I_2 in concentrated aqueous HI. The formulation $Tl^I(I_3^-)$ rather than $Tl^{III}(I^-)_3$ is consistent with the standard reduction potentials $E^\circ(Tl^{III}/Tl^I) + 1.26$ V and $E^\circ(\frac{1}{2}I_2/I^-) + 0.54$ V,

40 K. KRAUSZE, H. OPPERMANN, U. BRUHN and M. BALARIN, *Z. anorg. allg. Chem.* **550**, 116–22 (1987).

[†] Note that this X-ray evidence by itself does not rule out the possibility that the compound is $[I–Tl^{III}–I]^+I^-$.

which shows that uncomplexed Tl^{III} is susceptible to rapid and complete reduction to Tl^I by I^- in acid solution. The same conclusion follows from a consideration of the $I_3^-/3I^-$ couple for which $E° = +0.55\,V$. Curiously, however, in the presence of an excess of I^-, the Tl^{III} state is stabilized by complex formation

$$Tl^I I_3(s) + I^- \rightleftharpoons [Tl^{III} I_4]^-$$

Moreover, solutions of TlI_3 in MeOH do not show the visible absorption spectrum of I_3^- and, when shaken with aqueous Na_2CO_3, give a precipitate of Tl_2O_3, i.e.:

$$2TlI_3 + 6OH^- \rightleftharpoons Tl_2O_3 + 6I^- + 3H_2O$$

This is due partly to the great insolubility of Tl_2O_3 ($2.5 \times 10^{-10}\,g\,l^{-1}$ at $25°$) and partly to the enhanced oxidizing power of iodine in alkaline solution as a result of the formation of hypoiodate:

$$I_3^- + 2OH^- \rightleftharpoons OI^- + 2I^- + H_2O$$

Consistent with this, even KI_3 is rapidly decolorized in alkaline solution. The example is a salutory reminder of the influence of pH, solubility, and complex formation on the standard reduction potentials of many elements.

Numerous tetrahedral halogeno complexes $[Tl^{III}X_4]^-$ (X = Cl, Br, I) have been prepared by reaction of quaternary ammonium or arsonium halides on TlX_3 in nonaqueous solution, and octahedral complexes $[Tl^{III}X_6]^{3-}$ (X = Cl, Br) are also well established. The binuclear complex $Cs_3[Tl_2^{III}Cl_9]$ is an important structural type which features two $TlCl_6$ octahedra sharing a common face of 3 bridging Cl atoms (Fig. 7.9); the same binuclear complex structure is retained when Tl^{III} is replaced by Ti^{III}, V^{III}, Cr^{III} and Fe^{III} and also in $K_3W_2Cl_9$ and $Cs_3Bi_2I_9$, etc.

Lower halides of gallium, indium and thallium

Like AlX (p. 233), GaF and InF are known as unstable gaseous species. The other monohalides are more stable. GaX can be obtained as reactive sublimates by treating GaX_3 with

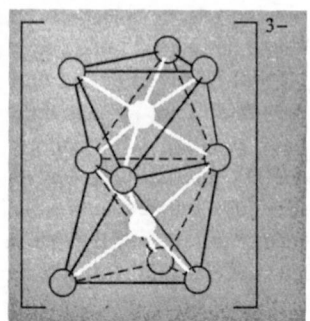

Figure 7.9 The structure of the ion $[Tl_2Cl_9]^{3-}$ showing two octahedral $TlCl_6$ units sharing a common face: $Tl-Cl_t$ 254 pm, $Tl-Cl_\mu$ 266 pm. The $Tl \cdots Tl$ distance is nonbonding (281 pm. cf. $2 \times Tl^{III} =$ 177 pm).

2Ga: stability increases with increasing size of the anion and GaI melts at $271°$. Stability is still further enhanced by coordination of the anion with, for example, AlX_3 to give $Ga^I[Al^{III}X_4]$. Likewise, the very stable "dihalides" $Ga^I[Ga^{III}Cl_4]$, $Ga[GaBr_4]$, and $Ga[GaI_4]$ can be prepared by heating equimolar amounts of GaX_3 and Ga, or more conveniently by halogenation of Ga with the stoichiometric amount of Hg_2X_2 or HgX_2. They form complexes of the type $[Ga^IL_4]^+[Ga^{III}X_4]^-$ with a wide range of N, As, O, S and Se donors. See also p. 264 for arene complexes of the type $[Ga^I(ar)_n]^+[Ga^{III}X_4]^-$. Note, however, that the complexes with dioxan $[Ga_2X_4(C_4H_8O_2)_2]$, do in fact contain Ga^{II} and a Ga–Ga bond, e.g. the chloro complex is a discrete molecule with Ga–Ga 240.6 pm (cf. 239.0 pm in $Ga_2Cl_6^{2-}$);[41] the coordination about each Ga atom is essentially tetrahedral and the compound surprisingly adopts an essentially eclipsed structure rather than the staggered structure of $Ga_2Cl_6^{2-}$. Likewise $[Ga_2I_4.2L]$, where L is a wide range of organic ligands with N, P, O or S donor atoms, have been shown by vibration spectroscopy to have a Ga–Ga bond.[42]

[41] J. C. BEAMISH, R. W. H. SMALL and I. J. WORRALL, *Inorg. Chem.* **18**, 220–3 (1979).

[42] J. C. BEAMISH, A. BOARDMAN and I. J. WORRALL, *Polyhedron* **10**, 95–9 (1991).

Indium monohalides, InX, can be prepared as red crystals either directly from the elements or by heating In metal with HgX_2 at 320–350°. They have a TlI-type structure (p. 242) with $[1 + 4 + 2]$ rather than 6-fold coordination of In by X, leading to rather close $In^I \ldots In^I$ contacts of 362, 356 and 357 pm respectively for X = Cl, Br and I.[43] Again, InI is the most stable, and mixed halides of the type $In^I[Al^{III}Cl_4]$, $In^I[Ga^{III}Cl_4]$ and $Tl^I[In^{III}Cl_4]$ are known. Numerous intermediate halides have also been reported and structural assignments of varying degrees of reliability have been suggested, e.g. $In^I[In^{III}X_4]$ for InX_2 (Cl, Br, I); and $In_3^I[In^{III}Cl_6]$ for In_2Cl_3. In contrast to the chloride, In_2Br_3 has the unexpected structure $[(In^+)_2 (In_2^{II}Br_6)^{2-}]$.[44] The compounds In_4X_7 and In_5X_7 (Cl, Br) and In_7Br_9 are also known. In all of these halides the observed stoichiometry is achieved by varying the ratio of In^I to In^{II} or In^{III}, e.g. $[(In^+)_5(InBr_4^-)_2(InBr_6^{3-})]$, $[(In^+)_3(In_2Br_6^{2-})Br^-]$ and $[(In^+)_6(InBr_6^{3-})-(Br^-)_3]$.[45,46] Compounds containing In^{II} were unknown until 1976 when the $[In_2X_6]^{2-}$ dianions having an ethane-like structure were prepared:[47]

$$2Bu_4NX + In_2X_4 \xrightarrow{\text{xylene}} [NBu_4]^+{}_2[X_3In\text{–}InX_3]^{2-}$$

$$(X = Cl, Br, I)$$

[43] G. MEYER and T. STAFFEL, *Z. anorg. allg. Chem.* **574**, 114–8 (1989).

[44] T. STAFFEL and G. MEYER, *Z. anorg. allg. Chem.* **552**, 113–22 (1987).

[45] J. E. DAVIES, L. G. WATERWORTH and I. J. WORRALL, *J. Inorg. Nucl. Chem.* **36**, 805–7 (1974).

[46] T. STAFFEL and G. MEYER, *Z. anorg. allg. Chem.* **563** 27–37 (1988). See also correction in R. E. MARSH and G. MEYER, *Z. anorg. allg. Chem.* **582**, 128–30 (1990).

[47] B. H. FREELAND, J. L. HENCHER, D. G. TUCK and J. G. CONTRERAS, *Inorg. Chem.* **15**, 2144–6 (1976). See also D. G. TUCK, *Polyhedron* **9**, 377–86 (1990).

The analogous Ga compounds, e.g. $[NEt_4]_2[Cl_3$-Ga–$GaCl_3]$, have been known for rather longer (1965). Oxidation of $In_2X_6^{2-}$ with halogens Y_2 yields the mononuclear mixed halide complexes InX_3Y^- and $InX_2Y_2^-$ ($X \neq Y = Cl, Br, I$).[48]

Thallium(I) is the stable oxidation state for the halides of this element (p. 226) and some physical properties are in Table 7.7. TlF is readily obtained by the action of aqueous HF on Tl_2CO_3; it is very soluble in water (in contrast to the other TlX) and has a distorted NaCl structure in which there are 3 pairs of Tl–F distances at 259, 275 and 304 pm. TlCl, TlBr and TlI are all prepared by addition of the appropriate halide ion to acidified solutions of soluble Tl^I salts (e.g. perchlorate, sulfate, nitrate). TlCl and TlBr have the CsCl structure (p. 80) as befits the large Tl^I cation and both salts (and TlI) are photosensitive (like AgX). Yellow TlI has a curious orthorhombic layer structure related to NaCl (Fig. 7.10), and this transforms at 175° or at 4.7 kbar to a metastable red cubic form with 8-iodine neighbours at 364 pm (CsCl type). This transformation is accompanied by 3% reduction in volume. Further application of pressure steadily reduces the volume and at pressures above about 160 kbar, when the volume has decreased by about 35%, the compound becomes a metallic conductor with a resistivity of the order of 10^{-4} ohm cm at room temperature and a positive temperature coefficient. TlCl and TlBr behave similarly. All three compounds are excellent insulators at normal pressures with negligible conductivity and an energy gap between the valence band and conduction band

[48] J. E. DRAKE, J. L. HENCHER, L. N. KHASROU, D. G. TUCK and L. VICTORIANO, *Inorg. Chem.* **19**, 34–8 (1980).

Table 7.7   Some properties of TlX

Property	TlF	TlCl	TlBr	TlI
MP/°C	322	431	460	442
BP/°C	826	720	815	823
Colour	White	White	Pale yellow	Yellow
Crystal structure	Distorted NaCl	CsCl	CsCl	See text
Solubility/g per 100 g H_2O (°C)	80 (15°)	0.33 (20°)	0.058 (25°)	0.006 (20°)
$\Delta H_f°/kJ\,mol^{-1}$	−326	−204	−173	−124

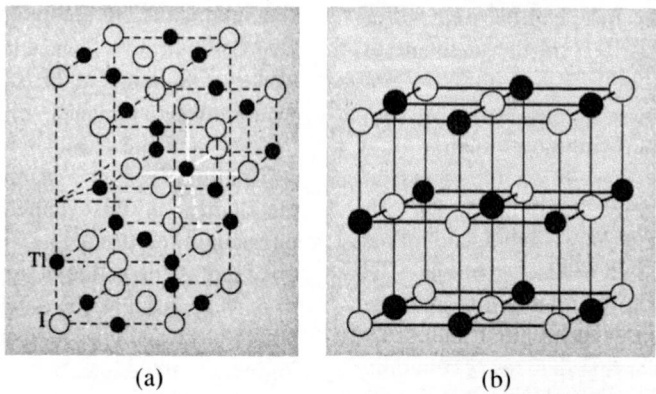

(a)   (b)

Figure 7.10   Structure of yellow TlI (a) showing its relation to NaCl (b). Tl has 5 nearest-neighbour I atoms at 5 of the vertices of an octahedron and then 2I + 2Tl as next-nearest neighbours; there is one I at 336 pm. 4 at 349 pm, and 2 at 387 pm, and the 2 close Tl–Tl approaches, one at 383 pm. InX (X = Cl, Br, I) have similar structures in their red forms.[43]

of about 3 eV ($\sim$300 kJ mol^{-1}), and the onset of metallic conduction is presumably due to the spreading and eventual overlap of the two bands as the atoms are forced closer together.[49]

Several other lower halides of Tl are known: $TlCl_2$ and $TlBr_2$ are $Tl^I[Tl^{III}X_4]$, Tl_2Cl_3 and Tl_2Br_3 are $Tl_3^I[Tl^{III}X_6]$. In addition there is Tl_3I_4, which is formed as an intermediate in the preparation of $Tl^I I_3$ from TlI and I_2 (p. 239).

7.3.3 Oxides and hydroxides

The structural relations between the many crystalline forms of aluminium oxide and hydroxide are exceedingly complex but they are of exceptional scientific interest and immense technological importance. The principal structural types are listed in Table 7.8 and many intermediate and related structures are also known. Al_2O_3 occurs as the mineral corundum (α-Al_2O_3, d 4.0 g cm^{-3}) and as emery, a granular form of corundum contaminated with iron oxide and silica. Because of its great hardness (Mohs 9),[†] high mp (2045°C), involatility (10^{-6} atm at 1950°), chemical inertness and good electrical

insulating properties, it finds many applications in abrasives (including toothpaste), refractories, and ceramics, in addition to its major use in the electrolytic production of Al metal (p. 219). Larger crystals, when coloured with metal-ion impurities, are prized as gemstones, e.g. ruby (Cr^{III} red), sapphire ($Fe^{II/III}$, Ti^{IV} blue), oriental emerald (?Cr^{III}/V^{III} green), oriental amethyst (Cr^{III}/Ti^{IV} violet) and oriental topaz (Fe^{III}, yellow). Many of these gems are also made industrially on a large scale by the fusion process first developed at the turn of the century by A. Verneuil. Pure α-Al_2O_3 is made industrially by igniting $Al(OH)_3$ or $AlO(OH)$ at high temperatures ($\sim$1200°); it is also formed by the combustion of Al and by calcination of various Al salts. It has a rhombohedral crystal structure comprising a hcp array of oxide ions with Al ordered on two-thirds of the octahedral interstices as shown in Fig. 7.11.[26] The same α-M_2O_3 structure is adopted by several other elements with small M^{III} (r 62–67 pm), e.g. Ga, Ti, V, Cr, Fe and Rh.[‡]

[49] G. A. SAMARA and H. G. DRICKAMER, *J. Chem. Phys.* **37**, 408–10 (1962); see also E. A. PEREZ-ALBUERNE and H. G. DRICKAMER, *J. Chem. Phys.* **43**, 1381–7 (1965).

[†] On the Mohs scale diamond is 10 and quartz 7. An alternative measure is the Knoop hardness (kg mm^{-2}) as measured with a 100-g load: typical values on this scale are diamond 7000, boron carbide 2750, corundum 2100, topaz 1340, quartz 820, hardened tool steel 740.

[‡] For somewhat larger cations (r 70–96 pm) the C-type rare-earth M_2O_3 structure (p. 1238) is adopted, e.g. for In,

Table 7.8 The main structural types of aluminium oxides and hydroxides[a]

Formula	Mineral name	Idealized structure
α-Al_2O_3	Corundum	hcp O with Al in two-thirds of the octahedral sites
α-AlO(OH)	Diaspore	hcp O (OH) with chains of octahedra stacked in layers interconnected with H bonds, and Al in certain octahedral sites
α-Al(OH)$_3$	Bayerite	hcp (OH) with Al in two-thirds of the octahedral sites
γ-Al_2O_3	—	ccp O defect spinel with Al in $21\frac{1}{3}$ of the 16 octahedral and 8 tetrahedral sites
γ-AlO(OH)	Boehmite	ccp O (OH) within layers; details uncertain
γ-Al(OH)$_3$	Gibbsite (Hydrargillite)	ccp OH within layers of edge-shared Al(OH)$_6$; octahedra stacked vertically via H bonds

[a]The Greek prefixes α- and γ- are not used consistently in the literature, e.g. bayerite is sometimes designated as β-Al(OH)$_3$ and gibbsite as α-Al(OH)$_3$. The UK usage adopted here is consistent with Wells[26] and emphasizes the structural relations between the hcp α-series and the ccp γ-series. Numerous other intermediate crystalline phases have been characterized during partial dehydration and designated as γ', δ, ζ, η, θ, κ, κ', ρ, χ, etc.

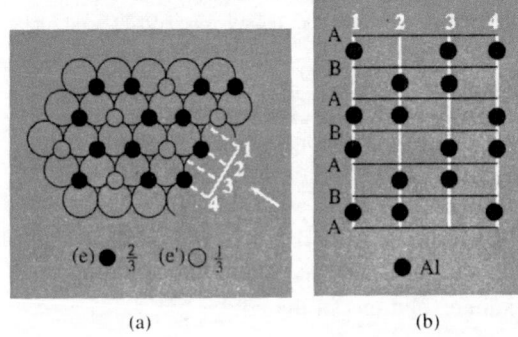

(a)   (b)

Figure 7.11 Schematic representation of the structure of α-Al_2O_3. (a) pattern of occupancy by Al (●) of the octahedral sites between hcp layers of oxide ion (○), and (b) stacking sequence of successive planes of Al atoms viewed in the direction of the arrow in (a).

The second modification of alumina is the less compact cubic γ-Al_2O_3 (d 3.4 g cm^{-3}); it is formed by the low-temperature dehydration (<450°) of gibbsite, γ-Al(OH)$_3$, or boehmite, γ-AlO(OH). It has a defect spinel-type structure (p. 248) comprising a face-centred cubic (fcc) arrangement of 32 oxide ions and a random occupation of $21\frac{1}{3}$ of the 24 available cation sites (16 octahedral, 8 tetrahedral). This structure forms the basis of the so-called "activated aluminas" and progressive dehydration in the γ-series leads to open-structured materials of great value as catalysts, catalyst-supports, ion exchangers and chromatographic media. Calcination of γ-Al_2O_3 above 1000° converts it irreversibly to the more stable and compact α-form ($\Delta H_{trans} - 20$ kJ mol^{-1}). Yet another form of Al_2O_3 occurs as the protective surface layer on the metal: it has a defect NaCl-type structure with Al occupying two-thirds of the octahedral (Na) interstices in the fcc oxide lattice. Perhaps the most ingenious and sophisticated development in aluminium technology has been the recent production of Al_2O_3 fibres which can be fabricated into a variety of textile forms, blankets, papers, and boards. Some idea of the many possibilities of such high-temperature inert fabrics is indicated in the Panel on p. 244.

Diaspore, α-AlO(OH) occurs in some types of clay and bauxite; it is stable in the range 280–450° and can be made by hydrothermal treatment of boehmite, γ-AlO(OH), in 0.4% aqueous NaOH at 380° and 500 atm. Crystalline boehmite is readily prepared by warming the amorphous, gelatinous white precipitate which first forms when aqueous NH$_3$ is added to cold solutions of Al salts. In α-AlO(OH) the O atoms are arranged in hcp; continuous chains of edge-shared octahedra are stacked in layers

Tl, Sc, Y, Sm and the subsequent lanthanoids, and perhaps surprisingly for Mn^{III} (r 65 pm); the largest lanthanoids La, Ce, Pr and Nd (r 106–100 pm) adopt the A-type rare-earth M_2O_3 structure (p. 1238).

Fibrous Alumina and Zirconia[50,51]

A new family of lightweight inorganic fibres made its commercial debut in 1974 when ICI announced the production of "Saffil", fibrous Al_2O_3 and ZrO_2 on an initial scale of 100 tonnes pa. Du Pont also has a process for α-Al_2O_3 fibres and the current world production of fibrous Al_2O_3 is of the order of 1000 tonnes per annum. The price is about $60/kg (1986). The fibres, which have no demonstrable toxic effects (cf. asbestos), have a diameter of $\sim 3\,\mu$m (cf. human hair $\sim 70\,\mu$m), and each fibre is extremely uniform along its length (2–5 cm). The fibres are microcrystalline (5–50 pm diam) and are both flexible and resilient with a high tensile strength. They have a soft, silky feel and can be made into rope, yarn, cloth, blankets, fibre matts, paper of various thickness, semi-rigid and rigid boards, and vacuum-formed objects of any required shape. The surface area of Saffil alumina is 100–$150\,\mathrm{m}^2\,\mathrm{g}^{-1}$ due to the presence of small pores 2–10 pm diameter between the microcrystals, and this enhances its properties as an insulator, filtration medium, and catalyst support. The fibres withstand extended heating to 1400° (Al_2O_3) or 1600°C (ZrO_2) and are impervious to attack by hot concentrated alkalis and most hot acids except conc H_2SO_4, conc H_3PO_4 and aq HF. This unique combination of properties provides the basis for their use in high-temperature insulation, heat shields, thermal barriers, and expansion joints and seals. Fibrous alumina and zirconia are also valuable in thermocouple protection, electric-cable sheathing, and heating-element supports in addition to their use in the high-temperature filtration of corrosive liquids. Both oxides are stabilized by incorporation of small amounts of other inorganic oxides which inhibit disruptive transformation to other crystalline forms.

Alumina fibres can also be used to strengthen metals. Molten metals (e.g. Al, Mg, Pb) or their alloys are forced into moulds containing up to 70% by volume of α-Al_2O_3 fibre. For example, fibre-reinforced Al containing 55% fibre by volume is 4–6 times stiffer than unreinforced Al even up to 370°C and has 2–4 times the fatigue strength. Potential applications for which high structural stiffness, heat resistance, and low weight are required include helicopter housings, automotive and jet engines, aerospace structures and lead-acid batteries. For example, fibre reinforced composites of Al or Mg could eventually replace much of the steel used in car bodies without decreasing safety, since the composite has the stiffness of steel but only one-third of its density.

In addition to the production of stabilized Al_2O_3 fibres there is also a huge production of melt-spun glassy fibres containing approximately equal proportions by weight of Al_2O_3 and SiO_2. This is used mainly for thermal insulation at temperatures up to 1400°C and current world production exceeds 20 000 tonnes per annum.

and are further interconnected by H bonds. The underlying hcp structure ensures that diaspore dehydrates directly to α-Al_2O_3 (corundum) which has the same basic hcp arrangement of O atoms. The structure is also adopted by several other α-MO(OH) (M = Ga, V, Mn and Fe); this contrasts with the structure of boehmite, γ-AlO(OH), which as a whole is not close-packed, though within each layer the O atoms are arranged in cubic close packing. Dehydration at temperatures up to 450° proceeds via a succession of phases to the cubic γ-Al_2O_3 and the α (hexagonal) structure cannot be attained without much more reconstruction of the lattice at 1100–1200° as noted above [and of γ-ScO(OH) and γ-FeO(OH)].

Bayerite, α-$Al(OH)_3$, does not occur in nature but can be made by rapid precipitation from alkaline solutions in the cold:

$$2[Al(OH)_4]^- aq + CO_2(g) \longrightarrow$$
$$2Al(OH)_3 + CO_3{}^{2-}(aq) + H_2O$$

Gibbsite (or hydrargillite), γ-$Al(OH)_3$, is a more stable form and can be prepared by slow precipitation from warm alkaline solutions or by digesting the α-form in aqueous sodium aluminate solution at 80°. In both bayerite (α) and gibbsite (γ) there are layers of composition $Al(OH)_3$ built up by the edge sharing of $Al(OH)_6$ octahedra to give a pair of approximately close-packed OH layers with Al atoms in two-thirds of the octahedral interstices (Fig. 7.12a). The two crystalline modifications differ in the way this layer is stacked: it is approximately hcp in α-$Al(OH)_3$ but in the γ-form the OH groups on the under side of one layer rest directly above the OH groups of the layer below as shown in Fig. 7.12b. A third form of $Al(OH)_3$, nordstrandite, is obtained from the gelatinous

[50] J. D. BIRCHALL, J. A. A. BRADBURY and J. DINWOODIE, Chap IV in W. WATT and B. V. PEROV (eds.), *Handbook of Composites, Vol. 1, Strong Fibres*, Elsevier, Amsterdam, 1985, pp. 115–54. J. D. BIRCHALL, in M. B. BEVER (ed.) *Encyclopedia of Materials Science and Engineering*, Pergamon Press, Oxford, 1986, pp. 2333–5.

[51] W. BÜCHNER, R. SCHLIEBS, G. WINTER and K. H. BÜCHEL, *Industrial Inorganic Chemistry*, VCH, Weinheim, 1989, pp. 362–4.

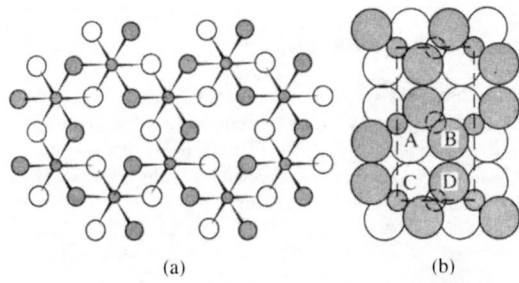

    (a)   (b)

Figure 7.12   (a) Part of a layer of $Al(OH)_3$ (idealized); the heavy and light open circles represent OH groups above and below the plane of the Al atoms. In α-$Al(OH)_3$ the layers are stacked to give approximately hcp. (b) Structure of γ-$Al(OH)_3$ viewed in a direction parallel to the layers; the OH groups labelled C and D are stacked directly beneath A and B. The six OH groups A, B, C, D and B', D' (behind B and D), form a distorted H-bonded trigonal prism.

hydroxide by ageing it in the presence of a chelating agent such as ethylenediamine, ethylene glycol, or edta; this aligns the OH to give a stacking arrangement which is intermediate between those of the α- and γ-forms.

As expected from the foregoing structural discussion, gibbsite can be dehydrated to boehmite at 100° and to anhydrous γ-Al_2O_3 at 150°, but ignition above 800° is required to form α-Al_2O_3. Numerous recipes have been devised for preparing catalysts of differing reactivity and absorptive power, based on the partial dehydration and progressive reconstitution of the Al/O/OH system.[1] In addition to pore size, surface area and general reactivity, the basic character of the surface diminishes (and its acidic character increases) in the following series as indicated by the pH of the isoelectric point:

(amorph. Al oxide hydrate)	$> \gamma$-AlO(OH) boehmite	$> \alpha$-$Al(OH)_3$ bayerite	$> \gamma$-$Al(OH)_3$ gibbsite	$> \gamma$-Al_2O_3
pH: 9.45 (isoelec. pt.)	9.45–9.40	9.20	–	8.00

The aqueous solution chemistry of Al and the other group 13 metals is rather complicated. The aquo ions are acidic with

$pK_A \approx 10^{-5}$, 10^{-3}, 10^{-4} and 10^{-1}, respectively, for $[M(H_2O)_6]^{3+} \rightleftharpoons [M(OH)(H_2O)_5]^{2+} + H^+$ (M = Al, Ga, In, Tl). The solution chemistry of Al in particular has been extensively investigated because of its industrial importance in water treatment plants, its use in many toiletry formulations, its possible implication in both Altzheimer's disease and the deleterious effects of acid rain, and the ubiquity of Al cooking utensils.[52–54] For example, hydrated aluminium sulphate ($10–30\,g\,m^{-3}$) can be added to turbid water supplies at pH 6.5–7.5 to flocculate the colloids, some 3 million tonnes per annum being used worldwide for this application alone. Likewise kilotonne amounts of "$Al(OH)_{2.5}Cl_{0.5}$" in concentrated (6M) aqueous solution are used in the manufacture of deodorants and antiperspirants.

The use of ^{27}Al nmr (see Panel) has been particularly valuable in characterizing the species present in aqueous solution of Al salts.[55] These depend very much on both concentration and pH and include the mononuclear ions $[Al(OH)_4]^-$, $[Al(H_2O_6)]^{3+}$ and $[Al(OH)(H_2O)_5]^{2+}$. This latter species can deprotonate further to $[Al(OH)_2(H_2O)_4]^+$ and readily dimerizes via hydroxyl bridges to $[(H_2O)_4Al(\mu\text{-}OH)_2Al(H_2O)_4]^{4+}$, i.e. $[H_{18}Al_2O_{10}]^{4+}$, which has also been found in several crystalline salts. Higher oligomers probably include appropriately hydrated forms of $[Al_3(OH)_{11}]^{2-}$, $[Al_6(OH)_{15}]^{3+}$ and $[Al_8(OH)_{22}]^{2+}$. A particularly important species is the well-characterized tridecameric cation $[Al_{13}O_4(OH)_{24}(H_2O)_{12}]^{7+}$ which has the well-known Keggin structure (p. 1014),

[52] H. SIGEL and A. SIGEL (eds), *Metal Ions in Biological Systems*, Vol. 24, *Aluminium and its Role in Biology*, Marcel Dekker, New York, 1988, 440 pp.

[53] R. C. MASSEY and D. TAYLOR (eds.), *Aluminium in Food and the Environment*. Royal Society of Chemistry (London) Special Publ. No. 73, 1989, 116 pp.

[54] G. H. ROBINSON (ed.), *Coordination Chemistry of Aluminium*, VCH, Cambridge, 1993, 234 pp.

[55] J. W. AKITT, *Prog. NMR Spectroscopy* **21**, 1–149 (1989). See also J. W. AKITT, Chap 9 in J. MASON (ed.), *Multinuclear NMR*, Plenum Press, New York, 1987, pp. 259–92, which also includes nmr of Ga, In and Tl isotopes.

^{27}Al in Nuclear Magnetic Resonance Spectroscopy

Aluminium is a very convenient element for nmr spectroscopy because ^{27}Al is 100% abundant and has a high nmr sensitivity, its receptivity being 0.206 when compared to ^{1}H and 1170 when compared to ^{13}C. It also has a high operating frequency (26.077 MHz when scaled to 100 MHz for ^{1}H) and a wide range of chemical shifts, δ (>300 ppm). The nuclear spin quantum number is 5/2 and the magnetogyric ratio γ is 6.9763 rad s^{-1}T^{-1}. The only disadvantage is the presence of a nuclear quadrupole moment ($Q = 0.149 \times 10^{-28}$ m^2) which leads to substantial line broadening for many species. The narrowest lines ($\omega_{1/2} \sim 2$ Hz) are obtained for highly symmetrical species such as [Al(H$_2$O)$_6$]$^{3+}$ and [Al(OH)$_4$]$^-$, but line widths of 1000 Hz or more are not uncommon and the use of special curve-analysis techniques is needed to extract the required parameters.

As expected, chemical shifts depend on coordination number (CN) and also on the nature of the atoms directly bonded to Al. Organometallic species, i.e. those with Al–C bonds, resonate at low field (high frequency): those with CN 3 have δ in the range 275–220 ppm, those with CN 4 have δ 220–140 ppm and those with CN 5 have δ 140–110 ppm. Tetrahalogenoaluminates, AlX$_4{}^-$, AlX$_n$Y$_{4-n}{}^-$, and 4-coordinate ligand adducts in general have δ in the range 120–50 ppm with the curious exception of AlI$_4{}^-$ which shows a resonance at a higher field than for any other Al species so far, δ being -26.7 ppm. Five-coordinate adducts have δ in the range 65–25 ppm and octahedral species have δ in the range +40 to -25 ppm. Typical parameters for some of the species mentioned in the main text are:

Species	[Al(OH)$_4$]$^-$	[Al(H$_2$O)$_6$]$^{3+}$	[Al$_2$(OH)$_2$(H$_2$O)$_8$]$^{4+}$	[Al$_{13}$O$_4$(OH)$_{24}$(H$_2$O)$_{12}$]$^{7+}$
δ/ppm	80	0.00 (std)	4	12Al @ $\sim$12, 1Al @ 625
$\omega_{1/2}$/Hz	10	2	500	8000, 25

These values show some dependence on concentration, pH and temperature. Note also the much smaller linewidth for the central, symmetrically 4-coordinated Al of the tridecameric Al$_{13}$ species when compared with that of the twelve less symmetrically coordinated octahedral Al atoms, and the possibility of extracting a reasonably precise value of δ for this latter resonance which has a linewidth of some 8000 Hz.

Solid-state ^{27}Al nmr spectroscopy has been much used in recent years to study the composition and structure of aluminisilcates (pp. 351–9) and other crystalline or amorphous Al compounds. The technique of magic angle spinning (MAS) must be used in such cases.[55]

[AlO$_4$\{Al(OH)$_2$(H$_2$O)\}$_{12}$]$^{7+}$, in which the central tetrahedral AlO$_4$ group is surrounded by corner- and edge-shared AlO$_6$ octahedra. The ion, which is almost spherical, has been further characterized by an X-ray diffraction study of crystalline Na[Al$_{13}$O$_4$(OH)$_{24}$(H$_2$O)$_{12}$](SO$_4$)$_4$.13H$_2$O.

The binary oxides and hydroxides of Ga, In and Tl have been much less extensively studied. The Ga system is somewhat similar to the Al system and a diagram summarizing the transformations in the systems is in Fig. 7.13. In general the α- and γ-series have the same structure as their Al counterparts. β-Ga$_2$O$_3$ is the most stable crystalline modification (mp 1740°); it has a unique crystal structure with the oxide ions in distorted ccp and Ga^{III} in distorted tetrahedral and octahedral sites. The structure appears to owe its stability to these distortions and, because of the lower coordination of half the Ga^{III}, the density is $\sim$10% less than for the α-(corundum-type) form. This preference of Ga^{III} for fourfold coordination despite the fact that it is larger than Al^{III} may again indicate the polarizing influence of the d^{10} core; a similar tetrahedral site preference is observed for Fe^{III}.

In$_2$O$_3$ has the C-type M$_2$O$_3$ structure (p. 1238) and InO(OH) (prepared hydrothermally from In(OH)$_3$ at 250–400°C and 100–1500 atm) has a deformed rutile structure (p. 961) rather than the layer lattice structure of AlO(OH) and GaO(OH). Crystalline In(OH)$_3$ is best prepared by addition of NH$_3$ to aqueous InCl$_3$ at 100° and ageing the precipitate for a few hours at this temperature; it has the simple ReO$_3$-type structure distorted somewhat by multiple H bonds.[26]

Thallium is notably different. Tl$_2^{I}$O forms as black platelets when Tl$_2$CO$_3$ is heated in N$_2$ at 700° (mp 596°, d 10.36 g cm^{-3}); it is hygroscopic and gives TlOH with water. Tl$_2^{III}$O$_3$ is brown-black (mp 716°, d 10.04 g cm^{-3}) and can be made by oxidation of aqueous TlNO$_3$ with Cl$_2$ or Br$_2$ followed by precipitation

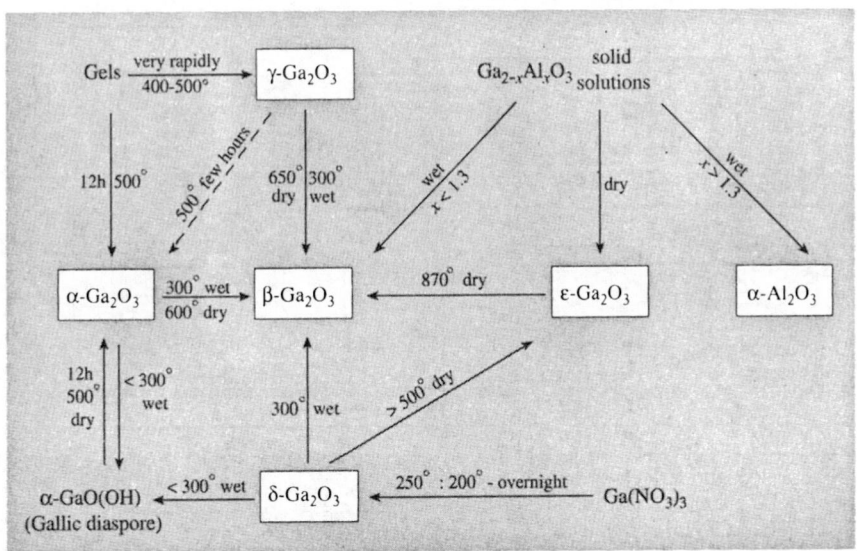

Figure 7.13   Chart illustrating transformation relationships among the forms of gallium oxide and its hydrates. Conversion (wet) of the phase designated as $Ga_{2-x}Al_xO_3$ to β-Ga_2O_3 occurs only where $x < 1.3$; where $x > 1.3$ an α-Al_2O_3 structure forms.

of the hydrated oxide $Tl_2O_3.1\frac{1}{2}H_2O$ and desiccation; single crystals have a very low electrical resistivity (e.g. 7×10^{-5} ohm cm at room temperature). A mixed oxide Tl_4O_3 (black) is known and also a violet peroxide Tl^IO_2 made by electrolysis of an aqueous solution of Tl_2SO_4 and oxalic acid between Pt electrodes. TlOH has been mentioned previously (p. 226).

7.3.4 Ternary and more complex oxide phases

This section considers a number of extremely important structure types in which Al combines with one or more other metals to form a mixed oxide phase. The most significant of these from both a theoretical and an industrial viewpoint are spinel ($MgAl_2O_4$) and related compounds, Na-β-alumina ($NaAl_{11}O_{17}$) and related phases, and tricalcium aluminate ($Ca_3Al_2O_6$) which is a major constituent of Portland cement. Each of these compounds raises points of fundamental importance in solid-state chemistry and each possesses properties of crucial significance to

modern technology. For aluminosilicates see p. 351 and for aluminophosphates see p. 526.

Spinels and related compounds [56]

Spinels form a large class of compounds whose crystal structure is related to that of the mineral spinel itself, $MgAl_2O_4$. The general formula is AB_2X_4 and the unit cell contains 32 oxygen atoms in almost perfect ccp array, i.e. $A_8B_{16}O_{32}$. In the normal spinel structure (Fig. 7.14) 8 metal atoms (A) occupy tetrahedral sites and 16 metal atoms (B) occupy octahedral sites, and the structure can be regarded as being built up of alternating cubelets of ZnS-type and NaCl-type structures. The two factors that determine which combinations of atoms can form a spinel-type structure are (a) the total formal cation charge, and (b) the relative sizes of the 2 cations with respect both to each other and to the

[56] N. N. GREENWOOD, *Ionic Crystals, Lattice Defects and Nonstoichiometry*, Butterworths, London, 1968, 194 pp. See also J. K. BURDETT, G. D. PRICE and S. L. PRICE, *J. Am. Chem. Soc.* **104**, 92–5 (1982).

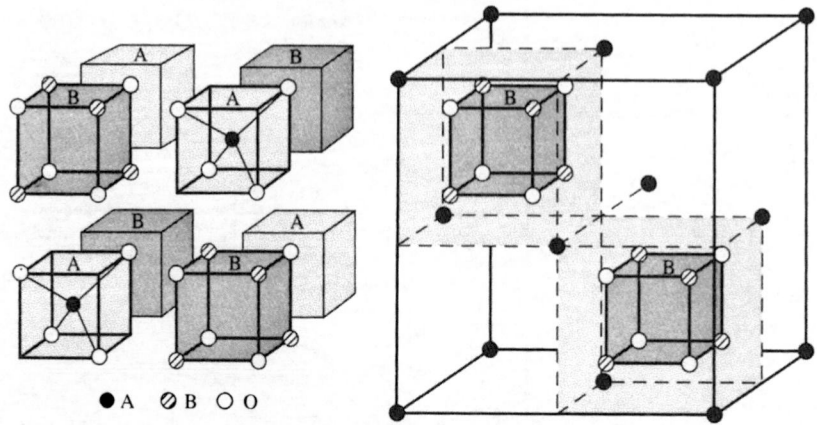

●A ⊘B ○O

Figure 7.14 Spinel structure AB_2O_4. The structure can be thought of as 8 octants of alternating AO_4 tetrahedra and B_4O_4 cubes as shown in the left-hand diagram; the 4O have the same orientation in all 8 octants and so build up into a fcc lattice of 32 ions which coordinate A tetrahedrally and B octahedrally. The 4 A octants contain 4 A ions and the 4 B octants contain 16 B ions. The unit cell is completed by an encompassing fcc of A ions (●) as shown in the right-hand diagram; this is shared with adjacent unit cells and comprises the remaining 4 A ions in the complete unit cell $A_8B_{16}O_{32}$. The location of two of the B_4O_4 cubes is shown for orientation.

anion. For oxides of formula AB_2O_4 charge balance can be achieved by three combinations of cation oxidation state: $A^{II}B_2^{III}O_4$, $A^{IV}B_2^{II}O_4$, and $A^{VI}B_2^IO_4$. The first combination is the most numerous and examples are known with

$$A^{II} = Mg, (Ca); Cr, Mn, Fe, Co, Ni, Cu;$$

$$Zn, Cd, (Hg); Sn$$

$$B^{III} = Al, Ga, In;$$

$$Ti, V, Cr, Mn, Fe, Co, Ni; Rh$$

The anion can be O, S, Se or Te. Most of the A^{II} cations have radii (6-coordinate) in the range 65–95 pm and larger cations such as Ca^{II} (100 pm) and Hg^{II} (102 pm) do not form oxide spinels. The radii of B^{III} fall predominantly in the range 60–70 pm though Al^{III} (53 pm) is smaller, and In^{III} (80 pm) normally forms sulfide spinels only.

Examples of spinels with other combinations of oxidation state are:

$$A^{IV}B_2^{II}X_4^{-II} : TiMg_2O_4, PbFe_2O_4, SnCu_2S_4$$

$$A^{VI}B_2^IX_4^{-II} : MoAg_2O_4, MoNa_2O_4, WNa_2O_4$$

$$A^{II}B_2^IX_4^{-1} : NiLi_2F_4, ZnK_2(CN)_4, CdK_2(CN)_4$$

Many of the spinel-type compounds mentioned above do not have the normal structure in which A are in tetrahedral sites (t) and B are in octahedral sites (o); instead they adopt the inverse spinel structure in which half the B cations occupy the tetrahedral sites whilst the other half of the B cations and all the A cations are distributed on the octahedral sites, i.e. $(B)_t[AB]_oO_4$. The occupancy of the octahedral sites may be random or ordered. Several factors influence whether a given spinel will adopt the normal or inverse structure, including (a) the relative sizes of A and B, (b) the Madelung constants for the normal and inverse structures, (c) ligand-field stabilization energies (p. 1131) of cations on tetrahedral and octahedral sites, and (d) polarization or covalency effects.[56]

Thus, if size alone were important it might be expected that the smaller cation would occupy the site of lower coordination number, i.e. $Al_t[MgAl]_oO_4$; however, in spinel itself this is outweighed by the greater lattice energy achieved by having the cation of higher charge, (Al^{III}) on the site of higher coordination and the normal structure is adopted: $(Mg)_t[Al_2]_oO_4$. An additional factor must be considered in a spinel such as $NiAl_2O_4$ since the crystal field stabilization energy of Ni^{II} is greater in octahedral than tetrahedral coordination; this redresses the balance, making the normal and inverse structures almost equal in energy and there is almost complete randomization of all the cations on all the available sites: $(Al_{0.75}Ni_{0.25})_t[Ni_{0.75}Al_{1.25}]_oO_4$.

Inverse and disordered spinels are said to have a defect structure because all crystallographically identical sites within the unit cell are not occupied by the same cation. A related type of defect structure occurs in valency disordered spinels where, for example, the divalent A^{II} cations in AB_2O_4 are replaced by equal numbers of M^I and M^{III} of appropriate size. Thus, in spinel itself, which can be written $Mg_8Al_{16}O_{32}$, the $8Mg^{II}$ (72 pm) can be replaced by $4Li^I$ (76 pm) and $4Al^{III}$ (53 pm) to give Li_4-$Al_{20}O_{32}$, i.e. $LiAl_5O_8$. This has a defect spinel structure in which two-fifths of the Al occupy all the tetrahedral sites: $(Al_2^{III})_t[Li^IAl_3^{III}]_oO_8$. Other compounds having this cation-disordered spinel structure are $LiGa_5O_8$ and $LiFe_5O_8$. Disordering on the tetrahedral sites occurs in $CuAl_5S_8$, $CuIn_5S_8$, $AgAl_5S_8$ and $AgIn_5S_8$, i.e. $(Cu^IAl^{III})_t[Al_4^{III}]_oS_8$, etc. Valency disordering can also be achieved by replacing A^{II} completely by M^I, thus necessitating replacement of half the B^{III} by M^{IV}, e.g. $(Li^I)_t[Al^{III}Ti^{IV}]_oO_4$. Even more extensive substitution of cations has been achieved in many cubic spinel phases, e.g. $Li_5^IZn_8^{II}Al_5^{III}Ge_9^{IV}O_{36}$ (and the Ga^{III} and Fe^{III} analogues), and the possibilities are virtually limitless.

The sensitive dependence of the electrical and magnetic properties of spinel-type compounds on composition, temperature, and detailed cation arrangement has proved a powerful incentive for the extensive study of these compounds in connection with the solid-state electronics industry. Perhaps the best-known examples are the ferrites, including the extraordinary compound magnetite Fe_3O_4 (p. 1080) which has an inverse spinel structure $(Fe^{III})_t[Fe^{II}Fe^{III}]_oO_4$.

It will also be recalled that γ-Al_2O_3 (p. 243) has a defect spinel structure in which not all of the cation sites are occupied, i.e. $Al_{21\frac{1}{3}}^{III}\square_{2\frac{2}{3}}O_{32}$: the relation to spinel ($Mg_8^{II}Al_{16}^{III}O_{32}$) is obvious, the $8Mg^{II}$ having been replaced by the isoelectronically equivalent $5\frac{1}{3}Al^{III}$. This explains why $MgAl_2O_4$ can form a complete range of solid solutions with γ-Al_2O_3: the oxygen builds on to the complete fcc oxide ion lattice and the Al^{III} gradually replaces Mg^{II}, electrical neutrality being achieved simply by leaving 1 cation site vacant for each $3Mg^{II}$ replaced by $2Al^{III}$.

Sodium-β-alumina and related phases [57]

Sodium-β-alumina has assumed tremendous importance as a solid-state electrolyte since its very high electrical conductivity was discovered at the Ford Motor Company by J. T. Kummer and N. Weber in 1967. The compound, which has the idealized formula $NaAl_{11}O_{17}(Na_2O.11Al_2O_3)$ was originally thought to be a form of Al_2O_3 and hence called β-alumina (1916); the presence of Na, which was at first either undetected or ignored, is now known to be essential for stability. X-ray analysis shows that the structure is closely related to that of spinel, no fewer than 50 of the 58 atoms in the unit cell being arranged exactly as in spinel. The large Na atoms are situated exclusively in loosely packed planes together with an equal number of O atoms as shown in Fig. 7.15; these planes are 1123 pm apart, being separated by the "spinel blocks". The close-packed oxygen layers above and below the Na planes are mirror images of each other 476 pm apart and they are bound together not only by the Na atoms but by an equal number of Al–O–Al bonds. There are several other sites in the mirror plane which can physically accommodate Na and this permits rapid two-dimensional diffusion of Na within the basal

[57] J. T. KUMMER, *Prog. Solid State Chem.* **7**, 141–75 (1972). J. H. KENNEDY, *Topics in Applied Physics* **21**, 105–41 (1977).

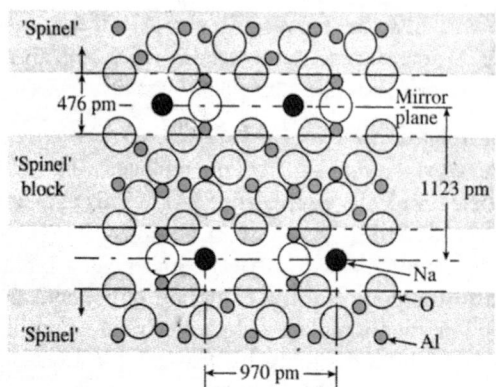

Figure 7.15 Crystal structure of Na-β-alumina (see text). This section, which is a plane parallel to the c-axis, does not show the closest Na–Na distance.

plane; it also explains the very low resistivity of the order of 30 ohm cm. The structure can also accommodate supernumerary Na ions, and the compound, even in the form of single crystals, is massively defective, having typically 20–30% more Na than indicated by the idealized formula; this is probably compensated by additional Al vacancies in the "spinel blocks" adjacent to the mirror planes, e.g. $Na_{2.58}Al_{21.8}O_{34}$.

Sodium-β-alumina can be prepared by heating Na_2CO_3 (or $NaNO_3$ or $NaOH$) with any modification of Al_2O_3 or its hydrates to ~1500° in a Pt vessel suitably sealed to avoid loss of Na_2O (as $Na + O_2$). In the presence of NaF or AlF_3 a temperature of 1000° suffices. Na-β-alumina melts at ~2000° (probably incongruently) and has d 3.25 g cm^{-3}. The Na can be replaced by Li, K, Rb, Cu^I, Ag^I, Ga^I, In^I or Tl^I by heating with a suitable molten salt, and Ag^I can be replaced by NO$^+$ by treatment with molten $NOCl/AlCl_3$. The ammonium compound is also known and H_3O^+-β-alumina can be prepared by reduction of the Ag compound. Similarly, Al^{III} can be replaced by Ga^{III} or Fe^{III} in the preparation, leading to compounds of (idealized) formulae $Na_2O.11Ga_2O_3$, $Na_2O.11Fe_2O_3$, $K_2O.11Fe_2O_3$, etc. Altervalent substitution is also possible, e.g. in Na-β''-alumina, $Na_{1+x}M_xAl_{11-x}O_{17}$, in which M is a divalent cation such as Mg, Ni or Zn. A typical composition is $Na_{1.67}Mg_{0.67}Al_{10.33}O_{17}$ and the excess Na charge is compensated for by substituting the divalent or univalent cation into the lattice sites normally occupied by Al.[58]

Apart from the intriguing structural implications of these fast-ion solid-state conductors, Na-β-alumina and related phases have been extensively used as permeable membranes in the Na/S battery system (p. 678): this requires an air-stable membrane that is readily permeable to Na ions but not to Na atoms or S, that is non-reactive with molten Na and S, and that is not an electronic conductor. Not surprisingly, few compounds have been found to compete with Na-β-alumina in this field, although Na-β''-alumina has the remarkable additional property of enabling the rapid diffusion of a large proportion of cations in the periodic table (whereas Na-β-alumina itself is restricted mainly to univalent cations). Indeed, the β''-aluminas are the first family of high conductivity solid electrolytes which permit fast ion transport of multivalent cations in solids.[58]

Unrelated to the β- and β''-aluminas are a group of white, hygroscopic sodium-rich aluminates which have recently been prepared by heating Na_2O and Al_2O_3 in appropriate stoichiometric ratios at 700°C for 18–24 hours.[59] Na_5AlO_4, which is isostructural with Na_5FeO_4, contains isolated $[AlO_4]$ tetrahedra with Al–O 176–179 pm. $Na_7Al_3O_8$ features a novel ring structure made up of six AlO_4 tetrahedra sharing corners to form a non-planar 12-membered ring which is then joined by pairs of oxygen atom bridges to adjacent rings, thus generating an infinite chain of alternating 12- and 8-membered rings with Al–O$_\mu$ 175–179 pm and Al–O$_t$ 173–4 pm. Finally, $Na_{17}Al_5O_{16}$ has discrete chains composed of five AlO_4 tetrahedra sharing corners with almost linear angles (160° and 173°) at the bridging O atoms and with

---

[58] D. F. SHRIVER and G. C. FARRINGTON, *Chem. and Eng. News*, May 20, 42–57 (1985), and references cited therein.

[59] M. G. BARKER, P. G. GADD and M. J. BEGLEY, *J. Chem. Soc., Chem. Commun.*, 379–81 (1981). M. G. BARKER, P. G. GADD and S. C. WALLWORK, *J. Chem. Soc., Chem. Commun.*, 516–7 (1982).

the various Al–O distances again falling in the range 170–180 pm. Note that the unusual formula $Na_{17}Al_5O_{16}$ (i.e. $Na_{3.4}AlO_{3.2}$) is nearly the same as Na_3AlO_3 which would have been the stoichiometry if the chains of AlO_4 tetrahedra had been infinite.

Tricalcium aluminate, $Ca_3Al_2O_6$

Tricalcium aluminate is an important component of Portland cement yet, despite numerous attempts dating back over the preceding 50 y, its structure remained unsolved until 1975.[60] The basic unit is now known to be a 12-membered ring of 6 fused {AlO_4} tetrahedra $[Al_6O_{18}]^{18-}$ as shown in Fig. 7.16; there are 8 such rings per unit cell surrounding holes of radius 147 pm, and the rings are held together by Ca ions in distorted sixfold coordination to give the structural formula $Ca_9Al_6O_{18}$. The rather short Ca–O distance (226 pm) and the observed compression of the {CaO_6} octahedra may indicate some strain and this, together with the large holes in the lattice, facilitate the rapid reaction with water. The products of hydration depend sensitively on the temperature. Above 21° $Ca_3Al_2O_6$ gives the hexahydrate $Ca_3Al_2O_6.6H_2O$, but below this temperature hydrated di- and tetra-calcium aluminates are formed of empirical composition $2CaO.Al_2O_3.5–9H_2O$ and $4CaO.Al_2O_3.12–14H_2O$. This is of great importance in cement technology (see Panel) since, in the absence of a retarder, cement reacts rapidly with water giving a sharp rise in temperature and a "flash set" during which the various calcium aluminate hydrates precipitate and congeal into an unmanageable mass. This can be avoided by grinding in 2–5% of gypsum ($CaSO_4.2H_2O$) with the cement clinker; this reacts rapidly with dissolved aluminates in the presence of $Ca(OH)_2$ to give the calcium sulfatoaluminate, $3CaO.Al_2O_3.3CaSO_4.31H_2O$, which is much less soluble than the hydrated calcium aluminates and

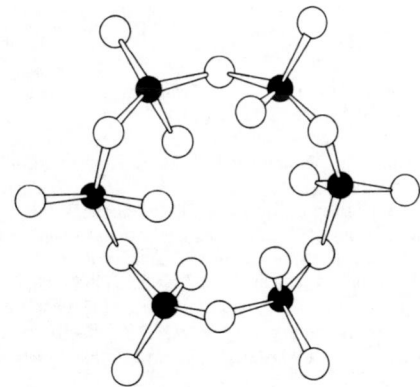

Figure 7.16　Structure of the $[Al_6O_{18}]^{18+}$ unit in $Ca_3Al_2O_6$ (i.e. $Ca_9Al_6O_{18}$). The Al–O distances are all in the range 175 ± 2 pm.

therefore preferentially precipitates and prevents the premature congealing.

Another important calcium aluminate system occurs in high-alumina cement (*ciment fondu*). This is not a Portland cement but is made by *fusing* limestone and bauxite with small amounts of SiO_2 and TiO_2 in an open-hearth furnace at 1425–1500°; rotary kilns with tap-holes for the molten cement can also be used. Typical analytical compositions for a high-alumina cement are ∼40% each of Al_2O_3 and CaO and about 10% each of Fe_2O_3 and SiO_2; the most important compounds in the cement are $CaAl_2O_4$, $Ca_2Al_2SiO_7$ and $Ca_6Al_8FeSiO_{21}$. Setting and hardening of high-alumina cement are probably due to the formation of calcium aluminate gels such as $CaO.Al_2O_3.10H_2O$, and the more basic $2CaO.Al_2O_3.8H_2O$, $3CaO.Al_2O_3.6H_2O$ and $4CaO.Al_2O_3.13H_2O$, though these empirical formulae give no indication of the structural units involved. The most notable property of high-alumina cement is that it develops very high strength at a very early stage (within 1 day). Long exposure to warm, moist conditions may lead to failure but resistance to corrosion by sea water and sulfate brines, or by weak mineral acids, is outstanding. It has also been much used as a refractory cement to withstand temperatures up to 1500°.

---

[60] P. MONDAL and J. W. JEFFREY, *Acta Cryst.* **B31**, 689–97 (1975).

Portland Cement[61]

The name "Portland cement" was first used by J. Aspdin in a patent (1824) because, when mixed with water and sand the powder hardened into a block that resembled the natural limestone quarried in the Isle of Portland, England. The two crucial discoveries which led to the production of strong, durable, hydraulic cement that did not disintegrate in water, were made in the eighteenth and nineteenth centuries. In 1756 John Smeaton, carrying out experiments in connection with building the Eddystone Lighthouse (UK), recognized the importance of using limes which contained admixed clays or shales (i.e. aluminosilicates), and by the early 1800s it was realized that firing must be carried out at sintering temperatures in order to produce a clinker now known to contain calcium silicates and aluminates. The first major engineering work to use Portland cement was in the tunnel constructed beneath the Thames in 1828. The first truly high-temperature cement (1450–1600°C) was made in 1854, and the technology was revolutionized in 1899 by the introduction of rotary kilns.

The important compounds in Portland cement are dicalcium silicate (Ca_2SiO_4) 26%, tricalcium silicate (Ca_3SiO_5) 51%, tricalcium aluminate ($Ca_3Al_2O_6$) 11% and the tetracalcium species $Ca_4Al_2Fe_2^{III}O_{10}$ (1%). The principal constituent of moistened cement paste is a tobermorite gel which can be represented schematically by the following idealized equations:

$$2Ca_2SiO_4 + 4H_2O \longrightarrow 3CaO.2SiO_2.3H_2O + Ca(OH)_2$$

$$2Ca_3SiO_5 + 6H_2O \longrightarrow 3CaO.2SiO_2.3H_2O + 3Ca(OH)_2$$

The adhesion of the tobermorite particles to each other and to the embedded aggregates is responsible for the strength of the cement which is due, ultimately, to the formation of $-Si-O-Si-O$ bonds.

Portland cement is made by heating a mixture of limestone (or chalk, shells, etc.) with aluminosilicates (derived from sand, shales, and clays) in carefully controlled amounts so as to give the approximate composition $CaO \sim 70\%$, $SiO_2 \sim 20\%$, $Al_2O_3 \sim 5\%$, $Fe_2O_3 \sim 3\%$. The presence of Na_2O, K_2O, MgO and P_2O_5 are detrimental and must be limited. The raw materials are ground to pass 200-mesh sieves and then heated in a rotary kiln to $\sim 1500°$ to give a sintered clinker; this is reground to 325-mesh and mixed with 2–5% of gypsum. An average-sized kiln can produce 1000–3000 tonnes of cement per day and the world's largest plants can produce up to 8000 tonnes per day. The vast scale of the industry can be gauged from the US production figures in the table below. Price (1990) was $45–55 per tonne for bulk supplies. In the same year China emerged as the world's largest cement producer (200 million tonnes per annum). Total world production continues to grow dramatically, from 590 Mtpa in 1970 and 881 Mtpa in 1980 to nearly 1200 Mtpa in 1990, of which Europe (including the European parts of the former Soviet Union) accounted for some 40%.

Production of Portland Cement in the USA/million tonnes (Mt)

1890	1900	1910	1920	1930	1940	1950	1960	1970	1980	1990
0.057	1.45	13.1	17.1	27.5	22.2	38.5	56.0	66.4	68.2	70.0

7.3.5 Other inorganic compounds

Chalcogenides

At normal temperatures the only stable chalcogenides of Al are Al_2S_3 (white), Al_2Se_3 (grey) and Al_2Te_3 (dark grey). They can be prepared by direct reaction of the elements at $\sim 1000°$ and all hydrolyse rapidly and completely in aqueous solution to give $Al(OH)_3$ and H_2X (X = S, Se, Te). The small size of Al relative to the chalcogens dictates tetrahedral coordination and the various polymorphs are related to wurtzite (hexagonal ZnS, p. 1210), two-thirds of the available

metal sites being occupied in either an ordered (α) or a random (β) fashion. Al_2S_3 also has a γ-form related to γ-Al_2O_3 (p. 243), and very recently a novel high-temperature hexagonal modification of Al_2S_3 containing 5-coordinate Al has been obtained by annealing α-Al_2S_3 at 550°C;[62] in this new form half the Al atoms are tetrahedrally coordinated (Al–S 223–227 pm) whereas the other half are in trigonal bipyramidal coordination with Al–S_{eq} 227–232 pm and Al–S_{ax} 250–252 pm.

The chalcogenides of Ga, In and Tl are much more numerous and at least a dozen different structure types have been established by X-ray

61 *Kirk–Othmer Encyclopedia of Chemical Technology*, 4th edn., Vol. 5, Interscience, New York, 564–98 (1993).

62 B. KREBS, A. SCHIEMANN and M. LÄGE, *Z. anorg. allg. Chem.* **619**, 983–8 (1993).

crystallography.[63] The compounds have been extensively studied not only because of their intriguing stoichiometries, but also because many of them are semiconductors, semi-metals, photoconductors or light emitters, and Tl_5Te_3 has been found to be a superconductor at low temperatures. (See p. 1182 for high-temperature super conductors, including $Tl_2Ca_2Ba_2Cu_3O_{10+x}$ which has one of the highest known superconducting transition temperatures, $T_c = 125$ K.) The chalcogenides, as expected from their position in the

periodic table, are far from ionic, but formal oxidation states remain a useful device for electron counting and for checking the overall charge balance. Well-established compounds are summarized in Table 7.9. The following points are noteworthy. The hexagonal α- and β-forms of Ga_2S_3 are isostructural with the Al analogues and an additional form, γ-Ga_2S_3, adopts the related defect sphalerite structure derived from cubic ZnS (zinc blende, p. 1210). The same structure is found for Ga_2Se_3 and Ga_2Te_3 but for the larger In^{III} atom octahedral coordination also becomes possible. The corresponding Tl^{III} sesquichalcogenides Tl_2X_3 are either

[63] L. I. MAN, R. M. IMANOV and S. A. SEMILETOV, *Sov. Phys. Crystallogr.* **21**, 255–63 (1976).

Table 7.9   Stoichiometries and structures of the crystalline chalcogenides of Group 13 elements

Ga_2S	Ga_2Se	
GaS (yellow) layer structure with Ga–Ga bonds	GaSe (like GaS)	GaTe (like GaS)
Ga_4S_5		(Ga_3Te_2)
α-Ga_2S_3 (yellow) ordered defect wurtzite (hexagonal ZnS)		
β-Ga_2S_3 defect wurtzite		
γ-Ga_2S_3 defect sphalerite (cubic ZnS)	Ga_2Se_3 defect sphalerite	Ga_2Te_3 defect sphalerite
		Ga_2Te_5 chains of linked {$GaTe_4$} plus single Te atoms
	In_4Se_3 contains $[(In^{III})_3]^V$ groups: $In^I[In_3^{III}]Se_3$	In_4Te_3 like In_4Se_3
InS (red) like GaS	InSe distorted NaCl, somewhat like GaS	InTe like TlSe (cubes and tetrahedra)
In_6S_7 see text	In_6Se_7 like In_6S_7	In_3Te_4
α-In_2S_3 (yellow) cubic γ'-Al_2O_3	α-In_2Se_3 defect wurtzite, but $\frac{1}{16}$ of In octahedral	α-In_2Te_3 defect sphalerite (cubic ZnS)
β-In_2S_3 (red) defect spinel, γ-Al_2O_3	β-In_2Se_3 ordered defect wurtzite (hexagonal ZnS)	β-In_2Te_3
In_6S_7 see text		In_3Te_5
		In_2Te_5
Tl_2S (black) distorted CdI_2 layer lattice (Tl^I in threefold coordination)		
Tl_4S_3 chains of linked {$Tl^{III}S_4$} tetrahedra $(Tl^I)_3[Tl^{III}S_3]$	Tl_5Se_3 complex Cr_5B_3-type structure	Tl_5Te_3 Cr_5B_3 layer structure, CN of Tl varies up to 9 and Te up to 10
TlS (black) like TlSe, $Tl^I[Tl^{III}S_2]$	TlSe (black) chains of edgeshared {$Tl^{III}Se_4$} tetrahedra $Tl^I[Tl^{III}Se_2]$	TlTe (variant of W_5Si_3 (complex)
[No Tl_2S_3 known]	Tl_2Se_3	(Tl_2Te_3)
TlS_2 Tl^I polysulfide		
Tl_2S_5 (red and black forms) Tl^I polysulfide		
Tl_2S_9 Tl^I polysulfide		

non-existent or of dubious authenticity, perhaps because of the ready reduction to Tl^I (see TlI_3, p. 239).

GaS (yellow, mp 970°) has a hexagonal layer structure with Ga–Ga bonds (248 pm); each Ga is coordinated by 3S and 1Ga, and the sequence of layers along the *c*-axis is··· SGaGaS,SGaGaS··· ; the compound can therefore be considered as an example of Ga^{II}. The structures of GaSe, GaTe, red InS and InSe are similar. By contrast, InTe, TlS (black) and TlSe (black, metallic) have a structure which can be formalized as $M^I[M^{III}X_2]$; each Tl^{III} is tetrahedrally coordinated by 4 Se at 268 pm and the tetrahedra are linked into infinite chains by edge sharing along the *c*-axis (see structure), whereas each Tl^I lies between these chains and is surrounded by a distorted cube of 8 Se at 342 pm. This explains the marked anisotropy of properties, especially the metallic conductivity in the (001) plane and the semiconductivity along the *c*-axis. Similar edge-linked {GeSe$_4$} tetrahedra are found in $Cs_{10}Ga_6Se_{14}$ which was obtained as transparent pale-yellow crystals by heating an equimolar mixture of GaSe and Cs in a carefully controlled temperature programme; the compound features the unprecedented finite complex anion $[Se_2Ga(\mu\text{-}Se_2Ga)_5Se_2]^{10-}$ which is 1900 pm long.[64]

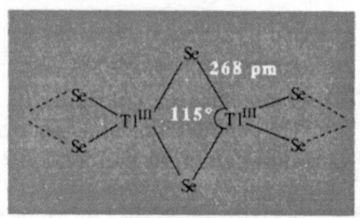

In_6S_7 (and the isostructural In_6Se_7) have a curious structure comprising two separate blocks of almost ccp S which are rotated about the *b*-axis by 61° with respect to each other; the In is in octahedral coordination. The compound can be formulated as $In^I(In_2^{III})^{IV}In_3^{III}S_7^{-II}$. There are also numerous ternary In/Tl sulfides in which In^I has been replaced by Tl^I, e.g.: $Tl^IIn_5^{III}S_8$, $Tl^IIn_3^{III}S_5$, $Tl^IIn^{III}S_2$, $Tl_3^IIn^{III}S_3$, $Tl^I(In_2^{III})_2^{IV}In^{III}S_6$, $Tl_3^IIn^IIn_4^{III}S_8$ and $Tl^I(In_2^{III})^{IV}In_3^{III}S_7$.[64a]

The crystal structures of In_4Se_3 and In_4Te_3 show that they can be regarded to a first approximation as $In^I[In_3]^V(X^{-II})_3$ but the compound does not really comprise discrete ions. The triatomic unit $[In^{III}\!-\!In^{III}\!-\!In^{III}]$ is bent, the angle at the central atom being 158° and the In–In distances 279 pm (cf. 324–326 pm in metallic In). However, it is also possible to discern non-planar 5-membered heterocycles in the structure formed by joining 2 In from 1 {In$_3$} to the terminal In of an adjacent {In$_3$} via 2 bridging Se (or Te) atoms so that the structure can be represented schematically as in Fig. 7.17. The In^{III}–Se distances average

[64] H. J. DEISEROTH and HAN FU-SON, *Angew. Chem. Int. Edn. Engl.* **20**, 962–3 (1981).

[64a] H. J. DIESEROTH and R. WALTHER, *Z. anorg. allg. Chem.* **622**, 611–16 (1996).

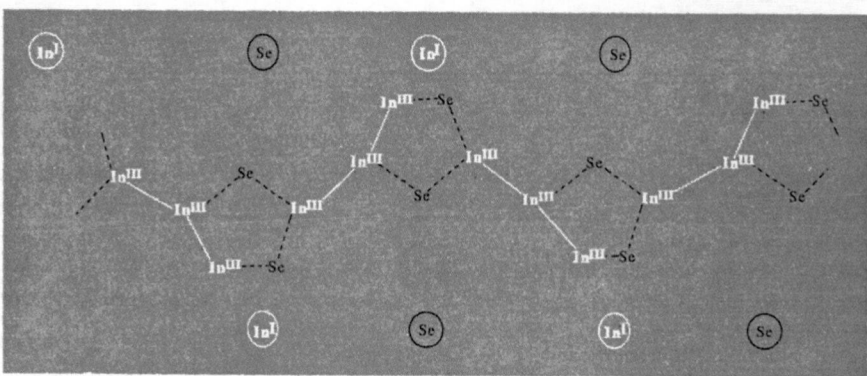

Figure 7.17 Schematic structure of In$_4$Se$_3$.

269 pm compared with the closest In^I–Se contact of 297 pm. The $[In_3^{III}]^V$ unit can be compared with the isoelectronic species $[Hg_3^{II}]^{II}$. The compound Tl_4S_3, which has the same stoichiometry as In_4X_3, has a different structure in which chains of corner-shared $\{Tl^{III}S_4\}$ tetrahedra of overall stoichiometry $[TlS_3]$ are bound together by Tl^I; within the chains the Tl^{III}–S distance is 254 pm whereas the Tl^I–S distances vary between 290–336 pm. A comparison of the formal designation of the two structures $In^I[(In_3^{III})]^V(Se^{-II})_3$ and $(Tl^I)_3[Tl^{III}S_3]^{-III}$ again illustrates the increasing preference of the heavier metal for the +1 oxidation state. The trend continues with the polysulfides Tl^IS_2, $Tl_2^IS_5$ and $Tl_2^IS_9$ already alluded to on p. 253.

Compounds with bonds to N, P, As, Sb or Bi

The binary compounds of the Group 13 metals with the elements of Group 15 (N, P, As, Sb, Bi) are structurally less diverse than the chalcogenides just considered but they have achieved considerable technological application as III–V semiconductors isoelectronic with Si and Ge (cf. BN isoelectronic with C, p. 207). Their structures are summarized in Table 7.10: all adopt the cubic ZnS structure except the nitrides of Al, Ga and In which are probably more ionic (less covalent or metallic) than the others. Thallium does not form simple compounds

Table 7.10 Structures of III–V compounds $MX^{(a)}$

X ↓ M →	B	Al	Ga	In
N	L, S	W	W	W
P	S	S	S	S
As	S	S	S	S
Sb	—	S	S	S

$^{(a)}$L = BN layer lattice (p. 208).
  S = sphalerite (zinc blende), cubic ZnS (p. 1210).
  W = wurtzite, hexagonal ZnS structure (p. 1210).

$M^{III}X^V$: the explosive black nitride Tl_3^IN is known, and the azides Tl^IN_3 and $Tl^I[Tl^{III}(N_3)_4]$; the phosphides Tl_3P, TlP_3 and TlP_5 have been reported but are not well characterized. With As, Sb and Bi thallium forms alloys and intermetallic compounds Tl_3X, Tl_7Bi_2 and $TlBi_2$.

The III–V semiconductors can all be made by direct reaction of the elements at high temperature and under high pressure when necessary. Some properties of the Al compounds are in Table 7.11 from which it is clear that there are trends to lower mp and energy band-gap E_g with increasing atomic number.

Analogous compounds of Ga and In are grey or semi-metallic in appearance and show similar trends (Table 7.12). These data should be compared with those for Si, Ge, Sn and Pb on p. 373 and for the isoelectronic II–VI semiconductors of Zn, Cd and Hg with S, Se and Te (p. 1210). In addition, GaN is obtained by reacting Ga and NH_3 at 1050° and InN by reducing and nitriding In_2O_3 with NH_3 at 630°. The

Table 7.11 Some properties of Al III–V compounds

Property	AlN	AlP	AlAs	AlSb
Colour	Pale yellow	Yellow	Orange	—
MP/°C	>2200 decomp	2000	1740	1060
E_g/kJ mol$^{-1(a)}$	411	236	208	145

$^{(a)}$Energy gap between top of (filled) valence band and bottom of (empty) conduction band (p. 332). To convert from kJ mol^{-1} to eV atom^{-1} divide by 96.485.

Table 7.12 Comparison of some III–V semiconductors

Property	GaP	GaAs	GaSb	InP	InAs	InSb
MP/°C	1465	1238	712	1070	942	525
E_g/kJ mol$^{-1(a)}$	218	138	69	130	34	17

$^{(a)}$See note to Table 7.11.

nitrides show increasing susceptibility to chemical attack, AlN being inert to both acids and alkalis, GaN being decomposed by alkali, but not acid, and InN being decomposed by both acids and alkalis. Most of the other III–V compounds decompose slowly in moist air, e.g. AlP gives $Al(OH)_3$ and PH_3. As a consequence, semiconductor devices must be completely encapsulated to prevent reaction with the atmosphere. The great value of III–V semiconductors is that they extend the range of properties of Si and Ge and by judicious mixing in ternary phases they permit a continuous interpolation of energy band gaps, current-carrier mobilities and other characteristic properties. Some of their uses are summarized in the Panel on p. 258.

Other compounds containing Al–N or Ga–N bonds, including heterocyclic compounds and cluster organometallic compounds, are considered in section 7.3.6.

Some unusual stereochemistries

While it remains true that tetrahedral and octahedral coordination modes are the predominant stereochemistries adopted by the group 13 metals, nevertheless increasing diversity is being achieved by carefully selecting appropriate electronic and geometric features to enhance the stabilization of unusual stereochemistries. Some representative examples follow.

Trigonal planar Al is found in the $[AlSb_3]^{6-}$ "anions" in $[Cs_6K_3Sb(AlSb_3)]$, which is formed by heating a stoichiometric mixture of 6Cs, 3KSb and AlSb in a sealed Nb ampoule at 677°C.[65] The Ga analogue was prepared similarly. The planar anions are embedded between columns of condensed icosahedra $(Cs_6K_{6/2})^{9+}$ which in turn are centred by the remaining unique monatomic Sb^{3-} anion.

The indium molybdate $In_{11}Mo_{40}O_{62}$, prepared by heating the appropriate mixture of In, Mo and MoO_2 at 1100°C, features novel quasi-linear chain cations. In_5^{7+} and In_6^{8+} in channels between condensed clusters of Mo_6 octahedra.[66] The intrachain distances are 262–266 pm in In_5^{7+} and 265–269 pm in In_6^{8+}, which are the shortest known In–In interatomic distances cf. 325 and 337 pm in In metal itself, and 333 pm for the closest distances between In atoms in neighbouring chains in the molybdate. Interatomic angles within the chains are 158° and 163° respectively and, when the coordination around each In atom by contiguous In and O atoms is considered, the chains can be formulated as $[In^{2+}(In^+)_n In^{2+}]$, $n = 3, 4$.

Square-pyramidal 5-coordinate In^{III} occurs in certain organoindium compounds such as the bis(2-methylaminopyridino-) adduct [MeIn{MeNC(CH)$_4$N}$_2$][67] — cf. $InCl_5^{2-}$ (p. 238). The less familiar pentagonal planar coordination has been established for the $InMn_5$ group in the dianion $[(\mu_5\text{-In})\{Mn(CO)_4\}_5]^{2-}$ which is readily prepared by treatment of $InCl_3$ with the manganese carbonyl cluster compound $K_3[Mn_3(\mu\text{-CO})_2(CO)_{10}]$.[68] The mean Mn–Mn distance in the encircling plane-pentagonal "ligand" $\{Mn(CO)_4\}_5$ is 317 pm; the mean In–Mn distance is 265 pm, and the In atom is only 4.6 pm from the best plane of the five Mn atoms. Note also that the ligand is isolobal with cyclopentadienyl, C_5H_5.

Seven-coordinate pentagonal-bipyramidal In^{III} has been found in the chloroindium complex of 1,4,7-triazacyclononanetriacetic acid [{-(CH$_2$)$_2$N(CH$_2$CO$_2$H)}$_3$], (LH$_3$).[69] The neutral, monoprotonated 7-coordinate complex [InCl(LH)] features Cl and one N in axial positions (angle Cl–In–N 168°) with the other two N atoms and three carboxylate O atoms in the pentagonal plane. Interest in such compounds stems

---

[65] M. Somer, K. Peters, T. Popp and H. G. von Schnering, *Z. anorg. allg. Chem.* **597**, 201–8 (1991).

[66] H. Mattausch, A. Simon and E.-M. Peters, *Inorg. Chem.* **25**, 3428–33 (1986).

[67] A. M. Aria, D. C. Bradley, D. M. Frigo, M. B. Hursthouse and B. Hussain, *J. Chem. Soc., Chem. Commun.*, 783–4 (1985).

[68] M. Schollenberger, B. Nuber and M. L. Ziegler, *Angew. Chem. Int. Edn. Engl.* **31**, 350–1 (1992).

[69] A. S. Craig, I. M. Helps, D. Parker, H. Adams, N. A. Bailey, M. G. Williams, J. M. A. Smith and G. Ferguson, *Polyhedron* **8**, 2481–4 (1989).

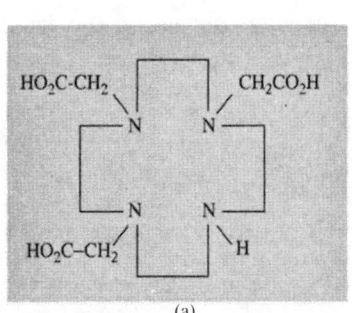

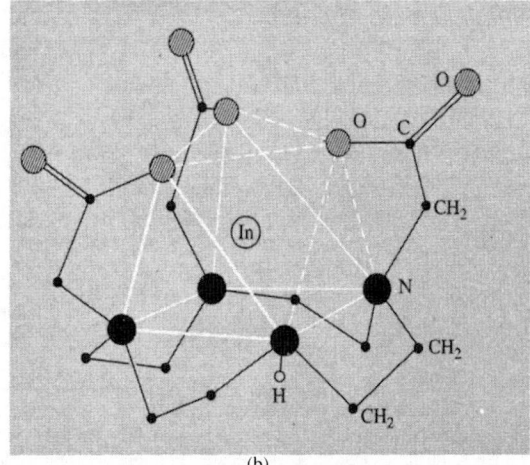

(a)   (b)

Figure 7.18   (a) 1,4,7,10-tetraazacyclododecane triacetic acid, (LH₃). (b) Structure of the 7-coordinate complex [InL]; the coordination polyhedron (shown in white) comprises a trigonal prism of 4N and 2O capped on one of its quadrilateral faces by the third O atom.

from the use of the γ-active ^{111}In isotope (E_γ 173, 247 keV, $t_{1/2}$ 2.81 d) in radio-labelled monoclonal antibodies to detect tumours. Interestingly, the 7-coordinate crystalline complex reverts to a stable neutral hexacoordinate species in aqueous solution. Other 7-coordinate macrocyclic In^{III} complexes of potential relevance in radiopharmaceutical applications have been prepared, including [InL] where L is the triacetate of the tetraaza macrocycle shown in Fig. 7.18(a).[70] In this case the coordination polyhedron is a trigonal prism with one of its quadrilateral faces capped by a carboxylate O atom as shown schematically in Fig. 7.18(b).

Indium clusters have also recently been characterized, notably in intermetallic compounds. Thus, the Zintl phase, Rb₂In₃, (prepared by direct reaction between the two metals at 1530°C) has layers of octahedral *closo*-In₆ clusters joined into sheets through exo bonds at four coplanar vertices.[71] These four In atoms are therefore each bonded to five neighbouring In atoms at the corners of a square-based pyramid, whereas the remaining two (*trans*) In atoms in the In₆ cluster

show pyramidal 4-fold bonding only, to contiguous In atoms in the same cluster. Cs₂In₃ is isostructural. The intermetallic compound K₃Na₂₆In₄₈ (synthesized from the elements in sealed Nb ampoules at 600°C) has a more complicated structure in which the In forms both *closo* icosahedral In₁₂ clusters and hexagonal antiprismatic In₁₂ clusters.[72] All the various In₁₂ clusters are interconnected by 12 exo bonds forming a covalent 3D network (In–In 291–315 pm) and the In₁₂ hexagonal antiprisms are additionally centred by single Na atoms. The phase contains several other interesting structural features and the original paper (in English) makes rewarding reading.

7.3.6 Organometallic compounds

Many organoaluminium compounds are known which contain 1, 2, 3 or 4 Al–C bonds per Al atom and, as these have an extensive reaction chemistry of considerable industrial importance, they will be considered before the organometallic compounds of Ga, In and Tl are discussed.

[70] A. RIESEN, T. A. KADEN, W. RITTER and H. A. MACKE, *J. Chem. Soc., Chem. Commun.*, 460–2 (1989).

[71] S. C. SEVEOV and J. D. CORBETT, *Z. anorg. allg. Chem.* **619**, 128–32 (1993).

[72] W. CARRILLO-CABRERA, N. CAROCA-CANALES, K. PETERS and H. G. VON SCHNERING, *Z. anorg. allg. Chem.* **619**, 1556–63 (1993).

Organoaluminium Compounds

Aluminium trialkyls and triaryls are highly reactive, colourless, volatile liquids or low-melting solids which ignite spontaneously in air and react violently with water; they should therefore be handled circumspectly and with suitable precautions. Unlike the boron trialkyls and triaryls they are often dimeric, though with branched-chain alkyls such as Pr^i, Bu^i and Me_3CCH_2 this tendency is less marked. Al_2Me_6 (mp 15°, bp 126°) has the methyl-bridged structure shown and the same dimeric structure is found for Al_2Ph_6 (mp 225°).

Applications of III–V Semiconductors

The 9 compounds that Al, Ga and In form with P, As and Sb have been extensively studied because of their many applications in the electronics industry, particularly those centred on the interconversion of electrical and optical (light) energy. For example, they are produced commercially as light-emitting diodes (LEDs) familiar in pocket calculators, wrist watches and the alpha-numeric output displays of many instruments; they are also used in infrared-emitting diodes, injection lasers, infrared detectors, photocathodes and photomultiplier tubes. An extremely elegant chemical solid-state technology has evolved in which crystals of the required properties are deposited, etched and modified to form the appropriate electrical circuits. The ternary system $GaAs_{1-x}P_x$ now dominates the LED market for α-numeric and graphic displays following the first report of this activity in 1961. $GaAs_{1-x}P_x$ is grown epitaxially on a single-crystal substrate of GaAs or GaP by chemical vapour deposition and crystal wafers as large as $20\,cm^2$ have been produced commercially. The colour of the emitted radiation is determined by the energy band gap E_g; for GaAs itself E_g is $138\,kJ\,mol^{-1}$ corresponding to an infrared emission (λ 870 nm), but this increases to $184\,kJ\,mol^{-1}$ for $x \sim 0.4$ corresponding to red emission (λ 650 nm). For $x > 0.4$ E_g continues to increase until it is $218\,kJ\,mol^{-1}$ for GaP (green, λ 550 nm). Commercial yellow and green LEDs contain the added isoelectronic impurity N to improve the conversion efficiency. A schematic cross-section of a typical $GaAs_{1-x}P_x$ epitaxial wafer doped with Te and N is shown in the diagram: Te (which has one more valence electron per atom than As or P) is the most widely used dopant to give n-type impurities in this system at concentrations of 10^{16}–10^{18} atoms cm^{-3} (0.5–50 ppm). The p–n junction is then formed by diffusing Zn (1 less electron than Ga) into the crystal to a similar concentration.

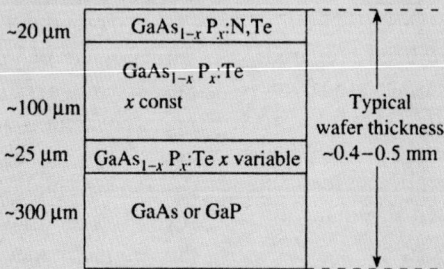

An even more recent application is the construction of semiconductor lasers. In normal optical lasers light is absorbed by an electronic transition to a broad band which lies above the upper laser level and the electron then drops into this level by a non-radiative transition. By contrast the radiation in a semiconductor laser originates in the region of a p–n junction and is due to the transitions of injected electrons and holes between the low-lying levels of the conduction band and the uppermost levels of the valence band. (Impurity levels may also be involved.) The efficiency of these semiconductor injection lasers is very much higher than those of optically pumped lasers and the devices are much smaller; they are also easily adaptable to modulation. As implied by the band gaps on p. 255, emission wavelengths are in the visible and near infrared. A heterostructure laser based on the system $GaAs–Al_xGa_{1-x}As$ was the first junction laser to run continuously at 3000 K and above (1970).

In the two types of device just considered, namely light emitting diodes and injection lasers, electrical energy is converted into optical energy. The reverse process of converting optical energy into electrical energy (photoconductivity and photovoltaic effects) has also been successfully achieved by III–V semiconductor systems. For example, the small band-gap compound InSb is valuable as a photoconductive infrared detector, and several compounds are being actively studied for use in solar cells to convert sunlight into useful sources of electrical power. The maximum photon flux in sunlight occurs at 75–95 $kJ\,mol^{-1}$ and GaAs shows promise, though other factors make Cu_2S–CdS cells more attractive commercially at the present time.

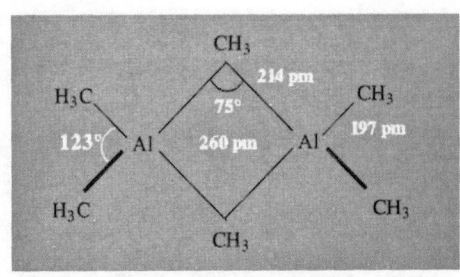

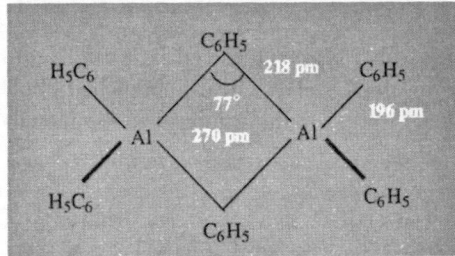

In each case $Al–C_\mu$ is about 10% longer than $Al–C_t$ (cf. Al_2X_6, p. 235; B_2H_6, p. 157). The enthalpy of dissociation of Al_2Me_6 into monomers is $84\,kJ\,mol^{-1}$. Al_2Et_6 (mp $-53°$) and $Al_2Pr^n_6$ (mp $-107°$) are also dimeric at room temperature but crystalline trimesitylaluminium (mesityl = 2,4,5-trimethylphenyl) is monomeric with planar 3-coordinate Al; the mesityl groups adopt a propeller-like configuration with a dihedral angle of 56° between the aromatic ring and the AlC_3 plane and with $Al–C$ 199.5 pm.[73]

As with $Al(BH_4)_3$ and related compounds (p. 230), solutions of Al_2Me_6 show only one proton nmr signal at room temperature due to the rapid interchange of bridging and terminal Me groups; at $-75°$ this process is sufficiently slow for separate resonances to be observed.

Al_2Me_6 can be prepared on a laboratory scale by the reaction of $HgMe_2$ on Al at $\sim90°C$. Al_2Ph_6 can be prepared similarly using $HgPh_2$ in boiling toluene or by the reaction of LiPh on Al_2Cl_6. On the industrial (kilotonne) scale Al is alkylated by means of RX or by alkenes plus H_2. In the first method the sesquichloride $R_3Al_2Cl_3$ is formed in equilibrium with its disproportionation

products:[†]

$$2Al + 3RCl \xrightarrow[\text{AlCl}_3 \text{ or AlR}_3]{\text{trace of I}_2} R_3Al_2Cl_3 \rightleftharpoons$$

$$\tfrac{1}{2}R_4Al_2Cl_2 + \tfrac{1}{2}R_2Al_2Cl_4$$

Addition of NaCl removes $R_2Al_2Cl_4$ as the complex ($2NaAlCl_3R$) and enables $R_4Al_2Cl_2$ to be distilled from the mixture. Reaction with Na yields the trialkyl, e.g.:

$$3Me_4Al_2Cl_2 + 6Na \longrightarrow 2Al_2Me_6 + 2Al + 6NaCl$$

Higher trialkyls are more readily prepared on an industrial scale by the alkene route (K. Ziegler et al., 1960) in which H_2 adds to Al in the presence of preformed AlR_3 to give a dialkylaluminium hydride which then readily adds to the alkene:

$$2Al + 3H_2 + 2Al_2Et_6 \xrightarrow{150°} \{6Et_2AlH\}$$

$$\xrightarrow[70°]{6CH_2CH_2} 3Al_2Et_6$$

Similarly, Al, H_2 and $Me_2C{=}CH_2$ react at 100° and 200 atm to give $AlBu^i_3$ in a single-stage process, provided a small amount of this compound is present at the start; this is required because Al does not react directly with H_2 to form AlH_3 prior to alkylation under these conditions. Alkene exchange reactions can be used to transform $AlBu^i_3$ into numerous other trialkyls. $AlBu^i_3$ can also be reduced by potassium metal in hexane at room temperature to give the novel brown compound $K_2Al_2Bu^i_6$ (mp 40°) which is notable in providing a rare example of an Al–Al bond in the diamagnetic anion $[Bu^i_3AlAlBu^i_3]^{2-}$.[74]

Al_2R_6 (or AlR_3) react readily with ligands to form adducts, $LAlR_3$. They are stronger Lewis acids than are organoboron compounds, BR_3, and can be considered as 'hard' (or class a)

[73] J. J. JERIUS, J. M. HAHN, A. F. M. M. RAHMAN, O. MOLS, W. H. ISLEY and J. P. OLIVER, *Organometallics* **5**, 1812–14 (1986).

[†] It is interesting to note that the reaction of EtI with Al metal to give the sesqui-iodide "$Et_3Al_2I_3$" was the first recorded preparation of an organoaluminium compound (W. Hallwachs and A. Schafarik, 1859).

[74] H. HOBERG and S. KRAUSE, *Angew. Chem. Int. Edn. Engl.* **17**, 949–50 (1979).

acids; for example, the stability of the adducts LAlMe$_3$ decreases in the following sequence of L: Me$_3$N > Me$_3$P > Me$_3$As > Me$_2$O > Me$_2$S > Me$_2$Se. With protonic reagents they react to liberate alkanes:

$$Al_2R_6 + 6HX \longrightarrow 6RH + 2AlX_3$$

$$(X = OH, OR, Cl, Br)$$

Reaction with halides or alkoxides of elements less electropositive than Al affords a useful route to other organometallics:

$$MX_n \xrightarrow{\text{excess } AlR_3} MR_n + \tfrac{n}{3}AlX_3$$

$$(M = B, Ga, Si, Ge, Sn, etc.)$$

The main importance of organoaluminium compounds stems from the crucial discovery of alkene insertion reactions by K. Ziegler,[75] and an industry of immense proportions based on these reactions has developed during the past 40 y. Two main processes must be distinguished: (a) "growth reactions" to synthesize unbranched long-chain primary alcohols and alkenes (K. Ziegler *et al.*, 1955), and (b) low-pressure polymerization of ethene and propene in the presence of organometallic mixed catalysts (1955) for which K. Ziegler (Germany) and G. Natta (Italy) were jointly awarded the Nobel Prize for Chemistry in 1963.

In the first process alkenes insert into the Al–C bonds of monomeric AlR$_3$ at ~150° and 100 atm to give long-chain derivatives whose composition can be closely controlled by the temperature, pressure and contact time:

$$Al\text{–}Et_3 \xrightarrow{C_2H_4} Et_2AlCH_2Et \xrightarrow{nC_2H_4} Al\underset{(C_2H_4)_zEt}{\overset{(C_2H_4)_xEt}{-}(C_2H_4)_yEt}$$

The reaction is thought to occur by repeated η^2-coordination of ethene molecules to Al followed by migration of an alkyl group from Al to the alkene carbon atom (see Scheme).

Unbranched chains up to C$_{200}$ can be made, but prime importance attaches to chains of 14–20 C

[75] K. ZIEGLER, *Adv. Organometallic Chem.* **6**, 1–17 (1968).

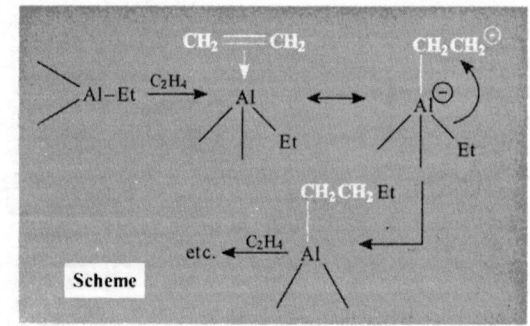

Scheme

atoms which are synthesized industrially in this way and then converted to unbranched aliphatic alcohols for use in the synthesis of biodegradable detergents:

$$Al(CH_2CH_2R)_3 \xrightarrow{\text{(i) } O_2,\ \text{(ii) } H_3O^+} 3RCH_2CH_2OH$$

Alternatively, thermolysis yields the terminal alkene RCH=CH$_2$. Note that, if propene or higher alkenes are used instead of ethene, then only single insertion into Al–C occurs. This has been commercially exploited in the catalytic dimerization of propene to 2-methylpentene-1, which can then be cracked to isoprene for the production of synthetic rubber (*cis*-1,4-polyisoprene):

$$2MeCH=CH_2 \xrightarrow{AlPr^n_3} CH_2=C\overset{Me}{\underset{Pr^n}{}}$$

cracking | –CH$_4$

rubber ← polym

Even more important is the stereoregular catalytic polymerization of ethene and other alkenes to give high-density polyethene ("polythene") and other plastics. A typical Ziegler–Natta catalyst can be made by mixing TiCl$_4$ and Al$_2$Et$_6$ in heptane: partial reduction to Ti^{III} and alkyl transfer occur, and a brown suspension forms which rapidly absorbs and polymerizes ethene even at room temperature and atmospheric pressure. Typical industrial conditions are 50–150°C and 10 atm. Polyethene produced at the surface of such a catalyst is 85–95% crystalline and has a density of 0.95–$0.98 \, g \, cm^{-3}$ (compared with low-density polymer $0.92 \, g \, cm^{-3}$); the product is stiffer, stronger, has a higher resistance to penetration by gases and liquids, and has a higher softening temperature (140–$150°$). Polyethene is produced in megatonne quantities and used mainly in the form of thin film for packaging or as molded articles, containers and bottles; electrical insulation is another major application. Stereoregular (isotactic) polypropene and many copolymers of ethene are also manufactured. Much work has been done in an attempt to elucidate the chemical nature of the catalysts and the mechanism of their action; the active site may differ in detail from system to system but there is now general agreement that polymerization is initiated by η^2 coordination of ethene to the partly alkylated lower-valent transition-metal atom (e.g. Ti^{III}) followed by migration of the attached alkyl group from transition-metal to carbon (the Cossee mechanism, see Scheme below). An alternative suggestion involves a metal–carbene species generated by α-hydrogen transfer from carbon to the transition metal.[76]

Coordination of the ethene or propene to Ti^{III} polarizes the C–C bond and allows ready migration of the alkyl group with its bonding electron-pair. This occurs as a concerted process, and transforms the η^2-alkene into a σ-bonded alkyl group. As much as 1 tonne of polypropylene can be obtained from as little as 5 g Ti in the catalyst.

Finally, in this subsection, we mention a few recent examples of the use of specific ligands to stabilize particular coordination geometries about the organoaluminium atom (see also p. 256). Trigonal planar stereochemistry has been achieved in $R_2AlCH_2AlR_2$ {R = $(Me_3Si)_2CH-$}, which was prepared as colourless crystals by reacting $CH_2(AlCl_2)_2$ with 4 moles of $LiCH(SiMe_3)_2$ in pentane.[77] It is also noteworthy that the bulky R groups permit the isolation for the first time of a molecule having the $AlCH_2Al$ grouping, by preventing the dismutation which spontaneously occurs with the Me an Et derivatives.

The linear cation $[AlMe_2]^+$ has been stabilized by use of crown ethers (p. 96).[78] For example, 15-crown-5 gives overall pentagonal bipyramidal 7-fold coordination around Al with axial Me groups having Al–C 200 pm and angle Me–Al–Me 178° (see Fig. 7.19a). With the larger ligand 18-crown-6, the Al atom is bonded to only three of the six O atoms to give unsymmetrical 5-fold coordination with Al–C 193 pm and angle Me–Al–Me 141°. Symmetrical (square-pyramidal) 5-coordinate Al is found

[76] M. L. H. GREEN, *Pure Appl. Chem.* **50**, 27–35 (1978). K. J. IVIN, J. J. ROONEY, C. D. STEWART, M. L. H. GREEN and R. MAHTAB, *J. Chem. Soc., Chem. Commun.*, 604–6 (1978).

[77] M. LAYH and W. UHL, *Polyhedron* **9**, 277–82 (1990).

[78] S. G. BOTT, A. ALVANIPOUR, S. D. MORLEY, D. A. ATWOOD, C. M. MEANS, A. W. COLEMAN and J. L. ATWOOD, *Angew. Chem. Int. Edn. Engl.* **26**, 485–6 (1987).

Scheme

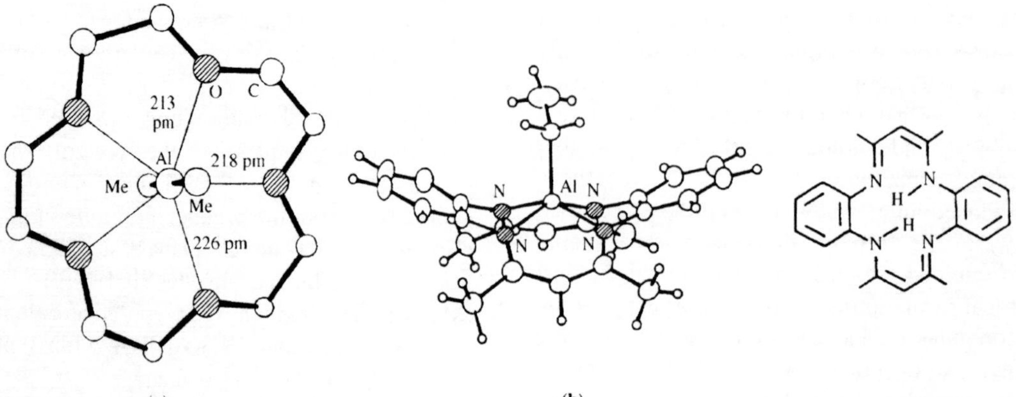

Figure 7.19 (a) Structure of the cation in $[AlMe_2(15\text{-}crown\text{-}5)]^+[AlMe_2Cl_2]^-$ showing pentagonal bipyramidal coordination of Al with axial Me groups. (b) Structure of [AlEtL] where L is the bis(deprotonated) form of the macrocycle $H_2[C_{22}H_{22}N_4]$ shown in (c).

in the complex [AlEt.L] (Fig. 7.19b) formed by reacting Al_2Et_6 in hexane solution with $H_2[C_{22}H_{22}N_4]$, i.e. H_2L, shown in Fig. 7.19c.[79] The average Al–N distance is 196.7 pm, Al–C is 197.6 pm (close to the value for the terminal Al–C in Al_2Me_6, p. 259) and the Al atom is 57 pm above the N_4 plane. A further notable feature is the great stability of the Al–C bond: the compound can be recrystallized unchanged from hydroxyllic or water-containing solvents and does not decompose even when heated to 300°C in an inert atmosphere.

Heterocyclic and cluster organoaluminium compounds containing various sequences of Al–N bonds are discussed on p. 265.

Organometallic compounds of Ga, In and Tl

Organometallic compounds of Ga, In and Tl have been less studied than their Al analogues. The trialkyls do not dimerize and there is a general tendency to diminishing thermal stability with increasing atomic weight of M. There is also a general decrease of chemical reactivity of the M–C bond in the sequence Al > Ga ≈ In > Tl, and this is particularly noticeable for compounds of the type R_2MX; indeed, Tl gives air-stable non-hydrolysing ionic derivatives of the type $[TlR_2]X$, where X = halogen, CN, NO_3, $\frac{1}{2}SO_4$, etc. For example, the ion $[TlMe_2]^+$ is stable in aqueous solution, and is linear like the isoelectronic $HgMe_2$ and $[PbMe_2]^{2+}$.

GaR_3 can be prepared by alkylating Ga with HgR_2 or by the action of RMgBr or AlR_3 on $GaCl_3$. They are low-melting, mobile, flammable liquids. The corresponding In and Tl compounds are similar but tend to have higher mps and bps; e.g.

Compound	GaMe₃	InMe₃	TlMe₃
MP	−16°	88.4°	38.5°
BP	56°	136°	147° (extrap)

Compound	GaEt₃	InEt₃	TlEt₃
MP	−82°	–	−63°
BP	143°	84°/12 mmHg	192° (extrap)

The triphenyl analogues are also monomeric in solution but tend to associate into chain structures in the crystalline state as a result of weak intermolecular M···C interactions: GaPh₃ mp

79 V. L. GOEDKEN, H. ITO and T. ITO, *J. Chem. Soc., Chem. Commun.*, 1453–5 (1984).

166°, $InPh_3$ mp 208°, $TlPh_3$ mp 170°. For Ga and In compounds the primary M–C bonds can be cleaved by HX, X_2 or MX_3 to give reactive halogen-bridged dimers $(R_2MX)_2$. This contrasts with the unreactive ionic compounds of Tl mentioned above, which can be prepared by suitable Grignard reactions:

$$TlX_3 + 2RMgX \longrightarrow [TlR_2]X + 2MgX_2$$

As in the case of organoaluminium compounds, unusual stereochemistries can be imposed by suitable design of ligands. Thus, reaction of $GaCl_3$ with 3,3′,3″-nitrilotris(propylmagnesium chloride), $[N\{(CH_2)_3MgCl\}_3]$, yields colourless crystals of $[\overline{Ga(CH_2)_3N}]$ in which intramolecular N→Ga coordination stabilizes a planar trigonal monopyramidal geometry about Ga as shown schematically in Fig. 7.20(a).[80] Because of steric constraints, the Ga–N distance of 209.5 pm is about 7% longer than the sum of the covalent radii (195 pm), although not so long as in Me_3GaNMe_3 (220 pm). Long bonds are also a feature of the unique 6-coordinate complex of $InMe_3$ with the heterocyclic triazine ligand $(Pr^iNCH_2)_3$. The air-sensitive adduct, $[Me_3In\{\eta^3-(Pr^iNCH_2)_3\}]$, can be prepared by

direct reaction of the donor and acceptor in ether solution, and is the first example of a tridentate cyclotriazine complex; it is also the first example of $InMe_3$ accepting three lone pairs of electrons rather than the more usual one or two.[81] The structure (Fig. 7.20b) features a shallow InC_3 pyramid with C–In–C angles of 114°–117° and extremely acute N–In–N angles (48.6°) associated with the long In–N bonds (278 pm). The three Pr^i groups are all in equatorial positions.

Cyclopentadienyl and arene complexes of Ga, In and Tl have likewise attracted increasing attention during the past decade and provide a rich variety of structural types and of chemical diversity. $[Ga(C_5H_5)_3]$, prepared directly from $GaCl_3$ and an excess of LiC_5H_5 in Et_2O, was found to have simple trigonal planar Ga bonded to three η^1-C_5H_5 groups. The more elusive C_5Me_5 derivative was finally prepared from $GaCl_3$ and an excess of the more reactive NaC_5Me_5 in thf solution, or by reduction of $Ga(C_5Me_5)_nCl_{3-n}$ ($n = 1, 2$) with sodium naphthalenide in thf.[82] $[Ga(C_5Me_5)_3]$

80 H. SCHUMANN, U. HARTMANN, A. DIETRICH and J. PICKARDT, *Angew. Chem. Int. Edn. Engl.* **27**, 1077–8 (1988).

81 D. C. BRADLEY, D. M. FRIGO, I. S. HARDING, M. B. HURSTHOUSE and M. MOTEVALLI, *J. Chem. Soc., Chem. Commun.*, 577–8 (1992).

82 O. T. BEACHLEY and R. B. HALLOCK, *Organometallics* **6**, 170–2 (1987).

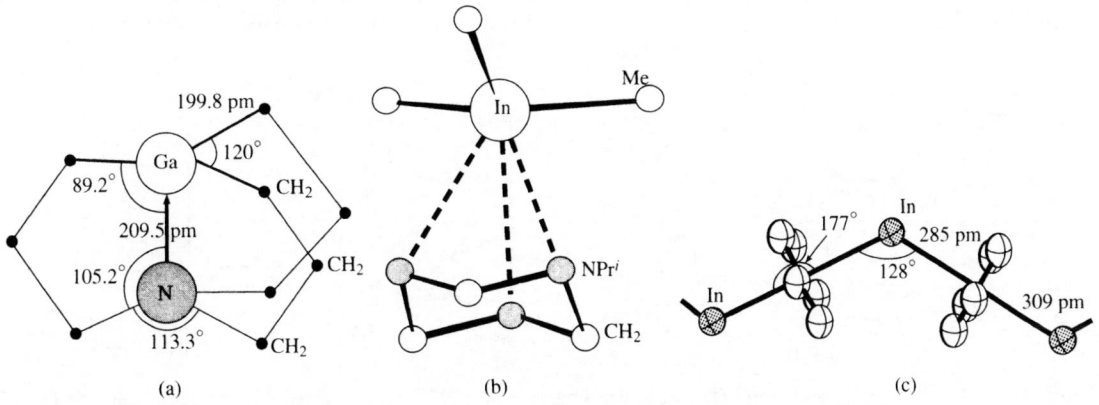

Figure 7.20   (a) Structure of $[\overline{Ga(CH_2)_3N}]$ showing trigonal planar monopyramidal 4-fold coordination about Ga and tetrahedral coordination about N. (b) Structure of $[Me_3In\{\eta^3-(Pr^iNCH_2)_3\}]$ — see text for dimensions. (c) Structure of polymeric $[In(\eta^5-C_5H_5)]$.

is a colourless, sublimable, crystalline solid, mp 168°, and appears to be a very weak Lewis acid.

As distinct from the cyclopentadienyls of Ga^{III}, those of In and Tl involve the +1 oxidation state of the metal and pentahapto bonding of the ligand. $[In(\eta^5\text{-}C_5H_5)]$ is best prepared by metathesis between LiC_5H_5 and a slurry of InCl in Et_2O.[83] It is monomeric in the gas phase with a 'half-sandwich' structure, the In–C_5(centroid) distance being 232 pm, but in the solid state it is a zig-zag polymer with significantly larger In–C_5(centroid) distances as shown in Fig. 7.20c.[84] The crystalline pentamethyl derivative, by contrast, is hexameric and features an octahedral In_6 cluster each vertex of which is η^5-coordinated by C_5Me_5.[85] $[Tl(\eta^5\text{-}C_5H_5)]$ precipitates as air-stable yellow crystals when aqueous TlOH is shaken with cyclopentadiene. In the gas phase the compound is monomeric with C_{5v} symmetry, the Tl atom being 241 pm above the plane of the ring (microwave), whereas in the crystalline phase there are zig-zag chains of equispaced alternating

C_5H_5 rings and Tl atoms similar to the In homologue.

Hexahapto (η^6-arene) complexes of Ga^I and In^I can be obtained from solutions of the lower halides (p. 240) in aromatic solvents, and some of these have surprisingly complex structures.[86] With bulky ligands such as C_6Me_6 simple adducts crystallize in which the cations $[M(\eta^6\text{-}C_6Me_6)]^+$ have the C_{6v} 'half-sandwich' structure shown in Fig. 7.21a, e.g. $[Ga(\eta^6\text{-}C_6Me_6)][GaCl_4]$ mp 168° and $[Ga(\eta^6\text{-}C_6Me_6)][GaBr_4]$ mp 146°.[87] With less bulky ligands such as mesitylene (1,3,5-$C_6H_3Me_3$), a 2:1 stoichiometry is possible to give cations $[M(\eta^6\text{-}C_6H_3Me_3)_2]^+$ shown schematically in Fig. 7.21b, although further ligation from the anion may also occur; e.g. $[In(\eta^6\text{-}C_6H_3Me_3)_2][InBr_4]$ features polymeric helical chains in which bridging $[\mu\text{-}\eta^1,\eta^2\text{-}InBr_4]$ units connect the cations as shown in Fig. 7.21c.[88] With still less bulky ligands such as benzene itself, discrete dimers can be formed as in the solvated complex $[Ga(\eta^6\text{-}C_6H_6)_2][GaCl_4].3C_6H_6$. This features tilted bis(arene)Ga^I units linked through bridging $GaCl_4$ units to form the dimeric structure shown in Fig. 7.22a.[86] Mixed adducts can also be prepared. Thus, when

[83] C. PEPPE, D. G. TUCK and L. VICTORIANO, *J. Chem. Soc., Dalton Trans.*, 2592 (1981).

[84] O. T. BEACHLEY, J. C. PAZIK, T. E. GLASSMAN, M. R. CHURCHILL, J. C. FETTINGER and R. BLOM, *Organometallics* **7**, 1051–9 (1988).

[85] O. T. BEACHLEY, M. R. CHURCHILL, J. C. FETTINGER, J. C. PAZIK and L. VICTORIANO, *J. Am. Chem. Soc.* **108**, 4666–8 (1986).

[86] H. SCHMIDBAUR, *Angew. Chem. Int. Edn. Engl.* **24**, 893–904 (1985).

[87] H. SCHMIDBAUR, U. THEWALT and T. ZAFIROPOULOS, *Angew. Chem. Int. Edn. Engl.* **23**, 76–7 (1984).

[88] J. EBENHÖCH, G. MÜLLER, J. RIEDE and H. SCHMIDBAUR, *Angew. Chem. Int. Edn. Engl.* **23**, 386–8 (1984).

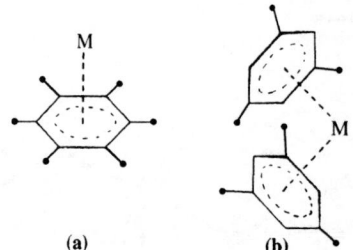 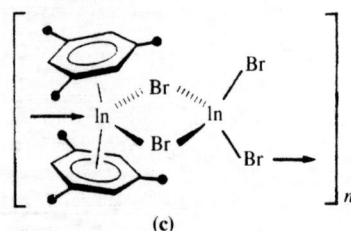

(a)   (b)   (c)

Figure 7.21 (a) The 'half-sandwich' C_{6v} structure characteristic of $[Ga(\eta^6\text{-}C_6Me_6)]^+$. (b) The 'bent-sandwich' structure found in ions of the type $[In(\eta^6\text{-}C_6H_3Me_3)_2]^+$. (c) A section of the helical chain in $[In(\eta^6\text{-}mes)_2][InBr_4]$ showing the $[\mu\text{-}\eta^1,\eta^2\text{-}InBr_4]$ unit bridging ions of the type shown in (b); the tilting angle is 133° and the ring-centres of the two arene ligands are almost equidistant from In (283 and 289 pm).

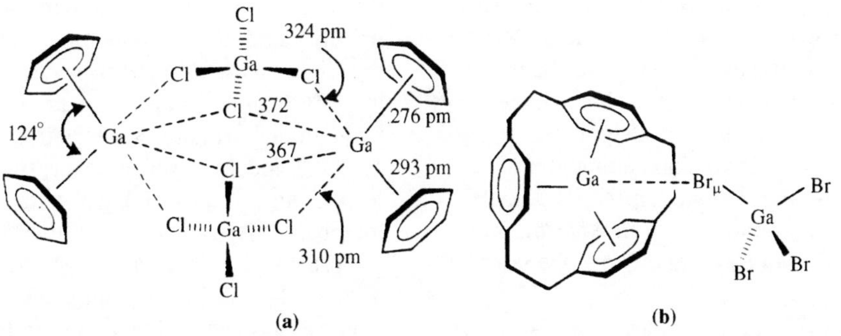

Figure 7.22 (a) Structure of the dimeric unit in the solvated complex $[Ga(\eta^6\text{-}C_6H_6)_2][GaCl_4].3C_6H_6$ indicating the principal dimensions; the six benzene molecules of solvation per dimer lie outside the coordination spheres of the gallium atoms. (b) Structure of the ion-pair $[Ga(\eta^{18}\text{-}[2.2.2] \text{ paracyclophane})][GaBr_4]$; the four Ga–Br distances within the tetrahedral anion are in the range 230.5–233.3 pm, the distance for Ga–Br$_\mu$ being 231.9 pm; the Ga$^I \cdots$ Br$_\mu$ distance is 338.8 pm.

dilute toluene solutions of Ga_2Cl_4 and durene $(1,2,4,5\text{-}C_6H_2Me_4)$ are cooled to 0°, crystals containing the centrosymmetric dimer $[\{Ga(\eta^6\text{-dur})(\eta^6\text{-tol})\}GaCl_4]_2$ are obtained.[89] The structure resembles that in Fig. 7.22a, with each Ga^I centre η^6-bonded to one durene molecule at 264 pm and one toluene molecule at 304 pm. These bent-sandwich moieties are then linked into dimeric units via three of the four Cl atoms of each of the two GaCl$_4$ tetrahedra.

An even more remarkable structure emerges for the monomeric complex of Ga_2Br_4 with the tris(arene) ligand [2.2.2]paracyclophane (Fig. 7.22b):[90] the Ga^I centre is encapsulated in a unique η^{18} environment which has no parallels even in transition-metal coordination chemistry. The Ga$^+$ cation is almost equidistant from the three ring centres (265 pm) but is displaced away from the ligand centre by 43 pm towards the GaBr$_4^-$ counter anion. The complex was prepared by dissolving the dimeric benzene complex $[\{(C_6H_6)_2Ga.GaBr_4\}_2]$ (cf. Fig. 7.22a) in benzene and adding the cyclophane.

Al–N heterocycles and clusters

Finally, in this chapter, attention should be drawn to a remarkable range of heterocyclic and cluster organoaluminium compounds containing various sequences of Al–N bonds[91] (cf. B–N compounds, p. 207). Thus the adduct $[AlMe_3(NH_2Me)]$ decomposes at 70°C with loss of methane to give the cyclic amido trimers *cis*- and *trans*-$[Me_2AlNHMe]_3$ (structures 2 and 3) and at 215° to give the oligomeric imido cluster compounds $(MeAlNMe)_7$ (structure 6) and $(MeAlNMe)_8$ (structure 7), e.g.:

$$21AlMe_3 + 21NH_2Me \xrightarrow[-21CH_4]{70°} 7(Me_2AlNHMe)_3$$

$$\xrightarrow[-21CH_4]{215°} 3(MeAlNMe)_7$$

Similar reactions lead to other oligomers depending on the size of the R groups and the conditions of the reaction, e.g. *cyclo*-$(Me_2AlNMe_2)_2$ (structure 1) and the imido-clusters $(PhAlNPh)_4$, $(HAlNPr^i)_4$ or 6,

89 H. SCHMIDBAUR, R. NOWAK, B. HUBER and G. MÜLLER, *Polyhedron* **9**, 283–7 (1990).

90 H. SCHMIDBAUR, R. HAGER, B. HUBER and G. MÜLLER, *Angew. Chem. Int. Edn. Engl.* **26**, 338–40 (1987). See also H. SCHMIDBAUR, W. BUBLAK, B. HUBER and G. MÜLLER, *Organometallics* **5**, 1647–51 (1986).

91 S. AMIRKHALILI, P. B. HITCHCOCK and J. D. SMITH, *J. Chem. Soc., Dalton Trans.*, 1206–12 (1979); and references 1–9 therein. See also P. P. POWER, *J. Organometallic Chem.* **400**, 49–69 (1990); K. M. WAGGONER, M. M. OLMSTEAD and P. P. POWER, *Polyhedron* **9**, 257–63 (1990); A. J. DOWNS, D. DUCKWORTH, J. C. MACHELL and C. R. PULHAM, *Polyhedron* **11**, 1295–304 (1992).

$(HAlNPr^n)_6$ or $_8$, $(HAlNBu^t)_4$, and $(MeAlN-Pr^i)_{4 or 6}$ (see structures 4, 5, 7). Intermediate amido-imido compounds have also been isolated from the reaction, e.g. $[Me_2AlNHMe)_2$ $(MeAlNMe)_6]$ (structure 8). Oligomers up to $(RAlNR')_{16}$ have been obtained although not necessarily structurally characterized. The known structures are all built up from varying numbers of fused 4-membered and 6-membered AlN heterocycles.

Until recently tetramers such as (4) were the smallest oligomers involving alternating Al and N atoms. It will be noted, however, that the hexamer (5) comprises a hexagonal prism formed by conjoining two plane six-membered rings. By increasing the size of the exocyclic groups it has proved possible to isolate a planar trimer, $(MeAlNAr)_3$, which is isoelectronic with borazine (p. 210). Thus, thermolysis of a mixture of $AlMe_3$ and $ArNH_2$

$(Ar = 2, 6-Pr_2^iC_6H_3)$ in toluene at 110° results in the smooth elimination of CH_4 to give the dimer, $(Me_2AlNHAr)_2$, which, when heated to 170°, loses more methane to give a high yield of the trimer, $(MeAlNAr)_3$, as colourless, air- and moisture-sensitive crystals.[92] The six *ipso*-C atoms are coplanar with the planar 6-membered Al_3N_3 ring and the Al–N distance of 178 pm is significantly shorter than in the higher (4-coordinate) oligomers (189–196 pm). Comparison with other 3-coordinate Al and N centres is difficult because of the paucity of examples but the homoleptic monomer $[Al\{N(SiMe_3)_2\}_3]$ has also been reported to have Al–N distances of 178 pm.

Several analogous gallium compounds are also known, e.g. $[(Me_2GaNHMe)_2(MeGaNMe)_6]$

92 K. M. WAGGONER, H. HOPE and P. P. POWER, *Angew. Chem. Int. Edn. Engl.* **27**, 1699–700 (1988).

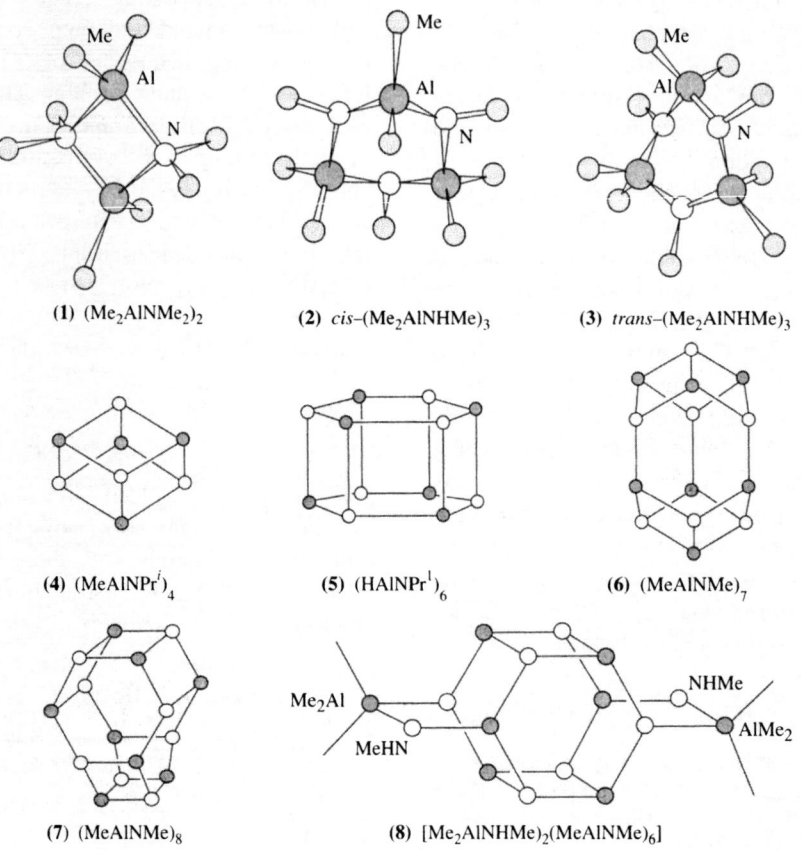

(1) $(Me_2AlNMe_2)_2$

(2) *cis*–$(Me_2AlNHMe)_3$

(3) *trans*–$(Me_2AlNHMe)_3$

(4) $(MeAlNPr^i)_4$

(5) $(HAlNPr^1)_6$

(6) $(MeAlNMe)_7$

(7) $(MeAlNMe)_8$

(8) $[Me_2AlNHMe)_2(MeAlNMe)_6]$

(structure 8).[91] Likewise, $(R_2GaPBu^t_2)_2$ and $(R_2GaAsBu^t_2)_2$ (R = Me, Bu^n) have structures analogous to (1).[93] A more complex 12-membered Ga_5As_7 cluster has been characterized in $[(PhAsH)(R_2Ga)(PhAs)_6(RGa)_4]$ (R = Me_3SiCH_2).[94] The cyclic trimer, $[\{(triph)\text{-}GaP(chex)\}_3]$, (where triph = $2,4,6\text{-}Ph_3C_6H_2$ and chex = cyclo-C_6H_{11}) is of interest in being the first well characterized heterocycle consisting entirely of heavier main-group elements. It is obtained as pale yellow crystals by reacting (triph)$GaCl_2$ with Li_2P(chex) and is formally iso-electronic with borazine (p. 210). Indeed, it has short Ga–P distances (mean 229.7 pm) but the ring is markedly non-planar and there is a slight, statistically significant alternation in Ga–P distances with three averaging at 228.5(4) pm and three at 230.8(4) pm.[95] Much of the burgeoning interest in this area of volatile compounds of Group 13 elements has come from attempts to devise effective routes to thin films of III–V semiconductors such as GaP, GaAs, etc. via MOCVD (metal-organic chemical vapour deposition).

93 A. M. ARIF, B. L. BENAC, A. H. COWLEY, R. GEERTS, R. A. JONES, K. B. KIDD, J. M. POWER and S. T. SCHWAB, *J. Chem. Soc., Chem. Commun.*, 1543–5 (1986).

94 R. L. WELLS, A. P. PURDY, A. T. McPHAIL and C. G. PITT, *J. Chem. Soc., Chem. Commun.*, 487–8 (1986).

95 H. HOPE, D. C. PESTANA and P. P. POWER, *Angew. Chem. Int. Edn. Engl.* **30**, 691–3 (1991).

8

Carbon

8.1 Introduction

One thing is absolutely certain — it is quite impossible to do justice to the chemistry of carbon in a single chapter; or, indeed, a single book. The areas of chemistry traditionally thought of as organic chemistry will largely be omitted except where they illuminate the general chemistry of the element. The field of organometallic chemistry is discussed in Section 19.7: this has been one of the most rapidly developing areas of the subject during the past 40 y and has led to major advances in our understanding of the structure, bonding and reactivity of molecular compounds. In fact, the unifying concepts emerging from organometallic chemistry emphasize the dangers of erecting too rigid a barrier between various branches of the subject, and nowhere is the boundary between inorganic and organic chemistry more arbitrary and less helpful than here. The present chapter gives a general account of the chemistry of carbon and its compounds; a more detailed discussion of specific organometallic systems will be found under the individual elements. Discussion of Group trends and the comparative chemistry of the Group 14 elements C, Si, Ge, Sn and Pb is deferred until Chapter 10.

Carbon was known as a substance in prehistory (charcoal, soot) though its recognition as an element came much later, being the culmination of several experiments in the eighteenth century.[1] Diamond and graphite were known to be different forms of the element by the close of the eighteenth century, and the relationship between carbon, carbonates, carbon dioxide, photosynthesis in plants, and respiration in animals was also clearly delineated by this time (see Panel). The great upsurge in synthetic organic chemistry began in the 1830s and various structural theories developed following the introduction of the concept of valency in the 1850s. Outstanding achievements in this area were F. A. Kekulé's use of structural formulae for organic compounds and his concept of the benzene ring, L. Pasteur's work on optical activity and the concept of tetrahedral carbon (J. H. van't Hoff).[†]

---

[1] M. E. WEEKS, *Discovery of the Elements*, Chaps. 1 and 2, pp. 58–89. J. Chem. Educ. Publ., 1956.

[†] J. A. Le Bel, whose name is often also associated with this concept, did indeed independently suggest a 3-dimensional model for the 4-coordinate C atom, but vigorously opposed the tetrahedral stereochemistry of van't Hoff for many years and favoured an alternative square pyramidal arrangement of the bonds.

Early History of Carbon and Carbon Dioxide

—	Carbon known as a substance in prehistory (charcoal, soot) but not recognized as an element until the second half of the eighteenth century.
BC	"Indian inks' made from soot used in the oldest Egyptian hieroglyphs on papyrus.
AD 1273	Ordinance prohibiting use of coal in London as prejudicial to health — the earliest known attempt to reduce smoke pollution in Britain.
~1564	Lead pencils first manufactured commercially during Queen Elizabeth's reign, using Cumberland graphite.
1752/4	CO_2 ("fixed air"), prepared by Joseph Black (aged 24–26), was the first gas other than air to be characterized: (i) chalk when heated lost weight and evolved CO_2 (genesis of quantitative gravimetric analysis), and (ii) action of acids on carbonates liberates CO_2.
1757	J. Black showed that CO_2 was produced by fermentation of vegetables, by burning charcoal and by animals (humans) when breathing; turns lime water turbid.
1771	J. Priestley established that green plants use CO_2 and "purify air" when growing. He later showed that the "purification" was due to the new gas oxygen (1774).
1779	Elements of photosynthesis elucidated by J. Ingenhousz: green plants in daylight use CO_2 and evolve oxygen; in the dark they liberate CO_2.
1789	The word "carbon" (Fr. *carbone*) coined by A. L. Lavoisier from the Latin *carbo*, charcoal. The name "graphite" was proposed by A. G. Werner and D. L. G. Harsten in the same year: Greek γραφίεν (*graphein*), to write. The name "diamond" is probably a blend of Greek δίαφανής (*diaphanes*), transparent, and αδαμας (*adamas*), indomitable or invincible, in reference to its extreme hardness.
1796	Diamond shown to be a form of carbon by S. Tennant who burned it and weighed the CO_2 produced; graphite had earlier been shown to be carbon by C. W. Scheele (1779); carbon recognized as essential for converting iron to steel (R.-A.-F de Réaumur and others in the late eighteenth century).
1805	Humphry Davy showed carbon particles are the source of luminosity in flames (lamp black).

The first metal carbonyl compounds $Ni(CO)_4$ and $Fe(CO)_5$ were prepared and characterized by L. Mond and his group in 1889–91 and this work has burgeoned into the huge field of metal carbonyl cluster compounds which is still producing results of fundamental importance. Even more extensive is the field of organometallic chemistry which developed rapidly after the seminal papers on the "sandwich" structure of ferrocene (E. O. Fischer and W. Pfab, 1952; G. Wilkinson, M. Rosenblum, M. C. Whiting and R. B. Woodward, 1952) and the "π bonding" of ethylene complexes (M. J. S. Dewar 1951, J. Chatt, and L. A. Duncanson, 1953). The constricting influence of classical covalent-bond theory was finally overcome when it was realized that carbon in many of its compounds can be 5-coordinate (Al_2Me_6, p. 258), 6-coordinate ($C_2B_{10}H_{12}$, p. 185) or even 7-coordinate (Li_4Me_4, p. 104). A compound featuring an 8-coordinate carbon atom is shown on p. 1142. In parallel with these developments in synthetic chemistry and bonding theory have been technical and instrumental advances of great significance; foremost amongst these have

been the development of ^{14}C radioactive dating techniques (W. F. Libby, 1949), the commercial availability of ^{13}C nmr instruments in the early 1970s, and the industrial production of artificial diamonds (General Electric Company, 1955). These and other notable dates in carbon chemistry are summarized in the Panel on p. 270.

The most exciting recent development in the chemistry of carbon has been the intriguing discovery of a whole new range of soluble molecular forms of elemental carbon, the fullerenes, of which C_{60} and C_{70} are the most prominent members. This was recognized by the 1996 Nobel Prize for Chemistry and has stimulated an enormous amount of research which is discussed in Section 8.2.4 (p. 279).

8.2 Carbon

8.2.1 Terrestrial abundance and distribution

Carbon occurs both as the free element (graphite, diamond) and in combined form (mainly as the

Some Notable Dates in Carbon Chemistry

1807   J. J. Berzelius classified compounds as "organic" or "inorganic" according to their origin in living matter or inanimate material.

1825-7   W. C. Zeise prepared $K[Pt(C_2H_4)Cl_3]$ and related compounds; though of unknown structure at the time they later proved to be the first organometallic compounds.

1828   The vitalist theory of Berzelius challenged by F. Wöhler (aged 28) who synthesized urea, $(NH_2)_2CO$, from $NH_4(OCN)$.

1830+   Rise of synthetic organic chemistry.

1848   L. Pasteur (aged 26) began work on optically active sodium ammonium tartrate.

1849   First metal alkyls, e.g. $ZnEt_2$, made by E. Frankland (aged 24); he also first propounded the theory of valency (1852).

1858   F. A. Kekulé's structural formulae for organic compounds; ring structure of benzene 1865.

1874   Tetrahedral, 4-coordinate carbon proposed by J. H. van't Hoff (aged 22) see also footnote to p. 268.

1890   First paper on metal carbonyls $[Ni(CO)_4]$ by L. Mond, C. Langer and F. Quincke.

1891   Carborundum, SiC, made by E. G. Acheson.

1900   First paper by V. Grignard (aged 29) on RMgX syntheses. Nobel Prize 1912.

1924   Solid CO_2 introduced commercially as a refrigerant.

1926 C_8K prepared — the first alkali metal-graphite intercalation compound.

1929   Isotopes of C (^{12}C and ^{13}C) discovered by A. S. King and R. T. Birge in the band spectrum of C_2, CO and CN (previously undetected by mass spectrometry).

1932   First metal halide-graphite intercalation compound made with $FeCl_3$.

1936   Radiocarbon $^{14}_6C^*$ established as the product of an (n,p) reaction on $^{14}_7N$ by W. E. Burcham and M. Goldhaber.

1940   Chemically significant amounts of ^{14}C synthezied by S. Ruben and M. D. Kamen.

1947-9   Concept and feasibility of ^{14}C dating established by W. F. Libby (awarded Nobel Prize in 1960).

1952   Structure of ferrocene elucidated; organometallic chemistry burgeons: Nobel Prize awarded jointly to E. O. Fischer and G. Wilkinson 1973.

1953   First authentic production of artificial diamonds by ASEA, Sweden; commercial production achieved by General Electric (USA) in 1955.

1955   Stereoregular polymerization of ethene and propene by catalysts developed by K. Ziegler and by G. Natta (shared Nobel Prize 1963).

1956   Cyclobutadiene-transition metal complexes predicted by H. C. Longuet-Higgins and L. E. Orgel 3 y before they were first synthesized.

1960 π-allylic metal complexes first recognized.

1961 $^{12}C = 12$ internationally adopted as the unified atomic weight standard by both chemists and physicists.

1964   6-coordinate carbon established in various carboranes by W. N. Lipscomb and others. (Nobel Prize 1976 for structure and bonding of boranes).

1965   Mass spectrometric observation of CH_5^+ by F. H. Field and M. S. B. Munson, and subsequent extensive study of hypercoordinate C compounds by G. A. Olah *et al.*

1966 CS_2 complexes such as $[Pt(CS_2)(PPh_3)_2]$ first prepared in G. Wilkinson's laboratory.

1971 ^{13}C fourier-transform nmr commercially available following first observation of ^{13}C nmr signal by P. C. Lauterbur and by C. H. Holm in 1957.

1976   8-coordinate carbon established in $[Co_8C(CO)_{18}]^{2-}$ by V. G. Albano, P. Chini *et al.* (Cubic coordination of C in the antifluorite structure of Be_2C known since 1948.)

1985   Discovery of C_{60} and C_{70} molecules (fullerenes) by H. Kroto, R. E. Smalley and their colleagues.

1989   Large-scale synthesis of C_{60} and C_{70} by D. Huffmann and W. Krätschmer.

1994   Nobel Prize to G. A. Olah for contributions to carbocation chemistry.

1996   Nobel Prize to R. Curl, H. Kroto and R. E. Smalley for discovery of the fullerenes.

carbonates of Ca, Mg and other electropositive elements). It also occurs as CO_2 a minor but crucially important constituent of the atmosphere. Estimates of the overall abundance of carbon in crustal rocks vary considerably, but a value of 180 ppm can be taken as typical; this places the element seventeenth in order of abundance after Ba, Sr and S but before Zr, V, Cl and Cr.

Graphite is widely distributed throughout the world though much of it is of little economic importance. Large crystals or "flake" occur in metamorphosed sedimentary silicate rocks such as quartz, mica schists and gneisses; crystal size varies from <1 mm up to about 6 mm (average ~4 mm) and the deposits form lenses up to 30 m thick stretching several

Production and Uses of Graphite[2]

There is a world shortage of natural graphite which is particularly marked in North America and Europe. As a result, prices have risen steeply; they vary widely in the range $500–1500 per tonne (1989) depending on crystalline quality; "amorphous" graphite is $220–440 per tonne. The annual world production of 649 ktonnes was distributed as follows in 1988: China 200 kt, South Korea 108, the former Soviet Union 84, India 52, Mexico 42, Brazil 32, North Korea 25, Czechoslovakia 25, Others 81 kt.

The USA used 37 ktonnes of natural graphite in 1989, nearly all imported; in addition, over 300 ktonnes of graphite was manufactured. Natural graphite is used in refractories (27%), lubricants (17%), foundries (14%), brake linings (12%), pencils (5.3%), crucibles, retorts, stoppers, sleeves and nozzles (4.0%) etc.

Artificial graphite was first manufactured on a large scale by A. G. Acheson in 1896. In this process coke is heated with silica at $\sim$2500°C for 25–35 h:

$$SiO_2 + 2C \xrightarrow{-2CO} \{SiC\} \xrightarrow{2500°} Si(g) + C(graphite)$$

In the USA artificial graphite is now made on a scale exceeding 300 kilotonnes pa (1989), and is used mainly for electrodes, crucibles and vessels, and various unmachined shapes; specialist uses include motor brushes and contacts and refractories of various sorts.

Carbon (graphite) fibres are also being manufactured on an increasing scale: The global market (1990) is of the order of 6 million kg per annum and prices range from $20–2000/kg depending on specifications (diameter, strength, stiffness, etc.). The two main production methods are the oxidative thermolysis of polyacrilonitrile fibres at 200–300°C under tension or the thermolysis of pitch at 370° followed by die-extrusion and stretching to give filaments which are then heated progressively in dry air to 2500°. Ultra-high-purity graphite is made on a substantial scale for use as a neutron moderator in nuclear reactors. Carbon whiskers grown from highly purified graphite are finding increasing use in high-strength composites; the whiskers are manufactured by striking a carbon arc at 3600°C under 90 atm Ar — the maximum length is $\sim$50 mm and the average diameter 5 μm.

kilometres across country. Average carbon content is 25% but can rise as high as 60% (Malagasy). Beneficiation is by flotation followed by treatment with HF and HCl, and then by heating to 1500°C *in vacuo*. Microcrystalline graphite (sometimes referred to as "amorphous") occurs in carbon-rich metamorphosed sediments and some deposits in Mexico contain up to 95% C. World production has remained fairly constant for the past few years and was 649 ktonnes in 1988 (see Panel above).

Diamonds are found in ancient volcanic pipes embedded in a relatively soft, dark coloured basic rock called "blue ground" or "kimberlite", from the South African town of Kimberley where such pipes were first discovered in 1870. Diamonds are also found in alluvial gravels and marine terraces to which they have been transported over geological ages by the weathering and erosion of pipes. The original mode of formation of the diamond crystals is still a subject of active investigation. The diamond content of a typical kimberlite pipe is extremely low, of the order of 1 part in 15 million, and the mineral must be isolated mechanically by crushing, sluicing and passing the material over greased belts to which the diamonds stick. This, in part, accounts for the very high price of gem-quality diamonds which is about 1 million times the price of flake graphite. The pattern of world production has changed dramatically over the past few decades as indicated in the Panel on p. 272.

Three other forms of carbon are manufactured on a vast scale and used extensively in industry: coke, carbon black, and activated carbon. The production and uses of these impure forms of carbon are briefly discussed in the Panel on p. 274.

In addition to its natural occurrence as the free element, carbon is widely distributed in the

² *Kirk–Othmer Encyclopedia of Chemical Technology*, 4th edn., Interscience, New York, 1992, Vol. 4: Carbon and artificial graphite, pp. 949–1015; Activated carbon, pp. 1015–37; Carbon black, pp. 1037–74; Diamond, natural and synthetic, pp. 1074–96; Natural graphite, pp. 1097–117; Carbon and graphite fibres, vol 5, pp. 1–19 (1993). See also H. O. PIERSON, *Handbook of Carbon, Graphite, Diamond and Fullerenes: Properties, Processing and Applications*, Noyes Publications, Park Ridge, N.J., 1993, 399 pp.

Production and Uses of Diamond[2, 2a]

Gemstone diamonds have been greatly prized in eastern countries for over 2000 y though their introduction and recognition in Europe is more recent. The only sources were from India and Borneo until they were also found in Brazil in 1729. In South Africa diamonds were discovered in alluvial deposits in 1867 and the first kimberlite pipe was identified in 1870 with dramatic consequences. Many other finds of economic importance were made in Africa during the first half of this century: most notably in Tanzania where large-scale production began in 1940 following the discovery of the enormous Williamson pipe — still the largest in the world and covering an area of $1.4 \, km^2$. During the 1950s 99% of the world output of diamonds was from Africa but then the USSR began to emerge as a major producer following the discovery of alluvial diamonds in Siberia in 1948 and the first kimberlite-type pipe at Yakutia later the same year. Within a decade more than 20 pipes had been located in the great basin of the Vilyui River 4000 km east of the Urals, and Siberia was established as a major producer of both gem-quality and industrial diamonds. However, year-round production in Siberian conditions posed severe developmental problems, and production is now supplemented by newer finds in the Urals near Sverdlovsk. Impressive finds of kimberlite pipes have also been made in North-western Australia since 1978 and this area is now one of the world's largest producers of industrial diamonds.

Diamond is the hardest and least perishable of all minerals, and these qualities, coupled with its brilliant sparkle, which derives from its transparency and high refractive index, make it the most prized of gemstones. By far the largest natural diamond ever found (25 January 1905) was the Cullinan: it weighed 3106 carats (621.2 g) and measured $\sim 10 \times 6.5 \times 5 \, cm^3$ (the size of a man's clenched fist). Other famous stones are in the range 100–800 carats though specimens larger than 50 carats are only rarely encountered. Most naturally occurring diamonds, however, are of industrial rather than gem-stone quality. They are used as single-point tools for engraving or cutting, and for surgical knives, bearings and wire dies, as well as for industrial abrasives for grinding and polishing. Other uses are as thermistors and radiation detectors, and as optical windows for lasers, etc.

Since the late 1950s the supply of natural diamonds has been progressively augmented by diamonds synthesized at high pressures and temperatures (p. 278) and this source now accounts for 90% of all industrial diamonds. The price for such diamond grit is relatively low, about $5–25 per g, the higher prices being for the largest crystals (0.3–1 mm on edge). Total world production (1990) approached 100 tonnes (500 megacarats) and was worth about 10^9. In 1985, Sumitomo Electric (Japan) began commercial production of diamond crystals of up to 2 carats (as large as 8 mm in length) and de Beer's (South Africa) have made single crystals up to 17 mm long. Such diamonds, which are pale yellow due to nitrogen inclusions, are used as heat sinks in the electronics industry because of the very high thermal conductivity of diamond. The synthetic stones are machined and laser cut to about $3 \times 3 \times 1 \, mm^3$ and are commercially available for $150 a piece. Synthetic industrial diamonds are manufactured in 16 countries, the major producers being in USA, Japan, China and Russia.

Exciting developments are also occurring in the emerging technology of large-area thin films of synthetic diamond. Such films are of interest as heat sinks for components in the electronics industry and, when bonded to inexpensive non-diamond surfaces, can also provide the unexcelled hardness, wear resistance and chemical inertness of diamond at lower cost than that of the bulk element. The films are made by low pressure (50 mbar) chemical vapour deposition of metastable diamond at 1000°C, the crucial feature of the method being the simultaneous presence of a plasma of atomic H to prevent the concurrent deposition of graphite from the decomposing organic vapours (see p. 278).

form of coal and petroleum, and as carbonates of the more electropositive[†] elements (e.g. Group 1, p. 88, Group 2, pp. 109, 122). The great bulk of carbon is immobilized in the form of coal, limestone, chalk, dolomite and other deposits, but there is also a dynamic equilibrium as a result of the numerous natural processes which constitute the so-called carbon cycle. The various

reservoirs of carbon and the flow between them are illustrated in Fig. 8.1 from which it is clear that there are two distinct cycles — one on land and one in the sea, dynamically inter-connected by the atmosphere. CO_2 in the atmosphere ($\sim 6.7 \times 10^{11}$ tonnes) accounts for only 0.003% of carbon in the earth's crust ($\sim 2 \times 10^{16}$ tonnes). It is in rapid circulation with the biosphere being removed by plant photosynthesis and added to by plant and animal respiration, and the decomposition of dead organic matter; it is also produced by the activities of man, notably the combustion of fossil fuels for energy and the calcination of limestone for cement. These last

---

[2a] R. M. HAZEN, *The New Alchemists: Breaking Through the Barriers of High Pressure*, Times Books, New York, 1994, 286 pp. P. W. MAY, *Endeavour* **19**, 101–6 (1995).

[†] Note that the *weight* of diamonds is usually quoted in carats (1 carat = 0.200 g); this unit is quite different from the carat used to describe the *quality* of gold (p. 1176).

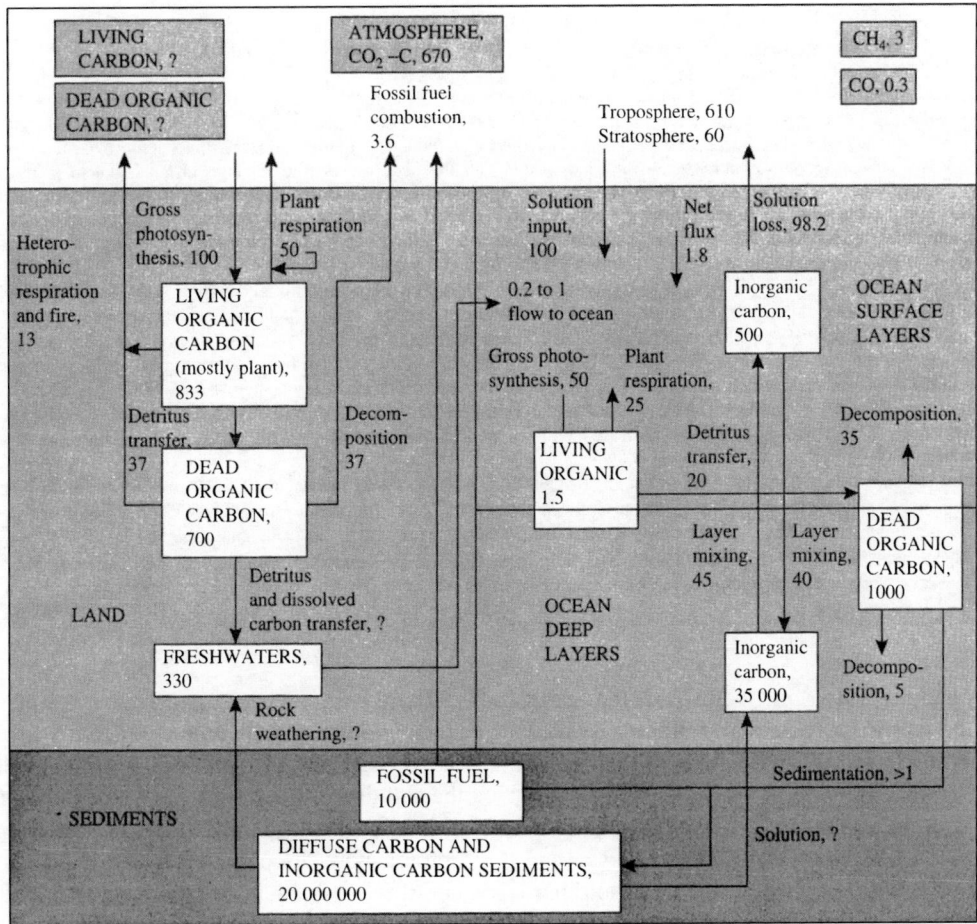

Figure 8.1 Diagrammatic model of the global carbon cycle. Questions marks indicate that no estimates are available. Figures are in units of 10^9 tonnes of contained carbon but estimates from various sources sometimes differ by factors of 3 or more. The diagram is based on one by B. Bolin[3] modified to include more recent data.[4]

two activities have increased dramatically in recent years and give some cause for concern. Interchange on a similar scale occurs between the atmosphere and ocean waters, and the total residence time of CO_2 in the atmosphere is ~10–15 y (as measured by ^{14}C experiments).

An increase in the concentration of atmospheric CO_2 has been thought by some to expose the planet to the dangers of a "greenhouse

effect" whereby the temperature is raised due to the trapping of the earth's thermal radiation by infrared absorption in the CO_2 molecules. In fact, the greenhouse gases, especially water vapour and CO_2, play a crucial role in regulating the temperature of the earth and its atmosphere. In the absence of these gases the average surface temperature would be $-18°C$ instead

[3] B. BOLIN, The carbon cycle, *Scientific American*, September 1970, reprinted in *Chemistry in the Environment*, pp. 53–61, W. H. Freeman, San Francisco, 1973.

[4] *SCOPE Report 10 on Environmental Issues*, Carbon, pp. 55–8, Wiley, New York, 1977. SCOPE is the Scientific Committee on Problems of the Environment; it reports to ICSU, the International Council of Scientific Unions.

Production and Uses of Coke, Carbon Black and Activated Carbon[2]

The high-temperature carbonization of coal yields metallurgical coke, a poorly graphitized form of carbon; most of this (92%) is used in blast furnaces for steel manufacture (p. 1072). World production of coke is of the order of 400 million tonnes per annum and was dominated, as expected, by the large industrial nations. Carbon black (soot) is made by the incomplete combustion of liquid hydrocarbons or natural gas; the scale of operations is enormous, world production in 1992 being nearly 7 million tonnes. The particle size of carbon black is exceedingly small ($0.02-0.30\,\mu$m) and its principal application (90%) is in the rubber industry where it is used to strengthen and reinforce the rubber in a way that is not completely understood. For example, each car tyre uses 3 kg carbon black and each truck tyre ~9 kg. Its other main uses are as a pigment in plastics (4.4%) in printing inks (3.6%) and paints (0.7%).

Activated carbons, being highly specialized products, are produced on a correspondingly smaller scale. World production capacity in 1990 being some 400 kilotonnes (USA 146, Western Europe 108, Japan 72 kt). They are distinguished by their enormous surface area which is typically in the range $300-2000\,\text{m}^2\,\text{g}^{-1}$. Activated carbon can be made either by chemical or by gas activation. In chemical activation the carbonaceous material (sawdust, peat, etc.) is mixed or impregnated with materials which oxidize and dehydrate the organic substrate when heated to $500-900°$, e.g. alkali metal hydroxides, carbonates or sulfates, alkaline earth metal chlorides, carbonates or sulfates, $ZnCl_2$, H_2SO_4 or H_3PO_4. In gas activation, the carbonaceous matter is heated with air at low temperature or with steam, CO_2 or flue gas at high temperature ($800-1000°$).

Activated carbon is used extensively in the sugar industry as a decolorizing agent and this accounts for some 20% of the output; related applications are in the purification of chemicals and gases including air pollution (15%), and in water and waste water treatment (50%). Notable catalytic uses are the aerial oxidation in aqueous solutions of Fe^{II}, $[Fe^{II}(CN)_6]^{4-}$, $[As^{III}O_3]^{3-}$ and $[N^{III}O_2]^-$, the manufacture of $COCl_2$ from CO and Cl_2, and the production of SO_2Cl_2 from SO_2 and Cl_2. The cost of activated carbon (USA, 1990) was $0.70-5.50 per kg depending on the grade.

of the present value of $+15°$ and the earth would be a frozen, essentially lifeless planet. However, there is legitimate concern that atmospheric temperatures may rise still further due to the steadily increasing concentration of CO_2 and other gases (e.g. CH_4, N_2O, CFCs and O_3) although reliable estimates are extraordinarily difficult to obtain and depend sensitively on the computer modelling of the many interacting effects.[5] Perhaps the most reliable estimate is that there will be a temperature rise from the greenhouse effect of $1.5 \pm 1.0°$C and a resulting average rise in sea level of 20 ± 14 cm by the year AD 2030, though even this assumes that other unrelated effects of potentially similar magnitude will not occur. The best estimates of all the various counterbalancing effects leads to the conclusion that the change in sea level will probably not exceed ± 10 cm during the next century.

There has also been concern that the increased concentration of CO_2 will significantly lower the pH of surface ocean waters thereby modifying the solution properties of $CaCO_3$ with potentially disastrous consequences to marine life. Informed opinion now discounts such global catastrophes but there has undoubtedly been a measurable perturbation of the carbon cycle in the last few decades, and the prudent course is to conserve resources, minimize wasteful practices and improve efficiency, whilst simultaneously collecting reliable data on the magnitude of the various carbon-containing reservoirs and the rates of transfer between them.[6]

8.2.2 Allotropic forms

Carbon can exist in at least 6 crystalline forms in addition to the many newly prepared fullerenes described in Section 8.2.4: α- and β-graphite, diamond, Lonsdaleite (hexagonal

---

[5] THE ROYAL SOCIETY (LONDON), *The Greenhouse Effect: the scientific basis for policy*, Submission to the House of Lords Select Committee, 40 pp. (1989). See also *Global Climate Change*, Information Pamphlet (12 pp.) issued by the American Chemical Society (1990); B. HILEMAN, Global Warming, *Chem. & Eng. News*, April 27, 7–19 (1992); and references cited therein.

[6] B. BOLIN, B. R. DÖÖS, J. JÄGER and R. A. WARRICK (eds.), SCOPE 29, *The Greenhouse Effect, Climatic Change and Ecosystems*, 2nd edn., 1989, 574 pp.

diamond), chaoite, and carbon(VI). Of these, α- (or hexagonal) graphite is thermodynamically the most stable form at normal temperatures and pressures. The various modifications differ either in the coordination environment of the carbon atoms or in the sequence of stacking of layers in the crystal. These differences have a profound effect on both the physical and the chemical properties of the element.

Graphite is composed of planar hexagonal nets of carbon atoms as shown in Fig. 8.2. In normal α- (or hexagonal) graphite the layers are arranged in the sequence $\cdots$ABAB$\cdots$ with carbon atoms in alternate layers vertically above each other, whereas in β- (or rhombohedral) graphite the stacking sequence is $\cdots$ABCABC$\cdots$. In both forms the C–C distance within the layer is 141.5 pm and the interlayer spacing is much greater, 335.4 pm. The two forms are interconvertible by grinding ($\alpha \rightarrow \beta$) or heating above 1025°C ($\beta \rightarrow \alpha$), and partial conversion

leads to an increase in the average spacing between layers; this reaches a maximum of 344 pm for turbostratic graphite in which the stacking sequence of the parallel layers is completely random. The enthalpy difference between α- and β-graphite is only $0.59 \pm 0.17 \, \text{kJ mol}^{-1}$.

In diamond, each C atom is tetrahedrally surrounded by 4 equidistant neighbours at 154.45 pm, and the tetrahedra are arranged to give a cubic unit cell with a_0 356.68 pm as in Fig. 8.3. Note that, although the diamond structure itself is not close-packed, it is built up of 2 interpenetrating fcc lattices which are off-set along the body diagonal of the unit cell by one-quarter of its length. Nearly all naturally occurring diamonds ($\sim$98%) are of this type but contain, in addition, a small amount of nitrogen atoms (0.05–0.25%) in platelets of approximate composition C_3N (type Ia) or, very occasionally ($\sim$1%), dispersed throughout the

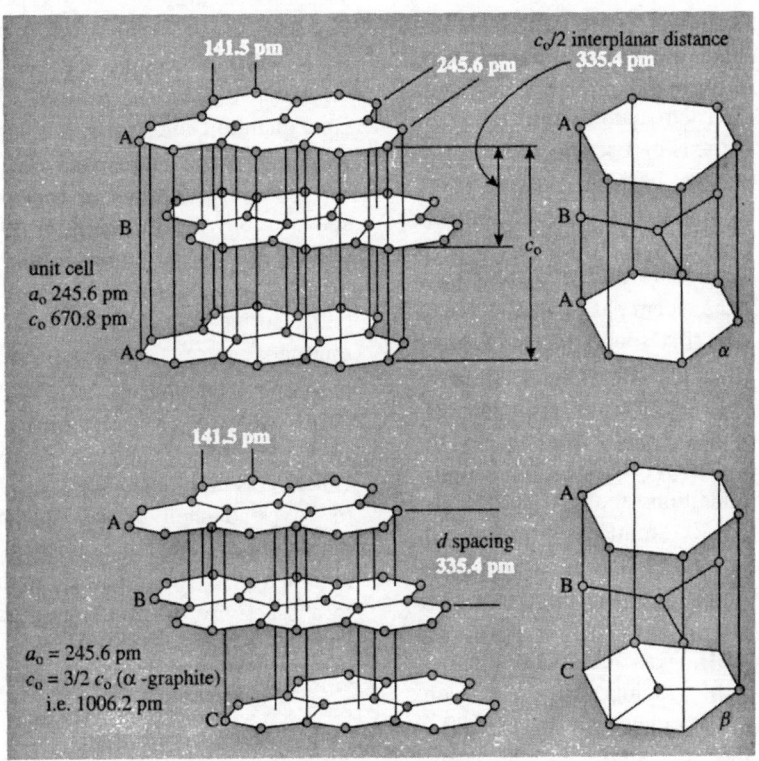

Figure 8.2   Structure of the α (hexagonal) and β (rhombohedral) forms of graphite.

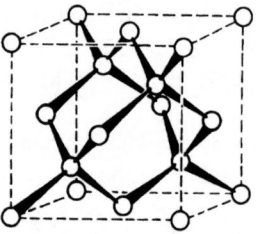

Figure 8.3 Structure of diamond showing the tetrahedral coordination of C; the dashed lines indicate the cubic unit cell containing 8 C atoms.

crystal (type Ib). A small minority of natural diamonds contain no significant amount of N (type IIa) and a very small percentage of these (including the highly valued blue diamonds, type IIb), contain Al. The exceedingly rare hexagonal modification of diamond, Lonsdaleite, was first found in the Canyon Diablo Meteorite, Arizona, in 1967: each C atom is tetrahedrally coordinated but the tetrahedra are stacked so as to give a hexagonal wurtzite-like lattice (p. 1210) rather than the cubic sphalerite-type lattice (p. 1210) of normal diamond. Lonsdaleite can be prepared at room temperature by static pressure along the c-axis of a single crystal of α-graphite, though it must be heated above 1000° under pressure to stabilize it (a_o 252 pm, c_o 412 pm, d_{obs} 3.3 g cm^{-3}, d_{calc} 3.51 g cm^{-3}).

Two other crystalline forms of carbon have been discovered in the recent past. Chaoite, a new white allotrope, was first found in shock-fused graphitic gneiss from the Ries Crater, Bavaria, in 1968; it can be synthesized artificially as white dendrites of hexagonal symmetry by the sublimation etching of pyrolytic graphite under free vaporization conditions above ~2000°C and at low pressure (~10^{-4} mmHg). The crystals were only 0.5 μm thick and 5–10 μm long and had a_o 894.5 pm, c_o 1407.1 pm and d_{calc} 3.43 g cm^{-3}. Finally, in 1972, a new hexagonal allotrope, carbon(VI), was obtained together with chaoite when graphitic carbons were heated resistively or radiatively at ~2300°C under any pressure of argon in the range 10^{-4} mmHg to 1 atm; laser heating was even

more effective (a_o 533 pm, c_o 1224 pm, $d >$ 2.9 g cm^{-3}). The detailed crystal structures of chaoite and carbon(VI) have not yet been determined but they appear to be based on a carbyne-type motif $-C\equiv C-C\equiv C;$[7] both are much more resistant to oxidation and reduction than graphite is and their properties are closer to those of diamond. Indeed, it now seems possible that there is a sequence of at least 6 stable carbyne allotropes in the region between stable graphite and the mp of carbon.

The structural differences between graphite and diamond are reflected in their differing physical and chemical properties, as outlined in the following sections.

8.2.3 Atomic and physical properties

Carbon occurs predominantly as the isotope ^{12}C but there also is a small amount of ^{13}C; the concentration of ^{13}C varies slightly from 0.99 to 1.15% depending on the source of the element, the most usual value being 1.10% which leads to an atomic weight for "normal" carbon of 12.0107(8). Like the proton, ^{13}C has a nuclear spin quantum number $I = \frac{1}{2}$, and this has been exploited with increasing effectiveness during the past two decades in fourier transform nmr spectroscopy.[8] In addition to ^{12}C and ^{13}C, carbon dioxide in the atmosphere contains 1.2 × 10^{-10}% of radioactive ^{14}C which is continually being formed by the $^{14}_7$N(n,p)$^{14}_6$C reaction with thermal neutrons resulting from cosmic ray activity. ^{14}C decays by β^- emission (E_{max} 0.156 MeV, E_{mean} 0.049 MeV) with a half-life of 5715 ± 30 y,[9] and this is sufficiently long to enable a steady-state equilibrium concentration to be established in the biosphere. Plants and animals therefore contain 1.2 × 10^{-10}% of their carbon as ^{14}C whilst they are living, and this leads to a β-activity of 15.3 counts per min per gram

[7] A. G. WHITTAKER, *Science* **200**, 763–4 (1978). See also Anon, *Chem. & Eng. News*, 29 Sept., p. 12 (1980).

[8] H.-O. KALINOWSKI, S. BERGER and S. BRAUN, *Carbon-13 NMR Spectroscopy*, Wiley, Chichester, 1988.

[9] N.E. HOLDEN, *Pure Appl. Chem.* **62**, 941–58 (1990).

of contained C. However, after death the dynamic interchange with the environment ceases and the ^{14}C concentration decreases exponentially. This is the basis of W. F. Libby's elegant radio-carbon dating technique for which he was awarded the Nobel Prize for Chemistry in 1960. It is particularly valuable for archeological dating.[10] (A modern variant is to count the number of ^{14}C atoms directly in a mass spectrometer.) The practical limit is about 50 000 y since by this time the ^{14}C activity has fallen to about 0.2% of its original valuable and becomes submerged in the background counts. ^{14}C is also extremely valuable as a radioactive tracer for mechanistic studies using labelled compounds, and many such compounds, particularly organic ones, are commercially available (p. 310).

Carbon is the sixth element in the periodic table and its ground-state electronic configuration is [He]$2s^2 2p^2$. The first 4 ionization energies of C are 1086.5, 2352.6, 4620.5 and 6222.7 kJ mol^{-1}, all much higher than those for the other Group 14 elements Si, Ge, Sn and Pb (p. 372). Excitation energies from the ground-state to various low-lying electron configurations of importance in valence theory are also well established:

Configuration	$2s^2 2p^2$	$2s^2 2p^2$	$2s^2 2p^2$
Term symbol	^3P	^1D	^1S
Energy/kJ mol^{-1}	0.000	121.5	258.2
Configuration	$2s^1 2p^3$	$2s^1 2p^3$	
Term symbol	$^5S°$	$^5S_{\text{valence state}}$	
Energy/kJ mol^{-1}	402.3	~632	

Of these, all are experimentally observable except the $^5S_{\text{valence state}}$ level which is a calculated value for a carbon atom with 4 unpaired and uncorrelated electron spins; this is a hypothetical state, not amenable to experimental observation, but is helpful in some discussions of bond energies and covalent bonding theory.

The electronegativity of C is 2.5, which is fairly close to the values for other members of the group (1.8–1.9) and for several other elements: B, As (2.0); H, P (2.1); Se (2.4); S, I (2.5); many of the second- and third-row transition metals also have electronegativities in the range 1.9–2.4.

The "single-bond covalent radius" of C can be taken as half the interatomic distance in diamond, i.e. $r(C) = 77.2$ pm. The corresponding values for "doubly-bonded" and "triply-bonded" carbon atoms are usually taken to be 66.7 and 60.3 pm respectively though variations occur, depending on details of the bonding and the nature of the attached atom (see also p. 292). Despite these smaller perturbations the underlying trend is clear: the covalent radius of the carbon atom becomes smaller the lower the coordination number and the higher the formal bond order.

Some properties of α-graphite and diamond are compared in Table 8.1. As expected from its structure, graphite is less dense than diamond and many of its properties are markedly anisotropic. It shows ready cleavage parallel to the basal plane, and this accounts for its flaky appearance, softness, and use as a lubricant although this latter property is due not so much to weak interplanar forces on an atomic scale as to the presence of adsorbed gases, since the coefficient of friction of graphite increases 5-fold at high altitudes and by a factor of 8 in a vacuum. By contrast, diamond can be cleaved in many directions, thus enabling many facets to be cut in gem-stones, but it is extremely hard and involatile because of the strong C–C bonding throughout the crystal. Interestingly, diamond has the highest thermal conductivity of any known substance (more than 5 times that of Cu) and for this reason the points of diamond cutting tools do not become overheated. Diamond also has one of the lowest known coefficients of thermal expansion: 1.06×10^{-6} at room temperature.

The optical and electrical properties of the two forms of carbon likewise reflect their differing structures. Graphite is a black, highly reflecting semi-metal with a resistivity $\rho \sim 10^{-4}$ ohm cm within the basal plane though this increases by a factor of ~5000 along the c-axis. Diamond, on the other hand, is transparent and has a high refractive index; there is a band energy gap of

[10] J. M. Michels, *Dating Methods in Archeology*, Seminar Press, New York, 1973, 230 pp., S. Fleming, *Dating in Archeology: A Guide to Scientific Techniques*, Dent, London, 1976, 272 pp.

Table 8.1   Some properties of α-graphite and diamond

Property	α-Graphite	Diamond
Density/g cm^{-3}	2.266 (ideal) varies from 2.23 (petroleum coke) to 1.48 (activated C)	3.514
Hardness/Mohs	<1	10
MP/K	4100 $\pm$ 100 (at 9 kbar)	4100 $\pm$ 200 (at 125 kbar)
ΔH_{subl}/kJ mol^{-1}	715[a]	~710[a]
Refractive index, n (at 546 nm)	2.15 (basal) 1.81 (c-axis)	2.41
Band gap E_g/kJ mol^{-1}	—	~580
ρ/ohm cm	(0.4–5.0) $\times$ 10^{-4} (basal) 0.2–1.0 (c-axis)	10^{14}–10^{16}
$\Delta H_{combustion}$/kJ mol^{-1}	393.51	395.41
ΔH_f°/kJ mol^{-1}	0.00 (standard state)	1.90

[a]Sublimation to monatomic C(g).

~580 kJ mol^{-1} so that diamond has a negligible electrical conductivity, the specific resistivity being of the order 10^{14}–10^{16} ohm cm. (For other properties and industrial applications of diamond, see ref. 11.)

As may be seen from the heats of combustion, α-graphite is more stable than diamond at room temperature, the heat of transformation being about 1.9 kJ mol^{-1}. However, as the molar volume of diamond (3.418 cm^3) is much smaller than that of graphite (5.301 cm^3), it follows that diamond can be made from graphite by application of a suitably high pressure, provided that the temperature is also sufficiently high to permit movement of the atoms. Such transformations were first successfully achieved in 1953–5, using pressures up to 100 kbar and temperatures in the range 1200–2800 K;[2a] the presence of molten-metal catalysts such as Cr, Fe, or Ni was also found to be necessary, suggesting that the transformation may proceed via the formation of unstable metal carbide intermediates. Very recently red phosphorus has also been shown to catalyse the conversion of graphite to diamond at 77 kbar and 1800°C.[12] The use of kinetically controlled non-equilibrium processes to deposit thin films of crystalline

diamond has already been mentioned (p. 272). The relationship between the conditions for these various processes is summarized in Fig. 8.4 which shows the phase diagram of carbon near its triple point.[13] This schematic representation does not explicitly include the several carbyne-like carbon phases[7] which have been identified at very low pressures (10^{-4}–10^{-8} kbar) in the region marked X.

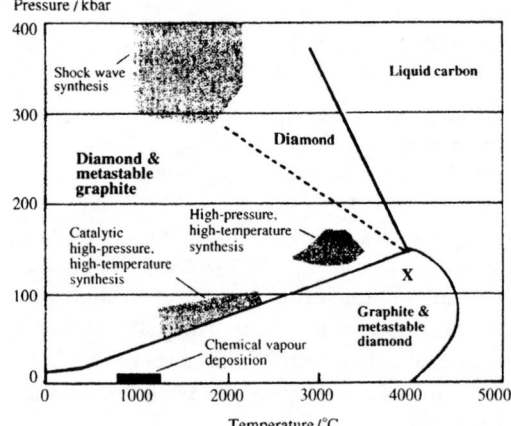

Figure 8.4   Phase diagram of carbon showing regions of importance for the production of synthetic diamond.[13]

[11] J. E. FIELD (ed.), *The Properties of Diamond*, Academic Press, London, 1979, 660 pp.

[12] M. AKAISHI, H. KANDA and S. YAMAOKA, *Science* **259**, 1592–3 (1993).

[13] P. K. BACHMANN and R. MESSLER, *Chem. & Eng. News*, May 15, 24–39 (1989).

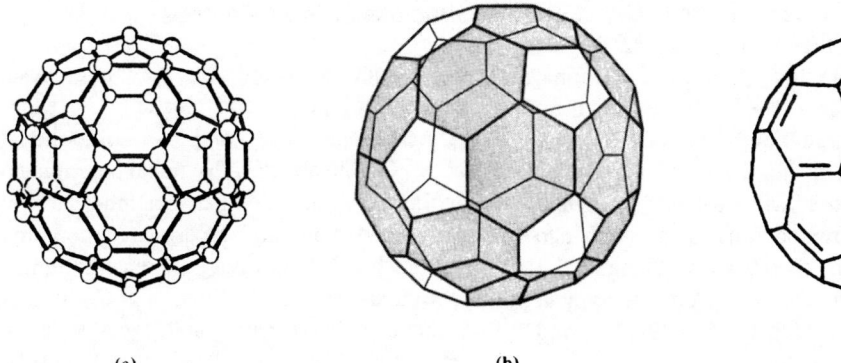

(a)　　　　　　　　　　　　　　(b)　　　　　　　　　　　　　　(c)

Figure 8.5 Three representations of the structure of C_{60}. (a) normal "ball-and-stick" model; (b) the polyhedron derived by truncating the 12 vertices of an icosahedron to form 12 symmetrically separated pentagonal faces; (c) a conventional bonding model.

8.2.4 Fullerenes

One of the most exciting and challenging developments in recent chemistry has been the synthesis and characterization of many new, soluble, *molecular* modifications of carbon. As a result, the number of identified allotropes of this element has increased enormously and their intriguing chemistry is gradually being elucidated. The new allotopes form an extensive series of polyhedral cluster molecules, C_n (*n* even), comprising fused pentagonal and hexagonal rings of C atoms. The first member to be characterized was C_{60} which features 12 pentagons separated by 20 fused hexagons as shown in Fig. 8.5. It has full icosahedral symmetry (p. 141) and was given the name buckminsterfullerene in honour of the architect R. Buckminster Fuller whose buildings popularized the geodesic dome, which uses the same tectonic principle. Other fullerenes which have been isolated and characterized include C_{70}, C_{76} (chiral), C_{78} (3 isomers), C_{84} (3 isomers), C_{90} and C_{94}, but there is mass spectrometric evidence for all even C_n from C_{30} to $C_{>600}$, (m.wt. 7206.6).

The fullerene story began in September 1985 when a group lead by H. W. Kroto (Sussex, UK) and R. E. Smalley (Rice, Texas) laser-blasted graphite at T > 10^4 °C and showed mass spectrometrically that the product contained a series of molecules with even numbers of atoms

from C_{44} to C_{90}.[14] Concentrations of the individual molecules varied with conditions but the peak for C_{60} was always by far the strongest, followed by C_{70}. This experiment showed the existence of new molecular forms of carbon but was not a bulk preparation. However, in a brilliant flash of insight it was conjectured that the stability of C_{60} might result from the football-like "spherical" structure of a truncated icosahedron, the most symmetrical of all possible structures in 3-dimensional space (Nobel Prize, 1996, see p. 270).

Three years later two astrophysicists, W. Krätschmer (Heidelberg, Germany) and D. R. Huffman (Tucson, Arizona), remembered an unusual and unexpected UV spectrum they had obtained in 1983 from soot obtained by striking an arc between graphite electrodes at about 3500°C under a low pressure of helium gas. They re-examined the material mass-spectrometrically and found it contained high concentrations of C_{60} and C_{70} which were soluble in aromatic hydrocarbon solvents such as benzene and toluene.[15] Here was a stunningly simple preparation of fullerenes in bulk, although separation of individual members proved to

[14] H. W. Kroto, J. R. Heath, S. C. O'Brien and R. E. Smalley, *Nature* **318**, 162–4 (1985).
[15] W. Krätschmer, L. D. Lamb, K. Fostiropoulos and D. R. Huffman, *Nature* **347**, 354–8 (1990).

be more difficult. Pure C_{60} and C_{70} were obtained for the first time on 22 August 1990 by chromatographic separation (alumina, hexane).[16] The process can easily be scaled up using multi-rod apparatus to give about 20 g/day of soot containing up to 10% of fullerenes; this can be extracted with toluene to yield about 15 g/week of mixed fullerenes which can be further separated if required. Commercial availability has also assisted progress, typical prices (1994) being £150/g for C_{60} (99.9%) and £2000/g for C_{70} (98%).

Other routes to C_{60} and C_{70} are being developed, e.g. (*i*) heating naphthalene vapour ($C_{10}H_8$) in argon at about 1000°C followed by extraction with CS_2; (*ii*) burning soot in a benzene/oxygen flame at about 1500°C with argon as a diluent. C_{60} and C_{70} have also been detected in several naturally occurring minerals, e.g. in carbon-rich semi-anthracite deposits from the Yarrabee mine in Queensland, Australia;[17a] in shungite, a highly metamorphosed meta-anthracite from Shunga, Karelia, Russia;[17b] and in a Colorado, USA fulgurite (a glassy mineral which can be formed when lightning strikes the ground).[17c] Most recently, significant finds of naturally occurring fullerenes have been made in Sudbury (Canada) and New Zealand.[17d]

The purified fullerenes have very attractive colours. Thin films of C_{60} are mustard-coloured (dark brown in bulk) and solutions in aromatic hydrocarbons are a beautiful magenta. Thin films of C_{70} are reddish brown (greyish black in bulk) and solutions are port-wine red. C_{76}, C_{78} and C_{84} are yellow.[16]

---

[16] R. TAYLOR, J. P. HARE, A. K. ABDUL-SADA and H. W. KROTO, *J. Chem. Soc., Chem. Commun.*, 1423–5 (1990). R. TAYLOR (and 12 others), *Pure Appl. Chem.* **65**, 135–42 (1993).

[17a] M. A. WILSON, L. S .K. PANG and A. M. VASSALLO, *Nature* **355**, 117–8 (1992).

[17b] P. R. BUSEK, S. J. TSIPURSKI and R. HETTICH, *Science* **257**, 215–17 (1992).

[17c] T. K. DALT, P. R. BUSECK, P. W. WILLIAMS and C. F. LEWIS, *Science* **259**, 1599–601 (1993).

[17d] R. DAGANI, *Chem. & Eng. News*, Aug. 1, 1994, pp. 4,5. See also L. BECKER, R. J. POREDA and J. L. BADA, *Science* **272**, 249–52 (1996).

Structure of the fullerenes

The structural motif of the fullerenes is a sequence of polyhedral clusters, C_n, each with 12 pentagonal faces and ($\frac{1}{2}n - 10$) hexagonal faces. C_{60} itself has 20 hexagonal faces and, significantly, is the first member for which all 12 pentagonal faces are non-adjacent. Smaller homologues have increasing numbers of contiguous pentagonal faces; e.g. C_{32} is expected to have only 6 hexagonal faces. As can be seen from Fig. 8.5, all C atoms in C_{60} are structurally identical and, consistent with this, only one signal is observed in the ^{13}C nmr spectrum (at 142.68 ppm). However, there are two geometrically distinct types of C–C bond: those at an edge shared between two fused hexagons, and those at an edge between a hexagon and a pentagon.

By contrast, C_{70} has 25 hexagonal faces and D_{5h} symmetry (Fig. 8.6a) with 5 types of C atom (a, b, c, d, e) and 8 types of C–C bond. Five ^{13}C nmr signals are therefore expected, with intensities in the ratio 10:10:20:20:10, and these are observed in the range 150.77–130.28 ppm.[16] Again, a ^{13}C nmr study of chromatographically isolated of C_{76} showed it to have 28 hexagonal faces and a fascinating chiral structure of D_2 symmetry, consisting of a spiralling double helical arrangement of edge-sharing pentagons and hexagons (Fig. 8.6b and c) uniquely consistent with the observed 19 ^{13}C nmr signals in the range 150.03–129.56 ppm, and each of equal intensity (19 × 4 = 76).[18]

The total potential number of geometric isomers increases enormously with increase in cluster size, being, for example, three for C_{30}, 40 for C_{40}, 271 for C_{50} and no fewer than 1812 for C_{60}.[19] However, the number becomes much more manageable if one considers only those isomers that have no contiguous pentagons. The theoretical justifications for this

---

[18] R. ETTL, I. CHAO, F. DIEDERICH and R. L. WHETTEN, *Nature* **353**, 149–53 (1991). D. E. MANOLOPOULOS, *J. Chem. Soc., Faraday Trans.*, **87**, 2861–2 (1991).

[19] D. E. MANOLOPOULOS and P. W. FOWLER, *J. Chem. Phys.* **96**, 7603–14 (1991).

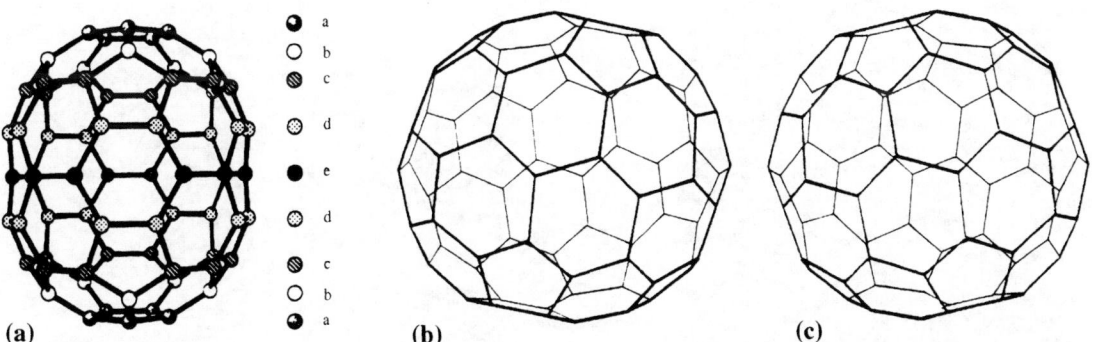

(a)   (b)   (c)

Figure 8.6   (a) The D_{5h} structure of C_{70} with the 5-fold rotation axis vertical; the five sets of geometrically distinct C atoms are labelled a-e (see text). (b), (c) Line drawings of the two enantiomers of C_{76} viewed along the short C_2 rotation axis and illustrating the chiral D_2 symmetry of the molecule.

restriction would be (a) that isomers with fused pentagons are expected to have greater σ-bonding strain energy and (b) that, since two fused pentagons have an 8-cycle around their periphery, there would be a further Hückel antiaromatic destabilizing effect on the overall π electron system. In fact, in the range $C_{20}-C_{70}$ this restriction of isolated pentagons eliminates all structures except the observed $C_{60}(I_h)$ and $C_{70}(D_{5h})$. From mass-spectrometric evidence other oligomers clearly exist, though not yet in isolable concentrations. Above C_{70} the number of distinct geometric isomers (i) with isolated pentagons increases rather rapidly with n as indicated below:[19]

n	72	74	76	78	80	82	84	86
i	1	1	2	5	7	9	24	19

n	88	90	92	94	96	98	100
i	35	46	86	134	187	259	450

Numerous other fullerenes have been isolated by the same techniques and their structures elucidated by ^{13}C nmr spectroscopy, e.g. C_{76} (see above); C_{78} [3 isomers: $C_{2v}\{18(4C) + 3(2C)$ nmr lines}, $D_3\{13(6C)\}$ and $C_{2v}\{17(4C) + 5(2C)\}$]; C_{82} [3 isomers: $C_2\{41(2C)\}$, $C_{2v}\{17(4C) + 7(2C)\}$ and $C_{3v}\{12(6C) + 3(3C) + 1(1C)\}$]; and C_{84} [2 isomers: $D_2\{21(4C)\}$ and $D_{2d}\{10(8C)$

+ 1(4C)}].[20] A copiously illustrated atlas of fullerenes elaborating and enumerating the numbers and structures of all possible fullerenes and fullerene isomers C_n as a function of n up to high n has recently been published.[20a]

Except for C_{60},[†] lack of sufficient quantities of pure material has prevented more detailed structural characterization of the fullerenes by X-ray diffraction analysis, and even for C_{60} problems of orientational disorder of the quasi-spherical molecules in the lattice have exacerbated the situation. At room temperature C_{60} crystallizes in a face-centred cubic lattice ($Fm\bar{3}$) but below 249 K the molecules become orientationally ordered and a simple cubic lattice ($Pa\bar{3}$) results. A neutron diffraction analysis of the ordered phase at 5 K led to the structure shown in Fig. 8.7a;[21] this reveals that the ordering results from the fact that

[20] F. DIEDERICH, R. L. WHETTEN, C. THILGEN, R. ETTL, I. CHAO and M. M. ALVAREZ, *Science* **254**, 1768–70 (1991). R. TAYLOR, G. J. LANGLEY, T. J. S. DENNIS, H. W. KROTO and D. R. M. WALTON, *J. Chem. Soc., Chem. Commun.*, 1043–6 (1992). K. KIKUCHI, Y. ACHIBA (and eight others) *Nature* **357**, 142–5 (1992).

[20a] P. W. FOWLER and D. E. MANOLOPOULOS, *An Atlas of Fullerenes*, Clarendon Press, Oxford, 1995, 392 pp.

[†] Gram amounts of purified C_{70} can now also be obtained by column chromatography (see *J. Am. Chem. Soc.* **116**, 6939 (1994)) and are available commercially.

[21] W. I. F. DAVID, R. M. IBBERSON, J. C. MATHEWMAN, K. PRASSIDES, T. J. S. DENNIS, J. P. HARE, H. W. KROTO, R. TAYLOR and D. R. M. WALTON, *Nature* **353**, 147–9 (1992).

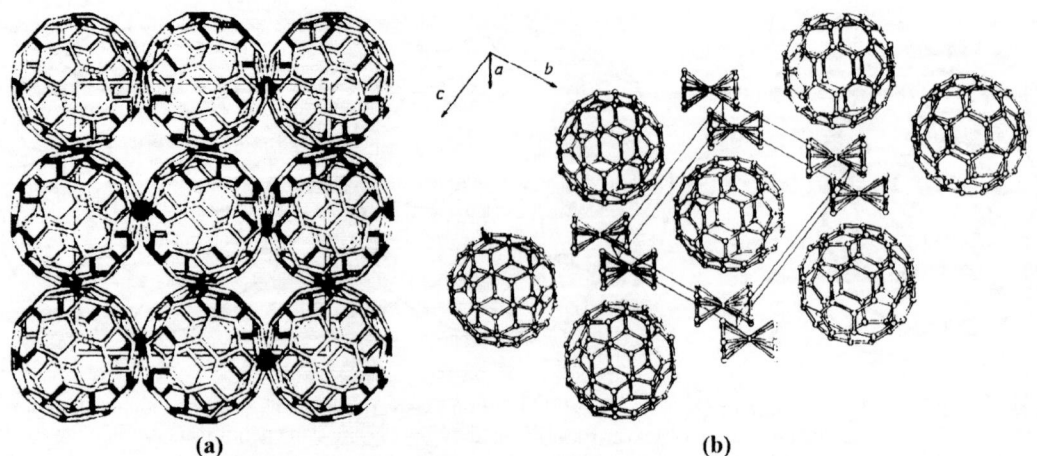

(a)   (b)

Figure 8.7   (a) The low-temperature, ordered, simple cubic arrangement of C_{60} molecules as revealed by neutron diffraction at 5 K; above 249 K the molecules become orientationally disordered and the lattice becomes fcc. (b) The packing arrangement for $[C_{60}(\text{ferrocene})_2]$ in the *bc* plane.

the electron-rich short bonds *between* pentagons (139.1 ± 1.8 pm) are positioned directly above the electron-poor pentagon face-centres of adjacent C_{60} units. The bonds *within* a given pentagon are somewhat longer (145.5 ± 1.2 pm).

The structures of the black crystalline benzene solvate $C_{60}.4C_6H_6$,[22] the black charge-transfer complex with bis(ethylenedithio)tetrathiafulvene, $[C_{60}(\text{BEDT-TTF})_2]$,[23] and the black ferrocene adduct $[C_{60}\{\text{Fe}(\text{Cp})_2\}_2]$ (Fig. 8.7b)[24] have also been solved and all feature the packing of C_{60} clusters.

Other molecular allotropes of carbon

Quite apart from the fullerene cluster molecules, numerous other molecular allotropes of carbon, C_n, have been discovered in the gases formed by the laser vaporization/supersonic expansion of graphite. The products are detected by mass

spectrometry after separation into identifiable series by gas-ion chromatography.[25] The technique suggests that linear oligomers exist from $n = 3{-}10$ and an overlapping series of monocyclic planar ring isomers from $n = 7{-}36$. Planar bicyclic rings appear for $n = 21{-}44$ and yet other series of condensed rings occur in the ranges $n = 37{-}54$ and $55{-}61$. Three-dimensional fused ring clusters form a series with $n = 28{-}35$, and the fullerenes from $C_{30}{-}C_{70}$ were seen as a quite distinct series. For each value of n from $29{-}41$ there are at least three isomers: e.g. $C_{32}{}^{+}$ comprises 23% monocyclic ring, 71% bicyclic ring, 2.4% open 3D cluster and 3.2% fullerene. The structural assignments are tentative.

Chemistry of the fullerenes

The tremendous burst of excitement which attended the initial isolation in 1990 of weighable amounts of separated fullerenes has been followed by an unparalleled and sustained surge of activity as chemists throughout the world rushed to investigate the chemical reactivity of these novel molecular forms of carbon.

[22] M. F. MEIDINE,   P. B. HITCHCOCK,   H. W. KROTO, R. TAYLOR and D. R. M. WALTON, *J. Chem. Soc., Chem. Commun.*, 1534–7 (1992).

[23] A. IZUOKA, T. TACHIKAWA, T. SUGAWARA, Y. SUZUKI, M. KONO, Y. SAITO and H. SINOHARA, *J. Chem. Soc., Chem. Commun.*, 1472–3 (1992).

[24] J. D. CRANE, P. B. HITCHCOCK, H. W. KROTO, R. TAYLOR and D. R. M. WALTON, *J. Chem. Soc., Chem. Commun.*, 1764–5 (1992).

[25] G. VON HELDEN, M.-T. HSU, P. R. KEMPER and M. T. BOWERS, *J. Chem. Phys.* **95**, 3835–7 (1991).

Considerable attention has been paid to possible mechanisms of formation[26,27] since a firm understanding of this aspect could lead to the development of more effective synthetic routes to the individual fullerenes. It is also known that, when thin films of C_{60} and C_{70} are laser-vaporized into a rapid stream of an inert gas, individual molecules of C_{60} or C_{70} can themselves coalesce to form stable larger fullerenes such as C_{120} or C_{140}, and higher multiples. Even more dramatically, when a sample of C_{60} is subjected to a pressure of 20 GPa (i.e. 200 kbar), it apparently immediately transforms into polycrystalline diamond.

Most solvents will only dissolve a few mg/l of the fullerenes. Solubility in benzene, toluene or CS_2 is somewhat higher but even so the acquisition of ^{13}C nmr data is still a lengthy and tedious business. By far the best solvents to date for C_{60} at 25°C are o-dichlorobenzene (25 mg cm^{-3}), 1-methylnaphthalene (33 mg cm^{-3}) and 1-Br-2-Me-naphthalene (35 mg cm^{-3}).[28] Colours in a range of some 30 solvents are variously pink, magenta, magenta-brown, brown-yellow, brown-green and brown, no doubt reflecting the varying interaction of the solute with the solvent (cf. I_2, p. 807).

Hydrogenation — One of the first chemical reactions of C_{60} to be studied was its Birch reduction. In a typical procedure, Li metal was added under an argon atmosphere to a suspension of C_{60} in liquid NH_3/thf, followed after 30 min by addition of Bu^tOH. Initially the off-white product was thought to be $C_{60}H_{36}$ but subsequent work using a variety of techniques[29] has shown that the product at low temperatures is a mixture of polyhydrofullerenes ranging from $C_{60}H_{18}$ to $C_{60}H_{36}$ with $C_{60}H_{32}$ being the

predominant species. This mixture is thermally labile and in the mass spectrometer probe (>250°C) $C_{60}H_{36}$ predominates, consistent with a molecule in which the 12 isolated pentagons of the C_{60} cluster each retain one double bond, i.e. $[(C_2)_{12}(CH)_{36}]$. A cleaner route to pure, white $C_{60}H_{36}$ is by using a 120-fold molar excess of 9,10-dihydroanthracene (1) as a H-transfer reagent at 350°C for 30 min. Prolonging the reaction time to 24 h produces $C_{60}H_{18}$ as a second product and the method has the added advantage that it permits the ready synthesis of $C_{60}D_{36}$, by use of 9,9′,10,10′[D_4]dihydroanthracene.[30]

(1)

Oxidation reactions — Direct fluorination of solid C_{60} with F_2 gas at 70° proceeds slowly in a stepwise manner *via* several coloured partially fluorinated materials to give, after a period of several days, the colourless fully fluorinated product $C_{60}F_{60}$.[31] Rapid fluorination under more forcing conditions (F_2 gas/UV irradiation/250°) yields $C_{60}F_{48}$ as the main product, plus an intractable mixture of other fluorides $C_{60}F_{2n}$ including some hyperfluorinated materials ($2n > 60$) which would require the opening of some skeletal C–C bonds.[32] $C_{60}F_{48}$ itself has over 20 million possible isomers but, astonishingly, the high-yield synthesis of just one of these has recently been achieved by heating a mixture of C_{60} and NaF under F_2 at 275° for several days.[33] Actually a racemic mixture of the two

[26] R. F. CURL, *Phil. Trans. Roy. Soc.* **343**, 119–32 (1993).

[27] H. SCHWARZ, *Angew. Chem. Int. Edn. Engl.* **32**, 1412–5 (1993). R. M. BAUM, *Chem. & Eng. News*, May 17, 32–4 (1993) and references cited therein.

[28] W. A. SCRIVENS and J. M. TOUR, *J. Chem. Soc., Chem. Commun.*, 1207–9 (1993).

[29] M. R. BANKS (and 14 others), *J. Chem. Soc., Chem. Commun.*, 1149–52 (1993).

[30] C. RÜCHARDT (and 8 others), *Angew. Chem. Int. Edn. Engl.* **32**, 584–6 (1993).

[31] J. H. HOLLOWAY (and 8 others), *J. Chem. Soc., Chem. Commun.*, 966–9 (1991).

[32] A. A. TUINMAN, A. A. GAKH, J. L. ADCOCK and R. N. COMPTON, *J. Am. Chem. Soc.* **115**, 5885–6 (1993).

[33] A. A. GAKH, A. A. TUINMAN J. L. ADCOCK, R. A. SACHLEBEN and R. N. COMPTION, *J. Am. Chem. Soc.* **116**, 819–20 (1994).

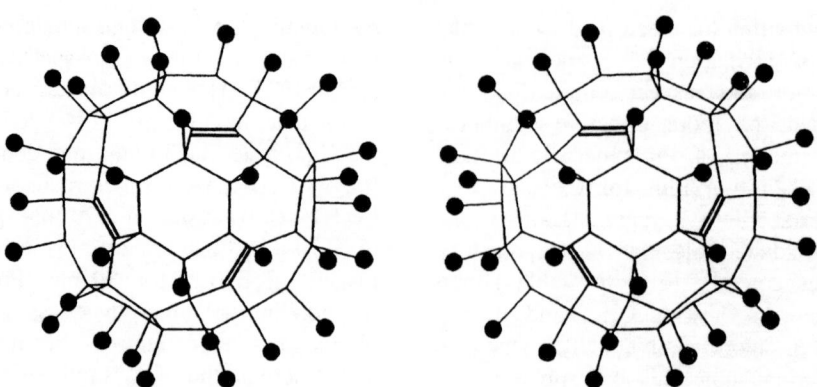

Figure 8.8 The enantiomeric pair of isomers of $C_{60}F_{48}$.[33]

chiral enantiomers shown in Fig. 8.8 is obtained. Shorter reaction times give complex mixtures of $C_{60}F_{46}$ and $C_{60}F_{48}$ isomers.

Direct chlorination of C_{60} with Cl_2 gas at 250–400°C led to an intractable pale orange mixture of polychlorinated species having on average about 24 Cl atoms per cluster molecule, but milder conditions using Cl_2 at various temperatures in a range of chloro organic solvents produced no detectable reaction.[34] By contrast, treatment of C_{60} with an excess of ICl in benzene or toluene at room temperature gave a quantitative yield of deep orange $C_{60}Cl_6$[35] which is isostructural with $C_{60}Br_6$ (see below).

Bromination of C_{60} in solution gives $C_{60}Br_6$ (magenta plates) and $C_{60}Br_8$ (dark brown prisms). The former has a structure involving one monobrominated pentagon with a long C–Br bond (203 pm) itself adjacent to five other monobrominated pentagons (C–Br 196 pm) as shown in Fig. 8.9a. It disproportionates on being warmed to give C_{60} and $C_{60}Br_8$ which has a C_{2v} structure with pairs of Br atoms arranged *meta* on four 6-membered rings (Fig. 8.9b).[36]

Bromination with liquid Br_2 yields the somewhat more stable $C_{60}Br_{24}$ which has T_h symmetry (Fig. 8.9c) with 12 hexagons disubstituted *para* and in pairs with boat conformation but mutually *meta* on the other 8 hexagons which have the chair conformation. The structure has 18 C=C arranged one per pentagon (12) and one at each 6:6 bond (6).[37] All three bromides can be completely dehalogenated on strong heating, as can the polychlorides. Iodine appears not to add directly to C_{60} but forms an intercalation product.

Fullerene epoxide, $C_{60}O$, is formed by the UV irradiation of an oxygenated benzene solution of C_{60}.[38] The O atom bridges a 6:6 bond of the closed fullerene structure. The same compound is also formed as one of the products of the reaction of C_{60} with dimethyldioxirane, $Me_2\overline{COO}$ (see later).[39]

Fullerols, $C_{60}(OH)_n$ ($n = 24-26$), can be synthesized directly by aerobic oxidation of a benzene solution of C_{60} using an aqueous solution of NaOH containing a few drops of Bu_4NOH as the most efficient catalyst: the deep violet benzene solution rapidly decolorizes and a brown sludge precipitates; further reaction with more water over a period of 10 h gives a clear red-brown solution from which the

[34] G. A. OLAH, I. BUSCI, C. LAMBERT, R. ANISFELD, N. J. TRIVEDI, D. K. SENSHARMA and G. K. S. PRAKASH, *J. Am. Chem. Soc.* **113**, 9385–7 (1991).

[35] P. R. BIRKETT, A. G. AVENT, A. D. DARWISH, H. W. KROTO, R. TAYLOR and D. R. M. WALTON, *J. Chem. Soc., Chem. Commun.*, 1230–2 (1993).

[36] P. R. BIRKETT, P. B. HITCHCOCK, H. W. KROTO, R. TAYLOR and D. R. M. WALTON, *Nature* **357**, 479–81 (1992).

[37] F. N. TEBBE (and 8 others), *Science* **256**, 822–5 (1992).

[38] K. M. CREEGAN (and 10 others), *J. Am. Chem. Soc.* **114**, 1103–5 (1992).

[39] Y. ELEMES (and 6 others), *Angew. Chem. Int. Edn. Engl.* **31**, 351–3 (1992).

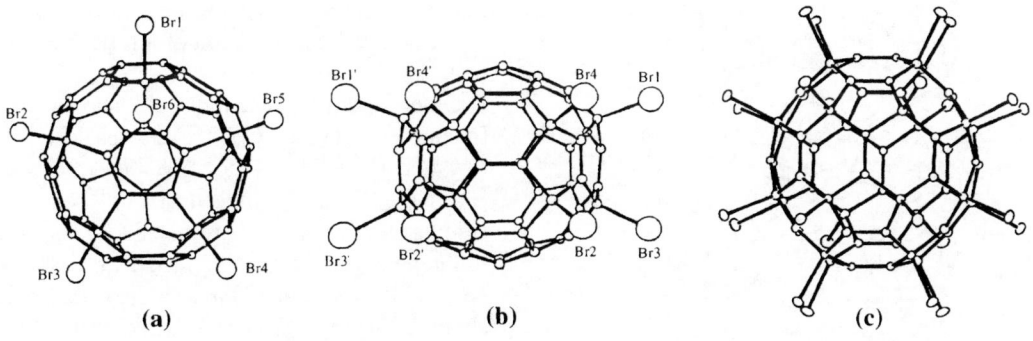

Figure 8.9   Structures of (a) $C_{60}Br_6$; (b) $C_{60}Br_8$; (c) $C_{60}Br_{24}$.

brown solid product is obtained by vacuum evaporation.[40] Hydroboration of C_{60} followed by treatment either with glacial acetic acid or aqueous $NaOH/H_2O_2$ affords another route to water-soluble fullerols, suggesting that C–H bonds on the fullerene cluster are readily oxidized to C–OH groups.[41]

Reduction of fullerenes to fullerides — Reversible electrochemical reduction of C_{60} in anhydrous dimethylformamide/toluene mixtures at low temperatures leads to the air-sensitive coloured anions $C_{60}{}^{n-}$, $(n = 1–6)$. The successive mid-point reduction potentials, $E_{1/2}$, at $-60°C$ are -0.82, -1.26, -1.82, -2.33, -2.89 and -3.34 V, respectively.[42] Liquid NH_3 solutions can also be used.[43] C_{60} is thus a very strong oxidizing agent, its first reduction potential being at least 1 V more positive than those of polycyclic aromatic hydrocarbons. C_{70} can also be reversibly reduced and various ions up to $C_{70}{}^{6-}$ have been detected.

Chemical reduction by alkali metals leads to solid fullerides which are sometimes solvated.

Thus, fullerides M_nC_{60} are known for $n = 1$ when M = Rb, Cs and for $n = 2, 3, 4$ and 6 when M = Na, K, Rb and Cs. An important alternative route treats C_{60} in toluene with a solution of $Na[Mn(\eta^5\text{-}C_5Me_5)_2]$ in thf to give an 80% yield of the dark-purple, air- and moisture-sensitive crystalline solvate $NaC_{60}.5thf$.[44]

Interest in the unsolvated compounds M_nC_{60} increased dramatically when several were found to be good electrical conductors. C_{60} films when doped with alkali metal vapour become organic metals, some of which show superconductivity at low temperatures. For example, K_3C_{60}, prepared from stoichiometric amounts of solid C_{60} and potassium vapour, has T_c 19.3 K: it has an fcc structure derived from that of C_{60} itself by incorporating K ions into all the octahedral and tetrahedral interstices of the host lattice as shown in Fig. 8.10.[45] Rb_3C_{60} has an even higher superconducting critical temperature, $T_c \sim 28$ K. It seems that, when electrons are added to C_{60} from an alkali metal, they enter a conduction band composed of the triply degenerate t_{1u} π orbitals of the individual C_{60} molecules. Maximum conductivity is observed when this band is half-filled (at $C_{60}{}^{3-}$) after which the conductivity gradually decreases until the composition M_6C_{60} when it is full, consistent

[40] J. Li, A. Takeuchi, M. Ozawa, X. Li, K. Saigo and K. Kitazawa, *J. Chem. Soc., Chem. Commun.*, 1784–5 (1993) and references cited therein.

[41] N. S. Schneider, A. D. Darwish, H. W. Kroto, R. Taylor and D. R. M. Walton, *J. Chem. Soc., Chem. Commun.*, 463–4 (1994).

[42] Y. Oshawa and T. Saji, *J. Chem. Soc., Chem. Commun.*, 781–2 (1992).

[43] W. K. Fullagar, I. R. Gentle, G. A. Heath and J. W. White, *J. Chem. Soc., Chem. Commun.*, 525–7 (1993).

[44] R. H. Douthwaite, A. R. Brough and M. L. H. Green, *J. Chem. Soc., Chem. Commun.*, 267–8 (1994).

[45] P. W. Stephens (and 7 others), *Nature* **351**, 632–4 (1991). See also H. H. Wang (and 13 others), *Inorg. Chem.* **30**, 2838–9 (1991).

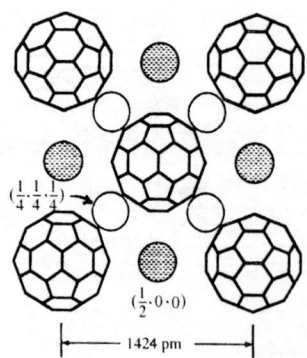

Figure 8.10 The fcc structure of K_3C_{60}, showing potassium ions occupying the tetrahedral (○) and octahedral (◉) sites. The shortest K–K distance is 617 pm (much larger than in metallic K) and the diameter of C_{60}^{3-} is 708 pm.

with the observation that K_6C_{60} (bcc lattice) is an insulator.[46]

Addition reactions — The fullerenes C_{60} and C_{70} react as electron-poor olefins with fairly localized double bonds. Addition occurs preferentially at a double bond common to two annelated 6-membered rings (a 6:6 bond) and a second addition, when it occurs is generally in the opposite hemisphere. The first characterizable mono adduct was $[C_{60}OsO_4(NC_5H_4Bu^t)_2]$, formed by reacting C_{60} with an excess of OsO_4 in 4-butylpyridine. The structure is shown in

Fig. 8.11 and was, in fact, the first definitive X-ray structural determination of a fullerene derivative.[47]

Other addition reactions are shown in the scheme.[48] Thus, C_{60} reacts as an olefin towards $[Pt^0(PPh_3)_2]$ to give the η^2 adduct $[Pt(\eta^2-C_{60})(PPh_3)_2]$. Indeed six M^0 centres can simultaneously be coordinated by a single fullerene cluster to give $[C_{60}\{M(PEt_3)_2\}_6]$, (M = Ni, Pd, Pt), with the 6M arranged octahedrally about the $(\eta^2)_6-C_{60}$ core.[49] Likewise, reaction of C_{60} with $[Ir(CO)Cl(PMe_2Ph)_2]$ provides two conformational isomers of $[(\eta^2,\eta^2-C_{60})-\{Ir(CO)Cl(PMe_2Ph)_2\}_2]$ in both of which the Ir atoms are ligated by 6:6 double bonds at diametrically opposite sides of the fullerene. Similarly,[50] C_{70} reacts with $[Ir(CO)Cl(PPh_3)_2]$ in benzene solution to give brown crystals of $[Ir(\eta^2-C_{70})(CO)Cl(PPh_3)_2]$, ligation occurring from a 6:6 double bond near one of the poles (i.e. an a–b bond in Fig. 8.6), and the bis-adduct $[(\eta^2,\eta^2-C_{70}\{Ir(CO)Cl(PPh_3)_2\}_2]$ involves a–b bonds at opposite poles. Very recently, in addition to η^2 dihapto and

[46] R. C. HADDON, *Pure Appl. Chem.* **65**, 11–15 (1993) and refs. cited therein.

[47] J. M. HAWKINS, A. MEYER, T. LEWIS, S. LOREN and F. J. HOLLANDER, *Science* **252**, 312–4 (1991).

[48] A. HIRSCH, *Angew. Chem. Int. Edn. Engl.* **32**, 1138–41 (1993) and references cited therein.

[49] P. J. FAGAN, J. C. CALABRESE and B. MALONE, *J. Am. Chem. Soc.* **113**, 9408–9 (1991). P. J. FAGAN, J. C. CALABRESE and B. MALONE, *Acc. Chem. Res.* **25**, 134–42 (1992).

[50] A. L. BALCH V. J. CATALANO, J. W. LEE, M. M. OLMSTEAD and S. R. PARKIN, *J. Am. Chem. Soc.* **113**, 8953–5 (1991).

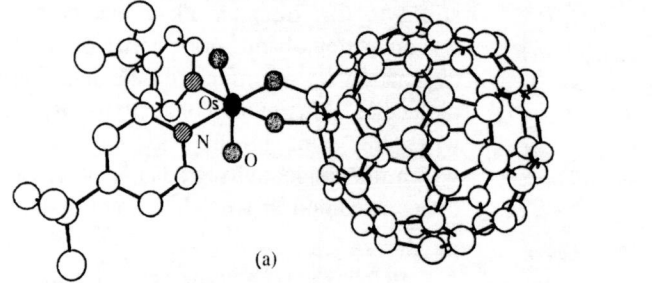

(a)   (b)

Figure 8.11 (a) Structure of $C_{60}OsO_4(NC_5H_4Bu^t)_2$ as determined by X-ray diffraction analysis.[47] (b) A schematic representation of the structure.

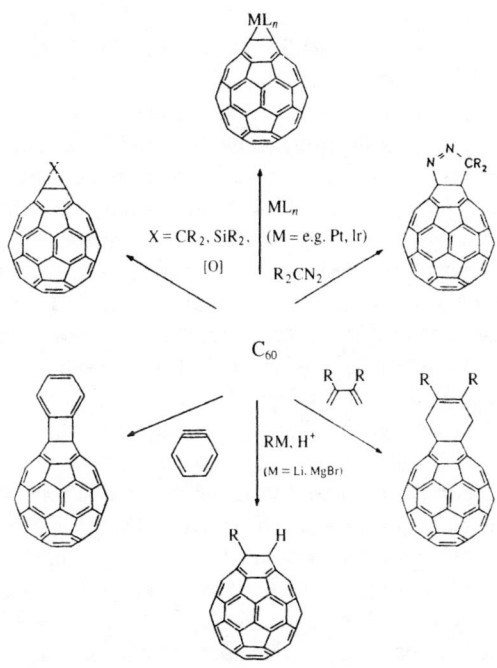

Scheme   Syntheses of exohedral fullerene derivatives. For clarity only the front sides of the fullerenes are shown.[48]

η^2,η^2 tetrahapto ligation of C_{60}, an example of η^2,η^2,η^2 hexahapto coordination has been identified in the red crystalline complex $[Ru_3[\mu_3-\eta^2,\eta^2,\eta^2-C_{60})(CO)_9]$, formed by heating C_{60} with $Ru_3(CO)_{12}$ in n-hexane, the three $C=C$ bonds from one hexagonal face displacing one CO from each Ru atom in the cluster.[50a][50b] Extensive cluster opening can also occur, as in the cobalt(I) cyclopentadienyl adduct of the purple C_{60}/butadiene fulleroid, $[Co(\eta^5-C_5H_5)(\eta^2,\eta^2-C_{60}C_4H_4)]$, which features an unprecedented fifteen-membered "trimethano[15]annulene" opening within the C_{60} framework.

Returning now to the reactions in the scheme it can be seen that carbenes and silenes

yield the derivatives $C_{60}CR_2$ and $C_{60}SiR_2$. The structurally related epoxide $C_{60}O$ has already been mentioned (p. 284). Benzyne yields a $[2+2]$ adduct as shown, since the $[4+2]$ adduct would require the formation of an energetically unfavourable 5:6 double bond. Nucleophilic reactions with Grignard reagents and Li alkyls yield intermediates which, after protonolysis, afford 1,9-$C_{60}RH$ derivatives, whereas hydroboration (not shown) yields $C_{60}H(BH_2)$ which on protonolysis gives the parent 1,9-dihydrofullerene, $C_{60}H_2$. Diels–Alder reactions give highly regiospecific addition products which can be isolated in high yield. By contrast, diphenyldiazomethane and related diazoalkanes and diazoacetates give substituted dihydropyrazole intermediates (via a $[3+2]$ cycloaddition reaction) which then lose N_2 to form the thermally stable final products; these may be *opened* π homoaromatic structures bridged at either a 5:6 or a 6:6 ring junction (Fig. 8.12a,b), or a *closed* σ homoaromatic fullerene bridged at a 6:6 ring junction (Fig. 8.12c). In the special case of diazomethane, $C_{60}(CH_2N_2)$ is formed as a thermally unstable brown solution in toluene; this loses N_2 when heated under reflux and $C_{61}H_2$ can be isolated as a dark powder from the now purple solution.[51] Structure type a (Fig. 8.12) in which the CH_2 group bridges an opened 5:6 junction is assigned on the basis of spectroscopic evidence. The opened azafulleroids $C_{60}NR$ (Fig. 8.12d) can be

50a H.-F. HSU and J. R. SHAPLEY, *J. Am. Chem. Soc.* **118**, 9192–3 (1996).

50b M.-J. ARCE, A. L. VIADO, Y.-Z. AN, S. I. KHAN and Y. RUBIN, *J. Am. Chem. Soc.* **118**, 3775–6 (1996).

51 T. SUZUKI, Q. C. LI, K. C. KHEMANI and F. WUDL, *J. Am. Chem. Soc.* **114**, 7301–2 (1992).

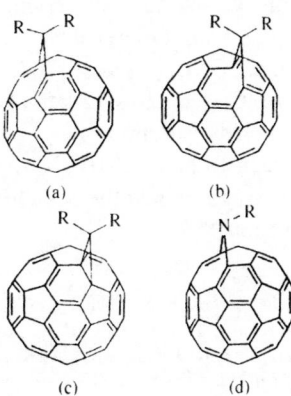

Figure 8.12   Structures (a), (b), (c) and (d); see text.

obtained from C_{60} and organic azides, RN_3, by [3 + 2] cycloaddition and subsequent loss of N_2.

Heteroatom fullerene-type clusters — The possibility of incorporation of hetero atoms into C_n clusters has excited the attention of both theoreticians and experimentalists since the earliest days of fullerene chemistry, particularly in view of the known stability and ubiquity of organic heterocycles. The structural relationship between C_{60} and β-rhombohedral boron has already been alluded to (p. 142).

Laser vaporization of a composite pressed disc of graphite and BN using He as carrier gas, followed by mass spectrometric analysis, gave a range of clusters with even numbers of atoms from less than 50 to well above 72:[52] the peak with 60 atoms was the most abundant and, in a typical run, was shown to be a mixture of clusters: C_{60} (22%), $C_{59}B$ (21%), $C_{58}B_2$ (24%), $C_{57}B_3$ (18%), $C_{56}B_4$ (9%), $C_{55}B_5$ (4%) and $C_{54}B_6$ (2%). Brief exposure of this mixture of 60-atom clusters to NH_3 at 1 µtorr for 2 s led, typically, to the formation of $C_{60-x}\{B.NH_3\}_x$ ($x = 0-4$).

Preliminary experiments with contact-arc vaporization of graphite in a stream of He containing N_2 or NH_3 yielded nitrogen-containing products tentatively assigned to species such as $C_{70}N_2$ and $C_{59}N_x$ ($x = 2, 4, 6$) of as yet undetermined structure.

The possibility of the isoelectronic replacement of pairs of C atoms by contiguous BN groups (p. 207) in fullerenes is particularly intriguing, e.g. $C_{58}BN$, $C_{60-2x}(BN)_x$. Because each fullerene, C_n, contains 12 pentagonal faces, the limit of such substitution of C_2 by alternating BN would seem to be at $C_{12}B_{24}N_{24}$, since there is a structural frustration at the odd (fifth) C atom of each pentagon.[54]

Encapsulation of metal atoms by fullerene clusters — It is readily apparent that there is sufficient space inside fullerene clusters to accommodate several other atoms: the trick has been in learning how to synthesize such species. When a composite rod of graphite/La_2O_3 was vaporized at 1200°C in argon and the resulting "soot" extracted with pyridine, the products included not only C_{60} and C_{70} but also LaC_{60}, LaC_{70}, LaC_{74} and LaC_{82}.[55] Photo fragmentation by laser irradiation can then strip off C atoms pairwise to "shrink wrap" the metal with ever smaller clusters down to about LaC_{44}. In each of these compounds the La is encapsulated by C_n, i.e. it is an *endo* compound, in contradistinction to the alkali metal fullerides discussed on p. 285. The accepted symbolism for this novel type of compound is $[La@C_{60}]$ etc., and esr shows that the correct electronic formulation is $[La^{3+}@C_{60}^{3-}]$. The smallest endohedral metallafullerene so far is $[U@C_{28}]$.[56] It is notable that C_{28} would have its 12 pentagons as 4 sets of 3, plus 4 hexagons, all arranged tetrahedrally to give T_d symmetry. MO calculations suggest that neutral C_{28} lacks $4e^-$ to fill completely its bonding MOs and these are supplied by M in $[M^{4+}@C_{28}^{4-}]$, (M = U, Ti, Zr, Hf).

The first dimetalla analogue to be characterized was $[La_2@C_{60}]$, and mixed metal and trimetalla compounds are also known, e.g. $[YLa@C_{80}]$[57] and $[Sc_3@C_{82}]$.[58] Other known compounds include the monometalla species $[M@C_{82}]$ for M = La, Ce, Nd, Sm, Eu, Gd, Tb, Dy, Ho and Er,[59] the dimetalla compounds $[Ce_2@C_{80}]$, $[Tb_2@C_{80}]$, $[Sc_2@C_{82}]$, $[Y_2@C_{82}]$, $[La_2@C_{82}]$ and $[Sc_2@C_{84}]$, and the trimetalla species $[La_3@C_{106}]$ and $[La_3@C_{112}]$. The products

[52] T. GUO, C. JIN and R. E. SMALLEY, *J. Phys. Chem.* **95**, 4948–50 (1991).

[53] T. PRADEEP, V. VIJAYAKRISHNAN, A. K. SANTRA and C. N. R. RAO, *J. Phys. Chem.* **95**, 10564–5 (1991).

[54] J. R. BOWSER, D. A. JELSKI and T. F. GEORGE, *Inorg. Chem.* **31**, 156–7 (1992).

[55] R. E. SMALLEY (and 8 others), *J. Phys. Chem.* **95**. 7564–8 (1991).

[56] R. E. SMALLEY (and 9 others), *Science* **257**, 1661–4 (1992).

[57] M. M. ROSS, H. H. NELSON, J. H. CALLAHAN and S. W. MCELVANEY, *J. Phys. Chem.* **96**, 5231–4 (1992).

[58] H. SHINOHARA (and 7 others), *Nature* **357**, 52–4 (1992).

[59] E. G. GILLAN, C. YERETZIAN, K. S. MIN, M. M. ALVAREZ, R. L. WHETTEN and R. B. KANER, *J. Phys. Chem.* **96**, 6869–71 (1992).

obtained depend sensitively on the relative concentrations of metal oxide and carbon in the electrode material.[59] Note also that only metals from the left-hand side of the periodic table have so far been encapsulated and there are no substantiated examples with M = Fe, Cu, Ag, Au, etc.

Some recent books and general reviews on the preparation, properties and chemical reactions of the fullerenes and their derivatives are in ref. 60.

The endohedral metallofullarenes just described (and the alkali metal fullerides described on p. 285) are all formally examples of metal carbides, M_xC_y, but they have entirely different structure motifs and properties from the classical metal carbides and the more recently discovered metallacarbohedrenes (metcars) on the one hand (both to be considered in Section 8.4) and the graphite intercalation compounds to be discussed in Section 8.3. Before that, however, we must complete this present section on the various forms of the element carbon by describing and comparing the chemical properties of the two most familiar forms of the element, diamond and graphite.

8.2.5 Chemical properties of carbon

Carbon in the form of diamond is extremely unreactive at room temperature. Graphite, although thermodynamically more stable than diamond under normal conditions, tends to react more readily due to its more vulnerable

layer structure. For example, it is oxidized by hot concentrated HNO_3 to mellitic acid, $C_6(CO_2H)_6$, in which planar-hexagonal C_{12} units are preserved. Graphite reacts with a suspension of $KClO_4$ in a 1:2 mixture (by volume) of conc HNO_3/H_2SO_4 to give "graphite oxide" an unstable, pale lemon-coloured product of variable stoichiometry and structure. Similar products can be prepared by anodic oxidation of graphite or by reaction with $NaNO_3/KMnO_4/$conc H_2SO_4. Graphite oxide decomposes slowly at 70°C, and at 200° it undergoes a spectacular deflagration with the formation of CO, CO_2, H_2O and soot. Infrared and X-ray evidence suggest that the structure-motif is a puckered hexagonal network of C_6 rings predominantly in the "chair" conformation but with a few remaining C=C bonds; in addition there are terminal and bridging O atoms and pendant OH groups; keto-enol tautomerism is implied and the empirical formula can be represented as $C_6O_x(OH)_y$ with $x \sim 1.0$–1.7 and $y \sim 2.25$–1.7.

Graphite reacts with an atmosphere of F_2 at temperatures between 400–500°C to give "graphite monofluoride" CF_x ($x \sim 0.68$–0.99). The reaction is catalysed by HF and can then occur at much lower temperatures (leading, on occasion, to the destruction of graphite electrodes during the preparation of F_2 by the electrolysis of KF/HF melts, p. 797). At $\sim 600°$ the reaction proceeds with explosive violence to give a mixture of CF_4, C_2F_6, and C_5F_{12}. The colour of CF_x depends on the reaction temperature and on the fluorine content, becoming progressively lighter from black ($x \sim 0.7$) to grey ($x \sim 0.8$), silver ($x \sim 0.9$) and transparent white ($x > 0.98$).[61] The structure has not been definitely established but the idealized layer lattice shown in Fig. 8.13a accounts for the observed interplanar spacings, infrared data, colour, and lack of electrical conductivity ($\rho > 3000$ ohm cm). CF is very unreactive, but when heated slowly between

[60] J. BAGGOTT, *Perfect Symmetry* (the discovery of buckminsterfullerene), Oxford University Press, Oxford, 1994, 300 pp. H. ALDERSLEY-WILLIAMS, *The Most Beautiful Molecule*, Aurum Press, London, 1995, 340 pp. T. BRAUN, A. SCHUBERT, H. MACZELKA and L. VASVÁRI, *Fullerene Research 1985–1993* (A computer-generated cross-indexed bibliography of the Journal literature), World Scientific Singapore, 1995, 480 pp. R. TAYLOR, *The Chemistry of the Fullerenes* (vol. 4 in *Advanced Series in Fullerenes*), World Scientific, Singapore, 1995, 260 pp. T. BRAUN (ed.) *Fullerene Science and Technology*, [now a regular Journal, vol. 3 (1995)], Marcel Dekker, New York, W. E. BILLUPS, and W. E. CIUFOLINI (eds.) *Buckminsterfullerenes*, VCH, New York, 1993, 308 pp. H. W. KROTO, J. E. FISCHER and D. E. COX (eds.), *The Fullerenes*, Pergamon Press, Oxford, 1993. 318 pp.

[61] Y. KITA, N. WATANABE and Y. FUJII, *J. Am. Chem. Soc.* **101**, 3832–41 (1979) and refs cited therein. See also H. TOUHARA, K. KADONO, Y. FUJII and N. WATANABE, *Z. anorg. allg. Chem.* **544**, 7–20 (1987) for structure of $(C_2F)_n$.

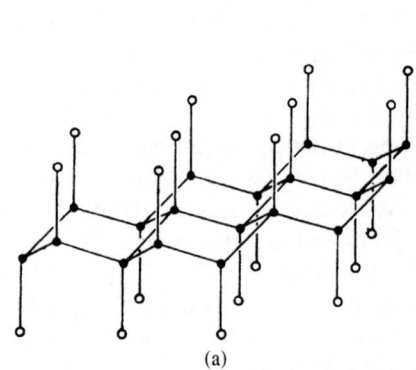

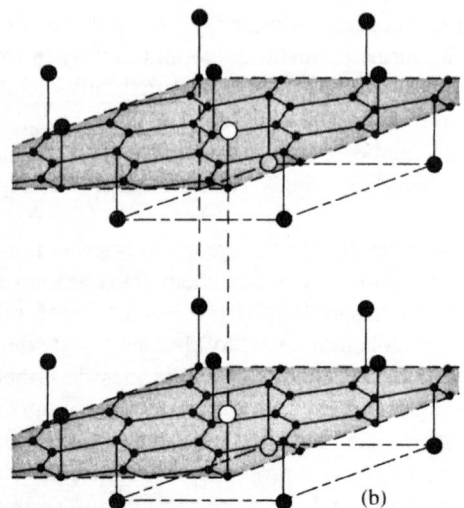

Figure 8.13   (a) Idealized structure of CF showing puckered layer lattice of fused C_6 rings in "chair" conformation and axial F atoms. The spacing between successive C layers is ~817 pm (cf. graphite 335.4 pm) and the density 2.43 g cm^{-3}. (b) Proposed structure for C_4F showing retention of the planar graphite sheets but with regularly spaced F atoms above and below each layer. The spacing between successive C layers is ~534 pm and the density is 2.077 g cm^{-3}.

600–1000° it gradually liberates fluorocarbons, C_nF_{2n+2}.

When gaseous mixtures of F_2/HF are allowed to react with finely powdered graphite at room temperature an inert bluish-black compound with a velvety appearance is formed with a composition which varies in the range C_4F to $C_{3.57}F$. The in-plane C–C distance remains as in graphite but the interlayer spacing increases to 534–550 pm depending on the F content. The infrared and X-ray data are best interpreted in terms of the structure shown in Fig. 8.13b. The electrical conductivity, though less than that of graphite, is still appreciable, the resistivity being ~2–4 ohm cm. Other chemical and electrochemical routes to C_xF $(x < 2)$ and $C_{14}F(HF)_y$ have also been explored.[62]

At high temperatures, C reacts with many elements including H (in the presence of a finely divided Ni catalyst), F (but not the other halogens), O, S, Si (p. 334), B (p. 149) and many metals (p. 297). It is an active reducing agent and reacts readily with many oxides to liberate the element or form a carbide. These reactions, which reflect the high enthalpy of formation of CO and CO_2, are of great industrial importance (p. 307).

Carbon is known with all coordination numbers from 0 to 8 though compounds in which it is 3- or 4-coordinate are the most numerous. Some typical examples are summarized in the Panel (p. 291). Particular mention should also be made of hypercoordinate "non-classical" carbonium ions such as 5-coordinate CH_5^+, square pyramidal $C_5H_5^+$ (cf. the isoelectronic cluster B_5H_9, p. 154), pentagonal pyramidal $C_6Me_6^{2+}$ (cf. iso-electronic B_6H_{10}, p. 154) and the bicyclic cation 2-norbornyl, $C_7H_{11}^+$.[63]

[62] R. Hagiwara, M. Lerner and N. Bartlett, *J. Chem. Soc., Chem. Commun.*, 573–4 (1989); H. Takenaka, M. Kawaguchi, M. Lerner and N. Bartlett, *J. Chem. Soc., Chem. Commun.*, 1431–2 (1987).

[63] G. A. Olah, *J. Am. Chem. Soc.* **94**, 808–20 (1972); G. A. Olah, G. K. S. Prakash, R. E. Williams, L. D. Field and K. Wade, *Hypercarbon Chemistry*, Wiley, New York, 1987, 311 pp.

Coordination Numbers of Carbon

CN	Examples	Comments
0	C atoms	High-temp, low-press, gas phase
1	CO	Stable gas
	CH$^{\bullet}$ (carbynes)	Reactive free-radical intermediates
2 (linear)	CO_2, CS_2	Stable gas, liquid
	HCN, HC$\equiv$CH, NCO$^-$, NCS$^-$	The ions are isoelectronic with CO_2 and COS respectively
	M(CO)$_n$	Terminal M–CO groups sometimes <180°
	RP$\equiv$C$\equiv$PR (R = 2,4,6-Bu$^t_3$C$_6$H$_2$)	Angle PCP 172.6°[63]
2 (bent)	Ph$_3$P:C:PPh$_3$	A bis(ylide) with angle PCP 130.1° (and 143.8°)[64]
	:CH$_2$, :CX$_2$ (carbenes)	Reactive intermediates with 1 lone-pair and 1 vacant orbital; (carbenes are bent for X = H, F, OH, OMe, NH$_2$, but linear if X is less electronegative, e.g. BH$_2$, BeH, Li)[65]
	$\bullet$CH$_2\bullet$, $\bullet$CPh$_2\bullet$ (methylenes)	Reactive intermediates with 2 unpaired electrons
3 (planar)	COXY (X = H. hal, OH. O$^-$ R, Ar)	Stable oxohalides, carbonates, carboxylic acids, aldehydes, ketones, etc.
	[C(N$=$PCl$_3$)$_3$]$^+$ [SbCl$_6$]$^-$	Colourless crystals prepared from [C(N$_3$)$_3$]$^+$ + PCl$_3$[66]
	M$_m$(CO)$_n$	Metal carbonyl clusters with bridging CO groups M–C(O)–M
	[PhC(OMe)M(CO)$_5$]	Stable metal — carbene complexes. e.g. M = Cr, W
	CH$_3^+$ (carbonium ions)	Unstable reaction intermediates with 1 vacant orbital[67]
3 (pyramidal)	CH$_3^-$, CPh$_3^-$ (carbanions), RMgX	Unstable reaction intermediates with 1 lone pair of electrons
	Ph$_3$C$^{\bullet}$, R$_3$C$^{\bullet}$ (free radicals)	Paramagnetic species of varying stability
3 (T-shaped)	[Ta($=$CHCMe$_3$)$_2$(2,4,6-Me$_3$C$_6$H$_2$)(PMe$_3$)$_2$]	The unique H is equatorial and angle Ta$=$C–CMe$_3$ is 169°[68]
4 (tetrahedral)	CX$_4$, etc.	4-coord covalent compds such as CF$_4$, C$_2$H$_6$, CHXYZ, etc.
	M$_m$(CO)$_n$	Metal carbonyl clusters with triply bridging CO groups (p. 928)
4 (see-saw, C$_{2v}$)	[Fe$_4$C(CO)$_{13}$]	The μ_4-carbido C caps Fe$_4$ "butterfly"[69]
5	Al$_2$Me$_6$	Alkyl-bridged organometallics involving 3c–2e, bonds (pp. 259, etc.)
	C$_2$B$_4$H$_6$, etc.	Several stable carboranes (p. 183)
	[(η^5-C$_5$H$_5$)NiRu$_3$(CO)$_9$CCHBu^t]	The C atom bonds to CHBu and to M$_4$ "butterfly"[70]
	[Os$_5$C(CO)$_{13}$HL$_2$]	The μ_5-carbido C bonds to all 5 Os[71]
	[C{AuPPh$_3$}$_5$]$^+$ BF$_4^-$	trigonal bipyramidal cation[72]
6	C$_2$B$_{10}$H$_{12}$, etc.	Several stable carboranes (p. 185)
	[C(AuPPh$_3$)$_6$]$^{2+}$[BF$_3$(OMe)]$_2^-$	octahedral dication[73]
7	(LiMe)$_4$ crystals	See structure, p. 104
8	Be$_2$C (antifluorite),	See structure. p. 118
	[Co$_8$C(CO)$_{18}$]$^{2-}$	See structure. p. 1142

[64] A. T. VINCENT and P. J. WHEATLEY, *J. Chem. Soc., Dalton Trans.*, 617–22 (1972). G. E. HARDY, J. I. ZINK, W. C. KASKA and J. C. BALDWIN, *J. Am. Chem. Soc.* **100**, 8001–2 (1978). see also E. FLUCK, B. NEUMÜLLER, R. BRAUN, G. HECKMANN, A. SIMON and H. BORRMANN, *Z. anorg. allg. Chem.* **567**, 23–38 (1988) and the many references cited therein.

[65] W. W. SCHOELLER, *J. Chem. Soc., Chem. Commun.*, 124–5 (1980).

[66] U. MÜLLER, I. LORENZ, and F. SCHMOCK, *Angew. Chem. Int. Edn. Engl.* **18**, 693–4 (1979).

[67] Note, however, that an X-ray structure analysis of the stable, crystalline carbocation 3,5,7-trimethyladamantyl showed the 3-coordinate C(1) atom as a considerably flattened pyramid 21 pm above the plane of the 3 adjacent C atoms and with bond angles 120°, 118° and 116° (Σ = 354°). T. LAUBE, *Angew. Chem. Int. Edn. Engl.* **25**, 349–51 (1986).

[68] M. R. CHURCHILL and W. J. YOUNGS, *J. Chem. Soc., Chem. Commun.*, 1048–9 (1978).

[69] J. S. BRADLEY, G. B. ANSELL, M. E. LEONOWICZ and E. W. HILL, *J. Am. Chem. Soc.* **103**, 4968–70 (1981).

[70] E. SAPPA, A. TIRIPICCHIO and M. T. CAMELLINI, *J. Chem. Soc., Chem. Commun.*, 154 (1979).

[71] J. M. FERNANDEZ, B. F. G. JOHNSON, J. LEWIS and P. RAITHBY, *J. Chem. Soc., Dalton Trans.*, 2250–7 (1981).

[72] F. SCHERBAUM, A. GROHMANN, G. MÜLLER and H. SCHMIDBAUR, *Angew. Chem. Int. Edn. Engl.* **28**, 463–5 (1989).

[73] F. SCHERBAUM, A. GROHMANN, B. HÜBER, C. KRÜGER and H. SCHMIDBAUR, *Angew. Chem. Int. Edn. Engl.* **27**, 1544–6 (1988).

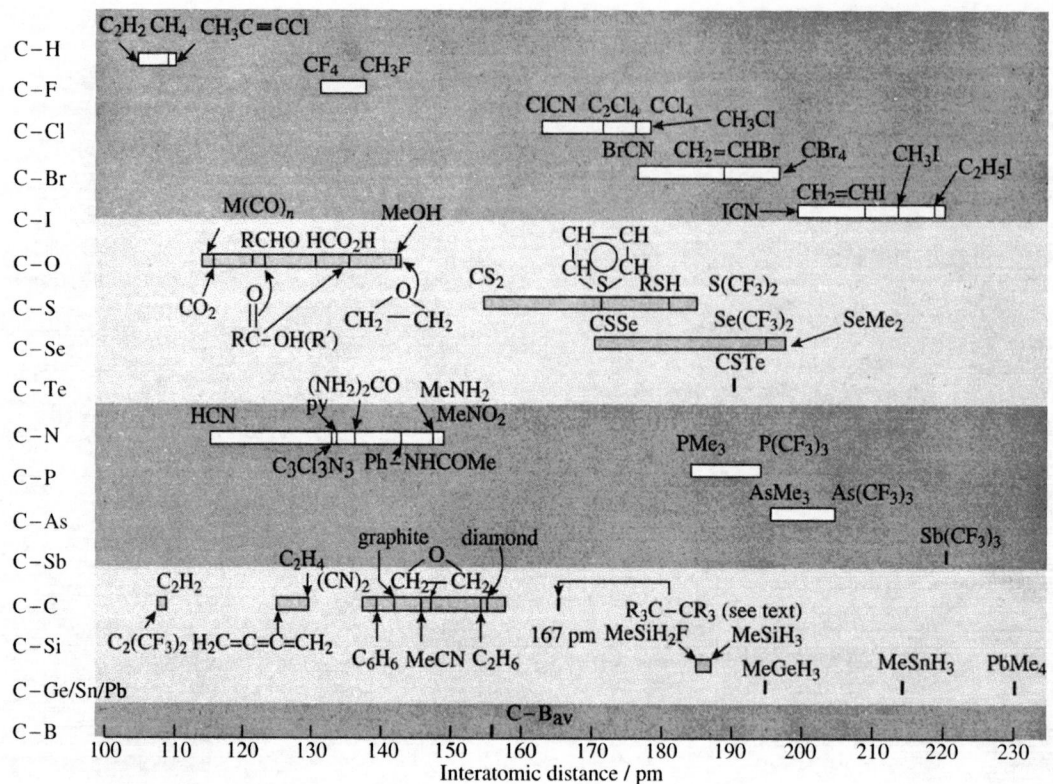

Figure 8.14   Some interatomic distances involving carbon.

Interatomic distances vary with the type of bond and the nature of the other atoms or groups attached to the bonded atoms. For example, the formally single-bonded C–C distance varies from 146 pm in Me–CN to 163.8 pm in $Bu_2^n PhC–CPhBu_2^{n(74)}$ and 167 pm in 3,5-Bu_2^t-$C_6H_3)_2C–C(C_6H_3$-3,5-$Bu_2^t)_3$ and $(CF_3)_2(4-FC_6H_4)C–C(C_6H_4$-4-F)$(CF_3)_2$.[75] Some typical examples are in Fig. 8.14. Note that because of the breadth of some of these ranges the interatomic distance between quite different pairs of atoms can be identical. For example, the value 133 pm includes C–F, C–O, C–N and C–C; likewise the value of 185 pm includes C–Br, C–S, C–Se, C–P and C–Si. The conventional classification into single, double and triple bonds is adopted for simplicity, but bonding is frequently more subtle and more extended than these localized descriptions imply. Bond energies are listed on p. 374, where they are compared with those for other elements of Group 14. It should perhaps be emphasized that interatomic distances are experimentally observable, whereas bond orders depend on theoretical models and the estimation of bond energies in polyatomic molecules depends additionally on various assumptions as to how the total energy is apportioned. Nevertheless, taken together, the data indicate that an increase in the order of a bond between 2 atoms is accompanied both by a decrease in bond length and by an increase in bond energy. Similarly, for a given bond order between C and a series of other elements (e.g. C–X), the bond energy increases as the bond length decreases.

[74] W. LITTKE and U. DRÜCK, *Angew Chem. Int. Edn. Engl.* **18**, 406–7 (1979).

[75] B. KAHR, D. VAN EUGEN and K. MISLOW, *J. Am. Chem. Soc.* **108**, 8305–7 (1986), and references cited therein.

8.3 Graphite Intercalation Compounds[76]

The large interlayer distance between the parallel planes of C atoms in graphite implies that the interlayer bonding is relatively weak. This accounts for the ready cleavage along the basal plane and the remarkable softness of the crystals. It also enables a wide range of substances to intercalate between the planes under mild conditions to give lamellar compounds of variable composition. These reactions are often reversible (unlike those with O and F discussed above) and the graphitic nature of the host lattice is retained. The compounds have quite different structures and properties from those previously encountered in this book and so will be described in some detail. They may be compared with the materials formed by intercalation into certain sheet silicates (p. 349).

The first alkali–metal graphite compound was reported in 1926: bronze-coloured C_8K was formed by direct reaction of graphite with K vapour at 300°C. Rubidium and Cs behave similarly. When heated at $\sim$360° under reduced pressure the metal is removed in stages to give a series of intercalation compounds C_8M (bronze-red), $C_{24}M$ (steel-blue), $C_{36}M$ (dark blue), $C_{48}M$ (black) and $C_{60}M$ (black). The compounds can also be prepared by electrolysis of fused melts with graphite electrodes, by reaction of graphite with solutions of M in liquid ammonia or amines, and by exchange reactions using M/aromatic radical anions. Intercalation is more difficult to achieve with Li and Na though direct reaction with highly purified graphite at 500° yields C_6Li (brass coloured), $C_{12}Li$ (copper), and $C_{18}Li$ (steel), and reaction with Li/naphthalene in thf yields $C_{16}Li$ and $C_{40}Li$. Corresponding reaction of graphite and molten Na at 450° gives $C_{64}Na$ (deep violet) whereas Na/naphthalene gives $C_{32}Na$ and $C_{120}Na$.

The crystal structure of C_8K is shown in Fig. 8.15(a); the graphite layers remain intact but are stacked vertically above each other instead of in the sequence $\cdots ABAB \cdots$ found in α-graphite itself. Each graphite layer is interleaved by a layer of K atoms having a commensurate lattice in which the spacing between each K is twice the spacing between the centres of the graphite hexagons (Fig. 8.15(b)). The stoichiometries of the other stages can then be achieved by varying the frequency of occurrence of the intercalated M layers in the host lattice. An idealized representation of this model is shown in Fig. 8.16. Difficulties are encountered in devising a plausible mechanistic route to the formation of these compounds since the direct preparation of one stage from an adjacent stage apparently requires both the complete emptying and the complete filling of inserted layers. It may be that the situation is more complex, with distributions of stages rather than a single uniform arrangement for each stoichiometry. Very recently a new metal-rich phase has been prepared by reacting graphite with molten potassium; the composition is very close to C_4K and the structure comprises double planes of K atoms intercalated between each graphite sheet, with a consequent increase in the interplanar spacing to 850 pm.[77]

The electrical resistance of graphite intercalation compounds is even lower than for graphite itself, resistance along the *a*-axis dropping by a factor of $\sim$10 and that along the *c*-axis by $\sim$100; moreover, in contrast to graphite, which is diamagnetic, the compounds have a temperature-independent (Pauli) paramagnetism and also behave as true metals in having a resistivity that increases with increase in temperature. This is illustrated by the comparative data shown in Table 8.2.

These data, and the other properties of C_nM, suggest that bonding occurs by transfer of electrons from the alkali metal atoms to the conduction band of the host graphite. Consistent with

[76] L. B. EBERT, *A. Rev. Materials Sci.* **6**, 181–211 (1976). A. HÉROLD, in F. LEVY (ed.), *Intercalated Layered Materials*, pp. 323–421, Reidel, 1979. H. SELIG and L. B. EBERT, *Adv. Inorg. Chem. Radiochem.* **23**, 281–327 (1980); a review with $\sim$350 references.

[77] M. EL GADI, C. HÉROLD and P. LAGRANGE, *Compt. Rend. Acad. Sci. Paris* **316**, 763–9 (1993).

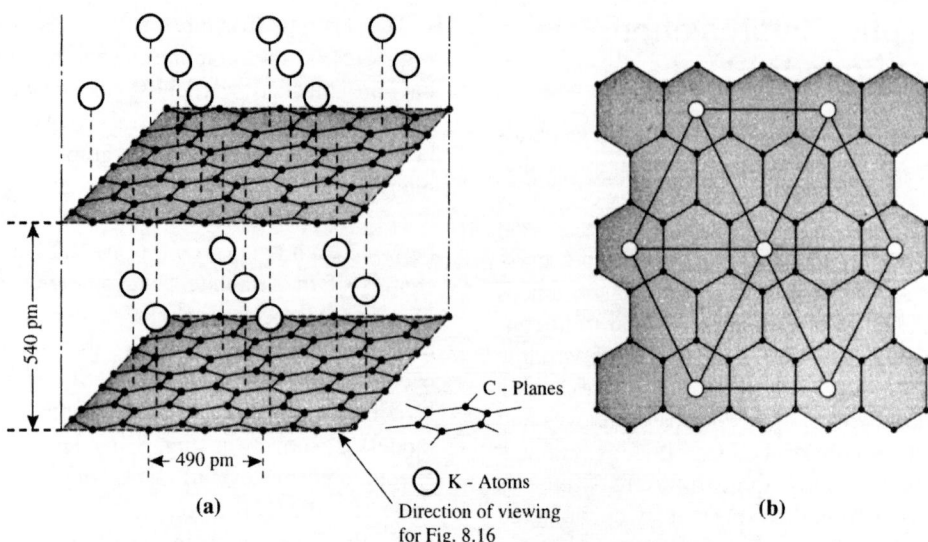

Figure 8.15 (a) Crystal lattice of C_8K showing the vertical packing of graphitic layers. The C–C distance within layers almost identical to that in graphite itself but the interplanar spacing (540 pm) is much larger than for graphite (335 pm) due to the presence of K atoms. The spacing increases still further to 561 pm for C_8Rb and to 595 pm for C_8Cs. (b) Triangular location of K atoms in C_8K showing the relation to the host graphite layers. In the other alkali-metal graphite compounds $C_{12n}M$ the central M atom is missing, leading to a stoichiometry of $C_{12}M$ if every alternate layer is M, $C_{24}M$ if each third layer is M, etc.

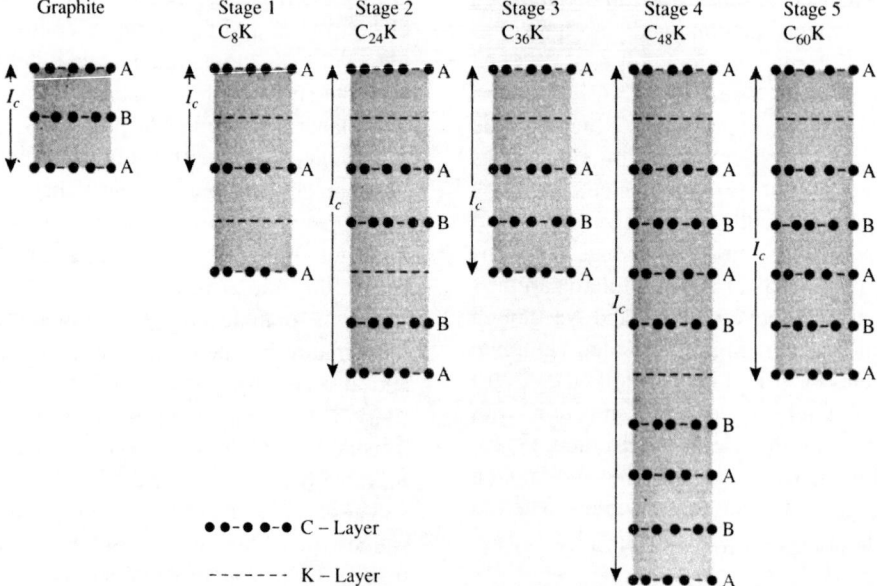

Figure 8.16 Layer-plane sequence along the c-axis for graphite in various stage 1–5 of alkali-metal graphite intercalation compounds. Comparison with Fig. 8.15 shows that the horizontal planes are being viewed diagonally across the figure. I_c is the interlayer repeat distance along the c-axis.

Table 8.2   Resistivity of graphite and its intercalates

Material	ρ (90 K)/ohm cm	ρ (285 K)/ohm cm	ρ_{90}/ρ_{285}
α-graphite	37.7	28.4	1.33
C_8K	0.768	1.02	0.75
$C_{12}K$	0.932	1.15	0.81

this, direct metal intercalation has only been observed with the most electropositive elements (Group 1) though Ba, with a first-stage ionization energy intermediate between those of Li and Na, was recently (1974) found to give C_6Ba.

Alkali-metal graphites are extremely reactive in air and may explode with water. In general, reactivity decreases with ease of ionization of M in the sequence Li > Na > K > Rb > Cs. Under controlled conditions H_2O or ROH produce only H_2, MOH and graphite, unlike the alkali-metal carbides M_2C_2 (p. 297) which produce hydrocarbons such as acetylene. In an important new reaction C_8K has been found to react smoothly with transition metal salts in tetrahydrofuran at room temperature to give the corresponding transition metal lamellar compounds:[78]

$$n C_8K + MX_n \xrightarrow{\text{thf}} C_{8n}M + nKX$$

Examples include reaction of $Ti(OPr^i)_4$, $MnCl_2$-$4H_2O$, $FeCl_3$, $CoCl_2.6H_2O$, $CuCl_2.2H_2O$, and $ZnCl_2$ to give $C_{32}Ti$, $C_{16}Mn$, $C_{24}Fe$, $C_{16}Co$, $C_{16}Cu$ and $C_{16}Zn$, respectively.

A quite different sort of graphite intercalation compound is formed by the halides of many elements, particularly those halides which themselves have layer structures or weak intermolecular binding. The first such compound (1932) was with $FeCl_3$; chlorides, in general, have been the most studied, but fluoride and bromide intercalates are also known. Halides which have been reported to intercalate include the following:

HF; ClF_3, BrF_3, IF_5; XeF_6, $XeOF_4$; CrO_2F_2, SbF_3Cl_2, TiF_4

78 D. Braga, A. Ripamonti, D. Savoia, C. Trombini and A. Umani-Ronchi, *J. Chem. Soc., Dalton Trans.*, 2026–8 (1979).

MF_5 (M = As, Sb, Nb, Ta); UF_6
MCl_2: M = Be; Mn, Co, Ni, Cu; Zn, Cd, Hg
MCl_3: M = B, Al, Ga, In, Tl; Y; Sm, Eu, Gd, Tb, Dy; Cr, Fe, Co; Ru, Rh, Au; I
MCl_4: M = Zr, Hf; Re, Ir; Pd, Pt
MCl_5: M = Sb; Mo; U
MCl_6: M = W, U; also CrO_2Cl_2, UO_2Cl_2
Mixtures of $AlCl_3$ plus Br_2, I_2, ICl_3, $FeCl_3$, WCl_6
Bromides: $CuBr_2$; $AlBr_3$, $GaBr_3$; $AuBr_3$

The intercalates are usually prepared by heating a mixture of the reactants though sometimes the presence of free Cl_2 is also necessary, particularly for "non-oxidizing" chlorides such as $MnCl_2$, $NiCl_2$, $ZnCl_2$, $AlCl_3$, etc. Many of the compounds appear to show various stages of intercalation, the first stage usually exhibiting a typical blue colour. A common feature of many of the intercalated halides is their ability to act as electron-pair acceptors (Lewis acids). Low heat of sublimation is a further characteristic of most of the intercalating compounds. It may be that an important feature is an ability of the guest molecule to form a layer lattice commensurate with the host graphite. For example, in $C_{6.69}FeCl_3$ the intercalated $FeCl_3$ has a layer structure similar to that in $FeCl_3$ itself with Cl in approximately close-packed arrangement though with some distortion, and with extensive stacking disorder. The "first-stage" compound varies in composition in the range $C_{\sim6-7}FeCl_3$; in addition a "second-stage" compound corresponding to $C_{\sim12}FeCl_3$ is known, and also a "third-stage" with composition in the range $C_{\sim24-30}FeCl_3$. Another well-characterized phase occurs with $MoCl_5$: layers of close-packed Mo_2Cl_{10} molecules alternate with sets of 4 graphite layers along the c-axis.

There appears to be a small but definite transfer of electron charge from the graphite to the guest species and this has led to formulations such as $C_{70}^+Cl^-.FeCl_2.5FeCl_3$. Similarly, the intercalate of $AlCl_3$ (which is formed in the presence of free Cl_2) has been formulated as $C_{27}^+Cl^-.3AlCl_3$ or $C_{27}^+AlCl_4^-.2AlCl_3$. This would explain the enhanced conductivity of the graphite–metal halide compounds, due to the formation of positive holes near the top of the valence band. However, despite extensive work using a variety of techniques, many structural problems remain unresolved and there is still no consensus on the detailed description of the bonding. Recent work includes studies on intercalation and staging in main-group element fluoride systems, e.g. (using ionic formulations)

$$2C_{12}^+AsF_6^- + AsF_3 \rightleftharpoons 3C_8AsF_5 \quad ^{(79)}$$

$$C_{12}^+GeF_5^- + \tfrac{1}{2}F_2 \rightleftharpoons C_{12}^{2+}GeF_6^{2-} \quad ^{(80)}$$

$$C_{24}^+SiF_5^- + 2PF_5 \longrightarrow SiF_4(g)$$
$$+ [C_{24}^+PF_6^-.PF_5]^{(81)}$$

$$20° \quad \big\Updownarrow \quad \pm PF_5(g)$$

$$24C + PF_5 + \tfrac{1}{2}F_2 \xrightarrow{20°/24-32\,h} C_{24}^+PF_6^-$$

The halogens themselves show a curious alternation of behaviour towards graphite. F_2 gives the compounds CF, C_2F and C_4F (p. 289) whereas liquid Cl_2 reacts slowly to give C_8Cl, and I_2 appears not to intercalate at all. By contrast, Br_2 readily intercalates in several stages to give compounds of formula C_8Br, $C_{12}Br$, $C_{16}Br$ and $C_{20}Br$; the compounds $C_{14}Br$ and $C_{28}Br$ have also been well-characterized crystallographically but may be metastable phases. A notable feature of the Br_2 intercalation reaction is that it is completely prevented by prior coating of the *basal* plane of the sample of graphite with a layer impervious to Br_2. The lamellar character of blue C_8Br has been confirmed by X-ray diffraction and the intercalation of bromine, is accompanied by a marked decrease in the resistivity of the graphite — more than tenfold along the *a*-axis and twofold along the *c*-axis. C_8ICl and $C_{36}ICl$ have also been prepared.

Numerous oxides, sulfides and oxoacids have been found to intercalate into graphite. For example, lamellar compounds with SO_3, N_2O_5 and Cl_2O_7 are known (but not with SO_2, NO or NO_2). CrO_3 and MoO_3 readily intercalate as do several sulfides such as V_2S_3, $Cr_2S_3(+S)$, WS_2, $PdS(+S)$ and Sb_2S_5. Metal nitrates and oxonitrates can also form intercalates, e.g. $Cu(NO_3)_2$, $Zn(NO_3)_2$, $Zr(NO_3)_4$, $CrO_2(NO_3)_2$, $NbO(NO_3)_3$ and $TaO(NO_3)_3$. A recent example is $[C_{28}MoO_2(NO_3)_2.0.3N_2O_5]^{(82)}$

The reversible intercalation of various oxoacids under oxidizing conditions leads to lamellar graphite "salts" some of which have been known for over a century and are now particularly well characterized structurally. For example, the formation of the blue, "first-stage" compound with conc H_2SO_4 can be expressed by the idealized equation

$$24C + 3H_2SO_4 + \tfrac{1}{4}O_2 \longrightarrow$$
$$C_{24}^+HSO_4^-.2H_2SO_4 + \tfrac{1}{2}H_2O$$

The overall stoichiometry is thus close to $C_8H_2SO_4$ and the structure is very similar to that of C_8K (p. 293) except for the detail of vertical alignment of the carbon atoms in the *c* direction which is $\cdots ABAB\cdots$. Several later stages (2, 3, 4, 5, 11) have been established and their properties studied. Intercalation is accompanied by a marked decrease in electrical resistance. A series of graphite nitrates can be prepared similarly, e.g. $C_{24}^+NO_3^-.2HNO_3$ (blue), $C_{48}^+NO_3^-.3HNO_3$ (black), etc. Other oxoacids which intercalate (particularly under electrolytic conditions) include $HClO_4$, HSO_3F, HSO_3Cl, H_2SeO_4, H_3PO_4, $H_4P_2O_7$, H_3AsO_4, CF_3CO_2H, CCl_3CO_2H, etc. The extent of intercalation depends both on the strength of the acid and its concentration, and the reactions are of considerable technological importance because they can lead to the swelling and eventual destruction of the graphite electrodes used in many electrochemical processes.

[79] E. M. McCarron and N. Bartlett, *J. Chem. Soc., Chem. Commun.*, 404–6 (1980).

[80] E. M. McCarron, J. Grannec and N. Bartlett, *J. Chem. Soc., Chem. Commun.*, 890–1 (1980).

[81] G. L. Rosenthal, T. E. Mallouk and N. Bartlett, *Synthetic Metals* **9**, 433–40 (1984).

[82] E. Stumpp and H. Griebel, *Z. anorg. allg. Chem.* **579**, 205–10 (1989).

8.4 Carbides

Carbon forms binary compounds with most elements: those with metals are considered in this section whilst those with H, the halogens, O, and the chalcogens are discussed in subsequent sections. Alkali metal fullerides and encapsulated (endohedral) metallafullerenes have already been considered (pp. 285, 288 respectively) and metallacarbohedrenes (metcars) will be dealt with later in this section (p. 300). Silicon carbide is discussed on p. 334. General methods of preparation of metal carbides are:[83]

(1) Direct combination of the elements above ~2000°C.
(2) Reaction of the metal oxide with carbon at high temperature.
(3) Reaction of the heated metal with gaseous hydrocarbon.
(4) Reaction of acetylene with electropositive metals in liquid ammonia.

Attempts to classify carbides according to structure or bond type meet the same difficulties as were encountered with hydrides (p. 64) and borides (p. 145) and for the same reasons. The general trends in properties of the three groups of compounds are, however, broadly similar, being most polar (ionic) for the electropositive metals, most covalent (molecular) for the electronegative non-metals and somewhat complex (interstitial) for the elements in the centre of the d block. There are also several elements with poorly characterized, unstable, or non-existent carbides, namely the later transition elements (Groups 11 and 12), the platinum metals, and the post transition-metal elements in Group 13.

Salt-like carbides containing individual C "anions" are sometimes called "methanides" since they yield predominantly CH_4 on hydrolysis. Be_2C and Al_4C_3 are the best-characterized examples, indicating the importance of small compact cations. Be_2C is prepared from BeO and C at 1900–2000°C; it is brick-red, has the antifluorite structure (p. 118), and decomposes to graphite when heated above 2100°. *Ab initio* calculations suggest that the structure is predominantly ionic with charges close to the nominal $Be^{2+}_2C^{4-}$.[84] Al_4C_3, prepared by direct union of the elements in an electric furnace, forms pale-yellow crystals, mp 2200°C. It has a complex structure in which {AlC_4} tetrahedra of two types are linked to form a layer lattice: this defines two types of C atom, one surrounded by a deformed octahedron of 6 Al at 217 pm and the other surrounded by 4 Al at 190–194 pm and a fifth Al at 221 pm. The closest C···C approach is at the nonbonding distance of 316 pm. Although it is formally possible to describe the structure as ionic, $(Al^{3+})_4(C^{4-})_3$, such a gross separation of charges is unlikely to occur over the observed interatomic distances.

Carbides containing a C_2 unit are well known; they are exemplified by the acetylides (ethynides) of the alkali metals, $M^I_2C_2$, alkaline earth metals, $M^{II}C_2$, and the lanthanoids LnC_2 and Ln_2C_3 i.e. $Ln_4(C_2)_3$. The corresponding compounds of Group 11 (Cu, Ag, Au) are explosive and those of Group 12 (Zn, Cd, Hg) are poorly characterized. $M^I_2C_2$ are best prepared by the action of C_2H_2 on a solution of alkali metal in liquid NH_3; they are colourless crystalline compounds which react violently with water and oxidize to the carbonate on being heated in air. $M^{II}C_2$ can be prepared by heating the alkaline earth metal with ethyne above 500°C. By far the most important compound in this group is CaC_2 — it is manufactured on a huge scale, 6.4 million tonnes worldwide in 1982 and is used as a major source of ethyne for the chemical industry and for oxyacetylene welding. US production peaked at 1.03 Mt in 1964 but then declined substantially as ethyne became available from petrochemical feedstocks, from the thermal cracking of hydrocarbons and as a byproduct of C_2H_4 manufacture. US production of CaC_2

[83] Reference 2, pp. 841–911: Carbides (p. 841); Cemented carbides (p. 848); Industrial hard carbides (p. 861); Calcium carbide (p. 878); Silicon carbide (p. 891).

[84] P. W. FOWLER and P. TOLE, *J. Chem. Soc., Chem. Commun.*, 1652–4 (1989).

has been below 250 000 tonnes per annum for the past 20 years and was 236 000 tonnes in 1990 (price \$515/t). Europe (3.25 Mtpa) and Asia/Australia (2.42 Mtpa) are currently the major producers.

Industrially, CaC_2 is produced by the endothermic reaction of lime and coke:

$$CaO + 3C \xrightarrow{2200-2250°C} CaC_2 + CO;$$

$$\Delta H = 465.7 \text{ kJ mol}^{-1}$$

Subsequent hydrolysis is highly exothermic and must be carefully controlled:

$$CaC_2 + 2H_2O \longrightarrow C_2H_2 + Ca(OH)_2;$$

$$\Delta H = -120 \text{ kJ mol}^{-1}$$

Another industrially important reaction of CaC_2 is its ability to fix N_2 from the air by formation of calcium cyanamide:

$$CaC_2 + N_2 \xrightarrow{1000°-1200°} CaCN_2 + C;$$

$$\Delta H = -296 \text{ kJ mol}^{-1}$$

$CaCN_2$ is widely used as a fertilizer because of its ready hydrolysis to cyanamide, H_2NCN (p. 323).

Pure CaC_2 is a colourless solid, mp 2300°C. It can be prepared on the laboratory scale by passing ethyne into a solution of Ca in liquid NH_3, followed by decomposition of the complex so formed, under reduced pressure at ~325°:

$$Ca(\text{liq } NH_3) + 2C_2H_2 \xrightarrow{-80°} H_2 + CaC_2.C_2H_2$$

$$\xrightarrow{325°} CaC_2 + C_2H_2$$

It exists in at least four crystalline forms, the one stable at room temperature being a tetragonally distorted NaCl-type structure (Fig. 8.17) in which the C_2 units are aligned along the c-axis. The ethynides of Mg, Sr and Ba have the same structure and also hydrolyse to give ethyne. In addition, BaC_2 absorbs N_2 from the atmosphere to give $Ba(CN)_2$ (cf. CaC_2 above).

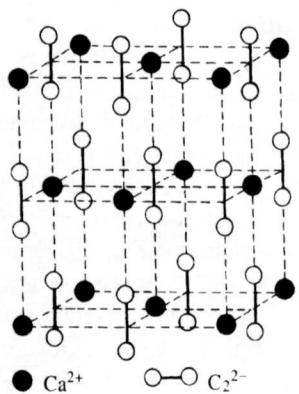

$\bullet$ Ca^{2+} $\circ\!-\!\circ$ C_2^{2-}

Figure 8.17 Crystal structure of tetragonal CaC_2 showing the resemblance to NaCl (p. 242). Above 450°C the parallel alignment of the C_2 units breaks down and the structure becomes cubic.

Carbides containing the essentially linear C_3^{4-} unit are known, e.g. Li_4C_3, Mg_2C_3, and the recently characterized $Ca_3C_3Cl_2$ and Sc_3C_4.[85] Thus $Ca_3C_3Cl_2$ forms as transparent red crystals when $CaCl_2$ is heated with graphite in sealed Ta capsules at 900°C for 1 day (C–C 134.6 pm, angle 169.0°). By contrast Sc_3C_4 is a grey-black metallic substance with Pauli paramagnetism: it contains C^{4-} and C_2^{2-} ions, and supernumerary electrons e^- in addition to C_3^{4-} (C–C 134.2 pm, angle 175.8°). It can best be represented as $10Sc_3C_4 \equiv [(Sc^{3+})_{30}(C^{4-})_{12}(C_2^{2-})_2(C_3^{4-})_8(e^-)_6]$.[85]

The carbides of the lanthanoids and actinoids can be prepared by heating M_2O_3 with C in an electric furnace or by arc-melting compressed pellets of the elements in an inert atmosphere. They contain the C_2 unit and have a stoichiometry MC_2 or $M_4(C_2)_3$. MC_2 have the CaC_2 structure or a related one of lower symmetry in which the C_2 units lie at right-angles to the c-axis of an orthogonal NaCl-type cell.[86] They are more reactive than the alkaline-earth metal

[85] R. HOFFMANN and H.-J. MEYER, *Z. anorg. allg. Chem.* **607**, 57–71 (1992).

[86] A. F. WELLS, *Structural Inorganic Chemistry*, 5th edn., Oxford University Press, Oxford, 1984, 1382 pp.

carbides, combining readily with atmospheric oxygen and hydrolysing to a complex mixture of hydrocarbons. This derives from their more complicated electronic structure and, indeed, LnC_2 are metallic conductors (not insulators like CaC_2); they are best regarded as ethynides of Ln^{III} with the supernumerary electron partly delocalized in a conduction band of the crystal. This would explain the evolution of H_2 as well as C_2H_2 on hydrolysis, and the simultaneous production of the reduced species C_2H_4 and C_2H_6 together with various other hydrocarbons up to C_6H_{10}:

$$LnC_2 + 3H_2O \longrightarrow Ln(OH)_3 + C_2H_2 + [H]$$

An interesting feature of the ethynides MC_2 and $M_4(C_2)_3$ is the variation in the C–C distance as measured by neutron diffraction. Typical values (in pm) are:

CaC_2	YC_2	CeC_2	LaC_2	UC_2
119.2	127.5	128.3	130.3	135.0

$La_4(C_2)_3$	$Ce_4(C_2)_3$	$U_4(C_2)_3$
123.6	127.6	129.5

The C–C distance in CaC_2 is close to that in ethyne (120.5 pm) and it has been suggested that the observed increase in the lanthanoid and actinoid carbides results from a partial localization of the supernumerary electron in the antibonding orbital of the ethynide ion $[C{\equiv}C]^{2-}$ (see p. 932). The effect is noticeably less in the sesquicarbides than in the dicarbides. The compounds EuC_2 and YbC_2 differ in their lattice parameters and hydrolysis behaviour from the other LnC_2 and this may be related to the relative stability of Eu^{II} and Yb^{II} (p. 1237).

The lanthanoids also form metal-rich carbides of stoichiometry M_3C in which individual C atoms occupy at random one-third of the octahedral Cl sites in a NaCl-like structure. Several of the actinoids (e.g. Th, U, Pu) form monocarbides, MC, in which all the octahedral Cl sites in the NaCl structure are occupied and this stoichiometry is also observed for several other carbides of the early transition elements, e.g. M = Ti, Zr, Hf; V, Nb, Ta; Mo, W. These

are best considered as interstitial carbides and in this sense the lanthanoids and actinoids occupy an intermediate position in the classification of the carbides, as they did with the hydrides (p. 66).

Interstitial carbides are infusible, extremely hard, refractory materials that retain many of the characteristic properties of metals (lustre, metallic conductivity).[87] Reported mps are frequently in the range 3000–4000°C. Interstitial carbides derive their name from the fact that the C atoms occupy octahedral interstices in a close-packed lattice of metal atoms, though the arrangement of metal atoms is not always the same as in the metal itself. The size of the metal atoms must be large enough to generate a site of sufficient size to accommodate C, and the critical radius of M seems to be ~135 pm: thus the transition metals mentioned in the preceding paragraph all have 12-coordinate radii >135 pm, whereas metals with smaller radii (e.g. Cr, Mn, Fe, Co, Ni) do not form MC and their interstitial carbides have a more complex structure (see below). If the close-packed arrangement of M atoms is hexagonal (h) rather than cubic (c) then the 2 octahedral interstices on either side of a close-packed M layer are located directly above one another and only one of these is ever occupied. This gives a stoichiometry M_2C as in V_2C, Nb_2C, Ta_2C and W_2C. Intermediate stoichiometries are encountered when the M atom stacking sequence alternates, e.g. Mo_3C_2 (hcc) and V_4C_3 (hhcc). Ordered defect NaCl-type structures are also known, e.g. V_8C_7 and V_6C_5, thus illustrating the wide range of stoichiometries which occur among interstitial carbides. Unlike the "ionic" carbides, interstitial carbides do not react with water and are generally very inert, though some do react with air when heated above 1000° and most are degraded by conc HNO_3 or HF. The extreme hardness and inertness of WC and TaC have led to their extensive use as high-speed cutting tools.

---

[87] H. H. JOHANSEN, *Survey of Progress in Chemistry* **8**, 57–81 (1977). See also A. COTTRELL, *Chemical Bonding in Transition Metal Carbides*, Inst. of Materials, London, 1995, 99 pp.

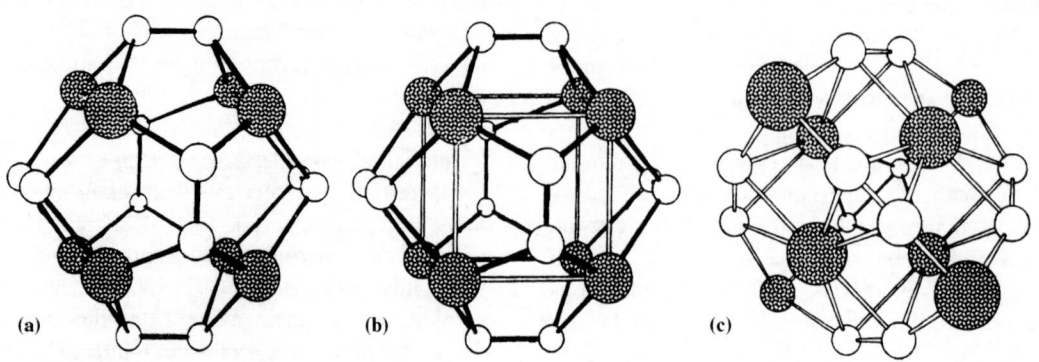

Figure 8.18   (a) Proposed pentagonal dodecahedral structure of Ti_8C_{12}. (b) The same structure viewed as a Ti_8 cube with each face capped by a C_2 group. (c) An alternative T_h structure (see text).

Table 8.3   Stoichiometries of some transition element carbides

V_2C, V_4C_3	$Cr_{23}C_6$	$Mn_{23}C_6$, $Mn_{15}C_4$	Fe_3C, Fe_7C_3	Co_3C	Ni_3C
V_6C_5, V_8C_7	Cr_7C_3	Mn_3C, Mn_5C_2	Fe_2C	Co_2C	
VC	Cr_3C_2	Mn_7C_3			

The carbides of Cr, Mn, Fe, Co and Ni are profuse in number, complicated in structure, and of great importance industrially. Cementite, Fe_3C, is an important constituent of steel (p. 1075). Typical stoichiometries are listed in Table 8.3 though it should be noted that several of the phases can exist over a range of composition.

The structures, particularly of the most metal-rich phases, are frequently related to those of the corresponding metal-rich borides (and silicides, germanides, phosphides, arsenides, sulfides and selenides), in which the non-metal is surrounded by a trigonal prism of M atoms with 0, 1, 2, or 3 additional neighbours beyond the quadrilateral prism faces (p. 148). e.g. Fe_3C (cementite), Mn_3C and Co_3B; Mn_5C_2 and Pd_5B_2; Cr_7C_3 and Re_7B_3. Numerous ternary carbides, carbonitrides, and oxocarbides are also known.

The carbides of Cr, Mn, Fe, Co and Ni are much more reactive than the interstitial carbides of the earlier transition metals. They are rapidly hydrolysed by dilute acid and sometimes even by water to give H_2 and a mixture of hydrocarbons. For example, M_3C give H_2 (75%), CH_4 (15%) and C_2H_6 (8%) together with small amounts of higher hydrocarbons.

Metallocarbohedrenes (met-cars)

An entirely novel group of binary metal carbides, reminiscent of the fullerenes (p. 279), were discovered by accident in 1992.[88] When Ti metal is vaporized in a laser plasma reactor in the presence of He gas containing a hydrocarbon such as methane, ethene, ethyne or benzene, the mass spectrum of the emerging beam contains a single dominant peak at 528 corresponding to Ti_8C_{12} [isotope ^{48}Ti 73.8% abundant: $(8 \times 48) + (12 \times 12) = 528$]. Detailed isotope distribution studies confirmed the molecular formula. The proposed structure, shown in Fig. 8.18a, is a pentagonal dodecahedron of T_h symmetry comprising 12 mutually fused Ti_2C_3 pentagons.

---
[88] B. C. GUO, K. P. KERNS and A. W. CASTLEMAN, *Science* **255**, 1411–3 (1992). B. C. GUO, S. WEI, J. PURNELL, S. BUZZA and A. W. CASTLEMAN, *Science* **256**, 515–6 and 818–20 (1992), *J. Chem. Phys.* **96**, 4166–8 (1992).

Table 8.4 Some properties of methane and CX_4

Property	CH_4	CF_4	CCl_4	CBr_4	CI_4
MP/°C	−182.5	−183.5	−22.9	90.1	171 (d)
BP/°C	−161.5	−128.5	76.7	189.5	~130 (subl)
Density/g cm^{-3}	0.424	1.96	1.594	2.961	4.32
(at T°C)	(−164°)	(−184°)	(20°)	(100°)	(20°) (s)
$-\Delta H_f^\circ$/kJ mol^{-1}	74.87	679.9	106.7 (g)	160 (l)	—
			139.3 (l)		
$D(X_3C–X)$/kJ mol^{-1}	435	515	295	235	—

Each Ti bonds to 3C via σ bonds and each C bonds to 2Ti and one C. The all-carbon analogue, C_{20}, is not expected to be stable because of severe internal strain; (it would be the smallest possible fullerene, p. 280). Note, however, that dodecahedrane, $C_{20}H_{20}$, is known.[89] An alternative description of the structure (Fig. 8.18b) would be as a weakly bonded cube, Ti_8, each face of which is capped by a C_2 unit. The calculated distances[90] are Ti$\cdots$Ti 302 pm, Ti–C 199 pm and C–C 140 pm (implying some multiple bonding: cf. 140 pm in benzene). An alternative T_h structure for Ti_8C_{12}, which is calculated to have a lower energy, has also been proposed.[90] In this, the Ti_8 array is a tetracapped tetrahedron containing six Ti_4 faces in butterfly conformation; each of these Ti_4 faces can then accommodate a C_2 unit as shown in Fig. 8.18c.

Other met-cars that have been detected mass spectrometrically are M_8C_{12} (M = V, Zr, Hf) and there is some evidence for higher members such as $Zr_{13}C_{22}$, $Zr_{14}C_{23}$, $Zr_{18}C_{29}$ and $Zr_{23}C_{32}$ which may feature fused clusters of clusters. The possibility of a super-pentagonal cluster, $M_{30}C_{45}$, of D_{5h} symmetry has also been mooted.[91]

As with the fullerenes, further detailed studies will depend on the discovery of viable bulk preparations of the met-cars. Macroscopic amounts of Ti_8C_{12} and V_8C_{12} have indeed been made by DC arc discharge techniques using electrodes of compacted metal and graphite powders and He as the quenching carrier gas.[92] The resulting soot contains about 1% of air-stable M_8C_{12} plus some C_{60} (unstable in air). Solution studies have not yet been reported but there is mass spectrometric evidence for $Ti_8C_{12}L_8$ (L = NH_3, ND_3, H_2O) as well as for $Ti_8C_{12}(MeOH)_4$.

8.5 Hydrides, Halides and Oxohalides

The ability of C to catenate (i.e. to form bonds to itself in compounds) is nowhere better illustrated than in the compounds it forms with H. Hydrocarbons occur in great variety in petroleum deposits and elsewhere, and form various homologous series in which the C atoms are linked into chains, branched chains and rings. The study of these compounds and their derivatives forms the subject of organic chemistry and is fully discussed in the many textbooks and treatises on that subject. The matter is further considered on p. 374 in relation to the much smaller ability of other Group 14 elements to form such catenated compounds. Methane, CH_4, is the archetype of tetrahedral coordination in molecular compounds; some of its properties are listed in Table 8.4 where they are compared with those of the

[89] R. J. TERNANSKY, D. W. BALOGH and L. A. PAQUETTE, *J. Am. Chem. Soc.* **104**, 4503–4 (1982). J. C. GALLUCCI, C. W. DOECKE and L. A. PAQUETTE *J. Am. Chem. Soc.* **108**, 1343–4 (1986).

[90] I. G. DANCE, *J. Chem. Soc., Chem. Commun.*, 1779–80 (1992).

[91] I. G. DANCE, *Aust. J. Chem.* **46**, 727–30 (1993).

[92] S. F. CARTIER, Z. Y. CHEN, G. J. WALDER and A. W. CASTLEMAN, *Science* **260**, 195–6 (1993).

corresponding halides. Unsaturated hydrocarbons such as ethene (C_2H_4), ethyne (C_2H_2), benzene (C_6H_6), cyclooctatetraene (C_8H_8) and homocyclic radicals such as cyclopentadienyl (C_5H_5) and cycloheptatrienyl (C_7H_7) are effective ligands to metals and form many organometallic complexes (pp. 930–43).

Methane is unique among hydrocarbons in being thermodynamically stable with respect to its elements. It follows that pyrolytic reactions to convert it to other hydrocarbons are energetically unfavourable and will be strongly equilibrium-limited. This is in marked contrast to the boranes where mild thermolysis of B_2H_6 or B_4H_{10}, for example, readily yields mixtures of the higher boranes (p. 164). Vast natural reserves of CH_4 gas exist but much is wasted

by flaring (direct burning off at the petroleum production site) because of the uneconomical cost of transport. However, in convenient locations such as the North Sea, natural gas is piped ashore for use as domestic or industrial fuel or as chemical feedstock. After CO_2, methane is the most important "greenhouse gas" (p. 273) accounting for an estimated 15–20% of the atmospheric global warming ($CO_2 > 50\%$). The major sources of atmospheric CH_4 are natural wetlands (25%), rice cultivation (22%), animals (mainly domestic ruminants) (17%) and the mining of fossil fuels (16%), the total "production" being some 460 million tonnes per annum.

Notable recent advances in the chemistry of hydrocarbons include the synthesis and

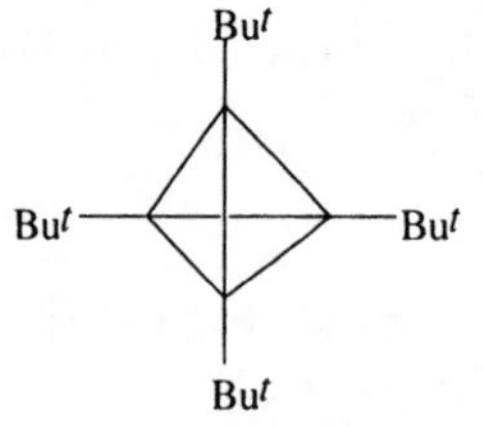

(1)

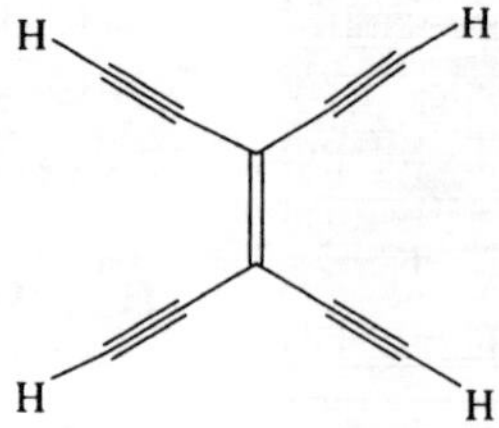

(2)

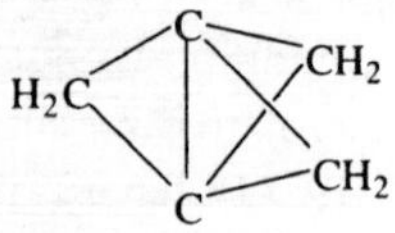

(3)

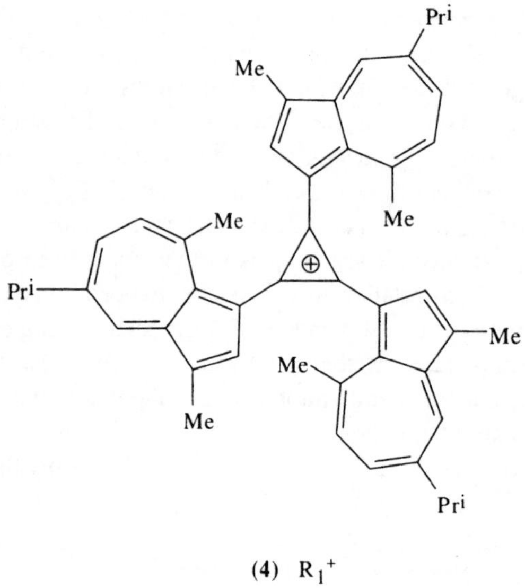

(4) R_1^+

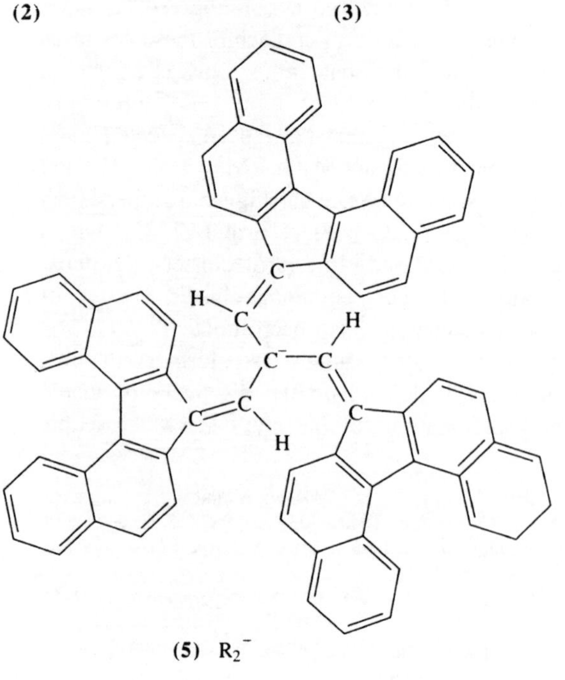

(5) R_2^-

(6) $R_3^- R_2$ (7) $R_3^+ R_2^-$

molecular structure determination of the tetrahedrane derivative, $C_4Bu_4^t$ (1),[93] the carbon-rich molecules tetraethynylmethane, $C(C{\equiv}CH)_4$ i.e. C_9H_4[94] and tetraethynylethene, $C_2(C{\equiv}CH)_4$ i.e. $C_{10}H_4$ (2),[95] the highly strained [1.1.1]propellane (3)[96] and the preparation of the largest discrete hydrocarbon molecules yet synthesized, the polyphenylethyne dendrimers $C_{1134}H_{1146}$ and $C_{1398}H_{1278}$ (mol wts 14 777.6 and 18 079.6).[97] There is also increasing interest in hydrocarbon salts $R_1^+R_2^-$. The first example was the stable, greenish-black crystalline compound $C_{48}H_{51}^+C_{61}H_{39}^-$ (mp 230°C decomp.) obtained by mixing thf solutions of Agranat's carbocation (4) and Kuhn's carbanion (5).[98] Of special interest is the covalent molecular hydrocarbon

$R_3{-}R_2$ (6) which exists in chloroform solution but which crystallizes on evaporation or cooling to give the ionic salt $R_3^+R_2^-$ (7).[99] This reversible ionic-covalent equilibrium is reminiscent of similar behaviour in certain halides such as $AlCl_3$ (p. 234), PCl_5 (p. 499) and $TeCl_4$ (p. 772), etc.

Fullerene derivatives such as $C_{60}H_n$ (p. 283), $C_{60}H_2$ (p. 287), and $C_{61}H_2$ (p. 287), and hypercoordinated non-classical carbonium ions (p. 290) have already been briefly mentioned.

Turning next to the simple halides of carbon: tetrafluoromethane (CF_4) is an exceptionally stable gas with mp close to that of CH_4 (see Table 8.4). It can be prepared on a laboratory scale by reacting SiC with F_2 or by fluorinating CO_2, CO or $COCl_2$ with SF_4. Industrially it is prepared by the aggressive reaction of F_2 on CF_2Cl_2 or CF_3Cl, or by electrolysis of MF or MF_2 using a C anode. CF_4 was first obtained pure in 1926; C_2F_6 was isolated in 1930 and C_2F_4 in 1933; but it was not until 1937 that the various homologous series of fluorocarbons were isolated and identified. Replacement of H by F greatly increases both thermal stability and chemical inertness because of the great strength of the C–F

[93] H. Irngartinger, A. Goldmann, R. Jahn, M. Nixdorf, H. Rodewald, G. Maier, K.-D. Malsch and R. Emrich, *Angew. Chem. Int. Edn. Engl.* **23**, 993–4 (1984).

[94] K. S. Feldman and C. M. Kraebel, *J. Am. Chem. Soc.* **115**, 3846–7 (1993).

[95] Y. Rubin, C. B. Knobler and F. Diederich, *Angew. Chem. Int. Edn. Engl.* **30**, 698–700 (1991).

[96] J. E. Jackson and L. C. Allen, *J. Am. Chem. Soc.* **106**, 591–9 (1984).

[97] Z. Xu and J. S. Moore, *Angew. Chem. Int. Edn. Engl.* **32**, 246–8 (1993), and *Abstracts*, ACS Denver Meeting, April 1993.

[98] K. Okamoto, T. Kitagawa, K. Takeuchi, K. Komatsu and K. Takahashi, *J. Chem. Soc., Chem. Commun.*, 173–4 (1985).

[99] K. Okamoto, T. Kitagawa, K. Takeuchi, K. Komatsu and A. Miyabo, *J. Chem. Soc., Chem. Commun.*, 923–4 (1988).

bond (Table 8.4). Accordingly, fluorocarbons are resistant to attack by acids, alkalis, oxidizing agents, reducing agents and most chemicals up to 600°. They are immiscible with both water and hydrocarbon solvents, and when combined with other groups they confer water-repellance and stain-resistance to paper, textiles and fabrics.[100] Tetrafluoroethene (C_2F_4) can be polymerized to a chemically inert, thermosetting plastic PTFE (polytetrafluoroethene); this has an extremely low coefficient of friction and is finding increasing use as a protective coating in non-stick kitchen utensils, razor blades and bearings. PTFE is made by partial fluorination of chloroform using HF in the presence of $SbFCl_4$ as catalyst, followed by thermolysis to C_2F_4 and subsequent polymerization:

$$CCl_3H \longrightarrow CF_2ClH \xrightarrow{\Delta} C_2F_4 \longrightarrow (C_2F_4)_n$$

As a ligand towards metals, C_2F_4 and other unsaturated fluorocarbons differ markedly from alkenes (p. 931).

CCl_4 is a common laboratory and industrial solvent with a distinctive smell, usually prepared by reaction of CS_2 or CH_4 with Cl_2. Its use as a solvent has declined somewhat because of its toxicity, but CCl_4 is still extensively used as an intermediate in preparing "Freons" such as $CFCl_3$, CF_2Cl_2 and CF_3Cl:[100]

$$CCl_4 + HF \xrightarrow{SbFCl_4} CFCl_3 + HCl$$

$$CFCl_3 + HF \xrightarrow{SbFCl_4} CF_2Cl_2 + HCl$$

The catalyst is formed by reaction of HF on $SbCl_5$. The Freons have a unique combination of properties which make them ideally suited for use as refrigerants and aerosol propellants. They have low bp, low viscosity, low surface tension and high density, and are non-toxic, non-flammable, odourless, chemically inert and thermally stable. The most commonly used is CF_2Cl_2, bp, −29.8°. The market for Freons

and other fluorocarbons expanded rapidly in the sixties: production in the USA alone exceeded 200 000 tonnes in 1964 (417 000 tonnes in 1990) and global production was about three times this amount. Already in 1977 there was an annual production of 2.4×10^9 spray-cans. However, there has been growing concern that chlorofluorocarbons from spray-cans gradually work their way into the upper atmosphere where they may, through a complex chemical reaction, deplete the earth's ozone layer (p. 608). For this reason there was an enforced progressive elimination of this particular application in the USA starting 15 October 1978 and production of CFCs will effectively be completely phased out following the Montreal Protocol of September 1981.

CBr_4 is a pale-yellow solid which is markedly less stable than the lighter tetrahalides. Preparation involves bromination of CH_4 with HBr or Br_2 or, more conveniently, reaction of CCl_4 with Al_2Br_6 at 100°. The trend to diminishing thermal stability continues to CI_4 which is a bright-red crystalline solid with a smell reminiscent of I_2. It is prepared by the $AlCl_3$-catalysed halogen exchange reaction between CCl_4 and EtI.

Carbon oxohalides are reactive gases or volatile liquids which feature planar molecules of C_{2v} symmetry; they are isoelectronic with BX_3 (p. 196) and the bonding is best described in terms of molecular orbitals spanning all 4 atoms rather than in terms of localized orbitals as implied by the formulation $\begin{matrix} X \\ \diagdown \\ \diagup \\ X \end{matrix} C{=}O$. Some physical properties and molecular dimensions are in Table 8.5. The values call for little comment except to note that the XCX angle is significantly less (as expected) than the value of 120° found for the more symmetrical isoelectronic species BX_3 and CO_3^{2-}. The C–Br distance is unusually long; it comes from a very early diffraction measurement and could profitably be checked.

Mixed oxohalides are also known and their volatilities are intermediate between those of the

---

[100] *Kirk–Othmer Encyclopedia of Chemical Technology*, 4th edn., Vol 11, 1994, pp. 467–729.

Table 8.5 Some physical properties and molecular dimensions of COX_2

Property	COF_2	$COCl_2$	$COBr_2$
MP/°C	$-114°$	$-127.8°$	—
BP/°C	$-83.1°$	$7.6°$	$64.5°$
Density (T°C)/g cm^{-3}	$1.139(-144°)$	$1.392(19°)$	—
Distance (C–O)/pm	117.4	116.6	113
Distance (C–X)/pm	131.2	174.6	(205)
Angle X–C–X	$108.0°$	$111.3°$	$110 \pm 5°$
Angle X–C–O	$126.0°$	$124.3°$	$\sim125°$

parent species, e.g. COFCl (bp $-42°$), COFBr (bp $-20.6°$). COI_2 is unknown but COFI has been prepared (mp $-90°$, bp $23.4°$). Synthetic routes are as follows: COFCl from $COCl_2$/HF; COFBr from CO/BrF_3; COFI from CO/IF_3; and COClBr from CCl_3Br/H_2SO_4.

COF_2 can be made by fluorinating $COCl_2$ with standard fluorinating agents such as NaF/MeCN or SbF_5/SbF_3; direct fluorination of CO with AgF_2 affords an alternative route. COF_2 is rapidly hydrolysed by water to CO_2 and HX, as are all the other COX_2. It is a useful laboratory reagent for producing a wide range of fluoroorganic compounds and the heavier alkali metal fluorides react in MeCN to give trifluoromethoxides $MOCF_3$.

$COCl_2$ (phosgene) is highly toxic and should be handled with great caution. It was first made in 1812 by John Davy (Sir Humphry Davy's brother) by the action of sunlight on $CO + Cl_2$, whence its otherwise surprising name (Greek $\phi\omega\varsigma$ *phos*, light; $-\gamma\varepsilon\nu\eta'\varsigma$, *-genes*, born of). It is now a major industrial chemical and is made on the kilotonne scale by combining the two gases catalytically over activated C (p. 274). It was used briefly and rather ineffectively as a chemical warfare gas in 1916 but is now principally used to prepare isocyanates as intermediates to polyurethanes. It also acts as a ligand (Lewis base) towards $AlCl_3$, $SnCl_4$, $SbCl_5$, etc., forming adducts $Cl_2CO \rightarrow MCl_n$, and is a useful chlorinating agent, converting metal oxides into highly pure chlorides. It reacts with NH_3 to form mainly urea, $CO(NH_2)_2$, together with more highly condensed products such as guanidine,

$C(NH)(NH_2)_2$; biuret, $NH_2CONHCONH_2$; and cyanuric acid, i.e. *cyclo*-$[CO(NH)]_3$ (p. 323).

$COBr_2$ has recently been shown to be a useful general brominating reagent for the preparation of d- and f-block bromides and oxide bromides.[101] Thus, when V_2O_5 is heated with an excess of $COBr_2$ in a sealed Carius tube at 125°C for 10 days, a quantitative yield of $VOBr_2$ is obtained by a reaction that is driven thermodynamically by the formation of CO_2: [$V_2O_5 + 3COBr_2 \longrightarrow 2VOBr_2 + 3CO_2 + Br_2$]. Similarly, MoO_2, Re_2O_7, Sm_2O_3 and UO_3 were smoothly converted to MoO_2Br_2, $ReOBr_4$, $SmBr_3$ and $UOBr_3$, respectively.

8.6 Oxides and Carbonates

Carbon forms 2 extremely stable oxides, CO and CO_2, 3 oxides of considerably lower stability, C_3O_2, C_5O_2 and $C_{12}O_9$, and a number of unstable or poorly characterized oxides including C_2O, C_2O_3 and the nonstoichiometric graphite oxide (p. 289). Of these, CO and CO_2 are of outstanding importance and their chemistry will be discussed in subsequent paragraphs after a few brief remarks about some of the others.

Tricarbon dioxide, C_3O_2, often called "carbon suboxide" and ponderously referred to in *Chemical Abstracts* as 1,2-propadiene-1,3-dione, is a foul-smelling gas obtained by dehydrating malonic acid, $CH_2(CO_2H)_2$, at

---

101 J. S. Yadav and V. R. Gadgil, *J. Chem. Soc., Chem. Commun.*, 1824–5 (1989).

Table 8.6 Some properties of CO, CO_2 and C_3O_2

Property	CO	CO_2	C_3O_2
MP/°C	−205.1	−56.6(5.2 atm)	−112.5
BP/°C	−191.5	−78.5 (subl)	6.7
ΔH_f°/kJ mol^{-1}	−110.5	−393.7	+97.8
Distance (C–O)/pm	112.8	116.3	116
Distance (C–C)/pm	—	—	128
D(C–O)/kJ mol^{-1}	1070.3	531.4	—

reduced pressure over P_4O_{10} at 140°, or by thermolysis of bis(trimethylsilyl) malonate, $CH_2(CO_2SiMe_3)_2$.[102] It has mp −112.5°, bp 6.7°, is stable at −78°, and polymerizes at room temperature to a yellow solid. C_3O_2 forms linear molecules ($D_{\infty h}$ symmetry) which can be written as O=C=C=C=O, consistent with the short interatomic distances C–C 128 pm and C–O 116 pm. Above 100°, polymerization yields a ruby-red solid; at 400° the product is violet and at 500° the polymer decomposes to C. The basic structure of all the polymers appears to be a polycyclic 6-membered lactone. C_3O_2 readily rehydrates to malonic acid, and reacts with NH_3 and HCl to give respectively the corresponding amide and acid chloride: $CH_2(CONH_2)_2$ and $CH_2(COCl)_2$. Thermolysis of C_3O_2 in a flow system has been reported to give a liquid product C_5O_2 though a better preparation is the photolysis or thermolysis of the tris(diazo)ketone, cyclo-1,3,5-$C_6O_3(N_2)_3$.[103] C_5O_2 is a yellow solid which decomposes above −90°; in solution it apparently remains unchanged for several days even at room temperature. Note that C_5O_2 is the next member after CO_2 and C_3O_2 of the linear catenated series OC_nO with n odd as required by simple π-bond theory. The other moderately stable lower oxide is $C_{12}O_9$, a white sublimable solid which is the anhydride of mellitic acid, $C_6(COOH)_6$.

Direct oxidation of C in a limited supply of oxygen or air yields CO; in a free supply CO_2

results. Some properties of these familiar gases and of C_3O_2 are in Table 8.6. The great strength of the C–O bond confers considerable thermal stability on these molecules but the compounds are also quite reactive chemically, and many of the reactions are of major industrial importance. Some of these are discussed more fully in the Panel.

The nature of the bonding, particularly in CO, has excited much attention because of the unusual coordination number (1) and oxidation state (+2) of carbon: it is discussed on p. 926 in connection with the formation of metal–carbonyl complexes.

Pure CO can be made on a laboratory scale by dehydrating formic acid (HCOOH) with conc H_2SO_4 at ∼140°. CO is a colourless, odourless, flammable gas; it has a relatively high toxicity due to its ability to form a complex with haemoglobin that is some 300 times more stable than the oxygen–haemoglobin complex (p. 1099): the oxygen-transport function of the red corpuscles in the blood is thereby impeded. This can result in unconsciousness or death, though recovery from mild poisoning is rapid and complete in fresh air and the effects are not cumulative. CO can be detected by its ability to reduce an aqueous solution of $PdCl_2$ to metallic Pd:

$$CO + PdCl_2 + H_2O \longrightarrow Pd + CO_2 + 2HCl$$

Quantitative estimation relies on the liberation of I_2 from I_2O_5 or (in the absence of C_2H_2) on absorption in an acid solution of CuCl to form the adduct $[Cu(CO)Cl(H_2O)_2]$.

[102] L. BIRKOFER and P. SOMMER, *Chem. Ber.* **109**, 1701–7 (1976).

[103] G. MAIER, H. P. REISENAUER, U. SCHÄFER and H. BALLI, *Angew. Chem. Int. Edn. Engl.* **27**, 566–8 (1988).

Industrially Important Reactions of Oxygen and Oxides with Carbon

Carbon monoxide is widely used as a fuel in the form of producer gas or water gas and is also formed during the isolation of many metals from their oxides by reduction with coke. Producer gas is obtained by blowing air through incandescent coke and consists of about 25% CO, 4% CO_2 and 70% N_2, together with traces of H_2, CH_4 and O_2. The reactions occurring during production are:

$$2C + O_2 \longrightarrow 2CO: \quad \Delta H° = -221.0 \text{ kJ/mol } O_2; \quad \Delta S° + 179.4 \text{ J K}^{-1} \text{ mol}^{-1}$$

$$C + O_2 \longrightarrow CO_2: \quad \Delta H° = -393.5 \text{ kJ mol}^{-1}; \quad \Delta S° + 2.89 \text{ J K}^{-1} \text{ mol}^{-1}$$

Water gas is made by blowing steam through incandescent coke: it consists of about 50% H_2, 40% CO, 5% CO_2 and 5% $N_2 + CH_4$. The oxidation of C by H_2O is strongly endothermic:

$$C + H_2O \longrightarrow CO + H_2; \quad \Delta H° = +131.3 \text{ kJ mol}^{-1}; \quad \Delta S° + 133.7 \text{ J K}^{-1} \text{ mol}^{-1}$$

Consequently, the coke cools down and the steam must be intermittently replaced by a flow of air to reheat the coke.

At high temperatures, particularly in the presence of metal catalysts, CO undergoes reversible disproportionation:[†]

$$2CO \rightleftharpoons C + CO_2: \quad \Delta H° = -172.5 \text{ kJ/mol } CO_2; \quad \Delta S° = -176.5 \text{ J K}^{-1} \text{ mol}^{-1}$$

The equilibrium concentration of CO is 10% at 550°C and 99% at 1000°. As the forward reaction involves a reduction in the number of gaseous molecules it is accompanied by a large decrease in entropy. Remembering that $\Delta G = \Delta H - T\Delta S$ this implies that the reverse reaction becomes progressively more favoured at higher temperatures. The thermodynamic data for the formation of CO and CO_2 can be represented diagramatically on an Ellingham diagram (Fig. 19) which plots standard free energy changes per mol of O_2 as a function of the absolute temperature. The oxidation of C to CO results in an increase in the number of gaseous molecules; it is therefore accompanied by a large increase in entropy and is favoured at high temperature. By contrast, oxidation to CO_2 leaves the number of gaseous molecules unchanged; there is little change in entropy ($\Delta S°$ 2.93 J K^{-1} mol^{-1}), and the free energy is almost independent of temperature. The two lines (and that for the oxidation of CO to CO_2) intersect at 983 K; it follows that ΔG for the disproportionation reaction is zero at this temperature. The diagram also includes the plots of ΔG (per mole of O_2) for the oxidation of several representative metals. On the left of the diagram (at $T = 0$ K) $\Delta G = \Delta H$ and the sequence of elements is approximately that of the electrochemical series. The slope of most of the lines is similar and corresponds to the loss of 1 mol of gaseous O_2; small changes of slope occur at the temperature of phase changes or the mp of the metal, and a more dramatic increase in slope signals the bp of the metal. For example, for MgO(s), the slope increases about three-fold at the bp of Mg since, above this temperature, reaction removes three gaseous species ($2Mg + O_2$) rather than one (O_2).

Such diagrams are of great value in codefying a mass of information of use in extractive metallurgy.[105] For example, it is clear that below 710°C (983 K) carbon is a stronger reducing agent when it is converted into CO_2 rather than CO, whereas above this temperature the reverse is true. Again, as reduction of metal oxides with C will occur when the accompanying ΔG is negative, such reduction becomes progressively more feasible the higher the temperature: Zn (and Cd) can be reduced at relatively low temperatures but MgO can only be reduced at temperatures approaching 2000 K. Caution should be exercised, however, in predicting the outcome of such reactions since a number of otherwise reasonable reductions cannot be used because the metal forms a carbide (e.g. Cr, Ti). The temperature at which the oxygen dissociation pressure of the various metal oxides reaches a given value can also be obtained from the diagram: as $-\Delta G = RT \ln K_p [= 2.303RT \log\{p(O_2)/\text{atm}\}$ for the reactions considered] it follows that the line drawn from the point $\odot(\Delta G = 0, T = 0)$ to the appropriate scale mark on the right-hand side of the diagram intercepts the free-energy line for the element concerned at the required temperature. (Establish to your own satisfaction that this statement is approximately true — what assumptions does it embody?)

[†] Note however that, at all pressures, there is a fairly wide range of temperatures in which CO_2 dissociates directly into CO and O_2 without precipitation of carbon:[104]

$$CO_2 \rightleftharpoons CO + \tfrac{1}{2}O_2$$

For example, the temperature range is 250–370°C at 10^{-2} atm, 320–480°C at 1 atm, and 405–630°C at 100 atm. At higher temperatures in each case, C is also formed, but always in the presence of some O_2.

---

[104] M. H. LIETZKE and C. MULLINS, *J. Inorg. Nucl. Chem.* **43**, 1769–71 (1981).
[105] C. B. ALCOCK, *Principles of Pyrometallurgy*, Academic Press, London, 1976, 348 pp.

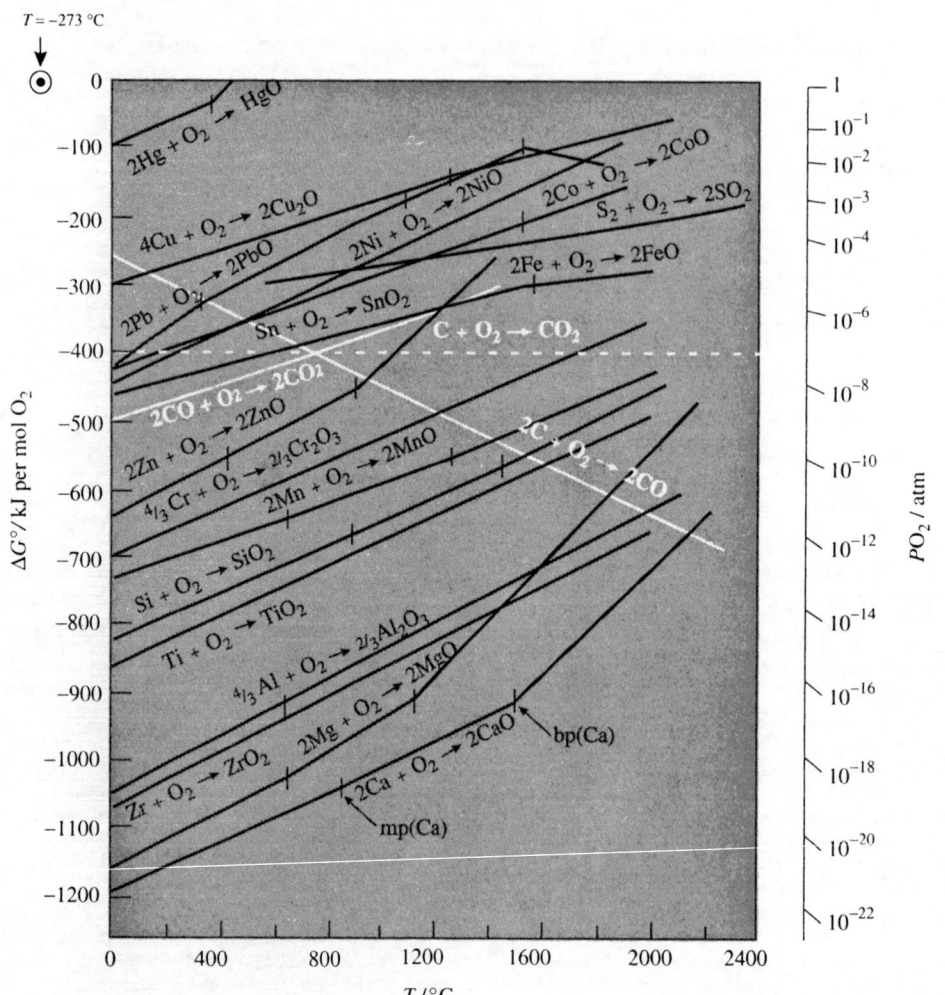

Figure 8.19 Ellingham diagram for the free energy of formation of metallic oxides. (After F. D. Richardson and J. H. E. Jeffes, *J. Iron Steel Inst.* **160**, 261 (1948).) The oxygen dissociation pressure of a given M–MO system at a given temperature is obtained by joining ⊙ on the top left hand to the appropriate point on the M–MO free-energy line, and extrapolating to the scale on the right hand ordinate for p_{O_2} (atm).

CO reacts at elevated temperatures to give formates with alkali hydroxides, and acetates with methoxides:

$$CO + NaOH \longrightarrow HCO_2Na;$$

$$CO + MeONa \longrightarrow MeCO_2Na$$

Reaction with alkali metals in liquid NH_3 leads to reductive coupling to give colourless crystals of the salt $Na_2C_2O_2$ which contains linear groups $NaOC{\equiv}CONa$ packed in chains. CO reacts with Cl_2 and Br_2 to give COX_2 (p. 305) and with liquid S to give COS. It cleaves B_2H_6 at high pressures to give the "symmetrical" adduct BH_3CO (p. 165), but in the presence of $NaBH_4$/thf the reaction takes a different course to yield the cyclic *B*-trimethylboroxine:

$$\tfrac{3}{2}B_2H_6 + 3CO \xrightarrow[\text{thf}]{\text{NaBH}_4/} Me\overline{BOB(Me)OB(Me)O}$$

With BR_3, CO inserts in successive stages to give, ultimately, the corresponding trialkyl-methylboroxine $(R_3CBO)_3$. Alternative products are obtained in the presence of other reagents, e.g. aqueous alkali yields R_3COH; water followed by alkaline peroxide yields R_2CO; and alkaline $NaBH_4$ yields RCH_2OH (p. 167). CO can also insert into M–C bonds (M = Mo, W; Mn, Fe, Co; Ni, Pd, Pt):

$$MeMn(CO)_5 + CO \longrightarrow MeC(O)Mn(CO)_5$$

A detailed discussion of CO as a ligand and the chemistry of metal carbonyls is on pp. 926–9. CO is a key intermediate in the catalytic production of a wide variety of organic compounds on an industrial scale. These include:[106,107]

1. Catalytic reduction to methanol (230–400°C, 50–100 atm):

$$CO + 2H_2 \longrightarrow CH_3OH$$

2. Homogeneous methanol carboxylation with I^-/Rh catalyst (175–195°C, 30 atm), this is now a leading route to acetic acid:

$$MeOH + CO \longrightarrow MeCO_2H$$

3. Hydroformylation of olefins to alcohols (the oxo process):[108]

$$RCH{=}CH_2 + CO + H_2$$
$$\longrightarrow RCH_2CH_2CHO \xrightarrow{H_2O} R(CH_2)_3OH$$

4. The Reppe synthesis of methyl acrylate and acrylic acid (100–190°C, 30 atm, Ni catalyst: **or** 40°C and 1 atm using $Ni(CO)_4$ as both the source of CO and the catalyst):

$$HC{\equiv}CH + MeOH + CO \longrightarrow$$
$$CH_2{=}CHCO_2Me \xrightarrow{H_2O} CH_2{=}CHCO_2H$$

5. Sabatier methanation (230–450°C, 1–100 atm, Ni catalyst):

$$CO + 3H_2 \longrightarrow CH_4 + H_2O$$

6. Fischer-Tropsch hydrogenation to a mixture of straight chain aliphatic, olefinic and oxygenated hydrocarbons.[109] Despite an enormous amount of research during the past two decades, this is still not an economically viable process except in special circumstances, such as in South Africa.[110]

Most industrial CO is produced and used on site. Prices for commercial supplies vary enormously depending on volume and purity required.[106] For large volumes (~28 000 m^3/day), "over the fence" prices can be as low as \$0.30/m^3 whereas for tube-trailer loads (1500–3000 m^3) prices are nearer \$1.40/m^3. For CO supplied in high-pressure cylinders current prices (1993) are \$15.00–35.00/m^3 for commercial grade (98–99% purity), \$63/m^3 for ultra high purity grade (99.8%) and \$68–1580/m^3 for research grades (99.97–99.98%).

Further reactions of CO of potential industrial or research significance are continually being explored. Recent examples include:

1. Amination with ammonia over zeolite catalysts at 350–400°C to give methylamine (and some dimethylamine):[111]

[106] *Kirk–Othmer Encyclopedia of Chemical Technology*, 4th ed., Wiley, New York, **5**, 97–122 (1993).

[107] W. KEIM, in H. GRÜNEWALD (ed.), *Chemistry for the Future* (Proc. 29th IUPAC Congress, Cologne, Germany, 5–10 June 1983) Pergamon Press, Oxford, 1984, pp. 53–62.

[108] R. L. PRUETT, *Adv. Organometallic Chem.* **17**, 1–60 (1979). See also G. P. COOLES and R. DAVIS, *Educ. in Chem.*, 48–50, March 1982.

[109] C. MASTERS, *Adv. Organometallic Chem.* **17**, 61–103 (1979). R. B. ANDERSON, *The Fischer-Tropsch Synthesis.* Academic Press, London, 1984, 320 pp.

[110] R. C. EVERSON and D. T. THOMPSON, *Platinum Metals Review* **25**, 50–6 (1981).

[111] M. SUBRAHMANYAM, S. J. KULKARNI and A. V. RAMA RAO, *J. Chem. Soc., Chem. Commun.*, 607–8 (1992).

$$CO + 3NH_3 \xrightarrow{\text{HZSM-5}} CH_3NH_2 + H_2O$$
$$+ N_2 + H_2$$

2. Reductive coupling of two CO ligands to form a coordinated alkyne derivative, e.g. treatment of the Ta^I complex $[Ta(CO)_2(dmpe)_2Cl]$ with activated Zn dust in thf and then with Me_3SiCl gave a 25% yield of $[Ta(Me_3SiOC\equiv COSiMe_3)(dmpe)_2Cl]$ which can in turn be hydrolysed to the corresponding complex of the novel dihydroxyacetylene, $HOC=COH$.[112]

CO_2 is much less volatile than CO (p. 306). It is a major industrial chemical but its uses, though occasionally chemical, more frequently depend on its properties as a refrigerant, as an inert atmosphere, or as a carbonating (gasifying) agent in drinks and foam plastic (see Panel).[113] Of more chemical interest is the synthesis of radioactive ^{14}C compounds from $^{14}CO_2$ which is conveniently stored as a carbonate. ^{14}C is generated by an (n,p) reaction on a nitride or nitrate in a nuclear reactor (see p. 1256). More than 500 compounds specifically labelled with ^{14}C are now available commercially, the starting point of many of the syntheses being one of the following reactions:

1. $NaH^{14}CO_3 + H_2/Pd/C \longrightarrow H^{14}CO_2H$
2. $^{14}CO_2 + RMgX \longrightarrow R^{14}CO_2H$
3. $^{14}CO_2 + LiAlH_4 \longrightarrow {}^{14}CH_3OH$
4. $Ba^{14}CO_3 + Ba \longrightarrow Ba^{14}C_2 \xrightarrow{H_2O} {}^{14}C_2H_2$
5. $Ba^{14}CO_3 + NH_3 \longrightarrow Ba^{14}CN_2 \longrightarrow$
$^{14}C/N$ compounds

When CO_2 dissolves in water at 25° it is only partly hydrated to carbonic acid according to the

equilibrium

$$H_2CO_3 \rightleftharpoons CO_2 + H_2O;$$
$$K = [CO_2]/[H_2CO_3] \approx 600$$

Interpretation of acid–base behaviour in this system is further complicated by the slowness of some of the reactions and their dependence on pH. The main reactions are:

$$CO_2 + H_2O \rightleftharpoons H_2CO_3 \text{ (slow)}$$
$$H_2CO_3 + OH^- \rightleftharpoons HCO_3^- + H_2O \text{ (fast)}$$
$$\left.\right\} \text{pH} < 8$$

$$CO_2 + OH^- \rightleftharpoons HCO_3^- \text{ (slow)}$$
$$HCO_3^- + OH^- \rightleftharpoons CO_3^{2-} + H_2O \text{ (fast)}$$
$$\left.\right\} \text{pH} > 10$$

In the range pH 8–10 both sets of equilibria are important. The apparent dissociation constant of carbonic acid is

$$K_1 = [H^+][HCO_3^-]/[CO_2 + H_2CO_3]$$
$$= 4.45 \times 10^{-7} \text{ mol l}^{-1}$$

As $[CO_2]/[H_2CO_3] = K \approx 600$, it follows that the true dissociation constant is:

$$K_a = [H^+][HCO_3^-]/[H_2CO_3]$$
$$= K_1(1 + K) \approx 2.5 \times 10^{-4} \text{ mol l}^{-1}$$

This value is in the range expected from an acid of structure $(HO)_2CO$ (p. 50). The second dissociation constant is given by

$$K_2 = [H^+][CO_3^{2-}]/[HCO_3^-]$$
$$= 4.84 \times 10^{-11} \text{ mol l}^{-1}$$

A hydrate $CO_2.8H_2O$ can be crystallized from aqueous solutions at 0° and $p(CO_2) \sim$ 45 atm. There is also evidence for a hydrogen-bonded sesquicarbonate ion, $H_3C_2O_6^-$; this was originally suggested to have the sandwich

---

[112] P. A. BIANCONI, I. D. WILLIAMS, M. P. ENGELER and S. J. LIPPARD, *J. Am. Chem. Soc.* **108**, 311–3 (1986). R. N. VRTIS, C. P. RAO, S. G. BOTT and S. J. LIPPARD, *J. Am. Chem. Soc.* **110**, 7564–6 (1988).

[113] Ref. 106, pp. 35–53. See also W. M. AYERS, (ed.) *Catalytic Activation of Carbon Dioxide*, ACS Symposium 363, Washington, DC (1988), 212 pp.

Production and Uses of CO_2

CO_2 can be readily obtained in small amounts by the action of acids on carbonates. On an industrial scale the main source is as a byproduct of the synthetic ammonia process in which the H_2 required is generated either by the catalytic reaction (a) or by the water-gas shift reaction (b):

$$\text{(a) } CH_4 + 2H_2O \longrightarrow CO_2 + 4H_2; \quad \text{(b) } CO + H_2O \rightleftharpoons CO_2 + H_2$$

CO_2 is also recovered economically from the flue gases resulting from combustion of carbonaceous fuels, from fermentation of sugars and from the calcination of limestone: recovery is by reversible absorption either in aqueous Na_2CO_3 or aqueous ethanolamine (Girbotol process).

$$Na_2CO_3 + H_2O + CO_2 \underset{\text{heat}}{\overset{\text{cool}}{\rightleftharpoons}} 2NaHCO_3$$

$$2HOC_2H_4NH_2 + H_2O + CO_2 \underset{100-150°}{\overset{25-65°}{\rightleftharpoons}} (HOC_2H_4NH_3)_2CO_3$$

In certain places CO_2 can be obtained from natural gas wells. H_2S impurity is removed by oxidation using a buffered alkaline solution saturated with $KMnO_4$:

$$3H_2S + 2KMnO_4 + 2CO_2 \longrightarrow 3S + 2MnO_2 + 2KHCO_3 + 2H_2O$$

The scale of production has increased rapidly in recent years and in 1980 exceeded 33 million tonnes in the USA alone though much of this is used in integrated plants, on site.

The most extensive application of CO_2 is as a refrigerant, some 52% of production being consumed in this way. CO_2 can be liquefied at any temperature between its triple point $-56.6°$ (5.11 atm) and its critical point $+31.1°$ (72.9 atm). The gas can either be pressurized to 75 atm and then water-cooled to room temperature, or precooled to about $-15°$ ($\pm5°$) and then pressurized to 15.25 atm. Solid CO_2 is obtained by expanding liquid CO_2 from cylinders to give a "snow" which is then mechanically compressed into blocks of convenient size. Until about 40 y ago the bulk of CO_2 refrigerant was in the form of solid CO_2, but since 1960 production of liquid CO_2 has overtaken the solid form because of lower production costs and ease of transporting and metering the material. Some typical production figures are shown in the Table. Supercritical CO_2 is also finding increasing use as a versatile solvent for chemical reactions.[113a]

USA production of CO_2

CO_2 production/kilotonnes	1955	1960	1962	1977	1987
Solid	520	426	406	340	310
Liquid and gas	185	432	522	1660	7310
Total	705	858	928	2000	7620

Solid CO_2 is used as a refrigerant for ice-cream, meat and frozen foods, and as a convenient laboratory cooling agent and refrigerant. Liquid CO_2 is extensively used to improve the grindability of low-melting metals (and hamburger meat), and for the rapid cooling of loaded trucks and rail cars; it is also used for inflating life rafts, in fire extinguishers, and in blasting shells for coal mining. A related application of growing importance is as a replacement for chlorofluorocarbon aerosol propellants (p. 304) though this application will never consume large amounts of the gas since the amount in each tin is extremely small.

Gaseous CO_2 is extensively used to carbonate soft drinks and this use alone accounts for 20% of production. Other quasi-chemical applications are its use as a gas purge, as an inert protective gas for welding, and for the neutralization of caustic and alkaline waste waters. Small amounts are also used in the manufacture of sodium salicylate, basic lead carbonate ("white lead"), and various carbonates such as $M_2^ICO_3$ and M^IHCO_3 (M^I = Na, K, NH_4, etc.). One of the most important uses of CO_2 is to manufacture urea via ammonium carbamate:

$$CO_2 + 2NH_3 \xrightarrow[200 \text{ atm}]{185°} NH_2CO_2NH_4 \xrightarrow{-H_2O} CO(NH_2)_2$$

Urea is used to make urea-formaldehyde plastics and resins and, increasingly, as a nitrogenous fertilizer (46.7% N). World production of urea was 23 million tonnes in 1984.

[113a]M. POLIAKOFF and S. HOWDLE, *Chem in Brit.*, February 1995, pp. 118–21, and references cited therein.

structure (1)[114] though later *ab initio* calculations favour the all-planar structure (2).[115] Solid alkali-metal peroxocarbonates Li_2CO_4, $MHCO_4$ and $M_2C_2O_6$ (M = Na, K, Rb, Cs) are known and the anion HCO_4^- (CO_4^{2-} at high pH) can be prepared in solution by reaction of HCO_3^- with aqueous H_2O_2.[116] The peroxodianion, $C_2O_6^{2-}$ (3), can be prepared in aprotic solvents such as MeCN, dmf and dmso, via nucleophilic oxidation of CO_2 by the superoxide ion $O_2^{\cdot-}$: $[2CO_2 + 2O_2^{\cdot-} \rightarrow C_2O_6^{2-} + O_2]$.[117] The amusing all-planar squarate ion, $C_4O_4^{2-}$ (4), although chemically unrelated to the preceding species, may be mentioned here as a further well-characterized binary C/O anion.[118,119] The short C–C and C–O distances have been interpreted in terms of π-electron delocalization.

(1)   (2)

(3)   (4)

The coordination chemistry of CO_2 is by no means as extensive as that of CO (p. 926) but some exciting developments have recently been published.[120] The first transition metal complexes with CO_2 were claimed by

M. E. Volpin's group in 1969: tertiary phosphine or N_2 ligands were displaced from Rh and Ni complexes to give binuclear products whose definitive structure has not yet been established. CO_2 also displaced N_2 from $[Co(N_2)(PPh_3)_3]$ to give $[Co(CO_2)(PPh_3)_3]$. The Ni^0 complexes $[Ni(PEt_3)_4]$ (violet) and $[Ni(PBu_3^n)_4]$ (red) react in toluene at room temperature with CO_2 (1 atm) to give the yellow complexes $[Ni(CO_2)L_3]$. The structure of the analogous complex with $P(C_6H_{11})_3$ was established by X-ray diffraction analysis; it features a pseudo-3-coordinate Ni atom μ-bonded to a bent CO_2 ligand as in Fig. 8.20a. The isoelectronic Rh^I appears to form two types of complex: an orange-red series $[Rh(CO_2)ClL_2]$ (L = tertiary phosphine) with a μ-bonded bent CO_2 as in Fig. 8.20a and a somewhat less-stable yellow series $[Rh(CO_2)ClL_3]$ which is thought to contain

the ligand configuration $Rh—C{\overset{O}{\underset{O}{\diagdown}}}$ A Pt

compound which had earlier (1965) been thought to contain CO_2 as a ligand was subsequently found to require the presence of O_2 for its formation and to be, in fact, a novel bidentate carbonato complex (Fig. 8.20b).

$$[Pt(PPh_3)_3] + CO_2 + O_2 \xrightarrow{C_6H_6/25°}$$
$$[Pt(CO_3)(PPh_3)_2] + Ph_3PO$$

If the starting material contains M–H or M–C bonds a further complication can arise due to the possibility of a CO_2 insertion reaction. Thus, both $[Ru(H)_2(N_2)(PPh_3)_3]$ and $[Ru(H)_2(PPh_3)_4]$ react to give the formate $[Ru(H)(OOCH)(PPh_3)_3]$, and similar CO_2 insertions into M–H are known for M = Co, Fe, Os, Ir, Pt. These "normal" insertion reactions are consistent with the expected bond polarities $M^{\delta+}-H^{\delta-}$ and $O^{\delta-}=C^{\delta+}=O$, but occasionally "abnormal" insertion occurs to give metal carboxylic acids

[114] A. K. COVINGTON, *Chem. Soc. Rev.* **14**, 265–81 (1985).

[115] N. V. RIGGS, *J. Chem. Soc., Chem. Commun.*, 137–8 (1987).

[116] J. FLANAGAN, D. P. JONES, W. P. GRIFFITH, A. C. SKAPSKI and A. P. WEST, *J. Chem. Soc., Chem. Commun.*, 20–1 (1986).

[117] J. L. ROBERTS, T. S. CALDERWOOD and D. T. SAWYER, *J. Am. Chem. Soc.* **106**, 4667–70 (1984).

[118] C. ROBL, V. GNUTZMANN and A. WEISS, *Z. anorg. allg. Chem.* **549**, 187–94 (1987), and references cited therein.

[119] R. SOULIS, F. DAHAN, J.-P. LAURENT and P. CASTAN, *J. Chem. Soc., Dalton Trans.*, 587–90 (1988).

[120] M. E. VOLPIN and I. S. KOLOMNIKOV, *Organometallic Reactions* **5**, 313–86 (1975). Further references to isolable CO_2-transition metal adducts are given in R. L. HARLOW,

J. B. KINNEY, and T. HERSKOVITZ, *J. Chem. Soc., Chem. Commun.*, 813–4. (1980). G. S. BRISTOW, P. B. HITCHCOCK and M. F. LAPPERT, *J. Chem. Soc., Chem. Commun.*, 1145–6 (1981).

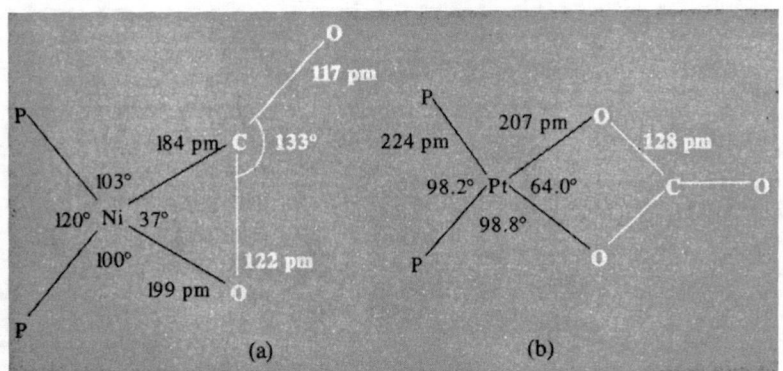

Figure 8.20   (a) Coordination about the Ni atom in the complex $[Ni(CO_2)\{P(C_6H_{11})_3\}_2].0.75C_6H_5Me$. (b) Coordination about the Pt atom in the complex $[Pt(CO_3)(PPh_3)_2].C_6H_6$.

M–COOH. Likewise, normal insertion into M–C yields alkyl carboxylates M–OOCR, though metalloacid esters M–COOR are sometimes obtained. The reactions have obvious catalytic implications and are being actively studied at the present time by several groups.[121]

CO_2 insertion into M–C bonds has, of course, been known since the first papers of V. Grignard in 1901 (p. 134). Organo-Li (and other M^I and M^{II}) also react extremely vigorously to give salts of carboxylic acids, RCO_2Li, $(RCO_2)_2Be$, etc. Zinc dialkyls are much less reactive towards CO_2, e.g.

$$ZnEt_2 + 2CO_2 \xrightarrow{150°} (EtCOO)_2Zn,$$

and organo-Cd and -Hg compounds are even less reactive. With AlR_3, one CO_2 inserts at room temperature and a second at 220° under pressure to give $R_2Al(OOCR)$ and $RAl(OOCR)_2$ respectively. B–C, Si–C, Ge–C, and Sn–C are rather inert to CO_2 but insertion readily occurs into bonds between these elements and N. A few examples are:

$$PhB(NHEt)_2 + CO_2 \xrightarrow{25°} PhB(OCONHEt)_2$$

$$Me_3SiNEt_2 + CO_2 \xrightarrow{Et_2NH/25°} Me_3SiOCONEt_2$$

$$Me_3SnNMe_2 + CO_2 \xrightarrow{20°} Me_3SnOCONMe_2$$

$$As(NMe_2)_3 + 1(3)CO_2 \xrightarrow{20° - 40°}$$

$$(Me_2N)_2AsOCONMe_2, \; As(OCONMe_2)_3$$

$$Ti(NMe_2)_4 + CO_2 \xrightarrow{20°} Ti(OCONMe_2)_4, \text{ etc.}$$

Returning briefly to CO_2 as a ligand: in addition to the various mono-CO_2 complexes referred to above, several bis(η^2-CO_2) transition-metal adducts are known, e.g. *trans*-$[Mo(\eta^2\text{-}CO_2)_2(PMe_3)_4]$ (5) and *trans,mer*-$[Mo(\eta^2\text{-}CO_2)_2(PMe_3)_3(CNPr^i)]$.[122] The first homo-bimetallic bridging-CO_2 complex has also been structurally characterized by X-ray analysis, *viz.* $[(dppp)(CO)_2Re(\mu,\eta^2\text{-}O,O':\eta'\text{-}C)Re(CO)_3(dppp)]$ (6) [dppp = 1,3-bis(diphenylphosphino)propane].[123]

The carbonate ion, CO_3^{2-}, by contrast, is a classic Werner ligand which forms innumerable complexes as a monohapto, dihapto or bridging donor. Examples of this latter mode

[121] A. BEHR, *Carbon Dioxide Activation by Metal Complexes*, VCH, Weinheim, 1988, 161 pp. See also J. D. MILLER in P. S. BRATERMAN (ed.), *Reactions of Coordinated Ligands*, Vol. 2., Plenum Press, New York, pp. 1–52 (1989) and J. L. GRANT, K. GOSWAMI, L. O. SPREER, J. W. OTVOS and M. CALVIN, *J. Chem. Soc., Dalton Trans.*, 2105–9 (1987) and references cited therein.

[122] R. ALVAREZ, E. CARMONA, M. L. POVEDA and R. SÁN-CHEZ-DELGADO, *J. Am. Chem. Soc.* **106**, 2731–2 (1984). R. ALVAREZ, E. CARMONA, E. GUTIERREZ-PUEBLA, J. M. MARIN, A. MONGE and M. L. POVEDA, *J. Chem. Soc., Chem. Commun.*, 1326–7 (1984).

[123] S. K. MANDAL, J. A. KRAUSE and M. ORCHIN, *Polyhedron* **12**, 1423–5 (1993).

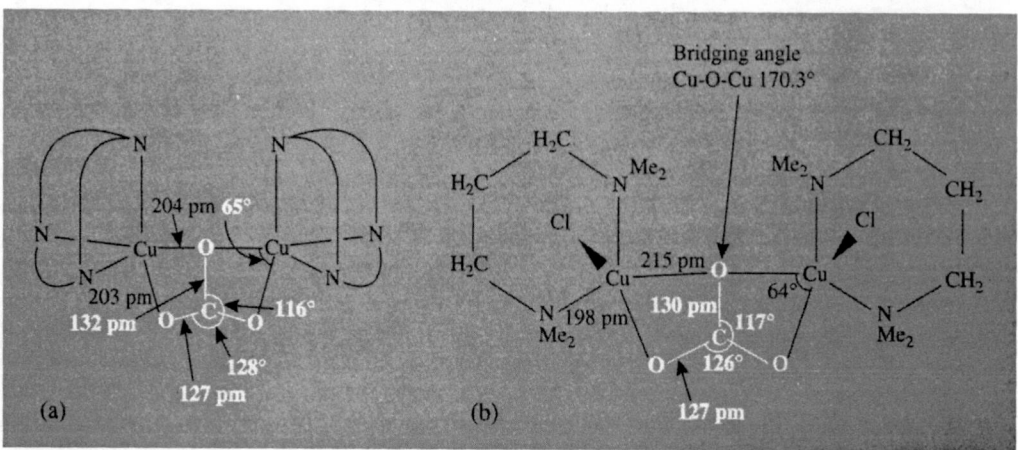

Figure 8.21   (a) The complex cation $[Cu(L_2)_2(\mu-\eta^2,\eta^2-CO_3)]^{2+}$. (b) The binuclear complex $[\{CuCl(Me_2N-CH_2CH_2CH_2NMe_2)\}_2(\mu-\eta^2,\eta^2-CO_3)]$.

(Fig. 8.22) features a unique tris(bidentate) sextuply bridging carbonato ligand as well as three bidentate μ_2-carbonato ligands. Other chelating and bridging coordination modes are also known.[126a]

8.7 Chalcogenides and Related Compounds

Carbon forms a great many sulfides in addition to the well known CS_2. CS (unlike CO) is an unstable reactive radical even at $-196°$: it reacts with the other chalcogens and with halogens to give CSSe, CSTe, and CSX_2. It is formed by action of a high-frequency discharge on CS_2 vapour. (See p. 319 for complexes of CS.) Passage of an electric discharge or arc through liquid or gaseous CS_2 yields C_3S_2, a red liquid mp $-5°$; it has a linear molecular structure, $S=C=C=C=S$, which polymerizes slowly at room temperature (cf. C_3O_2).[127]

are the complex cation $[(CuL_2)_2(\mu-CO_3)]^{2+}$, where L is a tridentate macrocylic triaza ligand (Fig. 8.21a),[124] and in the binuclear molecular complex molecule $[\{CuCl(Me_2NCH_2CH_2-CH_2NMe_2\}_2(\mu-CO_3)]$ (Fig. 8.21b).[125] This mode of coordination confers some unusual properties including diamagnetism on these Cu^{II} complexes. Even more extensive ligation occurs in the deep violet hexanuclear vanadium (IV) complex $(NH_4)_5[(VO)_6(CO_3)_4(OH)_9].10H_2O$ which was made by reacting $VOCl_2$ with aqueous NH_4HCO_3 under CO_2.[126] The novel anion

[124] A. R. DAVIS, F. W. P. EINSTEIN, N. F. CURTIS and J. W. L. MARTIN, *J. Am. Chem. Soc.* **100**, 6258–60 (1978).

[125] M. R. CHURCHILL, G. DAVIES, M. A. EL-SAYED, M. F. EL-SHAZLY, J. P. HUTCHINSON, M. RUPICH and K. O. WATKINS, *Inorg. Chem.* **18**, 2296–300 (1979).

[126] T. C. W. MAK, P. LI, C. ZHENG and K. HUANG, *J. Chem. Soc., Chem. Commun.*, 1597–8 (1986).

[126a] F. W. B. EINSTEIN and A. C. WILLIS, *Inorg. Chem.* **20**, 609–14 (1981). A. J. LINDSAY, M. MOTEVALLI, M. B. HURST-HOUSE and G. WILKINSON, *J. Chem. Soc., Chem. Commun.*, 433–4 (1986).

[127] M. T. BECH and G. B. KAUFFMAN, *Polyhedron* **5**, 775–81 (1985) and references cited therein. (This paper also gives an accessible account of the history of the discovery and applications of COS, i.e. $O=C=S$.)

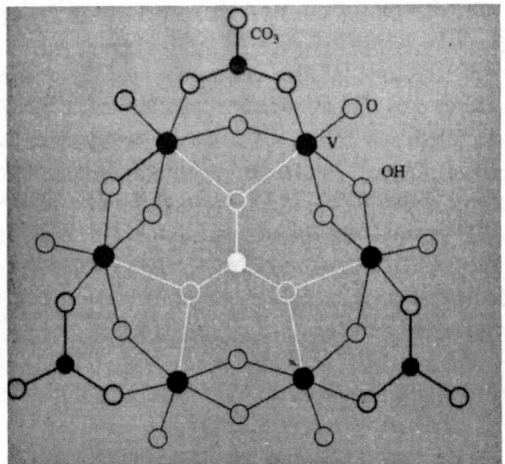

Figure 8.22 Perspective view of the hexanuclear anion $[(VO)_6(\mu_6\text{-}\eta^2,\eta^2,\eta^2\text{-}CO_3)(\mu\text{-}CO_3)_3\text{-}(\mu\text{-}OH)_9]^{5-}$. Averaged interatomic distances: vanadyl $V{=}O$ 161.6 pm, $V{-}OH(syn)$ 195.6 pm, $V{-}OH(anti)$ 201.2 pm, $V{-}O$ $(\mu_2\text{-}CO_3)$ 200.2 pm, $V{-}O$ $(\mu_6\text{-}CO_3)$ 228.7 pm, $C{-}O\mu)$ 129.1 pm, $C{-}O(exo)$ 126.6 pm.[126]

During the past decade there has been an astonishing proliferation of further binary carbon-sulfur species, both anionic and neutral.[128] Of the anions, the beige coloured dianion $C_3S_3^{2-}$ (made from tetrachlorocyclopropene) has the D_{3h} structure (1) and the yellow $C_4S_4^{2-}$ (made from squaric acid, p. 312) has the D_{4h} structure (2). The off-white $C_6S_6^{6-}$, (3), (made from

C_6Cl_6) is air-sensitive but can readily be protonated to give the more stable hexathiol $C_6(SH)_6$. Reduction of CS_2 either electrochemically or by alkali metals yields $C_3S_5^{2-}$ which can exist in two isomeric forms, (4) and (5):

$$4CS_2 \xrightarrow[\text{0 °C}]{4\,e^-} CS_3^{2-} + S$$

(4) $\alpha\text{-}C_3S_5^{2-}$

$\downarrow$ 130 °C

(5) $\beta\text{-}C_3S_5^{2-}$

Treatment of the primary product with a zinc salt leads to separation of $\alpha\text{-}C_3S_5^{2-}$ from its coproduct CS_3^{2-}, and multigram amounts of its complexes $[NR_4]_2[Zn(\alpha\text{-}C_3S_5)_2]$ and of the corresponding β-isomer's complexes afford convenient starting points for the synthesis of *molecular* binary sulfides as indicated below.

The sulfide C_4S_6 is known in three isomeric forms (6), (7) and (8).[128] The yellow-orange D_{2h} isomer (6) is readily prepared

168 pm
141 pm
(1)

166 pm
145 pm
(2)

(3)

(6)

(7)

(8)

128 C. P. GALLOWAY, T. B. RAUCHFUSS and X. YANG, in R. STEUDEL (ed.) *The Chemistry of Inorganic Ring Systems*, Studiees in Inorganic Chemistry, Vol. 14, Elsevier, Amsterdam, 1992, pp. 25–34. See also X. YANG, T. B. RAUCHFUSS and S. R. WILSON, *J. Am. Chem. Soc.* **111**, 3465–6 (1989) and *J. Chem. Soc., Chem. Commun.*, 34–5 (1990).

by the reaction of $CSCl_2$ with α-$C_3S_5{}^{2-}$, whilst the C_1 isomer (7) results from the corresponding reaction with β-$C_3S_5{}^{2-}$. The C_{2h} isomer (8) is less well characterized but is said to result from the reaction of hexachlorobutadiene, $CCl_2{=}CCl{-}CCl{=}CCl_2$, with polysulfide anions. The treatment of S_2Cl_2 with $[NBu_4]_2[Zn(\alpha\text{-}C_3S_5)_2]$ yields a mixture of C_3S_8 and C_6S_{12} which can be separated by fractional crystallization from CS_2:

$$[Zn(C_3S_5)_2]^{2-} + 2S_2Cl_2 \longrightarrow [ZnCl_4]^{2-}$$
$$+ 0.5C_6S_{12} + C_3S_8$$

C_3S_8 is a bicyclic species composed of the α-C_3S_5 unit capped by a polysulfide linkage (9), whereas C_6S_{12} features two cisoid eclipsed planar α-C_3S_5 units conjoined by further sulfur linkages to form a third ring (10); note that, if each of the two C_2 groups in this 10-membered ring are notionally replaced by an S atom, the conformation of the resulting S_8 ring is reminiscent of the familiar crown

configuration for this species (p. 655). Oxidation of $[NEt_4]_2[Zn(\beta\text{-}C_3S_5)_2]$ with $SOCl_2$ affords small amounts of the yellow C_6S_8 (11) which features an almost planar molecule with $S{\cdots}S$ fold angles $<3.8°$. By contrast, oxidation of $[NBu_4]_2[Zn(\alpha\text{-}C_3S_8)_2]$ with SO_2Cl_2 yields the orange dimer C_6S_{10} (12) in which the two planar C_3S_5 groups are interconnected by a pair of transoid S_2 linkages to give an overall chair configuration. Finally we should mention the two known isomers of C_9S_9. The simpler, formed by the reaction of $C_6S_6{}^{6-}$ (3) with $CSCl_2$, is the tris(trithiocarbonate) (13) which sublimes at $310°$ and can be recrystallized from $1,2\text{-}C_6H_4Cl_2$. The second C_9S_9 isomer is synthesized by

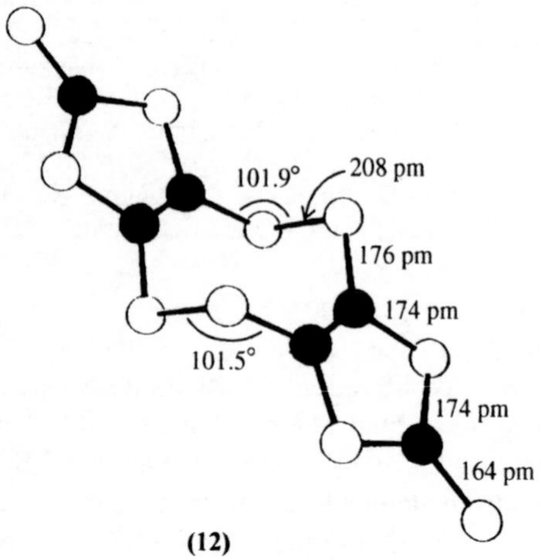

(12)

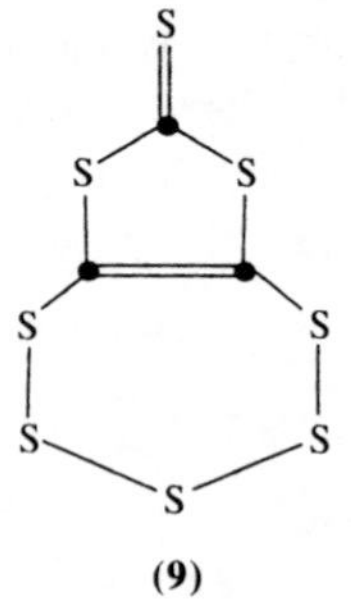

(9)

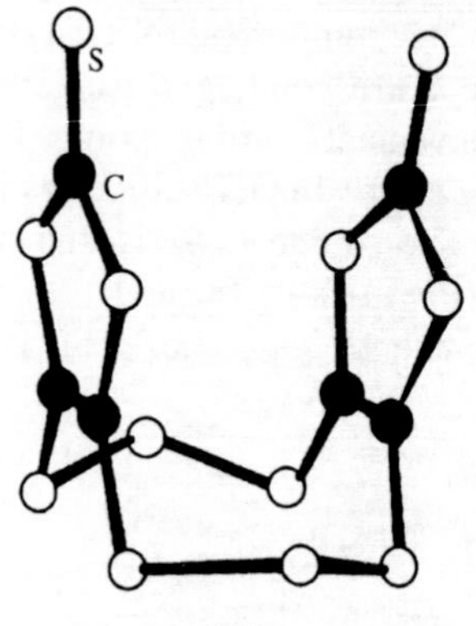

(10)

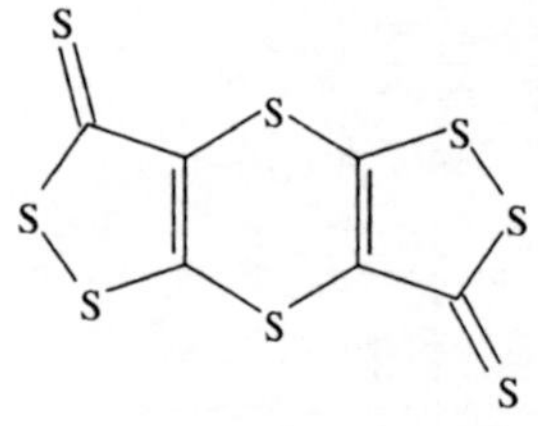

(11)

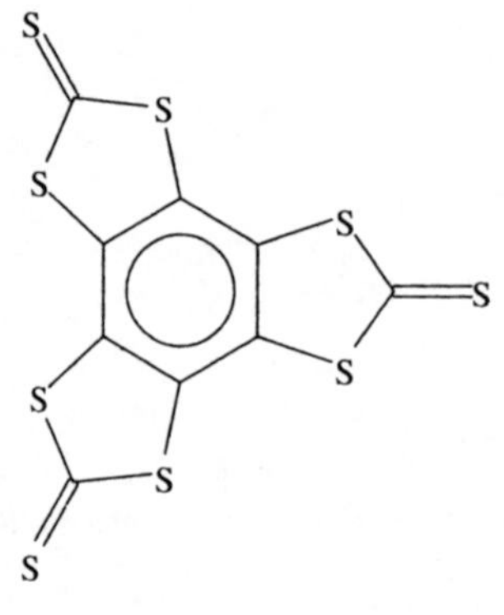

(13)

reaction of the benzene derivative 1,3,5-C_6Cl_3-2,4,6-$(CH_2NMe_2)_3$ with sulfur and H_2S in boiling quinoline; it forms red crystals of the planar D_{3h} molecule (14) which has a non-classical structure with three 3-coordinate S atoms. Both isomers are formally also oligomeric isomers of the diatomic monomer CS (p. 314).

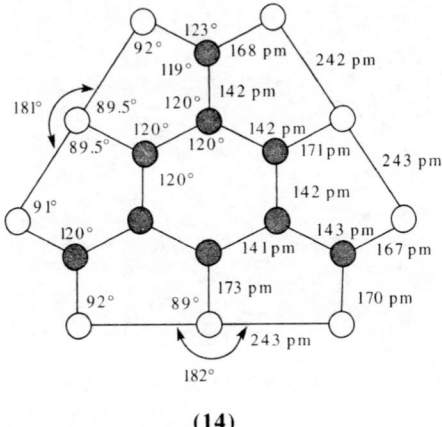

(14)

By far the most important sulfide is CS_2, a colourless, volatile, flammable liquid (mp $-111.6°$, bp $46.25°$, flash point $-30°$, auto-ignition temperature $100°$, explosion limits in air 1.25–50%). Impure samples have a fetid almost nauseating stench due to organic impurities but the purified liquid has a rather pleasant ethereal smell; it is very poisonous and can have disastrous effects on the nervous system and brain. CS_2 was formerly manufactured by direct reaction of S vapour and coke in Fe or steel retorts at 750–1000°C but, since the early 1950s, the preferred synthesis has been the catalysed reaction between sulfur and natural gas:

$$CH_4 + 4S \xrightarrow[\text{SiO}_2 \text{ gel or Al}_2\text{O}_3]{\sim 600°} CS_2 + 2H_2S$$

World production in 1991 was about 1 million tonnes the principal industrial uses being in the manufacture of viscose rayon (35–50%), cellophane films (15%) (see below), and CCl_4 (15–30%) depending on country. Indeed the CCl_4 application dropped to zero in USA in 1991 because of environmental concerns (p. 304).

CS_2 reacts with aqueous alkali to give a mixture of M_2CO_3 and the trithiocarbonate M_2CS_3. NH_3 gives ammonium dithiocarbamate $NH_4[H_2NCS_2]$; under more forcing conditions in the presence of Al_2O_3 the product is NH_4CNS and this can be isomerized at 160° to thiourea, $(NH_2)_2CS$. Water itself reacts only reluctantly, yielding COS at 200° and $H_2S + CO_2$ at higher temperatures; many other oxocompounds also convert CS_2 to COS, e.g. MgO, SO_3, HSO_3Cl and urea. With aqueous NaOH/EtOH carbon disulfide yields sodium ethyl dithiocarbonate (xanthate):

$$CS_2 + NaOH + EtOH \longrightarrow Na[SC(S)OEt]$$

When ethanol is replaced by cellulose, sodium cellulose xanthate is obtained; this dissolves in aqueous alkali to give a viscous solution (viscose) from which either viscose rayon or cellophane can be obtained by adding acid to regenerate the (reconstituted) cellulose. Trithiocarbonates (CS_3^{2-}), dithiocarbonates (COS_2^{2-}), xanthates (CS_2OR^-), dithiocarbamates ($CS_2NR_2^-$) and 1,2-dithiolates have an extensive coordination chemistry which has been reviewed.[129]

Chlorination of CS_2, when catalysed by $Fe/FeCl_3$, proceeds in two steps:

$$CS_2 + 3Cl_2 \longrightarrow CCl_4 + S_2Cl_2$$

$$CS_2 + 2S_2Cl_2 \longrightarrow CCl_4 + 6S$$

With I_2 as catalyst the main product is perchloromethylthiol (Cl_3CSCl). Reaction products with F_2 depend on the conditions used, typical products being SF_4, SF_6, S_2F_{10}, $F_2C(SF_3)_2$, $F_2C(SF_5)_2$, F_3CSF_5 and $F_3SCF_2SF_5$.

CS_2 is rather more reactive than CO_2 in forming complexes and in undergoing insertion reactions. The field was opened up by G. Wilkinson and his group in 1966 when they showed that $[Pt(PPh_3)_3]$ reacts rapidly and

129 G. D. THORN and R. A. LUDWIG, *The Dithiocarbamates and Related Compounds*, Elsevier 1962, 298 pp. J. A. MCCLEVERTY, *Prog. Inorg. Chem.* **10**, 49–221 (1968) (188 refs.). D. COUCOUVANIS, *Prog. Inorg. Chem.* **11**, 233–71 (1970) (516 refs.). R. E. EISENBERG, *Prog. Inorg. Chem.* **12**, 295–369 (1971) (173 refs.).

quantitatively with CS_2 at room temperature to give orange needles of $[Pt(CS_2)(PPh_3)_2]$, mp 170°. X-ray crystal diffraction analysis revealed the structure shown diagramatically in Fig. 8.23(a). The geometry of the bent CS_2 ligand is similar to that in the first excited state of the molecule and the CS_2 is almost coplanar with PtP_2 (dihedral angle 6°). Bonding is considered to involve a 1-electron transfer via the intermediary of Pt from the highest filled π MO of the ligand to its lowest antibonding MO, and the Pt can be thought of as being oxidized from Pt^0 to Pt^{II}. However, the substantial difference between the two Pt–P distances and the wide deviation of the angles of Pt from 90° emphasize the inadequacy of describing the bonding of such complicated species in terms of simple localized bonding theory. The orange complex $[Pd(CS_2)(PPh_3)_2]$ is isostructural and further work yielded deep-green $[V(\eta^5\text{-}C_5H_5)_2(CS_2)]$, dimeric $[(Ph_3P)Ni(\mu\text{-}CS_2)_2Ni(PPh_3)]$ and various CS_2 complexes of Fe, Ru, Rh and Ir. The deep-red complex $[Rh(CS_2)_2Cl(PPh_3)_2]$ probably involves pseudo-octahedral Rh^{III} with one of the CS_2 ligands η^2-bonded as above and the other one σ-bonded via a single S atom. By contrast, reaction of $[Fe_3(CO)_{12}]$ with an excess of CS_2 in hexane for several hours at 80°C under a 10 atm pressure of CO/Ar gave the orange complex $[\{Fe_2(CO)_6\}_2(\mu_4\text{-}C_2S_4)]$ as one of the products (1–2%). As can be seen from Fig. 8.23(b), the structure has two $\{Fe_2(CO)_6\}$ units bridged by a planar $\{S_2C{=}CS_2\}$ group, which can in turn be regarded as an ethenetetrathiol moiety formed by the C–C coupling of two CS_2 molecules.[130]

The numerous η^1, η^2, and bridging modes of coordination now known for CS_2 are indicated schematically below:[131]

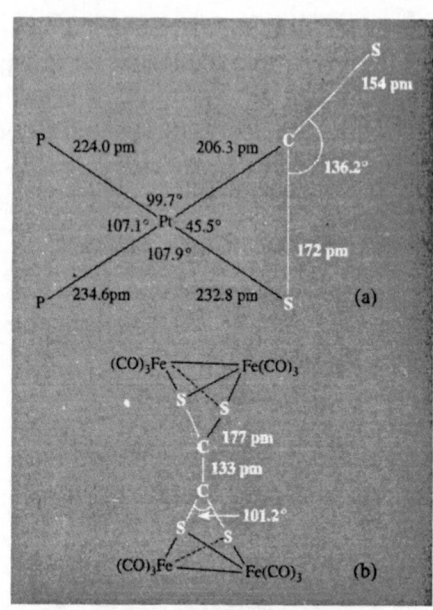

Figure 8.23 (a) Coordination about the Pt atom in $[Pt(CS_2)(PPh_3)_2]$. (b) Structure of $[\{Fe_2(CO)_6\}_2(\mu_4\text{-}C_2S_4)]$.

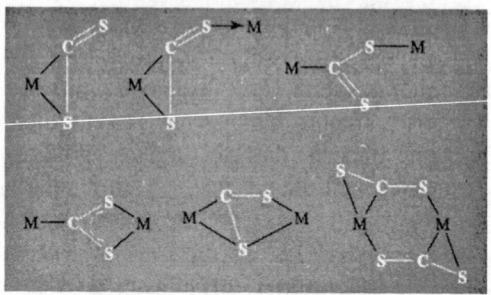

Insertion reactions of CS_2 are known for all the elements which undergo CO_2 insertion

[130] P. V. BROADHURST, B. F. G. JOHNSON, J. LEWIS and P. R. RAITHBY, *J. Chem. Soc., Chem. Commun.*, 140–1 (1982).

[131] T. G. SOUTHERN, U. OEHMICHEN, J. Y. LE MAROUILLE, H. LE BOZEC, D. GRANDJEAN and P. H. DIXNEUF, *Inorg. Chem.* **19**, 2976–80 (1980). Other key papers in this burgeoning field are: G. FACHINETTI, C. FLORIANI, A. CHIESI-VILLA and C. GUESTINI, *J. Chem. Soc., Dalton Trans.*, 1612–17 (1979). P. CONWAY, S. M. GRANT and A. R. MANNING, *J. Chem. Soc., Dalton Trans.*, 1920–4

(1979). P. J. VERGAMINI and P. G. ELLER, *Inorg. Chim. Acta* **34**, L291–2 (1979). C. BIANCHINI, A. MELI, A. ORLANDINI and L. SACCONI, *Inorg. Chim. Acta* **35**, L375–6 (1979). C. BIANCHINI, C. MEALLI, A. MELI, A. ORLANDINI and L. SACCONI, *Angew. Chem. Int. Edn. Engl.*, **18**, 673–4 (1979). C. BIANCHINI, C. MEALLI, A. MELLI, A. ORLANDINI and L. SACCONI, *Inorg. Chem.* **19**, 2968–75 (1980). W. P. FEHLHAMMER and H. STOLZENBERG, *Inorg. Chim. Acta* **44**, L151–2 (1980). C. BIANCHINI, C. A. GHILARDI, A. MELI, S. MIDOLLINI and A. ORLANDINI, *J. Chem. Soc., Chem. Commun.*, 753–4 (1983). D. H. FARRAR, R. R. GUKATHASAN and S. A. MORRIS, *Inorg. Chem.* **23**, 3258–61 (1984).

(p. 312) and also for M–N bonds involving Sb^{III}, Zr^{IV}, Nb^V, Ta^V, etc. Reaction of CS_2 with Au_2Cl_6 results in its novel insertion into Au–Cl bonds to form orange crystals of the chlorodithioformate complex $[AuCl_2(\eta^2\text{-}S_2CCl)]$.[132] The parent dithioformate ligand, HCS_2^-, has been prepared by insertion of CS_2 into the Ru–H bond of $[RuH(CO)Cl(PPh_3)_2(4\text{-vinyl pyridine})]$ to form the yellow complex $[Ru(CO)Cl(PPh_3)_2(\eta^2\text{-}S_2CH)].thf$.[133] Perhaps even more intriguingly, treatment of the orange *nido* 11-vertex metallathiaborane cluster $[8,8\text{-}(PPh_3)_2\text{-}8,7\text{-}nido\text{-}RhSB_9H_{10}]$ (cf. structure (42), p. 178) with CS_2 under reflux gives a 37% yield of the pale orange *nido* cluster $[8,8\text{-}(PPh_3)_2\text{-}\mu\text{-}8,9\text{-}(\eta^2\text{-}S_2CH)\text{-}8,7\text{-}RhSB_9H_9]$ which features a unique dithioformate bridge between Rh(8)–B(9), perhaps by addition of $B–H_t(9)$ across a C–S bond.[134]

Stable thiocarbonyl complexes containing the elusive CS ligand are also now well established and known coordination modes, which include terminal, bridging and polyhapto, are as shown at the top of the next column.[135]

Likewise complexes of CSe and CTe have been characterized.[136] The structure and reactivity of

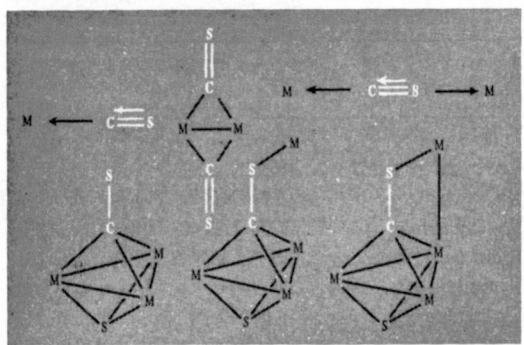

CS complexes has been well reviewed[137] and exciting work in this area continues.[138]

8.8 Cyanides and Other Carbon–Nitrogen Compounds

The chemistry of compounds containing the CN group is both extensive and varied. The types of compound to be discussed are listed in Table 8.7, which also summarizes some basic structural information. The names cyanide, cyanogen, etc., refer to the property of forming deep-blue pigments such as Prussian blue (p. 1094) with iron salts (Greek κύανος, *cyanos*, dark blue).

A useful theme for cohering much of the chemistry of compounds containing the CN group is the concept of pseudohalogens, a term introduced in 1925 for certain strongly bound, univalent radicals such as CN, OCN, SCN, SeCN, (and N_3, etc.). These groups can form anions X^-, hydracids HX, and sometimes neutral species X_2,

132 D. JENTSCH, P. G. JONES, C. THÖNE and E. SCHWARZMANN, *J. Chem. Soc., Chem. Commun.*, 1495–6 (1989).

133 V. G. PURANIK, S. S. TAVALE and T. N. G. ROW, *Polyhedron* **6**, 1859–61 (1987).

134 G. FERGUSON, M. C. JENNINGS, A. L. LOUGH, S. COUGHLAN, T. R. SPALDING, J. D. KENNEDY, X. L. R. FONTAINE and B. ŠTÍBR, *J. Chem. Soc., Chem. Commun.*, 891–4 (1990).

135 I. S. BUTLER, *Acc. Chem. Res.* **10**, 359–65 (1977). P. V. YANEFF, *Coord. Chem. Rev.* **23**, 183–220 (1977) (includes CS_2 complexes also). H. WERNER and K. LEONHARD, *Angew. Chem. Int. Edn. Engl.* **18**, 627–8 (1979). H. HERBERHOLD and P. H. SMITH, *Angew. Chem. Int. Edn. Engl.* **18**, 631–2 (1979). W. W. GREAVES, R. J. ANGELICI, B. J. HELLAND, R. KLIMA and R. A. JACOBSON, *J. Am. Chem. Soc.* **101**, 7618–20 (1979). F. FARONE, G. TRESOLDI, and G. A. LOPRETE, *J. Chem. Soc., Dalton Trans.*, 933–7 (1979); *J. Chem. Soc., Dalton Trans.*, 1053–6 (1979). P. V. BROADHURST, B. F. G. JOHNSON, J. LEWIS and P. R. RAITHBY, *J. Chem. Soc., Chem. Commun.*, 812–13 (1980); *J. Am. Chem. Soc.* **103**, 3198–200 (1981).

136 G. R. CLARK, K. MARSDEN, W. R. ROPER and L. J. WRIGHT, *J. Am. Chem. Soc.* **102**, 1206–7 (1981). J.-P. BATTIONI, D. MANSUY and J.-C. CHOTTARD, *Inorg. Chem.* **19**, 791–2 (1980).

137 P. V. BROADHURST, *Polyhedron* **4**, 1801–46 (1985).

138 K. J. KLABUNDE, M. P. KRAMER, A. SENNING and E. K. MOLTZEN, *J. Am. Chem. Soc.* **106**, 263–4 (1984). L. BUSETTO, V. ZANOTTI, V. G. ALBANO, D. BRAGA and M. MONARI, *J. Chem. Soc., Dalton Trans.*, 1791–4 (1986) and 1133–3 (1987). S. LOTZ, R. R. PILLE and P. H. VAN ROOYEN, *Inorg. Chem.* **25**, 3053–7 (1986). G. GERVASIO, R. ROSSETTI, P. L. STANGHELLINI and G. BOR, *J. Chem. Soc., Dalton Trans.*, 1707–11 (1987). A. R. MANNING, L. O'DWYER, P. A. MCARDLE and D. CUNNINGHAM, *J. Chem. Soc., Chem. Commun.*, 897–8 (1992).

Table 8.7 Some compounds containing the CN group

Name	Conventional formula	$r(C-N)$/pm	Remarks[a]
Cyanogen	N≡C–C≡N	115	Linear; $r(C-C)$ 138 pm (short)
Paracyanogen	(CN)$_x$	—	Involatile polymer, see text
diisocyanogen	CN–NC	118 (calc.)	Linear, symmetric, unstable[140]
isocyanogen	CN–CN	118 & 116 (calc.)	Zig-zag, unsymmetric, stable[140]
Hydrogen cyanide	H–C≡N	115.6	Linear; $r(C-H)$ 106.5 pm
Cyanide ion	(C≡N)$^-$	116	r_{eff} 192 pm when "freely rotating" in MCN
Cyanides (nitriles)	M–C≡N (R–C≡N)	115.8	Linear; $r(C-C)$ 146.0 pm (for MeCN)
Isocyanides	R–N≡C	116.7	Linear, $r(H_3C-N)$ 142.6 pm (for MeNC). Coordinated isocyanides are slightly bent, e.g. [M(←C≡N–C$_6$H$_5$)$_6$] angle CNC 173°. $r(C≡N)$ 117.6 pm: bridging modes are also known, e.g. structure (1), p. 321
Cyanogen halides (halogen cyanides)	X–C≡N	116	Linear
Cyanamide	H$_2$N–C≡N	115	Linear NCN; $r(C-NH_2)$ 131 pm
Dicyandiamide	N≡C–N=C(NH$_2$)$_2$	122–136	See structure (2), p. 321
Cyanuric compounds	{–C(X)=N–}$_3$	134	Cyclic trimers; X = halogen, OH, NH$_2$
Cyanate ion	(O–C≡N)$^-$	~121	Linear
Isocyanates	R–N=C=O	120	Linear NCO; ∠RNC ~ 126°
Fulminate ion	>(C=N–O)$^-$	109	Linear; another form of AgCNO has $r(C-N)$ 112 pm
Thiocyanate ion	(S–C≡N)$^-$	115	Linear
Thiocyanates	R–S–C≡N (M–S–C≡N)	116	Linear NCS; ∠RSC 100° in MeSCN; ∠MSC variable (80–107°)
Isothiocyanates	R–N=C=S	122	Linear NCS; ∠HNC 135° in HNCS; ∠MNC variable (111–180°)
Selenocyanate ion	(Se–C≡N)$^-$	~112	Linear NCSe

[a] Several groups can also act as bridging ligands in metal complexes, e.g. –CN–, >NCO, –SCN–

XY, etc. It is also helpful to recognize that CN$^-$ is isoelectronic with C$_2$$^{2-}$ (p. 299) and with several notable ligands such as CO, N$_2$ and NO$^+$. Similarly, the cyanate ion OCN$^-$ is isoelectronic with CO$_2$, N$_3$$^-$, fulminate (CNO$^-$), etc.[139]

Cyanogen, (CN)$_2$, is a colourless poisonous gas (like HCN) mp −27.9°, bp −21.2° (cf. Cl$_2$, Br$_2$). When pure it possesses considerable thermal stability (800°C) but trace impurities normally facilitate polymerization at 300–500° to paracyanogen a dark-coloured solid which may have a condensed polycyclic structure (3).

The polymer reverts to (CN)$_2$ above 800° and to CN radicals above 850°. (CN)$_2$ can be prepared in 80% yield by mild oxidation of CN$^-$ with aqueous Cu^{II}; the reaction is complex but can be idealized as

$$2CuSO_4 + 4KCN \xrightarrow{\text{H}_2\text{O}/60°} (CN)_2$$

$$+ 2CuCN + 2K_2SO_4$$

139 A. M. GOLUB, H. KÖHLER and V. V. SKOPENKO (eds.), *Chemistry of Pseudohalides*, Elsevier, Amsterdam, 1986, 479 pp., 4217 refs.

140 L. S. CEDERBAUM, F. TARANTELLI, H. G. WEIKERT, M. SCHELLER and H. KÖPPEL, *Angew. Chem. Int. Edn. Engl.* **28**, 761–2 (1989).

(1)   (2)

(3)

CO_2 which is also formed (20%) can be removed by passage of the product gas over solid NaOH and the byproduct CuCN can be further oxidized with hot aqueous Fe^{III} to complete the conversion:

$$2CuCN + 2FeCl_3 \xrightarrow{H_2O/heat} (CN)_2 + 2CuCl + 2FeCl_2$$

Industrially it is now made by direct gas-phase oxidation of HCN with O_2 (over a silver catalyst), or with Cl_2 (over activated charcoal), or NO_2 (over CaO glass). $(CN)_2$ is fairly stable in H_2O, EtOH and Et_2O but slowly decomposes in solution to give HCN, HNCO, $(H_2N)_2CO$ and $H_2NC(O)C(O)NH_2$ (oxamide). Alkaline solutions yield CN^- and $(OCN)^-$ (cf. halogens).

$$(CN)_2 + 2OH^- \longrightarrow CN^- + OCN^- + H_2O$$

Hydrogen cyanide, mp $-13.3°$ bp $25.7°$, is an extremely poisonous compound of very high dielectric constant (p. 55). It is miscible with H_2O, EtOH and Et_2O. In aqueous solution it is an even weaker acid than HF, the dissociation constant K_a being 7.2×10^{-10} at $25°C$. It was formerly produced industrially by acidifying NaCN or $Ca(CN)_2$ but the most modern catalytic processes are based on direct reaction between

CH_4 and NH_3, e.g.:[141]

Andrussow process:

$$CH_4 + NH_3 + 1\tfrac{1}{2}O_2 \xrightarrow[\text{2 atm/1000–1200°}]{\text{Pt/Rh or Pt/Ir}} HCN + 3H_2O$$

Degussa process:

$$CH_4 + NH_3 \xrightarrow[\text{1200–1300°}]{\text{Pt}} HCN + 3H_2$$

Both processes rely on a fast flow system and the rapid quenching of product gases; yields of up to 90% can be attained. It is salutory to note that US production of this highly toxic compound is 600 000 tonnes pa (1992) and world production exceeds one million tonnes pa. Of this, 41% is used to manufacture adiponitrile for nylon and 28% for acrylic plastics:

$$HCN + Me_2CO \longrightarrow \text{acetone cyanohydrin}$$

$$\xrightarrow{H_2SO_4} \text{methacrylamide sulfate} \xrightarrow{MeOH}$$

$$\text{methyl methacrylate}$$

HCN is now also used to make $(ClCN)_3$ for pesticides (9%), NaCN for gold recovery (13%), and chelating agents such as edta (4%), etc.

As noted above, CN^-(aq) is fairly easily oxidized to $(CN)_2$ or OCN^-; $E°$ values calculated from free energy data (p. 435) are:

$$\tfrac{1}{2}(CN)_2 + H^+ + e^- \rightleftharpoons HCN;$$

$$E° + 0.37 \text{ V}$$

$$OCN^- + 2H^+ + 2e^- \rightleftharpoons CN^- + H_2O;$$

$$E° - 0.14 \text{ V}$$

HCN can also be reduced to $MeNH_2$ by powerful reducing agents such as Pd/H_2 at $140°$.

The alkali metal cyanides MCN are produced by direct neutralization of HCN; they crystallize

---

141 Ref. 2, Vol. 7 (1993), Cyanides (including HCN, M^ICN, and $M^{II}(CN)_2$, pp. 753–82; Cyanamides including CaNCN, H_2NCN, dicyandiamide, and melamine), pp. 736–52; cyanuric and isocyanuric acids, pp. 834–51.

with the NaCl structure (M = Na, K, Rb) or the CsCl structure (M = Cs, Tl) consistent with "free" rotation of the CN⁻ group. The effective radius is ~190 pm, intermediate between those of Cl⁻ and Br⁻. At lower temperatures the structures transform to lower symmetries as a result of alignment of the CN⁻ ions. LiCN differs in having a loosely packed 4-coordinate arrangement and this explains its low density (1.025 g cm⁻³) and unusually low mp (160°, cf. NaCN 564°, KCN 634°C). World production of alkali metal cyanides was ~340 000 tonnes in 1989. NaCN readily complexes metallic Ag and Au under mildly oxidizing conditions and is much used in the extraction of these metals from their low-grade ores (first patented in 1888 by R. W. Forrest, W. Forrest and J. S. McArthur):

$$8NaCN + 4M + 2H_2O + O_2 \longrightarrow$$

$$4Na[M(CN)_2] + 4NaOH$$

Until the 1960s, when HCN became widely available, NaCN was made by the Castner process via sodamide and sodium cyanamide:

$$2Na + C + 2NH_3 \xrightarrow{750°} 2NaCN + 3H_2$$

The CN⁻ ion can act either as a monodentate or bidentate ligand.[142] Because of the similarity of electron density at C and N it is not usually possible to decide from X-ray data whether C or N is the donor atom in monodentate complexes, but in those cases where the matter has been established by neutron diffraction C is always found to be the donor atom (as with CO). Very frequently CN⁻ acts as a bridging ligand –CN– as in AgCN, and AuCN (both of which are infinite linear chain polymers), and in Prussian-blue type compounds (p. 1094). The same tendency for a coordinated M–CN group to form a further donor–acceptor bond using the lone-pair of electrons on the N atom is illustrated by the mononuclear BF₃ complexes

with tetracyanonickelates and hexacyanoferrates, e.g. K₂[Ni(CN.BF₃)₄] and K₄[Fe(CN.BF₃)₆].

The complex CuCN.NH₃ provides an unusual example of CN acting as a bridging ligand at C, a mode which is common in μ-CO complexes (p. 928); indeed, the complex is unique in featuring tridentate CN groups which link the metal atoms into plane nets via the grouping $\begin{matrix} Cu \\ | \\ Cu \end{matrix}\rangle C{-}N{-}Cu$ as shown in Fig. 8.24. Other cyanide complexes are discussed under the appropriate metals. In organic chemistry, both nitriles R–CN and isonitriles (isocyanides) R–NC are known. Isocyanides have been extensively studied as ligands (p. 926).[143] More

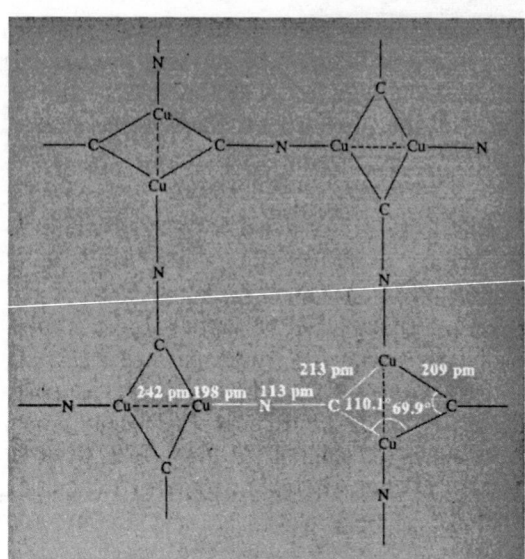

Figure 8.24 Schematic diagram of the layer structure of CuCN.NH₃ showing the tridentate CN groups; each Cu is also bonded to 1 NH₃ molecule at 207 pm. Note also the unusual 5-coordination of Cu including one near neighbour Cu at 242 pm (13 pm closer than Cu–Cu in the metal). The lines in the diagram delineate the geometry and do not represent pairs of electrons.

─────────────

[142] A. G. SHARPE, *The Chemistry of Cyano Complexes of the Transition Metals*, Academic Press, London, 1976, 302 pp.

[143] L. MALATESTA and F. BONATI, *Isocyanide Complexes of Metals*, Wiley, London, 1969, 199 pp.

Figure 8.25   The planar structure of various cyanuric compounds: all 6 C–N distances within the ring are equal.

Cyanuric halides   Cyanuric amide (melamine)   Cyanuric acid

keto ⇌ *enol*

complex coordination modes are now also well documented for CN^-, RCN and RNC.[144]

Cyanogen halides, X–CN, are colourless, volatile, reactive compounds which can be regarded as pseudohalogen analogues of the interhalogen compounds, XY (p. 824) (Table 8.8). All tend to trimerize to give cyclic cyanuric halides (Fig. 8.25) especially in the presence of free HX. FCN is prepared by pyrolysis of $(FCN)_3$ which in turn is made by fluorinating $(ClCN)_3$ with NaF in tetramethylene sulfone. ClCN and BrCN are prepared by direct reaction of X_2 on MCN in water or CCl_4, and ICN is prepared by a dry route from $Hg(CN)_2$ and I_2. Similarly, colourless crystals of cyanamide (H_2NCN mp 46°) result from the reaction of NH_3 on ClCN and trimerize to melamine at 150° (Fig. 8.25). The industrial preparation is by acidifying CaNCN (see Panel). The "dimer",

dicyandiamide, $CNC(NH_2)_2$, can be made by boiling calcium cyanamide with water: the colourless crystals are composed of nonlinear molecules which feature three different C–N distances (see Table 8.7).

The hydroxyl derivative of X–CN is cyanic acid HO–CN: it cannot be prepared pure due to rapid decomposition but it is probably present to the extent of about 3% when its tautomer, isocyanic acid (HNCO) is prepared from sodium cyanate and HCl. HNCO rapidly trimerizes to cyanuric acid (Fig. 8.25) from which it can be regenerated by pyrolysis. It is a fairly strong acid (K_a 1.2 × 10^{-4} at 0°) freezing at $-86.8°$ and boiling at 23.5°C. Thermolysis of urea is an alternative route to HNCO and $(HNCO)_3$; the reverse reaction, involving the isomerization of ammonium cyanate, is the classic synthesis of urea by F. Wöhler (1828):[145]

Table 8.8   Cyanogen halides

Property	FCN	ClCN	BrCN	ICN
MP/°C	−82	−6.9	51.3	146
BP/°C	−46	13.0	61.3	146 (subl)

---

[144] Some typical examples will be found in the following references. M. A. ANDREWS, C. B. KNOBLER and H. D. KAESZ, *J. Am. Chem. Soc.* **101**, 7260–4 (1979). M. I. BRUCE, T. W. HAMBLEY and B. K. NICHOLSON, *J. Chem. Soc., Chem. Commun.*, 353–5 (1982). V. CHEBOLU, R. R. WHITTLE and A. SEN, *Inorg. Chem.* **24**, 3082–5 (1985). T. C. WRIGHT, G. WILKINSON, M. MOTEVALLI and M. B. HURSTHOUSE, *J. Chem. Soc., Dalton Trans.*, 2017–9 (1986). K. S. RATLIFF, P. E. FANWICK and C. P. KUBIAK, *Polyhedron* **9**, 1487–9 (1990).

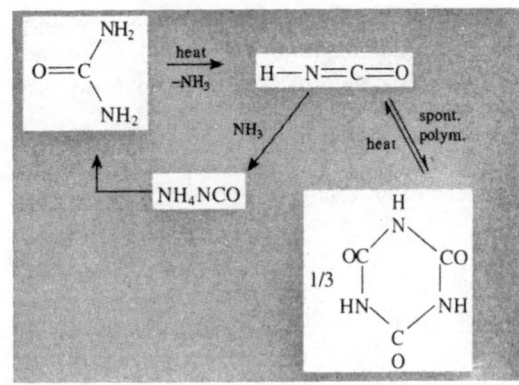

[145] J. SHORTER, *Chem. Soc. Revs.* **7**, 1–14 (1978).

The Cyanamide Industry[141]

The basic chemical of the cyanamide industry is calcium cyanamide CaNCN, mp 1340°, obtained by nitrogenation of CaC_2.

$$CaC_2 + N_2 \xrightarrow{1000°} CaNCN + C$$

CaNCN is used as a direct application fertilizer, weed killer, and cotton defoliant; it is also used for producing cyanamide, dicyandiamide and melamine plastics. Production formerly exceeded 1.3 million tonnes pa, but this has fallen considerably in the last few years, particularly in the USA where the use of CaNCN as a nitrogenous fertilizer has been replaced by other materials. In 1990 most of the world's supply was made in Japan, Germany and Canada.

Acidification of CaNCN yields free cyanamide, H_2NCN, which reacts further to give differing products depending on pH: at pH $\leq$ 2 or >12 urea is formed, but at pH 7–9 dimerization to dicyandiamide $NCNC(NH_2)_2$ occurs. Solutions are most stable at pH $\sim$ 5; accordingly commercial preparation of H_2NCN is by continuous carbonation of an aqueous slurry of CaNCN in the presence of graphite: the overall reaction can be represented

$$CaNCN + CO_2 + H_2O \longrightarrow H_2NCN + CaCO_3$$

Reaction of H_2NCN with H_2S gives thiourea, $SC(NH_2)_2$.

Dicyandiamide forms white, non-hygroscopic crystals which melt with decomposition at 209°. Its most important reaction is conversion to melamine (Fig. 8.25) by pyrolysis above the mp under a pressure of NH_3 to counteract the tendency to deammonation. Melamine is mainly used for melamine-formaldehyde plastics. Total annual production of both H_2NCN and $NCNC(NH_2)_2$ is on the 30 000 tonne scale.

Several of these compounds and their derivatives are commercially and industrially important. Urea has already been mentioned on p. 311. Again, world production of chloroisocyanurates, $(ClNC{=}O)_3$, in 1987 was ca. 80 000 tonnes (50 000 tonnes in USA alone, of which 75% went for swimming pool disinfection and most of the rest for scouring powders, household bleaches and dishwashing powder formulations).[141]

Alkali metal cyanates are stable and readily obtained by mild oxidation of aqueous cyanide solutions using oxides of Pb^{II} or Pb^{IV}. The commercial preparation of NaNCO is by reaction of urea with Na_2CO_3.

$$Na_2CO_3 + 2OC(NH_2)_2 \xrightarrow[\text{(dry)}]{\text{heat}} 2NaNCO$$
$$+ CO_2 + 2NH_3 + H_2O$$

The pseudohalogen concept (p. 319) might lead one to expect the existence of a cyanate analogue of cyanogen but there is little evidence for NCO–OCN, consistent with the known reluctance of oxygen to catenate. By contrast, thiocyanogen $(SCN)_2$ is moderately stable; it can be prepared as white crystals by suspending AgSCN in Et_2O or SO_2 and oxidizing the anion at low temperatures with Br_2 or I_2. $(SCN)_2$ melts at $\sim{-}7°$ to an unstable orange suspension which rapidly polymerizes to the brick-red solid parathiocyanogen $(SCN)_x$.[146] This ready polymerization hampers structural studies but it is probable that the molecular structure is $N{\equiv}C{-}S{-}S{-}C{\equiv}N$ with a nonlinear central $C{-}S{-}S{-}C$ group. $(SeCN)_2$ can be prepared similarly as a yellow powder which polymerizes to a red solid.

Thiocyanates and selenocyanates can be made by fusing the corresponding cyanide with S or Se. The SCN^- and $SeCN^-$ ions are both linear, like OCN^-. (See p. 779 for $TeCN^-$) Treatment of KSCN with dry $KHSO_4$ produces free isothiocyanic acid HNCS, a white crystalline solid which is stable below 0° but which decomposes rapidly at room temperatures to HCN and a yellow solid $H_2C_2N_2S_3$. Thiocyanic acid, HSCN, (like HOCN) has not been prepared

---

[146] F. CATALDO, *Polyhedron* **11**, 79–83 (1992).

Table 8.9 Modes of bonding established by X-ray crystallography

Mode	Example	Comment
Ag–NCO	$[AsPh_4]$ $[Ag(NCO)_2]$	Linear anion
Mo–OCN	$[Mo(OCN)_6]^{3-}$, $[Rh(OCN)(PPh_3)_3]$	Based on infrared data only
Ag⟍ NCO ⟋Ag	AgNCO	Cf. fulminate in Table 8.7
Ni⟍ OCN ⟋ NCO ⟍Ni	$[Ni_2(NCO)_2\{N(CH_2CH_2NH_2)_3\}_2]$ $[BPh_4]_2$	Note bent Ni–N–C
Co–NCS	$[Co(NH_3)_5(NCS)]Cl_2$	Linkage isomerism
Co–SCN	$[Co(NH_3)_5(SCN)]Cl_2$	
Pd–NCS / SCN	$[Pd(NCS)(SCN)\{Ph_2P(CH_2)_3PPh_2\}]$	Both *N* and *S* monodentate in a single crystal
Pd⟍ SCN ⟋Pd	$K_2[Pd(SCN)_4]$	Weak *S* bridging to a second Pd
SCN–Re–NCS / Re	$[NBu_4^n]_3[Re_2(NCS)_{10}]$	*N*-bonded bridging (and terminal)[154]
Co–NCS–Hg	$[Co(NCS)_4Hg]$	Bidentate, different metals
Pt⟍ SCN / NCS ⟋Pt	$[Pt_2(Cl)_2(PPr_3)_2(SCN)_2]$	Bidentate, same metal
Sb / S–C–N ⟍ Sb	Ph_2SbSCN	Spiral chain polymer[149]
Hg⟍ SCN–Co ⟋Hg	$[Co(NCS)_6Hg_2]\cdot C_6H_6$	Tridentate
Ni–NCSe	$[Ni(HCONMe_2)_4(NCSe)_2]$	*N* donor
Co–SeCN	$K[Co(Me_2glyoxime)_2(SeCN)_2]$	*Se* donor

pure but compounds such as MeSCN and Se(SCN)$_2$ are known.

The thiocyanate ion has been much studied as an ambidentate ligand (in which either S or N is the donor atom); it can also act as a bidentate bridging ligand –SCN–, and even as a tridentate ligand >SCN–.[147,148,149] The ligands OCN$^-$ and SeCN$^-$ have been less studied but appear to be generally similar. A preliminary indication of the mode of coordination can sometimes be obtained from vibrational spectroscopy since N coordination raises both $\nu(CN)$ and $\nu(CS)$ relative to the values of the uncoordinated ion, whereas S coordination leaves $\nu(CN)$ unchanged and increases $\nu(CS)$ only somewhat. The bridging mode tends to increase both $\nu(CN)$ and $\nu(CS)$. Similar trends are noted for OCN$^-$ and SeCN$^-$ complexes. However, these "group vibrations" are in reality appreciably mixed with other modes both in the ligand itself and in the complex as a whole, and vibrational spectroscopy is therefore not always a reliable criterion. Increasing use is being made of ^{14}N and ^{13}C nmr data[150] but the most reliable data, at least for crystalline complexes, come from X-ray diffraction studies.[151] The variety of coordination modes so revealed is illustrated in Table 8.9, which is based on one by A. H. Norbury.[147] Phenomenologically it is observed that class a metals tend to be N-bonded whereas class b tend to be S-bonded (see below), though it should be stressed that kinetic and solubility factors as well as relative thermodynamic stability are sometimes

implicated, and so-called 'linkage isomerism" is well established, e.g. [Co(NH$_3$)$_5$(NCS)]Cl$_2$ and [Co(NH$_3$)$_5$(SCN)]Cl$_2$. In terms of the a and b (or "hard" and "soft") classification of ligands and acceptors it is noted that metals in Groups 3–8 together with the lanthanoids and actinoids tend to form –NCS complexes; in the later transition groups Co, Ni, Cu and Zn also tend to form –NCS complexes whereas their heavier congeners Rh, Ir; Pd, Pt; Au; and Hg are predominantly S-bonded. Ag and Cd are intermediate and readily form both types of complex. See also refs. 152, 153. The interpretation to be placed on these observations is less certain. Steric influences have been mentioned (N bonding, which is usually linear, requires less space than the bent M–S–CN mode). Electronic factors also play a role, though the detailed nature of the bonding is still a matter of debate and devotees of the various types of electronic influence have numerous interpretations to select from. Solvent effects (dielectric constant ε, coordinating power, etc.) have also been invoked and it is clear that these various explanations are not mutually exclusive but simply tend to emphasize differing aspects of an extremely complicated and delicately balanced situation. The interrelation of these various interpretations is summarized in Table 8.10.

Table 8.10 Mode of bonding in thiocyanate complexes

Metal type[a]	σ-Donor ligand	High-ε solvent	Low-ε solvent	π-Acceptor ligand
Class a	–NCS	–NCS	–SCN	–SCN
Class b	–SCN	–SCN	–NCS	–NCS

[a] Sometimes discussed in terms of "hard" and "soft" acids and bases.

Fewer data are available for SeCN$^-$ complexes but similar generalizations seem to hold. By contrast, OCN$^-$ complexes are not so readily discussed in these terms: in fact, very few cyanato

[147] A. H. NORBURY, *Adv. Inorg. Chem. Radiochem.* **17**, 231–402 (1975) (825 refs.).

[148] A. A. NEWMAN (ed.), *Chemistry and Biochemistry of Thiocyanic Acid and its Derivatives*, Academic Press, London, 1975, 351 pp.

[149] G. E. FORSTER, I. G. SOUTHERINGTON, M. J. BEGLEY and D. B. SOWERBY, *J. Chem. Soc., Chem. Commun.*, 54–5 (1991).

[150] J. A. KARGOL, R. W. CRECELY and J. L. BURMEISTER, *Inorg. Chim. Acta* **25**, L109–L110 (1977), and references therein.

[151] S. J. ANDERSON, D. S. BROWN and K. J. FINNEY, *J. Chem. Soc., Dalton Trans.*, 152–4 (1979). (The compounds, originally thought to be O-bonded on the basis of infrared and ^{14}N nmr spectroscopy, now shown by X-ray analysis to be N-bonded.) See also ref. 154.

[152] W. KELM and W. PREETZ, *Z. anorg. allg. Chem.* **568**, 106–16 (1989).

[153] M. KAKOTI, S. CHAUDHURY, A. K. DEB and S. GOSWAMI, *Polyhedron* **12**, 783–9 (1993).

(−OCN) complexes have been characterized and the ligand is usually *N*-bonded (isocyanato).[151]

8.9 Organometallic Compounds

Compounds which contain direct M–C bonds comprise a vast field which spans the traditional branches of inorganic and organic chemistry. A general overview is given in Section 19.7

(p. 924) and specific aspects are treated separately under the chemistry of each individual element, e.g. alkali metals (pp. 102–6), alkaline earth metals (pp. 127–38), Group 13 metals (pp. 257–67) etc. In addition to the references cited on p. 924, useful general accounts can be found in refs. 155–160.

[154] F. A. COTTON, A. DAVISON, W. H. ISLEY and H. S. TROP, *Inorg. Chem.* **18**, 2719–23 (1979).

[155] A. W. PARKINS and R. C. POLLER, *An Introduction to Organometallic Chemistry*, Macmillan, Basingstoke, 1986, 252 pp.

[156] J. S. THAYER, *Organometallic Chemistry: An Overview*, VCH Publishers (UK), 1988, 250 pp.

[157] R. H. CRABTREE *The Organometallic Chemistry of the Transition Metals*, Wiley, New York, 1988, 440 pp.

[158] Ch. ELSCHENBROICH and A. SALZER, *Organometallics*, VCH Publishers (NY), 1989, 479 pp.

[159] T. J. MARKS (ed.) *Bonding Energetics in Organometallic Compounds*, ACS Symposium Series No. 428, Washington DC, 1990, 320 pp.

[160] E. W. ABEL, F. G. A. STONE and G. WILKINSON (eds.), *Comprehensive Organometallic Chemistry II:* A review of the literature 1982–1994 in 14 volumes, Pergamon, Oxford, 1995, approx 8750 pp.

9

Silicon

9.1 Introduction

Silicon shows a rich variety of chemical properties and it lies at the heart of much modern technology.[1] Indeed, it ranges from such bulk commodities as concrete, clays and ceramics, through more chemically modified systems such as soluble silicates, glasses and glazes to the recent industries based on silicone polymers and solid-state electronics devices. The refined technology of ultrapure silicon itself is perhaps the most elegant example of the close relation between chemistry and solid-state physics and has led to numerous developments such as the transistor, printed circuits and microelectronics (p. 332).

In its chemistry, silicon is clearly a member of Group 14 of the periodic classification but there are notable differences from carbon, on the one hand, and the heavier metals of the group on the other (p. 371). Perhaps the most obvious questions to be considered are why the vast covalent chemistry of carbon and its organic compounds finds such pallid reflection in the chemistry of silicon, and why the intricate and complex structural chemistry of the mineral silicates is not mirrored in the chemistry of carbon–oxygen compounds.[†]

Silica (SiO_2) and silicates have been intimately connected with the evolution of mankind from prehistoric times: the names derive from the Latin *silex*, gen. *silicis*, flint, and serve as a reminder of the simple tools developed in paleolithic times (~500 000 years ago) and the shaped flint knives and arrowheads of the neolithic age which began some 20 000 years ago. The name of the element, silicon, was proposed by Thomas Thomson in

---

[1] *Kirk–Othmer Encyclopedia of Chemical Technology*, 3rd edn., Vol. 20, pp. 748–973 (1982) (Silica, silicon and silicon alloys; Silicon compounds); 4th edn., Vol. 5 (1993) Cement pp. 564–98; Ceramics, pp. 599–697; Ceramics as electrical materials, pp. 698–728; Clays, Vol. 6, pp. 381–423 (1993).

[†] Throughout this chapter we will notice important differences between the chemical behaviour of carbon and silicon, and one is reminded of Grant Urry's memorable words: "It is perhaps appropriate to chide the polysilane chemist for milking the horse and riding the cow in attempting to adapt the success of organic chemistry in the study of polysilanes. A valid argument can be made for the point of view that the most effective chemistry of silicon arises from the differences with the chemistry of carbon compounds rather than the similarities" (see ref. 35 on p. 342).

1831, the ending *on* being intended to stress the analogy with carbon and boron.

The great affinity of silicon for oxygen delayed its isolation as the free element until 1823 when J. J. Berzelius succeeded in reducing K_2SiF_6 with molten potassium. He first made $SiCl_4$ in the same year, SiF_4 having previously been made in 1771 by C. W. Scheele who dissolved SiO_2 in hydrofluoric acid. The first volatile hydrides were discovered by F. Wöhler who synthesized $SiHCl_3$ in 1857 and SiH_4 in 1858, but major advances in the chemistry of the silanes awaited the work of A. Stock during the first third of the twentieth century. Likewise, the first organosilicon compound $SiEt_4$ was synthesized by C. Friedel and J. M. Crafts in 1863, but the extensive development of the field was due to F. S. Kipping in the first decades of this century.[2] The unique properties and industrial potential of siloxanes escaped attention at that time and the dramatic development of silicone polymers, elastomers, and resins has occurred during the past 50 years (p. 365).

The solid-state chemistry of silicon has shown similar phases. The bizarre compositions derived by analytical chemistry for the silicates only became intelligible following the pioneering X-ray structural work of W. L. Bragg in the 1920s[3] and the concurrent development of the principles of crystal chemistry by L. Pauling[4] and of geochemistry by V. M Goldschmidt.[5] More recently the complex crystal chemistry of the silicides has been elucidated and the solid-state chemistry of doped semiconductors has been developed to a level of sophistication that was undreamt of even in the 1960s.

---

[2] E. G. Rochow, Silicon, Chap. 15 in *Comprehensive Inorganic Chemistry*, Vol. 1, pp. 1323–467, Pergamon Press, Oxford, 1973. See also E. G. Rochow, *Silicon and Silicones*, Springer-Verlag, Newark, N.J., 1987, 181 pp.

[3] W. L. Bragg, *The Atomic Structure of Minerals*, Oxford University Press, 1937, 292 pp.

[4] L. Pauling, *The Nature of the Chemical Bond*, 3rd edn., pp. 543–62, Cornell University Press, 1960, and references cited therein.

[5] V. M. Goldschmidt, *Trans. Faraday Soc.* **25**, 253–83 (1929); *Geochemistry*, Oxford University Press, Oxford, 1954, 730 pp.

9.2 Silicon

9.2.1 Occurrence and distribution

Silicon (27.2 wt%) is the most abundant element in the earth's crust after oxygen (45.5%), and together these 2 elements comprise 4 out of every 5 atoms available near the surface of the globe. This implies that there has been a substantial fractionation of the elements during the formation of the solar system since, in the universe as a whole, silicon is only seventh in order of abundance after H, He, C, N, O and Ne (p. 4). Further fractionation must have occurred within the earth itself: the core, which has 31.5% of the earth's mass, is commonly considered to have a composition close to $Fe_{25}Ni_2Co_{0.1}S_3$; the mantle (68.1% of the mass) probably consists of dense oxides and silicates such as olivine $(Mg,Fe)_2SiO_4$, whereas the crust (0.4% of the mass) accumulates the lighter siliceous minerals which "float" to the surface. The crystallization of igneous rocks from magma (molten rock, e.g. lava) depends on several factors such as the overall composition, the lattice energy, mp and crystalline complexity of individual minerals, the rate of cooling, etc. This has been summarized by N. L. Bowen in a reaction series which gives the approximate sequence of appearance of crystalline minerals as the magma is cooled: olivine $[M_2^{II}SiO_4]$, pyroxene $[M_2^{II}Si_2O_6]$, amphibole $[M_7^{II}\{(Al,Si)_4O_{11}\}(OH)_2]$, biotite mica $[(K,H)_2(Mg,Fe)_2(Al,Fe)_2(SiO_4)_3]$, orthoclase feldspar $[KAlSi_3O_8]$, muscovite mica $[KAl_2(AlSi_3O_{10}(OH)_2]$, quartz $[SiO_2]$, zeolites and hydrothermal minerals. The structure of these mineral types is discussed later (p. 347), but it is clear that the reaction series leads to progressively more complex silicate structural units and that the later part of the series is characterized by the introduction of OH (and F) into the structures. Extensive isomorphous substitution among the metals is also possible. Subsequent weathering, transport and deposition leads to sedimentary rocks such as clays, shales and sandstones. Metamorphism at high temperatures and pressures can effect further changes during which the presence or absence of water plays a vital role.[6,7]

Silicon never occurs free: it invariably occurs combined with oxygen and, with trivial exceptions, is always 4-coordinate in nature. The $\{SiO_4\}$ unit may occur as an individual group or be linked into chains, ribbons, rings, sheets or three-dimensional frameworks (pp. 347–59).

9.2.2 Isolation, production and industrial uses

Silicon (96–99% pure) is now invariably made by the reduction of quartzite or sand with high purity coke in an electric arc furnace; the SiO_2 is kept in excess to prevent the accumulation of SiC (p. 334):

$$SiO_2 + 2C = Si + 2CO;$$

$$2SiC + SiO_2 = 3Si + 2CO$$

The reaction is frequently carried out in the presence of scrap iron (with low P and S content) to produce ferrosilicon alloys: these are used in the metallurgical industry to deoxidize steel, to manufacture high-Si corrosion-resistant Fe, and Si/steel laminations for electric motors. The scale of operations can be gauged from the 1980 world production figures which were in excess of 5 megatonnes. Consumption of high purity (semiconductor grade) Si leapt from less than 10 tonnes in 1955 to 2800 tonnes in 1980.

Silicon for the chemical industry is usually purified to ~98.5% by leaching the powdered 96–97% material with water. Very pure Si for semiconductor applications is obtained either from $SiCl_4$ (made from the chlorination of scrap Si) or from $SiHCl_3$ (a byproduct of the silicone industry, p. 338). These volatile compounds are purified by exhaustive fractional distillation and then reduced with exceedingly pure Zn or Mg; the resulting spongy Si is melted, grown into cylindrical single crystals, and then purified by zone refining. Alternative routes are the thermal decomposition of SiI_4/H_2 on a hot tungsten filament (cf. boron, p. 140), or the epitaxial growth of a single-crystal layer by thermal decomposition of SiH_4. A one-step process has also been developed to produce high-purity Si for solar cells at one-tenth of the cost of rival methods. In this process Na_2SiF_6 (which is a plentiful waste product from the phosphate fertilizer industry) is reduced by metallic Na; the reaction is highly exothermic and is self-sustaining without the need for external fuel.

Hyperfine Si is one of the purest materials ever made on an industrial scale: the production of transistors (p. 332) requires the routine preparation of crystals with impurity levels below 1 atom in 10^{10}, and levels below 1 atom in 10^{12} can be attained in special cases.

9.2.3 Atomic and physical properties

Silicon consists predominantly of ^{28}Si (92.23%) together with 4.67% ^{29}Si and 3.10% ^{30}Si. No other isotopes are stable. The ^{29}Si isotope (like the proton) has a nuclear spin $I = \frac{1}{2}$, and is being increasingly used in nmr spectroscopy.[8] ^{31}Si, formed by neutron irradiation of ^{30}Si, has $t_{\frac{1}{2}}$ 2.62 h; it can be detected by its characteristic β^- activity (E_{max} 1.48 MeV) and is very useful for the quantitative analysis of Si by neutron activation. The radioisotope with the longest half-life (~172 y) is the soft β^- emitter ^{32}Si (E_{max} 0.2 MeV).

In its ground state, the free atom Si has the electronic configuration $[Ne]3s^23p^2$. Ionization energies and other properties are compared with those of the other members of Group 14 on p. 372. Silicon crystallizes in the diamond

[6] B. MASON, *Principles of Geochemistry*, 3rd edn., Wiley, New York, 1966, 329 pp. P. HENDERSON, *Inorganic Geochemistry*, Pergamon Press, Oxford, 1982, 372 pp. S. R. ASTON (ed.), *Silicon Geochemistry and Biogeochemistry*, Academic Press, 1983, 272 pp.

[7] D. K. BAILEY and R. MACDONALD (eds.), *The Evolution of the Crystalline Rocks*, Academic Press, London, 1976, 484 pp.

[8] J.-P. KINTZINGER and H. MARSMANN, *Oxygen-17 and Silicon-29 NMR*, Vol. 17 of *NMR Basic Principles and Progress* (P. DIEHL, E. FLUCK and R. KOSFIELD, eds.), Springer-Verlag, Berlin, 1980, 250 pp.

lattice (p. 275) with a_0 543.10204 pm at 25°, corresponding to an Si–Si distance of 235.17 pm and a covalent atomic radius of 117.59 pm. The density and lattice constant of pure single-crystal Si are now known sufficiently accurately to give a direct value of the Avogadro constant ($N_A = 6.022\,1363 \times 10^{23}$ mol^{-1}) which is as precise as the best currently accepted value ($6.022\,1367 \times 10^{23}$ mol^{-1}).[9] There appear to be no allotropes of Si at ambient pressure but the 4-coordinate diamond lattice of Si–I transforms to several other modifications at higher pressures, of which distorted-diamond Si–II, primitive hexagonal Si–V and eventually hexagonal close packed Si–VII may be mentioned; the structural sequence corresponds to a systematic increase in coordination number:[10]

$$4(\text{Si–I}) \xrightarrow{8.8\ \text{GPa}} 6(\text{Si–II}) \xrightarrow{16\ \text{GPa}} 8(\text{Si–V})$$

$$\xrightarrow{\sim 40\ \text{GPa}} 12(\text{Si–VII})$$

[1 GPa = 10 kbar ≈ 9869 atm.]

Physical properties are summarized in Table 9.1 (see also p. 373). Silicon is notably more volatile than C and has a substantially lower energy of vaporization, thus reflecting the smaller

Table 9.1 Some physical properties of silicon

MP/°C	1420
BP/°C	~3280
Density (20°C)/g cm^{-3}	2.53259
ΔH_{fus}/kJ mol^{-1}	50.6 ± 1.7
ΔH_{vap}/kJ mol^{-1}	383 ± 10
ΔH_{f} (monatomic gas)/kJ mol^{-1}	454 ± 12
a_0/pm	543.10204
r (covalent)/pm	117.59
r ("ionic")/pm	26[a]
Pauling electronegativity	1.8

[a] This is the "effective ionic radius" for 4-coordinate Si^{IV} in silicates, obtained by subtracting $r(\text{O}^{-\text{II}}) = 140$ pm from the observed Si–O distance. The value for 6-coordinate Si^{IV} is 40 pm. [R. D. Shannon, *Acta Cryst.* **A32**, 751–67 (1976).]

[9] P. SEYFRIED and 13 others, *Z. Phys. B-Condensed Matter* **87**, 289–98 (1992).

[10] H. OLIJNYK, S. K. SIKKA and W. B. HOLZAPFEL, *Phys. Lett.* **103A**, 137–40 (1984).

Si–Si bond energy. The element is a semiconductor with a distinct shiny, blue–grey metallic lustre; the resistivity decreases with increase of temperature, as expected for a semiconductor. The actual value of the resistivity depends markedly on purity but is ~40 ohm cm at 25° for very pure material.

The immense importance of Si in transistor technology stems from the chance discovery of the effect in Ge at Bell Telephone Laboratories, New Jersey, in 1947, and the brilliant theoretical and practical development of the device by J. Bardeen, W. H. Brattain and W. Shockley for which they were awarded the 1956 Nobel Prize for Physics. A brief description of the physics and chemistry underlying transistor action in Si is given in the Panel (p. 332).

9.2.4 Chemical properties

Silicon in the massive, crystalline form is relatively unreactive except at high temperatures. Oxygen, water and steam all have little effect probably because of the formation of a very thin, continuous, protective surface layer of SiO_2 a few atoms thick (cf. Al, p. 224). Oxidation in air is not measurable below 900°; between 950° and 1160° the rate of formation of vitreous SiO_2 rapidly increases and at 1400° the N_2 in the air also reacts to give SiN and Si_3N_4. Sulfur vapour reacts at 600° and P vapour at 1000°. Silicon is also unreactive towards aqueous acids, though the aggressive mixture of conc HNO_3/HF oxidizes and fluorinates the element. Silicon dissolves readily in hot aqueous alkali due to reactions of the type $Si + 4OH^- = SiO_4^{4-} + 2H_2$. Likewise, the thin film of SiO_2 is no barrier to attack by halogens, F_2 reacting vigorously at room temperature, Cl_2 at ~300°, and Br_2, I_2 at ~500°. Even alkyl halides will react at elevated temperatures and, in the presence of Cu catalysts, this constitutes the preferred "direct" synthesis of organosilicon chlorides for the manufacture of silicones (p. 364).

In contrast to the relative inertness of solid Si to gaseous and liquid reagents, molten Si is an extremely reactive material: it forms alloys or

The Physics and Chemistry of Transistors

In ultrapure semiconductor grade Si there is an energy gap E_g between the highest occupied energy levels (the valence band) and the lowest unoccupied energy levels (the conduction band). This is shown diagrammatically in Fig. a: the valence band is completely filled, the conduction band is empty, the Fermi level (E_F), which is the energy at which the chance of a state being occupied by an electron is $\frac{1}{2}$, lies approximately midway between these, and the material is an insulator at room temperature. If the Si is doped with a Group 15 element such as P, As or Sb, each atom of dopant introduces a supernumerary electron and the impurity levels can act as a source of electrons which can be thermally or photolytically excited into the conduction band (Fig. b): the material is an n-type semiconductor with an activation energy ΔE_n (where n indicates negative current carriers, i.e. electrons). Conversely, doping with a Group 13 element such as B, Al or Ga introduces acceptor levels that can act as traps for electrons excited from the filled valence band (Fig. c): the material is a p-type semiconductor and the current is carried by the positive holes in the valence band.

When an n-type sample of Si is joined to a p-type sample, a p–n junction is formed having a common Fermi level as in Fig. d: electrons will flow from n to p and holes from p to n thereby producing a voltage drop V_0 across the space charge region. A p–n junction can thus act as a diode for rectifying alternating current, the current passing more easily in one direction than the other. In practise a large p–n junction might cover 10 mm², whereas in integrated circuits such a device might cover no more than 10^{-4} mm² (i.e. a square of side 10 μm).

A transistor, or n–p–n junction, is built up of two n-type regions of Si separated by a thin layer of weakly p-type (Fig. e). When the emitter is biased by a small voltage in the forward direction and the collector by a larger voltage in the reverse direction, this device acts as a triode amplifier. The relevant energy level diagram is shown schematically in Fig. f.

The large-scale reproducible manufacture of minute, electronically-stable, single-crystal transistor junctions is a triumph of the elegant techniques of solid-state chemical synthesis. The sequence of steps is illustrated in diagrams (i)–(v).

(i) A small wafer of single-crystal n-type Si is oxidized by heating it in O_2 or H_2O vapour to form a thin surface layer of SiO_2.

(ii) The oxide coating is covered by a photosensitive film called "photoresist".

(iii) A mask is placed over the photoresist to confine the exposure to the desired pattern and the chip is exposed to ultraviolet light; the exposed photoresist is then removed by treatment with acid, leaving a tough protective layer over the parts of the oxide coating that are to be retained.

(iv) The unprotected areas of Si are etched away with hydrofluoric acid and the remaining photoresist is also removed.

(v) The surface is exposed to the vapour of a Group 13 element and the impurity atoms diffuse into the unprotected area to form a layer of p-type Si.

(vi) Steps (i)–(v) are repeated, with a different mask, and then the newly exposed areas are treated with the vapour of a Group 15 element to produce a patterned layer of n-type Si.

(vii) Finally, again with a different mask, the surface is reoxidized and then re-etched to produce openings into which metal is deposited so as to connect the n- and p-regions into an integrated circuit.

Each individual p–n diode or n–p–n transistor can be made almost unbelievably minute by these techniques; for example computer memory units storing over 10^5 bits of information on a single small chip are routinely used. Further information can be obtained from textbooks of solid-state physics or electronic engineering.

silicides with most metals (see below) and rapidly reduces most metal oxides because of the very large heat of formation of SiO_2 ($\sim$900 kJ mol^{-1}). This presents problems of containment when working with molten Si, and crucibles must be made of refractories such as ZrO_2 or the borides of transition metals in Groups 4–6 (p. 146).

Chemical trends within Group 14 are discussed on p. 373. Silicon does not form binary compounds with the heavier members of the group (Ge, Sn, Pb) but its compound with carbon, SiC,

is of outstanding academic and practical interest, and is manufactured on a huge scale industrially (see Panel on p. 334).

In the vast majority of its compounds Si is tetrahedrally coordinated but sixfold coordination also occurs, and occasional examples of other coordination geometries are known as indicated in Table 9.2 (p. 335). Unstable 2-coordinate Si has been known for many years but in 1994 the stable, colourless, crystalline silylene [:SiNBu^{t}CH=CHNBu^t], structure (1), p. 336, was

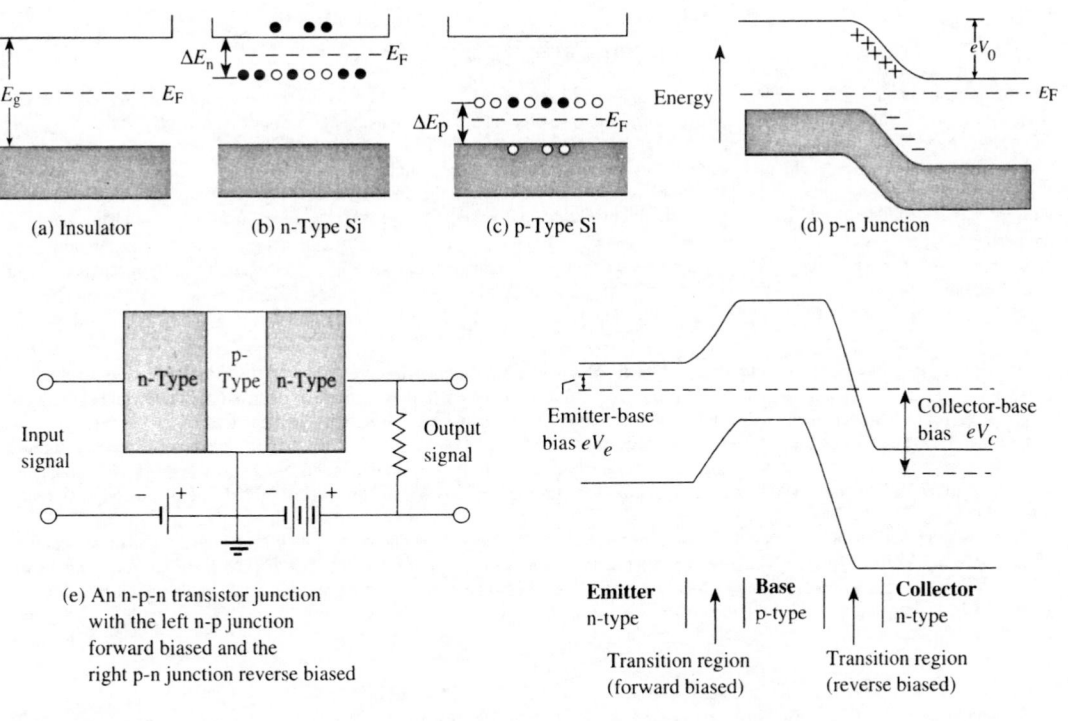

(a) Insulator   (b) n-Type Si   (c) p-Type Si   (d) p-n Junction

(e) An n-p-n transistor junction
with the left n-p junction
forward biased and the
right p-n junction reverse biased

(f) Energy level diagram

Figs. (a)–(f) mentioned in Panel opposite.

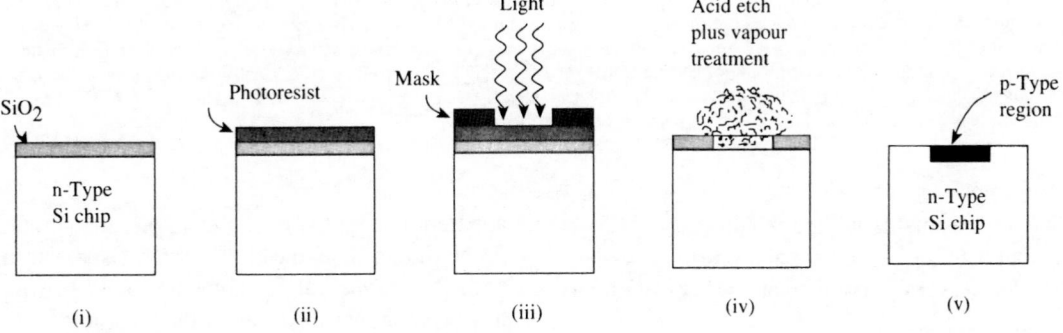

(i)   (ii)   (iii)   (iv)   (v)

Steps (i)–(v) mentioned in Panel opposite.

Silicon Carbide, SiC[11,12]

Silicon carbide was made accidently by E. G. Acheson in 1891; he recognized its abrasive power and coined the name "carborundum" from carbo(n) and (co)rundum (Al_2O_3) to indicate that its hardness on the Mohs scale (9.5) was intermediate between that of diamond (10) and Al_2O_3 (9). Within months he had formed the Carborundum Co. for its manufacture, and current world production approaches 1 million tonnes annually.

Despite its simple formula, SiC exists in at least 200 crystalline modifications based on hexagonal α-SiC (wurtzite-type ZnS, p. 1210) or cubic β-SiC (diamond or zincblende-type, p. 1210). The complexity arises from the numerous stacking sequences of the a and b "layers" in the crystal.[13] The α-form is marginally the more stable thermodynamically. Industrially, α-SiC is obtained as black, dark green or purplish iridescent crystals by reducing high-grade quartz sand with a slight excess of coke or anthracite in an electric furnace at 2000–2500°C:

$$SiO_2 + 2C \longrightarrow Si + 2CO; \quad Si + C \longrightarrow SiC$$

The dark colour is caused by impurities such as iron, and the iridescence is due to a very thin layer of SiO_2 formed by surface oxidation. Purer samples are pale yellow or colourless. Even higher temperatures (and vacuum conditions) are required to produce the β-form. Alternatively, very pure β-SiC can be obtained by heating grains of ultrapure Si with graphite at 1500° or by gas-phase plasma decomposition of Me_2SiCl_2, $MeSiCl_3$ or $SiCl_4/CH_4$ mixtures. Fibres of SiC are made by the progressive pyrolysis of organosilicon polymers such as $-CH_2SiHMe-$ or $-CH_2SiMe_2-$. Lattice constants for α-SiC are a 307.39 pm, c 1006.1 pm, c/a 3.273; for cubic β-SiC, a_0 435.02 pm (cf. diamond 356.68, Si 543.10, mean 449.89 pm).

SiC has greater thermal stability than any other binary compound of Si and decomposition by loss of Si only becomes appreciable at ~2700°. It resists attack by most aqueous acids (including HF but not H_3PO_4) and is oxidized in air only above 1000° because of the protective layer of SiO_2; this can be removed by molten hydroxides or carbonates and oxidation is much more rapid under these conditions, e.g.:

$$SiC + 2NaOH + 2O_2 \longrightarrow Na_2SiO_3 + H_2O + CO_2$$

Cl_2 attacks SiC vigorously, yielding $SiCl_4 + C$ at 100° and $SiCl_4 + CCl_4$ at 1000°.

Technical interest in SiC originally stemmed from its excellence as an abrasive powder; this derives not only from the great intrinsic hardness of the compound but also from its peculiar fracture to give sharp cutting edges. As a refractory, α-SiC combines great strength and chemical stability, with an extremely low thermal expansion coefficient (~6×10^{-6}) which shows no sudden discontinuities due to phase transitions. Pure α-SiC is an intrinsic semiconductor with an energy band gap sufficiently large (1.90 ± 0.10 eV) to make it a very poor electrical conductor (~10^{-13} ohm^{-1} cm^{-1}). However, the presence of controlled amounts of impurities makes it a valuable extrinsic semiconductor ($10^{-2} - 3$ ohm^{-1} cm^{-1}) with a positive temperature coefficient. This, combined with its mechanical and chemical stability, accounts for its extensive use in electrical heating elements. In recent years pure β-SiC has received much attention as a high-temperature semiconductor with applications in transistors, diode rectifiers, electroluminescent diodes, etc. (see p. 332). In fact, these various electrical and refractory uses account for only about 2% of the vast tonnages of SiC manufactured each year. About 43% is still used for its original application as an abrasive, and the remaining 55% is used in metallurgical processes, especially as a refining agent in the casting of iron and steel: the SiC reacts with free oxygen and with metal oxides to form CO and a siliceous slag.

isolated;[14] it distils without change at 85°C/0.1 torr and can be kept in solution in a sealed tube for several months at 150°C without

apparent change. A recent example of pyramidal 3-coordinate Si is the Si_4^{4-} anion (isoelectronic with the tetrahedral P_4 molecule, p. 479), which has been shown to occur in the long-known red silicide CsSi.[17] There has been much discussion about the possibility of planar 4-coordinate Si in orthosilicate esters of pyrocatechol (2) but this is

[11] *Kirk–Othmer Encyclopedia of Chemical Technology*, 4th edn., Vol. 4, Silicon Carbide, 1992, pp. 891–911.

[12] *Silicon Carbide*, World Business Publications, Ltd., 2nd edn., 1988, 340 pp.

[13] *Gmelin Handbook of Inorganic Chemistry*, 8th edn., Springer-Verlag, Berlin, *Silicon Suppl. B2*, 1984, 312 pp. See also *Suppl. B1*, 1986, 545 pp. for further information on occurrence of SiC in nature, its manufacture, chemical reactions, applications, etc.

[14] M. DENK and 8 others, *J. Am. Chem. Soc.* **116**, 2691–2 (1994).

[15] T. J. BARTON and G. T. BURNS, *J. Am. Chem. Soc.* **100**, 5246 (1978).

[16] C. L. KREIL, O. L. CHAPMAN, G. T. BURNS and T. J. BARTON, *J. Am. Chem. Soc.* **102**, 841–2 (1980).

[17] G. KLICHE, M. SCHWARZ and H. G. VON SCHNERING, *Angew. Chem. Int. Edn. Engl.* **26**, 349–51 (1987).

Table 9.2 Coordination geometries of silicon

Coordination number	Examples
2 (bent)	SiF_2(g), $SiMe_2$ (matrix, 77 K), $[:\overline{SiNBu^tCH{=}CHNBu^t}]$ (1)[14]
3 (planar)	Silabenzene, SiC_5H_6;[15] silatoluene, C_5H_5SiMe[16]
3 (pyramidal)	Si_4^{4-}, (?)SiH_3^- in $KSiH_3$ (NaCl structure)
4 (tetrahedral)	SiH_4, SiX_4, SiX_nY_{4-n}, SiO_2, silicates, etc.
4 (planar)	(see text)[18] (2)
4 (see-saw, C_{2v})	$SiLi_4$ (3)[19]
5 (trigonal bipyramidal)	SiX_5^-, cyclo-$[Me_2NSiH_3]_5$, $[Si(O_2C_6H_4)_2(OPPh_3)]$ (4)[20]
5 (square pyramidal)	$[Si(O_2C_6H_4)_2\{OP(NC_5H_{10})\}]$ (5),[20] $[SiF(O_2C_6H_4)_2]^-$[21]
6 (octahedral)	SiF_6^{2-}, $[Si(acac)_3]^+$, $[L_2SiX_4]$, SiO_2 (stishovite), SiP_2O
7 (capped trig. antiprism)	$[\{2\text{-}(Me_2NCH_2)C_6H_4\}_3SiH]$ (6)[22]
8 (cubic)	Mg_2Si (antifluorite)
9 (capped square antiprism)	$[\mu_8\text{-}SiCo_9(CO)_{21}]^{2-}$ (7)[23]
10 (various)	$TiSi_2$, $CrSi_2$, $MoSi_2$;[24] $[Si(\eta^5\text{-}C_5Me_5)_2]$ (8)[25]

still far from being unequivocally established.[18] However, a 'one-sided' C_{2v} geometry for $SiLi_4$ (3) seems probable.[19] Five-coordinate Si can be either trigonal bipyramidal or square pyramidal, e.g. (4), (5), etc.[20,21] Numerous examples of octahedral 6-coordination are known. A single example of 7-coordinate Si has been identified, (6)[22] and there are occasional examples of higher coordination numbers. Thus, Si has cubic 8-fold coordination in Mg_2Si which has the antifluorite structure, Si occupying the Ca sites and Mg the F sites of the fluorite lattice (p. 118). The capped square antiprismatic structure of the anion $[SiCo_9(CO)_{21}]^{2-}$ has essentially 9-fold coordination about the encapsulated Si atom (7), with $Si\text{-}Co_{base}$ 231 pm, $Si\text{-}Co_{upper}$ 228 pm and $Si\text{-}Co_{cap}$ 252.7 pm; each of the four basal Co atoms has two terminal CO ligands, each of the other five Co atoms has one, and there are eight bridging CO groups.[23] The coordination number 10 is found in the structures of several transition metal silicides[24] and in decamethylsilicocene (8). The crystal structure of this latter compound reveals two types of molecular geometry; one-third of the molecules have the two rings parallel and staggered as in $[Fe(C_5Me_5)_2]$ with Si–C 242 pm whereas the other two-thirds have non-parallel rings, implying a stereochemically active lone pair of electrons on the Si atom.[25] The bent (C_s) structure persists in the gas phase, the angle between the two C_5 planes being 22°.

9.3 Compounds

9.3.1 Silicides [26,27]

As with borides (p. 145) and carbides (p. 297) the formulae of metal silicides cannot be rationalized by the application of simple valency rules, and

[18] W. HÖNLE, U. DETTLAFF-WEGLIKOWSKA, L. WALZ and H. G. VON SCHNERING, *Angew. Chem. Int. Edn. Engl.* **28**, 623–4 (1989), and references cited therein.

[19] P. VON RAGUÉ SCHLEYER and A. E. REED, *J. Am. Chem. Soc.* **110**, 4453–4 (1988).

[20] E. HEY-HAWKINS, U. DETTLAFF-WEGLIAKOWSKA, D. THIERY and H. G. VON SCHNERING, *Polyhedron* **11**, 1789–94 (1992). See also T. VAN DEN ANKER, B. S. JOLLY, M. F. LAPPERT, C. L. RASTON, B. W. SKELTON and A. H. WHITE, *J. Chem. Soc., Chem. Commun.*, 1006–8 (1990).

[21] J. J. HARLAND, R. O. DAY, J. F. VOLLANO, A. C. SAU and R. R. HOLMES, *J. Am. Chem. Soc.* **103**, 5269–70 (1981).

[22] C. BRELLIERE, F. CARRÉ, R. J. P. CORRIU and G. ROYO, *Organometallics* **7**, 1006–8 (1988).

[23] K. M. MACKAY, B. K. NICHOLSON, W. T. ROBINSON and A. W. SIMS, *J. Chem. Soc., Chem. Commun.*, 1276–7 (1984).

[24] A. F. WELLS, *Structural Inorganic Chemistry*, 5th edn., Oxford University Press, Oxford, pp. 987–91 (1984).

[25] P. JUTZI, U. HOLTMANN, D. KANNE, C. KRÜGER, R. BLOM, R. GLEITER and I. HYLA-KRYSPIN *Chem. Ber.* **122**, 1629–39 (1989).

[26] A. S. BEREZHOI, *Silicon and its Binary Systems*, Consultants Bureau, New York, 1960, 275 pp.

[27] B. ARONSSON, T. LUNDSTRÖM and S. RUNDQVIST, *Borides, Silicides, and Phosphides*, Methuen, London, 1965, 120 pp.

the bonding varies from essentially metallic to ionic and covalent. Observed stoichiometries include M_6Si, M_5Si, M_4Si, $M_{15}Si_4$, M_3Si, M_5Si_2, M_2Si, M_5Si_3, M_3Si_2, MSi, M_2Si_3, MSi_2, MSi_3 and MSi_6. Silicon, like boron, is more electropositive than carbon, and structurally the silicides are more closely related to the borides than the carbides (cf. diagonal relation, p. 27). However, the covalent radius of Si (118 pm) is appreciably larger than for B (88 pm) and few silicides are actually isostructural with the corresponding borides. Silicides have been reported for virtually all elements in Groups 1–10 except Be, the greatest range of stoichiometries being shown by the transition metals in Groups 4–10 and uranium. No silicides are known for the metals in Groups 11–15 except Cu; most form simple eutectic mixtures, but the heaviest post-transition metals Hg, Tl, Pb and Bi are completely immiscible with molten Si.

Some metal-rich silicides have isolated Si atoms and these occur either in typical metal-like structures or in more polar structures. With increasing Si content, there is an increasing tendency to catenate into isolated Si_2 or Si_4, or into chains, layers or 3D networks of Si atoms. Examples are in Table 9.3 and further structural details are in refs. 24, 26 and 27.

Silicides are usually prepared by direct fusion of the elements but coreduction of SiO_2 and a metal oxide with C or Al is sometimes used. Heats of formation are similar to those of borides and carbides but mps are substantially lower; e.g. TiC 3140°, TiB$_2$ 2980°, TiSi$_2$ 1540°; and TaC 3800°, TaB$_2$ 3100°, TaSi$_2$ 1560°C. Few silicides melt as high as 2000–2500°, and above this temperature only SiC is solid (decomp ~2700°C).

Silicides of groups 1 and 2 are generally much more reactive than those of the transition elements (cf. borides and carbides). Hydrogen and/or silanes are typical products; e.g.:

$$Na_2Si + 3H_2O \xrightarrow[\text{complete}]{\text{rapid and}} Na_2SiO_3 + 3H_2$$

$$Mg_2Si + 2H_2SO_4(aq) \longrightarrow 2MgSO_4 + SiH_4$$

Products also depend on stoichiometry (i.e. structural type). For example, the polar, non-conducting Ca_2Si (anti-PbCl$_2$ structure with isolated Si atoms) reacts with water to give $Ca(OH)_2$, SiO_2 (hydrated), and H_2, whereas CaSi (which features zigzag Si chains) gives silanes and the polymeric SiH_2. By contrast CaSi$_2$, which has puckered layers of Si atoms, does not react with pure water, but with dilute hydrochloric acid it yields a yellow polymeric solid of overall composition Si_2H_2O. Transition metal silicides

Table 9.3   Structural units in metal silicides

Unit	Examples	
Isolated Si	Cu_5Si (β-Mn structure)	Metal structures
	M_3Si (β-W structure) M = V, Cr, Mo	(good electrical
	Fe_3Si (Fe_3Al superstructure)	conductors)
	Mn_3Si (random bcc)	
	M_2Si (anti-CaF_2); M = Mg, Ge, Sn, Pb	Non-metal structures
	M_2Si (anti-$PbCl_2$); M = Ca, Ru, Ce, Rh, Ir, Ni	(non-conductors)
Si_2 pairs	U_3Si_2 (Si–Si 230 pm), also for Hf and Th	
Si_4 tetrahedra	KSi (Si–Si 243 pm), i.e. $[M^+]_4[Si_4]^{4-}$ cf. isoelectronic P_4	
	(M = Li, K, Rb, Cs; also for M_4Ge_4)	
Si chains	USi (FeB structure) (Si–Si 236 pm); also for Ti, Zr, Hf, Th, Ce, Pu	
	$CaSi$ (CrB structure) (Si–Si 247 pm); also for Sr, Y	
Plane hexagonal Si nets	β-USi_2 (AlB_2 structure) (Si–Si 222–236 pm); also for other actinoids and	
	lanthanoids	
Puckered hexagonal Si nets	$CaSi_2$ (Si–Si 248 pm) — as in "puckered graphite" layer	
Open 3D Si frameworks	$SrSi_2$, α-$ThSi_2$ (Si–Si 239 pm; closely related to AlB_2), α-USi_2	

are usually inert to aqueous reagents except HF, but yield to more aggressive reagents such as molten KOH, or F_2 (Cl_2) at red heat.

9.3.2 Silicon hydrides (silanes)

The great development which occurred in synthetic organic chemistry from the 1830s onward encouraged early speculations that a similar extensive chemistry might be generated based on Si. The first silanes were made in 1857 by F. Wöhler and H. Buff who reacted Al/Si alloys with aqueous HCl; the compounds prepared were shown to be SiH_4 and $SiHCl_3$ by C. Friedel and A. Ladenburg in 1867 but it was not until 1902 that the first homologue, Si_2H_6, was prepared by H. Moissan and S. Smiles from the protonolysis of magnesium silicide. The thermal instability and great chemical reactivity of the compounds precluded further advances until A. Stock developed his greaseless vacuum techniques and first began to study them as contaminants of his boron hydrides in 1916. He proposed the names silanes and boranes (p. 151) by analogy with the alkanes.

Silanes Si_nH_{2n+2} are now known as unbranched and branched chains (up to $n = 8$) and as cyclic compounds Si_nH_{2n} ($n = 5, 6$). Silanes are colourless gases or volatile liquids; they

are extremely reactive and spontaneously ignite or explode in air. Thermal stability decreases with increasing chain length and only SiH_4 is stable indefinitely at room temperature; Si_2H_6 decomposes very slowly (2.5% in 8 months), Si_3H_8 slowly and the tetrasilanes more rapidly, at room temperature. Some physical properties are in Table 9.4 from which it can be seen that silanes are less volatile than both the alkanes and boranes (p. 163) of similar formula, but more volatile than the corresponding germanes (p. 375).

There are three general types of preparative route to the silanes and their derivatives. Early methods (pre-1945) treated materials such as metal silicides which contained negatively charged $Si^{\delta-}$ with a protonic reagent such as an aqueous acid. Concurrent hydrolysis of the products limited the yield but considerable improvement resulted from the use of nonaqueous systems such as NH_4Br/liq NH_3 (1934). The second general preparative route involves treatment of compounds such as SiX_4 ($Si^{\delta+}$) with hydridic reagents such as LiH, NaH, $LiAlH_4$, etc., in ether solvents at low temperatures. This is now the preferred route: e.g. reaction of Si_nCl_{2n+2} ($n = 1$, 2, 3) with $LiAlH_4$ gives essentially quantitative

---

[28] Ref. 13, Suppl. B1, 1982, 259 pp. (Si–H) and references cited therein.

Table 9.4 Some properties of silanes[28]

Property	MP/°C	BP(extrap)/°C	$d(20°)$/g cm^{-3}	Property	MP/°C	BP(extrap)/°C	$d(20°)$/g cm^{-3}
SiH_4	$-184.7°$	$-111.8°$	0.68 ($-185°$)	neo-Si_5H_{12}[b]	$-57.8°$	130°	—
Si_2H_6	$-132.5°$	$-14.3°$	0.686 ($-25°$)	n-Si_6H_{14}	$-44.7°$	193.6°	0.847
Si_3H_8	$-117.4°$	$+53.1°$	0.739	Si_6H_{14}[c]	$-78.4°$	185.2°	0.840
n-Si_4H_{10}	$-89.9°$	108.1°	0.792	Si_6H_{14}[(d]	$-57.8°$	134.3°	0.815
i-Si_4H_{10}	$-99.4°$	101.7°	0.793	n-Si_7H_{14}	$-30.1°$	226.8°	0.859
n-Si_5H_{12}	$-72.8°$	153.2°	0.827	$cyclo$-Si_5H_{10}[e]	$-10.5°$	194.3°	0.963
i-Si_5H_{12}[a]	$-109.8°$	146.2°	0.820	$cyclo$-Si_6H_{12}[f]	$+16.5°$	226°	—

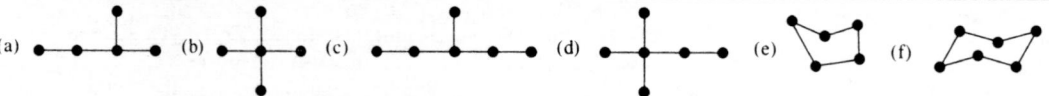

Table 9.5 Some typical bond energies/kJ mol^{-1}

X	=	C	Si	H	F	Cl	Br	I	O–	N<
C–X		368	360	435	453	351	293	216	~360	~305
Si–X		360	340	393	565	381	310	234	452	322

yields of SiH_4, Si_2H_6, and Si_3H_8. Organosilanes can be prepared similarly, e.g. Me_2SiCl_2 gives Me_2SiH_2. The third general method for preparing Si–H compounds involves direct reaction of HX or RX with Si or a ferrosilicon alloy in the presence of a catalyst such as Cu when necessary (p. 364), e.g.:

$$Si + 3HCl \xrightarrow{350°} SiHCl_3 + H_2$$

$$Si + 2MeCl \xrightarrow{Cu/300°} MeSiHCl_2 + H_2 + C$$

Combination of these various methods has led to a vast number of derivatives in which H is progressively replaced by one or more monofunctional group such as F, Cl, Br, I, CN, R, Ar, OR, SH, SR, NH_2, NR_2, etc.[1] The cyclic silanes Si_5H_{10} and Si_6H_{12} were prepared in the late 1970s[29] via $(SiPh)_n$ which were themselves the first known homocyclic silane derivatives (F. S. Kipping, 1921):

$$Ph_2SiCl_2 \xrightarrow{Na} (SiPh_2)_n$$

with Si_6Cl_{12} (via $AlCl_3$/HCl) $\xrightarrow{LiAlH_4}$ $cyclo$-Si_6H_{12}

and Si_5Br_{10} (via HBr) $\xrightarrow{LiAlH_4}$ $cyclo$-Si_5H_{10}

Silanes are much more reactive than the corresponding C compounds.[1,2,30] This has been ascribed to several factors including: (a) the larger radius of Si which would facilitate attack by nucleophiles, (b) the great polarity of Si–X bonds, and (c) the presence of low-lying d orbitals which permit the formation of 1:1 and 1:2 adducts, thereby lowering the activation energy of the reaction. The relative magnitude of the various bond energies is also an important factor in deciding which bonds will survive and which will be formed. Thus, it can be seen in Table 9.5, Si–Si < Si–C < C–C and Si–H < C–H, whereas for bonds for the other elements the energy C–X < Si–X. These data should

29 E. HENGGE and G. BAUER, *Monatshefte für Chemie* **106**, 503–12 (1975). E. HENGGE and D. KOVAR, *Z. anorg. allg. Chem.* **459**, 123–30 (1979).

30 E. WIBERG and E. AMBERGER, *Hydrides of the Elements of Main Groups I–IV*, Chap. 7, pp. 462–638, Elsevier, Amsterdam, 1971. A comprehensive review of compounds containing Si–H bonds; over 700 references.

be used only for broad comparisons since the estimated bond energies depend markedly on the particular compounds being studied and also on the experimental technique employed and the method of computation.

The pyrolysis of silanes leads to polymeric species and ultimately to Si and H_2; indeed, pyrolysis of SiH_4 is a commercial route to ultrapure Si. The reactions occurring have been less studied than those of alkanes (and boranes, p. 164), but it is clear that there are significant differences. Thus the initial step in the thermal decomposition of alkanes is the cleavage of a C–H or C–C bond with formation of radical intermediates $R_3C^{\bullet}$. However, studies using deuterium-substituted compounds suggest that the initial step in the decomposition of polysilanes is the elimination of silenes $:SiH_2$ or $:SiHR$.[31] Activation energies for this process ($\sim 210 \, kJ \, mol^{-1}$) are substantially less than Si–Si and Si–H bond energies and the reaction appears to involve a 1,2-H shift with a 5-coordinate transition state.

---

[31] I. M. T. Davidson and A. V. Howard, *J. Chem. Soc., Faraday I*, **71**, 69–77 (1975) and references therein. C. H. Haas and M. A. Ring, *Inorg. Chem.* **14**, 2253–6 (1975). A. J. Vanderwielen, M. A. Ring and H. E. O'Neal, *J. Am. Chem. Soc.* **97**, 993–8 (1975).

Pure silanes do not react with pure water or dilute acids in silica vessels, but even traces of alkali dissolved out of glass apparatus catalyse the hydrolysis which is then rapid and complete ($SiO_2 . nH_2O + 4H_2$). Solvolysis with MeOH can be controlled to give several products $SiH_{4-n}(OMe)_n$ ($n = 2, 3, 4$). Si–H adds (with difficulty) to alkenes though the reaction occurs more readily with substituted silanes. Similarly, SiH_4 adds to Me_2CO at 450° to give $C_3H_7OSiH_3$, and it ring-opens ethylene oxide at the same temperature to give $EtOSiH_3$ and other products. Silanes explode in the presence of Cl_2 or Br_2 but the reaction with Br_2 can be moderated at −80° to give good yields of SiH_3Br and SiH_2Br_2. More conveniently, halogenosilanes SiH_3X can be made by the catalysed reaction of SiH_4 and HX in the presence of Al_2X_6, or by the reaction with solid AgX in a heated flow reactor, e.g.:

$$SiH_4 + 2AgCl \xrightarrow{260°} SiH_3Cl + HCl + 2Ag$$

SiH_3I in particular is a valuable synthetic intermediate and some of its reactions are summarized in Table 9.6. SiH_3I is a dense, colourless, mobile liquid, mp −57.0°, bp +45.4°, $d(15°) \, 2.035 \, g \, cm^{-3}$.

Another valuable reagent is $KSiH_3$, a colourless crystalline compound with NaCl-type

Table 9.6 Some reactions of SiH_3I[a]

Reagent	Major Si product	Reagent	Major Si product
Na/Hg	Si_2H_6	N_2H_4	$(SiH_3)_2NN(SiH_3)_2$
H_2O	$O(SiH_3)_2$	$LiN(SiCl_3)_2$	$SiH_3N(SiCl_3)_2$
HgS	$S(SiH_3)_2$	P_4	$(SiH_3)_nPI_{3-n}$ ($n = 1, 2, 3$)
Ag_2Se	$Se(SiH_3)_2$	AgXCN (N_2 atm)	SiH_3NCX (X = O, Se)
Li_2Te	$Te(SiH_3)_2$	AgSCN	SiH_3NCS
$Si_2H_5Br + H_2O$	$SiH_3OSi_2H_5$	AgCN	SiH_3CN
$Hg(SCF_3)_2$	SiH_3SCF_3	Ag_2NCN	$(SiH_3)_2NCN$
$Hg(SeCF_3)_2$	SiH_3SeCF_3	$HC{\equiv}CMgBr$	$SiH_3C{\equiv}CH$
NH_3	$N(SiH_3)_3$	$NaMn(CO)_5$	$[Mn(CO)_5(SiH_3)]$
R_2NH	SiH_3NR_2	$Na_2Fe(CO)_4$	$[Fe(CO)_4(SiH_3)_2]$
NMe_3[b]	$SiH_3I.NMe_3$ and $SiH_3I.2NMe_3$	$[Co(CO)_4]^-$	$[Co(CO)_4(SiH_3)]$

[a] Detailed references to conditions, yields and other minor products are given in ref. 1 [2nd edn. Vol. 18, pp. 172–215 (1969)] which also summarizes the extensive reaction chemistry of $O(SiH_3)_2$, $S(SiH_3)_2$, and $N(SiH_3)_3$.

[b] Many other ligands (L) also give 1:1 and 1:2 adducts.

structure; it is stable up to $\sim 200°$ and is prepared by direct reaction of potassium on silane in monoglyme or diglyme:

$$SiH_4 + 2K \longrightarrow KSiH_3 + KH;$$

$$SiH_4 + K \longrightarrow KSiH_3 + \tfrac{1}{2}H_2$$

Table 9.7   Some reactions of $KSiH_3$[a]

Reagent	Major Si product	Reagent	Major Si product
H_2O	$SiO_2.nH_2O$	Me_3SiCl	$[SiMe_3(SiH_3)]$
MeOH	$Si(OMe)_4$	Me_3GeBr	$[GeMe_3(SiH_3)]$
HCl	SiH_4	Me_3SnBr	$[SnMe_3(SiH_3)]$
MeI	SiH_3Me	GeH_3Cl	GeH_3SiH_3
SiH_3Br	Si_2H_6, SiH_4	$MeOCH_2Cl$	$SiH_3(CH_2OMe)$
Si_2H_5Br	Si_3H_8, Si_2H_6		

[a]See footnote (a) to Table 9.6.

When hexamethylphosphoramide, $(NMe_2)_3PO$, is used as solvent only the second reaction occurs. The synthetic utility of $KSiH_3$ can be gauged from Table 9.7 which summarizes some of its reactions. In addition, PCl_3 gives polymeric $(PH)_x$, CO_2 gives CO plus HCO_2K (formate), and N_2O gives $N_2 + H_2$ (plus) some SiH_4 in each case.[32]

The hypervalent silicon hydride anion, SiH_5^- (cf. SiF_5^- below), has been synthesized as a reactive species in a low-pressure flow reactor:[33]

9.3.3 Silicon halides and related complexes

Silicon and silicon carbide both react readily with all the halogens to form colourless volatile reactive products SiX_4. $SiCl_4$ is particularly important and is manufactured on the multikilotonne scale for producing boron-free transistor grade Si, fumed silica (p. 345), and various silicon esters. When two different tetrahalides are heated together they equilibrate to form an approximately random distribution of silicon halides which, on cooling, can be separated and characterized:

$$nSiX_4 + (4-n)SiY_4 \rightleftharpoons 4SiX_nY_{4-n}$$

Mixed halides can also be made by halogen exchange reaction, e.g. by use of SbF_3 to successively fluorinate $SiCl_4$ or $SiBr_4$. The mps and bps of these numerous species are compared with those of the parent hydride and halides in Fig. 9.1. While there is a clear trend to higher mps and bps with increase in molecular weight, this is by no means always regular. More notable is the enormous drop in mp (bp) which occurs for the halides of Si when compared with Al and earlier elements in the same row of the periodic table, e.g.:

Compound	NaF	MgF_2	AlF_3	SiF_4	PF_5	SF_6
MP/°C	988	1266	1291 (subl)	-90	-94	-50

This is sometimes erroneously ascribed to a discontinuous change from "ionic" to "covalent" bonding, but the electronegativity and other bonding parameters of Al are fairly similar to those of Si and the difference is more convincingly seen merely as a consequence of the change from an infinite lattice structure (in which each Al is surrounded by 6 F) to a lattice of discrete SiF_4 molecules as dictated by stoichiometry and size. Several other examples of this effect will be noticed amongst compounds of the Group 14 elements. Another instructive trend is in the Si–F interatomic distance in binary Si/F species: in tetrahedral $SiF_4(c)$ it is 154.0 pm; in trigonal bipyramidal SiF_5^- it is 159.4 and 164.6 pm, respectively, for equatorial and axial bonds, and in SiF_6^{2-} it is 168.5 pm. The trend is to longer distances with increase in coordination number, presumably reflecting a gradual decrease in bond order. The 3.3% increase in going from

[32] V. A. WILLIAMS and D. M. RITTER, *Inorg. Chem.* **24**, 3278–80 (1985).

[33] D. J. HAJDASZ and R. R. SQUIRES, *J. Am. Chem. Soc.* **108**, 3139–40 (1986).

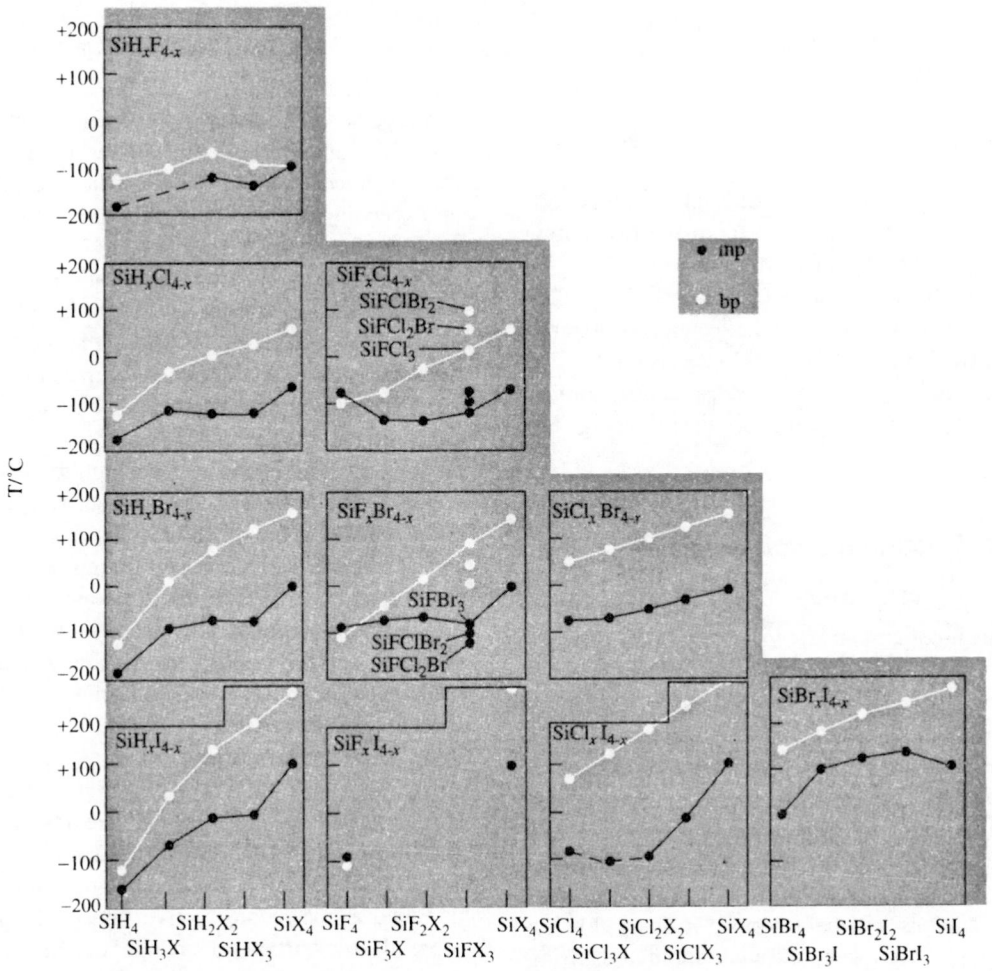

Figure 9.1 Trends in the mp and bp of silicon hydride halides and mixed halides.

equatorial to axial bonding in SiF_5^- is also in the usual direction.

The reactions of SiX_4 are straightforward and call for little comment.[1,2]

Higher homologues Si_nX_{2n+2} are volatile liquids or solids and, contrary to the situation in carbon chemistry, catenation in Si compounds reaches its maximum in the halides rather than the hydrides. This has been ascribed to additional back-bonding from filled halogen p_π orbitals into the Si d_π orbitals which thus synergically compensates for electron loss from Si via σ bonding to the electronegative halogens (cf. CO, pp. 926–8). Fluoropolysilanes up to $Si_{14}F_{30}$ and

other series up to at least Si_6Cl_{14} and Si_4Br_{10} are known. Preparative routes are exemplified by the following reactions:

$$Si + SiF_4 \xrightarrow[\text{system/1250°C}]{\text{low press. flow}} 2SiF_2(g) \xrightarrow[-196°]{\text{condense}}$$

$$(SiF_2)_x \text{ polymer} \xrightarrow{\sim 200°} Si_nF_{2n+2} \text{ mixture}$$

$$Si + SiCl_4 \xrightarrow{\text{red heat}} Si_2Cl_6 \text{ plus}$$

higher homologues

$$Si_2Cl_6 + ZnF_2 \longrightarrow Si_2F_6 + ZnCl_2$$

$$5Si_2Cl_6 \xrightarrow[\text{0.1 mol\% NMe}_3]{\text{heat with}} Si_6Cl_{14} + 4SiCl_4$$

$$3Si_2Cl_6 \xrightarrow{\text{NMe}_3 \text{ catalyst}} Si_5Cl_{12} + 2Si_2Cl_6$$

These compounds show many unusual reactions and reviews of their chemistry make fascinating reading.[34,35] Partial hydrolysis of $SiCl_4$ (or the reaction of $Cl_2 + O_2$ on Si at 700°) leads to a series of volatile chlorosiloxanes $Cl_3Si(OSiCl_2)_nOSiCl_3 (n = 0-5)$ and to the cyclic $(SiOCl_2)_4$. The corresponding bromo compounds are prepared similarly, using Br_2 and O_2.

9.3.4 Silica and silicic acids

Silica has been more studied than any other chemical compound except water. More than 22 phases have been described and, although some of these may depend on the presence of impurities or defects, at least a dozen polymorphs of "pure" SiO_2 are known. This intriguing structural complexity, coupled with the great scientific and technical utility of silica, have ensured continued interest in the compound from the earliest times. The various forms of SiO_2 and their structural inter relations will be described in the following paragraphs. By far the most commonly occurring form of SiO_2 is α-quartz which is a major mineral constituent of many rocks such as granite and sandstone; it also occurs alone as rock crystal and in impure forms as rose quartz, smoky quartz (red brown), morion (dark brown), amethyst (violet) and citrine (yellow). Poorly crystalline forms of quartz include chalcedony (various colours), chrysoprase (leek green), carnelian (deep red), agate (banded), onyx (banded), jasper (various), heliotrope (bloodstone) and flint (often black due to inclusions of carbon). Less-common crystalline modifications of SiO_2 are tridymite, cristobalite and the extremely rare

minerals coesite and stishovite. Earthy forms are particularly prevalent as kieselguhr and diatomaceous earth.[†]

Vitreous SiO_2 occurs as tectites, obsidian and the rare mineral lechatelierite. Synthetic forms include keatite and W-silica. Opals are an exceedingly complex crystalline aggregate of partly hydrated silica.

The main crystalline modifications of SiO_2 consist of infinite arrays of corner-shared $\{SiO_4\}$ tetrahedra. In α-quartz, which is thermodynamically the most stable form at room temperature, the tetrahedra form interlinked helical chains; there are two slightly different Si–O distances (159.7 and 161.7 pm) and the angle Si–O–Si is 144°. The helices in any one crystal can be either right-handed or left-handed so that individual crystals have non-superimposable mirror images and can readily be separated by hand. This enantiomorphism also accounts for the pronounced optical activity of α-quartz (specific rotation of the Na D-line 27.71°/mm). At 573°C α-quartz transforms into β-quartz which has the same general structure but is somewhat less distorted (Si–O–Si 155°): only slight displacements of the atoms are required so the transition is readily reversible on cooling and the "handedness" of the crystal is preserved throughout. This is called a non-reconstructive transformation. A more drastic structural change occurs at 867° when β-quartz transforms into β-tridymite. This is a reconstructive transformation which requires the breaking of Si–O bonds to enable the $\{SiO_4\}$

[†] The names of minerals often give a clue to their properties or discovery. Coesite, stishovite, and keatite are named after their discoverers (p. 343). Quartz derives from *kwardy*, a West Slav dialectal equivalent of the Polish *twardy*, hard. Tridymite was recognized as a new polymorph by von Rath in 1861 because of its typical occurrence as trillings or groups of 3 crystals (Greek τριδυμος, *tridymos*, threefold). Cristobalite was discovered by von Rath in 1884 on the slopes of Mt San Cristobal, Mexico, where tridymite had also first been discovered. Kieselguhr is a combination of the German *Kiesel*, flint, and *Guhr*, earthy deposit. Diatomaceous earth refers to its origin as the remains of minute unicellular algae called diatoms: these marine organisms (0.01–0.1 mm diam) have the astonishing property of accreting silica on their cell walls and this preserves the shape of the organism after death — enormous deposits occur in many places (see p. 345).

[34] J. L. MARGRAVE and P. W. WILSON, *Acc. Chem. Res.* **4**, 145–52 (1971).

[35] G. URRY, *Acc. Chem. Res.* **3**, 306–12 (1970).

tetrahedra to be rearranged into a simpler, more open hexagonal structure of lower density. For this reason the change is often sluggish and this enables tridymite to occur as a (metastable) mineral phase below the transition temperature. When β-tridymite is cooled to $\sim 120°$ it undergoes a fast, reversible, non-reconstructive transition to (metastable) α-tridymite by slight displacements of the atoms. Conversely, when β-tridymite is heated to 1470° it undergoes a sluggish reconstructive transformation into β-cristobalite and this, in turn, can retain its structure as a metastable phase when cooled below the transition temperature; further slight displacements occur rapidly and reversibly in the temperature range 200–280° to give α-cristobalite (Si–O 161 pm, Si–O–Si 147°). These transitions are summarized below.

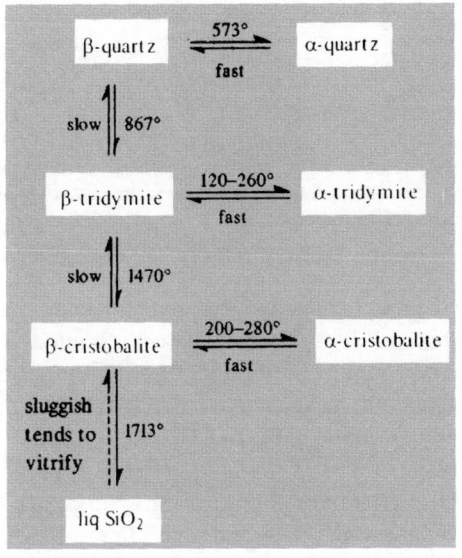

The α-form of each of the three minerals can thus be obtained at room temperature and, because of the sluggishness of the reconstructive interconversions of the β-forms, it is even possible to melt β-quartz (1550°) and β-tridymite (1703°) if they are heated sufficiently rapidly. The bp of SiO_2 is not accurately known but is about 2800°C.

Other forms of SiO_2 can be made at high pressure (Fig. 9.2). Coesite was first made by L. Coes in 1953 by heating dry Na_2SiO_3 and $(NH_4)_2HPO_4$ at 700° and 40 kbar, and was subsequently found in nature at Meteor Crater, Arizona (1960). Its structure consists of 4-connected networks of $\{SiO_4\}$ in which the smallest rings are 4- and 8-membered, and this compact structure explains its high density (Table 9.8). On being heated it rapidly converts to tridymite or cristobalite. At still higher pressures (40–120 kbar, 380–585°) keatite is formed under hydrothermal conditions from amorphous silica and dilute alkali (P. P. Keat, 1959); the $\{SiO_4\}$ are connected into 5-, 7-, and 8-membered rings as in ice(III) (p. 624). The highest density form of SiO_2 was predicted in 1952 by J. B. Thompson who visualized 6-coordinate Si in a rutile structure (p. 961). It was first synthesized in S. M. Stishov's laboratory (1961) at 1200–1400° and 160–180 kbar, and found to have the predicted structure. It was discovered in association with coesite at Meteor Crater in 1962: presumably both minerals were formed under transient shock pressures following meteorite impact and then preserved by rapid quenching from high temperature. The rapid melting and cooling of pre-existing silica phases also occurs during lightning strikes, and this leads to the formation of lechatelierite, a glassy or vitreous silica mineral.

Finally, a very low-density form of fibrous silica, W-SiO_2 has been made by the disproportionation of (metastable) crystalline SiO:

$$SiO_2 + Si \xrightarrow[10^{-4}\,mmHg]{1250-1300°} 2SiO \longrightarrow W\text{-}SiO_2 + Si$$

W-SiO_2 features $\{SiO_4\}$ tetrahedra linked by sharing opposite edges to form infinite parallel chains analogous to SiS_2 and $SiSe_2$; this edge-sharing of pairs of O atoms between pairs of Si atoms is not observed elsewhere in Si–O chemistry where linking is by corner sharing of single O atoms. The configuration is unstable, and fibrous SiO_2 rapidly reverts to amorphous SiO_2 on heating or in the presence of traces of moisture. It has also recently been shown that reaction of $(SiO)_2$ and O_2 in an argon matrix results in the formation of dimeric molecules

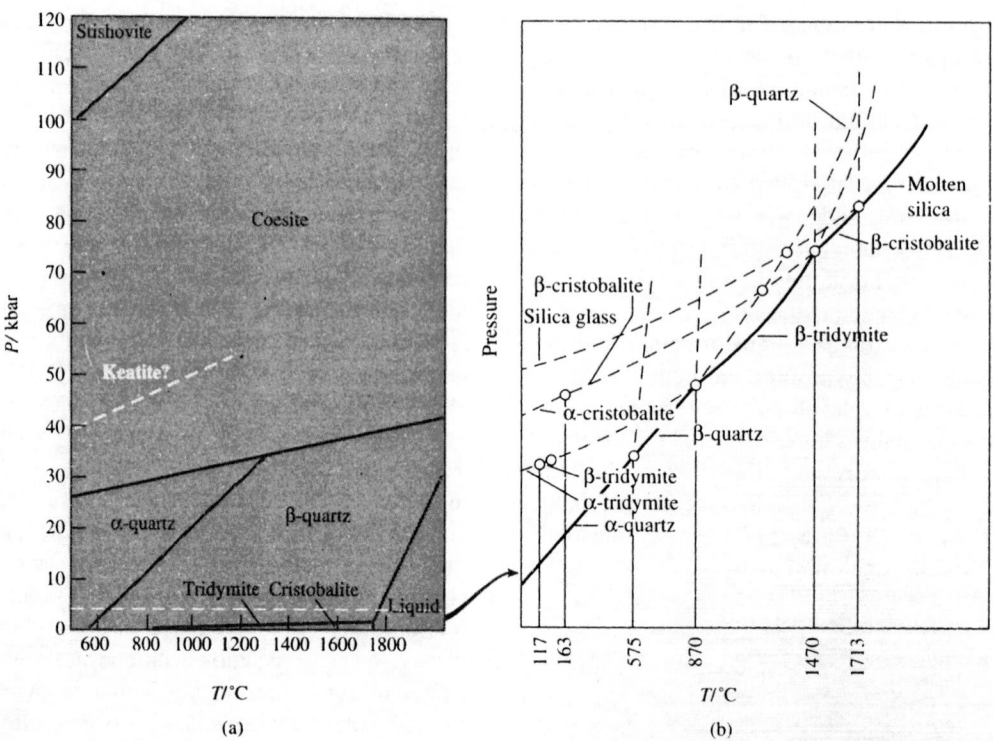

Figure 9.2   (a) Pressure-temperature phase diagram for SiO$_2$ showing the stability regions for the various polymorphs. The low-pressure segment below the broken line is shown in (b) using an (arbitrary) expanded
scale to illustrate the relationships described in the preceding paragraphs.

of silica, O=Si(μ-O)$_2$Si=O.[36] Interaction of
molecular SiO with Ag atoms in an argon matrix
gives cyclic $\overline{\text{AgSiO}}$ with the angle at Si being
$\leq 90°$.[37]

Table 9.8   Density of the main forms of SiO$_2$ (room
temperature)

	d/g cm^{-3}		d/g cm^{-3}
W (fibrous)	1.97	β-quartz (600°)	2.533
Lechatelierite	2.19	α-quartz	2.648
Vitreous	2.196	Coesite	2.911
Tridymite	2.265	Keatite	3.010
Cristobalite	2.334	Stishovite	4.287

---

[36] T. MEHNER, H. J. GÖCKE, S. SCHUNCK and H. SCHNÖCKEL,
Z. anorg. allg. Chem. **580**, 121–30 (1990).

[37] T. MEHNER,   H. SCHNÖCKEL,   M. J. ALMOND   and
A. J. DOWNS, *J. Chem. Soc., Chem. Commun.*, 117–9 (1988).

Silica is chemically resistant to all acids except
HF but dissolves slowly in hot concentrated alkali
and more rapidly in fused MOH or M$_2$CO$_3$ to give
M$_2$SiO$_3$. Of the halogens only F$_2$ attacks SiO$_2$
readily, forming SiF$_4$ and O$_2$. Above 1000° H$_2$
and C also react. Several varieties of crystalline,
cryptocrystalline and vitreous SiO$_2$ find extensive
applications and these are noted in the Panel. In
vitreous silica {SiO$_4$} tetrahedra are again linked
by sharing corners with each O linked to 2Si but
the extended three-dimensional network lacks the
symmetry and periodicity of the crystalline forms.
The Si–O distances are similar to those in other
forms of SiO$_2$ (158–162 pm) but the Si–O–Si
angles vary by as much as 15–20° on either side
of the mean value of 153°.

The detailed reactions of SiO$_2$ with the oxides
of the metals and semi-metals are of great
importance in glass technology and ceramics

but will not be treated here.[1,2,38] Suffice it to say that, in addition to innumerable crystalline compounds and vitreous phases, many water-soluble compositions are known and many of these find extensive commercial application.

38 S. FRANK, *Glass and Archaeology*, Academic Press, London, 1982, 156 pp. O. V. MAZURIN, M. V. STRELTSINA and T. P. SHVAIKO-SHVAIKOVSKAYA, *Handbook of Glass Data*, Elsevier, Amsterdam, Part **A**, 1983, 670 pp; **B**, 1985, 806 pp; **C**, 1987, 1110 pp; **D**, 1991, 992 pp; **E**, Supplements, to be published.

Perhaps the best known are the soluble sodium (and potassium) silicates which are made by fusing sand with the appropriate carbonate in a glass-making furnace at $\sim 1400°$. The resulting soluble glass is dissolved in hot water under pressure and any insoluble glass or unreacted sand filtered off. The ternary phase diagram for $Na_2O-SiO_2-H_2O$ (Fig. 9.3) indicates that only certain limited regions are of commercial interest, e.g. the stable liquid materials (area 9) in the composition range

Some Uses of Silica[1]

The main types of SiO_2 used in industry are high-purity α-quartz, vitreous silica, silica gel, fumed silica and diatomaceous earth. The most important application of quartz is as a piezoelectric material (p. 58); it is used in crystal oscillators and filters for frequency control and modulation, and in electromechanical devices such as transducers and pickups: tens of millions of such devices are made each year. There is insufficient natural quartz of adequate purity so it must be synthesized by hydrothermal growth of a seed crystal using dilute aqueous NaOH and vitreous SiO_2 at 400°C and 1.7 kbar. The technique was first successfully employed by G. R. Spezia in 1905. (Crystal growth from molten SiO_2 cannot be used — why?)

Vitreous silica combines exceptionally low thermal expansion[†] and high thermal shock resistance with high transparency to ultraviolet light, good refractory properties, and general chemical inertness. As a glass it is hard to work because of its very high softening point, high viscosity, short liquid range and high volatility at forming temperatures. It is familiar in high-quality laboratory glassware, particularly for photolysis experiments and as sample cells in ultraviolet/visible spectroscopy; it is also much used as a protective sheath in the form of tubing or as thin films deposited from the vapour.

Silica gel is an amorphous form of SiO_2 with a very porous structure, formed by acidification of aqueous solutions of sodium silicate; the gelatinous precipitate is washed free of electrolytes and then dehydrated either by roasting or spray drying. The properties of the resulting microporous material depend critically on the conditions of preparation, but typical samples have a pore diameter of 2200–2600 pm, a surface area of 750–800 $m^2 g^{-1}$, and an apparent bulk density of 0.67–0.75 $g\,cm^{-3}$. Such material finds extensive use as a desiccant, selective absorbant, chromatographic support, catalyst substrate and insulator (thermal and sound). It can absorb more than 40% of its own weight of water and, when stained with cobalt salts such as the nitrate or $(NH_4)_2CoCl_4$, is familiar as a self-indicating desiccant that can readily be regenerated by heating (anhydrous, blue; hydrated, pink). It is chemically inert, non-toxic and dimensionally stable, and finds a growing application in the food industry as an anticaking agent in cocoa, fruit juice powders, $NaHCO_3$ and powdered sugar and spices. It is also used as a flatting agent to produce an attractive matte finish on lacquers, varnishes and paints, and on the surface of vinyl plastics and synthetic fabrics.

Another manufactured form of ultrafine powdered SiO_2 is pyrogenic or fumed silica, formed by the high-temperature hydrolysis of $SiCl_4$ in an oxyhydrogen flame in specially designed burners; the SiO_2 is formed as a very fine white smoke which is collected on cooled rotating rollers. The bulk density is only 0.03–0.06 $g\,cm^{-3}$ and the surface area 150–500 $m^2 g^{-1}$. Its main use is as a thixotropic thickening agent in the processing of epoxy and polyester resins and plastics, and as a reinforcing filler in silicone rubbers where, in contrast to carbon black fillers (p. 271), its chemical inertness does not interfere with the peroxide initiated cure (p. 365).

Diatomaceous earth or kieselguhr (p. 342) is mined by open-cast methods on a very substantial scale, particularly in Europe and North America, which respectively account for 59% and 39% of the world production (1.8 million tonnes in 1977). The principal use is in filtration plants, and this accounts for about 60% of the supply; a further 20% is used in abrasives, fillers, light-weight aggregates and insulation material, and the remainder is used as an inert carrier, coating agent or in the manufacture of pozzolan.

[†] The linear coefficient of thermal expansion of vitreous silica is $\sim 0.25 \times 10^{-6}$. This can be compared with a value of $\sim 100 \times 10^{-6}$ for ordinary soda-lime glasses ($\sim 79\%$ SiO_2, $\sim 12.5\%$ Na_2O, $\sim 8.5\%$ CaO). Addition of B_2O_3 (as in Pyrex) sharply reduces this value to 3×10^{-6} (typical laboratory glassware has a composition 83.9% SiO_2, 10.6% B_2O_3, 1.2% Al_2O_3, 3.9% Na_2O, 0.4% K_2O).

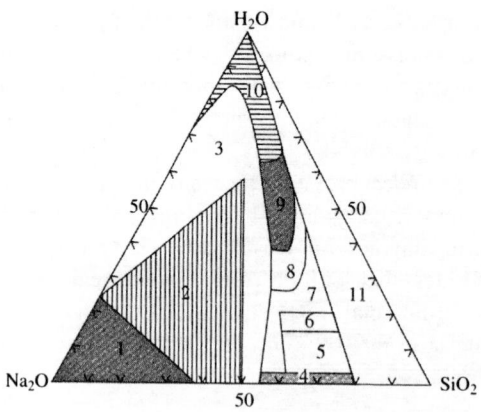

Figure 9.3 Simplified schematic ternary phase diagram for the system $Na_2O-SiO_2-H_2O$. Commercially important areas are shaded. (1) anhydrous "Na_4SiO_4" and its granular mixtures with NaOH; (2) granular crystalline alkaline silicates such as Na_2SiO_3 and its hydrates; (3) uneconomic partially crystallized mixtures; (4) glasses; (5) uneconomic hydrated glasses; (6) dehydrated liquids; (7) uneconomic semi-solids and gels; (8) uneconomic, unstable viscous liquids; (9) ordinary commercial liquids; (10) dilute liquids; (11) unstable liquids and gels. (From J. G. Vail, *Soluble Silicates*, Reinhold, New York, 1952.)

30–40% SiO_2, 10–20% Na_2O, 60–40% H_2O, i.e. $\sim Na_2Si_2O_5.6H_2O$. These find extensive use in industrial and domestic liquid detergents because they maintain high pH by means of their buffering ability and can saponify animal and vegetable oils and fats; they also emulsify mineral oils, deflocculate dirt ¹particles, and prevent redeposition of suspended dirt and soil. The more dilute solutions (area 10) are used in production of silica gels by acidification (pp. 345 and below). There are numerous other uses of soluble silicates including adhesives, glues and binders, especially for corrugated cardboard boxes, and as refractory acid-resistant cements and sealants. World production in 1981 was $\sim$3.0 million tonnes of which the sodium silicates formed the major part. Price range from \$220–450/tonne depending on composition.

Potassium silicate solutions are equally complex; for example, an aqueous solution prepared from KOH and SiO_2 in which the ratio K:Si is 1:1 contains 22 different discrete silicate anions as identified by ^{29}Si COSY nmr studies.[39]

The system SiO_2-H_2O, even in the absence of metal oxides, is particularly complex and of immense geochemical and industrial importance.[40] The mp of pure SiO_2 decreases dramatically by as much as 800° on addition of 1–2% H_2O (at high pressure), presumably as a result of the structure-breaking effect of replacing Si–O–Si links by "terminal" Si–OH groups. With increasing concentrations of H_2O one obtains hydrated silica gels and colloidal dispersions of silica; there are also numerous hydrates and distinct silicic acids in very dilute aqueous solutions, but these tend to be rather insoluble and rapidly precipitate with further condensation when aqueous solutions of soluble silicates are acidified. Structural information is sparse, particularly for the solid state, but in solution evidence has been claimed for at least 5 species (Table 9.9). It is unlikely that any of these species exist in the solid state since precipitation is accompanied by further condensation and cross-linking to form "polysilicic acids" of indefinite and variable composition $[SiO_x(OH)_{4-2x}]_n$ (cf B, Al, Fe, etc.). However, the crystal structure of $[(c\text{-}C_6H_{11})_7Si_7O_9\{O_3W(NMe_2)_3\}_3]$ has been

Table 9.9 Silicic acids in solution

Formula	n[a]	Name	Sol. (H_2O, 20°)/ mol l^{-1}
$H_{10}Si_2O_9$	2.5	Pentahydrosilicic acid	2.9×10^{-4}
H_4SiO_4	2	Orthosilicic acid	7×10^{-4}
$H_6Si_2O_7$	1.5	Pyrosilicic acid	9.6×10^{-4}
H_2SiO_3	1	Metasilicic acid	10×10^{-4}
$H_2Si_2O_5$	0.5	Disilicic acid	20×10^{-4}

[a] Number of mols H_2O per mol SiO_2, i.e. $SiO_2.nH_2O$.

[39] C. T. G. KNIGHT, *J. Chem. Soc., Dalton Trans.*, 1457–60 (1988).

[40] R. K. ILER, *The Chemistry of Silica: Solubility, Polymerization, Colloid and Surface Properties, and Biochemistry*, Wiley, New York, 1979, 866 pp.

determined[41] and various crystalline methyl and ethyl esters of cyclic silicic acids have been isolated.[42]

9.3.5 Silicate minerals [24,43,44]

The earth's crustal rocks and their breakdown products — the various soils, clays and sands — are composed almost entirely ($\sim$95%) of silicate minerals and silica. This predominance of silicates and aluminosilicates is reflected in the abundance of O, Si and Al, which are the commonest elements in the crust (p. 329). Despite the great profusion of structural types and the widely varying stoichiometries which are unmatched elsewhere in chemistry, it is possible to classify these structures on the basis of a few simple principles. Almost invariably Si is coordinated tetrahedrally by 4 oxygen atoms and these $\{SiO_4\}$ units can exist either as discrete structural entities or can combine by corner sharing of O atoms into larger units. The resulting O lattice is frequently close-packed, or approximately so, and charge balance is achieved by the presence of further cations in tetrahedral, octahedral, or other sites depending on their size. Typical examples are as follows (radii in pm):[†]

CN 4 : Li^I (59) Be^{II} (27) Al^{III} (39) Si^{IV} (26)
CN 6 : Na^I (102) Mg^{II} (72) Al^{III} (54) Ti^{IV} (61) Fe^{II} (78)
CN 8 : K^I (151) Ca^{II} (112)
CN 12: K^I (164)

The quoted radii, which in turn depend on the CN, are the empirical "effective ionic radii" deduced by R. D. Shannon (and C. T. Prewitt)[45] and do not imply full charge separation such as $\{Si^{4+}(O^{2-})_4\}$, etc. Note that Al^{III} can occupy either 4- or 6-coordinate sites so that it can replace either Si or M in the lattice — this is particularly important in discussing the structures of the aluminosilicates. Several other cations can occupy sites of differing CN, e.g. Li (4 and 6), Na (6 and 8), K (6–12), though they are most commonly observed in the CN shown.

As with the borates (p. 205) and to a lesser extent the phosphates (p. 526), the $\{SiO_4\}$ units can build up into chains, multiple chains (or ribbons), rings, sheets and three-dimensional networks as summarized below and elaborated in the following paragraphs.

Neso-silicates	discrete $\{SiO_4\}$	no O atoms shared
soro-silicates	discrete $\{Si_2O_7\}$	1 O atom shared
cyclo-silicates	closed ring structures	2 O atoms shared
ino-silicates	continuous chains or ribbons	
phyllo-silicates	continuous sheets	3 O atoms shared
tecto-silicates	continuous 3D frameworks	all 4 O atoms shared

Silicates with discrete units

Discrete $\{SiO_4\}$ units occur in the orthosilicates $M_2^{II}SiO_4$ (M = Be, Mg, Mn, Fe and Zn) and in $ZrSiO_4$ as well as in the synthetic orthosilicates Na_4SiO_4 and K_4SiO_4.[46] In phenacite, Be_2SiO_4, both Be and Si occupy sites of CN 4 and the structure could equally well be described as a 3D network M_3O_4. When octahedral sites are occupied, isomorphous replacement of M^{II} is often extensive as in olivine, $(Mg,Fe,Mn)_2SiO_4$ which derives its name from its olive-green colour (Fe^{II}). In zircon, $ZrSiO_4$, the stoichiometry

[41] M. H. CHISHOLM, T. A. BUDZICHOWSKI, F. J. FEHER and J. W. ZILLER, *Polyhedron* **11**, 1575–9 (1992).

[42] H. C. MARSMANN and E. MEYER, *Z. anorg. allg. Chem.* **548**, 193–203 (1987).

[43] W. A. DEER, R. A. HOWIE and J. ZUSSMAN, *An Introduction to the Rock-forming Minerals*, Longmans, London, 1966, 528 pp. B. MASON and L. G. BERRY, *Elements of Mineralogy*, W. H. Freeman, San Francisco, 1968, 550 pp.

[44] F. LIEBAU, Silicon, element 14, in K. H. WEDEPOHL (ed.), *Handbook of Geochemistry*, Vol. II-2, Chap. 14, Springer-Verlag, Berlin, 1978. F. LIEBAU, *Structural Chemistry of Silicates*, Springer-Verlag, Berlin, 1985, 347 pp.

[†] The metals which form silicate and aluminosilicate minerals are the more electropositive metals, i.e. those in Groups 1, 2 and the 3d transition series (except Co), together with Y, La and the lanthanoids, Zr, Hf, Th, U and to a much lesser extent the post-transition elements Sn^{II}, Pb^{II}, and Bi^{III}.

[45] R. D. SHANNON, *Acta Cryst.* **A32**, 751–67 (1976).

[46] M. G. BARKER and P. G. GOOD, *J. Chem. Research (S)*, 1981, 274, and references cited therein.

of the crystal and the larger radius of Zr (84 pm) dictate eightfold coordination of the cation. Another important group of orthosilicates is the garnets, $[M_3^{II}M_2^{III}(SiO_4)_3]$, in which M^{II} are 8-coordinate (e.g. Ca, Mg, Fe) and M^{III} are 6-coordinate (e.g. Al, Cr, Fe).[47] Orthosilicates are also vital components of Portland cement (p. 252): β-Ca_2SiO_4 has discrete $\{SiO_4\}$ groups with rather irregularly coordinated Ca in sixfold and eightfold environments (the α-form has the K_2SO_4 structure and the γ-form has the olivine structure). Again alite, Ca_3SiO_5, which is intimately involved in the "setting" process, has individual Ca, $\{SiO_4\}$ and O as the structural units.

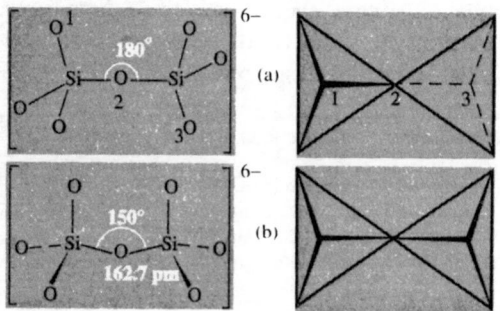

Figure 9.4   (a) Two representations of the $\{Si_2O_7\}$ unit in $Sc_2Si_2O_7$ showing the linear Si–O–Si link between the two tetrahedra and the D_{3d} (staggered) conformation, and (b) eclipsed (C_{2v}) conformation of the $\{Si_2O_7\}$ unit in hemimorphite, $[Zn_4Si_2O_7(OH)_2].H_2O$.

Disilicates, containing the discrete $\{Si_2O_7{}^{6-}\}$ unit, are rare. One example is the mineral thortveitite, $Sc_2Si_2O_7$, which features octahedral Sc^{III} (r 75 pm) and a linear Si–O–Si bond between staggered tetrahedra (Fig. 9.4a). There is also a series of lanthanoid disilicates $Ln_2Si_2O_7$ in which the Si–O–Si angle decreases progressively

from $180°$ to $133°$ and the CN of Ln increases from 6 through 7 to 8 as the size of Ln increases from 6-coordinated Lu^{III} (86 pm) to 8-coordinated Nd^{III} (111 pm). In the Zn mineral hemimorphite the angle is $150°$ but the conformation of the 2 tetrahedra is eclipsed (C_{2v}) rather than staggered (Fig. 9.4b); the mineral was originally formulated as $Zn_2SiO_4.H_2O$ or $H_2Zn_2SiO_5$, but X-ray studies showed that the correct formula was $[Zn_4(OH)_2Si_2O_7].H_2O$, i.e."$2H_2Zn_2SiO_5$". Two further features of importance also emerged. The first was that there was no significant difference between the Si–O distances to "bridging" and "terminal" O atoms as would be expected for isolated $\{Si_2O_7{}^{6-}\}$ groups, and the structure is best considered as a 3D framework of $\{ZnO_3(OH)\}$ and $\{SiO_4\}$ tetrahedra linked in threes to form 6-atom rings $\overline{Zn-O-Si-O-Zn-OH}$. The rings are linked into infinite sheets in the (010) planes which are themselves linked via Zn–O(H)–Zn or Si–O–Si bonds. The 3D framework so generated leaves large channels which open into large cavities that accommodate the removable H_2O molecules. The structure is thus very similar in principle to that of the framework aluminosilicates (p. 354) and its conventional description in terms of discrete $Si_2O_7{}^{6-}$ ions is rather misleading and uninformative.

Structures having triple tetrahedral units are extremely rare but they exist in aminoffite, $Ca_3(BeOH)_2(Si_3O_{10})$, and kinoite, $Cu_2Ca_2(Si_3O_{10}).2H_2O$. The first chain-tetrasilicate, $[O_3Si(OSiO_2)_2OSiO_3]^{10-}$, was synthesized as recently as 1979:[48] $Ag_{10}Si_4O_{13}$ was prepared as stable vermilion crystals by heating AgO and SiO_2 for 1–3 days at $500-600°C$ under a pressure of $2-4.5\,kbar$ of O_2. At lower temperatures ($<470°C$) the bright red mixed silicate $[Ag_{18}(SiO_4)_2(Si_4O_{13})]$ crystallizes.[49]

When every $\{SiO_4\}$ shares 2 O with contiguous tetrahedra, metasilicates of empirical

---

[47] See p. 500 of ref. 24 for a description of the garnet structure which is also adopted by many synthetic and non-silicate compounds; these have been much studied recently because of their important optical and magnetic properties, e.g. ferrimagnetic yttrium iron garnet (YIG), $Y_3^{III}Fe_2^{III}(Al^{III}O_4)_3$.

[48] M. JANSEN and H.-L. KELLER, *Angew. Chem. Int. Edn. Engl.* **18**, 464 (1979).

[49] K. HEIDEBRECHT and M. JANSEN, *Z. anorg. allg. Chem.* **597**, 79–86 (1991).

formula SiO_3^{2-} are formed. Cyclic metasilicates $[(SiO_3)_n]^{2n-}$ having 3, 4, 6 or 8 linked tetrahedra are known, though 3 and 6 are the most common. These anions are shown schematically in Fig. 9.5 and are exemplified by the mineral benitoite [BaTi{Si$_3$O$_9$}], the synthetic compound [K$_4$\{Si$_4$O$_8$(OH)$_4$\}], and by beryl [Be$_3$Al$_2$\{Si$_6$O$_{18}$\}] (p. 107) and murite [Ba$_{10}$(Ca,Mn,Ti)$_4$\{Si$_8$O$_{24}$\}(Cl,OH,O)$_{12}$].4H$_2$O.

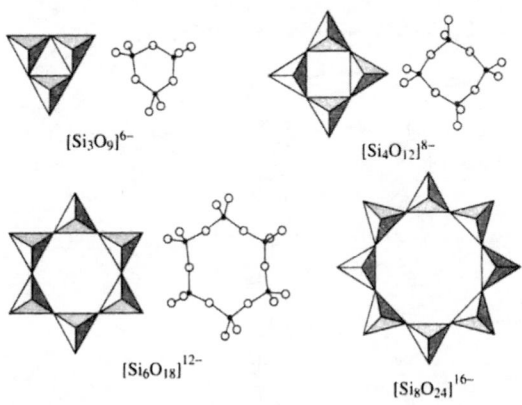

Figure 9.5   Schematic representations of the structures of cyclic metasilicate anions with $n = 3, 4, 6,$ and 8.

Silicates with chain or ribbon structures

Chain metasilicates $\{SiO_3^{2-}\}_\infty$ formed by corner-sharing of {SiO$_4$} tetrahedra are particularly prevalent in nature and many important minerals have this basic structural unit (cf. polyphosphates, p. 528). Despite the apparent simplicity of their structure motif and stoichiometry considerable structural diversity is encountered because of the differing conformations that can be adopted by the linked tetrahedra. As a result, the repeat distance along the c-axis can be (1), 2, 3, …, 7, 9 or 12 tetrahedra (T), as illustrated schematically in Fig. 9.6. The most common conformation for metasilicates is a repeat after every second tetrahedron (2T) with the chains stacked parallel so as to provide sites of 6- or 8-coordination for the cations; e.g. the pyroxene minerals enstatite [Mg$_2$Si$_2$O$_6$],

diopside [CaMgSi$_2$O$_6$], jadeite [NaAlSi$_2$O$_6$], and spodumene [LiAlSi$_2$O$_6$] (p. 69). The synthetic metasilicates Li$_2$SiO$_3$ and Na$_2$SiO$_3$ are similar; for the latter compound Si–O–Si is 134° and the Si–O distance is 167 pm within the chain and 159 pm for the other two O. The minerals wollastonite [Ca$_3$Si$_3$O$_9$] and pectolite [Ca$_2$NaHSi$_3$O$_9$] have a 3T repeat unit, haradaite [Sr$_2$(VO)Si$_4$O$_{12}$] is 4T, rhodonite [CaMn$_4$Si$_5$O$_{15}$] has a 5T repeat, etc.[24,44]

In the next stage of structural complexity the single $\{SiO_3^{2-}\}_\infty$ chains can link laterally to form double chains or ribbons whose stoichiometry depends on the repeat unit of the single chain (Fig. 9.7). By far the most numerous are the amphiboles or asbestos minerals which adopt the $\{Si_4O_{11}^{6-}\}$ double chain, e.g. tremolite [Ca$_2$Mg$_5$(Si$_4$O$_{11}$)$_2$(OH)$_2$]; the structure of this compound is very similar to that of diopside (above) except that the length of the b-axis of the unit cell is doubled. The fibrous nature of the asbestos minerals thus finds a ready interpretation on the basis of their crystal structures (see Panel on p. 351). In addition to these well-established double chains of linked {SiO$_4$} tetrahedra, examples of infinite one-dimensional structures consisting of linked triple, quadruple and even sextuple chains have been discovered in nephrite jade by means of electron microscopy,[50] and these form a satisfying link between the pyroxenes and amphiboles, on the one hand, and the sheet silicates (to be described in the next paragraph), on the other.

Silicates with layer structures

Silicates with layer structures include some of the most familiar and important minerals known to man, particularly the clay minerals [such as kaolinite (china clay), montmorillonite (bentonite, fuller's earth), and vermiculite], the micas (e.g. muscovite, phlogopite, and biotite), and others such as chrysotile (white asbestos),

[50] L. G. MALLINSON, J. L. HUTCHINSON, D. A. JEFFERSON and J. M. THOMAS, *J. Chem. Soc., Chem. Commun.*, 910–11 (1977).

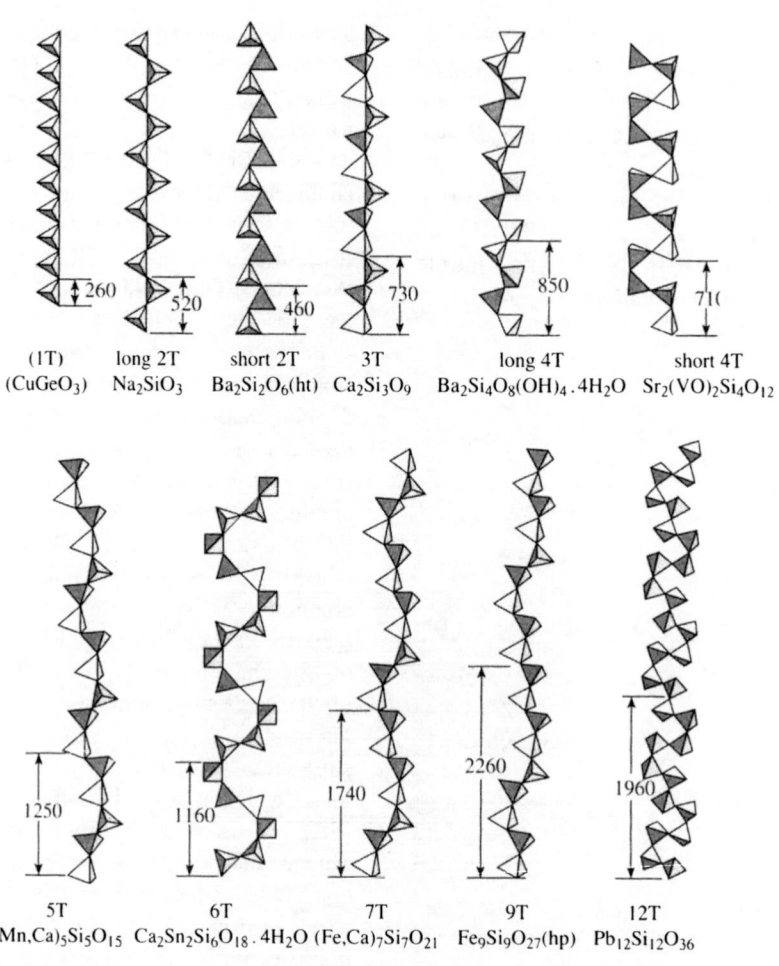

Figure 9.6   Schematic representation and examples of various chain metasilicates $\{SiO_3{}^{2-}\}_\infty$ with repeat distances (in pm) after 1, 2, ..., 7, 9 or 12 tetrahedra (T), [(ht) high-temperature form; (hp) high-pressure form].

talc, soapstone, and pyrophyllite. The physical and chemical properties of these minerals, which have made many of them so valued for domestic and industrial use for several milleniums (p. 328), can be directly related to the details of their crystal structure. The simplest silicate layer structure can be thought of as being formed either by the horizontal cross-linking of the 2T metasilicate chain $\{Si_2O_6{}^{4-}\}$ in Fig. 9.6 or by the planar condensation of the $\{Si_6O_{18}{}^{12-}\}$ unit in Fig. 9.5 to give a 6T network of composition $\{Si_2O_5{}^{2-}\}$ in which 3 of the 4 O atoms in each tetrahedron are shared; this is shown in both plan and elevation in Fig. 9.8. In fact, such a

structure with a completely planar arrangement is extremely rare though closely related puckered 6T networks are found in $M_2Si_2O_5$ (M=Li, Na, Ag, H) and in petalite ($LiAlSi_4O_{10}$, p. 69). More complex arrangements are also found in which the 6T rings forming the network are replaced by alternate 4T and 8T rings, or by equal numbers of 4T, 6T, and 8T rings, or even by a network of 4T, 6T and 12T rings.[24,44]

Double layers can be generated by sharing the fourth (apical) O atom between pairs of tetrahedra as in Fig. 9.9(a). This would give a stoichiometry SiO_2 (since each O atom is shared between 2 Si atoms) but if half the Si^{IV} were replaced by

Production and Uses of Asbestos

The fibrous silicate minerals known collectively as asbestos (Greek ἄσβεστος, unquenchable) have been used both in Europe and the Far East for thousands of years. In ancient Rome the wicks of the lamps of the vestal virgins were woven from asbestos, and Charlemagne astounded his barbarian guests by throwing the festive table cloth into the fire whence, being woven asbestos, it emerged cleansed and unburnt. Its use has accelerated during the past 100 y and it is now an important ingredient in over 3000 different products. Its desirable characteristics are high tensile strength, great flexibility, resistance both to heat and flame and also to corrosion by acids or alkalis, good thermal insulation properties and low cost.

Asbestos is derived from two large groups of rock-forming minerals — the serpentines and the amphiboles. Chrysotile, or white asbestos $[Mg_3(Si_2O_5)(OH)_4]$, is the sole representative of the serpentine layer silicate group (p. 352) but is by far the most abundant kind of asbestos and constitutes more than 98% of world production. The amphibole group includes the blue asbestos mineral crocidolite $[Na_2Fe_3^{II}Fe_2^{III}Si_8O_{22}(OH)_2]$ (<1% of world production) and the grey–brown mineral amosite $[(Mg,Fe)_7Si_8O_{22}(OH)_2]$. (<1%). Annual production in 1989 was 4.3 million tonnes having fallen from a maximum of 5 Mt in 1979.[51] The main producing countries are Russia (55%), Canada (20%), South Africa (4.7%) and Zimbabwe. China, Italy and Brazil (3–4% each).

Asbestos-reinforced cements (~12.5% asbestos) absorb nearly two-thirds of the world's annual production of chrysotile: it is used in corrugated and flat roofing sheets, pressure pipes and ducts, and many other hard-wearing, weather-proof, long-lasting products. About 8% is used in asbestos papers and a further 7% is used for making vinyl floor tiles. Other important uses include composites for brake linings, clutch facings, and other friction products. Long-fibred chrysotile (fibre length >20 mm) is woven into asbestos textiles for fire-fighting garments and numerous fire-proofing and insulating applications.

Prolonged exposure to airborne suspensions of asbestos fibre dust can be very dangerous and there has been increasing concern at the incidence of asbestosis (non-malignant scarring of lung tissue) and lung carcinoma among certain workers in the industry. Unfortunately, there is an extended latent period (typically 20–30 y) before these diseases are manifest. Stringent precautions are now enforced in many countries and the incidence of the disease appears to be falling steadily. There is also general (though not universal) agreement that white asbestos (chrysotile), which is the overwhelmingly predominant type of asbestos in use, is not implicated in the incidence of asbestosis and lung carcinoma which seems to be confined mainly (perhaps exclusively) to the blue crocidolite and brown amosite amphibole varieties. Asbestosis is dose-related and the best form of control is to reduce the level of dust exposure in places where the mineral is mined, processed or fabricated.

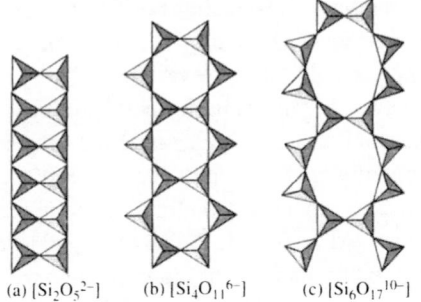

(a) $[Si_2O_5{}^{2-}]$ (b) $[Si_4O_{11}{}^{6-}]$ (c) $[Si_6O_{17}{}^{10-}]$

Figure 9.7 Double chains of {SiO₄} tetrahedra: (a) the double chain based on the 1T metasilicate structure, stoichiometry {$Si_2O_5{}^{2-}$} — it is found in the aluminosilicate sillimanite [Al(AlSiO₅)]; (b) {$Si_4O_{11}{}^{6-}$} chain based on the 2T metasilicate occurs in the amphiboles (see text); and (c) the rare 3T double chain $Si_6O_{17}{}^{10-}$ occurs in xonotlite [Ca₆Si₆O₁₇(OH)₂]. More complex 3T, 4T and 6T double chains are also known.[44]

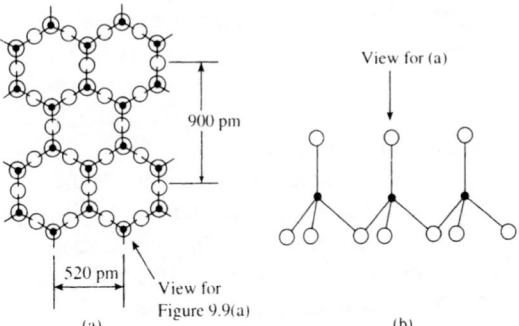

Figure 9.8 Planar network formed by extended 2D condensation of rings of 6 {SiO₄} tetrahedra to give {$Si_2O_5{}^{2-}$}. (a) Plan as seen looking down the O–Si direction, and (b) side elevation.

Al^{III} then the composition would be {$Al_2Si_2O_8{}^{2-}$} as found in Ca₂Al₂Si₂O₈ and Ba₂Al₂Si₂O₈ (Fig. 9.9b). Another way of building up double layers involves the interleaving of layers of the

⁵¹ Reference 1, 4th edn., Asbestos **3**, 659–88 (1992).

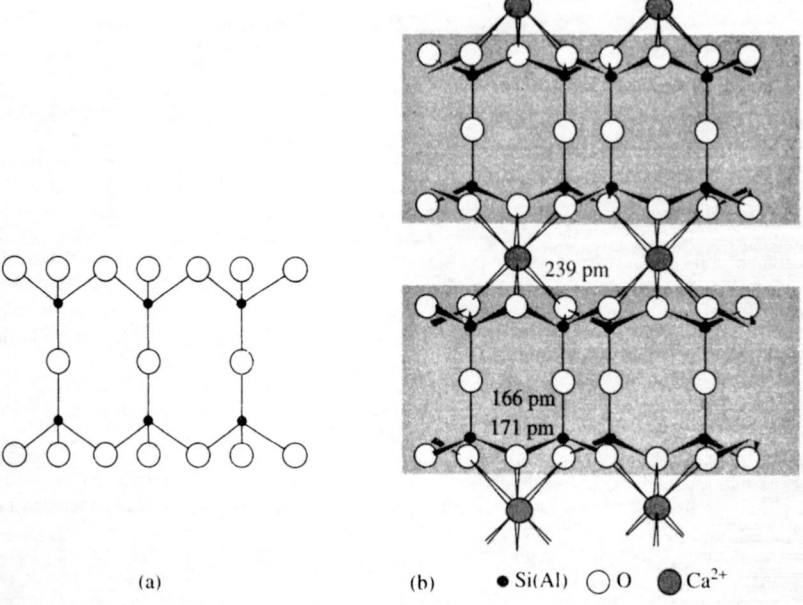

239 pm

166 pm
171 pm

(a)   (b)   ● Si(Al)   ○ O   ◉ Ca^{2+}

Figure 9.9   (a) Side elevation of double layers of formula {Al$_2$Si$_2$O$_8^{2-}$} formed by sharing the fourth (apical) O in Fig. 9.9(b). Sites marked ● are occupied by equal numbers of Al and Si atoms. (b) Structure of Ca$_2$Al$_2$Si$_2$O$_8$ formed by interleaving 6-coordinated Ca^{II} atoms between the double layers depicted in (a).

gibbsite Al(OH)$_3$ or brucite Mg(OH)$_2$ structure (pp. 243–5, 121) which happen to have closely similar dimensions and can thus share O atoms with the silicate network. This leads to the china-clay mineral kaolinite [Al$_2$(OH)$_4$Si$_2$O$_5$] illustrated in Figs. 9.10(a) and 9.11(a). [The mineral was so-named in 1867 from "kaolin", a corruption of the Chinese *kauling*, or high-ridge, the name of the hill where this china clay was found some 300 miles north of Hong Kong.]

Repetition of the process on the other side of the Al/O layer leads to the structure of pyrophyllite [Al$_2$(OH)$_2$Si$_4$O$_{10}$] (Fig. 9.10b,c). Replacement of 2Al^{III} by 3Mg^{II} in kaolinite [Al$_2$(OH)$_4$Si$_2$O$_5$] gives the serpentine asbestos mineral chrysotile [Mg$_3$(OH)$_4$Si$_2$O$_5$] and a similar replacement in pyrophyllite gives talc [Mg$_3$(OH)$_2$Si$_4$O$_{10}$]. The gibbsite series is sometimes called dioctahedral and the brucite series trioctahedral in obvious reference to the number of octahedral sites occupied in the "non-silicate" layer.

Alternative representations of the structures are given in Fig. 9.11, and it is well worth while looking carefully at these various diagrams since they have the pleasing property of becoming simpler and easier to understand the longer they are contemplated. It should be stressed that the formulae given are ideal limiting compositions and that Al^{III} or Mg^{II} can be replaced by several other cations of appropriate size. The stoichiometry is further complicated by the possibility that Si^{IV} can be partly replaced by Al^{III} in the tetrahedral sites thereby giving rise to charged layers. These layers can be interleaved with M^I or M^{II} cations to give the micas or by layers of 1hydrated cations to give montmorillonite. Alternatively, charge balance can be achieved by interleaving positively charged (Mg,Al)(OH)$_2$ layers as in the chlorites. These possibilities are shown schematically in Figs. 9.12 and 9.13 (p. 355) and elaborated in the following paragraphs.

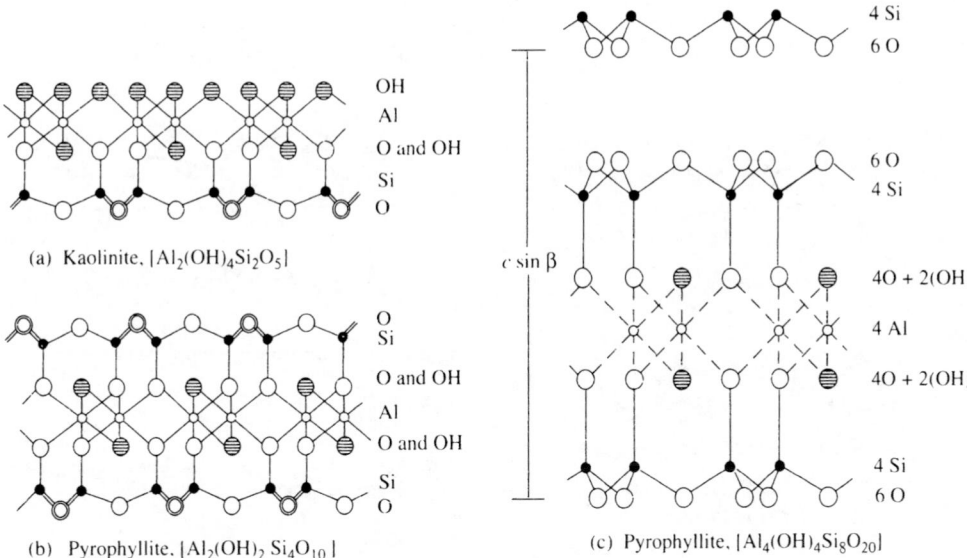

(a) Kaolinite, $[Al_2(OH)_4Si_2O_5]$

(b) Pyrophyllite, $[Al_2(OH)_2Si_4O_{10}]$

(c) Pyrophyllite, $[Al_4(OH)_4Si_8O_{20}]$

Figure 9.10   (a) Schematic representation of the structure of kaolinite (side elevation) showing $\{SiO_3O\}$ tetrahedra (bottom) sharing common O atoms with $\{Al(OH)_2O\}$ to give a composite layer of formula $[Al_2(OH)_4Si_2O_5]$. The double lines and double circles in the tetrahedra indicate bonds to 2 O atoms (one in front and one behind). (b) Similar representation of the structure of pyrophyllite, showing shared $\{SiO_3O\}$ tetrahedra above and below the $\{Al(OH)O_2\}$ layer to give a composite layer of formula $[Al_2(OH)_2Si_4O_{10}]$. (c) Alternative representation of pyrophyllite to be compared with (b), and showing the stoichiometry of each layer.

The technological importance of the clay minerals is outlined in the Panel on p. 356.

Micas are formed when one-quarter of the Si^{IV} in pyrophyllite and talc are replaced by Al^{III} and the resulting negative charge is balanced by K^I:

pyrophyllite $[Al_2(OH)_2Si_4O_{10}] \longrightarrow$

$[KAl_2(OH)_2(Si_3AlO_{10})]$ muscovite (white mica)

talc $[Mg_3(OH)_2Si_4O_{10}] \longrightarrow$

$[KMg_3(OH)_2(Si_3AlO_{10})]$ phlogopite

The OH can be partly replaced by F and, in phlogopite, partial replacement of Mg^{II} by Fe^{II} gives biotite (black mica) $[K(Mg,Fe^{II})_3-(OH,F)_2(Si_3AlO_{10})]$. The presence of K^I between the layers makes the micas appreciably harder than pyrophyllite and talc but the layers are still a source of weakness and micas show perfect cleavage parallel to the layers. With further

substitution of up to half the Si by Al charge balance can be restored by the more highly charged Ca^{II} and brittle micas result, such as margarite $[CaAl_2(OH)_2(Si_2Al_2O_{10})]$ which is even harder than muscovite.

Another set of minerals, the montmorillonites, result if, instead of replacing tetrahedral Si^{IV} by Al^{III} in phlogopite, the octahedral Al^{III} is *partially* replaced by Mg^{II} (not *completely* as in talc). The resulting partial negative charge per unit formula can be balanced by incorporating hydrated M^I or M^{II} between the layers; this leads to the characteristic swelling, cation exchange and thixotropy of these minerals (see Panel, p. 356). A typical sodium montmorillonite might be formulated $Na_{0.33}[Mg_{0.33}Al_{1.67}(OH)_2(Si_4O_{10})].nH_2O$, but more generally they can be written as $M_x[(Mg,Al,Fe)_2(OH)_2(Si_4O_{10})].nH_2O$ where $M=H$, Na, K, $\frac{1}{2}Mg$ or $\frac{1}{2}Ca$. Simultaneous altervalent substitution in both the octahedral and tetrahedral sites in talc leads to the vermiculites

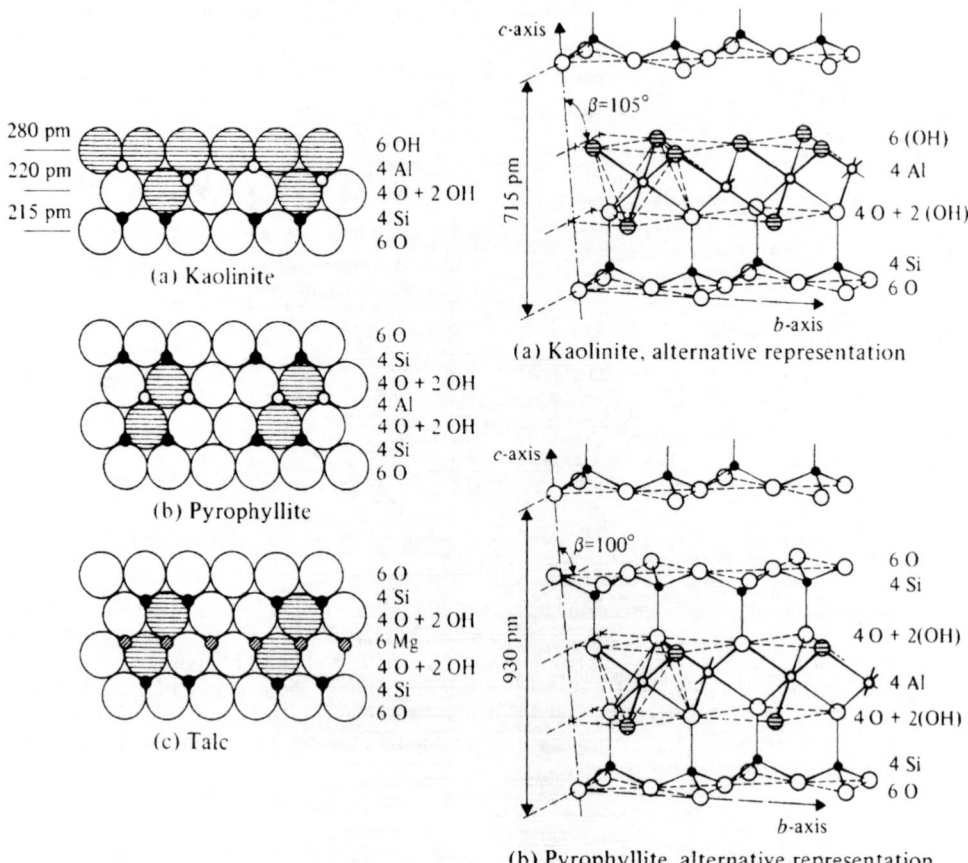

Figure 9.11 Alternative representations of the layer structures of (a) kaolinite, (b) pyrophyllite, and (c) talc. (After H. J. Eméleus and J. S. Anderson, 1960 and B. Mason and L. G. Berry, 1968.)

of which a typical formula is

$$[Mg_{0.32}(H_2O)_{4.32}]^{0.64+} \quad +$$

$$[(Mg_{2.36}Al_{0.16}Fe^{III}_{0.48})(OH)_2(Si_{2.72}Al_{1.20}O_{10})]^{0.64-}$$

total 3.00

When these minerals are heated they dehydrate in a remarkable way by extruding little worm-like structures as indicated by their name (Latin *vermiculus*, little worm); the resulting porous light-weight mass is much used for packing and insulation. The relationship between the various layer silicates is summarized with idealized formulae in Table 9.10 (on page 357).

Silicates with framework structures

The structural complexity of the 3D framework aluminosilicates precludes a detailed treatment here, but many of the minerals are of paramount importance. The group includes the feldspars (which are the most abundant of all minerals, and comprise ~60% of the earth's crust), the zeolites (which find major applications as molecular sieves, desiccants, ion exchangers and water softeners), and the ultramarines which, as their name implies, often have an intense blue colour. All are constructed from SiO_4 units in which each O atom is shared by 2 tetrahedra (as in the various forms of SiO_2 itself), but up to one-half of the Si

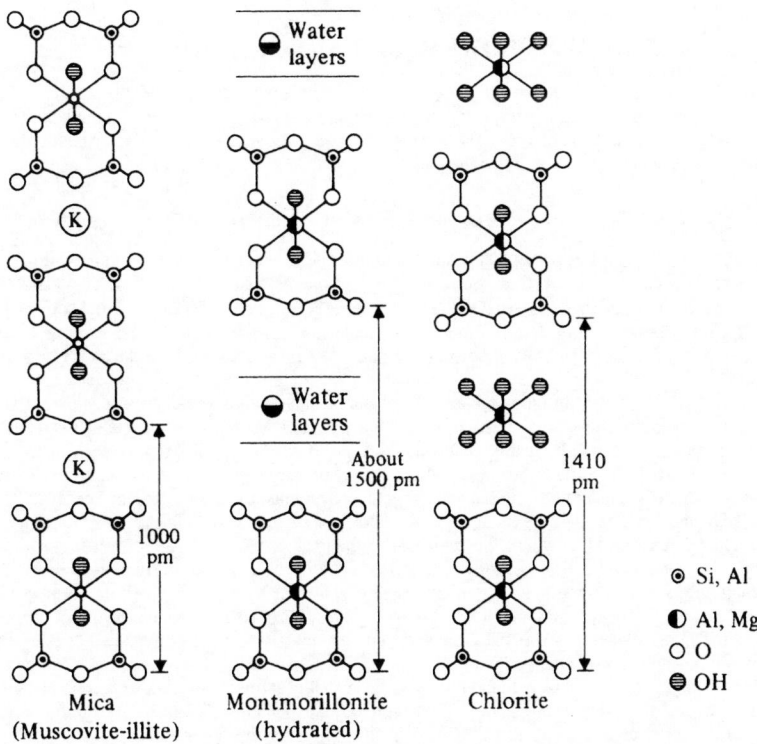

Figure 9.12   Schematic representation of the structures of muscovite mica, $[K_2Al_4(Si_6Al_2)O_{20}(OH)_4]$, hydrated montmorillonite, $[Al_4Si_8O_{20}(OH)_4].xH_2O$ and chlorite, $[Mg_{10}Al_2(Si_6Al_2)O_{20}(OH)_{16}]$, see text.

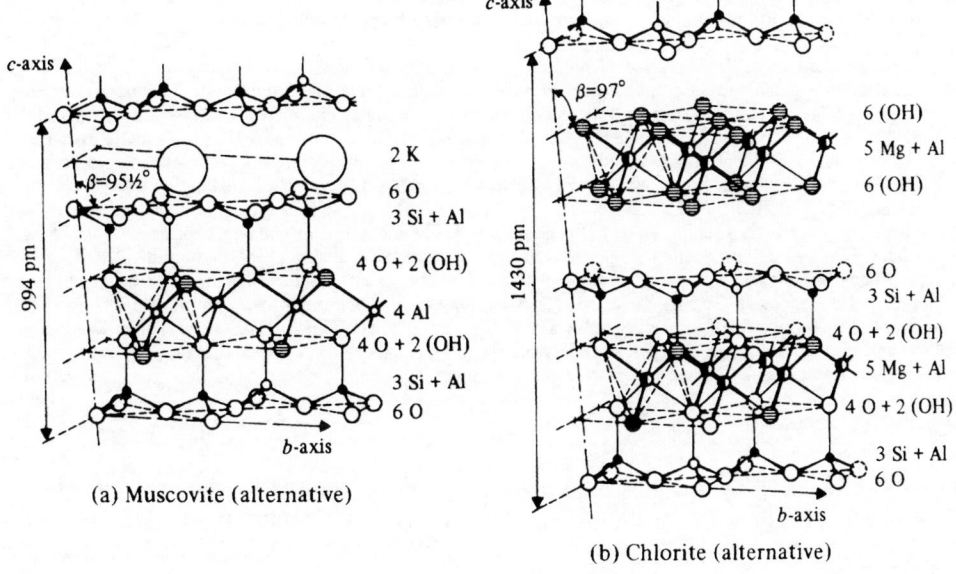

Figure 9.13   Alternative representations of muscovite and chlorite (after B. Mason and L. G. Berry[43]).

Clay Minerals and Related Aluminosilicates[1,52]

Clays are an essential component of soils, to which we owe our survival, and they are also the raw materials for some of mankind's most ancient and essential artefacts: pottery, bricks, tiles, etc. Clays are formed by the weathering and decomposition of igneous rocks and occur typically as very fine particles: e.g. kaolinite is formed as hexagonal plates of edge ~0.1–3 μm by the weathering of alkaline feldspar:

$$2[KAlSi_3O_8] + CO_2 + H_2O \xrightarrow{\text{idealized}} [Al_2(OH)_4Si_2O_5] + 4SiO_2 + K_2CO_3$$

When mixed with water, clays become soft, plastic and mouldable; the water of plasticity can be removed at ~100° and the clay then becomes rigid and brittle. Further heating (~500°) removes structural water of crystallization and results in the oxidation of any carbonaceous material or Fe^{II} (600–900°). Above about 950° mullite ($Al_6Si_2O_{13}$) begins to form and glassy phases appear. Common clay is mined on a huge scale (28 million tonnes in USA alone in 1991) and is used principally in the manufacture of bricks (12 Mt), portland cement (10 Mt) and concrete (2.4 Mt), as well as for paper filling and coating (3.7 Mt).

China clay or kaolin, which is predominantly kaolinite, is particularly valuable because it is essentially free from iron impurities (and therefore colourless). World production in 1991 was 24.7 Mt (USA 39%, UK 13%, Colombia, Korea and USSR ~7% each). In the USA over half of this vast tonnage is used for paper filling or paper coating and only 130 000 tonnes was used for china, crockery, and earthenware, which is now usually made from ball clay, a particularly fine-grained, highly plastic material which is predominantly kaolinite together with clay-mica and quartz. Some 800 000 tonnes of ball clay is used annually in the USA for white ware, table ware, wall and floor tiles, sanitary ware, and electrical porcelain.

Fuller's earth is a montmorillonite in which the principal exchangeable cation is calcium. It has a high absorbance and adsorptive capacity, and pronounced cation exchange properties which enable it to be converted to sodium-montmorillonite (bentonite). Nomenclature is confusing and, in American usage, the fibrous hydrated magnesium aluminosilicate attapulgite is also called fuller's earth. World production (1991) was 4.0 million tonnes (USA 68%, Germany 19%, UK 5%). Of the 2.74 Mt produced in the USA, two-thirds was used for what government statisticians coyly call "pet absorbant" and about one-eighth was for oil and grease absorbance.

Bentonite (sodium-montmorillonite) is extensively used as a drilling mud, but this apparently mundane application is based on the astonishing thixotropic properties of its aqueous suspensions. Thus, replacement of Ca by Na in the montmorillonite greatly enhances its ability to swell in one dimension by the reversible uptake of water; this effectively cleaves the clay particles causing a separation of the lamellar units to give a suspension of very finely divided, exceedingly thin plates. These plate-like particles have negative charges on the surface and positive charges on the edges and, even in a suspension of quite low solid content, the particles orient themselves negative to positive to give a jelly-like mass or gel; on agitation, however, the weak electrical bonds are broken and the dispersion becomes a fluid whose viscosity diminishes with the extent of agitation. This indefinitely reversible property is called thixotropy and is widely used in civil engineering applications, in oil-well drilling, and in non-drip paints. The plasticity of bentonite is also used in mortars, putties, and adhesives, in the pelletizing of iron ore and in foundry sands. World production was 9.3 Mt in 1991 (USA 37%, USSR 26% Greece 11%).

Micas occur as a late crystallization phase in igneous rocks. Usually the crystals are 1–5 mm on edge but in pegmatites (p. 108) they may considerably exceed this to give the valuable block mica. Uses of muscovite mica depend on its perfect basal cleavage, toughness, elasticity, transparency, high dielectric strength, chemical inertness and thermal stability to 500°. Phlogopite (Mg-mica) is less used except when stability to 850–1000° is required. Sheet mica is used for furnace windows, for electrical insulation (condensers, heating elements, etc.) and in vacuum tubes. Ground mica is used as a filler for rubber, plastics and insulating board, for silver glitter paints, etc. World production (excluding China) was ~240 000 tonnes in 1974 (USA 53%, India 20%, USSR 17%).

Talc, unlike the micas, consists of electrically neutral layers without the interleaving cations. It is valued for its softness, smoothness and dry lubricating properties, and for its whiteness, chemical inertness and foliated structure. Its most important applications are in ceramics, insecticides, paints and paper manufacture. The more familiar use in cosmetics and toilet preparations accounts for only 3% of world production which is about 5 Mt per annum. Half of this comes from Japan and the USA, and other major producers are Korea, the former Soviet Union, France and China. Talc and its more massive mineral form soapstone or steatite are widely distributed throughout the world and many countries produce it for domestic consumption either by open-cast or underground mining.

atoms have been replaced by Al, thus requiring the addition of further cations for charge-balance.

52 *Minerals Yearbook Vol. 1, 1991*, US Dept of the Interior, Bureau of Mines, Washington DC, pp. 403–45 (1991).

Most feldspars can be classified chemically as members of the ternary system $NaAlSi_3O_8$–$KAlSi_3O_8$–$CaAl_2Si_2O_8$. This is illustrated in Fig. 9.14, which also indicates the names of the mineral phases. Particularly notable

Table 9.10　Summary of layer silicate structures (idealized formulae)[44]

Dioctahedral (with gibbsite-type layers)	Trioctahedral (with brucite-type layers)
Two-layer structures	
Kaolinite, nacrite, dickite $[Al_4(OH)_8(Si_4O_{10})]$	Antigorite (platy serpentine) $[Mg_6(OH)_8(Si_4O_{10})]$
Halloysite $[Al_4(OH)_8(Si_4O_{10})]$	Chrysotile (fibrous serpentine) $[Mg_6(OH)_8(Si_4O_{10})]$
Three-layer structures	
Pyrophyllite $[Al_2(OH)_2(Si_4O_{10})]$	Talc $[Mg_3(OH)_2(Si_4O_{10})]$
Montmorillonite $[Al_2(OH)_2(Si_4O_{10})].xH_2O$[a]	Vermiculite $[Mg_3(OH)_2(Si_4O_{10})].xH_2O$[b]
Muscovite (mica) $[KAl_2(OH)_2(AlSi_3O_{10})]$	Phlogopite (mica) $[KMg_3(OH)_2(AlSi_3O_{10})]$
Margarite (brittle mica) $[CaAl_2(OH)_2(Al_2Si_2O_{10})]$	Clintonite $[CaMg_3(OH)_2(Al_2Si_2O_{10})]$
	Chlorite $[Mg_5Al(OH)_8(AlSi_3O_{10})]$[c]

[a] With partial replacement of octahedral Al by Mg and with adsorbed cations.

[b] With partial replacement of octahedral Mg by Al and with adsorbed cations.

[c] That is, regularly alternating talc-like and brucite-like sheets.

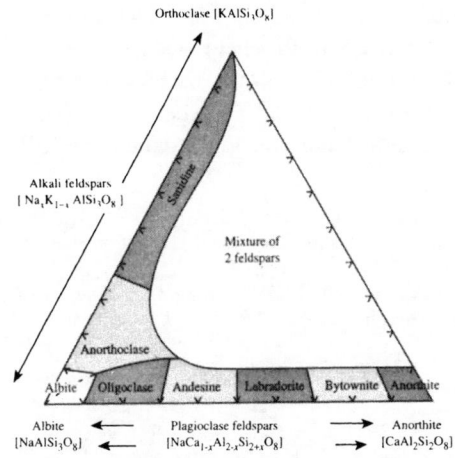

Figure 9.14　Ternary phase diagram for feldspars. The precise positions of the various phase boundaries depend on the temperature of formation.

is the continuous plagioclase series in which Na^I (102 pm) is replaced by Ca^{II} (100 pm) on octahedral sites, the charge-balance being maintained by a simultaneous substitution of Al^{III} for Si^{IV} on the tetrahedral sites. K^I (138 pm)

is too disparate in size to substitute for Ca^{II} and 2-phase mixtures result, though orthoclase does form a continuous series of solid solutions with the Ba feldspar celsian $[BaAl_2Si_2O_8]$ (Ba^{II} 136 pm). Likewise, most of the alkaline feldspars are not homogeneous but tend to contain separate K-rich and Na-rich phases unless they have crystallized rapidly from solid solutions at high temperatures (above $\sim 600°$). Feldspars have tightly constructed aluminosilicate frameworks that generate large interstices in which the large M^I or M^{II} are accommodated in irregular coordination.[43] Smaller cations, which are common in the chain and sheet silicates (e.g. Li^I, Mg^{II}, Fe^{III}), do not occur as major constituents in feldspars presumably because they are unable to fill the interstices adequately.

Pressure is another important variable in the formation of feldspars and at sufficiently high pressures there is a tendency for Al to increase its coordination number from 4 to 6 with consequent destruction of the feldspar lattice.† For example:

---

† In some compounds of course, octahedrally coordinated Al is stable at normal atmospheric pressure, e.g. in Al_2O_3,

$$NaAl_tSi_3O_8 \xrightarrow{\text{pressure}} NaAl_oSi_2O_6 + SiO_2$$
albite (feldspar)   jadeite (clinopyroxene) quartz

$$NaAl_tSi_3O_8 + NaAl_tSiO_4 \xrightarrow{\text{pressure}} 2NaAl_oSi_2O_6$$
albite   nepheline   jadeite

$$3Ca(Al_t)_2Si_2O_8 \xrightarrow{\text{pressure}} Ca_3(Al_o)_2(SiO_4)_3$$
anorthite (feldspar)   grossular (Ca garnet)

$$+ 2(Al_o)_2SiO_5 + SiO_2$$
kyanite   quartz

$$Ca(Al_t)_2Si_2O_8 + Ca_2(Al_t)_2SiO_7 + 3CaSiO_3$$
anorthite   gehlenite   wollastonite

$$\xrightarrow{\text{pressure}} 2Ca_3(Al_o)_2(SiO_4)_3$$
grossular

Such reactions marking the disappearance of plagioclase feldspars may be responsible for the Mohorovicic discontinuity between the earth's crust and mantle: this implies that the crust and mantle are isocompositional, the crustal rocks above having phases characteristic of gabbro rock (olivine, pyroxene, plagioclase) whilst the mantle rocks below are an eclogite-containing garnet, Al-rich pyroxene and quartz. Not all geochemists agree, however.

Zeolites have much more open aluminosilicate frameworks than feldspars and this enables them to take up loosely bound water or other small molecules in their structure. Indeed, the name zeolite was coined by the mineralogist

A. F. Cronstedt in 1756 (ζειν *zein*, to boil; λιθος *lithos*, stone) because the mineral appeared to boil when heated in the blow-pipe flame. Zeolite structures are characterized by the presence of tunnels or systems of interconnected cavities; these can be linked either in one direction giving fibrous crystals, or more usually in two or three directions to give lamellar and 3D structures respectively. Figure 9.15a shows the construction of a single cavity from 24 linked {SiO_4} tetrahedra and Fig. 9.15b shows how this can be conventionally represented by a truncated cubo-octahedron formed by joining the Si atom positions. Several other types of polyhedron have also been observed. These are then linked in three dimensions to build the aluminosilicate framework. A typical structure is shown in Fig. 9.15c for the synthetic zeolite "Linde A" which has the formula $[Na_{12}(Al_{12}Si_{12}O_{48})].27H_2O$.[53] Other cavity frameworks are found in other zeolites such as faujasite, which has the idealized formula $[NaCa_{0.5}(Al_2Si_5O_{14})].10H_2O$, and chabazite $[Ca(Al_2Si_4)O_{12}].6H_2O$. There is great current interest in this field since it offers scope for the reproducible synthesis of structures having cavities, tunnels and pores of precisely defined dimensions on the atomic scale.[54] By

Al(OH)_3, and spinels such as MgAl_2O_4. Much higher pressures still are required to transform 4-coordinated Si to 6-coordinated (p. 343).

[53] J. M. THOMAS, L. A. BURSILL, E. A. LODGE, A. K. CHEETHAM and C. A. FYFE, *J. Chem. Soc., Chem. Commun.*, 276–7 (1981).
[54] G. GOTTARD and E. GALLI, *Natural Zeolites*, Springer-Verlag, Berlin, 1985, 400 pp. P. A. JACOBS and

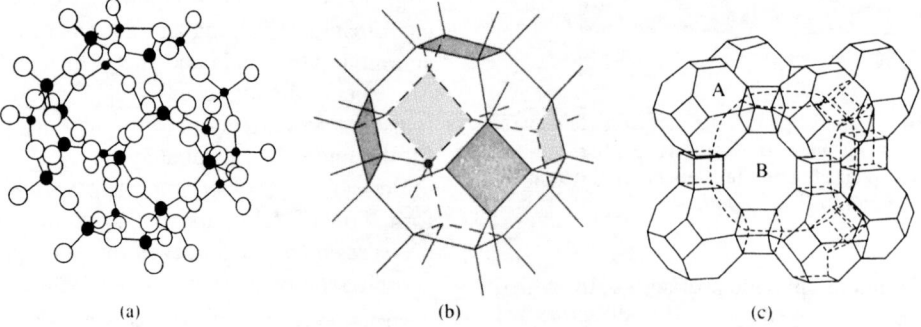

(a)   (b)   (c)

Figure 9.15   (a) 24 {SiO_4} tetrahedra linked by corner sharing to form a framework surrounding a truncated cubo-octahedral cavity; (b) conventional representation of the polyhedron in (a); and (c) space-filling arrangement of the polyhedra A which also generates larger cavities B.

appropriate design such molecular sieves can be used to selectively remove water or other small molecules, to separate normal from branched-chain paraffins, to generate highly dispersed metal catalysts, and to promote specific size-dependent chemical reactions.[55] Zeolites are made commercially by crystallizing aqueous gels of mixed alkaline silicates and aluminates at 60–100°. Zeolite-A is being increasingly used as a detergent builder to replace sodium tripolyphosphate (p. 528).

The final group of framework aluminosilicates are the ultramarines which have alternate Si and Al atoms at the corners of the polyhedra shown in Fig. 9.15a and b and, in addition, contain substantial concentrations of anions such as Cl^-, SO_4^{2-} or S_2^{2-}. These minerals tend to be anhydrous, like the feldspars, and in contrast to the even more open zeolites. Examples are sodalite $[Na_8Cl_2(Al_6Si_6O_{24})]$, noselite $[Na_8(SO_4)(Al_6Si_6O_{24})]$ and ultramarine $[Na_8(S_2)(Al_6Si_6O_{24})]$. Sodalite is colourless if the supernumerary anions are all chloride, but partial replacement by sulfide gives the brilliant blue mineral lapiz lazuli. Further replacement gives ultramarine which is now manufactured synthetically as an important blue pigment for oil-based paints and porcelain, and as a "blueing" agent to mask yellow tints in domestic washing,

paper making, starch, etc.[†] The colour is due to the presence of the sulfur radical anions S_2^- and S_3^- and shifts from green to blue as the ratio S_3^-/S_2^- increases; in ultramarine red the predominant species may be the neutral S_4 molecule though S_3^- and S_2^- are also present.[56]

9.3.6 Other inorganic compounds of silicon

This section briefly considers compounds in which Si is bonded to elements other than hydrogen, the halogens or oxygen, especially compounds in which Si is bonded to S, N or P. Silicon burns in S vapour at 100° to give SiS_2 which can be sublimed in a stream of N_2 to give long, white, flexible, asbestos-like fibres, mp 1090°, sublimation 1250°C. The structure consists of infinite chains of edge-shared tetrahedra (like W-silica, p. 343) and these transform at high temperature and pressure to a (corner-shared) cristobalite modification. The structural complexity of SiO_2 is not repeated, however. SiS_2 hydrolyses rapidly to SiO_2 and H_2S and is completely ammonolysed by liquid NH_3 to the imide

$$SiS_2 + 4NH_3 \longrightarrow Si(NH)_2 + 2NH_4SH$$

Sulfides of Na, Mg, Al and Fe convert SiS_2 into metal thiosilicates, and ethanol yields "ethylsilicate" $Si(OEt)_4$ and H_2S.[‡] Volatile

J. A. MARTENS, *Synthesis of High-Silica Aluminosilicate Zeolites*, Elsevier, Amsterdam, 1987, 390 pp. M. L. OCCELLI and H. E. ROBSON (eds.), *Zeolite Synthesis*, ACS Symposium Series No. 398, 1989, 664 pp. J. KLINOWSKI and P. J. BARRIE (eds.) *Recent Advances in Zeolite Science*, Elsevier, Amsterdam, 1990, 310 pp. G. V. TSITSISHVILI, T. G. ANDRONIKASHVILI, G. M. KIROV and L. D. FILIZOVA, *Natural Zeolites*, Ellis Horwood, Chichester, 1990, 274 pp.

55 D. W. BRECK, *Zeolite Molecular Sieves (Structure, Chemistry, and Uses)*, Wiley, New York, 1974, 771 pp. K. SEFF, *Acc. Chem. Res.* **9**, 121–8 (1976). R. M. BARRER, *Zeolites and Clay Minerals as Sorbents and Molecular Sieves*, Academic Press, London, 1978, 496 pp. W. HÖLDERICH, M. HESSE and F. NÄUMANN, *Angew. Chem. Int. Edn. Engl.* **27**, 226–46 (1988). G. A. OZIN, A. KUPEMAN and A. STEIN, *Angew. Chem. Int. Edn. Engl.* **28**, 359–76 (1989). See also K. B. YOON and J. K. KOCHI, *J. Chem. Soc., Chem. Commun.*, 510–11 (1988) for the novel synthesis of ionic clusters $[Na_4{}^{3+}]$, and P. A. ANDERSON, R. J. SINGER and P. P. EDWARDS, *J. Chem. Soc., Chem. Commun.*, 914–5 (1991) for the synthesis of $[Na_5{}^{4+}]$, $[Na_6{}^{5+}]$ and $[K_3{}^{2+}]$ by reaction of alkali metal vapours with zeolites.

[†] According to H. Remy the artificial production of ultramarine was first suggested by J. W. von Goethe in his *Italian Journey* (1786–8); it was first accomplished by L. Gmelin in 1828 and developed industrially by the Meissen porcelain works in the following year. It can be made by firing kaolin and sulfur with sodium carbonate; various treatments yield greens, reds and violets, as well as the deep blue, the colours being reminiscent of the highly coloured species obtained in nonaqueous solutions of S, Se and Te (pp. 664, 759).

56 R. J. H. CLARK and D. G. COBBOLD, *Inorg. Chem.* **17**, 3169–74 (1978).

[‡] $Si(OEt)_4$ is an important industrial chemical that is made on the kilotonne scale by the action of EtOH on $SiCl_4$. It has mp −77°, bp 168.5°, and d_{20} 0.9346 g cm^{-3}. Almost all uses depend on its controlled hydrolysis to produce silica in an adhesive or film-producing form. It is also a source of

thiohalides have been reported from the reaction of SiX_4 with H_2S at red heat; e.g. $SiCl_4$ yields $S(SiCl_3)_2$, cyclic $Cl_2Si(\mu\text{-}S)_2SiCl_2$ and crystalline $(SiSCl_2)_4$. The first normal thiocyanate derivative of Si, $RMe_2Si\text{-}SCN$, [R = $-C(SiMe_3)_2\{SiMe_2(OMe)\}$] was prepared from the corresponding chloride by treatment with AgSCN; it is more readily solvolysed than its isothiocyanate isomer, $RMe_2Si\text{-}NCS$.[57]

The elusive $Si=S$ grouping has been synthesized by reaction between solid Si and H_2S at $1200°C$ to give monomeric SiS; this high-temperature molecule can itself be reacted with Cl_2 or HCl in an argon matrix to yield monomeric $S=SiCl_2$ and $S=SiHCl$.[58] Synthesis of stable organosilanethiones, $RR'Si=S$ has been achieved by using the strategem of imparting additional stabilization through intramolecular coordination via an amine function; e.g. [(α-naphthyl)(8-Me$_2$NCH$_2$C$_{10}$H$_8$)Si=S] was prepared by heating the corresponding silane $RR'SiH_2$ with S_8; the $Si=S$ distance of 201.3 pm was noticeably shorter than the normal single bond $Si\text{-}S$ distance of 216 pm.[59]

The most important nitride of Si is Si_3N_4; this is formed by direct reaction of the elements above $1300°$ or more economically by heating SiO_2 and coke in a stream of N_2/H_2 at $1500°$. The compound is of considerable interest as an engineering material since it is almost completely inert chemically, and retains its strength, shape and resistance to corrosion and wear even above $1000°$.[60] Its great hardness (Mohs 9), high

dissociation temperature ($1900°$, 1 atm) and high density ($3.185\,g\,cm^{-3}$) can all be related to its compact structure which resembles that of phenacite (Be_2SiO_4, p. 347). It is an insulator with a resistivity at room temperature $\sim 6.6 \times 10^{10}\,ohm\,cm$. Another refractory, Si_2N_2O, is formed when $Si + SiO_2$ are heated to $1450°$ in a stream of Ar containing 5% N_2. The structure comprises puckered hexagonal nets of alternating Si and N atoms interlinked by nonlinear $Si\text{-}O\text{-}Si$ bonds to similar nets on either side; the Si atoms are thus each 4-coordinate and the N atoms 3-coordinate.

Volatile silylamides are readily prepared by reacting a silyl halide with NH_3, RNH_2 or R_2NH in the vapour phase or in Et_2O, e.g.:

$$3SiH_3Cl + 4NH_3 \longrightarrow N(SiH_3)_3 + 3NH_4Cl$$

$$SiH_3Br + 2Me_2NH \longrightarrow SiH_3NMe_2 + Me_2NH_2Br$$

$$4SiH_3I + 5N_2H_4 \longrightarrow (SiH_3)_2NN(SiH_3)_2 + 4N_2H_5I$$

Silicon-substituted derivatives may require the use of lithio or sodio reagents, e.g.:

$$Me_3SiCl + NaN(SiMe_3)_2 \longrightarrow N(SiMe_3) + NaCl$$

$$Ph_3SiLi + R_2NH \longrightarrow Ph_3SiNR_2 + LiH$$

The N atom is always tertiary in these compounds and no species containing the SiH–NH group is stable at room temperature. Apart from this restriction, innumerable such compounds have been prepared including cyclic and polymeric analogues, e.g. [cyclo-{Me$_2$SiN(SiMe$_3$)$_2$}] and [cyclo-(Me$_2$SiNH)$_4$]. Interest has focused on the stereochemistry of the N atom which is often planar, or nearly so.[61] Thus N(SiH$_3$)$_3$ features a planar N atom and this has been ascribed to p_π-d_π interaction between the "nonbonding" pair of electrons on N and the "vacant" d_π orbitals on Si as shown schematically in Fig. 9.16. Consistent with this trisilamines are notably weaker ligands than their tertiary amine analogues though replacement of one or two SiH$_3$ by CH$_3$ enhances the donor power again; e.g. N(SiH$_3$)$_3$ forms no adduct with BH$_3$ even at low temperature;

---

metal-free silica for use in phosphors in fluorescent lamps and TV tubes. In partly hydrolysed form it is used as a paint vehicle, a protective coating for porous stone, and as a vehicle for zinc-containing galvanic corrosion-preventing coatings. Many other orthoesters $Si(OR)_4$ are known but none are commercially important.

[57] C. EABORN and M. N. ROMANELLI, *J. Chem. Soc., Chem. Commun.*, 1616–7 (1984).

[58] H. SCHNÖCKEL, H. J. GÖCKE and R. KÖPPE, *Z. anorg. allg. Chem.* **578**, 159–65 (1989). R. KÖPPE and H. SCHNÖCKEL, *Z. anorg. allg. Chem.* **607**, 41–4 (1992).

[59] P. ARYA, J. BOYER, F. CARRÉ, R. CORRIU, G. LANNEAU, J. LAPASSET, M. PERROT and C. PRIOU, *Angew. Chem. Int. Edn. Engl.* **28**, 1016–7 (1989).

[60] *Silicon Nitride and the SIALONS* World Business Publications Ltd., (two vols.), 1989, 285 pp.

---

[61] E. A. V. EBSWORTH, *Volatile Silicon Compounds*, Pergamon Press, Oxford, 1963, 179 pp.

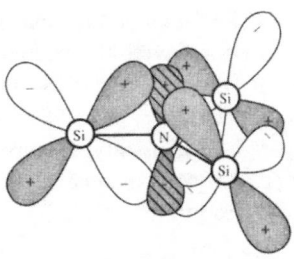

Figure 9.16 Symmetry relation between p_π orbital on N and d_π orbitals on the 3 Si atoms in planar {NSi$_3$} compounds such as N(SiH$_3$)$_3$.

MeN(SiH$_3$)$_2$ forms a 1:1 adduct with BH$_3$ at $-80°$ but this decomposes when warmed; Me$_2$N(SiH$_3$) gives a similar adduct which decomposes at room temperature into Me$_2$NBH$_2$ and SiH$_4$ (cf. the stability of Me$_3$NBH$_3$, p. 165). The linear skeleton of H$_3$SiNCO and H$_3$SiNCS has also been interpreted in terms of p_π–d_π N $\rightleftharpoons$ Si bonding.

Compounds containing an Si=N double bond are of very recent provenance. The first stable silanimine, Bu$'_2$Si=N–SiBu$'_3$, was prepared in 1986 as pale yellow crystals, mp 85° (decomp.);[62] it features a short Si=N distance (156.8 pm, cf. Si–N 169.5 pm) and almost linear coordination about the N atom (177.8°), suggesting some electronic delocalization as described above. The compound was made by reacting the azidosilane Bu$'_2$SiCl(N$_3$) with NaSiBu$'_3$ in Bu$_2$O at $-78°$. The related compound Pr$^i_2$Si=NR (R = 2,4,6-Bu$'_3$C$_6$H$_2{}^-$) forms stable orange crystals, mp 98°.[63]

Unusual Si/P compounds are also beginning to appear, for example, the tetrasilahexaphospha-adamantane derivative [(Pr^{i}Si)$_4$(PH)$_6$] (1), which is made by reacting Pr^{i}SiCl$_3$ with Li[Al(PH$_2$)$_4$].[64] Again, reaction of white phosphorus, P$_4$, with tetramesityldisilene, Mes$_2$Si=SiMes$_2$, in toluene

at 40° gives an 87% yield of the yellow bicyclo (Mes$_2$Si)$_2$P$_2$: this has a "butterfly" structure in which the "hinge" P atoms retain electron donor properties to give adducts such as the bis-W(CO)$_5$ complex (2) (P–P 234.2 pm; Si–P 224.4, 226.7 pm; P–W 256.0 pm; Si $\cdots$ Si 324.4 pm; angle Si–P–Si 91.9°).[65] The now extensive field of phosphorus-rich silaphosphanes has been reviewed.[66] Silaphosphenes, RR′Si=PAr are also known.[67]

(1)   (2)

9.3.7 Organosilicon compounds and silicones

Well over 100 000 organosilicon compounds have been synthesized. Of these, during the past few decades, silicone oils, elastomers and resins have become major industrial products. Many organosilicon compounds have considerable thermal stability and chemical inertness; e.g. SiPh$_4$ can be distilled in air at its bp 428°, as can Ph$_3$SiCl (bp 378°) and Ph$_2$SiCl$_2$ (bp 305°). These, and innumerable similar compounds, reflect the considerable strength of the Si–C bond which is, indeed, comparable with that of the C–C bond (p. 338). A further illustration is the compound SiC which closely resembles diamond in its properties (p. 334). Catenation and the formation of multiple bonds are further similarities with carbon chemistry, though these features are less prominent in organosilicon chemistry and much of the work in these areas is of recent

[62] N. WIBERG, K. SCHURZ, G. REBER and G. MÜLLER, *J. Chem. Soc., Chem. Commun.*, 591–2 (1986).

[63] M. HESSE and U. KLINGEBIEL, *Angew. Chem. Int. Edn. Engl.* **25**, 649–50 (1986).

[64] M. BAUDLER, W. OELERT and K.-F. TEBBE, *Z. anorg. allg. Chem.* **598/599**, 9–23 (1991).

[65] M. DRIESS, A. D. FANTA, D. R. POWELL and R. WEST, *Angew. Chem. Int. Edn. Engl.* **28**, 1038–40 (1989).

[66] G. FRITZ *Advances in Inorg. Chem.* **31**, 171–214 (1987).

[67] N. C. NORMAN, *Polyhedron* **12**, 2431–46 (1993) and references cited therein. M. DRIESS, *Adv. Organomet. Chem.* **39**, 193–229 (1996) — also deals with sila-arsenes containing Si=As bonds).

origin (e.g. pp. 338 and below). For example, although the word "silicone" was coined by F. S. Kipping in 1901 to indicate the similarity in *formula* of Ph$_2$SiO with that of the ketone benzophenone, Ph$_2$CO, he stressed that there was no chemical resemblance between them and that Ph$_2$SiO was polymeric.[68] It is now recognized that the great thermal and chemical stability of the silicones derives from the strength both of the Si–C bonds and of the Si–O–Si linkages. Many general reviews of the vast subject of organosilicon chemistry are available (e.g. refs 1, 2, 69–74) and only some of the salient or topical features will be touched on here. An interesting subset comprises the carbosilanes, that is compounds with a skeleton of alternating C and Si atoms.[75] These include chains, rings and polycyclic compounds, many of which can be made on a multigram or even larger scale by controlled thermolysis or by standard organometallic syntheses.

Transient reaction species containing Si=C bonds have been known since about 1966 and can be generated thermally, photolytically, or even chemically. A decade later Me$_2$Si=CHMe

was isolated in low-temperature matrices[76] but, despite concerted and well-planned attempts over many years, it was not until 1981 that a stable silene was reported.[77] A. G. Brook and his group prepared 2-adamantyl-2-trimethylsiloxy-1,1-bis(trimethylsilyl)-1-silaethene as very pale yellow needles, mp 92°:

$$(\text{Me}_3\text{Si})_3\text{SiC(O)(C}_{10}\text{H}_{15}) \overset{\text{ether}/h\nu}{\rightleftharpoons}$$

$$(\text{Me}_3\text{Si})_2\text{Si} = \text{C(OSiMe}_3)(\text{adamantyl})$$

The solid silaethene was stable indefinitely at room temperature in the absence of air or other reagents but in solution it slowly reverted (over several days) to the isomeric acylsilane starting material. An X-ray analysis confirmed the structure and revealed a short >Si=C< bond (176.4 pm, cf. 187–191 pm for single-bonded Si–C) and a planar disposition of *ipso* atoms, the two planes being slightly twisted with respect to each other (14.6°). The use of bulky groups to enhance the stability of the silaethene is also notable, though this is not a necessary feature, at least at the Si centre, since Me$_2$Si=C(SiMe$_3$)(SiMeBu$^t_2$) is stable as colourless crystals at room temperature (>Si=C< distance 170.2 pm, Si–C 189.0 pm and a planar C$_2$Si=CSi$_2$ skeleton).[78] The not unrelated planar heterocyclic compounds silabenzene, C$_5$SiH$_6$,[15] and silatoluene, C$_5$H$_5$SiMe,[16] should also be recalled.

Disilenes, containing the grouping >Si=Si<, can be isolated as thermally stable yellow or orange crystalline compounds provided that the substituents are sufficiently large to prevent

[68] F. S. KIPPING and L. L. LLOYD, *J. Chem. Soc. (Transactions)* **79**, 449–59 (1901).

[69] G. WILKINSON, F. G. A. STONE and E. W. ABEL (eds.), *Comprehensive Organometallic Chemistry*, Pergamon Press, Oxford, Vol. 2 (1982): D. A. ARMATAGE, Organosilanes, pp. 1–203; T. J. BARTON, Carbocyclic Silanes, pp. 205–303; F. O. STARK, J. R. FALENDER and A. P. WRIGHT, Silicones, pp. 305–63; R. WEST, Organopolysilanes, pp. 365–97.

[70] S. PAWLENKO, *Organosilicon Chemistry*, de Gruyter, Berlin, 1986, 186 pp.

[71] J. Y. COREY, E. J. COREY and P. P. GASPER (eds.), *Silicon Chemistry*, Ellis Horwood, Chichester, 1988, 565 pp.

[72] M. ZELDIN, K. J. WYNNE and H. R. ALCOCK (eds.), *Inorganic and Organometallic Polymers*, ACS Symposium Series **360** (1988) 512 pp.

[73] S. PATAI and Z. RAPPOPORT (eds.), *The Chemistry of Organic Silicon Compounds* (2 vols.), Wiley, Chichester, 1989, 892 pp. and 1668 pp.

[74] N. AUNER, W. ZICHE and R. WEST, *Heteroatom Chemistry* **2**, 335–55 (1991). This is a very readable account of current work, and includes an update of ref. 73 with a further 222 references.

[75] G. FRITZ, *Angew. Chem. Int. Edn. Engl.* **26**, 1111–32 (1987).

[76] O. L. CHAPMAN, C.-C. CHANG, J. KOLE, M. E. JUNG, J. A. LOWE, T. J. BARTON and M. L. TUMEY, *J. Am. Chem. Soc.* **98**, 7844–6 (1976). M. R. CHEDEKEL, M. SKOGLUND, R. L. KREEGER and H. SHECHTER, *ibid.*, 7846–8 (1976).

[77] A. G. BROOK, F. ABDESAKEN, B. GUTERKUNST, G. GUTERKUNST and R. K. KALLURY, *J. Chem. Soc., Chem. Commun.*, 191–2 (1981). A. G. BROOK and 8 others, *J. Am. Chem. Soc.*, **104**, 5667–72 (1982). For the most recent review of the chemistry of silenes see A. G. BROOK and M. A. BROOK, *Adv. Organomet. Chem.*, **39**, 71–158 (1996).

[78] N. WIBERG, G. WAGNER and G. MÜLLER, *Angew. Chem. Int. Edn. Engl.* **24**, 229–31 (1985). See also N. WIBERG *et al.*, *Organometallics* **6**, 32–5 and 35–41 (1987).

polymerization (e.g. mesityl, *t*-butyl, etc.)[79] The first such compound, Si_2Mes_4, was isolated in 1981 as orange crystals, mp 176°, following photolysis of the trisilane $SiMes_2(SiMe_3)_2$.[80] The $Si=Si$ distance in several such compounds falls in the range 214–216 pm, which is about 10% shorter than the normal single-bonded $Si-Si$ distance. Disilenes are chemically very reactive. Halogens and HX molecules give 1,2-addition products, e.g. $Mes_2Si(Cl)Si(Cl)$-Mes_2, whilst aldehydes and ketones undergo [2 + 2] cyclo-addition reactions to give 1,2,3-oxadisilenanes, $\overline{OSi(Mes)_2Si(Mes)_2CHR}$. Controlled oxidation gives predominantly the 1,2-dioxetane $\overline{OSiR_2SiR_2O}$ (80%), plus the 1,3-cyclodisiloxane $\overline{OSiR_2OSiR_2}$ as a minor product. Numerous other novel heterocyles have been prepared by controlled reactions of disilenes with chalcogens, N_2O, P_4 and organic nitro-, nitroso-, azo- and azido-compounds.[81] Transition metal complexes can give η^2-disilene adducts such as $[Pt(PR_3)_2)(\eta^2$-$Si_2Mes_4)]$.[79,82]

Another fertile area of current interest is the synthesis of stable homocyclic polysilane derivatives.[83] Typical examples are cyclo-$(SiMe_2)_7$,[84] (cyclo-Si_5Me_9)-$(SiMe_2)_n$-(cyclo-Si_5Me_9), $n = 2$–5,[85] and several new permethylated polycyclic silanes such as the colourless crystalline compounds bicyclo[3.2.1]-Si_8Me_{14} (mp 245°), bicyclo[3.3.1]-Si_9Me_{16} (mp $\geq 330°$) and bicyclo[4.4.0]-$Si_{10}Me_{18}$ (mp 165°.[86] Analogues of cubane and tetrahedrane have also been synthesized. Thus, the one-step condensation of $Br_2RSiSiRBr_2$ or even $RSiBr_3$ with Na in toluene at 90° gave yields of up to 72% of the cubane $(SiR)_8$ ($R = SiMe_2Bu^t$) as bright yellow, air-sensitive crystals which are stable up to at least $400°C$.[87] The synthesis of a molecular tetrasila-tetrahedrane has also finally been achieved by the following ingenious route ($R = SiBu^t_3$):[88]

$$2SiH_2Cl_2 \xrightarrow{2NaR} 2RSiH_2Cl \xrightarrow{2Na} RSiH_2SiH_2R$$

$$\longrightarrow RSiBr_2SiBr_2R$$

$$2RSiBr_2SiBr_2R + 4NaR \longrightarrow$$

$$Si_4R_4 + 4RBr + 4NaBr$$

The product, $Si_4(SiBu^t_3)_4$, forms intensely orange crystals that are stable to heat, light, water and air, and do not melt below 350°. The $Si-Si$ distances within the *closo*-Si_4 cluster are 232–234 pm and the *exo* $Si-Si$ distances are slightly longer, 235–237 pm (cf. $Si-Si$ 235.17 in crystalline Si). Comparison with the *closo*-anion Si_4^{4-}, which occurs in several metal silicides (p. 337) and is isoelectronic with the P_4 molecule, is also appropriate.

There are three general methods for forming $Si-C$ bonds. The most convenient laboratory method for small-scale preparations is by the reaction of $SiCl_4$ with organolithium, Grignard or organoaluminium reagents. A second attractive route is the hydrosilylation of alkenes, i.e. the catalytic addition of $Si-H$ across $C=C$ double bonds; this is widely applicable except for the crucially important methyl and phenyl silanes. Industrially, organosilanes are made by the direct reaction of RX or ArX with a fluidized bed of Si in the presence of about 10% by weight of metallic Cu as catalyst (cf. the direct preparation of organo compounds of

[79] R. WEST, *Angew. Chem. Int. Edn. Engl.* **26** 1201–11 (1987). R. OKAZAKI and R. WEST, *Adv. Organomet. Chem.* **39**, 232–73 (1996).

[80] R. WEST, M. J. FINK and J. MICHL, *Science* **214**, 1343–4 (1981). See also B. D. SHEPHERD, C. F. CAMPANA and R. WEST, *Heteroatom Chemistry*, **1**, 1–7 (1990).

[81] R. WEST, in R. STEUDEL (ed.), *The Chemistry of Inorganic Ring Systems*, Elsevier, Amsterdam, 1992, pp. 35–50. See also M. WEIDENBRUCH, *ibid.*, pp. 51–74.

[82] C. ZYBILL, *Topics in Current Chemistry* **160**, 1–45 (1992).

[83] E. HENGGE and H. STÜGER, in H. W. ROESKY (ed.), *Rings, Clusters and Polymers of Main Group and Transition Metals*, Elsevier, Amsterdam, 1989, pp. 107–38.

[84] F. SHAFIEE, J. R. DAMEWOOD, K. J. HALLER and R. WEST, *J. Am. Chem. Soc.* **107**, 6950–6 (1985).

[85] E. HENGGE and P. K. JENKNER, *Z. anorg. allg. Chem.* **560**, 27–34 (1988).

[86] E. HENGGE and P. K. JENKNER, *Z. anorg. allg. Chem.* **606**, 97–104 (1991).

[87] H. MATSUMOTO, K. HIGUCHI, Y. HOSHINO, H. KOIKE, Y. NAOI and Y. NAGAI, *J. Chem. Soc., Chem. Commun.*, 1083–4 (1988).

[88] N. WIBERG, C. M. M. FINGER and K. POLBORN, *Angew. Chem. Int. Edn. Engl.* **32**, 1054–6 (1993).

Ge, Sn, and Pb, pp. 396ff). The method was patented by E. G. Rochow in 1945 and ensured the commercial viability of the now extensive silicone industry.[2,69,72]

$$2\text{MeCl} + \text{Si} \xrightarrow[\sim 300°]{\text{Cu powder}} \text{Me}_2\text{SiCl}_2 \quad (70\% \text{ yield})$$

By-products are MeSiCl_3 (12%) and Me_3SiCl (5%) together with 1–2% each of SiCl_4, SiMe_4, MeSiHCl_2, etc. Relative yields can readily be altered by modifying the reaction conditions or by adding HCl (which increases MeSiHCl_2 and drastically reduces Me_2SiCl_2). The overall reaction is exothermic and heat must be removed from the fluidized bed. Because of their very similar bps, careful fractionation is necessary if pure products are required: Me_3SiCl 57.7°, Me_2SiCl_2 69.6°, MeSiCl_3 66.4°. Mixtures of ethylchlorosilanes or phenylchlorosilanes (or their bromo analogues) can be made similarly. All these compounds are mobile, volatile liquids (except Ph_3SiCl, mp 89°, bp 378°).

Innumerable derivatives have been prepared by the standard techniques of organic chemistry.[2,69−75] The organosilanes tend to be much more reactive than their carbon analogues, particularly towards hydrolysis, ammonolysis, and alcoholysis. Further condensation to cyclic oligomers or linear polymers generally ensues, e.g.:

$$\text{Ph}_2\text{SiCl}_2 \xrightarrow{\text{H}_2\text{O}} \text{Ph}_2\text{Si(OH)}_2 \text{ white crystals} \\ \text{mp} \sim 132° \text{ (d)}$$

$$\xrightarrow{>100°} \tfrac{1}{n}(\text{Ph}_2\text{SiO})_n + \text{H}_2\text{O} \\ n = 3(\text{cyclo}),\ 4(\text{cyclo}),\ \text{or } \infty$$

$$\text{Me}_2\text{SiCl}_2 \xrightarrow{\text{NH}_3/-35°} \{\text{Me}_2\text{Si(NH}_2)_2\} \longrightarrow \\ \text{not isolated}$$

$$[\text{cyclo-(Me}_2\text{SiNH)}_3] + [\text{cyclo-(Me}_2\text{SiNH)}_4]$$

For both economic and technical reasons, commercial production of such polymers is almost entirely restricted to the methyl derivatives (and to a lesser extent the phenyl derivatives) and hydrolysis of the various methylchlorosilanes has, accordingly, been much studied. Hydrolysis of Me_3SiCl yields trimethylsilanol as a volatile liquid (bp 99°); it is noticeably more acidic than

the corresponding Bu^tOH and can be converted to its Na salt by aqueous NaOH (12M). Condensation gives hexamethyldisiloxane which has a very similar bp (100.8°):

$$2\text{Me}_3\text{SiCl} \xrightarrow[(-2\text{HCl})]{+2\text{H}_2\text{O}} 2\text{Me}_3\text{SiOH} \xrightarrow{-\text{H}_2\text{O}} [\text{O(SiMe}_3)_2]$$

Hydrolysis of Me_2SiCl_2 usually gives high polymers, but under carefully controlled conditions leads to cyclic dimethylsiloxanes $[(\text{Me}_2\text{SiO})_n]$ ($n = 3, 4, 5, 6$). Linear siloxanes have also been made by hydrolysing Me_2SiCl_2 in the presence of varying amounts of Me_3SiCl as a "chain-stopping" group, i.e. $[\text{Me}_3\text{SiO(Me}_2\text{SiO})_x\text{SiMe}_3]$ ($x = 0, 1, 2, 3, 4$), etc. Cross-linking is achieved by hydrolysis and condensation in the presence of MeSiCl_3 since this generates a third Si–O function in addition to the two required for polymerization:

$$\text{Me}_3\text{SiCl} \xrightarrow{\text{H}_2\text{O}} \text{Me}_3\text{Si–O–} \quad \text{terminal group}$$

$$\text{Me}_2\text{SiCl}_2 \xrightarrow{\text{H}_2\text{O}} \text{–O–SiMe}_2\text{–O–}$$

chain-forming group

$$\text{MeSiCl}_3 \xrightarrow{\text{H}_2\text{O}} \text{MeSi(–O–)}_3$$

branching and bridging group

Comparison with the mineral silicates is instructive since there is a 1:1 correspondence between the two sets of compounds, the methyl groups in the silicones being replaced by the formally isoelectronic O^- in the silicates (see p. 366). This reminds us of the essentially covalent nature of the Si–O–Si linkage, but the analogy should not be taken to imply identity of structures in detail, particularly for the more highly condensed polymers. Some aspects of the technology of silicones are summarized in the concluding Panel.

While siloxanes and silicones are generally regarded as being unreactive, it is well to remember that they do indeed react with fluorinating agents and with concentrated hydroxide solutions. In certain cases they can even be employed as mild selective reagents for specific syntheses. For example, $(\text{Me}_3\text{Si})_2\text{O}$ is a useful reagent for the convenient high-yield

Silicone Polymers[1,2]

Silicones have good thermal and oxidative stability, valuable resistance to high and low temperatures, excellent water repellency, good dielectric properties, desirable antistick and antifoam properties, chemical inertness, prolonged resistance to ultraviolet irradiation and weathering, and complete physiological inertness. They can be made as fluids (oils), greases, emulsions, elastomers (rubbers) and resins.

Silicone oils are made by shaking suitable proportions of $[O(SiMe_3)_2]$ and $[cyclo-(Me_2SiO)_4]$ with a small quantity of 100% H_2SO_4; this randomizes the siloxane links by repeatedly cleaving the Si–O bonds to form HSO_4 esters and then reforming new Si–O bonds by hydrolysing the ester group:

$$\equiv Si\text{-}O\text{-}Si\equiv + H_2SO_4 \longrightarrow \equiv Si\text{-}O\text{-}SO_3H + \equiv Si\text{-}OH$$

$$\equiv Si\text{-}OH + HO_3S\text{-}O\text{-}Si\equiv \longrightarrow \equiv Si\text{-}O\text{-}Si\equiv + H_2SO_4$$

The molecular weight of the resulting polymer depends only on the initial proportion of the chain-ending groups (Me_3SiO- and Me_3Si-) and the chain-building groups ($-Me_2SiO-$) from the two components. Viscosity at room temperature is typically in the range 50–300 000 times that of water and it changes only slowly with temperature. These liquids are used as dielectric insulating media, hydraulic oils and compressible fluids for liquid springs. Pure methylsilicone oils are good lubricants at light loads but cannot be used for heavy-duty steel gears and shafts since they contain no polar film-forming groups and so are too readily exuded under high pressure. The introduction of some phenyl groups improves performance, and satisfactory greases can be made by thickening methyl phenyl silicone oil with Li soaps. Other uses are as heat transfer media in heating baths and as components in car polish, sun-tan lotion, lipstick and other cosmetic formulations. Their low surface tension leads to their extensive use as antifoams in textile dyeing, fermentation processes and sewage disposal: about 10^{-2} to 10^{-4}% is sufficient for these applications. Likewise their complete non-toxicity allows them to be used to prevent frothing in cooking oils, the processing of fruit juices and the production of potato crisps.

Silicone elastomers (rubbers) are reinforced linear dimethylpolysiloxanes of exceedingly high molecular weight (5×10^5–10^7). The reinforcing agent, without which the viscous gum is useless, is usually fumed silica (p. 345). Polymerization can be acid-catalysed but KOH produces a rubber with superior physical properties; in either case scrupulous care must be taken to avoid the presence of precursors of chain-blocking groups [$Me_3Si\text{-}O-$] or cross-linking groups [$MeSi(-O-)_3$]. The reinforced silicone rubber composition can be "vulcanized" by oxidative cross-linking using 1–3% of benzoyl peroxide or similar reagents; the mixture is heated to 150° for 10 min at the time of pressing or moulding and then cured for 1–10 h at 250°. Alternatively, and more elegantly, the process can be achieved at room temperature or slightly above by incorporating a small controlled concentration of Si–H groups which can be catalytically added across pre-introduced $Si\text{-}CH=CH_2$ groups in adjacent chains. Again, the cross-linking of 1-component silicone rubbers containing acetoxy groups can be readily effected at room temperature by exposure to moisture: Such rubbers generally have 1 cross-link for every 100–1000 Si atoms and are unmatched by any other synthetic or natural rubbers in retaining their inertness, flexibility, elasticity and strength up to 250° and down to −100°. They find use in cable-insulation sleeving, static and rotary seals, gaskets, belting, rollers, diaphragms, industrial sealants and adhesives, electrical tape insulation, plug-and-socket connectors, oxygen masks, medical tubing, space suits, fabrication of heart-valve implants, etc. They are also much used for making accurate moulds and to give rapid, accurate and flexible impressions for dentures and inlays.

Silicone resins are prepared by hydrolysing phenyl substituted dichloro- and trichloro-silanes in toluene. The Ph groups increase the heat stability, flexibility, and processability of the resins. The hydrolysed mixture is washed with water to remove HCl and then partly polymerized or "bodied" to a carefully controlled stage at which the resin is still soluble. It is in this form that the resins are normally applied, after which the final cross-linking to a 3D siloxane network is effected by heating to 200° in the presence of a heavy metal or quaternary ammonium catalyst to condense the silanol groups, e.g.:

$$3PhSiCl_3 + PhSiMeCl_2 \xrightarrow{H_2O/toluene} \left[HO-\underset{OH}{\underset{|}{\overset{Ph}{\overset{|}{Si}}}}-O-\underset{Me}{\underset{|}{\overset{Ph}{\overset{|}{Si}}}}-O-\underset{OH}{\underset{|}{\overset{Ph}{\overset{|}{Si}}}}-O-\underset{OH}{\underset{|}{\overset{Ph}{\overset{|}{Si}}}}-OH \right] \xrightarrow[\text{catalyst}]{200°} \text{[cross-linked resin]} \atop +nH_2O$$

a typical intermediate species

Silicone resins are used in the insulation of electrical equipment and machinery, and in electronics as laminates for printed circuit boards; they are also used for the encapsulation of components such as resistors and integrated circuits by means of transfer moulding. Non-electrical uses include high-temperature paints and the resinous release coatings familiar on domestic cooking ware and industrial tyre moulds. When one recalls the very small quantities of silicones needed in many of these individual applications, the global production figures are particularly impressive: they have grown from a few tonnes in the mid-1940s to over 100 000 tonnes in 1969 and an estimated production of 350 000 tonnes in 1982. About half of this is in the USA, distributed so that some 65–70% is as fluid silicones, 25–30% as elastomers, and 5–10% as resins. Over 1000 different silicone products are commercially available.

Orthosilicate

Tetramethylsilane

Disilicate

Hexamethyl-disiloxane

Pyroxenes

Polydimethyl-siloxane (silicone oil)

Cyclic metasilicates

Cyclic dimethylsiloxane

Amphiboles

Methylsil-sesquioxane ladder polymer

Infinite sheet silicates

Siloxenes

Framework silicates

Silicone resins

preparation of oxyhalide derivatives of Mo and W.[89] Thus, in CH_2Cl_2 solution, $(Me_3Si)_2O$ converts a suspension of WCl_6 quantitatively to red crystals of $W(O)Cl_4$ in less than 1 h at room temperature, and $W(O)Cl_4$ can then itself be converted to yellow $W(O)_2Cl_2$ in 95% yield (light petroleum, 100°, overnight). Likewise,

$Mo(O)Cl_4$ when treated with $(Me_3Si)_2O$ in CH_2Cl_2 gives $Mo(O)_2Cl_2$ in 97% yield at r.t. Even silicone high-vacuum grease has been found unexpectedly to react with the potassium salt of an organoindium hydride to give crystals of the pseudo-crown ether complex [cyclo-$(Me_2SiO)_7K^+](K^+)_3[HIn(CH_2CMe_3)_3^-]_4$.[90]

[89] V. C. Gibson, T. P. Kee and A. Shaw, *Polyhedron* **7**, 579–80 (1988).

[90] M. R. Churchill, C. H. Lake, S.-H. L. Chao and O. T. Beachley, *J. Chem. Soc., Chem. Commun.*, 1577–8 (1993).

10

Germanium, Tin and Lead

10.1 Introduction

Germanium was predicted as the missing element of a triad between silicon and tin by J. A. R. Newlands in 1864, and in 1871 D. I. Mendeleev specified the properties that "ekasilicon" would have (p. 29). The new element was discovered by C. A. Winkler in 1886 during the analysis of a new and rare mineral argyrodite, Ag_8GeS_6;[1] he named it in honour of his country, Germany.[†] By contrast, tin and lead are two of the oldest metals known

to man and both are mentioned in early books of the Old Testament. The chemical symbols for the elements come from their Latin names *stannum* and *plumbum*. Lead was used in ancient Egypt for glazing pottery (7000–5000 BC); the Hanging Gardens of Babylon were floored with sheet lead to retain moisture and the Romans used lead extensively for water-pipes and plumbing; they extracted some 6–8 million tonnes in four centuries with a peak annual production of 60 000 tonnes. Production of tin, though equally influential, has been on a more modest scale and dates back to 3500–3200 BC. Bronze weapons and tools containing 10–15% Sn alloyed with Cu have been found at Ur, and Pliny described solder as an alloy of Sn and Pb in AD 79.

Germanium and Sn are non-toxic (like C and Si). Lead is now recognized as a heavy-metal poison;[2] it acts by complexing with oxo-groups

---

[1] M. E. WEEKS, *Discovery of the Elements*, 6th edn., Journal of Chemical Education Publ. 1956, 910 pp. Germanium, pp. 683–93; Tin and lead, pp. 41–7.

[†] The astonishing correspondence between the predicted and observed properties of Ge (p. 29) has tempted later writers to overlook the fact that Winkler thought he had discovered a metalloid like As and Sb and he originally identified Ge with Mendeleev's (incorrectly) predicted "eka-stibium" between Sb and Bi; Mendeleev himself thought it was "eka-cadmium", which he had (again incorrectly) predicted as a missing element between Cd and Hg. H. T. von Richter thought it was "eka-silicon"; so did Lothar Meyer, and they proved to be correct. This illustrates the great difficulties encountered by chemists working only 100 y ago, yet three decades before the rationale which stemmed from the work of Moseley and Bohr.

---

[2] J. J. CHISHOLM, Lead poisoning, *Scientific American* **224**, 15–23 (1971). Reprinted as Chap. 36 in *Chemistry in the Environment*, Readings from *Scientific American*, pp. 335–43. W. H. Freeman, San Francisco, 1973. See also R. M. HARRISON and D. P. H. LAXEN, *Lead Pollution*, Chapman and Hall, London, 1981, 175 pp; T. C. HUTCHINSON and K. N. MEEMA (eds.), *Lead, Mercury, Cadmium and* (ctd.)

in enzymes and affects virtually all steps in the process of haem synthesis and porphyrin metabolism. It also inhibits acetylcholine-esterase, acid phosphatase, ATPase, carbonic anhydrase, etc. and inhibits protein synthesis probably by modifying transfer-RNA. In addition to O complexation (in which it resembles Tl^I, Ba^{II} and Ln^{III}), Pb^{II} also inhibits SH enzymes (though less strongly than Cd^{II} and Hg^{II}), especially by interaction with cysteine residues in proteins. Typical symptoms of lead poisoning are cholic, anaemia, headaches, convulsions, chronic nephritis of the kidneys, brain damage and central nervous-system disorders. Treatment is by complexing and sequestering the Pb using a strong chelating agent such as edta, $\{-CH_2N(CH_2CO_2H)_2\}_2$, or BAL i.e. British anti-Lewisite, $HSCH_2CH(SH)CH_2OH$.

10.2 The Elements

10.2.1 Terrestrial abundance and distribution

Germanium and Sn appear about half-way down the list of elements in order of abundance in crustal rocks, together with several other elements in the region of $1-2$ ppm:

Element	Br	U	Sn	Eu	Be	As
PPM	2.5	2.3	**2.1**	2.1	2	1.8
Order	46	47	**48**	=48	50	51
Element	Ta	**Ge**	Ho	Mo	W	Tb
PPM	1.7	**1.5**	1.4	1.2	1.2	1.2
Order	52	**53**	54	55	=55	=55

Germanium minerals are extremely rare but the element is widely distributed in trace amounts (like its neighbour Ga). Recovery has been achieved from coal ash but is now normally from the flue dusts of smelters processing Zn ores.

Arsenic in the Environment, SCOPE 31, Wiley, Chichester, 1987, 384 pp.

Tin occurs mainly as cassiterite, SnO_2, and this has been the only important source of the element from earliest times. Julius Caesar recorded the presence of tin in Britain, and Cornwall remained the predominant supplier for European needs until the present century (apart from a minor flourish from Bohemia between 1400 and 1550).[3] Today (1990s) world production approaches 200 000 tonnes per annum (see next section), of which the UK contributes less than 1%.[4]

Lead (13 ppm) is by far the most abundant of the heavy elements, being approached amongst these only by thallium (8.1 ppm) and uranium (2.3 ppm). This abundance is related to the fact that 3 of the 4 naturally occurring isotopes of lead (206, 207 and 208) arise primarily as the stable end products of the natural radioactive series. Only ^{204}Pb (1.4%) is non-radiogenic in origin. The variation in isotopic composition of Pb with its origin also accounts for the variability of atomic weight and the limited precision with which it can be quoted (p. 19). The most important Pb ore is the heavy black mineral galena, PbS. Other ore minerals are anglesite ($PbSO_4$), cerussite ($PbCO_3$), pyromorphite ($Pb_5(PO_4)_3Cl$) and mimetesite ($Pb_5(AsO_4)_3Cl$). Some 25 other minerals are known but are not economically important; all contain Pb^{II} in contrast to tin minerals which are invariably Sn^{IV} compounds. Lead ores are widely distributed and commercial deposits are worked in over fifty countries. Primary production (from mines) was 3.3 million tonnes (as Pb) in 1991 of which four-fifths came from the half dozen main producers: Australia 17.4%, USA 14.3%, the former Soviet Union 13.8%, China 9.6%, Canada 8.3% and Peru 6.0%.[4] Secondary production (from the resmelting of scrap) produces a further 5.6 Mtpa i.e. nearly two-thirds of the world's supply in 1991. The average price in 1992 was £306.4/tonne ($542/t).

---

[3] R. D. PENHALLURICK. *Tin in Antiquity*. Institute of Metals Publication, 1986, 271 pp.

[4] A. MACMILLAN (ed.) *Base Metals Handbook*, Woodhead Publ.. Cambridge. 1993 (loose leaf). See also refs. 6 and 9.

10.2.2 Production and uses of the elements

Recovery of Ge from flue dusts is complicated, not only because of the small concentration of Ge but also because its amphoteric properties are similar to those of Zn from which it is being separated.[5] Leaching with H_2SO_4, followed by addition of aqueous NaOH, results in the coprecipitation of the 2 elements at pH ~5 and enrichment of Ge from ~2 to 10%: GeO_2 begins to precipitate at pH 2.4, is 90% precipitated at pH 3, and 98% precipitated at pH 5. $Zn(OH)_2$ begins to precipitate at pH 4 and is completely precipitated at pH 5.5. The concentrate is heated with HCl/Cl_2 to drive off $GeCl_4$, bp 83.1° (cf. $ZnCl_2$, bp 756°). After further fractionation of $GeCl_4$, hydrolysis affords purified GeO_2, which can be slowly reduced to the element by H_2 at ~530°. Final purification for semiconductor-grade Ge is effected by zone refining. World production of Ge in 1991 was 80 000 kg (80 tonnes), about 10% less than a decade earlier. The largest use is in transistor technology and, indeed, transistor action was first discovered in this element (p. 331). This use is now diminishing somewhat whilst that in optics is growing — Ge is transparent in the infrared and is used in infrared windows, prisms and lenses. Magnesium germanate is a useful phosphor, and other small-scale applications are in special alloys, strain gauges and superconductors. Despite its spectacular increase in availability during the past few decades from a laboratory rarity to a general article of commerce Ge and its compounds are still relatively expensive. Zone-refined Ge was quoted at $850 per kg in 1991 and GeO_2 at $500 per kg.

The ready reduction of SnO_2 by glowing coals accounts for the knowledge of Sn and its alloys in the ancient world. Modern technology uses a reverberatory furnace at 1200–1300°.[6] The main chemical problem in reducing SnO_2 comes from the presence of Fe in the ores which leads to a hard product with unacceptable properties. Reference to Ellingham-type diagrams of the sort shown on p. 308 shows that $-\Delta G(SnO_2)$ is very close to that for FeO/Fe_3O_4 and only about 80 kJ mol^{-1} above the line for reducing FeO to Fe at 1000–2000°. It is therefore essential to reduce cassiterite/iron oxide ores at an oxygen pressure sufficiently high to prevent extensive reduction to Fe. This is achieved in a two-stage process, the impure molten Sn from the initial carbon reduction being stirred vigorously in contact with atmospheric O_2 to oxidize the iron — a process that can be effected by "poling" with long billets of green wood — or, alternatively, by use of steam or compressed air. The price of tin was formerly regulated by The International Tin Council, but the market became progressively less stable and the suspension of buffer stock interventions in October 1985 precipitated on immediate collapse in the market, from which it has not yet recovered. The ITC was superseded by The Association of Tin Producing Countries which attempts to limit production by the member countries. In 1991 there was an excess of tin on the world market for the 11th successive year and primary production was limited to 95 850 tonnes (Malaysia 29.8%, Indonesia 29.6%, Thailand 17.9%, Bolivia 13.2%, Australia 7.2%, Zaire 1.4%, Nigeria 0.9%). Additional production by China (43 000 t), the former USSR (13 500 t) and other countries brought the primary production of Sn in concentrates in 1991 to 196 700 tonnes. Prices hovered around $5700 per tonne, about half that of a few years earlier.[7,8] The many uses of metallic tin and its alloys are summarized in the Panel overleaf.

Lead is normally obtained from PbS. This is first concentrated from low-grade ores by froth flotation then roasted in a limited supply of air

---

[5] *Kirk–Othmer Encyclopedia of Chemical Technology* 4th edn. **12**, 540–55 (1994). Germanium and germanium compounds.

[6] *Kirk–Othmer Encyclopedia of Chemical Technology* 3rd edn. **23**, 18–42 (1983), Tin and tin alloys; 42–77, Tin compounds.

[7] *Minerals year book. Vol. 1: Metals and Minerals*, 1991. US Dept. of the Interior, Bureau of Mines. Ge pp. 649–54; Sn pp. 1591–612, Pb pp. 873–910.

[8] R. WOLFF, *Tin Market Report*, Metal Bulletin Books Ltd., Worcester Park, Surrey, 1991.

Uses of Metallic Tin and Its Alloys

Because of its low strength and high cost, Sn is seldom used by itself but its use as a coating, and as alloys, is familiar in a variety of domestic and technological applications. Tin-plate accounts for almost 27% of tin used — it provides a non-toxic corrosion-resistant cover for sheet steel and can be applied either by hot dipping in molten Sn or more elegantly and controllably by electrolytic tinning. The layer is typically $0.4-25\,\mu m$ thick. In addition to extensive use in food packaging, tin-plate is used increasingly for distributing beer and other drinks. In the USA alone 35 000 million of the 130 000 million drink cans sold annually are tin-plate, the rest being Al: this is a staggering per capita consumption of 500 pa.

The main alloys of tin together with an indication of the percentage of total Sn production for these alloys in the USA (1991) are:

Solder (37%)   (Sn/Pb) typically containing 33% Sn by weight but varying between 2–63% depending on use; sometimes Cd, Ga, In or Bi are added for increased fusibility.

Bronze (7%)   (Cu/Sn) typically 5–10% Sn often with added P or Zn to aid casting and impart superior elasticity and strain resistance. Gun metal is ~85% Cu, 5% Sn, 5% Zn and 5% Pb. Coinage metal and brass also often contain small amounts of Sn. World production of bronzes approaches 500 000 tonnes pa.

Babbitt (2%)   (heavy duty bearing metal introduced by I. Babbitt in 1839). The two main compositions are 80–90% Sn, 0–5% Pb, 5% Cu; and 75% Pb, 12% Sn, 13% Sb, 0–1% Cu. They have the characteristics of a hard compound embedded in a soft matrix and are used mainly in railway wagons, diesel locomotives, etc.

Pewter (3%)   (90–95% Sn, 1–8% Sb, 0.5–3% Cu); a decorative and servicable alloy that can be cast, bent, spun or formed into any shape; it is much used for coffee and tea services, trays, plates, jugs, tankards, candelabra, bowls and trophies. A related alloy of 90–95% Sn with Pb and other elements is highly prized and much used for organ pipes because of its tonal qualities, e.g. the Royal Albert Hall organ in London has 10 000 pipes containing some 150 tonnes Sn.

Other specialized uses of Sn and its alloys are as type metal, as the molten-metal bath in the manufacture of float glass and as the alloy Nb_3Sn in superconducting magnets. The many industrial and domestic uses of tin compounds are discussed in later sections; these compounds account for about 15% of the tin produced worldwide.

to give PbO which is then mixed with coke and a flux such as limestone and reduced in a blast furnace:[9]

$$PbS + 1.5O_2 \longrightarrow PbO + SO_2$$

$$PbO + C \longrightarrow Pb(liq) + CO;$$

$$PbO + CO \longrightarrow Pb(liq) + CO_2$$

Alternatively, the carbon reduction can be replaced by reduction of the roasted ore with fresh galena:

$$PbS + 2PbO \longrightarrow 3Pb(liq) + SO_2(g)$$

---

[9] *Kirk–Othmer Encyclopedia of Chemical Technology* 4th edn. **15**, 69–113 (1995), Lead; 113–32, Lead alloys; 132–58, Lead compounds.

In either case the Pb contains numerous undesirable metal impurities, notably Cu, Ag, Au, Zn, Sn, As and Sb, some of which are clearly valuable in themselves. Copper is first removed by liquation: the Pb bullion is melted and held just above its freezing point when Cu rises to the surface as an insoluble solid which is skimmed off. Tin, As and Sb are next removed by preferential oxidation in a reverberatory furnace and skimming off the oxides; alternatively, the molten bullion is churned with an oxidizing flux of molten $NaOH/NaNO_3$ (Harris process). The softened Pb may still contain Ag, Au and perhaps Bi. Removal of the first two depends on their preferential solubility in Zn: the mixed metals are cooled slowly from 480° to below 420° when the Zn (now containing nearly all the Ag and Au) solidifies as a crust which is skimmed off; the

Uses of Lead Alloys and Chemicals

Although much lead is used as an inert material in cast, rolled or extruded form, a far greater tonnage is consumed as alloys. Its major application is in storage batteries where an alloy of 91% Pb, 9% Sb forms the supporting grid for the oxidizing agent (PbO_2) and the reducing agent (spongy Pb).[10] Over 70% of this Pb is recovered and recycled. In addition, its use (with Sn) in solders, fusible alloys, bearing metals (babbitt) and type metals has been summarized on p. 370. Other mechanical as distinct from chemical applications are in ammunition, lead shot, lead weights and ballast.

The pattern of chemical usage of Pb compounds in a particular country depends very much on whether organolead compounds are allowed as antiknock additives in petrol for cars (gasoline for automobiles). In a growing number of developed countries such additives are considered to be wasteful, dangerous and unnecessary and environmental legislation is gradually achieving the elimination of $PbEt_4$ and $PbMe_4$ as antiknocks.[2] The presence of Pb additives in petrol also interferes with the catalytic converters that are being developed to reduce or eliminate CO, NO_x and hydrocarbons from exhaust fumes, and this has likewise encouraged the change to other antiknocks.

World production of mined lead was 3 331 000 tonnes in 1991 and a further 5 558 000 tonnes was refined by reprocessing. In the same year US consumption of Pb in metal products was 1 125 000 tonnes (including 967 000 tonnes in storage batteries). In addition, some 57 250 tonnes of other oxides and 29 750 tonnes of miscellaneous Pb-containing products were consumed. The US market price of Pb dropped from $1.05/kg in 1990 to $0.40/kg in 1993 due in part to the collapse in use of $PbEt_4$ in petrol.

Lead pigments are widely used as rust-inhibiting priming paints for iron and steel. Red lead (Pb_3O_4) is the traditional primer but Ca_2PbO_4 is finding increasing use, particularly for galvanized steel. Lead chromate, $PbCrO_4$, is a strong yellow pigment extensively used in yellow paints for road markings and as an ingredient (with iron blues) in many green paints and coloured plastics. Other pigments include $PbMoO_4$ (red-orange), litharge PbO (canary yellow), and white lead, $\sim 2PbCO_3.Pb(OH)_2$. Lead compounds are also used for ceramic glazes, e.g. $PbSi_2O_5$ (colourless), in crown glass manufacture, and as polyvinylchloride plastic stabilizers, e.g. "tribasic lead sulfate". $3PbO.PbSO_4.H_2O$. See also p. 386.

---

excess of dissolved Zn is then removed either by oxidation in a reverberatory furnace, or by preferential reaction with gaseous Cl_2, or by vacuum distillation. Final purification (which also removes any Bi) is by electrolysis using massive cast Pb anodes and an electrolyte of acid $PbSiF_6$ or a sulfamate;[10] this yields a cathode deposit of 99.99% Pb which can be further purified by zone refining to <1 ppm impurity if required. Total world production figures and the current price were given at the end of the preceding section, and the various uses for lead alloys and chemicals are summarized in the Panel.

10.2.3 Properties of the elements

The atomic properties of Ge, Sn and Pb are compared with those of C and Si in Table 10.1. Trends noted in previous groups are again apparent. The pairwise similarity in the ionization energies of Si and Ge (which can be related to the filling of the $3d^{10}$ shell) and of Sn and Pb

(which is likewise related to the filling of the $4f^{14}$ shell) are notable (Fig. 10.1). Tin has more stable isotopes than any other element (why?) and one of these, ^{119}Sn (nuclear spin $\frac{1}{2}$), is particularly valuable both for nmr experiments[11] and for Mössbauer spectroscopy.[12]

Some physical properties of the elements are compared in Table 10.2. Germanium forms brittle, grey-white lustrous crystals with the diamond structure; it is a metalloid with a similar electrical resistivity to Si at room temperature but with a substantially smaller band gap. Its mp, bp and associated enthalpy changes are also lower than for Si and this trend continues for Sn and Pb which are both very soft, low-melting metals.

Tin has two allotropes: at room temperature the stable modification is white, tetragonal

---

[10] A. T. KUHN (ed.), *The Electrochemistry of Lead*, Academic Press, London, 1977, 467 pp. H. BODE, *Lead-Acid Batteries*, Wiley, New York, 1977, 408 pp.

[11] J. D. KENNEDY and W. McFARLANE, in J. MASON (ed), *Multinuclear NMR*, Plenum Press, New York, 1987, Chap. 11, Si, Ge, Sn and Pb, pp. 305–33. See also B. WRACKMEYER, *Ann. Rept. NMR Spectrosc.* **16**, 73–186 (1985).

[12] N. N. GREENWOOD and T. C. GIBB, *Mössbauer Spectroscopy*, Chapman & Hall, London, 1971, 659 pp. T. C. GIBB, *Principles of Mössbauer Spectroscopy*, Chapman & Hall, London, 1976, 254 pp.

Table 10.1 Atomic properties of Group 14 elements

Property		C	Si	Ge	Sn	Pb
Atomic number		6	14	32	50	82
Electronic structure		[He]$2s^2 2p^2$	[Ne]$3s^2 3p^2$	[Ar]$3d^{10}$ $4s^2 4p^2$	[Kr]$4d^{10}$ $5s^2 5p^2$	[Xe]$4f^{14} 5d^{10}$ $6s^2 6p^2$
Number of naturally occurring isotopes		2 + 1	3	5	10	4
Atomic weight		12.0107(8)	28.0855(3)	72.61(2)	118.710(7)	207.2(1)
Ionization energy/kJ mol^{-1}	I	1086.1	786.3	761.2	708.4	715.4
	II	2351.9	1576.5	1537.0	1411.4	1450.0
	III	4618.8	3228.3	3301.2	2942.2	3080.7
	IV	6221.0	4354.4	4409.4	3929.3	4082.3
r^{IV}(covalent)/pm		77.2	117.6	122.3	140.5	146
r^{IV}("ionic"; 6-coordinate)/pm		(15) (CN 4)	40	53	69	78
r^{II}("ionic", 6-coordinate)/pm		—	—	73	118	119
Pauling electronegativity		2.5	1.8	1.8	1.8	1.9

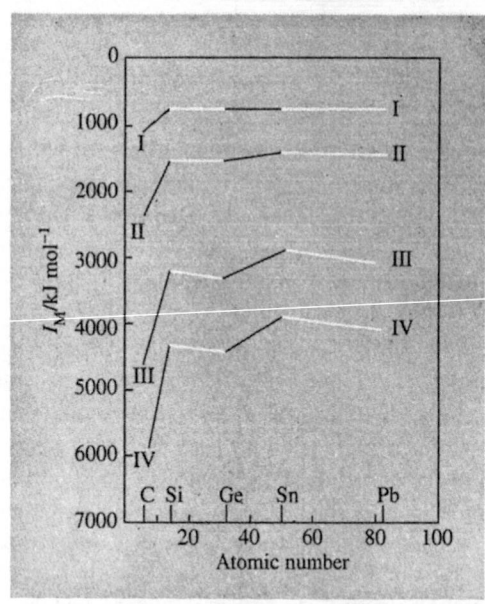

Figure 10.1 Successive ionization energies for Group 14 elements showing the influence of the $3d^{10}$ shell between Si and Ge and the $4f^{14}$ shell between Sn and Pb.

β-Sn, but at low temperatures this transforms into grey α-Sn which has the cubic diamond structure. The transition temperature is 13.2° but the transformation usually requires prolonged exposure at temperatures well below this.

The reverse transition from $\alpha \rightarrow \beta$ involves a structural distortion along the c-axis and is remarkable for the fact that the density increases by 26% in the high-temperature form. This arises because, although the Sn–Sn distances increase in the $\alpha \rightarrow \beta$ transition, the CN increases from 4 to 6 and the distortion also permits a closer approach of the 12 next-nearest neighbours:

Modification	α (grey, diamond)	β (white, tetragonal)
Bond angles	6 at 109.5°	4 at 94° 2 at 149.6°
Nearest neighbours	4 at 280 pm	4 at 302 pm 2 at 318 pm
Next nearest neighbours	12 at 459 pm	4 at 377 pm 8 at 441 pm

A similar transformation to a metallic, tetragonal β-form can be effected in Si and Ge by subjecting them to pressures of ~200 and ~120 kbar respectively along the c-axis, and again the density increases by ~25% from the value at atmospheric pressure. Lead is familiar as a blue-grey, malleable metal with a fairly high density (nearly 5 times that of Si and twice those of Ge and Sn, but only half that of Os and Ir).

Table 10.2 Some physical properties of Group 14 elements

Property	C	Si	Ge	Sn	Pb
MP/°C	4100	1420	945	232	327
BP/°C	—	~3280	2850	2623	1751
Density (20°C)/g cm^{-3}	3.514	2.336	5.323	α 5.769	11.342
		(β 2.905)$^{(a)}$	(β 6.71)$^{(a)}$	β 7.265$^{(b)}$	
a_0/pm	356.68$^{(c)}$	543.10$^{(c)}$	565.76	α 648.9$^{(b,c)}$	494.9$^{(d)}$
ΔH_{fus}/kJ mol^{-1}	—	50.6	36.8	7.07	4.81
ΔH_{vap}/kJ mol^{-1}	—	383	328	296	178
ΔH_f (monatomic gas)/kJ mol^{-1}	716.7	454	283	300.7	195.0
Electrical resistivity (20°)/ohm cm	10^{14}–10^{16}	~48	~47	β 11 × 10^{-6}	20 × 10^{-6}
Band gap E_g/kJ mol^{-1}	~580	106.8	64.2	α 7.7, β 0	0

[a] See text. [b] β-form (stable at room temperature) is tetragonal a_0 583.1 pm, c_0 318.1 pm.
[c] Diamond structure. [d] Face-centred cubic.

10.2.4 Chemical reactivity and group trends

Germanium is somewhat more reactive and more electropositive than Si: it dissolves slowly in hot concentrated H_2SO_4 and HNO_3 but does not react with water or with dilute acids or alkalis unless an oxidizing agent such as H_2O_2 or NaOCl is present; fused alkalis react with incandescence to give germanates. Germanium is oxidized to GeO_2 in air at red heat and both H_2S and gaseous S yield GeS_2; Cl_2 and Br_2 yield GeX_4 on moderate heating and HCl gives both $GeCl_4$ and $GeHCl_3$. Alkyl halides react with heated Ge (as with Si) to give the corresponding organogermanium halides.

Tin[13] is notably more reactive and electropositive than Ge though it is still markedly amphoteric in its aqueous chemistry. It is stable towards both water and air at ordinary temperatures but reacts with steam to give SnO_2 plus H_2 and with air or oxygen on heating to give SnO_2. Dilute HCl and H_2SO_4 show little, if any, reaction but dilute HNO_3 produces $Sn(NO_3)_2$ and NH_4NO_3. Hot concentrated HCl yields $SnCl_2$ and H_2 whereas hot concentrated H_2SO_4 forms $SnSO_4$ and SO_2. The occurrence of Sn^{II} compounds in these reactions is notable. By contrast, the action of hot aqueous alkali yields

hydroxostannate(IV) compounds, e.g.:

$$Sn + 2KOH + 4H_2O \longrightarrow K_2[Sn(OH)_6] + 2H_2$$

Tin reacts readily with Cl_2 and Br_2 in the cold and with F_2 and I_2 on warming to give SnX_4. It reacts vigorously with heated S and Se, to form Sn^{II} and Sn^{IV} chalcogenides depending on the proportions used, and with Te to form SnTe.

Finely divided Pb powder is pyrophoric but the reactivity of the metal is usually greatly diminished by the formation of a thin, coherent, protective layer of insoluble product such as oxide, oxocarbonate, sulfate or chloride. This inertness has been exploited as one of the main assets of the metal since early times: e.g. a temperature of 600–800° is needed to form PbO in air and Pb is widely used for handling hot concentrated H_2SO_4. Aqueous HCl does, in fact, react slowly to give the sparingly soluble $PbCl_2$ (<1% at room temperature) and nitric acid reacts quite rapidly to liberate oxides of nitrogen and form the very soluble $Pb(NO_3)_2$ (~50 g per 100 cm^3, i.e. 1.5 M). Organic acids such as acetic acid also dissolve Pb in the presence of air to give $Pb(OAc)_2$, etc.; this precludes contact with the metal when processing or storing wine, fruit juices and other drinks. The familiar soft metal protective caps covering the cork on quality wines is Pb-foil laminated between thin outer layers of non-toxic Sn metal to which coloured decorative finishes can be applied. Fluorine reacts at room temperatures to give PbF_2 and Cl_2 gives $PbCl_2$ on heating.

[13] P. G. HARRISON (ed.), *Chemistry of Tin*, Blackie, Glasgow, 1989, 461 pp.

Molten Pb reacts with the chalcogens to give PbS, PbSe and PbTe.

The steady trend towards increasing stability of M^{II} rather than M^{IV} compounds in the sequence Ge, Sn, Pb is an example of the so-called "inert-pair effect" which is well established for the heavier post-transition metals. The discussion on p. 226 is relevant here. A notable exception is the organometallic chemistry of Sn and Pb which is almost entirely confined to the M^{IV} state (pp. 399–405).

Catenation is also an important feature of the chemistry of Ge, Sn and Pb though less so than for C and Si. The discussion on p. 341 can be extended by reference to the bond energies in Table 10.3 from which it can be seen that there is a steady decrease in the M–M bond strength. In general, with the exception of M–H bonds, the strength of other M–X bonds diminishes less noticeably, though the absence of Ge analogues of silicone polymers speaks for the lower stability of the Ge–O–Ge linkage.

The structural chemistry of the Group 14 elements affords abundant illustrations of the trends to be expected from increasing atomic size, increasing electropositivity and increasing tendency to form M^{II} compounds, and these will become clear during the more detailed treatment of the chemistry in the succeeding sections. The often complicated stereochemistry of M^{II} compounds (which arises from the presence of a nonbonding electron-pair on the metal) is

particularly revealing as also is the propensity of Sn^{IV} to become 5- and 6-coordinate.[14] The ability of both Sn and Pb to form polyatomic cluster anions of very low formal oxidation state, (e.g. $M_5{}^{2-}$, $M_9{}^{4-}$, etc.) reflects the now well-established tendency of the heavier post-transition elements to form chain, ring or cluster homopolyatomic ions:[18] this was first established for the polyhalide anions and for $Hg_2{}^{2+}$ but is also prevalent in Groups 14, 15 and 16, e.g. $Pb_9{}^{4-}$ is isoelectronic with $Bi_9{}^{5+}$ (see Section 10.3.6, p. 391).

10.3 Compounds

10.3.1 Hydrides and hydrohalides

Germanes of general formula Ge_nH_{2n+2} are known as colourless gases or volatile liquids for $n = 1–5$ and their preparation, physical properties, and chemical reactions are very similar to those of silanes (p. 337). Thus GeH_4 was formerly made by the inefficient hydrolysis of Mg/Ge alloys with aqueous acids but is now generally made by the reaction of $GeCl_4$ with $LiAlH_4$ in ether or even more conveniently by the reaction of GeO_2 with aqueous solutions of $NaBH_4$. The higher germanes are prepared by the action of a silent electric discharge on GeH_4; mixed hydrides such as SiH_3GeH_3 can be prepared similarly by circulating a mixture of SiH_4 and GeH_4 but no cyclic or unsaturated hydrides have yet been prepared. The germanes are all less volatile than the corresponding silanes (see Table) and, perhaps surprisingly,

Table 10.3 Approximate average bond energies/kJ mol^{-1}(a)

M–	–M	–C	–H	–F	–Cl	–Br	–I
C	356	356	416	490	325	279	216
Si	226	360	323	596	400	325	248
Ge	188	255	289	471	339	281	216
Sn	151	226	253	—	315	261	187
Pb	98	130	205	411	308	—	—

(a)These values often vary widely (by as much as 50–100 kJ mol^{-1}) depending on the particular compound considered and the method of computation used. Individual values are thus less significant than general trends. The data represent a collation of values for typical compounds gleaned from refs 15–17.

[14] J. A. ZUBIETA and J. J. ZUCKERMAN, Structural tin chemistry, *Prog. Inorg. Chem.* **24**, 251–475 (1978). An excellent comprehensive review with full structural diagrams and data, and more than 750 references.

[15] J. A. KERR, Bond strengths in polyatomic molecules, *CRC Handbook of Chemistry and Physics*, 73rd edn., 1992–3, pp. **9**.138–**9**.145.

[16] W. E. DASENT, *Inorganic Energetics*, 2nd edn., Cambridge Univ. Press, 1982, 185 pp.

[17] C. F. SHAW and A. L. ALLRED, *Organometallic Chem. Rev.* **5A**, 95–142 (1970).

[18] J. D. CORBETT, *Prog. Inorg. Chem.* **21**, 129–55 (1976).

Property	GeH_4	Ge_2H_6
MP/°C	-164.8	-109
BP/°C	-88.1	29
Density $(T°C)/g\,cm^{-3}$	1.52 $(-142°)$	1.98 $(-109°)$

Property	Ge_3H_8	Ge_4H_{10}	Ge_5H_{12}
MP/°C	-105.6	–	–
BP/°C	110.5	176.9	234
Density $(T°C)/g\,cm^{-3}$	2.20 $(-105°)$	–	–

noticeably less reactive. Thus, in contrast to SiH_4 and SnH_4, GeH_4 does not ignite in contact with air and is unaffected by aqueous acid or 30% aqueous NaOH. It acts as an acid in liquid NH_3 forming NH_4^+ and GeH_3^- ions and reacts with alkali metals in this solvent (or in $MeOC_2H_4$-OMe) to give $MGeH_3$. Like the corresponding $MSiH_3$, these are white, crystalline compounds of considerable synthetic utility. X-ray diffraction analysis shows that $KGeH_3$ and $RbGeH_3$ have the NaCl-type structure, implying free rotation of GeH_3^-, and $CsGeH_3$ has the rare TlI structure (p. 242). The derived "ionic radius" of 229 pm emphasizes the similarity to SiH_3^- (226 pm) and this is reinforced by the bond angles deduced from broad-line nmr experiments: SiH_3^- 94 ± 4° (cf. isoelectronic PH_3, 93.5°); GeH_3^- 92.5 ± 4° (cf. isoelectronic AsH_3, 91.8°).[19]

The germanium hydrohalides GeH_xX_{4-x} (X = Cl, Br, I; x = 1, 2, 3) are colourless, volatile, reactive liquids. Preparative routes include reaction of Ge, GeX_2 or GeH_4 with HX. The compounds are valuable synthetic intermediates (cf. SiH_3I). For example, hydrolysis of GeH_3Cl yields $O(GeH_3)_2$, and various metatheses can be effected by use of the appropriate Ag salts or, more effectively, Pb^{II} salts, e.g. GeH_3Br with PbO, $Pb(OAc)_2$, and $Pb(NCS)_2$ affords $O(GeH_3)_2$, $GeH_3(OAc)$, and $GeH_3(SCN)$. Treatment of this latter compound with MeSH or $[Mn(CO)_5H]$ yields GeH_3SMe

and $[Mn(CO)_5(GeH_3)]$ respectively. An extensive phosphinogermane chemistry is also known, e.g. $R_nGe(PH_2)_{4-n}$, R = alkyl or H. The novel germaimine $CF_3N{=}GeH_2$ has been obtained as a colourless gas by reacting a 1:1 mixture of GeH_4 and CF_3NO in a sealed tube at 120° (the other product being H_2O). Addition of HI to the Ge=N double bond gave CF_3NHGeH_2I.[20]

Binary Sn hydrides are much less stable. Reduction of $SnCl_4$ with ethereal $LiAlH_4$ gives SnH_4 in 80–90% yield; $SnCl_2$ reacts similarly with aqueous $NaBH_4$. SnH_4 (mp $-146°$, bp $-52.5°$) decomposes slowly to Sn and H_2 at room temperature; it is unattacked by dilute aqueous acids or alkalis but is decomposed by more concentrated solutions. It is a potent reducing agent. Sn_2H_6 is even less stable, and higher homologues have not been obtained. By contrast, organotin hydrides are more stable, and catenation up to $H(SnPh_2)_6H$ has been achieved by thermolysis of Ph_2SnH_2. Preparation of R_nSnH_{4-n} is usually by $LiAlH_4$ reduction of the corresponding organotin chloride.

PbH_4 is the least well-characterized Group 14 hydride and it is unlikely that it has ever been prepared except perhaps in trace amounts at high dilution; methods which successfully yield MH_4 for the other Group 14 elements all fail even at low temperatures. The alkyl derivatives R_2PbH_2 and R_3PbH can be prepared from the corresponding halides and $LiAlH_4$ at $-78°$ or by exchange reactions with Ph_3SnH, e.g.:

$$Bu^n_3PbX + Ph_3SnH \longrightarrow Bu^n_3PbH + Ph_3SnX$$

Me_3PbH (mp $\sim -106°$, decomp above $-30°$) and Et_3PbH (mp $\sim -145°$, decomp above $-20°$) readily add to alkenes and alkynes (hydroplumbation) to give stable tetraorganolead compounds.

10.3.2 Halides and related complexes

Germanium, Sn and Pb form two series of halides: MX_2 and MX_4. PbX_2 are more stable than PbX_4, whereas the reverse is

[19] G. THIRASE, E. WEISS, H. J. HENNING and H. LECHERT, *Z. anorg. allg. Chem.* **417**, 221–8 (1975).

[20] H. G. ANG and F. KLEE, *J. Chem. Soc., Chem. Commun.*, 310–12 (1989).

true for Ge, consistent with the steady increase in stability of the dihalides in the sequence $CX_2 \ll SiX_2 < GeX_2 < SnX_2 < PbX_2$. Numerous complex halides are also known for both oxidation states.

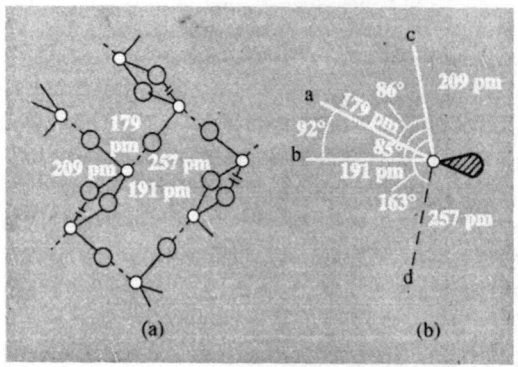

(a)   (b)

Figure 10.2 Crystal structure of GeF_2: (a) projection along the chains, and (b) environment of Ge (pseudo trigonal bipyramidal). The bond to the unshared F is appreciably shorter (179 pm) than those in the chain and there is a weaker interaction (257 pm) linking the chains into a 3D structure.

Germanium halides

GeF_2 is formed as a volatile white solid (mp 110°) by the action of GeF_4 on powdered Ge at 150–300°; it has a unique structure in which trigonal pyramidal {GeF_3} units share 2 F atoms to form infinite spiral chains (Fig. 10.2). Pale-yellow $GeCl_2$ can be prepared similarly at 300° or by thermal decomposition of $GeHCl_3$ at 70°. Typical reactions are summarized in the scheme:

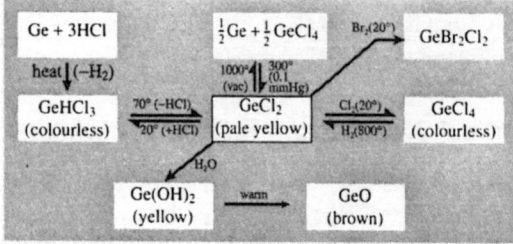

$GeBr_2$ is made by reduction of $GeBr_4$ or $GeHBr_3$ with Zn, or by the action of HBr on an excess of Ge at 400°; it is a yellow solid, mp 122°,

which disproportionates to Ge and $GeBr_4$ at 150°, adds HBr at 40°, and hydrolyses to the unstable yellow $Ge(OH)_2$. GeI_2 is best prepared by reduction of GeI_4 with aqueous H_3PO_2 in the presence of HI to prevent hydrolysis; it sublimes to give bright orange-yellow crystals, is stable in dry air and disproportionates only when heated above ~550°. The structure of the lemon-yellow, monomeric, pyramidal 3-coordinate Ge^{II} complex [Ge(acac)I] (1) has been determined.[21] GeI_2 is oxidized to GeI_4 in aqueous KI/HCl; it forms numerous adducts with nitrogen ligands, and reacts with C_2H_2 at 140° to give a compound that was originally formulated as a 3-membered heterocycle $\begin{matrix} CH \\ \| \\ CH \end{matrix}\!\!\!>\!GeI_2$ but which was subsequently shown by mass spectroscopy to have the unusual dimeric structure (2).

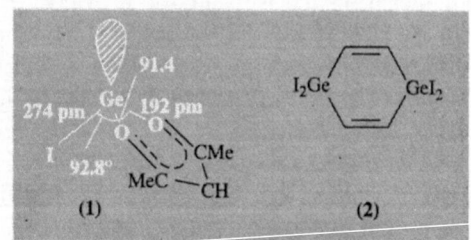

(1)   (2)

The ternary Ge^{II} halides, $MGeX_3$ (M = Rb, Cs; X = Cl, Br, I) are polymorphic with various distorted perovskite-like (p. 963) structures which reflect the influence of the "non-bonding" pair of electrons on the Ge^{II} centre.[22] Thus, at room temperature, rhombohedral $CsGeI_3$ has three Ge–I at 275 pm and three at 327 pm whereas in the high-temperature cubic form (above 277°C) there are six Ge–I distances at 320 pm as a result of position changes of the Ge atoms (reversible order–disorder transition). Again, $RbGeI_3$ has a lemon-yellow, orthorhombic form below −92°; an intermediate, bordeaux-red orthorhombic perovskite form (−92° to −52°); a black rhombohedral form (−52° to −29°); and

21 S. R. STOBART, M. R. CHURCHILL, F. J. HOLLANDER and W. J. YOUNGS, *J. Chem. Soc., Chem. Commun.*, 911–12 (1979).

22 G. THIELE, H. W. ROTTER and K. D. SCHMIDT, *Z. anorg. allg. Chem.* **545**, 148–56 (1987); **571**, 60–8 (1989).

a black, cubic perovskite form between $-29°$ and the decomposition temperature, $+61°$. In the yellow form there is one Ge–I at 281 pm, four at 306 pm and one at 327 pm, whereas in the red form there are three Ge–I at 287 pm and three at 324 pm. All the compounds are readily made simply by heating $Ge(OH)_2$ with MX in aqueous HX solutions.

Germanium tetrahalides are readily prepared by direct action of the elements or via the action of aqueous HX on GeO_2. The lighter members are colourless, volatile liquids, but GeI_4 is an orange solid (cf. CX_4, SiX_4). All hydrolyse readily and $GeCl_4$ in particular is an important intermediate in the preparation of organogermanium compounds via LiR or RMgX reagents. Many mixed halides and hydrohalides are also known, as are complexes of the type $GeF_6{}^{2-}$, $GeCl_6{}^{2-}$, *trans*-L_2GeCl_4 and L_4GeCl_4 (L = tertiary amine or pyridine). The curious mixed-valency complex Ge_5F_{12}, i.e. $[(GeF_2)_4GeF_4]$ has been shown to feature distorted square pyramids of $\{: Ge^{II}F_4\}$ with the "lone-pair" of electrons pointing away from the 4 basal F atoms which are at 181, 195, 220, and 245 pm from the apical Ge^{II}; the Ge^{IV} atom is at the centre of a slightly distorted octahedron (Ge^{IV}–F 171–180 pm, angle F–Ge–F 87.5–92.5°) and the whole structure is held together by F bridges.[23]

Property	GeF$_4$	GeCl$_4$
MP/°C	−15 (4 atm)	−49.5
BP/°C	−36.5 (subl)	83.1
Density (T°C)/g cm^{-3}	2.126 (0°)	1.844 (30°)

Property	GeBr$_4$	GeI$_4$
MP/°C	26	146
BP/°C	186	~400
Density (T°C)/g cm^{-3}	2.100 (30°)	4.322 (26°)

Tin halides

The structural chemistry of Sn^{II} halides is particularly complex, partly because of the stereochemical activity (or non-activity) of the nonbonding pair of electrons and partly because of the propensity of Sn^{II} to increase its CN by polymerization into larger structural units such as rings or chains. Thus, the first and second ionization energies of Sn (p. 372) are very similar to those of Mg (p. 111), but Sn^{II} rarely adopts structures typical of spherically symmetrical ions because the nonbonding pair of electrons, which is $5s^2$ in the free gaseous ion, readily distorts in the condensed phase; this can be described in terms of ligand-field distortions or the adoption of some "p character". Again, the "nonbonding" pair can act as a donor to vacant orbitals, and the "vacant" third 5p orbital and 5d orbitals can act as acceptors in forming further covalent bonds. A good example of this occurs with the adducts $[SnX_2(NMe_3)]$ (X = Cl, Br, I): the Sn^{II} atom, which has accepted a pair of electrons from the ligand NMe_3, can itself donate its own lone-pair to a strong Lewis acid to form a double adduct of the type $[BF_3\{\leftarrow SnX_2(\leftarrow NMe_3)\}]$ (X = Cl, Br, I).[24] Further examples, including more complicated interactions, are described later in this subsection.

SnF_2 (which is obtained as colourless monoclinic crystals by evaporation of a solution of SnO in 40% aqueous HF) is composed of Sn_4F_8 tetramers interlinked by weaker Sn–F interactions;[25] the tetramers are puckered 8-membered rings of alternating Sn and F as shown in Fig. 10.3 and each Sn is surrounded by a highly distorted octahedron of F (1 Sn–F$_t$ at ~205 pm, 2 Sn–F$_\mu$ at ~218 pm, and 3 much longer Sn$\cdots$F in the range 240–329 pm, presumably due to the influence of the nonbonding pair of electrons. In aqueous solutions containing F$^-$ the predominant species is the very stable pyramidal complex $SnF_3{}^-$ but crystallization is attended by further condensation. For example, crystallization of SnF_2 from aqueous solutions containing NaF does not give $NaSnF_3$ as previously supposed but

23 J. C. TAYLOR and P. W. WILSON, *J. Am. Chem. Soc.* **95**, 1834–8 (1973).

24 C. C. HSU and R. A. GEANANGEL, *Inorg. Chem.* **19**, 110–9 (1980).

25 R. C. MCDONALD, H. HO-KUEN HAU and K. ERIKS, *Inorg. Chem.* **15**, 762–5 (1976).

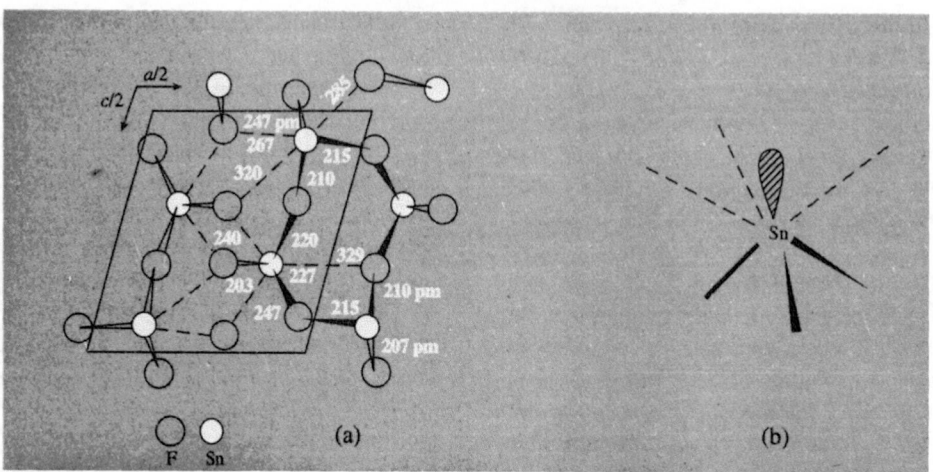

Figure 10.3 Structure of SnF_2 showing (a) interconnected rings of $\{Sn_4F_4(F_4)\}$, and (b) the unsymmetrical $3+3$ coordination around Sn.

$NaSn_2F_5$ or $Na_4Sn_3F_{10}$ depending on conditions. The $\{Sn_2F_5\}$ unit in the first compound can be thought of as a discrete ion $[Sn_2F_5]^-$ or as an F^- ion coordinating to 2 SnF_2 molecules (Fig. 10.4a): each Sn is trigonal pyramidal with two close F_t, one intermediate F_μ, and 3 more distant F at 253, 298, and 301 pm. By contrast the compound $Na_4Sn_3F_{10}$ features 3 corner-shared square-pyramidal $\{SnF_4\}$ units (Fig. 10.4b) though the wide range of Sn–F distances could be taken to indicate incipient formation of a central SnF_4^{2-} weakly bridged to two terminal SnF_3^- groups. In the corresponding system with KF the compound

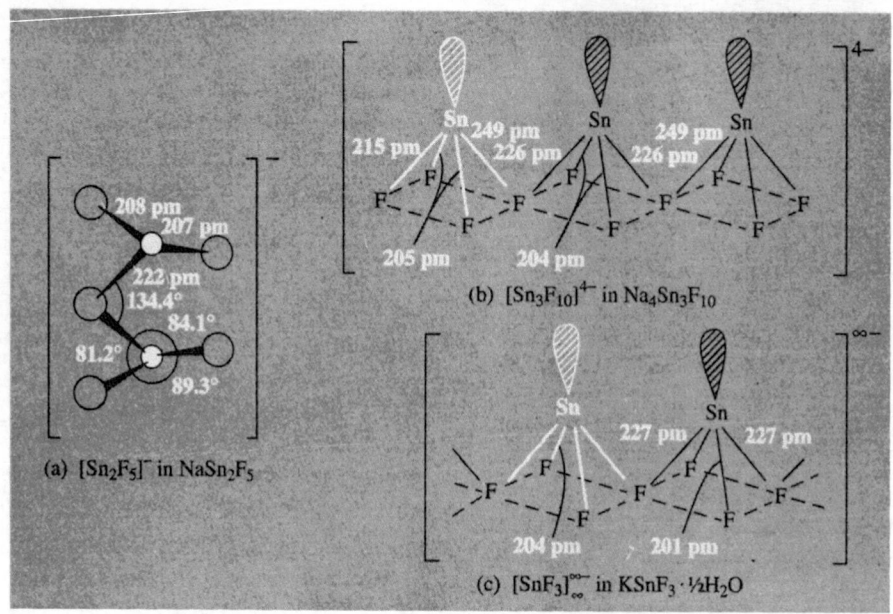

Figure 10.4 Structure of some fluoro-complexes of Sn^{II}.

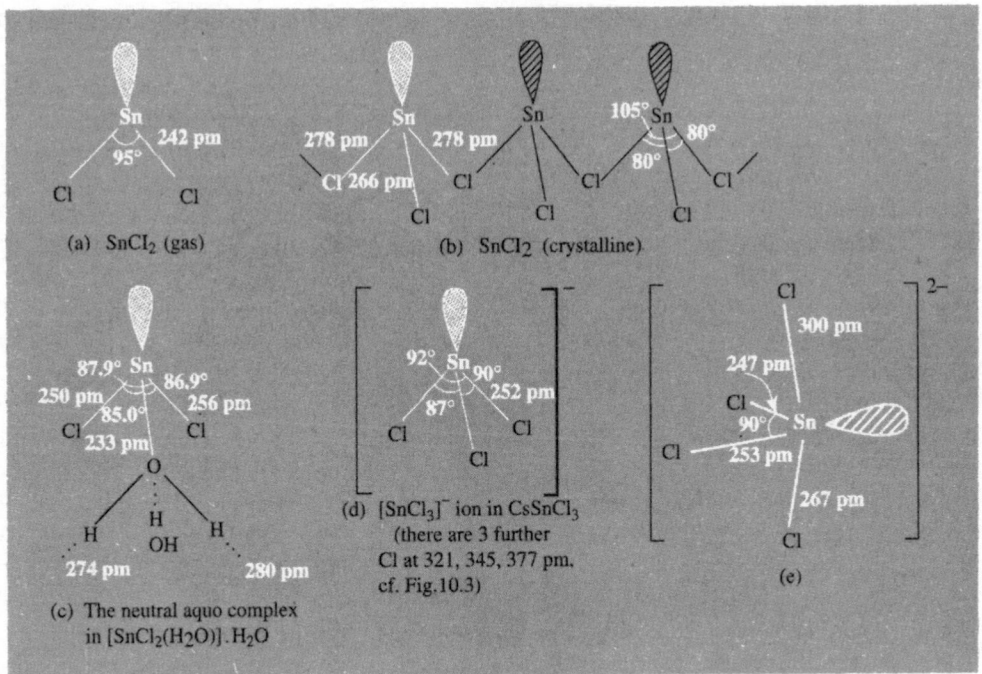

Figure 10.5   Structure of SnCl$_2$ and some chloro complexes of Sn^{II}.

that crystallizes is KSnF$_3 \cdot \frac{1}{2}$H$_2$O in which the bridging of square pyramids is extended to give infinite chain polymers (Fig. 10.4c). (The main commercial application of SnF$_2$ is in toothpaste and dental preparations where it is used to prevent demineralization of teeth and to lessen the development of dental caries.)

SnF$_4$ is described on p. 381. There are also some intriguing mixed valence compounds such as Sn$_3$F$_8$ (i.e. Sn$_2^{II}$Sn^{IV}F$_8$) which is formed when solutions of SnF$_2$ in anhydrous HF are oxidized at room temperature with F$_2$, O$_2$ or even SO$_2$; the structure features nearly regular {Sn^{IV}F$_6$} octahedra *trans*-bridged to {Sn^{II}F$_3$} pyramids which themselves form polymeric Sn^{II}F chains: Sn^{IV}–F 196 pm and Sn^{II}–F 210, 217, 225 pm with weaker Sn$^{II} \cdots$ F interactions in the range 255–265 pm.[26] Another example is α-Sn$_2$F$_6$ (i.e. Sn^{II}Sn^{IV}F$_6$) which transforms to β-Sn$_2$F$_6$ at 112° and to γ-Sn$_2$F$_6$ at 197°.

High-temperature neutron diffraction studies[27] have shown that this latter phase has the cubic ordered ReO$_3$-type structure (p. 1047) with octahedral coordination of both types of Sn atoms by F (Sn^{II}–F 229 pm, Sn^{IV}–F 186 pm). The β-phase also features octahedral coordination in a structure closely related to that of rhombohedral LiSbF$_6$.

Tin(II) chlorides are similarly complex (Fig. 10.5). In the gas phase, SnCl$_2$ forms bent molecules, but the crystalline material (mp 246°, bp 623°) has a layer structure with chains of corner-shared trigonal pyramidal {SnCl$_3$} groups. The dihydrate also has a 3-coordinated structure with only 1 of the H$_2$O molecules directly bonded to the Sn^{II} (Fig. 10.5c); the neutral aquo complexes are arranged in double layers with the second H$_2$O molecules interleaved between them to form a two-dimensional H-bonded network

[26] M. F. A. Dove, R. King and T. J. King, *J. Chem. Soc., Chem. Commun.*, 944–5 (1973).

[27] M. Ruchaud, C. Mirambet, L. Fournes, J. Grannec and J. L. Soubeyroux, *Z. anorg. allg. Chem.* **590**, 173–80 (1990).

with the coordinated H_2O (O—H$\cdots$O 274, 279, and 280 pm.[28] If the aquo ligand is replaced by Cl^- the pyramidal $SnCl_3^-$ ion (isoelectronic with $SbCl_3$) is obtained, e.g. in $CsSnCl_3$ Fig. 10.5d). There seems little tendency to add a second ligand: e.g. the compound $K_2SnCl_4.H_2O$ has been shown to contain pyramidal $SnCl_3^-$ and "isolated" Cl^- ions, i.e. $K_2[SnCl_3]Cl.H_2O$ with Sn—Cl 259 pm and the angle Cl–Sn–Cl $\sim$85°. Again, reaction of $[Co(en)_3]Cl_3$ and $SnCl_2.2H_2O$ in excess HCl gives $[Co(en)_3]^{3+}[SnCl_3]^-(Cl^-)_2$. However, reaction of the closely related complex $[Co(NH_3)_6]Cl_3$ with $SnCl_2$ in aqueous HCl/NaCl solution yields $[Co(NH_3)_6]^{3+}[SnCl_4]^{2-}(Cl)^-$ in which the novel $[SnCl_4]^{2-}$ anion has a distorted pseudo-trigonal bipyramidal structure as shown in Fig. 10.5(e), the axial angle Cl–Sn–Cl being 164.7°.[29] The bridged dinuclear anion $[Sn_2Cl_5]^-$ is also known known, i.e. $[Cl_2Sn(\mu$-$Cl)SnCl_2]^-$.[30] as in the corresponding $[Sn_2F_5]^-$ (Fig. 10.4a). The lone pair of electrons in $SnCl_3^-$ can itself act as a ligating bond: for example, $SnCl_3^-$ can replace PPh_3 from the central Au atom in the cluster cation $[Au_8(PPh_3)_8]^{2+}$ to give $[Au_8(PPh_3)_7(SnCl_3)]^+$.[31] Another interesting system involves crown complexes (p. 96) such as $[Sn(18\text{-crown-}6)Cl]^+[SnCl_3]^-$ in which the cation features 7-coordinate hexagonal-pyramidal Sn^{II}.[32]

Apart from its structural interest, $SnCl_2$ is important as a widely used mild reducing agent in acid solution. The dihydrate is commercially available for use in electrolytic tin-plating baths, as a sensitizer in silvering mirrors and in the plating of plastics, and as a perfume stabilizer in toilet soaps. The anhydrous material can be obtained either by dehydration using acetic anhydride or directly by reacting heated Sn with dry HCl gas.

$SnBr_2$ is a white solid when pure (mp 216°, bp 620°); it has a layer-lattice structure but the details are unknown. It forms numerous hydrates (e.g. $3SnBr_2.H_2O$, $2SnBr_2.H_2O$, $6SnBr_2.5H_2O$) all of which have a distorted trigonal prism of 6 Br about the Sn^{II} with a further Br and H_2O capping one or two of the prism faces and leaving the third face uncapped (presumably because of the presence of the nonbonding pair of electrons in that direction).[33] A similar pseudo-9-coordinate structure is adopted by $3PbBr_2.2H_2O$. By contrast, $NH_4SnBr_3.H_2O$ adopts a structure in which Sn^{II} is coordinated by a tetragonal pyramid of 5 Br atoms which form chains by edge sharing of the 4 basal Br; the Sn^{II} is slightly above the basal plane with Sn–Br 304–350 pm and Sn–Br_{apex} 269 pm. The NH_4^+ and H_2O form rows between the chains.

SnI_2 forms as brilliant red needles (mp 316°, bp 720°) when Sn is heated with I_2 in 2 M hydrochloric acid. It has a unique structure in which one-third of the Sn atoms are in almost perfect octahedral coordination in rutile-like chains (2 Sn–I 314.7 pm, 4 Sn–I 317.4 pm, and no significant distortions of angles from 90°); these chains are in turn cross-linked by double chains containing the remaining Sn atoms which are themselves 7-coordinate (5 Sn–I all on one side at 300.4–325.1 and 2 more-distant I at 371.8 pm).[34] There is an indication here of reduced distortion in the octahedral site and this has been observed more generally for compounds with the heavier halides and chalcogenides in which the nonbonding electron pair on Sn^{II} can delocalize into a low-lying band of the crystal. Accordingly, SnTe is a metalloid with cubic NaCl structure. Likewise, $CsSn^{II}Br_3$ has the ideal cubic perovskite structure (p. 963);[35] the compound forms black lustrous crystals with a semi-metallic

28 H. KIRIYAMA, K. KITAHAMA, O. NAKAMURA and R. KIRIYAMA, *Bull. Chem. Soc. Japan* **46**, 1389–95 (1973).

29 H. J. HAUPT, F. HUBER and H. PREUT, *Z. anorg. allg. Chem.* **422**, 97–103 (1976).

30 M. VEITH, B. GÜDICKE and V. HUCH, *Z. anorg. allg. Chem.* **579**, 99–110 (1989).

31 Z. DEMIDOWICZ, R. L. JOHNSTON, J. C. MACHELL, D. M. P. MINGOS and I. D. WILLIAMS, *J. Chem. Soc., Dalton Trans.*, 1751–6 (1988)..

32 M. G. B. DREW and D. G. NICHOLSON, *J. Chem. Soc., Dalton Trans.*, 1543–9 (1986).

33 J. ANDERSON, *Acta Chem. Scand.* **26**, 1730, 2543, 3813 (1973).

34 R. A. HOWIE, W. MOSER and I. C. TREVENA, *Acta Cryst.* **B28**, 2965–71 (1972).

35 J. D. DONALDSON, J. SILVER, S. HADJIMINOLIS and S. D. ROSS, *J. Chem. Soc., Dalton Trans.*, 1500–6 (1975) and

conductivity of $\sim 10^3 \, \text{ohm}^{-1} \, \text{cm}^{-1}$ at room temperature due, it is thought, to the population of a low-lying conduction band formed by the overlap of "empty" t_2 5d orbitals on Br. In this connection it is noteworthy that $Cs_2Sn^{IV}Br_6$ has a very similar structure to $CsSn^{II}Br_3$ (i.e. $Cs_2Sn^{II}_2Br_6$) but with only half the Sn sites occupied — it is white and non-conducting since there are no high-energy nonbonding electrons to populate the conduction band which must be present. Similarly, yellow $CsSn^{II}I_3$, $CsSn^{II}_2Br_5$, $Cs_4Sn^{II}Br_6$ and compositions in the system $CsSn^{II}_2X_5$ (X = Cl, Br) all transform to black metalloids on being warmed, and even yellow monoclinic $CsSnCl_3$ (Fig. 10.5d) transforms at 90° to a dark-coloured cubic perovskite structure. In solutions of SnX_2 in aqueous HX, however, the pyramidal SnX_3^- ions are formed and, by suitable mixtures of halides followed by extraction into Et_2O, all ten trihalogenostannate(II) anions $[SnCl_xBr_yI_z]^-$ $(x + y + z = 3)$ have been observed and characterized by ^{119}Sn nmr spectroscopy.[36]

Tin(IV) halides are more straightforward. SnF_4 (prepared by the action of anhydrous HF on $SnCl_4$) is an extremely hygroscopic, white crystalline compound which sublimes above 700°. The structure (unlike that of CF_4, SiF_4 and GeF_4) is polymeric with octahedral coordination

Property	SnF_4	$SnCl_4$
Colour	White	Colourless
MP/°C	–	−33.3
BP/°C	~705 (subl)	114
Density $(T°C)$/g cm^{-3}	4.78 (20°)	2.234(20°)
Sn–X/pm	188, 202	231

Property	$SnBr_4$	SnI_4
Colour	Colourless	Brown
MP/°C	31	144
BP/°C	205	348
Density $(T°C)$/g cm^{-3}	3.340(35°)	4.56(20°)
Sn–X/pm	244	264

about Sn: the $\{SnF_6\}$ units are joined into planar layers by edge-sharing of 4 equatorial F atoms ($Sn-F_\mu$ 202 pm) leaving 2 further (terminal) F in *trans* positions above and below each Sn ($Sn-F_t$ 188 pm). The other SnX_4 can be made by direct action of the elements and are unremarkable volatile liquids or solids comprising tetrahedral molecules. Similarities with the tetrahalides of Si and Ge are obvious. The compounds hydrolyse readily but definite hydrates can also be isolated from acid solution, e.g. $SnCl_4.5H_2O$, $SnBr_4.4H_2O$. Complexes with a wide range of organic and inorganic ligands are known, particularly the 6-coordinate *cis*- and *trans*-L_2SnX_4 and occasionally the 1:1 complexes $LSnX_4$. Stereochemistry has been deduced by infrared and Mössbauer spectroscopy and, when possible, by X-ray crystallography. The octahedral complexes SnX_6^{2-} (X = Cl, Br, I) are also well characterized for numerous cations. Five-coordinate trigonal bipyramidal complexes are less common but have been established for $SnCl_5^-$ and $Me_2SnCl_3^-$. A novel rectangular pyramidal geometry for Sn^{IV} has been revealed by X-ray analysis of the spirocyclic dithiolato complex anion $[(MeC_6H_3S_2)_2SnCl]^-$: the Cl atom occupies the apical position and the Sn atom is slightly above the plane of the 4 S atoms (mean angle Cl–Sn–Cl 103°).[37] A similar stereochemistry has also been established for Si^{IV} (p. 335) and for Ge^{IV} in $[(C_6H_4O_2)_2GeCl]^-$.

Lead halides

Lead continues the trends outlined in preceding sections, PbX_2 being much more stable thermally and chemically than PbX_4. Indeed, the only stable tetrahalide is the yellow PbF_4 (mp 600°); $PbCl_4$ is a yellow oil (mp −15°) stable below 0° but decomposing to $PbCl_2$ and Cl_2 above 50°; $PbBr_4$ is even less stable and PbI_4 is of doubtful existence (cf. discussion on TlI_3, p. 239). Stability can be markedly increased by coordination: e.g.

1980–3 (1975); see also J. D. DONALDSON and J. SILVER, *J. Chem. Soc., Dalton Trans.*, 666–9 (1973).

[36] J. M. CODDINGTON and M. J. TAYLOR, *J. Chem. Soc., Dalton Trans.*, 2223–7 (1989).

[37] A. C. SAU, R. O. DAY and R. R. HOLMES, *Inorg. Chem.* **20**, 3076–81 (1981); *J. Am. Chem. Soc.* **102**, 7972–3 (1980).

direct chlorination of $PbCl_2$ in aqueous HCl followed by addition of an alkali metal chloride gives stable yellow salts M_2PbCl_6 (M = Na, K, Rb, Cs, NH_4) which can serve as a useful source of Pb^{IV}. By contrast, PbX_2 are stable crystalline compounds which can readily be prepared by treating any water-soluble Pb^{II} salt with HX or halide ions to precipitate the insoluble PbX_2. As with Sn, the first two ionization energies of Pb are very similar to those of Mg; moreover, the 6-coordinate radius of Pb^{II} (119 pm) is virtually identical with that of Sr^{II} (118 pm) and there is less evidence of the structurally distorting influence of the nonbonding pair of electrons. Thus α-PbF_2, $PbCl_2$, and $PbBr_2$ all form colourless orthorhombic crystals in which Pb^{II} is surrounded by 9 X at the corners of a tricapped trigonal prism. There are, in fact, never 9 equidistant X neighbours but a range of distances in which one can discern 7 closer and 2 more distant neighbours. This (7 + 2)-coordination is also a feature of the structures of BaX_2 (X = Cl, Br, I), $EuCl_2$, CaH_2, etc.; see also hydrated tin(II) bromides, p. 380.

The high-temperature β-form of PbF_2 has the cubic fluorite (CaF_2) structure with 8-coordinated Pb^{II}. PbI_2 (yellow) has the CdI_2 hexagonal layer lattice structure. Like many other heavy-metal halides, $PbCl_2$ and $PbBr_2$ are photo-sensitive and deposit metallic Pb on irradiation with ultraviolet or visible light. PbI_2 is a photoconductor and decomposes on exposure to green light (λ_{max} 494.9 nm). Many mixed halides have also been characterized, e.g. PbFCl, PbFBr, PbFI, $PbX_2.4PbF_2$, etc. Of these PbFCl is an important tetragonal layer-lattice structure type frequently adopted by large cations in the presence of 2 anions of differing size;[38] its sparing solubility in water (37 mg per 100 cm^3 at 25°C) forms the basis of a gravimetric method of determining F. It is also interesting to note that PbF_2 was the first ionically conducting crystalline compound to be discovered (Michael Faraday, 1838).

Property	PbF_2	$PbCl_2$
MP/°C	818	500
BP/°C	1290	953
Density/g cm^{-3}	8.24 (α), 7.77 (β)	5.85
Solubility in H_2O (T°C)/ mg per 100 cm^3	64 (20°)	670 (0°) 3200 (100°)

Property	$PbBr_2$	PbI_2
MP/°C	367	400
BP/°C	916	860–950 (decomp)
Density/g cm^{-3}	6.66	6.2
Solubility in H_2O (T°C)/ mg per 100 cm^3	455 (0°) 4710 (100°)	44 (0°) 410 (100°)

Pb^{II} apparently forms complexes with an astonishing range of stoichiometries,[39] but structural information is frequently lacking. Cs_4PbX_6 (X = Cl, Br, I) have the K_4CdCl_6 structure with discrete $[Pb^{II}X_6]^{4-}$ units. $CsPb^{II}X_3$ also feature octahedral coordination (in perovskite-like structures, cf. p. 963) but there is sometimes appreciable distortion as in the yellow, low-temperature form of $CsPbI_3$ which adopts the NH_4CdCl_3 structure with three Pb–I distances, 301, 325, and 342 pm. Note also the orange-yellow crystalline compound of overall composition $[Co(en)_3PbCl_5.1.5H_2O]$ which in fact features a novel chain anion $[Pb_2Cl_9]_n^{5n-}$ and should be formulated $[Co(en)_3]_2[Pb_2Cl_9]$-$Cl.3H_2O$.[40] There are also many ternary solid state compounds, e.g. $Pb^{II}_{13}O_{10}Br_6$.[41]

10.3.3 Oxides and hydroxides

GeO is obtained as a yellow sublimate when powdered Ge and GeO_2 are heated to 1000°, and dark-brown crystalline GeO is obtained on further heating at 650°. The compound can also be obtained by dehydrating $Ge(OH)_2$

[38] N. N. GREENWOOD, *Ionic Crystals, Lattice Defects, and Nonstoichiometry*, pp. 59–60, Butterworths, London 1968.

[39] E. W. ABEL, Lead, Chap. 18 in *Comprehensive Inorganic Chemistry*, Vol. 2, pp. 105–46, Pergamon Press, Oxford, 1973.

[40] A. AQUILINO, M. CANNAS, A. CHRISTINI and G. MARONGIU, *J. Chem. Soc., Chem. Commun.*, 347–8 (1978).

[41] H.-J. RIEBE and H.-L. KELLER, *Z. anorg. allg. Chem.* **571**, 139–47 (1989).

(p. 376) but neither compound is particularly well characterized. Both are reducing agents and GeO disproportionates rapidly to Ge and GeO_2 above 700°. Much more is known about GeO_2 and there is an impressive resemblance between the oxide chemistry of Ge^{IV} and Si^{IV}. Thus hexagonal GeO_2 has the 4-coordinated β-quartz structure (p. 342), tetragonal GeO_2 has the 6-coordinated rutile-like structure of stishovite (p. 343), and vitreous GeO_2 resembles fused silica. Similarly, Ge analogues of all the major types of silicates and aluminosilicates (pp. 347–59) have been prepared. Be_2GeO_4 and Zn_2GeO_4 have the phenacite and willemite structures with "isolated" $\{GeO_4\}$ units; $Sc_2Ge_2O_7$ has the thortveitite structure; $BaTiGe_3O_9$ has the same type of cyclic ion as benitoite, and $CaMgGe_2O_6$ has a chain structure similar to diopside. Further, the two crystalline forms of Ca_2GeO_4 are isostructural with two forms of Ca_2SiO_4, and Ca_3GeO_5 crystallizes in no fewer than 4 of the known structures of Ca_3SiO_5. The reaction chemistry of the two sets of compounds is also very similar.

SnO exists in several modifications. The commonest is the blue-black tetragonal modification formed by the alkaline hydrolysis of Sn^{II} salts to the hydrous oxide and subsequent dehydration in the absence of air. The structure features square pyramids of $\{SnO_4\}$ arranged in parallel layers with Sn^{II} at the apex and alternately above and below the layer of O atoms as shown in Fig. 10.6. The Sn–Sn distance between tin atoms in adjacent layers is 370 pm, very close to the values in β-Sn (p. 372). The structure can also be described as a fluorite lattice with alternate layers of anions missing. A metastable, red modification of SnO is obtained by heating the white hydrous oxide; this appears to have a similar structure and it can be transformed into the blue-black form by heating, by pressure, by treatment with strong alkali or simply by contact with the stable form. Both forms oxidize to SnO_2 with incandescence when heated in air to $\sim300°$ but when heated in the absence of O_2, the compound disproportionates like GeO. Various mixed-valence oxides have also been reported of which the best characterized is Sn_3O_4, i.e. $Sn_2^{II}Sn^{IV}O_4$.

SnO and hydrous tin(II) oxide are amphoteric, dissolving readily in aqueous acids to give Sn^{II} or its complexes, and in alkalis to give the pyramidal $Sn(OH)_3^-$; at intermediate values of pH, condensed basic oxide–hydroxide species form, e.g. $[(OH)_2SnOSn(OH)_2]^{2-}$ and $[Sn_3(OH)_4]^{2+}$, etc. Analytically, the hydrous oxide frequently has a composition close to $3SnO.H_2O$ and an X-ray study shows it to

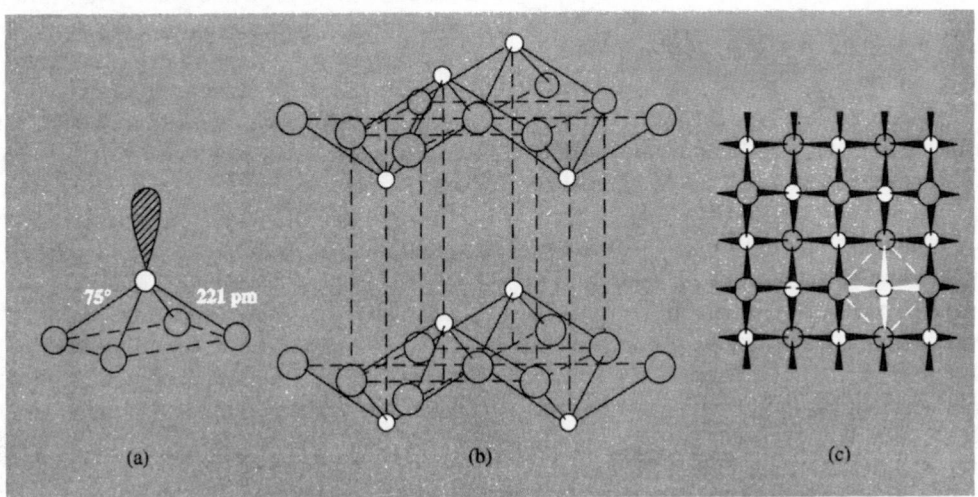

Figure 10.6   Structure of tetragonal SnO (and PbO) showing (a) a single square-based pyramid $\{:SnO_4\}$, (b) the arrangement of the pyramids in layers, and (c) a plane view of a single layer.

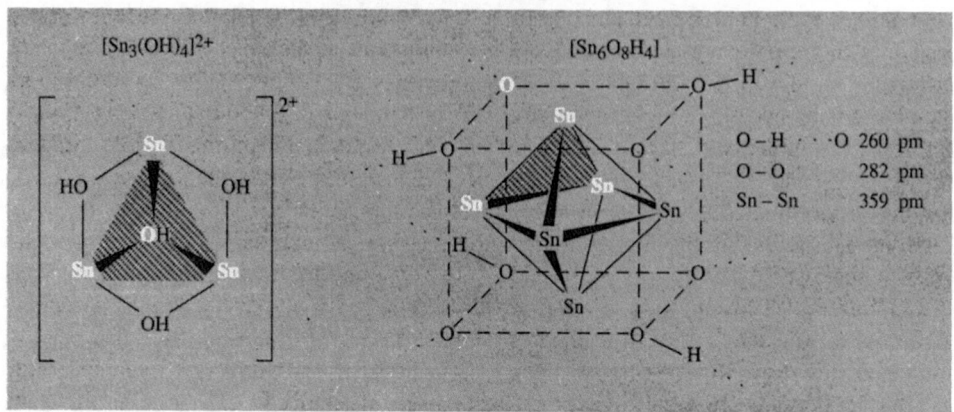

contain pseudo-cubic Sn_6O_8 clusters resembling $Mo_6Cl_8^{4+}$ (p. 1022) with 8 oxygen atoms centred above the faces of an Sn_6 octahedron and joined in infinite array by H bonds, i.e. $Sn_6O_8H_4$; the compound can be thought of as being formed by the deprotonation and condensation of $2[Sn_3(OH)_4]^{2+}$ units as the pH is raised:

$$2[Sn_3(OH)_4]^{2+} + 4OH^- \longrightarrow [Sn_6O_8H_4] + 4H_2O$$

(Hydrolysis of Pb^{II} salts leads to different structures, p. 395.) It seems unlikely that pure $Sn(OH)_2$ itself has ever been prepared from aqueous solutions but it can be obtained as a white, amorphous solid by an anhydrous organometallic method:[42]

$$2Me_3SnOH + SnCl_2 \xrightarrow{thf} Sn(OH)_2 + 2Me_3SnCl$$

SnO_2, cassiterite, is the main ore of tin and it crystallizes with a rutile-type structure (p. 961). It is insoluble in water and dilute acids or alkalis but dissolves readily in fused alkali hydroxides to form "stannates" $M_2^I Sn(OH)_6$. Conversely, aqueous solutions of tin(IV) salts hydrolyse to give a white precipitate of hydrous tin(IV) oxide which is readily soluble in both acids and alkalis thereby demonstrating the amphoteric nature of tin(IV). $Sn(OH)_4$ itself is not known, but a reproducible product of empirical formula $SnO_2.H_2O$ can be obtained by drying the hydrous gel at $110°$, and further dehydration

at temperatures up to $600°$ eventually yields crystalline SnO_2. Similarly, thermal dehydration of $K_2[Sn(OH)_6]$, i.e. "$K_2SnO_3.3H_2O$", yields successively $K_2SnO_3.H_2O$, $3K_2SnO_3.2H_2O$ and, finally, anhydrous K_2SnO_3; this latter compound also results when K_2O is heated directly with SnO_2, and variations in the ratio of the two reactants yield K_4SnO_4 and $K_2Sn_3O_7$. The structure of K_2SnO_3 does not have 6-coordinate Sn^{IV} but chains of 5-coordinate Sn^{IV} of composition $\{SnO_3\}$ formed by the edge sharing of tetragonal pyramids of $\{SnO_5\}$ as shown in Fig. 10.7. The colourless compound $RbNa_3SnO_4$, formed by heating RbSn and Na_2O_2 at $750°$ has tetrahedral SnO_4^{4-} units (Sn–O 196 pm); it is isotypic with $NaLi_3SiO_4$ and $NaLi_3GeO_4$.[43] Some industrial uses of tin(IV) oxide systems and other tin compounds are summarized in the Panel (opposite).

Much confusion exists concerning the number, composition, and structure of the oxides of lead. PbO exists as a red tetragonal form (litharge) stable at room temperature and a yellow orthorhombic form (massicot) stable above $488°C$. Litharge (mp $897°$, d $9.355\,g\,cm^{-3}$) is not only the most important oxide of Pb, it is also the most widely used inorganic compound of Pb (see Panel on p. 386); it is made by reacting molten Pb with air or O_2 above $600°$ and has the SnO structure (p. 383, Pb–O 230 pm). Massicot (d $9.642\,g\,cm^{-3}$) has

[42] W. D. HONNICK and J. J. ZUCKERMAN, *Inorg. Chem.* **15**, 3034–7 (1976).

[43] K. BERNET and R. HOPPE, *Z. anorg. allg. Chem.* **571**, 101–12 (1989).

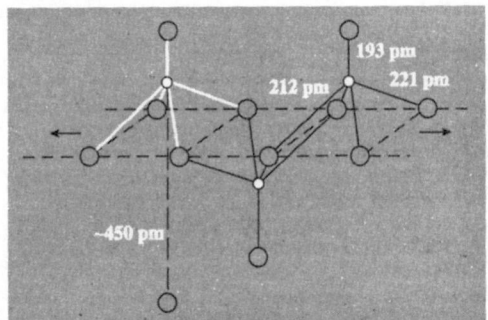

Figure 10.7 {SnO₃} chain in the structure of K₂SnO₃ (and K₂PbO₃).

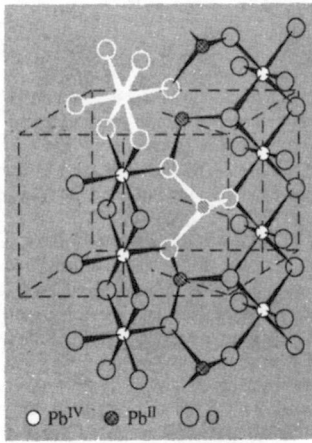

○ Pb^IV   ◉ Pb^II   ○ O

Figure 10.8 Portion of the crystal structure of Pb₃O₄ showing chains of edge-shared Pb^IVO₆ octahedra joined by pyramids of Pb^IIO₃; the mean O–Pb^II–O angle is 76° as in PbO.

a distorted version of the same structure. The mixed-valency oxide Pb₃O₄ (red lead, minium, d 8.924 g cm⁻³) is made by heating PbO in air in a reverberatory furnace at 450–500° and is important commercially as a pigment and primer (see Panel on p. 386). Its structure (Fig. 10.8) consists of chains of Pb^IVO₆ octahedra (Pb–O 214 pm) sharing opposite edges, these chains being linked by the Pb^II atoms which themselves

---

Some Industrial Uses of Tin Compounds

Tin(IV) oxide is much used an the ceramics industry as an opacifier for glazes and enamels. Because of its insolubility (or, rather, slow solubility) in glasses and glazes it also serves as a base for pigments, e.g. SnO₂/V₂O₅ yellows, SnO₂/Sb₂O₅ blue-greys and SnO₂/Cr₂O₃ pinks. These latter, which can vary from a delicate pale pink to a dark maroon, probably involve substitutional incorporation of Cr^III for Sn^IV with concomitant oxide-ion vacancies, i.e. [Sn^IV_{1−2x}Cr^III_{2x}O^{−}_{2−x} (□_−)_x]. The vanadium- and antimony-tin glazes, on the other hand, probably involve reductive substitution without vacant sites, e.g. [Sn^IV_{1−3x}Sn^II_{2x}Sb^V_x O^{−II}_2]. Some 3500 tonnes of SnO₂ are consumed annually for ceramic glazes.

A related application is the use of SnCl₄ vapour to toughen freshly fabricated glass bottles by deposition of an invisible transparent film of SnO₂ (<0.1 μm) which is then incorporated in the surface structure of the glass. This increases the strength of the glass and improves its abrasion resistance so that bottles so treated can be made considerably lighter without loss of robustness. When the thickness of the SnO₂ film is similar to the wavelength of visible light (0.1–1.0 μm), then thin-film interference effects occur and the glass acquires an attractive iridescence. Still thicker films give electrically conducting layers which, after suitable doping with Sb or F ions, can be used as electrodes, electro-luminescent devices (for low-intensity light panels and display signs, in aircraft, cinemas, etc.), fluorescent lamps, antistatic cover-glasses, transparent tube furnaces, deiceable windscreens (especially for aircraft), etc. Another property of these thicker films is their ability to reflect a high proportion of infrared (heat) radiation whilst remaining transparent to visible radiation — the application to heat insulation of windows is obvious.

Attention should be drawn to the use of tin oxide systems as heterogeneous catalysts. The oldest and most extensively patented systems are the mixed tin–vanadium oxide catalysts for the oxidation of aromatic compounds such as benzene, toluene, xylenes and naphthalene in the synthesis of organic acids and acid anhydrides. More recently mixed tin–antimony oxides have been applied to the selective oxidation and ammoxidation of propylene to acrolein, acrylic acid and acrylonitrile.

Homogeneous catalysis by tin compounds is also of great industrial importance. The use of SnCl₄ as a Friedel–Crafts catalyst for homogeneous acylation, alkylation and cyclization reactions has been known for many decades. The most commonly used industrial homogeneous tin catalysts, however, are the Sn(II) salts of organic acids (e.g. acetate, oxalate, oleate, stearate and octoate) for the curing of silicone elastomers and, more importantly, for the production of polyurethane foams. World consumption of tin catalysts for these last applications alone is over 1000 tonnes pa.

For uses of organotin compounds (i.e. compounds having at least one Sn–C bond), see p. 400.

The Oxides of Lead[(9,10)]

PbO (red, orange or yellow depending on the method of preparation) is amphoteric and dissolves readily in both acids and alkalis. It is much used in glass manufacture since a high Pb content leads to greater density, lower thermal conductivity, higher refractive index (greater brilliance), and greater stability and toughness. The replacement of the very mobile alkali ions by Pb also leads to high electrical capacities, comparable with mica. PbO is also used to form stable ceramic glazes and vitreous enamels (see SnO_2, p. 385). Electric storage batteries are the other major user of PbO (either as litharge or as "black oxide", i.e. PbO + Pb). The plates of the battery consist of an inactive grid or support onto which is applied a paste of PbO/H_2SO_4. The positive plates are activated by oxidizing PbO to PbO_2 and the negative plates by reducing PbO to Pb. Another use of PbO is in the production of pigments (p. 371).

Red lead (Pb_3O_4) is manufactured on the 20 000-tonne scale annually and is used primarily as a surface coating to prevent corrosion of iron and steel (check oxidation-reduction potentials). It is also used in the production of leaded glasses and ceramic glazes and, very substantially, as an activator, vulcanizing agent and pigment in natural and artificial rubbers and plastics.

PbO_2 is a strong oxidizing agent and, in addition to its *in situ* production in storage batteries, it is independently manufactured for use as an oxidant in the manufacture of chemicals, dyes, matches and pyrotechnics. It is also used in considerable quantity as a curing agent for sulfide polymers and in high-voltage lightning arresters. Because of the instability of Pb^{IV}, PbO_2 tends to give salts of Pb^{II} with liberation of O_2 when treated with acids, e.g.

$$PbO_2 + H_2SO_4 \xrightarrow{\text{warm}} PbSO_4 + H_2O + \tfrac{1}{2}O_2$$

$$PbO_2 + 2HNO_3 \longrightarrow Pb(NO_3)_2 + H_2O + \tfrac{1}{2}O_2$$

Warm HCl reacts similarly but in the cold $PbCl_4$ is obtained. PbO_2 is produced commercially by the oxidation of Pb_3O_4 in alkaline slurry with Cl_2 and the technical product is marketed in 90-kg drums.

Mixed oxides of Pb^{IV} with other metals find numerous applications in technology and industry. They are usually made by heating PbO_2 (or PbO) in air with the appropriate oxide, hydroxide or oxoacid salt, the product formed being dependent on the stoichiometry used, e.g. $M^{II}Pb^{IV}O_3$, $M_2^{II}Pb^{IV}O_4$ (M^{II} = Ca, Sr, Ba). $CaPbO_3$ in particular is increasingly replacing Pb_3O_4 as a priming pigment to protect steel against corrosion by salt water. Mixed oxides of Pb^{II} are also important. Ferrimagnetic oxides of general formula $PbO.nFe_2O_3$ (n = 6, 5, 2.5, 1, 0.5) can be prepared by direct reaction but have not proved to be as attractive, commercially, as the hard ferrite $BaFe_{12}O_{19}$. By contrast, the ferroelectric behaviour (p. 57) of several mixed oxides with Pb^{II} has excited considerable interest. Many of these compounds have a distorted perovskite-type structure (p. 963); e.g. yellow $PbTiO_3$ (ferroelectric below 490°C), colourless $PbZrO_3$ (230°), and $PbHfO_3$ (215°, antiferroelectric). Others have a tetragonal tungsten-bronze-type structure (p. 1016), e.g. $PbNb_2O_6$ (ferroelectric up to 560°C), $PbTi_2O_6$ (~215°). The mode of action and uses of hard ferroelectrics has been discussed on p. 58, and the high Curie temperature of many Pb^{II} ferroelectrics makes them particularly useful for high-temperature applications.

are pyramidally coordinated by 3 oxygen atoms (2 at 218 pm and 1 at 213 pm). The dioxide normally occurs as the maroon-coloured PbO_2(I) which has the tetragonal, rutile structure (Pb^{IV}–O 218 pm, d 9.643 g cm^{-3}), but there is also a high-pressure, black, orthorhombic polymorph, PbO_2(II) (d 9.773 g cm^{-3}).

When PbO_2 is heated in air it decomposes as follows:[(44)]

$$PbO_2 \xrightarrow{293°} Pb_{12}O_{19} \xrightarrow{351°} Pb_{12}O_{17}$$
$$\xrightarrow{374°} Pb_3O_4 \xrightarrow{605°} PbO$$

---

[44] W. B. WHITE and R. RAY, *J. Am. Ceram. Soc.* **47**, 242–7 (1964) and references therein.

In addition, a sesquioxide Pb_2O_3 can be obtained as vitreous black monoclinic crystals (d 10.046 g cm^{-3}) by decomposing PbO_2 (or PbO) at 580–620° under an oxygen pressure of 1.4 kbar: in this compound the Pb^{II} atoms are situated between layers of distorted $Pb^{IV}O_6$ octahedra (mean Pb^{IV}–O 218 pm) with 3 Pb^{II}–O in the range 231–246 pm and 3 in the range 264–300 pm. The monoclinic compound $Pb_{12}O_{19}$ (i.e. $PbO_{1.583}$) forms dark-brown or black crystals which have a pseudocubic defect-fluorite structure with 10 ordered anion vacancies according to the formulation $[Pb_{24}O_{38}(\square_-)_{10}]$ and no detectable variability of composition. It will be recalled that PbO can be considered as a defect fluorite structure in which each alternate layer of O atoms in the (001) direction is missing (p. 383), i.e. $[Pb_{24}O_{24}(\square_-)_{24}]$; it therefore seems reasonable to suppose that the anion vacancies in $[Pb_{24}O_{38}(\square_-)_{10}]$ are also confined to alternate layers, though it is not clear why this structure should show no variability in composition. Further heating above 350° (or careful oxidation of PbO) yields $Pb_{12}O_{17}$ (i.e. $PbO_{1.417}$) which is also a stoichiometric ordered defect fluorite structure $[Pb_{24}O_{34}(\square_-)_{14}]$. However, oxidation of this phase under increasing oxygen pressure leads to a nonstoichiometric phase of variable composition between $PbO_{1.42}$ and $PbO_{1.57}$ in which there appears to be a quasi-random array of anion vacancies.[45]

Lead does not appear to form a simple hydroxide, $Pb(OH)_2$, [cf. $Sn(OH)_2$, p. 384]. Instead, increasing the pH of solutions of Pb^{II} salts leads to hydrolysis and condensation, see $[Pb_6O(OH)_6]^{4+}$ (p. 395).

10.3.4 Derivatives of oxoacids

Oxoacid salts of Ge are usually unstable, generally uninteresting, and commercially unimportant. The tetraacetate $Ge(OAc)_4$ separates as white needles, mp 156°, when $GeCl_4$ is treated with TlOAc in acetic anhydride and the resulting solution is concentrated at low pressure and cooled. An unstable sulfate $Ge(SO_4)_2$ is formed in a curious reaction when $GeCl_4$ is heated with SO_3 in a sealed tube at 160°:

$$GeCl_4 + 6SO_3 \longrightarrow Ge(SO_4)_2 + 2S_2O_5Cl_2$$

Numerous oxoacid salts of Sn^{II} and Sn^{IV} have been reported and several basic salts are also known. Anhydrous $Sn(NO_3)_2$ has not been prepared but the basic salt $Sn_3(OH)_4(NO_3)_2$ can be made by reacting a paste of hydrous tin(II) oxide with aqueous HNO_3; the compound may well contain the oligomeric cation $[Sn_3(OH)_4]^{2+}$ illustrated on p. 384. $Sn(NO_3)_4$ can be obtained in anhydrous reactions of $SnCl_4$ with N_2O_5, $ClNO_3$ or $BrNO_3$; the compound readily oxidizes or nitrates organic compounds, probably by releasing reactive NO_3 radicals. Many phosphates and phosphato complexes have been described: typical examples for Sn^{II} are $Sn_3(PO_4)_2$, $SnHPO_4$, $Sn(H_2PO_4)_2$, $Sn_2P_2O_7$ and $Sn(PO_3)_2$. Examples with Sn^{IV} are $Sn_2O(PO_4)_2$, $Sn_2O(PO_4)_2.10H_2O$, SnP_4O_7, $KSn(PO_4)_3$, $KSnOPO_4$ and $Na_2Sn(PO_4)_2$. One remarkable compound is tin(IV) hypophosphite, $Sn(H_2PO_2)_4$ since it contains Sn^{IV} in the presence of the strongly reducing hypophosphorous anion; it has been suggested that the isolation of $Sn(H_2PO_2)_4$ (colourless crystals) by bubbling O_2 through a solution of SnO in hypophosphorous acid, $[H_2PO(OH)]$, may be due to a combination of kinetic effects and the low solubility of the product.

Treatment of SnO_2 with hot dilute H_2SO_4 yields the hygroscopic dihydrate $Sn(SO_4)_2.2H_2O$. In the Sn^{II} series $SnSO_4$ is a stable, colourless compound which is probably the most convenient laboratory source of Sn^{II} uncontaminated with Sn^{IV}; it is readily prepared by using metallic Sn to displace Cu from aqueous solutions of $CuSO_4$. $SnSO_4$ was at one time thought to be isostructural with $BaSO_4$ but this seemed unlikely in view of the very different sizes of the cations and the known propensity of Sn^{II} to form distorted structures; it is now known to consist of $\{SO_4\}$ groups linked into a framework by O–Sn–O bonds in such a way that Sn is pyramidally coordinated by 3 O atoms at 226 pm (O–Sn–O angles 77–79°); other Sn–O distances are much larger and fall in the range 295–334 pm.[46] A basic sulfate and oxosulfate are also known:

$$3Sn^{II}SO_4(aq) \xrightarrow{NH_3(aq)} [Sn_3^{II}(OH)_2O(SO_4)]$$

$$\xrightarrow{230°} [Sn_3^{II}O_2SO_4]$$

The crystal structures of the oxalates SnC_2O_4 and $K_2Sn(C_2O_4)_2.H_2O$ show interesting features[47]

[45] J. S. ANDERSON and M. STERNS, *J. Inorg. Nucl. Chem.* **11**, 272–85 (1959).

[46] J. D. DONALDSON and D. C. PUXLEY, *Acta Cryst.* **28B**, 864–7 (1972).

[47] A. D. CHRISTIE, R. A. HOWIE and W. MOSER, *Inorg. Chim. Acta.* **36**, L447–L448 (1979).

reminiscent of tetragonal SnO (Fig. 10.6). The organotin(IV) sulfate $(Me_3Sn)_2SO_4.2H_2O$ has trigonal bipyramidal Sn with trans-O_2SnMe_3 stereochemistry, i.e. $[H_2O-SnMe_3-(\mu-OSO_2O)-SnMe_3-OH_2]$; H-bonding between the two non-bridging O-atoms of the sulfate group and water molecules in neighbouring units produces a three-dimensional network.[48] In general, the product obtained by the thermal decomposition of Sn^{II} oxoacid salts depends on the coordinating strength of the oxoacid anion. For strong ligands such as formate, acetate and phosphite, other Sn^{II} compounds are formed (often SnO), whereas for less-strongly coordinating ligands such as the sulfate or nitrate internal oxidation to SnO_2 occurs, e.g.:

Strong ligands:

$$2Sn(HCO_2)_2 \xrightarrow{200°} 2SnO + H_2CO + CO_2$$

$$Sn(MeCO_2)_2 \xrightarrow{240°} SnO + Me_2CO + CO_2$$

$$5SnHPO_3 \xrightarrow{325°} Sn_2^{II}P_2O_7 + Sn_3^{II}(PO_4)_2 + PH_3 + H_2$$

$$2SnHPO_4 \xrightarrow{395°} Sn_2^{II}P_2O_7 + H_2O$$

Weak ligands:

$$2SnO \xrightarrow{350°} SnO_2 + Sn$$

$$SnSO_4 \xrightarrow{378°} SnO_2 + SO_2$$

$$Sn_3(OH)_4(NO_3)_2 \xrightarrow[\text{(explosive)}]{125°} 3SnO_2 + 2NO + 2H_2O$$

Most oxoacid derivatives of lead are Pb^{II} compounds, though $Pb(OAc)_4$ is well known and is extensively used as a selective oxidizing agent in organic chemistry.[49] It can be obtained as

colourless, moisture-sensitive crystals by treating Pb_3O_4 with glacial acetic acid. $Pb(SO_4)_2$ is also stable when dry and can be made by the action of conc H_2SO_4 on $Pb(OAc)_4$ or by electrolysis of strong H_2SO_4 between Pb electrodes. $PbSO_4$ is familiar as a precipitate for the gravimetric determination of sulfate (solubility 4.25 mg per $100\,cm^3$ at $25°C$); $PbSeO_4$ is likewise insoluble. By contrast $Pb(NO_3)_2$ is very soluble in water (37.7 g per $100\,cm^3$ at $0°$, 127 g at $100°$). The diacetate is similarly soluble (19.7 and 221 g per $100\,cm^3$ at $0°$ and $50°$ respectively). Both compounds find wide use in the preparation of Pb chemicals by wet methods and are made simply by dissolving PbO in the appropriate aqueous acid. A large number of basic nitrates and acetates is also known. The thermal decomposition of anydrous $Pb(NO_3)_2$ above $400°$ affords a convenient source of N_2O_4 (see p. 456).

Other important Pb^{II} salts are the carbonate, basic carbonate, silicates, phosphates and perchlorate, but little new chemistry is involved. $PbCO_3$ occurs as cerussite; the compound is made as a dense white precipitate by treating the nitrate or acetate with CO_2 in the presence of $(NH_4)_2CO_3$ or Na_2CO_3, care being taken to keep the temperature low to avoid formation of the basic carbonate $\sim2Pb(CO_3).Pb(OH)_2$. These compounds were formerly much used as pigments (white lead) but are now largely replaced by other white pigments such as TiO_2 which has higher covering power and lower toxicity. The highly soluble perchlorate [and even more the tetrafluoroborate $Pb(BF_4)_2$] are much used as electrolytic plating baths for the deposition of Pb to impart corrosion resistance or lubricating properties to various metal parts. Throughout the chemistry of the oxoacid salts of Pb^{II} the close correlation between anionic charge and aqueous solubility is apparent.

The complex coordination chemistry of Pb^{II} is also beginning to be actively explored and some unusual stereochemistries are emerging. Thus, the mononuclear $(\eta^2$-nitrato)bis(phenanthroline)(N-thiocyanato) complex $[Pb(phen)_2(NCS)(\eta^2-NO_3)]$ has 7-coordinate Pb^{II} with a large vacancy

[48] K. C. MOLLOY, K. QUILL, D. CUNNINGHAM, P. McARDLE and T. HIGGINS, *J. Chem. Soc., Dalton Trans.*, 267–73 (1989).

[49] R. N. BUTLER, in J. S. PIZEY (ed.), *Synthetic Reagents*, Vol. 3, pp. 278–419, Wiley Chichester, 1977.

in the coordination sphere, possibly indicating a stereochemically active lone pair.[50] Again, [Pb(phen)$_4$(OClO$_3$)]ClO$_4$ features 9-fold, capped square antiprismatic coordination about Pb,[51] whereas in [Pb[tpy]$_3$][ClO$_4$]$_2$ (tpy = 2, 2':6',2"-terpyridine) there is an unusual D_3 9-coordinate environment around the Pb^{II} centre.[52]

10.3.5 Other inorganic compounds

Few of the many other inorganic compounds of Ge, Sn and Pb call for special comment. Many pseudo-halogen derivatives of Sn^{IV}, Pb^{IV} and Pb^{II} have been reported, e.g. cyanides, azides, iso-cyanates, isothiocyanates, isoselenocyanates and alkoxides.[39,53]

All 9 chalcogenides MX are known (X = S, Se, Te). GeS and SnS are interesting in having layer structures similar to that of the isoelectronic black-P (p. 482). The former is prepared by reducing a fresh precipitate of GeS$_2$ with excess H$_3$PO$_2$ and purifying the resulting amorphous red-brown powder by vacuum sublimation. SnS is usually made by sulfide precipitation from Sn^{II} salts. PbS occurs widely as the black opaque mineral galena, which is the principal ore of Pb (p. 368). In common with PbSe, PbTe and SnTe, it has the cubic NaCl-type structure. Pure PbS can be made by direct reaction of the elements or by reaction of Pb(OAc)$_2$ with thiourea; the pure compound is an intrinsic semiconductor which, in the presence of impurities or stoichiometric imbalance, can develop either *n*-type or *p*-type semiconducting properties (p. 332). It is also a photoconductor (like PbSe and PbTe)

and is one of the most sensitive detectors of infrared radiation; the photovoltaic effect in these compounds is also widely used in photoelectric cells, e.g. PbS in photographic exposure meters. The three compounds are also unusual in that their colour diminishes with increasing molecular weight: PbS is black, PbSe grey, and PbTe white.

Of the selenides, GeSe (mp 667°) forms as a dark-brown precipitate when H$_2$Se is passed into an aqueous solution of GeCl$_2$. SnSe (mp 861°) is a grey-blue solid made by direct reaction of the elements above 350°. PbSe (mp 1075°) can be obtained by volatilizing PbCl$_2$ with H$_2$Se, by reacting PbEt$_4$ with H$_2$Se in organic solvents, or by reducing PbSeO$_4$ with H$_2$ or C in an electric furnace; thin films for semiconductor devices are generally made by the reaction of Pb(OAc)$_2$ with selenourea, (NH$_2$)$_2$CSe. The tellurides are best made by heating Ge, Sn or Pb with the stoichiometric amount of Te.

Other chalcogenides that have been described include GeS$_2$, GeSe$_2$, Sn$_2$S$_3$ and SnSe$_2$, but these introduce no novel chemistry or structural principles. Of more interest, perhaps, is the polymeric anion [Sn$_5$S$_{12}^{4-}$]$_\infty$ (1) which occurs in Cs$_4$Sn$_5$S$_{12}$.2H$_2$O and which contains both trigonal bipyramidal and octahedral Sn^{IV}.[54] The compound was prepared by hydrothermal reaction of Cs$_2$CO$_3$ with SnS$_2$ at 150°C. A similar reaction between Rb$_2$CO$_3$ and SnS$_2$ in saturated aqueous H$_2$S solution at 190°C afforded Rb$_2$Sn$_3$S$_7$.2H$_2$O in which the polymeric [Sn$_3$S$_7^{2-}$]$_\infty$ anion (2) features both SnS$_4$ tetrahedra and SnS$_6$ octahedra.[55] Another new structural form, in which a *commo*-Sn atom joins a double cube, is found in the discrete {Sn$_7$S$_6$O$_2$} cluster core (3) of [{Bu^{t}Sn(S)L}$_3$]$_2$Sn; the diphosphinate ligand L = μ-η^2-O$_2$PPh$_2$ bridges the three non-*commo* Sn atoms in each of the cubes.[56] Examples of

[50] L. M. Engelhardt, J. M. Patrick and A. H. White, *Aust. J. Chem.* **42**, 335–8 (1989). See also L. M. Engelhardt, B. M. Furphy, J. McB. Harrowfield, J. M. Patrick, B. W. Skelton and A. H. White, *J. Chem. Soc., Dalton Trans.*, 595–9 (1989).

[51] L. M. Engelhardt, D. L. Kepert, J. M. Patrick and A. H. White, *Aust. J. Chem.* **42**, 329–34 (1989).

[52] D. L. Kepert, J. M. Patrick, B. W. Skelton and A. H. White, *Aust. J. Chem.* **41**, 157–8 (1988).

[53] E. W. Abel, Tin, Chap. 17 in *Comprehensive Inorganic Chemistry*. Vol. 2, pp. 43–104, Pergamon Press, Oxford, 1973.

[54] W. S. Sheldrick *Z. anorg. allg. Chem.* **562**, 23–30 (1988).

[55] W. S. Sheldrick and B. Schaaf, *Z. anorg. allg. Chem.* **620**, 1041–5 (1994).

[56] K. C. K. Swamy, R. O. Day and R. R. Holmes, *J. Am. Chem. Soc.* **110**, 7543–4 (1988).

square-pyramidal 5-coordinate Sn^{IV} [57.58] and pentagonal bipyramidal 7-coordinate Sn^{IV} [59] have also been recently established in various thio-organotin complexes.

(1) $[Sn_5S_{12}{}^{4-}]_\infty$ **(2)** $[Sn_3S_7{}^{2-}]_\infty$

(3) $\{Sn_7S_6O_2\}$ core

(4) $[Sn_3Se_7{}^{2-}]_\infty$ **(5)** $Ge_4S_6Br_4$

(6) $[Sn\{C(PMe_2)_3\}_2]$

The discrete anions $[Sn_2Se_6]^{4-}$ and $[Sn_2Te_6]^{4-}$ have the B_2H_6-type structure (p. 154) and are known in $Rb_4(Sn_2Se_6)$,[55] $[enH_2]_2[Sn_2Se_6]$[60] and $[NMe_4]_4[Sn_2Te_6]$.[61] By contrast, $[enH_2]$-$[Sn_3Se_7].\frac{1}{2}en$ features a sheet polymeric anion $[Sn_3Se_7{}^{2-}]_\infty$ (4) in which the basic elements are $SnSe_5$ trigonal bipyramids.[60] The adamantane-like anion $[Ge_4Te_{10}]^{4-}$ was identified by X-ray diffraction analysis of the black crystalline salt $[NEt_4]_4[Ge_4Te_{10}]$, prepared in 72% yield by extraction of the alloy of composition $K_4Ge_4Te_{10}$ with ethylene diamine in the presence of Et_4NBr[61a]

The first sulfide halide of Ge was made by the apparently straightforward reaction:

$$4GeBr_4 + 6H_2S \xrightarrow{CS_2/Al_2Br_6} Ge_4S_6Br_4 + 12HBr$$

The unexpectedly complex product was isolated as an almost colourless air-stable powder, and a single-crystal X-ray analysis showed that it had the molecular adamantane-like structure (5).[62] This is very similar to the structure of the "iso-electronic" compound P_4O_{10} (p. 504).

There has been growing interest in the detailed structure and reaction chemistry of monomeric forms of two-coordinate derivatives of Ge^{II}, Sn^{II} and Pb^{II} since the first examples were unequiv-ocally established in 1980.[63.64] Thus, treat-ment of the corresponding chlorides MCl_2 with lithium di-*tert*-butyl phenoxide derivatives in thf affords a series of yellow (Ge^{II}, Sn^{II}) and red (Pb^{II}) compounds $M(OAr)_2$ in high yield.[63] The $O-M-O$ bond angle in $M(OC_6H_2Me-4-Bu'_2-2,6)_2$ was 92° for Ge and 89° for Sn. Similar reactions

[57] A. C. SAU, R. O. DAY and R. R. HOLMES, *J. Am. Chem. Soc.* **103**, 1264–5 (1981) and *Inorg. Chem.* **20**, 3076–81 (1981).

[58] S. W. NG, C. WEI, V. G. K. DAS and T. C. W. MAK, *J. Organometallic Chem.* **334**, 283–93 (1987).

[59] S. W. NG, C. WEI, V. G. K. DAS, G. B. JAMESON and R. J. BUTCHER, *J. Organometallic Chem.* **365**, 75–82 (1989).

[60] W. S. SHELDRICK and H. G. BRAUNBECK, *Z. anorg. allg. Chem.* **619**, 1300–6 (1993).

[61] J. C. HUFFMAN, J. P. HAUSHALTER, A. M. UMARJI, G. K. SHENOY and R. C. HAUSHALTER, *Inorg. Chem.* **23**, 2312–15 (1984).

[61a] S. S. DHINGRA and R. C. HAUSHALTER, *Polyhedron* **13**, 2775–9 (1994).

[62] S. POHL, *Angew. Chem. Int. Edn. Engl.* **15**, 162 (1976).

[63] B. CETINKAYA, I. GÜMRÜKÇÜ, M. F. LAPPERT, J. L. ATWOOD, R. D. ROGERS and M. J. ZAWOROTKO, *J. Am. Chem. Soc.* **102**, 2088–9 (1980). See also T. FJELDBERG, P. B. HITCHCOCK, M. F. LAPPERT, S. J. SMITH and A. J. THORNE, *J. Chem. Soc., Chem. Commun.*, 939–41 (1985).

[64] M. F. LAPPERT, M. J. SLADE, J. L. ATWOOD and M. J. ZAWOROTKO, *J. Chem. Soc., Chem. Commun.*, 621–2 (1980).

of MCl_2 with $LiNBu_2^t$ yielded the (less stable) monomeric di-*tert*-butylamide, $Ge(NBu_2^t)_2$ (orange), and $Sn(NBu_2^t)_2$ (maroon);[64] the more stable related bis(tetramethylpiperidino) compound $[Ge\{NCMe_2(CH_2)_3CMe_2\}_2]$ was found to have a somewhat larger bond angle at Ge (N–Ge–N = 111°) and a rather long Ge–N bond (189 pm). More recent examples are $[Ge\{N(SiMe_3)_2\}_2]$[65] and $[GeN(Bu^t)CH=CHN-(Bu^t)]$.[66] The first monomeric prochiral Sn^{II} complexes, $[Sn\{N(SiMe_3)_2\}X]$, have also been reported, where X is a bulky substituted phenoxy group or a tetramethylpiperidino moiety.[67] These are but illustrative examples of a large and burgeoning field.[68]

Turning finally to compounds with bonds from the heavier Group 14 elements to heavier Group 15 elements we may note compounds such as $[Sn\{C(PMe_2)_3\}_2]$ which has the pseudo trigonal bipyramidal structure (6). This complex, which has Sn bonded exclusively to four P atoms, is formed as yellow crystals by the reaction of $SnCl_2$ with $2Li\{C(PMe_2)_3\}$ in Et_2O at $-78°C$.[69] A notable feature of the structure is the substantial difference between the equatorial and axial Sn–P distances (260 pm *vs* 279 and 284 pm, respectively) and the small chelate bite angle of 62.9° at the Sn atom. The compound is fluxional in solution even at $-90°C$ due to pseudorotation (p. 499) which equilibrates the axial and equatorial positions. Several similar compounds are known.[69] Germanium analogues of (6) such as the stable crystalline complexes $[Ge\{C(PMe_2)_3\}_2]$ and $[Ge\{C(PMe_2)_2(SiMe_3)\}_2]$ can be made by similar procedures, starting from $GeCl_2$.dioxane:[70] see also next section.

A range of shiny metallic compounds featuring trigonal planar anions SnX_3^{5-} (X = As, Sb, Bi) have been characterized with composition $M_6(SnX_3)O_{0.5}$ (M = Rb, Cs); the Sn and X atoms in SnX_3^{5-} (isostructural with CO_3^{2-}) are coordinated by trigonal prisms of $6M^+$, and the O^{2-} ions occupy octahedral sites in the M^+ lattice.[70a]

Rather different is the X-ray structural characterization of the 'bare' Sn^{2+} ion in $[Sn^{2+}][SbF_6^-]_2.2AsF_3$ (prepared by treating the product of the direct reaction between SnF_2 and SbF_5 with AsF_3).[71] The crystal packing is such that each Sn^{2+} is surrounded by nine F atoms (tricapped trigonal prism) and the average Sn–F distance is 257 pm (cf. the sum of the ionic radii, 251 pm). The Mössbauer spectrum (p. 371) shows zero quadrupole splitting and the highest known chemical shift for any tin(II) species, consistent with the 'bare ion' formulation.

10.3.6 Metal–metal bonds and clusters

The catenation of Group 14 elements has been discussed on pp. 337–42 and 374–5,

[65] S. M. HAWKINS, P. B. HITCHCOCK, M. F. LAPPERT and A. K. RAI, *J. Chem. Soc., Chem. Commun.*, 1689–90 (1986) and references cited therein; C. GLIDEWELL, D. LLOYD, K. W. LUMBARD and J. S. MCKECHNIE, *J. Chem. Soc., Dalton Trans.*, 2981–7 (1987).

[66] W. A. HERRMANN, M. DENK, J. BEHM, W. SCHERER, F. R. KLINGAN, H. BOCK, B. SOLOUKI and M. WAGNER, *Angew. Chem. Int. Edn. Engl.* **31**, 1485–8 (1992).

[67] H. BRAUNSCHWEIG, R. W. CHORLEY, P. B. HITCHCOCK and M. F. LAPPERT, *J. Chem. Soc., Chem. Commun.*, 1311–13 (1992).

[68] M. VEITH and W. FRANK, *Angew. Chem. Int. Edn. Engl.* **24**, 223–4 (1985), C. GLIDEWELL, D. LLOYD and K. W. LUMBARD, *J. Chem. Soc., Dalton Trans.*, 501–8 (1987), J. KOCHER, M. LEHNIG and W. P. NEUMANN, *Organometallics* **7**, 1201–7 (1988), M. VEITH, L. STAHL and V. HUCH, *J. Chem. Soc., Chem. Commun.*, 359–61 (1990), P. B. HITCHCOCK, M. F. LAPPERT and A. J. THORNE, *J. Chem. Soc., Chem. Commun.*, 1587–9 (1990), A. MELLER, G. OSSIG, W. MARINGGELE, D. STALKE, R. HERBST-IRMER, S. FREITAG and G. M. SHELDRICK, *J. Chem. Soc., Chem. Commun.*, 1123–4 (1991), R. W. CHORLEY, P. B. HITCHCOCK, B. S. JOLLY, M. F. LAPPERT and G. A. LAWLESS, *J. Chem. Soc., Chem. Commun.*, 1302–3 (1991), R. W. CHORLEY, P. B. HITCHCOCK and M. F. LAPPERT, *J. Chem. Soc., Chem. Commun.*, 525–6 (1992), M. VEITH, M. NÖTZEL, L. STAHL and V. HUCH, *Z. anorg. allg. Chem.* **620**, 1264–70 (1994). See also Polyhedra Symposia-in-Print No. 12, M. J. HAMPDEN-SMITH (ed.), *Polyhedron* **10**, 1147–309 (1991).

[69] H. H. KARSCH, A. APPELT and G. MÜLLER, *Organometallics* **5**, 1664–70 (1986) and references cited therein.

[70] H. H. KARSCH, B. DEUBELLY, J. REIDE and G. MÜLLER, *Angew. Chem. Int. Edn. Engl.* **26**, 673–4 (1987).

[70a] M. ASBRAND and B. EISENMANN, *Z. anorg. allg. Chem.* **620**, 1837–43 (1994).

[71] A. J. EDWARDS and K. L. KHALLOW, *J. Chem. Soc., Chem. Commun.*, 50–1 (1984).

(7) $[Ge^{IV}\{C(PMe_2)_2X\}_2Cl_2]$

(8) $[Ge^I_2\{C(PMe_2)_2X\}_2]$

(9) $[Ge^I_2\{\mu\text{-}(PMe_2)_2CX\}_2_2Ge^{II}Cl_2(core)$

and further examples are in Section 10.3.7. In addition, when the reaction of GeCl₂.dioxane with 2Li[C{(PMe₂)₂X}₂] (mentioned above[70]) is varied by using a higher proportion of GeCl₂, concurrent redox disproportionation occurs to yield a mixture of $[Ge^{IV}\{C(PMe_2)_2X\}_2Cl_2]$ (7) and $[Ge^I_2\{C(PMe_2)_2X\}_2]$ (8) according to the optimized stoichiometry:[72]

$$3GeCl_2.diox + 4Li[\{C(PMe_2)_2X\}_2] = (7) + (8)$$

$$+ 4LiCl + 3C_4H_8O_2$$

where X + SiMe₃ (or PMe₂). The Ge–Ge distance in (8) is 254 pm, i.e. about 10 pm longer than in polygermanes. The stereochemically active lone pairs of electrons on Ge^I in (8) can be used as electron-pair donors to a further GeCl₂ moiety to form the homonuclear (germanediyl donor)–(germanediyl acceptor) complex $[Ge_2\{\mu\text{-}(PMe_2)_2CX\}_2]_2GeCl_2$ which features a mixed-valent Ge₅ chain as shown schematically in (9). The Ge–Ge distances along the Ge^I–Ge^I–Ge^{II}–Ge^I–Ge^I chain are 249.2, 255.4, 256.2 and 248.5 pm, respectively.

Heteroatomic metal–metal bonds can be formed by a variety of synthetic routes as illustrated below for tin:

Insertion: $SnCl_2 + Co_2(CO)_8 \longrightarrow$

$$(CO)_4Co\overset{\displaystyle Cl}{\underset{\displaystyle Cl}{-Sn-}}Co(CO)_4$$

Metathesis: $Me_2SnCl_2 + 2NaRe(CO)_5 \longrightarrow$

$$(CO)_5Re\overset{\displaystyle Me}{\underset{\displaystyle Me}{-Sn-}}Re(CO)_5 + 2NaCl$$

Elimination: $SnCl_2 + [Fe(\eta^5\text{-}C_5H_5)(CO)_2HgCl] \longrightarrow$

$$[(\eta^5\text{-}C_5H_5)Fe\overset{\displaystyle CO}{\underset{\displaystyle CO}{-SnCl_3}}] + Hg$$

Oxidative addition: $SnCl_4 + [Ir(CO)Cl(PPh_3)_2] \longrightarrow$

$$[(PPh_3)_2IrCl_2]\overset{\displaystyle CO}{\underset{\displaystyle SnCl_3}{|}}$$

Some representative examples, all featuring tetrahedral Sn, are in Fig. 10.9.[53] Several reactions are known in which the Sn–M bond remains intact, e.g.:

$$Ph_3SnMn(CO)_5 + 3Cl_2 \longrightarrow Cl_3SnMn(CO)_5$$

$$+ 3PhCl$$

$$Cl_2Sn\{Co(CO)_4\}_2 + 2RMgX \longrightarrow$$

$$R_2Sn\{Co(CO)_4\}_2 + 2MgClX$$

Others result in cleavage, e.g.:

$$Me_3SnCo(CO)_4 + I_2 \longrightarrow Me_3SnI + Co(CO)_4I$$

$$Me_3SnMn(CO)_5 + Ph_2PCl \longrightarrow Me_3SnCl$$

$$+ \tfrac{1}{2}[Ph_2PMn(CO)_4]_2 + CO$$

$$Me_3SnMn(CO)_5 + C_2F_4 \longrightarrow$$

$$Me_3SnCF_2CF_2Mn(CO)_4$$

[72] H. H. KARSCH, B. DEUBELLY, J. REIDE and G. MÜLLER, *Angew. Chem. Int. Edn. Engl.* **26**, 674–6 (1987).

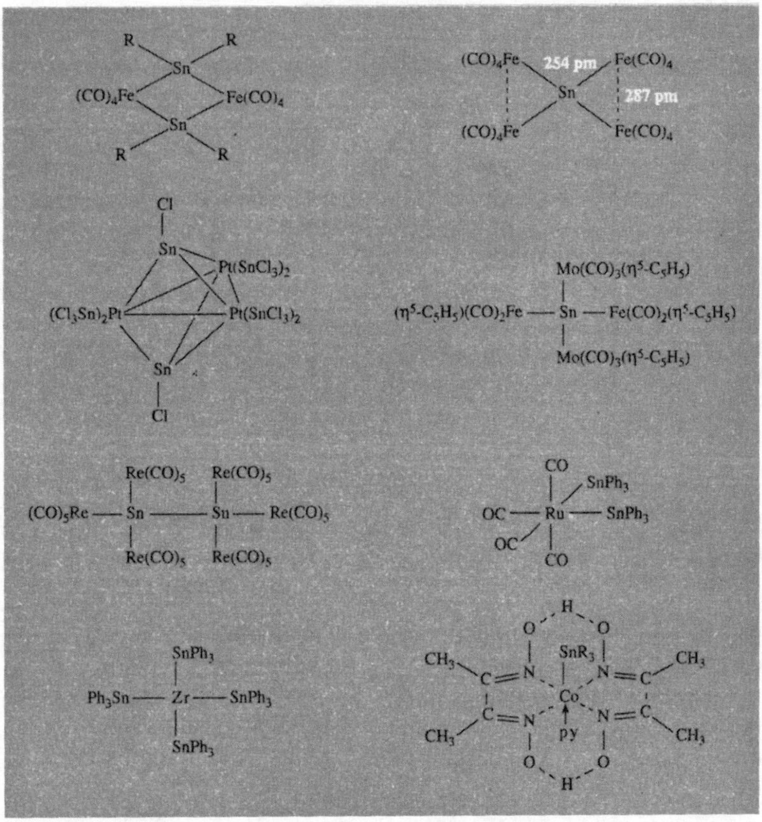

Figure 10.9   Some examples of metal sequences and metal clusters containing tin-transitional metal bonds.

A similar though less extensive range of Pb–M compounds has been established;[39] e.g. [Ph$_2$Pb{Mn(CO)$_5$}$_2$], [Ph$_3$PbRe(CO)$_5$], [Ph$_2$Pb-{Co(CO)$_4$}$_2$], [(PPh$_3$)$_2$Pt(PbPh$_3$)$_2$], [(CO)$_3$Fe(Pb-Et$_3$)$_2$], and the cyclic dimer [(CO)$_4$Fe–PbEt$_2$]$_2$. Reaction of these compounds with halogens results in fission of the Pb–M bonds. In the unique case of [Pb{Mn(η^5-C$_5$H$_5$)(CO)$_2$}$_2$] the linear central MnPbMn core (177.2°) and short Mn–Pb distance (246.3 pm) suggest that this is the first example of multiple bonding between Pb and a transition metal, Mn=Pb=Mn.[73] The compound is obtained in 20% yield as air-stable reddish-brown crystals by the reaction of PbCl$_2$ with the substitutionally labile complex [Mn(η^5-C$_5$H$_5$)(CO)$_2$(thf)].

It has been known since the early 1930s that reduction of Ge, Sn and Pb by Na in liquid ammonia gives polyatomic Group 14 metal anions, and crystalline compounds can be isolated using ethylenediamine, e.g. [Na$_4$(en)$_5$Ge$_9$] and [Na$_4$(en)$_7$Sn$_9$]. A dramatic advance was achieved[74] in the 1970s by means of the polydentate cryptand ligand [N{(C$_2$H$_4$)O(C$_2$H$_4$)-O(C$_2$H$_4$)}$_3$N] (p. 98). Thus, reaction of cryptand in ethylenediamine with the alloys NaSn$_{1-1.7}$ and NaPb$_{1.7-2}$ gave red crystalline salts [Na(crypt)]$_2^+$[Sn$_5$]$^{2-}$ and [Na(crypt)]$_2^+$[Pb$_5$]$^{2-}$ containing the D_{3h} cluster anions illustrated in Fig. 10.10. If each Sn or Pb atom is thought to have 1 nonbonding pair of electrons then the

73 W. A. HERRMANN, H.-J. KNEUPER and E. HERDTWECK, *Angew. Chem. Int. Edn. Engl.* **24**, 1062–3 (1985).

74 P. A. EDWARDS and J. D. CORBETT, *Inorg. Chem.* **16**, 903–7 (1977). J. D. CORBETT and P. A. EDWARDS, *J. Am. Chem. Soc.* **99**, 3313–7 (1977).

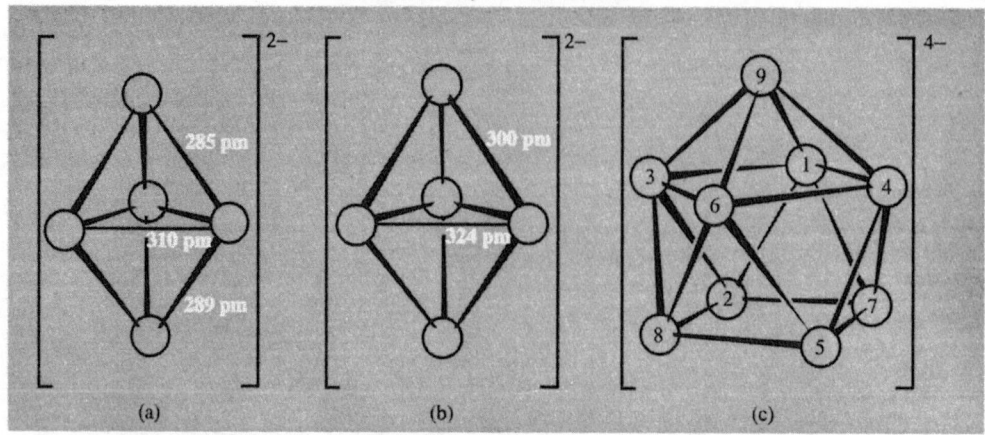

Figure 10.10   The structure of polystannide and polyplumbide anions: (a) the slightly distorted D_{3h} structure of $[Sn_5]^{2-}$, (b) the D_{3h} structure of $[Pb_5]^{2-}$, and (c) the unique C_{4v} structure of $[Sn_9]^{4-}$: all Sn–Sn distances are in the range 295–302 pm except those in the slightly longer upper square (1,3,6,4) which are in the range 319–331 pm; the angles within the two parallel squares are all 90° ($\pm 0.8°$).

$M_5{}^{2-}$ clusters have 12 framework bonding electrons as has $[B_5H_5]^{2-}$ (p. 161); the anions are also isoelectronic with the well-known cation $[Bi_5]^{3+}$. Similarly, the alloy $NaSn_{\sim 2.25}$ reacts with cryptand in ethylenediamine to give dark-red crystals of $[Na(crypt)]_4^+[Sn_9]^{4-}$; the anion is the first example of a C_{4v} unicapped Archimedian antiprism (Fig. 10.10c) and differs from the D_{3h} structure of the isoelectronic cation $[Bi_9]^{5+}$ which, in the salt $Bi^+[Bi_9]^{5+}[HfCl_6]_3^{2-}$ (p. 591), features a tricapped trigonal prism, as in $[B_9H_9]^{2-}$ (p. 153). The emerald green species $[Pb_9]^{4-}$, which is stable in liquid NH_3 solution, has not so far proved amenable to isolation via cryptand-complexed cations.

The influence of electron-count on cluster geometry has been very elegantly shown by a crystallographic study of the deep-red compound $[K(crypt)]_6^+[Ge_9]^{2-}[Ge_9]^{4-}.2.5en$, prepared by the reaction of KGe with cryptand in ethylenediamine. $[Ge_9]^{4-}$ has the C_{4v} unicapped square-antiprismatic structure (10.10c) whereas $[Ge_9]^{2-}$, with 2 less electrons, adopts a distorted D_{3h} structure which clearly derives from the tricapped trigonal prism (p. 153).[75] The field is one of

great interest and activity, as evidenced by papers describing the synthesis of and structural studies on tetrahedral $Ge_4{}^{2-}$ and $Sn_4{}^{2-}$,[76] tricapped trigonal-prismatic $TlSn_8{}^{3-}$,[77] bicapped square-antiprismatic $TlSn_9{}^{3-}$,[77] and the two *nido*-series $Sn_{9-x}Ge_x{}^{4-}$ ($x = 0$–9) and $Sn_{9-x}Pb_x{}^{4-}$ ($x = 0$–9).[78] Other theoretical studies on many of these polymetallic-cluster anions have also been published.[79] Recent synthetic and structural work includes the characterization of the octahedral *closo*-$[Ge_2Co_4]$ grouping in $[1,6-\{(CO)_4COGe\}_2Co_4(CO)_{11}]$,[80]

[75] C. H. E. Belin, J. D. Corbett and A. Cisar, *J. Am. Chem. Soc.* **99**, 7163–9 (1977).

[76] S. C. Critchlow and J. D. Corbett, *J. Chem. Soc., Chem. Commun.*, 236–7 (1981). M. J. Rothman, L. S. Bartell and L. L. Lohr, *J. Am. Chem. Soc.* **103**, 2482–3 (1981).

[77] R. C. Burns and J. D. Corbett, *J. Am. Chem. Soc.* **104**, 2804–10 (1982). See also *Inorg. Chem.* **24**, 1489–92 (1985) for $[KSn_9{}^{3-}]$.

[78] R. W. Rudolph, W. L. Wilson and R. C. Taylor *J. Am. Chem. Soc.* **103**, 2480–1 (1981), and references therein. See also W. L. Wilson, R. W. Rudolph, L. L. Lohr, R. C. Taylor and P. Pyykkö , *Inorg. Chem.* **25**, 1535–41 (1985).

[79] L. L. Lohr, *Inorg. Chem.* **20**, 4229–35 (1981); R. C. Burns, R. J. Gillespie, J. A. Barnes and M. J. McGlinchey, *Inorg. Chem.* **31**, 799–807 (1982). G. Kliche, H. G. von Schnering and M. Schwarz, *Z. anorg. allg. Chem.* **608**, 131–4 (1992).

[80] S. P. Foster, K. M. Mackay and B. K. Nicholson, *Inorg. Chem.* **24**, 909–13 (1985).

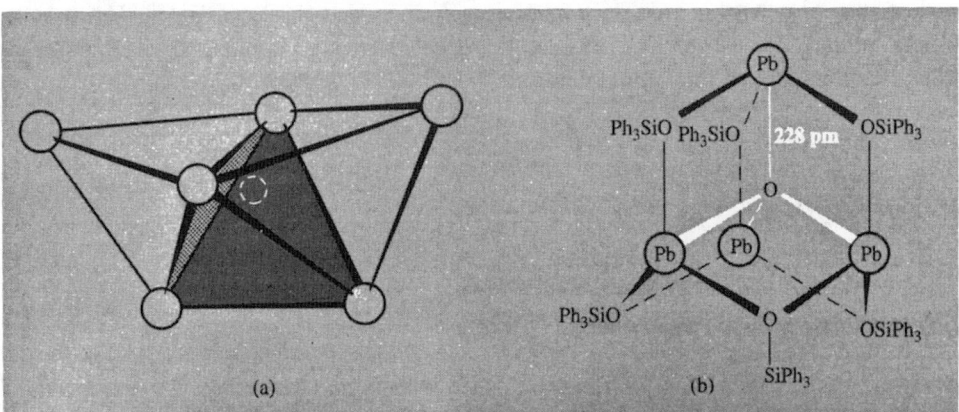

Figure 10.11   (a) The three face-sharing tetrahedra of Pb atoms in the $Pb_6O(OH)_6^{4+}$ cluster; only the unique 4-coordinate O atom at the centre of the central tetrahedron is shown (in white). (b) The adamantane-like structure of $[Pb_4O(OSiPh_3)_6]$ showing the fourfold coordination about the central O atom.

the *closo*-10 vertex cluster $[Sn_9Cr(CO)_3]^{4-}$ [81] and encapsulated Ge and Sn atoms (E) in species such as $[Ni_{12}(\mu_{12}\text{-}E)(CO)_{22}]^{2-}$ and $[Ni(\mu_{10}\text{-}Ge)(CO)_{20}]^{2-}$. [82]

The polymeric cluster compound $[Sn_6O_4(OH)_4]$ formed by hydrolysis of Sn^{II} compounds has been mentioned on p. 384. Hydrolysis of Pb^{II} compounds also leads to polymerized species; e.g. dissolution of PbO in aqueous $HClO_4$ followed by careful addition of base leads to $[Pb_6O(OH)_6]^{4+}[ClO_4]_4^-H_2O$. The cluster cation (Fig. 10.11a) consists of 3 tetrahedra of Pb sharing faces; the central tetrahedron encompasses the unique O atom and the 6 OH groups lie on the faces of the 2 end tetrahedra. [83] The extent of direct Pb–Pb interaction within the overall cluster has not been established but it is noted that the distance between "adjacent" Pb atoms falls in the range 344–409 pm (average 381 pm) which is appreciably larger than in the Pb_5^{2-} anion. The distance from the central O

to the 4 surrounding Pb atoms is 222–235 pm and the other Pb–O(H) distances are in the range 218–267 pm. The structure should be compared with the $[Sn_6O_4(OH)_4]$ cluster (p. 384), which also has larger Sn–Sn distances than in the polystannide anions in Fig. 10.10.

Another polycyclic structure in which a unique O atom is surrounded tetrahedrally by 4 Pb^{II} atoms is the colourless adamantane-like complex $[Pb_4O(OSiPh_3)_6]$, obtained as a 1:1 benzene solvate by reaction of Ph_3SiOH with $[Pb(C_5H_5)_2]$ (p. 404). The local geometry about Pb^{II} is also noteworthy: it comprises pseudo-trigonal bipyramidal coordination in which the bridging $OSiPh_3$ groups occupy the equatorial sites whilst the apical sites are occupied by the unique O atom and axially directed lone pairs of electrons. [84] The first heterometallic oxoalkoxide, $[Pb_6Nb_4O_4(OEt)_{24}]$, has also been prepared, by reacting $[Pb_4O(OEt)_6]$ and $[Nb_2(OEt)_{10}]$ in ethanol at room temperature. [85] X-ray structural analysis shows an octahedral Pb_6 framework, four of whose faces are capped by a μ_4-oxo ligand connected to 3Pb atoms and an $\{Nb(OEt)_5\}$ moiety; the remaining

[81] B. W. EICHHORN, R. C. HAUSHALTER and W. T. PENNINGTON, *J. Am. Chem. Soc.* **110**, 8704–6 (1988). B. W. EICHHORN and R. C. HAUSHALTER, *J. Chem. Soc., Chem. Commun.*, 937–8 (1990).

[82] A. CERIOTTI, F. DEMARTIN, B. T. HEATON, P. INGALLINA, G. LONGONI, M. MANASSERO, M. MARCHIONNA and N. MASCIOCCHI, *J. Chem. Soc., Chem. Commun.*, 786–7 (1989).

[83] T. G. SPIRO, D. H. TEMPLETON and A. ZALKIN. *Inorg. Chem.* **8**, 856–61 (1969).

[84] C. GAFFNEY, P. G. HARRISON, and T. J. KING, *J. Chem. Soc., Chem. Commun.*, 1251–2 (1980).

[85] R. PAPIERNIK, L. G. HUBERT-PFALZGRAF, J.-C. DARAN and Y. JEANNIN, *J. Chem. Soc., Chem. Commun.*, 695–7 (1990).

four faces of the Pb_6 octahedron are capped by (μ_3-OEt) groups. This leads, to the overall detailed formulation of the compound as $[Pb_6(\mu_4\text{-}O)_4\{Nb(OEt)_2\}_4(\mu_3\text{-}OEt)_4(\mu_2\text{-}OEt)_{12}]$. Alternatively the complex can be described as a tetradentate oxo ligand donating to $4\{Nb(OEt)_2(\mu_2\text{-}OEt)_3\}$ groups i.e. $[Pb_6O_4(OEt)_4\{Nb(OEt)_5\}_4]$.

10.3.7 Organometallic compounds [86]

Germanium [87]

Organogermanium chemistry closely resembles that of Si though the Ge compounds tend to be somewhat less thermally stable. They are also often rather more chemically reactive than their Si counterparts, e.g. in ligand scrambling reactions, Ge–C bond cleavage and hydrogermylation. However, GeR_4 compounds themselves are rather inert chemically and R_nGeX_{4-n} tend to be less prone to hydrolysis and condensation reactions than their Si analogues. Again, following expected group trends, germylenes (R_2Ge:) are more stable than silylenes. The table of comparative bond energies on p. 374 indicates that the Ge–C and Ge–H bonds are weaker than the corresponding bonds involving Si but are nevertheless quite strong; Ge–Ge is noticeably weaker. The electronegativity of both Si and Ge are similar to that of H, though the reactivity pattern towards organolithium reagents suggests a slight hydridic character ($H^{\delta-}$) for Ph_3SiH and some protic character ($H^{\delta+}$) for Ph_3GeH:

$$Ph_3Si\text{-}H + LiR \longrightarrow Ph_3Si\text{-}R + LiH$$

(metathesis)

$$Ph_3Ge\text{-}H + LiR \longrightarrow Ph_3Ge\text{-}Li + RH$$

(metallation)

---

[86] C. ELSCHENBROICH and A. SALZER, *Organometallics*, VCH, Weinheim, 1989, pp. 115–46.

[87] P. RIVIÈRE, M. RIVIÈRE-BAUDET and J. SATGÈ, Chap. 10 in G. WILKINSON, F. G. A. STONE and E. W. ABEL (eds.) *Comprehensive Organometallic Chemistry*, Pergamon Press, Oxford, Vol. 2, pp. 399–518 (1982) (716 refs.).

In fact, the polarity of the Ge–H bond can readily be reversed (umpolung) by an appropriate choice of constituents, e.g.:

$$Et_3Ge^{\delta+}\text{-}H^{\delta-} + {>}C{=}O \longrightarrow H\text{-}\overset{|}{\underset{|}{C}}\text{-}OGeEt_3$$

(germoxane)

$$Cl_3Ge^{\delta-}\text{-}H^{\delta+} + {>}C{=}O \longrightarrow Cl_3Ge\text{-}\overset{|}{\underset{|}{C}}\text{-}OH$$

(germylcarbinol)

Preparative routes to organogermanium compounds parallel those for organosilicon compounds (p. 363) and most of the several thousand known organogermanes can be considered as derivatives of R_nGeX_{4-n} or Ar_nGeX_{4-n} where X = hydrogen, halogen, pseudohalogen, OR, etc. The compounds are colourless, volatile liquids, or solids. Attempts to prepare $(-R_2GeO-)_x$ analogues of the silicones (p. 364) show that the system is different: hydrolysis of Me_2GeCl_2 is reversible and incomplete, but extraction of aqueous solutions of Me_2GeCl_2 with petrol leads to the cyclic tetramer $[Me_2GeO]_4$, mp 92°; the compound is monomeric in water. Organodigermanes and -polygermanes have also been made by standard routes, e.g.:

$$2Me_3GeBr + 2K \xrightarrow{\text{reflux}} 2KBr + Ge_2Me_6$$

(mp $-40°$, bp $140°$)

$$Et_3GeBr + NaGePh_3 \xrightarrow{\text{liq NH}_3} NaBr + Et_3GeGePh_3 \text{(mp 90°)}$$

$$2Ph_3GeBr + 2Na \xrightarrow[\text{xylene}]{\text{boiling}} 2NaBr + Ge_2Ph_6$$

(mp 340°)

$$Ph_2GeCl_2 + 2NaGePh_3 \longrightarrow 2NaCl + Ge_3Ph_8$$

(mp 248°)

In general, the Ge–Ge bond is readily cleaved by Br_2 either at ambient or elevated temperatures but the compounds are stable to thermal cleavage at moderate temperatures. Ge_2R_6 compounds can even be distilled unchanged in air (like Si_2R_6 but unlike the more reactive Sn_2R_6) and are stable towards hydrolysis and ammonolysis.

Considerable recent attention has focused on the preparation, structure and stability of germenes ($>Ge=C<$), germylenes ($R_2Ge:$), cyclo and polyhedral oligopolygermanes, and Ge^{II} species with coordination numbers greater than 4 (especially 5 and 10). Thus, evidence for fugitive germene species has been known for some 20 years[88] but stable germenes, $R_2Ge=CR'_2$, were first reported only in 1987,[89,90] the stabilization being achieved by use of bulky groups both on Ge [e.g. R = mesityl or $-N(SiMe_3)_2$] and on C [e.g. $R'_2 = -B(Bu^t)C(SiMe_3)_2B(Bu^t)-$ or $CR'_2 =$ fluorenylidene]. Numerous other stable germenes have since been characterized.[90]

The first germylene, R_2Ge: [R = $(SiMe_3)_2$-CH$-$], was reported in 1976. It can now be conveniently prepared from $GeCl_2$.diox and Grignard-type derivatives of the bulky bis(trimethylsilyl)methyl R group in Et_2O (e.g. ether complexes of RMgCl or MgR_2); gasphase electron diffraction at 155°C shows it to be a V-shaped monomer with the angle CGeC 107°.[91] In the solid phase the compound forms bright yellow crystals (mp 182°C) of the centrosymmetric dimer Ge_2R_4 which has a *trans*-folded framework (see structure on p. 403) with a fold angle θ of 32° and a Ge–Ge distance of 235 pm.[92] By contrast, reductive coupling reactions of R_2GeX_2 with a mixture of Mg/MgBr$_2$ in thf affords colourless crystals of cyclotrigermanes or cyclotetragermanes in moderate or good yield:[93]

$$R_2GeCl_2 \xrightarrow{MgBr_2} R_2Ge(Cl)Br \xrightarrow{Mg}$$

$$R_2Ge(Cl)MgBr \xrightarrow{dil\ HCl} (GeR_2)_n\ \ n = 3, 4$$

Bulky R groups such as mesityl, xylyl or 2,6-diethylphenyl lead to Ge_3 rings whereas sterically less demanding groups such as Pr, Ph or Me_3SiCH_2 yield Ge_4 rings. Note that the compounds $(GeR_2)_n$ feature Ge with the coordination number 2, 3 or 4 depending on whether $n = 1$, 2, or ≥ 3, respectively. Mixed derivatives can also be made: e.g., reductive coupling of $Mes(Bu)GeCl_2$ at room temperature affords [{Ge(Mes)Bu}$_3$], mp 201°. Thermolysis of [{Ge(Mes)$_2$}$_3$], (a) in the presence of Et_3SiH at 105° yields a mixture of dimesityl(triethylsilyl)germane (b) and tetramesityl(triethylsilyl)digermane (c) according to the subjoined scheme:[94]

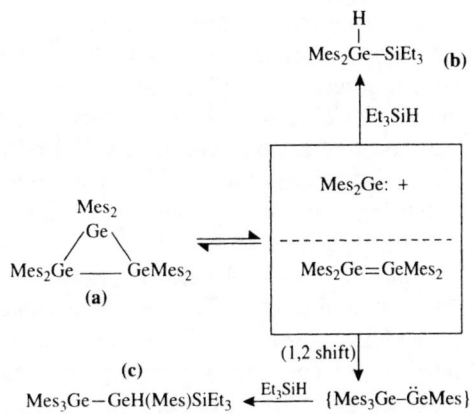

Polyhedral oligogermanes of varying complexity can be made by careful choice of the organo R group and the metal reductive coupling agent.[95] Thus, treatment of {(Me$_3$Si)$_2$CH}GeCl$_3$ with Li metal in thf gave thermochroic yellow-orange crystals of the hexamer [Ge$_6$[CH(SiMe$_3$)$_2$]$_6$] which were unexpectedly stable to atmospheric

88 T. J. BARTON, E. A. KLINE and P. M. GARVEY, *J. Am. Chem. Soc.* **95**, 3078 (1973). J. BARRAU, J. ESCUDIE and J. SATGÉ, *Chem. Rev.* **90**, 283–319 (1990) and references cited therein.

89 C. COURET, J. ESCUDIE, J. SATGÉ and M. LAZRAQ, *J. Am. Chem. Soc.* **109**, 4411–12 (1987).

90 M. LAZRAQ, C. COURET, J. ESCUDIE, J. SATGÉ and M. SOUFIAOUI, *Polyhedron* **10**, 1153–61 (1991) and references cited therein.

91 T. FJELDBERG, A. HAALAND, B. E. R. SCHILLING, M. F. LAPPERT and A. J. THORNE, *J. Chem. Soc., Dalton Trans.*, 1551–6 (1986).

92 D. E. GOLDBERG, P. B. HITCHCOCK, M. F. LAPPERT, K. M. THOMAS and A. J. THORNE, *J. Chem. Soc., Dalton Trans.*, 2387–94 (1986).

93 W. ANDO and T. TSUMURAYA, *J. Chem. Soc., Chem. Commun.*, 1514–5 (1987).

94 K. M. BAINES, J. A. COOKE and J. J. VITTAL, *J. Chem. Soc., Chem. Commun.*, 1484–5 (1992).

95 A. SEKIGUCHI and H. SAKURAI, Chap. 7 in R. STEUDEL (ed.), *The Chemistry of Inorganic Ring Systems*, Elsevier, Amsterdam, pp. 101–24 (1992).

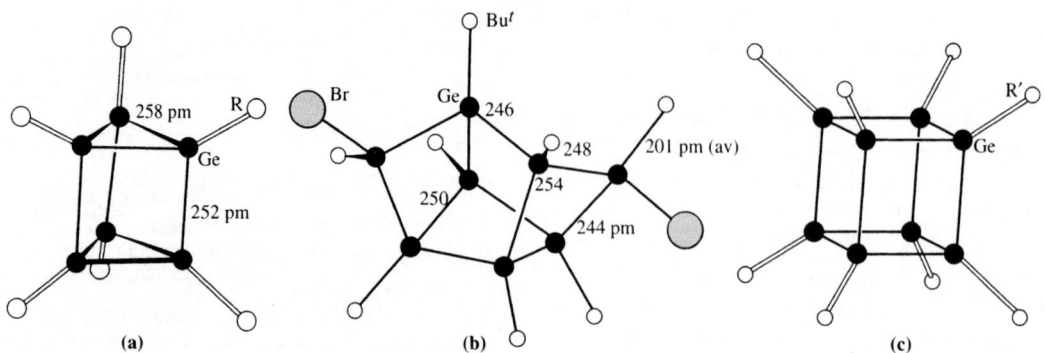

Figure 10.12   (a) Prismane structure of $[Ge_6\{CH(SiMe_3)_2\}_6]$ (for clarity only the *ipso* C atoms of the R groups are shown). (b) The tetracyclo structure of $[Ge_8Bu^t_8Br_2]$ with only the *ipso* C atoms of the Bu^t groups shown. (c) The cubane structure of $[Ge_8(CMeEt_2)_8]$ again with only the *ipso* C atoms of the *t*-hexyl groups shown.

O_2 and moisture.[96] X-ray analysis revealed a prismane structure (Fig. 10.12a) rather than a monocyclic benzenoid structure. The Ge–Ge distances within the two triangular faces (258 pm) are, perhaps surprisingly, longer than those in the prism quadrilateral edges (252 pm) and all the Ge–Ge distances are significantly longer than in other polygermanes (237–247 pm). Again, treatment of $GeBr_4$ with $LiBu^t$ yields a mixture of $Bu^t_2GeBr_2$ and $Bu^tBr_2Ge–GeBr_2Bu^t$, and treatment of this latter with an excess of Li/naphthalene afforded the polycyclic octagermane, $Ge_8Bu^t_8Br_2$, in 50% yield.[97] As shown in Fig 10.12b, the molecule is chiral with C_2 skeletal symmetry. The octagermacubane $[Ge_8(CHMeEt_2)_8]$ (Fig. 10.12c) was obtained as yellow crystals (mp > 215°) by a simple coupling reaction of R_3GeCl with $Mg/MgBr_2$, and numerous other cyclic, ladder and cluster polygermanes have been described.[95]

The coordination number of Ge in organogermanes is not limited to 2, 3 or 4, and higher coordination numbers are well documented. Examples are 5-coordinate Ge^{II} in the cation of $[Ge(\eta^5-C_5Me_5)]^+[BF_4]^-$ (10),[98]

6-coordinate Ge^{II} in the corresponding chloride $[(\eta^5-C_5Me_5)GeCl]$ (11)[98] and 10-coordinate Ge^{II} in $[Ge(\eta^5-C_5H_5)_2]$ (12)[99] and its $(\eta^5-C_5R_5)$ analogues.[98] These species can now readily be prepared by standard reactions, and structural details are in the leading references cited. Thus, reaction of NaC_5H_5 with $GeCl_2$.diox in thf gives a 60% yield of (12) as colourless crystals, mp 78°C. The angle of aperture between the two C_5H_5 planes in (12) is 50.4° compared with 45.9° or 48.4° for stannocene.[99] By contrast, 5-coordinate Ge^{IV} adopts a structure midway between trigonal bipyramidal and rectangular pyramidal in phenyl-substituted anionic germanates such as $[PhGe(\eta^2-C_6H_4O_2)_2]^-$ (13), the precise geometry being dictated by the co-cation, e.g. $[NEt_4]^+$, $[N(Et)_3H]^+$ or $[AsPh_4]^+$.[100]

Finally, brief mention should be made of the growing range of heterocyclic organogermanium compounds. Compounds with 3–13(+) atoms in the ring have recently been reviewed.[101] Cyclic organogermapolysilanes are also known, e.g.

[96] A. SEKIGUCHI, C. KABUTO and H. SAKURAI, *Angew. Chem. Int. Edn. Engl.* **28**, 55–6 (1989).

[97] M. WEIDENBRUCH, F.-T. GRIMM, S. POHL and W. SAAK, *Angew. Chem. Int. Edn. Engl.* **28**, 198–9 (1989).

[98] P. JUTZI, B. HAMPEL, M. B. HURSTHOUSE and A. J. HOWES, *Organometallics* **5**, 1944–8 (1986).

[99] M. GRENZ, E. HAHN, W.-W. DU MONT and J. PICKARDT, *Angew. Chem. Int. Edn. Engl.* **23**, 61–3 (1984).

[100] R. R. HOLMES, R. O. DAY, A. C. SAU, C. A. POUTASSE and J. M. HOLMES, *Inorg. Chem.* **25**, 607–11 (1986) and references cited therein.

[101] P. MAZEROLLES, pp. 139–93 in H. W. ROESKY (ed.), *Rings, Clusters and Polymers of Main Group and Transition Elements*, Elsevier, Amsterdam (1989).

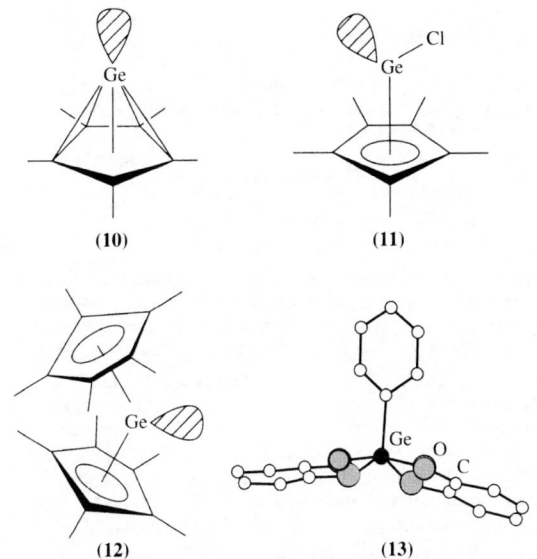

(10)   (11)

(12)   (13)

peralkyl-l-germa-2,3,4-trisilacyclobutanes.[102] Other variants include the novel telluradigermiranes, $Ar_2\overline{Ge-Te-Ge}Ar_2$,[103] a yellow phosphagermirene $Bu^t\overline{C=P-Ge}R_2$ [mp. 89° for R = $(Me_3Si)_2CH-$],[104] and a germaphosphetene featuring a $\overline{GeCCP}$ ring system.[105] The possibilities are clearly limitless.

Tin [106,107]

Organotin compounds have been much more extensively investigated than those of Ge and, as described in the Panel, many have important

industrial applications.[108] Syntheses are by standard techniques (pp. 134, 259, 363) of which the following are typical:

Grignard: $SnCl_4 + 4RMgCl \longrightarrow SnR_4$

$$+ 4MgCl_2 \text{ (also with } ArMgCl)$$

Organo Al: $3SnCl_4 + 4AlR_3 \longrightarrow 3SnR_4$

$$+ 4AlCl_3 \text{ (alkyl only)}$$

Direct (Rochow)[†] $Sn + 2RX \longrightarrow R_2SnX_2$

$$\text{(and } R_nSnX_{4-n}) \text{ (alkyl only)}.$$

All three routes are used on an industrial scale and the Grignard route (or the equivalent organo-Li reagent) is convenient for laboratory scale. Rather less used is the modified Wurtz-type reaction ($SnCl_4 + 4RCl \xrightarrow{8 \text{ Na}} SnR_4 + 8NaCl$). Conversion of SnR_4 to the partially halogenated species is readily achieved by scrambling reactions with $SnCl_4$. Reduction of R_nSnX_{4-n} with $LiAlH_4$ affords the corresponding hydrides and hydrostannation (addition of Sn–H) to C–C double and triple bonds is an attractive route to unsymmetrical or heterocyclic organotin compounds.

Most organotin compounds can be regarded as derivatives of $R_nSn^{IV}X_{4-n}$ ($n = 1$–4) and even compounds such as SnR_2 or $SnAr_2$ are in fact cyclic oligomers $(Sn^{IV}R_2)_x$ (p. 402). The physical properties of tetraorganostannanes closely resemble those of the corresponding hydrocarbons or tetraorganosilanes but with higher densities, refractive indices, etc. They are colourless, monomeric, volatile liquids or solids. Chemically they resist hydrolysis or oxidation under normal conditions though when

[102] H. SUZUKI, K. OKABE, N. SATO, Y. FUKUDA and H. WATANABE, *J. Chem. Soc., Chem. Commun.*, 1298–300 (1991).

[103] T. T. SUMURAYA, Y. KABE and W. ANDO, *J. Chem. Soc., Chem. Commun.*, 1159–60 (1990).

[104] A. H. COWLEY, S. W. HALL, C. M. NUNN and J. M. POWER, *J. Chem. Soc., Chem. Commun.*, 753–4 (1988).

[105] M. ANDRIANARISON, C. COURET, J.-P. DECLERCQ, A. DUBOURG, J. ESCUDIE and J. SATGÉ, *J. Chem. Soc., Chem. Commun.*, 921–3 (1987).

[106] A. G. DAVIES and P. J. SMITH, Chap. 11 in G. WILKINSON, F. G. A. STONE and E. W. ABEL (eds.) *Comprehensive Organometallic Chemistry*, Pergamon Press, Oxford, Vol. 2, pp 519–627 (1982), (722 refs.).

[107] I. OMAE, *Organotin Chemistry*, Elsevier, Amsterdam, 1989, 355 pp.

[108] C. J. EVANS and S. KARPEL, *Organotin Compounds in Modern Technology*, Journal of Organometallic Chemistry Library, **16** Elsevier, Amsterdam, 1985, 280 pp. S. J. BLUNDEN, P. A. CUSACK and R. HILL, *The Industrial Uses of Tin Chemicals*, Royal Society of Chemistry, London, 1985, 346 pp. K. DAS, S. W. NG and M. GIELEN, *Chemistry and Technology of Silicon and Tin*, Oxford University Press, Oxford, 1992, 608 pp.

[†] For example, with MeCl at 175° in the presence of catalytic amounts of CH_3I and NEt_3, the yields were Me_2SnCl_2 (39%), $MeSnCl_3$ (6.6%), Me_3SnCl (4.6%).

Uses of Organotin Compounds

Tin is unsurpassed by any other metal in the multiplicity of applications of its organometallic compounds. The first organotin compound was made in 1849 but large-scale applications have developed only recently; indeed, world production figures for organotin compounds increased more than 700-fold between 1950 and 1980:

Year	1950	1960	1965	1970	1975	1980
Tonnes pa	<50	2000	5000	15 000	25 000	35 000

The largest application for organotin compounds (75% by weight) is as stabilizers for PVC plastics; in their absence halogenated polymers are rapidly degraded by heat, light or oxygen to give discoloured, brittle products. The most effective stabilizers are R_2SnX_2, where R is an alkyl residue (typically n-octyl) and X is laurate, maleate, etc. For food packaging the cis-butenedioate polymer, $[Oct_2^iSn-OC(O)CH=CHC(O)O]_n$, and the S,S'-bis-(iso-octyl mercaptoethanoate), $Oct_2^iSn\{SCH_2C(O)OOct^i\}_2$ have been approved and are used when colourless non-toxic materials with high transparency are required. The compounds are thought to be such effective stabilizers because (i) they inhibit the onset of dehydrochlorination by exchanging their anionic groups X with reactive Cl sites in the polymer, (ii) they react with and hence scavenge the HCl which is produced and which would otherwise catalyse further elimination, and (iii) they act as antioxidants and thereby prevent breakdown of the polymer initiated by atmospheric O_2.

Another major use of organotin compounds is as curing agents for the room temperature "vulcanization" of silicones; the 3 most commonly used compounds are Bu_2SnX_2, where X is acetate, 2-ethylhexanoate or laurate. The same compounds are also used to catalyse the addition of alcohols to isocyanates to produce polyurethanes.

The next major use of organotin compounds (15–20%) is as agricultural biocides and here triorganotins are the most active materials; the importance of this application can readily be appreciated since, at present, over one-third of the world's food crops are lost annually to pests such as fungi, bacteria, insects or weeds. The great advantage of organotin compounds in these applications is that their toxic action is selective and there is little danger to higher (mammalian) life; furthermore, their inorganic degradation products are completely non-toxic. Bu_3^nSnOH and Ph_3SnOAc control fungal growths such as potato blight and related infections of sugar-beet, peanuts, and rice. They also eradicate red spider mite from apples and pears. Other R_3SnX are effective in controlling insects, either by acting as chemosterilants or by killing the larvae. Again, $O(SnBu_3^n)_2$ is an excellent wood preserver, and derivatives of Ph_3Sn- and (cyclohexyl)$_3Sn$- are also used for this. Related applications are as marine antifouling agents for timber-hulled boats; paints containing Bu_3^nSn- or Ph_3Sn- derivatives slowly release these groups and provide long-term protection against attachment of barnacles or attack by Teredo woodworm borers. Cellulose and woollen fabrics are likewise protected against fungal attack or destruction by moths. R_3SnX are also used as bacteriostats to control slime in paper and wood-pulp manufacture.

Me_2SnCl_2 is now used as an alternative to $SnCl_4$ for coating glass with a thin film of SnO_2 since it is a non-corrosive solid which is easier to handle. The glass (or ceramic) surface is treated with Me_2SnCl_2 vapour at temperatures above 450° and, depending on the thickness of the oxide film produced, the glass is toughened and the surface can be rendered scratch-resistant, lustrous, or electroconductive (p. 385).

Organotin reagents and intermediates are finding increasing use in organic syntheses.[109]

ignited they burn to SnO_2, CO_2 and H_2O. Ease of Sn–C cleavage by halogens or other reagents varies considerably with the nature of the organic group and generally increases in the sequence Bu (most stable) < Pr < Et < Me < vinyl < Ph < Bz < allyl < CH_2CN < CH_2CO_2R (least stable). The lability of Sn–C bonds and the ease of redistribution in mixed organostannane systems frustrated early attempts to prepare optically active tin compounds and

the first synthesis of a 4-coordinate Sn compound in which the metal is the sole chiral centre was only achieved in 1971 with the isolation and resolution of [MeSn(4-anisyl)(1-naphthyl)-$\{CH_2CH_2C(OH)Me_2\}$].[110]

The association of SnR_4 via bridging alkyl groups (which is such a notable feature of many organometallic compounds of Groups 1, 2 and 13) is not observed at all. However, many compounds of general formula R_3SnX or R_2SnX_2 are strongly associated via bridging X-groups

109 M. PEREYE, J.-P. QUINTARD and A. RAHM, *Tin in Organic Synthesis*, Butterworths, London, 1987, 342 pp. J. K. STILLE, *Angew. Chem. Int. Edn. Engl.* **25**, 508–24 (1986).

110 M. GIELEN, *Acc. Chem. Res.* **6**, 198–202 (1973).

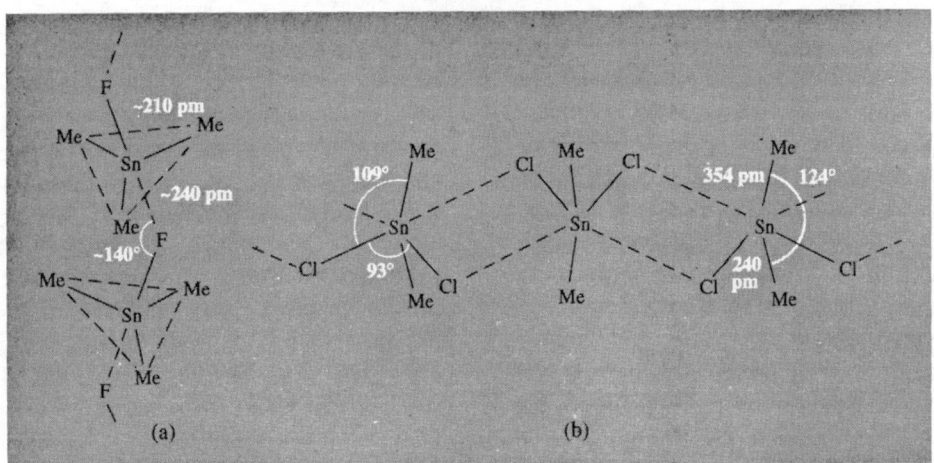

Figure 10.13 Crystal structure of (a) Me_3SnF, and (b) Me_2SnCl_2, showing tendency to polymerize via Sn—X···Sn bonds.

which thereby raise the coordination number of Sn to 5, 6 or even 7. As expected, F is more effective in this role than the other halogens (why?). For example, Ph_3SnF is a strictly linear polymer with 5-coordinate trigonal bipyramidal geometry about Sn; the angles Sn–F–Sn and F–Sn–F are both 180° and the Sn–F distances in the chain are identical (214.6 pm).[111] By contrast, Me_3SnF has a zig-zag chain structure (Fig. 10.13a) with unequal Sn–F distances and a pronounced bend at F (~140°). The volatile chlorine analogue (Me_3SnCl: mp 39.5°, bp 154°) also has a zig-zag chain structure with angle Sn–Cl–Sn 151° and essentially linear Cl–Sn–Cl (177°); The two Sn–Cl distances in the chain are 243 and 326 pm but even this longer distance is substantially shorter than the sum of the van der Waals radii (385 pm).[112] On the other hand crystalline Ph_3SnCl and Ph_3SnBr feature monomeric molecules with 4-coordinate Sn atoms.

Me_2SnF_2 has a layer structure with octahedral Sn and *trans*-Me groups above and below the F-bridged layers as in SnF_4 (p. 381). The weaker Cl bridging in Me_2SnCl_2 leads to the more distorted structure shown in Fig. 10.13b. The O atom is an even more effective ligand than F and, amongst the numerous compounds R_3SnOR' and $R_2Sn(OR')_2$ that have been studied by X-ray crystallography, the only ones with 4-coordinate tin (presumably because of the bulky ligands) are $1,4-(Et_3SnO)_2C_6Cl_4$ and $[Mn(CO)_3\{\eta^5\text{-}C_5Ph_4(OSnPh_3)\}]$.

The converse of polymerization is heterolytic bond scission leading either to R_3Sn^+ or R_3Sn^- species. Tricoordinate organotin(IV) cations can readily be synthesized at room temperature by hydride or halide abstraction reactions in benzene or other solvents.[113] For example, with R = Me, Bu or Ph:

$$R_3SnH + Ph_3CClO_4 \longrightarrow [R_3Sn]^+[ClO_4]^- + Ph_3CH$$

$$R_3SnCl + AgClO_4 \longrightarrow [R_3Sn]^+[ClO_4]^- + AgCl$$

$$R_3SnH + B(C_6F_5)_3 \longrightarrow [R_3Sn]^+[B(C_6F_5)_3H]^-$$

The highly ionic nature of these (presumably planar) species is revealed by cryoscopy, electrical conductance and the diagnostically large downfield ^{119}Sn nmr chemical shift. Salts of the corresponding anionic species Ph_3Sn^- are easily generated by heating either Ph_3SnH or Sn_2Ph_6

[111] D. TUDELA, E. GUTIÉRREZ-PUEBLA and A. MONGE, *J. Chem. Soc., Dalton Trans.*, 1069–71 (1992).

[112] M. B. HOSSAIN, J. L. LEFFERTS, K. C. MOLLOY, D. VAN DER HELM and J. J. ZUCKERMAN, *Inorg. Chim. Acta* **36**, L409–L410 (1979).

[113] J. B. LAMBERT and B. KUHLMANN, *J. Chem. Soc., Chem. Commun.*, 931–2 (1992).

with alkali metal, and an X-ray crystal structure of the crown ether complex (p. 97) [K(18-crown-6)]$^+$[Ph$_3$Sn]$^-$ revealed a naked pyramidal anion with Sn–C 222.4 pm (cf. 212 pm in SnPh$_4$) and the angle C–Sn–C 96.9°.[114] Seven-coordinate pentagonal bipyramidal organotin(IV) complexes are exemplified by [SnEt$_2$(η^5-dapt)] in which the two Et groups are axial and the planar 5-fold ligation (η^5-N$_3$O$_2$) is provided by the ligand (dapt), (H$_2$dapt = 2,6-diacetylpyridinebis-(2-thenoylhydrazone)].[115]

Catenation is well established in organotin chemistry and distannane derivatives can be prepared by standard methods (see Ge, p. 396). The compounds are more reactive than organodigermanes; e.g. Sn$_2$Me$_6$ (mp 23°) inflames in air at its bp (182°) and absorbs oxygen slowly at room temperature to give (Me$_2$Sn)$_2$O. Typical routes to higher polystannanes are:

$$2Me_3SnBr + NaMe_2SnSnMe_2Na \xrightarrow{\text{liq NH}_3}$$

$$Me_3Sn(SnMe_2)_2SnMe_3 \text{ (oil)}$$

$$3Ph_3SnLi + SnCl_2 \longrightarrow [(Ph_3Sn)_3SnLi]$$

$$\xrightarrow{Ph_3SnCl} Sn(SnPh_3)_4 (mp \sim 320°)$$

Unbranched chains up to at least Sn$_6$ are known, e.g. Ph$_3$Sn(Bu$_2^t$Sn)$_n$SnPh$_3$ ($n = 0$–4).[116] Cyclo-dialkyl stannanes(IV) can also be readily prepared, e.g. reaction of Me$_2$SnCl$_2$ with Na/liq NH$_3$ yields cyclo-(SnMe$_2$)$_6$ together with acyclic X(SnMe$_2$)$_n$X ($n = 12$–20). Yellow crystalline cyclo-(SnEt$_2$)$_9$ is obtained almost quantitatively when Et$_2$SnH$_2$, dissolved in toluene/pyridine, is catalytically dehydrogenated at 100° in the presence of a small amount of Et$_2$SnCl$_2$. Similarly, under differing conditions, the following have been prepared:[34] (SnEt$_2$)$_6$, (SnEt$_2$)$_7$, (SnBu$_2^i$)$_4$, (SnBu$_2^i$)$_4$, (SnBu$_2^i$)$_6$, and (SnPh$_2$)$_5$. The compounds are highly reactive

yellow or red oils or solids. A crystal structure of the colourless hexamer (SnPh$_2$)$_6$ shows that it exists in the chair conformation (I) with Sn–Sn distances very close to the value of 280 pm in α-Sn (p. 372). Small rings are also known, e.g. [cyclo-(SnR$_2$)$_3$] where R = 2,4,6-triisopropylphenyl,[117] and even the propellane [1.1.1]-Sn$_5$R$_6$ (structure II, R = 2,6-C$_6$H$_3$Et$_2$).[118] This latter compound was formed in 13% yield as dark blue-violet crystals by the thermolysis of cyclo-Sn$_3$R$_6$ in xylene at 200°. The axial Sn–Sn distance of 337 pm is substantially longer than the previously known longest Sn–Sn bond (305 pm) and may indicate significant singlet diradical character).

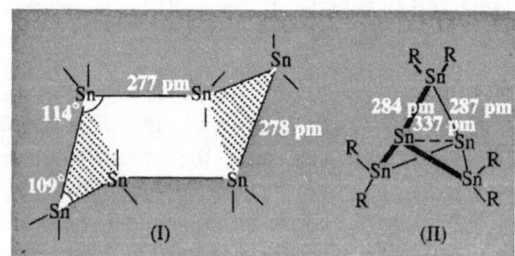

True monomeric organotin(II) compounds have proved rather elusive. The cyclopentadienyl compound [Sn(η^5-C$_5$H$_5$)$_2$] (which is obtained as white crystals mp 105° from the reaction of NaC$_5$H$_5$ and SnCl$_2$ in thf) has a structure similar to that of germanocene (12 pp. 398–9) with the angle subtended at Sn by the midpoints of the C$_5$ rings 143.7° and 148.0° in the two independent molecules.[119] Interestingly, the mean value of 146° is 1° larger than the value for [Sn(η^5-C$_5$Me$_5$)$_2$], suggesting that the angle is governed predominantly by electronic rather than steric factors. However, with the much more demanding η^5-C$_5$Ph$_5$ ligand, the two planar C$_5$ rings are exactly parallel and staggered, the opposed canting of the phenyl rings with respect to the C$_5$ rings giving overall

[114] T. BIRCHALL and J. A. VETRONE, *J. Chem. Soc., Chem. Commun.*, 877–9 (1988).

[115] C. CARINI, G. PELIZZI, P. TARASCONI, C. PELIZZI, K. C. MOLLOY and P. C. WATERFIELD, *J. Chem. Soc., Dalton Trans.*, 289–93 (1989).

[116] S. ADAMS and M. DRÄGER *Angew. Chem. Int. Edn. Engl.* **26**, 1255–6 (1987).

[117] S. MASAMUNE and L. R. SITA, *J. Am. Chem. Soc.* **107** 6390–1 (1985).

[118] L. R. SITA and R. D. BICKERSTAFF, *J. Am. Chem. Soc.* **111** 6454–6 (1989).

[119] J. L. ATWOOD and W. E. HUNTER, *J. Chem. Soc., Chem. Commun.*, 925–7 (1981).

S_{10} symmetry.[120] Heterostannocenes such as the pyrrole analogue, $[Sn(\eta^5\text{-}C_4Bu^t_2H_2N)_2]$, (in which a CH group has been replaced by the isoelectronic N atom) have also been reported, the angle subtended by the ring centres at Sn being 142.5° in this case.[121] The related "half-sandwich" cation, *nido*-$[(\eta^5\text{-}C_5Me_5)Sn:]^+$, which is isostructural with *nido*-B_6H_{10} (p. 154), can be made in moderate yield by treating $[Sn(\eta^5\text{-}C_5Me_5)_2]$ with an ethereal solution of HBF_4. The product, $[(\eta^5\text{-}C_5Me_5)Sn]BF_4$, forms colourless crystals which are somewhat sensitive to air and moisture.[122] As its trifluoromethanesulfonate salt $(X^- = CF_3SO_3^-)$, the cation undergoes a remarkable reaction with BI_3 which results in replacement of the apical Sn atom with the {BI} group to give a pentacarba analogue of *nido*-B_6H_{10}:[123]

$$nido\text{-}[(\eta^5\text{-}C_5Me_5)Sn]^+X^- + BI_3 \longrightarrow$$
$$nido\text{-}[(\eta^5\text{-}C_5Me_5)BI]^+X^- + SnI_2$$

The stabilization of σ-bonded dialkyltin(II) compounds, $R_2Sn:$, (and also those of Ge and Pb) can be achieved by the use of bulky R groups. The first such compound, $[Sn\{CH(SiMe_3)_2\}_2]$, was prepared by direct reaction of $LiCH(SiMe_3)_2$ with $SnCl_2$ or $[Sn\{N(SiMe_3)_2\}_2]$ in ether, and was obtained as air-sensitive red crystals (mp 136°).[124,125] It is monomeric in the gas phase and in benzene solution, and behaves chemically as a "stannylene", displacing CO from $M(CO)_6$ to give orange $[Cr(CO)_5(SnR_2)]$ and yellow $[Mo(CO)_5(SnR_2)]$.[124,126] However,

a crystal structure determination showed that the compound dimerizes in the solid state, perhaps by donation of the lone-pair of electrons on each Sn centre into the "vacant" orbital of its neighbour, to give a weak bent double bond as indicated schematically below;[125,127] this would interpret the orientation of the four $\{-CH(SiMe_3)_2\}$ groups.

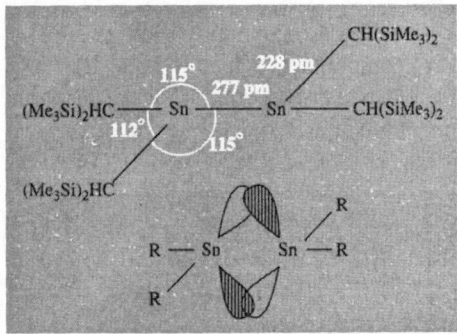

A synthetic strategy which ensures retention of the monomeric form of SnR_2 even in the crystalline state is to use functionalized R groups which contain a chelating substituent, e.g. by replacing the H atom in $\{-CH(SiMe_3)_2\}$ with a 2-pyridyl group.[128]

Stable stannaethenes, $>C{=}Sn{<}$,[129] and stannaphosphenes, $>Sn{=}P{<}$,[130] have been reported and these, again, exploit the use of bulky groups to prevent oligomerization.

[120] M. J. HEEG, C. JANIAK and J. J. ZUCKERMAN, *J. Am. Chem. Soc.* **106**, 4259–61 (1984).

[121] N. KUHN, G. HENKEL and S. STUBENRAUCH, *J. Chem. Soc., Chem. Commun.*, 760–1 (1992).

[122] P. JUTZI, F. KOHL and C. KRÜGER, *Angew. Chem. Int. Edn. Engl.* **18**, 59–61 (1979).

[123] F. KOHL and P. JUTZI, *Angew. Chem. Int. Edn. Engl.* **22**, 56 (1983).

[124] P. J. DAVIDSON and M. F. LAPPERT, *J. Chem. Soc., Chem. Commun.*, 317 (1973).

[125] D. E. GOLDBERG, D. H. HARRIS, M. F. LAPPERT and K. M. THOMAS, *J. Chem. Soc., Chem. Commun.*, 261–2 (1976).

[126] J. D. COTTON, P. J. DAVIDSON, D. E. GOLDBERG, M. F. LAPPERT and K. M. THOMAS, *J. Chem. Soc., Chem. Commun.*, 893–5 (1974).

[127] P. J. DAVIDSON, D. H. HARRIS and M. F. LAPPERT, *J. Chem. Soc., Dalton Trans.*, 2268–74 (1976). D. E. GOLDBERG, P. B. HITCHCOCK, M. F. LAPPERT, K. M. THOMAS, A. J. THORNE, T.FJELDBERG, A. HAALAND and B. E. R. SCHILLING, *J. Chem. Soc., Dalton Trans.*, 2387–94 (1986). See also U. LAY, H. PRITZKOW and H. GRÜTZMANN, *J. Chem. Soc., Chem. Commun.*, 260–2 (1992) for isomeric structures of crystalline $[Sn\{C_6H_2(CF_3)_3\text{-}2,4,6\}_2]$, *viz.* a yellow monomeric form (mp 76°) and a bright red form (mp 66°) which features a weakly associated dimer with a very long Sn–Sn interaction (364 pm).

[128] L. M. ENGELHARDT, B. S. JOLLY, M. F. LAPPERT, C. L. RASTON and A. H. WHITE, *J. Chem. Soc., Chem. Commun.*, 336–8 (1988).

[129] H. MEYER, G. BAUM, W. MASSA, S. BERGER and A. BERNDT, *Angew Chem. Int. Edn. Engl.* **26**, 546–8 (1987).

[130] H. RANAIVONJATOVO, J. ESCUDIE, C. COURET and J. SATGÉ, *J. Chem. Soc., Chem. Commun.*, 1047–8 (1992).

Lead[131]

The organic chemistry of Pb is much less extensive than that of Sn, though over 2000 organolead compounds are known and $PbEt_4$ has been produced on a larger tonnage than any other single organometallic compound (p. 371). The most useful laboratory-scale routes to organoleads involve the use of LiR, RMgX, or AlR_3 on lead(II) compounds such as $PbCl_2$, or lead(IV) compounds such as $R_2'PbX_2$, $R_3'PbX$, or K_2PbCl_6. On the industrial scale the reaction of RX on a Pb/Na alloy is much used; an alternative is the electrolysis of RMgX, M^IBR_4, or M^IAlR_4 using a Pb anode. The simple tetraalkyls are volatile, monomeric molecular liquids which can be steam-distilled without decomposition; $PbPh_4$ (mp 227–228°) is even more stable thermally: it can be distilled at 240° (15–20 mmHg) but decomposes above 270°. Diplumbanes Pb_2R_6 are much less stable and higher polyplumbanes are unknown except for the thermally unstable, reactive red solid, $Pb(PbPh_3)_4$.

The decreasing thermal stability of Group 14 organometallics with increasing atomic number of M reflects the decreasing M–C and M–M bond energies. This in turn is related to the increasing size of M and the consequent increasing interatomic distance (see table).

M	C	Si	Ge	Sn	Pb
M-C distance in MR$_4$/pm	154	194	199	217	227

Parallel with these trends and related to them is the increase in chemical reactivity which is further enhanced by the increasing bond polarity and the increasing availability of low-lying vacant orbitals for energetically favourable reaction pathways.

It is notable that the preparation of alkyl and aryl derivatives from Pb^{II} starting materials always results in Pb^{IV} organometallic compounds. The only well-defined examples of Pb^{II}

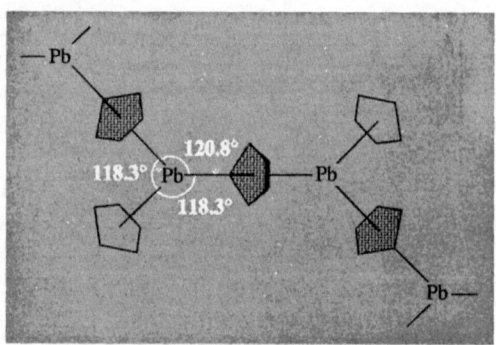

Figure 10.14 Schematic diagram of the chain structure of orthorhombic $Pb(\eta^5\text{-}C_5H_5)_2$. For the doubly coordinated C_5H_5 ring (shaded) Pb–C_{av} is 306 pm, and for the "terminal" C_5H_5 ring Pb–C_{av} is 276 pm; the Pb $\cdots$ Pb distance within the chain is 564 pm.

organometallics are purple compound $Pb[CH(SiMe_3)_2]_2$ (see refs on p. 403) and the cyclopentadienyl compound $Pb(\eta^5\text{-}C_5H_5)_2$ and its ring-methyl derivative. Like the Sn analogue (p. 402) $Pb(\eta^5\text{-}C_5H_5)_2$ features non-parallel cyclopentadienyl rings in the gas phase, the angle subtended at Pb being $135 \pm 15°$. Two crystalline forms are known and the orthorhombic polymorph has the unusual chain-like structure shown in Fig. 10.14:[132] one C_5H_5 is between 2 Pb and perpendicular to the Pb–Pb vector whilst the other C_5H_5 is bonded (more closely) to only 1 Pb. The chain polymer can be thought to arise as a result of the interaction of the lone-pair of electrons on a given Pb atom with a neighbouring (chain) C_5H_5 ring; a 3-centre bond is constructed by overlapping 2 opposite sp^2 hybrids on 2 successive Pb atoms in the chain with the σMO (A_2'') of the C_5H_5 group: this forms one bonding, one nonbonding, and one antibonding MO of which the first 2 are filled and the third empty. By contrast, the deep red crystalline compound $[Pb(\eta^5\text{-}C_5Me_5)_2]$ (mp 100–105°) is monomeric;[119] the angle subtended by the ring centres at Pb is 151° (i.e. even larger than in the Sn analogue) and there is a slight ring slippage

[131] P. G. HARRISON, Chap. 12 in G. WILKINSON, F. G. A. STONE and E. W. ABEL (eds.), *Comprehensive Organometallic Chemistry*, Pergamon Press, Oxford, Vol. 2, pp. 629–80 (1982), 419 refs.

[132] C. PANATTONI, G. BOMBIERI, and U. CROATO, *Acta Cryst.* **21**, 823–6 (1966).

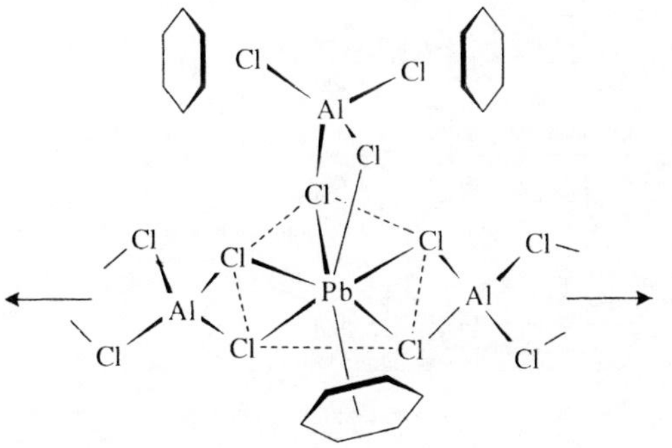

Figure 10.15   Schematic diagram of the chain structure of $[Pb^{II}(AlCl_4)_2(\eta^6\text{-}C_6H_6)].C_6H_6$: Pb–Cl varies from 285–322 pm, Pb–C_{av} (bound) 311 pm, Pb-centre of C_6H_6 (bound) 277 pm.

which leads to a range of Pb–C distances (269–290 pm) to the pentahapto rings.

Another unusual organo-Pb^{II} compound is the η^6-benzene complex $[Pb^{II}(AlCl_4)_2(\eta^6\text{-}C_6H_6)].$-

C_6H_6 in which Pb^{II} is in a distorted pentagonal bipyramidal site with 1 axial Cl and the other axial site occupied by the centre of the benzene ring (Fig. 10.15). The other C_6H_6 is a molecule of solvation far removed from the metal. One {AlCl$_4$} group chelates the Pb in an axial-equatorial configuration and the other {AlCl$_4$} chelates and bridges neighbouring Pb atoms to form a chain. There is a similar Sn^{II} compound with the same structure. The original paper should be consulted for a discussion of the bonding.[133]

The coordination chemistry of Pb^{II} with conventional ligands from groups 14–16 and with macrocyclic ligands has recently been reviewed.[134]

[133] A. G. Gash, P. F. Rodesiler and E. L. Amma, *Inorg. Chem.* **13**, 2429–4 (1974). See also J. L. Lefferts, M. B. Hossain, K. C. Molloy, D. van der Helm and J. J. Zuckerman, *Angew. Chem. Int. Edn. Engl.* **19**, 309–10 (1980).

[134] J. Parr, Polyhedron **16**, 551–66 (1997).

11
Nitrogen

11.1 Introduction

Nitrogen is the most abundant uncombined element accessible to man. It comprises 78.1% by volume of the atmosphere (i.e. 78.3 atom% or 75.5 wt%) and is produced industrially from this source on the multimegatonne scale annually. In combined form it is essential to all forms of life, and constitutes, on average, about 15% by weight of proteins. The industrial fixation of nitrogen for agricultural fertilizers and other chemical products is now carried out on a vast scale in many countries, and the number of moles of anhydrous ammonia manufactured exceeds that of any other compound. Indeed, of the top fifteen "high-volume" industrial chemicals produced in the USA, five contain nitrogen (Fig. 11.1).[1] This has important consequences, predominantly beneficial but occasionally detrimental, since of all man's recent interventions in the cycles of nature the industrial fixation of nitrogen is by far the most extensive. These aspects will be discussed further in later sections.

The "discovery" of nitrogen in 1772 is generally credited to Daniel Rutherford, though the gas was also isolated independently about the same time by both C. W. Scheele and H. Cavendish.[2] Rutherford (at the suggestion of his teacher Joseph Black who had earlier discovered CO_2, p. 269) was studying the properties of the residual "air" left after carbonaceous substances were burned in a limited supply of air; he removed the CO_2 by means of KOH and so obtained nitrogen which he thought was ordinary air that had taken up phlogiston from the combusted material. The elementary nature of nitrogen was disputed by some even as late as 1840 despite the work of A. L. Lavoisier. The name "nitrogen" was suggested by Jean-Antoine-Claude Chaptal in 1790 when it was realized that the element was a constituent of nitric acid and nitrates (Greek νίτρον, nitron; γεννᾶν, to form). Lavoisier preferred *azote* (Greek ἀζωτικός, no life) because

---

[1] Facts and Figures, *Chem. & Eng. News*, 23 June, 1997, pp. 40–1.

[2] M. E. WEEKS, in H. M. LEICESTER (ed.), *Discovery of the Elements*, 6th edn., Journal of Chemical Education Publication, 1956: Nitrogen, pp. 205–8; Rutherford, discoverer of nitrogen, pp. 235–51; Old compounds of nitrogen, pp. 188–95.

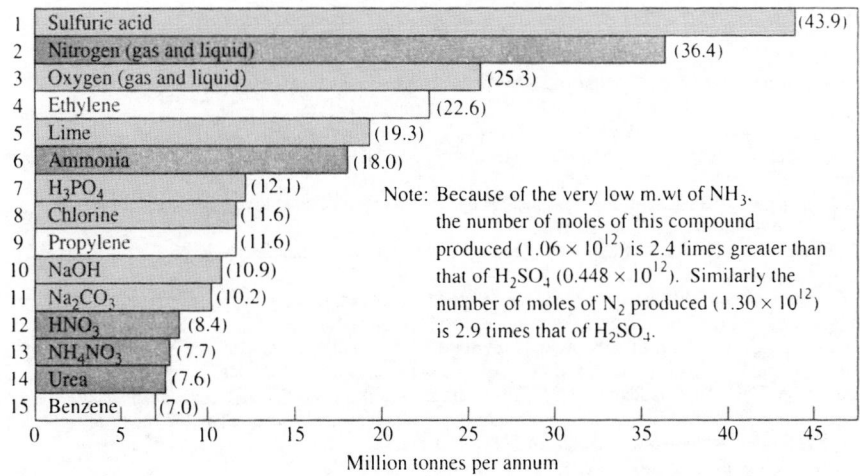

Figure 11.1   US production of the top 15 industrial chemicals (1996).

of the asphyxiating properties of the gas, and this name is still used in the French language and in such forms as azo, diazo, azide, etc. The German name *Stickstoff* refers to the same property (*sticken*, to choke or suffocate).

Compounds of nitrogen have an impressive history. Ammonium chloride was first mentioned in the *Historia* of Herodotus (fifth century BC)[†] and ammonium salts, together with nitrates, nitric acid and aqua regia, were well known to the early alchemists.[2] Some important dates in the subsequent development of the chemistry of nitrogen are given in the Panel on p. 408. Exciting discoveries are still being made at the present time and, indeed, the detailed mechanisms by which bacteria fix nitrogen at

ambient temperatures and pressures is still an active area of research. Several recent reviews, monographs, and proceedings of symposia have been published.[3−6]

11.2 The Element

11.2.1 Abundance and distribution

Despite its ready availability in the atmosphere, nitrogen is relatively unabundant in the crustal rocks and soils of the earth. At 19 ppm it is equal 33rd with Ga in the order of abundance, and similar to Nb (20 ppm) and Li (18 ppm). The only major minerals are KNO_3 (nitre, saltpetre) and $NaNO_3$ (sodanitre, Chile saltpetre). Both occur widespread, usually in small amounts as evaporites in arid regions, often as an efflorescence on soils or in caverns. $NaNO_3$ is isomorphous with calcite (p. 109) whereas KNO_3 is isomorphous with aragonite (p. 109), thus reflecting the similar size of NO_3^- and CO_3^{2-}, and the fact that K^+ is considerably larger than Na^+ and Ca^{2+}. Major deposits of KNO_3 occur in India and there are smaller amounts in Bolivia, Italy, Spain and the former Soviet Union. There are vast deposits of $NaNO_3$ in the desert regions of northern Chile where it occurs with other evaporites such as NaCl, Na_2SO_4 and

---

[†] "There are pieces of salt in large lumps on the hills of Libya and the Ammonians who live there worship the god Ammon in a temple resembling that of the Theban Jupiter." (Greek Άμμων, the name of the Egyptian diety Amun, whence *sal ammoniac* from άμμωνιακόν, belonging to Ammon.)

[3] R. W. F. HARDY, F. BOTTOMLEY and R. C. BURNS (eds.), *A Treatise on Dinitrogen Fixation*, Sections 1 and 2, Wiley, New York 1979, 812 pp.

[4] J. CHATT, L. M. DA C. PINA and R. L. RICHARDS, *New Trends in the Chemistry of Nitrogen Fixation*, Academic Press, London, 1980, 284 pp.

[5] J. CHATT, J. R. DILWORTH and R. L. RICHARDS, *Chem. Rev.* **78**, 589–625 (1978).

[6] A. E. SHILOV, *Pure Appl. Chem.* **64**, 1409–20 (1992).

Time Chart for Nitrogen Chemistry

1772	N_2 gas isolated by D. Rutherford (also by C. W. Scheele and H. Cavendish).
1772	N_2O prepared by J. Priestley who also showed it supported combustion.
1774	NH_3 gas isolated by Priestley using mercury in a pneumatic trough.
1809	First donor-acceptor adduct (coordination compound) $NH_3.BF_3$ prepared by J. L. Gay Lussac (A. Werner's theory, 1891–5).
1811	NCl_3 prepared by P. L. Dulong who lost an eye and three fingers studying its properties.
1828	Urea made from NH_4CNO by F. Wöhler.
1832	Phosphonitrilic chloride $(NPCl_2)_x$ prepared by J. von Liebig by heating NH_3 or NH_4Cl with PCl_5.
1835	S_4N_4 first prepared by M. Gregory.
1862	Importance of N *in soil* for agriculture recognized (despite von Liebig having incorrectly maintained, in the face of fierce opposition, that it came from the atmosphere directly).
1864	Ability of liquid NH_3 to dissolve metals giving coloured solutions reported by W. Weyl.
1886	Atmospheric N_2 shown to be "fixed" by organisms in certain root nodules.
1887	Hydrazine, N_2H_4, first isolated by T. Curtius; he also first made HN_3 (from N_2H_4) in 1890.
1895	First industrial process involving atmospheric N_2 — the Frank–Caro process for calcium cyanamide.
1900	Birkeland–Eyde industrial oxidation of N_2 to NO and hence HNO_3 (now obsolete).
1906	Crystalline sulfamic acid, H_3NSO_3, first obtained by F. Raschig.
1907	Raschig's industrial oxidation of NH_3 to N_2H_4 using hypochlorite.
1908	Catalytic oxidation of NH_3 to HNO_3 (1901) developed on an industrial scale by W. Ostwald (awarded the 1909 Nobel Prize in Chemistry for his work on catalysis).
1909	F. Haber's catalytic synthesis of NH_3 developed in collaboration with C. Bosch into a large-scale industrial process by 1913. (Haber was awarded the 1918 Nobel Prize in Chemistry "for the synthesis of ammonia from its elements"; Bosch shared the 1931 Nobel Prize for "contributions to the invention and development of chemical high-pressure methods", the Haber synthesis of NH_3 being the first high-pressure industrial process.)
1926	Borazine, $(HBNH)_3$, analogous to benzene prepared by A. Stock and E. Pohland.
1928	NF_3 first prepared by O. Ruff and E. Hanke, 117 y after NCl_3.
1925–35	Spectrum of atomic N gradually analysed.
1929	Discovery of a nitrogen isotope ^{15}N by S. M. Naudé following the discovery of isotopes of O and C by others earlier in the same year.
1934	Microwave absorption in NH_3 (due to molecular inversion) first observed — this marks the start of microwave spectroscopy.
1950	Nuclear magnetic resonance in compounds, containing ^{14}N and ^{15}N first observed by W. E. Proctor and F. C. Yu.
1957	N_2F_4 first made by C. B. Colburn and A. Kennedy and later (1961) shown to be in dissociative equilibrium with paramagnetic NF_2 above 100°C.
1958	$NH_3.BH_3$ isoelectronic with ethane prepared by S. G. Shore and R. W. Parry (direct reaction of NH_3 and B_2H_6 gives $[BH_2(NH_3)_2]^+[BH_4]^-$).
1962	First "bent" NO complex encountered, viz. $[Co(NO)(S_2CNMe_2)_2]$ (P. R. H. Alderman, P. G. Owston and J. M. Rowe).
1965	First N_2 ligand complex prepared by A. D. Allan and C. V. Senoff.
1966	ONF_3 (isoelectronic with CF_4) discovered independently by two groups.
1968	N_2 recognized as a bridging ligand in $[(NH_3)_5RuN_2Ru(NH_3)_5]^{4+}$ by D. F. Harrison, E. Weissberger, and H. Taube. (H. Taube, 1983 Nobel Prize for chemistry "for his work on the mechanisms of electron transfer reactions especially in metal complexes").
1974	First thionitrosyl (NS) complex isolated by J. Chatt and J. R. Dilworth.
1975	$(SN)_x$ polymer, known since 1910, found to be metallic (and a superconductor at temperatures below 0.33 K).
1979	Trigonal prismatic 6-fold coordination of N (Table 11.1, p. 413).
1980–90	Square pyramidal and trigonal bipyramidal 5-fold coordination of N (Table 11.1).

KNO_3 on the eastern slopes of the coastal ranges at an elevation of 1200–2500 m. Because of the development of the synthetic ammonia and nitric acid industries these large deposits are no longer a major source of nitrates, though they played an important role in agriculture until the 1920s (as also did guano, the massive deposits of bird excreta on certain islands).

The continuous interchange of nitrogen between the atmosphere and the biosphere is called the nitrogen cycle. Global estimates are difficult to obtain and there are frequently regional and local impacts which vary greatly from the mean. However, some indication of the size of the various "reservoirs" of nitrogen in the atmosphere, on land, and in the seas is given in Fig. 11.2 together with the estimated annual rate of transfer between these various pools.[7,8] Estimates frequently vary by a factor of 3 or more. Atmospheric nitrogen is fixed by biological action (p. 1035), industrial processes (p. 421), and to a significant extent by fires, lightning and other atmospheric discharges which produce NO_x. There is also a minute production (on the global scale) of NO_x from internal combustion engines and from coal-burning, though the local concentration in some urban environments can be very high and extremely unpleasant.[9-11] Absorption of fixed nitrogen by both terrestrial and aquatic plants leads to protein synthesis followed by death, decay, oxidation and denitrification by bacterial and other action which eventually returns the nitrogen to the seas and the atmosphere as N_2. An alternative sequence involves the digestion of plants by animals, the synthesis of animal proteins, excretion of nitrogenous material, and, again, ultimate death, decay and denitrification. Figure 11.2 indicates that the greatest anthropogenic impact on the cycle arises from the industrial fixation of nitrogen by the Haber and other processes. Much of this is used beneficially as fertilizers but the leaching of excess nitrogenous material can lead to eutrophication in freshwater systems, and the increased nitrate concentration in waters used for human consumption can pose a health hazard. Nevertheless, there is no doubt that the high yields of agriculture necessary to maintain even the present human population of the world cannot be achieved without the judicious application of manufactured nitrogenous fertilizers. Concern has also been expressed that increasing levels of N_2O following denitrification may eventually impoverish the ozone layer in the stratosphere. Much more data are required and the subject is being actively pursued by several international agencies as well as by national and local governments and individual scientists.

11.2.2 Production and uses of nitrogen

The only important large-scale process for producing N_2 is the liquefaction and fractional distillation of air[12] (see Panel on p. 411). Production has grown remarkably during the past few years, partly as a result of the increasing demand for its coproduct O_2 for steelmaking. For example, US domestic production has increased 250-fold in the past 25 y from 0.12 million tonnes in 1955 to 30 million tonnes in 1980. In 1991 world production was 56 million tonnes (USA 47%; Europe 35%; Asia 15%). Commercial N_2 is a highly purified product, typically containing less than 20 ppm O_2. Specially purified "oxygen-free" N_2, containing less than 2 ppm, is available commercially, and "ultrapure" N_2 (99.999%) containing less than 10 ppm Ar is also produced on the multitonne per day scale.

Laboratory routes to highly purified N_2 are seldom required. Thermal decomposition of sodium azide at 300°C under carefully controlled conditions is one possibility:

$$2NaN_3 \longrightarrow 2Na + 3N_2$$

Hot aqueous solutions of ammonium nitrite also decompose to give nitrogen though small amounts of NO and HNO_3 are also formed (p. 434) and must be removed by suitable absorbents such as dichromate in aqueous sulfuric acid:

$$NH_4NO_2 \xrightarrow{\text{aq}} N_2 + 2H_2O$$

Other routes are the thermal decomposition of $(NH_4)_2Cr_2O_7$, the reaction of NH_3 with bromine water, or the high-temperature reaction of NH_3

---

[7] C. C. DELWICHE, The nitrogen cycle, Chap. 5 in C. L. HAMILTON (ed.), *Chemistry in the Environment*, Readings from Scientific American, W. H. Freeman, San Francisco, 1973.

[8] SCOPE Report No. 10, *Environmental Issues*, Wiley, New York, 1977, 220 pp.

[9] J. HEICKLEN, *Atmospheric Chemistry*, Academic Press, 1976, 406 pp.

[10] I. M. CAMPBELL, *Energy and the Atmosphere*, 2nd edn. Wiley, London, 1986, Nitrogen cycles, pp 169–81.

[11] U. S. OZKAN, S. K. AGARWAL and G. MARCELIN (eds.), *Reduction of Nitrogen Oxide Emissions*, ACS Symposium Series No. 587, 1995, 260 pp.

[12] W. J. GRANT and S. L. REDFEARN, Industrial gases, in R. THOMPSON (ed.), *The Modern Inorganic Chemicals Industry*, Chem. Soc. Special Publ. **31**, 273–301 (1977).

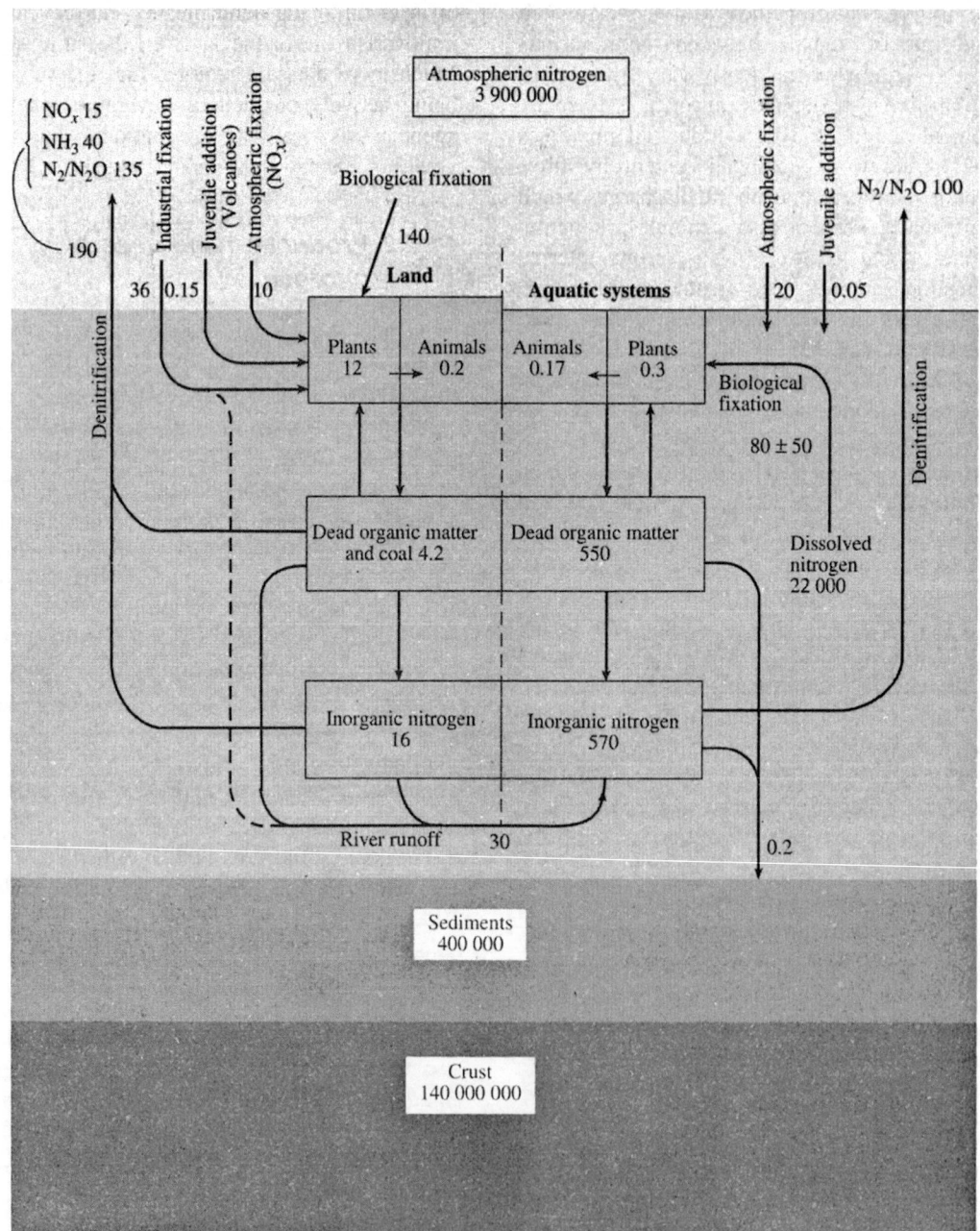

Figure 11.2   Distribution of nitrogen in the biosphere and annual transfer rates can be estimated only within broad limits. The two quantities known with high confidence are the amount of nitrogen in the atmosphere and the rate of industrial fixation. The inventories (within the boxes) are expressed in terms of 10^9 tonnes of N; the transfers (indicated by arrows) are in 10^6 tonnes of N. Taken from ref. 7 with some adjustments for more recent data.

Industrial Gases from Air

Air is the source of six industrial gases, N_2, O_2, Ne, Ar, Kr and Xe. As the mass of the earth's atmosphere is approximately 5×10^9 million tonnes, the supply is unlimited and the annual industrial production, though vast, is insignificant by comparison. The composition of air at low altitudes is remarkably constant, the main variable component being water vapour which ranges from $\sim 4\%$ by volume in tropical jungles to very low values in cold or arid climates. Other minor local variations result from volcanism or human activity. The main invariant part of the air has the following composition (% by volume, bp in parentheses):

N_2	78.03 (77.2 K)	CO_2	0.033 (194.7 K)	He	0.0005 (4.2 K)
O_2	20.99 (90.1 K)	Ne	0.0015 (27.2 K)	Kr	0.0001 (119.6 K)
Ar	0.93 (87.2 K)	H_2	0.0010 (20.2 K)	Xe	0.000008 (165.1 K)

Details of the production and uses of O_2 (p. 604) and the noble gases (p. 889) are in later chapters.

About two-thirds of the N_2 produced industrially is supplied as a gas, mainly in pipes but also in cylinders under pressure. The remaining one-third is supplied as liquid N_2 since this is also a very convenient source of the dry gas. The main use is as an inert atmosphere in the iron and steel industry and in many other metallurgical and chemical processes where the presence of air would involve fire or explosion hazards or unacceptable oxidation of products. Thus, it is extensively used as a purge in petrochemical reactors and other chemical equipment, as an inert diluent for chemicals, and in the float glass process to prevent oxidation of the molten tin (p. 370). It is also used as a blanketing gas in the electronics industry, in the packaging of processed foods and pharmaceuticals, and to pressurize electric cables, telephone wires, and inflatable rubber tyres, etc.

About 10% of the N_2 produced is used as a refrigerant. Typical of such applications are (a) freeze grinding of normally soft or rubbery materials, (b) low-temperature machining of rubbers, (c) shrink fitting and assembly of engineering components, (d) the preservation of biological specimens such as blood, semen, etc., and (e) as a constant low-temperature bath ($-196°C$). Liquid N_2 is also frequently used for convenience in applications where a very low temperature is not essential such as (a) food freezing (and hamburger meat grinding), (b) in-transit refrigeration, (c) freeze branding of cattle, (d) pipe-freezing for stopping flow in the absence of valves, and (e) soil-freezing for consolidating unstable ground in tunnelling or excavation.

The cost of N_2, like that of O_2, is particularly dependent on electricity costs, though plant maintenance and transport costs also obtrude. Typical prices in 1992 for N_2 in the USA were about $32 per tonne for bulk liquid (exclusive of transportation and handling charges). Costs for small-scale users of N_2 from gas cylinders are proportionately much higher.

with CuO; overall equations can be written as:

$$(NH_4)_2Cr_2O_7 \longrightarrow N_2 + Cr_2O_3 + 4H_2O$$

$$8NH_3 + 3Br_2 \xrightarrow{\text{aq}} N_2 + 6NH_4Br(aq)$$

$$2NH_3 + 3CuO \longrightarrow N_2 + 3Cu + 3H_2O$$

11.2.3 Atomic and physical properties

Nitrogen has two stable isotopes ^{14}N (relative atomic mass 14.003 07, abundance 99.634%) and ^{15}N (15.000 11, 0.366%); their relative abundance (272:1) is almost invariant in terrestrial sources and corresponds to an atomic weight of 14.006 74(7). Both isotopes have a nuclear spin and can be used in nmr experiments.[13] though the sensitivity at constant field is only one-thousandth that of ^1H. The ^{14}N nucleus has a spin quantum number of 1 and, in consequence, the spectra are broadened by quadrupole effects. The ^{15}N nucleus with spin $\frac{1}{2}$ does not have this difficulty though its low abundance poses problems.[14] Interestingly, the first chemical shift ever to be observed in nmr spectroscopy ("as an annoying ambiguity in the magnetic moment of ^{14}N") was in 1950 in an aqueous solution of NH_4NO_3.[15] Nowadays ^{14}N and ^{15}N nmr chemical shifts are widely used to probe the

13 G. J. MARTIN, M. L. MARTIN and J.-P. GOUESNARD, *NMR Volume 18: ^{15}N NMR Spectroscopy*, Springer-Verlag, Berlin,

1981, 382 pp. J. MASON, Nitrogen, in J. MASON (ed.), *Multinuclear NMR*, Plenum Press, New York, pp. 335–67 (1987).

14 G. C. LEVY and R. L. LICHTER, *Nitrogen-15 Nuclear Magnetic Resonance Spectroscopy*, Wiley, New York, 1979, 221 pp. W. VON PHILIPSBORN and R. MÜLLER, *Angew. Chem. Int. Edn. Engl.* **25**, 383–413 (1986).

15 W. G. PROCTOR and F. C. YU, *Phys. Rev.* **77**, 717 (1950).

nature of bonding in N-containing compounds, to study structural features (e.g. linear, bent, encapsulated N), to determine the site of coordination or protonation, to follow kinetically the course of chemical reactions and to detect new species.

Isotopic enrichment of ^{15}N is usually effected by chemical exchange, and samples containing up to 99.5% ^{15}N have been obtained from the 2-phase equilibrium

$$^{15}NO(g) + {}^{14}NO_3{}^-(aq) \rightleftharpoons {}^{14}NO(g) + {}^{15}NO_3{}^-(aq)$$

Other exchange reactions that have been used are:

$$^{15}NH_3(g) + {}^{14}NH_4{}^+(aq) \rightleftharpoons {}^{14}NH_3(g) + {}^{15}NH_4{}^+(aq)$$

$$^{15}NO(g) + {}^{14}NO_2(g) \rightleftharpoons {}^{14}NO(g) + {}^{15}NO_2(g)$$

Fractional distillation of NO provides another effective route and, as the heavier isotope of oxygen is simultaneously enriched, the product has a high concentration of $^{15}N^{18}O$. Many key nitrogen compounds are now commercially available with ^{15}N enriched to 5%, 30% or 95%, e.g. N_2, NO, NO_2, NH_3, HNO_3 and several ammonium salts and nitrates. Fortunately the use of these compounds in tracer experiments is simplified by the absence of exchange with atmospheric N_2 under normal conditions, in marked contrast with labelled H, C and O compounds where contract with atmospheric moisture and CO_2 must be avoided.

The ground state electronic configuration of the N atom is $1s^2 2s^2 2p_x^1 2p_y^1 2p_z^1$ with three unpaired electrons (^4S). The electronegativity of N ($\sim$3.0) is exceeded only by those of F and O. Its "single-bond" covalent radius ($\sim$70 pm) is slightly smaller than those of B and C, as expected; the nitride ion, N^{3-}, is much larger and has been assigned a radius in the range 140–170 pm. Ionization energies and other properties are compared with those of the other Group 15 elements (P, As, Sb and Bi) on p. 550.

Molecular N_2, i.e. dinitrogen (see p. 34), (mp $-210°C$, bp $-195.8°C$) is a colourless, odourless, tasteless, diamagnetic gas. The short interatomic distance (109.76 pm) and very high dissociation energy (945.41 kJ mol^{-1}) are both consistent with multiple bonding. The free-energy change for the equilibrium $N_2 \rightleftharpoons 2N$ is $\Delta G = 911.13$ kJ mol^{-1} from which it is clear that the dissociation constant $K_p = [N]^2/[N_2]$ atm is negligible under normal conditions; it is 1.6×10^{-24} atm at 2000 K and still only 1.3×10^{-12} atm at 4000 K. Detailed tabulations of other physical properties of nitrogen are available.[16]

11.2.4 Chemical reactivity

Gaseous N_2 is rather inert at room temperature presumably because of the great strength of the $N \equiv N$ bond and the large energy gap between the highest occupied molecular orbitals (HOMO) and the lowest unoccupied molecular orbitals (LUMO). Further contributory factors are the very symmetrical electron distribution in the molecule and the absence of bond polarity — when these are modified, as in the isoelectronic analogues CO, CN^- and NO^+, the reactivity is considerably enhanced. Nitrogen reacts readily with Li at room temperature (p. 76) and with several transition-element complexes (p. 414).

Reactivity increases rapidly with rising temperature and the element combines directly with Be, the alkaline earth metals, and B, Al, Si and Ge to give nitrides (p. 417); hydrogen yields ammonia (p. 421), and coke yields cyanogen, $(CN)_2$, when heated to incandescence (p. 320). Many finely divided transition metals also react directly at elevated temperatures to give nitrides of general formula MN (M = Sc, Y, lanthanoids; Zr, Hf; V; Cr, Mo, W; Th, U, Pu). Although not always directly preparable from N_2(g), many other nitrides are known (p. 417) and, indeed, nitrides as a class include some of the most stable compounds in the whole of chemistry. Nitrogen forms bonds with almost all elements in the periodic table, the only exceptions apparently being the noble gases (other than Xe and Kr, pp. 902, 904). A wide range of stereochemistries is observed and

---

[16] B. R. BROWN, Physical properties of nitrogen, in *Mellor's Comprehensive Treatise on Inorganic and Theoretical Chemistry*, Vol. 8, Suppl. 1, *Nitrogen*, Part 1, pp. 27–149, Longmans, London, 1964.

Table 11.1 Stereochemistry of nitrogen[a]

CN		Examples
0		N(g) in "active nitrogen"
1		N_2, NO, **NNO**, $[NNN]^-$, HNNN, $RC\equiv N$, $XC\equiv N$ (X = Hal), $[OsO_3N]^-$
2	Linear:	$[NO_2]^+$, NNO, $[NNN]^-$, HNNN; η^1-N_2 complexes, e.g. $[Ru(N_2)(NH_3)_5]^{2+}$; η^1-NO complexes, e.g. $[Fe(CN)_5(NO)]^{2-}$; μ_2-N complexes, e.g. $[(H_2O)Cl_4RuNRuCl_4(OH_2)]^{3-}$ and $[Cl_5WNWCl_5]^{2-}$ (ref. 18)
	Bent:	NO_2, $[NO_2]^-$, $[NH_2]^-$, HNNN, HNCO, RNCO, XNCO, N_2F_2, cyclo-$\overline{CH_2NN}$, cyclo-$[NSF(O)]_3$ $[W(CO)_5OPPh_2NPPh_3]$ (ref. 19)
3	Planar:	$[NO_3]^-$, N_2O_4, XNO_2, $(HO)NO_2$, $K[ON(NO)(SO_3)]$, $K_2[ON(SO_3)_2]$ (Fremy's salt), $N(SiH_3)_3$, $NMe(SiMe_3)_2$ (ref. 20), $N(GeH_3)_3$, $N(PF_2)_3$, Si_3N_4, and Ge_3N_4 (Be_2SiO_4 structure, p. 347), μ_3-N complexes, e.g. $[\{H_2O(SO_4)_2Ir\}_3N]^{4-}$
	Pyramidal:	NH_3, NF_3, NH_2F, NHF_2, $(HO)NH_2$, N_2H_4, N_2F_4, $[N_4(CH_2)_6]$
	T-shaped:	$[Mo_3(\mu_3\text{-}N)O(\eta^5\text{-}C_5H_5)_3(CO)_4]$ (ref. 21)
4	Tetrahedral:	$[NH_4]^+$, $[NH_3(OH)]^+$, $[NF_4]^+$, H_3NBF_3 and innumerable other coordination complexes of NH_3, NR_3, en, edta, etc., including Me_3NO and sulfamic acid (H_3NSO_3). BN (layer structure and Zn blende-type), AlN (wurtzite-type), $[PhAlNPh]_4$ (cubane-type)
	See-saw:	$[\{Fe(CO)_3\}_4(\mu_4\text{-}N)]^-$ (refs. 22, 23)
5	Square-pyramidal:	$[Fe_5(CO)_{14}H(\mu_5\text{-}N)]$ (ref. 23), $[(\eta^5\text{-}C_5Me_5)_2Mo_2Co_3(CO)_{10}(\mu_5\text{-}N)]$ (ref. 24), closo-NB_9H_{10} (p. 211)
	Trig. bipyramidal:	$[N(AuPPh_3)_5]^{2+}$ (ref. 25)
6	Octahedral:	MN (interstitial nitrides with NaCl or hcp structure, e.g. M = Sc, La; Ce, Pr, Nd; Ti, Zr, Hf; V, Nb, Ta; Cr, Mo, W; Th, U), Ti_2N (anti-rutile TiO_2-type), Cu_3N (ReO_3-type), Ca_3N_2 (anti-Mn_2O_3)
	Trigonal prism:	$[NCo_6(CO)_{15}]^-$ (ref. 26), $[Rh_{12}H(N)_2(CO)_{23}]^{3-}$ (ref. 27)
	Pentagonal prism:	closo-$NB_{11}H_{12}$ (p. 211)
8	Cubic:	Ternary nitrides with anti-CaF_2 structure, e.g. $BeLiN$, $AlLi_3N_2$, $TiLi_5N_3$, $NbLi_7N_4$, and $CrLi_9N_5$
	Square antiprism:	$[Rh_{12}H(N)_2(CO)_{23}]^{3-}$ (ref. 27)

[a] For coordination numbers 1, 2, and 3 the CN is sometimes increased in the condensed phase as a result of H bonding (p. 52), e.g. HCN, NH_2^-, NH_3, N_2H_4, $NH_2(OH)$, $NO_2(OH)$.

typical examples of coordination numbers 0, 1, 2, 3, 4, 5, 6, and 8 are given in Table 11.1.

A particularly reactive form of nitrogen can be obtained by passing an electric discharge through $N_2(g)$ at a pressure of 0.1–2 mmHg.[16,17] Atomic N is formed, and the process is accompanied by a peach-yellow emission which persists as an afterglow, often for several minutes after the discharge

[17] A. N. WRIGHT and C. A. WINKLER, *Active Nitrogen*, Academic Press, New York, 1968.

[18] F. WELLER, W. LIEBELT and K. DEHNICKE, *Angew. Chem. Int. Edn. Engl.* **19**, 220 (1980). [The W–N–W linkage is linear and the interatomic distances are 166 pm (W^{VI}-N) and 207 pm (W^V-N).

[19] D. J. DARENSBOURG, M. PALA, D. SIMMONS and A. L. RHEINGOLD, *Inorg. Chem.* **25**, 2537–41 (1986). See also H. G. ANG, Y. M. CAI, L. L. KOH and W. L. KWIK, *J. Chem. Soc., Chem. Commun.*, 850–2 (1991).

[20] D. W. H. RANKIN and H. E. ROBERTSON, *J. Chem. Soc., Dalton Trans.*, 785–8 (1987).

[21] N. D. FEASEY, S. A. R. KNOX and A. G. ORPEN, *J. Chem. Soc., Chem. Commun.*, 75–6 (1982).

[22] D. FJARE and W. L. GLADFELTER, *J. Am. Chem. Soc.* **103**, 1572–4 (1981); **106**, 4799–4810 (1984).

[23] M. TACHIKAWA, J. STEIN, E. L. MUETTERTIES, R. G. TELLER, M. A. BENO, E. GEBERT and J. M. WILLIAMS, *J. Am. Chem. Soc.* **102**, 6648–9 (1980).

[24] C. P. GIBSON and L. F. DAHL, *Organometallics* **7**, 543–52 (1988).

[25] A. GROHMANN, J. RIEDE and H. SCHMIDBAUR, *Nature* **345**, 140–2 (1990).

[26] S. MARTINENGO, G. CIANI, A. SIRONI, B. T. HEATON and J. MASON, *J. Am. Chem. Soc.* **101**, 7095–7 (1979).

[27] S. MARTINENGO, G. CIANI and A. SIRONI, *J. Chem. Soc., Chem. Commun.*, 1742–4 (1986).

has been stopped. Atoms of N in their ground state (^4S) have a relatively long lifetime since recombination involves either a 3-body collision on the surface of the vessel (first-order reaction in N at pressures below $\sim$3 mmHg) or a termolecular homogeneous association reaction (second order in N at pressures above $\sim$3 mmHg):

$$N(^4S) + N(^4S) \xrightarrow{M} N_2^* \longrightarrow N_2 + h\nu(\text{yellow}) \quad (1)$$

The molecules of N_2^* so formed are in an excited state ($B^3\Pi_g$) and give rise to the emission of the first positive band system of the spectrum of molecular N_2 in returning to the ground state ($A^3\Sigma_u^+$).

Several elements react with the N atoms in active nitrogen to form nitrides. The excited N_2 molecules are also highly reactive and can cause the dissociation of molecules that are normally stable to attack either by ordinary N_2 or even N atoms, e.g.:

$$N_2^* + CO_2 \longrightarrow N_2 + CO + O(^3P)$$

$$N_2^* + H_2O \longrightarrow N_2 + OH(^2\Pi) + H(^2S).$$

One of the most dramatic developments in the chemistry of N_2 during the past 30 years was the discovery by A. D. Allen and C. V. Senoff in 1965 that dinitrogen complexes such as $[Ru(NH_3)_5(N_2)]^{2+}$ could readily be prepared from aqueous $RuCl_3$ using hydrazine hydrate in aqueous solution.[28] Since that time virtually all transition metals have been found to give dinitrogen complexes and several hundred such compounds are now characterized.[5,29,30] Three general preparative methods are available:

(a) Direct replacement of labile ligands in metal complexes by N_2: such reactions proceed under mild conditions and are often reversible, e.g.:

$$[Ru(NH_3)_5(H_2O)]^{2+} + N_2 \underset{}{\overset{H_2O}{\rightleftharpoons}} H_2O$$
$$+ [Ru(NH_3)_5(N_2)]^{2+} \text{ pale yellow}$$

$$[CoH_3(PPh_3)_3] + N_2 \overset{EtOH}{\rightleftharpoons} H_2$$
$$+ [CoH(N_2)(PPh_3)_3] \text{ orange-red}$$

$$2[Cr(C_6Me_6)(CO)_3] + N_2 \xrightarrow{thf/h\nu} 2CO$$
$$+ [\{Cr(C_6Me_6)(CO)_2\}_2N_2] \text{ red-brown}$$

(b) Reduction of a metal complex in the presence of an excess of a suitable coligand under N_2, e.g.:

$$[MoCl_4(PMe_2Ph)_2] + 2N_2 \xrightarrow{Na/toluene/PMe_2Ph}$$
$$cis\text{-}[Mo(N_2)_2(PMe_2Ph)_4]$$

$$[WCl_4(PMe_2Ph)_2] + 2N_2 \xrightarrow{(Na/Hg)/PMe_2Ph}$$
$$cis\text{-}[W(N_2)_2(PMe_2Ph)_4] \text{ yellow}$$

$$[FeClH(depe)_2] + N_2 \xrightarrow{NaBH_4/Me_2CO}$$
$$NaCl + trans\text{-}[Fe(depe)_2H(N_2)] \text{ orange}$$

$$2[Ni(acac)_2] + 4PCy_3 + N_2 \xrightarrow{AlMe_3}$$
$$[\{Ni(N_2)(PCy_3)_2\}_2]$$

where depe is $Et_2PCH_2CH_2PEt_2$, acac is 3,5-pentanedionate, and PCy_3 is tris(cyclohexyl)phosphine. In some systems Mg/thf is a better reducing agent than Na, e.g.:

$$MoCl_5 + 4PMe_2PH + 2N_2 \xrightarrow{Mg/thf}$$
$$cis\text{-}[Mo(N_2)_2(PMe_2Ph)_4]$$

(c) Conversion of a ligand with N–N bonds into N_2; in the early development of N_2 complex chemistry this was the most successful and widely used route, e.g.:

$$[Mn(\eta^5\text{-}C_5H_5)(CO)_2(N_2H_4)] + 2H_2O_2$$
$$\xrightarrow{Cu^{II}/thf/-40°} 4H_2O$$
$$+ [Mn(\eta^5\text{-}C_5H_5)(CO)_2(N_2)] \text{ red-brown}$$

28 A. D. ALLEN and C. V. SENOFF, *Chem. Commun.*, 1965, 621–2. The unprecedented nature of the reaction can be gauged from the fact that this paper was rejected for publication by *J. Am. Chem. Soc.* on the grounds that it was impossible, before being accepted by *Chem. Commun.*, See also H. TAUBE, The researches of A. D. Allen — an appreciation, *Coord. Chem. Rev.* **26**, 1–5 (1978).

29 A. D. ALLEN, R. O. HARRIS, B. R. LOESCHER, J. R. STEVENS and R. N. WHITELEY, *Chem. Revs.* **73**, 11–20 (1973).

30 D. SELLMANN, *Angew. Chem. Int. Edn. Engl.* **13**, 639–49 (1974).

$$[(PPh_3)_2Cl_2Re\overset{\overset{\text{O}}{\overline{\qquad}}}{\longrightarrow}N{=}N{-}CPh] + 2PPh_3$$

$$\xrightarrow{\text{MeOH}} HCl + PhCO_2Me$$

$$+ \textit{trans-}[ReCl(N_2)(PPh_3)_4]\ \text{yellow}$$

$$[RuCl(das)_2(N_3)]PF_6 + NOPF_6 \longrightarrow$$

$$[RuCl(das)_2(N_2)]\ \text{white, plus byproducts}$$

$$(das = Ph_2AsCH_2CH_2AsPh_2)$$

$$\textit{trans-}[Ir(CO)Cl(PPh_3)_2] + PhCON_3$$

$$\xrightarrow{\text{CHCl}_3/0°} \textit{trans-}[IrCl(N_2)(PPh_3)_2]\ \text{yellow}$$

A related example is the reaction of NbCl$_5$ and thf with (Me$_3$Si)$_2$NN(SiMe$_3$)$_2$ in CH$_2$Cl$_2$ to give an 80% yield of [(μ-N$_2$){NbCl$_3$(thf)$_2$}$_2$].[31] Occasionally an N≡N triple bond can be formed within a metal complex, e.g. by reaction of coordinated NH$_3$ with HNO$_2$, but this method is of limited application, e.g.:

$$[Os(N_2)(NH_3)_5]^{2+} + HNO_2 \longrightarrow 2H_2O$$

$$+ \textit{cis-}[Os(N_2)_2(NH_3)_4]$$

Frequently dinitrogen complexes have colours in the range white-yellow-orange-red-brown but other colours are known, e.g. [{Ti(η^5-C$_5$H$_5$)$_2$}$_2$-(N$_2$)] is blue.

Dinitrogen might coordinate to metals in at least 4 ways,[32] but only the end-on modes, structures (1) and (2), are well established as common bonding modes by numerous well-defined examples:

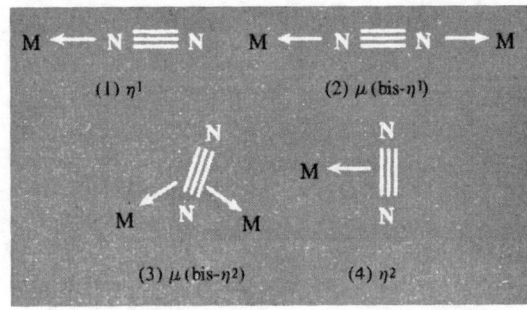

The side-on structure (3) has been established in two dinickel complexes which have very complicated structures involving lithium atoms also in association with the bridging N$_2$.[33] It also occurs in the first fully characterized N$_2$ complex of a lanthanide element, [(μ-η^2:η^2-N$_2$){Sm(η^5-C$_5$Me$_5$)$_2$}$_2$].[34] The "side-on" η^2 mode (structure 4) was at one time thought to be exemplified by the rhodium(I) complex [RhCl(N$_2$)(PPr$^i_3$)$_2$] but a reinvestigation of the X-ray structure by another group[35] showed conclusively that the N$_2$ ligand was coordinated in the "end-on" mode (1) — an instructive example of mistaken conclusions that can initially be drawn from this technique. The side on structure (4) has been postulated for the zirconium(III) complex [Zr(η^5-C$_5$H$_5$)(N$_2$)R] on the basis of its ^{15}N nmr spectrum.[36] A unique triply-coordinated bridging mode (μ_3-N$_2$) has also recently been established by X-ray crystallography.[37]

Complexes are known which feature more than one N$_2$ ligand, e.g. *cis*-[W(N$_2$)$_2$(PMe$_2$Ph)$_4$] and *trans*-[W(N$_2$)$_2$(diphos)$_2$] (where diphos = Ph$_2$PCH$_2$CH$_2$PPh$_2$) and some complexes feature more than one bonding mode, e.g.:[38]

$$[(\eta^5\text{-C}_5Me_5)_2(\eta^1\text{-N}_2)Zr{\leftarrow}N{\equiv}N{\rightarrow}Zr(\eta^1\text{-N}_2)\text{-}$$

$$(\eta^5\text{-C}_5Me_5)_2]$$

[31] J. R. DILWORTH, S. J. HARRISON, R. A. HENDERSON and D. R. M. WALTON, *J. Chem. Soc., Chem. Commun.*, 176–7 (1984).

[32] K. JONAS, D. J. BRAUER, C. KRÜGER, P. J. ROBERTS and Y.-H. TSAY, *J. Am. Chem. Soc.* **98**, 74–81 (1976). P. R. HOFFMAN, T. YOSHIDA, T. OKANO, S. OTSUKA and J. IBERS, *Inorg. Chem.* **15**, 2462–6 (1976).

[33] K. KRÜGER and Y.-H. TSAY, *Angew. Chem. Int. Edn. Engl.* **12**, 998–9 (1973).

[34] W. J. EVANS, T. A. ULIBARRI and J. W. ZILLER, *J. Am. Chem. Soc.* **110**, 6877–9 (1988).

[35] D. L. THORN, T. H. TULIP and J. A. IBERS, *J. Chem. Soc., Dalton Trans.*, 2022–5 (1979).

[36] M. J. S. GYNANE, J. JEFFREY and M. F. LAPPERT, *J. Chem. Soc., Chem. Commun.*, 34–6 (1978).

[37] G. P. PEZ, P. APGAR and R. K. CRISSEY, *J. Am. Chem. Soc.* **104**, 482–90 (1982).

[38] R. D. SANNER, J. M. MANRIQUEZ, R. E. MARSH and J. E. BERCAW, *J. Am. Chem. Soc.* **98**, 8351–7 (1976).

The first example of a tris-N_2 complex is the yellow crystalline compound *mer*-$[Mo(\eta^1\text{-}N_2)_3(PPr_2^n Ph)_3]$.[39]

X-ray structural studies have shown that for N_2 complexes with structure (1), the M–N–N group is linear or nearly so $(172–180°)$; the N–N internuclear distance is usually in the range $110–113\,pm$, only slightly longer than in gaseous N_2 $(109.8\,pm)$. Such complexes have a strong sharp, infrared absorption in the range $1900–2200\,cm^{-1}$, corresponding to the Raman-active band at $2331\,cm^{-1}$ in free N_2. Similarly, in complexes with structure (2), when both transition metals have a closed d-shell, the N–N distance falls in the range $112–120\,pm$ and $\nu(N–N)$ often occurs near $2100\,cm^{-1}$, i.e. little altered from that of the corresponding complexes of structure (1). On the other hand, if one of the M is a transition metal with a closed d-shell and the other is either a main-group metal such as Al in $AlMe_3$ or an open-shell transition metal such as Mo in $MoCl_4$, then the N–N bond is greatly lengthened and the N–N stretching frequency is lowered even to $1600\,cm^{-1}$. Compounds with structure (3) have N–N $\sim134–136\,pm$, and this very substantial lengthening has been attributed to interaction with the Li atoms in the structure.[33]

As implied above, N_2 is isoelectronic with both CO and C_2H_2, and the detailed description of the bonding in structures 1–4 follows closely along the lines indicated on pp. 927 and 932 though there are some differences in the detailed sequences of orbital energies. Crystallographic and vibrational spectroscopic data have been taken to indicate that N_2 is weaker than CO in both its σ-donor and π-acceptor functions. Theoretical studies suggest that σ donation is more important for the formation of the M–N bond than is π back-donation, which mainly contributes to the weakening of the N–N bond, and end-on (η^1) donation is more favourable than side-on (η^2).[40]

The chemical reactivity of coordinated N_2 has been extensively studied because of its potential relevance to the catalytic and biological fixation of N_2 to NH_3 (p. 1035). For other recent work on the reactions of coordinated dinitrogen see refs. 41–44

To conclude this section on the chemical reactivity of nitrogen it will be helpful to compare the element briefly with its horizontal neighbours C and O, and also with the heavier elements in Group 15, P, As, Sb and Bi. The diagonal relationship with S is vestigial. Nitrogen resembles oxygen in its high electronegativity and in its ability to form H bonds (p. 52) and coordination complexes (p. 198) by use of its lone-pair of electrons. Catenation is more limited than for carbon, the longest chain so far reported being the N_8 unit in $PhN{=}N{-}N(Ph){-}N{=}N{-}N(Ph){-}N{=}NPh$.

Nitrogen shares with C and O the propensity for multiple bonding via p_π–p_π interactions both with another N atom or with a C or O atom. In this it differs sharply from its Group 15 congeners which have no analogues of the oxides of nitrogen, nitrites, nitrates, nitro-, nitroso-, azo- and diazo-compounds, azides, cyanates, thiocyanates or imino-derivatives. Conversely, there are no nitrogen analogues of the various oxoacids of phosphorus (p. 510).

11.3 Compounds

This section deals with the binary compounds that nitrogen forms with metals, and then describes the extensive chemistry of the hydrides, halides, pseudohalides, oxides and oxoacids of the element. The chemistry of P–N compounds is deferred until Chapter 12 (p. 531) and S–N

[39] S. N. ANDERSON, D. L. HUGHES and R. L. RICHARDS, *J. Chem. Soc., Chem. Commun.*, 958–9 (1984).

[40] T. YAMABE, K. HORI, T. MINATO and K. FUKUI, *Inorg. Chem.* **19**, 2154–9 (1980).

[41] M. HIDAI and Y. MIZOBE, in P. S. BRATERMAN (ed.) *Reactions of Coordinated Ligands*, Vol. 2, Plenum Press, New York, 1989, pp. 53–114 (202 refs.)

[42] T. A. GEORGE, L. M. KOCZON and R. C. TISDALE, *Polyhedron* **9**, 545–51 (1990).

[43] J. O. DZIEGIELEWSKI and R. GRZYBEK, *Polyhedron* **9**, 645–51 (1990).

[44] S. NIELSON-MARSH, R. J. CROWTE and P. G. EDWARDS, *J. Chem. Soc., Chem. Commun.*, 699–700 (1992).

compounds are discussed in Chapter 15 (p. 721). Compounds with B (p. 207) and C (p. 319) have already been treated.

11.3.1 Nitrides, azides and nitrido complexes

Nitrogen forms binary compounds with almost all elements of the periodic table and for many elements several stoichiometries are observed, e.g. MnN, Mn_6N_5, Mn_3N_2, Mn_2N, Mn_4N and Mn_xN ($9.2 < x < 25.3$). Nitrides are frequently classified into 4 groups: "salt-like", covalent, "diamond-like" and metallic (or "interstitial"). The remarks on p. 64 concerning the limitations of such classifications are relevant here. The two main methods of preparation are by direct reaction of the metal with N_2 or NH_3 (often at high temperatures) and the thermal decomposition of metal amides, e.g.:

$$3Ca + N_2 \longrightarrow Ca_3N_2$$

$$3Mg + 2NH_3 \xrightarrow{900°} Mg_3N_2 + 3H_2$$

$$3Zn(NH_2)_2 \longrightarrow Zn_3N_2 + 4NH_3$$

Common variants include reduction of a metal oxide or halide in the presence of N_2 and the formation of a metal amide as an intermediate in reactions in liquid NH_3:

$$Al_2O_3 + 3C + N_2 \longrightarrow 2AlN + 3CO$$

$$2ZrCl_4 + N_2 + 4H_2 \longrightarrow 2ZrN + 8HCl$$

$$3Ca + 6NH_3 \xrightarrow{-3H_2} \{3Ca(NH_2)_2\}$$

$$\longrightarrow Ca_3N_2 + 4NH_3$$

Metal nitrides have also been prepared by adding KNH_2 to liquid-ammonia solutions of the appropriate metal salts in order to precipitate the nitride, e.g. Cu_3N, Hg_3N_2, AlN, Tl_3N and BiN.

"Salt-like" nitrides are exemplified by Li_3N (mp 548°C, decomp) and M_3N_2 (M = Be, Mg, Ca, Sr, Ba). It is possible to write ionic formulations of these compounds using the species N^{3-} though charge separation is unlikely to be complete, particularly for the corresponding compounds of Groups 11 and 12, i.e. Cu_3N, Ag_3N, and M_3N_2 (M = Zn, Cd, Hg). The N^{3-} ion has been assigned a radius of 146 pm, slightly larger than the value for the isoelectronic ions O^{2-} (140 pm) and F^- (133 pm), as expected. Stability varies widely; e.g. Be_3N_2 melts at 2200°C whereas Mg_3N_2 decomposes above 271°C. The existence of Na_3N is doubtful and the heavier alkali metals appear not to form analogous compounds, perhaps for steric reasons (p. 76). However the azides NaN_3 and KN_3 are well characterized as colourless crystalline salts which can be melted with little decomposition; they feature the symmetrical linear N_3^- group as do $Sr(N_3)_2$ and $Ba(N_3)_2$. The corresponding "B subgroup" metal azides such as AgN_3, $Cu(N_3)_2$, and $Pb(N_3)_2$ are shock-sensitive and detonate readily; they are far less ionic and have more complex structures. Further discussion of azides is on p. 433. Other stoichiometries are also known, e.g. Ca_2N (anti-$CdCl_2$ layer structure), Ca_3N_4, and $Ca_{11}N_8$.

The covalent binary nitrides are more conveniently treated under the appropriate element. Examples include cyanogen $(CN)_2$ (p. 320), P_3N_5 (p. 531), S_2N_2 (p. 725) and S_4N_4 (p. 722). The Group 13 nitrides MN (M = B, Al, Ga, In, Tl) are a special case since they are isoelectronic with graphite, diamond, SiC, etc., to which they are structurally related (p. 255). Their physical properties suggest a gradation of bond-type from covalent, through partially ionic, to essentially metallic as the atomic number increases. Si_3N_4 and Ge_3N_4 are also known and have the phenacite (Be_2SiO_4)-type structure. Si_3N_4, in particular, has excited considerable interest in recent years as a ceramic material with extremely desirable properties: high strength and wear resistance, high decomposition temperature and oxidation resistance, excellent thermal-shock properties and resistance to corrosive environments, low coefficient of friction, etc. Unfortunately it is extremely difficult to fabricate and sinter suitably shaped components, and considerable efforts have therefore been spent on developing related nitrogen ceramics by forming solid solutions between Si_3N_4 and Al_2O_3 to give the "sialons" (SiAlON) of general formula $Si_{6-0.75x}Al_{0.67x}O_xN_{8-x}(0 < x < 6)$.[45]

The most extensive group of nitrides are the metallic nitrides of general formulae MN, M_2N, and M_4N in which N atoms occupy some or all of the interstices in cubic or hcp metal lattices (examples are in Table 11.1, p. 413). These compounds are usually opaque, very hard, chemically inert, refractory materials with metallic lustre and conductivity and sometimes having variable composition. Similarities with borides (p. 145) and carbides (p. 297) are notable. Typical mps (°C) are:

TiN	ZrN	HfN	VN	NbN	TaN
2950	2980	2700	2050	2300	3090
CrN	ThN	UN			
d1770	2630	2800			

Hardness on the Mohs scale is often above 8 and sometimes approaches 10 (diamond). These properties commend nitrides for use as crucibles, high-temperature reaction vessels, thermocouple sheaths and related applications. Several metal nitrides are also used as heterogeneous catalysts, notably the iron nitrides in the Fischer-Tropsch hydriding of carbonyls. Few chemical reactions of metal nitrides have been studied; the most characteristic (often extremely slow but occasionally rapid) is hydrolysis to give ammonia or nitrogen:

$$2AlN + (n + 3)H_2O \longrightarrow Al_2O_3.nH_2O + 2NH_3$$
$$2VN + 3H_2SO_4 \longrightarrow V_2(SO_4)_3 + N_2 + 3H_2$$

The crystal chemistry of metal nitrides has been reviewed[45a] and there have recently been some intriguing developments in our understanding of the stoichiometries and structures of ternary and quaternary metal nitrides.[45b]

The nitride ion N^{3-} is an excellent ligand, particularly towards second- and third-row transition metals.[46] It is considered to be by far the strongest π donor known, the next strongest being the isoelectronic species O^{2-}. Nitrido complexes are usually prepared by the thermal decomposition of azides (e.g. those of phosphine complexes of V^V, Mo^{VI}, W^{VI}, Ru^{VI}, Re^V) or by deprotonation of NH_3 (e.g. $[OsO_4 \rightarrow OsO_3N]^-$). Most involve a terminal $\{\equiv N\}^{3-}$ group as in $[VCl_3N]^-$, $[MoO_3N]^-$, $[WCl_5N]^{2-}$, $[ReN(PR_3)_3X_2]$ and $[RuN(OH_2)X_4]^-$. The M–N distance is much shorter (by 40–50 pm) than the "normal" σ-(M–N) distance, consistent with strong multiple bonding. Other bonding modes feature linear symmetrical bridging as in $[(H_2O)Cl_4Ru-N-RuCl_4(OH_2)]^{3-}$, trigonal planar μ_3 bridging as in $[\{(H_2O)(SO_4)_2Ir\}_3N]^{4-}$, and tetrahedral coordination as in $[(MeHg)_4N]^+$ (Fig. 11.3). The nitrido ligand has a strong *trans* influence, e.g. in $[Os^{VI}NCl_5]^{2-}$ (p. 1085); likewise, in the octahedral complex. $[Tc^VNCl_2(PMe_2Ph)_3]$, the Tc–Cl distance *trans* to N is 266.5 pm whereas that *cis* to N is only 244.1 pm.[47]

Azidotrifluoromethylmethane, CF_3N_3, (mp $-152°$, bp $-285°$) is a colourless gas which is thermally stable at room temperature. It can be prepared in 90% yield by reacting CF_3NO with hydrazine in MeOH at $-78°$ and then treating the product with HCl gas.[48]

$$CF_3NO + H_2NNH_2 \longrightarrow CF_3-N=NNH_2$$
$$\longrightarrow CF_3NNN$$

The molecule has an almost linear N_3 group and an angle C–N–N of 112.4° (Fig. 11.4a).[49] The (linear) azide ion, N_3^-, is isoelectronic with N_2O, CO_2, OCN^-, etc. and forms numerous coordination complexes by standard ligand replacement reactions. Various coordination modes have been established, including end-on η^1, bridging

[45] K. H. JACK, *Trans. J. Br. Ceram. Soc.* **72**, 376–84 (1973). F. L. RILEY (ed.), *Nitrogen Ceramics,* Noordhoff-Leyden, 1977, 694 pp.

[45a] N. E. BRESE and M. O'KEEFE, *Structure and Bonding*, **79**, 307–78 (1992).

[45b] R. KNIEP, *Pure Appl. Chem.* **69**, 185–91 (1997).

[46] W. P. GRIFFITH, *Coord. Chem. Revs.* **8**, 369–96 (1972).

[47] A. S. BATSANOV, YU. T. STRUCHKOV, B. LORENZ and B. OLK, *Z. anorg. allg. Chem.* **564**, 129–34 (1988).

[48] K. O. CHRISTE, and C. J. SCHACK, *Inorg. Chem.* **20**, 2566–70 (1981).

[49] K. O. CHRISTE, D. CHRISTEN, H. OBERHAMMER and C. J. SCHACK, *Inorg. Chem.* **23**, 4283–8 (1984).

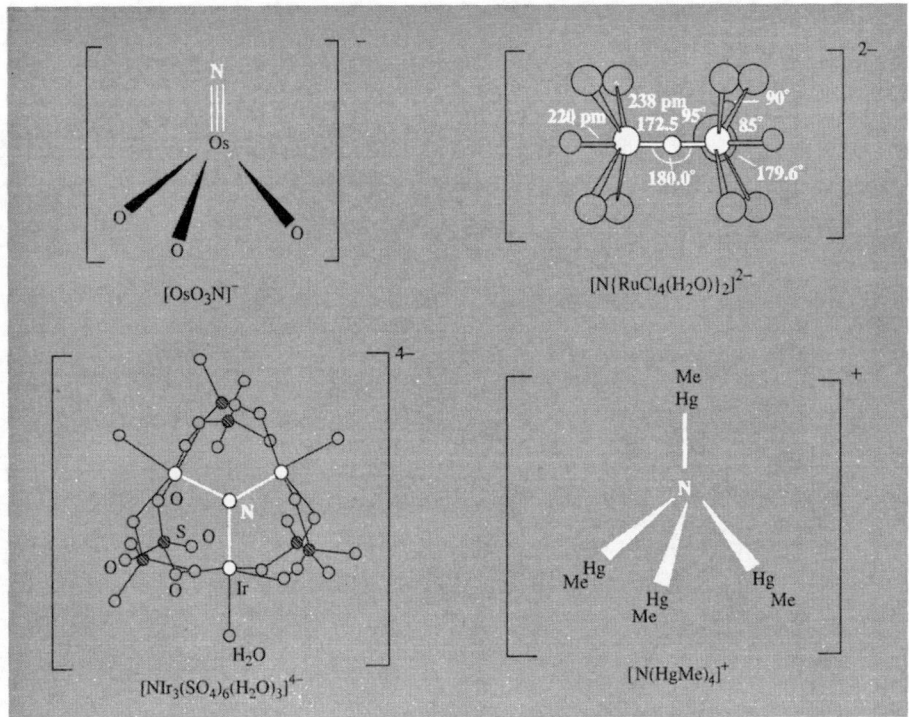

Figure 11.3   Structures of some nitrido complexes.[24]

μ,η^1 and bridging $\mu,\eta^1:\eta^1$ (Fig. 11.4).[50,51] The binuclear complex $[Mo_2Cl_2N_{20}]^{2-}$ features a terminal nitrido ligand, $N\equiv$, as well as terminal and bridging azido ligands, i.e. $[\{(MoCl(N)(\eta^1-N_3)_2(\mu,\eta^1-N_3)\}_2]^{2-}$.[52]

Concatenations larger than N_3 are rare. The planar bridging N_4^{4-} occurs in the binuclear W^{VI} dianion, $[Cl_5W(\mu,\eta^1:\eta^1-N_4)WCl_5]^{2-}$; this is formed during the thermolytic interconversion of $[W(N_3)Cl_5]$ to the corresponding nitrido complex $WNCl_3$ in the presence of Ph_4AsCl, the nitride reacting as it is formed with unreacted azide still present according to the simple stoichiometry:[53]

$$2Ph_4AsCl + WNCl_3 + W(N_3)Cl_5 \longrightarrow$$

$$[Ph_4AsCl]_2[Cl_5W(\mu-N_4)WCl_5]$$

It will be noted that N_4^{4-} is isosteric with the tetradeprotonated urea molecule, $(H_2N)_2C{=}O$, and is also isoelectronic and isostructural with CO_3^{2-} and NO_3^-. An X-ray analysis of the red single crystals shows that $N(\text{central})\text{-}N_\mu$ is long (149 pm) and that $N(\text{central})\text{-}N_t$ is short (123 pm). Unbranched N-catenation is observed in 2-tetrazenes such as $(Me_3Si)_2N\text{-}N{=}N\text{-}N(SiMe_3)_2$ (mp 46°) and its derivatives, e.g.

$$Me_3Si\text{-}N\text{-}N{=}N\text{-}N\text{-}N(SiMe_3)_2 \qquad (mp\ 40°)$$
$$\mathrel{\underset{\textstyle SiMe_2}{\rule{2em}{0.4pt}}}$$

and $(Me_3Si)_2N\text{-}N\text{-}N{=}N\text{-}N\text{-}N(SiMe_3)_2$ [54]
$$\mathrel{\underset{\textstyle SiMe_2}{\rule{2em}{0.4pt}}}$$

50 D. FENSKE, K. STEINER and K. DEHNICKE, *Z. anorg. allg. Chem.* **553**, 57–63 (1987).

51 P. CHAUDHURI, M. GUTTMANN, D. VENTUR, K. WIEGHARDT, B. NUBER and J. WEISS, *J. Chem. Soc., Chem. Commun.*, 1618–20 (1985).

52 K. JANSEN, J. SCHMITTE and K. DEHNICKE, *Z. anorg. allg. Chem.* **552**, 201–9 (1987).

53 W. MASSA, R. KUJANEK, G. BAUM and K. DEHNICKE, *Angew. Chem. Int. Edn. Engl.* **23**, 149 (1984).

54 N. WIBERG and G. ZIEGLEDER, *Chem. Ber.* **111**, 2123–9 (1978).

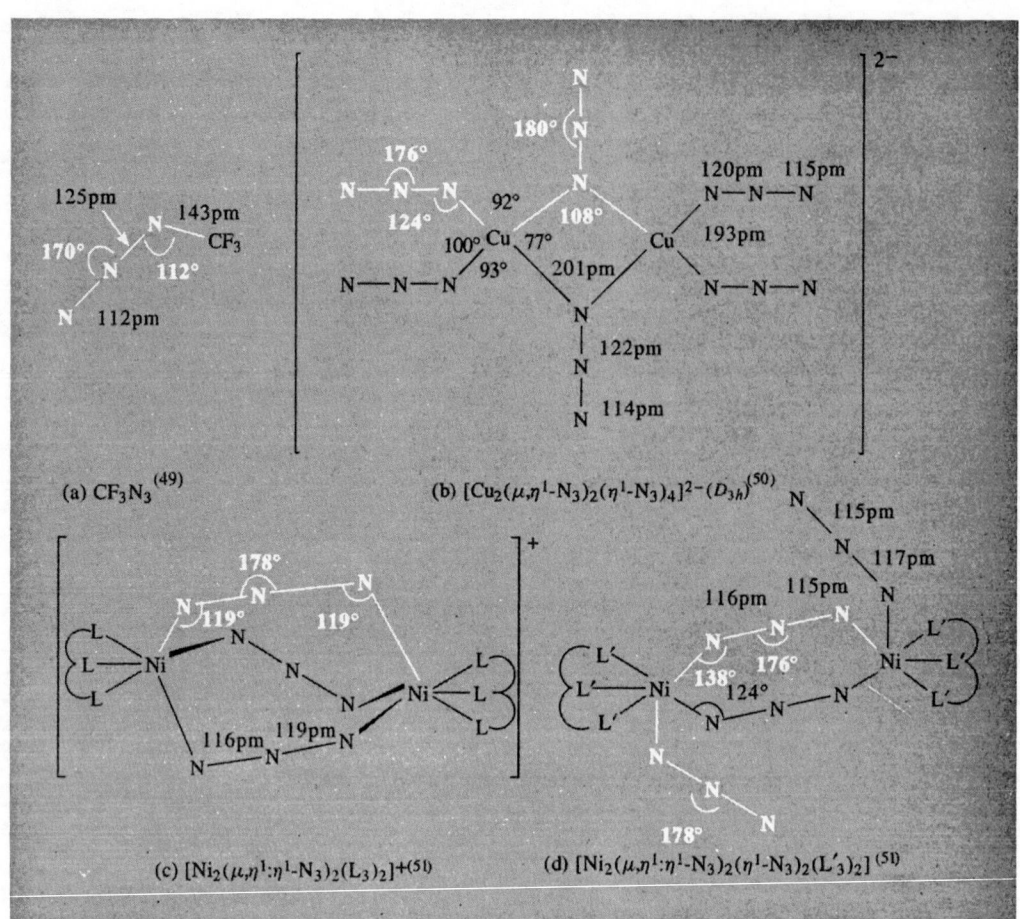

Figure 11.4 Structures of some azido complexes.

11.3.2 *Ammonia and ammonium salts*

NH_3 is a colourless, alkaline gas with a unique, penetrating odour that is first perceptible at concentrations of about 20–50 ppm. Noticeable irritation to eyes and the nasal passages begins at about 100–200 ppm, and higher concentrations can be dangerous.[55] NH_3 is prepared industrially in larger amounts (number of moles) than any other single compound (p. 407) and the production of synthetic ammonia is of major importance for several industries (see Panel).

---

55 T. A. CZUPPON, S. A. KNEZ and J. M. ROVNER, Ammonia, *Kirk–Othmer Encyclopedia of Chemical Technology*, 4th edn., Vol. 2, pp. 638–91, Wiley, New York, 1992

In the laboratory NH_3 is usually obtained from cylinders unless isotopically enriched species such as $^{15}NH_3$ or ND_3 are required. Pure dry $^{15}NH_3$ can be prepared by treating an enriched $^{15}NH_4^+$ salt with an excess of KOH and drying the product gas over metallic Na. Reduction of $^{15}NO_3^-$ or $^{15}NO_2^-$ with Devarda's alloy (50% Cu, 45% Al, 5% Zn) in alkaline solution provides an alternative route as does the hydrolysis of a nitride, e.g.:

$$3Ca + \,^{15}N_2 \longrightarrow Ca_3\,^{15}N_2 \xrightarrow{6H_2O} 2\,^{15}NH_3 + 3Ca(OH)_2$$

ND_3 can be prepared similarly using D_2O, e.g.:

$$Mg_3N_2 + 6D_2O \longrightarrow 2ND_3 + 3Mg(OD)_2$$

Industrial Production of Synthetic Ammonia[55-57]

The first industrial production of NH_3 began in 1913 at the BASF works in Ludwigshaven-Oppau, Germany. The plant, which had a design capacity of 30 tonnes per day, involved an entirely new concept in process technology; it was based on the Haber-Bosch high-pressure catalytic reduction of N_2 with H_2 obtained by electrolysis of water. Modern methods employ the same principles for the final synthesis but differ markedly in the source of hydrogen, the efficiency of the catalysts, and the scale of operations, many plants now having a capacity of 1650 tonnes per day or more. Great ingenuity has been shown not only in plant development but also in the application of fundamental thermodynamics to the selection of feasible chemical processes. Except where electricity is unusually cheap, reduction by electrolytic hydrogen has now been replaced either by coke/H_2O or, more recently, by natural gas (essentially CH_4) or naphtha (a volatile aliphatic petrol-like fraction of crude oil). The great advantages of modern hydrocarbon reduction methods over coal-based processes are that, comparing plant of similar capital costs, they occupy one-third the land area, use half the energy, and require one-tenth the manpower, yet produce 4 times the annual tonnage of NH_3.

The operation of a large synthetic ammonia plant based on natural gas involves a delicately balanced sequence of reactions. The gas is first *desulfurized* to remove compounds which will poison the metal catalysts, then compressed to ~30 atm and reacted with steam over a nickel catalyst at 750°C in the *primary steam reformer* to produce H_2 and oxides of carbon:

$$CH_4 + H_2O \underset{}{\overset{Ni/750°}{\rightleftharpoons}} CO + 3H_2; \quad CH_4 + 2H_2O \underset{}{\overset{Ni/750°}{\rightleftharpoons}} CO_2 + 4H_2$$

Under these conditions the issuing gases contain some 9% of unreacted methane; sufficient air is injected via a compressor to give a final composition of $1 : 3$ $N_2 : H_2$ and the air burns in the hydrogen thereby heating the gas to ~1100°C in the *secondary reformer:*

$$2H_2 + \underset{\text{air}}{(O_2 + 4N_2)} \overset{1100°}{\rightleftharpoons} 2H_2O + 4N_2; \quad CH_4 + H_2O \overset{Ni/1000°}{\rightleftharpoons} CO + 3H_2$$

The emerging gas, now containing only 0.25% CH_4, is cooled in heat exchangers which generate high-pressure steam for use first in the turbine compressors and then as a reactant in the primary steam reformer. Next, the CO is converted to CO_2 by the *shift reaction* which also produces more H_2:

$$CO + H_2O \overset{(a) + (b)}{\rightleftharpoons} CO_2 + H_2$$

Maximum conversion occurs by equilibration at the lowest possible temperature so the reaction is carried out sequentially on two beds of catalyst: (a) iron oxide (400°C) which reduces the CO concentration from 11% to 3%; (b) a copper catalyst (200°) which reduces the CO content to 0.3%. Removal of CO_2 (~18%) is effected in a *scrubber* containing either a concentrated alkaline solution of K_2CO_3 or an amine such as ethanolamine:

$$CO_2 + H_2O + K_2CO_3 \underset{\text{regeneration (heat)}}{\overset{\text{absorption}}{\rightleftharpoons}} 2KHCO_3$$

Remaining trace quantities of CO (which would poison the iron catalyst during ammonia synthesis) are converted back to CH_4 by passing the damp gas from the scrubbers over a Ni *methanation catalyst* at 325°: $CO + 3H_2 \rightleftharpoons CH_4 + H_2O$. This reaction is the reverse of that occurring in the primary steam reformer. The *synthesis gas* now emerging has the approximate composition H_2 74.3%, N_2 24.7%, CH_4 0.8%, Ar 0.3%, CO 1–2 ppm. It is *compressed* in three stages from 25 atm to ~200 atm and then passed over a *promoted iron catalyst* at 380–450°C:

$$N_2 + 3H_2 \overset{Fe/400°/200 \text{ atm}}{\rightleftharpoons} 2NH_3$$

The gas leaving the catalyst beds contains about 15% NH_3; this is condensed by refrigeration and the remaining gas mixed with more incoming synthesis gas and recycled. Variables in the final reaction are the synthesis pressure,

Panel continues

[56] S. P. S. ANDREW, in R. THOMPSON (ed.), *The Modern Inorganic Chemicals Industry*, pp. 201-31, The Chemical Society, London, 1977.
[57] S. D. LYON, *Chem. Ind.* 731-9 (1975).

synthesis temperature, gas composition, gas flow rate[†] and catalyst composition and particle size. Since the earliest days the "promoted" Fe catalysts have been prepared by fusing magnetite (Fe_3O_4) on a table with KOH in the presence of a small amount of mixed refractory oxides such as MgO, Al_2O_3 and SiO_2; the solidified sheet is broken up into chunks 5–10 mm in size. These chunks are then reduced inside the ammonia synthesis converter to give the active catalyst which consists of Fe crystallites separated by the amorphous refractory oxides and partly covered by the alkali promotor which increases its activity by at least an order of magnitude.

World production of synthetic ammonia has increased dramatically particularly during the period 1950–80. Production in 1950 was little more than 1 million tonnes; though this was huge when compared with the production of most other compounds, it is dwarfed by today's rate of production which exceeds 120 million tonnes pa. In 1990 world production capacity was 119.6 million tonnes distributed as follows: Asia 35.4%, the former Soviet Union 21.5%, North America 13.8%, Western Europe 11.3%, Eastern Europe 9.7% Latin America 5.3%, Africa 3.0%. The price of NH_3 (FOB Gulf Coast plants, USA) was $107/tonne in 1990.

The applications of NH_3 are dominated (over 85%) by its use in various forms as a fertilizer. Of these, direct application is the most common (28.7%), followed by urea (22.4%), NH_4NO_3 (15.8%), ammonium phosphates (14.6%), and $(NH_4)_2SO_4$ (3.4%). Industrial uses include (a) commercial explosives — such as NH_4NO_3, nitroglycerine, TNT and nitrocellulose, which are produced from NH_3 via HNO_3 — and (b) fibres/plastics e.g. in the manufacture of caprolactam for nylon-6, hexamethylenediamine for nylon-6.6, polyamides, rayon and polyurethanes. Other uses include a wide variety of applications in refrigeration, wood pulping, detinning of scrap-metal and corrosion inhibition; it is also used as a rubber stabilizer, pH controller, in the manufacture of household detergents, in the food and beverage industry, pharmaceuticals, water purification and the manufacture of numerous organic and inorganic chemicals. Indeed, synthetic ammonia is the key to the industrial production of most inorganic nitrogen compounds, as indicated in the subjoined Scheme.

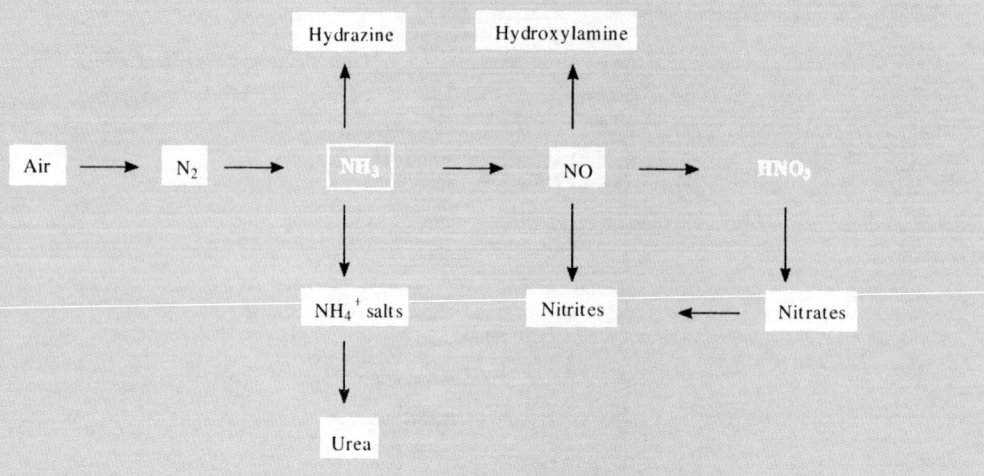

[†]Flow rate is usually quoted as "space velocity", i.e. the ratio of volumetric rate of gas at STP to volume of catalyst; typical values are in the range 8000–60 000 h^{-1}.

The chemical fixation of N_2 to NH_3 under less extreme conditions than those used industrially is a continuing area of active research and considerable progress has been made in elucidating mechanisms involving N_2 coordinated to Mo, W, V and other centres.[5,6,58–63]

Some physical and molecular properties of NH_3 are in Table 11.2. The influence of H

[58] T. A. GEORGE and R. C. TISDALE, *J. Am. Chem. Soc.* **107**, 5157–9 (1985).

[59] K. ALKA, *Angew. Chem. Int. Edn. Engl.* **25**, 558–9 (1986).

[60] R. L. RICHARDS, *Chem. in Britain*, Feb. 1988, pp. 133–6.

[61] M. Y. MOHAMMED and C. J. PICKETT, *J. Chem. Soc., Chem. Commun.*, 1119–21 (1988).

[62] R. R. EADY, *Polyhedron* **8**, 1695–1700 (1989).

[63] G. J. LEIGH, R. PRIETO-ALCÓN and J. R. SANDERS, *J. Chem. Soc., Chem. Commun.*, 921–2 (1991).

Table 11.2 Some properties of ammonia, NH_3

Physical properties		Molecular properties	
MP/K	195.42	Symmetry	C_{3v} (pyramidal)
BP/K	239.74	Distance (N–H)/pm	101.7
Density(l; 239 K)/g cm^{-3}	0.6826	Angle H–N–H	107.8°
Density(g; rel. air = 1)	0.5963	Pyramid height/pm	36.7
η(239.5 K)/centipoise[a]	0.254	μ/Debye[b]	1.46
Dielectric constant ε(239 K)	22	Inversion barrier kJ mol^{-1}	24.7
κ(234.3 K)/ohm^{-1} cm^{-1}	1.97×10^{-7}	Inversion frequency/GHz[c]	23.79
ΔH_f°(298 K)/kJ mol^{-1}	-46.1	$D(H–NH_2)$/kJ mol^{-1}	435
ΔG_f°(298 K)/kJ mol^{-1}	-16.5	Ionization energy/kJ mol^{-1}	979.7
S°(298 K)/J K^{-1} mol^{-1}	192.3	Proton affinity (gas)/kJ mol^{-1}	841

[a] 1 centipoise = 10^{-3} kg m^{-1} s^{-1}. [b] 1 Debye = 10^{-18} esu = $3.335\,64 \times 10^{-30}$ C m. [c] 1 GHz = 10^9 s^{-1}.

bonding on the bp and other properties has already been noted (p. 53). It has been estimated that 26% of the H bonding in NH_3 breaks down on melting, 7% on warming from the mp to the bp, and the final 67% on transfer to the gas phase at the bp. The low density, viscosity and electrical conductivity, and the high dielectric constant of liquid ammonia are also notable. Liquid NH_3 is an excellent solvent and a valuable medium for chemical reactions (p. 424); its high heat of vaporization (23.35 kJ mol^{-1} at the bp) makes it relatively easy to handle in simple vacuum flasks. The molecular properties call for little comment except to note that the rapid inversion frequency with which the N atom moves through the plane of the 3 H atoms has a marked effect on the vibrational spectrum of the molecule. The inversion itself occurs in the microwave region of the spectrum at 23.79 GHz (corresponding to a wavelength of 1.260 cm) and was, in fact, the first microwave absorption spectrum to be detected (C. E. Cleeton and N. H. Williams, 1934). The associated energy $(hc\bar{v})$ is 0.7935 cm^{-1} i.e. 9.49 J mol^{-1}. Inversion also occurs in ND_3 at a frequency of 1.591 GHz, i.e. less than for NH_3 by a factor of 14.95. The inversion can be stopped in NH_3 by increasing the pressure to $\sim$2 atm. The corresponding figure for ND_3 is $\sim$90 mmHg (i.e. again a factor of about 15).

Ammonia is readily absorbed by H_2O with considerable evolution of heat ($\sim$37.1 kJ per mol of NH_3 gas). Aqueous solutions are weakly basic due to the equilibrium

$$NH_3(aq) + H_2O \underset{H_2O}{\rightleftharpoons} NH_4^+(aq) + OH^-(aq);$$

$$K_{298.2} = [NH_4^+][OH^-]/[NH_3] = 1.81 \times 10^{-5}\ \text{mol}\,l^{-1}$$

The equilibrium constant at room temperature corresponds to $pK_b = 4.74$ and implies that a 1 molar aqueous solution of NH_3 contains only 4.25 mmol l^{-1} of NH_4^+ (or OH$^-$). Such solutions do not contain the undissociated "molecule" NH_4OH, though weakly bonded hydrates have been isolated at low temperature:

$NH_3.H_2O$ (mp 194.15 K) and $2NH_3.H_2O$

(mp 194.32 K)

These hydrates are not ionically dissociated but contain chains of H_2O molecules cross-linked by NH_3 molecules into a three-dimensional H-bonded network.

Ammonia burns in air with difficulty, the flammable limits being 16–25 vol%. Normal combustion yields nitrogen but, in the presence of a Pt or Pt/Rh catalyst at 750–900°C, the reaction proceeds further to give the thermodynamically less-favoured products NO and NO_2:

$$4NH_3 + 3O_2 \xrightarrow{\text{burn}} 2N_2 + 6H_2O$$

$$4NH_3 + 5O_2 \xrightarrow{\text{Pt/800}^\circ} 4NO + 6H_2O$$

$$2NO + O_2 \xrightarrow{\text{Pt/800}^\circ} 2NO_2$$

These reactions are very important industrially in the production of HNO_3 (p. 466). See also the industrial production of HCN by the Andrussov process (p. 321): $2NH_3 + 3O_2 + 2CH_4 \longrightarrow 2HCN + 6H_2O$.

Gaseous NH_3 burns with a greenish-yellow flame in F_2 (or ClF_3) to produce NF_3 (p. 439). Chlorine yields several products depending on conditions: NH_4Cl, NH_2Cl, $NHCl_2$, NCl_3, $NCl_3.NH_3$, N_2 and even small amounts of N_2H_4. The reaction to give chloramine, NH_2Cl, is important in urban and domestic water purification systems. Reactions with other non-metals and their halides or oxides are equally complex and lead to a variety of compounds, many of which are treated elsewhere (pp. 497, 501, 506, 535, 723, etc.). At red heat carbon reacts with NH_3 to give $NH_4CN + H_2$, whereas phosphorus yields PH_3 and N_2, and sulfur gives H_2S and N_4S_4. Metals frequently react at higher temperature to give nitrides (p. 417). Of particular importance is the attack on Cu in the presence of oxygen (air) at room temperature since this precludes the use of this metal and its alloys in piping and valves for handling either liquid or gaseous NH_3. Corrosion of Cu and brass by moist NH_3/air mixtures and by air-saturated aqueous solutions of NH_3 is also rapid. Contact with Ni and with polyvinylchloride plastics should be avoided for the same reason.

Liquid ammonia as a solvent [64–67]

Liquid ammonia is the best-known and most widely studied non-aqueous ionizing solvent. Its most conspicuous property is its ability to

dissolve alkali metals to form highly coloured, electrically conducting solutions containing solvated electrons, and the intriguing physical properties and synthetic utility of these solutions have already been discussed (p. 77). Apart from these remarkable solutions, much of the chemistry in liquid ammonia can be classified by analogy with related reactions in aqueous solutions. Accordingly, we briefly consider in turn, solubility relationships, metathesis reactions, acid-base reactions, amphoterism, solvates and solvolysis, redox reactions and the preparation of compounds in unusual oxidation states. Comparison of the physical properties of liquid NH_3 (p. 423) with those of water (p. 623) shows that NH_3 has the lower mp, bp, density, viscosity, dielectric constant and electrical conductivity; this is due at least in part to the weaker H bonding in NH_3 and the fact that such bonding cannot form cross-linked networks since each NH_3 molecule has only 1 lone-pair of electrons compared with 2 for each H_2O molecule. The ionic self-dissociation constant of liquid NH_3 at $-50°C$ is $\sim 10^{-33}$ mol^2 l^{-2}.

Most ammonium salts are freely soluble in liquid NH_3 as are many nitrates, nitrites, cyanides and thiocyanates. The solubilities of halides tend to increase from the fluoride to the iodide; solubilities of salts of multivalent ions are generally low suggesting that (as in aqueous systems) lattice-energy and entropy effects outweigh solvation energies. The possibility of H-bond formation also influences solubility and, in the case of NH_4I, an X-ray single-crystal analysis of the monosolvate shows the presence of an H-bonded cation $N_2H_7^+$ with an $N-H \cdots N$ distance of 269 ± 5 pm.[68] Some typical solubilities at 25°C expressed as g per 100 g solvent are: NH_4OAc 253.2, NH_4NO_3 389.6, $LiNO_3$ 243.7, $NaNO_3$ 97.6, KNO_3 10.4, NaF 0.35, NaCl 3.0, NaBr 138.0, NaI 161.9, NaSCN 205.5. Some of these solubilities are astonishingly high, particularly when expressed as the number of moles of solute per 10 mol

[64] W. L. JOLLY and C. J. HALLADA, Chap. 1 in T. C. WADDINGTON (ed.), *Non-Aqueous Solvent Systems*, pp. 1–45, Academic Press, London. 1965.

[65] G. W. A. FOWLES, Chap. 7, in C. B. COLBURN (ed.), *Developments in Inorganic Nitrogen Chemistry*, pp. 522–76, Elsevier, Amsterdam, 1966.

[66] J. J. LAGOWSKI and G. A. MOCZYGEMBA, Chap. 7 in J. J. LAGOWSKI (ed.), *The Chemistry of Non-aqueous Solvents*, Vol. 2, pp. 320–71, Academic Press, 1967.

[67] D. NICHOLLS, *Inorganic Chemistry in Liquid Ammonia: Topics in Inorganic and General Chemistry*, Monograph 17, Elsevier, Amsterdam, 1979, 238 pp.

[68] H. J. BERTHOLD, W. PREIBSCH and E. VONHOLDT, *Angew. Chem. Int. Edn. Engl.* **27**, 1524–5 (1988).

NH_3, e.g.: NH_4NO_3 8.3, $LiNO_3$ 6.1, $NaSCN$ 4.3. Further data at 25° and other temperatures are in ref. 69.

Metathesis reactions are sometimes the reverse of those in aqueous systems because of the differing solubility relations. For example because AgBr forms the complex ion $[Ag(NH_3)_2]^+$ in liquid NH_3 it is readily soluble, whereas $BaBr_2$ is not, and can be precipitated:

$$Ba(NO_3)_2 + 2AgBr \xrightarrow{\text{liq } NH_3} BaBr_2\downarrow + 2AgNO_3$$

Reactions analogous to the precipitation of AgOH and of insoluble oxides from aqueous solution are:

$$AgNO_3 + KNH_2 \xrightarrow{\text{liq } NH_3} AgNH_2\downarrow + KNO_3$$

$$3HgI_2 + 6KNH_2 \xrightarrow{\text{liq } NH_3} Hg_3N_2\downarrow + 6KI + 4NH_3$$

Acid-base reactions in many solvent systems can be thought of in terms of the characteristic cations and anions of the solvent (see also p. 831)

$$\text{solvent} \rightleftharpoons \text{characteristic cation (acid)}$$
$$+ \text{ characteristic anion (base)}$$
$$2H_2O \rightleftharpoons H_3O^+ + OH^-$$
$$2NH_3 \rightleftharpoons NH_4^+ + NH_2^-$$

On this basis NH_4^+ salts can be considered as solvo-acids in liquid NH_3 and amides as solvo-bases. Neutralization reactions can be followed conductimetrically, potentiometrically or even with coloured indicators such as phenolphthalein:

$$\underset{\text{solvo-acid}}{NH_4NO_3} + \underset{\text{solvo-base}}{KNH_2} \xrightarrow{\text{liq } NH_3} \underset{\text{salt}}{KNO_3} + \underset{\text{solvent}}{2NH_3}$$

Likewise, amphoteric behaviour can be observed. For example $Zn(NH_2)_2$ is insoluble in liquid NH_3 (as is $Zn(OH)_2$ in H_2O), but it dissolves on addition of the solvo-base KNH_2 due to the formation of $K_2[Zn(NH_2)_4]$; this in turn is decomposed by NH_4^+ salts (solvo-acids) with reprecipitation of the amide:

$$K_2[Zn(NH_2)_4] + 2NH_4NO_3 \xrightarrow{\text{liq } NH_3} Zn(NH_2)_2$$
$$+ 2KNO_3 + 4NH_3$$

Solvates are perhaps less prevalent in compounds prepared from liquid ammonia solutions than are hydrates precipitated from aqueous systems, but large numbers of ammines are known, and their study formed the basis of Werner's theory of coordination compounds (1891–5). Frequently, however, solvolysis (ammonolysis) occurs (cf. hydrolysis).[65] Examples are:

$$M^IH + NH_3 \longrightarrow MNH_2 + H_2$$
$$M_2^IO + NH_3 \longrightarrow MNH_2 + MOH$$
$$SiCl_4 \xrightarrow[\text{temp}]{\text{low}} [Si(NH_2)_4] \xrightarrow{0°} Si(NH)(NH_2)_2$$
$$\xrightarrow{1200°} Si_3N_4$$

Amides are one of the most prolific classes of ligand and the subject of metal and metalloid amides has been extensively reviewed.[70]

Redox reactions are particularly instructive. If all thermodynamically allowed reactions in liquid NH_3 were kinetically rapid, then no oxidizing agent more powerful than N_2 and no reducing agent more powerful than H_2 could exist in this solvent. Using data for solutions at 25°:[64]

Acid solutions (1 M NH_4^+)
$$NH_4^+ + e^- = NH_3 + \tfrac{1}{2}H_2 \qquad E° = 0.0\,V$$
$$3NH_4^+ + \tfrac{1}{2}N_2 + 3e^- = 4NH_3 \quad E° = -0.04\,V$$

Basic solutions (1 M NH_2^-)
$$NH_3 + e^- = NH_2^- + \tfrac{1}{2}H_2 \qquad E° = 1.59\,V$$
$$2NH_3 + \tfrac{1}{2}N_2 + 3e^- = 3NH_2^- \quad E° = 1.55\,V$$

Obviously, with a range of only 0.04 V available very few species are thermodynamically stable. However, both the hydrogen couple and the nitrogen couple usually exhibit "overvoltages" of ~1 V, so that in acid solutions the practical range of potentials for solutes is from +1.0 to −1.0 V. Similarly in basic solutions the practical range

---

69 K. JONES, Nitrogen, Chap. 19 in *Comprehensive Inorganic Chemistry* Vol. 2, pp. 147–388, Pergamon Press, Oxford, 1973.

70 M. F. LAPPERT, P. P. POWER, A. R. SANGER and R. C. SRIVASTAVA, *Metal and Metalloid Amides*, Ellis Horwood Ltd., Chichester, 1980, 847 pp. (approximately 3000 references).

extends from 2.6 to 0.6 V. It is thus possible to work in liquid ammonia with species which are extremely strong reducing agents (e.g. alkali metals) and also with extremely strong oxidizing agents (e.g. permanganates, superoxides and ozonides; p. 609). For similar reasons the NO_3^- ion is effectively inert towards NH_3 in acid solution but in alkaline solutions N_2 is slowly evolved:

$$3K^+ + 3NH_2^- + 3NO_3^- \longrightarrow 3KOH\downarrow + N_2$$
$$+ 3NO_2^- + NH_3$$

The use of liquid NH_3 to prepare compounds of elements in unusual (low) oxidation states is exemplified by the successive reduction of $K_2[Ni(CN)_4]$ with Na/Hg in the presence of an excess of CN^-: the dark-red dimeric Ni^I complex $K_4[Ni_2(CN)_6]$ is first formed and this can be further reduced to the yellow Ni^0 complex $K_4[Ni(CN)_4]$. The corresponding complexes $[Pd(CN)_4]^{4-}$ and $[Pt(CN)_4]^{4-}$ can be prepared similarly, though there is no evidence in these latter systems for the formation of the M^I dimer. A ditertiaryphosphine complex of Pd^0 has also been prepared:

$$[Pd\{1,2\text{-}(PEt_2)_2C_6H_4\}_2]Br_2 \xrightarrow{\text{Na/NH}_3}$$
$$[Pd\{1,2\text{-}(PEt_2)_2C_6H_4\}_2] + 2NaBr$$

$[Co^{III}(CN)_6]^{3-}$ yields the pale-yellow complex $[Co^I(CN)_4]^{3-}$ and the brown-violet complex $[Co_2^0(CN)_8]^{8-}$ (cf. the dimeric carbonyl $[Co_2(CO)_8]$).

Liquid NH_3 is also extensively used as a preparative medium for compounds which are unstable in aqueous solutions, e.g.:

$$2Ph_3GeNa + Br(CH_2)_xBr \xrightarrow{\text{liq NH}_3} Ph_3Ge(CH_2)_xGePh_3$$
$$+ 2NaBr$$

$$Me_3SnX + NaPEt_2 \xrightarrow{\text{liq NH}_3} Me_3SnPEt_2 + 2NaX$$

Alkali metal acetylides M_2C_2, MCCH and MCCR can readily be prepared by passing C_2H_2 or C_2HR into solutions of the alkali metal in liquid NH_3, and these can be used to synthesize a wide range of transition-element acetylides,[71] e.g.:

$$Ni(SCN)_2.6NH_3 + 5KC_2Ph \xrightarrow{\text{liq NH}_3}$$
$$K_2[Ni(C_2Ph)_4].2NH_3 + 2KSCN + 4NH_3$$

$$K_2[Ni(C_2Ph)_4].2NH_3 \xrightarrow{\text{vac}} K_2[Ni^{II}(C_2Ph)_4] + 2NH_3$$
$$\text{yellow}$$

Other examples are orange-red $K_3[Cr^{III}(C_2H)_6]$, rose-pink $Na_2[Mn^{II}(C_2Me)_4]$, dark-green $Na_4[Co^{II}(C_2Me)_6]$, orange $K_4[Ni^0(C_2H)_4]$, yellow $K_6[Ni_2^I(C_2Ph)_6]$. Such compounds are often explosive, though the analogues of Cu^I and Zn^{II} are not, e.g. yellow $Na[Cu(C_2Me)_2]$, colourless $K_2[Cu(C_2H)_3]$, and colourless $K_2[Zn(C_2H)_4]$.

Ammonium halides have been used as versatile reagents in low-temperature solid-state redox and acid-base reactions.[72] For example, direct reaction with the appropriate metal at 270–300° yields the ammonium salts of $ZnCl_4^{2-}$, $LaCl_5^{2-}$, YCl_6^{3-}, YBr_6^{3-}, $CuCl_3^{2-}$, etc., whereas Y_2O_3 yields either $(NH_4)_3YBr_6$ or YOBr depending on the stoichiometric ratio of the reagents. Solid-state reactions of ammonium sulfate, nitrate, phosphates and carbonate have also been studied.

11.3.3 Other hydrides of nitrogen

Nitrogen forms more than 20 binary compounds with hydrogen[73] of which ammonia (NH_3, p. 420), hydrazine (N_2H_4, p. 427) and hydrogen azide (N_3H, p. 432) are by far the most important. Hydroxylamine, $NH_2(OH)$, is closely related in structure and properties to both ammonia, $NH_2(H)$, and hydrazine, $NH_2(NH_2)$ and it will be convenient to discuss this compound in the present section also (p. 431). Several protonated cationic species such as NH_4^+, $N_2H_5^+$, etc, and deprotonated anionic species such as NH_2^-, $N_2H_3^-$, etc. also exist but ammonium hydride, NH_5, is unknown. Among

[71] R. NAST and coworkers; for summary of results and detailed refs., see pp. 568–71 of ref. 65.

[72] G. MEYER, T. STAFFEL, S.DÖTSCH and T. SCHLEID, *Inorg. Chem.* **24**, 3504–5 (1985).

[73] *Gmelin Handbook of Inorganic and Organometallic Chemistry*, 8th Edition, Nitrogen, Supplement B1, 280 pp., Supplement B2, 188 pp., Springer Verlag, Berlin, 1993.

Table 11.3 Some physical and thermochemical properties of hydrazine

MP/°C	2.0	Dielectric constant $\varepsilon(25°)$	51.7
BP/°C	113.5	$\kappa(25°)/\text{ohm}^{-1}\,\text{cm}^{-1}$	$\sim 2.5 \times 10^{-6}$
Density/(solid at $-5°$)/g cm^{-3}	1.146	$\Delta H_{combustion}/\text{kJ mol}^{-1}$	621.5
Density (liquid at $25°$)/g cm^{-3}	1.00	$\Delta H_f^\circ(25°)/\text{kJ mol}^{-1}$	50.6
$\eta(25°)$/centipoise[a]	0.9	$\Delta G_f^\circ(25°)/\text{kJ mol}^{-1}$	149.2
Refractive index n_D^{25}	1.470	$S^\circ(25°)/\text{J K}^{-1}\,\text{mol}^{-1}$	121.2

[a] 1 centipoise $= 10^{-3}\,\text{kg m}^{-1}\,\text{s}^{-1}$.

the less familiar (and less stable) neutral radicals which have been well characterized are the imidogen (NH), amidogen (NH$_2$), diazenyl (N$_2$H) and hydrazyl (N$_2$H$_3$) radicals. Such species are important in atmospheric chemistry and in combustion reactions. Of the neutral compounds the following can be mentioned:[73]

N$_2$H$_2$: *trans*-diazene, HN=NH (yellow), and its 1:1 isomer, H$_2$N=N

N$_3$H: hydrogen azide (p. 432) and cyclo-triazene (triazairine). $\overline{\text{N=N–NH}}$

N$_3$H$_3$: triazene, HN=N–NH$_2$ and cyclotri-azane (triaziridene) c-(NH)$_3$

N$_3$H$_5$: triazane (aminohydrazine), H$_2$NN(H)-NH$_2$

N$_4$H$_4$: *trans*-2-tetrazene, H$_2$N–N=N–NH$_2$, (colourless, low-melting crystals, N–N 143 pm, N=N 121 pm). and ammo-nium azide, NH$_4$N$_3$ (white crystals, subl. 133°C, d 1.350 g cm^{-3})

N$_4$H$_6$: tetrazane, H$_2$NN(H)N(H)NH$_2$, (bright yellow solid)

N$_5$H$_5$: hydrazinium azide, N$_2$H$_5$N$_3$, (explosive white crystals)

N$_6$H$_2$: Probably a cyclic dimer of N$_3$H

N$_7$H$_9$: hydrazinium azide monohydrazinate, N$_2$H$_5$N$_3$.N$_2$H$_4$

N$_9$H$_3$: cyclic trimer of N$_3$H, i.e. 1,3,5-N$_6$(NH)$_3$

Hydrazine [74]

Anhydrous N$_2$H$_4$ is a fuming, colourless liquid with a faint ammoniacal odour which is first

[74] E. W. SCHMIDT, *Hydrazine and its Derivatives, Prepa-ration, Properties, Application* Wiley, Chichester, 1984, 1059 pp. (over 4400 references).

detectable at a concentration of 70–80 ppm. Many of its physical properties (Table 11.3) are remarkably similar to those of water (p. 623); comparisons with NH$_3$ (p. 423) H$_2$O$_2$ (p. 634) are also instructive, and the influence of H bonding is apparent. In the gas phase four conformational isomers are conceivable (Fig. 11.5) but the large dipole (1.85 D) clearly eliminates the staggered *trans*-conformation; electron diffraction data (and infrared) indicate the *gauche*-conformation with an angle of rotation of 90–95° from the eclipsed position.

The most effective preparative routes to hydrazine are still based on the process introduced by F. Raschig in 1907: this involves the reaction of ammonia with an alkaline solution of sodium hypochlorite in the presence of gelatin or glue. The overall reaction can be written as

$$2NH_3 + NaOCl \xrightarrow{\text{aqueous alkali}} N_2H_4 + NaCl + H_2O \tag{1}$$

but it proceeds in two main steps. First there is a rapid formation of chloramine which proceeds to completion even in the cold:

$$NH_3 + OCl^- \longrightarrow NH_2Cl + OH^- \tag{2}$$

The chloramine then reacts further to produce N$_2$H$_4$ either by slow nucleophilic attack of NH$_3$ (3a) and subsequent rapid neutralization (3b), or by preliminary rapid formation of the chloramide ion (4a) followed by slow nucleophilic attack of NH$_3$ (4b):

$$NH_2Cl + NH_3 \xrightarrow{\text{slow}} N_2H_5^+ + Cl^- \tag{3a}$$

$$N_2H_5^+ + OH^- \xrightarrow{\text{fast}} N_2H_4 + H_2O \tag{3b}$$

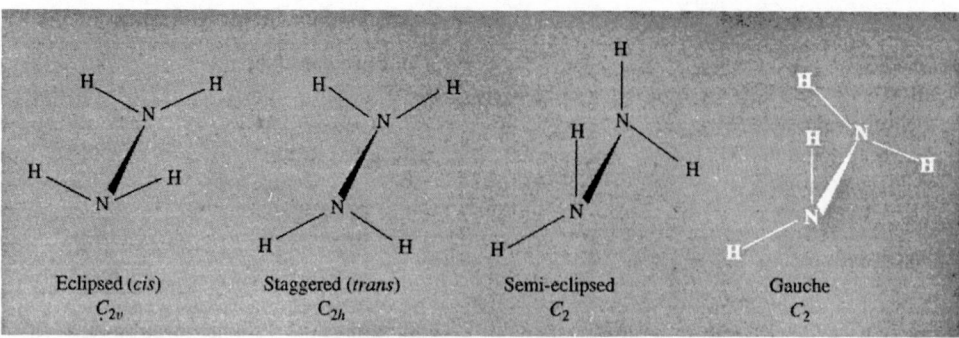

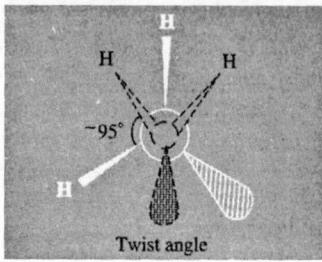

Figure 11.5   Possible conformations of N_2H_4 with pyramidal N. Hydrazine adopts the gauche C_2 form with N–N 145 pm, H–N–H 108°, and a twist angle of 95° as shown in the lower diagram.

$$NH_2Cl + OH^- \xrightarrow{fast} NHCl^- + H_2O \quad (4a)$$

$$NHCl^- + NH_3 \xrightarrow{slow} N_2H_4 + Cl^- \quad (4b)$$

In addition there is a further rapid but undesirable reaction with chloramine which destroys the N_2H_4 produced:

$$N_2H_4 + 2NH_2Cl \xrightarrow{fast} 2NH_4Cl + N_2 \quad (5)$$

This reaction is catalysed by traces of heavy metal ions such as Cu^{II} and the purpose of the gelatin is to suppress reaction (5) by sequestering the metal ions; it is probable that gelatin also assists the hydrazine-forming reactions between ammonia and chloramine in a way that is not fully understood. The industrial preparation and uses of N_2H_4 are summarized in the Panel.

At room temperature, pure N_2H_4 and its aqueous solutions are kinetically stable with respect to decomposition despite the endothermic nature of the compound and its positive free energy of formation:

$$N_2(g) + 2H_2(g) \longrightarrow N_2H_4(l); \ \Delta H_f^\circ = 50.6\,kJ\,mol^{-1}$$

$$\Delta G_f^\circ = 149.2\,kJ\,mol^{-1}$$

When ignited, N_2H_4 burns rapidly and completely in air with considerable evolution of heat (see Panel):

$$N_2H_4(l) + O_2(g) \longrightarrow N_2(g) + 2H_2O;$$

$$\Delta H = -621.5\,kJ\,mol^{-1}$$

In solution, N_2H_4 is oxidized by a wide variety of oxidizing agents (including O_2) and it finds use as a versatile reducing agent because of the variety of reactions it can undergo. Thus the thermodynamic reducing strength of N_2H_4 depends on whether it undergoes a 1-, 2-, or 4-electron oxidation and whether this is in acid or alkaline solution. Typical examples in acid solution are as follows:[†]

1-electron change (e.g. using Fe^{III}, Ce^{IV}, or MnO_4^-):

[†] See p. 435 for discussion of standard electrode potentials and their use. It is conventional to write the half-reactions as (oxidized form) $+ ne^- =$ (reduced form). Since $\Delta G = -nE^\circ F$ at unit activities, it follows that the reactions will occur spontaneously in the reverse direction to that written when E° is negative, i.e. hydrazine is oxidized by the reagents listed.

Industrial Production and Uses of Hydrazine[75]

Hydrazine is usually prepared in a continuous process based on the Raschig reaction. Solutions of ammonia and sodium hypochlorite (30:1) are mixed in the cold with a gelatin solution and then passed rapidly under pressure through a reactor at 150° (residence time 1 s). This results in a 60% conversion based on hypochlorite and produces a solution of $\sim$0.5% by weight of N_2H_4. The excess of NH_3 and steam are stripped off in stages and the solution finally distilled to give pure hydrazine hydrate $N_2H_4.H_2O$ (mp $-51.7°$, bp 118.5°, d 1.0305 g cm^{-3} at 21°). In the Olin Mathieson variation of this process, NH_2Cl is preformed from $NH_3 + NaOCl$ (3:1) and then anhydrous NH_3 is injected to a ratio of $\sim$30:1; this simultaneously raises the temperature and pressure in the reactor. An alternative industrial route, which is economical only for smaller plants, uses urea instead of ammonia in a process very similar to Raschig's:

$$(NH_2)_2CO + NaOCl + 2NaOH \xrightarrow[\text{protein inhibitor}]{\text{rapid heat/}} N_2H_4.H_2O + NaCl + Na_2CO_3$$

Hydrazine hydrate contains 64.0% by weight of N_2H_4 and is frequently preferred to the pure compound not only because it is cheaper but also because its much lower mp avoids problems of solidification. Anhydrous N_2H_4 can be obtained from concentrated aqueous solutions by distillation in the presence of dehydrating agents such as solid NaOH or KOH. Alternatively, hydrazine sulfate can be precipitated from dilute aqueous solutions using dilute H_2SO_4 and the precipitate treated with liquid NH_3 to liberate the hydrazine:

$$N_2H_4(aq) + H_2SO_4(aq) \longrightarrow N_2H_6SO_4 \xrightarrow[\text{(anhydr)}]{2NH_3} N_2H_4 + (NH_4)_2SO_4$$

World production capacity of hydrazine solutions in 1995 (expressed as N_2H_4) was about 40 000 tonnes, predominantly in USA 16 500 t, Germany 6400 t, Japan 6600 t and France 6100 t. In addition some 3200 t of anhydrous N_2H_4 was manufactured in USA for rocket fuels.

The major use (non-commercial) of anhydrous N_2H_4 and its methyl derivatives $MeNHNH_2$ and Me_2NNH_2 is as a rocket fuel in guided missiles, space shuttles, lunar missions, etc. For example the Apollo lunar modules were decelerated on landing and powered on blast-off for the return journey by the oxidation of a 1:1 mixture of $MeNHNH_2$ and Me_2NNH_2 with liquid N_2O_4; the landing required some 3 tonnes of fuel and 4.5 tonnes of oxidizer, and the relaunching about one-third of this amount. Other oxidants used are O_2, H_2O_2, HNO_3, or even F_2. Space vehicles propelled by anhydrous N_2H_4 itself include the Viking Lander on Mars, the Pioneer and Voyager interplanetary probes and the Giotto space probe to Halley's comet.

The major commercial applications of hydrazine solutions are as blowing agents ($\sim$40%), agricultural chemicals ($\sim$25%), medicinals ($\sim$5%), and — increasingly — in boiler water treatment now as much as 20%. The detailed pattern of usage, of course, depends to some extent on the country concerned.

Aqueous solutions of N_2H_4 are versatile and attractive reducing agents. They have long been used to prepare silver (and copper) mirrors, to precipitate many elements (such as the platinum metals) from solutions of their compounds, and in other analytical applications. A major application as noted above is now in the treatment of high-pressure boiler water: this was first introduced in about 1945 and has the following advantages over the previously favoured Na_2SO_3:

(a) N_2H_4 is completely miscible with H_2O and reacts with dissolved O_2 to give merely N_2 and H_2O:
   $N_2H_4 + O_2 \longrightarrow N_2 + 2H_2O$
(b) N_2H_4 does not increase the dissolved solids (cf. Na_2SO_3) since N_2H_4 itself and all its reaction and decomposition products are volatile.
(c) These products are either alkaline (like N_2H_4) or neutral, but never acidic.
(d) N_2H_4 is also a corrosion inhibitor (by reducing Fe_2O_3 to hard, coherent Fe_3O_4) and it is therefore useful for stand-by and idle boilers.

The usual concentration of O_2 in boiler feed water is $\sim$0.01 ppm so that, even allowing for a twofold excess, 1 kg N_2H_4 is sufficient to treat 50 000 tonnes of feed water (say $\sim$4 days' supply at the rate of 500 tonnes per hour).

Hydrazine and its derivatives find considerable use in the synthesis of biologically active materials, dyestuff intermediates and other organic derivatives. Reactions of aldehydes to form hydrazides ($RCH{=}NNH_2$) and azines ($RCH{=}NN{=}CHR$) are well known in organic chemistry, as is the use of hydrazine and its derivatives in the synthesis of heterocyclic compounds.

---

[75] Hydrazine and its derivatives, *Kirk–Othmer Encyclopedia of Chemical Technology*, 4th edn., Vol. 13, pp. 560–606 (1995).

$$NH_4^+ + \tfrac{1}{2}N_2 + H^+ + e^- = N_2H_5^+; \quad E° = -1.74\,V$$

2-electron change (e.g. using H_2O_2 or HNO_2):

$$\tfrac{1}{2}NH_4^+ + \tfrac{1}{2}HN_3 + \tfrac{5}{2}H^+ + 2e^- = N_2H_5^+;$$
$$E° = +0.11\,V$$

4-electron change (e.g. using IO_3^- or I_2):

$$N_2 + 5H^+ + 4e^- = N_2H_5^+; \quad E° = -0.23\,V$$

For basic solutions the corresponding reduction potentials are:

$$NH_3 + \tfrac{1}{2}N_2 + H_2O + e^- = N_2H_4 + OH^-;$$
$$E° = -2.42\,V$$

$$\tfrac{1}{2}NH_3 + \tfrac{1}{2}N_3^- + \tfrac{5}{2}H_2O + 2e^- = N_2H_4 + \tfrac{5}{2}OH^-;$$
$$E° = -0.92\,V$$

$$N_2 + 4H_2O + 4e^- = N_2H_4 + 4OH^-;$$
$$E° = -1.16\,V$$

In the 4-electron oxidation of acidified N_2H_4 to N_2, it has been shown by the use of N_2H_4 isotopically enriched in ^{15}N that both the N atoms of each molecule of N_2 originated in the same molecule of N_2H_4. This reaction is also the basis for the most commonly used method for the analytical determination of N_2H_4 in dilute aqueous solution:

$$N_2H_4 + KIO_3 + 2HCl \xrightarrow{\;H_2O/CCl_4\;} N_2 + KCl$$
$$+ ICl + 3H_2O$$

The IO_3^- is first reduced to I_2 which is subsequently oxidized to ICl by additional IO_3^-; the end-point is detected by the complete discharge of the iodine colour from the CCl_4 phase.

As expected, N_2H_4 in aqueous solutions is somewhat weaker as a base than is ammonia (p. 423):

$$N_2H_4(aq) + H_2O = N_2H_5^+ + OH^-;$$
$$K_{25°} = 8.5 \times 10^{-7}\,mol\,l^{-1}$$

$$N_2H_5^+(aq) + H_2O = N_2H_6^{2+} + OH^-;$$
$$K_{25°} = 8.9 \times 10^{-16}\,mol\,l^{-1}$$

The hydrate $N_2H_4.H_2O$ is an H-bonded molecular adduct and is not ionically dissociated. Two series of salts are known, e.g. N_2H_5Cl and $N_2H_6Cl_2$. (It will be noticed that $N_2H_6^{2+}$ is isoelectronic with ethane.) H bonding frequently influences the crystal structure and this is particularly noticeable in $N_2H_6F_2$ which features a layer lattice similar to CdI_2 though the structure is more open and the fluoride ions are not close packed. Sulfuric acid forms three salts, $N_2H_4.nH_2SO_4$ ($n = \tfrac{1}{2}$, 1, 2), i.e. $[N_2H_5]_2SO_4$, $[N_2H_6]SO_4$ and $[N_2H_6][HSO_4]_2$.

Hydrazido(2−)-complexes of Mo and W have been prepared by protonating dinitrogen complexes with concentrated solutions of HX and by ligand exchange.[76] For example several dozen complexes of general formulae $[MX_2(NNH_2)L_3]$ and *trans*-$[MX(NNH_2)L_4]$ have been characterized for M = Mo; X = halogen; L = phosphine or heterocyclic-N donor. Similarly, *cis*-$[W(N_2)_2(PMe_2Ph)_4]$ afforded *trans*-$[WF(NNH_2)(PMe_2Ph)_4][BF_4]$ when treated with HF/MeOH in a borosilicate glass vessel. Side-on coordination of a phenylhydrazido(1−) ligand has also been established in compounds such as the dark-red $[W(\eta^5\text{-}C_5H_5)_2(\eta^2\text{-}H_2NNPh)][BF_4]$;[77] these are synthesized by the ready isomerization of the first-formed yellow η^1-arylhydrazido(2−) tungsten hydride complex above −20° (X = BF_4, PF_6):

In these reactions R = Ph, p-MeOC$_6$H$_4$, p-MeC$_6$H$_4$ or p-FC$_6$H$_4$. Further bonding modes are as an isodiazene (i.e. M←N=NMe$_2$ rather than M=N−NMe$_2$)[78] and as a bridging diimido

[76] J. CHATT, A. J. PEARMAN and R. L. RICHARDS, *J. Chem. Soc., Dalton Trans.*, 1766–76 (1978).

[77] J. A. CARROLL, D. SUTTON, M. COWIE and M. D. GAUTHIER, *J. Chem. Soc., Chem. Commun.*, 1058–9 (1979).

[78] J. R. DILWORTH, J. ZUBIETA and J. R. HYDE, *J. Am. Chem. Soc.* **104**, 365–7 (1982).

group (M=N–N=M).[79] Both hydrazine itself and its dianion, HNNH^{2-}, act as bridging ligands in the pale yellow dinuclear tungsten(VI) complex shown in Fig. 11.6.[80] A selection of further recent work on the various coordination modes of substituted hydrazido, diazenido and related ligands is appended.[81]

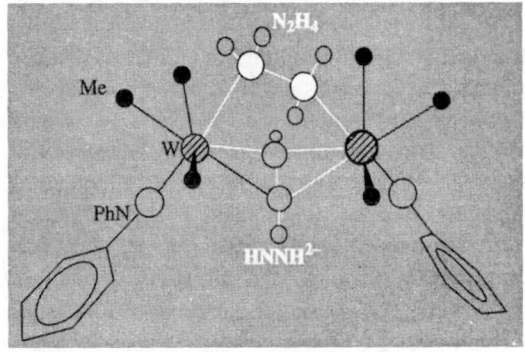

Figure 11.6 Structure of [{W(NPh)Me$_3$}$_2$(μ-η^1,η^1-NH$_2$NH$_2$)(μ-η^2,η^2-NHNH)].

Hydroxylamine

Anhydrous NH$_2$OH is a colourless, thermally unstable hygroscopic compound which is usually handled as an aqueous solution or in the form of one of its salts. The pure compound (mp 32.05°C, d 1.204 g cm^{-3} at 33°C) has a very high dielectric constant (77.63–77.85) and a vapour pressure of 10 mmHg at 47.2°. It can be regarded as water in which 1 H has been replaced by the more electronegative NH$_2$ group or as NH$_3$ in which

1 H has been replaced by OH. Aqueous solutions are less basic than either ammonia or hydrazine:

$$NH_2OH(aq) + H_2O = NH_3OH^+ + OH^-;$$
$$K_{25°} = 6.6 \times 10^{-9} \, mol \, l^{-1}$$

Hydroxylamine can be prepared by a variety of reactions involving the reduction of nitrites, nitric acid or NO, or by the acid hydrolysis of nitroalkanes. In the conventional Raschig synthesis, an aqueous solution of NH$_4$NO$_2$ is reduced with HSO$_4$$^-$/SO$_2$ at 0° to give the hydroxylamido-*N,N*-disulfate anion which is then hydrolysed stepwise to hydroxylammonium sulfate:

$$NH_4NO_2 + 2SO_2 + NH_3 + H_2O \longrightarrow$$
$$[NH_4]_2[N(OH)(OSO_2)_2]$$
$$[NH_4]^+{}_2[N(OH)(OSO_2)_2]^{2-} + H_2O \longrightarrow$$
$$[NH_4][NH(OH)(OSO_2)] + [NH_4][HSO_4]$$
$$2[NH_4]^+[NH(OH)(OSO_2)]^- + 2H_2O \longrightarrow$$
$$[NH_3(OH)]_2[SO_4] + [NH_4]_2[SO_4]$$

Aqueous solutions of NH$_2$OH can then be obtained by ion exchange, or the free compound can be prepared by ammonolysis with liquid NH$_3$; insoluble ammonium sulfate is filtered off and the excess of NH$_3$ removed under reduced pressure to leave solid NH$_2$OH.

Alternatively, hydroxylammonium salts can be made either (a) by the electrolytic reduction of aqueous nitric acid between amalgamated lead electrodes in the presence of H$_2$SO$_4$/HCl, or (b) by the hydrogenation of nitric oxide in acid solutions over a Pt/charcoal catalyst:

(a) $HNO_3(aq) + 6H^+(aq) \xrightarrow{6e^-} 2H_2O + NH_2OH$

$\xrightarrow{HCl(g)} [NH_3(OH)]Cl(s)$

(b) $2NO(g) + 3H_2(g) + H_2SO_4(aq) \xrightarrow{Pt/C}$

$[NH_3(OH)]_2SO_4$

A convenient laboratory route involves the reduction of an aqueous solution of nitrous acid or potassium nitrite with bisulfite under carefully

[79] M. R. CHURCHILL and H. J. WASSERMAN, *Inorg. Chem.* **20**, 2899–904 (1981).
[80] L. BLUM, I. D. WILLIAMS and R. R. SCHROCK, *J. Am. Chem. Soc.* **106**, 8316–7 (1984).
[81] M. D. FITZROY, J. M. FREDERIKSEN, K. S. MURRAY and M. R. SNOW, *Inorg. Chem.* **24**, 3265–70 (1985). J. BULTITUDE, L. F. LARKWORTHY, D. C. POVEY, G. W. SMITH, J. R. DILWORTH and G. J. LEIGH, *J. Chem. Soc., Chem. Commun.*, 1748–50 (1986). J. R. DILWORTH, R. A. HENDERSON, P. DAHLSTROM, T. NICHOLSON and J. S. ZUBIETA, *J. Chem. Soc., Dalton Trans.*, 529–40 (1987). T. NICHOLSON and J. ZUBIETA, *Polyhedron* **7**, 171–85 (1988). F. W. EINSTEIN, X. YAN and D. SUTTON, *J. Chem. Soc., Chem. Commun.*, 1466–7 (1990).

controlled conditions: The hydroxylamidodisulfate first formed, though stable in alkaline solution, rapidly hydrolyses to the monosulfate in acid solution and this can then subsequently be hydrolysed to the hydroxylammonium ion by treatment with aqueous HCl at 100° for 1 h:

$$HNO_2 + 2HSO_3^- \longrightarrow [N(OH)(OSO_2)_2]^{2-} + H_2O$$

$$\xrightarrow{\text{fast}} [NH(OH)(OSO_2)]^- + [HSO_4]^-$$

$$[NH(OH)(OSO_2)]^- + H_3O^+ \xrightarrow{100°/1\,h}$$

$$[NH_3(OH)]^+ + [HSO_4]^-$$

Anhydrous NH_2OH can be prepared by treating a suspension of hydroxylammonium chloride in butanol with NaOBu:

$$[NH_3(OH)]Cl + NaOBu \longrightarrow NH_2OH$$

$$+ NaCl + BuOH$$

The NaCl is removed by filtration and the NH_2OH precipitated by addition of Et_2O and cooling.

NH_2OH can exist as 2 configurational isomers (*cis* and *trans*) and in numerous intermediate *gauche* conformations as shown in Fig. 11.7. In the crystalline form, H bonding appears to favour packing in the *trans* conformation. The N–O distance is 147 pm consistent with its formulation as a single bond. Above room temperature the compound decomposes (sometimes explosively) by internal oxidation-reduction reactions into a complex mixture of N_2, NH_3, N_2O and H_2O. Aqueous solutions are much more stable, particularly acid solutions in which the compound

is protonated, $[NH_3(OH)]^+$. Such solutions can act as oxidizing agents particularly when acidified but are more generally used as reducing agents, e.g. as antioxidants in photographic developers, stabilizers of monomers, and for reducing Cu^{II} to Cu^I in the dyeing of acrylic fibres. Comparisons with the redox chemistry of H_2O_2 and N_2H_4 are also instructive (see, for example, pp. 272–3 of ref. 69). The ability of NH_2OH to react with N_2O, NO and N_2O_4 under suitable conditions (e.g. as the sulfate adsorbed on silica gel) makes it useful as an absorbent in combustion analysis. However, the major use of NH_2OH, which derives from its ability to form oximes with aldehydes and ketones, is in the manufacture of caprolactam, a key intermediate in the production of polyamide-6 fibres such as nylon. This consumes more than 97% of world production of NH_2OH, which is at least 650 000 tonnes per annum.

The extensive chemistry of the hydroxylamides of sulfuric acid is discussed later in the context of other H–N–O–S compounds (pp. 740–6).

Hydrogen azide

Aqueous solutions of HN_3 were first prepared in 1890 by T. Curtius who oxidized aqueous hydrazine with nitrous acid:

$$N_2H_5^+ + HNO_2 \longrightarrow HN_3 + H^+ + 2H_2O$$

Other oxidizing agents that can be used include nitric acid, hydrogen peroxide, peroxydisulfate, chlorate and the pervanadyl ion. The anhydrous

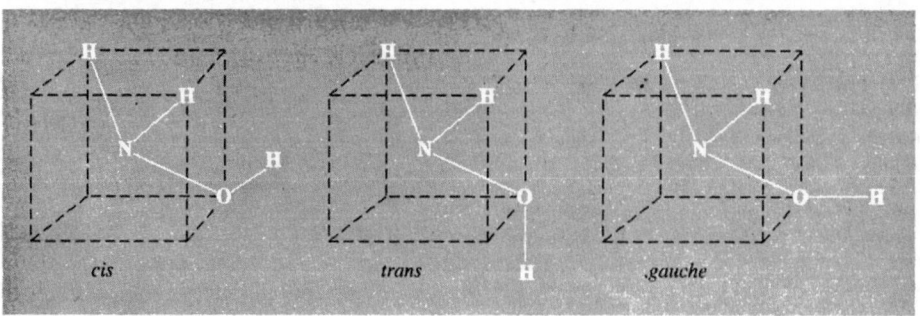

Figure 11.7   Configurations of NH_2OH.

compound is extremely explosive and even dilute solutions should be treated as potentially hazardous. Pure HN_3 is best prepared by careful addition of H_2SO_4 to NaN_3; it is a colourless liquid or gas (mp $\sim -80°$, estimated bp $35.7°$, d $1.126\,g\,cm^{-3}$ at $0°$). Its large positive enthalpy and free energy of formation emphasize its inherent instability: $\Delta H_f^\circ(1, 298\,K)$ 269.5, ΔG_f° $(1, 298\,K)$ $327.2\,kJ\,mol^{-1}$. It has a repulsive, intensely irritating odour and is a deadly (though non-cumulative) poison; even at concentrations less than 1 ppm in air it can be dangerous. In the gas phase the 3 N atoms are (almost) colinear, as expected for a 16 valence-electron species, and the angle HNN is $109°$; the two N–N distances are appreciably different, as shown in structure (1). The structure and dimensions of the isomeric molecule cyclotriazene are given in (2) for comparison; the N–H bond is tilted out of the plane of the N_3 ring by $74°$.

(1)   (2)

Similar differences are found for organic azides (e.g. MeN_3). In ionic azides (p. 417) the N_3^- ion is both linear and symmetrical (both N–N distances being 116 pm) as befits a 16-electron species isoelectronic with CO_2 (cf. also the cyanamide ion NCN^{2-}, the cyanate ion NCO^-, the fulminate ion CNO^- and the nitronium ion NO_2^+).

Aqueous solutions of HN_3 are about as strongly acidic as acetic acid:

$$HN_3(aq) = H^+(aq) + N_3^-(aq); \quad K_a \; 1.8 \times 10^{-5},$$

$$pK_a \; 4.77 \; at \; 298\,K$$

Numerous metal azides have been characterized (p. 417) and covalent derivatives of non-metals are also readily preparable by simple metathesis using either NaN_3 or aqueous solutions of

HN_3.[82,83] In these compounds the N_3 group behaves as a pseudohalogen (p. 319) and, indeed, the unstable compounds FN_3, ClN_3, BrN_3, IN_3 and NCN_3 are known, though potential allotropes of nitrogen such as N_3–N_3 (analogous to Cl_2) and $N(N_3)_3$ (analogous to NCl_3) have not been isolated. More complex heterocyclic compounds are, however, well established, e.g. cyanuric azide $\{-NC(N_3)-\}_3$, B,B,B-triazidoborazine $\{-NB(N_3)-\}_3$ and even the azidophosphazene derivative $\{-NP(N_3)_2-\}_3$.

Most preparative routes to HN_3 and its derivatives involve the use of NaN_3 since this is reasonably stable and commercially available. NaN_3 can be made by adding powdered $NaNO_3$ to fused $NaNH_2$ at $175°$ or by passing N_2O into the same molten amide at $190°$:

$$NaNO_3 + 3NaNH_2 \longrightarrow NaN_3 + 3NaOH + NH_3$$

$$N_2O + 2NaNH_2 \longrightarrow NaN_3 + NaOH + NH_3$$

The latter reaction is carried out on an industrial scale using liquid NH_3 as solvent; a variant uses Na/NH_3 without isolation of the $NaNH_2$:

$$3N_2O + 4Na + NH_3 \longrightarrow NaN_3 + 3NaOH + 2N_2$$

A remarkable new covalent azide is the pale yellow nitrosyl NNNNO, prepared by reacting gaseous NOCl (p. 441) with solid NaN_3 at low temperature.[84] $NNNN(SO_2F)_2$ has also very recently been made by a similar route from $(SO_2F)_2NCl$; it is a volatile yellow liquid which sometimes decomposes explosively.[84a]

The major use of inorganic azides exploits the explosive nature of heavy metal azides. $Pb(N_3)_2$ in particular is extensively used in detonators because of its reliability, especially in damp conditions; it is prepared by metathesis between $Pb(NO_3)_2$ and NaN_3 in aqueous solution.

---

[82] Pp. 276–93 of ref. 69.

[83] A. D. YOFFE, Chap. 2 in C. B. COLBURN (ed.), *Developments in Inorganic Nitrogen Chemistry*, Vol. 1, pp. 72–149, Elsevier, Amsterdam, 1966.

[84] A. SCHULZ, I. C. TORNIEPORTH-OETTING and T. M. KLAPÖTKE, *Angew. Chem. Int. Edn. Engl.* **32**, 1610–12 (1993).

[84a] H. HOLFTER, T. M. KLAPÖTKE and A. SCHULZ, *Polyhedron* **15**, 1405–7 (1996).

11.3.4 Thermodynamic relations between N-containing species

The ability of N to exist in its compounds in at least 10 different oxidation states from -3 to $+5$ poses certain thermodynamic and mechanistic problems that invite systematic treatment. Thus, in several compounds N exists in more than one oxidation state, e.g. $[N^{-III}H_4]^+[N^{III}O_2]^-$, $[N^{-III}H_4]^+[N^VO_3]^-$, $[N^{-II}_2H_5]^+[N^VO_3]^-$, $[N^{-III}H_4]^+[N^{-\frac{1}{3}}_3]^-$, etc. Furthermore, we have seen (p. 423) that, under appropriate conditions, NH_3 can be oxidized by O_2 to yield N_2, NO or NO_2, whereas oxidation by OCl^- yields N_2H_4 (p. 427). Likewise, using appropriate reagents, N_2H_4 can be oxidized either to N_2 or to HN_3 (in which the "average" oxidation number of N is $-\frac{1}{3}$). The thermodynamic relations between these various hydrido and oxo species containing N can be elegantly codified by means of their standard reduction potentials, and these can be displayed pictorially using the concept of the "volt equivalent" of each species (see Panel).

The standard reduction potentials in acidic aqueous solution are given in Table 11.4; these are shown diagrammatically in Fig. 11.8 (p. 437) which also includes the corresponding data for alkaline solutions. The reduction potentials are readily converted to volt equivalents (by multiplying by the appropriate oxidation state) and these are plotted against oxidation state in Fig. 11.9. This latter diagram is particularly valuable in giving a visual representation of the redox chemistry of the element. Thus, it follows from the definition of "volt equivalent" that the reduction potential of any couple is the *slope* of the line joining the two points: the greater the positive slope the stronger the oxidizing potential and the greater the negative slope the stronger the reducing power. Any pair of points can be joined. For example in acid solution N_2H_4 is a

Table 11.4 Standard reduction potentials for nitrogen species[a] in acidic aqueous solution (pH 0, 25°C)

Couple	$E°/V$	Corresponding half-reaction
N_2/HN_3	-3.09	$\frac{3}{2}N_2 + H^+(aq) + e^- \longrightarrow HN_3(aq)$
$N_2/N_2H_5^+$	-0.23	$N_2 + 5H^+ + 4e^- \longrightarrow N_2H_5^+$
$H_2N_2O_2/NH_3OH^+$	$+0.387$	$H_2N_2O_2 + 6H^+ + 4e^- \longrightarrow 2NH_3OH^+$
HN_3/NH_4^+	$+0.695$	$HN_3 + 11H^+ + 8e^- \longrightarrow 3NH_4^+$
$NO/H_2N_2O_2$	$+0.712$	$2NO + 2H^+ + 2e^- \longrightarrow H_2N_2O_2$
NO_3^-/N_2O_4	$+0.803$	$2NO_3^- + 4H^+ + 2e^- \longrightarrow N_2O_4 + 2H_2O$
$HNO_2/H_2N_2O_2$	$+0.86$	$2HNO_2 + 4H^+ + 4e^- \longrightarrow H_2N_2O_2 + 2H_2O$
NO_3^-/HNO_2	$+0.94$	$NO_3^- + 3H^+ + 2e^- \longrightarrow HNO_2 + H_2O$
NO_3^-/NO	$+0.957$	$NO_3^- + 4H^+ + 3e^- \longrightarrow NO + 2H_2O$
HNO_2/NO	$+0.983$	$HNO_2 + H^+ + e^- \longrightarrow NO + H_2O$
N_2O_4/NO	$+1.035$	$N_2O_4 + 4H^+ + 4e^- \longrightarrow 2NO + 2H_2O$
N_2O_4/HNO_2	$+1.065$	$N_2O_4 + 2H^+ + 2e^- \longrightarrow 2HNO_2$
$N_2H_5^+/NH_4^+$	$+1.275$	$N_2H_5^+ + 3H^+ + 2e^- \longrightarrow 2NH_4^+$
HNO_2/N_2O	$+1.29$	$2HNO_2 + 4H^+ + 4e^- \longrightarrow N_2O + 3H_2O$
NH_3OH^+/NH_4^+	$+1.35$	$NH_3OH^+ + 2H^+ + 2e^- \longrightarrow NH_4^+ + H_2O$
$NH_3OH^+/N_2H_5^+$	$+1.42$	$2NH_3OH^+ + H^+ + 2e^- \longrightarrow N_2H_5^+ + 2H_2O$
HN_3/NH_4^+	$+1.96$	$HN_3 + 3H^+ + 2e^- \longrightarrow NH_4^+ + N_2$
$H_2N_2O_2/N_2$	$+2.65$	$H_2N_2O_2 + 2H^+ + 2e^- \longrightarrow N_2 + 2H_2O$

[a]All the half-reactions listed in this table have only (Ox), H^+ and e^- on the left-hand side of the half-reaction. Others, such as $N_2/NH_3OH^+ - 1.87$ (i.e. $N_2 + 2H_2O + 4H^+ + 2e^- \longrightarrow 2NH_3OH^+$) can readily be calculated by appropriate combinations (in this case, for example, $N_2/N_2H_5^+ - NH_3OH^+/N_2H_5^+$). There are also simple electron addition reactions, e.g. NO^+/NO, $E° + 1.46\,V$ (i.e. $NO^+ + e^- \longrightarrow NO$) and more complex electron additions, e.g. $NO_3^-, NO/NO_2^-$, $E° + 0.49\,V$ (i.e. $NO_3^- + NO + e^- \longrightarrow 2NO_2^-$), etc.

Standard Reduction Potentials and Volt Equivalents

Chemical reactions can often formally be expressed as the sum of two or more "half-reactions" in which electrons are transferred from one chemical species to another. Conventionally these are now almost always represented as equilibria in which the forward reaction is a reduction (addition of electrons):

$$\text{(oxidized form)} + ne^- \rightleftharpoons \text{(reduced form)}$$

The electrochemical reduction potential (E volts) of such an equilibrium is given by

$$E = E° - \frac{2.3026RT}{nF} \log_{10} \frac{a(\text{red})}{a(\text{ox})} \tag{1}$$

where $E°$ is the "standard reduction potential" at unit activity a, R is the gas constant ($8.3144\,\text{J mol}^{-1}\,\text{K}^{-1}$), T is the absolute temperature, F is the Faraday constant ($96\,485\,\text{C mol}^{-1}$) and 2.3026 is the constant $\ln_e 10$ required to convert from natural to decadic logarithms. At 298.15 K (25°C) the factor $2.3026RT/F$ has the value $0.059\,16$ V and, replacing activities by concentrations, one obtains the approximate expression

$$E \approx E° - \frac{0.059\,16}{n} \log_{10} \frac{[\text{red}]}{[\text{ox}]} \tag{2}$$

By convention, $E°$ for the half-reaction (3) is taken as zero, i.e. $E°(H^+/\tfrac{1}{2}H_2) = 0.0$ V:

$$H^+(\text{aq}, a = 1) + e^- \rightleftharpoons \tfrac{1}{2}H_2(\text{g, 1 atm}) \tag{3}$$

Remembering that $\Delta G = -nEF$, it follows that the standard free energy change for the half reaction is $\Delta G° = -nE°F$, e.g.:

$$Fe^{3+}(\text{aq}) + e^- \rightleftharpoons Fe^{2+}(\text{aq}); \quad E°(Fe^{3+}/Fe^{2+}) = 0.771 \text{ V} \tag{4}$$

$$\Delta G° = -74.4\,\text{kJ mol}^{-1}$$

Coupling the half-reactions (3) and (4) gives the reaction (5) {i.e.(4) – (3)} which, because ΔG is negative, proceeds spontaneously from left to right as written:

$$Fe^{3+}(\text{aq}) + \tfrac{1}{2}H_2(\text{g}) \rightleftharpoons Fe^{2+}(\text{aq}) + H^+(\text{aq}); \quad E° = 0.771 \text{ V} \tag{5}$$

$$\Delta G° = -74.4\,\text{kJ mol}^{-1}$$

Again, $E°(Zn^{2+}/Zn) = -0.763$ V, hence reaction (6) occurs spontaneously in the reverse direction:

$$Zn^{2+}(\text{aq}) + H_2(\text{g}) \rightleftharpoons Zn(\text{s}) + 2H^+(\text{aq}); \quad E° = -0.763 \text{ V};$$

$$\Delta G° = +147.5\,\text{kJ mol}^{-1} \text{ (note the factor of 2 for } n\text{)} \tag{6}$$

In summary, at pH 0 a reaction is spontaneous from left to right if $E° > 0$ and spontaneous in the reverse direction if $E° < 0$. At other H-ion concentrations eqn. (2) indicates that the potential of the H electrode (3) will be

$$E = -0.05916 \log \frac{\{P_{H_2}/\text{atm}\}^{\frac{1}{2}}}{\{[H^+(\text{aq})]/\text{mol l}^{-1}\}} \text{ V}$$

and, in general, the potential of any half-reaction changes with the concentration of the species involved according to the Nernst equation (7):

$$E = E° - \frac{0.05916}{n} \log Q \tag{7}$$

where Q has the same form as the equilibrium constant but is a function of the actual activities of the reactants and products rather than those of the equilibrium state. Note also that the potential is independent of the coefficients of the half-reaction whereas the free energy is directly proportional to these, e.g.:

Panel continues

$$\tfrac{1}{2}I_2 + e^- \rightleftharpoons I^-; \quad E^c = 0.536 \text{ V}; \quad \Delta G^\circ = -51.5 \text{ kJ mol}^{-1}$$

$$I_2 + 2e^- \rightleftharpoons 2I^-; \quad E^\circ = 0.536 \text{ V}; \quad \Delta G^\circ = -103.0 \text{ kJ mol}^{-1}$$

It is vital to remember that, when half-reactions are added or subtracted, one should not add or subtract the corresponding E° values but rather nE°. (We shall return to this point later.)

Lists of standard reduction potentials are given in many books[85] and are extensively quoted throughout this text. Almost all lists now use the IUPAC sign conventions employed above, though some earlier American books (including, unfortunately, the classic early text on the subject[86]) use the opposite sign convention. When standard reduction potentials are listed in sequence from the most negative to the most positive the strongest reducing agents are at the top of the list and a reducing agent should, in principle, be capable of reducing all oxidizing agents lying below it in the table. Conversely, the oxidizing agents are listed in order of *increasing* strength and a given oxidizing agent should be able to oxidize all reducing agents lying above it in the table. Such lists are an extremely compact way of summarizing a great deal of predictive information. For example a list of 100 independent reduction potentials enables the free energy change for $100 \times 99/2 = 4950$ reactions to be calculated and indicates the direction in which a hypothetical reaction would occur under appropriate conditions (which might involve the use of a catalyst).

When an element can exist in several oxidation states it is sometimes convenient to display the various reduction potentials diagramatically, the corresponding half-reactions under standard conditions being implied. Thus, in acidic aqueous solutions

Note that the value of $E^\circ(\text{Fe}^{3+}/\text{Fe}) = -0.04$ V is equivalent to $\{(2 \times -0.44) + 0.77\}/3$. Because the quantity nE° is used in these calculations (rather than E°) it is convenient to define the "volt equivalent" of a species; the volt equivalent of a compound or ion is the reduction potential of the species relative to the element in its standard state multiplied by the oxidation state of the element in the compound (including its sign). The oxidation state is the number of electrons that must be added to an atom of an element to regain electroneutrality when all other atoms in the compound (ion) have been removed as their "normal" ions. For example the oxidation state of Fe is +6 in FeO_4^{2-}:

$$\text{FeO}_4^{2-} \xrightarrow{-4\text{O}^{2-}} \text{Fe}^{6+} \xrightarrow{+6e^-} \text{Fe}$$

It follows that, in the above example, the volt equivalents of Fe^{2+} and Fe^{3+} are -0.88 and -0.11 respectively and that of FeO_4^{2-} is $+6.49$ {i.e. $(2 \times -0.44) + 0.77 + (3 \times 2.20)$}. This leads to $E^\circ(\text{FeO}_4^{2-}/\text{Fe}) = +1.08$ V.

The power of these various concepts in codifying and rationalizing the redox chemistry of the elements is illustrated for the case of nitrogen in the present section. Standard reduction potentials and plots of volt equivalents against oxidation state for other elements are presented in later chapters.

stronger reducing agent than H_2 (slope of tie-line -0.23 V) and NH_2OH is even stronger (slope -1.87 V). By contrast, the couple N_2O/NH_3OH^+ has virtually the same reducing power as H_2 (slope -0.05 V).

It also follows that, when three (or more) oxidation states lie approximately on a straight line in the volt-equivalent diagram, they tend to form an equilibrium mixture rather than a reaction going to completion (provided that the attainment of thermodynamic equilibrium is not hindered kinetically). This is because the slopes joining the several points are almost the same, so that E° for the various couples (and hence ΔG°) are the same; there is consequently approximately zero change in free energy and a balanced

[85] A. J. BARD, R. PARSONS and J. JORDAN *Standard Potentials in Aqueous Solution*, Marcel Dekker, New York, 1985, 834 pp. G. MILAZZO and S. CAROLI, *Tables of Standard Electrode Potentials*, Wiley, New York, 1978, 421 pp.

[86] W. M. LATIMER, *The Oxidation States of the Elements and their Potentials in Aqueous Solutions*, 2nd edn., Prentice-Hall, New York, 1952, 392 pp.

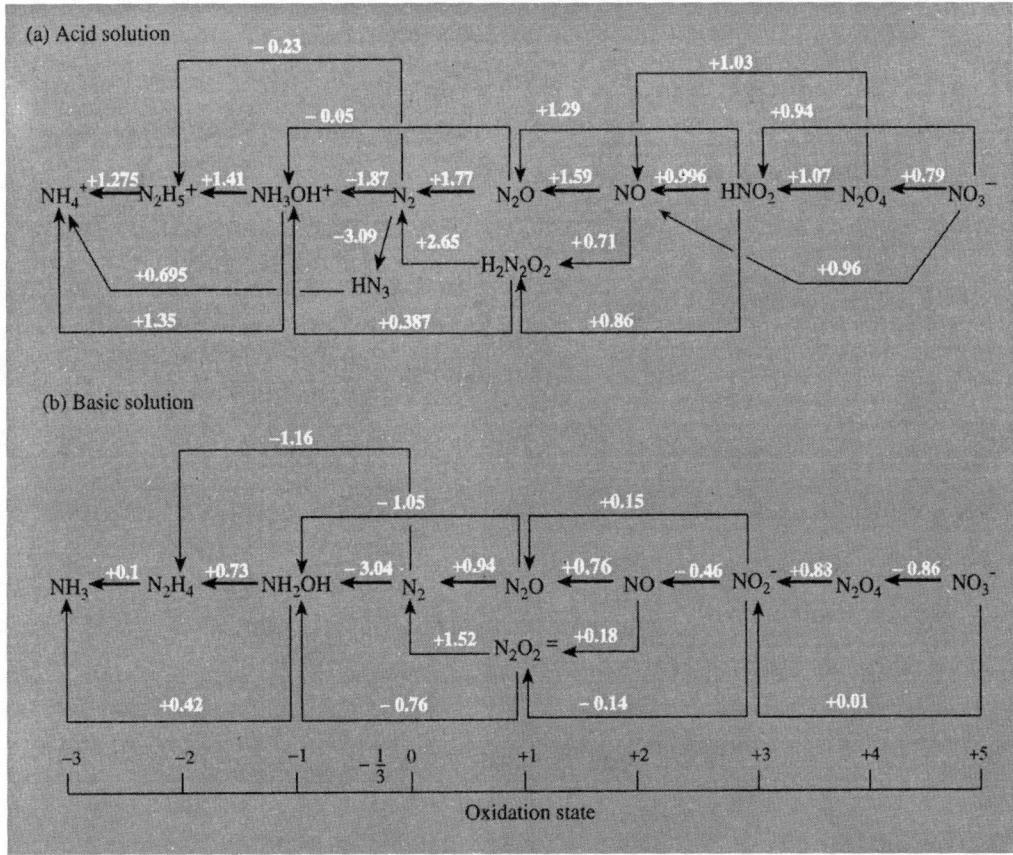

Figure 11.8 Oxidation states of nitrogen showing standard reduction potentials in volts: (a) in acid solution at pH 0, and (b) in basic solution at pH 14.

equilibrium is maintained between the several species. Indeed, the volt-equivalent diagram is essentially a plot of free energy versus oxidation state (as indicated by the right-hand ordinate of Fig. 11.9).

Two further points follow from these general considerations:

(a) a compound will tend to disproportionate into a higher and a lower oxidation state if it lies above the line joining the 2 compounds in these oxidation states, i.e. disproportionation is accompanied by a decrease in free energy and will tend to occur spontaneously if not kinetically hindered. Examples are the disproportionation of hydroxylamine in acidic solutions (slow) and alkaline solutions (fast):

$$4NH_3OH^+ \longrightarrow N_2O + 2NH_4^+ + 3H_2O + 2H^+$$

$$3NH_2OH \longrightarrow N_2 + NH_3 + 3H_2O$$

(b) Conversely, a compound can be formed by conproportionation of compounds in which the element has a higher and lower oxidation state if it lies below the line joining these two states. A particularly important example is the synthesis of $HN_3^{-\frac{1}{3}}$ by reacting $N_2^{-II}H_5^+$ and $HN^{+III}O_2$ (p. 432). It will be noted that the reduction potential of HN_3 (-3.09 V) is more negative than that of any other reducing agent in acidic aqueous solution so it is thermodynamically impossible to synthesize HN_3 by reduction of N_2 or any of its compounds in such media unless the reducing agent itself contains N (as does hydrazine).

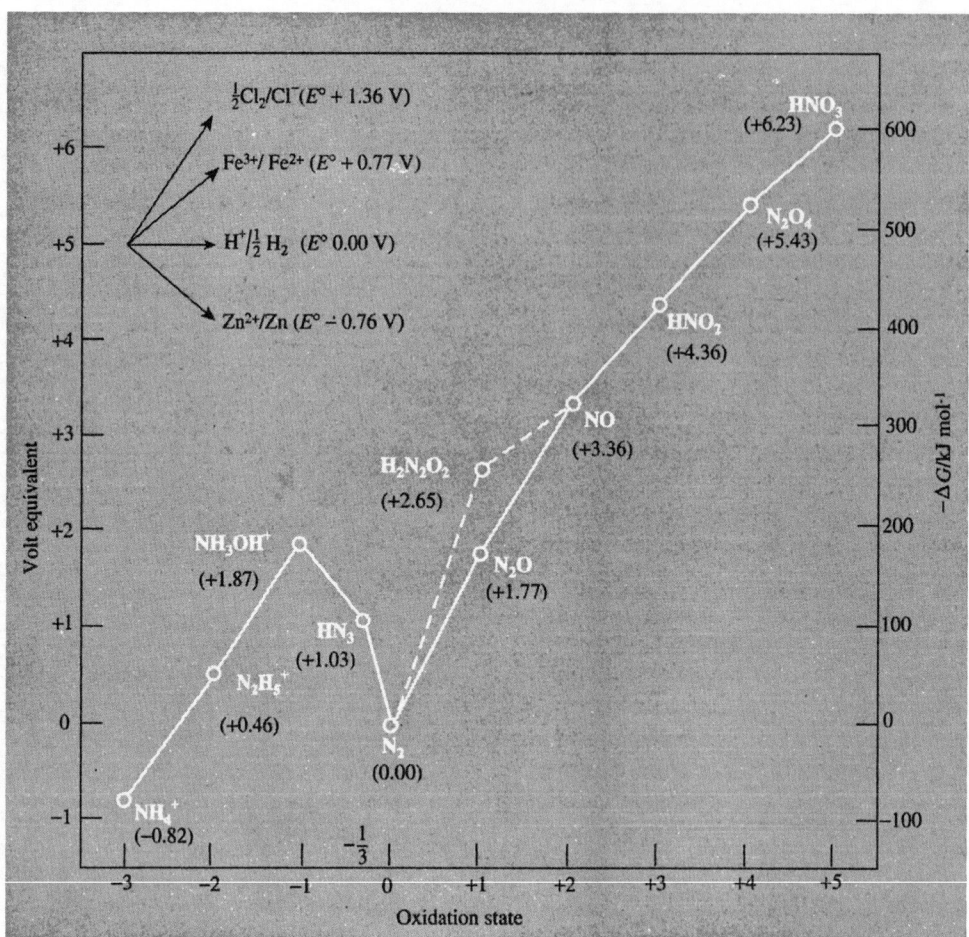

Figure 11.9 Plot of volt equivalent against oxidation state for various compounds or ions containing N in acidic aqueous solution. Note that values of $-\Delta G$ refer to N_2 as standard (zero) but are quoted per mol of N atoms and per mol of N_2; they refer to reactions in the direction (ox) $+ ne^- \rightarrow$ (red). Slopes corresponding to some common oxidizing and reducing agents are included for comparison.

In basic solutions a different set of redox equilibria obtain and a different set of reduction potentials must be used. For example:

	$E°$/V
$N_2 + 4H_2O + 2e^- = 2NH_2OH + 2OH^-$	-3.04
$N_2 + 4H_2O + 4e^- = N_2H_4 + 4OH^-$	-1.16
$N_2O + 5H_2O + 4e^- = 2NH_2OH + 4OH^-$	-1.05
$N_2O_2^{2-} + 6H_2O + 4e^- = 2NH_2OH + 6OH^-$	-0.73
$NO_3^- + H_2O + 2e^- = NO_2^- + 2OH^-$	$+0.01$
$N_2H_4 + 4H_2O + 2e^- = 2NH_4^+ + 4OH^-$	$+0.11$
$2NH_2OH + 2e^- = N_2H_4 + 2OH^-$	$+0.73$

A more complete compilation is summarized in Fig. 11.8. It is instructive to use these data to derive a plot of volt equivalent versus oxidation state in basic solution and to compare this with Fig. 11.9 which refers to acidic solutions.

11.3.5 Nitrogen halides and related compounds [69]

It is a curious paradox that NF_3, the most stable binary halide of N, was not prepared until 1928, more than 115 y after the highly unstable

NCl$_3$ was prepared in 1811 by P. L. Dulong (who lost three fingers and an eye studying its properties). Pure NBr$_3$ explodes even at $-100°$ and was not isolated until 1975[87] and NI$_3$ has not been prepared, though the explosive adduct NI$_3$.NH$_3$ was first made by B. Courtois in 1813 and several other ammines are known. In all, there are now 5 binary fluorides of nitrogen (NF$_3$, N$_2$F$_4$, *cis*- and *trans*-N$_2$F$_2$ and N$_3$F) and these, together with the cations NF$_4^+$ and N$_2$F$_3^+$ and various mixed halides, hydride halides and oxohalides are discussed in this section.

NF$_3$ was first prepared by Otto Ruff's group in Germany by the electrolysis of molten NH$_4$F/HF and this process is still used commercially. An alternative is the controlled fluorination of NH$_3$ over a Cu metal catalyst.

$$4NH_3 + 3F_2 \xrightarrow{\text{Cu}} NF_3 + 3NH_4F$$

NF$_3$ is a colourless, odourless, thermodynamically stable gas (mp $-206.8°$, bp $-129.0°$, $\Delta G_{298}° - 83.3\,\text{kJ mol}^{-1}$). The molecule is pyramidal with an F—N—F angle of $102.5°$, but the dipole moment (0.234 D) is only one-sixth of that of NH$_3$ (1.47 D) presumably because the N—F bond moments act in the opposite direction to that of the lone-pair moment:

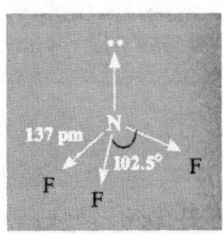

The gas is remarkably unreactive (like CF$_4$) being unaffected by water or dilute aqueous acid or alkali; at elevated temperatures it acts as a fluorinating agent and with Cu, As, Sb or Bi in a flow reactor it yields N$_2$F$_4$ (2NF$_3$ + 2Cu $\rightarrow$ N$_2$F$_4$ + 2CuF). As perhaps expected (p. 198) NF$_3$ shows little tendency to act as a

ligand, though NF$_4^+$ is known[88] and also the surprisingly stable isoelectronic species ONF$_3$ (mp $-160°$, bp $-87.6°$):

$$NF_3 + 2F_2 + SbF_3 \xrightarrow{200°/100\ \text{atm}} [NF_4]^+[SbF_6]^-$$

$$2NF_3 + O_2 \xrightarrow[-196°]{\text{electric discharge/}} 2ONF_3$$

$$3FNO + 2IrF_6 \xrightarrow{20°} ONF_3 + 2[NO]^+[IrF_6]^-$$

ONF$_3$ was discovered independently by two groups in 1966.[89] Although isoelectronic with BF$_4^-$, CF$_4$ and NF$_4^+$ it has excited interest because of the short N—O distance (115.8 pm), which implies some multiple bonding, and the correspondingly long N—F distances (143.1 pm). Similar partial double bonding to O and highly polar bonds to F have also been postulated for the analogous ion [OCF$_3$]$^-$ in Cs[OCF$_3$].[90]

FN$_3$ is one of the most explosive and thermally unstable covalent azides known. It can be prepared by reacting HN$_3$ with F$_2$ and is best handled as a gas at low pressure.[91] The molecular parameters (microwave) are N—F 144.4 pm, N$_\alpha$—N$_\beta$ 125.3 pm, N$_\alpha$—N$_\omega$ 113.2 pm, and angles FNN 103.8°, NNN 170.9° (cf HN$_3$ p. 433) The species NF is known only as a ligand, in the octahedral complex [ReF$_5$(NF)][92] the complex is made by treating ReF$_4$N or ReF$_3$N with XeF$_2$ and X-ray structural analysis revealed a linear Re—N—F group (178°) with N—F 126 pm.

Dinitrogen tetrafluoride, N$_2$F$_4$, is the fluorine analogue of hydrazine and exists in both the staggered (*trans*) C_{2h} and *gauche* C_2 conformations

[87] J. LANDER, J. KNACKMUSS and K.-U. THIEDEMANN, *Z. Naturforsch.* **B30**, 464–5 (1975).

[88] K. O. CHRISTE, C. H. SCHACK and R. D. WILSON, *Inorg. Chem.* **16**, 849–54 (1977), and references therein. See also K. O. CHRISTE, R. D. WILSON and I. R. GOLDBERG, *Inorg. Chem.* **18**, 2572–7 (1979). K. O. CHRISTE, R. D. WILSON and C. J. SCHACK, *Inorg. Chem.* **19**, 3046–9 (1980).

[89] See S. A. KINREAD and J. M. SHREEVE, *Inorg. Chem.* **23** 3109–12, 4174–7 (1984) for useful references to preparation and reactions of ONF$_3$.

[90] K. O. CHRISTE, E. C. CURTIS and C. J. SCHACK, *Spectrochim. Acta* **31A**, 1035–8 (1975).

[91] D. CHRISTEN, H. G. MACK, G. SCHATTE and H. WILLNER, *J. Am. Chem. Soc.* **110**, 707–12 (1988).

[92] J. FAWCETT, R. D. PEACOCK and D. R. RUSSELL, *J. Chem. Soc., Dalton Trans.*, 567–71 (1987).

(p. 428). It was discovered in 1957 and is now made either by partial defluorination of NF_3 (see above) or by quantitative oxidation of NF_2H with alkaline hypochlorite:

$$(NH_2)_2CO(aq) \xrightarrow[(70\% \text{ yield})]{F_2/N_2} NH_2CONF_2$$

$$\xrightarrow[(100\% \text{ yield})]{\text{conc } H_2SO_4} NF_2H \xrightarrow[(100\% \text{ yield})]{NaOCl (pH 12)} \tfrac{1}{2}N_2F_4$$

N_2F_4 is a colourless reactive gas (mp $-164.5°$, bp $-73°$, $\Delta G_{298}^{\circ} + 81.2\,\text{kJ mol}^{-1}$) which acts as a strong fluorinating agent towards many substances, e.g.:

$$SiH_4 + N_2F_4 \xrightarrow{25°} SiF_4 + N_2 + 2H_2$$

$$10Li + N_2F_4 \xrightarrow{-80 \text{ to } +250°} 4LiF + 2Li_3N$$

$$S + N_2F_4 \xrightarrow{110-140°} SF_4 + SF_5NF_2 + \dots$$

It forms adducts with strong fluoride-ion acceptors such as AsF_5 which can be formulated as salts, e.g. $[N_2F_3]^+[AsF_6]^-$. However, its most intriguing property is an ability to dissociate at room temperature and above to give the free radical NF_2. Thus, when N_2F_4 is frozen out from the warm gas at relatively low pressures the solid is dark blue whereas when it is frozen out from the cold gas at moderate pressures it is colourless. At 150°C the equilibrium constant for the dissociation $N_2F_4 \rightleftharpoons 2NF_2$ is $K = 0.03$ atm and the enthalpy of dissociation is $83.2\,\text{kJ mol}^{-1}$.[93] Such a dissociation, which interprets much of the reaction chemistry of N_2F_4,[94] is reminiscent of the behaviour of N_2O_4 (p. 455) but is not paralleled in the chemistry of N_2H_4:

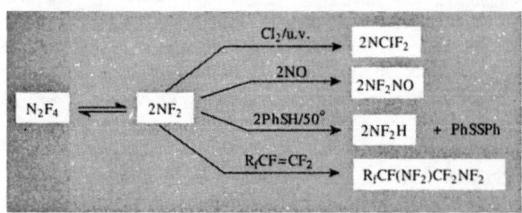

Dinitrogen difluoride, N_2F_2, was first identified in 1952 as a thermal decomposition product of the azide N_3F and it also occurs in small yield during the electrolysis of NH_4F/HF (p. 439), and in the reactions of NF_3 with Hg or with NF_3 in a Cu reactor (p. 439). Fluorination of NaN_3 gives good yields on a small scale but the compound is best prepared by the following reaction sequence:

$$KF + NF_2H \xrightarrow{-80°} KF.NF_2H$$

$$\xrightarrow[\sim 100\% \text{ yield}]{20°} N_2F_2 + KHF_2$$

All these methods give mixtures of the *cis*- and *trans*-isomers; these are thermally interconvertible but can be separated by low-temperature fractionation. The *trans*-form is thermodynamically more unstable than the *cis*-form but it can be stored in glass vessels whereas the *cis*-form reacts completely within 2 weeks to give SiF_4 and N_2O. *Trans*-N_2F_2 can be prepared free of the *cis*-form by the low-temperature reaction of N_2F_4 with $AlCl_3$ or MCl_2 (M = Mn, Fe, Co, Ni, Sn); thermal isomerization of *trans*-N_2F_2 at $70-100°$ yields an equilibrium mixture containing $\sim 90\%$ *cis*-N_2F_2 (ΔH_{isom} $12.5\,\text{kJ mol}^{-1}$). Pure *cis*-N_2F_2 can be obtained by selective complexation with AsF_5; only the *cis*-form reacts at room temperature to give $[N_2F]^+[AsF_6]^-$ and this, when treated with NaF/HF, yields pure *cis*-N_2F_2. Some characteristic properties are listed below.

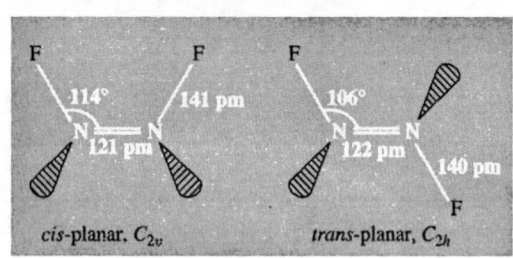

cis-planar, C_{2v} *trans*-planar, C_{2h}

Isomer	MP/°C	BP/°C	$\Delta H_f^{\circ}/\text{kJ mol}^{-1}$	μ/Debye
cis-N_2F_2	< -195	-105.7	69.5	0.18
trans-N_2F_2	-172	-111.4	82.0	0.00

93 F. H. JOHNSON and C. B. COLBURN, *J. Am. Chem. Soc.* **83**, 3043–7 (1961).

94 C. L. BAUMGARDNER and E. L. LAWTON, *Acc. Chem. Res.* **7**, 14–20 (1974).

Several mixed halides and hydrohalides of nitrogen are known but they tend to be unstable, difficult to isolate pure, and of little interest. Examples are[69] $NClF_2$, NCl_2F, $NBrF_2$, NF_2H, NCl_2H and $NClH_2$. The cation $NH_2F_2{}^+$ has also been prepared as its salts with $AsF_6{}^-$ and $SbF_6{}^-$.[95]

The well known compound NCl_3 is a dense, volatile, highly explosive liquid (mp $-40°$, bp $+71°$, $d(20°)$ $1.65\,g\,cm^{-3}$, μ 0.6 D) with physical properties which often closely resemble those of CCl_4 (p. 301). It is much less hazardous as a dilute gas and, indeed, is used industrially on a large scale for the bleaching and sterilizing of flour; for this purpose it is prepared by electrolysing an acidic solution of NH_4Cl at pH 4 and the product gas is swept out of the cell by means of a flow of air for immediate use. NCl_3 is rapidly hydrolysed by moisture and in alkaline solution can be used to prepare ClO_2:

$$NCl_3 + 3H_2O \longrightarrow NH_3 + 3HOCl \text{ (bleach, etc.)}$$

$$NCl_3 + 3H_2O + 6NaClO_2 \longrightarrow 6ClO_2 + 3NaCl$$
$$+ 3NaOH + NH_3$$

$$2NCl_3 + 6NaClO_2 \longrightarrow 6ClO_2 + 6NaCl + N_2$$

The elusive NBr_3 was finally prepared as a deep-red, very temperature-sensitive, volatile solid by the low-temperature bromination of bistrimethylsilylbromamine with BrCl:

$$(Me_3Si)_2NBr + 2BrCl \xrightarrow{\text{pentane}/-87°} NBr_3 + 2MeSiCl$$

It reacts instantly with NH_3 in CH_2Cl_2 solution at $-87°$ to give the dark-violet solid $NBrH_2$; under similar conditions I_2 yields the red-brown solid NBr_2I. The ligands NCl and NBr have been characterized in the purple complexes $[ReF_5(NCl)]$ (mp $\sim80°$, N–Cl 156 pm, angle Re–N–Cl 177°) and $[ReF_5(NBr)]$ (mp $\sim140°$); The preparation parallels that of $[ReF_5(NF)]$ (p. 439), the reagent XeF_2 being replaced by ClF_3 and BrF_3, respectively.[92] The complexes

$[VCl_3(NX)]$ (X = Cl, Br, I) have also been characterized.[96]

Pure NI_3 has not been isolated, but the structure of its well-known extremely shock-sensitive adduct with NH_3 has been elucidated — a feat of considerable technical virtuosity.[97] Unlike the volatile, soluble, molecular solid NCl_3, the involatile, insoluble compound $[NI_3.NH_3]_n$ has a polymeric structure in which tetrahedral NI_4 units are corner-linked into infinite chains of $-N-I-N-I-$ (215 and 230 pm) which in turn are linked into sheets by I–I interactions (336 pm) in the c-direction; in addition, one I of each NI_4 unit is also loosely attached to an NH_3 (253 pm) that projects into the space between the sheets of tetrahedra. The structure resembles that of the linked SiO_4 units in chain metasilicates (p. 349). A further interesting feature is the presence of linear or almost linear N–I–N groupings which suggest the presence of 3-centre, 4-electron bonds (pp. 63, 64) characteristic of polyhalides and xenon halides (pp. 835–8, 897).

Nitrogen forms two series of oxohalides — the nitrosyl halides XNO and the nitryl halides XNO_2. There are also two halogen nitrates $FONO_2$ (bp $-46°$) and $ClONO_2$ (bp 22.3°), but these do not contain N–X bonds and can be considered as highly reactive derivatives of nitric acid, from which they can be prepared by direct halogenation:

$$HNO_3 + F_2 \longrightarrow FONO_2 + HF$$

$$HNO_3 + ClF \longrightarrow ClONO_2 + HF$$

The nitrosyl halides are reactive gases that feature bent molecules; they can be made by direct halogenation of NO with X_2, though fluorination of NO with AgF_2 has also been used and ClNO can be more conveniently made by passing N_2O_4 over moist KCl:

$$2NO + X_2 \longrightarrow 2XNO$$

---

95 K. O. CHRISTE, *Inorg. Chem.* **14**, 2821–4 (1975).

96 J. STRÄHLE and K. DEHNICKE, *Z. anorg. allg. Chem.* **338**, 287–98 (1965). K. DEHNICKE and W. LIEBETT, *Z. anorg. allg. Chem.* **453**, 9–13 (1979).

97 J. JANDER, Recent chemistry and structure investigation of NI_3, NBr_3, NCl_3 and related compounds, *Adv. Inorg. Chem. Radiochem.* **19**, 1–63 (1976).

$$NO + AgF_2 \longrightarrow FNO + AgF$$

$$N_2O_4 + KCl \longrightarrow ClNO + KNO_3$$

Some physical properties are in Table 11.5. FNO is colourless, ClNO orange-yellow and BrNO red. The compounds, though generally less reactive than the parent halogens, are nevertheless extremely vigorous reagents. Thus FNO fluorinates many metals (nFNO + M → MF$_n$ + nNO) and also reacts with many fluorides to form salt-like adducts such as NOAsF$_6$, NOVF$_6$, and NOBF$_4$. ClNO acts similarly and has been used as an ionizing solvent to prepare complexes such as NOAlCl$_4$, NOFeCl$_4$, NOSbCl$_6$, and (NO)$_2$SnCl$_6$.[98] Aqueous solutions of XNO are particularly potent solvents for metals (like aqua regia, HNO$_3$/HCl) since the HNO$_2$ formed initially, reacts to give HNO$_3$:

$$XNO + H_2O \longrightarrow HNO_2 + HX$$

$$3HNO_2 \longrightarrow HNO_3 + 2NO + H_2O$$

Alkaline solutions contain a similar mixture:

$$4XNO + 3H_2O \longrightarrow HNO_3 + HNO_2 + 2NO + 4HX$$

$$4XNO + 6NaOH \longrightarrow NaNO_3 + NaNO_2 + 2NO$$
$$+ 4NaX + 3H_2O$$

With alcohols, however, the reaction stops at the nitrite stage:

$$XNO + ROH \longrightarrow RONO + HX$$

Nitryl fluoride and chloride, XNO$_2$, like their nitrosyl analogues, are reactive gases; they feature planar molecules, analogous to the

[98] V. GUTMANN (ed.), in *Halogen Chemistry*, Vol. 2, p. 399, Academic Press, London, 1967; and V. GUTMANN, *Coordination Chemistry in Nonaqueous Solutions*, Springer-Verlag, New York, 1968.

Table 11.5 Some physical properties of XNO[a]

Property	FNO	ClNO	BrNO
MP/°C	−132.5	−59.6	−56
BP/°C	−59.9	−6.4	∼0.
ΔH_f°(298 K)/kJ mol^{-1}	−66.5	+51.7	+82.2
ΔG_f°(298 K)/kJ mol^{-1}	−51.1	+66.0	+82.4
Angle X−N−O	110°	113°	117°
Distance N−O/pm	113	114	115
Distance N−X/pm	152	198	214
μ/D	1.81	0.42	—

[a]BrNO dissociates reversibly into NO and Br, the extent of dissociation being ∼7% at room temperature and 1 atm pressure. A similar reversible dissociation occurs with ClNO at higher temperatures.

isoelectronic nitrate anion, NO$_3^-$. Some physical properties are in Table 11.6. FNO$_2$ can be prepared by direct reaction of F$_2$ with NO$_2$ or NaNO$_2$ or by fluorination of NO$_2$ using CoF$_3$ at 300°. ClNO$_2$ can not be made by direct chlorination of NO$_2$ but is conveniently synthesized in high yield by reacting anhydrous nitric acid with chlorosulfuric acid at 0°C:

$$HNO_3 + ClSO_3H \longrightarrow ClNO_2 + H_2SO_4$$

Reactions of XNO$_2$ often parallel those of XNO; e.g. FNO$_2$ readily fluorinates many metals and reacts with the fluorides of non-metals to give nitryl "salts" such as NO$_2$BF$_4$, NO$_2$PF$_6$, etc. Likewise, ClNO$_2$ reacts with many chlorides in liquid Cl$_2$ to give complexes such as NO$_2$SbCl$_6$. Hydrolysis yields aqueous solutions of nitric and hydrochloric acids, whereas ammonolysis in liquid ammonia yields chloramine and ammonium nitrite:

$$ClNO_2 + H_2O \longrightarrow \{HOCl + HNO_2\}$$
$$\longrightarrow HNO_3 + HCl$$

$$ClNO_2 + 2NH_3 \longrightarrow ClNH_2 + NH_4NO_2$$

Table 11.6 Some physical properties of XNO$_2$

Property	FNO$_2$	ClNO$_2$	Property	FNO$_2$	ClNO$_2$
MP/°C	−166	−145	Angle X−N−O	118°	115°
BP/°C	−72.5	−15.9	Distance (N−O)/pm	123	120
ΔH_f°(298K)/kJ mol^{-1}	−80	+13	Distance (N−X)/pm	135	184
ΔG_f°(298K)/kJ mol^{-1}	−37.2	+54.4	μ/D	0.47	0.42

11.3.6 Oxides of nitrogen

Nitrogen is unique among the elements in forming no fewer than 8 molecular oxides, 3 of which are paramagnetic and all of which are thermodynamically unstable with respect to decomposition into N_2 and O_2. In addition there is evidence for fugitive species such as nitryl azide, N_3NO_2, but this decomposes rapidly below room temperature[99] and will not be considered further. Three of the oxides (N_2O, NO and NO_2) have been known for over 200 y and were, in fact, amongst the very first gaseous compounds to be isolated and identified (J. Priestley and others in the 1770s). The most recent addition, nitrosyl azide N_4O (p. 433), was isolated in 1993 as a pale yellow solid whose vibration spectrum at $-110°$ is consistent with the optimized computed structure (3).[84]

(3)

The physiological effects of N_2O (laughing gas, anaesthetic) and NO_2 (acrid, corrosive fumes) have been known from the earliest days, and the environmental problems of "NO_x" from automobile exhaust fumes and as a component in photochemical smog are well known in all industrial countries.[100,101] NO is now recognized as a key neuro transmitter in humans and other animals and its biologically triggered synthesis is implicated in cardiovascular pharmacology, hypertension, impotence, immunology and other vital functions.[102] NO and NO_2 are important in

[99] M. P. DOYLE, J. J. MACIEJKO and S. C. BUSMAN, *J. Am. Chem. Soc.* **95**, 952–3 (1973).

[100] S. D. LEE (ed.), *Nitrogen Oxides and their Effects on Health*, Ann Arbor Publishers, Michigan, 1980, 382 pp.

[101] H. BOSCH and F. J. J. JANSSEN, *Catalytic Reduction of Nitrogen Oxides*, Elsevier, Amsterdam, 1988, 164 pp.

[102] K. CULOTTA and D. E. KOSHLAND, *Science* **258**, 1862–5 (1992). J. S. STAMLER, D. J. SINGEL and J. S. LOSCALZO, *Science* **258**, 1898–901 (1992). P. L. FELDMAN, O. W. GRIFFITH

the commercial production of nitric acid (p. 466) and nitrate fertilizers and N_2O_4 has been used extensively as the oxidizer in rocket fuels for space missions (p. 429).

The oxides of nitrogen played an important role in exemplifying Dalton's law of multiple proportions which led up to the formulation of his atomic theory (1803–8), and they still pose some fascinating problems in bonding theory. Their formulae, molecular structure, and physical appearance are briefly summarized in Table 11.7 and each compound is discussed in turn in the following sections.

Nitrous oxide (Dinitrogen monoxide), N_2O

Nitrous oxide can be made by the careful thermal decomposition of molten NH_4NO_3 at about $250°C$:

$$NH_4NO_3 \xrightarrow{\Delta} N_2O + 2H_2O$$

Although the reaction has the overall stoichiometry of a dehydration it is more complex than this and involves a mutual redox reaction between N^{-III} and N^V. This is at once explicable in terms of the volt-equivalent diagram in Fig. 11.9 which also interprets why NO and N_2 are formed simultaneously as byproducts. It is probable that the mechanism involves dissociation of NH_4NO_3 into NH_3 and HNO_3, followed by autoprotolysis of HNO_3 to give NO_2^+, which is the key intermediate:

$$NH_4NO_3 \rightleftharpoons NH_3 + HNO_3$$

$$2HNO_3 \rightleftharpoons NO_2^+ + H_2O + NO_3^-$$

$$NH_3 + NO_2^+ \longrightarrow \{H_3NNO_2\}^+$$

$$\longrightarrow NNO + H_3O^+, \text{ etc.}$$

Consistent with this ^{15}NNO can be made from $^{15}NH_4NO_3$, and $N^{15}NO$ from $NH_4{}^{15}NO_3$. Alternative preparative routes (Fig. 11.9) are the reduction of aqueous nitrous acid with either hydroxylamine or hydrogen azide:

and D. J. STUEHR, *Chem. and Eng. News*, 26–38, 20 December 1993. C. R. TIGGLE, *Pharmaceutical News* **1** (3), 9–14 (1994).

Table 11.7   The oxides of nitrogen (See also structure 3, p. 443)

Formula	Name	Structure	Description
N_2O	Dinitrogen monoxide (nitrous oxide)	N—N—O linear ($C_{\infty v}$)	Colourless gas (bp −88.5°) (cf. isoelectronic CO_2, $NO_2{}^+$, $N_3{}^-$)
NO	(Mono) nitrogen monoxide	N—O	Colourless paramagnetic gas (bp −151.8°); liquid and solid are also colourless when pure
N_2O_3	Dinitrogen trioxide	planar (C_s)	Blue solid (mp −100.7°), dissociates reversibly in gas phase into NO and NO_2
NO_2	Nitrogen dioxide	bent (C_{2v})	Brown paramagnetic gas, dimerizes reversibly to N_2O_4
N_2O_4	Dinitrogen tetroxide	planar D_{2h}	Colourless liquid (mp −11.2°) dissociates reversibly in gas phase to NO_2
N_2O_5	Dinitrogen pentoxide	$[NO_2]^+[NO_3]^-$ planar C2v (~D_{2h})	Colourless ionic solid; sublimes at 32.4° to unstable molecular gas (angle N–O–N ~180°)
NO_3	Nitrogen trioxide	planar (D_{3h})	Unstable paramagnetic radical

$$HNO_2 + NH_2OH \xrightarrow{\text{aq}} N_2O + 2H_2O$$

$$HNO_2 + HN_3 \xrightarrow{\text{aq}} N_2O + N_2 + H_2O$$

Thermal decomposition of nitramide, H_2NNO_2, or hyponitrous acid $H_2N_2O_2$ (both of which have the empirical formula $N_2O.H_2O$) have also been used. The mechanisms of these and other reactions involving simple inorganic compounds of N have been reviewed.[103]

However, though N_2O can be made in this way it is not to be regarded as the anhydride of hyponitrous acid since $H_2N_2O_2$ is not formed when N_2O is dissolved in H_2O (a similar relation exists between CO and formic acid).

Nitrous oxide is a moderately unreactive gas comprised of linear unsymmetrical molecules, as expected for a 16-electron triatomic species (p. 433). The symmetrical structure N–O–N is precluded on the basis of orbital energetics. Some physical properties are in Table 11.8: it will be seen that the N–N and N–O distances are

[103] G. STEDMAN, *Adv. Inorg. Chem. Radiochem.* **22**, 114–70 (1979). See also F. T. BONNER and N.-Y. WANG, *Inorg. Chem.* **25**, 1858–62 (1986).

Table 11.8 Some physical properties of N_2O

MP/°C	−90.86	μ/D	0.166
BP/°C	−88.48	Distance (N–N)/pm	112.6
$\Delta H_f^\circ(298\,K)/kJ\,mol^{-1}$	82.0	Distance (N–O)/pm	118.6
$\Delta G_f^\circ(298\,K)/kJ\,mol^{-1}$	104.2		

both short and calculations[104] give the bond orders as N–N 2.73 and N–O 1.61. N_2O is thermodynamically unstable and when heated above ~600°C it dissociates by fission of the weaker bond ($N_2O \rightarrow N_2 + \frac{1}{2}O_2$). However, the reaction is much more complex than this simple equation might imply and the process involves a "forbidden" singlet-triplet transition in which electron spin is not conserved.[105] The activation energy for the process is high (~250 kJ mol^{-1}) and at room temperature N_2O is relatively inert: e.g. it does not react with the halogens, the alkali metals or even ozone. At higher temperatures reactivity increases markedly: H_2 gives N_2 and H_2O; many other non-metals (and some metals) react to form oxides, and the gas supports combustion. Perhaps its most remarkable reaction is with molten alkali metal amides to yield azides, the reaction with $NaNH_2$ being the commercial route to NaN_3 and hence all other azides (p. 433):

$$NaNH_2(1) + N_2O(g) \xrightarrow{200°} NaN_3 + H_2O(g)$$

$$NaNH_2 + H_2O \longrightarrow NaOH + NH_3(g)$$

It is also notable that N_2O (like N_2 itself) can act as a ligand by displacing H_2O from the aquo complex $[Ru(NH_3)_5(H_2O)]^{2+}$:[106]

$$[Ru(NH_3)_5(H_2O)]^{2+} + N_2O(aq) \longrightarrow$$
$$[Ru(NH_3)_5(N_2O)]^{2+} + H_2O$$

The formation constant K is 7.0 mol^{-1} l for N_2O and 3.3×10^4 mol^{-1} l for N_2.

[104] K. JUG, *J. Am. Chem. Soc.* **100**, 6581–6 (1978).

[105] I. R. BEATTIE, Nitrous Oxide, Section 24 in *Mellor's Comprehensive Treatise on Inorganic and Theoretical Chemistry*, Vol. 8, pp. 189–215, Supplement 2, *Nitrogen* (Part 2), Longmans, London, 1967.

[106] J. N. ARMOR and H. TAUBE, *J. Am. Chem. Soc.* **91**, 6874–6 (1969). A. A. DIAMANTIS and G. J. SPARROW, *J. Chem. Soc., Chem. Commun.*, 819–20 (1970). J. N. ARMOR and H. TAUBE, *J. Chem. Soc., Chem. Commun.*, 287–8 (1971).

Notwithstanding the fascinating reaction chemistry of N_2O it is salutory to remember that its largest commercial use is as a propellant and aerating agent for "whipped" ice-cream — this depends on its solubility under pressure in vegetable fats coupled with its non-toxicity in small concentrations and its absence of taste. It was also formerly much used as an anaesthetic.

Nitric oxide (Nitrogen monoxide), NO

Nitric oxide is the simplest thermally stable odd-electron molecule known and, accordingly, its electronic structure and reaction chemistry have been very extensively studied.[107] The compound is an intermediate in the production of nitric acid and is prepared industrially by the catalytic oxidation of ammonia (p. 466). On the laboratory scale it can be synthesized from aqueous solution by the mild reduction of acidified nitrites with iodide or ferrocyanide or by the disproportionation of nitrous acid in the presence of dilute sulfuric acid:

$$KNO_2 + KI + H_2SO_4 \xrightarrow{aq} NO + K_2SO_4$$
$$+ H_2O + \tfrac{1}{2}I_2$$

$$KNO_2 + K_4[Fe(CN)_6] + 2MeCO_2H \longrightarrow$$
$$NO + K_3[Fe(CN)_6] + H_2O + 2MeCO_2K$$

$$6NaNO_2 + 3H_2SO_4 \longrightarrow 4NO + 2HNO_3$$
$$+ 2H_2O + 3Na_2SO_4$$

The dry gas has been made by direct reduction of a solid mixture of nitrite and nitrate with chromium(III) oxide ($3KNO_2 + KNO_3 + Cr_2O_3 \rightarrow 4NO + 2K_2CrO_4$) but is now more conveniently obtained from a cylinder.

Nitric oxide is a colourless, monomeric, paramagnetic gas with a low mp and bp (Table 11.9). It is thermodynamically unstable and decomposes into its elements at elevated temperatures (1100–1200°C), a fact which militates against its direct synthesis from N_2 and O_2. At high pressures and moderate temperatures

[107] pp. 323–5 of ref. 69.

Table 11.9   Some physical properties of NO

MP/°C	−163.6	μ/D	0.15
BP/°C	−151.8	Distance (N–O)/pm	115
ΔH_f° (298 K)/			
kJ mol^{-1}	90.2	Ionization energy/eV	9.23
ΔG_f° (298 K)/		Ionization energy/	
kJ mol^{-1}	86.6	kJ mol^{-1}	890.6

($\sim 50°$) it rapidly disproportionates:

$$3NO \longrightarrow N_2O + NO_2; \quad -\Delta H = 3 \times 51.8 \, kJ \, mol^{-1}$$

$$-\Delta G = 3 \times 34.7 \, kJ \, mol^{-1}$$

However, when the gas is occluded by zeolites the disproportionation takes a different course:

$$4NO \longrightarrow N_2O + N_2O_3; \quad -\Delta H = 4 \times 48.8 \, kJ \, mol^{-1}$$

$$-\Delta G = 4 \times 25.7 \, kJ \, mol^{-1}$$

The molecular orbital description of the bonding in NO is similar to that in N_2 or CO (p. 927) but with an extra electron in one of the π^* antibonding orbitals. This effectively reduces the bond order from 3 to ~ 2.5 and accounts for the fact that the interatomic N–O distance (115 pm) is intermediate between that in the triple-bonded NO^+ (106 pm) and values typical of double-bonded NO species (~ 120 pm). It also interprets the very low ionization energy of the molecule (9.25 eV, compared with 15.6 eV for N_2, 14.0 eV for CO, and 12.1 eV for O_2). Similarly, the notable reluctance of NO to dimerize can be related both to the geometrical distribution of the unpaired electron over the entire molecule and to the fact that dimerization to O=N—N=O leaves the total bond order unchanged ($2 \times 2.5 = 5$). When NO condenses to a liquid, partial dimerization occurs, the *cis*-form being more stable than the *trans*-. The pure liquid is colourless, not blue as sometimes stated: blue samples owe their colour to traces of the intensely coloured N_2O_3.[108] Crystalline nitric oxide is also colourless (not blue) when pure,[108] and X-ray diffraction data are best interpreted in terms of weak association into

dimeric units. It seems probable that the dimers adopt the *cis*-(C_{2v}) structure[109] rather than the rectangular C_{2h} structure which was at one time favoured,[110] i.e.:

In either case each dimer has two possible orientations, and random disorder between these accounts for the residual entropy of the crystal (6.3 J mol^{-1} of dimer). More recently[111] an asymmetric dimer $\begin{smallmatrix} & N—O \\ O= & \quad =N \end{smallmatrix}$ has been characterized; this forms as a red species when NO is condensed in the presence of polar molecules such as HCl or SO_2, or Lewis acids such as BX_3, SiF_4, $SnCl_4$ or $TiCl_4$. Reaction of NO with either $[Pt(PPh_3)_3]$ or $[Pt(PPh_3)_4]$ yields $[Pt(NO)_2(PPh_3)_2]$ which has been shown by X-ray diffraction analysis to be an unstable planar *cis*-hyponitrite complex, $[(PPh_3)_2\overline{Pt—ON=NO}]$, with an N=N distance of 121 pm and N–O 132 and 139 pm.[112]

The reactivity of NO towards atoms, free radicals, and other paramagnetic species has been much studied, and the chemiluminescent reactions with atomic N and O are important in assaying atomic N (p. 414). NO reacts rapidly with molecular O_2 to give brown NO_2, and this gas is the normal product of reactions which produce NO if these are carried out in air. The oxidation is unusual in following third-order reaction kinetics and, indeed, is the classic

---

[108] J. MASON, *J. Chem. Educ.* **52**, 445–7 (1975).

[109] W. N. LIPSCOMB, F. E. WANG, W. R. MAY and E. L. LIPPERT, *Acta Cryst.* **14**, 1100–01 (1961).

[110] W. J. DULMAGE, E. A. MEYERS and W. N. LIPSCOMB, *Acta Cryst.* **6**, 760–4 (1953).

[111] J. R. OLSEN and J. LAANE, *J. Am. Chem. Soc.* **100**, 6948–55 (1978).

[112] S. BHADURI, B. F. G. JOHNSON, A. PICKARD, P. R. RAITHBY, G. M. SHELDRICK and C. I. ZUCCARO, *J. Chem. Soc., Chem. Commun.*, 354–5 (1977).

example of such a reaction (M. Bodenstein, 1918). The reaction is also unusual in having a negative temperature coefficient, i.e. the rate becomes progressively slower at higher temperatures. For example the rate drops by a factor of 2 between room temperature and 200°. This can be accounted for by postulating that the mechanism involves the initial equilibrium formation of an unstable dimer which then reacts with oxygen:

$$2NO \rightleftharpoons N_2O_2 \xrightarrow{O_2} 2NO_2$$

As the equilibrium concentration of N_2O_2 decreases rapidly with increase in temperature the decrease in rate is explained. However alternative mechanisms have also been suggested.[107]

Nitric oxide reacts with the halogens to give XNO (p. 441). Some other facile reactions are listed below:

$$ClNO_2 + NO \longrightarrow ClNO + NO_2$$

(?Cl transfer or O transfer)

$$NCl_3 + 2NO \longrightarrow ClNO + N_2O + Cl_2$$

(stepwise at $-150°$)

$$XeF_2 + 2NO \longrightarrow 2FNO + Xe$$

(occurs stepwise; also with XeF_4)

$$I_2O_5 + 5NO \longrightarrow \tfrac{5}{2}N_2O_4 + I_2$$

(N_2O_5 is also produced)

Reactions with sulfides, polysulfides, sulfur oxides and the oxoacids of sulfur are complex and the products depend markedly on reaction conditions (see also p. 745 for blue crystals in chamber acid). Some examples are:

$$SO_2 + 2NO \longrightarrow N_2O + SO_3$$

$$2SO_3 + NO \longrightarrow (SO_3)_2NO$$

$$2H_2SO_3 + 2NO \longrightarrow 2H_2SO_3NO \xrightarrow{-H_2SO_3}$$

$$H_2SO_3(NO)_2 \longrightarrow N_2O + H_2SO_4$$

$$K_2SO_3(aq) + NO \xrightarrow{0°}$$

$$\underset{\text{radical anion}}{K_2[ONSO_3]} \xrightarrow{NO} \underset{\substack{| \\ NO}}{K_2[ONSO_3]} \underset{\substack{\text{white} \\ \text{crystals}}}{}$$

Under alkaline conditions disproportionation reactions predominate. Thus with Na_2O the dioxonitrate(II) first formed, disproportionates into the corresponding nitrite(III) and dioxodinitrate($N-N$)(I) :

$$4Na_2O + 4N^{II}O \xrightarrow{100°C} 4Na_2N^{II}O_2 \longrightarrow$$

$$2Na_2O + 2NaN^{III}O_2 + Na_2N^I_2O_2$$

With alkali metal hydroxides, both N_2O and N_2 are formed in addition to the nitrite:

$$2MOH + 4N^{II}O \longrightarrow 2MN^{III}O_2 + N^I_2O + H_2O$$

$$4MOH + 6N^{II}O \longrightarrow 4MN^{III}O_2 + N^{(0)}_2 + 2H_2O$$

Nitric oxide complexes. NO readily reacts with many transition metal compounds to give nitrosyl complexes and these are also frequently formed in reactions involving other oxo-nitrogen species. Classic examples are the "brown-ring" complex $[Fe(H_2O)_5NO]^{2+}$ formed during the qualitative test for nitrates, Roussin's red and black salts (p. 1094), and sodium nitroprusside, $Na_2[Fe(CN)_5NO].2H_2O$. The field has been extensively reviewed[113-115] and only the salient features need be summarized here. A variety of preparative routes is available (see Panel). Most nitrosyl complexes are highly coloured — deep reds, browns, purples, or even black. Apart from the intrinsic interest in the structure and bonding of these compounds there

[113] B. F. G. JOHNSON and J. A. McCLEVERTY, *Progr. Inorg. Chem.* **7**, 277–359 (1966). W. P. GRIFFITH, *Adv. Organometallic Chem.* **7**, 211–39 (1968). J. H. ENEMARK and R. D. FELTHAM, *Coord. Chem. Revs.* **13**, 339–406 (1974).

[114] K. G. CAULTON, *Coord. Chem. Revs.* **14**, 317–55 (1975). J. A. McCLEVERTY, *Chem. Rev.* **79**, 53–76 (1979).

[115] R. EISENBERG and C. D. MEYER, *Acc. Chem. Res.* **8**, 26–34 (1975).

Synthetic Routes to NO Complexes[114]

The coordination chemistry of NO is often compared to that of CO but, whereas carbonyls are frequently prepared by reactions involving CO at high pressures and temperatures, this route is less viable for nitrosyls because of the thermodynamic instability of NO and its propensity to disproportionate or decompose under such conditions (p. 446). Nitrosyl complexes can sometimes be made by transformations involving pre-existing NO complexes, e.g. by ligand replacement, oxidative addition, reductive elimination or condensation reactions (reductive, thermal or photolytic). Typical examples are:

$$[Mn(CO)_3(NO)(PPh_3)] + PPh_3 \longrightarrow [Mn(CO)_2(NO)(PPh_3)_2] + CO$$

$$2[Cr(\eta^5\text{-}C_5H_5)Cl(NO)_2] \xrightarrow{BH_4^-} [\{Cr(\eta^2\text{-}C_5H_5)(NO)_2\}_2]$$

$$2[Mn(CO)_4(NO)] \xrightarrow{h\nu} [Mn_2(CO)_7(NO)_2]$$

$$[\{Mn(\eta^5\text{-}C_5H_5)(CO)(NO)\}_2] \xrightarrow{h\nu} [Mn_3(\eta^5\text{-}C_5H_5)_3(NO)_4]$$

Syntheses which *increase* the number of coordinated NO molecules can be classified into more than a dozen types, of which only the first three use free NO gas.

1. *Addition of NO to coordinatively unsaturated complexes:*

$$[CoCl_2L_2] + NO \longrightarrow [CoCl_2L_2(NO)]$$

$$[Co(OPPh_3)_2X_2] + 2NO \longrightarrow [Co(NO)_2(OPPh_3)_2X_2]$$

2. *Substitution (ligand replacement)*

Very frequently in these reactions 2NO replace 3CO. Alternatively, 1NO can replace 2CO with simultaneous formation of a metal–metal bond, or 1NO can replace CO + a halogen atom:

$$[Co(CO)_3(NO)] + 2NO \longrightarrow [Co(NO)_3] + 3CO$$

$$[Fe(CO)_5] + 2NO \longrightarrow [Fe(CO)_2(NO)_2] + 3CO$$

$$[Cr(CO)_6] + 4NO \longrightarrow [Cr(NO)_4] + 6CO$$

$$[CO(\eta^5\text{-}C_5H_5)(CO)_2] + NO \longrightarrow \tfrac{1}{2}[\{Co(\eta^5\text{-}C_5H_5)(NO)\}_2] + 2CO$$

$$[Mn(CO)_5I] + 3NO \longrightarrow [Mn(CO)(NO)_3] + 4CO + \{I\}$$

$$\tfrac{1}{2}[\{Mn(CO)_4I\}_2] + 3NO \longrightarrow [Mn(CO)(NO)_3] + 3CO + \{I\}$$

3. *Reductive nitrosylation* (cf. $MF_6 + NO \rightarrow NO^+MF_6^-$ for Mo, Tc, Re, Ru, Os, Ir, Pt)

$$CoCl_2 + 3NO + B + ROH \longrightarrow \tfrac{1}{2}[\{CoCl(NO)_2\}_2] + BH^+ + RONO$$

where B is a proton acceptor such as an alkoxide or amine.

4. *Addition of or substitution by NO+*

This method uses $NOBF_4$, $NOPF_6$, or $NO[HSO_4]$ in MeOH or MeCN, e.g.:

$$[Rh(CNR)_4]^+ + NO^+ \longrightarrow [Rh(CNR)_4(NO)]^{2+}$$

$$[Ir(CO)ClL_2] + NO^+ \longrightarrow [Ir(CO)ClL_2(NO)]^+$$

$$[Ni(CO)_2L_2] + NO^+ \longrightarrow [Ir(CO)L_2(NO)]^+ + CO$$

$$[Cr(CO)_4(diphos)] + 2NO^+ \xrightarrow{MeCN} [Cr(NO)_2(MeCN)_4]^{2+} + 4CO + diphos$$

5. *Oxidative addition of XNO*

The reaction may occur with either coordinatively unsaturated or saturated complexes, e.g.:

$$[PtX_4]^{2-} + ClNO \longrightarrow [PtCl(NO)(X)_4]^{2-} \ (X = Cl, CN, NO_2)$$

Panel continues

$$[Ni(PPh_3)_4] + ClNO \longrightarrow [Ni(Cl)(NO)(PPh_3)_2] + 2PPh_3$$

6. *Reaction of metal hydride complexes with N-nitrosoamides*, e.g. *N*-methyl-*N*-nitrosourea:

$$[Mn(CO)_5H] + MeN(NO)CONH_2 \longrightarrow [Mn(CO)_4(NO)] + CO + MeNHCONH_2$$

7. *Transfer of coordinated NO* (especially from dimethylglyoximate complexes)

$$[Co(dmg)_2(NO)] + [MClL_n] \longrightarrow [CoCl(dmg)_2] + [M(NO)L_n]$$

$$[Ru(NO)_2(PPh_3)_2] + [RuCl_2(PPh_3)_3] \xrightarrow[\text{dust}]{\text{Zn}} 2[RuCl(NO)(PPh_3)_2] + PPh_3$$

8. *Use of NH$_2$OH in basic solution* (especially for cyano complexes)

The net transformation can be considered as the replacement of CN^- (or X^-) by NO^- and the reaction can be formally represented as

$$2NH_2OH \longrightarrow NH_3 + H_2O + \{NOH\} \longrightarrow NO^- + H^+ \text{(removed by base)}$$

Examples are:

$$[Ni(CN)_4]^{2-} + 2NH_2OH \xrightarrow{\text{MOH}} [Ni(CN)_3(NO)]^{2-} + NH_3 + 2H_2O + MCN$$

$$[Cr(CN)_6]^{3-} + 2NH_2OH \xrightarrow{\text{MOH}} [Cr(CN)_5(NO)]^{3-} + NH_3 + 2H_2O + MCN$$

9. *Use of acidified nitrites* (i.e. $NO_2^- + 2H^+ \longrightarrow NO^+ + H_2O$), e.g.:

$$K[Fe(CO)_3(NO)] + KNO_2 + CO_2 + H_2O \longrightarrow [Fe(CO)_2(NO)_2] + 2KHCO_3$$

$$Na[Fe(CO)_4H] + 2NaNO_2 + 3MeCO_2H \longrightarrow [Fe(CO)_2(NO)_2] + 2CO + 2H_2O + 3MeCO_2Na$$

10. *Use of (acidified) nitrites RONO* (i.e. $RONO + H^+ \rightleftharpoons NO^+ + ROH$) e.g.:

$$[Fe(CO)_3(PPh_3)_2] + RONO + H^+ \longrightarrow [Fe(CO)_2(NO)(PPh_3)_2]^+ + CO + ROH$$

Alternatively in aprotic solvents such as benzene:

$$[\{Mn(CO)_4(PPh_3)\}_2] \xrightarrow{\text{RONO}} 2[Mn(CO)_3(NO)(PPh_3)] + 2CO$$

11. *Use of concentrated nitric acid* (i.e. $2HNO_3 \rightleftharpoons NO^+ + NO_3^- + H_2O$)

Some of these reactions result, essentially, in the oxidative addition of $NO^+NO_3^-$ to coordinatively unsaturated metal centres whereas in others ligand replacement by NO^+ occurs — this is a favoured route for producing "nitroprusside", i.e. nitrosylpentacyanoferrate(II):

$$[Pt(en)_2]^{2+} \xrightarrow{\text{HNO}_3} [Pt(en)_2(NO)(NO_3)]^{2+}$$

$$[Fe(CN)_6]^{4-} \xrightarrow{\text{HNO}_3} [Fe(CN)_5(NO)]^{2-}$$

12. *Oxide ion abstraction from coordinated NO$_2$*, i.e.

$$[ML_x(NO_2)]^{n+} + H^+ \longrightarrow [ML_x(NO)]^{(n+2)+} + OH^-$$

e.g.

$$cis\text{-}[Ru(bipy)_2(NO_2)X] \underset{2OH^-}{\overset{2H^+}{\rightleftharpoons}} cis\text{-}[Ru(bipy)_2(NO)X]^{2+} + H_2O$$

$$[Fe(CN)_5(NO_2)]^{4-} \xrightarrow{2H^+} [Fe(CN)_5(NO)]^{2-} + H_2O$$

13. *Oxygen atom abstraction*

$$[Fe(CO)_5] + KNO_2 \longrightarrow K[Fe(CO)_3(NO)] + CO + CO_2$$

Many variations on these synthetic routes have been devised and the field is still being actively developed. The reactions of NO coordinated to transition metals have been extensively reviewed.[114]

is much current interest in their potential use as homogeneous catalysts for a variety of chemical reactions.[115] See also p. 443.[102]

NO shows a wide variety of coordination geometries (linear, bent, doubly bridging, triply bridging and quadruply bridging — see p. 453) and sometimes adopts more than one mode within the same complex. NO has one more electron than CO and often acts as a 3-electron donor — this is well illustrated by the following isoelectronic series of compounds in which successive replacement of CO by NO is compensated by a matching decrease in atomic number of the metal centre:

$[Ni(CO)_4]$	$[Co(CO)_3(NO)]$	$[Fe(CO)_2(NO)_2]$
mp $-25°$	$-11°$	$+18.4°$
(colourless)	(red)	(deep red)
$[Mn(CO)(NO)_3]$	$[Cr(NO)_4]$	
$+27°$	decomp > rt	
(dark green)	(red-black)	

For the same reason 3CO can be replaced by 2NO; e.g.:

$$[Co(CO)_3(NO)] \longrightarrow [Co(NO)_3]$$

$$[Fe(CO)_5] \longrightarrow [Fe(CO)_2(NO)_2]$$

$$[Mn(CO)_4(NO)] \longrightarrow [Mn(CO)(NO)_3]$$

$$[Cr(CO)_6] \longrightarrow [Cr(NO)_4]$$

In these and analogous compounds the M–N–O group is linear or nearly so, the M–N and N–O distances are short, and the N–O infrared stretching modes usually occur in the range $1650-1900 \, cm^{-1}$. The bonding in such compounds is sometimes discussed in terms of the preliminary transfer of 1 electron from NO to the metal and the coordination of NO^+ to the reduced metal centre as a "2-electron σ donor, 2-electron π acceptor" analogous to CO (p. 926). This formal scheme, though useful in emphasizing similarities and trends in the coordination behaviour of NO^+, CO and CN^-, is unnecessary even for the purpose of "book-keeping" of electrons; it is also misleading in implying an unacceptably large separation of electronic charge in these covalent complexes and in leading to uncomfortably low

oxidation states for many metals. e.g. Cr(−IV) in $[Cr(NO)_4]$, Mn(−III) in $[Mn(CO)(NO)_3]$, etc. Many physical techniques (such as ESCA, Mössbauer spectroscopy, etc.) suggest a much more even distribution of charge and there is accordingly a growing trend to consider linear NO complexes in terms of molecular orbital energy level schemes in which an almost neutral NO contributes 3 electrons to the bonding system via orbitals of σ and π symmetry.[116] Nitrogen-15 nmr spectroscopy has also been developed as a powerful tool for characterizing and distinguishing between linear and bent nitrosyl complexes and, where appropriate for studying their interconversion.[117]

Compounds in which the {M–N–O} group is nominally linear often feature a slightly bent coordination geometry and M–N–O bond angles in the range $165-180°$ are frequently encountered. However, another group of compounds is known in which the angle M–N–O is close to $120°$. The first example, $[Co(NO)(S_2CNMe)_2]$, appeared in 1962[118] though there were problems in refining the structure, and a second example was found in 1968[119] when the cationic complex $[Ir(CO)Cl(NO)(PPh_3)_2]^+$ was found to have a bond angle of $124°$ (Fig. 11.10); values in the range $120-140°$ have since been observed in several other compounds (Table 11.10). The related complex $[RuCl(NO)_2(PPh_3)_2]^+$, in which the CO ligand has been replaced by a second NO molecule, is interesting in having both

116 H. W. CHEN and W. L. JOLLY, *Inorg. Chem.* **18**, 2548–51 (1979).

117 L. K. BELL, D. M. P. MINGOS, D. G. TEW, L. F. LARKWORTHY, B. SANDELL, D. C. POVEY and J. MASON, *J. Chem. Soc., Chem. Commun.*, 125–6 (1983). L. K. BELL, J. MASON, D. M. P. MINGOS, D. G. TEW, *Inorg. Chem.* **22**, 3497–502 (1983). J. MASON, D. M. P. MINGOS, D. SHERMAN and R. W. M. WARDLE, *J. Chem. Soc., Chem. Commun.*, 1223–5 (1984). J. MASON, D. M. P. MINGOS, J. SCHAEFER, D. SHERMAN and E. O. STEJSKAL, *J. Chem. Soc., Chem. Commun.*, 444–6 (1985). J. BULTITUDE, L. F. LARKWORTHY, J. MASON, D. C. POVEY and B. SANDELL, *Inorg. Chem.* **23**, 3629–33 (1984).

118 P. R. H. ALDERMAN, P. G. OWSTON and J. M. ROWE, *J. Chem. Soc.* 668–73 (1962).

119 D. J. HODGSON and J. A. IBERS, *Inorg. Chem.* **7**, 2345–52 (1968); see also *J. Am. Chem. Soc.* **90**, 4486–8 (1968).

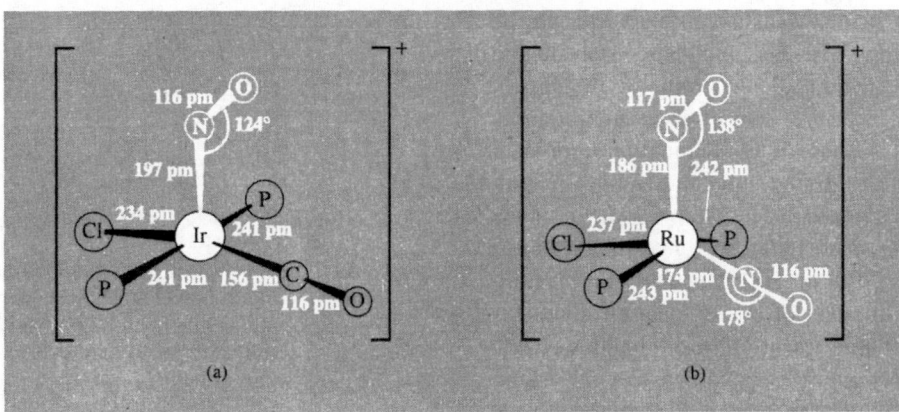

Figure 11.10 Complexes containing bent NO groups: (a) $[Ir(CO)Cl(NO)(PPh_3)_2]^+$, and (b) $[RuCl(NO)_2(PPh_3)_2]^+$. This latter complex also has a linearly coordinated NO group. The diagrams show only the coordination geometry around the metal (the phenyl groups being omitted for clarity).

Table 11.10 Some examples of "linear" and "bent" coordination of nitric oxide

Compound	Angle M–N–O	ν (N–O)/cm^{-1}
Linear		
$[Co(en)_3][Cr(CN)_5(NO)].2H_2O$	176°	1630
$[Cr(\eta^5\text{-}C_5H_5)Cl(NO)_2]$	171°, 166°	1823, 1715
$K_3[Mn(CN)_5(NO)].2H_2O$	174°	1700
$[Mn(CO)_2(NO)(PPh_3)_2]$	178°	1661
$[Fe(NO)(mnt)_2]^-$	180°	1867
$[Fe(NO)(mnt)_2]^{2-}$	165°	1645
$[Fe(NO)(S_2CNMe_2)_2]$	170°	1690
$Na_2[Fe(CN)_5(NO)].2H_2O$	178°	1935
$[Co(diars)(NO)]^{2+}$	179°	1852
$[Co(Cl)_2(NO)(PMePh_2)_2]$	165°	1735, 1630
$Na_2[Ru(NO)(NO_2)_4(OH)].2H_2O$	180°	1893
$[RuH(NO)(PPh_3)_3]$	176°	1645
$[Ru(diphos)_2(NO)]^+$	174°	1673
$[Os(CO)_2(NO)(PPh_3)_2]^+$	177°	1750
$[IrH(NO)(PPh_3)_3]^+$	175°	1715
Bent		
$[CoCl(en)_2(NO)]ClO_4$	124°	1611
$[Co(NH_3)_5NO]^{2+}$	119°	1610
$[Co(NO)(S_2CNMe_2)_2]^{(a)}$	~135°	1626
$[Rh(Cl)_2(NO)(PPh_3)_2]$	125°	1620
$[Ir(Cl)_2(NO)(PPh_3)_2]$	123°	1560
$[Ir(CO)Cl(NO)(PPh_3)_2]BF_4$	124°	1680
$[Ir(CO)I(NO)(PPh_3)_2]BF_4.C_6H_6$	124°	1720
$[Ir(CH_3)I(NO)(PPh_3)_2]$	120°	1525
Both		
$[RuCl(NO)_2(PPh_3)_2]^+$	178°, 138°	1845, 1687
$[Os(NO)_2(OH)(PPh_3)_2]^+$	~180°, 127°	1842, 1632
$[Ir(\eta^3\text{-}C_3H_5)(NO)(PPh_3)_2]^+$ (see text)	~180°, 129°	1763, 1631

mnt = maleonitriledithiolate. diars = 1,2-bis(dimethylarsino)benzene. diphos = $Ph_2PCH_2CH_2PPh_2$.
$^{(a)}$Value imprecise because of crystal twinning (see ref. 118).

linear and bent {M–NO} groups: as can be seen in Fig. 11.10 the nonlinear coordination is associated with a lengthening of the Ru–N and N–O distances. This is consistent with a weakening of these bonds and it is significant that the N–O infrared stretching mode in such compounds tends to occur at lower wave numbers $(1525-1690\,\mathrm{cm}^{-1})$ than for linearly coordinated NO $(1650-1900\,\mathrm{cm}^{-1})$. In such systems neutral NO can be thought of as a 1-electron donor, as in the analogous (bent) nitrosyl halides, XNO (p. 442); it is unnecessary to consider the ligand as an NO^- 2-electron donor. The implication is that the other pair of electrons on NO is placed in an essentially non-bonding orbital on N (which is thus approximately described as an sp^2 hybrid) rather than being donated to the metal as in the linear, 3-electron-donor mode (Fig. 11.11). Consistent with this, non-linear coordination is generally observed with the later transition elements in which the low-lying orbitals on the metal are already filled, whereas linear coordination tends to occur with earlier transition elements which can more readily accommodate the larger number of electrons supplied by the ligand. However, the energetics are frequently finely balanced and other factors must also be considered — a good example is supplied by the two "isoelectronic" complexes shown in Fig. 11.12: $[Co(diars)_2(NO)]^{2+}$ has a linear NO equatorially coordinated to a trigonal bipyramidal cobalt atoms whereas $[IrCl_2(NO)(PPh_3)_2]$ has a bent NO axially coordinated to a square-pyramidal iridium atom, even though both Co and Ir are in the same group in the periodic table. Indeed, the complex cation $[Ir(\eta^3\text{-}C_3H_5)(NO)(PPh_3)_2]^+$ shows a facile equilibrium (in CH_2Cl_2 or MeCN solutions) between the linear and the bent NO modes of coordination and, with appropriate counter anions, either the linear –NO (light brown) or bent –NO (red-brown) isomer can be crystallized.[120] Some further examples of the two coordination geometries are in Table 11.10.

[120] M. W. SCHOONOVER, E. C. BAKER and R. EISENBERG, *J. Am. Chem. Soc.* **101**, 1880–2 (1979).

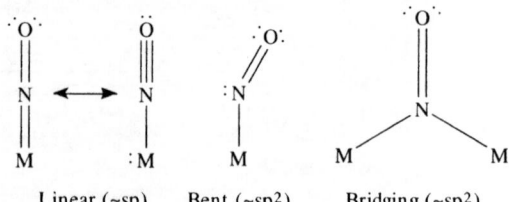

Figure 11.11   Schematic representation of the bonding in NO complexes. Note that bending would withdraw an electron-pair from the metal centre to the N atom thus creating a vacant coordination site: this may be a significant factor in the catalytic activity of such complexes.[115,121].

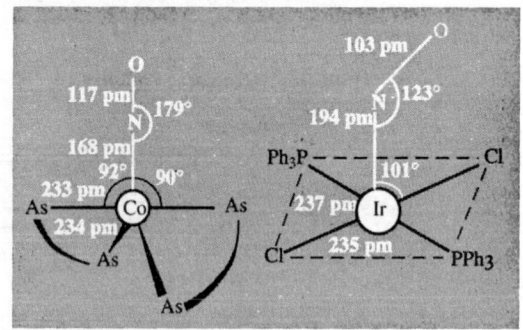

Figure 11.12   Comparison of the coordination geometries of $[Co(diars)_2(NO)]^{2+}$ and $[IrCl_2(NO)(PPh_3)]$; diars = 1,2-bis(dimethylarsino)benzene.

Like CO, nitric oxide can also act as a bridging ligand between 2 or 3 metals. Examples are the Cr and Mn complexes in Fig. 11.13. In $[\{Cr(\eta^5\text{-}C_5H_5)(NO)(\mu_2\text{-}NO)\}_2]$ the linear terminal NO has an infrared band at $1672\,\mathrm{cm}^{-1}$ whereas for the doubly bridging NO the vibration drops to $1505\,\mathrm{cm}^{-1}$. In both geometries NO can be considered as a 3-electron donor and there is also a Cr–Cr bond thereby completing an 18-electron configuration around each Cr atom. In $[Mn_3(\eta^5\text{-}C_5H_5)_3(\mu_2\text{-}NO)_3(\mu_3\text{-}NO)]$ the 3 Mn

[121] J. P. COLLMAN, N. W. HOFFMAN and D. E. MORRIS, *J. Am. Chem. Soc.* **91**, 5659–60 (1969). See also F. BOTTOMLEY in P. S. BRATERMAN, *Reactions of Coordinated Ligands*, Vol 2, Plenum Press, New York, 1989, pp. 115–222.

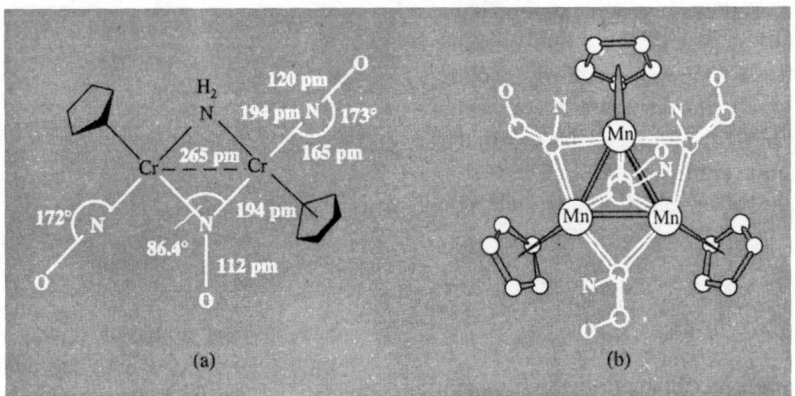

Figure 11.13 Structures of polynuclear nitrosyl complexes: (a) [{Cr(η^5-C$_5$H$_5$)(NO)}$_2$(μ_2-NH$_2$)(μ_2-NO)] showing linear-terminal and doubly bridging NO; and (b) [Mn$_3$(η^5-C$_5$H$_5$)$_3$(μ_2-NO)$_3$(μ_3-NO)] showing double-and triply-bridging NO; the molecule has virtual C_{3v} symmetry and the average Mn–Mn distance is 250 pm (range 247–257 pm).

form an equilateral triangle each edge of which is bridged by an NO group (ν 1543, 1481 cm^{-1}); the fourth NO is normal to the MN$_3$ plane and bridges all 3 Mn to form a triangular pyramid; the N–O stretching vibration moves to even lower wave numbers (1328 cm^{-1}). Again, each metal is associated with 18 valency electrons if each forms Mn–Mn bonds with its 2 neighbours and each NO is a 3-electron donor.

An unprecedented quadruply bridging mode for NO has been established in the violet cluster anion [{Re$_3$(μ-H)$_3$(CO)$_{10}$}$_2$(μ_4-η^2-NO)]$^-$ (see Fig. 11.14a).[122] The complex was isolated as its [NEt$_4$]$^+$ salt after its formation by reaction of NOBF$_4$ with the trinuclear hydrido anion [Re$_3$(μ-H)$_4$(CO)$_{10}$]$^-$. The rather long N–O distance (132–135 pm) is consistent with its formulation as NO$^-$. Another novel complex is [Os(CO)Cl$_2$(HNO)(PPh$_3$)$_2$] (Fig. 11.14b) which is formed by direct reaction of HCl with [Os(CO)(NO)(PPh$_3$)$_2$].[123] The complex is the first to contain the HNO ligand which is itself thermally unstable as a free molecule. The ligand is *N*-coordinated and coplanar with the

[Os(Co)Cl$_2$] moiety and has H–N 94 pm, N–O 119 pm and angle HNO 99°.

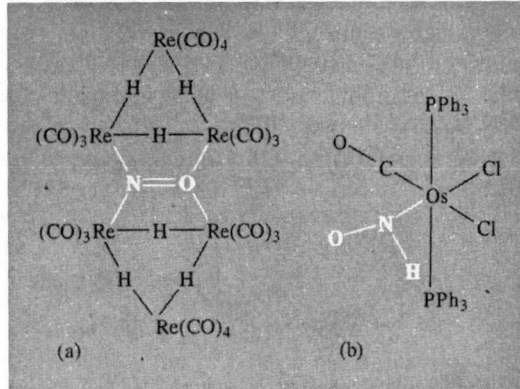

Figure 11.14 (a) Quadruply bridging NO in the anion [{Re$_3$(μ-H)$_3$(CO)$_{10}$}$_2$(μ_4-η^2-NO)]$^-$. (b) The neutral complex [Os(CO)Cl$_2$(HNO)(PPh$_3$)$_2$].

In contrast to the numerous complexes of NO which have been prepared and characterized, complexes of the thionitrosyl ligand (NS) are virtually unknown, as is the free ligand itself. The first such complex [Mo(NS)(S$_2$CNMe$_2$)$_3$] was obtained as orange-red air-stable crystals by treating [MoN(S$_2$CNMe$_2$)$_3$] with sulfur in

[122] T. BERINGHELLI, G. CIANI, G. D'ALFONSO, H. MOLINARI, A. SIRONI and M. FRENI, *J. Chem. Soc., Chem. Commun.*, 1327–9 (1984).

[123] R. D. WILSON and J. A. IBERS, *Inorg. Chem.* **18**, 336–43 (1979).

refluxing MeCN, and was shown later to have an M–N–S angle of $172.1°$.[124] More recently $[Cr(\eta^5\text{-}C_5H_5)(CO)_2(NS)]$ was made by reacting $Na[Cr(\eta^5\text{-}C_5H_5)(CO)_3]$ with $S_3N_3Cl_3$ and again the NS group was found to adopt an essentially linear coordination with Cr–N–S $176.8°$.[125] See also pp. 721–46 for other sulphur–nitrogen species.

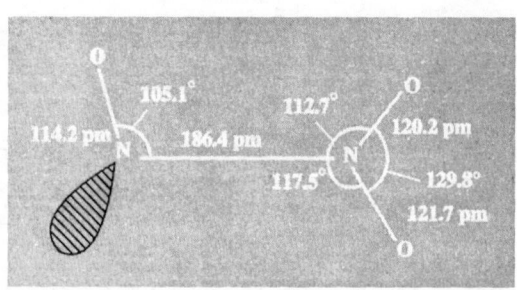

Dinitrogen trioxide, N_2O_3

Pure N_2O_3 can only be obtained at low temperatures because, above its mp ($-100.1°C$), it dissociates increasingly according to the equilibria:

$$N_2O_3 \rightleftharpoons NO + NO_2;$$
  Blue   Colourless Brown

$$2NO_2 \rightleftharpoons N_2O_4$$
  Brown   Colourless

The solid is pale blue; the liquid is an intense blue at low temperatures but the colour fades and becomes greenish due to the presence of NO_2 at higher temperatures. The dissociation also limits the precision with which physical properties of the compound can be determined. At $25°C$ the dissociative equilibrium in the gas phase is characterized by the following thermodynamic quantities:

$$N_2O_3(g) \rightleftharpoons NO(g) + NO_2(g); \quad \Delta H = 40.5 \text{ kJ mol}^{-1};$$
$$\Delta G = -1.59 \text{ kJ mol}^{-1}$$

Hence $\Delta S = 139 \text{ J K}^{-1} \text{ mol}^{-1}$ and the equilibrium constant $K(25°C) = 1.91$ atm. Molecules of N_2O_3 are planar with C_s symmetry.

Structural data are in the diagram; these data were obtained from the microwave spectrum of the gas at low temperatures. The long (weak) N–N bond is notable (cf. 145 pm in hydrazine, p. 428). In this N_2O_3 resembles N_2O_4 (p. 455).

[124] J. CHATT and J. R. DILWORTH, *J. Chem. Soc., Chem. Commun.*, 508 (1974): crystal structure by M. B. HURSTHOUSE and M. MONTEVALLI quoted by J. CHATT in *Pure Appl. Chem.* **49**, 815–26 (1977). See also M. W. BISHOP, J. CHATT and J. R. DILWORTH, *J. Chem. Soc., Dalton Trans.*, 1–5 (1979).
[125] T. J. GREENOUGH, B. W. S. KOLTHAMMER, P. LEGZDINS and J. TROTTER, *J. Chem. Soc., Chem. Commun.*, 1036–7 (1978).

N_2O_3 is best prepared simply by condensing equimolar amounts of NO and NO_2 at $-20°C$ or by adding the appropriate amount of O_2 to NO in order to generate the NO_2 *in situ*:

$$2NO + N_2O_4 \xrightarrow{\text{cool}} 2N_2O_3$$
$$4NO + O_2 \longrightarrow 2N_2O_3$$

Alternative preparations involve the reduction of 1:1 nitric acid by As_2O_3 at $70°$, or the reduction of fuming HNO_3 with SO_2 followed by hydrolysis:

$$2HNO_3 + 2H_2O + As_2O_3 \longrightarrow N_2O_3 + 2H_3AsO_4$$
$$2HNO_3 + 2SO_2 \longrightarrow 2NOHSO_4 \xrightarrow{2H_2O}$$
$$N_2O_3 + H_2SO_4$$

However, these methods do not yield a completely anhydrous product and dehydration can prove difficult.

Studies of the chemical reactivity of N_2O_3 are complicated by its extensive dissociation into NO and NO_2 which are themselves reactive species. With water N_2O_3 acts as the formal anhydride of nitrous acid and in alkaline solution it is converted essentially quantitatively to nitrite:

$$N_2O_3 + H_2O \xrightarrow{\text{aq}} 2HNO_2$$
$$N_2O_3 + 2OH^- \longrightarrow 2NO_2^- + H_2O$$

Reaction with concentrated acids provides a preparative route to nitrosyl salts such as $NO[HSO_4]$, $NO[HSeO_4]$, $NO[ClO_4]$, and $NO[BF_4]$, e.g.:

$$N_2O_3 + 3H_2SO_4 \longrightarrow 2NO^+ + H_3O^+ + 3HSO_4^-$$

Nitrogen dioxide, NO_2, and dinitrogen tetroxide, N_2O_4

The facile equilibrium $N_2O_4 \rightleftharpoons 2NO_2$ makes it impossible to study the pure individual compounds in the temperature range $-10°$ to $+140°$ though the *molecular* properties of each species in the equilibrium mixture can often be determined. At all temperatures below the freezing point $(-11.2°)$ the solid consists entirely of N_2O_4 molecules but the liquid at this temperature has 0.01% NO_2. At the bp $(21.5°C)$ the liquid contains 0.1% NO_2 but the gas is more extensively dissociated and contains 15.9% NO_2 at this temperature and 99% NO_2 at 135°. The increasing dissociation can readily be followed by a deepening of the brown colour due to NO_2 and an increase in the paramagnetism; the thermodynamic data for the dissociation of $N_2O_4(g)$ at 25°C are:

$$\Delta H° \ 57.20\,kJ\,mol^{-1}; \Delta G° \ 4.77\,kJ\,mol^{-1};$$

$$\Delta S° \ 175.7\,J\,K^{-1}mol^{-1}$$

The unpaired electron in NO_2 appears to be more localized on the N atom than it is in NO and this may explain the ready dimerization. NO_2 is also readily ionized either by loss of an electron (9.91 eV) to give the nitryl cation NO_2^+ (iso-electronic with CO_2) or by gain of an electron to give the nitrite ion NO_2^- (isoelectronic with O_3). These changes are accompanied by a dramatic diminution in bond angle and an increase in N–O distance as the number of valence electrons increases from 16 to 18 (top diagram).

The structure of N_2O_4 in the gas phase is planar (D_{2h}) with a remarkably long N–N bond, and these features persist in both the monoclinic crystalline form near the mp and the more stable low-temperature cubic form. Data for the monoclinic form are in the lower diagram[†] together with those for the isoelectronic species B_2F_4 and

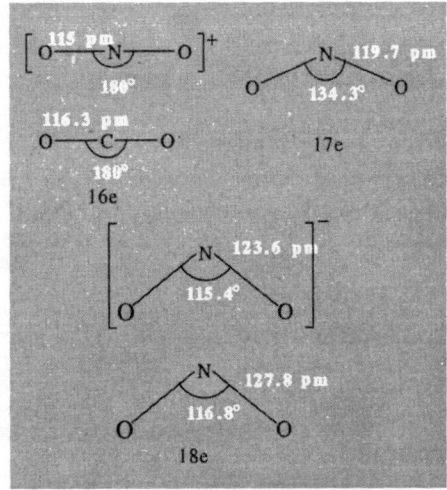

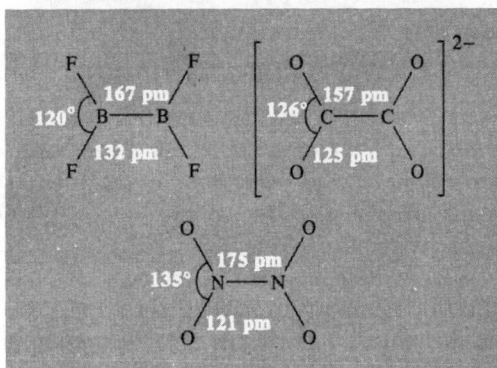

the oxalate ion $C_2O_4^{2-}$. The trends in bond angles and terminal bond distances are clear but the long central bond in N_2O_4 is not paralleled in the other 2 molecules where the B–B distance (p. 148) and C–C distance (p. 292) are normal. However, the B–B bond in B_2Cl_4 is also long (175 pm).

In addition to the normal homolytic dissociation of N_2O_4 into $2NO_2$, the molecule sometimes reacts as if by heterolytic fission: thus in media of high dielectric constant the compound often reacts as though dissociated according to the equilibrium $N_2O_4 \rightleftharpoons NO^+ + NO_3^-$ (see p. 457). This has sometimes been taken to imply

[†] Values for the gas phase are similar but there is a noticeable contraction in the cubic crystalline form (in parentheses). N–N 175 pm (164 pm), N–O 118 pm (117 pm), angle O–N–O 133.7° (126°). In addition, infrared studies on N_2O_4 isolated in a low-temperature matrix at liquid nitrogen temperature ($-196°C$) have been interpreted in terms of a twisted

(non-planar) molecule O_2N–NO_2, and similar experiments at liquid helium temperature ($-269°C$) have been interpreted in terms of the unstable oxygen-bridged species $ONONO_2$.

the presence in liquid N_2O_4 of oxygen-bridged species such as $ONONO_2$ or even

$$ON\underset{O}{\overset{O}{\diamondsuit}}NO$$

but there is no evidence for such species in solution and it seems unnecessary to invoke them since similar reactions also occur with the oxalate ion:
Thus

$$N_2O_4 \longrightarrow NO^+ + NO_3{}^- \xrightarrow{2H^+} NO^+ +$$

$$H_2NO_3{}^+ \xrightarrow{H^+} NO^+ + NO_2{}^+ + H_3O^+$$

Compare

$$C_2O_4{}^{2-} \longrightarrow CO + CO_3{}^{2-} \xrightarrow{2H^+} CO +$$

$$H_2CO_3 \xrightarrow{H^+} CO + CO_2 + H_3O^+$$

There is no noticeable tendency for pure N_2O_4 to dissociate into ions and the electrical conductivity of the liquid is extremely low (1.3×10^{-13} ohm^{-1} cm^{-1} at $0°$). The physical properties of N_2O_4 are summarized in Table 11.11.

N_2O_4 is best prepared by thermal decomposition of rigorously dried $Pb(NO_3)_2$ in a steel reaction vessel, followed by condensation of the effluent gases and fractional distillation:

$$2Pb(NO_3)_2 \xrightarrow{\sim 400°} 4NO_2 + 2PbO + O_2$$

Other methods (which are either more tedious or more expensive) include the reaction of nitric acid with SO_2 or P_4O_{10} and the reaction of nitrosyl chloride with $AgNO_3$:

$$2HNO_3 + SO_2 \longrightarrow N_2O_4 + H_2SO_4$$

$$4HNO_3 + P_4O_{10} \longrightarrow 2N_2O_4 + O_2 + 4HPO_3$$

$$NOCl + AgNO_3 \longrightarrow N_2O_4 + AgCl$$

The compound is also formed when NO reacts with oxygen:

$$2NO + O_2 \rightleftharpoons 2NO_2 \underset{warm}{\overset{cool}{\rightleftharpoons}} N_2O_4$$

These equilibria limit the temperature range in which reactions of N_2O_4 and NO_2 can be studied since dissociation of N_2O_4 into NO_2 is extensive above room temperature and is virtually complete by $140°$ whereas decomposition of NO_2 into NO and O_2 becomes significant above $150°$ and is complete at about $600°$.

N_2O_4/NO_2 react with water to form nitric acid (p. 466) and the moist gases are therefore highly corrosive:

$$N_2O_4 + H_2O \longrightarrow HNO_3 + HNO_2;$$

$$3HNO_2 \longrightarrow HNO_3 + 2NO + H_2O$$

The oxidizing action of NO_2 is illustrated by the following:

$$NO_2 + 2HCl \longrightarrow NOCl + H_2O + \tfrac{1}{2}Cl_2$$

$$NO_2 + 2HX \xrightarrow{heat} NO + H_2O + X_2 \ (X = Cl, Br)$$

$$2NO_2 + F_2 \longrightarrow 2FNO_2$$

$$NO_2 + CO \longrightarrow NO + CO_2$$

N_2O_4 has been extensively studied as a nonaqueous solvent system[126] and it is uniquely useful for preparing anhydrous metal nitrates and nitrato complexes (p. 468). Much of the chemistry can be rationalized in terms of a self-ionization equilibrium similar to that observed for

---

126 C. C. ADDISON, in G. JANDER, H. SPANDAU and C. C. ADDISON (eds.), *Chemistry in Non-aqueous Ionizing Solvents*, Vol. 3, Part 1, pp. 1–78, Pergamon Press, London, 1967. C. C. ADDISON, *Chem. Rev.* **80**, 21–39 (1980).

Table 11.11 Some physical properties of N_2O_4

MP/°C	−11.2	Density($-195°C$)/g cm^{-3}	1.979 (s)
BP/°C	+21.15	Density($0°C$)/g cm^{-3}	1.4927 (l)
$\Delta H_f°$(298 K)/kJ mol^{-1}	9.16	$\eta(0°C)$/poise	0.527
$\Delta G_f°$(298 K)/kJ mol^{-1}	97.83	$\kappa(0°C)$/ohm^{-1} cm^{-1}	1.3×10^{-13}
$S°$(298 K)/J K^{-1} mol^{-1}	304.2	Dielectric constant ε	2.42

liquid ammonia (p. 425):

$$N_2O_4 \rightleftharpoons NO^+ + NO_3^-$$
Solvent   Solvo-acid   Solvo-base

As noted above, there is no physical evidence for this equilibrium in pure N_2O_4, but the electrical conductivity is considerably enhanced when the liquid is mixed with a solvent of high dielectric constant such as nitromethane ($\varepsilon \approx 37$), or with donor solvents (D) such as $MeCO_2Et$, Et_2O, Me_2SO, or Et_2NNO (diethylnitrosamine):

$$N_2O_4 + nD \rightleftharpoons \{D_n.N_2O_4\}$$
$$\rightleftharpoons [D_nNO]^+ + NO_3^-$$

Typical solvent system reactions are summarized below together with the analogous reactions from the liquid ammonia solvent system:

"Neutralization"

$$NOCl + AgNO_3 \xrightarrow{N_2O_4} AgCl + N_2O_4$$
$$NH_4Cl + NaNH_2 \xrightarrow{NH_3} NaCl + 2NH_3$$

"Acid"

$$2NOCl + Sn \xrightarrow{N_2O_4} SnCl_2 + 2NO$$
$$2NH_4Cl + Sn \xrightarrow{NH_3} SnCl_2 + 2NH_3 + H_2$$

"Base/amphoterism"

$$2[EtNH_3][NO_3] + 2N_2O_4 + Zn \xrightarrow{N_2O_4}$$
$$[EtNH_3]_2[Zn(NO_3)_4] + 2NO$$
$$2NaNH_2 + 2NH_3 + Zn \xrightarrow{NH_3} Na_2[Zn(NH_2)_4] + H_2$$

"Solvolysis"

$$CaO + 2N_2O_4 \xrightarrow{N_2O_4} Ca(NO_3)_2 + N_2O_3$$
$$Na_2O + NH_3 \xrightarrow{NH_3} NaNH_2 + NaOH$$

Similarly :

$$ZnCl_2 + N_2O_4 \xrightarrow{N_2O_4} Zn(NO_3)_2 + 2NOCl$$

Such reactions provide an excellent route to anhydrous metal nitrates, particularly when metal bromides or iodides are used, since then the nitrosyl halide decomposes and this prevents the possible

formation of nitrosyl compounds, e.g.:

$$TiI_4 + 4N_2O_4 \rightleftharpoons Ti(NO_3)_4 + 4NO + 2I_2$$

Many carbonyls react similarly, e.g.:

$$[Mn_2(CO)_{10}] + N_2O_4 \longrightarrow [Mn(CO)_5(NO_3)]$$
$$+ [Mn(CO)_x(NO)_y]$$
$$[Fe(CO)_5] + 4N_2O_4 \longrightarrow [Fe(NO_3)_3.N_2O_4] +$$
$$5CO + 3NO$$

Solvates are frequently formed in these various reactions, e.g.:

$$Cu + 3N_2O_4 \xrightarrow{MeNO_2} [Cu(NO_3)_2.N_2O_4] + 2NO$$

Some of these may contain undissociated solvent molecules N_2O_4 but structural studies have revealed that often such "solvates" are actually nitrosonium nitrato-complexes. For example it has been shown[127] that $[ScNO_3)_3.2N_2O_4]$ is, in fact, $[NO]_2^+[Sc(NO_3)_5]^{2-}$. Similarly, X-ray crystallography revealed[128] that $[Fe(NO_3)_3.1\frac{1}{2}N_2O_4]$ is $[NO]^+_3[Fe(NO_3)_4]^-_2[NO_3]^-$, in which there is a fairly close approach of 3 NO^+ groups to the "uncoordinated" nitrate ion to give a structural unit of stoichiometry $[N_4O_6]^{2+}$ (see also p. 472).

In contrast to the wealth of reactions in which N_2O_4 tends to behave as $NO^+NO_3^-$, there is no evidence for reactions based on the alternative heterolytic dissociation $NO_2^+NO_2^-$.[129] Earlier claims[129a] to have identified BF_3 adducts such as $[NO_2]^+[ONOBF_3]^-$ have been shown to be incorrect and the predominant products of the reaction of BF_3 with N_2O_4 (and also with N_2O_3 and with N_2O_5) are, in fact, $NO^+BF_4^-$ and $NO_2^+BF_4^-$.[129b] This latter compound had

---

[127] C. C. ADDISON, A. J. GREENWOOD, M. J. HALEY and N. LOGAN, *J. Chem. Soc., Chem. Commun.*, 580–1 (1978).
[128] L. J. BLACKWELL, E. K. NUNN and S. C. WALLWORK, *J. Chem. Soc., Dalton Trans.*, 2068–72 (1975).
[129] C. C. ADDISON, S. ARROWSMITH, M. F. A. DOVE, B. F. G. JOHNSON, N. LOGAN and S. A. WOOD, *Polyhedron* **15**, 781–4 (1996).
[129a] R. W. SPRAGUE, A. B. GARRETT and H. H. SISLER, *J. Am. Chem. Soc.* **82**, 1059–64 (1960).
[129b] J. C. EVANS, H. W. RINN, S. J. KUHN and G. A. OLAH, *Inorg. Chem.* **3**, 857–61 (1964).

earlier (1956) been introduced by G. A. Olah as a powerful, stable nitrating agent in organic chemistry and it has been widely used since then.[130]

N_2O_4 has also been used extensively as a hypogolic oxidizer for hydrazine-based fuels in spacecraft. For example, the Apollo manned lunar landing modules (1969–72) used 5.0 tonnes of liquid N_2O_4 during descent to the lunar surface and 1.5 tonnes during the return ascent, the fuel being a 1:1 mixture of $MeNHNH_2$ and Me_2NNH_2.

Dinitrogen pentoxide, N_2O_5, and nitrogen trioxide, NO_3

N_2O_5 is the anhydride of nitric acid and is obtained as a highly reactive deliquescent, light-sensitive, colourless, crystalline solid by carefully dehydrating the concentrated acid with P_4O_{10} at low temperatures:

$$4HNO_3 + P_4O_{10} \xrightarrow{-10°} 2N_2O_5 + 4HPO_3$$

The solid has a vapour pressure of 100 mmHg at 7.5°C and sublimes (1 atm) at 32.4°C, but is thermally unstable both as a solid and as a gas above room temperature. Thermodynamic data at 25°C are:

	$\Delta H_f°$/kJ mol^{-1}	$\Delta G_f°$/kJ mol^{-1}	$S°$/J K^{-1} mol^{-1}
N_2O_5 (cryst)	−43.1	113.8	178.2
N_2O_5 (g)	11.3	115.1	355.6

X-ray diffraction studies show that solid N_2O_5 consists of an ionic array of linear NO_2^+ (N–O 115.4 pm) and planar NO_3^- (N–O 124 pm). In the gase phase and in solution (CCl_4, $CHCl_3$, $OPCl_3$) the compound is molecular; the structure is not well established but may be $O_2N–O–NO_2$ with a central N–O–N angle close to 180°. The molecular form can also be obtained in the solid phase by rapidly quenching the gas to −180°, but it rapidly reverts to the more stable ionic form

on being warmed to −70°. [cf. ionic and covalent forms of $BF_3.2H_2O$ (p. 198), $AlCl_3$ (p. 234), PCl_5 (p. 498), etc.]

N_2O_5 is readily hydrated to nitric acid and reacts with H_2O_2 to give pernitric acid as a coproduct:

$$N_2O_5 + H_2O \longrightarrow 2HONO_2$$

$$N_2O_5 + H_2O_2 \longrightarrow HONO_2 + HOONO_2$$

It reacts violently as an oxidizing agent towards many metals, non-metals and organic substances, e.g.:

$$N_2O_5 + Na \longrightarrow NaNO_3 + NO_2$$

$$N_2O_5 + NaF \longrightarrow NaNO_3 + FNO_2$$

$$N_2O_5 + I_2 \longrightarrow I_2O_5 + N_2$$

Like N_2O_4 (p. 457) it dissociates ionically in strong anhydrous acids such as HNO_3, H_3PO_4, H_2SO_4, HSO_3F and $HClO_4$, and this affords a convenient source of nitronium ions and hence a route to nitronium salts, e.g.:

$$N_2O_5 + 3H_2SO_4 \longrightarrow 2NO_2^+ + H_3O^+ + 3HSO_4^-$$

$$N_2O_5 + HSO_3F \longrightarrow [NO_2]^+[FSO_3]^- + HNO_3$$

$$N_2O_5 + 2SO_3 \longrightarrow [NO_2]^+_2[S_2O_7]^{2-}$$

In the gas phase, N_2O_5 decomposes according to a first-order rate law which can be explained by a dissociative equilibrium followed by rapid reaction according to the scheme

$$N_2O_5 \rightleftharpoons NO_2 + \{NO_3\} \longrightarrow NO_2 + O_2 + NO$$

$$N_2O_5 + NO \rightleftharpoons 3NO_2$$

The fugitive, paramagnetic species $\{NO_3\}$ is also implicated in several other gas-phase reactions involving the oxides of nitrogen and, in the N_2O_5-catalysed decomposition of ozone, its concentration is sufficiently high for its absorption spectrum to be recorded, thereby establishing its integrity as an independent chemical species. Such reactions are the subject of considerable current interest for environmental reasons. NO_3 probably has a symmetrical planar structure (like NO_3^-) but it has not been isolated as a pure compound.

---

[130] G. A. OLAH, R. MALHOTRA and S. C. NARANG, *Nitration: Methods and Mechanisms* VCH Publishers, New York, 1989.

11.3.7 Oxoacids, oxoanions and oxoacid salts of nitrogen

Nitrogen forms numerous oxoacids, though several are unstable in the free state and are known only in aqueous solution or as their salts. The principal species are summarized in Table 11.12; of these by far the most stable is nitric acid and this compound, together with its salts the nitrates, are major products of the chemical industry (p. 466).

Hyponitrous acid and hyponitrites [131]

Hyponitrous acid crystallizes from ether solutions as colourless crystals which readily decompose

---

[131] M. N. Hughes, *Q. Rev.* **22**, 1–13 (1968).

Table 11.12   Oxoacids of nitrogen and related species

Formula	Name	Remarks
$H_2N_2O_2$	Hyponitrous acid	Weak acid HON=NOH, isomeric with nitramide, H_2N-NO_2;[a] salts are known (p. 460)
{HNO}	Nitroxyl	Reactive intermediate (p. 461), salts are known (see also p. 453).
$H_2N_2O_3$	Hyponitric acid [trioxodinitric(II) acid]	Known in solution and as salts, e.g. Angeli's salt $Na_2[ON=NO_2]$ (p. 460)
$H_4N_2O_4$	Nitroxylic (hydronitrous) acid	Explosive; sodium salt known $Na_4[O_2NNO_2]$[b]
HNO_2	Nitrous acid	Unstable weak acid, HONO (p. 461); stable salts (nitrites) are known
HOONO	Peroxonitrous acid	Unstable, isomeric with nitric acid; some salts are more stable[c]
HNO_3	Nitric acid	Stable strong acid $HONO_2$; many stable salts (nitrates) are known (p. 465)
HNO_4	Peroxonitric acid	Unstable, explosive crystals, $HOONO_2$; no solid salts known. (For "orthonitrates", NO_4^{3-}, i.e. salts of the unknown orthonitric acid H_3NO_4, see p. 471–2)

[a] The structure of nitramide is as shown, the dihedral angle between NH_2 and NNO_2 is 52°. Nitramide is a weak acid pK_1 6.6 (K_1 2.6×10^{-7}) and it decomposes into N_2O and H_2O by a base-catalysed mechanism:

$$H_2NNO_2 + B \xrightarrow{\text{slow}} BH^+ + [HNNO_2]^- \xrightarrow{\text{fast}} N_2O + OH^-$$

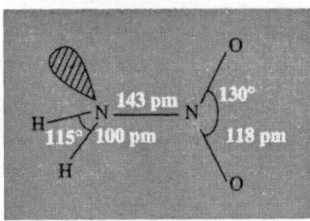

[b] Sodium nitroxylate can be prepared as a yellow solid by reduction of sodium nitrite with Na/NH_3(liq.):

$$2NaNO_2 + 2Na \xrightarrow{NH_3} Na_4\left[\begin{array}{c} O \\ O \end{array} \!\!\!\!> N - N <\!\!\!\! \begin{array}{c} O \\ O \end{array} \right]$$

[c] Peroxonitrous acid is formed as an unstable intermediate during the oxidation of acidified aqueous solutions of nitrites to nitrates using H_2O_2; such solutions are orange-red and are more highly oxidizing than either H_2O_2 or HNO_3 alone (e.g. they liberate Br_2 from Br^-). Alkaline solutions are more stable but the yellow peroxonitrites M[OONO] have not been isolated pure. The chemistry of peroxonitrites has recently been reviewed J. O. Edwards and R. C. Plumb, in K. D. Karlin (ed). *Progr. Inorg. Chem.* **41**, 599–635 (1994).

(explosively when heated). Its structure has not been determined but the molecular weight indicates a double formula $H_2N_2O_2$, i.e. $HON=NOH$; consistent with this the compound yields N_2O when decomposed by H_2SO_4, and hydrazine when reduced. The free acid is obtained by treating $Ag_2N_2O_2$ with anhydrous HCl in ethereal solution. It is a weak dibasic acid: pK_1 6.9, pK_2 11.6. Aqueous solutions are unstable between pH 4–14 due to base catalysed decomposition via the hydrogen-hyponitrite ion:

$$HONNOH \xrightarrow{\text{base}} [HONNO]^- \xrightarrow[\text{(minutes)}]{\text{fast}} N_2O + OH^-$$

At higher acidities (lower pH) decomposition is slower ($t_{1/2}$ days or weeks) and the pathways are more complex. The stoichiometry, kinetics and mechanisms of several other reactions of $H_2N_2O_2$ with, for example, NO and with HNO_2 have also been studied.[132]

Hyponitrites can be prepared in variable (low) yields by several routes of which the commonest are reduction of aqueous nitrite solutions using sodium (or magnesium) amalgam, and condensation of organic nitrites with hydroxylamine in NaOEt/EtOH:

$$2NaNO_3 + 8Na/Hg + 4H_2O \longrightarrow$$
$$Na_2N_2O_2 + 8NaOH + 8Hg$$

$$2AgNO_3 + 2NaNO_2 + 4Na/Hg + 2H_2O \longrightarrow$$
$$Ag_2N_2O_2 + 2NaNO_3 + 4NaOH + 4Hg$$

$$Ca(NO_3)_2 + 4Mg/Hg + 4H_2O \longrightarrow$$
$$CaN_2O_2 + 4Mg(OH)_2 + 4Hg$$

$$NH_2OH + RONO + 2NaOEt \xrightarrow{\text{EtOH}}$$
$$Na_2N_2O_2 + ROH + 2EtOH$$

Vibrational spectroscopy indicates that the hyponitrite ion has the *trans-* (C_{2h}) configuration (1) in the above salts.

As implied by the preparative methods employed, hyponitrites are usually stable towards

(1)   (2)

reducing agents though under some conditions they can be reduced (p. 434). More frequently they themselves act as reducing agents and are thereby oxidized, e.g. the analytically useful reaction with iodine:

$$[ONNO]^{2-} + 3I_2 + 3H_2O \longrightarrow [NO_3]^- +$$
$$[NO_2]^- + 6HI$$

There is also considerable current environmental interest in hyponitrite oxidation because it is implicated in the oxidation of ammonia to nitrite, an important step in the nitrogen cycle (p. 410). Specifically, it seems likely that the oxidation proceeds from ammonia through hydroxylamine and hyponitrous acid to nitrite (or N_2O).

With liquid N_2O_4 stepwise oxidation of hyponitrites occurs to give $Na_2N_2O_x$ ($x = 3$–6):

$$Na_2N_2O_2 \xrightarrow{\text{fast}} Na_2N_2O_3 \xrightarrow{\text{slow}}$$

$$Na_2N_2O_5 \xrightarrow[100°]{\text{slow}} Na_2N_2O_6$$

Angeli's salt $Na_2N_2O_3$ has been shown by vibration spectroscopy to contain the trioxodinitrate(II) anion structure (2). Its decomposition and reactions in aqueous solutions have been extensively studied by ^{15}N nmr spectroscopy and other techniques.[133]

In contrast to the stepwise oxidation of sodium hyponitrite in liquid N_2O_4, the oxidation goes rapidly to the nitrate ion in an inert solvent of high dielectric constant such as nitromethane:

$$[ON=NO]^{2-} + 2N_2O_4 \xrightarrow{\text{MeNO}_2} 2[NO_3]^- +$$
$$\{ONON=NONO\} \longrightarrow N_2 + 2NO_2$$

---

[132] M. N. Hughes *et al.*, *Inorg. Chem.* **24**, 1934–5 (1985); *J. Chem. Soc., Dalton Trans.*, 527–32 and 533–7 (1989).

[133] M. J. Akhtar, C. A. Lutz and F. T. Bonner, *Inorg. Chem.* **18**, 2369–75 (1979). F. T. Bonner, H. Degani and M. J. Akhtar, *J. Am. Chem. Soc.* **103**, 3739–42 (1981). D. A. Bazylinski and T.C. Hollocher, *Inorg. Chem.* **24**, 4285–8 (1985).

More recently it has been found that the hyponitrite ion can act as a bidentate ligand in either a bridging or a chelating mode. Thus, the controversy about the nature of the black and red isomers of nitrosyl pentammine cobalt(III) complexes has been resolved by X-ray crystallographic studies which show that the black chloride $[Co(NH_3)_5NO]Cl_2$ contains a mononuclear octahedral Co^{III} cation with a linear Co–N–O group whereas the red isomer, in the form of a mixed nitrate-bromide, is dinuclear with a bridging *cis*-hyponitrite-(*N,O*) group as shown in Fig. 11.15.[134] The *cis*-configuration is probably adopted for steric reasons since this is the only configuration that allows the bridging of two $\{Co(NH_3)_5\}$ groups by an ONNO group without steric interference between them. The *cis*-chelating mode (*O,O*) was found in the air-sensitive yellow crystalline complex $[Pt(O_2N_2)(PPh_3)_2]$ which has already been mentioned on p. 446. The presence of the *cis*-configuration in this complex invites speculation as to whether *cis*-$[ON–NO]^{2-}$ can also exist in simple hyponitrites. Likely candidates appear to be the "alkali metal nitrosyls" MNO prepared by the action of NO on Na/NH$_3$; infrared data suggest they are not $M^+[NO]^-$ and might indeed contain the *cis*-hyponitrite ion. They would therefore not be salts

of nitroxyl HNO which has often been postulated as an intermediate in reactions which give N$_2$O and which is well known in the gas phase. Nitroxyl can be prepared by the action of atomic H or HI on NO and decomposes to N$_2$O and H$_2$O. As expected, the molecule is bent (angle H—N=O 109°). See also Fig. 11.14(b), p. 453.

Nitrous acid and nitrites

Nitrous acid, HNO$_2$, has not been isolated as a pure compound but it is a well known and important reagent in aqueous solutions and has also been studied as a component in gas-phase equilibria. Solutions of the free acid can readily be obtained by acidification of cooled aqueous nitrite solutions but even at room temperature disproportionation is noticeable:

$$3HNO_2(aq) \rightleftharpoons H_3O^+ + NO_3^- + 2NO$$

It is a fairly weak acid with pK_a 3.35 at 18°C, i.e. intermediate in strength between acetic (4.75) and chloroacetic (2.85) acids at 25°, and very similar to formic (3.75) and sulfanilic (3.23) acids. Salt-free aqueous solutions can be made by choosing combinations of reagents which give insoluble salts, e.g.:

$$Ba(NO_2)_2 + H_2SO_4 \xrightarrow{\ aq\ } 2HNO_2 + BaSO_4$$

$$AgNO_2 + HCl \xrightarrow{\ aq\ } HNO_2 + AgCl$$

[134] B. F. HOSKINS,   F. D. WHILLANS,   D. H. DALE   and D. C. HODGKIN, *J. Chem. Soc., Chem. Commun.*, 69–70 (1969).

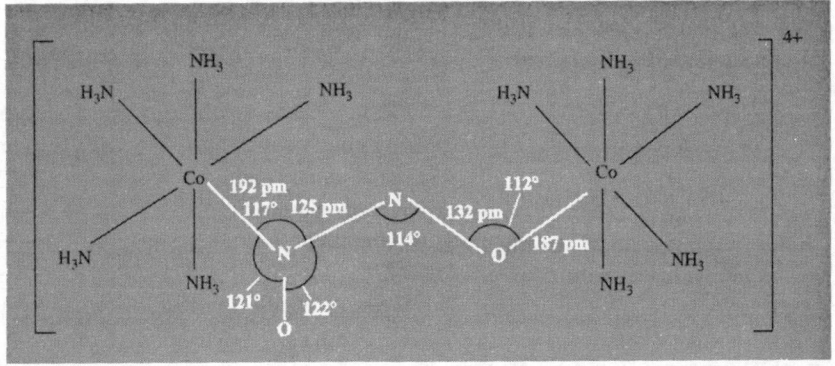

Figure 11.15   Structure of the dinuclear cation in the red isomer $[\{Co(NH_3)_5NO\}_2](Br)_{2.5}(NO_3)_{1.5}.2H_2O$; (mean Co–NH$_3$ 194 ± 2 pm, mean angle 90 ± 4°).

When the presence of salts in solution is unimportant, the more usual procedure is simply to acidify $NaNO_2$ with hydrochloric acid below 0°.

In the gas phase, an equilibrium reaction producing HNO_2 can be established by mixing equimolar amounts of H_2O, NO and NO_2:

$$2HNO_2(g) \rightleftharpoons H_2O(g) + NO(g) + NO_2(g);$$

$$\Delta H°(298\,K)\ 38\,kJ/2\,mol\ HNO_2;$$

$$K_p(298\,K)\ 8.0 \times 10^5\ N\,m^{-2}\ (7.9\ atm)$$

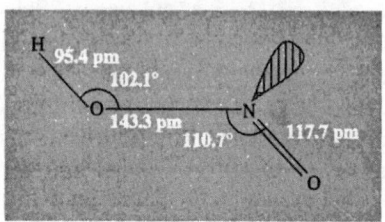

Microwave spectroscopy shows that the gaseous compound is predominantly in the *trans*-planar (C_s) configuration with the dimensions shown. The differences between the two N–O distances is notable. Despite the formal single-bond character of the central bond the barrier to rotation is $45.2\,kJ\,mol^{-1}$. Infrared data suggest that the *trans*-form is ∼$2.3\,kJ\,mol^{-1}$ more stable ($\Delta G°$) than the *cis*- form at room temperature.

Nitrites are usually obtained by the mild reduction of nitrates, using C, Fe or Pb at moderately elevated temperatures, e.g.:

$$NaNO_3 + Pb \xrightarrow{melt} NaNO_2 + PbO$$

On the industrial scale, impure $NaNO_2$ is made by absorbing "nitrous fumes" in aqueous alkali or carbonate solutions and then recrystallizing the product:

$$NO + NO_2 + 2NaOH\ (or\ Na_2CO_3) \xrightarrow{aq}$$

$$2NaNO_2 + H_2O\ (or\ CO_2)$$

The sparingly soluble $AgNO_2$ can be obtained by metathesis, and simple variants yield the other stable nitrites, e.g.:

$$NaNO_2 + AgNO_3 \xrightarrow{aq} AgNO_2 + NaNO_3$$

$$NaNO_2 + KCl \xrightarrow{aq} KNO_2 + NaCl$$

$$2NH_3 + H_2O + N_2O_3 \longrightarrow 2NH_4NO_2$$

$$Ba(OH)_2 + NO + NO_2 \xrightarrow{aq} Ba(NO_2)_2 + H_2O$$

Many stable metal nitrites (Li, Na, K, Cs, Ag, Tl^I, NH_4, Ba) contain the bent $[O–N–O]^-$ anion (p. 413) with N–O in the range 113–123 pm and the angle 116–132°. Nitrites of less basic metals such as Co(II), Ni(II) and Hg(II) are often highly coloured and are probably essentially covalent assemblies. Solubility (g per 100 g H_2O at 25°) varies considerably, e.g. $AgNO_2$ 0.41, $NaNO_2$ (hygroscopic) 85.5, KNO_2 (deliquescent) 314. Thermal stability also varies widely: e.g. the alkali metal nitrites can be fused without decomposition (mp $NaNO_2$ 284°, KNO_2 441°C), whereas $Ba(NO_2)_2$ decomposes when heated above 220°, $AgNO_2$ above 140° and $Hg(NO_2)_2$ above 75°. Such trends are a general feature of oxoacid salts (pp. 469, 863, 868). NH_4NO_2 can decompose explosively.

The aqueous solution chemistry of nitrous acid and nitrites has been extensively studied. Some reduction potentials involving these species are given in Table 11.4 (p. 434) and these form a useful summary of their redox reactions. Nitrites are quantitatively oxidized to nitrate by permanganate and this reaction is used in titrimetric analysis. Nitrites (and HNO_2) are readily reduced to NO and N_2O with SO_2, to $H_2N_2O_2$ with Sn(II), and to NH_3 with H_2S. Hydrazinium salts yield azides (p. 432) which can then react with further HNO_2:

$$HNO_2 + N_2H_5{}^+ \longrightarrow HN_3 + H_2O + H_3O^+$$

$$HNO_2 + HN_3 \longrightarrow N_2O + N_2 + H_2O$$

This latter reaction is most unusual in that it simultaneously involves an element (N) in four different oxidation states. Use of ^{15}N-enriched reagents shows that all the N from HNO_2 goes quantitatively to the internal N of N_2O:[135]

$$HN_3 + HO^{15}NO \xrightarrow{-H_2O} \{NNN^{15}NO\}$$

$$\longrightarrow NN + N^{15}NO$$

─────────────

[135] K. CLUSIUS and H. KNOFF, *Chem. Ber.* **89**, 681–5 (1956).

$NaNO_2$ is mildly toxic (tolerance limit ~100 mg/kg body weight per day, i.e. 4–8 g/day for humans). $NaNO_2$ (or a precursor such as $NaNO_3$, which is itself harmless) has been much used for curing meat and for treating preserved foods stuffs to prevent bacterial spoilage and consequent poisoning by the (often deadly) toxins produced by *Clostridium botulinum* etc., (normal dietary intake of NO_2^- 10–15 μg per day). $NaNO_2$ is used industrially on a large scale for the synthesis of hydroxylamine (p. 431), and in acid solution for the diazotization of primary *aromatic* amines:

$$ArNH_2 + HNO_2 \xrightarrow{HCl/aq} [ArNN]Cl + 2H_2O$$

The resulting diazo reagents undergo a wide variety of reactions including those of interest in the manufacture of azo dyes and pharmaceuticals. With primary *aliphatic* amines the course of the reaction is different: N_2 is quantitatively evolved and alcohols usually result:

$$RNH_2 + HNO_2 \xrightarrow{-H_2O} RNHNO \longrightarrow RN{=}NOH$$
$$\xrightarrow{-OH^-} RN_2^+ \longrightarrow N_2 + R^+ \longrightarrow products$$

The reaction is generally thought to involve carbonium-ion intermediates but several puzzling features remain.[136] Secondary aliphatic amines give nitrosamines without evolution of N_2:

$$R_2NH + HONO \longrightarrow R_2NNO + H_2O$$

Tertiary aliphatic amines react in the cold to give nitrite salts and these decompose on warming to give nitrosamines and alcohols:

$$R_3N + HNO_2 \xrightarrow{cold} [R_3NH][NO_2]$$
$$\xrightarrow{warm} R_2NNO + ROH$$

In addition to their general use in synthetic organic chemistry, these various reactions afford the major route for introducing ^{15}N into organic compounds by use of $Na^{15}NO_2$.

The nitrite ion, NO_2^-, is a versatile ligand and can coordinate in at least five different ways (i)–(v):

(i) Nitro   (ii) Nitrito   (iii) Chelating

(iv) Unsymmetrical   (v) η^1-O bridging
bridging (N,O)

Nitro-nitrito isomerism (i), (ii), was discovered by S. M. Jörgensen in 1894–9 and was extensively studied during the classic experiments of A. Werner (p. 912); the isomers usually have quite different colours, e.g. $[Co(NH_3)_5(NO_2)]^{2+}$, yellow, and $[Co(NH_3)_5(ONO)]^{2+}$, red. The nitrito form is usually less stable and tends to isomerize to the nitro form. The change can also be effected by increase in pressure since the nitro form has the higher density. For example application of 20 kbar pressure converts the violet nitrito complex $[Ni(en)_2(ONO)_2]$ to the red nitro complex $[Ni(en)_2(NO_2)_2]$ at 126°C, thereby reversing the change from nitro to nitrito which occurs on heating the complex from room temperature at atmospheric pressure.[137] An X-ray study of the thermally induced nitrito → nitro isomerization and the photochemically induced nitro → nitrito isomerization of Co(III) complexes has shown that both occur intra-molecularly by rotation of the NO_2 group in its own plane, probably via a 7-coordinated cobalt intermediate.[138] Similarly, the base-catalysed nitrito → nitro isomerization of $[M^{III}(NH_3)_5(ONO)]^{2+}$ (M = Co,

---

[136] C. J. COLLINS, *Acc. Chem. Res.* **4**, 315–22 (1971).

[137] J. R. FERRARO and L. FABBRIZZI, *Inorg. Chim. Acta* **26**, L15–L17 (1978).

[138] I. GRENTHE and E. NORDIN, *Inorg. Chem.* **18**, 1109–16 and 1869–74 (1979).

Rh, Ir) is intramolecular and occurs without ^{18}O exchange of the coordinated ONO^-
with $H_2^{18}O$, $^{18}OH^-$ or "free" $N^{18}O_2^-$.[139]
However, an elegant ^{17}O nmr study using
specifically labelled $[Co(NH_3)_5(^{17}ONO)]^{2+}$ and
$[Co(NH_3)_5(ON^{17}O)]^{2+}$ established that spontaneous intramolecular O-to-O exchange in the
nitrite ligand occurs at a rate comparable to that
of the spontaneous *O*-to-*N* isomerization.[140]

A typical value for the N–O distance in
nitro complexes is 124 pm whereas in nitrito
complexes the terminal N–O (121 pm) is
shorter than the internal N–O(M) ~129 pm.
In the bidentate chelating mode (iii) the 2
M–O distances may be fairly similar as in
$[Cu(bipy)_2(O_2N)]NO_3$ or quite different as in
$[Cu(bipy)(O_2N)_2]$:

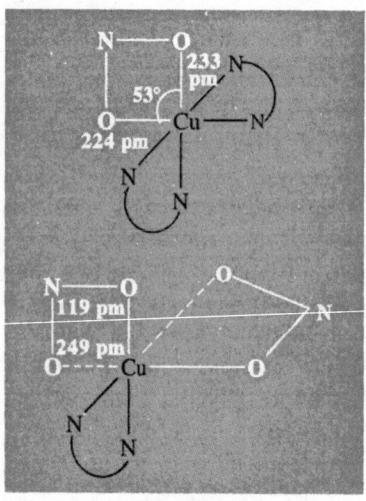

Examples of the unsymmetrical bridging mode
(iv) are shown in the top diagram.

The oxygen-bridging mode (v) is less common
but occurs together with modes (iii) and (iv) in
the following centrosymmetrical trimeric Ni complex and related compounds.[141]

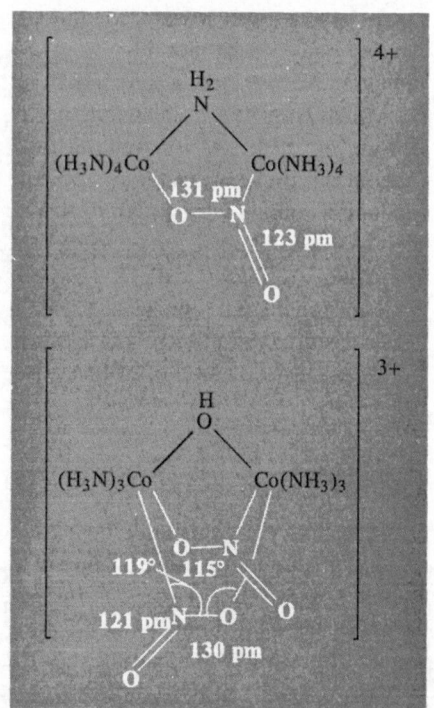

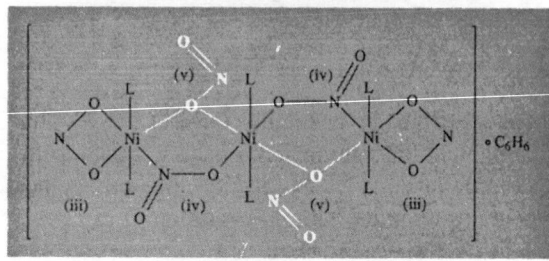

It is possible that a sixth (symmetrical
bridging) mode M—O
N
O—M occurs in

some complexes such as $Rb_3Ni(NO_2)_5$ but
this has not definitely been established; an
unsymmetrical bridging mode with a *trans*-
configuration of metal atoms is also possible, i.e.

O   M
‖   /
N—O   [compare with (iv)].
/
M

The familiar problem of misleading stoichiometries, and the frequent impossibility of
deducing the correct structural formula from the
empirical composition is well illustrated by the

139 W. G. JACKSON,   G. A. LAWRANCE,   P. A. LAY   and
A. M. SARGESON, *Inorg. Chem.* **19**, 904–10 (1980).
140 W. G. JACKSON,   G. A. LAWRANCE,   P. A. LAY   and
A. M. SARGESON, *J. Chem. Soc., Chem. Commun.*, 70–2
(1982).
141 D. M. L. GOODGAME, M. A. HITCHMAN, D. F. MARSHAM,
P. PHAVANANTHA and D. ROGERS, *Chem. Commun.*, 1383–4
(1969); see also *J. Chem. Soc. A*, 259–64 (1971).

recent synthesis of the novel alkali metal oxide nitrites $Na_4N_2O_5$ (yellow) and $K_4N_2O_5$ (red).[142] These compounds are made by heating powdered mixtures of M_2O and MNO_2 at 340° for 8 days in a silver crucible and have an anti-K_2NiF_4 type structure, $[(NO_2)_2OM_4]$, i.e $M_4O(NO_2)_2$, with N–O 122.1 pm, angle O–N–O 114.5° and octahedrally coordinated O^{2-} (i.e OM_6 with K–O 260 pm.

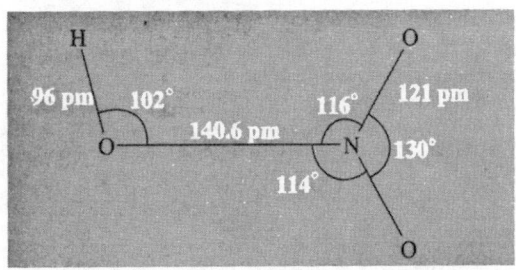

Nitric acid and nitrates

Nitric acid is one of the three major acids of the modern chemical industry and has been known as a corrosive solvent for metals since alchemical times in the thirteenth century.[143,144] It is now invariably made by the catalytic oxidation of ammonia under conditions which promote the formation of NO rather than the thermodynamically more favoured products N_2 or N_2O (p. 423). The NO is then further oxidized to NO_2 and the gases absorbed in water to yield a concentrated aqueous solution of the acid. The vast scale of production requires the optimization of all the reaction conditions and present-day operations are based on the intricate interaction of fundamental thermodynamics, modern catalyst technology, advanced reactor design, and chemical engineering aspects of process control (see Panel). Production in the USA alone now exceeds 7 million tonnes annually, of which the greater part is used to produce nitrates for fertilizers, explosives and other purposes (see Panel).

Anhydrous HNO_3 can be obtained by low-pressure distillation of concentrated aqueous nitric acid in the presence of P_4O_{10} or anhydrous H_2SO_4 in an all-glass, grease-free apparatus in the dark. The molecule is planar in the gas phase

with the dimensions shown (microwave). The difference in N–O distances, the slight but real tilt of the NO_2 group away from the H atom by 2°, and the absence of free rotation are notable features. The same general structure obtains in the solid state but detailed data are less reliable. Physical properties are shown in Table 11.13. Despite its great thermodynamic stability (with respect to the elements) pure HNO_3 can only be obtained in the solid state; in the gas and liquid phases the compound decomposes spontaneously to NO_2 and this occurs more rapidly in daylight (thereby accounting for the brownish colour which develops in the acid on standing):

$$2HNO_3 \rightleftharpoons 2NO_2 + H_2O + \tfrac{1}{2}O_2$$

Table 11.13 Some physical properties of anhydrous liquid HNO_3 at 25°C

MP/°C	−41.6	Vapour pressure/mmHg	57
BP/°C	82.6	Density/g cm^{-3}	1.504
ΔH_f°/kJ mol^{-1}	−174.1	η/centipoise	7.46
ΔG_f°/kJ mol^{-1}	−80.8	κ/ohm^{-1}cm^{-1} (20°)	3.72×10^{-2}
S°/J K^{-1} mol^{-1}	155.6	Dielectric constant ε (14°)	50 ± 10

In addition, the liquid undergoes self-ionic dissociation to a greater extent than any other nominally covalent pure liquid (cf. $BF_3.2H_2O$, p. 198); initial autoprotolysis is followed by rapid loss of water which can then react with a further molecule of HNO_3:

$$2HNO_3 \rightleftharpoons H_2NO_3^+ + NO_3^- \rightleftharpoons H_2O$$
$$+ [NO_2]^+ + [NO_3]^-$$

$$HNO_3 + H_2O \rightleftharpoons [H_3O]^+ + [NO_3]^-$$

[142] W. MULLER and M. JANSEN, *Z. anorg. allg. Chem.* **610**, 28–32 (1992).

[143] J. W. MELLOR, *A Comprehensive Treatise on Inorganic and Theoretical Chemistry*, Vol. 8, pp. 555–8, Longmans, Green, London, 1928.

[144] T. K. DERRY and T. I. WILLIAMS, *A Short History of Technology from the Earliest Times to AD 1900*, Oxford University Press, Oxford, 1960, 782 pp.

Production and Uses of Nitric Acid[56,145,146]

Before 1900 the large-scale production of nitric acid was based entirely on the reaction of concentrated sulfuric acid with $NaNO_3$ and KNO_3 (p. 407). The first successful process for making nitric acid directly from N_2 and O_2 was devised in 1903 by E. Birkeland and S. Eyde in Norway and represented the first industrial fixation of nitrogen:

$$\tfrac{1}{2}N_2 + 1\tfrac{1}{4}O_2 + \tfrac{1}{2}H_2O(l) \longrightarrow HNO_3(l); \quad \Delta H°(298\,K) - 30.3\,kJ\,mol^{-1}$$

The overall reaction is exothermic but required the use of an electric arc furnace which, even with relatively cheap hydroelectricity, made the process very expensive. The severe activation energy barrier, though economically regrettable, is in fact essential to life since, in its absence, all the oxygen in the air would be rapidly consumed and the oceans would be a dilute solution of nitric acid and its salts. [Dilution of $HNO_3(l)$ to $HNO_3(aq)$ evolves a further $33.3\,kJ\,mol^{-1}$ at 25°C.]

The modern process for manufacturing nitric acid depends on the catalytic oxidation of NH_3 over heated Pt to give NO in preference to other thermodynamically more favoured products (p. 423). The reaction was first systematically studied in 1901 by W. Ostwald (Nobel Prize 1909) and by 1908 a commercial plant near Bochum, Germany, was producing 3 tonnes/day. However, significant expansion in production depended on the economical availability of synthetic ammonia by the Haber–Bosch process (p. 421). The reactions occurring, and the enthalpy changes per mole of N atoms at 25°C are:

$$NH_3 + 1\tfrac{1}{4}O_2 \longrightarrow NO + 1\tfrac{1}{2}H_2O(l); \quad \Delta H° - 292.5\ kJ\,mol^{-1}$$

$$NO + \tfrac{1}{2}O_2 \longrightarrow NO_2; \quad \Delta H° - 56.8\ kJ\,mol^{-1}$$

$$NO_2 + \tfrac{1}{3}H_2O(l) \longrightarrow \tfrac{2}{3}HNO_3(l) + \tfrac{1}{3}NO; \quad \Delta H° - 23.3\ kJ\,mol^{-1}$$

Whence, multiplying the second and third reactions by $\tfrac{3}{2}$ and adding:

$$NH_3(g) + 2O_2(g) \longrightarrow HNO_3(l) + H_2O(l); \quad \Delta H° - 412.6\ kJ\,mol^{-1}$$

In a typical industrial unit a mixture of air with 10% by volume of NH_3 is passed very rapidly over a series of gauzes (Pt, 5–10% Rh) at ~850°C and 5 atm pressure; contact time with the catalyst is restricted to ≤ 1 ms in order to minimize unwanted side reactions. Conversion efficiency is ~96% (one of the most efficient industrial catalytic reactions known) and the effluent gases are passed through an absorption column to yield 60% aqueous nitric acid at about 40°C. Loss of platinum metal from the catalyst under operating conditions is reduced by alloying with Rh but tends to increase with pressure from about 50–100 mg/tonne of HNO_3 produced at atmospheric pressure to about 250 mg/tonne at 10 atm; though this is not a major part of the cost, the scale of operations means that about 0.5 tonne of Pt metals is lost annually in the UK from this cause and more than twice this amount in the USA.

Concentration by distillation of the 60% aqueous nitric acid produced in most modern ammonia-burning plants is limited by the formation of a maximum-boiling azeotrope (122°) at 68.5% by weight; further concentration to 98–9% can be effected by countercurrent dehydration using concentrated H_2SO_4, or by distillation from concentrated $Mg(NO_3)_2$ solutions. Alternatively 99% pure HNO_3 can be obtained directly from ammonia oxidation by incorporating a final oxidation of N_2O_4 with the theoretical amounts of air and water at 70°C and 50 atm over a period of 4 h:

$$N_2O_4 + \tfrac{1}{2}O_2 + H_2O \longrightarrow 2HNO_3$$

The largest use of nitric acid (~75%) is in the manufacture of NH_4NO_3 and of this, about 75% is used for fertilizer production. Many plants have a capacity of 2000 tonnes/day or more and great care must be taken to produce the NH_4NO_3 in a readily handleable form (e.g. prills of about 3 mm diameter); about 1% of a "conditioner" is usually added to improve storage and handling properties. NH_4NO_3 is thermally unstable (p. 469) and decomposition can become explosive. For this reason a temperature limit of 140°C is imposed on the neutralization step and pH is strictly controlled. The decomposition is catalysed by many inorganic materials including chloride, chromates, hypophosphites, thiosulfates and powdered metals (e.g. Cu, Zn, Hg). Organic materials (oil, paper, string, sawdust, etc.) must also be rigorously excluded during neutralization since their oxidation releases additional heat. Indeed, since the mid-1950s NH_4NO_3 prills mixed with fuel oil have been extensively used as a direct explosive in mining and quarrying operations (p. 469) and this use now accounts for up to 15% of the NH_4NO_3 produced.

Panel continues

[145] C. KELETI (ed), *Nitric Acid and Fertilizer Nitrates*, Marcel Dekker, N.Y. 1985, 392 pp.
[146] S. I. CLARKE and W. J. MAZZAFRO Nitric acid, in *Kirk–Othmer Encyclopedia of Chemical Technology*, 4th edn., Vol. 17, pp. 80–107 (1996).

Some 8–9% of HNO_3 goes to make cyclohexanone, the raw material for adipic acid and ε-caprolactam, which are the monomers for nylon-6,6 and nylon-6 respectively. A further 7–10% is used in other organic nitration reactions to give nitroglycerine, nitrocellulose, trinitrotoluene and numerous other organic intermediates. Minor uses (which still consume large quantities of the acid) include the pickling of stainless steel, the etching of metals, and its use as the oxidizer in rocket fuels. In Europe nitric acid is sometimes used to replace sulfuric acid in the treatment of phosphate rock to give nitrophosphate fertilizers according to the idealized equation:

$$Ca_{10}(PO_4)_6F_2 + 14HNO_3 \longrightarrow 3Ca(H_2PO_4)_2 + 7Ca(NO_3)_2 + 2HF$$

Another minority use is in the manufacture of nitrates (other than NH_4NO_3) for use in explosives, propellants, and pyrotechnics generally; typical examples are:

explosives: gun powder, KNO_3/S/powdered C (often reinforced with powdered Si)
white smokes: $ZnO/CaSi_2/KNO_3/C_2Cl_6$
incendiary agents: $Al/NaNO_3$/methylmethacrylate/benzene
local heat sources: $Al/Fe_3O_4/Ba(NO_3)_2$; $Mg/Sr(NO_3)_2/SrC_2O_4$/thiokol polysulfide
photoflashes: $Mg/NaNO_3$
flares (up to 10 min): $Mg/NaNO_3/CaC_2O_4$/polyvinyl chloride/varnish; $Ti/NaNO_3$/boiled linseed oil
coloured flares: $Mg/Sr(NO_3)_2$/chlorinated rubber (red); $Mg(Ba(NO_3)_2)$/chlorinated rubber (green).

These equilibria effect a rapid exchange of N atoms between the various species and only a single ^{15}N nmr signal is seen at the weighted average position of HNO_3, $[NO_2]^+$ and $[NO_3]^-$. They also account for the high electrical conductivity of the "pure" (stoichiometric) liquid (Table 11.13), and are an important factor in the chemical reactions of nitric acid and its non-aqueous solutions see below.

The phase diagram HNO_3–H_2O shows the presence of two hydrates, $HNO_3.H_2O$ mp $-37.68°$, and $HNO_3.3H_2O$ mp $-18.47°$. A further hemihydrate, $2HNO_3.H_2O$, can be extracted into benzene or toluene from 6 to 16 M aqueous solutions of nitric acid, and a dimer hydrate, $2HNO_3.3H_2O$, is also known, though neither can be crystallized. The structure of the two crystalline hydrates is dominated by hydrogen bonding as expected; e.g. the monohydrate is $[H_3O]^+[NO_3]^-$ in which there are puckered layers comprising pyramidal $[H_3O]^+$ hydrogen bonded to planar $[NO_3]^-$ so that there are 3 H bonds per ion. The trihydrate forms a more complex three-dimensional H-bonded framework. (See also p. 468 for the structure of hydrogen-nitrates.)

The solution chemistry of nitric acid is extremely varied. Redox data are summarized in Table 11.4 and Fig. 11.9 (pp. 434–8). In dilute aqueous solutions (<2 M) nitric acid is extensively dissociated into ions and behaves as a typical strong acid in its reactions with metals, oxides, carbonates, etc. More concentrated aqueous solutions are strongly oxidizing and attack most metals except Au, Pt, Rh and Ir, though some metals which react at lower concentrations are rendered passive, probably because of the formation of an oxide film (e.g. Al, Cr, Fe, Cu). Aqua regia (a mixture of concentrated hydrochloric and nitric acids in the ratio of ∼3:1 by volume) is even more aggressive, due to the formation of free Cl_2 and ClNO and the superior complexing ability of the chloride ion; it has long been known to "dissolve" both gold and the platinum metals, hence its name. In concentrated H_2SO_4 the chemistry of nitric acid is dominated by the presence of the nitronium ion (pp. 458, 465):

$$HNO_3 + 2H_2SO_4 \rightleftharpoons NO_2^+ + H_3O^+ + 2HSO_4^-;$$

$$K \sim 22 \text{ mol l}^{-1}$$

Such solutions are extensively used in aromatic nitration reactions in the heavy organic chemicals industry. See also pp. 457–8.

Anhydrous nitric acid has been studied as a nonaqueous ionizing solvent, though salts tend to be rather insoluble unless they produce NO_2^+ or

NO_3^- ions.[147] Addition of water to nitric acid at first diminishes its electrical conductivity by repressing the autoprotolysis reactions mentioned above. For example, at $-10°$ the conductivity decreases from 3.67×10^{-2} ohm^{-1} cm^{-1} to a minimum of 1.08×10^{-2} ohm^{-1} cm^{-1} at 1.75 molal H_2O (82.8% N_2O_5) before rising again due to the increasing formation of the hydroxonium ion according to the acid-base equilibrium

$$HNO_3 + H_2O \rightleftharpoons H_3O^+ + NO_3^-$$

By contrast, Raman spectroscopy and conductivity measurements show that N_2O_4 ionizes almost completely in anhydrous HNO_3 to give NO^+ and NO_3^- and such solutions show no evidence for the species N_2O_4, NO_2^+ or NO_2^-.[126] N_2O_5 is also extremely soluble in anhydrous nitric acid in which it is completely ionized as $NO_2^+NO_3^-$.

Nitrates, the salts of nitric acid, can readily be made by appropriate neutralization of the acid, though sometimes it is the hydrate which crystallizes from aqueous solution. Anhydrous

---

147 W. H. LEE, in J. J. LAGOWSKI (ed.), *The Chemistry of Non-aqueous Solvents*, Vol. 2, pp. 151–89, Academic Press, New York, 1967.

nitrates and nitrato complexes are often best prepared by use of donor solvents containing N_2O_4 (p. 456). The reaction of liquid N_2O_5 with metal oxides and chlorides affords an alternative route, e.g.:

$$TiCl_4 + 4N_2O_5 \longrightarrow Ti(NO_3)_4 + 2N_2O_4 + 2Cl_2$$

Many nitrates are major items of commerce and are dealt with under the appropriate metal (e.g. $NaNO_3$, KNO_3, NH_4NO_3, etc.). In addition, various hydrogen dinitrates and dihydrogen trinitrates are known of formula $M[H(NO_3)_2]$ and $M[H_2(NO_3)_3]$ where M is a large cation such as K, Rb, Cs, NH_4 or AsPh$_4$. In [AsPh$_4$][H(NO$_3$)$_2$] 2 coplanar NO_3^- ions are linked by a short H bond as shown in (a) whereas [*trans*-RhBr$_2$(py)$_4$][H(NO$_3$)$_2$] features a slightly distorted tetrahedral group of 4 oxygen atoms in which the position of the H atom is not obvious [structure (b)]. In [NH$_4$][H$_2$(NO$_3$)$_3$] there is a more extended system of H bonds in which 2 coplanar molecules of HNO_3 are symmetrically bridged by an NO_3^- ion at right angles as shown in (c).

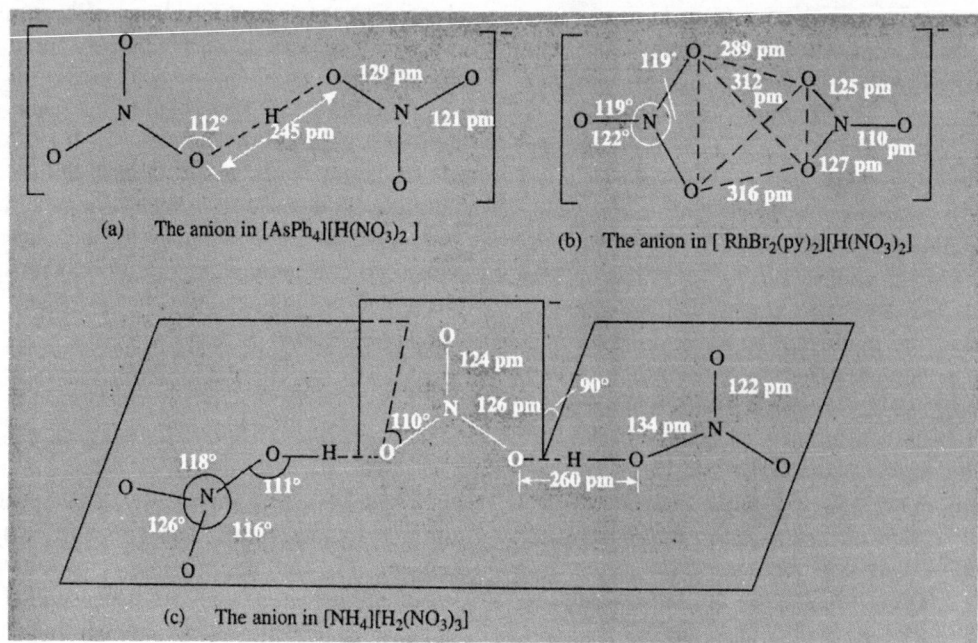

(a) The anion in [AsPh$_4$][H(NO$_3$)$_2$]

(b) The anion in [RhBr$_2$(py)$_2$][H(NO$_3$)$_2$]

(c) The anion in [NH$_4$][H$_2$(NO$_3$)$_3$]

As with the salts of other oxoacids, the thermal stability of nitrates varies markedly with the basicity of the metal, and the products of decomposition are equally varied.[148] Thus the nitrates of Group 1 and 2 metals find use as molten salt baths because of their thermal stability and low mp (especially as mixtures). Representative values of mp and the temperature (T_d) at which the decomposition pressure of O_2 reaches 1 atm are:

M	Li	Na	K	Rb	Cs	Ag	Tl
MP of MNO_3/°C	255	307	333	310	414	212	206
T_d/°C		474	525	533	548	584	–	–

The product of thermolysis is the nitrite or, if this is unstable at the temperature employed, the oxide (or even the metal if the oxide is also unstable):[149]

$$2NaNO_3 \longrightarrow 2NaNO_2 + O_2 \qquad \text{(see p. 462)}$$

$$2KNO_3 \longrightarrow K_2O + N_2 + \tfrac{5}{2}O_2$$

$$Pb(NO_3)_2 \longrightarrow PbO + 2NO_2 + \tfrac{1}{2}O_2 \quad \text{(see p. 456)}$$

$$2AgNO_3 \longrightarrow Ag + 2NO_2 + O_2$$

As indicated in earlier sections, NH_4NO_3 can be exploded violently at high temperatures or by use of detonators (p. 466), but slow controlled thermolysis yields N_2O (p. 443):

$$2NH_4NO_3 \xrightarrow{>300°} 2N_2 + O_2 + 4H_2O$$

$$NH_4NO_3 \xrightarrow{200-260°} N_2O + 2H_2O$$

The presence of organic matter or other reducible material also markedly affects the thermal stability of nitrates and the use of KNO_3 in gunpowder has been known for centuries (p. 645).

The nitrate group, like the nitrite group, is a versatile ligand and numerous modes of coordination have been found in nitrato complexes.[150] The "uncoordinated" NO_3^- ion (isoelectronic with BF_3, BO_3^{3-}, CO_3^{2-}, etc.) is planar with N–O near 122 pm; this value increases to 126 pm in $AgNO_3$ and 127 pm in $Pb(NO_3)_2$. The most common mode of coordination is the symmetric bidentate mode Fig. 11.16a, though unsymmetrical bidentate coordination (b) also occurs and, in the limit, unidentate coordination (c). Bridging modes include the *syn-syn* conformation (d) (and the *anti-anti* analogue), and also geometries in which a single O atom bridges 2 or even 3 metal atoms (e), (f). Sometimes more than one mode occurs in the same compound.

Symmetrical bidentate coordination (a) has been observed in complexes with 1–6 nitrates coordinated to the central metal, e.g. [Cu(NO_3)(PPh_3)_2]; [Cu(NO_3)_2], [Co(NO_3)_2(OPMe_3)_2]; [Co(NO_3)_3] in which the 6 coordinating O atoms define an almost regular octahedron (Fig. 11.17a), [La(NO_3)_3(bipy)_2]; [Ti(NO_3)_4], [Mn(NO_3)_4]^{2-}, [Fe(NO_3)_4]^- and [Sn(NO_3)_4], which feature dodecahedral coordination about the metal; [Ce(NO_3)_5]^{2-} in which the 5 bidentate nitrate groups define a trigonal bipyramid leading to tenfold coordination of cerium (Fig. 11.17b); [Ce(NO_3)_6]^{2-} and [Th(NO_3)_6]^{2-}, which feature nearly regular icosahedral (p. 141) coordination of the metal by 12 O atoms; and many lanthanide and uranyl [UO_2]^{2+} complexes. It seems, therefore, that the size of the metal centre is not necessarily a dominant factor.

Unsymmetrical bidentate coordination (Fig. 11.16b) is observed in the high-spin d^7 complex [Co(NO_3)_4]^{2-} (Fig. 11.17c), in [SnMe_2(NO_3)_2] and also in several Cu^{II} complexes of formula [CuL_2(NO_3)_2], where L is MeCN, H_2O, py or 2-MeC_5H_4N (α-picoline). An example of unidentate coordination is furnished by K[Au(NO_3)_4] as shown in Fig. 11.18(a), and further examples are in *cis*-[Pd(NO_3)_2(OSMe_2)_2], [Re(CO)_5(NO_3)], [Ni(NO_3)_2(H_2O)_4], [Zn(NO_3)_2(H_2O)_4] and several Cu^{II} complexes such as [CuL_2(NO_3)_2] where L is pyridine *N*-oxide or 1,4-diazacycloheptane. It appears that a combination of steric effects and the limited availability of coordination sites in these already highly coordinated late-transition-metal complexes restricts each nitrate group to one coordination site. When more

[148] B. O. Field and C. J. Hardy, *Q. Rev.* **18**, 361–88 (1964).

[149] K. J. Mysels, *J. Chem. Educ.* **36** 303–4 (1959).

[150] C. C. Addison, N. Logan, S. C. Wallwork and C. D. Garner, *Q. Rev.* **25**, 289–322 (1971).

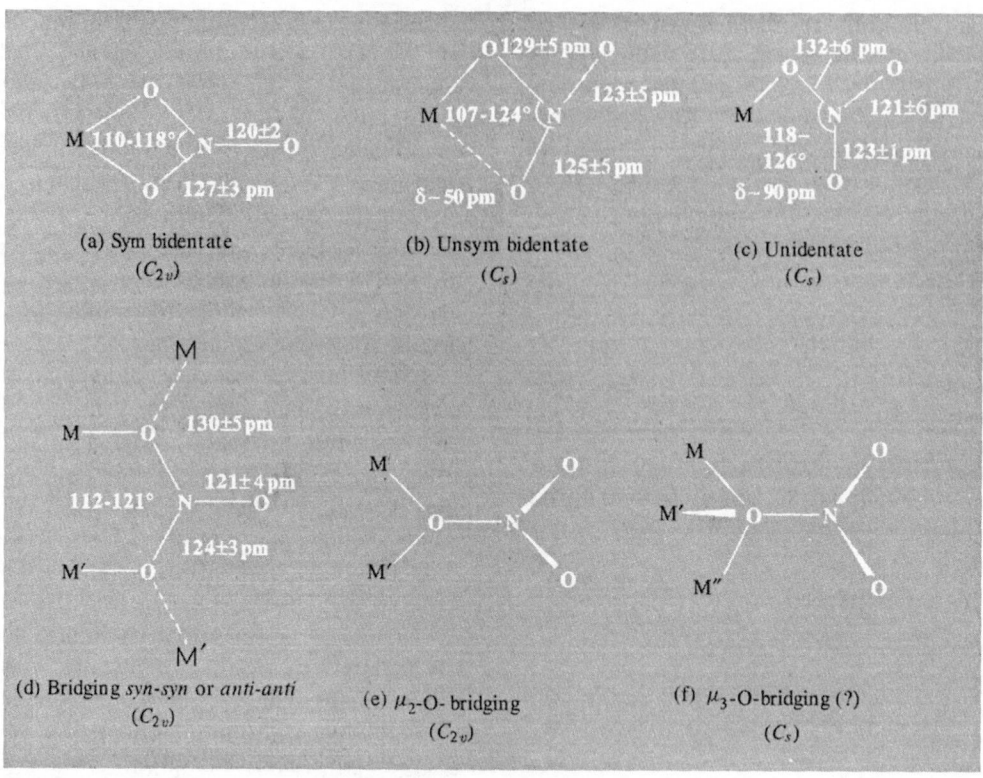

Figure 11.16 Coordination geometries of the nitrate group showing typical values for the interatomic distances and angles. Further structural details are in ref. 150.

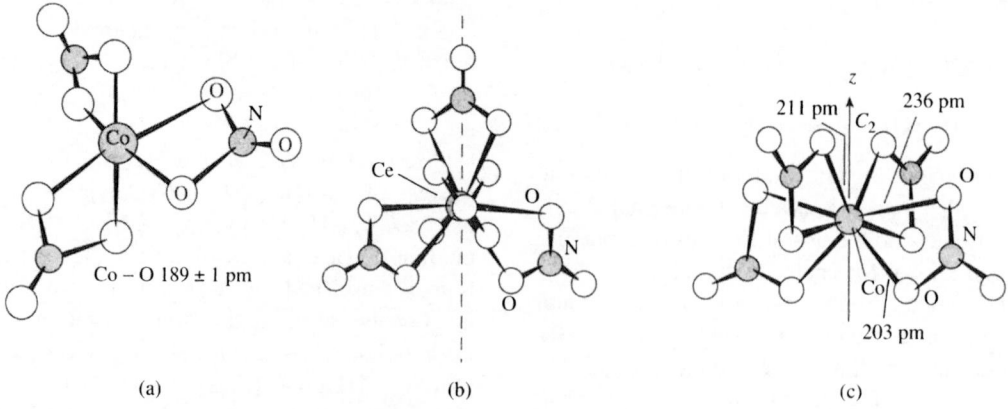

Figure 11.17 Structures of (a) $Co(NO_3)_3$, (b) $[Ce(NO_3)_5]^{2-}$ and (c) $[Co(NO_3)_4]^{2-}$.

sites become available, as in $[Ni(NO_3)_2(H_2O)_2]$ and $[Zn(NO_3)_2(H_2O)_2]$, or when the co-ligands are less bulky, as in $[CuL_2(NO_3)_2]$, where L is H_2O, MeCN or $MeNO_2$, then the nitrate groups become bidentate bridging (mode d in Fig. 11.16) and a further example of this is seen in $[\alpha\text{-}Cu(NO_3)_2]$, which forms a more extensive network of bridging nitrate groups, as

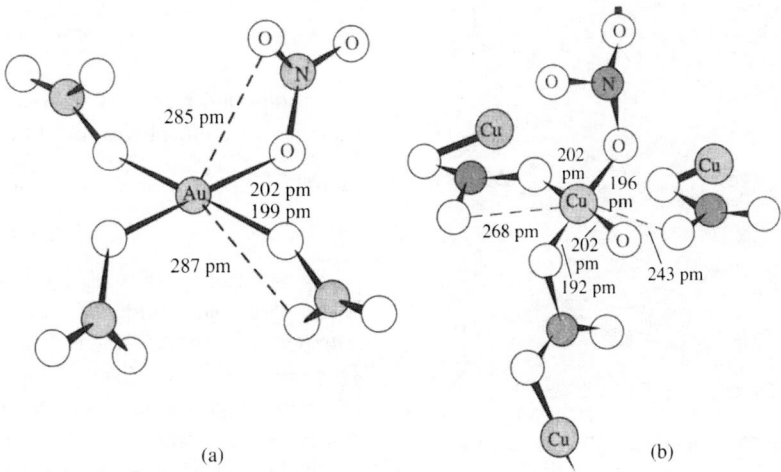

Figure 11.18   (a) Structure of $[Au(NO_3)_4]^-$, (b) α-$Cu(NO_3)_2$.

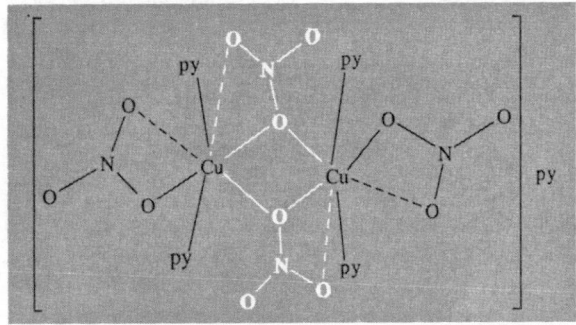

Figure 11.19   Schematic diagram of the centrosymmetric dimer in $[Cu_2(NO_3)_4(py)_4]py$ showing the two bridging nitrato groups each coordinated to the 2 Cu atoms by a single O atom; the dimer also has an unsymmetrical bidentate nitrate group on each Cu.

shown in Fig. 11.18(b). The single oxygen atom bridging mode (e) occurs in $[Cu(NO_3)_2(py)_2]_2py$ (Fig. 11.19) and the triple-bridge (f) may occur in $[Cu_4(NO_3)_2(OH)_6]$ though there is some uncertainty about this structure and further refinement would be desirable. Finally, the structure of the unique yellow solvate of formula $[Fe(NO_3)_3.1\frac{1}{2}N_2O_4]$ (p. 457) has been shown[128] to be $[N_4O_6]^{2+}[Fe(NO_3)_4]^-_2$. Each anion has 4 symmetrically bidentate NO_3 groups in which the coordinating O atoms lie at the corners of a trigonal dodecahedron, as is commonly found in tetranitrato species (N–O_t 120 pm, N–O(Fe) 127 pm, angles O–N–O 113.4° and O–Fe–O 60.0°). The $[N_4O_6]^{2+}$ cation comprises a central planar nitrate group (N–O 123 pm) surrounded by 3 NO groups at distances which vary from 241 to 278 pm (Fig. 11.20); the interatomic distance in the NO groups is very short (90–99 pm) implying NO^+ and the distances of these to the central NO_3 group are slightly less than the sum of the van der Waals radii for N and O.

Orthonitrates, $M_3^I NO_4$

There is no free acid H_3NO_4 analogous to orthophosphoric acid H_3PO_4 (p. 516), but the alkali metal orthonitrates Na_3NO_4 and K_3NO_4

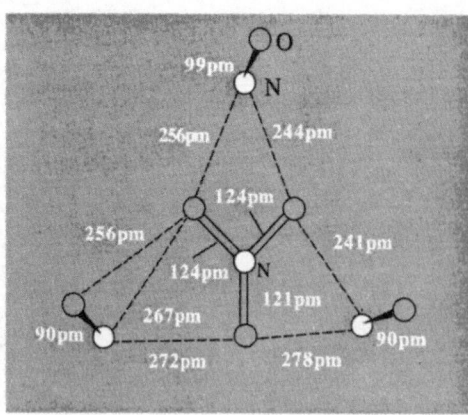

Figure 11.20 The $[N_4O_6]^{2+}$ cation.

have been synthesized by direct reaction at elevated temperatures, e.g.:[151,152]

$$NaNO_3 + Na_2O \xrightarrow[\text{300°C for 7 days}]{\text{Ag crucible}} Na_3NO_4$$

The compound forms white crystals that are very sensitive to atmospheric moisture and CO_2:

$$Na_3NO_4 + H_2O + CO_2 \longrightarrow NaNO_3$$
$$+ NaOH + NaHCO_3$$

X-ray structural analyses have shown that the NO_4^{3-} ion has regular T_d symmetry with the unexpectedly small N–O distance of 139 pm. This suggests that substantial polar interactions are superimposed on the N–O single bonds since the d_π orbitals on N are too high in energy to contribute significantly to multiple covalent bonding. It further implies that d_π–p_π interactions need not necessarily be invoked to explain the observed short interatomic distance in the isoelectronic oxoanions PO_4^{3-}, SO_4^{2-} and ClO_4^-.

[151] M. JANSEN, *Angew. Chem. Int. Edn. Engl.* **16**, 534 (1977); **18**, 698 (1979).

[152] T. BREMM and M. JANSEN, *Z. anorg. allg. Chem.* **608**, 56–9 (1992).

			1 H	2 He				

(periodic table graphic)

12
Phosphorus

12.1 Introduction

Phosphorus has an extensive and varied chemistry which transcends the traditional boundaries of inorganic chemistry not only because of its propensity to form innumerable covalent "organophosphorus" compounds, but also because of the numerous and crucial roles it plays in the biochemistry of all living things. It was first isolated by the alchemist Hennig Brandt in 1669 by the unsavoury process of allowing urine to putrify for several days before boiling it down to a paste which was then reductively distilled at high temperatures; the vapours were condensed under water to give the element as a white waxy substance that glowed in the dark when exposed to air.[1] Robert Boyle improved the process (1680) and in subsequent years made the oxide and phosphoric acid; he referred to the element as "aerial noctiluca", but the name phosphorus soon became generally accepted (Greek φως *phos*, light; Greek φορος *phoros*, bringing).

As shown in the Panel on the next page, phosphorus is probably unique among the elements in being isolated first from animal (human) excreta, then from plants, and only a century later being recognized in a mineral.

C 6	N 7	O 8
Si 14	P 15	S 16
Ge 32	As 33	Se 34

In much of its chemistry phosphorus stands in relation to nitrogen as sulfur does to oxygen. For example, whereas N_2 and O_2 are diatomic gases, P and S have many allotropic modifications which reflect the various modes of catenation adopted. Again, the ability of P and S to form multiple bonds to C, N and O, though it exists, is less highly developed than for N (p. 416), whereas the ability to form extended networks of $-P-O-P-O-$ and $-S-O-S-O-$ bonds is greater; this is well illustrated by comparing the oxides and oxoanions of N

---

[1] M. E. WEEKS, *Discovery of the Elements*, Journal of Chemical Education Publ., Easton, Pa., 1956; Phosphorus, pp. 109–39.

Time Chart for Phosphorus Chemistry

1669	Phosphorus isolated from urine by H. Brandt.
1680	R. Boyle improved the process and showed air was necessary for the phosphorescence of P.
1688	Phosphorus first detected in the vegetable kingdom (by B. Albino).
1694	P_4O_{10} and H_3PO_4 first made by R. Boyle.
1769	Phosphorus shown by J. G. Gahn and C. W. Scheele to be an essential constituent in the bones of man and animals, thereby revealing a plentiful source of fertilizers.
1779	Phosphorus first discovered in a mineral by J. G. Gahn (pyromorphite, a lead phosphate); subsequently found in the much more abundant apatite by T. Bergman and J. L. Proust.
1783	PH_3 first prepared by P. Gengembre (and independently in 1786 by R. Kirwan).
1808	PCl_3 and PCl_5 made by J. L. Gay Lussac and L. J. Thenard (and by H. Davy).
1811	N. L. Vauquelin isolated the first organic P compound (lethicin) from brain fat; it was characterized as a phospholipid by Gobbley in 1850.
1816	P. L. Dulong first clearly demonstrated the existence of two oxides of P.
1820	First synthesis of an organo-P compound by J. L. Lassaigne who made alkyl phosphites from H_3PO_4 + ROH.
1833	T. Graham (who later became the first President of the Chemical Society) classified phosphates as ortho, pyro or meta, following J. J. Berzelius's preparation of pyrophosphoric acid by heat.
1834	$(PNCl_2)_n$ made by F. Wöhler and J. von Liebig (originally formulated as $P_3N_2Cl_5$).
1843	J. Murray patented his production of "superphosphate" fertilizer (a name coined by him for the product of H_2SO_4 on phosphate rock).
1844	A. Albright started the manufacture of elemental P in England (for matches); 0.75 tonne in 1844, 26.5 tonnes in 1851.
1845	Polyphosphoric acids made by T. Fleitmann and W. Henneberg.
1848	Red (amorphous) P discovered by A. Schrötter.
1850	First commercial production of "wet process" phosphoric acid.
1868	E. F. Hoppe-Seyler and F. Miescher isolated "nuclein", the first nucleic acid, from pus.
1880	Modern cyclic formulation of tetrametaphosphate anion suggested by A. Glatzel. (Ring structure of metaphosphate definitely established by L. Pauling and J. Sherman 1937.)
1888	Electrothermal process for manufacturing P introduced by J. B. Readman (Edinburgh).
1898	"Strike-anywhere" matches devised by H. Sévène and E. D. Cahen in France; previously the brothers Lundström had exhibited "safety matches" in 1855, and the first P-containing striking match had been invented by F. Dérosne in 1812.
1929	C. H. Fiske and Y. Subbarow discovered adenosine triphosphate (ATP) in muscle fibre; it was synthesized some 20 y later by A. Todd *et al.* (Nobel Prize 1957).
1932	Elucidation of the glycolysis process (by G. Embden and by O. Meyerhof) followed by the glucose oxidation process (H. A. Krebs, 1937) established the intimate involvement of P compounds in many biochemical reactions.
1935	Radioactive ^{32}P made by (n, γ) reaction on ^{31}P.
~1940	Highly polymeric phosphate esters (nucleic acids) present in all cells and recognized as essential constituents of chromosomes.
1951	First ^{31}P nmr chemical shifts measured by W. C. Dickinson (for $POCl_3$, PCl_3, etc. relative to aq. H_3PO_4).
1952	Detergents (using polyphosphates) overtake soap as main washing agent in the USA. (Heavy duty liquid detergents with polyphosphates introduced in 1955.)
1953	F. H. C. Crick, J. B. Watson and M. H. F. Wilkins (with Rosalind Franklin) establish the double helix structure of nucleic acids (Nobel Prize 1962).
1960	Concept of "pseudorotation" introduced by R. S. Berry to interpret the stereochemical non-rigidity of trigonal bipyramidal PF_5 (and SF_4, ClF_3); the 5 F atoms are equivalent (1953) due to interconversion via a square pyramidal intermediate.
1961	First 2-coordinate compound of P prepared by A. B. Burg ($Me_3P=PCF_3$). First 1-coordinate P compound ($HC\equiv P$) made by T. E. Gier.
1966	First heterocyclic aromatic analogue of pyridine ($Ph_3C_5H_2P$) prepared by G. Märkl, followed by the parent compound C_5H_5P in 1971 (A. J. Ashe).
1977+	P_4 as an η^1, η^2, etc. ligand (see Fig. 12.9, p. 488).
1979	G. Wittig shared the Chemistry Nobel Prize for his development of the Wittig reaction (first published with G. Geissler in 1953).
1981	First stable phospha-alkyne, $Bu^tC\equiv P$ (cf. RCN).
1983+	Characterization of extended *conjuncto*-polyphosphide clusters (p. 491) and polyphosphanes (p. 492).

and P. "Valency expansion" is another point of difference between the elements of the first and second periods of the periodic table for, although compounds in which N has a formal oxidation state of $+5$ are known, no simple "single-bonded" species such as NF_5 or NCl_6^- have been prepared, analogous to PF_5 and PCl_6^-. This finds interpretation in the availability of 3d orbitals for bonding in P (and S) but not for N (or O). The extremely important Wittig reaction for olefin synthesis (p. 545) is another manifestation of this property. Discussion of more extensive group trends in which N and P are compared with the other Group 15 elements As, Sb and Bi, is deferred until the next chapter (pp. 550–4).

Because of the great importance of phosphorus and its compounds in the chemical industry, several books and reviews on their preparation and uses are available.[2–10] Some of these applications reflect the fact that P is a vital element for the growth and development of all plants and animals and is therefore an important constituent in many fertilizers. Phosphorus compounds are involved in energy transfer processes (such as photosynthesis (p. 126), metabolism, nerve function and muscle action), in heredity (via DNA), and in the production of bones and teeth.[11–14] Topics in phosphorus chemistry are regularly reviewed.[15]

12.2 The Element

12.2.1 Abundance and distribution

Phosphorus is the eleventh element in order of abundance in crustal rocks of the earth and it occurs there to the extent of $\sim$1120 ppm (cf. H $\sim$1520 ppm, Mn $\sim$1060 ppm). All its known terrestrial minerals are orthophosphates though the reduced phosphide mineral schreibersite $(Fe,Ni)_3P$ occurs in most iron meteorites. Some 200 crystalline phosphate minerals have been described, but by far the major amount of P occurs in a single mineral family, the apatites, and these are the only ones of industrial importance, the others being rare curiosities.[16] Apatites (p. 523) have the idealized general formula $3Ca_3(PO_4)_2.CaX_2$, that is $Ca_{10}(PO_4)_6X_2$, and common members are fluorapatite $Ca_5(PO_4)_3F$, chloroapatite $Ca_5(PO_4)_3Cl$, and hydroxyapatite $Ca_5(PO_4)_3(OH)$. In addition, there are vast deposits of amorphous phosphate rock, phosphorite, which approximates in composition to fluoroapatite.[11,17] These deposits are widely

[2] J. EMSLEY and D. HALL, *The Chemistry of Phosphorus*, Harper & Row, London 1976, 534 pp.

[3] A. F. CHILDS, Phosphorus, phosphoric acid and inorganic phosphates, in *The Modern Inorganic Chemicals Industry*, (R. THOMPSON, ed.), pp. 375–401, The Chemical Society, London, 1977.

[4] *Proceedings of the First International Congress on Phosphorus Compounds and their Non-fertilizer Applications, 17–21 October 1977 Rabat, Morocco*, IMPHOS (Institut Mondial du Phosphat), Rabat, 1978, 767 pp.

[5] L. D. QUIN and J. D. VERKADE (eds.), *Phosphorus Chemistry: Proceedings of the 1981 International Conference*, ACS Symposium Series No. 171, 1981, 640 pp.

[6] H. GOLDWHITE, *Introduction to Phosphorus Chemistry*, Cambridge University Press, Cambridge, 1981, 113 pp.

[7] E. C. ALYEA and D. W. MEEK (eds.), *Catalytic Aspects of Metal Phosphine Complexes*, ACS Symposium Series No. 196, 1982, 421 pp.

[8] D. E. C. CORBRIDGE, *Phosphorus: An Outline of its Chemistry, Biochemistry and Technology*, 5th edn. Elsevier, Amsterdam, 1995, 1208 pp.

[9] A. D. F. TOY and E. N. WALSH, *Phosphorus Chemistry in Everyday Living*, (2nd edn). Washington, ACS, 1987, 362 pp.

[10] E. N. WALSH, E. J. GRIFFITH, R. W. PARRY and L. D. QUIN (eds.), *Phosphorus Chemistry: Developments in American Science*, ACS Symposium Series No. 486, 1992, 288 pp.

[11] J. R. VAN WAZER (ed.), *Phosphorus and its Compounds*, Vol. 2, *Technology, Biological Functions and Applications*, Interscience, New York, 1961, 2046 pp.

[12] F. H. PORTUGAL and J. S. COHEN, *A Century of DNA. A History of the Discovery of the Structure and Function of the Genetic Substance*, MIT Press, Littleton, Mass., 1977, 384 pp.

[13] R. L. RAWLS, *Chem. and Eng. News*, Dec. 21, 1987, pp. 26–39.

[14] J. K. BARTON, *Chem. and Eng. News*, Sept. 26, 1988, pp. 30–42.

[15] *Topics in Phosphorus Chemistry*, Wiley, New York, Vol. 1 (1964)–Vol. 11 (1983).

[16] J. O. NRIAGU and P. B. MOORE (eds.), *Phosphate Minerals*, Springer Verlag, Berlin, 1984, 442 pp.

[17] W. BÜCHNER, R. SCHLIEBS, G. WINTER and K. H. BÜCHEL, *Industrial Inorganic Chemistry*, (transl. D. R. TERRELL), VCH, Weinheim, 1989, Phosphorus, pp. 68–105.

Table 12.1 Estimated reserves of phosphate rock (in gigatonnes of contained P)

Continent	Main areas	Reserves/10^9 tonnes P
Africa	Morocco, Senegal, Tunisia, Algeria, Sahara, Egypt, Togo, Angola, South Africa	4.6
North America	USA (Florida, Georgia, Carolina, Tennessee, Idaho, Montana, Utah, Wyoming), Mexico	1.6
South America	Peru, Brazil, Chile, Columbia	0.4
Europe	Western and Eastern	0.7
Asia/Middle East	Kola Peninsula, Kazakhstan, Siberia, Jordan, Israel, Saudi Arabia, India, Turkey	1.4
Australasia	Queensland, Nauru, Makatea	0.4
Total		9.1

spread throughout the world as indicated in Table 12.1 and reserves (1982 estimates) are adequate for several centuries with present technology. The phosphate content of commercial phosphate rock generally falls in the range $(72 \pm 10)\%$ BPL [i.e. "bone phosphate of lime", $Ca_3(PO_4)_2$] corresponding to $(33 \pm 5)\%$ P_4O_{10} or 12–17% P. The USA is the principal producer, having produced one-third of the total world output in 1985, and Morocco is the largest exporter, mainly to the UK and continental Europe. World production is a staggering 151 million tonnes of phosphate rock per annum (1985), equivalent to some 20 million tonnes of contained phosphorus (p. 480).

Phosphorus also occurs in all living things and the phosphate cycle, including the massive use of phosphatic fertilizers, is of great current interest.[18-20] The movement of phosphorus through the environment differs from that of the other non-metals essential to life (H, C, N, O and S) because it has no volatile compounds that can circulate via the atmosphere. Instead, it circulates via two rapid biological cycles on land and sea (weeks and years) superimposed on a much slower primary geological inorganic cycle (millions of years). In the inorganic cycle, phosphates are slowly leached from the igneous or sedimentary rocks by weathering, and transported by rivers to the lakes and seas where they are precipitated as insoluble metal phosphates or incorporated into the aquatic food chain. The solubility of metal phosphates clearly depends on pH, salinity, temperature, etc., but in neutral solution $Ca_3(PO_4)_2$ (solubility product $\sim 10^{-29}$ $mol^5 \, l^{-5}$) may first precipitate and then gradually transform into the less soluble hydroxyapatite [$Ca_5(PO_4)_3(OH)$], and, finally, into the least-soluble member, fluoroapatite (solubility product $\sim 10^{-60}$ $mol^9 \, l^{-9}$). Sedimentation follows and eventually, on a geological time scale, uplift to form a new land mass. Some idea of actual concentrations of ions involved may be obtained from the fact that in sea water there is one phosphate group per million water molecules; at a salinity of 3.3%, pH 8 and 20°C, 87% of the inorganic phosphate exist as [HPO_4]$^{2-}$, 12% as [PO_4]$^{3-}$ and 1% as [H_2PO_4]$^-$. Of the [PO_4]$^{3-}$ species, 99.6% is complexed with cations other than Na^+.[21]

The secondary biological cycles stem from the crucial roles that phosphates and particularly organophosphates play in all life processes. Thus organophosphates are incorporated into the backbone structures of DNA and RNA which regulate the reproductive processes of cells, and they

[18] B. H. SVENSSON and R. SÖDERLUND (eds.), *Nitrogen, Phosphorus, and Sulfur–Global Biogeochemical Cycles*, SCOPE Report, No. 7, Sweden 1976, 170 pp.; also SCOPE Report No. 10, Wiley, New York, 1977, 220 pp, and SCOPE Newsletter 47, Jan. 1995, pp. 1–4.

[19] E. J. GRIFFITH, A. BEETON, J. M. SPENCER, and D. T. MITCHELL (eds.), *Environmental Phosphorus Handbook*, Wiley, New York, 1973, 718 pp.

[20] Ciba Foundation Symposium 57 (New Series), *Phosphorus in the Environment: Its Chemistry and Biochemistry*, Elsevier, Amsterdam, 1978, 320 pp.

[21] E. T. DEGENS, *Topics in Current Chem.* **64**, 1–112 (1976).

are also involved in many metabolic and energy-transfer processes either as adenosine triphosphate (ATP) (p. 528) or other such compounds. Another role, restricted to higher forms of life, is the structural use of calcium phosphates as bones and teeth. Tooth enamel is nearly pure hydroxyapatite and its resistance to dental caries is enhanced by replacement of OH^- by F^- (fluoridation) to give the tougher, less soluble $[Ca_5(PO_4)_3F]$. It is also commonly believed that the main inorganic phases in bone are hydroxyapatite and an amorphous phosphate, though many crystallographers favour an isomorphous solution of hydroxyapatite and the carbonate–apatite mineral dahlite, $[(Na,Ca)_5(PO_4,CO_3)_3(OH)]$, as the main crystalline phase with little or no amorphous material. Young bones also contain brushite, $[CaHPO_4.2H_2O]$, and the hydrated octacalcium phosphate $[Ca_8H_2(PO_4)_6.5H_2O]$ which

is composed, essentially, of alternate layers of apatite and water oriented parallel to (001).[21]

The land-based phosphate cycle is shown in Fig. 12.1.[22] The amount of phosphate in untilled soil is normally quite small and remains fairly stable because it is present as the insoluble salts of Ca^{II}, Fe^{III} and Al^{III}. To be used by plants, the phosphate must be released as the soluble $[H_2PO_4]^-$ anion, in which form it can be taken up by plant roots. Although acidic soil conditions will facilitate phosphate absorption, phosphorus is the nutrient which is often in shortest supply for the growing plant. Most mined phosphate is thus destined for use in fertilizers and this accounts for up to 75% of phosphate rock in technologically advanced countries and over 90% in less advanced (more

---

[22] J. EMSLEY, *Chem. Br.* **13**, 459–63 (1977).

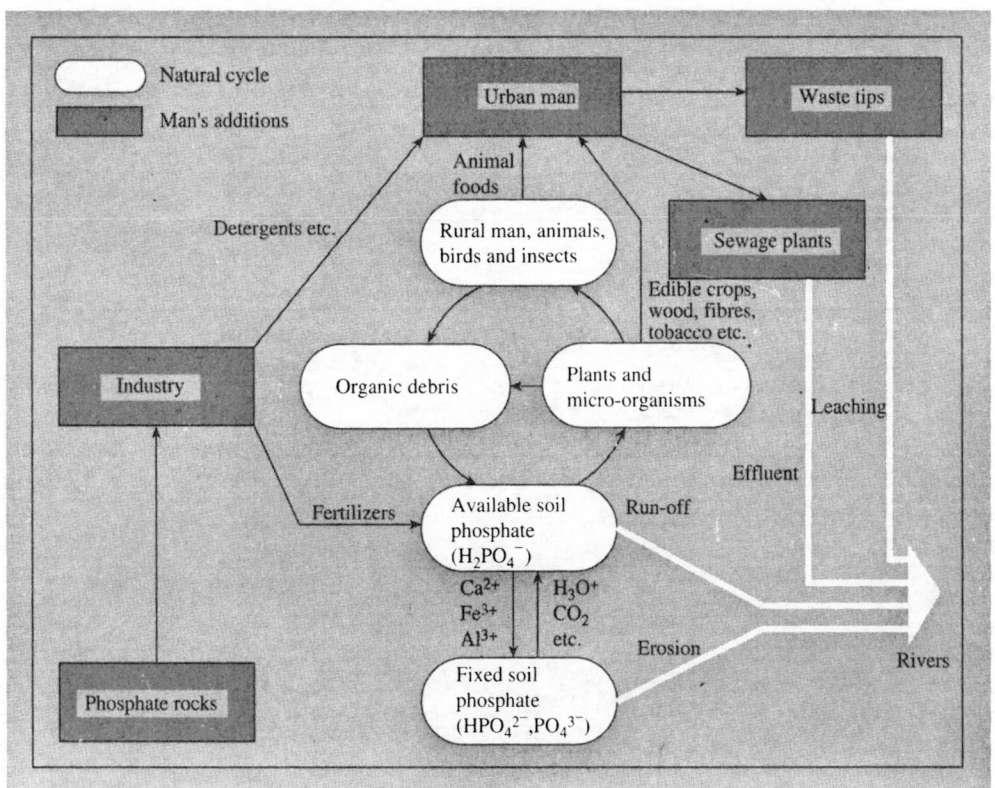

Figure 12.1   The land-based phosphate cycle.

agriculturally based) countries. Moderation in all things, however: excessive fertilization of natural waters due to detergents and untreated sewage in run-off water can lead to heavy overgrowth of algae and higher plants, thus starving the water of dissolved oxygen, killing fish and other aquatic life, and preventing the use of lakes for recreation, etc. This unintended over-fertilization and its consequences has been termed eutrophication (Greek εὖ, *eu*, well; τρέφειν, *trephein*, to nourish) and is the subject of active environmental legislation in several countries. Reclamation of eutrophied lakes can best be effected by addition of soluble Al^{III} salts to precipitate the phosphates.

As just implied, the land-based phosphorus cycle is connected to the water-based cycle via the rivers and sewers. It has been estimated that, on a global scale, about 2 million tonnes of phosphate are washed into the seas annually from natural processes and rather more than this amount is dumped from human activities. For example in the UK some 200 000 tonnes of phosphate enters the sewers each year: 100 000 tonnes from detergents (now decreasing), 75 000 from human excreta, and 25 000 tonnes from industrial processes. Details of the subsequent water-based phosphate cycle are shown schematically in Fig. 12.2. The water-based cycle is the most rapid of the three phosphate cycles and can be completed within weeks (or even days). The first members of the food chain are the algae and experiments with radioactive ^{32}P (p. 482) have shown that, within minutes of entering an aquatic environment, inorganic phosphate is absorbed by algae and bacteria (50% uptake in 1 min. 80% in 3 min). In the seas and oceans the various phosphate anions

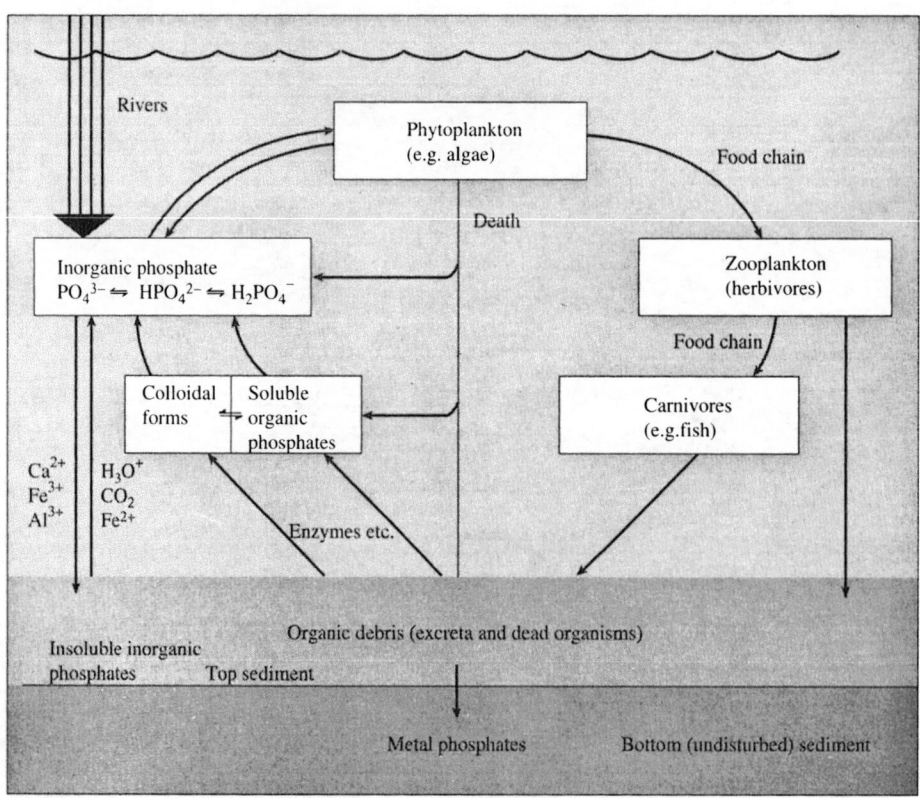

Figure 12.2 The water-based phosphate cycle.[22]

form insoluble inorganic phosphates which gradually sink to the sea bed. The concentration of phosphate therefore increases with depth (down to about 1000 m, below which it remains fairly constant); by contrast the sunlight, which is necessary for the primary photosynthesis in the food chain, is greatest at the surface and rapidly diminishes with depth. It is significant that those regions of the sea where the deeper phosphate-rich waters come welling up to the surface support by far the greatest concentration of the world's fish population; such regions, which occur in the mid-Pacific, the Pacific coast of the Americas, Arabia and Antarctica, account for only 0.1% of the sea's surface but support 50% of the world's fish population.

12.2.2 Production and uses of elemental phosphorus

For a century after its discovery the only source of phosphorus was urine. The present process of heating phosphate rock with sand and coke was proposed by E. Aubertin and L. Boblique in 1867 and improved by J. B. Readman who introduced the use of an electric furnace. The reactions occurring are still not fully understood, but the overall process can be represented by the idealized equation:

$$2Ca_3(PO_4)_2 + 6SiO_2 + 10C \xrightarrow[1500°]{1400-} 6CaSiO_3$$

$$+ 10CO + P_4; \quad \Delta H = -3060 \, kJ/mol \, P_4$$

The presence of silica to form slag which is vital to large-scale production was perceptively introduced by Robert Boyle in his very early experiments. Two apparently acceptable mechanisms have been proposed and it is possible that both may be occurring. In the first, the rock is thought to react with molten silica to form slag and P_4O_{10} which is then reduced by the carbon:

$$2Ca_3(PO_4)_2 + 6SiO_2 \longrightarrow 6CaSiO_3 + P_4O_{10}$$

$$P_4O_{10} + 10C \longrightarrow 10CO + P_4$$

In the second possible mechanism, the rock is considered to be directly reduced by CO and the CaO so formed then reacts with the silica to form slag:

$$2Ca_3(PO_4)_2 + 10CO \longrightarrow 6CaO + 10CO_2 + P_4$$

$$6CaO + 6SiO_2 \longrightarrow 6CaSiO_3$$

$$10CO_2 + 10C \longrightarrow 20CO$$

Whatever the details, the process is clearly energy intensive and, even at 90% efficiency, requires ~ 15 MWh per tonne of phosphorus (see Panel).

12.2.3 Allotropes of phosphorus [23]

Phosphorus (like C and S) exists in many allotropic modifications which reflect the variety of ways of achieving catenation. At least five crystalline polymorphs are known and there are also several "amorphous" or vitreous forms (see Fig. 12.3). All forms, however, melt to give the same liquid which consists of symmetrical P_4 tetrahedral molecules, P–P 225 pm. The same molecular form exists in the gas phase (P–P 221 pm), but at high temperatures (above $\sim 800°C$) and low pressures P_4 is in equilibrium with the diatomic form $P\equiv P$ (189.5 pm). At atmospheric pressure, dissociation of P_4 into $2P_2$ reaches 50% at $\sim 1800°C$ and dissociation of P_2 into 2P reaches 50% at $\sim 2800°$.

The commonest form of phosphorus, and the one which is usually formed by condensation from the gaseous or liquid states, is the waxy, cubic, white form α-P_4 (d 1.8232 g cm^{-3} at 20°C). This, paradoxically, is also the most volatile and reactive solid form and thermodynamically the least stable. It is the slow phosphorescent oxidation of the vapour above these crystals that gives white phosphorus its most characteristic property. Indeed, the emission of yellow-green light from the oxidation of P_4 is one of the earliest recorded examples of chemiluminescence, though the details of the reaction

―――――――――
[23] D. E. C. CORBRIDGE, *The Structural Chemistry of Phosphorus*, Elsevier, Amsterdam, 1974, 542 pp.

Production of White Phosphorus[3,11,17]

A typical modern phosphorus furnace (12 m diameter) can produce some 4 tonnes per hour and is rated at 60–70 MW (i.e. 140 000 A at 500 V). Three electrodes, each weighing 60 tonnes, lead in the current. The amounts of raw material required to make 1 tonne of white phosphorus depend on their purity but are typically 8 tonnes of phosphate rock, 2 tonnes of silica, 1.5 tonnes of coke, and 0.4 tonnes of electrode carbon. The phosphorus vapour is driven off from the top of the furnace together with the CO and some H_2; it is passed through a hot electrostatic precipitator to remove dust and then condensed by water sprays at about 70° (P_4 melts at 44.1°). The byproduct CO is used for supplementary heating.

As most phosphate rock approximates in composition to fluoroapatite, $[Ca_5(PO_4)_3F]$, it contains 3–4 wt% F. This reacts to give the toxic and corrosive gas SiF_4 which must be removed from the effluent. The stoichiometry of phosphate rock might suggest that about 1 mole of SiF_4 is formed for each 3 moles of P_4, but only about 20% of the fluorine reacts in this way, the rest being retained in the slag. Nevertheless, since a typical furnace can produce over 30 000 tonnes of phosphorus per year this represents a substantial waste of a potentially useful byproduct (~5000 tonnes SiF_4 yearly per furnace). In some plants the SiF_4 is recovered by treatment with water and soda ash (Na_2CO_3) to give Na_2SiF_6 which can be used in the fluoridation of drinking water.

Another troublesome impurity in phosphate rock (1–5%) is Fe_2O_3 which is reduced in the furnace to "ferrophosphorus", an impure form of Fe_2P. This is a dense liquid at the reaction temperature; it sinks beneath the slag and can be drained away at intervals. As every tonne of ferrophosphorus contains ~0.25 tonne of P, this is a major loss, but is unavoidable since the Fe_2O_3 cannot economically be removed beforehand. The few uses of ferrophosphorus depend on its high density (~6.6 g cm^{-3}). It can be mixed with dynamite for blasting or used as a filler in high-density concrete and in radiation shields for nuclear reactors. It is also used in the manufacture of special steels and cast-irons, especially for non-sparking railway brake-shoes. The other substantial byproduct, $CaSiO_3$ slag, has little economic use and is sold as hard core for road-fill or concrete aggregate; about 7–9 tonnes are formed per tonne of P produced.

World capacity for the production of elemental P is ~1.5 million tonnes per year. Some figures for 1984 are as follows:

Country	USSR	USA	Germany	Netherlands	Canada	France
ktonne/y	615	412	95	90	90	39
Country	China	Japan	Mexico	India	South Africa	
ktonne/y	35	20	10	10	6	

About 80–90% of the elemental P produced is reoxidized to (pure) phosphoric acid (p. 521). The rest is used to make phosphorus oxides (p. 503), sulfides (p. 506), phosphorus chlorides and oxochloride (p. 496), and organic P compounds. A small amount is converted to red phosphorus (see below) for use in the striking surface of matches for pyrotechnics and as a flame retarding agent (in polyamides). Bulk price for P_4 is ~\$2.00/kg.

mechanism are still not fully understood: the primary emitting species in the visible region of the spectrum are probably $(PO)_2$ and HPO; ultraviolet emission from excited states of PO also occurs.[24] At −76.9° and atmospheric pressure the α-form of P_4 converts to the very similar white hexagonal β-form (d 1.88 g cm^{-3}), possibly by loss of rotational disorder; $\Delta H(\alpha \rightarrow \beta)$ −15.9 kJ (mol P_4)$^{-1}$. White phosphorus is insoluble in water but exceedingly soluble (as P_4) in CS_2 (~880 g per 100 g CS_2 at 10°C). It is also very soluble in PCl_3, $POCl_3$, liquid SO_2, liquid

NH$_3$ and benzene, and somewhat less soluble in numerous other organic solvents. The β-form can be maintained as a solid up to 64.4°C under a pressure of 11 600 atm, whereas the α-form melts at 44.1°C. White phosphorus is highly toxic and ingestion, inhalation or even contact with skin must be avoided; the fatal dose when taken internally is about 50 mg.

Amorphous red phosphorus was first obtained in 1848 by heating white P_4 out of contact with air for several days, and is now made on a commercial scale by a similar process at 270°–300°C. It is denser than white P_4 (~2.16 g cm^{-3}), has a much higher m.p.

24 R. J. van Zee and A. U. Khan, *J. Am. Chem. Soc.* **96**, 6805–6 (1974).

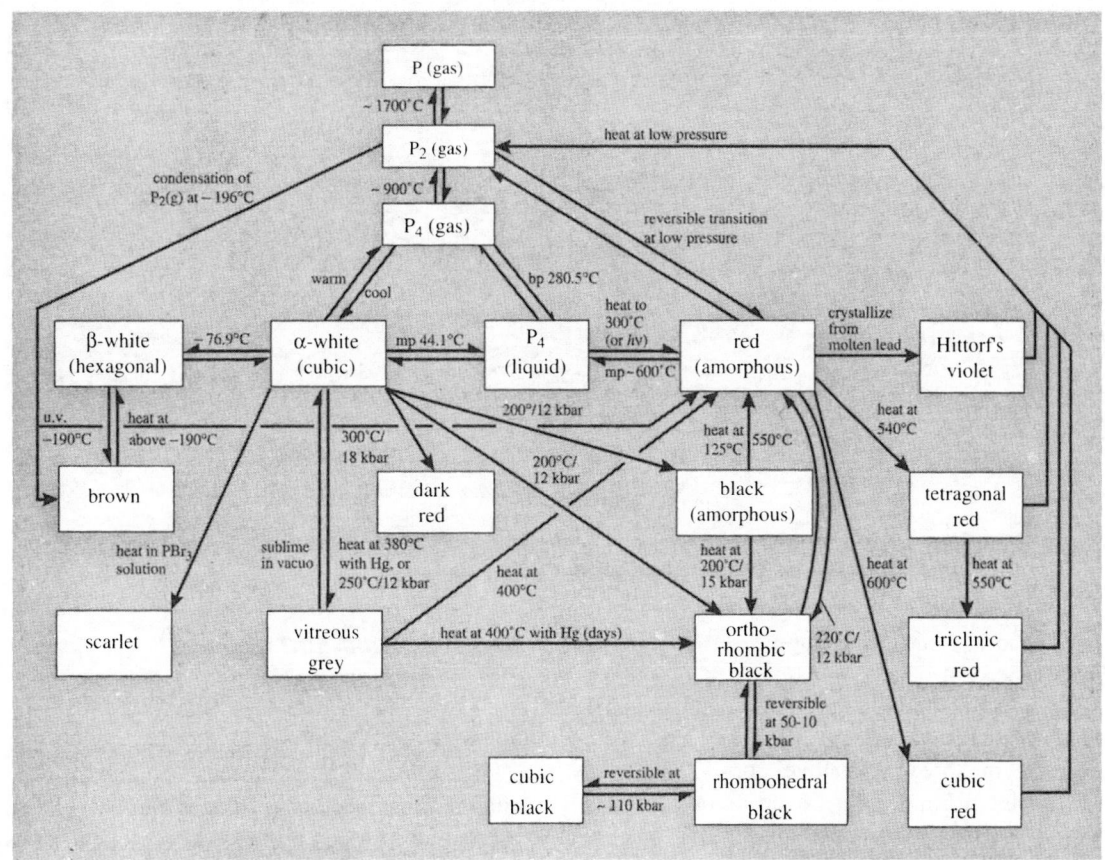

Figure 12.3 Interconversion of the various forms of elemental phosphorus (1 kbar $= 10^8$ Pa $= 987.2$ atm).

($\sim 600°C$), and is much less reactive; it is therefore safer and easier to handle, and is essentially non-toxic. The amorphous material can be transformed into various crystalline red modifications by suitable heat treatment, as summarized on the right hand side of Fig. 12.3. It seems likely that all are highly polymeric and contain three-dimensional networks formed by breaking one P–P bond in each P_4 tetrahedron and then linking the remaining P_4 units into chains or rings of P atoms each of which is pyramidal and 3 coordinate as shown schematically below:

This is well illustrated by the crystal structure of Hittorf's violet monoclinic allotrope (d 2.35 g cm^{-3}) which was first made in 1865 by crystallizing phosphorus in molten lead. The structure is exceedingly complex[25] and consists of P_8 and P_9 groups linked alternately by pairs of P atoms to form tubes of pentagonal cross-section and with a repeat unit of 21P (Fig. 12.4). These tubes, or complex chains, are stacked (without direct covalent bonding) to form sheets and are linked by P–P bonds to similar chains which lie at right angles to the first set in an adjacent parallel layer. These pairs of composite parallel sheets are then stacked to form the crystal. The average P–P distance is 222 pm (essentially the

---

[25] VON H. THURN and H. KREBS. *Acta Cryst.* **B25**, 125–35 (1969).

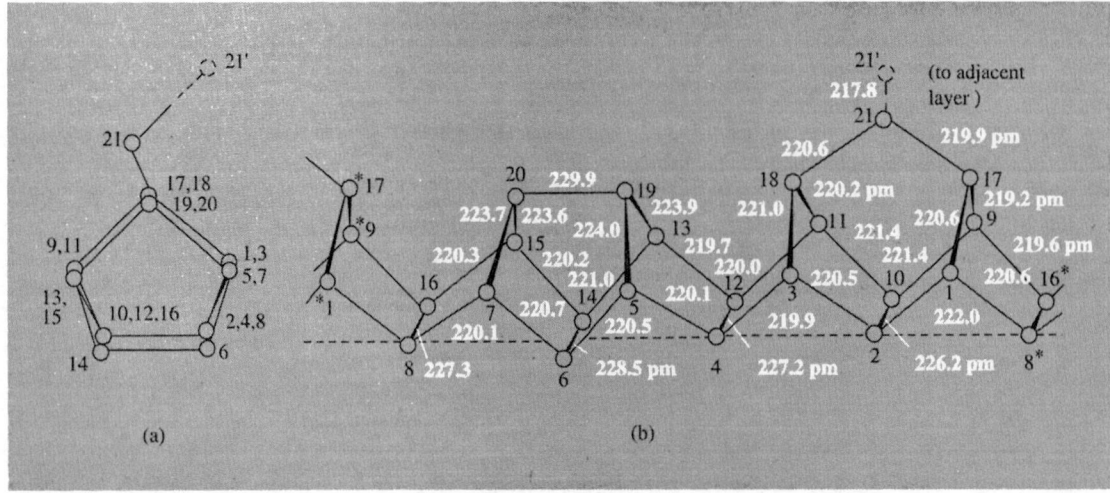

Figure 12.4   Structure of Hittorf's violet monoclinic phosphorus showing (a) end view of one pentagonal tube, (b) the side view of a single tube (dimensions in pm).

same as in P_4) but the average P–P–P angle is 101° (instead of 60°).

Black phosphorus, the thermodynamically most stable form of the element, has been prepared in three crystalline forms and one amorphous form. It is even more highly polymeric than the red form and has a correspondingly higher density (orthorhombic 2.69, rhombohedral 3.56, cubic 3.88 g cm^{-3}). Black phosphorus (orthorhombic) was originally made by heating white P_4 to 200° under a pressure of 12 000 atm (P. W. Bridgman, 1916). Higher pressures convert it successively to the rhombohedral and cubic forms (Fig. 12.3). Orthorhombic black P (mp ∼610°) has a layer structure which is based on a puckered hexagonal net of 3-coordinate P atoms with 2 interatomic angles of 102° and 1 of 96.5° (P–P 223 pm). The relation of this form to the rhombohedral and cubic forms is shown in Fig. 12.5. Comparison with the rhombohedral forms of As, Sb and Bi is also instructive in showing the increasing tendency towards octahedral coordination and metallic properties (p. 551). Black P is semiconducting but its electrical properties are probably significantly affected by impurities introduced during its preparation.

12.2.4 Atomic and physical properties [26]

Phosphorus has only one stable isotope, $^{31}_{15}$P, and accordingly (p. 17) its atomic weight is known with extreme accuracy, 30.973 762(4). Sixteen radioactive isotopes are known, of which ^{32}P is by far the most important; it is made on the multikilogram scale by the neutron irradiation of ^{32}S(n,p) or ^{31}P(n,γ) in a nuclear reactor, and is a pure β-emitter of half life 14.26 days, E_{max} 1.709 MeV, E_{mean} 0.69 MeV. It finds extensive use in tracer and mechanistic studies. The stable isotope ^{31}P has a nuclear spin quantum number of $\frac{1}{2}$ and this is much used in nmr spectroscopy.[27] Chemical shifts and coupling constants can both be used diagnostically to determine structural information.

In the ground state, P has the electronic configuration [Ne]$3s^2 3p_x^1 3p_y^1 3p_z^1$ with 3 unpaired

[26] *Mellor's Comprehensive Treatise on Inorganic and Theoretical Chemistry*, Vol. 8, Suppl. 3, *Phosphorus*, Longman, London, 1971, 1467 pp.

[27] D. G. GORENSTEIN (ed.) *Phosphorus-31 NMR; Principles and Applications* Academic Press, London, 1984, 604 pp. J. G. VERKADE and L. D. QUIN (eds.), *Phosphorus-31 NMR Spectroscopy in Stereochemical Analysis*, VCH Publishers, Weinheim, 1987, 717 pp.

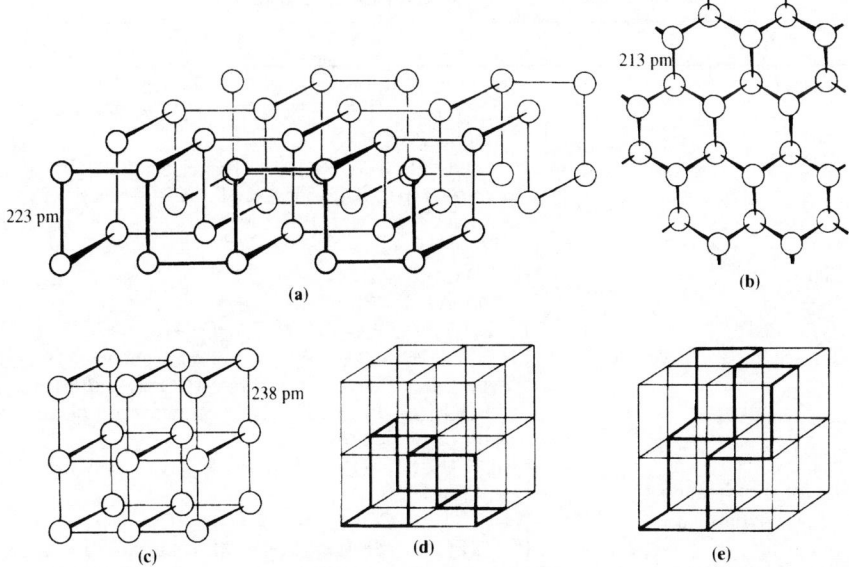

Figure 12.5 The structures of black phosphorus: (a) portion of one layer of orthorhombic P (idealized), (b) rhombohedral form, portion of one hexagonal layer, (c) cubic form, 4 unit cells, (d) distortion of (a) to the cubic form, and (e) distortion of (b) to the cubic form.

electrons; this, together with the availability of low-lying vacant 3d orbitals, accounts for the predominant oxidation states III and V in phosphorus chemistry. Ionization energies, electronegativity, and atomic radii are compared with those of N, As, Sb and Bi on p. 550. White phosphorus (α-P_4) has mp 44.1° (or 44.25° when ultrapure), bp 280.5° and a vapour pressure of 0.122 mmHg at 40°C. It is an insulator with an electrical resistivity of $\sim 10^{11}$ ohm cm at 11°C, a dielectric constant of 4.1 (at 20°) and a refractive index n_D (29.2°) 1.8244. The heat of combustion of P_4 to P_4O_{10} is -2971 kJ mol^{-1} and the heat of transition to amorphous red phosphorus is -29 kJ (mol P_4)$^{-1}$.

12.2.5 Chemical reactivity and stereochemistry

The spontaneous chemiluminescent reaction of white phosphorus with moist air was the first property of the element to be observed and was the origin of its name (p. 473); its spontaneous ignition temperature in air is $\sim 35°$. We have already seen (p. 481) that the reactivity

of phosphorus depends markedly upon which allotrope is being studied and that increasing catenation of the polymeric red and black forms notably diminishes both reactivity and solubility. The preference of phosphorus for these forms rather than for the gaseous form P_2, which is its most obvious distinction from nitrogen, can be rationalized in terms of the relative strengths of the triple and single bonds for the 2 elements. Reliable values are hard to obtain but generally accepted values are as follows:

$E(N{\equiv}N)$/kJ		$E(P{\equiv}P)$/kJ	
per mol of N	946	per mol of P	490
$E({>}N{-}N{<})$/kJ	159	$E({>}P{-}P{<})$/kJ	200
per mol of N	(or 296)	per mol of P	200
Ratio	5.95	Ratio	2.45
	(or 3.20)		

It is clear that, for nitrogen, the triple bond is preferred since it has more than 3 times the energy of a single bond, whereas for phosphorus the triple-bond energy is less than 3 times the single-bond energy and so allotropes having 3 single bonds per P atom are more stable than that with a triple bond.

Table 12.2 Stereochemistry of phosphorus

CN	Geometry	Examples
0	—	P(g) — in equilibrium with P_2(g) above 2200°C
1	—	P_2(g) — in equilibrium with P_4(g) above 800°C; HC≡P; FC≡P; MeC≡P (p. 544)
2	Bent[28]	HP=CH_2,[29] $[P(CN)_2]^-$,[30] $[\{C_6H_4S(NR)C\}_2P]^+X^-$ (p. 544), *cyclo*-C_5H_5P, 2,4,6-$Ph_3C_5H_2P$; Me_3P=PCF_3; $P_7{}^{3-}$ anion[31] (isoelectronic with P_4S_3) in Sr_3P_{14}; $P_{11}{}^{3-}$ anion in Na_3P_{11}; diazaphospholes[32]
3	Planar	$[PhP\{Mn(\eta^5\text{-}C_5H_5)(CO)_2\}_2]$[33], $[(\text{fluorenyl})=P\{=C(SiMe_3)_2\}]^{-[33a]}$
	Pyramidal	P_4, PH_3, PX_3, P_4O_6, $[PhP\{Co(CO)_4\}_2]$[34]
4	Tetrahedral	$PH_4{}^+$, Cl_3PO, P_4O_{10}, $PO_4{}^{3-}$, polyphosphates, MP (zinc-blende type, M = B, Al, Ga, In), $[Co_3(CO)_9(\mu_3\text{-}PPh)]$,[35] $[(P_4)Ni\{(Ph_2PCH_2CH_2)_3N\}]$;[36] many complexes of PR_3 etc., with metal centres
	Local C_{2v}	$PBr_4{}^-$, $[PBr_2(CN)_2]^-$.[37] $[\mu(\eta^3\text{-}P_3)\{Ni(triphos)\}_2]^{2+}$[38]
5	Trigonal bipyramidal	PF_5, PPh_5
	Square pyramidal	$[Co_4(CO)_8(\mu\text{-}CO)_2(\mu_4\text{-}PPh)_2]$, $[Os_5(CO)_{15}(\mu_4\text{-}POMe)]$[39]
6	Octahedral	$PF_6{}^-$, $PCl_6{}^-$, MP (NaCl-type, M = La, Sm, Th, U etc.)
	Trigonal prismatic	Rh_4P_3, Hf_3P_2 (also contains seven- and eight-fold coordination of P by M), $[(\mu_6\text{-}P)\{Os(CO)_3\}_6]^-$[40]
	Irregular (4 + 2)	$[Co_6(CO)_{14}(\mu\text{-}CO)_2P]^-$
7	Capped trigonal prismatic	Ta_2P, Hf_2P (contains P in seven-, eight-, and nine-fold coordination by M)
8	Cubic	M_2P (antifluorite type (p. 118), M = Ir, Rh)
	Bicapped trigonal prismatic	Hf_2P
9	Tricapped trigonal prismatic	M_3P (M = Ti, V, Cr, Mn, Fe, Ni, Zr, Nb, Ta) M_2P ($PbCl_2$-type, M = Fe, Co, Ru)
	Monocapped square antiprismatic	$[Rh_9(CO)_{21}P]^{2-}$[41]

[28] E. FLUCK, *Topics in Phosphorus Chemistry* **10**, 193–284 (1980).

[29] H. W. KROTO, J. F. NIXON, K. OHNO and N. P. C. SIMMONS, *J. Chem. Soc., Chem. Commun.*, 709 (1980).

[30] W. S. SHELDRICK, J. KRONER, F. ZWASCHKA and A. SCHMIDPETER, *Angew. Chem. Int. Edn. Engl.* **18**, 934–5 (1979).

[31] W. DAHLMANN and H. G. VON SCHNERING, *Naturwissenschaften* **59**, 420 (1972). W. WICHELHAUS and H. G. VON SCHNERING, ibid. **60**, 104 (1973).

[32] J. H. WEINMAIER, A. SCHMIDPETER, *et al.*, *Angew. Chem. Int. Edn. Engl.* **18**, 412 (1979); *Chem. Ber.* **113**, 2278–90 (1980); *J. Organometallic Chem.* **185**, 53–68 (1980).

[33] G. HUTTNER, H.-D. MÜLLER, A. FRANK, and H. LORENZ, *Angew. Chem. Int. Edn. Engl.* **14**, 705–6 (1975).

[33a] R. APPEL, E. GAITZSCH and F. KNOCH, *Angew. Chem. Int. Edn. Engl.* **24**, 589–90 (1985).

[34] J. C. BURT and G. SCHMID, *J. Chem. Soc., Dalton Trans.*, 1385–7 (1978).

[35] L. MARKÓ and B. MARKÓ, *Inorg. Chim. Acta* **14**, L39 (1975).

[36] P. DAPPORTO, S. MIDOLLINI and L. SACCONI, *Angew. Chem. Int. Edn. Engl.* **18**, 469 (1979).

[37] W. S. SHELDRICK, A. SCHMIDPETER, F. ZWASCHKA, K. B. DILLON, A. W. G. PLATT and T. C. WADDINGTON, *J. Chem. Soc., Dalton Trans.*, 413–8 (1981) see also *Angew. Chem. Int. Edn. Engl.* **18**, 935–6 (1979).

[38] M. DI VAIRA, S. MIDOLLINI and L. SACCONI, *J. Am. Chem. Soc.* **101**, 1757–63 (1979). For analogous complexes in which μ-$(\eta^3$-$P_3)$ bridges RhCo, RhNi, IrCo, and RhRh, see C. BIANCHINI, M. DI VAIRA, A. MELI and L. SACCONI, *Angew. Chem. Int. Edn. Engl.* **19**, 405–6 (1980).

[39] J. M. FERNANDEZ, B. F. G. JOHNSON, J. LEWIS and P. R. RAITHBY, *J. Chem. Soc., Chem. Commun.*, 1015–6 (1978).

[40] S. B. COLBRAN, C. M. HAY, B. F. G. JOHNSON, F. J. LAHOZ, J. LEWIS and P. R. RAITHBY, *J. Chem. Soc., Chem. Commun.*, 1766–8 (1986).

[41] J. L. VIDAL, W. E. WALKER, R. L. PRUETT and R. C. SCHOENING, $[Rh_9P(CO)_{21}]^{2-}$. *Inorg. Chem.* **18**, 129–36 (1979).

Phosphorus forms binary compounds with all elements except Sb, Bi and the noble gases. It reacts spontaneously with O_2 and the halogens at room temperature, the mixtures rapidly reaching incandescence. Sulfur and the alkali metals also react vigorously with phosphorus on warming, and the element combines directly with all metals (except Bi, Hg, Pb) frequently with incandescence (e.g. Fe, Ni, Cu, Pt). White phosphorus (but not red) also reacts readily with heated aqueous solutions to give a variety of products (pp. 493 and 513ff), and with many other aqueous and nonaqueous reagents.

The stereochemistry and bonding of P are very varied as will become apparent in later sections: the element is known in at least 14 coordination geometries with CN up to 9, though the most frequently met have CN 3, 4, 5 and 6. Some typical coordination geometries are summarized in Table 12.2 and illustrated in Fig. 12.6. Many of these compounds will be more fully discussed in later sections.

The great propensity of P atoms to catenate into chains, rings and clusters, P_n, has already been noted during the discussion on allotropy (pp. 479–83). These groupings and other similar ones also feature in the structures of metal phosphides (p. 489), polyphosphanes (p. 492) and organopolyphosphanes (p. 542). Moreover, neutral or charged groupings, P_n, ($n = 2$–6, 10) can also serve as ligands[42–44], as can isolated P atoms in anions such as $[(\mu_6\text{-P})\{Os(CO)_3\}_6]^{-}$ [40] and other structures shown at the foot of Fig. 12.6. Two decades ago virtually nothing was known about this aspect of phosphorus chemistry, but it is now a burgeoning field, and the substantial progress which has been made in recent years now permits a general overview to be given.

The P_2 group is isoelectronic with ethyne (p. 932) and with N_2 (pp. 414–6) and As_2. It has emerged as a versatile ligand with several well characterized coordination modes as shown schematically in Fig 12.7. The first compound containing the P_2 ligand, $[\{Co(CO)_3\}_2(\mu,\eta^2\text{-}P_2)]$, was isolated as a red oil in 1973 and was clearly similar to the already known alkyne and As_2 complexes $[\{Co(CO)_3\}_2\{\mu,\eta^2\text{-}(CR)_2\}]$ and $[\{Co(CO)_3\}_2(\mu,\eta^2\text{-}As_2)]$. It was formed by reaction of $Na[Co(CO)_4]$ with PCl_3 or PBr_3 in thf. The tetrahedrane-like core (Fig. 12.7a) was confirmed by X-ray analysis on the related PPh_3 derivative $[Co_2(CO)_5(PPh_3)(\mu,\eta^2\text{-}P_2)]$.[45] Direct action of P_4 with appropriate carbonyl, cyclopentadienyl or alkoxide derivatives of Cr, Mo, W, etc. has yielded a wide range of such compounds of P_2 acting as a 4e-donor, in all of which the two ML_n vertices can be considered as 15e-acceptors (i.e $d^{10} + 5e$, "isoelectronic" with P in Group 15) e.g., $\{Cr(Cp)(CO)_2\}$,[46] $\{Mo(Cp)(CO)_2\}$, $\{W(py)(OPr^i)_2(\mu\text{-}OPr^i)\}$[47], etc., where Cp is $(\eta^5\text{-}C_5H_5)$ or one of its derivatives. With 14e or 16e metal–vertex acceptors the core adopts the more open "butterfly" configuration (Fig 12.7b) without direct M–M bonding, e.g $[\{Ni(Et_2PCH_2CH_2PEt_2)\}_2(\mu,\eta^2\text{-}P_2)]$[48] and its $\{Ni(PEt_3)_2\}$ and $[Pt(PEt_3)_2]$ analogues. Further electron-pair donation from one or both of the P atoms can also occur to give compounds such as $[Cr_2(\eta^5\text{-}C_5H_5)_2(CO)_4(\mu,\eta^2\text{-}P_2)\{M(CO)_5\}_{1 \text{ or } 2}]$ (M = Cr, Mo, W) (see Figs. 12.7 c, d).[49] In these, the P_2 group acts as a 6e or 8e donor, and bridges 3 or 4 M atoms respectively. See below — p. 488 — for examples cf. bis-P_2, i.e. pseudo-P_4 complexes.)

[42] M. DI VAIRA and P. STOPPIONI, *Polyhedron* **6**, 351–82 (1987). (Review)

[43] O. J. SCHERER, *Angew. Chem. Int. Edn. Engl.* **24**, 924–43 (1985); **29** 1104–22 (1990). (Reviews)

[44] O. J. SCHERER (and 9 others), in R. STEUDEL (ed.), *The Chemistry of Inorganic Ring Systems*, Elsevier, Amsterdam, 1992, pp. 193–208.

[45] C. F. CAMPANA, A. VIZI-OROSZ, G. PÀLYI, L. MARKÒ and L. F. DAHL, *Inorg. Chem.* **18**, 3054–9 (1979).

[46] L. Y. GOH, C. K. CHU, R. C. S. WONG and T. W. HAMBLEY, *J. Chem. Soc., Chem. Commun.*, 1951–6 (1979).

[47] M. H. CHISHOLM, K. FOLTING, J. C. HUFFMAN and J. J. KOH, *Polyhedron* **4**, 893–5 (1985).

[48] H. SCHÄFFER, D. BINDER and D. FENSKE, *Angew. Chem. Int. Edn. Engl.* **24**, 522–4 (1985).

[49] L. Y. GOH, R. C. S. WONG and T. C. W. MAK, *J. Organometallic Chem.* **364**, 363–71 (1989) and **373**, 71–6 (1989).

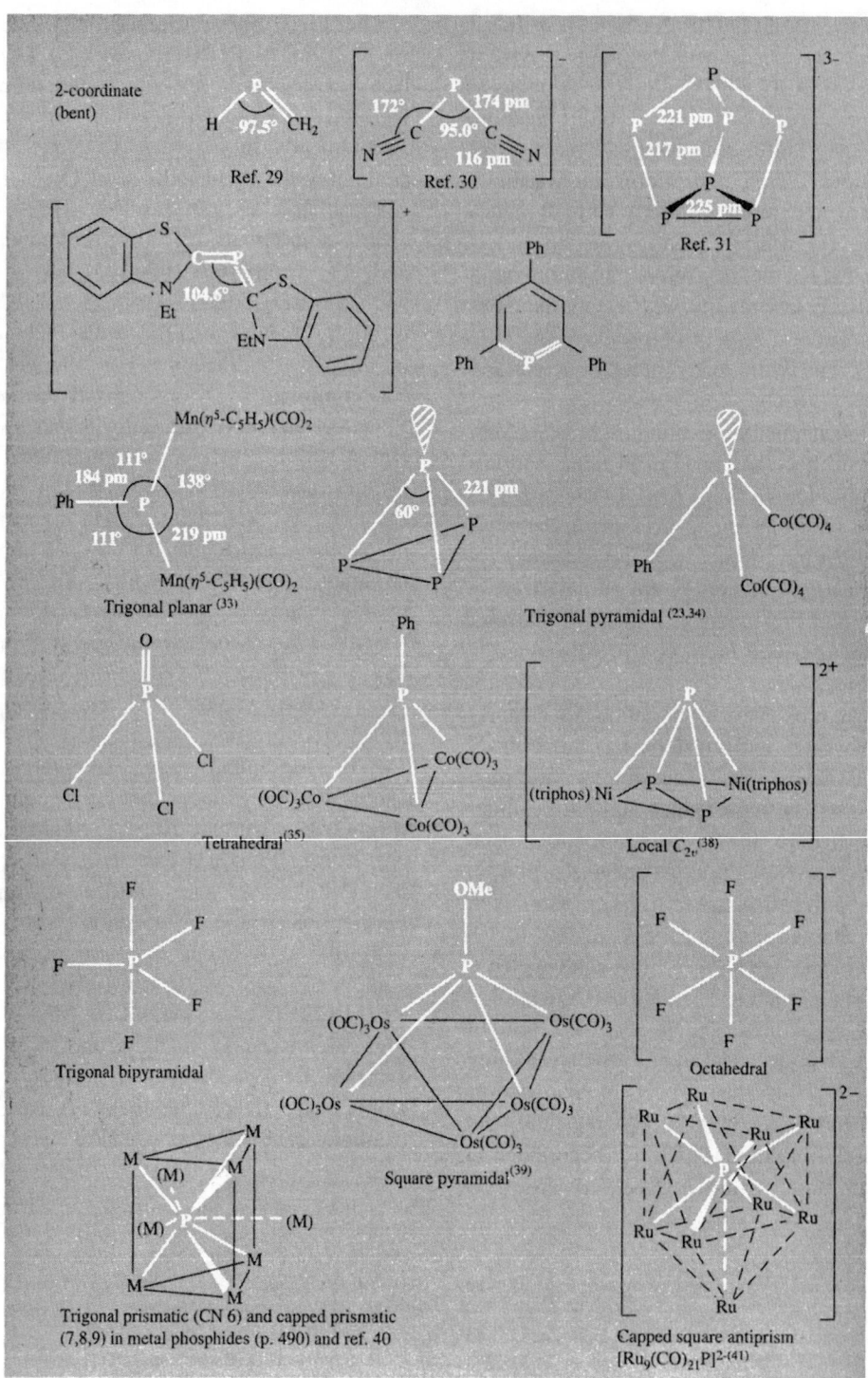

Figure 12.6 Schematic representation of some of the coordination geometries of phosphorus.

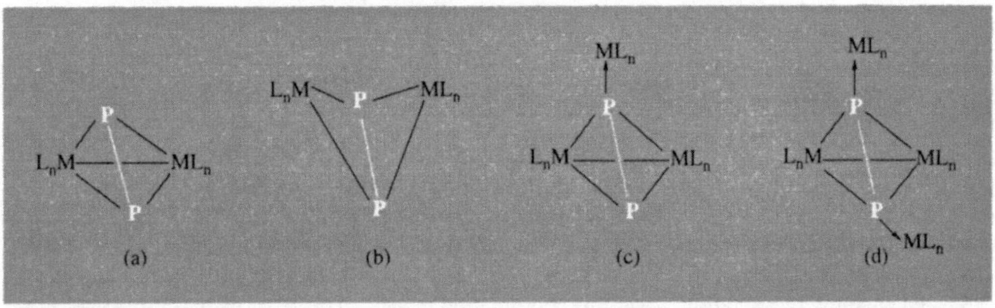

Figure 12.7 (a) $(\mu,\eta^2\text{-}P_2)$ 4e-donor to 15e ML_n vertices. (b) $(\mu,\eta^2\text{-}P_2)$4e-donor to 14e or 16e ML_n. (c) Triply bridging $(\mu_3,\eta^2\text{-}P_2)$, a formal 6e-donor. (d) Quadruply bridging $(\mu_4,\eta^2\text{-}P_2)$ 8e-donor.

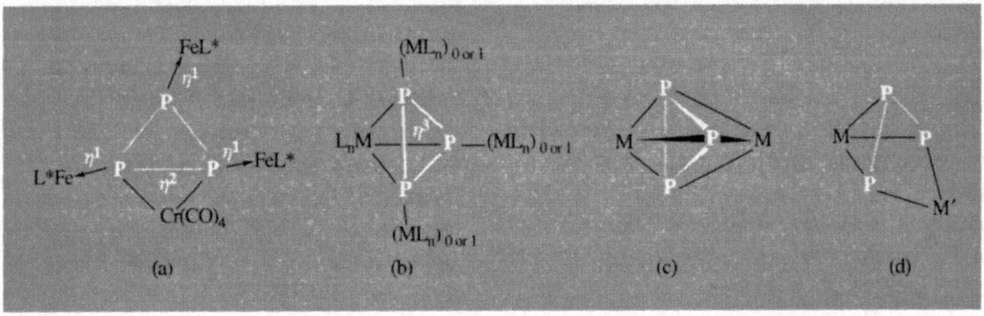

Figure 12.8 (a) *Cyclo*-P_3 as an η^1 and η^2 donor (see text). (b) *Cyclo*-P_3 as an η^3 donor; addition of η^1 donation to 1, 2 or 3 further metal centres is possible. (c) Bis-η^3 ligation of *cyclo*-P_3 to coordinated metal centres $M(L_n)$. (d) More open η^2,η^3 coordination of P_3 to different metal centres, e.g. $M = \{Ni(triphos)\}^+$, $M' = \{Pt(PPh_3)_2\}$ (see text).

The *cyclo*-P_3 ligand can act in either the η^1,η^2 or η^3 mode as shown schematically in Fig. 12.8(a)–(c).[42,50] Each of the three P atoms in 8(b) can also have a further pendant ML_n group attached thereby making the *cyclo*-P_3 ligand μ_2, μ_3 or μ_4. In addition, the more open structure 8(d) is known in the binuclear cation $[(triphos)Ni\{P_3Pt(PPh_3)_2\}]^+$, where triphos is 1,1,1-tris(diphenylphosphinomethyl)-ethane, $\{CH_3C(CH_2PPh_2)_3\}$.[42] The η^1 and η^2 modes in Fig. 12.8(a) have only recently been established (in $[\{(\eta^5\text{-}C_5Me_5)(CO)_2Fe-P\}_3\text{-}Cr(CO)_4])$[50] but the η^3 mode in Fig. 12.8(b) has been known since 1976 when it was found that one of the main products of the reaction between P_4 and $[Co_2(CO)_8]$ was the reactive

pale-yellow solid $[Co(CO)_3(\eta^3\text{-}P_3)]$.[51] Numerous other examples featuring Co, Rh and Ir, and the isoelectronic cationic metal centres with Ni, Pd and Pt are now known. Metals in earlier groups require more electron donation from pendant ligands to achieve the 15-electron vertex configuration isolobal with the subrogated P atom in P_4, e.g. $\{Mo(\eta^5\text{-}C_5Me_5)(CO)_2\}$. The binuclear η^3,η^3 mode of *cyclo*-P_3 (Fig. 12.8c) and its As_3 homologues were extensively studied by L. Sacconi and others in the early 1980s.[38,42,43]

As a ligand, P_4 can adopt various geometries,[42,43] including the P_4 tetrahedron, planar *cyclo*-P_4 (both square and trapezoidal), and a planar zig-zag chain. In principle, the tetrahedral cluster P_4 could ligate in η^1,η^2 and η^3 modes,

[50] L. WEBER, U. SONNENBERG, H.-G. STAMMLER and B. NEUMANN, *Z. anorg. allg. Chem.* **605**, 87–99 (1991).

[51] A. VIZI-OROSZ *J. Organomet. Chem.* **111**, 61–4 (1976).

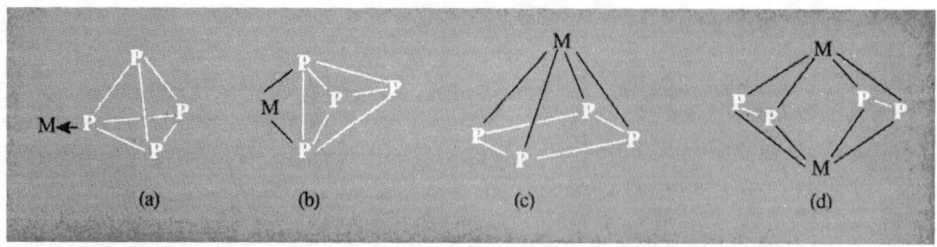

Figure 12.9 Schematic representation of various coordination modes: (a) η^1-P_4; (b) η^2-P_4; (c) η^4-*cyclo*-P_4; (d) (μ, η^2-P_2)$_2$ (see text).

though only the first two have so far been established (Fig. 12.9 (a), (b)). [Note, however, the face-coordinated η^3 configuration in the Bi_4 complex [(CO)$_4$Fe(μ_4,η^3-Bi_4){Fe(CO)$_3$}$_3$]$^{2-}$.][52] The first example of what turned out to be a complex involving the η^1 mode was the unstable red-brown compound [{Fe(CO)$_4$}$_3$(μ_3-P_4)] which was made in 1977 by reacting P_4 with Fe$_2$(CO)$_9$ in benzene at room temperature:[53] one vertex of the P_4 tetrahedron was coordinated η^1 to one of the {Fe(CO)$_4$} groups while opposite edges of the P_4 cluster were bonded η^2 to the other two {Fe(CO)$_4$} groups. The first η^1-P_4 complex to be characterized by X-ray structural analysis was [(η^3-np$_3$)Ni(η^1-P_4)],[54] formed by direct reaction of white P_4 with the Ni^0 complex [Ni(η^4-np$_3$)] in thf at 0°C where np$_3$ is N(CH$_2$CH$_2$PPh$_2$)$_3$. Coordination results in a slight elongation of the tetrahedron with P$_{basal}$–P$_{apical}$ 220 pm and P$_{basal}$–P$_{basal}$ 209 pm (cf. 221 pm in α-P_4. The η^2-P_4 mode of coordination is featured in many complexes with Rh, Ir, etc., for example [RhCl(η^2-P_4)(PPh$_3$)$_2$],[55] formed by direct reaction of P_4 with [RhCl(PPh$_3$)$_3$] in CH$_2$Cl$_2$ at −78°C. The coordinated edge is almost perpendicular to the {RhClL$_2$} plane and is lengthened by

about 25 pm to 246.2 pm, whereas the other P–P distances are essentially unchanged from those in uncoordinated P_4.[56]

Square planar *cyclo*-P_4 features as a ligand in [Nb(η^5-C$_5$H$_3$Bu$_2^t$-1,3)(CO)$_2$(η^4-P_4)][57] and the corresponding Ta analogue.[58] The compounds are formed by uv photolysis of P_4 with [M(cp*)(CO)$_4$] and the square-pyramidal *nido* structure of the MP$_4$ cluster (Fig. 12.9c) is consistent with its 14e ($2n + 4$) cluster-electron count (p. 161). The P–P distances in the coplanar P_4 ligand are in the range 214–218 pm for the Nb complex, with Nb–P_4(centre) being 142 pm and the basal PPP angles being 92.6° and 88.4°. In the Ta complex, the P–P distances are 215–217 pm. A co-product of the photolysis reaction is the related bis-(P_2) complex [{Ta(C$_5$H$_3$Bu$_2^t$)(CO)(μ,η^2-P_2)}$_2$], Fig. 12.9d, in which the P–P distance is 212 pm within each P_2 ligand and 357 pm between the coplanar P_2 ligands. Several similar binuclear bis-(P_2) complexes are known, including Rh/Rh, and mixed metal species involving Nb/Ta and Ta/Co.[58]

A still more open configuration occurs in the zig-zag P_4 chain shown in Fig. 12.10(a).[59] This was found in the dianion of the deep

[52] K. H. Whitmire, T. A. Albright, S. K. Kang, M. R. Churchill and J. C. Fettinger, *Inorg. Chem.* **25**, 2799–805 (1986).

[53] G. Schmid and H. P. Kempny, *Z. anorg. allg. Chem.* **432**, 160–6 (1977).

[54] P. Dapporto, S. Midollini and L. Sacconi, *Angew. Chem. Int. Edn. Engl.* **18**, 469 (1979).

[55] W. E. Lindsell, K. J. McCullough and A. J. Welch, *J. Am. Chem. Soc.* **105**, 4487–9 (1983).

[56] A. P. Ginsberg, W. E. Lindsell, K. J. McCullough, C. R. Sprinkle and A. J. Welch, *J. Am. Chem. Soc.* **108**, 403–16 (1986).

[57] O. J. Scherer, J. Vondung and G. Wolmershäuser, *Angew. Chem. Int. Edn. Engl.* **28**, 1355–7 (1989).

[58] O. J. Scherer, R. Winter and G. Wolmershäuser, *Z. anorg. allg. Chem.* **619**, 827–35 (1993).

[59] G. Fritz, E. Layher, H. Krautscheid, B. Mayer, E. Matern, W. Hönle and H. G. von Schnering, *Z. anorg. allg. Chem.* **611**, 56–60 (1992).

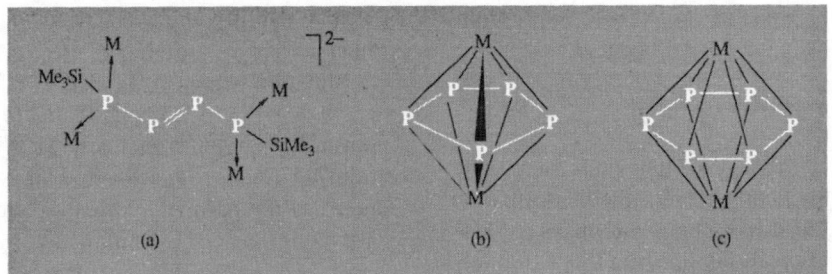

Figure 12.10   (a) Zig-zag P_4 chain, M = {$Cr(CO)_5$}; (b) η^5-*cyclo*-P_5, M various; (c) η^6-*cyclo*-P_6, M various (see text).

red crystalline compound $[Li(dme)_3]^+{}_2[(SiMe_3)\text{-}\{Cr(CO)_5\}_2P\text{-}P{=}P\text{-}P\{Cr(CO)_5\}_2(SiMe_3)]^{2-}$ which was obtained by reacting $Li[P(SiMe_3)_2\text{-}\{Cr(CO)_5\}]$ with $BrCH_2CH_2Br$ in 1,2-dimethoxyethane (dme). The interatomic distances P–P 221.9 pm and P=P 202.5 pm reflect the bond orders indicated.

Because *cyclo*-P_5 and *cyclo*-P_6 can be considered as isoelectronic with C_5H_5 and C_6H_6 their appearance as ligands is not entirely unexpected, but the recent synthesis and characterization of such complexes was nevertheless a noteworthy achievement.[43] Typical examples are $[(Mn(CO)_3(\eta^5\text{-}P_5)]^{[60]}$ (formed by the direct action of KP_5 on $[Mn(CO)_5Br]$ in dmf at 155°C) and $[Fe(\eta^5\text{-}C_5H_5)(\mu{:}\eta^5,\eta^5\text{-}P_5)Fe(\eta^5\text{-}C_5Me_4R)]^{[43]}$ (Fig. 12.10(b)) for *cyclo*-P_5; and $[\{Mo(\eta^5\text{-}C_5Me_5)\}_2(\mu{:}\eta^5,\eta^5\text{-}P_6)]^{[43]}$ (Fig. 12.10(c)) for planar *cyclo*-P_6. Several *cyclo*-As_5 and -As_6 analogues are also known. The complex $[\{Ti(\eta^5\text{-}C_5Me_5)\}_2(\mu{:}\eta^3,\eta^3\text{-}P_6)]$ features a puckered P_6 ring in the chair conformation, so that the overall cluster core has a distorted cubane geometry.[61]

The most complex P_n ligand so far characterized is the astonishing μ_5 hexadentate P_{10} unit in $[\{Cr(\eta^5\text{-}C_5H_5)(CO)_2\}_5P_{10}]$ (see ref. 62 for details).

12.3 Compounds

12.3.1 Phosphides[63-65]

Phosphorus forms stable binary compounds with almost every element in the periodic table and those with metals are called phosphides. Like borides (p. 145) they are known in a bewilderingly large number of stoichiometries, and typical formulae are M_4P, M_3P, $M_{12}P_5$, M_7P_3, M_2P, M_7P_4, M_5P_3, M_3P_2, M_4P_3, M_5P_4, M_6P_5, MP, M_3P_4, M_2P_3, MP_2, M_3P_7, M_2P_5, MP_3, M_3P_{11}, M_3P_{14}, MP_5, M_3P_{16}, M_4P_{26}, MP_7, M_2P_{16} and MP_{15}. Many metals (e.g. Ti, Ta, W, Rh) form as many as 5 or 6 phosphides and Ni has at least 8 (Ni_3P, Ni_5P_2, $Ni_{12}P_5$, NiP_2, Ni_5P_4, NiP, NiP_2 and NiP_3). Ternary and more complex metal phosphides are also known.

The most general preparative route to phosphides (Faraday's method) is to heat the metal with the appropriate amount of red P at high temperature in an inert atmosphere or an evacuated sealed tube:

$$n\text{M} + m\text{P} \xrightarrow{\text{heat}} \text{M}_n\text{P}_m$$

An alternative route (Andrieux's method) is the electrolysis of fused salts such as molten

[60] M. BAUDLER and T. ETZBACH, *Angew. Chem. Int. Edn. Engl.* **30**, 580–2 (1991).

[61] O. J. SCHERER, H. SWAROWSKY, G. WOLMERSHÄUSER, W. KAIM and S. KOHLMANN, *Angew. Chem. Int. Edn. Engl.* **26**, 1153–5 (1987).

[62] L. Y. GOH, R. C. S. WONG and E. SINN, *Organometallics* **12**, 888–94 (1993).

[63] A. WILSON, The metal phosphides, Chap. 3 (pp. 289–363) in ref. 23, see also p. 256.

[64] A. D. F. TOY, in *Comprehensive Inorganic Chemistry*, Vol. 2, Pergamon Press, Oxford, 1973 (Section 20.2, Phosphides, pp. 406–14).

[65] D. E. C. CORBRIDGE, *Phosphorus* (3rd edn.), Elsevier, Amsterdam, 1985, Section 2.2 Metallic Phosphides, pp. 56–69. (See also 5th edn. 1995.)

alkali-metal phosphates to which appropriate metal oxides or halides have been added:

$$\{(NaPO_3)_n/NaCl/WO_3\} \text{ fused } \xrightarrow{\text{electrol}} W_3P$$

Variation in current, voltage and electrolyte composition frequently results in the formation of phosphides of different stoichiometries. Less-general routes (which are nevertheless extremely valuable in specific instances) include:

(a) Reaction of PH_3 with a metal, metal halide or sulfide, e.g.:

$$PH_3 + 2Ti \xrightarrow{800°} Ti_2P$$

$$2PH_3 + 3Ni(O_2CMe)_2 \xrightarrow{H_2O} Ni_3P_2$$

$$+ 6HOAc \xrightarrow[\text{reaction}]{\text{further}} Ni_5P_2$$

(b) Reduction of a phosphate such as apatite with C at high temperature, e.g.:

$$Ca_3(PO_4)_2 + 8C \xrightarrow{1200°} Ca_3P_2 + 8CO$$

(c) Reaction of a metal phosphide with further metal or phosphorus to give a product of different stoichiometry, e.g.:

$$Th_3P_4 + Th \xrightarrow{900°} 4ThP$$

$$4RuP + P_4(g) \xrightarrow{650°} 4RuP_2$$

$$4IrP_2 \xrightarrow[\text{(low press)}]{1150°} 2Ir_2P + 1\tfrac{1}{2}P_4(g)$$

Phosphides resemble in many ways the metal borides (p. 145), carbides (p. 297), and nitrides (p. 417), and there are the same difficulties in classification and description of bonding. Perhaps the least-contentious procedure is to classify according to stoichiometry, i.e. (a) metal-rich phosphides (M/P > 1), (b) monophosphides (M/P = 1), and (c) phosphorus-rich phosphides (M/P < 1):

(a) *Metal-rich phosphides* are usually hard, brittle, refractory materials with metallic lustre, high thermal and electrical conductivity, great thermal stability and general chemical inertness. Phosphorus is often in trigonal prismatic coordination being surrounded by 6 M, or by 7, 8 or 9 M (see Fig. 6.7 on p. 148 and Fig. 12.6). The antifluorite structure of many M_2P also features eightfold (cubic) coordination of P by M. The details of the particular structure adopted in each case are influenced predominantly by size effects.

(b) *Monophosphides* adopt a variety of structures which appear to be influenced by both size and electronic effects. Thus the Group 3 phosphides MP adopt the zinc-blende structure (p. 1210) with tetrahedral coordination of P, whereas SnP has the NaCl-type structure (p. 242) with octahedral coordination of P, VP has the hexagonal NiAs-type structure (p. 556) with trigonal prismatic coordination of isolated P atoms by V, and MoP has the hexagonal WC-type structure (p. 299) in which both Mo and P have a trigonal prismatic coordination by atoms of the other kind. More complicated arrangements are also encountered, e.g.:[65]

TiP, ZrP, HfP: half the P trigonal prismatic and half octahedral;

MP (M = Cr, Mn, Fe, Co, Ru, W): distorted trigonal prismatic coordination of P by M plus two rather short contacts to P atoms in adjacent trigonal prisms, thus building up a continuous chain of P atoms; NiP is a distortion of this in which the P atoms are grouped in pairs rather than in chains (or isolated as in VP).

(c) *Phosphorus-rich phosphides* are typified by lower mps and much lower thermal stabilities when compared with monophosphides or metal-rich phosphides. They are often semiconductors rather than metallic conductors and feature increasing catenation of the P atoms (cf. boron rich borides, p. 148). P_2 units occur in FeP_2, RuP_2 and OsP_2 (marcasite-type, p. 680) and in PtP_2 (pyrites type, p. 680) with P–P 217 pm. Planar P_4 rings (square or rectangular) occur in several MP_3 (M = Co, Ni, Rh, Pd, Ir) with P–P typically 223 pm in the square ring of RhP_3. Structures are also known in which the P atoms form chains (PdP_2, NiP_2, CdP_2, BaP_3),

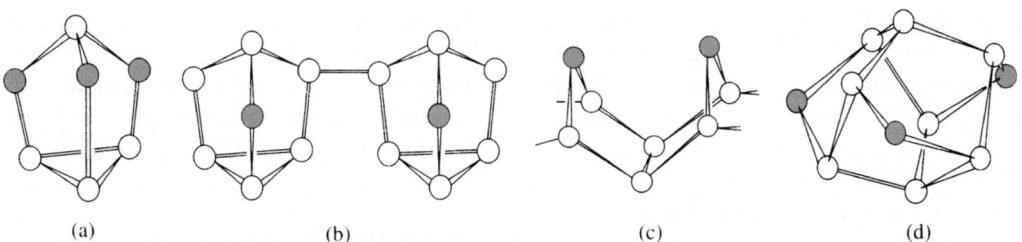

    (a)   (b)   (c)   (d)

Figure 12.11   Schematic representation of the structures of polycyclic polyphosphide anions (open circles P, shaded circles P^-) (a) P_7^{3-}, (b) $\{P_7^-\}_x$, (c) $\{P_8^{2-}\}_x$, (d) P_{11}^{3-}

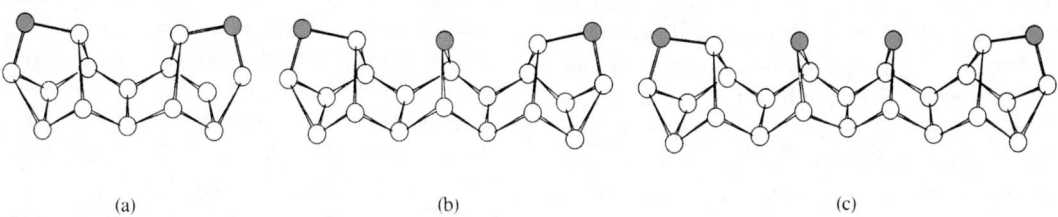

    (a)   (b)   (c)

Figure 12.12   Schematic representation of the structures of (a) P_{16}^{2-}, (b) P_{21}^{3-}, (c) P_{26}^{4-}, (open circles P, shaded circles P^-)

double chains ($ZnPbP_{14}$, $CdPbP_{14}$, $HgPbP_{14}$), or layers (CuP_2, AgP_2, CdP_4); in the last 3 phosphides the layers are made up by a regular fusion of puckered 10-membered rings of P atoms with the metal atoms in the interstices. The double-chained structure of $MPbP_{14}$ is closely related to that of violet phosphorus (p. 482).

In addition, phosphides of the electropositive elements in Groups 1, 2 and the lanthanoids form phosphides with some degree of ionic bonding. The compounds Na_3P_{11} and Sr_3P_{14} have already been mentioned (p. 484) and other somewhat ionic phosphides are M_3P (M = Li, Na), M_3P_2 (M = Be, Mg, Zn, Cd), MP (M = La, Ce) and Th_3P_4. However, it would be misleading to consider these as fully ionized compounds of P^{3-} and there is extensive metallic or covalent interaction in the solids. Such compounds are characterized by their ready hydrolysis by water or dilute acid to give PH_3.

Recent extensive structural studies by X-ray crystallography and by ^{31}P nmr spectroscopy have revealed an astonishing variety of *conjuncto*-polyphosphides with quasi-ionic cluster structures.[66,67] Thus, the yellow compound Li_3P_7 (which has been known since 1912) and its Na–Cs analogues have been found to contain the P_7^{3-} cluster shown schematically in Fig. 12.11(a). The cluster can be regarded as being related to the P_4 tetrahedron (p. 479) by the notional insertion of three 2-connected P^- atoms (cf. the structure of P_4S_3, p. 507, with which it is precisely isoelectronic). Substitution of P by As leads to a series of closely related anions $[P_{7-x}As_x]^{3-}$ $x = 1–5$, (?6),[68] and As_7^{3-} is also known for Na, Rb, Cs. Catenation of the P_7^{3-} unit, as shown in Fig. 12.11(b), leads to the stoichiometry $M^+P_7^-$. The repeating unit $=P_8=$, which is clearly related to a segment in the structure of Hittorf's allotrope (p. 482), is shown in Fig. 12.11(c). A more complex

[66] H. G. VON SCHNERING, in A. H. COWLEY (ed.) *Rings, Clusters and Polymers of the Main Group Elements,* ACS Symposium Series No. **232**, Washington D. C. 1983, pp. 69–80.

[67] M. BAUDLER, *Angew. Chem. Int. Edn. Engl.* **21**, 492–512 (1982); **26**, 419–41 (1987).

[68] W. HÖNLE and H. G. VON SCHNERING, *Angew. Chem. Int. Edn. Engl.* **25**, 352–3 (1986).

cluster occurs in the yellow/orange compounds $M_3^+P_{11}^{3-}$ (Fig. 12.11d): P_{11}^{3-} can be thought of as comprising two axial PP_3 tetrahedra joined by a central belt of three 2-connected P^- atoms, so that the sequence of cluster planes contains 1,3,(3),3,1 P atoms, respectively.

Even more complex *conjuncto*-polyphosphide anions can be constructed, such as those of stoichiometry P_{16}^{2-}, P_{21}^{3-} and P_{26}^{4-}, Fig. 12.12(a)(b)(c).[66,67] These bear an obvious structural relationship to $=P_8=$ (Fig. 12.11c) and to Hittorf's phosphorus (Fig. 12.4) and can be viewed as ladders of P atoms with alternate P–P and P(P^-)P rungs, terminated at each end by a ring-closing P(P^-) unit. The P–P distances and PPP angles in these various species are much as expected. These cluster anions, and those mentioned in the preceding paragraphs, can be partially or completely protonated (see next subsection) and they also occur in neutral organopolyphosphanes (p. 495).

A completely different structural motif has very recently been found in the red-brown phosphide Ca_5P_8, formed by direct fusion of Ca metal and red P in the correct atom ratio in a corundum crucible at $1000°C$.[69] The structure comprises Ca^{2+} cations and P_8^{10-} anions, the latter adopting a staggered ethane conformation. (Note that P^+ is isolobal with C and P^{2-} with H so that $C_2H_6 = [(P^+)_2(P^{2-})_6] = P_8^{10-}$.) The internal P–P distance is 230.1 pm and the terminal P–P distances 214.9–216.9 pm, while the internal PPP angles are 104.2–106.4° and the outer angles are 103.4–103.7°.

Few industrial uses have so far been found for phosphides. "Ferrophosphorus" is produced on a large scale as a byproduct of P_4 manufacture, and its uses have been noted (p. 480). Phosphorus is also much used as an alloying element in iron and steel, and for improving the workability of Cu. Group 3 monophosphides are valuable semiconductors (p. 255) and Ca_3P_2 is an important ingredient in some navy sea-flares since its reaction with water releases spontaneously flammable

phosphines. By contrast the phosphides of Nb, Ta and W are valued for their chemical inertness, particularly their resistance to oxidation at very high temperatures, though they are susceptible to attack by oxidizing acids or peroxides.

12.3.2 Phosphine and related compounds

The most stable hydride of P is phosphine (phosphane), PH_3. It is the first of a homologous open-chain series P_nH_{n+2} ($n = 1-9$) the members of which rapidly diminish in thermal stability, though P_2H_4 and P_3H_5 have been isolated pure. There are ten other (unstable) homologous series: P_nH_n ($n = 3-10$), P_nH_{n-2} ($n = 4-12$), and P_nH_{n-4} ($n = 5-13$) and so on up to P_nH_{n-18} ($n = 19-22$)[67]; in all of these there is a tendency to form cyclic and condensed polyphosphanes at the expense of open-chain structures. Some 85 phosphanes have so far been identified and structurally characterized by nmr spectroscopy and other techniques, although few have been obtained pure because of problems involving thermal instability, ready disproportionation, light-sensitivity and great chemical reactivity.[67,70,71] Phosphorane, PH_5, has not been prepared or even detected, despite numerous attempts, although HPF_4, H_2PF_3 and H_3PF_2 have recently been well characterized.[72,73]

PH_3 is an extremely poisonous, highly reactive, colourless gas which has a faint garlic odour at concentrations above about 2 ppm by volume. It is intermediate in thermal stability between NH_3 (p. 421) and AsH_3 (p. 557). Several convenient routes are available for its preparation:

1. Hydrolysis of a metal phosphide such as AlP or Ca_3P_2; the method is useful even

[69] C. HADENFELDT and F. BARTELS, *Z. anorg. allg. Chem.* **620**, 1247–52 (1994).

[70] M. BAUDLER and K. GLINKA, *Chem. Rev.* **93**, 1623–67 (1993).

[71] M. BAUDLER and K. GLINKA, *Chem. Rev.* **94**, 1273–97 (1994). See also *Z. anorg. allg. Chem.* **621**, 1133–9 (1995).

[72] A. J. DOWNS G. S. MCGRADY, E. A. BARNFIELD and D. W. H. RANKIN, *J. Chem. Soc., Dalton Trans.*, 545–50 (1989).

[73] A. BECHERS, *Z. anorg. allg. Chem.* **619**, 1869–79 (1993).

up to the 10-mole scale and can be made almost quantitative

$$Ca_3P_2 + 6H_2O \longrightarrow 2PH_3 + 3Ca(OH)_2$$

2. Pyrolysis of phosphorous acid at $205-210°$; under these conditions the yield of PH_3 is 97% though at higher temperatures the reaction can be more complex (p. 512)

$$4H_3PO_3 \xrightarrow{200°} PH_3 + 3H_3PO_4$$

3. Alkaline hydrolysis of PH_4I (for very pure phosphine):

$$P_4 + 2I_2 + 8H_2O \longrightarrow 2PH_4I + 2HI$$
$$+ 2H_3PO_4$$
$$PH_4I + KOH(aq) \longrightarrow PH_3 + KI + H_2O$$

4. Reduction of PCl_3 with $LiAlH_4$ or LiH:

$$PCl_3 + LiAlH_4 \xrightarrow{Et_2O/ < 0°} PH_3 + \dots$$
$$PCl_3 + 3LiH \xrightarrow{warm} PH_3 + 3LiCl$$

5. Alkaline hydrolysis of white P_4 (industrial process):

$$P_4 + 3KOH + 3H_2O \longrightarrow PH_3 + 3KH_2PO_2$$

Phosphine has a pyramidal structure, as expected, with P–H 142 pm and the H–P–H angle $93.6°$ (see p. 557). Other physical properties are mp $-133.5°$, bp $-87.7°$, dipole moment 0.58 D, heat of formation $\Delta H_f°$ $-9.6\,kJ\,mol^{-1}$ (uncertain) and mean P–H bond energy $320\,kJ\,mol^{-1}$. The free energy change (at 25°C) for the reaction $\frac{1}{4}P_4(\alpha\text{-white}) + \frac{3}{2}H_2(g) = PH_3(g)$ is $-13.1\,kJ\,mol^{-1}$, implying a tendency for the elements to combine, though there is negligible reaction unless H_2 is energized photolytically or by a high-current arc. The inversion frequency of PH_3 is about 4000 times less than for NH_3 (p. 423); this reflects the substantially higher energy barrier to inversion for PH_3 which is calculated to be $\sim155\,kJ\,mol^{-1}$ rather than $24.7\,kJ\,mol^{-1}$ for NH_3.

Phosphine is rather insoluble in water at atmospheric pressure but is more soluble in organic liquids, and particularly so in CS_2 and CCl_3CO_2H. Some typical values are:

Solvent ($T°C$)	H_2O (17°)	CH_3CO_2H (20°)	C_6H_6 (22°)
Solubility/ml PH_3 (g) per 100 ml solvent	26	319	726

Solvent ($T°C$)	CS_2(21°)	CCl_3CO_2H
Solubility/ml PH_3 (g) per 100 ml solvent	1025	1590

[Note:1 ml PH_3(g) $\simeq 1.5$ mg]

Aqueous solutions are neutral and there is little tendency for PH_3 to protonate or deprotonate:

$$PH_3 + H_2O \rightleftharpoons PH_2^- + H_3O^+;$$
$$K_A = 1.6 \times 10^{-29}$$
$$PH_3 + H_2O \rightleftharpoons PH_4^+ + OH^-;$$
$$K_B = 4 \times 10^{-28}$$

In liquid ammonia, however, phosphine dissolves to give $NH_4^+PH_2^-$ and with potassium gives KPH_2 in the same solvent. Again, phosphine reacts with liquid HCl to give the sparingly soluble $PH_4^+Cl^-$ and this reacts further with BCl_3 to give PH_4BCl_4. The corresponding bromides and PH_4I are also known.

More generally, phosphine readily acts as a ligand to numerous Lewis acids and typical coordination complexes are $[BH_3(PH_3)]$, $[BF_3(PH_3)]$, $[AlCl_3(PH_3)]$, $[Cr(CO)_2(PH_3)_4]$, $[Cr(CO)_3(PH_3)_3]$, $[Co(CO)_2(NO)(PH_3)]$, $[Ni(PF_3)_2(PH_3)_2]$ and $[CuCl(PH_3)]$. Further details are in the Panel and other aspects of the chemistry of PH_3 have been extensively reviewed.[74]

Phosphine is also a strong reducing agent: many metal salts are reduced to the metal and PCl_5 yields PCl_3. The pure gas ignites in air at about 150° but when contaminated with traces of P_2H_4 it is spontaneously flammable:

$$PH_3 + 2O_2 \longrightarrow H_3PO_4$$

When heated with sulfur, PH_3 yields H_2S and a mixture of phosphorus sulfides. Probably the most important reaction industrially is

---

[74] E. FLUCK, Chemistry of phosphine, *Topics in Current Chem.* **35**, 1–64 (1973). A review with 493 references.

Phosphine and its Derivatives as Ligands[7,75-78]

A wide variety of 3-coordinate phosphorus(III) compounds are known and these have been extensively studied as ligands because of their significance in improving our understanding of the stability and reactivity of many coordination complexes. Among the most studied of these ligands are PH_3, PF_3 (p. 495), PCl_3 (p. 496). PR_3 (R = alkyl), PPh_3 and $P(OR)_3$, together with a large number of "mixed" ligands such as Me_2NPF_2, $PMePh_2$, etc., and many multidentate (chelating) ligands such as $Ph_2PCH_2CH_2PPh_2$, etc.

In many of their complexes PF_3 and PPh_3 (for example) resemble CO (p. 926) and this at one time encouraged the belief that their bonding capabilities were influenced not only by the factors (p. 198) which affect the stability of the σ P→M interaction which uses the lone-pair of electrons on P^{III} and a vacant orbital on M, but also by the possibility of synergic π back-donation from a "nonbonding" d_π pair of electrons on the metal into a "vacant" $3d_\pi$ orbital on P. It is, however, not clear to what extent, if any, the σ and π bonds reinforce each other, and more recent descriptions are based on an MO approach which uses all (σ and π) orbitals of appropriate symmetry on both the phosphine and the metal-containing moiety. To the extent that σ and π bonding effects on the stability of metal-phosphorus bonds can be isolated from each other and from steric factors (see below) the accepted sequence of effects is as follows:

σ bonding: $PBu_3^t > P(OR)_3 > PR_3 \approx PPh_3 > PH_3 > PF_3 > P(OPh)_3$

π bonding: $PF_3 > P(OPh)_3 > PH_3 > P(OR)_3 > PPh_3 \approx PR_3 > PBu_3^t$

Steric interference: $PBu_3^t > PPh_3 > P(OPh)_3 > PMe_3 > P(OR)_3 > PF_3 > PH_3$

Steric factors are frequently dominant, particularly with bulky ligands, and their influence on the course of many reactions is crucial. One measure of the "size" of a ligand in so far as it affects bond formation is C. A. Tolman's cone angle (1970) which is the angle at the metal atom of the cone swept out by the van der Waals radii of the groups attached to P. This will, of course, be dependent on the actual interatomic distance between M and P. For the particular case of Ni, for which a standard value of 228 pm was adopted for Ni–P, the calculated values for the cone angle are:

Ligand	PH_3	PF_3	$P(OMe)_3$	$P(OEt)_3$	PMe_3	$P(OPh)_3$	PCl_3
Cone angle	87°	104°	107°	109°	118°	121°	125°

Ligand	PEt_3	PPh_3	PPr_3^i	PBu_3^t	$P(o\text{-tol})_3$	$P(\text{mesityl})_3$
Cone angle	132°	145°	160°	182°	195°	212°

Bulky tertiary phosphine ligands exert both steric and electronic influences when they form complexes (since an increase in bulkiness of a substituent on P increases the inter-bond angles and this in turn can be thought of as an increase in "p-character" of the lone-pair of electrons on P). For example, the sterically demanding di-t-butylphosphines, PBu_2^tR (R = alkyl or aryl), promote spatially less-demanding features such as hydride formation, coordinative unsaturation at the metal centre, and even the stabilization of unusual oxidation states, such as Ir^{II}. They also favour internal C– or O– metallation reactions for the same reasons. Indeed, the metallation of C–H and C–P bonds of coordinated tertiary phosphines can be considered as examples of intramolecular oxidative addition, and these have important mechanistic implications for homogeneous and heterogeneous catalysis.[79]

Other notable examples are the orthometallation (orthophenylation) reactions of many complexes of aryl phosphines (PAr_3) and aryl phosphites $P(OAr)_3$ with platinum metals in particular, e.g.:

$$[RuClH\{P(OPh)_3\}_4] \underset{H_2}{\overset{heat(-H_2)}{\rightleftharpoons}} (PhO)_2\overline{PO-C_6H_4-Ru}Cl\{P(OPh)_3\}_3$$

[75] Chapter 5 in ref. 2, Phosphorus(III) ligands in transition-metal complexes, pp. 177–207.

[76] C. A. MCAULIFFE and W. LEVASON, *Phosphine, Arsine and Stibine Complexes of the Transition Elements*, Elsevier, Amsterdam, 1979, 546 pp. A review with over 2700 references. See also C. A. MCAULIFFE (ed.), *Transition-Metal Complexes of Phosphorus, Arsenic and Antimony Donor Ligands*, Macmillan, London, 1972.

[77] O. STELZER, *Topics in Phosphorus Chemistry* **9**, 1–229 (1977). An extensive review with over 1700 references arranged by element and by technique but with no assessment or generalizations.

[78] R. MASON and D. W. MEEK, *Angew. Chem. Int. Edn. Engl.* **17**, 183–94 (1978).

[79] G. PARSHALL, Homogeneous catalytic activation of C–H bonds, *Acc. Chem. Res.* **8**, 113–7 (1975).

its hydrophosphorylation of formaldehyde in aqueous hydrochloric acid solution:

$$PH_3 + 4HCHO + HCl \longrightarrow [P(CH_2OH)_4]Cl$$

The tetrakis(hydroxymethyl)phosphonium chloride so formed is the major ingredient with urea-formaldehyde or melamine-formaldehyde resins for the permanent flame-proofing of cotton cloth.

Of the many other hydrides of phosphorus, diphosphane (diphosphine), P_2H_4, is the most studied. It is best made[71] by treating CaP with cold oxygen-free water. Passage of PH_3 through an electric discharge at 5–10 kV is an alternative method for small amounts. P_2H_4 is a colourless, volatile liquid (mp −99°) which is thermally unstable even below room temperature and is decomposed slowly by water. Its vapour pressure at 0°C is 70.2 mmHg but partial decomposition precludes precise determination of the bp (63.5° extrap); $d \simeq 1.014 \, \text{g cm}^{-3}$ at 20°C. Electron-diffraction measurements on the gas establish the *gauche*-C_2 configuration (p. 428) with P–P 222 pm, P–H 145 pm, and the angle H–P–H 91.3°, though vibration spectroscopy suggests a *trans*-C_{2h} configuration in the solid phase. These results can be compared with those for the halides P_2X_4 on p. 498.

The next member of the open-chain series P_nH_{n+2} is P_3H_5, i.e. PH_2PHPH_2, a colourless liquid that can be stored in the dark at −80° for several days.[67,71] It can be made by disproportionation ($2P_2H_4 \longrightarrow P_3H_5 + PH_3$) but it is difficult to purify because of its own fairly ready disproportionation and reactivity, e.g. $2P_3H_5 \longrightarrow P_4H_6 + P_2H_4$; and $P_3H_5 + P_2H_4 \longrightarrow P_4H_6 + PH_3$. Tetraphosphane(6), P_4H_6, exists as an equilibrium mixture of the two structural isomers $H_2PPHPHPH_2$ (*n*) and $P(PH_2)_3$ (*i*), and itself reacts with P_3H_5 at −20° according to the idealized stoichiometry $P_4H_6 + P_3H_5 \longrightarrow 2PH_3 + P_5H_5$, i.e. *cyclo*-$(PH)_5$. All members of the series *cyclo*-P_nH_n ($n = 3$–10) have been detected mass spectrometrically in the thermolysis products from P_2H_4.[70]

Polycyclic polyphosphanes are often best prepared by direct protonation of the corresponding polyphosphide anions (Figs. 12.11 and 12.12)

with HX, though other routes are also available. Thus, treatment of P_7^{3-} yields P_7H^{2-}, $P_7H_2^-$ and P_7H_3 by sucessive protonation of the three 2-connected P^- sites. The alkyl derivatives are more stable than the parent polycyclic phosphanes and provide many examples of the elegant solution of complex conformational problems by the use of nmr spectroscopy.[67,70]

12.3.3 Phosphorus halides

Phosphorus forms three series of halides P_2X_4, PX_3 and PX_5. All 12 compounds may exist, although there is considerable doubt about PI_5.[80] Numerous mixed halides PX_2Y and PX_2Y_3 are also known as well as various pseudohalides such as $P(CN)_3$, $P(CNO)_3$, $P(CNS)_3$ and their mixed halogeno-counterparts. The compounds form an extremely useful extended series with which to follow the effect of progressive substitution on various properties, and the pentahalides are particularly significant in spanning the "ionic-covalent" border, so that they exist in various structural forms depending on the nature of the halogen, the phase of aggregation, or the polarity of the solvent. Some subhalides such as P_4X_2 and P_7X_3, and some curious polyhalides such as PBr_7 and PBr_{11} have also been characterized. Physical properties of the binary halides are summarized in Table 12.3 (on the next page). Ternary (mixed) halides tend to have properties intermediate between those of the parent binary halides.

Phosphorus trihalides

All 4 trihalides are volatile reactive compounds which feature pyramidal molecules. The fluoride is best made by the action of CaF_2, ZnF_2 or AsF_3 on PCl_3, but the others are formed by direct halogenation of the element. PF_3 is colourless, odourless and does not fume in air, but is very hazardous due to the formation of a complex with blood haemoglobin (cf.

---

80 I. Tornieporth-Oetting and T. Klapötke, *J. Chem. Soc., Chem. Commun.*, 132–3 (1990).

Table 12.3 Some physical properties of the binary phosphorus halides

Compound	Physical State at 25°C	MP/°C	BP/°C	P–X/pm	Angle X–P–X
PF_3	Colourless gas	−151.5	−101.8	156	96.3°
PCl_3	Colourless liquid	−93.6	76.1	204	100°
PBr_3	Colourless liquid	−41.5	173.2	222	101°
PI_3	Red hexagonal crystals	61.2	decomp > 200	243	102°
P_2F_4	Colourless gas	−86.5	−6.2	159 (P–P 228)	99.1° (F–P–P 95.4°)
P_2Cl_4	Colourless oily liquid	−28	~180 (d)	—	—
P_2Br_4	?	—	—	—	—
P_2I_4	Red triclinic needles	125.5	decomp	248 (P–P 221)	102.3° (I–P–P 94.0°)
PF_5	Colourless gas	−93.7	−84.5	153 (eq) 158 (ax)	120° (eq-eq) 90° (eq-ax)
PCl_5	Off-white tetragonal crystals	167	160 (subl)	See text	
PBr_5	Reddish-yellow rhombohedral crystals	<100 (d)	106 (d)	See text	
PI_5?	Brown-black crystals	41	—	However, see ref. 80	

CO, p. 1101). It is about as toxic as $COCl_2$. The similarity of PF_3 and CO as ligands was first noted by J. Chatt[81] and many complexes with transition elements are now known,[82] e.g. $[Ni(CO)_n(PF_3)_{4-n}]$ ($n = 0-4$), $[Pd(PF_3)_4]$, $[Pt(PF_3)_4]$, $[CoH(PF_3)_4]$, $[Co_2(\mu-PF_2)_2(PF_3)_6]$, etc. Such complexes can be prepared by ligand replacement reactions, by fluorination of PCl_3 complexes, by direct reaction of PF_3 with metal salts or even by direct reaction of PF_3 with metals at elevated temperatures and pressures.

PF_3, unlike the other trihalides of phosphorus, hydrolyses only slowly with water, the products being phosphorous acid and HF: $PF_3 + 3H_2O \rightarrow H_3PO_3 + 3HF$.

The reaction is much more rapid in alkaline solutions, and in dilute aqueous $KHCO_3$ solutions the intermediate monofluorophosphorous acid is formed:

$$PF_3 + 2H_2O \xrightarrow{\text{2% aq } KHCO_3} O{=}PH(OH)F + 2HF$$

PCl_3 is the most important compound of the group and is made industrially on a large scale[†] by direct chlorination of phosphorus suspended in a precharge of PCl_3 — the reaction is carried out under reflux with continuous take-off of the PCl_3 formed. PCl_3 undergoes many substitution reactions, as shown in the diagram, and is the main source of organophosphorus compounds. Particularly notable are PR_3, PR_nCl_{3-n}, $PR_n(OR)_{3-n}$, $(PhO)_3PO$, and $(RO)_3PS$. Many of these compounds are made on the 1000-tonne scale pa, and the major uses are as oil additives, plasticizers, flame retardants, fuel additives and intermediates in the manufacture of insecticides.[83] PCl_3 is also readily oxidized to the important phosphorus(V) derivatives PCl_5, $POCl_3$ and $PSCl_3$. It is oxidized by As_2O_3 to P_2O_5 though this is not the commercial route to this compound (p. 505). It fumes in moist air and is more readily hydrolysed (and oxidized) by water than is PF_3. With cold N_2O_4 (−10°) it undergoes a curious oxidative coupling reaction to give $Cl_3P{=}N{-}POCl_2$,

[81] J. Chatt, *Nature* **165**, 637–8 (1950); J. Chatt and A. A. Williams, *J. Chem. Soc.* 3061–7 (1951).

[82] T. Kruck, *Angew. Chem. Int. Edn. Engl.* **6**, 53–67 (1967); J. F. Nixon, *Adv. Inorg. Chem. Radiochem.* **13**, 363–469 (1970); R. J. Clarke and M. A. Busch, *Acc. Chem. Res.* **6**, 246–52 (1973).

[†] World production exceeds one third of a million tonnes pa; of this USA produces ~155 000 tonnes, Western Europe ~115 000 and Japan ~35 000 tonnes pa.

[83] D. H. Chadwick and R. S. Watt, Chap. 19 in ref. 11, pp. 1221–79.

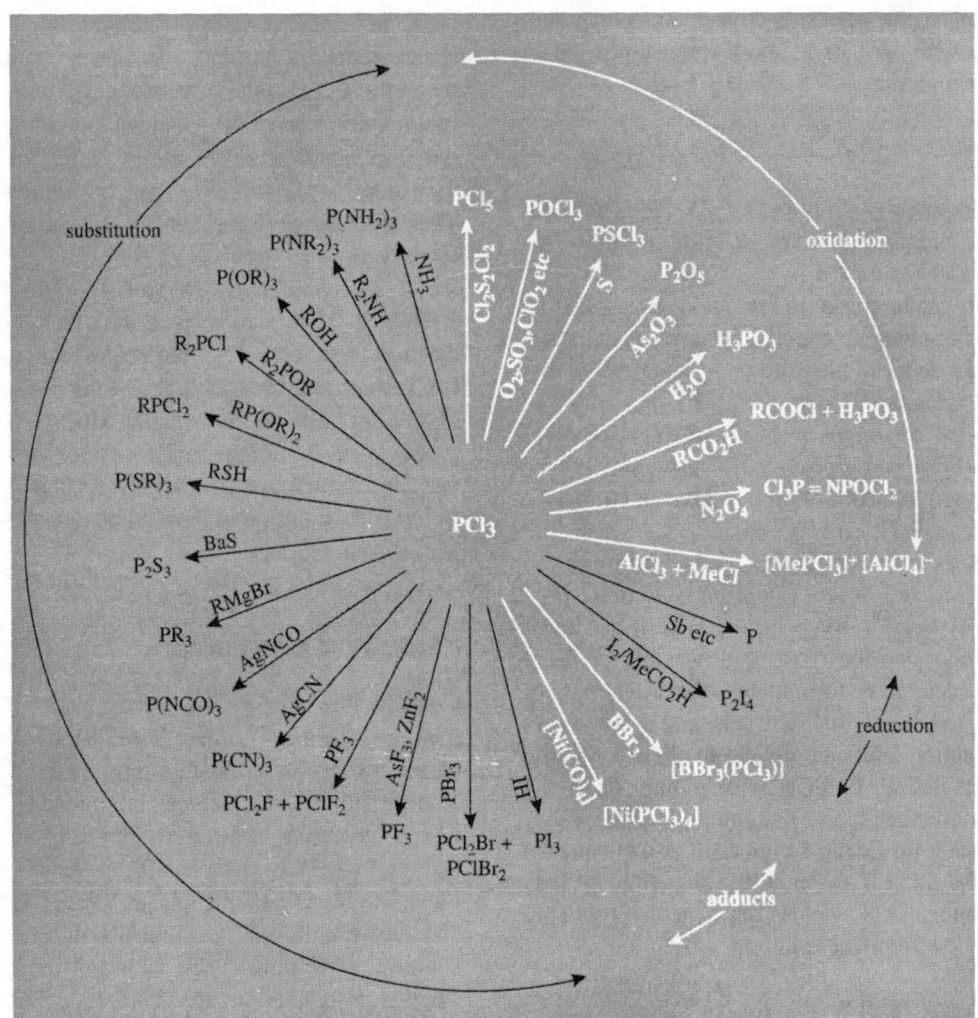

mp 35.5°; (note the presence of two different 4-coordinate P^V atoms).[84] Other notable reactions of PCl_3 are its extensive use to convert alcohols to RCl and carboxylic acids to RCOCl, its reduction to P_2I_4 by iodine, and its ability to form coordination complexes with Lewis acids such as BX_3 and Ni^0.

PI_3 is emerging as a powerful and versatile deoxygenating agent.[85] For example solutions of PI_3 in CH_2Cl_2 at or below room temperature convert sulfoxides (RR'SO) into diorganosulfides, selenoxides (RR'SeO) into selenides, aldehyde oximes (RCH=NOH) into nitriles, and primary nitroalkanes (RCH$_2$NO$_2$) into nitriles, all in high yield (75–95%). The formation of nitriles, RCN, in the last two reactions requires the presence of triethylamine in addition to the PI_3.

Diphosphorus tetrahalides and other lower halides of phosphorus

The physical properties of P_2X_4, in so far as they are known, are summarized in Table 12.3. P_2F_4 was first made in other than trace amounts in

[84] M. BECKE-GOEHRING, A. DEBO, E. FLUCK and W. GOETZE, *Chem. Ber.* **94**, 1383–7 (1961).

[85] J. N. DENIS and A. KRIEF, *J. Chem. Soc., Chem. Commun.*, 544–5 (1980).

1966, using the very effective method of coupling two PF_2 groups at room temperature under reduced pressure:

$$2PF_2I + 2Hg \xrightarrow{86\% \text{ yield}} P_2F_4 + Hg_2I_2$$

The compound hydrolyses to F_2POPF_2 which can also be prepared directly in good yield by the reaction of O_2 on P_2F_4.

P_2Cl_4 can be made (in low yield) by passing an electric discharge through a mixture of PCl_3 and H_2 under reduced pressure or by microwave discharge through PCl_3 at $1-5$ mmHg pressure. The compound decomposes slowly at room temperature to PCl_3 and an involatile solid, and can be hydrolysed in basic solution to give an equimolar mixture of P_2H_4 and $P_2(OH)_4$.

Little is known of P_2Br_4, said to be produced by an obscure reaction in the system C_2H_4- $PBr_3-Al_2Br_6$.[86] By contrast, P_2I_4 is the most stable and also the most readily made of the 4 tetrahalides; it is formed by direct reaction of I_2 and red P at $180°$ or by I_2 and white P_4 in CS_2 solution, and can also be made by reducing PI_3 with red P, or PCl_3 with iodine. Its X-ray crystal structure shows that the molecules of P_2I_4 adopt the *trans-*, centrosymmetric (C_{2h}) form (see N_2H_4, p. 428, N_2F_4, p. 439). Reaction of P_2I_4 with sulfur in CS_2 yields $P_2I_4S_2$, which probably has the symmetrical structure

but most reactions of P_2I_4 result in cleavage of the P–P bond, e.g. Br_2 gives $PBrI_2$ in 90% yield. Hydrolysis yields various phosphines and oxoacids of P, together with a small amount of hypophosphoric acid, $(HO)_2(O)PP(O)(OH)_2$.

Several ternary diphosphorus tetrahalides, $P_2X_nY_{4-n}$, (X, Y = Cl, Br, I) have recently been detected in CS_2 solutions by ^{31}P nmr spectroscopy.[87] It has also been found that reactions CS_2 solution between P_4 and half a mole-equivalent of Br_2 yielded not only P_2Br_4 but also small amounts of the new "butterfly" molecules *exo,exo-*P_4Br_2 and *exo,endo-*P_4Br_2. The structure of these can be viewed as being formed by the scission of one P–P bond in the P_4 tetrahedron by Br_2 (cf. the structure of B_4H_{10}, p. 154) which is also a 22 *valence-electron* species. The molecules P_4BrCl and P_4Cl_2 were also identified, following chlorination of the bromide solution using Me_3SnCl. Other products of the initial reactions included P_7Br_3 and P_7I_3 which are structurally related to P_7H_3 (p. 495). None of these novel subhalides has been isolated pure.[87]

Phosphorus pentahalides

Considerable theoretical and stereochemical interest attaches to these compounds because of the variety of structures they adopt; PCl_5 is also an important chemical intermediate. Thus, PF_5 is molecular and stereochemically non-rigid (see below), PCl_5 is molecular in the gas phase, ionic in the crystalline phase, $[PCl_4]^+[PCl_6]^-$, and either molecular or ionically dissociated in solution, depending on the nature of the solvent. PBr_5 is also ionic in the solid state but exists as $[PBr_4]^+[Br]^-$ rather than $[PBr_4]^+[PBr_6]^-$. The pentaiodide does not exist[80] (except perhaps as $PI_3.I_2$, but certainly not as $PI_4^+I^-$ as originally claimed[88]).

PF_5 is a thermally stable, chemically reactive gas which can be made either by fluorinating PCl_5 with AsF_3 (or CaF_2), or by thermal decomposition of $NaPF_6$, $Ba(PF_6)_2$ or the corresponding diazonium salts. Single-crystal X-ray analysis (at $-164°C$) indicates a trigonal bipyramidal structure with $P-F_{ax}$ (158.0 pm) being

[86] R. I. Pyrkin, Ya. A. Levin and E. I. Goldfarb, *J. Gen. Chem. USSR* **43**, 1690–6 (1973). See also A. Hinke, W. Kuchen and J. Kutter, *Angew. Chem. Int. Edn. Engl.* **20**, 1060 (1981).

[87] B. W. Tattershall and N. L. Kendall, *Polyhedron* **13**, 1517–21 (1994).

[88] N. G. Feshchenko V. G. Kostina and A. V. Kirsanov, *J. Gen. Chem. USSR* **48**, 195–6 (1978).

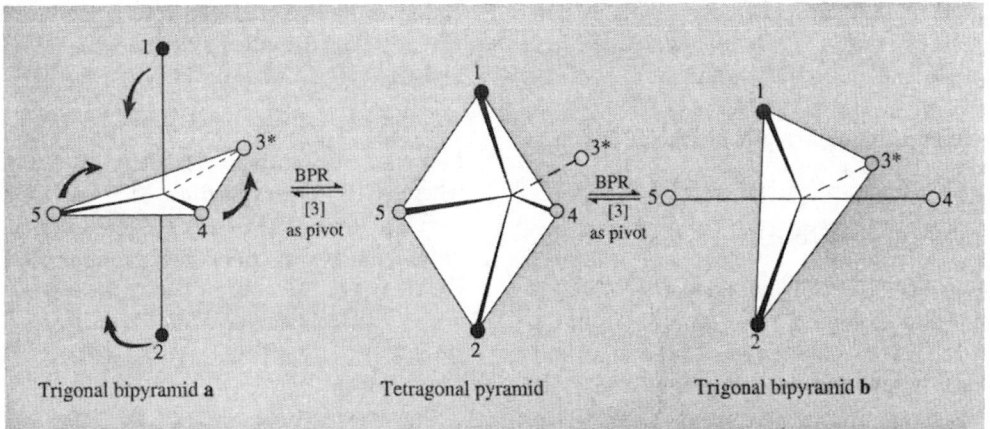

Figure 12.13   Interchange of axial and equatorial positions by Berry pseudorotation (BPR).

significantly longer than P–F_{eq} (152.2 pm).[89] This confirms the deductions from a gas phase electron-diffraction study (D_{3h}: P–F_{ax} 158 pm, P–F_{eq} 153 pm). However, the ^{19}F nmr spectrum, as recorded down to $-100°$C, shows only a single fluorine resonance peak (split into a doublet by ^{31}P–^{19}F coupling) implying that on this longer time scale (milliseconds, as distinct from "instantaneous" for electron diffraction) all 5 F atoms are equivalent. This can be explained if the axial and equatorial F atoms interchange their positions more rapidly than this, a process termed "pseudorotation" by R. S. Berry (1960); indeed, PF$_5$ was the first compound to show this effect.[90] The proposed mechanism is illustrated in Fig. 12.13 and is discussed more fully in ref. 91; the barrier to notation has been calculated as 16 ± 2 kJ mol^{-1} [92]

The mixed chlorofluorides PCl$_4$F (mp $-59°$, bp $+67°$) and PCl$_3$F$_2$ (mp $-63°$) are also trigonal bipyramidal with axial F atoms; likewise PCl$_2$F$_3$ (mp $-125°$, bp $+7.1°$) has 2 axial and 1 equatorial F atoms and PClF$_4$ (mp $-132°$,

bp $-43.4°$) has both axial positions occupied by F atoms.[93] These compounds are obtained by addition of halogen to the appropriate phosphorus(III) chlorofluoride, but if PCl$_5$ is fluorinated in a polar solvent, ionic isomers are formed, e.g. [PCl$_4$]$^+$[PCl$_4$F$_2$]$^-$ (colourless crystals, subl 175°) and [PCl$_4$]$^+$[PF$_6$]$^-$ (white crystals, subl 135° with decomposition). The crystalline hemifluoride [PCl$_4$]$^+$[PCl$_5$F]$^-$ has also been identified. The analogous parallel series of covalent and ionic bromofluorides is less well characterized but PBr$_2$F$_3$ is known both as an unstable molecular liquid (decomp 15°) and as a white crystalline powder [PBr$_4$]$^+$[PF$_6$]$^-$ (subl 135° decomp). It can be noted that PF$_3$(NH$_2$)$_2$ is a trigonal bipyramidal molecule with C_{2v} symmetry (i.e. equatorial NH$_2$ groups),[94] whereas the most stable form of tetra-arylfluorophosphoranes is ionic, [PR$_4$]$^+$F$^-$, although molecular monomers R$_4$PF and an ionic dimer [PR$_4$]$^+$[PR$_4$F$_2$]$^-$ also exist.[95]

PCl$_5$ is even closer to the ionic-covalent borderline than is PF$_5$, the ionic solid [PCl$_4$]$^+$[PCl$_6$]$^-$ melting (or subliming) to give a covalent molecular

[89] D. Mootz and M. Wiebcke, *Z. anorg. allg. Chem.* **545**, 39–42 (1987).

[90] R. S. Berry, *J. Chem. Phys.* **32**, 933–8 (1960).

[91] R. Luckenbach, *Dynamic Stereochemistry of Pentacoordinate Phosphorus and Related Elements*, G. Thieme, Stuttgart, 1973, 259 pp.

[92] C. J. Marsden, *J. Chem. Soc., Chem. Commun.*, 401–2 (1984).

[93] C. Macho, R. Minkwitz, J. Rohman, B. Steger, W. Wölfel and H. Oberhammer, *Inorg. Chem.* **25**, 2828–35 (1986), and references cited therein.

[94] C. J. Marsden, K. Hedberg, J. M. Shreeve and K. D. Gupta, *Inorg. Chem.* **23**, 3659–62 (1984).

[95] S. J. Brown, J. H. Clark and D. J. Macquarrie, *J. Chem. Soc., Dalton Trans.*, 277–80 (1988).

liquid (or gas). Again, when dissolved in non-polar solvents such as CCl_4 or benzene, PCl_5 is monomeric and molecular, whereas in ionizing solvents such as $MeCN$, $MeNO_2$ and $PhNO_2$ there are two competing ionizing equilibria:[96]

$$2PCl_5 \rightleftharpoons [PCl_4]^+ + [PCl_6]^-$$

$$PCl_5 \rightleftharpoons [PCl_4]^+ + Cl^-$$

As might be expected, the former equilibrium predominates at higher concentrations of PCl_5 (above about $0.03\,mol\,l^{-1}$) whilst the latter predominates below this concentration. The P–Cl distances (pm) in these various species are: PCl_5 214 (axial), 202 (equatorial); $[PCl_4]^+$ 197; $[PCl_6]^-$ 208 pm. Ionic isomerism is also known and, in addition to $[PCl_4]^+[PCl_6]^-$, another (metastable) crystalline phase of constitution $[PCl_4]_2^+[PCl_6]^-Cl^-$ can be formed either by application of high pressure or by crystallizing PCl_5 from solutions of dichloromethane containing Br_2 or SCl_2.[97] When gaseous PCl_5 (in equilibrium with $PCl_3 + Cl_2$) is quenched to 15 K the trigonal-bipyramidal molecular structure is retained; this forms an ordered molecular crystalline lattice on warming to $\sim 130\,K$, but further warming towards room temperature results in chloride-ion transfer to give $[PCl_4]^+[PCl_6]^-$.[98] The first alkali metal salt of $[PCl_6]^-$, $CsPCl_6$, has only recently been made.[99]

The delicate balance between ionic and covalent forms is influenced not only by the state of aggregation (solid, liquid, gas) or the nature of the solvent, but also by the effect of substituents. Thus $PhPCl_4$ is molecular with Ph equatorial whereas the corresponding methyl derivative is ionic, $[MePCl_3]^+Cl^-$. Despite this the $[PhPCl_3]^+$ cation is known and can readily be formed by reacting $PhPCl_4$ with a chlorine ion acceptor such as BCl_3, $SbCl_5$, or even PCl_5 itself:[100]

$$PhPCl_4 + PCl_5 \longrightarrow [PhPCl_3]^+[PCl_6]^-$$

Likewise crystalline Ph_2PCl_3 is molecular whereas the corresponding Me and Et derivatives are ionic $[R_2PCl_2]^+Cl^-$. However, all 3 triorganophosphorus dihalides are ionic $[R_3PCl]^+Cl^-$ (R = Ph, Me, Et). The pale-yellow, crystalline mixed halide P_2BrCl_9 appears to be $[PCl_4]_6^+[PCl_3Br]_2^+[PCl_6]_4^-[Br]_4^-$ (i.e. $P_{12}Br_6Cl_{54}$).[101]

Phosphorus pentabromide is rather different. The crystalline solid is $[PBr_4]^+Br^-$ but this appears to dissociate completely to PBr_3 and Br_2 in the vapour phase; rapid cooling of this vapour to 15 K results in the formation of a disordered lattice of PBr_3 and PBr_7 (i.e. $[PBr_4]^+[Br_3]^-$) and this mixture reverts to $[PBr_4]^+Br^-$ on being warmed to 180 K.[98] The corresponding trichloride, $[PBr_4]^+[Cl_3]^-$ is also known.[102] $[PI_4]^+$ has been identified only as its salt $[PI_4]^+[AsF_6]^-$.[80]

PCl_5 is made on an industrial scale by the reaction of Cl_2 on PCl_3 dissolved in an equal volume of CCl_4. World production probably exceeds 20 000 tonnes pa. On the laboratory scale Cl_2 gas (or liquid) can be passed directly into PCl_3. PCl_5 reacts violently with water to give HCl and H_3PO_4 but in equimolar amounts the reaction can be moderated to give $POCl_3$:

$$PCl_5 + H_2O \longrightarrow POCl_3 + 2HCl$$

PCl_5 chlorinates alcohols to alkyl halides and carboxylic acids to the corresponding RCOCl. When heated with NH_4Cl the phosphonitrilic chlorides are obtained (p. 536). These and other reactions are summarized in the diagram.[8]

[96] R. W. SUTER, H. C. KNACHEL, V. P. PETRO, J. H. HOWATSON and S. G. SHORE, *J. Am. Chem. Soc.* **95**, 1474–9 (1973).
[97] A. FINCH, P. N. GATES, H. D. B. JENKINS and K. P. THAKUR, *J. Chem. Soc., Chem. Commun.*, 579–80 (1980). See also H. D. B. JENKINS, L. SHARMAN, A. FINCH and P. N. GATES, *Polyhedron* **13**, 1481–2 (1994) and references cited therein.
[98] A. FINCH, P. N. GATES and A. S. MUIR, *J. Chem. Soc., Chem. Commun.*, 812–4 (1981). See also H. D. B. JENKINS, K. P. THAKUR, A. FINCH and P. N. GATES, *Inorg. Chem.* **21**, 423–6 (1982).
[99] A. S. MUIR, *Polyhedron* **10**, 2217–9 (1991).

[100] K. B. DILLON, R. J. LYNCH, R. N. REEVE and T. C. WADDINGTON, *J. Chem. Soc., Dalton Trans.*, 1243–8 (1976). See also M. A. H. A. AL-JUBOORI, P. N. GATES and A. S. MUIR, *J. Chem. Soc., Chem. Commun.*, 1270–1 (1991).
[101] F. F. BENTLEY, A. FINCH, P. N. GATES, F. J. RYAN and K. B. DILLON. *J. Inorg. Nucl. Chem.* **36**, 457–9 (1974). See also *J. Chem. Soc., Dalton Trans.*, 1863–6 (1973).
[102] K. B. DILLON, M. P. NISBET and R. N. REEVE, *Polyhedron* **7**, 1725–6 (1988). See also H. D. B. JENKINS, *Polyhedron* **15**, 2831–4 (1996).

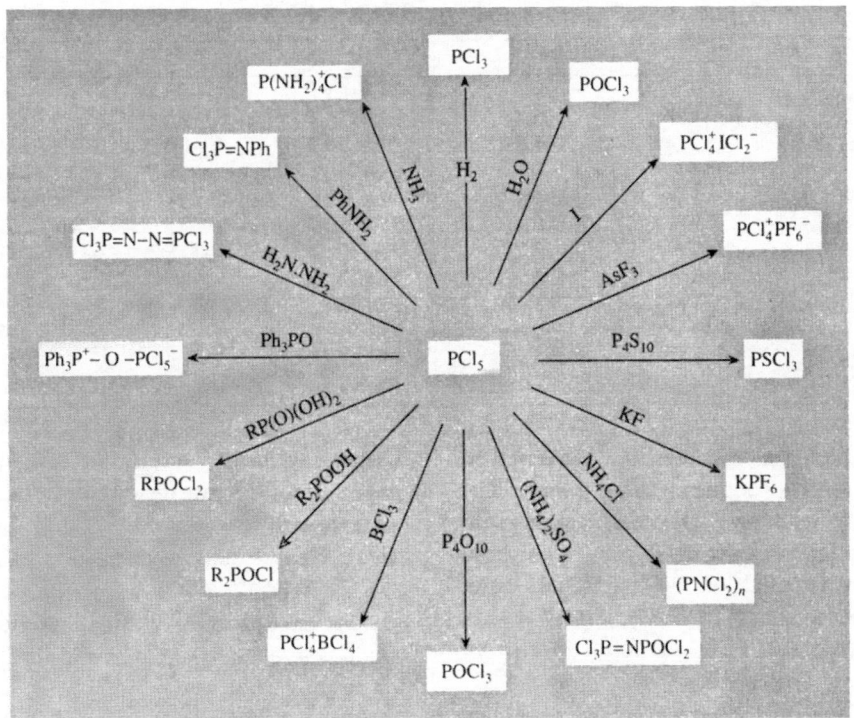

The chlorination of phosphonic and phosphinic acids and esters are of considerable importance. PCl_5 can also act as a Lewis acid to give 6-coordinate P complexes, e.g. $pyPCl_5$, and pyz-PCl_5, where $py = C_5H_5N$ (pyridine) and $pyz = cyclo$-1,4-$C_4H_4N_2$ (pyrazine).[103]

Pseudohalides of phosphorus(III)

Paralleling the various phosphorus trihalides are numerous pseudohalides and mixed pseudohalide-halides of which the various isocyanates and isothiocyanates are perhaps the best known. Most are volatile liquids, e.g.

Compound	$P(NCO)_3$	$PF(NCO)_2$	$PF_2(NCO)$
MP/°C	−2	−55	$\sim$ −108
BP/°C	169.3	98.7	12.3

103 B. N. MEYER,   J. N. ISHLEY,   A. V. FRATINI   and H. C. KNACHEL, *Inorg. Chem.* **19**, 2324–7 (1980) and references therein.

Compound	$PCl(NCO)_2$	$PCl_2(NCO)$	$P(NCS)_3$
MP/°C	−50	−99	−4
BP/°C	134.6	104.5	$\sim$120/1 mmHg

Compound	$PF_2(NCS)$	$PCl_2(NCS)$
MP/°C	−95	−76
BP/°C	90.3	148(decomp)

The corresponding phosphoryl and thiophosphoryl pseudohalides are also known, i.e. $PO(NCO)_3$, $PS(NCO)_3$, etc. Preparations are by standard procedures such as those on the diagram for PCl_3 (p. 497). As indicated there, $P(CN)_3$ has also been made: it is a highly reactive white crystalline solid mp 203° which reacts violently with water to give mainly phosphorous acid and HCN.

12.3.4 Oxohalides and thiohalides of phosphorus

The propensity of phosphorus(III) compounds to oxidize to phosphorus(V) by formation of an additional P=O bond is well illustrated by the

Table 12.4   Some phosphoryl and thiophosphoryl halides and pseudohalides

Compound	MP/°C	BP/°C	Compound	MP/°C	BP/°C
POF_3	−39.1	−39.7	POF_2Cl	−96.4	3.1
$POCl_3$	1.25	105.1	$POFCl_2$	−80.1	52.9
$POBr_3$	55	191.7	POF_2Br	−84.8	31.6
POI_3	53	—	$POFBr_2$	−117.2	110.1
$PO(NCO)_3$	5.0	193.1	$POCl_2Br$	11	52/3 mmHg
$PO(NCS)_3$	13.8	300.1	$POClBr_2$	31	49/12 mmHg
PSF_3	−148.8	−52.2	PSF_2Cl	−155.2	6.3
$PSCl_3$	−35	−125	$PSFCl_2$	−96.0	64.7
$PSBr_3$	37.8	212 (d)	PSF_2Br	−136.9	35.5
PSI_3	48	decomp	$PSFBr_2$	−75.2	125.3
$PS(NCO)_3$	8.8	215	$PO(NCO)FCl$	—	103
$PS(NCS)_3$	—	123/0.3 mmHg	$PS(NCS)F_2$	—	90

ease with which the trihalides are converted to their phosphoryl analogues POX_3. Thus, PCl_3 reacts rapidly with pure O_2 (less rapidly with air) at room temperature or slightly above and this reaction is used on an industrial scale. Alternatively, a slurry of P_4O_{10} in PCl_3 can be chlorinated, the PCl_5 so formed reacting instantaneously with the P_4O_{10}:

$$P_4O_{10} + 6PCl_5 \longrightarrow 10POCl_3$$

$POBr_3$ can be made by similar methods, but POF_3 is usually made by fluorination of $POCl_3$ using a metal fluoride (e.g. M = Na, Mg, Zn, Pb, Ag, etc.). POI_3 was first made in 1973 by iodinating $POCl_3$ with LiI, or by reacting $ROPI_2$ with iodine ($ROPI_2 + I_2 \rightarrow RI + POI_3$).[104] Mixed phosphoryl halides, POX_nY_{3-n}, and pseudohalides (e.g. X = NCO, NCS) are known, as also are the thiophosphoryl halides PSX_3, e.g.:

$$P_2S_5 + 3PCl_5 \longrightarrow 5PSCl_3$$

$$PCl_3 + S \xrightarrow{AlCl_3} PSCl_3; \quad PI_3 + S \xrightarrow{CS_2/dark} PSI_3$$

Most of the phosphoryl and thiophosphoryl compounds are colourless gases or volatile liquids though $PSBr_3$ forms yellow crystals, mp 37.8°, POI_3 is dark violet, mp 53°, and PSI_3 is red-brown, mp 48°. All are monomeric tetrahedral (C_{3v}) or pseudotetrahedral. Some physical properties are in Table 12.4. The P–O interatomic

distance in these compounds generally falls in the range 154–158 pm, the small value being consistent with considerable "double-bond character". Likewise the P–S distance is relatively short (185–194 pm).

The phosphoryl and thiophosphoryl halides are reactive compounds that hydrolyse readily on contact with water. They form adducts with Lewis acids and undergo a variety of substitution reactions to form numerous organophosphorus derivatives and phosphate esters. Thus, alcohols give successively $(RO)POCl_2$, $(RO)_2POCl$ and $(RO)_3PO$; phenols react similarly but more slowly. Likewise, amines yield $(RNH)POCl_2$, $(RNH)_2POCl$ and $(RNH)_3PO$ whereas Grignard reagents yield R_nPOCl_{3-n} ($n = 1-3$). Many of these compounds find extensive use as oil additives, insecticides, plasticizers, surfactants or flame retardants, and are manufactured on the multikilotonne scale.

In addition to the monophosphorus phosphoryl and thiophosphoryl compounds discussed above, several poly-phosphoryl and -thiophosphoryl halides have been characterized. Pyrophosphoryl fluoride, $O{=}PF_2{-}O{-}P({=}O)F_2$ (mp −0.1°, bp 72° extrap) and the white crystalline cyclic tetramer $[O{=}P(F){-}O]_4$ were

obtained by subjecting equimolar mixtures of PF_3 and O_2 to a silent electric discharge at −70°. Pyrophosphoryl chloride, $O{=}PCl_2{-}O{-}P({=}O)Cl_2$ is conveniently prepared by passing Cl_2 into a boiling suspension

[104] A. V. KIRSANOV, ZH. K. GORBATENKO and N. G. FESHCHENKO, *Pure Appl. Chem.* **44**, 125–39 (1975).

of P_4O_{10} in PCl_3 diluted with CCl_4:

$$P_4O_{10} + 4PCl_3 + 4Cl_2 \longrightarrow 2P_2O_3Cl_4 + 4POCl_3$$

It is a colourless, odourless, non-fuming, oily liquid, mp $-16.5°$, bp $215°$ (decomp), with reactions similar to those of $POCl_3$. Sealed-tube reactions between P_4O_{10} and $POCl_3$ at $200–230°$ give more highly condensed cyclic and open-chain polyphosphoryl chlorides. A rather different structural motif occurs in $P_2S_4F_4$; this compound is obtained by fluorinating P_4S_{10} with an alkali-metal fluoride to give the anion $[S_2PF_2]^-$ which is then oxidized by bromine to $P_2S_4F_4$ (bp $60°$ at $10\,mmHg$). Vibrational and nmr spectra are consistent with the structure $F_2(S)PSSP(S)F_2$.

Bromination of P_4S_7 in cold CS_2 yields, in addition to PBr_3 and $PSBr_3$, two further thiobromides $P_2S_6Br_2$ (mp $118°$ decomp) and $P_2S_5Br_4$ (mp $90°$ decomp). The first of these has the cyclic structure shown in which the ring adopts a skew-boat configuration. An even more complex, bicyclic arrangement is found in the orange-yellow compound $P_4S_3I_2$ (mp $120°$ decomp) which is formed (together with several other products) when equiatomic amounts of P, S and I are allowed to react. The P and S atoms are arranged in two 5-membered rings having a common $P–S–P$ group as shown; in each there is a $P–P$ group and the I atoms are bonded in *cis*-configuration to the P atoms not common to the two rings. The orange compound $P_2S_2I_4$ (mp $94°$) was mentioned on p. 498.

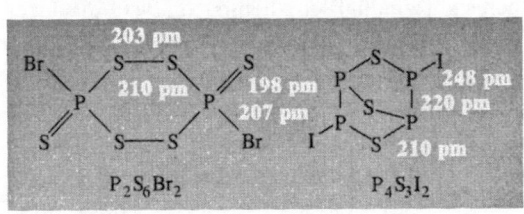

$P_2S_6Br_2$ $P_4S_3I_2$

By contrast to the plethora of simple oxo-halides and thiohalides of P^V, the corresponding derivatives of P^{III} are fugitive species that require matrix isolation techniques for preparation and characterization:[105] ClPO, BrPO, FPS and BrPS all form non-linear triatomic molecules, as expected. The corresponding oxosulfide, BrP(O)S,[106] and its thio-analogue, FP(S)S,[107] have also recently been isolated.

12.3.5 Phosphorus oxides, sulfides, selenides and related compounds

The oxides and sulfides of phosphorus are amongst the most important compounds of the element. At least 6 binary oxides and 9 well-defined sulfides are known, together with a similar number of selenides and several oxo-sulfides. It will be convenient to discuss first the preparation and structure of each group of compounds and then to mention the chemical reactions of the more important members in so far as they are known. It is notable that, in contrast to the ubiquitous NO and its many complexes (pp. 445 ff), little is known about its analogue, PO (see p. 506), although it is probably the most abundant P-containing molecule in interstellar clouds.[108] The first complex with a PO ligand was first synthesized as recently as 1991, when dark green crystals of the square-based pyramidal hetero-atom cluster $[W(CO)_4\{Ni(\eta^5\text{-}C_5HPr^i_4)\}_2(\mu:\eta^2,\eta^2\text{-}P_2)]$ was oxidized with bis(trimethylsilyl) peroxide, $(Me_3Si)_2O_2$, to yield black crystals of the corresponding $[W(CO)_4\{Ni(\eta^5\text{-}C_5HPr^i_4)\}_2(\mu:\eta^2,\eta^2\text{-}PO)_2]$.[108]

Oxides

P_4O_6 is obtained by controlled oxidation of P_4 in an atmosphere of 75% O_2 and 25% N_2 at $90\,mmHg$ and $\sim50°$ followed by distillation of the product from the mixture. Careful

[105] H. SCHNÖCKEL and S. SCHUNCK, *Z. anorg. allg. Chem.* **548**, 161–4 (1987); **552**, 155–62 and 63–70 (1987). M. BINNEWIES and H. BORRMANN, *ibid.* **552**, 147–54 (1987).

[106] S. SCHUNCK, H.-J. GÖCKE and H. SCHNÖCKEL, *Z. anorg. allg. Chem.* **583**, 78–84 (1990).

[107] H. BOK, M. KREMER, B. SOLOUKI, M. BINNEWIES and M. MEISEL, *J. Chem. Soc., Chem. Commun.*, 9–11 (1992).

[108] O. J. SCHERER, J. BRAUN, P. WALTHER, G. HECKMANN and G. WOLMERSHÄUSER, *Angew. Chem. Int. Edn. Engl.* **30**, 852–4. (1991).

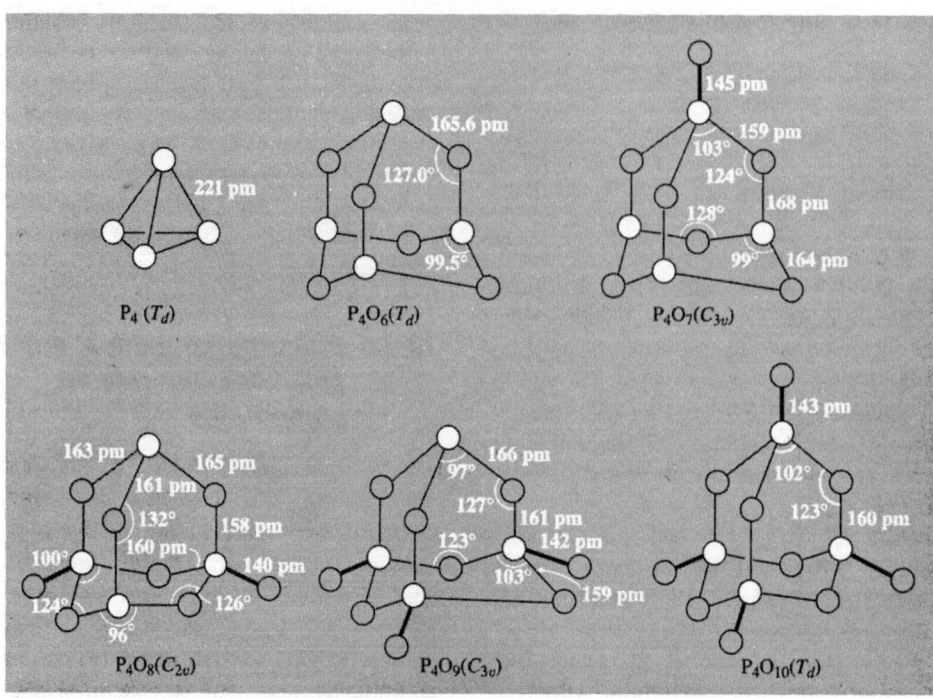

Figure 12.14   Molecular structures, symmetries and dimensions of the 5 oxides P_4O_{6+n} ($n = 0-4$) compared with α-P_4. The P···P distances in the oxides are ~280–290 pm, i.e. essentially nonbonding.

precautions are necessary if good yields are to be obtained.[109] It forms soft white crystals, mp 23.8°, bp 175.4°, and is soluble in many organic solvents. The molecular structure has tetrahedral symmetry and comprises 4 fused 6-membered P_3O_3 heterocycles each with the chair conformation as shown in Fig. 12.14.[110] When P_4O_6 is heated to 200–400° in a sealed, evacuated tube it disproportionates into red phosphorus and a solid-solution series of composition P_4O_n depending on conditions. The α-phase has a composition in the range $P_4O_{8.1}$–$P_4O_{9.2}$ and comprises a solid solution of oxides in which one or two of the "external" O atoms in P_4O_{10} have been removed. The β-phase has a composition range $P_4O_{8.0}$-$P_4O_{7.7}$

and appears to be a solid solution of P_4O_8 and P_4O_7, the latter compound having only one O atom external to the P_4O_6 cluster (C_{3v} symmetry). P_4O_7 is now best prepared from P_4O_6 dissolved in thf, using Ph_3PO as a catalyst (not an oxidant) at room temperature. The molecular structure and dimensions of P_4O_7 are given in Fig. 12.14 from which it is apparent that there is a gradual lengthening of P–O distances in the sequence P^V–O_t < P^V–O_μ < P^{III}–O_μ. Similar trends are apparent in the dimensions of the other members of the series P_4O_{6+n} shown in Fig. 12.14.[110] In addition, ring angles at P (96–103°) are always less than those at O (122–132°), as expected.

P_4O_6 hydrolyses in cold water to give H_3PO_3 i.e. $HP(O)(OH)_2$; this is interesting in view of the structure of P_4O_6 and implies an oxidative rearrangement of {P–OH} to {H–P=O} (p. 514). The oxide itself ignites and burns when heated in air; the progress of the reaction depends very much on the

109 D. Heinze, *Pure Appl. Chem.* **44**, 141–72 (1975).

110 M. Jansen and M. Voss, *Angew. Chem. Int. Edn. Engl.* **20**, 100–1, 965 (1981), and references therein to crystal structure determinations on the other members of the series P_4O_{6+n}. See also M. Jansen and M. Moebs, *Inorg. Chem.* **23**, 4486–8 (1984).

Table 12.5 Some properties of crystalline polymorphs of P_2O_5

Polymorph	Density/g cm^{-3}	MP/°C	Pressure at triple pt/mmHg	ΔH_{subl}/kJ (mol P$_4$O$_{10}$)$^{-1}$
H: hexagonal P$_4$O$_{10}$	2.30	420	3600	95
O: metastable (P$_2$O$_5$)$_n$	2.72	562	437	152
O': stable (P$_2$O$_5$)$_n$	2.74–3.05	580	555	142

purity of the oxide and the conditions employed, and, when traces of elemental phosphorus are present in the oxide, the reaction is spontaneous even at room temperature. P_4O_6 reacts readily (often violently) with many simple inorganic and organic compounds but well-characterized products have rarely been isolated until recently.[109] It behaves as a ligand and successively displaces CO from [Ni(CO)$_4$] to give compounds such as [P$_4$O$_6${Ni(CO)$_3$}$_4$], [Ni(CO)$_2$(P$_4$O$_6$)$_2$] and [Ni(CO)(P$_4$O$_6$)$_3$]. With diborane adducts of formula [P$_4$O$_6$(BH$_3$)$_n$] (n = 1–3) are obtained.

"Phosphorus pentoxide", P_4O_{10}, is the commonest and most important oxide of phosphorus. It is formed as a fine white smoke or powder when phosphorus burns in air and, when condensed rapidly from the vapour phase in this way, is obtained in the H (hexagonal) form comprising tetrahedral molecules as shown in Fig. 12.14. This compound and the other phosphorus oxides are the first we have considered that feature the {PO$_4$} group as a structural unit; this group dominates most of phosphate chemistry and will recur repeatedly during the rest of this chapter. The common hexagonal form of P_4O_{10} is, in fact, metastable and can be transformed into several other modifications by suitable thermal or high-pressure treatment. A metastable orthorhombic (O) form is obtained by heating H for 2 h at 400° and the stable orthorhombic (O') form is obtained after 24 h at 450°. Both consist of extensive sheet polymers of interlocking heterocyclic rings composed of fused {PO$_4$} groups. There is also a high-pressure form and a glass, which probably consists of an irregular three-dimensional network of linked {PO$_4$} tetrahedra. These polymeric forms are hard and brittle because of the P–O–P bonds throughout the lattice and, as

expected, they are much less volatile and reactive than the less-dense molecular H form. For example, whilst the common H form hydrolyses violently, almost explosively, with evolution of much heat, the polymeric forms react only slowly with water to give, finally, H_3PO_4. Some properties of the various polymorphs are compared in Table 12.5. The limpid liquid obtained by rapidly heating the H form contains P_4O_{10} molecules but these rapidly polymerize and rearrange to layer or three-dimensional polymeric forms with a concomitant drop in the vapour pressure and an increase in the viscosity and mp.

Because of its avidity for water, P_4O_{10} is widely used as a dehydrating agent, but its efficacy as a desiccant is greatly impaired by the formation of a crusty surface film of hydrolysis products unless it is finely dispersed on glass wool. Its largest use is in the industrial production of ortho- and poly-phosphoric acids (p. 520) but it is also an intermediate in the production of phosphate esters. Thus, triethylphosphate is made by reacting P_4O_{10} with diethyl ether to form ethylpolyphosphates which, on subsequent pyrolysis and distillation, yield the required product:

$$P_4O_{10} + 6Et_2O \xrightarrow{\text{heat}} 4PO(OEt)_3$$

Direct reaction with alcohols gives mixed mono- and di-alkyl phosphoric acids by cleavage of the P–O–P bonds:

$$P_4O_{10} + 6ROH \xrightarrow{65°} 2(RO)PO(OH)_2$$
$$+ 2(RO)_2PO(OH)$$

Under less-controlled conditions P_4O_{10} dehydrates ethanol to ethene and methylarylcarbinols to the corresponding styrenes. H_2SO_4 is dehydrated to SO_3, HNO_3 gives N_2O_5 and amides

(RCONH$_2$) yield nitriles (RCN). In each of these reactions metaphosphoric acid HPO$_3$ is the main P-containing product. P$_4$O$_{10}$ reacts vigorously with both wet and dry NH$_3$ to form a range of amorphous polymeric powdery materials which are used industrially for water softening because of their ability to sequester Ca ions; composition depends markedly on the preparative conditions employed but most of the commercial products appear to be condensed linear or cyclic amido-polyphosphates which can be represented by formulae such as:

The annual production/consumption of P$_4$O$_{10}$ in USA and Western Europe totals about 15 000 tonnes.

Other oxides of phosphorus are less well characterized though the suboxide PO and the peroxide P$_2$O$_6$ seem to be definite compounds. PO was obtained as a brown cathodic deposit when a saturated solution of Et$_3$NHCl in anhydrous POCl$_3$ was electrolysed between Pt electrodes at 0°. Alternatively it can be made by the slow reaction of POBr$_3$ with Mg in Et$_2$O under reflux:

$$2POBr_3 + 3Mg \longrightarrow 2PO + 3MgBr_2$$

Its structure is unknown but is presumably based on a polymeric network of P–O–P links. It reacts with water to give PH$_3$ and is quantitatively oxidized to P$_2$O$_5$ by oxygen at 300°. The peroxide P$_2$O$_6$ is thought to be the active ingredient in the violet solid obtained when P$_4$O$_{10}$ and O$_2$ are passed through a heated discharge tube at low pressure. The compound has not been obtained pure but liberates I$_2$ from aqueous KI, hydrolyses to a peroxophosphoric acid, and liberates O$_2$ when heated to 130° under reduced pressure. Its structure may be (O=)$_2$P–O–O–P(=O)$_2$ or, in view of the variable composition of the product, it may be a mixture of P$_4$O$_{11}$ and P$_4$O$_{12}$ obtained by replacing P–O–P links by P–O–O–P in P$_4$O$_{10}$.

Sulfides [111]

The sulfides of phosphorus form an intriguing series of compounds which continue to present puzzling structural features. The compounds P$_4$S$_{10}$, P$_4$S$_9$, P$_4$S$_7$, α-P$_4$S$_5$, β-P$_4$S$_5$, α-P$_4$S$_4$, β-P$_4$S$_4$, P$_4$S$_3$ and P$_4$S$_2$ are all based on the P$_4$ tetrahedron but only P$_4$S$_{10}$ (and possibly P$_4$S$_9$) is structurally analogous to the oxide. P$_4$S$_6$ is conspicuous by its absence. Structural data are summarized in Fig. 12.15 and some physical properties are in Table 12.6.

P$_4$S$_3$ is the most stable compound in the series and can be prepared by heating the required amounts of red P and sulfur above 180° in an inert atmosphere and then purifying the product by distillation at 420° or by recrystallization from toluene. The retention of a P$_3$ ring in the structure is notable. Its reactions and commercial application in match manufacture are discussed on p. 509.

The curious phase relations between phosphorus, sulfur and their binary compounds are worth noting. Because both P$_4$ and S$_8$ are stable molecules the phase diagram, if studied below 100°, shows only solid solutions with a simple eutectic at 10° (75 atom % P). By contrast, when the mixtures are heated above 200° the elements react and an entirely different phase diagram is obtained; however, as only the most stable compounds P$_4$S$_3$, P$_4$S$_7$ and P$_4$S$_{10}$

[111] H. HOFFMANN and M. BECKE-GOEHRING, *Topics in Phosphorus Chemistry* **8**, 193–271 (1976); J. G. RIESS in A. H. COWLEY (ed.), *Rings, Clusters and Polymers of the Main Group Elements*, ACS Symposium Series No. **232**, 17–47 (1983).

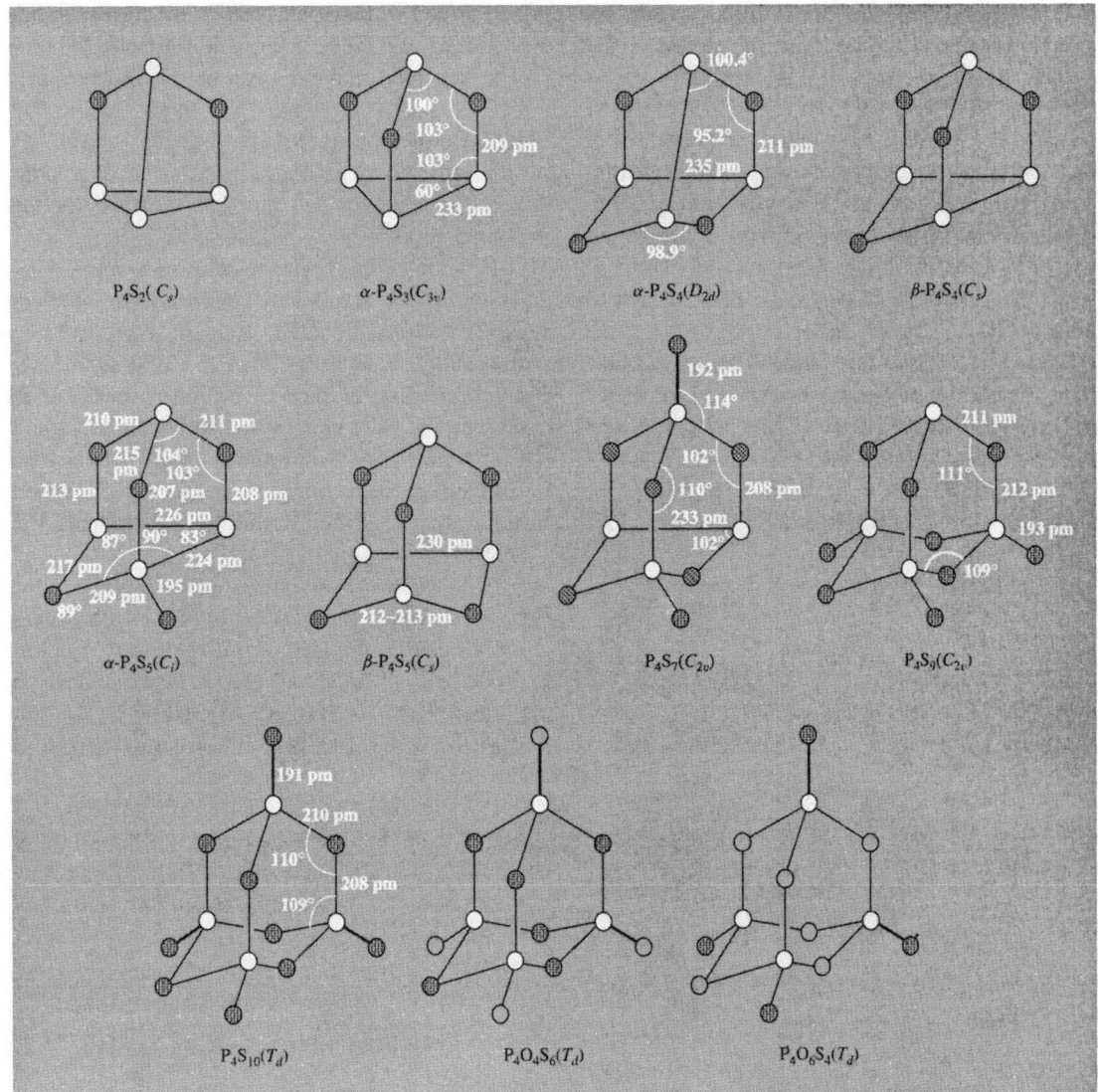

Figure 12.15   Structures of phosphorus sulfides and oxosulfides (schematic).

Table 12.6   Physical properties of some phosphorus sulfides

Property	α-P_4S_3	α-P_4S_4	α-P_4S_5	P_4S_7	P_4S_{10}
Colour	Yellow green	Pale yellow	Bright yellow	Very pale yellow	Yellow
MP/°C	174	230 (d)	170–220 (d)	308	288
BP/°C	408	—	—	523	514
Density/g cm^{-3}	2.03	2.22	2.17	2.19	2.09
Solubility in CS_2(17°)/ g per 100 g CS_2	100	sol	0.5	0.029	0.222

melt congruently, only these three appear as compounds in equilibrium with the melt. Careful work at lower temperatures is needed to detect peritectic equilibria involving P_4S_9, P_4S_5 (and possibly even P_4S_2),[112] and it is notable that these compounds are normally prepared by low-temperature reactions involving addition of 2S to P_4S_7 and P_4S_3 respectively. Likewise there is no sign of P_4S_4 on the phase diagram, and claims to have detected it in this way have been shown to be erroneous.[113]

P_4S_4 is one of the most recent binary sulfides to be isolated and characterized and it exists in two structurally distinct forms.[113,114] Each can be made in quantitative yield by reacting the appropriate isomer of $P_4S_3I_2$ (p. 503) with $[(Me_3Sn)_2S]$ in CS_2 solution:

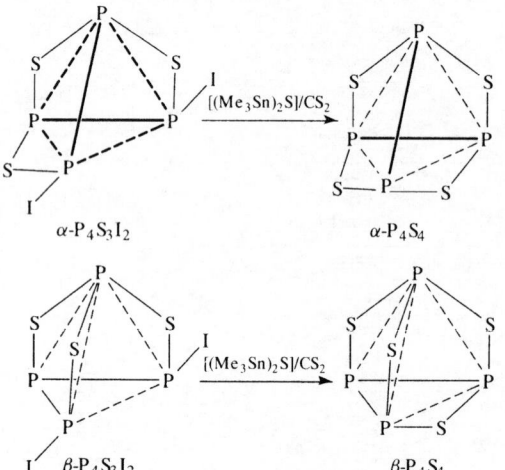

As seen from Fig. 12.15 the structure of α-P_4S_4 resembles that of As_4S_4 (p. 579) rather than N_4S_4 (p. 723). The 4 P atoms are in tetrahedral array and the 4 S atoms form a slightly distorted square. The 2 P–P bonds are long (as also in P_4S_3

and P_4S_7) when compared with corresponding distances in P_4S_5 (225 pm) and P_4 itself (221 pm). The structure of β-P_4S_4 has not been determined by X-ray crystallography but spectroscopic data indicate the absence of P=S groups and the C_s structure shown in Fig. 12.15 is the only other possible arrangement of 3 coordinate P for this composition.

P_4S_5 disproportionates below its mp ($2P_4S_5 \rightleftharpoons P_4S_3 + P_4S_7$) and so cannot be obtained directly from the melt. It is best prepared by irradiating a solution of P_4S_3 and S in CS_2 solution using a trace of iodine as catalyst. Its structure is quite unexpected and features a single exocyclic P=S group and 3 fused heterocycles containing, respectively, 4, 5 and 6 atoms; there are 2 short P–P bonds and the 4-membered P_3S ring is almost square planar.

P_4S_7 is the second most stable sulfide (after P_4S_3) and can be obtained by direct reaction of the elements. Perhaps surprisingly the structure retains a P–P bond and has two exocyclic P=S groups. P_4S_9 is formed reversibly by heating $P_4S_7 + 2P_4S_{10}$ and has the structure shown in Fig. 12.15.

P_4S_{10} is commercially the most important sulfide of P and is formed by direct reaction of liquid white P_4 with a slight excess of sulfur above 300°. It can also be made from byproduct ferrophosphorus (p. 480).

$$4Fe_2P + 18FeS_2 \xrightarrow{heat} P_4S_{10} + 26FeS$$

$$4Fe_2P + 18S \longrightarrow P_4S_{10} + 8FeS$$

It has essentially the same structure as the H form of P_4O_{10} and hydrolyses mainly according to the overall equation

$$P_4S_{10} + 16H_2O \longrightarrow 4H_3PO_4 + 10H_2S$$

Presumably intermediate thiophosphoric acids are first formed and, indeed, when the hydrolysis is carried out in aqueous NaOH solution at 100°, substantial amounts of the mono- and di-thiophosphates are obtained. P–S bonds are also retained during reaction of P_4S_{10} with alcohols or phenols and the products formed are used extensively in industry for a wide variety of

[112] H. VINCENT, *Bull. Soc. Chim. France* 1972, 4517–21; R. FÖRTHMANN and A. SCHNEIDER, *Z. Phys. Chem.* (NF) **49**, 22–37 (1966).

[113] A. M. GRIFFIN, P. C. MINSHALL and G. M. SHELDRICK, *J. Chem. Soc., Chem. Commun.*, 809–10 (1976).

[114] C.-C. CHANG, R. C. HALTIWANGER and A. D. NORMAN, *Inorg. Chem.* **17**, 2056–62 (1978). See also B. W. TATTERSHALL *J. Chem. Soc., ·Dalton Trans.*, 1515–20 (1987); B. W. TATTERSHALL and N. L. KENDALL, *Polyhedron* **13**, 2629–37 (1994).

Phosphorus Sulfides in Industry

The two compounds of importance are P_4S_3 and P_4S_{10}. The former is made on a large scale for use in "strike anywhere" matches according to a formula evolved by Sévène and Cahen in France in 1898. The ignition results from the violent reaction between P_4S_3 and $KClO_3$ which is initiated by friction of the match against glass paper (on the side of the box) or other abrasive material. A typical formulation for the match head is:

Reactants		Fillers (moderators)			Adhesives	
$KClO_3$	P_4S_3	Ground glass	Fe_2O_3	ZnO	Glue	Water
20%	9%	14%	11%	7%	10%	29%

Formulations of this type have completely replaced earlier "strike anywhere" matches based on (poisonous) white P_4, sulfur, and $KClO_3$, though "safety matches" still use a match head which is predominantly $KClO_3$ struck against the side of the match-box which has been covered with a paste of (non-toxic) red P (49.5%), antimony sulfide (27.6%), Fe_2O_3 (1.2%) and gum arabic (21.7%). About 10^{11} matches are used annually in the UK alone.

P_4S_{10} is made on an even larger scale than P_4S_3 and is the primary source of a very wide range of organic P–S compounds. World production of P_4S_{10} exceeds 250 000 tonnes annually of which about half is made in the USA, one-third in the UK/Europe, and the remaining 30 000 tonnes elsewhere (Japan, Romania, the former Soviet Union, Mexico, etc.). The most important reaction of P_4S_{10} is with alcohols or phenols to give dialkyl or diaryl dithiophosphoric acids:

$$P_4S_{10} + 8ROH \longrightarrow 4(RO)_2P(S)SH + 2H_2S$$

The zinc salts of these acids are extensively used as additives to lubricating oils to improve their extreme-pressure properties. The compounds also act as antioxidants, corrosion inhibitors and detergents. Short-chain dialkyl dithiophosphates and their sodium and ammonium salts are used as flotation agents for zinc and lead sulfide ores. The methyl and ethyl derivatives $(RO)_2P(S)SH$ and $(RO)_2P(S)Cl$ are of particular interest in the large-scale manufacture of pesticides such as parathion, malathion, dimethylparathion, etc.[83] For example parathion, which first went into production as an insecticide in Germany in 1947, is made by the following reaction sequence:

$$(EtO)_2P(S)SH + Cl_2 \longrightarrow HCl + S + (EtO)_2P(S)Cl$$

$$(EtO)_2P(S)Cl + NaOC_6H_4-p-NO_2 \longrightarrow (EtO)_2P(S)OC_6H_4-p-NO_2 \text{ (parathion)}$$

Methylparathion is the corresponding dimethyl derivative. Later (1952) malathion found favour because of its decreased toxicity to mammals; it is readily made in 90% yield by the addition of dimethyldithiophosphate to diethylmaleate in the presence of NEt_3 as a catalyst and hydroquinone as a polymerization inhibitor:

$$(MeO)_2P(S)SH + \begin{matrix} CHCO_2Et \\ \| \\ CHCO_2Et \end{matrix} \quad \xrightarrow[60\%]{NEt_3/HQ} \quad \begin{matrix} (MeO)_2P(S)SCHCO_2Et \\ | \\ CH_2CO_2Et \end{matrix} \text{ (malathion)}$$

The scale of manufacture of these organophosphorus pesticides can be guaged from data referring to the USA annual production in 1975 (tonnes): methylparathion 46 000, parathion 36 000 and malathion 16 000. In addition, some 15 other thioorganophosphorus insecticides are manufactured in the USA on a scale exceeding 2000 tonnes pa each.[4] They act by inhibiting cholinesterase, thus preventing the natural hydrolysis of the neurotransmitter acetylcholine in the insect.[20]

applications (see Panel). P_4S_{10} is also widely used to replace O by S in organic compounds to form, e.g., thioamides $RC(S)NH_2$, thioaldehydes RCHS and thioketones R_2CS. Methanolysis yields $(MeO)_2P(S)SH$ plus H_2S,[115] and the related anions $(RO)_2PS_2^-$ are known as versatile ligands with a remarkable variety of coordination modes.[116]

A rather different series of cyclic thiophosphate(III) anions $[(PS_2)_n]^{n-}$ is emerging from a study of the reaction of elemental phosphorus with polysulfidic sulfur. Anhydrous compounds

[115] P. BOURDAUDUCQ and M. C. DÉMARCQ, *J. Chem. Soc., Dalton Trans.,* 1897–900 (1987).

[116] M. G. B. DREW, R. J. HOBSON, P. P. E. M. MUMBA and D. A. RICE, *J. Chem. Soc., Dalton Trans.,* 1569–71 (1987).

$M_5^I[cyclo\text{-}P_5S_{10}]$ and $M_6^I[cyclo\text{-}P_6S_{12}]$ were obtained using red phosphorus, whereas white P_4 yielded $[NH_4]_4[cyclo\text{-}P_4S_8].2H_2O$ as shiny platelets. This unique $P_4S_8^{4-}$ anion is the first known homocycle of 4 tetracoordinated P atoms and X-ray studies reveal that the P atoms form a square with rather long P–P distances (228 pm).[117]

The new planar anion PS_3^- (cf. the nitrate ion, NO_3^-) has been isolated as its tetraphenylarsonium salt, mp 183°, following a surprising reaction of P_4S_{10} with KCN/H_2S in MeCN, in which the coproduct was the known dianion $[(NC)P(S)_2\text{–}S\text{–}P(S)_2(CN)]^{2-}$.[118] The first sulfido heptaphosphane cluster anions, $[P_7(S)_3]^{3-}$ and $[HP_7(S)_2]^{2-}$ (cf. P_7^{3-}, p. 491), have also recently been characterized.[119]

Oxosulfides

When P_4O_{10} and P_4S_{10} are heated in appropriate proportions above 400°, $P_4O_6S_4$ is obtained as colourless hygroscopic crystals, mp 102°.

$$3P_4O_{10} + 2P_4S_{10} \longrightarrow 5P_4O_6S_4$$

The structure is shown in Fig. 12.15. The related compound $P_4O_4S_6$ is said to be formed by the reaction of H_2S with $POCl_3$ at 0° (A. Besson, 1897) but has not been recently investigated. An amorphous yellow material of composition $P_4O_4S_3$ is obtained when a solution of P_4S_3 in CS_2 or organic solvents is oxidized by dry air or oxygen. Other oxosulfides of uncertain authenticity such as $P_6O_{10}S_5$ have been reported but their structural integrity has not been established and they may be mixtures. However, the following series can be prepared by appropriate redistribution reactions: $P_4O_6S_n$ ($n = 1-4$), $P_4O_6Se_n$ ($n = 1-3$), P_4O_6SSe, $P_4O_7S_n$

($n = 1-3$), P_4O_7Se, $P_4O_8S_n$ ($n = 1, 2$).[120] the crystal and molecular structures of $P_4O_6S_2$ and $P_4O_6S_3$ have recently been determined.[121] Two isomers each of $\beta\text{-}P_4S_2SeI_2$ and $\beta\text{-}P_4SSe_2I_2$, prepared by reaction of $P_4S_{3-n}Se_n$ with I_2 in CS_2 have been structurally identified by ^{31}P nmr spectroscopy.[122]

12.3.6 Oxoacids of phosphorus and their salts

The oxoacids of P are more numerous than those of any other element, and the number of oxoanions and oxo-salts is probably exceeded only by those of Si. Many are of great importance technologically and their derivatives are vitally involved in many biological processes (p. 528). Fortunately, the structural principles covering this extensive array of compounds are very simple and can be stated as follows:[†]

(i) All P atoms in the oxoacids and oxoanions are 4-coordinate and contain at least one P–O unit (1).

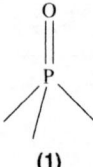

(1)

(ii) All P atoms in the oxoacids have at least one P–OH group (2a) and this often occurs in the anions also; all such groups are ionizable as proton donors (2b).

[117] H. FALIUS, W. KRAUSE and W. S. SHELDRICK, *Angew. Chem. Int. Edn. Engl.* **20**, 103–4 (1981).

[118] H. W. ROESKY, R. AHLRICHS and S. BRODE, *Angew. Chem. Int. Edn. Engl.* **25**, 82–3 (1986)

[119] M. BAUDLER and A. FLORUSS, *Z. anorg. allg. Chem.* **620**, 2070–6 (1994).

[120] M. L. WALKER, D. E. PECKENPAUGH and J. L. MILLS, *Inorg. Chem.* **18**, 2792–6 (1979).

[121] F. FRICK and M. JANSEN, *Z. anorg. allg. Chem.* **619**, 281–6 (1993). See M. JANSEN and S. STROJEK, *Z. anorg. allg. Chem.* **621**, 479–83 (1995) for X-ray structures of P_4O_7S, i.e. $P_4O_6(O)_t(S)_t$.

[122] P. LÖNNECKE and R. BLACHNIK, *Z. anorg. allg. Chem.* **619**, 1257–61 (1993). See also M. RUCK, *ibid.* **620**, 1832–6 (1994) R. BLACHNIK, A. HEPP, P. LÖNNECKE, J. A. DONKIN and B. W. TATTERSHALL, *ibid.* **620**, 1925–31 (1994).

[†] Heteropolyacids containing P fall outside this classification and are treated, together with the isopolyacids and their salts, on pp. 1010–16. Organic esters such as $P(OR)_3$ are also excluded.

(iii) Some species also have one (or more) P–H group (3); such directly bonded H atoms are not ionizable.

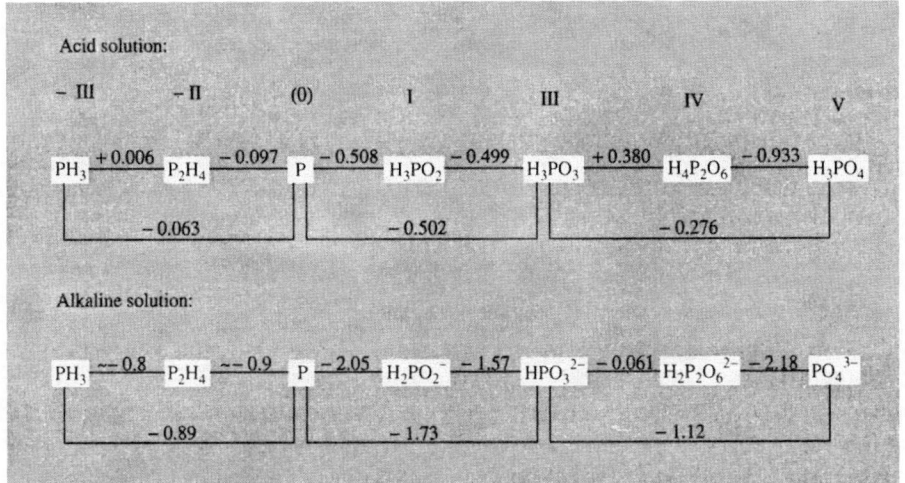

(2a)　　　**(2b)**　　　**(3)**

(iv) Catenation is by P–O–P links (4a) or via direct P–P bonds (4b); with the former both open chain ("linear") and cyclic species are known but only corner sharing of tetrahedra occurs, never edge- or face-sharing.

(4a)　　　　**(4b)**

(v) Peroxo compounds feature either $\geqslant$P—OOH groups or $\geqslant$POOP$\leqslant$ links.

It follows from these structural principles that each P atom is 5-covalent. However, the oxidation state of P is 5 only when it is directly bound to 4 O atoms; the oxidation state is reduced by 1 each time a P–OH is replaced by a P–P bond and by 2 each time a P–OH is replaced by a P–H. Some examples of phosphorus oxoacids are listed in Table 12.7 together with their recommended and common names. It will be seen that the numerous structural types and the variability of oxidation state pose several problems of nomenclature which offer a rich source of confusion in the literature.

The oxoacids of P are clearly very different structurally from those of N (p. 459) and this difference is accentuated when the standard reduction potentials (p. 434) and oxidation-state diagrams (p. 437) for the two sets of compounds are compared. Some reduction potentials ($E°/V$) in acid solution are in Table 12.8[123] (p. 513) and these are shown schematically below, together with the corresponding data for alkaline solutions.

The alternative presentation as an oxidation state diagram is in Fig. 12.16 which shows the dramatic difference to N (p. 438).

The fact that the element readily dissolves in aqueous media with disproportionation into PH_3 and an oxoacid is immediately clear from the fact that P lies above the line joining PH_3 and either H_3PO_2 (hypophosphorous acid), H_3PO_3 (phosphorous acid) or H_3PO_4 (orthophosphoric acid). The reaction is even

---

[123] G. MILAZZO and S. CAROLI, *Tables of Standard Electrode Potentials*, Wiley, New York, 1978, 421 pp. A. J. BARD, R. PARSONS and J. JORDAN, *Standard Potentials in Aqueous Solution*, Marcel Dekker, New York, 1985, 834 pp.

Table 12.7 Some phosphorus oxoacids[a]

Formula/Name	Structure[a]	Formula/Name	Structure[a]
H_3PO_4 (Ortho)phosphoric acid		H_3PO_5 Peroxomonophosphoric acid	
$H_4P_2O_7$ Diphosphoric acid (pyrophosphoric acid)		$H_4P_2O_8$ Peroxodiphosphoric acid	
$H_5P_3O_{10}$ Triphosphoric acid		$H_4P_2O_6$ Hypophosphoric acid [diphosphoric(IV) acid]	
$H_{n+2}P_nO_{3n+1}$ Polyphosphoric acid (n up to 17 isolated)		$H_4P_2O_6$ Isohypophosphoric acid [diphosphoric(III,V) acid]	
$(HPO_3)_3$ Cyclo-trimetaphosphoric acid		$H_3PO_3\ (2)^{[b]}$ Phosphonic acid (phosphorous acid)	
$(HPO_3)_4$ Cyclo-tetrametaphosphoric acid (anions known in both "boat" and "chair" forms)		$H_4P_2O_5\ (2)^{[b]}$ Diphosphonic acid (diphosphorous or pyrophosphorous acid)	
$(HPO_3)_n$ Polymetaphosphoric acid (see text for salts)		$H_3PO_2\ (1)^{[b]}$ Phosphinic acid (hypophosphorous acid)	

[a] Some acids are known only as their salts in which one or more −OH group has been replaced by O⁻.

[b] The number in parentheses after the formula indicates the maximum basicity, where this differs from the total number of H atoms in the formula.

more effective in alkaline solution. Similarly, $H_4P_2O_6$ disproportionates into H_3PO_3 and H_3PO_4. Figure 12.16 also illustrates that H_3PO_2 and H_3PO_3 are both effective reducing agents, being readily oxidized to H_3PO_4, but this latter compound (unlike HNO_3) is not an oxidizing agent.

A comprehensive treatment of the oxoacids and oxoanions of P is inappropriate but selected examples have been chosen to illustrate

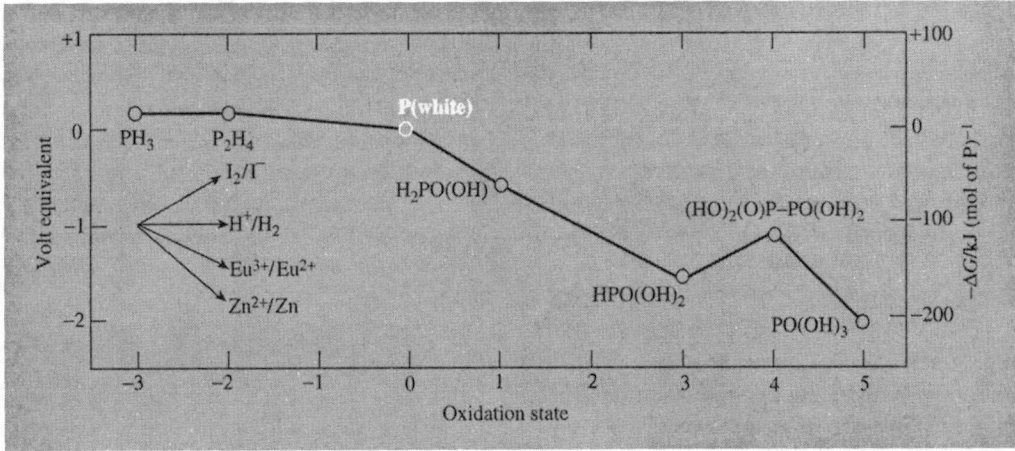

Figure 12.16   Oxidation state diagram for phosphorus. (Note that all the oxoacids have a phosphorus covalency of 5.)

interesting points of stereochemistry, reaction chemistry or technological applications. The treatment begins with the lower oxoacids and their salts (in which P has an oxidation state less than +5) and then considers phosphoric acid, phosphates and polyphosphates. The peroxoacids H_3PO_5 and $H_4P_2O_8$ and their salts will not be treated further[124] (except peripherally) nor will the peroxohydrates of orthophosphates, which are obtained from aqueous H_2O_2 solutions.[64]

Hypophosphorous acid and hypophosphites [$H_2PO(OH)$ and $H_2PO_2^-$]

The recommended names for these compounds (phosphinic acid and phosphinates) have not yet gained wide acceptance for inorganic compounds but are generally used for organophosphorus derivatives. Hypophosphites can be made by heating white phosphorus in aqueous alkali:

$$P_4 + 4OH^- + 4H_2O \xrightarrow[\text{[NaOH/Ca(OH)}_2]}{\text{warm}} 4H_2PO_2^- + 2H_2$$

Phosphite and phosphine are obtained as byproducts (p. 493) and the former can be removed via

124 I. I. CREASER and J. O. EDWARDS, *Topics in Phosphorus Chemistry* **7**, 379–435 (1972).

its insoluble calcium salt:

$$P_4 + 4OH^- + 2H_2O \xrightarrow{2Ca^{2+}} Ca(HPO_3)_2 + 2PH_3$$

Table 12.8   Some reduction potentials in acid solution (pH 0)[a]

Reaction	$E°$/V
$P + 3H^+ + 3e^- \rightleftharpoons PH_3(g)$	−0.063
$P + 2H^+ + 2e^- \rightleftharpoons \frac{1}{2}P_2H_4(g)$	−0.097
$\frac{1}{2}P_2H_4 + H^+ + e^- \rightleftharpoons PH_3$	+0.006
$H_3PO_2 + H^+ + e^- \rightleftharpoons P + 2H_2O$	−0.508
$H_3PO_3 + 3H^+ + 3e^- \rightleftharpoons P + 3H_2O$	−0.502
$H_3PO_4 + 5H^+ + 5e^- \rightleftharpoons P + 4H_2O$	−0.411
$H_3PO_3 + 2H^+ + 2e^- \rightleftharpoons H_3PO_2 + H_2O$	−0.499
$H_3PO_4 + 2H^+ + 2e^- \rightleftharpoons H_3PO_3 + H_2O$	−0.276
$H_3PO_4 + H^+ + e^- \rightleftharpoons \frac{1}{2}H_4P_2O_6 + H_2O$	−0.933
$\frac{1}{2}H_4P_2O_6 + H^+ + e^- \rightleftharpoons H_3PO_3$	+0.380

[a] P refers to white phosphorus, $\frac{1}{4}P_4(s)$.

Free hypophosphorous acid is obtained by acidifying aqueous solutions of hypophosphites but the pure acid cannot be isolated simply by evaporating such solutions because of its ready oxidation to phosphorous and phosphoric acids and disproportionation to phosphine and phosphorous acid (Fig. 12.16). Pure H_3PO_2 is obtained by continuous extraction from aqueous solutions into Et_2O; it forms white crystals mp

26.5° and is a monobasic acid pK_a 1.244 at 25°.[125]

During the past few decades hydrated sodium hypophosphite, $NaH_2PO_2.H_2O$, has been increasingly used as an industrial reducing agent, particularly for the electroless plating of Ni onto both metals and non-metals.[126] This developed from an accidental discovery by A. Brenner and Grace E. Riddel at the National Bureau of Standards, Washington, in 1944. Acid solutions ($E \sim -0.40$ V at pH 4–6 and $T > 90°$) are used to plate thick Ni layers on to other metals, but more highly reducing alkaline solutions (pH 7–10; T 25–50°) are used to plate plastics and other non-conducting materials:

$$HPO_3{}^{2-} + 2H_2O + 2e^- \rightleftharpoons H_2PO_2{}^- + 3OH^-;$$

$$E \sim -1.57 \text{ V}$$

Typical plating solutions contain 10–30 g/l of nickel chloride or sulfate and 10–50 g/l NaH_2PO_2; with suitable pump capacities it is possible to plate up to 10 kg Ni per hour from such a bath (i.e. 45 m² surface to a thickness of 25 μm). Chemical plating is more expensive than normal electrolytic plating but is competitive when intricate shapes are being plated and is essential for non-conducting substrates. (See also the use of $BH_4{}^-$ in this connection, p. 167.)

Phosphorous acid and phosphites [HPO(OH)₂ and HPO₃²⁻]

Again, the recommended names (phosphonic acid and phosphonates) have found more general acceptance for organic derivatives such as $RPO_3{}^{2-}$, and purely inorganic salts are still usually called phosphites. The free acid is readily made by direct hydrolysis of PCl_3 in cold CCl_4 solution:

$$PCl_3 + 3H_2O \longrightarrow HPO(OH)_2 + 3HCl$$

On an industrial scale PCl_3 is sprayed into steam at 190° and the product sparged of residual water and HCl using nitrogen at 165°. Phosphorous acid forms colourless, deliquescent crystals, mp 70.1°, in which the structural units shown form four essentially linear H bonds (O···H 155–160 pm) which stabilize a complex 3D network. The molecular dimensions were determined by low-temperature single-crystal neutron diffraction at 15 K.[127]

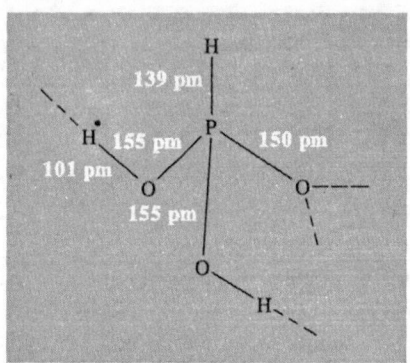

In aqueous solutions phosphorous acid is dibasic (pK_1 1.257, pK_2 6.7)[125] and forms two series of salts: phosphites and hydrogen phosphites (acid phosphites), e.g.

"normal": $[NH_4]_2[HPO_3].H_2O$, $Li_2[HPO_3]$, $Na_2[HPO_3].5H_2O$, $K_2[HPO_3]$

"acid": $[NH_4][HPO_2(OH)]$, $Li[HPO_2(OH)]$, $Na[HPO_2(OH)].2\frac{1}{2}H_2O$, $K[HPO_2(OH)]$ and $M[HPO_2(OH)]_2$ (M = Mg, Ca, Sr).

Dehydration of these acid phosphites by warming under reduced pressure leads to the corresponding pyrophosphites $M_2^I[HP(O)_2-O-P(O)_2H]$ and $M^{II}[HP(O)_2-O-P(O)_2H]$.

Organic derivatives fall into 4 classes $RPO(OH)_2$, $HPO(OR)_2$, $R'PO(OR)_2$ and the phosphite esters $P(OR)_3$; this latter class has no purely inorganic analogues, though it is, of course, closely related to PCl_3. Some preparative routes have already been indicated. Reactions with alcohols depend on conditions:

$$PCl_3 + 3ROH \longrightarrow HPO(OR)_2 + RCl + 2HCl$$

[125] J. W. LARSON and M. PIPPIN, *Polyhedron* **8**, 527–30 (1989).

[126] H. NIEDERPRÜM, *Angew. Chem. Int. Edn. Engl.* **14**, 614–20 (1975); G. A. KRULIK, *Kirk–Othmer Encyclopedia of Chemical Technology*, 4th edn., Vol. 9, pp. 198–218, Wiley, New York, 1994.

[127] G. BECKER, H.-D. HAUSEN, O. MUNDT, W. SCHWARZ, C. T. WAGNER and T. VOGT, *Z. anorg. allg. Chem.* **591**, 17–31 (1990).

$$PCl_3 + 3ROH + 3R'_3N \longrightarrow P(OR)_3 + 3R'_3NHCl$$

Phenols give triaryl phosphites $P(OAr)_3$ directly at $\sim 160°$ and these react with phosphorous acid to give diaryl phosphonates:

$$2P(OAr)_3 + HPO(OH)_2 \longrightarrow 3HPO(OAr)_2$$

Trimethyl phosphite $P(OMe)_3$ spontaneously isomerizes to methyl dimethylphosphonate $MePO(OMe)_2$, whereas other trialkyl phosphites undergo the Michaelis–Arbusov reaction with alkyl halides via a phosphonium intermediate:

$$P(OR)_3 + R'X \longrightarrow \{[R'P(OR)_3]X\}$$
$$\longrightarrow R'PO(OR)_2 + RX$$

Further discussion of these fascinating series of reactions falls outside our present scope.[2]

Hypophosphoric acid ($H_4P_2O_6$) and hypophosphates

There has been much confusion over the structure of these compounds but their diamagnetism has long ruled out a monomeric formulation, H_2PO_3. In fact, as shown in Table 12.7, isomeric forms are known: (a) hypophosphoric acid and hypophosphates in which both P atoms are identical and there is a direct P–P bond; (b) isohypophosphoric acid and isohypophosphates in which 1 P has a direct P–H bond

and the 2 different P atoms are joined by a P^{III}–O–P^V link.[23]

Hypophosphoric acid, $(HO)_2P(O)$–$P(O)(OH)_2$, is usually prepared by the controlled oxidation of red P with sodium chlorite solution at room temperature: the tetrasodium salt, $Na_4P_2O_6.10H_2O$, crystallizes at pH 10 and the disodium salt at pH 5.2:

$$2P + 2NaClO_2 + 8H_2O \longrightarrow Na_2H_2P_2O_6.6H_2O$$
$$+ 2HCl$$

Ion exchange on an acid column yields the crystalline "dihydrate" $H_4P_2O_6.2H_2O$ which is actually the hydroxonium salt of the dihydrogen hypophosphate anion $[H_3O]_2^+[(HO)P(O)_2$–$P(O)_2(OH)]^{2-}$; it is isostructural with the corresponding ammonium salt for which X-ray diffraction studies establish the staggered structure shown.

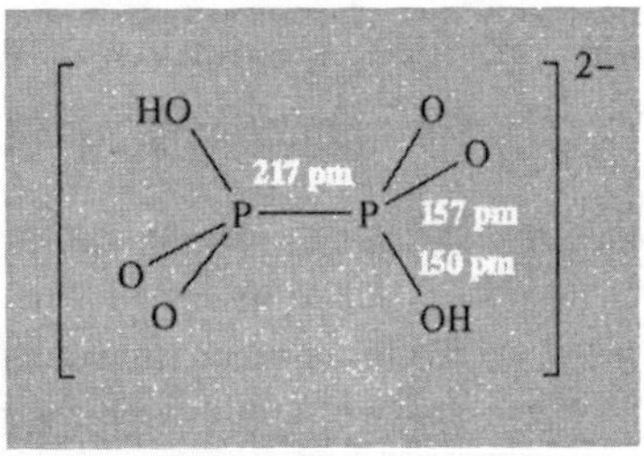

The anhydrous acid is obtained either by the vacuum dehydration of the dihydrate over P_4O_{10}

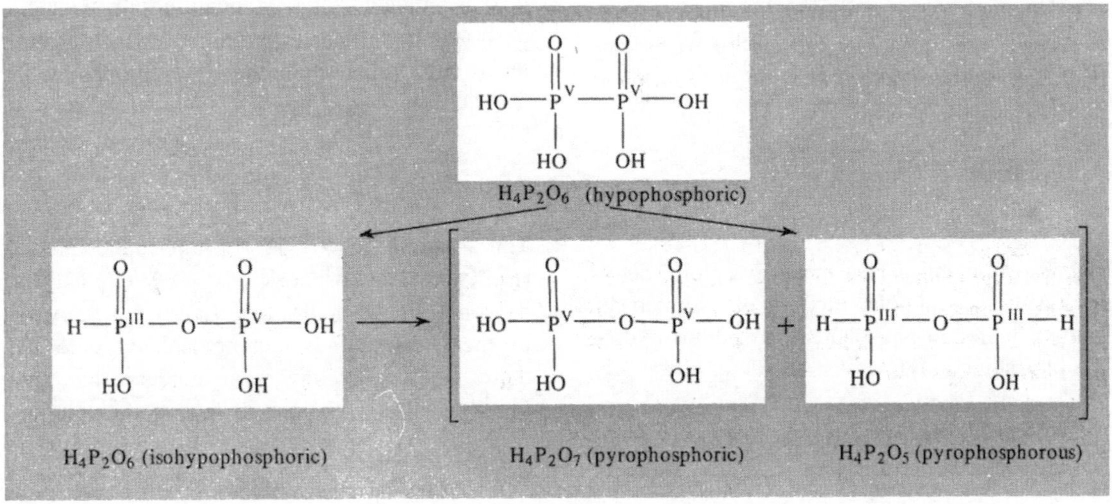

$H_4P_2O_6$ (hypophosphoric)

$H_4P_2O_6$ (isohypophosphoric) $H_4P_2O_7$ (pyrophosphoric) $H_4P_2O_5$ (pyrophosphorous) or by the action of H_2S on the insoluble lead salt $Pb_2P_2O_6$. As implied above, the first proton on each $-PO(OH)_2$ unit is more readily removed than the second and the successive dissociation constants at $25°$ are pK_1 2.2, pK_2 2.8, pK_3 7.3, pK_4 10.0. Both $H_4P_2O_6$ and its dihydrate are stable at $0°$ in the absence of moisture. The acid begins to melt (with decomposition) at $73°$ but even at room temperature it undergoes rearrangement and disproportionation to give a mixture of isohypophosphoric, pyrophosphoric, and pyrophosphorous acids as represented schematically on the previous page.

Hypophosphoric acid is very stable towards alkali and does not decompose even when heated with 80% NaOH at $200°$. However, in acid solution it is less stable and even at $25°$ hydrolyses at a rate dependent on pH (e.g. $t_{\frac{1}{2}}$ 180 days in 1 M HCl, $t_{\frac{1}{2}} < 1$ h in 4 M HCl):

$$(HO)_2P(O)-P(O)(OH)_2 + H_2O \xrightarrow{\text{pH} < 0}$$

$$HP(O)(OH)_2 + P(O)(OH)_3$$

The presence of P–H groups amongst the products of these reactions was one of the earlier sources of confusion in the structures of hypophosphoric and isohypophosphoric acids.

The structure of isohypophosphoric acid and its salts can be deduced from ^{31}P nmr which shows the presence of 2 different 4-coordinate P atoms, the absence of a P–P bond and the presence of a P–H group (also confirmed by Raman spectroscopy). It is made by the careful hydrolysis of PCl_3 with the stoichiometric amounts of phosphoric acid and water at $50°$:

$$PCl_3 + H_3PO_4 + 2H_2O \xrightarrow{50°}$$

$$\textit{iso-}[H_3(HP_2O_6)] + 3HCl$$

The trisodium salt is best made by careful dehydration of an equimolar mixture of hydrated disodium hydrogen phosphate and sodium hydrogen phosphite at $180°$:

$$Na_2HPO_4.12H_2O + NaH_2PO_3.2\tfrac{1}{2}H_2O \xrightarrow{180°}$$

$$Na_3[HP_2O_6] + 15\tfrac{1}{2}H_2O$$

The structural relation between the reacting anions and the product is shown schematically below:

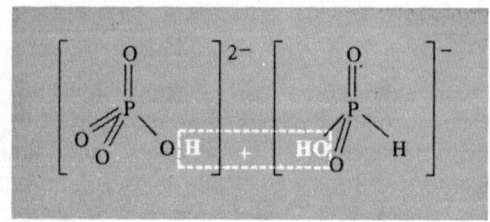

Other lower oxoacids of phosphorus

The possibility of P–H and P–P bonds in phosphorus oxoacids, coupled with the ease of polymerization via P–O–P linkages enables innumerable acids and their salts to be synthesized. Frequently mixtures are obtained and these can be separated by paper chromatography, paper electrophoresis, thin-layer chromatography, ion exchange or gel chromatography.[128] Much ingenuity has been expended in designing appropriate syntheses but no new principles emerge. A few examples are listed in Table 12.9 to illustrate both the range of compounds available and also the abbreviated notation, which proves to be more convenient than formal systematic nomenclature in this area. In this notation the sequence of P–P and P–O–P links is indicated and the oxidation state of each P is shown as a superscript numeral which enables the full formula (including P–H groups) to be deduced.

The phosphoric acids

This section deals with orthophosphoric acid (H_3PO_4), pyrophosphoric acid ($H_4P_2O_7$) and the polyphosphoric acids ($H_{n+2}P_nO_{3n+1}$). Several of these compounds can be isolated pure but their facile interconversion renders this area of phosphorus chemistry far more complex

[128] S. OHASHI, *Pure Appl. Chem.* **44**, 415–38 (1975).

Table 12.9 Some lower oxoacids of phosphorus (Superscript numerals in the abbreviated notation indicate oxidation states)

Formula (basicity)	Structure	Abbreviated notation	Formula (basicity)	Structure	Abbreviated notation
$H_4P_2O_4$ (2)		$\overset{2}{P}-\overset{2}{P}$	$H_5P_3O_9$ (5)		$\overset{5}{P}-O-\overset{4}{P}-\overset{4}{P}$
$H_4P_2O_5$ (3)		$\overset{2}{P}-\overset{4}{P}$	$H_6P_4O_{11}$ (6)		$\overset{4}{P}-\overset{4}{P}-O-\overset{4}{P}-\overset{4}{P}$
$H_4P_2O_6$ (3)		$\overset{3}{P}-O-\overset{5}{P}$	$H_4P_4O_{10}$ (10)		$(-\overset{4}{P}-\overset{4}{P}-O-)_2$ ring
$H_5P_3O_7$ (4)		$\overset{3}{P}-O-\overset{4}{P}-\overset{4}{P}$	$H_6P_6O_{12}$ (6)		$(-\overset{3}{P}-)_6$ ring
$H_5P_3O_8$ (5)		$\overset{4}{P}-\overset{3}{P}-\overset{4}{P}$			

than might otherwise appear. The corresponding phosphate salts are discussed in subsequent sections as also are the cyclic metaphosphoric acids $(HPO_3)_n$, the polymetaphosphoric acids $(HPO_3)_n$, and their salts.

Orthophosphoric acid is a remarkable substance: it can only be obtained pure in the crystalline state (mp 42.35°C) and when fused it slowly undergoes partial self-dehydration to diphosphoric acid:

$$2H_3PO_4 \rightleftharpoons H_2O + H_4P_2O_7$$

The sluggish equilibrium is obtained only after several weeks near the mp but is more rapid at higher temperatures. This process is accompanied by extremely rapid autoprotolysis (see below) which gives rise to several further (ionic) species in the melt. As the concentration of these various species builds up the mp slowly drops until at equilibrium it is 34.6°, corresponding to about 6.5 mole% of diphosphate.[129] Slow crystallization of stoichiometric molecular H_3PO_4 from this isocompositional melt gradually reverses the equilibria and the mp eventually rises again to the initial value. Crystalline H_3PO_4 has a hydrogen-bonded layer structure in which each $PO(OH)_3$ molecule is linked to 6 others by H bonds which are of two lengths, 253 and 284 pm. The shorter bonds link OH and O=P groups whereas the longer H bonds are between 2 OH groups on adjacent molecules.

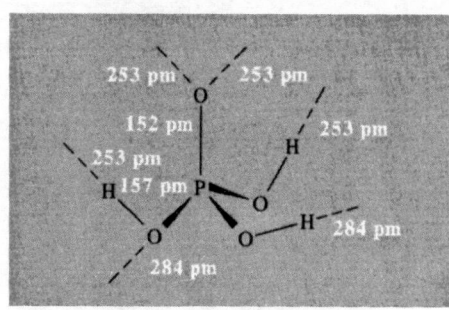

Extensive H bonding persists on fusion and phosphoric acid is a viscous syrupy liquid that

readily supercools. At 45°C (just above the mp) the viscosity is 76.5 centipoise (cP) and this increases to 177.7 cP at 25°. These values can be compared with 1.00 cP for H_2O at 20° and 24.5 cP for anhydrous H_2SO_4 at 25°. As shown in the Table[129] trideuterophosphoric acid has an even higher viscosity and deuteration also raises the mp and density.

Property	H_3PO_4	D_3PO_4
MP/°C	42.35	46.0
Density (25°C); supercooled/g cm^{-3}	1.8683	1.9083
η (25°C)/centipoise	177.5	231.8
κ/ohm^{-1} cm^{-1}	4.68×10^{-2}	2.82×10^{-2}

Property	$H_3PO_4 \cdot \frac{1}{2}H_2O$
MP/°C	29.30
Density (25°C); supercooled/g cm^{-3}	1.7548
η (25°C)/centipoise	70.64
κ/ohm^{-1} cm^{-1}	7.01×10^{-2}

Despite this enormous viscosity, fused H_3PO_4 (and D_3PO_4) conduct electricity extremely well and this has been shown to arise from extensive self-ionization (autoprotolysis) coupled with a proton-switch conduction mechanism for the $H_2PO_4^-$ ion:[129,130]

$$2H_3PO_4 \rightleftharpoons H_4PO_4^+ + H_2PO_4^- \qquad (1)$$

In addition, the diphosphate group is also deprotonated:

$$2H_3PO_4 \rightleftharpoons H_2O + H_4P_2O_7$$
$$\rightleftharpoons H_3O^+ + H_3P_2O_7^-$$
$$H_3P_2O_7^- + H_3PO_4 \rightleftharpoons H_4PO_4^+$$
$$+ H_2P_2O_7^{2-}$$

i.e. $\qquad 3H_3PO_4 \rightleftharpoons H_3O^+ + H_4PO_4^+$
$$+ H_2P_2O_7^{2-} \qquad (2)$$

At equilibrium, the concentration of H_3O^+ and $H_2P_2O_7^{2-}$ are each $\sim$0.28 molal and $H_2PO_4^-$ is $\sim$0.26 molal, thereby implying a

[129] N. N. GREENWOOD and A. THOMPSON, *J. Chem. Soc.* 3485–92 and 3864–7 (1959).

[130] R. A. MUNSON, *J. Phys. Chem.* **68**, 3374–7 (1964).

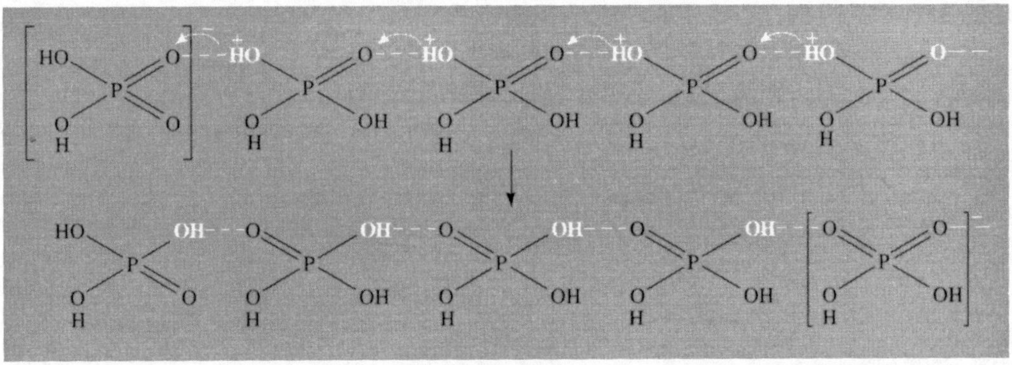

Figure 12.17 Schematic representation of proton-switch conduction mechanism involving $[H_2PO_4]^-$ in molten phosphoric acid.

concentration of 0.54 molal for $H_4PO_4^+$. These values are about 20–30 times greater than the concentrations of ions in molten H_2SO_4, namely $[HSO_4^-]$ 0.0178 molal, $[H_3SO_4^+]$ 0.0135 molal and $[HS_2O_7^-]$ 0.0088 molal (see p. 711). Because of the very high viscosity of molten H_3PO_4 electrical conduction by normal ionic migration is negligible and the high conductivity is due almost entirely to a rapid proton-switch followed by a relatively slow reorientation involving the $H_2PO_4^-$ ion, H-bonded to the solvent structure (Fig. 12.17).[129] Note that the tetrahedral $H_4PO_4^+$ ion, i.e. $[P(OH)_4]^+$, like the NH_4^+ ion in liquid NH_3, does not contribute to the proton-switch conduction mechanism in H_3PO_4 because, having no dipole moment, it does not orient preferentially in the applied electric field; accordingly any proton switching will occur randomly in all directions independently of the applied field and therefore will not contribute to the electrical conduction.

Addition of the appropriate amount of water to anhydrous H_3PO_4, or crystallization from a concentrated aqueous solution of syrupy phosphoric acid, yields the hemihydrate $2H_3PO_4.H_2O$ as a congruently melting compound (mp 29.3°). The crystal structure[131] shows the presence of 2 similar H_3PO_4 molecules which, together with the H_2O molecule, are linked into

a three-dimensional H-bonded network: each of the nine O atoms participates in at least 1 relatively strong O–H⋯O bond (255–272 pm) and the interatomic distances P=O (149 pm) and P–OH (155 pm) are both slightly shorter than the corresponding distances in H_3PO_4. Hydrogen bonding persists in the molten compound, and the proton-switch conductivity is even higher than in the anhydrous acid (See Table on p. 518).

In dilute aqueous solutions H_3PO_4 behaves as a strong acid but only one of the hydrogens is readily ionizable, the second and third ionization constants decreasing successively by factors of $\sim 10^5$ (see p. 50). Thus, at 25°:

$$H_3PO_4 + H_2O \rightleftharpoons H_3O^+ + H_2PO_4^-;$$
$$K_1 = 7.11 \times 10^{-3}; \quad pK_1 = 2.15$$
$$H_2PO_4^- + H_2O \rightleftharpoons H_3O^+ + HPO_4^{2-};$$
$$K_2 = 6.31 \times 10^{-8}; \quad pK_2 = 7.20$$
$$HPO_4^{2-} + H_2O \rightleftharpoons H_3O^+ + PO_4^{3-};$$
$$K_3 = 4.22 \times 10^{-13}; \quad pK_3 = 12.37$$

Accordingly, the acid gives three series of salts, e.g. NaH_2PO_4, Na_2HPO_4, and Na_3PO_4 (p. 523). A typical titration curve in this system is shown in Fig. 12.18: there are three steps with two inflexions at pH 4.5 and 9.5. The first inflexion, corresponding to the formation of NaH_2PO_4, can be detected by an indicator such as methyl

---

[131] A. D. MIGHELL, J. P. SMITH, and W. E. BROWN, *Acta Cryst.* **B25**, 776–81 (1969).

Industrial production and uses of H_3PO_4 [3−5.8.9.11.132]

Phosphoric acid[132] is manufactured on a vast scale and is produced in a wide variety of concentrations and purities. It is therefore convenient to express production figures in terms of the amount of contained P_4O_{10} (the figures based on the equivalent amount of contained anhydrous H_3PO_4 can be obtained by multiplying by the factor 1.380, though these may be misleading if they are taken to imply that it is the anhydrous acid that is being produced). World production capacity in 1986 exceeded 43 million tonnes of contained P_4O_{10} and was distributed as follows:

Production   capacity of phosphoric acid (million tonnes/year of contained P_4O_{10})

Region	North America	USSR & East.Eur.	Africa	Western Europe	Asia and Australasia	Central/S. America	Middle East
"P_4O_{10}"/Mtpa	13.1	10.6	6.1	5.0	3.9	2.4	1.5

Production is still increasing steadily in many countries "Thermal" acid (made by oxidation of phosphorus in the presence of water vapour) is about 3 times as expensive as "wet" acid (made by treating rock phosphate with sulfuric acid). The present approximate pattern of production and uses is shown in the following scheme:

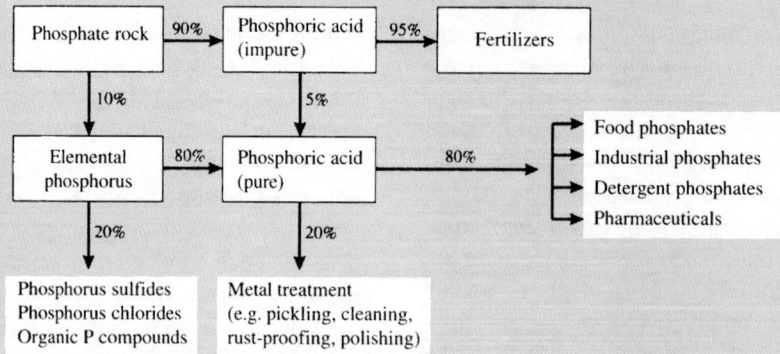

Many of these uses have already been discussed, or will be in later sections (pp. 524, 527).

Applications of phosphoric acid in metal treatment date from 1869 when a British patent was granted for the prevention of rusting of corset stays by damp air or perspiration. Improvements followed the incorporation of certain metal ions in the phosphatizing solution (notably Mn, Fe and Zn), and today corrosion resistance is imparted in this way to innumerable metal objects such as nuts, bolts, screws, tools, car-engine parts, gears, etc. In addition, car-bodies, refrigerators, washing machines and other electrical appliances with painted or enamelled surfaces all use phosphatized undercoatings to prevent the paint from blistering or peeling. The simple immersion process may take up to 2 h at 90°C but can be accelerated 25-fold by adding small amounts of oxidizing agent such as $NaNO_3$ and $Cu(NO_3)_2$. A zinc phosphatized coating is usually about $0.6\,\mu$m thick (i.e. $2.2\,\mathrm{g\,m^{-2}}$). Another important process is "bright dip" or chemical polishing of Al metal which has replaced chrome plating for car trims and other uses: the metal is immersed at 91–99°C in a solution containing 95 parts by weight of 85% H_3PO_4, 4 parts of 68% HNO_3, and 0.01% $Cu(NO_3)_2$, followed by electrolytic anodization to give the mirror-like surface a protective coating of transparent Al_2O_3.

Polyphosphoric acid supported on diatomaceous earth (p. 342) is a petrochemicals catalyst for the polymerization, alkylation, dehydrogenation, and low-temperature isomerization of hydrocarbons. Phosphoric acid is also used in the production of activated carbon (p. 274). In addition to its massive use in the fertilizer industry (p. 524) free phosphoric acid can be used as a stabilizer for clay soils: small additions of H_3PO_4 under moist conditions gradually leach out Al and Fe from the clay and these form polymeric phosphates which bind the clay particles together. An allied, though more refined use is in the setting of dental cements.

By far the greatest consumption of pure aqueous phosphoric acid is in the preparation of various salts for use in the food, detergent and tooth-paste industries (p. 524). When highly diluted the free acid is non-toxic and devoid of odour, and is extensively used to impart the sour or tart taste to many soft drinks ("carbonated beverages") such as the various colas (~0.05% H_3PO_4, pH 2.3), root beers (~0.01% H_3PO_4, pH 5.0), and sarsaparilla (~0.01% H_3PO_4, pH ~4.5).

---

[132]P. BECKER, *Phosphates and Phosphoric Acid*, Marcel Dekker, New York, 1988, 760 pp.

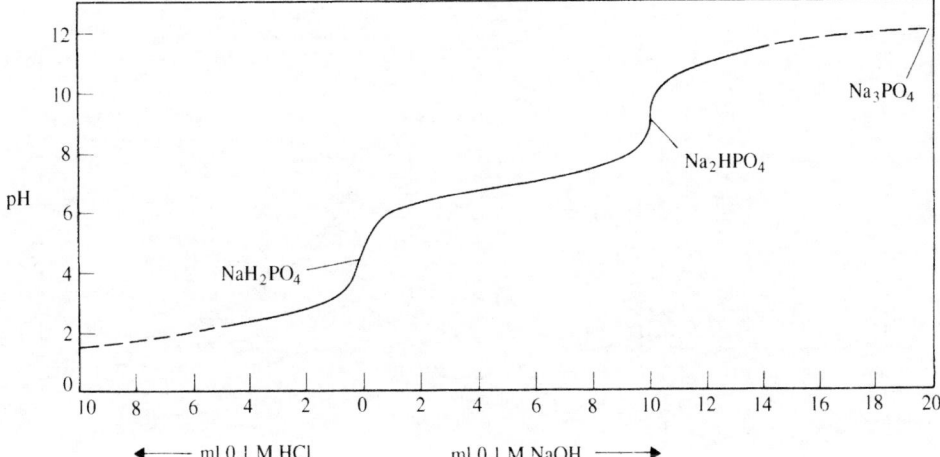

Figure 12.18 Neutralization curve for aqueous orthophosphoric acid. For technical reasons the curve shown refers to $10\,cm^3$ of $0.1\,M\,NaH_2PO_4$ titrated (to the left) with $0.1\,M$ aqueous HCl and (to the right) with $0.1\,M$ NaOH solutions. Extrapolations to points corresponding to $0.1\,M\,H_3PO_4$ (pH 1.5) and $0.1\,M$ Na_3PO_4 (pH 12.0) are also shown.

orange (pK_i 3.5) and the second, corresponding to Na_2HPO_4, is indicated by the phenolphthalein end point (pK_i 9.5). The third equivalence point cannot be detected directly by means of a coloured indicator. Between the two inflexions the pH changes relatively slowly with addition of NaOH and this is an example of buffer action.[†] Indeed, one of the standard buffer solutions used in analytical chemistry comprises an equimolar mixture of Na_2HPO_4 and KH_2PO_4. Another important buffer, which has been designed to have a pH close to that of blood, consists of $0.030\,43\,M\,Na_2HPO_4$ and $0.008\,695\,M\,KH_2PO_4$, i.e. a mole ratio of 3.5:1 (pH 7.413 at 25°).

Concentrated H_3PO_4 is one of the major acids of the chemical industry and is manufactured on the multimillion-tonne scale for the production of phosphate fertilizers and for many other purposes (see Panel). Two main processes (the so-called "thermal" and "wet" processes) are used depending on the purity required. The "thermal" (or "furnace") process yields concentrated acid essentially free from impurities and is used in applications involving products destined for human consumption (see also p. 524); in this process a spray of molten phosphorus is burned in a mixture of air and steam in a stainless steel combustion chamber:

$$P_4 + 5O_2 \longrightarrow P_4O_{10} \xrightarrow{6H_2O} 4H_3PO_4$$

Acid of any concentration up to 84 wt% P_4O_{10} can be prepared by this method (72.42% P_4O_{10} corresponds to anhydrous H_3PO_4) but the usual commercial grades are 75–85% (expressed as anhydrous H_3PO_4). The hemihydrate (p. 518) corresponds to 91.58% H_3PO_4 (66.33% P_4O_{10}). The somewhat older "wet" (or "gypsum") process involves the treatment of rock phosphate (p. 476) with sulfuric acid, the idealized stoichiometry being:

$$Ca_5(PO_4)_3F + 5H_2SO_4 + 10H_2O \longrightarrow 3H_3PO_4$$
$$+ 5CaSO_4.2H_2O + HF$$

[†] A buffer solution is one that resists changes in pH on dilution or on addition of acid or alkali. It consists of a solution of a weak acid (e.g. $H_2PO_4{}^-$) and its conjugate base ($HPO_4{}^{2-}$) and is most effective when the concentration of the two species are the same. For example at 25° an equimolar mixture of Na_2HPO_4 and KH_2PO_4 has pH 6.654 when each is $0.2\,M$ and pH 6.888 when each is $0.01\,M$. The central section of Fig. 12.18 shows the variation in pH of an equimolar buffer of Na_2HPO_4 and NaH_2PO_4 at a concentration of $0.033\,M$ (you should check this statement). Further discussion of buffer solutions is given in standard textbooks of volumetric analysis.

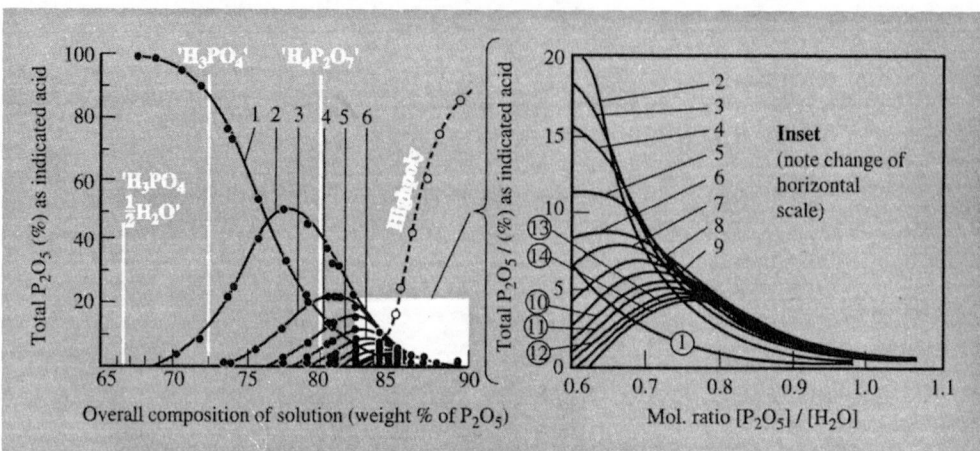

Figure 12.19 The composition of the strong phosphoric acids shown as the weight per cent of P_2O_5 present in the form of each acid plotted against the overall stoichiometric composition of the mixture. The overall stoichiometries corresponding to the three congruently melting species $H_3PO_4 \cdot \frac{1}{2}H_2O$, H_3PO_4 and $H_4P_2O_7$ are indicated. Compositions above 82 wt P_2O_5 are shown on an expanded scale in the inset using the mole ratio $[P_2O_5]/[H_2O]$ as the measure of stoichiometry. (For comparison, $H_4P_2O_7$ corresponds to a mole ratio of 0.500, $H_5P_3O_{10}$ to a ratio 0.600, $H_6P_4O_{13}$ to 0.667, etc.). In both diagrams the curves labelled 1,2,3, . . . refer to ortho-, di-, tri- . . . phosphoric acids, and "highpoly" refers to highly polymeric material hydrolysed from the column.

The gypsum is filtered off together with other insoluble matter such as silica, and the fluorine is removed as insoluble Na_2SiF_6. The dilute phosphoric acid so obtained (containing 35–70% H_3PO_4 depending on the plant used) is then concentrated by evaporation. It is usually dark green or brown in colour and contains many metal impurities (e.g. Na, Mg, Ca, Al, Fe, etc.) as well as residual sulfate and fluoride, but is suitable for the manufacture of phosphatic fertilizers, metallurgical applications, etc. (see Panel on p. 520).

Diphosphoric acid $H_4P_2O_7$ becomes an increasingly prevalent species as the system P_4O_{10}/H_2O becomes increasingly concentrated: indeed, the phase diagram shows that, in addition to the hemihydrate (mp 29.30°) and orthophosphoric acid (mp 42.35°) the only other congruently melting phase in the system is $H_4P_2O_7$. The compound is dimorphic with a metastable modification mp 54.3° and a stable form mp 71.5°, but in the molten state it comprises an isocompositional mixture of various polyphosphoric acids and their autoprotolysis

products. Equilibrium is reached only sluggishly and the actual constitution of the melt depends sensitively both on the precise stoichiometry and the temperature (Fig. 12.19)[133] For the nominal stoichiometry corresponding to $H_4P_2O_7$ typical concentrations of the species $H_{n+2}P_nO_{3n+1}$ from $n = 1$ (i.e. H_3PO_4) to $n = 8$ are as follows:

n	1	2	3	4	5	6	7	8
mole%	35.0	42.6	14.6	5.0	1.8	0.7	0.3	0.1

Thus, although $H_4P_2O_7$ is marginally the most abundant species present, there are substantial amounts of H_3PO_4, $H_5P_3O_{10}$, $H_6P_4O_{13}$ and higher polyphosphoric acids. Note that the table indicates mole% of each molecular species present whereas the graphs in Fig. 12.19 plot weight percentage of P_2O_5 present as each acid shown.

In dilute aqueous solution $H_4P_2O_7$ is a somewhat stronger acid than H_3PO_4: the 4 dissociation constants at 25° are: $K_1 \sim 10^{-1}$,

[133] R. F. JAMESON, *J. Chem. Soc.* 752–9 (1959).

Table 12.10   Factors affecting the rate of polyphosphate degradation

Factor	Effect on rate	Factor	Effect on rate
Temperature	$10^5 - 10^6$ faster from $0°$ to $100°$	Complexing cations	Often much faster
pH	$10^3 - 10^4$ faster from base to acid	Concentration	Roughly proportional
Enzymes	Up to $10^5 - 10^6$ faster	Ionic environment in solution	Several-fold change
Colloidal gels	Up to $10^4 - 10^5$ faster		

$K_2 \sim 1.5 \times 10^{-2}$, K_3 2.7×10^{-7} and K_4 2.4×10^{-10}, and the corresponding negative logarithms are: $pK_1 \sim 1.0$, $pK_2 \sim 1.8$, pK_3 6.57 and pK_4 9.62. The P—O—P linkage is kinetically stable towards hydrolysis in dilute neutral solutions at room temperature and the reaction half-life can be of the order of years. Such hydrolytic breakdown of polyphosphate is of considerable importance in certain biological systems and has been much studied. Some factors which affect the rate of degradation of polyphosphates are shown in Table 12.10.

Orthophosphates [23,64]

Phosphoric acid forms several series of salts in which the acidic H atoms are successively replaced by various cations; there is considerable commercial application for many of these compounds.

Lithium orthophosphates are unimportant and differ from the other alkali metal phosphates in being insoluble. At least 10 crystalline hydrated or anhydrous sodium orthophosphates are known and these can be grouped into three series:

$Na_3PO_4.nH_2O$ ($n = 0$, $\frac{1}{2}$, 6, 8, 12)
$Na_2HPO_4.nH_2O$ ($n = 0$, 2, 7, 8, 12)
$NaH_2PO_4.nH_2O$ ($n = 0$, 1, 2),
     $NaH_2PO_4.H_3PO_4$ [i.e. $NaH_5(PO_4)_2$]
     $NaH_2PO_4.Na_2HPO_4$ [i.e. $Na_3H_3(PO_4)_2$]
     and $2NaH_2PO_4.Na_2HPO_4.2H_2O$

Likewise, there are at least 10 well-characterized potassium orthophosphates and several ammonium analogues. The presence of extensive H bonding in many of these compounds leads to considerable structural complexity and frequently confers important properties (see later). The

mono- and di-sodium phosphates are prepared industrially by neutralization of aqueous H_3PO_4 with soda ash (anhydrous Na_2CO_3, p. 89). However, preparation of the trisodium salts requires the use of the more expensive NaOH to replace the third H atom. Careful control of concentration and temperature are needed to avoid the simultaneous formation of pyrophosphates (diphosphates). Some indication of the structural complexity can be gained from the compound $Na_3PO_4.12H_2O$ which actually crystallizes with variable amounts of NaOH up to the limiting composition $4(Na_3PO_4.12H_2O).NaOH$. The structure is built from octahedral $[Na(H_2O)_6]$ units which join to form "hexagonal" rings of 6 octahedra which in turn form a continuous two-dimensional network of overall composition $\{Na(H_2O)_4\}$; between the sheets lie $\{PO_4\}$ connected to them by H bonds. [134] Some industrial, domestic, and scientific applications of Na, K and NH_4 orthophosphates are given in the Panel.

Calcium orthophosphates are particularly important in fertilizer technology, in the chemistry of bones and teeth, and in innumerable industrial and domestic applications (see Panel). They are also the main source of phosphorus and phosphorus chemicals and occur in vast deposits as apatites and rock phosphate (p. 475). The main compounds occurring in the $CaO-H_2O-P_4O_{10}$ phase diagram are: $Ca(H_2PO_4)_2$, $Ca(H_2PO_4)_2.H_2O$, $Ca(HPO_4).nH_2O$ ($n = 0$, $\frac{1}{2}$, 2), $Ca_3(PO_4)_2$, $Ca_2PO_4(OH).2H_2O$, $Ca_5(PO_4)_3OH$ (i.e. apatite), $Ca_4P_2O_9$ [probably $Ca_3(PO_4)_2.CaO$] and $Ca_8H_2(PO_4)_6.5H_2O$.

In all of these alkali-metal and alkaline earth-metal orthophosphates there are discrete, approximately regular tetrahedral PO_4 units in

---

[134] E. TILLMANNS and W. H. BAUR, *Inorg. Chem.* **9**, 1957–8 (1970).

Uses of Orthophosphates[9]

Phosphates are used in an astonishing variety of domestic and industrial applications but their ubiquitous presence and their substantial impact on everyday life is frequently overlooked. It will be convenient first to indicate the specific uses of individual compounds and the properties on which they are based, then to conclude with a brief summary of many different types of application and their interrelation. The most widely used compounds are the various phosphate salts of Na, K, NH_4 and Ca. The uses of di-, tri- and poly-phosphates are mentioned on pp. 527–29.

Na_3PO_4 is strongly alkaline in aqueous solution and is thus a valuable constituent of scouring powders, paint strippers and grease saponifiers. Its complex with NaOCl [$(Na_3PO_4.11H_2O)_4$ NaOCl], is also strongly alkaline (a 1% solution has pH 11.8) and, in addition, it releases active chlorine when wetted; this combination of scouring, bleaching and bacteriocidal action makes the adduct valuable in formulations of automatic dishwashing powders.

Na_2HPO_4 is widely used as a buffer component (p. 521). The use of the dihydrate ($\sim$2% concentration) as an emulsifier in the manufacture of pasteurized processed cheese was patented by J. L. Kraft in 1916 and is still used, together with insoluble sodium metaphosphate or the mixed phosphate $Na_{15}Al_3(PO_4)_8$, to process cheese on the multikilotonne scale daily. Despite much study, the reason why phosphate salts act as emulsifiers is still not well understood in detail. Na_2HPO_4 is also added ($\sim$0.1%) to evaporated milk to maintain the correct Ca/PO_4 balance and to prevent gelation of the milk powder to a mush. Its addition at the 5% level to brine (15–20% NaCl solution) for the pickling of ham makes the product more tender and juicy by preventing the exudation of juices during subsequent cooking. Another major use in the food industry is as a starch modifier: small additions enhance the ability to form stable cold-water gels (e.g. instant pudding mixes), and the addition of 1% to farinaceous products raises the pH to slightly above 7 and provides "quick-cooking" breakfast cereals.

NaH_2PO_4 is a solid water-soluble acid, and this property finds use (with $NaHCO_3$) in effervescent laxative tablets and in the pH adjustment of boiler waters. It is also used as a mild phosphatizing agent for steel surfaces and as a constituent in the undercoat for metal paints.

K_3PO_4 (like Na_3PO_4) is strongly alkaline in aqueous solution and is used to absorb H_2S from gas streams; the solution can be regenerated simply by heating. K_3PO_4 is also used as a regulating electrolyte to control the stability of synthetic latex during the polymerization of styrenebutadiene rubbers. The buffering action of K_2HPO_4 has already been mentioned (p. 521) and this is the reason for its addition as a corrosion inhibitor to car-radiator coolants which otherwise tend to become acidic due to slow oxidation of the glycol antifreeze. KH_2PO_4 is a piezoelectric (p. 57) and finds use in submarine sonar systems. For many applications, however, the cheaper sodium salts are preferred unless there is a specific advantage for the potassium salt; one example is the specialist balanced commercial fertilizer formulation [$KH_2PO_4.(NH_4)_2HPO_4$] which contains 10.5%, N, 53% P_2O_5 and 17.2% K_2O (i.e. N–P–K 10–53–17).

$(NH_4)_2HPO_4$ and $(NH_4)H_2PO_4$ can be used interchangeably as specialist fertilizers and nutrients in fermentation broths; though expensive, their high concentration of active ingredients ameliorate this, particularly in localities where transportation costs are high. Indeed, $(NH_4)_2HPO_4$ in granulated or liquid form consumes more phosphate rock than any other single end-product (over 8 million tonnes pa in the USA alone in 1974). Ammonium phosphates are also much used as flame retardants for cellulosic materials, about 3–5% gain in dry weight being the optimum treatment. Their action probably depends on their ready dissociation into NH_3 and H_3PO_4 on heating; the H_3PO_4 then catalyses the decomposition of cellulose to a slow-burning char (carbon) and this, together with the suppression of flammable volatiles, smothers the flame. As the ammonium phosphates are soluble, they are used mainly for curtains, theatre scenery and disposable paper dresses and costumes. The related compound urea phosphate ($NH_2CONH_2.H_3PO_4$) has also been used to flameproof cotton fabrics: the material is soaked in a concentrated aqueous solution, dried (15% weight gain) and cured at 160° to bond the retardant to the cellulose fibre. The advantage is that the retardant does not wash out, but the strength of the fabric is somewhat reduced by the process.

Calcium phosphates have a broad range of applications both in the food industry and as bulk fertilizers. The vast scale of the phosphate rock industry has already been indicated (p. 476) and this is further elaborated for the particular case of the USA in the Scheme on the page opposite (kilotonnes pa and %, 1974).

The crucial importance of Ca and PO_4 as nutrient supplements for the healthy growth of bones, teeth, muscle and nerve cells has long been recognized. The non-cellular bone structure of an average adult human consists of $\sim$60% of some form of "tricalcium phosphate" [$Ca_5(PO_4)_3OH$]; teeth likewise comprise $\sim$70% and average persons carry 3.5 kg of this material in their bodies. Phosphates in the body are replenished by a continuous cycle, and used P is carried by the blood to the kidneys and then excreted in urine, mainly as $Na(NH_4)HPO_4$. An average adult eliminates 3–4 g of PO_4 equivalent daily (cf. the discovery of P in urine by Brandt, p. 473).

Calcium phosphates are used in baking acids, toothpastes, mineral supplements and stock feeds. $Ca(H_2PO_4)_2$ was introduced as a leavening acid in the late nineteenth century (to replace "cream of tartar" $KHC_4H_4O_6$) but the monohydrate (introduced in the 1930s) finds more use today. "Straight baking powder", a mixture of $Ca(H_2PO_4)_2.H_2O$ and $NaHCO_3$ with some 40% starch coating, tends to produce CO_2 too quickly during dough mixing and so "combination baking

Panel continues

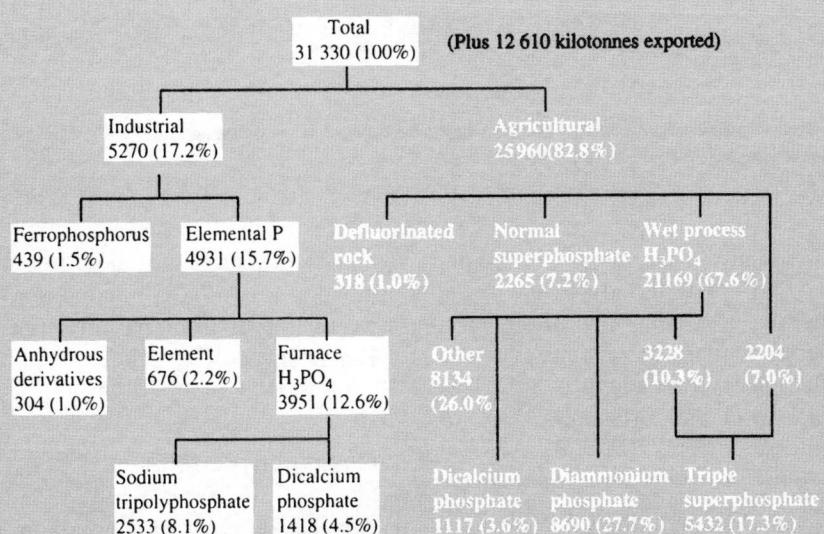

* Note that ammoniation of H_3PO_4 to give granulated or liquid ammonium phosphates consumes more phosphate rock in the USA than any other single end product.

powder", which also incorporates a slow-acting acid such as $NaAl(SO_4)_2$, is preferred. Nearly 90% of all US household baking powders now use such combinations, e.g.:

$$Ca(H_2PO_4)_2.H_2O + 2NaHCO_3 \longrightarrow 2CO_2 + 3H_2O + \text{'}Na_2Ca(HPO_4)_2\text{'}$$

$$NaAl(SO_4)_2 + 3NaHCO_3 \xrightarrow{H_2O} 3CO_2 + Al(OH)_3 + 2Na_2SO_4$$

A typical powder contains 28% $NaHCO_3$, 10.7% $Ca(H_2PO_4)_2.H_2O$, 21.4% $NaAl(SO_4)_2$ and 39.9% starch and the scale of manufacture approaches 10^5 tonnes pa.

In toothpastes, $CaHPO_4.2H_2O$ was first used to replace chalk as a mild abrasive and polishing agent in the early 1930s. It is still widely used provided the toothpaste does not also contain fluoride, since this would precipitate as CaF_2 and effectively eliminate the desired anion. Some 25 000 tonnes of $CaHPO_4.H_2O$ are used in this way annually in the USA and the compound typically comprises 50% by weight of the paste. The first important fluoride toothpaste contained 39% of the diphosphate $Ca_2P_2O_7$ which is the most insoluble and inert of all calcium phosphates. It is made by careful dehydration of $CaHPO_4.2H_2O$ at 150° and then above 400°. It was first used in Procter and Gamble's "Crest" which also contained 0.4% SnF_2 and 1% $Sn_2P_2O_7$.

Synthetic $Ca_5(PO_4)_3OH$ is added to table salt (1–2%) to impart free-flowing properties and it is likewise added to granulated sugar, baking powders and even fertilizers. It is prepared by adding H_3PO_4 to a slurry of hydrated lime — this is the reverse order of addition to that used for making $Ca(H_2PO_4)_2$ and $CaHPO_4$ since the aim is to deprotonate all three OH groups. The compound is extremely insoluble and precipitates as very fine particles (~0.5–3 μm diameter).

The idea of converting insoluble "tricalcium phosphate" or phosphate rock into soluble "monocalcium phosphate" $Ca(H_2PO_2)_2$ dates back to the 1830s when J. von Liebig observed that acidulated bones made good fertilizer. The limited supply of bones (including those from old battlefields!) was soon replaced by Suffolk coprolites and apatites, though the vast North African deposits were still unknown. The phosphate fertilizer industry originated in England (Lawes, 1843); it grew rapidly as shown by the dramatic increase in world production of phosphate rock, which leapt from 500 tonnes in 1847 to 500 kilotonnes in 1880, 3.1 million tonnes in 1900, and now exceeds 150 Mt (p. 476). This unprecedented demand for phosphatic fertilizers is, of course, closely related to the demand for food from an exploding world population of humans which reached 1 billion (10^9) in 1830, 2 billion in 1930, 3 billion in 1960, 4 billion in 1974 and will be over 8 billion by the end of the century.

"Superphosphate" is now made by the (highly exothermic) addition of H_2SO_4 to fine-ground phosphate rock:

$$2Ca_5(PO_4)_3F + 7H_2SO_4 + H_2O \longrightarrow 7CaSO_4 + 3Ca(H_2PO_4)_2.H_2O + 2HF$$

Panel continues

The CaSO$_4$ or its hydrate (gypsum) acts only as an unwanted diluent. Its presence can be avoided by using H$_3$PO$_4$ instead of H$_2$SO$_4$ for the acidulation, thus giving rise to "triple superphosphate"

$$Ca_5(PO_4)_3F + 7H_3PO_4 + H_2O \longrightarrow 5Ca(H_2PO_4)_2.H_2O + HF$$

Commercial triple superphosphate contains almost 3 times the amount of available (soluble) P$_2$O$_5$ as ordinary superphosphate, hence its name (45–50 wt% vs. 18–20 wt%).

which P–O is usually in the range 153 ± 3 pm and the angle O–P–O is usually in the range $109 \pm 5°$. Extensive H-bonding and M–O interactions frequently induce substantial deviations from a purely ionic formulation (p. 81). This trend continues with the orthophosphates of tervalent elements $M^{III}PO_4$ (M = B, Al, Ga, Cr, Mn, Fe) which all adopt structures closely related to the polymorphs of silica (p. 342). NaBePO$_4$ is similar, and YPO$_4$ adopts the zircon (ZrSiO$_4$) structure. The most elaborate analogy so far revealed is for AlPO$_4$ which can adopt each of the 6 main polymorphs of silica as indicated in the scheme below. The analogy covers not only the structural relations between the phases but also the sequence of transformation temperatures (°C) and the fact that the α–β-transitions occur readily whilst the others are sluggish (p. 343). Similarly, the orthophosphates of B, Ga and Mn are known in the β-quartz and the α- and β-cristobalite forms whereas FePO$_4$ adopts either the α- or β-quartz structure. Numerous hydrated forms are also known. The Al–PO$_4$–H$_2$O system is used industrially as the basis for many adhesives, binders and cements.[135] Novel chain

and sheet aluminium phosphate anions of composition [H$_2$AlP$_2$O$_8$] and [Al$_5$P$_4$O$_{16}$]$^{3-}$, respectively, have also recently been structurally characterized.[136]

Chain polyphosphates[23.64]

A rather different structure-motif is observed in the chain polyphosphates: these feature corner-shared {PO$_4$} tetrahedra as in the polyphosphoric acids (p. 522). The general formula for such anions is $[P_nO_{3n+1}]^{(n+2)-}$, of which the diphosphates, P$_2$O$_7^{4-}$, and tripolyphosphates, P$_3$O$_{10}^{5-}$, constitute the first two members. Chain polyphosphates have been isolated with n up to 10 and with n "infinite", but those of intermediate chain length ($10 < n < 50$) can only be obtained as glassy or amorphous mixtures. As the chain length increases, the ratio $(3n + 1)/n$ approaches 3.00 and the formula approaches that of the polymetaphosphates $[PO_3^-]_\infty$.

Diphosphates (pyrophosphates) are usually prepared by thermal condensation of dihydrogen

135 J. H. Morris, P. G. Perkins, A. E. A. Rose and W. E. Smith, *Chem. Soc. Revs.* **6**, 173–94 (1977).

136 J .M. Thomas *et al.*, *J. Chem. Soc., Chem. Commun.*, 1170–2 (1992), 929–31 and 1266–8 (1992). See also R. Kniep, *Angew. Chem. Int. Edn. Engl.* **25**, 525–34 (1986).

SiO$_2$ $\begin{cases} \text{quartz} \xrightleftharpoons{867°} \text{tridymite} \xrightleftharpoons{1470°} \text{cristobalite} \xrightleftharpoons{1713°} \text{melt} \\ \beta \xrightleftharpoons{573°} \alpha \quad \beta \xrightleftharpoons{117°} \alpha_1 \xrightleftharpoons{163°} \alpha_2 \quad \beta \xrightleftharpoons{220°} \alpha \end{cases}$

AlPO$_4$ $\begin{cases} \text{berlinite} \xrightleftharpoons{705°} \text{tridymite-form} \xrightleftharpoons{1025°} \text{cristobalite-form} \xrightleftharpoons{>1600°} \text{melt} \\ \beta \xrightleftharpoons{586°} \alpha \quad \beta \xrightleftharpoons{93°} \alpha_1 \xrightleftharpoons{130°} \alpha_2 \quad \beta \xrightleftharpoons{210°} \alpha \end{cases}$

phosphates or hydrogen phosphates:

$$2MH_2PO_4 \xrightarrow{\Delta} M_2H_2P_2O_7 + H_2O$$

$$2M_2HPO_4 \xrightarrow{\Delta} M_4P_2O_7 + H_2O$$

They can also be prepared in specialized cases by (a) metathesis, (b) the action of H_3PO_4 on an oxide, (c) thermolysis of a metaphosphate, (d) thermolysis of an orthophosphate, or (e) reductive thermolysis, e.g.:

(a) $Na_4P_2O_7 + 4AgNO_3$

$$\longrightarrow Ag_4P_2O_7\downarrow + 4NaNO_3$$

(b) $2H_3PO_4 + PbO_2 \longrightarrow PbP_2O_7\downarrow + 3H_2O$

(c) $\quad 4Cr(PO_3)_3 \xrightarrow{\Delta} Cr_4(P_2O_7)_3 + 3P_2O_5$

(d) $\quad 2Hg_3(PO_4)_2 \xrightarrow{\Delta} 2Hg_2P_2O_7 + 2Hg + O_2$

(e) $\quad 2FePO_4 + H_2 \longrightarrow Fe_2P_2O_7 + H_2O$

Many diphosphates of formula $M^{IV}P_2O_7$, M_2^{II}-P_2O_7 and hydrated $M_4^{I}P_2O_7$ are known and there has been considerable interest in the relative orientation of the two linked {PO_4} groups and in the P–O–P angle between them.[137] For small cations the 2 {PO_4} are approximately staggered whereas for larger cations they tend to be nearly eclipsed. The P–O–P angle is large and variable, ranging from $130°$ in $Na_4P_2O_7.10H_2O$ to $156°$ in α-$Mg_2P_2O_7$. The apparent colinearity in the higher-temperature (β) form of many diphosphates, which was previously ascribed to a P–O–P angle of $180°$, is now generally attributed to positional disorder. Bridging P–O distances are invariably longer than terminal P–O distances, typical values (for $Na_4P_2O_7.10H_2O$) being P–O_μ 161 pm, P–O_t 152 pm. Note that bridging can also be via a peroxo group as in ammonium peroxodiphosphate[138] which features the zig-zag anion $[O_3P-O-O-PO_3]^{4-}$ with P–O_μ 165.8 pm, P–O_t 150.8 pm and O–O

150.1 pm (cf. 145.3 pm in H_2O_2 and 148–150 pm in $S_2O_5^{2-}$).

As diphosphoric acid is tetrabasic, four series of salts are possible though not all are always known, even for simple cations. The most studied are those of Na, K, NH_4 and Ca, e.g.:

$Na_4P_2O_7.10H_2O$(mp 79.5°), $Na_4P_2O_7$(mp 985°)

$$Na_3HP_2O_7.9H_2O \xrightarrow{30-35°} Na_3HP_2O_7.H_2O$$

$$\xrightarrow{150°} Na_3HP_2O_7$$

$$Na_2H_2P_2O_7.6H_2O \xrightarrow{\sim27°} Na_2H_2P_2O_7$$

$NaH_3P_2O_7$(mp 185°)

Before the advent of synthetic detergents, $Na_4P_2O_7$ was much used as a dispersant for lime soap scum which formed in hard water, but it has since been replaced by the tripolyphosphate (see below). However, the ability of diphosphate ions to form a gel with soluble calcium salts has made $Na_4P_2O_7$ a useful ingredient for starch-type instant pudding which requires no cooking. The main application of $Na_2H_2P_2O_7$ is as a leavening acid in baking: it does not react with $NaHCO_3$ until heated, and so large batches of dough or batter can be made up and stored. $Ca_2P_2O_7$, because of its insolubility, inertness, and abrasive properties, is used as a toothpaste additive compatible with Sn^{II} and fluoride ions (see Panel on p. 525).

Of the tripolyphosphates only the sodium salt need be mentioned. It was introduced in the mid-1940s as a "builder" for synthetic detergents, and its production for this purpose is now measured in megatonnes per annum (see Panel on the next page). On the industrial scale $Na_5P_3O_{10}$ is usually made by heating an intimate mixture of powdered Na_2HPO_4 and NaH_2PO_4 of the required stoichiometry under carefully controlled conditions:

$$2Na_2HPO_4 + NaH_2PO_4 \longrightarrow Na_5P_3O_{10} + 2H_2O$$

The low-temperature form (I) converts to the high-temperature form (II) above $417°C$ and both forms react with water to give the crystalline hexahydrate. All three materials contain the

---

[137] G. M. CLARK and R. MORLEY, *Chem. Soc. Revs.* **5**, 269–95 (1976).

[138] W. P. GRIFFITH, R. D. POWELL and A. C. SKAPSKI, *Polyhedron* **7**, 1305–10 (1988).

Uses of Sodium Tripolyphosphate

Many synthetic detergents contain 25–45% $Na_5P_3O_{10}$ though the amount is lower in the USA than in Europe because of the problems of eutrophication in some areas (p. 478). It acts mainly as a water softener, by chelating and sequestering the Mg^{2+} and Ca^{2+} in hard water. Indeed, the formation constants of its complexes with these ions are nearly one million-fold greater than with Na^+: ($NaP_3O_{10}^{4-}$ pK ~2.8; $MgP_3O_{10}^{3-}$ pK ~8.6; $CaP_3O_{10}^{3-}$ pK ~8.1). In addition, $Na_5P_3O_{10}$ increases the efficiency of the surfactant by lowering the critical micelle concentration, and by its ability to suspend and peptize dirt particles by building up a large negative charge on the particles by adsorption; it also furnishes a suitable alkalinity for cleansing action without irritating eyes or skin and it provides effective buffering action at these pHs. The dramatic growth of synthetic detergent powders during the 1950s was accompanied by an equally dramatic drop in the use of soap powders.[11]

$Na_5P_3O_{10}$ is also used as a dispersing agent in clay suspensions used in oil-well drilling. Again, addition of <1% $Na_5P_3O_{10}$ to the slurries used in manufacturing cement and bricks enables much less water to be used to attain workability, and thus less to be removed during the setting or calcining processes.

tripolyphosphate ion $P_3O_{10}^{5-}$ with a *trans*-configuration of adjacent tetrahedra and a twofold symmetry axis; forms (I) and (II) differ mainly in the coordination of the sodium ions and the slight differences in the dimensions of the ion in the three crystals are probably within experimental error. Typical values are:

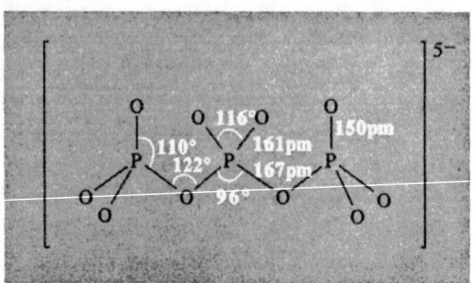

The complicated solubility relations, rates of hydrolysis, self-disproportionation and interconversion with other phosphates depends sensitively on pH, concentration, temperature and the presence of impurities.[139] Though of great interest academically and of paramount importance industrially these aspects will not be further considered here.[11,23,64,140] Triphosphates such as adenosine triphosphate (ATP) are also of vital importance in living organisms (see text books on biochemistry, and also ref. 141).

The stoichiometric formula of a chain-polyphosphate can sometimes be an unreliable guide to its structure. for example, the crystalline compound "$CaNb_2P_6O_{21}$" has been shown by X-ray crystal structure analysis to contain equal numbers of oxide(2−), diphosphate(4−) and tetraphosphate(6−) anions, i.e. $CaNb_2O[P_2O_7][P_4O_{13}]$.[142] By contrast, $CsM_2P_5O_{16}$ (M = V, Fe) does contain the anticipated homologous *catena*-pentaphosphate $[P_nO_{3n+1}]^{(n+2)-}$ anion (p. 512) with $n = 5$.[143]

Long-chain polyphosphates, $M^I_{n+2}P_nO_{3n+1}$, approach the limiting composition M^IPO_3 as $n \to \infty$ and are sometimes called linear metaphosphates to distinguish them from the cyclic metaphosphates of the same composition (p. 529). Their history extends back over 150 y to the time when Thomas Graham described the formation of a glassy sodium polyphosphate mixture now known as Graham's salt. Various heat treatments converted this to crystalline compounds known as Kurrol's salt, Maddrell's salt, etc., and it is now appreciated, as a result of X-ray crystallographic studies, that these and many related substances all feature unbranched chains of corner-shared {PO_4} units which differ only in the mutual orientations and

[139] G. P. HAIGHT, T. W. HAMBLEY, P. HENDRY, G. A. LAWRANCE and A. M. SARGESON, *J. Chem. Soc., Chem. Commun.*, 488–91 (1985), and references cited therein.

[140] E. J. GRIFFITH, *Pure Appl. Chem.* **44**, 173–200 (1975).

[141] I. S. KULAEV, *The Biochemistry of Inorganic Polyphosphates*, Wiley, Chichester, 1980, 225 pp.

[142] M.-T. AVERBUCH-POUCHOT, *Z. anorg. allg. Chem.* **545**, 118–24 (1987).

[143] B. KLINKERT and M. JANSEN, *Z. anorg. allg. Chem.* **567**, 87–94 (1988).

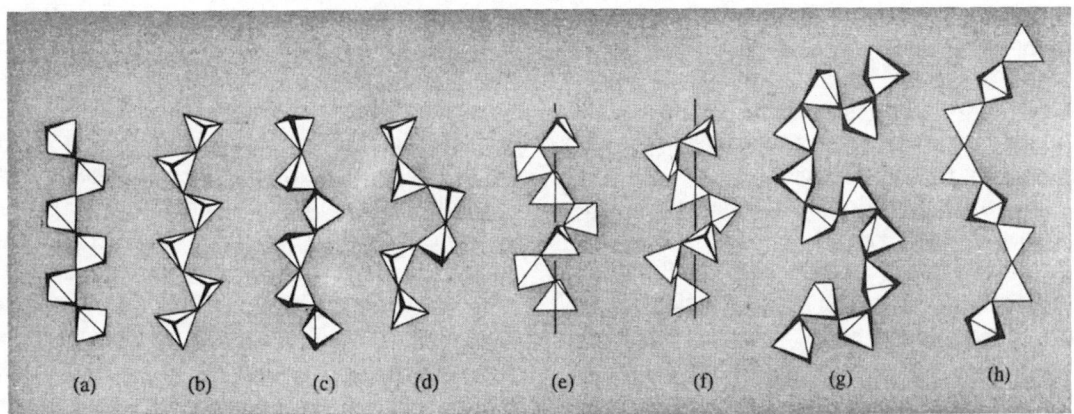

Figure 12.20   Types of polyphosphate chain configuration. The diagrams indicate the relative orientations of adjacent PO_4 tetrahedra, extended along the chain axes. (a) $(RbPO_3)_n$ and $(CsPO_3)_n$, (b) $(LiPO_3)_n$ low temp, and $(KPO_3)_n$, (c) $(NaPO_3)_n$ high-temperature Maddrell salt and $[Na_2H(PO_3)_3]_n$, (d) $[Ca(PO_3)_2]_n$ and $[Pb(PO_3)_2]_n$, (e) $(NaPO_3)_n$, Kurrol A and $(AgPO_3)_n$, (f) $(NaPO_3)_n$, Kurrol B, (g) $[CuNH_4(PO_3)_3]_n$ and isomorphous salts, (h) $[CuK_2(PO_3)_4]_n$ and isomorphous salts. Each crystalline form of Kurrol salt contains equal numbers of right-handed and left-handed spiralling chains.

repeat units of the constituent tetrahedra.[144] These, in turn, are dictated by the size and coordination requirements of the counter cations present (including H). Some examples are shown schematically in Fig. 12.20 and the geometric resemblance between these and many of the chain metasilicates (p. 350) should be noted. In most of these polyphosphates $P-O_\mu$ is $161 \pm 5\,pm$, $P-O_t$ $150 \pm 2\,pm$, $P-O_\mu-P$ $125-135°$ and O_t-P-O_t $115-120°$ (i.e. very similar to the dimensions and angles in the tripolyphosphate ion, p. 528).

The complex preparative interrelationships occurring in the sodium polyphosphate system are summarized in Fig. 12.21 (p. 531). Thus anhydrous NaH_2PO_4, when heated to $170°$ under conditions which allow the escape of water vapour, forms the diphosphate $Na_2H_2P_2O_7$, and further dehydration at $250°$ yields either Maddrell's salt (closed system) or the cyclic trimetaphosphate (water vapour pressure kept low). Maddrell's salt converts from the low-temperature to the high-temperature form above $300°$, and above $400°$ reverts to the cyclic

trimetaphosphate. The high-temperature form can also be obtained (via Graham's and Kurrol's salts) by fusing the cyclic trimetaphosphate (mp $526°C$) and then quenching it from $625°$ (or from $580°$ to give Kurrol's salt directly). All these linear polyphosphates of sodium revert to the cyclic trimetaphosphate on prolonged annealing at $\sim400°C$.

Fuller treatments of the phase relations and structures of polyphosphates, and their uses as glasses, ceramics, refractories, cements, plasters and abrasives, are available.[144,145]

Cyclo-*polyphosphoric acids and* cyclo-*polyphosphates* [146]

These compounds were formerly called metaphosphoric acids and metaphosphates but the IUPAC *cyclo-* nomenclature is preferred as being structurally more informative. The only

[144] J. MALING and F. HANIC, *Topics in Phosphorus Chemistry* **10**, 341–502 (1980).

[145] A. E. R. WESTMAN, *Topics in Phosphorus Chemistry* **9**, 231–405, 1977. A comprehensive account with 963 references.

[146] S. Y. KALLINEY, *Topics in Phosphorus Chemistry* **7**, 255–309, 1972.

two important acids in the series are *cyclo*-triphosphoric acid $H_3P_3O_9$ and *cyclo*-tetra-phosphoric acid $H_4P_4O_{12}$, but well-characterized salts are known with heterocyclic anions [*cyclo*-$(PO_3)_n]^{n-}$ ($n = 3$–8, 10),[147] and larger rings are undoubtedly present in some mixtures.

The structural relationship between the *cyclo*-phosphates and P_4O_{10} (p. 504) is shown schematically below. In P_4O_{10} all 10 P–O(–P) bridges are equivalent and hydrolytic cleavage of any one leads to "$H_2P_4O_{11}$" in which P–O(–P) bridges are now of two types. Cleavage of "type a" leads to *cyclo*-tetraphosphoric acid or its salts (as shown in the upper line of the scheme), whereas cleavage of any of the other bridges leads to a *cyclo*-triphosphate ring with a pendant –OP(O)OH group which can subsequently be hydrolysed off to leave $(HPO_3)_3$

or its salts (lower line of scheme). *Cyclo*-$(HPO_3)_4$ can, indeed, be made by careful hydrolysis of hexagonal P_4O_{10} with ice-water, and similar treatment with iced NaOH or $NaHCO_3$ gives a 75% yield of the corresponding salt *cyclo*-$(NaPO_3)_4$. The preparation of *cyclo*-$(NaPO_3)_3$ by controlled thermolytic dehydration of NaH_2PO_4 was mentioned in the preceding section and acidification yields *cyclo*-triphosphoric acid. The *cyclo*-$(PO_3)_3^{3-}$ anion adopts the chair configuration with dimensions as shown; *cyclo*-$(PO_3)_4^{4-}$ is also known in this configuration though this can be modified by changing the cation.

The crystal structure of the *cyclo*-hexaphosphate anion in $Na_6P_6O_{18}.6H_2O$ shows that all 6 P atoms are coplanar and that bond lengths are similar to those in the $P_3O_9^{3-}$ and $P_4O_{12}^{4-}$ anions. See ref. 147 for the structure of the hydrated *cyclo*-decaphosphate $K_{10}P_{10}O_{30}.4H_2O$. Higher *cyclo*-metaphosphates can be isolated by

[147] U. SCHÜLKE, M. T. AVERBUCH-POUCHOT and A. DURIF, *Z. anorg. allg. Chem.* **612**, 107–12 (1992).

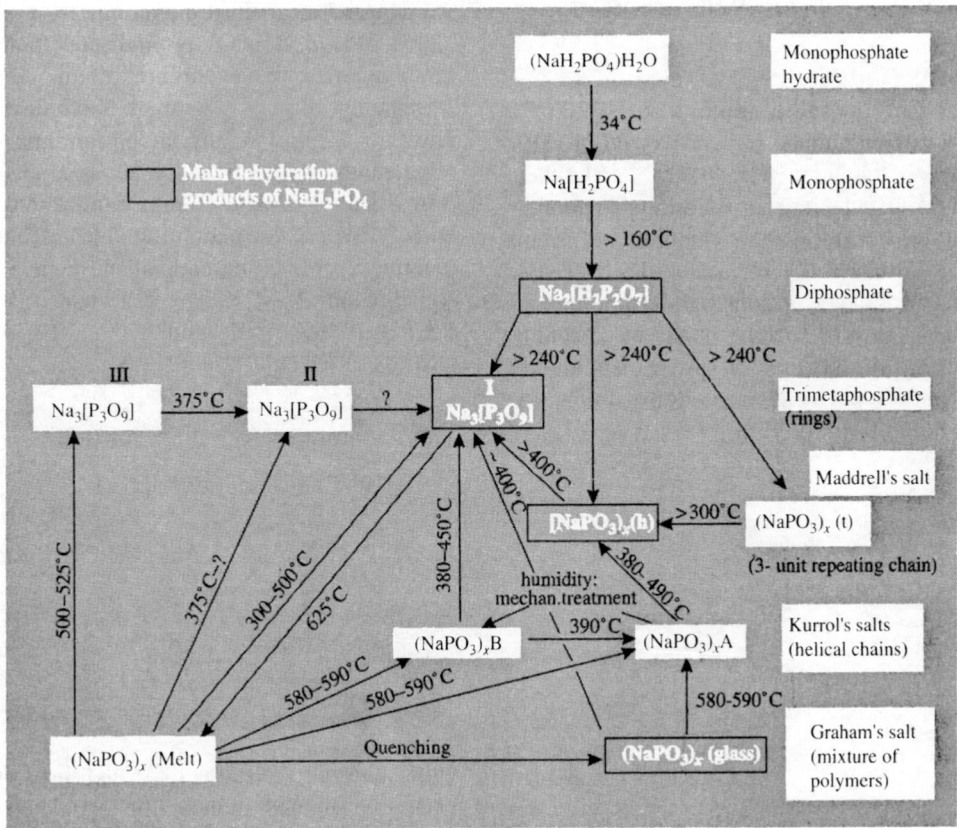

Figure 12.21 Interrelationship of metaphosphates. (From CIC, Vol. 2, p. 521.)

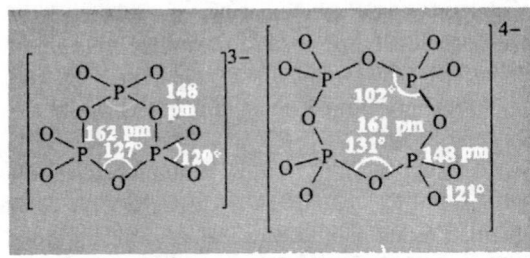

chromatographic separation from Graham's salt in which they are present to the extent of ~1%.

12.3.7 Phosphorus–nitrogen compounds

The P–N bond is one of the most intriguing in chemistry and many of its more subtle aspects

still elude a detailed and satisfactory description. It occurs in innumerable compounds, frequently of great stability, and in many of these the strength of the bond and the shortness of the interatomic distance have been interpreted in terms of "partial double-bond character". In fact, the conventional symbols P–N and P=N are more an aid to electron counting than a description of the bond in any given compound (see p. 538).

Many compounds containing the P–N link can be considered formally as derivatives of the oxoacids of phosphorus and their salts (pp. 510–31) in which there has been isoelectronic replacement of:

PH [or P(OH)] by $P(NH_2)$ or $P(NR_2)$;

P=O [or P=S] by P=NH or P=NR;

P–O–P by P–NH–P or P–NR–P, etc.[(148,149)]

Examples are phosphoramidic acid, $H_2NP(O)(OH)_2$; phosphordiamidic acid, $(H_2N)_2P(O)(OH)$; phosphoric triamide, $(H_2N)_3PO$; and their derivatives. There are an enormous number of compounds featuring the 4-coordinate group shown in structure (1) including the versatile nonaqueous solvent hexamethylphosphoramide $(Me_2N)_3PO$; this is readily made by reacting $POCl_3$ with $6Me_2NH$, and dissolves metallic Na to give paramagnetic blue solutions similar to those in liquid NH_3 (p. 77).

(1)

(2)

(3)

Another series includes the *cyclo*-metaphosphimic acids, which are tautomers of the *cyclo*-polyphosphazene hydroxides (p. 541). Similarly, halogen atoms in PX_3 or other P–X compounds can be successively replaced by the isoelectronic groups $-NH_2$, $-NHR$, $-NR_2$, etc., and sometimes a pair of halogens can be replaced by $=NH$ or $=NR$. These, in turn, can be used to prepare a large number of other derivatives as indicated schematically opposite for $P(NMe_2)_3^{(2)}$.

Although such compounds all formally contain P–N single bonds, they frequently display properties consistent with more extensive bonding. A particularly clear example is $PF_2(NMe_2)$

which features a short interatomic P–N distance and a *planar* N atom as indicated in the diagram below. (In the absence of this additional π bonding the P^{III}–N single-bond distance is close to 177 pm.) Again, the proton nmr of such compounds sometimes reveals restricted rotation about P–N at low temperatures and typical energy barriers to rotation (and coalescence temperatures of the non-equivalent methyl proton signals) are $PCl_2(NMe_2)$ 35 kJ mol^{-1} ($-120°$), $P(CF_3)_2(NMe_2)$ 38 kJ mol^{-1} ($-120°$), PClPh-(NMe_2) 50 kJ mol^{-1} ($-50°$).

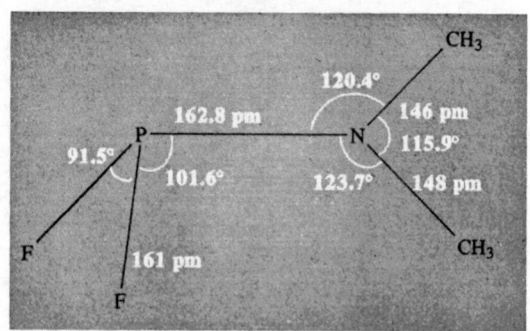

Other unusual P/N systems which have recently been investigated include the crystalline compound HPN_2, i.e. PN(NH), which is formed by ammonolysis of P_3N_5 at 580°C and which has a β-cristobalite (SiO_2) type structure;[(150)] PNO (cf. N_2O), which can be studied as a matrix-isolated species;[(151)] various phosphine azides, $RR'PN_3$, and their reactions;[(152)] and numerous substituted phosphonyl triphenylphosphazenes, $Ph_3P=N-PX_2$, (X=Cl, F, OPh, SEt, NEt_2, etc.).[(153)] The iminophosphenium ion, $[ArN\equiv P]^+$ (Ar = 2,4,6-$Bu^t_3C_6H_2$) has been obtained as its pale yellow $AlCl_4^-$ salt by reaction of the corresponding covalently bonded chloride, ArN=PCl, with $AlCl_3$; the ion is notable

[148] D. A. PALGRAVE, Section 28, pp. 760–815, in ref. 26
[149] M. L. NIELSEN, Chap. 5 in C. B. COLBURN (ed.), *Developments in Inorganic Nitrogen Chemistry*, Vol. 1, pp. 307–469, Elsevier, Amsterdam, 1966.

[150] W. SCHNICK and J. LÜCKE, *Z. anorg. allg. Chem.* **610**, 121–6 (1992).
[151] R. AHLRICHS, S. SCHUNK and H.-G. SCHNÖCKEL, *Angew. Chem. Int. Edn. Engl.* **27**, 421–2 (1988).
[152] J. BÖSKE, E. NIECKE, E. OCANDO-MAVEREZ, J.-P. MAJORAL and G. BERTAND, *Inorg. Chem.* **25**, 2695–8 (1986).
[153] L. RIESEL and R. FRIEBE, *Z. anorg. allg. Chem.* **604**, 85–91 (1991).

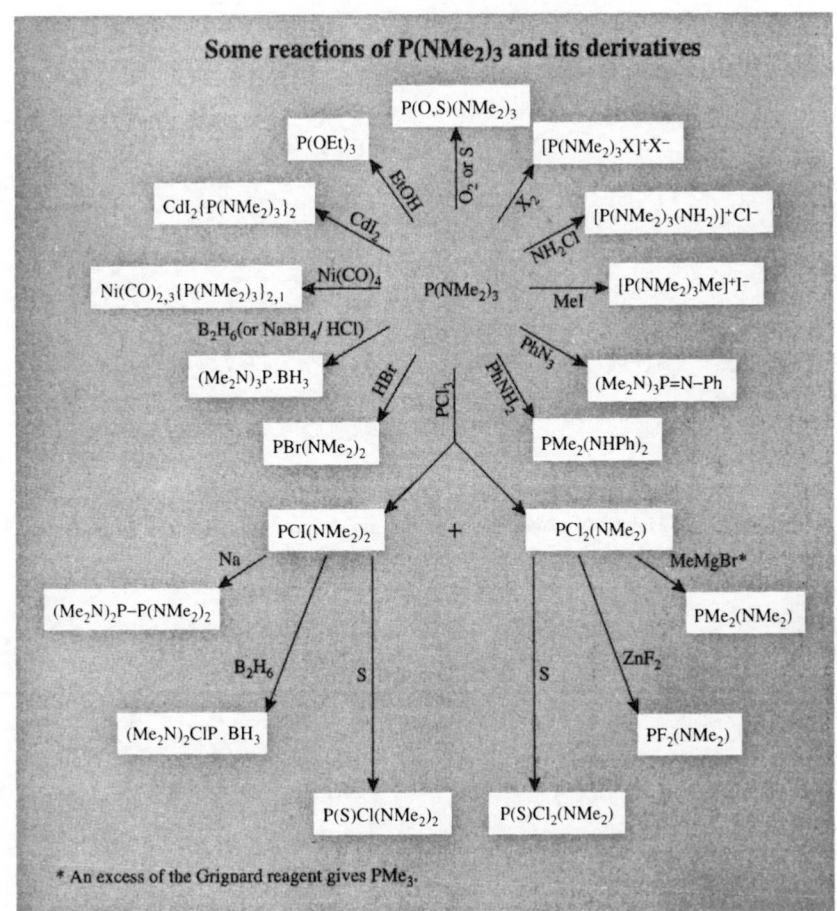

Some reactions of P(NMe₂)₃ and its derivatives

* An excess of the Grignard reagent gives PMe₃.

as the first stable species having a P≡N triple bond (P–N 148 pm, angle C–N–P 177°).[154] The coordination chemistry of phosphorane iminato complexes (containing the R_3PN^- ligand) of transition metals has been reviewed.[155]

Cyclophosphazanes

Many heterocyclic compounds contain formally single-bonded P–N groups, the simplest being the *cyclo*-diphosphazanes $(X_3PNR)_2$ and $\{X(O,S)PNR\}_2$. These contain P^V and have the structures shown in Fig. 12.22. A few

phosph(III)azane dimers are also known, e.g. $(RPNR')_2$. A more complex example, containing fused heterocycles of alternating P^{III} and N atoms, is the interesting hexamethyl derivative $P_4(NMe)_6$ mp 122°. This stable compound (Fig. 12.23a) is readily obtained by reacting PCl_3 with $6MeNH_2$; it is isoelectronic with and isostructural with P_4O_6 (p. 504) and undergoes many similar reactions. The stoichiometrically similar compound $P_4(NPr^i)_6$ can be prepared in the non-adamantane-type structure shown in Fig. 12.23b, though it converts to structure-type a on being heated at 157° for 12 days.[156] A different sequence of atoms occurs in $P_2(NMe)_6$

[154] E. NIECKE, M. NIEGER and F. REICHERT *Angew. Chem. Int. Edn. Engl.* **27**, 1715–6 (1988).

[155] K. DEHNICKE and J. STRÄHLE, *Polyhedron* **8**, 707–26 (1989).

[156] O. J. SCHERER, K. ANDRES, C. KRÜGER, Y.-H. TSAY and G. WOLMERSHÄUSER, *Angew. Chem. Int. Edn. Engl.* **19**, 571–2 (1980).

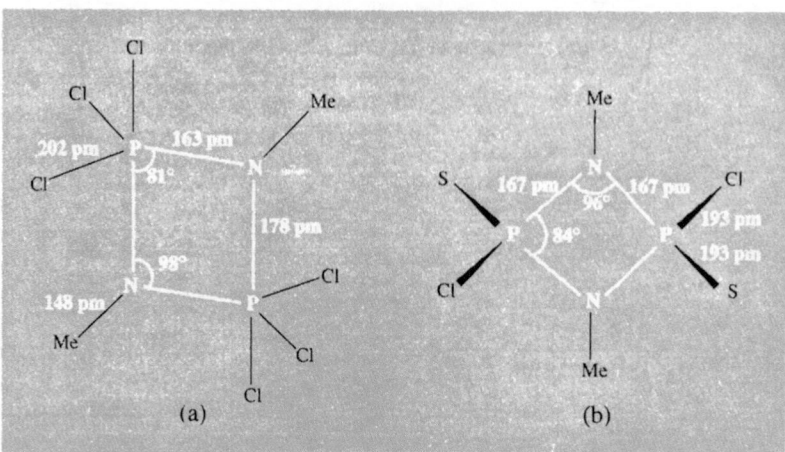

Figure 12.22   Structures of (a) (Cl$_3$PNMe)$_2$, and (b) {Cl(S)PNMe}$_2$. Note the difference in length of the axial P–N and equatorial P–N bonds (and of the axial and equatorial P–Cl bonds) about the trigonal bipyramidal P atoms in (a).

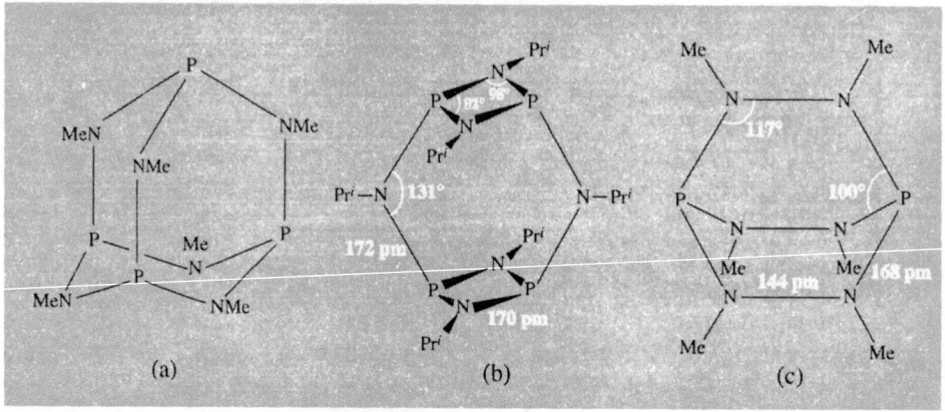

Figure 12.23   Structures of (a) P$_4$(NMe)$_6$, (b) P$_4$(NPr^i)$_6$, and (c) P$_2$(NMe)$_6$ (see text).

(Fig. 12.23c) and many other "saturated" hetero-cycles featuring either P^{III} or P^V have been made. A typical example, made by slow addition of PCl$_3$ to PhNH$_2$ in toluene at 0°, is [PhNHP$_2$(NPh)$_2$]$_2$NPh; the crystal structure of the 1:1 solvate of this compound with CH$_2$Cl$_2$ (mp 250°) reveals that all N atoms are essentially planar with distances to P as indicated in the following diagram.[157]

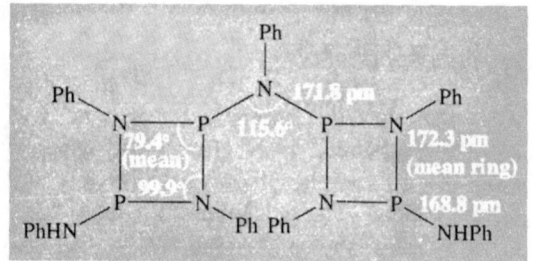

Phosphazenes

Formally "unsaturated" PN compounds are called phosphazenes and contain P^V in the

[157] M. L. THOMPSON, R. C. HALTIWANGER, and A. D. NORMAN, *J. Chem. Soc., Chem. Commun.*, 647–8 (1979).

grouping $\diagup$ P=N–. A few phosph(III)azenes are also known. Phosphazenes can be classified into monophosphazenes (e.g. X_3P=NR), diphosphazenes (e.g. X_3P=N–P(O)X_2), polyphosphazenes containing $2,3,4,\ldots\infty$ –X_2P=N– units, and the *cyclo*-polyphosphazenes $[-X_2P$=N–$]_n$, $n = 3,4,5\ldots 17$.

Monophosphazenes, particularly those with organic substituents, R_3P=NR′, derive great interest from being the N analogues of phosphorus ylides R_3P=CR_2 (p. 545). They were first made by H. Staudinger in 1919 by reacting an organic azide such as PhN_3 with PR_3 (R=Cl, OR, NR_2, Ar, etc.), e.g.:

$$PPh_3 + PhN_3 \longrightarrow N_2 + Ph_3P{=}NPh; \quad mp\ 132°$$

More recently they have been made via a reaction associated with the name of A. V. Kirsanov (1962), e.g.:

$$Ph_3PCl_2 + PhNH_2 \longrightarrow Ph_3P{=}NPh + 2HCl$$

As expected, the P–N distance is short and the angle at N is $\sim 120°$, e.g. (a) and (b) above. Over 600 such compounds are now known, especially those with the Cl_3P=N— group.[158]

Diphosphazenes can be made by reacting PCl_5 with NH_4Cl in a chlorohydrocarbon solvent under mild conditions:

$$3PCl_5 + NH_4Cl \xrightarrow{\text{solvent}} 4HCl$$
$$+ [Cl_3P{=}N{-}PCl_3]^+PCl_6^-; \quad mp\ 310°$$
$$\downarrow {\scriptstyle NH_4Cl}$$
$$4HCl + [Cl_3P{=}N{-}PCl_2{=}N{-}PCl_3]^+Cl^-$$

The inverse of these compounds are the phosphadiazene cations, prepared by halide ion abstraction from diaminohalophosphoranes in CH_2Cl_2 or SO_2 solution, e.g.:

$$(R_2N)_2PCl + AlCl_3 \longrightarrow [(R_2N)_2P]^+[AlCl_4]^-$$

An X-ray crystal structure of the Pr^i_2N-derivative shows the presence of a bent, 2-coordinate P atom, equal P–N distances, and accurately planar 3-coordinate N atoms as in (c) above.[159] In liquid ammonia ammonolysis also occurs:

$$2PCl_5 + 16NH_3(\text{liq.}) \longrightarrow$$
$$[(H_2N)_3P{=}N{-}P(NH_2)_3]^+Cl^- + 9NH_4Cl$$

The P=N and P–N bonds are equivalent in these compounds and they could perhaps better be written as $[X_3P\stackrel{\cdots}{\cdots}N\stackrel{\cdots}{\cdots}PX_3]^+$, etc. Like the parent phosphorus pentahalides (p. 498), these diphosphazenes can often exist in ionic and covalent forms and they are part of a more extended group of compounds which can be classified into several general series $Cl(Cl_2PN)_nPCl_4$, $[Cl(Cl_2PN)_nPCl_3]^+Cl^-$,

[158] M. BERMANN, *Topics in Phosphorus Chemistry* **7**, 311–78, 1972.

[159] A. H. COWLEY, M. C. CASHNER and J. S. SZOBOTA, *J. Am. Chem. Soc.* **100**, 7784–6 (1978).

$$
\begin{array}{ccc}
& \underset{\underset{Cl}{|}}{\overset{\overset{Cl}{|}}{Cl-P}}=N-PCl_2 & \underset{\underset{Cl}{|}}{\overset{\overset{Cl}{|}}{Cl-P}}=N-\underset{\underset{Cl}{|}}{\overset{\overset{Cl}{|}}{P}}=N-PCl_2 \\
\end{array}
$$

(a)   (b)

(c)

$[Cl(Cl_2PN)_nPCl_3]^+PCl_6{}^-$, $\quad Cl(Cl_2PN)_nPOCl_2$, etc., where $n = 0, 1, 2, 3\ldots$. Some examples of the first series are PCl_5 (i.e. $n = 0$), P_2NCl_7 (a), $P_3N_2Cl_9$ (b), and $P_4N_3Cl_{11}$ (c) (above).

Some of these can exist in the ionic form represented by the second series (d):

$$
[\cdots\cdots\overset{\overset{Cl}{|}}{\underset{\underset{Cl}{|}}{P}}-Cl]^+Cl^- \qquad [Cl(-\overset{\overset{Cl}{|}}{P}=N-)_4\underset{\underset{Cl}{|}}{\overset{\overset{Cl}{|}}{P}}-Cl]^+PCl_6{}^-
$$

(d)   (e)

Likewise, the third series runs from $n = 0$ (i.e. $PCl_4{}^+PCl_6{}^-$) through P_3NCl_{12}, $P_4N_2Cl_{14}$, and $P_5N_3Cl_{16}$ to $P_6N_4Cl_{18}$ (e). In the limit, polymeric phosphazene dichlorides are formed $(-NPCl_2-)_n$, where n can exceed 10^4 and these polyphosphazenes and their *cyclo*-analogues form by far the most extensive range PN compounds.

Polyphosphazenes

The grouping

$$
-N=\overset{\overset{R}{|}}{\underset{\underset{R}{|}}{P}}- \quad \text{is isoelectronic with the}
$$

silicone grouping $-O-\overset{\overset{R}{|}}{\underset{\underset{R}{|}}{Si}}-$ (p. 364)

and, after the silicones, the polyphosphazenes form the most extensive series of covalently bonded polymers with a non-carbon skeleton. This section will describe their

preparation, structure, bonding and potential applications.[2,8,160,161]

Preparation and structure. Polyphosphazenes have a venerable history. $(NPCl_2)_n$ oligomers were first made in 1834 by J. von Liebig and F. Wöhler who reacted PCl_5 with NH_3, but their stoichiometry and structure were not elucidated until much later. The fluoro analogues $(NPF_2)_n$ were first made in 1956 and the bromo compounds $(NPBr_2)_n$ in 1960. The synthesis of $(NPCl_2)_n$ was much improved by R. Schenk and G. Römer in 1924 and their method remains the basis for present-day production on both the laboratory and industrial scales:

$$
n\,PCl_5 + n\,NH_4Cl \xrightarrow[120-150°]{\text{solvent}} (NPCl_2)_n + 4n\,HCl
$$

Appropriate solvents are 1,1,2,2-tetrachloroethane (bp 146°), PhCl (bp 132°) and 1,2-dichlorobenzene (bp 179°). By varying the conditions, yields of the cyclic trimer or tetramer and other oligomers can be optimized and the compounds then separated by fractionation. Highly polymeric $(NPCl_2)_\infty$ can be made by heating *cyclo*-$(NPCl_2)_3$ to 150–300°, though heating to 350° induces depolymerization. Polycyclic compounds are rarely obtained in

---

[160] H. R. ALLCOCK, *Phosphorus Nitrogen Compounds*, Academic Press, New York, 1972, 498 pp.; H. R. ALLCOCK, *Chem. Rev.* **72**, 315–56 (1972) (475 refs.). H. R. ALLCOCK, Chap. 3 in A. H. COWLEY (ed.) *Rings, Clusters and Polymers of the Main Group Elements*, ACS Symposium Series No. **282**, Washington, DC, 49–67 (1982). H. R. ALLCOCK in J. E. MARK, R. WEST and H. R. ALLCOCK, *Inorganic Polymers*, Prentice Hall, 1991, 304 pp. H. R. ALLCOCK, Chap. 9 in R. STEUDEL (ed.) *The Chemistry of Inorganic Ring Systems*, Elsevier, Amsterdam, 145–69 (1992).

[161] S. S. KRISNAMURTHY, A. C. SAU and M. WOODS, *Adv. Inorg. Chem. Radiochem.* **21**, 41–112 (1978) (499 refs.).

these preparations, one exception being $N_7P_6Cl_9$, mp 237.5°, which can be obtained in modest yields from the direct thermolytic reaction of PCl_5 and NH_4Cl. The tricyclic structure is strongly distorted from planarity though the central NP_3 group features an accurately planar 3-coordinate N atom with much longer N–P bonds than those in the peripheral macrocycle. The 2 sorts of P–Cl bonds are also noticeably different in length and the 3 central Cl atoms are all on one side of the NP_3 plane with ∠NPCl 104°.

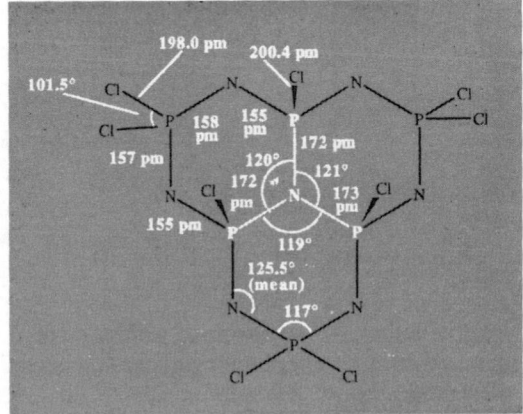

Many details of the preparative reaction mechanism remain unclear but it is thought that NH_4Cl partly dissociates into NH_3 and HCl, and that PCl_5 reacts in its ionic form $PCl_4^+PCl_6^-$ (p. 499). Nucleophilic attack by NH_3 on PCl_4^+ then occurs with elimination of HCl and the $\{HN{=}PCl_3\}$ attacks a second PCl_4^+ to give $[Cl_3P{=}N{-}PCl_3]^+$ and HCl. After 1 h the major (insoluble) intermediate product is $[Cl_3P{=}N{-}PCl_3]^+PCl_6^-$ (i.e. P_3NCl_{12}, p. 536) and this then slowly reacts with more NH_3 to give HCl and $\{Cl_3P{=}N{-}PCl_2{=}NH\}$, etc. It is probable that NH_4Br and $PBr_4^+Br^-$ react similarly to give $(NPBr_2)_n$ but NH_4F fluorinates PCl_5 to NH_4PF_4 and the fluoroanalogues $(NPF_2)_n$ are best prepared by fluorinating $(NPCl_2)_n$ with KSO_2F/SO_2 (i.e. KF in liquid SO_2). Similarly, standard substitution reactions lead to many derivatives in which all (or some) of the Cl atoms are replaced by OMe, OEt, OCH_2CF_3, OPh, NHPh, NMe_2, NR_2, R, Ar, etc. Partial

replacement leads to geminal derivatives (in which both Cl atoms on 1 P atom are replaced) and to non-geminal derivatives which, in turn, can exist as *cis*- or *trans*- isomers.

The cyclic trimer $(NPF_2)_3$, mp 28°, has an accurately planar 6-membered ring (D_{3h} symmetry) in which all 6 P–N distances are equal (156 pm) and the angles NPN and PNP are all 120 ±1°. Most other trimers are also more-or-less planar with equal P–N distances: for example, $(NPCl_2)_3$ is almost planar (pseudo-chair with P–N 158 pm, P–Cl 197 pm, ∠NPN 118.4°, ∠PNP 121.4°, ∠ClPCl 102°. Perhaps surprisingly, the cyclic tetramer $(NPF_2)_4$, mp 30.4°, is also a planar heterocycle (D_{4h} symmetry) with even shorter P–N bonds (151 pm) and with ring angles of 122.7° and 147.4° at P and N respectively. However, other conformations are found in other derivatives, e.g. chair (C_{2h}), saddle (D_{2d}), boat (S_4), crown tetrameric (C_{4v}) and hybrid. Thus $(NPCl_2)_4$ exists in the metastable K form (in which it has the boat conformation) and the stable T form (chair configuration) as shown in Fig. 12.24. The remarkable diversity of molecular conformations observed for the 8-membered heterocycle $\{P_4N_4\}$ suggests that the particular structure adopted in each case results from a delicate balance of intra- and inter-molecular forces including the details of skeletal bonding, the orientation of substituents and their polar and steric nature, crystal-packing effects, etc. The mps for various series of *cyclo*-$(NPX_2)_n$ frequently show an alternation, with values for n even being greater than those for adjacent n odd. Some examples are in Fig. 12.25. The crystal structures of the four compounds $(NPMe_2)_{9-12}$ have recently been determined.[162]

Bonding. All phosphazenes, whether cyclic or chain, contain the formally unsaturated

group   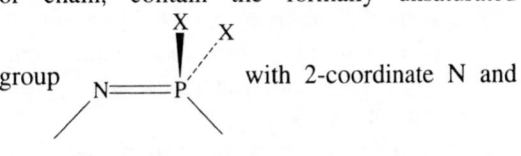   with 2-coordinate N and

[162] R. T. OAKLEY, S. J. RETTIG, N. L. PADDOCK and J. TROTTER, *J. Am. Chem. Soc.* **107**, 6923–36 (1985).

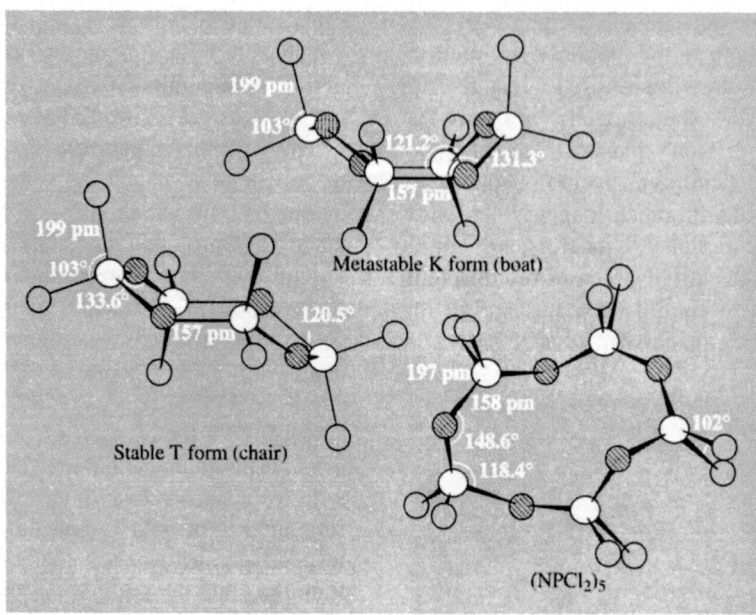

Figure 12.24   Molecular structure and dimensions of the two forms of $(NPCl_2)_4$ and of $(NPCl_2)_5$.

4-coordinate P. The experimental facts that have to be interpreted by any acceptable theory of bonding are:

(i) the rings and chains are very stable;

(ii) the skeletal interatomic distances are equal around the ring (or along the chain) unless there is differing substitution at the various P atoms;

(iii) the P–N distances are shorter than expected for a covalent single bond (~177 pm) and are usually in the range 158 ± 2 pm (though bonds as short as 147 pm occur in some compounds);

(iv) the N–P–N angles are usually in the range 120 ± 2° but the P–N–P angles in various compounds span the range from 120–148.6°;

(v) skeletal N atoms are weakly basic and can be protonated or form coordination complexes, especially when there are electron-releasing groups on P;

(vi) unlike many aromatic systems the phosphazene skeleton is hard to reduce electrochemically;

(vii) spectral effects associated with organic π-systems (such as the bathochromic ultra-violet shift that accompanies increased electron delocalization) are not found.

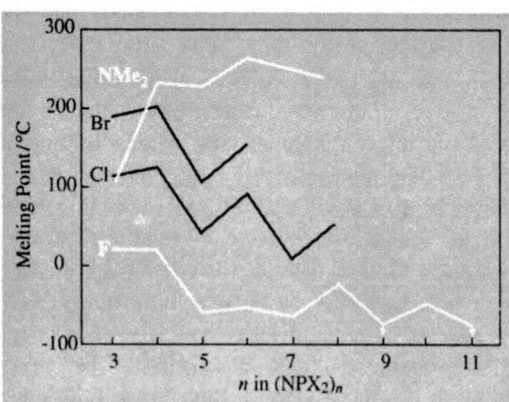

Figure 12.25   Melting points of various series of *cyclo*-polyphosphazenes $(NPX_2)_n$ showing the higher values for n even.

In short, the bonding in phosphazenes is not adequately represented by a sequence of alternating double and single bonds –N═P–N═P– yet it

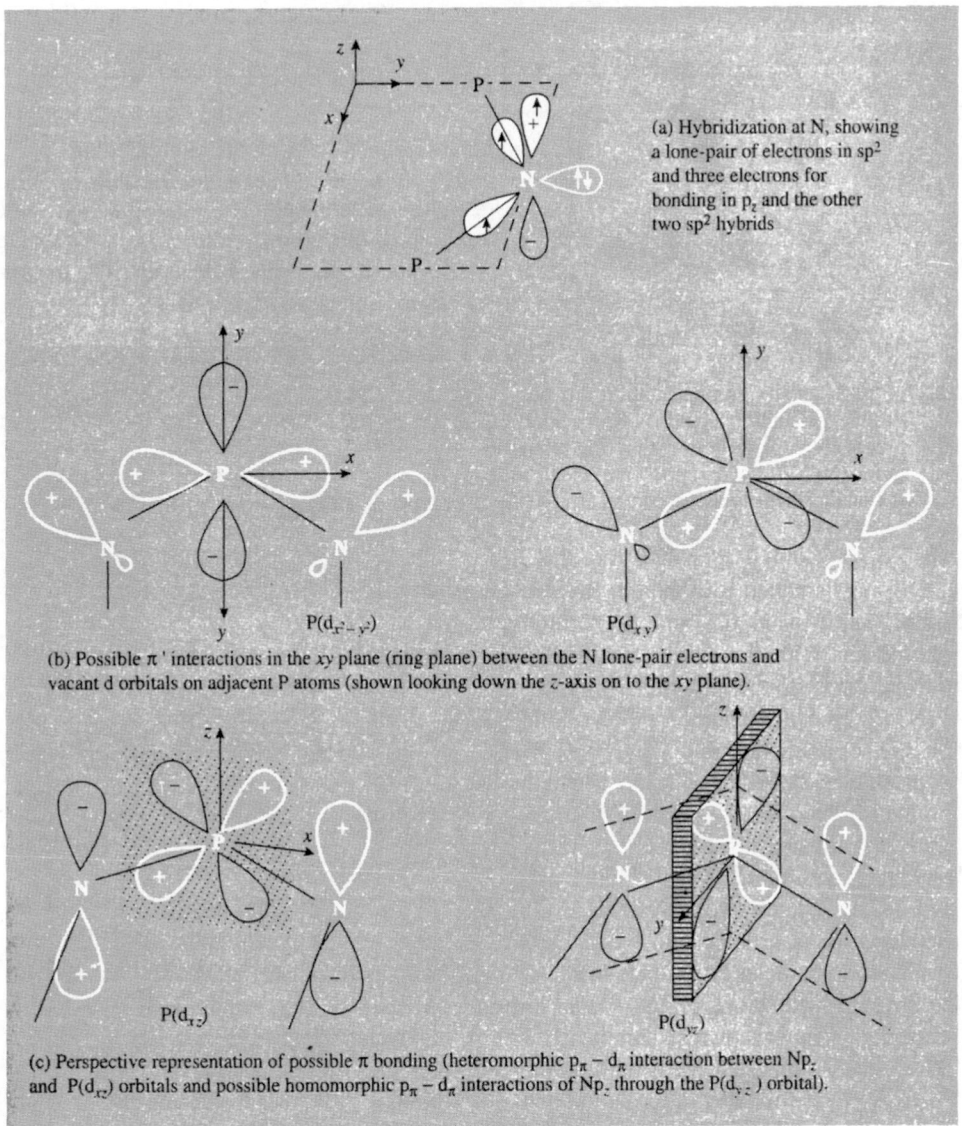

(a) Hybridization at N, showing a lone-pair of electrons in sp^2 and three electrons for bonding in p$_z$ and the other two sp^2 hybrids

(b) Possible π' interactions in the *xy* plane (ring plane) between the N lone-pair electrons and vacant d orbitals on adjacent P atoms (shown looking down the *z*-axis on to the *xy* plane).

P(d$_{x^2-y^2}$)   P(d$_{xy}$)

(c) Perspective representation of possible π bonding (heteromorphic p$_\pi$ – d$_\pi$ interaction between Np$_z$ and P(d$_{xz}$) orbitals and possible homomorphic p$_\pi$ – d$_\pi$ interactions of Np$_z$ through the P(d$_{yz}$) orbital).

P(d$_{xz}$)   P(d$_{yz}$)

Figure 12.26   A possible description of bonding in phosphazenes.

differs from aromatic σ–π system in which there is extensive electron delocalization via p$_\pi$–p$_\pi$ bonding. The possibility of p$_\pi$–d$_\pi$ bonding in N–P systems has been considered by many authors since the mid-1950s but there is still no consensus, and for nearly every argument that can be mounted in favour of P(3d)-orbital contributions another can be raised against it. It seems generally agreed that 2 electrons on

N occupy an sp^2 lone-pair in the plane of the ring (or the plane of the local PNP triangle) as in Fig. 12.26a. The situation at P is less clear mainly because of uncertainties concerning the d-orbital energies and the radial extent (size) of these orbitals in the *bonding situation* (as distinct from the free atom). In so far as symmetry is concerned, the sp^2 lone-pair on each N can be involved in coordinate bonding in the *xy* plane

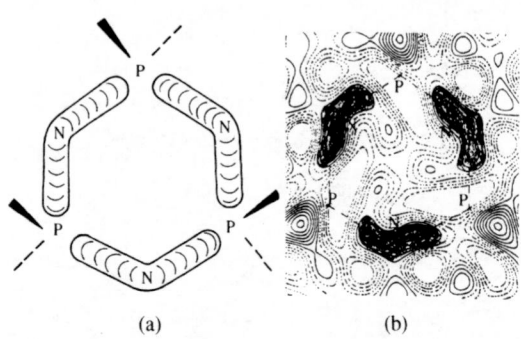

(a)   (b)

Figure 12.27 (a) Schematic representation of possible 3-centre islands of π bonding above and below the ring plane for $(NPX_2)_3$. (b) experimental electron bonding density (see text).

to "vacant" $d_{x^2-y^2}$ and d_{xy} orbitals on the P (Fig. 12.26b); this is called π'-bonding. Involvement of the out-of-plane d_{xz} and d_{yz} orbitals on the phosphorus with the singly occupied p_z orbital on N gives rise to the possibility of heteromorphic (N–P) "pseudoaromatic" p_π–d_π bonding (with d_{xz}), or homomorphic (N–N) p_π–p_π bonding (through d_{yz}) as in Fig. 12.26c. The controversy hinges in part on the relative contributions of the π' in-plane and of the two π out-of-plane interactions; approximately equal contributions from these latter two π systems would tend to separate the π orbitals into localized 3-centre islands of π character interrupted at each P atom, and broad delocalization effects would not then be expected. This is shown schematically in Fig. 12.27(a) and is consistent with the bonding electron density (b) as found by deformation density studies on the benzene clathrate of hexa(1-aziridinyl)cyclotriphosphazene, $2(\overline{CH_2CH_2N})_6$-$P_3N_3.C_6H_6$.[163] The possibility of exocyclic π bonding between $P(d_{z^2})$ and appropriate orbitals on the substituents X has also been envisaged.

Reactions. The N atom in *cyclo*-polyphosphazenes can act as a weak Brønsted base (proton acceptor) towards such strong acids as HF

and $HClO_4$; compounds with alkyl or NR_2 substituents on P are more basic than the halides, as expected, and their adducts with HCl have been well characterized. There is usually a substantial lengthening of the two N–P bonds adjacent to the site of protonation and a noticeable contraction of the next-nearest N–P bonds. For example, the relevant distances in $[HN_3P_3Cl_2(NHPr^i)_4]Cl$ and the parent compound are:[164]

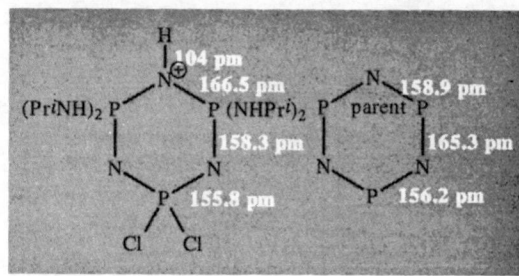

Typical basicities (pK'_a measured against $HClO_4$ in $PhNO_2$) for ring-N protonation are:

$N_3P_3(NHMe)_6$	$N_3P_3(NEt_2)_6$	$N_3P_3Et_6$
8.2	8.2	6.4

$N_3P_3Ph_6$	$N_3P_3(OEt)_6$	*trans*-$N_3P_3Cl_3(NMe_2)_3$
1.5	−0.2	−5.4

Cyclo-polyphosphazenes can also act as Lewis bases (N donor-ligands) to form complexes such as $[TiCl_4(N_3P_3Me_6)]$, $[SnCl_4(N_3P_3Me_6)]$, $[AlBr_3(N_3P_3Br_6)]$ and $[2AlBr_3.(N_3P_3Br_6)]$. Not all such adducts are necessarily ring-N donors and the 1:1 adduct of $(NPCl_2)_3$ with $AlCl_3$ is thought to be a chloride ion donor, $[N_3P_3Cl_5]^+$-$[AlCl_4]^-$. By contrast, the complex $[Pt^{II}Cl_2(\eta^2$-$N_4P_4Me_8)].MeCN$ features transannular bridging of 2 N atoms by the $PtCl_2$ moiety.[165] An intriguing example of a *cyclo*-polyphosphazene acting as a multidentate macrocyclic ligand occurs in the bright orange complex formed when $N_6P_6(NMe_2)_{12}$ reacts with equal amounts of $CuCl_2$ and $CuCl$. The crystal structure of

[163] T. S. CAMERON and B. BORECKA, *Phosphorus, Sulfur, Silicon and Related Elements,* **64**, 121–8 (1992).

[164] N. V. MANI and A. J. WAGNER, *Acta Cryst.* **27B**, 51–8 (1971).

[165] J. P. O'BRIEN, R. W. ALLEN and H. R. ALLCOCK, *Inorg. Chem.* **18**, 2230–5 (1979).

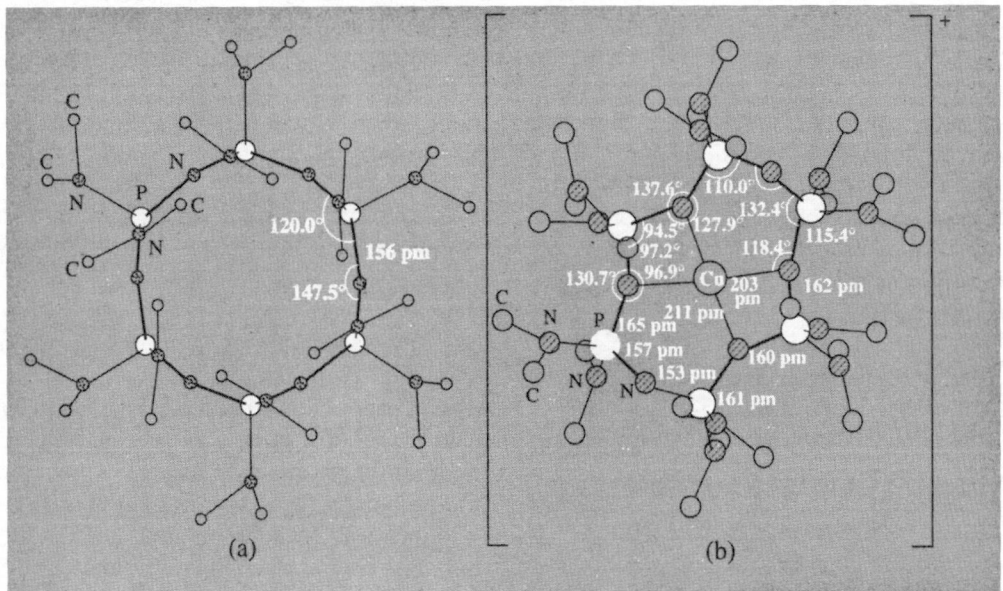

Figure 12.28 Structure of (a) the free ligand $N_6P_6(NMe_2)_{12}$, and (b) the η^4 complex cation $[CuCl\{N_6P_6(NMe_2)_{12}\}]^+$ showing changes in conformation and interatomic distances in the phosphazene macrocycle. The Cl is obscured beneath the Cu and can be regarded as occupying either the apical position of a square pyramid or, since ∠N(1)-Cu-N(1′) is large (160.9°), an equatorial position of a distorted trigonal bipyramid. Note that coordination tightens the ring, already somewhat crowded in the uncomplexed state, the mean angles at P being reduced from 120.0° to 107.5°, and the mean angles at N being reduced from 147.5° to 133.6°. The lengthening of the 8 P–N bonds contiguous to the 4 donor N atoms from 156 to 162 pm is significant, the other P–N distances (mean 156 pm) remaining similar to those in the free ligand.

the resulting $[N_6P_6(NMe_2)_{12}CuCl]^+[CuCl_2]^-$ has been determined (Fig. 12.28b) and detailed comparison with the conformation and interatomic distances in the parent heterocycle (Fig. 12.28a) gives important clues as to the relative importance of the various π and π' bonding interactions involving N (and P) atoms.[166] Incidentally, the compound also affords the first example of the linear 2-coordinate Cu^I complex $[CuCl_2]^-$. The related (and more extensive) organometallic chemistry of the phosphazenes has been reviewed.[167]

As P is isoelectronic with N, it has been found possible to prepare 8-membered diazahexaphos-

phocins such as $\overline{NPPh_2PPPh_2NPPh_2PPPh_2}$, analogous to $(NPPh_2)_4$.[168] The two subrogated **P** atoms can chelate to $PdCl_2$ to form a square planar complex.[169]

Many of the cyclic and chain dichloro derivatives $(NPCl_2)_n$ can be hydrolysed to n-basic acids and the lower members form well-defined salts frequently in the tautomeric metaphosphimic-acid form, e.g.:

$$
\left[\begin{array}{c} QH \quad OH \\ \diagup \\ N{=}P \\ \diagup \quad \diagdown \end{array}\right]_{3,4}
\rightleftharpoons
\left[\begin{array}{c} H \quad O \quad OH \\ | \quad || \\ N{-}P \\ \diagup \quad \diagdown \end{array}\right]_{3,4}
$$

[166] W. C. MARSH, N. L. PADDOCK, C. J. STEWART and J. TROTTER, *J. Chem. Soc., Chem. Commun.*, 1190–1 (1970).
[167] H. R. ALLCOCK, J. L. DESORCIE and G. H. RIDING, *Polyhedron* **6**, 119–57 (1987).

[168] A. SCHMIDPETER and G. BURGET, *Angew. Chem. Int. Edn. Engl.* **24**, 580–1 (1985).
[169] A. SCHMIDPETER, F. STEINMÜLLER and W. S. SHELDRICK, *Z. anorg. allg. Chem.* **579**, 158–72 (1989).

The dihydrate of the tetramer is particularly stable and is, in fact, the bishydroxonium salt of tetrametaphosphimic acid $[H_3O]_2^+[(NH)_4P_4O_6(OH)_2]^{2-}$ the anion of which has a boat configuration and is linked by short H bonds (246 pm) into a two-dimensional sheet (Fig. 12.29). The related salts $M_4^I[NHPO_2)_4].nH_2O$ show considerable variation in conformation of the tetrametaphosphimate anion, as do the 8-membered heterocyclic tetraphosphazenes $(NPX_2)_4$ (p. 537), e.g.

[NH$_4$]$_4$[N$_4$H$_4$P$_4$O$_8$].2H$_2$O   boat conformation

K$_4$[N$_4$H$_4$P$_4$O$_8$].4H$_2$O   chair conformation

Cs$_4$[N$_4$H$_4$P$_4$O$_8$].6H$_2$O   saddle conformation.

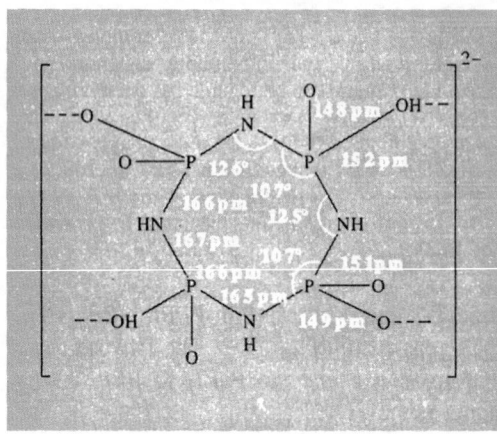

Figure 12.29 Schematic representation of the boat-shaped anion $[(NH)_4P_4O_6(OH)_2]^{2-}$ showing important dimensions and the positions of H bonds.

Applications. Many applications have been proposed for polyphosphazenes, particularly the non-cyclic polymers of high molecular weight, but those with the most desirable properties are extremely expensive and costs will have to drop considerably before they gain widespread use (cf. silicones, p. 365). The cheapest compounds are the chloro series

$(NPCl_2)_n$ but these readily hydrolyse in moist air to polymetaphosphimic acids. Greater stability is displayed by amino, alkoxy, phenoxy and especially fluorinated derivatives, and these are attracting increasing interest as rigid plastics, elastomers, plastic films, extruded fibres and expanded foams.[160,170] Such materials (MW >500 000) are water-repellent, solvent-resistant, flame-resistant and flexible at low temperatures (Fig. 12.30). Possible applications are as fuel hoses, gaskets and O-ring seals for use in high-flying aircraft or for vehicles in Arctic climates. Their extraordinary dielectric strength makes them good candidates for metal coatings and wire insulation. Other applications of polyphosphazenes include their use to improve the high-temperature properties of phenolic resins and their use as composites with asbestos or glass for non-flammable insulating material. Some of the more reactive derivatives have been proposed as pesticides and even as ultra-high capacity fertilizers.

12.3.8 Organophosphorus compounds

A general treatment of the vast domain of organic compounds of phosphorus[171] falls outside the scope of this book though several important classes of compound have already been briefly mentioned, e.g. tertiary phosphine ligands (p. 494), alkoxyphosphines and their derivatives (p. 496), organophosphorus halides (p. 500), phosphate esters in life processes (p. 528) and organic derivatives of PN compounds (preceding section). There are also innumerable organic derivatives of the polycyclic polyphosphanes (p. 495),[67,70,172] and vast numbers of heterocyclic organophosphorus

[170] H. R. ALLCOCK, *Sci. Progr. Oxf.* **66**, 355–69 (1980).

[171] R. S. EDMONDSON (ed.) *Dictionary of Organophosphorus Compounds*, Chapman and Hall, New York, 1988, 1347 pp.

[172] G. FRITZ, H.-G. VON SCHERING *et al.*, *Z. anorg. allg. Chem.* **552**, 34–49 (1987); **584** 21–50, 51–70 (1990); **585**, 51–64 (1990); **595**, 67–94 (1991); and references cited therein.

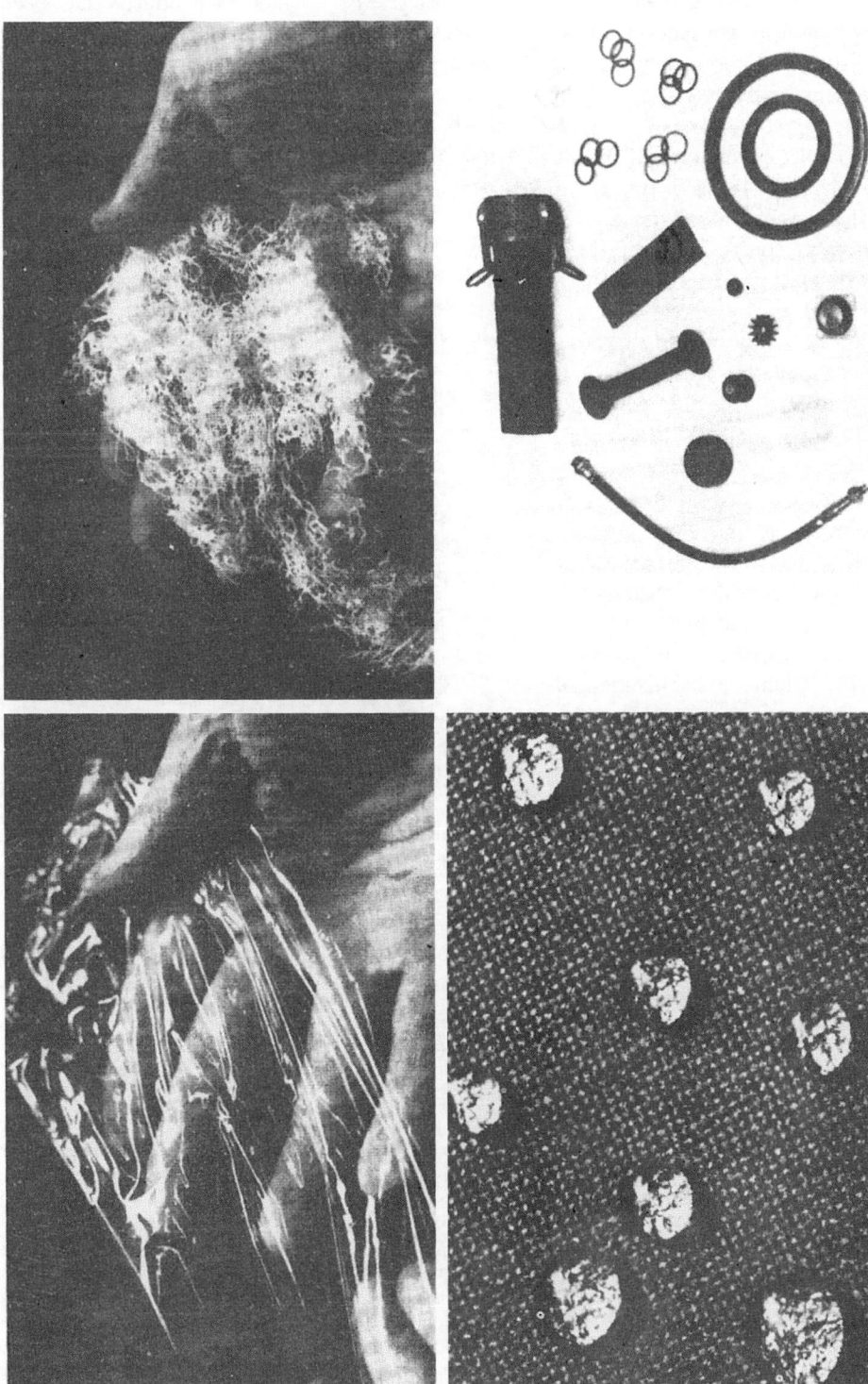

Figure 12.30   Potential uses of polyphosphazenes: (a) A thin film of a poly(aminophosphazene); such materials are of interest for biomedical applications. (b) Fibres of poly[bis(trifluoroethoxy)phosphazene]; these fibres are water-repellant, resistant to hydrolysis or strong sunlight, and do not burn. (c) Cotton cloth treated with a poly(fluoroalkoxyphosphazene) showing the water repellancy conferred by the phosphazene. (d) Polyphosphazene elastomers are now being manufactured for use in fuel lines, gaskets, O-rings, shock absorbers, and carburettor components; they are impervious to oils and fuels, do not burn, and remain flexible at very low temperatures. Photographs by courtesy of H. R. Allcock (Pennsylvania State University) and the Firestone Tire and Rubber Company.

compounds.[173,174] Within the general realm of organic compounds of phosphorus it is convenient to distinguish organophosphorus compounds as a particular group, i.e. those which contain one or more direct P–C bond. In such compounds the coordination number of P can be 1, 2, 3, 4, 5 or 6 (p. 484). Examples of coordination number 1 were initially restricted to the relatively unstable compounds HCP, FCP and MeCP (cf. HCN, FCN and MeCN). HC≡P was first made in 1961 by subjecting PH_3 gas at 40 mmHg pressure to a low-intensity rotating arc struck between graphite electrodes;[175] it is a colourless, reactive gas, stable only below its triple point of −124° (30 mmHg). Monomeric HCP slowly polymerizes at −130° (more rapidly at −78°) to a black solid, and adds 2HCl at −110° to give $MePCl_2$ as the sole product. Both monomer and polymer are pyrophoric in air even at room temperature. More recently[176] MeCP was made by pyrolysing $MeCH_2PCl_2$ at 930° in a low-pressure flow reactor and trapping the products at −78°. Dramatic stabilization of a phospha-alkyne has been achieved by η^2-complexation to a metal centre:[177]

$$Bu^tC{\equiv}P + [Pt(C_2H_4)(PPh_3)_2] \xrightarrow[\text{room temp}]{C_6H_6} C_2H_4$$
$$+ [Pt(\eta^2\text{-}Bu^tCP)(PPh_3)_2].C_6H_6$$

The translucent, cream-coloured benzene solvate was characterized by single-crystal X-ray analysis and by ^{31}P nmr spectroscopy. The first free phospha-alkyne stable to polymerization

was $Bu^tC{\equiv}P$,[178] and its chemistry has been extensively investigated.[179,180] The similarly bulky $ArC{\equiv}P$ (Ar = 2,4,6,-$Bu^t_3C_6H_2$) has been studied by X-ray crystallography[182] and the C–P distance found to be 152 pm, similar to the short C–P distance of 154 pm deduced from the microwave spectrum of HCP and MeCP. The most studied reactions of phospha-alkynes are cyclo-additions to give organo-P heterocycles,[179−181] and reactions with nucleophiles to give phospha-alkenes and 1,3-diphosphabutadienes.[182]

As with coordination number 1, the first 2-coordinate P compound also appeared in 1961:[183] $Me_3P{=}PCF_3$ was made as a white solid by cleaving cyclo-[P(CF_3)]_4 or 5 with PMe_3; it is stable at low temperatures but readily dissociates into the starting materials above room temperature. More stable is the bent 2-coordinate phosphocation occurring in the orange salt[184]

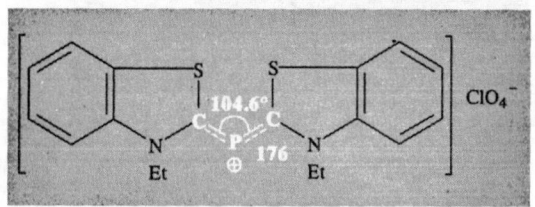

The aromatic heterocycle phosphabenzene C_5H_5P (analogous to pyridine) was reported in 1971,[185] some years after its triphenyl derivative 2,4,6-$Ph_3C_5H_2P$. See also $HP{=}CH_2$[29] and $[P(CN)_2]^{-}$[30] (p. 484). The burgeoning field of heterocyclic phosphorus compounds featuring

173 E. FLUCK and B. NEUMÜLLER, in H. W. ROESKY (ed.), *Rings, Clusters and Polymers of Main Group and Transition Metals*, Elsevier, Amsterdam, 1989, pp. 193–5.

174 A. SCHMIDPETER and K. KARAGHIOSOFF, in H. W. ROESKY (ed.), *Rings, Clusters and Polymers of Main Group and Transition Metals*, Elsevier, Amsterdam, 1989, pp. 307–43.

175 T. E. GIER, *J. Am. Chem. Soc.* **83**, 1769–70 (1961).

176 N. P. C. WESTWOOD, H. W. KROTO, J. F. NIXON and N. P. C. SIMMONS, *J. Chem. Soc., Dalton Trans.*, 1405–8 (1979).

177 J. C. T. R. BURKETT-ST. LAURENT, P. B. HITCHCOCK, H. W. KROTO and J. F. NIXON, *J. Chem. Soc., Chem. Commun.*, 1141–3 (1981).

178 G. BECKER, G. GRESSER and W. UHL, *Z. Naturforsch., Teil B* **36**, 16 (1981).

179 J. F. NIXON, *Chem. Rev.* **88**, 1327–62 (1988).

180 M. REGITZ, *Chem. Rev.* **90**, 191–213 (1990). See also M. REGITZ and O. J. SCHERER, *Multiple Bonds and Low Coordination in Phosphorus Chemistry*, Georg Thieme Verlag, Stuttgart, (1990).

181 R. BARTSCH and J. F. NIXON, *Polyhedron*, **8**, 2407 (1989).

182 A. M. ARIF, A. F. BARRON, A. H. COWLEY and S. W. HALL, *J. Chem. Soc., Chem. Commun.*, 171–2 (1988).

183 A. BURG and W. MAHLER, *J. Am. Chem. Soc.* **83**, 2388–9 (1961).

184 K. DIMROTH and P. HOFFMANN, *Chem. Ber.* **99**, 1325–31 (1966); R. ALLMANN, *Chem. Ber.* **99**, 1332–40 (1966).

185 A. J. ASHE, *J. Am. Chem. Soc.* **93**, 3293–5 (1971).

2-coordinate and 3-coordinate P has been fully reviewed,[173,174] as has the equally active field of phospha-alkenes $\left(-P{=}C\diagup^{\diagup}_{\diagdown}\right)$ and diphosphenes $(-P{=}P-)$.[179,180,186,187]

The most common coordination numbers for organophosphorus compounds are 3 and 4 as represented by tertiary phosphines and their complexes, and quaternary cations such as $[PMe_4]^+$ and $[PPh_4]^+$. Also of great significance are the 4-coordinate P ylides[†] $R_3P{=}CH_2$; indeed, few papers have created so much activity as the report by G. Wittig and G. Geissler in 1953 that methylene triphenylphosphorane reacts with benzophenone to give Ph_3PO and 1,1-diphenylethylene in excellent yield.[188]

$$Ph_3P{=}CH_2 + Ph_2CO \longrightarrow Ph_3PO + Ph_2C{=}CH_2$$

The ylide $Ph_3P{=}CH_2$ can readily be made by deprotonating a quaternary phosphonium halide with *n*-butyllithium and many such ylides are now known:

$$[Ph_3PCH_3]^+Br^- \xrightarrow{\text{LiBu}^n} Ph_3P{=}CH_2$$
$$+ LiBr + Bu^nH$$

$$[PMe_4]^+Br^- + NaNH_2 \xrightarrow{\text{thf/0°}} Me_3P{=}CH_2$$
$$+ NaBr + NH_3$$

The enormous scope of the Wittig reaction and its variants in affording a smooth, high-yield synthesis of $C{=}C$ double bonds, etc., has been amply delineated by the work of Wittig

---

[186] R. APPEL, F. KNOLL and I. RUPPERT, *Angew. Chem. Int. Edn. Engl.* **20**, 731–44 (1981).

[187] N. C. NORMAN, *Polyhedron* **12**, 2431–6 (1993).

[†] An ylide can be defined as a compound in which a carbanion is attached directly to a heteroatom carrying a high degree of positive charge:

$$\diagup^{\diagup}_{\diagdown}C^-{-}X\Big\}^+ \longleftrightarrow \diagup^{\diagup}_{\diagdown}C{=}X\Big\}$$

Thus $Ph_3P{=}CH_2$ is triphenylphosphonium methylide (see pp. 274–304 of reference 2, or textbooks of organic chemistry for a fuller treatment of the Wittig reaction).

[188] G. WITTIG and G. GEISSLER, *Annalen* **580**, 44–57 (1953).

and others and culminated in the award of the 1979 Nobel Prize for Chemistry (jointly with H. C. Brown for hydroboration, p. 166). The reaction of P ylides with many inorganic compounds has also led to some fascinating new chemistry.[189] The curious yellow compound $Ph_3P{=}C{=}PPh_3$ should also be noted:[190] unlike allene, $H_2C{=}C{=}CH_2$, which has a linear central carbon atom, the molecules are bent and the structure is strikingly unusual in having 2 crystallographically independent molecules in the unit cell which have substantially differing bond angles, 130.1° and 143.8°. The short $P{=}C$ distances (163 pm as compared with 183.5 pm for $P{-}C(Ph)$) suggest double bonding, but the nonlinear $P{=}C{=}P$ unit and especially the two values of the angle, are hard to rationalize (cf. the isoelectronic cation $[Ph_3P{=}N{=}PPh_3]^+$ which has various angles in different compounds).

Pentaorgano derivatives of P are rare. The first to be made (by G. Wittig and M. Rieber in 1948) was PPh_5:

$$Ph_3PO \xrightarrow[\text{(2) HCl}]{\text{(1) LiPh}} [PPh_4]^+Cl^- \xrightarrow{\text{HI}}$$
$$[PPh_4]^+I^- \xrightarrow{\text{LiPh}} PPh_5 \text{ (d. 124°)}$$

Unlike $SbPh_5$ (which has a square-pyramidal structure p. 598), PPh_5 adopts a trigonal bipyramidal coordination with the axial $P{-}C$ distances (199 pm) being appreciably longer than the equatorial $P{-}C$ distances (185 pm). More recently (1976) $P(CF_3)_3Me_2$ and $P(CF_3)_2Me_3$ were obtained by methylating the corresponding chlorides with $PbMe_4$. There are also many examples of 5-coordinate P in which not all the directly bonded atoms are carbon. One such is the dioxaphenylspiro-phosphorane shown in Fig. 12.31; the local symmetry about P is essentially square pyramidal, and the factors which affect the choice between this geometry and trigonal bipyramidal is a topic of active

---

[189] H. SCHMIDBAUR, *Acc. Chem. Res.* **8**, 62–70 (1975).

[190] A. T. VINCENT and P. J. WHEATLEY, *J. Chem. Soc. (D), Chem. Commun.*, 592 (1971).

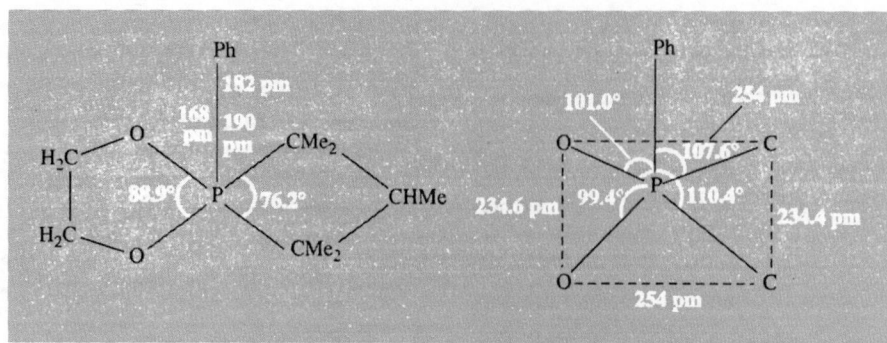

Figure 12.31   Schematic representation of the molecular structure of $[P(C_3HMe_5)(O_2C_2H_4)Ph]$ showing the rectangular-based pyramidal disposition of the 5 atoms bonded to P; the P atom is 44 pm above the C_2O_2 plane.

current interest.[39,191] It should also be noted that the compounds, Ph_3PBr_2 and Ph_3PI_2, which might have been thought to involve 5-coordinate P, feature instead 4-coordinate P and an unusual end-on bonding of the dihalogen moiety, i.e. $Ph_3P-Br-Br$,[192] and Ph_3P-I-I.[193]

The corresponding interhalogen adducts Ph_3PIX (X = Cl, Br) appear to be 4-coordinate but ionic, i.e. $[Ph_3PI]^+X^-$.[194]

Many organophosphorus compounds are highly toxic and frequently lethal. They have been actively developed for herbicides, pesticides and more sinister purposes such as nerve gases which disorient, harass, paralyse or kill.[9]

[191] W. ALTHOFF,   R. O. DAY,   R. K. BROWN   and R. R. HOLMES, *Inorg. Chem.* **17**, 3265–70 (1978); see also the immediately following two papers, pp. 3270–6 and 3276–85.
[192] N. BRICKLEBANK,   S. M. GODFREY,   A. G. MACKIE, C. A. MCAULIFFE and R. G. PRITCHARD, *J. Chem. Soc., Chem. Commun.*, 355–6 (1992).
[193] S. M. GODFREY,   D. G. KELLY,   C. S. MCAULIFFE, A. G. MACKIE, R. G. PRITCHARD and S. M. WATSON, *J. Chem. Soc., Chem. Commun.*, 1163–4 (1991).

[194] K. B. DILLON and J. LINCOLN, *Polyhedron*, **8**, 1445–6 (1989).

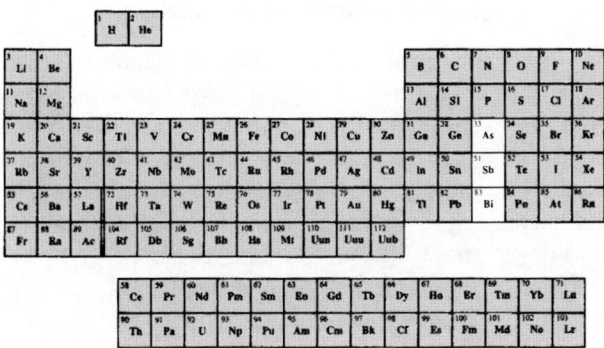

13

Arsenic, Antimony and Bismuth

13.1 Introduction

The three elements arsenic, antimony and bismuth, which complete Group 15 of the periodic table, were amongst the earliest elements to be isolated and all were known before either nitrogen (1772) or phosphorus (1669) had been obtained as the free elements. The properties of arsenic sulfide and related compounds have been known to physicians and professional poisoners since the fifth century BC though their use is no longer recommended by either group of practitioners. Isolation of the element is sometimes credited to Albertus Magnus (AD 1193–1280) who heated orpiment (As_2S_3) with soap, and its name reflects its ancient lineage. [Arsenic, Latin *arsenicum* from Greek ἀρσενικόν (*arsenicon*) which was itself derived (with addition of όν) from Persian *az-zarnīkh*, yellow orpiment (*zar* = gold).] Antimony compounds were also known to the ancients and the black sulfide, stibnite, was used in early biblical times as a cosmetic to darken and beautify women's eyebrows; a rare Chaldean vase of cast antimony dates from 4000 BC and antimony-coated copper articles were used in Egypt 2500–2200 BC. Pliny (~AD 50) gave it the name *stibium* and writings attributed to Jabir (~AD 800) used the form *antimonium*; indeed, both names were used for both the element and its sulfide until the end of the eighteenth century (Lavoisier). The history of the element, like that of arsenic, is much obscured by the intentionally vague and misleading descriptions of the alchemists, though the elusive Benedictine monk Basil Valentine may have prepared it in 1492 (about the time of Columbus). N. Lémery published his famous *Treatise on Antimony* in 1707. Bismuth was known as the metal at least by 1480 though its previous history in the Middle Ages is difficult to unravel because the element was sometimes confused with Pb, Sn, Sb or even Ag. The Gutenberg printing presses (1440 onwards) used type that had been cut from brass or cast from Pb, Sn or Cu, but about 1450 a secret method of casting type from Bi alloys came into use and this particular use is, still an important application of the element (p. 549). The name derives from the German *Wismut* (possibly white metal or meadow mines) and this was latinized to *bisemutum* by the sixteenth-century German scientist G. Bauer (Agricola) about 1530. Despite the difficulty of

547

assigning precise dates to discoveries made by alchemists, miners and metal workers (or indeed even discerning what those discoveries actually were), it seems clear that As, Sb and Bi became increasingly recognized in their free form during the thirteenth to fifteenth centuries; they are therefore contemporary with Zn and Co, and predate all other elements except the 7 metals and 2 non-metallic elements known from ancient times (Au, Ag, Cu, Fe, Hg, Pb, Sn; C and S).[1]

Arsenic and antimony are classed as metalloids or semi-metals and bismuth is a typical B subgroup (post-transition-element) metal like tin and lead.

13.2 The Elements

13.2.1 Abundance, distribution and extraction

None of the three elements is particularly abundant in the earth's crust though several minerals contain them as major constituents. As can be seen from Table 13.1, arsenic occurs about halfway down the elements in order of abundance, grouped with several others near 2 ppm. Antimony has only one-tenth of this abundance and Bi, down by a further factor of 20 or more, is about as unabundant as several of the commoner platinum metals and gold. In common with all the post-transition-element metals, As, Sb and Bi are chalcophiles, i.e. they occur in association with the chalcogens S, Se and Te rather than as oxides and silicates.

Arsenic minerals are widely distributed throughout the world and small amounts of the free element have also been found. Common

minerals include the two sulfides realgar (As_4S_4) and orpiment (As_2S_3) and the oxidized form arsenolite (As_2O_3). The arsenides of Fe, Co and Ni and the mixed sulfides with these metals form another set of minerals, e.g. loellingite (FeAs$_2$), safforlite (CoAs), niccolite (NiAs), rammelsbergite (NiAs$_2$), arsenopyrite (FeAsS), cobaltite (CoAsS), enargite (Cu$_3$AsS$_4$), gersdorffite (NiAsS) and the quaternary sulfide glaucodot [(Co,Fe)AsS]. Elemental As is obtained on an industrial scale by smelting FeAs$_2$ or FeAsS at 650–700°C in the absence of air and condensing the sublimed element: FeAsS $\longrightarrow$ FeS + As(g) $\longrightarrow$ As(s). Residual As trapped in the sulfide residues can be released by roasting them in air and trapping the sublimed As_2O_3 in the flue system. The oxide can then either be used directly for chemical products or reduced with charcoal at 700–800° to give more As. As_2O_3 is also obtained in large quantities as flue dust from the smelting of Cu and Pb concentrates; because of the huge scale of these operations (pp. 1174, 371) this represents the most important industrial source of As. Some production figures and major uses of As and its compounds are listed in the Panel.

Stibnite, Sb_2S_3, is the most important ore of antimony and it occurs in large quantities in China, South Africa, Mexico, Bolivia and Chile. Other sulfide ores include ullmanite (NiSbS), livingstonite (HgSb$_4$S$_8$), tetrahedrite (Cu$_3$SbS$_3$), wolfsbergite (CuSbS$_2$) and jamesonite (FePb$_4$Sb$_6$S$_{14}$). Indeed, complex ores containing Pb, Cu, Ag and Hg are an important industrial source of Sb. Small amounts of oxide minerals formed by weathering are also known, e.g. valentinite (Sb_2O_3), cervantite (Sb_2O_4), and stibiconite (Sb_2O_4.H_2O), and minor finds of native Sb have occasionally been reported. Commercial ores have 5–60% Sb, and recovery methods depend on the

---

[1] M. E. WEEKS, *Discovery of the Elements*, Chap. 3, pp. 91–119, Journal of Chemical Education, Easton, Pa, 1956.

Table 13.1 Abundances of elements in crustal rocks (g tonne^{-1})

Element	Sn	Eu	Be	**As**	Ta	Ge	In	**Sb**	Cd	Pd	Pt	**Bi**	Os	Au
PPM	2.1	2.1	2.0	**1.8**	1.7	1.5	0.24	**0.2**	0.16	0.015	0.01	**0.008**	0.005	0.004
Order	48 =	48 =	50	**51**	52	53	61	**62**	63	67	68	**69**	70	71

Production and Uses of Arsenic, Antimony and Bismuth[2]

Until the late 1980s the USA was the principal supplier of "white arsenic" (i.e. As_2O_3) but it now relies entirely on imports. World production has been steady for many years at about 52 000 tonnes pa and the main producers are France (10 000 tpa), Sweden (10 000 tpa), Russia (8 000 tpa) and Chile (7 000 tpa). The price of refined oxide was about $480 per tonne in 1989 and commercial grade As metal (99%+) was about $2.20/kg in 1990. High purity As (99.99%+) was $45.00/kg and zone-refined semiconductor grade even more expensive.

The main use of elemental As is in alloys with Pb and to a lesser extent Cu. Addition of small concentrations of As improves the properties of Pb/Sb for storage batteries (see below), up to 0.75% improves the hardness and castability of type metal, and 0.5–2.0% improves the sphericity of Pb ammunition. Automotive body solder is Pb (92%), Sb (5.0%), Sn (2.5%) and As (0.5%). Intermetallic compounds with Al, Ga and In give the III–V semiconductors (p. 255) of which GaAs and InAs are of particular value for light-emitting diodes (LEDs), tunnel diodes, infrared emitters, laser windows and Hall-effect devices (p. 258).

The use of As compounds as herbicides and pest controls in agriculture is now considerably restricted because of environmental considerations though arsenic acid itself, $AsO(OH)_3$, is still used in the formulation of wood preservatives. The oxide is widely used to decolorize glass.

World production capacity for antimony and its compounds (as contained Sb) was 116 000 tonnes in 1988, plus a similar amount of secondary (recycled) Sb obtained by smelting. However, actual production was somewhat below this. Typical prices (1988) were $3.50/kg for high-grade Sb_2O_3 and $2.30/kg for 99.5%+ Sb metal ($1.80/kg in 1990). Lead storage batteries use alloys containing 2.5–3% Sb and a trace of As, to minimize self-discharge, gassing and poisoning of the negative electrode. Other typical uses of Sb alloys in the USA, 1975 (tonnes of contained Sb), are shown in the Table.

Use	Sb/Pb batteries	Bearings	Ammuni-tion	Solder	Type metal	Sheet pipe	Other metal	Non-metal products
Sb/tonnes	4143	365	216	121	68	55	144	6657
Percentage	35.2	3.5	1.8	1.0	0.6	0.5	1.2	56.5

As with arsenic, semiconductor grade Sb is prepared by chemical reduction of highly purified compounds. AlSb, GaSb and InSb have applications in infrared devices, diodes and Hall-effect devices. ZnSb has good thermoelectric properties. Applications of various *compounds* of Sb will be mentioned when the compounds themselves are discussed.

World annual production of bismuth and its compounds has hovered around 4000 tonnes of contained Bi for many years and a similar amount of secondary (refinery) Bi is also produced. Production has been dominated by China, Japan, Peru, Bolivia, Mexico, Canada, USA and Australia which, between them, account for almost of all supplies. Prices for the free element have fluctuated wildly since the 1970s, from <$4.00/kg to >$44.00/kg; at the end of 1990 it was $6.30/kg. Consumption of the metal and its compounds has also been unusual, usage in the USA dropping by a factor of 2 from 1973 to 1975, for example. The main uses are in pharmaceuticals, fusible alloys (including type metal, p. 547), and metallurgical additives.

No industrial poisoning by Bi metal has ever been reported but ingestion of compounds and inhalation of dust should be avoided.

grade. Low-grade sulfide ores (5–25% Sb) are volatilized as the oxide (any As_2O_3 being readily removed first by virtue of its greater volatility). The oxide can be reduced to the metal by heating it in a reverberatory furnace with charcoal in the presence of an alkali metal carbonate

---

[2] *Kirk–Othmer Encyclopedia of Chemical Technology*, 4th edn., Vol. 3, Wiley, New York, 1992; Arsenic and arsenic alloys (pp. 624–33); Arsenic compounds (633–59); Antimony and antimony alloys (367–81); Antimony compounds (382–412); Bismuth and bismuth alloys (Vol. 4, 1992 (pp. 237–45); Bismuth compounds (246–70).

or sulfate as flux. Intermediate ores (25–40%) are smelted in a blast furnace and the oxide recovered from the flue system. Ores containing 40–60% Sb are liquated at 550–600° under reducing conditions to give Sb_2S_3 and then treated with scrap iron to remove the sulfide: $Sb_2S_3 + 3Fe \longrightarrow 2Sb + 3FeS$. Some complex sulfide ores are treated by leaching and electro-winning, e.g. the electrolysis of alkaline solutions of the thioantimonate Na_3SbS_4, and the element is also recovered from the flue dusts of Pb smelters. Impure Sb contains Pb, As, S, Fe and

Cu; the latter two can be removed by stibnite treatment or heating with charcoal/Na_2SO_4 flux; the As and S can be removed by an oxidizing flux of $NaNO_3$ and NaOH (or Na_2CO_3); Pb is hard to remove but this is unnecessary if the Sb is to be used in Pb alloys (see below). Electrolysis yields >99.9% purity and remaining impurities can be reduced to the ppm level by zone refining. The scale of production and the various uses of Sb and its compounds are summarized in the Panel.

Bismuth occurs mainly as bismite (α-Bi_2O_3), bismuthinite (Bi_2S_3) and bismutite [$(BiO)_2CO_3$]; very occasionally it occurs native, in association with Pb, Ag or Co ores. The main commercial source of the element is as a byproduct from Pb/Zn and Cu plants, from which it is obtained by special processes dependent on the nature of the main product.[2] Sulfide ores are roasted to the oxide and then reduced by iron or charcoal. Because of its low mp, very low solubility in Fe, and fairly high oxidative stability in air, Bi can be melted and cast (like Pb) in iron and steel vessels. Like Sb, the metal is too brittle to roll, draw, or extrude at room temperature, but above 225°C Bi can be worked quite well.

13.2.2 Atomic and physical properties

Arsenic and Bi (like P) each have only 1 stable isotope and this occurs with 100% abundance in all natural sources of the elements. Accordingly (p. 17) their atomic weights are known with great precision (Table 13.2). Antimony has 2 stable isotopes (like N); however, unlike N, which has 1 predominantly abundant isotope, the 2 isotopes of Sb are approximately equal in abundance (^{121}Sb 57.21%, ^{123}Sb 42.79%) and consequently (p. 17) the atomic weight is known with somewhat less accuracy. It is also noteworthy that ^{209}Bi is the heaviest stable isotope of any element; all nuclides beyond $^{209}_{83}$Bi are radioactive.

The ground-state electronic configuration of each element in the group is ns^2np^3 with an unpaired electron in each of the three p orbitals, and much of the chemistry of the group can be interpreted directly on this basis. However, smooth trends are sometimes modified (or even absent altogether), firstly, because of the lack of low-lying empty d orbitals in N, which differentiates it from its heavier congeners, and, secondly, because of the countervailing influence of the underlying filled d and f orbitals in As, Sb and Bi. Such perturbations are apparent when the various ionization energies in Table 13.2 are plotted as a function of atomic number. Table 13.2 also contains approximate data on the conventional covalent single-bond radii for threefold coordination though these values vary by about ±4 pm in various tabulations and should only be used as a rough guide. The 6-coordinate "effective ionic radii" for the +3 and +5

Table 13.2 Atomic properties of Group 15 elements

Property		N	P	As	Sb	Bi
Atomic number		7	15	33	51	83
Atomic weight (1997)		14.00674(7)	30.973762(4)	74.92160(2)	121.760(1)	208.98038(2)
Electronic configuration		[He]$2s^2 2p^3$	[Ne]$3s^2 3p^3$	[Ar]$3d^{10}4s^2 4p^3$	[Kr]$4d^{10}5s^2 5p^3$	[Xe]$4f^{14}5d^{10}$-$6s^2 6p^3$
Ionization energies/MJ mol^{-1}	(I)	1.402	1.012	0.947	0.834	0.703
	(II)	2.856	1.903	1.798	1.595	1.610
	(III)	4.577	2.910	2.736	2.443	2.466
Sum (I+II+III)/MJ mol^{-1}		8.835	5.825	5.481	4.872	4.779
Sum (IV+V)/MJ mol^{-1}		16.920	11.220	10.880	9.636	9.776
Electronegativity χ		3.0	2.1	2.0	1.9	1.9
r_{cov} (M^{III} single bond)/pm		70	110	120	140	150
r_{ionic} (6-coordinate) (M^{III})/pm		(16)	44	58	76	103
(6-coordinate) (M^V)/pm		(13)	38	46	60	76

oxidation states are taken from R. D. Shannon's tabulation,[3] but should not be taken to imply the presence of M^{3+} and M^{5+} cations in many of the compounds of these elements.

Arsenic, Sb and Bi each exist in several allotropic forms[4,5] though the allotropy is not so extensive as in P (p. 481). There are three crystalline forms of As, of which the ordinary, grey, "metallic", rhombohedral, α-form is the most stable at room temperature. It consists of puckered sheets of covalently bonded As stacked in layers perpendicular to the hexagonal c-axis as shown in Fig. 13.1. Within each layer each As has 3 nearest neighbours at 251.7 pm and the angle As–As–As is 96.7°; each As also has a further 3 neighbours at 312 pm in an adjacent layer. The α-forms of Sb and Bi are isostructural with α-As and have the dimensions shown in Table 13.3. It can be seen that there is a progressive diminution in the difference between intra-layer and inter-layer distances though the inter-bond angles remain almost constant.

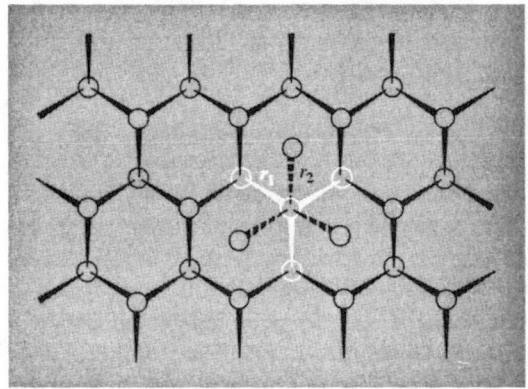

Figure 13.1 Puckered layer structure of As showing pyramidal coordination of each As to 3 neighbours at a distance r_1 (252 pm). The disposition of As atoms in the next layer (r_2 312 pm) is shown by dashed lines.

[3] R. D. Shannon, *Acta Cryst.* **A32**, 751–67 (1976).

[4] J. Donohue, *The Structure of the Elements*, Wiley, 1974, 436 pp.

[5] H. G. von Schnering, *Angew. Chem. Int. Edn. Engl.* **20**, 33–51 (1981).

Table 13.3 Comparison of black P and α-rhombohedral As, Sb and Bi

	r_1/pm	r_2/pm	r_2/r_1	$\angle$ M–M–M
Black P	223.1 (av)	332.4 (av)	1.490	2 at 96.3° (1 at 102.1°)
α-As	251.7	312.0	1.240	96.7°
α-Sb	290.8	335.5	1.153	96.6°
α-Bi	307.2	352.9	1.149	95.5°

In the vapour phase As is known to exist as tetrahedral As_4 molecules with (As–As 243.5 pm) and when the element is sublimed, a yellow, cubic modification is obtained which probably also contains As_4 units though the structure has not yet been determined because the crystals decompose in the X-ray beam. The mineral arsenolamprite is another polymorph, ε-As; it is possibly isostructural with "metallic" orthorhombic P.

Antimony exists in 5 forms in addition to the ordinary α-form which has been discussed above. The yellow form is unstable above $-90°$; a black form can be obtained by cooling gaseous Sb, and an explosive (impure?) form can be made electrolytically. The two remaining crystalline forms are made by high-pressure techniques: Form I has a primitive cubic lattice with a_0 296.6 pm: it is obtained from α-Sb at 50 kbar (5GPa, i.e. 5×10^9 N m^{-2}) by increasing the rhombohedral angle from 57.1° to 60.0° together with small shifts in atomic position so that each Sb has 6 equidistant neighbours. Further increase in pressure to 90 kbar yields Form II which is hcp with an interatomic distance of 328 pm for the 12 nearest neighbours.

Several polymorphs of Bi have been described but there is as yet no general agreement on their structures except for α-Bi (above) and ζ-Bi which forms at 90 kbar and has a bcc structure with 8 nearest neighbours at 329.1 pm.

The physical properties of the α-rhombohedral form of As, Sb and Bi are summarized in Table 13.4. Data for N_2 and P_4 are included for comparison. Crystalline As is rather volatile and the vapour pressure of the solid reaches 1 atm at 615° some 200° below its mp of 816°C (at 38.6 atm, i.e. 3.91 MPa). Antimony and Bi are

Table 13.4 Some physical properties of Group 15 elements

Property	N_2	P_4	α-As	α-Sb	α-Bi
MP/°C	−210.0	44.1	816 (38.6 atm)	630.7	271.4
BP/°C	−195.8	280.5	615 (subl)	1753	1564
Density (25°C)/g cm^{-3}	0.879 (−210°)	1.823	5.778[a]	6.684	9.808
Hardness (Mohs)	—	—	3.5	3–3.5	2.5
Electrical resistivity (20°C)/μohm cm	—	—	33.3	41.7	120
Contraction on freezing/%	—	—	10	0.8	−3.32

[a]Yellow As$_4$ has d_{25} 1.97 g cm^{-3}; cf. difference between the density of rhombohedral black P (3.56 g cm^{-3}) and white P$_4$ (1.823 g cm^{-3}) (p. 479).

much less volatile and also have appreciably lower mps than As, so that both have quite long liquid ranges at atmospheric pressure.

Arsenic forms brittle steel-grey crystals of metallic appearance. However, its lack of ductility and comparatively high electrical resistivity (33.3 μohm cm), coupled with its amphoterism and intermediate chemical nature between that of metals and non-metals, have led to its being classified as a metalloid rather than a "true" metal. Antimony is also very brittle and forms bluish-white, flaky, lustrous crystals of high electrical resistivity (41.7 μohm cm). These values of resistivity can be compared with those for "good" metals such as Ag (1.59), Cu (1.72), and Al (2.82 μohm cm), and with "poor" metals such as Sn (11.5) and Pb (22 μohm cm). Bismuth has a still higher resistivity (120 μohm cm) which even exceeds that of commercial resistors such as Nichrome alloy (100 μohm cm). Bismuth is a brittle, white, crystalline metal with a pinkish tinge. It is the most diamagnetic of all metals (mass susceptibility 17.0×10^{-9} m^3 kg^{-1} — to convert this SI value to cgs multiply by $10^3/4\pi$, i.e. 1.35×10^{-6} cm^3 g^{-1}). It also has the highest Hall effect coefficient of any metal and is unusual in expanding on solidifying from the melt, a property which it holds uniquely with Ga and Ge among the elements.

13.2.3 Chemical reactivity and group trends

Arsenic is stable in dry air but the surface oxidizes in moist air to give a superficial golden bronze tarnish which deepens to a black surface coating on further exposure. When heated in air it sublimes and oxidizes to As$_4$O$_6$ with a garlic like odour (poisonous). Above 250–300° the reaction is accompanied by phosphorescence (cf. P$_4$, p. 473). When ignited in oxygen, As burns brilliantly to give As$_4$O$_6$ and As$_4$O$_{10}$. Metals give arsenides (p. 554), fluorine enflames to give AsF$_5$ (p. 561), and the other halogens yield AsX$_3$ (p. 559). Arsenic is not readily attacked by water, alkaline solutions or non-oxidizing acids, but dilute HNO$_3$ gives arsenious acid (H$_3$AsO$_3$), hot conc HNO$_3$ yields arsenic acid (H$_3$AsO$_4$), and hot conc H$_2$SO$_4$ gives As$_4$O$_6$. Reaction with fused NaOH liberates H$_2$:

$$\text{As} + 3\text{NaOH} \longrightarrow \text{Na}_3\text{AsO}_3 + \tfrac{3}{2}\text{H}_2$$

One important property which As has in common with its neighbouring elements immediately following the 3d transition series (i.e. Ge, As, Se, Br) and which differentiates it from its Group 15 neighbours P and Sb, is its notable reluctance to be oxidized to the group valence of +5. Consequently As$_4$O$_{10}$ and H$_3$AsO$_4$ are oxidizing agents and arsenates are used for this purpose in titrimetric analysis (p. 577).

The ground-state electronic structure of As, as with all Group 15 elements features 3 unpaired electrons ns^2np^3; there is a substantial electron affinity for the acquisition of 1 electron but further additions must be effected against considerable coulombic repulsion, and the formation of As^{3-} is highly endothermic. Consistent with this there are no "ionic" compounds containing the arsenide ion and compounds such as Na_3As are intermetallic or alloy-like. However, despite the metalloidal character of the free element, the ionization energies and electronegativity of As are similar to those of P (Table 13.2) and the element readily forms strong covalent bonds to most non-metals. Thus AsX_3 (X = H, hal, R, Ar etc.) are covalent molecules like PX_3 and the tertiary arsines have been widely used as ligands to b-class transition elements (p. 909).[6] Similarly, As_4O_6 and As_4O_{10} resemble their P analogues in structure; the sulfides are also covalent heterocyclic molecules though their stoichiometry and structure differ from those of P.

Antimony is in many ways similar to As, but it is somewhat less reactive. It is stable to air and moisture at room temperature, oxidizes on being heated under controlled conditions to give Sb_2O_3, Sb_2O_4 or Sb_2O_5, reacts vigorously with Cl_2 and more sedately with Br_2 and I_2 to give SbX_3, and also combines with S on being heated. H_2 is without direct reaction and SbH_3 (p. 557) is both very poisonous and thermally very unstable. Dilute acids have no effect on Sb; concentrated oxidizing acids react readily, e.g. conc HNO_3 gives hydrated Sb_2O_5, aqua regia gives a solution of $SbCl_5$, and hot conc H_2SO_4 gives the salt $Sb_2(SO_4)_3$.

Bismuth continues the trend to electropositive behaviour and Bi_2O_3 is definitely basic, compared with the amphoteric oxides of Sb and As and the acidic oxides of P and N. There is also a growing tendency to form salts of oxoacids by reaction of either the metal or its oxide with the acid, e.g. $Bi_2(SO_4)_3$ and $Bi(NO_3)_3$. Direct reaction of Bi with O_2, S and X_2 at elevated temperatures yields Bi_2O_3, Bi_2S_3 and BiX_3 respectively, but the increasing size of the metal atom results in a steady decrease in the strength of covalent linkages in the sequence P > As > Sb > Bi. This is most noticeable in the instability of BiH_3 and of many organobismuth compounds (p. 599).

Most of the trends are qualitatively understandable in terms of the general atomic properties in Table 13.2 though they are not readily deducible from them in any quantitative sense. Again, the +5 oxidation state in Bi is less stable than in Sb for the reasons discussed on p. 226; not only is the sum of the 4th and 5th ionization energies for Bi greater than for Sb (9.78 vs. 9.63 MJ mol^{-1}) but the promotion energies of one of the ns^2 electrons to a vacant nd orbital is also greater for Bi (and As) than for Sb. The discussions on redox properties (p. 577) and the role of d orbitals (p. 222) are also relevant. Finally, Bi shows an interesting resemblance to La in the crystal structures of the chloride oxide, MOCl, and in the isomorphism of the sulfates and double nitrates; this undoubtedly stems from the very similar ionic radii of the 2 cations: Bi^{3+} 103, La^{3+} 103.2 pm.

All coordination numbers from 1–10 (and 12) are known for the sub-group, though 3, 4, 5 and 6 are by far the most frequently met. CN 1 is exemplified by $RC{\equiv}As$[7] (R = 2,4,6-$Bu^t_3C_6H_2$; cf $RC{\equiv}P$, p. 544) and by the isolated tetrahedral anions $SiAs_4^{8-}$ and $GeAs_4^{8-}$ (isoelectronic with SiO_4^{4-} and GeO_4^{4-}) which occur in the lustrous dark metallic Zintl phases Ba_4MAs_4.[8] CN 2 (bent) is quite common in heterocyclic organic compounds (p. 592) and in cluster anions such as As_7^{3-}, Sb_7^{3-} and As_{11}^{3-} and their derivates (p. 588). A rare example of linear 2-coordinate As was recently established in the bis(manganese) complex $[(\eta^5\text{-}C_5H_4Me)(CO)_2Mn{=}As{=}Mn(CO)_2(\eta^5\text{-}C_5H_4Me)]^+$, isolated as its dark brown salt with $CF_3SO_3^-$: the angle at As was found to be 176.3° and the As–Mn distance was 215 pm.[9] Likewise, examples of pyramidal 3-coordinate As, Sb and Bi are endemic, but planar CN 3 is extremely rare; examples occur in

[6] C. A. McAuliffe (ed.), *Transition Metal Complexes of Phosphorus, Arsenic and Antimony Ligands*, Macmillan, London, 1973, 428 pp.

[7] G. Märkl and H. Sejpka, *Angew. Chem. Int. Edn. Engl.* **25**, 264 (1986).

[8] B. Eisenmann, H. Jordan and H. Schäfer, *Angew. Chem. Int. Edn. Engl.* **20**, 197–8 (1981).

[9] A. Strube, G. Huttner and L. Zsolnai, *Angew. Chem. Int. Edn. Engl.* **27**, 1529–30 (1988).

compounds such as $[PhAs(Cr(CO)_5)_2]$ and $[PhSb(Mn(\eta^5\text{-}C_5H_5)(CO)_2)_2]$ (p. 597) See later, also, for examples of CN 4 (tetrahedral, flattened tetrahedral and see-saw), CN 5 (trigonal bipyramidal and square pyramidal) and CN 6 (octahedral, 3 + 3, and pentagonal pyramidal).

Higher coordination numbers are less common and are mainly confined to Bi. CN 7 has been found in the tetradendate crown-ether bismuth complex $[BiCl_3(12\text{-crown-}4)]$[10] and in the bismuth complex, [BiL], of the novel heptadentate anionic ligand of 'saltren', (H_3L), i.e. $(N(CH_2CH_2N{=}CHC_6H_4OH)_3)$.[11] The first example of CN 8 was found in the colourless 2:1 adduct $[2BiCl_3.18\text{-crown-}6]$ which was shown by X-ray analysis to involve an unexpected ionic structure featuring 8-coordinate Bi cations, viz. $[BiCl_2(18\text{-crown-}6)]^+{}_2[Bi_2Cl_8]^{2-}$.[10] CN 9 is represented by the discrete tris(tridentate) complex $[Bi(-O{-}C(Bu^t){=}C{-}N{=}C{-}C(Bu^t){=}O{\rightarrow})_3]$ in which Bi has a face-capped, slightly-twisted trigonal-prismatic coordination environment.[12] Still higher coordination numbers are exemplified by encapsulated As and Sb atoms in rhodium carbonyl cluster anions: for example As is surrounded by a bicapped square antiprism of 10 Rh atoms in $[Rh_{10}As(CO)_{22}]^{3-}$,[13] and Sb is surrounded by an icosahedron of 12 Rh in $[Rh_{12}Sb(CO)_{27}]^{3-}$.[14] In each case the anion is the first example of a complex in which As or Sb acts as a 5-electron donor (cf. P as a 5-electron donor in $[Rh_9P(CO)_{21}]^{3-}$): all these clusters then have precisely the appropriate number of valence electrons for *closo* structures on the basis of Wade's rules (pp. 161, 174).

13.3 Compounds of Arsenic, Antimony and Bismuth[15]

13.3.1 Intermetallic compounds and alloys[16,17]

Most metals form arsenides, antimonides and bismuthides, and many of these command attention because of their interesting structures or valuable physical properties. Like the borides (p. 145), carbides (p. 297), silicides (p. 335), nitrides (p. 417) and phosphides (p. 489), classification is difficult because of the multitude of stoichiometries, the complexities of the structures and the intermediate nature of the bonding. The compounds are usually prepared by direct reaction of the elements in the required proportions and typical compositions are M_9As, M_5As, M_4As, M_3As, M_5As_2, M_2As, M_5As_3, M_3As_2, M_4As_3, M_5As_4, MAs, M_3As_4, M_2As_3, MAs_2 and M_3As_7. Antimony and bismuth are similar. Many of these intermetallic compounds exist over a range of composition, and nonstoichiometry is rife.

The (electropositive) alkali metals of Group 1 form compounds M_3E (E = As, Sb, Bi) and the metals of Groups 2 and 12 likewise form M_3E_2. These can formally be written as $M^+{}_3E^{3-}$ and $M^{2+}{}_3E^{3-}{}_2$ but the compounds are even less ionic than Li_3N (p. 76) and have many metallic properties. Moreover, other stoichiometries are found (e.g. $LiBi$, KBi_2, $CaBi_3$) which are not readily accounted for by the ionic model and, conversely, compounds M_3E are formed by many metals that are not usually thought of as univalent, e.g. Ti, Zr, Hf; V, Nb, Ta; Mn. There are clearly also strong additional interactions between unlike atoms as indicated by the structures adopted and the high mp of many of the compounds, e.g. Na_3Bi melts

[10] N. W. ALCOCK, M. RAVINDRAN and G. R. WILLEY, *J. Chem. Soc.. Chem. Commun.*, 1063–5 (1989).

[11] P. K. BHARADWAJ, A. M. LEE, S. MANDAL, B. W. SKELTON and A. H. WHITE, *Aust. J. Chem.* **47**, 1799–803 (1994).

[12] C. A. STEWART, J. C. CALABRESE and A. J. ARDUENGO, *J. Am. Chem. Soc.* **107**, 3397–8 (1985).

[13] J. L. VIDAL *Inorg. Chem.* **20**, 243–9 (1981).

[14] J. L. VIDAL and J. M. TROUP, *J. Organometallic Chem.* **213**, 351–63 (1981).

[15] C. A. MCAULIFFE and A. G. MACKIE *Chemistry of Arsenic, Antimony and Bismuth*, Ellis Horwood, Chichester, 1990, 350 pp.

[16] J. D. SMITH, Chap. 21 in *Comprehensive Inorganic Chemistry*, Vol. 2, pp. 547–683, Pergamon Press, Oxford, 1973.

[17] F. HULLIGER, *Struct. Bond.* **4**, 83–229 (1968). A comprehensive review with 532 references.

at 840°, compared with Na 98° and Bi 271°C. Many of the M_3E compounds have the hexagonal Na_3As (anti-LaF_3) structure in which equal numbers of Na and As form hexagonal nets as in boron nitride and the remaining Na atoms are arranged in layers on either side of these nets. Each As has 5 Na neighbours at the corners of a trigonal bipyramid (3 at 294 and 2 at 299) and 6 other Na atoms at 330 pm form a trigonal prism (i.e. 11-coordinate). The Na atoms are of two sorts, both of high mixed CN to As and Na, and all the Na–Na distances (328–330 pm) are less than in Na metal (371.6 pm). The compounds show either metallic conductivity or are semiconductors. An even more compact metal structure (cubic) is adopted by β-Li_3Bi, β-Li_3Sb, and by M_3E, where M = Rb, Cs, and E = Sb, Bi.

Some of the alkali metal–group 15 element systems give compounds of stoichiometry ME. Of these, LiBi and NaBi have typical alloy structures and are superconductors below 2.47 K and 2.22 K respectively. Others, like LiAs, NaSb and KSb, have parallel infinite spirals of As or Sb atoms, and it is tempting to formulate them as $M^+_n(E_n)^{n-}$ in which the $(E_n)^{n-}$ spirals are isoelectronic with those of covalently catenated Se and Te (p. 752); however, their metallic lustre and electrical conductivity indicate at least some metallic bonding. Within the spiral chains As–As is 246 pm (cf. 252 pm in the element) and Sb–Sb is ~285 pm (cf. 291 pm in the element).

Compounds with Sc, Y, lanthanoids and actinoids are of three types. Those with composition ME have the (6-coordinated) NaCl structure, whereas M_3E_4 (and sometimes M_4E_3) adopt the body-centred thorium phosphide structure (Th_3P_4) with 8-coordinated M, and ME_2 are like $ThAs_2$ in which each Th has 9 As neighbours. Most of these compounds are metallic and those of uranium are magnetically ordered. Full details of the structures and properties of the several hundred other transition metal–Group 15 element compounds fall outside the scope of this treatment, but three particularly important structure types should be mentioned because of their widespread occurrence and relation to other structure types, namely $CoAs_3$,

NiAs and structures related to those adopted by FeS_2 (marcasite, pyrites, loellingite, etc.).

$CoAs_3$ occurs in the mineral skutterudite; it is a diamagnetic semiconductor and has a cubic structure related to that of ReO_3 (p. 1047) but with a systematic distortion which results in the generation of well-defined *planar* rings of As_4. The same structure motif is found in MP_3 (M = Co, Ni, Rh, Pd), MAs_3 (M = Co, Rh, Ir) and MSb_3 (M = Co, Rh, Ir). The unit cell (Fig. 13.2) contains 8Co and 24As (i.e. $6As_4$), and it follows from the directions in which the various sets of atoms move, that 2 of the 8 original ReO_3 cells do not contain an As_4 group. Each As has a nearly regular tetrahedral arrangement of 2 Co and 2 As neighbours and each Co has a slightly distorted octahedral coordination group of 6 As. The planar As_4 groups are not quite square, the sides of the rectangle being 246 and 257 pm (cf. 244 pm in the tetrahedral As_4 molecule). The distortions from the ReO_3 structure (in which each As would have had 8 equidistant neighbours at about 330 pm) thus permit the closer approach of the As atoms in groups of 4 though this does not proceed so far as to form 6 equidistant As–As links as in the tetrahedral As_4 molecule. The P–P distances in the P_4 rectangles of the isostructural phosphides are 223 and 231 pm (cf. 225 pm in the tetrahedral P_4 molecule).

The NiAs structure is one of the commonest MX structure types, the number of compounds adopting it being exceeded only by those with the NaCl structure. It is peculiar to compounds formed by the transition elements with either As, Sb, Bi, the chalcogens (p. 748) or occasionally Sn. Examples with the Group 15 elements are Ti(As, Sb), V(P, Sb), CrSb, Mn(As, Sb, Bi), FeSb, Co(As, Sb), Ni(As, Sb, Bi), RhBi, Ir(Sb, Bi), PdSb, Pt(Sb, Bi). The structure is illustrated in Fig. 13.3a: each Ni is 8-coordinate, being surrounded by 6 As and by 2 Ni (which are coplanar with 4 of the As); the As atoms form a hcp lattice in which the interstices are occupied by Ni atoms in such a way that each As is surrounded by a trigonal prism of 6 Ni. Another important feature of the NiAs structure is the close approach of Ni atoms

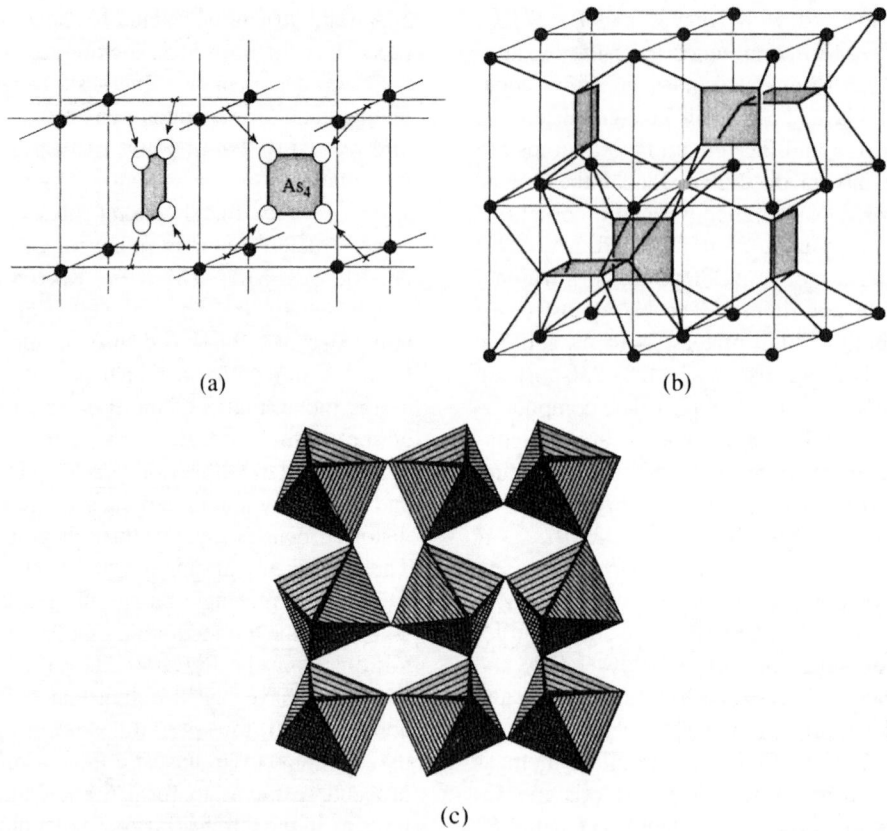

(a)

(b)

(c)

Figure 13.2 The cubic structure of skutterudite (CoAs$_3$). (a) Relation to the ReO$_3$ structure; (b) unit cell (only sufficient Co–As bonds are drawn to show that there is a square group of As atoms in only 6 of the 8 octants of the cubic unit cell, the complete 6-coordination group of Co is shown only for the atom at the body-centre of the cell); and (c) section of the unit cell showing {CoAs$_6$} octahedra corner-linked to form As$_4$ squares.

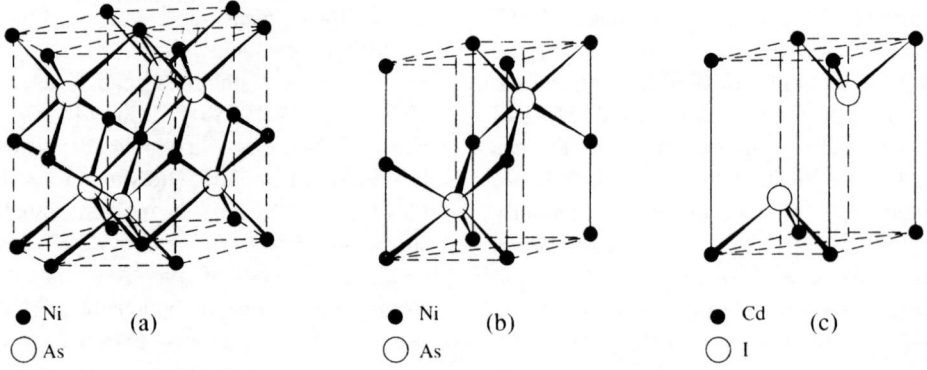

● Ni   (a)

○ As

● Ni   (b)

○ As

● Cd   (c)

○ I

Figure 13.3 Structure of nickel arsenide showing (a) 3 unit cells, (b) a single unit cell Ni$_2$As$_2$ and its relation to (c) the unit cell of the layer lattice compound CdI$_2$ (see text).

in chains along the (vertical) *c*-axis. The unit cell (Fig. 13.3b) contains Ni_2As_2, and if the central layer of Ni atoms is omitted the CdI_2 structure is obtained (Fig. 13.3c). This structural relationship accounts for the extensive ranges of composition frequently observed in compounds with this structure, since partial filling of the intermediate layer gives compositions in the range $M_{1+x}X_2$ ($0 < x < 1$). With the chalcogens the range sometimes extends the whole way from ME to ME_2 but for As, Sb and Bi it never reaches ME_2 and intermetallic compounds of this composition usually have either the marcasite or pyrites structures of FeS_2 (p. 680) or the compressed marcasite (loellingite) structure of $FeAs_2$. All three structure types contain the E_2 group. Examples are:

marcasite type:	$NiAs_2$, $NiSb_2$
pyrites type:	$PdAs_2$, $PdSb_2$, $PtAs_2$, $PtSb_2$, $PtBi_2$, $AuSb_2$
loellingite type:	$CrSb_2$, FeP_2, $FeAs_2$, $FeSb_2$, RuP_2, $RuAs_2$, $RuSb_2$, OsP_2, $OsAs_2$, $OsSb_2$
ternary compounds:	$CoAsS$ (i.e. "pyrites" $Co_2As_2S_2$), $NiSbS$ {i.e. "pyrites" $Ni(Sb-S)$}, $NiAsS$ (i.e. pyrites with random As and S on the S positions)

Compounds of As, Sb and Bi with the metals in Group 13 (Al, Ga, In, Tl) comprise the important III–V semiconductors whose structures, properties, and extensive applications have already been discussed (pp. 255–8). Group 14 elements also readily form compounds of which the following serve as examples: GeAs mp 737°C, $GeAs_2$ mp 732°C, SnAs

(NaCl structure, superconductor below 3.5 K), Sn_4As_3 (defect NaCl structure, superconductor below 1.2 K). The many important industrial applications of dilute alloys of As, Sb and Bi with tin and lead were mentioned on pp. 370 and 371.

13.3.2 Hydrides of arsenic, antimony and bismuth

AsH_3, SbH_3 and BiH_3 are exceedingly poisonous, thermally unstable, colourless gases whose physical properties are compared with those of NH_3 (p. 423) and PH_3 (p. 492) in Table 13.5. The absence of H bonding is apparent; in addition, the proton affinity is very low and there is little tendency to form the onium ions MH_4^+ analogous to NH_4^+. However, very recently the thermally unstable salts $[AsH_4]^+[SbF_6]^-$ (decomp. $-40°C$), $[AsH_4]^+[AsF_6]^-$ (d. $-75°$) and $[SbH_4]^+[SbF_6]^-$ (d. $-70°$), have been isolated as colourless air- and moisture-sensitive crystals by protonation of the hydrides MH_3 with the appropriate superacids. HF/MF_5 (M = As, Sb).[18] The gradually increasing densities of the liquids near their bp is expected, as is the increase in M–H distance. There is a small diminution in the angle H–M–H with increasing molecular weight though the difference for AsH_3 and SbH_3 is similar to the experimental uncertainty. The rapid diminution in thermal stability is reflected in the standard heats of formation ΔH_f°; AsH_3 decomposes to the elements on being warmed to 250–300°, SbH_3 decomposes steadily

---

[18] R. MINKWITZ, A. KORNATH, W. SAWODNY and H. HÄRT-NER, *Z. anorg. allg. Chem.* **620** 753–6 (1994).

Table 13.5 Comparison of the physical properties of AsH_3, SbH_3 and BiH_3 with those of NH_3 and PH_3

Property	NH_3	PH_3	AsH_3	SbH_3	BiH_3
MP/°C	-77.8	-133.5	-116.3	-88	—
BP/°C	-34.5	-87.5	-62.4	-18.4	$+16.8$ (extrap)
Density/g cm^{-3}(T°C)	0.683 ($-34°$)	0.746 ($-90°$)	1.640 ($-64°$)	2.204 ($-18°$)	—
ΔH_f°/kJ mol^{-1}	-46.1	$-9.6(?)$	66.4	145.1	277.8
Distance (M–H)/pm	101.7	141.9	151.9	170.7	—
Angle H–M–H	107.8°	93.6°	91.8°	91.3°	—

at room temperature, and BiH_3, cannot be kept above $-45°$.

Arsine, AsH_3, is formed when many As-containing compounds are reduced with nascent hydrogen and its decomposition on a heated glass surface to form a metallic mirror formed the basis of Marsh's test for the element. The low-temperature reduction of $AsCl_3$ with $LiAlH_4$ in diethyl ether solution gives good yields of the gas as does the dilute acid hydrolysis of many arsenides of electropositive elements (Na, Mg, Zn, etc.). Similar reactions yield stibine, e.g.:

$$Zn_3Sb_2 + 6H_3O^+ \xrightarrow[\text{14\% yield}]{\text{aq HCl}} 2SbH_3$$

$$+ 3Zn^{2+} + 6H_2O$$

$$SbO_3{}^{3-} + 3Zn + 9H_3O^+ \longrightarrow SbH_3$$

$$+ 3Zn^{2+} + 12H_2O$$

$$SbCl_3(\text{in aq NaCl}) + NaBH_4 \longrightarrow SbH_3$$

(high yield)

Both AsH_3 and SbH_3 oxidize readily to the tri-oxide and water, and similar reactions occur with S and Se. AsH_3 and SbH_3 form arsenides and antimonides when heated with metals and this reaction also finds application in semiconductor technology; e.g. highly purified SbH_3 is used as a gaseous n-type dopant for Si (p. 332).

Bismuthine, BiH_3, is extremely unstable and was first detected in minute traces by F. Paneth using a radiochemical technique involving $^{212}Bi_2Mg_3$. These experiments, carried out in 1918, were one of the earliest applications of radiochemical tracer experiments in chemistry. Later work using $BH_4{}^-$ to reduce $BiCl_3$ was unsuccessful in producing macroscopic amounts of the gas and the best preparation (1961) is the disproportionation of $MeBiH_2$ at $-45°$ for several hours; Me_2BiH can also be used:

$$Me_{3-n}BiH_n \xrightarrow{-45°} \frac{n}{3}BiH_3 + \frac{3-n}{3}BiMe_3$$

Lower hydrides such as As_2H_4 have occasionally been reported as fugitive species but little is known of their properties (see p. 583;

cf. also N_2H_4, p. 427; P_2H_4, p. 495). Recent fully optimized *ab initio* calculations (including relativistic core potentials) suggest that the double-bonded species HM=MH (M = P, As, Sb, Bi) should all exist as *trans* planar (C_{2v}) molecules;[19] close agreement with experimental interatomic distances in known organic diphosphenes (p. 544) and diarsenes adds confidence to the computed distances for $-Sb=Sb-$ (260.8 pm) and $-Bi=Bi-$ (271.9 pm) which are both about 9% shorter than the corresponding single-bond distances (cf. also $-P=P-$ 200.5 pm and $-As=As-$ 222.7 pm). The computed bond angles H–M–M in M_2H_2 (M = P, As, Sb, Bi) are $96.2°$, $94.4°$, $93.0°$ and $91.8°$, respectively.

13.3.3 Halides and related complexes

The numerous halides of As, Sb and Bi show highly significant gradations in physical proper-ties, structure, bonding and chemical reactivity. Distinctions between ionic, coordinate and cova-lent (molecular) structures in the halides and their complexes frequently depend on purely arbitrary demarcations and are often more a hindrance than a help in discerning the underlying structural and bonding principles. Alternations in the stability of the +5 oxidation state are also illuminating. It will be convenient to divide the discussion into five subsections dealing in turn with the trihalides MX_3, the pentahalides MX_5, other halides, halide complexes of M^{III} and M^V, and oxohalides.

Trihalides, MX_3

All 12 compounds are well known and are available commercially; their physical properties are summarized in Table 13.6 Comparisons with the corresponding data for NX_3 (p. 438) and PX_3 (p. 496) are also instructive. Trends in mp, bp and density are far from regular and reflect the differing structures and bond types.

---

[19] S. NAGASE, S. SUSUKI and T. KURAKAKE, *J. Chem. Soc., Chem. Commun.*, 1724–6 (1990).

Table 13.6 Some physical properties of the trihalides of arsenic, antimony and bismuth

Compound	Colour and state at 25°C	MP/°C	BP/°C	$d/\text{g cm}^{-3}$ (T°C)	$\Delta H_f^\circ/$ kJ mol^{-1}
AsF$_3$	Colourless liquid	−6.0	62.8	2.666 (0°)	−956.5
AsCl$_3$	Colourless liquid	−16.2	130.2	2.205 (0°)	−305.0
AsBr$_3$	Pale-yellow crystals	+31.2	221	3.66 (15°)	−197.0
AsI$_3$	Red crystals	140.4	∼400	4.39 (15°)	−58.2
SbF$_3$	Colourless crystals	290	∼345	4.38 (25°)	−915.5
SbCl$_3$	White, deliquescent crystals	73.4	223	3.14 (20°)	−382.2
SbBr$_3$	White, deliquescent crystals	96.0	288	4.15 (25°)	−259.4
SbI$_3$	Red crystals	170.5	401	4.92 (22°)	−100.4
BiF$_3$	Grey-white powder	649[a]	900	∼5.3	−900
BiCl$_3$	White, deliquescent crystals	233.5	441	4.75	−379
BiBr$_3$	Golden, deliquescent crystals	219	462	5.72	−276
BiI$_3$	Green-black crystals	408.6	∼542 (extrap)	5.64	−150

[a] BiF$_3$ is sometimes said to be "infusible" or to have mp at varying temperatures in the range 725–770°, but such materials are probably contaminated with the oxofluoride BiOF (p. 572).

Thus AsF$_3$, AsCl$_3$, AsBr$_3$, SbCl$_3$ and SbBr$_3$ are clearly volatile molecular species, whereas AsI$_3$, SbF$_3$ and BiX$_3$ have more extended interactions in the solid state. Trends in the heats of formation from the elements are more regular being *ca.* −925 kJ mol^{-1} for MF$_3$, *ca.* −350 kJ mol^{-1} for MCl$_3$, *ca.* −245 kJ mol^{-1} for MBr$_3$ and *ca.* −100 kJ mol for MI$_3$. Within these average values, however, AsF$_3$ is noticeably more exothermic than SbF$_3$ and BiF$_3$, whereas the reverse is true for the chlorides; there is also a regular trend towards increasing stability in the sequence As < Sb < Bi for the bromides and for the iodides of these elements.

The trifluorides are all readily prepared by the action of HF on the oxide M$_2$O$_3$ (direct fluorination of M or M$_2$O$_3$ with F$_2$ gives MF$_5$, p. 561). Because AsF$_3$ hydrolyses readily, the reaction is best done under anhydrous conditions using H$_2$SO$_4$/CaF$_2$ or HSO$_3$F/CaF$_2$, but aqueous HF can be used for the others. The trichlorides, tribromides and triiodides of As and Sb can all be prepared by direct reaction of X$_2$ with M or M$_2$O$_3$, whereas the less readily hydrolysed BiX$_3$ can be obtained by treating Bi$_2$O$_3$ with the aqueous HX. Many variants of these reactions are possible: e.g., AsCl$_3$ can be made by chlorination of As$_2$O$_3$ with Cl$_2$, S$_2$Cl$_2$, conc HCl or H$_2$SO$_4$/MCl.

The trihalides of As are all pyramidal molecular species in the gas phase with angle X–As–X in the range 96–100°. This structure persists in the solid state, and with AsI$_3$ the packing is such that each As is surrounded by an octahedron of six I with 3 short and 3 long As–I distances (256 and 350 pm; ratio 1.37, mean 303 pm). The I atoms form a regular hcp lattice. A similar layer structure is adopted by SbI$_3$ and BiI$_3$ but with the metal atoms progressively nearer to the centre of the I$_6$ octahedra:

3 Sb–I at 287 pm and 3 at 332 pm; ratio 1.16, mean 310 pm
all 6Bi–I at 310 pm; "ratio" 1.00

This is sometimes described as a trend from covalent, molecular AsI$_3$ through intermediate SbI$_3$ to ionic BiI$_3$, but this exaggerates the difference in bond-type. Arsenic, Sb and Bi have very similar electronegativities (p. 550) and it seems likely that the structural trend reflects more the way in which the octahedral interstices in the hcp iodine lattice are filled by atoms of gradually increasing size. The size of these interstices is about constant (see mean M–X distance) but only Bi is sufficiently large to fill them symmetrically.

Discrete molecules are apparent in the crystal structure of the higher trihalides of Sb, and,

Table 13.7 Structural data for antimony trihalides

	SbF_3	$SbCl_3$	α-$SbBr_3$	β-$SbBr_3$	SbI_3
Sb–X in gas molecule/pm	?	233	251	251	272
Three short Sb–X in crystal/pm	192	236	250	249	287
Three long Sb–X in crystal/pm	261	≥ 350	≥ 375	≥ 360	332
Ratio (long/short)	1.36	≥ 1.48	≥ 1.50	≥ 1.44	1.16
Angle X–Sb–X in crystal	87°	95°	96°	95°	96°

again, these pack to give 3 longer and 3 shorter interatomic distances (Table 13.7).

The structure of BiF_3 is quite different: β-BiF_3 has the "ionic" YF_3 structure with tricapped trigonal prismatic coordination of Bi by 9 F. $BiCl_3$ has an essentially molecular structure (like SbX_3) but there is a significant distortion within the molecule itself, and the packing gives 5 (not 3) further Cl at 322–345 pm to complete a *bi*capped trigonal prism. As a consequence of this structure $BiCl_3$ has smaller unit cell dimensions than $SbCl_3$ despite the longer Bi–Cl bond (250 pm, as against 236 pm for Sb–Cl). The eightfold coordination has been rationalized by postulating that the ninth position is occupied by the stereochemically active lone-pair of electrons on Bi^{III}. On this basis, the 3 long and 3 short M–X distances in octahedrally coordinated structures can also be understood, the lone-pair being directed towards the centre of the more distant triangle of 3X. However, it is hard to quantify this suggestion, particularly as the X–M–X angles are fairly constant at $97 \pm 2°$ (rather than 109.5° for sp^3 hybrids), implying little variation in hybridization and a lone-pair with substantial s^2 character. The effect is less apparent in SbI_3 and absent BiI_3 (see above) and this parallels the diminishing steric influence of the lone-pair in some of the complexes of the heavier halides with Sn^{II} (p. 380) and Te^{IV} (p. 757).

Many of the trihalides of As, Sb and Bi hydrolyse readily but can be handled without great difficulty under anhydrous conditions. AsF_3 and SbF_3 are important reagents for converting non-metal chlorides to fluorides. SbF_3 in particular is valuable for preparing organofluorine compounds (the Swarts reaction):

$$CCl_3CCl_3 + SbF_3 \longrightarrow CCl_2FCCl_2F$$

$$SiCl_4 + SbF_3 \longrightarrow SiCl_3F, SiCl_2F_2, SiClF_3$$

$$CF_3PCl_2 + SbF_3 \longrightarrow CF_3PF_2$$

$$R_3PS + SbF_3 \longrightarrow R_3PF_2$$

Sometimes the reagents simultaneously act as mild oxidants:

$$3PhPCl_2 + 4SbF_3 \longrightarrow 3PhPF_4 + 2Sb + 2SbCl_3$$

$$3Me_2P(S)P(S)Me_2 + 6SbF_3 \longrightarrow 6Me_2PF_3$$
$$+ 2Sb + 2Sb_2S_3$$

AsF_3, though a weaker fluorinating agent than SbF_3, is preferred for the preparation of high-boiling fluorides since $AsCl_3$ (bp 130°) can be distilled off. SbF_3 is preferred for low-boiling fluorides, which can be readily fractionated from $SbCl_3$ (bp 223°). Selective fluorinations are also possible, e.g.:

$$[PCl_4]^+[PCl_6]^- + 2AsF_3 \longrightarrow [PCl_4]^+[PF_6]^-$$
$$+ 2AsCl_3$$

$AsCl_3$ and $SbCl_3$ have been used as non-aqueous solvent systems for a variety of reactions.[20,21] They are readily available, have convenient liquid ranges (p. 559), are fairly easy to handle, have low viscosities η, moderately high dielectric constants ε and good solvent properties (Table 13.8).

[20] D. S. Payne, Chap. 8 in T. C. Waddington (ed.), *Nonaqueous Solvent Systems*, pp. 301–25, Academic Press, London, 1965.
[21] E. C. Baughan, Chap. 5 in J. J. Lagowski (ed.), *The Chemistry of Nonaqueous Solvents*, Vol. 4, pp. 129–65, Academic Press, London, 1976.

Table 13.8 Some properties of liquid $AsCl_3$ and $SbCl_3$

	η/centipoise	ε	κ/ohm^{-1} cm^{-1}
$AsCl_3$ at 20°C	1.23	12.8	1.4×10^{-7}
$SbCl_3$ at 75°C	2.58	33.2	1.4×10^{-6}

The low conductivities imply almost negligible self-ionization according to the formal scheme:

$$2MCl_3 \rightleftharpoons MCl_2^+ + MCl_4^-$$

Despite this, they are good solvents for chloride-ion transfer reactions, and solvo-acid–solvo-base reactions (p. 827) can be followed conductimetrically, voltametrically or by use of coloured indicators. As expected from their constitution, the trihalides of As and Sb are only feeble electron-pair donors (p. 198) but they have marked acceptor properties, particularly towards halide ions (p. 564) and amines.

AsX_3 and SbX_3 react with alcohols (especially in the presence of bases) and with sodium alkoxide to give arsenite and antimonite esters, $M(OR)_3$ (cf. phosphorus, (p. 515):

$$AsCl_3 + 3PhOH \longrightarrow As(OPh)_3 + 3HCl$$

$$SbCl_3 + 3Bu^tOH + 3NH_3 \longrightarrow Sb(OBu^t)_3$$
$$+ 3NH_4Cl$$

$$SbCl_3 + 3NaOSiEt_3 \longrightarrow Sb(OSiEt_3)_3 + 3NaCl$$

Halide esters $(RO)_2MX$ and $(RO)MX_2$ can be made similarly:

$$AsCl_3 + 2NaOEt \longrightarrow (EtO)_2AsCl + 2NaCl$$

$$AsCl_3 + EtOH \xrightarrow{CO_2} (EtO)AsCl_2 + HCl$$

$$As(OPr)_3 + MeCOCl \longrightarrow (PrO)_2AsCl + MeCO_2Pr$$

Amino derivatives are obtained by standard reactions with secondary amines, lithium amides or by transaminations:

$$AsCl_3 + 6Me_2NH \longrightarrow As(NMe_2)_3 + 3[Me_2NH_2]Cl$$

$$SbCl_3 + 3LiNMe_2 \longrightarrow Sb(NMe_2)_3 + 3LiCl$$

$$As(NMe_2)_3 + 3Bu_2NH \longrightarrow As(NBu_2)_3 + 3Me_2NH$$

As with phosphorus (p. 533) there is an extensive derivative chemistry of these and related compounds.[15,16]

Pentahalides, MX$_5$

Until fairly recently only the pentafluorides and $SbCl_5$ were known, but the exceedingly elusive $AsCl_5$ was finally prepared in 1976 by ultraviolet irradiation of $AsCl_3$ in liquid Cl_2 at $-105°C$.[22] Some properties of the 5 pentahalides are given in Table 13.9.

The pentafluorides are prepared by direct reaction of F_2 with the elements (As, Bi) or their oxides (As_2O_3, Sb_2O_3). $AsCl_5$, as noted above, has only a fugitive existence and decomposes to $AsCl_3$ and Cl_2 at about $-50°$. $SbCl_5$ is more stable and is made by reaction of Cl_2 on $SbCl_3$. No pentabromides or pentaiodides have been characterized, presumably because M^V is too highly oxidizing for these heavier halogens (cf. TlI_3, p. 239). The relative instability of $AsCl_5$ when compared with PCl_5 and $SbCl_5$ is a further example of the instability of the highest valency state of p-block elements following the completion of the first (3d) transition series (p. 552). This can be understood in terms of incomplete shielding of the nucleus which leads to a "d-block contraction" and a consequent lowering of the energy of the 4s orbital in As and $AsCl_3$, thereby making it more difficult to promote one of the $4s^2$ electrons

---

[22] K. SEPPELT, *Angew. Chem. Int. Edn. Engl.* **15**, 377–8 (1976).

Table 13.9 Some properties of the known pentahalides

Property	AsF$_5$	SbF$_5$	BiF$_5$	AsCl$_5$	SbCl$_5$
MP/°C	−79.8	8.3	154.4	~ -50 (d)	4
BP/°C	−52.8	141	230	—	140 (d)
Density (T°C)/g cm^{-3}	2.33 (−53°)	3.11 (25°)	5.40 (25°)	—	2.35 (21°)

for the formation of $AsCl_5$. There is no evidence that the As–Cl bond strength itself, in $AsCl_5$, is unduly weak. The non-existence of $BiCl_5$ likewise suggests that it is probably less stable than $SbCl_5$, due the analogous "f-block contraction" following the lanthanide elements (p. 1232).

Evidence from vibration spectroscopy suggests that gaseous AsF_5, solid $AsCl_5$ and liquid $SbCl_5$ are trigonal bipyramidal molecules like PF_5 (D_{3h}), and this is confirmed for AsF_5 by a low-temperature X-ray crystal structure which also indicates that the As-F(axial) distances (171.9 pm) are slightly longer than the As–F (equatorial) distances (166.8 pm).[23] By contrast SbF_5 is an extremely viscous, syrupy liquid with a viscosity approaching 850 centipoise at 20°: the liquid features polymeric chains of cis-bridged {SbF_6} octahedra in which the 3 different types of F atom (a, b, c) can be distinguished by low-temperature ^{19}F nmr spectroscopy.[24] As shown in Fig. 13.4(a), F_a are the bridging atoms and are cis to each other in any one octahedron; F_b are

also cis to each other and are, in addition, cis to 1 F_a and trans to the other, whereas F_c are trans to each other and cis to both F_a. In the crystalline state the cis bridging persists but the structure has tetrameric molecular units (Fig. 13.4(b)) rather than high polymers.[25] There are two different Sb–F–Sb bridging angles, 141° and 170°, and the terminal $Sb–F_t$ distances (mean 182 ± 5 pm) are noticeably less than the bridging $Sb–F_\mu$ distances (mean 203 ± 5 pm). (See p. 569 for the ionic structures of Sb_8F_{30}, i.e. $Sb^V{}_3Sb^{III}{}_5F_{30}$.) Yet another structure motif is adopted in BiF_5; this crystallizes in long white needles and has the α-UF_5 structure in which infinite linear chains of trans-bridged {BiF_6} octahedra are stacked parallel to each other. The Bi–F–Bi bridging angle between adjacent octahedra in the chain is 180°.

The pentafluorides are extremely powerful fluorinating and oxidizing agents and they also have a strong tendency to form complexes with electron-pair donors. This latter property has already been presaged by the propensity of SbF_5 to polymerize and is discussed more fully on p. 569.

[23] J. KÖHLER, A. SIMON and R. HOPPE, *Z. anorg. allg. Chem.* **575**, 55–60 (1989).

[24] T. K. DAVIES and K. C. MOSS, *J. Chem. Soc.*, (A), 1054–8 (1970).

[25] A. J. EDWARDS and P. TAYLOR, *J. Chem. Soc., Chem. Commun.*, 1376–7 (1971).

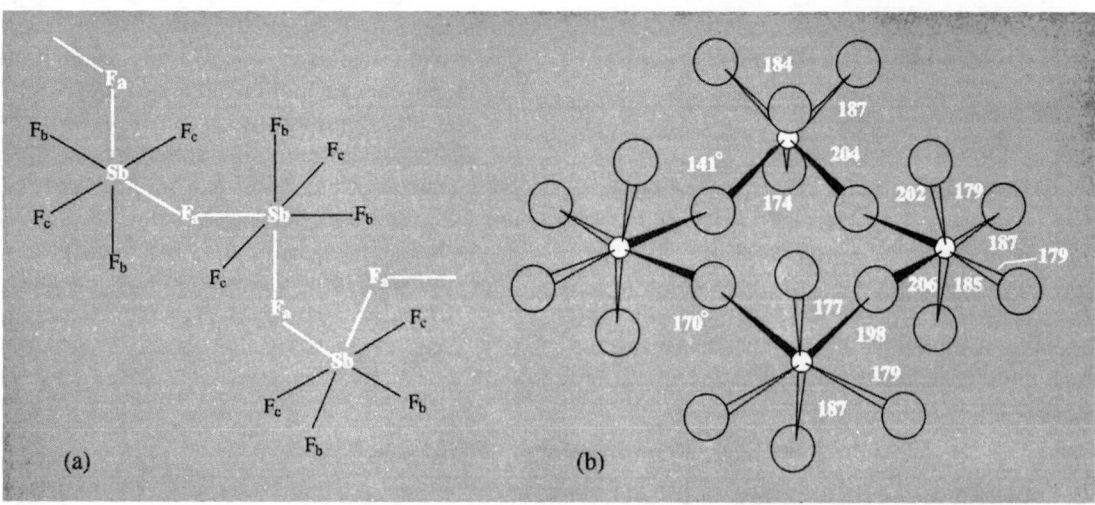

Figure 13.4 (a) The cis-bridged polymeric structure of liquid SbF_5 (schematic) showing the three sorts of F atom.[24] (b) Structure of the tetrameric molecular unit in crystalline $(SbF_5)_4$ showing the cis-bridging of 4 {SbF_6} octahedra (distances in pm).[25]

See also "superacids" on p. 570. Some typical reactions of SbF_5 and $SbCl_5$ are as follows:

$$ClCH_2PCl_2 + SbF_5 \longrightarrow ClCH_2PF_4$$

$$Me_3As + SbCl_5 \longrightarrow Me_3AsCl_2 + SbCl_3$$

$$R_3P + SbCl_5 \longrightarrow [R_3PCl]^+[SbCl_6]^-$$

$$(R = Ph, Et_2N, Cl)$$

$$SbCl_5 \xrightarrow{\text{5NaOR}} Sb(OR)_5 \xrightarrow{\text{NaX}} Na[Sb(OR)_5X]$$

$$(X = OR, Cl)$$

Perhaps the most reactive compound of the group is BiF_5. It reacts extremely vigorously with H_2O to form O_3, OF_2 and a voluminous brown precipitate which is probably a hydrated bismuth(V) oxide fluoride. At room temperature BiF_5 reacts vigorously with iodine or sulfur; above 50° it converts paraffin oil to fluorocarbons; at 150° it fluorinates UF_4 to UF_6; and at 180° it converts Br_2 to BrF_3 and BrF_5, and Cl_2 to ClF.

Mixed halides and lower halides

Unlike phosphorus, which forms a large number of readily isolable mixed halides of both P^{III} and P^V, there is apparently less tendency to form such compounds with As, Sb and Bi, and few mixed halides have so far been characterized. AsF_3 and $AsCl_3$ are immiscible below 19°C, but at room temperature ^{19}F nmr indicates some halogen exchange; however equilibrium constants for the formation of AsF_2Cl and $AsFCl_2$ are rather small. Likewise, Raman spectra show the presence of $AsCl_2Br$ and $AsClBr_2$ in mixtures of the parent trihalides, though rapid equilibration prevents isolation of the mixed halides. It is said that $SbBrI_2$ (mp 88°) can be obtained by eliminating EtBr from $EtSbI_2Br_2$.

Mixed pentahalides are more readily isolated and are of at least three types: ionic, tetrameric, and less stable molecular trigonal-bipyramidal monomers. Thus, chlorination of a mixture of $AsF_3/AsCl_3$ with Cl_2, or fluorination of $AsCl_3$ with ClF_3 (p. 828) gives $[AsCl_4]^+[AsF_6]^-$ [mp 130°(d)] whose X-ray crystal structure has recently been redetermined.[26] Similarly, $AsCl_3 + SbCl_5 + Cl_2 \rightarrow [AsCl_4]^+[SbCl_6]^-$. It also appears that all members of the monomeric molecular series $AsCl_{5-n}F_n$ ($n = 1-4$) can be made either by thermolysis of $[AsCl_4]^+[AsF_6]^-$ or, in the case of $AsCl_3F_2$ (D_{3h}), by gas-solid reaction of $AsCl_2F_3$ (g) with $CaCl_2$ (s); the compounds were characterized as trigonal-bipyramidal molecules by low-temperature matrix ir and Raman spectra.[27] The mixed bromofluoride $[AsBr_4]^+[AsF_6]^-$, made by reaction of $AsBr_3$, Br_2 and AsF_5 at low temperature was also characterized by Raman spectroscopy.[28]

Antimony chloride fluorides have been known since the turn of the century but the complexity of the system, the tendency to form mixtures of compounds, and their great reactivity have conspired against structural characterization until fairly recently.[29] It is now clear that fluorination of $SbCl_5$ depends crucially on the nature of the fluorinating agent. Thus, with AsF_3 it gives $SbCl_4F$ (mp 83°) which is a *cis*-F-bridged tetramer as in Fig. 13.4(b) with the terminal F atoms replaced by Cl. Fluorination of $SbCl_5$ with HF also gives this compound but, in addition, $SbCl_3F_2$ mp 68° (*cis*-F-bridged tetramer) and $SbCl_2F_3$ mp 62°, which turns out to be $[SbCl_4]^+[Sb_2Cl_2F_9]^-$. The anion is F-bridged, i.e. $[ClF_4Sb-F-SbF_4Cl]^-$ with angle Sb-F-Sb 163°. Even more extensive fluorination occurs when $SbCl_5$ is reacted with SbF_5 and the product is $[SbCl_4]^+[Sb_2F_{11}]^-$. By contrast, fluorination of $(SbCl_4F)_4$ with SbF_5 in liquid SO_2 yields $Sb_4Cl_{13}F_7$ (mp $\sim$ 50°) which is a *cis*-F-bridged tetramer of $SbCl_3F_2$ with two of the Sb atoms having a Cl atom partially replaced by F, i.e. $(Sb_2Cl_{6.5}F_{3.5})_2$ and bridge angles Sb-F-Sb of 166–168°.

[26] R. MINKWITZ, J. NOWICKI and H. BORRMANN, *Z. anorg. allg. Chem.* **596**, 93–8 (1991).

[27] R. MINKWITZ and H. PRENZEL, *Z. anorg. allg. Chem.* **548**, 103–7 (1987).

[28] T. KLAPÖTKE, J PASSMORE and E. G. AWERE, *J. Chem. Soc., Chem. Commun.*, 1426–7 (1988).

[29] J. G. BALLARD, T. BIRCHALL and D. R. SLIM, *J. Chem. Soc., Dalton Trans.*, 62–5 (1979), and references therein.

The attention which has been paid to the mixed chloride fluorides of Sb^V is due not only to the intellectual problem of their structures but also to their importance as industrial fluorinating agents (Swarts reaction). Addition of small amounts of $SbCl_5$ to SbF_5 results in a dramatic decrease in viscosity (due to the breaking of Sb–F–Sb links) and a substantial increase in electrical conductivity (due to the formation of fluoro-complex ions). Such mixed halides are often more effective fluorinating agents than SbF_3, provided that yields are not lowered by oxidation, e.g. $SOCl_2$ gives SOF_2; $POCl_3$ gives $POFCl_2$; and hexachlorobutadiene is partially fluorinated and oxidized to give $CF_3CCl{=}CClCF_3$ which can then be further oxidized to CF_3CO_2H:

$$CCl_2{=}CClCCl{=}CCl_2 \xrightarrow{\text{``SbF}_3\text{Cl}_2\text{''}} CF_3CCl{=}CClCF_3$$

$$\xrightarrow[\text{KOH}]{\text{KMnO}_4/} 2CF_3CO_2H$$

The use of SbF_5 in the preparation of "superacids" such as $(HSO_3F + SbF_5 + SO_3)$ is described in the following subsection (p. 570).

The only well-established lower halide of As is As_2I_4 which is formed as red crystals (mp 137°) when stoichiometric amounts of the 2 elements are heated to 260° in a sealed tube in the presence of octahydrophenanthrene. The compound hydrolyses and oxidizes readily and disproportionates in warm CS_2 solution but is stable up to 150° in an inert atmosphere. Disproportionation is quantitative at 400°:

$$3As_2I_4 \longrightarrow 4AsI_3 + 2As$$

Sb_2I_4 is much less stable: it has been detected by emf or vapour pressure measurements on solutions of Sb in SbI_3 at 230° but has not been isolated as a pure compound.

The lower halides of Bi are rather different. The diatomic species BiX (X = Cl, Br, I) occur in the equilibrium vapour above heated $Bi–BiX_3$ mixtures. A black crystalline lower chloride of composition $BiCl_{1.167}$ is obtained by heating $Bi–BiCl_3$ mixtures to 325° and cooling them during 1–2 weeks to 270° before removing excess $BiCl_3$ by sublimation or extraction into benzene. The compound is diamagnetic and has an astonishing structure which involves cationic clusters of bismuth and 2 different chloro-complex anions:[30] $[(Bi_9{}^{5+})_2(BiCl_5{}^{2-})_4(Bi_2Cl_8{}^{2-})]$, i.e. $Bi_{24}Cl_{28}$ or Bi_6Cl_7. The $Bi_9{}^{5+}$ cluster is a tricapped trigonal prism (p. 591); the anion $BiCl_5{}^{2-}$ has square pyramidal coordination of the 5 Cl atoms around Bi with the sixth octahedral position presumably occupied by the lone-pair of electrons, and $Bi_2Cl_8{}^{2-}$ has two such pyramids *trans*-fused at a basal edge (p. 565). The compound is stable in vacuum below 200° but disproportionates at higher temperatures. It also disproportionates in the presence of ligands which coordinate strongly to $BiCl_3$ and hydrolyses readily to the oxide chloride.

Bismuth also forms an intriguing family of subiodides, Bi_4I_4, $Bi_{14}I_4$ and $Bi_{18}I_4$, which comprise a series of infinite one-dimensional quasi-molecular ribbons of Bi atoms $[Bi_mI_4]_\infty$ of different width (m = 4, 14, 18). There are two sorts of Bi atom in these structures: "internal" atoms (Bi_{in}) surrounded by three other Bi atoms only, at 300–312 pm (cf. 307 pm in Bi metal), and "external" Bi_{ex}, connected to differing numbers of Bi and I atoms depending on m.[31] Bi_4Br_4 has a similar structure. The first unambiguous identification of Bi^+ in the solid state came in 1971 when the structure of the complex halide $Bi_{10}Hf_3Cl_{18}$ was shown by X-ray diffraction analysis[32] to be $(Bi^+)(Bi_9{}^{5+})(HfCl_6{}^{2-})_3$. The compound was made by the oxidation of Bi with $HfCl_4/BiCl_3$.

Halide complexes of M^{III} and M^V

The trihalides of As, Sb and Bi are strong halide-ion acceptors and numerous complexes have been isolated with a wide variety of compositions. They are usually prepared by direct reaction of the trihalide with the appropriate

[30] A. HERSHAFT and J. D. CORBETT, *Inorg. Chem.* **2**, 979–85 (1963).

[31] E. V. DIKAREV, B. A. POPOVKIN and A. V. SHEVELKOV, *Z. anorg. allg. Chem.* **612** 118–22 (1992).

[32] R. M. FRIEDMAN and J. D. CORBETT, *J. Chem. Soc., Chem. Commun.*, 422–3 (1971).

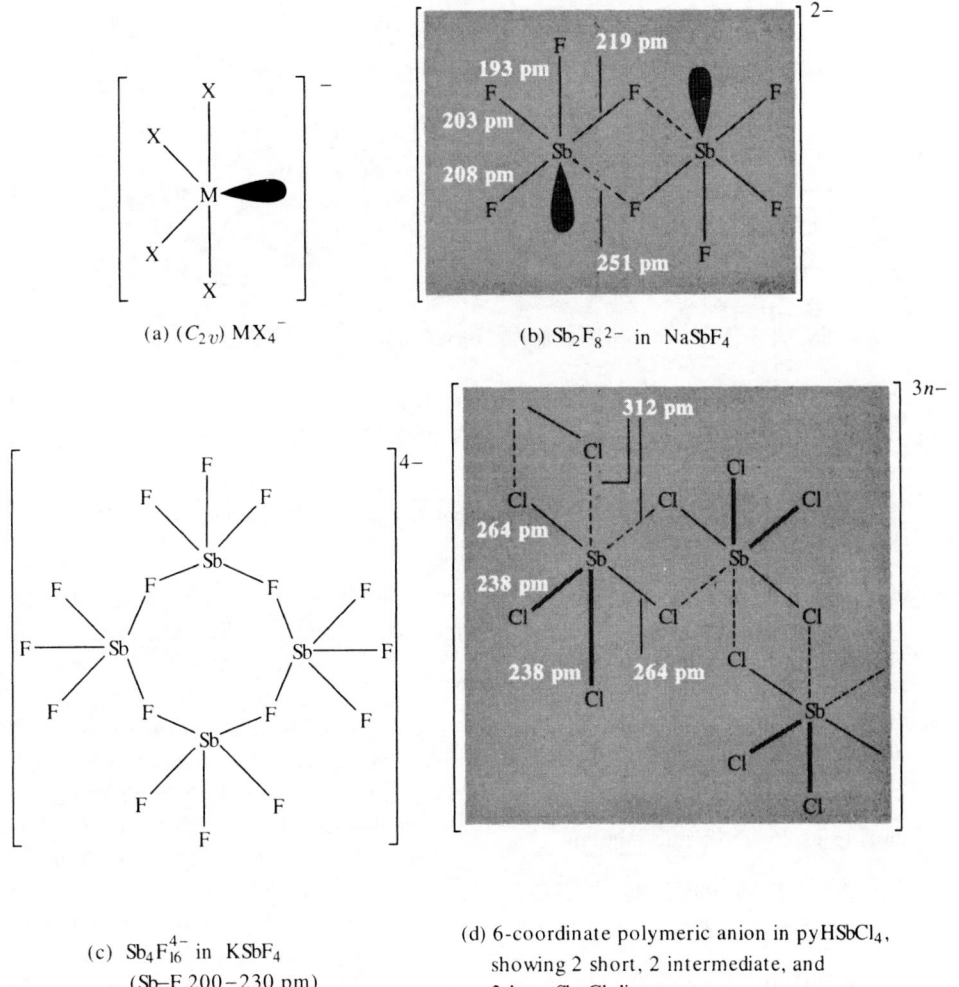

(a) (C_{2v}) MX_4^-

(b) $Sb_2F_8^{2-}$ in $NaSbF_4$

(c) $Sb_4F_{16}^{4-}$ in $KSbF_4$
(Sb–F 200–230 pm)

(d) 6-coordinate polymeric anion in $pyHSbCl_4$,
showing 2 short, 2 intermediate, and
2 long Sb–Cl distances

Figure 13.5 Structures of some complex halide anions of stoichiometry MX_4^-.

halide-ion donor. However, stoichiometry is not always a reliable guide to structure because of the possibility of oligomerization which depends both on the nature of M and X, and often also on the nature of the counter cation.[16,33] Thus the tetra-alkylammonium salts of MCl_4^-, MBr_4^-, and MI_4^- may contain the monomeric C_{2v} ion as shown in Fig. 13.5a (cf. isoelectronic SeF_4, p. 773), whereas in $NaSbF_4$

there is a tendency to dimerize by formation of subsidiary F···Sb interactions (Fig. 13.5b) cf. $Bi_2Cl_8^{2-}$ in the preceding subsection. With $KSbF_4$ association proceeds even further to give tetrameric cyclic anions (Fig. 13.5c). In both $NaSbF_4$ and $KSbF_4$ the Sb atoms are 5-coordinate but coordination rises to 6 in the polymeric chain anions of the pyridinium and 2-methylpyridinium salts $pyHSbCl_4$, $(2\text{-}MeC_5H_4NH)BiBr_4$ and $(2\text{-}MeC_5H_4NH)BiI_4$. The structure of $(SbCl_4)_n^{n-}$ is shown schematically in Fig. 13.5d and the three differing Sb–Cl distances reflect, in part,

[33] A. F. Wells, *Structural Inorganic Chemistry*, 5th edn., pp. 879–88 and 894–9, Oxford University Press, Oxford, 1984.

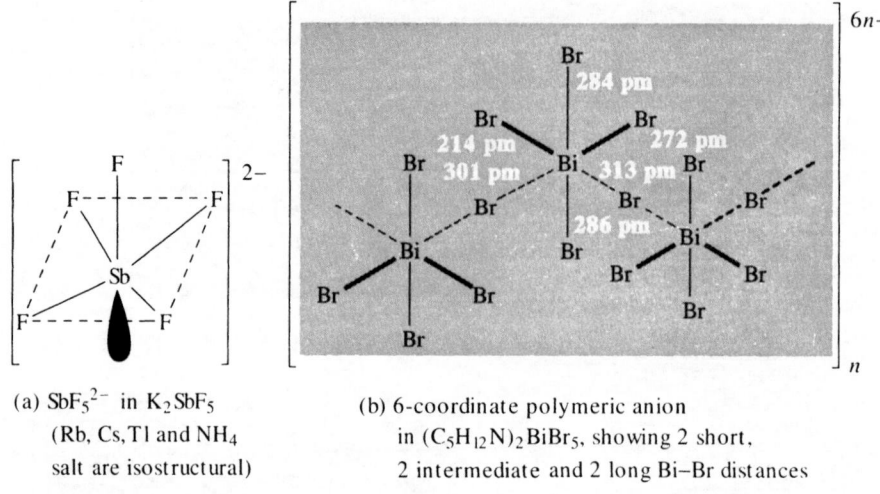

(a) SbF_5^{2-} in K_2SbF_5
(Rb, Cs, Tl and NH_4
salt are isostructural)

(b) 6-coordinate polymeric anion
in $(C_5H_{12}N)_2BiBr_5$, showing 2 short,
2 intermediate and 2 long Bi–Br distances

Figure 13.6 Structures of some complex halide anions of stoichiometry MX_5^{2-}.

the influence of the lone-pair of electrons on Sb^{III}. It will be noted that the shortest bonds are *cis* to each other, whereas the intermediate bonds are *trans* to each other; the longest bonds are *cis* to each other and *trans* to the short bonds. Corresponding distances in the Bi^{III} analogues are:

$(BiBr_4)_n^{n-}$: short (2 at 264 pm); intermediate

(283, 297 pm); long (308, 327 pm)

$(BiI_4)_n^{n-}$: short (2 at 289 pm); intermediate

(2 at 310 pm); long (331, 345 pm).

Complexes of stoichiometry MX_5^{2-} can feature either discrete 5-coordinate anions as in K_2SbF_5 and $(NH_4)_2SbCl_5$ (Fig. 13.6a), or 6-coordinate polymeric anions as in the piperidinium salt $(C_5H_{10}NH_2)_2BiBr_5$ (Fig. 13.6b). In the discrete anion $SbCl_5^{2-}$ the Sb–Cl_{apex} distance (236 pm) is shorter than the Sb–Cl_{base} distances (2 at 258 and 2 at 269 pm) and the Sb atom is slightly below the basal plane (by 22 pm). The same structure is observed in K_2SbCl_5.

In addition to the various complex fluoroantimonate(III) salts M^ISbF_4 and $M_2^ISbF_5$ mentioned above, the alkali metals form complexes of stoichiometry $M^ISb_2F_7$, $M^ISb_3F_{10}$ and $M^ISb_4F_{13}$, i.e. $[SbF_4^-(SbF_3)_n]$ ($n = 1, 2, 3$)

but the mononuclear complexes $M_3^ISbF_6$ have not been found. The structure of $M^ISb_2F_7$ depends on the strength of the Sb–$F\cdots Sb$ bridge between the 2 units and this, in turn is influenced by the cation. Thus, in KSb_2F_7 there are distorted trigonal-bipyramidal SbF_4^- ions (Fig. 13.7a) and discrete pyramidal SbF_3 molecules (Sb–F 194 pm) with 2 (rather than 3) contacts between these and neighbouring SbF_4^- units of 241 and 257 pm (cf. SbF_3 itself, p. 560). By contrast $CsSb_2F_7$ has well-defined $Sb_2F_7^-$ anions (Fig. 13.7b) formed from 2 distorted trigonal bipyramidal $\{SbF_4\}$ groups sharing a common axial F atom with long bridge bonds.

Similar structural diversity characterizes the heavier halide complexes of the group. The

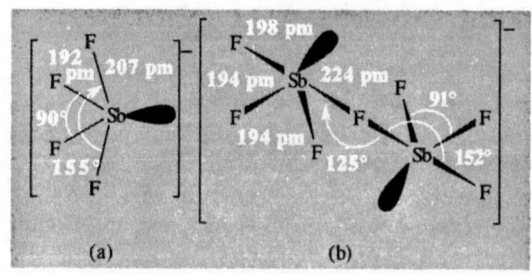

Figure 13.7 Structures of SbF_4^- and $Sb_2F_7^-$ ions in $KSbF_4(SbF_3)$ and $CsSb_2F_7$ respectively.

$[MX_6]^{3-}$ group occurs in several compounds, and these frequently have a regular octahedral structure like the isoelectronic $[Te^{IV}X_6]^{2-}$ ions (p. 776), despite the formal 14-electron configuration on the central atom. For example the jet-black compound $(NH_4)_2SbBr_6$ is actually $[(NH_4^+)_4(Sb^{III}Br_6)^{3-}(Sb^VBr_6)^-]$ with alternating octahedral Sb^{III} and Sb^V ions. The undistorted nature of the $SbBr_6^{3-}$ octahedra suggests that the lone-pair is predominantly $5s^2$ but there is a sense in which this is still stereochemically active since the Sb–Br distance in $[Sb^{III}Br_6]^{3-}$ (279.5 pm) is substantially longer than in $[Sb^VBr_6]^-$ (256.4 pm). Similar dimensional changes are found in $(pyH)_6Sb_4Br_{24}$ which is $[(pyH^+)_6(Sb^{III}Br_6)^{3-}(Sb^VBr_6^-)_3]$. In $(Me_2NH_2)_3BiBr_6$ the $(Bi^{III}Br_6)^{3-}$ octahedron is only slightly distorted. Sixfold coordination also occurs in compounds such as $Cs_3Bi_2I_9$ and $[(pyH^+)_5(Sb_2Br_9)^{3-}(Br^-)_2]$ in which $M_2X_9^{3-}$ has the confacial bioctahedral structure of $Tl_2Cl_9^{3-}$ (p. 240) (Fig. 13.8). In β-$Cs_3Sb_2Cl_9$ and $Cs_3Bi_2Cl_9$, however, there are close-packed Cs^+ and Cl^- with Sb^{III} (or Bi^{III}) in octahedral interstices. In $Cs_3As_2Cl_9$ the $\{AsCl_6\}$ groups are highly distorted so that there are discrete $AsCl_3$ molecules (As–Cl 225 pm) embedded between Cs^+ and Cl^- ions (As–Cl$^-$ 275 pm).

Irregular 6- and 7-fold coordination of Sb occurs in the complexes of $SbCl_3$ with crown thioethers,[34] and 8-fold coordination has been established in its complex with the η^5-ether

ligand 15-crown-5.[35] Crown ethers have also been used to stabilize the first complexed (9-coordinate) trications of Sb^{III} and Bi^{III}, viz. $[Sb(12\text{-crown-}4)_2(MeCN)]^{3+}[SbCl_6]_3^-$ and $[Bi(12\text{-crown-}4)_2(MeCN)]^{3+}[SbCl_6]_3^-$.[36] The complicated 9- and 10-fold coordination around Bi^{III} in the novel 1:1 and 1:2 arene complexes of $BiCl_3$ with $1,3,5\text{-Me}_3C_6H_3$ (i.e. mesitylene) and C_6Me_6, respectively, should also be noted, viz. $[(\eta^6\text{-mes})_2Bi_2Cl_6]$ in which each Bi is coordinated by $6C + 3Cl + (2Cl)$, and $[(\mu:\eta^6,\eta^6\text{-ar})_2Bi_4Cl_{12}]$ in which each Bi is coordinated by $6C + 2Cl + 2Cl + (2Cl)$ and each C_6Me_6 ligand bridges two Bi atoms.[37] A planar 6-membered $[Bi_3Cl_3]$ ring occurs in $[\{Fe(\eta^5\text{-}C_5H_4Me)(CO)_2\}_2BiCl]_3$.[38]

A fascinating variety of discrete (or occasionally polymeric) polynuclear halogeno complexes of As^{III}, Sb^{III} and Bi have recently been characterized. A detailed discussion would be inappropriate here, but structural motifs include face-shared and edge-shared distorted $\{MX_6\}$ octahedral units fused into cubane-like and other related clusters or cluster fragments. Examples (see also preceding paragraph) are:

$[As_3Br_{12}]^{3-}$,[39] $[As_6Br_8]^{2-}$,[40] $[As_6I_8]^{2-}$,[41]

$[As_8I_{28}]^{4-}$;[39] $[Sb_2Cl_8]^{2-}$,[42] $[Sb_2I_8]^{2-}$,[43]

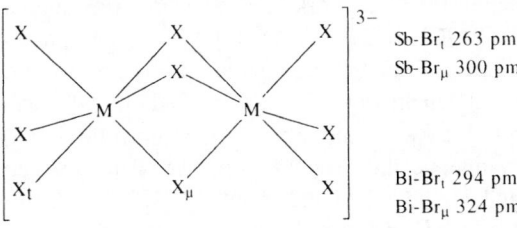

Sb-Br$_t$ 263 pm
Sb-Br$_\mu$ 300 pm

Bi-Br$_t$ 294 pm
Bi-Br$_\mu$ 324 pm

Figure 13.8 Structure of $M_2X_9^{3-}$.

[34] G. R. WILLEY, M. T. LAKIN, M. RAVINDRAN and N. W. ALCOCK, *J. Chem. Soc., Chem. Commun.*, 271–2 (1991).

[35] E. HOUGH, D. G. NICHOLSON and A. K. VASUDEVAN, *J. Chem. Soc., Dalton Trans.*, 427–30 (1987).

[36] R. GARBE, B. VOLLMER, B. NEUMÜLLER, J. PEBLER and K. DENICKE, *Z. anorg. allg. Chem.* **619**, 272–6 (1993).

[37] A. SCHIER, J. M. WALLIS, G. MÜLLER and H. SCHMIDBAUR, *Angew. Chem. Int. Edn. Engl.* **25**, 757–9 (1986).

[38] W. CLEGG, N. A. COMPTON, R. J. ERRINGTON and N. C. NORMAN, *Polyhedron* **6**, 2031–3 (1987). See also W. CLEGG, N. A. COMPTON, R. J. ERRINGTON, G. A. FISHER, C. R. HOCKLESS, N. C. NORMAN and A. G. ORPEN, *Polyhedron* **10**, 123–6 (1991).

[39] W. S. SHELDRICK and H.-J. HÄUSLER, *Angew. Chem. Int. Edn. Engl.* **26**, 1172–4 (1987).

[40] U. MÜLLER and H. SINNINO, *ibid.* **28**, 185–6 (1989).

[41] C. A. GHILARDI, S. MIDOLLINI, S. MONETI and A. ORLANDINI, *J. Chem. Soc., Chem. Commun.*, 1241–2 (1988).

[42] M. G. B. DREW, P. P. K. CLAIRE and G. R. WILLEY, *J. Chem. Soc., Dalton Trans.*, 215–8 (1988).

[43] S. POHL, W. SAAK and D. HASSE, *Angew. Chem. Int. Edn. Engl.* **26**, 467–8 (1987).

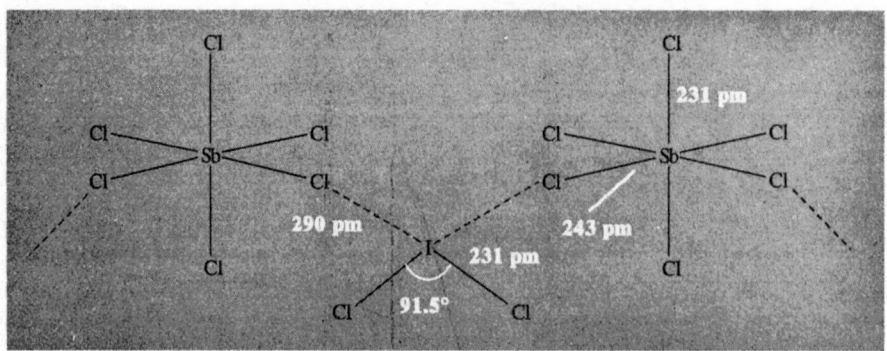

Figure 13.9   Schematic representation of the structure of $ISbCl_8$ (see text).

$[Sb_3I_{10}]^-$,[44] $[Sb_3I_{11}]^{2-}$,[45] $[Sb_5I_{18}]^{3-}$,[45,46] $[Sb_6I_{22}]^{4-}$,[45] $[Sb_8I_{28}]^{4-}$;[46] $[Bi_2I_8L_2]^{2-}$,[47] $[Bi_4I_{14}L_2]^{2-}$,[48] $[Bi_5I_{19}]^{4-}$,[48] and $[Bi_6I_{22}]^{4-}$.[48]

The detailed coordination geometry about As, Sb or Bi in these clusters varies substantially, and is of considerable significance in describing the nature of the bonding in these species.

No completely general and quantitative theory of the stereochemical activity of the lone-pair of electrons in complex halides of tervalent As, Sb and Bi has been developed but certain trends are discernible. The lone-pair becomes less decisive in modifying the stereochemistry (a) with increase in the coordination number of the central atom from 4 through 5 to 6, (b) with increase in the atomic weight of the central atom (As > Sb > Bi), and (c) with increase in the atomic weight of the halogen (F > Cl > Br > I). The relative energies of the various valence-level orbitals may also be an important factor: the $F(\sigma)$ orbital of F lies well below both the s and the p valence orbitals of Sb (for example) whereas the σ orbital energies of Cl, Br and I lie between these two levels, at least in the free atoms. It follows that the lone pair is likely to be in a (stereochemically active) metal-based sp^x hybrid orbital in fluoro complexes of Sb but in a (stereochemically inactive) metal-based a_1 orbital for the heavier halogens.[49]

In the +5 oxidation state, halide complexes of As, Sb and Bi are also well established and the powerful acceptor properties of SbF_5 in particular have already been noted (p. 562). Such complexes are usually made by direct reaction of the pentahalide with the appropriate ligand. Thus $KAsF_6$ and $NOAsF_6$ have octahedral AsF_6^- groups and salts of SbF_6^- and $SbCl_6^-$ (as well as $[Sb(OH)_6]^-$) are also known. Frequently, however, there is strong residual interaction between the "cation" and the "complex anion" and the structure is better thought of as an extended three-dimensional network. For example the adduct $SbCl_5.ICl_3$ (i.e. $ISbCl_8$) comprises distorted octahedra of $\{SbCl_6\}$ and angular $\{ICl_2\}$ groups but, as shown in Fig. 13.9, there is additional interaction between the groups which links them into chains and the structure is intermediate between $[ICl_2]^+[SbCl_6]^-$ and $[SbCl_4]^+[ICl_4]^-$. Complexes are also formed by a variety of oxygen-donors, e.g. $[SbCl_5(OPCl_3)]$ and $[SbF_5(OSO)]$ as

[44] S. Pohl, W. Saak, P. Mayer and A. Schmidpeter, *Angew. Chem. Int. Edn. Engl.*, **25**, 825 (1986).

[45] S. Pohl, R. Lotz, W. Saak and D. Haase, *ibid.* **28**, 344–5 (1989).

[46] C. J. Camalt, N. C. Norman and L. J. Farrugia, *Polyhedron* **12**, 2081–90 (1993).

[47] W. Clegg, N. C. Norman and N. L. Pickett, *ibid.* **12** 1251–2 (1993).

[48] H. Krautschied, *Z. anorg. allg. Chem.* **620**, 1559–64 (1994).

[49] E. Shustorovich and P. A. Dobosh, *J. Am. Chem. Soc.* **101**, 4090–5 (1979). B. M. Gimarc, *Molecular Structure and Bonding*, Academic Press, New York, 1979, 240 pp.

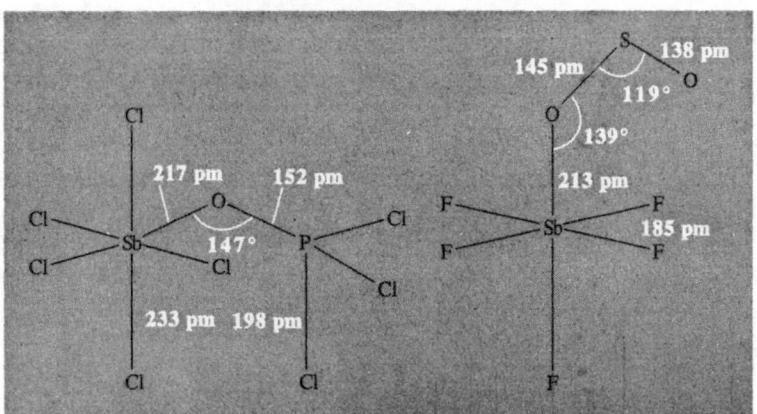

Figure 13.10　Schematic representation of the pseudo-octahedral structures of [SbCl$_5$(OPCl$_3$)] and [SbF$_5$(OSO)].

shown in Fig. 13.10. Fluoro-complexes in particular are favoured by large non-polarizing cations, and polynuclear complex anions sometimes then result as a consequence of fluorine bridging. For example irradiation of a mixture of SbF$_5$, F$_2$ and O$_2$ yields white crystals of O$_2$Sb$_2$F$_{11}$ which can be formulated[50] as O$_2$$^+$[Sb$_2F_{11}$]$^-$, and this complex, when heated under reduced pressure at 110°, loses SbF$_5$ to give O$_2$$^+SbF_6$$^-$. The dinuclear anion probably has a linear Sb–F–Sb bridge as in [BrF$_4$]$^+$[Sb$_2$F$_{11}$]$^-$ (p. 834), but in [XeF]$^+$[Sb$_2$F$_{11}$]$^-$ and [XeF$_3$]$^+$[Sb$_2$F$_{11}$]$^-$ (p. 898) the bridging angle is reduced to 150° and 155° respectively. Even more extended coordination occurs in the 1:3 adduct PF$_5$.3SbF$_5$ which has been formulated as [PF$_4$]$^+$[Sb$_3$F$_{16}$]$^-$ on the basis of vibrational spectroscopy.[51] The same anion occurs in the scarlet paramagnetic complex [Br$_2$]$^+$[Sb$_3$F$_{16}$]$^-$ for which X-ray crystallography has established the *trans*-bridged octahedral structure [F$_5$SbFSb(F$_4$)FSbF$_5$]$^-$ with a bridging angle SbF$_\mu$Sb of 148°; the Sb–F$_t$ distances (181–184 pm) are significantly less than the asymmetrical Sb–F$_\mu$ distances (197 and 210 pm 4 pm).[52] The compound (mp 69°) was prepared

by adding a small amount of BrF$_5$ to a mixture of Br$_2$ and SbF$_5$. The structure of the compound AsF$_3$.SbF$_5$ can be described either as a molecular adduct, F$_2$AsF→SbF$_5$, or as an ionic complex, [AsF$_2$]$^+$[SbF$_6$]$^-$; in both descriptions the alternating As and Sb units are joined into an infinite network by further F bonding.[53]

The 1:1 adduct SbF$_3$.SbF$_5$ has the pseudo-ionic structure [Sb$_2$^{III}F$_4$]$^{2+}$[Sb^{V}F$_6$$^-$]$_2$; however, the [F$_2$Sb–F··· SbF]$^{2+}$ cation features 5 different Sb–F distances (185, 187, 199, 201 and 215 pm) and can be regarded either as an SbF^{2+} cation coordinated by SbF$_3$, or as a fluorine-bridged dinuclear cation [F$_2$Sb–F–SbF]$^{2+}$, or even as part of an infinite three-dimensional polymer [(SbF$_4$)$_4$]$_n$ when still longer Sb^{III}–F contacts are considered.[54] Several other "adducts" have been prepared leading to the binary fluorides Sb$_3$F$_{11}$, Sb$_4$F$_{14}$, Sb$_7$F$_{29}$, Sb$_8$F$_{30}$ and Sb$_{11}$F$_{43}$. The fluoride Sb$_8$F$_{30}$ (i.e. 5SbF$_3$.3SbF$_5$) is unusual in having more than one structure, depending on its method of preparation. Reduction of SbF$_3$.SbF$_5$ or of SbF$_5$ itself with a stoichiometric amount of PF$_3$ in AsF$_3$ solutions yields crystals of α-Sb$_8$F$_{30}$ comprised of a 3D cross-linked polymeric cation, [Sb$_5$F$_{12}$$^{3+}$]$_\infty$, and [SbF$_6$]$^-$ anions. The polymeric cation can be viewed as strongly interacting

[50] D. E. McKee and N. Bartlett, *Inorg. Chem.* **12**, 2738–40 (1973).

[51] G. S. H. Chen and J. Passmore, *J. Chem. Soc., Chem. Commun.*, 559 (1973).

[52] A. J. Edwards and G. R. Jones, *J. Chem. Soc. A* 2318–20 (1971).

[53] A. J. Edwards and R. J. C. Sills, *J. Chem. Soc. A* 942–5 (1971).

[54] R. J. Gillespie, D. R. Slim and J. E. Vekris, *J. Chem. Soc., Dalton Trans.*, 971–4 (1977).

$\{Sb_2F_5\}^+$, $\{SbF_3\}$ and $\{Sb_2F_3\}^{3+}$ units, and there are also significant cation-anion interactions.[55] Alternatively, the less obvious preparative route of oxidative bromination of MeSCN with Br_2 and SbF_5 in liquid SO_2 yields crystals of β-Sb_8F_{30} which were shown by X-ray structure analysis to be best formulated as $[Sb_2F_5]^+$-$[Sb_3F_7]^{2+}[SbF_6]_3^-$.[56] The compound $Sb_{11}F_{43}$ (i.e. $6SbF_3.5SbF_5$) was prepared as a white high-melting solid by direct fluorination of Sb; it contains the polymeric chain cation $[Sb_6F_{13}{}^{5+}]_\infty$ and $[SbF_6]^-$ anions.[57]

The great electron-pair acceptor capacity (Lewis acidity) of SbF_5 has been utilized in the production of extremely strong proton donors (Brønsted acids, p. 48). Thus the acidity of anhydrous HF is substantially increased in the presence of SbF_5:

$$2HF + SbF_5 \rightleftharpoons [H_2F]^+[SbF_6]^-$$

Crystalline compounds isolated from such solutions at $-20°$ to $-30°C$ have been shown by X-ray analysis to be the fluoronium salts $[H_3F_2]^+[Sb_2F_{11}]^-$ and $[H_2F]^+[Sb_2F_{11}]^-$.[58]

An even stronger acid ("Magic Acid") results from the interaction of SbF_5 with an oxygen atom in fluorosulfuric acid HSO_3F (i.e. HF/SO_3):

$$SbF_5 + HSO_3F \rightleftharpoons HOS\!\!\!\underset{\substack{\| \\ F}}{\overset{O}{=}}\!\!\!O\rightarrow SbF_5$$

$$\underset{HSO_3F}{\rightleftharpoons} [HOSOH]^+ + [O\!=\!\!\!\underset{\substack{| \\ F}}{\overset{\substack{O \\ \|}}{S}}\!\!\!=\!O\rightarrow SbF_5]^-$$

Such acids, and those based on oleums, $H_2SO_4.nSO_3$, are extremely strong proton donors with acidities up to 10^{12} times that of H_2SO_4 itself, and have been given the generic name 'superacids'.[59-63] They have been extensively studied, particularly as they are able to protonate virtually all organic compounds. In addition, they have played a vital rôle in the preparation and study of stable long-lived carbocations:

$$RH + HSO_3F/SbF_5 \longrightarrow R^+ + [FSO_3.SbF_5]^- + H_2$$

The imaginative exploitation of these and related reactions by G. A. Olah and his group[60-62,64,65] have had an enormous impact on our understanding of organic catalytic processes and on their industrial application, as recognized by the award to Olah of the 1994 Nobel Prize for Chemistry.[66]

Oxide halides

The stable molecular nitrosyl halides NOX (p. 442) and phosphoryl halides POX_3 (p. 501) find few counterparts in the chemistry of As, Sb and Bi. AsOF has been reported as a product of the reaction of As_4O_6 with AsF_3 in a sealed tube at $320°$ but has not been fully characterized. $AsOF_3$ is known only as a polymer. Again, just as $AsCl_5$ eluded preparation for over 140 y after Liebig's first attempt to make it in 1834, so

[55] W. A. S. NANDANA, J. PASSMORE, P. S. WHITE and C.-M. WONG, *J. Chem. Soc., Dalton Trans.*, 1989–98 (1987).

[56] R. MINKWITZ, J. NOWICKI and H. BORRMANN, *Z. anorg. allg. Chem.* **605**, 109–16 (1991).

[57] A. J. EDWARDS and D. R. SLIM, *J. Chem. Soc., Chem. Commun.*, 178–9 (1974).

[58] D. MOOTZ and K. BARTMANN, *Angew. Chem. Int. Edn. Engl.* **27**, 391–2 (1988).

[59] R. J. GILLESPIE, *Acc. Chem. Res.* **1**, 202–9 (1968).

[60] G. A. OLAH, A. M. WHITE and D. H. O'BRIEN, *Chem. Rev.* **70**, 561–91 (1970).

[61] G. A. OLAH, G. K. S. PRAKASH and J. SOMMER, *Science* **206**, 13–20 (1979).

[62] G. A. OLAH, G. K. S. PRAKASH, and J. SOMMER, *Superacids*, Wiley, New York, 1985, 371 pp.

[63] T. A. O'DONNELL, *Superacids and Acidic Melts as Inorganic Chemical Reaction Media*, VCH, New York, 1992, 243 pp.

[64] G. A. OLAH, *Aldrichimica Acta* **6**, 7–16 (1973).

[65] G. A. OLAH, D. G. PARKER and Y. YONEDA, *Angew. Chem. Int. Edn. Engl.* **17**, 909–31 (1978). See also Chapters 1 and 7 in G. A. OLAH, G. K. S. PRAKASH, R. E. WILLIAMS L. D. FIELD and K. WADE, *Hypercarbon Chemistry*, Wiley, New York, 1987, 311 pp.

[66] G. A. OLAH, *Angew. Chem. Int. Edn. Engl.*, **34**, 1393–405. (Nobel Lecture.)

AsOCl$_3$ defied synthesis until 1976 when it was made by ozonization of AsCl$_3$ in CFCl$_3$/CH$_2$Cl$_2$ at $-78°$: it is a white, monomeric, crystalline solid and is one of the few compounds that can be said to contain a "real" As=O double bond.[67] AsOCl$_3$ is thermally more stable than AsCl$_5$ (p. 561) but decomposes slowly at $-25°$ to give As$_2$O$_3$Cl$_4$:

$$3AsOCl_3 \xrightarrow[\text{(rapid)}]{0°} AsCl_3 + Cl_2 + As_2O_3Cl_4$$

The compound As$_2$O$_3$Cl$_4$ is polymeric and is thus not isostructural with Cl$_2$P(O)OP(O)Cl$_2$.

SbOF and SbOCl can be obtained as polymeric solids by controlled hydrolysis of SbX$_3$. Several other oxide chlorides can be obtained by varying the conditions, e.g.:

$$SbCl_3 \xrightarrow[\text{H}_2\text{O}]{\text{limited}} SbOCl \xrightarrow[\text{H}_2\text{O}]{\text{more}} Sb_4O_5Cl_2$$

$$\xrightarrow{460°/\text{Ar}} Sb_8O_{11}Cl_2$$

An alternative dry-way preparation which permits the growth of large, colourless, single crystals suitable for ferroelectric studies (pp. 55–8) has been devised:[68]

$$5Sb_2O_3 + 2SbCl_3 \xrightarrow[\text{vac}]{75°} 3Sb_4O_5Cl_2 (\text{mp } 590°)$$

The compounds Sb$_4$O$_3$(OH)$_3$Cl$_2$ and Sb$_8$OCl$_{22}$ have also been reported. SbOCl itself comprises polymeric sheets of composition [Sb$_6$O$_6$Cl$_4$]$^{2+}$ (formed by linking Sb atoms via O and Cl bridges) interleaved with layers of chloride ions. In addition to polymeric species, finite heterocyclic complexes can also be obtained. For example partial hydrolysis of the polymeric [pyH]$_3$[Sb$_2^{III}$Cl$_9$] in ethanol leads to [pyH$^+$]$_2$[Sb$_2^{III}$OCl$_6$]$^{2-}$ in which the anion contains 2 pseudo-octahedral {:SbOCl$_4$} units sharing a common face {μ_3-OCl$_2$} with the lone-pairs *trans* to the bridging oxygen atom

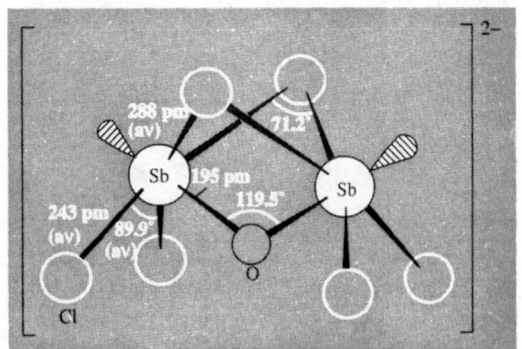

Figure 13.11 Structure of the binuclear anion [Sb$_2^{III}$OCl$_6$]$^{2-}$ showing the bridging oxygen and chlorine atoms and the pseudooctahedral coordination about Sb; the O atom is at the common apex of the face-shared square pyramids and the lone-pairs are *trans*- to this below the {SbCl$_4$} bases. The bridging distances Sb–Cl$_\mu$ are substantially longer than the terminal distances Sb–Cl$_t$.

(Fig. 13.11).[69] Another novel polynuclear anti-mony oxide halide anion has been established in the dark-blue ferrocenium complex {[Fe(η^5-C$_5$H$_5$)]$_2$[Sb$_4$Cl$_{12}$O]}$_2$.2C$_6$H$_6$ which was made by photolysis of benzene solutions of ferrocene (p. 1109) and SbCl$_3$ in the presence of oxygen:[70] the anion (Fig. 13.12) contains 2 square-pyramidal {Sb^{III}Cl$_5$} units sharing a common edge and joined via a unique quadruply bridging Cl atom to 2 pseudo trigonal bipyramidal {Sb^{III}Cl$_3$O} units which share a common bridging O atom and the unique Cl atom. The structure implies the presence of a lone-pair of electrons beneath the basal plane of the first 2 Sb atoms and in the equatorial plane (with O$_\mu$ and Cl$_t$) of the second 2 Sb atoms.

Other finite-complex anions occur in the oxyfluorides. For example the hydrated salts K$_2$[As$_2$F$_{10}$O].H$_2$O and Rb$_2$[As$_2$F$_{10}$O].H$_2$O

[67] K. Seppelt, *Angew Chem. Int. Edn. Engl.* **15**, 766–7 (1976).

[68] Ya. P. Kutsenko, *Kristallografiya* (Engl. transl.) **24**, 349–51 (1979).

[69] M. Hall and D. B. Sowerby, *J. Chem. Soc., Chem. Commun.,* 1134–5 (1979).

[70] A. L. Rheingold, A. G. Landers, P. Dahlstrom and J. Zubieta, *J. Chem. Soc., Chem. Commun.,* 143–4 (1979).

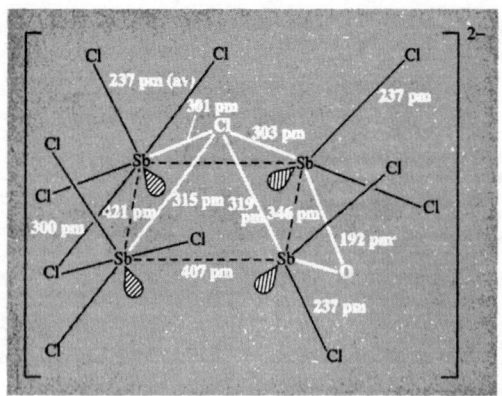

Figure 13.12   Schematic representation of the structure of the complex anion $[Sb_4Cl_{12}O]^{2-}$ showing the two different coordination geometries about Sb and the unique quadruply bridging Cl atom.

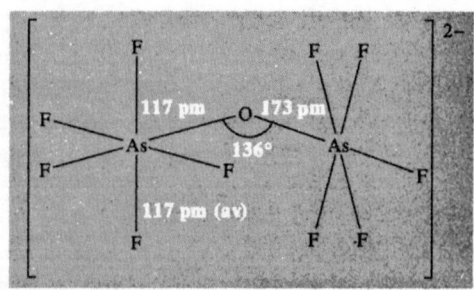

Figure 13.13   Schematic representation of the anion structure in $M_2[As_2F_{10}O].H_2O$.

contain the oxo-bridged binuclear anion $[F_5As-OAsF_5]^{2-}$ as shown in Fig. 13.13[71] and the anhydrous salt $Rb_2[Sb_2F_{10}O]$ contains a similar anion with angle Sb–O–Sb 133°, Sb–F 188 pm, and Sb–O 191 pm.[72] The compound of empirical formula $CsSbF_4O$ is, in fact, trimeric with a 6-membered heterocyclic anion in the boat configuration, i.e. $Cs_3[Sb_3F_{12}O_3]$,[73] whereas the corresponding arsenic compound[74] has a dimeric

anion $[As_2F_8O_2]^{2-}$ (Fig. 13.14). In both cases the Group 15 element is octahedrally coordinated by 4 F and 2 O atoms in the *cis-* configuration.

Bismuth oxide halides BiOX are readily formed as insoluble precipitates by the partial hydrolysis of the trihalides (e.g. by dilution of solutions in concentrated aqueous HX). BiOF and BiOI can also be made by heating the corresponding BiX_3 in air. BiOI, which itself decomposes above 300°, is brick-red in colour; the other 3 BiOX are white. All have complex layer-lattice structures.[33] When BiOCl or BiOBr are heated above 600° oxide halides of composition $Bi_{24}O_{31}X_{10}$ are formed, i.e. replacement of 5 O atoms by 10 X in $Bi_{24}O_{36}$, (Bi_2O_3).

13.3.4 Oxides and oxo compounds

The amphoteric nature of As_2O_3 and the trends in properties of several of the oxides and oxoacids

[71] W. HAASE, *Acta Cryst.* **B30**, 1722–7 (1974).
[72] W. HAASE, *Acta Cryst.* **B30**, 2508–10 (1974).
[73] W. HAASE, *Acta Cryst.* **B30**, 2465–9 (1974).
[74] W. HAASE, *Chem. Ber.* **107**, 1009–18 (1974).

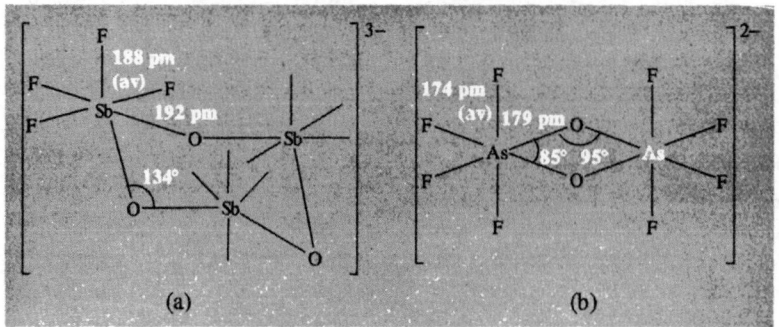

Figure 13.14   Schematic representation of the structure of (a) the trimeric anion $[Sb_3F_{12}O_3]^{3-}$, and (b) the dimeric anion $[As_2F_8O_2]^{2-}$.

of As, Sb and Bi have already been mentioned briefly on pp. 552–3. Because of the trend towards greater basicity in the sequence As < Sb < Bi and the trend towards greater acidity in the sequence $M^{III} < M^V$, coupled with the difficulty of isolating some of the oxides from their "hydrated" forms, it is not convenient to have separate sections on oxides, hydrous oxides, hydroxides, acids, oxoacid salts, polyacid salts and mixed oxides. Accordingly, all these types of compound will be considered in the present

section: M^{III} compounds will be discussed first then intermediate M^{III}/M^V systems and, finally, M^V oxo- compounds.

Oxo compounds of M^{III}

As_2O_3 (diarsenic trioxide) is the most important compound of As (Panel, p. 549). It is made (a) by burning As in air, (b) by hydrolysis of $AsCl_3$ or (c) industrially, by roasting sulfide

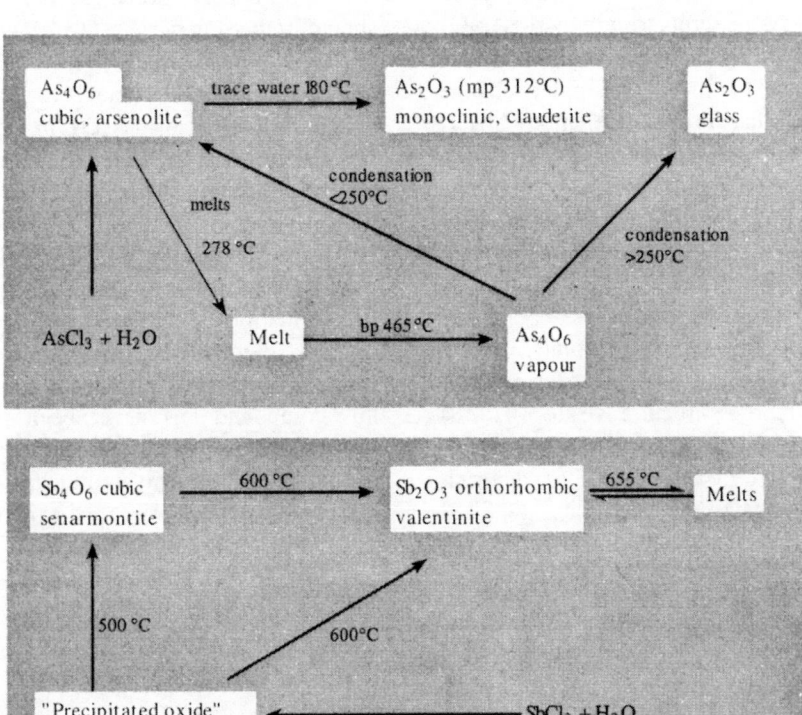

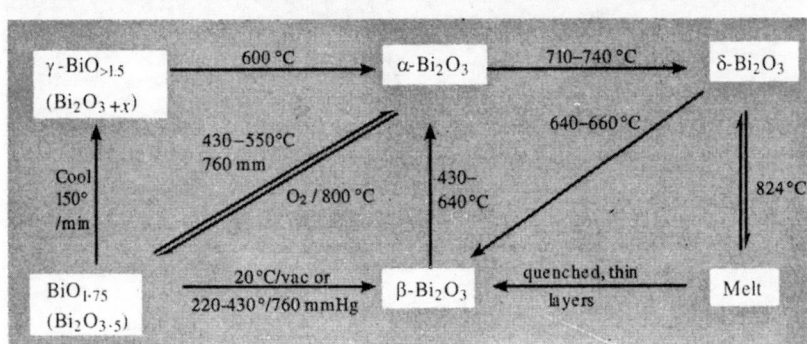

ores such as arsenopyrite, FeAsS. Sb_2O_3 and Bi_2O_3 are made similarly. All 3 oxides exist in several modifications as shown in the schemes on p. 573.[16] In the vapour phase As_2O_3 exists as As_4O_6 molecules isostructural with P_4O_6 (p. 504), and this unit also occurs in the cubic crystalline form. Above 800° gaseous As_4O_6 partially dissociates to an equilibrium mixture containing both As_4O_6 and As_2O_3 molecules. The less-volatile monoclinic form of As_2O_3 has a sheet-like structure of pyramidal $\{AsO_3\}$ groups sharing common O atoms. This transformation from molecular As_4O_6 units to polymeric As_2O_3 is accompanied by an 8.7% increase in density from 3.89 to $4.23\,g\,cm^{-3}$. A similar change from cubic, molecular Sb_4O_6 to polymeric Sb_2O_3 results in an 11.3% density increase from 5.20 to $5.79\,g\,cm^{-3}$.

The structural relationships in Bi_2O_3 are more complex. At room temperature the stable form is monoclinic α-Bi_2O_3 which has a polymeric layer structure featuring distorted, 5-coordinate Bi in pseudo-octahedral $\{:BiO_5\}$ units. Above 717°C this transforms to the cubic δ-form which has a defect fluorite structure (CaF_2, p. 118) with randomly distributed oxygen vacancies, i.e. $[Bi_2O_3\square]$. The β-form and several oxygen-rich forms (in which some of the vacant sites are filled

by O^{2-} with concomitant oxidation of some Bi^{III} to Bi^V) are related to the δ-Bi_2O_3 structure. There are also numerous double oxides $pMO_n.qBi_2O_3$, e.g. $Bi_{12}GeO_{20}$ (i.e. $GeO_2.6Bi_2O_3$), and other mixed oxides can be made by fusing Bi_2O_3 with oxides of Ca, Sr, Ba, Cd or Pb; these latter have $(BiO)_n$ layers as in the oxide halides, interleaved with M^{II} cations. $Bi_2Sr_2CaCu_2O_8$ is a superconductor with $T_c = 85\,K$ (cf. p. 1182).

The oxides M_2O_3 are convenient starting points for the synthesis of many other compounds of As, Sb and Bi. Some reactions of As_2O_3 are shown in the scheme; Sb_2O_3 reacts similarly, but Bi_2O_3 is more basic, being insoluble in aqueous alkali but dissolving in acids to give Bi^{III} salts.

The solubility of As_2O_3 in water, and the species present in solution, depend markedly on pH. In pure water at 25°C the solubility is 2.16 g per 100 g; this diminishes in dilute HCl to a minimum of 1.56 g per 100 g at about $3\,M$ HCl and then increases, presumably due to the formation of chloro-complexes. In neutral or acid solutions the main species is probably pyramidal $As(OH)_3$, "arsenious acid", though this compound has never been isolated either from solution or otherwise (cf. carbonic acid, p. 310). The solubility is much greater in basic solutions and spectroscopic evidence points to

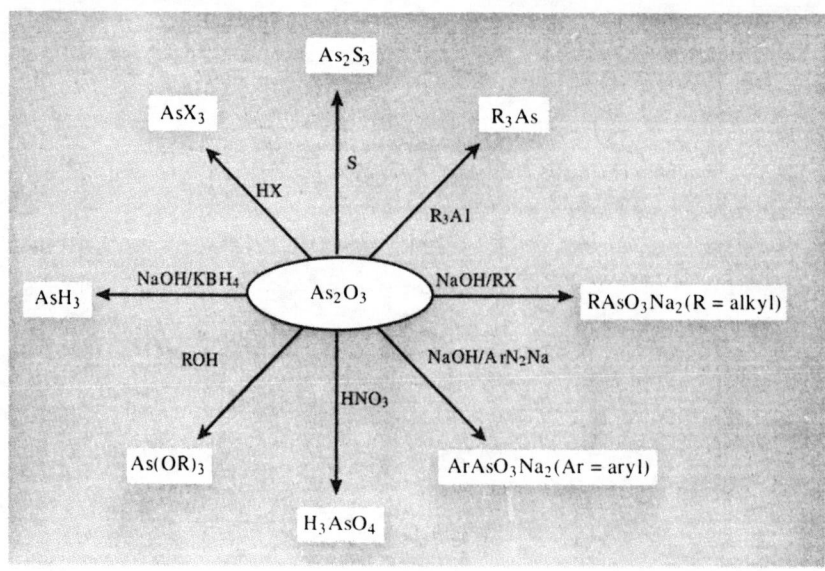

the presence of such anions as $[AsO(OH)_2]^-$, $[AsO_2(OH)]^{2-}$ and $[AsO_3]^{3-}$, corresponding to successive deprotonation of H_3AsO_3. The first stage dissociation constant at 25° is $K_a = [AsO(OH)_2^-][H^+]/[H_3AsO_3] \simeq 6 \times 10^{-10}$, pK_a 9.2; ortho-arsenious acid is therefore a very weak acid (as expected from Pauling's rules, p. 50) and is comparable in strength to boric acid (p. 203). Dissociation as a base is even weaker: $K_b = [As(OH)_2^+][OH^-]/[As(OH)_3] \simeq 10^{-14}$. There now seems to be less evidence for other species that were formerly considered to be present in solution, e.g. the monomeric meta-acid $HAsO_2$, i.e. $[AsO(OH)]$ (by loss of 1 H_2O) and the hexahydroxoacid $H_3[As(OH)_6]$ or its hydrate.

Arsenites of the alkali metals are very soluble in water, those of the alkaline earth metals less so, and those of the heavy metals are virtually insoluble. Many of the salts are obtained as meta-arsenites, e.g. $NaAsO_2$, which comprises polymeric chain anions formed by corner linkage of pyramidal $\{AsO_3\}$ groups and held together by Na ions:

$$\left[\begin{array}{c} \text{polymeric arsenite chain anion} \end{array} \right]_\infty$$

The sparingly soluble yellow Ag_3AsO_3 is an example of an orthoarsenite. Copper(II) arsenites were formerly used as fine green pigments, e.g. Paris green, which is an acetate arsenite $[Cu_2(MeCO_2)(AsO_3)]$, and Scheele's green, which approximates to the hydrogen arsenite $CuHAsO_3$ or the dehydrated composition $Cu_2As_2O_5$.

Antimonious acid H_3SbO_3 and its salts are less well characterized but a few meta-antimonites and polyantimonites are known, e.g. $NaSbO_2$, $NaSb_3O_5.H_2O$ and $Na_2Sb_4O_7$. The oxide itself finds extensive use as a flame retardant in fabrics, paper, paints, plastics, epoxy resins, adhesives and rubbers. The scale of industrial use can be gauged from the US statistics which indicate an annual consumption of Sb_2O_3 of some 10 000 tonnes in that country.

The corresponding Bi compound $Bi(OH)_3$ is definitely basic rather than acidic. It dissolves readily in acid giving solutions of Bi^{III} ions but an increase in pH causes precipitation of oxo-salts. Before precipitation, however, polymeric oxocations can be detected in solution of which the best characterized is $[Bi_6(OH)_{12}]^{6+}$ in perchlorate solution. The species (Fig. 13.15) resembles $[Ta_6Cl_{12}]^{2+}$ and has 6 Bi at the corners of an octahedron with bridging OH groups above each of the 12 edges. The shortest Bi–O distance is 233 pm and the (nonbonding) $Bi \cdots Bi$ distance is 370 pm (307 and 353 in Bi metal). This contrasts with the bicapped tetrahedral distribution of metal atoms in $[Pb_6O(OH)_6]^{4+}$ (p. 395) where there is an O atom at the centre of the central tetrahedron and OH groups above the faces of the capping tetrahedra. A different arrangement of oxygen atoms around the Bi_6 octahedron has been found by X-ray and neutron diffraction studies on $[Bi_6O_4(OH)_4]^{6+}[ClO_4]^-{}_6.7H_2O$, which can be crystallized from solutions prepared by dissolving Bi_2O_3 in 3 M $HClO_4$.[75] The eight oxygen atoms (4 O and 4 OH) are disposed, respectively, on two tetrahedra above the eight triangular faces of the octahedron, thus giving the cluster overall

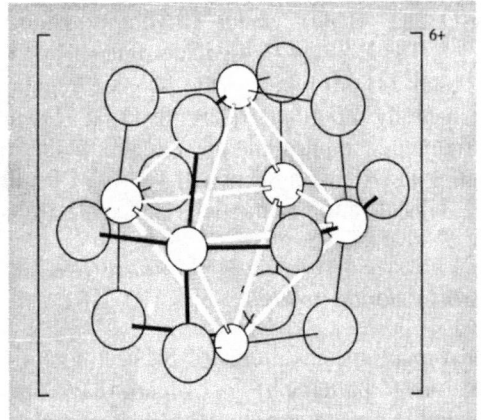

Figure 13.15 The structure of the oxocation $[Bi_6(OH)_{12}]^{6+}$; the white lines indicate geometry but do not imply Bi–Bi bonds (see text).

75 B. SUNDVALL. *Inorg. Chem.* **22**, 1906–12 (1983).

T_d symmetry and with average distances Bi–O 215 pm, Bi–O(H) 240 pm and Bi $\cdots$ Bi 368 pm.

The tendency of Bi^{III} oxo-groups to aggregate is also found in Li$_3$BiO$_3$, which is formed as colourless crystals by heating a mixture of Li$_2$O and Bi$_2$O$_3$ (in a 3.1:1 mole ratio) in Ag capsules (bombs!) at 750°C for 20 days.[76] The "isolated" pyramidal BiO$_3^{3-}$ ions are arranged in apparently electrostatically unfavourable groups of eight with the 8 Bi atoms at the corners of a cube, all 24 O atoms pointing outwards and the eight lone pairs of electrons pointing inwards; Bi–O 205 pm (av), Bi $\cdots$ Bi 368 pm (av); cf. Bi–Bi 307.2 and 352.9 pm in Bi metal (p. 551). Likewise, colourless crystals of Ag$_3$BiO$_3$ and of Ag$_5$BiO$_4$, prepared by heating Ag$_2$O and Bi$_2$O$_3$ at 500°–530°C under 100 MPa (1 kbar) of O$_2$ or hydrothermally at 350°C and 10 MPa of O$_2$, both feature Bi$_2$O$_8^{10-}$ units. In Ag$_5$BiO$_4$ (i.e. Ag$_{10}$Bi$_2$O$_8$) the units are "isolated" and comprise two square-based pyramidal {BiO$_5$} groups *trans*-fused at a common basal edge and with Bi–O$_b$ 231 pm (av), Bi–O$_a$ 214 pm, Bi $\cdots$ Bi 379 pm. In Ag$_3$BiO$_3$ these {Bi$_2$O$_8$} groups are further linked by the remaining terminal basal O atoms to form a 3D network.[77] A fascinating mixed valence bismuthate Ag$_{25}$Bi$_3$O$_{18}$ (i.e. Bi$_2^{III}$Bi^V has been prepared as black crystals by heating Ag$_2$O and 'Bi$_2$O$_5$' under 10 MPa pressure of O$_2$.[78] The Bi^{III} are (3 + 3)-coordinated by O at 221 and 231 pm whereas the Bi^V are regularly octahedrally coordinated by 6 O at 213 pm. Intriguingly, application of pressure induces a change in oxidation states (III $\longrightarrow$ V) leading to a delocalization of the 6s^2 valence electrons.

Mixed-valence oxides

The vapour species produced by heating As$_2$O$_5$ (see next paragraph) *in vacuo* have been isolated in low-temperature matrices and shown by vibration spectroscopy to comprise the complete series of stable molecules As$_4$O$_n$ ($n = 6$–10),[79] analogous in structures to the phosphorus series (p. 504) The intermediate diamagnetic oxide α-Sb$_2$O$_4$ (i.e. Sb^{III}Sb^{V}O$_4$) has long been known as the massive, fine-grained, yellow, orthorhombic mineral cervantite and more recently a monoclinic β-form has been recognized. α-Sb$_2$O$_4$ can also be obtained by heating Sb$_2$O$_3$ in dry air at 460–540°C, and further heating in air or oxygen at 1130° produces β-Sb$_2$O$_4$. Both forms have similar structures with equal numbers of Sb^{III} and Sb^V. α-Sb$_2$O$_4$ is isostructural with SbNbO$_4$ and SbTaO$_4$ and consists of corrugated sheets of slightly distorted {Sb^{V}O$_6$} octahedra sharing all their vertices (as in the plane layer in K$_2$NiF$_4$); the Sb^{III} lie between the layers in positions of irregular pyramidal fourfold coordination, all four O atoms lying on the same side of the Sb^{III}. Further oxidation to anhydrous Sb$_2$O$_5$ has not been achieved (see below). For oxygen-rich Bi$_2$O$_{3+x}$ see pp. 573–4 and also the preceding paragraph.

Oxo compounds of M^V

Arsenic(V) oxide, As$_2$O$_5$, is one of the oldest-known oxides, but structural analysis has been thwarted until recently because of poor thermal stability, ease of hydrolysis and the difficulty of growing a single crystal. It is now known to consist of equal numbers of {AsO$_6$} octahedra and {AsO$_4$} tetrahedra completely linked by corner sharing to give cross-linked strands which define tubular cavities (cf. the corner sharing in ReO$_3$ octahedra, p. 1047, and SiO$_2$ tetrahedra, p. 343).[80] The structure accounts for the reluctance of the compound to crystallize and also for the observation that only half the As atoms can be replaced by Sb (6-coordinate) and P (4-coordinate) respectively. As$_2$O$_5$ can be prepared either by heating As (or As$_2$O$_3$) with O$_2$ under pressure or by dehydrating crystalline

[76] R. HOPPE and R. HÜBENTHAL, *Z. anorg. allg. Chem.* **576**, 159–78 (1989).

[77] M. BORTZ and M. JANSEN, *Z. anorg. allg. Chem.* **619**, 1446–54 (1993).

[78] M. BORTZ and M. JANSEN, *Z. anorg. allg. Chem.* **612**, 113–7 (1992).

[79] A. K. BRISDON, R. A. GOMME and J. S. OGDEN, *J. Chem. Soc., Dalton Trans.*, 2725–30 (1986).

[80] M. JANSEN, *Angew. Chem. Int. Edn. Engl.* **16**, 214 (1977).

H_3AsO_4 at about $200°C$. It is deliquescent, exceedingly soluble in water ($230 g$ per $100 g$ H_2O at $20°$), thermally unstable (loosing O_2 near the mp, *ca.* $300°C$) and a strong oxidizing agent (liberating Cl_2 from HCl).

Arsenic acid, H_3AsO_4, can be obtained in aqueous solution by oxidizing As_2O_3 with concentrated HNO_3 or by dissolving As_2O_5 in water. Crystallization below $30°$ yields $2H_3AsO_4.H_2O$ (cf. phosphoric acid hemihydrate, p. 519), whereas crystallization at $100°C$ or above results in loss of water and the formation of $As_2O_5.\frac{5}{3}H_2O$, i.e. ribbon-like polymeric $(H_5As_3O_{10})_n$. All these materials are strongly H-bonded. Arsenic acid, like H_3PO_4 (p. 519), is tribasic with pK_1 2.2, pK_2 6.9, pK_3 11.5 at $25°$. $M^IH_2AsO_4$ (M = K, Rb, Cs, NH_4) are ferroelectric (p. 57). The corresponding sodium salt readily dehydrates to give meta-arsenate $NaAs^VO_3$:

$$NaH_2AsO_4 \longrightarrow NaAsO_3 + H_2O$$

$NaAsO_3$ has an infinite polymeric chain anion similar to that in diopside (pp. 349, 529) but with a trimeric repeat unit; $LiAsO_3$ is similar but with a dimeric repeat unit whereas β-$KAsO_3$ appears to have a cyclic trimeric anion $As_3O_9^{3-}$ which resembles the *cyclo*-trimetaphosphates (p. 530). There is thus a certain structural similarity between arsenates and phosphates, though arsenic acid and the arsenates show less tendency to catenation (p. 526). The tetrahedral $\{As^VO_4\}$ group also resembles $\{PO_4\}$ in forming the central unit in several heteropolyacid anions (p. 1014).

One striking difference between arsenates and phosphates is the appreciable oxidizing tendency of the former. This is clear from the oxidation state diagram for the Group V elements shown in Fig. 13.16, which summarizes a great deal of relevant information (p. 435). Antimony is seen to resemble arsenic quite closely but Bi^V–Bi^{III} is a much more strongly oxidizing couple and, indeed (as is clear from Fig. 13.16), it is able to oxidize water to oxygen. It is also clear that the $+3$ oxidation states of As, Sb and Bi do not disproportionate in solution. Nor do the elements themselves, so there are no reactions comparable to that of P_4 with alkali to give phosphine and hypophosphite (p. 513). Redox reactions have proved a useful volumetric method of analysis for both As and Sb. For example As^{III} is quantitatively oxidized in aqueous solution by I_2, or by potassium bromate, iodate or permanganate. Such reactions can be formally represented as follows:

$$As^{III} + I_2 \longrightarrow As^V + 2I^-, \text{ etc.}$$

Thus, in an acid buffer such as borax-boric acid or Na_2HPO_4–NaH_2PO_4 (p. 521):

$$\frac{1}{2}As_2O_3(aq) + I_2 + H_2O \longrightarrow \frac{1}{2}As_2O_5(aq)$$
$$+ 2H^+(aq) + 2I^-$$

Such reactions are not available for Bi^{III} but this can readily be determined by complexometric titration using ethylenediaminetetraacetic acid or similar complexones:

$$Bi^{III} + H_4edta \xrightarrow{aq} [Bi(edta)]^- + 4H^+$$

Antimony(V) oxide has been obtained as a poorly characterized pale-yellow powder of ill-defined stoichiometry by hydrolysing $SbCl_5$ with aqueous ammonia solution and dehydrating the product at $275°$. Antimonates generally feature pseudooctahedral $\{SbO_6\}$ units but polymerization by corner, edge or face sharing is rife. Some compounds which have been structurally characterized are $NaSb(OH)_6$, $LiSbO_3$ (edge-shared), Li_3SbO_4 (NaCl superstructure with isolated lozenges of $\{Sb_4O_{16}\}^{12-}$), $NaSbO_3$ (ilmenite, p. 963), $MgSb_2O_6$ (trirutile, p. 961), $AlSbO_4$ (rutile, $2MO_2$ with random occupancy) and $Zn_7Sb_2O_{12}$ (defect spinel, i.e. $3AB_2O_4$, p. 248).

Bismuth(V) oxide and bismuthates are even less well established though a recent important development has been the synthesis and structural characterization of Li_5BiO_5, prepared by heating an intimate mixture of Li_2O and α-Bi_2O_3 at $650°$ for $24 h$ in dry O_2. The structure is of the defect rock-salt type with an ordering of

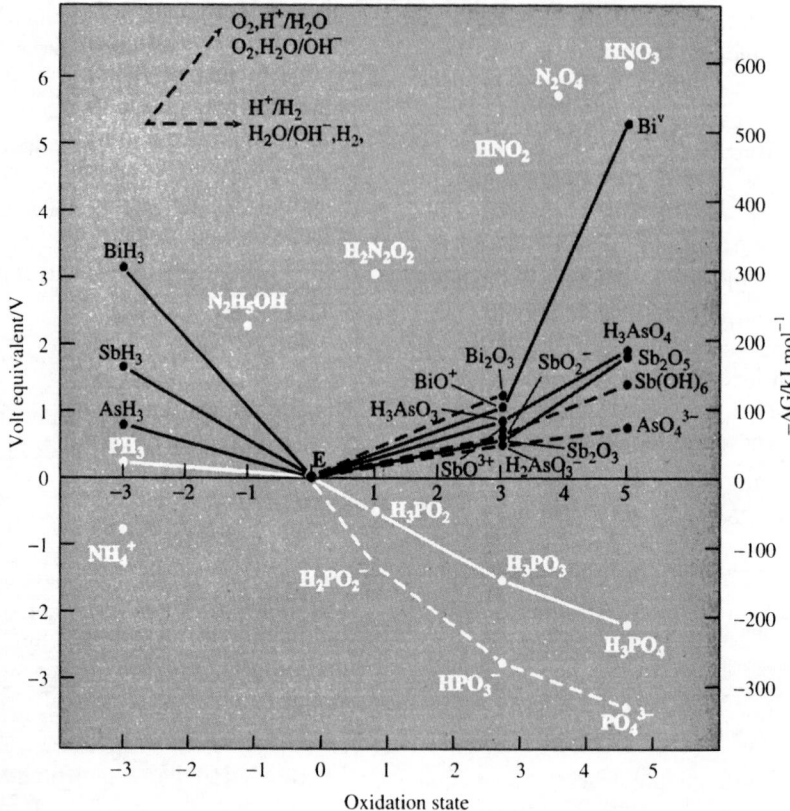

Figure 13.16 Oxidation state diagram for As, Sb and Bi in acid and alkaline solutions, together with selected data on N and P for comparison.

cations and anion vacancies similar to that found in the ordered low-temperature phase of TiO (p. 962).[81] Note that the nominal ionic radii of Li^+ and Bi^{5+} are equal (76 pm). Strong oxidizing agents give brown or black precipitates with alkaline solutions of Bi^{III}, which may be an impure higher oxide, and $NaBi^VO_3$ can be made by heating Na_2O and Bi_2O_3 in O_2. Such bismuthates of alkali and alkaline earth metals, though often poorly characterized, can be used as strong oxidizing agents in acid solution. Thus Mn in steel can be quantitatively determined by oxidizing it directly to permanganate and estimating the concentration colorometrically.

[81] C. GREAVES and S. M. A. KATIB, *J. Chem. Soc., Chem. Commun.*, 1828–9 (1987).

13.3.5 Sulfides and related compounds

Despite the venerable history of the yellow mineral orpiment, As_2S_3, and the orange-red mineral realgar, As_4S_4 (p. 547), it is only during the past two or three decades that the structural interrelation of the numerous arsenic sulfides has emerged. As_2S_3 has a layer-structure analogous to As_2O_3 (p. 574) with each As bonded pyramidally to 3 S atoms at 224 pm and angle S–As–S 99°. It can be made by heating As_2O_3 with S or by passing H_2S into an acidified solution of the oxide. It sublimes readily, even below its mp of 320°, and the vapour has been shown by electron diffraction studies to comprise As_4S_6 molecules isostructural with P_4O_6 (p. 504). The structure can be thought

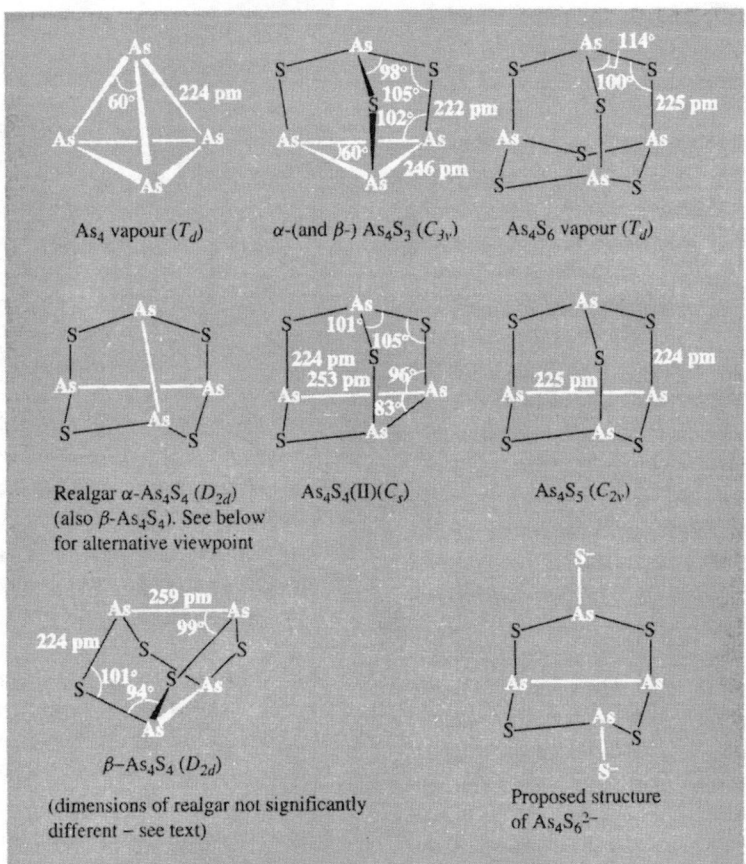

Figure 13.17 Molecular structure of some sulfides of arsenic, stressing the relationship to the As_4 tetrahedron (point group symmetry in parentheses).

of as being derived from the As_4 tetrahedron by placing a bridging S atom above each edge thereby extending the $As \cdots As$ distance to a nonbonding value of ~290 pm. If instead of 6 As–S–As bridges there are 3, 4 or 5, then, as illustrated in Fig. 13.17, the compounds As_4S_3, As_4S_4 (2 isomers) and As_4S_5 are obtained. The molecule As_4S_3 is seen to be isostructural with P_4S_3 and P_4Se_3 (p. 507); it occurs in both the α- and the β-form of the orange-yellow mineral dimorphite (literally "two forms", discovered by A. Scacchi in volcanic fumaroles in Italy in 1849), the two forms differing only in the arrangement of the molecular units.[82] The

compound can be synthesized by heating As and S in the required proportions and purifying the product by sublimation, the β-form being the stable modification at room temperature and the α-form above 130°. The same molecular form occurs in the recently synthesized isoelectronic cationic clusters $As_3S_4^+$ (yellow) and $As_3Se_4^+$ (orange)[83] and in the isoelectronic clusters P_7^{3-}, As_7^{3-} and Sb_7^{3-} (p. 588).

With As_4S_4 there are two possible geometrical isomers of the molecule depending on whether the 2 As–As bonds are skew or adjacent, as shown in Fig. 13.17. Realgar (mp 307°) adopts the more symmetric D_{2d} form with skew As–As

[82] H. J. WHITFIELD, *J. Chem. Soc.* (A), 1800–3 (1970); 1737–8 (1973).

[83] B. H. CHRISTIAN, R. J. GILLESPIE and J. F. SAWYER, *Inorg. Chem.* **20**, 3410–20 (1981).

bonds and, depending on how the molecules pack in the crystal, either α- or β-As$_4$S$_4$ results.[84] In addition to the tetrahedral disposition of the 4 As atoms, note that the 4 S atoms are almost coplanar; this is precisely the inverse of the D_{2d} structure adopted by N$_4$S$_4$ (p. 723) in which the 4 S atoms form a tetrahedron and the 4 N atoms a coplanar square. It is also instructive to compare As$_4$S$_4$ with S$_8$ (p. 655): each S atom has 2 unpaired electrons available for bonding whereas each As atom has 3; As$_4$S$_4$ thus has 4 extra valency electrons for bonding and these form the 2 transannular As–As bonds. The structure of the second molecular isomer As$_4$S$_4$(II) parallels[85] the analogous geometrical isomerism of P$_4$S$_4$ (p. 507). It was obtained as yellow-orange platy crystals by heating equi-atomic amounts of the elements to 500–600°, then rapidly cooling the melt to room temperature and recrystallizing from CS$_2$.

Orange needle-like crystals of As$_4$S$_5$ occasionally form as a minor product when As$_4$S$_4$ is made by heating As$_4$S$_3$ with a solution of sulfur in CS$_2$. Its structure[86] (Fig. 13.17) differs from that of P$_4$S$_5$ and P$_4$Se$_5$ (p. 507) in having only 1 As–As bond and no exocyclic chalcogen As=S; this is a further illustration of the reluctance of As to oxidize beyond As^{III} (p. 552). The compound can also be made by heterolytic cleavage of the As$_4$S$_6^{2-}$ anion. This anion, which is itself made by base cleavage of one of the As–As bonds in realgar, probably has the structure shown in Fig. 13.17 and this would certainly explain the observed sequence of reactions:[87]

$$\text{As}_4\text{S}_4 \xrightarrow[\text{in MeNHCH}_2\text{CH}_2\text{OH}]{\substack{\text{piperidine (or hexa-}\\\text{methylenetetramine)}}} [\text{pipH}^+]_2[\text{As}_4\text{S}_6]^{2-}$$

$$\xrightarrow{2\text{HX}} 2\text{pipHX} + \text{H}_2\text{S} + \text{As}_2\text{S}_5$$

[84] E. J. PORTER and G. M. SHELDRICK, *J. Chem. Soc., Dalton Trans.*, 1347–9 (1972).

[85] A. KUTOGLU, *Z. anorg. allg. Chem.* **419**, 176–84 (1976).

[86] H. J. WHITFIELD, *J. Chem. Soc., Dalton Trans.*, 1740–2 (1973).

[87] W. LAUER, M. BECKE-GOEHRING and K. SOMMER *Z. anorg allg. Chem.* **371**. 193–200 (1969).

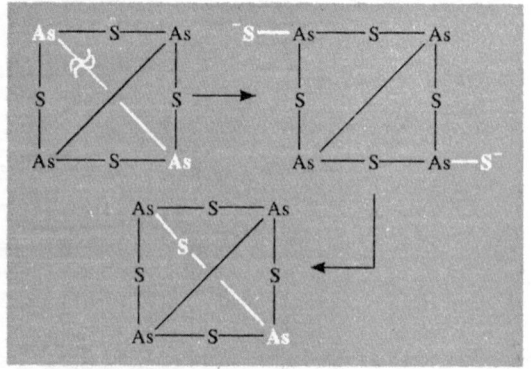

The structure of As$_2^V$S$_5$ is unknown. It is said to be formed as a yellow solid by passing a rapid stream of H$_2$S gas into an ice-cold solution of an arsenate in conc HCl; slower passage of H$_2$S at room temperature results in reduction of arsenate to arsenite and consequent precipitation of As$_2$S$_3$. It decomposes in air above 95° to give As$_2$S$_3$ and sulfur.

Reactions of the various sulfides of arsenic call for little further comment. As$_2$S$_3$ burns when heated in air to give As$_2$O$_3$ and SO$_2$. Chlorine converts it to AsCl$_3$ and S$_2$Cl$_2$. It is insoluble in water but dissolves readily in aqueous alkali or alkali-metal sulfide solutions to give thioarsenites:

$$\text{As}_2\text{S}_3 + \text{Na}_2\text{S} \xrightarrow{\text{aq}} 2\text{NaAs}^{III}\text{S}_2$$

Reacidification reprecipitates As$_2$S$_3$ quantitatively. With alkali metal or ammonium polysulfides thioarsenates are formed which are virtually insoluble even in hot conc HCl:

$$\text{As}_2\text{S}_3 \xrightarrow{\text{aq (NH}_4)_2\text{S}_n} (\text{NH}_4)_3\text{As}^V\text{S}_4$$

When As$_2$S$_3$ is treated with boiling sodium carbonate solution it is converted to As$_4$S$_4$; this latter compound can also be made by fusing As$_2$O$_3$ with sulfur or (industrially) by heating iron pyrites with arsenical pyrites. As$_4$S$_4$ is scarcely attacked by water, inflames in Cl$_2$, and is used in pyrotechny as it violently enflames when heated with KNO$_3$. Above about 550° As$_4$S$_4$ begins to dissociate reversibly and at 1000° the molecular weight corresponds to As$_2$S$_2$ (of unknown structure).

As_2S_3 and As_4S_4 have also provided a wealth of new ligands for transition-metal complexes, e.g. AsS, AsS_3, As_2S and, more recently, the geometrically novel bridging η^2,η^2-SAsSAsS ligand.[88] Further diversity is emerging with the synthesis and structural characterization of a range of (halogenated)polythiopolyarsenate(III) ions such as cyclo-$[As_3S_3X_4]^-$, (i.e. cyclo-$[(XAs)_3S_3(\mu_3\text{-}X)]^-$; X = Cl, Br, I), cyclo-$[S{=}AsS_5]^-$, bicyclo-$[Br_2As(S)_2As_2(S)_2(CH_2)]^-$ and $[As_2SBr_6]^{2-}$ {i.e. *fac*-$[Br_2As(\mu\text{-}S,Br,Br)\text{-}AsBr_2]^{2-}$}, all isolated as their $[PPh_4]^+$ salts.[89]

Three selenides of arsenic are known: As_2Se_3, As_4Se_3 and As_4Se_4; each can be made by direct heating of the elements in appropriate proportions at about 500° followed by annealing at temperatures between 220–280°. As_2Se_3 is a stable, brown, semiconducting glass which crystallizes when annealed at 280°; it melts at 380° and is isomorphous with As_2S_3. α-As_4Se_3 forms fine, dark-red crystals isostructural with α-$As_4S_3(C_{3v})$ and the lighter-coloured β-form almost certainly contains the same molecular units.[90] Similarly, As_4Se_4 is isostructural with realgar, α-As_4S_4, and the directly linked As–As distances are very similar in the 2 molecules (257 and 259 pm respectively);[91] other dimensions are As–Se(av) 239 pm, angle Se–As–Se 95°, angle As–Se–As 97° and angle As–As–Se 102° (cf. Fig. 13.17). The cationic cluster $As_3Se_4^+$ was mentioned on p. 579, and the heterocyclic anion $As_2Se_6^{2-}$ has been isolated as its orange $[Na(crypt)]^+$ salt:[92] the anion comprises a 6-membered heterocycle {As_2Se_4} in the chair conformation and each As carries a further exocyclic Se atom to give overall C_{2h} symmetry, i.e.

$$Se^-\!\!\diagdown\!\!As(\mu\text{-}Se_2)_2As\!\!\diagdown\!\!Se^-.$$

Methanolothermal reactions of As_2Se_3 with alkali metal carbonates at 130° yield polymetaselenoarsenites, $MAsSe_2$ (M = K, Rb, Cs), in which the polymeric anions consist of tetrahedral {$AsSe_3$} units linked by corner sharing into infinite chains.[93] Complexes of the triangulo-η^3 ligands As_2Se^- and As_2Te^-, such as $[(triphos)Co(As_2E)]^+$, can be made by reacting $[Co(H_2O)_6]^{2+}[BF_4]_2^-$ with the appropriate arsenic chalcogenide in the presence of the tridentate ligand $CH_3C(CH_2PPh_3)_3$, (triphos).[94]

The binary chalcogenides of Sb and Bi are also readily prepared by direct reaction of the elements at 500–900°. They have rather complex ribbon or layer-lattice structures and have been much studied because of their semiconductor properties. Both n-type and p-type materials can be obtained by appropriate doping (pp. 258, 332) and for the compounds M_2X_3 the intrinsic band gap decreases in the sequence As > Sb > Bi for a given chalcogen, and in the sequence S > Se > Te for a given Group 15 element. Some typical properties of these highly coloured compounds are in Table 13.10, but it should be mentioned that mp, density and even colour are often dependent on crystalline form and purity. The large thermoelectric effect of the selenides and tellurides of Sb and Bi finds use in solid-state refrigerators. Sb_2S_3 occurs as the black or steely grey mineral stibnite and is made industrially on a moderately large scale for use in the manufacture of safety matches, military ammunition, explosives and pyrotechnic products, and in the production of ruby-coloured glass. It reacts vigorously when heated with oxidizing agents but is also useful as a pigment in plastics such as

[88] H. Brunner, H. Kauermann, B. Nuber, J. Wachter and M. L. Ziegler, *Angew. Chem. Int. Edn. Engl.* **25**, 557–8 (1986) and references cited therein.

[89] U. Müller and coworkers, *Z. anorg. allg. Chem.* **557**, 91–7 (1987); **566**, 18–24 (1988); **568**, 49–54 (1989); **609**, 82–8 (1992).

[90] T. J. Bastow and H. J. Whitfield, *J. Chem. Soc., Dalton Trans.*, 959–61 (1977).

[91] T. J. Bastow and H. J. Whitfield, *J. Chem. Soc., Dalton Trans.*, 1739–40 (1973).

[92] C. H. E. Belin and M. M. Charbonnel, *Inorg. Chem.* **21**, 2504–6 (1982).

[93] W. S. Sheldrick and H.-J. Häusler, *Z. anorg. allg. Chem.* **561**, 139–48 (1988). See also pp. 149–56 for the similarly prepared $Cs_3Sb_5S_9$ and $Cs_3Sb_5Se_9$.

[94] M. di Vaira, M. Peruzzini and P. Stoppioni, *Polyhedron* **5**, 945–50 (1986).

Table 13.10   Some properties of Group 15 chalcogenides M_2X_3

Property	As_2S_3	Sb_2S_3	Bi_2S_3	As_2Se_3	Sb_2Se_3	Bi_2Se_3	As_2Te_3	Sb_2Te_3	Bi_2Te_3
Colour	Yellow	Black	Brown-black	Brown	Grey	Black	Grey	Grey	Grey
MP/°C	320	546	850	380	612	706	360	620	580
Density/g cm^{-3}	3.49	4.61	6.78	4.80	5.81	7.50	6.25	6.50	7.74
E_g/eV[a]	2.5	1.7	1.3	2.1	1.3	0.35	$\sim$1	0.3	0.15

[a] 1 eV per atom = 96.485 kJ mol^{-1}.

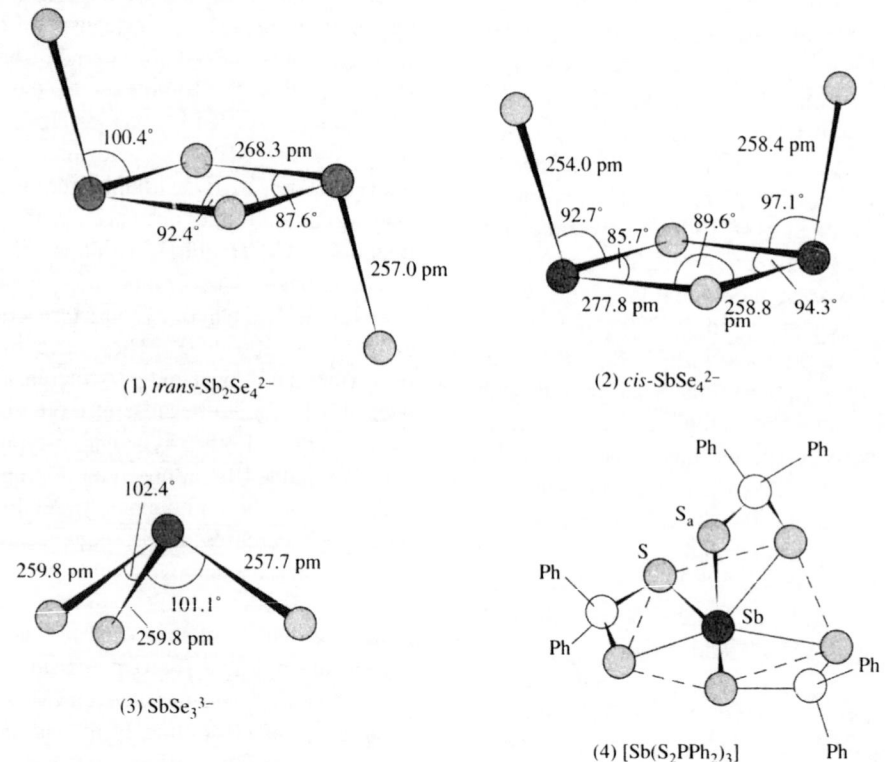

(1) *trans*-Sb$_2$Se$_4^{2-}$

(2) *cis*-SbSe$_4^{2-}$

(3) SbSe$_3^{3-}$

(4) [Sb(S$_2$PPh$_2$)$_3$]

polythene or polyvinylchloride because of its flame-retarding properties. Golden and crimson antimony sulfides (which comprise mixtures of Sb_2S_3, Sb_2S_4 and Sb_2OS_3) are likewise used as flame-retarding pigments in plastics and rubbers. A poorly characterized higher sulfide, sometimes said to be Sb_2S_5, can be obtained as a red solid by methods similar to those outlined for As_2S_5 (p. 580). It is used in fireworks, as a pigment, and to vulcanize red rubber.

Of the more complex chalcogenide derivatives of the Group 15 elements two examples must suffice to indicate the great structural versatility of these elements, particularly in the +3 oxidation state where the nonbonding electron pair can play an important stereochemical role. Thus, the compound of unusual stoichiometry Ba$_4$Sb$_4^{III}$Se$_{11}$ was found to contain within 1 unit cell: one *trans*-[Sb$_2$Se$_4$]$^{2-}$ (1), two *cis*-[Sb$_2$Se$_4$]$^{2-}$ (2), two pyramidal [SbSe$_3$]$^{3-}$ (3), and two Se$_2^{2-}$ ions (Se−Se 236.7 pm) together with the requisite 8 Ba^{2+} cations.[95] Conversely, the apparently simple 6-coordinate tris(dithiophosphinate), [Sb(η^2-S$_2$PPh$_2$)$_3$] (4), features pentagonal pyramidal coordination

95 G. CORDIER, R. COOK and H. SCHAFER, *Angew. Chem. Int. Edn. Engl.* **19**, 324–5 (1980).

geometry, which is most unusual for a main-group element and may result from the comparatively 'small bite' of the ligand, the lone pair of electrons presumably occupying the seventh coordination position below the pentagonal plane.[96] The tris(oxalato) anion, $[Sb^{III}(C_2O_4)_3]^{3-}$, is perhaps the only other example of this geometry.[97]

13.3.6 Metal–metal bonds and clusters

The somewhat limited tendency of N and P to catenate into homonuclear chains has already been noted. The ability to form long chains is even less with As, Sb and Bi, though numerous compounds containing one M–M bond are known and many stable ring and cluster compounds featuring M_n groups have been emerging in recent years. The Group 15 elements therefore differ only qualitatively from C and the other Group 14 elements, on the one hand (p. 374), and S and the Group 16 elements, on the other (p. 751). The elements As, Sb and Bi (like P, p. 487) form well-defined sets of *triangulo*-M_3 and *tetrahedro*-M_4 compounds, whilst Bi in particular has a propensity to form cluster cations Bi_m^{n+} reminiscent of Sn and Pb clusters (p. 394) and *closo*-borane anions (p. 153). Before discussing these various classes of compound, however, it is convenient to recall that a particular grouping of atoms may well have strong interatomic bonds yet still be unstable because of disproportionation into even more stable groupings. A pertinent example concerns the bond dissociation energies of the diatomic molecules of the Group 15 elements themselves in the gas phase. Thus, the ground state electronic configuration of the atoms (ns^2np^3) allows the possibility of triple bonding between pairs of atoms $M_2(g)$, and it is notable that the bond dissociation energy of each of the Group 15 diatomic molecules

is much greater than for those of neighbouring molecules in the same period (Fig. 13.18). Despite this, only N_2 is stable in the condensed phase because of the even greater stability of M_4 or M_{metal} for the heavier congeners (p. 551). A notable advance has, however, been signalled in the isolation and X-ray structural characterization of Sb homologues of N_2 and azobenzene as complex ligands: the red compounds $[(\mu_3\eta^2\text{-Sb}\equiv\text{Sb})\{W(CO)_5\}_3]$ and $[(\eta^1,\eta^1,(\mu,\eta^2)\text{-}(PhSb=SbPh)\{W(CO)_5\}_3]$ are both stable at room temperature, even on exposure to air.[98] The dihapto distibene complex $[Fe(CO)_4\text{-}(\eta^2\text{-RSb}=SbR)]$ {R=$(Me_3Si)_2CH$} has also been characterized.[99]

Diarsane, As_2H_4, is obtained in small yield as a byproduct of the formation of AsH_3 when an alkaline solution of arsenite is reduced by BH_4^- upon acidification:

$$2H_2AsO_3^- + BH_4^- + 3H^+ \longrightarrow As_2H_4$$
$$+ B(OH)_3 + H_2O + H_2$$

Diarsane is a thermally unstable liquid with an extrapolated bp $\sim100°$; it readily decomposes at room temperature to a mixture of AsH_3 and a polymeric hydride of approximate composition $(As_2H)_x$. Sb_2H_4 ($SbCl_3$ + $NaBH_4$/dil HCl) is even less stable. Both compounds can also be prepared by passing a silent electric discharge through MH_3 gas in an ozonizer at low temperature. Mass spectrometric measurements give the thermochemical bond energy E°_{298} (M–M) as $128\,kJ\,mol^{-1}$ for Sb_2H_4 and $167\,kJ\,mol^{-1}$ for As_2H_4, compared with $183\,kJ\,mol^{-1}$ for P_2H_4. Of the halides, As_2I_4 is known (p. 564) but no corresponding compounds of Sb or Bi have yet been isolated (cf. P_2X_4, p. 497).

Organometallic derivatives M_2R_4 are rather more stable than the hydrides and, indeed, dicacodyl, $Me_2AsAsMe_2$, was one of the very first organometallic compounds to be made

[96] M. J. BEGLEY, D. B. SOWERBY and I. HAIDUC, *J. Chem. Soc., Chem. Commun.*, 64–5 (1980).

[97] M. D. POORE and D. R. RUSSELL, *J. Chem. Soc., Chem. Commun.*, 18–9 (1971).

[98] G. HUTTNER, U. WEBER, B. SIGWARTH and O. SCHEIDSTEGER, *Angew. Chem. Int. Edn. Engl.* **21**, 215–6 (1982).

[99] A. H. COWLEY, N. C. NORMAN, M. PAKULSKI, D. L. BRICKER and D. H. RUSSELL, *J. Am. Chem. Soc.* **107** 8211–18 (1985).

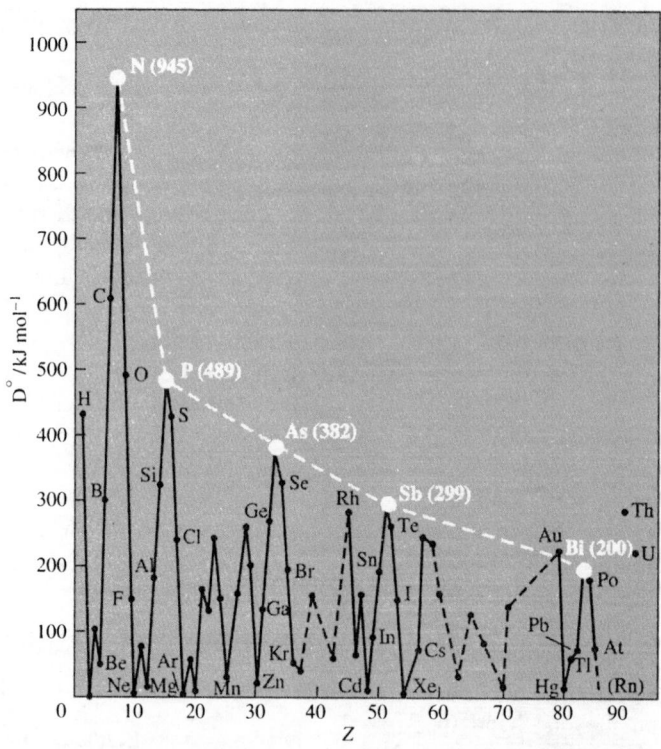

Figure 13.18 Bond dissociation energies for gaseous, homonuclear diatomic molecules (from J. A. Kerr in *Handbook of Chemistry and Physics*, 73rd edn., 1992–3, CRC Press, Boca Raton, Florida). pp. **9**.129–**9**.137.

(L. C. Cadet, 1760; R. Bunsen, 1837): it has mp −1°, bp 78°, is extremely poisonous, and has a revolting smell, as indicated by its name (Greek καϰωδία, *cacodia*, stink). It is now readily made by the reaction of Li metal on Me_2AsI in thf. Other preparative routes to As_2R_4 include reaction of R_2AsH with either R_2AsX or R_2AsNH_2, and the reaction of R_2AsCl with $MAsR_2$ (M = Li, Na, K). In addition to alkyl derivatives numerous other compounds are known, e.g. As_2Ph_4 mp 127°. $As_2(CF_3)_4$ bp 106° has the *trans* (C_{2h}) structure whereas As_2Me_4 has a temperature-dependent mixture of *trans* and *gauche* isomers (p. 428). Corresponding Sb compounds are of more recent lineage, the first to be made (1931) being the yellow crystalline Sb_2Ph_4 mp 122°. Other derivatives have R = Me, Bu^t, CF_3, cyclohexyl, *p*-tolyl, cyclopentadienyl, etc. Little is known of organodibismuthanes Bi_2R_4 despite sporadic attempts to prepare them.

More extensive catenation occurs in the *cyclo*-polyarsanes $(RAs)_n$ which can readily be prepared from organoarsenic dihalides or from arsonic acids as follows:

$$6PhAsCl_2 \xrightarrow{Na/Et_2O} (PhAs)_6 + 12NaCl$$

$$6PhAsI_2 \xrightarrow{Hg\ (fast)} 3PhIAsAsIPh \xrightarrow{Hg\ (slow)} (PhAs)_6$$

$$nPhAsO(OH)_2 \xrightarrow{H_3PO_2} (PhAs)_n \quad n = 5, 6$$

In addition to the 6-membered ring in $(PhAs)_6$, 5-membered rings have been obtained with R = Me, Et, Pr, Ph, CF_3, SiH_3, GeH_3 and 4-membered rings occur with R = CF_3, Ph. A 3-membered As_3 ring has also been made and is the first *all-cis* organocyclotriarsane to be characterized.[100]

―――――――――
[100] J. ELLERMANN and H. SCHOSSNER, *Angew. Chem. Int. Edn. Engl.* **13**, 601–2 (1974).

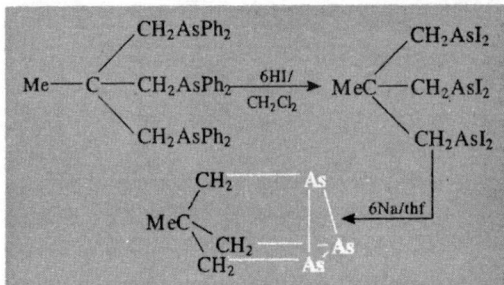

The factors influencing ring size and conformation have not yet become clear. Thus, the yellow $(MeAs)_5$ has a puckered As_5 ring with As–As 243 pm and angle As–As–As 102°; there is also a more stable red form. $(PhAs)_6$ has a puckered As_6 (chair form) with As–As 246 pm and angle As–As–As 91°. Numerous polycyclic compounds As_nR_m have also been characterized, for example the bright-yellow crystalline *tricyclo*-$As_{12}Bu^t_8$.[100a]

In view of the excellent donor properties of tertiary arsines, it is of interest to inquire whether these *cyclo*-polyarsanes can also act as ligands. Indeed, $(MeAs)_5$ can displace CO from metal carbonyls to form complexes in which it behaves as a uni-, bi- or tridentate ligand. For example, direct reaction of $(MeAs)_5$ with $M(CO)_6$ in benzene at 170° (M = Cr, Mo, W) yielded red crystalline compounds $[M(CO)_3(\eta^3\text{-}As_5Me_5)]$ for which the structure

in Fig. 13.19a has been proposed,[101] whereas reaction at room temperature with the ethanol derivative $[M(CO)_5(EtOH)]$ gave the yellow dinuclear product $[\{M(CO)_5\}_2\text{-}\mu\text{-}(\eta^1\eta^1\text{-}As_5Me_5)]$ for which a possible structure is given in Fig. 13.19b. Reaction can also lead to ring degradation; e.g. reaction with $Fe(CO)_5$ cleaves the ring to give dark-orange crystals of the *catena*-tetraarsane $[\{Fe(CO)_3\}_2(As_4Me_4)]$ whose structure (Fig. 13.20a) has been established by X-ray crystallography.[102] Even further degradation of the *cyclo*-polyarsane occurs when $(C_6F_5As)_4$ reacts with $Fe(CO)_5$ in benzene at 120° to give yellow plates of $[Fe(CO)_4\{(AsC_6F_5)_2\}]$ mp 150° (Fig. 13.20b).[103] In other reactions homoatomic ring expansion or chain extension can occur. For example $(AsMe)_5$ when heated with $Cr(CO)_6$ in benzene at 150° gives crystals of $[Cr_2(CO)_6\text{-}\mu\text{-}\{\eta^6\text{-}cyclo(AsMe)_9\}]$, whereas $(AsPr^n)_5$ and $Mo(CO)_6$ under similar conditions yield crystals of $[Mo_2(CO)_6\text{-}\mu\text{-}\{\eta^4\text{-}catena(AsPr^n)_8\}]$. The molecular structures were determined by X-ray analysis and are shown in Fig. 13.21.[104] In the first, each Cr is 6-coordinate and the As_9 ring is hexahapto, donating 3 pairs of electrons to

100a M. BAUDLER and S. WIETFELDT-HALTENHOFF, *Angew. Chem. Int. Edn. Engl.* **24**, 991–2 (1985).

101 P. S. ELMES and B. O. WEST, *Coord. Chem. Rev.* **3**, 279–91 (1968).

102 B. M. GATEHOUSE, *J. Chem. Soc., Chem. Commun.*, 948–9 (1969).

103 P. S. ELMES, P. LEVERET and B. O. WEST, *J. Chem. Soc., Chem. Commun.*, 747–8 (1971).

104 P. S. ELMES, B. M. GATEHOUSE, D. J. LLOYD and B. O. WEST, *J. Chem. Soc., Chem. Commun.*, 953–4 (1974).

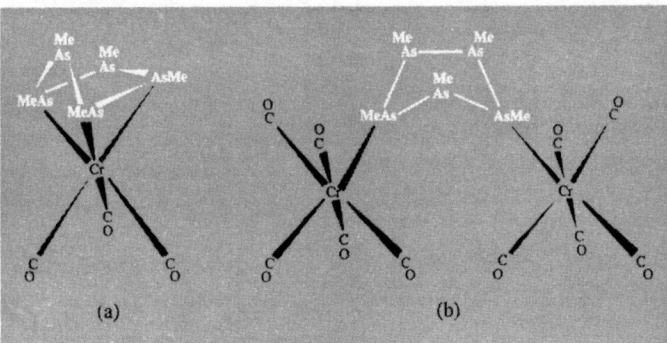

Figure 13.19 Proposed structures for (a) the tridentate *cyclo*-polyarsane complex $[Cr(CO)_3(As_5Me_5)]$, and (b) the bismonodentate binuclear complex $[\{Cr(CO)_5\}_2(As_5Me_5)]$.

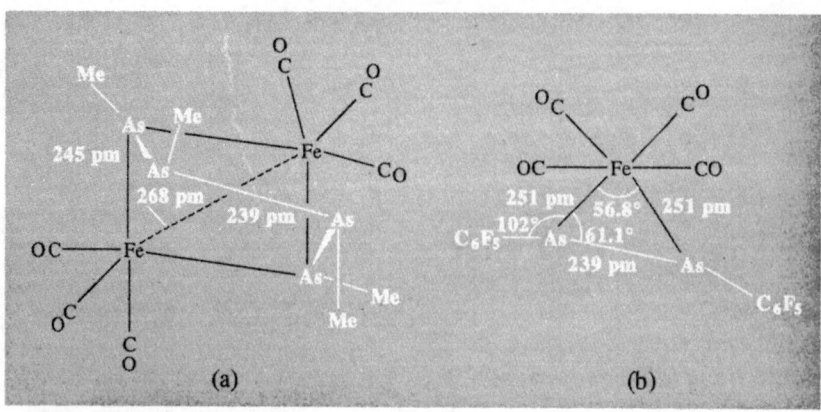

Figure 13.20 Crystal structures of (a) $[\{Fe(CO)_3\}_2\{(AsMe)_4\}]$, and (b) $[Fe(CO)_4\{(AsC_6F_5)_2\}]$. In (a) the distance between the 2 terminal As atoms is 189 pm, suggesting some "residual interaction" but no direct σ bond.

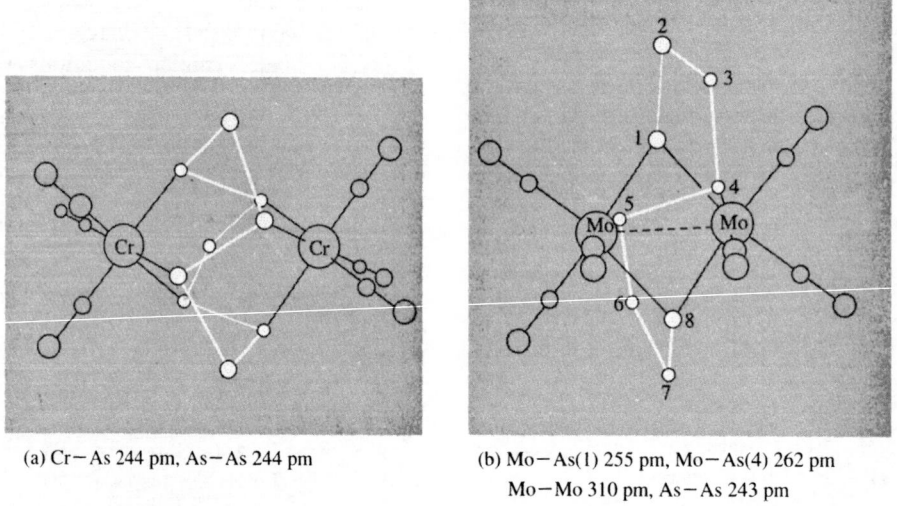

(a) Cr—As 244 pm, As—As 244 pm

(b) Mo—As(1) 255 pm, Mo—As(4) 262 pm
Mo—Mo 310 pm, As—As 243 pm

Figure 13.21 Structures of (a) $[Cr_2(CO)_6\text{-}\mu\text{-}\{\eta^6\text{-}cyclo(AsMe)_9\}]$, and (b) $[Mo_2(CO)_6\text{-}\mu\text{-}\{\eta^4\text{-}catena(AsPr^n)_8\}]$. In both structures the alkyl group attached to each As atom has been omitted for clarity.

each Cr atom. In the second the As atom at each end of the As_8 chain bridges the 2 Mo atoms whereas the 2 central As atoms each bond to 1 Mo atom only and there is an Mo—Mo bond. Complexes of $cyclo\text{-}As_8$ with niobium cyclopentadienyls have also been synthesized,[105] and it

is noteworthy that this ligand is "isoelectronic" with cyclooctatetraene, C_8H_8. The analogy holds for smaller rings, too, and $cyclo\text{-}As_n$ complexes are known for As_3, As_4, As_5^-, As_6 and As_7^-,

105 O. J. SCHERER, R. WINTER, G. HECKMANN and G. WOLMERSHAUSER, *Angew. Chem. Int. Edn. Engl.* **30**, 850–2 (1991). See also H.-G. VON SCHNERING, J. WOLF,

D. WEBER, R. RAMIREZ and T. MEYER, *Angew. Chem. Int. Edn. Engl.* **25**, 353–4 (1986) for the first example of this octahapto $cyclo\text{-}As_8^{8-}$ ligand in the deep red complex $[Rb(crypt)]^+{}_2[Rb\{Nb^VAs_8\}]^{2-}$ (Nb–As 261–9 pm, As–As 2434 pm, angle AsAsAs 93.7°).

(norbornadiene analogue) as well as for *cyclo*-As_8^{8-} (crown-shaped S_8 analogue).

Some of the compounds mentioned in the preceding paragraph can be thought of as heteronuclear cluster compounds and it is convenient to consider here other such heteronuclear cluster species before discussing compounds in which there are homonuclear clusters of Group 15 atoms. Compounds structurally related to the As_4 cluster include the complete series $[As_{4-n}\{Co(CO)_3\}_n]$ $n = 0$, 1, 2, 3, 4. It will be noted that the atom As and the group $\{Co(CO)_3\}$ are "isoelectronic" in the sense that each requires 3 additional electrons to achieve a stable 8- or 18-electron configuration respectively. Yellow crystals of $[As_3Co(CO)_3]$ are obtained by heating $(MeAs)_5$ with $Co_2(CO)_8$ in hexane at 200° under a high pressure of CO.[106]. The red air-sensitive liquid $[As_2\{Co(CO)_3\}_2]$ mp $-10°$ is obtained by the milder reaction of $AsCl_3$ with $Co_2(CO)_8$ in thf.[107] Substitution of some carbonyls by tertiary phosphines is also possible under ultraviolet irradiation. Typical structural details are in Fig. 13.22. In the first compound the η^3-*triangulo*-As_3 group can be thought of as a 3-electron donor to the cobalt atom; in the second, the very short As–As bond suggests multiple bonding and the structure closely resembles

that of the "isoelectronic" acetylene complex $[\{Co(CO)_3\}_2PhC{\equiv}CPh]$ (p. 933). Phosphorus analogues are also known, e.g. the sand-coloured or colourless complexes $[M(\eta^3\text{-}P_3)L^*]$, where $M = Co$, Rh or Ir and L^* is the tripod-like tris(tertiary phosphine) ligand $MeC(CH_2\text{-}PPh_2)_3$.[108] Likewise the first example of an η^2-P_2 ligand symmetrically bonded to 2 metal atoms to give a tetrahedral $\{P_2Co_2\}$ cluster was established by the X-ray structure determination of $[(\mu\text{-}P_2)\{Co(CO)_3\}\{Co(CO)_2(PPh_3)\}]$.[109] If the μ-P_2 (or μ-As_2) ligand is replaced by μ-S_2^- (or μ-Se_2), then isoelectronic and isostructural clusters can be obtained by replacing Co by Fe, as in $[(\mu\text{-}S_2)\{Fe(CO)_3\}_2]$ and $[(\mu\text{-}Se_2)\{Fe(CO)_3\}_2]$ (p. 758).

Even more intriguing are the "double sandwich" complexes which feature $\{\eta^3\text{-}P_3\}$ and $\{\eta^3\text{-}As_3\}$ as symmetrically bridging 3-electron donors. Thus As_4 reacts smoothly with Co^{II} or Ni^{II} aquo ions and the triphosphane ligand $L^* = MeC(CH_2PPh_2)_3$ in thf/ethanol/acetone mixtures to give the exceptionally air-stable dark-green paramagnetic cation $[L^*Co\text{-}\mu\text{-}(\eta^3\text{-}As_3)CoL^*]^{2+}$ with the dimensions shown in Fig. 13.23.[110] The structure of the related P_3 complex $[L^*\text{-}\mu\text{-}(\eta^3\text{-}P_3)\text{-}NiL^*]^{2+}$ (prepared in the same way using white

[106] A. S. FOUST, M. F. FOSTER and L. F. DAHL, *J. Am. Chem. Soc.* **91**, 5631–3 and 5633–5 (1969).

[107] A. S. FOUST, C. F. CAMPANA, J. D. SINCLAIR and L. F. DAHL, *Inorg. Chem.* **18**, 3047–54 (1979).

[108] C. BIANCHINI, C. MEALLI, A. MELI and L. SACCONI, *Inorg. Chim. Acta* **37**, L543–L544 (1979).

[109] C. F. CAMPANA, A. VIZI-OROSZ, G. PALYI, L. MARKÓ and L. F. DAHL, *Inorg. Chem.* **18**, 3054–9 (1979).

[110] M. DI VAIRA, S. MIDOLLINI, L. SACCONI and F. ZANOBINI, *Angew. Chem. Int. Edn. Engl.* **17**, 676–7 (1978).

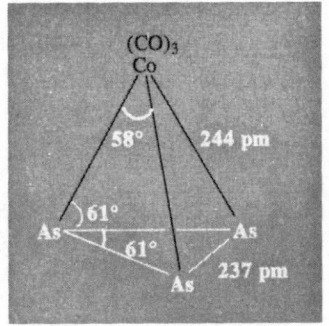 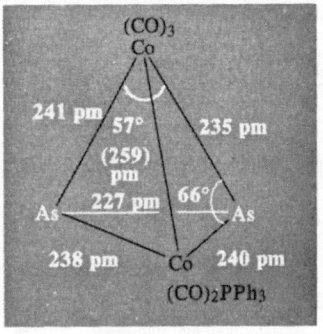

Figure 13.22 Structures of $[As_3Co(CO)_3]$ and $[As_2\{Co(CO)_3\}\{Co(CO)_2(PPh_3)\}]$.

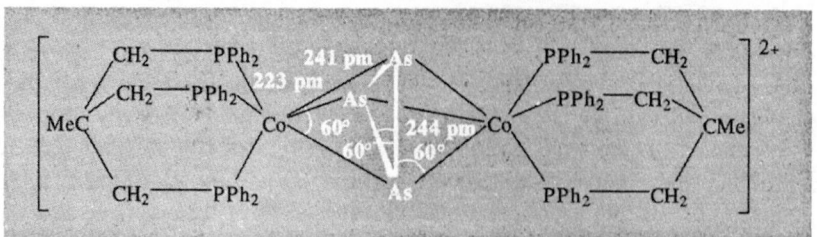

Figure 13.23 Structure of the cation $[L^*Co\text{-}\mu\text{-}(\eta^3\text{-}As_3)CoL^*]^{2+}$.

Table 13.11 Electronic configurations of the isostructural series of complexes containing bridging $\eta^3\text{-}P_3$ and $\eta^3\text{-}As_3$ ligands {L^* is the tridentate tertiary phosphine $MeC(CH_2PPh_2)_3$}

($\eta^3\text{-}P_3$) complex	Colour	Valence electrons	Unpaired electrons	Electrons in highest (e) orbital	Colour	($\eta^3\text{-}As_3$) complex
$[L^*_2Co_2(P_3)]^{3+}$	Bright green	**30**	0	0		$[L^*_2Co_2(As_3)]^{3+}$
$[L^*_2Co_2(P_3)]^{2+}$		**31**	1	1	Dark green	$[L^*_2Co_2(As_3)]^{2+}$
$[L^*_2Co_2(P_3)]^{+}$		**32**	2	2		$[L^*_2Co_2(As_3)]^{+}$
$[L^*_2CoNi(P_3)]^{2+}$	Red-brown	**32**	2	2		—
$[L^*_2Ni_2(P_3)]^{2+}$		**33**	1	3		$[L^*_2Ni_2(As_3)]^{2+}$
$[L^*_2Ni_2(P_3)]^{+}$	Dark	**34**	0	4		$[L^*_2Ni_2(As_3)]^{+}$

P_4) is closely similar[111] with P–P distances of 216 pm (smaller than for P_4 itself, 221 pm). Indeed, a whole series of complexes has now been established with the same structure-motif and differing only in the number of valency electrons in the cluster; some of these are summarized in Table 13.11.[111,112] The number of valence electrons in all these complexes falls in the range 30–34 as predicted by R. Hoffmann and his colleagues.[113] Many other cluster types incorporating differing numbers of Group 15 and transition metal atoms are now known and have been fully reviewed.[114,115]

With Sb even larger clusters can be obtained. For example reaction of $Co(OAc)_2.4H_2O$ and SbCl$_3$ in pentane at 150° under a pressure of H_2/CO gave black crystals of $[Sb_4\{Co(CO)_3\}_4]$ which was found to have a cubane like structure with Sb and Co at alternate vertices of a grossly distorted cube (Fig. 13.24).[116]

In addition to the heteronuclear clusters considered in the preceding paragraphs, As, Sb and Bi also form homonuclear clusters. We have already seen that alkaline earth phosphides $M^{II}_3P_{14}$ contain the $[P_7]^{3-}$ cluster isoelectronic and isostructural with P_4S_3, and the analogous clusters $[As_7]^{3-}$ and $[Sb_7]^{3-}$ have also been synthesized. Thus, when As was heated with metallic Ba at 800°C, black lustrous prisms of Ba_3As_{14} were obtained, isotypic with Ba_3P_{14}; these contained the $[As_7]^{3-}$ anion with dimensions as shown in Fig. 13.25(a).[117] Again,

[111] M. DI VAIRA, S. MIDOLLINI and L. SACCONI, *J. Am. Chem. Soc.* **101**, 1757–63 (1979).

[112] F. FABBRIZZI and L. SACCONI, *Inorg. Chim. Acta*, **36**, L407–L408 (1979).

[113] J. W. LAUHER, M. ELIAN, R. H. SUMMERVILLE and R. HOFFMANN, *J. Am. Chem. Soc.* **98**, 3219–24 (1976).

[114] O. J. SCHERER (and 9 others), in R. STEUDEL (ed.), *The Chemistry of Inorganic Ring Systems*, Elsevier, Amsterdam, 1992 pp. 193–208.

[115] K. H. WHITMIRE, in H. W. ROESKY (ed.), *Rings, Clusters and Polymers of Main Group and Transition Elements*, Elsevier, Amsterdam, 1989, pp. 503–41.

[116] A. S. FOUST and L. F. DAHL, *J. Am. Chem. Soc.* **92**, 7337–41 (1970).

[117] W. SCHMETTOW and H. G. VON SCHNERING, *Angew. Chem. Int. Edn. Engl.* **16**, 857 (1977).

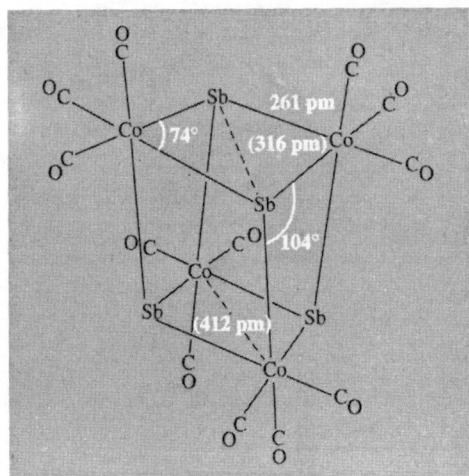

Figure 13.24   Structure of the cubane-like mixed metal-metal cluster complex $[Sb_4\text{-}\{Co(CO)_3\}_4]$.

when powdered NaSb or NaSb$_3$ were treated with crypt, $[N(C_2H_4OC_2H_4OC_2H_4)_3N]$ (p. 98) in dry ethylenediamine, a deep-brown solution was obtained from which brown needles of $[Na(crypt)^+]_3[Sb_7]^{3-}$ were isolated with a C_{3v} anion like $[As_7]^{3-}$ and Sb–Sb distances 286 pm (base), 270 pm (side) and 278 pm (cap).[118]

Isostructural, neutral molecular clusters can be obtained by replacing the 3 S or 3 Se atoms in P_4S_3 or As_4Se_3 by PR or AsR rather than by P^- or As^-. For example reaction of Na/K alloy with white P_4 and Me_3SiCl in monoglyme gave P_7R_3, $P_{14}R_4$ and $P_{13}R_5$. Similarly, Cs_3P_{11} and Rb_3As_7 react with Me_3SiCl in toluene to give good yields of the bright-yellow crystalline compounds $P_{11}(SiMe_3)_3$ and $As_7(SiMe_3)_3$. This latter compound is stable to air and moisture for several hours and has the structure shown in Fig. 13.25b.[119] Other examples include $As_{11}{}^{3-}$[120] and $Sb_{11}{}^{3-}$[121] which both have the structure indicated in Fig. 13.26(a). This is very similar to the structure of $P_{11}{}^{3-}$ [Fig. 12.11(d)] and has approximately D_3 symmetry with eight 3-coordinate As(Sb) atoms forming a bicapped twisted triangular prism with a "waist" of three 2-coordinate bridging atoms. The related $As_{22}{}^{4-}$ anion comprises two such $\{As_{11}\}$ units conjoined by linking two of these equatorial "waist"

---

[118] J. D. CORBETT, D. G. ADOLPHSON, D. J. MERRIMAN, P. A. EDWARDS and F. J. ARMATIS, *J. Am. Chem. Soc.* **97**, 6267–8 (1975). S. C. CRITCHLOW and J. D. CORBETT, *Inorg.*

Chem. **23**, 770–4 (1994); this also describes the synthesis and structure of $[K(crypt)]^+{}_2[Sb_4]^{2-}$ which features the square planar $[Sb_4]^{2-}$ anion with Sb–Sb 275 pm.

[119] H. G. VON SCHNERING, D. FENSKE, W. HÖNLE, M. BINNEWIES and K. PETERS, *Angew. Chem. Int. Edn. Engl.* **18**, 679 (1979).

[120] C. H. E. BELIN, *J. Am. Chem. Soc* **102**, 6036–40 (1980).

[121] U. BOLLE and W. TREMEL, *J. Chem. Soc., Chem. Commun.*, 91–3 (1992).

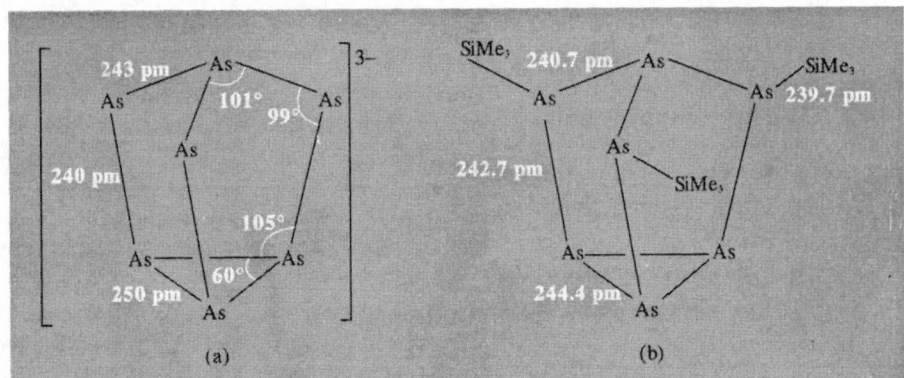

Figure 13.25   (a) Structure of the anion $As_7{}^{3-}$, isoelectronic with As_4Se_3 (p. 581). The sequence of As–As distances (base>cap>side) is typical for such cluster anions but this alters to the sequence base >side>cap for neutral species such as $As_7(SiMe_3)_3$ shown in (b).

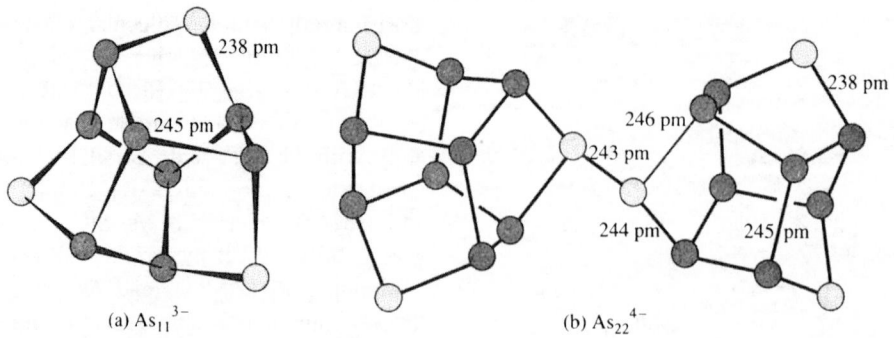

Figure 13.26   (a) Structure of the anion As_{11}^{3-}; note that the As–As distances involving the three 2-coordinate As atoms are significantly shorter than those between pairs of 3-coordinate As atoms. (b) Structure of the anion As_{22}^{4-} i.e. $[As_{11}-As_{11}]^{4-}$ (see text).

atoms as shown in Fig. 13.26(b)[122] Many other homonuclear and heteronuclear clusters have also been prepared, of which $[As_7Se_4]^{3-}$ [123], $[As_{10}Te_3]^{2-}$ [124] and $[As_{11}Te]^{3-}$ [125] can serve as examples. They were made, respectively, by reduction of As_4Se_4 with $K/C_2H_4(NH_2)_2$ in the presence of $[Ph_4P]Br$, the oxidation of polyarsenides with Te (or reduction of As_2Te_3 with K), and the reaction of the alloy $K_{1.6}As_{1.6}Te$ with a cryptand ligand in ethylenediamine.

In all the cluster compounds discussed above there are sufficient electrons to form 2-centre 2-electron bonds between each pair of adjacent atoms. Such is not the case, however, for the cationic bismuth species now to be discussed and these must be considered as "electron deficient". The unparalleled ability of $Bi/BiCl_3$ to form numerous low oxidation-state compounds in the presence of suitable complex anions has already been mentioned (p. 564) and the cationic species shown in Table 13.12 have been unequivocally identified.

The structure of the last 3 cluster cations are shown in Fig. 13.27. In discussing the structure and bonding of these clusters it will be noted that $Bi^+(6s^26p^2)$ can contribute $2p$ electrons to the framework bonding just as {BH} contributes 2 electrons to the cluster bonding in boranes (p. 158). Hence, using the theory developed for the boranes, it can be seen that $[B_nH_n]^{2-}$ is electronically equivalent to $(Bi^+)_n^{2-}$ i.e. $[Bi_n]^{n-2}$. This would account for the stoichiometries Bi_3^+ and Bi_5^{3+} but would also lead one to expect Bi_8^{6+} and Bi_9^{7+} for the larger clusters. However, these charges are very large and it seems likely that the lowest-lying nonbonding orbital would also be occupied in $(Bi^+)_n^{2-}$. For $(Bi^+)_8^{2-}$ this is an e_1 orbital which can accommodate 4 electrons, thereby reducing the charge from Bi_8^{6+} to Bi_8^{2+} as observed. In $(Bi^+)_9^{2-}$ the lowest nonbonding orbital is a_2'' which can accommodate 2 electrons, thus reducing the charge from Bi_9^{7+} to Bi_9^{5+} as observed.[126] It will also be noted that Bi_5^{3+} is isoelectronic with Sn_5^{2-} and Pb_5^{2-} (p. 394); these penta-atomic species all have 12 valence electrons (not counting the "inert" s^2 electrons on each atom), i.e. $n+1$ pairs ($n = 5$) hence a *closo*-structure would be expected by Wade's rules (p. 161).

The Bi_9^{5+} ion was discovered in 1963 as a result of work by A. Herschaft and J. D. Corbett on the structure of the black subhalide "BiCl" (p. 564) and subsequently was

[122] R. C. HAUSHALTER, B. W. EICHHORN, A. L. RHEINGOLD and S. J. GIBB, *J. Chem. Soc., Chem. Commun.*, 1027–8 (1988).

[123] V. ANGILELLA H. MERCIA and C. BELIN, *J. Chem. Soc., Chem. Commun.*, 1654–5 (1989).

[124] R. C. HAUSHALTER, *J. Chem. Soc., Chem. Commun.*, 196–7 (1987).

[125] C. BELIN and H. MERCIER, *J. Chem. Soc., Chem. Commun.*, 190–1 (1987).

[126] J. D. CORBETT, *Prog. Inorg. Chem.* **21**, 129–58 (1976).

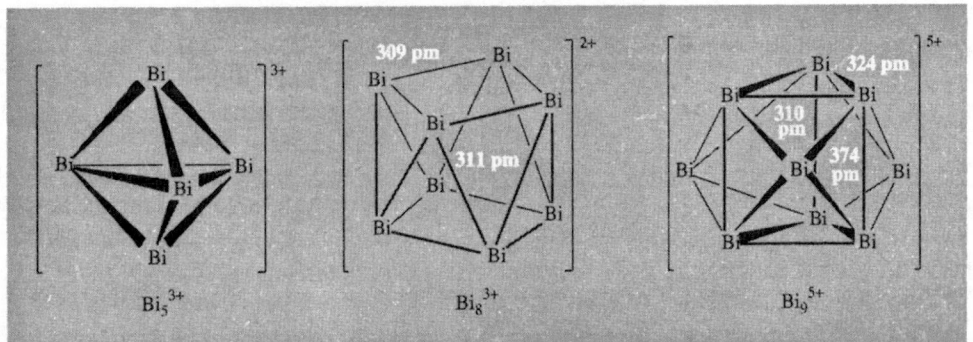

Figure 13.27   The structures of cationic clusters of Bi_m^{n+}. The dimensions cited for Bi_9^{5+} were obtained from an X-ray study on $[(Bi_9^{5+})(Bi^+)(HfCl_6^{2-})_3]$; the corresponding average distances for Bi_9^{5+} in $BiCl_{1.167}$ i.e. $[(Bi_9^{5+})_2(BiCl_5^{2-})_4(Bi_2Cl_8^{2-})]$ are 310, 320 and 380 pm respectively. The square antiprismatic structure of Bi_8^{2+} was established by an X-ray study of $Bi_8[AlCl_4]_2$.[127]

Table 13.12   Cationic bismuth clusters

Cation	Formal oxidation state	Cluster structure	Point group symmetry
Bi^+	1.00	—	—
Bi_3^+	0.33	Triangle	D_{3h}
Bi_5^{3+}	0.60	Trigonal bipyramid	D_{3h}
Bi_8^{2+}	0.25	Square antiprism	D_{4h}
Bi_9^{5+}	0.56	Tricapped trigonal prism	$C_{3h}(\sim D_{3h})$

also found in $Bi_{10}HfCl_{18}$.[32] The diamagnetic compound $Bi_5(AlCl_4)_3$ was prepared by reaction of $BiCl_3/AlCl_3$ with the stoichiometric amount of Bi in fused $NaAlCl_4$ (mp 151°).[128] With an excess of Bi under the same conditions $Bi_8(AlCl_4)_2$ was obtained. More recently it has been found that AsF_5 and other pentafluorides oxidize Bi in liquid SO_2 first to Bi_8^{2+} and then to Bi_5^{3+}:[129]

$$10Bi + 9AsF_5 \xrightarrow{SO_2} 2Bi_5(AsF_6)_3.2SO_2 + 3AsF_3$$

(bright yellow)

[127] B. Krebs, M. Hucke and C. J. Brendel, *Angew. Chem. Int. Edn. Engl.* **21**, 445–6 (1982).

[128] J. D. Corbett, *Inorg. Chem.* **7**, 198–208 (1968).

[129] R. C. Burns, R. J. Gillespie and Woon-Chung Luk, *Inorg. Chem.* **17**, 3596–604 (1978).

13.3.7 Other inorganic compounds

The ability to form stable oxoacid salts such as sulfates, nitrates, perchlorates, etc., increases in the order $As \ll Sb < Bi$. As^{III} is insufficiently basic to enable oxoacid salts to be isolated though species such as $[As(OH)(HSO_4)_2]$ and $[As(OH)(HSO_4)]^+$ have been postulated in anhydrous H_2SO_4 solutions of As_2O_3. In oleum, species such as $[As(HSO_4)_3]$, $[\{(HSO_4)_2As\}_2O]$ and $[\{(HSO_4)_2As\}_2SO_4]$ may be present. By contrast, $Sb_2(SO_4)_3$ can be isolated, as can the hydrates $Bi_2(SO_4)_3.nH_2O$ and the double sulfate $KBi(SO_4)_2$, though all are readily hydrolysed to basic salts.

The pentahydrate $Bi(NO_3)_3.5H_2O$ can be crystallized from solutions of Bi^{III} oxide or carbonate in conc HNO_3. Dilution causes the basic salt $BiO(NO_3)$ to precipitate. Attempts at thermal dehydration yield complex oxocations by reactions which have been formulated as follows:

$$Bi(NO_3)_3.5H_2O \xrightarrow{50-60°} [Bi_6O_6]_2(NO_3)_{11}-$$

$$(OH).6H_2O \xrightarrow{77-130°} [Bi_6O_6](NO_3)_6.3H_2O$$

$$\xrightarrow{400-450°} \alpha\text{-}Bi_2O_3$$

The $[Bi_6O_6]^{6+}$ ion is the dehydrated form of $[Bi_6(OH)_{12}]^{6+}$ (p. 575). Treatment of the pentahydrate with N_2O_4 yields an adduct which decomposes to oxide nitrates on heating:

$$Bi(NO_3)_3.N_2O_4 \xrightarrow{200°} Bi_2O(NO_3)_4$$

$$\xrightarrow{415°} Bi_4O_5(NO_3)_2$$

N_2O_5 also yields a 1:1 adduct and this has been formulated as $[NO_2]^+[Bi(NO_3)_4]^-$. Bi reacts with NO_2 in dimethyl sulfoxide to give the solvate $Bi(NO_3)_3.3Me_2SO$, whereas Sb gives the basic salt $SbO(NO_3).Me_2SO$. $Bi(ClO_4)_3.5H_2O$ dissolves in water to give complex polymeric oxocations such as $[Bi_6(OH)_{12}]^{6+}$ (p. 575).

The first stable arsazene [dark red ArN(H)-As=NAr, mp 173°C, $Ar = C_6H_2Bu^t_3$-2,4,6)] and its orange P analogue (mp 203°C) have been prepared by treating $AsCl_3$ (or PCl_3) with $Li[NHAr]$; an X-ray study found As–N 175 pm, As=N 171 pm and the angle NAsN 98.9° (compared with 163 pm, 157 pm and 103.8° for the N–P=N system.[130] The first 2-coordinate iminoarsine (containing an As=N double bond) was prepared by reacting AsH_3 with O-nitrosobis(trifluoromethyl)hydroxylamine at room temperature, and isolated as a volatile white solid at $-86°$:[131]

$$AsH_3 + (CF_3)_2NONO \longrightarrow$$

$$(CF_3)_2NON{=}AsH + H_2O$$

Numerous Sb–N and Bi–N containing species are also beginning to appear in the literature, for example:

(a) the Sb-subrogated cyclo-triphosphazene, $NPX_2NPX_2NSb(OOCMe)_2$, which was obtained as a white moisture-sensitive solid, the 4-coordinate Sb being pseudo trigonal bipyramidal with the lone pair of electrons in the N_2Sb: plane;[132]

(b) the azastibacubane cluster compound, $(MeNSbCl_3)_4$, which was obtained in good yield as pale yellow crystals by the stoichiometric reaction of $SbCl_5$ with $MeNR_2$ (R = $SiMe_3$);[133]

(c) the homoleptic bismuth amide $Bi(NPh_2)_3$; an X-ray examination of the orange crystals found pyramidal Bi with Bi–N 220 pm (av) and angle NBiN 97° (av).[134]

13.3.8 Organometallic compounds [2.6.15,16,135–139]

All 3 elements form a wide range of organometallic compounds in both the +3 and the +5 state, those of As being generally more stable and those of Bi less stable than their Sb analogues. For example, the mean bond dissociation energies $\overline{D}$(M–Me)/kJ mol^{-1} are 238 for $AsMe_3$, 224 for $SbMe_3$ and 140 for $BiMe_3$. For the corresponding MPh_3, the values are 280, 267, and 200 kJ mol^{-1} respectively, showing again that the M–C bond becomes progressively weaker in the sequence As>Sb>Bi. Comparison with organophosphorus compounds (p. 542) is also apposite. In most of the compounds the metals are 3, 4, 5 or 6 coordinate though a few multiply-bonded compounds are known in which they have a coordination number of 2. In view of the vast range of compounds which have been studied, only a representative selection of structure types will be given in this section.

[130] P. B. HITCHCOCK, M. F. LAPPERT, A. K. RAI and H. D. WILLIAMS, J. Chem. Soc., Chem. Commun., 1633–4 (1986).
[131] H. G. ANG and F. K. LEE, Polyhedron **8**, 1461–2 (1989).
[132] S. K. PANDEY, R. HASSELBRING, A. STEINER, D. STALKE and H. W. ROESKY, Polyhedron **12**, 2941–5 (1993).

[133] W. NEUBERT, H. PRITZKOW and H. P. LATSCHA Angew. Chem. Int. Edn. Engl. **27**, 287–8 (1988).
[134] W. CLEGG, N. A. COMPTON R. J. ERRINGTON, N. C. NORMAN and N. WISHART, Polyhedron **8**, 1579–80 (1989).
[135] G. E. COATES and K. WADE, Organometallic Compounds, Vol. 1, The Main Group Elements, 3rd edn., pp. 510–44, Methuen, London, 1967.
[136] B. J. AYLETT, Organometallic Compounds, 4th edn., Vol. 1, The Main Group Elements, Part 2, pp. 387–521, Chapman & Hall, London, 1979.
[137] G. E. COATES, M. L. H. GREEN, P. POWELL and K. WADE, Principles of Organometallic Chemistry, pp. 143–9, Methuen, London, 1968.
[138] F. G. MANN, The Heterocyclic Derivatives of P, As, Sb and Bi, 2nd edn., Wiley, New York, 1970, 716 pp.
[139] S. PATAI (ed.) The Chemistry of Organic As, Sb and Bi Compounds, Wiley, Chichester, 1994, 962 pp.

Organoarsenic(III) compounds

The first 1-coordinate organoarsenic(III) compound, $RC\equiv As$, $(R = 2,4,6\text{-tri-}t\text{-butylphenyl})$ was isolated in 1986 as pale yellow crystals, mp. 114°C.[7]

Some examples of 2-coordinate organoarsenic(III) compounds are:

Arsabenzene   1-Arsanaphthalene

9-Arsa-anthracene

The first such compound to be prepared was the deep-yellow unstable compound 9-arsa-anthracene[140] but the thermally stable colourless arsabenzene (arsenin) can now conveniently be made by a general route from 1,4-pentadiyne:[141]

AsC_5H_5 is somewhat air sensitive but is distillable and stable to hydrolysis by mild acid or base. Using the same route, PBr_3 gave PC_5H_5 as a colourless volatile liquid (p. 544), $SbCl_3$ gave SbC_5H_5 as an isolable though rather

labile substance which rapidly polymerized at room temperature, and $BiCl_3$ gave the even less-stable BiC_5H_5 which could only be detected spectroscopically by chemical trapping.[141,142] Arsanaphthalene is an air-sensitive yellow oil.[143] Complexes of some of these heterocycles are also known, e.g. $[Cr(\eta^6\text{-}C_5H_5As)_2]$,[144] $[Mo(\eta^6\text{-}C_5H_5As)(CO)_3]$,[145] and $[Fe(\eta^5\text{-}C_4H_4As)_2]$, i.e. diarsaferrocene.[146]

Most organoarsenic(III) compounds are readily prepared by standard methods (p. 497) such as the treatment of $AsCl_3$ with Grignard reagents, organolithium reagents, organoaluminium compounds, or by sodium-alkyl halide (Wurtz) reactions. As_2O_3 can also be used as starting material as indicated in the scheme on p. 595. AsR_3 and $AsAr_3$ are widely used as ligands in coordination chemistry.[6] Common examples are the 4 compounds $AsMe_{3-n}Ph_n (n = 0, 1, 2, 3)$. Multidentate ligands have also been extensively studied particularly the chelating ligand "o-phenylenebis(dimethylarsine)" i.e. 1,2-bis(dimethylarseno)benzene which can be prepared from cacodylic acid (dimethylarsinic acid) $Me_2AsO(OH)$ (itself prepared as indicated in the general scheme on p. 595):

Arsine complexes are especially stable for b-class metals such as Rh, Pd and Pt, and such complexes have found considerable industrial use in hydrogenation or hydroformylation of alkenes,

[140] P. JUZI and K. DEUCHERT, *Angew. Chem. Int. Edn. Engl.* **8**, 991 (1969). H. VERMEER and F. BICKELHAUPT, ibid. 992.

[141] A. J. ASHE, *J. Am. Chem. Soc.* **93**, 3293–5 (1971).

[142] A. J. ASHE, *Acc. Chem. Res.* **11**, 153–7 (1978).

[143] A. J. ASHE, D. L. BELLVILLE and H. S. FRIEDMAN, *J. Chem. Soc., Chem. Commun.*, 880–1 (1979).

[144] C. ELSCHENBROICH, J. KROKER, W. MASSA, M. WÜNSCH and A. J. ASHE, *Angew. Chem. Int. Edn. Engl.* **25**, 571–2 (1986).

[145] A. J. ASHE and J. C. COLBURN, *J. Am. Chem. Soc.* **99**, 8099–100 (1977).

[146] A. J. ASHE, S. MAHMOUD, C. ELSCHENBROICH and M. WÜNSCH, *Angew. Chem. Int. Edn. Engl.* **26**, 229–30 (1987), and references cited therein.

oligomerization of isoprene, carbonylation of α-olefins, etc.

Halogenoarsines R_2AsX and dihalogenoarsines $RAsX_2$ are best prepared by reducing the corresponding arsinic acids $R_2AsO(OH)$ or arsonic acid $RAsO(OH)_2$ with SO_2 in the presence of HCl or HBr and a trace of KI. The actual reducing agent is I^- and the resulting I_2 is in turn reduced by the SO_2. Fluoro compounds are best prepared by metathesis of the chloro derivative with a metal fluoride, e.g. AgF. Interestingly, the compound Ph_3AsI_2 has been shown by X-ray analysis to contain 4-coordinate As and an almost linear As–I–I group with As–I 264 pm, I–I 300.5 pm and angle As–I–I 174.8°.[147]

Hydrolysis of R_2AsX yields arsinous acids R_2AsOH or their anhydrides $(R_2As)_2O$. An alternative route employs a Grignard reagent and As_2O_3, e.g. PhMgBr affords $(Ph_2As)_2O$. Hydrolysis of $RAsX_2$ yields either arsonous acids $RAs(OH)_2$ or their anhydrides $(RAsO)_n$. These latter are not arsenoso compounds $RAs{=}O$ analogous to nitroso compounds (p. 416) but are polymeric. Indeed, all these As^{III} compounds feature pyramidal 3-coordinate As as do the formally As^I compounds $(RAs)_n$ discussed on p. 584. A series of *planar* 3-coordinate arsenic(I) compounds have also been prepared and these are discussed on p. 597.

Organoarsenic(V) compounds

Among the compounds of As^V can be noted the complete series $R_{5-n}AsX_n$ ($n = 0–5$) where R can be alkyl or aryl. Thus $AsPh_5$ (mp 150°) can be prepared by direct reaction of LiPh on either $[AsPh_4]I$, Ph_3AsCl_2 or $Ph_3As{=}O$. Similarly, $AsMe_5$ has been prepared as a colourless, volatile, mobile liquid (mp $-6°$):[148]

$$Me_3AsCl_2 \xrightarrow[(-LiCl)]{LiMe} [AsMe_4]Cl \xrightarrow[(-LiCl)]{LiMe} AsMe_5$$

The preparation is carried out in Me_2O at $-60°$ to avoid formation of the ylide $Me_3As{=}CH_2$ (mp 35°) by elimination of CH_4. $AsMe_5$ decomposes above 100° by one of two routes:

It is stable in air and hydrolyses only slowly:

The aryl analogues are rather more stable.

Of the quaternary arsonium compounds, methyltriaryl derivatives are important as precursors of arsonium ylides, e.g.

$$[Ph_3AsMe]Br + NaNH_2 \xrightarrow{thf}$$

$$Ph_3As{=}CH_2(mp\ 74°) + NaBr + NH_3$$

Such ylides are unstable and react with carbonyl compounds to give both the Wittig product (p. 545) as well as $AsPh_3$ and an epoxide. However, this very reactivity is sometimes an advantage since As ylides often react with carbonyl compounds that are unresponsive to P ylides. Substituted quaternary arsonium compounds are also a useful source of heterocyclic organoarsanes, e.g. thermolysis of 4-(1,7-dibromoheptyl)trimethylarsonium bromide to 1-arsabicyclo[3.3.0]octane:

[147] C. A. McAuliffe, B. Beagley, G. A. Gott, A. G. Mackie, P. M. MacRory . and R. G. Pritchard, *Angew. Chem. Int. Edn. Engl.* **26**, 264–5 (1987).
[148] K.-H. Mitschke and H. Schmidbaur, *Chem. Ber.* **106**, 3645–51 (1973).

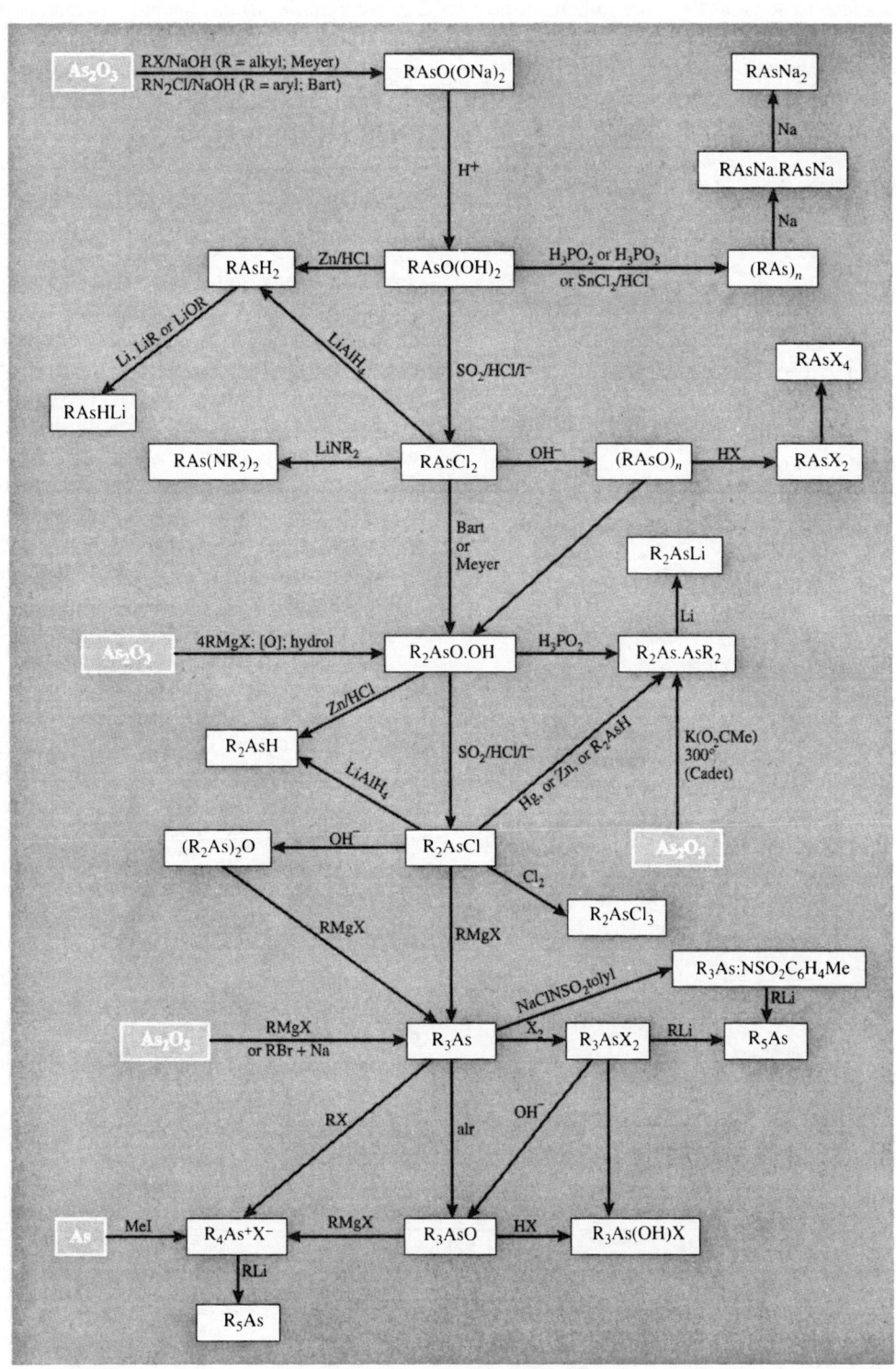

Some routes to organoarsenic compounds[137]

Arsonic acids $RAsO(OH)_2$ are amongst the most important organoarsonium compounds. Alkyl arsonic acids are generally prepared by the Meyer reaction in which an alkaline solution of As_2O_3 is heated with an alkyl halide:

$$As(ONa)_3 + RX \xrightarrow{\text{heat}} NaX + RAsO(ONa)_2$$

$$\xrightarrow{\text{acidify}} RAsO(OH)_2$$

Aryl arsonic acids can be made from a diazonium salt by the Bart reaction:

$$As(ONa)_3 + ArN_2X \longrightarrow NaX + N_2$$

$$+ ArAsO(ONa)_2$$

Similar reactions on alkyl or aryl arsonites yield the arsinic acids $R_2AsO(OH)$ and $Ar_2AsO(OH)$. Arsine oxides are made by alkaline hydrolysis of R_3AsX_2 (or Ar_3AsX_2) or by oxidation of a tertiary arsine with $KMnO_4$, H_2O_2 or I_2.

Physiological activity of arsenicals

In general As^{III} organic derivatives are more toxic than As^V derivatives. The use of organoarsenicals in medicine dates from the discovery in 1905 by H. W. Thomas that "atoxyl" (first made by A. Béchamp in 1863) cured experimental trypanosomiasis (e.g. sleeping sickness). In 1907 P. Erlich and A. Bertheim showed that "atoxyl" was sodium hydrogen 4-aminophenylarsonate

$$H_2N-\underset{}{\bigcirc}-As\overset{O}{\underset{ONa}{\overset{|}{-}}}OH$$

and the field was systematically developed especially when some arsenicals proved effective against syphilis. Today such treatment is obsolete but arsenicals are still used against amoebic dysentery and are indispensable for treatment of the late neurological stages of African trypanosomiasis.

Organoantimony and organobismuth compounds

Organoantimony and organobismuth compounds are closely related to organoarsenic compounds but have not been so extensively investigated. Similar preparative routes are available and it will suffice to single out a few individual compounds for comment or comparison. MR_3 (and MAr_3) are colourless, volatile liquids or solids having the expected pyramidal molecular structure. Some properties are in Table 13.13. As expected (p. 198) tertiary stibines are much weaker ligands than phosphines or arsines.[6] Tertiary bismuthines are weaker still: among the very few coordination complexes that have been reported are $[Ag(BiPh_3)]ClO_4$, $Ph_3BiNbCl_5$, and $Ph_3BiM(CO)_5$ (M = Cr, Mo, W).

An intriguing 3-coordinate organoantimony compound, which is the first example of trigonal-planar Sb^I, has been characterized.[149] The stibinidene complex $[PhSb\{Mn(CO)_2(\eta^5-C_5H_5)\}_2]$ has been isolated as shiny golden metallic crystals (mp 128°) from the crown-ether catalysed reaction:

$$[(\eta^5-C_5H_5)(CO)_2MnSbPhI_2]$$

$$+ [(\eta^5-C_5H_5)Mn(CO)_2].thf \xrightarrow[\text{18-crown-6}]{\text{K/thf}}$$

$$[PhSb\{Mn(CO)_2(\eta^5-C_5H_5)\}_2] + 2KI + \cdots$$

---

149 J. VON SEYERL and G. HUTTNER, *Angew. Chem. Int. Edn. Engl.* **17**, 843–4 (1978).

Table 13.13   Some physical properties of MMe₃ and MPh₃

Property	$AsMe_3$	$SbMe_3$	$BiMe_3$	$AsPh_3$	$SbPh_3$	$BiPh_3$
MP/°C	−87	−62	−86	61	55	78
BP/°C	50	80	109	—	—	—
Bond angle at M	96°	—	97°	102°	—	94°
Mean M–C bond energy/kJ mol⁻¹	229	215	143	267	244	177

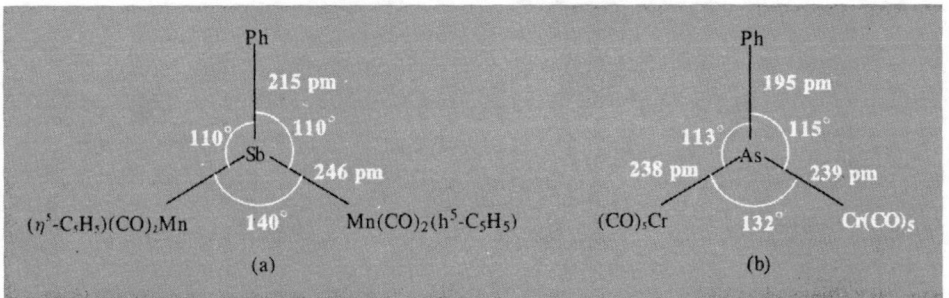

Figure 13.28   Planar structure of (a) [PhSb{Mn(CO)$_2$(η^5-C$_5$H$_5$)$_2$}], and (b) [PhAs{Cr(CO)$_5$}$_2$]. Note the relatively short Sb–Mn and As–Cr bonds.

The structure is shown in Fig. 13.28a: the interatomic angles and distances suggest that the bridging {PhSb^I} group is stabilized by Sb–Mn π interactions. A similar route leads to 3-coordinate planar organoarsinidine complexes which can also be prepared by the following reaction sequence:

$$[Cr(CO)_6] \xrightarrow{\ PhAsH_2\ } [Cr(CO)_5(AsPhH_2)] \text{ yellow}$$

$$\xrightarrow{\ LiBu\ } [Cr(CO)_5(AsPhLi_2)] \text{ orange} \xrightarrow[\text{NCl}_2]{\text{cyclohexyl-}}$$

$$[\{Cr(CO)_5\}_2AsPh] \text{ dark violet (mp } 104°)$$

The chloro-derivative [ClAs{Mn(CO)$_2$-(η^5-C$_5$H$_5$)}$_2$] (shiny black crystals, mp 124°) can now be much more readily obtained by direct reaction of AsCl$_3$ with [Mn(CO)$_2$-(η^5-C$_5$H$_5$)].thf.[150]

Halogenostibines R$_2$SbX and dihalogenostibines RSbX$_2$ (R = alkyl, aryl) can be prepared by standard methods. The former hydrolyse to the corresponding covalent molecular oxides (R$_2$Sb)$_2$O, whereas RSbX$_2$ yield highly polymeric "stiboso" compounds (RSbO)$_n$. The stibonic acids, RSbO(OH)$_2$, and stibinic acids, R$_2$SbO(OH), differ in structure from phosphonic and phosphinic acids (p. 512) or arsonic and arsinic acids (p. 594) in being high molecular weight materials of unknown structure. They are probably best considered as oxide hydroxides

of organoantimony(V) cations. Indeed, throughout its organometallic chemistry Sb shows a propensity to increase its coordination number by dimerization or polymerization. Thus Ph$_2$SbF consists of infinite chains of F-bridged pseudo trigonalbipyramidal units as shown in Fig. 13.29.[151] The compound could not be prepared by the normal methods of fluorinating Ph$_2$SbCl or phenylating SbF$_3$ but can be obtained as a white, air-stable, crystalline solid mp 154° by the following sequence of steps:

$$PhSiCl_3 \xrightarrow[\text{(anhydr)}]{\text{SbF}_3/80°} PhSiF_3 \xrightarrow{\ aq\ NH_4F\ }$$

$$[NH_4]_2[PhSiF_5] \xrightarrow{\ aq\ SbF_3\ } Ph_2SbF$$

Again, Me$_2$SbCl$_3$ is monomeric with equatorial methyl groups (C_{2v}) in solution (CH$_2$Cl$_2$, CHCl$_3$ or C$_6$H$_6$) but forms Cl-bridged dimers with *trans* methyl groups (D_{2h}) in the solid:[152]

[150] J. VON SEYERL, U. MOERING, A. WAGNER, A. FRANK and G. HUTTNER, *Angew Chem. Int. Edn. Engl.* **17**, 844–5 (1978).

[151] S. P. BONE and D. B. SOWERBY, *J. Chem. Soc., Dalton Trans.*, 1430–3 (1979).

[152] N. BERTAZZI, T. C. GIBB and N. N. GREENWOOD, *J. Chem. Soc., Dalton Trans.*, 1153–7 (1976) K. DEHNICKE and H. G. NADLER, *Chem. Ber.* **109**, 3034–8 (1976).

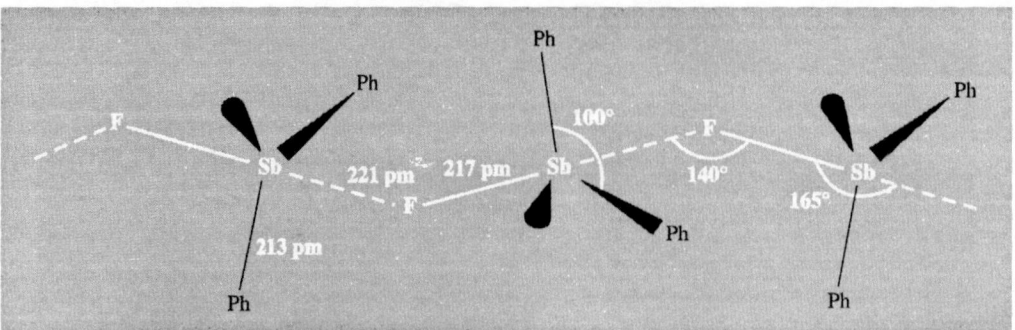

Figure 13.29   Structure of Ph_2SbF_2 showing polymeric chains of apex-shared pseudo trigonal bipyramidal units {$Ph_2FSb...F$}.

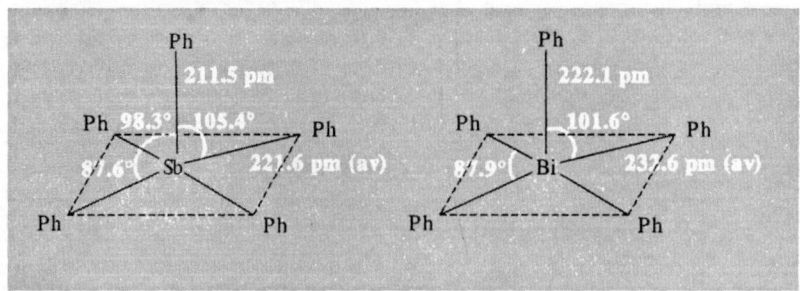

Figure 13.30   (a) Molecular geometry of $SbPh_5$ showing the slightly distorted square-pyramidal structure.[155] (b) Similar data obtained at $-96°$ for the slightly more regular square-pyramidal $BiPh_5$.[159].

A similar Cl-bridged dimeric structure was established by X-ray analysis for Ph_2SbCl_3.[153]

Pentaphenylantimony, $SbPh_5$ (mp 171°), has attracted much attention as the first known example of a 10-valence-electron molecule of a main group element that has a square pyramidal structure[154,155] rather than the usual trigonal bipyramidal structure (as found in PPh_5 and $AsPh_5$). $BiPh_5$ is now also known to have a square pyramidal structure (see below) as does the *anion* $InCl_5^{2-}$ (p. 238). $SbPh_5$ can conveniently be prepared as colourless crystals from $SbPh_3$ by chlorination to give Ph_3SbCl_2 and

then reaction wtih LiPh:

$$Ph_3SbCl_2 + 3LiPh \longrightarrow 2LiCl + Li[SbPh_6]$$

$$\xrightarrow{H_2O} LiOH + C_6H_6 + SbPh_5$$

The structure, shown in Fig. 13.30(a), is based on a slightly distorted square–pyramidal coordination around the Sb atom (C_{2v} instead of C_{4v}), the *ipso*–C_{ax}–Sb–C_b angles being alternately 98.3° and 105.4°.[155] Vibrational spectroscopy suggests that the molecule retains its square-pyramidal structure even in solution, so the structure is not an artefact of crystal packing forces. The yellow cyclopropyl analogue, $Sb(C_3H_5)_5$, apparently has the same geomentry,[156] while the solvate $SbPh_5 \cdot \frac{1}{2}C_6H_{12}$

[153] J. BORDNER, G. O. DOAK and J. R. PETERS, *J. Am. Chem. Soc.* **96**, 6763–5 (1974).

[154] P. J. WHEATLEY, *J. Chem. Soc.* 3718–23 (1964).

[155] A. L. BEAUCHAMP, M. J. BENNETT and F. A. COTTON, *J. Am. Chem. Soc.* **90**, 6675–80 (1968).

[156] A. H. COWLEY, J. L. MILLS, T. M. LOEHR and T. V. LONG, *J. Am. Chem. Soc.* **93**, 2150–3 (1971).

and the *p*-tolyl derivative $Sb(4\text{-}MeC_6H_4)_5$ have almost undistorted trigonal bipyramidal structures.[157]

$BiPh_5$ is even more remarkable. Not only is it square pyramidal (Fig. 13.30b) but it is also highly coloured. It can be prepared as violet crystals by the direct reaction of Ph_3BiCl_2 with two moles of LiPh in ether at $-75°$.[158] The colour is retained in solution, and is due to a weak broad absorption in the green-yellow region (λ_{max} 532 nm, $\log \varepsilon$ 2.4).[159] Substitution on the phenyl rings modifies the colour and may also alter the structure, e.g.:[160] $[BiPh_3(2\text{-}FC_6H_4)_2]$, which is square pyramidal with the *o*-fluorophenyl groups *trans-* basal, forms violet crystals but is reddish in solution, whereas $[Bi(4\text{-}Me\text{-}C_6H_4)_3(2\text{-}F\text{-}C_6H_4)_2]$ is trigonal bipyramidal with axial fluorophenyl groups; it forms yellow crystals but again gives reddish solutions. The structures and colours have been interpreted in terms of relativistic effects which lower the energy of the a_1 LUMO in the C_{4v} structure.[161]

The pentamethyl compound, $SbMe_5$, is surprisingly stable in view of the difficulty of obtaining $AsMe_5$ and $BiMe_5$; it melts at $-19°$, boils at $127°$, and does not inflame in air, though it oxidizes quickly and is hydrolysed by water. It resembles $SbPh_5$ in reacting with LiMe (LiPh) to give $Li^+[SbR_6]^-$ and in reacting with BPh_3 to give $[SbR_4]^+[RBPh_3]^-$.

Organobismuth(V) compounds are in general similar to their As and Sb analogues but are less stable and there are few examples known; e.g. $[BiR_4]X$ and R_3BiX_2 are known but not R_2BiX_3 or $RBiX_4$, whereas all 4 classes of compound are known for P, As and Sb. Similarly, no pentaalkylbismuth compound is known, though as noted above $BiPh_5$ and its derivatives have been prepared. It decomposes spontaneously over a period of days at room temperature and reacts readily with HX, X_2 or even BPh_3 by cleaving 1 phenyl to form quaternary bismuth compounds $[BiPh_4]X$ and $[BiPh_4][BPh_4]$; this latter compound (mp 228°) is the most stable bismuthonium salt yet known.

[157] C. BRABANT, J. HUBERT and A. L. BEAUCHAMP, *Can. J. Chem.* **51**, 2952–7 (1973).

[158] G. WITTIG and K. CLAUSS, *Liebig's Ann. Chem.* **578**, 136–46 (1952).

[159] A. SCHMUCK, J. BUSCHMANN, J. FUCHS and K. SEPPELT, *Angew. Chem. Int. Edn. Engl.* **26**, 1180–2 (1987).

[160] A. SCHMUCK, P. PYYKKÖ and K. SEPPELT, *Angew. Chem. Int. Edn. Engl.* **29**, 213–5 (1990).

[161] B. D. EL-ISSA, P. PYYKKÖ and H. M. ZANATI, *Inorg. Chem.* **30**, 2781–7 (1991).

1 H																	2 He
3 Li	4 Be											5 B	6 C	7 N	8 O	9 F	10 Ne
11 Na	12 Mg											13 Al	14 Si	15 P	16 S	17 Cl	18 Ar
19 K	20 Ca	21 Sc	22 Ti	23 V	24 Cr	25 Mn	26 Fe	27 Co	28 Ni	29 Cu	30 Zn	31 Ga	32 Ge	33 As	34 Se	35 Br	36 Kr
37 Rb	38 Sr	39 Y	40 Zr	41 Nb	42 Mo	43 Tc	44 Ru	45 Rh	46 Pd	47 Ag	48 Cd	49 In	50 Sn	51 Sb	52 Te	53 I	54 Xe
55 Cs	56 Ba	57 La	72 Hf	73 Ta	74 W	75 Re	76 Os	77 Ir	78 Pt	79 Au	80 Hg	81 Tl	82 Pb	83 Bi	84 Po	85 At	86 Rn
87 Fr	88 Ra	89 Ac	104 Rf	105 Db	106 Sg	107 Bh	108 Hs	109 Mt	110 Uun	111 Uuu	112 Uub						

58 Ce	59 Pr	60 Nd	61 Pm	62 Sm	63 Eu	64 Gd	65 Tb	66 Dy	67 Ho	68 Er	69 Tm	70 Yb	71 Lu
90 Th	91 Pa	92 U	93 Np	94 Pu	95 Am	96 Cm	97 Bk	98 Cf	99 Es	100 Fm	101 Md	102 No	103 Lr

14
Oxygen

14.1 The Element

14.1.1 Introduction

Oxygen is the most abundant element on the earth's surface: it occurs both as the free element and combined in innumerable compounds, and comprises 23% of the atmosphere by weight, 46% of the lithosphere and more than 85% of the hydrosphere (~85.8% of the oceans and 88.81% of pure water). It is also, perhaps paradoxically, by far the most abundant element on the surface of the moon where, on average, 3 out of every 5 atoms are oxygen (44.6% by weight).

The "discovery" of oxygen is generally credited to C. W. Scheele and J. Priestley (independently) in 1773–4, though several earlier investigators had made pertinent observations without actually isolating and characterizing the gas.[1−4] Indeed, it is difficult to ascribe a precise meaning to the word "discovery" when applied to a substance so ubiquitously present

as oxygen; particularly when (a) experiments on combustion and respiration were interpreted in terms of the phlogiston theory, (b) there was no clear consensus on what constituted "an element", and (c) the birth of Dalton's atomic theory was still far in the future. Moreover, the technical difficulties before the mid-eighteenth century of isolating and manipulating gases compounded the problem still further, and it seems certain that several investigators had previously prepared oxygen without actually collecting it or recognizing it as a constituent of "common air". Scheele, a pharmacist in Uppsala, Sweden, prepared oxygen at various times between 1771–3 by heating KNO_3, $Mg(NO_3)_2$, Ag_2CO_3, HgO and a mixture of H_3AsO_4 and

---

[1] J. W. MELLOR, *A Comprehensive Treatise on Inorganic and Theoretical Chemistry*, Vol. 1, pp. 344–51, Longmans, Green, 1922. History of the discovery of oxygen.

[2] M. E. Weeks, *Discovery of the Elements*, 6th edn., pp. 209–23, Journal of Chemical Education, Easton, Pa, 1956. (Oxygen.)

[3] J. R. PARTINGTON, *A History of Chemistry*, Vol. 3, Macmillan, London, 1962; Scheele and the discovery of oxygen (pp. 219–22); Priestley and the discovery of oxygen (pp. 256–63); Lavoisier and the rediscovery of oxygen (pp. 402–10).

[4] *Gmelin's Handbuch der Anorganischen Chemie*, 8th edn., pp. 1–82. "Sauerstoff" System No. 3, Vol. 1, Verlag Chemie, 1943. (Historical.)

MnO_2. He called the gas "vitriol air" and reported that it was colourless, odourless and tasteless, and supported combustion better than common air, but the results did not appear until 1777 because of his publisher's negligence. Priestley's classic experiment of using a "burning glass" to calcine HgO confined in a cylinder inverted over liquid mercury was first performed in Colne, England, on 1 August 1774; he related this to A. L. Lavoisier and others at a dinner party in Paris in October 1774 and published the results in 1775 after he had shown that the gas was different from nitrous oxide. Priestley's ingenious experiments undoubtedly established oxygen as a separate substance ("dephlogisticated air") but it was Lavoisier's deep insight which recognized the new gas as an element and as the key to our present understanding of the nature of combustion. This led to the overthrow of the phlogiston theory and laid the foundations

Oxygen: Some Important Dates

15th century	Leonardo da Vinci noted that air has several constituents, one of which supports combustion.
1773–4	C. W. Scheele and J. Priestley independently discovered oxygen, prepared it by several routes, and studied its properties.
1775–7	A. L. Lavoisier recognized oxygen as an element, developed the modern theory of combustion, and demolished the phlogiston theory.
1777	A. L. Lavoisier coined the name "oxygen" (acid former).
1781	Composition of water as a compound of oxygen and hydrogen established by H. Cavendish.
1800	W. Nicholson and A. Carlisle decomposed water electrolytically into hydrogen and oxygen which they then recombine by explosion to resynthesize water.
1818	Hydrogen peroxide discovered by L.-J. Thenard.
1840	C. F. Schönbein detected and named ozone from its smell (see 1857).
1848	M. Faraday noted that oxygen was paramagnetic, correctly ascribed to the triplet $^3\Sigma_g^-$ ground state by R. S. Mulliken (in 1928).
1857	W. Siemens constructed the first machine to use the ozonator-discharge principle to generate ozone.
1877	Oxygen first liquefied by L. Cailletet and R. Pictet (independently).
1881	Oxygen gas first produced industrially (from BaO_2) by A. Brin and L. W. Brin's Oxygen Company.
1896	First production of liquid oxygen on a technical scale (C. von Linde).
1903	Ozonolysis of alkenes discovered and developed by C. D. Harries.
1921–3	The water molecule, previously thought to be linear, shown to be bent.
1929	Isotopes ^{17}O and ^{18}O discovered by W. F. Giauque and H. L. Johnston (see 1961).
1931	Singlet state of O_2, $^1\Sigma_g^+$, discovered by W. H. J. Childe and R. Mecke.
1934	A lower lying singlet state $^1\Delta_g$ discovered by G. Herzberg.
1931–9	H. Kautsky showed the significance of singlet O_2 in organic reactions; his views were discounted at the time but the great importance of singlet O_2 was rediscovered in 1964 by (a) C. S. Foote and S. Wexler, and (b) E. J. Corey and W. C. Taylor.
1941	^{18}O-tracer experiments by S. Ruben and M. D. Kamen showed that the oxygen atoms in photosynthetically produced O_2 both come from H_2O and not CO_2; confirmed in 1975 by A. Stemler.
1951	First detection of ^{17}O nmr signal by H. E. Weaver, B. M. Tolbert and R. C. La Force.
1952	Introduction (in Austria) of the "basic oxygen process", now by far the most common process for making steel.
1961	Dual atomic-weight scales based on oxygen = 16 (chemical) and ^{16}O = 16 (physical) abandoned in favour of the present unified scale based on ^{12}C = 12.
1963	First successful launch of a rocket propelled by liquid H_2/liquid O_2 (Cape Kennedy, USA).
1963	Reversible formation of a dioxygen complex by direct reaction of O_2 with trans-$[Ir(CO)Cl(PPh_3)_2]$ discovered by L. Vaska.
1967	Many crown ethers synthesized by C. J. Pederson (Nobel Prize for Chemistry, 1987) who also studied their use as complexing agents for alkali metal and other cations.
1974	F. S. Rowland and M. Molina showed that man-made chlorofluorocarbons, CFCs, could catalytically destroy ozone in the stratosphere (Nobel Prize for Chemistry, with P. Crutzen, 1995).
1985	J. C. Farman discovered the "ozone hole" (substantial seasonal depletion of ozone) over Halley Bay, Antarctica.

of modern chemistry.[5] Lavoisier named the element "oxygéne" in 1777 in the erroneous belief that it was an essential constituent of all acids (Greek όξύς, *oxys*, sharp, sour; γείνòμαι, *geinomai*, I produce; i.e. acid forming). Some other important dates in oxygen chemistry are in the Panel.

14.1.2 Occurrence

Oxygen occurs in the atmosphere in vast quantities as the free element O_2 (and O_3, p. 607) and there are also substantial amounts dissolved in the oceans and surface waters of the world. Virtually all of this oxygen is of biological origin having been generated by green-plant photosynthesis from water (and carbon dioxide).[6,7] The net reaction can be represented by:

$$H_2O + CO_2 + h\nu \xrightarrow[\text{enzymes}]{\text{chlorophyl}} O_2 + \{CH_2O\}$$

(i.e. carbohydrates, etc.)

However, this is misleading since isotope-tracer experiments using ^{18}O have shown that both of the oxygen atoms in O_2 originate from H_2O, whereas those in the carbohydrates come from CO_2. The process is a complex multistage reaction involving many other species,[8] and requires $469 \, kJ \, mol^{-1}$ of energy (supplied by the light). The reverse process, combustion of organic materials with oxygen, releases this energy again. Indeed, except for very small amounts of energy generated from wind or water power, or from nuclear reactors, all the energy used by man comes ultimately from the combustion of wood or fossil fuels such as coal, peat, natural gas and oil. Photosynthesis thus converts inorganic compounds into organic material, generates atmospheric oxygen, and converts light energy (from the sun) into chemical energy. The $1.5 \times 10^9 \, km^3$ of water on the earth is split by photosynthesis and reconstituted by respiration and combustion once every 2 million years or so.[9] The photosynthetically generated gas temporarily enters the atmosphere and is recycled about once every 2000 years at present rates. The carbon dioxide is partly recycled in the atmosphere and oceans after an average residence time of 300 years and is partly fixed by precipitation of $CaCO_3$, etc. (p. 273).

There was very little, if any, oxygen in the atmosphere 3000 million years ago. Green-plant photosynthesis probably began about 2500 My ago and O_2 first appeared in the atmosphere in geochemically significant amounts about 2000 My ago (this is signalled by the appearance of red beds of iron-containing minerals that have been weathered in an oxygen-containing atmosphere).[6-8] The O_2 content of the atmosphere reached ~2% of the present level some 800 My ago and ~20% of the present level about 580 My ago. This can be compared with the era of rapid sea-floor spreading to give the separated continents which occurred 110–85 My ago. The concentration of O_2 in the atmosphere has probably remained fairly constant for the past 50 My, a period of time which is still extensive when compared with the presence of *homo sapiens*, <1 My. The composition of the present atmosphere (excluding water vapour which is present in variable amounts depending on locality, season of the year, etc., is given in Table 14.1.[6] The oxygen content corresponds to 21.04 atom% and 23.15 wt% (see also ref. 10). The question of atmospheric ozone and pollution of the stratosphere is discussed on p. 608.

[5] A. L. LAVOISIER, *La Traité Elémentaire de Chimie*, Paris, 1789, translated by R. Kerr, *Elements of Chemistry*, London, 1790; facsimile reprint by Dover Publications, Inc., New York, 1965.

[6] J. C. G. WALKER, *Evolution of the Atmosphere*, pp. 318, Macmillan, New York, 1977.

[7] R. P. WAYNE, Chemistry of Atmospheres, 2nd edn. Oxford Univ. Press, Oxford, 1991, 456 pp (See especially Chap. 9).

[8] R. Govindgee, Photosynthesis, *McGraw Hill Encyclopedia of Science and Technology*, 4th edn., Vol. 10, pp. 200–10, 1977.

[9] P. CLOUD and A. GIBOR, The oxygen cycle, Article 4 in *Chemistry in the Environment*, pp. 31–41, Readings from Scientific American, W. H. Freeman, San Francisco, 1973.

[10] P. BRIMBLECOMBE, *Air Composition and Chemistry*, Cambridge Univ. Press, Cambridge, 1986, 224 pp.

Table 14.1　Composition of the atmosphere[a] (excluding H_2O, variable)

Constituent	Vol%	Total mass/tonnes	Constituent	Vol%	Total mass/tonnes
Dry air	100.0	$5.119(8) \times 10^{15}$	CH_4	$\sim 1.5 \times 10^{-4}$	$\sim 4.3 \times 10^9$
N_2	78.084(4)	$3.866(6) \times 10^{15}$	H_2	$\sim 5 \times 10^{-5}$	$\sim 1.8 \times 10^8$
O_2	**20.948(2)**	$\mathbf{1.185(2) \times 10^{15}}$	N_2O	$\sim 3 \times 10^{-5}$	$\sim 2.3 \times 10^9$
			CO	$\sim 1.2 \times 10^{-5}$	$\sim 5.9 \times 10^8$
Ar	0.934(1)	$6.59(1) \times 10^{13}$	NH_3	$\sim 1 \times 10^{-6}$	$\sim 3 \times 10^7$
CO_2	0.0315(10)	$2.45(8) \times 10^{12}$	NO_2	$\sim 1 \times 10^{-7}$	$\sim 8 \times 10^6$
Ne	$1.818(4) \times 10^{-3}$	$6.48(2) \times 10^{10}$	SO_2	$\sim 1 \times 10^{-8}$	$\sim 2 \times 10^6$
He	$5.24(5) \times 10^{-4}$	$3.71(4) \times 10^9$	H_2S	$\sim 1 \times 10^{-8}$	$\sim 1 \times 10^6$
Kr	$1.14(1) \times 10^{-4}$	$1.69(2) \times 10^{10}$	**O_3**	**Variable**	$\mathbf{\sim 3.3 \times 10^9}$
Xe	$8.7(1) \times 10^{-6}$	$2.02(2) \times 10^9$			

[a]Total mass: $5.136(7) \times 10^{15}$ tonnes; H_2O $0.017(1) \times 10^{15}$ tonnes; dry atmosphere $5.119(8) \times 10^{15}$ tonnes. Figures in parentheses denote estimated uncertainty in last significant digit.

In addition to its presence as the free element in the atmosphere and dissolved in surface waters, oxygen occurs in combined form both as water, and a constituent of most rocks, minerals, and soils. The estimated abundance of oxygen in the crustal rocks of the earth is 455 000 ppm (i.e. 45.5% by weight): see silicates, p. 347; aluminosilicates, p. 347; carbonates, p. 109; phosphates, p. 475, etc.

14.1.3 Preparation

Oxygen is now separated from air on a vast scale (see below) and is conveniently obtained for most laboratory purposes from high-pressure stainless steel cylinders. Small traces of N_2 and the rare gases, particularly argon, are the most persistent impurities. Occasionally, small-scale laboratory preparations are required and the method chosen depends on the amount and purity required and the availability of services. Electrolysis of degassed aqueous electrolytes produces wet O_2, the purest gas being obtained from 30% potassium hydroxide solution using nickel electrodes. Another source is the catalytic decomposition of 30% aqueous hydrogen peroxide on a platinized nickel foil.

Many oxoacid salts decompose to give oxygen when heated (p. 864). A convenient source is $KClO_3$ which evolves oxygen when heated to 400–500° according to the simplified equation

$$2KClO_3 \xrightarrow{\Delta} 2KCl + 3O_2$$

The decomposition temperature is reduced to 150° in the presence of MnO_2 but then the product is contaminated with up to 3% of ClO_2 (p. 847). Small amounts of breathable oxygen for use in emergencies (e.g. failure of normal supply in aircraft or submarines) can be generated by decomposition of $NaClO_3$ in "oxygen candles". The best method for the controlled preparation of very pure O_2 is the thermal decomposition of recrystallized, predried, degassed $KMnO_4$ in a vacuum line. Mn^{VI} and Mn^{IV} are both formed and the reaction can formally be represented as:

$$2KMnO_4 \xrightarrow{215-235°} K_2MnO_4 + MnO_2 + O_2$$

Oxygen gas and liquid oxygen are manufactured on a huge scale by the fractional distillation of liquid air at temperatures near $-183°C$. Although world production exceeds 100 million tonnes pa this is still less than one ten-millionth part of the oxygen in the atmosphere; moreover, the oxygen is continuously being replenished by photosynthesis. Further information on the industrial production and uses of oxygen are in the Panel.

Industrial Production and Uses of Oxygen[11]

Air can be cooled and eventually liquified by compressing it isothermally and then allowing it to expand adiabatically to obtain cooling by the Joule-Thompson effect. Although this process was developed by C. von Linde (Germany) and W. Hampson (UK) at the end of the last century, it is thermodynamically inefficient and costly in energy. Most large industrial plants now use the method developed by G. Claude (France) in which air is expanded isentropically in an engine from which mechanical work can be obtained; this produces a much greater cooling effect than that obtained by the Joule-Thompson effect alone. Because N_2 (bp $-195.8°C$) is more volatile than O_2 (bp $-183.0°C$) there is a higher concentration of N_2 in the vapour phase above boiling liquid air than in the liquid phase, whilst O_2 becomes progressively enriched in the liquid phase. Fractional distillation of the liquefied air is usually effected in an ingeniously designed double-column dual-pressure still which uses product oxygen from the upper column at a lower pressure (lower bp) to condense vapour for reflux at a higher pressure in the lower column. The most volatile constituents of air (He, H_2, Ne) do not condense but accumulate as a high-pressure gaseous mixture with N_2 at the top of the lower column. Argon, which has a volatility between those of O_2 and N_2, concentrates in the upper column from which it can be withdrawn for further purification in a separate column, whilst the least-volatile constituents (Kr, Xe) accumulate in the oxygen boiler at the foot of the upper column. Typical operating pressures are 5 atm at the top of the lower column and 0.5 atm at the bottom of the upper column. A large plant might produce 1700 tonnes per day of separated products. A rather different design is used if liquid (rather than gaseous) N_2 is required in addition to the liquid and/or gaseous O_2.

From modest beginnings at the turn of the century, oxygen has now become the third largest volume chemical produced in the USA (after H_2SO_4 and N_2 and ahead of ethylene, lime and NH_3, see p. 407). Production in 1995 was 23.3 million tonnes (USA), over 3 Mt (UK), and 100 Mt worldwide. About 20% of the USA production is as liquid O_2. This phenomenal growth derived mainly from the growing use of O_2 in steelmaking; the use of O_2 rather than air in the Bessemer process was introduced in the late 1950s and greatly increased the productivity by hastening the reactions. In many of the major industrial countries this use alone now accounts for 65–85% of the oxygen produced. Much of this is manufactured on site and is simply piped from the air-separation plant to the steel converter.

Oxygen is also used to an increasing extent in iron blast furnaces since enrichment of the blast enables heavy fuel oil to replace some of the more expensive metallurgical coke. Other furnace applications are in ferrous and non-ferrous metal smelting and in glass manufacture, where considerable benefits accrue from higher temperatures, greater productivity, and longer furnace life. Related, though smaller-scale applications, include steel cutting, oxy-gas welding, and oxygen lancing (concrete drilling).

In the chemical industry oxygen is used on a large scale in the production of TiO_2 by the chloride process (p. 959), in the direct oxidation of ethene to ethylene oxide, and in the manufacture of synthesis gas (H_2 + CO), propylene oxide, vinyl chloride, vinyl acetate, etc. Environmental and biomedical uses embrace sewage treatment, river revival, paper-pulp bleaching, fish farming, artificial atmospheres for diving and submarine work, oxygen tents in hospitals, etc. Much of the oxygen for these applications is transported either in bulk liquid carriers or in high-pressure steel cylinders.

A final, somewhat variable outlet for large-scale liquid oxygen is as oxidant in rocket fuels for space exploration, satellite launching and space shuttles. For example, in the Apollo mission to the moon (1979), each Saturn 5 launch rocket used 1270 m^3 (i.e. 1.25 million litres or 1450 tonnes) of liquid oxygen in Stage 1, where it oxidized the kerosene fuel (195 000 l, or about 550 tonnes) in the almost unbelievably short time of 2.5 min. Stages 2 and 3 had 315 and 76.3 m^3 of liquid O_2 respectively, and the fuel was liquid H_2.

14.1.4 Atomic and physical properties

Oxygen has 3 stable isotopes of which ^{16}O (relative atomic mass 15.994 915) is by far the most abundant (99.762 atom%). Of the others, ^{17}O (16.999 134) has an abundance of only 0.038% and ^{18}O (17.999 160) is 0.200% abundant. These values vary slightly in differing natural sources (the ranges being 0.0350–0.0407% for ^{17}O and 0.188–0.215% for ^{18}O) and this variability prevents the atomic weight of oxygen being quoted more precisely than 15.9994 ± 0.0003 (see p. 17). Artificial enrichment of ^{17}O and ^{18}O can be achieved by several physical or chemical processes such as the fractional distillation of water, the electrolysis of water, and the thermal diffusion of oxygen gas. Heavy water enriched to 20 atom% ^{17}O or 98% ^{18}O is available commercially, as is oxygen gas enriched to 95% in ^{17}O or 99% in ^{18}O. The ^{18}O isotope has been much used in kinetic and

---

[11] W. J. GRANT and S. L. REDFEARN, Industrial Gases, in R. Thompson (ed.), *The Modern Inorganic Chemicals Industry*, pp. 273–301. Chem. Soc. Special Publ. No. 31, 1978.

mechanistic studies.[12] Ten radioactive isotopes are also known but their very short half-lives make them unsuitable for tracer work. The longest lived, ^{15}O, decays by positron emission with $t_{\frac{1}{2}}$ 122.2 s; it can be made by bombarding ^{16}O with ^3He particles: $^{16}O(^3He,\alpha)^{15}O$.

The isotope ^{17}O is important in having a nuclear spin ($I = \frac{5}{2}$) and this enables it to be used in nmr studies.[13] The nuclear magnetic moment is -1.8930 nuclear magnetons (very similar to the value for the free neutron, -1.9132 NM) and the relative sensitivity for equal numbers of nuclei is 0.0291, compared with ^1H 1.00, ^{11}B 0.17, ^{13}C 0.016, ^{31}P 0.066, etc. In addition to this low sensitivity, measurements are made more difficult because the quadrupolar nucleus leads to very broad resonances, typically $10^2 - 10^3$ times those for ^1H. The observing frequency is ~0.136 times that for proton nmr. The resonance was first observed in 1951[14] and the range of chemical shifts extended in 1955.[15] The technique has proved particularly valuable for studying aqueous solutions and the solvation equilibria of electrolytes. Thus the hydration numbers for the diamagnetic cations Be^{II}, Al^{III}, and Ga^{III} have been directly measured as 4, 6 and 6 respectively, and several exchange reactions between "bound" and "free" water have been investigated. Chemical shifts for ^{17}O in a wide range of oxoanions $[XO_n]^{m-}$ have been studied and it has been found that the shifts for terminal and bridging O atoms in $[Cr_2O_7]^{2-}$ differ by as much as 760 ppm. The technique is proving increasingly valuable in the structure determination of complex polyanions in solution; for example all seven different types of O atoms

in $[V_{10}O_{28}]^{6-}$ (p. 986) have been detected.[16] The exchange of ^{17}O between $H_2{}^{17}O$ and various oxoanions has also been studied. Less work has been done so far on transition metal complexes of CO and NO though advances in techniques are now beginning to yield valuable structural and kinetic data.[17]

The electronic configuration of the free O atom is $1s^2 2s^2 2p^4$, leading to a $^3P_2$ ground state. The ionization energy of O is 1313.5 kJ mol^{-1} (cf. S on p. 662 and the other Group 16 elements on p. 754). The electronegativity of O is 3.5; this is exceeded only by F and the high value is reflected in much of the chemistry of oxygen and the oxides. The single-bond atomic radius of O is usually quoted as 73–74 pm, i.e. slightly smaller than for C and N, and slightly larger than for F, as expected. The ionic radius of O^{2-} is assigned the standard value of 140 pm and all other ionic radii are derived from this.[18]

Molecular oxygen, O_2, is unique among gaseous diatomic species with an even number of electrons in being paramagnetic. This property, first observed by M. Faraday in 1848, receives a satisfying explanation in terms of molecular orbital theory. The schematic energy-level diagram is shown in Fig. 14.1; this indicates that the 2 least-strongly bound electrons in O_2 occupy degenerate orbitals of π symmetry and have parallel spins. This leads to a triplet ground state, $^3\Sigma_g^-$. As there are 4 more electrons in bonding MOs than in antibonding MOs, O_2 can be formally said to contain a double bond. If the 2 electrons, whilst remaining unpaired in separate orbitals, have opposite spin, then a singlet excited state of zero resultant spin results, $^1\Delta_g$. A singlet state also results if the 2 electrons occupy a single π^* orbital with opposed spins, $^1\Sigma_g^+$. These 2 singlet states lie 94.72 and 157.85 kJ mol^{-1} above the ground state and are extremely important in gas-phase oxidation reactions (p. 614). The excitation is

[12] I. D. DOSTROVSKY and D. SAMUEL, in R. H. HERBER (ed.), *Inorganic Isotopic Syntheses*, Chap. 5, pp. 119–42, Benjamin, New York, 1962.

[13] C. ROGER, N. SHEPPARD, C. MCFARLANE and W. MCFARLANE, Chap. 12A in R. H. HARRIS and B. E. MANN (eds.). *NMR and the Periodic Table*, pp. 383–400, Academic Press, London, 1978. H. C. E. MCFARLANE and W. MCFARLANE, in J. MASON (ed.), *Multinuclear NMR*, Plenum Press, New York, 1987, pp. 403–16.

[14] F. ALDER and F. C. YU, *Phys. Rev.* **81**, 1067–8 (1951).

[15] H. E. WEAVER, B. M. TOLBERT and R. C. LAFORCE, *J. Chem. Phys.* **23**, 1956–7 (1955).

[16] W. G. KLEMPERER and W. SHUM, *J. Am. Chem. Soc.* **99**, 3544–5 (1977).

[17] R. L. KUMP and L. J. TODD, *J. Chem. Soc., Chem. Commun.*, 292–3 (1980).

[18] R. D. SHANNON, *Acta Cryst.* **A32**, 751–67 (1976).

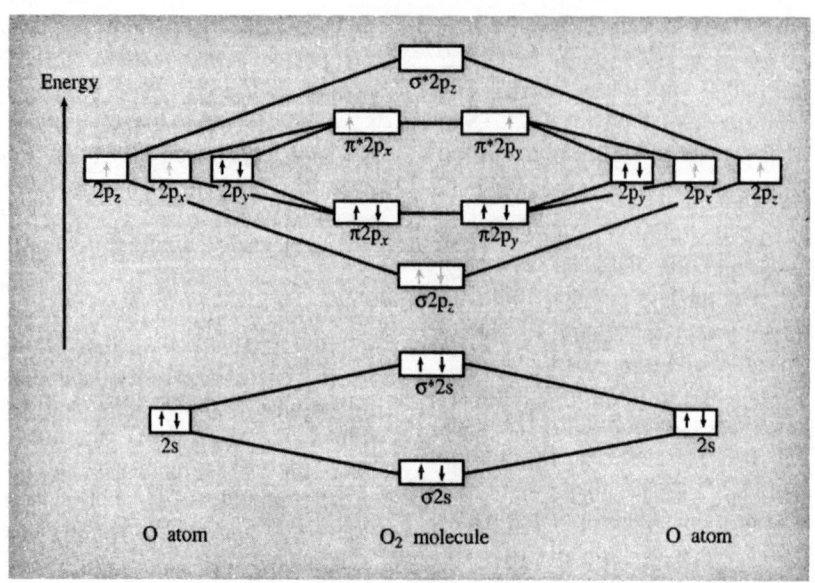

Figure 14.1   Schematic molecular–orbital energy level diagram for the molecule O_2 in its ground state, $^3\Sigma_g^-$. The internuclear vector is along the z-axis.

accompanied by a slight but definite increase in the internuclear distance from 120.74 pm in the ground state to 121.55 and 122.77 pm in the excited states. The bond dissociation energy of O_2 is 493.4(2) kJ mol^{-1}; this is substantially less than for the triply bonded species N_2 (945.4 kJ mol^{-1}) but is much greater than for F_2 (158.8 kJ mol^{-1}). See also the discussion on p. 616.

Oxygen is a colourless, odourless, tasteless highly reactive gas. It dissolves to the extent of 3.08 cm^3 (gas at STP) in 100 cm^3 H_2O at 20° and this drops to 2.08 cm^3 at 50°. Solubility in salt water is slightly less but is still sufficient for the vital support of marine and aquatic life. Solubility in many organic solvents is about 10 times that in water and necessitates careful degassing if these solvents are to be used in the preparation and handling of oxygen-sensitive compounds. Typical solubilities (expressed as gas volumes dissolved in 100 cm^3 of solvent at 25°C and 1 atm pressure) are Et_2O 45.0, CCl_4 30.2, Me_2CO 28.0 and C_6H_6 22.3 cm^3.

Oxygen condenses to a pale blue, mobile paramagnetic liquid (bp −183.0°C at 1 atm).

The viscosity (0.199 centipoise at −183.5° and 10.6 atm) is about one-fifth that of water at room temperature. The critical temperature, above which oxygen cannot be liquefied by application of pressure alone, is −118.4°C and the critical pressure is 50.15 atm. Solid oxygen (pale blue, mp −218.8°C) also comprises paramagnetic O_2 molecules but, in the cubic γ-phase just below the mp, these are rotationally disordered and the solid is soft, transparent, and only slightly more dense than the liquid. There is a much greater increase in density when the solid transforms to the rhombohedral β-phase at −229.4° and there is a further phase change to the monoclinic α-form at −249.3°C; these various changes and the accompanying changes in molar volume ΔV_M are summarized in Table 14.2.

The blue colour of oxygen in the liquid and solid phases is due to electronic transitions by which molecules in the triplet ground state are excited to the singlet states. These transitions are normally forbidden in pure gaseous oxygen and, in any case, they occur in the infrared region of the spectrum at 7918 cm^{-1} ($^1\Delta_g$) and 13 195 cm^{-1} ($^1\Sigma_g^+$). However, in the condensed phases a

Table 14.2 Densities and molar volumes of liquid and solid O_2

Transition	bp/1 (atm)	mp (triple pt)	$\gamma \longleftrightarrow \beta$	$\beta \longleftrightarrow \alpha$	
T/K	90.18	54.35	43.80	23.89	
$d/g\,cm^{-3}$					
	1.1407(1)	1.3215(1)	1.334(γ)	1.495(β)	1.53(α)
$\Delta V_M/cm^3\,mol^{-1}$	3.84	0.23	2.58	0.49	

single photon can elevate 2 colliding molecules simultaneously to excited states, thereby requiring absorption of energy in the visible (red-yellow-green) regions of the spectrum.[19] For example:

$$2O_2(^3\Sigma_g^-) + h\nu \longrightarrow 2O_2(^1\Delta_g);$$

$$\bar{\nu} = 15\,800\,cm^{-1},\ i.e.\ \lambda = 631.2\,nm$$

$$2O_2(^3\Sigma_g^-) + h\nu \longrightarrow O_2(^1\Delta_g) + O_2(^1\Sigma_g^+);$$

$$\bar{\nu} \sim 21\,100\,cm^{-1},\ i.e.\ \lambda = 473.7\,nm$$

The blue colour of the sky is, of course, due to Rayleigh scattering and not to electronic absorption by O_2 molecules.

14.1.5 Other forms of oxygen

Ozone [20]

Ozone, O_3, is the triatomic allotrope of oxygen. It is an unstable, blue diamagnetic gas with a characteristic pungent odour: indeed, it was first detected by means of its smell, as reflected by its name (Greek ὄζειν, *ozein*, to smell) coined by C. F. Schönbein in 1840. Ozone can be detected by its smell in concentrations as low as 0.01 ppm; the maximum permissible concentration for continuous exposure is 0.1 ppm but levels as high as 1 ppm are considered non-toxic if breathed for less than 10 min.

The molecule O_3 is bent, as are the iso-electronic species $ONCl$ and ONO^-. Microwave measurements lead to a bond angle of $116.8 \pm 0.5°$ and an interatomic distance of 127.8 (±0.3) pm between the central O and each of the 2 terminal O atoms as shown in Fig. 14.2a. This implies an O$\cdots$O distance of only 218 pm between the 2 terminal O atoms, compared with the normal van der Waals O$\cdots$O distance of 280 pm. A valence-bond description of the molecule is given by the resonance hybrids in Fig. 14.2b and a MO description of the bonding is indicated in Fig. 14.2c: in this, each O atom forms a σ bond to its neighbour using an sp^2-type orbital, and the 3 atomic p_π orbitals can combine to give the 3 MOs shown. There are just sufficient electrons to fill the bonding and nonbonding MOs so that the π system can be termed a 4electron 3-centre bond. The total bond order for each O–O bond is therefore approximately 1.5 (1 σ bond and half of 1 π-bonding MO). It is instructive to note that SO_2 has a similar structure (angle O–S–O 120°): the much greater stability of this molecule when compared with O_3 has been ascribed, in part, to the possible involvement of d_π orbitals on the S atom which would allow the filled nonbonding orbital in O_3 to become bonding in SO_2 (see also p. 700). Other comparisons of O–O bond orders, interatomic distances and bond energies are in Table 14.4 (p. 616).

Ozone condenses to a deep blue liquid (bp $-111.9°C$) and to a violet-black solid (mp $-192.5°C$). The colour is due to an intense absorption band in the red region of the spectrum between 500–700 nm (λ_{max} 557.4 and 601.9 nm). Both the liquid and the solid are explosive

[19] E. A. OGRYZLO, Why liquid oxygen is blue, *J. Chem. Educ.* **42**, 647–8 (1965).

[20] M. HORVÁTH, L. BILITZKY and J. HÜTTNER (eds.), *Ozone*, Elsevier, Amsterdam, 1985, 350 pp.

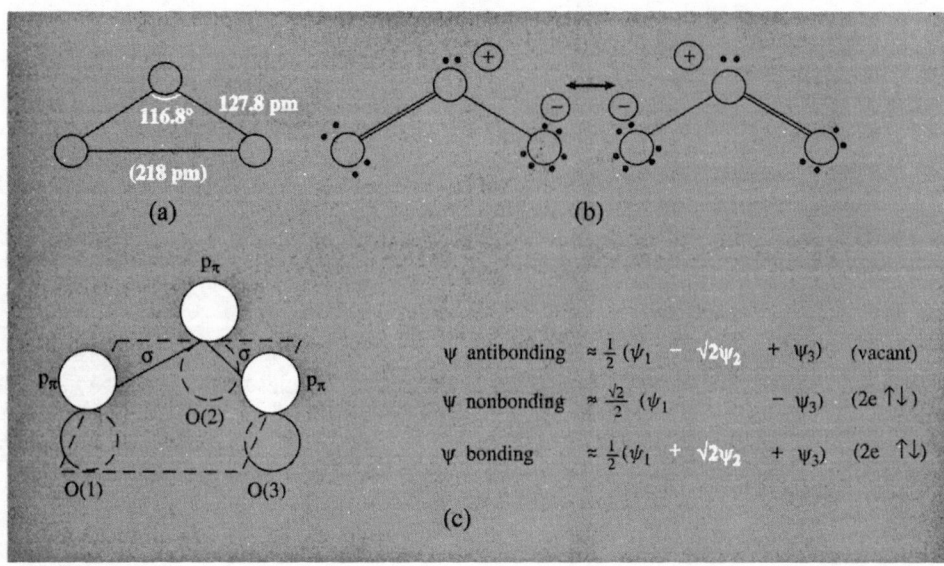

Figure 14.2 (a) Geometry of the O_3 molecule, (b) valence-bond resonance description of the bonding in O_3, and (c) orbitals used in the MO description of the bonding in O_3, where ψ_1 is the $2p_\pi$ orbital of O(1), etc.

due to decomposition into gaseous O_2. Gaseous ozone is also thermodynamically unstable with respect to decomposition into dioxygen though it decomposes only slowly, even at 200°, in the absence of catalysts or ultraviolet light:

$$\tfrac{3}{2}O_2(g) \longrightarrow O_3(g); \quad \Delta H_f^\circ + 142.7\,\text{kJ mol}^{-1};$$

$$\Delta G_f^\circ + 163.2\,\text{kJ mol}^{-1}$$

Other properties of ozone (which can be compared with those of dioxygen on p. 606) are: density at $-119.4°C$ $1.354\,\text{g cm}^{-3}$ (liquid), density at $-195.8°C$ $1.728\,\text{g cm}^{-3}$ (solid), viscosity at $-183°C$ 1.57 centipoise, dipole moment 0.54 D. Liquid ozone is miscible in all proportions with CH_4, CCl_2F_2, $CClF_3$, CO, NF_3, OF_2 and F_2 but forms two layers with liquid Ar, N_2, O_2 and CF_4.

A particularly important property of ozone is its strong absorption in the ultraviolet region of the spectrum between 220–290 nm ($\lambda_{\max}255.3$ nm); this protects the surface of the earth and its inhabitants from the intense ultraviolet radiation of the sun. Indeed, it is this absorption of energy, and the consequent rise in temperature, which is the main cause for the existence of the stratosphere in the first place.

Thus, the mean temperature of the atmosphere, which is about 20°C at sea level, falls steadily to about $-55°$ at an altitude of 10 km and then rises to almost 0°C at 50 km before dropping steadily again to about $-90°$ at 90 km. Concern was expressed in 1974[21] that interaction of ozone with man-made chlorofluorocarbons would deplete the equilibrium concentration of ozone with potentially disastrous consequences, and this was dramatically confirmed by the discovery of a seasonally recurring "ozone hole" above Antarctica in 1985.[22] A less prominent ozone hole was subsequently detected above the Arctic Ocean. The detailed physical and chemical conditions required to generate these large seasonal depletions of ozone are extremely complex but the main features have now been elucidated (see p. 848). Several accounts of various aspects of the emerging story, and of the consequent international governmental actions to

---

[21] M. J. MOLINA and F. S. ROWLAND, *Nature* **249**, 810–12 (1974). (Shared 1995 Nobel Prize for Chemistry with P. Crutzen.)

[22] J. C. FARMAN, B. G. GARDINER and J. D. SHANKLIN, *Nature* **315**, 207–10 (1985).

ameliorate or reverse the depletion have been published.[7.23−27]

Ozone is best prepared by flowing O_2 at 1 atm and 25° through concentric metallized glass tubes to which low-frequency power at 50–500 Hz and 10–20 kV is applied to maintain a silent electric discharge (see also p. 611). The ozonizer tube, which becomes heated by dielectric loss, should be kept cooled to room temperature and the effluent gas, which contains up to 10% O_3 at moderate flow rates, can be used directly or fractionated if higher concentrations are required. Reaction proceeds via O atoms at the surface M, via excited $O_2{}^*$ molecules, and by dissociative ion recombination:

$$O_2 + O + M \longrightarrow O_3 + M^*; \quad \Delta H^\circ_{298} - 109 \, \text{kJ mol}^{-1}$$

$$O_2 + O_2{}^* \longrightarrow O_3 + O$$

$$O_2{}^+ + O_2{}^- \longrightarrow O_3 + O$$

However, the reverse reaction of ozone with atomic oxygen is highly exothermic and must be suppressed by trapping out the ozone if good yields are to be obtained:

$$O_3 + O \longrightarrow 2O_2; \quad \Delta H^\circ_{298} - 394 \, \text{kJ mol}^{-1}$$

An alternative route to O_3 is by ultraviolet irradiation of O_2: this is useful for producing low concentrations of O_3 for sterilization of foodstuffs and disinfection, and also occurs during the generation of photochemical smog. The electrolysis of cold aqueous H_2SO_4 (or $HClO_4$) at very high anode current densities also affords modest concentrations of O_3, together with O_2 and $H_2S_2O_8$

[23] D. G. COGAN, *Stones in a Glass House: CFCs and Ozone Depletion, Investor Responsibility Research Center Inc.*, Washington, DC, 1988, 147 pp.

[24] ARJUN MAKHIJANI, ANNIE MAKHIJANI and A. BICKEL, *Saving our Skins: Technical Potential and Policies for the Elimination of Ozone-Depleting Compounds*, Environmental Policy Institute and Institute for Energy and Environmental Research, Washington, DC, 1988, 167 pp.

[25] R. P. WAYNE, *Proc. Royal Institution* **61**, 13–49 (1989).

[26] M. J. MOLINA and L. T. MOLINA, Chap. 2 in D. A. DUNNETTE and R. J. O'BRIEN (eds.), *The Science of Global Change: The Impact of Human, Activities on the Environment*, ACS Symposium Series, Am. Chem. Soc., Washington, DC, 1992, pp. 24–35.

[27] P. S. ZURER, *Chem. and Eng. News*, May 24, 1993, pp. 8–18.

(p. 712) as byproducts. Other reactions in which O_3 is formed are the reaction of elementary F_2 with H_2O (p. 804) and the thermal decomposition of periodic acid at 130° (p. 872).

The concentration of ozone in O_2/O_3 mixtures can be determined by catalytic decomposition to O_2 in the gas phase and measurement of the expansion in volume. More conveniently it can be determined iodometrically by passing the gas mixture into an alkaline boric-acid-buffered aqueous solution of KI and determining the I_2 so formed by titration with sodium thiosulfate in acidified solution:

$$O_3 + 2I^- + H_2O \longrightarrow O_2 + I_2 + 2OH^-$$

The reaction illustrates the two most characteristic chemical properties of ozone: its strongly oxidizing nature and its tendency to transfer an O atom with coproduction of O_2. Standard reduction potentials in acid and in alkaline solution are:

$$O_3 + 2H^+ + 2e^- \rightleftharpoons O_2 + H_2O; \quad E^\circ + 2.075 \, \text{V}$$

$$O_3 + H_2O + 2e^- \rightleftharpoons O_2 + 2OH^-; \quad E^\circ + 1.246 \, \text{V}$$

The acid potential is exceeded only by fluorine (p. 804), perxenate (p. 901), atomic O, the OH radical, and a few other such potent oxidants. Decomposition is rapid in acid solutions but the allotrope is much more stable in alkaline solution. At 25° the half-life of O_3 in 1 M NaOH is ~2 min; corresponding times for 5 M and 20 M NaOH are 40 min and 83 h respectively.

The highly reactive nature of O_3 is further typified by the following reactions:

$$CN^- + O_3 \longrightarrow OCN^- + O_2$$

$$2NO_2 + O_3 \longrightarrow N_2O_5 + O_2$$

$$PbS + 4O_3 \longrightarrow PbSO_4 + 4O_2$$

$$3I^- + O_3 + 2H^+ \longrightarrow I_3{}^- + O_2 + H_2O$$

$$2Co^{2+} + O_3 + 2H^+ \longrightarrow 2Co^{3+} + O_2 + H_2O$$

An important reaction of ozone is the formation of ozonides MO_3. The formation of a red coloration when O_3 is passed into concentrated aqueous alkali was first noted by C. F. Schönbein in 1866, but the presence of O_3^- was not established until 1949.[28] The compounds are best prepared by action of gaseous O_3 on dry, powdered MOH below $-10°$ (or O_3/O_2 mixtures on CsO_2) followed by extraction with liquid ammonia (which may also catalyse their formation). The compounds are red-brown paramagnetic solids ($\mu = 1.74-1.80$ BM)[29] and they decrease in stability in the sequence Cs > Rb > K > Na; unsolvated LiO_3 has not been prepared but the ammine $LiO_3.4NH_3$ is known. Likewise the stability of $M^{II}(O_3)_2$ decreases in the sequence Ba > Sr > Ca. Above room temperature MO_3 decomposes to the superoxide MO_2 (p. 616) and the compounds are also hydrolytically unstable:

$$MO_3 \xrightarrow{\text{warm}} MO_2 + \tfrac{1}{2}O_2$$

$$KO_3 + H_2O \longrightarrow KOH + O_2 + \{OH\}$$

$$2\{OH\} \longrightarrow H_2O + \tfrac{1}{2}O_2$$

The ozonide ion O_3^- has the expected C_{2v} symmetry like O_3 itself and the isoelectronic, paramagnetic molecule ClO_2 (p. 845). Early attempts at X-ray structural analysis were frustrated by the thermal instability of the compounds, their great reactivity, the difficulty of growing single crystals and the tendency to rotational disorder.[30] However, it is now clear that the O_3^- ion is indeed bent, the most accurate data being obtained on crystals of the surprisingly stable red compound $[NMe_4]O_3$ (decomp. 75°, cf. CsO_3 53°):[31] the angle O-O-O is 119.5(5)°, only slightly larger than for O_3 itself, and the O-O and O$\cdots$O distances

are 126.4(4) and 222.2(4) pm, respectively (cf. Fig. 14.2).

Ozone adds readily to unsaturated organic compounds[32] and can cause unwanted cross-linking in rubbers and other polymers with residual unsaturation, thereby leading to brittleness and fracture. Addition to alkenes yields "ozonides" which can be reductively cleaved by Zn/H_2O (or $I^-/MeOH$, etc.) to yield aldehydes or ketones. This smooth reaction, discovered by C. D. Harries in 1903, has long been used to determine the position of double bonds in organic molecules, e.g.:

Ozonide formation occurs by a three-step mechanism along the lines first proposed in 1951 by R. Criegee:[33,34]

[28] I. A. KAZARNOVSKII, G. P. NIKOL'SKII and T. A. ABLETSOVA, *Dokl. Akad. Nauk SSSR* **64**, 69–72 (1949).

[29] H. LUEKEN, M. DEUSSEN, M. JANSEN, W. HESSE and W. SCHNICK, *Z. anorg. allg. Chem.* **553**, 179–86 (1981).

[30] L. V. AZAROV and I. CORVIN, *Proc. Natl. Acad. Sci. (US)* **49**, 1–5 (1963). M. JANSEN and W. HESSE, *Z. anorg. allg. Chem.* **560**, 47–54 (1988).

[31] W. HESSE and M. JANSEN, *Angew. Chem. Int. Edn. Engl.* **27**, 1341–2 (1988). See also W. ASSENMACHER and M. JANSEN, *Z. anorg. allg. Chem.* **621**, 431–4 (1995) for information on the newest ionic ozonides, $[PMe_4]O_3$ and $[AsMe_4]O_3$.

[32] P. S. BAILEY, *Ozonation in Organic Chemistry*, Vol. 1, Olefinic Compounds, Academic Press, New York, 1978, 272 pp.; Vol. 2, Nonolefinic Compounds, 1982, 496 pp. S. D. RAZUMOVSKI and G. E. ZAIKOV, *Ozone and Its Reactions with Organic Compounds*, Elsevier, Amsterdam, 1984, 404 pp.

[33] R. CRIEGEE, *Rec. Chem. Prog.* **18**, 111–20 (1957). *Angew. Chem. Int. Edn. Engl.* **14**, 745–52 (1975).

[34] R. L. KUCZKOWSKI, *Chem. Soc. Revs.* **21**, 79–83 (1992).

The primary ozonides (1), which are 1,2,3-trioxolanes, are formed by a concerted 1,3-dipolar cycloaddition between ozone and the alkene and are detectable only at very low temperatures. For example, at $-175°C$ ethene gives $\overline{CH_2CH_2OOO}$ which was shown by microwave spectroscopy to be non-planar with O–O 145 pm, angle O–O–O 100° and a dihedral angle between the C_2O_2 and O_3 planes of 51°.[35] At higher temperatures the primary ozonides spontaneously rearrange to secondary ozonides: these have a 1,2,4-trioxolane structure (2) and can be studied by a variety of techniques including ^{17}O nmr spectroscopy.[36] Normally, however, the ozonide is not isolated but is reductively cleaved to aldehydes and ketones in solution. Oxidative cleavage (air or O_2) yields carboxylic acids and, indeed, the first large-scale application of the reaction was the commercial production of pelargonic and azelaic acids from oleic acid:

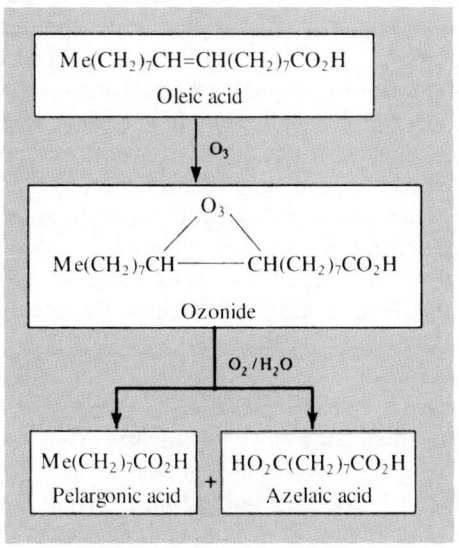

Esters of these acids are used as plasticizers for PVC (polyvinylchloride) and other plastics.

Because of the reactivity, instability and hazardous nature of O_3 it is always generated on site. Typical industrial ozone generators operate at 1 or 2 atm, 15–20 kV, and 50 or 500 Hz. The concentration of O_3 in the effluent gas depends on the industrial use envisaged but yields of up to 10 kg per hour or 150 kg per day from a single apparatus are not uncommon and some plants yield over 1 tonne per day. In addition to pelargonic and azelaic acid production, O_3 is used to make peroxoacetic acid from acetaldehyde and for various inorganic oxidations. At low concentrations it is used (particularly in Europe) to purify drinking water, since this avoids the undesirable taste and smell of chlorinated water, and residual ozone decomposes to O_2 soon after treatment.[37] Of the 1039 plants operating in 1977 all but 40 were in Europe, with the greatest numbers in France (593), Switzerland (150), Germany (136), and Austria (42). Other industrial uses include the preservation of goods in cold storage, the treatment of industrial waste and the deodorizing of air and sewage gases.[38]

Atomic oxygen

Atomic oxygen is an extremely reactive, fugitive species which cannot be isolated free from other substances. Many methods of preparing oxygen atoms also yield other reactive or electronically excited species, and this somewhat complicates the study of their properties. Passage of a microwave or electric discharge through purified O_2 gas diluted with argon produces O atoms in the ^3P ground state (2 unpaired electrons). Mercury-sensitized photolysis of N_2O is perhaps a more convenient route to ground state O atoms (plus inert N_2 molecules) though they can also be made by photolysis of O_2 or NO_2. Photolysis of N_2O in the absence of Hg gives O atoms in the spin-paired ^1D excited state, and this species can also be obtained by photolysis of O_3 or CO_2.

[35] J. Z. GILLIES, C. W. GILLIES, R. D. SUENRAM and F. J. LOVAS, *J. Am. Chem. Soc.* **110**, 1991–9 (1988).

[36] J. LAUTERWEIN, K. GRIESBAUM, P. KRIEGER-BECK, V. BALL and K. SCHLINDWEIN, *J. Chem. Soc., Chem. Commun.*, 816–7 (1991).

[37] J. KATZ (ed.), *Ozone and Chlorine Dioxide Technology for Disinfection of Drinking Water*, Noyes Data Corp., Park Ridge, New Jersey, 1980, 659 pp. R. G. RICE and M. E. BROWNING, *Ozone Treatment of Industrial Wastewater*, Noyes Data Corp., Park Ridge, New Jersey, 1981, 371 pp.

[38] J. A. WOJTOWICZ, Ozone, *Kirk–Othmer Encyclopedia of Chemical Technology*, 4th edn. **17**, 953–95. Wiley, New York, 1996.

The best method for determining the concentration of O atoms is by their extremely rapid reaction with NO_2 in a flow system:

$$O + NO_2 \longrightarrow O_2 + NO$$

The NO thus formed reacts more slowly with any excess of O atoms to reform NO_2 and this reaction emits a yellow-green glow.

$$NO + O \longrightarrow NO_2^* \longrightarrow NO_2 + h\nu$$

The system is thus titrated with NO_2 until the glow is sharply extinguished.

As expected, atomic O is a strong oxidizing agent and it is an important reactant in the chemistry of the upper atmosphere.[17,18] Typical reactions are:

$$H_2 + O \longrightarrow OH + H$$

$$OH + O \longrightarrow O_2 + H$$

$$O_2 + O \longrightarrow O_3$$

$$Cl_2 + O \longrightarrow Cl_2O, \ ClO_2$$

$$CO + O \longrightarrow CO_2$$

$$CH_4 + O \longrightarrow CO_2, \ H_2O$$

$$HCN + O \longrightarrow CO, \ CO_2, \ NO, \ H_2O$$

$$H_2S + O \longrightarrow H_2O, \ SO_2, \ SO_3, \ H_2SO_4$$

$$NaCl + O \xrightarrow{\text{aq}} NaClO_3, \ Cl_2, \ NaOH$$

Many of these reactions are explosive and/or chemiluminescent.

14.1.6 Chemical properties of dioxygen, O_2

Oxygen is an extremely reactive gas which vigorously oxidizes many elements directly, either at room temperature or above. Despite the high bond dissociation energy of O_2 ($493.4 \, kJ \, mol^{-1}$) these reactions are frequently highly exothermic and, once initiated, can continue spontaneously (combustion) or even explosively. Familiar examples are its reactions with carbon (charcoal) and hydrogen. Some elements do not combine with oxygen *directly*, e.g. certain refractory or noble metals such as

W, Pt, Au and the noble gases, though oxo compounds of all elements are known except for He, Ne, Ar and possibly Kr. This great range of compounds was one of the reasons why Mendeleev chose oxides to exemplify his periodic law (p. 20) and why oxygen was chosen as the standard element for the atomic weight scale in the early days when atomic weights were determined mainly by chemical stoichiometry (p. 16).

Many inorganic compounds and all organic compounds also react directly with O_2 under appropriate conditions. Reaction may be spontaneous, or may require initiation by heat, light, electric discharge, chemisorption or various catalytic means. Oxygen is normally considered to be divalent, though the oxidation state can vary widely and includes the values of $+\frac{1}{2}$, 0, $-\frac{1}{3}$, $-\frac{1}{2}$, -1 and -2 in isolable compounds of such species as O_2^+, O_3, O_3^-, O_2^-, O_2^{2-} and O^{2-} respectively. The coordination number of oxygen in its compounds also varies widely, as illustrated in Table 14.3 and numerous examples of stable compounds are known which exemplify each coordination number from 1 to 8 (with the possible exception of 7, for which unambiguous examples are more difficult to find). Most of these examples are straightforward and structural details will be found at appropriate points in the text. Linear 2-coordinate O occurs in the silyl ether molecule $[O(SiPh_3)_2]$.[39] Planar 3-coordinate O occurs in the neutral gaseous molecular species OLi_3 and ONa_3[40] and in both cationic and anionic complexes (Fig. 14.3a, b). It also occurs in two-dimensional layer lattices such as tunellite, $[OB_6O_8(OH)_2]^{2n-}$ (cf. Fig. 14.3b) and in the three-dimensional rutile structure (p. 961).

Planar 4-coordinate O occurs uniquely in NbO which can be considered as a defect-NaCl-type structure with O and Nb vacancies at (000) and $\left(\frac{1}{2}\frac{1}{2}\frac{1}{2}\right)$ respectively, thereby having only 3

[39] C. GLIDEWELL and D. C. LILES, *J. Chem. Soc., Chem. Commun.*, 682 (1977).

[40] E.-U. WÜRTHWEIN, P. von R. SCHLEYER and J. A. POPLE, *J. Am. Chem. Soc.*, **106**, 6973–8 (1984).

Table 14.3 Coordination geometry of oxygen

CN	Geometry	Examples
0	—	Atomic O
1	—	O_2, CO, CO_2, NO, NO_2, SO_3(g), OsO_4; terminal O_t in P_4O_{10}, [VO(acac)$_2$], and many oxoanions $[MO_n]^{m-}$ (M = C, N, P, As, S, Se, Cl, Br, Cr, Mn, etc.)
2	Linear	Some silicates, e.g. $[O_3Si\text{-}O\text{-}SiO_3]^{6-}$ in $Sc_2Si_2O_7$; $[Cl_5Ru\text{-}O\text{-}RuCl_5]^{4-}$; ReO$_3$(WO$_3$)-type structures; coesite (SiO$_2$); [O(SiPh$_3$)$_2$][39]
2	Bent	O$_3$, H$_2$O, H$_2$O$_2$, F$_2$O; silica structures, GeO$_2$; P$_4$O$_6$ and many heterocyclic compounds with O_μ; complexes of ligands which have O_t as donor atom, e.g. [BF$_3$(OSMe$_2$)], [SnCl$_4$(OSeCl$_2$)$_2$], [{TiCl$_4$(OPCl$_3$)}$_2$], [HgCl$_2$(OAsPh$_3$)$_2$]; complexes of O$_2$, e.g. [Pt(O$_2$)(PPh$_3$)$_2$]
3	Planar	OLi$_3$, ONa$_3$;[40] [O(HgCl)$_3$]$^+$Cl$^-$, Mg[**OB$_6$O$_6$(OH)$_6$**].4$\frac{1}{2}$H$_2$O (macallisterite); Sr[**OB$_6$O$_8$(OH)$_2$**].3H$_2$O, (tunellite); rutile-type structures, e.g. MO$_2$ (M = Ti; V, Nb, Ta; Cr, Mo, W; Mn, Tc, Re; Ru, Os; Rh, Ir; Pt; Ge, Sn, Pb; Te)
3	Pyramidal	[H$_3$O]$^+$; hydrato-complexes, e.g. [M(H$_2$O)$_6$]$^{n+}$; complexes of R$_2$O and crown ethers; organometallic clusters such as [(η-C$_5$H$_5$)$_5$(O)V$_6$(μ_3-**O**)$_8$][41]
4	Square planar	NbO (see text)
4	Tetrahedral	[**OBe$_4$**(O$_2$CMe)$_6$]; CuO, AgO, PdO; wurtzite structures, e.g. BeO, ZnO; corundum structures, e.g. M$_2$O$_3$ (M = Al, Ga, Ti, V, Cr, Fe, Rh); fluorite structures, e.g. MO$_2$ (M = Zr, Hf; Ce, Pr, Tb; Th, U, Np, Pu, Am, Cm; Po)
4	See-saw	[Fe$_3$Mn(CO)$_{12}$(μ_4-**O**)]$^-$[42]
5	Square pyram.	[LCu$_4$(OH)]$^{3+}$[43], [(InOPr^i)$_5$(μ_5-**O**)(μ_2-OPr^i)$_4$(μ_3-OPr^i)$_4$][44]
6	Octahedral	Central O in [Mo$_6$O$_{19}$]$^{2-}$; many oxides with NaCl-type structure, e.g. MO (M = Mg, Ca, Sr, Ba; Mn, Fe, Co, Ni; Cd; Eu)
7		—
8	Cubic	Anti-fluorite-type structure, e.g. M$_2$O (M = Li, Na, K, Rb)

NbO (rather than 4) per unit cell (see p. 983). Tetrahedral, 4–coordinate O is featured in "basic beryllium acetate" (p. 122) and in many binary oxides as mentioned in Table 14.3. The detailed structure depends both on the stoichiometry and on the coordination geometry of the metal, which is planar in CuO, AgO and PdO, tetrahedral in BeO and ZnO, octahedral in M$_2$O$_3$ and cubic in MO$_2$. Tetrahedral coordination of O also occurs in the unusual species ONa$_4$ and HONa$_3$.[40] The less common see-saw (C_{2v}) coordination mode occurs in the "butterfly" oxo cluster anion [Fe$_3$Mn(CO)$_{12}$(μ_4-**O**)]$^-$, in which the O atom bridges the [Mn(CO)$_3$] and {Fe(CO)$_3$} wingtips and the two [Fe(CO)$_3$] hinge groups.[42]

Five-fold coordination of O has only recently been established, in the μ_4-hydroxo bridged Cu$_4^{II}$ cluster, [Cu$_4$(μ_4-**OH**)(η^8-L*)], in which the central planar OCu$_4$ group is supported by a circum-annular octadentate macrocyclic ligand, L*, with the H atom of the OH group vertically above (or below) this plane.[43] Square pyramidal coordination of O also occurs in the indium *iso*-propoxide cluster [(InOPr^i)$_5$(μ_5-**O**)(μ_2-OPr^i)$_4$(μ_3-OPr^i)$_4$][44] and in some complicated [Ba$_5$(μ_5-**O**)] oxobarium clusters supported by μ_2 and μ_3 phenoxide of *t*-butoxide ligands.[45]

[41] F. BOTTOMLEY, D. F. DRUMMOND, D. E. PAEZ and P. S. WHITE, *J. Chem. Soc., Chem. Commun.*, 1752–3 (1986).
[42] C. K. SCHAUER and D. F. SHRIVER, *Angew. Chem. Int. Edn. Engl.* **26**, 255–6 (1987).

[43] V. McKEE and S. S. TANDON, *J. Chem. Soc., Chem. Commun.*, 385–7 (1988). See also K. P. McKILLOP, S. M. NELSON, J. NELSON and V. McKEE, *ibid.*, 387–9 (1988).
[44] D. C. BRADLEY, H. CHUDZYNSKA, D. M. FRIGO, M. B. HURSTHOUSE and M. A. MAZID, *J. Chem. Soc., Chem. Commun.*, 1258–9 (1988).
[45] K. G. CAULTON, M. H. CHISHOLM, S. R. DRAKE and K. FOLTING, *J. Chem. Soc., Chem. Commun.*, 1349–51 (1990).

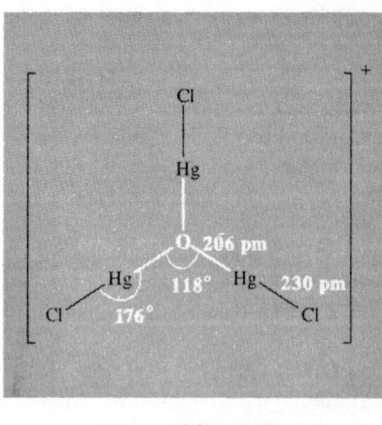 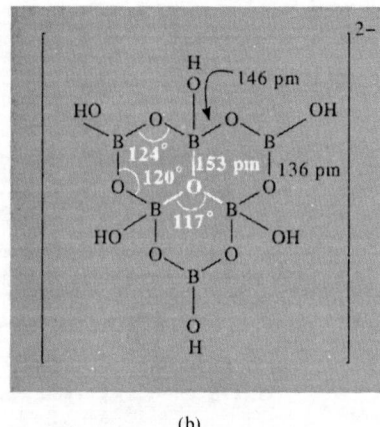

(a)   (b)

Figure 14.3   Examples of planar 3-coordinate O: (a) the cation in [O(HgCl)₃]Cl, (b) the central O atom in the
discrete borate anion $[OB_6O_6(OH)_6]^{2-}$ in macallisterite — the three heterocycles are coplanar but
the 6 pendant OH groups lie out of the plane.

A recent addition to the many examples of octahedral coordination of O (Table 14.3) is the unusual volatile, hydrocarbon-soluble, crystalline oxo-alkoxide of barium $[H_4Ba_6(\mu_6\text{-}O)(OCH_2\text{-}CH_{2l}OMe)_{14}]$, which forms rapidly when Ba granules are reacted with $MeOCH_2CH_2OH$ in toluene suspension.[46]

Much of the chemistry of oxygen can be rationalized in terms of its electronic structure ($2s^2 2p^4$), high electronegativity (3.5) and small size. Thus, oxygen shows many similarities to nitrogen (p. 412) in its covalent chemistry, and its propensity to form H bonds (p. 52) and p_π double bonds (p. 416), though the anionic chemistry of O^{2-} and OH^- is much more extensive than for the isoelectronic ions N^{3-}, NH^{2-} and NH_2^-. Similarities to fluorine and fluorides are also notable. Comparisons with the chemical properties of sulfur (p. 662) and the heavier chalcogens (p. 754) are deferred to Chapters 15 and 16.

One of the most important reactions of dioxygen is that with the protein haemoglobin which forms the basis of oxygen transport in blood (p. 1099).[47] Other coordination complexes of O_2 are discussed in the following section (p. 615).

Another particularly important aspect of the chemical reactivity of O_2 concerns the photochemical reaction of singlet O_2 (p. 605) with unsaturated or aromatic organic compounds.[48-51] The pioneering work was done in 1931–9 by H. Kautsky who noticed that oxygen could quench the fluorescence of certain irradiated dyes by excitation to the singlet state, and that such excited O_2 molecules could oxidize compounds which did not react with oxygen in its triplet ground state. Although Kautsky gave essentially the correct explanation of his observations, his views were not accepted at the time and the work remained unnoticed by organic chemists for 25 years until the reactivity of singlet oxygen was rediscovered independently by two other groups in 1964 (p. 601). With the wisdom of hindsight it seems remarkable that Kautsky's elegant experiments

[46] K. G. CAULTON, M. H. CHISHOLM, S. R. DRAKE and J. C. HUFFMAN, *J. Chem. Soc., Chem. Commun.*, 1498–9 (1990).

[47] T. G. SPIRO (ed.), *Metal Ion Activation of Dioxygen*, Wiley, New York, 1980, 247 pp.

[48] B. RANBY and J. F. RABEK (eds.) *Singlet Oxygen: Reactions with Organic Compounds and Polymers*, Wiley, Chichester, 1978, 331 pp.

[49] A. A. FRIMER, *Chem. Rev.* **79**, 359–87 (1979).

[50] H. H. WASSERMAN and R. W. MURRAY (eds.), *Singlet Oxygen*, Academic Press, New York, 1979, 688 pp.

[51] A. A. FRIMER (ed.), *Singlet O₂*. Vol. 1, 236 pp., Vol. 2, 284 pp.; Vol. 3, 269 pp.; Vol. 4, 208 pp.; CRC Press, Boca Raton, Florida, 1985.

and careful reasoning failed to convince his contemporaries.

Singlet oxygen, $^1O_2$, can readily be generated by irradiating normal triplet oxygen, $^3O_2$ in the presence of a sensitizer, S, which is usually a fluorescein-type dye, a polycyclic hydrocarbon or other strong absorber of light. A spin-allowed transition then occurs:

$$^3O_2 + {}^1S \xrightarrow{h\nu} {}^1O_2 + {}^3S$$

Provided that the energy gap in the sensitizer is greater than $94.7\,kJ\,mol^{-1}$, the $^1\Delta_g$ singlet state of O_2 is generated (p. 605). Above $157.8\,kJ\,mol^{-1}$ some $^1\Sigma_g^+O_2$ is also produced and this species predominates above $200\,kJ\,mol^{-1}$. The $^1\Delta_g$ singlet state can also be conveniently generated chemically in alcoholic solution by the reaction

$$H_2O_2 + ClO^- \longrightarrow Cl + H_2O + O_2(^1\Delta_g)$$

Another chemical route is by decomposition of solid adducts of ozone with triaryl and other phosphites at subambient temperatures:

$$O_3 + P(OPh)_3 \xrightarrow{-78°} O_3P(OPh)_3 \xrightarrow{-15°} O_2(^1\Delta_g)$$
$$+ \; OP(OPh)_3$$

Reactions of $^1O_2$ can be classified into three types: 1,2 addition, 1,3 addition and 1,4 addition (see refs. 48–51 for details). In addition to its great importance in synthetic organic chemistry, singlet oxygen plays an important role in autoxidation (i.e. the photodegradation of polymers in air), and methods of improving the stability of commercial polymers and vulcanized rubbers to oxidation are of considerable industrial significance. Reactions of singlet oxygen also feature in the chemistry of the upper atmosphere.

14.2 Compounds of Oxygen

14.2.1 Coordination chemistry: dioxygen as a ligand

Few discoveries in synthetic chemistry during the past three decades have caused more excitement or had more influence on the direction of subsequent work than L. Vaska's observation in 1963 that the planar 16-electron complex *trans*-$[Ir(CO)Cl(PPh_3)_2]$ can act as a reversible oxygen carrier by means of the equilibrium[52]

$$[Ir(CO)Cl(PPh_3)_2] + O_2 \rightleftharpoons$$
$$[Ir(CO)Cl(O_2)(PPh_3)_2]$$

Not only were the structures, stabilities and range of metals that could form such complexes of theoretical interest, but there were manifest implications for an understanding of the biochemistry of the oxygen-carrying metalloproteins haemoglobin, myoglobin, haemerythrin and haemocyanin. Such complexes were also seen as potential keys to an understanding of the interactions occurring during homogeneous catalytic oxidations, heterogeneous catalysis and the action of metalloenzymes. Several excellent reviews are available:[47.53–64]

Dioxygen–metal complexes in which there is a 1:1 stoichiometry of O_2:M are of two main types, usually designated Ia (or superoxo) and IIa (or

[52] L. VASKA, *Science* **140**, 809–10 (1963).

[53] J. A. CONNOR and E. A. V. EBSWORTH, *Adv. Inorg. Chem. Radiochem.* **6**, 279–381 (1964).

[54] V. J. CHOY and C. J. O'CONNOR, *Coord. Chem. Rev.* **9**, 145–70 (1972/3).

[55] J. S. VALENTINE, *Chem. Revs.* **73**, 235–45 (1973).

[56] M. J. NOLTE, E. SINGLETON and M. LAING, *J. Am. Chem. Soc.* **97**, 6396–400 (1975). An important paper showing how errors can arise even in careful single crystal X-ray studies, leading to incorrect inferences.

[57] R. W. ERSKINE and B. O. FIELD, Reversible oxygenation, *Struct. Bond.* **28**, 1–50 (1976).

[58] J. P. COLLMAN, *Acc. Chem. Res.* **10**, 265–72 (1977).

[59] A. B. P. LEVER and H. B. GRAY, *Acc. Chem. Res.* **11**, 348–55 (1978).

[60] R. D. JONES, D. A. SUMMERVILLE and F. BASOLO, *Chem. Revs.* **79**, 139–79 (1979).

[61] A. B. P. LEVER, G. A. OZIN and H. B. GRAY, *Inorg. Chem.* **19**, 1823–4 (1980).

[62] T. G. SPIRO (ed.), *Metal Ion Activation of Dioxygen*, Wiley-Interscience, New York, 1980, 247 pp.

[63] A. E. MARTELL and D. T. SAWYER (eds.), *Oxygen Complexes and Oxygen Activation by Transition Metals*, Plenum, New York, 1988, 341 pp.

[64] T. VÄNNGÅRD (ed.), *Biophysical Chemistry of Dioxygen Reactions in Respiration and Photosynthesis*, Cambridge Univ. Press, New York, 1988, 131 pp.

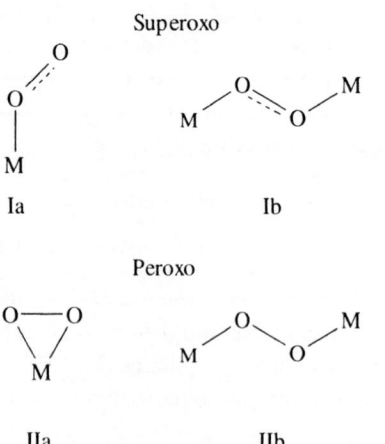

Superoxo

Ia   Ib

Peroxo

IIa   IIb

Figure 14.4   The four main types of O_2–M geometry. The bridging modes Ib and IIb appear superficially similar but differ markedly in dihedral angles and other bonding properties. See also footnote to Table 14.5 for the recently established unique μ,η^1-superoxide bridging mode.

peroxo) for reasons which will shortly become apparent (Fig. 14.4). Dioxygen can also form 1:2 complexes in which O_2 adopts a bidentate bridging geometry, labelled Ib and IIb in Fig. 14.4. Of these four classes of complex, the Vaska-type IIa peroxo complexes, are by far the most widespread amongst the transition metals, though many are not reversible oxygen carriers and some are formed by deprotonation of H_2O_2 (p. 636) rather than coordination of molecular O_2. By contrast, the bridging superoxo type Ib is known only for the green cobalt complexes formed by 1-electron oxidation of the corresponding IIb peroxo compounds. In all cases complex formation

is accompanied by a significant increase in the O–O interatomic distances and a considerable decrease in the ν(O–O) vibrational stretching frequency. Both effects are more marked for the peroxo (type II) complexes than for the superoxo (type I) complexes and have been interpreted in terms of a transfer of electrons from M into the antibonding orbitals of O_2 (p. 606) thereby weakening the O–O bond. The magnitude of the effects to be expected can be gauged from Table 14.4.[60] Note that the O–O bond in O_2^+ is stronger than in O_2 but this does not mean that O_2^+ is more stable than O_2 since energy must be supplied to remove an electron from O_2 and this energy is greater than that released in forming the stronger bond: it is important not to confuse bond energy with stability. Comparative data for a wide range of dioxygen-metal complexes is in Table 14.5.[60,65] It will be noted also that the O–O distances and vibrational frequencies are rather insensitive to the nature of the metal or its other attached ligands, or, indeed, as to whether the O_2 is coordinated to 1 or 2 metal centres. Both classes of superoxo complex, however, have d(O–O) and ν(O–O) close to the values for the superoxide ion, whereas both classes of peroxo complex have values close to those for the peroxide ion. (However, see footnote to Table 14.5 for an important caveat to this generalization.)

Superoxo complexes having a nonlinear M–O–O configuration are known at present only for Fe, Co, Rh and perhaps a few other transition metals, whereas the Vaska-type (IIa) complexes are known for almost all the transition metals

[65] L. VASKA, *Acc. Chem. Res.* **9**, 175–83 (1976).

Table 14.4   Effect of electron configuration and charge on the bond properties of dioxygen species

Species	Bond order	Compound	d(O–O)/pm	Bond energy/ kJ mol^{-1}	ν(O–O)/cm^{-1}
O_2^+	2.5	$O_2[AsF_6]$	112.3	625.1	1858
$O_2(^3\Sigma_g^-)$	2	O_2(g)	120.7	490.4	1554.7
$O_2(^1\Delta_g)$	2	O_2(g)	121.6	396.2	1483.5
O_2^-(superoxide)	1.5	$K[O_2]$	128	—	1145
O_2^{2-}(peroxide)	1	$Na_2[O_2]$	149	204.2	842
–OO–	1	H_2O_2 (cryst)	145.3	213	882

Table 14.5 Summary of properties of known dioxygen–metal complexes[a]

Complex type	O_2:M ratio	Structure	d(O–O)/pm (normal range)	ν(O–O)/cm^{-1} (normal range)
superoxo Ia	1:1		125–135	1130–1195
superoxo Ib	1:2		126–136	1075–1122
peroxo IIa	1:1		130–155	800–932
peroxo IIb	1:1		144–149	790–884

[a] Reaction of K_2O with Al_2Me_6 in the presence of dibenzo-18-crown-6 (p. 96) yields the surprisingly stable anion $[(\mu,\eta^1$-$O_2)(AlMe_3)_2]^-$ in which one O of the superoxo ion bridges the 2 Al atoms (angle Al–O–Al 128°):

 In this new type of coordination mode d(O–O) is long (147 pm) and the weakness of the O–O linkage is also shown by the very low value of 851 cm^{-1} for ν(O–O), both values being more characteristic of peroxo than of superoxo complexes.[66]

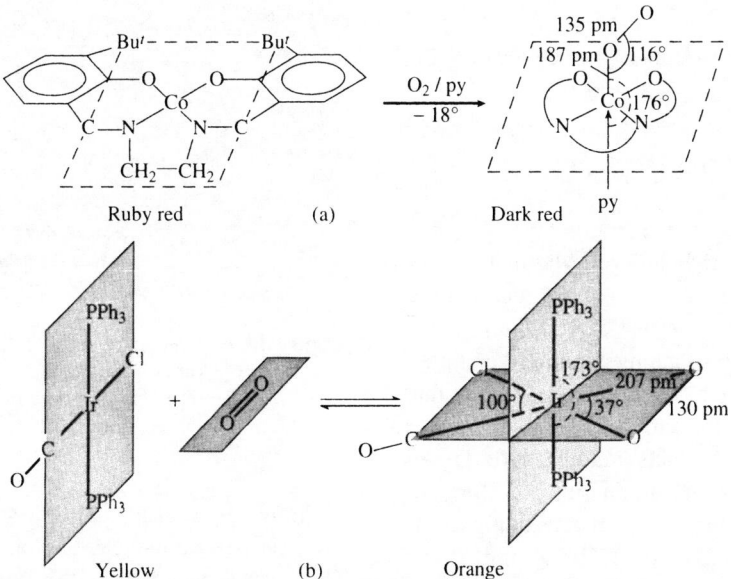

Figure 14.5 (a) Reaction of N,N'-ethylenebis(3-Bu^t-salicylideniminato)cobalt(II) with dioxygen and pyridine to form the superoxo complex [Co(3-Bu^{t}Salen)$_2$(O$_2$)py]; the py ligand is almost coplanar with the Co–O–O plane, the angle between the two being 18°.[67] (b) Reversible formation of the peroxo complex [Ir(CO)Cl(O$_2$)(PPh$_3$)$_2$]. The more densely shaded part of the complex is accurately coplanar.[68]

[66]D. C. HRNCIR, R. D. ROGERS and J. L. ATWOOD, *J. Am. Chem. Soc.* **103**, 4277–8 (1981). see also P. FANTUCCI and G. PACCHIONI, *J. Chem. Soc., Dalton Trans.*, 355–60 (1987).
[67]W. P. SCHAEFFER, B. T. HUIE, M. G. KURILLA and S. E. EALICK, *Inorg. Chem.* **19**, 340–4 (1980).
[68]S. J. LAPLACA and J. A. IBERS, *J. Am. Chem. Soc.* **87**, 2581–6 (1965).

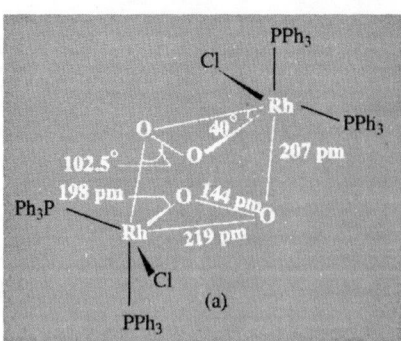
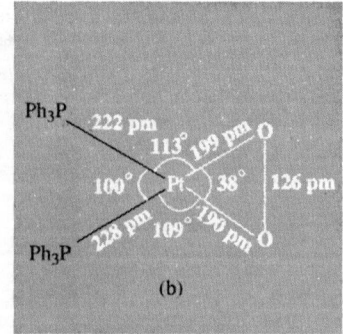

Figure 14.6 Structure and key dimensions of (a) the complex $[(Ph_3P)_2RhCl(\mu\text{-}O_2)]_2$ and (b) the complex $[Pt(O_2)(PPh_3)_2]$. The data in (b) are of poor quality because of the difficulty of growing suitable crystals and their instability in the X-ray beam (distances ± 5 pm angles $\pm 2°$).

except those in the Sc and Zn groups and possibly Mn, Cr and Fe. The two modes of formation are illustrated in Fig. 14.5 for the two reactions:

$$[Co(3\text{-}Bu^tSalen)_2] \xrightarrow{O_2/py}$$

$$[Co(3\text{-}Bu^tSalen)_2(\eta^1\text{-}O_2)py], \quad \text{(Ia)}$$

$$[Ir(CO)Cl(PPh_3)_2] \xrightarrow{O_2/C_6H_6}$$

$$[Ir(CO)Cl(\eta^2\text{-}O_2)(PPh_3)_2], \quad \text{(IIa)}$$

The sensitivity of the reaction type to the detailed nature of the bonding in the metal complex can be gauged from the fact that neither the PMe₃ analogue of Vaska's iridium complex, nor the corresponding rhodium complex $[Rh(CO)Cl(PPh_3)_2]$ react with dioxygen in this way. By contrast, the closely related red complex $[RhCl(PPh_3)_3]$ reacts readily with O_2 in CH_2Cl_2 solution with elimination of PPh_3 to give the brown dinuclear doubly bridging complex $[(Ph_3P)_2RhCl(\mu\text{-}O_2)]_2.CH_2Cl_2$ the structure of which is shown in Fig. 14.6a.[69] With $[Pt(PPh_3)_4]$ reaction also occurs with elimination of PPh_3 but the product is the yellow, planar, mononuclear complex $[Pt(\eta^2\text{-}O_2)(PPh_3)_2]$ (Fig. 14.6b).[70]

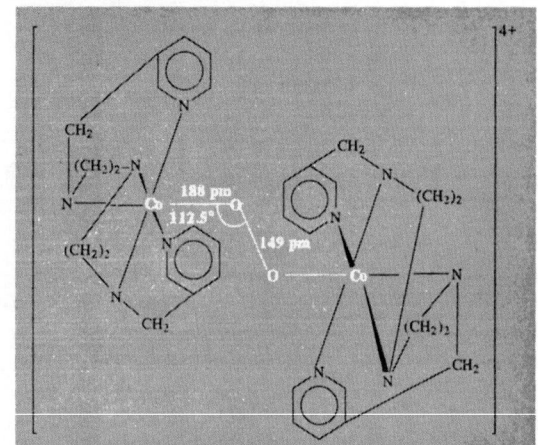

Figure 14.7 Schematic representation of the structure of the dinuclear cation in $[\{Co(pydien)\}_2O_2]I_4$ showing some important dimensions.

An example of a singly-bridging peroxo complex is the dinuclear cation $[\{Co(pydien)\}_2\text{-}O_2]^{4+}$ where pydien is the pentadentate ligand 1,9-bis(2-pyridyl)-2,5,8-triazanonane, $NC_5H_4\text{-}CH_2N(CH_2CH_2N)_2CH_2C_5H_4N$. The complex is readily formed by mixing ethanolic solutions of $CoCl_2.6H_2O$, NaI and the ligand, and then exposing the resulting solution to oxygen.[71] Some structural details are in Fig. 14.7. Such

[69] M. J. BENNETT and P. B. DONALDSON, *J. Am. Chem. Soc.* **93**, 3307–8 (1971).

[70] C. D. COOK, P.-T. CHENG and S. C. NYBURG, *J. Am. Chem. Soc.* **91**, 2123 (1969).

[71] J. H. TIMMONS, R. H. NISWANDER, A. CLEARFIELD and A. E. MARTELL, *Inorg. Chem.* **18**, 2977–82 (1979).

μ-O_2 complexes are formed generally among the "Group VIII" metals (Fe), Ru, Os; Co, Rh, Ir: Ni, Pd, Pt. A unique example from main-group element chemistry is in the doubly-bridged $R_2Sn(\mu$-O$)(\mu$:η^1,η^1-**O_2**$)SnR_2$, (R = CH(SiMe$_3$)$_2$), in which O–O is 154 pm, Sn–O_2 201 pm, angle Sn–O–O 103.3°; Sn–O 198 pm angle Sn–O–Sn 110.3°.[72]

Many mono- and di-nuclear peroxo-type dioxygen complexes can also be made by an alternative route involving direct reaction of transition metal compounds with H_2O_2 and it is, in fact, quite arbitrary to distinguish these complexes from those made directly from O_2. Many such compounds are discussed further on p. 637 and under the chemistry of individual transition metals, but one example calls for special mention since it was the first structurally characterized peroxo derivative to feature a symmetrical, doubly bidentate (side on) bridge linking two metal centres.[73] The local coordination geometry and dimensions of the central planar {LaO$_2$La} group are shown in Fig. 14.8; the very long O–O distance is particularly notable, being substantially longer than in the O_2^{2-} ion itself (p. 616). The compound [La{N(SiMe$_3$)$_2$}$_2$(OPPh$_3$)]$_2$O$_2$, which is colourless, was made by treating [La{N(SiMe$_3$)$_2$}$_3$]

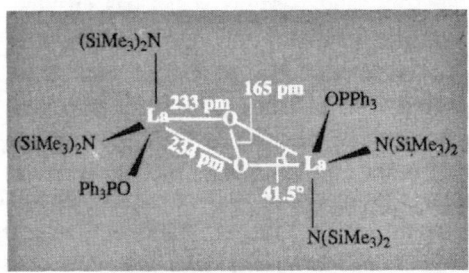

Figure 14.8   Schematic representation of the planar central portion of the μ-peroxo complex [La{N(SiMe$_3$)$_2$}$_2$(OPPh$_3$)]$_2$O$_2$.

with Ph$_3$PO, but the origin of the peroxo group remains obscure. Similar complexes of Pr (which is also, surprisingly, colourless), Sm (pale yellow), Eu (orange-red) and Lu (colourless), were obtained in good yield either by a similar reaction or by treating [Ln{N(SiMe$_3$)$_2$}$_3$] with a half-molar proportion of (Ph$_3$PO)$_2$.H$_2$O$_2$.

The nature of the metal–oxygen bonding in the various types of dioxygen complex has been the subject of much discussion.[56,58,59,60,65,74] The electronic structure of the O_2 molecule (p. 606) makes it unlikely that coordination would be by the usual donation of an "onium" lone-pair (from O_2 to the metal centre) which forms an important component of most other donor–acceptor adducts (p. 198). Most discussion has centred on the extent of electron transfer from the metal into the partly occupied antibonding orbitals of O_2. There now seems general agreement that there is substantial transfer of electron density from the metal d_{z^2} orbital into the π^* antibonding orbitals of O_2 with concomitant increase in the formal oxidation state of the metal, e.g. {Co^{II}} + O_2 → {Co^{III}(O_2^-)}. Whether the resulting bonding between dioxygen and the metal atom is predominantly ionic or partly covalent may well depend to some extent on the nature of the metal centre and is largely a semantic problem which gradually disappears the more precisely one can define the detailed MOs or the actual electron distribution,[75] cf. the discussion on p. 79.

A dramatic discovery in this area was made in 1996 when a dicopper–dioxygen adduct was found to have two isomeric forms which featured either a side-on bridging unit {Cu(μ:η^2,η^2-O_2)-Cu}$^{2+}$ or a cyclic {Cu(μ-O)$_2$Cu}$^{2+}$ core depending on whether it was crystallized from CH$_2$Cl$_2$ or thf, respectively. The two forms could be readily interconverted by reversible O–O bond cleavage and reformation, the O–O distance being ~141 pm and 229 pm in the two isomers.[75a] The

[72] C. J. CARDIN, D. J. CARDIN, M. M. DEVEREUX and MAIRE A. CONVERY, *J. Chem. Soc., Chem. Commun.*, 1461–2 (1990).

[73] D. C. BRADLEY, J. S. GHOTRA, F. A. HART, M. B. HURST-HOUSE and P. R. RAITHBY, *J. Chem. Soc., Dalton Trans.*, 1166–72 (1977).

[74] R. S. DRAGO, T. BEUGELSDIJK, J. A. BREESE and J. P. CANNADY *J. Am. Chem. Soc.* **100**, 5374–82 (1978).

[75] S. SAKAKI, K. HORI and A. OHYOSHI, *Inorg. Chem.* **17**, 3183–8 (1978).

[75a] W. B. TOLMAN and 7 others, *Science* **271**, 1397–400 (1996).

biochemical implications for reductive cleavage of O_2 by metalloenzymes and for O_2 evolution during photosynthesis are particularly exciting.

In addition to their great importance for structural and bonding studies, dioxygen complexes undergo many reactions. As already indicated, some of these reactions are of unique importance in biological chemistry[76] and in catalytic systems. Some of the simpler inorganic reactions can be summarized as follows: aqueous acids yield H_2O_2 and reducing agents give coordinatively unsaturated complexes. Frequently the dioxygen complex can oxidize species that do not readily react directly with free molecular O_2, e.g. CO, CO_2, CS_2, NO, NO_2, SO_2, RNC, RCHO, R_2CO, PPh_3, etc. Illustrative examples of these reactions are:

$$[Pt(O_2)(PPh_3)_2] \xrightarrow{CO} [(Ph_3P)_2Pt\underset{O}{\overset{O}{<}}C{=}O]$$

$$[Pt(O_2)(PPh_3)_2] \xrightarrow{CO_2} [(Ph_3P)_2Pt\underset{O}{\overset{O-O}{<}}C{=}O]$$

$$[Pt(O_2)(PPh_3)_2] \xrightarrow{CS_2} [Pt(PPh_3)_2(S_2CO)]$$

$$[Pd(O_2)(PPh_3)_2] \xrightarrow{NO} [Pt(NO_2)_2(PPh_3)_2]$$

$$[Ir(CO)Cl(O_2)(PPh_3)_2] \xrightarrow{2NO_2} [Ir(CO)Cl(NO_3)_2(PPh_3)_2]$$

$$[Ir(CO)Cl(O_2)(PPh_3)_2] \xrightarrow{SO_2} [Ir(CO)Cl(PPh_3)_2(SO_4)]$$

$$[RuCl(NO)(O_2)(PPh_3)_2] \xrightarrow{SO_2} [RuCl(NO)(PPh_3)_2(SO_4)]$$

$$[Ni(CNBu^t)_2(O_2)] \xrightarrow{4Bu^tNC} [Ni(CNBu^t)_4] + 2RNCO$$

$$[Pt(O_2)(PPh_3)_2] \xrightarrow{MeCHO} [(Ph_3P)_2Pt\underset{O}{\overset{O-O}{<}}CHMe]$$

$$[Ni(CNBu^t)_2(O_2)] \xrightarrow{4PPh_3} [Ni(CNBu^t)_2(PPh_3)_2]$$
$$+ 2Ph_3PO$$

Explanations that have been advanced to explain the enhanced reactivity of coordinated dioxygen include:

(1) The diamagnetic nature of most O_2 complexes might facilitate reactions to form diamagnetic products which would otherwise be hindered by the requirement of spin conservation;

(2) the metal may hold O_2 and the reactant in *cis* positions thereby lowering the activation energy for oxidation, particularly with coordinatively unsaturated complexes;

(3) coordinated O_2 is usually partially reduced (towards O_2^- or O_2^{2-}) and this increased electron density might activate it.

Detailed kinetic and mechanistic studies will be required to assess the relative importance of these and other possible factors in specific instances.

14.2.2 Water

Introduction

Water is without doubt the most abundant, the most accessible and the most studied of all chemical compounds. Its omnipresence, its crucial importance for man's survival and its ability to transform so readily from the liquid to the solid and gaseous states has ensured its prominence in man's thinking from the earliest times. Water plays a prominent role in most creation myths and has a symbolic purifying or regenerating significance in many great religions even to the present day. In the religion of ancient Mesopotamia, the oldest of which we have written records (*ca.* 2000 BC), Nammu, goddess of the primaeval sea, was "the mother who gave birth to heaven and earth"; she was also the mother of the god of water, Enki, one of the four main gods controlling the major realms of the universe. In the Judaic-Christian tradition[77] "the Spirit of God moved upon the face of the waters" and creation proceeded via "a firmament in the midst of the waters" to divide heaven from

[76] E.-I. OCHIAI, *J. Inorg. Nucl. Chem.* **37**, 1503–9 (1975). See also *Oxygen and Life: Second BOC Priestley Conference*, Roy. Soc. Chem. Special Publ. No. 39, London, 1981, 224 pp.

[77] Holy Bible, Genesis, Chap. 1, verses 1–10.

earth. Again, the Flood figures prominently[78] as it does in the legends of many other peoples. The activities of John the Baptist[79] and the obligatory washing practised by Muslims before prayers are further manifestations of the deep ritual significance of water.

Secular philosophers also perceived the unique nature of water. Thus, Thales of Miletus, who is generally regarded as the initiator of the Greek classical tradition of philosophy, *ca.* 585 BC, considered water to be the sole fundamental principle in nature. His celebrated dictum maintains: "It is water that, in taking different forms, constitutes the earth, atmosphere, sky, mountains, gods and men, beasts and birds, grass and trees, and animals down to worms, flies and ants. All these are but different forms of water. Meditate on water!" Though this may sound quaint or even perverse to modern ears, we should reflect that some marine invertebrates are, indeed, 96–97% water, and the human embryo during its first month is 93% water by weight. Aristotle considered water to be one of the four elements, alongside earth, air and fire, and this belief in the fundamental and elementary nature of water persisted until the epoch-making experiments of H. Cavendish and others in the second half of the eighteenth century (pp. 32, 601) showed water to be a compound of hydrogen and oxygen.[80]

Distribution and availability

Water is distributed very unevenly and with very variable purity over the surface of the earth (Table 14.6). Desert regions have little rainfall and no permanent surface waters, whereas oceans, containing many dissolved salts, cover vast tracts of the globe; they comprise 97% of the available water and cover an area of $3.61 \times 10^8 \, km^2$ (i.e. 70.8% of the surface of the

Table 14.6   Estimated world water supply

Source	Volume/$10^3 \, km^3$	% of total
Salt water		
Oceans	1 348 000	97.33
Saline lakes and inland seas	105[a]	0.008
Fresh water		
Polar ice and glaciers	28 200	2.04
Ground water	8 450	0.61
Lakes	125[b]	0.009
Soil moisture	69	0.005
Atmospheric water vapour	13.5	0.001
Rivers	1.5	0.0001
Total	1 385 000	100.0

[a] The Caspian Sea accounts for 75% of this.
[b] More than half of this is in the four largest lakes: Baikal 26 000; Tanganyika 20 000; Nyassa 13 000; and Superior 12 000 km^3.

earth). Less than 2.7% of the total surface water is fresh and most of this is locked up in the Antarctic ice cap and to a much lesser extent the Arctic. The Antarctic ice cap covers some $1.5 \times 10^7 \, km^2$, i.e. larger than Continental Europe to the Urals ($1.01 \times 10^7 \, km^2$), the USA including Alaska and Hawaii ($0.94 \times 10^7 \, km^2$), or Australia ($0.77 \times 10^7 \, km^2$): it comprises some $2.5–2.9 \times 10^7 \, km^3$ of fresh water which, if melted, would supply all the rivers of the earth for more than 800 years. Every year some 5000 icebergs, totalling $10^{12} \, m^3$ of ice (i.e. 10^{12} tonnes), are calved from the glaciers and ice shelves of Antarctica. Each iceberg consists (on average) of ~200 Mtonnes of pure fresh water and, if towed at $1–2 \, km \, h^{-1}$, could arrive 30% intact in Australia to provide water at one-tenth of the cost of current desalination procedures.[81] Transportation of crushed ice by ship from the polar regions is an alternative that was used intermittently towards the end of the last century.

Surface freshwater lakes contain $1.25 \times 10^5 \, km^3$ of water, more than half of which

[78] Holy Bible, Genesis, Chaps. 6–8.

[79] Holy Bible, Gospels according to St. Matthew, Chap. 3; St. Mark, Chap. 1; St. Luke, Chap. 3, St. John, Chap. 1.

[80] J. W. MELLOR, *A Comprehensive Treatise on Inorganic and Theoretical Chemistry*, Vol. 1, Chap. 3. pp. 122–46, Longmans Green, London, 1922.

[81] F. FRANKS, *Introduction — Water, the Unique Chemical*, Vol. 1, Chap. 1, of F. FRANKS (ed.), *Water, a Comprehensive Treatise in 7 Volumes*, Plenum Press, New York, 1972–82. Continued as F. FRANKS (ed.) *Water Science Reviews* published by Cambridge University Press: Vol. 1, 1985 etc.

is in the four largest lakes. Though these huge lacustrine sources dwarf the innumerable smaller lakes, springs and rivers of the earth, human habitation depends more on these widely distributed smaller sources which, in total, still far exceed the needs of man and the animal and plant kingdoms. Despite this, severe local problems can arise due to prolonged drought, the pollution of surface waters, or the extension of settlements into more arid regions. Indeed, droughts have been endemic since ancient times, and even pollution of local sources has been a cause of concern and the subject of legislation since at least 1847 (UK). Fortunately, it now appears that the quality of water supplies and amenities is rising steadily in most communities since the nadir of some 40 years ago, and public concern is now increasingly ensuring that funds are available on an appropriate scale to deal with the massive problems of water pollution.[82-85] (See also p. 478.)

Water purification and recycling is now a major industry.[86] The method of treatment depends on the source of the water, the use envisaged and the volume required. Luckily the human body is very tolerant to changes in the composition of drinking water, and in many communities this may contain $0.5\,\mathrm{g\,l^{-1}}$ or more of dissolved solids (Table 14.7). Prior treatment may consist of coagulation (by addition of alum or chlorinated $FeSO_4$ to produce flocs of $Al(OH)_3$ or $Fe(OH)_3$), filtration, softening (removal of

Table 14.7 World Health Organization standards for drinking water

Material	Maximum desirable conc/mg l^{-1}	Maximum permissible conc/mg l^{-1}
Total dissolved solids	500	1500
Mg	30	150
Ca	75	200
Chlorides	20	60
Sulfates	200	400

Mg^{II} and Ca^{II} by ion exchange) and disinfection (by chlorination, p. 793, or addition of ozone, p. 611). In most developed countries industrial needs for water are at least 10 times the volume used domestically. Moreover, some industrial processes require much purer water than that for human consumption, and for high-pressure boiler feedwater in particular the purity standard is 99.999 998%, i.e. no more than 0.02 ppm impurities. This is far purer than for reactor grade uranium, the finest refined gold or the best analytical reagents, and is probably exceeded only by semiconductor grade germanium and silicon. In contrast to Ge and Si, however, water is processed on a megatonne-per-day scale at a cost of only about £1 per tonne.

The beneficiation of sea water and other saline sources to produce fresh water is also of increasing importance. Normal freshwater supplies from precipitation cannot meet the needs of the increasing world population, particularly in the semi-arid regions of the world, and desalination is being used increasingly to augment normal water supplies, or even to provide all the fresh water in some places such as the arid parts of the Arabian Peninsula. The most commonly used methods are distillation (e.g. multistage flash distillation processes) and ion-exchange techniques, including electrodialysis and reverse osmosis (hyperfiltration). The enormous importance of the field can be gauged from the fact that Gmelin's volume on *Water Desalting*,[87] which reviewed 14 000 papers published up to 1973/4, has already

[82] H. B. N. HYNES, *The Biology of Polluted Waters*, Liverpool Univ. Press, 4th impression 1973, 202 pp.

[83] A. D. MCKNIGHT, P. K. MARSTRAND and T. C. SINCLAIR (eds.), *Environmental Pollution Control*, Chap. 5: Pollution of inland waters; Chap. 6: The Law relating to pollution of inland waters; George, Allen and Unwin, London, 1974.

[84] C. E. WARREN, *Biology and Water Pollution Control*, Saunders, Philadelphia, 1971, 434 pp.

[85] B. COMMONER, The killing of a great lake, in *The 1968 World Book Year Book*, Field Enterprises Educ. Corp., 1968; Lake Erie water, Chap. 5 in *The Closing Circle*, London, Jonathan Cape, 1972. See also A. NISBETT *New Scientist*, 23 March 1972, pp. 650-2, who argues that B. Commoner's views are unfounded: Lake Erie is not dead but it is damaged.

[86] T. V. ARDEN, in R. THOMPSON (ed.), *The Modern Inorganic Chemicals Industry*, pp. 69-105, Chemical Society Special Publication, No. 31, 1977.

[87] *Gmelin Handbook of Inorganic Chemistry*, 8th edn. (in English), *O: Water Desalting*, 1974, 339 pp.

Table 14.8   Some physical properties of H_2O, D_2O and T_2O (at 25°C unless otherwise stated)[a]

Property	H_2O	D_2O	T_2O
Molecular weight	18.0151	20.0276	22.0315
MP/°C	0.00	3.81	4.48
BP/°C	100.00	101.42	101.51
Temperature of maximum density/°C	3.98	11.23	13.4
Maximum density/g cm^{-3}	1.0000	1.1059	1.2150
Density(25°)/g cm^{-3}	0.997 01	1.1044	1.2138
Vapour pressure/mmHg	23.75	20.51	~19.8
Viscosity/centipoise	0.8903	1.107	—
Dielectric constant ε	78.39	78.06	—
Electrical conductivity(20°C)/ohm^{-1} cm^{-1}	5.7×10^{-8}	—	—
Ionization constant $[H^+][OH^-]$/mol^2 l^{-2}	1.008×10^{-14}	1.95×10^{-15}	$\sim 6 \times 10^{-16}$
Ionic dissociation constant $K = [H^+][OH^-]/[H_2O]$/mol l^{-1}	1.821×10^{-16}	3.54×10^{-17}	$\sim 1.1 \times 10^{-17}$
Heat of ionization/kJ mol^{-1}	56.27	60.33	—
ΔH_f°/kJ mol^{-1}	−285.85	−294.6	—
ΔG_f° kJ mol^{-1}	−237.19	−243.5	—

[a] Heavy water (p. 39) is now manufactured on the multikilotonne scale for use both as a coolant and neutron-moderator in nuclear reactors: its absorption cross-section for neutrons is much less than for normal water: σ_H 332, σ_D 0.46 mb (1 millibarn = 10^{-21} cm^2)

had to be supplemented by a further 360-page volume[88] dealing with the 4000 papers appearing during the following 4 years. A far cry from the first recorded use of desalination techniques in biblical times.[89]

Physical properties and structure

Water is a volatile, mobile liquid with many curious properties, most of which can be ascribed to extensive H bonding (p. 52). In the gas phase the H_2O molecule has a bond angle of 104.5° (close to tetrahedral) and an interatomic distance of 95.7 pm. The dipole moment is 1.84 D. Some properties of liquid water are summarized in Table 14.8 together with those of heavy water

---

[88] *Gmelin Handbook of Inorganic Chemistry*, 8th edn., O: *Water Desalting*, Supplement Vol. 1, 1979, 360 pp.

[89] Holy Bible, Exodus, Chap. 15, verses 22–25: "... so Moses brought the sons of Israel from the Red Sea and they went into the desert of Sur. And they marched three days in the wilderness and found no water to drink. And then they arrived at Merra and they could not drink from the waters' of Merra because they were bitter. ... And the people murmured against Moses saying: What shall we drink? And Moses cried unto the Lord. And the Lord showed him a wood and he put it into the water and the water became sweet".

D_2O and the tritium analogue T_2O (p. 41). The high bp is notable (cf. H_2S, etc.) as is the temperature of maximum density and its marked dependence on the isotopic composition of water. The high dielectric constant and measurable ionic dissociation equilibrium are also unusual and important properties. The ionic mobilities of $[H_3O]^+$ and $[OH]^-$ in water are abnormally high (350×10^{-4} and 192×10^{-4} cm s^{-1} per V cm^{-1} at 25° compared with $50–75 \times 10^{-4}$ cm^2 V^{-1} s^{-1} for most other ions). This has been ascribed to a proton switch and reorientation mechanism involving the ions and chains of H-bonded solvent molecules. Other properties which show the influence of H bonding are the high heat and entropy of vaporization (ΔH_{vap} 44.02 kJ mol^{-1}, ΔS_{vap} 118.8 J deg^{-1} mol^{-1}), high surface tension (71.97 dyne cm^{-1}, i.e. 71.97 mN m^{-1}) and relatively high viscosity. The strength of the H bonds has been variously estimated at between 5–50 kJ per mol of H bonds and is most probably close to 20 kJ mol^{-1}. The structured nature of liquid water in which the molecules are linked to a small number of neighbours (2–3) by H bonds also accounts for its anomalously low density compared with a value of ~ 1.84 g cm^{-3} calculated for a normal close-packed liquid with molecules of similar size and mass. Details of the structure of liquid water have been probed for more than six decades since the classic paper of J. D. Bernal and R. H. Fowler proposed the first plausible model.[90] Despite extensive work by X-ray and neutron diffraction, Raman and infrared spectroscopy, and the theoretical calculation of thermodynamic properties based on various models, details are still controversial and there does not even appear to be general agreement on whether water consists of a mixture of two or more species of varying degrees of polymerization or whether it is better described on a continuous model of highly bent H-bond configurations.[91]

When water freezes the crystalline form adopted depends upon the detailed conditions employed. At least nine structurally distinct forms of ice are known and the phase relations between them are summarized in Fig. 14.9. Thus, when liquid or gaseous water crystallizes at atmospheric pressure normal hexagonal ice I_h forms, but at very low temperatures ($-120°$ to $-140°$) the vapour condenses to the cubic form, ice I_c. The relation between these structures is the same as that between the tridymite and cristobalite forms of SiO_2 (p. 342), though in both forms of ice the protons are disordered.

Many of the high-pressure forms of ice are also based on silica structures (Table 14.9) and in ice II, VIII and IX the protons are ordered, the last 2 being low-temperature forms of ice VII and III respectively in which the protons are disordered. Note also that the high-pressure polymorphs VI and VII can exist at temperatures as high as 80°C and that, as expected, the high-pressure forms have substantially greater densities than that for ice I. A vitreous form of ice can be obtained by condensing water vapour at temperatures of $-160°C$ or below.

In "normal" hexagonal ice I_h each O is surrounded by a nearly regular tetrahedral arrangement of 4 other O atoms (3 at 276.5 pm and 1, along the c-axis, at 275.2 pm). The O–O–O angles are all close to 109.5° and neutron diffraction shows that the angle H–O–H is close to 105°, implying that the H atoms lie slightly off the O–O vectors. The detailed description of the disordered H atom positions is complex. In the proton-ordered phases II and IX neutron diffraction again indicates an angle H–O–H close to 105° but the O–O–O angles are now 88° and 99° respectively. More details are in the papers mentioned in ref. 92.

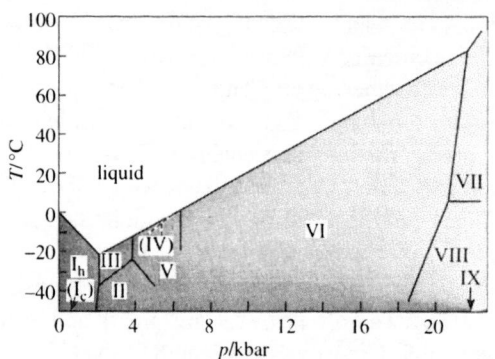

Figure 14.9 Partial phase diagram for ice (metastable equilibrium shown by broken lines).

Table 14.9 Structural relations in the polymorphs of ice[92]

Polymorph	Analogous silica polymorph	$d/(\text{g cm}^{-3})$	Ordered (O) or disordered (D) positions
I_h	Tridymite	0.92	D
I_c	Cristobalite	0.92	D
II	—	1.17	O
III⎫	Keatite	1.16	D⎫
IX⎭	Keatite		O⎭
IV	See footnote[a]	—	—
V	No obvious analogue	1.23	D
VI	Edingtonite[b,c]	1.31	D
VII ⎫	Cristobalite[c]	1.50	D⎫
VIII⎭	Cristobalite[c]		O⎭

[a]Metastable for H_2O, but firmly established for D_2O.
[b]Edingtonite is $BaAl_2Si_3O_{10}.4H_2O$ (see p. 1037 of ref. 93).
[c]Structure consists of two interpenetrating frameworks.

[90] J. D. BERNAL and R. H. FOWLER, *J. Chem. Phys.* **1**, 515–48 (1933).

[91] P. KRINDEL and I. ELIEZER, *Coord. Chem. Rev.* **6**, 217–46 (1971).

[92] A. F. WELLS, Water and hydrates, Chap. 15 in *Structural Inorganic Chemistry*, 5th edn., pp. 653–98, Oxford University Press, Oxford, 1984.

As indicated in Tables 14.8 and 14.9, ice I_h is unusual in having a density less than that of the liquid phase with which it is in equilibrium (a property which is of crucial significance for the preservation of aquatic life). When ice I_h melts some of the H bonds (possibly about 1 in 4) in the fully H-bonded lattice of 4-coordinate O atoms begin to break, and this process continues as the liquid is warmed, thereby enabling the molecules to pack progressively more closely with a consequent *increase* in density. This effect is opposed by the thermal motion of the molecules which tends to expand the liquid, and the net result is a maximum in the density at 3.98°C. Further heating reduces the density, though only slowly, presumably because the effects of thermal motion begin to outweigh the countervailing influence of breaking more H bonds. Again the qualitative explanation is clear but quantitative calculations of the density, viscosity, dielectric constant, etc., of H_2O, D_2O and their mixtures remain formidable.

It was previously thought that pure ice had a low but measurable electrical conductivity of about 1×10^{-10} ohm^{-1} cm^{-1} at -10°C. However, this conductivity is now thought to arise almost exclusively from surface defects, and when these have been removed ice is essentially an insulator with an immeasurably small conductivity.[93]

Water of crystallization, aquo complexes and solid hydrates

Many salts crystallize from aqueous solution not as the anhydrous compound but as a well-defined hydrate. Still other solid phases have variable quantities of water associated with them, and there is an almost continuous gradation in the degree of association or "bonding" between the molecules of water and the other components of the crystal. It is convenient to recognise five limiting types of interaction though the boundaries between them are vague

and undefined and many compounds incorporate more than one type.

(a) *H_2O coordinated in a cationic complex.* This is perhaps the most familiar class and can be exemplified by complexes such as $[Be(OH_2)_4]SO_4$, $[Mg(OH_2)_6]Cl_2$, $[Ni(OH_2)_6]$-$(NO_3)_2$, etc.; the metal ion is frequently in the $+2$ or $+3$ oxidation state and tends to be small and with high coordination power. Sometimes there is further interaction via H bonding between the aquocation and the anion, particularly if this derives from an oxoacid, e.g. the alums $\{[M(OH_2)_6]^+[Al(OH_2)_6]^{3+}[SO_4]_2^{2-}\}$ and related salts of Cr^{3+}, Fe^{3+}, etc. The species H_3O^+, $H_5O_2^+$, $H_7O_3^+$ and $H_9O_4^+$ are a special case in which the cation is a proton, i.e. $[H(OH_2)_n]^+$, and are discussed on p. 630.

(b) *H_2O coordinated by H bonding to oxoanions.* This mode is relatively uncommon but occurs in the classic case of $CuSO_4.5H_2O$ and probably also in $ZnSO_4.7H_2O$. Thus, in hydrated copper sulfate, 1 of the H_2O molecules is held much more tenaciously than the other 4 (which can all be removed over P_4O_{10} or by warming under reduced pressure); the fifth can only be removed by heating the compound above 350°C (or to 250° *in vacuo*). The crystal structure shows that each Cu atom is coordinated by $4H_2O$ and $2SO_4$ groups in a *trans* octahedral configuration (Fig. 14.10) and that the fifth H_2O molecule is not bound to Cu but forms H (donor) bonds to 2 SO_4 groups on neighbouring Cu atoms and 2 further H (acceptor) bonds with *cis*-H_2O molecules on 1 of the Cu atoms. It therefore plays a cohesive role in binding the various units of the structure into a continuous lattice.

(c) *Lattice water.* Sometimes hydration of either the cation or the anion is required to improve the size compatibility of the units comprising the lattice, and sometimes voids in the lattice so formed can be filled by additional molecules of water. Thus, although LiF and NaF are anhydrous, the larger alkali metal fluorides can form definite hydrates $MF.nH_2O$ ($n = 2$ and 4 for K; $1\frac{1}{2}$ for Rb; $\frac{2}{3}$ and $1\frac{1}{2}$ for Cs). Conversely, for the chlorides: KCl, RbCl and CsCl are always anhydrous whereas LiCl can form hydrates with

---

[93] A. VON HIPPEL, *Mat. Res. Bull.* **14**, 273–99 (1979).

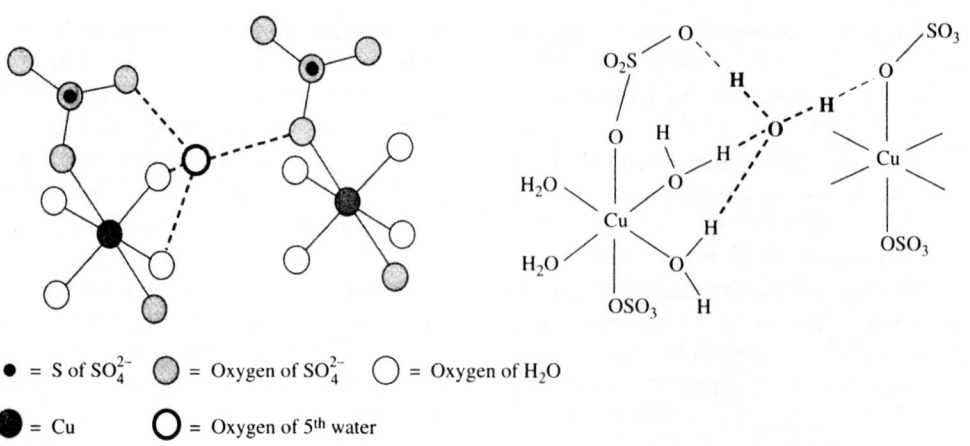

● = S of SO_4^{2-} ◉ = Oxygen of SO_4^{2-} ○ = Oxygen of H_2O

⬤ = Cu   ⭕ = Oxygen of 5th water

Figure 14.10   Two representations of the repeating structural unit in $CuSO_4.5H_2O$ showing the geometrical distribution of ligands about Cu and the connectivity of the unique H_2O molecule.

1, 2, 3 and $5H_2O$, and $NaCl.2H_2O$ is also known. The space-filling role of water molecules is even more evident with very large anions such as those of the heteropoly acids (p. 1013), e.g. $H_3[PW_{12}O_{40}].29H_2O$.

(d) *Zeolitic water.* The large cavities of the framework silicates (p. 354) can readily accommodate water molecules, and the lack of specific strong interactions enables the "degree of hydration" to vary continuously over very wide ranges. The swelling of ion-exchange resins and clay minerals (p. 353) are further examples of non-specific hydrates of variable composition.

(e) *Clathrate hydrates.*[94] The structure motif of zeolite "hosts" accommodating "guest" molecules of water can be inverted in an intriguing way: just as the various forms of ice (p. 624) are formally related to those of silica (p. 342), so $(H_2O)_n$ can be induced to generate various cage-like structures with large cavities, thereby enabling the water structure itself to act as host to various guest molecules. Thus, polyhedral frameworks, sometimes with cavities of more than one size, can be generated from unit cells containing $12H_2O$, $46H_2O$, $136H_2O$, etc. In

94 E. BERECZ and M. BALLA-ACHS, *Gas Hydrates*, Elsevier, Amsterdam, 1983, 343 pp.

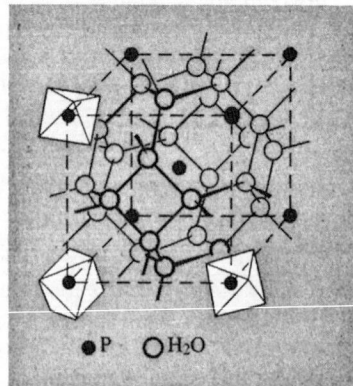

●P   ○H_2O

Figure 14.11   Crystal structure of $HPF_6.6H_2O$ showing the cavity formed by 24 H_2O molecules disposed with their O atoms at the vertices of a truncated octahedron. The PF_6 octahedra occupy centre and corners of the cubic unit cell, i.e. one PF_6 at the centre of each cavity.[92]

the first of these (Fig. 14.11) there is a cubic array of 24-cornered cavities, each cavity being a truncated octahedron with square faces of O atoms and each H_2O being common to 2 adjacent cavities (i.e. $24/2 = 12H_2O$). There is space for a guest molecule G at the centre of each cavity, i.e. at the centre of the cube and at each corner resulting in a stoichiometry $G(8G)_{1/8}.12H_2O$, i.e. $G.6H_2O$ as in $HPF_6.6H_2O$. The structure should be compared with the aluminosilicate framework in ultramarine (p. 358).

With the more complicated framework of $46H_2O$ there are 6 cavities of one size and 2 slightly smaller. If all are filled one has $46/8H_2O$ per guest molecule, i.e. $G.5\frac{3}{4}H_2O$ as in the high-pressure clathrates with $G = Ar$, Kr, CH_4 and H_2S. If only the larger cavities are filled, the stoichiometry rises to $G.7\frac{2}{3}H_2O$: this is approximated by the classic chlorine hydrate phase discovered by Humphry Davy and studied by Michael Faraday. The compound is now known to be $Cl_2.7\frac{1}{4}H_2O$, implying that up to 20% of the smaller guest sites are also occupied.

With the $136H_2O$ polyhedron there are 8 larger and 16 smaller voids. If only the former are filled, then $G.17H_2O$ results $(17 = 136/8)$ as in $CHCl_3.17H_2O$ and $CHI_3.17H_2O$, whereas if both sets are filled with molecules of different sizes, compounds such as $CHCl_3.2H_2S.17H_2O$ result. Many more complicated arrays are possible, resulting from partial filling of the voids or partial replacement of H_2O in the framework by other species capable of being H-bonded into the network, e.g. $[NMe_4]F.4H_2O$, $[NMe_4]OH.5H_2O$, $Bu_3^nSF.20H_2O$ and $[N(i\text{-}C_5H_{11})_4]F.38H_2O$. Further structural details are in ref. 92, and industrial applications are discussed in the comprehensive ref. 94.

Chemical properties

Water is an excellent solvent because of its high dielectric constant and very strong solvating power. Many compounds, whether hydrated or anhydrous, dissolve to give electrolytic solutions of hydrated cations and anions. However, detailed treatments of solubility relations, free energies and enthalpies of ionic hydration, temperature dependence of solubility and the influence of dissolved ions on the H-bonded structure of the solvent, fall outside the scope of the present treatment. Even predominantly covalent compounds such as $EtOH$, $MeCO_2H$, Me_2CO, $(CH_2)_4O$, etc. can have high solubility or even complete miscibility with water due to H-bonded interaction with the solvent. Again, covalent

compounds such as HCl can dissolve to give ionic solutions by heterolytic cleavage (e.g. to aquated $H_3O^+Cl^-$), and the process of dissolution sometimes also results in ionic cleavage of the solvent itself, e.g. $[H_3O]^+[BF_3(OH)]^-$ (p. 198). Because of the great affinity that many elements have for oxygen, solvolytic cleavage (hydrolysis) of "covalent" or "ionic" bonds frequently ensues, e.g.:

$$P_4O_{10}(s) + xH_2O \longrightarrow 4H_3PO_4(aq) \qquad \text{(p. 505)}$$

$$AlCl_3(s) + xH_2O \longrightarrow [Al(OH_2)_6]^{3+}(aq)$$
$$+ 3Cl^-(aq) \quad \text{(p. 225)}$$

Such reactions are discussed at appropriate points throughout the book as each individual compound is being considered. A particularly important set of reactions in this category is the synthesis of element hydrides by hydrolysis of certain sulfides (to give H_2S), nitrides (to give NH_3), phosphides (PH_3), carbides (C_nH_m), borides (B_nH_m), etc. Useful reviews are available on hydrometallurgy (the recovery of metals by use of aqueous solutions at relatively low temperatures),[94a] hydrothermal syntheses[94b] and the use of supercritical water as a reaction medium for chemistry.[94c]

Another important reaction (between H_2O, I_2 and SO_2) forms the basis of the quantitative determination of water when present in small amounts. The reaction, originally investigated by R. Bunsen in 1835, was introduced in 1935 as an analytical reagent by Karl Fischer who believed, incorrectly, that each mole of I_2 was equivalent to 2 moles of H_2O:

$$2H_2O + I_2 + SO_2 \xrightleftharpoons{\text{MeOH/py}} 2HI + H_2SO_4$$

In fact, the reaction is only quantitative in the presence of pyridine, and the methanol solvent

[94a] F. HABASHI, *Chem. and Eng. News*, 8 Feb. 1982, pp. 46–58.

[94b] A. RABENAU, *Angew. Chem. Int. Edn. Engl.* **24**, 1026–40 (1985).

[94c] R. W. SHAW, T. B. BRILL, A. A. CLIFFORD, C. A. ECKERT and E. U. FRANCK, *Chem. and Eng. News*, 23 Dec. 1991, pp. 26–39.

is also involved leading to a 1:1 stoichiometry between I_2 and H_2O:

$$H_2O + I_2 + SO_2 + 3py \longrightarrow 2pyHI + C_5H_5N\diagdown\begin{matrix}SO_2 \\ | \\ O\end{matrix}$$

$$\xrightarrow{\text{MeOH}} [pyH][MeOSO_3]$$

The stability of the reagent is much improved by replacing MeOH with $MeOCH_2CH_2OH$, and this forms the basis of the present-day Karl Fischer reagent.[95]

In addition to simple dissolution, ionic dissociation and solvolysis, two further classes of reaction are of pre-eminent importance in aqueous solution chemistry, namely acid-base reactions (p. 48) and oxidation–reduction reactions. In water, the oxygen atom is in its lowest oxidation state (-2). Standard reduction potentials (p. 435) of oxygen in acid and alkaline solution are listed in Table 14.10[96] and shown diagramatically in the scheme opposite. It is important to remember that if H^+ or OH^- appear in the electrode half-reaction, then the electrode potential will change markedly with the pH. Thus for the first reaction in Table 14.10: $O_2 + 4H^+ + 4e^- \rightleftharpoons 2H_2O$, although $E^\circ = 1.229$ V, the actual potential at 25°C will be given by

$$E/\text{volt} = 1.229 + 0.05916\log\{[H^+]/\text{mol}\,l^{-1}\} \times \{P_{O_2}/\text{atm}\}^{\frac{1}{4}}$$

which diminishes to 0.401 V at pH 14 (Fig. 14.12). Likewise, for the half-reaction

[95] E. SCHOLZ, *Karl Fischer Titration Determination of Water*, Springer Verlag, Berlin, 1984, 150 pp.

[96] G. MILAZZO and S. CAROLI, *Tables of Standard Electrode Potentials*, p. 229, Wiley-Interscience, New York, 1978.

$H^+ + e^- \rightleftharpoons \frac{1}{2}H_2$, E° is zero by definition at pH 0, whereas at other concentrations

$$E/\text{volt} = -0.05916\log\{P_{H_2}/\text{atm}\}^{\frac{1}{2}}/ \{[H^+]/\text{mol}\,l^{-1}\}$$

and the value falls to -0.828 at pH 14. Theoretically no oxidizing agent whose reduction potential lies above the O_2/H_2O line and no reducing agent whose reduction potential falls below the H^+/H_2 line can exist in thermodynamically stable aqueous solutions. However, for kinetic reasons associated with the existence of over-potentials, these lines can be extended by about 0.5 V as shown by the dotted lines in Fig. 14.12, and these are a more realistic estimate of the region of stability of oxidizing and reducing agents in aqueous solution. Outside these limits more strongly oxidizing species (e.g. F_2, E° 2.866 V) oxidize water to O_2 and more strongly reducing agents (e.g. K_{metal}, E° -2.931 V) liberate H_2. Sometimes even greater activation energies have to be overcome and reaction only proceeds at elevated temperatures (e.g. $C + H_2O \rightarrow CO + H_2$; p. 307).

The acid-base behaviour of aqueous solutions has already been discussed (p. 48). The ionic self-dissociation of water is well established (Table 14.8) and can be formally represented as

$$2H_2O \rightleftharpoons H_3O^+ + OH^-$$

On the Brønsted theory (p. 51), solutions with concentrations of H_3O^+ greater than that in pure water are acids (proton donors), and solutions rich in OH^- are bases (proton acceptors). The same classifications follow from the solvent-system theory of acids and bases

Table 14.10　Standard reduction potentials of oxygen

Acid solution (pH 0)	E°/V	Alkaline solution (pH 14)	E°/V
$O_2 + 4H^+ + 4e^- \rightleftharpoons 2H_2O$	1.229	$O_2 + 2H_2O + 4e^- \rightleftharpoons 4OH^-$	0.401
$O_2 + 2H^+ + 2e^- \rightleftharpoons H_2O_2$	0.695	$O_2 + H_2O + 2e^- \rightleftharpoons HO_2^- + OH^-$	-0.076
$O_2 + H^+ + e^- \rightleftharpoons HO_2$	-0.105	$O_2 + e^- \rightleftharpoons O_2^-$	-0.563
$HO_2 + H^+ + e^- \rightleftharpoons H_2O_2$	1.495	$O_2^- + H_2O + e^- \rightleftharpoons HO_2^- + OH^-$	0.413
$H_2O_2 + 2H^+ + 2e^- \rightleftharpoons 2H_2O$	1.776	$HO_2^- + H_2O + 2e^- \rightleftharpoons 3OH^-$	0.878
$H_2O_2 + H^+ + e^- \rightleftharpoons OH + H_2O$	0.71	$HO_2^- + H_2O + e^- \rightleftharpoons OH + 2OH^-$	-0.245
$OH + H^+ + e^- \rightleftharpoons H_2O$	2.85	$OH + e^- \rightleftharpoons OH^-$	2.02

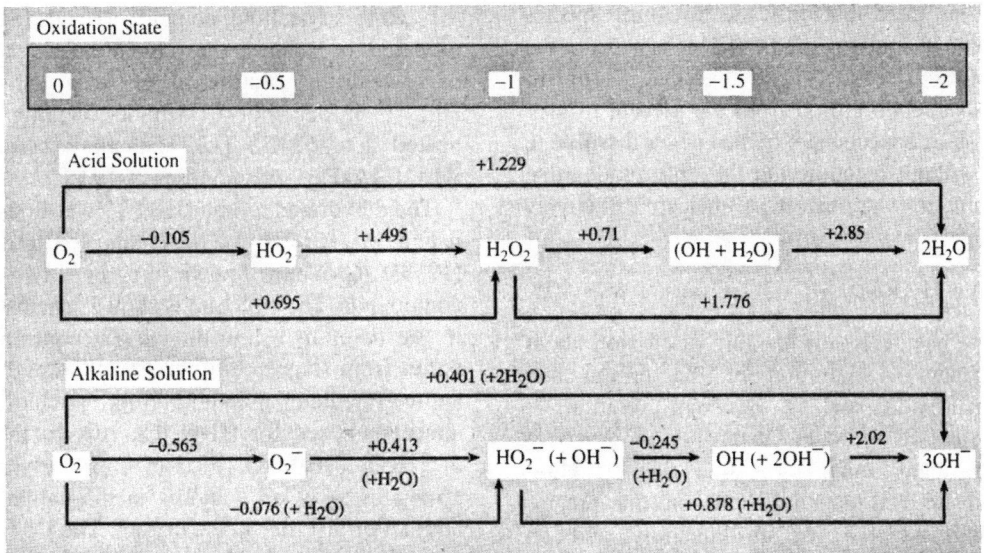

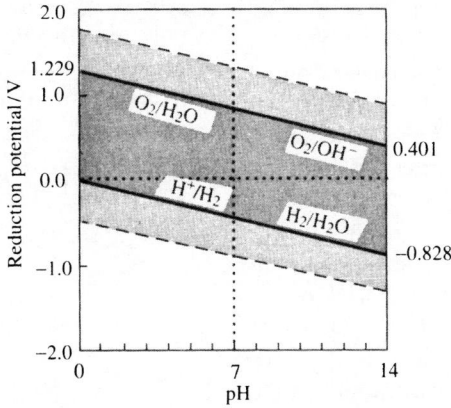

Figure 14.12 Variation of the reduction potentials of the couples O_2/H_2O and H^+/H_2 (or O_2/OH^- and H_2/H_2O) as a function of pH (full lines). The broken lines lie 0.5 V above and below these full lines and give the approximate practical limits of oxidants and reductants in aqueous solution beyond which the solvent itself is oxidized to $O_2(g)$ or reduced to $H_2(g)$.

since compounds enhancing the concentrations of the characteristic solvent cation (H_3O^+) and anion (OH^-) are solvo-acids and solvo-bases (p. 425). On the Lewis theory, H^+ is an electron-pair acceptor (acid) and OH^- an electron-pair donor (base, or ligand) (p. 198). The various definitions tend to diverge only in other systems (either nonaqueous or solvent-free), particularly when aprotic media are being considered (e.g. N_2O_4, p. 456; BrF_3, p. 831; etc.).

In considering the following isoelectronic sequence (8 valence electrons) and the corresponding gas-phase proton affinities ($A_{H^+}/$ kJ mol^{-1}):[97]

$$O^{2-} \xrightarrow[(-2860)]{H^+} OH^- \xrightarrow[(-1650)]{H^+} H_2O \xrightarrow[(-695)]{H^+} H_3O^+$$

[97] R. E. KARI and I. G. CSIZMADIA, *J. Am. Chem. Soc.* **99**, 4539–45 (1977).

it will be noted that only the last three species are stable in aqueous solution. This is because the proton affinity of O^{2-} is so huge that it immediately abstracts a proton from the solvent to give OH^-; as a consequence, oxides never dissolve in water without reaction and the only oxides that are stable to water are those that are effectively completely insoluble in it:

$$O^{2-}(s) + H_2O(aq) \longrightarrow 2OH^-(aq); \quad K > 10^{22}$$

There has been considerable discussion about the extent of hydration of the proton and the hydroxide ion in aqueous solution.[98] There is little doubt that this is variable (as for many other ions) and the hydration number derived depends both on the precise definition adopted for this quantity and on the experimental method used to determine it. H_3O^+ has definitely been detected by vibration spectroscopy, and by ^{17}O nmr spectroscopy on a solution of $HF/SbF_5/H_2^{17}O$ in SO_2; a quartet was observed at $-15°$ which collapsed to a singlet on proton decoupling, $J(^{17}O-^1H)$ 106 Hz.[99] In crystalline hydrates there are a growing number of well-characterized hydrates of the series H_3O^+, $H_5O_2^+$, $H_7O_3^+$, $H_9O_4^+$ and $H_{13}O_6^+$, i.e. $[H(OH_2)_n]^+$ $n = 1-4, 6$.[100] Thus X-ray studies have established the presence of H_3O^+ in the monohydrates of HCl, HNO₃ and HClO₄, and in the mono- and di-hydrates of sulfuric acid, $[H_3O][HSO_4]$ and $[H_3O]_2[SO_4]$. As expected, H_3O^+ is pyramidal like the isoelectronic molecule NH_3, but the values of the angles H–O–H vary considerably due to extensive H bonding throughout the crystal, e.g. $117°$ in the chloride, $112°$ in the nitrate, and $101°$, $106°$ and $126°$ in $[H_3O][HSO_4]$.[92] Likewise the H-bonded distance $O-H \cdots O$ varies: it is 266 pm in the nitrate, 254–265 in $[H_3O]$-$[HSO_4]$ and 252–259 in $[H_3O]_2[SO_4]$. The most stable hydroxonium salt yet known is

the white crystalline complex $[H_3O]^+[SbF_6]^-$, prepared by adding the stoichiometric amount of H_2O to a solution of SbF_5 in anhydrous HF;[101] it decomposes without melting when heated to $357°C$. The analogous compound $[H_3O]^+[AsF_6]^-$ decomposes at $193°C$.

The dihydrated proton $[H_5O_2]^+$ was first established in $HCl.2H_2O$ (1967) and $HClO_4.2H_2O$ (1968), and is now known in perhaps two dozen compounds. The structure is shown schematically in the diagram below though the conformation varies from staggered in the perchlorate, through an intermediate orientation for the chloride to almost eclipsed for $[H_5O_2]Cl.H_2O$. In the case of $[H_5O_2]_3^+[PW_{12}O_{40}]^{3-}$, an apparently planar arrangement of all 7 atoms in the cation is an artefact of disorder in the crystal. The $O-H \cdots O$ distance is usually in the range 240–245 pm though in the deep-yellow crystalline compound $[NEt_4]_3[H_5O_2][Mo_2Cl_8H][MoCl_4O(OH_2)]$ it is only 234 pm, one of the shortest $O-H \cdots O$ bonds known.[102] The detailed crystal structures of the hydrated hexafluorosilicic acids, $H_2SiF_6.nH_2O$ ($n = 4, 6, 9.5$) have shown them to be, respectively, $[H_5O_2]_2SiF_6$, $[H_5O_2]_2SiF_6.2H_2O$ and $[H_5O_2][H_7O_3]SiF_6.4.5H_2O$.[103]

The ions $[H_7O_3]^+$ and $[H_9O_4]^+$ are both featured in the compound $HBr.4H_2O$ which has the unexpectedly complicated formulation $[H_9O_4]^+[H_7O_3]^+[Br]_2^-.H_2O$. The structures of the cations are shown schematically in Fig. 14.13

[98] P. A. GIGUÈRE, *J. Chem. Educ.* **56**, 571–5 (1979).

[99] G. D. METEESCU and G. M. BENEDIKT, *J. Am. Chem. Soc.* **101**, 3959–60 (1979). See also G. A. OLAH, G. K. S. PRAKASH, M. BARZAGHI, K. LAMMERTSMA, P. von R. SCHLEYER and J. A. POPLE, *J. Am. Chem. Soc.* **108**, 1032–5 (1986).

[100] E. KOCHANSKI, *J. Am. Chem. Soc.* **107**, 7869–73 (1985).

[101] K. O. CHRISTE, C. J. SCHACK and R. D. WILSON, *Inorg. Chem.* **14**, 2224–30 (1975). See also K. O. CHRISTE, P. CHARPIN, E. SOULIE, R. BOUGON, J. FAWCETT and D. R. RUSSELL, *Inorg. Chem.* **23**, 3756–66 (1984).

[102] A. BINO and F. A. COTTON, *J. Am. Chem. Soc.* **101**, 4150–4 (1979). See also G. J. KEARLEY, H. A. PRESSMAN and R. C. T. SLADE, *J. Chem. Soc., Chem. Commun.*, 1801–2 (1986).

[103] D. MOOTZ and E.-J. OELLERS, *Z. anorg. allg. Chem.* **559**, 27–39 (1988).

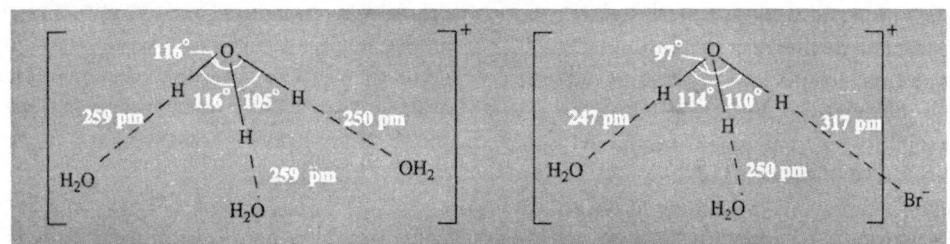

Figure 14.13 Schematic representation of the structures of the $[H_9O_4]^+$ and $[H_7O_3]^+ \cdots Br^-$ units in HBr.4H$_2$O, showing bond angles and O-H $\cdots$ O (O-H $\cdots$ Br) distances.

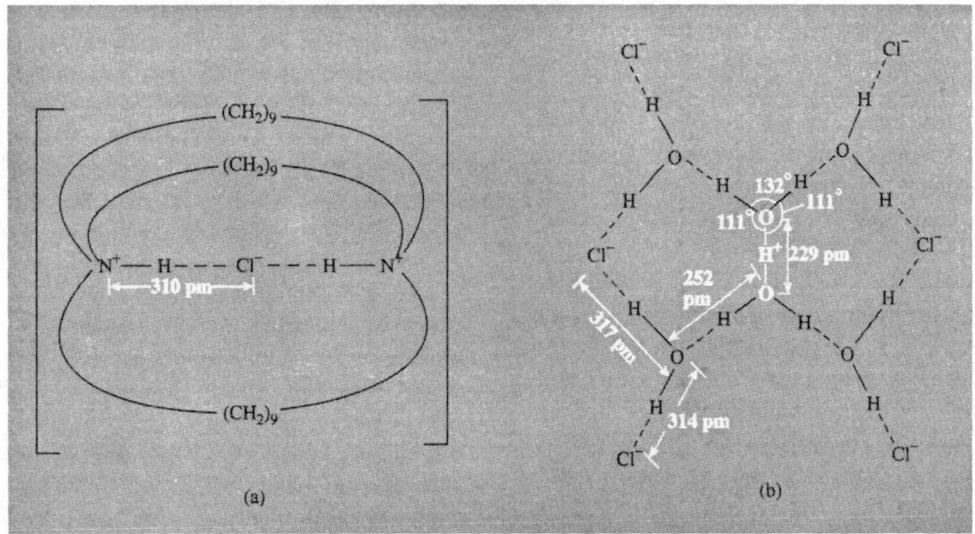

Figure 14.14 (a) Schematic representation of the structure of the cage cation $[(C_9H_{18})_3(NH)_2Cl]^+$, and (b) detailed structure of the $[H_{13}O_6]^+$ ion showing its H bonding to surrounding Cl$^-$ anions. The ion has C_{2h} symmetry with the very short central O-H-O lying across the centre of symmetry.

which indicates that a bromide ion has essentially displaced the fourth water molecule of the second cation to give an effectively neutral H-bonded unit $[(H_3O)_2H^+Br^-]$. The discrete $[H_7O_3]^+$ ion is now known in about a dozen complexes of which a good example is the deep-green complex $[NEt_4]_2[H_7O_3]_2[Ru_3Cl_{12}]$ in which the 2 O-H $\cdots$ O distances are 245 and 255 pm and the O-O $\cdots$ O angle is 115.9°.[104] Similar dimensions were found in the hexafluorosilicate.[103]

The largest protonated cluster of water molecules yet definitively characterized is the discrete unit $[H_{13}O_6]^+$ formed serendipitously when the cage compound $[(C_9H_{18})_3(NH)_2Cl]^+Cl^-$ was crystallized from a 10% aqueous hydrochloric acid solution.[105] The structure of the cage cation is shown in Fig. 14.14 and the unit cell contains $4\{[(C_9H_{18})_3(NH)_2Cl]Cl[H_{13}O_6]Cl\}$. The hydrated proton features a short symmetrical O-H-O bond at the centre of symmetry and 4 longer unsymmetrical O-H $\cdots$ O bonds to 4

[104] A. Bino and F. A. Cotton, *J. Am. Chem. Soc.* **102**, 608-11 (1980).

[105] R. A. Bell, G. G. Christoph, F. R. Fronczek and R. E. Marsh, *Science* **190**, 151-2 (1975).

further H_2O molecules, the whole $[H_{13}O_6]^+$ unit being connected to the rest of the lattice by H bonds of normal length to surrounding chloride ions. It is clear from these various examples that the stability of the larger proton hydrates is enhanced by the presence of large co-cations and/or counter-anions in the lattice. Stability can also be enhanced by structural features of the cluster cation itself, as beautifully exemplified by the species $[H_{41}O_{20}]^+$ and $[H_{43}O_{21}]^+$:[106] these stable groupings comprise a central {H} or {H_3O} bonded to an encapsulating pentagonal dodecahedron of H-bonded {$(H_2O)_{20}$} over which the positive charge can move by proton switching, i.e $[H(OH_2)_{20}]^+$ and $[H_3O(OH_2)_{20}]^+$.

Hydrated forms of the hydroxide ion have been much less well characterized though the monohydrate $[H_3O_2]^-$ has been discovered in the mixed salt $Na_2[NEt_3Me][Cr\{PhC(S)=N-(O)\}_3].\frac{1}{2}NaH_3O_2.18H_2O$ which formed when $[NEt_3Me]I$ was added to a solution of tris(thiobenzohydroximato)chromate(III) in aqueous NaOH.[107] The compound tended to lose water at room temperature but an X-ray study identified the centro-symmetric $[HO-H-OH]^-$ anion shown in Fig. 14.15. The central O–H–O bond is very short indeed (229 pm) and is

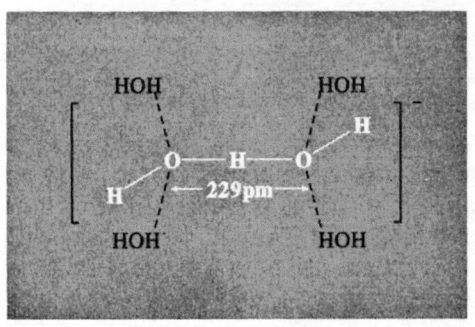

Figure 14.15 Structure of the centrosymmetric $[H_3O_2]^-$ ion showing the disposition of longer H bonds to neighbouring water molecules.

probably symmetrical, though the central H was not located on the electron density map. It will be noted that $[H_3O_2]^-$ is isoelectronic with the bifluoride ion $[F-H-F]^-$ which also features a very short, symmetrical H bond with $F \cdots F$ 227 pm (p. 60).

Polywater

The saga of polywater forms a fascinating and informative case history of the massive amount of work that can be done, even in modern times, on the preparation and characterization of a compound which was eventually found not to exist. Between 1966 and 1973 over 500 scientific papers were published on polywater following B. V. Deryagin's description of work done in the USSR during the preceding years.[108] The supposed compound, variously called anomalous water, orthowater, polywater, superwater, cyclimetric water, superdense water, water II and water-X, was prepared in minute amounts by condensing purified "ordinary water" into fine, freshly drawn glass capillaries of diameter $1-3\,\mu m$. The thermodynamic difficulties inherent in the very existence of such a compound were soon apparent and it was proposed that polywater was, in fact, a dispersion of a silica gel leached from the glass capillaries,[109] despite the specific rejection of this possibility by several groups of earlier workers. The full panoply of physicochemical techniques was brought to bear on the problem, and it was finally conceded that the anomalous properties were caused by a mixture of colloidal silicic acid and dissolved compounds of Na, K, Ca, B, Si, N (nitrate), O (sulfate) and Cl leached from the glass by the aggressive action of freshly condensed water.[110] A very informative annotated bibliography is available

[106] S. Wei, Z. Shi and A. W. Castleman, *J. Chem. Phys.* **94**, 3268–70 (1991).

[107] J. Abu-Dari, K. N. Raymond and D. P. Freyberg, *J. Am. Chem. Soc.* **101**, 3688–9 (1979).

[108] B. V. Deryagin, *Discussions Faraday Soc.* **42**, 109–19 (1966).

[109] A. Cherkin, *Nature* **224**, 1293 (1969). (See also *Nature* **222**, 159–61 (1969)).

[110] B. V. Deryagin and N. V. Churaev, *Nature* **244**, 430–1 (1973); B. V. Deryagin, *Recent Advances in Adhesion*, 1973, 23–31.

which traces the course of this controversy and analyses the reasons why it took so long to resolve.[111]

14.2.3 Hydrogen peroxide

Hydrogen peroxide was first made in 1818 by J. L. Thenard who acidified barium peroxide (p. 121) and then removed excess H_2O by evaporation under reduced pressure. Later the compound was prepared by hydrolysis of peroxodisulfates obtained by electrolytic oxidation of acidified sulfate solutions at high current densities:

$$2HSO_4^-(aq) \xrightarrow{-2e^-} HO_3SOOSO_3H(aq)$$
$$\xrightarrow{2H_2O} 2HSO_4^- + H_2O_2$$

Such processes are now no longer used except in the laboratory preparation of D_2O_2, e.g.:

$$K_2S_2O_8 + 2D_2O \longrightarrow 2KDSO_4 + D_2O_2$$

On an industrial scale H_2O_2 is now almost exclusively prepared by the autoxidation of 2-alkylanthraquinols (see Panel on next page).

Physical properties

Hydrogen peroxide, when pure, is an almost colourless (very pale blue) liquid, less volatile than water and somewhat more dense and viscous. Its more important physical properties are in Table 14.11 (cf. H_2O, p. 623). The compound is miscible with water in all proportions and forms a hydrate $H_2O_2.H_2O$, mp $-52°$. Addition of water increases the already high dielectric constant of H_2O_2 (70.7) to a maximum value of 121 at $\sim 35\%$ H_2O_2, i.e. substantially higher than the value of water itself (78.4 at $25°$).

In the gas phase the molecule adopts a skew configuration with a dihedral angle of $111.5°$ as

Table 14.11 Some physical properties of hydrogen peroxide[a]

Property	Value
MP/°C	-0.41
BP/°C (extrap)	150.2
Vapour pressure(25°)/mmHg	1.9
Density (solid at $-4.5°$)/g cm^{-3}	1.6434
Density (liquid at 25°)/g cm^{-3}	1.4425
Viscosity(20°)/centipoise	1.245
Dielectric constant $\varepsilon(25°)$	70.7
Electric conductivity(25°)/Ω^{-1} cm^{-1}	5.1×10^{-8}
$\Delta H_f°$/kJ mol^{-1}	-187.6
$\Delta G_f°$/kJ mol^{-1}	-118.0

[a]For D_2O_2: mp $+1.5°$; d_{20} 1.5348 g cm^{-3}; η_{20} 1.358 centipoise.

shown in Fig. 14.16a. This is due to repulsive interaction of the O–H bonds with the lone-pairs of electrons on each O atom. Indeed, H_2O_2 is the smallest molecule known to show hindered rotation about a single bond, the rotational barriers being 4.62 and 29.45 kJ mol^{-1} for the *trans* and *cis* conformations respectively. The skew form persists in the liquid phase, no doubt modified by H bonding, and in the crystalline state at $-163°C$ a neutron diffraction study[112] gives the dimensions shown in Fig. 14.16b. The dihedral angle is particularly sensitive to H bonding, decreasing from $111.5°$ in the gas phase to $90.2°$ in crystalline H_2O_2; in fact, values spanning the complete range from $90°$ to $180°$ (i.e. *trans* planar) are known for various solid phases containing molecular H_2O_2 (Table 14.12). The O–O distance in H_2O_2 corresponds to the value expected for a single bond (p. 616).

Chemical properties

In H_2O_2 the oxidation state of oxygen is -1, intermediate between the values for O_2 and H_2O, and, as indicated by the reduction potentials on p. 628, aqueous solutions of H_2O_2 should spontaneously disproportionate. For the pure

[111] F. PERCIVAL and A. H. JOHNSTONE, *Polywater — A Library Exercise for Chemistry Degree Students*, The Chemical Society, London, 1978, 24 pp. [See also B. F. POWELL, *J. Chem. Educ.* **48**, 663–7 (1971). H. FREIZER, *J. Chem. Educ.* **49**, 445 (1972). F. FRANKS, *Polywater*, MIT Press, Cambridge, Mass., 1981, 208 pp.]

[112] J.-M. SAVARIAULT and M. S. LEHMANN, *J. Am. Chem. Soc.* **102**, 1298–303 (1980).

Preparation and Uses of Hydrogen Peroxide[113]

Hydrogen peroxide is a major industrial chemical manufactured on a multikilotonne scale by an ingenious cycle of reactions introduced by I. G. Farbenindustrie about 60 years ago. Since the value of the solvents and organic substrates used are several hundred times that of the H_2O_2 produced, the economic viability of the process depends on keeping losses very small indeed. The basic process consists of dissolving 2-ethylanthraquinone in a mixed ester/hydrocarbon or alcohol/hydrocarbon solvent and reducing it by a Raney nickel or supported palladium catalyst to the corresponding quinol. The catalyst is then separated and the quinol non-catalytically reoxidized in a stream of air:

$$+ H_2 \xrightarrow{\text{Catalyst}}$$

Separate and redissolve

air

$$+ H_2O_2 \ (\sim 1\% \ \text{conc}) \xrightarrow{\text{Extract and concentrate}}$$

The H_2O_2 is extracted by water and concentrated to ~30% (by weight) by distillation under reduced pressure. Further low-pressure distillation to concentrations up to 85% are not uncommon.

World production expressed as 100% H_2O_2 approached 1.9 million tonnes in 1994 of which half was in Europe and one-fifth in the USA. The earliest and still the largest industrial use for H_2O_2 is as a bleach for textiles, paper pulp, straw, leather, oils and fats, etc. Domestic use as a hair bleach and a mild disinfectant has diminished somewhat. Hydrogen peroxide is also extensively used to manufacture chemicals, notably sodium perborate (p. 206) and percarbonate, which are major constituents of most domestic detergents at least in the UK and Europe. Normal formulations include 15–25% of such peroxoacid salts, though the practice is much less widespread in the USA, and the concentrations, when included at all, are usually less than 10%.

In the organic chemicals industry, H_2O_2 is used in the production of epoxides, propylene oxide, and caprolactones for PVC stabilizers and polyurethanes, in the manufacture of organic peroxy compounds for use as polymerization initiators and curing agents, and in the synthesis of fine chemicals such as hydroquinone, pharmaceuticals (e.g. cephalosporin) and food products (e.g. tartaric acid).

One of the rapidly growing uses of H_2O_2 is in environmental applications such as control of pollution by treatment of domestic and industrial effluents, e.g. oxidation of cyanides and obnoxious malodorous sulfides, and the restoration of aerobic conditions to sewage waters. Its production in the USA for these and related purposes has trebled during the past decade (from 126 kt in 1984 to 360 kt in 1994) and it has substantially replaced chlorine as an industrial bleach because it yields only H_2O and O_2 on decomposition. An indication of the proportion of H_2O_2 production used for various applications in North America (1991) is: pulp and paper treatment 49%, chemicals manufacture 15%, environmental uses 15%, textiles 8%, all other uses 13%. The price per kg for technical grade aqueous H_2O_2 in tank-car lots (1994) is $0.54 (30%), $0.75 (50%) and $1.05 (70%), i.e. essentially a constant price of $1.50 per kg on a "100% basis."

[113] W. T. HESS, Hydrogen Peroxide in *Kirk–Othmer Encyclopedia of Chemical Technology*, 4th Edn., Wiley, New York, Vol. 13, 961–95 (1995).

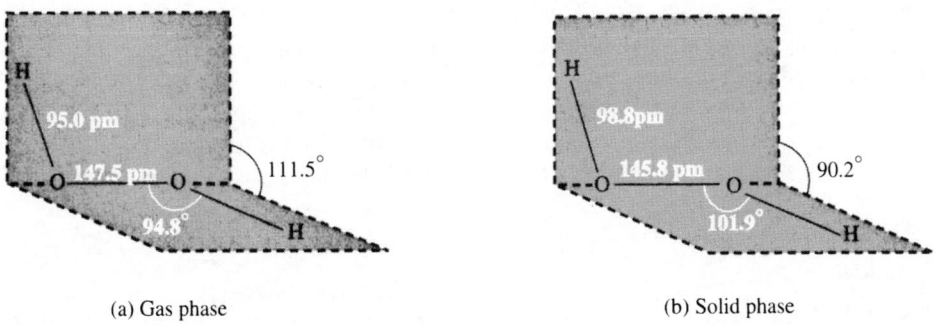

(a) Gas phase   (b) Solid phase

Figure 14.16   Structure of the H_2O_2 molecule (a) in the gas phase, and (b) in the crystalline state.

Table 14.12   Dihedral angle of H_2O_2 in some crystalline phases

Compound	Dihedral angle	Compound	Dihedral angle
$H_2O_2(s)$	90.2°	$Li_2C_2O_4.H_2O_2$	180°
$K_2C_2O_4.H_2O_2$	101.6°	$Na_2C_2O_4.H_2O_2$	180°
$Rb_2C_2O_4.H_2O_2$	103.4°	$NH_4F.H_2O_2{}^{(114)}$	180°
$H_2O_2.2H_2O$	129°		

liquid: $H_2O_2(l) \longrightarrow H_2O(l) + \frac{1}{2}O_2(g)$; $\Delta H° = -98.2\,kJ\,mol^{-1}$, $\Delta G° = -119.2\,kJ\,mol^{-1}$.   In fact, in the absence of catalysts, the compound decomposes negligibly slowly but the reaction is strongly catalysed by metal surfaces (Pt, Ag), by MnO_2 or by traces of alkali (dissolved from glass), and for this reason H_2O_2 is generally stored in wax-coated or plastic vessels with stabilizers such as urea; even a speck of dust can initiate explosive decomposition and all handling of the anhydrous compound or its concentrated solutions must be carried out in dust-free conditions and in the absence of metal ions. A useful "carrier" for H_2O_2 in some reactions is the adduct $(Ph_3PO)_2.H_2O_2$.

Hydrogen peroxide has a rich and varied chemistry which arises from (i) its ability to act either as an oxidizing or a reducing agent in both acid and alkaline solution, (ii) its ability to undergo proton acid/base reactions to form peroxonium salts $(H_2OOH)^+$, hydroperoxides $(OOH)^-$ and peroxides $(O_2)^{2-}$, and (iii) its reactions to give peroxometal complexes and peroxoacid anions.

The ability of H_2O_2 to act both as an oxidizing and a reducing agent is well known in analytical chemistry. Typical examples (not necessarily of analytical utility) are:

Oxidizing agent in acid solution:

$$2[Fe(CN)_6]^{4-} + H_2O_2 + 2H^+ \longrightarrow$$
$$2[Fe(CN)_6]^{3-} + 2H_2O$$

Likewise $Fe^{2+} \rightarrow Fe^{3+}$, $SO_3^{2-} \rightarrow SO_4^{2-}$,
$$NH_2OH \rightarrow HNO_3 \text{ etc.}$$

Reducing agent in acid solution:

$$MnO_4{}^- + 2\tfrac{1}{2}H_2O_2 + 3H^+ \longrightarrow$$
$$Mn^{2+} + 4H_2O + 2\tfrac{1}{2}O_2$$

$$2Ce^{4+} + H_2O_2 \longrightarrow 2Ce^{3+} + 2H^+ + O_2$$

Oxidizing agent in alkaline solution:

$$Mn^{2+} + H_2O_2 \longrightarrow Mn^{4+} + 2OH^-$$

Reducing agent in alkaline solution:

$$2[Fe(CN)_6]^{3-} + H_2O_2 + 2OH^- \longrightarrow$$
$$2[Fe(CN)_6]^{4-} + 2H_2O + O_2$$

$$2Fe^{3+} + H_2O_2 + 2OH^- \longrightarrow$$
$$2Fe^{2+} + 2H_2O + O_2$$

$$KIO_4 + H_2O_2 \longrightarrow KIO_3 + H_2O + O_2$$

[114] V. A. SARIN, V. YA. DUDAREV, T. A. DOBRYNINA and V. E. ZAVODNIK, *Soviet Phys. Crystallogr.* **24**, 472–3 (1979), and references therein.

It will be noted that O_2 is always evolved when H_2O_2 acts as a reducing agent, and sometimes this gives rise to a red chemiluminescence if the dioxygen molecule is produced in a singlet state (p. 605), e.g.:

Acid solution:

$$HOCl + H_2O_2 \longrightarrow H_3O^+ + Cl^- + {}^1O_2{}^* \longrightarrow h\nu$$

Alkaline solution:

$$Cl_2 + H_2O_2 + 2OH^- \longrightarrow 2Cl^- + 2H_2O$$
$$+ {}^1O_2{}^* \longrightarrow h\nu$$

The catalytic decomposition of aqueous solutions H_2O_2 alluded to on p. 635 can also be viewed as an oxidation–reduction process and, indeed, most homogeneous catalysts for this reaction are oxidation–reduction couples of which the oxidizing agent can oxidize (be reduced by) H_2O_2 and the reducing agent can reduce (be oxidized by) H_2O_2. Thus, using the data on p. 628, any complex with a reduction potential between $+0.695$ and $+1.776$ V in acid solution should catalyse the reaction. For example:

$$\underline{Fe^{3+}/Fe^{2+}, E° + 0.771 \text{ V}}$$

$$2Fe^{3+} + H_2O_2 \xrightarrow{-2H^+} 2Fe^{2+} + O_2$$

$$2Fe^{2+} + H_2O_2 \xrightarrow{+2H^+} 2Fe^{3+} + 2H_2O$$

$$Net : 2H_2O_2 \longrightarrow 2H_2O + O_2$$

$$\underline{Br_2/2Br^-, E° + 1.078}$$

$$Br_2 + H_2O_2 \xrightarrow{-2H^+} 2Br^- + O_2$$

$$2Br^- + H_2O_2 \xrightarrow{+2H^+} Br_2 + 2H_2O$$

$$Net : 2H_2O_2 \longrightarrow 2H_2O + O_2$$

In many such reactions, experiments using ^{18}O show negligible exchange between H_2O_2 and H_2O, and all the O_2 formed when H_2O_2 is used as a reducing agent comes from the H_2O_2, implying that oxidizing agents do not break the O–O bond but simply remove electrons. Not all reactions are heterolytic, however, and free radicals are sometimes involved, e.g. Ti^{3+}/H_2O_2 and Fenton's

reagent (Fe^{2+}/H_2O_2). The most important free radicals are OH and O_2H.

Hydrogen peroxide is a somewhat stronger acid than water, and in dilute aqueous solutions has $pK_a(25°) = 11.65 \pm 0.02$, i.e. comparable with the third dissociation constant of H_3PO_4 (p. 519):

$$H_2O_2 + H_2O \rightleftharpoons H_3O^+ + OOH^-;$$

$$K_a = \frac{[H_3O^+][OOH^-]}{[H_2O_2]} = 2.24 \times 10^{-12} \text{ mol l}^{-1}$$

Conversely, H_2O_2 is a much weaker base than H_2O (perhaps by a factor of 10^6), and the following equilibrium lies far to the right:

$$H_3O_2{}^+ + H_2O \rightleftharpoons H_2O_2 + H_3O^+$$

As a consequence, salts of $H_3O_2{}^+$ cannot be prepared from aqueous solutions but they have been obtained as white solids from the strongly acid solvent systems anhydrous HF/SbF_5 and HF/AsF_5, e.g.:[115]

$$H_2O_2 + HF + MF_5 \longrightarrow [H_3O_2]^+[MF_6]^-$$

$$H_2O_2 + HF + 2SbF_5 \longrightarrow [H_3O_2]^+[Sb_2F_{11}]^-$$

The salts decompose quantitatively at or slightly above room temperature, e.g.:

$$2[H_3O_2][SbF_6] \xrightarrow{45°} 2[H_3O][SbF_6] + O_2$$

The ion $[H_2OOH]^+$ is isoelectronic with H_2NOH and vibrational spectroscopy shows it to have the same (C_s) symmetry.

Deprotonation of H_2O_2 yields OOH^-, and hydroperoxides of the alkali metals are known in solution. Liquid ammonia can also effect deprotonation and NH_4OOH is a white solid, mp $25°$; infrared spectroscopy shows the presence of $NH_4{}^+$ and OOH^- ions in the solid phase but the melt appears to contain only the H-bonded species NH_3 and H_2O_2.[116] Double deprotonation yields the peroxide ion $O_2{}^{2-}$, and this is a standard route to transition metal peroxides.[53]

115 K. O. Christe, W. W. Wilson and E. C. Curtis, *Inorg. Chem.* 18, 2578–86 (1979).
116 O. Knop and P. A. Giguère, *Canad. J. Chem.* 37, 1794–7 (1959).

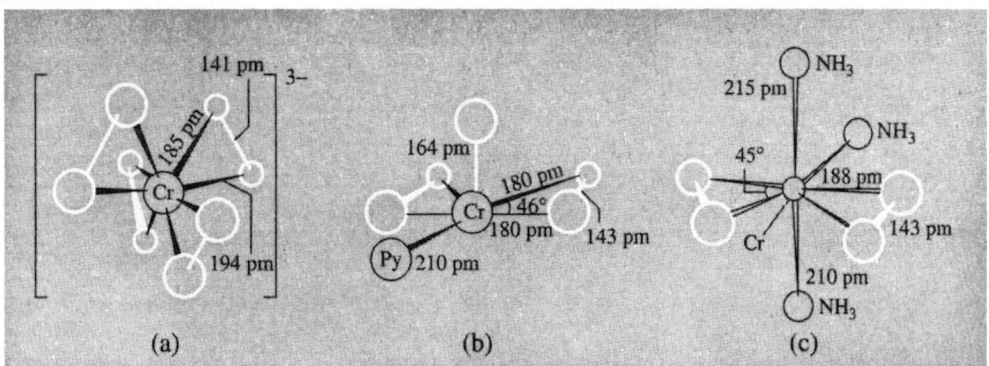

Figure 14.17   Structures of (a) the tetraperoxochromate(V) ion $[Cr^V(O_2)_4]^{3-}$, (b) the pyridine oxodiperoxo-chromium(VI) complex $[Cr^{VI}O(O_2)_2py]$, and (c) the triamminodiperoxochromium(IV) complex $[Cr^{IV}(NH_3)_3(O_2)_2]$ showing important interatomic distances and angles. (This last compound was originally described as a chromium(II) superoxo complex $[Cr^{II}(NH_3)_3(O_2)_2]$ on the basis of an apparent O–O distance of 131 pm,[117] and is a salutary example of the factual and interpretative errors that can arise even in X-ray diffraction studies.[118]

Many such compounds are discussed under the individual transition elements and it is only necessary here to note that the chemical identity of the products obtained is often very sensitive to the conditions employed because of the combination of acid-base and redox reactions in the system. For example, treatment of alkaline aqueous solutions of chromate(VI) with H_2O_2 yields the stable red paramagnetic tetraperoxochromate(V) compounds $[Cr^V(O_2)_4]^{3-}$ (μ 1.80 BM), whereas treatment of chromate(VI) with H_2O_2 in acid solution followed by extraction with ether and coordination with pyridine yields the neutral peroxochromate(VI) complex $[CrO(O_2)_2py]$ which has a small temperature-independent paramagnetism of about 0.5 BM. The structure of these two species is in Fig. 14.17 which also includes the structure of the brown diperoxochromium(IV) complex $[Cr^{IV}(NH_3)_3(O_2)_2]$ (μ 2.8 BM) prepared by treating either of the other two complexes with an excess of aqueous ammonia or more directly by treating an aqueous ammonical solution of $[NH_4]_2[Cr_2O_7]$ with H_2O_2. Besides deprotonation of H_2O_2, other routes to metal peroxides include the direct reduction of O_2 by combustion of the electropositive alkali and alkaline earth metals in oxygen (pp. 84, 119) or by reaction of O_2 with transition metal complexes in solution (p. 616).[119] Very recently K_2O_2 has been obtained as a colourless crystalline biproduct of the synthesis of the orthonitrate K_3NO_4 (p. 472) by prolonged heating of KNO_3 and K_2O in a silver crucible at temperatures up to 400°C.[120] The O–O distance was found to be 154.1(6) pm, significantly longer than the values of ∼150 pm previously obtained for alkali metal peroxides (Table 14.4, p. 616).

Another recent development is the production of HOOOH (the ozone analogue of H_2O_2) in 40% yield by the simple expedient of replacing O_2 by O_3 in the standard synthesis via 2-ethylanthraquinone at −78° (cf. p. 634); H_2O_3 begins to decompose appreciably around −40° to give single oxygen, Δ^1O_2, but is much more stable (up to +20°) in MeOBu^t and similar solvents.[121]

[117] E. H. McLaren and L. Helmholz, *J. Chem. Phys.* **63**, 1279–83 (1959).

[118] R. Stromberg, *Arkiv Kemi* **22**, 49–64 (1974).

[119] N.-G. Vannerberg, *Prog. Inorg. Chem.* **4**, 125–97 (1962).

[120] T. Bremm and M. Jansen, *Z. anorg. allg. Chem.* **610**, 64–6 (1992).

[121] J. Cerkovnik and B. Plesničar, *J. Am. Chem. Soc.* **115**, 12169–70 (1993).

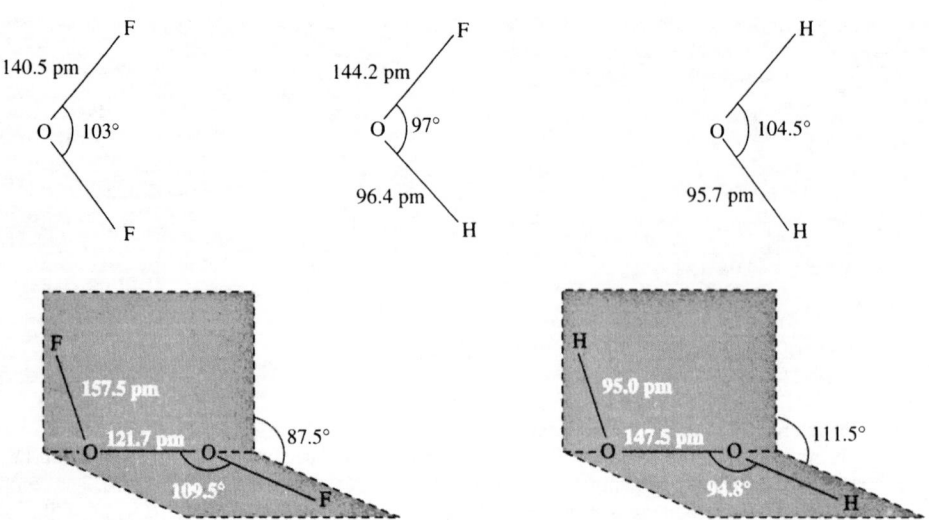

Figure 14.18   Comparison of the molecular dimensions of various gaseous molecules having O–F and O–H bonds.

Peroxoanions are described under the appropriate element, e.g. peroxoborates (p. 206), peroxonitrates (p. 459), peroxophosphates (p. 512), peroxosulfates (p. 712), and peroxodisulfates (p. 713).

14.2.4 Oxygen fluorides[122]

Oxygen forms several binary fluorides of which the most stable is OF_2. This was first made in 1929 by the electrolysis of slightly moist molten KF/HF but is now generally made by reacting F_2 gas with 2% aqueous NaOH solution:

$$2F_2 + 2NaOH \longrightarrow OF_2 + 2NaF + H_2O$$

Conditions must be controlled so as to minimize loss of the product by the secondary reaction:

$$OF_2 + 2OH^- \longrightarrow O_2 + 2F^- + H_2O$$

Oxygen fluoride is a colourless, very poisonous gas that condenses to a pale-yellow liquid (mp

−223.8°, bp −145.3°C). When pure it is stable to 200° in glass vessels but above this temperature it decomposes by a radical mechanism to the elements. Molecular dimensions (microwave) are in Fig. 14.18, where they are compared with those of related molecules. The heat of formation has been given as ΔH_f° 24.5 kJ mol^{-1}, leading to an average O–F bond energy of 187 kJ mol^{-1}. Though less reactive than elementary fluorine, OF_2 is a powerful oxidizing and fluorinating agent. Many metals give oxides and fluorides, phosphorus yields PF_5 plus POF_3, sulfur SO_2 plus SF_4, and xenon gives XeF_4 and oxofluorides (p. 900). H_2S explodes on being mixed with OF_2 at room temperature. OF_2 is formally the anhydride of hypofluorous acid, HOF, but there is no evidence that it reacts with water to form this compound. Indeed, HOF had been sought for many decades but has only relatively recently been prepared and fully characterized.[123]

HOF was first identified by P. N. Noble and G. C. Pimentel in 1968 using matrix isolation techniques: F_2/H_2O mixtures were frozen in solid

[122] E. A. V. EBSWORTH, J. A. CONNOR and J. J. TURNER, in J. C. BAILAR, H. J. EMELÉUS, R. S. NYHOLM and A. F. TROTMAN-DICKENSON (eds.), *Comprehensive Inorganic Chemistry*, Vol. 2, Chap. 22, Section 5, pp. 747–71. Pergamon Press, Oxford, 1973.

[123] E. H. APPELMAN, Nonexistent compounds: two case histories, *Acc. Chem. Res.* **6**, 113–7 (1973).

N_2 and photolysed at 14–20 K:

$$F_2 + H_2O \rightleftharpoons HOF + HF$$

A more convenient larger-scale preparation was devised in 1971 by M. H. Studier and E. H. Appleman, who circulated F_2 rapidly through a Kel-F U-tube filled with Räschig rings of polytetrafluoroethylene (Teflon) which had been moistened with water and cooled to −40°. An essential further condition was the presence of traps at −50° and −79° to remove H_2O and HF (both of which react with HOF), and the product was retained in a trap at −183°. HOF is a white solid, melting at −117° to a pale yellow liquid which boils below room temperature. Molecular dimensions are in Fig. 14.18; the small bond angle is particularly notable, being the smallest yet recorded for 2-coordinate O in an open chain. HOF is stable with respect to its elements: $\Delta H_f^\circ(298) =$ −98.2, $\Delta G_f^\circ(298) = -85.7 \, kJ \, mol^{-1}$. However, HOF decomposes fairly rapidly to HF and O_2 at room temperature ($t_{1/2} \sim 30$ min at 100 mmHg in Kel-F or Teflon). Decomposition is accelerated by light and by the presence of F_2 or metal surfaces. HOF reacts rapidly with water to produce HF, H_2O_2 and O_2; with acid solutions H_2O is oxidized primarily to H_2O_2, whereas in alkaline solutions O_2 is the principal oxygen-containing product. Ag^I is oxidized to Ag^{II} and, in alkaline solution, BrO_3^- yields the elusive perbromate ion BrO_4^- (p. 871). All these reactions parallel closely those of F_2 in water, and it may well be that HOF is the reactive species produced when F_2 reacts with water (p. 856). No ionic salts of hypofluorous acid have been isolated but covalent hypofluorites have been known for several decades as highly reactive (sometimes explosive) gases, e.g.:

$$KNO_3 + F_2 \longrightarrow KF + O_2NOF \ (bp \ -45.9°)$$

$$SOF_2 + 2F_2 \xrightarrow{CsF} F_5SOF \ (bp \ -35.1°)$$

$$HClO_4(conc) + F_2 \longrightarrow HF + O_3ClOF \ (bp \ -15.9°)$$

Dioxygen difluoride, O_2F_2, is best prepared by passing a silent electric discharge through a low-pressure mixture of F_2 and O_2: the products obtained depend markedly on conditions, and the yield of O_2F_2 is optimized by using a 1:1 mixture at 7–17 mmHg and a discharge of 25–30 mA at 2.1–2.4 kV. Alternatively, pure O_2F_2 can be synthesized by subjecting a mixture of liquid O_2 and F_2 in a stainless steel reactor at −196° to 3 MeV bremsstrahlung radiation for 1–4 h. O_2F_2 is a yellow solid and liquid, mp −154°, bp −57° (extrapolated). It is much less stable than OF_2 and even at −160° decomposes at a rate of some 4% per day. Decomposition by a radical mechanism is rapid above −100°. The structure of O_2F_2 (Fig. 14.18) resembles that of H_2O_2 but the remarkably short O–O distance is a notable difference in detail (cf. O_2 gas 120.7 pm). Conversely, the O–F distance is unusually long when compared to those in OF_2 and HOF (Fig. 14.18). These features are paralleled by the bond dissociation energies:

$$D(FO-OF) \ 430 \, kJ \, mol^{-1},$$

$$D(F-OOF) \sim 75 \, kJ \, mol^{-1}.$$

Consistent with this, mass spectrometric, infrared and electron spin resonance studies confirm dissociation into F and OOF radicals, and low-temperature studies have also established the presence of the dimer O_4F_2, which is a dark red-brown solid, mp −191°C. Impure O_4F_2 can also be prepared by silent electric discharge but the material previously thought to be O_3F_2 is probably a mixture of O_4F_2 and O_2F_2. Dioxygen difluoride, as expected, is a very vigorous and powerful oxidizing and fluorinating agent even at very low temperatures (−150°). It converts ClF to ClF_3, BrF_3 to BrF_5, and SF_4 to SF_6. Similar products are obtained from HCl, HBr and H_2S, e.g.:

$$H_2S + 4O_2F_2 \longrightarrow SF_6 + 2HF + 4O_2$$

Interest in the production of high-energy oxidizers for use in rocket motors has stimulated the study of peroxo compounds bound to highly electronegative groups during the past few decades. Although such applications have not yet materialized, numerous new compounds of this type

Table 14.13 Properties of some fluorinated peroxides

Compound	MP/°C	BP/°C	Compound	MP/°C	BP/°C
FO_2SOOSO_2F	−55.4	67.1	F_3COONO_2	—	0.7
FO_2SOOF	—	0	$F_3COOP(O)F_2$	−88.6	15.5
FO_2SOOSF_5	—	54.1	F_3COOCl	−132	−22
F_5SOOSF_5	−95.4	49.4	$(F_3C)_3COOC(CF_3)_3$	12	98.6
F_5SOOCF_3	−136	7.7	$F_3COOOCF_3$	−138	−16

have been synthesized and characterized, e.g.:

$$2SO_3 + F_2 \xrightarrow[90\% \text{ yield}]{160°/AgF_2 \text{ catalyst}} FO_2SOOSO_2F$$

$$2SF_5Cl + O_2 \xrightarrow{h\nu} F_5SOOSF_5 + Cl_2$$

$$2COF_2 + OF_2 \xrightarrow{CsF} F_3COOOCF_3$$

Such compounds are volatile liquids or gases (Table 14.13) and their extensive reaction chemistry has been very fully reviewed.[124]

14.2.5 Oxides

Various methods of classification

Oxides are known for all elements of the periodic table except the lighter noble gases and, indeed, most elements form more than one binary compound with oxygen. Their properties span the full range of volatility from difficultly condensible gases such as CO (bp −191.5°C) to refractory oxides such as ZrO_2 (mp 3265°C, bp ~4850°C). Likewise, their electrical properties vary from being excellent insulators (e.g. MgO), through semi-conductors (e.g. NiO), to good metallic conductors (e.g. ReO_3). They may be precisely stoichiometric or show stoichiometric variability over a narrow or a wide range of composition. They may be thermodynamically stable or unstable with respect to their elements, thermally stable or unstable, highly reactive to common reagents or almost completely inert even at very high temperatures. With such a vast array

of compounds and such a broad spectrum of properties any classification of oxides is likely to be either too simplified to be reliable or too complicated to be useful. One classification that is both convenient and helpful at an elementary level stresses the acid–base properties of oxides; this can be complemented and supplemented by classifications which stress the structural relationships between oxides. General classifications based on redox properties or on presumed bonding models have proved to be less helpful, though they are sometimes of use when a more restricted group of compounds is being considered.

The acid–base classification[125] turns essentially on the thermodynamic properties of hydroxides in aqueous solution, since oxides themselves are not soluble as such (p. 630). Oxides may be:

acidic: e.g. most oxides of non-metallic elements (CO_2, NO_2, P_4O_{10}, SO_3, etc.);
basic: e.g. oxides of electropositive elements (Na_2O, CaO, Tl_2O, La_2O_3, etc.);
amphoteric: oxides of less electropositive elements (BeO, Al_2O_3, Bi_2O_3, ZnO, etc.);
neutral: oxides that do not interact with water or aqueous acids or bases (CO, NO, etc.).

Periodic trends in these properties are well documented (p. 27). Thus, in a given period, oxides progress from strongly basic, through weakly basic, amphoteric, and weakly acidic, to strongly acidic (e.g. Na_2O, MgO, Al_2O_3, SiO_2, P_4O_{10}, SO_3, ClO_2). Acidity also increases with increasing oxidation state (e.g. MnO < Mn_2O_3 < MnO_2 < Mn_2O_7). A similar trend is

[124] R. A. DE MARCO and J. M. SHREEVE, *Adv. Inorg. Chem. Radiochem.*, **16**, 109–76 (1974); J. M. SHREEVE, *Endeavour* xxxv, No. 125, 79–82 (1976).

[125] C. S. G. PHILLIPS and R. J. P. WILLIAMS, *Inorganic Chemistry*, Vol. 1, Oxford University Press, Oxford, 1965; Section 14.1, see also pp. 722–9 of ref. 122.

the decrease in basicity of the lanthanide oxides with increase in atomic number from La to Lu. In the main groups, basicity of the oxides increases with increase in atomic number down a group (e.g. $BeO < MgO < CaO < SrO < BaO$), though the reverse tends to occur in the later transition element groups. Acid–base interactions can also be used to classify reaction types of (a) oxides with each other (eg. CaO with SiO_2), (b) oxides with oxysalts (eg. CaO with $CaSiO_3$), and (c) oxysalts with each other (eg. Ca_2SiO_4 and $Ca_3(PO_4)_2$), and to predict the products of such reactions.[126]

The thermodynamic and other physical properties of binary oxides (e.g. ΔH_f°, ΔG_f°, mp, etc.) show characteristic trends and variations when plotted as a function of atomic number, and the preparation of such plots using readily available compilations of data[127] can be a revealing and rewarding exercise.[128]

Structural classifications of oxides recognize discrete molecular species and structures which are polymeric in one or more dimensions leading to chains, layers, and ultimately, to three-dimensional networks. Some typical examples are in Table 14.14; structural details are given elsewhere under each individual element. The type of structure adopted in any particular case depends (obviously) not only on the

Table 14.14　Structure types for binary oxides in the solid state

Structure type	Examples
Molecular structures	CO, CO_2, OsO_4, Tc_2O_7, Sb_2O_6, P_4O_{10}
Chain structures	HgO, SeO_2, CrO_3, Sb_2O_3
Layer structures	SnO, MoO_3, As_2O_3, Re_2O_7
Three-dimensional structures	See text

[126] L. S. DENT-GLASSER and J. A. DUFFR, *J. Chem. Soc., Dalton Trans.*, 2323–8 (1987).

[127] M. C. BALL and A. H. NORBURY, *Physical Data for Inorganic Chemists*, Longmans, London, 1974, 175 pp. G. H. AYLWARD and T. J. V. FINDLAY, *SI Chemical Data*, 2nd edn., Wiley, Sydney, 1975, 136 pp.

[128] R. V. PARISH, *The Metallic Elements*, Longmans, London 1977, 254 pp. (see particularly pp. 25–8, 40–44, 66–74, 128–33, 148–50, 168–77, 188–98.

stoichiometry but also on the relative sizes of the atoms involved and the propensity to form p_π double bonds to oxygen. In structures which are conventionally described as "ionic", the 6-coordinate radius of O^{2-} (140 pm) is larger than all 6-coordinate cation radii except for Rb^I, Cs^I, Fr^I, Ra^{II}, and Tl^I though it is approached by K^I (138 pm) and Ba^{II} (135 pm).[129] Accordingly, many oxides are found to adopt structures in which there is a close-packed oxygen lattice with cations in the interstices (frequently octahedral). For "cations", which have very small effective ionic radii (say < 50 pm), particularly if they carry a high formal charge, the structure type and bonding are usually better described in covalent terms, particularly when π interactions enhance the stability of terminal M=O bonds (M = C, N, P^V, S^{VI}, etc.). Thus, for oxides of formula MO, a coordination number of 1 (molecular) is found for CO and NO, though the latter tends towards a coordination number of 2 (dimers, p. 446). With the somewhat larger Be^{II} and Zn^{II} the wurtzite (4:4) structure is adopted, whereas monoxides of still larger divalent cations tend to adopt the sodium chloride (6:6) structure (e.g. M^{II} = Mg, Ca, Sr, Ba, Co, Ni, Cd, Eu, etc.).

A similar trend is observed for oxides of $M^{IV}O_2$ in Group 14 of the periodic table. The small C atom, with its propensity to form p_π–p_π bonds to oxygen, adopts a linear, molecular structure O=C=O. Silicon, being somewhat larger and less prone to double bonding (p. 361), is surrounded by 4 essentially single-bonded O in most forms of SiO_2 (p. 342) and the coordination geometry is thus 4:2. Similarly, GeO_2 adopts the quartz structure; in addition a rutile form (p. 961) is known in which the coordination is 6:3. SnO_2 and PbO_2 also have rutile structures as has TiO_2, but the largest Group 4 cations Zr and Hf adopt the fluorite (8:4) structure (p. 118) in their dioxides. Other large cations with a fluorite structure for MO_2 are Po; Ce, Pr, Tb; Th, U, Np, Pu, Am and Cm. Conversely, the antifluorite structure is found for

[129] R. D. SHANNON, *Acta Cryst.* **A32**, 751–67 (1976).

the alkali metal monoxides M_2O (p. 84). Such simple ideas are capable of considerable further elaboration.[130]

Nonstoichiometry

Transition elements, for which variable valency is energetically feasible, frequently show non-stoichiometric behaviour (variable composition) in their oxides, sulfides and related binary compounds. For small deviations from stoichiometry a thermodynamic approach is instructive, but for larger deviations structural considerations supervene, and the possibility of thermodynamically unstable but kinetically isolable phases must be considered. These ideas will be expanded in the following paragraphs but more detailed treatment must be sought elsewhere.[131-134]

Any crystal in contact with the vapour of one of its constituents is potentially a nonstoichiometric compound since, for true thermodynamic equilibrium, the composition of the solid phase must depend on the concentration (pressure) of this constituent in the vapour phase. If the solid and vapour are in equilibrium with each other ($\Delta G = 0$) at a given temperature and pressure, then a change in this pressure will lead to a change (however minute) in the composition of the solid, provided that the activation energy for the reaction is not too high at the temperature being used. Such deviations from ideal stoichiometry imply a change in valency of at least some of the ions in the crystal and

are readily detected for many oxides using a range of techniques such as pressure-composition isotherms, X-ray diffraction, neutron diffraction, electrical conductivity (semi-conductivity), visible and ultraviolet absorption spectroscopy (colour centres)[131] and Mössbauer (γ-ray resonance) spectroscopy.[135]

If the pressure of O_2 above a crystalline oxide is increased, the oxide-ion activity in the solid can be increased by placing the supernumerary O^{2-} ions in the interstitial positions, e.g.:

$$UO_2 + \frac{x}{2}O_2 \xrightarrow{1150°C} UO_{2+x} \quad 0 < x < 0.25$$

The electrons required to reduce $\frac{1}{2}O_2$ to O^{2-} come from individual cations which are thereby oxidized to a higher oxidation state. Alternatively, if suitable interstitial sites are not available, the excess O^{2-} ions can build on to normal lattice sites thereby creating cation vacancies which diffuse into the crystal, e.g.:

$$\left(1 - \frac{x}{2}\right)Cu_2O + \frac{x}{4}O_2 \longrightarrow Cu_{2-x}O$$

In this case the requisite electrons are provided by $2Cu^I$ becoming oxidized to $2Cu^{II}$.

Conversely, if the pressure of O_2 above a crystalline oxide is decreased below the equilibrium value appropriate for the stoichiometric composition, oxygen "boils out" of the lattice leaving supernumerary metal atoms or lower-valent ions in interstitial positions, e.g.:

$$(1 + x)ZnO \longrightarrow Zn_{1+x}O + \frac{x}{2}O_2$$

The absorption spectrum of this nonstoichiometric phase forms the basis for the formerly much-used qualitative test for zinc oxide: "yellow when hot, white when cold". Alternatively, anion sites can be left vacant, e.g.:

$$TiO \longrightarrow TiO_{1-x} + \frac{x}{2}O_2$$

In both cases the average oxidation state of the metal is reduced. It is important to appreciate that,

[130] A. F. WELLS, *Structural Inorganic Chemistry*, 5th edn., Oxford University Press, Oxford, 1984; Chap. 12, Binary metal oxides, pp. 531-74; Chap. 13, Complex oxides, pp. 575-625.

[131] N. N. GREENWOOD, *Ionic Crystals, Lattice Defects, and Nonstoichiometry*, Chaps. 6 and 7, pp. 111-81, Butterworths, London, 1968.

[132] D. J. M. BEVAN, Chap. 49 in J. C. BAILAR, H. J. EMELÉUS, R. S. NYHOLM and A. F. TROTMAN-DICKENSON (eds.), *Comprehensive Inorganic Chemistry*, Vol. 4, pp. 453-40, Pergamon Press, Oxford, 1973.

[133] T. SØRENSEN, *Nonstoichiometric Oxides*, Academic Press, New York, 1981, 441 pp.

[134] S. TRASATTI, *Electrodes of Conductive Metallic Oxides*, Elsevier, Amsterdam, Part A, 1980, 366 pp.; Part B, 1981, 336 pp.

[135] N. N. GREENWOOD and T. C. GIBB, *Mössbauer Spectroscopy*, Chapman & Hall, London, 1971, 659 pp.

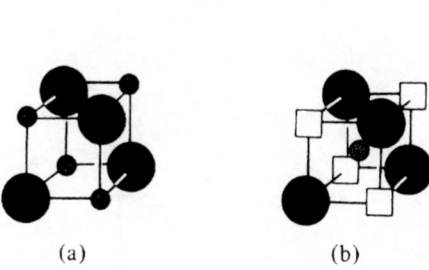

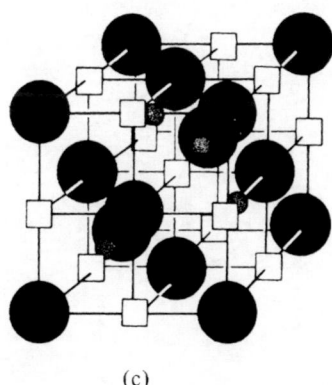

(a)   (b)

(c)

Figure 14.19   Schematic representation of defect clusters in $Fe_{1-x}O$. The normal NaCl-type structure (a) has Fe^{II} (small open circles) and O^{-II} (large dark circles) at alternate corners of the cube. In the 4:1 cluster (b), four octahedral Fe^{II} sites are left vacant and an Fe^{III} ion (grey) occupies the cube centre, thus being tetrahedrally coordinated by the $4O^{-II}$. In (c) a more extended 13:4 cluster is shown in which, again, all anion sites are occupied but the 13 octahedral Fe^{II} sites are vacant and four Fe^{III} occupy a tetrahedral array of cube centres.

in all such examples, the resulting nonstoichiometric compound is a homogeneous phase which is thermodynamically stable under the prevailing ambient conditions.

Sometimes the lattice defects form clusters amongst themselves rather than being randomly distributed throughout the lattice. A classic example is "ferrous oxide", which is unstable as FeO at room temperature but exists as $Fe_{1-x}O$ ($0.05 < x < 0.12$): the NaCl-type lattice has a substantial number of vacant Fe^{II} sites and these tend to cluster so that Fe^{III} can occupy tetrahedral sites within the lattice as shown schematically in Fig. 14.19. Such clustering can sometimes nucleate a new phase in which "vacant sites" are eliminated by being ordered in a new structure type. For example, PrO_{2-x} forms a disordered nonstoichiometric phase ($0 < x < 0.25$) at 1000°C but at lower temperatures (400–700°C) this is replaced by a succession of intermediate phases with only very narrow (and non-overlapping) composition ranges of general formula Pr_nO_{2n-2} with $n = 4, 7, 9, 10, 11, 12$ and ∞ as shown in Fig. 14.20 and Table 14.15. There is now compelling evidence that oxide-ion vacancies, $\square$, in these and other such fluorite-related lattices do not exist in

isolation but occur as octahedral 'coordination defects' of composition $\{M_2^{III}M_{1.5}^{IV}\square O_6\}$. The structure-forming topology of these coordination defects and their role in generating more extensive defects has recently been brilliantly expounded.[136]

Table 14.15   Intermediate phases formed by ordering of defects in the praseodymium–oxygen system

n	Formula Pr_nO_{2n-2}	y in PrO_y	Nonstoichiometric limits of x at T°C	T°C
4	Pr_2O_3	1.500	1.500–1.503	1000
7	Pr_7O_{12}	1.714	1.713–1.719	700
9	Pr_9O_{16}	1.778	1.776–1.778	500
10	Pr_5O_9	1.800	1.799–1.801	450
11	$Pr_{11}O_{20}$	1.818	1.817–1.820	430
12	Pr_6O_{11}	1.833	1.831–1.836	400
∞	PrO_2	2.000	1.999–2.000	400
			1.75 –2.00	1000

Oxygen (oxide ions) in crystal lattices can be progressively removed by systematically

---

[136] B. F. Hoskins and R. L. Martin, *Aust. J. Chem.* **48**, 709–39 (1995). R. L. Martin, *J. Chem. Soc., Dalton Trans.*, 3659–70 (1997).

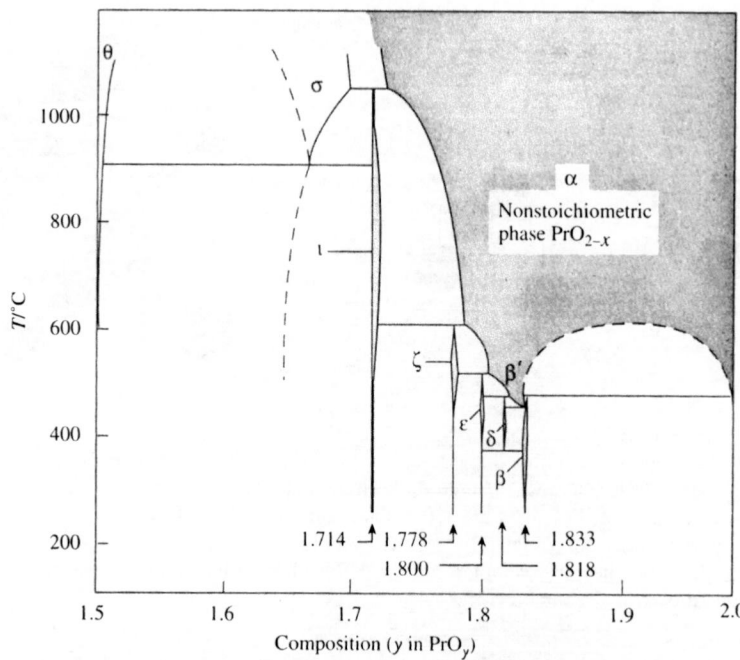

Figure 14.20 Part of the Pr–O phase diagram showing the extended nonstoichiometric α phase PrO_{2-x} at high temperatures (shaded) and the succession of phases Pr_nO_{2n-2} at lower temperatures.

replacing corner-shared $\{MO_6\}$ octahedra with edge-shared octahedra. The geometrical principles involved in the conceptual generation of such successions of phases (chemical-shear structures) are now well understood, but many mechanistic details of their formation remain unresolved. Typical examples are the rutile series Ti_nO_{2n-1} ($n = 4, 5, 6, 7, 8, 9, 10, \infty$) between $TiO_{1.75}$ and TiO_2 and the ReO_3 series M_nO_{3n-1} which leads to a succession of 6 phases with $n = 8, 9, 10, 11, 12$ and 14 in the narrow composition range $MO_{2.875}$ to $MO_{2.929}$ (M = Mo or W).

Nonstoichiometric oxide phases are of great importance in semiconductor devices, in heterogeneous catalysis and in understanding photoelectric, thermoelectric, magnetic and diffusional properties of solids. They have been used in thermistors, photoelectric cells, rectifiers, transistors, phosphors, luminescent materials and computer components (ferrites, etc.). They are crucially implicated in reactions at electrode surfaces, the performance of batteries, the tarnishing and corrosion of metals, and many other reactions of significance in catalysis.[131–134]

15

Sulfur

15.1 The Element

15.1.1 Introduction

Sulfur occurs uncombined in many parts of the world and has therefore been known since pre-historic times. Indeed, sulfur and carbon were the only two non-metallic elements known to the ancients. References to sulfur occur throughout recorded history from the legendary destruction of Sodom and Gomorrah by brimstone[1] to its recent discovery (together with H_2SO_4) as a major component in the atmosphere of the planet Venus. The element was certainly known to the Egyptians as far back as the sixteenth century BC and Homer refers to its use as a fumigant.[2] Pliny the Elder[3] mentioned the occurrence of sulfur in volcanic islands and other Mediterranean locations, spoke of its use in religious ceremonies and in the fumigation of houses, described its use by fullers, cotton-bleachers, and match-makers, and indicated fourteen supposed medicinal virtues of the element.

Gunpowder, which revolutionized military tactics in the thirteenth century, was the sole known propellant for ammunition until the mid-nineteenth century when smokeless powders based on guncotton (1846), nitroglycerine (1846), and cordite (1889) were discovered. Gunpowder, an intimate mixture of saltpeter (KNO_3), powdered charcoal and sulfur in the approximate ratios 75:15:10 by weight, was discovered by Chinese alchemists more than 1000 years ago:[4] The earliest known recipe for explosive gunpowder (as distinct from incendiary mixtures and fireworks) appeared in a Chinese military manual of AD 1044 and its use in a gun (bombard) dates from at least as early as 1128. Arab and European formulae and technology were derived from this. The first use of gunpowder

---

[1] Genesis *19*, 24: "Then the Lord rained upon Sodom and Gomorrah brimstone and fire from the Lord out of heaven." Other biblical references to brimstone are in Deuteronomy *29*, 23; Job *18*, 15; Psalm *11*, 6; Isaiah *30*, 33; Ezekiel *38*, 22; Revelation *19*, 20; etc.

[2] HOMER, *Odyssey*, Book 22, 481: "Bring me sulfur, old nurse, that cleanses all pollution and bring me fire, that I may purify the house with sulfur."

[3] G. PLINY (the Elder), AD 23–79, mentions sulfur in several of the many books of his posthumously published major work, *Naturalis Historia*.

[4] A. R. BUTLER, *Chem. in Britain*, 1119–21 (1988); and research by Joseph Needham, Cambridge, UK.

Developments in the Chemistry of Sulfur

Prehistory	Sulfur (brimstone) mentioned frequently in the Bible.[1]
~800 BC	Fumigating power of burning S mentioned by Homer.[2]
~ AD 79	Occurrence and many uses of S recorded by G. Pliny.[3]
AD 940	Sulfuric acid mentioned by Persian writer Abu Bekr al Rases.
1044	Earliest known (Chinese) recipe for explosive gunpowder.[4]
1128	Gunpowder used by Chinese military in a bombard.
~1245	Gunpowder "discovered" independently in Europe by Roger Bacon (England) and Berthold Swartz.
1661	Effects of SO_2 pollution in London dramatically described to Charles II by John Evelyn (p. 698).
1746	Lead chamber process for H_2SO_4 introduced by John Roebuck (Birmingham, UK); this immediately superseded the cumbersome small-scale glass bell-jar process (p. 708).
1777	Elemental character of S proposed by A.-L. Lavoisier though even in 1809 experiments (presumably on impure samples) led Humphry Davy to contend that oxygen and hydrogen were also essential constituents of S.
1781	Sulfur compounds first detected in plants by N. Deyeux (roots of the dock, horse-radish, and cochlearia).
1809	Sulfur firmly established as an element by J. L. Gay Lussac and L. J. Thenard.
1813	Sulfur detected in the bile and blood of animals by H. A. Vogel.
1822	Xanthates (e.g. EtOCSSK) discovered by W. C. Zeise who also prepared the first mercaptan (EtSH) in 1834 (see also p. 930).
1831	Contact process for SO_3/H_2SO_4 patented by P. Philips of Bristol, UK (the original platinum catalyst was subsequently replaced by ones based on V_2O_5).
1835	S_4N_4 first made by M. Gregory (S_2Cl_2 + NH_3); X-ray structure by M. J. Bueger, 1936.
1839	Vulcanization of natural rubber latex by heating it with S discovered by Charles Goodyear (USA).
1865	Prospectors boring for petroleum in Louisiana discovered a great S deposit beneath a 150-m thick layer of quicksand.
1891–4	H. Frasch developed commercial recovery of S by superheated water process.
1912	E. Beckmann showed that rhombohedral sulfur was S_8 by cryoscopy in molten iodine.
1923	V. B. Goldschmid's geochemical classification includes "chalcophiles" (p. 648).
1926	Isotopes ^{33}S and ^{34}S discovered by F. W. Aston who previously (1920) had only detected ^{32}S in his mass spectrometer.
1935	Molecular structure of *cyclo*-S_8 established by X-ray methods (B. E. Warren and J. T. Burwell).
1944	Sulfur first produced from sour natural gas; by 1971 this source, together with crude oil, accounted for nearly one-third of world production.
1950	SF_4 first isolated by G. A. Silvery and G. H. Cady.
1951	Sulfur nmr signals (from ^{33}S) first detected by S. S. Dharmatti and H. E. Weaver.
1972	Sulfur and H_2SO_4 detected in the atmosphere of the planet Venus by USSR Venera 8 (subsequently confirmed in 1978 by US Venus Pioneer 2).
1973	S_{18} and S_{20} synthesized and characterized by M. Schmidt, A. Kutoglu, and their coworkers.
1975	The metallic and superconducting properties of polymeric $(SN)_x$ discovered independently by two groups in the USA (p. 727).

in a major compaign in the West was at the Battle of Crécy (26 August 1346), but the guns lacked all power of manoeuvre and the devastating victory of Edward III was due chiefly to the long-bow men whom the French were also encountering for the first time. By 1415, however, gunpowder was decisive in Henry V's siege of Harfleur, and its increasing use in mobile field guns, naval artillery, and hand-held firearms was a dominant feature of world history for the next 500 y. Parallel with these activities, but largely independent of them, was the European development of the alchemy and chemistry of sulfur, and the growth of the emerging chemical industry based on sulfuric acid (p. 708). Some of the key points in this story are summarized in the Panel and a fuller treatment can be found in standard references.[5−8]

[5] J. W. MELLOR, *A Comprehensive Treatise on Inorganic and Theoretical Chemistry*, Vol. 10, Chap. 57, pp. 1–692, Longmans, Green, London, 1930.

[6] *Gmelins Handbuch der Anorganischen Chemie*, System Number 9A *Schwefel*, pp. 1–60, Verlag Chemie, Weinheim/Bergstrasse, 1953.

[7] M. E. WEEKS, *Discovery of the Elements*, Sulfur, pp. 52–73, Journal of Chemical Education, Easton, 1956.

[8] T. K. DERRY and T. I. WILLIAMS, *A Short History of Technology*, Oxford University Press, Oxford, 1960 (consult index).

15.1.2 Abundance and distribution

Sulfur occurs, mainly in combined form, to the extent of about 340 ppm in the crustal rocks of the earth. It is the sixteenth element in order or abundance, closely following barium (390 ppm) and strontium (384 ppm), and being about twice as abundant as the next element carbon (180 ppm). Earlier estimates placed its global abundance in the range 300–1000 ppm. Sulfur is widely distributed in nature but only rarely is it sufficiently concentrated to justify economic mining. Its ubiquity is probably related to its occurrence in nature in both inorganic and organic compounds, and to the fact that it can occur in at least five oxidation states: -2 (sulfides, H_2S and organosulfur compounds), -1 (disulfides, S_2^{2-}), 0 (elemental S), $+4$ (SO_2) and $+6$ (sulfates). The three most important commercial sources are:

(1) elemental sulfur in the caprock salt domes in the USA and Mexico, and the sedimentary evaporite deposits in south-eastern Poland;

(2) H_2S in natural gas and crude oil, and organosulfur compounds in tar sands, oil shales and coal (the latter two also contain pyrites inclusions);

(3) pyrites (FeS_2) and other metal-sulfide minerals.

Volcanic sources of the free element are also widespread; they have been of great economic importance until this century but are now little used. They occur throughout the mountain ranges bordering the Pacific Ocean, and also in Iceland and the Mediterranean region, notably in Turkey, Italy and formerly also in Sicily and Spain.

Elemental sulfur in the caprock of salt domes was almost certainly produced by the anaerobic bacterial reduction of sedimentary sulfate deposits (mainly anhydrite or gypsum, p. 648). The strata are also associated with hydrocarbons; these are consumed as a source of energy by the anaerobic bacteria, which use sulfur instead of O_2 as a hydrogen acceptor to produce $CaCO_3$, H_2O and H_2S. The H_2S

may then be oxidized to colloidal sulfur, or may form calcium hydrosulfide and polysulfide, which reacts with CO_2 generated by the bacteria to precipitate crystalline sulfur and secondary calcite. Alternatively, H_2S may escape from the system and the limestone caprock will then be free of sulfur. Indeed, of over 400 salt-dome structures known to exist in the coastal and offshore area of the Gulf of Mexico, only about 12 contain commercial deposits of sulfur (5 in Louisiana, 5 in Texas and 2 in Mexico). The mining operations are described in the Section 15.1.3.

The great evaporite basin deposits of elemental sulfur in Poland were discovered only in 1953 but have since had a dramatic impact on the economy of that country which, by 1985, was one of the world's leading producers (p. 649). The sulfur occurs in association with secondary limestone, gypsum and anhydrite, and is believed to be derived from hydrocarbon reduction of sulfates assisted by bacterial action. The H_2S so formed is consumed by other bacteria to produce sulfur as waste — this accumulates in the bodies of the bacteria until death, when the sulfur remains.

The next great natural occurrence of sulfur is as H_2S in sour natural gas and as organosulfur compounds in crude oil. Again, distribution is widespread. Although commercial production of elemental sulfur from such sources was first effected only in 1944 (in the USA) it now represents a major source of the element in the USA, Canada and France, and this growth has been one of the most significant trends in world sulfur production during the past few decades. Sulfur, of course, also occurs in many plant and animal proteins, and three of the principal amino-acid residues contain sulfur: cysteine, $\mathbf{HS}CH_2CH(NH_2)CO_2H$; cystine $\{-\mathbf{S}CH_2CH(NH_2)CO_2H\}_2$; and methionine, $\mathbf{MeS}CH_2CH_2CH(NH_2)CO_2H$.

Oil shales represent a further source of sulfur though here (unlike the tar sands which yield crude oil and H_2S) the sulfur is predominantly in the form of pyrites. US oil shales contain about 0.7% S of which about 80% is pyritic; other major reserves are in Brazil, the former USSR, China and Africa, though these do not at present seem to be used as an industrial source of sulfur. Coal also contains about 1–2% S and is thus as huge a potential source of the element as it is an actual present source of air pollution (p. 698). From over 3×10^9 tonnes of coal mined annually, only some 500 000 tonnes of sulfur are recovered (as H_2SO_4) from a potential 50 million tonnes.

The third great source of sulfur and its compounds is from the mineral sulfides. V. M. Goldschmid's geochemical classification of the elements (1923), which has formed the basis of all subsequent developments in the field, proposed four main groups of elements: chalcophile, siderophile, lithophile and atmophile.[9] Of these the chalcophiles (Greek χαλκος, *chalcos*, copper; φιλος, *philos*, loving) are associated with copper, specifically as sulfides. Elements which occur mainly as sulfide minerals are predominantly from Groups 11–16 of the periodic table (together with iron, molybdenum and, to a lesser extent, some of the platinum metals as shown in Fig. 15.1. Some

examples of the more important sulfide minerals are listed in Table 15.1, and a further discussion of the structural chemistry and reactivity of metal sulfides is on p. 676. Pyrites (fool's gold, FeS_2) is one of the most abundant of all sulfur minerals and is a major source of the element (see above). It often occurs in massive lenses but may also appear in veins or in disseminated zones. The largest commercial deposits extend from Seville (Spain) westward into Portugal and, at the Rio Tinto mines in Huelva Province, one of the lenses is 1.5 km long and 240 m wide with a sulfur content of 48% (pure FeS_2 has 53.4% S). Other major deposits are in the former USSR, Japan, Italy, Cyprus and Scandinavia. The most important non-ferrous metal sulfides are those of Cu, Ni, Zn, Pb and As.

Finally, sulfur occurs in many localities as the sulfates of electropositive elements (see Chapters 4 and 5) and to a lesser extent as sulfates of Al, Fe, Cu and Pb, etc. Gypsum ($CaSO_4.2H_2O$) and anhydrite ($CaSO_4$) are particularly notable but are little used as a source of sulfur because of high capital and operating costs. Similarly, by far the largest untapped source of sulfur is in the oceans as the dissolved sulfates of Mg, Ca and K. It has been estimated that there are some 1.5×10^9 cubic km of water in the oceans of the world and that 1 cubic km of sea-water contains approximately 1 million tonnes of sulfur combined as sulfate.

---

[9] R. W. FAIRBRIDGE, *Encyclopedia of Geochemistry and Environmental Sciences*, Van Nostrand, New York, 1972. See sections on Geochemical Classification of the Elements; Sulfates; Sulfate Reduction–Microbial; Sulfides; Sulfosalts; Sulfur; Sulfur Cycle; Sulfur Isotope Fractionation in Biological Processes, etc., pp. 1123–58.

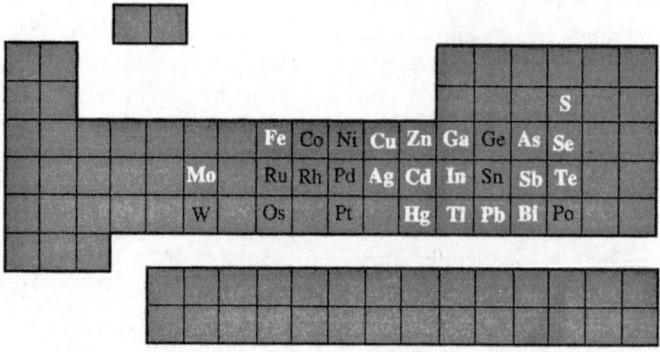

Figure 15.1 Position of the chalcophilic elements in the periodic table: these elements (particularly those in white) tend to occur in nature as sulfide minerals; the tendency is much less pronounced for the elements in normal black type.

Table 15.1 Some sulfide minerals (those in bold are the more prevalent or important)

Name	Idealized formula	Name	Idealized formula
Molybdenite	MoS_2	**Galena** (Pb glance)	**PbS**
Tungstenite	WS_2	**Realgar**	As_4S_4
Alabandite	MnS	**Orpiment**	As_2S_3
Pyrite (fool's gold)	FeS_2	Dimorphite	As_4S_3
Marcasite	FeS_2	**Stibnite**	Sb_2S_3
Pyrrhotite	$Fe_{1-x}S$	Bismuthinite	Bi_2S_3
Laurite	RuS_2	Pentlandite	$(Fe,Ni)_9S_8$
Linnaeite	Co_3S_4	**Chalcopyrite**	$CuFeS_2$
Millerite	NiS	**Bornite**	Cu_5FeS_4
Cooperite	PtS	**Arsenopyrite**	**FeAsS**
Chalcocite (Cu glance)	Cu_2S	Cobaltite	CoAsS
Argentite (Ag glance)	Ag_2S	Enargite	Cu_3AsS_4
Sphalerite (Zn blende)	**ZnS**	Bournoite	$CuPbSbS_3$
Wurtzite	ZnS	Proustite	Ag_3AsS_3
Greenockite	CdS	Pyrargyrite	Ag_3SbS_3
Cinnabar (vermillion)	**HgS**	**Tetrahedrite**[a]	$Cu_{12}As_4S_{13}$[a]

[a]There is a second series in which As is replaced by Sb; in both series Cu is often substituted in part by Fe, Ag, Zn, Hg or Pb.

The gloabal geochemical sulfur cycle has been extensively studied in recent years for both commercial and environmental reasons.[10-17]

15.1.3 Production and uses of elemental sulfur

Sulfur is produced commercially from one or more sources in over seventy countries of

Table 15.2 Main producers of sulfur in 1985 (in megatonnes)[18]

World	USA	USSR	Canada	Poland	China	Japan	Others
54.0	11.4	9.7	6.7	5.1	2.9	2.5	15.7

the world, and production of all forms in 1985 amounted to 54.0 million tonnes. The main producers are shown in Table 15.2. Until the beginning of this century, sulfur was obtained mainly by mining volcanic deposits of the element, but this now accounts for less than 5% of the total. During the first half of this century the prime method of production was the process developed by H. Frasch in 1891–4. This involves forcing superheated water into submerged sulfur-bearing strata and then forcing the molten element to the surface by compressed air (see Panel). This is the method used to obtain sulfur from the caprock of salt domes in the

10 M. V. IVANOV and J. R. FRENET (eds.), *The Global Biogeochemical Sulfur Cycle*, SCOPE Report 19, Wiley, Chichester, 1983, 495 pp.

11 A. MÜLLER and B. KREBS (eds.), *Sulfur: Its Significance for Chemistry, for the Geo-, Bio-, and Cosmo-sphere and Technology*, Elsevier, Amsterdam, 1984, 512 pp.

12 P. BRIMBLECOMBE and A. Y. LEIN (eds.), *Evolution of the Global Biogeochemical Sulfur Cycle*, SCOPE Report 39, Wiley, Chichester, 1989, 276 pp.

13 E. S. SALZMAN and W. J. COOPER (eds.), *Biogenic Sulfur in the Environment*, ACS Symposium Series No. 393, Amer. Chem. Soc., Washington, DC, 1989, 584 pp.

14 W. L. ORR and C. M. WHITE (eds.), *Geochemistry of Sulfur in Fossil Fuels*, ACS Symposium Series, No. 429, Amer. Chem. Soc., Washington, DC, 1990, 720 pp.

15 H. R. KROUSE and V. A. GRINENKO (eds.), *Stable Isotopes; Natural and Anthropogenic Sulfur in the Environment*, SCOPE Report 43, Wiley, Chichester, 1991, 466 pp.

16 R. W. HOWARTH, J. W. B. STEWART and M. V. IVANOV (eds.), *Sulfur Cycling on the Continents*, SCOPE Report 48, Wiley, Chichester, 1992, 372 pp.

17 D. A. DUNNETTE and R. J. O'BRIEN (eds.), *The Science of Global Change: The Impact of Human Activities on the Environment*, ACS Symposium Series No. 483, Amer. Chem. Soc., Washington, DC, 1992, 498 pp.

18 W. BÜCHNER, R. SCHLIEBS, G. WINTER and K. H. BÜCHEL, (transl. by D. R. TERRELL), *Industrial Inorganic Chemistry*, VCH, Weinheim, 1989, pp. 105–8.

The Frasch Process for Mining Elemental Sulfur[19]

The ingenious process of melting subterranean sulfur with superheated water and forcing it to the surface with compressed air was devised and perfected by Herman Frasch in the period 1891–4. Originally designed to overcome the problems of recovering sulfur from the caprock of salt domes far below the swamps and quicksands of Louisiana, the method is now also extensively used elsewhere to extract native sulfur.

The caprock typically occurs some 150–750 m beneath the surface and the sulfur-bearing zone is typically about 30 m thick and contains 20–40% S. Using oil-well drilling techniques a cased 200 mm (8-inch) pipe is sunk through the caprock to the bottom of the S-bearing layer. Its lower end is perforated with small holes. Inside this pipe a 100 mm (4-inch) pipe is lowered to within a short distance of the bottom and, finally, a concentric 25-mm (1-inch) compressed-air pipe is lowered to a point rather more than half-way down to the bottom of the well as shown in Fig. **a**. Superheated water at 165°C is forced down the two outer pipes and melts the surrounding sulfur (mp 119°C). As liquid sulfur is about twice as dense as water under these conditions, it flows to the bottom of the well; the pumping of water down the 100-mm pipe is discontinued, but the static pressure of the hot water being pumped down the outer 200-mm pipe forces the liquid sulfur some 100 m up the 100-mm pipe as shown in Fig. **b**. Compressed air is then forced down the central 25-mm pipe to aerate the molten sulfur and carry it to the surface where it emerges from the 100-mm annulus Fig. (**c**). One well can extract sulfur (~35 000 tonnes) from an area of about 2000 m^2 (0.5 acre) and new wells must continually be sunk. Bleed-water wells must also be sunk to remove the excess of water pumped into the strata.

A Frasch mine can produce as much as 2.5 million tonnes of sulfur per annum. Such massive operations clearly require huge quantities of mining water (up to 5 million gallons daily) and abundant power supplies for the drilling, pumping and superheating operations.

The sulfur can be piped long distances in liquid form or transported molten in ships, barges or rail cars. Alternatively it can be prilled or handled as nuggets or chunks. Despite the vast bulk of liquid sulfur mined by the Frasch process it is obtained in very pure form. There is virtually no selenium, tellurium or arsenic impurity, and the product is usually 99.5–99.9% pure.

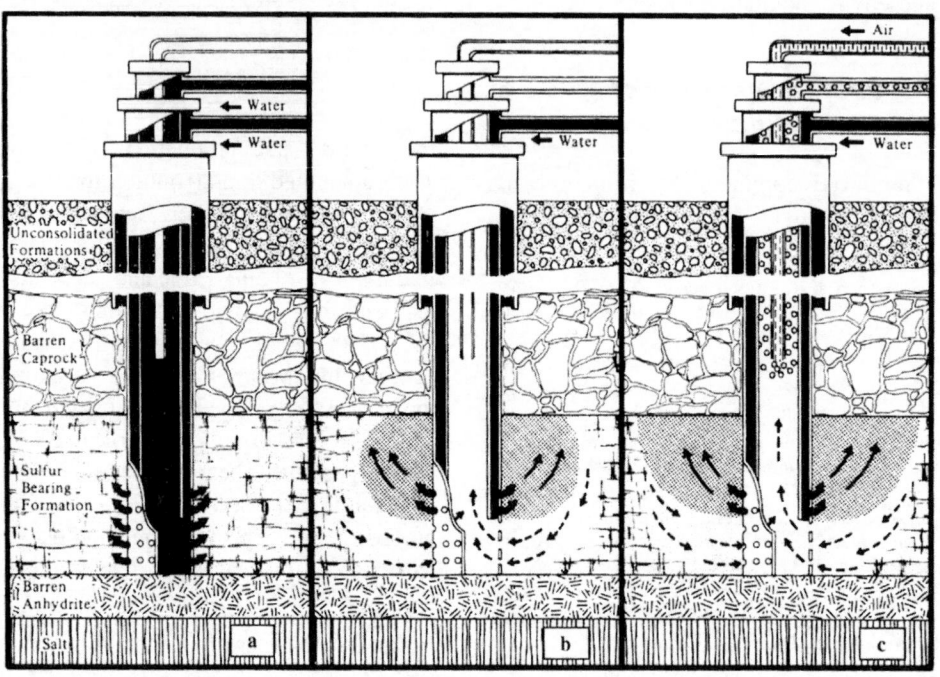

[19] W. HAYNES, *Brimstone: The Stone that Burns*, Van Nostrand, Princeton, 1959, 308 pp. (The story of the Frasch sulfur industry.)

Gulf Coast region of the USA and Mexico, and from the evaporite basin deposits in west Texas, Poland, the former USSR and Iran.

Recovery from sour natural gas and from crude oil was first developed in the USA in 1944, and by 1970 these sources exceeded the total volume of Frasch-mined sulfur for the first time. Canada (Alberta) and France are the principal producers from sour natural gas, which contains 15–20% H_2S. The USA and Japan are the largest producers from petroleum refineries. The phenomenal growth of these sources is clear from the following figures (in 10^6 tonnes): <0.5 (1950); 2.5 (1960); 15 (1972); >25 (1985). Recovery from sour natural gas involves first separating out the H_2S by absorption in mono-ethanolamine and then converting it to sulfur by a process first developed by C. F. Claus in Germany about 1880. In this process one-third of the H_2S is burned to produce SO_2, water vapour, and sulfur vapour; the SO_2 then reacts with the remaining H_2S in the presence of oxide catalysts such as Fe_2O_3 or Al_2O_3 to produce more H_2O and S vapour:

$$H_2S + 1\tfrac{1}{2}O_2 \longrightarrow SO_2 + H_2O$$

$$2H_2S + SO_2 \xrightarrow[\text{catalyst/300}^\circ]{\text{oxide}} \tfrac{3}{8}S_8 + 2H_2O$$

Overall reaction: $3H_2S + 1\tfrac{1}{2}O_2 \longrightarrow \tfrac{3}{8}S_8 + 3H_2O;$

$$-\Delta H = 664 \text{ kJ mol}^{-1}$$

Multiple reactors achieve 95–96% conversion and recovery, and stringent air pollution legislation has now pushed this to 99%. A similar sequence of reactions is used for sulfur production from crude oil except that the organosulfur compounds must first be removed from the refinery feed and converted to H_2S by a hydrogenation process before the sulfur can be recovered.

The third major source of sulfur is pyrite and related sulfide minerals. The ore is roasted to secure SO_2 gas which is then usually used directly for the manufacture of H_2SO_4 (p. 708). Again air pollution by SO_2 gas emissions has been the subject of increasing legislation and control during the past three decades (p. 698).

The proportion of sulfur and S-containing compounds recovered by these various methods has been changing rapidly and frequently depends on the nature of local sources available. The comparative figures for 1985 are: sour natural gas 38%, Frasch S 28%, pyrites 18%, miscellaneous 16% (includes metallurgy, crude oil, coal, gypsum, tar sands and flue gases). Estimated reserves on the basis of present technology and prices are summarized in Table 15.3; these can increase more than tenfold if coal, gypsum, anhydrite and sea-water are included. At present these latter sources are economic only under special conditions though, as we have already seen (p. 648), vast quantities of SO_2 are lost from industrial coal each year. Recovery of useful sulfur compounds from anhydrite (and gypsum) can be achieved by two main routes. The Müller–Kühne process used in the UK and Austria involves the roasting of anhydrite with clay, sand and coke in a rotary kiln at 1200–1400°:

$$2CaSO_4 + C \longrightarrow 2CaO + 2SO_2 + CO_2$$

The emergent SO_2 is then fed into a contact process for H_2SO_4 (p. 708). Alternatively, ammonia and CO_2 can be passed into a gypsum slurry to give ammonium sulfate for use in fertilizers:

$$CaSO_4 + (NH_4)_2CO_3 \rightarrow CaCO_3 + (NH_4)_2SO_4$$

This double decomposition route was developed in Germany and has been used in the UK since 1971.

The pattern of uses of sulfur and its compounds in the chemical industry is illustrated in the

Table 15.3   Estimated world reserves of sulfur

Source	Natural gas	Petroleum	Native ore	Pyrite	Sulfide ore	Dome	**Total**
S/10^6 tonne	690	450	560	380	270	150	**2500**

flow chart below. Most sulfur is converted via SO_2/SO_3 into sulfuric acid which accounts, for example, for some 88% of the contained sulfur used in the USA. The proportion of sulfur used in making the extensive number of end products is shown in Fig. 15.2. Indeed, the uses of sulfur and its principal compounds are so widely spread throughout industry that a nation's consumption of sulfur is often used as a reliable measure of its economic development. Thus, the USA, the former USSR, Japan and Germany lead the world in industrial production and rank similarly in the consumption of sulfur. Further details of industrial uses will be found in subsequent sections dealing with specific compounds of sulfur, and various review books are available.[20-22]

[20] J. R. WEST (ed.), *New Uses of Sulfur*, Advances in Chemistry Series No. 140, Am. Chem. Soc., Washington, DC, 1975, 230 pp.

[21] D. J. BOURNE (ed.), *New Uses of Sulfur — II*, Advances in Chemistry Series No. 165, Am. Chem. Soc., Washington, DC 1978, 282 pp.

[22] U. H. F. SANDER, H. FISCHER, U. ROTHE and R. KOLA, (Engl. edn. prepared by A. I. MORE), *Sulfur, Sulfur Dioxide, Sulfuric Acid: Industrial Chemistry and Technology*, British Sulfur Corporation, London, 1984, 428 pp.

15.1.4 Allotropes of sulfur [23-25]

The allotropy of sulfur is far more extensive and complex than for any other element (except perhaps carbon, after the synthesis of the innumerable fullerene clusters, p. 279). This arises partly because of the great variety of molecular forms that can be achieved by $-S-S-$ catenation and partly because of the numerous ways in which the molecules so formed can be arranged within the crystal. In fact, S–S bonds are very variable and flexible: interatomic distances cover an enormous range, 180–260 pm (depending to some extent on the amount of multiple bonding), whilst bond angles S–S–S vary from 90° to 180° and dihedral angles S–S–S–S from 0° to 180° (Fig. 15.3). Estimated S–S bond energies may be as high as 430 kJ mol^{-1} and the unrestrained $-S-S-$ *single-bond* energy of 265 kJ mol^{-1} is exceeded amongst homonuclear single bonds only by those of H_2 (435 kJ mol^{-1}) and C–C

[23] J. DONOHUE, *The Structures of the Elements*, Sulfur, pp. 324–69, Wiley, New York, 1974.

[24] B. MEYER, *Chem. Revs.* **76**, 367–88, (1976).

[25] M. SCHMIDT, Chap. 1, pp. 1–12, in ref. 21.

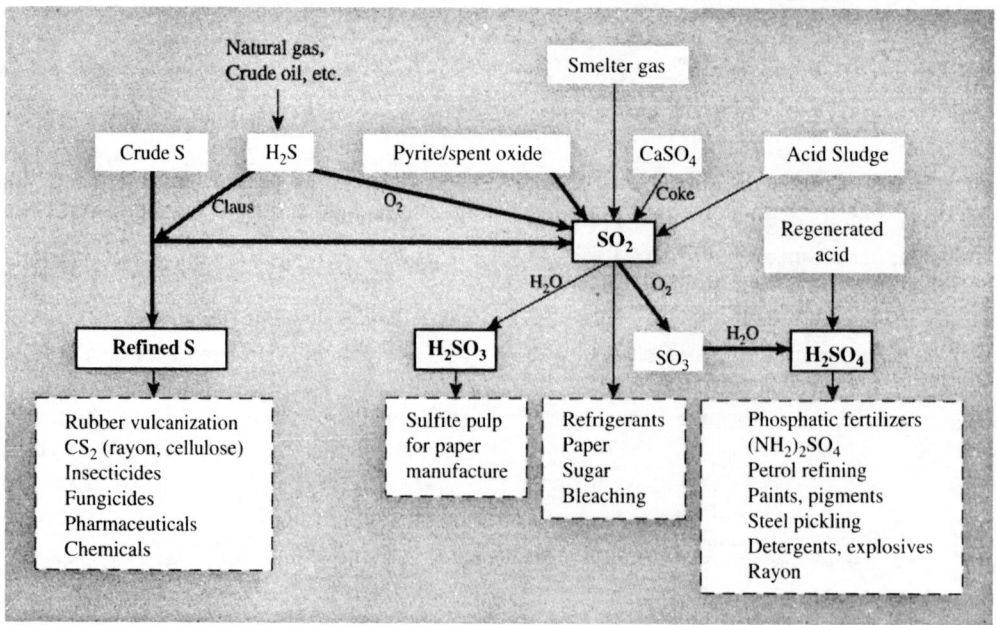

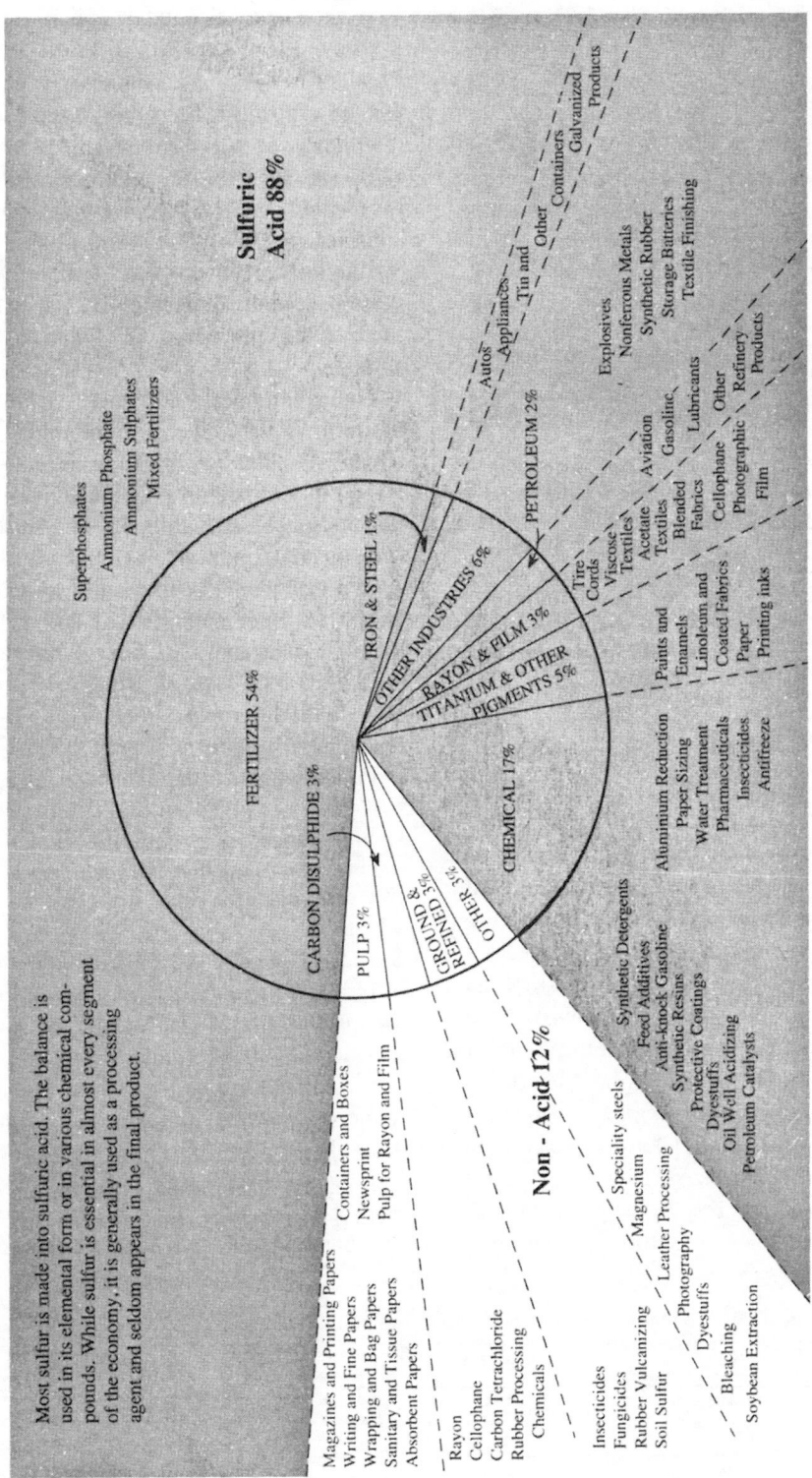

Figure 15.2 Sulfur's uses as acid and as non-acid.

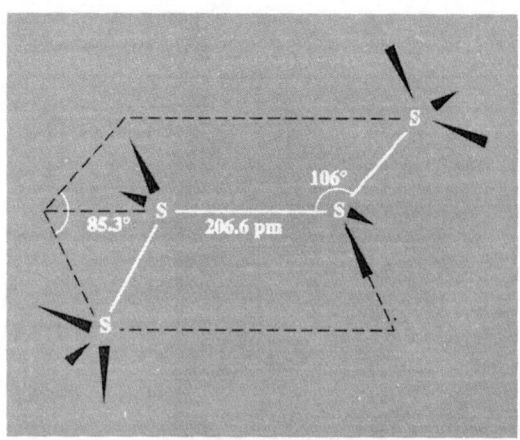

Figure 15.3 Portion of an unrestrained-S_n-chain showing typical values for the S–S–S bond angle (106°) and S–S–S–S dihedral angle (85.3°). Possible alternative orientations of the bonds from the 2 inner S atoms, and possible directions for extensions of the chain from the 2 outer S atoms are indicated by the black lines. (See also p. 656.)

(330 kJ mol^{-1}). Again, the amazing temperature dependence of the properties of liquid sulfur have attracted attention for over a century since the rapid and reversible gelation of liquid sulfur was first observed in the temperature range 160–195°C. Major advances have been achieved during the past 25 y in our knowledge of the molecular structure of many of the crystalline allotropes of sulfur and of the complex molecular equilibria occurring in the liquid and gaseous states. Sulfur is also unique in the extent to which new allotropes can now be purposefully synthesized using kinetically controlled reactions that rely on the great strength of the S–S bond once it is formed, and over

a dozen new elemental sulfur rings, *cyclo*-S_n, have been synthesized. Fortunately, several excellent reviews are available,[23–25] and these can be consulted for fuller details and further references. It will be convenient to start with some of the classic allotropes (now known to contain *cyclo*-S_8 molecules), and then to consider in turn other cyclic oligomers (*cyclo*-S_n) various chain polymers (*catena*-S_n), certain unstable small molecules S_n ($n = 2$–5) and, finally, the properties of liquid and gaseous sulfur.

The commonest (and most stable) allotrope of sulfur is the yellow, orthorhombic α-form to which all other modifications eventually revert at room temperature. Commercial roll sulfur, flowers of sulfur (sublimed) and milk of sulfur (precipitated) are all of this form. It was shown to contain S_8 molecules by cryoscopy in iodine (E. Beckmann, 1912) and was amongst the first substances to be examined by X-ray crystallography (W. H. Bragg, 1914), but the now familiar crown structure of *cyclo*-S_8 was not finally established until 1935.[23] Various representations of the idealized D_{4d} molecular structure are given in Fig. 15.4. The packing of the molecules within the crystal has been likened to a crankshaft arrangement extending in two different directions and leads to a structure which is very complex.[23] Orthorhombic α-S_8 has a density of 2.069 g cm^{-3}, is a good electrical insulator when pure, and is an excellent thermal insulator, the extremely low thermal conductivity being similar to those of the very best insulators such as mica (p. 356) and wood. Some solubilities in common solvents are in Table 15.4.

At about 95.3° α-S_8 becomes unstable with respect to β-monoclinic sulfur in which the packing of the S_8 molecules is altered and their

Table 15.4 Solubilities of α-orthorhombic sulfur (at 25°C unless otherwise stated)

Solvent	CS$_2$	S$_2$Cl$_2$	Me$_2$CO	C$_6$H$_6$	CCl$_4$	Et$_2$O	C$_6$H$_{14}$	EtOH
g S per 100 g solvent (T°C)	35.5[a]	17[b] (21°)	2.5	2.1	0.86[c]	0.283 (23°)	0.25 (20°)	0.065

[a] 55.6 at 60°. [b] 97 at 110°. [c] 1.94 at 60°.

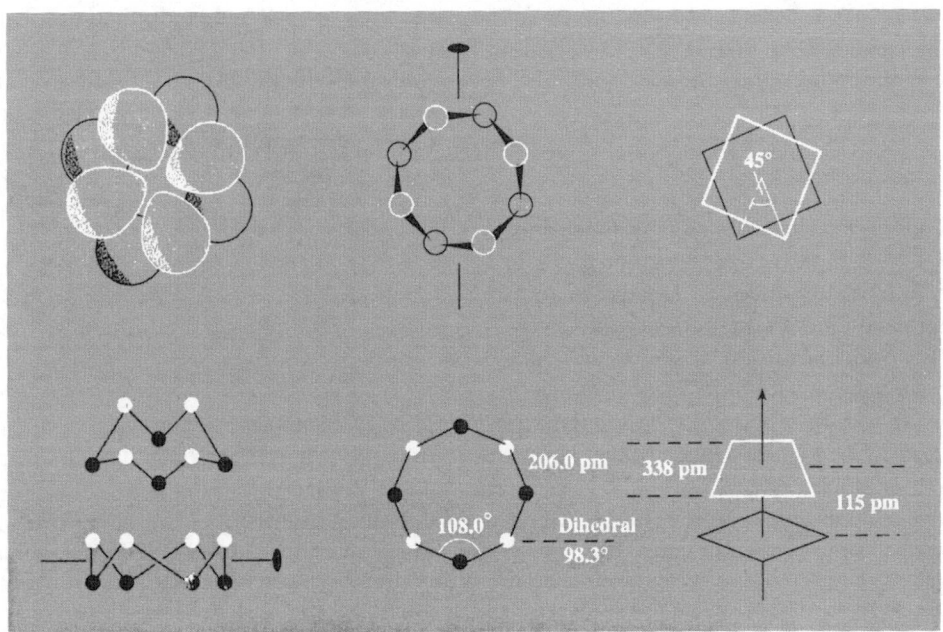

Figure 15.4   Various representations of the molecule *cyclo*-S_8 found in α-orthorhombic, β-monoclinic, and γ-monoclinic sulfur.

orientation becomes partly disordered.[26] This results in a lower density (1.94–2.01 g cm^{-3}), but the dimensions of the S_8 rings in the two allotropes are very similar. The transition is somewhat sluggish even above 100°, and this enables a mp of metastable single crystals of α-S_8 to be obtained: a value of 112.8° is often quoted but microcrystals may melt as high as 115.1°. Monoclinic β-S_8 has a "mp" which is usually quoted as 119.6° but this can rise to 120.4° in microcrystals or may be as low as 114.6°. The uncertainty arises because the S_8 ring is unstable above ~119° and begins to form other species which progressively depress the mp. The situation is reminiscent of the equilibria accompanying the melting of anhydrous phosphoric acid (p. 518). Monoclinic β-S_8 is best prepared by crystallizing liquid sulfur at about 100° and then cooling it rapidly to room temperature to retard the formation of orthorhombic α-S_8; under these conditions

β-S_8 can be kept for several weeks at room temperature before reverting to the more stable α-form.

A third crystalline modification, γ-monoclinic sulfur, was first obtained by W. Muthmann in 1890. It is also called nacreous or mother-of-pearl sulfur and can be made by slowly cooling a sulfur melt that has been heated above 150°, or by chilling hot concentrated solutions of sulfur in EtOH, CS$_2$ or hydrocarbons. However, it is best prepared as pale-yellow needles by the mechanistically obscure reaction of pyridine with copper(I) ethyl xanthate, CuSSCOEt. Like α- and β-sulfur, γ-monoclinic sulfur comprises *cyclo*-S_8 molecules but the packing is more efficient and leads to a higher density (2.19 g cm^{-3}). It reverts slowly to α-S_8 at room temperature but rapid heating leads to a mp of 106.8°.

We now consider other homocyclic polymorphs of sulfur containing 6–20 S atoms per ring. A rhombohedral form, ϵ-sulfur, was first prepared by M. R. Engel in 1891 by the reaction of concentrated HCl on a saturated solution of thiosulfate HS$_2$O$_3^-$ at 0°. It was shown to be

[26] L. K. TEMPLETON, D. H. TEMPLETON and A. ZALKIN, *Inorg. Chem.* **15**, 1999–2001 (1976).

hexameric in 1914 but its structure as *cyclo*-S_6 was not established until 1958–61.[23] The allotrope is best prepared by the reaction

$$H_2S_4 + S_2Cl_2 \xrightarrow[87\% \text{ yield}]{\text{dil solns in Et}_2O} cyclo\text{-}S_6 + 2HCl$$

The ring adopts the chair form and its dimensions are compared with those of other polymorphs in Table 15.5. Note that *cyclo*-S_6 has the smallest bond angle and dihedral angle of all poly-sulfur species for which data are available and this, together with the small "hole" at the centre of the molecule and the efficient packing within the crystal, lead to the highest density of any known polymorph of sulfur (Table 15.6).

In *cyclo*-S_6 and *cyclo*-S_8 all the S atoms are equivalent with essentially equal interatomic

distances, angles and conformations. This is not necessarily so for all homocyclic molecules. Thus, in building up cumulated $-S_n-$ bonds, addition of S atoms to an S_3 unit can occur in three ways: *cis* (c), d-*trans* (dt), and l-*trans* (lt):

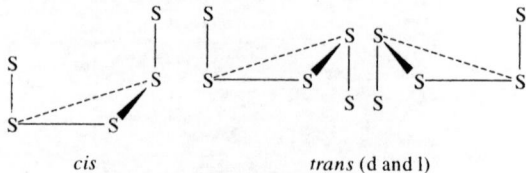

cis   *trans* (d and l)

Both S_6 (chair) and S_8 (crown) are all -*cis* conformations, but larger rings have more complex motifs.

At least eight further cyclic modifications of sulfur have been synthesized during the past 25 y

Table 15.5 Dimensions of some sulfur molecules. Average values are given except for S_7 where deviations from the mean are more substantial (see text)

Molecule	Interatomic distance/pm	Bond angle	Dihedral angle
S_2 (matrix at 20 K)	188.9	—	—
cyclo-S_6	205.7	102.2°	74.5°
cyclo-S_7	199.3–218.1	101.5°–107.5°	0.3°–107.6°
cyclo-$S_8(\alpha)$	203.7	107.8°	98.3°
cyclo-$S_8(\beta)$	204.5	107.9°	—
cyclo-S_{10}	205.6	106.2°	−77° and +123°
cyclo-S_{12}	205.3	106.5°	86.1°
cyclo-S_{18}	205.9	106.3°	84.4°
cyclo-S_{20}	204.7	106.5°	83.0°
catena-S_x	206.6	106.0°	85.3°

Table 15.6 Some properties of sulfur allotropes

Allotrope	Colour	Density/g cm^{-3}	Mp or decomp. point/°C
S_2(g) or matrix at 20 K	Blue-violet	—	Very stable at high temp
S_3(g)	Cherry red	—	Stable at high temp
S_6	Orange red	2.209	d > 50°
S_7	Yellow	2.182 (−110°)	d 39°
α-S_8	Yellow	2.069	112.8° (see text)
β-S_8	Yellow	1.94–2.01	119.6° (see text)
γ-S_8	Light yellow	2.19	106.8° (see text)
S_9	Intense yellow	—	Stable below rt
S_{10}	Pale yellow green	2.103 (−110°C)	d > 0°
S_{11}	—	—	—
S_{12}	Pale yellow	2.036	148°
S_{18}	Lemon yellow	2.090	m 128°(d)
S_{20}	Pale yellow	2.016	m 124°(d)
S_∞	Yellow	2.01	104°(d)

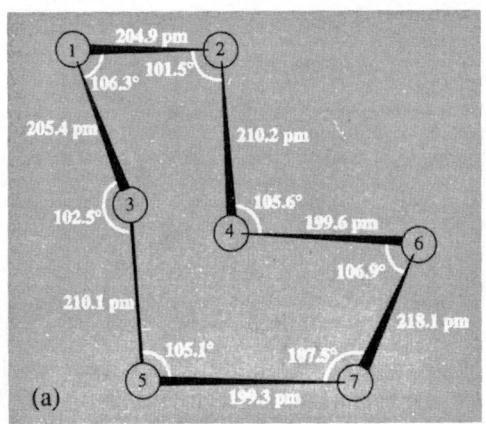
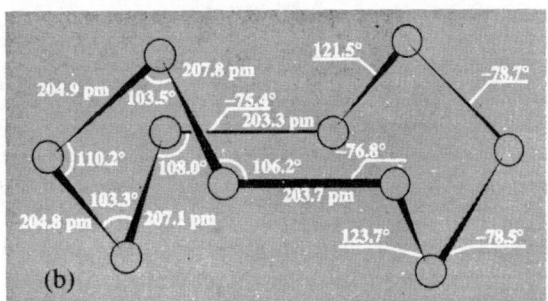

Figure 15.5   (a) Molecular structure of *cyclo*-S_7 showing the large distance S(6)-(7) and alternating interatomic distances away from this bond; the point group symmetry is approximately C_s. (b) Molecular structure of *cyclo*-S_{10} showing interatomic distances, bond angles and dihedral angles; the distance between the 2 "horizontal" bonds is 541 pm.

by the elegant work of M. Schmidt and his group. The method is to couple two compounds which have the desired combined number of S atoms and appropriate terminal groups, e.g.:

$$S_{12-n}Cl_2 + H_2S_n \longrightarrow cyclo\text{-}S_{12} + 2HCl$$

[also for S_6, S_{10}, S_{18}, S_{20}]

$$S_xCl_2 + [Ti(\eta^5\text{-}C_5H_5)_2(S_5)] \longrightarrow cyclo\text{-}S_{x+5}$$

$$+ [Ti(\eta^5\text{-}C_5H_5)_2Cl_2] \quad [\text{for } S_7, S_9, S_{10}, S_{11}]$$

A variant is the ligand displacement and coupling reaction:

$$2[Ti(\eta^5\text{-}C_5H_5)_2(S_5)] + 2SO_2Cl_2 \xrightarrow[\substack{35\%\text{yield}}]{-78°}$$

$$cyclo\text{-}S_{10} + 2[Ti(\eta^5\text{-}C_5H_5)_2Cl_2] + 2SO_2$$

The preparation and structures of the reactants are on p. 683 (H_2S_n), p. 689 (S_xCl_2), and p. 670 [$Ti(\eta^5\text{-}C_5H_5)_2(S_5)$].

S_7 is known in four crystalline modifications; one of these, obtained by crystallization from CS_2 at $-78°$, rapidly disintegrates to a powder at room temperature, but an X-ray study at $-110°$ showed it to consist of *cyclo*-S_7 molecules with

the dimensions shown in Fig. 15.5(a).[27] Notable features are the very large interatomic distance S(6)–S(7) (218.1 pm) which probably arises from the almost zero dihedral angle between the virtually coplanar atoms S(4) S(6) S(7) S(5), thus leading to maximum repulsion between nonbonding lone-pairs of electrons on adjacent S atoms. As a result of this weakening of S(6)–S(7), the adjacent bonds are strengthened (199.5 pm) and there are further alternations of bond lengths (210.2 and 205.2 pm) throughout the molecule.

The structure of *cyclo*-S_{10} is shown in Fig. 15.5(b).[28] The molecule belongs to the very rare point group symmetry D_2 (three orthogonal twofold axes of rotation as the only symmetry elements). The mean interatomic distance and bond angle are close to those in *cyclo*-S_{12} (Table 15.5) and the molecule can be regarded as composed of two identical S_5 units obtained from the S_{12} molecule (Fig. 15.6).

Cyclo-S_{12} occupies an important place amongst the cyclic oligomers of sulfur. In a

[27] R. STEUDEL, R. REINHARDT and F. SCHUSTER, *Angew. Chem. Int. Edn. Engl.* **16**, 715 (1977).
[28] R. REINHARDT, R. STEUDEL and F. SCHUSTER, *Angew. Chem. Int. Edn. Engl.* **17**, 57–8 (1978).

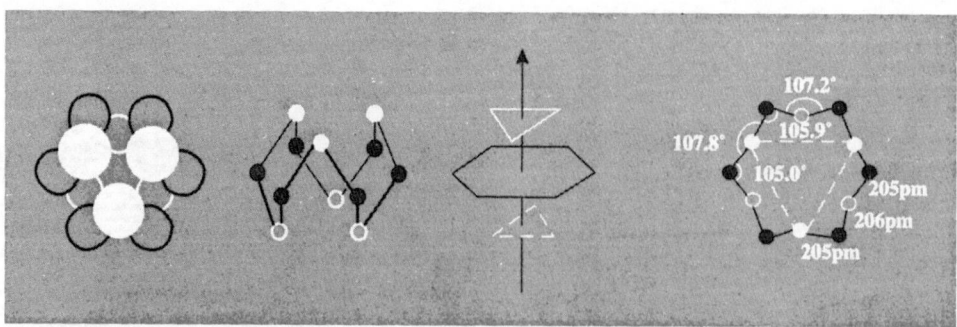

Figure 15.6 Various representations of the molecular structure of *cyclo*-S_{12} showing S atoms in three parallel planes. The idealized point group symmetry is D_{3d} and the mean dihedral angle is $86.1 \pm 5.5°$. In the crystal the symmetry is slightly distorted to C_{2h} and the central group of 6 S atoms deviate from coplanarity by ± 14 pm.

classic paper by L. Pauling[29] the molecule had been predicted to be unstable, though subsequent synthesis showed it to be second only to *cyclo*-S_8 in stability. In fact, the basic principles underlying Pauling's prediction remain valid but he erroneously applied them to two sets of S atoms in two parallel planes whereas the configuration adopted has S atoms in three parallel planes. Several representations of the structure are in Fig. 15.6. Using the nomenclature of p. 656 it can be seen that, unlike S_6 and S_8, the conformation of all S atoms is not *cis*: the S atoms in upper and lower planes do indeed have this conformation but the 6 atoms in the central plane are alternately d-*trans* and l-*trans* leading to the sequence:

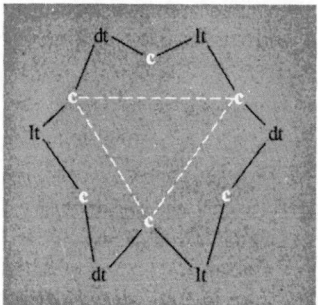

Cyclo-S_{12} was first prepared in 1966 in 3% yield by reacting H_2S_4 with S_2Cl_2 but a better

route is the reaction between dilute solutions of H_2S_8 and S_4Cl_2 in Et_2O (18% yield). It can also be extracted from liquid sulfur. The stability of the allotrope can be gauged from its mp (148°), which is higher than that of any other allotrope and nearly 30° above the temperature at which the S_8 ring begins to decompose.

Two allotropes of *cyclo*-S_{18} are known. The structure of the first is shown in Fig. 15.7(a): if we take 3 successive atoms out of the S_{12} ring then the 9-atom fragment combines with a second one to generate the structure. Alternatively, the structure can be viewed as two parallel 9-atom helices (see below), one right-handed and one left-handed, mutually joined at each end by the *cis* atoms S(5) and S(14). Interatomic distances vary between 204–211 pm (mean 206 pm), bond angles between 103.7–108.3° (mean 106.3°), and dihedral angles between 79.1–90.0° (mean 84.5°). This form of *cyclo*-S_{18} is formed by the reaction between H_2S_8 and $S_{10}Cl_2$ and forms lemon-coloured crystals, mp 128°, which can be stored in the dark for several days without apparent change. The second form of *cyclo*-S_{18} has the molecular structure shown in Fig. 15.7(b): this has twice the 8-atom repeat motif *cis-cis-trans-cis-trans-cis-trans-cis* (one with d-*trans* and the other with l-*trans*) joined at each end by further bridging single *trans*-sulfur atoms which constitute the 2 extreme atoms of the elongated ring.

[29] L. PAULING, *Proc. Natl. Acad. Sci. USA* **35**, 495–9 (1949).

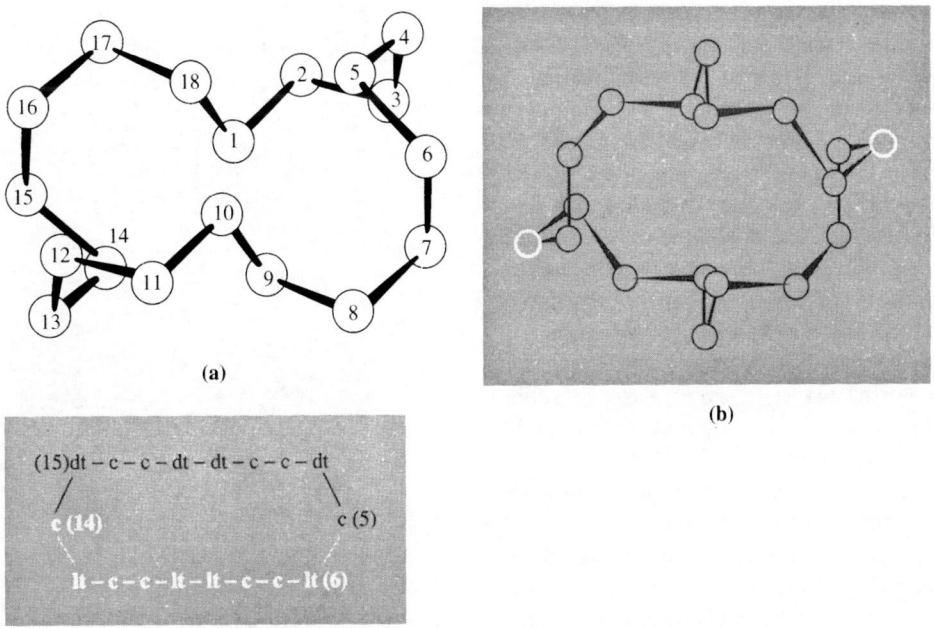

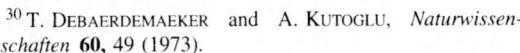

Figure 15.7 (a) The molecular structure of one form of *cyclo*-S_{18}, together with the conformational sequence of the two helical subunits.[30] (b) The molecular structure of the second form of *cyclo*-S_{18} showing the *trans*-configuration of the S atoms at the extreme ends of the elongated rings.[25]

Pale yellow crystals of *cyclo*-S_{20}, mp 124° (decomp), *d* 2.016 g cm^{-3}, have been made by the reaction of H_2S_{10} and $S_{10}Cl_2$. The molecular structure is shown in Fig. 15.8[31] The interatomic S–S distances vary between 202.3–210.4 pm (mean 204.2 pm), the angles S–S–S between 104.6–107.7° (mean 106.4°), and the dihedral angles between 66.3–89.9° (mean 84.7°). In this case the conformation motif is -c-lt-lt-lt-c- repeated 4 times and the abnormally long bond required to achieve ring closure is notable; it is also this section of the molecule which has the smallest dihedral angles thereby incurring increased repulsion between adjacent nonbonding lone-pairs of electrons. Consistent with this the adjacent bonds are the shortest in the molecule.

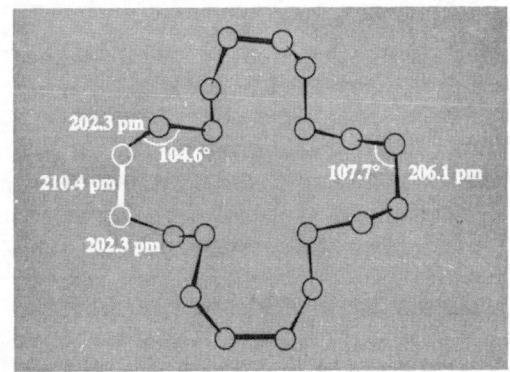

Figure 15.8 Molecular structure of *cyclo*-S_{20} viewed along the [001] direction.[31] The 2 adjacent S atoms with the longest interatomic distance are shown in white.

Solid poly*catena*sulfur comes in many forms: it is present in rubbery S, plastic (χ)S, lamina S, fibrous (ψ,ϕ), polymeric (μ) and insoluble (ω)S, supersublimation S, white S and the commercial product Crystex. All these are metastable mixtures of allotropes containing more or less

[30] T. DEBAERDEMAEKER and A. KUTOGLU, *Naturwissenschaften* **60**, 49 (1973).
[31] T. DEBAERDEMAEKER, E. HELLNER, A. KUTOGLU, M. SCHMIDT and E. WILHELM, *Naturwissenschaften* **60**, 300 (1973).

defined concentrations of helices (S_∞), *cyclo*-S_8, and other molecular forms. The various modifications are prepared by precipitating S from solution or by quenching *hot* liquid S (say from 400°C). The best-defined forms are fibrous ($d \sim 2.01\,\mathrm{g\,cm^{-3}}$) in which the helices are mainly parallel, and lamella S in which they are partly criss-crossed. When carefully prepared by drawing filaments from hot liquid sulfur, fibrous rubbery or plastic S can be repeatedly stretched to as much as 15 times its normal length without substantially impairing its elasticity. All these forms revert to *cyclo*-$S_8(\alpha)$ at room temperature and this has caused considerable difficulty in obtaining their X-ray structures.[23] However, it is now established that fibrous S consists of infinite chains of S atoms arranged in parallel helices whose axes are arranged on a close-packed (hexagonal) net 463 pm apart. The structure contains both left-handed and right-handed helices of radius 95 pm and features a repeat distance of 1380 pm comprising 10 S atoms in three turns as shown in Fig. 15.9. Within each helix the interatomic distance S–S is 206.6 pm, the bond angle S–S–S is 106.0°, and the dihedral angle S–S–S–S is 85.3°.

The constitution of liquid sulfur has been extensively investigated, particularly in the region just above the remarkable transition at 159.4°. At this temperature virtually all properties of liquid sulfur change discontinuously, e.g. specific heat (λ point), density, velocity of sound, polarizability, compressibility, colour, electrical conductivity, surface tension and, most strikingly, viscosity, which increases over 10 000-fold within the temperature range 160–195°C before gradually decreasing again. The phenomena can now be interpreted at least semi-quantitatively by a 2-step polymerization theory involving initiation and propagation:

$$cyclo\text{-}S_8 \rightleftharpoons catena\text{-}S_8$$

$$catena\text{-}S_8 + cyclo\text{-}S_8 \longrightarrow catena\text{-}S_{16}, \text{ etc.}$$

The polymerization is photosensitive, involves diradicals and leads to chain lengths that exceed 200 000 S atoms at $\sim$180°C before dropping slowly to $\sim$1000 S at 400° and $\sim$100 S at 600°.

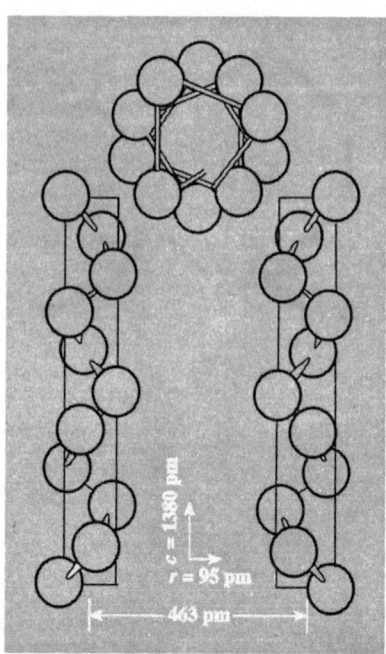

Figure 15.9   The structure of right-handed and left-handed S_∞ helices in fibrous sulfur (see text).

Polymeric S_∞ is dark yellow with an absorption edge at 350 nm (cf. H_2S_n, p. 683) but the colour is often obscured either by the presence of trace organic impurities or, in pure S, by the presence of other highly coloured species such as the dark cherry-red trimer S_3 or the deeper-coloured diradicals S_4 and S_5.

The saturated vapour pressure above solid and liquid sulfur is given in Table 15.7. The molecular composition of the vapour has long been in contention but, mainly as a result of the work of J. Birkowitz and others[24] is now known to contain all molecules S_n with $2 \leq n \leq 10$ including odd-numbered species. The actual concentration

Table 15.7   Vapour pressure of crystalline *cyclo*-$S_8(\alpha)$ and liquid sulfur

p/mmHg[a]	10^{-5}	10^{-3}	10^{-1}	1	10	100	760
T/°C	39.0	81.1	141	186	244.9	328	444.61

p/atm[a]	1	2	5	10	50	100	200
T/°C	444.61	495	574	644	833	936	1035

[a] 1 mmHg $\approx$ 133.322 Pa; 1 atm = 101 325 Pa

of each species depends on both temperature and pressure. In the saturated vapour up to 600°C S_8 is the most common species followed by S_6 and S_7, and the vapour is green. Between 620–720°C S_7 and S_6 are slightly more prevalent than S_8 but the concentration of all three species falls rapidly with respect to those of S_2, S_3 and S_4, and above 720°C S_2 is the predominant species. At lower pressures S_2 is even more prominent, accounting for more than 80% of all vapour species at 530°C and 100 mmHg, and 99% at 730°C and 1 mmHg. This vapour is violet. The vapour above FeS_2 at 850°C is also S_2.

The best conditions for observing S_3 are 440°C and 10 mmHg when 10–20% of vapour species comprise this deep cherry-red bent triatomic species; like ozone, p. 607, it has a singlet ground state. The best conditions for S_4 are 450°C and 20 mmHg (concentration ~20%) but the structure is still not definitely established and may, in fact be a strained ring, an unbranched diradical chain, or a branched-chain isostructural with $SO_3(g)$ (p. 703).

The great stability of S_2 in the gas phase at high temperature is presumably due to the essentially double-bond character of the molecule and to the increase in entropy ($T\Delta S$) consequent on the breaking up of the single-bonded S_n oligomers. As with O_2 (p. 606) the ground state is a triplet level $^3\Sigma_g^-$ but the splitting within the triplet state is far larger than with O_2 and the violet colour is due to the transition $B^3\Sigma_u^- \leftarrow X^3\Sigma_g^-$ at 31 689 cm^{-1}. The corresponding B→X emission is observed whenever S compounds are burned in a reducing flame and the transition can be used for the quantitative analytical determination of the concentration of S compounds. There is also a singlet $^1\Delta$ excited state as for O_2. The dissociation energy $D_0^\circ(S_2)$ is 421.3 kJ mol^{-1}, and the interatomic distance in the gas phase 188.7 pm (cf. Table 15.5).

15.1.5 Atomic and physical properties

Several physical properties of sulfur have been mentioned in the preceding section; they vary markedly with the particular allotrope and its physical state.

Sulfur ($Z = 16$) has 4 stable isotopes of which ^{32}S is by far the most abundant in nature (95.02%). The others are ^{33}S (0.75%), ^{34}S (4.21%), and ^{36}S (0.02%). These abundances vary somewhat depending on the source of the sulfur, and this prevents the atomic weight of sulfur being quoted for general use more precisely than 32.066(6) (p. 17). The variability is a valuable geochemical indication of the source of the sulfur and the isotope ratios of sulfur-containing impurities can even be used to identify the probable source of petroleum samples.[15,32] In such work it is convenient to define the abundance ratio of the 2 most abundant isotopes ($R = {}^{32}S/{}^{34}S$) and to take as standard the value of 22.22 for meteoritic troilite (FeS). Deviations from this standard ratio are then expressed in parts per thousand (sometimes confusingly called "per mil" or ‰):

$$\delta^{34}S = 1000(R_{sample} - R_{std})/R_{std}$$

On this definition, $\delta^{34}S$ is zero for meteoritic troilite; dissolved sulfate in ocean water is enriched +20‰ in ^{34}S, as are contemporary evaporite sulfates, whereas sedimentary sulfides are depleted in ^{34}S by as much as −50‰ due to fractionation during bacterial reduction to H_2S.

In addition to the 4 stable isotopes sulfur has at least 9 radioactive isotopes, the one with the longest half-life being ^{35}S which decays by β^- activity (E_{max} 0.167 MeV, $t_{\frac{1}{2}}$ 87.5 d). ^{35}S can be prepared by $^{35}Cl(n,p)$, $^{34}S(n,\gamma)$ or $^{34}S(d,p)$ and is commercially available as $S_{element}$, H_2S, $SOCl_2$ and KSCN. The β^- radiation has a similar energy to that of ^{14}C (E_{max} 0.155 MeV) and similar counting techniques can be used (p. 276). The maximum range is 300 mm in air and 0.28 mm in water, and effective shielding is provided by a perspex screen 3–10 mm thick. The preparation of many ^{35}S-containing compounds has been

---

[32] H. NIELSEN, Sulfur isotopes, in E. JÄGER and J. C. HUNZIKER (eds.), *Lectures in Isotope Geology*, pp. 283–312, Springer-Verlag, Berlin, 1979.

reviewed[33] and many of these have been used for mechanistic studies, e.g. the reactions of the specifically labelled thiosulfate ions $^{35}SSO_3{}^{2-}$ and $S^{35}SO_3{}^{2-}$. Another ingenious application, which won Barbara B. Askins the US Inventor of the Year award for 1978, is the use of ^{35}S for intensifying under-exposed photographic images: prints or films are immersed in dilute aqueous alkaline solutions of ^{35}S-thiourea, which complexes all the silver in the image (including invisibly small amounts), and the alkaline medium converts this to immobile, insoluble $Ag^{35}S$; the film so treated is then overlayed with unexposed film which reproduces the image with heightened intensity as a result of exposure to the β^- activity.

The isotope ^{33}S has a nuclear spin quantum number $I = \frac{3}{2}$ and so is potentially useful in nmr experiments (receptivity to nmr detection 17×10^{-6} that of the proton). The resonance was first observed in 1951 but the low natural abundance of $^{33}S(0.75\%)$ and the quadrupolar broadening of many of the signals has so far restricted the amount of chemically significant work appearing on this resonance.[34] However, more results are expected now that pulsed fourier-transform techniques have become generally available.

The S atom in the ground state has the electronic configuration $[Ne]3s^23p^4$ with 2 unpaired p electrons $(^3P_1)$. Other atomic properties are: ionization energy $999.30\,kJ\,mol^{-1}$, electron affinities $+200$ and $-414\,kJ\,mol^{-1}$ for the addition of the first and second electrons respectively, electronegativity (Pauling) 2.5, covalent radius 103 pm and ionic radius of S^{2-} 184 pm. These properties can be compared with those of the other elements in Group 16 on p. 754.

[33] R. H. HERBER, Sulfur-35, in R. H. HERBER (ed.), *Inorganic Isotopic Syntheses*, pp. 193–214, Benjamin, New York, 1962.
[34] C. RODGER, N. SHEPPARD, C. MCFARLANE and W. MCFARLANE, in R. H. HARRIS and B. E. MANN (eds.), *NMR and the Periodic Table*, pp. 401–2, Academic Press, London, 1978. H. C. E. MCFARLANE and W. MCFARLANE, in J. MASON (ed.) *Multinuclear NMR*, Plenum Press, New York, 1987, pp. 417–35.

15.1.6 Chemical reactivity

Sulfur is a very reactive element especially at slightly elevated temperatures (which presumably facilitates cleavage of S–S bonds). It unites directly with all elements except the noble gases, nitrogen, tellurium, iodine, iridium, platinum and gold, though even here compounds containing S bonded directly to N, Te, I, Ir, Pt and Au are known. Sulfur reacts slowly with H_2 at 120°, more rapidly above 200°, and is in reversible thermodynamic equilibrium with H_2 and H_2S at higher temperatures. It ignites in F_2 and burns with a livid flame to give SF_6; reaction with chlorine is more sedate at room temperature but rapidly accelerates above this to give (initially) S_2Cl_2 (p. 689). Sulfur dissolves in liquid Br_2 to form S_2Br_2, which readily dissociates into its elements; iodine has been used as a cryoscopic solvent for sulfur (p. 654) and no binary compound is formed (directly) even at elevated temperature (see, however, p. 691). Oxidation of sulfur by (moist?) air is very slow at room temperature though traces of SO_2 are formed; the ignition temperature of S in air is 250-260°. Pure dry O_2 does not react at room temperature though O_3 does. Likewise direct reaction with N_2 has not been observed but, in a discharge tube, activated N reacts. All other non-metals (B, C, Si, Ge; P, As, Sb; Se) react at elevated temperatures. Of the metals, sulfur reacts in the cold with all the main group representatives of Groups 1, 2, 13, Sn, Pb and Bi, and also Cu, Ag and Hg (which even tarnishes at liquid-air temperatures). The transition metals (except Ir, Pt and Au) and the lanthanides and actinides react more or less vigorously on being heated with sulfur to form binary metal sulfides (p. 676).

The reactivity of sulfur clearly depends sensitively on the molecular complexity of the reacting species. Little systematic work has been done. *Cyclo*-S_8 is obviously less reactive than the diradical *catena*-S_8, and smaller oligomers in the liquid or vapour phase also complicate the picture. In the limit atomic sulfur, which can readily be generated photolytically, is an extremely reactive species. As with atomic oxygen and the various

Table 15.8   Coordination geometries of sulfur

CN	Examples
1	S_2(g), CS_2, HNCS, K[SCN] and "covalent" isothiocyanates, $P_4O_6S_4$, P_4S_n (terminal S), SSF_2, $SSO_3{}^{2-}$, $Na_3SbS_4.9H_2O$, Tl_3VS_4, M_2MoS_4, $(NH_4)_2WS_4$, $S{=}WCl_4$
2 (linear)	$[(\eta^5\text{-}C_5H_5)(CO)_2Cr{\equiv}S{\equiv}Cr(CO)_2(\eta^5\text{-}C_5H_5)]^{(a)}$
2 (bent)	S_n, H_2S, H_2S_n, Me_2S_n, S_nX_2 (Cl, Br), SO_2, P_4S_n (briding S), $Se(SCN)_2$ and "covalent" thiocyanates
3 (planar, D_{3h})	SO_3 (g), $[\{(\eta^5\text{-}C_5H_5)(CO)_2\,Mn\}SO_2]$, $[\{\eta^5\text{-}C_5H_5)(CO)_2Mn\}_2SO]^{(b)}$
3 (T-shaped planar)	
3 (pyramidal)	SSF_2, $OSCl_2$, S_8O(1 S), $SO_3{}^{2-}$, $S_2O_4{}^{2-}$, $S_2O_5{}^{2-}$ (1 S), Me_3S^+, $SF_3{}^+$
4 (tetrahedral)	SO_3 (s) [i.e. cyclic S_3O_9 or fibrous $(SO_3)_\infty$], SO_2Cl_2, $SO_4{}^{2-}$, $S_2O_6{}^{2-}$ $(O_3SSO_3{}^{2-})$, $S_2O_7{}^{2-}$ $(O_3SOSO_3{}^{2-})$, $S_3O_{10}{}^{2-}$, $S_5O_{16}{}^{2-}$, ZnS (blende, and M = Be, Cd, Hg), ZnS(wurtzite, and M = Cd, Mn)
4 (seesaw) (ψ-tbp)	SF_4
4 (pyramidal)	$[(\mu_4\text{-}S)(OsL_n)_4]$ pyramidal clusters,$^{(d)}$ $[(\mu_4\text{-}S)_2Ru_8L_m]$ bioctahedral cluster$^{(e)}$, $[(\mu_4\text{-}S)_2Nb_4(SPh)_{12}]^{4-}$ octahedral $\{S_2Nb_4\}$ cluster$^{(f)}$
5 (square pyramidal) (ψ-octahedral)	$SF_5{}^-$, SOF_4, NiS (millerite structure)
6 (octahedral)	SF_6, S_2F_{10}, MS(NaCl-type, M = Mg, Ca, Sr, Ba, Mn, Pb, Ln, Th, U, Pu)
6 (trigonal prismatic)	MS(NiAs-type), (M = Ti, V, Fe, Co, Ni), Hf_2S
7 (mono-capped trigonal prismatic)	Ta_6S,$^{(g)}$ $Ti_2S^{(h)}$
8 (cubic)	M_2S (antifluorite-type, M = Li, Na, K, Rb)
9 (mono-capped square antiprismatic)	$[Rh_{17}(CO)_{32}(S)_2]^{3-}$ (encapsulated S)$^{(i)}$
10 (bicapped square antiprismatic)	$[Rh_{10}(CO)_{10}(\mu\text{-}CO)_{12}S]^{2-}$ (encapsulated S)$^{(j)}$

[a]Ref. 35. [b]Ref. 36. [c]Ref. 37. [d]Ref. 38. [e]Ref. 39. [f]Ref. 40. [g]Ref. 41. [h]Ref. 42. [i]Ref. 43. [j]Ref. 44.

[35]T. J. GREENHOUGH, B. W. S. KOLTHAMMER, P. LEGZDINS and J. TROTTER, *Inorg. Chem.* **18**, 3543–8 (1979). See also L. Y. GOH and T. C. W. MAK, *J. Chem. Soc., Chem. Commun.*, 1474–5 (1986).

[36]I.-P. LORENZ, J. MESSELHÄUSER, W. HILLER and K. HAUG, *Angew. Chem. Int. Edn. Engl.* **24**, 228–9 (1985).

[37]P. H. W. LAU and J. C. MARTIN, *J. Am. Chem. Soc.* **100**, 7077–9 (1978).

[38]R. D. ADAMS, *Polyhedron* **4**, 2003–25 (1985).

[39]R. D. ADAMS, J. E. BABIN and M. TASI, *Inorg. Chem.* **25**, 4460–1 (1986).

[40]J. L. SEELA, J. C. HUFFMAN and G. CHRISTOU, *J. Chem. Soc., Chem. Commun.*, 1258–60 (1987).

[41]H. F. FRANZEN and J. G. SMEGGIL, *Acta Cryst.* **B26**, 125–9 (1970).

[42]J. P. OWENS, B. R. CONARD and H. F. FRANZEN, *Acta Cryst.* **23**, 77–82 (1967).

[43]J. L. VIDAL, R. A. FIATO, L. A. CROSBY and R. L. PRUETT, *Inorg. Chem.* **17**, 2574–82 (1978).

[44]G. CIANI, L. GARLASCHELLI, A. SIRONI and S. MARTINENGO, *J. Chem. Soc., Chem. Commun.*, 563–5 (1981).

methylenes, both singlet and triplet states are possible and these have different reactivities. The ground state is $^3P_2$, and the singlet state $^1D_2$ lies $110.52 \, \text{kJ mol}^{-1}$ above this. Triplet state S atoms (with 2 unpaired electrons) can be generated by the Hg-photosensitized irradiation of COS:

$$Hg + h\nu \; (253.7 \, \text{nm}) \longrightarrow Hg(^3P_1)$$

$$Hg(^3P_1) + COS \longrightarrow Hg + CO + S(^3P)$$

Triplet S can also be generated by direct photolysis of CS_2 ($h\nu < 210 \, \text{nm}$) or ethylene episulfide $\overline{CH_2CH_2S}$ ($h\nu$ 220–260 nm). Photolysis of SPF_3 ($h\nu$ 210–230 pm) generates singlet state S atoms (with no unpaired electrons) but the best syntheses of these is the direct primary photolysis of COS in the absence of Hg; this generates mainly singlet S (75%) with the rest being in the triplet state (^3P):

$$COS + h\nu \longrightarrow CO + S(^1D_2)$$

Generation of (excited state) singlet S in the presence of paraffins yields the corresponding mercaptan by a concerted single-step insertion: $RH + S(^1D_2) \longrightarrow RSH$. By contrast, paraffins are inert to triplet (ground state) S atoms. Singlet S undergoes analogous insertion reactions with $MeSiH_3$, $SiMe_4$ and B_2H_6. Olefins can undergo insertion of singlet S atoms on stereospecific addition of triplet S atoms; according to experimental conditions, the products are alkenyl mercaptans, vinylic mercaptans or episulfides. Analogous reactions with inorganic compounds appear to be a very promising field for future research. Generation of the reactive diatomic species S_2 for synthetic purposes is also currently an active field.[45,46]

Sulfur compounds exhibit a rich and multifarious variety which derives not only from the numerous possible oxidation states of the element (from -2 to $+6$) but also from the range of bond types utilized (covalent, coordinate,

ionic and even metallic) and the multiplicity of coordination geometries adopted by the element. Oxidation states and their interrelationships as codified by oxidation state diagrams are dealt with more fully in the section on oxoacids of sulfur (p. 706) though the existence of several other series of compounds, notably the halides, also illustrates the element's versatility. The range of bond types, as reflected in the physical and chemical properties of the various compounds of the element, will become increasingly apparent throughout the rest of the chapter. The multiplicity of coordination geometries is amply demonstrated by the examples in Table 15.8. Most of these can be readily rationalized by the numerous variants of elementary bonding theory. See ref. 47 for a VSEPR treatment.

Polyatomic sulfur cations

As long ago as 1804 C. F. Bucholz observed that sulfur dissolves in oleum to give clear, brightly coloured solutions which could be yellow, deep blue or red (or intermediate colours) depending on the strength of the oleum and the time of the reaction. These solutions are now known to contain S_n^{2+} cations, the structure of which has been elucidated during the past two decades mainly by elegant synthetic, Raman spectroscopic and crystallographic studies.[48−50] Selenium and tellurium behave similarly (p. 759). Sulfur can most conveniently be quantitatively oxidized using SbF_5 or AsF_5 in an inert solvent such as SO_2, e.g.:

$$S_8 + 3AsF_5 \xrightarrow{SO_2} [S_8]^{2+}[AsF_6]_2^- + AsF_3$$

$$S_8 + 6AsF_5 \longrightarrow 2[S_4]^{2+}[AsF_6]_2^- + 2AsF_3$$

[45] M. SCHMIDT and U. GÖRL, *Angew. Chem. Int. Edn. Engl.* **26** 887–8 (1987).

[46] T. L. GILCHRIST and J. E. WOOD, *J. Chem. Soc., Chem. Commun.*, 1460–1 (1992).

[47] I. HARGITTAI, *The Structure of Volatile Sulfur Compounds*, D. Reidel Publ. Co., (Kluwer Academic Publ.), Dordrecht, 1985, 301 pp.

[48] R. J. GILLESPIE, *Chem. Soc. Rev.* **8**, 315–52 (1979).

[49] T. A. O'DONNELL, *Chem. Soc. Rev.* **16**, 1–43 (1987).

[50] N. BURFORD, J. PASSMORE and J. C. P. SANDERS, Chap. 2 in J .F. LIEBMAN and A. GREENBERG (eds.), *From Atoms to Polymers: Isoelectronic Analogies*, 1989, pp. 53–108.

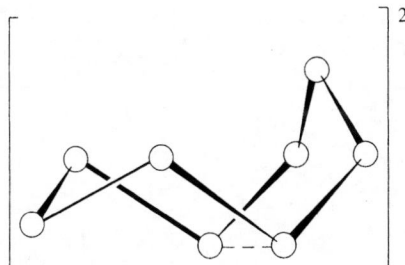

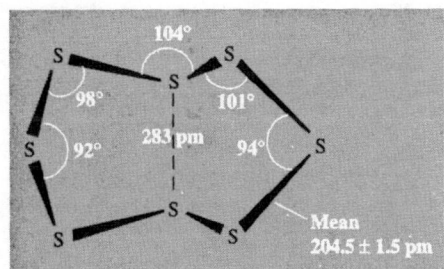

Figure 15.10 The structure and dimensions of the S_8^{2+} cation in $[S_8]^{2+}[AsF_6]_2^-$.

The bright-yellow solutions contain S_4^{2+}, a square-planar ring whose structure has been confirmed by an X-ray study on the unusual crystalline compound $As_6F_{36}I_4S_{32}$, i.e. $[S_4]^{2+}[S_7I]^+_4[AsF_6]^-_6$ (p. 692). The S–S interatomic distance is 198 pm compared with 204 pm for a single-bonded species. Note also that S_4^{2+} is isoelectronic with the known heterocyclic compound S_2N_2 (p. 725). The pale-yellow compound $[S_4]^{2+}[SbF_6]^-_2$ has also been isolated.

The deep-blue solutions contain S_8^{2+}, and the X-ray structure of $[S_8]^{2+}[AsF_6]^-_2$ reveals that the cation has an *exo-endo* cyclic structure with a long transannular bond as shown in Fig. 15.10 (see also p. 724). The bright-red solutions were originally thought to contain the S_{16}^{2+} cation and a compound thought to be $S_{16}(AsF_6)_2$ was isolated; however, crystallographic study has shown[51] that the compound has the totally unexpected formulation $[S_{19}]^{2+}[AsF_6]^-_2$ which could not have been distinguished from the earlier stoichiometry on the basis of the original analytical data. This astonishing cation consists of two 7-membered rings joined by a 5-atom chain. As shown in Fig. 15.11, one of the rings has a boat conformation whilst the other is disordered, existing as a 4:1 mixture of chair and boat conformations. S–S distances vary greatly from 187 to 239 pm and S–S–S angles vary from 91.9° to 127.6°. See also p. 692 for $[S_7X]^+$ cations.

Solutions of sulfur in oleum also give rise to paramagnetic species, probably S_n^+, but the

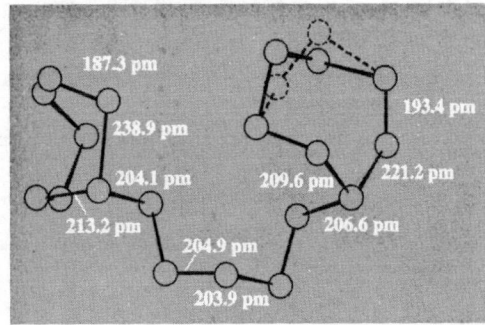

Figure 15.11 The structure and some of the dimensions of the disordered cation S_{19}^{2+} (see text).

nature of these has not yet been fully established. For polysulfur anions S_n^{2-}, see p. 681.

Sulfur as a ligand

The S atom can act either as a terminal or a bridging ligand. The dianion S_2^{2-} is also an effective ligand, and chelating polysulfides $-S_n-$ are well established. These various sulfur ligands will be briefly considered before dealing with the broad range of compounds in which S acts as the donor atom, e.g. H_2S, R_2S, dithiocarbamates and related anions, 1,2-dithiolenes etc. Ligands in which S acts as a donor atom are usually classified as class-b ligands ("soft" Lewis bases), in contrast to oxygen donor-atom ligands which tend to be class-a or hard (p. 909). The larger size of the S atom and the consequent greater deformability of its electron cloud give a qualitative rationalization of this difference and the possible participation

[51] R. C. BURNS, R. J. GILLESPIE and J. F. SAWYER, *Inorg. Chem.* **19**, 1423–32 (1980).

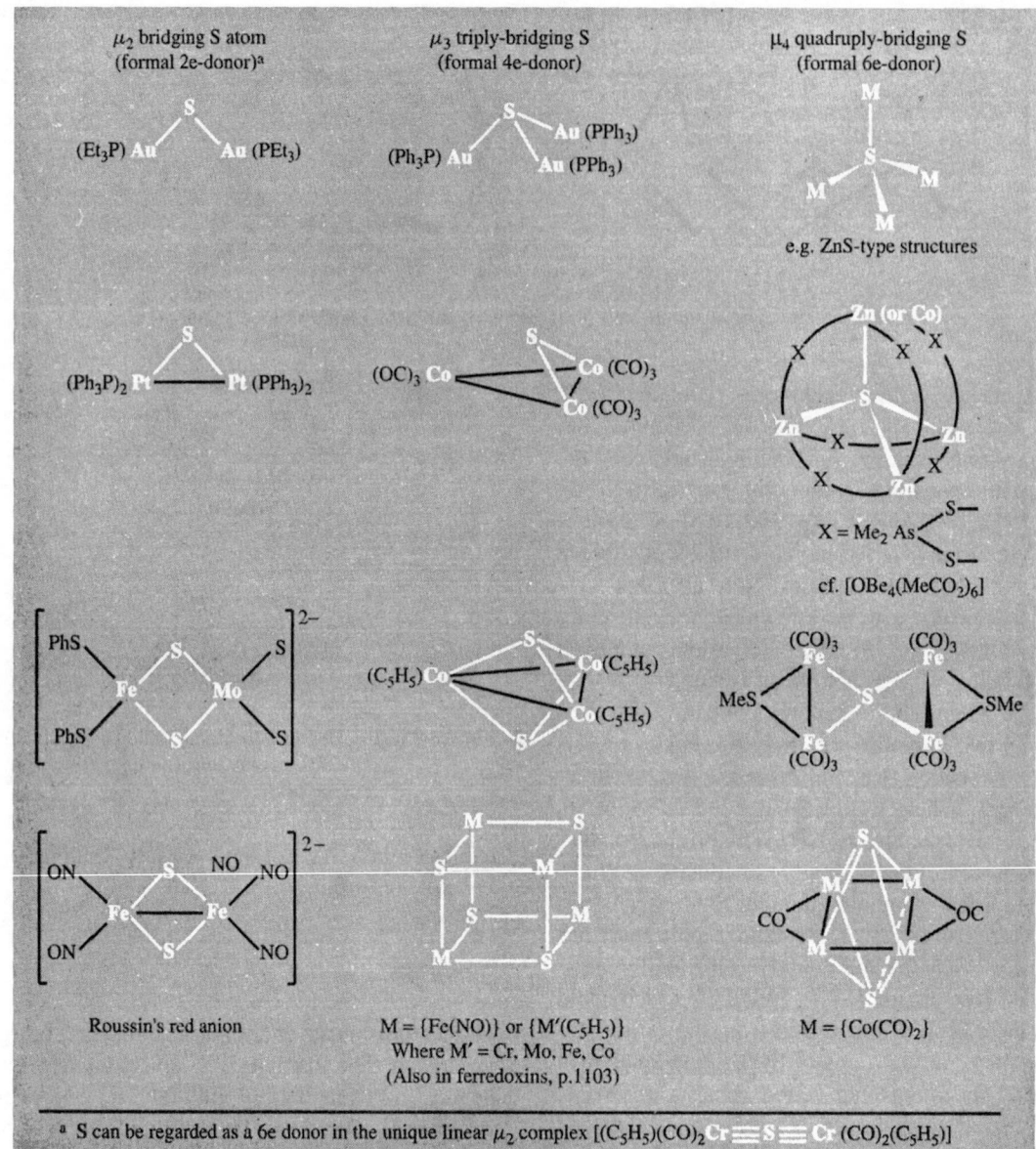

Figure 15.12   The S atom as a bridging ligand.

of d_π orbitals in bonding to sulfur has also been invoked (see comparison of N and P, p. 416).

Some examples of the S atom as a bridging ligand are given in Fig. 15.12. In the μ_2 bridging mode S is usually regarded as a 2-electron donor, though in the linear bridge $[\{(C_5H_5)(CO)_2Cr\}_2S]$ it is probably best regarded as a 6-electron donor.[35] In the μ_3 triply bridging mode S can be regarded as a 4-electron donor, using both its unpaired electrons and one lone-pair.[52] If the 3 bridged metal atoms

---

[52] H. Vahrenkamp, *Angew. Chem. Int. Edn. Engl.* **14**, 322–9 (1975).

are different then a chiral tetrahedrane molecule results and this has permitted the recent (1980) resolution of the enantiomers of the first optically active metal cluster compound, the red complex [{Co(CO)$_3$}{Fe(CO)$_3$}{Mo(η^5-C$_5$H$_5$)(CO)$_2$}S].[53] The pseudo-cubane structure adopted by some of the μ_3-S compounds is assuming added significance as a crucial structural unit in many biologically important systems, e.g. the {(RS)FeS}$_4$ units which cross-link the polypeptide chains in ferredoxins (p. 1103). In the μ_4-mode 6-electrons are involved, if the bonding is considered to be predominantly covalent, though metal-sulfides are sometimes treated as compounds of S^{2-}. No *molecular* compounds are known in which S bridges 6 or 8 metal atoms though, again, these coordinations are prevalent in solid-state compounds, many of which have interatomic bonding which is far from being purely ionic.

The disulfur ligand S$_2$ (sometimes more helpfully considered as S$_2{}^{2-}$) is attracting increasing attention since no other simple ligand is as versatile in the variety of its modes of coordination. Moreover, in one particular mode (see Type III, p. 669) it is particularly effective in stabilizing metal clusters. Many of the complexes of S$_2$ were first obtained accidentally, and their seemingly bizarre stoichiometries only became intelligible after structural elucidation by X-ray crystallography. The complexes can be prepared by reacting metals or their compounds with: (a) a positive S$_2$ group as in S$_2$Cl$_2$;[54] (b) a neutral S$_2$ group, usually derived from S$_8$; (c) a negative S$_2{}^{2-}$ group such as an alkaline polysulfide solution. Examples are:

$$Nb + S_2Cl_2 \xrightarrow{\text{heat}} NbS_2Cl_2 \text{ (see Fig. 15.14a), (p. 671)}$$

$$Nb + \tfrac{1}{4}S_8 + X_2 \xrightarrow{500°C} NbS_2X_2 \text{ (X = Cl, Br, I)}$$

$$(NH_4)_6Mo_7O_{24}.4H_2O + H_2S + (NH_4)_2S_n$$

$$\xrightarrow{\text{aq NH}_3} (NH_4)_2[Mo_2(S_2)_6] \text{ (see Fig. 15.13g)}$$

The S–S bond can also be formed by a direct coupling reaction, e.g.:

$$2[(H_2O)_5Cr(SH)]^{2+} + I_2 \longrightarrow$$
$$[(H_2O)_5CrSSCr(OH_2)_5]^{4+} + 2HI$$

At least 8 modes of coordination are known (Table 15.9);[55] they are all based on either side-on S$_2$ or bridging –S–S– with possible further ligation via one or two lone-pairs as shown schematically below:

Frequently, more than one type of coordination occurs in a given complex, e.g. Figs. 15.13b, c and g. Interestingly, there appear to be no known example of terminal "end-on" coordination, M–S–S (see dioxygen complexes, p. 615). Detailed descriptions of all the structures and their bonding are beyond the scope of this treatment but it will be noted from Table 15.9 that the S–S interatomic distances in disulfide complexes range from 201 to 209 pm. The following specific points of interest may also be mentioned. The orange-red anion [Mo$_4$(NO)$_4$S$_{13}$]$^{4-}$ (Fig. 15.13b) features two triangular arrays of Mo atoms joined by a common edge and with an angle of 127.6° between the two Mo$_3$ planes; each plane has a μ_3-bonded S atom above it (Mo–S 250.1 pm) and there is a further unique μ_4-bonded S atom which is 261.6 pm from each of the 4 Mo atoms. Four of the 5 S$_2{}^{2-}$ ligands are simultaneously bonded both end on (Mo–S 246.5 pm) and side on (Mo–S 249.2 pm) whilst the fifth is side-on only. The complex therefore has sulfur in five different bonding states. In the red complex [Mn$_4$(CO)$_{15}$(S$_2$)$_2$] (Fig. 15.13c) the 2 S$_2{}^{2-}$ ligands are different (Types Ic and Id); the 4 Mn

[53] F. RICHTER and H. VAHRENKAMP, *Angew. Chem. Int. Edn. Engl.* **19**, 65 (1980).

[54] M. J. ATHERTON and J. H. HOLLOWAY, *Adv. Inorg. Chem. Radiochem.* **22**, 171–98 (1979).

[55] A. MULLER and W. JAEGERMANN, *Inorg. Chem.* **18**, 2631–3 (1979).

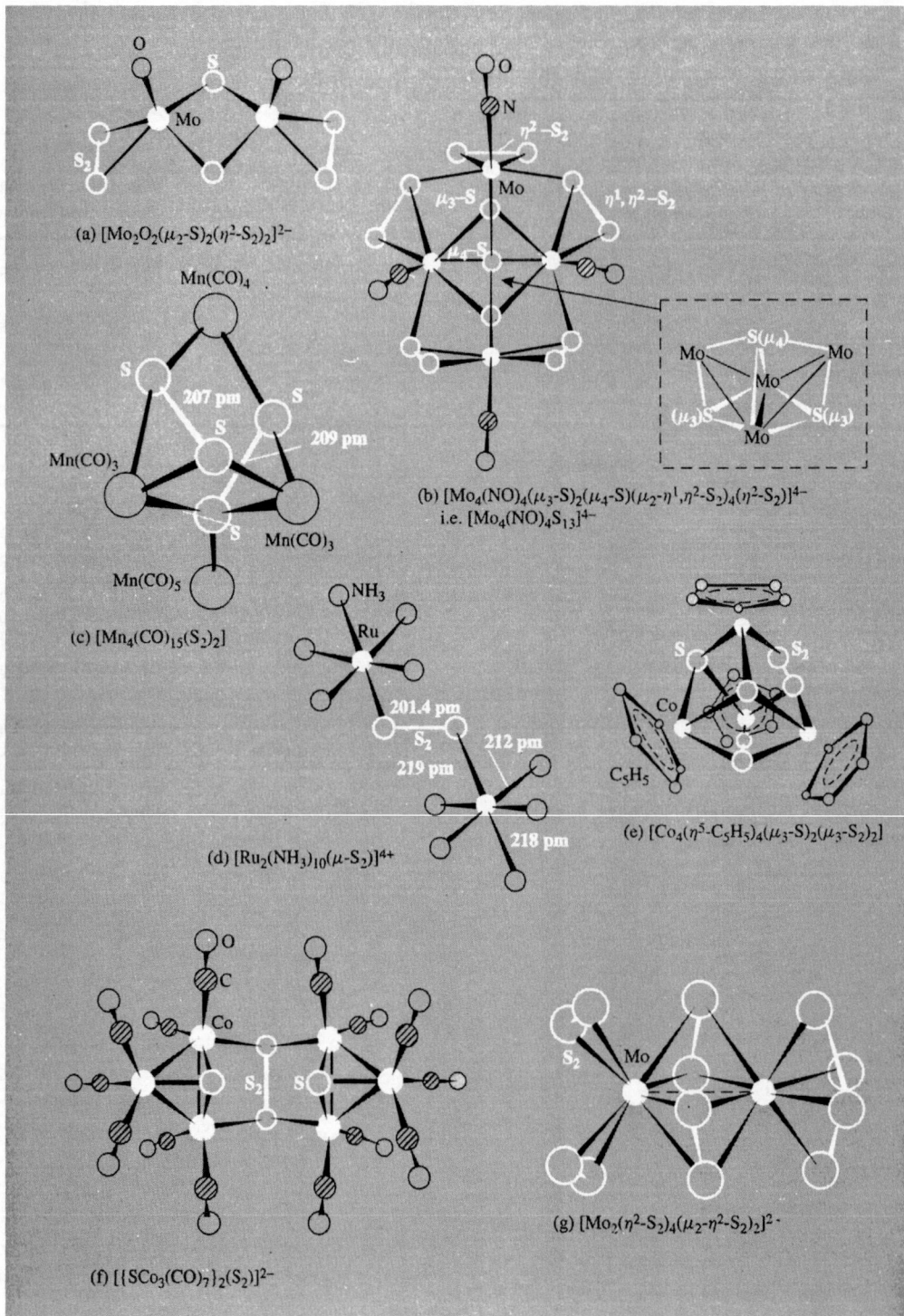

(a) $[Mo_2O_2(\mu_2\text{-}S)_2(\eta^2\text{-}S_2)_2]^{2-}$

(b) $[Mo_4(NO)_4(\mu_3\text{-}S)_2(\mu_4\text{-}S)(\mu_2\text{-}\eta^1,\eta^2\text{-}S_2)_4(\eta^2\text{-}S_2)]^{4-}$
i.e. $[Mo_4(NO)_4S_{13}]^{4-}$

(c) $[Mn_4(CO)_{15}(S_2)_2]$

(d) $[Ru_2(NH_3)_{10}(\mu\text{-}S_2)]^{4+}$

(e) $[Co_4(\eta^5\text{-}C_5H_5)_4(\mu_3\text{-}S)_2(\mu_3\text{-}S_2)_2]$

(f) $[\{SCo_3(CO)_7\}_2(S_2)]^{2-}$

(g) $[Mo_2(\eta^2\text{-}S_2)_4(\mu_2\text{-}\eta^2\text{-}S_2)_2]^{2-}$

Figure 15.13 Structures of some disulfide complexes.

Table 15.9   Types of metal-disulfide complex

Type	Example	$d(S–S)$/pm	Structure
Ia	$[Mo_2O_2S_2(S_2)_2]^{2-}$	208(1)	Figure 15.13a[56]
Ib	$[Mo_4(NO)_4S_{13}]^{4-}$	204.8(7)	Figure 15.13b[57]
Ic	$[Mn_4(CO)_{15}(S_2)_2]$	207	Figure 15.13c[58]
Id	$[Mn_4(CO)_{15}(S_2)_2]$	209	Figure 15.13c[58]
IIa	$[Ru_2(NH_3)_{10}S_2]^{4+}$	201.4(1)	Figure 15.13d[59]
IIb	$[Co_4(\eta^5\text{-}C_5H_5)_4(\mu_3\text{-}S)_2(\mu_3\text{-}S_2)_2]$	201(3)	Figure 15.13e[60]
IIc	$[\{SCo_3(CO)_7\}_2S_2]$	204.2(14)	Figure 15.13f[61]
III	$[Mo_2(S_2)_6]^{2-}$	204.3(5)	Figure 15.13g[62]

[56] W. CLEGG, N. MOHAN, A. MÜLLER, A. NEUMAN, W. RITTNER and G. M. SHELDRICK, *Inorg. Chem.* **19**, 2066–9 (1980).

[57] A. MÜLLER, W. ELTZNER and N. MOHAN, *Angew. Chem. Int. Edn. Engl.* **18**, 168–9 (1979).

[58] V. KÜLLMER, E. RÖTTINGER and H. VAHRENKAMP, *J. Chem. Soc., Chem. Commun.*, 782–3 (1977).

[59] R. C. ELDER and M. TRKULA, *Inorg. Chem.* **16**, 1048–51 (1977).

[60] V. A. UCHTMAN and L. F. DAHL, *J. Am. Chem. Soc.* **91**, 3756–63 (1969).

[61] D. L. STEVENSON, V. R. MAGNUSON and L. F. DAHL, *J. Am. Chem. Soc.* **89**, 3727–32 (1967).

[62] A. MÜLLER, W.-O. NOLTE and B. KREBS, *Angew. Chem. Int. Edn. Engl.* **17**, 279 (1978); A. MÜLLER, W.-O. NOLTE and B. KREBS, *Inorg. Chem.* **19**, 2835–6 (1980).

atoms are bonded, respectively, to 3, 3, 4 and 5 carbonyl ligands, but each achieves a distorted octahedral coordination by being bonded also to 3, 3, 2 and 1 S atoms respectively. There seems no reason to suppose that the diamagnetic bridged dinuclear anion $[(NC)_5Co^{III}SSCo^{III}(CN)_5]^{6-}$ is not a formal Type IIa disulfido S_2^{2-} complex, but there is evidence[59] that the superficially analogous paramagnetic dinuclear ruthenium cation in Fig. 15.13d is, in fact, a mixed-valence supersulfido S_2^- complex: $[(H_3N)_5Ru^{II}SSRu^{III}(NH_3)_5]^{4+}$. The bridged dinuclear cobalt anion undergoes a remarkable aerial oxidation in aqueous ethanol solutions at $-15°C$; one of the bridging S atoms only is oxidized and this results in the formation of a bridging thiosulfito group $[(NC)_5CoSSO_2Co(CN)_5]^{6-}$ coordinated through the two S atoms to the two Co atoms.[63]. Other recent examples of S_2-complexes include $[V(\eta^5-C_5Me_5)_2(\eta^2-S_2)]$,[64] $[W_2(S)_2(SH)(\mu-\eta^3-S_2)(\eta^2-S_2)_3]^-$,[65] $[(\eta^5-C_5Me_5)_2Fe_2(\mu-\eta^2,\eta^2-S_2)]$[66] and $[Ru_2\{P(OMe)_3\}_2(\eta^5-C_5H_5)_2(\mu-\eta^1,-\eta^1-S_2)_2]$.[67].

Not all disulfide complexes are discrete molecular or ionic species and several solid-state compounds of S_2^{2-} are known in addition to the familiar pyrites and marcasite-type disulfides (p. 680). Examples are the chlorine-bridged polymeric NbS_2Cl_2 mentioned on p. 667 (Fig. 15.14a) and the curious series of brown and red compounds formed by heating Mo or MoS_3 with S_2Cl_2, e.g.[54] MoS_2Cl_2, MoS_2Cl_3 (Fig. 15.14b), $Mo_2S_4Cl_5$ (Fig. 15.14c), $Mo_2S_5Cl_3$ and $Mo_3S_7Cl_4$.

Complexes with chelating polysulfide ligands can be made either by reacting complex metal halides with solutions of polysulfides or by reacting hydrido complexes with elemental

sulfur, e.g.:

$$H_2PtCl_6 + (NH_4)_2S_x(aq)$$

$$\xrightarrow{\text{boil}} (NH_4)_2[Pt^{IV}(S_5)_3]$$

$$[Ti(\eta^5-C_5H_5)_2Cl_2] + Na_2S_5$$

$$\longrightarrow [Ti^{IV}(\eta^5-C_5H_5)_2(S_5)] + 2NaCl$$

$$[W(\eta^5-C_5H_5)_2H_2] + \tfrac{5}{8}S_8$$

$$\longrightarrow [W^{IV}(\eta^5-C_5H_5)_2(S_4)] + H_2S$$

The red dianion $[PtS_{15}]^{2-}$ was first made in 1903 but its structure as a chiral tris chelating pentasulfido complex (Fig. 15.15a) was not established until 1969.[68] It is a rare example of a "purely inorganic" (carbon-free) optically active species.[69] [Other examples are S. Heřmánek and J. Plešek's resolution of the main group element cluster compound i-$B_{18}H_{22}$,[70] A. Werner's first-row transition-metal complex cation $[Co\{(\mu-OH)_2Co(NH_3)_4\}_3]^{6+}$,[71] and F. G. Mann's second-row complex anion cis-$[Rh\{\eta^2-(NH)_2-SO_2\}_2(OH_2)_2]^-]$.[72] The structure of the complex $[Ti(\eta^5-C_5H_5)_2(S_5)]$ is in Fig. 15.15b; it has previously been mentioned in connection with the synthesis of *cyclo*-polysulfur allotropes (p. 657). The chair conformation of the 6-membered TiS_5 ring undergoes chair-to-chair inversion above room temperature with an activation energy of about $69\,kJ\,mol^{-1}$.[73] A similar ring inversion in $[Pt(S_5)_3]^{2-}$ is even more facile and ^{195}Pt n.m.r. studies lead to a value of $50.5 \pm 1.3\,kJ\,mol^{-1}$ for $\Delta G^{\ddagger}$ at $0°C$.[74] Other recent examples of chelating S_n^{2-} ligands occur in the dark red-brown dianion[75] $[(\eta^2-S_5)Fe(\mu-S)_2Fe(\eta^2-S_5)]^{2-}$ and in the intriguing black

[63] F. R. FRONCZEK, R. E. MARSH and W. P. SCHAEFER, *J. Am. Chem. Soc.* **104**, 3382–5 (1982).

[64] C. FLORIANO, S. GAMBAROTTA, A. CHIESI-VILLA and C. GUASTINI, *J. Chem. Soc., Dalton Trans.*, 2099–103 (1987).

[65] F. SÉCHERESSE, J. M. MANOLI and C. POTVIN, *Inorg. Chem.* **25**, 3967–71 (1986).

[66] H. OGINO, H. TOBITA, S. INOMATA, and M. SHIMOI, *J. Chem. Soc., Chem. Commun.*, 586–7 (1988).

[67] P. M. TREICHEL, R. A. CRANE and K. J. HALLER, *Polyhedron* **9**, 1893–9 (1990).

[68] P. E. JONES and L. KATZ, *Acta Cryst.* **B25**, 745–52 (1969).

[69] R. D. GILLARD and F. L. WIMMER, *J. Chem. Soc., Chem. Commun.*, 936–7 (1978).

[70] S. HEŘMÁNEK and J. PLEŠEK, *Coll. Czech. Chem. Comm.* **35**, 2488–93 (1970).

[71] A. WERNER, *Ber.* **47**, 3057–94 (1914).

[72] F. G. MANN, *J. Chem. Soc.* 412–19 (1933).

[73] E. W. ABEL, M. BOOTH and K. G. ORRELL, *J. Organometall. Chem.* **160**, 75–9 (1978).

[74] F. G. RIDDELL, R. D. GILLARD and F. L. WIMMER, *J. Chem. Soc., Chem. Commun.*, 332–3 (1982).

[75] D. COUCOUVANIS, D. SWENSON, P. STREMPLE and N. C. BAENZIGER, *J. Am. Chem. Soc.* **101**, 3392–4 (1979).

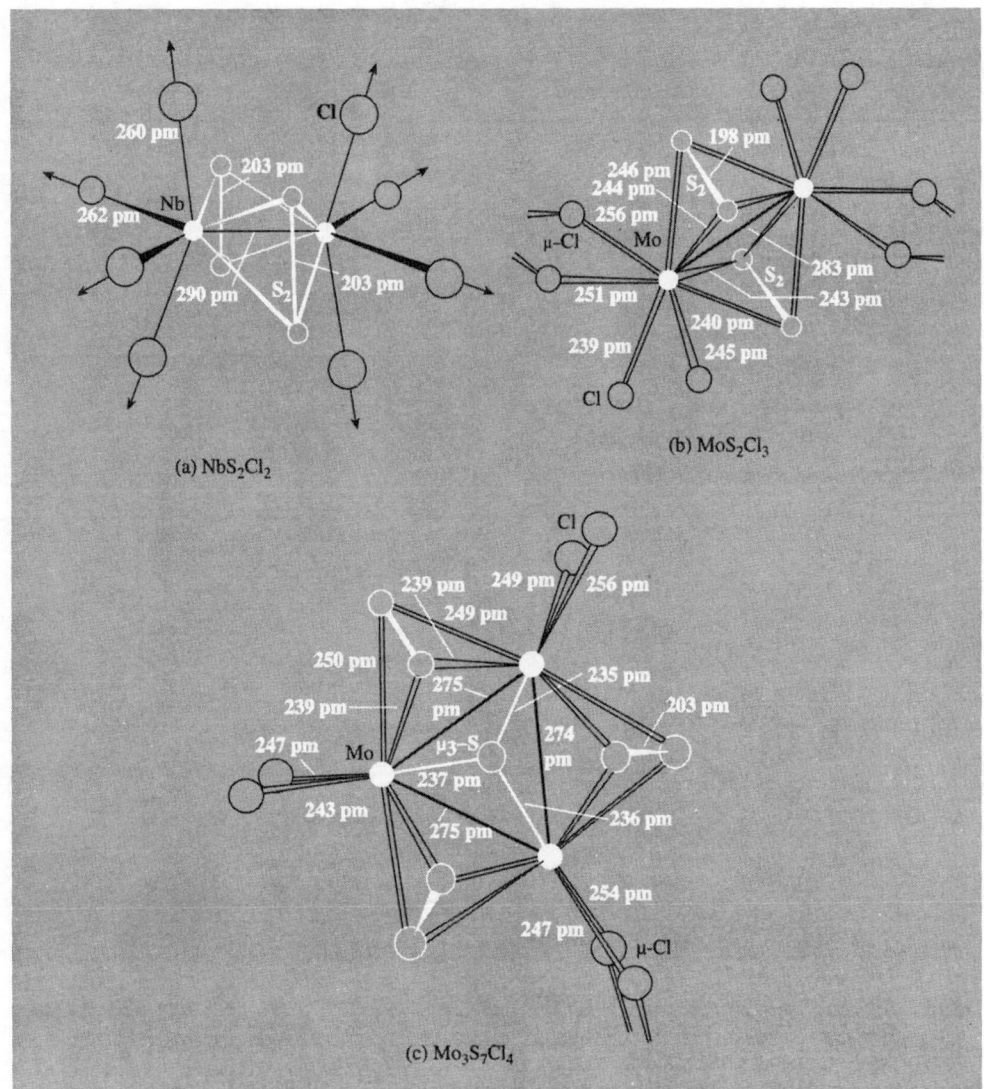

Figure 15.14   Chlorine bridged polymeric structures of (a) NbS_2Cl_2, (b) MoS_2Cl_3 and (c) $Mo_3S_7Cl_4$.

dianion $[Mo_2S_{10}]^{2-}$ which features 4 different sorts of sulfur ligand and at least 6 different S-atom environments (Fig. 15.15c).[76] More complicated structures, including those featuring multidentate polymers or metal-sulfur clusters are continually being discovered in polysulfides whose apparently simple stoichiometry often conceals on amazing structural complexity. Some recent examples are: $[(\eta^5\text{-}C_5Me_5)_2Th(\eta^4\text{-}S_5)]$,[77] $[NMe_4]^+[Ag(S_5)]_\infty^-$,[78] $[Cu_4(S_5)_2(py)_4]$,[79]

[76] W. CLEGG, G. CHRISTOU, C. D. GARNER and G. M. SHELDRICK, *Inorg. Chem.* **20**, 1562–6 (1981).

[77] D. A. WROBLESKI, D. T. CROMER, J. V. ORTIZ, T. B. RAUCHFUSS, R. R. RYAN and A. P. SATTELBERGER, *J. Am. Chem. Soc.* **108**, 174–5 (1986).

[78] R. M. H. BANDA, D. C. CRAIG, I. G. DANCE and M. L. SCUDDER, *Polyhedron* **8** 2379–83 (1989).

[79] E. RAMLI, T. B. RAUCHFUSS and C. L. STERN, *J. Am. Chem. Soc.* **112** 4043–4 (1990).

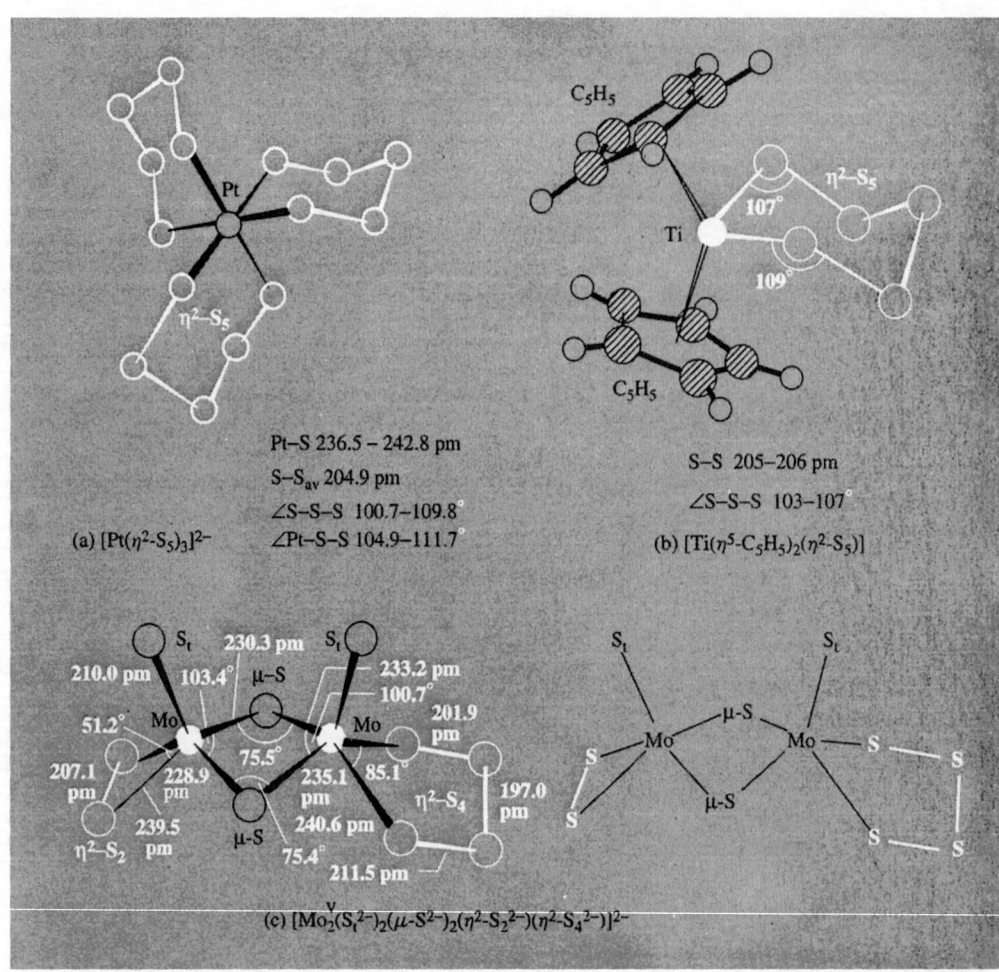

Figure 15.15 Structure and dimensions of (a) $[Pt(\eta^2\text{-}S_5)_3]^{2-}$, (b) $[Ti(\eta^5\text{-}C_5H_5)_2(\eta^2\text{-}S_5)]$ and (c) $[Mo_2S_{10}]^{2-}$: this last complex can be considered as an Mo^V derivative on the basis of the formulation $[Mo_2^V(S_t^{2-})_2(\mu\text{-}S^{2-})_2(\eta^2\text{-}S_2^{2-})(\eta^2\text{-}S_4^{2-})]^{2-}$. Note that the angles subtended by S atoms at Mo vary from $51.2°$ through $85.1°$ to $100.7°$ and $103.4°$, the M–S distances from $211\,pm$ through 229 and $235\,pm$ to $241\,pm$, and the S–S distances from 197 to $211.5\,pm$ with the S_2^{2-} group being $207\,pm$.

$[PPh_4]_2[In(\eta^2\text{-}S_4)(\eta^2\text{-}S_6)Br]$,[80] $[Li_2(\mu\text{-}S_6)\text{-}(tmeda)_2]$,[81] $[Cu_3(\mu\text{-}S_4)_3]^{3-}$,[82] $[(\eta^2\text{-}S_6)Cu\text{-}$ $(\mu\text{-}\eta^1,\eta^1\text{-}S_8)Cu(\eta^2\text{-}S_6)]^{4-}$,[82] $[Cu_6S_{17}]^{2-}$[83] and $[M_6S_{17}]^{4-}$ (M = Nb, Ta).[84] The original papers should be consulted for preparative routes and structural details. A review is also available.[85]

[80] S. DHINGRA and M. G. KANATZIDS, *Polyhedron* **10**, 1069–73 (1991). See also W. BUBENHEIM and U. MÜLLER, *Z. anorg. allg. Chem.* **620**, 1607–12 (1994) for $[In(\eta^2\text{-}S_4)(\eta^2\text{-}S_6)Cl]^-$.

[81] A. J. BANISTER (and 12 others), *J. Chem. Soc., Chem. Commun.*, 105–7 (1990).

[82] A. MÜLLER, F.-W. BAUMANN, H. BÖGGE, M. RÖMER, E. KRICKEMEYER and K. SCHMITZ, *Angew. Chem. Int. Edn. Engl.* **23**, 632–3 (1984).

[83] A. MÜLLER, M. RÖMER, H. BÖGGE, E. KRICKEMEYER and D. BERGMANN, *J. Chem. Soc., Chem. Commun.*, 384–5 (1984).

[84] J. SOLA, Y. DO, J. M. BERG and R. H. HOLM, *J. Am. Chem. Soc.* **105**, 7784–6 (1983).

[85] M. DRAGANJAC and T. B. RAUCHFUSS, *Angew. Chem. Int. Edn. Engl.* **24** 742–57 (1985).

Other ligands containing sulfur as donor atom

H_2S, the simplest compound of sulfur, differs markedly from its homologue H_2O in complex-forming ability: whereas aquo complexes are extremely numerous and frequently very stable (p. 625), H_2S rarely forms simple adducts due to its ready oxidation to sulfur or its facile deprotonation to SH^- or S^{2-}. $[AlBr_3(SH_2)]$ has long been known as a stable compound of tetrahedral $Al^{(86)}$ but the few transition metal complexes having some degree of stability at room temperature are of more recent vintage: examples include $[Mn(\eta^5\text{-}C_5H_5)(CO)_2(SH_2)]$, $[W(CO)_5(SH_2)]$, and the *triangulo* cluster complexes $[Ru_3(CO)_9(SH_2)]$ and $[Os_3(CO)_9(SH_2)]$.$^{(52,87)}$ Action of H_2S on acidic aqueous solutions frequently precipitates the metal sulfide (cf. qualitative analysis separation schemes) but, in the presence of a reducing agent such as Eu^{II}, H_2S can displace H_2O from the pale-yellow aquopentammine ruthenium(II) ion:

$$[Ru(NH_3)_5(OH_2)]^{2+} + H_2S \rightleftharpoons [Ru(NH_3)_5(SH_2)]^{2+};$$

$$K_{298} = 1.5 \times 10^3 \, l \, mol^{-1}$$

In the absence of Eu^{II}, oxidative deprotonation of the pale-yellow H_2S complex occurs to give the orange ruthenium(III) complex $[Ru(NH_3)_5(SH)]^{2+}$. Other examples of complexes containing the SH^- ligand are $[Cr(OH_2)_5(SH)]^{2+}$, $[W(\eta^5\text{-}C_5H_5)(CO)_3(SH)]$, $[Ni(\eta^5\text{-}C_5H_5)(PBu_3^n)(SH)]$, *trans*-$[PtH(PEt_3)_2(SH)]$ and *trans*-$[Pt(PEt_3)_2(SH)_2]$.$^{(52,88,89)}$

The S-donor ligands SO, S_2O_2 and SO_2 are mentioned in Section 15.2.5 and S–N ligands in Section 15.2.7. Thiocyanate (SCN^-) is ambidentate, but towards heavier metals it tends to be S-bonded rather than N-bonded. Bridging modes are also known (p. 324), including M–SCN–M and the rare S-only bridged MS(CN)M.$^{(90)}$

Organic thio ligands are well established, examples being the thiols RSH (R = Et, Pr^n, Bu^t, Ph),$^{(91)}$ the thioethers SMe_2, SEt_2, tetrahydrothiophene, etc., the chelating dithioethers, e.g. $MeS(CH_2)_2SMe$, and macro-cyclic ligands such as $\{-(CH_2)_3S-\}_n$ with $n = 3, 4$ etc.$^{(92)}$ Thiourea, $(H_2N)_2C{=}S$, affords a further example. Factors affecting the stability of the resulting complexes have already been reviewed (p. 198). It is also notable that when $B_{10}H_{14}$ reacts with solutions of thioethers in OEt_2, tetrahydrofuran, etc., it is the thio ligand rather than the oxygen-containing species which forms the stable *arachno*-bis adducts $[B_{10}H_{12}(SR_2)_2]$ (p. 176).

Another large class of S-donor ligands comprises the dithiocarbamates $R_2NCS_2^{2-}$ and related anions YCS_2^-, e.g. dithiocarboxylates RCS_2^-, xanthates $ROCS_2^-$, thioxanthates $RSCS_2^-$, dithiocarbonate OCS_2^{2-}, trithiocarbonate SCS_2^{2-} and dithiophosphinates $R_2PS_2^-$ (see p. 509 for applications). Dithiocarbamates can function either as unidentate or bidentate (chelating) ligands:

^{86} A. WEISS, R. PLASS, and AL. WEISS, *Z. anorg. allg. Chem.* **283**, 390–400 (1956).

^{87} C. G. KUEHN and H. TAUBE, *J. Am. Chem. Soc.* **98**, 689–702 (1976).

^{88} T. RAMASAMI and A. G. SYKES, *Inorg. Chem.* **15**, 1010–14 (1976).

^{89} I. M. BLACKLAWS, E. A. V. EBSWORTH, D. W. H. RANKIN and H. E. ROBERTSON, *J. Chem. Soc., Dalton Trans.*, 753–8 (1978).

^{90} S. M. NELSON, F. S. ESHO and M. G. B. DREW, *J. Chem. Soc., Chem. Commun.*, 388–9 (1981).

^{91} F. M. CONROY-LEWIS and S. J. SIMPSON, *J. Chem. Soc., Chem. Commun.*, 388–9 (1991) and references cited therein.

^{92} S. CRAWLE, J. R. HARTMAN, D. J. WATKIN and S. R. COOPER, *J. Chem. Soc., Chem. Commun.*, 1083–4 (1986); C. M. THORNE, S. C. RAWLE, G. A. ADMANS and S. R. COOPER, *ibid.*, 306–7 (1987); S. C. RAWLE and S. R. COOPER, *ibid.*, 308–9 (1987); T. YOSHIDA, T. ADACHI, M. KAMINAKA and T. UEDA, *J. Am. Chem. Soc.* **110**, 4872–3 (1988). See also W. TREMEL, B. KREBS and G. HENKEL, *J. Chem. Soc., Chem. Commun.*, 1527–9 (1986).

In the chelating mode they frequently stabilize the metal centre in an unusually high apparent formal oxidation state, e.g. $[Fe^{IV}(S_2CNR_2)_3)]^+$ and $[Ni^{IV}(S_2CNR_2)_3]^+$. They also have a propensity for stabilizing novel stereochemical configurations, unusual mixed oxidation states (e.g. of Cu), intermediate spin states (e.g. Fe^{III}, $S = \frac{3}{2}$), and for forming a variety of tris chelated complexes of Fe^{III} which lie at the $^2T_2 - {}^6A_1$ spin crossover (p. 1096).[93]

Dithiocarbamates and their analogues have 2 potential S-donor atoms joined to a single C atom and their complexes are sometimes called 1,1-dithiolato complexes. If the 2 S atoms are joined to adjacent C atoms then the equally numerous class of 1,2-dithiolato complexes results. Examples of chelating dithiolene ligands (drawn for convenience with localized valence bonds and ionic charges) are:

R = alkyl, aryl, CF₃, H   R = Me, F, Cl, H

Complexes of these ligands have been extensively studied during the past few decades not only because of the intrinsically interesting structural and bonding problems that they pose but also because of their varied industrial applications.[94-96] These include their use as highly specific analytical reagents, chromatographic supports, polarizers in sunglasses, mode-locking additives in neodymium lasers, semiconductors, fungicides, pesticides, vulcanization accelerators, high-temperature wear-inhibiting additives in lubricants, polymerization and oxidation catalysts and even fingerprint developers in forensic investigations.

Complexes in which dithiolenes are the only ligands present can be classified according to six structural types as shown schematically in Fig. 15.16. For bis(dithiolato) complexes the planar structure (a) with D_{2h} local symmetry about the metal is the commonest mode but occasionally 5-coordinate dimers (b) are observed. The very rare metal–metal bonded 5-coordinate dimeric bis(dithiolato) structure (c) has been found for the palladium and platinum complexes $[\{M(S_2C_2H_2)_2\}_2]$ with Pd–Pd 279 pm and Pt–Pt 275 pm. For tris(dithiolato) complexes two limiting geometries are possible: trigonal prismatic (Fig. 15.16d) and octahedral (Fig. 15.16f). The two geometries are related by a 30° twist of one triangular S_3 face with respect to the other, and intermediate twists are also known (Fig. 15.16e). As a rough generalization, the less-common trigonal prismatic geometry (local D_{3h} symmetry) is adopted by "ligand-controlled" complexes which are often neutral or highly oxidized [e.g. $M(S_2C_2R_2)_3$, where M = V, Cr, Mo, W, Re], whereas the more usual octahedral (D_3) geometry tends to be formed when the central metal dominates the stereochemistry as in the reduced anionic complexes. Thus reduction of the trigonal prismatic $[V\{S_2C_2(CN)_2\}_3]$ to the dianion $[V\{S_2C_2(CN)_2\}_3]^{2-}$ results in distortion to an intermediate geometry, whereas the iron analogue $[Fe\{S_2C_2(CN)_2\}_3]^{2-}$ has the chelated octahedral D_3 structure. Intermediate geometries (Fig. 15.16e) have also been found for $[Mo\{S_2C_2(CN)_2\}_3]^{2-}$ and its W analogue.

There has been much discussion about the detailed bonding in 1,2-dithiolene complexes because of the alternative ways that the ring system can be described, e.g.:

The formal oxidation state of the metal differs by 2 in these two limiting formulations (or

[93] R. L. MARTIN, in D. BANERJEA (ed.), *Coordination Chemistry — 20*, (International Conf. Calcutta, 1979) pp. 255–65, Pergamon Press, Oxford, 1980.

[94] R. EISENBERG, *Prog. Inorg. Chem.* **12**, 295–369 (1970).

[95] R. P. BURNS and C. A. MCAULIFFE, *Adv. Inorg. Chem. Radiochem.* **22**, 303–48 (1979); R. P. BURNS, F. P. MCCULLOUGH and C. A. MCAULIFFE, *Adv. Inorg. Chem. Radiochem.* **23**, 211–80 (1980).

[96] A. M. BOND and R. L. MARTIN, *Coord. Chem. Revs.* **54**, 23–98 (1984).

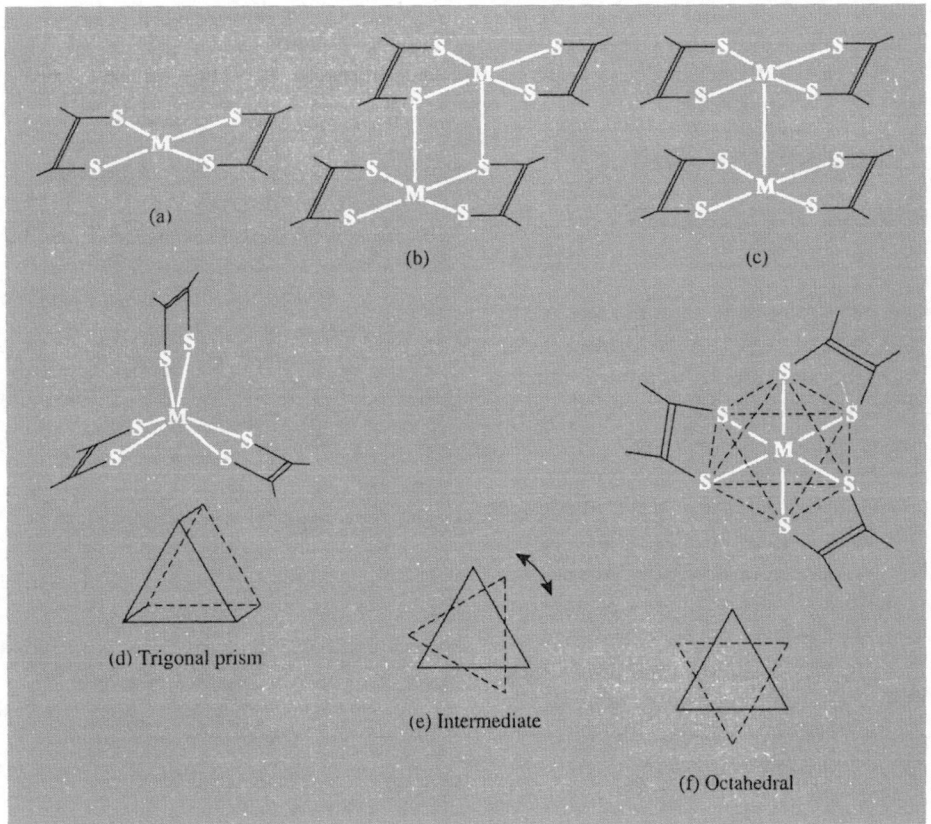

Figure 15.16 Coordination geometries of bis- and tris-1,2-dithiolene complexes (see text).

by 6 in a tris complex). On this basis it is unclear whether the complex $[V\{S_2C_2(CN)_2\}_3]$ mentioned in the preceding paragraph should be formulated as $V^{VI}(!)$ or V^0: it seems probable that an intermediate value would be more likely, but the example emphasizes the difficulty of assigning meaningful oxidation numbers to metal atoms in a redox series when the electronic configuration of the ligands themselves may also be undergoing change during reduction. Such reversible oxidation–reduction sequences are a characteristic feature of many 1,2-dithiolene complexes, e.g. for $L = \{S_2C_2(CN)_2\}$:

$$[CrL_3]^0 \underset{-e}{\overset{+e}{\rightleftharpoons}} [CrL_3]^{1-} \overset{+e}{\underset{-e}{\rightleftharpoons}}$$

$$[CrL_3]^{2-} \underset{-e}{\overset{+e}{\rightleftharpoons}} [CrL_3]^{3-}$$

$$[NiL_2]^0 \underset{-e}{\overset{+e}{\rightleftharpoons}} [NiL_2]^{1-} \underset{-e}{\overset{+e}{\rightleftharpoons}}$$

$$[NiL_2]^{2-} \underset{-e}{\overset{+e}{\rightleftharpoons}} [NiL_2]^{3-}$$

and similarly for the Pd, Pt and other analogues.[97] Likewise for dimeric species with $L = \{S_2C_2(CF_3)_2\}$:

$$[\{CoL_2\}_2]^0 \underset{-e}{\overset{+e}{\rightleftharpoons}} [\{CoL_2\}_2]^{1-} \underset{-e}{\overset{+e}{\rightleftharpoons}}$$

$$[\{CoL_2\}_2]^{2-} \underset{-2e}{\overset{+2e}{\rightleftharpoons}} 2[CoL_2]^{2-}$$

---

[97] W. E. GEIGER, T. E. MINES and F. E. SENFTLEBER, *Inorg. Chem.* **14**, 2141–7 (1975); W. E. GEIGER, C. S. ALLEN, T. E. MINES and F. C. SENFTLEBER, *Inorg. Chem.* **16**, 2003–8 (1977).

Mixed complexes in which a metal is coordinated by a dithiolene and by other ligands such as (η^5-C_5H_5), CO, NO, R_3P, etc., are also known.

15.2 Compounds of Sulfur

15.2.1 Sulfides of the metallic elements [98,99]

Many of the most important naturally occurring minerals and ores of the metallic elements are sulfides (p. 648), and the recovery of metals from these ores is of major importance. Other metal sulfides, though they do not occur in nature, can be synthesized by a variety of preparative methods, and many have important physical or chemical properties which have led to their industrial production. Again, the solubility relations of metal sulfides in aqueous solution form the basis of the most widely used scheme of elementary qualitative analysis. These various more general considerations will be briefly discussed before the systematic structural chemistry of metal sulfides is summarized.

General considerations

When sulfide ores are roasted in air two possible reactions may occur:

(a) conversion of the material to the oxide (as a preliminary to metal extraction, e.g. lead sulfide roasting);

(b) formation of water-soluble sulfates which can then be used in hydrometallurgical processes.

The operating conditions (temperature, oxygen pressure, etc.) required to achieve each of these results depend on the thermodynamics of the system and the duration of the roast is determined by the kinetics of the gas–solid reactions. [100] According to the Gibbs' phase rule:

$$F + P = C + 2$$

where F is the number of degrees of freedom (pressure, temperature, etc.), P is the number of phases in equilibrium and C is the number of components (independently variable chemical entities) in the system. It follows that, for a 3-component system (metal-sulfur-oxygen) at a given temperature and total pressure of the gas phase, a maximum of *three* condensed phases can coexist in equilibrium. The ranges of stability of the various solid phases at a fixed temperature can be shown on a stability diagram which plots the equilibrium pressure of SO_2 against the pressure of oxygen on a log–log graph. An idealized stability diagram for a divalent metal M is shown in Fig. 15.17a, and actual stability diagrams for copper at 950 K and lead at 1175 K are in Fig. 15.17b, and c. Note that, ideally, all boundaries are straight lines: those between M/MO and MS/MSO_4 are vertical whereas the others have slopes of 1.0 (M/MS), 1.5 (MS/MO), and -0.5 (MO/MSO_4).[†]

The application of these generalizations to the extractive metallurgy of individual metals is illustrated at appropriate points in the text dealing with the chemistry of the various elements.

---

[98] F. JELLINEK, Sulfides, Chap. 19 in G. NICKLESS (ed.), *Inorganic Sulfur Chemistry*, pp. 669–747, Elsevier, Amsterdam, 1968. A comprehensive review with 631 references.

[99] D. J. VAUGHAN and J. R. CRAIG, *Mineral Chemistry of Metal Sulfides*, Cambridge University Press, Cambridge, 1978, 493 pp. A comprehensive account of the structure bonding and properties of mineral sulfides.

[100] C. B. ALCOCK, *Principles of Pyrometallurgy*, Chap. 2, pp. 15 ff., Academic Press, London, 1967.

[†] These simple relations can readily be deduced from the equilibria being represented. Thus at constant temperature:

M/MO boundary: $MO = M + \frac{1}{2}O_2(g)$; $K = p^{\frac{1}{2}}(O_2)$. Hence $\log p(O_2) = 2 \log K = $ constant [i.e. independent of $p(SO_2)$].

MS/MSO_4 boundary: $MSO_4 = MS + 2O_2(g)$; $K = p^2(O_2)$. Hence $\log p(O_2) = \frac{1}{2} \log K = $ constant.

M/MS boundary: $MS + O_2(g) = M + SO_2(g)$; $K = p(SO_2)/p(O_2)$. Hence $\log p(SO_2) = \log K + \log p(O_2)$, i.e. slope $= 1.0$.

MS/MO boundary: $MS + \frac{3}{2}O_2(g) = MO + SO_2(g)$; $K = p(SO_2)/p^{3/2}(O_2)$. Hence $\log p(SO_2) = \log K + \frac{3}{2} \log p(O_2)$, i.e. slope $= 1.5$.

MO/MSO_4 boundary: $MSO_4 = MO + SO_2(g) + \frac{1}{2}O_2(g)$; $K = p(SO_2) \cdot p^{\frac{1}{2}}(O_2)$. Hence $\log p(SO_2) = \log K - \frac{1}{2} \log p(O_2)$, i.e. slope $= -0.5$.

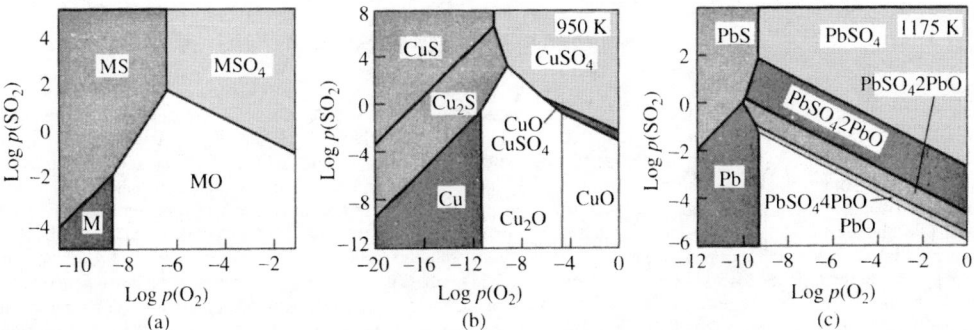

Figure 15.17 Stability diagrams for the systems (a) metal (M)–sulfur–oxygen (idealized), (b) Cu–S–O and (c) Pb–S–O.

As noted above, the roasting of most metal sulfides yields either the oxide or sulfate. However, a few metals can be obtained directly by oxidation of their sulfides, and these all have the characteristic property that their oxides are much less stable than SO_2. Examples are Cu, Ag, Hg and the platinum metals. In addition, metallic Pb can be extracted by partial oxidation of galena to form a sulfate (the "Scotch hearth" or Newnham process, p. 370). The oversimplified reaction is:

$$PbS + PbSO_4 \longrightarrow 2Pb + 2SO_2$$

However, as indicated in Fig. 15.17c, the system is complicated by the presence of several stable "basic sulfates" $PbSO_4.nPbO$ ($n = 1, 2, 4$), and these can react with gaseous PbS at lower metal-making temperatures, e.g.:

$$PbSO_4.2PbO(s) + 2PbS(g) \longrightarrow 5Pb(l) + 3SO_2(g)$$

Metal sulfides can be prepared in the laboratory or on an industrial scale by a number of reactions; pure products are rarely obtained without considerable refinement and nonstoichiometric phases abound (p. 679). The more important preparative routes include:

(a) direct combination of the elements (e.g. $Fe + S \longrightarrow FeS$);
(b) reduction of a sulfate with carbon (e.g. $Na_2SO_4 + 4C \longrightarrow Na_2S + 4CO$);
(c) precipitation from aqueous solution by treatment with either acidified H_2S (e.g. the platinum metals; Cu, Ag, Au; Cd, Hg;

Ge, Sn, Pb; As, Sb, Bi; Se, Te) or alkaline $(NH_4)_2S$ (e.g. Mn, Fe, Co, Ni, Zn; In, Tl);
(d) saturation of an alkali hydroxide solution with H_2S to give MHS followed by reaction with a further equivalent of alkali (e.g. $KOH(aq) + H_2S \longrightarrow KHS + H_2O$; $KHS + KOH \longrightarrow K_2S + H_2O$).

This last method is particularly suitable for water-soluble sulfides, though frequently it is the hydrate that crystallizes, e.g. $Na_2S.9H_2O$, $K_2S.5H_2O$. The hydrogensulfides MHS can also be made by passing H_2S into solutions of metals in liquid NH_3. The colourless hygroscopic mixed metal sulfide RbKS was recently made by annealing a mixture of K_2S and Rb_2S.[100a]

Industrial applications of metal sulfides span the full time-scale from the earliest rise of the emerging chemical industry in the eighteenth century to the most recent developments of Li/S and Na/S power battery systems (see Panel). Reduction of Na_2SO_4 by C was the first step in the now defunct Leblanc process (1791) for making Na_2CO_3 (p. 71). Na_2S (or NaHS) is still used extensively in the leather industry for removal of hair from hides prior to tanning, for making organo-sulfur dyes, as a reducing agent for organic nitro compounds in the production of amines, and as a flotation agent for copper ores. It is readily oxidized by atmospheric O_2 to give

---

[100a] H. SABROWSKY and P. VOGT, *Z. anorg. allg. Chem.*, **616**, 183–5 (1992).

Sodium-Sulfur Batteries

Alternatives to coal and hydrocarbon fuels as a source of power have been sought with increasing determination over the past three decades. One possibility is the Hydrogen Economy (p. 40). Another possibility, particularly for secondary, mobile sources of power, is the use of storage batteries. Indeed, electric vehicles were developed simultaneously with the first internal-combustion-engined vehicles, the first being made in 1888. In those days, over a century ago, electric vehicles were popular and sold well compared with the then noisy, inconvenient and rather unreliable petrol-engined vehicles. In 1899 an electric car held the world land-speed record at 105 km per hour. In the early years of this century, taxis in New York, Boston and Berlin were mainly electric; there were over 20 000 electric vehicles in the USA and some 10 000 cars and commercial vehicles in London. Even today (silent) battery-powered milk delivery vehicles are still operated in the UK. These use the traditional lead-sulfuric acid battery (p. 371), but this is extremely heavy and rather expensive.

The Na/S system has the potential to store 5-times as much energy (for the same weight) as the conventional lead battery and, in addition, shares with it the advantages of being silent, cheap to run, and essentially pollution-free; in general it is also reliable, has a long life and has extremely low maintenance costs. However, until recently it lacked the mileage range between successive chargings when compared with the highly developed petrol- or diesel-powered vehicles and it has a rather low performance (top speed and acceleration). A further disadvantage is the very long time taken to recharge the batteries (15–20 h) compared with the average time required to refill a petrol tank (1–2 min). Mixed power sources (petrol/electric battery) are a possible mode for development.

Conventional batteries consist of a liquid electrolyte separating two solid electrodes. In the Na/S battery this is inverted: a solid electrolyte separates two liquid electrodes: a ceramic tube made from the solid electrolyte sodium β-alumina (p. 249) separates an inner pool of molten sodium (mp 98°) from an outer bath of molten sulfur (mp 119°) and allows Na^+ ions to pass through. The whole system is sealed and is encased in a stainless steel canister which also serves as the sulfur-electrode current collector. Within the battery, the current is passed by Na^+ ions which pass through the solid electrolyte and react with the sulfur. The cell reaction can be written formally as

$$2Na(l) + \frac{n}{8}S_8(l) \longrightarrow Na_2S_n(l)$$

In the central compartment molten Na gives up electrons which pass through the external circuit and reduce the molten S_8 to polysulfide ions $S_n{}^{2-}$ (p. 681). The open circuit voltage is 2.08 V at 350°C. Since sulfur is an insulator the outer compartment is packed with porous carbon to provide efficient electrical conduction: the electrode volume is partially filled with sulfur when fully charged and is completely filled with sodium sulfide when fully discharged. To recharge, the polarity of the electrodes is changed and the passage of current forces the Na^+ ions back into the central compartment where they are discharged as Na atoms.

Typical dimensions for the β-alumina electrolyte tube are 380 mm long, with an outer diameter of 28 mm, and a wall thickness of 1.5 mm. A typical battery for automotive power might contain 980 of such cells (20 modules each of 49 cells) and have an open-circuit voltage of 100 V. Capacity exceeds 50 kWh. The cells operate at an optimum temperature of 300–350°C (to ensure that the sodium polysulfides remain molten and that the β-alumina solid electrolyte has an adequate Na^+ ion conductivity). This means that the cells must be thermally insulated to reduce wasteful loss of heat and to maintain the electrodes molten even when not in operation. Such a system is about one-fifth of the weight of an equivalent lead-acid traction battery and has a similar life (~1000 cycles).

thiosulfate:

$$2Na_2S + 2O_2 + H_2O \longrightarrow Na_2S_2O_3 + 2NaOH$$

World production of Na_2S exceeds 150 000 tonnes pa and that of NaHS approaches 100 000 tpa. Barium sulfide (from $BaSO_4 + C$) is the largest volume Ba compound manufactured but little of it is sold; almost all commercial Ba compounds are made by first making BaS and then converting it to the required compound.

Metal sulfides vary enormously in their solubility in water. As expected, the (predominantly ionic) alkali metal sulfides and alkaline earth metal sulfides are quite soluble though there is appreciable hydrolysis which results in strongly alkaline solutions ($M_2S + H_2O \longrightarrow$ MSH + MOH). Accordingly, solubilities depend sensitively not only on temperature but also on pH and partial pressure of H_2S. Thus, by varying the acidity, As can be separated from Pb, Pb from Zn, Zn from Ni, and Mn from Mg. In pure water the solubility of Na_2S is said to be 18.06 g per 100 g H_2O and for Ba_2S it is 7.28 g. In the case of some less-basic elements (e.g. Al_2S_3, Cr_2S_3) hydrolysis is complete and action of H_2S on solutions of the metal cation results in the precipitation of the hydroxide; likewise these sulfides (and SiS_2, etc.) react rapidly with water with evolution of H_2S.

By contrast with the water-soluble sulfides of Groups 1 and 2, the corresponding heavy metal sulfides of Groups 11 and 12 are amongst the least-soluble compounds known. Literature values are often wildly discordant, and care should be taken in interpreting the data. Thus, for black HgS the most acceptable value of the solubility product $[Hg^{2+}][S^{2-}]$ is $10^{-51.8}$ mol^2 l^{-2}, i.e.

$$HgS(s) \rightleftharpoons Hg^{2+}(aq) + S^{2-}(aq); \ pK = 51.8 \pm 0.5$$

However, this should not be taken to imply a concentration of only $10^{-25.9}$ mol l^{-1} for mercury in solution (i.e. less than 10^{-2} of 1 atom of Hg per litre!) since complex formation can simultaneously occur to give species such as $[Hg(SH)_2]$ in weakly acid solutions and $[HgS_2]^{2-}$ in alkaline solutions:

$$HgS(s) + H_2S(1 \ atm) \rightleftharpoons [Hg(SH)_2](aq); \ pK = 6.2$$

$$HgS(s) + S^{2-}(aq) \rightleftharpoons [HgS_2]^{2-}(aq); \ pK = 1.5$$

Hydrolysis also sometimes obtrudes.

Structural chemistry of metal sulfides

The predominantly ionic alkali metal sulfides M_2S (Li, Na, K, Rb, Cs) adopt the antifluorite structure (p. 118) in which each S atom is surrounded by a cube of 8 M and each M by a tetrahedron of S. The alkaline earth sulfides MS (Mg, Ca, Sr, Ba) adopt the NaCl-type 6:6 structure (p. 242) as do many other monosulfides of rather less basic metals (M = Pb, Mn, La, Ce, Pr, Nd, Sm, Eu, Tb, Ho, Th, U, Pu). However, many metals in the later transition element groups show substantial trends to increasing covalency leading either to lower coordination numbers or to layer-lattice structures.[101] Thus MS (Be, Zn, Cd, Hg) adopt the 4:4 zinc blende structure (p. 1210) and ZnS, CdS and MnS also crystallize in the 4:4 wurtzite modification (p. 1210). In both of these structures both M and S are tetrahedrally coordinated, whereas PtS, which also has 4:4

coordination, features a square-planar array of 4 S atoms about each Pt, thus emphasizing its covalent rather than ionic bonding. Group 13 sulfides M_2S_3 (p. 252) have defect ZnS structures with various patterns of vacant lattice sites.

The final major structure type found amongst monosulfides is the NiAs (nickel arsenide) structure (Fig. 15.18a). Each S atom is surrounded by a trigonal prism of 6 M atoms whilst each M has eightfold coordination, being surrounded octahedrally by 6 S atoms and by 2 additional M atoms which are coplanar with 4 of the S atoms. A significant feature of the structure is the close approach of the M atoms in chains along the (vertical) c-axis (e.g. 260 pm in FeS) and the structure can be regarded as transitional between the 6:6 NaCl structure and the more highly coordinated structures typical of metals. The NiAs structure is adopted by most first row transition-metal monosulfides MS (M = Ti, V, Cr, Fe, Co, Ni) as well as by many selenides and tellurides of these elements.

The NiAs structure is closely related to the hexagonal layer-lattice CdI$_2$ structure shown in Fig. 15.18b, this stoichiometry being achieved simply by leaving alternate M layers of the NiAs structure vacant. Disulfides MS$_2$ adopting this structure include those of Ti, Zr, Hf, Ta, Pt and Sn; conversely, Tl$_2$S has the anti-CdI$_2$ structure. Progressive partial filling of the alternate metal layers leads to phases of intermediate composition as exemplified by the Cr/S system (Table 15.10). For some elements these intermediate phases have quite extensive ranges of composition, the limits depending on the temperature of the system. For example, at 1000°C there is a succession of non-stoichiometric titanium sulfides TiS$_{0.97}$–TiS$_{1.06}$, TiS$_{1.204}$–TiS$_{1.333}$, TiS$_{1.377}$–TiS$_{1.594}$, TiS$_{1.810}$–TiS$_{1.919}$.[101] Many diselenides and ditellurides also adopt the CdI$_2$ structure and in some there is an almost continuous nonstoichiometric variation in composition, e.g. CoTe $\longrightarrow$ CoTe$_2$. A related 6:3 layer structure is the CdCl$_2$-type adopted by TaS$_2$, and the layer structures of MoS$_2$ and WS$_2$ are mentioned on p. 1018.

[101] N. N. Greenwood, *Ionic Crystals, Lattice Defects, and Nonstoichiometry*, Chap. 3, pp. 37–61; also pp. 153–5, Butterworths, London, 1968.

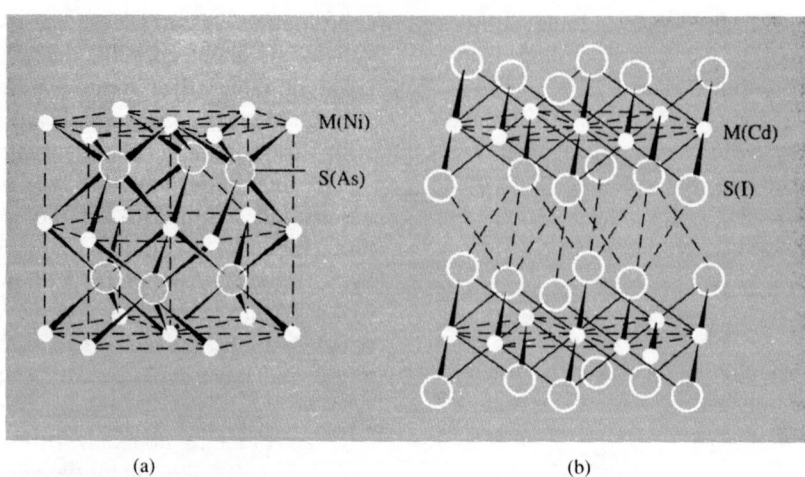

Figure 15.18 Comparison of the nickel arsenide structure (a) adopted by many monosulfides MS with the cadmium iodide structure (b) adopted by some disulfides MS_2. The structures are related simply by removing alternate layers of M from MS to give MS_2.

Table 15.10 Some sulfides of chromium (see text)

Nominal formula	Ratio Cr/S		Proportion of sites occupied in alternate layers	Random or ordered vacancies[a]
	calculated	observed		
CrS[b]	1.000	≈ 0.97	1:1	None
Cr_7S_8	0.875	0.88–0.87	$1:\frac{3}{4}$	Random
Cr_5S_6	0.833	0.85	$1:\frac{2}{3}$	Ordered
Cr_3S_4	0.750	0.79–0.76	$1:\frac{1}{2}$	Ordered
Cr_2S_3	0.667	0.69–0.67	$1:\frac{1}{3}$	Ordered
(CrS_2)	0.500	Not observed	1:0	—

[a] Refers to the vacancies in the alternate metal layers.

[b] CrS has a unique monoclinic structure intermediate between NiAs and PtS types.

Finally, many disulfides have a quite different structure motif, being composed of infinite three-dimensional networks of M and discrete S_2 units. The predominate structural types are pyrites, FeS_2 (also for M = Mn, Co, Ni, Ru, Os), and marcasite (known only for FeS_2 among the disulfides). Pyrites can be described as a distorted NaCl-type structure in which the rod-shaped S_2 units (S–S 217 pm) are centred on the Cl positions but are oriented so that they are inclined away from the cubic axes. The marcasite structure is a variant of the rutile structure (TiO_2, p. 961) in which the columns of edge-shared octahedra are rotated to give close approaches between pairs of S atoms in adjacent columns (S–S 221 pm).

Many metal sulfides have important physical properties.[98,102] They range from insulators, through semiconductors to metallic conductors of electricity, and some are even superconductors,

---

[102] F. HULLIGER, *Struct. Bonding* (Berlin) **4**, 83–229 (1968). A comprehensive review with 532 references, 65 structural diagrams, and a 34-page appendix tabulating the known phases and their physical properties.

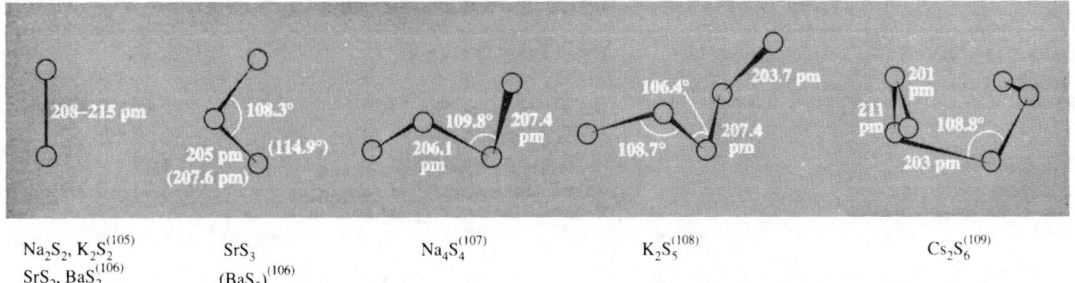

Figure 15.19   Structures of polysulfide anions S_n^{2-} in $M_2^1 S_n$ and BaS_n.

e.g. NbS_2 (<6.2 K), TaS_2 (<2.1 K), $Rh_{17}S_{15}$ (<5.8 K), CuS (<1.62 K) and CuS_2 (<1.56 K). Likewise they can be diamagnetic, paramagnetic, temperature-independent paramagnetic, ferro-magnetic, antiferromagnetic or ferrimagnetic.

The structures of more complex ternary metal sulfides such as $BaZrS_3$ (perovskite-type, p. 963), $ZnAl_2S_4$ (spinel type, p. 247), and $NaCrS_2$ (NaCl superstructure) introduce no new principles. Likewise, thiosalts, which may feature finite anions (e.g. $Tl_3[VS_4]$), vertex-shared chains (e.g. Ba_2MnS_3), edge-shared chains (e.g. $KFeS_2$), double chains (e.g. Ba_2ZnS_3), double layers (e.g. KCu_4S_3) or three-dimensional frameworks (e.g. $NH_4Cu_7S_4$).[103] Finite clusters also abound.[104]

Anionic polysulfides

The pyrites and marcasite structures can be thought of as containing S_2^{2-} units though the variability of the interatomic distance and other properties suggest substantial deviation from a purely ionic description. Numerous higher polysulfides S_n^{2-} have been characterized, particularly for the more electropositive elements Na, K, Ba, etc. They are yellow at room temperature, turn dark red on being heated, and may be thought of as salts of the polysulfanes

(p. 683). Typical examples are M_2S_n ($n = 2-5$ for Na, 2–6 for K, 6 for Cs), BaS_2, BaS_3, BaS_4, etc. The polysulfides, unlike the monosulfides, are low melting solids: published values for mps vary somewhat but representative values (°C) are:

Na_2S 1180°	Na_2S_2 484°		Na_2S_4 294°	Na_2S_5 255°
K_2S_3 292°	K_2S_4 ~145°	K_2S_5 211°	K_2S_6 196°	BaS_3 554°

Structures are in Fig. 15.19. The S_3^{2-} ion is bent (C_{2v}) and is isoelectronic with SCl_2 (p. 689). The S_4^{2-} ion has twofold symmetry, essentially tetrahedral bond angles, and a dihedral angle of 97.8° (see p. 654). The S_5^{2-} ion also has approximately twofold symmetry (about the central S atom); it is a contorted but unbranched chain with bond angles close to tetrahedral and a small but significant difference between the terminal and internal S–S distances. The S_6^{2-} ion has alternating S–S distances, and bond angles in the range 106.4–110.0° (mean 108.8°). Several of the references in Fig. 15.19 give preparative details: these can involve direct reaction of

[103] A. F. WELLS, *Structural Inorganic Chemistry*, 5th edn., Chap. 17 pp. 748–87, Oxford University Press, 1984.

[104] I. DANCE and K. FISHER, *Prog. Inorg. Chem.* **41**, 637–803 (1994). A comprehensive review with 503 references, 100 structural diagrams and 40 pages of tabulated material.

[105] H. FÖPPL, E. BUSMANN, and F.-K. FRORATH, *Z. anorg. allg. Chem.* **314**, 12–30 (1962).

[106] H. G. VON SCHNERING and N.-K. GOH, *Naturwissenschaften* **61**, 272 (1974).

[107] R. TEGMAN, *Acta Cryst.* **B29**, 1463–9 (1973).

[108] B. KELLY and P. WOODWARD, *J. Chem. Soc., Dalton Trans.*, 1314–6 (1976).

[109] S. C. ABRAHAMS and E. GRISON, *Acta Cryst.* **6**, 206–13 (1953).

Table 15.11 Some molecular and physical properties of H_2S

Distance (S–H)/pm	133.6(g)	$\Delta H_f^\circ/\text{kJ mol}^{-1}$	20.1(g)
Angle H–S–H	92.1°(g)	Density (s)/g cm^{-3}	1.12 (−85.6°)
MP/°C	−85.6	Density (l)/g cm^{-3}	0.993 (−85.6°)
BP/°C	−60.3	Viscosity/centipoise	0.547 (−82°)
Critical temperature/°C	100.4	Dielectric constant ε	8.99 (−78°)
Critical pressure/atm	84	Electrical conductivity/ohm^{-1} cm^{-1}	3.7×10^{-11} (−78°)

stoichiometric amounts of the elements in sealed tubes or reaction of MSH with S in ethanol.[110] It is interesting that, despite the unequivocal presence of the S_3^{2-} ion in K_2S_3, BaS_3, etc., a Raman spectroscopic study of *molten* "Na_2S_3" showed that the ion had disproportionated into S_2^{2-} and S_4^{2-}.[111]

15.2.2 Hydrides of sulfur (sulfanes)

Hydrogen sulfide is the only thermodynamically stable sulfane; it occurs widely in nature as a result of volcanic or bacterial action and is, indeed, a prime source of elemental S (p. 647). It has been known since earliest times and its classical chemistry has been extensively studied since the seventeenth century.[112] H_2S is a foul smelling, very poisonous gas familiar to all students of chemistry. Its smell is noticeable at 0.02 ppm but the gas tends to anaesthetize the olefactory senses and the intensity of the smell is therefore a dangerously unreliable guide to its concentration. H_2S causes irritation at 5 ppm, headaches and nausea at 10 ppm and immediate paralysis and death at 100 ppm; it is therefore as toxic and as dangerous as HCN.

H_2S is readily prepared in the laboratory by treating FeS with dilute HCl in a Kipp apparatus. Purer samples can be made by hydrolysing CaS, BaS or Al_2S_3, and the purest gas is prepared by direct reaction of the elements at 600°C.

Some physical properties are in Table 15.11:[113] comparison with the properties of water (p. 623) shows the absence of any appreciable H bonding in H_2S.[114] Comparisons with H_2Se, H_2Te and H_2Po are on p. 767.

H_2S is readily soluble in both acidic and alkaline aqueous solutions. Pure water dissolves 4.65 volumes of the gas at 0° and 2.61 volumes at 20°; in other units a saturated solution is 0.1 M at atmospheric pressure and 25°, i.e.

$$H_2S(g) \rightleftharpoons H_2S(aq); \quad K = 0.1023 \text{ mol l}^{-1} \text{ atm}^{-1};$$
$$pK = 0.99$$

In aqueous solution H_2S is a weak acid (p. 49). At 20°:[115]

$$H_2S(aq) \rightleftharpoons H^+(aq) + SH^-(aq);$$
$$pK_{a_1} = 6.88 \pm 0.02$$
$$SH^-(aq) \rightleftharpoons H^+(aq) + S^{2-}(aq);$$
$$pK_{a_2} = 14.15 \pm 0.05$$

The chemistry of such solutions has been alluded to on p. 678. At low temperatures a hydrate $H_2S.5\frac{3}{4}H_2O$ crystallizes. In acid solution H_2S is also a mild reducing agent; e.g. even on standing in air solutions slowly precipitate sulfur. The gas burns with a bluish flame in air to give H_2O and SO_2 (or H_2O and S if the air supply is restricted). For adducts, see p. 673.

In very strongly acidic nonaqueous solutions (such as HF/SbF_5) H_2S acts as a base (proton acceptor) and the white crystalline

[110] G. WEDDIDEN, H. KLEINSCHMAGER and S. HOPPE, *J. Chem. Res. (S)*, 1978, 96; (*M*), 1978, 1101–12.
[111] G. J. JANZ et al., *Inorg. Chem.* **15**, 1751–4, 1755–9, 1759–63 (1976).
[112] J. W. MELLOR, *A Comprehensive Treatise on Inorganic and Theoretical Chemistry*, Vol. 10, pp. 114–61, Longmans, London, 1930.

[113] F. FEHÉR, Liquid hydrogen sulfide, Chap. 4 in J. J. LAGOWSKI (ed.), *The Chemistry of Nonaqueous Solvents*, Vol. 3, pp. 219–40, Academic Press, New York, 1970.
[114] A. N. FITCH and J. K. COCKROFT, *J. Chem. Soc., Chem. Commun.*, 515–6 (1990).
[115] M. WIDMER and G. SCHWARZENBACH, *Helv. Chim. Acta* **47**, 266–71 (1964).

solid $[SH_3]^+[SbF_6]^-$ has been isolated from such solutions.[116] The compound, which is the first known example of a stable salt of SH_3^+, can be stored at room temperature in Teflon or Kel-F containers but attacks quartz. Vibrational spectroscopy confirms the pyramidal C_{3v} structure expected for a species isoelectronic with PH_3 (p. 492). In the presence of an excess of H_2S at $-80°C$, the trimercaptosulfonium salts $[S(SH)_3]^+AsF_6^-$ and $[S(SH)_3]^+SbCl_6^-$ can be prepared;[117] the cation is isoelectronic with $P(PH_2)_3$ (p. 495) and is expected to have C_{3v} symmetry.

Polysulfanes, H_2S_n, with $n = 2-8$ have been prepared and isolated pure, and many higher homologues have been obtained as mixtures with variable n. Our modern knowledge of these numerous compounds stems mainly from the elegant work of F. Fehér and his group in the 1950s. All polysulfanes have unbranched chains of n sulfur atoms thus reflecting the well-established propensity of this element towards catenation (p. 652). The polysulfanes are reactive liquids whose density d, viscosity η, and bp increase with increasing chain length. H_2S_2, the analogue of H_2O_2, is colourless but the others are yellow, the colour deepening with increasing chain length.

The polysulfanes were at one time made by fusing crude $Na_2S.9H_2O$ with various amounts of sulfur and pouring the resulting polysulfide solution into an excess of dilute hydrochloric acid at $-10°C$. The resulting crude yellow oil is a mixture mainly of H_2S_n ($n = 4-7$). Polysulfanes can now also be readily prepared by a variety of other reactions, e.g.:

$$Na_2S_n(aq) + 2HCl(aq) \longrightarrow 2NaCl(aq)$$
$$+ H_2S_n \ (n = 4-6)$$

$$S_nCl_2(l) + 2H_2S(l) \longrightarrow 2HCl(g) + H_2S_{n+2}(l)$$

$$S_nCl_2(l) + 2H_2S_m(l) \longrightarrow 2HCl(g)$$
$$+ H_2S_{n+2m}(H_2S_6-H_2S_{18})$$

Purification is by low-pressure distillation. Some physical properties are in Table 15.12. Polysulfanes are readily oxidized and all are thermodynamically unstable with respect to disproportionation:

$$H_2S_n(l) \longrightarrow H_2S(g) + \frac{n-1}{8}S_8(s)$$

Table 15.12 Some physical properties of poly-sulfanes[118]

Compound	$d_{20}/g\,cm^{-3}$	$P_{20}/mmHg$	BP/°C (extrap)
H_2S_2	1.334	87.7	70
H_2S_3	1.491	1.4	170
H_2S_4	1.582	0.035	240
H_2S_5	1.644	0.0012	285
H_2S_6	1.688	—	—
H_2S_7	1.721	—	—
H_2S_8	1.747	—	—

This disproportionation is catalysed by alkali, and even traces dissolved from the surface of glass containers is sufficient to effect deposition of sulfur. They are also degraded by sulfite and by cyanide ions:

$$H_2S_n + (n-1)SO_3^{2-} \longrightarrow H_2S + (n-1)S_2O_3^{2-}$$

$$H_2S_n + (n-1)CN^- \longrightarrow H_2S + (n-1)SCN^-$$

The former reaction, in particular, affords a convenient means of quantitative analysis by determination of the H_2S (precipitated as CdS) and iodometric determination of the thiosulfate produced.

15.2.3 Halides of sulfur

Sulfur fluorides

The seven known sulfur fluorides are quite different from the other halides of sulfur in their stability, reactivity and to some extent even in their stoichiometries; it is therefore convenient to

[116] K. O. CHRISTE, *Inorg. Chem.* **14**, 2230-3 (1975).

[117] R. MINKWITZ, R. KRAUSE, H. HÄRTNER and W. SAWODNY, *Z. anorg. allg. Chem.* **593**, 137-46 (1991).

[118] M. SCHMIDT and W. SIEBERT in *Comprehensive Inorganic Chemistry*, Vol. 2, Chap. 23, pp. 826-42, Pergamon Press, Oxford, 1973.

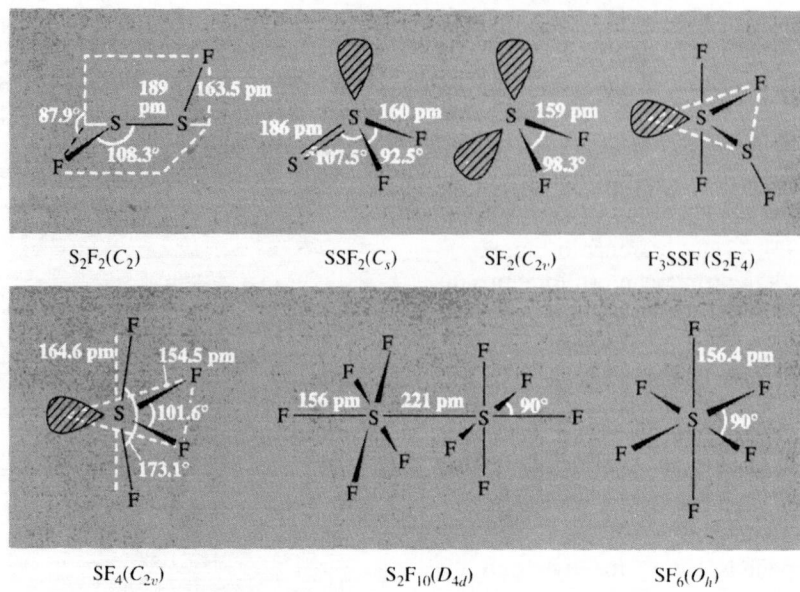

$S_2F_2(C_2)$ $SSF_2(C_s)$ $SF_2(C_{2v})$ $F_3SSF\ (S_2F_4)$

$SF_4(C_{2v})$ $S_2F_{10}(D_{4d})$ $SF_6(O_h)$

Figure 15.20   Molecular structures of the sulfur fluorides.

consider them separately. Moreover, they have proved a rich field for both structural and theoretical studies since they form an unusually extensive and graded series of covalent molecular compounds in which S has the oxidation states 1, 2, 3, 4, 5 and 6, and in which it also exhibits all coordination numbers from 1 to 6 (if SF_5^- is also included). The compounds feature a rare example of structural isomerism amongst simple molecular inorganic compounds (FSSF and SSF$_2$) and also a monomer–dimer pair (SF$_2$ and F$_3$SSF). The structures and physical properties will be described first, before discussing the preparative routes and chemical reactions.

Structures and physical properties. The molecular structure, point group symmetries, and dimensions of the sulfur fluorides are summarized in Fig. 15.20[119] S_2F_2 resembles H_2O_2, H_2S_2, O_2F_2 and S_2X_2, and detailed comparisons of bond distances, bond angles and dihedral angles are instructive. The isomer SSF$_2$ (thiothionylfluoride) features 3-coordinate S^{IV} and 1-coordinate S^{II} and it is notable that the formally

double-bonded S–S distance is very close to that in the singly bonded isomer. The fugitive species SF$_2$ has the expected bent configuration in the gas phase but is unique in readily undergoing dimerization by insertion of a second SF$_2$ into an S–F bond. The structure of the resulting molecule F$_3$SSF is, in a sense, intermediate between those of S$_2$F$_2$ and SF$_4$, being based on a trigonal bipyramid with the equatorial F atom replaced by an SF group. The fact that the ^{19}F nmr spectrum at $-100°$ shows four distinct F resonances indicates that the 2 axial F atoms are non-equivalent, implying restricted rotation about the S–S bond.

The structure of SF$_4$ is particularly significant. It is based on a trigonal bipyramid with one equatorial position occupied by the lone-pair; this distorts the structure by reducing the equatorial F–S–F bond angle bond angle from $120°$ to $101.6°$ and by repelling the axial F_{ax} atoms towards F_{eq}. There is also a significant difference between the (long) S–F_{ax} and (short) S–F_{eq} distances. Again, the low-temperature ^{19}F nmr spectrum is precisely diagnostic of the C_{2v} structure, since the observed doublet of 1:2:1 triplets is consistent only with the two sets of 2 equivalent F atoms in this point group symmetry

[119] F. SEEL, *Adv. Inorg. Chem. Radiochem.* **16**, 297–333 (1974).

Halides of sulfur

Table 15.13 Physical properties of some sulfur fluorides

	FSSF	S=SF$_2$	SF$_4$	SF$_6$	S$_2$F$_{10}$
MP/°C	−133	−164.6	−121	−50.54	−52.7
BP/°C	+15	−10.6	−38	−63.8 (subl)	+30
Density(T°C)/g cm^{-3}	—	—	1.919(−73°)	1.88(−50°)	2.08(0°)

(^{19}F, like ^{1}H, has nuclear spin $\frac{1}{2}$).[120] Thus, an axial lone-pair (C_{3v}) would lead to a doublet and a quartet of integrated relative intensity 3:1, whereas all other conceivable symmetries (T_d, C_{4v}, D_{4h}, D_{2d}, D_{2h}) would give a sharp singlet from the 4 equivalent F atoms. Above −98° the 30 MHz ^{19}F nmr spectrum of SF$_4$ gradually broadens and it coalesces at −47° into a single broad resonance which gradually sharpens again to a narrow singlet at higher temperatures; this is due to molecular fluxionality which permits intramolecular interchange of the axial and equatorial F atoms.

The structure of SF$_4$ can be rationalized on most of the simple bonding theories; the environment of S has 10 valency electrons and this leads to the observed structure in both valence-bond and electron-pair repulsion models. However, the rather high energy of the 3d orbitals on S make their full participation in bonding via sp^{3}d$_{z^2}$ unlikely and, indeed, calculations[121] show that there may be as little as 12% d-orbital participation rather than the 50% implied by the scheme sp$_x$p$_y$ + p$_z$d$_{z^2}$. Thus charge-transfer configurations or bonding via sp$_x$p$_y$ + p$_z$ seem to be better descriptions, the p$_z$ orbital on S being involved in a 3-centre 4-electron bond with the 2 axial F atoms (cf. XeF$_2$, p. 897).

The regular octahedral structure of SF$_6$ and the related structure of S$_2$F$_{10}$ (Fig. 15.20) call for little comment except to note the staggered (D_{4d}) arrangement of the two sets of F$_{eq}$ in S$_2$F$_{10}$ and the unusually long S–S distance, both features presumably reflecting interatomic repulsion between the F atoms. SF$_6$ is also of

interest in establishing conclusively that S can be hexavalent. Its great stability (see below) contrasts with the non-existence of SH$_4$ and SH$_6$ despite the general similarity in S–F and S–H bond strengths; its existence probably reflects (a) the high electronegativity of F (p. 26), which facilitates the formation of either polar or 3-centre 4-electron bonds as discussed above for SF$_4$, and (b) the lower bond energy of F$_2$ compared to H$_2$, which for SH$_4$ and SH$_6$ favours dissociation into H$_2$S + nH$_2$.[122] For descriptions of the bonding which involve the use of 3d orbitals on sulfur, a net positive charge on the central atom would contract the d orbitals thereby making them energetically and spatially more favourable for overlap with the fluorine orbitals.

Some physical properties of the more stable sulfur fluorides are in Table 15.13. All are colourless gases or volatile liquids at room temperature. SF$_6$ sublimes at −63.8° (1 atm) and can only be melted under pressure (−50.8°). It is notable both for its extreme thermal and chemical stability (see below), and also for having a higher gas density than any other substance that boils below room temperature (5.107 times as dense as air).

Synthesis and chemical reactions. Disulfur difluoride, S$_2$F$_2$, can be prepared by the mild fluorination of sulfur with AgF in a rigorously dried apparatus at 125°. It is best handled in the gas phase at low pressures and readily isomerizes to thiothionylfluoride, SSF$_2$, in the presence of alkali metal fluorides. SSF$_2$ can be made either by isomerizing S$_2$F$_2$ or directly by the fluorination of S$_2$Cl$_2$ using KF in SO$_2$:

$$2KSO_2F + S_2Cl_2 \longrightarrow SSF_2 + 2KCl + 2SO_2$$

[120] F. A. COTTON, J. W. GEORGE and J. S. WAUGH, *J. Chem. Phys.* **28**, 994–5 (1958); E. MUETTERTIES and W. D. PHILLIPS, *J. Am. Chem. Soc.* **81**, 1084–8 (1959).

[121] P. J. HAY, *J. Am. Chem. Soc.* **99**, 1003–12 (1977).

[122] G. M. SCHWENZER and H. F. SCHAEFFER, *J. Am. Chem. Soc.* **97**, 1393–7 (1975).

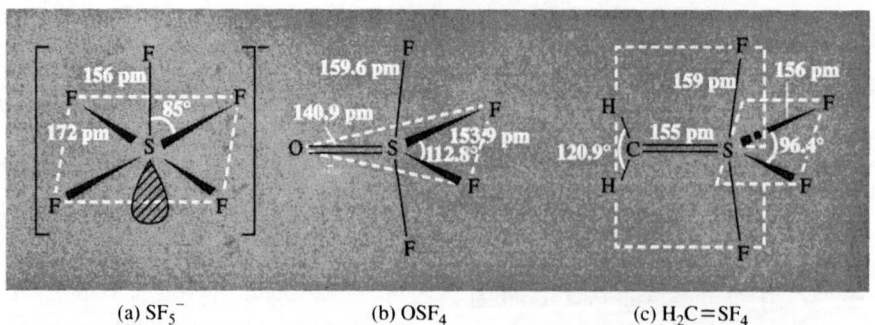

(a) SF_5^- (b) OSF_4 (c) $H_2C=SF_4$

Figure 15.21   Comparison of the structures of three species in which S has 12 valence electrons: (a) the SF_5^- ion in $RbSF_5$, as deduced from X-ray analysis,[123] (b) OSF_4 as deduced from gas-phase electron diffraction[124] (note the wider angle $F_{eq}SF_{eq}$ when compared with SF_4 (Fig. 15.20) and the shorter distance $S-F_{ax}$; the angle $F_{ax}SF_{ax}$ is 164.6°), and (c) H_2CSF_4 (X-ray crystal structure at $-160°$).[125] The angle $F_{eq}SF_{eq}$ is significantly smaller than in SF_4 as is the angle $F_{ax}SF_{ax}$ (170.4°); the methylene group is coplanar with the axial SF_2 group as expected for $p_\pi-d_\pi$ C=S overlap and, unlike SF_4, the molecule is non-fluxional.

SSF_2 can be heated to 250° but is, in fact, thermodynamically unstable with respect to disproportionation, being immediately transformed to SF_4 in the presence of acid catalysts such as BF_3 or HF:

$$2SSF_2 \longrightarrow \tfrac{3}{8}S_8 + SF_4$$

Both S_2F_2 and SSF_2 are rapidly hydrolysed by pure water to give S_8, HF and a mixture of polythionic acids $H_2S_nO_6$ (n 4–6), e.g.:

$$5S_2F_2 + 6H_2O \longrightarrow \tfrac{3}{4}S_8 + 10HF + H_2S_4O_6$$

Alkaline hydrolysis yields predominantly thiosulfate. SSF_2 burns with a pale-blue flame when ignited, to yield SO_2, SOF_2 and SO_2F_2.

Sulfur difluoride, SF_2, is a surprisingly fugitive species in view of its stoichiometric similarity to the stable compounds H_2S and SCl_2 (p. 689). It is best made by fluorinating gaseous SCl_2 with activated KF (from KSO_2F) or with HgF_2 at 150°, followed by a tedious fractionation from the other sulfur fluorides (FSSF, SSF_2 and SF_4) which form the predominant products. The chlorofluorides ClSSF and $ClSSF_3$ are also formed. The compound can only be handled as a dilute gas under rigorously anhydrous conditions or at very low temperatures in a matrix of solid argon, and it rapidly dimerizes to give F_3SSF.

Sulfur tetrafluoride, SF_4, though extremely reactive (and valuable) as a selective fluorinating agent, is much more stable than the lower fluorides. It is formed, together with SF_6, when a cooled film of sulfur is reacted with F_2, but is best prepared by fluorinating SCl_2 with NaF in warm acetonitrile solution:

$$3SCl_2 + 4NaF \xrightarrow[75°]{MeCN} S_2Cl_2 + SF_4 + 4NaCl$$

SF_4 is unusual in apparently acting both as an electron-pair acceptor and an electron-pair donor (amphoteric Lewis acid-base). Thus pyridine forms a stable 1:1 adduct $C_5H_5NSF_4$ which presumably has a pseudooctahedral (square-pyramidal) geometry. Likewise CsF (at 125°) and Me_4NF (at $-20°$) form $CsSF_5$ and $[NMe_4]^+[SF_5]^-$ (Fig. 15.21a). By contrast, SF_4 behaves as a donor to form 1:1 adducts with many Lewis acids; the stability decreases in the sequence $SbF_5 > AsF_5 > IrF_5 > BF_3 > PF_5 > AsF_3$. In view of the discussion on

[123] J. BITTNER, J. FUCHS and K. SEPPELT, *Z. anorg. allg. Chem.* **551**, 182–90 (1988).
[124] L. HEDBERG and K. HEDBERG, *J. Phys. Chem.* **86**, 598–602 (1982).
[125] H. BOCK, J. E. BOGGS, G. KLEEMANN, D. LENTZ, H. OBERHAMMER, E. M. PETERS, K. SEPELT, A. SIMON and B. SOLOUKI, *Angew. Chem. Int. Edn. Engl.* **18**, 944–5 (1979).

p. 198 it seems likely that SF_4 is acting here not as an S lone-pair donor but as a fluoride ion lone-pair donor and there is, indeed, infrared evidence to suggest that $SF_4.BF_3$ is predominantly $[SF_3]^+[BF_4]^-$.

SF_4 rapidly decomposes in the presence of moisture, being instantly hydrolysed to HF and SO_2. Despite this it has been increasingly used as a powerful and highly selective fluorinating agent for both inorganic and organic compounds. In particular it is useful for converting ketonic and aldehyde $>C{=}O$ groups to $>CF_2$, and carboxylic acid groups $-COOH$ to $-CF_3$. Similarly, $\equiv P{=}O$ groups are smoothly converted to $\equiv PF_2$, and $>P(O)OH$ groups to $>PF_3$. It also undergoes numerous oxidative addition reactions to give derivatives of S^{VI}. The simplest of these are direct oxidation of SF_4 with F_2 or ClF (at $380°$) to give SF_6 and $SClF_5$ respectively. Analogous reactions with $N_2F_4(h\nu)$ and F_5SOOSF_5 yield SF_5NF_2 and *cis*-$SF_4(OSF_5)_2$ respectively; likewise F_5SOF (p. 688) yields F_5SOSF_5. Direct oxidation of SF_4 with O_2, however, proceeds only slowly unless catalysed by NO_2: the product is OSF_4, which has a trigonal bipyramidal structure like SF_4 itself, but with the equatorial lone-pair replaced by the oxygen atom (Fig. 15.21b). A similar structure is adopted by the more recently prepared methylene compound $H_2C{=}SF_4$ (Fig. 15.21c);[125] this is made by treating SF_5-CH_2Br with $LiBu^n$ at $-110°$ and is more stable than the isoelectronic P or S ylides or metal carbene complexes, being stable in the gas phase up to $650°$ at low pressures.

Some other reactions of SF_4 are:

$$Cl_2 + CsF + SF_4 \xrightarrow{110°} SClF_5 + CsCl$$

$$I_2O_5 + 5SF_4 \longrightarrow 2IF_5 + 5OSF_2$$

$$4BCl_3 + 3SF_4 \longrightarrow 4BF_3 + 3SCl_2 + 3Cl_2$$

$$RCN + SF_4 \longrightarrow RCF_2N{=}SF_2$$

$$NaOCN + SF_4 \longrightarrow CF_3N{=}SF_2 + \cdots$$

$$CF_3CF{=}CF_2 + SF_4 \xrightarrow{CsF/150°} (CF_3)_2CFSF_3$$

$$(bp\,46°)$$

$$2CF_3CF{=}CF_2 + SF_4 \xrightarrow{CsF/150°} \{(CF_3)_2CF\}_2SF_2$$

$$(bp \sim 111°)$$

Disulfur decafluoride, S_2F_{10}, is obtained as a byproduct of the direct fluorination of sulfur to SF_6 but is somewhat tedious to separate and is more conveniently made by the photolytic reduction of $SClF_5$ (prepared as above):

$$2SClF_5 + H_2 \xrightarrow{h\nu} S_2F_{10} + 2HCl$$

It is intermediate in reactivity between SF_4 and the very inert SF_6. Unlike SF_4 it is not hydrolysed by water or even by dilute acids or alkalis and, unlike SF_6, it is extremely toxic. It disproportionates readily at $150°$ probably by a free radical mechanism involving $SF_5^{\bullet}$ (note the long, weak S–S bond; Fig. 15.20):

$$S_2F_{10} \xrightarrow{150°} SF_4 + SF_6$$

Similarly it reacts readily with Cl_2 and Br_2 to give $SClF_5$ and $SBrF_5$. It oxidizes KI (and I_3^-) in acetone solution to give iodine (note SF_4 converts acetone to Me_2CF_2). S_2F_{10} reacts with SO_2 to give F_5SSO_2F and with NH_3 to give $N{\equiv}SF_3$.

Sulfur hexafluoride is unique in its stability and chemical inertness: it is a colourless, odourless, tasteless, unreactive, non-flammable, non-toxic, insoluble gas prepared by burning sulfur in an atmosphere of fluorine. Because of its extraordinary stability and excellent dielectric properties it is extensively used as an insulating gas for high-voltage generators and switch gear: at a pressure of $2-3$ bars it withstands $1.0-1.4$ MV across electrodes 50 mm apart without breakdown, and at 10 bars it is used for high-power underground electrical transmission systems at 400 V and above. However, there is now some environmental concern at its use as an electrical transformer fluid and as an inert blanketing gas in magnesium metal casting, since even minute amounts may contribute to an atmospheric greenhouse effect (it is 6800 times as potent as CO_2).

SF_6 can be heated to $500°$ without decomposition, and is unattacked by most metals, P, As, etc., even when heated. It is also unreactive towards high-pressure steam presumably as a result of kinetic factors since the gas-phase reaction $SF_6 + 3H_2O \longrightarrow SO_3 + 6HF$ should release some $460 \, kJ \, mol^{-1}$ ($\Delta G° \sim 200 \, kJ \, mol^{-1}$). By contrast, reaction with H_2S yields sulfur and HF. Hot HCl and molten KOH at 500° are without effect. Boiling Na attacks SF_6 to yield Na_2S and NaF; indeed, this reaction can be induced to go rapidly even at room temperature or below in the presence of biphenyl dissolved in glyme (1,2-dimethoxyethane). It is also reduced by Na/liq NH_3 and, more slowly, by $LiAlH_4/Et_2O$. Al_2Cl_6 at 200° yields AlF_3, Cl_2, and sulfur chlorides. Recent experiments[126] indicate that SF_6 becomes much more reactive at higher temperatures and pressures; for example PF_3 is quantitatively oxidized to PF_5 at 500° and 300 bars, and to a mixture of PF_5 and SPF_3 at ~380° and 1800–3600 bars.

Derivatives of SF_6 are rather more reactive: S_2F_{10} and $SClF_5$ have already been mentioned. Further synthetically useful reactions of this latter compound are:

$$RC \equiv N \xrightarrow{h\nu} RCCl = NSF_5$$

$$HC \equiv CH \longrightarrow HCCl = CHSF_5$$

$$RCH = CH_2 \longrightarrow RCHClCH_2SF_5$$

$$CH_2 = C = O \xrightarrow{SClF_5} SF_5CH_2COCl$$

$$SF_5CH_2COCl \xrightarrow{H_2O/Ag^+} SF_5CH_2CO_2Ag$$

$$SF_5CH_2CO_2Ag \xrightarrow[-CO_2]{Br_2} SF_5CH_2Br$$

$$SF_5Me \xleftarrow{Zn/HCl} SF_5CH_2Br$$

$$SF_5CH_2Br \xrightarrow{LiBu^n \, (-LiF)} SF_4 = CH_2$$

p. 687

$$SClF_5 + O_2 \xrightarrow{h\nu} F_5SOSF_5 + F_5SOOSF_5$$

$SClF_5$ is readily attacked by other nucleophiles, e.g. OH^- but is inert to acids. SF_5OH and SF_5OOH are known.

The very reactive yellow SF_5OF, which is one of the few known hypofluorites, can be made by the catalytic reaction:

$$SOF_2 + 2F_2 \xrightarrow{CsF/25°} SF_5OF$$

In the absence of CsF the product is SOF_4 (p. 687) and this can then be isomerized in the presence of CsF to give a second hypofluorite, SF_3OF. Derivatives of $-SF_5$ are usually reactive volatile liquids or gases, e.g.:

Compound	F_5SCl	F_5SBr	$(F_5S)_2O$	$(F_5SO)_2$
MP/°C	−64	−79	−118	−95.4
BP/°C	−21	+3.1	+31	+49.4

Compound	F_5SNF_2[(a)]	$(F_5S)_2$	F_5SOF
MP/°C	−	−52.7	−86
BP/°C	−18	+30.0	−35.1

[(a)]See ref. 127 for F_5SNClF, F_5SNHF and $F_4S{=}NF$, and ref. 128 for $F_5SN{=}SClF$

Of these, $(F_5SO-)_2$ is an amusing example of a compound accidentally prepared as a byproduct of SF_6 and S_2F_{10} due to the fortuitous presence of traces of molecular oxygen in the gaseous fluorine used to fluorinate sulfur. A small amount of material boiling somewhat above S_2F_{10} and having a molecular weight some 32 units higher was isolated. [How would you show that it was not S_3F_{10}, and that its structure was F_5SOOSF_5 rather than one of the 8 possible isomers of $F_4S(OF)-SF_4(OF)$ or $F_4S(OF)-OSF_5$?][129]

Numerous other highly reactive oxofluorosulfur compounds have been prepared but their chemistry, though sometimes hazardous because of a tendency to explosion, introduces no new principles. Some examples are:

Thionyl fluorides: OSF_2, $OSFCl$, $OSFBr$, $OSF(OM)$.
Sulfuryl fluorides: O_2SF_2, FSO_2-O-SO_2F, $FSO_2-O-SO_2-O-SO_2F$, $FSO_2-OO-SO_2F$, $FSO_2-OO-SF_5$.

[126] A. P. HAGEN and D. L. TERRELL, *Inorg. Chem.* **20**, 1325–6 (1981).

[127] D. D. DESMARTEAU, H. H. EYSEL, H. OBERHAMMER and H. GÜNTHER, *Inorg. Chem.* **21**, 1607–16 (1982).

[128] J. S. THRASHER, N. S. HOSMANE, D. E. MAURER and A. F. CLIFFORD, *Inorg. Chem.* **21**, 2506–8 (1982).

[129] R. B. HARVEY and S. H. BAUER, *J. Am. Chem. Soc.* **76**, 859–64 (1954).

Other peroxo compounds:[130] $SF_5OOC(O)F$, $SF_5OSF_4OOSF_5$, $SF_5OSF_4OOSF_4OSF_5$, $CF_3OSF_4OOSF_5$, $CF_3OSF_4OOSF_4OCF_3$, $(CF_3SO_2)_2O_2$, $HOSO_2OOCF_3$, $CF_3OOSO_2OCF_3$.

Fluorosulfuric acid:[131] $FSO_2(OH)$, FSO_3^-.

Of these the most extensively studied is fluorosulfuric acid, made by direct reaction of SO_3 and HF. Its importance derives from its use as a solvent system and from the fact that its mixtures with SbF_5 and SO_3 are amongst the strongest known acids (superacids, p. 570). Anhydrous HSO_3F is a colourless, dense, mobile liquid which fumes in moist air: mp $-89.0°$, bp $162.7°$; d_{25} $1.726\,g\,cm^{-3}$, η_{25} $1.56\,centipoise$, κ_{25} $1.085 \times 10^{-4}\,ohm^{-1}\,cm^{-1}$.

Attention should also be directed to the growing number of perfluorocarbon–sulfur species which feature single, double or even triple C–S bonds, e.g.:

Single: $(F_5S)_2CF_2$,[132] $F_4\overline{SCF_2SF_4}CF_2$,[132] $[(F_5S)C(CF_3)_2]^-$,[133] $[(F_5S)_2C(CF_3)]^-$,[133] $[F_3\overline{SCF_2S(F_3)}F]^-$;[134] see also footnote on p. 690;

Double: $(F_5S)(F_3C)C{=}SF_2$,[135] $(F_3C)_2C{=}SF_2$;[135] Triple: $(F_3C)C{\equiv}SF_3$,[136–138] $(F_5S)C{\equiv}SF_3$.[139]

---

[130] R. A. DE MARCO and J. M. SHREEVE, *Adv. Inorg. Chem. Radiochem.* **16**, 109–76 (1974).

[131] A. W. JACHE, *Adv. Inorg. Chem. Radiochem.* **16**, 177–200 (1974).

[132] K. D. GUPTA, R. MEWS, A. WATERFELD, J. M. SHREEVE and H. OBERHAMMER, *Inorg. Chem.* **25**, 275–8 (1986).

[133] J. BITTNER, R. GERHARDT, K. MOOCK and K. SEPPELT, *Z. anorg. allg. Chem.* **602**, 89–96 (1991).

[134] D. VIETS, W. HEILEMANN, A. WATERFELD, R. MEWS, S. BESSER, R. HERBST-IRMER, G. M. SHELDRICK and W.-D. STOHRER, *J. Chem. Soc., Chem. Commun.*, 1017–9 (1992).

[135] R. DAMERIUS, K. SEPPELT and J. S. THRASHER, *Angew. Chem. Int. Edn. Engl.* **28**, 769–70 (1989).

[136] W. SAAK, G. HENKEL and S. POHL, *Angew. Chem. Int. Edn. Engl.* **23**, 150 (1984).

[137] B. PÖTTER, K. SEPPELT, A. SIMON, E.-M. PETERS and B. HETTICH, *J. Am. Chem. Soc.* **107**, 980–5 (1985).

[138] D. A. DIXON and B. E. SMART, *J. Am. Chem. Soc.* **108**, 2688–91 (1986).

[139] R. GERHARDT, T. GRELBIG, J. BUSCHMANN, P. LUGER and K. SEPPELT, *Angew. Chem. Int. Edn. Engl.* **27**, 1534–6 (1988).

Also notable are sulfur cyanide fluorides such as SF_3CN,[140] $SF_2(CN)_2$[140] and SF_5CN[141,142] and the sulfinyl cyanide fluoride $FS(O)CN$.[140]

Chlorides, bromides and iodides of sulfur

Sulfur is readily chlorinated by direct reaction with Cl_2 but the simplicity of the products obtained belies the complexity of the mechanisms involved. The reaction was first investigated by C. W. Scheele in 1774 and has been extensively studied since because of its economic importance (see below) and its intrinsic physicochemical interest. Direct chlorination of molten S followed by fractional distillation yields disulfur dichloride (S_2Cl_2) a toxic, golden-yellow liquid of revolting smell: mp $-76°$, bp $138°$, $d(20°)$ $1.677\,g\,cm^{-3}$. The molecule has the expected C_2 structure (like S_2F_2, H_2O_2, etc.) with S–S $195\,pm$, S–Cl $206\,pm$, angle Cl–S–S $107.7°$, and a dihedral angle of $85.2°$.[143] Further chlorination of S_2Cl_2, preferably in the presence of a trace of catalyst such as $FeCl_3$, yields the more-volatile, cherry-red liquid sulfur dichloride, SCl_2: mp $-122°$, bp $59°$, $d(20°)$ $1.621\,g\,cm^{-3}$. SCl_2 resembles S_2Cl_2 in being foul-smelling and toxic, but is rather unstable when pure due to the decomposition equilibrium $2SCl_2 \rightleftharpoons S_2Cl_2 + Cl_2$. However, it can be stabilized by the presence of as little as 0.01% PCl_5 and can be purified by distillation at atmospheric pressure in the presence of 0.1% PCl_5.[144] The sulfur dichloride molecule is nonlinear (C_{2v}) as expected, with S–Cl $201\,pm$ and angle Cl–S–Cl $103°$.

S_2Cl_2 and SCl_2 both react readily with H_2O to give a variety of products such as

---

[140] J. JACOBS and H. WILLNER, *Z. anorg. allg. Chem.* **619**, 1221–6 (1993).

[141] O. LÖSKING and H. WILLNER, *Angew. Chem. Int. Edn. Engl.* **28**, 1255–6 (1989).

[142] J. S. THRASHER and K. V. MADAPPAT *Angew. Chem. Int. Edn. Engl.* **28**, 1256–8 (1989).

[143] C. J. MARSDEN, R. D. BROWN, and P. D. GODFREY, *J. Chem. Soc., Chem. Commun.*, 399–401 (1979).

[144] R. J. ROSSEN and F. R. WHITT, *J. Appl. Chem.* **10**, 229–37 (1960); see also the following paper (pp. 237–46) for large-scale distillation unit.

H_2S, SO_2, H_2SO_3, H_2SO_4 and the polythionic acids $H_2S_xO_6$. Oxidation of SCl_2 yields thionyl chloride ($OSCl_2$) and sulfuryl chloride (O_2SCl_2) (see Section 15.2.4). Reaction with F_2 produces SF_4 and SF_6 (p. 686), whereas fluorination with NaF is accompanied by some disproportionation:

$$3SCl_2 + 4NaF \longrightarrow SF_4 + S_2Cl_2 + 4NaCl$$

As indicated on p. 686, fluorination of S_2Cl_2 with KF/SO_2 occurs with concurrent isomerization to SSF_2. Both S_2Cl_2 and SCl_2 react with atomic N (p. 413) to give NSCl as the first step, and this can then react further with S_2Cl_2 to give the ionic heterocyclic compound $S_3N_2Cl^+Cl^-$ (p. 739). By contrast, reaction of S_2Cl_2 with NH_4Cl at 160° (or with $NH_3 + Cl_2$ in boiling CCl_4) yields the cluster compound S_4N_4 (p. 722). Treatment of S_2Cl_2 with $Hg(SCN)_2$ yields colourless crystals of $S_4(CN)_4$, mp $-2°$, which are composed of unbranched chain molecules NCSSSSCN with essentially linear NCS groups (177.5°, 178.4°) and the angles CSS 98.6° and SSS 106.5°; interatomic distances are within the expected ranges, *viz.* $N{\equiv}C$ 113.4, C–S 169.6, outer S–S 206.8 and inner S–S 201.7 pm.[145] SCl_2 acts as a ligand to Pd and Pt in the yellow 4-coordinate complex *trans*-$[PdCl_2(SCl_2)_2]$ and the red 6-coordinate complex *trans*-$[PtCl_4(SCl_2)_2]$.[146] These are formed when either Pd or Pt metal is heated in a quartz ampoule with elemental S and Cl_2 at 200°C for 4 days, and they decompose into SCl_2 and $PdCl_2$ or $PtCl_4$, respectively, on being heated.

S_2Cl_2 and SCl_2 are important industrial chemicals. The main use for S_2Cl_2 is in the vapour-phase vulcanization of certain rubbers, but other uses include its chlorinating action in the preparation of mono- and di-chlorohydrins, and the opening of some minerals in extractive metallurgy. Some idea of the scale of production can be gauged from the fact that S_2Cl_2 is shipped in 50-tonne tank cars; smaller quantities are transported in drums containing 300 or 60 kg

of the liquid. Its less-stable homologue SCl_2 is notable for its ready addition across olefinic double bonds: e.g., thiochlorination of ethene yields the notorious vesicant, mustard gas:

$$SCl_2 + 2CH_2{=}CH_2 \longrightarrow S(CH_2CH_2Cl)_2$$

The compounds SCl_2 and S_2Cl_2 can be thought of as the first two members of an extended series of dichlorosulfanes S_nCl_2. The lower electronegativity of Cl (compared with F) and the lower S–Cl bond energy (compared with S–F) enable the natural catenating propensity of S to have full reign and a series of dichlorosulfanes can be prepared in which S–S bonds in sulfur chains (and rings) can be broken and the resulting $-S_n-$ oligomers stabilized by the formation of chain-terminating S–Cl bonds. The first eight members with $n = 1 - 8$ have been isolated as pure compounds, and mixtures up to perhaps $S_{100}Cl_2$ are known.[†] Specific compounds have been made by F. Fehér's group using the polysulfanes as starting materials (p. 683):[147]

$$H_2S_x + 2S_2Cl_2 \longrightarrow 2HCl + S_{4+x}Cl_2$$

$$H_2S_x + 2SCl_2 \xrightarrow{-80°} 2HCl + S_{2+x}Cl_2$$

The dichlorosulfanes are yellow to orange-yellow viscous liquids with an irritating odour. They are thermally and hydrolytically unstable. S_3Cl_2 boils at 31° (10^{-4} mmHg) and has a density of 1.744 g cm^{-3} at 20°. Higher homologues have

---

[†] Several related series of compounds are also known in which Cl is replaced by a pseudohalogen such as $-CF_3$ or $-C_2F_5$, e.g. $S_n(CF_3)_2$ ($n = 1-4$), $CF_3S_nC_2F_5$ ($n = 2-4$), and $S_n(C_2F_5)_2$ ($n = 2-4$). These can be prepared by the reaction of CF_3I and S vapour in a glow discharge followed by fractionation and glc separation; other routes include reaction of CS_2 with IF_5 at 60–200°, reaction of CF_3I with sulfur at 310°, and fluorination of $SCCl_2$ or related compounds with NaF or KF at 150–250°. (See, for example, T. Yasumura and R. J. Lagow, *Inorg. Chem.* **17**, 3108–10 (1978).)

[145] R. STEUDEL, K. BERGEMANN and M. KUSTOS, *Z. anorg. allg. Chem.* **620**, 117–20 (1994).

[146] M. PAULUS and G. THIELE, *Z. anorg. allg. Chem.* **588**, 69–76 (1990).

[147] F. FEHÉR, pp. 370–9 in G. BRAUER (ed.), *Handbook of Preparative Inorganic Chemistry*, 2nd edn., Vol. 1, Academic Press, New York, 1963.

even higher densities:

n in S_nCl_2	1	2	3	4
Density(20°)/g cm^{-3}	1.621	1.677	1.744	1.777

n in S_nCl_2	5	6	7	8
Density(20°)/g cm^{-3}	1.802	1.822	1.84	1.85

The higher chlorides of S (unlike the higher fluorides) are very unstable and poorly characterized. There is no evidence for molecular chloro analogues of SF_4, S_2F_{10} and SF_6, though $SClF_5$ is known (p. 687). Chlorination of SCl_2 by liquid Cl_2 at $-78°$ yields a powdery off-white solid which begins to decompose when warmed above $-30°$. It analyses as SCl_4 and is generally formulated as $SCl_3^+Cl^-$, but little reliable structural work has been done on it. Consistent with this ionic formulation, reaction of SCl_4 with Lewis acids results in the formation of stable adducts; e.g. $AlCl_3$ yields the white solid $SCl_4.AlCl_3$ which has been shown by vibrational spectroscopy on both the solid and the melt (125°) to be $[SCl_3]^+[AlCl_4]^-$.[148] The compound $[SCl_3]^+[ICl_4^-]$ is also known (p. 693).[149] As expected from a species that is isoelectronic with PCl_3 the cation is pyramidal; dimensions are: S–Cl (average) 198.5 pm, angle Cl–S–Cl 101.3° (cf. PCl_3: P–Cl 204.3 pm, angle Cl–P–Cl 100.1°). Other compounds containing $[SCl_3]^+$ which have been characterized spectroscopically and by X-ray crystallography include those with $[SbCl_6]^-$, $[UCl_6]^-$ and $[AsF_6]^-$.[150]

Sulfur bromides are but poorly characterized and there are few reliable data on them. SBr_2 probably does not exist at room temperature but has been claimed as a matrix-isolated product when a mixture of $S_2Cl_2/SCl_2:Br_2:Ar$ in the ratio 1:1:150 is passed through an 80-W microwave discharge and the product condensed on a CsI

window at 9 K.[151] The dibromosulfanes S_nBr_2 ($n = 2$–8) are formed by the action of anhydrous HBr on the corresponding chlorides.[147] The best characterized compound (which can also be made directly from the elements at 100°C) is the garnet-red oily liquid S_2Br_2 isostructural with S_2Cl_2 (S–S 198 pm, S–Br 224 pm, angle Br–S–S 105°, dihedral angle $84 \pm 11°$). It has mp $-46°$, bp(0.18 mmHg) 54°, and $d(20°)$ 2.629 g cm^{-3}, but even at room temperature S_2Br_2 tends to dissociate into its elements. Interestingly, the higher homologues have progressively lower densities (cf. S_nCl_2). The unusual ionic compound $[BrSSSBr_2]^+[AsF_6]^-$ can be formed by reacting stoichiometric amounts of S, Br_2 and AsF_5 in liquid SO_2.

n in S_nBr_2	2	3	4	5	6	7	8
Density(20°)/ g cm^{-3}	2.629	2.52	2.47	2.41	2.36	2.33	2.30

Sulfur iodides are a topic of considerable current interest, although compounds containing S–I bonds were, in fact, unknown until fairly recently. The failure to prepare sulfur iodides by direct reaction of the elements probably reflects the comparative weakness of the S–I bond: an experimental value is not available but extrapolation from representative values for the bond energies of other S–X bonds leads to a value of ~ 170 kJ mol^{-1}:

Bond	S–F	S–Cl	S–Br	S–I	S–S	I–I
Energy/ kJ mol^{-1}	327	271	218	(~ 170)	225	150

The data indicate that formation of SI_2 from $\frac{1}{8}S_8 + I_2$ and the formation of S_2I_2 from $\frac{1}{4}S_8 + I_2$ are both endothermic to the extent of ~ 35 kJ mol^{-1}, implying that successful synthesis of these compounds must employ kinetically controlled routes to obviate decomposition back to the free elements.

Pure S_2I_2 was first isolated (as a dark reddish-brown solid) following the reaction of S_2Cl_2 with

[148] G. MAMANTOV, R. MARASSI, F. W. POULSON, S. E. SPRINGER, J. P. WIAUX, R. HUGLEN and N. R. SMYNL, *J. Inorg. Nuclear Chem.* **41**, 260–1 (1979).

[149] A. J. EDWARDS, *J. Chem. Soc., Dalton Trans.*, 1723–5 (1978).

[150] B. H. CHRISTIAN, M. J. COLLINS, R. J. GILLESPIE and J. F. SAWYER, *Inorg. Chem.* **25**, 777–88 (1986), and references cited therein.

[151] M. FEUERHAN and G. VAHL, *Inorg. Nuclear Chem. Lett.* **16**, 5–8 (1980).

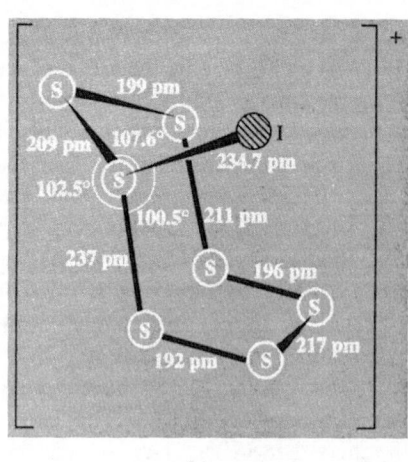
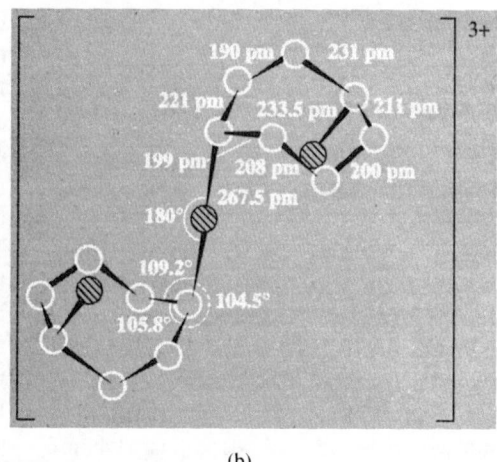

(a)   (b)

Figure 15.22 (a) Structure of the iodocycloheptasulfur cation in $[S_7I]^+[SbF_6]^-$. The S–S–S angles in the S_7 ring are in the range 102.5–108.4° (mean 105.6°).[154] (b) Structure of the centrosymmetric cation $[(S_7I)_2I]^{3+}$ showing similar dimensions to those in $[S_7I]^+$.[156]

HI/N_2 in a freon solvent of $-78°$ in the presence of catalytic amounts of added I_2.[152] The darker brown solid OSI_2 was formed similarly from $OSCl_2$. S_2I_2 and OSI_2 are both thermally unstable and decompose rapidly above about $-30°$ into S, I_2 (and also SO_2 in the case of OSI_2).[152] S_2I_2 was assigned C_2 symmetry (like S_2F_2, p. 684) on the basis of its vibrational spectrum.[153]

The first X-ray crystal structure of a species containing an S–I bond was of the curious and unexpected cation $[S_7I]^+$ which was found in the dark-orange compound $[S_7I]^+[SbF_6]^-$ formed when iodine and sulfur react in SbF_5 solution.[154] The structure of the cation is shown in Fig. 15.22a and features an S_7 ring with alternating S–S distances and a pendant iodine atom; the conformation of the ring is the same as in S_7, S_8, and S_8O (p. 696). The same cation was

found in $[S_7I]_4^+[S_4]^{2+}[AsF_6]_6^-$ [155] and a similar motif forms part of the iodo-bridged species $[(S_7I)_2I]^{3+}$ (Fig. 15.22b);[156] this latter cation was formed during the reaction of S_8 and I_2 with SbF_5 in the presence of AsF_3 according to the reaction stoichiometry:

$$3\tfrac{1}{2}S_8 + 3I_2 + 10SbF_5 \xrightarrow{2AsF_3} 2[S_{14}I_3]^{3+}[SbF_6]_3^- .2AsF_3$$
$$+ (SbF_3)_3SbF_5$$

The very long S–I_μ bonds in the linear S–I–S bridge (267.5 pm) are notable and have been interpreted in terms of an S–I bond order of $\tfrac{1}{2}$. Even weaker S$\cdots$I interactions occur in the cation $[S_2I_4]^{2+}$ which could, indeed, alternatively be regarded as an S_2^{2+} cation coordinated side-on by two I_2 molecules (Fig. 15.23).[157] This

[152] D. K. Padma, *Indian Journal of Chemistry* **12**, 417–8 (1974).

[153] V. G. Vahl and R. Minkwitz, *Inorg. Nuclear Chem. Lett.* **13**, 213–5 (1977).

[154] J. Passmore, P. Taylor, T. K. Whidden and P. S. White, *J. Chem. Soc., Chem. Commun.*, 689 (1976). J. Passmore, G. Sutherland, P. Taylor, T. K. Whidden and P. S. White, *Inorg. Chem.* **20**, 3839–45 (1981). The cation is also one of the products formed when an excess of S reacts with $[I_3]^+[AsF_6]^-$ or $[I_3]^+[As_2F_{11}]^-$ or AsF_5/I_2, or when $[S_{16}]^{2+}[SbF_6]_2^-$ is iodinated with an excess of iodine.

[155] J. Passmore, G. Sutherland and P. S. White, *J. Chem. Soc., Chem. Commun.*, 330–1 (1980). (See also *Inorg. Chem.* **21**, 2717–23 (1982).)

[156] J. Passmore, G. Sutherland and P. S. White, *J. Chem. Soc., Chem. Commun.*, 901–2 (1979). (See also *Inorg. Chem.* **21**, 2717–23 (1982).)

[157] J. Passmore, G. Sutherland, T. Whidden and P. S. White, *J. Chem. Soc., Chem. Commun.*, 289–90 (1980). M. P. Murchie, J. P. Johnson, J. Passmore, G. W. Sutherland, M. Tajik, T. K. Whidden, P. S. White and F. Grein, *Inorg. Chem.* **31**, 273–83 (1992). See also T. Klapötke and J. Passmore, *Accounts Chem. Research* **22**, 234–240 (1989).

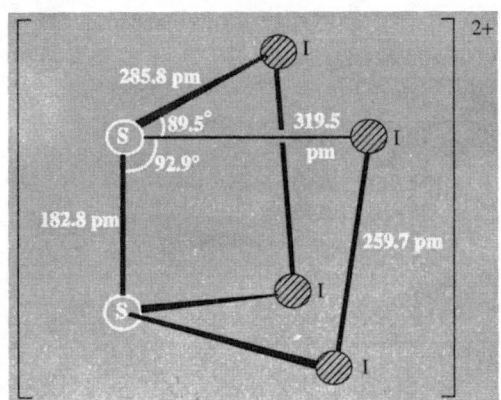

Figure 15.23 Structure of the $[S_2I_4]^{2+}$ cation of C_2 symmetry, showing the very short S–S distance and the rather short I–I distances; note also the S–I distances which are even longer than in the weak charge transfer complex $[(H_2N_2CS)_2I]^+$ (262.9 pm). The nonbonding I···I distance is 426.7 pm.

curious right triangular prismatic conformation (notably at variance with that in the isoelectronic P_2I_4 molecule) is associated with a very short S–S bond (bond order $2\frac{1}{3}$) and rather short I–I distances (bond order $1\frac{1}{3}$). The cation is formed in AsF_5/SO_2 solution according to the equation:

$$\tfrac{1}{4}S_8 + 2I_2 + 3AsF_5 \xrightarrow{SO_2} [S_2I_4]^{2+}[AsF_6]_2^- + AsF_3$$

Other species containing S–I bonds that have been characterized include the pseudopolyhalide anions $[I(SCN)_2]^-$ and $[I_2(SCN)]^-$,[158] and the dimethyliodosulfonium(IV) salts of $[Me_2SI]^+$ with $[AsF_6]^-$ and $[SbCl_6]^-$ (which latter are thermally unstable above about $-20°$).[159]

We conclude this section with an amusing cautionary tale which illustrates the type of blunder that can still appear in the pages of a refereed journal (1975) when scientists (in this

case physicists) attempt to deduce the structure of a compound by spectroscopic techniques alone, without ever analysing the substance being investigated. The work[160] purported to establish the presence of a new molecule Cl_3SI in solid solution with an ionic complex $[SCl_3]^+[ICl_2]^-$, thus leading to an overall formula for the crystals of $S_2Cl_8I_2$. The mixed compound had apparently been made originally by M. Jaillard in 1860: he obtained it as beautiful transparent yellow-orange prismatic crystals by treating a mixture of sulfur and iodine with a stream of dry Cl_2. R. Weber obtained the same material in 1866 by passing Cl_2 into a solution of I_2 in CS_2 but he reported a composition of S_2Cl_7I rather than Jaillard's SCl_4I ($S_2Cl_8I_2$). The implausibility of forming a stable compound containing an S–I bond in this way, coupled with the perceptive recognition that the published Raman spectrum had bands that could be assigned to $[ICl_4]^-$ rather than $[ICl_2]^-$, led P. N. Gates and A. Finch to reinvestigate the compound.[161] It transpired that the nineteenth-century workers had used S=16 as the atomic weight of sulfur so the true chemical composition of the crystals was, in fact, SCl_7I. The previous spectroscopic interpretation[160] was therefore totally incorrect and the compound was shown to be $[SCl_3]^+[ICl_4]^-$. This was later confirmed by a single-crystal X-ray diffraction study (p. 691).[149] In short, far from containing the new iodo-derivative Cl_3SI, the compound did not even contain an S–I bond.

15.2.4 Oxohalides of sulfur

Sulfur forms two main series of oxohalides, the thionyl dihalides $OS^{IV}X_2$ and the sulfuryl dihalides $O_2S^{VI}X_2$. In addition, various other oxofluorides and peroxofluorides are known (p. 688). Thionyl fluorides and chlorides are colourless volatile liquids (Table 15.14); $OSBr_2$ is rather less volatile and is orange-coloured.

158 G. A. BOWMAKER and D. A. ROGERS, *J. Chem. Soc., Dalton Trans.*, 1146–51 (1981).

159 R. MINKWITZ and H. PRENZEL, *Z. anorg. allg. Chem.* **548**, 91–102 (1987).

160 Y. TAVARES-FORNERIS and R. FORNERIS, *J. Mol. Structure* **24**, 205–13 (1975).

161 A. FINCH, P. N. GATES and T. H. PAGE, *Inorg. Chim. Acta* **25**, L49–L50 (1977).

Table 15.14 Some properties of thionyl dihalides,

Property	OSF$_2$	OSFCl	OSCl$_2$	OSBr$_2$
MP/°C	−110	−120	−101	−50
BP/°C	−44	12	76	140
d(O–S)/pm	141.2	—	145	145 (assumed)
d(S–X)/pm	158.5	—	207	227
angle O–S–X	106.8°	—	106°	108°
angle X–S–X	92.8°	—	114°(?)	96°

All have pyramidal molecules (C_s point group for OSX$_2$), and OSFCl is chiral though stereochemically labile. Dimensions are in Table 15.14: the short O–S distance is notable. The unstable compound OSI$_2$ was mentioned on p. 692.

The most important thionyl compound is OSCl$_2$ — it is readily prepared by chlorination of SO$_2$ with PCl$_5$ or, on an industrial scale, by oxygen-atom transfer from SO$_3$ to SCl$_2$:

$$SO_2 + PCl_5 \longrightarrow OSCl_2 + OPCl_3$$

$$SO_3 + SCl_2 \longrightarrow OSCl_2 + SO_2$$

OSCl$_2$ reacts vigorously with water and is particularly valuable for drying or dehydrating readily hydrolysable inorganic halides:

$$MX_n.mH_2O + mOSCl_2 \longrightarrow MX_n + mSO_2 + 2mHCl$$

Examples are MgCl$_2$.6H$_2$O, AlCl$_3$.6H$_2$O, FeCl$_3$.-6H$_2$O, etc. Thionyl chloride begins to decompose above its bp (76°) into S$_2$Cl$_2$, SO$_2$, and Cl$_2$; it is therefore much used as an oxidizing and chlorinating agent in organic chemistry. Fluorination with SbF$_3$/SbF$_5$ gives OSF$_2$; use of NaF/MeCN gives OSFCl or OSF$_2$ according to conditions. Thionyl chloride also finds some use as a nonaqueous ionizing solvent as does SO$_2$ (p. 700) and the formally related dimethylsulfoxide (dmso), Me$_2$SO (mp 18.6°, bp 189°, viscosity η_{25} 1.996 centipoise, dielectric constant ε_{25} 46.7). OSF$_2$ is a useful low-temperature fluorinating agent in organic chemistry: it converts active C–H and P–H groups into C–F and P–F, and replaces N–H with N–S(O)F.[162]

Sulfuryl halides, like their thionyl analogues, are also reactive, colourless, volatile liquids or gases (Table 15.15). The most important compound is O$_2$SCl$_2$, which is made on an industrial scale by direct chlorination of SO$_2$ in the presence of a catalyst such as activated charcoal (p. 274) or FeCl$_3$. It is stable to 300° but begins to dissociate into SO$_2$ and Cl$_2$ above this: it is a useful reagent for introducing Cl or O$_2$SCl into organic compounds. O$_2$SCl$_2$ can be regarded as the acid chloride of H$_2$SO$_4$ and, accordingly, slow hydrolysis (or ammonolysis) yields O$_2$S(OH)$_2$ or O$_2$S(NH$_2$)$_2$. Fluorination yields O$_2$SF$_2$ (also prepared by SO$_2$ + F$_2$) and comproportionation of this with O$_2$SCl$_2$ and O$_2$SBr$_2$ yield the corresponding O$_2$SFX species.

Table 15.15 Some properties of sulfuryl dihalides,

Property	O$_2$SF$_2$	O$_2$SFCl	O$_2$SCl$_2$	O$_2$SFBr
MP/°C	−120	−125	−54	−86
BP/°C	−55	7	69	41
d(O-S)/pm	140.5	—	143	—
d(S-X)/pm	153.0	—	199	—
angle O–S–O	124°	—	120°	—
angle X–S–X	96°	—	111°	—

---

162 T. Mahmood and J. M. Shreeve, *Inorg. Chem.* **24**, 1395-8 (1985).

All these compounds have (distorted) tetrahedral molecules, those of formula O_2SX_2 having C_{2v} symmetry and the others C_s. Dimensions are in Table 15.15: the remarkably short O–S and S–F distances in O_2SF_2 should be noted (cf. above). Indeed, the implied strength of bonding in this molecule is reflected by the fact that it can be made by reacting the normally extremely inert compound SF_6 (p. 687) with the fluoro-acceptor SO_3:

$$SF_6 + 2SO_3 \longrightarrow 3O_2SF_2; \quad \Delta G_{298}^{\circ} = -202\,\text{kJ mol}^{-1}$$

A 20% conversion can be effected by heating the two compounds at 250° for 24 h.

15.2.5 Oxides of sulfur

At least thirteen proven oxides of sulfur are known to exist[163] though this profusion should not obscure the fact that SO_2 and SO_3 remain by far the most stable and unquestionably the most important economically. The six homocyclic polysulfur monoxides $S_nO(5 < n < 10)$ are made by oxidizing the appropriate cyclo-S_n (p. 656) with trifluoroperoxoacetic acid, $CF_3C(O)OOH$, at −30°. The dioxides S_7O_2 and S_6O_2 are also known. In addition there are the thermally unstable acyclic oxides S_2O, S_2O_2, SO and the fugitive species SOO and SO_4. Several other compounds were described in the older literature (pre-1950s) but these reports are now known to be in error. For example, the blue substance of composition "S_2O_3" prepared from liquid SO_3 and sulfur now appears to be a mixture of salts of the cations S_4^{2+} and S_8^{2+} (p. 664) with polysulfate anions. Likewise a "sulfur monoxide" prepared by P. W. Schenk in 1933 was shown by D. J. Meschi and R. J. Meyers in 1956 to be a mixture of S_2O and SO_2. The well-established lower oxides of S will be briefly reviewed before SO_2 and SO_3 are discussed in more detail.

Lower oxides [163]

Elegant work by R. Steudel and his group in Berlin has shown that, when cyclo-S_{10}, -S_9, and -S_8 are dissolved in CS_2 and oxidized by freshly prepared $CF_3C(O)O_2H$ at temperatures below −10°, modest yields (10–20%) of the corresponding crystalline monoxides S_nO are obtained. Similar oxidation of cyclo-S_7, and α- and β-S_6 in CH_2Cl_2 solution yields crystalline S_7O, S_7O_2, and α- and β-S_6O. Crystals of S_6O_2 and S_5O (d > −50°) have not yet been isolated but the compounds have been made in solution by the same technique. S_8O had previously been made (1972) by the reaction of $OSCl_2$ and H_2S_7 in CS_2 at −40°: it is one of the most stable compounds in the series and melts (with decomposition) at 78°. All the compounds are orange or dark yellow and decompose with liberation of SO_2 and sulfur when warmed to room temperature or slightly above. Structures are in Fig. 15.24. It will be noted that S_7O is isoelectronic and isostructural with $[S_7I]^+$ (p. 692). This invites the question as to whether S_7S can be prepared as a new structural isomer of cyclo-S_8.

S_8O reacts with $SbCl_5$ in CS_2 over a period of 9 days at −50° to give a 71% yield of the unstable orange adduct $S_8O.SbCl_5$:[164] its structure and dimensions are in Fig. 15.25a. It will be noted that the S_8O unit differs from molecular S_8O in having an equatorially bonded O atom and significantly different S–O and S–S interatomic distances. The X-ray crystal structure was determined at −100°C as the adduct decomposes within 5 min at 25° to give $OSCl_2$, $SbCl_3$ and S_8. When a similar reaction was attempted with β-S_6O, the novel dimer $S_{12}O_2.2SbCl_5.3CS_2$ was obtained as orange crystals in 10% yield after 1 week at −50°[165] (Fig. 15.25b). Formation of the centrosymmetric $S_{12}O_2$ molecule, which is still unknown in the uncoordinated state, can be

163 *Gmelin Handbuch der Anorganischen Chemie*, 8th edn., Schwefel Oxide, Ergänzungsband **3**, 1980, 344 pp.

164 R. STEUDEL, T. SANDOW and J. STEIDEL, *J. Chem. Soc., Chem. Commun.*, 180–1 (1980).

165 R. STEUDEL, J. STEIDEL and J. PICKARDT, *Angew. Chem. Int. Edn. Engl.* **19**, 325–6 (1980).

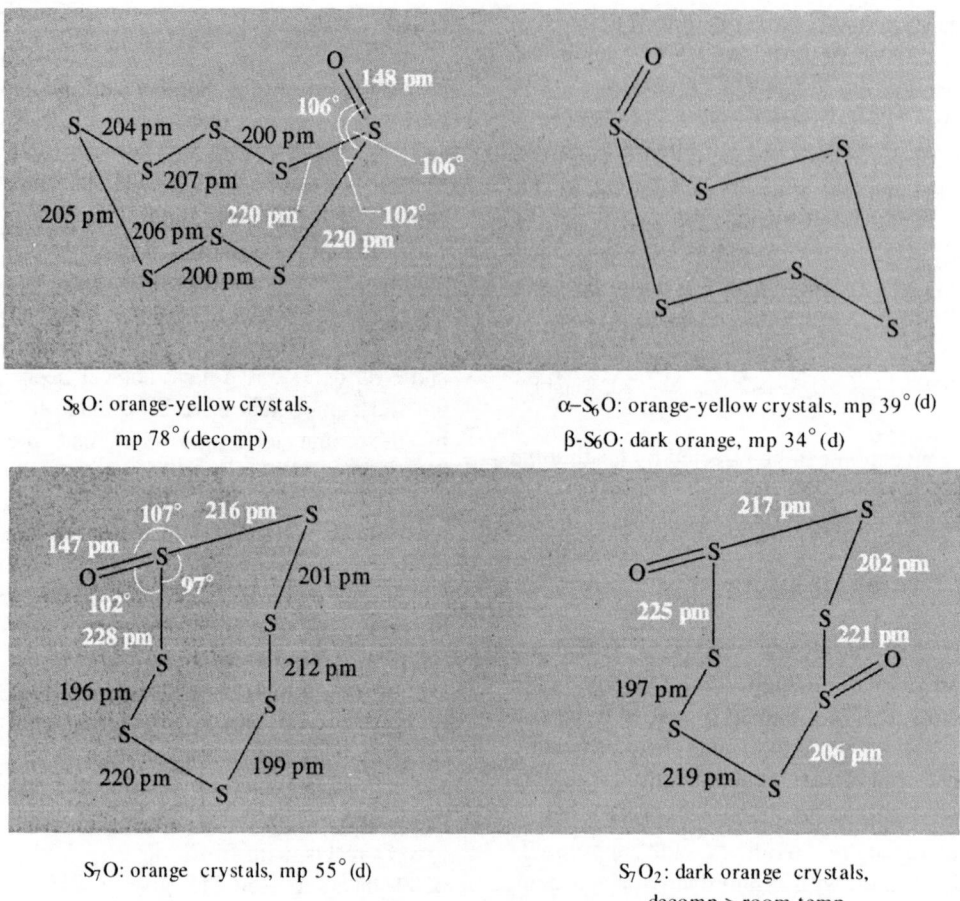

S$_8$O: orange-yellow crystals,
mp 78° (decomp)

α-S$_6$O: orange-yellow crystals, mp 39° (d)
β-S$_6$O: dark orange, mp 34° (d)

S$_7$O: orange crystals, mp 55° (d)

S$_7$O$_2$: dark orange crystals,
decomp > room temp

Figure 15.24   Structures of S$_8$O, S$_7$O, S$_7$O$_2$ and S$_6$O; in each case the O atom adopts an axial conformation. For S$_8$O there is an alternation of S–S distances, the longest being adjacent to the exocyclic O atoms; S–S–S angles are in the range 102–108° and dihedral angles (p. 654) vary from 95° to 112° (+ and −). For S$_7$O there is again an alternation in S–S distances; ring angles are in the range 97–106° the smallest angle again being at the S atom carrying the pendant O. The structure of S$_7$O$_2$ was deduced from its Raman spectrum, the interatomic distances (d/pm) being computed from the relation $\log(d/\text{pm}) = 2.881 - 0.213 \log(\nu/\text{cm}^{-1})$. The two modifications α- and β-S$_6$O have the same Raman spectrum in solution.

explained in terms of a dipolar addition reaction (Fig. 15.25c). Its conformation differs drastically from the D_{3d} symmetry of the parent *cyclo*-S$_{12}$ (p. 658).

The fugitive species SO was first identified by its ultraviolet spectrum in 1929 but it is thermodynamically unstable and decomposes completely in the gas phase in less than 1 s. It is formed by reduction of SO$_2$ with sulfur vapour in a glow discharge and its spectroscopic properties

have excited interest because of its relation to O$_2$ ($^3\Sigma^-$ ground state, p. 605). Molecular properties include internuclear distance 148.1 pm, dipole moment 1.55 D, equilibrium bond energy D_e 524 kJ mol^{-1}. The use of transition-metal complexes to trap SO has received considerable attention.[166] It can bond in several modes including

166 W. A. SCHENK, *Angew. Chem. Int. Edn. Engl.* **26**, 98–109 (1987).

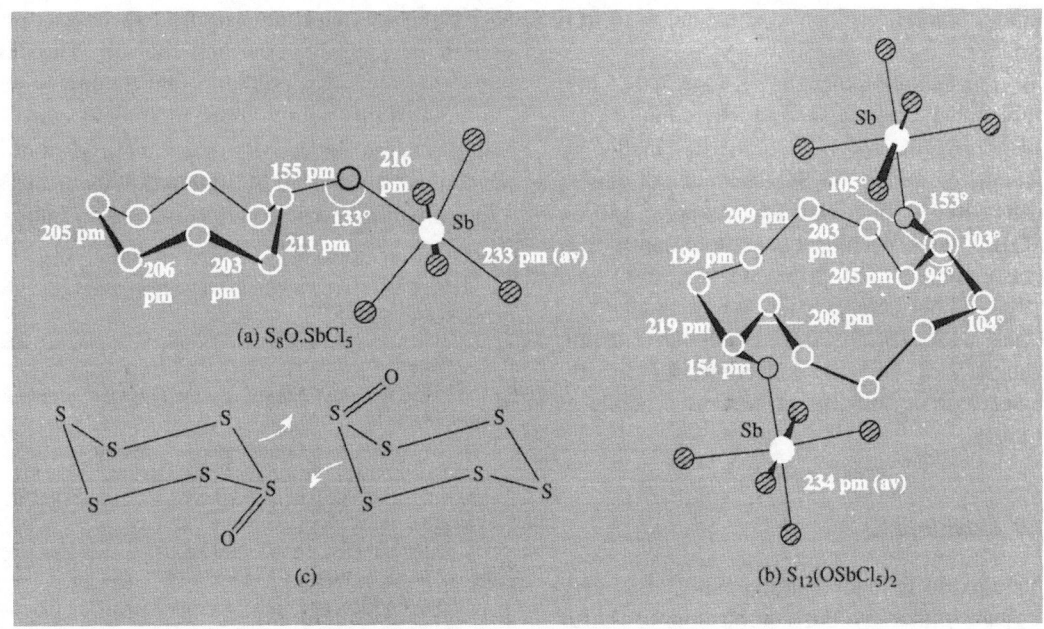

Figure 15.25   Molecular structure and dimensions of (a) the adduct $S_8O.SbCl_5$ at $-100°$, and (b) the dimeric unit $Sb_{12}O_2.2SbCl_5$ in $Sb_{12}O_2.2SbCl_5.3CS_2$ at $-115°C$. (c) Possible dipolar addition of $2S_6O$ to form $S_{12}O_2$.

4-centre-2 electron (4c–2e) as in $[Fe_3(CO)_9S(\mu_3$-SO)]$,^{(167)}$ 2c–2e as in $[IrCl(SO)(PR_3)_2]$,$^{(168)}$ and also 3c–4e and 3c–2e in several dinuclear transition-metal complexes.$^{(169,170)}$ A novel and unprecedented route to this last class of μ-SO complexes involves the direct oxidative addition of $OSCl_2$ to the Ni^0 complex $[Ni(cod)_2]$ in the presence of dppm (cod = cycloocta-1,5-diene, dppm = $Ph_2PCH_2PPh_2$) to form the purple crystalline dinickel A-frame complex, $[Ni_2(\mu\text{-SO})(dppm)_2Cl_2]$.$^{(171)}$ X-ray analysis reveals two slightly differing geometries, with SO

144 and 145.9 pm, respectively (both shorter than in the free molecule, 148.1 pm), and with the SO ligand being tilted with respect to the $Ni\cdots Ni$ vector.

S_2O is also an unstable species but survives for several days in the gas phase at <1 mmHg pressure. It is formed by decomposition of SO (above) and by numerous other reactions between S- and O-containing species but cannot be isolated as a pure compound. Typical recipes include: (a) passing a stream of $OSCl_2$ at 0.1–0.5 mmHg over heated Ag_2S at 160°, (b) burning S_8 in a stream of O_2 at ~8 mmHg pressure, and (c) passing SO_2 at 120° and <1 mmHg through a high-voltage discharge (~5 kV). Spectroscopic studies in the gas phase have shown it to be a nonlinear molecule (like O_3 and SO_2) with angle S–S–O 118° and the interatomic distances S–S 188, S–O 146 pm. S_2O readily decomposes at room temperature to SO_2 and sulfur. As with SO, the fugitive S_2O species can be trapped with transition-metal complexes (of Mn and Ir, for

^{167} L. MARKÓ, B. MARKÓ-MONOSTORY, T. MADACH and H. VAHRENKAMP, *Angew. Chem. Int. Edn. Engl.* **19**, 226–7 (1980).

^{168} W. A. SCHENK, J. LEISSNER and C. BURSCHKA, *Angew. Chem. Int. Edn. Engl.* **23**, 806–7 (1984).

^{169} I.-P. LORENZ, J. MESSELHAUSER, W. HILLER and K. HAUG, *Angew. Chem. Int. Edn. Engl.* **3**, 24–5 (1985).

^{170} G. BESENEI, C. L. LEE, J. GULINSKI, S. J. RETTIG, B. R. JAMES, D. A. NELSON and M. A. LILGA, *Inorg. Chem.* **26**, 3622–8 (1987).

^{171} J. K. GONG, P. E. FANWICK and C. P. KUBIAK, *J. Chem. Soc., Chem. Commun.*, 1190–1 (1990).

example) wherein it behaves as an η^2-SS(O) ligand.[172]

The unstable molecule S_2O_2 was first unambiguously characterized by microwave spectroscopy in 1974. It can be made by subjecting a stream of SO_2 gas at 0.1 mmHg pressure to a microwave discharge (80 W, 2.45 GHz): the effluent gas is predominantly SO_2 but also contains 20–30% SO, 5% S_2O and 5% S_2O_2. This latter species has a planar C_{2v} structure with r(S–S) 202 pm, r(S–O) 146 pm, and angle S–S–O 113°; it decomposes directly into SO with a half-life of several seconds at 0.1 mmHg.

Sulfur dioxide, SO_2

Sulfur dioxide is made commercially on a very large scale either by the combustion of sulfur or H_2S or by roasting sulfide ores (particularly pyrite, FeS_2) in air (p. 651). It is also produced

as a noxious and undesirable byproduct during the combustion of coal and fuel oil. The ensuing environmental problems and the urgent need to control this pollution are matters of considerable concern and activity (see Panel). Most of the technically produced SO_2 is used in the manufacture of sulfuric acid (p. 708) but it also finds use

[172] G. A. UROVE and M. E. WELKER, *Organometallics* **7**, 1013–4 (1988).

[173] I. M. CAMPBELL, *Energy and the Atmosphere*, pp. 202–9, Wiley, London, 1977.

[174] J. HEICKLEN, *Atmospheric Chemistry*, Academic Press, New York, 1976, 406 pp.

[175] B. MEYER, *Sulfur, Energy, and the Environment*, Elsevier, Amsterdam, 1977, 448 pp.

[176] R. B. HUSAR, J. P. LODGE, and D. J. MOORE (eds.), *Sulfur in the Atmosphere*, Pergamon Press, Oxford, 1978, 816 pp. Proceedings of the International Symposium at Dubrovnik, September 1977.

[177] J. O. NRIAGU (ed.), *Sulfur in the Environment. Part 2. Ecological Impacts*, Wiley, Chichester, 1979, 494 pp.

[178] R. W. JOHNSON and G. E. GORDON (eds.), *The Chemistry of Acid Rain*, ACS Symposium **349**, 337 pp. (1987). See also M. Freemantle, *Chem. and Eng. News*, pp. 10–17, May 1, 1995.

[179] D. J. LITTLER (ed.), *Acid Rain*, CEGB Research, Special Issue No. 20, 64 pp. (1987), published by the Central Electricity Generating Board, Southampton SO4 4ZB. See also W. D. Halstead, *CEGB Research* **22**, 3–11 (1988).

Atmospheric SO_2 and Environmental Pollution[173–179]

The pollution of air by smoke and sulfurous fumes is no new problem[†] but the quickening pace of industrial development during the nineteenth century, and the growing concern for both personal health and protection of the environment generally since the 1950s, has given added impetus to measures required to eliminate or at least minimize the hazard.

As indicated on p. 647, there are vast amounts of volatile sulfur compounds in the environment as a result of natural processes. Geothermal activity (especially volcanic) releases large amounts of SO_2 together with smaller quantities of H_2S, SO_3, elemental S and particulate sulfates. From a global viewpoint, however, this accounts for less than 1% of the naturally formed volatile S compounds (Fig. A). By far the most important source is the biological reduction of S compounds which occurs most readily in the presence of organic matter and under oxygen-deficient conditions. Much of this is released as H_2S but other compounds such as Me_2S are probably also implicated. The final natural source of atmospheric S compounds is sea-spray (sulfate is the second most abundant anion in sea-water being about one-seventh the concentration of chloride). Though much sulfur is transported as sulfate by wind-driven sea spray and by river run off, its environmental impact is not severe.

[†] One of the earliest tracts on the matter was John Evelyn's *Fumifugium, or the Inconvenience of the Aer and Smoake of London Dissipated* which he submitted (with little effect) to Charles II in 1661. Evelyn, a noted diarist and a founder Fellow of the Royal Society, outlined the problem as follows: "For when in all other places the Aer is most Serene and Pure, it is here [in London] Eclipsed with such a Cloud of Sulphure, as the Sun itself, which gives day to all the World besides, is hardly able to penetrate and impart it here; and the weary Traveller, at many Miles distance, sooner smells than sees the City to which he repairs. This is that pernicious Smoake which sullyes all her Glory, superinducing a sooty Crust or Fur upon all that it lights, spoyling the moveables, tarnishing the Plate, Gildings, and Furniture, and corroding the very Iron-bars and hardest Stones with these piercing and acrimonious Spirits which accompany its Sulphure; and executing more in one year than exposed to the pure Aer of the Country it could effect in some hundreds."

Panel continues

Much more serious is the effect of volatile S compounds (mainly SO_2) released into the atmosphere as a result of man's domestic and industrial activities. This has been estimated to be some 200 million tonnes pa, and is comparable in amount to all the sulfur released by natural processes ($\sim 310 \times 10^6$ tonnes pa). Unfortunately, by the very nature of its origin, this SO_2 is released in the heart of densely populated areas and does great damage to the respiratory organs of man and animals, to buildings, and perhaps most seriously to plants, lake-waters and aquatic life as a result of "acid rain". Dispersal by means of high chimney stacks is inadequate since this merely transfers the problem to neighbouring regions. For example, only one-tenth of the serious SO_2/H_2SO_4 pollution of lakes and streams in Sweden is as a result of atmospheric SO_2 emissions in Sweden itself; one-tenth is due to emissions from the UK, and the remaining four-fifths is from industrial regions in northern Europe.

In Europe and the USA (and presumably elsewhere) the major source of SO_2 pollution is in coal-based power generation; this, together with other coal consumption and coking operations accounts for some 60% of the emissions. A further 25% arises from oil-refinery operations, oil-fired power generation, and other oil consumption. Copper-smelting (together with much smaller amounts from zinc and lead ore processing) accounts for some 12% of the annual release of SO_2. The sulfuric acid manufacturing industry, which is the only one designed actually to make SO_2 on a large scale, only contributes <2% to the total, probably because of the efficient design of the process.

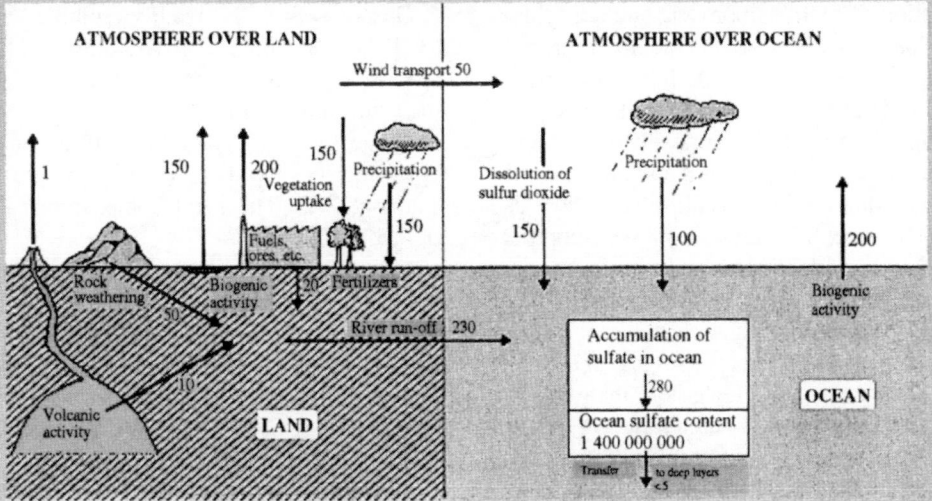

Figure A   The sulfur budget for the land–atmosphere–ocean system. Annual turnover rates are indicated in units of 10^6 tonnes (as estimated for 1977).[173]

Ultimately, pollution can only be avoided by complete removal of SO_2 from the effluent gases, but this council of perfection is both technologically and economically unattainable. Many processes are available to reduce the SO_2 concentration to very low figures, but the vast scale of power generation and domestic heating by coal and oil still results in substantial emission. SO_2 can be removed by scrubbing with a slurry of "milk of lime", $Ca(OH)_2$. Alternatively, partial reduction to H_2S using natural gas (CH_4), naphtha or coal, followed by catalytic conversion to elemental sulfur by the Claus process can be used:

$$2H_2S + SO_2 \xrightarrow[\text{Al}_2\text{O}_3]{\text{activated}} 3S\downarrow + 2H_2O$$

The detection of SO_2 in the atmosphere has become a refined analytical procedure. Several techniques are available such as (a) absorption in aqueous H_2O_2 and titration (or conductimetric determination) of the resulting H_2SO_4 ($H_2O_2 + SO_2 \longrightarrow H_2SO_4$); and (b) reaction with $Na_2[HgCl_4]$ or $K_2[HgCl_4]$:

$$[HgCl_4]^{2-} + 2SO_2 + 2H_2O \longrightarrow [Hg(SO_3)_2]^{2-} + 4Cl^- + 4H^+$$

The resulting disulfitomercurate is determined colorimetrically after addition of acidic pararosaniline and formaldehyde (P. W. West and G. C. Gaeke, 1956). Other methods are (c) flame-photometric monitoring of the gas stream using a reducing H_2/air flame and emission of S_2 at 394 nm sensitive down to 1 part in 10^9 by volume and (d) pulsed fluorescent analyser using radiation in the region of 214 nm; this is specific for SO_2 and response is linear over wide ranges down to 1 in 10^9. Commercial instruments are available.

Table 15.16 Some molecular and physical properties of SO_2

Property	Value	Property	Value
MP/°C	−75.5	Electrical conductivity κ/ohm^{-1}cm^{-1}	$<10^{-8}$
BP/°C	−10.0	Dielectric constant ε (0°)	15.4
Critical temperature/°C	157.5	Dipole moment μ/D	1.62
Critical pressure/atm	77.7	Angle O–S–O	119°
Density(−10°)/g cm^{-3}	1.46	Distance r(S–O)/pm	143.1
Viscosity η(0°)/centipoise	0.403	ΔH_f°(g)/kJ mol^{-1}	−296.9

as a bleach, disinfectant (Homer, p. 645), food preservative, refrigerant and nonaqueous solvent. Other chemical uses are in the preparation of sulfites and dithionites (p. 716) and, with Cl_2, in the derivatization of hydrocarbons via sulfochlorination reactions. There is also much current interest in its properties as a multimode ligand (p. 701).

SO_2 is a colourless, toxic gas with a choking odour. Maximum permitted atmospheric concentration for humans is 5 ppm but many green plants suffer severe distress in concentrations as low as 1–2 ppm. SO_2 neither burns in air nor supports combustion. Some molecular and physical properties of the compound are in Table 15.16. Comparison of these properties with those of ozone (p. 607) is instructive. Note also that the S–O distance of 143.1 pm in SO_2 is less than that in unstable SO (148.1 pm) whereas the O–O distance of 127.8 pm in O_3 is greater than that in stable O_2 (120.7 pm). Furthermore the mean bond energy in SO_2 is 548 kJ mol^{-1} which is greater than that for SO (524 kJ mol^{-1}) whereas the mean bond energy in O_3 is 297 kJ mol^{-1} which is less than the value for O_2 (490 kJ mol^{-1}). This has been taken to imply an S–O bond order of at least 2 in SO_2, compared with only 1.5 for O–O in O_3 (p. 607).

By far the most important chemical reaction of SO_2 is its further oxidation to SO_3 according to the equilibrium:

$$SO_2 + \tfrac{1}{2}O_2 \rightleftharpoons SO_3; \quad \Delta H^\circ = -95.6 \text{ kJ mol}^{-1}$$

The equilibrium constant, $K_p = p(SO_3)/[p(SO_2).p^{\frac{1}{2}}(O_2)]$, decreases rapidly with increasing temperature; for example: $\log K_p = 3.49$ at 800°C and −0.52 at 1100°C. Thus for maximum oxidation during the manufacture of H_2SO_4 it is necessary to work at lower temperatures and to increase the rate of reaction by use of catalysts.

Typical conditions would be to pass a mixture of SO_2 and air over Pt gauze or more commonly a V_2O_5/K_2O contact catalyst supported on Kieselguhr or zeolite.

Gaseous SO_2 is readily soluble in water (3927 cm^3 SO_2 in 100 g H_2O at 20°). Numerous species are present in this aqueous solution of "sulfurous acid" (p. 717). At 0° a cubic clathrate hydrate also forms with a composition $\sim SO_2.6H_2O$; its dissociation pressure reaches 1 atm at 7.1°. The ideal composition would be $SO_2.5\tfrac{3}{4}H_2O$ (p. 627).

In addition to the role of gaseous SO_2 in the manufacture of H_2SO_4, pure (liquid) SO_2 is manufactured on a large scale for the uses mentioned above. Typical production levels (in 1985) were 162 000 tonnes in USA and 65 000 tonnes in (West) Germany. About half of this is used in the manufacture of S-containing chemicals such as sulfites, hydrogen sulfites, thiosulfates, dithionites, salts of hydroxalkane-sulfinic acids and alkane sulfonates. It is also used in cellulose manufacture, in the chemical dressing of Mn-ores, in the removal of S-containing impurities from mineral oils, for food disinfection and preservation, and for treatment of water.

Liquid SO_2 has been much studied as a nonaqueous solvent.[180] Some of the early work (particularly on the physical properties of the solutions) is now known to be in error but

---

[180] T. C. WADDINGTON, Liquid sulfur dioxide, Chap. 6 in T. C. WADDINGTON (ed.), *Nonaqueous Solvent Systems*, pp. 253–84, Academic Press, London, 1965. W. KARCHER and H. HECHT, *Chemie in Flussigem Schwefeldioxid*, Vol. 3, Part 2, of G. JANDER, H. SPAUNDAU and C. C. ADDISON, *Chemistry in Nonaqueous Ionizing Solvents*, pp. 79–193, Pergamon Press, Oxford, 1967. See also D. F. BUROW, Liquid sulfur dioxide, in J. J. LAGOWSKI (ed.), *Nonaqueous Solvents*, Vol. 3, pp. 138–85, Academic Press, New York, 1970.

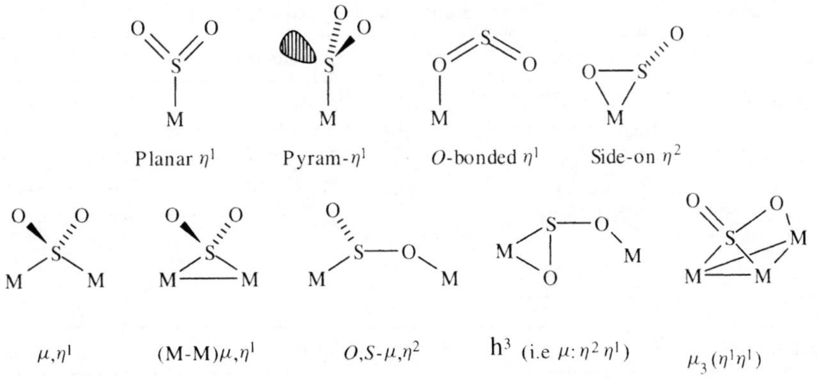

Figure 15.26   Various bonding modes of SO_2 as a ligand.

the solvent is especially useful for carrying out a range of inorganic reactions. It is also an excellent solvent for proton nmr studies. In general, covalent compounds are very soluble: e.g. Br_2, ICl, OSX_2, BCl_3, CS_2, PCl_3, $OPCl_3$ and $AsCl_3$ are completely miscible, and most organic amines, ethers, esters, alcohols, mercaptans and acids are readily soluble. Many uni-univalent salts are moderately soluble, and those with ions such as the tetramethylammonium halides and the alkali metal iodides are freely so. The low dielectric constant of liquid SO_2 leads to extensive ion-pair and ion-triplet formation but the solutions have limiting molar conductances in the range $190{-}250\,ohm^{-1}\,cm^2\,mol^{-1}$ at $0°$. Solvate formation is exemplified by compounds such as $SnBr_4.SO_2$ and $2TiCl_4.SO_2$ (see below for SO_2 as a ligand). Solvolysis reactions are also documented, e.g.:

$$NbCl_5 + SO_2 \longrightarrow NbOCl_3 + OSCl_2$$
$$WCl_6 + SO_2 \longrightarrow WOCl_4 + OSCl_2$$
$$UCl_5 + 2SO_2 \longrightarrow UO_2Cl_2 + 2OSCl_2$$

Several other reaction types have also appeared in the literature but are sometimes purely formal schemes dating from the time when the solvent was (incorrectly) thought to undergo self-ionic dissociation into SO^{2+} and SO_3^{2-} or SO^{2+} and $S_2O_5^{2-}$. More recently it has been shown that, whereas neither SO_2 nor $OSMe_2$ (dmso) react with first-row transition metals, the mixed solvent smoothly effects

dissolution of the metals with simultaneous oxidation of S^{IV} to S^{VI}, thereby enabling the production of crystalline solvated metal disulfates ($S_2O_7^{2-}$) in high yield.[181] Examples are: colourless $[Ti^{IV}(OSMe_2)_6][S_2O_7]_2$, green $[V^{III}(OSMe_2)_6]_2[S_2O_7]_3$ and the salts $[M^{II}(OSMe_2)_6][S_2O_7]$, where M = Mn (yellow), Fe (pale green), Co (pale pink), Ni (green), Cu (pale blue), Zn (white) and Cd (white). This is by far the most convenient way to prepare pure disulfates. Dissolution of metals in SO_2 mixed with other solvents such as dmf, dma, or hmpa also occurs, but in these cases there is no oxidation of the S^{IV}, and the product is usually the metal dithionite, $M^{II}[S_2O_4]$.

Sulfur dioxide as a ligand

The coordination chemistry of SO_2 has been extensively studied during the past two decades and at least 9 different bonding modes have been established.[166] These are illustrated schematically in Fig. 15.26 and typical examples are given in Table 15.17.[166,182] It is clear that nearly all the transition-metal complexes involve the metals in oxidation state zero or +1. Moreover, SO_2 in the pyramidal η^1-clusters tends to be reversibly bound (being eliminated when

---

[181] W. D. HARRISON, J. B. GILL and D. C. GOODALL, *J. Chem. Soc., Dalton Trans.*, 847–50 (1979). See also *ibid.*, 2995–7 (1987); 728–9 (1988).

Table 15.17   Example of structurally characterized complexes containing SO_2

Planar η^1	Pyramidal η^1	O-bonded η^1	Side-on η^2
$[Mn(C_5H_5)(CO)_2(SO_2)]$	$[RhCl(CO)(PPh_3)_2(SO_2)]$	$[SbF_5(OSO)]$	$[Mo(CO)_2(PMe_3)_2(\eta^2\text{-}SO_2)]$
$[RuCl(NH_3)_4(SO_2)]Cl$	$[\{RhCl(PPh_3)_2(SO_2)\}_2]$	$[\{Mg(OSO)_2(AsF_6)_2\}_n]$	$[Mo(CO)_2(bpy)(\eta^2\text{-}SO_2)]$
$[Os(CO)ClH(PCy_3)_2(SO_2)]$	$[IrCl(CO)(PPh_3)_2(SO_2)]$	$[\{Ti(\eta^6\text{-}C_6H_6)Cl_4(OSO)\}_2]$	$[Mo(\eta^2\text{-}S_2CNEt_2)_3(\eta^2\text{-}SO_2)]$
$[Co(NO)(PPh_3)_2(SO_2)]$	$[Ir(SPh)(CO)\text{-}$	$[Mn(OPPh_3)_4(OSO)_2]I_2$	$[RuCl(\eta^2\text{-}S_2CNEt_2)_3(\eta^2\text{-}SO_2)]$
$[Rh(C_5H_5)(C_2H_4)(SO_2)]$	$(PPh_3)_2(SO_2)]$		$[Rh(NO)(\eta^2\text{-}S_2CNEt_2)_3\text{-}$
			$(\eta^2\text{-}SO_2)]$
$[Ni(PPh_3)_3(SO_2)]$	$[Pt(PPh_3)_3(SO_2)]$		
$[Ni(PPh_3)_2(SO_2)_2]$	$[Pt(PPh_3)_2(SO_2)_2]$		

Bridging η^1	M–M bridging η^1	Others
$[\{Fe(C_5H_5)(CO)_2\}_2(\mu\text{-}SO_2)]$	$[Fe_2(CO)_8(\mu\text{-}SO_2)]$	$O,S\text{-}\mu,\eta^2$: $[Rh_2(PPh_3)_4(\mu\text{-}Cl)\text{-}$
$[\{Co(\eta^5\text{-}C_5H_5)(\mu\text{-}PR_2)\}_2(\mu SO_2)]$	$[Fe_2(C_5H_5)_2(CO)_3(\mu\text{-}SO_2)]$	$(\mu\text{-}OSO)_2]_2(SO_4)$
$[\{IrH(CO)_2(PPh_3)\}_2(\mu\text{-}SO_2)]$	$[Pd_2Cl_2(dpm)_2(\mu\text{-}SO_2)]$	$\eta^3(\mu\text{:}\eta^2\eta^1)$: $[\{Mo(CO)_2(PPh_3)\text{-}$
$[\{IrI(CO)(PPh_3)\}_2(\mu\text{-}SO_2)]$	$[Pd_3(CNBu^t)_5(\mu\text{-}SO_2)_2]$	$(py)(\mu\eta^3\text{-}SO_2)\}_2].2CH_2Cl_2$
	$[Pt_3(PPh_3)_3(\mu\text{-}SO_2)_3]$	$\mu_3(\eta^1\eta^1)$: $[Rh_4(\mu\text{-}CO)_4(\mu_3\text{-}$
	$[Pt(PPh_3)_3(\mu,\eta^1\text{-}Ph)(\mu\text{-}$	$SO_2)\{P(OPh)_3\}_4].\frac{1}{2}C_6H_6$
	$PPh_2)(\mu\text{-}SO_2)]$	$[Pd_5(PMe_3)_5(\mu_2\text{-}SO_2)_2\text{-}$
		$(\mu_3\text{-}SO_2)_2]$

the complex is heated to $<200°$ and recombining when the system is cooled to room temperature) whereas this tends not to be the case for the other bonding modes. Facile oxidation of the SO_2 by molecular O_2 to give coordinated sulfato complexes $(SO_4{}^{2-})$ is also a characteristic of pyramidal $\eta^1\text{-}SO_2$ which is not shared by the other types.

In the absence of X-ray crystallographic data vibrational spectroscopy can sometimes provide information concerning the mode of ligation, the position of the two $\nu(SO)$ stretching modes in particular often providing a useful but not always reliable diagnostic:[182]

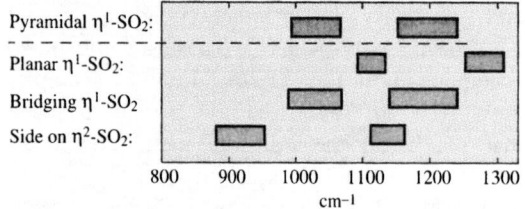

With such structural diversity it is perhaps not surprising that no certain method has been devised for theoretically predicting the mode of bonding to be expected in specific cases, although plausible *post hoc* rationalization of the observed structure is sometimes possible.

Sometimes coordination of SO_2 to an organometallic complex is followed by intramolecular insertion of SO_2 into the M–C σ bond, e.g.

trans-$[PtClPh(PEt_3)_2] + SO_2]$ ⟶
(4 coordinate Pt)

$[PtClPh(PEt_3)_2(SO_2)]$ (5-coordinate)

↓

trans-$[PtCl(PEt_3)_2\{S(O)_2Ph\}]$ (4-coordinate)

Intermolecular insertion of SO_2 can also occur (without prior formation of an isolable complex) and the general reaction can be represented by the equation:[183]

[182] G. J. KUBAS, *Inorg. Chem.* **18**, 182–8 (1979) and references therein. R. R. RYAN, G. J. KUBAS, D. C. MOODY and P. G. ELLER, *Structure and Bonding*, **46**, 47–100 (1981). More recent work can be found in the following references: J. SIELER *et al*. *Z. anorg. allg. Chem.* **549**, 171–6 (1987); E. WENSCHUH *et al*., *Z. anorg. allg. Chem.* **600**, 55–60 (1991) and **603**, 21–4 (1991); E. SOLARI, C. FLORIANI and K. SCHENK, *J. Chem. Soc., Chem. Commun.*, 963–4 (1990); D. M. P. MINGOS *et al*. *J. Chem. Soc., Chem. Commun.*, 1048–9 (1988); *J. Chem. Soc., Dalton Trans.*, 1535–41 (1986); 1509–22 (1988); 261–8 (1992).

[183] A. WOJCICKI, *Adv. Organomet. Chem.* **12**, 31–81 (1974).

$$\}M–R + SO_2 \longrightarrow \}M–(SO_2)–R$$

where $\}M$ represents a metal atom and its pendant ligands and R is an alkyl, aryl or related σ-bonded carbon group. The reaction is more flexible (though less important industrially) than the analogous carbonylation reaction of CO (p. 306) and can, in principle, lead to four different types of product:

M—S—R (S-sulfinate, with two O double bonds on S)

M—S—OR (O-alkyl-S-sulfoxylate, with two O double bonds on S)

S-sulfinate   *O-alkyl-S-sulfoxylate*

M—O—S—R (O-sulfinate, with one O double bond on S)

M / O–S–R \ O (O-O'-sulfinate, four-membered ring)

O-sulfinate   *O-O'-sulfinate*

Examples of all except possibly the second mode are known.

Sulfur trioxide

SO_3 is made on a huge scale by the catalytic oxidation of SO_2 (p. 700): it is not usually isolated but is immediately converted to H_2SO_4 (p. 708). It can also be obtained by the thermolysis of sulfates though rather high temperatures are required. SO_3 is available commercially as a liquid: such samples contain small amounts (0.03–1.5%) of additives to inhibit polymerization. Typical additives are simple compounds of boron (e.g. B_2O_3, $B(OH)_3$, HBO_2, BX_3, MBF_4, $Na_2B_4O_7$), silica, siloxanes, $SOCl_2$, sulfonic acids, etc. The detailed mode of action of these additives remains obscure. SO_3 is also readily available as fuming sulfuric acid (or oleum) which is a solution of 25–65% SO_3 in H_2SO_4 (p. 707). Because of its extremely aggressive reaction with most materials, pure anhydrous SO_3 is difficult to handle although it is made in the USA (for example) on a

scale approaching 90 000 tonnes per annum. It can be obtained on a laboratory scale by the double distillation of oleum in an evacuated all-glass apparatus; a small amount of $KMnO_4$ is sometimes used to oxidize any traces of SO_2.

In the gas phase, monomeric SO_3 has a planar (D_{3h}) structure with S–O 142 pm. This species is in equilibrium with the cyclic trimer S_3O_9 in both the gaseous and liquid phases: $K_p \approx$ 1 atm^{-2} at 25°, $\Delta H° \approx 125$ kJ (mole $S_3O_9)^{-1}$. Bulk properties therefore often refer to this equilibrium mixture, e.g. bp 44.6°C, $d(25°)$ 1.903 g cm^{-3}, $\eta(25°)$ 1.820 centipoise. Below the mp (16.86°), colourless crystals of ice-like orthorhombic γ-SO_3 separate and structural studies reveal that the only species present is the trimer S_3O_9 (Fig. 15.27). Traces of water (10^{-3} mole%) lead to the rapid formation of glistening, white, needle-like crystals of β-SO_3 which is actually a mixture of fibrous, polymeric polysulfuric acids $HO(SO_2O)_xH$, where x is very large ($\approx 10^5$). The helical chain structure of β-SO_3 is shown in Fig. 15.27 (cf. polyphosphates, p. 528). A third and still more stable form, α-SO_3, also requires traces of moisture or other polymerizing agent for its formation but involves some cross-linking between the chains to give a complex layer structure (mp 62°). The standard enthalpies of formation ($\Delta H_f°/kJ$ mol^{-1}) of the various forms of SO_3 at 25°C are: gas -395.2, liquid -437.9, γ-crystals -447.4, β-crystals -449.6, α-solid -462.4.

SO_3 reacts vigorously and extremely exothermically with water to give H_2SO_4. Substoichiometric amounts yield oleums and mixtures of various polysulfuric acids (p. 712). Hydrogen halides give the corresponding halogenosulfuric acids HSO_3X. SO_3 extracts the elements of H_2O from carbohydrates and other organic matter leaving a carbonaceous char. It acts as a strong Lewis acid towards a wide variety of inorganic and organic ligands to give adducts: e.g. oxides give SO_4^{2-}, Ph_3P gives $Ph_3P.SO_3$ (with a rather long P–S bond, 217.6 pm)[184]

184 R. L. BEDDOES and O. S. MILLS, *J. Chem. Research* (M) 2772–89 (1981); (S) 233 (1981); see also *J. Chem. Soc., Chem. Commun.*, 789–90 (1981).

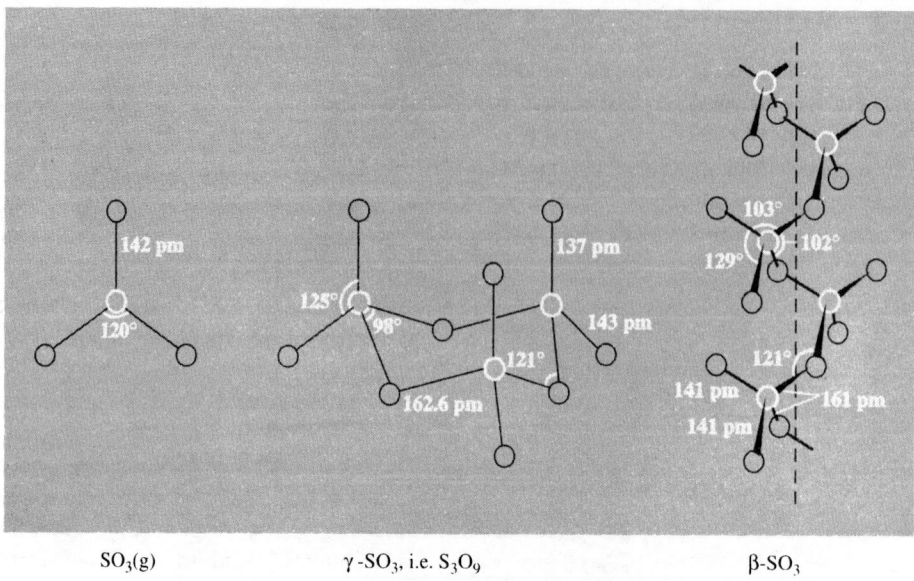

Figure 15.27   Structure of the monomeric, trimeric and chain-polymeric forms of sulfur trioxide.

Ph$_3$AsO gives Ph$_3$AsO.SO$_3$ etc. Frequently further reaction ensues: thus, under various conditions reaction with NH$_3$ yields H$_2$NSO$_3$H, HN(SO$_3$H)$_2$, HN(SO$_3$NH$_4$)$_2$, NH$_4$N(SO$_3$NH$_4$)$_2$, etc. SO$_3$ can also act as a ligand towards strong electron-pair acceptors such as AsF$_3$, SbF$_3$ and SbCl$_3$. It is reduced to SO$_2$ by activated charcoal or by metal sulfides. The reaction with metal oxides (particularly Fe$_3$O$_4$) to give sulfates is used industrially to rid stack-gases of unwanted byproduct SO$_3$.

Higher oxides

The reaction of gaseous SO$_2$ or SO$_3$ with O$_2$ in a silent electric discharge gives colourless polymeric condensates of composition SO$_{3+x}$ ($0 < x < 1$). These materials are derived from β-SO$_3$ by random substitution of oxo-bridges by peroxo-bridges:

$$\begin{array}{c} O \\ \parallel \\ -O-S-O-O-S-O- \\ \parallel \\ O \end{array}$$

Hydrolysis of the polymers yields H$_2$SO$_4$ and H$_2$SO$_5$ (p. 712), with H$_2$O$_2$ and O$_2$ as secondary products.

Monomeric neutral SO$_4$ can be obtained by reaction of SO$_3$ and atomic oxygen; photolysis of SO$_3$/ozone mixtures also yields monomeric SO$_4$, which can be isolated by inert-gas matrix techniques at low temperatures (15–78 K). Vibration spectroscopy indicates either an open peroxo C_s structure or a closed peroxo C_{2v} structure, the former being preferred by the most recent study, on the basis of agreement between observed and calculated frequencies and reasonable values for the force constants:[185]

The compound decomposes spontaneously below room temperature.

185 P. LA BONVILLE, R. KUGEL, and J. R. FERRARO, *J. Chem. Phys.* **67**, 1477–81 (1977).

Table 15.18   Oxoacids of sulfur

Formula	Name	Ox. states	Schematic structure*	Salt
H_2SO_4	sulfuric	VI	(structure)	sulfate, SO_4^{2-} H-sulfate, $HOSO_3^-$
$H_2S_2O_7$	disulfuric	VI	(structure)	disulfate, $O_3SOSO_3^{2-}$
$H_2S_2O_3$	thiosulfuric	IV, 0, (or VI, −II)	(structure)	thiosulfate, SSO_3^{2-}
H_2SO_5	peroxomonosulfuric	VI	(structure)	peroxomonosulfate, $OOSO_3^{2-}$
$H_2S_2O_8$	peroxodisulfuric	VI	(structure)	peroxodisulfate, $O_3SOOSO_3^{2-}$
$H_2S_2O_6$	dithionic*	V	(structure)	dithionate, $O_3SSO_3^{2-}$
$H_2S_{n+2}O_6$	polythionic	V,0	(structure)	polythionate, $O_3S(S)_nSO_3^{2-}$
H_2SO_3	sulfurous*	IV	(structure)	sulfite, SO_3^{2-} H-sulfite, $HOSO_2^-$
$H_2S_2O_5$	disulfurous*	V, III	(structure)	disulfite, $O_3SSO_2^{2-}$
$H_2S_2O_4$	dithionous*	III	(structure)	dithionite, $O_2SSO_2^{2-}$

*Acids marked with an asterisk do not exist in the free state but are known as salts.

15.2.6 Oxoacids of sulfur

Sulfur, like nitrogen and phosphorus, forms many oxoacids though few of these can be isolated as the free acid and most are known either as aqueous solutions or as crystalline salts of the corresponding oxoacid anions. Sulfuric acid, H_2SO_4, is the most important of all industrial chemicals and is manufactured on an enormous scale, greater than for any other compound of any element (p. 407). Other compounds, such as thiosulfates, sulfites, disulfites and dithionites, are valuable reducing agents with a wide variety of applications. Nomenclature is somewhat confusing but is summarized in Table 15.18 which also gives an indication of the various oxidation states of S and a schematic representation of the structures. Previously claimed species such as "sulfoxylic acid" (H_2SO_2), "thiosulfurous acid" ($H_2S_2O_2$), and their salts are now thought not to exist.

Table 15.19 Some standard reduction potentials of sulfur species (25°, pH 0)

Couple	$E°/V$
$2H_2SO_3 + H^+ + 2e^- \rightleftharpoons HS_2O_4^- + 2H_2O$	-0.082
$S + 2H^+ + 2e^- \rightleftharpoons H_2S$	$+0.142$
$HSO_4^- + 7H^+ + 6e^- \rightleftharpoons S + 4H_2O$	0.339
$H_2SO_3 + 4H^+ + 4e^- \rightleftharpoons S + 3H_2O$	0.449
$S_2O_3^{2-} + 6H^+ + 4e^- \rightleftharpoons 2S + 3H_2O$	0.465
$4H_2SO_3 + 4H^+ + 6e^- \rightleftharpoons S_4O_6^{2-} + 6H_2O$	0.509
$S_2O_6^{2-} + 4H^+ + 2e^- \rightleftharpoons 2H_2SO_3$	0.564
$S_2O_8^{2-} + 2H^+ + 2e^- \rightleftharpoons 2HSO_4^-$	2.123

Many of the sulfur oxoacids and their salts are connected by oxidation-reduction equilibria: some of the more important standard reduction potentials are summarized in Table 15.19 and displayed in graphic form as a volt-equivalent diagram (p. 435) in Fig. 15.28. By use of the couples in Table 15.19 data for many other oxidation-reduction equilibria can readily be calculated. (Indeed, it is an instructive exercise to check the derivation of the numerical data

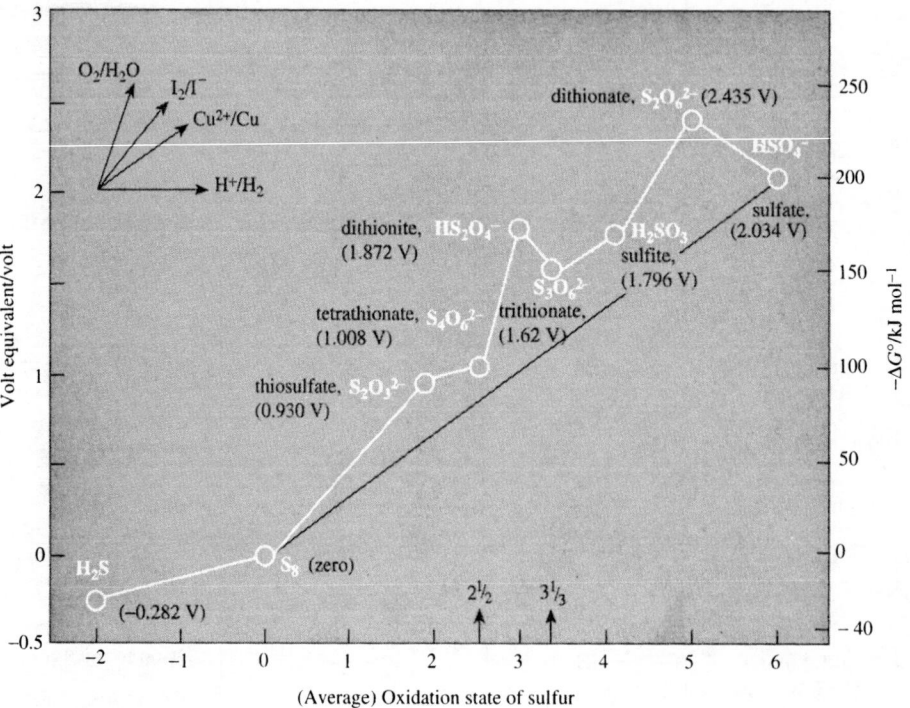

Figure 15.28 Volt-equivalent diagram for sulfur-containing species in acid solution.

given in parentheses in Fig. 15.28 from the data given in Table 15.19 and to calculate the standard reduction potentials of other couples, e.g. HSO_4^-/H_2S 0.289 V, HSO_4^-/H_2SO_3 0.119 V, $H_2SO_3/S_2O_3^{2-}$ 0.433 V, etc.) Several important points emerge which are immediately apparent from inspection of Fig. 15.28. For example, it is clear that, in acid solutions, the gradient between H_2S and S_8 is less than between S_8 and any positive oxidation state, so that H_2S is thermodynamically able to reduce any oxoacid of sulfur to the element. Again, as all the intermediate oxoacids lie above the line joining HSO_4^- and S_8, it follows that all can ultimately disproportionate into sulfuric acid and the element. Similarly, any moderately powerful oxidizing agent should be capable of oxidizing the intermediate oxoacids to sulfuric acid (sometimes with concurrent precipitation of sulfur) though by suitable choice of conditions it is often possible to obtain kinetically stable intermediate oxidation states (e.g. the polythionates with the stable S–S linkages). It follows that all the oxoacids except H_2SO_4 are moderately strong reducing agents (see below).

The formal interrelationship between the various oxoacids of sulfur can also be illustrated in a scheme[186] which places less emphasis on oxidation–reduction reactions but which is useful in suggesting possible alternative synthetic routes

to these oxoacids. Thus successive addition of SO_3 or SO_2 to H_2O can be represented by the scheme:

$$H_2O \xrightarrow{SO_3} \underset{\text{sulfuric}}{H_2SO_4} \xrightarrow{SO_3} \underset{\text{disulfuric}}{H_2S_2O_7}$$

$$\downarrow SO_2$$

$$\underset{\text{dithionic}}{H_2S_2O_6}$$

$$\uparrow SO_3$$

$$H_2O \xrightarrow{SO_2} \underset{\text{sulfurous}}{H_2SO_3} \xrightarrow{SO_2} \underset{\text{disulfurous}}{H_2S_2O_5}$$

Likewise addition of SO_3 to H_2O_2, H_2S and H_2S_n generates the formulae of the other oxoacids as follows:

$$H_2O_2 \xrightarrow{SO_3} \underset{\text{peroxomonosulfuric}}{H_2SO_5} \xrightarrow{SO_3} \underset{\text{peroxodisulfuric}}{H_2S_2O_8}$$

$$H_2S \xrightarrow{SO_3} \underset{\text{thiosulfuric}}{H_2S_2O_3} \xrightarrow{SO_3} \underset{\text{trithionic}}{H_2S_3O_6}$$

$$H_2S_n \xrightarrow{SO_3} H_2S_{n+1}O_3 \xrightarrow{SO_3} \underset{\text{polythionic}}{H_2S_{n+2}O_6}$$

It should be emphasized that not all the processes in these schemes represent viable syntheses, and other routes are frequently preferred. The following sections give a fuller discussion of the individual oxoacids and their salts.

186 M. SCHMIDT and W. SIEBERT, Oxyacids of sulfur, Section 2.4 in *Comprehensive Inorganic Chemistry*, Vol. 2, Chapter 23, pp. 868–98, Pergamon Press, Oxford, 1973.

187 R. L. KUCZKOWSKI, R. D. SUENRAM and F. J. LOVAS, *J. Am. Chem. Soc.* **103**, 2561–6 (1981).

Table 15.20 Some physical properties of anhydrous H_2SO_4 and D_2SO_4[a]

Property	H_2SO_4	D_2SO_4
MP/°C	10.371	14.35
BP/°C	~300 (decomp)	—
Density(25°)/g cm^{-3}	1.8267	1.8572
Viscosity(25°)/centipoise	24.55	24.88
Dielectric constant ε	100	—
Specific conductivity κ(25°)/ohm^{-1}cm^{-1}	1.0439×10^{-2}	0.2832×10^{-2}

(a) In the gas phase H_2SO_4 and D_2SO_4 adopt the C_2 conformation with r(O–H) 97 pm, r(S–OH) 157.4 pm, r(S–O) 142.2 pm; the various interatomic and dihedral angles were also determined and the molecular dipole moment calculated to be 2.73 D.[187]

Industrial Manufacture of Sulfuric Acid

Sulfuric acid is the world's most important industrial chemical and is the cheapest bulk acid available in every country of the world. It was one of the first chemicals to be produced commercially in the USA (by John Harrison, Philadelphia, 1793); in Europe the history of its manufacture goes back even further — by at least two centuries.[188,189] Concentrated sulfuric acid ("oil of vitriol") was first made by the distillation of "green vitriol", $FeSO_4.nH_2O$ and was needed in quantity to make Na_2SO_4 from NaCl for use in the Leblanc Process (p. 71). This expensive method was replaced in the early eighteenth century by the burning of sulfur and Chile saltpetre ($NaNO_3$) in the necks of large glass vessels containing a little water. The process was patented in 1749 by Joshua Ward (the Quack of Hogarth's *Harlot's Progress*) though it had been in use for several decades previously in Germany, France and England. The price plumetted 20-fold from £2 to 2 shillings per pound. It dropped by a further factor of 10 by 1830 following firstly John Roebuck's replacement (*ca.* 1755) of the fragile glass jars by lead-chambers of 200 ft^3 (5.7 m^3) capacity, and, secondly, the discovery (by N. Clement and C. B. Désormes in 1793) that the amount of $NaNO_3$ could be substantially reduced by admitting air for the combustion of sulfur. By 1860 James Muspratt (UK) was using lead chambers of 56 000 ft^3 capacity (1585 m^3) and the process was continuous. The maximum concentration of acid that could be produced by this method was about 78% and until 1870 virtually the only source of oleum was the Nordhausen works (distillation of $FeSO_4.nH_2O$). Today both processes have been almost entirely replaced by the modern contact process. This derives originally from Peregrine Philips' observation (patented in 1831) that SO_2 can be oxidized to SO_3 by air in the presence of a platinum catalyst.

The modern process uses a potassium-sulfate-promoted vanadium(V) oxide catalyst on a silica or kieselguhr support.[190] The SO_2 is obtained either by burning pure sulfur or by roasting sulfide minerals (p. 651) notably iron pyrite, or ores of Cu, Ni and Zn during the production of these metals. On a worldwide basis about 65% of the SO_2 comes from the burning of sulfur and some 35% by the roasting of sulfide ores but in some countries (e.g. the UK) over 95% comes from the former.

The oxidation of SO_2 to SO_3 is exothermic and reversible:

$$SO_2 + \tfrac{1}{2}O_2 \rightleftharpoons SO_3: \quad \Delta H° - 98 \text{ kJ mol}^{-1}$$

According to le Chatelier's principle the *yield* of SO_3 will increase with increase in pressure, increase in excess O_2 concentration, and removal of SO_3 from the reaction zone; each of these factors will also increase the *rate* of conversion somewhat (by the law of mass action). Reaction rate will also increase substantially with increase in temperature but this will simultaneously decrease the yield of the exothermic forward reaction. Accordingly, a catalyst is required to accelerate the reaction without diminishing the yield. Optimum conditions involve an equimolar feed of O_2/SO_2 (i.e. air/SO_2:5/1) and a 4-stage catalytic converter operating at the temperatures shown in the Figure.[123] (The V_2O_5 catalyst is inactive below 400°C and breaks down above 620°C; it is dispersed as a thin film of molten salt on the catalyst support.) Such a converter may be 13 m high, 9 m in diameter, contain 80 tonnes of catalyst pellets and produce 500 tonnes per day of acid. The gas temperature rises during passage through the catalyst bed and is recooled by passage through external heat-exchanger loops between the first three stages. In the most modern "double-absorption" plants (IPA) the SO_3 is removed at this stage before the residual SO_2/O_2 is passed through a fourth catalyst bed for final conversion. The SO_3 gas cannot be absorbed directly in water because it would first come into contact with the water-vapour above the absorbant and so produce a stable mist of fine droplets of H_2SO_4 which would then pass right through the absorber and out into the atmosphere. Instead, absorption is effected by 98% H_2SO_4 in ceramic-packed towers and sufficient water is added to the circulating acid to maintain the required concentration. Commercial conc H_2SO_4 is generally 96-98% to prevent undesirable solidification of the product. The main construction materials of the sulfur burner, catalytic converter, absorption towers and ducting are mild steel and stainless steel, and the major impurity in the acid is therefore Fe^{II} (10 ppm) together with traces of SO_2 and NO_x.

Some idea of the accelerating demand for sulfuric acid can be gained from the following UK production figures:

Year	1860	1870	1880	1890	1900	1917	1960	1980
10^3 tonnes	260	560	900	870	1100	1400	2750	4750

[188] T. K. DERRY and T. I. WILLIAMS, *A Short History of Technology from the Earliest Times to AD 1900*, pp. 268, and 534-5, Oxford University Press, Oxford, 1960.

[189] L. F. HABER, *The Chemical Industry During the Nineteenth Century*, Oxford University Press, Oxford, 1958, 292 pp; L. F. HABER, *The Chemical Industry 1900-1930*, Oxford University Press, Oxford, 1971, 452 pp.

[190] A. PHILLIPS, in R. THOMPSON (ed.), *The Modern Inorganic Chemicals Industry*, pp. 183-200, The Chemical Society, London, 1977. See also W. BÜCHNER, R. SCHLIEBS, G. WINTER and K. H. BÜCHEL, *Industrial Inorganic Chemistry*, VCH Publishers, New York, pp. 108-20 (1989).

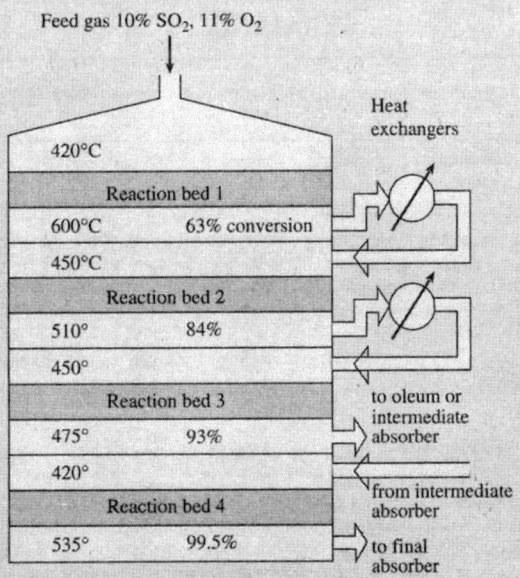

Schematic diagram of converter

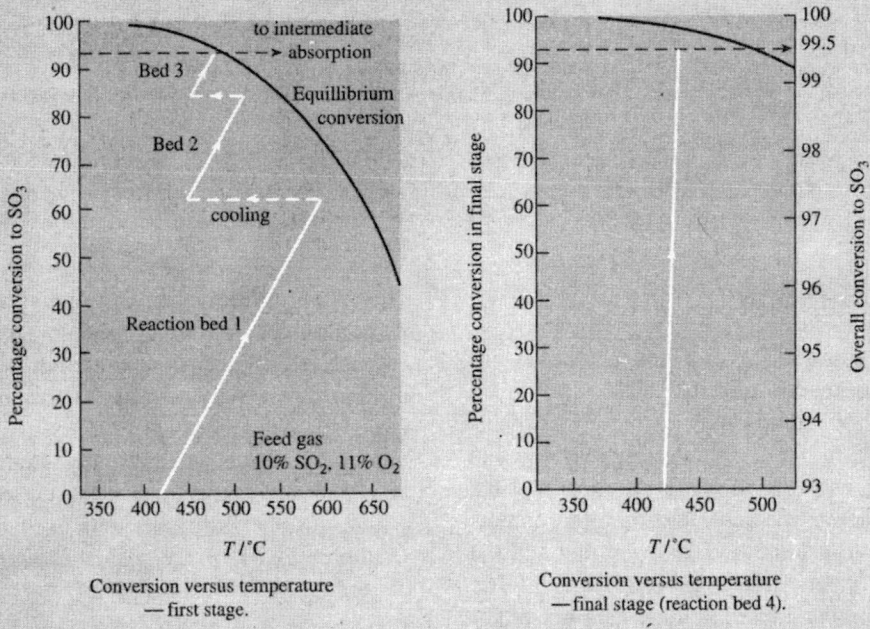

Conversion versus temperature
— first stage.

Conversion versus temperature
— final stage (reaction bed 4).

Double absorption (IPA) sulfuric acid plant.

Figures for France, Germany and the USA were lower than these until the turn of the century, but then the USA began to outstrip the rest. At about the same time superphosphate manufacture overtook the Leblanc soda process as the main user of H_2SO_4. H_2SO_4 production is now often taken as a reliable measure of a nation's industrial strength because it enters into so many industrial and manufacturing processes. Thus in 1900 production was equivalent to 4.05 million tonnes of 100% H_2SO_4 distributed as follows (%):

UK	USA	Germany	France	Austria	Belgium	Russia	Japan
25.9	23.2	21.0	15.5	4.9	4.0	3.1	1.2

By 1976 world production was 113 million tonnes and the distribution changed to the following (%):

USA	USSR	Japan	Germany	France	Poland	UK	Canada	Spain	Italy	Others
25.6	17.7	5.4	4.1	3.5	3.2	2.9	2.8	2.5	2.4	29.9

This had increased to 145 million tonnes by 1986 (Europe 44%, USA/Canada 24%, Asia/Oceania 18%, Africa 9%, Latin America 5%). Such vast quantities require huge plants: these frequently have a capacity in excess of 2000 tonnes per day in the USA but are more commonly in the range 300–750 tonnes per day in Europe and smaller still in less industrialized countries. Even so, the energy flows are enormous as can be appreciated by scaling up the following reactions:

$$S + O_2 \longrightarrow SO_2, \qquad \Delta H° - 297 \text{ kJ mol}^{-1}$$

$$SO_2 + \tfrac{1}{2}O_2 \longrightarrow SO_3, \qquad \Delta H° - 9.8 \text{ kJ mol}^{-1}$$

$$SO_3 + H_2O \text{ (in 98\%} H_2SO_4) \longrightarrow H_2SO_4, \qquad \Delta H° - 130 \text{ kJ mol}^{-1}$$

For example, the oxidation of S to SO_3 liberates nearly 4×10^9 J per tonne of H_2SO_4 of which ~3 GJ can be sold as energy in the form of steam and much of the rest used to pump materials around the plant, etc. A plant producing 750 tonnes per day of H_2SO_4 produces ~25 MW of byproduct thermal energy, equivalent to ~7 MW of electricity if the steam is used to drive generators. Effective utilization of this energy is an important factor in minimizing the cost of sulfuric acid which remains a remarkably cheap commodity despite inflation (of the order of $150 per tonne in 1994).

Environmental legislation in the USA requires that sulfur emitted from the stack (SO_2 and persistent H_2SO_4 mist) must not exceed 0.3% of the sulfur burned (0.5% in the UK). Despite this, because of the vast scale of the industry, large quantities of unconverted SO_2 are vented to the atmosphere each year (say 0.3% of 145×10^6 tonnes $\times \frac{64}{98} = 284\,000$ tonnes SO_2 pa). It is a testament to the efficiency of the process that this represents a global impact of only some 780 tonnes SO_2 per day, which is minute compared with other sources of this pollution (p. 698).

The pattern of use of H_2SO_4 varies from country to country and from decade to decade. Current US usage is dominated by fertilizer production (70%) followed by chemical manufacture, metallurgical uses, and petroleum refining (~5% each). In the UK the distribution of uses is more even: only 30% of the H_2SO_4 manufactured is used in the fertilizer industry but 18% goes on paints, pigments and dyestuff intermediates, 16% on chemicals manufacture, 12% on soaps and detergents, 10% on natural and manmade fibres, and 2.5% on metallurgical applications.

Sulfuric acid, H_2SO_4

Anhydrous sulfuric acid is a dense, viscous liquid which is readily miscible with water in all proportions: the reaction is extremely exothermic (~880 kJ mol^{-1} at infinite dilution) and can result in explosive spattering of the mixture if the water is added to the acid; it is therefore important always to use the reverse order and add the acid to the water, slowly and with stirring. The large-scale preparation of sulfuric acid is a major industry in most countries and is described in the preceding Panel.

Some physical properties of anhydrous H_2SO_4 (and D_2SO_4) are in Table 15.20 (p. 707).[191,192] In addition, several congruently melting hydrates,

$H_2SO_4.nH_2O$, are known with $n = 1$, 2, 3, 4 (mps 8.5°, −39.5°, −36.4° and −28.3°, respectively). Other compounds in the H_2O/SO_3 system are $H_2S_2O_7$ (mp 36°) and $H_2S_4O_{13}$ (mp 4°). Anhydrous H_2SO_4 is a remarkable compound with an unusually high dielectric constant, and a very high electrical conductivity which results from the ionic self-dissociation (autoprotolysis) of the compound coupled with a proton-switch mechanism for the rapid

---

[191] R. J. GILLESPIE and E. A. ROBINSON, Sulfuric acid, Chap. 4 in T. C. WADDINGTON (ed.), *Nonaqueous Solvent Systems*, pp. 117–210, Academic Press, London, 1965. A definitive review with some 250 references.
[192] N. N. GREENWOOD and A. THOMPSON, *J. Chem. Soc.* 3474–84 (1959).

conduction of current through the viscous H-bonded liquid. For example, at 25° the single-ion conductances for $H_3SO_4^+$ and HSO_4^- are 220 and 150 respectively, whereas those for Na^+ and K^+ which are viscosity-controlled are only 3–5. Anhydrous H_2SO_4 thus has many features in common with anhydrous H_3PO_4 (p. 518) but the equilibria are reached much more rapidly (almost instantaneously) in H_2SO_4:

$$2H_2SO_4 \rightleftharpoons H_3SO_4^+ + HSO_4^-$$

$$K_{ap}(25°) = [H_3SO_4^+][HSO_4^-] = 2.7 \times 10^{-4}$$

This value is compared with those for other acids and protonic liquids in Table 15.21:[191] the extent of autoprotolysis in H_2SO_4 is greater than that in water by a factor of more than 10^{10} and is exceeded only by anhydrous H_3PO_4 and $[HBF_3(OH)]$ (p. 198). In addition to autoprotolysis, H_2SO_4 undergoes ionic self-dehydration:

$$2H_2SO_4 \rightleftharpoons H_3O^+ + HS_2O_7^-; \quad K_{id}(25°)5.1 \times 10^{-5}$$

This arises from the primary dissociation of H_2SO_4 into H_2O and SO_3 which then react with further H_2SO_4 as follows:

$$H_2O + H_2SO_4 \rightleftharpoons H_3O^+ + HSO_4^-;$$

$$K_{H_2O}(25°) = [H_3O^+][HSO_4^-]/[H_2O] \sim 1$$

$$SO_3 + H_2SO_4 \rightleftharpoons H_2S_2O_7$$

$$H_2S_2O_7 + H_2SO_4 \rightleftharpoons H_3SO_4^+ + HS_2O_7^-;$$

$$K_{H_2S_2O_7}(25°) = [H_3SO_4^+][HS_2O_7^-]/[H_2S_2O_7]$$

$$= 1.4 \times 10^{-2}$$

It is clear that "pure" anhydrous sulfuric acid, far from being a single substance in the bulk liquid phase, comprises a dynamic equilibrium involving at least seven well-defined species. The concentration of the self-dissociation products in H_2SO_4 and D_2SO_4 at 25° (expressed in millimoles of solute per kg solvent) are:

HSO_4^-	$H_3SO_4^+$	H_3O^+	$HS_2O_7^-$	$H_2S_2O_7$	H_2O	Total
15.0	11.3	8.0	4.4	3.6	0.1	42.4

DSO_4^-	$D_3SO_4^+$	D_3O^+	$DS_2O_7^-$	$D_2S_2O_7$	D_2O	Total
11.2	4.1	11.2	4.9	7.1	0.6	39.1

As the molecular weight of H_2SO_4 is 98.078 it follows that 1 kg contains 10.196 mol; hence the predominant ions are present to the extent of about 1 millimole per mole of H_2SO_4 and the total concentration of species in equilibrium with the parent acid is 4.16 millimole per mole. Many of the physical and chemical properties of anhydrous H_2SO_4 as a nonaqueous solvent stem from these equilibria.

In the sulfuric acid solvent system, compounds that enhance the concentration of the solvo-cation HSO_4^- will behave as bases and those that give rise to $H_3SO_4^+$ will behave as acids (p. 425). Basic solutions can be formed in several ways of which the following examples are typical:

(a) Dissolution of metal hydrogen sulfates:

$$KHSO_4 \xrightarrow{H_2SO_4} K^+ + HSO_4^-$$

(b) Solvolysis of salts of acids that are weaker than H_2SO_4:

$$KNO_3 + H_2SO_4 \longrightarrow K^+ + HSO_4^- + HNO_3$$

$$NH_4ClO_4 + H_2SO_4 \longrightarrow NH_4^+ + HSO_4^-$$
$$+ HClO_4$$

(c) Protonation of compounds with lone-pairs of electrons:

$$H_2O + H_2SO_4 \longrightarrow H_3O^+ + HSO_4^-$$

$$Me_2CO + H_2SO_4 \longrightarrow Me_2COH^+ + HSO_4^-$$

Table 15.21   Autoprotolysis constants at 25°

Compound	$-\log K_{ap}$	Compound	$-\log K_{ap}$	Compound	$-\log K_{ap}$
$HBF_3(OH)$	~ -1	HCO_2H	6.2	H_2O_2	12
H_3PO_4	~ 2	HF	9.7	H_2O	14.0
H_2SO_4	3.6	$MeCO_2H$	12.6	D_2O	14.8
D_2SO_4	4.3	EtOH	18.9	NH_3	29.8

$$MeCOOH + H_2SO_4 \longrightarrow MeC(OH)_2{}^+ + HSO_4{}^-$$

(d) Dehydration reactions:

$$HNO_3 + 2H_2SO_4 \longrightarrow NO_2{}^+ + H_3O^+ + 2HSO_4{}^-$$

$$N_2O_5 + 3H_2SO_4 \longrightarrow 2NO_2{}^+ + H_3O^+ + 3HSO_4{}^-$$

The reaction with HNO_3 is quantitative, and the presence of large concentrations of the nitronium ion, $NO_2{}^+$, in solutions of HNO_3, MNO_3 and N_2O_5 in H_2SO_4 enable a detailed interpretation to be given of the nitration of aromatic hydrocarbons by these solutions.

Because of the high acidity of H_2SO_4 itself, bases form the largest class of electrolytes and only few acids (proton donors) are known in this solvent system. As noted above, $H_2S_2O_7$ acts as a proton donor to H_2SO_4 and HSO_3F is also a weak acid:

$$HSO_3F + H_2SO_4 \rightleftharpoons H_3SO_4{}^+ + SO_3F^-$$

One of the few strong acids is tetra(hydrogen sulfato)boric acid $HB(HSO_4)_4$; solutions of this can be obtained by dissolving boric acid in oleum:

$$B(OH)_3 + 3H_2S_2O_7 \longrightarrow H_3SO_4{}^+ + [B(HSO_4)_4]^- + H_2SO_4$$

Other strong acids are $H_2Sn(HSO_4)_6$ and $H_2Pb(HSO_4)_6$.

Sulfuric acid forms salts (sulfates and hydrogen sulfates) with many metals. These are frequently very stable and, indeed, they are the most important mineral compounds of several of the more electropositive elements. They have been discussed in detail under the appropriate elements. Sulfates can be prepared by:

(a) dissolution of metals in aqueous H_2SO_4 (e.g. Fe);
(b) neutralization of aqueous H_2SO_4 with metal oxides or hydroxides (e.g. MOH);
(c) decomposition of salts of volatile acids (e.g. carbonates) with aqueous H_2SO_4;
(d) metathesis between a soluble sulfate and a soluble salt of the metal whose (insoluble) sulfate is required (e.g. $BaSO_4$);
(e) oxidation of metal sulfides or sulfites.

The sulfate ion is tetrahedral (S–O 149 pm) and can act as a monodentate, bidentate (chelating) or bridging ligand. Examples are in Fig. 15.29. Vibrational spectroscopy is a useful diagnostic, as the progressive reduction in local symmetry of the SO_4 group from C_{3v} to C_{3v} and eventually C_{2v} increases the number of infrared active modes from 2 to 6 and 8 respectively, and the number of Raman active modes from 4 to 6 and 9.[193] (The effects of crystal symmetry and the overlapping of bands complicates the analysis but correct assignments are frequently still possible.)

Pairs of corner-shared SO_4 tetrahedra are found in the disulfates, $S_2O_7{}^{2-}$ ($S-O_\mu-S$ 124°, $S-O_\mu$ 164.5 pm, $S-O_t$ 144 pm); they are made by thermal dehydration of $MHSO_4$. Likewise the trisulfate ion $S_3O_{10}{}^{2-}$ is known and also the pentasulfate ion, $S_5O_{16}{}^{2-}$ whose structure indicates an alternation of S–O interatomic distances and very long O–S distances to the almost planar terminal SO_3 groups:

Peroxosulfuric acids, H_2SO_5 and $H_2S_2O_8$

Anhydrous peroxomonosulfuric acid (Caro's acid) can be prepared by reacting chlorosulfuric acid with anhydrous H_2O_2

$$HOOH + ClSO_2(OH) \longrightarrow HOOSO_2(OH) + HCl$$

---

193 K. NAKAMOTO, *Infrared Spectra of Inorganic and Coordination Compounds*, 2nd edn., Wiley, New York, 1970, 338 pp. (See also *J. Am. Chem. Soc.* **79**, 4904–8 (1957) for detailed correlation table.)

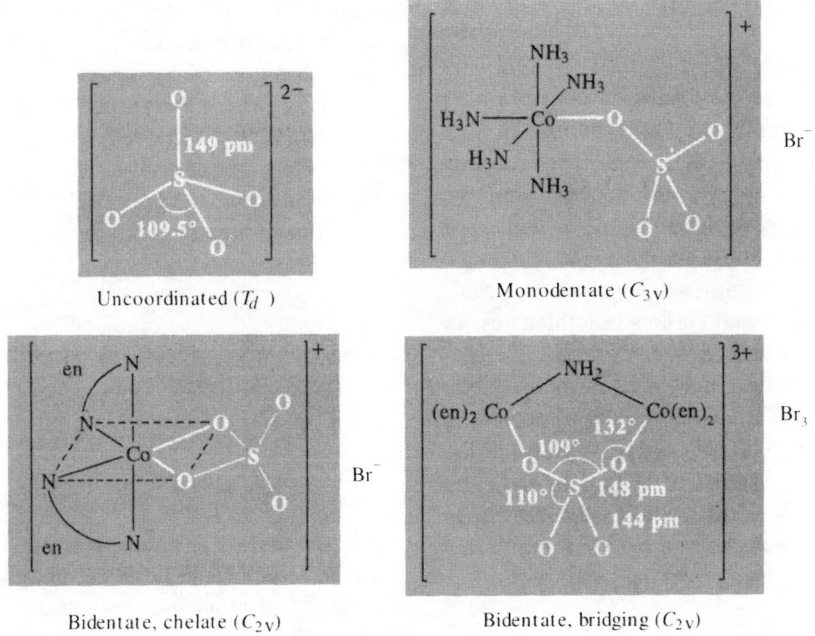

Figure 15.29   Examples of $SO_4{}^{2-}$ as a ligand.

It is colourless, beautifully crystalline, and melts at 45°, but should be handled carefully because of the danger of explosions. It can also be made by the action of conc H_2SO_4 on peroxodisulfates and is formed as a byproduct during the preparation of $H_2S_2O_8$ by electrolysis of aqueous H_2SO_4 (N. Caro, 1898). Its salts, which are preferably called trioxoperoxosulfates(2−) rather than peroxomonosulfates,[194] are unstable and the compound has few uses except those dependent on the formation of the H_2O_2 during its decomposition. The structure of the anion $[HOOSO_3]^-$, which is the active principle of Caro's acid, has been determined by X-ray analysis of the hydrated salt $KHSO_5.H_2O$; selected dimensions are O–O 140.0, S–O₂ 163.2, S–Oₜ 143.5–144.4 pm, angle OOS 109.4°.[195]

Peroxodisulfuric acid, $H_2S_2O_8$, is a colourless solid mp 65° (with decomposition). The acid is soluble in water in all proportions and its most important salts, $(NH_4)_2S_2O_8$ and $K_2S_2O_8$, are also freely soluble. These salts are, in fact, easier to prepare than the acid and both are made on an industrial scale by anodic oxidation of the corresponding sulfates under carefully controlled conditions (high current density, $T < 30°$, bright Pt electrodes, protected cathode). The structure of the peroxodisulfate ion [now preferably called hexaoxo-μ-peroxodisulfate(2-)][194] is $O_3SOOSO_3{}^{2-}$ with O–O 131 pm and S–O 150 pm. The compounds are used as oxidizing and bleaching agents. Thus, as can be seen from Table 15.19, the standard reduction potential $S_2O_8{}^{2-}/HSO_4{}^-$ is 2.123 V, and $E°(S_2O_8{}^{2-}/SO_4{}^{2-})$ is similar (2.010 V); these are more positive than for any other aqueous couples except $H_2N_2O_2$, $2H^+/N_2$, $2H_2O$ (2.85 V), $F_2/2F^-$ (2.87 V) and $F_2,2H^+/2HF(aq)$ (3.06) — see also O(g), $2H^+/H_2O$ (2.42 V), $OH,H^+/H_2O$ (2.8 V).

[194] G. J. Leigh (ed.), *Nomenclature of Inorganic Chemistry* (The IUPAC 'Red Book'), Blackwell Scientific Publications, Oxford, 1990, pp. 268, 269.

[195] J. Flanagan, W. P. Griffith and A. C. Skapski, *J. Chem. Soc., Chem. Commun.*, 1574–5 (1984).

Thiosulfuric acid, $H_2S_2O_3$

Attempts to prepare thiosulfuric acid by acidification of stable thiosulfates are invariably thwarted by the ready decomposition of the free acid in the presence of water. The reaction is extremely complex and depends on the conditions used, being dominated by numerous redox interconversions amongst the products: these can include sulfur (partly as *cyclo*-S_6), SO_2, H_2S, H_2S_n, H_2SO_4 and various polythionates. In the absence of water, however, these reactions are avoided and the parent acid is more stable: it decomposes quantitatively below 0° according to the reaction $H_2S_2O_3 \longrightarrow H_2S + SO_3$ (cf. the analogous decomposition of H_2SO_4 to H_2O and SO_3 above its bp ~300°). Successful anhydrous syntheses have been devised by M. Schmidt and his group (1959–61), e.g.:

$$H_2S + SO_3 \xrightarrow{Et_2O/-78°} H_2S_2O_3.nEt_2O$$

$$Na_2S_2O_3 + 2HCl \xrightarrow{Et_2O/-78°} 2NaCl + H_2S_2O_3.2Et_2O$$

$$HSO_3Cl + H_2S \xrightarrow[\text{low temp}]{\text{no solvent}} HCl + H_2S_2O_3$$
$$\text{(solvent-free acid)}$$

Combination of stoichiometric amounts of H_2S and SO_3 at low temperature yields the white crystalline adduct $H_2S.SO_3$ which is isomeric with thiosulfuric acid.

In contrast to the free acid, stable thiosulfate salts can readily be prepared by reaction of H_2S on aqueous solutions of sulfites:

$$2HS^- + 4HSO_3^- \longrightarrow 3S_2O_3^{2-} + 3H_2O$$

The reaction appears to proceed first by the formation of elemental sulfur which then equilibrates with more HSO_3^- to form the product:[196]

$$2HS^- + HSO_3^- \longrightarrow 3S + 3OH^-$$

$$3S + 3HSO_3^- \longrightarrow 3S_2O_3^{2-} + 3H^+$$

---

[196] G. W. HEUNISH, *Inorg. Chem.* **16,** 1411–13 (1979) and references therein.

Consistent with this, experiments using HS^- labelled with radioactive ^{35}S (p. 661) show that acid hydrolysis of the $S_2O_3^{2-}$ produces elemental sulfur in which two-thirds of the ^{35}S activity is concentrated. Thiosulfates can also be made by boiling aqueous solutions of metal sulfites (or hydrogen sulfites) with elemental sulfur according to the stoichiometry

$$Na_2SO_3 + \tfrac{1}{8}S_8 \xrightarrow{H_2O/100°} Na_2S_2O_3$$

Aerial oxidation of polysulfides offers an alternative industrial route:

$$Na_2S_5 + \tfrac{3}{2}O_2 \longrightarrow Na_2S_2O_3 + \tfrac{3}{x}S_x$$

$$CaS_2 + \tfrac{3}{2}O_2 \longrightarrow CaS_2O_3$$

The thiosulfate ion closely resembles the SO_4^{2-} ion in structure and can act as monodentate η^1-S ligand, a monhapto bidentate bridging ligand $(\mu,\eta^1$-$S)$, or a dihapto chelating η^2-S,O ligand as illustrated in Fig. 15.30.[197] Hydrated sodium thiosulfate $Na_2S_2O_3.5H_2O$ ("hypo") forms large, colourless, transparent crystals, mp 48.5°; it is readily soluble in water and is used as a "fixer" in photography to dissolve unreacted $AgBr$ from the emulsion by complexation:

$$AgBr(cryst) + 3Na_2S_2O_3(aq) \longrightarrow$$
$$Na_5[Ag(S_2O_3)_3](aq) + NaBr(aq)$$

The thiosulfate ion is a moderately strong reducing agent as indicated by the couple

$$S_4O_6^{2-} + 2e^- \rightleftharpoons 2S_2O_3^{2-}; \quad E° = 0.169 \text{ V}$$

Thus the quantitative oxidation of $S_2O_3^{2-}$ by I_2 to form tetrathionate and iodide is the basis for the iodometric titrations in volumetric analysis

$$2S_2O_3^{2-} + I_2 \longrightarrow S_4O_6^{2-} + 2I^-$$

Stronger oxidizing agents take the reaction through to sulfate, e.g.:

$$S_2O_3^{2-} + 4Cl_2 + 5H_2O \longrightarrow$$
$$2HSO_4^- + 8H^+ + 8Cl^-$$

---

[197] See p. 723 of ref. 103 for detailed references.

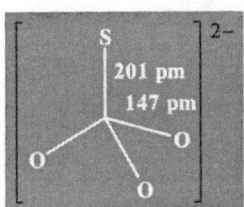

(a) Uncoordinated

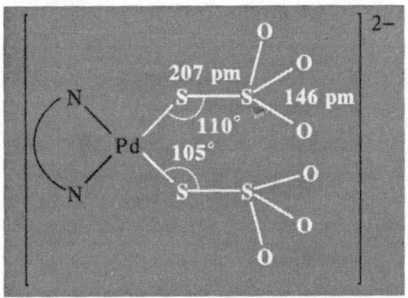

(b) Monodentate (η^1-S): the S^{VI} atoms are not coplanar with the {PdN_2S_2} group

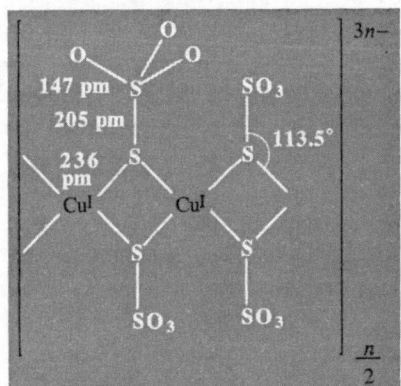

(c) Monohapto bidentate bridging (μ,η^1-S)

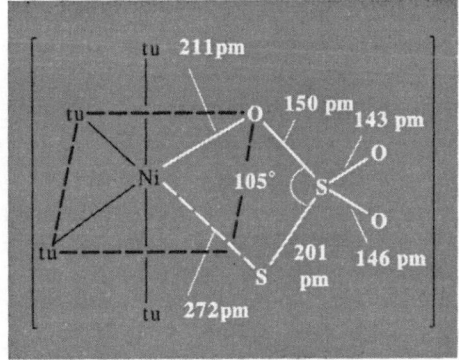

(d) Dihapto bidentate chelating (η^2-S,O)

Figure 15.30   Structure of the thiosulfate ion and its various modes of coordination: (a) uncoordinated $S_2O_3{}^{2-}$; (b) monodentate (η^1-S) in the anion of the orange complex [Pd^{II}(en)$_2$][Pd^{II}(en)(S_2O_3)$_2$]; (c) monohapto bidentate bridging (μ,η^1-S) in the polymeric anion of the pale-violet mixed valence copper complex Na_4[Cu^{II}(NH_3)$_4$][Cu^{I}(S_2O_3)$_2$]$_2$; and (d) dihapto chelating (η^2-S,O) in the thiourea nickel complex [Ni(S_2O_3)(tu)$_4$].H_2O.

This reaction is the basis for the use of thiosulfates as "antichlorine" in the bleaching industry where they are used to destroy any excess of Cl_2 in the fibres. Bromine, being intermediate between iodine and chlorine, can cause $S_2O_3{}^{2-}$ to act either as a 1-electron or an 8-electron reducer according to conditions. For example, in an amusing and instructive experiment, if concentrated aqueous solutions of $S_2O_3{}^{2-}$ and Br_2 are titrated, and the titration is then repeated after having diluted both the $S_2O_3{}^{2-}$ and Br_2 solutions 100-fold, then the titre will be found to have increased by a factor of exactly 8.

Dithionic acid, $H_2S_2O_6$

In dithionic acid and dithionates, $S_2O_6{}^{2-}$, the oxidation state of the 2 S atoms has been reduced from VI to V by the formation of an S–S bond (Table 15.18, p. 705). The free acid has not been obtained pure, but quite concentrated aqueous solutions can be prepared by treatment of the barium salt with the stoichiometric amount of H_2SO_4:

$$BaS_2O_6(aq) + H_2SO_4(aq) \longrightarrow$$
$$H_2S_2O_6(aq) + BaSO_4\downarrow$$

Crystalline dithionates are thermally stable above room temperature (e.g. $K_2S_2O_6$ decomp 258° to $K_2SO_4 + SO_2$). They are commonly made by oxidizing the corresponding sulfite. On a technical scale aqueous solutions of SO_2 are oxidized by a suspension of hydrated MnO_2 or Fe_2O_3:

$$2MnO_2 + 3SO_2 \xrightarrow{aq/0°C} MnSO_4 + MnS_2O_6$$

$$Fe_2O_3 + 3SO_2 \xrightarrow{aq} \{Fe_2^{III}(SO_3)_3\} \longrightarrow$$
$$Fe^{II}SO_3 + Fe^{II}S_2O_6$$

All the dithionates are readily soluble in water and can be made by standard metathesis reactions. For example, addition of an excess of Ba^{II} ions to the Mn^{II} solution above precipitates $BaSO_4$, after which $BaS_2O_6.2H_2O$ can be crystallized. The $[O_3SSO_3]^{2-}$ ion is centrosymmetric (staggered) D_{3d} in $Na_2S_2O_6.2H_2O$ but in the anhydrous potassium salt some of the $S_2O_6^{2-}$ ions have an almost eclipsed configuration for the two SO_3 groups (D_{3h}). Dimensions are unremarkable: S–S 215 pm, S–O 143 pm, and angle S–S–O 103°. In a curious reaction between dibenzenechromium(0) and dry, oxygen-free SO_2 in toluene, a red precipitate is formed which subsequently turns black. The unexpected product is $[(\eta^6\text{-}C_6H_6)_2Cr]_2[S_4O_{10}]$, which contains the dianion $[S_4O_{10}]^{2-}$ formed by coordination of two SO_2 molecules to a dithionate ion, $[O_2S{\to}OS(O)_2{-}S(O)_2O{\leftarrow}SO_2]^{2-}$ with S–S 221.8 pm, S${\to}$O 243.3 pm and angle S${\to}$O–S 129.3°.[198]

Dithionates are relatively stable towards oxidation in solution though strong oxidants such as the halogens, dichromate and permanganate oxidize them to sulfate. Powerful reductants (e.g. Na/Hg) reduce dithionates to sulfites and dithionites ($S_2O_4^{2-}$). In neutral and slightly acidic aqueous solutions dithionite itself decomposes by pH-dependent routes to thiosulfite ($S_2O_3^{2-}$), sulfite (SO_3^{2-}), sulfide (S^{2-}), etc. These, and the products of the reactions of dithionites with polythionates ($S_nO_6^{2-}$, $n = 3{-}5$) have been studied by ion-pair chromotography:[199]

$$S_2O_4^{2-} + S_nO_6^{2-} + 2H_2O \longrightarrow S_2O_3^{2-}$$
$$+ S_{n-3}SO_3^{2-} + 4H^+ + 2SO_3^{2-}$$

Polythionic acids, $H_2S_nO_6$

The numerous acids and salts in this group have a venerable history and the chemistry of systems in which they occur goes back to John Dalton's studies (1808) of the effect of H_2S on aqueous solutions of SO_2. Such solutions are now named after H. W. F. Wackenroder (1846) who subjected them to systematic study. Work during the following 60–80 y indicated the presence of numerous species including, in particular, the tetrathionate $S_4O_6^{2-}$ and pentathionate $S_5O_6^{2-}$ ions. New perceptions have emerged during the past few decades as a result of the work of H. Schmidt and others in Germany: just as H_2S can react with SO_3 or HSO_3Cl to yield thiosulfuric acid, $H_2S_2O_3$ (p. 714), so reaction with H_2S_2 yields "disulfane monosulfonic acid", HS_2SO_3H; likewise polysulfanes H_2S_n ($n = 2{-}6$) yield HS_nSO_3H. Reaction at both ends of the polysulfane chain would yield "polysulfane disulfonic acids" $HO_3SS_nSO_3H$ which are more commonly called polythionic acids ($H_2S_{n+2}O_6$). Many synthetic routes are available, though mechanistic details are frequently obscure because of the numerous simultaneous and competing redox, catenation and disproportionation reactions that occur. Typical examples include:

(a) Interaction of H_2S and SO_2 in Wackenroder's solution (see above).

(b) Reaction of chlorosulfanes with HSO_3^- or $HS_2O_3^-$, e.g.:

$$SCl_2 + 2HSO_3^- \longrightarrow [O_3SSSO_3]^{2-} + 2HCl$$
$$S_2Cl_2 + 2HSO_3^- \longrightarrow [O_3SS_2SO_3]^{2-} + 2HCl$$

[198] C. ELSCHENBROICH, R. GONDRUM and W. MASSA, *Angew. Chem. Int. Edn. Engl.* **24**, 967–8 (1985).

[199] V. MÜNCHOW and R. STEUDEL, *Z. anorg. allg. Chem.* **620**, 121–6 (1994).

$$SCl_2 + 2HS_2O_3^- \longrightarrow [O_3SS_3SO_3]^{2-}$$
$$+ 2HCl, \text{ etc.}$$

(c) Oxidation of thiosulfates with mild oxidants (p. 714) such as I_2, Cu^{II}, $S_2O_8^{2-}$, H_2O_2.

(d) Specific syntheses as noted below.

Sodium trithionate, $Na_2S_3O_6$, can be made by oxidizing sodium thiosulfate with cooled hydrogen peroxide solution

$$2Na_2S_2O_3 + 4H_2O_2 \longrightarrow Na_2S_3O_6$$
$$+ Na_2SO_4 + 4H_2O$$

The potassium (but not the sodium) salt is obtained by the obscure reaction of SO_2 on aqueous thiosulfate. Aqueous solutions of the acid $H_2S_3O_6$ can then be obtained from $K_2S_3O_6$ by treatment with tartaric acid or perchloric acid.

Sodium (and potassium) tetrathionate, $M_2S_4O_6$, can be made by oxidation of thiosulfate by I_2 (p. 714) and the free acid liberated (in aqueous solution) by addition of the stoichiometric amount of tartaric acid.

Potassium pentathionate, $K_2S_5O_6$, can be made by adding potassium acetate to Wackenroder's solution and solutions of the free acid $H_2S_5O_6$ can then be obtained by subsequent addition of tartaric acid.

Potassium hexathionate, $K_2S_6O_6$, is best synthesized by the action of KNO_2 on $K_2S_2O_3$ in conc HCl at low temperatures, though the ion is also a constituent of Wackenroder's solution.

Anhydrous polythionic acids can be made in ether solution by three general routes:

$$HS_nSO_3H + SO_3 \longrightarrow H_2S_{n+2}O_6$$
$$(n + 2 = 3, 4, 5, 6, 7, 8)$$

$$H_2S_n + 2SO_3 \longrightarrow H_2S_{n+2}O_6$$
$$(n + 2 = 3, 4, 5, 6, 7, 8)$$

$$2HS_nSO_3H + I_2 \longrightarrow H_2S_{2n+2}O_6 + 2HI$$
$$(2n + 2 = 4, 6, 8, 10, 12, 14)$$

The structure of the trithionate ion (in $K_2S_3O_6$) is shown in Fig. 15.31a and calls for little comment (cf. the disulfate ion $O_3SOSO_3^{2-}$, p. 712). The tetrathionate ion (in $BaS_4O_6.2H_2O$ and $Na_2S_4O_6.2H_2O$) has the configuration shown in Fig. 15.31b with dihedral angles close to $90°$ and a small, but definite, alternation in S–S distances. The pentathionate ion in $BaS_5O_6.2H_2O$ has the *cis* configuration in which the S_5 unit can be regarded as part of an S_8 ring (p. 655) from which 3 adjacent S atoms have been removed (Fig. 15.31c). By contrast, in the potassium salt $K_2S_5O_6.1\frac{1}{2}H_2O$ the pentathionate ion adopts the *trans* configuration in which the two terminal SO_3 groups are on opposite sides of the central S_3 plane (Fig. 15.31d). These structural differences persist in the seleno- and telluro-analogues $O_3SSSeSSO_3^{2-}$ and $O_3SSTeSSO_3^{2-}$, the dihydrated Ba salts being *cis* and the potassium hemihydrates being *trans*.[200] There are three possible rotameric forms of the hexathionate ion $S_6O_6^{2-}$: the extended *trans-trans* form analogous to spiral chains of fibrous sulfur (p. 660) occurs in the *trans*-$[Co^{III}(en)_2Cl_2]^+$ salt (Fig. 15.31e), whereas the *cis-cis* form (analogous to *cyclo*-S_8) occurs in the potassium barium salt (Fig. 15.31f); the *cis-trans* form of $S_6O_6^{2-}$ has not yet been observed in crystals but presumably occurs in equilibrium with the other two forms in solution since the energy barrier to rotation about the S–S bonds is only some $40\,kJ\,mol^{-1}$.

Sulfurous acid, H_2SO_3

Sulfurous acid has never been isolated as a pure compound, although it has recently been detected in the gas phase by neutralization reionization mass spectrometry (NRMS) following the facile dissociative ionization (70 eV) of either diethyl sulfite or ethanesulfonic acid:[201]

---

200 O. Foss, *IUPAC Additional Publication* (24th International Congress, Hamburg, 1973), Vol. 4, *Compounds of Non-Metals*, pp. 103–13, Butterworths, London, 1974, and references therein.
201 D. Sülzle, M. Verhoeven, J. K. Terlouw and H. Schwarz, *Angew. Chem. Int. Edn. Engl.* **27**, 1533–4 (1988).

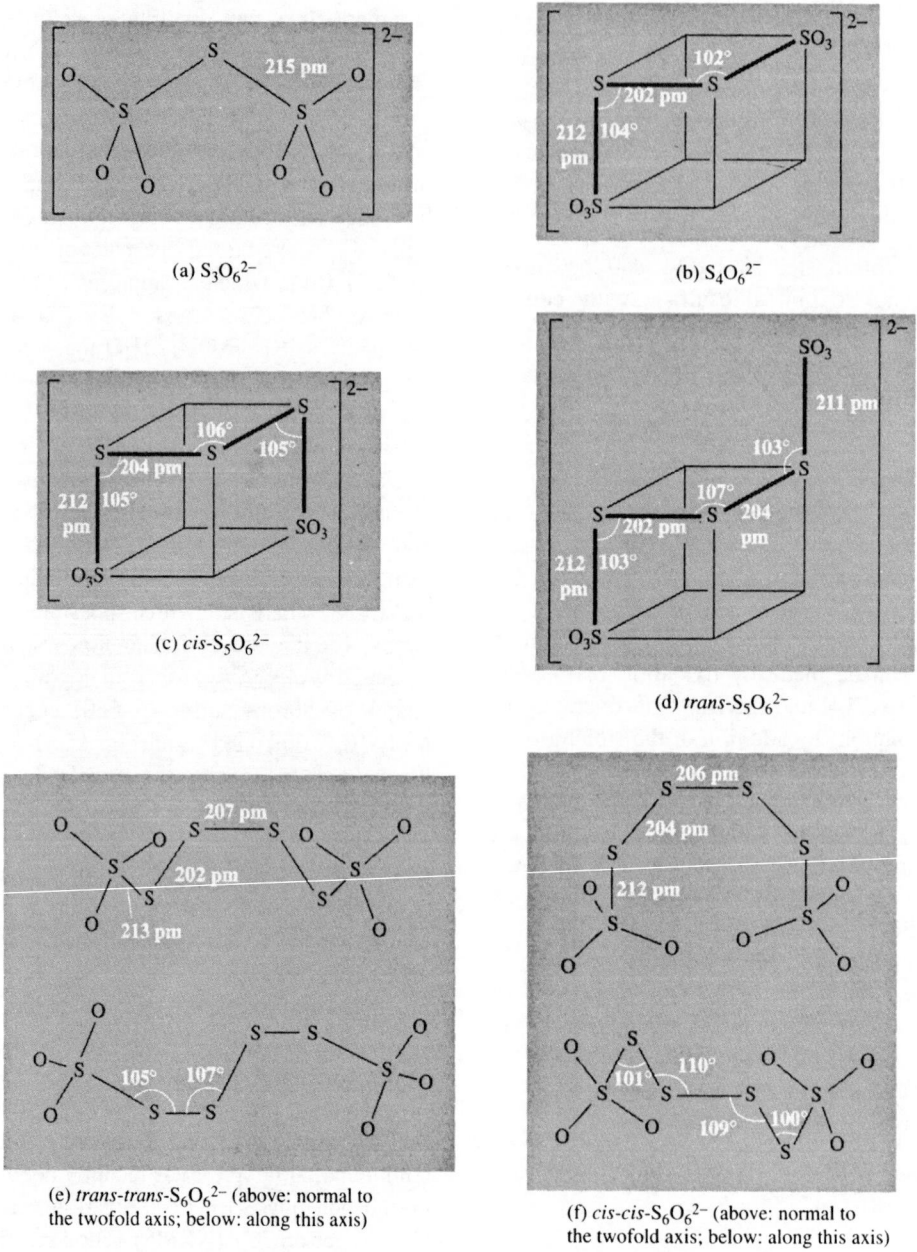

(a) $S_3O_6^{2-}$

(b) $S_4O_6^{2-}$

(c) *cis*-$S_5O_6^{2-}$

(d) *trans*-$S_5O_6^{2-}$

(e) *trans-trans*-$S_6O_6^{2-}$ (above: normal to the twofold axis; below: along this axis)

(f) *cis-cis*-$S_6O_6^{2-}$ (above: normal to the twofold axis; below: along this axis)

Figure 15.31   Structures of some polythionate ions.[200]

The experimental finding was substantiated by high-level *ab initio* calculations. The unionized acid exists in only minute concentrations (if at all) in aqueous solutions of SO_2. However, its salts, the sulfites, are quite stable and many are known in crystalline form; a second series of salts, the hydrogen sulfites HSO_3^-, are known in solution. Spectroscopic studies of aqueous solutions of SO_2 suggest that the predominant species are various hydrates, $SO_2.nH_2O$; depending on the concentration, temperature and pH, the ions present are H_3O^+, HSO_3^- and $S_2O_5^{2-}$ together with traces of SO_3^{2-}. The undissociated acid $OS(OH)_2$ has not been detected:

$$SO_2.nH_2O \rightleftharpoons H_2SO_3(aq); \quad K \ll 10^{-9}$$

The first acid dissociation constant of "sulfurous acid" in aqueous solution is therefore defined as:

$$SO_2.nH_2O \overset{H_2O}{\rightleftharpoons} H_3O^+(aq) + HSO_3^-(aq);$$

$$K_1(25°) = 1.6 \times 10^{-2} \text{ mol } l^{-1}$$

where

$$K_1 = \frac{[H_3O^+][HSO_3^-]}{[\text{total dissolved } SO_2] - [HSO_3^-] - [SO_3^{2-}]}$$

The second dissociation constant is given by the equation

$$HSO_3^-(aq) \rightleftharpoons H_3O^+(aq) + SO_3^{2-}(aq);$$

$$K_2(25°) = 1.0 \times 10^{-7} \text{ mol } l^{-1}$$

$$K_2 = [H_3O^+][SO_3^{2-}]/[HSO_3^-]$$

Most sulfites (except those of the alkali metals and ammonium) are rather insoluble; as indicated above such solutions contain the HSO_3^- ion predominantly, but attempts to isolate M^IHSO_3 tend to produce disulfites (p. 720) by "dehydration":

$$2HSO_3^- \rightleftharpoons S_2O_5^{2-} + H_2O$$

Only with large cations such as Rb, Cs and $NR_4(R = Et, Bu^n, n\text{-pentyl})$ has it proved possible to isolate the solid sulfites $MHSO_3$.[202]

The sulfite ion SO_3^{2-} is pyramidal with C_{3v} symmetry: angle O–S–O 106°, S–O 151 pm. The hydrogen sulfite ion also appears to have C_{3v} symmetry both in the solid state and in solution, i.e. protonation occurs at S rather than

O to give $H–SO_3^-$ rather than $HO–SO_2^-(C_s$ symmetry). However, recent ^{17}O nmr studies appear to provide evidence for the existence in solution of a dynamic equilibrium between the two isomers: $H–SO_3^- \rightleftharpoons HO–SO_2^-$.[203] The sulfite ion also coordinates through S in transition-metal complexes, e.g. $[Pd(NH_3)_3(\eta^1\text{-}SO_3)]$, *cis*- and *trans*-$[Pt(NH_3)_2(\eta^1\text{-}SO_3)_2]^{2-}$. The structure of hydrogen-sulfito complex *trans*-$[Ru^{II}(NH_3)_4(SO_3H)_2]$ is also *S*-bonded, implying a 1,2 proton shift to give $M\{SO_2(OH)\}$.[204]

Sulfites and hydrogen sulfites are moderately strong reducing agents (p. 706) and, depending on conditions, are oxidized either to dithionate or sulfate. The reaction with iodine is quantitative and is used in volumetric analysis:

$$HSO_3^- + I_2 + H_2O \longrightarrow HSO_4^- + 2H^+ + 2I^-$$

Conversely, sulfites can act as oxidants in the presence of strong reducing agents; e.g. sodium amalgam yields dithionite, and formates (in being oxidized to oxalates) yield thiosulfate:

$$2SO_3^{2-} + 2H_2O + 2Na/Hg \longrightarrow S_2O_4^{2-}$$
$$+ 4OH^- + 2Na^+$$

$$2SO_3^{2-} + 4HCO_2^- \longrightarrow SSO_3^{2-} + 2C_2O_4^{2-}$$
$$+ 2OH^- + H_2O$$

Thiosulfates also result from reduction of SO_3^{2-} or HSO_3^- with elemental sulfur (p. 714), whereas reduction with H_2S in Wackenroder's solution (pp. 716–7) yields polythionates. It is also notable that the sulfite ion is involved in the 6-electron sulfite reductase reaction: $SO_3^{2-} + 6H^+ + 6e^- \longrightarrow S^{2-} + 3H_2O$; $E° = 0.380$ V. Indeed, there are only three such $6e^-$ reductions known in the whole of biology, the other two being nitrite reductase $(NO_2^- + 7H^+ + 6e^- \longrightarrow NH_3 + 2H_2O)$ and nitrogenase $(N_2 + 6H^+ + 6e^- \longrightarrow 2NH_3)$.

On a technical scale, solutions of sodium hydrogen sulfite are prepared by passing SO_2

202 R. MAYLOR, J. B. GILL and D. C. GOODALL, *J. Chem. Soc., Dalton Trans.*, 2001–3 (1972) and references therein.

203 D. A. HORNER and R. E. CONNICK, *Inorg. Chem.* **25**, 2414–7 (1986).
204 D. K. BREITINGER and R. BREITER, *Z. Naturforsch.* **45b**, 1651–6 (1990).

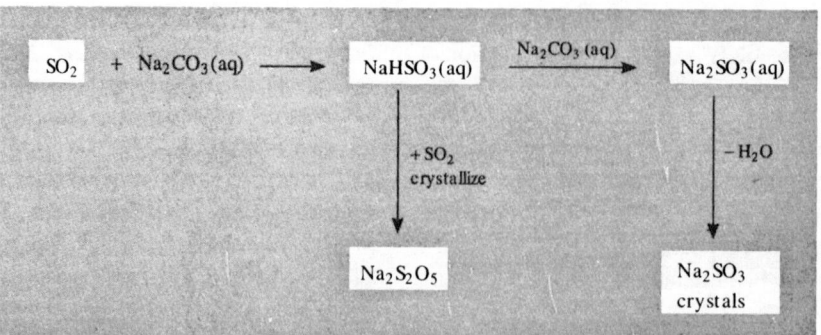

into aqueous Na_2CO_3. As shown in the Scheme above, addition of a further equivalent of Na_2CO_3 allows the normal sulfite to be crystallized, whereas addition of more SO_2 yields the disulfite (see the next subsection below).

Crystallization of Na_2SO_3 above 37° gives the anhydrous salt; below this temperature $Na_2SO_3.7H_2O$ is obtained. World production of the anhydrous salt exceeds 1 million tonnes pa; most is used in the paper pulp industry, but other applications are as an O_2 scavenger in boiler-water treatment, and as a reducing agent in photography. Similarly, $K_2SO_3.2H_2O$ is obtained by passing SO_2 into aqueous KOH until samples of the solution are neutral to phenolphthalein. For a compilation of critically evaluated solubility data, see ref. 205

Disulfurous acid, $H_2S_2O_5$

Like "sulfurous acid", disulfurous acid is unknown either in the free state or in solution. However, as indicated in the preceding section, its salts, are readily obtained from concentrated solutions of hydrogen sulfite: $2HSO_3^- \rightleftharpoons S_2O_5^{2-} + H_2O$. Unlike disulfates (p. 712), diphosphates (p. 522), etc., disulfites condense by forming an S–S bond. As indicated in Fig. 15.32a this S–S bond is rather long, but the S–O distances are unexceptional.

---

[205] M. R. MASSON, H. D. LUTZ and B. ENGELEN (eds.) *Sulfites, Selenites and Tellurites*, Pergamon Press, Oxford, 1986, 474 pp.

Acidification of solutions of disulfites regenerates HSO_3^- and SO_2 again, and the solution chemistry of $S_2O_5^{2-}$ is essentially that of the normal sulfites and hydrogen sulfites, despite the formal presence of S^V and S^{III} (rather than S^{IV}) in the solid state.

Dithionous acid, $H_2S_2O_4$

Dithionites, $S_2O_4^{2-}$ are quite stable when anhydrous, but in the presence of water they disproportionate (slowly at pH $\geq$ 7, rapidly in acid solution):

$$\overset{III}{2S_2O_4^{2-}} + H_2O \longrightarrow \overset{IV}{2HSO_3^-} + \overset{-II/VI}{SSO_3^{2-}}$$

The parent acid has no independent existence and has not been detected in aqueous solution either. Sodium dithionite is widely used as an industrial reducing agent and can be prepared by reduction of sulfite using Zn dust, Na/Hg or electrolytically, e.g.:

$$\overset{IV}{2HSO_3^-} + \overset{IV}{SO_2.nH_2O} + 2Zn \longrightarrow \overset{IV}{ZnSO_3}$$
$$+ \overset{III}{ZnS_2O_4} + (n+2)H_2O$$

The dihydrate $Na_2S_2O_4.2H_2O$ can be precipitated by "salting out" with NaCl. Air and oxygen must be excluded at all stages in the process to avoid reoxidation. The dithionite ion can also be produced *in situ* on an industrial scale by reaction

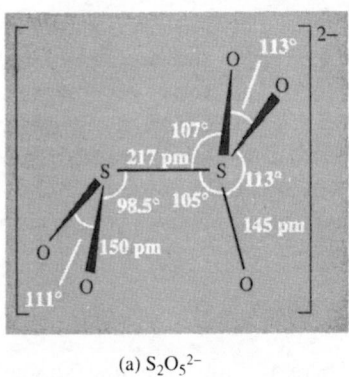

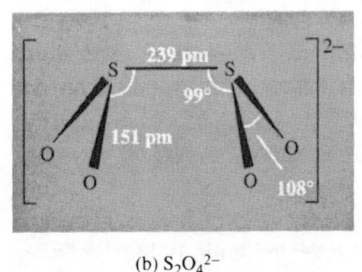

(a) $S_2O_5^{2-}$ (b) $S_2O_4^{2-}$

Figure 15.32   Structure of (a) the disulfite ion $S_2O_5^{2-}$ in $(NH_4)_2S_2O_5$, and (b) the dithionite ion $S_2O_4^{2-}$ in $Na_2S_2O_4 \cdot 2H_2O$.

between $NaHSO_3$ and $NaBH_4$ (p. 167). Its main use is as a reducing agent in dyeing, bleaching of paper pulp, straw, clay, soaps, etc., and in chemical reductions (see below). Current worldwide demand is about 300 000 tonnes per annum.

The dithionite ion has a remarkable eclipsed structure of approximate C_{2v} symmetry (Fig. 15.32b). The extraordinarily long S–S distance (239 pm) and the almost parallel SO_2 planes (dihedral angle 30°) are other unusual features. Electron-spin-resonance studies have shown the presence of the $SO_2^{\cdot}$ radical ion in solution (~300 ppm), suggesting the establishment of a monomer-dimer equilibrium $S_2O_4^{2-} \rightleftharpoons 2SO_2^-$. Consistent with this, air-oxidation of alkaline dithionite solutions at 30–60° are of order one-half with respect to $[S_2O_4^{2-}]$. Acid hydrolysis (second order with respect to $[S_2O_4^{2-}]$) yields thiosulfate and hydrogen sulfite, whereas alkaline hydrolysis produces sulfite and sulfide:

$$2S_2O_4^{2-} + H_2O \longrightarrow S_2O_3^{2-} + 2HSO_3^-$$

$$3Na_2S_2O_4 + 6NaOH \longrightarrow 5Na_2SO_3 + Na_2S + 3H_2O$$

Hydrated dithionites can be dehydrated by gentle warming, but the anhydrous salts themselves decompose on further heating. For example, $Na_2S_2O_4$ decomposes rapidly at 150° and violently at 190°:

$$2Na_2S_2O_4 \longrightarrow Na_2S_2O_3 + Na_2SO_3 + SO_2$$

Dithionites are strong reducing agents and will reduce dissolved O_2, H_2O_2, I_2, IO_3^- and MnO_4^-

Likewise Cr^{VI} is reduced to Cr^{III} and TiO^{2+} to Ti^{III}. Heavy metal ions such as Cu^I, Ag^I, Pb^{II}, Sb^{III} and Bi^{III} are reduced to the metal. Many of these reactions are useful in water-treatment and pollution control.

15.2.7 Sulfur–nitrogen compounds [206-210]

The study of S–N compounds is one of the most active areas of current inorganic research: many novel cyclic and acyclic compounds are being prepared which have unusual structures and which pose considerable problems in terms of simple bonding theory. The discovery in 1975 that the polymer $(SN)_x$ is a metal whose conductivity *increases* with decrease in

[206] M. BECKE-GOEHRING and E. FLUCK, Chap. 3 in C. B. COLBURN (ed.), *Developments in Inorganic Nitrogen Chemistry*, Vol. 1, pp. 150–240, Elsevier, Amsterdam, 1966.

[207] I. HAIDUC, *The Chemistry of Inorganic Ring Systems*, Part 2, (sulfur–nitrogen heterocycles), pp. 909–83, Wiley, London, 1970.

[208] H. G. HEAL, *The Inorganic Heterocyclic Chemistry of Sulfur, Nitrogen and Phosphorus*, Academic Press, London, 1981, 288 pp.

[209] H. W. ROESKY, *Adv. Inorg. Chem. Radiochem.* **22**, 239–301 (1979).

[210] *Gmelin Handbook of Inorganic Chemistry*, Sulfur–Nitrogen Compounds: Part 1, 288 pp (1977); Part 2, 333 pp (1985); Part 3, 325 pp (1987); Part 4, 272 pp (1987); Part 5, 276 pp (1990), Springer Verlag, Berlin.

temperature and which becomes superconducting below 0.33 K aroused tremendous additional interest and has stimulated still further the already substantial activity in this area of synthetic and structural chemistry. The field is not new. S_4N_4 was first prepared in an impure form by W. Gregory in 1835,[†] though the stoichiometry and tetrameric nature of the pure compound were not established until 1851 and 1896 respectively, and its cyclic, pseudo-cluster structure was not revealed until 1944.[211] Other important compounds containing S–N bonds that date from the first half of the nineteenth century include sulfamic acid $H[H_2NSO_3]$, imidosulfonic acid $HSO_3N{=}NH$, sulfamide $SO_2(NH_2)_2$, nitrilotrisulfonic acid $N(HSO_3)_3$, hydroxy nitrilosulfonic acids $HSO_3NH(OH)$ and $(HSO_3)_2N(OH)$, and their many derivatives (p. 743).

It will be convenient to describe first the binary sulfur nitrides S_xN_y and then the related cationic and anionic species, $S_xN_y^{n\pm}$. The sulfur imides and other cyclic S–N compounds will then be discussed and this will be followed by sections on S–N–halogen and S–N–O compounds. Several compounds which feature isolated $S{\leftarrow}N$, S–N, $S{=}N$ and $S{\equiv}N$ bonds have already been mentioned in the section on SF_4; e.g. $F_4S{\leftarrow}NC_5H_5$, $F_5S{-}NF_2$, $F_2S{=}NCF_3$, and $F_3S{\equiv}N$ (p. 687). However, many SN compounds do not lend themselves to simple bond diagrams,[212] and formal oxidation states are often unhelpful or even misleading.

Nitrogen and sulfur are diagonally related in the periodic table and might therefore be expected to have similar electronic charge densities for similar coordination numbers (p. 76). Likewise, they have similar electronegativities (N 3.0, S 2.5) and these become even more similar when additional electron-withdrawing groups are bonded to the S atoms. Extensive covalent bonding into acyclic, cyclic and polycyclic molecular structures is thus not unexpected.

(i) Binary sulfur nitrides

There is little structural similarity between the sulfur nitrides and the oxides of nitrogen (p. 443). The instability of NS when compared with the great stability of NO, and the paucity of thionitrosyl complexes have already been mentioned (p. 453), as has the difference between diatomic O_2 and oligomeric or polymeric S_n. The compounds to be considered in this section are S_4N_4, cyclo-S_2N_2 and catena-$(SN)_x$ polymer, together with cyclo-S_4N_2, bicyclo-$S_{11}N_2$, and the higher homologues $S_{15}N_2$, $S_{16}N_2$, $S_{17}N_2$ and $S_{19}N_2$. More recently, crystalline S_5N_6 (the first binary sulfur nitride with more atoms of N than S) has been synthesized. The fugitive radicals SN• and $S_3N_3^•$ have also been characterized.

(a) *Tetrasulfur tetranitride*, S_4N_4. This is the most readily prepared sulfur nitride and is an important starting point for the preparation of many S–N compounds. It is obtained as orange-yellow, air-stable crystals[†] by passing NH_3 gas into a warm solution of S_2Cl_2 (or SCl_2) in CCl_4 or benzene; the overall stoichiometries of the mechanistically obscure reactions are:

$$6S_2Cl_2 + 16NH_3 \xrightarrow{50°} S_4N_4 + 8S + 12NH_4Cl$$

$$6SCl_2 + 16NH_3 \longrightarrow S_4N_4 + 2S + 14NH_4Cl$$

Alternatively, NH_4Cl can be heated with S_2Cl_2 at 160°:

$$6S_2Cl_2 + 4NH_4Cl \xrightarrow{26\% \text{ yield}} S_4N_4 + 8S + 16HCl$$

[†] Disulfur dichloride was added to an aqueous solution of ammonia to give a yellow precipitate of sulfur contaminated with S_4N_4; *J. Pharm. Chim.* **21**, 315 (1835).

[211] CHIA-SI LU and J. DONOHUE, *J. Am. Chem. Soc.* **66**, 818–27 (1944). D. CLARK, *J. Chem. Soc.* 1615–20 (1952).

[212] R. GLEITER, *Angew. Chem. Int. Edn. Engl.* **20**, 444–52 (1981); R. D. HARCOURT and H. M. HÜGEL, *J. Inorg. Nuclear Chem.* **43**, 239–52 (1981); A. A. BATTACHARYYA, A. BATTACHARYYA, R. R. ADKINS and A. G. TURNER, *J. Am. Chem. Soc.* **103**, 7458–65 (1981); R. C. HADDON, S. R. WASSERMAN, F. WUDL and G. R. J. WILLIAMS, *J. Am. Chem. Soc.* **102**, 6687–93 (1980).

[†] Crystalline S_4N_4 is thermochromic, being pale yellow below about $-30°$; the colour deepens to orange at room temperature and to a deep red at 100° (cf. sulfur, p. 656).

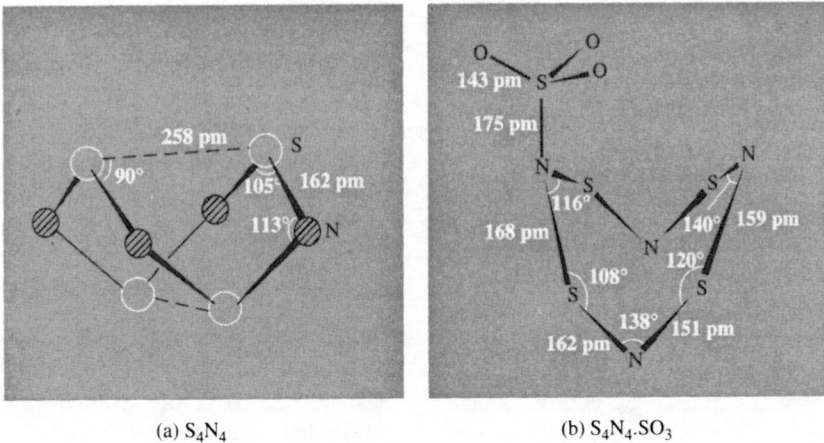

(a) S$_4$N$_4$ (b) S$_4$N$_4$.SO$_3$

Figure 15.33 Structure of (a) S$_4$N$_4$, and (b) S$_4$N$_4$.SO$_3$.

The compound also results from the reversible equilibrium reaction of sulfur with anhydrous liquid ammonia:

$$10S + 4NH_3 \rightleftharpoons S_4N_4 + 6H_2S$$

The H$_2$S, of course, reacts with further ammonia to form ammonium sulfides but the reaction can be made to proceed in the forward direction as written by addition of (soluble) AgI to precipitate AgS and form NH$_4$I.

S$_4$N$_4$ is kinetically stable in air but is endothermic with respect to its elements (ΔH_f° 460 $\pm$ 8 kJ mol^{-1}) and may detonate when struck or when heated rapidly. This is due more to the stability of elementary sulfur and the great bond strength of N$_2$ rather than to any inherent weakness in the S–N bonds. On careful heating S$_4$N$_4$ melts at 178.2°. The structure (Fig. 15.33a) is an 8-membered heterocycle in the extreme cradle configuration; it has D_{2d} symmetry and resembles that of As$_4$S$_4$ (p. 579) but with the sites of the Group 15 and Group 16 elements interchanged. The S–N distance of 162 pm is rather short when compared with the sum of the covalent radii (178 pm) and this, coupled with the equality of all the S–N bond distances in the molecule, has been attributed to some electron delocalization in the heterocycle. The trans-annular S$\cdots$S distances (258 pm) are intermediate between bonding S–S (208 pm) and

nonbonding van der Waals (330 pm) distances; this suggests a weak but structurally significant bonding interaction between the pairs of S atoms. A study by gas-phase electron diffraction yields similar dimensions except that the trans-annular S$\cdots$S distance is slightly longer (266.6 pm) probably because of the absence of constraining crystal packing forces.[213]

It is not possible to write down a single, satisfactory, classical bonding diagram for S$_4$N$_4$ and, in valence-bond theory, numerous resonance hybrids must be considered of which the following are typical:

The extent to which each hybrid is incorporated into the full bonding description of the molecule will depend on the extent to which 3d orbitals

213 A. J. DOWNS, T. L. JEFFERY and K. HAGEN, *Polyhedron* **8**, 2631–6 (1989).

on S are involved and the extent of trans-annular S–S bonding. More recent MO-calculations lead to semiquantitative estimates of these features and to electron charge densities on the individual atoms.[212] It is also instructive to compare the structure of the 44-(valence)electron species S_4N_4 with those of the 46-electron species S_8^{2+} (p. 665) and the 48-electron species S_8 (p. 655): successive formal addition of 2 and then 4 electron results in the progressive opening of the S_4N_4 pseudocluster first to the *bicyclic*-S_8^{2+} with a single weak trans-annular S–S bond and then to the open-crown structure of S_8 with no trans-annular bonding at all.

Interestingly, in the N-donor adducts $S_4N_4.BF_3$ and $S_4N_4.SbCl_5$ the S_4N_4 ring adopts the alternative D_{2d} configuration of As_4S_4, with the 4 S atoms now coplanar instead of the 4 N atoms; the mean S–N distance increases slightly to 168 pm but the (nonbonding) trans-annular S···S distances are 380 pm. The same interchange occurs in $S_4N_4.SO_3$ and Fig. 15.33b shows the substantial alternations in S–N distances and angles that are concurrently introduced into the ring. Likewise in the burgundy red salt $[S_4N_4H]^+[BF_4]^-$, formed by direct protonation of S_4N_4 by $HBF_4.Et_2O$ (S–N 157 pm, S–NH$^+$ 165 pm).[214] By contrast, in $S_4N_4.CuCl$ the heterocycle acts as a bridging ligand between zigzag chains of $(-Cu-Cl-)_\infty$; the S_4N_4 retains the same conformation and almost the same dimensions as in the free molecule, with 2 of the 4 planar N atoms acting as a *cisoid* bridge and the 2 trans-annular S···S distances remaining short (259 and 263 pm).[215] It is not yet clear in detail what factors determine the ring conformation adopted (see also p. 656). Other complexes are mentioned below.

S_4N_4 is insoluble in and unreactive towards water but readily undergoes base hydrolysis with dilute NaOH solutions to give thiosulfate,

[214] A. W. CORDES, C. G. MARCELLUS, M. C. NOBLE, R. T. OAKLEY and W. T. PENNINGTON, *J. Am. Chem. Soc.* **105**, 6008–12 (1983).

[215] U. THEWALT, *Angew. Chem. Int. Edn. Engl.* **15**, 765–6 (1976).

trithionate and ammonia:

$$2S_4N_4 + 6OH^- + 9H_2O \longrightarrow S_2O_3^{2-}$$
$$+ 2S_3O_6^{2-} + 8NH_3$$

More concentrated alkali yields sulfite instead of trithionate:

$$S_4N_4 + 6OH^- + 3H_2O \longrightarrow S_2O_3^{2-}$$
$$+ 2SO_3^{2-} + 4NH_3$$

Milder bases such as Et_2NH leave some of the S–N bonds intact to yield, for example, $S(NEt_2)_2$. The value of S_4N_4 as a synthetic intermediate can be gauged from the representative reactions in the Scheme below[210] and in Table 15.22. It can be seen that these reactions embrace:

(a) conservation of the 8-membered heterocycle and attachment of substituents to S or N (or subrogation of N by S);
(b) ring contraction to a 7-, 6-, 5- or 4-membered heterocycle with or without attachment of substituents;
(c) ring fragmentation into non-cyclic S–N groups (which sometimes then coordinate to metal centres);
(d) complete cleavage of all S–N bonds;
(e) formation of more complex heterocycles with 3 (or more) different heteroatoms.

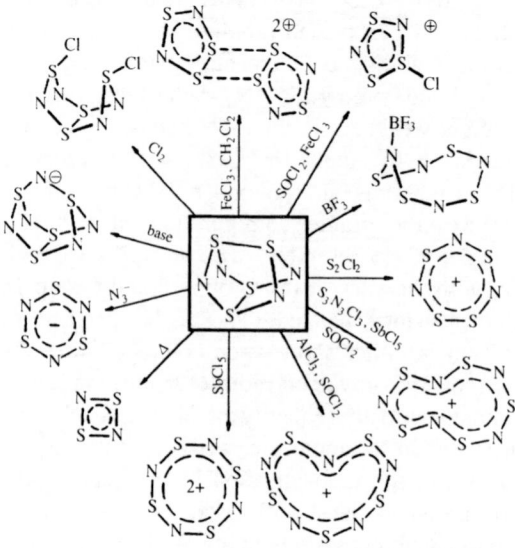

Table 15.22   Some further reactions of $S_4N_4^{(206-210)}$

Reagents and conditions	Products	Ref. for structure, etc.
Vacuum thermolysis (Ag wool 300°)	S_2N_2, $(SN)_x$	pp. 726, 727
$SnCl_2$ (boiling C_6H_6 + EtOH)	$S_4(NH)_4$	p. 735
NH_3	$S_2N_2.NH_3$	
$N_2H_4/SiO_2(C_6H_6, 46°)$	$S_{8-n}(NH)_n$, $n = 1-4$	p. 735
S/CS_2 (heat in autoclave)	S_4N_2	
S_2Cl_2	$[S_4N_3]^+Cl^-$	
AgF_2 (cold CCl_4)	$N_4(SF)_4$	
AgF_2 (hot CCl_4)	NSF, NSF_3	
$Cl_2(CCl_4)$	$N_3(SCl)_3$	
Br_2 (neat, heat in sealed tube)	$[S_4N_3]^+Br_3^-$	100% yield[216]
$HX(CCl_4)$ X = F, Cl, Br	$[S_4N_3]^+X^-$	
HI	H_2S, NH_3, I_2	
$OSCl_2$	$S_3N_2O_2$	Fig. 15.34a
$NiCl_2/MeOH$	$[Ni(S_2N_2H)_2]$ (also Co, Pd)	Fig. 15.34b
H_2PtCl_6	$[Pt(S_2N_2H)_2]$	Fig. 15.34b
PbI_2/NH_3	$[\overline{Pb(NSNS})(NH_3)]$	Fig. 15.34c

The molecular structures of the products are described as indicated at appropriate points in the text. $S_3N_2O_2$ was at one time thought to be cyclic but X-ray diffraction analysis has revealed an open chain structure (Fig. 15.34a).[217] The structure of $[Pt(S_2N_2H)_2]$ (Fig. 15.34b) is typical of several such compounds. When S_4N_4 reacts with metal carbonyls in aprotic media, the products are the structurally similar $[M(S_2N_2)_2]$ (M = Fe, Co, Ni). The pyramidal Pb^{II} complex (Fig. 15.34c) is also notable, and features unequal S–N distances consistent with the bonding indicated. Still further reaction types are continually being discovered. For example, with the diphosphines $Ph_2P(X)PPh_2$ (X = CH_2CH_2 or NC_4H_8N), S_4N_4 yields $(N_3S_3)-NPPh_2(X)-PPh_2N-(S_3N_3)$[218] whereas with platinum-metal complexes it forms adducts of the tridentate *S,S,N*-ligand *catena*-$S_4N_4^{2-}$, e.g. *fac*-$[Ir(CO)Cl(\eta^3-S_4N_4)(PPh_3)]$, Fig. 15.34d,[219]

fac-$[PtX_3(\eta^3-S_4N_4)]^-$ (X = Cl, Br, I)[220] and *mer*-$[PtCl_2(\eta^3-S_4N_4)(PMe_2Ph)]$, (Fig 15.34e).[220]

(b) *Disulfur dinitrogen*, S_2N_2. When S_4N_4 is carefully depolymerized by passing the heated vapour over Ag wool at 250–300° and 0.1–1.0 mmHg, the unstable cyclic dimer S_2N_2 is obtained. The main purpose of the silver is to remove sulfur generated by the thermal decomposition of S_4N_4; the Ag_2S so formed then catalyses the depolymerization of further S_4N_4:

$$S_4N_4 + 8Ag \longrightarrow 4Ag_2S + 2N_2$$

$$S_4N_4 \xrightarrow{Ag_2S} 2S_2N_2$$

In the absence of Ag/Ag_2S the product is contaminated with S_4N_2 (p. 728) formed by the reaction of the excess sulfur with either S_4N_4 or S_2N_2. (See next subsection for discussion of possible mechanisms.) S_2N_2 forms large colourless crystals which are insoluble in water but soluble in many organic solvents. The molecular structure is a square-planar ring (D_{2h}) analogous to the isoelectronic cation

216 G. WOLMERSHÄUSER and G. B. STREET, *Inorg. Chem.* **17**, 2685–6 (1978).

217 J. WEISS, *Z. Naturforsch.* **16b**, 477 (1961); J. WEISS, *Fortsch. Chem. Forsch.* **5**, 635–62 (1966).

218 C. J. THOMAS and M. N. S. RAO, *Z. anorg. allg. Chem.* **619**, 433–6 (1993), and references cited therein.

219 F. EDELMANN, H. W. ROESKY, C. SPANG, M. NOLTE-MEYER and G. M. SHELDRICK, *Angew. Chem. Int. Edn. Engl.* **25**, 931 (1986).

220 V. C. GINN, P. F. KELLY, A. M. Z. SLAWIN, D. J. WILLIAMS and J. D. WOOLLINS, *Polyhedron* **12**, 1135–9 (1993). P. F. KELLY, R. N. SHEPPARD and J. D. WOOLLINS, *Polyhedron* **11**, 2605–9 (1992). See also P. F. KELLY and J. D. WOOLLINS, *Polyhedron* **8**, 2907–10 (1989).

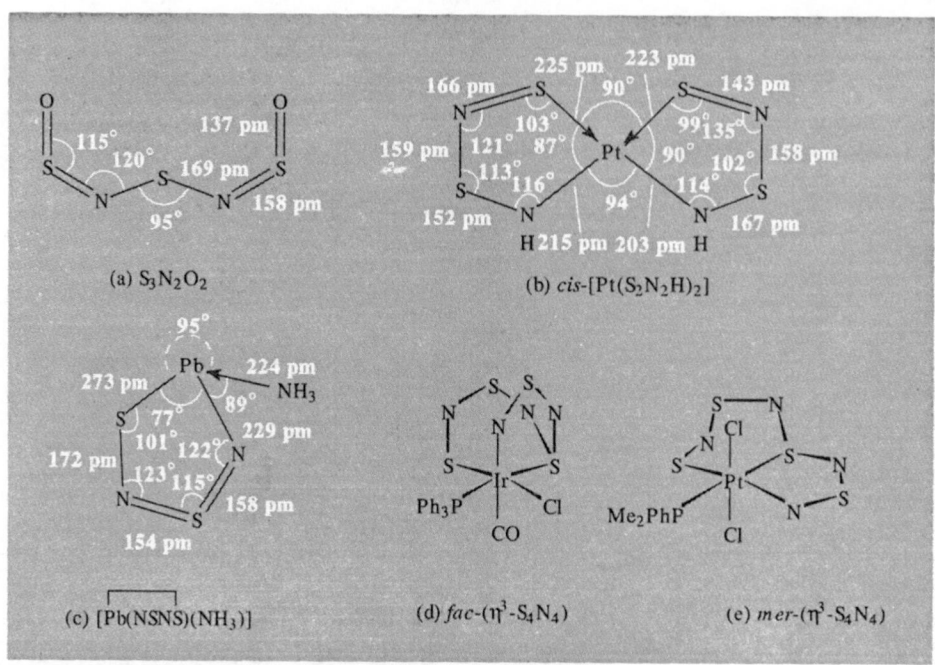

Figure 15.34   Structures of some SN compounds mentioned in Table 15.22 and the text.

S_4^{2+} (D_{4h}, p. 665). Figure 15.35 shows the structure obtained by X-ray diffraction at $-130°^{(221)}$ together with typical valence-bond representations.$^{(212)}$

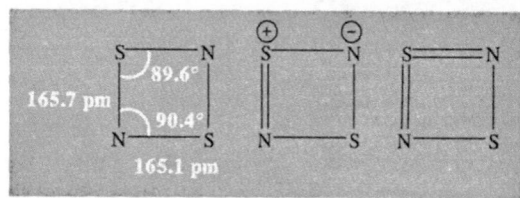

(a) S_2N_2 (b) Four hybrids   (c) Two hybrids

Figure 15.35   (a) Molecular structure and dimensions of S_2N_2,$^{(220)}$ together with (b) minimal valence-bond representation and (c) additional valence-bond representation involving 3d S orbitals. (Note that the molecule has 6 π electrons and 4 unshared electron-pairs superimposed on the square-planar σ-bonded structure.)

S_2N_2 decomposes explosively when struck or when warmed above 30°. Its chemistry

has therefore not been extensively studied. Reactions with NH_3 and with aqueous alkali are similar to those of S_4N_4. It also forms adducts with Lewis bases, e.g. $S_2N_2(SbCl_5)_2$; this latter is a yellow crystalline *N*-bonded complex which reacts with further S_2N_2 to give the orange crystalline monoadduct $S_2N_2.SbCl_5$. The heterocycle remains planar and the S–N distances are almost the same as in the free S_2N_2 molecule.

Undoubtedly the most exciting reaction of S_2N_2 is its slow spontaneous polymerization in the solid state at room temperature to give crystalline $(SN)_x$. Crystals up to several millimetres in length can be grown. Not only is this an unusually facile topochemical reaction for a solid at low temperature but it results in an unprecedented metallic superconducting polymer, as discussed in the following subsection.

^{221} A. G. MacDiarmid,   C. M. Mikulski,   P. J. Russo, M. S. Saran, A. F. Garito and A. J. Heeger, *J. Chem. Soc., Chem. Commun.*, 476–7 (1975).

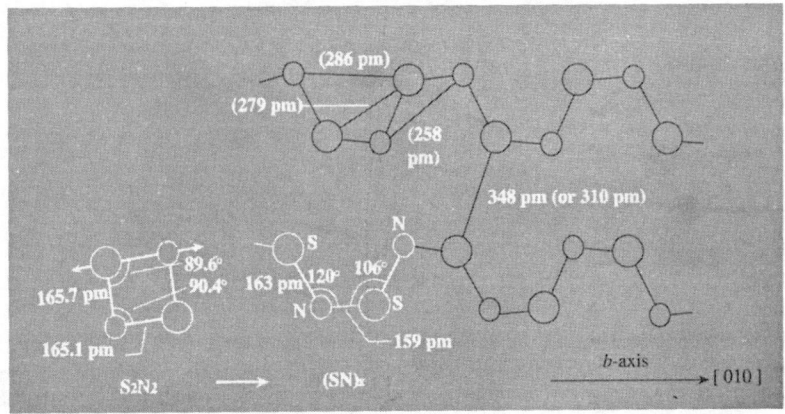

Figure 15.36   Structure of fibrous $(SN)_x$ and its relation to S_2N_2.

(c) *Polythiazyl*, $(SN)_x$.[222] Polymeric sulfur nitride, also known as polythiazyl, was first prepared by F. B. Burt in 1910 using a method that is still often used today — the solid-state polymerization of crystalline S_2N_2 at room temperature (or preferably at 0°C over several days). Despite the bronze colour and metallic lustre of the polymer, over 50 y were to elapse before its metallic electrical conductivity, thermal conductivity and thermoelectric effect were investigated. By 1973 it had been established that $(SN)_x$ was indeed a metal down to liquid helium temperatures, and in 1975 the polymer was shown to be a superconductor below 0.26 K. (For higher-quality crystals the transition temperature rises to 0.33 K.) Values of the conductivity σ depend on the purity and crystallinity of the polymer and on the direction of measurement, being much greater along the fibres (b-axis) than across them. At room temperature typical values of $\sigma_\parallel$ are 1000–4000 ohm^{-1} cm^{-1}, and this increases by as much as 1000-fold on cooling to 4.2 K. Typical values of the anisotropy ratio $\sigma_\parallel / \sigma_\perp$ are ∼50 at room temperature and ∼1000 at 40 K.

The mechanism of formation of S_2N_2 from S_4N_4 and of the subsequent polymerization to $(SN)_x$ have been much studied and are very

sensitive to the exact conditions employed.[223] The use of the explosive intermediates S_4N_4 and S_2N_2 can be avoided by various alternative high-yield syntheses employing nonaqueous solvents. For example, $(SN)_x$ can be made in 65% yield by the reaction of $SiMe_3(N_3)$ with $N_3S_3Cl_3$, $N_2S_3Cl_2$ or N_2S_3Cl (pp. 738, 739) in MeCN solution at −15°C or by the reaction of $N_3S_3Cl_3$ with an excess of NaN_3.[224] More recently still, the electrolytic reduction of $S_5N_5{}^+Cl^-$ (p. 732) in liquid SO_2 using a silver electrode has been used to deposit thin films of $(SN)_x$ on a variety of surfaces.[225]

$(SN)_x$ is much more stable than its precursor S_2N_2. When heated in air it decomposes explosively at about 240°C but it sublimes readily in vacuum at about 135°. The crystal structure reveals an almost planar chain polymer with the dimensions shown in Fig. 15.36. The S and N atoms deviate by about 17 pm from the mean plane. The structure should be compared

[222] M. M. Labes, P. Love and L. F. Nichols, *Chem. Revs.* **79**, 1–15 (1979). A definitive review with 150 references.

[223] H. Bock, B. Solouki and H. W. Roesky, *Inorg. Chem.* **24**, 4425–7 (1985); E. Besenyei, G. K. Eigendorf and D. C. Frost, *Inorg. Chem.* **25**, 4404–8 (1986); M. J. Almond, A. J. Downs and T. L. Jeffery, *Polyhedron* **7**, 629–34 (1988).

[224] F. A. Kennett, G. K. MacLean, J. Passmore and M. N. S. Rao, *J. Chem. Soc., Dalton Trans*, 851–7 (1982); A. J. Banister, Z. V. Hauptman, J. Passmore, C-M. Wong and P. S. White, *J. Chem. Soc., Dalton Trans.*, 2371–9 (1986).

[225] A. J. Banister, Z. V. Hauptman, J. M. Rawson and S. T. Wait, *J. Materials Chem.*, **6**, 1161–4 (1996).

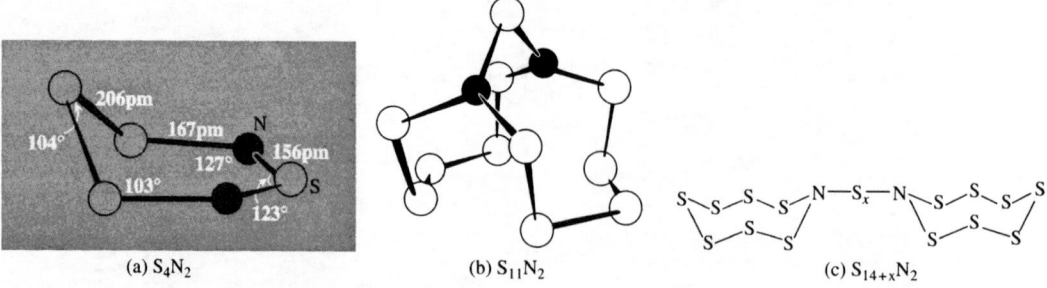

(a) S_4N_2 (b) $S_{11}N_2$ (c) $S_{14+x}N_2$

Figure 15.37   Structures of (a) S_4N_2[226] showing the "half-chair" conformation with the central S of the S_3 unit tilted out of the plane of the SNSNS group by 55°; (b) $S_{11}N_2$[227] showing the two planar N atoms; (c) $S_{14+x}N_2$ ($x = 1, 2, 3, 5$) — for $x = 2$ the linking S–S distance is 190 pm and S–N is 170 pm; for $x = 3$ the linking S–S is 204 pm and S–N 171 pm[228].

with that of helical S_∞ (p. 660), the (formal) replacement of alternate S atoms by N resulting both in a conformational change in the position of the atoms and an electronic change whereby 1 valence electron is removed for each SN unit in the chain. Polymerization is thought to occur by a one-point ring cleavage of each S_2N_2 molecule followed by the formation of the *cis-trans*-polymer along the *a*-axis of the S_2N_2 crystal which thereby transforms to the *b*-axis of the $(SN)_x$ polymer.

There is intense current interest in these one-dimensional metals and several related partially halogenated derivatives have also been made, some of which have an even higher metallic conductivity, e.g. partial bromination of $(SN)_x$ with Br_2 vapour yields blue-black single crystals of $(SNBr_{0.4})_x$ having a room-temperature conductivity of 2×10^4 ohm^{-1} cm^{-1} i.e. an order of magnitude greater than for the parent $(SN)_x$ polymer. An even more facile preparation involves direct bromination of S_4N_4 crystals ($\sigma \sim 10^{-14}$ ohm^{-1} cm^{-1} at 25°) with Br_2 vapour at 180 mmHg over a period of hours; subsequent pumping at room temperature gives stoichiometries in the range $(SNBr_{1.5})_x$ to $(SNBr_{0.4})_x$ and further pumping at 80°C for 4 h reduces the halogen content to $(SNBr_{0.25})_x$. Similar highly conducting nonstoichiometric polymers can be obtained by treating S_4N_4 with ICl, IBr and I_2, the increase in conductivity being more than 16 orders of magnitude.

(d) *Other binary sulfur nitrides.* Six further sulfur nitrides can be briefly mentioned: S_4N_2, $S_{11}N_2$ and $(S_7N)_2S_x$ ($x = 1,2,3,5$); as can be seen from Fig. 15.37, these belong to three distinct structural classes. (For a fourth structure class, exemplified by S_5N_6, see p. 729.)

S_4N_2 is usually prepared by heating S_4N_4 with a solution of sulfur in CS_2 under pressure at 100–120°, though a more convenient laboratory preparation is now available by the reaction of activated Zn on N_3S_4Cl.[226] The compound also results from the thermolytic loss of N_2 from S_4N_4 which occurs when S_4N_4 is heated under reflux in xylene for some hours. An alternative preparation (42% yield), which involves neither high pressure or high temperature, is the smooth reaction of solutions of $Hg_5(NS)_8$ and S_2Cl_2 in CS_2:

$$Hg_5(NS)_8 + 4S_2Cl_2 \xrightarrow{CS_2/20°} Hg_2Cl_2$$
$$+ 3HgCl_2 + 4S_4N_2$$

In all these reactions only the 1,3-diazahetero-cycle (Fig. 15.37a) is obtained: the 1,1- and

226 R. W. H. SMALL, A. J. BANISTER and Z. V. HAUPTMAN, *J. Chem. Soc., Dalton Trans.*, 2188–91 (1981). T. CHIVERS, P. W. CODDING and R. T. OAKLEY, *J. Chem. Soc., Chem. Commun.*, 584–5 (1981). T. CHIVERS, P. W. CODDING, W. G. LAIDLAW, S. W. LIBLONG, R. T. OAKLEY and M. TRSIC, *J. Am. Chem. Soc.* **105**, 1186–92 (1983).

227 H. GARCIA-FERNANDEZ, H. G. HEAL and G. TESTE DE SAGEY, *Compt. Rend.* **C275**, 323–6 (1972).

228 H. GARCIA-FERNANDEZ, H. G. HEAL and G. TESTE DE SAGEY, *Compt. Rend.* **C282**, 241–3 (1976).

1,4-heterocycles and acyclic isomers are unknown (cf. N_2O_4, p. 455). S_4N_2 forms opaque red-grey needles or transparent dark red prisms which melt at 25° to a dark-red liquid resembling Br_2. It decomposes explosively above 100°. S_4N_2 appears to be a weaker ligand than either S_4N_4 or S_2N_2: it does not react with BCl_3 in CS_2 solution, and $SbCl_5$ gives a complex reaction mixture which contains $S_4N_4 \cdot SbCl_5$ and $[S_4N_3]^+[SbCl_6]^-$ in addition to a poorly defined 1:1 adduct.

$S_{11}N_2$ is obtained as pale amber-coloured crystals by the double condensation of 1,3-$S_6(NH)_2$ with an equimolar amount of S_5Cl_2 in the presence of pyridine:

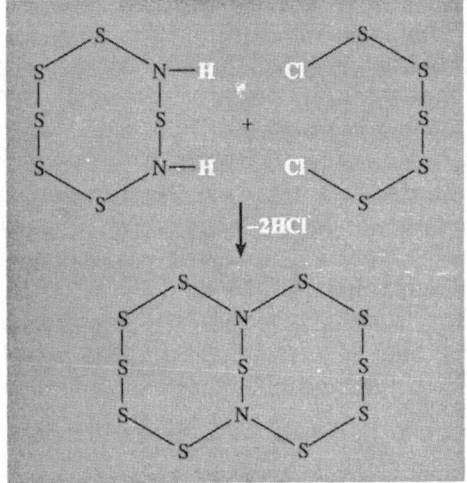

Some polymer is also formed but this can be converted into the bicyclic $S_{11}N_2$ by refluxing in CS_2. The X-ray crystal structure (Fig. 15.37b) shows that the 2 N atoms are planar.[227] This has been interpreted in terms of sp^2 hybridization at N, with some delocalization of the p_π lone-pair of electrons into S-based orbitals, thus explaining the considerably diminished donor power of the molecule. $S_{11}N_2$ is stable at room temperature but begins to decompose when heated above 145°.

The sulfur nitrides $S_{15}N_2$ and $S_{16}N_2$ are (formally) derived from cyclo-S_8 (or S_7NH) and can be prepared by reacting S_7NH with SCl_2 and S_2Cl_2 respectively:

$$2S_7NH + S_xCl_2 \longrightarrow S_7N-S_x-NS_7 + 2HCl$$

Both are yellow crystalline materials, stable at room temperature, and readily soluble in CS_2 (Fig. 15.37c).[228] Compounds with $x = 3$ and 5 can be prepared similarly.

Finally, in this subsection we mention the discovery of S_5N_6 which is best prepared (73% yield) by the reaction of $S_4N_5^-$ (p. 733) with Br_2 in CH_2Cl_2 at 0°C for several hours[229] Iodine reacts similarly but chlorine affords S_4N_5Cl (p. 731). S_5N_6 forms orange crystals which are stable for prolonged periods at room temperature in an inert atmosphere, though they immediately blacken in air. It can be sublimed unchanged at 45° (10^{-2} mmHg) and decomposes above 130°. The structure (Fig. 15.38) features a molecular basket in which an $-N=S-N-$ group bridges 2 S atoms of an S_4N_4 cradle. Comparison with S_4N_4 itself (p. 723) shows little change in the S–N distances in the cradle (161 pm) but the trans-annular $S \cdots S$ distances are markedly different: one is opened up from 258 pm to 394 pm (nonbonding) whereas the other contracts to 243 pm suggesting stronger trans-annular bonding between these 2 S atoms and the incipient formation of 2 fused 5-membered S_3N_2 rings.

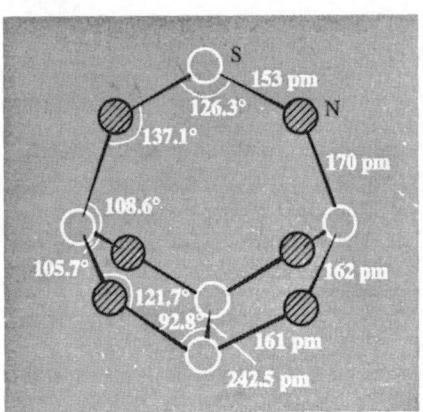

Figure 15.38 Structure of S_5N_6.

[229] T. CHIVERS and J. PROCTOR, *J. Chem. Soc., Chem. Commun.*, 642–3 (1978) and *Can. J. Chem.* **57**, 1286–93 (1979). See also W. S. SHELDRICK, M. N. S. RAO and H. W. ROESKY, *Inorg. Chem.* **19**, 538–43 (1980).

(ii) Sulfur–nitrogen cations and anions

Numerous charged sulfur–nitrogen species have been synthesized in recent years, particularly those having an odd number of N atoms which would otherwise be paramagnetic. However, thio analogues of nitrites (NO_2^-, p. 461) and nitrates (NO_3^-, p. 465) are unknown.

The simplest stable sulfur–nitrogen species is the cation $[SN]^+$ which was first prepared by the direct fluoride-ion transfer reaction between NSF and AsF_5 or SbF_5.[230] $[NS]^+[AsF_6]^-$ can also be prepared by reaction of an excess of AsF_5 with $S_3N_3F_3$ or by thermal decomposition of $[S_3N_2F_2]^+[AsF_6]^-$, but the simplest high-yield synthesis is by the reaction of $S_3N_3Cl_3$ with an excess of $AgAsF_6$ in liquid SO_2:[231]

$$AgAsF_6 + 1/3 S_3N_3Cl_3 \longrightarrow AgCl + [SN]^+[AsF_6]^-$$

(75% yield)

The cation has considerable synthetic potential for a wide range of S/N compounds, e.g.[231,232]

$$[SN]^+[AsF_6]^- + 1/8 S_8 \xrightarrow{SO_2} [S_2N]^+[AsF_6]^-$$

(50% yield)

$$[SN]^+[AsF_6]^- + CsF \xrightarrow{110^\circ} NSF + CsAsF_6$$

(80% yield)

$$[SN]^+[SbF_6]^- + [Re(CO)_5Br] \longrightarrow$$

$$[Re(CO)_5NS]^+[SbF_6]^- \text{ (100% yield)}$$

Thionitrosyl complexes have already been briefly mentioned on p. 453 and have recently been reviewed.[233] They were first made[234] by reacting azido complexes directly with

sulfur {e.g. $[(Et_2NCS)_3Mo{\equiv}N] + 1/8 S_8 \longrightarrow [(Et_2NCS)_3Mo(NS)]$}, but this reaction is not general. An alternative to direct metathesis with $[SN]^+$ is dissociative oxidative addition {e.g. $[MCl_2(PPh_3)_2] + 1/3(S_3N_3Cl_3) \longrightarrow [MCl_3(NS)(PPh_3)_2]$}. In the few complexes for which X-ray structural data are available the M–N–S group is essentially linear (170–177°) (see p. 453 and refs. 233, 235) but spectroscopic data on others suggest that bent and even η^1-bridging modes may be possible.

The dithionitronium cation $[S_2N]^+$, which is the sulfur analogue of the nitronium cation (p. 458), was first prepared as the crystalline salt $[S_2N]^+[SbCl_6]^-$ by the complex oxidative reaction of S_7NH, S_7NBCl_2 or $1,4-S_6(NH)_2$ (p. 735) with $SbCl_3$.[236] It can be more conveniently prepared, in 30% yield, by reaction of $S_3N_3Cl_3$ with $3SbCl_5 + 3/8 S_8$ using $OSCl_2$ or CH_2Cl_2 as solvent.[237] An X-ray structure determination on $[S_2N]^+[SbCl_6]^-$ showed the cation to be linear ($D_{\infty h}$) as expected for a species isoelectronic with CS_2 and NO_2^+.[236] The rather short N–S distance of 146.4 pm is consistent with the formulation $[S{=}N{=}S]^+$.

The radical cation $S_3N_2^+$ is formed in high yield from the oxidation of S_4N_4 with the anhydride $(CF_3SO_2)_2O$:[238]

$$(CF_3SO_2)_2O + S_4N_4 \longrightarrow [S_3N_2]^+[CF_3SO_3]^-$$

$$+ CF_3SO_2S_3N_3$$

The product is a black-brown solid that is very sensitive to oxygen. The same cation can be obtained by oxidation of S_4N_4 with AsF_5 and is unusual in being the only sulfur–nitrogen (paramagnetic) radical that has been obtained as a stable crystalline salt. X-ray diffraction analysis shows the structure to be a planar 5-membered ring with approximate

[230] O. GLEMSER and W. KOCH, *Angew. Chem. Int. Edn. Engl.* **10**, 127 (1971).

[231] A. APBLETT, A. J. BANISTER, D. BIRON, A. G. KENDRICK, J. PASSMORE, M. SCHRIVER and M. STOJANAC, *Inorg. Chem.* **25**, 4451–2 (1986).

[232] G. HARTMANN and R. MEWS, *Angew. Chem. Int. Edn. Engl.* **24**, 202–3 (1985).

[233] J. D. WOOLLINS, Chap. 18 in R. STEUDEL (ed.), *The Chemistry of Inorganic Ring Systems*, Elsevier, Amsterdam, 1992, pp. 349–72.

[234] J. CHATT and J. R. DILWORTH, *J. Chem. Soc., Chem. Commun.*, 508 (1974).

[235] J. BALDAS, J. BONNYMAN, M. F. MACKAY and G. A. WILLIAMS, *Aust. J Chem.* **37**, 751–9 (1984).

[236] R. FAGGIANI, R. J. GILLESPIE, C. J. L. LOCK and J. D. TYRER, *Inor. Chem.* **17**, 2975–8 (1978).

[237] A. J. BANISTER and A. G. KENDRICK, *J. Chem. Soc., Dalton Trans.*, 1565–7 (1987).

[238] R. J. GILLESPIE, J. P. KEMT and J. F. SAWYER, *Inorg. Chem.* **20**, 3784–99 (1981).

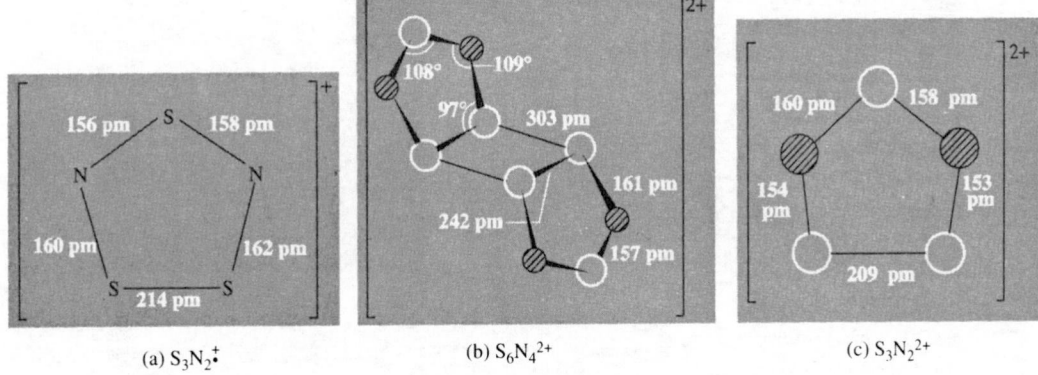

(a) $S_3N_2^{+\cdot}$ (b) $S_6N_4^{2+}$ (c) $S_3N_2^{2+}$

Figure 15.39 Structures of (a) the planar radical cation $S_3N_2^{+\cdot}$, (b) its dimer $S_6N_4^{2+}$ and (c) the corresponding planar diamagnetic dication $S_3N_2^{2+}$.

C_{2v} symmetry (Fig. 15.39a). The corresponding diamagnetic dimer $S_6N_4^{2+}$ was obtained in low yield by oxidation of S_3N_2Cl with $ClSO_3H$: its structure (Fig. 15.39b) consists of 2 symmetry-related planar $S_3N_2^+$ units linked by 2 very long S–S bonds. Alternatively, the central S_4 unit can be thought of as being bound by a 4-centre 6-electron bond. Even more remarkably, a diamagnetic 6π-electron dication, $[S_3N_2]^{2+}$, which is less stable than its paramagnetic 7π-electron analogue $[S_3N_2]^+$, has been prepared and characterized as the crystalline salt $[S_3N_2]^{2+}[AsF_6]_2^{-}$.[239] The planar conformation of the ring is retained, but the dimensions are significantly different (Fig. 15.39(c)) most notably in the shortening of the S–S and adjacent S–N bonds. The dictation is only stable in the crystalline phase; in SO_2 solutions it reversibly dissociates into the paramagnetic species $[SN]^+$ and $[SNS]^+$, the cycloaddition in the solid state apparently being driven by the high lattice energy of the 1:2 salt.

Cations containing 4 S atoms include $S_4N_3^+$, $S_4N_4^{2+}$ and $S_4N_5^+$, as well as the unique radical cation $S_4N_4^+$. The structures are in Fig. 15.40 and typical preparative routes are:[210, 240−241]

$$S_3N_3Cl_3 + S_2Cl_2 \longrightarrow [S_4N_3]^+Cl^- + SCl_2 + Cl_2$$

$$3S_3N_2Cl_2 + S_2Cl_2 \longrightarrow 2[S_4N_3]^+Cl^- + 3SCl_2$$

$$S_4N_4 + 4SbF_5 \xrightarrow{SO_2} [S_4N_4]^{2+}[SbF_6]^-[Sb_3F_{14}]^-$$

$$S_3N_3Cl_3 + (Me_3SiN)_2S \xrightarrow{CCl_4} [S_4N_5]^+Cl^- + \ldots$$

$$S_3N_3Cl_3 + FeCl_3 \xrightarrow{CH_2Cl_2} [S_4N_4]^+FeCl_4^- + \ldots$$

These compounds contain some fascinating and subtle structural and bonding problems. For example, the compound $[S_4N_4]^{2+}[SbF_6]^-$-$[Sb_3F_{11}]^-$ shows two structurally distinct cations, one with essentially equal S–N distances around the planar ring (Fig. 15.40b) and the other, also planar, but with alternating S–N distances of *ca.* 153 and 162 pm and with bond angles at S and N of 127° and 143°, respectively. By contrast, a non-planar boat-shaped structure was found for the dication in $[S_4N_4]^{2+}[SbCl_6]_2^{-}$.[240] The unusual radical cation $[S_4N_4]^{+\cdot}$ occurs in the brown, moisture-sensitive compound $[S_4N_4]^+[FeCl_4]^-$ and features a puckered 8-membered ring in which the four S atoms form an almost perfect square and all the S–N

[239] W. V. F. BROOKS, T. S. CAMERON, F. GREIN, S. PARSONS, J. PASSMORE and M. J. SCHRIVER, *J. Chem. Soc., Chem. Commun.*, 1079–81 (1991).

[240] R. J. GILLESPIE, D. R. SLIM and J. D. TYRER, *J. Chem. Soc., Chem. Commun.*, 253–5 (1977). R. J. GILLESPIE, J. P. KENT, J. F. SAWYER, D. R. SLIM and J. D. TYRER, *Inorg. Chem.* **20**, 3799–812 (1981).

[241] T. CHIVERS, L. FIELDING, W. G. LAIDLAW and M. TRSIC, *Inorg. Chem.* **18**, 3379–87 (1979).

[242] U. MÜLLER, E. CONRADI, U. DEMANT and K. DEHNICKE, *Angew. Chem. Int. Edn. Engl.* **23**, 237–8 (1984).

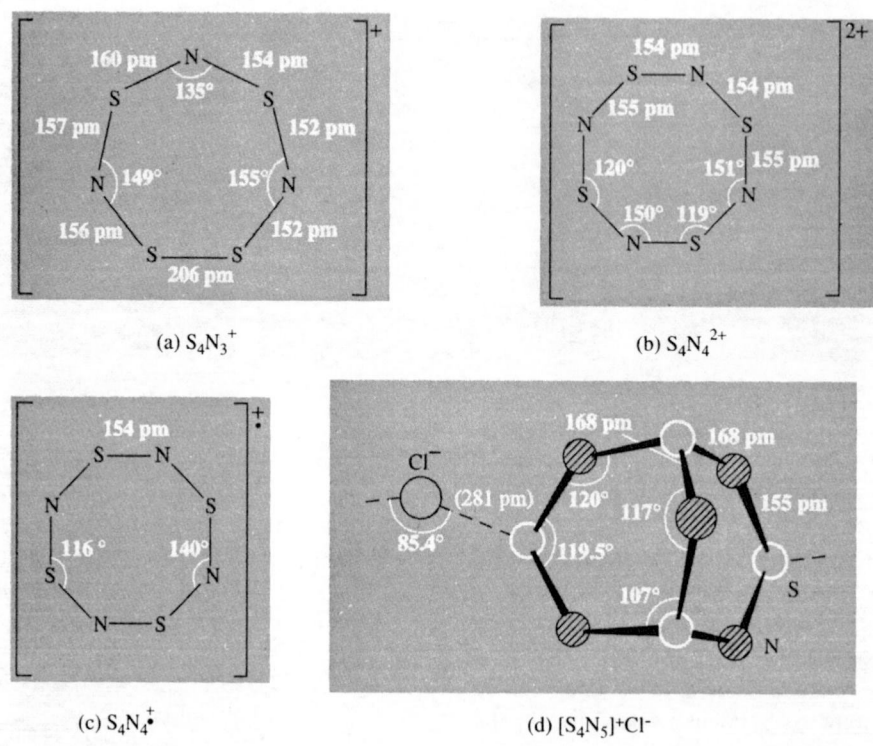

(a) $S_4N_3^+$

(b) $S_4N_4^{2+}$

(c) $S_4N_4^{+\cdot}$

(d) $[S_4N_5]^+Cl^-$

Figure 15.40   Structure of (a) planar $S_4N_3^+$; (b) planar $S_4N_4^{2+}$ (see text); (c) puckered $S_4N_4^{+\cdot}$; (d) a portion of the polymeric structure of $[S_4N_5]^+Cl^-$ showing the trans-annular bridging N atom.

distances are essentially equal at 154 pm, but in which the four N atoms are located alternately 34, −59, 45 and −38 pm above and below the plane of the four S atoms. The original papers should be consulted for further details.

An interesting structural problem also emerges from the study of the final sulfur–nitrogen cation to be considered, $S_5N_5^+$. First made in 1972, this was originally thought to contain a planar, heart shaped 10-membered heterocycle on the basis of X-ray diffraction studies on $[S_5N_5]^+[AlCl_4]^-$; however, it now seems likely that this is an artefact of disorder within the crystals and that the structure of the cation is as in Fig. 15.41[243] which is the

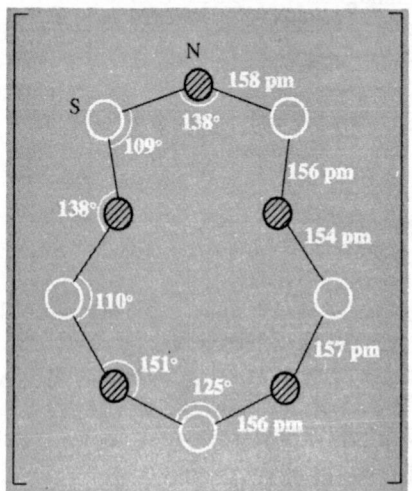

Figure 15.41   Structure of $S_5N_5^+$.

243 H. W. ROESKY,   W. G. BÖWING,   I. RAYMENT   and H. M. M. SHEARER, *J. Chem. Soc., Chem. Commun.*, 735–6 (1975); A. J. BANISTER, J. A. DURRANT, I. RAYMENT and H. M. M. SHEARER, *J. Chem. Soc., Dalton Trans.*, 928–30

(1976). See also R. J. GILLESPIE, J. F. SAWYER, D. R. SLIM and J. D. TYRER, *Inorg. Chem.* **21**, 1296–302 (1982).

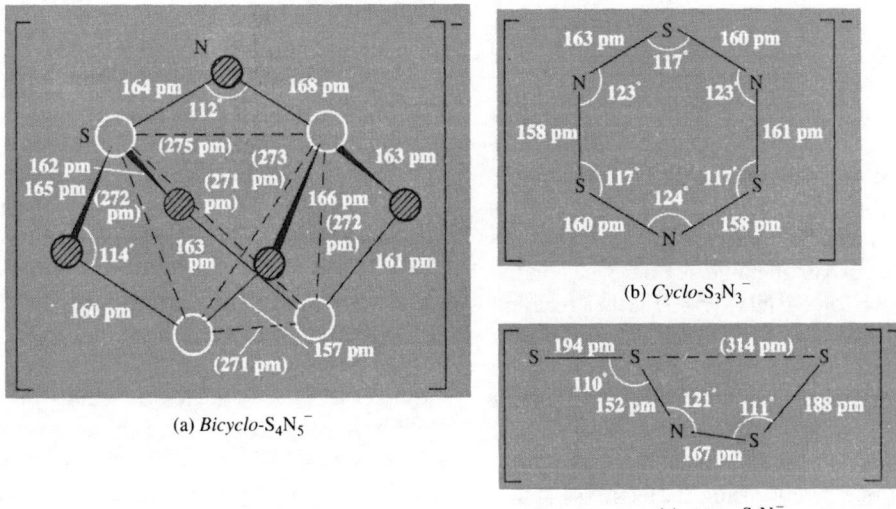

(a) *Bicyclo-*$S_4N_5^-$

(b) *Cyclo-*$S_3N_3^-$

(c) *catena-*S_4N^-

Figure 15.42　Structure of sulfur–nitrogen anions.

conformation observed in $[S_5N_5]^+[S_3N_3O_4]^-$ and $[S_5N_5]^+[SnCl_5(POCl_3)]^-$. Salts such as the yellow $[S_5N_5]^+[AlCl_4]^-$ and dark-orange $[S_5N_5]^+[FeCl_4]^-$ can readily be prepared in high yield by adding $AlCl_3$ (or $FeCl_3$) to $S_3N_3Cl_3$ in $SOCl_2$ solution and then treating the adduct so formed with S_4N_4; the overall stoichiometry can be represented as:

$$\tfrac{1}{3}(SNCl)_3 + AlCl_3 \longrightarrow \text{“}[NS]^+[AlCl_4]^-\text{”}$$

$$\xrightarrow{S_4N_4} [S_5N_5]^+[AlCl_4]^-$$

though the reaction is undoubtedly more complex and proceeds via the adduct $(SNCl)_3.2AlCl_3$.[244] Treatment of $[S_5N_5]^+[AlCl_4]^-$ with thf yields pure $[S_5N_5]Cl$ from which $[S_5N_5]^+[BF_4]^-$ can readily be prepared.[245] The planar azulene-shaped cation also occurs in the crystalline adduct $[S_5N_5]^+_4[As_8Cl_{28}]^{4-}.2S_4N_4$.[246] Uncoordinated sulfur–nitrogen anions are less common than

S–N cations and all are of recent preparation:[247] *bicyclo-*$S_4N_5^-$ (1976), *cyclo-*$S_3N_3^-$ (1977) and *catena-*S_4N^- (1979), as well as the more fugitive species S_3N^- and S_7N^-. Structures are in Fig. 15.42. $S_4N_5^-$ occurs as the product in a variety of reactions of S_4N_4 with nucleophiles:[248] e.g. liquid NH_3 or ethanolic solutions of R_2NH, MN_3 (M = Li, Na, K, Rb), KCN or even Na_2S. The course of these reactions suggests the initial formation of $S_3N_3^-$ which then reacts with further S_4N_4 to give $S_4N_5^-$. The ammonium salt $[NH_4]^+[S_4N_5]^-$ is a ubiquitous product of the reaction of ammonia with S_4N_4, $(SNCl)_3$, S_2Cl_2, SCl_2 or SCl_4.[249] Yet another route is the methanolysis of $(Me_3SiN)_2S$:

$$Me_3Si-N{=}S{=}N-SiMe_3 \xrightarrow{MeOH} [NH_4]^+[S_4N_5]^-$$

Subsequent metathesis with Bu_4^nNOH yielded yellow crystals suitable for X-ray structure analysis. The structure of $[S_4N_5]^-$ (Fig. 15.42a)

[244] A. J. BANISTER and H. G. CLARKE, *J. Chem. Soc., Dalton Trans.*, 2661–3 (1972). See also A. J. BANISTER, A. J. FIELDER, R. G. HEY, and N. R. M. SMITH, *ibid.*, 1457–60.

[245] A. J. BANISTER, Z. V. HAUPTMAN, A. G. KENDRICK and R. W. H. SMALL, *J. Chem. Soc., Dalton Trans.*, 915–24 (1987).

[246] W. WILLING, U. MULLER, J. EICHER and K. DEHNICKE, *Z. anorg. allg. Chem.* **537**, 145–53 (1986).

[247] T. CHIVERS and R. T. OAKLEY *Topics in Current Chemistry. Vol. 102, Inorganic Ring Systems*, Springer Verlag, Berlin, 1982, pp. 117–47 (114 references).

[248] J. BOJES, T. CHIVERS, I. DRUMMOND and G. MACLEAN, *Inorg. Chem.* **17**, 3668–72 (1978).

[249] O. J. SCHERER and G. WOLMERSHÄUSER, *Chem. Ber.* **110**, 3241–4 (1977).

is closely related to that of S_4N_4 (and $S_4N_5{}^+$), one trans-annular $S \cdots S$ being bridged by the fifth N atom.[250] One feature of the structure is that all the $S \cdots S$ distances become almost equal so that an alternative description is of an S_4 tetrahedron with 5 of the 6 edges bridged by N atoms, angle S–N–S 112–114°.

The anion $S_3N_3{}^-$ can be obtained by the action of azides (or metallic K) on S_4N_4 or the reaction of KH on $S_4(NH)_4$.[251] Further reaction of $S_3N_3{}^-$ with S_4N_4 yields $S_4N_5{}^-$ (as above). The structure of $S_3N_3{}^-$ (Fig. 15.42b) is a planar ring of approximate D_{3h} symmetry.[251] This has interesting bonding implications. Thus each S in a heterocycle forms a σ bond to each of its neighbours (thereby using 2 electrons) and it also has an exocyclic lone-pair of electrons: this leaves 2 electrons to contribute to the π system of the heterocycle (which might or might not involve S 3d orbitals). Likewise, each N atom has 2 electrons in σ bonds, one exocyclic lone pair, and contributes one electron to the π system. Planar S–N heterocycles having 4–10 ring atoms are now known and all except the radical cation $S_3N_2{}^{+\cdot}$ have $(4n + 2)\pi$ electrons where $n = 1, 2,$ or 3 as shown below:

Ringe/size	4	5	6	7	8	10
Species	S_2N_2	$S_3N_2{}^{+\cdot}$	$S_3N_3{}^-$	$S_4N_3{}^+$	$S_4N_4{}^{2+}$	$S_5N_5{}^+$
Number of π electrons	6	[7]	10	10	10	14

Thermal decomposition of $[N(PPh_3)_2]^+$-$[S_4N_5]^-$ in MeCN yields sequentially the corresponding salts of $S_3N_3{}^-$ and S_4N^- (50% yield). An X-ray crystallographic analysis of the dark-blue air-stable product $[N(PPh_3)_2]^+[S_4N]^-$ revealed the presence of the unique acyclic anion $[SSNSS]^-$ whose structure is in Fig. 15.42c. The anion is planar with *cis-trans* configuration,

though a different geometrical configuration occurs in the $[AsPh_4]^+$ salt.[252] The existence of $[S_4N]^-$ as well as of $[S_7N]^-$ and small amounts of $[S_3N]^-$ in sulfur-ammonia solutions has been demonstrated by ^{14}N nmr spectroscopy.[253]

The coordination chemistry of sulfur–nitrogen anions is also a burgeoning field.[254] Some complexes have already been mentioned (pp. 725–6) and others for which X-ray structural data are available include the chelate $[Pt(PPh_3)_2(\eta^2\text{-}SNSN)]^{[255]}$ and the bridged dimer $[\{(Ph_3P)_2Pt\}_2\text{-}(\mu,\eta^2\text{-}S_2N_2)_2]$ in which each Pt atom is chelated by –SNSN– and then bridged to the other Pt atom by the coordinated N atom to form a central planar Pt_2N_2 ring.[256] For coordinated $[S_3N_2]^{2-}$ and $[S_3N_4]^{2-}$ examples include the chelated titanocene derivatives $[Ti(\eta^5\text{-}C_5H_5)_2\text{-}(\eta^2\text{-}S_3N_2)]$ and $[Ti(\eta^5\text{-}C_5H_5)_2 (\eta^2\text{-}S_3N_4)]$ which feature the 6- and 8-membered ring systems $\overline{TiSSNSN}$ and $\overline{TiNSNSNSN}$, respectively.[257] The chelating trianion $[S_2N_3]^{3-}$ occurs in the 6-coordinate mixed ligand trisbidentate vanadium(V) complex $[V(dtbc)(phen)(\eta^2\text{-}N_3S_2)]$ (dtbc = di-t-butylcatecholate, $Bu_2^tC_6H_2O_2{}^{2-}$; phen = 1,10-phenanthroline)[258] and in the

[250] W. FLUES, O. J. SCHERER, J. WEISS and G. WOLMERS-HÄUSER, *Angew. Chem. Int. Edn. Engl.* **15**, 379–80 (1976).

[251] J. BOJES, T. CHIVERS, W. G. LAIDLAW and M. TRSIC, *J. Am. Chem. Soc.* **101**, 4517–22 (1979), and references therein. See also R. JONES, P. F. KELLY, D. J. WILLIAMS and J. D. WOOLLINS, *Polyhedron* **6**, 1541–6 (1987); and P. N. JAGG, P. F. KELLY, H. S. RZEPA, D. J. WILLIAMS, J. D. WOOLLINS and W. WYLIE *J. Chem. Soc., Chem. Commun.*, 942–4 (1991).

[252] N. BUFORD, T. CHIVERS, A. W. CORDES, R. T. OAKLEY, W. T. PENNINGTON and P. N. SWEPSTON, *Inorg. Chem.* **20**, 4430–2 (1981). See also T. CHIVERS and C. LAU. *Inorg. Chem.* **21**, 453–5 (1982).

[253] T. CHIVERS, D. D. McINTYRE, K. J. SCHMIDT and H. J. VOGEL, *J. Chem. Soc., Chem. Commun.*, 1341–2 (1990); see also T. CHIVERS and K. J. SCHMIDT, *ibid.* pp. 1342–3, for $S_2N_2H]^-$.

[254] P. F. KELLY and J. D. WOOLLINS, *Polyhedron* **5**, 607–32 (1986); T. CHIVERS and F. EDELMANN, *Polyhedron* **5** 1661–99 (1986); H. W. ROESKY, in H. W. ROESKY (ed.), *Rings Clusters and Polymers of Main Group and Transition Elements*, Elsevier, Amsterdam, 1989, pp. 369–408; J. D. WOOLLINS, in R. STEUDEL (ed.), *The Chemistry of Inorganic Ring Systems*, Elsevier, Amsterdam, 1992, pp. 349–72.

[255] R. JONES, P. F. KELLY, D. J. WILLIAMS and J. D. WOOLLINS, *Polyhedron* **4**, 1947–50 (1985). See also P. A. BATES, M. B. HURSTHOUSE, P. F. KELLY and J. D. WOOLLINS, *J. Chem. Soc., Dalton Trans.*, 2367–70 (1986).

[256] R. JONES, P. F. KELLEY, D. J. WILLIAMS and J. D. WOOLLINS, *J. Chem. Soc., Chem. Commun.*, 1325–6 (1985).

[257] C. G. MARCELLUS, R. T. OAKLEY, W. T. PENNINGTON and A. W. CORDES, *Organometallics* **5**, 1395–400 (1986).

[258] T. A. KABANOS, A. M. Z. SLAWIN, D. J. WILLIAMS and J. D. WOOLLINS, *J. Chem. Soc., Chem. Commun.*, 193–4

anionic complex $[WCl_2F_2(\eta^2\text{-}N_3S_2)]^{-}$.[259] Copper(I) and silver complexes of the $[S_3N]^{-}$ ion are of older vintage, e.g. $[Cu(PPh_3)_2(\eta^2\text{-}SSNS)]$ and $[Cu(\eta^2\text{-}SSNS)_2]^{-}$.[260]

(iii) Sulfur imides, $S_{8-n}(NH)_n$ [206]

The NH group is "isoelectronic" with S and so can successively subrogate S in *cyclo*-S_8. Thus we have already seen that reduction of S_4N_4 with dithionite or with $SnCl_2$ in boiling ethanol/benzene yields $S_4(NH)_4$. Again, whereas reaction of S_2Cl_2 or SCl_2 with NH_3 in non-polar solvents yields S_4N_4, heating these 2 reactants in

polar solvents such as dimethylformamide affords a range of sulfur imides. In a typical reaction 170 g S_2Cl_2 and the corresponding amount of NH_3 yielded:

S_8 (32 g)	1,3-S_6(NH)$_2$ (0.98 g)	1,3,5-S_5(NH)$_3$ (0.08 g)
S_7NH	1,4-S_6(NH)$_2$ (2.3 g)	1,3,6-S_5(NH)$_3$ (0.32 g)
(15.4 g)	1,5-S_6(NH)$_2$ (0.82 g)	

In no case have adjacent NH groups been observed.

S_7NH is a stable pale-yellow compound, mp 113.5°; the structure is closely related to that of *cyclo*-S_8 as shown in Fig. 15.43a. The proton is acidic and undergoes many reactions of which the following are typical (see also p. 729):

$$BX_3 \longrightarrow S_7N-BX_2 + HX \quad (X = Cl, Br)$$

$$NaCPh_3 \longrightarrow S_7NNa + Ph_3CH$$

$$(Me_3Si)_2NH \longrightarrow S_7N-SiMe_3 + NH_3$$

$$Hg(MeCO_2)_2 \longrightarrow Hg(NS_7)_2 + MeCO_2H$$

(1990). See also P. F. KELLY, A. M. Z. SLAWIN, D. J. WILLIAMS and J. D. WOOLLINS *Polyhedron* **10**, 2337–40 (1991).

[259] H. BORGHOLTE, K. DEHNICKE, H. GOESMANN and D. FENSKE, *Z. anorg. allg. Chem.*, **586**, 159–65 (1990).

[260] J. BOJES, T. CHIVERS and P. W. CODDING, *J. Chem. Soc., Chem. Commun.*, 1171–3 (1981).

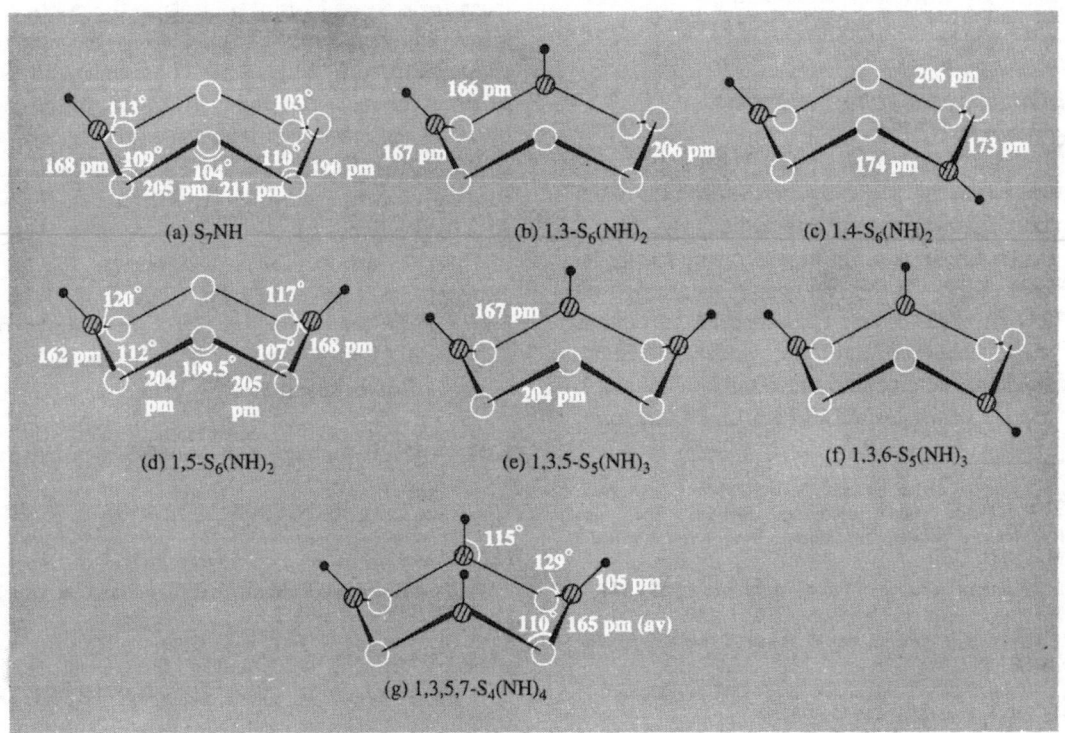

Figure 15.43 Structures of the various cyclo sulfur imides.

The 3 isomeric compounds $S_6(NH)_2$ form stable colourless crystals and have the structures illustrated in Fig. 15.43b, c, and d.[208,261] The 1,3-, 1,4-, and 1,5-isomers melt at 130°, 133°, and 155° respectively. The 1,3,5- and 1,3,6-triimides melt with decomposition at 128° and 133° (Fig. 15.43e and f). The tetraimide, $S_4(NH)_4$ (mp 145°) is structurally very similar (Fig. 15.43g):[262] the N atoms are each essentially trigonal planar and the heterocycle is somewhat flattened, the distance between the planes of the 4 N atoms and 4 S atoms being only 57 pm. The influence of extensive intermolecular H-bonding on the structure has been studied by electron deformation density techniques.[263].

Alkyl derivatives such as $1,4\text{-}S_6(NR)_2$ and $S_4(NR)_4$ can be synthesized by reacting S_2Cl_2 with primary amines RNH_2 in an inert solvent. Compounds such as $1,4\text{-}S_2(NR)_4$ ($R = -CO_2Et$) are now also well characterized.[264] The bis-adduct $[Ag(S_4N_4H_4)_2]^+$ has been isolated as its perchlorate; this has a sandwich-like structure and is unique in being S-bonded rather than N-bonded to the metal ion.[265]

(iv) Other cyclic sulfur–nitrogen compounds [207,209]

Incorporation of a third heteroatom into S–N compounds is now well established, e.g. for C, Si; P, As; O; Sn and Pb, together with the S_2N_2 chelates of Fe, Co, Ni, Pd and Pt mentioned on p. 725. The field is very extensive but introduces no new concepts into the general scheme of covalent heterocyclic molecular chemistry. Illustrative examples are in Fig. 15.44 and fuller

details including X-ray structures for many of the compounds are in the references cited above. A selenium analogue of the dimer $S_6N_4^{2+}$ (p. 731) has also been prepared and structurally characterized, viz. $[SN_2Se_2Se_2N_2S]^{2+}$.[266]

(v) Sulfur–nitrogen halogen compounds [267-9]

As with sulfur–halogen compounds (pp. 683–93) the stability of N–S–X compounds decreases with increase in atomic weight of the halogen. There are numerous fluoro and chloro derivatives but bromo and iodo derivatives are virtually unknown except for the nonstoichiometric $(SNX_x)_\infty$ polymers (p. 728) and $S(NX)_2$ (p. 740). Unlike the H atoms in the sulfur imides (p. 735) the halogen atoms are attached to S rather than N. Fluoro derivatives have been known since 1965 but some of the chloro compounds have been known for over a century. The simplest compounds are the nonlinear thiazyl halides $N\equiv S-F$ and $N\equiv S-Cl$: these form a noteworthy contrast to the nonlinear nitrosyl halides $O=N-X$. In all cases, the pairs of elements directly bonded are consistent with the rule that the most electronegative atom of the trio bonds to the least electronegative, i.e. $\{S(NH)\}_4$, $\{N(SF)\}_{1,3,4}$, $\{N(SCl)\}_{1,3}$, $O(NF)$, $O(NCl)$ (formal Pauling electronegativities: H 2.1, S 2.5, N 3.0, Cl 3.0, O 3.5, F 4.0).

Thiazyl fluoride, NSF, is a colourless, reactive, pungent gas (mp −89°, bp +0.4°). It is best prepared by the action of HgF_2 on a slurry of S_4N_4 and CCl_4 but it can also be made by a variety of other reactions:[267]

$$S_4N_4 + 4HgF_2 \text{(or } AgF_2) \xrightarrow{CCl_4} 4NSF + 2Hg_2F_2$$

$$S_4N_4 \xrightarrow{IF_5} \{S_4N_4(NSF)_4\} \xrightarrow{50°} S_4N_4 + 4NSF$$

[261] J. C. van de Grampel and A. Vos, *Acta Cryst.* **B25**, 611–17 (1969), and references therein. See also H. J. Postma, F. van Bolhuis and A. Vos, *Acta Cryst.* **B27**, 2480–6 (1971).

[262] T. M. Sabine and G. W. Cox, *Acta Cryst.* **28**, 574–7 (1967).

[263] D. Gregson, G. Klebe and H. Fuess, *J. Am. Chem. Soc.* **110**, 8488–93 (1988).

[264] J. Novosad, D. J. Williams and J. D. Woollins, *Z. anorg. allg. Chem.* **620**, 495–7 (1994).

[265] M. B. Hursthouse, K. M. A. Malik and S. N. Nabi, *J. Chem. Soc., Dalton Trans.*, 355–9 (1980).

[266] R. J. Gillespie, J. P. Kent and J. F. Sawyer, *Inorg. Chem.* **20**, 4053–60 (1981).

[267] O. Glemser and M. Fild, in V. Gutmann (ed.), *Halogen Chemistry*, Vol. 2, pp. 1–30, Academic Press, London, 1967.

[268] R. Mews, *Adv. Inorg. Chem. Radiochem.* **19**, 185–237 (1976).

[269] O. Glemser and R. Mews, *Angew. Chem. Int. Edn. Engl.* **19**, 883–99 (1980).

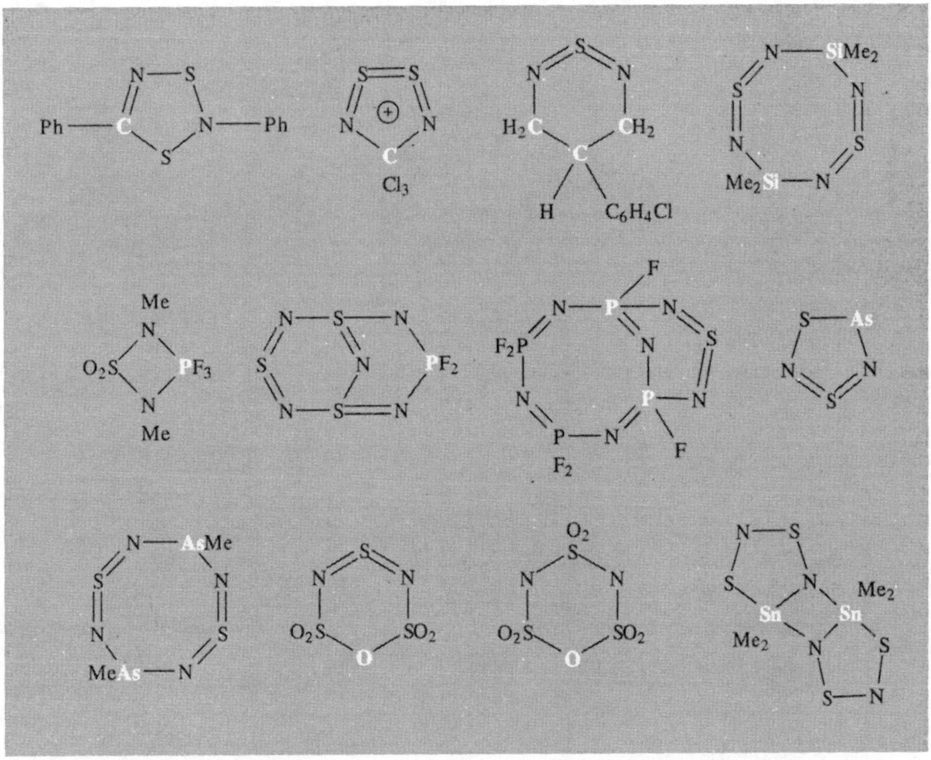

Figure 15.44   Some heterocyclic S–N compounds incorporating a third heteroelement.

$$SF_4 + NH_3 \longrightarrow NSF + 3HF$$

$$NF_3 + 3S \longrightarrow NSF + SSF_2$$

S_4N_4 can also be fluorinated to NSF (and other products) using F_2 at $-75°$, SeF_4 at $-10°$, or SF_4. The molecular dimensions of NSF have been determined by microwave spectroscopy: N–S 145 pm, S–F 164 pm, angle at S 116.5°. The angle at S is very close to the angle at N in ONX (110–117°, p. 442). NSF can be stored at room temperature in copper or teflon vessels but it slowly decomposes in glass (more rapidly at 200°) to form a mixture of OSF_2, SO_2, SiF_4, S_4N_4 and N_2. At room temperature and at pressures above 1 atm it trimerises to cyclo-$N_3S_3F_3$ (see below) but at lower pressures it affords S_4N_4 admixed with yellow-green crystals of $S_3N_2F_2$; this latter is of unknown structure but may well be the nonlinear acyclic species FSN=S=NSF. $N_3S_3F_3$ is best made by fluorinating cyclo-$N_3S_3Cl_3$ with AgF_2/CCl_4. The tetramer cyclo-$N_4S_4F_4$ is not obtained by polymerization of NSF monomer but can be readily made by fluorinating S_4N_4 with a hot slurry of AgF_2/CCl_4. Some physical properties of these and other N–S–F compounds (p. 725) are compared in the following table:

Compound	N≡S—F	$S_3N_2F_2$	$N_3S_3F_3$
MP/°C	−89	83	74.2
BP/°C	+0.4	–	92.5

Compound	$N_4S_4F_4$	N≡SF_3	FN=SF_2
MP/°C	153(d)	−72	–
BP/°C	–	27.1	−6.7

The structures of $N_3S_3F_3$ and $N_4S_4F_4$ are in Fig. 15.45. The former features a slightly puckered 6-membered ring (chair conformation) with essentially equal S–N distances around the ring and 3 eclipsed axial F atoms. By contrast,

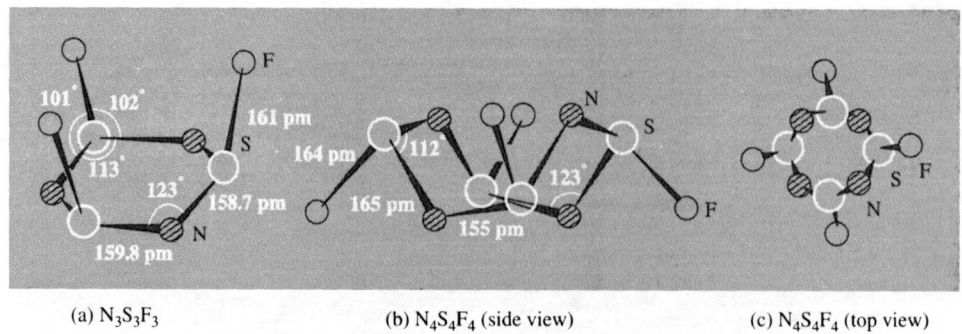

(a) $N_3S_3F_3$ (b) $N_4S_4F_4$ (side view)   (c) $N_4S_4F_4$ (top view)

Figure 15.45 Molecular structures of (a) $N_3S_3F_3$, (b) $N_4S_4F_4$ (side view), and (c) $N_4S_4F_4$ (top view).

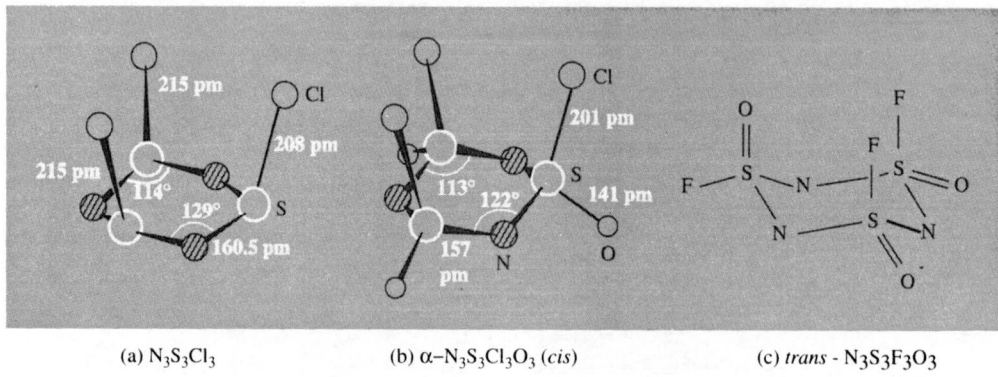

(a) $N_3S_3Cl_3$ (b) α-$N_3S_3Cl_3O_3$ (*cis*)   (c) *trans* - $N_3S_3F_3O_3$

Figure 15.46 Molecular structure of (a) $N_3S_3Cl_3$, (b) α-$N_3S_3Cl_3O_3$ (*cis*), and (c) *trans*-$N_3S_3F_3O_3$.

$N_4S_4F_4$ shows a pronounced alternation in S–N distances and only 2 of the F atoms are axial; it will also be noted that the conformation of the N_4S_4 ring is very different to that in S_4N_4 (p. 723) or $S_4(NH)_4$ (p. 735). It is an interesting intellectual exercise to attempt to rationalize these striking structural differences.[270] The chemistry of these various NSF oligomers has not been extensively studied. $N_3S_3F_3$ is stable in dry air but is hydrolysed by dilute aqueous NaOH to give NH_4F and sulfate. $N_4S_4F_4$ is reported to form an N-bonded 1:1 adduct with BF_3 whereas with AsF_5 or SbF_5 fluoride ion transfer occurs (accompanied by dethiazylation of the ring) to give $[N_3S_3F_2]^+[MF_6]^-$ and $[NS]^+[MF_6]^-$.

In the chloro series, the compounds to be considered are $N{\equiv}S{-}Cl$, *cyclo*-$N_3S_3Cl_3$, *cyclo*-$N_3S_3Cl_3O_3$, and *cyclo*-$N_4S_4Cl_2$; the ionic compounds $[S_4N_3]^+Cl^-$ and $[cyclo\text{-}N_2S_2Cl]^+Cl^-$ and $[catena\text{-}N(SCl)_2]^+[BCl_4]^-$; together with various isomeric oxo- and fluoro-chloro derivatives. Thiazyl chloride, NSCl, is best obtained by pyrolysis of the trimer in vacuum at 100°. It can also be made by the reaction of Cl_2 on NSF (note that $NSF + F_2 \longrightarrow NSF_3$) and by numerous other reactions.[267] It is a yellow-green gas that rapidly trimerizes at room temperature, and is isostructural with NSF.

By far the most common compound in the series is $N_3S_3Cl_3$ (yellow needles, mp 168°) which can be prepared by the direct action of Cl_2 (or $SOCl_2$) on S_4N_4 in CCl_4, and which is also obtained in all reactions leading to NSCl. The structure (Fig. 15.46a) is very

270 S. M. OWEN and A. T. BROOKER, *A Guide to Modern Inorganic Chemistry*, Longman Scientific and Technical, Harlow 1991, pp. 120–1.

similar to that of $N_3S_3F_3$ and comprises a slightly puckered ring with equal S–N distances of 160.5 pm and the N atoms only 18 pm above and below the plane of the 3 S atoms. $N_3S_3Cl_3$ is sensitive to moisture and is oxidized by SO_3 above 100° to $N_3S_3Cl_3O_3$; at lower temperatures the adduct $N_3S_3Cl_3.6SO_3$ is formed and this dissociates at 100° to $N_3S_3Cl_3.3SO_3$. A more efficient preparation of $N_3S_3Cl_3O_3$ is by thermal decomposition of the product obtained by the reaction of amidosulfuric acid with PCl_5:

$$H_2NSO_3H + 2PCl_5 \longrightarrow 3HCl + OPCl_3$$
$$+ ClSO_2-N{=}PCl_3$$
$$3ClSO_2-N{=}PCl_3 \xrightarrow{\text{heat}} 3OPCl_3 + (NSClO)_3$$

The compound is obtained in two isomeric forms from this reaction: α, mp 145° and β, mp 43°. The structure of the α-form is in Fig. 15.46b and is closely related to that of $(NSCl)_3$ with uniform S–N distances around the ring. The β-form may have a different ring conformation but more probably involves *cis-trans* isomerism of the pendant Cl and O atoms. Fluorination of α-$N_3S_3Cl_3O_3$ with KF in CCl_4 yields the two isomeric fluorides *cis*-$N_3S_3F_3O_3$ (mp 17.4°) and *trans*-$N_3S_3F_3O_3$ (mp $-12.5°$) (Fig. 15.46c). The structural assignment of the 2 isomers was made on the basis of ^{19}F nmr. Fluorination with SbF_3 under reduced pressure yields both the monofluoro and difluoro derivatives $N_3S_3Cl_2FO_3$ and $N_3S_3ClF_2O_3$, each having 3 isomers which can be separated chromatographically and assigned by ^{19}F nmr as indicated schematically in Fig. 15.47. Numerous other derivatives are known in which one or more halogen atom is replaced by $-NH_2$, $-N{=}SF_2$, $-N{=}PCl_3$, $-N{=}CHPh$, $-OSiMe_3$, etc.

A different structure motif occurs in S_4N_3Cl. This very stable yellow compound features the $S_4N_3^+$ cation (p. 732) and is obtained by many reactions, e.g.:

$$3S_4N_4 + 2S_2Cl_2 \xrightarrow{CCl_4/\text{heat}} 4[S_4N_3]^+Cl^-$$

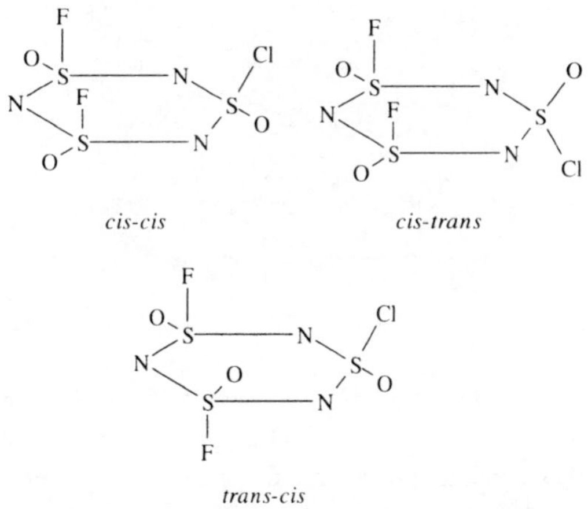

cis-cis   *cis-trans*

trans-cis

Figure 15.47 Schematic representation of the three geometric isomers of $N_3S_3ClF_2O_3$. The three isomers of the monofluoro derivative are similar but with Cl and F interchanged.

The chloride ion is readily replaced by other anions to give, for example, the orange-yellow $[S_4N_3]Br$, bronze-coloured $[S_4N_3]SCN$, $[S_4N_3]NO_3$, $[S_4N_3]HSO_4$, etc.

Chlorination of S_4N_4 with $NOCl$ or $SOCl_2$ in a polar solvent yields $S_3N_2Cl_2$:

$$S_4N_4 + 2NOCl \longrightarrow S_3N_2Cl_2 + \tfrac{1}{2}S_2Cl_2 + 2N_2O$$

The crystal structure again reveals an ionic formulation, $[N_2S_3Cl]^+Cl^-$, this time with a slightly puckered 5-membered ring carrying a single pendant Cl atom as shown in Fig. 15.48a; the alternation of S–N distances and the rather small angles at the 2 directly linked S atoms are notable features. Reaction of $[N_2S_3Cl]^+Cl^-$ with bis(trimethylsilyl)cyanamide, $(Me_3Si)_2NCN$, in MeCN yields dark red crystals of N_2S_3NCN (i.e. $\overline{SNSNS}{=}NCN$) in which the essentially linear NCN group (176.4°) lies diagonally above the N_2S_3-ring with the angle S=N–C being 119.0°.[271] Yet a further chloride can be obtained by the partial chlorination of S_4N_4 with Cl_2 in CS_2 solution below room temperature: one of the

[271] A. J. BANISTER, W. CLEGG, I. B. GORRELL, Z. V. HAUPT-MAN and R. W. H. SMALL, *J. Chem. Soc., Chem. Commun.*, 1611–13 (1987).

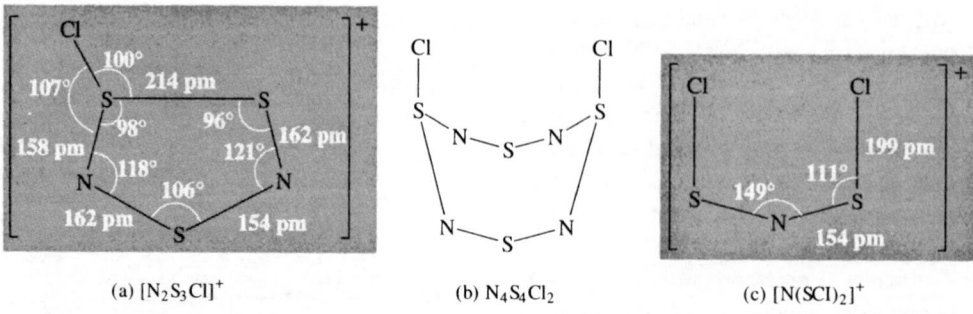

(a) $[N_2S_3Cl]^+$ (b) $N_4S_4Cl_2$ (c) $[N(SCl)_2]^+$

Figure 15.48 Structure of (a) the cation in $[N_2S_3Cl]^+Cl^-$, (b) $N_4S_4Cl_2$, and (c) $[N(SCl)_2]^+$.

trans-annular $S\cdots S$ "bonds" is opened to give yellow crystals of $N_4S_4Cl_2$ (Fig. 15.48b) and this derivatized heterocycle can be used to prepare several other compounds.[272]

Reaction of NSF_3 with BCl_3 yields the acyclic cation $[N(SCl)_2]^+$ as its BCl_4^- salt (Fig. 15.48c); the compound is very hygroscopic and readily decomposes to BCl_3, SCl_2, S_2Cl_2, and N_2.

The formation of highly conducting nonstoichiometric bromo and iodo derivatives of polythiazyl has already been mentioned (p. 728). It has been found that, whereas bromination of solid S_4N_4 with gaseous Br_2 yields conducting $(SNBr_{0.4})_x$, reaction with liquid bromine leads to the stable tribromide $[S_4N_3]^+[Br_3]^-$.[273] In contrast, the reaction of S_4N_4 with Br_2 in CS_2 solution results in a (separable) mixture of $[S_4N_3]^+[Br_3]^-$, $[S_4N_3]^+Br^-$ and the novel ionic compound $CS_3N_2Br_2$ which may be $[S{=}\overline{C{-}S{=}N{-}S{=}N}]^{2+}[Br^-]_2$ or $[S{=}\overline{C{-}S{=}N{-}S(Br){=}N}]^+Br^-$. The binary halides SN_2Br_2 and SN_2I_2 are also known. Thus SF_4 reacts with $(Me_3Si)_2NI$ in $C_2F_4Cl_2$ at $0°C$ to give $S(NI)_2$ as a shock-sensitive yellow crystalline powder composed of $I{-}N{=}S{=}N{-}I$ molecules in *syn-anti* configuration:[274]

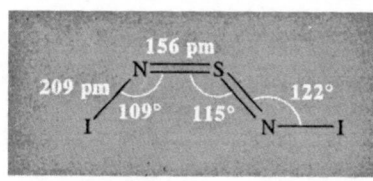

(vi) Sulfur–nitrogen–oxygen compounds [207]

This is a classic area of inorganic chemistry dating back to the middle of the last century and only a brief outline will be possible. It will be convenient first to treat the sulfur nitrogen oxides and then the amides, imides and nitrides of sulfuric acid. Hydrazides and hydroxylamides of sulfuric acid will also be considered. Some of these compounds have remarkable properties and some are implicated in the lead-chamber process for the manufacture of H_2SO_4 (p. 708). The field is closely associated with the names of the great German chemists E. Frémy ($\sim$1845), A. Claus ($\sim$1870), F. Raschig ($\sim$1885–1925), W. Traube ($\sim$1890–1920), F. Ephraim ($\sim$1910), P. Baumgarten ($\sim$1925) and, in more recent years, M. Becke-Goehring ($\sim$1955) and F. Seel ($\sim$1955–65).

(a) *Sulfur–nitrogen oxides.* Trisulfur dinitrogen dioxide, $S_3N_2O_2$, is best made by treating S_4N_4 with boiling $OSCl_2$ under a stream of SO_2:

$$S_4N_4 + 2OSCl_2 \longrightarrow S_3N_2O_2 + 2Cl_2 + S_2N_2 + S$$

It is a yellow solid with an acyclic structure (Fig. 15.49a), cf N_2O_5 (p. 458). Moist air converts $S_3N_2O_2$ to SO_2 and S_4N_4 whereas SO_3

[272] H. W. ROESKY, C. GRAF, M. N. S. RAO, B. KREBS and G. HENKEL, *Angew. Chem. Int. Edn. Engl.* **18**, 780–1 (1979)), and references therein. H. W. ROESKY, M. N. S. RAO, C. GRAF, A. GIEREN and E. HÄDICKE, *Angew. Chem. Int. Edn. Engl.* **20**, 592–3 (1981).

[273] G. WOLMERSHÄUSER, G. B. STREET and R. D. SMITH, $CS_3N_2Br_2$, *Inorg. Chem.* **18**, 383–5 (1979).

[274] M. ROCK, P. BRAVIN and K. SEPPELT, *Z. anorg. allg. Chem.* **618**, 89–92 (1992).

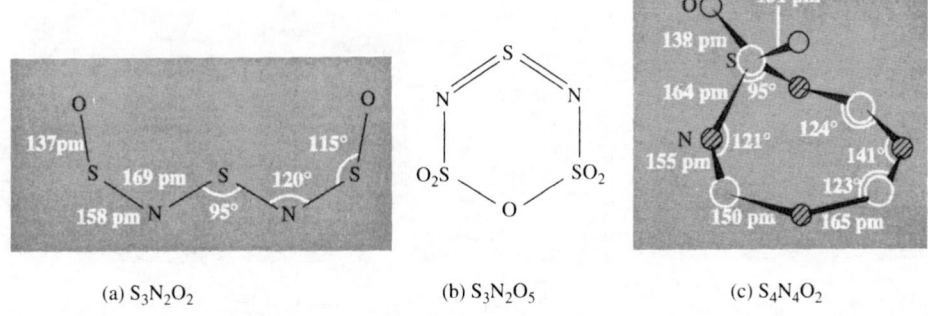

(a) $S_3N_2O_2$ (b) $S_3N_2O_5$ (c) $S_4N_4O_2$

Figure 15.49   Structures of sulfur–nitrogen oxides.

oxidizes it smoothly to $S_3N_2O_5$:

$$S_3N_2O_2 + 3SO_3 \longrightarrow S_3N_2O_5 + 3SO_2$$

The pentoxide $S_3N_2O_5$ can also be made directly from S_4N_4 and SO_3. It forms colourless, strongly refracting crystals which readily hydrolyse to sulfamic acid:

$$S_3N_2O_5 + 3H_2O \longrightarrow 2H_2NSO_3H + SO_2$$

It has a cyclic structure and may be regarded as a substituted diamide of disulfuric acid, $H_2S_2O_7$ (Fig. 15.49b).

An alternative synthetic strategy for sulfur-nitrogen oxides is exemplified by the more recent reaction:[275]

$$S_3N_2Cl_2 + SO_2(NH_2)_2 \xrightarrow[\text{reflux}]{CCl_4} S_4N_4O_2$$

The product forms orange-yellow crystals, mp 166 (d), having a structure in which 1 S atom of an S_4N_4 ring carries both O atoms. X-ray diffractometry shows substantial deviation from the parent S_4N_4 structure, a notable feature being the coplanarity of the S_3N_2 moiety furthest removed from the SO_2 group (Fig. 15.49c). If $S_4N_4O_2$ is allowed to react with 2 mols of SO_3 in liquid SO_2, two further compounds are formed: the known $S_3N_2O_5$ (Fig. 15.49b) and the novel greenish-black $S_6N_5O_4$, which is composed of separately stacked tricyclic radical cation dimers

$[\{S_3N_2^{\bullet}\}_2]^{2+}$ (Fig. 15.39b)) and the cyclic anion $S_3N_3O_4^-$, i.e. $[O_2\overline{SNSNS(O)_2O}]^-$.[276] Numerous other *cyclic-* and *polycyclic-*N/S/O species have recently been prepared and structurally characterized.[277]

(b) *Amides of sulfuric acid.* Amidosulfuric acid (better known as sulfamic acid, $H[H_2NSO_3]$), is a classical inorganic compound and an important industrial chemical. Formal replacement of both hydroxyl groups in sulfuric acid leads to sulfamide $(H_2N)_2SO_2$ (p. 742) which is also clearly related structurally to the sulfuryl halides X_2SO_2 (p. 694).

Sulfamic acid can be made by many routes, including addition of hydroxylamine to SO_2 and addition of NH_3 to SO_3:

$$H_2NOH + SO_2 \longrightarrow H[H_2NSO_3]$$

$$NH_3 + SO_3 \longrightarrow H[H_2NSO_3]$$

The industrial synthesis uses the strongly exothermic reaction between urea and anhydrous H_2SO_4 (or dilute oleum):

$$(H_2N)_2CO + 2H_2SO_4 \longrightarrow CO_2$$
$$+ H[H_2NSO_3] + NH_4[HSO_4]$$

[275] H. W. ROESKY, W. SCHAPER, O. PETERSEN and T. MÜLLER, *Chem. Ber.* **110**, 2695–8 (1977).

[276] H. ROESKY, M. WITT, J. SCHIMKOWIAK, M. SCHMIDT, M. NOLTEMEYER and G. M. SHELDRICK, *Angew. Chem. Int. Edn. Engl.* **21**, 538–9 (1982).

[277] T. CHIVERS, R. T. OAKLEY, A. W. CORDES and W. T. PENNINGTON, *J. Chem. Soc., Chem. Commun.*, 1214–5 (1981). T. CHIVERS, A. W. CORDES, R. T. OAKLEY and W. T. PENNINGTON, *Inorg. Chem.* **22**, 2429–35 (1983). T. CHIVERS and M. HOJO, *Inorg. Chem.* **23**, 4088–93 (1984).

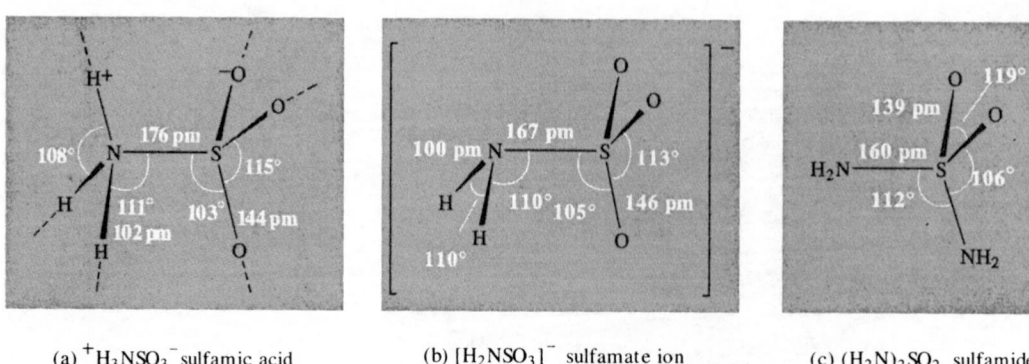

(a) $^+H_3NSO_3^-$ sulfamic acid   (b) $[H_2NSO_3]^-$ sulfamate ion   (c) $(H_2N)_2SO_2$ sulfamide

Figure 15.50 The structures of (a) sulfamic acid, (b) the sulfamate ion, and (c) sulfamide.

Salts are obtained by direct neutralization of the acid with appropriate oxides, hydroxides, or carbonates. Sulfamic acid is a dry, non-volatile, non-hygroscopic, colourless, white, crystalline solid of considerable stability. It melts at 205°, begins to decompose at 210°, and at 260° rapidly gives a mixture of SO_2, SO_3, N_2, H_2O, etc. It is a strong acid (dissociation constant 1.01×10^{-1} at 25° solubility ~25 g per 100 g H_2O) and, because of its physical form and stability, is a convenient standard for acidimetry. Over 50 000 tonnes are manufactured annually and its principal applications are in formulations for metal cleaners, scale removers, detergents and stabilizers for chlorine in aqueous solution.[278] Its salts are used in flame retardants, weed killers and for electroplating.

In the solid state sulfamic acid forms a strongly H-bonded network which is best described in terms of zwitterion units $^+H_3NSO_3^-$ rather than the more obvious formulation as aminosulfuric acid, $H_2NSO_2(OH)$. The zwitterion has the staggered configuration shown in Fig. 15.50a and the S–N distance is notably longer than in the sulfamate ion or sulfamide.

Dilute aqueous solutions of sulfamic acid are stable for many months at room temperature but at higher temperatures hydrolysis to $NH_4[HSO_4]$ sets in. Alkali metal salts are stable in neutral and

alkaline solutions even at the bp. Sulfamic acid is a monobasic acid in water (see Fig. 15.50b for structure of the sulfamate ion). In liquid ammonia solutions it is dibasic and, with Na for example, it forms $NaNH.SO_3Na$. Sulfamic acid is oxidized to nitrogen and sulfate by Cl_2, Br_2 and ClO_3^-, e.g.:

$$2H[H_2NSO_3] + KClO_3 \longrightarrow N_2 + 2H_2SO_4$$
$$+ KCl + H_2O$$

Concentrated HNO_3 yields pure N_2O whilst aqueous HNO_2 reacts quantitatively to give N_2:

$$H[H_2NSO_3] + HNO_3 \longrightarrow H_2SO_4 + H_2O + N_2O$$
$$H[H_2NSO_3] + NaNO_2 \xrightarrow{acidify} NaHSO_4 + H_2O + N_2$$

This last reaction finds use in volumetric analysis. The use of sulfamic acid to stabilize chlorinated water depends on the equilibrium formation of *N*-chlorosulfamic acid, which reduces loss of chlorine by evaporation, and slowly re-releases hypochlorous acid by the reverse hydrolysis:

$$Cl_2 + H_2O \rightleftharpoons HOCl + HCl$$
$$H[H_2NSO_3] + HOCl \rightleftharpoons HN(Cl)SO_3H + H_2O$$
$$HOCl \longrightarrow HCl + \tfrac{1}{2}O_2$$

Sulfamide, $(H_2N)_2SO_2$, can be made by ammonolysis of SO_3 or O_2SCl_2. It is a colourless crystalline material, mp 93°, which begins to decompose above this temperature. It is soluble in water to give a neutral non-electrolytic solution but in boiling water it decomposes to ammonia and sulfuric acid. The structure (Fig. 15.50c)

278 E. B. BELL, Sulfamic acid and sulfamates, *Kirk–Othmer Encyclopedia of Chemical Technology*, 3rd edn., Vol. 21, pp. 940–60, Wiley, New York, 1983.

can be compared with those of sulfuric acid, $(HO)_2SO_2$ (p. 710) and the sulfuryl halides X_2SO_2 (p. 694).

(c) *Imido and nitrido derivatives of sulfuric acid*. In the preceding section the sulfamate ion and related species were regarded as being formed by replacement of an OH group in $(HO)SO_3^-$ or $(HO)_2SO_3$ by an NH_2 group. They could equally well be regarded as sulfonates of ammonia in which each H atom is successively replaced by SO_3^- (or SO_3H):

H—N(—H)—H　　　Ammonia

[O₃S—N(—H)—H]⁻

(Sulfamate)
Amidosulfate
Aminosulfonate

[O₃S—N(—H)—SO₃]²⁻

Imidodisulfate
Imidodisufonate

[O₃S—N(—SO₃)—SO₃]³⁻

Nitridotrisulfate
Nitrilotrisulfonate

Both sets of names are used in the literature. Free imidodisulfuric acid $HN(SO_3H)_2$ (which is isoelectronic with disulfuric acid $H_2S_2O_7$, p. 705) and free nitridotrisulfuric acid $N(SO_3H)_3$ are unstable, but their salts are well characterized and have been extensively studied.

Imidodisulfuric acid derivatives can be prepared from urea by using less sulfuric acid than required for sulfamic acid (p. 741):

$$4(H_2N)_2CO + 5H_2SO_4 \xrightarrow{\text{warm}} 4CO_2$$
$$+ 2HN(SO_3NH_4)_2 + (NH_4)_2SO_4$$

Addition of aqueous KOH liberates NH_3 and affords crystalline $HN(SO_3K)_2$ on evaporation. All 3 H atoms in $HN(SO_3H)_2$ can be replaced by NH_4 or M^I, e.g. the direct reaction of NH_3 and SO_3 yields the triammonium salt:

$$4NH_3 + 2SO_3 \longrightarrow NH_4[N(SO_3NH_4)_2]$$

Imidodisulfates can also be obtained by hydrolysis of nitridotrisulfates (see below). Figure 15.51 compares the structure of the imidodisulfate and parent disulfate ions, as determined from the potassium salts. Comparison with the hydroxylamine derivative $K[HN(OH)SO_3]$ (below) is also instructive.

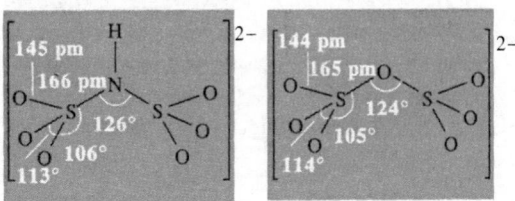

Figure 15.51 Comparison of the structures of the imidodisulfate and disulfate ions in their potassium salts.

Fluoro and chloro derivatives of imidodisulfuric acid can be made by reacting HSO_3F or HSO_3Cl (rather than H_2SO_4) with urea:

$$(H_2N)_2CO + 3HSO_3F \longrightarrow CO_2 + HN(SO_2F)_2$$
$$+ [NH_4][HSO_4] + HF$$

$HN(SO_2F)_2$ melts at $17°$, boils at $170°$ and can be further fluorinated with elemental F_2 at room temperature to give $FN(SO_2F)_2$, mp $-79.9°$, bp $60°$. The chloro derivative $HN(SO_2Cl)_2$ is a white crystalline compound, mp $37°$: it is made in better yield from sulfamic acid by the following reaction sequence:

$$2PCl_5 + H_2NHSO_3 \longrightarrow Cl_3P{=}NSO_2Cl$$
$$+ OPCl_3 + HCl$$

$$Cl_3P{=}NSO_2Cl + ClSO_3H \longrightarrow$$
$$HN(SO_2Cl)_2 + OPCl_3$$

Salts of nitridotrisulfuric acid, $N(SO_3M^I)_3$, are readily obtained by the exothermic reaction of nitrites with sulfites or hydrogen sulfites in hot aqueous solution:

$$KNO_2 + 4KHSO_3 \longrightarrow N(SO_3K)_3$$
$$+ K_2SO_3 + 2H_2O$$

The dihydrate crystallizes as the solution cools. Such salts are stable in alkaline solution but hydrolyse in acid solution to imidodisulfate (and then more slowly to sulfamic acid):

$$[N(SO_3)_3]^{3-} + H_3O^+ \longrightarrow$$
$$[HN(SO_3)_2]^{2-} + H_2SO_4$$

(d) *Hydrazine and hydroxylamine derivatives of sulfuric acid.* Hydrazine sulfonic acid, $H_2NNH.HSO_3$ is obtained as its hydrazinium salt by reacting anhydrous N_2H_4 with diluted gaseous SO_3 or its pyridine adduct:

$$C_5H_5NSO_3 + 2N_2H_4 \longrightarrow C_5H_5N$$
$$+ [N_2H_5]^+[H_2NNHSO_3]^-$$

The free acid is monobasic, pK 3.85; it is much more easily hydrolysed than sulfamic acid and has reducing properties comparable with those of hydrazine. Like sulfamic acid it exists as a zwitterion in the solid state: $^+H_3NNHSO_3^-$.

Symmetrical hydrazine disulfonic acid can be made by reacting a hydrazine sulfonate with a chlorosulfate:

$$H_2NNHSO_3^- + ClSO_3^- \longrightarrow HCl$$
$$+ [O_3SNHNHSO_3]^{2-}$$

Oxidation of the dipotassium salt with HOCl yields the azodisulfonate $KO_3SN{=}NSO_3K$. Numerous other symmetrical and unsymmetrical hydrazine polysulfonate derivatives are known.

With hydroxylamine, $HONH_2$, 4 of the 5 possible sulfonate derivatives have been prepared as anions of the following acids:

$HONHSO_3H$: hydroxylamine N-sulfonic acid
$HON(SO_3H)_2$: hydroxylamine N,N-disulfonic acid
$(HSO_3)ONHSO_3H$: hydroxylamine O,N-disulfonic acid
$(HSO_3)ON(SO_3H)_2$: hydroxylamine trisulfonic acid

The first of these can be made by careful hydrolysis of the N,N-disulfonate which is itself made by the reaction of SO_2 and a nitrite in cold alkaline solution:

$$KNO_2 + KHSO_3 + SO_2 \longrightarrow HON(SO_3K)_2$$

The potassium salt readily crystallizes from the cold solution thus preventing further reaction with the hydrogen sulfate to give nitridotrisulfate (p. 743). The structure of the hydroxylamine N-sulfonate ion is shown in Fig. 15.52a. The closely related N-nitrosohydroxylamine N-sulfonate ion (Fig. 15.52b) can be made directly by absorbing NO in alkaline K_2SO_3 solution: the 6 atoms ONN(O)SO all lie in one plane and the interatomic distances suggest an S–N single bond but considerable additional π bonding in the N–N bond.

Oxidation of hydroxylamine N,N-disulfonate with permanganate or PbO_2 yields the intriguing

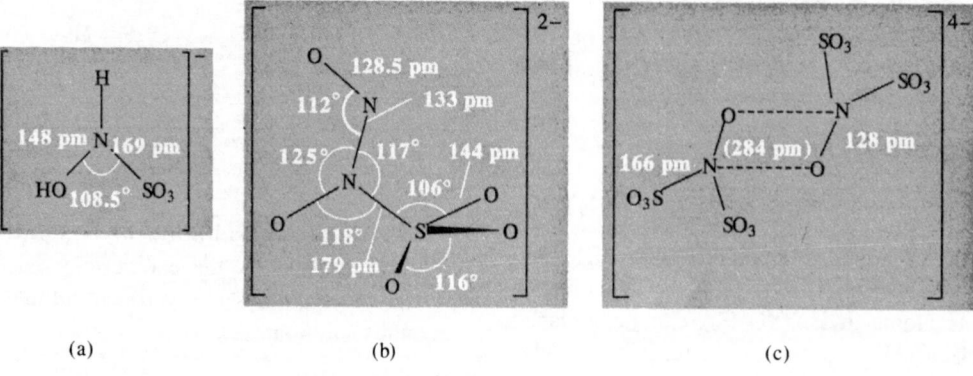

Figure 15.52 Structures of various S–N oxoanions: (a) hydroxylamine-N-sulfonate, (b) N-nitrosohydroxylamine N-sulfonate and (c) the dimeric anion in Frémy's salt {$K_2[ON(SO_3)_2]$}$_2$.

nitrosodisulfonate $K_2[ON(SO_3)_2]$: this was first isolated by Frémy as a yellow solid which was subsequently shown to be dimeric and diamagnetic due to the formation of long $N \cdots O$ bonds in the crystal (Fig. 15.52c). However, in aqueous solution the anion dissociates reversibly into the deep violet, paramagnetic monomer $[ON(SO_3)_2]^{2-}$.

Hydroxylamine trisulfonates, e.g. $(KO_3S)ON(SO_3K)_2$ are made by the reaction of K_2SO_3 with potassium nitrosodisulfonate (Frémy's salt). Acidification of the product results in rapid hydrolysis to the *O,N*-disulfonate which can be isolated as the exclusive product:

$$(KO_3S)ON(SO_3K)_2 + H_2O \longrightarrow$$

$$(KO_3S)ONH(SO_3K) + KHSO_4$$

Sulfonic acids containing nitrogen have long been implicated as essential intermediates in the synthesis of H_2SO_4 by the lead-chamber process (p. 708) and, as shown by F. Seel and his group, the crucial stage is the oxidation of sulfite ions by the nitrosyl ion NO^+:

$$SO_3^{2-} + NO^+ \longrightarrow [ONSO_3]^- \xrightarrow{NO^+} 2NO + SO_3$$

The NO^+ ions are thought to be generated by the following sequence of reactions:

$$NO + \tfrac{1}{2}O_2 \longrightarrow NO_2 \quad \text{(gas phase)}$$

$$\left.\begin{array}{l} NO_2 + NO + H_2O \longrightarrow 2\{ONOH\} \\ SO_2 + H_2O \longrightarrow H_2SO_3 \end{array}\right\} \text{(surface reactions)}$$

$$H_2SO_3 \longrightarrow H^+ + HSO_3^-$$

$$\{ONOH\} + H^+ \longrightarrow NO^+ + H_2O$$

The nitrososulfonate intermediate $[ONSO_3]^-$ can also react with SO_3^{2-} to give the hydroxylamine disulfonate ion which can likewise be oxidized by NO^+:

$$[ON(SO_3)_2]^{3-} + NO^+ \longrightarrow N_2O + SO_3 + SO_4^{2-}$$

In a parallel reaction the $[ONSO_3]^-$ intermediate can react with SO_2 to form nitrilotrisulfonate:

$$[ON(SO_3)_2]^{3-} + SO_2 \longrightarrow [N(SO_3)_3]^{3-}$$

This then reacts with NO^+ to form N_2, SO_3 and SO_4^{2-}.

(e) *Selected other sulfur–nitrogen compounds.* There are innumerable organo–sulfur–nitrogen compounds which fall outside the scope of the present treatment. Even without the presence of skeletal carbon atoms, a rich variety of novel reactions and structural types is being explored as briefly indicated on the preceding page by a selection of examples which is itself far from complete:[279-282] (E = S, Se).

[279] N. BURFORD,   T. CHIVERS,   M. N. S. RAO   and J. F. RICHARDSON, *Inorg. Chem.* **23**, 1946–52 (1984).

[280] M. HEBERHOLD, K. GULDAR, A. GIEREN, C. RUIZ-PÉREZ and T. HÜBNER, *Angew. Chem. Int. Edn. Engl.* **26**, 82–3 (1987).

[281] P. F. KELLY,   A. M. Z. SLAWIN,   D. J. WILLIAMS   and J. D. WOOLLINS, *Polyhedron* **9**, 2659–62 (1990).

[282] T. CHIVERS, D. D. DOXSEE, M. EDWARDS and R. W. HILTS, in R. STEUDEL (ed.), *The Chemistry of Inorganic Ring Systems*, Elsevier, Amsterdam, 1992, Chap. 15, pp. 271–94.

16

Selenium, Tellurium and Polonium

16.1 The Elements[1-4]

16.1.1 Introduction: history, abundance, distribution

Tellurium was the first of these three elements to be discovered. It was isolated by the Austrian chemist F. J. Müller von Reichenstein in 1782 a few years after the discovery of oxygen by J. Priestley and C. W. Scheele (p. 600), though the periodic group relationship between the elements was not apparent until nearly a century later (p. 20). Tellurium was first observed in ores mined in the gold districts of Transylvania; Müller called it *metallum problematicum* or *aurum paradoxum* because it showed none of the properties of the expected antimony.[5] The name tellurium (Latin *tellus*, earth) is due to another Austrian chemist, M. H. Klaproth, the discoverer of zirconium and uranium.

Selenium was isolated some 35 y after tellurium and, since the new element resembled tellurium, it was named from the Greek σελήνη, *selene*, the moon. The discovery was made in 1817 by the Swedish chemist J. J. Berzelius (discoverer of Si, Ce and Th) and J. G. Gahn (discoverer of Mn);[5] they observed a reddish-brown deposit during the burning of sulfur obtained from Fahlun copper pyrites, and showed it to be volatile and readily reducible to the new element.

The discovery of polonium by Marie Curie in 1898 is a story that has been told many

[1] K. W. BAGNALL, Selenium, tellurium and polonium, Chap. 24 in *Comprehensive Inorganic Chemistry*, Vol. 2, pp. 935–1008, Pergamon Press, Oxford, 1973.

[2] R. A. ZINGARO and W. C. COOPER (eds.), *Selenium*, Van Nostrand, Reinhold, New York, 1974, 835 pp.

[3] W. C. COOPER (ed.), *Tellurium*, Van Nostrand, Reinhold, New York, 1971, 437 pp.

[4] N. B. MIKEEV, Polonium, *Chemiker Zeitung* **102**, 277–86 (1978). See also K. W. BAGNALL, *Radiochim. Acta*. **32**, 153–61 (1983). Polonium, *Gmelin Handbook of Inorganic and Organometallic Chemistry*, Suppl. Vol. 1, Springer-Verlag, Berlin, 1990, 425 pp.

[5] M. E. WEEKS, *Discovery of the Elements*, 6th edn., Journal of Chemical Education, Easton, Pa., 1956: pp. 303–37.

times.[6] The immense feat of processing huge quantities of uranium ore and of following the progress of separation by the newly discovered phenomenon of radioactivity (together with her parallel isolation of radium by similar techniques, p. 108), earned her the Nobel Prize for Chemistry in 1911. She had already shared the 1902 Nobel Prize for Physics with H. A. Becquerel and her husband P. Curie for their joint researches on radioactivity. Indeed, this was the first time, though by no means the last, that invisible quantities of a new element had been identified, separated, and investigated solely by means of its radioactivity. The element was named after Marie Curie's home country, Poland.

Selenium and tellurium are comparatively rare elements, being sixty-sixth and seventy-third respectively in order of crustal abundance; polonium, on account of its radioactive decay, is exceedingly unabundant. Selenium comprises some 0.05 ppm of the earth's crust and is therefore similar to Ag and Hg, which are each about 0.08 ppm, and Pd (0.015 ppm). Tellurium, at about 0.002 ppm can be compared with Au (0.004 ppm) and Ir (0.001 ppm). Both elements are occasionally found native, in association with sulfur, and many of their minerals occur together with the sulfides of chalcophilic metals (p. 648),[2,3] e.g. Cu, Ag, Au; Zn, Cd, Hg; Fe, Co, Ni; Pb, As, Bi. Sometimes the minerals are partly oxidized, e.g. $MSeO_3.2H_2O$ (M = Ni, Cu, Pb); $PbTeO_3$, $Fe_2(TeO_3)_3.2H_2O$, $FeTeO_4$, Hg_2TeO_4, $Bi_2TeO_4(OH)_4$, etc. Selenolite, SeO_2, and tellurite, TeO_2, have also been found.

Polonium has no stable isotopes, all 27 isotopes being radioactive; of these only ^{210}Po occurs naturally, as the penultimate member of the radium decay series:

$$^{210}_{82}Pb \xrightarrow[22.3\ y]{\beta^-} {}^{210}_{83}Bi \xrightarrow[5.01\ d]{\beta^-} {}^{210}_{84}Po \xrightarrow[138.38\ d]{\alpha} {}^{206}_{82}Pb$$

RaD   RaE   RaF   RaG

Because of the fugitive nature of ^{210}Po, uranium ores contain only about 0.1 mg Po per tonne of ore (i.e. 10^{-4} ppm). The overall abundance of Po in crustal rocks of the earth is thus of the order of 3×10^{-10} ppm.

16.1.2 Production and uses of the elements [2-4,7]

The main source of Se and Te is the anode slime deposited during the electrolytic refining of Cu (p. 1175); this mud also contains commercial quantities of Ag, Au and the platinum metals. Direct recovery from minerals is not usually economically viable because of their rarity. Selenium is also recovered from the sludge accumulating in sulfuric acid plants and from electrostatic precipitator dust collected during the processing of Cu and Pb. Detailed procedures for isolation and purification depend on the relative concentrations of Se, Te and other impurities, but a typical sequence involves oxidation by roasting in air with soda ash followed by leaching:

$$Ag_2Se + Na_2CO_3 + O_2 \xrightarrow{650°}$$
$$2Ag + Na_2SeO_3 + CO_2$$

$$Cu_2Se + Na_2CO_3 + 2O_2 \longrightarrow$$
$$2CuO + Na_2SeO_3 + CO_2$$

$$Cu_2Te + Na_2CO_3 + 2O_2 \longrightarrow$$
$$2CuO + Na_2TeO_3 + CO_2$$

In the absence of soda ash, SeO_2 can be volatilized directly from the roast:

$$Cu_2Se + \tfrac{3}{2}O_2 \xrightarrow{300°} CuO + CuSeO_3 \xrightarrow{650°}$$
$$2CuO + SeO_2$$

$$Ag_2SeO_3 \xrightarrow{700°} 2Ag + SeO_2 + \tfrac{1}{2}O_2$$

[6] Ref. 5, Chap. 29, pp. 803–43. See also E. FARBER, *Nobel Prize Winners in Chemistry 1901–1961*, Abelard-Schuman, London, Marie Sklodowska Curie, pp. 45–8. F. C. WOOD, Marie Curie, in E. FARBER (ed.), *Great Chemists*, pp. 1263–75. Interscience, New York, 1961.

[7] *Kirk–Othmer Encyclopedia of Chemical Technology*, 4th edn., 1997, Selenium and Selenium Compounds, Vol. 21, pp. 686–719, Tellurium and tellurium compounds, Vol. 22, pp. 659–79, 1983.

Separation of Se and Te can also be achieved by neutralizing the alkaline selenite and tellurite leach with H_2SO_4; this precipitates the tellurium as a hydrous dioxide and leaves the more acidic selenous acid, H_2SeO_3, in solution from which 99.5% pure Se can be precipitated by SO_2:[†]

$$H_2SeO_3 + 2SO_2 + H_2O \longrightarrow Se + 2H_2SO_4$$

Tellurium is obtained by dissolving the dioxide in aqueous NaOH followed by electrolytic reduction:

$$Na_2TeO_3 + H_2O \longrightarrow Te + 2NaOH + O_2$$

The NaOH is regenerated and only make-up quantities are required. However, the detailed processes adopted industrially to produce Se and Te are much more complex and sophisticated than this outline implies.[2,3,7]

World production of refined Se in 1995 was ~2000 tonnes the largest producers being Japan (600 t), USA (360 t) and Canada (300 t). The pattern of use no doubt varies somewhat from country to country, but in the USA the largest single use of the element (35%) is as a decolorizor of glass (0.01–0.15 kg/tonne). Higher concentrations (1–2 kg/tonne) yield delicate pink glasses. The glorious selenium ruby glasses, which are the most brilliant reds known to glass-makers, are obtained by incorporating solid particles of cadmium sulfoselenide in the glass; the deepest ruby colour is obtained when Cd(S,Se) has about 10% CdS, but as the relative concentration of CdS increases the colour moderates to red (40% CdS), orange (75%) and yellow (100%). Cadmium sulfoselenides are also widely used as heat-resistant red pigments in plastics, paints, inks and enamels. Another very important application of elemental Se is in xerography, which has developed during the past four decades into the pre-eminent process for document copying, as witnessed by

the ubiquitous presence of xerox machines in offices and libraries (see Panel). Related uses are as a photoconductor (selenium photoelectric cells) and as a rectifier in semiconductor devices (p. 258). Small amounts of ferroselenium are used to improve the casting, forging and machinability of stainless steels, and the dithiocarbamate $[Se(S_2CNEt_2)_4]$ finds some use in the processing of natural and synthetic rubbers. Selenium pharmaceuticals comprise a further small outlet. In addition to Se, Fe/Se, Cd(S,Se) and $[Se(S_2CNEt_2)_4]$ the main commercially available compounds of Se are SeO_2, Na_2SeO_3, Na_2SeO_4, H_2SeO_4 and $SeOCl_2$ (q.v.).

Production of Te is on a much smaller scale: *ca.* 350 tonnes in 1978, dominated by USA, Canada and Japan. More than 70% of the Te is used in iron and steel production and in non-ferrous metals and alloys, and 25% for chemicals. A small amount of TeO_2 is used in tinting glass, and Te compounds find some use as catalysts and as curing agents in the rubber industry. In addition to Te, Fe/Te and TeO_2, commercially important compounds include Na_2TeO_4 and $[Te(S_2CNEt_2)_4]$.

Polonium, because of its very low abundance and very short half-life, is not obtained from natural sources. Virtually all our knowledge of the physical and chemical properties of the element come from studies on ^{210}Po which is best made by neutron irradiation of ^{209}Bi in a nuclear reactor:

$$^{209}_{83}Bi(n,\gamma)^{210}_{83}Bi \xrightarrow[t_{\frac{1}{2}}5.01\,d]{\beta^-} {}^{210}_{84}Po \xrightarrow[t_{\frac{1}{2}}138.38\,d]{\alpha} \cdots$$

It will be recalled that ^{209}Bi is 100% abundant and is the heaviest stable nuclide of any element (p. 550), but it is essential to use very high purity Bi to prevent unwanted nuclear side-reactions which would contaminate the product ^{210}Po; in particular Sc, Ag, As, Sb and Te must be <0.1 ppm and Fe <10 ppm. Polonium can be obtained directly in milligram amounts by fractional vacuum distillation from the metallic bismuth. Alternatively, it can be deposited spontaneously by electrochemical replacement onto the surface of a less electropositive metal

---

[†] Very pure Se can be obtained by heating the crude material in H_2 at 650° and then decomposing the H_2Se so formed by passing the gas through a silica tube at 1000°. Any H_2S present, being more stable than H_2Se, passes through the tube unchanged, whereas hydrides which are less stable than H_2Se, such as those of Te, P, As, Sb, are not formed in the initial reaction at 650°.

Xerography

The invention of xerography by C. F. Carlson (USA) in the period 1934–42 was the culmination of a prolonged and concerted attack on the problem of devising a rapid, cheap and dry process for direct document copying without the need for the intermediate formation of a permanent photographic "negative", or even the use of specially prepared photographic paper for the "print". The discovery that vacuum-deposited amorphous or vitreous selenium was the almost ideal photoconductor for xerography was made in the Battelle Memorial Institute (Ohio, USA) in 1948. The dramatic success of these twin developments is witnessed by the vast number of xerox machines in daily use throughout the world today. However, early xerox equipment was not automatic. Models introduced in 1951 became popular for making offset masters, and rotary xerographic machines were introduced in 1959, but it was only after the introduction of the Xerox 914 copier in the early 1960s that electrophotography came of age. The word "xerography" derives from the Greek ξηρό, *xero* dry, γραφή, *graphy*, writing.

The sequential steps involved in commercial machines which employ reusable photoreceptors for generating xerox copies are shown in the figure[2] and further elucidated below.

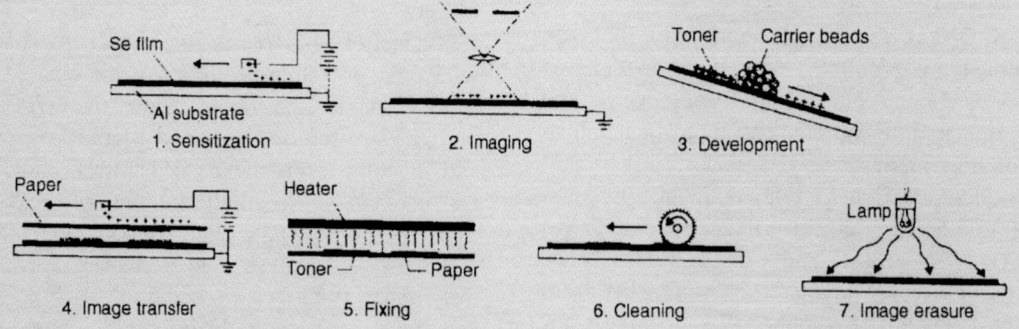

1. Sensitization   2. Imaging   3. Development

4. Image transfer   5. Fixing   6. Cleaning   7. Image erasure

1. *Sensitization of the photoreceptor*. The photoreceptor consists of a vacuum-deposited film of amorphous Se, $\sim$50 μm thick, on an Al substrate; this is sensitized by electrostatic charging from a corona discharge using a field of $\sim$10^5 V cm^{-1}.

2. *Exposure and latent image formation*. The sensitized photoreceptor is exposed to a light and dark image pattern; in the light areas the surface potential of the photoconductor is reduced due to a photoconductive discharge. Since current can only flow perpendicular to the surface, this step produces an electrostatic-potential distribution which replicates the pattern of the image.

3. *Development of the image*. This is done using a mixture of black (or coloured) toner particles, typically 10 μm in diameter, and spherical carrier beads ($\sim$100 μm diameter). The toner particles become charged triboelectrically (i.e. by friction) and are preferentially attracted either by the surface fringe field at light–dark boundaries or (in systems with a developing electrode) by the absolute potential in the dark areas; they adhere to the photoreceptor, thus forming a visible image corresponding to the latent electrostatic image.

4. *Image transfer*. This is best done electrostatically by charging the print paper to attract the toner particles.

5. *Print fixing*. The powder image is made permanent by fusing or melting the toner particles into the surface of the paper, either by heat, by heat and pressure, or by solvent vapours.

6. *Cleaning*. Any toner still left on the photoreceptor after the transfer process is removed with a cloth web or brush, or by a combination of electrostatic and mechanical means.

7. *Image erasure*. The potential differences due to latent image formation are removed by flooding the photoreceptors with a sufficiently intense light source to drive the surface potential to some uniformly low value (typically $\sim$100 V corresponding to fields of $\sim$10^4 V cm^{-1}); the photoreceptor is then ready for another print cycle.

The elegance, cheapness and convenience of xerography for document copying has led to rapid commercial development on a colossal scale throughout the world.

such as Ag. Solution techniques are unsuitable except on the trace scale (submicrogram amounts) because of the radiation damage caused by the intense radioactivity (p. 753). All

applications of Po depend on its radioactivity: it is an almost pure α-emitter (E_α 5.30 MeV) and only 0.0011% of the activity is due to γ-rays (E_{max} 0.803 MeV). Because of its short half-life (138.38 d) this entails a tremendous energy output of 141 W per gram of metal: in consequence, there is considerable self-heating of Po and its compounds. The element can therefore be used as a convenient light-weight heat source, or to generate spontaneous and reliable thermoelectric power for space satellites and lunar stations, since no moving parts are involved. Polonium also finds limited use as a neutron generator when combined with a light element of high α,n cross-section such as beryllium: $^{9}_{4}Be(\alpha,n)^{12}_{6}C$. The best yield (93 neutrons per $10^6\alpha$-particles) is obtained with a BeO target.

16.1.3 Allotropy

At least eight structurally distinct forms of Se are known: the three red monoclinic polymorphs (α, β and γ) consist of Se_8 rings and differ only in the intermolecular packing of the rings in the crystals. Other ring sizes have recently been synthesized in the red allotropes *cyclo*-Se_6 and *cyclo*-Se_7, and the heterocyclic analogues *cyclo*-Se_5S and *cyclo*-Se_5S_2.[8] The grey, "metallic", hexagonal crystalline form features helical polymeric chains and these also occur, somewhat deformed, in amorphous red Se. Finally, vitreous black Se, the ordinary commercial form of the element, comprises an extremely complex and irregular structure of large polymeric rings having up to 1000 atoms per ring.

The α- and β-forms of red crystalline Se_8 are obtained respectively by the slow and rapid evaporation of CS_2 or benzene solutions of black vitreous Se and more recently a third (γ) form of red crystalline Se_8 was obtained from the reaction

of dipiperidinotetraselane with solvent CS_2:[9]

$$[Se_4(NC_5H_{10})_2] \xrightarrow{2CS_2} [Se(S_2CNC_5H_{10})_2] + \tfrac{3}{8}Se_8$$

All three allotropes consist of almost identical puckered Se_8 rings similar to those found in *cyclo*-S_8 (p. 658) and of average dimensions Se–Se 233.5 pm, angle Se–Se–Se 105.7°, dihedral angle 101.3° (Fig. 16.1a). The intermolecular packing is most efficient for the α-form. [It is interesting to note that β-Se_8 was at one time thought, on the basis of an X-ray crystal structure determination, to be an 8-membered *chain* with the configuration of a puckered ring in which 1 Se-Se bond had been broken; the error was corrected in a very perceptive paper by L. Pauling and his co-workers.[10]] Both α- and β-Se_8 (and presumably also γ-Se_8) are appreciably soluble in CS_2 to give red solutions.

Grey, hexagonal, "metallic" selenium is thermodynamically the most stable form of the element and can be formed by warming other modifications; it can also be obtained by slowly cooling molten Se or by condensing Se vapour at a temperature just below the mp (220.5°). It is a photoconductor (p. 750) and is the only modification which conducts electricity. The structure (Fig. 16.1b) consists of unbranched helical chains with Se–Se 237.3 pm, angle Se–Se–Se 103.1°, and a repeat unit every 3 atoms (cf. fibrous sulfur, p. 660). The closest Se $\cdots$ Se distance between chains is 343.6 pm, which is very close to that in Te_x (350 pm) (see below). Grey Se_x is insoluble in CS_2 and its density, 4.82 g cm^{-3}, is the highest of any modification of the element. A related allotrope is red amorphous Se, formed by condensation of Se vapour onto a cold surface or by precipitation from aqueous solutions of selenous acid by treatment with SO_2 (p. 755) or other reducing agents such as hydrazine hydrate. It is slightly soluble in CS_2, and has a deformed chain structure but does not conduct electricity. The heat of transformation to the stable hexagonal

[8] R. STEUDEL and E.-M. STRAUSS, in H. J. EMELÉUS and A. G. SHARPE, *Adv. Inorg. Chem. Radiochem.* **28**, 135–66 (1984). R. STEUDEL, M. PAPAVASSILIOU, E.-M. STRAUSS and R. LAITINEN, *Angew. Chem. Int. Edn. Engl.* **25**, 99–101 (1986) and references cited therein. See also R. STEUDEL and M. PAPAVASSILIOU, *Polyhedron* **7**, 581–3 (1988). R. STEUDEL, M. PRIDÖHL, H. HARTL and I. BRÜGAM, *Z. anorg. allg. Chem.* **619**, 1589–96 (1993).

[9] O. FOSS and V. JANICKIS, *J. Chem. Soc., Chem. Commun.*, 834–5 (1977).
[10] R. E. MARSH, L. PAULING and J. D. MCCULLOUGH, *Acta Cryst.* **6**, 71–5 (1953).

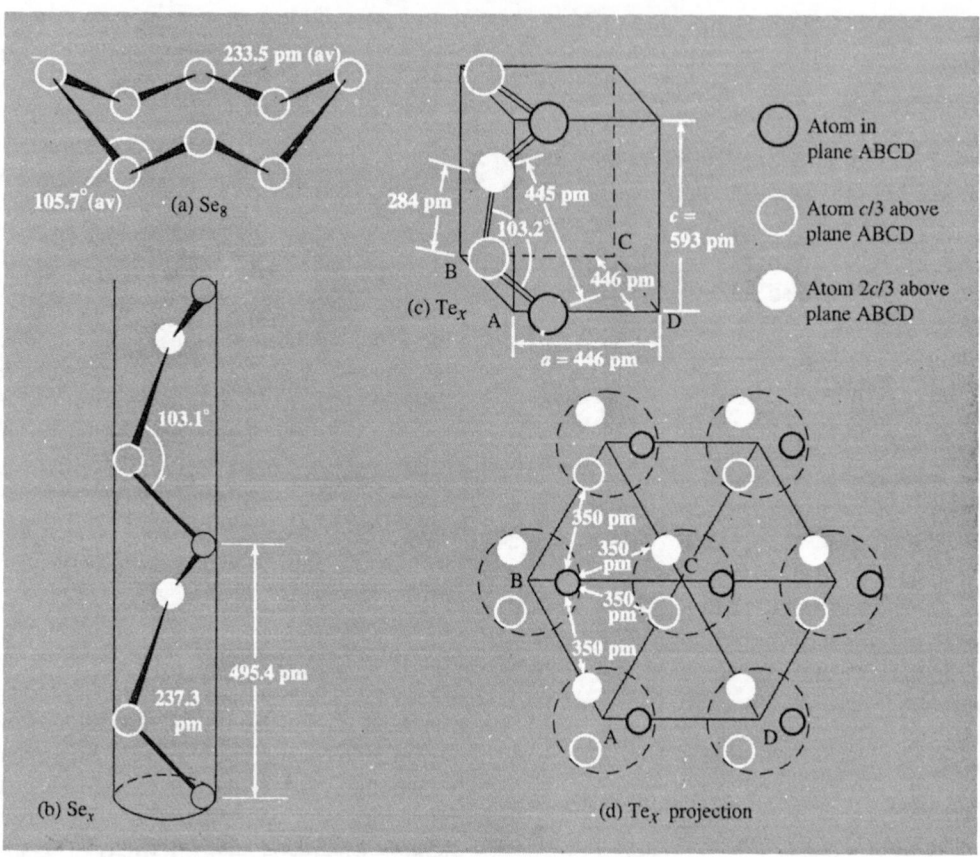

Figure 16.1   Structures of various allotropes of selenium and the structure of crystalline tellurium: (a) the Se_8 unit in α-, β- and γ-red selenium; (b) the helical Se chain along the c-axis in hexagonal grey selenium; (c) the similar helical chain in crystalline tellurium shown in perspective; and (d) projection of the tellurium structure on a plane perpendicular to the c-axis.

grey form has been variously quoted but is in the region of 5–10 kJ per mole of Se atoms.

Vitreous, black Se is the ordinary commercial form of the element, obtained by rapid cooling of molten Se; it is a brittle, opaque, bluish-black lustrous solid which is somewhat soluble in CS_2. It does not melt sharply but softens at about $50°$ and rapidly transforms to hexagonal grey Se when heated to $180°$ (or at lower temperatures when catalysed by halogens, amines, etc.). There has been much discussion about the structure but it seems to comprise rings of varying size up to quite high molecular weights. Presumably these rings cleave and polymerize into helical chains under the influence of thermal soaking or

catalysts. The great interest in the various allotropes of selenium and their stabilization or interconversion, stems from its use in photocells, rectifiers, and xerography (p. 750).[2]

Tellurium has only one crystalline form and this is composed of a network of spiral chains similar to those in hexagonal Se (Fig. 16.1c and d). Although the intra-chain Te–Te distance of 284 pm and the c dimension of the crystal (593 pm) are both substantially greater than for Se_x (as expected), nevertheless the closest inter-atomic distance between chains is almost identical for the 2 elements (Te $\cdots$ Te 350 pm). Accordingly the elements form a continuous range of solid solutions in which there is a random

Atomic and physical properties

Table 16.1 Production and properties of long-lived Po isotopes

Isotope	Production	$t_{\frac{1}{2}}$	E_γ/MeV	A_r (relative atomic mass)
^{208}Po	^{209}Bi(d,3n) or (p,2n)	2.898 y	5.11	207.9812
^{209}Po	^{209}Bi(d,2n) or (p,n)	102 y	4.88	208.9824
^{210}Po	^{209}Bi(n,γ)	138.376 d	5.305	209.9828

alternation of Se and Te atoms in the helical chains.[11] The homogeneous alloys Se_xTe_{1-x} can also, most remarkably, be prepared directly by hydrazine reduction of glycol solutions of $xSeO_2$ and $(1 - x)TeO_2$ or other compounds of Se^{IV} and Te^{IV} such as dialkylselenites and tetraalkoxytelluranes); the lattice parameters and mp of the alloys vary steadily between those of the two end members Se and Te.[12] The rapid diminution in allotropic complexity from sulfur through selenium to tellurium is notable.

Polonium is unique in being the only element known to crystallize in the simple cubic form (6 nearest neighbours at 335 pm). This α-form distorts at about 36° to a simple rhombohedral modification in which each Po also has 6 nearest neighbours at 335 pm. The precise temperature of the phase change is difficult to determine because of the self-heating of crystalline Po (p. 751) and it appears that both modifications can coexist from about 18° to 54°. Both are silvery-white metallic crystals with substantially higher electrical conductivity than Te.

16.1.4 Atomic and physical properties

Selenium, Te and Po are the three heaviest members of Group 16 and, like their congenors O and S, have two p electrons less than the next following noble gases. Selenium is normally said to have 6 stable isotopes though the heaviest of these (^{82}Se, 8.73% abundant) is actually an extremely long-lived β^- emitter,

$t_{\frac{1}{2}}$ 1.4×10^{20} y. The most abundant isotope is ^{80}Se (49.61%), and all have zero nuclear spin except the 7.63% abundant ^{77}Se $(I = \frac{1}{2})$, which is finding increasing use in nmr experiments.[13] Because of the plethora of isotopes the atomic weight is only known to about 1 part in 2600 (p. 16). Tellurium, with 8 naturally occurring stable isotopes, likewise suffers some imprecision in its atomic weight (1 part in 4300). The most abundant isotopes are ^{130}Te (33.87%) and ^{128}Te (31.70%), and again all have zero nuclear spin except the nmr active isotopes ^{123}Te (0.905%) and ^{125}Te (7.12%), which have spin $\frac{1}{2}$.[13] ^{125}Te also has a low-lying nuclear isomer ^{125m}Te which decays by pure γ emission (E_γ 35.48 keV, $t_{\frac{1}{2}}$ 58 d) — this has found much use in Mössbauer spectroscopy.[14] Polonium, as we have seen (p. 748), has no stable isotopes. The 3 longest lived, together with their modes of production and other properties, are as shown in Table 16.1.

Several atomic and physical properties of the elements are given in Table 16.2. The trends to larger size, lower ionization energy and lower electronegativity are as expected. The trend to metallic conductivity is also noteworthy; indeed, Po resembles its horizontal neighbours Bi, Pb and Tl not only in this but in its moderately high density and notably low mp and bp.

[11] A. A. Kudryavtsev, *The Chemistry and Technology of Selenium and Tellurium*, Collet's Publishers, London, 1974, 278 pp.

[12] T. W. Smith, S. D. Smith and S. S. Badesha, *J. Am. Chem. Soc.* **106**, 7247–8 (1984).

[13] C. Rodger, N. Sheppard, H. C. E. McFarlane, and W. McFarlane, in R. K. Harris and B. R. Mann (eds.), *NMR and the Periodic Table*, pp. 402–19. Academic Press, London, 1978. H. C. E. McFarlane and W. McFarlane, in J. Mason (ed.) *Multinuclear NMR* pp. 417–35, Plenum Press, New York, 1987.

[14] N. N. Greenwood and T. C. Gibb, *Mössbauer Spectroscopy*, pp. 452–62, Chapman & Hall, London, 1971. F. J. Berry, Chap. 8 in G. J. Long (ed.) *Mössbauer Spectroscopy Applied to Inorganic Chemistry*, Vol. 2, Plenum Press, New York 1987, pp. 343–90.

Table 16.2 Some atomic and physical properties of selenium, tellurium and polonium

Property	Se	Te	Po
Atomic number	34	52	84
Number of stable isotopes	6	8	0
Electronic structure	$[Ar]3d^{10}4s^24p^4$	$[Kr]4d^{10}5s^25p^4$	$[Xe]4f^{14}5d^{10}6s^26p^4$
Atomic weight	78.96($\pm$ 0.03)	127.60($\pm$ 0.03)	(210)
Atomic radius (12-coordinate)/pm[a]	140[a]	160[a]	164[a]
Ionic radius/pm (M^{2-})	198	221	(230?)
(M^{4+})	50	97	94
(M^{6+})	42	56	67
Ionization energy/kJ mol^{-1}	940.7	869.0	813.0
Pauling electronegativity	2.4	2.1	2.0
Density(25°)/g cm^{-3})	Hexag 4.189 α-monoclinic 4.389 Vitreous 4.285	6.25	α9.142 β9.352
MP/°C	217	452	246–254
BP/°C	685	990	962
$\Delta H_{atomization}$/kJ mol^{-1}	206.7	192	—
Electrical resistivity(25°)/ohm cm	$10^{10[b]}$	1	α4.2 $\times 10^{-5}$ β4.4 $\times 10^{-5}$
Band energy gap E_g/kJ mol^{-1}	178	32.2	0

[a]The 2-coordinate covalent radius is 119 pm for elemental Se and 142 pm for Te; the 6-coordinate metallic radius of Po is 168 pm.

[b]Depends markedly on purity, temperature and photon flux; resistivity of liquid Se at 400° is 1.3×10^5 ohm cm.

16.1.5 Chemical reactivity and trends

The elements in Group 16 share with the preceding main-group elements the tendency towards increasing metallic character as the atomic weight increases within the group. Thus O and S are insulators, Se and Te are semiconductors and Po is a metal. Parallel with this trend is the gradual emergence of cationic (basic) properties with Te, and these are even more pronounced with Po. For example, Se is not appreciably attacked by dilute HCl whereas Te dissolves to some extent in the presence of air; Po dissolves readily to yield pink solutions of Po^{II} which are then rapidly oxidized further to yellow Po^{IV} by the products of radiolytic decomposition of the solvent. Likewise, the structure and bonding of the halides of these elements depends markedly on both the electronegativity of the halogen and on the oxidation state of the central element, thereby paralleling the "ionic-covalent" transition which has already been discussed for the halides of P (p. 499), As and Sb (p. 558), and S (p. 691).

Selenium, Te and Po combine directly with most elements, though less readily than do O and S. The most stable compounds are (a) the selenides, tellurides and polonides (M^{2-}) formed with the strongly positive elements of Groups 1, 2 and the lanthanides, and (b) the compounds with the electronegative elements O, F and Cl in which the oxidation states are +2, +4 and +6. The compounds tend to be less stable than the corresponding compounds of S (or O), and there are few analogues of the extensive range of sulfur–nitrogen compounds (p. 721). A similar trend (also noted in the preceding groups) is the decreasing thermal stability of the hydrides: $H_2O > H_2S > H_2Se > H_2Te > H_2Po$. Selenium and tellurium share to a limited extent sulfur's great propensity for catenation (see allotropy of the elements, polysulfanes, halides, etc.).

As found in preceding groups, there is a diminution in the stability of multiple bonds (e.g. to C, N, O) and a corresponding decrease in their occurrence as the atomic number of the group element increases. Thus O=C=O and (to a lesser extent) S=C=S are stable, whereas

Se=C=Se polymerizes readily, Se=C=Te is unstable and Te=C=Te is unknown. Again, SO$_2$ is a (nonlinear) gaseous molecule, $\underset{O}{\overset{S}{\diagup}}\underset{O}{\diagdown}$, whereas SeO$_2$ is a chain polymer −O−Se(=O)− (p. 779) and TeO$_2$ features 4-coordinate pseudo-trigonal-bipyramidal units {:TeO$_4$} which are singly-bonded into extended layer or 3D structures (p. 779); in PoO$_2$ the coordination number increases still further to 8 and the compound adopts the typical "ionic" fluorite structure (p. 118). It can be seen that double bonds are less readily formed between 2 elements the greater the electronegativity difference between them and the smaller the sum of their individual electronegativities; this is paralleled by a diminution in double-bond formation with increasing size of the more electropositive element and the consequent decrease in bond energy.

The redox properties of the elements also show interesting trends. In common with several

elements immediately following the first (3d) transition series (especially Ge, As, Se, Br) selenium shows a marked resistance to oxidation up to its group valency, i.e. Se^{VI}. For example, whereas HNO$_3$ readily oxidizes S to H$_2$SO$_4$, selenium gives H$_2$SeO$_3$. Again dehydration of H$_2$SO$_4$ with P$_2$O$_5$ yields SO$_3$ whereas H$_2$SeO$_4$ gives SeO$_2$ + $\frac{1}{2}$O$_2$. Likewise S forms a wide range of sulfones, R$_2$SO$_2$, but very few selenones are known; thus, Ph$_2$SeO is not oxidized either by HNO$_3$ or by acidified K$_2$Cr$_2$O$_7$, and alkaline KMnO$_4$ is required to produce Ph$_2$SeO$_2$ (mp 155°). As noted in the isolation of the element (p. 749), SO$_2$ precipitates Se from acidified solutions of Se^{IV}.

The standard reduction potentials of the elements in acid and alkaline solutions are summarized in the schemes below.[15] It is

15 A. J. BARD, R. PARSONS and J. JORDAN, (eds.) *Standard Potentials in Aqueous Solution*, (IUPAC) Marcel Dekker, New York, 1985, 834 pp.

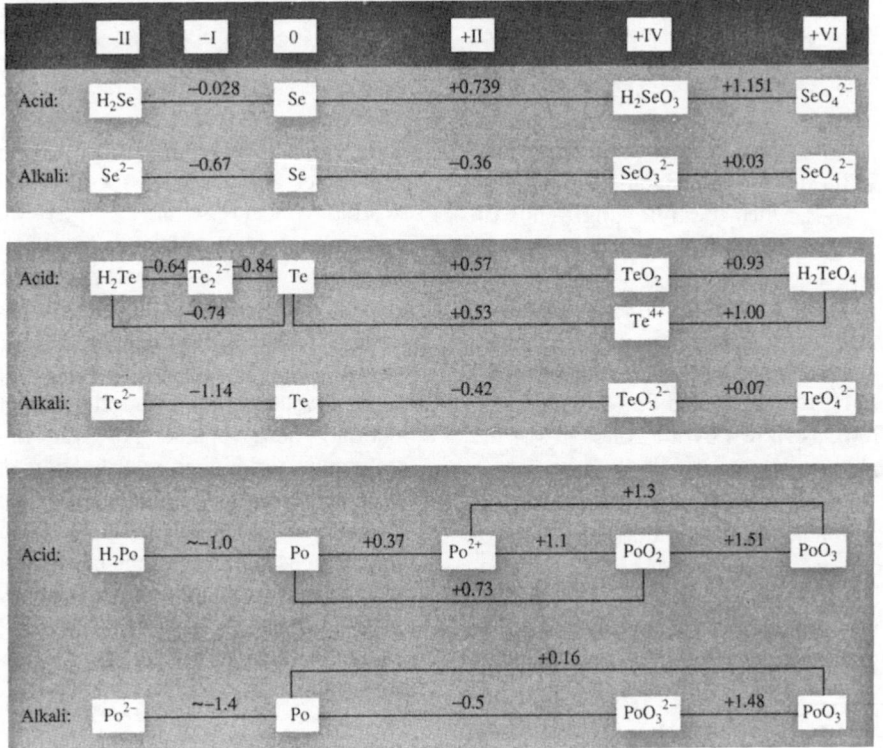

Standard reduction potentials of Se, Te and Po.[15]

Table 16.3   Coordination geometries of selenium, tellurium and polonium

Coordination number	Se	Te	Po
1	$COSe$, CSe_2, $NCSe^-$, $MoSe_4^{2-}$, WSe_4^{2-}	$COTe$, $CSTe$ Te_3^{2-}	
2 (bent)	Se_x, H_2Se, R_2Se *cyclo*-Se_4^{2+}	Te_x, H_2Te, R_2Te, $TeBr_2$ *cyclo*-Te_4^{2+}	
(linear)	$[L_nCr{\equiv}Se{\equiv}CrL_n]^{(a)}$		
3 (trigonal planar)	$[(L_nCr)_3(\mu_3\text{-}Se)]^{-(a)}$	$TeO_3(g)$	
(pyramidal)	$(SeO_2)_x$, $SeOX_2$, $SeMe_3^+$	TeO_3^{2-}, $TeMe_3^+$	
4 (planar)	—	$[TeBr_2\{SC(NH_2)_2\}_2]$	
(tetrahedral)	SeO_4^{2-}, SeO_2Cl_2	—	$CdPo$ (ZnS)
(pseudo-trigonal bipyramidal)	R_2SeX_2	TeO_2, Me_2TeCl_2	
5 (square pyramidal)	$[SeOCl_2py_2]$	TeF_5^-, $[TeI_4Me]^+$	
(pentagonal planar)	—	$[Te(S_2COEt)_3]^-$ (Fig. 16.2a)	
6 (octahedral)	SeF_6, $SeBr_6^{2-}$	$Te(OH)_6$, $TeBr_6^{2-}$	PoI_6^{2-}, Po metal $CaPo$ (NaCl)
(trigonal prismatic)	VSe, $CrSe$, $MnSe$ (NiAs)	$ScTe$, VTe, $MnTe$, (NiAs)	$MgPo$ (NiAs)
(pentagonal pyramidal)	—	$[Me\,Te(I)\{S_2CNEt_2\}_2]$ (Fig. 16.2b)	
7 (pentagonal bipyramidal)	—	$[PhTe\{S_2CNEt_2\}_2\text{-}\{S_2P(OEt)_2\}]$ (Fig. 16.2c)	
8 (cubic)	—	TeF_8^{2-}(?)	Na_2Po, PoO_2 (CaF$_2$)

$^{(a)}\{CrL_n\} = \{Cr(\eta^5\text{-}C_5H_5)(CO)_2\}^{(16)}$

instructive to plot these data, and the equivalent values for sulfur, as volt-equivalents *vs* oxidation state (pp. 435–8), when the following trends (in acid solution) become obvious:

   (i) the decreasing stability of H_2M from H_2S to H_2Po;

   (ii) the greater stability of M^{IV} relative to M^0 and M^{VI} for Se, Te and Po (but not for S, p. 706), as shown by the concavity of the graph;

   (iii) the anomalous position of Se in its higher oxidation states, as mentioned in the preceding paragraph.

The known coordination geometries of Se, Te and Po are summarized in Table 16.3 together

with typical examples. Most of the common geometries are observed for Se and Te, though twofold (linear) is rare and fivefold (trigonal bipyramidal) is conspicuous by its absence. The smaller range of established geometries for compounds of Po undoubtedly reflects the paucity of structural data occasioned by the rarity of this element and the extreme difficulty of obtaining X-ray crystallographic or other structural information. There appears, however, to be a clear preference for higher coordination numbers, as expected from the larger size of the Po atom. The various examples will be discussed more fully in subsequent sections but the rare pentagonal planar coordination formed in the ethyl xanthato complex $[Te(\eta^2\text{-}S_2COEt)_2(\eta^1\text{-}S_2COEt)]^-$ should be noted (Fig. 16.2a);[17] Other unusual stereochemistries are the pentagonal pyramidal

[16] W. A. HERRMANN,   J. ROHRMANN,   E. HERDTWECK, H. BOCK and A. VELTMANN, *J. Am. Chem. Soc.* **108**, 3134–5 (1986).

[17] B. F. HOSKINS and C. D. PANNAN, *J. Chem. Soc., Chem. Commun.*, 408–9 (1975).

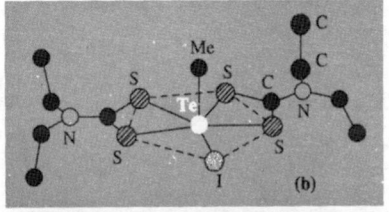

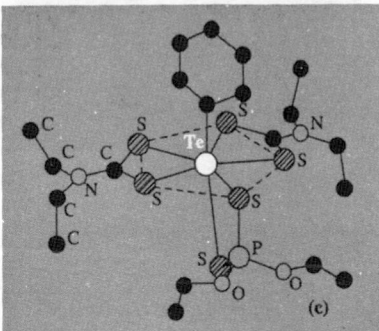

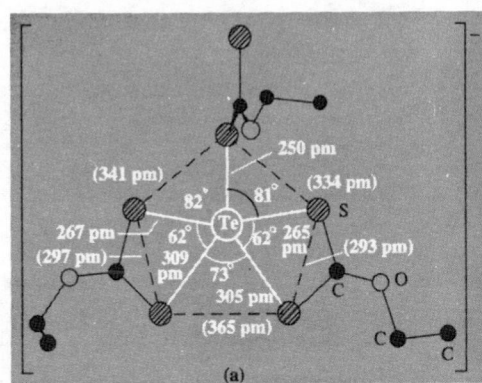

Figure 16.2   Structure of (a) the anion $[Te(S_2COEt)_3]^-$, the first authentic example of 5-coordinate pentagonal planar geometry;[17] (b) $[MeTe(I)\{S_2CNEt_2\}_2]$[18] and (c) $[PhTe\{S_2CNEt_2\}_2\{S_2P(OEt)_2\}]$[18] (see text).

6-coordinate Te^{IV} in $[MeTe(I)\{S_2CNEt_2\}_2]$[18] and pentagonal bipyramidal 7-coordinate Te^{IV} in $[PhTe\{S_2CNEt_2\}_2\{S_2P(OEt)_2\}]$;[18] in both cases the crystallographic data suggest the presence of a stereochemically active lone pair of electrons which distorts the regular geometry of the coordination sphere. This structure is consistent with a pentagonal bipyramidal set of orbitals on Te^{II}, 2 of which are occupied by stereochemically active lone-pairs directed above and below the TeS_5 plane. By contrast, the single lone-pairs in $Se^{IV}X_6{}^{2-}$, $Te^{IV}X_6{}^{2-}$ and $Po^{IV}I_6{}^{2-}$ are sterically inactive and the 14-(valence)electron anions are accurately octahedral (see p. 776), as in molecular $Se^{VI}F_6$, which has only 12 valence electrons.

Other less-symmetrical coordination geometries for Se and Te occur in the μ-Se_2 and μ-Te_2 complexes and the polyatomic cluster cations $Se_{10}{}^{2+}$ and $Te_6{}^{4+}$, as mentioned below.

The coordination chemistry of complexes in which Se is the donor atom has been extensively studied.[2,19] Ligands with Te as donor atom have been less widely investigated but both sets of ligands resemble S-donor ligands (p. 673) rather than O-donor ligands in favouring b-class acceptors such as Pd^{II}, Pt^{II} and Hg^{II}. The linear selenocyanate ion $SeCN^-$, like the thiocyanate ion (p. 324) is ambidentate, bonding via Se to heavy metals and via N (isoselenocyanate) to first-row transition metals, e.g. $[Ag^I(SeCN)_3]^{2-}$, $[Cd^{II}(SeCN)_4]^{2-}$ $[Pb^{II}(SeCN)_6]^{4-}$, but $[Cr^{III}(NCSe)_6]^{3-}$ and $[Ni(NCSe)_4]^{2-}$. The isoselenocyanate ligand often features nonlinear coordination

$$M\diagup \overset{\displaystyle N=C=Se}{}$$

but in the presence of bulky ligands it tends to become linear $M-\overset{+}{N}\equiv C-\overset{-}{Se}$. A bidentate bridging mode is also well established, e.g. $\{Cd-Se-C-N-Cd\}$ and $\{Ag-Se-C-N-Cr\}$. Monodentate organoselenium ligands include

[18] D. DAKTERNIEKS, R. D. GIACOMO, R. W. GABLE and B. F. HOSKINS, *J. Am. Chem. Soc.* **110**, 6762–8 (1988). Later papers are reviewed in S. HUSEBYE and S. V. LINDEMAN, *Main Group Chemistry News*, **3**(4), 8–16 (1996).

[19] S. E. LIVINGSTONE, *Q. Rev.* **19**, 386–425 (1965).

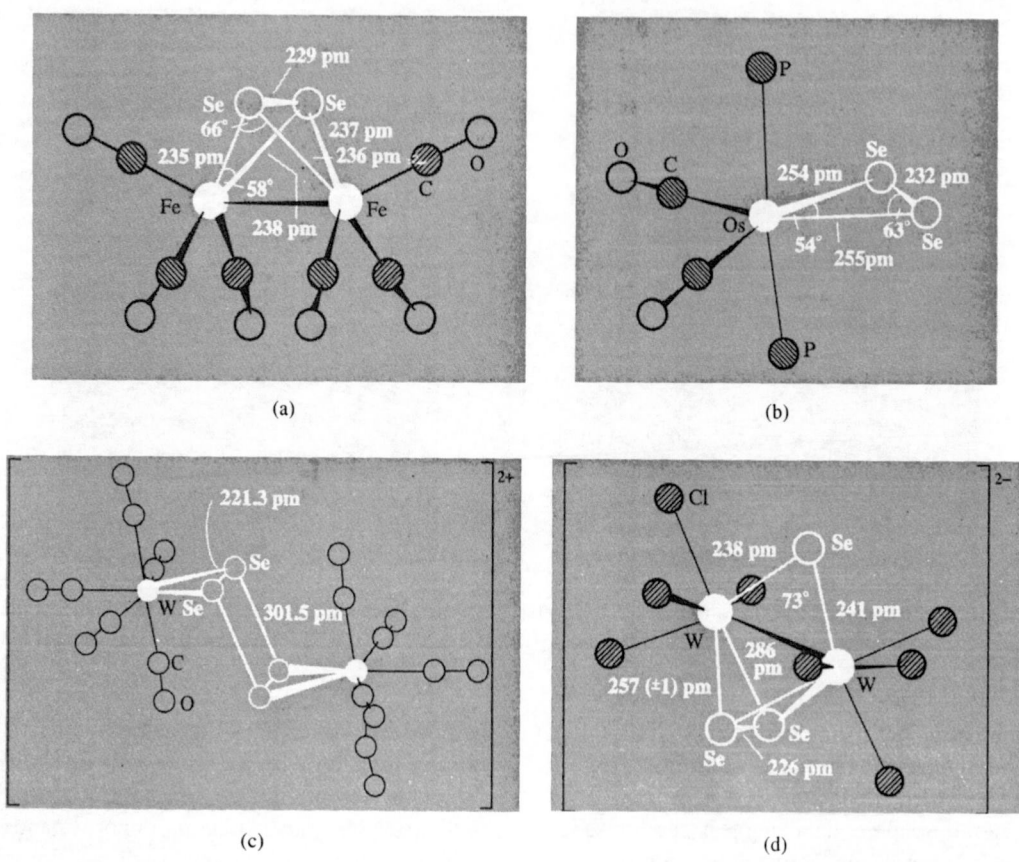

Figure 16.3 Structures of some η^2-Se$_2$ complexes. (a) red [Fe$_2$(CO)$_6$(μ,η^2-Se$_2$)],[20] (b) reddish-purple [Os(CO)$_2$(PPh$_3$)$_2$(η^2-Se$_2$)],[22] (c) the purple-black dication [W$_2$(CO)$_8$(μ:η^2,η^2-Se$_4$)]$^{2+}$ [23] and (d) brown [W$_2$Cl$_8$(μ-Se)(μ-Se$_2$)]$^{2-}$.[24]

R$_2$Se, Ar$_2$Se, R$_3$P=Se and selenourea (H$_2$N)$_2$C=Se, all of which bond well to heavy metal acceptors. Tellurium appears to be analogous:[3] e.g. Me$_2$Te.HgX$_2$, C$_4$H$_8$Te.HgCl$_2$, Ph$_2$Te.HgX$_2$, etc.

The structure of complexes containing the η^2-Se$_2$ ligand have recently been determined and, where appropriate, compared with analogous η^2-S$_2$, η^2-P$_2$ and η^2-As$_2$ complexes (p. 587). Examples are in Fig. 16.3 and the original papers should be consulted for further details.[20–25] Complexes

which feature side-on η^2-Te$_2$ such as [Ni(ppp)(η^2-Te$_2$)] (ppp = Ph$_2$PC$_2$H$_4$P(Ph)C$_2$H$_4$PPh$_2$), analogous to the η^2-Se$_2$ complex in Fig. 16.3b are also

[20] C. F. CAMPANA, F. Y.-K. LO, and L. F. DAHL, *Inorg. Chem.* **18**, 3060–4 (1979); see also pp. 3047 and 3054. The mixed-metal cationic complex [FeW(CO)$_8$(μ,η^2-Se$_2$)]$^{2+}$ has a similar structure.[21]

[21] D. J. JONES, T. MAKANI and J. ROZIÈRE, *J. Chem. Soc., Chem. Commun.*, 1275–80 (1986).

[22] D. H. FARRAR, K. R. GRUNDY, N. C. PAYNE, W. R. ROPER and A. WALKER, *J. Am. Chem. Soc.* **101**, 6577–82 (1979).

[23] M. J. COLLINS, R. J. GILLESPIE, J. W. KOLIS and J. F. SAWYER, *Inorg. Chem.* **25**, 2057–61 (1986).

[24] M. G. B. DREW, G. W. A. FOWLES, E. M. PAGE and D. A. RICE, *J. Am. Chem. Soc.* **101**, 5827–8 (1979). The dark green rhodium complex [Rh$_2$(η^5-C$_5$Me$_5$)$_2$(μ-Se)(μ-Se$_2$)] and the violet-brown osmium analogue [Os$_2$(η^5-C$_5$Me$_5$)$_2$(μ-Se)(μ-Se$_2$)] have a similar structure.[25]

[25] H. BRUNNER, W. MEIER, B. NUBER, J. WACHTER and M. L. ZIEGLER, *Angew. Chem. Int. Edn. Engl.* **25** 907–8 (1986).

known,[26] as well as those which feature the $\mu:\eta^2,\eta^2$ bridging mode:[27]

$$L_n Ni \underset{Te}{\overset{Te}{\diagup\!\!\!\diagdown}} NiL_n$$

The tridentate triangulo ligand η^3-cyclo-Te_3 has been characterized in the cationic complex $[W(CO)_4(\eta^3\text{-}Te_3)]^{2+}$ [28] [cf. η^3-P_3 (p. 487), η^3-As_3 (p. 588), etc.], and μ_3- and μ_4-bridging Te atoms have been found in the heptanuclear trimetallic cluster $[\{Fe_2(CO)_6\}(\mu_4\text{-}Te)(\mu_3\text{-}Te)\{Re_3(CO)_{11}\}]$ [29] The core geometry of this latter cluster can be described as a $\{Fe_2Te_2\}$ 'butterfly' with wing-tip Te atoms bridging a bent Ru_3 unit.

The compounds of Se, Te and Po should all be treated as potentially toxic. Volatile compounds such as H_2Se, H_2Te and organo derivatives are particularly dangerous and maximum permissible limits for air-borne concentrations are $0.1\,mg\,m^{-3}$ (cf. $10\,mg\,m^{-3}$ for HCN). The elements are taken up by the kidneys, spleen and liver, and even in minute concentrations cause headache, nausea and irritation of mucous membrane.

Organoselenium compounds in particular, once ingested, are slowly released over prolonged periods and result in foul-smelling breath and perspiration. The element is also highly toxic towards grazing sheep, cattle and other animals, and, at concentrations above about 5 ppm, causes severe disorders. Despite this, Se was found (in 1957) to play an essential dietary role in animals and also in humans — it is required in the formation of the enzyme glutathione peroxidase which is involved in fat metabolism. It has also been found that the incidence of kwashiorkor (severe protein malnutrition) in children is associated with inadequate uptake of Se, and it may well be involved in protection against certain cancers. The average dietary intake of Se in the USA is said to be $\sim150\,\mu g$ daily, usually in meat and sea food. Considerable caution should be taken in handling compounds of Se and Te, but the hazards should also be kept in perspective — no human fatalities directly attributable to either Se or Te poisoning have ever been recorded. The biochemistry and dietary aspects of Se have been reviewed.[30]

Polonium is extremely toxic at all concentrations and is never beneficial. Severe radiation damage of vital organs follows ingestion of even the minutest concentrations and, for the most commonly used isotope, ^{210}Po, the maximum permissible body burden is $0.03\,\mu Ci$, i.e. 1100 Bq ($\equiv 1100\,s^{-1}$), equivalent to $\sim 7 \times 10^{-12}\,g$ of the element. Concentrations of airborne Po compounds must be kept below $4 \times 10^{-11}\,mg\,m^{-3}$.

16.1.6 Polyatomic cations, M_x^{n+}

The brightly coloured solutions obtained when sulfur is dissolved in oleums (p. 664) are paralleled by similar behaviour of Se and Te. Indeed, the bright-red solutions of Te in H_2SO_4 were noted by M. H. Klaproth in 1798 and the coloured solutions of Se in the same solvent were reported by G. Magnus in 1827. Systematic studies in a range of nonaqueous solvents have since shown that the polycations of Se and Te are less electropositive than their S analogues and can be prepared in a variety of strong acids such as H_2SO_4, $H_2S_2O_7$, HSO_3F, SO_2/AsF_5, SO_2/SbF_5 and molten $AlCl_3$.[31,32] Typical reactions for Se are:

[26] M. Di. Vaira, M. Peruzzini and P. Stoppioni, *Angew. Chem. Int. Edn. Engl.* **26**, 916–7 (1987).

[27] M. Di. Vaira, M. Peruzzini and P. Stoppioni, *J. Chem. Soc., Chem. Commun.*, 374–5 (1986).

[28] R. Faggiani, R. J. Gillespie, C. Campana and J. W. Kolis, *J. Chem. Soc., Chem. Commun.*, 485–6 (1987).

[29] P. Mathur, I. J. Mavunkal and A. L. Rheingold, *J. Chem. Soc., Chem. Commun.*, 382–4 (1989).

[30] R. J. Shamberger, *Biochemistry of Selenium*, Plenum Press, New York, 1983, 334 pp. C. Reilly, *Selenium in Food and Health*, Blackie, London, 1996, 338 pp.

[31] R. J. Gillespie and J. Passmore, *Adv. Inorg. Chem. Radiochem.* **17**, 49–87 (1975). M. J. Taylor, *Metal–Metal Bonded States in Main Group Elements*, Academic Press, London, 1975, 211 pp. J. D. Corbett, *Prog. Inorg. Chem.* **21**, 121–58 (1976). T. A. O'Donnell, *Chem. Soc. Rev.* **16**, 1–43 (1987).

[32] N. Burford, J. Passmore and J. C. P. Sanders, Chap. 2, Preparation, Structure and Energetics of the Homopolyatomic Cations of Groups 16 and 17, in J. F. Liebman and A. Greenburg (eds.), *From Atoms to Polymers: Isoelectronic Analogies*, VCH Publ., Florida, 1989, pp. 53–108. J. Passmore, Chap. 19 Homopolyatomic Selenium Cations

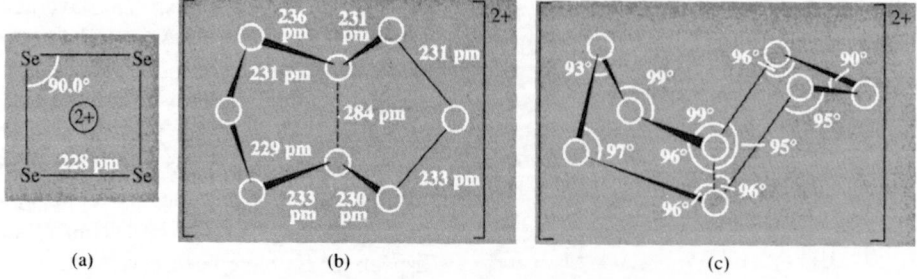

Figure 16.4   (a) Structure of $[Se_4]^{2+}$; (b) and (c) views of $[Se_8]^{2+}$

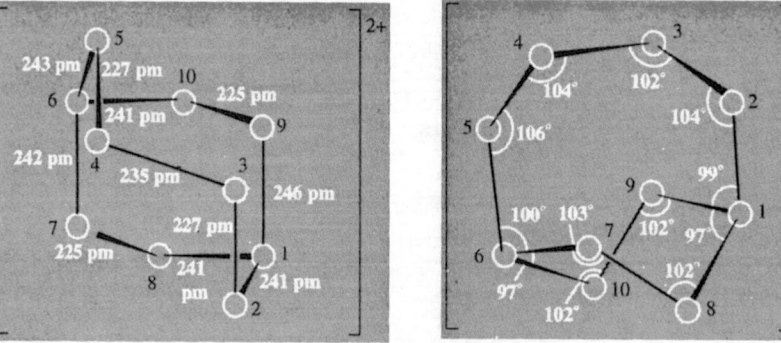

Figure 16.5   Structure of the $[Se_{10}]^{2+}$ cation in $Se_{10}(SbF_6)_2$ along the *b*- and *c*-axes of the crystal; angles Se(2)-Se(1)-Se(9) and Se(5)-Se(6)-Se(10) are each 101.7°.

$$4Se + S_2O_6F_2 \xrightarrow{HSO_3F} [Se_4]^{2+}[SO_3F]^-{}_2 \text{ (yellow)}$$

$$[Se_4]^{2+} + 4Se \xrightarrow{HSO_3F} [Se_8]^{2+} \text{ (green)}$$

$$Se_8 + 6AsF_5 \xrightarrow[(-2AsF_3)]{SO_2/80°} 2[Se_4]^{2+}[AsF_6]^-{}_2 \text{ (yellow)}$$

$$Se_8 + 5SbF_5 \xrightarrow[(-SbF_3)]{SO_2/-23°} [Se_8]^{2+}[Sb_2F_{11}]^-{}_2 \text{ (green)}$$

$$7\tfrac{1}{2}Se + \tfrac{1}{2}SeCl_4 + 2AlCl_3 \xrightarrow{\text{fuse at }250°} [Se_8]^{2+}[AlCl_4]^-{}_2$$

$$\text{(green-black)}$$

X-ray crystal structure studies on $[Se_4]^{2+}$-$[HS_2O_7]^-{}_2$ show that the cation is square planar (like S_4^{2+}, p. 665) as in Fig. 16.4a. The Se–Se distance of 228 pm is significantly less than the value of 234 pm in Se_8 and 237 pm in

Se_∞, consistent with some multiple bonding. The structure of $[Se_8]^{2+}$ in the salt $[Se_8]^{2+}[AlCl_4]^-{}_2$ is in Fig. 16.4b and c: it comprises a bicyclo C_s structure with the *endo-exo* configuration with a long trans-annular link of 284 pm. Other Se–Se distances are very similar to those in Se_8 itself, but the Se–Se–Se angles are significantly smaller in the cation, being ~96° rather than 106°. More recently[33] the deep-red crystalline compound $Se_{10}(SbF_6)_2$ has been isolated from the reaction of SbF_5 with an excess of Se in SO_2 under pressure at ~50°. Two views of the bicyclic cation are shown in Fig. 16.5; it features a 6-membered boat-shaped ring linked across the middle of a zigzag chain of 4 further Se atoms. The Se–Se distances vary from 225 to 240 pm and Se–Se–Se angles range from

and Related Halo-polyselenium Cations, in R. Steudel (ed.), *The Chemistry of Inorganic Ring Systems*, Elsevier, Amsterdam, 1992, pp. 373–407.

[33] R. C. BURNS, W.-L. CHAN, R. J. GILLESPIE, W.-C. LUK, J. F. SAWYER and D. R. SLIM, *Inorg. Chem.* **19**, 1432–9 (1980).

97° to 106°, with 6 angles at the bridgehead atoms Se(1) and Se(6) being significantly smaller than the other 8 in the linking chains. The low-temperature disproportionation of Se_{10}^{2+} into Se_8^{2+} and a second species, probably Se_{17}^{2+}, i.e $[Se_8–Se–Se_8]^{2+}$, has been studied by ^{77}Se nmr spectroscopy.[34] Heteronuclear species such as $[S_xSe_{4-x}]^{2+}$ have also been identified by nmr techniques and characterized by X-ray structure analysis.[35] Analogous Se/Te heteronuclear cations are described below.

Polyatomic tellurium cations can be prepared by similar routes. The bright-red species Te_4^{2+}, like S_4^{2+} and Se_4^{2+}, is square planar with the Te–Te distance (266 m) somewhat less than in the element (284 m) (Fig. 16.6a). Oxidation of Te with AsF_5 in AsF_3 as solvent yields the brown crystalline compound $Te_6(AsF_6)_4.2AsF_3$: X-ray studies reveal the presence of $[Te_6]^{4+}$ which is the first example of a simple trigonal prismatic cluster cation (Fig. 16.6b). The Te–Te distances between the triangular faces (313 pm) are substantially larger than those within the triangle (267 pm).[36] No Te analogue of S_8^{2+} and Se_8^{2+} had been identified until 1997 when the reaction of $ReCl_4$ with Te and $TeCl_4$ at 230° yielded silvery crystals of $[Te_8]^{2+}[ReCl_6]^{2-}$ with Te–Te 272 pm (av), the shortest Te $\cdots$ Te distance being 315 pm.[36a] Previously (1990), oxidation

of Te with WCl_6 had yielded $[Te_8][WCl_6]_2$ in which the Te_8^{2+} dication was found to have a more pronounced bicyclic structure of C_2 symmetry with Te–Te 275.2 pm and the central transannular link being 299.3 pm.[36a]

Mixed Se/Te polatomic cations are also known. For example, when Se and Te are dissolved in 65% oleum at room temperature the resulting orange-brown solutions were shown by ^{125}Te and ^{123}Te nmr spectroscopy to contain the four species $[Te_nSe_{4-n}]^{2+}$ ($n = 1–4$) and the species $[Se_4]^{2+}$ was also presumably present.[37] Likewise ^{77}Se and ^{125}Te multinuclear magnetic resonance studies on solutions obtained by oxidizing equimolar mixtures of Se and Te with AsF_5 in SO_2 reveal not only $[Se_4]^{2+}$, $[Te_4]^{2+}$ and $[Te_6]^{4+}$ but also $[TeSe_3]^{2+}$, *cis*- and *trans*-$[Te_2Se_2]^{2+}$, $[Te_3Se]^{2+}$, $[Te_2Se_4]^{2+}$ and $[Te_3Se_3]^{2+}$.[38] The molecular structures of the sulfur analogue $[Te_3S_3]^{2+}$ and of $[Te_2Se_4]^{2+}$ have also been determined by X-ray diffractometry and found to have a boat-shaped 6-membered heterocyclic structure with a cross-ring bond as shown in Fig. 16.7. As expected, these M_6^{2+} species are more open than the corresponding Te_6^{4+} cluster because of the presence of 2 extra valency-shell electrons (p. 724). Other mixed species that have been characterized include $[Te_2Se_6]^{2+}$ (cube, with diagonally placed Te)[39]

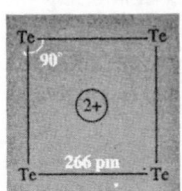
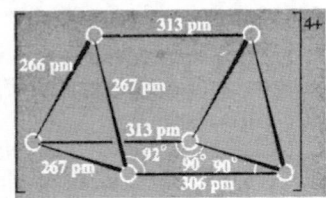

Figure 16.6 Structure of the cations $[Te_4]^{2+}$ and $[Te_6]^{4+}$.

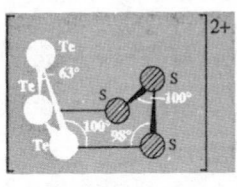
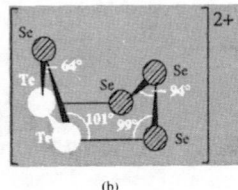

Figure 16.7 Structures of the heteroatomic cluster cations (a) $[Te_3S_3]^{2+}$ and (b) $[Te_2Se_4]^{2+}$.

[34] R. C. BURNS, M. J. COLLINS, R. J. GILLESPIE and G. J. SCHROBILGEN, *Inorg. Chem.* **25**, 4465–9 (1986); but see *Z. anorg. allg. Chem.* **623**, 780–4 (1977).

[35] M. J. COLLINS, R. J. GILLESPIE, J. F. SAWYER and G. J. SCHROBILGEN, *Inorg. Chem.* **25**, 2053–7 (1986).

[36] R. C. BURNS, R. J. GILLESPIE, W.-C. LUK and D. R. SLIM, *Inorg. Chem.* **18**, 3086–94 (1979).

[36a] J. BECK and K. MÜLLER-BUSCHBAUM, *Z. anorg. allg. Chem.* **623**, 409–13 (1997) and references therein.

[37] C. R. LASSIGNE and E. J. WELLS, *J. Chem. Soc., Chem. Commun.*, 956–7 (1978).

[38] G. J. SCHROBILGEN, R. C. BURNS and P. GRANGER, *J. Chem. Soc., Chem. Commun.*, 957–60 (1978). P. BOLDRINI, I. D. BROWN, M. J. COLLINS, R. J. GILLESPIE, E. MAHRAJH, D. R. SLIM and J. F. SAWYER, *Inorg. Chem.* **24**, 4302–7 (1985).

[39] M. J. COLLINS and R. J. GILLESPIE, *Inorg. Chem.* **23**, 1975–8 (1984).

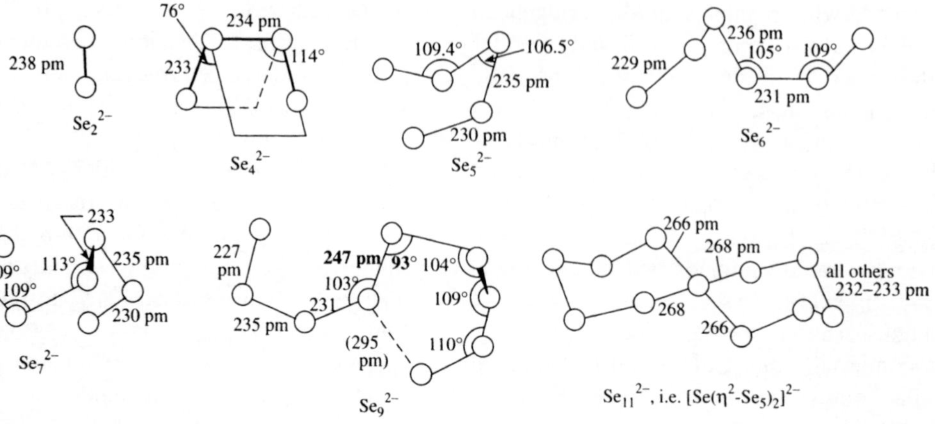

Figure 16.8 Structures of some dianions Se_x^{2-} (see text).

and $[Te_4S_4]^{2+}$ (electron-rich S_4N_4 cluster but with coplanar S atoms as in As_4S_4).[40]

The mixed *anionic* species $[Tl_2Te_2]^{2-}$ (20 valence electrons) is butterfly-shaped with Tl_2 at the "hinge" and 2Te at the "wing tips",[41] in contrast to the 22 valence-electron *cationic* species Te_4^{2+} and Se_4^{2+} which are square planar. The remarkable cationic cluster species $[(NbI_2)_3-O(Te_4)(Te_2)_2]^+$ should also be noted: this was formed serendipitously in low yield as the monoiodide during the high-temperature reaction between $NbOI_3$, Te and I_2 and features the bridging groups $(\mu,\eta^2{:}\eta^2\text{-}Te_4)^{2+}$ and two $(\mu,\eta^2\text{-}Te_2)$ in addition to $(\mu_3\text{-}O)^{2-}$ and six terminal I^-. This implies a mixed $Nb^{III} Nb^{IV} Nb^{IV}$ oxidation state with two localized Nb–Nb single bonds.[42]

16.1.7 Polyatomic anions, M_x^{2-}

The synthesis, structural characterization and coordination chemistry of polyselenides, Se_x^{2-}, and polytellurides, Te_x^{2-}, is a burgeoning field which has sprung into prominence during the past decade. The seminal studies by E. Zintl and his group during the 1930s showed that such species could be prepared by reduction of the elements with alkali metals in liquid ammonia, but it was the advent of ^{77}Se and ^{125}Te nmr techniques, and the use of crown and crypt complexes (p. 96) to prepare crystalline derivatives for X-ray structural analysis which provided the firm bases for further advances. The rich reaction chemistry and coordination properties soon followed. Comparisons with polysulfides and polysulfanes (pp. 681–3) are instructive. Thus, little is known about H_2Se_2 and H_2Te_2, and nothing at all about the higher homologues H_2Se_x and H_2Te_x; however, compounds containing the dianions Se_x^{2-} ($x = 2$–11) and Te_x^{2-} ($x = 2$–5, 8...) are considerably more stable both in solution and in the crystalline state than are the parent hydrides.

Reaction of Na_2Se and Na_2Se_2 with Se in the presence of ethanolic solutions of tetraalkyl-ammonium halides and catalytic amounts of I_2 yields dark green or black crystalline polyselenides ($x = 3, 5$–9) depending on the conditions used and the particular cation selected.[43] Tetraphenylphosphonium salts and crown ether complexes of alkali or alkaline earth cations in dimethylformamide solution can also be used.[44]

[40] R. FAGGIANI, R. J. GILLESPIE and J. E. VEKRIS, *J. Chem. Soc., Chem. Commun.*, 902–4 (1988).

[41] R. C. BURNS and J. D. CORBETT, *J. Am. Chem. Soc.* **103**, 2627–32 (1981).

[42] W. TREMEL, *J. Chem. Soc., Chem. Commun.*, 126–8 (1992).

[43] F. WELLER, J. ADEL and K. DEHNICKE, *Z. anorg. allg. Chem.* **548**, 125–32 (1987).

[44] D. FENSKE, C. KRAUS and K. DEHNICKE, *Z. anorg. allg. Chem.* **607**, 109–12 (1992). V. MÜLLER, A. AHLE,

Typical structures and dimensions of the resulting polyselenide dianions are shown in Fig. 16.8, though it should be emphasized that torsion angles, interatomic angles and even to some extent interatomic distances may depend on the countercation chosen. Detailed references have been tabulated.[45] The triselenide ion, $Se_3{}^{2-}$ has been identified as a moderately stable species in solution and in the solid state, but its X-ray structure has not been reported; it is presumably angular like $S_3{}^{2-}$ and $Te_3{}^{2-}$. The evolution of the chains up to $Se_7{}^{2-}$ is clear. The structure of $Se_8{}^{2-}$ has also been determined in $[Na(crown)]^+{}_2[Se_8]^{2-}$·$(Se_6.Se_7)$ which features a curious packing of the cation and the anion with an equimolar amount of neutral *cyclo*-Se_n comprising variable amounts of Se_6 and Se_7.[46] The structure of *catena*-$Se_9{}^{2-}$ has a relatively long central Se–Se bond (247 pm) which forms, at one end, a sharp angle of 93° to the adjacent Se atom; the Se at other end of the bond is approached rather closely by one of the terminal Se atoms (295 pm) to form an incipient 6-membered ring. The process continues in $Se_{11}{}^{2-}$ which has a centrosymmetric spiro-bicyclic structure involving a central square-planar Se atom common to the two chair-conformation rings. The central bonds are again rather long (266–268 pm) and the structure may be described as a central Se^{2+} chelated by two η^2-$Se_5{}^{2-}$ ligands (see below). The structure also has similarities with the anion in $Cs^+{}_4[Se_{16}]^{4-}$,[47] which has a central planar formal Se^{2+} coordinated by one chelating η^2-$Se_5{}^{2-}$ ligand (Se–Se 243 pm) and by two monohapto η^1-$Se_5{}^{2-}$ ligands (Se–Se 299 pm), i.e. $[Se(\eta^2$-$Se_5)(\eta^1$-$Se_5)_2]^{2-}$.

Several of the *catena*-$Se_x{}^{2-}$ anions have proved to be effective chelating ligands to both main-group and transition metals. Synthesis of the complexes is usually via direct reaction with the preformed anion or by synthesis of the anion in the presence of the appropriate metal centre. Examples are $[Sn(\eta^2$-$Se_4)_3]^{2-}$,[48] $[M(\eta^2$-$Se_4)_2]^{2-}$ (M = Zn, Cd, Hg, Ni, Pb^{II}),[49] $[Mo^{IV}(\eta^5$-$C_5H_5)(\eta^2$-$Se_4)_2]^{-}$[50] and $[M_3(Se_4)_6]^{3-}$, i.e. $[\{M(Se_4)_3\}M\{(Se_4)_3M\}]^{3-}$ (M = Cr,[51] Co[52]), in which the two terminal M^{III} atoms have approximately *tris*-tetraselenide chelate coordination whilst the central M^{III} atom (also approximately octahedral) has $(\mu$-$Se)_6$ coordination, achieved by sharing one 'terminal' Se atom from each of the six Se_4 groups. The complex $[Ti(\eta^5$-$C_5H_5)_2(\eta^2$-$Se_5)]$ reacts with SCl_2, S_2Cl_2 and $SeCl_2$ to form, respectively, Se_5S, Se_5S_2 and Se_7.[53] Heterocyclic chelating ligands are also known, e.g. in $[PtCl(PMe_2Ph)(\eta^2$-$Se_3N)]$.[54] Note also the extraordinary 1900 pm long hexameric anion, $[Ga_6Se_{14}]^{10-}$, which is composed of a linear array of edge-sharing $\{GaSe_4\}$ units, i.e. $[Se_2\{Ga(\mu$-$Se)_2\}_5GaSe_2]^{10-}$.[55]

Polytellurides, $Te_x{}^{2-}$, are less straightforward and often form complex units coordinated to metal centres.[56] The isolated ions $Te_2{}^{2-}$ and

G. Frenzen, B. Neumüller and K. Dehnicke, *Z. anorg. allg. Chem.* **619**, 1247–56 (1993). V. Müller, C. Grebe, U. Müller and K. Dehnicke, *Z. anorg. allg. Chem.* **619**, 416–20 (1993).

[45] J. Cusick and I. Dance, *Polyhedron* **10**, 2629–40 (1991).

[46] R. Staffel, U. Müller, A. Ahle and K. Dehnicke, *Z. Naturforsch.* **46b**, 1287–92 (1992).

[47] W. S. Sheldrick and H. G. Braunbeck, *Z. Naturforsch*, **44b** 1397–401 (1989).

[48] S.-P. Huang, S. Dhingra and M. G. Kanatzidis, *Polyhedron* **9**, 1389–95 (1990).

[49] R. M. H. Banda, J. Cusick, M. L. Scudder, D. C. Craig and I. G. Dance, *Polyhedron* **8**, 1995–8 (1989). S. Magull, K. Dehnicke and D. Fenske, *Z. anorg. allg. Chem.* **608**, 17–22 (1992).

[50] R. M. H. Banda, J. Cusick, M. L. Scudder, D. C. Craig and I. G. Dance, *Polyhedron* **8**, 1999–2001 (1989). See also J. Cusick, M. L. Scudder, D. C. Craig and I. G. Dance, *Polyhedron* **8**, 1139–41 (1989) for the more complex structures of tetranuclear Cu and Ag polyselenides.

[51] W. A. Flomer, S. C. O'Neal, W. T. Pennington, D. Jeter, A. W. Cordes and J. W. Kolis, *Angew. Chem. Int. Edn. Engl.* **27**, 1702–3 (1988).

[52] J. Cusick, M. L. Scudder, D. C. Craig and I. G. Dance, *Aust. J. Chem.* **43**, 209–11 (1990).

[53] R. Steudel, M. Papavassiliou, E.-M. Strauss and R. Laitinen, *Angew. Chem. Int. Edn. Engl.* **25**, 99–101 (1986).

[54] P. F. Kelly, A. M. Z. Slawin, D. J. Williams and J. D. Woollins, *J. Chem. Soc., Chem. Commun.*, 408–9 (1989).

[55] E. Niecke, K. Schwichtenhövel, H. G. Schäfer and B. Krebs, *Angew. Chem. Int. Edn. Engl.* **20**, 962–3 (1981).

[56] P. Böttcher, *Angew. Chem. Int. Edn. Engl.* **27**, 759–72 (1988).

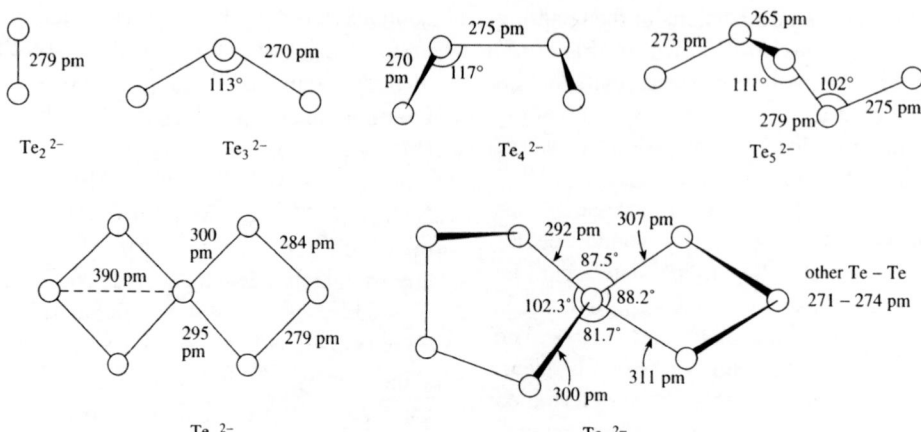

Figure 16.9 Structures of some dianions Te_x^{2-} (see text).

Te_3^{2-} are found in K_2Te_2, Rb_2Te_2[57] and $[K(crypt)]_2Te_3$[58] — see Fig. 16.9. Likewise, Te_4^{2-} has been characterized in salts of crown ether complexes of Ca, Sr and Ba, and Te_5^{2-} as its salt with $[Ph_3PNPPh_3]^{+}$[59] (Fig. 16.9). The bicyclic polytellurides Te_7^{2-}[60] and Te_8^{2-}[61] are also known (Fig. 16.9). However, simple stoichiometry often conceals structural complexity as in the many alkali metal tellurides MTe_x ($x = 1, 1.5, 2.5, 3, 4$).[56,62]

There is also a bewildering variety of structural motifs in polytelluride–ligand complexes as the brief selection in Fig. 16.10 indicates; the original papers should be consulted for preparative routes and other details. Thus, dissolution of the alloy $K_2Hg_2Te_3$ in ethylenediamine, followed by treatment with a methanolic solution of $[NBu_4^n]Br$, yields the dark brown compound $[NBu_4^n]_4[Hg_4Te_{12}]$;[63] this features the remarkable anion $[Hg_4Te_{12}]^{4-}$ in which the four Hg atoms, which are coplanar, are coordinated in distorted tetrahedral fashion to an array of two Te^{2-}, two Te_2^{2-} and two Te_3^{2-} ligands (Fig. 16.10). By contrast, use of $[PPh_4]^{+}$ as the counter-cation yields the unbranched, approximately planar, polymeric anion $[\{Hg_2Te_5\}^{2-}]_\infty$ (Fig. 16.10) which contains $\{Hg_2Te_3\}$ heterocycles joined by bridging Te_2^{2-} units.[63] Cu^I and Ag^I form discrete polytelluride complexes in $[PPh_4]_2[M_2Te_{12}]$[64] (Fig. 16.10) containing two chelating and one bridging Te_4^{2-} groups. A similar chelating mode occurs in $[Pd(\eta^2\text{-}Te_4)_2]^{2-}$.[65] Discrete $[HgTe_7]^{2-}$ ions occur in the $[K(crown)_2]^{+}$ salt whereas the corresponding Zn derivative has a polymeric structure[66] (Fig. 16.10). The soluble cluster anion $NbTe_{10}^{3-}$ is also notable; its structure has been determined in the black, crystalline tetraphenylphosphonium salt.[67] Cubane-like clusters occur

[57] P. BÖTTCHER, J. GETZSCHMANN and R. KELLER, *Z. anorg. allg. Chem.* **619**, 476–88 (1993).

[58] A. CISAR and J. D. CORBETT, *Inorg. Chem.* **16**, 632–5 (1977).

[59] D. FENSKE, G. BAUM, H. WOLKERS, B. SCHREINER, F. WELLER and K. DEHNICKE, *Z. anorg. allg. Chem.* **619**, 489–99 (1993).

[60] B. HARBRECHT and A. SELMER, *Z. anorg. allg. Chem.* **620**, 1861–6 (1994).

[61] B. SCHREINER, K. DEHNICKE, K. MACZEK and D. FENSKE, *Z. anorg. allg. Chem.* **619**, 1414–8 (1993).

[62] J. BERNSTEIN and R. HOFFMANN, *Inorg. Chem.* **24**, 4100–8 (1985).

[63] R. C. HAUSHALTER, *Angew. Chem. Int. Edn. Engl.* **24**, 433–5 (1985).

[64] D. FENSKE, B. SCHREINER and K. DEHNICKE, *Z. anorg. allg. Chem.* **619**, 253–60 (1993).

[65] R. D. ADAMS, T. A. WOLFE, B. W. EICHHORN and R. C. HAUSHALTER, *Polyhedron* **8**, 701–3 (1989).

[66] U. MÜLLER, C. GREBE, B. NEUMÜLLER, B. SCHREINER and K. DEHNICKE, *Z. anorg. allg. Chem.* **619**, 500–6 (1993).

[67] W. A. FLOMER and J. W. KOLIS, *J. Am. Chem. Soc.* **110**, 3682–3 (1988).

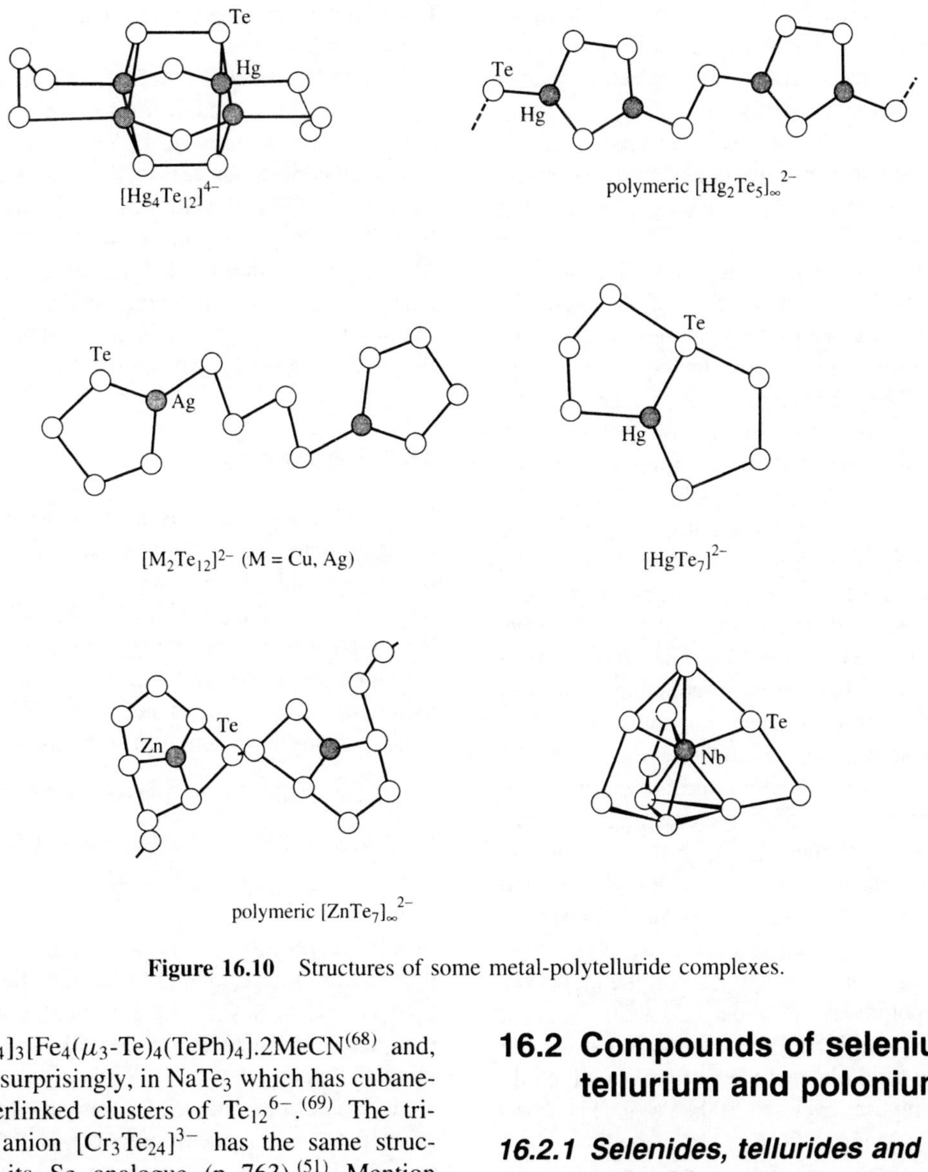

$[Hg_4Te_{12}]^{4-}$

polymeric $[Hg_2Te_5]_\infty^{2-}$

$[M_2Te_{12}]^{2-}$ (M = Cu, Ag)

$[HgTe_7]^{2-}$

polymeric $[ZnTe_7]_\infty^{2-}$

Figure 16.10   Structures of some metal-polytelluride complexes.

in $[NEt_4]_3[Fe_4(\mu_3\text{-}Te)_4(TePh)_4].2MeCN^{(68)}$ and, perhaps surprisingly, in $NaTe_3$ which has cubane-like interlinked clusters of $Te_{12}^{6-}.^{(69)}$ The trinuclear anion $[Cr_3Te_{24}]^{3-}$ has the same structure as its Se analogue (p. 763).$^{(51)}$ Mention could also be made of the planar ion $[TeS_3]^{2-}$ and the spiro-bicyclic $[Te(\eta^2\text{-}S_5)_2]^{2-}$ in which the Te atom is also planar$^{(70)}$ (cf. Se_{11}^{2-} in Fig. 16.8).

---

^{68} W. SIMON, A. WILK, B. KREBS and G. HENKEL, *Angew. Chem. Int. Edn. Engl.* **26**, 1009–10 (1987).

^{69} P. BÖTTCHER and R. KELLER, *Z. anorg. allg. Chem.* **542**, 144–52 (1986).

^{70} W. BUBENHEIM G. FRENZEN and U. MÜLLER, *Z. anorg. allg. Chem.* **620** 1046–50 (1994).

16.2 Compounds of selenium, tellurium and polonium

16.2.1 Selenides, tellurides and polonides

All three elements combine readily with most metals and many non-metals to form binary chalcogenides. Indeed, selenides and tellurides are the most common mineral forms of these elements (p. 748). Nonstoichiometry abounds, particularly for compounds with the transition elements (where electronegativity differences are minimal and variable valency is favoured), and many of the chalcogenides can be considered as metallic alloys. Many such compounds have important technological potentialities for solid-state optical, electrical and thermoelectric devices and have been extensively studied. For the more electropositive elements (e.g. Groups 1 and 2), the chalcogenides can be considered as "salts" of the acids, H_2Se, H_2Te, and H_2Po (see next subsection).

The alkali metal selenides and tellurides can be prepared by direct reaction of the elements at moderate temperatures in the absence of air, or more conveniently in liquid ammonia solution. They are colourless, water soluble, and readily oxidized by air to the element. The structures adopted are not unexpected from general crystallochemical principles. Thus Li_2Se, Na_2Se and K_2Se have the antifluorite structure (p. 118); MgSe, CaSe, SrSe, BaSe, ScSe, YSe, LuSe, etc., have the rock-salt structure (p. 242); BeSe, ZnSe and HgSe have the zinc-blende structure (p. 1210); and CdSe has the wurtzite structure (p. 1210). The corresponding tellurides are similar, though there is not a complete 1:1 correspondence. Polonides can also be prepared by direct reaction and are amongst the stablest compounds of this element: Na_2Po has the antifluorite structure; the NaCl structure is adopted by the polonides of Ca, Ba, Hg, Pb and the lanthanide elements; BePo and CdPo have the ZnS structure and MgPo the nickel arsenide structure (p. 556). Decomposition temperatures of these polonides are about $600 \pm 50°C$ except for the less-stable HgPo (decomp 300°) and the extremely stable lanthanide derivatives which do not decompose even at 1000° (e.g. PrPo mp 1253°, TmPo mp 2200°C).

Transition-element chalcogenides are also best prepared by direct reaction of the elements at 400–1000°C in the absence of air. They tend to be metallic nonstoichiometric alloys though intermetallic compounds also occur, e.g. $Ti_{\sim 2}Se$, $Ti_{\sim 3}Se$, $TiSe_{0.95}$, $TiSe_{1.05}$, $Ti_{0.9}Se$, Ti_3Se_4, $Ti_{0.7}Se$, Ti_5Se_8, $TiSe_2$, $TiSe_3$, etc.[71,72]

Fuller details of these many compounds are in the references cited.

Most selenides and tellurides are decomposed by water or dilute acid to form H_2Se or H_2Te but the yields, particularly of the latter, are poor.

Polychalcogenides are less stable than polysulfides (p. 681). Reaction of alkali metals with Se in liquid ammonia affords M_2Se_2, M_2Se_3 and M_2Se_4, and analogous polytellurides have also been reported (see preceding section). However many of these compounds are rather unstable thermally and tend to be oxidized in air.

16.2.2 Hydrides

H_2Se (like H_2O and H_2S) can be made by direct combination of the elements (above 350°), but H_2Te and H_2Po cannot be made in this way because of their thermal instability. H_2Se is a colourless, offensive-smelling poisonous gas which can be made by hydrolysis of Al_2Se_3, the action of dilute mineral acids on FeSe or the surface-catalysed reaction of gaseous Se and H_2:

$$Al_2Se_3 + 6H_2O \longrightarrow 3H_2Se + 2Al(OH)_3$$

$$FeSe + 2HCl \longrightarrow H_2Se + FeCl_2$$

$$Se + H_2 \rightleftharpoons H_2Se$$

In this last reaction, conversion at first rises with increase in temperature and then falls because of increasing thermolysis of the product: conversion exceeds ~40% between 350–650° and is optimum (64%) at 520°.

H_2Te is also a colourless, foul-smelling toxic gas which is best made by electrolysis of 15–50% aqueous H_2SO_4 at a Te cathode at −20°, 4.5 A and 75–110 V. It can also be made by hydrolysis of Al_2Te_3, the action of hydrochloric acid on the tellurides of Mg, Zn or Al, or by reduction of Na_2TeO_3 with $TiCl_3$ in a buffered solution. The compound is unstable above 0° and decomposes in moist air and on exposure to light. H_2Po is even less stable and has only been made in trace amounts (~10^{-10} g scale) by reduction of Po using Mg foil/dilute HCl and the reaction followed by radioactive tracer techniques.

[71] D. M. CHIZHIKOV and V. P. SHCHASTLIVYI, *Selenium and Selenides*, Collet's, London, 1968, 403 pp.

[72] F. HULLIGER, *Struct. Bonding (Berlin)*, **4**, 83–229 (1968).

Table 16.4   Some physical properties of H_2O, H_2S, H_2Se, H_2Te and H_2Po

Property	H_2O	H_2S	H_2Se	H_2Te	H_2Po
MP/°C	0.0	−85.6	−65.7	−51	−36(?)
BP/°C	100.0	−60.3	−41.3	−4	+37(?)
ΔH_f°/kJ mol^{-1}	−285.9	+20.1	+73.0	+99.6	—
Bond length (M–H)/pm	95.7	133.6	146	169	—
Bond angle (H–M–H) (g)	104.5°	92.1°	91°	90°	—
Dissociation constant:					
HM$^-$, K_1	1.8×10^{-16}	1.3×10^{-7}	1.3×10^{-4}	2.3×10^{-3}	—
M^{2-}, K_2	—	7.1×10^{-15}	$\sim 10^{-11}$	1.6×10^{-11}	—

Physical properties of the three gases are compared with those of H_2O and H_2S in Table 16.4. The trends are obvious, as is the "anomalous" position of water (p. 623). The densities of liquid and solid H_2Se are 2.12 and 2.45 g cm^{-3}. H_2Te condenses to a colourless liquid (d 4.4 g cm^{-3}) and then to lemon-yellow crystals. Both gases are soluble in water to about the same extent as H_2S, yielding increasingly acidic solutions (cf. acetic acid $K_1 \sim 2 \times 10^{-5}$). Such solutions precipitate the selenides and tellurides of many metals from aqueous solutions of their salts but, since both H_2Se and H_2Te are readily oxidized (e.g. by air), elementary Se and Te are often formed simultaneously.

H_2Se and H_2Te burn in air with a blue flame to give the dioxide (p. 779). Halogens and other oxidizing agents (e.g. HNO_3, $KMnO_4$) also rapidly react with aqueous solutions to precipitate the elements. Reaction of H_2Se with aqueous SO_2 is complex, the products formed depending critically on conditions (cf. Wackenroder's solution, p. 716): addition of the selenide to aqueous SO_2 yields a 2:1 mixture of S and Se together with oxoacids of sulfur, whereas addition of SO_2 to aqueous H_2Se yields mainly Se:

$$H_2Se + 5SO_2 + 2H_2O \longrightarrow 2S + Se + 3H_2SO_4$$

$$H_2Se + 6SO_2 + 2H_2O \longrightarrow 2S + Se + H_2S_2O_6$$
$$+ 2H_2SO_4$$

$$H_2Se + 6SO_2 + 2H_2O \longrightarrow Se + H_2S_4O_6$$
$$+ 2H_2SO_4$$

H_2Te undergoes oxidative addition to certain organometallic compounds, e.g. [Re(η^5-C$_5$Me$_5$)-(CO)$_2$(thf)] reacts in thf solution at 25°C to give [HRe(η^5-C$_5$Me$_5$)(CO)$_2$(TeH)] and related dinuclear complexes.[73] The Te analogue of the hydroxide ion, TeH$^-$, has been reported from time to time but has only recently been properly characterized crystallographically, in [PPh$_4$]$^+$[TeH]$^-$.[74]

16.2.3 Halides

As with sulfur, there is a definite pattern to the stoichiometries of the known halides of the heavier chalcogens. Selenium forms no binary iodides whereas the more electropositive Te and Po do. Numerous chlorides and bromides are known for all 3 elements, particularly in oxidation states +1, +2 and +4. In the highest oxidation state, +6, only the fluorides MF$_6$ are known for the 3 elements; in addition SeF$_4$ and TeF$_4$ have been characterized but no fluorides of lower oxidation states except the fugitive FSeSeF, Se=SeF$_2$ and SeF$_2$ which can be trapped out at low temperature.[75,76] The compound previously thought to be Te$_2$F$_{10}$ is now known to be O(TeF$_5$)$_2$[76,77] (p. 778). Finally, Te forms a range of curious lower halides which

[73] W. A. HERRMANN, C. HECHT, E. HERDTWECK and H.-J. KNEUPER, *Angew. Chem. Int. Edn. Engl.* **26**, 132–4 (1987).

[74] J. C. HUFFMAN and R. C. HAUSHALTER, *Polyhedron* **8**, 531–2 (1989).

[75] B. COHEN and R. D. PEACOCK, *Adv. Fluorine Chem.* **6**, 343–85 (1970).

[76] E. ENGELBRECHT and F. SLADKY, *Adv. Inorg. Chem. Radiochem.* **24**, 189–223 (1981). This review also includes oxofluorides of Se and Te, and related anions.

[77] P. M. WATKINS, *J. Chem. Educ.*, **51**, 520–1 (1974).

are structurally related to the Te_x chains in elementary tellurium.

The known compounds are summarized in Table 16.5 which also lists their colour, mp, bp and decomposition temperature where these have been reported. It will be convenient to discuss the preparation, structure and chemical properties of these various compounds approximately in ascending order of formal oxidation state. For comparable information on the halides of S, see pp. 683–93.

Lower halides

The phase relations in the tellurium-halogen systems have only recently been elucidated

Table 16.5　Halides of selenium, tellurium and polonium

Oxidation state	Fluorides	Chlorides	Bromides	Iodides
< 1		Te_2Cl Te_3Cl_2 silver grey mp 238° (peritectic)	Te_2Br grey needles mp 224 (peritectic)	Te_2I silver grey $[(Te_2)_2(I_2)_x](X \leq_i$ metallic black
+1	(FSeSeF) and (Se=SeF₂) trapped at low temperature	Se_2Cl_2 yellow-brown liquid mp −85°, bp 130° (d)	$(\beta\text{-})Se_2Br_2$ blood-red liquid bp 225° (d) (α-SeBr, mp +5°)	$\alpha\text{-}Te_4I_4$ black mp 185°(peritectic) β-TeI black
+2	(SeF₂) trapped at low temperature	(SeCl₂) d in vapour ("TeCl₂") black eutectic $PoCl_2$ dark ruby red mp 355°, subl 130°	(SeBr₂) d in vapour ("TeBr₂") brown d (see text) $PoBr_2$ purple-brown mp 270° (d)	(PoI₂) impure (from decomp of PoI₄ at 200°)
+4	SeF_4 colourless liquid mp −10°, bp 101° TeF_4 colourless mp 129° d > 194° $PoF_4(?)$ solid from decomp of PoF₆	Se_4Cl_{16} colourless mp 305°, subl 196° Te_4Cl_{16} pale-yellow solid. maroon liquid mp 223°, bp 390° $PoCl_4$ yellow d > 200° to PoCl₂ mp 300°, bp ∼ 390° extrapolated	$\alpha\text{-}Se_4Br_{16}$ orange-red mp 123° (also β-Se₄Br₁₆) Te_4Br_{16} yellow mp 388° (under Br₂) bp 414° (under Br₂) $PoBr_4$ bright red mp 330°, bp 360°/200 mmHg	Te_4I_{16} black mp 280°, d 100° PoI_4 black d > 200°
+6	SeF_6 colourless gas mp −35° (2 atm), subl −47° TeF_6 colourless gas mp −38°, subl −39°		*Mixed halides* $TeBr_2Cl_2$　yellow solid, ruby-red liquid mp 292°, bp 415° $TeBr_2I_2$　garnet-red crystals mp 325°, d 420° $PoBr_2Cl_2$　salmon pink (PoCl₂ + Br₂ vap)	

and the results show a series of subhalides with various structural motifs based on the helical-chain structure of Te itself.[78] These are summarized in Fig. 16.11. Thus, reaction of Te and Cl_2 under carefully controlled conditions in a sealed tube[79] results in Te_3Cl_2 (Fig. 16.11b) in which every third Te atom in the chain is oxidized by addition of 2 Cl atoms, thereby forming a series of 4-coordinate pseudo-trigonal-bipyramidal groups with axial Cl atoms linked by pairs of unmodified Te atoms $-Te-Te-TeCl_2-Te-Te-TeCl_2-$.[80] Te_2Br and Te_2I consist of zigzag chains of Te in planar arrangement (Fig. 16.11c); along the chain is an alternation of trigonal pyramidal (pseudo-tetrahedral) and square-planar (pseudo-octahedral) Te atoms. These chains are joined in pairs by cross-linking at the trigonal pyramidal Te atoms, thereby forming a ribbon of fused 6-membered Te rings in the boat configuration.[80] A similar motif occurs in β-TeI (Fig. 16.11d) which is formed by rapidly cooling partially melted α-TeI (see below) from 190°: in this case the third bond from the trigonal pyramidal Te atoms carries an I atom instead of being cross-linked to a similar chain.[81] The second, more stable modification, α-TeI, features tetrameric molecules Te_4I_4 which are themselves very loosely associated into chains by $Te-I\cdots Te$ links (Fig. 16.11e); the non-planar Te_4 ring comprises two non-adjacent 3-coordinate trigonal pyramidal Te atoms bridged on one side by a single 2-coordinate Te atom and on the other by a 4-coordinate planar $>TeI_2$ group. An unrelated structure motif is found in the unusual intercalation compound, $[(Te_2)_2(I_2)_x]$ ($x = 0.42-1.0$),[82] which is obtained as shiny, metallic-black air-stable crystals by hydrothermal reaction of 67% HI (aq.) on a 1:1 mixture of Te and GeTe at *ca.* 170° followed by slow cooling (18 h). The structure comprises planar double layers of Te_2 units intercalated by I_2 up to the limiting formula $[(Te_2)_2I_2]$. The Te atoms within the double layers exhibit distorted tetragonal pyramidal coordination with one short and four longer Te–Te distances (271.3 and 332.3 pm, respectively; cf. distances in Fig. 16.11). The I–I distance within the I_2 molecules is 286.6 pm (cf. 271.5 pm in solid iodine, p. 803). The semiconductivity and nonlinear optical properties of these various tellurium subhalides have been much studied for possible electronic applications.

The only other "monohalides" of these chalcogens are the highly coloured heavy liquids Se_2Cl_2 (d_{25} 2.774 g cm^{-3}) and Se_2Br_2 (d_{15} 3.604 g cm^{-3}). Both can be made by reaction of the stoichiometric amounts of the elements or better, by adding the halogen to a suspension of powdered Se in CS_2. Reduction of SeX_4 with 3Se in a sealed tube at 120° is also effective. Se_2Br_2 has a structure similar to that of S_2Cl_2 and S_2F_2 (pp. 689, 684) with a dihedral angle of 94°, angle Br–Se–Se 104° and a rather short Se–Se bond (224 pm, cf. 233.5 pm in monoclinic Se_8 and 237.3 pm in hexagonal Se_∞).[83] The structure of Se_2Cl_2 has not been determined but is probably similar. Se_2Br_2 is, in fact, the metastable molecular form (also known as β-SeBr); the structure of the more stable α-SeBr is as yet unknown.

Several mixed species have been identified in nonaqueous solutions by ^{77}Se nmr spectroscopy. These include BrSeSeCl. Se_3X_2 and Se_4X_2;[84] and ClSeSCl, BrSeSCl, ClSeSBr and

[78] R. KNIEP and A. RABENAU, *Topics in Current Chemistry* **111**, 145–92 (1983).

[79] A. RABENAU and H. RAU, *Z. anorg. allg. Chem.* **395**, 273–9 (1973).

[80] R. KNIEP, D. MOOTZ and A. RABENAU, *Angew. Chem. Int. Edn. Engl.* **12**, 499–500 (1973). M. TAKEDA and N. N. GREENWOOD, *J. Chem. Soc., Dalton Trans.*, 631–6 (1976).

[81] R. KNIEP, D. MOOTZ and A. RABENAU, *Angew. Chem. Int. Edn. Engl.* **13**, 403–4 (1973). More complex chain and ribbon structures are observed for the ternary compounds α-AsSeI, β-AsSeI, α-AsTeI and β-AsTeI, all of which are isoelectronic with Se_∞ and Te_∞ (R. KNIEP and H. D. RESKI, *Angew. Chem. Int. Edn. Engl.* **20**, 212–4 (1981)).

[82] R. KNIEP and H.-J. BEISTER, *Angew. Chem. Int. Edn. Engl.* **24**, 393–4 (1985).

[83] D. KATRYNIOK and R. KNIEP, *Angew. Chem. Int. Edn. Engl.* **19**, 645 (1980).

[84] M. LAMOUREUX and J. MILNE, *Polyhedron* **9**, 589–95 (1990).

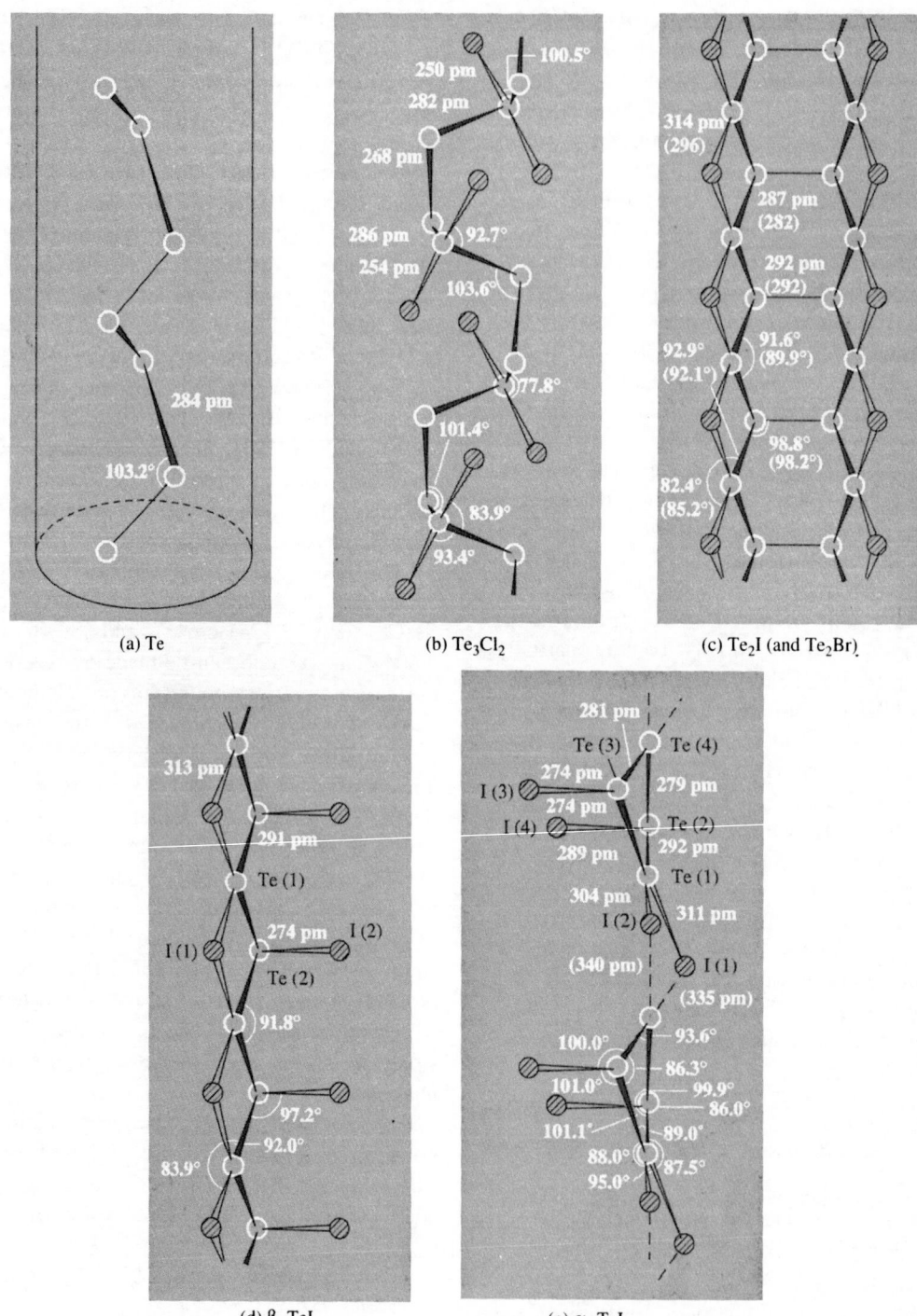

Figure 16.11 Structural relations between tellurium and its subhalides: (a) tellurium, (b) Te₃Cl₂, (c) Te₂Br and Te₂I, (d) β-TeI, and (e) α-TeI.

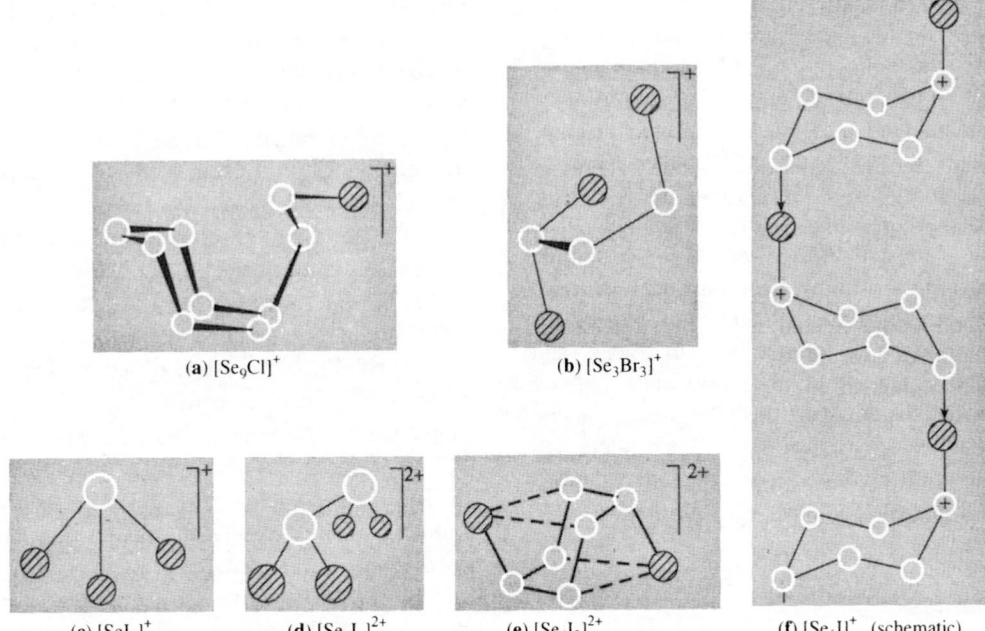

Figure 16.12 Structures of some selenium subhalide cations.

BrSeSBr.[85] ClSeSCl, formed by mixing solutions of S_2Cl_2 and Se_2Cl_2, has been reacted with titanocene pentasulfide (p. 672) to give mainly S_7, SeS_6 and 1,2-Se_2S_5, plus smaller amounts of 6-, 8-, 9- and 12-membered Se/S ring molecules.[86] The related reaction with $SeBr_2$ ($SeBr_4 + Se$) in MeCN yields similar Se/S heterocycles.[87]

It is also convenient to mention here several cationic subhalide species that have recently been synthesized. Reaction of Se with [NO][SbCl$_6$] in liquid SO_2 yields lustrous dark red crystals of $[Se_9Cl]^+[SbCl_6]^-$ which is the first example of a 7-membered Se ring, [cyclo-Se_7-SeSeCl]$^+$ (Fig. 16.12a).[88] Again, reaction of stoichiometric amounts of Se (or S), Br$_2$

and AsF_5 in liquid SO_2 yields dark red crystals or $[Br_2Se-SeSeBr]^+[AsF_6]^-$ (Fig. 16.12b)[89] or its S analogue. The first known binary Se/I species (albeit cationic rather than neutral) have been prepared[90] by reaction of Se_4^{2+} and I_2 in SO_2: The species SeI_3^+, $Se_2I_4^{2+}$, $Se_6I_2^{2+}$ were identified by ^{77}Se nmr spectroscopy and subsequently assigned the definitive structures shown in Fig. 16.12c,d,e after X-ray diffraction analysis.[91] The polymeric cation $[Se_6I]_\infty^+$ is also shown, (f).

Paradoxically, the most firmly established dihalides of the heavier chalcogens are the dark ruby-red $PoCl_2$ and the purple-brown $PoBr_2$ (Table 16.5). Both are formed by direct reaction of the elements or more conveniently by reducing $PoCl_4$ with SO_2 and $PoBr_4$ with H_2S at 25°.

[85] J. Milne, *J. Chem. Soc., Chem. Commun.*, 1048–9 (1991).

[86] R. Steudel, B. Plinke, D. Jensen and F. Baumgart, *Polyhedron*, **10**, 1037–48 (1991).

[87] R. Steudel, D. Jensen and F. Baumgart, *Polyhedron* **9**, 1199–208 (1990).

[88] R. Faggiani, R. J. Gillespie, J. W. Kolis and K. C. Malhotra, *J. Chem. Soc., Chem. Commun.*, 591–2 (1987).

[89] J. Passmore, M. Tajik and P. S. White, *J. Chem. Soc., Chem. Commun.*, 175–7 (1988).

[90] M. M. Carnell, F. Grein, M. Murchie, J. Passmore and C.-M. Wong, *J. Chem. Soc., Chem. Commun.*, 225–7 (1986).

[91] T. Klapötke and J. Passmore *Acc Chem. Res.* **22**, 234–40 (1989).

Doubt has been cast on "TeCl$_2$" and "TeBr$_2$" mentioned in the older literature since no sign of these was found in the phase diagrams.[79] However, this is not an entirely reliable method of establishing the existence of relatively unstable compounds between covalently bonded elements (cf. P/S, p. 506, and S/I, p. 691). It has been claimed that TeCl$_2$ and TeBr$_2$ are formed when fused Te reacts with CCl$_2$F$_2$ or CBrF$_3$,[92] though these materials certainly disproportionate to TeX$_4$ and Te on being heated and may indeed be eutectic-type phases in the system. SeCl$_2$ and SeBr$_2$ are unknown in the solid state but are thought to be present as unstable species in the vapour above SeX$_4$ and have been identified in equilibrium mixtures in nonaqueous solutions (see preceding paragraph).

Tetrahalides

All 12 tetrahalides of Se, Te and Po are known except, perhaps, for SeI$_4$. As with PX$_5$ (p. 498) and SX$_4$ (p. 691) these span the "covalent-ionic" border and numerous structural types are known; the stereochemical influence of the lone-pair of electrons (p. 377) is also prominent. SeF$_4$ is a colourless reactive liquid which fumes in air and crystallizes to a white hygroscopic solid (Table 16.5). It can be made by the controlled fluorination of Se (using F$_2$ at 0°, or AgF) or by reaction of SF$_4$ with SeO$_2$ above 100°. SeF$_4$ can be handled in scrupulously dried borosilicate glassware and is a useful fluorinating agent. Its structure in the gas phase, like that of SF$_4$ (p. 684), is pseudo-trigonal-bipyramidal with C_{2v} symmetry; the dimensions shown in Fig. 16.13a were obtained by microwave spectroscopy. The same structure persists in solution but, with increasing concentration there is an increasing tendency to association *via* intermolecular F-bridges. The structure in the crystalline phase also has Se bonded to 4F atoms in a distorted pseudo-trigonal bipyramidal configuration as shown in

Fig. 16.13b (Se–F$_{ax}$ 180 pm, Se–F$_{eq}$ 167 pm, with axial and equatorial angles subtended at Se of 169.3° and 96.9°, respectively).[93] However, these pseudo-tbp molecules are arranged in layers by weaker intermolecular interactions to neighbouring molecules so as to form an overall distorted octahedral environment with two further Se···F at 266 pm (Fig. 16.13b) somewhat reminiscent of the structure found earlier for TeF$_4$ (see Fig. 16.13c and below).

TeF$_4$ can be obtained as colourless, hygroscopic, sublimable crystals by controlled fluorination of Te or TeX$_2$ with F$_2$/N$_2$ at 0°, or more conveniently by reaction of SeF$_4$ with TeO$_2$ at 80°. It decomposes above 190° with formation of TeF$_6$ and is much more reactive than SeF$_4$. For example, it readily fluorinates SiO$_2$ above room temperature and reacts with Cu, Ag, Au and Ni at 185° to give the metal tellurides and fluorides. Adducts with BF$_3$, AsF$_5$ and SbF$_5$ are known (see also p. 776). Although probably monomeric in the gas phase, crystalline TeF$_4$ comprises chains of *cis*-linked square-pyramidal TeF$_5$ groups (Fig. 16.13c) similar to those in the isoelectronic (SbF$_4^-$)$_n$ ions (p. 565). The lone-pair is alternately above and below the mean basal plane and each Te atom is displaced some 30 pm in the same direction. However, the local Te environment is somewhat less symmetrical than implied by this idealized description, and the Te–F distances span the range 183–228 pm.[93]

The other tetrahalides can all readily be made by direct reactions of the elements. Crystalline SeCl$_4$, TeCl$_4$ and β-SeBr$_4$ are isotypic and the structural unit is a cubane-like tetramer of the same general type as [Me$_3$Pt(μ_3-Cl)]$_4$ (p. 1168). This is illustrated schematically for TeCl$_4$ in Fig. 16.13d: each Te is displaced outwards along a threefold axis and thus has a distorted octahedral environment. This can be visualized as resulting from repulsions due to the Te lone-pairs directed towards the cube centre and, in the limit, would result in the separation into

[92] E. E. AYNSLEY, *J. Chem. Soc.* 3016–9 (1953). E. E. AYNSLEY and R. H. WATSON, *J. Chem. Soc.* 2603–6 (1955).

[93] R. KNIEP, L. KORTE, R. KRYSCHI and W. POLL, *Angew. Chem. Int. Edn. Engl.* **23**, 388–9 (1984).

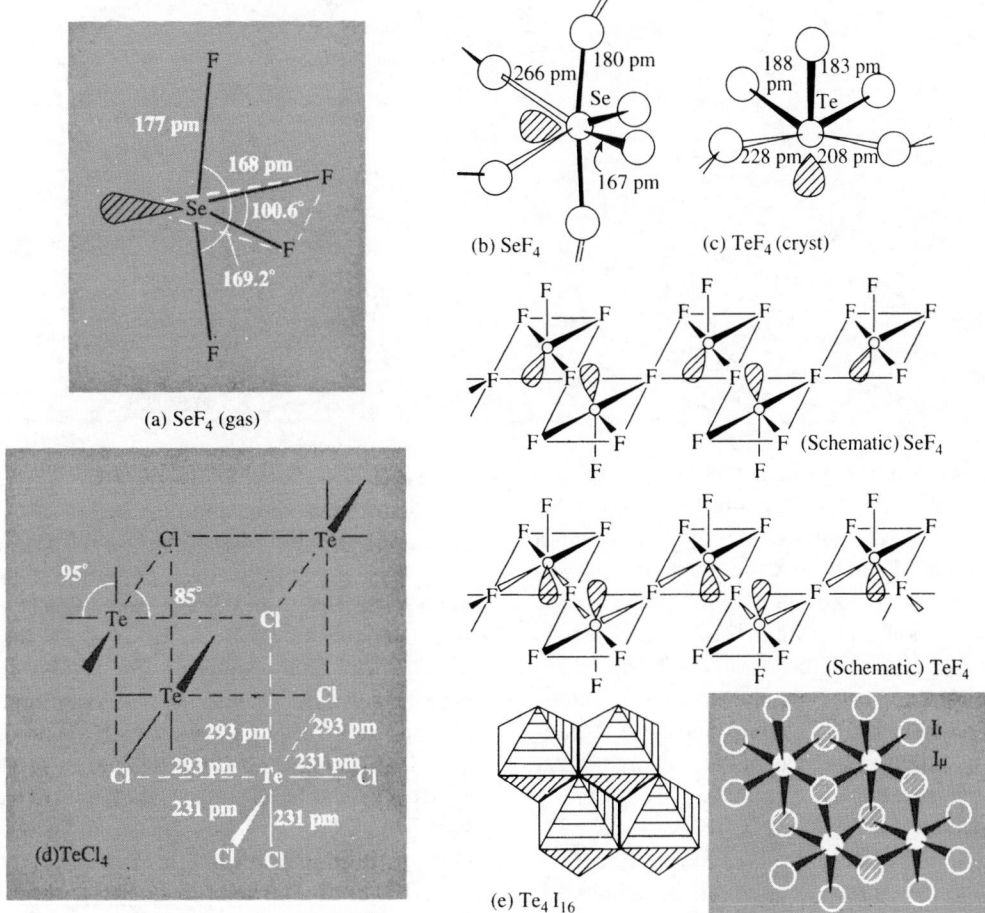

Figure 16.13 Structures of some tetrahalides of Se and Te: (a) SeF_4 (gas), (b) crystalline SeF_4, and schematic representation of the association of the pseudo-tbp molecules (see text), (c) coordination environment of Te in crystalline TeF_4 and schematic representation of the polymerized square pyramidal units, (d) the tetrameric unit in crystalline $(TeCl_4)_4$, and (e) two representations of the tetrameric molecules in Te_4I_{16} showing the shared edges of the $\{TeI_6\}$ octahedral subunits.

$TeCl_3^+$ and Cl^- ions. Accordingly, the 3 tetrahalides are good electrical conductors in the fused state, and salts of SeX_3^+ and $TeCl_3^+$ can be isolated in the presence of strong halide ion acceptors, e.g. $[SeCl_3]^+[GaCl_4]^-$, $[SeBr_3]^+[AlBr_4]^-$, $[TeCl_3]^+[AlCl_4]^-$. In solution, however, the structure depends on the donor properties of the solvent:[94] in donor solvents such as MeCN, Me_2CO and EtOH the electrical conductivity

and vibrational spectra indicate the structure $[L_2TeCl_3]^+Cl^-$, where L is a molecule of solvent, whereas in benzene and toluene the compound dissolves as a non-conducting molecular oligomer which is tetrameric at a concentration of 0.1 molar but which is in equilibrium with smaller oligomeric units at lower concentrations. Removal of one $TeCl_3^+$ unit from the cubane-like structure of Te_4Cl_{16} leaves the trinuclear anion $Te_3Cl_{13}^-$ which can be isolated from benzene solutions as the salt of the large counter-cation Ph_3C^+; the anion has the expected C_{3v} structure

[94] N. N. GREENWOOD, B. P. STRAUGHAN and A. E. WILSON, *J. Chem. Soc.* (A) 2209–12 (1968).

$$Te_4Cl_{16} \xrightarrow{-TeCl_3^+} [Te_3Cl_{13}]^- \xrightarrow{-TeCl_3^+} [Te_2Cl_{10}]^{2-} \xrightarrow{-TeCl_4} [TeCl_6]^{2-}$$

comprising three edge-shared octahedra with a central triply bridging Cl atom.[95] Removal of a further $TeCl_3^+$ unit yields the edge-shared bi-octahedral dianion $Te_2Cl_{10}{}^{2-}$ which was isolated as the crystalline salt $[AsPh_4]_2^+[Te_2Cl_{10}]^{2-}$. Notional removal of a final $\{TeCl_4\}$ unit leaves the octahedral anion $TeCl_6{}^{2-}$ (p. 776) as in the scheme above.

Numerous crystal structures have been published of compounds containing the pyramidal cations $Se^{IV}Cl_3^+$, $Se^{IV}Br_3^+$, $Te^{IV}Cl_3^+$, etc.[96] and the anions $Se^{II}Cl_4{}^{2-}$, $Se_2^{II}Cl_6{}^{2-}$;[97] $Se_3Cl_{13}^-$, $Se_3Br_{13}^-$;[98] $SeCl_5^-$, $TeCl_5^-$, $TeCl_6{}^{2-}$, etc.[99] The anion structures are much as expected with the Se^{II} species featuring square planar (pseudo-octahedral) units, and the trinuclear Se^{IV} anions as in the tellurium analogue above. See also p. 776. There are, in addition, a fascinating series of bromoselenate(II) dianions based on fused planar $\{SeBr_4\}$ units, e.g. $Se_3Br_8{}^{2-}$, $Se_4Br_{14}{}^{2-}$,

and $Se_5Br_{12}{}^{2-}$, (see Fig. 16.14a,b,c)[100]. Access has also been gained to a series of novel mixed-valence bromopolyselenate (II,IV) dianions by exploiting the dissociation equilibria $\frac{1}{4}Se_4Br_{16} \rightleftharpoons SeBr_4 \rightleftharpoons SeBr_2 + Br_2$ and $2SeBr_2 \rightleftharpoons Se_2Br_2 + Br_2$. Careful addition of Br_2 to such solutions in weakly polar organic solvents displaces these equilibria and permits the isolation of tetraalkylammonium or tetraphenylphosphonium salts of $Se_2Br_8{}^{2-}$, $Se_3Br_{10}{}^{2-}$, and $Se_4Br_{12}{}^{2-}$, as dark red crystalline salts featuring fused square planar and octahedral units as illustrated in Fig. 16.15a,b,c.[101]

$SeBr_4$ itself is dimorphic: the α-form, like β-$SeBr_4$ mentioned on p. 772, has a cubane-like tetrameric unit (Se–Br_t 237 pm, Se–Br_μ 297 pm) but the two forms differ in the spacial arrangement of the tetramers.[102] TeI_4 has yet another structure which involves a tetrameric arrangement of edge-shared $\{TeI_6\}$ octahedra not previously encountered in binary inorganic compounds (Fig. 16.13e).[103] The molecule is close to idealized C_{2h} symmetry with each terminal octahedron sharing 2 edges with the 2 neighbouring central octahedra

[95] B. KREBS and V. PAULAT, *Z. Naturforsch.* **34b**, 900–5 (1979), and references therein.

[96] B. H. CHRISTIAN, M. J. COLLINS, R. J. GILLESPIE and J. F. SAWYER, *Inorg. Chem.* **25**, 777–88 (1986). B. NEUMÜLLER, C. LAU and K. DEHNICKE, *Z. anorg. allg. Chem.* **622**, 1847–53 (1996).

[97] B. KREBS, E. LÜHRS, R. WILLMER and F.-P. AHLERS, *Z. anorg. allg. Chem.* **592**, 17–34 (1991). See also H. FOLKERTS, K. DEHNICKE, J. MAGULL, H. GOESMANN and D. FENSKE, *Z. anorg. allg. Chem.* **620**, 1301–6 (1994).

[98] F.-P. AHLERS, E. LÜHRS and B. KREBS, *Z. anorg. allg. Chem.* **594**, 7–22 (1991).

[99] B. BORGSEN, F. WELLER and K. DEHNICKE, *Z. anorg. allg. Chem.* **596**, 55–61 (1991), and 2nd part of ref. 96.

[100] B. KREBS, F.-P. AHLERS and E. LÜHRS, *Z. anorg. allg. Chem.* **597**, 115–32 (1991).

[101] B. KREBS, E. LÜHRS and F.-P. AHLERS, *Angew. Chem. Int. Edn. Engl.* **28**, 187–9 (1989).

[102] P. BORN, R. KNIEP and D. MOOTZ, *Z. anorg. allg. Chem.* **451**, 12–24 (1979).

[103] V. PAULAT and B. KREBS, *Angew. Chem. Int. Edn. Engl.* **15**, 39–40 (1976).

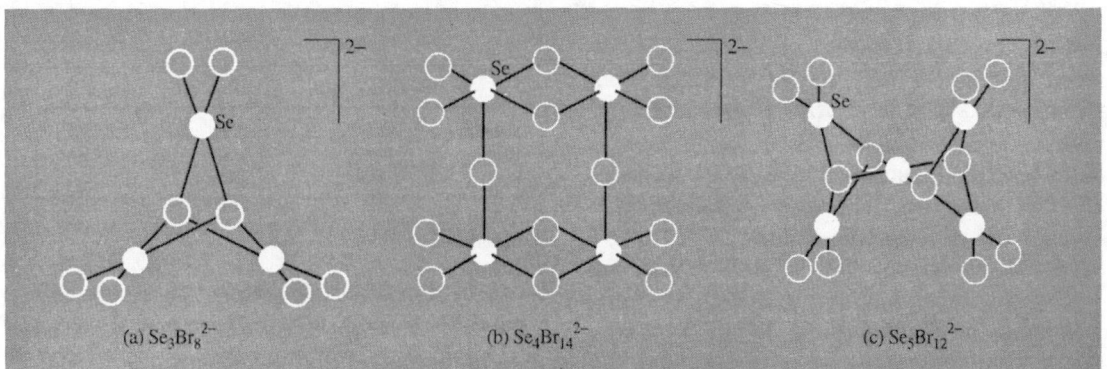

Figure 16.14   Structures of some bromoselenate(II) anions.

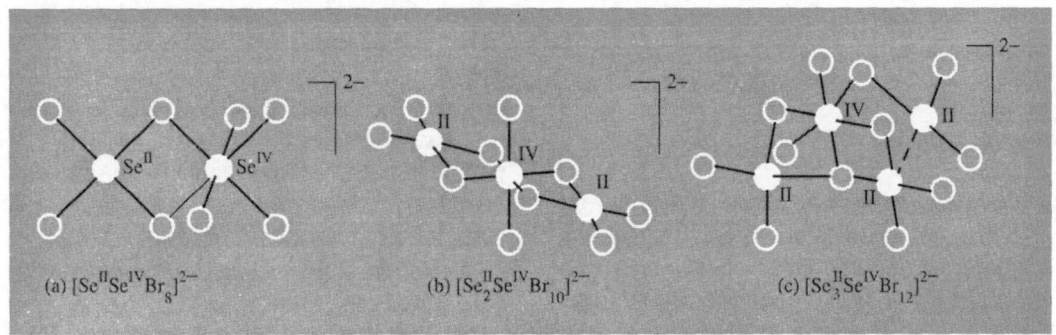

Figure 16.15   Structures of some mixed-valence bromopolyselenate(II,IV) anions.

and each central octahedron sharing 3 edges with its 3 neighbours (Te–I_t 277 pm. Te–I_{μ_2} 311 pm, Te–I_{μ_3} 323 pm). There is no significant intermolecular I$\cdots$I bonding. Comparison of the structures and bond data for the homologous series TeF_4, $TeCl_4$($TeBr_4$), TeI_4 reveals an increasing delocalization of the Te^{IV} lone-pair. This effect is also observed in the compounds of other ns^2 elements (e.g. Sn^{II}, Pb^{II}, As^{III}, Sb^{III}, Bi^{III}, I^V; see pp. 380, 383, 568) and correlates with the gradation of electronegativities and the polarizing power of the halogens.

The detailed structures of PoX_4 are unknown. Some properties are in Table 16.5. PoF_4 is not well characterized. $PoCl_4$ forms bright-yellow monoclinic crystals which can be melted under an atmosphere of chlorine, and $PoBr_4$ has a fcc lattice with $a_0 = 560$ pm. These compounds and PoI_4 can be made by direct combination of the elements or indirectly, e.g. by the chlorination of PoO_2 with HCl, PCl_5 or $SOCl_2$, or by the reaction of PoO_2 with HI and 200°. Similar methods are used to prepare the tetrahalides of Se and Te, e.g.:

$TeCl_4$: Cl_2 + Te; $SeCl_2$ on Te, TeO_2 or $TeCl_2$;
                  CCl_4 + TeO_2 at 500°
$TeBr_4$:   Te + Br_2 at room temp;   aq HBr on TeO_2
TeI_4:   Heat Te + I_2;   Te + MeI; $TeBr_4$ + EtI

The two mixed tellurium(IV) halides listed in Table 16.5 were prepared by the action of liquid Br_2 on $TeCl_2$ to give the yellow solid $TeBr_2Cl_2$, and by the action of I_2 on $TeBr_2$ in ether solution to give the red crystalline $TeBr_2I_2$; their structures are as yet unknown.

Hexahalides

The only hexahalides known are the colourless gaseous fluorides SeF_6 and TeF_6 and the volatile liquids TeClF$_5$ and TeBrF$_5$. The hexafluorides are prepared by direct fluorination of the elements or by reaction of BrF$_3$ on the dioxides. Both are octahedral with Se–F 167–170 pm and Te–F 184 pm. SeF$_6$ resembles SF$_6$ in being inert to water but it is decomposed by aqueous solutions of KI or thiosulfate. TeF$_6$ hydrolyses completely within 1 day at room temperature.

The mixed halides TeClF$_5$ and TeBrF$_5$ are made by oxidative fluorination of TeCl$_4$ or TeBr$_4$ in a stream of F$_2$ diluted with N$_2$ at 25°. Under similar conditions TeI$_4$ gave only TeF$_6$ and IF$_5$. TeCiF$_5$ can also be made by the action of ClF on TeF$_4$, TeCl$_4$ or TeO$_2$ below room temperature; it is a colourless liquid, mp −28°, bp 13.5°, which does not react with Hg, dry metals or glass at room temperature.

Halide complexes

It is convenient to include halide complexes in this section on the halides of Se, Te and Po and, indeed, some have already been alluded to above. In addition, pentafluoroselenates(IV) can be obtained as rather unstable white solids MSeF$_5$ by dissolving alkali metal fluorides or TlF in SeF$_4$. The crystal structure of Me$_4$NSeF$_5$ features square-pyramidal SeF$_5^-$ ions,[104] with Se–F$_{apex}$ 171 pm Se–F$_{base}$ 185 pm and the angle F$_a$–Se–F$_b$ 84°, implying that the Se atom and its lone pair of electrons lies some 20 pm below the basal plane (cf. Fig. 16.13b). The tellurium analogues are best prepared by dissolving MF and TeO$_2$ in aqueous HF or SeF$_4$; they are white crystalline solids. The TeF$_5^-$ ion (like SeF$_5^-$) has a distorted square-based pyramidal structure (C_{4v}) in which the Te atom (and pendant lone-pair of electrons) is about 30 pm below the basal plane with Te–F$_{apex}$ 184 pm, Te–F$_{base}$ 196 pm and the angle F$_a$–Te–F$_b$ 81°[104] (cf. TeF$_4$, Fig. 16.13c). The resemblance to other isoelectronic MF$_5^{n\pm}$ species is illustrated in Table 16.6; in each case, the fact that the distance M–F$_{base}$ is greater than M–F$_{apex}$ and that the angle F$_{apex}$–M–F$_{base}$ is less than 90°

Table 16.6 Dimensions of some isoelectronic square-pyramidal species

Species	M–F$_{apex}$/pm	M–F$_{base}$/pm	∠F$_{apex}$–M–F$_{base}$
SbF$_5^{2-}$	200	204	83°
TeF$_5^-$	184	196	81°
BrF$_5$	168	181	84°
XeF$_5^+$	181	188	79°

can be ascribed to repulsive interaction of the basal M–F bonds with the lone-pair of electrons.

Attempts to prepare compounds containing the TeF$_6^{2-}$ ion have not been successful though numerous routes have been tried. However, reaction of Me$_4$NF with TeF$_6$ in anhydrous MeCN affords the novel 7- and 8-coordinated species TeF$_7^-$ (D_{5h}, pentagonal bipyramid)[105,106] and TeF$_8^{2-}$ (D_{4d}, square antiprism),[105] There is also a remarkable heterolytic reaction of TeF$_4$ with 4-coordinated rhodium complexes [Rh(CO)X(PEt$_3$)$_2$], (X = Cl, Br, NCS, NCO) at −78°C to give the unusual ionic complex [Rh(CO)X(PEt$_3$)$_2$(TeF$_3$)]$^+$(TeF$_5$)]$^-$.[107] Note that the TeF$_3^+$ ligand is isoelectronic with PF$_3$, SbF$_3$, etc.

By contrast to the absence of TeF$_6^{2-}$, compounds of the complex anions SeX$_6^{2-}$ and TeX$_6^{2-}$ (X = Cl, Br, I) are readily prepared in crystalline form by direct reaction (e.g. TeX$_4$ + 2MX) or by precipitating the complex from a solution of SeO$_2$ or TeO$_2$ in aqueous HX. Their most notable feature is a regular octahedral structure despite the fact that they are formally 14-electron species; it appears that with large monatomic ligands of moderate electronegativity the stereochemistry is dominated by inter-ligand repulsions and the lone-pair then either resides in an ns^2 orbital for isolated ions or is delocalized in a low-energy solid-state band.[108] Similar results

104 A. R. MAHJOUB, D. LEOPOLD and K. SEPPELT, *Z. anorg. allg. Chem.* **618**, 83–8 (1992).

105 K. O. CHRISTE, J. P. C. SANDERS, G. J. SCHROBILGEN and W. W. WILSON, *J. Chem. Soc., Chem. Commun.*, 837–40 (1991) and references cited therein.

106 A. R. MAHJOUB and K. SEPPELT, *J. Chem. Soc., Chem. Commun.*, 840–1 (1991).

107 E. A. V. EBSWORTH, J. H. HOLLOWAY and P. G. WATSON, *J. Chem. Soc., Chem. Commun.*, 1443–4 (1991).

108 For experimental results and theoretical discussion see I. D. BROWN, *Can. J. Chem.* **42**, 2758–67 (1964);

Table 16.7   Some physical properties of selenium oxohalides

Property	$SeOF_2$	$SeOCl_2$	$SeOBr_2$	SeO_2F_2	$(SeOF_4)_2$	F_5SeOF	$F_5SeOOSF_5$
MP/°C	15	10.9	41.6	−99.5	−12	−54	−62.8
BP/°C	125	177.2	~220 (d)	−8.4	65	−29	76.3
Density/g cm^{-3} (T°C)	2.80 (21.5°)	2.445 (16°)	3.38 (50°)	—	—	—	—

were noted for octahedral Sn^{II} (p. 380) and Sb^{III} (p. 568).

16.2.4 Oxohalides and pseudohalides [1]

Numerous oxohalides of Se^{IV} and Se^{VI} are known, $SeOF_2$ and $SeOCl_2$ are colourless, fuming, volatile liquids, whereas $SeOBr_2$ is a rather less-stable orange solid which decomposes in air above 50° (Table 16.7). The compounds can be conveniently made by reacting SeO_2 with the appropriate tetrahalide and their molecular structure is probably pyramidal (like SOX_2, p. 694). $SeOF_2$ is an aggressive reagent which attacks glass, reacts violently with red phosphorus and with powdered SiO_2 and slowly with Si. In the solid state, X-ray studies have revealed that the pyramidal $SeOF_2$ units are linked by O and F bridges into layers thereby building a distorted octahedral environment around each Se with 3 close contacts (to O and 2F) and 3 (longer) bridging contacts grouped around the lone-pair to neighbouring units.[109] This contrasts with the discrete

molecular structure of SOF_2 and affords yet another example of the influence of preferred coordination number on the structure and physical properties of isovalent compounds, e.g. molecular BF_3 and 6-coordinate AlF_3, molecular GeF_4 and the 6-coordinate layer lattice of SnF_4 and, to a less extent, molecular AsF_3 and F-bridged SbF_3. (See also the Group 14 dioxides, etc.)

$SeOCl_2$ (Table 16.7) is a useful solvent: it has a high dielectric constant (46.2 at 20°), a high dipole moment (2.62 D in benzene) and an appreciable electrical conductivity (2 × 10^{-5} ohm^{-1} cm^{-1} at 25°). This last has been ascribed to self-ionic dissociation resulting from chloride-ion transfer: $2SeOCl_2 \rightleftharpoons SeOCl^+ + SeOCl_3^-$.

Oxohalides of Se^{VI} are known only for fluorine (Table 16.7). SeO_2F_2 is a readily hydrolysable colourless gas which can be made by fluorinating SeO_3 with SeF_4 (or KBF_4 at 70°) or by reacting $BaSeO_4$ with HSO_3F under reflux at 50°. Its vibrational spectra imply a tetrahedral structure with C_{2v} symmetry as expected. By contrast, $SeOF_4$ is a dimer $[F_4Se(\mu\text{-}O)_2SeF_4]$ in which each Se achieves octahedral coordination via the 2 bridging O atoms: the planar central Se_2O_2 ring has Se–O 178 pm and angle Se–O–Se 97.5°, and Se–F$_{eq}$ and Se–F$_{ax}$ are 167 and 170 pm respectively.[110]

Two further oxofluorides of Se^{VI} can be prepared by reaction of SeO_2 with a mixture of F_2/N_2: at 80° the main product is the "hypofluorite" F_5SeOF whereas at 120° the peroxide $F_5SeOOSeF_5$ predominates. The compounds (Table 16.7) can be purified by

D. S. URCH, *J. Chem. Soc.* 5775–81 (1964); N. N. GREEN-WOOD and B. P. STRAUGHAN, *J. Chem. Soc.* (A) 962–4 (1966); T. C. GIBB, R. GREATREX, N. N. GREENWOOD and A. C. SARMA, *J. Chem. Soc.* (A) 212–17 (1970). J. D. DONALDSON, S. D. ROSS, J. SILVER and P. WATKISS, *J. Chem. Soc., Dalton Trans.*, 1980–3 (1975), and references therein. There is, however, some very recent X-ray crystallographic evidence that the anion in $[Bu^tNH_3]_2^+[TeBr_6]^{2-}$ is trigonally distorted, with 3 long bonds of 276 pm (av.) and 3 shorter bonds of 261 pm, although the corresponding $TeCl_6^{2-}$ salt had regular octahedral O_h symmetry: see L.-J. BAKER, C. E. F. RICKARD and M. J. TAYLOR, *Polyhedron* **14**, 401–5 (1995).

[109] J. C. DEWAN and A. J. EDWARDS, *J. Chem. Soc., Dalton Trans.*, 2433–5 (1976).

[110] H. OBERHAMMER and K. SEPPELT, *Inorg. Chem.* **18**, 2226–9 (1979).

fractional sublimation and are reactive, volatile, colourless solids. The analogous sulfur compounds were discussed on p. 688. The colourless liquid $F_5SeOSeF_5$ (mp $-85°$, bp $53°$) is made by a somewhat more esoteric route as follows:[111]

$$Xe(OSeF_5)_2 \xrightarrow{130°} Xe + \tfrac{1}{2}O_2 + F_5SeOSeF_5$$

The corresponding tellurium analogue, F_5Te-$TeOF_5$, is made by fluorinating TeO_2 in a copper vessel at $60°$ using a stream of F_2/N_2 (1:10); it is a colourless, mobile, unreactive liquid, mp $-36.6°$ bp $59.8°$.[76,77] The Se–O–Se angle in $F_5SeOSeF_5$ is $142.4°$ ($\pm 1.9°$) as in the sulfur analogue, and the Te–O–Te angle is very similar ($145.5 \pm 2.1°$). The fluorination of Te in the presence of oxygen yields (in addition to $Te_2F_{10}O$, p. 767) the dense colourless liquids $Te_3^{VI}O_2F_{14}$ and $Te_6^{VI}O_5F_{26}$. More purposeful synthetic routes have also been devised, leading to the isolation and structural characterization of the 6-coordinate Te^{VI} oxofluorides cis- and trans-$F_4Te(OTeF_5)_2$, cis- and trans-$F_2Te(OTeF_5)_4$, $FTe(OTeF_5)_5$ and even $Te(OTeF_5)_6$.[112] Similarly, thermolysis of $B(OTeF_5)_3$ at $600°$ in a flow system yields the oxygen-bridged dimer $Te_2O_2F_8$ analogous to $Se_2O_2F_8$ above. $Te_2O_2F_8$ is a colourless liquid with a garlic-like smell, mp $28°$, bp $77.5°$. The planar central Te_2O_2 ring has Te–O 192 pm and angle Te–O–Te $99.5°$, and again the equatorial Te–F distances (180 pm) are shorter than the axial ones (185 pm).[110]

The $-OTeF_5$ group (like the $-OSeF_5$ group) has a very high electronegativity as can be seen, for example, by the reactions of the ligand transfer reagent $[B(OTeF_5)_3]$:[113]

$$IF_5 + B(OTeF_5)_3 \longrightarrow FI(OTeF_5)_4$$

$$XeF_4 + B(OTeF_5)_3 \longrightarrow Xe(OTeF_5)_4$$

(see also p. 899)

Direct fluorination of $B(OTeF_5)_3$ at $115°$ gives a 95% yield of the hypofluorite, F_5TeOF, as a colourless gas which condenses to a colourless liquid below $0°$ and finally to a glass at about $-80°$; the extrapolated bp is $0.6°$.[114] The chlorine derivative, $ClOTeF_5$, the so-called teflic acid, $HOTeF_5$, and the teflate anion, F_5TeO^- (as caesium or tetraalkylammonium salts) are also useful synthons for a variety of metal derivatives, e.g. $[Fe(OTeF_5)_3]$,[115] $[Nb(OTeF_5)_6]^-$ and $[Ta(OTeF_5)_6]^-$.[116] Other examples are $[Mn(CO)_5(OTeF_5)]$ and $[Pt(norbornadiene)(OTeF_5)_2]$. The $-OTeF_5$ group can also act as a bridging ligand, as in the dimeric Ag^I and Tl^I complexes, $[\{(\eta^2\text{-tol})Ag\}_2(\mu\text{-}OTeF_5)_2]$[117] and $[\{(\eta^6\text{-mes})_2Tl\}_2(\mu(OTeF_5)_2]$,[118] which both feature a central planar M_2O_2 core (tol = toluene, C_6H_5Me; mes = mesitylene, $1,3,5\text{-}C_6H_3Me_3$). The H-bonded anion $[H(OTeF_5)_2]^-$ is also notable.[119]

Pseudohalides of Se in which the role of halogen is played by cyanide, thiocyanate or selenocyanate are known and, in the case of Se^{II} are much more stable with respect to disproportionation than are the halides themselves. Examples are $Se(CN)_2$, $Se_2(CN)_2$, $Se(SeCN)_2$, $Se(SCN)_2$, $Se_2(SCN)_2$. The selenocyanate ion $SeCN^-$ is ambidentate like the thiocyanate ion, etc., p. 325), being capable of ligating to metal centres via either N or Se, as in the osmium(IV) complexes $[OsCl_5(NCSe)]^{2-}$, $[OsCl_5(SeCN)]^{2-}$, and trans-$[OsCl_4(NCSe)(SeCN)]^{2-}$.[120] Tellurium and polonium pseudohalogen analogues include $Te(CN)_2$ and $Po(CN)_4$ but have been much

[111] H. OBERHAMMER and K. SEPPELT, *Inorg. Chem.* **17**, 1435–9 (1978).

[112] D. LENTZ, H. PRITZKOW and K. SEPPELT, *Inorg. Chem.* **17**, 1926–31 (1978).

[113] D. LENZ and K. SEPPELT, *Angew. Chem. Int. Edn. Engl.* **17**, 355–6 and 356–61 (1978).

[114] C. J. SCHACK and K. O. CHRISTE, *Inorg. Chem.* **23**, 2922 (1984).

[115] T. DREWS and K. SEPPELT, *Z. anorg. allg. Chem.* **606**, 201–7 (1991).

[116] K. MOOCK and K. SEPPELT, *Z. anorg. allg. Chem.* **561**, 132–8 (1988).

[117] S. H. STRAUSS, N. D. NOIROT and O. P. ANDERSON, *Inorg. Chem.* **24**, 4307–11 (1985).

[118] S. H. STRAUSS, N. D. NOIROT and O. P. ANDERSON, *Inorg. Chem.* **25**, 3851–3 (1986).

[119] S. H. STRAUSS, K. D. ABNEY and O. P. ANDERSON, *Inorg. Chem.* **25**, 2806–12 (1986).

[120] W. PREETZ and U. SELLERBERG, *Z. anorg. allg. Chem.* **589**, 158–66 (1988).

less studied than their Se counterparts. The long-sought tellurocyanate ion TeCN⁻ has finally been made, and isolated in crystalline form by the use of large counter-cations;[121] as expected, the anion is essentially linear (angle Te–C–N 175°), and the distances Te–C and C–N are 202 and 107 pm respectively.

The selenohalides and tellurohalides of both main-group elements and transition metals have been compared with the corresponding thiohalides in two extensive reviews.[122] Other inorganic compounds of Se and Te, with bonds to N, P etc are described on pp. 783–6.

16.2.5 Oxides

The monoxides SeO and TeO have transient existence in flames but can not be isolated as stable solids. PoO has been obtained as a black, easily oxidized solid by the spontaneous radiolytic decomposition of the sulfoxide $PoSO_3$.

The dioxides of all 3 elements are well established and can be obtained by direct

---

[121] A. S. FOUST, *J. Chem. Soc., Chem. Commun.*, 414–5 (1979).

[122] M. J. ATHERTON and J. H. HOLLOWAY, *Adv. Inorg. Chem. Radiochem.* **22**, 171–98 (1979). J. FENNER, A. RABENAU and G. TRAGESER, *Adv. Inorg. Chem. Radiochem.* **23**, 329–425 (1980).

combination of the elements. SeO_2 is a white solid which melts in a sealed tube to a yellow liquid at 340° (sublimes at 315°/760 mmHg). It is very soluble in water to give selenous acid H_2SeO_3 from which it can be recovered by dehydration. It is also very soluble (as a trimer) in $SeOCl_2$ and in H_2SO_4 in which it behaves as a weak base. SeO_2 is thermodynamically less stable than either SO_2 or TeO_2 and is readily reduced to the elements by NH_3, N_2H_4 or aqueous SO_2 (but not gaseous SO_2). It also finds use as an oxidizing agent in organic chemistry. In the solid state SeO_2 has a polymeric structure of corner-linked flattened {SeO_3} pyramids each carrying a pendant terminal O atom:

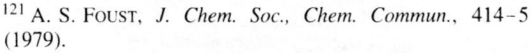

TeO_2 is dimorphic: the yellow, orthorhombic mineral tellurite (β-TeO_2) has a layer structure in which pseudo-trigonal bipyramidal {TeO_4} groups form edge-sharing pairs (Fig. 16.16a) which then further aggregate into layers (Fig. 16.16b) by sharing the remaining vertices. By contrast, synthetic α-TeO_2 ("paratellurite")

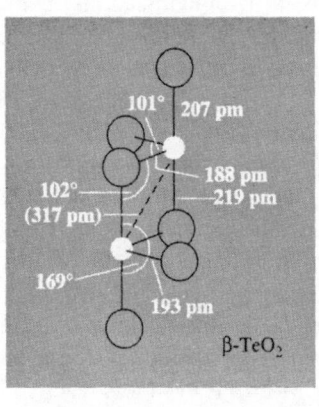

(a)

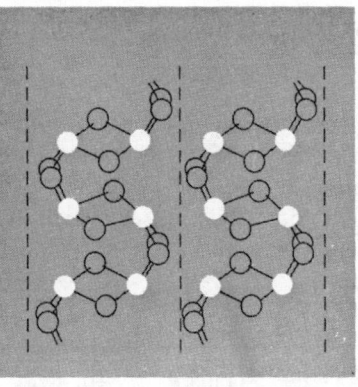

(b)

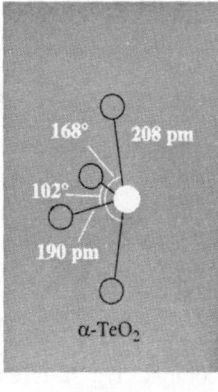

(c)

Figure 16.16 Structural units in crystalline TeO_2: (a) pair of edge-sharing pseudo-trigonal bipyramidal {TeO_4} groups in tellurite (β-TeO_2) which aggregate into layers as shown in (b) by sharing the remaining vertices with neighbouring pairs, and (c) the {TeO_4} unit in paratellurite (α-TeO_2).

forms colourless tetragonal crystals in which very similar {TeO$_4$} units (Fig. 16.16c) share all vertices (angle Te–O–Te 140°) to form a rutile-like (p. 961) three-dimensional structure. TeO$_2$ melts to a red liquid at 733° and is much less volatile than SeO$_2$. It can be prepared by the action of O$_2$ on Te, by dehydrating H$_2$TeO$_3$ or by thermal decomposition of the basic nitrate above 400°. TeO$_2$ is not very soluble in water; it is amphoteric and shows a minimum in solubility (at pH ∼ 4.0). It is, however, very soluble in SeOCl$_2$.

PoO$_2$ is obtained by direct combination of the elements at 250° or by thermal decomposition of polonium(IV) hydroxide, nitrate, sulfate or selenate. The yellow (low-temperature) fcc form has a fluorite lattice; it becomes brown when heated and can be sublimed in a stream of O$_2$ at 885°. However, under reduced pressure it decomposes into the elements at almost 500°. There is also a high-temperature, red, tetragonal form. PoO$_2$ is amphoteric, though appreciably more basic than TeO$_2$: e.g. it forms the disulfate Po(SO$_4$)$_2$ for which no Te analogue is known.

It is instructive to note the progressive trend to higher coordination numbers in the Group 16 dioxides, and the consequent influence on structure:

Compound	SO$_2$	SeO$_2$
Coordination number	2	3
Structure	molecule	chain polymers

Compound	TeO$_2$	PoO$_2$
Coordination number	4	8
Structure	layer or 3D	3D "fluorite"

The difficulty of oxidizing Se to the +6 state has already been mentioned (p. 755). Indeed, unlike SO$_3$ and TeO$_3$, SeO$_3$ is thermodynamically unstable with respect to the dioxide:

$$SeO_3 \longrightarrow SeO_2 + \tfrac{1}{2}O_2; \quad \Delta H° = -46 \text{ kJ mol}^{-1}$$

Some comparative figures for the standard heats of formation $-\Delta H_f°$ are in Table 16.8. Accordingly, SeO$_3$ can not be made by direct oxidation of Se or SeO$_2$ and is even hard to make by the dehydration of H$_2$SeO$_4$ with P$_2$O$_5$; a better

Table 16.8 $-\Delta H_f°$ (298)/kJ mol^{-1} for MO$_n$ from elements in standard states

SO$_2$	297	SeO$_2$	230	TeO$_2$	325
SO$_3$	432	SeO$_3$	184	TeO$_3$	348

route is to treat anhydrous K$_2$SeO$_4$ with SO$_3$ under reflux, followed by vacuum sublimation at 120°. SeO$_3$ is a white, hygroscopic solid which melts at 118°, sublimes readily above 100° (40 mmHg) and decomposes above 165°. The crystal structure is built up from cyclic tetramers, Se$_4$O$_{12}$, which have a configuration very similar to that of (PNCl$_2$)$_4$ (p. 538). In the vapour phase, however, there is some dissociation into the monomer. In the molten state SeO$_3$ is probably polymeric like the isoelectronic polymetaphosphate ions (p. 528).

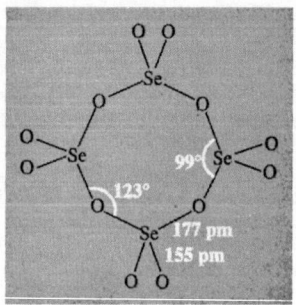

TeO$_3$ exists in two modifications. The yellow-orange α-form and the more stable, less reactive, grey β-form. The α-TeO$_3$ is made by dehydrating Te(OH)$_6$ (p. 782) at 300–360°; the β-TeO$_3$ is made by heating α-TeO$_3$ or Te(OH)$_6$ in a sealed tube in the presence of H$_2$SO$_4$ and O$_2$ for 12 h at 350°. α-TeO$_3$ has a structure like that of FeF$_3$, in which TeO$_6$ octahedra share all vertices to give a 3D lattice. It is unattacked by water, but is a powerful oxidizing agent when heated with a variety of metals or non-metals. It is also soluble in hot concentrated alkalis to form tellurates (p. 782). The β-form is even less reactive but can be cleaved with fused KOH.

PoO$_3$ may have been detected on a tracer scale but has not been characterized with weighable amounts of the element.

16.2.6 Hydroxides and oxoacids

The rich oxoacid chemistry of sulfur (pp. 705–21) is not paralleled by the heavier elements of the group. The redox relationships have already been summarized (p. 755). Apart from the dark-brown hydrated monoxide "Po(OH)$_2$", which precipitates when alkali is added to a freshly prepared solution of Po(II), only compounds in the +4 and +6 oxidation states are known.

Selenous acid, $O{=}Se(OH)_2$, i.e. H_2SeO_3, and tellurous acid, H_2TeO_3, are white solids which can readily be dehydrated to the dioxide (e.g. in a stream of dry air). H_2SeO_3 is best prepared by slow crystallization of an aqueous solution of SeO_2 or by oxidation of powdered Se with dilute nitric acid:

$$3Se + 4HNO_3 + H_2O \longrightarrow 3H_2SeO_3 + 4NO$$

The less-stable H_2TeO_3 is obtained by hydrolysis of a tetrahalide or acidification of a cooled aqueous solution of a telluride. Crystalline H_2SeO_3 is built up of pyramidal SeO_3 groups (Se–O 174 pm) which are hydrogen-bonded to give an orthorhombic layer lattice. The detailed structure of H_2TeO_3 is unknown. Both acids form acid salts $MHSeO_3$ and $MHTeO_3$ by reaction of the appropriate aqueous alkali. The neutral salts M_2SeO_3 and M_2TeO_3 can be obtained similarly or by heating the metal oxide with the appropriate dioxide. Dissociation constants have not been precisely determined but approximate values are:

H_2SeO_3: $K_1 \sim 3.5 \times 10^{-3}$ $K_2 \sim 5 \times 10^{-8}$
H_2TeO_3: $K_1 \sim 3 \times 10^{-3}$ $K_2 \sim 2 \times 10^{-8}$

Alkali diselenites $M_2^I Se_2O_5$ are also known and appear (on the basis of vibrational spectroscopy) to contain the ion $[O_2Se{-}O{-}SeO_2]^{2-}$, with C_{2v} symmetry and a nonlinear Se–O–Se bridge (cf. disulfite $O_3S{-}SO_2^{2-}$, p. 720). Selenous acid, in contrast to H_2TeO_3, can readily be oxidized to H_2SeO_4 by ozone in strongly acid solution; it is reduced to elementary selenium by H_2S, SO_2 or aqueous iodide solution.

Hydrated polonium dioxide, $PoO(OH)_2$, is obtained as a pale-yellow flocculent precipitate by addition of dilute aqueous alkali to a solution containing Po(IV). It is appreciably acidic, e.g.:

$$PoO(OH)_2 + 2KOH \underset{22°}{\rightleftharpoons} K_2PoO_3 + 2H_2O;$$

$$K_a = \frac{[PoO_3{}^{2-}]}{[OH^-]^2} = 8.2 \times 10^{-5}$$

In the +6 oxidation state the oxoacids of Se and Te show little resemblance to each other. H_2SeO_4 resembles H_2SO_4 (p. 710) whereas orthotelluric acid $Te(OH)_6$ and polymetatelluric acid $(H_2TeO_4)_n$ are quite different.

Anhydrous H_2SeO_4 is a viscous liquid which crystallizes to a white deliquescent solid (mp 62°). It loses water on being heated and combines readily with SeO_3 to give "pyroselenic acid", $H_2Se_2O_7$ (mp 19°), and triselenic acid, $H_4Se_3O_{11}$ (mp 25°). It also resembles H_2SO_4 in forming several hydrates: $H_2SeO_4 \cdot H_2O$ (mp 26°) and $H_2SeO_4 \cdot 4H_2O$ (52°). Crystalline H_2SeO_4 (d 2.961 g cm^{-3}) comprises tetrahedral SeO_4 groups strongly H-bonded into layers through all 4 O atoms (Se–O 161 pm, O–H$\cdots$O 261–268 pm). H_2SeO_4 can be prepared by several routes:

(i) Oxidation of H_2SeO_3 with H_2O_2, $KMnO_4$ or $HClO_3$, which can be formally represented by the equations:

$$H_2SeO_3 + H_2O_2 \longrightarrow H_2SeO_4 + H_2O$$

$$8H_2SeO_3 + 2KMnO_4 \longrightarrow 5H_2SeO_4$$
$$+ K_2SeO_3 + 2MnSeO_3 + 3H_2O$$

$$5H_2SeO_3 + 2HClO_3 \longrightarrow 5H_2SeO_4$$
$$+ Cl_2 + H_2O$$

(ii) Oxidation of Se with chlorine or bromine water, e.g.:

$$Se + 3Cl_2 + 4H_2O \longrightarrow H_2SeO_4 + 6HCl$$

(iii) Action of bromine water on a suspension of silver selenite:

$$Ag_2SeO_3 + Br_2 + H_2O \longrightarrow$$
$$H_2SeO_4 + 2AgBr$$

The acid dissociation constants of H_2SeO_4 are close to those of H_2SO_4, e.g. K_2 (H_2SeO_4)

1.2×10^{-2}. Selenates resemble sulfates and both acids form a series of alums (p. 76). Selenic acid differs from H_2SO_4, however, in being a strong oxidizing agent: this is perhaps most dramatically shown by its ability to dissolve not only Ag (as does H_2SO_4) but also Au, Pd (and even Pt in the presence of Cl^-):

$$2Au + 6H_2SeO_4 \longrightarrow Au_2(SeO_4)_3$$
$$+ 3H_2SeO_3 + 3H_2O$$

It oxidizes halide ions (except F^-) to free halogen. Solutions of S, Se, Te and Po in H_2SeO_4 are brightly coloured (cf. p. 664).

By contrast, the two main forms of telluric acid do not resemble H_2SO_4 and H_2SeO_4 and tellurates are not isomorphous with sulfates and selenates. Orthotelluric acid is a white solid, mp 136°, whose crystal structure is built up of regular octahedral molecules, $Te(OH)_6$. This structure, which persists in solution (Raman spectrum), is also reflected in its chemistry; e.g. breaks occur in the neutralization curve at points corresponding to NaH_5TeO_6, $Na_2H_4TeO_6$, $Na_4H_2TeO_6$ and Na_6TeO_6. Similar salts include Ag_6TeO_6 and Hg_3TeO_6. Moreover diazomethane converts it to the hexamethyl ester $Te(OMe)_6$. In this respect Te resembles its horizontal neighbours in the periodic table Sn, Sb and I which form the isoelectronic species $[Sn(OH)_6]^{2-}$, $[Sb(OH)_6]^-$ and $IO(OH)_5$. Orthotelluric acid can be prepared by oxidation of powdered Te with chloric acid solution or oxidation of TeO_2 with permanganate in nitric acid:

$$5Te + 6HClO_3 + 12H_2O \longrightarrow 5H_6TeO_6 + 3Cl_2$$

$$5TeO_2 + 2KMnO_4 + 6HNO_3 + 12H_2O \longrightarrow$$
$$5H_6TeO_6 + 2KNO_3 + 2Mn(NO_3)_2$$

Alternatively, Te or TeO_2 can be oxidized by CrO_3/HNO_3 or by 30% H_2O_2 under reflux. Acidification of a tellurate with an appropriate precipitating acid offers a further convenient route:

$$BaTeO_4 + H_2SO_4 + 2H_2O \longrightarrow BaSO_4\downarrow + H_6TeO_6$$

$$Ag_2TeO_4 + 2HCl + 2H_2O \longrightarrow 2AgCl\downarrow + H_6TeO_6$$

Crystallization from aqueous solutions below 10° gives the tetrahydrate $H_6TeO_6.4H_2O$. The anhydrous acid is stable in air at 100° but above 120° gradually loses water to give polymetatelluric acid and allotelluric acid (see below). Unlike H_2SO_4 and H_2SeO_4, H_6TeO_6 is a weak acid, approximate values of its successive dissociation constants being $K_1 \sim 2 \times 10^{-8}$, $K_2 \sim 10^{-11}$, $K_3 \sim 3 \times 10^{-15}$. It is a fairly strong oxidant, being reduced to the element by SO_2 and to H_2TeO_3 in hot HCl:

$$H_6TeO_6 + 3SO_2 \longrightarrow Te + 3H_2SO_4$$

$$H_6TeO_6 + 2HCl \longrightarrow H_2TeO_3 + 3H_2O + Cl_2$$

Polymetatelluric acid $(H_2TeO_4)_{\sim 10}$ is a white, amorphous hygroscopic powder formed by incomplete dehydration of H_6TeO_6 in air at 160°. Alternatively, in aqueous solution the equilibrium $nH_6TeO_6 \rightleftharpoons (H_2TeO_4)_n + 2nH_2O$ can be shifted to the right by increasing the temperature; rapid cooling then precipitates the sparingly soluble polymetatelluric acid. The structure is unknown but appears to contain 6-coordinate Te. Allotelluric acid "$(H_2TeO_4)_3(H_2O)_4$" is an acid syrup obtained by heating $Te(OH)_6$ in a sealed tube at 305°: the compound has not been obtained pure but tends to revert to H_6TeO_6 at room temperature or to $(H_2TeO_4)_n$ when heated in air; indeed, it may well be a mixture of these two substances.

Tellurates are prepared by fusing a tellurite with a corresponding nitrate, by oxidizing a tellurite with chlorine, by or neutralizing telluric acid with a hydroxide.[123] An interesting variant is to heat intimate mixtures of TeO_3 with metal oxides. For example, with Rb_2O at 680° for several weeks, colourless crystals having the unusual stoichiometry $Rb_6Te_2^{VI}O_9$ were formed which contained both tetrahedral TeO_4^{2-} and trigonal bipyramidal TeO_5^{4-} groups, i.e. $Rb_6[TeO_5][TeO_4]$.[124]

Numerous peroxoacid or thioacid derivatives of Se and Te have been reported[1] but these add little to the discussion of the reaction chemistry or the structure types already

---

[123] Ref. 11, pp. 94–7.

[124] T. WISSER and R. HOPPE, *Z. anorg. allg. Chem.* **584**, 105–13 (1990).

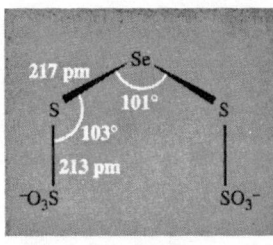
(a) *cis*-[Se(S₂O₃)₂]²⁻

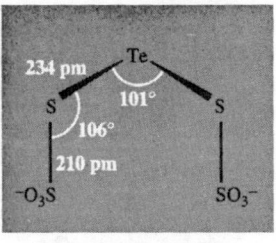
(b) *cis*-[Te(S₂O₃)₂]²⁻

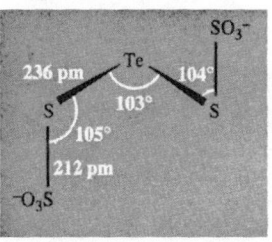
(c) *trans*-[Te(S₂O₃)₂]²⁻

Figure 16.17 Structures and conformations of unbranched chain anions in (a) $Ba[Se(S_2O_3)_2].2H_2O$, (b) $Ba[Te(S_2O_3)_2].2H_2O$, and (c) $(NH_4)_2[Te(S_2O_3)_2]$.

described. Examples are peroxoselenous acid HOSeO(OOH) (stable at $-10°$) and potassium peroxo-orthotellurate $K_2H_4TeO_7$ which also loses oxygen at room temperature. Isomeric selenosulfates, $M_2^ISO_3Se$, and thioselenates, $M_2^ISeO_3S$, are known and can be made by the obvious routes of $[SO_3^{2-}(aq) + Se]$ and $[SeO_3^{2-}(aq) + S]$. Likewise, colourless or yellow-green crystalline selenopolythionates $M_2Se_xS_yO_6$ ($x = 1, 2$; $y = 2, 4$) and orange-yellow telluropentathionates $M_2^ITeS_4O_6$ are known. X-ray structure analysis reveals unbranched chains with various conformations as found for the polythionates themselves (p. 718).[125] Typical examples are in Fig. 16.17. It will be seen that these compounds contain Se and Te bonded to S rather than O and they therefore form a natural link with the Group 16 sulfides to be described in the next section.

16.2.7 Other inorganic compounds

The red compound Se_4S_4, obtained by fusing equimolar amounts of the elements, is a covalent molecular species which can be crystallized from benzene. Similar procedures yield Se_2S_6, SeS_7 and TeS_7, all of which are structurally related to S_8 (p. 654; see also p. 763).

PoS forms as a black precipitate when H_2S is added to acidic solutions of polonium compounds. Its solubility product is $\sim5 \times 10^{-29}$. The

action of aqueous ammonium sulfide on polonium(IV) hydroxide gives the same compound. It decomposes to the elements when heated to $275°$ under reduced pressure and is of unknown structure.

The chemistry of compounds containing Se–N and Te–N bonds has been very activity developed during the past decade and many new and unusual species are emerging.[126,127] Se_4N_4 is an orange, shock sensitive crystalline compound which decomposes violently at $160°$. It resembles its sulfur analogue (p. 722) in being thermochroic (yellow-orange at $-195°$, red at $+100°$) and in having the same D_{2d} molecular structure. Se_4N_4 can be made by reacting anhydrous NH_3 with $SeBr_4$ (or with SeO_2 at $70°$ under pressure). A new red-brown crystalline modification, β-Se_4N_4, which has a very similar cluster structure but differs in the packing arrangement, has recently been prepared by reacting SeO_2 with the phosphane imine, $Me_3SiNPMe_3$.[128] Tellurium nitride can be prepared similarly ($TeBr_4$ + NH_3); it is a lemon-yellow, violently explosive compound with a formula that might be Te_3N_4 rather than Te_4N_4; its structure is unknown.

Se_4N_4 reacts with $[PtCl_2(PMe_2Ph)_2]$ in liquid ammonia (50 atm.) to give a quantitative yield of $[Pt(\eta^2$-$Se_2N_2)(PMe_2Ph)_2]$ which features a

[125] A. F. WELLS, *Structural Inorganic Chemistry*, 5th edn., pp. 726–35, Oxford University Press, Oxford, 1984. See also *J. Chem. Soc., Dalton Trans.*, 1528–32 (1978) ($Pb_2Te_3O_8$). *Inorg. Chem.* **19**, 1040–3, 1044–8, 1063–4 (1980) ($SeS_3O_6^{2-}$, $Se_2S_2O_6^{2-}$, $SeS_2O_6^{2-}$).

[126] M. BJÖRGVINSSON and H. W. ROESKY, *Polyhedron* **10**, 2353–70 (1991).

[127] P. F. KELLY A. M. Z. SLAWIN, D. J. WILLIAMS and J. D. WOOLLINS, *Chem. Soc. Rev.* **21**, 245–52 (1992). T. M. KLAPÖTKE, in R. STEUDEL (ed.), *The Chemistry of Inorganic Ring Systems*, Elsevier, Amsterdam, 1992, pp. 409–27.

[128] H. FOLKERTS, B. NEUMÜLLER and K. DEHNICKE, *Z. anorg. allg. Chem.* **620**, 1011–15 (1994).

(1) $(Se_3N_2^{+\bullet})_2$

(2) $Se_3N_2^{2+}$

(3) $ClSe_3N_2^+$

(4) $[N(SeCl_2)_2]^+$

(5) $Se(NSO)_2$

(6) $ClSe_2N_2S^+$

(7) $Cl_2Se_2N_2S$

(8) $S_3SeN_5^+$

5-membered $\overline{Pt-SeNSeN}$ heterocycle at the planar Pt centre.[129] A similar reaction with [Pt(PPh$_3$)$_3$] in CH$_2$Cl$_2$ gives the analogous PPh$_3$ complex—plus the related dark-green dimer, [(Ph$_3$P)Pt(μ,η^2-Se$_2$N$_2$)$_2$Pt(PPh$_3$)], in which the chelating ligand also bridges the two Pt atoms via the ipso-N atoms so as to form a central planar Pt$_2$N$_2$ core which is also coplanar with the two planar 5-membered heterocycles.[130] Innumerable other Se/N species have been synthesized and characterized by X-ray diffraction analysis, e.g. the 7π-electron radical cation Se$_3$N$_2^{+\bullet}$ (1),[131] the 6π-electron dication Se$_3$N$_2^{2+}$ (2),[131] ClSe$_3$N$_2$ (3),[132] [N(SeCl$_2$)$_2$]$^+$ (4),[133] Se(NSO)$_2$ (5),[134] ClSe$_3$N$_2$S$^+$ (6),[134] Cl$_2$Se$_2$N$_2$S (7),[134] [S$_3$SeN$_5$]$^+$ (8),[134] etc. The original papers should be consulted for preparative procedures.

Metal complexes with Se/N ligands are also appearing in increasing numbers in the literature. Thus, *cyclo*-Se$_4$N$_2$ forms the red-brown donor–acceptor complexes [SnCl$_4$(η^1-N$_2$Se$_4$)$_2$] (9) and [TiCl$_4$(η^2-N$_2$Se$_4$)],[135] whereas reaction of [Se$_2$SN$_2$]$_2$Cl$_2$ with *cis*-[PtCl$_2$(PMe$_2$Ph)$_2$] in liquid ammonia gives [Pt(η^2-SeSN$_2$)(PMe$_2$Ph)$_2$] which in turn can be protonated with HBF$_4$ to give [Pt(η^2-SeSN$_2$H)(PMe$_2$Ph)$_2$]$^+$ (10).[136] The di-Se analogues with η^2-Se$_2$N$_2^{2-}$ and η^2-Se$_2$N$_2$H$^-$ have also been characterized.[137]

Heterocycles involving P^V include [1,5-(Ph$_2$P)$_2$N$_4$(SeMe)$_2$] (11), which has an 8-membered chair configuration with the two Se atoms displaced on either side of the P$_2$N$_4$ plane, and the related [1,5-(Ph$_2$P)$_2$N$_4$Se$_2$] (12).[138] The reaction of (12) with [PtCl$_2$(PEt$_3$)$_2$] gives the η^1-complexes (13), (14) which, in turn, can be oxidatively added to [Pt(η^2-C$_2$H$_4$)(PPh$_3$)$_2$] to give the η^2-Se,Se$'$ complexes (15) and (16),[139]

[129] P. F. KELLY J. D. WOOLLINS, *Polyhedron* **12**, 1129–33 (1993).

[130] P. F. KELLY A. M. Z. SLAWIN, D. J. WILLIAMS and J. D. WOOLLINS, *Polyhedron* **9**, 1567–71 (1990).

[131] E. G. AWERE, J. PASSMORE, P. S. WHITE and T. M. KLAPÖTKE, *J. Chem. Soc., Chem. Commun.*, 1415–7 (1989).

[132] R. WOLLERT, B. NEUMÜLLER and K. DEHNICKE, *Z. anorg. allg. Chem.* **616**, 191–4 (1992).

[133] M. BROSCHAG, T. M. KLAPÖTKE, I. C. TORNIEPORTH-OETTING and P. S. WHITE, *J. Chem. Soc., Chem. Commun.*, 1390–1 (1992).

[134] A. HAAS, J. KASPROWSKI, K. ANGERMUND, P. BETZ, C. KRÜGER, Yi-H. TSAY and S. WERNER, *Chem. Ber.* **124**, 1895–906 (1991).

[135] S. VOGLER, M. SCHÄFER and K. DEHNICKE, *Z. anorg. allg. Chem.* **606**, 73–8 (1991).

[136] C. A. O'MAHONEY, I. P. PARKIN, D. J. WILLIAMS and J. D. WOOLLINS, *Polyhedron* **8**, 2215–7 (1989).

[137] P. F. KELLY, I. P. PARKIN, A. M. Z. SLAWIN, D. J. WILLIAMS and J. D. WOOLLINS, *Angew. Chem., Int. Edn. Engl.* **28**, 1047–9 (1989).

[138] T. CHIVERS, D. D. DOXSEE and J. F. FAIT, *J. Chem. Soc., Chem. Commun.*, 1703–5 (1989).

[139] T. CHIVERS, D. D. DOXSEE, R. W. HILTS, A. MEETSMA, M. PARVEZ and J. C. VAN DE GRAMPEL, *J. Chem. Soc., Chem. Commun.*, 1330–2 (1992).

(9) [SnCl$_4$(N$_2$Se$_4$)$_2$]

(10) [Pt(SeSN$_2$H)(PMe$_2$Ph)$_2$]$^+$

(11) [(Ph$_2$P)$_2$N$_4$(SeMe)$_2$]

(12) [(Ph$_2$P)$_2$N$_4$Se$_2$]

(13)

(14)

(15)

(16)

(17) P$_2$Se$_8^{2-}$

(18) [Fe$_2$(CO)$_4$(PSe$_5$)$_2$]

Reaction of P$_4$Se$_4$ with soluble polyselenides afforded the first isolated P/Se anion, the yellow P$_2$Se$_8^{2-}$ (17) which further reacts with Fe(CO)$_5$ to generate the novel brown cluster anion [Fe$_2$(CO)$_4$(PSe$_5$)$_2$] (18).[140] Numerous other examples are known; indeed, the whole field is still rapidly developing and many new types of compound are being synthesized and characterized each year.

Tellurium-chalcogen-nitrogen chemistry is also burgeoning. Typical examples include the red crystalline Te(NSO)$_2$,[141] isomorphous with Se(NSO)$_2$ (5), and the cationic heterocycle [FTeNSNSeNSN]$^+$[TeF$_5$]$^-$, which is formed, together with [{SeNSNSe$^•$}$_2$]$^{2+}$[TeF$_5$]$^-{}_2$, when Se(NSO)$_2$ reacts with TeF$_4$ in CH$_2$Cl$_2$.[142] The first stable tellurophosphorane complexes [M(CO)$_5$(Te=PBu$^t_3$)] (M = Cr, Mo, W) were prepared as dark-red crystals by photolysis of the hexacarbonyls in the presence of Bu$^t_3$P=Te, and the expected bent coordination at Te was confirmed by X-ray analysis (angle W−Te−P 120.1°.[143] By Contrast, reaction of Et$_3$P=Te with [Mn(CH$_2$Ph)(CO)$_5$] in refluxing toluene results in the insertion of Te into

140 J. ZHAO, W. T. PENNINGTON and J. W. KOLIS, *J. Chem. Soc., Chem. Commun.*, 265–6 (1992).

141 A. HAAS and R. POHL, *Chimia* **43**, 261–2 (1989). See also R. BOESE, F. DWORAK, A. HAAS and M. PRYKA, *Chem. Ber.* **128**, 477–80 (1995).

142 A. HAAS and M. PRYKA, *Chem. Ber.* **128**, 11–22 (1995).

143 N. KUHN, H. SCHUMANN and G. WOLMERSHÄUSER, *J. Chem. Soc., Chem. Commun.*, 1595–7 (1985).

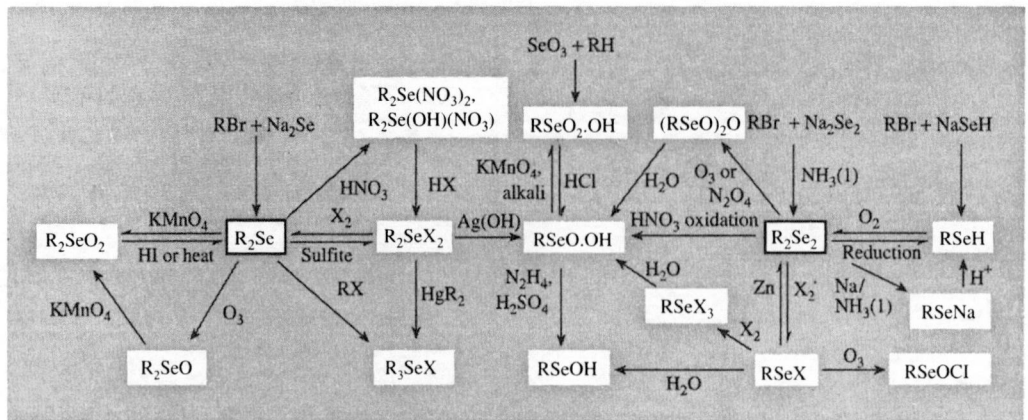

Reaction scheme for the formation of organo-selenium compounds (X = halogen).

the Mn–CH$_2$ bond and the displacement of two CO ligands to yield the red crystalline solid [Mn(CO)$_3$(PEt$_3$)$_2$(TeCH$_2$Ph)], in which the three carbonyls are *mer* and the two tertiary phospine ligands are *trans* to each other.[144]

The increasing basicity of the heavier members of Group 16 is reflected in the increasing incidence of oxoacid salts. Thus polonium forms Po(NO$_3$)$_4$.xN$_2$O$_4$, Po(SO$_4$)$_2$.xH$_2$O, and a basic sulfate and selenate 2PoO$_2$.SO$_3$ and 2PoO$_2$.SeO$_3$ all of which are white, and a hydrated yellow chromate Po(CrO$_4$)$_2$.xH$_2$O. There is also fragmentary information on the precipitation of an insoluble polonium(IV) carbonate, iodate, phosphate and vanadate.[4] Tellurium(IV) forms a white basic nitrate 2TeO$_2$.HNO$_3$ and a basic sulfate and selenate 2TeO$_2$.XO$_3$, and there are indications of a white, hygroscopic basic sulfate of selenium(IV), SeO$_2$.SO$_3$ or SeOSO$_4$. Most of these compounds have been prepared by evaporation of aqueous solutions of the oxide or hydrated oxide in the appropriate acid. There is no doubt that more imaginative nonaqueous synthetic routes could be devised, but the likely products seem rather uninteresting and the field has attracted little recent attention.

16.2.8 Organo-compounds [145–149]

Organoselenium and organotellurium chemistry is a large and expanding field which parallels but is distinct from organosulfur chemistry. The biochemistry of organoselenium compounds has also been much studied (p. 759). Organopolonium chemistry is almost entirely restricted to trace-level experiments because of the charring and decomposition of the compounds by the intense α activity of polonium (pp. 749ff.).

The principal classes of organoselenium compound are summarized in the scheme above which indicates the central synthetic role of

[144] K. McGREGOR, G. B. DEACON, R. S. DICKSON, G. D. FALLON, R. S. ROWE and B. O. WEST, *J. Chem. Soc., Chem. Commun.*, 1293–4 (1990).

[145] K. J. IRGOLIC and M. V. KUDCHADKER, The organic chemistry of selenium, Chap. 8 in ref. 2, pp. 408–545. H. E. GANTHER, Biochemistry of selenium, Chap. 9 in ref. 2, pp. 546–614. W. C. COOPER and J. R. GLOVER, The toxicology of selenium and its compounds, Chap. 11 in ref. 2, pp. 654–74.

[146] R. A. ZINGARO and K. IRGOLIC, Organic compounds of tellurium, Chap 5 in ref. 3, pp. 184–280. W. C. COOPER. Toxicology of tellurium and its compounds, Chap. 7 in ref. 3, pp. 313–72.

[147] P. D. MAGNUS, Organic selenium and tellurium compounds, in D. BARTON and W. D. OLLIS (eds.), *Comprehensive Organic Chemistry*, Vol. 3, Chap. 12, pp. 491–538, Pergamon Press, Oxford, 1979.

[148] Specialist Periodical Reports of the Chemical Society (London), *Organic Compounds of Sulfur, Selenium and Tellurium*, Vols. 1–5 (1970–79).

[149] S. PATAI and Z. RAPPAPORT (eds.) *The Chemistry of Organic Selenium and Tellurium Compounds*, John Wiley (Interscience), Chichester, Vol. 1, 1986, 939 pp. Vol. 2 (S. PATAI, ed.), 1987, 864 pp.

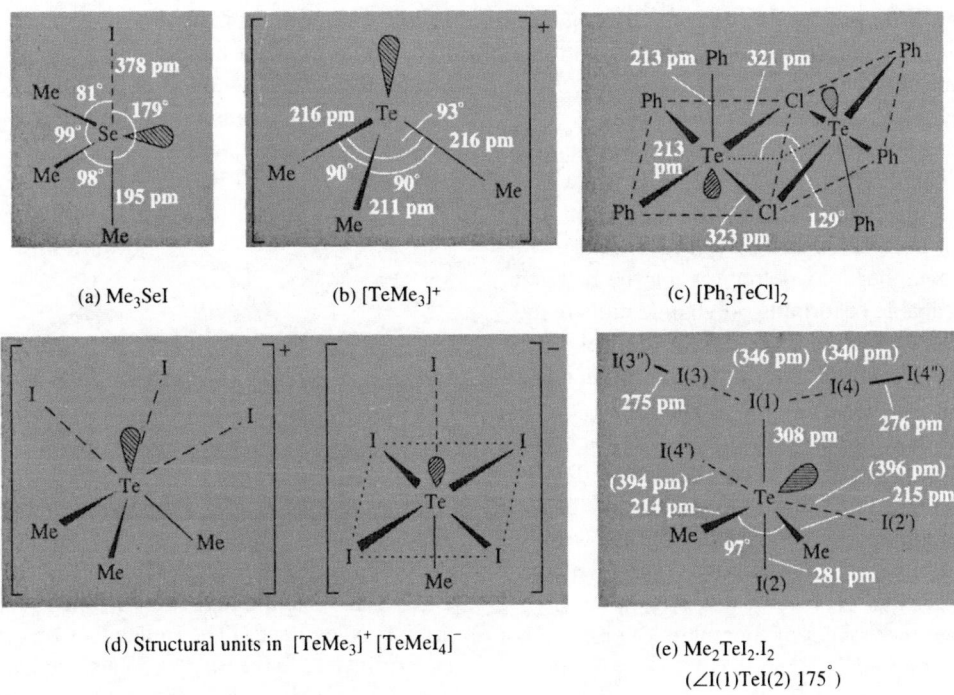

(a) Me$_3$SeI   (b) [TeMe$_3$]$^+$ (c) [Ph$_3$TeCl]$_2$

(d) Structural units in [TeMe$_3$]$^+$ [TeMeI$_4$]$^-$

(e) Me$_2$TeI$_2$.I$_2$
($\angle$I(1)TeI(2) 175°)

Figure 16.18   Some coordination environments of Se and Te in their organohalides.

the selenides R$_2$Se and diselenides R$_2$Se$_2$.[1] Detailed discussion of these and related tellurium compounds falls outside the scope of the present treatment. Other compounds such as the cyano derivatives (p. 778) and CSe$_2$, COSe, COTe and CSTe (p. 754) have already been briefly mentioned.

Tellurocarbonyl derivatives R^{1}C($=$Te)OR^2 and telluroamides, e.g. PhC($=$Te)NMe$_2$ (mp 73°) have been prepared[150] and shown to be similar to, though more reactive than, the corresponding seleno derivatives.

Reaction of [Se$_4$]$^{2+}$[AsF$_6$]$_2^-$ with Ph$_2$Se$_2$ in liquid SO$_2$ gives the bright orange compound [Se$_6$Ph$_2$]$^{2+}$[AsF$_6$]$_2^-$.SO$_2$ in which the Se$_6$ ring adopts the boat conformation with pendent Ph groups in the 1- and 4-positions.[151] By contrast the reaction of K$_2$CO$_3$ with red-Se in acetone in

the presence of [(Ph$_3$P)$_2$N]Cl yields red crystals of [(Ph$_3$P)$_2$N]$^+$[Se$_5$C(Se)C(O)Me]$^-$; the anion, which adopts the chair conformation, is the first example of an Se$_5$C ring, and the C atom has exocyclic $=$Se and $-$C(O)Me groups attached.[152]

Stoichiometry is frequently an inadequate guide to structure in organo-derivatives of Se and Te particularly when other elements (such as halogens) are also present. This arises from the incipient tendency of many of the compounds to undergo ionic dissociation or, conversely, to increase the coordination number of the central atom by dimerization or other oligomeric interactions. Thus Me$_3$SeI features pyramidal ions [SeMe$_3$]$^+$ but these are each associated rather closely with 1 iodide which is colinear with 1 Me$-$Se bond to give a distorted pseudotrigonal bipyramidal configuration (Fig. 16.18a).[125] A regular pyramidal cation can, however, be obtained by use of a large non-coordinating counteranion, as in

[150] K. A. LERSTRUP and L. HENRIKSEN, *J. Chem. Soc., Chem. Commun.*, 1102–3 (1979) and references therein.

[151] R. FAGGIANI R. J. GILLESPIE and J. W. KOLIS *J. Chem. Soc., Chem. Commun.*, 592–3 (1987).

[152] T. CHIVERS, M. PARVEZ, M. PEACH and R. VOLLMERHAUS, *J. Chem. Soc., Chem. Commun.*, 1539–40 (1992).

$[TeMe_3]^+[BPh_4]^-$ (Fig. 16.18b).[153] By contrast, Ph_3TeCl is a chloride-bridged dimer with 5-coordinate square-pyramidal Te (Fig. 16.13c).[154] The possibility of isomerism also exists: e.g. 4-coordinate, monomeric molecular Me_2TeI_2 and its ionic counterpart $[TeMe_3]^+[TeMeI_4]^-$ in which interionic interactions make both the cation and the anion pseudo-6-coordinate (Fig. 16.18d).[125] Further complications obtrude when the halogen itself is capable of forming polyhalide units in the crystal. Thus reaction of molecular Me_2TeI_2 with iodine readily affords Me_2TeI_4 but the chemical behaviour and spectra of the product give no evidence for oxidation to Te(VI), and X-ray analysis indicates the formation of an adduct $Me_2TeI_2.I_2$ in which the axially disposed iodine atoms of the pseudo-trigonal-bipyramidal Me_2TeI_2 are weakly bonded to molecules of iodine to form a network as shown in Fig. 16.18e[155] (cf. TlI_3, p. 239).

Among the range of homoleptic organotellurium compounds that have recently been synthesized are the perfluoroalkyl derivatives $Te(C_nF_{2n+1})_4$, $(n = 1-4)$.[156] Of these, the yellow oily liquid $Te(CF_3)_4$ is the least stable, being both light- and temperature-sensitive. It reacts with fluorides to give the complex anion $[Te(CF_3)_4F]^-$ and with fluoride-ion acceptors to form the cation $[Te(CF_3)_3]^+$. $Te(CF_3)_4$ is made by reacting $Te(CF_3)_2Cl_2$ with $Cd(CF_3)_2$ in MeCN. The higher members can be made directly form $TeCl_4$ and $Cd(CF_3)_2$ are also viscous yellow liquids. The related $TeMe_4$ was first made in 1989 as a yellow pyrophoric liquid by treating $TeCl_4$ with LiMe in ether at $-78°$;[157] it can be oxidized by XeF_2 to the volatile white solid Me_4TeF_2 which, when treated with $ZnMe_2$, gave $TeMe_6$ as a white

solid.[158] $TeMe_6$, the first peralkylated derivative of a hexavalent main-group element, can be heated for several hours at $140°$ without decomposition, and is thus much more stable than $TeMe_4$.

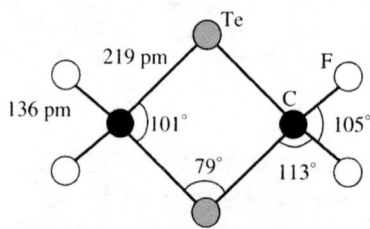

(19) $F_2C(\mu\text{-Te})_2CF_2$

Organopolytellurides (and polyselenides) are also known, e.g. $ArTeTeAr$ (Ar = 2, 4, 6-$Ph_3C_6H_2$-)[159] and $RTeTeTeR$ (R = $(Me_3Si)_3$-C);[160] the stabilizing rôle of the bulky end groups is evident. [The related "isoelectronic" cation $Bu^t_3PTeTeTePBu^t_3{}^{2+}$ can also be noted;[161] it is prepared by oxidizing the tellurophosphorane $Bu^t_3P=Te$ (see p. 785) using ferricenium salts.] Related compounds are R_2Se_x $(x = 2-7)$ and $(RSe)_2S_y$ $(y = 1-15)$.[162] Other compounds of note are the first "telluroketone", $Te=CF_2$,[163] a thermally unstable violet compound which readily dimerizes even below room temperature to the dark-red crystalline 1,3-ditelluretane (19). Cocondensation with its analogue, $Se=CF_2$ yields the corresponding volatile orange solid, 1-selena-3-telluretane, $F_2\overline{CTeCF_2}Se$.

[153] R. F. ZIOLO and J. M. TROUP, *Inorg. Chem.* **18**, 2271–4 (1979). See also, however, M. J. COLLINS, J. A. RIPMEESTER and J. F. SAWYER, *J. Am. Chem. Soc.* **110**, 8583–90 (1988).

[154] R. F. ZIOLO and M. EXTINE, *Inorg. Chem.* **19**, 2964–7 (1980).

[155] H. PRITZKOW, *Inorg. Chem.* **18**, 311–13 (1979).

[156] D. NAUMANN, H. BUTLER, J. FISCHER, J. HANKE, J. MOGIAS and B. WILKES, *Z. anorg. allg. Chem.* **608**, 69–72 (1992).

[157] R. W. GEDRIDGE,   D. C. HARRIS,   K. T. HIGA   and R. A. NISSAN, *Organometallics* **8**, 2817–20 (1989).

[158] L. AHMED and J. A. MORRISON, *J. Am. Chem. Soc.* **112**, 7411–13 (1990).

[159] E. S. LANG, C. MAICHLE-MÖSSMER and J. STRÄHLE, *Z. anorg. allg. Chem.* **620**, 1678–85 (1994).

[160] F. SLADKY,   B. BILDSTEIN,   C. RIEKER,   A. GIEREN, H. BETZ and T. HÜBNER, *J. Chem. Soc., Chem. Commun.*, 1800–1 (1985).

[161] N. KUHN, H. SCHUMANN and R. BOESE, *J. Chem. Soc., Chem. Commun.*, 1257–8 (1987).

[162] M. PRIDÖHL and R. STEUDEL, *Polyhedron* **12**, 2577–85 (1993).

[163] R. BOESE, A. HAAS and C. LIMBBERG, *J. Chem. Soc., Chem. Commun.*, 1378–9 (1991) and *J. Chem. Soc., Dalton Trans.*, 2547–56 (1993).

17

The Halogens: Fluorine, Chlorine, Bromine, Iodine and Astatine

17.1 The Elements

17.1.1 Introduction

Compounds of the halogens have been known from earliest times and the elements have played a particularly important role during the past two hundred years in the development of both experimental and theoretical chemistry.[1] Some of this early history is summarized in Table 17.1. The name "halogen" was introduced by J. S. C. Schweigger in 1811 to describe the property of chlorine, at that time unique among the elements, of combining directly with metals to give salts (Greek $\dot{\alpha}\lambda\varsigma$, sea salt, plus the root -$\gamma\varepsilon\nu$, produce). The name has since been extended to cover all five members of Group 17 of the periodic table.

---

[1] M. E. WEEKS, *Discovery of the Elements*, 6th edn., Journal of Chemical Education, Easton, 1956, Chap. 27, 'The halogen family', pp. 729–77.

Fluorine

Fluorine derives its name from the early use of fluorspar (CaF_2) as a flux (Latin *fluor*, flowing). The name was suggested to Sir Humphry Davy by A.-M. Ampère in 1812. The corrosive nature of hydrofluoric acid and the curious property that fluorspar has of emitting light when heated ("fluorescence") were discovered in the seventeenth century. However, all attempts to isolate the element either by chemical reactions or by electrolysis were foiled by the extreme reactivity of free fluorine. Success was finally achieved on 26 June 1886 by H. Moissan who electrolysed a cooled solution of KHF_2 in anhydrous liquid HF, using Pt/Ir electrodes sealed into a platinum U-tube sealed with fluorspar caps: the gas evolved immediately caused crystalline silicon to burst into flames, and Moissan reported the results to the Academy two days later in the following cautious words: "One can indeed make various hypotheses on the nature of the liberated gas; the simplest would be that *we are in the*

Table 17.1   Early history of the halogens and their compounds

3000 BC	Archaeological evidence for the use of rock-salt
~400 BC	Written records on salt (ascribed to Herodot)
~200 BC	Use of salt as part payment for services (salary)
~21 AD	Strabo described dyeworks for obtaining tyrian purple (dibromoindigo) in his *Geographica*
~100	Use of salt to purify noble metals
~900	Dilute hydrochloric acid prepared by Arabian alchemist Rhazes
~1200	Development of *aqua regia* (HCl/HNO$_3$) to dissove gold — presumably Cl$_2$ was also formed
1529	Georgius Agricola described use of fluorspar as a flux
~1630	Chlorine recognized as a gas by Belgian physician J. B. van Helmont (see Scheele, 1774)
1648	Concentrated HCl prepared by J.L. Glauber (by heating hydrated ZnCl$_2$ and sand)
1670	H. Schwanhard (Nürnberg) found that CaF$_2$ + strong acid gave acid vapours (HF) that etched glass (used decoratively)
1678	J. S. Elsholtz described emission of bluish-white light when fluorspar was heated. Also described by J. G. Wallerius, 1750; the name "fluorescence" was coined in 1852 by G. G. Stokes
1768	First chemical study of fluorite undertaken by A. S. Marggraf
1771	Crude hydrofluoric acid prepared by C. W. Scheele
1772	Gaseous HCl prepared over mercury by J. Priestley
1774	C. W. Scheele prepared and studied gaseous chlorine (MnO$_2$ + HCl) but thought it was a compound
1785	Chemical bleaching (eau de Javel: aqueous KOH + Cl$_2$) introduced by C.-L. Berthollet
1787	N. Leblanc devised a technical process for obtaining NaOH from NaCl (beginnings of the chemical industry)
1798	Bleaching powder patented by C. Tennant (Cl$_2$ + slaked lime) following preparation of bleaching liquors from Cl$_2$ and lime solutions by T. Henry (1788)
1801	W. Cruickshank recommended use of Cl$_2$ as a disinfectant (widely used in hospitals by 1823; notably effective in the European cholera epidemic, 1831, and in the outbreak of puerperal fever, Vienna, 1845)
1802	Fluoride found in fossil ivory and teeth by D. P. Morichini (soon confirmed by J. J. Berzelius who found it also in bones)
1810	H. Davy announced proof of the elementary nature of chlorine to the Royal Society (15 November) and suggested the name "chlorine" (1811)
1811	B. Courtois isolated iodine by sublimation (H$_2$SO$_4$ + seaweed ash)
1811	The term "halogen" introduced by J. S. C. Schweigger to denote the (then) unique property of the element chlorine to combine directly with metals to give salts
1812	A.-M. Ampère wrote to H. Davy (12 August) suggesting the name *le fluore* (fluorine) for the presumed new element in CaF$_2$ and HF (by analogy with *le chlore*, chlorine). Adapted by Davy in 1813
1814	Starch/iodine blue colour-reaction described by J.-J. Colin and H.-F. Gaultier de Claubry; developed by F. Stromeyer in the same year as an analytical test sensitive to 2–3 ppm iodine
1814	First interhalogen compound (ICl) prepared by J.L. Gay Lussac
1819	Potassium iodide introduced as a remedy for goitre by J.-F. Coindet (Switzerland), the efficacy of extracts from kelp having been known in China and Europe since the sixteenth century
1823	M. Faraday showed that "solid chlorine" was chlorine hydrate (Cl$_2$.~10H$_2$O using present-day nomenclature). He also liquefied Cl$_2$ (5 March) by warming the hydrate in a sealed tube
1825	First iodine containing mineral (AgI) identified by A. M. del Rio (Mexico) and N.-L. Vauquelin (Paris)
1826	Bromine isolated by A.-J. Balard (aged 23 y)
1835	L. J. M. Daguerre's photographic process (silver plate sensitized by exposure to iodine vapour)
~1840	Introduction of (light sensitive) AgBr into photography
1840	Iodine (as iodate) found in Chilean saltpetre by A. A. Hayes
1841	First mineral bromide (bromyrite, AgBr) discovered in Mexico by P. Berthier — later also found in Chile and France
1851	Diaphragm cell for the electrolytic generation of Cl$_2$ invented by C. Watt (London) but lack of electric generators delayed exploitation until 1886–90 (Matthes and Weber of Duisberg)
1857	Bromide therapy introduced by Lacock as a sedative and anticonvulsant for treatment of epilepsy
1858	Discovery of Stassfurt salt deposits opened the way for bromine production (for photography and medicine) as a by-product of potash
1863	Alkali Act (UK) prohibited atmospheric pollution and enforced the condensation of by-product HCl from the Leblanc process
1886	H. Moissan isolated F$_2$ by electrolysis of KHF$_2$/HF (26 June) after over 70 y of unsuccessful attempts by others (Nobel Prize for Chemistry 1906 — he died 2 months later)
1892–5	H. Y. Castner (US/UK) and C. Kellner (Vienna) independently developed commercial mercury-cathode cell for chlor-alkali production

Introduction

Table 17.2 Halogens in the twentieth century

~1900	First manufacture of inorganic fluorides for aluminium industry
1902	J. C. Downs (of E. I. du Pont de Nemours, Delaware) patented the first practical molten-salt cell for Cl_2 and Na metal
1908	HCl shown to be present in gastric juices of animals by P. Sommerfeld
1909	P. Friedländer showed that Tyrian Purple from *Murex brandaris* was 6,6'-dibromoindigo (previously synthesized by F. Sachs in 1904)
1920	Bromine detected in blood and organs of humans and other animals and birds by A. Damiens
1928	T. Midgley, A. L. Henne and R. R. McNary synthesized Freon (CCl_2F_2) as a non-flammable, non-toxic gas for refrigeration
1928	ClF made by O. Ruff *et al.* ($Cl_2 + F_2$ at 250°)
1930	IF_7 made by O. Ruff and R. Keim (IF_5 having been made in 1871 by G. Gore)
1930+	H. T. Dean *et al.* put the correlation between decreased incidence of dental caries and the presence of fluoride ions in drinking water on a quantitative basis
1931	First bulk shipment of commercial anhydrous HF (USA)
1938	R. J. Plunket discovered Teflon (polytetrafluoroethylene, PTFE)
1940	Astatine made via $^{209}Bi(\alpha,2n)$ by D. R. Corson, K. R. Mackenzie and E. Segré
1940–1	Industrial production of $F_2(g)$ begun (in the UK and the USA for manufacture of UF_6 and in Germany for ClF_3)
1950	Chemical shifts for ^{19}F and nmr signals for ^{35}Cl and ^{37}Cl first observed
1962	ClF_5 (the last halogen fluoride to be made) synthesized by W. Maya
1965	LaF_3 crystals developed by J. W. Ross and M. S. Frant as the first non-glass membrane electrode (for ion-selective determination of F^-)
1965	Perchlorate ion established as a monodentate ligand (to Co) by X-ray crystallography, following earlier spectrosopic and conductimetric indications of coordination (1961)
1968	Perbromates first prepared by E. H. Appelman
1967	First example of $\mu(\eta^1,\eta^1)$-ClO_4^- as a bidentate bridging ligand (to Ag^+); chelating η^2-ClO_4^- identified in 1974
1971	HOF first isolated in weighable amounts (p. 856)
1986	First chemical synthesis of F_2 gas (p. 821)

presence of fluorine, but it would be possible, of course, that it might be a perfluoride of hydrogen or even a mixture of hydrofluoric acid and ozone. ..." For this achievement, which had eluded some of the finest experimental chemists of the nineteenth century [including H. Davy (1813–14), G. Aimé (1833), M. Faraday (1834), C. J. and T. Knox (1836), P. Louyet (1846), E. Frémy (1854), H. Kammerer (1862) and G. Gore (1870)], and for his development of the electric furnace, Moissan was awarded the Nobel Prize for Chemistry in 1906.

Fluorine technology and the applications of fluorine-containing compounds have developed dramatically during the twentieth century.[2,3] Some highlights are included in Table 17.2 and will be discussed more fully in later sections.

Noteworthy events are the development of inert fluorinated oils, greases and polymers: Freon gases such as CCl_2F_2 (1928) were specifically developed for refrigeration engineering; others were used as propellants in pressurized dispensers and aerosols; and the non-stick plastic polytetrafluoroethylene (PTFE or Teflon) was made in 1938. Inorganic fluorides, especially for the aluminium industry (p. 219) have been increasingly exploited from about 1900, and from 1940 UF_6 has been used in gaseous diffusion plants for the separation of uranium isotopes for nuclear reactor technology. The great oxidizing strength of F_2 and many of its compounds with N and O have attracted the attention of rocket

---

[2] *Kirk–Othmer Encyclopedia of Chemical Technology*, 4th edn., Vol. 11, 1994: Fluorine pp. 241–67; In- organic fluorine

compounds, pp. 267–466; Organic fluorine compounds, pp. 467–729.

[3] R. E. BANKS, D. W. A. SHARP and J. C. TATLOW (eds.), *Fluorine: the First Hundred years*, Elsevier, New York, 1987 399 pp.

engineers and there have been growing large-scale industrial applications of anhydrous HF (p. 810).

The aggressive nature of HF fumes and solutions has been known since Schwanhard of Nürnberg used them for the decorative etching of glass. Hydrofluoric acid inflicts excruciatingly painful skin burns (p. 810) and any compound that might hydrolyse to form HF should be treated with great caution.[4] Maximum allowable concentration for continuous exposure to HF gas is 2–3 ppm (cf. HCN 10 ppm). The free element itself is even more toxic, maximum allowable concentration for a daily 8-h exposure being 0.1 ppm. Low concentrations of fluoride ion in drinking water have been known to provide excellent protection against dental caries since the classical work of H. T. Dean and his colleagues in the early 1930s; as there are no deleterious effects, even over many years, providing the total fluoride ion concentration is kept at or below 1 ppm, fluoridation has been a recommended and adopted procedure in several countries for many years (p. 810). However, at 2–3 ppm a brown mottling of teeth can occur and at 50 ppm harmful toxic effects are noted. Ingestion of 150 mg of NaF can cause nausea, vomiting, diarrhoea and acute abdominal pains though complete recovery is rapid following intravenous or intramuscular injection of calcium ions. The deliberate fluoridation of domestic water supplies has been a controversial, even polemical subject for several decades, though it is important to separate out the biological and toxicological aspects from the moral and philosophical aspects concerning the "right" of individuals to drink untreated water if they wish.[5-7]

---

[4] A. J. FINKEL, Treatment of hydrogen fluoride injuries, *Adv. Fluorine Chem.* **7**, 199–203 (1973).

[5] G. L. WALDBOTT (with A. W. BURGSTAHLER and H. L. MCKINNEY, *Fluoridation: The Great Dilemma*, Coronado Press, Lawrence, Kansas, 1978, 423 pp.

[6] B. HILEMAN, Fluoridation of Water: A Special Report, *C & E News* August 1, 26–42 (1988). See also B. HILEMAN, *C & E News* February 25, 6–7 (1991).

[7] B. MARTIN, *Scientific Knowledge in Controversy: The Social Dynamics of the Fluoridation Debate*, State University of New York Press, Albany, N.Y. 1991, 256 pp.

Chlorine

Chlorine was the first of the halogens to be isolated and common salt (NaCl) has been known from earliest times (see Table 17.1). Its efficacy in human diet was well recognized in classical antiquity and there are numerous references to its importance in the Bible. On occasion salt was used as part payment for the services of Roman generals and military tribunes (salary) and, indeed, it is an essential ingredient in mammalian diets (p. 68). The alchemical use of *aqua regia* (HCl/HNO$_3$) to dissolve gold is also well documented from the thirteenth century onwards. Concentrated hydrochloric acid was prepared by J. L. Glauber in 1648 by heating hydrated ZnCl$_2$ and sand in a retort and the pure gas, free of water, was collected over mercury by J. Priestley in 1772. This was closely followed by the isolation of gaseous chlorine by C. W. Scheele in 1774: he obtained the gas by oxidizing nascent HCl with MnO$_2$ in a reaction which would now formally be written as:

$$4NaCl + 2H_2SO_4 + MnO_2 \xrightarrow{\text{heat}} 2Na_2SO_4$$
$$+ MnCl_2 + 2H_2O + Cl_2$$

However, Scheele believed he had prepared a *compound* (dephlogisticated marine acid air) and the misconception was compounded by C.-L. Berthollet who showed in 1785 that the action of chlorine on water releases oxygen: [Cl$_2$(g) + H$_2$O $\longrightarrow$ 2HCl(soln) + $\frac{1}{2}$O$_2$(g)]; he concluded that chlorine was a loose compound of HCl and oxygen and called it oxymuriatic acid.[†]

[†] *Muriatic* acid and *marine* acid were synonymous terms for what is now called hydrochloric acid, thus signifying its relation to the sodium chloride contained in brine (Latin *muria*) or sea water (Latin *mare*). Both names were strongly criticized by H. Davy in a scathing paper entitled "Some reflections on the nomenclature of oxymuriatic compounds" in *Phil. Trans. R. Soc.* for 1811: "To call a body which is not known to contain oxygen, and which cannot contain muriatic acid, oxymuriatic acid, is contrary to the principles of that nomenclature in which it is adopted; and an alteration of it seems necessary to assist the progress of the discussion, and to diffuse just ideas on the subject. If the great discoverer of this substance (i.e. Scheele) had signified it by any simple name it would have been proper to have referred to it; but

The two decades from 1790 to 1810 were characterized by two major advances in chemical theory: Lavoisier's demolition of the phlogiston theory of combustion, and Davy's refutation of Lavoisier's contention that oxygen is a necessary constituent of all acids. Only when both these transformations had been achieved could the elementary nature of chlorine and the true composition of hydrochloric acid be appreciated, though some further time was to elapse (Dalton, Avogadro, Cannizaro) before gaseous chlorine was universally recognized to consist of diatomic molecules, Cl_2, rather than single atoms, Cl. The name, proposed by Davy in 1811, refers to the colour of the gas (Greek χλωρός, *chloros*, yellowish or light green — cf. chlorophyl).

The bleaching power of Cl_2 was discovered by Scheele in his early work (1774) and was put to technical use by Berthollet in 1785. This was a major advance on the previous time-consuming, labour-intensive, weather-dependent method of solar bleaching, and numerous patents followed (see Table 17.1). Indeed, the use of chlorine as a bleach remains one of its principal industrial applications (bleaching powder, elemental chlorine, hypochlorite solutions, chlorine dioxide, chloramines, etc.).[8] Another all-pervading use of chlorine, as a disinfectant and germicide, also dates from this period (1801), and the chlorination of domestic water supplies is now almost universal in developed countries. Again, as with fluoride, higher concentrations are toxic to humans: the gas is detectable by smell at 3 ppm, causes throat irritation at 15 ppm, coughing at 30 ppm, and rapid death at 1000 ppm. Prolonged exposure to concentrations above 1 ppm should be avoided.

Sodium chloride, by far the most abundant compound of chlorine, occurs in extensive evaporite deposits, saline lakes and brines, and in the ocean (p. 795). It has played a dominant role in the chemical industry since its inception in the late eighteenth century (p. 71). The now defunct Leblanc process for obtaining NaOH from NaCl signalled the beginnings of large-scale chemical manufacture, and NaCl remains virtually the sole source of chlorine and hydrochloric acid for the vast present-day chlorine-chemicals industry.[8] This embraces not only the large-scale production and distribution of Cl_2 and HCl, but also the manufacture of chlorinated methanes and ethanes, vinyl chloride, aluminium trichloride catalysts and the chlorides of Mg, Ti, Zr, Hf, etc., for production of the metals. Details of many of these processes are to be found either in other chapters or in later sections of the present chapter. About 15 000 chlorinated compounds are currently used to varying degrees in commerce. Of these, the environmental and health hazards posed by certain polychlorinated hydrocarbons is now well established, though not all such compounds are dangerous: focused selective restrictions rather than a blanket banning of all organochlorine compounds is advocated.[9] The rôle of chlorofluorocarbons in the depletion of stratospheric ozone above the polar regions has already been mentioned (p. 608).

Bromine

The magnificent purple pigment referred to in the Bible[10] and known to the Romans as Tyrian purple after the Phoenician port of Tyre (Lebanon), was shown by P. Friedländer in 1909 to be 6,6'-dibromoindigo. This precious dye was extracted in the early days from the small purple snail *Murex brandaris*, as many as 12 000 snails being required to prepare 1.5 g of dye. The element itself was isolated by A.-J. Balard in 1826 from the mother liquors remaining after the crystallization of sodium chloride and sulfate from the waters of the Montpellier salt marshes;

'dephlogisticated marine acid' is a term which can hardly be adopted in the present advanced area of the science. After consulting some of the most eminent chemical philosophers in the country, it has been judged most proper to suggest a name founded upon one of its most obvious and characteristic properties — its colour, and to call it *Chlorine*."

[8] J. S. SCONCE, *Chlorine: Its Manufacture, Properties and Uses*, Reinhold, New York, 1962, 901 pp.

---

[9] B. HILEMAN, *C & E News*, April 19, 11–20 (1993). See also B. HILEMAN, J. R. LONG and E. M. KIRSCHNER, *C & E News*, November 21, 12–26 (1994).

[10] Holy Bible, Ezekiel **27**:7, 16.

the liquor is rich in $MgBr_2$, and the young Balard, then 23 y of age, noticed the deep yellow coloration that developed on addition of chlorine water. Extraction with ether and KOH, followed by treatment of the resulting KBr with H_2SO_4/MnO_2, yielded the element as a red liquid. Astonishingly rapid progress was possible in establishing the chemistry of bromine and in recognizing its elemental nature because of its similarity to chlorine and iodine (which had been isolated 15 y earlier). Indeed, J. von Liebig had missed discovering the element several years previously by misidentifying a sample of it as iodine monochloride.[1] Balard had proposed the name *muride*, but this was not accepted by the French Academy, and the element was named bromine (Greek βρῶμος, stink) because of its unpleasant, penetrating odour. It is perhaps ironic that the name fluorine had already been pre-empted for the element in CaF_2 and HF (p. 789) since bromine, as the only non-metallic element that is liquid at room temperature, would pre-eminently have deserved the name.

The first mineral found to contain bromine (bromyrite, AgBr) was discovered in Mexico in 1841, and industrial production of bromides followed the discovery of the giant Stassfurt potash deposits in 1858. The major use at that time was in photography and medicine: AgBr had been introduced as the light-sensitive agent in photography about 1840, and the use of KBr as a sedative and anti-convulsant in the treatment of epilepsy was begun in 1857. Other major uses of bromine-containing compounds include their application as flame retardants and as phase-transfer catalysts. The scale of the present-day production of bromine and bromine chemicals will become clear in later sections of this chapter.[11]

Iodine

The lustrous, purple-black metallic sheen of resublimed crystalline iodine was first observed by the industrial chemist B. Courtois in 1811, and the name, proposed by J. L. Gay Lussac in 1813, reflects this most characteristic property (Greek ἰώδης, violet-coloured). Courtois obtained the element by treating the ash of seaweed (which had been calcined to extract saltpetre and potash) with concentrated sulfuric acid. Extracts of the brown kelps and seaweeds *Fucus* and *Laminaria* had long been known to be effective for the treatment of goitre and it was not long before J. F. Coindet and others introduced pure KI as a remedy in 1819.[12] It is now known that the thyroid gland produces the growth-regulating hormone thyroxine, an iodinated aminoacid: p-(HO)-$C_6H_2(I)_2$-O-$C_6H_2(I)_2$-$CH_2CH(NH_2)CO_2H$.

If the necessary iodine input is insufficient the thyroid gland enlarges in an attempt to garner more iodine: addition of 0.01% NaI to table salt (iodized salt) prevents this condition. Tincture of iodine is a useful antiseptic.

The first iodine-containing mineral (AgI) was discovered in Mexico in 1825 but the discovery of iodate as an impurity in Chilean saltpetre in 1840 proved to be more significant industrially. The Chilean nitrate deposits provided the largest proportion of the world's iodine until overtaken in the late 1960s by Japanese production from natural brines (pp. 796, 799).

In addition to its uses in photography and medicine, iodine and its compounds have been much exploited in volumetric analysis (iodometry and iodimetry, p. 864). Organoiodine compounds have also played a notable part in the development of synthetic organic chemistry, being the first compounds used in A. W. von Hofmann's alkylation of amines (1850), A. W. Williamson's synthesis of ethers (1851), A. Wurtz's coupling reactions (1855) and V. Grignard's reagents (1900).

Astatine

From its position in the periodic table, all isotopes of element 85 would be expected to

---

[11] D. PRICE, B. IDDON and B. J. WAKEFIELD, *Bromine Compounds: Chemistry and Applications*, Elsevier, Amsterdam 1988, 422 pp.

[12] E. BOOTH, *Chem. Ind. (Lond.)* 31 and 52–5 (1979).

be radioactive. Those isotopes that occur in the natural radioactive series all have half-lives of less than 1 min and thus occur in negligible amounts in nature (p. 796). Astatine (Greek $\overset{''}{\alpha}\sigma\tau\alpha\tau$-$o\varsigma$, unstable) was first made and characterized by D. R. Corson, K. R. Mackenzie and E. Segré in 1940: they synthesized the isotope ^{211}At ($t_{\frac{1}{2}}$ 7.21 h) by bombarding ^{209}Bi with α-particles in a large cyclotron:

$$^{209}_{83}Bi + ^{4}_{2}He \longrightarrow ^{211}_{85}At + 2^{1}_{0}n$$

In all, some 27 isotopes from ^{194}At to ^{220}At have now been prepared by various routes but all are short-lived. The only ones besides ^{211}At having half-lives longer than 1 h are ^{207}At (1.80 h), ^{208}At (1.63 h), ^{209}At (5.41 h), and ^{210}At (8.1 h): this means that weighable amounts of astatine or its compounds cannot be isolated, and nothing is known of the bulk physical properties of the element. For example, the least-unstable isotope (^{210}At) has a specific activity corresponding to 2 curies per μg, i.e. 7×10^{10} disintegrations per second per μg. The largest preparations of astatine to date have involved about $0.05\,\mu$g and our knowledge of the chemistry of this element comes from extremely elegant tracer experiments, typically in the concentration range 10^{-11}–10^{-15} M. The most concentrated aqueous solutions of the element or its compounds ever investigated were only $\sim 10^{-8}$ M.

17.1.2 Abundance and distribution

Because of their reactivity, the halogens do not occur in the free elemental state but they are both widespread and abundant in the form of their ions, X^-. Iodine also occurs as iodate (see below). In addition to large halide mineral deposits, particularly of NaCl and KCl, there are vast quantities of chloride and bromide in ocean waters and brines.

Fluorine is the thirteenth element in order of abundance in crustal rocks of the earth, occurring to the extent of 544 ppm (cf. twelfth Mn, 1060 ppm; fourteenth Ba, 390 ppm; fifteenth Sr, 384 ppm). The three most important minerals are

fluorite CaF_2, cryolite Na_3AlF_6 and fluorapatite $Ca_5(PO_4)_3F$. Of these, however, only fluorite is extensively processed for recovery of fluorine and its compounds (p. 809). Cryolite is a rare mineral, the only commercial deposit being in Greenland, and most of the Na_3AlF_6 needed for the huge aluminium industry (p. 219) is now synthetic. By far the largest amount of fluorine in the earth's crust is in the form of fluorapatite, but this contains only about 3.5% by weight of fluorine and the mineral is processed almost exclusively for its phosphate content. Despite this, about 7% of the domestic requirement for fluorine compounds in the USA was obtained from fluorosilicic acid recovered as a by-product of the huge phosphate industry (pp. 476, 520). Minor occurrences of fluorine are in the rare minerals topaz $Al_2SiO_4(OH,F)_2$, sellaite MgF_2, villiaumite NaF and bastnaesite $(Ce,La)(CO_3)F$ (but see p. 1229). The insolubility of alkaline-earth and other fluorides precludes their occurrence at commercially useful concentrations in ocean water (1.2 ppm) and brines.

Chlorine is the twentieth most abundant element in crustal rocks where it occurs to the extent of 126 ppm (cf. nineteenth V, 136 ppm, and twenty-first Cr, 122 ppm). The vast evaporite deposits of NaCl and other chloride minerals have already been described (pp. 69, 73). Dwarfing these, however, are the inconceivably vast reserves in ocean waters (p. 69) where more than half the total average salinity of 3.4 wt% is due to chloride ions (1.9 wt%). Smaller quantities, though at higher concentrations, occur in certain inland seas and in subterranean brine wells, e.g. the Great Salt Lake, Utah (23% NaCl) and the Dead Sea, Israel (8.0% NaCl, 13.0% $MgCl_2$, 3.5% $CaCl_2$).

Bromine is substantially less abundant in crustal rocks than either fluorine or chlorine; at 2.5 ppm it is forty-sixth in order of abundance being similar to Hf 2.8, Cs 2.6, U 2.3, Eu 2.1 and Sn 2.1 ppm. Like chlorine, the largest natural source of bromine is the oceans, which contain $\sim 6.5 \times 10^{-3}$%, i.e. 65 ppm or 65 mg/l. The mass ratio Cl:Br is ~ 300:1 in the oceans, corresponding to an atomic ratio of $\sim$660:1. Salt lakes and brine wells are also rich sources of bromine, and these are usually proportionately richer in bromine than are the oceans: the atom ratio Cl:Br spans the range $\sim$200–700. Typical bromide-ion concentrations in such waters are: Dead Sea 0.4% (4 g/l), Sakskoe Ozoro (Crimea) 0.28% and Searle's Lake (California) 0.085%.

Iodine is considerably less abundant than the lighter halogens both in the earth's crust and in the hydrosphere. It comprises 0.46 ppm of the crustal rocks and is sixtieth in order of abundance (cf. Tl 0.7, Tm 0.5, In 0.24, Sb 0.2). It occurs but rarely as iodide minerals, and commercial deposits are usually as iodates, e.g. lautarite, $Ca(IO_3)_2$ and dietzeite, $7Ca(IO_3)_2.8CaCrO_4$. Thus the caliche nitrate beds of Chile contain iodine in this form ($\sim$0.02–1 wt% I). These mine workings soon replaced calcined seaweeds as the main source of iodine during the last century, but have recently been themselves overtaken by iodine recovered from brines. Brines associated with oil-well drillings in Louisiana and California were found to contain 30–40 ppm iodine in the 1920s, and independent subterranean brines were located at Midland, Michigan, in the 1960s, and in Oklahoma (1977), which is now the main US source. Natural brine wells in Japan (up to 100 ppm I) were discovered after the Second World War, and exploitation of these now ensures Japan first place among the world's iodine producers. The concentration of iodine in ocean waters is only 0.05 ppm, too low for commercial recovery, though brown seaweeds of the *Laminaria* family (and to a lesser extent *Fucus*) can concentrate this up to 0.45% of their dry weight (see above).

The fugitive radioactive element astatine can hardly be said to exist in nature though the punctillious would rightly point to its temporary participation in the natural radioactive series. Thus ^{219}At ($t_{\frac{1}{2}}$ 54 s) occurs as a rare and inconspicuous branch (4×10^{-3}%) of another minor branch (1.2%) of the ^{235}U ($4n + 3$) series (see scheme). Another branch (5×10^{-4}%) at ^{215}Po yields ^{215}At by β emission before itself decaying by α emission ($t_{\frac{1}{2}}$ 1.0 $\times$ 10^{-4} s); likewise ^{218}At ($t_{\frac{1}{2}} \sim$ 72 s) is a descendant of the ^{238}U ($4n +$ 2) series, and traces have been detected of ^{217}At ($t_{\frac{1}{2}}$ 0.0323 s) and ^{216}At ($t_{\frac{1}{2}}$ 3.0 $\times$ 10^{-4} s). Estimates suggest that the outermost kilometre of the earth's crust contains no more than 44 mg of astatine compared with 15 g of francium (p. 69) or the relatively abundant polonium (2500 tonnes) and actinium (7000 tonnes). Astatine can therefore be regarded as the rarest naturally occurring terrestrial element.

17.1.3 Production and uses of the elements

The only practicable large-scale method of preparing F_2 gas is Moissan's original procedure based on the electrolysis of KF dissolved in anhydrous HF; (see however p. 821). Moissan used a mole ratio KF:HF of about 1:13, but this has a high vapour pressure of HF and had to be operated at $-24°$. Electrolyte systems having mole ratios of 1:2 and 1:1 melt at $\sim$72° and $\sim$240°C respectively and have much lower vapour pressures of HF; accordingly these compositions were subsequently favoured. Nowadays, medium-temperature cells (80–100°) are universally employed, being preferred over the high-temperature cells because (a) they have a lower pressure of HF gas above the cell, (b) there are fewer corrosion problems, (c) the anode has a longer life and (d) the composition of the electrolyte can vary within fairly wide limits without impairing the operating conditions or efficiency. The highly corrosive nature of the electrolyte, coupled with the aggressive oxidizing power of F_2, pose considerable problems of handling, and these are exacerbated by the explosive reaction of F_2 with its co-product H_2, so that accidental mixing of the gases must be prevented at all costs. Scrupulous absence of grease and other flamable contaminants must also be ensured since they can lead to spectacular fires which puncture the protective fluoride coating of the metal containers and cause the whole system to enflame. Another hazard in early generators was the formation of explosive graphite-fluorine compounds at the anode (p. 289). All these problems have now been overcome and F_2 can be routinely generated with safety both in the laboratory and on a large industrial scale.[2,13] A typical generator (Fig. 17.1) consists of a mild-steel pot (cathode) containing the electrolyte KF.2HF which is kept at 80–100°C either by a heating jacket when the cell is quiescent or by a cooling system when the cell is working. The anode consists of a central rod of compacted, ungraphitized carbon, and the product gases are kept separate by a skirt or diaphragm dipping below the electrolyte surface. The temperature is automatically controlled, as is the level of the electrolyte by controlled addition of make-up anhydrous HF. Laboratory generators usually operate at about 10–50 A whereas industrial production, employing banks of cells, may operate at 4000–6000 A and 8–12 V. An individual cell in such a bank might typically be $3.0 \times 0.8 \times 0.6$ m and hold 1 tonne of electrolyte; it might have 12 anode

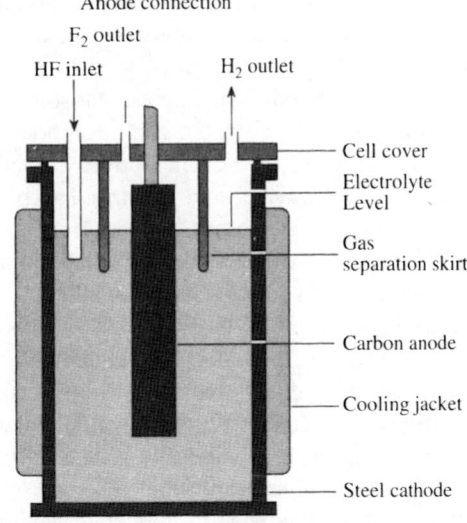

Figure 17.1 Schematic diagram of an electrolytic fluorine-generating cell.

assemblies each holding two anode blocks and produce 3–4 kg F_2 per hour. A large-scale plant can produce *ca.* 9 tonnes of liquefied F_2 per day. The total annual production in the USA and Canada exceeds 5000 tonnes, and similar though somewhat smaller amounts are produced in several European countries (UK, France, Germany, Italy, Russia). Production in Japan approaches 1000 tpa.

Cylinders of F_2 are now commercially available in various sizes from 230-g to 2.7-kg capacity; 1993 price ~$110–260 per kg depending on cylinder size. The gas pressure is 2.86 MPa (~28 atm.) at 21°C. Liquid F_2 is shipped in tank trucks of 2.27 tonnes capacity, the container being itself cooled by a jacket of liquid N_2 which boils 8° below F_2. Alternatively, it can be converted to ClF_3, bp 11.7°C (p. 828), which is easier to handle and transport than F_2. In fact, about 70–80% of the elemental F_2 produced is used captively for the manufacture of UF_6 for nuclear power generation (p. 1259). Another important use is in the production of SF_6 for dielectrics (p. 687). The captive use to manufacture the versatile fluorinating agents ClF_3, BrF_3 and IF_5 is a third important outlet. Fluorination of W and Re to

13 H. C. FIELDING and B. E. LEE, in R. THOMPSON (ed.), *The Modern Inorganic Chemicals Industry*, pp. 149–67, Chemical Society Special Publication No. 31, 1977.

their hexafluorides is also industrially important since these volatile compounds are used in chemical vapour deposition of W and Re films on intricately shaped components. Most other fluorinations of inorganic and organic compounds avoid the direct use of F_2. The former demand for liquid F_2 as a rocket-fuel oxidizer has now ceased.

Chlorine is rarely generated on a laboratory scale since it is so readily available in cylinders of all sizes from 450 g (net) to 70 kg. When required it can also be generated by adding concentrated, air-free hydrochloric acid (d 1.16 g cm^{-3}) dropwise on to precipitated hydrated manganese dioxide in a flask fitted with a dropping funnel and outlet tube: the gas formation can be regulated by moderate heating and the Cl_2 thus formed can be purified by passage through water (to remove HCl) and H_2SO_4 (to remove H_2O). The gas, whether generated in this way or obtained from a cylinder, can be further purified if necessary by passage through successive tubes containing CaO and P_2O_5, followed by condensation in a bath cooled by solid CO_2 and fractionation in a vacuum line.

Industrial production of Cl_2 and chlorine chemicals is on a vast scale and comprises a major section of the heavy chemical industry.[8,9,14,15] Some aspects have already been discussed on p. 793, and further details are in the Panel.

Bromine is invariably made on an industrial scale by oxidation of bromide ion with Cl_2. The main sources of Br$^-$ are Arkansas brines (4000–5000 ppm) which account for most of US production, various brines and bitterns in Europe, the Dead Sea (4000–6000 ppm), and ocean waters (65 ppm). Following the oxidation of Br$^-$ the Br_2 is removed from the solution either by passage of steam ("steaming out") or air ("blowing out"), and then condensed and purified. Although apparently simple, these unit operations must deal with highly reactive and corrosive materials, and the industrial processes have been ingeniously developed and refined

---

[14] R. W. PURCELL, The chor-alkali industry, in ref. 13, pp. 106–33. A. CAMPBELL, Chlorine and chlorination, *ibid.*, pp. 134–48.
[15] *Kirk–Othmer Encyclopedia of Chemical Technology*, 4th edn., **1**, 938–1025 (1991).

Industrial Production and Uses of Chlorine

The large-scale production of Cl_2 is invariably achieved by the electrolytic oxidation of the chloride ion. Natural brines or aqueous solutions of NaCl can be electrolysed in an asbestos diaphragm cell or a mercury cathode cell, though these latter are being phased out for environmental and other reasons (p. 1225). Electrolysis of molten NaCl is also carried out on a large scale: in this case the co-product is Na rather than NaOH. Electrolysis of by-product HCl is also used where this is cheaply available. World consumption of Cl_2 in 1987 exceeded 35 million tonnes. Production is dominated by the USA, but large tonnages are produced in all industrial countries: USA 30%, Western Europe 29%, Eastern Europe 15%, Japan 8.5%, Asia/Pacific 6.8%. Cl_2 was ranked eighth among the large-volume chemicals manufactured in the USA during 1996. Diaphragm cells predominated though there is a growing interest in membrane cells in which the anolyte and catholyte are separated by a porous Nafion membrane (Nafion is a copolymer of tetrafluoroethylene and a perfluorosulfonylethoxy ether and the membrane is reinforced with a Teflon mesh).[15] In addition to cylinders of varying capacity up to 70 kg, chlorine can be transported in drums (865 kg), tank wagons (road: 15 tonnes; rail 27–90 tonnes), or barges (600–1200 tonnes).

The three main categories of use for Cl_2 are:

(a) Production of organic compounds by chlorination and/or oxychlorination using a fluidized bed of copper chloride catalyst (pre-eminent amongst these are vinyl chloride monomer and propylene oxide which in the USA alone are produced on a scale of 9.0 and 2.0 million tonnes respectively). Production of chlorinated organic compounds accounts for about 63% of the Cl_2 produced.

(b) Bleaches (for paper, pulp and textiles) sanitation and disinfection of municipal water supplies and swimming pools, sewage treatment and control. These uses account for about 19% of the Cl_2 produced.

(c) Production of inorganic compounds, notably HCl, Cl_2O, HOCl, $NaClO_3$, chlorinated isocyanurates, $AlCl_3$, $SiCl_4$, $SnCl_4$, PCl_3, PCl_5, $POCl_3$, $AsCl_3$, $SbCl_3$, $SbCl_5$, $BiCl_3$, S_2Cl_2, SCl_2, $SOCl_2$, ClF_3, ICl, ICl_3, $TiCl_3$, $TiCl_4$, $MoCl_5$, $FeCl_3$, $ZnCl_2$, Hg_2Cl_2, $HgCl_2$, etc. (see index for page references to production and uses). About 18% of Cl_2 production is used to manufacture inorganic chemicals.

to give optimum yields at the lowest possible operating costs.[16,17]

World production of Br_2 in 1990 was about 438 000 tonnes pa, i.e. about one-hundredth of the scale of the chlorine industry. The main producing countries are (tonnes): USA 177 000, Israel 135 000, Russia 60 000, UK 28 000, France 18 000 and Japan 15 000. The production capacity of Israel has recently increased almost threefold because of expanded facilities on the Dead Sea. Historically, bromine was shipped in individual 3-kg (net) bottles to minimize damage due to breakage, but during the 1960s bulk transport in monel metal drums (100-kg capacity) or lead-lined tanks (24 or 48 tonnes) was developed and these are now used for transport by road, rail and ship. The price of Br_2 in tank-car lots was $975/kg in 1990.

The industrial usage of bromine has been dominated by the single compound ethylene dibromide which has been (with ethylene dichloride) a valuable gasoline (petrol) additive where it acts as a scavenger for lead from the anti-knock additive $PbEt_4$. Environmental legislation has dramatically reduced the amount of leaded petrol produced and, accordingly, ethylene dibromide, which accounted for 90% of US bromine production in 1955, declined to 75% a decade later and now represents a mere 16% of the total bromine consumption in the USA (1990). Fortunately this decline has been matched by a steady increase in other applications and the industry worldwide has shown a modest growth. Most of these large-volume applications involve organic compounds, notably MeBr, which is one of the most effective nematocides known (i.e. kills worms) and is also used as a general pesticide (herbicide, fungicide and insecticide). Ethylene dibromide and dibromochloropropane are also used as pesticides. Bromine compounds are extensively used as fire retardants, especially for fibres, carpets, rugs and plastics; they are about 3–4 times as effective (weight for

weight) as chlorocompounds which gives them a substantial cost advantage.

Other uses of bromo-organics include high-density drilling fluids, dyestuffs and pharmaceuticals. Bromine is also used in water sanitation and to synthesize a wide range of inorganic compounds, e.g. AgBr for photography, HBr, alkali metal bromides, bromates, etc. (see later sections). An indication of the overall pattern of use (USA, 1990) is as follows: flame retardants 29%, ethylene dibromide 16%, agrochemicals 16% drilling fluids 11% inorganic bromides 5.5%, water treatment chemicals 5.5%, other 17%.

The commercial recovery of iodine on an industrial scale depends on the particular source of the element.[18] From natural brines, such as those at Midland (Michigan) or in Russia or Japan, chlorine oxidation followed by air blow-out as for bromine (above) is much used, the final purification being by resublimation. Alternatively the brine, after clarification, can be treated with just sufficient $AgNO_3$ to precipitate the AgI which is then treated with clean scrap iron or steel to form metallic Ag and a solution of FeI_2; the Ag is redissolved in HNO_3 for recycling and the solution is treated with Cl_2 to liberate the I_2:

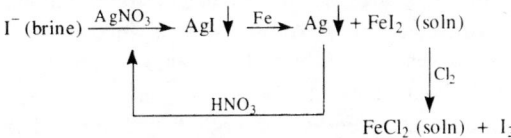

The newest process to be developed oxidizes the brine with Cl_2 and then treats the solution with an ion-exchange resin: the iodine is adsorbed in the form of polyiodide which can be eluted with alkali followed by NaCl to regenerate the column. About 65% of the iodine consumed in the world comes from brines.

Recovery of iodine from Chilean saltpetre differs entirely from its recovery from brine since it is present as iodate. $NaIO_3$ is extracted from the caliche and is allowed to accumulate in the mother liquors from the crystallization of $NaNO_3$

---

[16] R. B. McDonald and W. R. Merriman, pp. 168–82 of ref. 13.
[17] Ref. 2, Vol. 4 (1992), Bromine, pp. 536–60; Bromine compounds, pp. 560–89.

[18] Ref. 2, Vol. 14 (1995), Iodine and Iodine compounds, pp. 709–37.

until its concentration is about 6 g/l. Part is then drawn off and treated with the stoichiometric amount of sodium hydrogen sulfite required to reduce it to iodide:

$$IO_3^- + 3HSO_3^- \longrightarrow I^- + 3SO_4^{2-} + 3H^+$$

The resulting acidic mixture is treated with just sufficient fresh mother liquor to liberate all the contained iodine:

$$5I^- + IO_3^- + 6H^+ \longrightarrow 3I_2\downarrow + 3H_2O$$

The precipitated I_2 is filtered off and the iodine-free filtrate returned to the nitrate-leaching cycle after neutralization of any excess acid with Na_2CO_3.

World production of I_2 in 1992 approached 15 000 tonnes, the dominant producers being Japan 41%, Chile 40%, USA 10% and the former Soviet Union 9%. Crude iodine is packed in double polythene-lined fibre drums of 10–50-kg capacity. Resublimed iodine is transported in lined fibre drums (11.3 kg) or in bottles containing 0.11, 0.45 or 2.26 kg. The price of I_2 has traditionally fluctuated wildly. Thus, because of acute over-supply in 1990 the price for I_2 peaked at $22/kg in 1988, falling to $12/kg in 1990 and $9.50/kg in 1992. Unlike Cl_2 and Br_2, iodine has no predominant commercial outlet. About 50% is incorporated into a wide variety of organic compounds and about 15% each is accounted for as resublimed iodine, KI, and other inorganics. The end uses include catalysts for synthetic rubber manufacture, animal- and fowl-feed supplements, stabilizers, dyestuffs, colourants and pigments for inks, pharmaceuticals, sanitary uses (tincture of iodine, etc.) and photographic chemicals for high-speed negatives. Uses of iodine compounds as smog inhibitors and cloud-seeding agents are small. In analytical chemistry $KHgI_3$ forms the basis for Nessler's reagent for the detection of NH_3, and Cu_2HgI_4 was used in Mayer's reagent for alkaloids. Iodides and iodates are standard reagents in quantitative volumetric analysis (p. 864). Ag_2HgI_4 has the highest ionic electrical conductivity of any known solid at room temperature but this has not yet been exploited on a large scale in any solid-state device.

17.1.4 Atomic and physical properties

The halogens are volatile, diatomic elements whose colour increases steadily with increase in atomic number. Fluorine is a pale yellow gas which condenses to a canary yellow liquid, bp $-188.1°C$ (intermediate between N_2, bp $-195.8°$, and O_2, bp $-183.0°C$). Chlorine is a greenish-yellow gas, bp $-34.0°$, and bromine a dark-red mobile liquid, bp $59.5°$: interestingly the colour of both elements diminishes with decrease in temperature and at $-195°$ Cl_2 is almost colourless and Br_2 pale yellow. Iodine is a lustrous, black, crystalline solid, mp $113.6°$, which sublimes readily and boils at $185.2°C$.

Atomic properties are summarized in Table 17.3 and some physical properties are in Table 17.4.

Table 17.3 Atomic properties of the halogens

Property	F	Cl	Br	I	At
Atomic number	9	17	35	53	85
Number of stable isotopes	1	2	2	1	0
Atomic weight	18.998 4032(9)	35.4527(9)	79.904(1)	126.90447(3)	(210)
Electronic configuration	$[He]2s^22p^5$	$[Ne]3s^23p^5$	$[Ar]3d^{10}4s^24p^5$	$[Kr]4d^{10}5s^25p^5$	$[Xe]4f^{14}5d^{10}6s^26p^5$
Ionization energy/kJ mol^{-1}	1680.6	1255.7	1142.7	1008.7	[926]
Electron affinity/kJ mol^{-1}	332.6	348.7	324.5	295.3	[270]
ΔH_{dissoc}/kJ mol$(X_2)^{-1}$	158.8	242.58	192.77	151.10	—
Ionic radius, X$^-$/pm	133	184	196	220	—
van der Waals radius/pm	135	180	195	215	—
Distance X–X in X_2/pm	143	199	228	266	—

Table 17.4　Physical properties of the halogens

Property	F_2	Cl_2	Br_2	I_2
MP/°C	−219.6	−101.0	−7.25	113.6[a]
BP/°C	−188.1	−34.0	59.5	185.2[a]
d (liquid, T°C)/g cm^{-3}	1.516(−188°)	1.655(−70°)	3.187 (0°)	3.960[b] (120°)
ΔH_{fusion}/kJ mol$(X_2)^{-1}$	0.51	6.41	10.57	15.52
ΔH_{vap}/kJ mol$(X_2)^{-1}$	6.54	20.41	29.56	41.95
Temperature (°C) for 1% dissoc at 1 atm	765	975	775	575

[a]Solid iodine has a vapour pressure of 0.31 mmHg (41 Pa) at 25°C and 90.5 mmHg (12.07 kPa) at the mp (113.6°).

[b]Solid iodine has a density of 4.940 g cm^{-3} at 20°C.

As befits their odd atomic numbers, the halogens have few naturally occurring isotopes (p. 3). Only one isotope each of F and I occurs in nature and the atomic weights of these elements are therefore known very accurately indeed (p. 17). Chlorine has two naturally occurring isotopes (^{35}Cl 75.77%, ^{37}Cl 24.23%) as also does bromine (^{79}Br 50.69%, ^{81}Br 49.31%). All isotopes of At are radioactive (p. 795). The ionization energies of the halogen atoms show the expected trend to lower values with increase in atomic number. The electronic configuration of each atom (ns^2np^5) is one p electron less than that of the next succeeding noble gas, and energy is evolved in the reaction X(g) + e$^-$ ⟶ X$^-$(g). The electron affinity, which traditionally (though misleadingly) is given a positive sign despite the negative enthalpy change in the above reaction, is maximum for Cl, the value for F being intermediate between those for Cl and Br. Even more noticeable is the small enthalpy of dissociation for F_2 which is similar to that of I_2 and less than two-thirds of the value for Cl_2.[19] In this connection it can be noted that N−N single bonds in hydrazines are weaker than the corresponding P−P bonds and that O−O single bonds in peroxides are weaker than the corresponding S−S bonds. This was explained (R. S. Mulliken and others, 1955) by postulating that partial pd hybridization imparts some double-bond character

to the formal P−P, S−S and Cl−Cl single bonds thereby making them stronger than their first-row counterparts. However, following C. A. Coulson and others (1962), it seems unnecessary to invoke substantial d-orbital participation and the weakness of the F−F single bond is then ascribed to decreased overlap of bonding orbitals, appreciable internuclear repulsion and the relatively large electron−electron repulsions of the lone-pairs which are much closer together in F_2 than in Cl_2.[20] The rapid diminution of bond-dissociation energies in the sequence $N_2 \gg O_2 \gg F_2$ is, of course, due to successive filling of the antibonding orbitals (p. 606), thus reducing the formal bond order from triple in N≡N to double and single in O=O and F−F respectively.

Radioactive isotopes of the halogens have found use in the study of isotope-exchange reactions and the mechanisms of various other reactions.[21,22] The properties of some of the most used isotopes are in Table 17.5. Many of these isotopes are available commercially. A fuller treatment with detailed references

[19] J. BERKOWITZ and A. C. WAHL, Adv. Fluorine Chem. **7**, 147–74 (1973). A. A. WOOLF, Adv. Inorg. Chem. Radiochem. **24**, 1–55 (1981). J. J. TURNER, MTP International Review of Science: Inorganic Chemistry Series 1, Vol. 3, pp. 253–91, Butterworths, London, 1972.

[20] P. POLITZER, Anomalous properties of fluorine, J. Am. Chem. Soc. **91**, 6235–7 (1969); Some anomalous properties of oxygen and nitrogen, Inorg. Chem. **16**, 3350–1 (1977).

[21] M. F. A. DOVE and D. B. SOWERBY, in V. GUTMANN (ed.), Halogen Chemistry, Vol. 1, pp. 41–132, Academic Press, London, 1967.

[22] R. H. HERBER (ed.), Inorganic Isotopic Syntheses, W. H. Benjamin, New York, 1962; Radio-chlorine (B. J. MASTERS), pp. 215–26; Iodine-131 (M. KAHN), pp. 227–42. See also G. ANGELINI, M. SEPERANZA, C.-Y. SHIUE and A. P. WOLF, J. Chem. Soc., Chem. Commun., 924–5 (1986) for radio fluorine (^{18}F).

Table 17.5 Some radioactive isotopes of the halogens

Isotope	Nuclear spin and parity	Half-life	Principal mode of decay (E/MeV)	Principal source
^{18}F	1+	109.77 min	β^+ (0.649)	$^{19}F(n,2n)$
^{36}Cl	2+	3.01×10^5 y	β^- (0.714)	$^{35}Cl(n,\gamma)$
^{38}Cl	2−	37.24 min	β^- (4.81, 1.11, 2.77)	$^{37}Cl(n,\gamma)$
^{80m}Br	5−	4.42 h	γ (internal trans) (0.086)	$^{79}Br(n,\gamma)$
^{80}Br	1+	17.68 min	β^- (2.02, 1.35)	^{80m}Br (IT)
^{82}Br	5−	35.30 h	β^- (0.44)	^{81}Br (n,γ)
^{125}I	$\frac{5}{2}+$	60.2 d	Electron capture (0.035)	$^{123}Sb(\alpha,2n)$, $^{124}Te(d,n)$, or $^{125}Xe(\beta^-)$
^{128}I	1+	24.99 min	β^- (2.12, 1.66)	$^{127}I(n,\gamma)$
^{129}I	$\frac{7}{2}+$	1.57×10^7 y	β^- (0.189)	U fission
^{131}I	$\frac{7}{2}+$	8.04 d	β^- (0.806)	$^{130}Te(n,\gamma)$, U or Pu fission

of the use of radioactive isotopes of the halogens, including exchange reactions, tracer studies of other reactions, studies of diffusion phenomena, radiochemical methods of analysis, physiological and biochemical applications, and uses in technology and industry is available.[23] Excited states of ^{127}I and ^{129}I have also been used extensively in Mössbauer spectroscopy.[24]

The nuclear spin of the stable isotopes of the halogens has been exploited in nmr spectroscopy. The use of ^{19}F in particular, with its 100% abundance, convenient spin of $\frac{1}{2}$ and excellent sensitivity, has resulted in a vast and continually expanding literature since ^{19}F chemical shifts were first observed in 1950.[25] The resonances for ^{35}Cl and ^{37}Cl were also first observed in 1950.[26] Appropriate nuclear parameters are in Table 17.6. From this it is clear that the ^{19}F resonance can be observed with high receptivity at a frequency fairly close to that for ^1H. Furthermore, since $I < 1$ there is no nuclear quadrupole moment and hence no quadrupolar broadening of the resonance. The observed range of ^{19}F chemical shifts is more than an order of magnitude greater than for ^1H and spans more than 800 ppm of the resonance frequency.[27,28] The signal moves to higher frequency with increasing electronegativity and oxidation state of the attached atom thus following the usual trends. Results are regularly reviewed.[29] For other halogens, as seen from Table 17.6, the nuclear spin I is greater than $\frac{1}{2}$ which means that the nuclear charge distribution is non-spherical; this results in a nuclear quadrupole moment, and resonance broadening due to quadrupolar relaxation severely restricts the use of the technique except for the halide ions X^- or for tetrahedral species such as ClO_4^- which have zero electric field gradient at the halogen nucleus. The receptivity is also much less

[23] A. J. DOWNS and C. J. ADAMS, in J. C. BAILAR, H. J. EMELÉUS, R. S. NYHOLM and A. F. TROTMAN-DICKENSON, Comprehensive Inorganic Chemistry, Vol. 2, pp. 1148–61 (Isotopes), Pergamon Press, Oxford, 1973.

[24] N. N. GREENWOOD and T. C. GIBB, Mössbauer Spectroscopy, pp. 462–82, Chapman & Hall, London, 1971. R. V. PARISH in G. J. LONG (ed.), Mössbauer Spectroscopy Applied to Inorganic Chemistry, Vol. 2, Chap. 9, 391–428 (1987). Plenum Press, New York.

[25] W. C. DICKENSON, Phys. Rev. 77, 736–7 (1950). H. S. GUTOWSKY and C. J. HOFFMAN, Phys. Rev. 80, 110–11 (1950).

[26] W. G. PROCTOR and F. C. YU, Phys. Rev. 77, 716–7 (1950).

[27] J. W. EMSLEY, J. FEENEY and L. H. SUTCLIFFE, High Resolution Nuclear Magnetic Resonance Spectroscopy, Vols. 1 and 2, Pergamon Press, Oxford, 1966, Chap. 11, Fluorine-19, pp. 871–968.

[28] C. J. JAMESON in J. MASON (ed.) Multinuclear NMR, Plenum Press, New York, 1987. Fluorine, pp. 437–46. See also J. H. CLARK, E. M. GOODMAN, D. K. SMITH, S. J. BROWN and J. M. MILLER, J. Chem. Soc., Chem. Commun., 657–8 (1986).

[29] Annual Reports on NMR Spectroscopy, Vol. 1 (1968)–Vol. 10b (1980) (Fluorine).

Table 17.6 Nuclear magnetic resonance parameters for the halogen isotopes

Isotope	Nuclear spin quantum no. I	NMR frequency rel to $^1H(SiMe_4)$ = 100.000	Relative receptivity $D_p^{(a)}$	Nuclear quadrupole moment $Q/$ ($e\ 10^{-28}\ m^2$)
^1H	1/2	100.000	1.000	0
^{19}F	1/2	94.094	0.8328	0
^{35}Cl	3/2	9.809	3.55×10^{-3}	-8.2×10^{-2}
^{37}Cl	3/2	8.165	6.44×10^{-4}	-6.5×10^{-2}
$(^{79}Br)^{(b)}$	3/2	25.140	3.97×10^{-2}	0.33
^{81}Br	3/2	27.100	4.87×10^{-2}	0.27
^{127}I	5/2	20.146	9.34×10^{-2}	-0.79

[a] Receptivity D is proportional to $\gamma^3 NI(I+1)$ where γ is the magnetogyric ratio, N the natural abundance of the isotope, and I the nuclear spin quantum number; D_p is the receptivity relative to that of the proton taken as 1.000.
[b] Less-favourable isotope.

Table 17.7 Interatomic distances in crystalline halogens (pm)

X	X–X	X···X Within layer	X···X Between layers	X···X Ratio $\frac{X···X}{X-X}$
F	149	324	284	(1.91)
Cl	198	332, 382	374	1.68
Br	227	331, 379	399	1.46
I	272	350, 397	427	1.29

than for ^1H or ^{19}F which accordingly renders observation difficult. Despite these technical problems, much useful information has been obtained, especially in physicochemical and biological investigations.[30,31] The quadrupole moments of Cl, Br and I have also been exploited successfully in nuclear quadrupole resonance studies of halogen-containing compounds in the solid state.[32]

The molecular and bulk properties of the halogens, as distinct from their atomic and nuclear properties, were summarized in Table 17.4 and have to some extent already been briefly discussed. The high volatility and relatively low enthalpy of vaporization reflect the diatomic molecular structure of these elements. In the solid state the molecules align to give a layer lattice: F_2 has two modifications (a low-temperature, α-form and a higher-temperature, β-form) neither of which resembles the orthorhombic layer lattice of the isostructural Cl_2, Br_2 and I_2. The layer lattice is illustrated below for I_2 the I–I distance of 271.5 pm is appreciably longer than in gaseous I_2 (266.6 pm) and the closest interatomic approach between the molecules is 350 pm within the layer and 427 pm between layers (cf the van der Waals radius of 215 pm). These values are

[30] B. LINDMAN and S. FORSEN, Chap. 13 in R. K. HARRIS and B. E. MANN (eds.), *NMR and the Periodic Table*, pp. 421–38, Academic Press, London, 1978. B. LINDMAN and S. FORSEN, Physicochemical and biological applications, Vol. 12 of P. DIEHL, E. FLUCK and R. KOSFELD (eds.), *NMR Basic Principles and Progress*, Springer-Verlag, Berlin, 1976, 365 pp.
[31] J. W. AKITT, in ref. 28, The quadrupolar halides Cl, Br and I, pp. 447–61.
[32] T. P. DAS and E. L. HAHN, *Nuclear Quadrupole Resonance Spectroscopy*, Academic Press, New York, 1958, 223 pp; E. A. C. LUCKEN, *Nuclear Quadrupole Coupling Constants*, Academic Press, London, 1969, 360 pp.

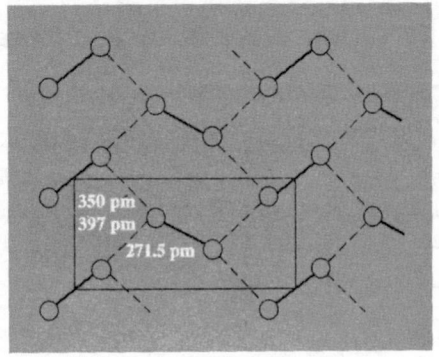

compared with similar data for the other halogens in Table 17.7 from which two further features of interest emerge: (a) the intralayer intermolecular distances $Cl \cdots Cl$ and $Br \cdots Br$ are almost identical, and (b) the differences between intra- and inter-layer $X \cdots X$ distances decreases with increase in atomic number. (Fluorine is not directly comparable because of its differing structure.)

As expected from their structures, the elements are poor conductors of electricity: solid F_2 and Cl_2 have negligible conductivity and Br_2 has a value of $\sim 5 \times 10^{-13}$ ohm^{-1} cm^{-1} just below the mp. Iodine single crystals at room temperature have a conductivity of 5×10^{-12} ohm^{-1} cm^{-1} perpendicular to the bc layer plane but this increases to 1.7×10^{-8} ohm^{-1} cm^{-1} within this plane; indeed, the element is a two-dimensional semiconductor with a band gap $E_g \sim 1.3$ eV (125 kJ mol^{-1}). Even more remarkably, when crystals of iodine are compressed they become metallic, and at 350 kbar have a conductivity of $\sim 10^4$ ohm^{-1} cm^{-1}.[33] The metallic nature of the conductivity is confirmed by its negative temperature coefficient.

The ease of dissociation of the X_2 molecules follows closely the values of the enthalpy of dissociation since the entropy change for the reaction is almost independent of X. Thus F_2 at 1 atm pressure is 1% dissociated into atoms at 765°C but a temperature of 975°C is required to achieve the same degree of dissociation for Cl_2; thereafter, the required temperature drops to 775°C for Br_2 and 575°C for I_2 (see also next section for atomic halogens).

17.1.5 Chemical reactivity and trends

General reactivity and stereochemistry

Fluorine is the most reactive of all elements. It forms compounds, under appropriate conditions, with every other element in the periodic table except He, Ar and Ne, frequently combining

---

[33] A. S. BALCHIN and H. G. DRICKAMER, *J. Chem. Phys.* **34**, 1948–9 (1961).

directly and with such vigour that the reaction becomes explosive. Some elements such as O_2 and N_2 react less readily with fluorine (pp. 639, 438) and some bulk metals (e.g. Al, Fe, Ni, Cu) acquire a protective fluoride coating, though all metals react exothermically when powdered and/or heated. For example, powdered Fe (0.84 mm size, 20 mesh) is not attacked by liquid F_2 whereas at 0.14 mm size (100 mesh) it ignites and burns violently. Perhaps the most striking example of the reactivity of F_2 is the ease with which it reacts directly with Xe under mild conditions to produce crystalline xenon fluorides (p. 894). This great reactivity of F_2 can be related to its small dissociation energy (p. 801) (which leads to low activation energies of reaction), and to the great strength of the bonds that fluorine forms with other elements. Both factors in turn can be related to the small size of the F atom and ensure that enthalpies of fluorination are much greater than those of other halogenations. Some typical average bond energies (kJ mol^{-1}) illustrating these points are:

X	XX	HX	BX$_3$	AlX$_3$	CX$_4$
F	159	574	645	582	456
Cl	243	428	444	427	327
Br	193	363	368	360	272
I	151	294	272	285	239

The tendency for F_2 to give F^- ions in solution is also much greater than for the other halogens as indicated by the steady decrease in oxidation potential ($E°$) for the reaction $X_2(soln) + 2e^- \rightleftharpoons 2X^-$ (aq):

X$_2$	F$_2$	Cl$_2$	Br$_2$	I$_2$	At$_2$
$E°$/V	2.866	1.395	1.087	0.615	~ 0.3

The corresponding free energy changes can be calculated from the relation $\Delta G = -nE°F$ where $n = 2$ and $F = 96.485$ kJ mol^{-1}. Note that $E°(F_2/2F^-)$ is greater than the decomposition potential for water (p. 629). Note also the different sequence of values for $E°(X_2/2X^-)$ and for the electron affinities of X(g) (p. 800). A similar "anomaly" was observed (p. 75) for $E°$ (Li$^+$/Li) and the ionization energy of Li(g), and in both cases the reason is the same, namely the enhanced enthalpy of hydration of the smaller ions. Other redox properties of the halogens are compared on pp. 853–6.

It follows from the preceding paragraph that F_2 is an extremely strong oxidizing element that can engender unusually high oxidation states in the elements with which it reacts, e.g. IF_7, PtF_6, PuF_6, BiF_5, TbF_4, CmF_4, $KAg^{III}F_4$ and AgF_2. Indeed, fluorine (like the other first-row elements Li, Be, B, C, N and O) is atypical of the elements in its group and for the same reasons. For all 7 elements deviations from extrapolated trends can be explained in terms of three factors:

(1) their atoms are small;
(2) their electrons are tightly held and not so readily ionized or distorted (polarized) as in later members of the group;
(3) they have no low-lying d orbitals available for bonding.

Thus the ionization energy I_M is much greater for F than for the other halogens, thereby making formal positive oxidation states virtually impossible to attain. Accordingly, fluorine is exclusively univalent and its compounds are formed either by gain of 1 electron to give F^- ($2s^2 2p^6$) or by sharing 1 electron in a covalent single bond. Note, however, that the presence of lone-pairs permits both the fluoride ion itself and also certain molecular fluorides to act as Lewis bases in which the coordination number of F is greater than 1, e.g. it is 2 for the bridging F atoms in $As_2F_{11}^-$, $Sb_3F_{16}^-$, Nb_4F_{20}, $(HF)_n$ and $(BeF_2)_\infty$. The coordination number of F^- can rise to 3 (planar) in compounds with the rutile structure (e.g. MgF_2, MnF_2, FeF_2, CoF_2, NiF_2, ZnF_2 and PdF_2). Likewise, fourfold coordination (tetrahedral) is found in the zinc-blende-type structure of CuF and in the fluorite structure of CaF_2, SrF_2, BaF_2, RaF_2, CdF_2, HgF_2 and PbF_2. A coordination number of 6 occurs in the alkali metal fluorides MF (NaCl type). In many of these compounds F^- resembles O^{2-} stereochemically rather than the other halides, and the radii of the 2 ions are very similar (F^- 133, O^{2-} 140 pm, cf. Cl^- 184, Br^- 196 pm).

The heavier halogens, though markedly less reactive than fluorine, are still amongst the most reactive of the elements. Their reactivity diminishes in the sequence $Cl_2 > Br_2 > I_2$. For example, Cl_2 reacts with CO, NO and SO_2 to give $COCl_2$, NOCl and SO_2Cl_2, whereas iodine does not react with these compounds. Again, in the direct halogenation of metals, Cl_2 and Br_2 sometimes produce a higher metal oxidation state than does I_2, e.g. Re yields $ReCl_6$, $ReBr_5$ and ReI_4 respectively. Conversely, the decreasing ionization energies and increasing ease of oxidation of the elements results in the readier formation of iodine cations (p. 842) and compounds in which iodine has a higher stable oxidation state than the other halogens (e.g. IF_7). The general reactivity of the individual halogens with other elements (both metals and non-metals) is treated under the particular element concerned. Reaction between the halogens themselves is discussed on p. 824. In general, reaction of X_2 with compounds containing M–M, M–H or M–C bonds results in the formation of M–X bonds (M = metal or non-metal). Reaction with metal oxides sometimes requires the presence of C and the use of elevated temperatures.

The stereochemistry of the halogens in their various compounds is summarized in Table 17.8 and will be elucidated in more detail in subsequent sections.

Reactivity is enhanced in conditions which promote the generation of halogen atoms, though this does not imply that all reactions proceed via the intermediacy of X atoms. The reversible thermal dissociation of gaseous $I_2 \rightleftharpoons 2I$ was first demonstrated by Victor Meyer in 1880 and has since been observed for the other halogens as well (p. 804). Atomic Cl and Br are more conveniently produced by electric discharge though, curiously, this particularly method is not successful for I. Microwave and radiofrequency discharges have also been used as well as optical dissociation by ultraviolet light. At room temperature and at pressures below 1 mmHg, up to 40% atomization can be achieved, the mean lives of the Cl and Br atoms in glass apparatus being of the order of a few milliseconds. The

Table 17.8   Stereochemistry of the halogens

CN	Geometry	F	Cl	Br	I
0	—	$F^\bullet$(g), F^- (soln)	$Cl^\bullet$(g), Cl^- (soln)	$Br^\bullet$(g), Br^- (soln)	$I^\bullet$(g), I^- (soln)
1	—	F_2, ClF, BrF_3, BF_3, RF	Cl_2, ICl, BCl_3, RCl	Br_2, IBr, BBr_3, RBr	I_2, IX, PI_3, RI
2	Linear	Nb_4F_{20}, NbF_3(ReO$_3$-type)	ClF_2^-, YCl_3(ReO$_3$-type)	Br_3^-, $(MeCN)_2Br_2$, $CrBr_3$(ReO$_3$-type)	I_3^-, ICl_2^-, $BrICl^-$, Me_3NI_2 BiI_3(ReO$_3$-type)
	Bent	$(BeF_2)_\alpha$, $(HF)_n$, Sn_4F_8	ClO_2, ClO_2^-, Al_2Cl_6, $[Nb_6Cl_{12}]^{2+}$, ClF_2^+ $BeCl_2$ (polym), $PdCl_2$	BrF_2^+, Al_2Br_6	IR_2^+, Al_2I_6, AuI(polymeric)
3	Trigonal pyramidal		ClO_3^-, $CdCl_2$, $[Mo_6Cl_8]^{4+}$	BrO_3^-, $MgBr_2$	HIO_3, IO_3^-, CdI_2
	T-shaped		ClF_3	BrF_3	$RICl_2$
	Planar	MgF_2 (rutile)			
4	Tetrahedral	CaF_2 (fluorite) CuF (blende)	$SrCl_2$ (fluorite), ClO_4^-, $FClO_3$, $CuCl$	BrO_4^-, $FBrO_3$ $CuBr$	IO_4^- CuI
	Square planar			BrF_4^-	ICl_4^-, I_2Cl_6
	See-saw (C_{2v}, or C_s)		F_3ClO, $[F_2ClO_2]^-$	F_3BrO, $[F_2BrO_2]^-$	$[F_2IO_2]^-$, IF_4^+
5	Square pyramidal		ClF_5, $[F_4ClO]^-$	BrF_5, $[F_4BrO]^-$	IF_5, $[(F_5TeO)_4IO]^-$
	Trigonal bipyramidal		F_3ClO_2		IO_5^{3-} (?)
6	Octahedral	NaF	$NaCl$	$NaBr$	IO_6^{5-}, F_5IO, NaI, IF_6^+
	Distorted octahedral			BrF_6^-	IF_6^- (?)
7	Pentagonal bipyramidal				IF_7
	Hexagonal pyramidal		$C_6H_6.Cl_2$	$C_6H_6.Br_2$	
8	Cubic		$CsCl$, $TlCl$	$CsBr$, $TlBr$	CsI, TlI,
	Square antiprismatic				$Zr(IO_3)_4$

reason for the slow and relatively inefficient reversion to X_2 is the need for a 3-body collision in order to dissipate the energy of combination: $X^\bullet + X^\bullet + M \longrightarrow X_2 + M^*$. A fuller account of the production, detection and chemical reactions of atomic Cl, Br and I is on pages 1141–8 and 1165–72 of reference 23.

Solutions and charge-transfer complexes [34]

The halogens are soluble to varying extents in numerous solvents though their great reactivity

sometimes results in solvolysis or in halogenation of the solvent. Reactions with water are discussed on pp. 855ff. Iodine is only slightly soluble in water (0.340 g/kg at 25°, 4.48 g/kg at 100°). It is more soluble in aqueous iodide solutions due to the formation of polyiodides (p. 835) and these can achieve astonishing concentrations; e.g. the solution in equilibrium with solid iodine and $KI_7.H_2O$ at 25° contains 67.8 wt% of iodine, 25.6% KI and 6.6% H_2O. Iodine is also readily soluble in many organic solvents, typical values of its solubility at 25°C being (gI/kg solvent): Et_2O 337.3, EtOH 271.7, mesitylene 253.1, *p*-xylene 198.3, CS_2 197.0, toluene 182.5, benzene 164.0, ethyl acetate 157, EtBr 146, EtCN 141,

---

[34] Ref. 23, pp. 1196–220.

$C_2H_4Br_2$ 115.1, Bu^iOH 97, $CHBr_3$ 65.9, $CHCl_3$ 49.7, cyclohexane 27.9, CCl_4 19.2, n-hexane 13.2, perfluoroheptane 0.12.

The most notable feature of such solutions is the dramatic dependence of their colour on the nature of the solvent chosen. Thus, solutions in aliphatic hydrocarbons or CCl_4 are bright violet (λ_{max} 520–540 nm), those in aromatic hydrocarbons are pink or reddish brown, and those in stronger donors such as alcohols, ethers or amines are deep brown (λ_{max} 460–480 nm). This variation can be understood in terms of a weak donor–acceptor interaction leading to complex formation between the solvent (donor) and I_2 (acceptor) which alters the optical transition energy. Thus, referring to the conventional molecular orbital energy diagram for I_2 (or other X_2) as shown in Fig. 17.2, the violet colour of I_2 vapour can be seen to arise as a result of the excitation of an electron from the highest occupied MO (the antibonding π_g level) into the lowest unoccupied MO (the antibonding σ_u level). In non-coordinating solvents such as aliphatic hydrocarbons or their fluoro- or chloro-derivatives the transition energy (and hence the colour) remains essentially unmodified.

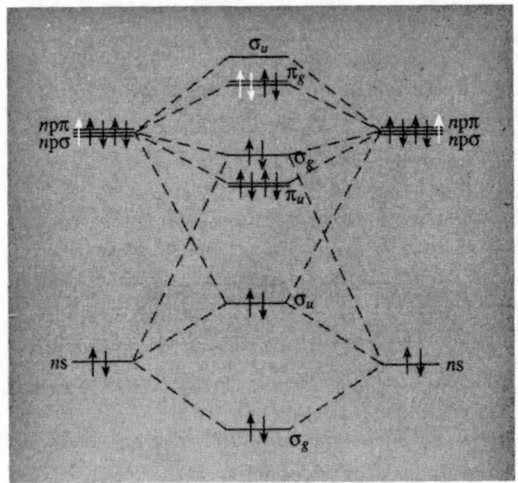

Figure 17.2   Schematic molecular orbital energy diagram for diatomic halogen molecules. (For F_2 the order of the upper σ_g and π_u bonding MOs is inverted.).

However, in electron-donor solvents, L, the vacant antibonding σ_u orbital of I_2 acts as an electron acceptor thus weakening the I–I bond and altering the energy of the electronic transitions:

$$\sigma_g^2\pi_u^4\pi_g^3\sigma_u^1(^3\Pi_u \text{ and } ^1\Pi_u) \leftarrow \sigma_g^2\pi_u^4\pi_g^4(^1\Sigma_g^+)$$

Consistent with this: (a) the solubility of iodine in the donor solvents tends to be greater than in the non-donor solvents (see list of solubilities), (b) brown solutions frequently turn violet on being heated, and brown again on cooling, due to the ready dissociation and reformation of the complex, and (c) addition of a small amount of a donor solvent to a violet solution turns the colour brown. Such donor solvents can be classified as (i) weak π donors (e.g. the aromatic hydrocarbons and alkenes), (ii) stronger σ donors such as nitrogen bases (amines, pyridines, nitriles), oxygen bases (alcohols, ethers, carbonyls), and organic sulfides and selenides.

The most direct evidence for the formation of a complex L→I_2 in solution comes from the appearance if an intense new charge-transfer band in the near ultraviolet spectrum. Such a band occurs in the region 230–330 nm with a molar extinction coefficient ε of the order of $5 \times 10^3 - 5 \times 10^4 \, l\,mol^{-1}\,cm^{-1}$ and a half-width typically of 4000–8000 cm^{-1}. Detailed physico-chemical studies further establish that the formation constants of such complexes span the range $10^{-1} - 10^4 \, l\,mol^{-1}$ with enthalpies of formation 5–50 kJ mol^{-1}. Some typical examples are in Table 17.9. The donor strength of the various solvents (ligands) is rather independent of the particular halogen (or interhalogen) solute and follows the approximate sequence benzene < alkenes < polyalkylbenzenes ≈ alkyl iodides ≈ alcohols ≈ ethers ≈ ketones < organic sulfides < organic selenides < amines. Conversely, for a given solvent the relative acceptor strength of the halogens increases in the sequence Cl_2 < Br_2 < I_2 < IBr < ICl, i.e. they are class b or "soft" acceptors (p. 909). Further interactions may also occur in polar solvents leading to ionic dissociation which

Table 17.9   Some iodine complexes in solution

Donor solvent	Formation constant $K(20°C)/1\ mol^{-1}$	$-\Delta H_f/$ kJ mol^{-1}	Charge-transfer band		
			λ_{max}/nm	ε_{max}	$\Delta \nu_{\frac{1}{2}}/cm^{-1}$
Benzene	0.15	5.9	292	16 000	5100
Ethanol	0.26	18.8	230	12 700	6800
Diethyl ether	0.97	18.0	249	5 700	6900
Diethyl sulfide	210	32.7	302	29 800	5400
Methylamine	530	29.7	245	21 200	6400
Dimethylamine	6 800	41.0	256	26 800	6450
Trimethylamine	12 100	50.6	266	31 300	8100
Pyridine	269	32.6	235	50 000	5200

renders the solutions electrically conducting, e.g.:

$$2pyI_2 \rightleftharpoons [py_2I]^+ + I_3^-$$

Numerous solid complexes have been crystallized from brown solutions of iodine and extensive X-ray structural data are available. Complexes of the type L→I–X and L→I–X←L

(L = Me$_3$N, py, etc.; X = I, Br, Cl, CN) feature a linear configuration as expected from the involvement of the σ_u antibonding orbital of IX (Fig. 17.3a, b, c). When the ligand has two donor atoms (as in dioxan) or the donor atom has more than one lone-pair of electrons (as in acetone) the complexes can associate

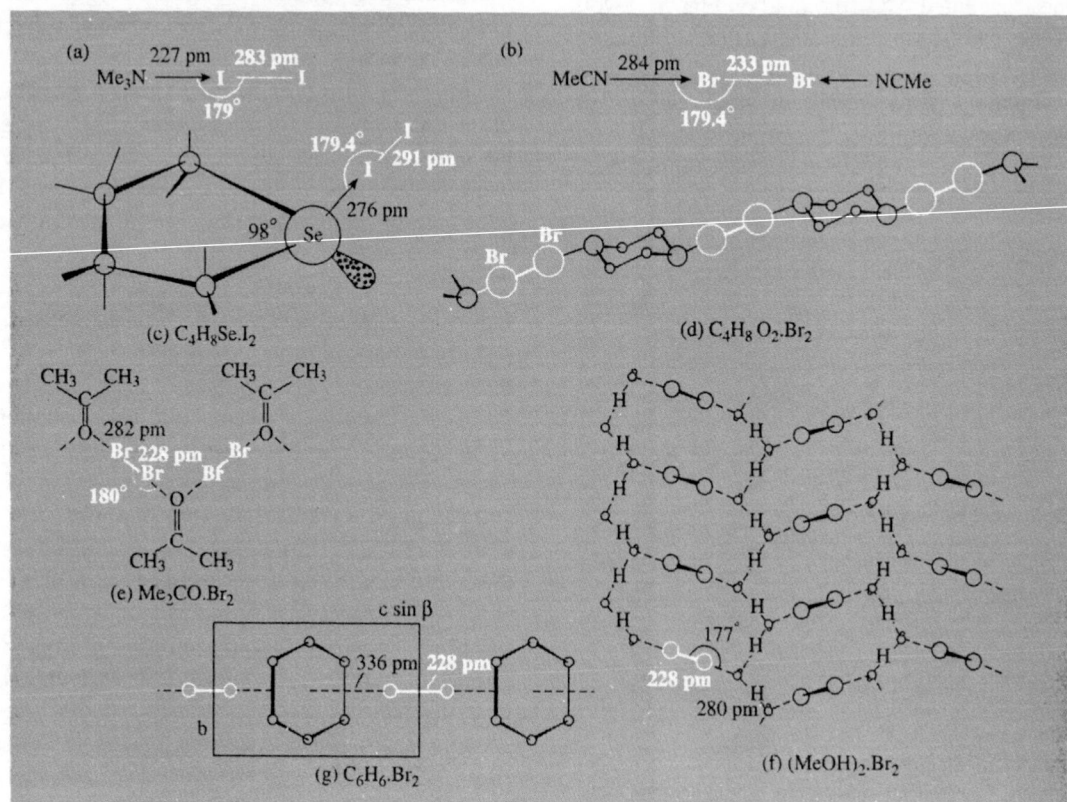

Figure 17.3   Structures of some molecular complexes of the halogens.

into infinite chains (Fig. 17.3d, e), whereas with methanol, the additional possibility of hydrogen bonding permits further association into layers (Fig. 17.3f). The structure of $C_6H_6.Br_2$ is also included in Fig. 17.3(g). In all these examples, the lengthening of the X–X bond from that in the free halogen molecule is notable.

The intense blue colour of starch-iodine was mentioned on p. 790.

17.2 Compounds of Fluorine, Chlorine, Bromine and Iodine

17.2.1 Hydrogen halides, HX

It is common practice to refer to the molecular species HX and also the pure (anhydrous) compounds as hydrogen halides, and to call their aqueous solutions hydrohalic acids. Both the anhydrous compounds and their aqueous solutions will be considered in this section. HCl and hydrochloric acid are major industrial chemicals and there is also a substantial production of HF and hydrofluoric acid. HBr and hydrobromic acid are made on a much smaller scale and there seems to be little industrial demand for HI and hydriodic acid. It will be convenient to discuss first the preparation and industrial uses of the compounds and then to consider their molecular and bulk physical properties. The chemical reactivity of the anhydrous compounds and their acidic aqueous solutions will then be reviewed, and the section concludes with a discussion of the anhydrous compounds as nonaqueous solvents.

Preparation and uses

Anhydrous HF is almost invariably made by the action of conc H_2SO_4 ($\geq 95\%$) on "acid grade" fluorspar ($\geq 98\%$ CaF_2):

$$CaF_2(s) + H_2SO_4(l) \longrightarrow CaSO_4(s) + 2HF(g)$$

As the reaction is endothermic heat must be supplied to obtain good yields in reasonable

time (e.g. 30–60 min at 200–250°C). Silica is a particularly undesirable impurity in the fluorspar since it consumes up to 6 moles of HF per mole of SiO_2 by reacting to form SiF_4 and then H_2SiF_6. A typical unit, producing up to 20 000 tonnes of HF pa, consists of an externally heated, horizontal steel kiln about 30 m long rotating at 1 revolution per minute. The product gas emerges at 100–150°C and, after appropriate treatment to remove solid, liquid and gaseous impurities, is condensed to give a 99% pure product which is then redistilled to give a final product of 99.9% purity. The technical requirements to enable the safe manufacture and handling of so corrosive a product are considerable.[2,13] In principle, HF could also be obtained from the wet-processing of fluorapatite to give phosphoric acid (p. 521) but the presence of SiO_2 preferentially yields SiF_4 and H_2SiF_6 from which HF can only be recovered uneconomically.

$$Ca_5(PO_4)_3F + 5H_2SO_4 \longrightarrow 5CaSO_4 + 3H_3PO_4$$
$$+ HF$$

$$SiO_2 + 4HF \longrightarrow SiF_4 + 2H_2O \xrightarrow{\text{aq HF}} \text{aq } H_2SiF_6$$

Some of the H_2SiF_6 so produced finds commercial outlets (p. 810), but it has been estimated that ~500 000 tonnes of H_2SiF_6 is discarded annually by the US phosphoric acid industry, equivalent to ~1 million tonnes of fluorspar — enough to supply that nation's entire requirements for HF. Production figures and major uses are in the Panel.

Hydrogen chloride is a major industrial chemical and is manufactured on a huge scale. It is also a familiar laboratory reagent both as a gas and as an aqueous acid. The industrial production and uses of HCl are summarized in the Panel on p. 811. One important method for synthesis on a large scale is the burning of H_2 in Cl_2: no catalyst is needed but economic sources of the two elements are obviously required. Another major source of HCl is as a by-product of the chlorination of hydrocarbons (p. 798). The traditional "salt-cake" process of treating NaCl with conc H_2SO_4 also remains an important industrial source of the acid. On a small laboratory scale, gaseous HCl can be made by treating concentrated aqueous hydrochloric acid

Production and Uses of Hydrogen Fluoride

Anhydrous HF was first produced commercially in the USA in 1931 and in the UK from about 1942. By 1992 some eighteen countries were each producing at least 3000 tonnes pa with North America accounting for some 330 000 tonnes of the estimated annual world production of about 875 000 tonnes. A further 205 000 tonnes was used captively for production of AlF$_3$. Price in 1990 was about $1.50/kg for the anhydrous acid and somewhat less for 70% acid. The primary suppliers ship HF in tank-cars of 20–91-tonne capacity and the product is also repackaged in steel cylinders holding 8.0–900 kg (2.7–635 kg in the UK). Lecture bottles contain 340 g HF. The 70% acid is shipped in tank-cars of 32–80-tonne capacity, tank trucks of 20-tonne capacity, and in polyethylene-lined drums holding 114 or 208 l.

The early need for HF was in the production of chlorofluorocarbons for refrigeration units and pressurizing gases. The large increase in aluminium production in 1935–40 brought an equivalent requirement for HF (for synthetic cryolite, p. 219) and these two uses still account for the bulk of HF produced in North America (comprising the single market of USA, Canada and Mexico), namely 53.0% and 24.3%, respectively. Other outlets are petroleum alkylation catalysts and steel pickling (3.8% each) and the nuclear industry (3.0%). The remaining 12.1% is distributed amongst traditional uses (such as glass etching and the frosting of light bulbs and television tubes, and the manufacture of fluoride salts), and newer applications such as rocket-propellant stabilizers, preparation of microelectronic circuits, laundry sours and stain removers.

Probably about 50 000 tonnes of HF are used worldwide annually to make inorganic compounds other than UF$_4$/UF$_6$ for the nuclear industry. Prominent amongst these products are:

NaF: for water fluoridation, wood preservatives, the formulation of insecticides and fungicides, and use as a fluxing agent. It is also used to remove HF from gaseous F$_2$ in the manufacture and purification of F$_2$.

SnF$_2$: in toothpastes to prevent dental caries.

HBF$_4$ (aq) and metal fluoroborates: electroplating of metals, catalysts, fluxing in metal processing and surface treatment.

H$_2$SiF$_6$ and its salts: fluoridation of water, glass and ceramics manufacture, metal-ore treatment.

The highly corrosive nature of HF and aqueous hydrofluoric acid solutions have already been alluded to (pp. 792, 797) and great caution must be exercised in their handling. The salient feature of HF burns is the delayed onset of discomfit and the development of a characteristic white lesion that is excruciatingly painful. The progressive action of HF on skin is due to dehydration, low pH and the specific toxic effect of high concentrations of fluoride ions: these remove Ca^{2+} from tissues as insoluble CaF$_2$ and thereby delay healing; in addition the immobilization of Ca^{2+} results in a relative excess of K$^+$ within the tissue, so that nerve stimulation ensues. Treatment of HF burns involves copious sluicing with water for at least 15 min followed either by (a) immersion in (or application of wet packs of) cold MgSO$_4$, or (b) subcutaneous injection of a 10% solution of calcium gluconate (which gives rapid relief from pain), or (c) surgical excision of the burn lesion.[4] Medical attention is essential, even if the initial effects appear slight, because of the slow onset of the more serious symptoms.

with conc H$_2$SO$_4$. Preparation of DCl is best effected by the action of D$_2$O on PhCOCl or a similar organic acid chloride; PCl$_3$, PCl$_5$, SiCl$_4$, AlCl$_3$, etc., have also been used.

Similar routes are available for the production of HBr and HI. The catalysed combination of H$_2$ and Br$_2$ at elevated temperatures (200–400°C in the presence of Pt/asbestos, etc.) is the principal industrial route for HBr, and is also used, though on a relatively small scale, for the energetically less-favoured combination of H$_2$ and I$_2$ (Pt catalyst above 300°C). Commercially HI is more often prepared by the reaction of I$_2$ with H$_2$S or hydrazine, e.g.:

$$2I_2 + N_2H_4 \xrightarrow{H_2O} 4HI + N_2 \text{ (quantitative)}$$

Reduction of the parent halogen with red phosphorus and water provides a convenient laboratory preparation of both HBr and HI:

$$2P + 6H_2O + 3X_2 \longrightarrow 6HX + 2H_3PO_3$$

$$H_3PO_3 + H_2O + Br_2 \longrightarrow 2HBr + H_3PO_4$$

The rapid reaction of 1,2,3,4-tetrahydronaphthalene (tetralin) with Br$_2$ at 20° affords an alternative small-scale preparation though only half the Br$_2$ is converted, the other half being lost in brominating the tetralin:

$$C_{10}H_{12} + 4Br_2 \longrightarrow 4HBr + C_{10}H_8Br_4.$$

The action of conc H$_2$SO$_4$ on metal bromides or iodides (analogous to the "salt-cake" process of HCl) causes considerable oxidation of the product HX but conc H$_3$PO$_4$ is satisfactory. Dehydration of the aqueous acids with P$_2$O$_5$ is a viable alternative. DBr and DI are obtained by reaction of D$_2$O on PBr$_3$ and PI$_3$ respectively.

Industrial Production and Uses of Hydrogen Chloride[35]

World production of HCl is of the order of 10 million tonnes pa, thus making it one of the largest volume chemicals to be manufactured. Four major processes account for the bulk of HCl produced, the choice of method invariably being dictated by the ready availability of the particular starting materials, the need for the co-products, or simply the availability of by-product HCl which can be recovered as part of an integrated process.

1. The classic salt-cake method was introduced with the Leblanc process towards the end of the eighteenth century and is still used to produce HCl where rock-salt mineral is cheaply available (as in the UK Cheshire deposits). The process is endothermic and takes place in two stages:

$$NaCl + H_2SO_4 \xrightarrow{\sim150°} NaHSO_4 + HCl; \text{ and } NaCl + NaHSO_4 \xrightarrow{540-600°} Na_2SO_4 + HCl$$

2. The Hargreaves process (late 19th C) is a variant of the salt-cake process in which NaCl is reacted with a gaseous mixture of SO_2, air and H_2O (i.e. "H_2SO_4") in a self-sustaining exothermic reaction:

$$2NaCl + SO_2 + \tfrac{1}{2}O_2 + H_2O \xrightarrow{430-450°} Na_2SO_4 + 2HCl$$

Again the economic operation of the process depends on abundant rock-salt or the need for the by-product Na_2SO_4 for the paper and glass industries.

3. Direct synthesis of HCl by the burning of hydrogen in chlorine is the favoured process when high-purity HCl is required. The reaction is highly exothermic (~92 kJ/mol HCl) and requires specially designed burners and absorption systems.

4. By-product HCl from the heavy organic-chemicals industry (p. 798) now accounts for over 90% of the HCl produced in the USA. Where such petrochemical industries are less extensive this source of HCl becomes correspondingly smaller. The crude HCl so produced may be contaminated with unreacted Cl_2, organics, chloro-organics or entrained solids (catalyst supports, etc.), all of which must be removed.

Most of the byproduct HCl is used captively, primarily in oxyhydrochlorination processes for making vinyl chloride and chlorinated solvents or for Mg processing (p. 110). The scale of the industry is enormous; for example, 5.2 million tonnes of HCl per annum in the US alone (1993). HCl gas for industrial use can be transmitted without difficult over moderate distances in mild-steel piping or in tank cars or trailers. It is also available in cylinders of varying size down to laboratory scale lecture bottles containing 225 g. Aqueous hydrochloric acid consumption (1993) was 1.57 Mt (100% basis). Price for anhydrous HCl is $\sim\$330$/tonne and for 31.4% aqueous acid $\sim\$73$/tonne (1993) depending on plant location and amount required.

Industrial use of HCl gas for the manufacture of inorganic chemicals includes the preparation of anhydrous NH_4Cl by direct reaction with NH_3 and the synthesis of anhydrous metal chlorides by reaction with appropriate carbides, nitrides, oxides or even the free metals themselves, e.g.:

$$SiC \xrightarrow[\text{(NiCl}_2\text{ catal)}]{\text{HCl/700°}} SiCl_4$$

$$MN_y \xrightarrow{\text{HCl/heat}} MCl_x(\text{pure}) \quad (Ti, Zr, Hf; Nb, Ta; Cr, Mo, W, \text{etc.})$$

$$MO + 2HCl \longrightarrow MCl_2 + H_2O \quad \begin{array}{l}\text{(especially for removal of impurities or}\\\text{waste recovery)}\end{array}$$

$$Al + 3HCl \longrightarrow AlCl_3 + \tfrac{3}{2}H_2$$

HCl is also used in the industrial synthesis of ClO_2 (p. 846):

$$NaClO_3 + 2HCl \longrightarrow ClO_2 + \tfrac{1}{2}Cl_2 + NaCl + H_2O$$

The reaction is catalysed by various salts of Ti, Mn, Pd and Ag which promote the formation of ClO_2 rather than the competing reaction which otherwise occurs:

$$NaClO_3 + 6HCl \longrightarrow 3Cl_2 + NaCl + 3H_2O$$

Panel continues

---

[35] *Kirk–Othmer's Encyclopedia of Chemical Technology*, 4th Edn., Vol. 13, pp. 894–925 (1995).

HCl is also used in the production of Al_2O_3 (p. 242) and TiO_2 (p. 959), the isolation of Mg from sea water (p. 110), and in many extractive metallurgical processes for isolating or refining metals, e.g. Ge, Sn, V, Mn, Ta, W and Ra.

Aqueous HCl is also produced on a vast scale (e.g. 1.57 Mt/yr in the USA, 1993). Most of this is made and consumed captively at the site of production, predominantly for brine acidification prior to electrolysis in Cl_2/alkali cells. The largest merchant market use is for pickling steel and other metals to remove adhering oxide scale, and for the desulfurization of petroleum. It is also used in pH control (effluent neutralization, etc.), the desliming of hides and chrome tanning, ore beneficiation, the coagulation of latex and the production of aniline from $PhNO_2$ for dyestuffs intermediates. The manufacture of gelatine requires large quantities of hydrochloric acid to decompose the bones used as raw materials — high purity acid must be used since much of the gelatine is used in foodstuffs for human consumption. Another food-related application is the hydrolysis of starch to glucose under pressure: this process is catalysed by small concentrations of HCl and is extensively used to produce "maple syrup" from maize (corn) starch. At higher concentrations of HCl wood (lignin) can be converted to glucose.

Other uses of HCl are legion and range from the purification of fine silica for the ceramics industry, and the refining of oils, fats and waxes, to the manufacture of chloroprene rubbers, PVC plastics, industrial solvents and organic intermediates, the production of viscose rayon yarn and staple fibre, and the wet processing of textiles (where hydrochloric acid is used as a sour to neutralize residual alkali and remove metallic and other impurities).

Anhydrous HBr is available in cylinders (6.8-kg and 68-kg capacity) under its own vapour pressure (24 atm at 25°C) and in lecture bottles (450-g capacity). Its main industrial use is in the manufacture of inorganic bromides and the synthesis of alkyl bromides either from alcohols or by direct addition to alkenes. HBr also catalyses numerous organic reactions. Aqueous HBr (48% and 62%) is available as a corrosive pale-yellow liquid in drums or in large tank trailers (15 000 l and 38 000 l).

There seem to be no large-scale uses for HI outside the laboratory, where it is used in various iodination reactions (lecture bottles containing 400 g HI are available). Commercial solutions contain 40–55 wt% of HI (cf. azeotrope at 56.9% HI, p. 815) and these solutions are thermodynamically much more stable than pure HI as indicated by the large negative free energy of solution.

Physical properties of the hydrogen halides

HF is a colourless volatile liquid and an oligomeric H-bonded gas $(HF)_x$, whereas the heavier HX are colourless diatomic gases at room temperature. Some molecular and bulk physical properties are summarized in Table 17.10. The influence of H bonding on the (low) vapour pressure, (long) liquid range and (high) dielectric constant of HF have already been discussed

(pp. 53–5). Note also that the viscosity of liquid HF is lower than that of water (or indeed of the other HX) and this has been taken to imply the absence of a three-dimensional network of H bonds such as occurs in H_2O, H_2SO_4, H_3PO_4, etc. However, it should be remembered that the viscosity of HF is quoted for 0°C, i.e. some 80° above its mp and only 20° below its bp; a more relevant comparison might be its value of 0.772 centipoise at −62.5° (i.e. 19° above its mp) compared with a value of 1.00 centipoise for water at 20°. Hydrogen bonding is also responsible for the association of HF molecules in the vapour phase: the vapour density of the gas over liquid HF reaches a maximum value of ∼86 at −34°. At atmospheric pressure the value drops from 58 at 25° to 20.6 at 80° (the limiting vapour density of monomeric HF is $\frac{20.0063}{2.0159} = 9.924$). These results, together with infrared and electron diffraction studies, indicate that gaseous HF comprises an equilibrium mixture of monomers and cyclic hexamers, though chain dimers may also occur under some conditions of temperature and pressure:

$$6HF \rightleftharpoons (HF)_6; \quad 2HF \rightleftharpoons (HF)_2$$

The crystal structure of HF shows it to consist of planar zigzag chain polymers with an $F–H \cdots F$ distance of 249 pm and an angle at F of 120.1°.

The other HX are not associated in the gaseous or liquid phases but the low-temperature forms of crystalline HCl and HBr both feature weakly

Table 17.10   Physical properties of the hydrogen halides

Property	HF	HCl	HBr	HI
MP/°C	−83.5	−114.2	−88.6	−51.0
BP/°C	19.5[a]	−85.1	−67.1	−35.1
Liquid range (1 atm)/°C	103.0	29.1	21.5	15.9
Density(T°C)/g cm^{-3}	1.002(0°)[b]	1.187(−114°)	2.603(−84°)	2.85(−47°)
Viscosity(T°C)/centipoise	0.256(0°)	0.51(−95°)	0.83(−67°)	1.35(−35.4°)
Dielectric constant, ε	83.6(0°)[c]	9.28(−95°)	7.0(−85°)	3.39(−50°)
Electrical conductivity (T°C)/ohm^{-1} cm^{-1}	~10^{-6}(0°)	~10^{-9}(−85°)	~10^{-9}(−85°)	~10^{-10}(−50°)
ΔH_f°(298°)/kJ mol^{-1}	−271.12	−92.31	−36.40	26.48
ΔG_f°(298°)/kJ mol^{-1}	−273.22	−95.30	−53.45	1.72
S°(298°)/J mol^{-1}K^{-1}	173.67	186.80	198.59	206.48
$\Delta H_{\mathrm{dissoc}}$(H−X)/kJ mol^{-1}	573.98	431.62	362.50	294.58
r_e(H−X)/pm	91.7	127.4	141.4	160.9
Vibrational frequency ω_e/cm^{-1}	4138.33	2990.94(H^{35}Cl) 2988.48(H^{37}Cl)	2649.65	2309.53
Dipole moment μ/D	1.86	1.11	0.788	0.382

[a] Vapour pressure of HF 363.8 mmHg (48.50 kPa) at 0°.
[b] Density of liquid HF 1.23 g cm^{-3} near melting point. [c] Dielectric constant ε(HF) 175 at −73°C.

H-bonded zigzag chains similar to those in solid HF. At higher temperatures substantial disorder sets in.

The standard heats of formation ΔH_f° of gaseous HX diminish rapidly with increase in molecular weight and HI is endothermic. The very small (and positive) value for the standard free energy of formation ΔG_f° of HI indicates that (under equilibrium conditions) this species is substantially dissociated at room temperature and pressure. However, dissociation is slow in the absence of a catalyst. The bond dissociation energies of HX show a similar trend from the very large value of 574 kJ mol^{-1} for HF to little more than half this (295 kJ mol^{-1}) for HI.

Chemical reactivity of the hydrogen halides

Anhydrous HX are versatile and vigorous reagents for the halogenation of metals, non-metals, hydrides, oxides and many other classes of compound, though reactions that are thermodynamically permissible do not always occur in the absence of catalysts, thermal initiation or photolytic encouragement, because of kinetic factors. For example,[36] reaction of HX(g) with elements (M) can thermodynamically proceed according to the equation

$$M + nHX = MX_n + \tfrac{1}{2}nH_2$$

providing that ΔG for the reaction [i.e. $\Delta G_f^\circ(MX_n) - n\Delta G_f^\circ$ (HX, g)] is negative. From the data in Table 17.10 this means that M could be oxidized to the n-valent halide MX_n if:

for the fluoride $\Delta G_f^\circ(MF_n)$ is $< -274n$ kJ mol^{-1}
for the chloride $\Delta G_f^\circ(MCl_n)$ is $< -96n$ kJ mol^{-1}
for the bromide $\Delta G_f^\circ(MBr_n)$ is $< -54n$ kJ mol^{-1}
for the iodide $\Delta G_f^\circ(MI_n)$ is $<\sim 0$ kJ mol^{-1}

Using tables of free energies of formation it is clear that most metals will react with most HX. Moreover, in many cases, e.g. with the alkali metals, alkaline earth metals, Zn, Al and the lanthanide elements, such reactions are extremely exothermic. It is also clear that Ag should react with HCl, HBr and HI but not with HF, and

---

[36] T. C. Waddington, in V. Gutmann (ed.), *Main Group Elements: Group VII and Noble Gases*, MTP International Review of Science: Inorganic Chemistry Series 1, Vol. 3, pp. 85–125, Butterworths, London, 1972.

Cu should form CuF_2 with HF but not CuX_2 with the other HX. Iron should give $FeCl_3$ but in practice the reaction only proceeds to $FeCl_2$. TiX_4 can be made, but only at high temperatures. Reactions of Si to form SiX_4 are very favourable for X = F, Cl, Br, but only HF reacts at room temperature. With As, reaction with HF to give AsF_3 is thermodynamically favourable but reactions with the other HX are not. Similar, though more complicated, schemes can be worked out for the reactions of HX with oxides, other halides, hydrides, etc.

HF is miscible with water in all proportions and the phase diagram (Fig. 17.4a) shows the presence of three compounds: $H_2O.HF$ (mp $-35.5°$), $H_2O.2HF$ (mp $-75.5°$) and $H_2O.4HF$ (mp $-100.4°$, i.e. $17°$ below the mp of pure HF). Recent X-ray studies have confirmed earlier conjectures that these compounds are best formulated as H-bonded oxonium salts $[H_3O]F$, $[H_3O][HF_2]$, and $[H_3O][H_3F_4]$ with three very strong H bonds per oxonium ion and average $O \cdots F$ distances of 246.7, 250.2

and 253.6 pm respectively.[37] More recently, the low-temperature crystal structure of $Me_4NF.5HF$ (decomp. $-76°C$) has revealed the presence of $H_5F_6^-$, i.e $[(FH)_2FHF(HF)_2]^-$, with four terminal $F-H \cdots F$ of 248.4 pm and a very strong central $F-H \cdots F$ of 226.6 pm. $Me_4NF.7HF$ was also identified (decomp. $-110°C$).[38] Another significant crystal structure, that of tris(ethylenediamine)zinc(II) fluoride dihydrate reveals the strongly H-bonded difluoride cluster $[F_2(H_2O)_2]^{2-}$ which adopts a diamond-shaped cyclic structure $\overline{F \cdots HOH \cdots F \cdots HOH \cdots}^{2-}$ with $O-H \cdots F$ distances of 258.6 and 267.9 pm and non-bonded distances across the lozenge of $O \cdots O$ 335 pm and $F \cdots F$ 406 pm.[39] Such H bonds are very relevant to the otherwise surprising observation that, unlike

---

[37] D. MOOTZ, *Angew. Chem. Int. Edn. Engl.* **20**, 791 (1981). See also J. EMSLEY and D. A. JOHNSON, *Polyhedron* **5**, 1109–10 (1986).

[38] D. MOOTZ and D. BOENIGK, *Z. anorg. allg. Chem.* **544**, 159–66 (1987).

[39] J. EMSLEY, M. ARIF, P. A. BATES and M. B. HURSTHOUSE, *J. Chem. Soc., Chem. Commun.*, 738–9 (1989).

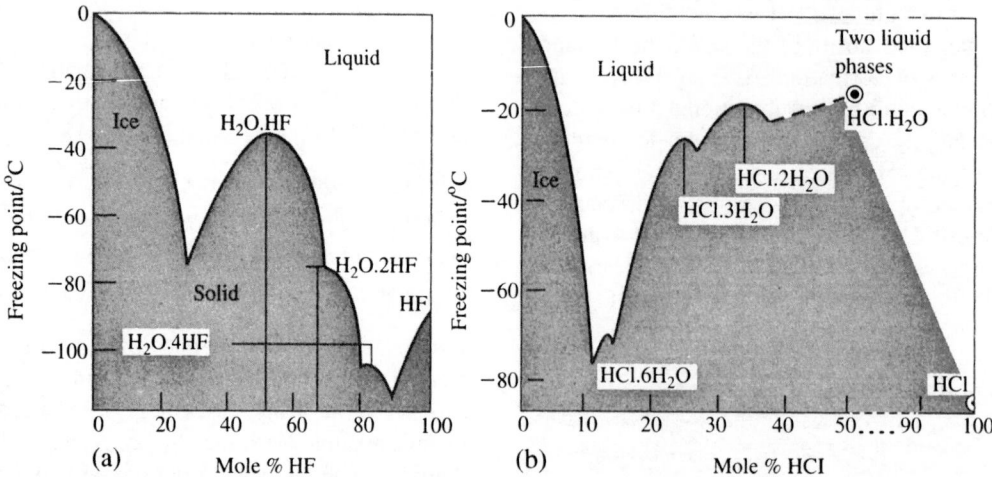

Figure 17.4 The phase diagrams of the systems (a) HF/H_2O and (b) HCl/H_2O. Note that for hydrofluoric acid all the solvates contain $\geq 1HF$ per H_2O, whereas for hydrochloric acid they contain $\leq 1HCl$ per H_2O. This is because the H bonds $F-H \cdots F$ and $F-H \cdots O$ are *stronger* than $O-H \cdots O$, whereas $Cl-H \cdots Cl$ and $Cl-H \cdots O$ are *weaker* than $O-H \cdots O$. Accordingly the solvates in the former system have the crystal structures $[H_3O]^+F^-$, $[H_3O]^+[HF_2]^-$ and $[H_3O]^+[H_3F_4]^-$, whereas the latter are $[H_3O]^+Cl^-$, $[H_5O_2]^+Cl^-$ and $[H_5O_2]^+Cl^-$. H_2O. The structures of $HCl.6H_2O$ and the metastable $HCl.4H_2O$ are not known.

the other aqueous hydrohalic acids which are extremely strong, hydrofluoric acid is a very weak acid in aqueous solution. Indeed, the behaviour of such solutions is remarkable in showing a dissociation constant (as calculated from electrical conductivity measurements) that *diminishes* continuously on dilution. Detailed studies reveal the presence of two predominant equilibria:[40]

$$H_2O + HF \longrightarrow [(H_3O)^+F^-] \rightleftharpoons$$
$$[H_3O]^+(aq) + F^-(aq); \quad pK_a \ 2.95$$

$$F^-(aq) + HF \rightleftharpoons HF_2^-(aq); \quad K_2 = \frac{[HF_2^-]}{[HF][F^-]}$$

The dissociation constant for the first process is only $1.1 \times 10^{-3}\,l\,mol^{-1}$ at 25°C; this corresponds to pK_a 2.95 and indicates a rather small free hydrogen-ion concentration (cf. $ClCH_2CO_2H$, pK_a 2.85) as a result of the strongly H-bonded, undissociated ion-pair $[(H_3O)^+F^-]$. By contrast, $K_2 = 2.6 \times 10^{-1}\,l\,mol^{-1}$ (pK_2 0.58), indicating that an appreciable number of the fluoride ions in the solution are coordinated by HF to give HF_2^- rather than by H_2O despite the very much higher concentration of H_2O molecules.

Numerous hydrates also occur in the HCl/H_2O system (Fig. 17.4b), e.g. $HCl.H_2O$ (mp $-15.4°$), $HCl.2H_2O$ (mp $-17.7°$), $HCl.3H_2O$ (mp $-24.9°$), $HCl.4H_2O$ and $HCl.6H_2O$ (mp $-70°$). The system differs from HF/H_2O not only in the stoichiometry of the hydrates but also in separating into two liquid phases at HCl concentrations higher than 1:1. The weakness of the $O-H\cdots Cl$ hydrogen bond also ensures that there is very little impediment to complete ionic dissociation, and aqueous solutions of HCl (and also of HBr and HI) are strong acids; approximate values of pK_a are HCl -7, HBr -9, HI -10. The systems HBr/H_2O and HI/H_2O also show a miscibility gap at high concentrations of HX and also numerous hydrates which feature hydrated oxonium ions:

[40] L. G. SILLÉN and A. E. MARTELL, *Stability Constants of Metal–Ion Complexes*, Special Publication No. 17, pp. 256–7, The Chemical Society, London, 1964; *Supplement No. 1* (Special Publication No. 17), pp. 152–3 (1971). See also P. McTIGUE, T. A. O'DONNELL and B. VERITT, *Aust. J. Chem.* **38**, 1797–807 (1985).

$HBr.H_2O$: stable under pressure between $-3.3°$ and $-15.5°$; $[H_3O]^+Br^-$

$HBr.2H_2O$: mp $-11.3°$; presumably $[H_5O_2]^+Br^-$, i.e. $[(H_2O)_2H]^+Br^-$

$HBr.3H_2O$: decomp $-47.9°$; structure unknown

$HBr.4H_2O$: mp $-55.8°$; $\{[(H_2O)_3H]^+\text{-}[(H_2O)_4H]^+(Br^-)_2.H_2O\}$ (p. 630)

$HBr.6H_2O$: decomposes at $-88.2°$

The compound $HI.H_2O$ does not appear as a stable hydrate in the phase diagram, but the vibrational spectra of frozen solutions of this composition indicate the formulation $[H_3O]^+I^-$. Higher hydrates appear at $HI.2H_2O$ (mp $\sim -43°$), $HI.3H_2O$ (mp $\sim -48°$), and $HI.4H_2O$ (mp $-36.5°$C).

Just as the solid/liquid phase equilibria in the systems HX/H_2O show several points of interest, so too do the liquid/gas phase equilibria. When dilute aqueous solutions of HX are heated to boiling the concentration of HX in the vapour is less than that in the liquid phase, so that the liquid becomes progressively more concentrated and the bp progressively rises until a point is reached at which the liquid has the same composition as the gas phase so that it boils without change in composition and at constant temperature. This mixture is called an azeotrope (Greek α, without; ζεῖη, *zein*, to boil; τροπή, *trope*, change). The phenomenon is illustrated for HF and HCl in Fig. 17.5. Conversely, when more concentrated aqueous solutions are boiled, the concentration of HX in the vapour is greater than that in the liquid phase which thereby becomes progressively diluted by distillation until the azeotropic mixture is again reached, whereupon distillation continues without change of composition and at constant temperature. The bps and azeotropic compositions at atmospheric pressure are listed below, together with the densities of the azeotropic acids at 25°C:

Azeotrope	HF	HCl	HBr	HI
BP (1 atm)/°C	112	108.58	124.3	126.7
g(HX)/100 g soln	38	20.22	47.63	56.7
Density(25°)/g cm^{-3}	1.138	1.096	1.482	1.708

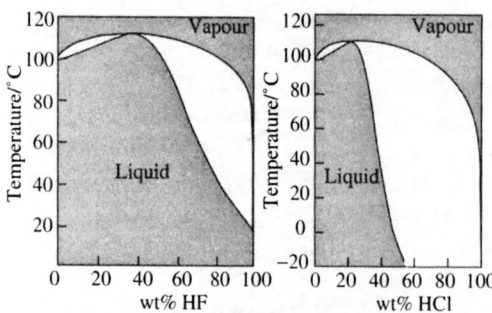

Figure 17.5 Liquid/gas phase equilibria for the systems HF/H₂O and HCl/H₂O showing the formation of maximum boiling azeotropes as described in the text.

Of course, the bp and composition of the azeotrope both vary with pressure, as illustrated below for the case of hydrochloric acid (1 mmHg = 0.1333 kPa):

P/mmHg	50	250	500	700
BP/°C	48.72	81.21	97.58	106.42
g(HX)/100 g soln	23.42	21.88	20.92	20.36
Density(25°)/g cm⁻³	1.112	1.104	1.099	1.097

P/mmHg	**760**	800	1000	1200
BP/°C	**108.58**	110.01	116.19	122.98
g(HX)/100 g soln	**20.222**	20.16	19.73	19.36
Density(25°)/g cm⁻³	**1.0959**	1.095₅	1.093	1.091₅

The occurrence of such azeotropes clearly restricts the degree to which aqueous solutions of HX can be concentrated by evaporation. However, they do afford a ready means of obtaining solutions of precisely known concentration: in the case of hydrochloric acid, its azeotrope is particularly stable over long periods of time and has found much use in analytical chemistry.

The hydrogen halides as nonaqueous solvents

The great synthetic value of liquid NH₃ as a nonaqueous solvent (p. 424) has encouraged the extensive study of the other neighbour of H₂O in the periodic table, namely, HF.[36,41−44] Early studies were hampered by the aggressive nature of anhydrous HF towards glass and quartz,

but the pure acid can now be safely handled without contamination using fluorinated plastics such as polytetrafluoroethylene. The self-ionic dissociation of the solvent, as evidenced by the residual electrical conductivity of highly purified HF, can be represented as $HF \rightleftharpoons H^+ + F^-$; however, since both ions will be solvated it is more usual to represent the equilibrium as

$$3HF \rightleftharpoons H_2F^+ + HF_2^-$$

The fluoride ion has an anomalously high conductance, λ_∞, as shown by the following values obtained at 0°:

Ion λ_∞/ohm⁻¹ cm² mol⁻¹	Na⁺	K⁺	**H₂F⁺**	BF₄⁻	SbF₆⁻	**HF₂⁻**
	117	117	**79**	183	196	**273**

As the specific conductivity of pure HF is ~10^{-6} ohm⁻¹ cm² at 0°, these values imply concentrations of $H_2F^+ = HF_2^- \simeq 2.9 \times 10^{-6}$ mol l⁻¹ and an ionic product for the liquid of ~8×10^{-12} mol² l⁻² (cf. values of ~10^{-33} for NH₃ and ~10^{-14} for H₂O).

The high dielectric constant, low viscosity and long liquid range of HF make it an excellent solvent for a wide variety of compounds. Whilst most inorganic fluorides give fluoride ions when dissolved (see next paragraph), a few solutes dissolve without ionization, e.g. XeF₂, SO₂, HSO₃F, SF₆ and MF₆ (M = Mo, W, U, Re and Os). It is also probable that VF₅ and ReF₇ dissolve without ionizing. Perhaps more surprisingly liquid HF is now extensively used in biochemical research: carbohydrates, amino acids and proteins dissolve readily, frequently with only minor chemical consequences. In particular, complex organic compounds that are potentially

[41] H. H. HYMAN and J. J. KATZ, Chap. 2 in T. C. WADDINGTON (ed.), *Nonaqueous Solvent Systems*, pp. 47–81, Academic Press. London, 1965.

[42] M. KILPATRICK and J. G. JONES. Chap. 2 in J. J. LAGOWSKI (ed.), *The Chemistry of Nonaqueous Solvents*, pp. 43–99, Vol. 2, Academic Press, New York, 1967.

[43] T. A. O'DONNELL, Chap. 25 in *Comprehensive Inorganic Chemistry*, Vol. 2, pp. 1009–106, Pergamon Press, Oxford, 1973.

[44] R. J. GILLESPIE and J. LIANG, *J. Am. Chem. Soc.* **110**, 6053–7 (1988).

capable of eliminating the elements of water (e.g. cellulose, sugar esters, etc.) often dissolve without dehydration. Likewise globular proteins and many fibrous proteins that are insoluble in water, such as silk fibroin. These solutions are remarkably stable: e.g. the hormones insulin and ACTH were recovered after 2 h in HF at $0°$ with their biological activity substantially intact.

Many of the ionic fluorides of M^{I}, M^{II} and M^{III} dissolve to give highly conducting solutions due to ready dissociation. Some typical values of the solubility of fluorides in HF are in Table 17.11: the data show the expected trend towards greater solubility with increase in ionic radius within the alkali metals and alkaline earth metals, and the expected decrease in solubility with increase in ionic charge so that $MF > MF_2 > MF_3$. This is dramatically illustrated by AgF which is 155 times more soluble than AgF_2 and TlF which is over 7000 times more soluble than TlF_3.

With inorganic solutes other than fluorides, solvolysis usually occurs. Thus chlorides, bromides and iodides give the corresponding fluorides with evolution of HX, and fluorides are also formed from oxides, hydroxides, carbonates and sulfites. Indeed, this is an excellent synthetic route for the preparation of anhydrous metal fluorides and has been used with good effect for TiF_4, ZrF_4, UF_4, SnF_4, VOF_3, VF_3, NbF_5, TaF_5, SbF_5, MoO_2F_2, etc. (Note, however, that $AgCl$, $PdCl_2$, $PtCl_4$, Au_2Cl_6 and ICl are apparently exceptions.[42]) Less-extensive solvolysis occurs with sulfates, phosphates and certain other oxoanions. For example, a careful cryoscopic study of

solutions of K_2SO_4 in HF (at $\sim -84°C$) gave a value of $\nu = 5$ for the number of solute species in solution, but this increased to about 6 when determined by vapour-pressure depressions at $0°$. These observations can be rationalized if un-ionized H_2SO_4 is formed at the lower temperature and if solvolysis of this species to unionized HSO_3F sets in at the higher temperatures:

$$K_2SO_4 + 4HF \xrightarrow{-80°} 2K^+ + 2HF_2^- + H_2SO_4$$

$$H_2SO_4 + 3HF \xrightarrow{0°} H_3O^+ + HSO_3F + HF_2^-$$

Consistent with this, the ^{19}F nmr spectra of solutions at $0°$ showed the presence of HSO_3F, and separate cryoscopic experiments with pure H_2SO_4 as the sole solute gave a value of ν close to unity.

Solvolysis of phosphoric acids in the system $HF/P_2O_5/H_2O$ gave successively H_2PO_3F, HPO_2F_2 and $H_3O^+PF_6^-$, as shown by ^{19}F and ^{31}P nmr spectroscopy. Raman studies show that KNO_3 solvolyses according to the reaction

$$KNO_3 + 6HF \longrightarrow K^+ + NO_2^+ + H_3O^+ + 3HF_2^-$$

Permanganates and chromates are solvolysed by HF to oxide fluorides such as MnO_3F and CrO_2F_2.

Acid–base reactions in anhydrous HF are well documented. Within the Brønsted formalism, few if any acids would be expected to be sufficiently strong proton donors to be able to protonate the very strong proton-donor HF (p. 51), and this is borne out by observation. Conversely, HF can protonate many Brønsted bases, notably water,

Table 17.11 Solubility of some metal fluorides in anhydrous HF (in g/100 g HF and at 12°C unless otherwise stated)

LiF	NaF(11°)	NH₄F(17°)	KF(8°)	RbF(20°)	CsF(10°)	**AgF**	**TlF**
10.3	30.1	32.6	36.5	110	199	**83.2**	**580**
Hg_2F_2	BeF_2(11°)	MgF_2	CaF_2	SrF_2	BaF_2	**AgF_2**	CaF_2
0.87	0.015	0.025	0.817	14.83	5.60	**0.54**	0.010
HgF_2	CdF_2(14°)	ZnF_2(14°)	CrF_2(14°)	FeF_2	NiF_2	PbF_2	
0.54	0.201	0.024	0.036	0.006	0.037	2.62	
AlF_3	CeF_3	**TlF_3**	MnF_3	FeF_3	CoF_3	SbF_3	BrF_3
0.002	0.043	**0.081**	0.164	0.008	0.257	0.536	0.010

alcohols, carboxylic acids and other organic compounds having one or more lone-pairs on O, N, etc.:

$$H_2O + 2HF \rightleftharpoons H_3O^+ + HF_2^-$$

$$RCH_2OH + 2HF \longrightarrow RCH_2OH_2^+ + HF_2^-$$

$$RCO_2H + 2HF \longrightarrow RC(OH)_2^+ + HF_2^-$$

Alternatively, within the Lewis formalism, acids are fluoride-ion acceptors. The prime examples are AsF_5 and SbF_5 (which give MF_6^-) and to a lesser extent BF_3 which yields BF_4^-. A greater diversity is found amongst Lewis bases (fluoride-ion donors), typical examples being XeF_6, SF_4, ClF_3 and BrF_3:

$$MF_n + HF \longrightarrow MF_{n-1}^+ + HF_2^-$$

Such solutions can frequently be "neutralized" by titration with an appropriate Lewis acid, e.g.:

$$BrF_2^+HF_2^- + H_2F^+SbF_6^- \longrightarrow BrF_2^+SbF_6^- + 3HF$$

Oxidation-reduction reactions in HF form a particularly important group of reactions with considerable industrial application. The standard electrode potentials $E^\circ(M^{n+}/M)$ in HF follow the same sequence as for H_2O though individual values in the two series may differ by up to ± 0.2 V. Early examples showed that CrF_2 and UF_4 reduced HF to H_2 whereas VCl_2 gave VF_3, $2HCl$ and H_2. Of more significance is the very high potential needed for the anodic oxidation of F^- in HF:

$$F^- \rightleftharpoons \tfrac{1}{2}F_2 + e^-; \quad E^\circ(F_2/2F^-) = 2.71 \text{ V at } 0^\circ C$$

This enables a wide variety of inorganic and organic fluorinations to be effected by the electrochemical insertion of fluorine. For example, the production of NFH_2, NF_2H and NF_3 by electrolysis of NH_4F in liquid HF represents the only convenient route to these compounds. Again, CF_3CO_2H is most readily obtained by electrolysis of CH_3CO_2H in HF. Other examples of anodic oxidations in HF are as follows:

Reactant	Products	Reactant	Products
NH_4F	NF_3, NF_2H, NFH_2	NMe_3	$(CF_3)_3N$
H_2O	OF_2	$(MeCO)_2O$	CF_3COF
SCl_2, SF_4	SF_6	SMe_2, CS_2	CF_3SF_5, $(CF_3)_2SF_4$
$NaClO_4$	ClO_3F	$MeCN$	CF_3CN, $C_2F_5NF_2$

The other hydrogen halides are less tractable as solvents, as might be expected from their physical properties (p. 813), especially their low bps, short liquid ranges, low dielectric constants and negligible self-dissociation into ions. Nevertheless, they have received some attention, both for comparison with HF and as preparative media with their own special advantages.[36,45,46] In particular, because of their low bp and consequent ease of removal, the liquid HX solvent systems have provided convenient routes to BX_4^-, BF_3Cl^-, $B_2Cl_6^{2-}$, NO_2Cl, $Al_2Cl_7^-$, R_2SCl^+, $RSCl_2^+$, PCl_3Br^+, $Ni_2Cl_4(CO)_3$ (from nickel tetracarbonyl and Cl_2) and $Ni(NO)_2Cl_2$ (from nickel tetracarbonyl and NOCl). Solubilities in liquid HX are generally much smaller than in HF and tend to be restricted to molecular compounds (e.g. NOCl, PhOH, etc.) or salts with small lattice energies, e.g. the tetraalkylammonium halides. Concentrations rarely attain 0.5 mol l^{-1} (i.e. $0.05 \text{ mol}/100 \text{ g HF}$). Ready protonation of compounds containing lone-pairs or π bonds is observed, e.g. amines, phosphines, ethers, sulfides, aromatic olefins, and compounds containing $-C\equiv N$, $-N=N-$, $>C=O$, $>P=O$ etc. Of particular interest is the protonation of phosphine in the presence of BX_3 to give $PH_4^+BCl_4^-$, $PH_4^+BF_3Cl^-$, and $PH_4^+BBr_4^-$. $Fe(CO)_5$ affords $[Fe(CO)_5H]^+$ and $[Fe(\eta^5\text{-}C_5H_5)(CO)_2]_2$ yields $[Fe(\eta^5\text{-}C_5H_5)(CO)_2]_2H^+$. Solvolysis is also well established:

$$Ph_3SnCl + HCl \longrightarrow Ph_2SnCl_2 + PhH$$

$$Ph_3COH + 3HCl \longrightarrow Ph_3C^+HCl_2^- + H_3O^+Cl^-$$

[45] M. E. PEACH and T. C. WADDINGTON, Chap. 3 in T. C. WADDINGTON (ed.), *Nonaqueous Solvent Systems*, pp. 83–115, Academic Press, London, 1965.

[46] F. KLANBERG, Chap. 1 in J. J. LAGOWSKI (ed.), *The Chemistry of Nonaqueous Solvents*, Vol. 2, pp. 1–41, Academic Press, New York, 1967.

Likewise ligand replacement reactions and oxidations, e.g.:

$$Me_4N^+HCl_2^- + BCl_3 \longrightarrow Me_4N^+BCl_4^- + HCl$$

$$PCl_3 + Cl_2 + HCl \longrightarrow PCl_4^+HCl_2^-$$

The preparation and structural characterization of the ions HX_2^- has been an important feature of such work.[36] As expected, these H-bonded ions are much less stable than HF_2^- though crystalline salts of all three anions and of the mixed anions HXY^- (except $HBrI^-$) have been isolated by use of large counter cations, typically Cs^+ and NR_4^+ (R = Me, Et, Bu^n) — see pp. 1313–21, of ref. 23 for further details. Neutron and X-ray diffraction studies suggest that $[Cl-H \cdots Cl]^-$ can be either centrosymmetric or non-centrosymmetric depending on the crystalline environment. An example of the latter mode involves interatomic distances of 145 and 178 pm respectively and a bond angle of $\sim 168°$ (Cl$\cdots$Cl 321.2 pm).[47]

17.2.2 Halides of the elements

The binary halides of the elements span a wide range of stoichiometries, structure types and properties which defy any but the most grossly oversimplified attempt at a unified classification. Indeed, interest in the halides as a class of compound derives in no small measure from this very diversity and from the fact that, being so numerous, there are many examples of well-developed and well-graded trends between the limiting cases. Thus the fluorides alone include OF_2, one of the most volatile molecular compounds known (bp $-145°$), and CaF_2, which is one of the least-volatile "ionic" compounds (bp $2513°C$). Between these extremes of discrete molecules on the one hand, and 3D lattices on the other, is a continuous sequence of oligomers, polymers and extended layer lattices which may be either predominantly covalent [e.g. ClF, $(MoF_5)_4$,

$(CF_2)_\infty$, $(CF)_\infty$, p. 289] or substantially ionic [e.g. Na^+F^-(g), $(SnF_2)_4$, $(BeF_2)_\infty$ (quartz type), SnF_4, NaF (cryst)], or intermediate in bond type with secondary interactions also complicating the picture. The problems of classifying binary compounds according to presumed bond types or limiting structural characteristics have already been alluded to for the hydrides (p. 64), borides (p. 145), oxides, sulfides, etc. Such diversity and gradations are further compounded by the existence of four different halogens (F, Cl, Br, I) and by the possibility of numerous oxidation states of the element being considered, e.g. CrF_2, Cr_2F_5, CrF_3, CrF_4, CrF_5 and CrF_6, or S_2F_2, SF_2, SF_4, S_2F_{10} and SF_6.

A detailed discussion of individual halides is given under the chemistry of each particular element. This section deals with more general aspects of the halides as a class of compound and will consider, in turn, general preparative routes, structure and bonding. For reasons outlined on p. 805, fluorides tend to differ from the other halides either in their method of synthesis, their structure or their bond-type. For example, the fluoride ion is the smallest and least polarizable of all anions and fluorides frequently adopt 3D "ionic" structures typical of oxides. By contrast, chlorides, bromides and iodides are larger and more polarizable and frequently adopt mutually similar layer-lattices or chain structures (cf. sulfides). Numerous examples of this dichotomy can be found in other chapters and in several general references.[48−52] Because of this it is convenient to discuss fluorides as a group first, and then the other halides.

[47] W. KUCHEN, D. MOOTZ, H. SOMBERG, H. WUNDERLICH and H.-G. WUSSOW, *Angew. Chem. Int. Edn. Engl.* **17**, 869–70 (1978).

[48] V. GUTMANN (ed.), *Halogen Chemistry*, Academic Press, London, 1967; Vol. 1. 473 pp.; Vol. 2, 481 pp; Vol. 3, 471 pp.

[49] R. COLTON and J. H. CANTERFORD, *Halides of the First Row Transition Elements*, Wiley, London, 1969, 579 pp.; *Halides of the Second and Third Row Transition Elements*, Wiley, London, 1968, 409 pp.

[50] Ref. 43, pp. 1062–1106; ref. 23, pp. 1232–80.

[51] A. F. WELLS, *Structural Inorganic Chemistry*, 5th edn. pp. 407–44, Oxford University Press, Oxford, 1984.

[52] B. MÜLLER, *Angew. Chem. Int. Edn. Engl.* **26**, 1081–97 (1987).

Fluorides

Binary fluorides are known with stoichiometries that span the range from C_4F to IF_7 (or even, possibly, XeF_8). Methods of synthesis turn on the properties of the desired products.[50,53-57] If hydrolysis poses no problem, fluorides can be prepared by halide metathesis in aqueous solution or by the reactions of aqueous hydrofluoric acid with an appropriate oxide, hydroxide, carbonate, or the metal itself. The following non-hydrated fluorides precipitate as easily filterable solids: LiF, NaF, NH_4F; MgF_2, CaF_2, SrF_2, BaF_2; SnF_2, PbF_2; SbF_3. Gaseous SiF_4 and GeF_4 can also be prepared from aqueous HF. Furthermore, the following fluorides separate as hydrates that can readily be dehydrated thermally, though an atmosphere of HF is required to suppress hydrolysis except in the case of the univalent metal fluorides:

$KF.2H_2O$	$CuF_2.4H_2O$	$AlF_3.H_2O$
$RbF.3H_2O$	$ZnF_2.4H_2O$	$GaF_3.3H_2O$
$CsF.1\frac{1}{2}H_2O$	$CdF_2.4H_2O$	$InF_3.3H_2O$
$TlF.2HF.\frac{1}{2}H_2O$	$HgF_2.2H_2O$	$LnF_3.xH_2O$
$AgF.4H_2O$	$MF_2.6H_2O$	(Ln = lanthanide
	(M = Fe,	metal)
	Co, Ni)	

By contrast $BeF_2.xH_2O$, $TiF_4.2H_2O$ and $ThF_4.4H_2O$ cannot be dehydrated without hydrolysis.

When hydrolysis is a problem then the action anhydrous HF on the metal (or chloride) may prove successful (e.g. the difluorides of Zn, Cd, Ge, Sn, Mn, Fe, Co, Ni; the trifluorides of Ga, In, Ti and the lanthanides; the tetrafluorides of Ti, Zr, Hf, Th, U; and the pentafluorides of Nb and Ta). However, many higher fluorides require the use of a more aggressive fluorinating agent or even F_2 itself. Typical of the fluorides prepared by oxidative fluorination with F_2 are:

difluorides:	Ag, Xe
trifluorides:	Cl, Br, Mn, Co
tetrafluorides:	Sn, Pb, Kr, Xe, Mo, Mn, Ce, Am, Cm
pentafluorides:	As, Sb, Bi, Br, I, V, Nb, Ta, Mo
hexafluorides:	S, Se, Te, Xe, Mo, W, Tc, Ru, Os, Rh, Ir, Pt, U, Np, Pu
heptafluorides:	I, Re
octafluorides:	Xe(?)

Wherever possible the use of elementary F_2 is avoided because of its cost and the difficulty of handling it; instead one of a graded series of halogen fluorides can often be used, the fluorinating power steadily diminishing in the sequence: $ClF_3 > BrF_5 > IF_7 > ClF > BrF_3 > IF_5$. Other "hard" oxidizing fluorinating agents are AgF_2, CoF_3, MnF_3, PbF_4, CeF_4, BiF_5 and UF_6. When selective fluorination of certain groups in organic compounds is required, then "moderate" fluorinating agents are employed, e.g. HgF_2, SbF_5, $SbF_3/SbCl_5$, AsF_3, CaF_2 or KSO_2F. Such nucleophilic reagents may replace other halogens in halohydrocarbons by F but rarely substitute F for H. An electrophilic variant is ClO_3F. Most recently XeF_2, which is available commercially, has been used to effect fluorinations via radical cations: it can oxidatively fluorinate CC double bonds and can replace either aliphatic or aromatic H atoms with F. Even gentler are the "soft" fluorinating agents which do not cause fragmentation of functional groups, do not saturate double bonds, and do not oxidize metals to their highest oxidation states; typical of such mild fluorinating agents are the monofluorides of H, Li, Na, K, Rb, Cs, Ag and Tl and compounds such as SF_4, SeF_4, COF_2, SiF_4 and Na_2SiF_6.

The fluorination reactions considered so far can be categorized as metathesis, oxidation or substitution. Occasionally reductive fluorination is the preferred route to a lower fluoride. Examples are:

$$2PdF_3 + SeF_4 \xrightarrow{\text{warm}} 2PdF_2 + SeF_6$$

$$6ReF_6 + W(CO)_6 \xrightarrow{\text{room temp}} 6ReF_5 + WF_6 + 6CO$$

[53] E. L. Muetterties and C. W. Tullock, Chap. 7 in W. L. Jolly (ed.), *Preparative Inorganic Reactions*, Vol. 2, pp. 237-99 (1965). R. J. Lagow and L. J. Margrave, *Prog. Inorg. Chem.* **26**, 161-210 (1979). M. R. C. Gerstenberger and A. Haas, *Angew. Chem. Int. Edn. Engl.* **20**, 647-67 (1981).

[54] J. Portier, *Angew. Chem. Int. Edn. Engl.* **15**, 475-86 (1976).

[55] R. D. Peacock, *Adv. Fluorine Chem.* **7**, 113-45 (1973).

[56] B. Zemva, K. Lutar, A. Jesih, W. J. Casteel and N. Bartlett, *J. Chem. Soc., Chem. Commun.*, 346-7 (1989).

[57] G. A. Olah, G. K. S. Prakash and R. D. Chambers (eds.), *Synthetic Fluorine Chemistry*, Wiley, Chichester, 1992, 416 pp.

$$2RuF_5 + \tfrac{1}{x}I_2 \xrightarrow{50°} 2RuF_4 + \tfrac{2}{x}IF_x$$

$$2EuF_3 + H_2 \xrightarrow{1100°} 2EuF_2 + 2HF$$

$$6ReF_7 + Re \xrightarrow{400°} 7ReF_6$$

Further examples of this last type of reductive fluorination in which the element itself is used to reduce its higher fluoride are:

Product	ClF	CrF$_2$	GeF$_2$
Reactants	Cl$_2$/ClF$_3$	Cr/CrF$_3$	Ge/GeF$_4$
T/°C	350	1000	300

Product	MoF$_3$	UF$_3$	IrF$_4$	TeF$_4$
Reactants	Mo/MoF$_5$	U/UF$_4$	Ir/IrF$_6$	Te/TeF$_6$
T/°C	400	1050	170	180

The final route to fluorine compounds is electrofluorination (anodic fluorination) usually in anhydrous or aqueous HF. The preparation of NF$_x$H$_{3-x}$ ($x = 1, 2, 3$) has already been described (p. 818). Likewise a reliable route to OF$_2$ is the electrolysis of 80% HF in the presence of dissolved MF (p. 638). Perchloryl fluoride has been made by electrolysing NaClO$_4$ in HF but a simpler route (p. 879) is the direct reaction of a perchlorate with fluorosulfuric acid:

$$KClO_4 + HSO_3F \longrightarrow KHSO_4 + ClO_3F$$

Electrolysis of organic sulfides in HF affords a variety of fluorocarbon derivatives:

$$Me_2S \text{ or } CS_2 \longrightarrow CF_3SF_5 \text{ and } (CF_3)_2SF_4$$

$$(-CH_2S-)_3 \longrightarrow (-CF_2SF_4-)_3, CF_3SF_5$$
$$\text{and } SF_5CF_2SF_5$$

$$R_2S \longrightarrow R_fSF_5 \text{ and } (R_f)_2SF_4$$

where R$_f$ is a perfluoroalkyl group.

The application of the foregoing routes has led to the preparation and characterization of fluorides of virtually every element in the periodic table except the three lightest noble gases, He, Ne and Ar. The structures, bonding, reactivity, and industrial applications of these compounds will be found in the treatment of the individual elements and it is an instructive exercise to gather this information together in the form of comparative tables.[(2.50.53−62)]

One important postscript can be added — the achievement by K. O. Christe in 1986 of synthesizing fluorine itself by chemical means alone, a goal that had eluded chemists for at least 173 years.[(63)] In this context, the term *chemical synthesis* excludes techniques such as electrolysis, photolysis, discharge, etc., or the use of F$_2$ in the synthesis of any of the starting materials. It is well known that high oxidation states can often be stabilized by complex-ion formation. Christe's ingenious strategy was to treat just such a complex fluoride with a strong fluoride-ion acceptor, thus liberating the unstable metal fluoride which then spontaneously decomposed to a lower oxidation state with the liberation of F$_2$. He chose to use K$_2$MnF$_6$ and SbF$_5$, both of which can be readily prepared from HF solutions without the use of F$_2$ itself:

$$K_2MnF_6 + 2SbF_5 \longrightarrow 2KSbF_6 + [MnF_4]$$
$$\longrightarrow MnF_3 + \tfrac{1}{2}F_2$$

The reaction was carried out in a passivated Teflon-stainless steel reactor at 150°C for 1 hour, and the yield was >40%. Fluorine pressures of more than 1 atm were generated in this way.

Chlorides, bromides and iodides

A similar set of preparative routes is available as were outlined above for the fluorides, though the range of applicability of each method and the products obtained sometimes vary from halogen to halogen. When hydrolysis is not a problem

58 A. J. EDWARDS, *Adv. Inorg. Chem. Radiochem.* **27**, 83–112 (1983).

59 P. HAGENMÜLLER (ed.), *Inorganic Solid Fluorides*, Academic Press, N.Y., 1985, 628 pp.

60 J. F. LIEBMAN, A. GREENBERG and W. R. DOLBIER (eds.), *Fluorine-containing Molecules: Structure, Reactivity, Synthesis and Applications*, VCH Publishers, N.Y. 1988, 350 pp.

61 A. E. COMYNS (ed.), *Fluoride Glasses*, Wiley, Chichester, 1989, 219 pp.

62 J. S. THRASHER and S. H. STRAUSS (eds.) *Inorganic Fluorine Chemistry Towards the 21st Century*, ACS Symposium Series **555**, 1994, 437 pp.

63 K. O. CHRISTE, *Inorg. Chem.* **25**, 3721–2 (1986). See also *C & E News*, March 2, pp. 4–5 (1987) for discussion of the implications.

or when hydrated halides are sought, then wet methods are available, e.g. dissolution of a metal or its oxide, hydroxide or carbonate in aqueous hydrohalic acid followed by evaporative crystallization:

$$Fe + 2HCl \text{ (aq)} \longrightarrow [Fe(H_2O)_6]Cl_2 + H_2$$

$$CoCO_3 + 2HI \text{ (aq)} \longrightarrow [Co(H_2O)_6]I_2 + H_2O$$
$$+ CO_2$$

Dehydration can sometimes be effected by controlled removal of water using a judicious combination of gentle warming and either reduced pressure or the presence of anhydrous HX:

$$[M(H_2O)_6]Br_3 \xrightarrow[\text{reduced press}]{70-170°} MBr_3 + 6H_2O$$

$$(M = Ln \text{ or actinide})$$

$$CuCl_2.2H_2O \xrightarrow{HCl(g)/150°} CuCl_2 + 2H_2O$$

Hydrated chlorides that are susceptible to hydrolysis above room temperature can often be dehydrated by treating them with $SOCl_2$ under reflux:

$$[Cr(H_2O)_6]Cl_3 + 6SOCl_2 \xrightarrow{79°} CrCl_3 + 12HCl$$
$$+ 6SO_2$$

Alternative wet routes to hydrolytically stable halides are metathetical precipitation and reductive precipitation reactions, e.g.:

$$Ag^+(aq) + Cl^-(aq) \longrightarrow AgCl$$

$$Cu^{2+}(aq) + 2I^-(aq) \longrightarrow CuI + \tfrac{1}{2}I_2$$

More complex is the hydrolytic disproportionation of the molecular halogens themselves in aqueous alkali which is a commercial route to several alkali-metal halides:

$$3X_2 + 6OH^- \longrightarrow 5X^- + XO_3^- + 3H_2O$$

When the desired halide is hydrolytically unstable then dry methods must be used, often at elevated temperatures. Pre-eminent amongst these methods is the oxidative halogenation of metals (or non-metals) with X_2 or HX; when more than one oxidation state is available X_2 sometimes gives the higher and HX the lower, e.g.:

$$Cr + \tfrac{3}{2}Cl_2 \xrightarrow{600°} CrCl_3$$

$$Cr + 2HCl(g) \xrightarrow{\text{red heat}} CrCl_2 + H_2$$

Similarly, Cl_2 sometimes yields a higher and Br_2 a lower oxidation state, e.g. $MoCl_5$ and $MoBr_3$.

Other routes include the high-temperature halogenation of metal oxides, sometimes in the presence of carbon, to assist removal of oxygen; the source of halogen can be X_2, a volatile metal halide CX_4 or another organic halide. A few examples of the many reactions that have been used industrially or for laboratory scale preparations are:

$$ZrO_2 \xrightarrow{Cl_2} ZrCl_4$$

$$Ta_2O_5 \xrightarrow[>460°]{C + Br_2} TaBr_5$$

$$Nb_2O_5 \xrightarrow[370°]{CBr_4} NbBr_5$$

$$UO_3 \xrightarrow[\text{reflux}]{CCl_2 = CClCCl_3} UCl_4$$

$$MoO_2 \xrightarrow[230°]{AlI_3} MoI_2$$

The last two of these reactions also feature a reduction in oxidation state. A closely related route is halogen exchange usually in the presence of an excess of the "halogenating reagent", e.g.:

$$FeCl_3 + BBr_3(\text{excess}) \longrightarrow FeBr_3 + BCl_3$$

$$MCl_3 + 3HBr \text{ (excess)} \xrightarrow{400°-600°} MBr_3 + 3HCl$$
$$(M = Ln \text{ or } Pu)$$

$$3TaCl_5 + 5AlI_3(\text{excess}) \xrightarrow{400°} 3TaI_5 + 5AlCl_3$$

Reductive halogenation can be achieved by reducing a higher halide with the parent metal, another metal or hydrogen:

$$TaI_5 + Ta \xrightarrow[630° \to 575°]{\text{thermal gradient}} Ta_6I_{14}$$

$$3WBr_5 + Al \xrightarrow[475° \to 240°]{\text{thermal gradient}} 3WBr_4 + AlBr_3$$

$$MX_3 + \tfrac{1}{2}H_2 \longrightarrow MX_2 + HX$$

$$(M = Sm, Eu, Yb, etc., X = Cl, Br, I)$$

Alternatively, thermal decomposition or disproportionation can yield the lower halide:

$$ReCl_5 \xrightarrow{\text{ at "bp" }} ReCl_3 + Cl_2$$

$$MoI_3 \xrightarrow{\;100°\;} MoI_2 + \tfrac{1}{2}I_2$$

$$AuCl_3 \xrightarrow{\;160°\;} AuCl + Cl_2$$

$$2TaBr_4 \xrightarrow{\;500°\;} TaBr_3 + TaBr_5$$

Many significant trends are apparent in the structures of the halides and in their physical and chemical properties. The nature of the element concerned, its position in the periodic table, the particular oxidation state, and, of course, the particular halogen involved, all play a role. The majority of pre-transition metals (Groups 1, 2) together with Group 3, the lanthanides and the actinides in the +2 and +3 oxidation states form halides that are predominantly ionic in character, whereas the non-metals and metals in higher oxidation states ($\geq +3$) tend to form covalent molecular halides. The "ionic-covalent transition" in the halides of Group 15 (P, As, Sb, Bi) and 16 (S, Se, Te, Po) has already been discussed at length (pp. 498, 558, 772) as has the tendency of the refractory transition metals to form cluster halides (pp. 991, 1021, etc.). The problems associated with the ionic bond model and its range of validity were considered in Chapter 4 (p. 79). Presumed bond types tend to show gradual rather than abrupt changes within series in which the central element, the oxidation state or the halogen are systematically varied. For example, in a sequence of chlorides of isoelectronic metals such as KCl, $CaCl_2$, $ScCl_3$ and $TiCl_4$ the first member is predominantly ionic with a 3D lattice of octahedrally coordinated potassium ions; $CaCl_2$ has a framework structure (distorted rutile) in which Ca is surrounded by a distorted octahedron of 6Cl; $ScCl_3$ has a layer structure and $TiCl_4$ is a covalent molecular liquid.

The sudden discontinuity in physical properties at $TiCl_4$ is more a function of stoichiometry and coordination number than a sign of any discontinuous or catastrophic change in bond type. Numerous other examples can be found amongst the transition metal halides and the halides of the post-transition elements. In general, the greater the difference in electronegativity between the element and the halogen the greater will be the tendency to charge separation and the more satisfactory will be the ionic bond model. With increasing formal charge on the central atom or with decreasing electronegativity difference the more satisfactory will be the various covalent bond models. The complexities of the situation can be illustrated by reference to the bp (and mp) of the halides: for the more ionic halides these generally follow the sequence $MF_n > MCl_n > MBr_n > MI_n$, being dominated by coulombic interactions which are greatest for the small F^- and least for the large I^-, whereas for molecular halides the sequence is usually the reverse, viz. $MI_n > MBr_n > MCl_n > MF_n$ being dictated rather by polarizability and London dispersion forces which are greatest for I and least for F. As expected, intermediate halides are less regular as the first sequence yields to the reverse, and no general pattern can be discerned. Physical techniques such as $^{35,37}Cl$ nmr spectroscopy and nuclear quadrupole resonance spectroscopy are being increasingly used to probe such trends.[64]

Similar observations hold for solubility. Predominantly ionic halides tend to dissolve in polar, coordinating solvents of high dielectric constant, the precise solubility being dictated by the balance between lattice energies and solvation energies of the ions, on the one hand, and on entropy changes involved in dissolution of the crystal lattice, solvation of the ions and modification of the solvent structure, on the other: $[\Delta G(\text{cryst} \to \text{saturated soln}) = 0 = \Delta H - T\Delta S]$. For a given cation (e.g. K^+, Ca^{2+}) solubility in water typically follows the sequence

---

64 T. L. WEEDING and W. S. VEEMAN, *J. Chem. Soc., Chem. Commun.*, 946–8 (1989).

$MF_n < MCl_n < MBr_n < MI_n$. By contrast for less-ionic halides with significant non-coulombic lattice forces (e.g. Ag) solubility in water follows the reverse sequence $MI_n < MBr_n < MCl_n < MF_n$. For molecular halides solubility is determined principally by weak intermolecular van der Waals' and dipolar forces, and dissolution is commonly favoured by less-polar solvents such as benzene, CCl_4 or CS_2.

Trends in chemical reactivity are also apparent, e.g. ease of hydrolysis tends to increase from the non-hydrolysing predominantly ionic halides, through the intermediate halides to the readily hydrolysable molecular halides. Reactivity depends both on the relative energies of M–X and M–O bonds and also, frequently, on kinetic factors which may hinder or even prevent the occurrence of thermodynamically favourable reactions. Further trends become apparent within the various groups of halides and are discussed at appropriate points throughout the text.

17.2.3 Interhalogen compounds [65-67]

The halogens combine exothermically with each other to form interhalogen compounds of four stoichiometries: XY, XY_3, XY_5 and XY_7 where X is the heavier halogen. A few ternary compounds are also known, e.g. $IFCl_2$ and IF_2Cl. For the hexatomic series, only the fluorides are known (ClF_5, BrF_5, IF_5), and IF_7 is the sole example of the octatomic series. All the interhalogen compounds are diamagnetic and contain an even number of halogen atoms. Similarly, the closely related polyhalide anions XY_{2n}^- and polyhalonium cations XY_{2n}^+ ($n = 1, 2, 3$) each have an odd

number of halogen atoms: these ions will be considered in subsequent sections (pp. 835, 839).

Related to the interhalogens chemically, are compounds formed between a halogen atom and a pseudohalogen group such as CN, SCN, N_3. Examples are the linear molecules ClCN, BrCN, ICN and the corresponding compounds XSCN and XN_3. Some of these compounds have already been discussed (p. 319) and need not be considered further. A microwave study[68] shows that chlorine thiocyanate is ClSCN (angle Cl–S–C 99.8°) rather than ClNCS, in contrast to the cyanate which is ClNCO. The corresponding fluoro compound, FNCO, can be synthesized by several low-temperature routes but is not stable at room temperature and rapidly dimerizes to $F_2NC(O)NCO$.[69] The chemistry of iodine azide has been reviewed[70] — it is obtained as volatile, golden yellow, shock-sensitive needles by reaction of I_2 with AgN_3 in non-oxygen-containing solvents such as CH_2Cl_2, CCl_4 or benzene: the structure in the gas phase (as with FN_3, ClN_3 and BrN_3 also) comprises a linear N_3 group joined at an obtuse angle to the pendant X atom, thereby giving a molecule of C_s symmetry.

Diatomic interhalogens, XY

All six possible diatomic compounds between F, Cl, Br and I are known. Indeed, ICl was first made (independently) by J. L. Gay Lussac and H. Davy in 1813–4 soon after the isolation of the parent halogens themselves, and its existence led J. von Liebig to miss the discovery of the new element bromine, which has similar properties (p. 794). The compounds vary considerably in thermal stability: ClF is extremely robust; ICl and IBr are moderately stable and can be obtained in very pure crystalline form at room temperature; BrCl readily dissociates reversibly into its

[65] Ref. 23, pp. 1476–1563, see also D. M. MARTIN, R. ROUSSON and J. M. WEULERSSE, in J. J. LAGOWSKI (ed.), *The Chemistry of Nonaqueous Solvents*, Chap. 3, pp. 157–95, Academic Press, New York, 1978.

[66] A. I. POPOV, Chap. 2, in V. GUTMANN (ed.), *MTP International Review of Science: Inorganic Chemistry Series* 1, Vol. 3, pp. 53–84, Butterworths, London, 1972.

[67] K. O. CHRISTE, *IUPAC Additional Publication 24th Int. Congr. Pure Appl. Chem.*, Hamburg, 1973, Vol. 4. *Compounds of Non-Metals*, pp. 115–41, Butterworths, London, 1974.

[68] R. J. RICHARDS, R. W. DAVIS and M. C. L. GERRY, *J. Chem. Soc., Chem. Commun.*, 915–6 (1980).

[69] K. GHOLIVAND and H. WILLNER, *Z. anorg. allg. Chem.* **550**, 27–34 (1987).

[70] K. DEHNICKE, *Angew. Chem. Int. Edn. Engl.* **18**, 507–14 (1979).

elements; BrF and IF disproportionate rapidly and irreversibly to a higher fluoride and Br_2 (or I_2). Thus, although all six compounds can be formed by direct, controlled reaction of the appropriate elements, not all can be obtained in pure form by this route. Typical preparative routes (with comments) are as follows:

$$Cl_2 + F_2 \xrightarrow{225°} 2ClF;$$

must be purified from ClF_3 and reactants

$$Cl_2 + ClF_3 \xrightarrow{300°} 3ClF;$$

must be purified from excess ClF_3

$$Br_2 + F_2 \xrightarrow{\text{gas phase}} 2BrF;$$

disproportionates to $Br_2 + BrF_3$ (and BrF_5) at room temp

$$Br_2 + BrF_3 \longrightarrow 3BrF;$$

BrF favoured at high temp

$$I_2 + F_2 \xrightarrow[\text{at } -45°]{\text{in } CCl_3F} 2IF;$$

disproportionates rapidly to $I_2 + IF_5$ at room temp

$$I_2 + IF_3 \xrightarrow[\text{at } -78°]{\text{in } CCl_3F} 3IF$$

$$I_2 + AgF \xrightarrow{0°} IF + AgI$$

$$Br_2 + Cl_2 \underset{\text{or in } CCl_4}{\overset{\text{gas phase}}{\rightleftharpoons}} 2BrCl;$$

compound cannot be isolated free from Br_2 and Cl_2

$$I_2 + X_2 \xrightarrow{\text{room temp}} 2IX;(X = Cl, Br)$$

purify by fractional crystallization of the molten compound

In general the compounds have properties intermediate between those of the parent halogens, though a combination of aggressive chemical reactivity and/or thermal instability militates against the determination of physical properties such as mp, bp, etc., in some instances. However, even for such highly dissociated species as BrCl, precise molecular (as distinct from bulk) properties can be determined by spectroscopic techniques. Table 17.12 summarizes some of the more important physical properties of the

Table 17.12   Physical properties of interhalogen compounds XY

Property	ClF	BrF	IF	BrCl	ICl	IBr
Form at room temperature	Colourless gas	Pale brown (Br_2)	Unstable	Red brown gas	Ruby red crystals	Black crystals
MP/°C	−155.6	*ca.* −33 Disprop[a]	— Disprop[a]	*ca.* −66 Dissoc[a]	27.2(α) 13.9(β)	41 Some dissoc
BP/°C	−100.1	*ca.* 20	—	*ca.* 5	97–100[b]	~116[b]
ΔH_f°(298 K)/kJ mol^{-1}	−56.5	−58.6	−95.4	+14.6	−35.3(α)	−10.5 (cryst)
ΔG_f°(298 K)/kJ mol^{-1}	−57.7	−73.6	−117.6	−1.0	−13.95(α)	+3.7(gas)
Dissociation energy/ kJ mol^{-1}	252.5	248.6	~277	215.1	207.7	175.4
d(liq. T°C)/g cm^{-3}	1.62(−100°)	—	—	—	3.095(30°)	3.762(42°)
r(X–Y)/pm	162.81	175.6	190.9	213.8	232.07	248.5
Dipole moment/D	0.881	1.29	—	0.57	0.65	1.21
κ(liq, T°C)/ ohm^{-1} cm^{-1}	1.9 × 10^{-7} (−128°)	—	—	—	5.50 × 10^{-3}	3.4 × 10^{-4}

[a]Substantial disproportionation or dissociation prevents meaningful determination of mp and bp; the figures merely indicate the approximate temperature range over which the (impure) compound is liquid at atmospheric pressure.
[b]Fused ICl and IBr both dissociate into the free halogens to some extent: ICl 0.4% at 25° (supercooled) and 1.1% at 100°C; IBr 8.8% at 25° (supercooled) and 13.4% at 100°C.

diatomic interhalogens. The most volatile compound, ClF, is a colourless gas which condenses to a very pale yellow liquid below $-100°$. The least volatile is IBr; it forms black crystals in which the IBr molecules pack in a herringbone pattern similar to that in I_2 (p. 803) and in which the internuclear distance $r(I-Br)$ is 252 pm. i.e. slightly longer than in the gas phase (248.5 pm). ICl is unusual in forming two crystalline modifications: the stable (α) form crystallizes as large, transparent ruby-red needles from the melt and features zigzag chains of molecules (Fig. 17.6) with two different ICl units and appreciable interchain intermolecular bonding. The packing is somewhat different in the yellow, metastable (β) form (Fig. 17.6) which can be obtained as brownish-red crystals from strongly supercooled melts.

The chemical reactions of XY can be conveniently classified as (a) halogenation reactions, (b) donor-acceptor interactions and (c) use as solvent systems. Reactions frequently parallel those of the parent halogens but with subtle and revealing differences. ClF is an effective fluorinating agent (p. 820) and will react with many metals and non-metals either at room temperature or above, converting them to fluorides and liberating chlorine, e.g.:

$$W + 6ClF \longrightarrow WF_6 + 3Cl_2$$

$$Se + 4ClF \longrightarrow SeF_4 + 2Cl_2$$

It can also act as a chlorofluorinating agent by addition across a multiple bond and/or by oxidation, e.g.:

$$(CF_3)_2CO + ClF \xrightarrow{MF} (CF_3)_2CFOCl$$
$$(M = K, Rb, Cs)$$

$$CO + ClF \longrightarrow COFCl$$

$$RCN + 2ClF \longrightarrow RCF_2NCl_2$$

$$SO_3 + ClF \longrightarrow ClOSO_2F$$

$$SO_2 + ClF \longrightarrow ClSO_2F$$

$$SF_4 + ClF \xrightarrow{CsF} SF_5Cl$$

$$N{\equiv}SF_3 + 2ClF \longrightarrow Cl_2NSF_5$$

Reaction with OH groups or NH groups results in the exothermic elimination of HF and the (often violent) chlorination of the substrate, e.g.:

$$HOH + 2ClF \longrightarrow 2HF + Cl_2O$$

$$HONO_2 + ClF \longrightarrow HF + ClONO_2$$

$$HNF_2 + ClF \longrightarrow HF + NF_2Cl$$

Lewis acid (fluoride-ion acceptor) behaviour is exemplified by reactions with NOF and MF to give $[NO]^+[ClF_2]^-$ and $M^+[ClF_2]^-$ respectively (M = alkali metal or NH_4). Lewis base (fluoride ion donor) activity includes reactions with BF_3 and AsF_5:

$$BF_3 + 2ClF \longrightarrow [Cl_2F]^+[BF_4]^-$$

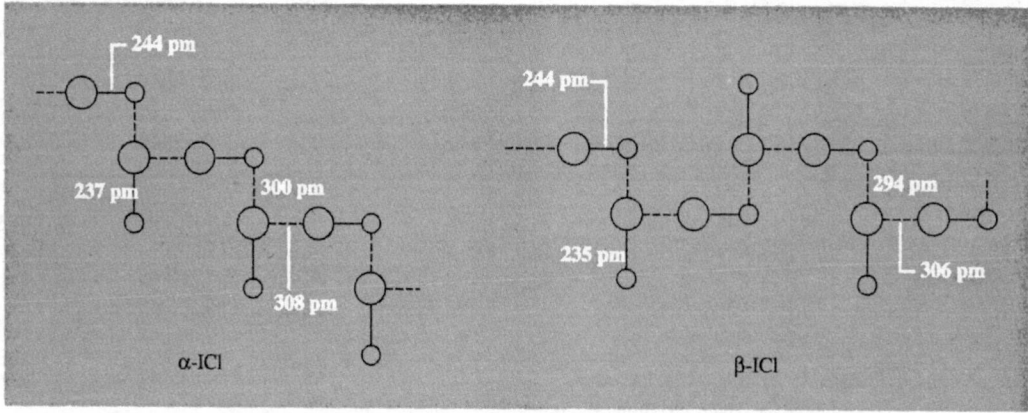

Figure 17.6   Structures of α- and β-forms of crystalline ICl.

$$AsF_5 + 2ClF \longrightarrow [Cl_2F]^+[AsF_6]^-$$

The linear polyhalide anion $[F-Cl-F]^-$ and the angular polyhalonium cation $[F{\diagup}{\overset{Cl}{}}{\diagdown}Cl]^+$ are members of a more extensive set of ions to be treated on pp. 835ff. ClF is commercially available in steel lecture bottles of 500-g capacity but must be handled with extreme circumspection in scrupulously dried and degreased apparatus constructed in steel, copper, Monel metal or nickel; fluorocarbon polymers such as Teflon can also be used, but not at elevated temperatures.

The reactivity of ICl and IBr, though milder than that of ClF is nevertheless still extremely vigorous and the compounds react with most metals including Pt and Au, but not with B, C, Cd, Pb, Zr, Nb, Mo or W. With ICl, phosphorus yields PCl_5 and V conveniently yields VCl_3 (rather than VCl_4). Reaction with organic substrates depends subtly on the conditions chosen. For example, phenol and salicylic acid are chlorinated by ICl *vapour*, since homolytic dissociation of the ICl molecule leads to chlorination by Cl_2 rather than iodination by the less-reactive I_2. By contrast, in CCl_4 solution (low dielectric constant) iodination predominates, accompanied to a small extent by chlorination: this implies heterolytic fission and rapid electrophilic iodination by I^+ plus some residual chlorination by Cl_2 (or ICl). In a solvent of high dielectric constant, e.g. $PhNO_2$, iodination occurs exclusively.[71] Likewise BrF, in the presence of EtOH, rapidly and essentially quantitatively monobrominates aromatics such as PhX: when X = Me, Bu^t, OMe or Br, substitution is mainly or exclusively *para*, whereas with deactivating substituents (X = $-CO_2Et$, $-CHO$, $-NO_2$) exclusively *meta*-bromination occurs.[72] A similar interpretation explains why IBr almost invariably brominates rather than iodinates aromatic compounds due to its appreciable dissociation into Br_2 and I_2 in

solution and the much greater rate of reaction of bromination by Br_2 compared with iodination by iodine.

Both ICl and IBr are partly dissociated into ions in the fused state, and this gives rise to an appreciable electrical conductivity (Table 17.12). The ions formed by this heterolytic dissociation of IX are undoubtedly solvated in the melt and the equilibria can be formally represented as

$$3IX \rightleftharpoons I_2X^+ + IX_2^- \quad (X = Cl, Br)$$

The compounds can therefore be used as nonaqueous ionizing solvent systems (p. 424). For example the conductivity of ICl is greatly enhanced by addition of alkali metal halides or aluminium halides which may be considered as halide-ion donors and acceptors respectively:

$$ICl + MCl \longrightarrow M^+[ICl_2]^-$$

$$2ICl + AlCl_3 \longrightarrow [I_2Cl]^+[AlCl_4]^-$$

Similarly pyridine gives $[pyI]^+[ICl_2]^-$ and $SbCl_5$ forms a 2:1 adduct which can be reasonably formulated as $[I_2Cl]^+[SbCl_6]^-$. By contrast, the 1:1 adduct with PCl_5 has been shown by X-ray studies to be $[PCl_4]^+[ICl_2]^-$. Solvoacid–solvobase reactions have been monitored by conductimetric titration; e.g. titration of solutions of RbCl and $SbCl_5$ in ICl (or of KCl and $NbCl_5$) shows a break at 1:1 molar proportions, whereas titration of NH_4Cl with $SnCl_4$ shows a break at the 2:1 mole ratio:

$$Rb^+[ICl_2]^- + [I_2Cl]^+[SbCl_6]^- \longrightarrow$$
$$Rb^+[SbCl_6]^- + 3ICl$$

$$K^+[ICl_2]^- + [I_2Cl]^+[NbCl_6]^- \longrightarrow$$
$$K^+[NbCl_6]^- + 3ICl$$

$$2NH_4{}^+[ICl_2]^- + [I_2Cl]^+{}_2[SnCl_6]^{2-} \longrightarrow$$
$$[NH_4]^+{}_2[SnCl_6]^{2-} + 6ICl$$

The preparative utility of such reactions is, however, rather limited, and neither ICl or IBr has been much used except to form various mixed polyhalide species. Compounds must frequently

---

[71] F. W. BENNETT and A. G. SHARPE, *J. Chem. Soc.* 1383–4 (1950).

[72] S. ROZEN and M. BRAND, *J. Chem. Soc., Chem. Commun.*, 752–3 (1987).

be isolated by extraction rather than by precipitation, and solvolysis is a further complicating factor.

Tetra-atomic interhalogens, XY₃

The compounds to be considered are ClF_3, BrF_3, IF_3 and ICl_3 (I_2Cl_6). All can be prepared by direct reaction of the elements, but conditions must be chosen so as to avoid formation of mixtures of interhalogens of different stoichiometries. ClF_3 is best formed by direct fluorination of Cl_2 or ClF in the gas phase at 200–300° in Cu, Ni or Monel metal apparatus. BrF_3 is formed similarly at or near room temperature and can be purified by distillation to give a pale straw-coloured liquid. With IF_3, which is only stable below −30° the problem is to avoid the more facile formation of IF_5; this can be achieved either by the action of F_2 on I_2 suspended in CCl_3F at −45° or more elegantly by the low-temperature fluorination of I_2 with XeF_2:

$$I_2 + 3XeF_2 \longrightarrow 2IF_3 + 3Xe$$

I_2Cl_6 is readily made as a bright-yellow solid by reaction of I_2 with an excess of liquid chlorine at −80° followed by the low-temperature evaporation of the Cl_2; care must be taken with this latter operation, however, because of the very ready dissociation of I_2Cl_6 into ICl and Cl_2.

Physical properties are summarized in Table 17.13. Little is known of the unstable IF_3 but ClF_3 and BrF_3 are well-characterized volatile molecular liquids. Both have an unusual T-shaped structure of C_{2v} symmetry, consistent with the presence of 10 electrons in the valency shell of the central atom (Fig. 17.7a,b). A notable feature of both structures is the slight deviation from colinearity of the apical F–X–F bonds, the angle being 175.0° for ClF_3 and 172.4° for BrF_3; this reflects the greater electrostatic repulsion of the nonbonding pair of electrons in the equatorial plane of the molecule. For each molecule the X–F$_{apical}$ distance is some 5–6% greater than the X–F$_{equatorial}$ distance but the mean X–F distance is very similar to that in the corresponding monofluoride. The structure of crystalline ICl_3 is quite different, being built up of planar I_2Cl_6 molecules separated by normal van der Waals' distances between the Cl atoms (Fig. 17.7c). The terminal I–Cl distances are similar to those in ICl but the bridging I–Cl distances are appreciably longer.

ClF_3 is one of the most reactive chemical compounds known[73] and reacts violently with many substances generally thought of as inert. Thus it spontaneously ignites asbestos, wood, and other building materials and was used in incendiary bomb attacks on UK cities during the Second World War. It reacts explosively with water and with most organic substances, though

---

[73] L. STEIN, in V. GUTMANN (ed.), *Halogen Chemistry*, Vol. 1, pp. 133–224, Academic Press, London, 1967.

Table 17.13   Physical properties of interhalogen compounds XY₃

Property	ClF_3	BrF_3	IF_3	I_2Cl_6
Form at room temperature	Colourless gas/liquid	Straw-coloured liquid	Yellow solid (decomp above −28°)	Bright yellow solid
MP/°C	−76.3	8.8	—	101 (16 atm)
BP/°C	11.8	125.8	—	—
ΔH_f°(298 K)/kJ mol⁻¹	−164 (g)	−301 (l)	*ca.* −485 (g) calc	−89.3 (s)
ΔG_f°(298 K)/kJ mol⁻¹	−124 (g)	−241 (l)	*ca.* −460 (g) calc	−21.5 (s)
Mean X–Y bond energy of XY₃/kJ mol⁻¹	174	202	*ca.* 275 (calc)	—
Density(T°C)/g cm⁻³	1.885 (0°)	2.803 (25°)	—	3.111 (15°)
Dipole moment/D	0.557	1.19	—	—
Dielectric constant $\varepsilon(T°)$	4.75 (0°)	—	—	—
κ(liq, T°C)/ ohm⁻¹cm⁻¹	6.5×10^{-9}(0°)	8.0×10^{-3}(25°)	—	8.6×10^{-3}(102°)

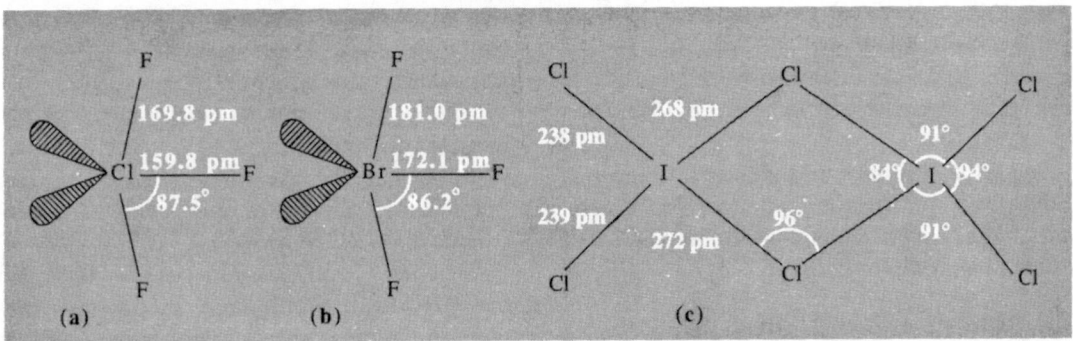

Figure 17.7   Molecular structures of (**a**) ClF_3 and (**b**) BrF_3 as determined by microwave spectroscopy. An X-ray study of crystalline ClF_3 gave slightly longer distances (171.6 and 162.1 pm) and a slightly smaller angle (87.0°). (**c**) Structure of I_2Cl_6 showing planar molecules of approximate D_{2h} symmetry.

reaction can sometimes be moderated by dilution of ClF_3 with an inert gas, by dissolution of the organic compound in an inert fluorocarbon solvent or by the use of low temperatures. Spontaneous ignition occurs with H_2, K, P, As, Sb, S, Se, Te, and powdered Mo, W, Rh, Ir and Fe. Likewise, Br_2 and I_2 enflame and produce higher fluorides. Some metals (e.g. Na, Mg, Al, Zn, Sn, Ag) react at room temperature until a fluoride coating is established; when heated they continue to react vigorously. Palladium, Pt and Au are also attacked at elevated temperatures and even Xe and Rn are fluorinated. Mild steel can be used as a container at room temperature and Cu is only slightly attacked below 300° but the most resistant are Ni and Monel metal. Very pure ClF_3 has no effect on Pyrex or quartz but traces of HF, which are normally present, cause slow etching.

ClF_3 converts most chlorides to fluorides and reacts even with refractory oxides such as MgO, CaO, Al_2O_3, MnO_2, Ta_2O_5 and MoO_3 to form higher fluorides, e.g.:

$$AgCl + ClF_3 \longrightarrow AgF_2 + \tfrac{1}{2}Cl_2 + ClF$$

$$NiO + \tfrac{2}{3}ClF_3 \longrightarrow NiF_2 + \tfrac{1}{3}Cl_2 + \tfrac{1}{2}O_2$$

$$Co_3O_4 + 3ClF_3 \longrightarrow 3CoF_3 + \tfrac{3}{2}Cl_2 + 2O_2$$

With suitable dilution to moderate the otherwise violent reactions. NH_3 gas and N_2H_4 yield HF and the elements:

$$NH_3 + ClF_3 \longrightarrow 3HF + \tfrac{1}{2}N_2 + \tfrac{1}{2}Cl_2$$

$$N_2H_4 + \tfrac{4}{3}ClF_3 \longrightarrow 4HF + N_2 + \tfrac{2}{3}Cl_2$$

At one time this latter reaction was used in experimental rocket motors, the ClF_3 oxidizer reacting spontaneously with the fuel (N_2H_4 or $Me_2N_2H_2$). At low temperatures NH_4F and NH_4HF_2 react with liquid ClF_3 when allowed to warm from -196 to $-5°$ but the reaction is hazardous and may explode above $-5°$:

$$NH_4F + \tfrac{5}{3}ClF_3 \longrightarrow NF_2Cl + 4HF + \tfrac{1}{3}Cl_2$$

The same products are obtained more safely by reacting gaseous ClF_3 with a suspension of NH_4F or NH_4HF_2 in a fluorocarbon oil.

ClF_3 is manufactured on a moderately large scale, considering its extraordinarily aggressive properties which necessitate major precautions during handling and transport. Production plant in Germany had a capacity of ~5 tonnes/day in 1940 (~1500 tonnes pa). It is now used in the USA, the UK, France and Russia primarily for nuclear fuel processing. ClF_3 is used to produce $UF_6(g)$:

$$U(s) + 3ClF_3(l) \xrightarrow{50-90°} UF_6(l) + 3ClF(g)$$

It is also invaluable in separating U from Pu and other fission products during nuclear fuel reprocessing, since Pu reacts only to give the (involatile) PuF_4 and most fission products (except Te, I and Mo) also yield involatile fluorides from which the UF_6 can readily be separated. ClF_3 is available in steel cylinders of up to 82 kg capacity and the price in 1992 was $100 per kg.

Liquid ClF_3 can act both as a fluoride ion donor (Lewis base) or fluoride ion acceptor (Lewis acid) to give difluorochloronium compounds and tetrafluorochlorides respectively, e.g.:

$$MF_5 + ClF_3 \longrightarrow [ClF_2]^+[MF_6]^-;$$

colourless solids: M = As, Sb

$$PtF_5 + ClF_3 \longrightarrow [ClF_2]^+[PtF_6]^-;$$

orange, paramagnetic solid, mp 171°

$$BF_3 + ClF_3 \longrightarrow [ClF_2]^+[BF_4]^-;$$

colourless solid, mp 30°

$$MF + ClF_3 \longrightarrow M^+[ClF_4]^-;$$

white or pink solids, decomp $\sim$ 350° :

M = K, Rb, Cs

$$NOF + ClF_3 \longrightarrow [NO]^+[ClF_4]^-;$$

white solid, dissociates below 25°

Despite these reaction products there is little evidence for an ionic self-dissociation equilibrium in liquid ClF_3 such as may be formally represented by $2ClF_3 \rightleftharpoons ClF_2^+ + ClF_4^-$, and the electrical conductivity of the pure liquid (p. 828) is only of the order of 10^{-9} ohm^{-1} cm^{-1}. The structures of these ions are discussed more fully in subsequent sections.

Bromine trifluoride, though it reacts explosively with water and hydrocarbon tap greases, is somewhat less violent and vigorous a fluorinating agent than is ClF_3. The sequence of reactivity usually quoted for the halogen fluorides is:

$$ClF_3 > BrF_5 > IF_7 > ClF > BrF_3 >$$

$$IF_5 > BrF > IF_3 > IF$$

It can be seen that, for a given stoichiometry of XF_n, the sequence follows the order Cl > Br > I and for a given halogen the reactivity of XF_n diminishes with decrease in n, i.e. $XF_5 > XF_3 >$

XF. (A possible exception is ClF_5; this is not included in the above sequence but, from the fragmentary data available, it seems likely that it should be placed near the beginning — perhaps between ClF_3 and BrF_5.) BrF_3 reacts vigorously with B, C, Si, As, Sb, I and S to form fluorides. It has also been used to prepare simple fluorides from metals, oxides and other compounds: volatile fluorides such as MoF_6, WF_6 and UF_6 distil readily from solutions in which they are formed whereas less-volatile fluorides such as AuF_3, PdF_4, RhF_4, PtF_4 and BiF_5 are obtained as residues on removal of BrF_3 under reduced pressure. Reaction with oxides often evolves O_2 quantitatively (e.g. B_2O_3, Tl_2O_3, SiO_2, GeO_2, As_2O_3, Sb_2O_3, SeO_3, I_2O_5, CuO, TiO_2, UO_3):

$$B_2O_3 + 2BrF_3 \longrightarrow 2BF_3 + Br_2 + \tfrac{3}{2}O_2$$

$$SiO_2 + \tfrac{4}{3}BrF_3 \longrightarrow SiF_4 + \tfrac{2}{3}Br_2 + O_2$$

The reaction can be used as a method of analysis and also as a procedure for determining small amounts of O (or N) in metals and alloys of Li, Ti, U, etc. In cases when BrF_3 itself only partially fluorinates the refractory oxides, the related reagents $KBrF_4$ and BrF_2SbF_6 have been found to be effective (e.g. for MgO, CaO, Al_2O_3, MnO_2, Fe_2O_3, NiO, CeO_2, Nd_2O_3, ZrO_2, ThO_2). Oxygen in carbonates and phosphates can also be determined by reaction with BrF_3. Sometimes partial fluorination yields new compounds, e.g. perrhenates afford tetrafluoroperrhenates:

$$MReO_4 + \tfrac{4}{3}BrF_3 \xrightarrow{\text{liq}} MReO_2F_4 + \tfrac{2}{3}Br_2 + O_2$$

M = K, Rb, Cs, Ag, $\tfrac{1}{2}$Ca, $\tfrac{1}{2}$Sr, $\tfrac{1}{2}$Ba

Likewise, $K_2Cr_2O_7$ and $Ag_2Cr_2O_7$ yield the corresponding $MCrOF_4$ (i.e. reduction from Cr^{VI} to Cr^V). Other similar reactions, which nevertheless differ slightly in their overall stoichiometry, are:

$$KClO_3 + \tfrac{5}{3}BrF_3 \longrightarrow KBrF_4 + \tfrac{2}{3}Br_2$$

$$+ \tfrac{3}{2}O_2 + ClO_2F$$

$$ClO_2 + \tfrac{1}{3}BrF_3 \longrightarrow ClO_2F + \tfrac{1}{6}Br_2$$

$$N_2O_5 + \tfrac{1}{3}BrF_3 \longrightarrow \tfrac{1}{3}Br(NO_3)_3 + NO_2F$$

$$IO_2F + \tfrac{4}{3}BrF_3 \longrightarrow IF_5 + \tfrac{2}{3}Br_2 + O_2$$

As with ClF_3, BrF_3 is used to fluorinate U to UF_6 in the processing and reprocessing of nuclear fuel. It is manufactured commercially on a multitonne pa scale and is available as a liquid in steel cylinders of varying size up to $91\,kg$ capacity. The US price in 1992 was $\sim\$80$ per kg.

In addition to its use as a straight fluorinating agent, BrF_3 has been extensively investigated and exploited as a preparative nonaqueous ionizing solvent. The appreciable electrical conductivity of the pure liquid (p. 828) can be interpreted in terms of the dissociative equilibrium

$$2BrF_3 \rightleftharpoons BrF_2^+ + BrF_4^-$$

Electrolysis gives a brown coloration at the cathode but no visible change at the anode:

$$2BrF_2^+ + 2e^- \longrightarrow BrF_3 + BrF \text{ (brown)}$$

$$2BrF_4^- \longrightarrow BrF_3 + BrF_5 + 2e^- \text{ (colourless)}$$

The specific conductivity decreases from $8.1 \times 10^{-3}\,ohm^{-1}\,cm^{-1}$ at $10°$ to $7.1 \times 10^{-3}\,ohm^{-1}\,cm^{-1}$ at $55°$ and this unusual behaviour has been attributed to the thermal instability of the BrF_2^+ and BrF_4^- ions at higher temperatures. Consistent with the above scheme KF, BaF_2 and numerous other fluorides (such as NaF, RbF, AgF, NOF) dissolve in BrF_3 with enhancement of the electrical conductivity due to the formation of the solvobases $KBrF_4$, $Ba(BrF_4)_2$, etc. Likewise, Sb and Sn give solutions of the solvoacids BrF_2SbF_6 and $(BrF_2)_2SnF_6$. Conductimetric titrations between these various species can be carried out, the end point being indicated by a sharp minimum in the conductivity:

$$BrF_2^+SbF_6^- + Ag^+BrF_4^- \longrightarrow$$
$$Ag^+SbF_6^- + 2BrF_3$$
$$(BrF_2^+)_2SnF_6^{2-} + 2Ag^+BrF_4^- \longrightarrow$$
$$(Ag^+)_2SnF_6^{2-} + 4BrF_3$$

Other solvoacids that have been isolated include the BrF_2^+ compounds of AuF_4^-, BiF_6^-, NbF_6^-,

TaF_6^-, RuF_6^- and PdF_6^{2-} and reactions of BrF_3 solutions have led to the isolation of large numbers of such anhydrous complex fluorides with a variety of cations.[73] Solvolysis sometimes complicates the isolation of a complex by evaporation of BrF_3 and solvates are also known, e.g. $K_2TiF_6.BrF_3$ and $K_2PtF_6.BrF_3$. It is frequently unnecessary to isolate the presumed reaction intermediates and the required complex can be obtained by the action of BrF_3 on an appropriate mixture of starting materials:

$$Ag + Au \xrightarrow{\ BrF_3\ } \{AgBrF_4 + BrF_2AuF_4\}$$
$$\xrightarrow{\ -2BrF_3\ } Ag[AuF_4]$$

$$N_2O_4 + Sb_2O_3 \xrightarrow{\ BrF_3\ } [NO_2][SbF_6]$$

$$Ru + KCl \xrightarrow{\ BrF_3\ } K[RuF_6]$$

In these reactions BrF_3 serves both as a fluorinating agent and as a nonaqueous solvent reaction medium.

Molten I_2Cl_6 has been much less studied as an ionizing solvent because of the high dissociation pressure of Cl_2 above the melt. The appreciable electrical conductivity may well indicate an ionic self-dissociation equilibrium such as

$$I_2Cl_6 \rightleftharpoons ICl_2^+ + ICl_4^-$$

Such ions are known from various crystal-structure determinations, e.g. $K[ICl_2].H_2O$, $[ICl_2][AlCl_4]$ and $[ICl_2][SbCl_6]$ (p. 839). I_2Cl_6 is a vigorous chlorinating agent, no doubt due at least in part to its ready dissociation into ICl and Cl_2. Aromatic compounds, including thiophen, C_4H_4S, give chlorosubstituted products with very little if any iodination. By contrast, reaction of I_2Cl_6 with aryl–tin or aryl–mercury compounds yield the corresponding diaryliodonium derivatives, e.g.:

$$2PhSnCl_3 + ICl_3 \longrightarrow Ph_2ICl + 2SnCl_4$$

Hexa-atomic and octa-atomic interhalogens, XF_5 and IF_7

The three fluorides ClF_5, BrF_5 and IF_5 are the only known hexa-atomic interhalogens, and IF_7 is the sole representative of the octa-atomic class. The first to be made (1871) was IF_5 which is the most readily formed of the iodine fluorides, whereas the more vigorous conditions required for the others delayed the synthesis of BrF_5 and IF_7 until 1930/1 and ClF_5 until 1962. The preferred method of preparing all four compounds on a large scale is by direct fluorination of the element or a lower fluoride:

$$Cl_2 + 5F_2 \xrightarrow{\text{excess } F_2,\ 350°C,\ 250\ atm} 2ClF_5$$

$$ClF_3 + F_2 \xrightarrow{h\nu,\ \text{room temp. 1 atm}} ClF_5$$

$$Br_2 + 5F_2 \xrightarrow{\text{excess } F_2,\ \text{above } 150°} BrF_5$$

$$I_2(s) + 5F_2 \xrightarrow{\text{room temp}} IF_5$$

$$I_2(g) + 7F_2 \xrightarrow{250-300°} IF_7$$

Small-scale preparations can conveniently be effected as follows:

$$MCl(s) + 3F_2 \xrightarrow{100-300°} MF(s) + ClF_5$$

$$KBr + 3F_2 \xrightarrow{25°} KF(s) + BrF_5$$

$$I_2 \xrightarrow{\text{AgF, } ClF_3 \text{ or } BrF_3} IF_5$$

$$I_2O_5 \xrightarrow{ClF_3,\ BrF_3 \text{ or } SF_4} IF_5$$

$$KI + 4F_2 \xrightarrow{250°} KF(s) + IF_7$$

$$PdI_2 + 8F_2 \longrightarrow PdF_2 + 2IF_7$$

This last reaction is preferred for IF_7 because of the difficulty of drying I_2. (IF_7 reacts with SiO_2, I_2O_5 or traces of water to give OIF_5 from which it can be separated only with difficulty.)

ClF_5, BrF_5 and IF_7 are extremely vigorous fluorinating reagents, being excelled in this only by ClF_3. IF_5 is (relatively) a much milder fluorinating agent and can be handled in glass apparatus: it is manufactured in the USA on a scale of several hundred tonnes pa. It is available as a liquid in steel cylinders up to 1350 kg capacity (i.e. $1\frac{1}{3}$ tonnes) and the price in 1992 was *ca.* \$50 per kg. All four compounds are colourless, volatile molecular liquids or gases at room temperature and their physical properties are given in Table 17.14. It will be seen that the liquid range of IF_5 resembles that of BrF_3 and that BrF_5 is similar to ClF_3. The free energies of formation of these and the other halogen fluorides in the gas phase are compared in Fig. 17.8. The trends are obvious; it is also clear from the convexity (or concavity) of the lines that BrF and IF might be expected to disproportionate into the trifluoride and the parent halogen, whereas ClF_3, BrF_3 and IF_5 are thermodynamically the most stable fluorides of Cl, Br and I respectively. Plots of average bond energies are in Fig. 17.9: for a

Table 17.14   Physical properties of the higher halogen fluorides

Property	ClF_5	BrF_5	IF_5	IF_7
MP/°C	−103	−60.5	9.4	6.5 (triple point)
BP/°C	−13.1	41.3	104.5	4.8 (subl 1 atm)
$\Delta H_f°$(gas, 298 K)/kJ mol^{-1}	−255	429[a]	−843[b]	−962
$\Delta G_f°$(gas, 298 K)/kJ mol^{-1}	−165	−351[a]	−775[b]	−842
Mean X–F bond energy/ kJ mol^{-1}	154	187	269	232
$d_{liq}(T°C)$/g cm^{-3}	2.105 (−80°)	2.4716 (25°)	3.207 (25°)	2.669 (25°)
Dipole moment/D	—	1.51	2.18	0
Dielectric constant $\varepsilon(T°C)$	4.28 (−80°)	7.91 (25°)	36.14 (25°)	1.75 (25°)
κ(liq at $T°C$)/ohm^{-1} cm^{-1}	3.7×10^{-8} (−80°)	9.9×10^{-8} (25°)	5.4×10^{-6} (25°)	$<10^{-9}$(25°)

[a]For liquid BrF_5: $\Delta H_f°$(298 K) −458.6 kJ mol^{-1}, $\Delta G_f°$(298 K) −351.9 kJ mol^{-1}.

[b]For liquid IF_5: $\Delta H_f°$(298 K) −885 kJ mol^{-1}, $\Delta G_f°$(298 K) −784 kJ mol^{-1}.

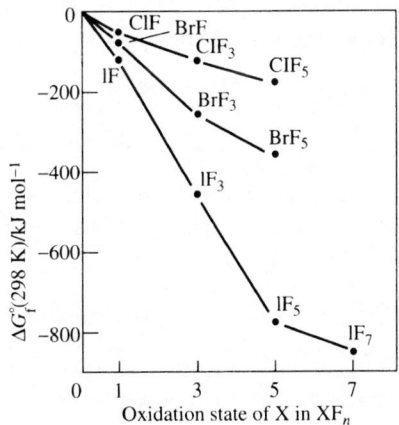

Figure 17.8   Free energies of formation of gaseous halogen fluorides at 298 K.

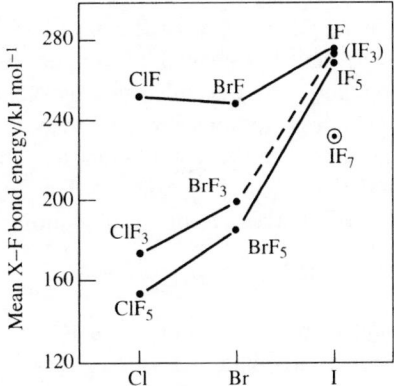

Figure 17.9   Mean bond energies of halogen fluorides.

given value of n in XF_n the sequence of energies is $ClF_n < BrF_n < IF_n$, reflecting the increasing

difference in electronegativity between X and F. ClF is an exception. As expected, for a given halogen, the mean bond energy decreases as n increases in XF_n, the effect being most marked for Cl and least for I. Note that high bond energy (as in BrF and IF) does not necessarily confer stability on a compound (why?).

The molecular structure of XF_5 has been shown to be square pyramidal (C_{4v}) with the central atom slightly below the plane of the four basal F atoms (Fig. 17.10). The structure is essentially the same in the gaseous, liquid and crystalline phases and has been established by some (or all) of the following techniques: electron diffraction, microwave spectroscopy, infrared and Raman spectroscopy, ^{19}F nmr spectroscopy and X-ray diffraction analysis. This structure immediately explains the existence of a small permanent dipole moment, which would be absent if the structure were trigonal bipyramidal (C_{3v}), and is consistent with the presence of 12 valence-shell electrons on the central atom X. Electrostatic effects account for the slight displacement of the four F_b away from the lone-pair of electrons and also the fact that $X-F_b > X-F_a$. The ^{19}F nmr spectra of both BrF_5 and IF_5 consist of a highfield doublet (integrated relative area 4) and a 1:4:6:4:1 quintet of integrated area 1: these multiplets can immediately be assigned on the basis of $^{19}F-^{19}F$ coupling and relative area to the 4 basal and the unique apical F atom respectively. The molecules are fluxional at higher temperatures: e.g. spin–spin coupling disappears in IF_5 at 115° and further heating leads to broadening and coalescence of the two signals, but a sharp singlet could not be attained at still

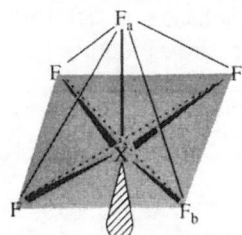

	ClF_5	BrF_5		IF_5	
	(gas)	(gas)	(cryst)	(gas)	(cryst)
$X–F_b$/pm	~172	177.4	178	186.9	189
$X–F_a$/pm	~162	168.9	168	184.4	186
$\angle F_a–X–F_b$	~90° (assumed)	84.8°	84.5°	81.9°	80.9°

Figure 17.10   Structure of XF_5 (X = Cl, Br, I) showing X slightly below the basal plane of the four F_b.

higher temperatures because of accelerated attack of IF_5 on the quartz tube.

The structure of IF_7 is generally taken to be pentagonal bipyramidal (D_{5h} symmetry) as originally suggested on the basis of infrared and Raman spectra (Fig. 17.11). Electron diffraction data have been interpreted in terms of slightly differing axial and equatorial distances and a slight deformation from D_{5h} symmetry due to a 7.5° puckering displacement and a 4.5° axial bending displacement. An assessment of the diffraction data permits the Delphic pronouncement[74] that, on the evidence available, it is not possible to demonstrate that the molecular symmetry is different from D_{5h}.

The very great chemical reactivity of ClF_5 is well established but few specific stoichiometric reactions have been reported. Water reacts vigorously to liberate HF and form $FClO_2$ ($ClF_5 + 2H_2O \longrightarrow FClO_2 + 4HF$). AsF_5 and SbF_5 form 1:1 adducts which may well be ionic: $[ClF_4]^+[MF_6]^-$. A similar reaction with BrF_5 yields a 1:2 adduct which has been shown by X-ray crystallography to be $[BrF_4]^+[Sb_2F_{11}]^-$ (p. 841). Fluoride ion transfer probably also occurs with SO_3 to give $[BrF_4]^+[SO_3F]^-$, but adducts with BF_3, PF_5 or TiF_4 could not be formed. Conversely, BrF_5 can act as a fluoride ion acceptor (from CsF) to give $CsBrF_6$ as a white, crystalline solid stable

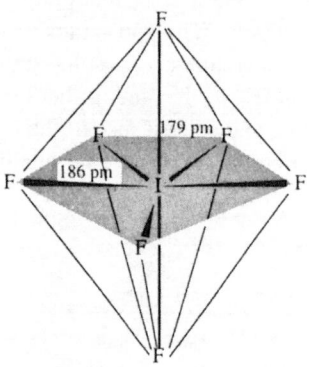

Figure 17.11   Approximate structure of IF_7 (see text).

---

[74] J. D. DONOHUE, *Acta Cryst.* **18**, 1018–21 (1965).

to about 300°, and this solvobase can be titrated with the solvoacid $[BrF_4]^+[Sb_2F_{11}]^-$ according to the following stoichiometry:

$$[BrF_4]^+[Sb_2F_{11}]^- + 2Cs^+[BrF_6]^- \longrightarrow$$
$$3BrF_5 + 2CsSbF_6$$

BrF_5 reacts explosively with water but when moderated by dilution with MeCN gives bromic and hydrofluoric acids:

$$BrF_5 + 3H_2O \longrightarrow HBrO_3 + 5HF$$

The vigorous fluorinating activity of BrF_5 is demonstrated by its reaction with silicates, e.g.:

$$KAlSi_3O_8 + 8BrF_5 \xrightarrow{450°C} KF + AlF_3 + 3SiF_4$$
$$+ 4O_2 + 8BrF_3$$

The chemical reactions of IF_5 have been more extensively and systematically studied because the compound can be handled in glass apparatus and is much less vigorous a reagent than the other pentafluorides. The (very low) electrical conductivity of the pure liquid has been ascribed to slight ionic dissociation according to the equilibrium

$$2IF_5 \rightleftharpoons IF_4^+ + IF_6^-$$

Consistent with this, dissolution of KF increases the conductivity and KIF_6 can be isolated on removal of the solvent. Likewise NOF affords $[NO]^+[IF_6]^-$. Antimony compounds yield $ISbF_{10}$, i.e. $[IF_4]^+[SbF_6]^-$, which can be titrated with $KSbF_6$. However, the milder fluorinating power of IF_5 frequently enables partially fluorinated adducts to be isolated and in some of these the iodine is partly oxygenated. Complete structural identification of the products has not yet been established in all cases but typical stoichiometries are as follows:

$CrO_3 \longrightarrow CrO_2F_2$	$V_2O_5 \longrightarrow 2VOF_3.3IOF_3$	
$MoO_3 \longrightarrow 2MoO_3.3IF_5$	$Sb_2O_5 \longrightarrow SbF_5.3IO_2F$	
$WO_3 \longrightarrow WO_3.2IF_5$	$KMnO_4 \longrightarrow MnO_3$	
		$+ IOF_3 + KF$

Potassium perrhenate reacts similarly to $KMnO_4$ to give ReO_3F. Similarly, the mild fluorinating action of IF_5 enables substituted iodine fluorides to be synthesized, e.g.:

$$Me_3SiOMe + IF_5 \longrightarrow IF_4OMe + Me_3SiF$$

IF_5 is unusual as an interhalogen in forming adducts with both XeF_2 and XeF_4:

$$XeF_2 + 2IF_5 \xrightarrow{5°} XeF_2.2IF_5$$

$$XeF_4 + IF_5 \xrightarrow{\text{room temp}} XeF_4.IF_5$$

$$\xrightarrow{>92°} XeF_4 + IF_5$$

It should be emphasized that the reactivity of IF_5 is mild only in comparison with the other halogen fluorides (p. 830). Reaction with water is extremely vigorous but the iodine is not reduced and oxygen is not evolved:

$$IF_5 + 3H_2O \longrightarrow HIO_3 + 5HF;$$

$$\Delta H = -92.3 \, kJ \, mol^{-1}$$

$$IF_5 + 6KOH(aq) \longrightarrow 5KF(aq) + KIO_3(aq) + 3H_2O;$$

$$\Delta H = -497.5 \, kJ \, mol^{-1}$$

Boron enflames in contact with IF_5; so do P, As and Sb. Molybdenum and W enflame when heated and the alkali metals react violently. KH and CaC_2 become incandescent in hot IF_5. However, reaction is more sedate with many other metals and non-metals, and compounds such as $CaCO_3$ and $Ca_3(PO_4)_2$ appear not to react with the liquid.

IF_7 is a stronger fluorinating agent that IF_5 and reacts with most elements either in the cold or on warming. CO enflames in IF_7 vapour but NO reacts smoothly and SO_2 only when warmed. IF_7 vapour hydrolyses without violence to HIO_4 and HF; with small amounts of water at room temperature the oxyfluoride can be isolated:

$$IF_7 + H_2O \longrightarrow IOF_5 + 2HF$$

The same compound is formed by action of IF_7 on silica (at $100°$) and Pyrex glass:

$$2IF_7 + SiO_2 \longrightarrow 2IOF_5 + SiF_4$$

IF_7 acts as a fluoride ion donor towards AsF_5 and SbF_5 and the compounds $[IF_6]^+[MF_6]^-$ have

been isolated. Few complexes with alkali metal fluorides have been isolated but CsF and NOF form adducts which have been characterized by X-ray powder data, and formulated on the basis of Raman spectroscopy as $Cs^+[IF_8]^-$ and $[NO]^+[IF_8]^-$.[75]

17.2.4 Polyhalide anions

Polyhalides anions of general formula XY_{2n}^- ($n = 1, 2, 3, 4$) have been mentioned several times in the preceding section. They can be made by addition of a halide ion to an interhalogen compound, or by reactions which result in halide-ion transfer between molecular species. Ternary polyhalide anions $X_mY_nZ_p^-$ ($m + n + p$ odd) are also known as are numerous polyiodides I_n^-. Stability is often enhanced by use of a large counter-cation, e.g. Rb^+, Cs^+, NR_4^+, PCl_4^+, etc.; likewise, for a given cation, thermal stability is enhanced the more symmetrical the polyhalide ion and the larger the central atom (i.e. stability decreases in the sequence $I_3^- > IBr_2^- > ICl_2^- > I_2Br^- > Br_3^- > BrCl_2^- > Br_2Cl^-$). The structures of many of these polyhalide anions have been established by X-ray diffraction analysis or inferred from vibrational spectroscopic data and in all cases the gross stereochemistry is consistent with the expectations of simple bond theories (p. 897); however, subtle deviations from the highest expected symmetry sometimes occur, probably due to crystal-packing forces and residual interactions between the various ions in the condensed phase.

Typical examples of linear (or nearly linear) triatomic polyhalides are in Table 17.15;[67,76] the structures are characterized by considerable variability of interatomic distances and these distances are individually always substantially greater than for the corresponding diatomic interhalogen (p. 825). Note also that for

[75] C. J. ADAMS, *Inorg. Nuclear Chem. Letters* **10**, 831–5 (1974).

[76] Ref. 23, pp. 1534–63 (Polyhalide anions) and references therein.

Table 17.15 Triatomic polyhalides $[X-Y-Z]^-$

Polyhalide	Cations	Structure	Dimensions x/pm, y/pm	Angle
ClF_2^-	NO^+	$[F^xCl^yF]^-$	$x = y$	~180°
	Rb^+, Cs^+	$[F-Cl-F]^-$	$x \neq y$	
Cl_3^-	NEt_4^+, NPr_4^{n+}, NBu_4^{n+}	$[Cl-Cl-Cl]^-$	$x = y$	~180°
BrF_2^-	Cs^+	$[F-Br-F]^-$		
$BrCl_2^-$	Cs^+, NR_4^+ (R = Me, Et, Pr^n, Bu^n)	$[Cl-Br-Cl]^-$	$x = y$	~180°
Br_2Cl^-		$[Br-Br-Cl]^-$	$x \neq y$	
Br_3^-	$Me_3NH^{+(a)}$	$[Br-Br-Br]^-$	$x = y = 254$	171°
	Cs^+ (and PBr_4^+)	$[Br-Br-Br]^-$	244(239) 270(291)	177.5° (177.3°)
IF_2^-	NEt_4^+	$[F-I-F]^-$		
$IBrF^-$		$[F-I-Br]^-$		
$IBrCl^-$	NH_4^+	$[Cl-I-Br]^-$	291 251	179°
ICl_2^-	NMe_4^+ (and PCl_4^+)	$[Cl-I-Cl]^-$	$x = y = 255$	180°
	piperazinium$^{(b)}$	$[Cl-I-Cl]^-$	247 269	180°
	triethylenediammonium$^{(c)}$	$[Cl-I-Cl]^-$	254(253) 267(263)	180° (180°)
IBr_2^-	Cs^+	$[Br-I-Br]^-$	262 278	178°
I_2Cl^-		$[Cl-I-I]^-$		
I_2Br^-	Cs^+	$[Br-I-I]^-$	291 278	178°
I_3^-	$AsPh_4^+$	$[I-I-I]^-$	$x = y = 290$	176°
	$[PhCONH_2]_2H^+$	$[I-I-I]^-$	291 295	177°
	NEt_4^+ (form I)	$[I-I-I]^-$	293 294	180°
	(form II)		291 (& 289), 296 (& 298)	180° (& 178°)
	Cs^+ (and NH_4^+)	$[I-I\cdots I]^-$	283(282) 303(310)	176° (177°)

$^{(a)}$In the compound $[Me_3NH]^+{}_2Br^-Br_3^-$; same dimensions for Br_3^- in PhN_2Br_3 and in $[C_6H_7NH]_2[SbBr_6][Br_3]$. Other known values summarized in ref. 77
$^{(b)}$piperazinium, $[H_2NC_4H_8NH_2]^{2+}$.
$^{(c)}$triethylenediammonium, $[HN(C_2H_4)_3NH]^{2+}$: compound contains 2 non-equivalent ICl_2^- ions.

$[Cl-I-Br]^-$ the I–Cl distance is greater than the I–Br distance, and in $[Br-I-I]^-$ I–Br is greater than I–I. On dissociation, the polyhalide yields the solid monohalide corresponding to the smaller of the halogens present, e.g. $CsICl_2$ gives CsCl and ICl rather than $CsI + Cl_2$. Likewise for CsIBrCl the favoured products are CsCl(s) + IBr(g) rather than CsBr(s) + ICl(g) or CsI(s) + BrCl(g). Thermochemical cycles have been developed to interpret these results.$^{(76)}$

Penta-atomic polyhalide anions $[XY_4]^-$ favour the square-planar geometry (D_{4h}) as expected for species with 12 valence-shell electrons on the central atom. Examples are the Rb^+ and Cs^+ salts of $[ClF_4]^{-1}$, and $KBrF_4$ (in which Br–F is 189 pm and adjacent angles F–Br–F are 90° ($\pm 2°$). The symmetry of the anion is slightly

lowered in $CsIF_4$(C_{2v}) and also in $KICl_4.H_2O$ (in which I–Cl is 242, 247, 253, and 260 pm and the adjacent angles Cl–I–Cl are 90.6°, 90.7°, 89.2° and 89.5°. Other penta-atomic polyhalide anions for which the structure has not yet been determined are $[ICl_3F]^-$, $[IBrCl_3]^-$, $[I_2Cl_3]^-$, $[I_2BrCl_2]^-$, $[I_2Br_2Cl]^-$, $[I_2Br_3]^-$, $[I_4Br]^-$ and $[I_4Cl]^-$. Some of these may be "square planar" but the polyiodo species might well be more closely related to I_5^-: the tetramethylammonium salt of this anion features a planar V-shaped array in which two I_2 units are bonded to a single iodide ion, i.e. $[I(I_2)_2]^-$ as in Fig. 17.12. The V-shaped ions are arranged in a planar array which bear an interesting relation to a (hypothetical) array of planar IX_4^- ions.

Hepta-atomic polyhalide anions are exemplified by BrF_6^- (K^+, Rb^+ and Cs^+ salts) and IF_6^- (K^+, Cs^+, NMe_4^+ and NEt_4^+ salts). The

^{77} F. A. COTTON, G. E. LEWIS and W. SCHWOTZER, *Inorg. Chem.* **25**, 3528–9 (1986).

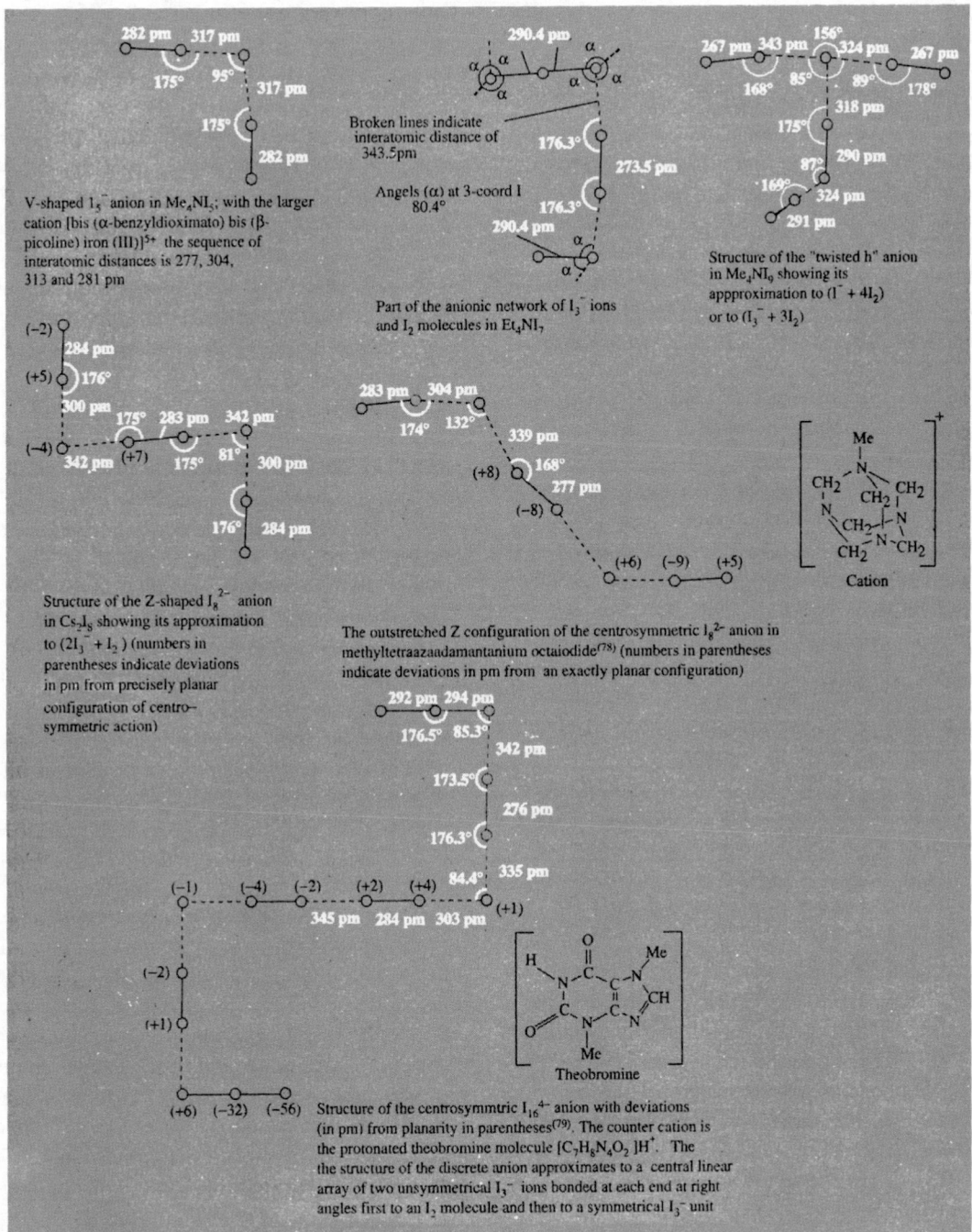

Figure 17.12   Structure of some polyiodides.

[78] P. K. Hon, T. C. M. Mak and J. Trotter, *Inorg. Chem.* **18**, 2916–7 (1979) and references therein.

[79] F. H. Herstein and M. Kapon, *J. Chem. Soc., Chem. Commun.*, 677–8 (1975).

anions have 14 valence-shell electrons on the central atom and spectroscopic studies indicate non-octahedral geometry (D_{3d} for BrF_6^-). Other possible examples are Br_6Cl^- and I_6Br^- but these have not been shown to contain discrete hepta-atomic species and may be extended anionic networks such as that found in Et_4NI_7 (Fig. 17.12).

IF_7 has been shown to act as a weak Lewis acid towards CsF and NOF, and the compounds $CsIF_8$ and $NOIF_8$ have been characterized by X-ray powder patterns and by Raman spectroscopy; they are believed to contain the IF_8^- anion.[75] A rather different structure motif occurs in the polyiodide Me_4NI_9; this consists of discrete units with a "twisted h" configuration (Fig. 17.12). Interatomic distances within these units vary from 267 to 343 pm implying varying strengths of bonding, and the anions can be thought of as being built up either from $I^- + 4I_2$ or from a central unsymmetrical I_3^- and $3I_2$. (The rather arbitrary recognition of discrete I_9^- anions is emphasized by the fact that the closest interionic $I \cdots I$ contact is 349 pm which is only slightly greater than the 343 pm separating one I_2 from the remaining I_7^- in the structure.)

The propensity for iodine to catenate is well illustrated by the numerous polyiodides which crystallize from solutions containing iodide ions and iodine. The symmetrical and unsymmetrical I_3^- ions (Table 17.15) have already been mentioned as have the I_5^- and I_9^- anions and the extended networks of stoichiometry I_7^- (Fig. 17.12). The stoichiometry of the crystals and the detailed geometry of the polyhalide depend sensitively on the relative concentrations of the components and the nature of the cation. For example, the linear I_4^{2-} ion may have the following dimensions:

$$[I \text{-----} I \text{———} I \text{-----} I]^{2-}$$
$$\overset{334\,pm \qquad 280\,pm \qquad 334\,pm}{}$$

$$\text{in } [Cu(NH_3)_4]I_4^{(80)}$$

$$[I \text{———} I \text{———} I \text{———} I]^{2-}$$
$$\overset{318\,pm \qquad 314\,pm \qquad 318\,pm}{}$$

$$\text{in } Tl_6PbI_{10}^{(81)}$$

(Note, however, that the overall length of the two I_4^{2-} ions is virtually identical.) Again, the I_8^{2-} anion is found with an acute-angled planar Z configuration in its Cs^+ salt but with an outstretched configuration in the black methyltetraazaadamantanium salt (Fig. 17.12). The largest discrete polyiodide ion so far encountered is the planar centro-symmetric I_{16}^{4-} anion; this was shown by X-ray diffractometry[79] to be present in the dark-blue needle-shaped crystals of (theobromine)$_2$.H_2I_8 which had first been prepared over a century earlier by S. M. Jorgensen in 1869.

The bonding in these various polyiodides as in the other polyhalides and neutral interhalogens has been the subject of much speculation, computation and altercation. The detailed nature of the bonds probably depends on whether F is one of the terminal atoms or whether only the heavier halogens are involved. There is now less tendency than formerly to invoke much d-orbital participation (because of the large promotion energies required) and Mössbauer spectroscopic studies in iodine-containing species[82] also suggest rather scant s-orbital participation. The bonding appears predominantly to involve p orbitals only, and multicentred (partially delocalized) bonds such as are invoked in discussions of the isoelectronic xenon halides (p. 897) are currently favoured. However, no bonding model yet comes close to reproducing the range of interatomic distances and angles observed in the crystalline polyhalides.[76] There has also been much interest in the bis(ethylenedithio)tetrathiafulvalene layer-like compounds with polyhalide anions. For example, [(BEDT–TTF)(ICl$_2$)] is a one-dimensional metal down to $\sim$22 K at which temperature it transforms to an insulator. The [BrICl]$^-$ salt is similar, whereas with the larger

[80] E. DUBLER and L. LINOWSKY, Helv. Chim. Acta 58, 2604–9 (1978).

[81] A. RABENAU, H. SCHULZ and W. STOEGER, Naturwissenschaften 63, 245 (1976).

[82] N. N. GREENWOOD and T. C. GIBB, Mössbauer Spectroscopy, pp. 462–82, Chapman & Hall, London, 1971.

anions IBr_2^- and I_3^- the salts become ambient pressure superconductors.[83]

17.2.5 Polyhalonium cations XY$_{2n}$$^+$

Numerous polyhalonium cations have already been mentioned in Section 17.2.3 during the discussion of the self-ionization of interhalogen compounds and their ability to act as halide-ion donors. The known species are summarized in Table 17.16.[84,85] Preparations are usually by addition of the appropriate interhalogen and halide-ion acceptor, or by straightforward modification of this general procedure in which the interhalogen or halogen is also used as an oxidant. For example Au dissolves in BrF_3 to give $[BrF_2][AuF_4]$, BrF_3 fluorinates and oxidizes $PdCl_2$ and $PdBr_2$ to $[BrF_2][PdF_4]$; ClF_3 converts

---

[83] T. J. EMGE and 12 others, *J. Am. Chem. Soc.* **108**, 695–702 (1986).

[84] J. SHAMIR, *Struct. Bonding* **37**, 141–210 (1979).

[85] T. BIRCHALL and R. D. MEYERS, *Inorg. Chem.* **21**, 213–7 (1982).

$AsCl_3$ to $[ClF_2][AsF_6]$; stoichiometric amounts of I_2, Cl_2 and $2SbCl_5$ yield $[ICl_2][SbCl_6]$. The fluorocations tend to be colourless or pale yellow but the colour deepens with increasing atomic weight so that compounds of ICl_2^+ are wine-red or bright orange whilst I_2Cl^+ compounds are dark brown or purplish black.

Structures are as expected from simple valency theory and the isoelectronic principle (20 valency electrons). Thus the triatomic species are bent, rather than linear, as illustrated in Fig. 17.13 for ClF_2^+, BrF_2^+ and ICl_2^+; there is frequently some residual interionic interaction due to close approach of the cation and anion and this sometimes complicates the interpretation of vibrational spectroscopic data. In the case of $[ICl_2][SbF_6]$ (Fig. 17.13c) the very short $I \cdots F$ distance implies one of the strongest secondary interactions known between these two elements and the $Sb-F \cdots I$ angle deviates appreciably from linearity.[86] The ion $[Cl_2F]^+$ was originally thought to have the symmetrical

---

[86] T. BIRCHALL and R. D. MEYERS, *Inorg. Chem.* **20**, 2207–10 (1981).

Table 17.16   Polyhalonium cations, XY_{2n}^+

Cation	(Date)[a]	Examples of co-anions (mp of compound in parentheses)
ClF_2^+	(1950)	BF_4^- (30°), PF_6^-, AsF_6^-, SbF_6^- (78°), PtF_6^- (171°), SnF_6^{2-}
Cl_2F^+	(1969)	BF_4^-, AsF_6^-
BrF_2^+	(1949)	PdF_4^-, AuF_4^-, AsF_6^-, SbF_6^- (130°), $Sb_2F_{11}^-$ (33.5°), BiF_6^-, NbF_6^-, TaF_6^-, GeF_6^{2-} (subl 20°), SnF_6^{2-}, PtF_6^{2-} (136°), SO_3F^-
IF_2^+	(1968)	BF_4^-, AsF_6^- (d − 22°), SbF_6^- (d 45°)
ICl_2^+	(1959)	$AlCl_4^-$ (105°), $SbCl_6^-$ (83.5°), $Sb_2F_{11}^-$ (62°), SO_3F^- (42°), SO_3Cl^- (8°)
I_2Cl^+	(1972)	$AlCl_4^-$ (53°), $SbCl_6^-$ (70°), $TaCl_6^-$ (102°), SO_3F^- (40°)
IBr_2^+	(1971)	$Sb_2F_{11}^-$ (65°), SO_3F^- (97°), $SO_3CF_3^-$ (75°)
I_2Br^+	(1974)	SO_3F^- (70°)
$IBrCl^+$	(1973)	$SbCl_6^-$, SO_3F^- (65°)
ClF_4^+	(1967)	AsF_6^-, SbF_6^- (88°), $Sb_2F_{11}^-$ (64°), PtF_6^-
BrF_4^+	(1957)	AsF_6^-, $Sb_2F_{11}^-$ (60°), SnF_6^{2-}
IF_4^+	(1950)	SbF_6^- (103°), $Sb_2F_{11}^-$, PtF_6^-, SO_3F^-, SnF_6^{2-}
$I_3Cl_2^+$	(1982)	$SbCl_6^-$ (47°)
ClF_6^+	(1972)	PtF_6^- (d140°)
BrF_6^+	(1973)	AsF_6^-, $Sb_2F_{11}^-$
IF_6^+	(1958)	BF_4^-, AsF_6^- (subl 120°), SbF_6^- (175°), $Sb_2F_{11}^-$, $[(SbF_5)_3F]^-$ (94°), AuF_6^-

[a] The date given refers to the first isolation of a compound containing the cation, or the characterization of the cation in solution.

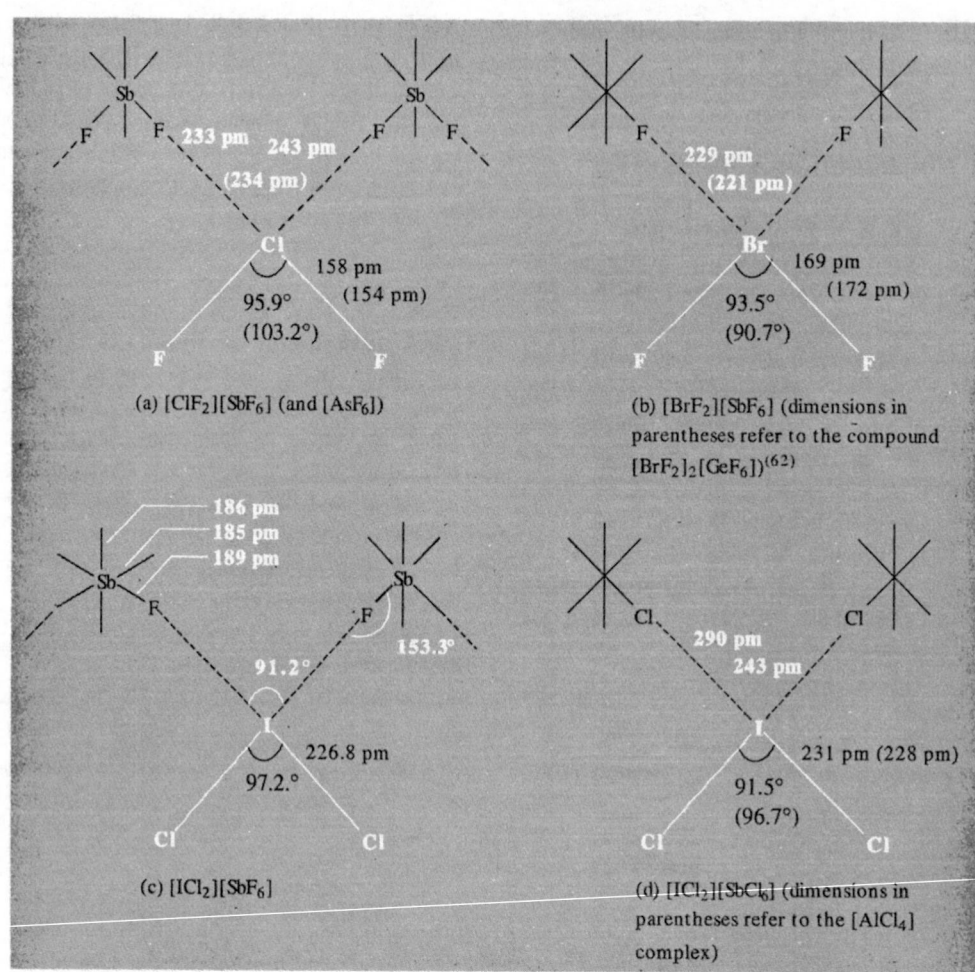

Figure 17.13 Chain structures of compounds containing the triatomic cations XY_2^+: (a) $[ClF_2][SbF_6]$ (with dimensions for $[ClF_2][AsF_6]$ in parentheses); (b) $[BrF_2][SbF_6]$; (c) $[ICl_2][SbF_6]$ indicating slightly bent Sb–F$\cdots$I configuration and very short I$\cdots$F distance; and (d) $[ICl_2][SbCl_6]$ (with dimensions for the $[AlCl_4]^-$ salt in parentheses).

bent C_{2v} structure $[Cl–F–Cl]^+$ but later Raman spectroscopic studies were interpreted on the basis of the unsymmetrical bent structure $[Cl–Cl–F]^+$. Calculations[87] suggest that the symmetrical C_{2v} structure is indeed the more stable form at least for the isolated cation and the question must be regarded as still open:

it may well be that the configuration adopted is determined by residual interactions in the solid state or in solution. In fact the ion is rather unstable in solution and disproportionates completely in SbF$_5$/HF even at $-76°$:

$$2Cl_2F^+ \longrightarrow ClF_2^+ + Cl_3^+$$

The pentaatomic cations ClF_4^+, BrF_4^+ and IF_4^+ are precisely isoelectronic with SF_4, SeF_4 and TeF_4 and adopt the same T-shaped (C_{2v}) configuration. This is illustrated in Fig. 17.14

[87] B. D. JOSHI and K. MOROKUMA, *J. Am. Chem. Soc.* **101**, 1714–7 (1979), and references therein.

[88] A. J. EDWARDS and K. G. CHRISTE. *J. Chem. Soc., Dalton Trans.*, 175–7 (1976)

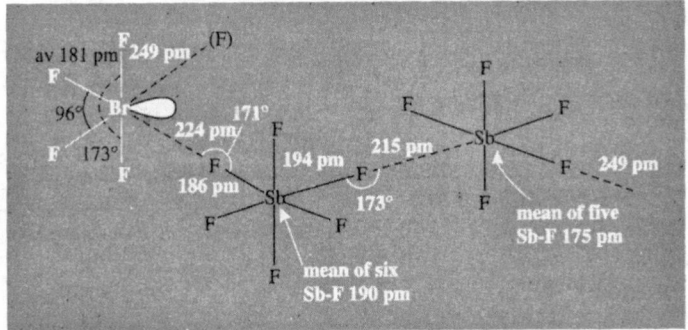

Figure 17.14   Structure of [BrF$_4$][Sb$_2$F$_{11}$] (see text).

for the case of [BrF$_4$][Sb$_2$F$_{11}$]: again there are strong subsidiary interactions, the coordination about Br being pseudooctahedral with four short Br–F distances and two longer Br $\cdots$ F distances which are no doubt influenced by the presence of the stereochemically active nonbonding pair of electrons on the Br atom. In addition, the mean Sb–F distance in the central SbF$_6$ unit is substantially longer than the mean of the five "terminal" Sb–F distances in the second unit and the structure can be described approximately as [BrF$_4^+ \cdots$ SbF$_6^- \cdots$ SbF$_5$]. The structure of the final pentaatomic cation, I$_3$Cl$_2^+$ (1), is different and resembles that of I$_5^+$ (p. 844) in being a planar centrosymmetric species with C_{2h} symmetry:[85]

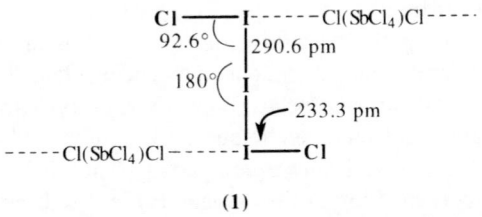

(1)

It will be noted that the central I–I distance is close to that in I$_5^+$ and that the terminal I–Cl distance is very similar to that in β-ICl (p. 826). There are also strong secondary interactions so as to form infinite zig-zag chains via *trans*-Cl atoms of the octahedral SbCl$_6^-$ anions (I $\cdots$ Cl 294.1 pm, angle Cl–I $\cdots$ I 177.6°).

Of the heptaatomic cations, IF$_6^+$ has been known for some time since it can be made

by fluoride-ion transfer from IF$_7$. Because ClF$_7$ and BrF$_7$ do not exist, alternative preparative procedures must be devised and compounds of ClF$_6^+$ and BrF$_6^+$ are of more recent vintage (Table 17.16). The cations have been made by oxidation of the pentafluorides with extremely strong oxidizers such as PtF$_6$, KrF$^+$, or KrF$_3^+$, e.g.:[84]

$$ClF_5(excess) + PtF_6(red\ gas) \xrightarrow[\text{room temp}]{\text{sapphire reactor}}$$

$$ClF_6^+PtF_6^- + ClF_4^+PtF_6^-$$

(bright yellow solids)

$$BrF_5(excess) + KrF^+AsF_6^- \longrightarrow$$

$$Kr + BrF_6^+AsF_6^-$$

Vibrational spectra and ^{19}F nmr studies on all three cations XF$_6^+$ and the ^{129}I Mössbauer spectrum of [IF$_6$][AsF$_6$] establish octahedral (O_h) symmetry as expected for species isoelectronic with SF$_6$, SeF$_6$ and TeF$_6$ respectively.

Attempts to prepare ClF$_7$ and BrF$_7$ by reacting the appropriate cation with NOF failed; instead the following reactions occurred:

$$ClF_6^+PtF_6^- + NOF \longrightarrow NO^+PtF_6^-$$

$$+ ClF_5 + F_2$$

$$BrF_6^+AsF_6^- + 2NOF \xrightarrow{-78°} NO^+AsF_6^-$$

$$+ NO^+BrF_6^- + F_2$$

As expected, the cations are extremely powerful oxidants, e.g.:

$$O_2 + BrF_6^+AsF_6^- \longrightarrow O_2^+AsF_6^- + BrF_5 + \tfrac{1}{2}F_2$$

$$Xe + BrF_6^+AsF_6^- \longrightarrow XeF^+AsF_6^- + BrF_5$$

$$Rn + IF_6^+SbF_6^- \longrightarrow RnF^+SbF_6^- + IF_5$$

17.2.6 Halogen cations[84.89]

It has been known for many years that iodine dissolves in strongly oxidizing solvents such as oleum to give bright blue paramagnetic solutions, but only in 1966 was this behaviour unambiguously shown to be due to the formation of the diiodine cation I_2^+. (The production of similar brightly coloured solutions of S, Se and Te has already been discussed on pp. 664, 759.) The ionization energies of Br_2 and Cl_2, whilst greater than that for I_2 (Table 17.17), are nevertheless smaller than for O_2, which can likewise be oxidized to O_2^+ (p. 616). Accordingly, compounds of the bright-red cationic species Br_2^+ are now well established, but Cl_2^+ is known only from its electronic band spectrum obtained in a low-pressure discharge tube. Some properties of the three diatomic cations X_2^+ are compared with those of the parent halogen molecules X_2 in Table 17.17; as expected, ionization reduces the interatomic distance and increases the vibration frequency (v cm^{-1}) and

Table 17.17 Comparison of diatomic halogens X_2 and their cations X_2^+

Species	I/kJ mol^{-1}	r/pm	v/cm^{-1}	k/N m^{-1}[a]	λ_{max}/nm
Cl_2	1110	199	554	316	330
Cl_2^+	—	189	645	429	—
Br_2	1014	228	319	238	410
Br_2^+	—	213	360	305	510
I_2	900	267	215	170	520
I_2^+	—	256	238	212	640

[a] Force constant k in newton/metre: 1 millidyne/Å = 100 N m^{-1}.

force constant (k N m^{-1}). The principal synthetic routes to crystalline compounds of Br_2^+ and I_2^+ have been either (a) the comproportionation of BrF_3, BrF_5 or IF_5 with the stoichiometric amount of halogen in the presence of SbF_5, or (b) the direct oxidation of the halogen by an excess of SbF_5 or by SbF_5 dissolved in SO_2, e.g.:

$$2I_2 + 5SbF_5 \xrightarrow{SO_2/20^\circ} 2[I_2]^+[Sb_2F_{11}]^- + SbF_3$$

More recently[90] a simpler route has been devised which involves oxidation of Br_2 or I_2 with the peroxide $S_2O_6F_2$ (p. 640) followed by solvolysis using an excess of SbF_5, e.g.:

$$Br_2 + \tfrac{1}{2}S_2O_6F_2 \xrightarrow{rt} \left(\tfrac{1}{2}Br_2 \text{ dissolved in } BrSO_3F\right)$$

$$\xrightarrow{3SbF_5} [Br_2]^+[Sb_3F_{16}]^-$$

The bright-red crystals of $[Br_2]^+[Sb_3F_{16}]^-$ melt at 85.5°C to a cherry-red liquid. Dark-blue crystals of $[I_2]^+[Sb_2F_{11}]^-$ melt sharply at 127°C and the corresponding blue solid $[I_2]^+[Ta_2F_{11}]^-$ melts at 120°C. When solutions of I_2^+ in HSO_3F are cooled below -60°C there is a dramatic colour change from deep blue to red as the cation dimerizes: $2I_2^+ \rightleftharpoons I_4^{2+}$. There is a simultaneous drop in the paramagnetic susceptibility of the solution and in its electrical conductivity. The changes are rapid and reversible, the blue colour appearing again on warming.

During the past 20 y numerous other highly coloured halogen cations have been characterized by Raman spectroscopy, X-ray crystallography, and other techniques, as summarized in Table 17.18. Typical preparative routes involve direct oxidation of the halogen (a) in the absence of solvent, (b) in a solvent which is itself the oxidant (e.g. AsF_5) or (c) in a non-reactive solvent (e.g. SO_2). Some examples are listed below:

$$Cl_2 + ClF + AsF_5 \xrightarrow{-78^\circ} Cl_3^+AsF_6^-$$

$$\tfrac{3}{2}Br_2 + O_2^+AsF_6^- \longrightarrow Br_3^+AsF_6^- + O_2$$

[89] R. J. GILLESPIE and J. PASSMORE *Adv. Inorg. Chem. Radiochem.* **17**, 49–87 (1975).

[90] W. W. WILSON, R. C. THOMPSON and F. AUBKE, *Inorg. Chem.* **19**, 1489–93 (1980).

Table 17.18 Summary of known halogen cations

(Cl_2^+)	Br_2^+ cherry red	I_2^+ bright blue
Cl_3^+ yellow	Br_3^+ brown	I_3^+ dark brown/black
	—	I_4^{2+} red-brown
	Br_5^+ dark brown	I_5^+ green/black[a]
	—	(I_7^+) black

[a] $[I_5][AlCl_4]$ is described as greenish-black needles, dark brown-red in thin sections.

$$4Br_2 + BrF_3 + 3AsF_5 \longrightarrow$$

$$3Br_3^+AsF_6^- \text{(subl 50°, decomp 70°)}$$

$$3I_2 + 3AsF_5 \xrightarrow{\text{in AsF}_5 \text{ or SO}_2} 2I_3^+AsF_6^- + AsF_3$$

$$3I_2 + S_2O_6F_2 \longrightarrow 2I_3^+SO_3F^- \text{ (mp 101.5°)}$$

$$I_2 + ICl + AlCl_3 \longrightarrow I_3^+AlCl_4^- \text{ (mp 45°)}$$

$$2I_2 + ICl + AlCl_3 \longrightarrow I_5^+AlCl_4^- \text{ (mp 50°)}$$

$$7I_2 + S_2O_6F_2 \longrightarrow 2I_7SO_3F \text{ (mp 90.5°)}$$

Other compounds that have been prepared[91] include the dark-brown gold(III) complexes

[91] K. C. LEE and F. AUBKE, *Inorg. Chem.* **19**, 119–22 (1980).

$Br_3[Au(SO_3F)_4]$ (decomp ~150°C) and $Br_5[Au(SO_3F)_4]$ (mp 65°).

The triatomic cations X_3^+ are nonlinear and thus isostructural with other 20-electron species such as XY_2^+ (p. 839) and SCl_2 (p. 689). The contrast in bond lengths and angles between I_3^+ (Fig. 17.15)[92] and the linear 22-electron anion I_3^- (p. 836) is notable, as is its similarity with the isoelectronic Te_3^{2-} anion (p. 764). Likewise, Br_3AsF_6 is isomorphous with I_3AsF_6 and the non-linear cation has Br–Br 227.0 pm and an angle of 102.5°[93] (cf. Br_3^-, Table 17.15). The structures of the penta-atomic cations Br_5^+ (2)[94] and I_5^+ (3)[95] have been determined by X-ray analysis of their AsF_6^- salts and shown to have centrosymmetric C_{2h} symmetry like the

[92] J. PASSMORE, G. SUTHERLAND and P. S. WHITE, *Inorg. Chem.* **20**, 2169–71 (1981).

[93] K. O. CHRISTE, R. BAU and D. ZHAO, *Z. anorg. allg. Chem.* **593**, 46–60 (1991).

[94] H. HARTL, J. NOWICKI and R. MINKWITZ, *Angew. Chem. Int. Edn. Engl.* **30**, 328–9 (1991). See also K. O. CHRISTE, D. A. DIXON and R. MINKWITZ, *Z. anorg. allg. Chem.* **612**, 51–5 (1992).

[95] A. APBLETT, F. GREIN, J. P. JOHNSON, J. PASSMORE and P. S. WHITE, *Inorg. Chem.* **25**, 422–6 (1986).

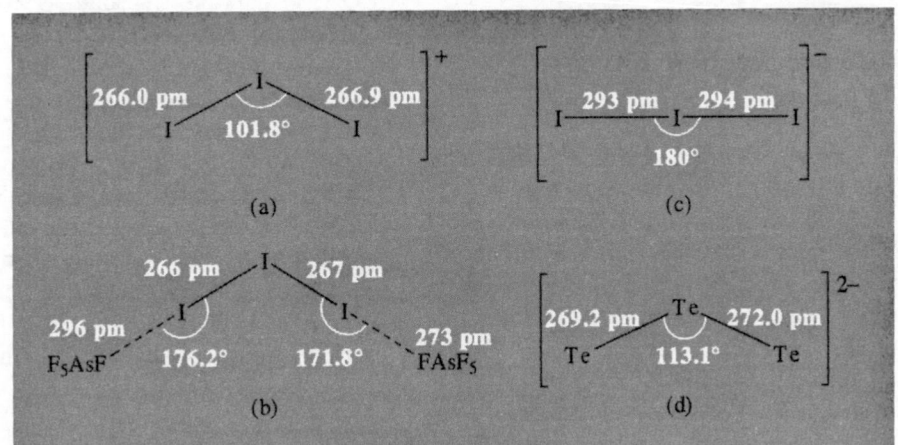

Figure 17.15 The structure of (a) the nonlinear I_3^+ cation in I_3AsF_6 and (b) the weaker cation–anion interactions along the chain (cf. Fig. 17.13). For comparison, the dimensions of (c) the linear 22-electron cation I_3^- and (d) the nonlinear 20-electron cation Te_3^{2-} are given. The data for this latter species refer to the compound $[K(crypt)]_2Te_3.en$; in K_2Te_3 itself, where there are stronger cation–anion interactions, the dimensions are $r = 280$ pm and angle = 104.4°).

analogous cation $I_3Cl_2^+$ (1) (p. 841). The figures in parenthesis in (2) refer to the SbF_6^- salt.

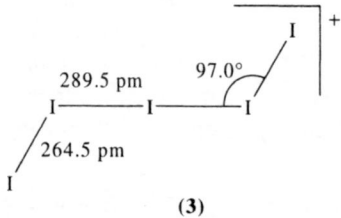

(2)

(3)

The black compound I_7SO_3F (mp 90.5°) was established[96] as a local mp maximum in the phase diagram of the system $I_2/S_2O_6F_2$, together with the known compounds I_3SO_3F (mp 101.5°), ISO_3F (mp 50.2°), and $I(SO_3F)_3$ (mp 33.7°), but its structure has not been determined and there is at present no evidence for the presence of the discrete heptaatomic cation I_7^+ in the crystals.

17.2.7 Oxides of chlorine, bromine and iodine

Perhaps nowhere else are the chemical differences between the halogens so pronounced as in their binary compounds with oxygen. This stems partly from the factors that distinguish F from its heavier congeners (p. 804) and partly from the fact that oxygen is less electronegative than F but more electronegative than Cl, Br and I. The varying relative strengths of O–X bonds and the detailed redox properties of the halogens also ensure considerable diversity in stoichiometry, structure, thermal stability and chemical reactivity of the various species. The binary

compounds between O and F have already been described (p. 638). About 25 further binary halogen oxide species are known, which vary from shock-sensitive liquids and short-lived free radicals to rather stable solids. It will be convenient to treat the 3 halogens separately though intercomparison of corresponding species is instructive and the chemistry is also, at times, related to that of the oxoacids (p. 853) and the halogen oxide fluorides (p. 875).

Oxides of chlorine [97,98]

Despite their instability (or perhaps because of it) the oxides of chlorine have been much studied and some (such as Cl_2O and particularly ClO_2) find extensive industrial use. They have also assumed considerable importance in studies of the upper atmosphere because of the vulnerability of ozone in the stratosphere to destruction by the photolysis products of chlorofluorocarbons (p. 848). The compounds to be discussed are:

Cl_2O: a brownish-yellow gas at room temperature (or red-brown liquid and solid at lower temperatures) discovered in 1834; it explodes when heated or sparked.

Cl_2O_3: a dark-brown solid (1967) which explodes even below 0°.

ClO_2: a yellow paramagnetic gas (deep-red paramagnetic liquid and solid) discovered in 1811 by H. Davy; the liquid explodes above $-40°$ and the gas at room temperature may explode at pressures greater than 50 mmHg (6.7 kPa); despite this more than half a million tonnes are made for industrial use each year in North America alone.

Cl_2O_4: a pale-yellow liquid (1970), $ClOClO_3$, which readily decomposes at room temperature into Cl_2, O_2, ClO_2 and Cl_2O_6.

---

[96] C. CHUNG and G. H. CADY, *Inorg. Chem.* **11**, 2528–31 (1972).

[97] Ref. 23, pp. 1361–86. The oxides of the halogens.

[98] J. A. WOJTOWICZ, Dichlorine monoxide, hypochlorous acid and hypochlorites. *Kirk–Othmer Encyclopedia of Chemical Technology*, 4th edn., Wiley, New York, 1993, Vol. 5, pp. 932–68. J. J. KACZUR and D. W. CAWLFIELD, Chlorine dioxide, chlorous acid and chlorites, *ibid.*, pp. 968–91.

Cl_2O_6: a dark-red liquid (1843) which is in equilibrium with its monomer ClO_3 in the gas phase; it decomposes to ClO_2 and O_2.

Cl_2O_7: a colourless oily liquid (1900) which can be distilled under reduced pressure.

In addition, there are the short-lived radical ClO, the chlorine peroxide radical ClOO (cf. OClO above). and the tetroxide radical ClO_4 (p. 850).

Some physical and molecular properties are summarized in Table 17.19. All the compounds are endothermic, having large positive enthalpies and free energies of formation. Structural data are in Fig. 17.16. Cl_2O has C_{2v} symmetry, as expected for a molecule with 20 valency-shell electrons; the dimensions indicate normal single bonds, and the bond angle can be compared with those for similar molecules such as OF_2, H_2O, SCl_2, etc. Chlorine dioxide, ClO_2, also has C_{2v} symmetry but there are only 19 valency-shell electrons and this is reflected in the considerable shortening of the Cl–O bonds and the increase in the bond angle, which is only 1.7° less than in the 18-electron species SO_2 (p. 700). ClO_2 is an interesting example of an odd-electron molecule which is stable towards dimerization (cf. NO, p. 445); calculations suggest that the odd electron is delocalized throughout the molecule and this probably explains the reluctance to dimerize. Indeed, there is no evidence of dimerization even

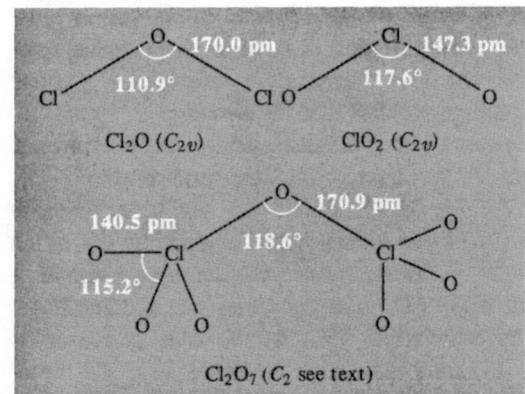

Figure 17.16 Molecular structure and dimensions of gaseous molecules of chlorine oxides as determined by microwave spectroscopy (Cl_2O and ClO_2) or electron diffraction (Cl_2O_7).

in the liquid or solid phases, or in solution. This contrasts with the precisely isoelectronic thionite ion SO_2^- which exists as dithionite, $S_2O_4^{2-}$, albeit with a rather long S–S bond (p. 721). The trioxide ClO_3 is also predominantly dimeric in the condensed phase (see below) as probably is BrO_2 (p. 850).

The gaseous molecule of Cl_2O_7 has C_2 symmetry (Fig. 17.16) the ClO_3 groups being twisted 15° from the staggered (C_{2v}) configuration; the $Cl-O_\mu$ bonds are also inclined

Table 17.19 Physical and molecular properties of the oxides of chlorine

Property	Cl_2O	ClO_2	$ClOClO_3$	Cl_2O_6(l) ($\rightleftharpoons 2ClO_3$ (g))	Cl_2O_7
Colour and form at room temperature	Yellow-brown gas	Yellow-green gas	Pale yellow liquid	Dark red liquid	Colourless liquid
Oxidation states of Cl	+1	+4	+1, +7	+6	+7
MP/°C	−120.6	−59	−117	3.5	−91.5
BP/°C	2.0	11	44.5 (extrap)	203 (extrap)	81
d(liq, 0°C)/g cm^{-3}	—	1.64	1.806	—	2.02
ΔH_f°(gas, 25°C)/ kJ mol^{-1}	80.3	102.6	~180	(155)	272
ΔG_f°(gas, 25°C)/ kJ mol^{-1}	97.9	120.6	—	—	—
S°(gas, 25°C)/ J K^{-1} mol^{-1}	265.9	256.7	327.2	—	—
Dipole moment μ/D$^{(a)}$	0.78 ± 0.08	1.78 ± 0.01	—	—	0.72 ± 0.02

$^{(a)}$1 D ≡ 3.3356 × 10^{-30} C m.

at an angle of 4.7° to the three-fold axis of the ClO_3 groups and there is a substantial decrease from the (single-bonded) $Cl-O_\mu$ to the (multiple-bonded) $Cl-O_t$ distance. A recent X-ray crystal structure analysis at $-160°$ confirmed the C_2 symmetry of Cl_2O_7 and found $Cl-O_\mu$ 172.3 pm, $Cl-O_t$ (av.) 141.6 pm.[99] By contrast an X-ray examination of crystalline Cl_2O_6 at $-70°$ revealed a mixed-valence ionic compound $[Cl^VO_2]^+[Cl^{VII}O_4]^-$ in which the angular ClO_2^+ and tetrahedral ClO_4^- ions were arranged in a distorted CsCl-type structure:[100] ClO_2^+ has $Cl-O$ 140.8 pm, angle OClO 118.9°; ClO_4^- has $Cl-O$ (av) 144.3 pm. The structures of the other oxides of chlorine have not been rigorously established.

We next consider the synthesis and chemical reactions of the oxides of chlorine. Because the compounds are strongly endothermic and have large positive free energies of formation it is not possible to prepare them by direct reaction of Cl_2 and O_2. Dichlorine monoxide, Cl_2O, is best obtained by treating freshly prepared yellow HgO and Cl_2 gas (diluted with dry air or by dissolution in CCl_4):

$$2Cl_2 + 2HgO \longrightarrow HgCl_2.HgO + Cl_2O(g)$$

The reaction is convenient for both laboratory scale and industrial preparations. Another large-scale process is the reaction of Cl_2 gas on moist Na_2CO_3 in a tower or rotary tube reactor:

$$2Cl_2 + 2Na_2CO_3 + H_2O \longrightarrow 2NaHCO_3$$
$$+ 2NaCl + Cl_2O(g)$$

Cl_2O is very soluble in water, a saturated solution at $-9.4°C$ containing 143.6 g Cl_2O per 100 g H_2O; in fact the gas is the anhydride of hypochlorous acid, with which it is in equilibrium in aqueous solutions:

$$Cl_2O + H_2O \rightleftharpoons 2HOCl$$

Much of the Cl_2O manufactured industrially is used to make hypochlorites, particularly $Ca(OCl)_2$, and it is an effective bleach for wood-pulp and textiles. Cl_2O is also used to prepare chloroisocyanurates (p. 324) and chlorinated solvents (via mixed chain reactions in which Cl and OCl are the chain-propagating species).[101] Its reactions with inorganic reagents are summarized in the scheme opposite.

Gaseous mixtures of Cl_2O and NH_3 explode violently: the overall stoichiometry of the reaction can be represented as

$$3Cl_2O + 10NH_3 \longrightarrow 2N_2 + 6NH_4Cl + 3H_2O$$

Chlorine dioxide, ClO_2, was the first oxide of chlorine to be discovered and is now manufactured on a massive scale for the bleaching of wood-pulp and for water treatment;[98,102] however, because of its explosive character as a liquid or concentrated gas, it must be made at low concentrations where it is to be used. For this reason, production statistics can only be estimated, but it is known that its use in the US wood-pulp and paper industry increased ten-fold from 7800 tonnes in 1955 to 78 800 tonnes in 1970; thereafter captive production for this purpose increased less rapidly but the total US production of this gas for all purposes reached 361 000 tonnes in 1990. Production in Canada paralled this growth and was 200 000 tonnes in 1990. Prices in 1992 were in the range $1100–1800/tonne. Usually ClO_2 is prepared by reducing $NaClO_3$ with NaCl, HCl, SO_2 or MeOH in strongly acid solution; other reducing agents that have been used on a laboratory scale include oxalic acid, N_2O, EtOH and sugar. With Cl^- as reducing agent the formal reaction can be written:

$$ClO_3^- + Cl^- + 2H^+ \longrightarrow ClO_2 + \tfrac{1}{2}Cl_2 + H_2O$$

[99] A. SIMON and H. BORRMANN, *Angew. Chem. Int. Edn. Engl.* **27**, 1339–41 (1988).
[100] K. M. TOBIAS and M. JANSEN, *Z. anorg. allg. Chem.* **550**, 16–26 (1987).

[101] J. J. RENARD and H. I. BOLKER, *Chem. Revs.* **76**, 487–505 (1976).
[102] W. J. MASSCHELEIN, *Chlorine Dioxide: Chemistry and Environmental Impact of Oxychlorine Compounds*, Ann Arbor Science Publishers, Ann Arbor, 1979, 190 pp. J. KATZ (ed.), *Ozone and Chlorine Dioxide Technology for Disinfection of Drinking Water*, Noyes Data Corp., Park Ridge, New Jersey, 1980, 659 pp.

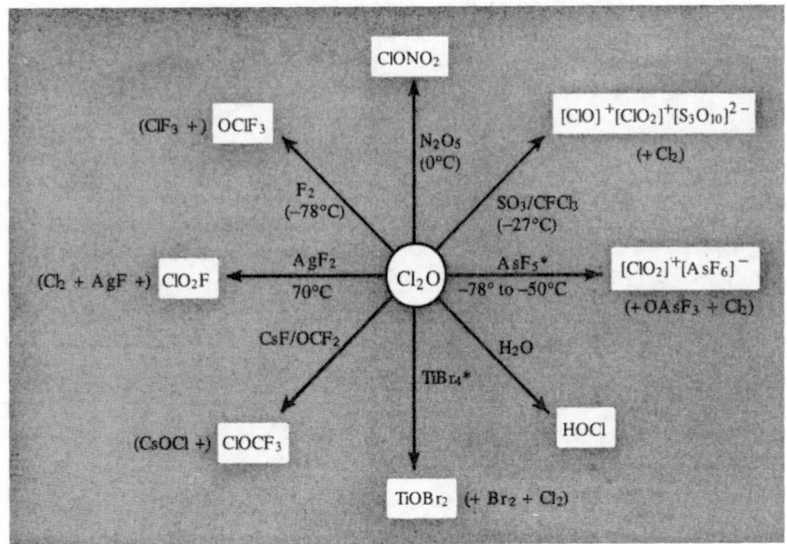

Scheme   Some reactions of dichlorine monoxide. *[In addition $AsCl_3 \rightarrow AsO_2Cl$; $SbCl_5 \rightarrow SbO_2Cl$; $VOCl_3 \rightarrow VO_2Cl$; $TiCl_4 \rightarrow TiOCl_2$.][101]

Contamination of the product with Cl_2 gas is not always undesirable but can be avoided by using SO_2:

$$2ClO_3^- + SO_2 \xrightarrow[\text{solution}]{\text{acid}} 2ClO_2 + SO_4^{2-}$$

On a laboratory scale reduction of $KClO_3$ with moist oxalic acid generates the gas suitably diluted with oxides of carbon:

$$ClO_3^- + \tfrac{1}{2}C_2O_4^{2-} + 2H^+ \longrightarrow ClO_2 + CO_2 + H_2O$$

Samples of pure ClO_2 for measurement of physical properties can be obtained by chlorine reduction of silver chlorate at 90°C:

$$2AgClO_3 + Cl_2 \longrightarrow 2ClO_2 + O_2 + 2AgCl$$

Chlorine oxidation of sodium chlorite has also been used on both an industrial scale (by mixing concentrated aqueous solutions) or on a laboratory scale (by passing Cl_2/air through a column packed with the solid chlorite):

$$2NaClO_2 + Cl_2 \longrightarrow 2ClO_2 + 2NaCl$$

The production of ClO_2 obviously hinges on the redox properties of oxochlorine species (p. 853)

and, indeed, the gas was originally obtained simply by the (extremely hazardous) disproportionation of chloric acid liberated by the action of concentrated sulfuric acid on a solid chlorate:

$$3HClO_3 \longrightarrow 2ClO_2 + HClO_4 + H_2O$$

ClO_2 is a strong oxidizing agent towards both organic and inorganic materials and it reacts readily with S, P, PX_3 and KBH_4. Some further reactions are in the scheme overleaf:[97]

ClO_2 dissolves exothermically in water and the dark-green solutions, containing up to 8 g/l, decompose only very slowly in the dark. At low temperatures crystalline clathrate hydrates, $ClO_2 \cdot nH_2O$, separate ($n \approx 6{-}10$). Illumination of neutral aqueous solutions initiates rapid photodecomposition to a mixture of chloric and hydrochloric acids:

$$ClO_2 \xrightarrow{h\nu} ClO + O$$

$$ClO + H_2O \longrightarrow H_2ClO_2 \xrightarrow{ClO} HCl + HClO_3$$

By contrast, alkaline solutions hydrolyse vigorously to a mixture of chlorite and chlorate (see scheme overleaf).

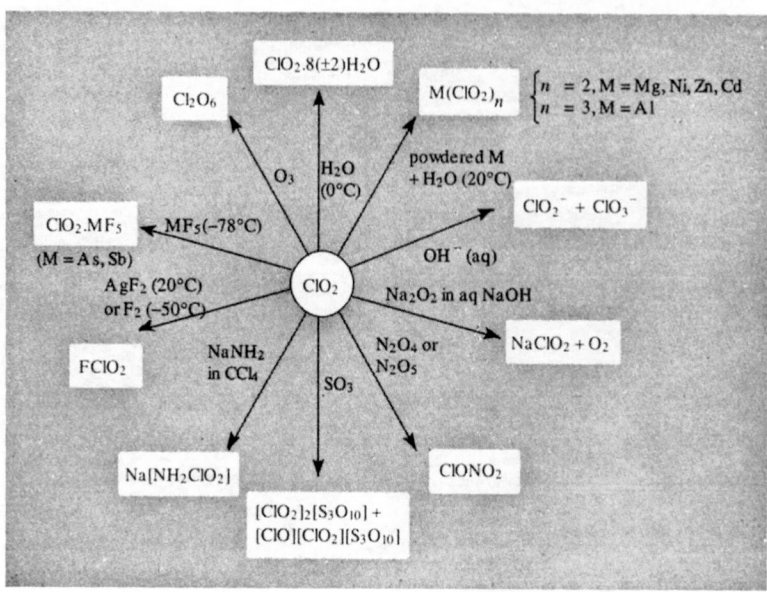

The photochemical and thermal decomposition of ClO_2 both begin by homolytic scission of a Cl–O bond:

$$ClO_2 \xrightarrow{\Delta \text{ or } h\nu} ClO + O; \quad \Delta H_{298}^{\circ} = 278 \text{ kJ mol}^{-1}$$

Subsequent reactions depend on conditions. Ultraviolet photolysis of isolated molecules in an inert matrix yields the radicals ClO and ClOO. At room temperature, photolysis of dry gaseous ClO_2 yields Cl_2, O_2, and some ClO_3 which either dimerizes or is further photolysed to Cl_2 and O_2:

$$ClO_2 + O \longrightarrow ClO_3$$
$$ClO + ClO \longrightarrow Cl_2 + O_2$$
$$2ClO_3 \longrightarrow Cl_2O_6$$
$$2ClO_3 \longrightarrow Cl_2 + 3O_2$$

By contrast, photolysis of solid ClO_2 at $-78°C$ produces some Cl_2O_3 as well as Cl_2O_6:

$$ClO_2 + ClO \rightleftharpoons O-Cl\cdots Cl\begin{matrix} O \\ \diagup \\ \diagdown \\ O \end{matrix}$$

The ClO radical in particular is implicated in environmentally sensitive reactions which lead to depletion of ozone and oxygen atoms in the stratosphere.[103] Thus (as was first pointed out by M. J. Molina and F. S. Rowland in 1974[104]) chlorofluorocarbons such as $CFCl_3$ and CF_2Cl_2, which have been increasingly used as aerosol spray propellants, refrigerants, solvents and plastic foaming agents (p. 304), have penetrated the stratosphere (10–50 km above the earth's surface) where they are photolysed or react with electronically excited $O(^1D)$ atoms to yield Cl atoms and chlorine oxides; this leads to the continuous removal of O_3 and O atoms via such reactions as:

$$Cl + O_3 \longrightarrow ClO + O_2$$
$$ClO + O \longrightarrow Cl + O_2$$

i.e. $O + O_3 \longrightarrow 2O_2$ plus regeneration of Cl

Depletion of O_3 results in an increased penetration of ultraviolet light with wavelengths in the range 290–320 nm which may in time effect changes in climate and perhaps lead also to an increased incidence of skin cancer in

103 R. J. DONOVAN, *Educ. in Chem.* **15**, 110–13 (1978). B. A. THRUSH, *Endeavour* (New Series) **1**, 3–6 (1977), and references therein.
104 M. J. MOLINA and F. S. ROWLAND, *Nature* **249**, 810–12 (1974).

humans. Because of these concerns, the alarming increase in global sales of chlorofluorocarbons, which grew 15-fold between 1948 and 1973, has since been drastically reduced as shown by the following illustrative figures for CFC-11 and CFC-12 (tonnes):

	1948	1973	1983
$CFCl_3$ (CFC-11)	2 270	302 000	93 000
CF_2Cl_2 (CFC-12)	2 220	383 000	120 000

The decrease is continuing due to global adherence to the provisions of the Montreal (1989) and London (1990) Protocols, and it is hoped that the most deleterious CFCs will eventually be phased out completely. As a result of their work, Rowland and Molina were awarded the Nobel Prize for Chemistry for 1995 (together with P. Crutzen, who showed how NO and NO_2 could similarly act as catalysts for the depletion of stratospheric ozone). Several excellent accounts giving more details of the chemistry and meteorology involved are available.[105−108]

The great importance of the short-lived ClO radical has stimulated numerous investigations of its synthesis and molecular properties. Several routes are now available to this species (some of which have already been indicated above):

(a) thermal decomposition of ClO_2 or ClO_3;

(b) decomposition of $FClO_3$ in an electric discharge;

(c) passage of a microwave or radio-frequency discharge through mixtures of Cl_2 and O_2;

(d) reactions of Cl atoms with ClO or O_3 at 300 K;

(e) gas-phase photolysis of Cl_2O, ClO_2 or mixtures of Cl_2 and O_2.

It is an endothermic species with $\Delta H_f^\circ(298\,K)$ 101.8 kJ mol⁻¹, $\Delta G_f^\circ(298\,K)$ 98.1 kJ mol⁻¹, $S^\circ(298\,K)$ 226.5 J K⁻¹ mol⁻¹. The interatomic distance Cl–O is 156.9 pm, its dipole moment is 1.24 D, and the bond dissociation energy D_0 is 264.9 kJ mol⁻¹ (cf. BrO p. 851, IO p. 853).

Chlorine perchlorate $ClOClO_3$ is made by the following low-temperature reaction:

$$MClO_4 + ClOSO_2F \xrightarrow{-45^\circ} MSO_3F + ClOClO_3$$

$$(M = Cs, NO_2)$$

Little is known of its structure and properties; it is even less stable than ClO_2 and decomposes at room temperature to Cl_2, O_2 and Cl_2O_6.

Dichlorine hexoxide, Cl_2O_6, is best made by ozonolysis of ClO_2:

$$2ClO_2 + 2O_3 \longrightarrow Cl_2O_6 + 2O_2$$

The dark-red liquid freezes to a solid which is yellow at −180°C. The structure in the liquid phase is not known but two possibilities have been considered. The Cl–Cl linked structure is superficially attractive as the product of dimerization of the paramagnetic gaseous species ClO_3, but magnetic susceptibility studies of the equilibrium $Cl_2O_6 \rightleftharpoons 2ClO_3$ in the liquid phase were flawed by the subsequent finding that there was no esr signal from ClO_3 and that ClO_2 (as an impurity) was the sole paramagnetic species present. Accordingly, the much-quoted value of 7.24 kJ mol⁻¹ for the derived heat of dimerization is without foundation. The alternative oxygen-bridged dimer, though requiring more electronic and geometric rearrangement of the presumed pyramidal ˙ClO_3 monomers, is rather closer to the ionic structure $[ClO_2]^+[ClO_4]^-$ which has been established by X-ray analysis (p. 846) of the solid. Cl_2O_6 does, in fact, frequently behave as chloryl perchlorate in its reactions though experience with N_2O_4 as "nitrosyl nitrate" (p. 455) engenders caution in attempting to deduce a geometrical structure from chemical reactions (cf. however, diborane, p. 165).

[105] F. S. ROWLAND and M. J. MOLINA, *Chem. & Eng. News*, August 15, 8–13 (1994).

[106] M. J. MOLINA and L. T. MOLINA, Chap. 2 in D. A. DUNNETTE and R. J. O'BRIEN (eds.), *The Science of Global Change: The Impact of Human Activities on the Environment*, ACS Symposium Series **483**, 24–35 (1992).

[107] R. P. WAYNE, *Chemistry of Atmospheres*, (2nd. edn.), Oxford University Press, Oxford, 1991, 456 pp.

[108] P. S. ZURER, *Chem. & Eng. News*, May 24, 8–18 (1993). See also P. S. ZURER, *Chem. & Eng News*, Jan. 2, 30–2 (1989) and Mar. 6, 29–31 (1989).

Hydrolysis of Cl_2O_6 gives a mixture of chloric and perchloric acids, whereas anhydrous HF sets up an equilibrium:

$$Cl_2O_6 + H_2O \longrightarrow HClO_2 + HClO_4$$

$$Cl_2O_6 + HF \rightleftharpoons FClO_2 + HClO_4$$

Nitrogen oxides and their derivatives displace ClO_2 to form nitrosyl and nitryl perchlorates. These and other reactions are summarized in the scheme below.

Dichlorine heptoxide, Cl_2O_7, is the anhydride of perchloric acid (p. 865) and is conveniently obtained by careful dehydration of $HClO_4$ with H_3PO_4 at $-10°C$ followed by cautious low-pressure distillation at $-35°C$ and 1 mmHg. The compound is a shock-sensitive oily liquid with physical properties and structure as already described (p. 845). Cl_2O_7 is less reactive than the lower oxides of chlorine and does not ignite organic materials at room temperature. Dissolution in water or aqueous alkalis regenerates perchloric acid and perchlorates respectively. Thermal decomposition (which can be explosive) is initiated by rupture of a $Cl–O_\mu$ bond, the activation energy being $\sim135\,kJ\,mol^{-1}$:

$$Cl_2O_7 \xrightarrow{\Delta} ClO_3 + ClO_4$$

Oxides of bromine

The oxides of Br are less numerous, far less studied, and much less well characterized than the ten oxide species of chlorine discussed in the preceding section. The reasonably well established compounds are listed below.

Br_2O: a dark-brown solid moderately stable at $-60°$ (mp $-17.5°$ with decomposition), prepared by reaction of Br_2 vapour on HgO (cf. Cl_2O p. 846) or better, by low-temperature vacuum decomposition of BrO_2. The molecule has C_{2v} symmetry in both the solid and vapour phase with Br–O 185 ± 1 pm and angle BrOBr $112 \pm 2°$ as determined by EXAFS (extended X-ray absorption fine structure).[109] It oxidizes I_2 to I_2O_5, benzene to 1,4-quinone, and yields OBr^- in alkaline solution.

"BrO_2": a pale yellow crystalline solid formed quantitatively by low-temperature ozonolysis of Br_2:[†]

[109] W. LEVASON, J. S. OGDEN, M. D. SPICER and N. A. YOUNG, *J. Am. Chem. Soc.* **112**, 1019–22 (1990).

[†] Ozonolysis of Br_2 at $0°C$ yields white, poorly characterized solids which, depending on the conditions used, have compositions close to Br_2O_5, Br_3O_8, and BrO_3; no structural data are available.

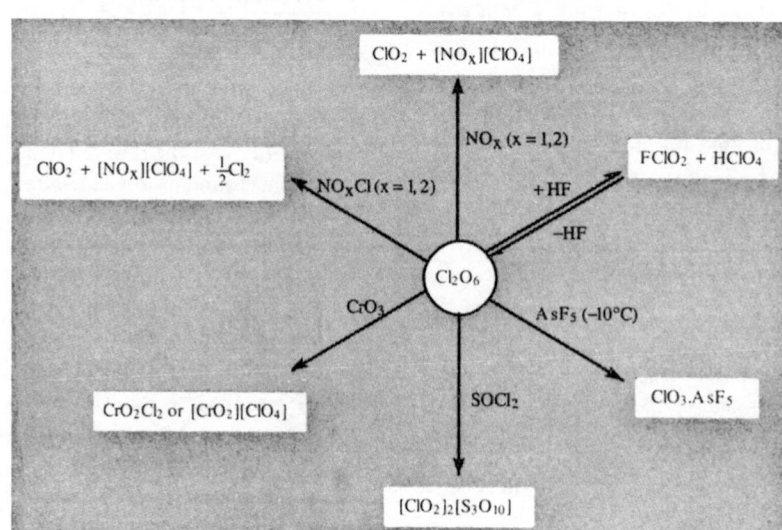

$$Br_2 + 4O_3 \xrightarrow{CF_3Cl/-78°C} 2BrO_2 + 4O_2$$

The structure has recently been shown by EXAFS to be bromine perbromate $BrOBrO_3$ with Br^I-O 186.2 pm, $Br^{VII}-O$ 160.5 pm and angle BrOBr $110 \pm 3°$;[110] (cf. $ClOClO_3$ and $BrOClO_3$). $BrOBrO_3$ is thermally unstable above $-40°C$ and decomposes violently to the elements at $0°C$; slower warming yields BrO_2 (see above). Alkaline hydrolysis leads to disproportionation:

$$6BrO_2 + 6OH^- \longrightarrow 5BrO_3^- + Br^- + 3H_2O$$

Reaction with F_2 yields $FBrO_2$ and with N_2O_4 yields $[NO_2]^+[Br(NO_3)_2]^-$.

Br_2O_3: an orange crystalline solid very recently isolated at $-90°$ from CH_2Cl_2 solution after ozonization of Br_2 in $CFCl_3$. It decomposes above $-40°$, detonates if warmed rapidly to $0°$, and was shown by X-ray analysis to be *syn*-$BrOBrO_2$ with Br^I-O 184.5 pm, Br^V-O 161.3 pm and angle BrOBr $111.6°$.[111] It is thus, formally, the anhydride of hypobromous and bromic acids.

In addition to these compounds the unstable monomeric radicals BrO, BrO_2 and BrO_3 have been made by γ-radiolysis or flash photolysis of the anions OBr^-, BrO_2^- and BrO_3^-. For BrO the interatomic distance is 172.1 pm, the dipole moment 1.55 D, and the thermodynamic properties $\Delta H_f°(298\,K)$ 125.8 kJ mol^{-1}, $\Delta G_f°(298\,K)$ 108.2 kJ mol^{-1} and $S°(298\,K)$ 237.4 J K^{-1} mol^{-1}. Most recently[112] it has been shown that flash pyrolysis at $800-1000°C$ of a mixture containing $Br_2/O_2/Ar$ yields bromine superoxide, $[BrOO]^•$, which can be trapped at 12 K and shown by ir-and uv-spectroscopy to be non-linear. Irradiation of this species at 254 nm results in isomerization to bromine dioxide, $[OBrO]^•$, which is also non-linear (angle $\sim110°$) and which can be reconverted to the superoxide by irradiating the matrix at wavelengths greater than 360 nm.

Oxides of iodine

Iodine forms the most stable oxides of the halogens and I_2O_5 was made (independently) by J. L. Gay Lussac and H. Davy in 1813. However, despite this venerable history the structure of the compound was not determined unambiguously until 1970. It is most conveniently prepared by dehydrating iodic acid (p. 863) at $200°C$ in a stream of dry air but it also results from the direct oxidation of I_2 with oxygen in a glow discharge. The structure (Fig. 17.17) features molecular units of O_2IOIO_2 formed by joining two pyramidal IO_3 groups at a common oxygen. The bridging I–O distances correspond to single bonds, whereas the terminal I–O distances are substantially shorter.[113] There are also appreciable intermolecular interactions which join the molecular units into cross-linked chains; this gives each iodine pseudo-fivefold coordination, the sixth position of the distorted

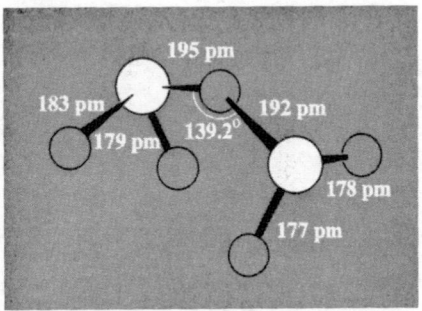

Figure 17.17 The structure of I_2O_5 showing the dimensions and conformation of a single molecular unit. Note that the molecule has no mirror plane of symmetry so is not C_{2v}.

[110] T. R. Gilson, W. Levason, J. S. Ogden, M. D. Spicer and N. A. Young, *J. Am. Chem. Soc.* **114**, 5469–70 (1992).

[111] R. Kuschel and K. Seppelt, *Angew. Chem. Int. Edn. Engl.* **32**, 1632–3 (1993).

[112] G. Maier and A. Bothur, *Z. anorg. allg. Chem.* **621**, 743–6 (1995).

[113] K. Selte and A. Kjekshus, *Acta Chem. Scand.* **24**, 1912–24 (1970).

octahedron presumably being occupied by the lone-pair of electrons on the iodine atom.

I_2O_5 forms white, hygroscopic, thermodynamically stable crystals: $\Delta H_f^{\circ} -158.1\,\text{kJ}\,\text{mol}^{-1}$, d $4.980\,\text{g}\,\text{cm}^{-3}$. The compound is very soluble in water, reforming the parent acid HIO_3. So great is the affinity for water that commercial "I_2O_5" consists almost entirely of HI_3O_8, i.e. $I_2O_5.HIO_3$. The interrelations between these compounds and the rather less stable oxides I_4O_9 and I_2O_4 are shown in the scheme below. I_4O_9 is a hygroscopic yellow powder which decomposes to I_2O_5 when heated above 75°; I_2O_4 forms diamagnetic lemon-yellow crystals (d 4.2 g cm^{-3}) which start to decompose above 85° and which rapidly yield I_2O_5 at 135°:

$$2I_4O_9 \xrightarrow{75°} 3I_2O_5 + I_2 + \tfrac{3}{2}O_2$$

$$5I_2O_4 \xrightarrow{135°} 4I_2O_5 + I_2$$

The structure of these oxides are unknown but I_4O_9 has been formulated as $I^{III}(I^{V}O_3)_3$ and I_2O_4 as $[IO]^+[IO_3]^-$.

I_2O_5 is notable in being one of the few chemicals that will oxidize CO rapidly and completely at room temperature:

$$5CO + I_2O_5 \longrightarrow I_2 + 5CO_2$$

The reaction forms the basis of a useful analytical method for determining the concentration of CO in the atmosphere or in other gaseous mixtures. I_2O_5 also oxidizes NO, C_2H_4 and H_2S. SO_3 and $S_2O_6F_2$ yield iodyl salts, $[IO_2]^+$, whereas concentrated H_2SO_4 and related acids reduce I_2O_5 to iodosyl derivatives, $[IO]^+$. Fluorination of I_2O_5 with F_2, BrF_3, SF_4 or $FClO_2$ yields IF_5 which itself reacts with the oxide to give OIF_3. It is also convenient to note here other related compounds which have recently been characterized: $I(OTeF_5)_3$, $O{=}I(OTeF_5)_3$, $I(OTeF_5)_5$, $[I(OTeF_5)_4]^-$ and $[O{=}I(OTeF_5)_4]^-$;[114] all have the expected structures (cf. pp. 688, 777, 899, 904).

[114] L. TUROWSKY and K. SEPPELT, *Z. anorg. allg. Chem.* **602**, 79–87 (1991), and references cited therein.

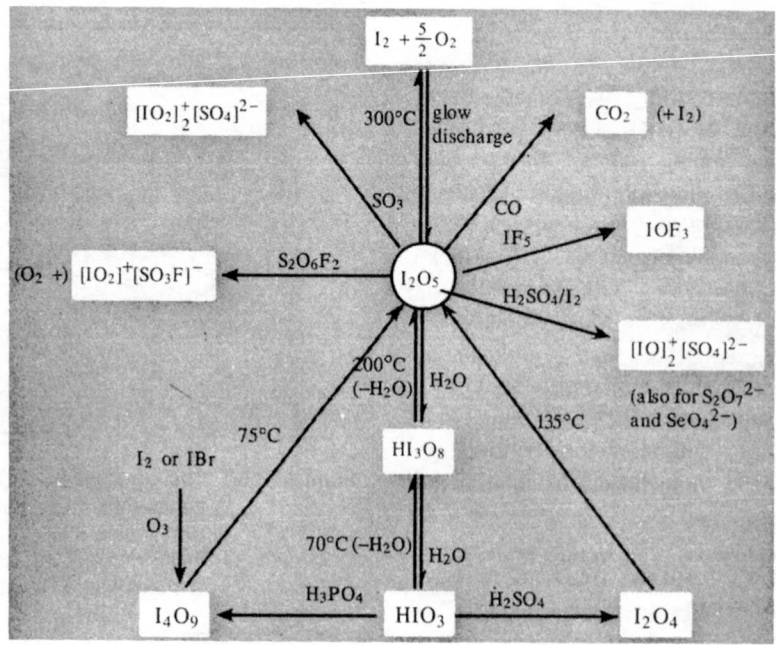

SCHEME: Preparation of reactions of iodine oxides.

In addition to the stable I_2O_5 and moderately stable I_4O_9 and I_2O_4, several short-lived radicals have been detected and characterized during γ-radiolysis and flash photolysis of iodates in aqueous alkali:

$$IO_3^- \xrightarrow{h\nu} IO_2 + O^-$$

$$IO_3^- + O^- \xrightarrow{H_2O} IO_3 + 2OH^-$$

$$IO_3^- + IO_2 \longrightarrow IO + IO_4^-$$

The endothermic radical IO has also been studied in the gas phase: the interatomic distance is 186.7 pm and the bond dissociation energy $\sim 175 \pm 20\,$kJ mol^{-1}. It thus appears that, although the higher oxides of iodine are much more stable than any oxide of Cl or Br, nevertheless, IO is much less stable than ClO (p. 849) or BrO (p. 851). Its enthalpy of formation and other thermodynamic properties are: $\Delta H_f^\circ(298\,\text{K})$ 175.1 kJ mol^{-1}, $\Delta G_f^\circ(298\,\text{K})$ 149.8 kJ mol^{-1}, $S^\circ(298\,\text{K})$ 245.5 J K^{-1}mol^{-1}.

17.2.8 Oxoacids and oxoacid salts

General considerations [115]

The preparative chemistry and technical applications of the halogen oxoacids and their salts have been actively pursued and developed for over two centuries (p. 790) and can now be very satisfactorily systematized in terms of general

___

[115] Ref. 23, Chemical properties of the halogens — redox properties: aqueous solutions, pp. 1188–95; Oxoacids and oxoacid salts of the halogens, pp. 1396–1465.

thermodynamic principles. The thermodynamic data are codified in the form of reduction potentials and equilibrium constants and these, coupled with the relative rates of competing reactions, allow a vast range of aqueous solution chemistry of the halogens to be interrelated. Thus, although all the halogens are to some extent soluble in water, extensive disproportionation reactions and/or mutual redox reactions with the solvent can occur to an extent that depends crucially on conditions such as pH and concentration (which influence the thermodynamic variables) and the presence of catalysts or light quanta (which can overcome kinetic activation barriers). Fluorine is again exceptional and, because of its very high standard reduction potential, $E^\circ(\frac{1}{2}F_2/F^-) + 2.866$ V, reacts very strongly with water at all values of pH (p. 629). Its inability to achieve formal oxidation states higher than $+1$ also limits the available oxoacids to hypofluorous acid HOF (p. 856). Numerous other oxoacids are known for the heavier halogens (Table 17.20) though most cannot be isolated pure and are stable only in aqueous solution or in the form of their salts. Anhydrous perchloric acid ($HClO_4$), iodic acid (HIO_3), paraperiodic acid (H_5IO_6) and metaperiodic acid (HIO_4) have been isolated as pure compounds.

The standard reduction potentials for Cl, Br and I species in acid and in alkaline aqueous solutions are summarized in Fig. 17.18. The couples $\frac{1}{2}X_2/X^-$ are independent of pH and, together with the value for F_2, indicate a steadily decreasing oxidizing power of the halogens in the sequence $F_2(+2.866$ V$) > Cl_2(+1.358$ V$) > Br_2(+1.066$ V$) > I_2(+0.536$V$)$. Remembering

Table 17.20 Oxoacids of the halogens

Generic name	Chlorine	Bromine	Iodine	Salts
Hypohalous acids[b]	HOCl[a]	HOBr[a]	HOI[a]	Hypohalites
Halous acids	HOClO[a]	(HOBrO?)[a]	—	Halites
Halic acids	HOClO$_2$[a]	HOBrO$_2$[a]	HOIO$_2$	Halates
Perhalic acids	HOClO$_3$	HOBrO$_3$[a]	HOIO$_3$, (HO)$_5$IO, H$_4$I$_2$O$_7$	Perhalates

[a]Stable only in aqueous solution.

[b]HOF also known (p. 856).

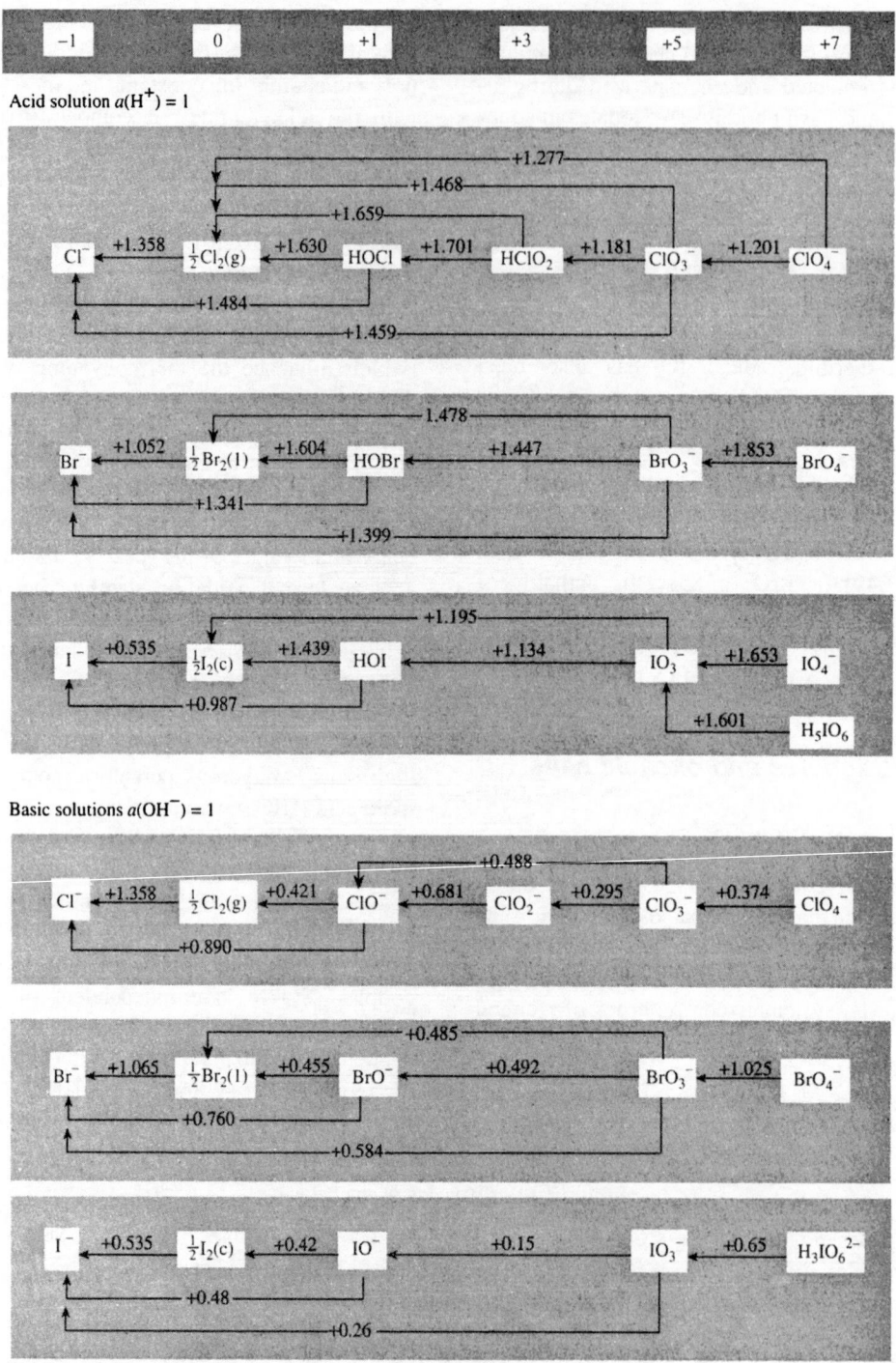

Figure 17.18   Standard reduction potentials for Cl, Br and I species in acid and alkaline solutions. For At see p. 886.

that $E^\circ(\frac{1}{2}O_2/H_2O) = 1.229\,V$ these values indicate that the potentials for the reaction.

$$X_2 + H_2O \longrightarrow \tfrac{1}{2}O_2 + 2H^+ + 2X^-$$

decrease in the sequence $F_2(+1.637\,V) > Cl_2(+0.129\,V) > Br_2(-0.163\,V) > I_2(-0.693\,V)$. As already mentioned, this implies that F_2 will oxidize water to O_2 and the same should happen with chlorine in the absence of sluggish kinetic factors. In fact, were it not for the further fortunate circumstance of an appreciably higher overvoltage for oxygen, chlorine would not be evolved during the electrolysis of aqueous chloride solutions at low current densities: the phenomenon is clearly of great technical importance for the industrial preparation of chlorine by electrolysis of brines (p. 798).

For all other couples in Fig. 17.18 (i.e. for all couples involving oxygenated species) an increase in pH causes a dramatic reduction in E° as expected (p. 435). For example, in acid solution the couple $BrO_3^-/\frac{1}{2}Br_2(l)$ refers to the

equilibrium reaction

$$BrO_3^- + 6H^+ + 5e^- \rightleftharpoons \tfrac{1}{2}Br_2 + 3H_2O;$$

$$(E^\circ\ 1.478\ V)$$

The equilibrium constant clearly depends on the sixth power of the hydrogen-ion concentration and, when this is reduced (say to 10^{-14} in $1\,M$ alkali), the potential is likewise diminished by an amount $\sim(RT/nF)\log_{10}[H^+]^6$, i.e. by *ca.* $(0.0592/5) \times 14 \times 6 \simeq 0.99V$. In agreement with this (Fig. 17.18) the potential at pH 14 is $0.485\,V$ (calc $\sim0.49\,V$) for the reaction

$$BrO_3^- + 3H_2O + 5e^- \rightleftharpoons \tfrac{1}{2}Br_2(1) + 6OH^-$$

The data in Fig. 17.18 are presented in graphical form in Fig. 17.19 which shows the volt-equivalent diagrams (p. 436) for acid and alkaline solutions. It is clear from these that Cl_2 and Br_2 are much more stable towards disproportionation in acid solution (concave angle at X_2) than in alkaline solutions (convex angle). In terms of

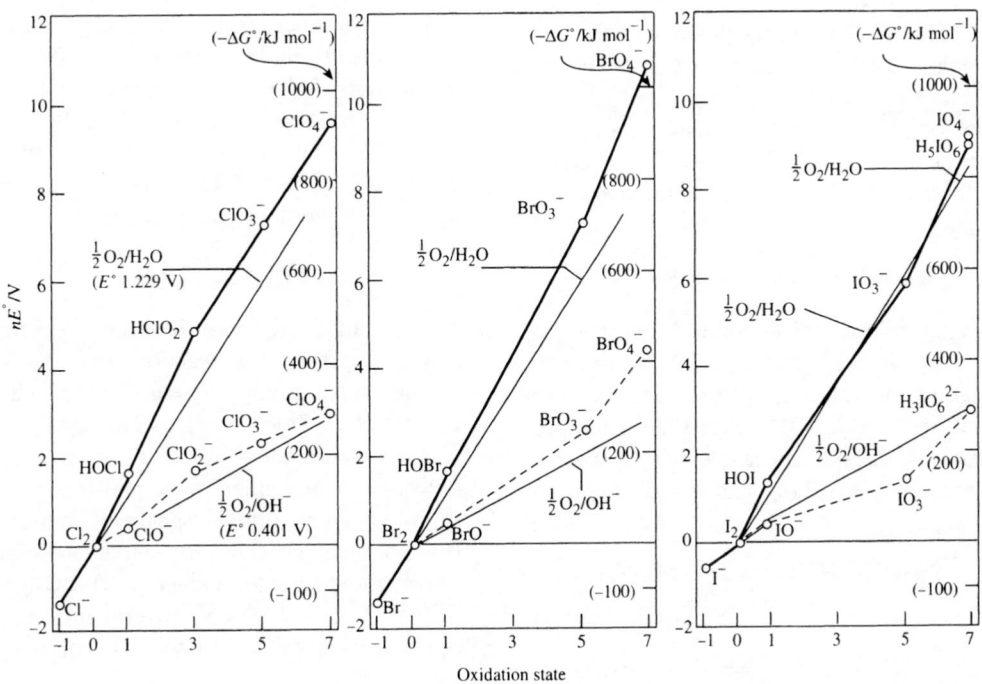

Figure 17.19 Volt-equivalent diagrams for Cl, Br and I.

equilibrium constants:

acid solution :

$$X_2 + H_2O \rightleftharpoons HOX + H^+ + X^-;$$

$$K_{ac} = \frac{[HOX][H^+][X^-]}{[X_2]}$$

alkaline solution :

$$X_2 + 2OH^- \rightleftharpoons OX^- + H_2O + X^-;$$

$$K_{alk} = \frac{[OX^-][X^-]}{[X_2][OH^-]^2}$$

For Cl_2, Br_2 and I_2, K_{ac} is $4.2 \times 10^{-4}, 7.2 \times 10^{-9}$ and 2.0×10^{-13} mol^2 l^{-2} respectively, thereby favouring the free halogens, whereas K_{alk} is $7.5 \times 10^{15}, 2 \times 10^8$ and 30 mol^{-1} l respectively, indicating a tendency to disproportionation which is overwhelming for Cl_2 but progressively less pronounced for Br_2 and I_2. In actuality the situation is somewhat more complicated because of the tendency of the hypohalite ions themselves to disproportionate further to produce the corresponding halite ions:

$$3XO^- \rightleftharpoons 2X^- + XO_3^-$$

The equilibrium constant for this reaction is very favourable in each case: 10^{27} for ClO^-, 10^{15} for BrO^-, and 10^{20} for IO^-. However, particularly in the case of ClO^-, the rate of disproportionation is slow at room temperature and only becomes appreciable above 70°. Similarly, the disproportionation

$$4ClO_3^- \rightleftharpoons Cl^- + 3ClO_4^-$$

has an equilibrium constant of 10^{20} but the reaction is very slow even at 100°. By contrast, as indicated by the concavity of the volt-equivalent curve at BrO_3^- and IO_3^- (Fig. 17.19), the bromate and iodate ions are stable with respect to disproportionation (in both acid and alkaline solutions), e.g.:

$$7IO_3^- + 9H_2O + 7H^+ \rightleftharpoons I_2 + 5H_5IO_6;$$

$$K = 10^{-85} \text{ mol}^{-8} \text{ l}^8$$

$$4IO_3^- + 3OH^- + 3H_2O \rightleftharpoons I^- + 3H_3IO_6^{2-};$$

$$K = 10^{-44} \text{ mol}^{-3} \text{ l}^3$$

More detailed consideration of these various equilibria and other redox reactions of the halogen oxoacids will be found under the separate headings below. As expected, the *rates* of redox reactions of the halogen oxyanions will depend, sometimes crucially, on the precise conditions used. However, as a very broad generalization, they tend to become progressively faster as the oxidation state of the halogen decreases, i.e.:

$$ClO_4^- < ClO_3^- < ClO_2^- \ll ClO^- \approx Cl_2;$$

$$BrO_4^- < BrO_3^- \ll BrO^- \approx Br_2;$$

$$IO_4^- < IO_3^- < I_2; \text{ and } ClO_4^- < BrO_4^- < IO_4^-.$$

The strengths of the monobasic acids increase rapidly with increase in oxidation state of the halogen in accordance with Pauling's rules (p. 50). For example, approximate values of pK_a are: HOCl 7.52, HOClO 1.94, HOClO$_2$ − 3, HOClO$_3$ − 10. The pK_a values of related acids increase in the sequence Cl < Br < I.

Hypohalous acids, HOX, and hypohalites, XO$^-$ [98,115]

Hypofluorous acid is the most recent of the halogen oxoacids to be prepared.[116] Traces were obtained in 1968 by photolysis of a mixture of F_2 and H_2O in a matrix of solid N_2 at 14–20 K but weighable amounts of the compound were first obtained by M. H. Studier and E. H. Appelman in 1971 by the fluorination of ice:

$$F_2 + H_2O \underset{-40°C}{\rightleftharpoons} HOF + HF$$

The isolation of HOF depends on removing it rapidly from the reaction zone so that it is prevented from reacting further with HF, F_2 or H_2O (see below). The method used was to recirculate F_2 at ~100 mmHg through a Kel-F U-tube filled with moistened Räschig rings cut from Teflon "spaghetti" tubing (Kel-F is polymerized chlorotrifluoroethene; Teflon is polymerized tetrafluoroethene). The U-tube was held at about −40°C and the effluent was passed through U-tubes cooled to −50° and −79° to

116 E. H. APPELMAN, *Acc. Chem. Res.* **6**, 113–7 (1973).

remove water and HF, and, finally, through a U-tube at $-183°$ to trap the HOF. The use of the $-50°$ trap was found to be critical because without it all of the HOF was caught in the $-79°$ with the H_2O, from which it could not be isolated because of subsequent reaction.

HOF is a white solid which melts at $-117°$ to a pale-yellow liquid. Its bp (extrap) is somewhat below room temperature and its volatility is thus comparable to that of HF with which it is always slightly contaminated. Spectroscopic data establish a nonlinear structure with H–O 96.4 pm, O–F 144.2 pm, and bond angle H–O–F $97.2°$: this is the smallest known bond angle at an unrestricted O atom (cf. H–O–H $104.7°$, F–O–F $103.2°$). It has been suggested that this arises in part from electrostatic attraction of the 2 terminal atoms, since nmr data lead to a charge of $\sim+0.5e$ on H and $\sim-0.5e$ on F. The negative charge on F is intermediate between those estimated for F in HF and OF_2 and this emphasizes the strictly formal nature of the +1 oxidation state for F in HOF. Subsequently, the crystal structure of HOF was determined at $-160°$ in an experimental *tour de force*.[117] The dimensions were similar to those found for the gaseous molecule except for the expected artefact of a slightly shorter H–O distance due to the X-ray method (H–O 0.78 pm, O–F 144.2 pm, angle HOF $101°$). The molecules are arranged in chains along a screw axis parallel to the *b* axis of the crystal as a result of almost linear O–H···O bonds (angle $163°$, O···O 289.5 pm).

The most prominent chemical property of HOF is its instability. It decomposes spontaneously (sometimes explosively) to HF and O_2 with a half-life of *ca.* 30 min in a Teflon apparatus at room temperature and 100 mmHg. It reacts rapidly with water to produce HF, H_2O_2 and O_2; in dilute aqueous acid H_2O_2 is the predominant product whereas in alkaline solution O_2 is the principal O-containing product. The kinetics of these processes have been studied and, by use of ^{18}O-enriched H_2O_2, it has

been shown, uniquely, that the O_2 formed in the reaction, $[HOF + H_2O_2 \rightarrow O_2 + HF + H_2O]$, contains a substantial amount of oxygen from the HOF.[118]

HOF reacts with HF to reverse the equilibrium used in its preparation. It does not dehydrate to its formal anhydride OF_2 but in the presence of H_2O it reacts with F_2 to form this species.

$$F_2 + HOF \xrightarrow{H_2O} OF_2 + HF$$

This reaction does not occur in the gas phase, however, in the absence of H_2O.

By contrast with the elusive though isolable HOF, the history of HOCl goes back over two centuries to the earliest experiments of C. W. Scheele with Cl_2 in 1774 (p. 792), and the bleaching and sterilizing action of hypochlorites have long been used both industrially and domestically. HOCl, HOBr and HOI are all highly reactive, relatively unstable compounds that are known primarily in aqueous solutions. The most convenient preparation of such solutions is by perturbing the hydrolytic disproportionation equilibrium (p. 856):

$$X_2 + H_2O \rightleftharpoons H^+ + X^- + HOX$$

by addition of HgO or Ag_2O so as to remove the halide ions. On an industrial scale, aqueous solutions of HOCl (containing Cl^-) are readily prepared by reacting Cl_2 with aqueous alkali. With strong bases {NaOH, $Ca(OH)_2$} the reaction proceeds via the intermediate formation of hypochlorite, but this intermediate product is not formed with weaker bases such as $NaHCO_3$ or $CaCO_3$:

$$Cl_2 + 2OH^- \xrightarrow{aq} \{ClO^- + Cl^- + H_2O\}$$

$$\xrightarrow{Cl_2} 2HOCl + 2Cl^-$$

Chloride-free solutions (up to 5 M concentration) can be made by treating Cl_2O with water at $0°$ or industrially by passing Cl_2O gas into water. In fact, concentrated solutions of HOCl also contain appreciable amounts of Cl_2O which can form a

117 W. POLL, G. PAWELKE, D. MOOTZ and E. H. APPELMAN, *Angew. Chem. Int. Edn. Engl.* **27**, 392–3 (1988).

118 E. H. APPELMAN and R. C. THOMPSON, *J. Am. Chem. Soc.*, **106**, 4167–72 (1984).

separate layer and which is probably the source of the yellow colour of such solutions:

$$2HOCl(aq) \rightleftharpoons Cl_2O(aq) + H_2O(l);$$

$$K(0°C) = 3.55 \times 10^{-3} mol^{-1} l$$

Organic solutions can be obtained in high yield by extracting HOCl from Cl^--containing aqueous solutions into polar solvents such as ketones, nitriles or esters. Electrodialysis using semipermeable membranes affords an alternative route.

Solutions of the corresponding hypohalites can be made by the rapid disproportionation of the individual halogens in cold alkaline solutions (p. 856):

$$X_2 + 2OH^- \rightleftharpoons X^- + OX^- + H_2O$$

Such solutions are necessarily contaminated with halide ions and with the products of any subsequent decomposition of the hypohalite anions themselves. Alternative routes are the electrochemical oxidation of halides in cold dilute solutions or the chemical oxidation of bromides and iodides:

$$X^- + OCl^- \longrightarrow OX^- + Cl^- \quad (X = Br, I)$$

$$I^- + OBr^- \longrightarrow OI^- + Br^-$$

Hypochlorites can also be made by careful neutralization of aqueous solutions of hypochlorous acid or Cl_2O.

The most stable solid hypochlorites are those of Li, Ca, Sr and Ba (see below). NaOCl has only poor stability and cannot be isolated pure; KOCl is known only in solution, Mg yields a basic hypochlorite and impure Ag and Zn hypochlorites have been reported. Hydrated salts are also known. Solid, yellow, hydrated hypobromites $NaOBr.xH_2O$ ($x = 5, 7$) and $KOBr.3H_2O$ can be crystallized from solutions obtained by adding Br_2 to cold conc solutions of MOH but the compounds decompose above 0°C. No solid metal hypoiodites have yet been isolated.

HOCl is more stable than HOBr and HOI and its microwave spectrum in the gas phase confirms the expected nonlinear geometry with H–O 97 pm, O–Cl 169.3 pm, and angle H–O–Cl $103 \pm 3°$ (cf. HOF, p. 857). All three

hypohalous acids are weak and solutions of their salts are therefore alkaline since the equilibrium

$$OX^- + H_2O \rightleftharpoons HOX + OH^-$$

lies well to the right. Except at high pH, hypohalite solutions contain significant amounts of the undissociated acid. Approximate values for the acid dissociation constants K_a at room temperature are HOCl 2.9×10^{-8}, HOBr 5×10^{-9}, HOI $\sim 10^{-11}$: these values are close to those of many α-aminoacids and may also be compared with carbonic acid K_a 4.3×10^{-7}, which is some 10 times stronger than HOCl, and phenol, which has K_a 1.3×10^{-10}.

The manner and rate of decomposition of hypohalous acids (and hypohalite ions) in solution are much influenced by the concentration, pH and temperature of the solutions, by the presence or absence of salts which can act as catalysts, promotors or activators, and by light quanta. The main competing modes of decomposition are:

$$2HOX \longrightarrow 2H^+ + 2X^- + O_2$$

$$(\text{or } 2OX^- \longrightarrow 2X^- + O_2)$$

and $\quad 3HOX \longrightarrow 3H^+ + 2X^- + XO_3^-$

$$(\text{or } 3OX^- \longrightarrow 2X^- + XO_3^-)$$

The acids decompose more readily than the anions so hypohalites are stabilized in basic solutions. The stability of the anions diminishes in the sequence $ClO^- > BrO^- > IO^-$.

Hypochlorites are amongst the strongest of the more common oxidizing agents and they react with inorganic species, usually by the net transfer of an O atom. Kinetic studies suggest that the oxidizing agent can be either HOCl or OCl^- in a given reaction, but rarely both simultaneously. Some typical examples are in Table 17.21. Hypochlorites react with ammonia and organic amino compounds to form chloramines. The characteristic "chlorine" odour of water that has been sterilized with hypochlorite is, in fact, due to chloramines produced from attack on bacteria. By contrast, hypobromites

Table 17.21   Oxidation of inorganic substrates with HOCl or OCl⁻

HOCl		OCl⁻	
Substrate	Products	Substrate	Products
HCO_2^-	CO_3^{2-}	ClO^-	ClO_2^-
$HC_2O_4^-$	CO_2	ClO_2^-	ClO_3^-
OCN^-	CO_3^{2-}, N_2, NO_3^-	CN^-	OCN^-
NH_3	NCl_3	NH_3	NH_2Cl
NO_2^-	NO_3^-	SO_3^{2-}	SO_4^{2-}
H_2O_2	O_2	IO_3^-	IO_4^-
S	SO_4^{2-}	Mn^{2+}	MnO_4^-
Br^-	Br_2 (acid)	Br^-	OBr^-, BrO_3^- (alkaline)
I^-	I_2 (acid)	I^-	OI^-, IO_3^- (alkaline)

oxidize amines quantitatively to N_2, a reaction that is exploited in the analysis of urea:

$$(NH_2)_2CO + 3OBr^- + 2OH^- \longrightarrow N_2 + CO_3^{2-}$$
$$+ 3Br^- + 3H_2O$$

Other uses of hypohalous acids and hypohalites are described in the Panel.

This section concludes with a reminder that, in addition to the hypohalous acids HOX and metal hypohalites $M(OX)_n$, various covalent (molecular) hypohalites are known. Hypochlorites are summarized in Table 17.22. All are volatile liquids or gases at room temperature and are discussed elsewhere (see Index). Organic hypohalites are unstable and rapidly expel HX or RX to form the corresponding aldehyde or ketone:

$$ROH + HOX \longrightarrow ROX + H_2O$$

$$RCH_2OX \longrightarrow RCHO + HX$$

$$RR'CHOX \longrightarrow RR'C{=}O + HX$$

$$RR'R''COX \xrightarrow{hv} RR'C{=}O + R''X$$

Halous acids, HOXO, and halites, XO_2^- [98,115,119,120]

Chlorous acid is the least stable of the oxoacids of chlorine; it cannot be isolated but is known in dilute aqueous solution. HOBrO and HOIO are even less stable, and, if they exist at all, have only a fleeting presence in aqueous solutions. Several chlorites have been isolated and $NaClO_2$ is sufficiently stable to be manufactured as an article of commerce on the kilotonne pa scale. Little reliable information is available on bromites and still less is established for iodites which are essentially non-existent.

$HClO_2$ is formed (together with $HClO_3$) during the decomposition of aqueous solutions of ClO_2 (p. 847) but the best laboratory preparation is to treat an aqueous suspension of $Ba(ClO_2)_2$ with

[119] G. GORDON, R. G. KIEFFER and D. H. ROSENBLATT, *Progr. Inorg. Chem.* **15**, 201–86 (1972). The first half of this review deals with the aqueous solution chemistry of chlorous acid and chlorites.
[120] F. SOLYMOSI, *Structure and Stability of Salts of the Halogen Oxyacids in the Solid Phase*, Wiley, UK, 1978, 468 pp.

Table 17.22   Physical properties of some molecular hypochlorites

Compound	MP/°C	BP/°C	Compound	MP/°C	BP/°C
$ClONO_2$	−107	18	$ClOSeF_5$	−115	31.5
$ClOClO_3$	−117	44.5	$ClOTeF_5$	−121	38.5
$ClOSO_2F$	−84.3	45.1	$ClOOSF_5$	−130	26.4
$ClOSF_5$	—	8.9	$ClOOCF_3$	−132	−22

Some Uses of Hypohalous Acids and Hypohalites

In addition to the applications indicated on p. 858, hypohalous acids are useful halogenating agents for both aromatic and aliphatic compounds. HOBr and HOI are usually generated *in situ*. The ease of aromatic halogenation increases in the sequence $OCl^- < OBr^- < OI^-$ and is facilitated by salts of Pb or Ag. Another well-known reaction of hypohalites is their cleavage of methyl ketones to form carboxylates and haloform:

$$RCOCH_3 + 3OX^- \longrightarrow RCO_2^- + 2OH^- + CHX_3$$

This is the basis of the iodoform test for the CH_3CO group. In addition to these reactions there is considerable industrial use for HOCl and hypochlorites in the manufacture of hydrazine (p. 427), chlorhydrins and α-glycols:

By far the largest tonnage of hypochlorites is used for bleaching and sterilizing. "Liquid bleach" is an alkaline solution of NaOCl (pH $\geq$ 11); domestic bleaches have about 5% "available chlorine" content[†] whereas small-scale commercial installations such as laundries use ~12% concentration. Chlorinated trisodium phosphate, which is a crystalline efflorescent product of approximate empirical composition $(Na_3PO_4.11H_2O)_4.NaOCl$, has 3.5–4.5% available Cl and is used in automatic dishwasher detergents, scouring powders, and acid metal cleaners for dairy equipment. Paper and pulp bleaching is effected by "bleach liquor", a solution of $Ca(OCl)_2$ and $CaCl_2$, yielding ~85 g l^{-1} of "available chlorine". Powdered calcium hypochlorite, $Ca(OCl)_2.2H_2O$ (70% available Cl), is used for swimming-pool sanitation whereas "bleaching powder", $Ca(OCl)_2.CaCl_2.Ca(OH)_2.2H_2O$ (obtained by the action of Cl_2 gas on slaked lime) contains 35% available Cl and is used for general bleaching and sanitation:

$$3Ca(OH)_2 + 2Cl_2 \longrightarrow Ca(OCl)_2.CaCl_2.Ca(OH)_2.2H_2O$$

The speciality chemical LiOCl (40% "Cl") is used when calcium is contra-indicated, such as in the sanitation of hard water and in some dairy applications. Some idea of the scale of these applications can be gained from the following production figures which relate to the USA:[98]

LiOCl ~ 2500 tonnes pa. Price (1993) ~\$ 2.80/kg.

NaOCl ~ 250 000 tpa (on a dry basis) used mainly for household liquid bleach, laundries, disinfection of swimming pools, municipal water supplies and sewage, and the industrial manufacture of N_2H_4 and organic chemicals.

NaOCl.$(Na_3PO_4.11H_2O)_4$ was commercialized in 1930 and demand rose to 81 000 tonnes in 1973. Use has dropped sharply since about 1980 (37 000 tonnes in 1988, price \$0.70/kg).

$Ca(OCl)_2$ ~ 85 000 tpa plus production facilities in numerous other countries (e.g. the USSR, Japan, South Africa and Canada).

Bleaching power is now much less used than formerly in highly industrialized countries but is still manufactured on a large scale in less-developed regions. In the USA its production peaked at 133 000 tonnes in 1923 but had fallen to 23 600 tonnes by 1955 and has not been reported since, though ~1160 tonnes per annum were imported during the 1980s.

[†] "Available chlorine" content is defined as the weight of Cl_2 which liberates the same amount of I_2 from HI as does a given weight of the compound; it is often expressed as a percentage. For example, from the two (possibly hypothetical) stoichiometric equations $Cl_2 + 2HI \rightarrow I_2 + 2HCl$ and $LiOCl + 2HI \rightarrow I_2 + LiCl + H_2O$ it can be seen that 1 mol of I_2 is liberated by 70.92 g Cl_2 or by 58.4 g LiOCl. Whence the "available chlorine" content of pure LiOCl is $(70.92/58.4) \times 100 = 121\%$. The commercial product is usually diluted by sulfates to about one-third of this strength (see below).

dilute sulfuric acid:

$$Ba(OH)_2(aq) + H_2O_2 + ClO_2 \longrightarrow$$
$$Ba(ClO_2)_2 + 2H_2O + O_2$$

$$Ba(ClO_2)_2(suspension) + dil\ H_2SO_4 \longrightarrow$$
$$BaSO_4 \downarrow + 2HClO_2$$

Evidence for the undissociated acid comes from spectroscopic data but the solutions cannot be concentrated without decomposition. $HClO_2$ is a moderately strong acid $K_a(25°C)$ 1.1×10^{-2} (cf H_2SeO_4 K_a 1.2×10^{-2}, $H_4P_2O_7$ K_a 2.6×10^{-2}).

The decomposition of chlorous acid depends sensitively on its concentration, pH and the presence of catalytically active ions such as Cl^- which is itself produced during the decomposition. The main mode of decomposition (particularly if Cl^- is present) is to form ClO_2:

$$5HClO_2 \longrightarrow 4ClO_2 + Cl^- + H^+ + 2H_2O;$$
$$\Delta G° -144\ kJ\ mol^{-1}$$

Competing modes produce ClO_3^- or evolve O_2:

$$3HClO_2 \longrightarrow 2ClO_3^- + Cl^- + 3H^+;$$
$$\Delta G° -139\ kJ\ mol^{-1}$$

$$HClO_2 \longrightarrow Cl^- + O_2 + H^+;$$
$$\Delta G° -123\ kJ\ mol^{-1}$$

Metal chlorites are normally made by reduction of aqueous solutions of ClO_2 in the presence of the metal hydroxide or carbonate. As with the preparation of $Ba(ClO_2)_2$ above, the reducing agent is usually a peroxide since this adds no contaminant to the resulting chlorite solution:

$$2ClO_2 + O_2^{2-} \longrightarrow 2ClO_2^- + O_2$$

The ClO_2^- ion is nonlinear, as expected, and X-ray studies of NH_4ClO_2 (at $-35°$) and of $AgClO_2$ lead to the dimensions Cl–O 156 pm, angle O–Cl–O 111°. The chlorites of the alkali metals and alkaline earth metals are colourless or pale yellow. Heavy metal chlorites tend to explode or detonate when heated or struck (e.g. those of Ag^+, Hg^+, Tl^+, Pb^{2+} and also those of Cu^{2+} and NH_4^+). Sodium chlorite is the only one to

have sufficient stability and to be sufficiently inexpensive to be a major article of commerce (see below).

Anhydrous $NaClO_2$ crystallizes from aqueous solutions above 37.4° but below this temperature the trihydrate is obtained. The commercial product contains about 80% $NaClO_2$. The anhydrous salt forms colourless deliquescent crystals which decompose when heated to 175–200°: the reaction is predominantly a disproportionation to ClO_3^- and Cl^- but about 5% of molecular O_2 is also released (based on the ClO_2^- consumed). Neutral and alkaline aqueous solutions of $NaClO_2$ are stable at room temperature (despite their thermodynamic instability towards disproportionation as evidenced by the reduction potentials on p. 854). This is a kinetic activation-energy effect and, when the solutions are heated near to boiling, slow disproportionation occurs:

$$3ClO_2^- \longrightarrow 2ClO_3^- + Cl^-$$

Photochemical decomposition is rapid and the products obtained depend on the pH of the solution;

$$\text{at pH 8.4:}\ \ 6ClO_2^- \xrightarrow{h\nu} 2ClO_3^- + 4Cl^- + 3O_2$$

$$\text{at pH 4.0:}\ 10ClO_2^- \xrightarrow{h\nu} 2ClO_3^- + 6Cl^-$$
$$+ 2ClO_4^- + 3O_2$$

The stoichiometry in acid solution implies that, in addition to the more usual disproportionation into ClO_3^- and Cl^-, the following disproportionation also occurs:

$$2ClO_2^- \longrightarrow Cl^- + ClO_4^-$$

The mechanisms of these various reactions have been the object of many studies.[98,115,119]

The main commercial applications of $NaClO_2$ are in the bleaching and stripping of textiles, and as a source of ClO_2 where required volumes are comparatively small. It is also used as an oxidant for removal of nitrogen oxide pollutants from industrial off-gases. The specific oxidizing properties of $NaClO_2$ towards certain malodorous or toxic compounds such as unsaturated aldehydes, mercaptans, thioethers,

H_2S and HCN have likewise led to its use for scrubbing the off-gases of processes where these noxious pollutants are formed. Production statistics are rather sparse but the main production plants are in Europe, which produced some 11 000 tonnes pa in 1990 and the USA, where production is expected to exceed 10 000 tpa in 1995. Other major producers are in Japan ($\sim$5000 tpa) and Canada (2700 tpa in 1990). The 1991 price for technical grade $NaClO_2$ in the USA was \$2.65/kg.

Crystalline barium bromite $Ba(BrO_2)_2.H_2O$ was first isolated in 1959; it can be made by treating the hypobromite with Br_2 at pH 11.2 and 0°C, followed by slow evaporation. $Sr(BrO_2)_2.2H_2O$ was obtained similarly.

Halic acids, $HOXO_2$, and halates, XO_3^{-} [121,122]

Disproportionation of X_2 in hot alkaline solution has long been used to synthesize chlorates and bromates (see oxidation state diagrams, p. 855):

$$3X_2 + 6OH^- \longrightarrow XO_3^- + 5X^- + 3H_2O$$

For example, J. von Liebig developed the technical preparation of $KClO_3$ by passing Cl_2 into a warm suspension of $Ca(OH)_2$ and then adding KCl to enable the less-soluble chlorate to crystallize on cooling:

$$6Ca(OH)_2 + 6Cl_2 \longrightarrow Ca(ClO_3)_2 + 5CaCl_2$$
$$+ 6H_2O$$
$$Ca(ClO_3)_2 + 2KCl \longrightarrow 2KClO_3 + CaCl_2$$

However, only one-sixth of the halogen present is oxidized and alternative routes are more generally preferred for large-scale manufacture. Thus, the most important halate, $NaClO_3$, is manufactured

on a huge scale[†] by the electrolysis of brine in a diaphragmless cell which promotes efficient mixing. Under these conditions, the Cl_2 produced by anodic oxidation of Cl^- reacts with cathodic OH^- to give hypochlorite which then either disproportionates or is itself further anodically oxidized to ClO_3^-:

anode: $Cl^- \rightarrow \frac{1}{2}Cl_2 + e^-$;

cathode: $H_2O + e^- \rightarrow \frac{1}{2}H_2 + OH^-$

mixing: $Cl_2 + 2OH^- \rightarrow Cl^- + OCl^- + H_2O$

further disproportionation:

$$3OCl^- \rightarrow ClO_3^- + 2Cl^-$$

further anodic oxidation:

$$OCl^- + 2H_2O \rightarrow ClO_3^- + 2H_2$$

Modern cells employ arrays of anodes (TiO_2 coated with a noble metal) and cathodes (mild steel) spaced 3 mm apart and carrying current at 2700 A m^{-2} into brine (80–100 g l^{-1}) at 60–80°C. Under these conditions current efficiency can reach 93% and 1 tonne of $NaClO_3$ can be obtained from 565 kg NaCl and 4535 kWh of electricity. The off-gas H_2 is also collected.

Bromates and iodates are prepared on a much smaller scale, usually by chemical oxidation. For example, Br^- is oxidized to BrO_3^- by aqueous hypochlorite (conveniently effected by passing

[121] Ref. 23, pp. 1418–35, Halic acids and halates.
[122] S. K. MENDIRATTA and B. L. DUNCAN, Chloric acid and chlorates, *Kirk–Othmer Encyclopedia of Chemical Technology*, 4th edn., Vol. 5, pp. 998–1016, Wiley, New York, 1993.

[†] World production of $NaClO_3$ (1989–91) exceeds 2 billion tonnes pa, Canada alone producing some 872 000 tpa, USA 630 000 tpa and Europe 421 000 tpa. Consumption in the USA exceeds production by some 50%, the rest being imported. The 1991 price ($\sim$\$480/tonne) was similar in both North America and Europe where, interestingly, the main consumers are Finland (156 800 tpa) and Sweden (109 700 tpa). The overwhelming use of $NaClO_3$ (95% in the USA) is in the manufacture of ClO_2, mainly for bleaching paper pulp (p. 846). Other uses are to make perchlorates and other chlorates (3%), in uranium production (1% but declining sharply) and for agricultural uses (0.7%) such as herbicides, cotton defoliants and soya-bean desiccants. The use of $NaClO_3$ in pyrotechnic formulations is hampered by its hygroscopicity. $KClO_3$ does not suffer this disadvantage and is unexcelled as an oxidizer in fireworks and flares, the colours being obtained by admixture with salts of Sr (red), Ba (green), Cu (blue), etc. In addition $KClO_3$ is a crucial component in the head of "safety matches" ($KClO_3$, S, Sb_2S_3, powdered glass and dextrin paste). Its price in very similar to that of $NaClO_3$.

Cl_2 into alkaline solutions of Br^-). Iodates can be prepared either by direct high-pressure oxidation of alkali metal iodides with oxygen at $600°$ or by oxidation of I_2 with chlorates:

$$I_2 + NaClO_3 \longrightarrow 2NaIO_3 + Cl_2$$

Salts of other metals are obtained by metathesis, and aqueous solutions of the corresponding acids are obtained by controlled addition of sulfuric acid to the barium salts:

$$Ba(XO_3)_2 + H_2SO_4 \longrightarrow 2HXO_3 + BaSO_4$$

Chloric acid, $HClO_3$, is fairly stable in cold water up to about 30% concentration but, on being warmed, such solutions evolve Cl_2 and ClO_2. Evaporation under reduced pressure can increase the concentration up to about 40% ($\sim HClO_3.7H_2O$) but thereafter it is accompanied by decomposition to $HClO_4$ and the evolution of Cl_2, O_2 and ClO_2:

$$8HClO_3 \longrightarrow 4HClO_4 + 2H_2O + 2Cl_2 + 3O_2$$

$$3HClO_3 \longrightarrow HClO_4 + H_2O + 2ClO_2$$

Likewise, aqueous $HBrO_3$ can be concentrated under reduced pressure to about 50% concentration ($\sim HBrO_3.7H_2O$) before decomposition obtrudes:

$$4HBrO_3 \longrightarrow 2H_2O + 2Br_2 + 5O_2$$

Both chloric and bromic acids are strong acids in aqueous solution ($pK_a \lesssim 0$) whereas iodic acid is slightly weaker, with pK_a 0.804, i.e. K_a 0.157.

Iodic acid is more conveniently synthesized by oxidation of an aqueous suspension of I_2 either electrolytically or with fuming HNO_3. Crystallization from acid solution yields colourless, orthorhombic crystals of $\alpha\text{-}HIO_3$ which feature H-bonded pyramidal molecules of $HOIO_2$: $r(I-O)$ 181 pm, $r(I-OH)$ 189 pm, angle $O-I-O$ 101.4°, angle $O-I-(OH)$ 97°. When heated to $\sim 100°C$ iodic acid partly dehydrates to HI_3O_8 (p. 852); this comprises an H-bonded array of composition $HOIO_2.I_2O_5$ in which the HIO_3 has almost identical dimensions to those in $\alpha\text{-}HIO_3$. Further heating to 200° results in complete dehydration to I_2O_5. In concentrated aqueous solutions of HIO_3, the iodate ions formed by deprotonation react with undissociated acid according to the equilibrium

$$IO_3^- + HIO_3 \rightleftharpoons [H(IO_3)_2]^-; \quad K \approx 4\,l\,mol^{-1}$$

Accordingly, crystallization of iodates from solutions containing an excess of HIO_3 sometimes results in the formation of hydrogen biiodates, $M^I H(IO_3)_2$, or even dihydrogen triiodates, $M^I H_2(IO_3)_3$.

Chlorates and bromates feature the expected pyramidal ions XO_3^- with angles close to the tetrahedral (106–107°). With iodates the interatomic angles at iodine are rather less (97–105°) and there are three short $I-O$ distances (177–190 pm) and three somewhat longer distances (251–300 pm) leading to distorted perovskite structures (p. 963) with pseudo-sixfold coordination of iodine and piezoelectric properties (p. 58). In $Sr(IO_3)_2.H_2O$ the coordination number of iodine rises to 7 and this increases still further to 8 (square antiprism) in $Ce(IO_3)_4$ and $Zr(IO_3)_4$.

The modes of thermal decomposition of the halates and their complex oxidation-reduction chemistry reflect the interplay of both thermodynamic and kinetic factors. On the one hand, thermodynamically feasible reactions may be sluggish, whilst, on the other, traces of catalyst may radically alter the course of the reaction. In general, for a given cation, thermal stability decreases in the sequence iodate > chlorate > bromate, but the mode and ease of decomposition can be substantially modified. For example, alkali metal chlorates decompose by disproportionation when fused:

$$4ClO_3^- \longrightarrow Cl^- + 3ClO_4^-$$

e.g. $LiClO_3$, mp 125° (d 270°); $NaClO_3$, mp 248° (d 265°); $KClO_3$, mp 368° (d 400°).[†] However, in

---

[†] Note, however, that thermal decomposition of NH_4ClO_3 begins at 50°C and the compound explodes on further heating; this much lower decomposition temperature may result from prior proton transfer to give the less-stable acid: [$NH_4ClO_3 \longrightarrow NH_3 + HClO_3$].

A similar thermal instability afflicts NH_4BrO_3 (d $-5°$) and NH_4IO_3 (d $\sim 100°$).

the presence of a transition-metal catalyst such as MnO_2 decomposition of $KClO_3$ to KCl and oxygen begins at about $70°$ and is vigorous at $100°$

$$2ClO_3^- \longrightarrow 2Cl^- + 3O_2$$

This is, indeed, a classic laboratory method for preparing small amounts of oxygen (p. 603). For bromates and iodates, disproportionation to halide and perhalate is not thermodynamically feasible and decomposition occurs either with formation of halide and liberation of O_2 (as in the catalysed decomposition of ClO_3^- just considered), or by formation of the oxide:

$$4XO_3^- \longrightarrow 2O^{2-} + 2X_2 + 5O_2$$

For all three halates (in the absence of disproportionation) the preferred mode of decomposition depends, again, on both thermodynamic and kinetic considerations. Oxide formation tends to be favoured by the presence of a strongly polarizing cation (e.g. magnesium, transition-metal and lanthanide halates), whereas halide formation is observed for alkali-metal, alkaline- earth and silver halates.

The oxidizing power of the halate ions in aqueous solution, as measured by their standard reduction potentials (p. 854), decreases in the sequence bromate $\gtrsim$ chlorate > iodate but the rates of reaction follow the sequence iodate > bromate > chlorate. In addition, both the thermodynamic oxidizing power and the rate of reaction depend markedly on the hydrogen-ion concentration of the solution, being substantially greater in acid than in alkaline conditions (p. 855).

An important series of reactions, which illustrates the diversity of behaviour to be expected, is the comproportionation of halates and halides. Bromides are oxidized quantitatively to bromine and iodides to iodine, this latter reaction being much used in volumetric analysis:

$$XO_3^- + 5X^- + 6H^+ \longrightarrow 3X_2 + 3H_2O$$

$$(X = Cl, Br, I)$$

Numerous variants are possible, e.g.:

$$ClO_3^- + 6Br^-(or\ I^-) + 6H^+ \longrightarrow Cl^- + 3Br_2(or\ I_2) + 3H_2O$$

$$BrO_3^- + 6I^- + 6H^+ \longrightarrow Br^- + 3I_2 + 3H_2O$$

$$IO_3^- + 5Br^- + 6H^+ \longrightarrow 2Br_2 + IBr + 3H_2O$$

$$2ClO_3^- + 2Cl^- + 4H^+ \longrightarrow Cl_2 + 2ClO_2 + 2H_2O \quad (p.\ 846)$$

$$2BrO_3^- + 2Cl^- + 12H^+ \longrightarrow Br_2 + Cl_2 + 6H_2O$$

$$IO_3^- + 3Cl^- + 6H^+ \longrightarrow ICl + Cl_2 + 3H_2O$$

The greater thermodynamic stability of iodates enables iodine to displace Cl_2 and Br_2 from their halates:

$$I_2 + 2XO_3^- \longrightarrow X_2 + 2IO_3^- \quad (X = Cl, Br)$$

With bromate at pH 1.5–2.5 the reaction occurs in four stages:

(1) an induction period in which a catalyst (probably HOBr) is produced;

(2) $$I_2 + BrO_3^- \longrightarrow IBr + IO_3^-;$$

(3) $$3IBr + 2BrO_3^- + 3H_2O \longrightarrow 5Br^- + 3IO_3^- + 6H^+;$$

(4) $$5Br^- + BrO_3^- + 6H^+ \longrightarrow 3Br_2 + 3H_2O.$$

The dependence of reaction rates on pH and on the relative and absolute concentrations of reacting species, coupled with the possibility of autocatalysis and induction periods, has led to the discovery of some spectacular kinetic effects such as H. Landolt's "chemical clock" (1885): an acidified solution of Na_2SO_3 is reacted with an excess of iodic acid solution in the presence of starch indicator — the induction period before the appearance of the deep-blue starch-iodine colour can be increased systematically from seconds to minutes by appropriate dilution of the solutions before mixing. With an excess of sulfite, free iodine may appear and then disappear as a single pulse due to the following sequence of reactions:

$$IO_3^- + 3SO_3^{2-} \longrightarrow I^- + 3SO_4^{2-}$$

$$5I^- + IO_3^- + 6H^+ \longrightarrow 3I_2 + 3H_2O$$

$$3I_2 + 3SO_3^{2-} + 3H_2O \longrightarrow 6I^- + 6H^+ + 3SO_4^{2-}$$

A true periodic reaction was discovered by W. C. Bray in 1921 and involves the reduction of iodic acid to I_2 by H_2O_2 followed by the reoxidation of I_2 to HIO_3:

$$2HIO_3 + 5H_2O_2 \longrightarrow 5O_2 + I_2 + 6H_2O$$

$$I_2 + 5H_2O_2 \longrightarrow 2HIO_3 + 4H_2O$$

The net reaction is the disproportionation of H_2O_2 to $H_2O + \frac{1}{2}O_2$ and the starch indicator oscillates between deep blue and colourless as the iodine concentration pulsates.

Even more intriguing is the Belousov–Zhabotinskii class of oscillating reactions some of which can continue for hours. Such a reaction was first observed in 1959 by B. P. Belousov who noticed that, in stirred sulfuric acid solutions containing initially $KBrO_3$, cerium(IV) sulfate and malonic acid, $CH_2(CO_2H)_2$, the concentrations of Br^- and Ce^{4+} underwent repeated oscillations of major proportions (e.g. tenfold changes on a time-scale which was constant but which could be varied from a few seconds to a few minutes depending on concentrations and temperature). These observations were extended by A. M. Zhabotinskii in 1964 to the bromate oxidation of several other organic substrates containing a reactive methylene group catalysed either by Ce^{IV}/Ce^{III} or Mn^{III}/Mn^{II}. Not surprisingly these reactions have attracted considerable attention, but detailed studies of their mechanisms are beyond the scope of this chapter.[123−125]

The various reactions of bromates and iodates are summarized in the schemes on p. 866.[121]

The oxidation of halates to perhalates is considered further in the next section.

Perhalic acid and perhalates

Because of their differing structures, chemical reactions and applications, perchloric acid and the perchlorates are best considered separately from the various periodic acids and their salts; the curious history of perbromates also argues for their individual treatment.

Perchloric acid and perchlorates [126−128]

The most stable compounds of chlorine are those in which the element is in either its lowest oxidation state $(-I)$ or its highest (VII): accordingly perchlorates are the most stable oxo-compounds of chlorine (see oxidation-state diagram, (p. 855) and most are extremely stable both as solids and as solutions at room temperature. When heated they tend to decompose by loss of O_2 (e.g. $KClO_4$ above $400°$). Aqueous solutions of perchloric acid and perchlorates are not notable oxidizing agents at room temperature but when heated they become vigorous, even violent, oxidants. Considerable CAUTION should therefore be exercised when handling these materials, and it is crucial to avoid the presence of readily oxidizable organic (or inorganic) matter since this can initiate reactions of explosive intensity.

On an industrial scale, perchlorates are now invariably produced by the electrolytic oxidation of $NaClO_3$ (see Panel, p. 867). Alternative routes have historical importance but are now only rarely used, even for small-scale laboratory syntheses.

Perchloric acid is best made by treating anhydrous $NaClO_4$ or $Ba(ClO_4)_2$ with concentrated HCl, filtering off the precipitated chloride and concentrating the filtrate by distillation. The azeotrope (p. 815) boils at $203°C$ and contains 71.6% $HClO_4$ (i.e. $HClO_4.2H_2O$). The anhydrous acid is obtained by low-pressure distillation of the azeotrope ($p < 1$ mmHg $= 0.13$ kPa) in an all-glass apparatus in the presence of fuming sulfuric acid. Commercially available perchloric acid is usually $60–62\%$ ($\sim 3.5H_2O$) or $70–72\%$

123 R. J. FIELD, E. KÖRÖS and R. M. NOYES, *J. Am. Chem. Soc.* **94**, 8649–64 (1972).
124 R. M. NOYES, *J. Phys. Chem.* **94**, 4404–12 (1990).
125 S. K. SCOTT, *Oscillations, Waves and Chaos in Chemical Kinetics*, Oxford Univ. Press, Oxford, 1994, 96 pp.

126 Ref. 23, pp. 1435–60, Perhalic acids and perhalates.
127 F. SOLYMOSI, *Structure and Stability of Salts of Halogen Oxyacids in the Solid Phase*, Wiley, New York, 1978, 468 pp.
128 A. A. SCHILT, *Perchloric Acid and Perchlorates*, Northern Illinois University Press, 1979, 189 pp.

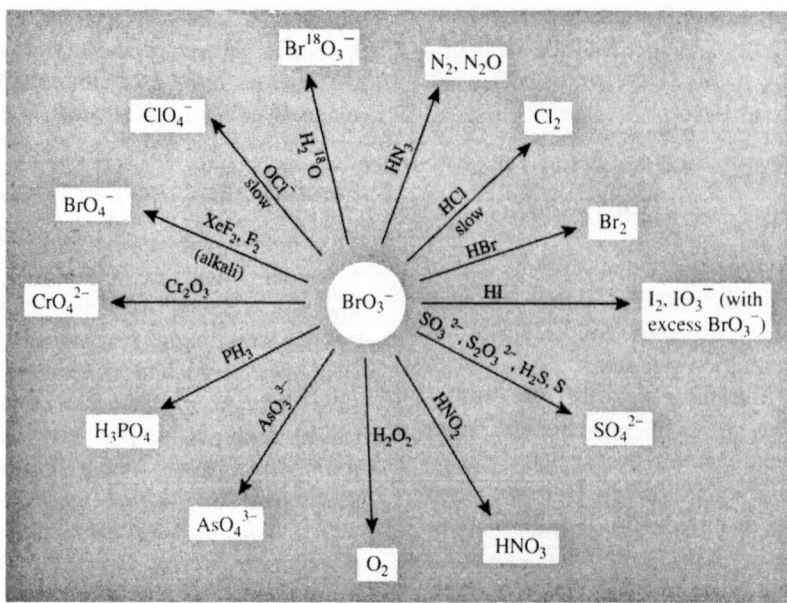

Some reactions of aqueous bromates.

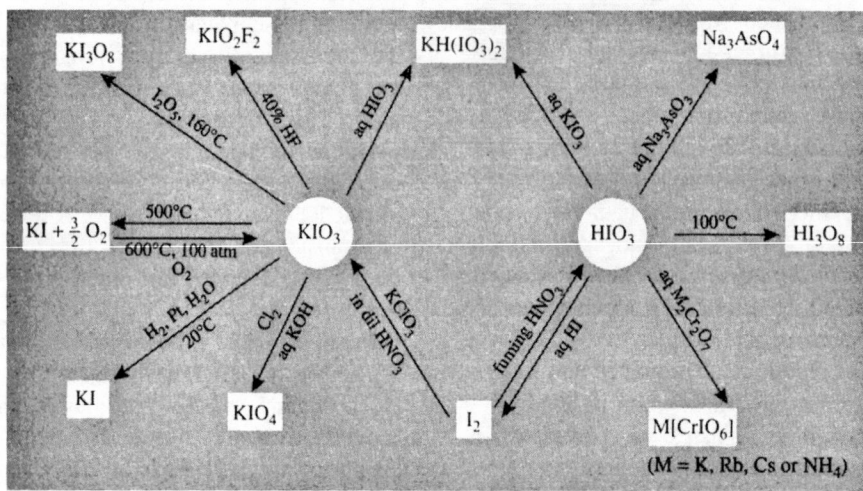

Some reactions of iodates.

($\sim 2H_2O$); more concentrated solutions are hygroscopic and are also unstable towards loss of Cl_2O_7 or violent decomposition by accidental impurities.

Pure $HClO_4$ is a colourless mobile, shock-sensitive, liquid: $d(25°)$ 1.761 g cm^{-3}. At least 6 hydrates are known (Table 17.23). The structure of $HClO_4$, as determined by electron diffraction in the gas phase, is as shown in Fig. 17.20. This

molecular structure persists in the liquid phase, with some H bonding, and also in the crystalline phase, where an X-ray study at $-160°$ found three Cl–O distances of 142 pm and one of 161 pm[99] (very close to the dimensions of the extremely stable "isoelectronic" molecule, $FClO_3$ (140.4 and 161.9 pm, p. 879)). The (low) electrical conductivity and other physical properties of anhydrous $HClO_4$ have been interpreted on the

Production and Uses of Perchlorates

$NaClO_4$ is made by the electrolytic oxidation of aqueous $NaClO_3$ using smooth Pt or PbO_2 anodes and a steel cathode which also acts as the container. All other perchlorates, including $HClO_4$, are made either directly or indirectly from this $NaClO_4$. In a typical cell $NaClO_3$ (600 g/l pH 6.5) is oxidized at 30–50°C with 90% current efficiency at 5000 A and 6.0 V with an anode current density of 3100 A m^{-2} and an electrode separation of ∼5 mm. The process can be either batch or continuous and energy consumption is ∼2.5 kWh/kg. A small concentration of $Na_2Cr_2O_7$ (1–5 g/l) is found to be extremely beneficial in inhibiting cathodic reduction of ClO_4^-.

World production of perchlorates was less than 1800 tonnes pa until 1940 when wartime missile and rocket requirements boosted this tenfold. World production capacity peaked at around 40 000 tpa in 1963 but is now still above 30 000 tpa. More than half of this is converted to NH_4ClO_4 for use as a propellant:

$$NaClO_4 + NH_4Cl \longrightarrow NH_4ClO_4 + NaCl$$

US production was severely disrupted by a series of devastating explosions in May 1988 which killed 2 people and injured several hundred.[129] Ultrapure NH_4ClO_4 for physical measurements and research purposes can be made by direct neutralization of aqueous solutions of NH_3 and $HClO_4$. One of the main current uses of NH_4ClO_4 is in the Space Shuttle Programme: the two booster rockets use a solid propellant containing 70% by weight of NH_4ClO_4, this being the oxidizer for the "fuel" (powdered Al metal) which comprises most of the rest of the weight. Each shuttle launch requires about 770 tonnes of NH_4ClO_4.

The annual consumption of 70% $HClO_4$ is about 450 tonnes mainly for making other perchlorates. Most of the $NaClO_4$ produced is used captively to make NH_4ClO_4 and $HClO_4$, but about 725 tpa is used for explosives, particularly in slurry blasting formulations.

The two other perchlorates manufactured on a fairly large scale industrially are $Mg(ClO_4)_2$ and $KClO_4$. The former is used as the electrolyte in "dry cells" (batteries), whereas $KClO_4$ is a major constituent in pyrotechnic devices such as fireworks, flares, etc. Thus the white flash and thundering boom in fireworks displays are achieved by incorporating a compartment containing $KClO_4$/S/Al, whereas the flash powder commonly used in rock concerts and theatricals comprises $KClO_4$/Mg. Vivid blues, perhaps the most difficult pyrotechnic colour to achieve, are best obtained from the low temperature (< 1200° C) flame emission of CuCl in the 420–460 nm region: because of the instability of copper chlorate and perchlorate this colour is generated by ignition of a mixture containing 38% $KClO_4$, 29% NH_4ClO_4, and 14% $CuCO_3$ bound with red gum (14%) and dextrin (5%).

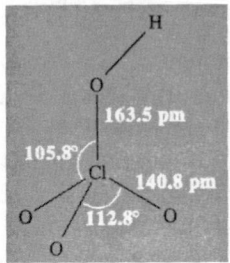 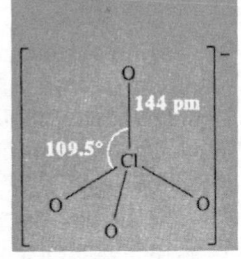

Figure 17.20   Structure of the gaseous molecule $HClO_4$ and of the ClO_4^- anion.

basis of slight dissociation according to the overall equilibrium:

$$3HClO_4 \rightleftharpoons Cl_2O_7 + H_3O^+ + ClO_4^-;$$

$$K(25°)\ 0.68 \times 10^{-6}$$

---

[129] R. J. SELTZER, *Chem. & Eng. News*, August 8, 7–15 (1988).

(cf. H_2SO_4, p. 711; H_3PO_4, p. 518, etc.). The monohydrate forms an H-bonded crystalline lattice $[H_3O]^+[ClO_4]^-$ that undergoes a phase transition with rotational disorder above −30°; it melts to a viscous, highly ionized liquid at 49.9°. The other hydrates also feature hydroxonium ions $[(H_2O)_nH]^+$ as described more fully on p. 630. It is particularly notable that hydration does not increase the coordination number of Cl and in this perchloric acid differs markedly from periodic acid (p. 872). This parallels the difference between sulfuric and telluric acids in the preceding group (p. 782).

Anhydrous $HClO_4$ is an extremely powerful oxidizing agent. It reacts explosively with most organic materials, ignites HI and $SOCl_2$ and rapidly oxidizes Ag and Au. Thermal decomposition in the gas phase yields a mixture of HCl, Cl_2, Cl_2O, ClO_2 and O_2 depending on the conditions. Above 310° the decomposition is first

Table 17.23　Perchloric acid and its hydrates

n in $HClO_4.nH_2O$	Structure	MP/°C	BP/°C	$\Delta H_f^{\circ}/kJ\,mol^{-1}$
0	$HOClO_3$	−112	110 (expl)	−40.6 (liq)
0.25	$(HClO_4)_4.H_2O$	d−73.1	—	—
1	$[H_3O]^+[ClO_4]^-$	49.9	decomp	−382.2 (cryst)
2	$[H_5O_2]^+[ClO_4]^-$	−20.7	203	−688 (liq)
2.5	—	−33.1	—	—
3	$[H_7O_3]^+[ClO_4]^-$	−40.2	—	—
3.5	—	−45.9	—	—

order and homogeneous, the rate-determining step being homolytic fission of the Cl–OH bond:

$$HOClO_3 \longrightarrow HO^\bullet + ClO_3^\bullet$$

The hydroxyl radical rapidly abstracts an H atom from a second molecule of $HClO_4$ to give H_2O plus $ClO_4^\bullet$ and the 2 radicals $ClO_3^\bullet$ and $ClO_4^\bullet$ then decompose to the elements via the intermediate oxides. Above 450° the Cl_2 produced reacts with H_2O to give 2HCl plus $\frac{1}{2}O_2$ whilst in the low-temperature range (150–310°) the decomposition is heterogeneous and second order in $HClO_4$.

Aqueous perchloric acid solutions exhibit very little oxidizing power at room temperature, presumably because of kinetic activation barriers, though some strongly reducing species slowly react, e.g. Sn^{II}, Ti^{III}, V^{II} and V^{III}, and dithionite. Others do not, e.g. H_2S, SO_2, HNO_2, HI and, surprisingly, Cr^{II} and Eu^{II}. Electropositive metals dissolve with liberation of H_2 and oxides of less basic metals also yield perchlorates. e.g. with 72% acid:

$$Mg + 2HClO_4 \xrightarrow{20°} [Mg(H_2O)_6](ClO_4)_2 + H_2$$

$$Ag_2O + 2HClO_4 \longrightarrow 2AgClO_4 + H_2O$$

NO and NO_2 react to give $NO^+ClO_4^-$ and F_2 yields $FOClO_3$ (p. 639). P_2O_5 dehydrates the acid to Cl_2O_7 (p. 850).

Perchlorates are known for most metals in the periodic table.[128] The alkali-metal perchlorates are thermally stable to several hundred degrees above room temperature but NH_4ClO_4 deflagrates with a yellow flame when heated to 200°:

$$2NH_4ClO_4 \longrightarrow N_2 + Cl_2 + 2O_2 + 4H_2O$$

NH_4ClO_4 has a solubility in water of 20.2 g per 100 g solution at 25° and 135 g per 100 g liquid NH_3 at the same temperature. Aqueous solubilities decrease in the sequence Na > Li > NH_4 > K > Rb > Cs; indeed, the low solubility of the last 3 perchlorates in this series has been used for separatory purposes and even for gravimetric analysis (e.g. $KClO_4$ 1.99 g per 100 g H_2O at 20°). Many of these perchlorates and those of M^{II} can also be obtained as hydrates. $AgClO_4$ has the astonishing solubility of 557 g per 100 g H_2O at 25° and even in toluene its solubility is 101 g per 100 g PhMe at 25°. This has great advantages in the metathetic preparation of other perchlorates, particularly organic perchlorates, e.g. RI yields $ROClO_3$, Ph_3CCl yields $Ph_3C^+ClO_4^-$, and CCl_4 affords CCl_3OClO_3.

Oxidation-reduction reactions involving perchlorates have been mentioned in several of the preceding sections and the reactivity of aqueous solutions is similar to that of aqueous solutions of perchloric acid.

The perchlorate ion was for long considered to be a non-coordinating ligand and has frequently been used to prepare "inert" ionic solutions of constant ionic strength for physicochemical measurements. Though it is true that ClO_4^- is a weaker ligand than H_2O it is not entirely toothless and, as shown schematically in Fig. 17.21, examples are known in which the perchlorate acts as a monodentate (η^1), bidentate chelating (η^2) and bidentate bridging (μ,η^2) ligand. The first unambiguous structural evidence for coordinated ClO_4^- was obtained in 1965 for the 5 coordinate cobalt(II)

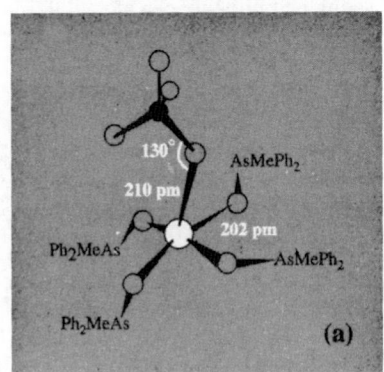

Figure 17.21 Coordination modes of ClO_4^- as determined by X-ray crystallography.

complex $[Co(OAsMePh_2)_4(\eta^1\text{-}OClO_3)_2]^{(130)}$ and this was quickly followed by a second example, the red 6-coordinate *trans* complex $[Co(\eta^2\text{-}MeSCH_2CH_2SMe)_2(\eta^1\text{-}OClO_3)_2]$.[131] The two structures are shown in Fig. 17.22. The perchlorate ion has now been established as a monodentate ligand towards an s-block element (Ba),[132]

a p-block element (Sn^{II} and Sn^{IV}),[133] and an f-block element (Sm^{III})[134] as well as to the d-block elements Co^{II}, Ni^{II}, Cu^{II} and Ag^{I}.[131,135] It is also known to function as a bidentate ligand towards Na,[136] Ba,[132] Sn^{IV},[133] Sm^{III},[134] Ti^{IV} in $[Ti(\eta^2\text{-}ClO_4)_4]^{(137)}$ and Ni^{II} in $[Ni(\eta^2\text{-}ClO_4)L_2]^+$ where L is a chiral bidentate organic ligand.[138] Sometimes both η^1 and η^2 modes occur in the same compound. The bidentate bridging mode occurs in the silver complex $[Ag\{\mu,\eta^2\text{-}OCl(O)_2O\text{-}\}(m\text{-}xylene)_2]$.[139] The structure of appropriate segments of some of these compounds are in Fig. 17.23. The distinction between coordinated and non-coordinated ("ionic") perchlorate is sometimes hard to make and there is an almost continuous

[130] P. PAULING, G. B. ROBERTSON and G. A. RODLEY, *Nature* **207**, 73–74 (1965).

[131] F. A. COTTON and D. L. WEAVER, *J. Am. Chem. Soc.* **87**, 4189–90 (1965).

[132] D. L. HUGHES, C. L. MORTIMER and M. R. TRUTER, *Acta Cryst.* **B34**, 800–7 (1978). *Inorg. Chim. Acta* **29**, 43–55 (1978).

[133] R. C. ELDER, M. J. HEEG and E. DEUTSCH, *Inorg. Chem.* **17**, 427–31 (1978). C. BELIN, M. CHAABOUNI, J.-L. PASCAL, J. POTIER and J. ROZIERE, *J. Chem. Soc., Chem. Commun.*, 105–6 (1980).

[134] M. CIAMPOLINI, N. NARDI, R. CINI, S. MANGANI and P. ORIOLI, *J. Chem. Soc., Dalton Trans.*, 1983–6 (1979).

[135] F. MADAULE-AUBRY and G. M. BROWN, *Acta Cryst.* **B24**, 745–53 (1968). F. BIGOLI, M. A. PELLINGHELLI and A. TIRIPICCHIO, *Cryst. Struct. Comm.* **4**, 123–6 (1976). E. A. HALL GRIFFITH and E. L. AMMA, *J. Am. Chem. Soc.* **93**, 3167–72 (1971).

[136] H. MILBURN, M. R. TRUTER and B. L. VICKERY, *J. Chem. Soc., Dalton Trans.*, 841–6 (1974).

[137] M. FOURATI, M. CHAABOUNI, C. H. BELIN, M. CHARBONNEL, J.-L. PASCAL and J. POTIER, *Inorg. Chem.* **25**, 1386–90 (1986).

[138] D. A. HOUSE, P. J. STEEL and A. A. WATSON, *J. Chem. Soc., Chem. Commun.*, 1575–6 (1987).

[139] I. F. TAYLOR, E. A. HALL and E. L. AMMA, *J. Am. Chem. Soc.* **91**, 5745–9 (1969).

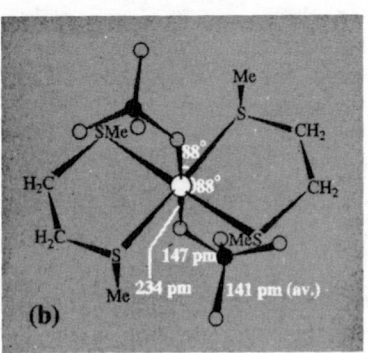

Figure 17.22 The structures of monodentate perchlorate complexes (see text).

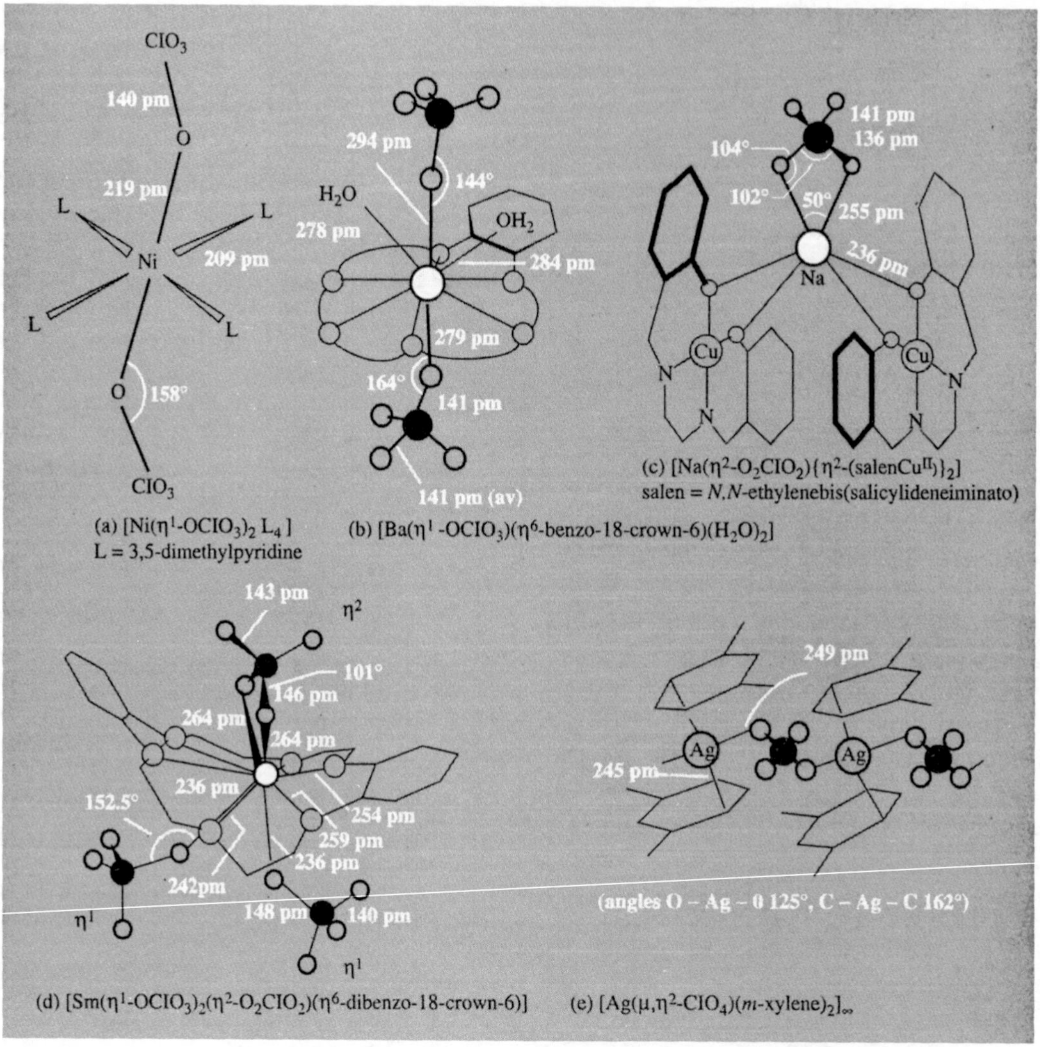

ClO3
140 pm
O
219 pm
L
L
Ni
209 pm
L
L
O
158°
ClO3
(a) [Ni(η1-OClO3)2 L4]
L = 3,5-dimethylpyridine
294 pm
144°
H2O
278 pm
OH2
284 pm
279 pm
164°
141 pm
141 pm (av)
(b) [Ba(η1-OClO3)(η6-benzo-18-crown-6)(H2O)2]
141 pm
136 pm
104°
102°
50°
255 pm
236 pm
Na
Cu
Cu
N
N
N
N
(c) [Na(η2-O2ClO2){η2-(salenCuII)}2]
salen = N,N-ethylenebis(salicylideneiminato)
143 pm
η2
101°
146 pm
264 pm
264 pm
236 pm
152.5°
254 pm
259 pm
236 pm
242pm
148 pm
140 pm
η1
η1
(d) [Sm(η1-OClO3)2(η2-O2ClO2)(η6-dibenzo-18-crown-6)]
249 pm
Ag
Ag
245 pm
(angles O – Ag – O 125°, C – Ag – C 162°)
(e) [Ag(μ,η2-ClO4)(m-xylene)2]∞

Figure 17.23 Examples of monodentate, chelating and bridging perchlorate ligands.

gradation between the two extremes. Similarly it is sometimes difficult to distinguish unambiguously between η^1 and unsymmetrical η^2 and, in the colourless complex $[Ag(cyclohexylbenzene)_2(ClO_4)]$, the η^1 bonding between Ag and $OClO_3$ (Ag–O 266 pm) is accompanied by a further weak symmetrical η^2 bonding from each ClO_4 to the neighbouring Ag (2Ag–O 284 pm) thereby generating a weakly-bridged chain-like structure involving pseudo-η^3 coordination of the perchlorate group:[135]

O
266 pm
Cl
O
Ag
O
O
284 pm
O
Cl
O
284 pm
Ag
O
O

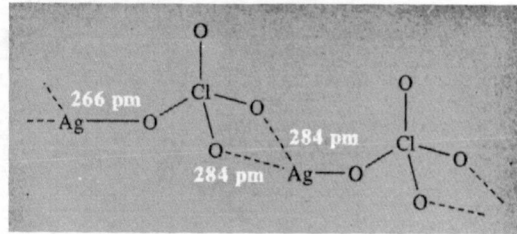

Because of its generally rather weak coordinating ability quite small changes can determine whether or not a perchlorate group coordinates and if so, in which mode. For example, the barium crown-ether dihydrate complex illustrated in Fig. 17.23 features 10-coordinate Ba with 6 oxygen atoms from the crown ring (Ba–O 280–285 pm), two H_2O molecules (Ba–O 278 and 284 pm), and one of the perchlorates (Ba–O 294 pm) all on one side of the ring, and the other perchlorate (Ba–O 279 pm) below it. By contrast, the analogous strontium complex is a trihydrate with 9-coordinate Sr (six Sr–O from the crown ring at 266–272 pm, plus two H_2O at 257, 259 pm, on one side of the ring, and one H_2O on the other side at 255 pm); the ClO_4^- ions are uncoordinated though they are H-bonded to the water molecules.

An even more dramatic change occurs with nickel(II) perchlorate complexes. Thus, the complex with 4 molecules of 3,5-dimethylpyridine (Fig. 17.23a) is blue, paramagnetic, and 6-coordinate with *trans*-$(\eta^1$-$OClO_3)$ ligands, whereas the corresponding complex with 3,4-dimethylpyridine is yellow and diamagnetic with square-planar Ni^{II} and uncoordinated ClO_4^- ions.[135,140] There is no steric feature of the structure which prevents the four 3,4-ligands from adopting the propeller-like configuration of the four 3,5-ligands thereby enabling Ni to accept two η^1-$OClO_3$, or vice versa, and one must conclude that subtle differences in secondary valency forces and energies of packing are sufficient to dictate whether the complex that crystallizes is blue, paramagnetic and octahedral, or yellow, diamagnetic and square planar.

Perbromic acid and perbromates

The quest for perbromic acid and perbromates and the various reasons adduced for their apparent non-existence make fascinating and salutary reading.[116] The esoteric radiochemical synthesis of BrO_4^- in 1968 using the β-decay of radioactive ^{83}Se, whilst not providing a viable route to macroscopic quantities of perbromate,

proved that this previously elusive species could exist:

$$^{83}SeO_4^{2-} \xrightarrow[t_{\frac{1}{2}}\ 22.5\ \text{min}]{-\beta^-} {}^{83}BrO_4^- \xrightarrow[t_{\frac{1}{2}}\ 2.39\ \text{h}]{-\beta^-}$$

$$\{^{83}Kr + 2O_2\}$$

This stimulated the search for a chemical synthesis. Electrolytic oxidation of aqueous $LiBrO_3$ produced a 1% yield of perbromate, but the first isolation of a solid perbromate salt ($RbBrO_4$) was achieved by oxidation of BrO_3^- with aqueous XeF_2:[141]

$$BrO_3^- + XeF_2 + H_2O \xrightarrow{10\%\ \text{yield}} BrO_4^- + Xe + 2HF$$

The best synthesis is now by oxidation of alkaline solutions of BrO_3^- using F_2 gas under rather specific conditions:[142]

$$BrO_3^- + F_2 + 2OH^- \xrightarrow{20\%\ \text{yield}} BrO_4^- + 2F^- + H_2O$$

In practice, F_2 is bubbled in until the solution is neutral, at which point excess bromate and fluoride are precipitated as $AgBrO_3$ and CaF_2; the solution is then passed through a cation exchange column to yield a dilute solution of $HBrO_4$. Several hundred grams at a time can be made by this route. The acid can be concentrated up to 6 M (55%) without decomposition and such solutions are stable for prolonged periods even at 100°. More concentrated solutions of $HBrO_4$ can be obtained but they are unstable; a white solid, possibly $HBrO_4.2H_2O$, can be crystallized.

Pure $KBrO_4$ is isomorphous with $KClO_4$ and contains tetrahedral BrO_4^- anions (Br–O 161 pm, cf. Cl–O 144 pm in ClO_4^- and I–O 179 pm in IO_4^-). Oxygen-18 exchange between 0.14 M $KBrO_4$ and H_2O proceeds to less than 7% completion during 19 days at 94° in either acid or basic solutions and there is no sign of any increase in coordination number of Br; in this BrO_4^- resembles ClO_4^- rather than IO_4^-. $KBrO_4$ is stable to 275–280° at which

140 F. MADAULE-AUBRY, W. R. BUSING and G. M. BROWN, *Acta Cryst.* **B24**, 754–60 (1968).

141 E. H. APPELMAN, *J. Am. Chem. Soc.* **90**, 1900–1 (1968); *Inorg. Chem.* **8**, 223–7 (1969).

142 E. H. APPELMAN, *Inorg. Synth.* **13**, 1–9 (1972).

temperature it begins to dissociate into $KBrO_3$ and O_2. Even NH_4BrO_4 is stable to 170°. Dilute solutions of BrO_4^- show little oxidizing power at 25°; they slowly oxidize I^- and Br^- but not Cl^-. More concentrated $HBrO_4$ (3 M) readily oxidizes stainless steel and 12 M acid rapidly oxidizes Cl^-. The general inertness of BrO_4^- at room temperature stands in sharp contrast to its high thermodynamic oxidizing power, which is greater than that of any other oxohalogen ion that persists in aqueous solution. The oxidation potential is

$$BrO_4^- + 2H^+ + 2e^- \longrightarrow BrO_3^- + H_2O;$$

$$E° + 1.853 \text{ V}$$

(cf. 1.201 V for ClO_4^- and 1.653 for IO_4^-). Accordingly, only the strongest oxidants would be expected to convert bromates to perbromates. As seen above, F_2/H_2O ($E°$ ~2.87 V) and XeF_2/H_2O ($E°$ ~2.64 V) are effective, but ozone ($E°$ 2.07 V) and $S_2O_8^{2-}$ ($E°$ 2.01 V) are not, presumably for kinetic reasons. Thermochemical measurements[143] further show that $KBrO_4$ is thermodynamically stable with respect to its elements, but less so than the corresponding $KClO_4$ and KIO_4: this is not due to any significant difference in entropy effects or lattice energies and implies that the Br–O bond in BrO_4^- is substantially weaker than the X–O bond in the other perhalates. Some comparative data (298.15 K) are:

	$KClO_4$	$KBrO_4$	KIO_4
$\Delta H_f°/\text{kJ mol}^{-1}$	−431.9	**−287.6**	−460.6
$\Delta G_f°/\text{kJ mol}^{-1}$	−302.1	**−174.1**	−349.3

No entirely satisfactory explanation of these observations has been devised, though they are paralleled by the similar reluctance of other elements following the completion of the 3d subshell to achieve their highest oxidation states — see particularly Se (p. 755) and As (p. 552) immediately preceding Br in the periodic table. The detailed kinetics of several oxidation reactions involving aqueous solutions of BrO_4^-

have been studied.[144] In general, the reactivity of perbromates lies between that of the chlorates and perchlorates which means that, after the perchlorates, perbromates are the least reactive of the known oxohalogen compounds. It has even been suggested[116] that earlier investigators may actually have made perbromates, but not realized this because they were expecting a highly reactive product rather than an inert one.

Periodic acids and periodates [126]

At least four series of periodates are known, interconnected in aqueous solutions by a complex series of equilibria involving deprotonation, dehydration and aggregation of the parent acid H_5IO_6 — cf. telluric acids (p. 782) and antimonic acids (p. 577) in the immediately preceding groups. Nomenclature is summarized in Table 17.24, though not all of the fully protonated acids have been isolated in the free state. The structural relationship between these acids, obtained mainly from X-ray studies on their salts, are shown in Fig. 17.24. H_5IO_6 itself (mp 128.5° decomp) consists of molecules of $(HO)_5IO$ linked into a three-dimensional array by O–H···O bonds (10 for each molecule, 260–278 pm).

Periodates can be made by oxidation of I^-, I_2 or IO_3^- in aqueous solution. Industrial processes involve oxidation of alkaline $NaIO_3$ either electrochemically (using a PbO_2 anode) or with Cl_2:

$$IO_3^- + 6OH^- - 2e^- \longrightarrow IO_6^{5-} + 3H_2O$$

Table 17.24 Nomenclature of periodic acids

Formula	Name	Alternative	Formal relation to H_5IO_6
H_5IO_6	*Ortho*periodic	*Para*periodic	Parent
HIO_4	Periodic	*Meta*periodic	$H_5IO_6 - 2H_2O$
"H_3IO_5"	*Meso*periodic	Diperiodic	$\begin{cases} 2H_5IO_6 - 2H_2O \\ 2H_5IO_6 - 3H_2O \end{cases}$
$H_7I_3O_{14}$	Triperiodic		$3H_5IO_6 - 4H_2O$

[143] F. Schreiner, D. W. Osborne, A. V. Pocius and E. H. Appelman, *Inorg. Chem.* **9**, 2320–4 (1970).

[144] E. H. Appelman, U. K. Kläning and R. C. Thompson, *J. Am. Chem. Soc.* **101**, 929–34 (1979).

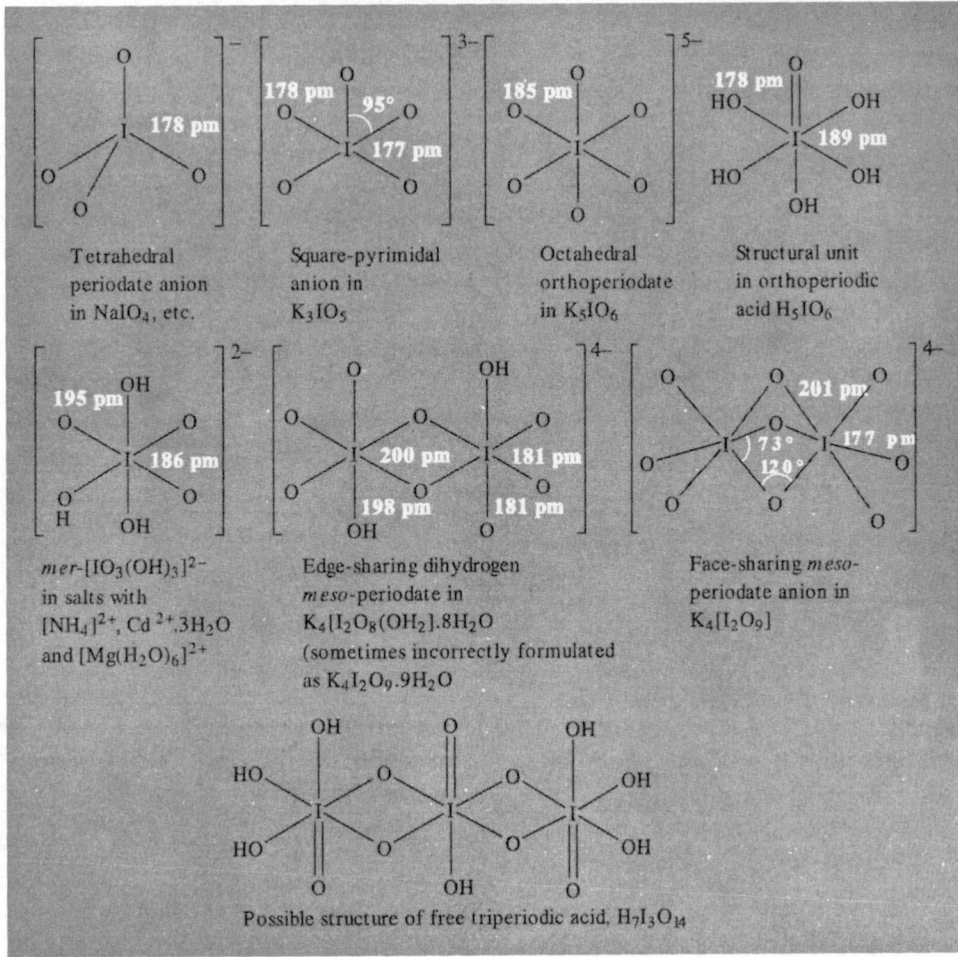

Figure 17.24   Structures of periodic acids and periodate anions.

$$IO_3^- + 6OH^- + Cl_2 \longrightarrow IO_6^{5-} + 2Cl^- + 3H_2O$$

The product is the dihydrogen orthoperiodate $Na_3H_2IO_6$, which is a convenient starting point for many further preparations (see Scheme on next page). Paraperiodates of the alkaline earth metals can be made by the thermal disproportionation of the corresponding iodates, e.g.:

$$5Ba(IO_3)_2 \xrightarrow{\;\Delta\;} Ba_5(IO_6)_2 + 4I_2 + 9O_2$$

Aqueous solutions of periodic acid are best made by treating this barium salt with concentrated nitric acid. White crystals of

H_5IO_6 can be obtained from these solutions. Dehydration of H_5IO_6 at $120°$ yields $H_7I_3O_{14}$, whereas heating to $100°$ under reduced pressure affords HIO_4. Attempts to dehydrate further do not yield the non-existent I_2O_7 (p. 852); oxygen is progressively evolved to form the mixed oxide $I_2O_5.I_2O_7$ and finally I_2O_5. Protonation of orthoperiodic acid with concentrated $HClO_4$ yields the cation $[I(OH)_6]^+$. Similarly, dissolution of crystalline H_5IO_6 in 95% H_2SO_4 (or H_2SeO_4) at $120°$ yields colourless crystals of $[I(OH)_6][HSO_4]$ on slow cooling to room temperature and prolonged digestion of these with trichloroacetic acid extracts H_2SO_4 to give the

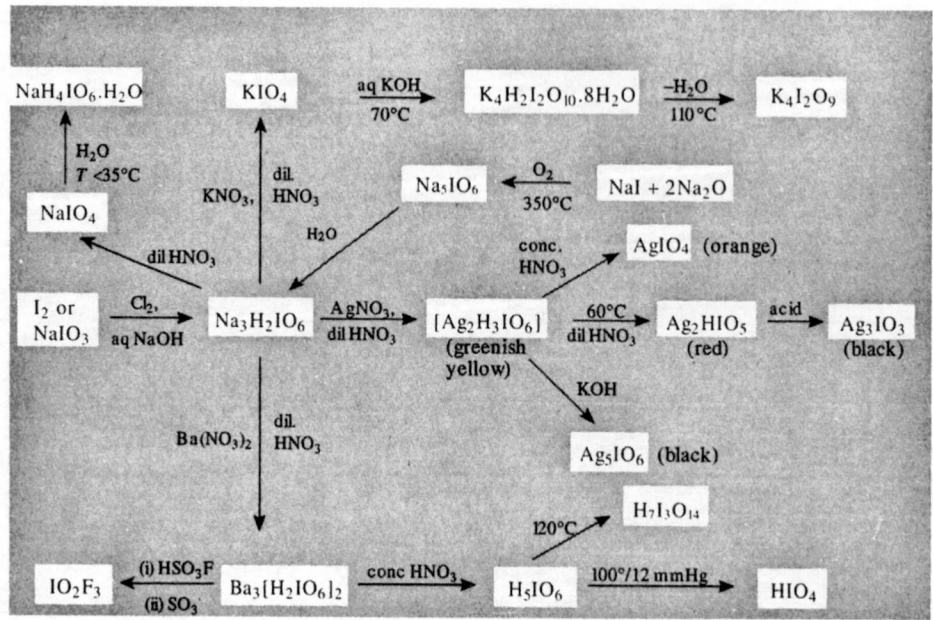

white, hygroscopic powder $[I(OH)_6]_2SO_4$.[145] These compounds thus complete the series of octahedral hexahydroxo species $[Sn(OH)_6]^{2-}$, $[Sb(OH)_6]^-$, $[Te(OH)_6]$ and $[I(OH)_6]^+$.

In aqueous solution increase in pH results in progressive deprotonation, dehydration and dimerization, the principal species being $[(HO)_4IO_2]^-$, $[(HO)_3IO_3]^{2-}$, $[(HO)_2IO_4]^{3-}$, $[IO_4]^-$ and $[(HO)_2I_2O_8]^{4-}$. The various equilibrium constants are:

	$K(25°C)$	pK
$H_6IO_6^+ \rightleftharpoons H_5IO_6 + H^+$	6.3	-0.80
$H_5IO_6 \rightleftharpoons H_4IO_6^- + H^+$	5.1×10^{-4}	3.29
$H_4IO_6^- \rightleftharpoons H_3IO_6^{2-} + H^+$	4.9×10^{-9}	8.31
$H_3IO_6^{2-} \rightleftharpoons H_2IO_6^{3-} + H^+$	2.5×10^{-12}	11.60
$H_4IO_6^- \rightleftharpoons IO_4^- + 2H_2O$	29	-1.46
$2H_4IO_6^{2-} \rightleftharpoons H_2I_2O_{10}^{4-} + 2H_2O$	~ 820	-2.91

Periodates are both thermodynamically potent and kinetically facile oxidants. The oxidation potential is greatest in acid solution (p. 855) and can be progressively diminished by increasing the pH of the solution. In acid solution it is one of the

few reagents that can rapidly and quantitatively convert Mn^{II} to $Mn^{VII}O_4^-$. In organic chemistry it specifically cleaves 1,2-diols (glycols) and related compounds such as α-diketones, α-ketols, α-aminoalcohols, and α-diamines, e.g.:

In rigid systems only *cis*-difunctional groups are oxidized, the specificity arising from the

145 H. SIEBERT and U. WOERNER, Z. anorg. allgem. Chem. **398**, 193–7 (1973).

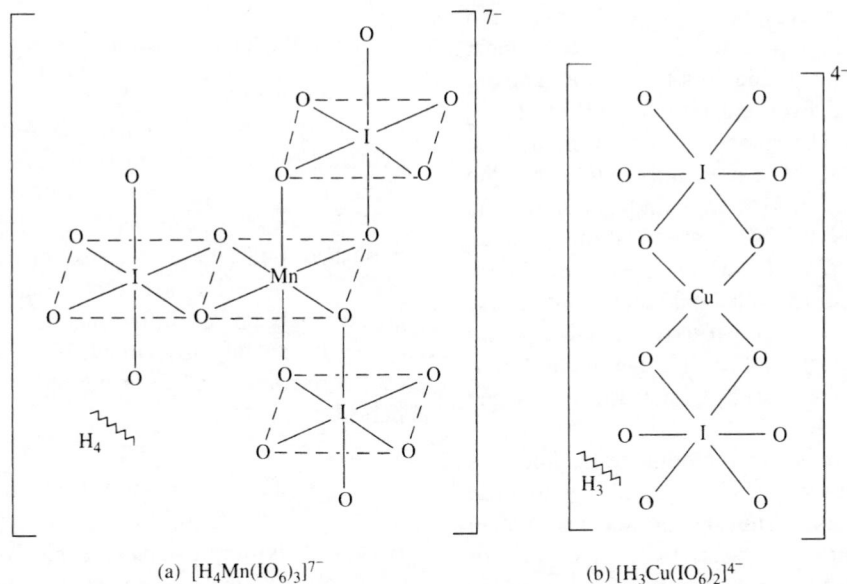

(a) $[H_4Mn(IO_6)_3]^{7-}$ (b) $[H_3Cu(IO_6)_2]^{4-}$

Figure 17.25   Structure of anions in $Na_7[H_4Mn(IO_6)_3].17H_2O$ and $Na_3K[H_3Cu(IO_6)_2].14H_2O$.

formation of the cyclic intermediate. Such reactions have been widely used in carbohydrate and nucleic acid chemistry.

Periodates form numerous complexes with transition metals in which the octahedral IO_6^{5-} unit acts as a bidentate chelate. Examples are:

$[Mn^{IV}(IO_6)]^-$, $[Ni^{IV}(IO_6)]^-$, $[Fe^{III}(IO_6)]^{2-}$, $[Co^{III}(IO_6)]^{2-}$
$[M^{IV}(IO_6)_2]^{6-}$ (M^{IV} = Pd, Pd, Ce);
$[M^{III}(IO_6)_2]^{7-}$ (M^{III} = Fe, Co, Cu, Ag, Au)
$[Mn^{IV}(IO_6)_3]^{11-}$; $[Fe_4^{III}(IO_6)_3]^{3-}$,
$[Co_4^{III}(IO_6)_3]^{3-}$

The stabilization of Ni^{IV}, Cu^{III} and Ag^{III} is notable and many of the complexes have very high formation constants, e.g. $[Cu(IO_6)_2]^{7-} \sim 10^{10}$, $[Co(IO_6)_2]^{7-} \sim 10^{18}$. The high formal charge on the anion is frequently reduced by protonation of the $\{I(\mu\text{-}O)_2O_4\}$ moiety, as in orthoperiodic acid itself. For example $H_{11}[Mn(IO_6)_3]$ is a heptabasic acid with pK_1 and $pK_2 < 0$, pK_3 2.75, pK_4 4.35, pK_5 5.45, pK_6 9.55, and pK_7 10.45. The crystal structure of $Na_7[H_4Mn(IO_6)_3].17H_2O$ features a 6-coordinate paramagnetic Mn^{IV} anion (Fig. 17.25a) whereas

the diamagnetic compound $Na_3K[H_3Cu(IO_6)_2]-14H_2O$ has square-planar Cu^{III} (Fig. 17.25b).

17.2.9 Halogen oxide fluorides and related compounds [146]

This section considers compounds in which X (Cl, Br or I) is bonded to both O and F, i.e. F_nXO_m. Oxofluorides –OF and peroxofluorides –OOF have already been discussed (p. 638) and halogen derivatives of oxoacids, containing –OX bonds are treated in the following section (p. 883).

Chlorine oxide fluorides [147]

Of the 6 possible oxide fluorides of Cl, 5 have been characterized: they range in stability from the thermally unstable $FCl^{III}O$ to the chemically rather inert perchloryl fluoride $FCl^{VII}O_3$. The others are FCl^VO_2, F_3Cl^VO and $F_3Cl^{VII}O_2$.

[146] Ref. 23, pp. 1386–96, The oxyfluorides of the halogens.
[147] K. O. Christe and C. J. Schack, *Adv. Inorg. Chem. Radiochem.* **18**, 319–98 (1976).

The remaining compound $F_5Cl^{VII}O$ has been claimed but the report could not be confirmed. Fewer bromine oxide fluorides are known, only $FBrO_2$, F_3BrO and possibly $FBrO_3$ being characterized. The compounds of iodine include the I^V derivatives FIO_2 and F_3IO and the I^{VII} derivatives FIO_3, F_3IO_2 and F_5IO. All the halogen oxide fluorides resemble the halogen fluorides (p. 824), to which they are closely related both structurally and chemically. Thus they tend to be very reactive oxidizing and fluorinating agents and several can act as Lewis acids or bases (or both) by gain or loss of fluoride ions, respectively.

The structures of the chlorine oxide fluorides are summarized in Fig. 17.26, together with those of related cationic and anionic species formed from the neutral molecules by gain or loss or F^-. The first conclusive evidence for free FClO in the gas phase came in 1972 during a study of the hydrolysis of ClF_3 with substoichiometric amounts of H_2O in a flow reactor:

$$ClF_3 + H_2O \longrightarrow FClO + 2HF$$

The compound is thermally unstable, and decomposes with a half-life of about 25 s at room temperature:

$$2FClO \xrightarrow{\text{rt}/t_{\frac{1}{2}}\ 25\ s} FClO_2 + ClF$$

The compound can also be made by photolysis of a mixture of ClF and O_3 in Ar at 4–15 K; evidence for the expected nonlinear by structure comes from vibration spectroscopy (Fig. 17.26a).

F_3ClO was discovered in 1965 but not published until 1972 because of US security classification. It has low kinetic stability and is an extremely powerful fluorinating and oxidizing agent. It can be made in yields of up to 80% by fluorination of Cl_2O in the presence of metal fluorides, e.g. NaF:

$$Cl_2O + 2F_2 \xrightarrow[-78°]{MF} F_3ClO + ClF$$

However, the unpredictably explosive nature of Cl_2O in the liquid state renders this process somewhat hazardous and the best large-scale preparation is the low-temperature fluorination of $ClONO_2$ (p. 884):

$$ClONO_2 + 2F_2 \xrightarrow[(>80\%\ \text{yield})]{-35°} F_3ClO + FNO_2$$

F_3ClO is a colourless gas or liquid: mp $-43°$, bp $28°$ $d(l, 20°)$ $1.865\,g\,cm^{-3}$. The compound

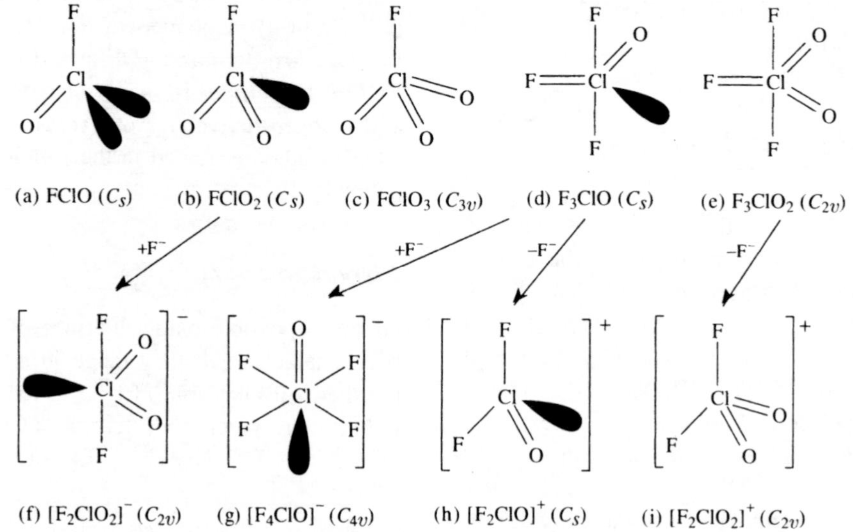

(a) FClO (C_s)   (b) FClO$_2$ (C_s)   (c) FClO$_3$ (C_{3v})   (d) F$_3$ClO (C_s)   (e) F$_3$ClO$_2$ (C_{2v})

(f) [F$_2$ClO$_2$]$^-$ (C_{2v})   (g) [F$_4$ClO]$^-$ (C_{4v})   (h) [F$_2$ClO]$^+$ (C_s)   (i) [F$_2$ClO$_2$]$^+$ (C_{2v})

Figure 17.26   Structures of chlorine oxide fluorides and related cations and anions.

is stable at room temperature: $\Delta H_f^\circ(g) = -148\,kJ\,mol^{-1}$, $\Delta H_f^\circ(l) = -179\,kJ\,mol^{-1}$. Its C_s structure (Fig. 17.26d) has been established by gas electron diffraction which also led to the dimensions $Cl=O$ 140.5 pm, $Cl-F_{eq}$ 160.3 pm, $Cl-F_{ax}$ 171.3 pm, and angle $F_{ax}-Cl-F_{ax}$ 171°; other angles are $F_{ax}-Cl-F_{eq}$ 88°, $F_{ax}-Cl-O$ 95° and $F_{eq}-Cl-O$ 109°.[148] F_3ClO can be handled in well-passivated metal, Teflon or Kel-F but reacts rapidly with glass or quartz. Its thermal stability is intermediate between those of ClF_3 and ClF_5 (p. 832) and it decomposes above 300°C according to

$$F_3ClO \longrightarrow ClF_3 + \tfrac{1}{2}O_2$$

F_3ClO tends to react slowly at room temperature but rapidly on heating or under ultraviolet irradiation. Typical of its fluorinating reactions are:

$$Cl_2 + F_3ClO \xrightarrow{200°} 3ClF + \tfrac{1}{2}O_2$$

$$Cl_2O + F_3ClO \xrightarrow{rt} 2ClF + FClO_2$$

$$ClOSO_2F + F_3ClO \longrightarrow SO_2F_2 + FClO_2 + ClF$$

$$2ClOSO_2F + F_3ClO \longrightarrow S_2O_5F_2 + FClO_2 + 2ClF$$

Combined fluorinating and oxygenating capacity is exemplified by the following (some of the reactions being complicated by further reaction of the products with F_3ClO):

$$SF_4 + F_3ClO \xrightarrow{CsF/25°} SF_6, FClO_2, SF_5Cl, SF_4O$$

$$MoF_5 + F_3ClO \longrightarrow MoF_6, MF_4O$$

$$2N_2F_4 + F_3ClO \xrightarrow{100°} 3NF_3 + FNO + ClF$$

$$HNF_2 + F_3ClO \xrightarrow{low\ temp} NF_3O, NF_2Cl,$$
$$N_2F_4, FClO_2, HF$$

$$F_2NC(O)F + F_3ClO \longrightarrow NF_3O, ClNF_2, N_2F_4$$

It reacts as a reducing agent towards the extremely strong oxidant PtF_6:

$$F_3ClO + PtF_6 \longrightarrow [F_2ClO]^+[PtF_6]^- + \tfrac{1}{2}F_2$$

---

[148] H. OBERHAMMER and K. O. CHRISTIE, *Inorg. Chem.* **21**, 273–5 (1982).

Hydrolysis with small amounts of water yields HF but this can react further by fluoride ion abstraction:

$$F_3ClO + H_2O \longrightarrow FClO_2 + 2HF$$

$$F_3ClO + HF \longrightarrow [F_2ClO]^+[HF_2]^-$$

This last reaction is typical of many in which F_3ClO can act as a Lewis base by fluoride ion donation to acceptors such as MF_5 (M = P, As, Sb, Bi, V, Nb, Ta, Pt, U), MoF_4O, SiF_4, BF_3, etc. These products are all white, stable, crystalline solids (except the canary yellow PtF_6^-) and contain the $[F_2ClO]^+$ cation (see Fig. 17.26h) which is isostructural with the isoelectronic F_2SO. Chlorine trifluoride oxide can also act as a Lewis acid (fluoride ion acceptor) and is therefore to be considered as amphoteric (p. 225). For example KF, RbF and CsF yield $M^+[F_4ClO]^-$ as white solids whose stabilities increase with increasing size of M^+. Vibration spectroscopy establishes the C_{4v} structure of the anion (Fig. 17.29g).

The other Cl^V oxide fluoride $FClO_2$ (1942) can be made by the low-temperature fluorination of ClO_2 but is best prepared by the reaction:

$$6NaClO_3 + 4ClF_3 \xrightarrow[\text{(high yield)}]{rt/1\ day} 6FClO_2 + 6NaF$$
$$+ 2Cl_2 + 3O_2$$

The C_s structure and dimensions (Fig. 17.26b) were established by microwave spectroscopy which also yielded a value for the molecular dipole moment μ 1.72 D. Other physical properties of this colourless gas are mp $-115°$ (or $-123°$), bp $\sim -6°$, ΔH_f°(g, 298 K) $-34 \pm 10\,kJ\,mol^{-1}$ [or $-273\,kJ\,mol^{-1}$ when corrected for ΔH_f°(HF, g)!]. $FClO_2$ is thermally stable at room temperature in dry passivated metal containers and quartz. Thermal decomposition of the gas (first-order kinetics) only becomes measurable above 300° in quartz and above 200° in Monel metal:

$$FClO_2(g) \xrightarrow{300°} ClF(g) + O_2(g)$$

It is far more chemically reactive than $FClO_3$ (p. 879) despite the lower oxidation state of Cl.

Hydrolysis is slow at room temperature and the corresponding reaction with anhydrous HNO_3 results in dehydration to the parent N_2O_5:

$$2FClO_2 + H_2O \longrightarrow 2HF + 2ClO_2 + \tfrac{1}{2}O_2$$

$$2FClO_2 + 2HONO_2 \longrightarrow 2HF + 2ClO_2$$
$$+ \tfrac{1}{2}O_2 + N_2O_5$$

Other reactions with protonic reagents are:

$$2OH^-(aq) + FClO_2 \longrightarrow ClO_3^- + F^- + H_2O$$

$$NH_3(l) + FClO_2 \xrightarrow[\text{ignites}]{-78°} NH_4Cl, NH_4F$$

$$HCl(l) + FClO_2 \xrightarrow{-110°} HF + ClO_2 + \tfrac{1}{2}Cl_2$$

$$HOSO_2F + FClO_2 \xrightarrow{-78°} HF + ClO_2OSO_2F$$

$$HOClO_3(\text{anhydrous}) + FClO_2 \longrightarrow HF$$
$$+ ClO_2OClO_3$$

$$SO_3 + FClO_2 \xrightarrow{-10°} ClO_2OSO_2F \text{ (insertion)}$$

$FClO_2$ explodes with the strong reducing agent SO_2 even at $-40°$ and HBr likewise explodes at $-110°$.

Chlorine dioxide fluoride is a good fluorinating agent and a moderately strong oxidant: SF_4 is oxidized to SF_6, SF_4O and SF_2O_2 above $50°$, whereas N_2F_4 yields NF_3, FNO_2 and FNO at $30°$. UF_4 is oxidized to UF_5 at room temperature and to UF_6 at $100°$. Chlorides (and some oxides) are fluorinated and the products can react further to form fluoro complexes. Thus, whereas $AlCl_3$ yields AlF_3, B_2O_3 affords $[ClO_2]^+BF_4^-$, and the Lewis acid chlorides $SbCl_5$, $SnCl_4$ and $TiCl_4$ yield $[ClO_2]^+[SbF_6]^-$, $[ClO_2]^+_2[SnF_6]^{2-}$ and $[ClO_2]^+_2[TiF_6]^{2-}$. Such complexes, and many others can, of course, be prepared directly from the corresponding fluorides either with or without concurrent oxidation, e.g.:

$$AsF_3 + 3FClO_2 \longrightarrow [ClO_2]^+[AsF_6]^- + 2ClO_2$$

$$SbF_5 + FClO_2 \longrightarrow [ClO_2]^+[SbF_6]^- \text{ (mp 220°)}$$

$$2SbF_5 + FClO_2 \longrightarrow [ClO_2]^+[Sb_2F_{11}]^-$$

An X-ray study on this last compound showed the chloryl cation to have the expected nonlinear structure, with angle OClO 122° and Cl–O 131 pm. $FClO_2$ can also act as a fluoride ion acceptor, though not so readily as F_3ClO above. For example CsF reacts at room temperature to give the white solid $Cs[F_2ClO_2]$; this is stable at room temperature but dissociates reversibly into its components above 100°. The C_{2v} structure of $[F_2ClO_2]^-$ (Fig. 17.26f) is deduced from its vibration spectrum.

The two remaining Cl^{VII} oxide fluorides are F_3ClO_2 and $FClO_3$. At one time F_3ClO_2 was thought to exist in isomeric forms but the so-called violet form, previously thought to be the peroxo compound F_2ClOOF has now been discounted.[147] The well-defined compound F_3ClO_2 was first made in 1972 as an extremely reactive colourless gas: mp $-81.2°$, bp $-21.6°$. It is a very strong oxidant and fluorinating agent and, because of its corrosive action, must be handled in Teflon or sapphire apparatus. It thus resembles the higher chlorine fluorides. The synthesis of F_3ClO_2 is complicated and depends on an ingenious sequence of fluorine-transfer reactions as outlined below:

$$2FClO_2 + 2PtF_6$$
$$\downarrow$$
$$[F_2ClO_2]^+[PtF_6]^- + [ClO_2]^+[PtF_6]^-$$
$$F_3ClO_2 + FClO_2 + 2[NO_2]^+[PtF_6]^- \xleftarrow{\quad} \Big\} 2FNO_2$$

Fractional condensation at $-112°$ removes most of the $FClO_2$, which is slightly less volatile than F_3ClO_2. The remaining $FClO_2$ is removed by complexing with BF_3 and then relying on the greater stability of the F_3ClO_2 complex:

$$[ClO_2]^+[BF_4]^- \text{ (dissoc press 1 atm at 44°C)}$$

$$\left. \begin{array}{l} FClO_2 \\ (\text{mixture}) \\ F_3ClO_2 \end{array} \right\} + 2BF_3 \nearrow$$
$$\searrow$$

$$[F_2ClO_2]^+[BF_4]^- \text{ stable at room temperature}$$

Pumping at 20° removes $[ClO_2]^+[BF_4]^-$ as its component gases, leaving $[F_2ClO_2]^+[BF_4]^-$ which, on treatment with FNO_2, releases the desired product:

$$[F_2ClO_2]^+[BF_4]^- + FNO_2 \longrightarrow [NO_2]^+[BF_4]^-$$
$$+ F_3ClO_2$$

The whole sequence of reactions represents a *tour de force* in the elegant manipulation of extremely reactive compounds. F_3ClO_2 is a violent oxidizing reagent but forms stable adducts by fluoride ion transfer to Lewis acids such as BF_3, AsF_5 and PtF_6. The structures of F_3ClO_2 and $[F_2ClO_2]^+$ have C_{2v} symmetry as expected (Fig. 17.26e and i).

In dramatic contrast to F_3ClO_2, perchloryl fluoride ($FClO_3$) is notably inert, particularly at room temperature. This colourless tetrahedral molecular gas (Fig. 17.26c) was first synthesized in 1951 by fluorination of $KClO_3$ at $-40°$ and it can also be made (in 50% yield) by the action of F_2 on an aqueous solution of $NaClO_3$. Electrolysis of $NaClO_4$ in anhydrous HF has also been used but the most convenient route for industrial scale manufacture is the fluorination of a perchlorate with SbF_5, SbF_5/HF, $HOSO_2F$ or perhaps best of all $HOSO_2F/SbF_5$:

$$KClO_4 \xrightarrow[\text{rt (or above)}]{HOSO_2F/SbF_5} FClO_3 \quad (97\% \text{ yield})$$

Because of its remarkably low reactivity at room temperature and its very high specific impulse, the gas has been much studied as a rocket propellent oxidizer (e.g. it compares favourably with N_2O_4 and with ClF_3 as an oxidizer for fuels such as N_2H_4, Me_2NNH_2 and LiH). $FClO_3$ has mp $-147.8°$, bp $-46.7°$, $d(1, -73°C)$ 1.782 g cm^{-3}, viscosity $\eta(-73°)$ 0.55 centipoise. The extremely low dipole moment ($\mu = 0.023$ D) is particularly noteworthy. $FClO_3$ has high kinetic stability despite its modest thermodynamic instability: $\Delta H_f°(g, 298 \text{ K})$ -23.8 kJ mol^{-1}, $\Delta G_f°(g, 298 \text{ K})$ $+48.1$ kJ mol^{-1}. $FClO_3$ offers the highest known resistance to dielectric breakdown for any gas (30% greater than for SF_6, p. 687) and has been used as an insulator in high-voltage systems.

Perchloryl fluoride is thermally stable up to about $400°$. Above $465°$ it undergoes decomposition with first-order kinetics and an activation energy of 244 kJ mol^{-1}. Hydrolysis is slow even at $250-300°$ and quantitative reaction is only achieved with concentrated aqueous hydroxide in a sealed tube under high pressure at $300°C$:

$$FClO_3 + 2NaOH \longrightarrow NaClO_4 + NaF + H_2O$$

However, alcoholic KOH effects a similar quantitative reaction at $25°C$. Reaction with liquid NH_3 is also smooth particularly in the presence of a strong nucleophile such as $NaNH_2$:

$$FClO_3 + 3NH_3 \longrightarrow [NH_4]^+[HNClO_3]^- + NH_4F$$

Metallic Na and K react only above $300°$.

$FClO_3$ shows no tendency to form adducts with either Lewis acids or bases. This is in sharp contrast to most of the other oxide fluorides of chlorine discussed above and has been related to the preferred tetrahedral (C_{3v}) geometry as compared with the planar (D_{3h}) and trigonal bipyramidal (D_{3h}) geometries expected for $[ClO_3]^+$ and $[F_2ClO_3]^-$ respectively. Conversely the pseudo-trigonal bipyramidal C_s structure F_3ClO gains stability when converted to the pseudo-tetrahedral $[F_2ClO]^+$ or pseudo-octahedral $[F_4ClO]^-$ (see Fig. 17.26).

In reactions with organic compounds $FClO_3$ acts either as an oxidant or as a 1- or 2-centre electrophile which can therefore be used to introduce either F, a $-ClO_3$ group, or both F and O into the molecule. As $FClO_3$ is highly susceptible to nucleophilic attack at Cl it reacts readily with organic anions:

$$FClO_3 + Li^+Ph^- \longrightarrow PhClO_3 + LiF$$

Compounds having a cyclic double bond conjugated to an aromatic ring (e.g. indene) undergo oxofluorination, with $FClO_3$ acting as a 2-centre electrophile:

$FClO_3$ also acts as a mild fluorinating agent for compounds possessing a reactive methylene group, e.g.:

$$CH_2(CO_2R)_2 \xrightarrow{FClO_3} CF_2(CO_2R)_2$$

It is particularly useful for selective fluorination of steroids.

Bromine oxide fluorides[149]

These compounds are less numerous and rather less studied than their chlorine analogues; indeed, until fairly recently only $FBrO_2$ was well characterized. The known species are:

Oxidation state of Br	Cations	**Neutral species**	Anions
V	$[BrO_2]^+$	**$FBrO_2$** (1955)	$[F_2BrO_2]^-$
	$[F_2BrO]^+$	**F_3BrO** (1976)	$[F_4BrO]^-$
VII		**$FBrO_3$** (1969)	

Despite several attempts at synthesis, there is little or no evidence for the existence of $FBrO$, F_3BrO_2 or F_5BrO. The bromine oxide fluorides are somewhat less thermally stable than their chlorine analogues and somewhat more reactive chemically. The structures are as already described for the chlorine oxide fluorides (Fig. 17.26).

Bromyl fluoride, $FBrO_2$, is a colourless liquid, mp $-9°$, which attacks glass at room temperature and which undergoes rapid decomposition

[149] R. J. GILLESPIE and P. H. SPEKKENS, *Israel J. Chem.* **17**, 11–19 (1978). R. BOUGON, T. B. HUY, P. CHARPIN, R. J. GILLESPIE and P. H. SPEKKENS, *J. Chem. Soc., Dalton Trans.*, 6–12 (1979).

above 55°:

$$3FBrO_2 \xrightarrow{\Delta} BrF_3 + Br_2 + 3O_2$$

It is best prepared by fluorine transfer reactions such as

$$K[F_2BrO_2] + HF(l) \longrightarrow KHF_2 + FBrO_2$$

The $K[F_2BrO_2]$ can be prepared by fluorination of $KBrO_3$ with BrF_5 in the presence of a trace of HF:

$$KBrO_3 + BrF_5 \longrightarrow FBrO_2 + K[F_4BrO]$$

$$K[F_4BrO] + KBrO_3 \longrightarrow 2K[F_2BrO_2]$$

However, the most convenient method of preparation of $K[F_2BrO_2]$ is by reaction of $KBrO_3$ with $KBrF_6$ in MeCN:

$$KBrO_3 + KBrF_6 \xrightarrow{MeCN} K[F_2BrO_2]\downarrow$$
$$+ K[F_4BrO] \text{ (sol)}$$

Bromyl fluoride is also produced by fluorine-oxygen exchange between BrF_5 and oxoiodine compounds (p. 881), e.g.:

$$FIO_2 + BrF_5 \longrightarrow FBrO_2 + IF_5$$

$$2F_3IO + BrF_5 \longrightarrow FBrO_2 + 2IF_5$$

$$2I_2O_5 + 5BrF_5 \longrightarrow 5FBrO_2 + 4IF_5$$

As with $FClO_2$ and FIO_2, hydrolysis regenerates the halate ion, the reaction with $FBrO_2$ being of explosive violence. Hydrolysis in basic solution at 0° can be represented as

$$FBrO_2 + 2OH^- \longrightarrow BrO_3^- + F^- + H_2O$$

Organic substances react vigorously, often enflaming. Co-condensation of $FBrO_2$ with the Lewis acid AsF_5 produced $[BrO_2]^+[AsF_6]^-$. Vibrational spectra establish the expected non-linear structure of the cation (3 bands active in both Raman and infrared). $FBrO_2$ can also react as a fluoride ion acceptor (from KF).

Bromine oxide trifluoride, F_3BrO, is made by reaction of $K[F_4BrO]$ with a weak Lewis acid:

$$K[F_4BrO] + [O_2]^+[AsF_6]^- \longrightarrow F_3BrO$$
$$+ KAsF_6 + O_2 + \tfrac{1}{2}F_2$$

$$K[F_4BrO] + HF(anhydr) \xrightarrow{-72°} F_3BrO + KHF_2$$

The product is a white solid which melts to a clear liquid at about $-5°$; it is only marginally stable at room temperature and slowly decomposes with loss of oxygen:

$$F_3BrO \longrightarrow BrF_3 + \tfrac{1}{2}O_2$$

The molecular symmetry is C_s (like F_3ClO; Fig. 17.26d) and there is some evidence for weak intermolecular association via F_{ax}–$Br\cdots F_{ax}$ bonding. Fluoride ion transfer reactions have been established and yield compounds such as $[F_2BrO]^+[AsF_6]^-$, $[F_2BrO]^+[BF_4]^-$ and $K[F_4BrO]$, though this last compound is more conveniently made independently, e.g. by the reaction of $KBrO_3$ with $KBrF_6$ mentioned above, or by direct fluorination of $K[F_2BrO_2]$:

$$K[F_2BrO_2] + F_2 \longrightarrow K[F_4BrO] + \tfrac{1}{2}O_2$$

Perbromyl fluoride, $FBrO_3$, is made by fluorinating the corresponding perbromate ion with AsF_5, SbF_5, BrF_5 or $[BrF_6]^+[AsF_6]^-$ in HF solutions. The reactions are smooth and quantitative at room temperature:

$$KBrO_4 + 2AsF_5 + 3HF \longrightarrow FBrO_3$$
$$+ [H_3O]^+[AsF_6]^- + KAsF_6$$

$$2KBrO_4 + BrF_5 + 2HF \longrightarrow 2FBrO_3$$
$$+ FBrO_2 + 2KHF_2$$

$$KBrO_4 + [BrF_6]^+[AsF_6]^- \longrightarrow FBrO_3 + BrF_5$$
$$+ \tfrac{1}{2}O_2 + KAsF_6$$

Perbromyl fluoride is a reactive gas which condenses to a colourless liquid (bp $2.4°$) and then solidifies to a white solid (mp *ca.* $-110°$). It has the expected C_{3v} symmetry Fig. 17.27 and decomposes slowly at room temperature; it is more reactive than $FClO_3$ and, unlike that compound, it reacts rapidly with water, aqueous base and even glass:

$$FBrO_3 + H_2O \longrightarrow BrO_4^- + HF + H^+$$
$$FBrO_3 + 2OH^- \longrightarrow BrO_4^- + F^- + H_2O$$

Fluoride ion transfer reactions have not been established for $FBrO_3$ and may be unlikely, (see p. 879).

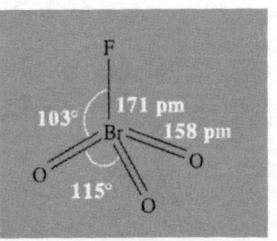

Figure 17.27   Structure of $FBrO_3$ as determined by gas-phase electron diffraction.

Iodine oxide fluorides

The compounds to be considered are the I^V derivatives FIO_2 and F_3IO and the I^{VII} derivatives FIO_3, F_3IO_2 and F_5IO. Note that, unlike Cl, no I^{III} compound FIO has been reported and that, conversely, F_5IO (but not F_5ClO) has been characterized.

FIO_2 has been prepared both by direct fluorination of I_2O_5 in anhydrous HF at room temperature and by thermal dismutation of F_3IO:

$$I_2O_5 + F_2 \xrightarrow{\text{HF}/20°} 2FIO_2 + \tfrac{1}{2}O_2$$

$$2F_3IO \xrightarrow{110°} FIO_2 + IF_5$$

Unlike gaseous molecular $FClO_2$, it is a colourless polymeric solid which decomposes without melting when heated above $200°$. Like the other halyl fluorides it readily undergoes alkaline hydrolysis and also forms a complex with F^-:

$$FIO_2 + 2OH^- \longrightarrow IO_3^- + F^- + H_2O$$

$$FIO_2 + KF \xrightarrow{\text{HF}} K^+[F_2IO_2]^-$$

An X-ray study of this latter complex reveals a C_{2v} anion as in the chlorine analogue (Fig. 17.28a). This is closely related to the C_s structure of the neutral molecule F_3IO (Fig. 17.28b).

F_3IO is prepared as colourless crystals by dissolving I_2O_5 in boiling IF_5 and then cooling the mixture:

$$I_2O_5 + 3IF_5 \xrightarrow{105°} 5F_3IO$$

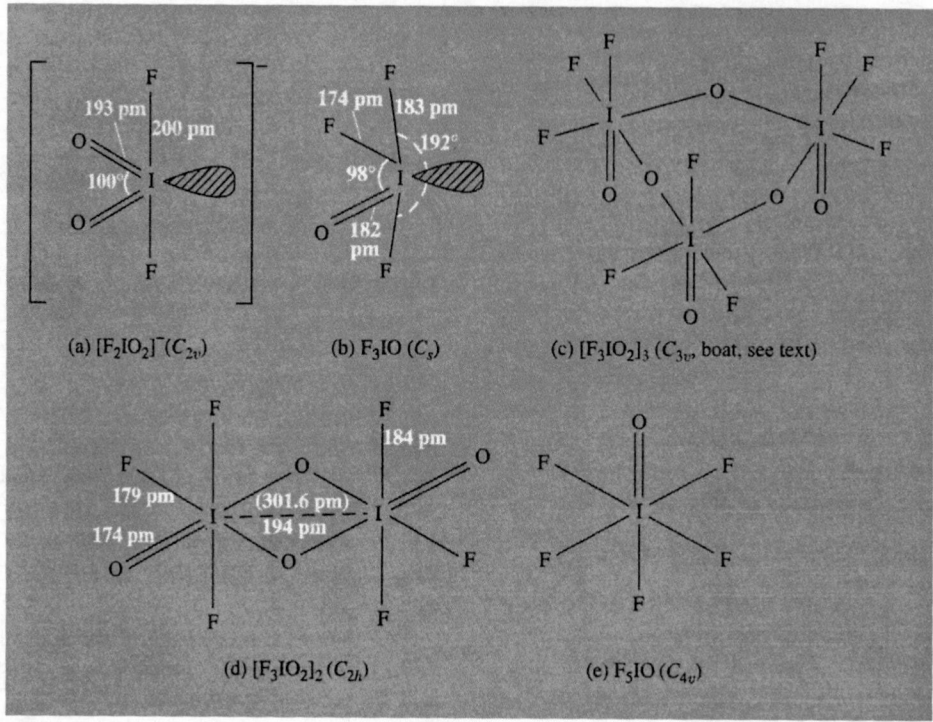

Figure 17.28   Structures of iodine oxide fluorides.

Above 110° it dismutates into FIO_2 and IF_5 as mentioned above.

Of the I^{VII} oxide fluorides FIO_3 has been prepared by the action of F_2/liquid HF on HIO_4. It is a white, crystalline solid, stable in glass but decomposing with loss of oxygen on being heated:

$$FIO_3 \xrightarrow{100°} FIO_2 + \tfrac{1}{2}O_2$$

Unlike its analogue $FClO_3$ it forms adducts with BF_3 and AsF_5, possibly by F^- donation to give $[IO_3]^+[BF_4^-]$ and $[IO_3]^+[AsF_6]^-$, though the structures have not yet been determined. Alternatively, the coordination number of the central I atom might be increased. SO_3 reduces FIO_3 to iodyl fluorosulfate:

$$FIO_3 + SO_3 \longrightarrow IO_2SO_2F + O_2$$

Like $FClO_3$ it reacts with NH_3 but the products have not been fully characterized.

F_3IO_2, first made in 1969, has posed an interesting structural problem. The yellow solid, mp 41°, can be prepared by partial fluorination of a periodate with fluorosulfuric acid:

$$Ba_3H_4(IO_6)_2 \xrightarrow{HSO_3F} [HIO_2F_4] \xrightarrow{SO_3} F_3IO_2$$

Unlike monomeric F_3ClO_2 (p. 878) the structure is oligomeric not only in the solid state but also in the gaseous and solution phases. This arises from the familiar tendency of iodine to increase its coordination number to 6. Fluorine-19 nmr and Raman spectroscopy of F_3IO_2 dissolved in BrF_3 at $-48°$ have been interpreted in terms of a *cis*-oxygen-bridged trimer with axial terminal O atoms and a C_{3v} boat conformation (Fig. 17.28c).[150] On warming the solution to 50° there is a fast interconversion between this and the C_s chair conformer. The vibration spectrum of the gas phase at room temperature has been interpreted in terms of a centrosymmetric dimer

150 R. J. GILLESPIE and J. P. KRASZNAI, *Inorg. Chem.* **15**, 1251–6 (1976).

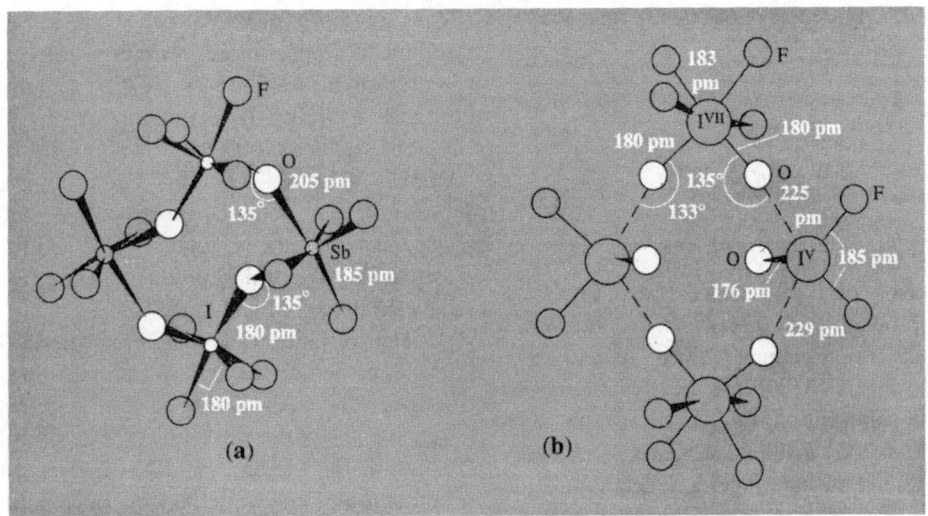

Figure 17.29 Structures of dimeric adducts of F_3IO_2.

(Fig. 17.28d). There is significant dissociation into monomers at 100° and this is almost complete at 185°. The centrosymmetric dimer has also been found in an X-ray study of the crystalline solid at −80° (Fig. 17.28d).[151] Complexes of F_3IO_2 with AsF_5, SbF_5, NbF_5 and TaF_5 have been studied:[152] they are oxygen-bridged polymers with alternating $\{F_4IO_2\}$ and $\{O_2MF_4\}$ groups. For example, the crystal structure of the complex with SbF_5 shows it to be dimeric (Fig. 17.29a).[153] A similar structure motif is found in the adduct $F_3IO.F_3IO_2$ which features alternating 5- and 6-coordinate I atoms (Fig. 17.29b);[154] the structure can be regarded as a cyclic dimer of the ion pair $[F_2IO]^+[F_4IO_2]^-$. See also p. 885 for the mixed valence oxo-iodine polymeric cation in $[(IO_2)_3]^+HSO_4^-$.

Finally in this section we mention iodine oxide pentafluoride, F_5IO, obtained as a colourless liquid, mp 45°, when IF_7 is allowed to react with water, silica, glass or I_2O_5. As implied by its preparation from water, F_5IO is not readily hydrolysed. Vibrational spectroscopy and ^{19}F nmr studies point to the 6-coordinate C_{4v} geometry in Fig. 17.28e (i.e. I^{VII}) rather than the alternative 5-coordinate structure F_4I^VOF. Microwave spectroscopy yields a value of 1.08 D for the molecular dipole moment.

17.2.10 Halogen derivatives of oxoacids

Numerous compounds are known in which the H atom of an oxoacid has been replaced by a halogen atom. Examples are:

halogen(I) perchlorates $XOClO_3$ (X=F, Cl, Br, ?I)
halogen(I) fluorosulfates $XOSO_2F$ (X=F, Cl, Br, I)
halogen(I) nitrates $XONO_2$ (X=F, Cl, Br, I)

In addition, halogen(III) derivatives such as $Br(ONO_2)_3$, $I(ONO_2)_3$, $Br(OSO_2F)_3$ and $I(OSO_2-F)_3$ are known, as well as complexes M^I-$[X^I(ONO_2)_2]$, $M^I[I^{III}(ONO_2)_4]$, $M^I[X^{III}(OSO_2-F)_4]$ (X=Br, I). In general, thermal stability decreases with increase in atomic number of the halogen.

The properties of halogen(I) perchlorates are in Table 17.25. $FOClO_3$ was originally prepared

151 L. E. SMART, *J. Chem. Soc., Chem. Commun.*, 519–20 (1977).
152 R. J. GILLESPIE and J. P. KRASZNAI, *Inorg. Chem.* **16**. 1384–92 (1977).
153 A. J. EDWARDS and A. A. K. HANA. *J. Chem. Soc., Dalton Trans.*, 1734–6 (1980).
154 R. J. GILLESPIE, J. P. KRASZNAI and D. R. SLIM, *J. Chem. Soc., Dalton Trans.*, 481–3 (1980).

Table 17.25   Properties of halogen(I) perchlorates

Property		$FOClO_3$	$ClOClO_3$	$BrOClO_3$	$IOClO_3$
Colour	Colourless		Pale yellow	Red	Not obtained pure
MP/°C		-167.3	-117	< -78	
BP/°C		-15.9	44.5	—	
Decomp temp /°C		~ 100	20	-20	

by the action of F_2 on concentrated $HOClO_3$, but the product had a pronounced tendency to explode on freezing. More recently,[155] extremely pure $FOClO_3$ has been obtained by thermal decomposition of NF_4ClO_4 and such samples can be manipulated and repeatedly frozen without mishap. Thermal decomposition occurs via two routes:

$$ClF + 2O_2 \longleftarrow FOClO_3 \longrightarrow FClO_2 + O_2$$

It readily oxidizes iodide ions: $FOClO_3 + 2I^- \longrightarrow ClO_4^- + F^- + I_2$. $FOClO_3$ also adds to C=C double bonds in fluorocarbons to give perfluoroalkyl perchlorates:

$$CF_2{=}CF_2 + FOClO_3 \xrightarrow{-45°} CF_3CF_2OClO_3$$

$$CF_3CF{=}CF_2 + FOCl_3 \xrightarrow{-45°} \underset{68\%}{CF_3CF_2CF_2OClO_3}$$

$$+ \underset{32\%}{CF_3CF(OClO_3)CF_3}$$

The formation of isomers in this last reaction implies a low bond polarity of FO– in $FOClO_3$.

Chlorine perchlorate, $ClOClO_3$, is made by low-temperature metathesis:

$$MClO_4 + ClOSO_2F \xrightarrow{-45°} ClOClO_3 + MSO_3F$$

$$(M{=}Cs, NO_2)$$

The bromine analogue can be made similarly using $BrOSO_2F$ at $-20°$ or by direct bromination of $ClOClO_3$ with Br_2 at $-45°$. Both compounds

155 C. J. SCHACK and K. O. CHRISTE, *Inorg. Chem.* **18**, 2619-20 (1979). For vibrational spectra, thermodynamic properties and confirmation of C_s structure see K. O. CHRISTE and E. C. CURTIS, *Inorg. Chem.* **21**, 2938-45 (1982).

are thermally unstable and shock sensitive; e.g. $ClOClO_3$ decomposes predominantly to Cl_2O_6 with smaller amounts of ClO_2, Cl_2 and O_2 on gentle warming. Direct iodination of $ClOClO_3$ at $-50°$ yields the polymeric white solid $I(OClO_3)_3$ rather than $IOClO_3$; this latter compound has never been obtained pure but is among the products of the reaction of I_2 with $AgClO_4$ at $-85°$, the other products being $I(OClO_3)_3$, $Ag[I(OClO_3)_2)]$ and AgI.

Halogen nitrates are even less thermally stable than the perchlorates: they are made by the action of $AgNO_3$ on an alcoholic solution of the halogen at low temperature. With an excess of $AgNO_3$, bromine and iodine yield $X(ONO_2)_3$. Numerous other routes are available; e.g., the reaction of ClF on $HONO_2$ gives a 90% yield of $ClONO_2$ and the best preparation of this compound is probably the reaction

$$Cl_2O + N_2O_5 \xrightarrow{0°} 2ClONO_2$$

Some physical properties are in Table 17.26. Both $FONO_2$ and $ClONO_2$ feature planar NO_3 groups with the halogen atom out of the plane. $ClONO_2$ has been used to convert metal chlorides to anhydrous metal nitrates, e.g. $Ti(NO_3)_4$. Likewise ICl_3 at $-30°$ yields $I(ONO_2)_3$. $ClONO_2$ and $IONO_2$ add across C=C double bonds, e.g.:

$$CH_2{=}CMe_2 + Cl{-}ONO_2 \xrightarrow{-78°} ClCH_2C(Me_2)ONO_2$$

Table 17.26   Some properties of halogen(I) nitrates

Property	$FONO_2$	$ClONO_2$	$BrONO_2$	$IONO_2$
Colour	Colourless	Colourless	Yellow	Yellow
MP/°C	-175	-107	-42	—
BP/°C	-45.9	18	—	—
Decomp temp/°C	Ambient	Ambient	<0	<0
$\Delta H_f^\circ(g, 298\ K)/$ kJ mol^{-1}	$+10.5$	$+29.2$	—	—
$\Delta G_f^\circ(g, 298\ K)/$ kJ mol^{-1}	$+73.5$	$+92.4$	—	—

Several other reactions have been studied but the overall picture is one of thermal instability, hazardous explosions, and vigorous chemical reactivity leading to complex mixtures of products.

The halogen fluorosulfates are amongst the most stable of the oxoacid derivatives of the halogens. $FOSO_2F$ is made by direct addition of F_2 to SO_3 and the others are made by direct combination of the halogen with an equimolar quantity of peroxodisulfuryl difluoride, $S_2O_6F_2$ (p. 640). With an excess of $S_2O_6F_2$, bromine and iodine yield $X(OSO_2F)_3$. An alternative route to $ClOSO_2F$ is the direct addition of ClF to SO_3, whilst $BrOSO_2F$ and $IOSO_2F$ can be made by thermal decomposition of the corresponding $X(OSO_2F)_3$. The halogen fluorosulfates are thermally unstable, moisture sensitive, highly reactive compounds. Some physical properties are summarized in Table 17.27. The vibrational spectra of $FOSO_2$ and $ClOSO_2F$ are consistent with C_s molecular symmetry as in $HOSO_2F$:

Much of the chemistry of the halogen fluorosulfates resembles that of the interhalogens (p. 824) and in many respects the fluorosulfate group can be regarded as a pseudohalogen (p. 319). There is some evidence of ionic self-dissociation and reactions can be classified as exchange, addition, displacement and complexation. This is illustrated for the iodine fluorosulfates in the following scheme:[156]

Table 17.27 Some physical properties of halogen fluorosulfates[a]

Property	$FOSO_2F$	$ClOSO_2F$	$BrOSO_2F$	$IOSO_2F$
Colour	Colourless	Yellow	Red-brown	Black
State at room temp	Gas	Liquid	Liquid	Solid
MP/°C	−158.5	−84.3	−31.5	51.5
BP/°C	−31.3	45.1	117.3	—

[a] $Br(OSO_2F)_3$ is a pale yellow solid, mp 59°; $I(OSO_2F)_3$ is a pale yellow solid, mp 32°.

---

[156] Ref. 23, pp. 1466–75, Halogen derivatives of oxyacids.

$BrOSO_2F$ has also been used to prepare new *N*-bromo sulfonimides such as $(CF_3SO_2)_2NBr$.[157] Other novel compounds include $[I(OSO_2F)_2]^+$-I^-[158] and the mixed valent iodine (III,V) polycation in $[(IO_2)_3]^+HSO_4^-$.[159]

17.3 The Chemistry of Astatine[160,161]

All isotopes of element 85, astatine, are intensely radioactive with very short half-lives (p. 795). As a consequence weighable amounts of the element or its compounds cannot be prepared and no bulk properties are known. The chemistry of the element must, of necessity, be studied by tracer techniques on extremely dilute solutions, and this introduces the risk of experimental errors and the consequent possibility of erroneous

---

[157] S. SINGH and D. D. DESMARTEAU, *Inorg. Chem.* **25**, 4596–7 (1986).

[158] M. J. COLLINS, G. DÉNÈS and R. J. GILLESPIE, *J. Chem. Soc., Chem. Commun.*, 1296–7 (1984).

[159] A. REHR and M. JANSEN, *Z. anorg. allg. Chem.* **608**, 159–65 (1992).

[160] E. H. APPELMAN, Astatine, Chap. 6 in *MTP International Review of Science, Inorganic Chemistry*, Series 1. Vol. 3, *Main Group Elements Group VII and Noble Gases*, pp. 181–98, Butterworths, London, 1972; see also ref. 23, pp. 1573–94, Astatine.

[161] T. J. RUTH, M. DOMBSKY, J. M. D'AURIA and T. E. WARD, *Radiochemistry of Astatine*, US Dept. of Energy, Nuclear Science Series NAS-NS-3064 (DE 880 15386), Washington, DC, 1988, 80 pp.

conclusions. Nevertheless, a picture of the element is emerging, as outlined below. The synthesis of the element (p. 795), its natural occurrence in rare branches of the ^{235}U decay series (p. 796), and its atomic properties (p. 800) have already been mentioned.

The chemistry of At is most conveniently studied using ^{211}At ($t_{\frac{1}{2}}$ 7.21 h). This isotope is prepared by α-particle bombardment of ^{209}Bi using acceleration energies in the range 26–29 MeV. Higher energies result in the concurrent formation of ^{210}At and ^{209}At which complicate the subsequent radiochemical assays. The Bi is irradiated either as the metal or its oxide and the target must be cooled to avoid volatilization of the At produced. Astatine is then removed by heating the target to 300–600° (i.e. above the mp of Bi, 217°) in a stream of N_2 and depositing the sublimed element on a glass cold finger or cooled Pt disc. Aqueous solutions of the element can be prepared by washing the cold finger or disc with dilute HNO_3 or HCl. Alternatively, the irradiated target can be dissolved in perchloric acid containing a little iodine as carrier for the astatine; the Bi is precipitated as phosphate and the aqueous solution of AtI used as it is or the activity can be extracted into CCl_4 or $CHCl_3$.

Five oxidation states of At have been definitely established (−I, 0, +I, V, VII) and one other (III) has been postulated. The standard oxidation potentials connecting these states in 0.1 M acid solution are $E°/V$:

$$\text{At}^- \xleftarrow{+0.3} \text{At(0)} \xleftarrow{+1.0} \text{HOAt} \xleftarrow{+1.5} \text{AtO}_3^-$$
$$\xleftarrow[\quad]{> +1.6} \text{AtO}_4^-$$

These values should be compared with those for the other halogens (in 1 M acid) (p. 854). Noteworthy features are that At is the only halogen with an oxidation state between 0 and V that is thermodynamically stable towards disproportionation, and that the smooth trends in the values of $E°(\frac{1}{2}X_2/X^-)$ and $E°(HOX/\frac{1}{2}X_2)$ continue to At.

The astatide ion At^- (which coprecipitates with AgI, TlI, PtI_2 or PdI_2) can be obtained from At(0) or AtI using moderately powerful reducing agents, e.g. Zn/H^+, SO_2, SO_3^{2-}/OH^-, $[Fe(CN)_6]^{4-}$ or As^{III}. Reoxidation to At(0) can be effected by the weak oxidants $[Fe(CN)_6]^{3-}$, As^V or dilute HNO_3. Oxidants of intermediate power (e.g. Cl_2, Br_2, Fe^{3+}, $Cr_2O_7^{2-}$, VO^{2+}) convert astatine to an intermediate oxidation state which is most probably AtO^- or At^+ and which does not extract into CCl_4. Powerful oxidants (Ce^{IV}, $NaBiO_3$, $S_2O_8^{2-}$, IO_4^-) convert At(0) directly to AtO_3^- (carried by $AgIO_3$, $Ba(IO_3)_2$, etc., and not extractable into CCl_4). The perastatate ion, AtO_4^-, was first conclusively prepared by V. A. Khalkin's group in the USSR in 1970 using solid XeF_2 in hot NaOH solution at pH ~ 10. It is unstable in acid solutions, being completely decomposed to AtO_3^- within 5–10 minutes at pH 1 and 90°C, for example.

At(0) reacts with halogens X_2 to produce interhalogen species AtX, which can be extracted into CCl_4, whereas halide ions X^- yield polyhalide ions AtX_2^- which are not extracted by CCl_4 but can be extracted into Pr_2^iO. The equilibrium formation constants of the various trihalide ions are intercompared in Table 17.28.

A rudimentary chemistry of organic derivatives of astatine is emerging, but the problems of radiation damage, product separation and tracer

Table 17.28 Formation constants for trihalide ions at 25°C

Reaction	$K/\text{l mol}^{-1}$	Reaction	$K/\text{l mol}^{-1}$
$Cl_2 + Cl^- \rightleftharpoons Cl_3^-$	0.12	**AtI + Br$^-$ $\rightleftharpoons$ AtIBr$^-$**	**120**
$Br_2 + Cl^- \rightleftharpoons Br_2Cl^-$	1.4	$ICl + Cl^- \rightleftharpoons ICl_2^-$	170
$I_2 + Cl^- \rightleftharpoons I_2Cl^-$	3	**AtBr + Br$^-$ $\rightleftharpoons$ AtBr$_2^-$**	**320**
AtI + Cl$^-$ $\rightleftharpoons$ AtICl$^-$	**9**	$IBr + Br^- \rightleftharpoons IBr_2^-$	440
$Br_2 + Br^- \rightleftharpoons Br_3^-$	17	$I_2 + I^- \rightleftharpoons I_3^-$	800
$IBr + Cl^- \rightleftharpoons IBrCl^-$	43	**AtI + I$^-$ $\rightleftharpoons$ AtI$_2^-$**	**2000**

identification, already severe for inorganic compounds of astatine, are even worse with organic derivatives. Two reviews are available.[162,163] Various compounds of the type RAt, $RAtCl_2$, R_2AtCl and $RAtO_2$ (R = phenyl or *p*-tolyl) have been synthesized using astatine-labelled iodine reagents, e.g.:

$$Ph_2I.I \xrightarrow{At^-} Ph_2IAt \xrightarrow{175°} PhI + PhAt$$

$$PhI \xrightarrow{AtI} PhAt$$

$$PhI \xrightarrow[130-200°]{At^-} PhAt$$

$$PhN_2Cl \xrightarrow{At^-} PhAt$$

[162] K. BEREI and L. VASAROS, The Organic Chemistry of Astatine, in S. PATAI and Z. RAPPAPORT (eds.), *The Chemistry of Organic Functional Groups*, Wiley, New York, 1983.

[163] H. H. COENEN, S. M. MOERLEIN and G. STÖCKLIN, *Radiochem. Acta* **34**, 47–68 (1983).

$$PhAt \xrightarrow{Cl_2} PhAtCl_2 \begin{cases} \xrightarrow{HgPh_2} Ph_2AtCl \\ \xrightarrow[70-100°]{NaOCl} PhAtO_2 \end{cases}$$

In addition, demercuriation reactions have resulted in a wide variety of rather complex compounds including aromatic aminoacids, steroids, imidazols, etc. in good yields (at the tracer level). The driving force in these studies has been the hope of incorporating ^{211}At into biologically active compounds for therapautic use.

Astatine has been shown to be superior to radio-iodine for the destruction of abnormal thyroid tissue (p. 794) because of the localized action of the emitted α-particles which dissipate 5.9 MeV within a range of 70 μm of tissue, whereas the much less energetic β-rays of radio-iodine have a maximum range of *ca.* 2000 μm. However, its general inaccessibility and high cost render its extensive application unlikely.

1 H	2 He																
3 Li	4 Be											5 B	6 C	7 N	8 O	9 F	10 Ne
11 Na	12 Mg											13 Al	14 Si	15 P	16 S	17 Cl	18 Ar
19 K	20 Ca	21 Sc	22 Ti	23 V	24 Cr	25 Mn	26 Fe	27 Co	28 Ni	29 Cu	30 Zn	31 Ga	32 Ge	33 As	34 Se	35 Br	36 Kr
37 Rb	38 Sr	39 Y	40 Zr	41 Nb	42 Mo	43 Tc	44 Ru	45 Rh	46 Pd	47 Ag	48 Cd	49 In	50 Sn	51 Sb	52 Te	53 I	54 Xe
55 Cs	56 Ba	57 La	72 Hf	73 Ta	74 W	75 Re	76 Os	77 Ir	78 Pt	79 Au	80 Hg	81 Tl	82 Pb	83 Bi	84 Po	85 At	86 Rn
87 Pr	88 Ra	89 Ac	104 Rf	105 Db	106 Sg	107 Bh	108 Hs	109 Mt	110 Uun	111 Uuu	112 Uub						

58 Ce	59 Pr	60 Nd	61 Pm	62 Sm	63 Eu	64 Gd	65 Tb	66 Dy	67 Ho	68 Er	69 Tm	70 Yb	71 Lu
90 Th	91 Pa	92 U	93 Np	94 Pu	95 Am	96 Cm	97 Bk	98 Cf	99 Es	100 Fm	101 Md	102 No	103 Lr

18

The Noble Gases: Helium, Neon, Argon, Krypton, Xenon and Radon

18.1 Introduction

In 1785 H. Cavendish in his classic work on the composition of air (p. 406) noted that, after repeatedly sparking a sample of air with an excess of O_2, there was a small residue of gas which he was unable to remove by chemical means and which he estimated with astonishing accuracy to be "not more than $\frac{1}{120}$th part of the whole". He could not further characterize this component of air, and its identification as argon had to wait for more than a century. But first came the discovery of helium, which is unique in being the only element discovered extraterrestrially before being found on earth. During the solar eclipse of 18 August 1868, a new yellow line was observed close to the sodium D lines in the spectrum of the sun's chromosphere. This led J. N. Lockyer (founder in 1869 of the journal *Nature*) and E. Frankland to suggest the existence of a new element which, appropriately, they named helium (Greek ἥλιος, the sun). The same line was observed by L. Palmieri in 1881

in the spectrum of volcanic gas from Mount Vesuvius, and the terrestrial existence of helium was finally confirmed by W. Ramsay[1] in the course of his intensive study of atmospheric gases which led to the recognition of a new group in the periodic table. This work was initiated by the physicist, Lord Rayleigh, and was recognized in 1904 by the award of the Nobel Prizes for Chemistry and Physics to Ramsay and Rayleigh respectively.

In order to test Prout's hypothesis (that the atomic weights of all elements are multiples of that of hydrogen) Rayleigh made accurate measurements of the densities of common gases and found, to his surprise, that the density of nitrogen obtained from air by the removal of O_2, CO_2 and H_2O was consistently about 0.5% higher than that of nitrogen obtained chemically from ammonia. Ramsay then treated "atmospheric nitrogen" with heated magnesium ($3Mg + N_2 \longrightarrow Mg_3N_2$), and was left with a small amount of a much

---

[1] M. W. TRAVERS, *Life of Sir William Ramsay*. E. Arnold, London, 1956.

denser, monatomic gas[†] which, in a joint paper [*Proc. R. Soc.* **57**, 265 (1895)], was identified as a new element which was named *argon* (Greek ἀργόν, idle or lazy) because of its inert nature. Unfortunately there was no space for a new and unreactive, gaseous, element in the periodic table (p. 20), which led to Ramsay's audacious suggestion that a whole new group might be accommodated. By 1898 Ramsay and M. W. Travers had isolated three further new elements by the low-temperature distillation of liquid air (which had only recently become available) and characterized them by spectroscopic analysis: krypton (Greek κρυπτόν, hidden, concealed), neon (Greek νέον, new) and xenon (Greek ξένον, strange).

In 1895 Ramsay also identified helium as the gas previously found occluded in uranium minerals and mistakenly reported as nitrogen. Five years later he and Travers isolated helium from samples of atmospheric neon.

Element 86, the final member of the group, is a short-lived, radioactive element, formerly known as radium-emanation or niton or, depending on which radioactive series it originates in (i.e. which isotope) as radon, thoron, or actinon. It was first isolated and studied in 1902 by E. Rutherford and F. Soddy and is now universally known as radon (from radium and the termination-on adopted for the noble gases; Latin *radius*, ray).

Once the existence of the new group had been established it was apparent that it not only fitted into the periodic table but actually improved it by providing a bridge between the strongly electronegative halogens and strongly electropositive alkali metals. The elements became known as "inert gases" comprising Group 0, though A. von Antropoff suggested that a maximum valency of eight might be attainable and designated them as Group VIIIB. They have also been described as

the "rare gases" but, since the lighter members are by no means rare and the heavier ones are not entirely inert, "noble" gases seems a more appropriate name and has come into general use during the past three decades as has their designation as Group 18 of the periodic table.

The apparent inertness of the noble gases gave them a key position in the electronic theories of valency as developed by G. N. Lewis (1916) and W. Kossel (1916) and the attainment of a "stable octet" was regarded as a prime criterion for bond formation between atoms (p. 21). Their monatomic, non-polar nature makes them the most nearly "perfect" gases known, and has led to continuous interest in their physical properties.

18.2 The Elements

18.2.1 Distribution, production and uses [2,3]

Helium is the second most abundant element in the universe (76% H, 23% He) as a result of its synthesis from hydrogen (p. 9) but, being too light to be retained by the earth's gravitational field, all primordial helium has been lost and terrestrial helium, like argon, is the result of radioactive decay (^{4}He from α-decay of heavier elements, ^{40}Ar from electron capture by ^{40}K (p. 18).

The noble gases make up about 1% of the earth's atmosphere in which their major component is Ar. Smaller concentrations are occluded in igneous rocks, but the atmosphere is the principal commercial source of Ne, Ar, Kr and Xe, which are obtained as by-products of the liquefaction and separation of air (p. 604). Some Ar is also obtained from synthetic ammonia plants in which it accumulates after entering as impurity in the N_2 and H_2 feeds. World production of

---

[†] The molecular weight (mean relative molecular mass) was obtained by determination of density but, in order to determine that the gas was monatomic and its atomic and molecular weights identical, it was necessary to measure the velocity of sound in the gas and to derive from this the ratio of its specific heats: kinetic theory predicts that $C_p/C_v = 1.67$ for a monatomic and 1.40 for a diatomic gas.

[2] Helium-group gases, in *Kirk–Othmer Encyclopedia of Chemical Technology*, 4th edn, Vol. 13, pp. 1–53. Wiley-Interscience, New York, 1995.

[3] W. J. GRANT and S. L. REDFEARN, Industrial gases, in R. THOMPSON (ed.), *The Modern Inorganic Chemicals Industry*, pp. 273–301. The Chemical Society, London, 1977.

Ar in 1975 was 700 000 tonnes for use mainly as an inert atmosphere in high-temperature metallurgical processes and, in smaller amounts, for filling incandescent lamps. By 1993, production had increased considerably and 716 000 tonnes (427×10^6 m^3) were produced in the USA alone. The price was \$0.76/m^3 for bulk supplies and \$2.6–8.5/m^3 for laboratory quantities, depending on purity. Along with Ne, Kr and Xe, which are produced on a much smaller scale, Ar is also used in discharge tubes — the so-called neon lights for advertisements — (the colour produced depending on the particular mixture of gases used). They are also used in fluorescent tubes, though here the colour produced depends not on the gas but on the phosphor which is coated on the inside walls of the tube. Lasers are another important application, though the actual amount of gas required for this use is minute compared with the other uses.

Although the concentration of He in the atmosphere is five times that of Kr and sixty times that of Xe (see Table 18.1), its recovery from this source is uneconomical compared to that from natural gas if more than 0.4% He is present. This concentration is attained in a number of gases in the USA (concentrations as high as 7% are known) and in eastern Europe (mainly Poland). Some 99×10^6 m^3 (16 800 tonnes) of He was produced in the USA in 1993, the bulk price being \$1.77/m^3 (\$2.30 m^3 for liquid He). Laboratory quantities were in the range \$5.00–45.00/m^3 depending on purity. The former use of He as a non-flammable gas (it has a lifting power of approximately 1 kg per m^3) in airships is no longer important, though it is still employed in meteorological balloons. The primary domestic use of He (30%) in as a cryogenic fluid for temperatures at or below 4.2 K; as much as two-thirds of this is for magnetic resonance imaging and other nmr instruments. Other major uses are in arc welding (21%), pressurizing and purging (11%). The choice between Ar and He for these purposes is determined by cost and, except in the USA, this generally favours Ar. Smaller, but important, uses for He are:

(a) as a substitute for N$_2$ in synthetic breathing gas for deep-sea diving (its low solubility in blood minimizes the degassing which occurs with N$_2$ when divers are depressurized and which produces the sometimes fatal "bends");

(b) as a leak detector;

(c) as a coolant in HTR nuclear reactors (p. 1258);

(d) as a flow-gas in gas–liquid chromatography;

(e) for deaeration of solutions and as a general inert diluent or inert atmosphere.

The price per m^3 of the other noble gases is considerably higher (Ne \$70, Kr \$350 and Xe \$3500, and this tends to restrict their usage to specialist applications only. Radon has been used in the treatment of cancer and as a radioactive source in testing metal castings but, because of its short half-life (3.824 days) it has been superseded by more convenient materials. Such small quantities as are required are obtained as a decay product of ^{226}Ra (1 g of which yields 0.64 cm^3 in 30 days).

18.2.2 Atomic and physical properties of the elements [2-4]

Some of the important properties of the elements are given in Table 18.1. The imprecision of the atomic weights of Kr and Xe reflects the natural occurrence of several isotopes of these elements. For He, however, and to a lesser extent Ar, a single isotope predominates (^{4}He, 99.999 863%; ^{40}Ar, 99.600%) and much greater precision is possible. The natural preponderance of ^{40}Ar is indeed responsible for the well-known inversion of atomic weight order of Ar and K in the periodic table, and the position of Ar in front of K was only finally accepted when it was shown that the atomic weight of He placed it in front of Li. The second isotope of helium, ^{3}He, has only been available in significant amounts since

---

[4] A. H. COCKETT and K. C. SMITH, Chap. 5 in *Comprehensive Inorganic Chemistry*, Vol. 1, pp. 139–211, Pergamon Press, Oxford, 1973. G. A. COOK (ed.), *Argon, Helium and the Rare Gases*, 2 vols, Interscience, New York, 1961, 818 pp.

Table 18.1   Some properties of the noble gases

Property	He	Ne	Ar	Kr	Xe	Rn
Atomic number	2	10	18	36	54	86
Number of naturally occurring isotopes	2	3[a]	3	6	9	(1)
Atomic weight	4.002 602(2)	20.179 7(6)	39.948(1)	83.80(1)	131.29(2)	(222)[b]
Abundance in dry air/ppm by vol	5.24	18.21	9340	1.14	0.087	Variable traces[c]
Abundance in igneous rocks/ppm by wt	3×10^{-3}	7×10^{-5}	4×10^{-2}	—	—	1.7×10^{-10}
Outer shell electronic configuration	$1s^2$	$2s^2 2p^6$	$3s^2 3p^6$	$4s^2 4p^6$	$5s^2 5p^6$	$6s^2 6p^6$
First ionization energy/kJ mol^{-1}	2372	2080	1520	1351	1170	1037
BP/K	4.215	27.09	87.28	119.80	165.03	211
/°C	−268.93	−246.06	−185.86	−153.35	−108.13	−62
MP/K	—[d]	24.56	83.80	115.76	161.37	202
/°C	—	−248.61	−189.37	−157.20	−111.80	−71
ΔH_{vap}/kJ mol^{-1}	0.08	1.74	6.52	9.05	12.65	18.1
Density at STP/mg cm^{-3}	0.178 50	0.899 94	1.7838	3.7493	5.8971	9.73
Thermal conductivity at 0°C/J s^{-1} m^{-1} K^{-1}	0.1418	0.0461	0.0169	0.008 74	0.005 06	
Solubility in water at 20°C/cm^3 kg^{-1}	8.61	10.5	33.6	59.4	108.1	230

[a] In the pioneering work of J. J. Thomson and F. W. Aston on mass-spectrometry, neon was the first non-radioactive element shown to exist in different isotopic forms.

[b] The relative atomic mass of this nuclide is 222.0176.

[c] Mean value ~6×10^{-14}.

[d] Helium is the only liquid which cannot be frozen by the reduction of temperature alone. Pressure must also be applied. It is also the only substance lacking a "triple point", i.e. a combination of temperature and pressure at which solid, liquid and gas coexist in equilibrium.

the 1950s when it began to accumulate as a β-decay product of tritium stored for thermonuclear weapons.

All the elements have stable electronic configurations ($1s^2$ or $ns^2 np^6$) and, under normal circumstances are colourless, odourless and tasteless monatomic gases. The non-polar, spherical nature of the atoms which this implies, leads to physical properties which vary regularly with atomic number. The only interatomic interactions are weak van der Waals forces. These increase in magnitude as the polarizabilities of the atoms increase and the ionization energies decrease, the effect of both factors therefore being to increase the interactions as the sizes of the atoms increase. This is shown most directly by the enthalpy of vaporization, which is a measure of the energy required to overcome the interactions, and increases from He to Rn by a factor of over 200. However, ΔH_{vap} is in all cases small and bps are correspondingly low, that of He being the lowest of any substance.

The stability of the electronic configuration is indicated by the fact that each element has the highest ionization energy in its period, though the value decreases down the group as a result of increasing size of the atoms. For the heavier elements is it actually smaller than for first-row elements such as O and F with consequences for the chemical reactivities of the noble gases which will be considered in the next section. Nuclear properties, particularly for xenon, have been exploited for nmr spectroscopy[5] and Mössbauer

---

[5] C. J. JAMESON in J. MASON (ed.), *Multinuclear NMR*, Plenum Press, New York, 1987, pp. 463–77.

spectroscopy[6] (p. 896). The environmental health hazard posed by the natural generation of radioactive radon gas should also be noted.[7]

As the first member of this unusual group He has, of course, a number of unique properties. Among these is the astonishing transition from so-called HeI to HeII which occurs around 2.2 K (the λ-point temperature) when liquid He (^{4}He to be precise, since ^{3}He does not behave in this way until 1–3 millikelvin) is cooled by continuous pumping. The transition is clearly seen as the sudden cessation of turbulent boiling, even though evaporation continues. HeI is a normal liquid but at the transition the specific heat increases abruptly by a factor of 10, the thermal conductivity by the order of 10^6, and the viscosity, as measured by its flow through a fine capillary, becomes effectively zero (hence its description as a "superfluid"). HeII also has the curious ability to cover, with a film a few hundred atoms thick, all solid surfaces which are connected to it and are below the λ point. This can be spectacularly demonstrated by dipping the bottom of a suitable container into a bath of HeII. Once the vessel has cooled, liquid He flows, apparently without friction, up and over the edge of the container until the levels inside and outside are equal. These phenomena are evidently the result of quantum effects on a macroscopic scale, and HeII is believed to consist of two components: a true superfluid with zero viscosity and entropy, together with a normal fluid, the fraction of the former increasing to 1 at absolute zero. No completely satisfactory explanation of these phenomena is yet available.

Finally, a property of practical importance which may be noted is the ability of noble gases, especially He, to diffuse through many materials commonly used in laboratories. Rubber and PVC

are cases in point, and He will even diffuse through most glasses so that glass Dewar vessels cannot be used in cryoscopic work involving liquid He.

18.3 Chemistry of the Noble Gases[8-12]

The discovery of the noble gases was a direct result of their unreactive nature, and early unsuccessful attempts to induce chemical reactions reinforced the belief in their inertness. Nevertheless, attempts were made to make the heavier gases react, and in 1933 Linus Pauling, from a consideration of ionic radii, suggested that KrF_6 and XeF_6 should be preparable. D. M. Yost and A. L. Kaye attempted to prepare the latter by passing an electric discharge through a mixture of Xe and F_2 but failed[†] and, until "$XePtF_6$" was prepared in 1962, the only compounds of the noble gases which could be prepared were clathrates.

While investigating the chemistry of PtF_6, N. Bartlett noticed that its accidental exposure to air produced a change in colour, and with D. H. Lohmann he later showed this to be O_2^+-$[PtF_6]^-$.[13] Recognizing that PtF_6 must therefore be an oxidizing agent of unprecedented power, he noted that Rn and Xe should similarly be oxidizable by this reagent since the first ionization energy of Rn is less than, and that of

[6] N. N. Greenwood and T. C. Gibb, *Mössbauer Spectroscopy*, Chapman and Hall, London 1971, ^{83}Kr pp. 437–41; ^{129}Xe, ^{131}Xe pp. 482–6.

[7] P. K. Hopke (ed.), *Radon and its Decay Products: Occurrence, Properties and Health Effects* ACS Symposium Series No. 331, 1986, 586 pp. D. J. Hanson, *Chem. & Eng. News*, Feb. 6, 1989, pp. 7–13. A. F. Gardner, R. S. Gillett and P. S. Phillips, *Chem. in Britain*, April 1992, pp. 344–8.

[8] N. Bartlett and F. E. Sladky, Chap. 6, in *Comprehensive Inorganic Chemistry*, Vol. 1, pp. 213–330, Pergamon Press, Oxford. 1973.

[9] D. T. Hawkins, W. E. Falconer and N. Bartlett, *Noble Gas Compounds, A Bibliography 1962–1976*. Plenum Press, New York, 1978.

[10] J. H. Holloway, *Noble-gas Chemistry*, Methuen, London, 1968, 213 pp. See also *Chem. in Britain*, July 1987, pp. 658–64.

[11] K. Seppelt and D. Lentz, *Progr. Inorg. Chem.* **29**, 167–202 (1982).

[12] pp. 38–53 of ref. 2.

[13] N. Bartlett and D. H. Lohmann, *Proc. Chem. Soc.* 1962, 115–6.

[†] By what must have seemed to these workers a cruel irony, essentially the same method, but using sunlight instead of a discharge, when tried 30 years later produced XeF_2.

Xe is comparable to, that of molecular oxygen ($1175\,kJ\,mol^{-1}$ for $O_2 \rightarrow O_2^+ + e^-$). He quickly proceeded to show that deep-red PtF_6 vapour spontaneously oxidized Xe to produce an orange-yellow solid and announced this in a brief note.[14] Within a few months XeF_4 and XeF_2 had been synthesized in other laboratories.[15,16] Noble-gas chemistry had begun.

Isolable compounds are obtained only with the heavier noble gases Kr and Xe; radon also reacts with F_2 but isolation and characterization of products is hampered by its intense radioactivity which is not only hazardous but also decomposes the reagents involved. The compounds usually involve bonds to F or O, in most cases exclusively so. However, a growing number of compounds involving bonds to Cl, N and even C are becoming known (p. 901). Chemical combinations involving the lighter noble gases have been observed but are very unstable, and frequently occur only as transient species (p. 903).

18.3.1 Clathrates

Probably the most familiar of all clathrates are those formed by Ar, Kr and Xe with quinol, $1,4-C_6H_4(OH)_2$, and with water. The former are obtained by crystallizing quinol from aqueous or other convenient solution in the presence of the noble gas at a pressure of 10–40 atm. The quinol crystallizes in the less-common β-form, the lattice of which is held together by hydrogen bonds in such a way as to produce cavities in the ratio 1 cavity: 3 molecules of quinol. Molecules of gas (G) are physically trapped in these cavities, there being only weak van der Waals interactions between

"guest" and "host" molecules. The clathrates are therefore nonstoichiometric but have an "ideal" or "limiting" composition of $[G\{C_6H_4(OH)_2\}_3]$. Once formed they have considerable stability but the gas is released on dissolution or melting. Similar clathrates are obtained with numerous other gases of comparable size, such as O_2, N_2, CO and SO_2 (the first clathrate to be fully characterized, by H. M. Powell in 1947) but not He or Ne, which are too small or insufficiently polarizable to be retained.

Noble gas hydrates are formed similarly when water is frozen under a high pressure of gas (p. 626). They have the ideal composition, $[G_8(H_2O)_{46}]$, and again are formed by Ar, Kr and Xe but not by He or Ne. A comparable phenomenon occurs when synthetic zeolites (molecular sieves) are cooled under a high pressure of gas, and Ar and Kr have been encapsulated in this way (p. 358). Samples containing up to 20% by weight of Ar have been obtained.

Clathrates provide a means of storing noble gases and of handling the various radioactive isotopes of Kr and Xe which are produced in nuclear reactors.

18.3.2 Compounds of xenon

The chemistry of Xe is much the most extensive in this group and the known oxidation states of Xe range from +2 to +8. Details of some of the more important compounds are given in Table 18.2. There is clearly a rich variety of stereochemistries, though the description of these depends on whether only nearest-neighbour atoms are considered or whether the supposed disposition of lone-pairs of electrons is also included. Weaker secondary interactions in crystalline compounds also tend to increase the number of atoms surrounding a central Xe atom. For example, $[XeF_5]^+[AsF_6]^-$ has 5 F at 179–182 pm and *three* further F at 265–281 pm, whereas $[XeF_5]^+[RuF_6]^-$ has 5 F at 179–184 pm and *four* further F at 255–292 pm. If only the most closely bonded atoms are counted, then Xe is known with all coordination numbers from 0 to 8 as shown schematically in Table 18.3.

[14] N. BARTLETT, *Proc. Chem. Soc.* 1962, 218.

[15] H. H. CLAASSEN, H. SELIG and J. G. MALM, *J. Am. Chem. Soc.* **84**, 3593 (1962). See also P. LAZLO and G. J. SCHROBILGEN, *Angew. Chem. Int. Edn. Engl.* **28**, 636 (1989) for further detailed chronology of the first synthesis of XeF_4.

[16] R. HOPPE, W. DÄHNE, H. MATTAUCH and K. H. RÖDDER, *Angew. Chem.* **74**, 903 (1962). See also note on priorities by W. KLEMM, *Nachr. Chem. Tech. Lab.* **30**, 963 (1982).

Table 18.2 Some compounds of xenon with fluorine and oxygen

Oxidation State	Compound	MP/°C	Stereochemistry of Xe	
			Actual	Pseudo, i.e. with electron lone-pairs (in parentheses) included
+2	XeF_2	129	$D_{\infty h}$, linear	Trigonal bipyramidal (3)
+4	XeF_4	117.1	D_{4h}, square planar	Octahedral (2)
+6	XeF_6	49.5	Distorted octahedral (fluxional)	Pentagonal bipyramidal or capped octahedral (1)
	$[XeF_5]^+[AsF_6]^-$	130.5	C_{4v}, square pyramidal	Octahedral (1)
	$CsXeF_7$	dec > 50		
	$[NO]^+_2[XeF_8]^{2-}$		D_{4d}, square antiprismatic	(Lone-pair inactive)
	$XeOF_4$	(−46)	C_{4v}, square pyramidal	Octahedral (1)
	XeO_2F_2	30.8	C_{2v}, "see-saw"	Trigonal bipyramidal (1)
	$CsXeOF_5$		Distorted octahedral	Capped octahedral (1)
	$KXeO_3F$		Square pyramidal (chain)	Octahedral (1)
+8	XeO_3	explodes	C_{3v}, pyramidal	Tetrahedral (1)
	XeO_4	−35.9	T_d, tetrahedral	(No lone-pairs on Xe)
	XeO_3F_2	−54.1	D_{3h}, trigonal bipyramidal	Trigonal bipyramidal
	Ba_2XeO_6	dec > 300	O_h, octahedral	(No lone-pairs on Xe)

The three fluorides of Xe can be obtained by direct reaction but conditions need to be carefully controlled if these are to be produced individually in pure form. XeF_2 can be prepared by heating F_2 with an excess of Xe to 400°C in a sealed nickel vessel or by irradiating mixtures of Xe and F_2 with sunlight. The product is a white, crystalline solid consisting of parallel linear XeF_2 units (Fig. 18.1). It is sublimable and its infrared and Raman spectra show that the linear molecular structure is retained in the vapour. XeF_2 is a versatile mild fluorinating agent and will, for instance, difluorinate olefins (alkenes). Oxidative fluorination of MeI yields $MeIF_2$, and similar reactions yield Me_2EF_2 (E = S, Se, Te) and Me_3EF_2 (E = P, As, Sb).[17] A related reaction was used to prepare the organotellurium(VI) compound *mer*-Ph_3TeF_3:[18]

$$Ph_3TeF + XeF_2 \xrightarrow[\text{r.t.}]{CHCl_3} Ph_3TeF_3 + Xe$$

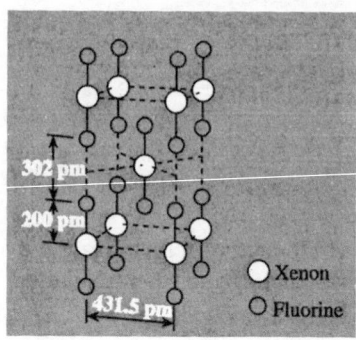

Figure 18.1 The until cell of crystalline XeF_2.

Reductive fluorination is exemplified by the high-yield synthesis of crystalline $CrOF_3$ at 275°C:[19]

$$2CrO_2F_2 + XeF_2 \longrightarrow 2CrOF_3 + Xe + O_2$$

XeF_2 sequentially fluorinates $Ir_4(CO)_{12}$ dissolved in anhydrous HF yielding, initially, the novel neutral complexes *mer*- and *fac*-$[Ir(CO)_3F_3]$.[20]

[17] A. M. FORSTER and A. J. DOWNS, *Polyhedron* **4**, 1625–35 (1985).

[18] A. S. SECCO,   K. ALAM,   B. J. BLACKBURN   and A. F. JANZEN, *Inorg. Chem.* **25** 2125–9 (1986).

[19] M. McHUGHES,   R. D. WILLETT,   H. B. DAVIS   and G. L. GARD, *Inorg. Chem.* **25**, 426–7 (1986).

[20] S. A. BREWER,   J. H. HOLLOWAY,   E. G. HOPE   and P. G. WATSON, *J. Chem. Soc., Chem. Commun.*, 1577–8 (1992).

Table 18.3 Stereochemistry of xenon

CN	Stereochemistry	Examples	Structure
0	—	Xe(g)	Xe
1	—	$[XeF]^+$, $[XeOTeF_5]^-$	Xe—
2	Linear	XeF_2, $[FXeFXeF]^+$, $FXeOSO_2F$	—Xe—
3	Pyramidal	XeO_3	
	T-shaped	$[XeF_3]^+$, $XeOF_2$	
4	Tetrahedral	XeO_4	
	Square	XeF_4	
	C_{2v}, "see-saw"	XeO_2F_2	
5	Trigonal bipyramidal	XeO_3F_2	
	Square pyramidal	$XeOF_4$, $[XeF_5]^+$	
6	Octahedral Distorted octahedral	$[XeO_6]^{4-}$ $XeF_6(g)$, $[XeOF_5]^-$	
7	(?)	$CsXeF_7$	
8	Square antiprismatic	$[XeF_8]^{2-}$	

By contrast, reaction of XeF_2 with the iridium carbonyl complex cation $[Ir(CO)_3(PEt_3)_2]^+$ in CH_2Cl_2 results in addition across one of the Ir–CO bonds to give the first example of a metal fluoroacyl complex:[21]

[21] A. J. BLAKE, R. W. COCKMAN, E. A. V. EBSWORTH and J. H. HOLLOWAY, *J. Chem. Soc., Chem. Commun.*, 529–30 (1988).

The product was isolated as white, air-sensitive crystals of the BF_4^- and PF_6^- salts.

XeF_2 dissolves in water to the extent of $25\,g\,dm^{-3}$ at $0°C$, the solution being fairly stable (half-life $\sim$7 h at $0°C$) unless base is present, in which case almost instantaneous decomposition takes place:

$$2XeF_2 + 2H_2O \longrightarrow 2Xe + 4HF + O_2$$

The aqueous solutions are powerful oxidizing agents, converting $2Cl^-$ to Cl_2, Ce^{III} to Ce^{IV}, Cr^{III} to Cr^{VI}, Ag^I to Ag^{II}, and even BrO_3^- to BrO_4^- (p. 871).

XeF_4 is best prepared by heating a 1:5 volume mixture of Xe and F_2 to 400°C under 6 atm pressure in a nickel vessel. It also is a white, crystalline, easily sublimed solid; the molecular shape is square planar (Xe–F 195.2 pm) and is essentially the same in both the solid and gaseous phases. Its properties are similar to those of XeF_2 except that it is a rather stronger fluorinating agent, as shown by the reactions:

$$2Hg + XeF_4 \longrightarrow Xe + 2HgF_2$$

$$Pt + XeF_4 \longrightarrow Xe + PtF_4$$

$$2SF_4 + XeF_4 \longrightarrow Xe + 2SF_6$$

It is also hydrolysed instantly by water, yielding a variety of products which include XeO_3:

$$XeF_4 + 2H_2O \longrightarrow \tfrac{1}{3}XeO_3 + \tfrac{2}{3}Xe + \tfrac{1}{2}O_2 + 4HF$$

This reaction is indeed a major hazard in Xe/F chemistry, since XeO_3 is highly explosive, and the complete exclusion of moisture is therefore essential (see p. 165 of ref. 10). Interestingly, the maximum yield of XeO_3 is 33% rather than the 50% that would be expected from a simple disproportionation of $2Xe^{IV} \rightarrow Xe^{VI} + Xe^{II}$, and the following reaction sequence has been suggested to explain this:

$$3Xe^{IV}F_4 + 6H_2O$$

$$\downarrow$$

$$2\{Xe^{II}O\} + \{Xe^{VIII}O_4\} + 12HF$$

$$\xrightarrow{\text{Decomposition}} Xe^{VI}O_3 + \tfrac{1}{2}O_2$$

$$\xrightarrow{\text{Decomposition in solution}} 2Xe^0 + O_2$$

The stoichiometry of the reaction also depends sensitively on the precise conditions of hydrolysis.[22]

XeF_6 is produced by the prolonged heating of 1:20 volume mixtures of Xe and F_2 at 250–300°C under 50–60 atm pressure in a nickel vessel. It is a crystalline solid, even more volatile than XeF_2

and XeF_4, and although colourless in the solid it is yellow in the liquid and gaseous phases. It is also more reactive than the other fluorides, being both a stronger oxidizing and a stronger fluorinating agent. Hydrolysis occurs with great vigour and the compound cannot be handled in glass or quartz apparatus because of a stepwise reaction which finally produces the dangerous XeO_3:

$$2XeF_6 + SiO_2 \longrightarrow 2XeOF_4 + SiF_4$$

$$2XeOF_4 + SiO_2 \longrightarrow 2XeO_2F_2 + SiF_4$$

$$2XeO_2F_2 + SiO_2 \longrightarrow 2XeO_3 + SiF_4$$

The structure of XeF_6 was the source of some controversy for more than a decade after its discovery in 1963. This was partly a result of the obvious problems associated with a substance which attacks most of the materials used to construct apparatus for structural determinations. It is now clear that in the gaseous phase this seemingly simple molecule⁻ is not a regular octahedron; it appears to be a non-rigid, distorted octahedron although, in spite of numerous theoretical studies, the precise nature of the distortion is uncertain (see, for instance, p. 299 of ref. 8). In the crystalline state at least four different forms of XeF_6 are known comprising square-pyramidal XeF_5^+ ions bridged by F^- ions. Three of these forms are tetramers, $[(XeF_5^+)F^-]_4$, while in the fourth and best-characterized cubic form,[23] the unit cell comprises 24 tetramers and 8 hexamers, $[(XeF_5^+)F^-]_6$ (Fig. 18.2).

The nature of the bonding in these xenon fluorides is discussed in the Panel opposite.

Apart from XeF, which is the light-emitting species in certain Xe/F_2 lasers, there is no evidence for the existence of any odd-valent fluorides. Reports of XeF_8 have not been confirmed. Of the other halides, $XeCl_2$, $XeBr_2$ and $XeCl_4$ have been detected by Mössbauer spectroscopy as products of the β-decay of their $^{129}_{53}I$

[22] J. L. Huston, *Inorg. Chem.* **21**, 685–8 (1982).

[23] R. D. Burbank and G. R. Jones, *J. Am. Chem. Soc.* **96**, 43–8 (1974).

Bonding in Noble Gas Compounds

As it was widely believed, prior to 1962, that the noble gases were chemically inert because of the stability, if not inviolability, of their electronic configurations, the discovery that compounds could in fact be prepared, immediately necessitated a description of the bonding involved. A variety of approaches has been suggested,[24] none of which is universally applicable. The simplest molecular-orbital description is that of the 3-centre, 4-electron σ bond in XeF_2, which involves only valence shell p orbitals and eschews the use of higher energy d orbitals. The orbitals involved are the colinear set comprising the $5p_x$ orbital of Xe, which contains 2 electrons, and the $2p_x$ orbitals from each of the F atoms, each containing 1 electron. The possible combinations of these orbitals are shown in Fig. A and yield 1 bonding, 1 nonbonding, and 1 antibonding orbital. A single bonding pair of electrons is responsible for binding all 3 atoms, and the occupation of the nonbonding orbital, situated largely on the F atoms, implies significant ionic character. The scheme should be compared with the 3-centre, 2-electron bonding proposed for boron hydrides (p. 158).

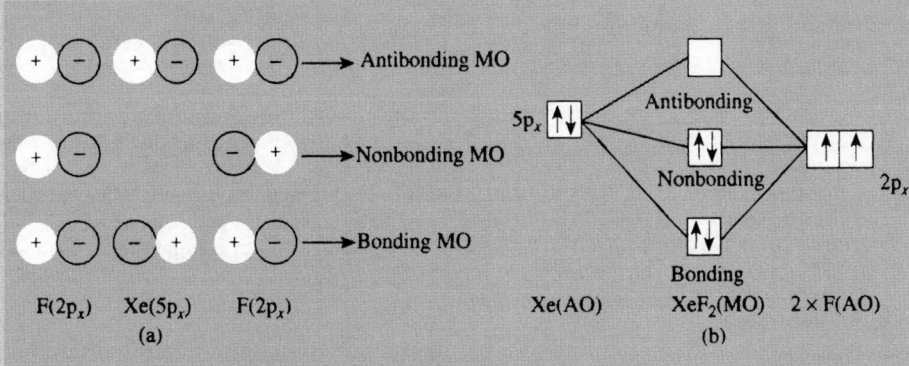

Fig. A. Molecular-orbital representation of the 3-centre F–Xe–F bond. (a) The possible combinations of colinear p_x atomic orbitals, and (b) the energies of the resulting MOs (schematic).

A similar treatment, involving two 3-centre bonds accounts satisfactorily for the planar structure of XeF_4 but fails when applied to XeF_6 since three 3-centre bonds would produce a regular octahedron instead of the distorted structure actually found. An improvement is possible if involvement of the Xe 5d orbitals is invoked,[25] since this produces a triplet level which would be subject to a Jahn–Teller distortion (p. 1021). However, the approach which has most consistently rationalized the stereochemistries of noble-gas compounds (as distinct from their bonding) is the electron-pair repulsion theory of Gillespie and Nyholm.[26] This assumes that stereochemistry is determined by the repulsions between valence-shell electron-pairs, both nonbonding and bonding, and that the former exert the stronger effect. Thus, in XeF_2 the Xe is surrounded by 10 electrons (8 from Xe and 1 from each F) distributed in 5 pairs; 2 bonding and 3 nonbonding. The 5 pairs are directed to the corners of a trigonal bipyramid and, because of their greater mutual repulsions, the 3 nonbonding pairs are situated in the equatorial plane at 120° to each other, leaving the 2 bonding pairs perpendicular to the plane and so producing a linear F–Xe–F molecule.

In the same way XeF_4, with 6 electron-pairs, is considered as pseudo-octahedral with its 2 nonbonding pairs trans to each other, leaving the 4 F atoms in a plane around the Xe. More distinctively, the 7 electron-pairs of XeF_6 suggest the possibility of a non-regular octahedral geometry and imply a distorted structure based on either a monocapped octahedral or a pentagonal pyramidal arrangement of electron-pairs, with the Xe–F bonds bending away from the projecting nonbonding pair.

It is an instructive exercise to devise similar rationalizations for the xenon oxides and oxofluorides listed in Table 18.3.

---

[24] C. A. COULSON, *J. Chem. Soc.* 1442–54 (1964). J. G. MALM, H. SELIG, J. JORTNER and S. A. RICE, *Chem. Revs.* **65**, 199–236 (1965)

[25] G. L. GOODMAN, *J. Chem. Phys.* **56**, 5038–41 (1972).

[26] R. J. GILLESPIE, *Molecular Geometry*, van Nostrand Rheinhold, London, 1972, 228 pp.

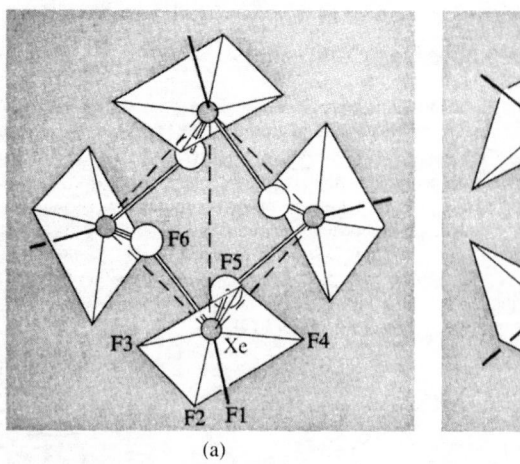
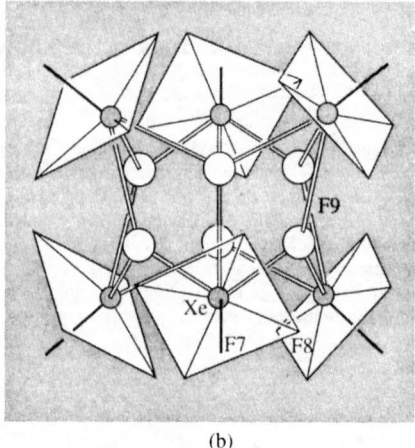

(a)   (b)

Figure 18.2   (a) Tetrameric, and (b) hexameric units in the cubic crystalline form of XeF_6. In (a) the Xe atoms (◯) form a tetrahedron, with the apical F atoms of the square-pyramidal XeF_5^+ ions pointing outwards, approximately from the centre, and the bridging F^- ions (○) near four of the six edges of the tetrahedron: Xe–F(1–5) 184 pm, Xe–F(6), 223 pm and 260 pm, angle Xe–F(6)–Xe 120.7°. In (b) the Xe atoms (◯) form an octahedron with the apical F atoms of the XeF_5^+ ions pointing outwards from the centre, and the bridging F^- ions (○) over six of the eight faces of the octahedron: Xe–F(7) 175 pm, Xe–F(8) 188 pm, Xe–F(9) 256 pm, angle Xe–F(9)–Xe 118.8°. XeF_5^+ ions are shown in skeletal form for clarity.

analogues, for instance:

$$\ce{^{129}_{53}ICl_2^- ->[-\beta^-] ^{129}_{54}XeCl_2}$$

$XeCl_2$ has also been trapped in a matrix of solid Xe after Xe/Cl_2 mixtures had been passed through a microwave discharge, but these halides are too unstable to be chemically characterized.

It is from the binary fluorides that other compounds of xenon are invariably prepared, by reactions which fall mostly into four classes:

(a) with F^- acceptors, yielding fluorocations of xenon;
(b) with F^- donors, yielding fluoroanions of xenon;
(c) F/H metathesis between XeF_2 and an anhydrous acid;
(d) hydrolysis, yielding oxofluorides, oxides and xenates.

(a) *Reactions with F^- acceptors.* XeF_2 has a more extensive F^- donor chemistry than has XeF_4; it reacts with the pentafluorides of P,

As, Sb, I, as well as with metal pentafluorides, to form salts of the types $[XeF]^+[MF_6]^-$, $[XeF]^+[M_2F_{11}]^-$ and $[Xe_2F_3]^+[MF_6]^-$. The $[XeF]^+$ ions are apparently always weakly attached to the counter-anion forming linear F–Xe···F–M units with one short and one long Xe–F bond, while the $[Xe_2F_3]^+$ ions are V-shaped (see p. 899; cf. isoelectronic I_5^- with central angle 95°, p. 837). With SbF_5 the bright-green paramagnetic Xe_2^+ cation has been identified as a further product.[27] MOF_4 (M = W, Mo) are also weak F^- acceptors and form $[XeF]^+[MOF_5]^-$, which again contain linear F–Xe···F–M units.[28] The XeF^+ cation is an excellent Lewis acid and this property has been used to prepare a range of compounds featuring Xe–N bonds[29] (see also p. 902).

[27] L. STEIN and W. H. HENDERSON, *J. Am. Chem. Soc.* **102**, 2856–7 (1980).

[28] J. H. HOLLOWAY and G. J. SCHROBILGEN, *Inorg. Chem.* **19**, 2632–40 (1980).

[29] G. J. SCHROBILGEN, Chap. 1 in G. A. OLAH, R. D. CHAMBERS and G. K. S. PRAKASH (eds.), *Synthetic Fluorine Chemistry*, John Wiley, New York, 1992, pp. 1–30.

Although the orange-yellow solid prepared by Bartlett (p. 892) was originally formulated as $Xe^+[PtF_6]^-$, it was subsequently found to have the variable composition $Xe(PtF_6)_x$, x lying between 1 and 2. The material has still not been fully characterized but probably contains both $[XeF]^+[PtF_6]^-$ and $[XeF]^+[Pt_2F_{11}]^-$.

XeF_4 forms comparable complexes only with the strongest F^- acceptors such as SbF_5 and BiF_5, but XeF_6 combines with a variety of pentafluorides to yield 1:1 adducts. In view of the structure of XeF_6 (see Fig. 18.2) it is not surprising that these adducts contain XeF_5^+ cations, as for instance in $[XeF_5]^+[AsF_6]^-$ and $[XeF_5]^+[PtF_6]^-$. In a similar manner, reactions with FeF_3 and CoF_3 yield $[XeF_5][MF_4]$ in which layers of corner-sharing FeF_6 octahedra are separated by $[XeF_5]^+$ ions.[30]

(b) *Reactions with F^- donors.* F^- acceptor behaviour of xenon fluorides is evidently confined to XeF_6 which reacts with alkali metal fluorides to form $MXeF_7$ (M = Rb, Cs) and M_2XeF_8 (M = Na, K, Rb, Cs). These compounds lose XeF_6 when heated:

$$2MXeF_7 \longrightarrow M_2XeF_8 + XeF_6$$

$$M_2XeF_8 \longrightarrow 2MF + XeF_6$$

Their thermal stability increases with molecular weight. Thus the Cs and Rb octafluoro complexes only decompose above 400°C, whereas the Na complex decomposes below 100°C. NaF can therefore conveniently be used to separate XeF_6 from XeF_2 and XeF_4, with which it does not react, the purified XeF_6 being regenerated on heating.

A similar product, $[NO]^+_2[XeF_8]^{2-}$, is formed with NOF and its anion has been shown by X-ray crystallography to be a slightly distorted square antiprism[31] (probably due to weak $F \cdots NO^+$ interactions). The absence of any clearly defined ninth coordination position for the lone-pair of valence electrons which is present, implies that this must be stereochemically inactive.

(c) *F/H metathesis between XeF_2 and an anhydrous acid:*

$$XeF_2 + nHL \longrightarrow F_{2-n}XeL_n + nHF \quad (n = 1, 2)$$

where L = $OTeF_5$, $OSeF_5$, OSO_2F, $OClO_3$, ONO_2, $OC(O)Me$, $OC(O)CF_3$, OSO_2Me and OSO_2CF_3 (see also p. 902 for an analogous reaction with $HN(OSO_2F)_2$). The compounds are colourless or pale yellow and many are thermodynamically unstable. The perchlorate (mp 16.5°) is dangerously explosive. The fluorosulfate (mp 36.6°) can be stored for many weeks at 0° but decomposes with a half-life of a few days at 20°.

$$2FXeOSO_2F \longrightarrow XeF_2 + Xe + S_2O_6F_2$$

The molecular structure of $FXeOSO_2F$ is in Fig. 18.3a. Many other such compounds have been made by similar routes e.g. $O_2Xe(F)(OTeF_5)$, $O_2Xe(OTeF_5)_2$, $OXeF_{4-n}(OTeF_5)_n$ ($n = 1-4$) and $XeF_{4-n}(OTeF_5)_n$ ($n = 1-4$);[32] $FXeOI(O)F_4$ and $Xe\{OI(O)F_4\}_2$;[33] $FXeOP(O)F_2$ and $Xe\{OP(O)F_2\}_2$ etc. Typical reactions are:

$$3O_2XeF_2 + 2B(OTeF_5)_3 \longrightarrow$$
$$3O_2Xe(OTeF_5)_2 + 2BF_3 \text{[32]}$$

$$OXe(OTeF_5)_4 \longrightarrow$$
$$O_2Xe(OTeF_5)_2 + O(TeF_5)_2 \text{[34]}$$

$$XeF_2 + (IO_2F_3)_2 \longrightarrow FXeOI(O)F_4$$
$$+ OIF_3 + \tfrac{1}{2}O_2 \text{[33]}$$

[30] J. SLIVNIK, B. ZEMVA, M. BOHINC, D. HANZEL, J. GRANNEC and P. HAGENMULLER, *J. Inorg. Nucl. Chem.* **38**, 997–1000 (1976).

[31] S. W. PETERSON, J. H. HOLLOWAY, B. A. COYLE and J. M. WILLIAMS, *Science*, **173**, 1238–9 (1971).

[32] G. A. SCHUMACHER and G. J. SCHROBILGEN, *Inorg. Chem.* **23**, 2923–9 (1984).

[33] R. G. STYRET and G. J. SCHROBILGEN, *J. Chem. Soc., Chem. Commun.*, 1529–30 (1985).

[34] L. TUROWSKY and K. SEPPELT, *Z. anorg. allg. Chem.* **609**, 153–6 (1992).

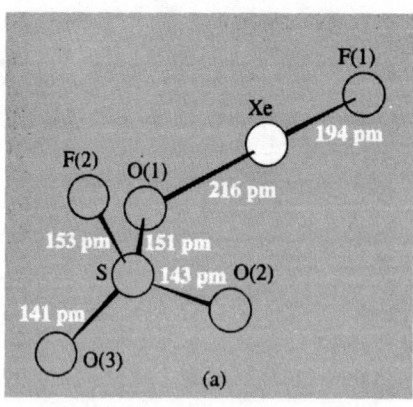
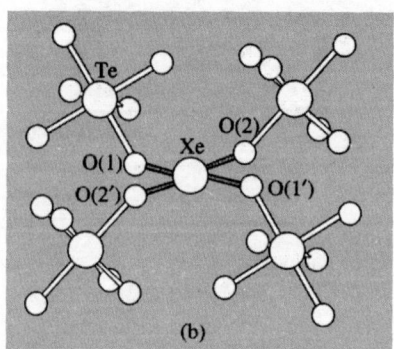

Figure 18.3 (a) The molecular structure of FXeOSO$_2$F. Precision of bond lengths is *ca.* 1 pm (uncorrected for thermal motion). The angle F(1)–Xe–O(1) is 177.5 ± 0.4° and angle Xe–O(1)–S is 123.4 ± 0.6°. (b) The molecular structure of Xe(OTeF$_5$)$_4$ (see text)

$$FXeOI(O)F_4 + (IO_2F_3)_2 \longrightarrow$$
$$Xe\{OI(O)F_4\}_2 + OIF_3 + \tfrac{1}{2}O_2 \quad ^{(33)}$$

$$Xe(OTeF_5)_2 + 2HOI(O)F_4 \longrightarrow$$
$$Xe\{OI(O)F_4\}_2 + 2HOTeF_5 \quad ^{(33)}$$

$$3XeF_2 + B(OSO_2CF_3)_3 \longrightarrow$$
$$3FXe(OSO_2CF_3) + BF_3 \quad ^{(35)}$$

$$3XeF_2 + 2B(OCOCF_3)_3 \longrightarrow$$
$$3Xe(OCOCF_3)_2 + 2BF_3 \quad ^{(35)}$$

The molecular structure of yellow crystalline Xe(OTeF$_5$)$_4$ has been determined by X-ray analysis (see Fig. 18.3b);[34] the Xe atom is surrounded by a square-planar array of four O atoms, with the adjacent TeF$_5$ groups pointing, curiously, pair-wise up and down from this plane (Xe–O 203.9(5) and 202.6(5) pm, Te–O 188.5 pm).

(d) *Hydrolysis and related reactions.* Two Xe^{VI} oxofluorides, XeOF$_4$ and XeO$_2$F$_2$, have been characterized, and the Xe^{VIII} derivative XeO$_3$F$_2$ (mp. −54.1°C)[22] is also known (see below). XeOF$_4$ is a colourless volatile liquid with a square-pyramidal molecular structure, the O atom being at the apex. It can be prepared by the controlled hydrolysis of XeF$_6$:

$$XeF_6 + H_2O \longrightarrow XeOF_4 + 2HF$$

Its most pronounced chemical characteristic is its propensity to hydrolyse further to XeO$_2$F$_2$ and then XeO$_3$ (p. 901). This reaction is difficult to control, and the low-melting, colourless solid, XeO$_2$F$_2$, is more reliably obtained by the reaction:

$$XeO_3 + XeOF_4 \longrightarrow 2XeO_2F_2$$

An analogous reaction with XeO$_4$ (see p. 901) is:

$$XeO_4 + XeF_6 \longrightarrow XeO_3F_2 + XeOF_4$$

Indeed, many of the reactions of the xenon oxides, fluorides and oxofluorides can be systematized in terms of generalized acid-base theory in which any acid (here defined as an oxide acceptor) can react with any base (oxide donor) lying beneath it in the sequence of descending acidity: XeF$_6$ > XeO$_2$F$_4$ > XeO$_3$F$_2$ > XeO$_4$ > XeOF$_4$ > XeF$_4$ > XeO$_2$F$_2$ > XeO$_3$ ≈ XeF$_2$.[22]

In addition, oxofluoro anions may be produced by treating hydrolysis products with F$^-$. Thus aqueous XeO$_3$ and MF (M = K, Cs) yield the stable white solids M[XeO$_3$F] in which the anion consists of chains of pseudo-octahedral Xe atoms (the lone-pair of valence electrons occupying one of the six positions) linked by angular F bridges.

[35] B. CREMER-LOBER, H. BUTLER, D. NAUMANN and W. TYRRA, *Z. anorg. allg. Chem.* **607**, 34–40 (1992).

Again, the reaction of $XeOF_4$ and dry CsF has been shown to yield the labile $Cs[(XeOF_4)_3F]$ in which the anion consists of three equivalent $XeOF_4$ groups attached to a central F^- ion.[36] The ready loss of $2XeOF_4$ produces the more stable $CsXeOF_5$, the anion of which has a distorted octahedral geometry, the lone-pair of electrons again being stereochemically active and apparently occupying an octahedral face.

Complete hydrolysis of XeF_6 is the route to XeO_3. The most effective control of this potentially violent reaction is achieved by using a current of dry N_2 to sweep XeF_6 vapour into water:[37]

$$XeF_6 + 3H_2O \longrightarrow XeO_3 + 6HF$$

The HF may then be removed by adding MgO to precipitate MgF_2 and the colourless deliquescent solid XeO_3 obtained by evaporation. The aqueous solution known as "xenic acid" is quite stable if all oxidizable material is excluded, but the solid is a most dangerous explosive (reported to be comparable to TNT) which is easily detonated. The X-ray analysis, made even more difficult by the tendency of the crystals to disintegrate in an X-ray beam, shows the solid to consist of trigonal pyramidal XeO_3 units, with the xenon atom at the apex[38] (cf. the isoelectronic iodate ion IO_3^-; p. 863).

In aqueous solution XeO_3 is an extremely strong oxidizing agent (for $XeO_3 + 6H^+ + 6e^- \rightleftharpoons Xe + 3H_2O; E° = 2.10$ V), but may be kinetically slow; the oxidation of Mn^{II} takes hours to produce MnO_2 and days before MnO_4^- is obtained. Treatment of aqueous XeO_3 with alkali produces xenate ions:

$$XeO_3 + OH^- \rightleftharpoons HXeO_4^-; \quad K = 1.5 \times 10^3$$

[36] G. J. SCHROBILGEN, D. MARTIN-ROVET, P. CHARPIN and M. LANCE, *J. Chem. Soc., Chem. Commun.*, 894–7 (1980). J. H. HOLLOWAY, V. KAUČIČ, D. MARTIN-ROVET, D. R. RUSSELL, G. J. SCHROBILGEN and H. SELIG, *Inorg. Chem.* **24**, 678–83 (1985).

[37] B. JASELSKIS, T. M. SPITTLER and J. L. HUSTON, *J. Am. Chem. Soc.* **88**, 2149–50 (1966).

[38] D. H. TEMPLETON, A. ZALKIN, J. D. FORRESTER and S. M. WILLIAMSON, *J. Am. Chem. Soc.* **85**, 817 (1963).

However, although some salts have been isolated, alkaline solutions are not stable and immediately, if slowly, begin to disproportionate into Xe^{VIII} (perxenates) and Xe gas by routes such as:

$$2HXeO_4^- + 2OH^- \longrightarrow XeO_6^{4-} + Xe + O_2 + 2H_2O$$

Similar results are obtained by the alkaline hydrolysis of XeF_6:

$$2XeF_6 + 16OH^- \longrightarrow XeO_6^{4-} + Xe + O_2 + 12F^- + 8H_2O$$

The most efficient production of perxenate is the treatment of XeO_3 in aqueous NaOH with ozone, when $Na_4XeO_6.2\frac{1}{5}H_2O$ precipitates almost quantitatively. The crystal structures of $Na_4XeO_6.6H_2O$ and $Na_4XeO_6.8H_2O$ show them to contain octahedral XeO_6^{4-} units with Xe–O 184 pm and 186.4 pm respectively. Perxenates of other alkali metals (Li^+, K^+) and of several divalent and trivalent cations (e.g. (Ba^{2+}, Am^{3+}) have also been prepared. They are colourless solids, thermally stable to over 200°C, and contain octahedral XeO_6^{4-} ions. They are powerful oxidizing agents, the reduction of Xe^{VIII} to Xe^{VI} in aqueous acid solution being very rapid. The oxidation of Mn^{II} to MnO_4^- by perxenates, unlike that by XeO_3, is thus immediate and is accompanied by evolution of O_2:

$$2H_2XeO_6^{2-} + 2H^+ \longrightarrow 2HXeO_4^- + O_2 + 2H_2O$$

The addition of solid Ba_2XeO_6 to cold conc H_2SO_4 produces the second known oxide of xenon, XeO_4. This is an explosively unstable gas which may be condensed in a liquid nitrogen trap. The solid tends to detonate when melted but small sublimed crystals have been shown to melt sharply at $-35.9°C$.[22] XeO_4 has only been incompletely studied, but electron diffraction and infrared evidence show the molecule to be tetrahedral.

Whilst the great bulk of noble-gas chemistry concerns Xe–F or Xe–O bonds, attempts to bond Xe to certain other atoms have also been successful. Compounds containing Xe–N bonds have been produced by the replacement of F atoms by $-N(SO_2F)_2$ groups.[39] The relevant reactions may be represented as:

$$2XeF_2 + 2HN(SO_2F)_2 \xrightarrow[\text{0°C, 4 days}]{\text{in } CF_2Cl_2} 2F-Xe-N(SO_2F)_2$$
white solid

$$\Big\downarrow \begin{array}{c} 2AsF_3 \\ -10°C \end{array}$$

2[FXe(NSO$_2$F)$_2$·AsF$_5$]
unstable, bright yellow solid

$$\Big\downarrow -AsF_5 \quad 22°C, \text{vacuum}$$

[F{Xe-N(SO$_2$F)$_2$}$_2$]$^+$ AsF$_6^-$
pale yellow solid

The first (white) product has been characterized by X-ray diffraction at $-55°$ and features a linear F–Xe–N group and a planar N atom (Fig. 18.4).[40] On the basis of Raman and ^{19}F nmr data, the cation of the final (pale yellow) product is believed to be essentially like the V-shaped [Xe$_2$F$_3$]$^+$ cation but with the 2 terminal F atoms replaced by

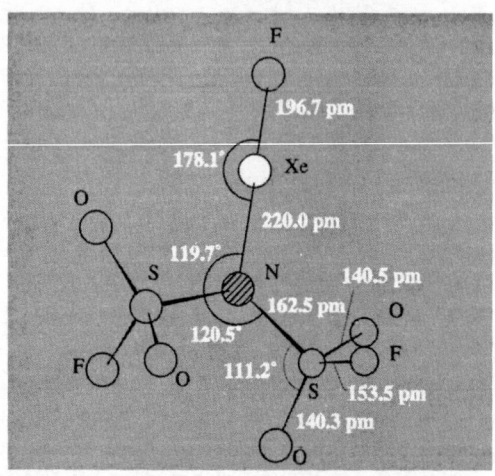

Figure 18.4 The structure of FXeN(SO$_2$F)$_2$ (C_2 symmetry) showing essentially linear Xe and planar N. Other bond angles are OSO 122.6°, OSF 106.3°, NSO 107.2° and 111.2°, NSF 101.2°.

$-N(SO_2F)_2$ groups.[40] The related compound [Xe{N(SO$_2$F)$_2$}$_2$] was the first to feature an Xe atom bonded to two N atoms.[41] The cations [XeN(SO$_2$F)$_2$]$^+$ and [F{XeN(SO$_2$F)$_2$}$_2$]$^+$ have also been characterized and the X-ray structure of [XeN(SO$_2$F)$_2$]$^+$[Sb$_3$F$_{16}$]$^-$ determined.[42] An important new synthetic strategy was introduced by G. J. Schrobilgen who exploited the Lewis acid (electron-pair acceptor) properties of the XeF$^+$ cation to prepare a wide range of stable nitrile adducts featuring Xe–N bonds, e.g. [RC≡NXeF]$^+$AsF$_6^-$ (R = H, Me, CH$_2$F, Et, C$_2$F$_5$, C$_3$F$_7$, C$_6$F$_5$).[43] Similarly, perfluoropyridine ligands have been used to prepare [4-RC$_5$F$_4$NXeF]$^+$ cations (R = F, CF$_3$) in HF or BrF$_5$ solutions at temperatures below $-30°$C.[44] Other cationic species involving Xe–N bonds include [F$_3$S≡NXeF]$^+$, [F$_4$S=NXe]$^+$, [F$_5$SN(H)Xe]$^+$, [F$_5$TeN(H)Xe]$^+$, [s-C$_3$F$_3$N$_2$NXeF]$^+$, [MeC≡NXeOTeF$_5$]$^+$, [C$_5$F$_5$-NXeOTeF$_5$]$^+$ and [F$_3$S≡NXeOSeF$_5$]$^+$. Over three dozen such compounds are now known and The field has been recently reviewed.[29]

Fewer compounds with Xe–C bonds have been characterized. The first to be claimed was synthesized by the plasma reaction of XeF$_2$ with CF$_3^•$ radicals; the volatile waxy white solid produced, Xe(CF$_3$)$_2$, decomposed at room temperature with a half-life of about 30 min.[45]

$$XeF_2 + C_2F_6 \xrightarrow{\text{plasma}} Xe(CF_3)_2 + F_2$$

$$Xe(CF_3)_2 \xrightarrow[t_{\frac{1}{2}} 30\,\text{min}]{20°} XeF_2 + C_nF_m$$

[39] D. D. DesMarteau, *J. Am. Chem. Soc.* **100**, 6270–1 (1978). D. D. DesMarteau, R. D. LeBlond, S. F. Hossain and D. Nothe, *J. Am. Chem. Soc.* **103**, 7734–9 (1981).

[40] J. F. Sawyer, G. J. Schrobilgen and S. J. Sutherland, *J. Chem. Soc., Chem. Commun.*, 210–11 (1982).

[41] G. A. Schumacher and G. J. Schrobilgen, *Inorg. Chem.* **22**, 2178–83 (1983).

[42] R. Faggiani, D. K. Kennepohl, C. J. L. Lock and G. J. Schrobilgen, *Inorg. Chem.* **25**, 563–71 (1986).

[43] A. A. A. Emara and G. J. Schrobilgen, *J. Chem. Soc., Chem. Commun.*, 1644–6 (1987).

[44] A. A. A. Emara and G. J. Schrobilgen, *J. Chem. Soc., Chem. Commun.*, 257–9 (1988).

[45] L. J. Turbini, R. E. Aikman and R. J. Lagow, *J. Am. Chem. Soc.* **101**, 5833–4 (1979).

However, the first compound to have a stable Xe–C bond was reported independently by two groups in 1989:[46] reaction of XeF_2 with an excess of $B(C_6F_5)_3$ in MeCN or CH_2Cl_2 yielded $[XeC_6F_5]^+[B(C_6F_5)_3F]^-$ which was characterized by its chemical reactions and by ^{129}Xe and ^{19}F nmr spectroscopy. The compound can be isolated as a colourless solid. Several other similar compounds have since been synthesized at temperatures below $-40°C$, e.g. $[XeC_6H_4R]^+[B(C_6H_4R)_nF_{4-n}]^-$ (R = *m*-F, *p*-F, *m*-CF_3, *p*-CF_3), (*n* = 0, 1, 2).[47] An X-ray structure analysis of the adduct, $[MeC\equiv N\rightarrow Xe-C_6F_5]^+[(C_6F_5)_2BF_2]^-$ at $-123°C$ established the Xe–C distance as 209.2(8) pm and the coordinate link $N\rightarrow Xe$ as 268.1(8) pm (substantially longer than the Xe–N distance in Fig. 18.4; the angle C–Xe–N is 174.5(3)°.[48] The alkynyl xenonium compound $[Bu^tC\equiv C-Xe]^+BF_4^-$ has also been characterized.[49]

The most recent extension of xenon chemistry is the formation of a compound containing a Xe–Xe bond.[49a] Thus, when the yellow compound $XeF^+Sb_2F_{11}^-$ was reacted with Xe in "magic acid" (HF/SbF_5), dark-green crystals of $Xe_2^+Sb_4F_{21}^-$ were formed at $-30°C$. An X-ray structure analysis at $-143°C$ revealed that the $Xe-Xe^+$ bond length was 308.7(1) pm, making it the longest element–element bond yet known [cf. 304.1(1) pm for Re–Re in $Re_2(CO)_{10}$].

18.3.3 Compounds of other noble gases

No stable compounds of He, Ne or Ar are known. Radon apparently forms a difluoride and some complexes such as $[RnF]^+X^-$ ($X^- = SbF_6^-$, TaF_6^-, BiF_6^-), but the evidence is based solely on radiochemical tracer techniques since Rn has no stable isotopes.[50] The remaining noble gas, Kr, has an emerging chemistry though this is less extensive than that of Xe.

Apart from the violet free radical KrF, which has been generated in minute amounts by γ-radiation of KrF_2 and exists only below $-153°C$, the chemistry of Kr was for some time confined to the difluoride and its derivatives. An early claim for KrF_4 remains unsubstantiated. The volatile, colourless solid, KrF_2, is produced when mixtures of Kr and F_2 are cooled to temperatures near $-196°C$ and then subjected to electric discharge, or irradiated with high-energy electrons or X-rays. It is a thermally (and thermodynamically) unstable compound which slowly decomposes even at room temperature. It has the same linear molecular structure as XeF_2 (Kr–F 188.9 pm) but, consistent with its lower stability, is a stronger fluorinating agent and is rapidly decomposed by water without requiring the addition of a base. KrF_2 has been used as a specialist reagent to prepare high oxidation state fluorides. Reaction with Ag or AgF in HF gave the new fluoride AgF_3;[51] high-purity MnF_4 was prepared from MnF_2/HF via the adducts $2KrF_2.MnF_4$ and $KrF_2.MnF_4$;[52] the square-pyramidal CrF_4O (mp. 55°C) was obtained by an improved route from CrO_2F_2/HF.[53] KrF_2 also affords an unusual and extremely useful room-temperature route to NpF_6 and PuF_6, thus avoiding the necessity of using F_2 at high temperatures, the compound O_2F_2 being the only other reagent known to do this.[54]

Complexes of KrF_2 are analogous to those of XeF_2 and are confined to cationic species

[46] D. NAUMANN and W. TYRRA, *J. Chem. Soc., Chem. Commun.*, 47–50 (1989). H. J. FROHN and S. JAKOBS, *J. Chem. Soc., Chem. Commun.*, 625–7 (1989).

[47] H. J. FROHN and C. ROSSBACH, *Z. anorg. allg. Chem.* **619**, 1672–8 (1993).

[48] H. J. FROHN, S. JACOBS and G. HENKEL, *Angew. Chem. Int. Edn. Engl.* **28**, 1506–7 (1989).

[49] V. V. ZHDANKIN, P. J. STANG and N. S. ZEFIROV, *J. Chem. Soc., Chem. Commun.*, 578–9 (1992).

[49a] T. DREWS and K. SEPPELT, *Angew. Chem. Int. Edn. Engl.* **36**, 273–4 (1997), and references cited therein.

[50] L. STEIN, *Inorg. Chem.* **23**, 3670–1 (1984).

[51] R. BOUGON, T. B. HUY, M. LANCE and H. ABAZLI, *Inorg. Chem.* **23**, 3667–8 (1984).

[52] K. LUTAR, A. JESIH and B. ŽEMVA, *Polyhedron* **7**, 1217–9 (1988).

[53] K. O. CHRISTE, W. W. WILSON and R. A. BOUGON, *Inorg. Chem.* **25**, 2163–9 (1986).

[54] L. B. ASPREY, P. G. ELLER and S. A. KINKEAD, *Inorg. Chem.* **25**, 670–2 (1986).

which can be generated by reaction with F^- acceptors. Thus, such compounds as $[KrF]^+[MF_6]^-$, $[Kr_2F_3]^+[MF_6]^+$ (M = As, Sb) are known, and also $[KrF]^+[MoOF_5]^-$ and $[KrF]^+[WOF_5]^-$ which have been prepared and characterized by ^{19}F nmr and Raman spectroscopy.[55] In addition, adducts of KrF^+ with nitrile donors have been synthesized, analogous to those of XeF^+ described in the preceding section, e.g. $[RC{\equiv}NKrF]^+$ (R = Me, CF_3, C_2F_5, n-C_3F_5).[29,56]

The formation of the first compound having Kr–O bonds has been documented by using ^{19}F and ^{17}O nmr spectroscopy of ^{17}O-enriched samples to follow the synthesis and decomposition of the thermally unstable compound, $[Kr(OTeF_5)_2]$, according to the reactions:[57]

$$3KrF_2 + 2B(OTeF_5)_3 \longrightarrow 3Kr(OTeF_5)_2 + 2BF_3$$

$$Kr(OTeF_5)_2 \longrightarrow Kr + F_5TeOOTeF_5$$

[55] J. H. Holloway and G. J. Schrobilgen, *Inorg. Chem.* **20**, 3363–8 (1981).

[56] G. J. Schrobilgen, *J. Chem. Soc., Chem. Commun.*, 863–5 and 1506–8 (1988).

[57] J. C. P. Saunders and G. J. Schrobilgen, *J. Chem. Soc., Chem. Commun.*, 1576–8 (1989).

19

Coordination and Organometallic Compounds

19.1 Introduction

The three series of elements arising from the filling of the 3d, 4d and 5d shells, and situated in the periodic table following the alkaline earth metals, are commonly described as "transition elements", though this term is sometimes also extended to include the lanthanide and actinide (or inner transition) elements. They exhibit a number of characteristic properties which together distinguish them from other groups of elements:

(i) They are all metals and as such are lustrous and deformable and have high electrical and thermal conductivities. In addition, their melting and boiling points tend to be high and they are generally hard and strong.

(ii) Most of them display numerous oxidation states which vary by steps of 1 rather than 2 as is usually the case with those main-group elements which exhibit more than one oxidation state.

(iii) They have an unparalleled propensity for forming coordination compounds with Lewis bases.

(i) and (ii) will be dealt with more fully in later chapters but it is the purpose of the present chapter to expand the theme of (iii).

A coordination compound, or complex, is formed when a Lewis base (ligand)[1] is attached to a Lewis acid (acceptor) by means of a "lone-pair" of electrons. Where the ligand is composed of a number of atoms, the one which is directly attached to the acceptor is called the "donor atom". This type of bonding has already been discussed (p. 198) and is exemplified by the addition compounds formed by the trihalides of the elements of Group 13 (p. 237); it is also the basis of much of the chemistry of the

---

[1] W. H. BROCK, K. A. JENSEN, C. K. JØRGENSEN and G. B. KAUFFMAN, *Ambix* **27**, 171–83 (1981).

transition elements. The precise nature of the bond between a transition metal ion and a ligand varies enormously and the term "donor atom" is often used in situations where its literal meaning should not be assumed. Although inevitably the line of demarcation is rather ill-defined, it is conventional to distinguish two extremes. On the one hand, are those cases in which the bond may be considered profitably as a single σ bond, or even a purely electrostatic interaction, and in which the metal has an oxidation state of +2 or higher. On the other hand, are those cases where the bonding is multiple, the ligand acting simultaneously as both a σ donor and a π acceptor (p. 922) and in which the metal usually has a formal oxidation state of +1 or less, though the significance of such values is often unclear. Compounds of the former type are commonly described as "classical" or "Werner" complexes since it was through the investigation of such materials that A. Werner in the period 1893–1913 laid the foundations of coordination chemistry[2] (see also p. 912). Compounds of the latter type are exemplified by the carbonyls and other organometallic compounds.

19.2 Types of Ligand

Ligands are most conveniently classified according to the number of potential donor atoms which they contain and are known as uni-, bi-, ter-, quadri-, quinqi- and sexi-dentate accordingly as the number is 1, 2, 3, 4, 5 or 6. Unidentate ligands may be simple monatomic ions such as halide ions, or polyatomic ions or molecules which contain a donor atom from Groups 16, 15 or even 14 (e.g. CN^-). Bidentate ligands are frequently chelating ligands (from Greek χηλή, crab's claw) and, with the metal ion, produce chelate rings[3]

[2] G. B. KAUFFMAN, *Alfred Werner Founder of Coordination Theory*, Springer, Berlin, 1966, 127 pp. G. B. Kauffman (ed.) *Coordination Chemistry: A Century of Progress*, ACS Symposium Series **565**, Washington DC, 1994, 464 pp.

[3] C. F. BELL, *Principles and Applications of Metal Chelation*, Oxford University Press, Oxford, 1977, 147 pp.

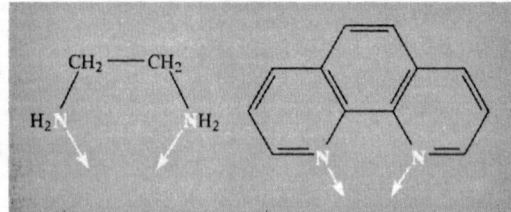

Ethylenediamine, en　　1,10-phenanthroline, phen

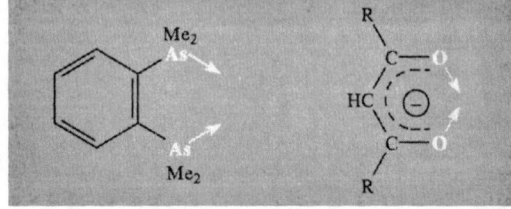

o-phenylenebis(dimethylarsine), diars: [1,2-bis(dimethylarsino)benzene]　　β-diketonates (e.g. R = Me: acetylacetonate, acac)

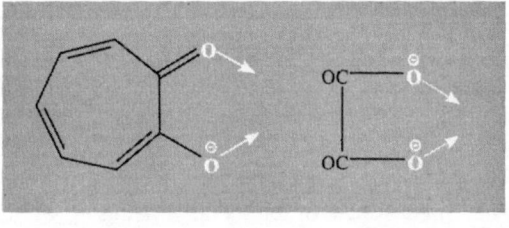

Tropolonate　　Oxalate

Figure 19.1　Some bidentate ligands.

which in the case of the most commonly occurring bidentate ligands are 5- or 6-membered, e.g.: see Fig. 19.1. Terdentate ligands produce 2 ring systems when coordinated to a single metal ion and in consequence may impose structural limitations on the complex, particularly where rigidity is introduced by the incorporation of conjugated double bonds within the rings. Thus diethylenetriamine, dien (1), being flexible is stereochemically relatively undemanding, whereas terpyridine, terpy (2), can only coordinate when the 3 donor nitrogen atoms and the metal ion are in the same plane.

Quadridentate ligands produce 3, and in some cases 4, rings on coordination, and so even greater restrictions on the stereochemistry of the complex may be imposed by an

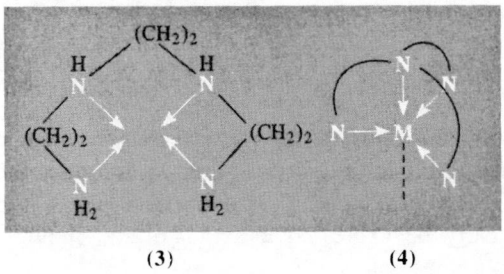

(1)   (2)

(3)   (4)

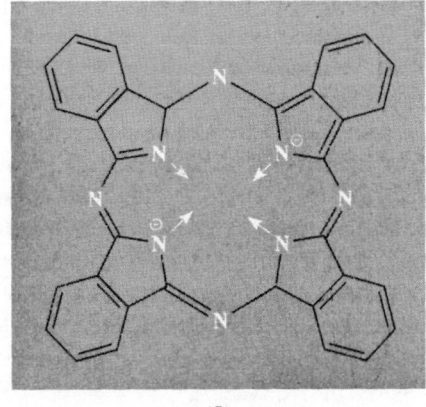

(5)

(6)   (7)

appropriate choice of ligand. The open-chain ligand triethylenetetramine, trien (3), is, like dien, flexible and undemanding, whereas tri-ethylaminetriamine, tren, i.e. $N(CH_2CH_2NH_2)_3$, is one of the so-called "tripod" ligands which are quite unable to give planar coordination but instead favour trigonal bipyramidal structures (4). By contrast, the highly conjugated phthalocya-nine[4] (5), which is an example of the class of macrocyclic ligands of which the crown ethers have already been mentioned (p. 96), forces the complex to adopt a virtually planar struc-ture and has proved to be a valuable model for the naturally occurring porphyrins which, for instance, are involved in haem (p. 1100), B_{12} (p. 1138) and the chlorophylls (p. 125). Another well-known ligand, which has been used to synthesize oxygen-carrying molecules, is bis(salicylaldehyde)ethylenediimine, salen (6). Quinquidenate and sexidentate ligands are most familiarly exemplified by the anions derived from ethylenediaminetetraacetic acid, edtaH$_4$ i.e. $(HO_2CCH_2)_2N(CH_2)_2N(CH_2CO_2H)_2$, which is used with remarkable versatility in the volumetric analysis of metal ions. As the fully ionized anion, edta^{4-}, it has 4 oxygen and 2 nitrogen donor atoms and has the flexibility to wrap itself around a variety of metal ions to produce a pseudo-octahedral complex involving five 5-membered rings as in (7).

In the incompletely ionized form, edtaH^{3-}, one of the oxygen atoms is no longer able to coordi-nate to the metal and the anion is quinquidentate.

Ambidentate ligands possess more than 1 donor atom and can coordinate through either one or the other. This leads to the possibility of "linkage" isomerism (p. 920). The commonest examples are the ions NO_2^- (p. 463) and SCN^- (p. 325). Such ligands can also coordinate via both donor sites simultaneously, thereby acting as bridging ligands.

In the case of organometallic compounds the most satisfactory way of classifying the ligands

---

[4] C. C. LEZNOFF and A. B. P. LEVER (eds.), *Phthalocyan-ines, Properties and Applications,* V.C.H., Weinheim, 1990, 336 pp.

is by the number of C atoms attached to (or closely associated with) the metal atom. This essentially structural criterion can be established by several techniques and is more definite than other features such as the presumed number of electrons involved in the bonding. The number of attached carbon atoms is called the *hapticity* of the organic group (Greek ηαπτειν, *haptein*, to fasten) and hapticities from 1 to 8 have been observed. Monohapto groups are specified as η^1, dihapto as η^2, etc. This classification will form the basis of the later discussion of organometallic compounds (pp. 924).

19.3 Stability of Coordination Compounds

Because complexes are not generally prepared from their components in the gaseous phase, measurements of their stability necessarily imply a comparison with the stability of some starting material. The overwhelming majority of quantitative measurements have been made in aqueous solutions when the complex in question is formed by the ligand displacing water from the aquo complex of the metal ion. If, for simplicity, we take the case where L is a unidentate ligand and ignore charge, then the process can be represented as a succession of steps for which the stepwise stability (or formation) constants K are as shown:[†]

[†] These constants are expressed here in terms of concentrations which means that the activity coefficients have been assumed to be unity. When pure water is the solvent this will only be true at infinite dilution, and so stability constants should be obtained by taking measurements over a range of concentrations and extrapolating to zero concentration. In practice, however, it is more usual to make measurements in the presence of a relatively high concentration of an inert electrolyte (e.g. 3 M NaClO₄) so as to maintain a constant ionic strength, thereby ensuring that the activity coefficients remain essentially constant. Stability constants obtained in this way (sometimes referred to as "concentration quotients" or "stoichiometric stability constants") are true thermodynamic stability constants referred to the standard state of solution in 3 M NaClO₄(aq), but they will, of course, differ from stability constants referred to solution in the pure solvent as standard state.

$$M(H_2O)_n + L \rightleftharpoons ML(H_2O)_{n-1} + H_2O;$$

$$K_1 = \frac{[ML(H_2O)_{n-1}]}{[M(H_2O)_n][L]}$$

$$ML_{n-1}(H_2O) + L \rightleftharpoons ML_n + H_2O;$$

$$K_n = \frac{[ML_n]}{[ML_{n-1}H_2O][L]}$$

$$M(H_2O)_n + nL \rightleftharpoons ML_n + nH_2O;$$

$$\beta_n = \frac{[ML_n]}{[M(H_2O)_n][L]^n}$$

By convention the displaced water is ignored since its concentration is essentially constant. The overall stability (or formation) constant β_n can clearly be expressed in terms of the stepwise constants:

$$\beta_n = K_1 \times K_2 \times \ldots \times K_n$$

These are thermodynamic constants which relate to the system when it has reached equilibrium, and must be distinguished from any considerations of kinetic lability or inertness which refer to the speed with which that equilibrium is attained.

A vast amount of data[5] has been accumulated from which a number of generalizations can be inferred concerning the factors which determine the stabilities of such complexes. Some of these are as follows:

(i) *The metal ion and its charge.* For a given metal and ligand the stability is generally greater if the oxidation state of the metal is +3 rather than +2. Furthermore, the stabilities of corresponding complexes of the bivalent ions of the first transition series, irrespective of the

---

[5] L. G. SILLÉN and A. E. MARTELL, *Stability Constants of Metal-ion Complexes*, The Chemical Society, London, Special Publications No. 17, 1964, 754 pp., and No. 25, 1971, 865 pp. *Stability Constants of Metal-Ion Complexes, Part A. Inorganic Ligands* (E. Högfeldt, ed.), 1982, pp. 310, *Part B. Organic Ligands* (D. Perrin, ed.), 1979, pp. 1263. Pergamon Press, Oxford. A continually updated database is now provided by: L. D. PETTIT and K. J. POWELL (eds.), *IUPAC Stability Constants Database*, IUPAC and Academic Software.

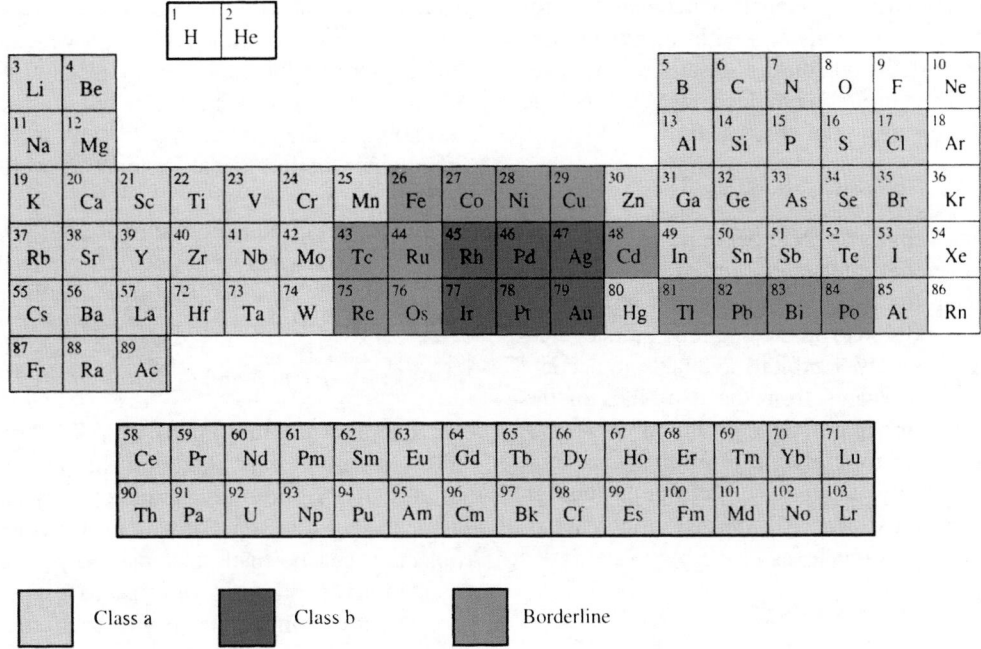

Figure 19.2   Classification of acceptor atoms in their common oxidation states.

particular ligand involved, usually vary in the Irving–Williams[6] order (1953):

$$Mn^{II} < Fe^{II} < Co^{II} < Ni^{II} < Cu^{II} > Zn^{II}$$

which is the reverse of the order for the cation radii (p. 1295). These observations are consistent with the view that, at least for metals in oxidation states +2 and +3, the coordinate bond is largely electrostatic. This was a major factor in the acceptance of crystal field theory (see pp. 921–3).

(ii) *The relationship between metal and donor atom.*[6a] Some metal ions (known as class-a acceptors or alternatively as "hard" acids) form their most stable complexes with ligands containing N, O or F donor atoms. Others (known as class-b acceptors or alternatively as "soft" acids) form their most stable complexes with ligands whose donor atoms are the heavier elements of the N, O or F groups. The metals of

Groups 1 and 2 along with the inner transition elements and the early members of the transition series (Groups 3 → 6) fall into class-a. The transition elements Rh, Pd, Ag and Ir, Pt, Au, Hg comprise class-b, while the remaining transition elements may be regarded as borderline (Fig. 19.2). The difference between the class-a elements of Group 2 and the borderline class-b elements of Group 12 is elegantly and colourfully illustrated by the equilibrium

$$[CoCl_4]^{2-} + 6H_2O \underset{Ca^{II}}{\overset{Zn^{II}}{\rightleftharpoons}} [Co(H_2O)_6]^{2+} + 4Cl^-$$
$$\text{Blue} \qquad\qquad\qquad\qquad \text{Pink}$$

If Ca^{II} is added it pushes the equilibrium to the left by bonding preferentially to H_2O, whereas Zn^{II}, with its partial b character (p. 1206), prefers the heavier Cl^- and so pushes the equilibrium to the right.

It seems that, as suggested by Ahrland *et al.*[7] in 1958, this distinction can be explained at least partly on the basis that class-a acceptors are the

[6] H. M. N. H. IRVING and R. J. P. WILLIAMS, *J. Chem. Soc.* 1953, 3192–210.
[6a] R. G. PEARSON, *Coord. Chem. Revs.* **100**, 403–25 (1990).

[7] S. AHRLAND, J. CHATT and N. R. DAVIES, *Q. Revs.* **12**, 265–76 (1958).

more electropositive elements which tend to form their most stable complexes with ligands favouring electrostatic bonding, so that, for instance, the stabilities of their complexes with halide ions should decrease in the order

$$F^- > Cl^- > Br^- > I^-$$

Class-b acceptors on the other hand are less electropositive, have relatively full d orbitals, and form their most stable complexes with ligands which, in addition to possessing lone-pairs of electrons, have empty π orbitals available to accommodate some charge from the d orbitals of the metal. The order of stability will now be the reverse of that for class-a acceptors, the increasing accessibility of empty d orbitals in the heavier halide ions for instance, favouring an increase in stability of the complexes in the sequence

$$F^- < Cl^- < Br^- < I^-$$

(iii) *The type of ligand.* In comparing the stabilities of complexes formed by different ligands, one of the most important factors is the possible formation of chelate rings. If L is a unidentate ligand and L-L a bidentate ligand, the simplest illustration of this point is provided by comparing the two reactions:

$$M(aq) + 2L(aq) \rightleftharpoons ML_2(aq)$$

for which $\beta_L = \dfrac{[ML_2]}{[M][L]^2}$

and

$$M(aq) + L\text{-}L(aq) \rightleftharpoons ML\text{-}L \ (aq)$$

for which $\beta_{L\text{-}L} = \dfrac{[ML\text{-}L]}{[M][L\text{-}L]}$

or alternatively by considering the replacement reaction obtained by combining them:

$$ML_2(aq) + L\text{-}L(aq) \rightleftharpoons ML\text{-}L(aq) + 2L(aq)$$

for which $K = \dfrac{[ML\text{-}L][L]^2}{[ML_2][L\text{-}L]} = \dfrac{\beta_{L\text{-}L}}{\beta_L}$

Experimental evidence shows overwhelmingly that, providing the donor atoms of L and L-L are the same element and that the chelate ring

formed by the coordination of L-L does not involve undue strain, L-L will replace L and the equilibrium of the replacement reaction will be to the right. This stabilization due to chelation is known as the *chelate effect*[8] and is of great importance in biological systems as well as in analytical chemistry.

The effect is frequently expressed as $\beta_{L\text{-}L} > \beta_L$ or $K > 1$ and, when values of ΔH° are available, ΔG° and ΔS° are calculated from the thermodynamic relationships

$$\Delta G^\circ = -RT \ln \beta \quad \text{and} \quad \Delta G^\circ = \Delta H^\circ - T\Delta S^\circ$$

On the basis of the values of ΔS° derived in this way it appears that the chelate effect is usually due to more favourable entropy changes associated with ring formation. However, the objection can be made that β_L and $\beta_{L\text{-}L}$ as just defined have different dimensions and so are not directly comparable. It has been suggested that to surmount this objection concentrations should be expressed in the dimensionless unit "mole fraction" instead of the more usual mol dm^{-3}. Since the concentration of pure water at $25^\circ C$ is approximately $55.5 \ mol \, dm^{-3}$, the value of concentration expressed in mole fractions = conc in $mol \, dm^{-3}/55.5$ Thus, while β_L is thereby increased by the factor $(55.5)^2$, $\beta_{L\text{-}L}$ is increased by the factor (55.5) so that the derived values of ΔG° and ΔS° will be quite different. The effect of this change in units is shown in Table 19.1 for the Cd^{II} complexes of L = methylamine and L-L = ethylenediamine. It appears that the entropy advantage of the chelate, and with it the chelate effect itself, virtually disappears when mole fractions replace $mol \, dm^{-3}$.

The resolution of this paradox lies in the assumptions about standard (reference), states which are unavoidably involved in the above definitions of β_L and $\beta_{L\text{-}L}$. In order to ensure that β_L and $\beta_{L\text{-}L}$ are dimensionless (as they have to be if their logarithms are to be used) when concentrations are expressed in units which have dimensions, it is necessary to use the ratios of the actual concentrations to the concentrations of

---

[8] D. C. MUNRO, *Chem. Br.* **13**, 100–5 (1977).

Table 19.1 Stability constants and thermodynamic functions for some complexes of Cd^{II} at 25°C

Complex	$\log \beta$	$\Delta H°$ (kJ mol^{-1})	$\Delta G°$ (kJ mol^{-1})	$T\Delta S°$ (kJ mol^{-1})
(a) $[Cd(NH_2Me)_4]^{2+}$	6.55	-57.32	-37.41	-19.91
	13.53		*-72.20*	*+19.98*
(b) $[Cd(en)_2]^{2+}$	10.62	-56.48	-60.67	+4.19
	14.11		*-80.51*	*+24.04*
Difference (b)-(a)	4.07	+0.84	-23.26	+24.1
	0.58		*-3.31*	*+4.06*

Values in roman type are based on concentrations expressed in mol dm^{-3}. Values in *italics* are based on concentrations expressed in mole fractions. The difference (b)-(a) refers to the replacement reaction

$$[Cd(NH_2Me)_4]^{2+}(aq) + 2en(aq) \rightleftharpoons [Cd(en)_2]^{2+}(aq) + 4NH_2Me(aq)$$

some standard state. Accordingly, the expression for any β should incorporate an additional factor composed of standard state concentrations, and the expression $\Delta G° = -RT \ln \beta$ should have an additional term involving the logarithm of this factor. Not to include this factor and this term inevitably implies the choice of standard states of concentration = 1 in whatever units are being used. Only in this way can the factor associated with β be 1 and its logarithm zero. It should be stressed, however, that irrespective of these definitional niceties, it remains true as stated above that chelating ligands which form unstrained complexes always tend to displace their monodentate counterparts under normally attainable experimental conditions.

Probably the most satisfactory model with which to explain the chelate effect is that proposed by G. Schwarzenbach[9] If L and L-L are present in similar concentrations and are competing for two coordination sites on the metal, the probability of either of them coordinating to the first site may be taken as equal. However, once one end of L-L has become attached it is much more likely that the second site will be won by its other end than by L, simply because its other end must be held close to the second site and its effective concentration where it matters is therefore much

higher than the concentration of L. Because $\Delta G°$ refers to the transfer of the separate reactants at concentrations = 1 to the products, also at concentrations = 1, it is clear from this model that the advantage of L-L over L, as denoted by $\Delta G°$ or β, will be greatest when the units of concentration are such that a value of 1 corresponds to a dilute solution. Conversely, where a value of 1 coresponds to an exceedingly high concentration, the advantage will be much less and may even disappear. In normal practice even a concentration of 1 mol dm^{-3} is regarded as high, and a concentration of 1 mole fraction is so high as to be of only hypothetical significance, so it need cause no surprise that the choice of the latter unit should lead to rather bizarre results.

The chelate effect is usually most pronounced for 5- and 6-membered rings. Smaller rings generally involve excessive strain while increasingly large rings offer a rapidly decreasing advantage for coordination to the second site. Naturally the more rings there are in a complex the greater the total increase in stability. If a multidentate ligand is also cyclic, and there are no unfavourable steric effects, a further increase in the stability of its complexes accrues. Favourable entropy changes can again be invoked to explain this *macrocyclic effect*. Since a macrocyclic ligand has very little rotational entropy even before coordination, the net increase in entropy when it does coordinate is expected to be even greater than in the case of a comparable non-cyclic ligand.

[9] G. SCHWARZENBACH. *Helv. Chim. Acta* **35**, 2344–59 (1952).

19.4 The Various Coordination Numbers[10]

In 1893 at the age of 26, Alfred Werner[†] produced his classic coordination theory.[2,11] It is said that, after a dream which crystallized his ideas, he set down his views and by midday had written the paper which was the starting point for work which culminated in the award of the Nobel Prize for Chemistry in 1913. The main thesis of his argument was that metals possess two types of valency: (i) the primary, or ionizable, valency which must be satisfied by negative ions and is what is now referred to as the "oxidation state"; and (ii) the secondary valency which has fixed directions with respect to the central metal and can be satisfied by either negative ions or neutral molecules. This is the basis for the various stereochemistries found amongst coordination compounds. Without the armoury of physical methods available to the modern chemist, in particular X-ray crystallography, the early workers were obliged to rely on purely chemical methods to identify the more important of these stereochemistries. They did this during the next 20 y or so, mainly by preparing vast numbers of complexes of various metals of such stoichiometry that the number of isomers which could be produced would distinguish between alternative stereochemistries.

The term "secondary valency" has been superseded by the term "coordination number". This may be defined as the number of donor atoms associated with the central metal atom or ion. For many years a distinction was made between coordination number in this sense and in the crystallographic sense, where it is the number of nearest-neighbour ions of opposite charge in an ionic crystal. Though the former definition applies to species which can exist independently in the solid or in solution, while the latter applies to extended lattice systems, the distinction is rather artificial, particularly in view of the fact that crystal field theory (one of the theories of bonding most commonly applied to coordination compounds) assumes that the coordinate bond is entirely ionic! Indeed, the concept can be extended to all molecules. $TiCl_4$, for instance, can be regarded as a complex of Ti^{4+} with 4 Cl^- ions in which one lone-pair of electrons on each of the latter is completely shared with the Ti^{4+} to give essentially covalent bonds.

The most commonly occurring coordination numbers for transition elements are 4 and 6, but all values from 2 to 9 are known and a few examples of even higher ones have been established. The more important factors determining the most favourable coordination number for a particular metal and ligand are summarized below. However it is important to realize that, with so many factors involved, it is not difficult to provide facile explanations of varying degrees of plausibility for most experimental observations, and it is therefore prudent to treat such explanations with caution.

(i) If electrostatic forces are dominant the attractions between the metal and the ligands should exceed the destabilizing repulsions between the ligands. The attractions are proportional to the product of the charges on the metal and the ligand whereas the repulsions are proportional to the square of the ligand charge. High cation charge and low ligand charge should consequently favour high coordination numbers, e.g. halide ions usually favour higher coordination numbers than does O^{2-}.

(ii) There must be an upper limit to the number of molecules (atoms) of a particular ligand which can physically be fitted around a particular cation. For monatomic ligands this limit will be dependent on the radius ratio of cation and anion, just as is the case with extended crystal lattices.

(iii) Where covalency is important the distribution of charge is equalized by the transference

[10] G. WILKINSON, R. D. GILLARD and J. A. McCLEVERTY (eds.), *Comprehensive Coordination Chemistry*, Pergamon Press, Oxford, Vol. 1, 1987, 613 pp. D. L. KEPERT, *Inorganic Stereochemistry*, Springer-Verlag, Berlin, 1982, 227 pp. J. A. DAVIES, C. M. HOCKENSMITH, V. YU. KUKUSHKIN and YU. N. KUKUSHKIN, *Synthetic Coordination Chemistry: Principles and Practise*, World Scientific Publ., Singapore, 1996, 452 pp.

[11] G. B. KAUFFMAN, *Inorganic Coordination Compounds*, Wiley, New York, 1981, 205 pp.

[†] Born in Mulhouse, Alsace, in 1866, he was French by birth, German in upbringing, and, working in Zürich, he became a Swiss citizen in 1894.

of charge in the form of lone-pairs of electrons from ligands to cation. The more polarizable the ligand the lower the coordination number required to satisfy the particular cation though, if back-donation of charge from cation to ligand via suitable π orbitals is possible, then more ligands can be accommodated. Thus the species most readily formed with Fe^{III} in aqueous solutions are $[FeF_5(H_2O)]^{2-}$ for the non-polarizable F^-, $[FeCl_4]^-$ for the more polarizable Cl^-, but $[Fe(CN)_6]^{3-}$ for CN^- which, though it is even more polarizable, also possesses empty antibonding π orbitals suitable for back-donation.

(iv) The availability of empty metal orbitals of suitable symmetries and energies to accommodate electron-pairs from the ligands must also be important in covalent compounds. This is probably one of the main reasons why the lowest coordination numbers (2 and 3) are to be found in the Ag, Au, Hg region of the periodic table where the d shell has been filled. However, it would be unwise to draw the converse conclusion that the highest coordinations are found amongst the early members of the transition and inner-transition series because of the availability of empty d or f orbitals. It seems more likely that these high coordination numbers are achieved by electrostatic attractions between highly charged but rather large cations and a large number of relatively non-polarizable ligands.

Representative examples of the stereochemistries associated with each of the various coordination numbers will now be discussed.

Coordination number 2

Examples of this coordination number are virtually confined to linear $D_{\infty h}$ complexes of Cu^I, Ag^I, Au^I, and Hg^{II} of which a well-known instance is the ammine formed when ammonia is added to an aqueous solution of Ag^+:

$$[H_3N-Ag-NH_3]^+$$

Coordination number 3 [12]

This is rather rare and even in $[HgI_3]^-$, the example usually cited, the coordination number is dependent on the counter cation. In $[SMe_3][HgI_3]$ the Hg^{II} lies at the centre of an almost equilateral triangle of iodide ions (D_{3h}) whereas in $[NMe_4][HgI_3]$ the anion apparently polymerizes into loosely linked chains of 4-coordinate Hg^{II}. Other examples feature bulky ligands, e.g. the trigonal planar complexes $[Fe\{N(SiMe_3)_2\}_3]$, $[Cu\{(SC(NH_2)_2\}_3]Cl$ and $[Cu(SPPh_3)_3]ClO_4$.

Coordination number 4

This is very common and usually gives rise to stereochemistries which may be regarded essentially as either tetrahedral T_d or (square) planar D_{4h}. Where a complex may be thought to have been formed from a central cation with a spherically symmetrical electron configuration, the ligands will lie as far from each other as possible, that is they will be tetrahedrally disposed around the cation. This has already been seen in complex anions such as BF_4^- and is also common amongst complexes of transition metals in their group oxidation states and of d^5 and d^{10} ions. $[MnO_4]^-$, $[Ni(CO)_4]$ and $[Cu(py)_4]^+$, respectively, exemplify these types. Central cations with other d configurations, in particular d^8, may give rise to a square-planar stereochemistry and the complexes of Pd^{II} and Pt^{II} are predominantly of this type. Then again, the difference in energy between tetrahedral and square-planar forms may be only slight, in which case both forms may be known or, indeed, interconversions may be possible as happens with a number of Ni^{II} complexes (p. 1159). In the $M_2^I CuX_4$ series of complexes of Cu^{II}, variation of M^I and X gives complex anions with stereochemistries ranging from square planar, e.g. $(NH_4)_2[CuCl_4]$, to almost tetrahedral, e.g. $Cs_2[CuBr_4]$. Figure 19.3 shows that the change from square planar to tetrahedral requires a $90°$ rotation of one L,L pair and a $19\frac{1}{2}°$ change in the LML angles, and a continuous range of distortions from one extreme to the other would appear to be feasible.

---
[12] P. G. ELLER, D. C. BRADLEY, M. B. HURSTHOUSE and D. W. MEEK, *Coord. Chem. Revs.* **24**, 1–95 (1977).

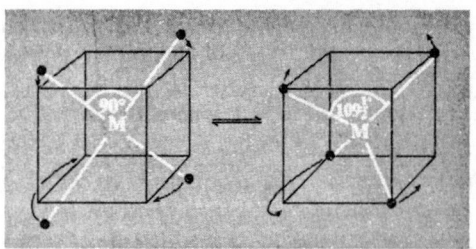

Figure 19.3 Schematic interconversion of square planar and tetrahedral geometries.

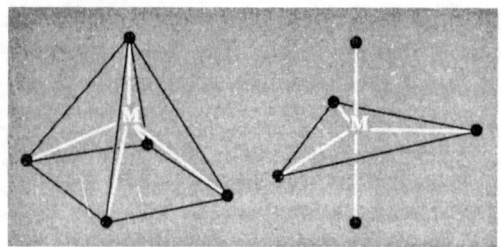

Square pyramidal   Trigonal bipyramidal

Figure 19.4 Limiting stereochemistries for 5-coordination.

Four-coordinate complexes provide good examples of the early use of preparative methods for establishing stereochemistry. For complexes of the type [Ma_2b_2], where a and b are unidentate ligands, a tetrahedral structure cannot produce isomerism whereas a planar structure leads to *cis* and *trans* isomers (see below). The preparation of 2 isomers of [$PtCl_2(NH_3)_2$], for instance, was taken as good evidence for their planarity.[†]

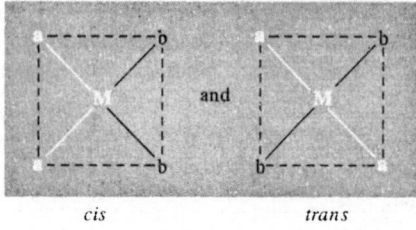

cis   *trans*

Coordination number 5

Five-coordinate complexes are far more common than was once supposed and are now known for all configurations from d^1 to d^9. Two limiting stereochemistries may be distinguished (Fig. 19.4). One of the first authenticated examples of 5-coordination was [$VO(acac)_2$] which has the square-pyramidal C_{4v} structure with the $=O$ occupying the unique apical site. However, many of the complexes with this coordination number have structures intermediate between the

two extremes and it appears that the energy required for their interconversion is frequently rather small. Because of this stereochemical non-rigidity a number of 5-coordinate compounds behave in a manner described as "fluxional". That is, they exist in two or more configurations which are chemically equivalent and which interconvert at such a rate that some physical measurement (commonly nmr) is unable to distinguish the separate configurations and instead "sees" only their time-average. If ML_5 has a trigonal bipyramidal D_{3h} structure then 2 ligands must be "axial" and 3 "equatorial", but interchange via a square-pyramidal intermediate is possible (Fig. 19.5). This mechanism has been suggested as the reason why the ^{13}C nmr spectrum of trigonal bipyramidal $Fe(CO)_5$ (p. 1104) fails to distinguish two different kinds of carbon nuclei. See also the discussion of PF_5 on p. 499.

Coordination number 6

This is the most common coordination number for complexes of transition elements. It can be seen by inspection that, for compounds of the type (Ma_4b_2), the three symmetrical structures (Fig. 19.6) can give rise to 3, 3 and 2 isomers respectively. Exactly the same is true for compounds of the type [Ma_3b_3]. In order to determine the stereochemistry of 6-coordinate complexes very many examples of such compounds were prepared, particularly with M = Cr^{III} and Co^{III}, and in no case was more than 2 isomers found. This, of course, was only negative evidence for the octahedral structure, though the

---

[†] On the basis of this evidence alone it is logically possible that one isomer could be tetrahedral. Early coordination chemists, however, assumed that the directions of the "secondary valencies" were fixed, which would preclude this possibility. X-ray structural analysis shows that, in the case of Pt^{II} complexes, they were correct.

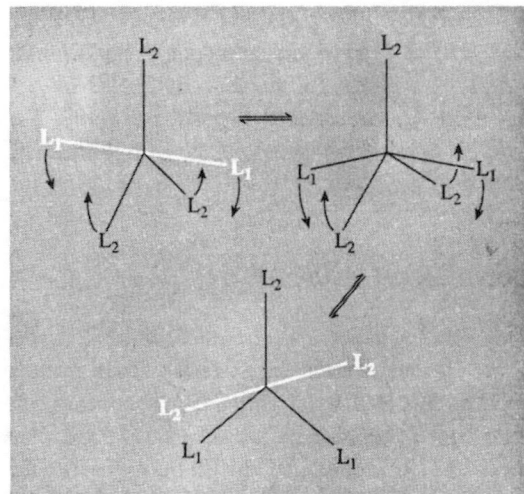

Figure 19.5 The interconversion of trigonal bipyramidal configurations via a square-pyramidal intermediate. Notice that the L_1 ligands, which in the left-hand tbp are axial, become equatorial in the right-hand tbp and simultaneously 2 of the L_2 ligands change from equatorial to axial.

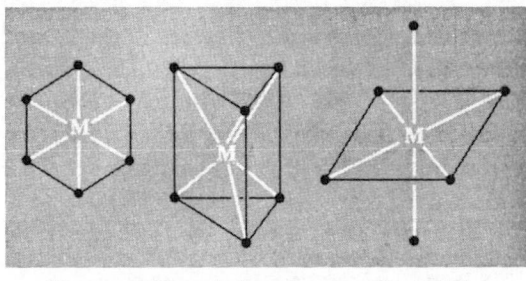

Planar   Trigonal prismatic   Octahedral

Figure 19.6 Possible stereochemistries for 6-coordination.

sheer volume of it made it rather compelling. More positive evidence was provided by Werner, who in 1914 achieved the first resolution into optical isomers of an entirely inorganic compound, since

$$\left[Co \left\langle \begin{array}{c} OH \\ \diagup \diagdown \\ \diagdown \diagup \\ OH \end{array} Co(NH_3)_4 \right\rangle_3 \right]^{6+}$$

neither the planar nor trigonal prismatic structures can give rise to such optical isomers.

Nevertheless, it cannot be assumed that every 6-coordinate complex is octahedral. In 1923 the first example of trigonal prismatic coordination was reported for the infinite layer lattices of MoS_2 and WS_2. A limited number of further examples are now known following the report in 1965 of the structure of $[Re(S_2C_2Ph_2)_3]$ (Fig. 19.7). Intermediate structures also occur and can be defined by the "twist angle" which is the angle through which one face of an octahedron has been rotated with respect to the opposite face as "viewed along" a threefold axis of the octahedron. A twist angle of $60°$ suffices to convert an octahedron into a trigonal prism:

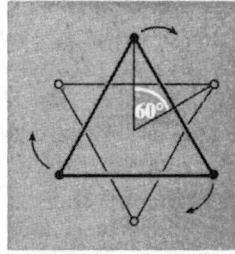

In fact the vast majority of 6-coordinate complexes are indeed octahedral or distorted octahedral. In addition to the twist distortion just considered distortions can be of two other types: trigonal and tetragonal distortions which mean compression or elongation along a threefold and a fourfold axis of the octahedron respectively (Fig. 19.8).

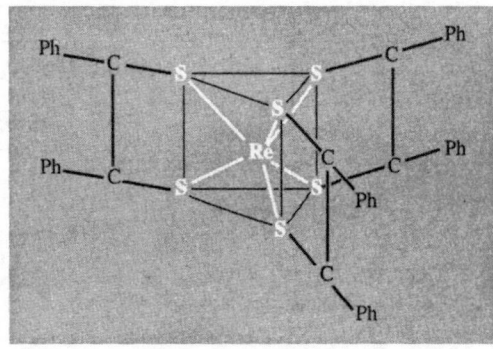

Figure 19.7 Trigonal prismatic structure of $[Re(S_2C_2Ph_2)_3]$.

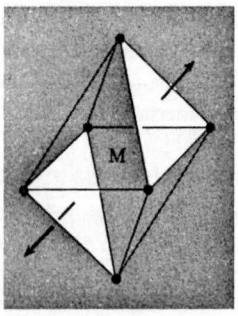 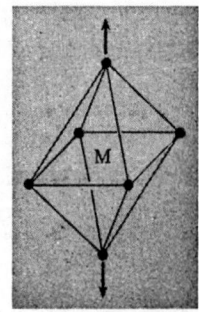

Trigonal elongation   Tetragonal elongation

Figure 19.8 Distortions of octahedral geometry.

Coordination number 7

There are three main stereochemistries for complexes of this coordination number: pentagonal bipyramidal D_{5h}, capped trigonal prismatic C_{2v} and capped octahedral C_{3v}, the last two being obtained by the addition of a seventh ligand either above one of the rectangular faces of a trigonal prism or above a triangular face of an octahedron respectively. These structures may conveniently be visualized as having the ligating atoms which form the coordination polyhedra on the surfaces of circumscribed spheres (Fig. 19.9).

As with other high coordination numbers, there seems to be little difference in energy between these structures. Factors such as the number of counter ions and the stereochemical requirements of chelating ligands are probably decisive and *a priori* arguments are unreliable in predicting the geometry of a particular complex. $[ZrF_7]^{3-}$ and $[HfF_7]^{3-}$ have the pentagonal bipyramidal structure, whereas the bivalent anions, $[NbF_7]^{2-}$ and $[TaF_7]^{2-}$ are capped trigonal prismatic. The capped octahedral structure is exemplified by $[NbOF_6]^{3-}$.

Coordination number 8 [13,14]

The most symmetrical structure possible is the cube O_h but, except in extended ionic lattices such as those of CsCl and CaF_2, it appears that inter-ligand repulsions are nearly always (but see p. 1275) reduced by distorting the cube, the two most important resultant structures being the square antiprism D_{4h} and the dodecahedron D_{2d} (Fig. 19.10).

Again, these forms are energetically very similar; distortions from the idealized structures make it difficult to specify one or other, and the particular structure actually found must result from the interplay of many factors. $[TaF_8]^{3-}$, $[ReF_8]^{2-}$ and $[Zr(acac)_4]$ are square antiprismatic, whereas $[ZrF_8]^{4-}$ and $[Mo(CN)_8]^{4-}$ are dodecahedral. The nitrates $[Co(NO_3)_4]^{2-}$ and $Ti(NO_3)_4$ may both be regarded as dodecahedral, the former with some distortion. Each nitrate ion is bidentate but the 2

[13] I. G. SHTEREV, G. St. NIKOLOV, N. TRENDAFILOVA and R. KIROV, *Polyhedron*, **10**, 393–402 (1991).
[14] C. W. HAIGH, *Polyhedron*, **15**, 605–43 (1996).

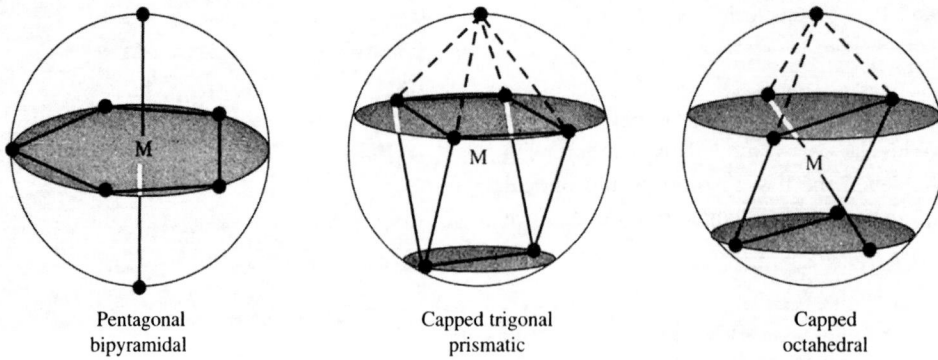

Pentagonal   Capped trigonal   Capped
bipyramidal   prismatic   octahedral

Figure 19.9 The three main stereochemistries for 7-coordination.

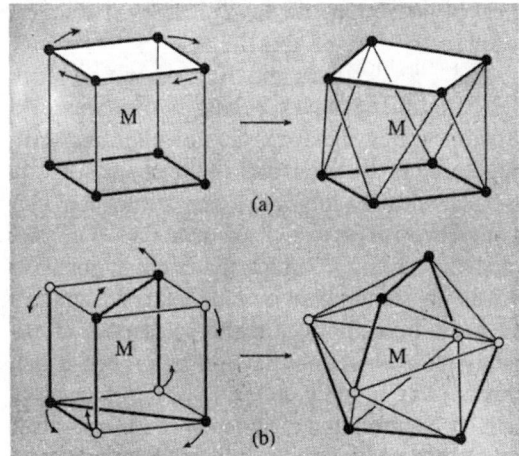

Figure 19.10 (a) Conversion of cube to square antiprism by rotation of one face through 45° (b) Conversion of cube into dodecahedron.

oxygen atoms are necessarily close together so that the structure of the complexes is probably more easily visualized from the point of view of the 4 nitrogen atoms which form a flattened tetrahedron around the metal (p. 966).

Coordination number 9

The stereochemistry of most 9-coordinate complexes approximates to the tri-capped trigonal prism D_{3h}, formed by placing additional ligands above the three rectangular faces of a trigonal prism:

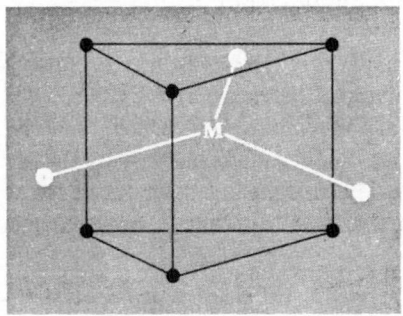

Amongst the known examples of this arrangement are a number of $[M(H_2O)_9]^{3+}$ hydrates of lanthanide salts and $[ReH_9]^{2-}$. The latter is interesting in that it is presumably only the small size of the H ligand which allows such a high coordination number for rhenium. Very occasionally 9-coordination results in a capped square antiprismatic C_{4v} arrangement in which the ninth ligand lies above one of the square faces, e.g. the Cl-bridged $[\{LaCl(H_2O)_7\}_2]^{4+}$.

Coordination numbers above 9

Such high coordination numbers are not common and it is difficult to generalize about their structures since so few have been accurately determined. They are found mainly with ions of the early lanthanide and actinide elements and it is therefore tempting to assume that the availability of empty and accessible f orbitals is necessary for their formation. However, it appears that the bonding is predominantly ionic and that the really important point is that these are the elements which provide stable cations with charges high enough to attract a large number of anions and yet are large enough to ensure that the inter-ligand repulsions are not unacceptably high. $K_4[Th(O_2CCO_2)_4(H_2O)_2].2H_2O$ (bicapped square antiprism D_{4d}) and $[La(edta)(H_2O)_4]$ afford examples of 10-coordination. Higher coordination numbers are reached only by chelating ligands such as NO_3^-, SO_4^{2-}, and 1,8-naphthyridine (8) with donor atoms close together (i.e. ligands with only a small "bite"). $[La(dapbaH)(NO_3)_3]$, is a good example (see

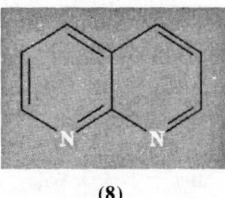

(8)

(9)

also p. 1276): in it the 5 donor atoms of the dapbaH, i.e. 2,6-diacetylpyridinebis(benzoic acid hydrazone) (9), are situated in a plane, with the N atoms (but not the donor oxygens) of the 3 bidentate nitrates in a second plane at right angles to the first. $Ce_2Mg_3(NO_3)_{12}.24H_2O$ contains 12-coordinate Ce in the complex ion $[Ce(NO_3)_6]^{3-}$. This has a distorted icosahedral stereochemistry, though it is more easily visualized as an octahedral arrangement of the nitrogen atoms around the Ce^{III}. Another example is $[Pr(naph)_6]^{3+}$ where naph is 1,8-naphthyridine (8).

Higher coordination numbers (up to 16) are known, particularly among organometallic compounds (pp. 940–3) and metal borohydrides (p. 168).

In addition to coordination compounds in which a central metal atom is surrounded by a polyhedral array of donor atoms, a large and rapidly increasing number of "cluster" compounds[15−18] is known in which a group of metal atoms is held together largely by M—M bonds. Where more than three metal atoms are involved, they themselves form polyhedral arrays which may be considered as conceptual intermediates between mononuclear classical complexes and the non-molecular lattice structures of binary and ternary compounds of transition metals. A distinction is sometimes made between "clusters" which owe their stability to M—M bonds, and "cages" which are held together by ligand bridges, but the distinction is not rigidly adhered to.

Cluster and cage structures are widespread in the chemistry of main group elements, being particularly extensive in the case of boron (Chap. 6). For transition elements the principal areas of interest are the lower halides of elements towards the left of the d-block, and carbonyls of elements towards the right of the d-block, the latter being an especially active area. The possibility that metal clusters of high nuclearity might mimic the behaviour of metal surfaces (the "surface-cluster analogy") has stimulated synthetic chemists to search for materials with high catalytic activity.[19] Such materials, particularly if soluble, should also provide better insight into the catalytic activity of metal surfaces. Unfortunately these objectives have so far proved largely elusive and in only a few cases can catalytic activity be attributed confidently to a cluster itself rather than to its fragmentation products.

These and other classes of cluster compounds will be dealt with more fully in later chapters devoted to the chemistry of the metals involved.

19.5 Isomerism[20]

Isomers are compounds with the same chemical composition but different structures, and the possibility of their occurrence in coordination compounds is manifest. Their importance in the early elucidation of the stereochemistries of complexes has already been referred to and, though the purposeful preparation of isomers is no longer common, the preparative chemist must still be aware of the diversity of the compounds which can be produced. The more important types of isomerism are listed below.

Conformational isomerism

In principle this type of isomerism (also known as "polytopal" isomerism) is possible with any coordination number for which there is more than one known stereochemistry. However, to actually occur the isomers need to be of comparable stability, and to be separable there

[15] M. Moskovits, *Metal Clusters*, Wiley, New York, 1986, 313 pp.

[16] I. G. Dance, Chap. 5 in *Comprehensive Coordination Chemistry*, Vol. 1, pp. 135–78, Pergamon Press, Oxford, 1987.

[17] D. F. Shriver, H. D. Kaesz and R. D. Adams, *The Chemistry of Metal Cluster Complexes*, VCH, New York, 1990, 439 pp.

[18] D. M. P. Mingos and D. I. Wales, *Introduction to Cluster Chemistry*, Prentice Hall, New York, 1990, 318 pp.

[19] B. C. Gates, L. Guczi and H. Knözinger (eds.) *Metal Clusters in Catalysis*, Vol. 29 of *Studies in Surface Science and Catalysis*, Elsevier, Amsterdam, 1986, 648 pp.

[20] J. MacB. Harrowfield, Chap. 6 in *Comprehensive Coordination Chemistry*, Vol. 1, pp. 179–212, Pergamon Press, Oxford, 1987.

must be a significant energy barrier preventing their interconversion. This behaviour is confined primarily to 4-coordinate nickel(II), an example being [NiCl$_2${P(CH$_2$Ph)Ph$_2$}$_2$] which is known in both planar and tetrahedral forms (p. 1160).

Geometrical isomerism

This is of most importance in square-planar and octahedral compounds where ligands, or more specifically donor atoms, can occupy positions next to one another (*cis*) or opposite each other (*trans*) (Fig. 19.11).

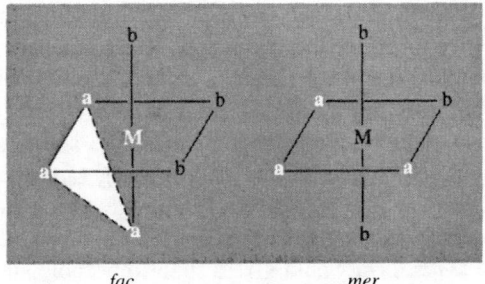

fac   *mer*

Figure 19.12   Facial and meridional isomers.

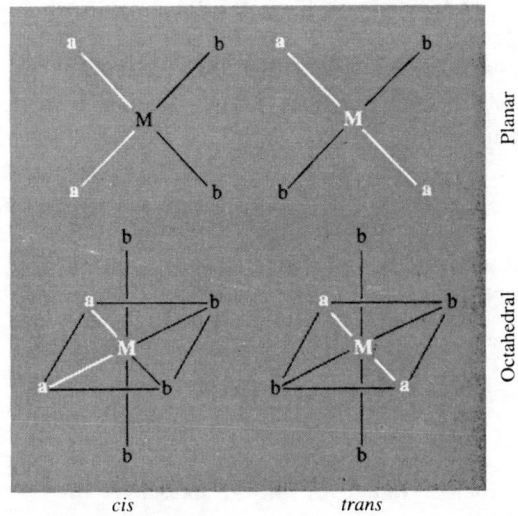

cis   *trans*

Figure 19.11   *Cis* and *trans* isomerism.

A similar type of isomerism occurs for [Ma$_3$b$_3$] octahedral complexes since each trio of donor atoms can occupy either adjacent positions at the corners of an octahedral face (*fac*ial) or positions around the meridian of the octahedron (*mer*idional). (Fig. 19.12.) Geometrical isomers differ in a variety of physical properties, amongst which dipole moment and visible/ultraviolet spectra are often diagnostically important.

Optical isomerism

Optical isomers, enantiomorphs or enantiomers, as they are also known, are pairs of molecules

which are non-superimposable mirror images of each other. Such isomers have the property of chirality (from Greek χειρ, hand), i.e. handedness, and virtually the only physical or chemical difference between them is that they rotate the plane of polarized light, one of them to the left and the other to the right. They are consequently designated as laevo (*l* or −) and dextro (*d* or +) isomers.

A few cases of optical isomerism are known for planar and tetrahedral complexes involving unsymmetrical bidentate ligands, but by far the most numerous examples are afforded by octahedral compounds of chelating ligands, e.g. [Cr(oxalate)$_3$]$^{2-}$ and [Co(edta)]$^-$ (Fig. 19.13).

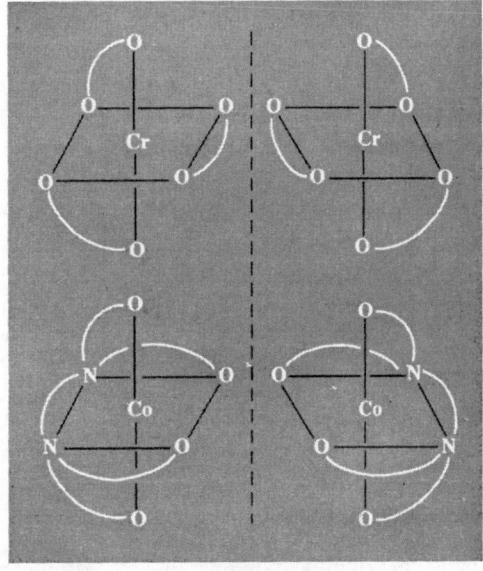

Figure 19.13   Non-superimposable mirror images.

Where unidentate ligands are present, the ability to effect the resolution of an octahedral complex (i.e. to separate 2 optical isomers) is proof that the 2 ligands are *cis* to each other. Resolution of $[PtCl_2(en)_2]^{2-}$ therefore shows it to be *cis* while of the 2 known geometrical isomers of $[CrCl_2en(NH_3)_2]^+$ the one which can be resolved must have the *cis-cis* structure since the *trans* form would give a superimposable, and therefore identical, mirror image:

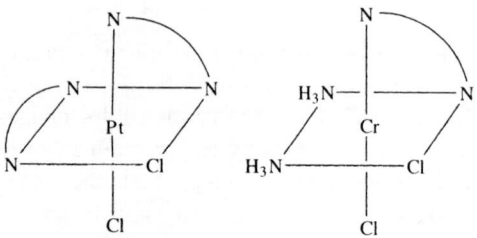

Ionization isomerism

This type of isomerism occurs when isomers produce different ions in solution, and is possible in compounds which consists of a complex ion with a counter ion which is itself a potential ligand. The pairs: $[Co(NH_3)_5(NO_3)]SO_4$, $[Co(NH_3)_5(SO_4)]NO_3$ and $[PtCl_2(NH_3)_4]Br_2$, $[PtBr_2(NH_3)_4]Cl_2$, and the series $[CoCl(en)_2(NO_2)]SCN$, $[CoCl(en)_2(SCN)]NO_2$, $[Co(en)_2(NO_2)(SCN)]Cl$ are examples of ionization isomers.

A subdivision of this type of isomerism, known as "hydrate isomerism", occurs when water may be inside or outside the coordination sphere. It is typified by $CrCl_3.6H_2O$ which exists in the three distinct forms $[Cr(H_2O)_6]Cl_3$ (violet), $[CrCl(H_2O)_5]Cl_2.H_2O$ (pale green), and $[CrCl_2(H_2O)_4]Cl.2H_2O$ (dark green). These are readily distinguished by the action of $AgNO_3$ in aqueous solution which immediately precipitates 3, 2 and 1 chloride ions respectively.

Linkage isomerism

This is in principle possible in any compound containing an ambidentate ligand. However, that

such a ligand can *under different circumstances* coordinate through either of the 2 different donor atoms is by no means a guarantee that it will form isolable linkage isomers with the same cation. In fact, in only a very small proportion of the complexes of ambidentate ligands can linkage isomers actually be isolated, and these are confined largely to complexes of NO_2^- (p. 463) and, to a lesser extent, SCN^- (p. 325). Examples are:

$$[Co(en)_2(NO_2)_2]^-, [Co(en)_2(ONO)_2]^-$$

and

$$[Pd(PPh_3)_2(NCS)_2], [Pd(PPh_3)_2(SCN)_2]$$

It should be noted that, by convention, the ambidentate ligand is always written with its donor atom first, i.e. NO_2 for the nitro, ONO for the nitrito, NCS for the *N*-thiocyanato and SCN for the *S*-thiocyanato complex. Differences in infrared spectra arising from the differences in bonding are often used to distinguish between such isomers.

Coordination isomerism

In compounds made up of both anionic and cationic complexes it is possible for the distribution of ligands between the ions to vary and so lead to isomers such as:

$$[Co(en)_3][Cr(CN)_6] \text{ and } [Cr(en)_3][Co(CN)_6]$$

$$[Cu(NH_3)_4][PtCl_4] \text{ and } [Pt(NH_3)_4][CuCl_4]$$

$$[Pt^{II}(NH_3)_4][Pt^{IV}Cl_6] \text{ and } [Pt^{IV}(NH_3)_4Cl_2][Pt^{II}Cl_4]$$

It can be seen that other intermediate isomers are feasible but in the above cases they have not been isolated. Substantial differences in both physical and chemical properties are to be expected between coordination isomers.

When the two coordinating centres are not in separate ions but are joined by bridging groups, the isomers are often distinguished as "coordination position isomers" as is the case for:

$$[NH_3)_4Co \overset{\displaystyle \underset{H}{O}}{\underset{\displaystyle \underset{H}{O}}{\Big\langle}} Co(NH_3)_2Cl_2]^{2+} \text{ and}$$

$$[Cl(NH_3)_3Co \overset{\displaystyle \underset{H}{O}}{\underset{\displaystyle \underset{H}{O}}{\Big\langle}} Co(NH_3)_3Cl]^{2+}$$

Polymerization isomerism

Compounds whose molecular compositions are multiples of a simple stoichiometry are polymers, strictly, only if they are formed by repetition of the simplest unit. However, the name "polymerization isomerism" is applied rather loosely to cases where the same stoichiometry is retained but where the molecular arrangements are different. The stoichiometry $PtCl_2(NH_3)_2$ applies to the 3 known compounds, $[Pt(NH_3)_4][PtCl_4]$, $[Pt(NH_3)_4][PtCl_3(NH_3)]_2$, and $[PtCl(NH_3)_3]_2[PtCl_4]$ (in addition to the *cis* and *trans* isomers of monomeric $[PtCl_2(NH_3)_2]$). There are actually 7 known compounds with the stoichiometry $Co(NH_3)_3(NO_2)_3$. Again it is clear that considerable differences are to be expected in the chemical properties and in physical properties such as conductivity.

Ligand isomerism

Should a ligand exist in different isomeric forms then of course the corresponding complexes will also be isomers, often described as "ligand isomers". In $[CoCl(en)_2(NH_2C_6H_4Me)]Cl_2$, for instance, the toluidine may be of the *o-*, *m-* or *p-* form.

19.6 The Coordinate Bond[21]

(see also p. 198)

The concept of the coordinate bond as an interaction between a cation and an ion or molecule possessing a lone-pair of electrons can be accepted before specifying the nature of that interaction. Indeed, it is now evident that in different complexes the bond can span the whole range from electrostatic to covalent character. This is why the various theories which have been accorded popular favour at different times have been acceptable and useful even though based on apparently incompatible assumptions. This dichotomy is reflected in the now obsolete adjectives "dative-covalent", "semi-polar" and "co-ionic", which have been used to describe the coordinate bond. The first of these descriptions arises from the idea advanced by N. V. Sidgwick in 1927, that the coordinate bond is a covalent bond formed by the donation of a lone-pair of electrons from the donor atom to the central metal. Since noble gases are extremely unreactive, and compounds in which atoms have attained the electronic configuration of a noble gas either by sharing or transferring electrons also tend to be stable, Sidgwick further suggested that, in complexes, the metal would tend to surround itself with sufficient ligands to ensure that the number of electrons around it (its "effective atomic number" or EAN) would be the same as that of the next noble gas. If this were true then a metal would have a unique coordination number for each oxidation state, which is certainly not always the case. However, the EAN rule is still of use in rationalizing the coordination numbers and structures of simple metal carbonyls.

In his *valence bond theory* (VB), L. Pauling extended the idea of electron-pair donation by considering the orbitals of the metal which would be needed to accommodate them, and the stereochemical consequences of their hybridization (1931–3). He was thereby able to account for much that was known in the 1930s about the stereochemistry and kinetic behaviour of complexes, and demonstrated the diagnostic value of measuring their magnetic properties. Unfortunately the theory offers no satisfactory explanation of spectroscopic properties and so was

[21] B. N. FIGGIS, Chap. 7 in *Comprehensive Coordination Chemistry*, Vol. 1, pp. 213–80, Pergamon Press, Oxford, 1987. S. F. A. KETTLE, *Physical Inorganic Chemistry, A Coordination Chemistry Approach*, pp. 95–237, Spektrum, Oxford, 1996.

eventually superseded by *crystal field theory* (CF).

About the same time that VB theory was being developed, CF theory was also being used by H. Bethe, J. H. van Vleck and other physicists to account for the colours and magnetic properties of hydrated salts of transition metals (1933–6). It is based on what, to chemists, appeared to be the outrageous assumption that the coordinate bond is entirely electrostatic. Nevertheless, in the 1950s a number of theoretical chemists used it to interpret the electronic spectra of transition metal complexes. It has since been remarkably successful in explaining the properties of M^{II} and M^{III} ions of the first transition series, especially when modifications have been incorporated to include the possibility of some covalency. (The theory is then often described as *ligand field theory*, but there is no general agreement on this terminology.)

In order to take full account of both ionic and covalent character, recourse must be made to *molecular orbital theory* (MO) which, like the VB and CF theories, originated in the 1930s. It has gained increasing ground with the development of powerful high-speed computers and the ready accessibility of software programmes which enable either semi-empirical or complex *ab initio* calculations to be carried out reliably and rapidly. There is still a place, however, for the pictorial representation of localized two-centre or three-centre bonds in elementary descriptions of bonding.

The fundamental assumption of MO theory is that metal and ligand orbitals will overlap and combine, providing they are of the correct symmetries to do so and have similar energies. In one approximation the appropriate AOs of the metal and atomic or molecular orbitals of the ligand, are used to produce the MOs by the linear combination of atomic orbitals (LCAO) method. Since combination of metal and ligand orbitals of widely differing energies can be neglected, only valence orbitals are considered.

In the case of an octahedral complex ML_6, the metal has six σ orbitals, i.e. the e_g pair of the nd set, together with the $(n+1)$s and the three $(n+1)$p. The ligands each have one

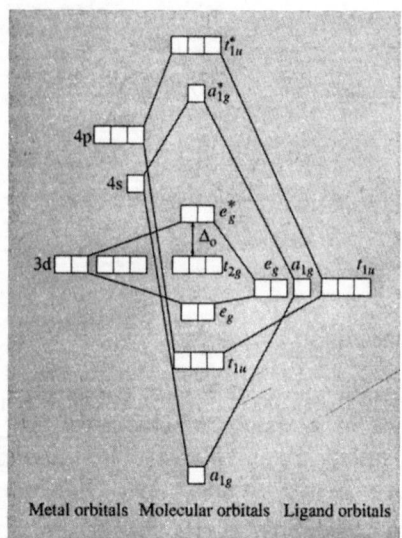

Figure 19.14 Molecular orbital diagram for an octahedral complex of a first series transition metal (only σ interactions are considered in this simplified diagram).

σ orbital (containing the lone-pair of electrons) and these are combined to give orbitals with the correct symmetry to overlap with the metal σ orbitals (Fig. 19.14). The 6 electron pairs from the ligands are placed in the six lowest MOs, leaving the non-axial, and hence non-σ-bonding, metal t_{2g} and the antibonding e_g^* orbitals to accommodate the electrons originally on the metal. This central portion of the figure is the same as the e_g/t_{2g} splitting defined in CF theory, with the difference that the e_g^* orbitals now have some ligand character which implies covalency. The lower in energy the ligand orbitals are with respect to the AOs of the metal the nearer is the bonding to the electrostatic extreme. Conversely, the nearer in energy the ligand orbitals are to the AOs of the metal the more nearly can the bonding be described as electron pair donation by the ligand as in VB theory. Indeed, the metal character of the bonding MOs is derived from just those metal orbitals used in VB theory to produce the d^2sp^3 hybrids which accommodate the electron pairs donated by the ligands.

If the ligand possesses orbitals of π as well as σ symmetry the situation is drastically changed because of the overlap of these orbitals with the t_{2g} orbitals of the metal. Two situations may arise. Either the ligand π orbitals are empty and of higher energy than the metal t_{2g}, or they are filled and of lower energy than the metal t_{2g} orbitals (Fig. 19.15). The former in effect increases Δ_o, the separation of the t_{2g} and e_g^* orbitals, and is the more important case, including ligands such as CO, NO^+ and CN^-. This type of covalency, called π bonding or back bonding, provides a plausible explanation for the stability of such compounds as the metal carbonyls (pp. 926–9).

If Δ_o is large enough then electrons which would otherwise remain unpaired in the e_g orbitals may instead be forced to pair in the lower t_{2g} orbitals. For metal ions with d^4, d^5, d^6 and d^7 configurations therefore two possibilities arise depending on the magnitude of Δ_o. If Δ_o is small (compared with electron–electron repulsion energies within one orbital) then the maximum possible number of electrons remain unpaired and the configurations are known as "spin-free" or "high-spin". If Δ_o is large then electrons are forced to pair in the lower t_{2g} set and the configurations are known as "spin-paired" or "low-spin". This is summarized in Fig. 19.16.

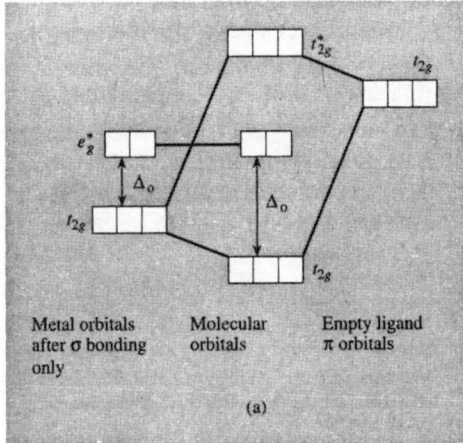

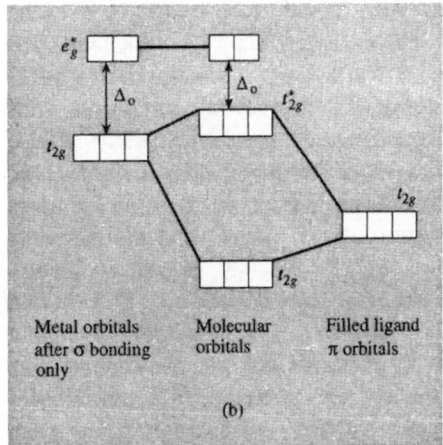

Figure 19.15 Possible effects of π bonding on Δ_o: (a) when ligand π orbitals are empty, and (b) when ligand π orbitals are filled.

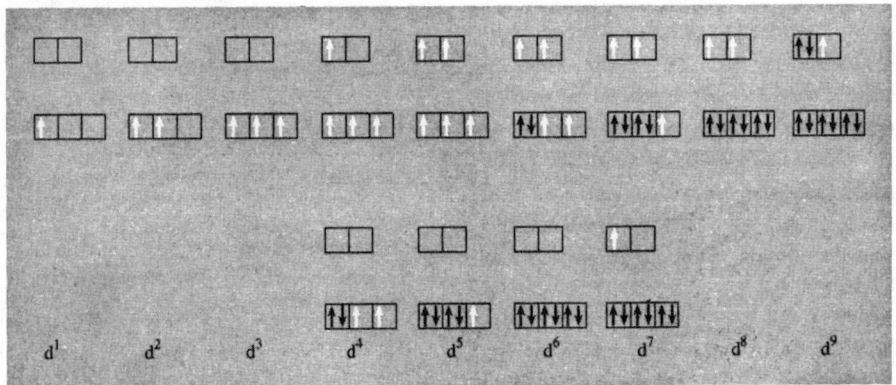

Figure 19.16 The possible high-spin and low-spin configurations arising as a result of the imposition of an octahedral crystal field on a transition metal ion.

Similar MO treatments are possible for tetrahedral and square planar complexes but are increasingly complicated.

19.7 Organometallic Compounds

This section gives a brief overview of the vast and burgeoning field of organometallic chemistry. The term *organometallic* is somewhat vague since definitions of *organo* and *metallic* are themselves necessarily imprecise. We use the term to refer to compounds that involve at least one close M–C interaction: this includes metal complexes with ligands such as CO, CO_2, CS_2 and CN^- but excludes "ionic" compounds such as NaCN or Na acetate; it also excludes metal alkoxides $M(OR)_n$ and metal complexes with organic ligands such as C_5H_5N, PPh_3, OEt_2, SMe_2, etc., where the donor atom is not carbon. A permissive view is often taken in the literature of what constitutes a "metal" and the elements B; Si, Ge; As, Sb; Se and Te are frequently included for convenience and to give added perspective. However, it is not helpful to include as metals all elements less electronegative than C since this includes I, S and P. Metal carbides (p. 297) and graphite intercalation compounds (p. 293) are also normally excluded. Further treatment of organometallic compounds will be found throughout the book under each individual element.

No area of chemistry produces more surprises and challenges and the whole field of organometallic chemistry continues to be one of great excitement and activity. A rich harvest of new and previously undreamed of structure types is reaped each year, the rewards of elegant and skilful synthetic programmes being supplemented by an unusual number of chance discoveries and totally unsuspected reactions. Synthetic chemists can take either a buccaneering or an intellectual approach (or both); structural chemists are able to press their various techniques to the limit in elucidating the products formed; theoretical chemists and reaction kineticists, though badly

outpaced in predictive work, provide an invaluable underlying rationale for various aspects of the continually evolving field and just occasionally run ahead of the experimentalists; industrial chemists can exploit and extend the results by developing numerous catalytic processes of immense importance. The field is not new, but was transformed in 1952 by the recognition of the "sandwich" structure of dicyclopentadienyliron (ferrocene).[22,23] Compendia and extended reviews[24-27] are available on various aspects, and continued progress is summarized in annual volumes.[28,29]

The various classes of ligands and attached groups that occur in organometallic compounds are summarized in Table 19.2, and these will be briefly discussed in the following paragraphs. Aspects which concern the general chemistry of carbon will be emphasized in order to give coherence and added significance to the more detailed treatment of the organometallic chemistry of individual elements given in other sections, e.g. Li (p. 102), Be (p. 127), Mg (p. 131), etc.

[22] G. WILKINSON, M. ROSENBLUM, M. C. WHITING and R. B. WOODWARD, *J. Am. Chem. Soc.* **74**, 2125-6 (1952). For some personal recollections on the events leading up to this paper, see G. WILKINSON, *J. Organometallic Chem.* **100**, 273-8 (1975).

[23] J. S. THAYER, *Adv. Organometallic Chem.* **13**, 1-49 (1975).

[24] G. WILKINSON, F. G. A. STONE and E. W. ABEL (eds.), *Comprehensive Organometallic Chemistry,* 9 Vols., Pergamon Press, Oxford, 1982, 9569 pp. E. W. ABEL, F. G. A. STONE and G. WILKINSON (eds.), *Comprehensive Organometallic Chemistry II,* 14 Vols, Pergamon Press, Oxford, 1995, approx. 8750 pp.

[25] F. A. COTTON and G. WILKINSON, *Advanced Inorganic Chemistry,* 5th edn., Wiley, New York, 1988, particularly Chaps. 22-29, pp. 1021-334.

[26] *Dictionary of Organometallic Compounds,* Chapman and Hall, London, Vols. 1-3, (1984), J. BUCKINGHAM (ed.); Supplement 1 (1985)-Supplement 5 (1989), Index (1990), J. F. MACINTYRE (ed).

[27] *The Chemistry of the Metal-Carbon Bond,* Wiley, Chichester, Vols. 1-3 (1985), F. R. HARTLEY and S. PATAI (eds.); Vol. 4 (1987), Vol. 5 (1989), F. R. HARTLEY (ed.).

[28] F. G. A. STONE and R. WEST (eds.), *Advances in Organometallic Chemistry,* Academic Press, New York, Vol. 1 (1964)-Vol. 40 (1996).

[29] *Organometallic Chemistry Reactions,* Wiley, Vol. 1, (1967)-Vol. 12 (1981).

Table 19.2   Classification of organometallic ligands according to the number of attached C atoms[a]

Number	Examples
η^1, monohapto	Alkyl ($-R$), aryl ($-Ar$), perfluoro ($-R_f$), acyl ($-\overset{\overset{O}{\|\|}}{C}R$), σ-allyl ($-CH_2CH=CH_2$), σ-ethynyl ($-C\equiv CR$), CO, CO$_2$, CS$_2$, CN$^-$, isocyanide (RNC), carbene ($=CR_2$, $=C\Big\langle{^{OR'}_{R}}$, $=C\Big\langle{^{OR}_{NHAr}}$, $=$Ccyclo, etc.) carbyne ($\equiv CR$, $\equiv CAr$), carbido (C)
η^2, dihapto	Alkene ($\rangle C=C\langle$), perfluoroalkene (e.g. C_2F_4), alkyne ($-C\equiv C-$), etc. [non-conjugated dienes are bis-dihapto]
η^3, trihapto	π-Allyl ($\rangle C\text{---}C\text{---}C\langle$)
η^4, tetrahapto	Conjugated diene (e.g. butadiene), cyclobutadiene derivatives
η^5, pentahapto	Dienyl (e.g. cyclopentadienyl derivatives, cycloheptadienyl derivatives)
η^6, hexahapto	Arene (e.g. benzene, substituted benzenes) cycloheptatriene, cycloocta-1,3,5-triene
η^7, heptahapto	Tropylium (cycloheptatrienyl)
η^8, octahapto	Cyclooctatetraene

[a] Many ligands can bond in more than one way: e.g. allyl can be η^1 (σ-allyl) or η^3 (π-allyl); cyclooctatetraene can be η^4 (1,3-diene), η^4 (chelating, 1,5-diene), η^6 (1,3,5-triene), η^6 (bis-1,2,3,–5,6,7-π-allyl), η^8 (1,3,5,7-tetraene), etc.

19.7.1 Monohapto ligands

Alkyl and aryl derivatives of many main-group metals have already been discussed in previous chapters, and compounds such as PbMe$_4$ and PbEt$_4$ are made on a huge scale, larger than all other organometallics put together (p. 371). The alkyl and aryl groups are usually regarded as 1-electron donors but it is important to remember that even a monohapto 1-electron donor can bond simultaneously to more than 1 metal atom, e.g. to 2 in Al$_2$Me$_6$ (p. 259), 3 in Li$_4$Bu$_4^t$ (p. 105) and 4 in [Li$_4$Me$_4$]$_n$. Similarly, an η^1 ligand such as CO, which is often regarded as a 2-electron donor, can bond simultaneously to either 1, 2 or 3 metal atoms (p. 928). There is thus an important distinction to be drawn between (a) hapticity (the number of C atoms in the organic group that are closely associated with a metal atom), (b) metal connectivity (the number of M atoms simultaneously bonded to the organic group), and (c) the number of ligand electrons formally involved in bonding to the metal atom(s). The metal connectivity is also to be distinguished from the coordination number of the C atom, which also includes all other atoms or groups attached to it: e.g. the bridging C atoms in Al$_2$Me$_6$ are monohapto with a metal connectivity of 2 and a coordination number of 5.

Although zinc alkyls were first described by E. Frankland in 1849 and the alkyls and aryls of most main group elements had been prepared and often extensively studied during the subsequent 100 y, very few such compounds were known for the transition metals even as recently as the late 1960s. The great burst of more recent activity stems from the independent suggestion[30,31] that M–C bonds involving transition elements are not inherently weak and that kinetically stable complexes can be made by a suitable choice of organic groups. In particular, the use of groups which have no β-hydrogen atom (e.g. $-CH_2Ph$,

[30] M. R. COLLIER, M. F. LAPPERT and M. M. TRUELOCK, *J. Organometallic Chem.* **25**, C36–8 (1970).
[31] G. YAGUPSKY, W. MOWAT, A. SHORTLAND and G. WILKINSON, *J. Chem. Soc., Chem. Commun.*, 1369–71 (1970).

–CH$_2$CMe$_3$, or –CH$_2$SiMe$_3$) often leads to stable complexes since this prevents at least one facile decomposition route namely β-elimination.

The reverse reaction (formation of metal alkyls by addition of alkenes to M–H) is the basis of several important catalytic reactions such as alkene hydrogenation, hydroformylation, hydroboration, and isomerization. A good example of decomposition by β-elimination is the first-order intramolecular reaction:

$$[Pt(Bu)_2(PPh_3)_2] \longrightarrow 1\text{-}C_4H_8$$

$$+ [Pt(Bu)(H)(PPh_3)_2] \longrightarrow n\text{-}C_4H_{10} + [Pt(PPh_3)_2]$$

β-Elimination reactions have been much studied but should not be over emphasized since other decomposition routes must also be considered. Amongst these are:

homolytic fission, e.g. HgPh$_2$ $\longrightarrow$ Hg + 2Ph
reductive elimination, e.g. [Au^{III}Me$_3$(PPh$_3$)]

$$\longrightarrow [Au^I Me(PPh_3)] + C_2H_6$$

binuclear elimination (or formation of Bu radicals) e.g.

$$2[Cu(Bu)(PBu_3)] \longrightarrow 2Cu + 2PBu_3$$

$$+ n\text{-}C_4H_{10} + 1\text{-}C_4H_8$$

α-Elimination to give a carbene complex, e.g.

$$[Ta(CH_2CMe_3)_3Cl_2] + 2LiCH_2CMe_3 \longrightarrow$$

$$2LiCl + \text{"}[Ta(CH_2CMe_3)_5]\text{"} \xrightarrow{\alpha\text{-elim}}$$

$$CMe_4 + [Ta(CH_2CMe_3)_3(=C\overset{H}{\underset{CMe_3}{<}})]$$

Stabilization of η^1-alkyl and -aryl derivatives of transition metals can be enhanced by the judicious inclusion of various other stabilizing ligands in the complex, even though such ligands are known not to be an essential prerequisite. Particularly efficacious are potential π acceptors (see below) such as AsPh$_3$, PPh$_3$,

CO or η^5-C$_5$H$_5$ in combination with the heavier transition metals since the firm occupation of coordination sites prevents their use for concerted decomposition routes. Steric protection may also be implicated. Similar arguments have been used to interpret the observed increase in stability of η^1 complexes in the sequence alkyl < aryl < o-substituted aryl < ethynyl (–C≡CH).

The next group of η^1 ligands comprise the isoelectronic species, CO, CN$^-$ and RNC. They are closely related to other 14-electron (10 valence electron) ligands such as N$_2$ and NO$^+$ (and also to tertiary phosphines and arsines, and to organic sulfides, selenides, etc.), and it is merely the presence of C as the donor atom which classifies their complexes as organometallics. All have characteristic donor properties that distinguish them from simple electron-pair donors (Lewis bases, p. 198) and these have been successfully interpreted in terms of a synergic or mutually reinforcing interaction between σ donation from ligand to metal and π back donation from metal to ligand as elaborated below. CO is undoubtedly the most important and most widely studied of all organometallic ligands and it is the prototype for this group of so-called π-acceptor ligands. The currently accepted view of the bonding is represented diagramatically in Figs. 19.17 and 19.18. Figure 19.17 shows a schematic molecular orbital energy level diagram for the heteronuclear diatomic molecule CO. The AOs lie deeper in O than in C because of the higher effective nuclear charge on O; consequently O contributes more to bonding MOs and C contributes more to the antibonding MOs. It can be seen that all the bonding MOs are filled and, in this description, the CO molecule can be said to have a triple bond :C≡O: with the lone-pair on carbon weakly available for donation to an acceptor. The top part (a) of Fig. 19.18 shows the formation of a σ bond by donation of the lone-pair into a suitably directed hybrid orbital on M, and the lower part (b) shows the accompanying back donation from a filled metal d orbital into the vacant antibonding CO orbital having π symmetry (one node) with respect to the bonding axis. This

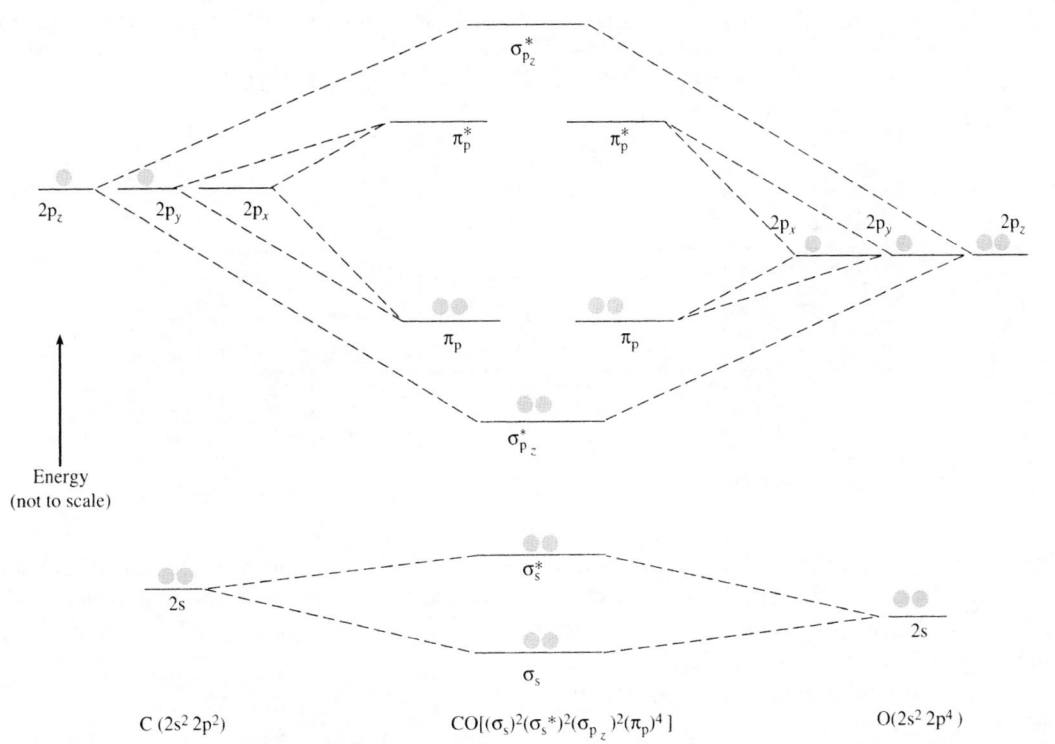

Figure 19.17 Schematic molecular energy level diagram for CO. The 1s orbitals have been omitted as they contribute nothing to the bonding. A more sophisticated treatment would allow some mixing of the 2s and $2p_z$ orbitals in the bonding direction (z) as implied by the orbital diagram in Fig. 19.18.

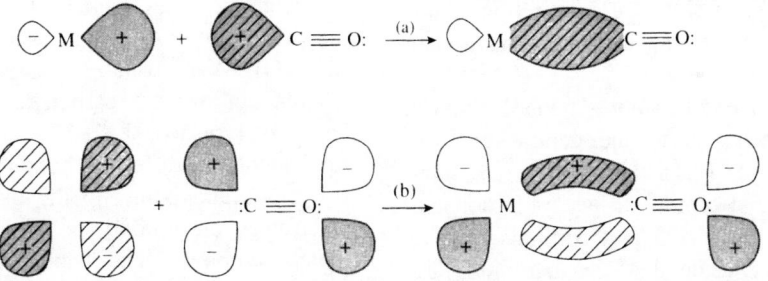

Figure 19.18 Schematic representation of the orbital overlaps leading to M–CO bonding: (a) σ overlap and donation from the lone-pair on C into a vacant (hybrid) metal orbital to form a σ M←C bond, and (b) π overlap and the donation from a filled d_{xz} or d_{yz} orbital on M into a vacant antibonding π_p^* orbital on CO to form a π M→C bond.

at once interprets why CO, which is a very weak σ donor to Lewis acids such as BF_3 and $AlCl_3$, forms such strong complexes with transition elements, since the drift of π-electron density from M to C tends to make the ligand more negative and so enhances its σ-donor power. The pre-existing negative charge on CN^- increases its σ-donor propensity but weakens its effectiveness as a π acceptor. It is thus possible to rationalize many chemical

Table 19.3 Known neutral binary metal carbonyls. Osmium also forms $Os_5(CO)_{16}$, $Os_5(CO)_{19}$, $Os_6(CO)_{18}$, $Os_6(CO)_{20}$, $Os_7(CO)_{21}$ and $Os_8(CO)_{23}$. Carbonyls of elements in the shaded area are either very unstable or anionic or require additional ligands besides CO for stabilization

3	4	5	6	7	8	9	10	11	12
	Ti	$V(CO)_6$	$Cr(CO)_6$	$Mn_2(CO)_{10}$	$Fe(CO)_5$ $Fe_2(CO)_9$ $Fe_3(CO)_{12}$	$Co_2(CO)_8$ $Co_4(CO)_{12}$ $Co_6(CO)_{16}$	$Ni(CO)_4$	Cu	
	Zr	Nb	$Mo(CO)_6$	$Tc_2(CO)_{10}$ $Tc_3(CO)_{12}$	$Ru(CO)_5$ $Ru_2(CO)_9$ $Ru_3(CO)_{12}$	$Rh_2(CO)_8$ $Rh_4(CO)_{12}$ $Rh_6(CO)_{16}$	Pd	Ag	
	Hf	Ta	$W(CO)_6$	$Re_2(CO)_{10}$	$Os(CO)_5$ $Os_2(CO)_9$ $Os_3(CO)_{12}$	$Ir_2(CO)_8$ $Ir_4(CO)_{12}$ $Ir_6(CO)_{16}$	Pt	Au	

observations by noting that effectiveness as a σ donor decreases in the sequence $CN^- > RNC > NO^+ \sim CO$ whereas effectiveness as a π acceptor follows the reverse sequence $NO^+ > CO \gg RNC > CN^-$. By implication, back donation into antibonding CO orbitals weakens the CO bond and this is manifest in the slight increase in interatomic distance from 112.8 pm in free CO to $\sim$115 pm in many complexes. There is also a decrease in the C–O force constant, and the drop in the infrared stretching frequency from 2143 cm^{-1} in free CO to 2125–1850 cm^{-1} for terminal COs in neutral carbonyls has been interpreted in the same way.

The occurrence of stable neutral binary carbonyls is restricted to the central area of the d block (Table 19.3), where there are low-lying vacant metal orbitals to accept σ-donated lone-pairs and also filled d orbitals for π back donation. Outside this area carbonyls are either very unstable (e.g. Cu, Ag, p. 1199), or anionic, or require additional ligands besides CO for stabilization. As with boranes and carboranes (p. 181), CO can be replaced by isoelectronic equivalents such as $2e^-$, H^-, $2H^\bullet$ or L. Mean bond dissociation energies $\overline{D}(M–CO)/kJ\,mol^{-1}$ increase in the sequence $Cr(CO)_6$ 109, $Mo(CO)_6$ 151, $W(CO)_6$ 176, and in the sequence $Mn_2(CO)_{10}$ 100, $Fe(CO)_5$ 121, $Co_2(CO)_8$ 138, $Ni(CO)_4$ 147.

CO can act as a terminal ligand, as an unsymmetrical or symmetrical bridging ligand (μ_2-CO) or as a triply bridging ligand (μ_3-CO):

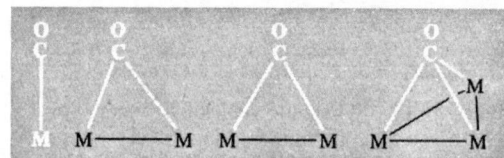

In all these cases CO is η^1 but the connectivity to metal increases from 1 to 3. It is notable that in the μ_2-bridging carbonyls the angle M–C(O)–M is usually very acute (77–80°), whereas in organic carbonyls the C–C(O)–C angle is typically 120–124°. This suggests a fundamentally differing bonding mode in the two cases and points to the likelihood of a 2-electron 3-centre bond (p. 158) for the bridging metal carbonyls. The hapticity can also rise, and structural determinations indicate that one or both of the π^* orbitals in CO contribute to η^2 bonding to 1 or 2 M atoms.[32] A bis-η^1-bridging mode has also been detected in an AlPh$_3$ adduct,[33] reminiscent of the bridging mode in the isoelectronic CN^- ligand (p. 322):

[32] C. P. HORWITZ and D. F. SHRIVER, *Adv. Organometallic Chem.* **23**, 219–305 (1984).

[33] J. M. BURLICH, M. E. LEONOWICZ, R. B. PETERSEN and R. E. HUGHES, *Inorg. Chem.* **18**, 1097–105 (1979).

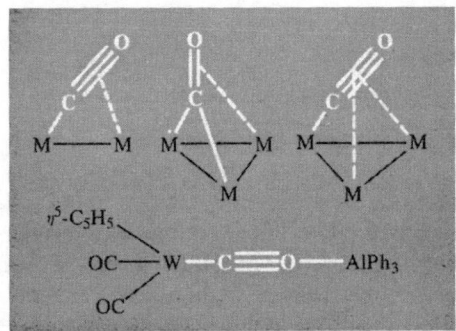

Numerous examples of metal carbonyls will be found in later chapters dealing with the chemistry of the individual transition metals. CO also has an unrivalled capacity for stabilizing metal clusters and for inserting into M–C bonds (p. 309). Synthetic routes include:

(a) direct reaction, e.g.:

$$Ni + 4CO \xrightarrow{30°/1\ atm} Ni(CO)_4$$

$$Fe + 5CO \xrightarrow{200°/200\ atm} Fe(CO)_5$$

(b) reductive carbonylation, e.g.:

$$OsO_4 + 9CO \xrightarrow{250°/350\ atm} Os(CO)_5 + 4CO_2$$

$$RuI_3 + 5CO + 3Ag \xrightarrow{175°/250\ atm} Ru(CO)_5 + 3AgI$$

$$WCl_6 + 3Fe(CO)_5 \xrightarrow{100°} W(CO)_6 + 3FeCl_2 + 9CO$$

(c) photolysis or thermolysis, e.g.:

$$2Fe(CO)_5 \xrightarrow{h\nu} Fe_2(CO)_9 + CO$$

$$2Co_2(CO)_8 \xrightarrow{70°} Co_4(CO)_{12} + 4CO$$

The remaining classes of monohapto organic ligands listed in Table 19.2 are carbene ($=CR_2$), carbyne ($\equiv CR$), and carbido (C). Stable carbene complexes were first reported in 1964 by E. O. Fischer and A. Maasböl.[34] Initially they were of the type $[W(CO)_5(:C\overset{OMe}{\underset{R}{\diagdown}})]$, and it was

not until 1968 that the first homonuclear carbene complex was reported $[Cr(CO)_5(:C\overset{CPh}{\underset{CPh}{\diagdown\!\!\!|\!\!\!\diagup}})]$; isolation of a carbene containing the parent methylene group $:CH_2$ was not achieved until 1975:[35]

$$[Ta(\eta^5\text{-}C_5H_5)_2Me_3] \xrightarrow{Ph_3CBF_4} [Ta(\eta^5\text{-}C_5H_5)_2Me_2]^+ \cdot$$

$$BF_4^- \xrightarrow{base} [Ta(\eta^5\text{-}C_5H_5)_2(Me)(:CH_2)]$$

Other preparative routes are:

$$[W(CO)_6] + LiR \xrightarrow{Et_2O} [W(CO)_5(C\overset{OLi(OEt_2)_n}{\underset{R}{\diagdown}})]$$

$$[W(CO)_5(:C\overset{OMe}{\underset{R}{\diagdown}})] \xleftarrow{Me_3OBF_4}$$

$$[cyclo\text{-}(PhC)_2CCl_2] + Na_2Cr(CO)_5$$

$$[Cr(CO)_5(:C\overset{CPh}{\underset{CPh}{\diagdown\!\!\!|\!\!\!\diagup}})] \xleftarrow[thf]{-20°}$$

The metal is in the formal oxidation state zero. As expected, the M–C bonds are somewhat shorter than M–R bonds to alkyls, but they are noticeably longer than M–CO bonds suggesting only limited double-bond character M=C, e.g.:

in $[Ta(\eta^5\text{-}C_5H_5)_2(Me)(CH_2)]$	Ta–CH$_2$ 220.6 pm
	Ta–CH$_3$ 225 pm
in $[W(CO)_5\{C(OMe)Ph\}]$	W–C(OMe)Ph 205 pm
	W–CO 189 pm
in $[Cr(CO)_4\{C(OMe)Me\}$-	Cr–C(OMe)Me 204 pm
(PPh$_3$)]	Cr–CO 186 pm

Carbene complexes are highly reactive species.[36]

Carbyne complexes were first made in 1973 by the unexpected reaction of methoxycarbene

---

[34] E. O. FISCHER, *Adv. Organometallic Chem.* **14**, 1–32 (1976).

[35] R. R. SCHROCK, *J. Am. Chem. Soc.* **97**, 6577–8 (1975); L. J. GUGGENBERGER and R. R. SCHROCK, ibid. 6578–9.

[36] K. H. DÖTZ, H. FISCHER, P. HOFMANN, F. R. KREISSL, U. SCHUBERT and K. WEISS, *Transition Metal Carbene Complexes*, Verlag Chemie, Weinheim, 1983, 264 pp.

complexes with boron trihalides:

$$[M(CO)_5\{C(OMe)R\}] + BX_3 \xrightarrow[\text{low temp}]{\text{pentane}}$$

$$[M(CO)_4(\equiv CR)X] + CO + BX_2(OMe)$$

M = Cr, Mo, W; R = Me, Et, Ph; X = Cl, Br, I

Several other routes are now also available in which BX_3 is replaced by $AlCl_3$, $GaCl_3$, Al_2Br_6, Ph_3PBr_2, e.g.:

$$[W(CO)_5\{C(OMe)Ph\}] + Al_2Br_6 \xrightarrow[-30°]{\text{pentane}}$$

$$[WBr(CO)_4(\equiv CPh)] + CO + Al_2Br_5(OMe)$$

X-ray studies reveal the expected short M–CR distance, but the bond angle at the carbyne C atom is not always linear. Some structural data are annexed, see below. A compound which features all three types of η^1 ligand, alkyl, alkylidene and alkylidyne, is the red, square-pyramidal tungsten(VI) complex $[W(\equiv CCMe_3)(=CHCMe_3)(CH_2CMe_3)(Me_2PCH_2CH_2PMe_2)]$ in which the W–C distance is 226 pm to neopentyl, 194 pm to neopentylidene, and 176 pm to the apical neopentylidyne ligand; the corresponding

W–C–C angles are 125°, 150° and 175° respectively.[37]

19.7.2 Dihapto ligands

Reference to Table 19.2 places this section in context. The first complex between a hydrocarbon and a transition metal was isolated by the Danish chemist W. C. Zeise in 1825 and in the following years he characterized the pale-yellow compound now formulated as $K[Pt(\eta^2\text{-}C_2H_4)Cl_3].H_2O$.[†] Zeise's salt, and a few closely related complexes such as the chloro-bridged binuclear compound $[Pt_2(\eta^2\text{-}C_2H_4)(\mu_2\text{-}Cl)_2Cl_2]$, remained as chemical curiosities and a considerable theoretical embarrassment for over 100 y but are now seen as the archetypes of a large family of complexes based on the bonding of unsaturated organic

---

[37] M. R. CHURCHILL and W. J. YOUNGS, *Inorg. Chem.* **18**, 2454–8 (1979).

[†] The original reaction was obscure: Zeise heated a mixture of $PtCl_2$ and $PtCl_4$ in EtOH under reflux and then treated the resulting black solid with aqueous KCl and HCl to give ultimately the cream-yellow product. Subsequently the compound was isolated by direct reaction of C_2H_4 with $K_2[PtCl_4]$ in aqueous HCl.

This is the shortest known Cr–C distance cf. 217–222 pm in Cr–C single bonds and 191 pm in $Cr(CO_6)$

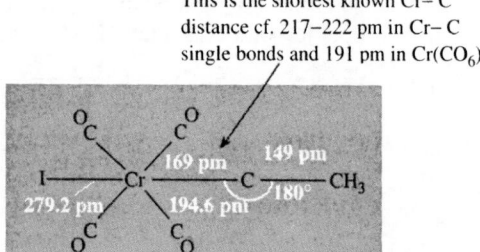

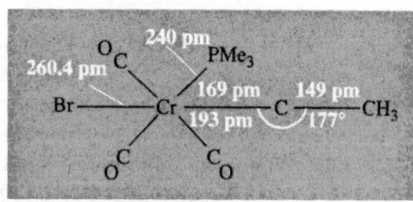

Cf. 227–232 pm for W–C single bond and 206 pm in $W(CO)_6$

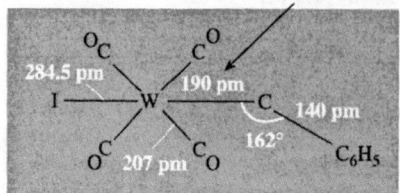

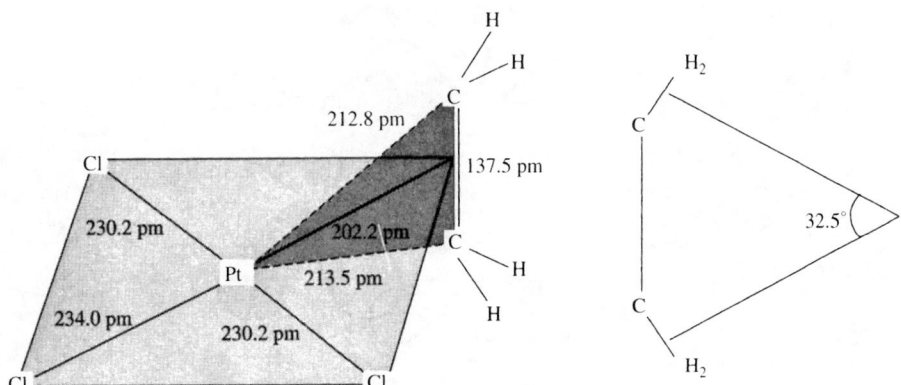

Figure 19.19　Structure of the anion of Zeise's salt, $[Pt(\eta^2\text{-}C_2H_2)Cl_3]^-$; standard deviations are Pt–Cl 0.2 pm; Pt–C 0.3 pm, and C–C 0.4 pm.

molecules to transition metals. The structure of the anion of Zeise's salt has been extensively studied and neutron diffraction data[38] are in Fig. 19.19. Significant features are (a) the C=C bond is perpendicular to the $PtCl_3$ plane and is only 3.8 pm longer than in free C_2H_4, (b) the C_2H_4 group is significantly distorted from planarity, each C being 16.4 pm from the plane of 4H, (c) the angle between the normals to the CH_2 planes is 32.5°, and (d) there is an unambiguous *trans*-effect (p. 1163), i.e. the Pt–Cl distance *trans* to C_2H_4 is longer than the 2 *cis*-Pt–Cl distances by 3.8 pm (19 standard deviations).

The key to our present understanding of the bonding in Zeise's salt and all other alkene complexes stems from the perceptive suggestion by M. J. S. Dewar in 1951 that the bonding involves electron donation from the π bond of the alkene into a vacant metal orbital of σ symmetry; this idea was modified and elaborated by J. Chatt and L. A. Duncanson in a seminal paper in 1953 and the Dewar–Chatt–Duncanson theory forms the basis for most subsequent discussion. The bonding is considered to arise from two interdependent components as illustrated schematically in Fig. 19.20 (a) and (b). In the first part, σ overlap between the filled π orbital of

ethene and a suitably directed vacant hybrid metal orbital forms the "electron-pair donor bond". This is reinforced by the second component, (b), which derives from overlap of a filled metal d orbital with the vacant antibonding orbital of ethene; these orbitals have π symmetry with respect to the bonding axis and allow $M{\rightarrow}C_2$ π back bonding to assist the $\sigma C_2{\rightarrow}M$ bond synergically as for CO (p. 927). The flexible interplay of these two components allows a wide variety of experimental observations to be rationalized: in particular the theory convincingly interprets the orientation of the alkene with respect to the metal and the observed lengthening of the C–C bond. However, the details of the distortion of the alkene from planarity are less easy to quantify on the model and evidence is accumulating which suggests that the extent of π back bonding may have been overemphasized for some systems in the past. At the other extreme back donation may become so dominant that C–C distances approach values to be expected for a single bond and the interaction would be described as oxidative addition to give a metallacyclopropane ring involving two 2-electron 2-centre M–C bonds (see Fig. 19.20(c)).

For example, tetracyanoethylene has a formal C=C double bond (133.9 pm) in the free ligand but in the complex $[Pt\{C_2(CN)_4\}(PPh_3)_2]$ the C–C distance (152 pm) is that of a single bond and the CN groups are bent away from the

[38] R. A. LOVE, T. F. KOETZLE, G. J. B. WILLIAMS, L. C. ANDREWS and R. BAU, *Inorg. Chem.* **14**, 2653–7 (1975).

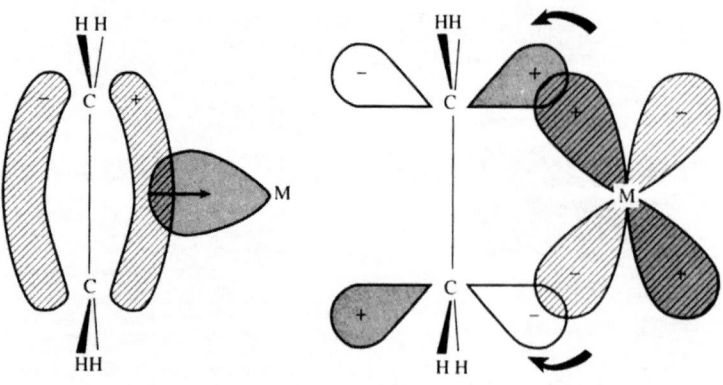
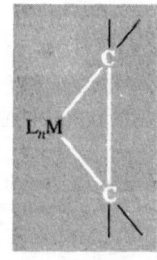

(a) σ donation from filled π orbital of alkene into vacant metal hybrid orbital.

(b) π–back donation from a filled metal d orbital (or hybrid) into the vacant antibonding orbit of alkene.

(c) Description in terms of two M–C σ bonds (see text).

Figure 19.20 Schematic representation of the two components, (a) and (b), of an η^2-alkene-metal bond.

Pt and 2P atoms; moroever, the 2P and 2C that are bonded to Pt are nearly coplanar, as expected for Pt^{II} but not as in (tetrahedral) 4-coordinate Pt^0 complexes. $[Rh(C_2F_4)Cl(PPh_3)_2]$ affords another example of the tendency to form a metallacylopropane-type complex (C–C 141 pm) with pseudo-5-coordinate Rh^{III} rather than a pseudo-4-coordinate η^2-alkene complex of Rh^I. However, the two descriptions are not mutually exclusive and, in principle, there can be a continuous gradation between them.

Compounds containing $M–\eta^2$-alkene bonds are generally prepared by direct replacement of a less strongly bound ligand such as a halide ion (cf. Zeise's salt), a carbonyl, or another alkene. Chelating dialkene complexes can be made similarly, e.g. with *cis-cis*-cycloocta-1,5-diene (cod):

$$Na_2[PtCl_4] + C_8H_{12} \xrightarrow{Pr^nOH} 2NaCl + \ \text{[diagram]} \ Pt \big\langle {}^{Cl}_{Cl}$$

Numerous examples are given in later sections dealing with the chemistry of individual transition metals. Few, if any, η^2-alkene or -diene complexes have been reported for the first three transition-metal groups (why?), but all later groups are well represented, including Cu^I, Ag^I and Au^I. Indeed, an industrial method for the

separation of alkenes uses the differing stabilities of their complexes with CuCl. For many metals it is found that increasing alkyl substitution of the alkene lowers the stability of the complex and that *trans*-substituted alkenes give less stable complexes than do *cis*-substituted alkenes. For Rh^I complexes F substitution of the alkene enhances the stability of the complex and Cl substitution lowers it.

Alkyne complexes have been less studied than alkene complexes but are similar. Preparative routes are the same and bonding descriptions are also analogous. In some cases, e.g. the pseudo-4-coordinate complex $[Pt(\eta^2-C_2Bu^t_2)Cl_2(4\text{-toluidine})]$ (Fig. 19.21) the C≡C bond remains short and the alkyne group is normal to the plane of coordination; in others, e.g. the pseudo-3-coordinate complex $[Pt(\eta^2-C_2Ph_2)-(PPh_3)_2]$ (Fig. 19.22), the alkyne group is almost in the plane (14°) and the attached substituents are bent back to an angle of 140° suggesting a formulation intermediate between 3-coordinate Pt^0 and 4-coordinate Pt^{II}. One important difference between alkynes and alkenes is that the former have a triple bond which can be described in terms of a σ bond and two mutually perpendicular π bonds. The possibility thus arises that η^2-alkynes can function as bridging ligands and several such complexes have been characterized.

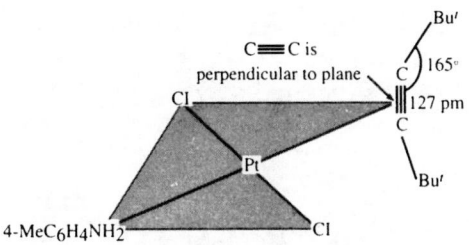

Figure 19.21 Structure of [Pt(η^2-C$_2$Bu$_2'$)Cl$_2$(4-tolui-dine)].

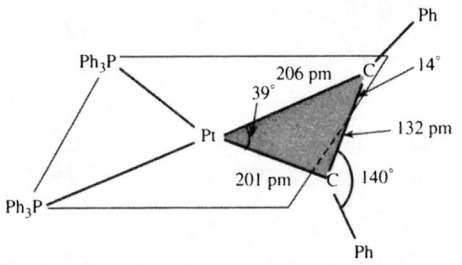

Figure 19.22 Structure of [Pt(η^2-C$_2$Ph$_2$)(PPh$_3$)$_2$].

The classic example is [Co$_2$(CO)$_6$(C$_2$Ph$_2$)] which is formed by direct displacement of the 2 bridging carbonyls in [Co$_2$(CO)$_8$] to give the structure sketched below:

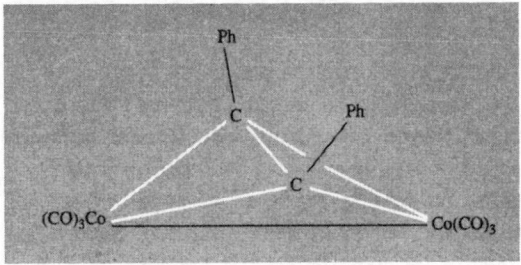

The C–C group lies above and at right angles to the Co–Co vector; the C–C distance is 146 pm (27 pm greater than in the free alkyne) and this has been taken to indicate extensive back donation from the 2 Co atoms. The Co–Co distance is 247 pm compared with 252 pm in Co$_2$(CO)$_8$. A rather different situation is found in [Ru$_4$(μ_4-η^1,η^2-C$_2$)(μ-PPh$_2$)$_2$(CO)$_{12}$], where a μ_4-η^1,η^2-acetylide dianion bridges two {Ru$_2$(μ-PPh$_2$)(CO)$_6$} units. Here, the steric demands of the other ligands make the C–C bridge almost coplanar with the two η^2-bonded

Ru atoms, and reduced π-bonding is indicated by a much shorter (127.5 pm) C–C distance.[38a]

19.7.3 Trihapto ligands

The possibility that the allyl group CH$_2$=CH–CH$_2$– can act as an η^3 ligand was recognized independently by several groups in 1960 and since then the field has flourished, partly because of its importance in homogeneous catalysis and partly because of the novel steric possibilities and interconversions that can be studied by proton nmr spectroscopy. Many synthetic routes are available of which the following are representative.

(a) Allyl Grignard reagent:

$$NiBr_2 + 2C_3H_5MgBr \longrightarrow 2MgBr_2$$
$$+ [Ni(\eta^3\text{-}C_3H_5)_2] \text{ (also Pd, Pt)}$$

A mixture of *cis* and *trans* isomers is obtained:

$$\text{—Ni—} \quad \text{—Ni—}$$

Tris-(η^3-allyl) complexes [M(C$_3$H$_5$)$_3$] can be prepared similarly for V, Cr, Fe, Co, Rh, Ir, and *tetrakis* complexes [M(η^3-C$_3$H$_5$)$_4$] for Zr, Th, Mo and W.

(b) Conversion of η^1-allyl to η^3-allyl:

$$Na[Mn(CO)_5] \xrightarrow{C_3H_5Cl} [Mn(CO)_5(\eta^1\text{-}C_3H_5)]$$
$$\xrightarrow[80°]{h\nu \text{ or}} [Mn(CO)_4(\eta^3\text{-}C_3H_5)] + CO$$

Similarly many other η^1-allyl carbonyl complexes convert to η^3-allyl complexes with loss of 1 CO.

(c) From allylic halides (e.g. 2-methylallyl chloride):

$$Na_2PdCl_4 + C_4H_7Cl + CO + H_2O \xrightarrow{MeOH}$$
$$\tfrac{1}{2}[Pd_2(\eta^3\text{-}C_4H_7)_2(\mu_2\text{-}Cl_2)] + 2NaCl + 2HCl + CO_2$$

[38a] M. I. BRUCE, M. R. SNOW, E. R. T. TIEKINK and M. L. WILLIAMS, *J. Chem. Soc., Chem. Commun.*, 701–2 (1986).

(d) Oxidative addition of allyl halides, e.g.:

$$[Fe^0(CO)_5] + C_3H_5I \longrightarrow$$
$$[Fe^{II}(\eta^3\text{-}C_3H_5)(CO)_3I] + 2CO$$
$$[Co^I(\eta^5\text{-}C_5H_5)(CO)_2] + C_3H_5I \longrightarrow$$
$$[Co^{III}(\eta^3\text{-}C_3H_5)(\eta^5\text{-}C_5H_5)I] + 2CO$$

(e) Elimination of HCl from an alkene metal halide complex, e.g.:

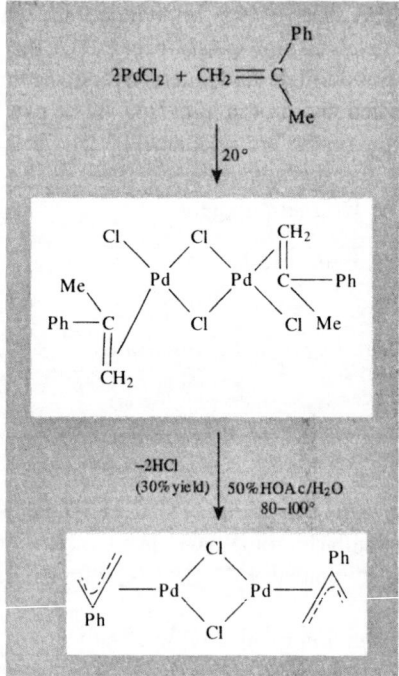

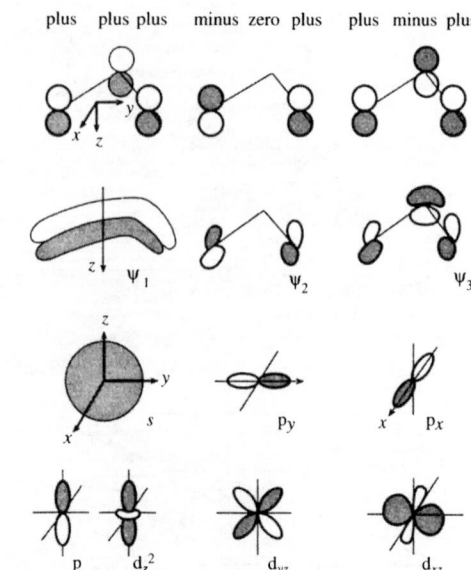

Figure 19.23 Schematic illustration of possible combinations of orbitals in the π-allytic complexes. The bonding direction is taken to be the z-axis with the M atom below the C_3 plane. Appropriate combinations of p_π orbitals on the 3 C are shown in the top half of the figure, and beneath them are the metal orbitals with which they are most likely to form bonding interactions.

The bonding in η^3-allylic complexes can be described in terms of the qualitative MO theory illustrated in Fig. 19.23. The p_z orbitals on the 3 allylic C atoms can be combined to give the 3 orbitals shown in the upper part of Fig. 19.23; each retains π symmetry with respect to the C_3 plane but has, in addition, 0, 1 or 2 nodes perpendicular to this plane. The metal orbitals of appropriate symmetry to form bonding MOs with these 3 combinations are shown in the lower part of Fig. 19.23. The extent to which these orbitals are, in fact, involved in bonding depends on their relative energies, their radial diffuseness and the actual extent of orbital overlap. Electrons to fill these bonding MOs can be thought of as coming both from the allylic π-electron cloud and

from the metal, and the possibility of "back donation" from filled metal hybrid orbitals also exists. Experimental observables which must be interpreted in any quantitative treatment are the variations (if any) in the M–C distances to the 3 C atoms and the tilt of the C_3 plane to the bonding plane of the metal atom.

In addition to acting as an η^1 and an η^3 ligand the allyl group can also act as a bridging ligand by η^1 bonding to one metal atom and η^2 bonding via the alkene function to a second metal atom. For example $[Pt_2(acac)_2(\eta^1,\eta^2\text{-}C_3H_5)_2]$ has the dimeric structure shown in Fig. 19.24. The compound was made from $[Pt(\eta^3\text{-}C_3H_5)_2]$ by treatment first with HCl to give polymeric $[Pt(C_3H_5)Cl]$ and then with thallium(I) acetylacetonate.

Many η^3-allyl complexes are fluxional (p. 914) at room temperature or slightly above,

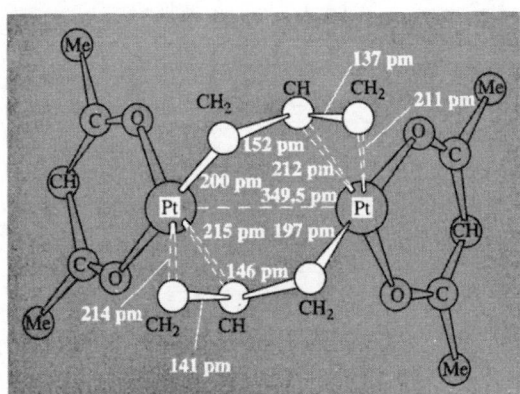

Figure 19.24 Structure of $[Pt_2(acac)_2(\mu\text{-}C_3H_5)_2]$ showing the bridging allyl groups, each η^1 bonded to 1 Pt and η^2-bonded to the other. Interatomic distances are in pm with standard deviations of $\sim$5 pm for Pt–C and $\sim$7 for C–C. The distance of Pt to the centre of the η^2-C_2 group is 201 pm, very close to the η^1-Pt–C distance of 199 pm.

and this property has been extensively studied by ^1H nmr spectroscopy. Exceedingly complex patterns can emerge. The simplest interchange that can occur is between those H atoms which are on the side nearer the metal (*syn*) and those which are on the side away from the metal (*anti*) probably via a short-lived η^1-allyl metal intermediate. The fluxional behaviour can be slowed down by lowering the temperature, and separate resonances from the various types of H atom are then observed. Fluxionality can also sometimes be quenched by incorporating the allylic group in a ring system which restricts its mobility.

19.7.4 Tetrahapto ligands

Conjugated dienes such as butadiene and its open-chain analogues can act as η^4 ligands; the complexes are usually prepared from metal carbonyl complexes by direct replacement of 2CO by the diene. Isomerization or rearrangement of the diene may occur as indicated schematically below:

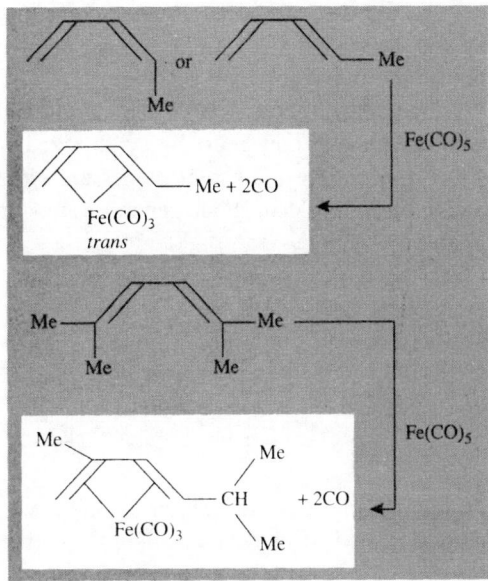

No new principles are involved in describing the bonding in these complexes and appropriate combinations of the $4p_\pi$ orbitals on the diene system can be used to construct MOs with the metal-based orbitals for donation and back donation of electron density.[39] As with ethene, two limiting cases can be envisaged which can be represented schematically as in Fig. 19.25. Consistent with

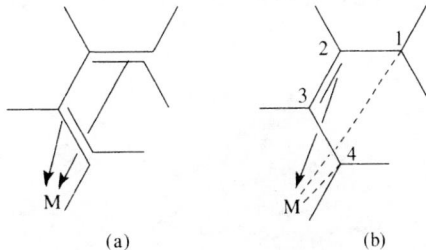

Figure 19.25 Schematic representation of the two formal extremes of bonding in 1,3-diene complexes. In (a) the bonding is considered as two almost independent η^2-alkene–metal bonds, whereas in (b) there are σ bonds to C(1) and C(4) and an η^2-alkene–metal bond from C(2)–C(3).

[39] D. M. P. MINGOS, *J. Chem. Soc., Dalton Trans.*, 20–35 (1977).

this view, the C–C distances in diene complexes vary and the central C(2)–C(3) distance is often less than the two outer C–C distances.

Cyclobutadiene complexes are also well established though they must be synthesized by indirect routes since the parent dienes are either unstable or non-existent. Four general routes are available:

(a) Dehalogenation of dihalocyclobutenes, e.g.:

(b) Cyclodimerization of alkynes, e.g. with cyclopentadienyl-(cycloocta-1,5-diene)cobalt:

(c) From metallacyclopentadienes:

(d) Ligand exchange from other cyclobutadiene complexes, e.g.:

A schematic interpretation of the bonding in cyclobutadiene complexes can be given within the framework outlined in the preceding sections and this is illustrated in Fig. 19.26.

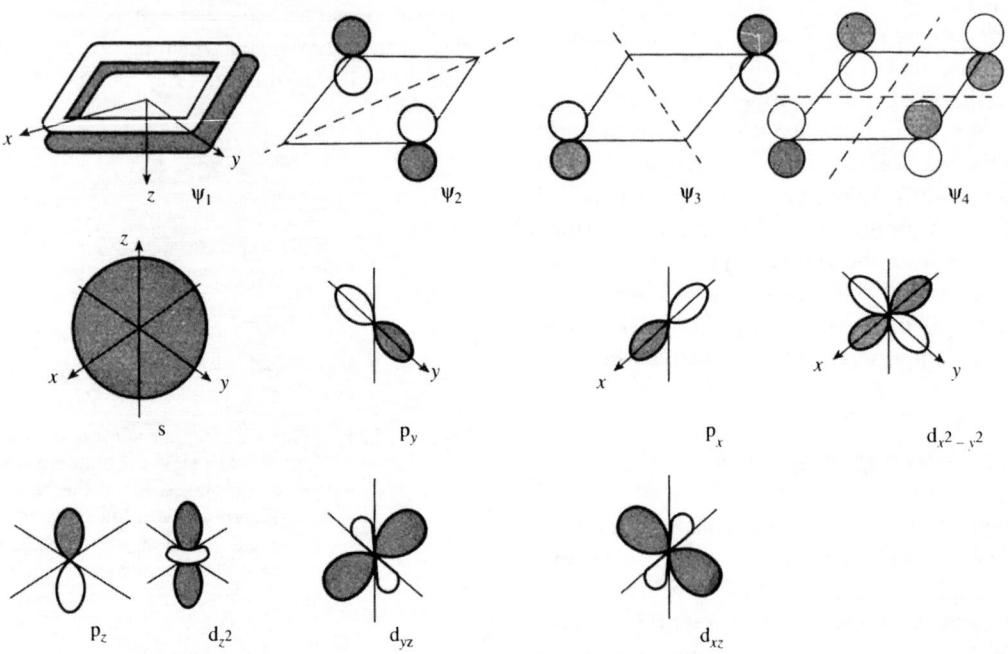

Figure 19.26   Orbitals used in describing the bonding in metal-η^2- cyclobutadiene complexes. The sign convention and axes are as in Fig. 19.23.

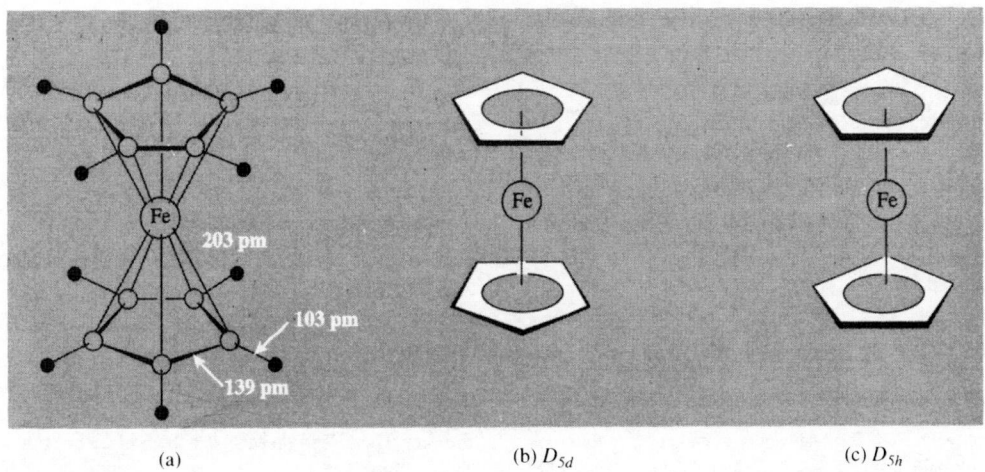

(a)   (b) D_{5d} (c) D_{5h}

Figure 19.27   Structure of ferrocene, $[Fe(\eta^5\text{-}C_5H_5)_2]$, and a conventional "shorthand" representation.

Cyclobutadiene complexes afford a classic example of the stabilization of a ligand by coordination to a metal and, indeed, were predicted theoretically on this basis by H. C. Longuet-Higgins and L. E. Orgel (1956) some 3 y before the first examples were synthesized. In the (hypothetical) free cyclobutadiene molecule 2 of the 4 π-electrons would occupy ψ_1 and there would be an unpaired electron in each of the 2 degenerate orbitals ψ_2, ψ_3. Coordination to a metal provides further interactions and avoids this unstable configuration. See also the discussion on ferraboranes (p. 174).

19.7.5 Pentahapto ligands

The importance of bis(cyclopentadienyl)iron $[Fe(\eta^5\text{-}C_5H_5)_2]$ in the development of organometallic chemistry has already been alluded to (p. 924). The compound, which forms orange crystals, mp 174°, has extraordinary thermal stability (>500°) and a remarkable structure which was unique when first established. It also has an extensive aromatic-type reaction chemistry which is reflected in its common name "ferrocene". The molecular structure of ferrocene in the crystalline state features two parallel cyclopentadienyl rings: at one time these rings were thought to be staggered (D_{5d}) as in Fig. 19.27a and b since only this was compatible with the molecular inversion centre required by the crystallographic space group (C_{2h}^5, $Z = 2$). However, gas-phase electron diffraction data suggest that the equilibrium structure of ferrocene is eclipsed (D_{5h}) as in Fig. 19.27c rather than staggered, with a rather low barrier to internal rotation of $\sim$4 kJ mol^{-1}. X-ray crystallographic[40] and neutron diffraction studies[41] confirm this general conclusion, the space-group symmetry requirement being met by a disordered arrangement of nearly eclipsed molecules (rotation angle between the rings $\sim$9° rather than 0° for precisely eclipsed or 36° for staggered conformation). Below 169 K the molecules become ordered, the rotation angle remaining $\sim$9°. The perpendicular distance between the rings is 325 pm (cf. graphite 335 pm) and the mean interatomic distances are Fe–C 203 ± 2 pm and C–C 139 ± 6 pm. The Ru and Os analogues $[M(\eta^5\text{-}C_5H_5)_2]$ have similar molecular structures with eclipsed parallel C_5 rings. A molecular-orbital description of the bonding can be developed along the lines indicated in

[40] P. Seiler and J. D. Dunitz, *Acta Cryst.* **B35**, 1068–74 (1979).

[41] F. Takusagawa and T. F. Koetzle, *Acta Cryst.* **B35**, 1074–81 (1979).

previous sections. Because of the importance of ferrocene, numerous calculations have been made of the detailed sequence of energy levels in the molecule; though these differ slightly depending on the assumptions made and the computational methods adopted, there is now a general consensus concerning the main features of the bonding as shown in the Panel.

A general preparative route to η^5-C_5H_5 compounds is the reaction of NaC_5H_5 with a metal halide or complex halide in a polar solvent such as thf, Me_2O (bp $-23°$), $(MeO)C_2H_4(OMe)$, or $HC(O)NMe_2$:

$$C_5H_6 + Na \xrightarrow{-\frac{1}{2}H_2} \{NaC_5H_5\} \xrightarrow{L_nMX} [M(\eta^5\text{-}C_5H_5)L_n] + NaX$$

A Molecular Orbital Description of the Bonding in [Fe(η^5-C_5H_5)$_2$]

The 5 p_π atomic orbitals on the planar C_5H_5 group can be combined to give 5 group MOs as shown in Fig. A; one combination has the full symmetry of the ring (a) and there are two doubly degenerate combinations (e_1 and e_2) having respectively 1 and 2 planar nodes at right angles to the plane of the ring. These 5 group MOs can themselves be combined in pairs with a similar set from the second C_5H_5 group before combining with metal orbitals. Each of the combinations [(ligand orbitals) + (metal orbitals)] leads, in principle, to a bonding MO of the molecule, providing that the energy of the two component sets is not very different. There are an equal number of antibonding combinations with the sign [(ligand orbitals) − (metal orbital)].

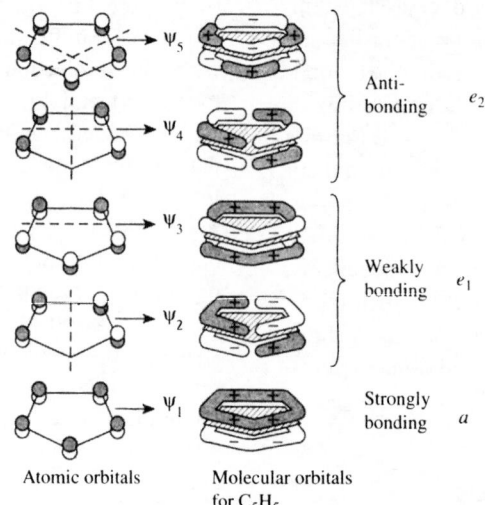

Figure A The π molecular orbitals formed from the set of p_π orbitals of the C_5H_5 ring.

Calculation of the detailed sequence of energy levels arising from these combinations poses severe computational problems but a schematic indication of the sequence (not to scale) is shown in Fig. B. Thus, starting from the foot of the figure, the a_{1a} bonding MO is mainly ligand-based with only a slight admixture of the Fe 4s and $3d_{z^2}$ orbitals. Similarly, the a_{2u} level has little, if any, admixture of the even higher-lying Fe $4p_z$ orbital with which it is formally able to combine. The e_{1g} MO arises from the bonding combination of the ligand e_{1g} orbitals with Fe $3d_{xz}$ and $3d_{yz}$ and this is the main contribution to the stability of the complex; the corresponding antibonding e_{1g}^* are unoccupied in the ground state but will be involved in optical transitions. The e_{1u} bonding MOs are again mainly ligand-based but with some contribution from Fe $4p_x$ and $4p_y$, etc. It can be seen that there is room for just 18 electrons in bonding and nonbonding MOs and that the antibonding MOs are unoccupied. In terms of electron counting the 18 electrons can be thought of as originating from the Fe atom (8e) and the two C_5H_5 groups (2 × 5e) or from an Fe^{II} ion (6e) and two $C_5H_5^-$ groups (2 × 6e).

Panel continues

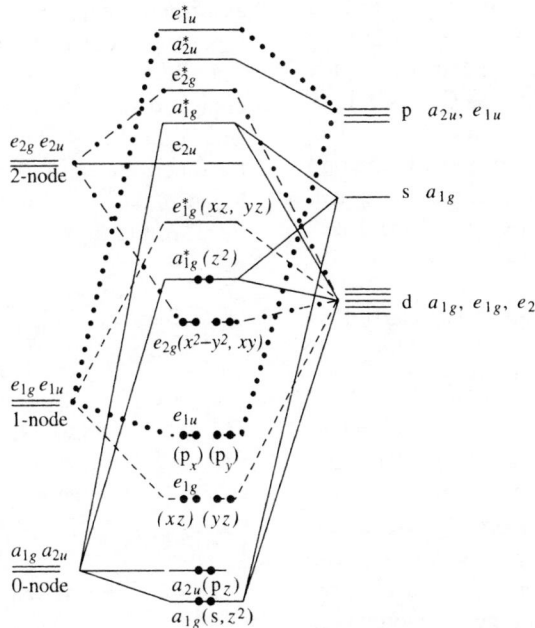

Figure B   A qualitative molecular orbital diagram for ferrocene. The subscripts *g* and *u* refer to the parity of the orbitals: *g* (German *gerade*, even) indicates that the orbital (or orbital combination) is symmetric with respect to inversion, whereas the subscript *u* (*ungerade*, odd) indicates that it is antisymmetric with respect to inversion. Only orbitals with the same parity can combine.

The stability of $[Fe(\eta^5\text{-}C_5H_5)_2]$ compared with the 19 electron system $[Co(\eta^5\text{-}C_5H_5)_2]$ and the 20-electron system $[Ni(\eta^5\text{-}C_5H_5)_2]$ is readily interpreted on this bonding scheme since these latter species have 1 and 2 easily oxidizable electrons in the antibonding e_{1g}^* orbitals. Similarly, $[Cr(\eta^5\text{-}C_5H_5)_2]$ (16e) and $[V(\eta^5\text{-}C_5H_5)_2]$ (15e) have unfilled bonding MOs and are highly reactive. However, attachment of additional groups or ligands destroys the D_{5d} (or D_{5h}) symmetry of the simple metallocene and this modifies the orbital diagram. This also happens when ferrocene is protonated to give the 18-electron cation $[Fe(\eta^5\text{-}C_5H_5)_2H]^+$ and when the (bent) isoelectronic neutral molecules $[Re(\eta^5\text{-}C_5H_5)_2H]$ (p. 1067) and $[Mo(\eta^5\text{-}C_5H_5)_2H_2]$ (p. 1038) are considered. An excellent discussion of the bonding in such "bent metallocenes" has been given.[42]

A very convenient though somewhat less general method is to use a strong nitrogen base to deprotonate the C_5H_6:

$$2C_5H_6 + 2NEt_2H + FeCl_2 \xrightarrow[\text{amine}]{\text{excess of}}$$

$$[Fe(\eta^5\text{-}C_5H_5)_2] + [NEt_2H_2]Cl$$

An enormous number of $\eta^5\text{-}C_5H_5$ complexes is now known. Thus the isoelectronic yellow

---
[42] J. W. LAUHER and R. HOFFMAN, *J. Am. Chem. Soc.* **98**, 1729–42 (1976), and references therein.

Co^I species $[Co(\eta^5\text{-}C_5H_5)_2]^+$ is stable in aqueous solutions and its salts are thermally stable to ~400°. The bright-green paramagnetic complex $[Ni(\eta^5\text{-}C_5H_5)_2]$, mp 173° (d), is fairly stable as a solid but is rapidly oxidized to $[Ni(\eta^5\text{-}C_5H_5)_2]^+$. In contrast, the scarlet, paramagnetic complex $[Cr(\eta^5\text{-}C_5H_5)_2]$, mp 173°, is very air sensitive; it dissolves in aqueous HCl to give C_5H_6 and a blue cation which is probably $[Cr(\eta^5\text{-}C_5H_5)Cl(H_2O)_n]^+$. Other stoichiometries are exemplified by $[Ti(\eta^5\text{-}C_5H_5)_3]$ and $[M(\eta^5\text{-}C_5H_5)_4]$, where M is Zr, Hf, Th.

Innumerable derivatives have been synthesized in which one or more η^5-C_5H_5 group is present in a ı ononuclear or polynuclear metal complex together with other ligands such as CO, NO, H or X. It should also be borne in mind that C_5H_5 can act as an η^1-ligand by forming a σ M–C bond and mixed complexes are sometimes obtained, e.g. $[Be(\eta^1$-$C_5H_5)(\eta^5$-$C_5H_5)]$ (see p. 130). Likewise:

$$MoCl_5 \xrightarrow{NaC_5H_5} [Mo(\eta^1\text{-}C_5H_5)_3(\eta^5\text{-}C_5H_5)]$$

$$NbCl_5 \xrightarrow{NaC_5H_5} [Nb(\eta^1\text{-}C_5H_5)_2(\eta^5\text{-}C_5H_5)_2]$$

Such η^1-C_5H_5 complexes are often found to be fluxional in solution at room temperature, the 5 H atoms giving rise to a single sharp ^{1}H nmr resonance. At lower temperatures the spectrum usually broadens and finally resolves into the expected complex spectrum at temperatures which are sufficiently low to prevent interchange on the nmr time scale ($\sim 10^{-3}$ s). Numerous experiments have been devised to elucidate the mechanism by which the H atoms become equivalent and, at least in some systems, it seems likely that a non-dissociative (unimolecular) 1,2-shift occurs.

19.7.6 Hexahapto ligands

Arenes such as benzene and its derivatives can form complexes precisely analogous to ferrocene and related species. Though particularly exciting when first recognized as η^6 complexes in 1955 these compounds introduce no new principles and need only be briefly considered here. Curiously, the first such compounds were made as long ago as 1919 when F. Hein reacted $CrCl_3$ with PhMgBr to give compounds which he formulated as "polyphenylchromium" compounds $[CrPh_n]^{0, +1}$ ($n = 2, 3$, or 4); their true nature

as η^6-arene complexes of benzene and diphenyl was not recognized until over 35 y later.[43] The best general method for making bis(η^6-arene) metal complexes is due to E. O. Fischer and W. Hafner (1955) who devised it originally for dibenzenechromium — the isoelectronic analogue of ferrocene: $CrCl_3$ was reduced with Al metal in the presence of C_6H_6, using $AlCl_3$ as a catalyst:

$$3CrCl_3 + 2Al + AlCl_3 + 6C_6H_6 \xrightarrow{140°/press}$$
$$3[Cr(\eta^6\text{-}C_6H_6)_2]^+[AlCl_4]^-$$

The yield is almost quantitative and the orange-yellow Cr^I cation can be reduced to the neutral species with aqueous dithionite:

$$[Cr(\eta^6\text{-}C_6H_6)_2]^+ + \tfrac{1}{2}S_2O_4{}^{2-} + 2OH^- \longrightarrow$$
$$[Cr(\eta^6\text{-}C_6H_6)_2] + SO_3{}^{2-} + H_2O$$

Dibenzenechromium(0) forms dark-brown crystals, mp 284°, and the molecular structure (Fig. 19.28) comprises plane parallel rings in eclipsed configuration above and below the Cr atom (D_{6h}); the C–H bonds are tilted slightly towards the metal and, most significantly, the C–C distances show no alternation around the rings. A bonding scheme can be constructed as for ferrocene (p. 938) using the six p_z orbitals on each benzene ring.

Bis (η^6-arene) metal complexes have been made for many transition metals by the Al/AlCl₃ reduction method and cationic species $[M(\eta^6\text{-}Ar)_2]^{n+}$ are also well established for $n = 1$, 2, and 3. Numerous arenes besides benzene have been used, the next most common being $1,3,5\text{-}Me_3C_6H_3$ (mesitylene) and C_6Me_6. Reaction of arenes with metal carbonyls in high-boiling solvents or under the influence of ultraviolet light results in the displacement of 3CO and the formation of arene–metal carbonyls:

$$Ar + [M(CO)_6] \xrightarrow[\text{or heat}]{h\nu} [M(\eta^6\text{-}Ar)(CO)_3] + 3CO$$

---

[43] H. ZEISS, P. J. WHEATLEY and H. J. S. WINKLER, *Benzenoid-Metal Complexes*, Ronald Press, New York, 1966, 101 pp.

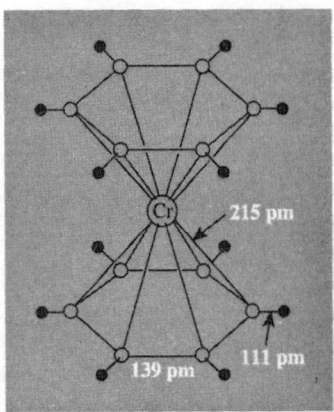

Figure 19.28   The eclipsed (D_{6h}) structure of [Cr(η^6-C$_6$H$_6$)$_2$] as revealed by X-ray diffraction, showing the two parallel rings 323 pm apart. Neutron diffraction shows the H atoms are tilted slightly towards the Cr, and electron diffraction on the gaseous compound shows that the eclipsed configuration is retained without rotation.

For Cr, Mo and W the benzenetricarbonyl complexes are yellow solids melting at 162°, 125°, and 140°, respectively. The structure of [Cr(η^6-C$_6$H$_6$)(CO)$_3$] is in Fig. 19.29. In general, η^6-arene complexes are more reactive than their η^5-C$_5$H$_5$ analogues and are thermally less stable.

19.7.7 Heptahapto and octahapto ligands

Treatment of cycloheptatriene complexes of the type [M(η^6-C$_7$H$_8$)(CO)$_3$] (M = Cr, Mo, W) with Ph$_3$C$^+$BF$_4^-$ results in hydride abstraction to give orange-coloured η^7-cycloheptatrienyl (or tropylium) complexes:

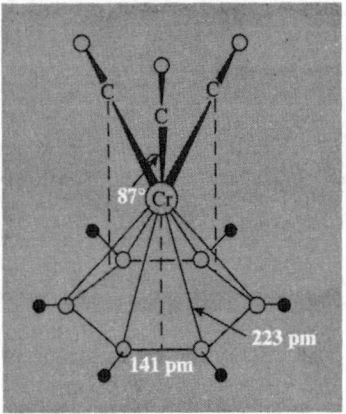

Figure 19.29   The structure of [Cr(η^6-C$_6$H$_6$)(CO)$_3$] showing the three CO groups in staggered configuration with respect to the benzene ring: the Cr–O distance is 295 pm and the plane of the 3 O atoms is parallel to the plane of the ring.

In some cases the loss of hydrogen may occur spontaneously, e.g.:

$$[V(\eta^5\text{-}C_5H_5)(CO)_4] + C_7H_8 \longrightarrow$$
$$[V(\eta^5\text{-}C_5H_5)(\eta^7\text{-}C_7H_7)] + 4CO + \tfrac{1}{2}H_2$$

$$3[V(CO)_6] + 3C_7H_8 \longrightarrow [V(\eta^7\text{-}C_7H_7)(CO)_3]$$
$$+ [V(\eta^6\text{-}C_7H_8)(\eta^7\text{-}C_7H_7)]^+[V(CO)_6]^- + 9CO + H_2$$

The purple paramagnetic complex [V(η^5-C$_5$H$_5$)-(η^7-C$_7$H$_7$)] and the dark-brown diamagnetic complex [V(η^7-C$_7$H$_7$)(CO)$_3$] both feature symmetrical planar C$_7$ rings as illustrated in Fig. 19.30. The bonding appears to be similar to that in η^5-C$_5$H$_5$ and η^6-C$_6$H$_6$ complexes but, as expected from the large number of bonding electrons formally provided by the ligand, its complexes are restricted to elements in the early part of the transition series, e.g. V, Cr, Mo, Mn[l]. For [V(η^5-C$_5$H$_5$) (η^7-C$_7$H$_7$)] the rings are "eclipsed" as shown, and a notable feature of the structure is the substantially closer approach of the C$_7$H$_7$ ring to the V atom, suggesting that equality of V–C distances to the 2 rings is the controlling factor; consistent with this V–C(7 ring) is 225 pm and V–C(5 ring) is 223 pm. In addition to acting as an

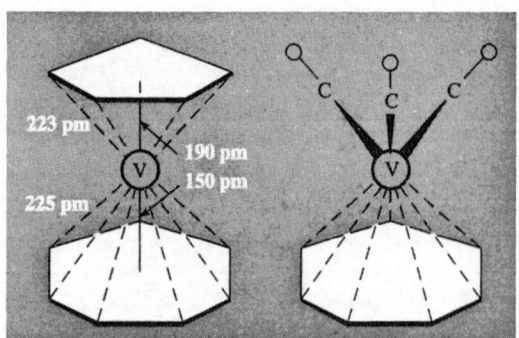

Figure 19.30 Schematic representation of the structures of $[V(\eta^5\text{-}C_5H_5)(\eta^7\text{-}C_7H_7)]$ and $[V(\eta^7\text{-}C_7H_7)(CO)_3]$ (see text).

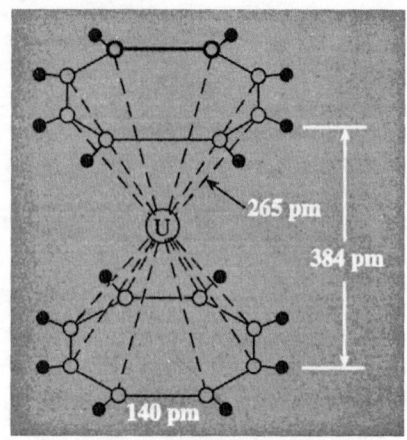

Figure 19.31 The structure of $[U(\eta^8\text{-}C_8H_8)_2]$ showing D_{8h} symmetry.

η^7 ligand, cycloheptatrienyl can also bond in the η^5, η^3, and even η^1 mode (see ref. 44 on p. 943).

Octahapto ligands are rare but cyclooctatetraene fulfils this role in some of its complexes — the metal must clearly have an adequate number of unfilled orbitals and be large enough to bond effectively with such a large ring. Th, Pa, U, Np and Pu satisfy these criteria and the complexes $[M(\eta^8\text{-}C_8H_8)_2]$ have been shown by X-ray crystallography to have eclipsed parallel planar rings (Fig. 19.31). The deep-green U complex can be made by reducing C_8H_8 with K in dry thf and then reacting the intense yellow

solution of $K_2C_8H_8$ with UCl_4:

$$2C_8H_8 + 4K \xrightarrow[-30°]{\text{thf}} 2K_2C_8H_8 \xrightarrow[0°]{UCl_4/\text{thf}}$$

$$[U(\eta^8\text{-}C_8H_8)_2] + 4KCl$$

The compound inflames in air but is stable in aqueous acid or alkali solutions. The colourless complex $[Th(\eta^8\text{-}C_8H_8)_2]$, yellow complexes $[Pa(\eta^8\text{-}C_8H_8)_2]$ and $[Np(\eta^8\text{-}C_8H_8)_2]$ and the cherry red compound $[Pu(\eta^8\text{-}C_8H_8)_2]$ are prepared similarly. One of the very few

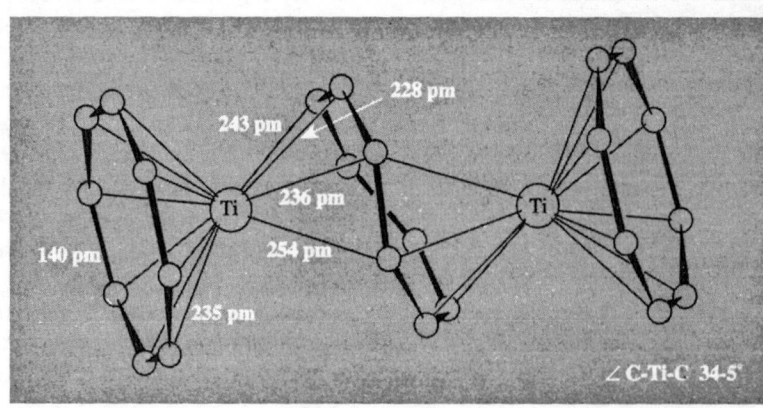

Figure 19.32 Structure of $[Ti_2(C_8H_8)_3]$ showing it to be $[\{Ti(\eta^8\text{-}C_8H_8)\}_2\mu\text{-}(\eta^4,\eta^4\text{-}C_8H_8)]$. Ti–C to outer 16C = 235 pm. H atoms are omitted for clarity.

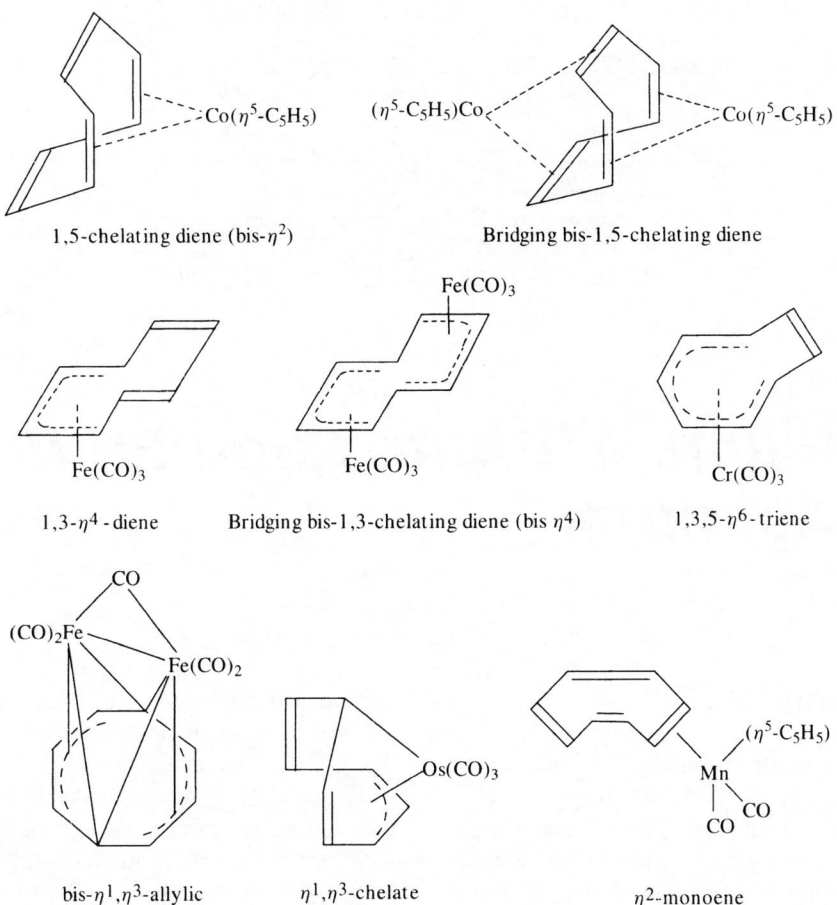

Figure 19.33   Some further coordinating modes of C_8H_8.

examples of η^8 bonding to a d-block element is in the curious complex $Ti_2(C_8H_8)_3$. As shown in Fig. 19.32, two of the ligands are planar η^8 donors whereas the central puckered ring bridges the 2 Ti atoms in a bis-η^4-mode. It is made by treating $Ti(OBu^n)_4$ with C_8H_8 in the presence of $AlEt_3$.

In addition to acting as an η^8 ligand, C_8H_8 can coordinate in other modes,[44] some of which are illustrated in Fig. 19.33. Many of these complexes show fluxional behaviour[45] in solution (p. 935) and the distinction between the various types of bonding is not as clear-cut as implied by the limiting structures in Fig. 19.33.

[44] G. DEGANELLO, *Transition Metal Complexes of Cyclic Polyolefins*. Academic Press, London, 1980, 476 pp.

[45] D. M. HEINEKEY and W. A. G. GRAHAM, *J. Am. Chem. Soc.* **101**, 6115–6 (1979).

20

Scandium, Yttrium, Lanthanum and Actinium

20.1 Introduction

In 1794 the Finnish chemist J. Gadolin, while examining a mineral that had recently been discovered in a quarry at Ytterby, near Stockholm, isolated what he thought was a new oxide (or "earth") which A. G. Ekeberg in 1797 named yttria. In fact it was a mixture of a number of metal oxides from which yttrium oxide was separated by C. G. Mosander in 1843. This is actually part of the fascinating story of the "rare earths" to which we shall return in Chapter 30. The first sample of yttrium metal, albeit very impure, was obtained by F. Wöhler in 1828 by the reduction of the trichloride by potassium.

Four years before isolating yttria, Mosander extracted lanthanum oxide as an impurity from cerium nitrate (hence the name from Greek λανθάνειν, to hide), but it was not until 1923 that metallic lanthanum in a relatively pure form was obtained, by electrolysis of fused halides.

Scandium, the first member of the group, is also present in the Swedish ores from which yttrium and lanthanum had been extracted, but in only very small amounts and, probably for this reason, its discovery was delayed until 1879 when L. F. Nilsen isolated a new oxide and named it scandia. A few years later and with larger amounts at his disposal, P. T. Cleve prepared a large number of salts from this oxide and was able to show that it was the oxide of a new element whose properties tallied very closely indeed with those predicted by D. I. Mendeleev for ekaboron, an element missing from his classification (p. 29). It was only in 1937 that the metal itself was prepared by the electrolysis of molten chlorides of potassium, lithium and scandium, and only in 1960 that the first pound of 99% pure metal was produced.

The final member of the group, actinium, was identified in uranium minerals by A. Debierne in 1899, the year after P. and M. Curie had discovered polonium and radium in the same minerals. However, the naturally occurring isotope, ^{227}Ac, is a β^- emitter with a half-life of 21.77 y and the intense γ activity of its decay products makes it difficult to study.

20.2 The Elements[1,2,3]

20.2.1 Terrestrial abundance and distribution

With the exception of actinium, which is found naturally only in traces in uranium ores, these elements are by no means rare though they were once thought to be so: Sc 25, Y 31, La 35 ppm of the earth's crustal rocks, (cf. Co 29 ppm). This was, no doubt, at least partly because of the considerable difficulty experienced in separating them from other constituent rare earths. As might be expected for class-a metals, in most of their minerals they are associated with oxoanions such as phosphate, silicate and to a lesser extent carbonate.

Scandium is very widely but thinly distributed and its only rich mineral is the rare thortveitite, $Sc_2Si_2O_7$ (p. 348), found in Norway, but since scandium has only small-scale commercial use, and can be obtained as a byproduct in the extraction of other materials, this is not a critical problem. Yttrium and lanthanum are invariably associated with lanthanide elements, the former (Y) with the heavier or "Yttrium group" lanthanides in minerals such as xenotime, $M^{III}PO_4$ and gadolinite, $M_2^{III}M_3^{II}Si_2O_{10}$ (M^{II} = Fe, Be), and the latter (La) with the lighter or "cerium group" lanthanides in minerals such as monazite, $M^{III}PO_4$ and bastnaesite, $M^{III}CO_3F$. This association of similar metals is a reflection of their ionic radii. While La^{III} is similar in size to the early lanthanides which immediately follow it in the periodic table, Y^{III}, because of the steady fall in ionic radius along the lanthanide series (p. 1234), is more akin to the later lanthanides.

[1] R. C. VICKERY, Scandium, yttrium and lanthanum, Chap. 31 in *Comprehensive Inorganic Chemistry*, Vol. 3, pp. 329–53, Pergamon Press, Oxford, 1973, and references therein. C. T. HOROVITZ (ed.), *Scandium: Its Occurrence, Chemistry, Physics, Metallurgy, Biology and Technology*, Academic Press, London, 1975, 598 pp.

[2] S. COTTON, *Lanthanides and Actinides*, Macmillan, Basingstoke, 1991, 192 pp.

[3] K. A. GSCHNEIDER and L. EYRING (eds) *Handbook of the Physics and Chemistry of Rare Earths*, Vols 1–21, 1978–1995, Elsevier, Amersterdam.

20.2.2 Preparation and uses of the metals

Some scandium is obtained from thortveitite, which contains 35–40% Sc_2O_3, but most is obtained as a byproduct in the processing of uranium ores which contain only about 0.02% Sc_2O_3, and in the production of tungsten. Its applications, for instance in laser crystals and coatings, are highly specialized and the amount consumed is low, though increasing.

Yttrium and lanthanum are both obtained from lanthanide minerals and the method of extraction depends on the particular mineral involved. Digestions with hydrochloric acid, sulfuric acid, or caustic soda are all used to extract the mixture of metal salts. Prior to the Second World War the separation of these mixtures was effected by fractional crystallizations, sometimes numbered in their thousands. However, during the period 1940–45 the main interest in separating these elements was in order to purify and characterize them more fully. The realization that they are also major constituents of the products of nuclear fission effected a dramatic sharpening of interest in the USA. As a result, ion-exchange techniques were developed and, together with selective complexation and solvent extraction, these have now completely supplanted the older methods of separation (p. 1228). In cases where the free metals are required, reduction of the trifluorides with metallic calcium can be used.

Yttrium has important roles in the field of electronics, providing the basis of the phosphors used to produce the red colour on television screens and, in the form of garnets such as $Y_3Fe_5O_{12}$, being employed as microwave filters in radar. Because of its low neutron absorption cross-section, yttrium has potential as a moderator in nuclear reactors though this use has yet to be developed. It was, however, the announcement in 1986/87 of the *high temperature superconductors*, $La_{2-x}Sr_xCuO_4$ and $YBa_2Cu_3O_{7-x}$ which produced the highest, though as yet unfulfilled, hopes of commercial exploitation. The latter compound has a critical temperature, $T_c \sim 95\,K$, below which it is superconducting. This temperature, crucially, can be attained using liquid nitrogen rather than liquid helium as refrigerant and a continuing spate of publications on these and related materials has been generated (p. 1182).

Lanthanum has also found modest uses. Its oxide is an additive in high-quality optical glasses to which it imparts a high refractive index (sparkle) and has been suggested for a variety of catalytic uses. "Mischmetal", an unseparated mixture of lanthanide metals containing about 25% La, is used in making lighter flints, and more importantly in the production of alloy steels. (p. 1232).

Actinium occurs naturally as a decay product of ^{235}U:

$$^{235}_{92}U \xrightarrow[7.04 \times 10^8 \, y]{\alpha} \, ^{231}_{90}Th \xrightarrow[25.52 \, h]{\beta^-} \, ^{231}_{91}Pa \xrightarrow[3.28 \times 10^4 \, y]{\alpha}$$

$$^{227}_{89}Ac \xrightarrow[21.77 \, y]{\beta^-} \, ^{227}_{90}Th \, \text{- - - -} \rightarrow$$

but the half-lives are such that one tonne of the naturally occurring uranium ore contains on average only about 0.2 mg of Ac. An alternative source is the neutron irradiation of ^{226}Ra in a nuclear reactor:

$$^{226}_{88}Ra + {}^1_0n \longrightarrow \, ^{227}_{88}Ra \xrightarrow[42.2 \, min]{\beta^-} \, ^{227}_{89}Ac \, \text{- - - -} \rightarrow$$

In either case, ion-exchange or solvent extraction techniques are needed to separate the element and, at best, it can be produced in no more than milligram quantities. Large-scale use is therefore impossible even if desired.

20.2.3 Properties of the elements

A number of the properties of Group 3 elements are summarized in Table 20.1. Each of the elements has an odd atomic number and so has few stable isotopes. All are rather soft, silvery-white metals, and they display the gradation in properties that might be expected for elements immediately following the strongly electropositive alkaline-earth metals and preceding the transition elements proper. Each is less electropositive than its predecessor in Group 2 but more electropositive than its successors in transition series, while the increasingly electropositive character of the heavier elements of the group is in keeping with the increase in size. The inverse trends in electronegativity are illustrated in Fig. 20.1.

As is the case for boron and aluminium (in Group 13), the underlying electron cores are those of the preceding noble gases and indeed, as was pointed out in Chapter 7, a much more

Table 20.1 Some properties of Group 3 elements

Property	Sc	Y	La	Ac
Atomic number	21	39	57	89
Number of naturally occurring isotopes	1	1	2	(2)
Atomic weight	44.955910(8)	88.90585(2)	138.9055(2)	227.0277[a]
Electronic configuration	$[Ar]3d^1 4s^2$	$[Kr]4d^1 5s^2$	$[Xe]5d^1 6s^2$	$[Rn]6d^1 7s^2$
Electronegativity	1.3	1.2	1.1	1.1
Metal radius (12-coordinate)/pm	162	180	187	—
Ionic radius (6-coordinate)/pm	74.5	90.0	103.2	112
$E°(M^{3+} + 3e^- = M(s))/V$	−2.03	−2.37	−2.37	−2.6
MP/°C	1539	1530	920	817
BP/°C	2748	3264	3420	2470
$\Delta H_{fus}/kJ\,mol^{-1}$	15.77	11.5	8.5	(10.5)
$\Delta H_{vap}/kJ\,mol^{-1}$	332.71	367	402	(293)
ΔH_f (monatomic gas)/kJ mol^{-1}	376 (±20)	425 (±8)	423 (±6)	—
Density (20°C)/g cm^{-3}	3.0	4.5	6.17	—
Electrical resistivity (20°C)/μohm cm	50–61	57–70	57–80	—

[a]This value is for the radioisotope with the longest half-life (^{227}Ac).

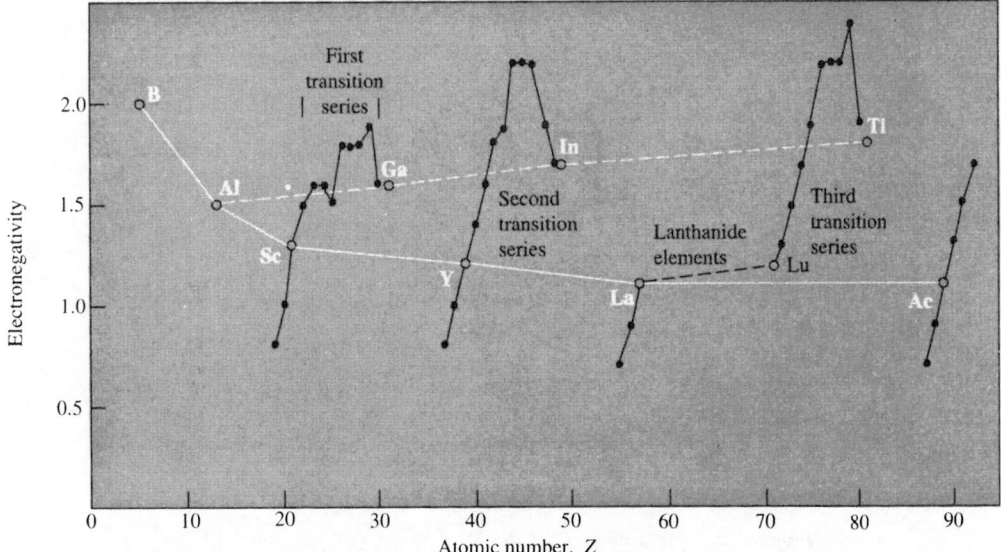

Figure 20.1　Electronegativity of the elements in Groups 3 and 13.

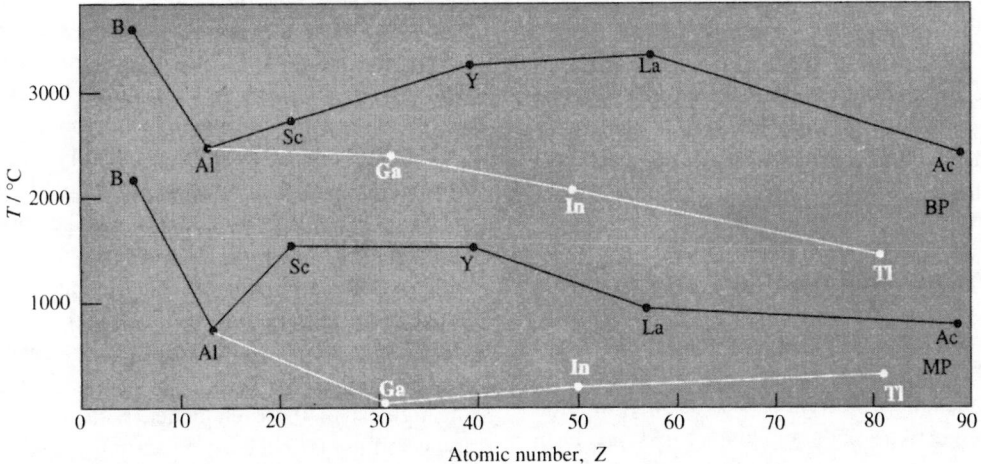

Figure 20.2　Mps and bps of the elements in Groups 3 and 13.

regular variation in atomic properties occurs in passing from B and Al to Group 3 than to heavier congeners in Group 13 (p. 223). However, the presence of a d electron on each of the atoms of this group (in contrast to the p electron in the atoms of B, Al and the other elements in Group 13) has consequences which can be seen in some of the bulk properties of the metals. For instance, the mps and bps (Fig. 20.2), along with

the enthalpies associated with these transitions, all show discontinuous increases in passing from Al to Sc rather than to Ga, indicating that the d electron has a more cohesive effect than the p electron. It appears that this is due to d electrons forming more localized bonds within the metals. Thus, although Sc, Y and La have typically metallic (hcp) structures (with other metallic modifications at higher temperatures),

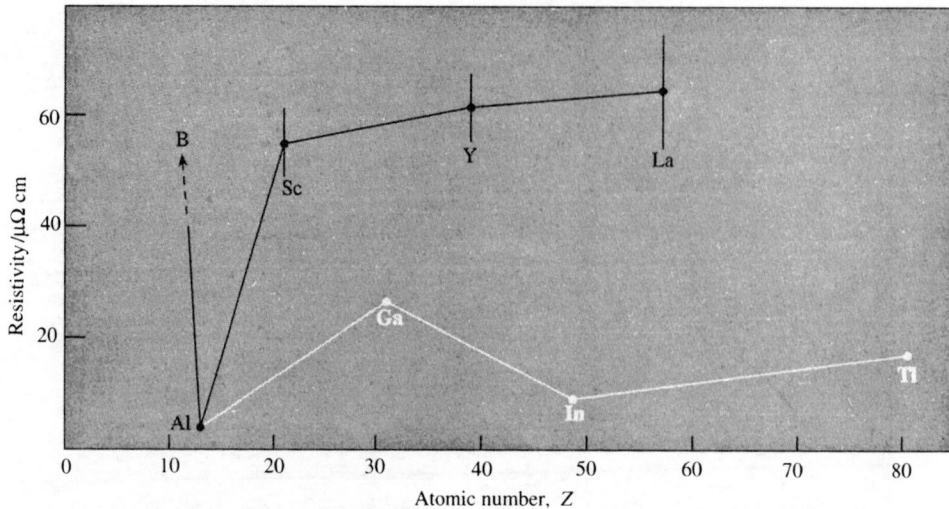

Figure 20.3 Resistivities of the elements in Groups 3 and 13.

their electrical resistivities are much higher than that of Al (Fig. 20.3). Admittedly, resistivity is a function of thermal vibrations of the crystal lattice as well as of the degree of localization of valence electrons, but even so the marked changes between Al and Sc seem to indicate a marked reduction in the mobility of the d electron of the latter.

20.2.4 Chemical reactivity and trends

The general reactivity of the metals increases down the group. They tarnish in air — La rapidly, but Y much more slowly because of the formation of a protective oxide coating — and all burn easily to give the oxides M_2O_3. They react with halogens at room temperature and with most non-metals on warming. They reduce water with evolution of hydrogen, particularly if finely divided or heated, and all dissolve in dilute acid. Strong acids produce soluble salts whereas weak acids such as HF, H_3PO_4 and $H_2C_2O_4$ produce sparingly soluble or insoluble salts.

In the main, the chemistry of these elements concerns the formation of a predominantly ionic +3 oxidation state arising from the loss of all 3 valence electrons and giving a well-defined cationic aqueous chemistry. Because of this, although each member of this group is the first member of a transition series, its chemistry is largely atypical of the transition elements. The variable oxidation states and the marked ability to form coordination compounds with a wide variety of ligands are barely hinted at in this group although materials containing the metals in low oxidation states can be prepared (see p. 949) and a limited organometallic (predominantly cyclopentadienyl) chemistry has developed. Differences in chemical behaviour within the group are largely a consequence of the differing sizes of the M^{III} ions. Scandium, the lightest of these elements, with the smallest ionic radius, is the least basic and the strongest complexing agent, with properties not unlike those of aluminium. Its aqueous solutions are appreciably hydrolysed and its oxide has some acidic properties. On the other hand, lanthanum and actinium (in so far as its properties have been examined) show basic properties approaching those of calcium.

Most structural studies have relied exclusively on the use of X-ray techniques but these elements have nuclei, ^{45}Sc, ^{89}Y and ^{139}La with abundances in excess of 99.9% and $I = \frac{7}{2}, \frac{1}{2}, \frac{7}{2}$ respectively. The application of nmr studies is therefore becoming increasingly important,[4] mainly on solutions but also for solid-state work.[5]

20.3 Compounds of Scandium, Yttrium, Lanthanum and Actinium

20.3.1 Simple compounds [6]

The oxides, M_2O_3, are white solids which can be prepared directly from the elements. In Sc_2O_3 and Y_2O_3 the metals are 6-coordinate but the larger La^{III} ion adopts this structure only at elevated temperatures, a 7-coordinate structure being normally more stable. When water is added to La_2O_3 it "slakes" like lime with evolution of much heat and a hissing sound. The hydroxides, $M(OH)_3$, (or in the case of scandium possibly the hydrated oxide) are obtained as gelatinous precipitates from aqueous solutions of the metal salts by addition of alkali hydroxide. In the case of scandium only, this precipitate can be dissolved in an excess of conc NaOH to give anionic species such as $[Sc(OH)_6]^{3-}$. Yttrium and lanthanum hydroxides possess only basic properties, and the latter especially will absorb atmospheric CO_2 to form basic carbonates.

Dissolution of the oxide or hydroxide in the appropriate acid provides the most convenient method for producing the salts of the colourless, diamagnetic M^{III} ions. Such solutions, especially those of Sc^{III}, are significantly hydrolysed with the formation of polymeric hydroxy species.

With the exception of the fluorides, the halides are all very water-soluble and deliquescent. Precipitation of the insoluble fluorides can be used as a qualitative test for these elements. The distinctive ability of Sc^{III} to form complexes is illustrated by the fact that an excess of F^- causes the first-precipitated ScF_3 to redissolve as

$[ScF_6]^{3-}$; indeed, $M_3[ScF_6]$, M = NH$_4$, Na, K, were isolated as long ago as 1914. The anhydrous halides are best prepared by direct reaction of the elements rather than by heating the hydrates which causes hydrolysis. Heating the hydrated chlorides, for instance, gives Sc_2O_3, YOCl and LaOCl respectively, though to produce AcOCl it is necessary to use superheated steam. The anhydrous halides illustrate nicely the effects of ionic size on the coordination number of the metal[2]. In all four of its halides scandium is 6-coordinate. So too is yttrium except in its fluoride where it has eight near neighbours and one slightly further away (8 + 1). The larger lanthanum however has 9 + 2 coordination in its fluoride, but is 9-coordinate in its chloride and bromide and 8-coordinate in its iodide.

Sulfates and nitrates are known and in all cases they decompose to the oxides on heating. Double sulfates of the type $M_2^{III}(SO_4)_3.3Na_2SO_4.12H_2O$ can be prepared, and La (unlike Sc and Y) forms a double nitrate, $La(NO_3)_3.2NH_4NO_3.4H_2O$, which is of the type once used extensively in fractional crystallization procedures for separating individual lanthanides.

Reaction of the metals with hydrogen produces highly conducting materials with the composition MH_2, similar to the metallic nonstoichiometric hydrides of the subsequent transition elements (pp. 66–7). Except in the case of ScH_2, further H_2 can then be absorbed causing a diminution of electrical conductivity until materials similar to the ionic hydrides of the alkaline-earth metals, and with the limiting composition MH_3, are produced. The dihydrides, though ostensibly containing the divalent metals, are probably best considered as pseudo-ionic compounds of M^{3+} and $2H^-$ with the extra electron in a conduction band. However, the question of the type of bonding is still controversial, as was explained more fully in Chapter 3 (p. 66).

Another example of a "divalent" metal of this group, but which in fact is probably entirely analogous to the dihydrides, is LaI_2. However, the most extensive set of examples of these metals in low formal oxidation states is provided by the binary and ternary halides produced by

[4] J. MASON, *Polyhedron* **8**, 1657–68 (1989).

[5] A. R. THOMPSON and E. OLDFIELD, *J. Chem. Soc., Chem. Commun.*, 27–9 (1987).

[6] G. MEYER and L. R. MORSS (eds.), *Synthesis of Lanthanide and Actinide Compounds*, Kluwer Acad. Publ., Dordrecht, 1991, 367 pp.

prolonged heating of the reactants in sealed tantalum or niobium vessels to temperatures sometimes in excess of 1000°C. Starting with ScX_3 and Sc metal along with the appropriate alkali metal halide, several compounds of the series $M^ISc X_3$ have been obtained containing octahedrally coordinated Sc^{II} in linear $[ScX_3^-]$ chains[7]. $ScCl_3 + Sc$ yield no less than five reduced phases, dark-coloured and sensitive to oxygen and moisture[8]:

Sc_7Cl_{12} consists of discrete $[Sc_6Cl_{12}]^{3-}$ clusters, similar to the M_6Cl_{12} clusters of Nb and Ta (p. 991), along with separate Sc^{3+} ions;

Sc_5Cl_8 is best regarded as $(ScCl_2^+)_n$-$(Sc_4Cl_6^-)_n$ in which edge-sharing $ScCl_6$ octahedra and edge-sharing Sc_6 octahedra lie in parallel chains;

Sc_2Cl_3 and its Br analogue are of unknown structure, as are reported La_2X_3 phases, though Y_2Cl_3 and Y_2Br_3 have been shown to consist of parallel chains of Y_6 octahedra, the chains being linked by Cl atoms;

Sc_7Cl_{10} is composed of a double chain of Sc_6 octahedra sharing edges, and a parallel chain of $ScCl_6$ octahedra[9];

ScCl, made up of close-packed layers of Sc and Cl atoms in the sequence Cl-Sc-Sc-Cl has, like analogous Y and La materials with Cl and Br, since been shown to have been stabilised by interstitial H impurity.[10]

The ability of B, C and N as well as H to stabilize many of these reduced phases is at once a major preparative problem[11] and also a source of an expanding area of cluster chemistry of which $Sc_7X_{12}Z$ (Z = C; X = Br, I. Z = B; X = I), best regarded as $Sc(Sc_6X_{12}Z)$, are examples.[12]

20.3.2 Complexes [13,14]

Compared to later elements in their respective transition series, scandium, yttrium and lanthanum have rather poorly developed coordination chemistries and form weaker coordinate bonds, lanthanum generally being even less inclined to form strong coordinate bonds than scandium. This is reflected in the stability constants of a number of relevant 1:1 metal-edta complexes:

Metal ion	Sc^{III}	Y^{III}	La^{III}	Fe^{III}	Co^{III}
$\log_{10} K_1$	23.1	18.1	15.5	25.5	36.0

This may seem somewhat surprising in view of the charge of +3 ions, but this is coupled with appreciably larger ionic radii and also with greater electropositive character which inhibits covalent contribution to their bonding. Lanthanum of course exhibits these characteristics more clearly than Sc, and, while La and Y closely resemble the lanthanide elements, Sc has more similarity with Al. Even Sc however is a class-a acceptor, complexing most readily with *O*-donor ligands particularly if chelating. Complexes with *N*-donor and halide ligands are less well-characterized and those with *S*-donors are largely confined to the Y and La complexes with dithiocarbamates and dithiophosphinates, $[M(S_2CNEt_2)_3]$ and $[M\{S_2P(C_6H_{11})_2\}_3]$.

The complex anion $[ScF_6]^{3-}$ has already been mentioned and, while there is a fairly extensive series of halo complexes with a

[7] A. Lachgar, D. S. Dudis, P. K. Dorhout and J. D. Corbett, *Inorg. Chem.* **30**, 3321–6 (1991).

[8] J. D. Corbett, *Acc. Chem. Res.* **14**, 239–46 (1981).

[9] F. J. Di Salvo, J. V. Waszczak, W. M. Walsh, Jr., L. W. Rupp and J. D. Corbett, *Inorg. Chem.* **24**, 4624–5 (1985).

[10] See p. 176 of A. Simon, *Angew. Chem. Int. Edn. Engl.*, **27**, 159–83 (1988). Hj. Mattausch, R. Eger, J. D. Corbett and A. Simon, *Z. anorg. allg. Chem.* **616**, 157–61 (1992).

[11] J. D. Corbett in *Synthesis of Lanthanide and Actinide Compounds*, pp. 159–73, Kluwer Acad. Publ., Dordrecht, (1991).

[12] D. S. Dudis, J. D. Corbett and S-J. Hwu, *Inorg. Chem.* **25**, 3434–8 (1986).

[13] G. A. Melson and R. W. Stotz, *Coord. Chem. Revs.* **7**, 133–60 (1971).

[14] F. A. Hart, Scandium, Yttrium and the Lanthanides, in *Comprehensive Coordination Chemistry*, Vol. 3, pp. 1059–127, Pergamon Press, Oxford, 1987.

variety of stereochemistries, they must normally be prepared[15] by dry methods to avoid hydrolysis, and iodo complexes are invariably unstable. Other complexes such as $[Sc(dmso)_6]^{3+}$ (where dmso is dimethylsulfoxide, Me_2SO), $[Sc(bipy)_3]^{3+}$, $[Sc(bipy)_2(NCS)_2]^+$ and $[Sc(bipy)_2Cl_2]^+$ exhibit scandium's usual coordination number of 6. Data for corresponding Y and La compounds are limited but in $[Y(OH)(H_2O)_2(phen)_2]_2Cl_4.2(phen).MeOH$ the yttrium is 8-coordinate with square antiprismatic geometry,[16] and in $[La(NO_3)_3(bipy)_2]$ the lanthanum is 10-coordinate. This is illustrative of the general trend in moving down the group that coordination numbers greater than 6 become the rule rather than the exception. It seems likely that in aqueous solutions, in the absence of other preferred ligands, Y^{III} is directly coordinated to 8 water molecules and La^{III} to 9 and in $M(OH)_3$, (M = Y, La) the metal ion is 9-coordinate with a stereochemistry approximating to tri-capped trigonal prismatic.

A coordination number of 8 is probably the most characteristic of La and possibly even of Y, with the square antiprism and the dodecahedron being the preferred stereochemistries. The acac complexes referred to below are good examples of the former type, while $Cs[Y(CF_3COCHCOCF_3)_4]$ typifies the latter. On the basis of ligand–ligand repulsions the cubic arrangement is expected to be much less favoured in discrete complexes, but, nonetheless, the complex $[La(bipyO_2)_4]ClO_4$, in which $bipyO_2$ is 2,2'-bipyridine dioxide, has been shown to be very nearly cubic.

The gradation of properties within this group is also illustrated by the oxalates and β-diketonates

which are formed. On addition of alkali-metal oxalate to aqueous solutions of M^{III}, oxalate precipitates form but their solubilities in an excess of the alkali-metal oxalate decrease very markedly down the group. Scandium oxalate dissolves readily with evidence of such anionic species as $[Sc(C_2O_4)_2]^-$. Yttrium oxalate also dissolves to some extent but lanthanum oxalate dissolves only slightly. All three elements form acetylacetonates: that of scandium is usually anhydrous, $[Sc(acac)_3]$, and presumably pseudo-octahedral: $[Y(acac)_3(H_2O)]$ is 7-coordinate with a capped trigonal prismatic structure (p. 916); $[Y(acac)_3(H_2O)_2].H_2O$ and $[La(acac)_3(H_2O)_2]$ are 8-coordinate with distorted square-antiprismatic structures (p. 917); the scandium compound can be sublimed without decomposition whereas the yttrium and lanthanum compounds decompose at about 500°C and dehydration without decomposition or polymerization is difficult.

The alkoxides and aryloxides, particularly of yttrium have excited recent interest.[17] This is because of their potential use in the production of electronic and ceramic materials,[18] in particular high temperature superconductors, by the deposition of pure oxides (metallo-organic chemical vapour deposition, MOCVD). They are moisture sensitive but mostly polymeric and involatile and so attempts have been made to inhibit polymerization and produce the required volatility by using bulky alkoxide ligands. $M(OR)_3$, R = 2,6-di-*tert*-butyl-4-methylphenoxide, are indeed 3-coordinate (pyramidal) monomers but still not sufficiently volatile. More success has been achieved with fluorinated alkoxides, prepared by reacting the parent alcohols with the metal tris-(bis-trimethylsilylamides):

$$[M\{N(SiMe_3)_2\}_3] + 3ROH \longrightarrow M(OR)_3$$
$$+ 3(Me_3Si)_2NH, \text{ eg } R = (CF_3)_2MeC-$$

The Y and La compounds, though polymeric, are surprisingly volatile but, using

---

[15] G. MEYER, p. 145–58 in ref. 6.

[16] M. D. GRILLONE, F. BENETOLLO and G. BOMBIERI *Polyhedron* **10**, 2171–7 (1991).

[17] R. C. MEHROTRA, A. SINGH and U. M. TRIPATHI, *Chem. Revs.* **91**, 1287–303 (1991).

[18] D. C. BRADLEY, *Chem. Revs.* **89**, 1317–22 (1989).

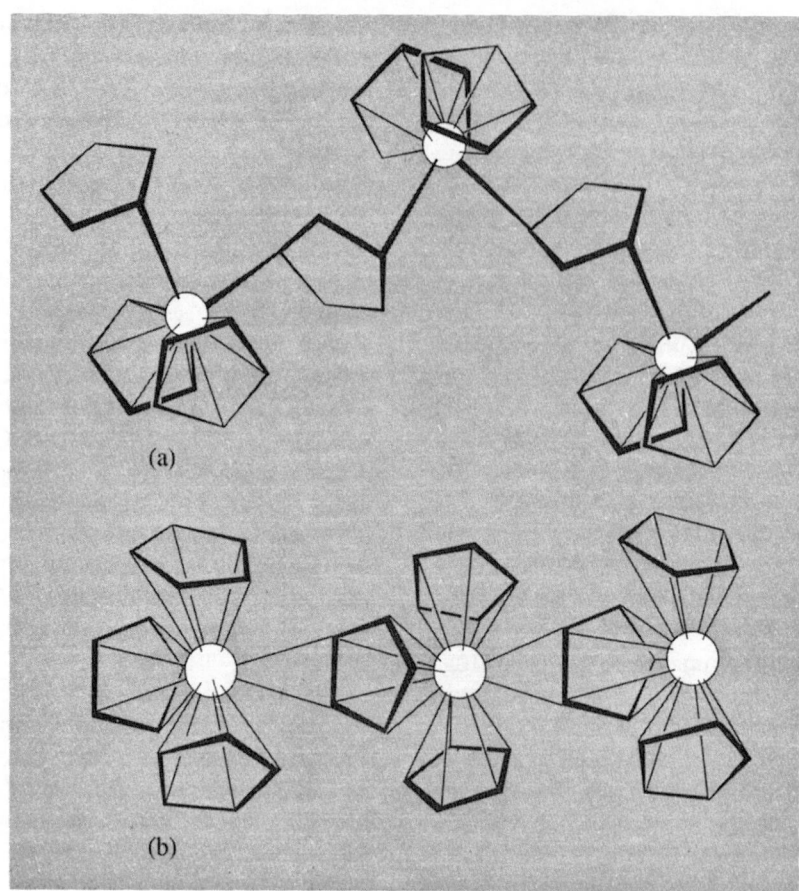

(a)

(b)

Figure 20.4   (a) The structure of [Sc(C$_5$H$_5$)$_3$]. (b) The structure of [La(C$_5$H$_5$)$_3$]. Note that the "total connectivity"
of the ligands around each Sc atom is 12 as compared to 17 for the larger La.

thf as solvent, volatile octahedral monomers
[M(OR)$_3$(thf)$_3$], M = Y, La, are obtained.[19]
With 2,6-diphenylphenolate ligands the coordination number 5 is stabilized in the distorted
trigonal-bipyramidal [La(Odpp)$_3$(thf)$_2$].(thf).[20]

EDTA complexes of La and the lanthanides
are known. K[La(edta)(H$_2$O)$_3$].5H$_2$O is a 9-co-
ordinate complex but steric constraints imposed
by the edta produce deviations from a
tricapped trigonal prismatic structure. [La(edtaH)-

(H$_2$O)$_4$].3H$_2$O is 10-coordinate and its structure
is probably best regarded as being based on the
same structure but with an extra water "squeezed"
between the three coordinated water molecules.

The highest coordination numbers of all are
attained with the aid of chelating ligands, such
as SO$_4$$^{2-}$ and NO$_3$$^-$, with very small "bites"
(p. 917). In La$_2$(SO$_4$)$_3$.9H$_2$O there are actually
two types of La^{III}, one being coordinated to
12 oxygens in SO$_4$$^{2-}$ ions while the other is
coordinated to 6 water molecules and 3 oxygens
in SO$_4$$^{2-}$ ions. In [Y(NO$_3$)$_5$]$^{2-}$ the Y^{III} is 10-
coordinate and in [Sc(NO$_3$)$_5$]$^{2-}$, even though one
of the nitrate ions is only unidentate (p. 469), the
coordination number of 9 is extraordinarily high
for scandium.

[19] D. C. BRADLEY,   H. CHUDZYNSKA,   M. E. HAMMOND,
M. B. HURSTHOLISE, M. MOTEVALLI and W. RUOWEN, *Polyhedron* **11**, 375–9 (1992).

[20] G. B. DEACON, B. M. GATEHOUSE, Q. SHEN, G. N. WARD
and E. R. T. TIEKINK, *Polyhedron* **12**, 1289–94 (1993).

The low symmetries of many of the above highly coordinated species, which appear to be determined largely by the stereochemical requirements of the ligands, together with the fact that these high coordination numbers are attained almost exclusively with oxygen-donor ligands, are consistent with the belief that the bonding is essentially of an electrostatic rather than a directional covalent character.

20.3.3 Organometallic compounds [2,21,22]

In view of the electronic structures of the elements of this group, little interaction with π-acceptor ligands is to be expected, though cocondensation of metal vapours with an excess of the bulky ligand, 1,3,5-tri-*tert*-butylbenzene at 77 K yields the unstable sandwich compounds $[M(\eta^6\text{-Bu}^t_3C_6H_3)_2]$, M = Sc, Y which are the first examples of these metals in oxidation state zero.[23] The organometallic chemistry of this group, as of the lanthanides, is instead dominated by compounds involving cyclopentadiene and its methyl-substituted derivatives.[23] Though many

are thermally stable, they are invariably sensitive to moisture and oxygen. The first to be prepared were the ionic cyclopentadienides, $M(C_5H_5)_3$, formed by the reactions of anhydrous MCl_3 with NaC_5H_5 in tetrahydrofuran and purified by vacuum sublimation at 200–250°C. The solids are polymeric, $[Sc(C_5H_5)_3]$ being made up of zig-zag chains of $\{Sc(\eta^5\text{-}C_5H_5)_2\}$ groups joined by $\eta^1:\eta^1\text{-}C_5H_5$ bridges,[24] (Fig. 20.4a), whereas in the lanthanum analogue the zig-zag chains of $\{La(\eta^5\text{-}C_5H_5)_2\}$ groups are joined by $\eta^5:\eta^2\text{-}C_5H_5$ bridges[25] (Fig. 20.4b). They are reactive compounds and form "tetrahedral" monomers, $[M(C_5H_5)_3L]$ with neutral ligands such as ammonia and phosphines.

The $M(C_5H_5)_2Cl$ compounds, which are actually Cl-bridged dimers, $[(C_5H_5)M(\mu\text{-Cl})_2M(C_5H_5)]$, provide an extensive substitution chemistry in which μ-Cl can be replaced by a variety of ligands including H, CN, NH_2, MeO and alkyl groups.

Monomeric alkyl compounds of the form MR_3 have also been obtained for Sc and Y, where the alkyl groups are of the types Me_3SiCH_2 and Me_3CCH_2 which are bulky and contain no β hydrogen atoms (p. 926).

[21] T. J. MARKS and R. D. ERNST, Chap 21 in *Comprehensive Organometallic Chemistry*, Vol. 3, pp. 173–270, Pergamon Press, Oxford, 1982.

[22] M. N. BOCHKAREV, L. N. ZAKHAROV and G. S. KALININA, *Organoderivatives of Rare Earth Elements*, Kluwer Academic Publishers, Dordrecht, 1995, 532 pp.

[23] F. G. N. CLOKE, K. KHAN and R. N. PERUTZ, *J. Chem. Soc., Chem. Commun.*, 1372–3 (1991).

[24] J. L. ATWOOD and K. D. SMITH, *J. Am. Chem. Soc.* **95**, 1488–91 (1973).

[25] S. H. EGGERS, J. KOPF and R. D. FISCHER, *Organometallics* **5**, 383–5 (1986).

The periodic table is shown at the top of the page.

21

Titanium, Zirconium and Hafnium

21.1 Introduction

In 1791 William Gregor, a Cornish vicar and amateur chemist, examined sand from the local river Helford. Using a magnet he extracted a black material (now called ilmenite) from which he removed iron by treatment with hydrochloric acid. The residue, which dissolved only with difficulty in concentrated sulfuric acid, was the impure oxide of a new element, and Gregor proceeded to discover the reactions which were to form the basis of the production of virtually all TiO_2 up to about 1960. Four years later the German chemist M. H. Klaproth independently discovered the same oxide (or "earth"), in a sample of ore now known to be rutile, and named the element titanium after the Titans who, in Greek mythology, were the children of Heaven and Earth condemned to live amongst the hidden fires of the earth. Klaproth had previously (1789) isolated the oxide of zirconium from a sample of zircon, $ZrSiO_4$. Various forms of zircon (Arabic *zargun*) have been known as gemstones since ancient times. Impure samples of the two metals were prepared by J. J. Berzelius (Sweden) in 1824 (Zr) and 1825 (Ti) but samples of high purity were not obtained until much later. M. A. Hunter (USA) reduced $TiCl_4$ with sodium in 1910 to obtain titanium, and A. E. van Arkel and J. H. de Boer (Netherlands) produced zirconium in 1925 by their iodide-decomposition process (see below).

The discovery of hafnium was one of chemistry's more controversial episodes[1]. In 1911 G. Urbain, the French chemist and authority on "rare earths", claimed to have isolated the element of atomic number 72 from a sample of rare-earth residues, and named it celtium. With hindsight, and more especially with an understanding of the consequences of H. G. J. Moseley's and N. Bohr's work on atomic structure, it now seems very unlikely that element 72 could have been found in the necessary concentrations along with rare earths. But this knowledge was lacking in the early part of the century and, indeed, in 1922 Urbain and A. Dauvillier claimed to have X-ray evidence to support the discovery. However, by that time Niels Bohr had developed his atomic theory and so was confident that element 72 would be a

---

[1] R. T. ALLSOP, *Educ. Chem.* **10**, 222–3 (1973).

member of Group 4 and was more likely to be found along with zirconium than with the rare earths. Working in Bohr's laboratory in Copenhagen in 1922/3, D. Coster (Netherlands) and G. von Hevesy (Hungary) used Moseley's method of X-ray spectroscopic analysis to show that element 72 was present in Norwegian zircon, and it was named hafnium (*Hafnia*, Latin name for Copenhagen). The separation of hafnium from zirconium was then effected by repeated recrystallizations of the complex fluorides and hafnium metal was obtained by reduction with sodium. For rutherfordium ($Z = 104$) see pp. 1280–82.

21.2 The Elements[2]

21.2.1 Terrestrial abundance and distribution

Titanium, which comprises 0.63% (i.e. 6320 ppm) of the earth's crustal rocks, is a very abundant element (ninth of all elements, second of the transition elements), and, of the transition elements, only Fe, Ti and Mn are more abundant than zirconium (0.016%, 162 ppm). Even hafnium (2.8 ppm) is as common as Cs and Br.

That these elements have in the past been considered unfamiliar has been due largely to the difficulties involved in preparing the pure metals and also to their rather diffuse occurrence. Like their predecessors in Group 3, they are classified as type-a metals and are found as silicates and oxides in many silicaceous materials. These are frequently resistant to weathering and so often accumulate in beach deposits which can be profitably exploited.

The two most important minerals of titanium are ilmenite ($FeTiO_3$) and rutile (TiO_2). The former is a black sandy material mined in Canada, the USA, Australia, Scandinavia and Malaysia, while the latter is mined principally in Australia. Zirconium's main minerals are zircon ($ZrSiO_4$)

and baddeleyite (ZrO_2) mined mainly in Australia, the Republic of S. Africa, USA and the former USSR and invariably containing hafnium, most commonly in quantities around 2% of the zirconium content. Only in a few minerals, such as alvite, $MSiO_4 \cdot xH_2O$ (M = Hf, Th, Zr), does the hafnium content occasionally exceed that of zirconium. As a result of the lanthanide contraction (p. 1232) the ionic radii of Zr and Hf are virtually identical and their association in nature parallels their very close chemical similarity.

21.2.2 Preparation and uses of the metals [3]

Viable methods of producing the metals from oxide ores have to surmount two problems. In the first place, reduction with carbon is not possible because of the formation of intractable carbides (p. 299), and even reduction with Na, Ca or Mg is unlikely to remove all the oxygen. In addition, the metals are extremely reactive at high temperatures and, unless prepared in the absence of air, will certainly be contaminated with oxygen and nitrogen.

In 1932 Wilhelm Kroll of Luxembourg produced titanium by reducing $TiCl_4$ with calcium and then later (1940) with magnesium and even sodium. The expense of this process was a severe deterrent to any commercial use of titanium. However, the metal has a very low density (~57% that of steel) combined with good mechanical strength and, in fact, when alloyed with small quantities of such metals as Al and Sn, has the highest strength:weight ratio of any of the engineering metals. Accordingly, about 1950, a demand developed for titanium for the manufacture of gas-turbine engines, and this demand has rapidly increased as production and fabrication problems have been overcome. Its major uses are still in the aircraft industry

[2] R. J. H CLARK, Chap. 32, pp. 355–417, and D. C. BRADLEY and P. THORNTON, Chap. 33, pp. 419–90, in *Comprehensive Inorganic Chemistry*, Vol. 3, Pergamon Press, Oxford, 1973.

[3] *Kirk–Othmer Encyclopedia of Chemical Technology*, 4th edn. Interscience. New York. For Ti, See Vol. 24, 1997, pp. 186–349; for Zr, See Vol. 25, 1998, pp. 853–96; for Hf, See Vol. 12, 1994, pp. 861–81.

for the production of both engines and airframes, but it is also widely used in chemical processing and marine equipment. Current world production capacity is estimated to exceed 120 000 tonnes pa though actual production is less than this. The Kroll method still dominates the industry: in this ilmenite or rutile is heated with chlorine and carbon, e.g.:

$$2FeTiO_3 + 7Cl_2 + 6C \xrightarrow{900°C} 2TiCl_4 + 2FeCl_3 + 6CO$$

The $TiCl_4$ is fractionally distilled from $FeCl_3$ and other impurities and then reduced with molten magnesium in a sealed furnace under Ar,

$$TiCl_4 + 2Mg \xrightarrow{900°C} Ti + 2MgCl_2$$

Molten $MgCl_2$ is tapped off periodically and, after cooling, residual $MgCl_2$ and any excess of magnesium are removed by leaching with water and dilute hydrochloric acid or by distillation, leaving titanium "sponge" which, after grinding and cleaning with aqua regia (1:3 mixture of concentrated nitric and hydrochloric acids), is melted under argon or vacuum and cast into ingots. The use of sodium instead of magnesium requires little change in the basic process but gives a more readily leached product. This yields titanium metal in a granular form which is fabricated by somewhat different techniques and has been preferred by some users.

Zirconium, too, is produced commercially by the Kroll process, but the van Arkel-de Boer process is also useful when it is especially important to remove all oxygen and nitrogen. In this latter method the crude zirconium is heated in an evacuated vessel with a little iodine, to a temperature of about 200°C when ZrI_4 volatilizes. A tungsten or zirconium filament is simultaneously electrically heated to about 1300°C. This decomposes the ZrI_4 and pure zirconium is deposited on the filament. As the deposit grows the current is steadily increased so as to maintain the temperatures. The method is applicable to many metals by judicious adjustment of the temperatures. Zirconium has a high corrosion resistance and in certain chemical plants is preferred to alternatives such as stainless

steel, titanium and tantalum. It is also used in a variety of alloy steels and, when added to niobium, forms a superconducting alloy which retains its superconductivity in strong magnetic fields. The small percentage of hafnium normally present in zirconium is of no detriment in these cases and may even improve its properties, but a further important use for zirconium is as a cladding for uranium dioxide fuel rods in water-cooled nuclear reactors. When alloyed with ~1.5% tin, its corrosion resistance and mechanical properties, which are stable under irradiation, coupled with its extremely low absorption of "thermal" neutrons, make it an ideal material for this purpose. Unfortunately, hafnium is a powerful absorber of thermal neutrons (600 times more so than Zr) and its removal, though difficult, is therefore necessary. Solvent extraction methods, taking advantage of the different solubilities of, for instance, the two nitrates in tri-*n*-butyl phosphate or the thiocyanates in hexone (methyl isobutyl ketone) have been developed and reduce the hafnium content to less than 100 ppm. The neutron absorbing ability of hafnium is not always disadvantageous, however, since it is the reason for hafnium's use for reactor control rods in nuclear submarines. Hafnium is produced in the same ways as zirconium but on a much smaller scale. For rutherfordium see p. 1281.

21.2.3 Properties of the elements

Table 21.1 summarizes a number of properties of these elements. The difficulties in attaining high purity has led to frequent revision of the estimates of several of these properties. Each element has a number of naturally occurring isotopes and, in the case of zirconium and hafnium, the least abundant of these is radioactive, though with a very long half-life ($^{96}_{40}Zr$, 2.76%, 3.6×10^{17} y; $^{174}_{72}Hf$, 0.162%, 2.0×10^{15} y).

The elements are all lustrous, silvery metals with high mps and they have typically metallic hcp structures which transform to bcc at high temperatures (882°, 870° and 1760°C for Ti, Zr and Hf). They are better conductors of

Table 21.1   Some properties of Group 4 elements

Property		Ti	Zr	Hf
Atomic number		22	40	72
Number of naturally occurring isotopes		5	5	6
Atomic weight		47.867(1)	91.224(2)	178.49(2)
Electronic configuration		[Ar]$3d^2 4s^2$	[Kr]$4d^2 5s^2$	[Xe]$4f^{14} 5d^2 6s^2$
Electronegativity		1.5	1.4	1.3
Metal radius/pm		147	160	159
Ionic radius (6-coordinate)/pm	M(IV)	60.5	72	71
	M(III)	67.0	—	—
	M(II)	86	—	—
MP/°C		1667	1857	2222 (or 2467)
BP/°C		3285	4200	4450
ΔH_{fus}/kJ mol^{-1}		18.8	19.2	(25)
ΔH_{vap}/kJ mol^{-1}		425 ($\pm$11)	567	571 ($\pm$25)
ΔH_f (monatomic gas)/kJ mol^{-1}		469 ($\pm$4)	612 ($\pm$11)	611 ($\pm$17)
Density (25°C)/g cm^{-1}		4.50	6.51	13.28
Electrical resistivity (20°C)/μohm cm		42.0	40.0	35.1

heat and electricity than their predecessors in Group 3 but are not to be regarded as "good" conductors in comparison with most other metals. The enthalpies of fusion, vaporization and atomization have also increased, indicating that the additional d electron has in each case contributed to stronger metal bonding. As was noticed in comparing groups 3 and 13, similarly for groups 4 and 14, the d electrons of the first group contribute more effectively to the metal–metal bonding in the bulk materials than do the p electrons of the heavier members of the latter group (Ge, Sn, Pb). Figure 21.1 illustrates the consequent discontinuous increases in mp, bp and enthalpy of atomization in passing from C

and Si to Ti, Zr and Hf, rather than to Ge, Sn and Pb.

The mechanical properties of these metals are markedly affected by traces of impurities such as O, N and C which have an embrittling effect on the metals, making them difficult to fabricate.

The effect of the lanthanide contraction on the metal and ionic radii of hafnium has already been mentioned. That these radii are virtually identical for zirconium and hafnium has the result that the ratio of their densities, like that of their atomic weights, is very close to Zr:Hf = 1:2.0. Indeed, the densities, the transition temperatures and the neutron-absorbing abilities are the only common properties of these two elements which differ

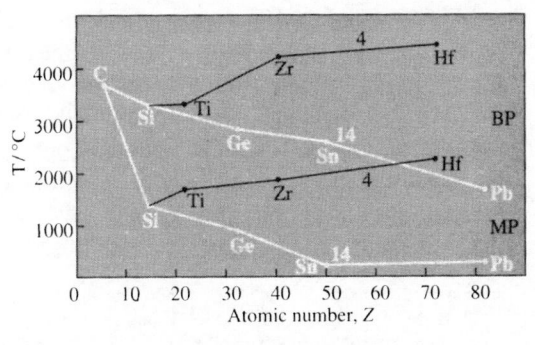

(a) Melting points and boiling points.

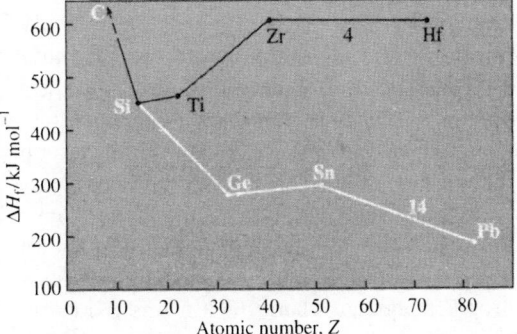

(b) Enthalpies of atomization..

Figure 21.1   Trends in some properties of elements of Groups 4 and 14.

significantly. This close similarity of second and third members is noticeable in all subsequent groups of the transition elements but is never more pronounced than here.

21.2.4 Chemical reactivity and trends

The elements of this group are relatively electropositive but less so than those of Group 3. If heated to high temperatures they react directly with most non-metals, particularly oxygen, hydrogen (reversibly), and, in the case of titanium, nitrogen (Ti actually burns in N_2). When finely divided the metals are pyrophoric and for this reason care is necessary when machining them to avoid the production of fine waste chips. In spite of this inherent reactivity, the most noticeable feature of these metals in the massive form at room temperature is their outstanding resistance to corrosion, which is due to the formation of a dense, adherent, self-healing oxide film. This is particularly striking in the case of zirconium. With the exception of hydrofluoric acid (which is the best solvent, probably because of the formation of soluble fluoro complexes) mineral acids have little effect unless hot. Even when hot, aqueous alkalis do not attack the metals. The presence of oxidizing agents such as nitric acid frequently reduces the reactivity of the metals by ensuring the retention of the protective oxide film.

The chemistry of hafnium has not received the same attention as that of titanium or zirconium, but it is clear that its behaviour follows that of zirconium very closely indeed with only minor differences in such properties as solubility and volatility being apparent in most of their compounds. The most important oxidation state in the chemistry of these elements is the group oxidation state of +4. This is too high to be ionic, but zirconium and hafnium, being larger, have oxides which are more basic than that of titanium and give rise to a more extensive and less-hydrolysed aqueous chemistry. In this oxidation state, particularly in the case of the dioxide and tetrachloride, titanium shows many similarities with tin which is of much the same size. A large

number of coordination compounds of the M^{IV} metals have been studied[4] and complexes such as $[MF_6]^{2-}$ and those with O- or N- donor ligands are especially stable.

The M^{IV} ions, though much smaller than their triply charged predecessors in Group 3, are, nonetheless, sufficiently large, bearing in mind their high charge, to attain a coordination number of 8 or more, which is certainly higher than is usually found for most transition elements. Eight is not a common coordination number for the first member, titanium, but is very well known for zirconium and hafnium, and the spherical symmetry of the d^0 configuration allows a variety of stereochemistries.

Lower oxidation states are rather sparsely represented for Zr and Hf. Even for Ti they are readily oxidized to +4 but they are undoubtedly well defined and, whatever arguments may be advanced against applying the description to Sc, there is no doubt that Ti is a "transition metal". In aqueous solution Ti^{III} can be prepared by reduction of Ti^{IV}, either with Zn and dilute acid or electrolytically, and it exists in dilute acids as the violet, octahedral $[Ti(H_2O)_6]^{3+}$ ion (p. 970). Although this is subject to a certain amount of hydrolysis, normal salts such as halides and sulfates can be separated. Zr^{III} and Hf^{III} are known mainly as the trihalides or their derivatives and have no aqueous chemistry since they reduce water. Table 21.2 (p. 960) gives the oxidation states and stereochemistries found in the complexes of Ti, Zr and Hf along with illustrative examples. (See also pp. 1281–2.)

M–C σ bonds are not strong and, as might be expected for metals with so few d electrons, little help is available from synergic π bonding: for instance, of the simple carbonyls only $Ti(CO)_6$ has been reported, and that only on the basis of spectroscopic evidence. However, as will be seen on p. 972, the discovery that titanium compounds can be used to

---

[4] C. H. MCAULIFFE and D. S. BARRATT, Chap. 31, pp. 323–61, and R. J. FAY, Chap. 32, pp. 363–451, in *Comprehensive Coordination Chemistry*, Vol. 3, Pergamon Press, Oxford, 1987.

Titanium Dioxide as a Pigment (See page 961)

Of all white pigments, TiO_2 is now the most widely used: the impressive growth in demand is shown in Table A.[5]

Table A Annual world production of TiO_2

Year	1925	1937	1975	1993
TiO_2/tonnes	5000	100 000	2 000 000	3 730 000

Its major use is in the manufacture of paint, and other important uses are as a surface coating on paper and as a filler in rubber and plastics.

The value of TiO_2 as a pigment is due to its exceptionally high refractive index in the visible region of the spectrum. Thus although large crystals are transparent, fine particles scatter light so strongly that they can be used to produce films of high opacity[†]. Table B gives the refractive indices of a number of relevant materials. In the manufacture of TiO_2 either the anatase or the rutile form is produced depending on modifications in the process employed. Because of its slightly higher refractive index, rutile has a somewhat greater opacity and most of the TiO_2 currently produced is of this form.

In addition to these optical properties, TiO_2 is chemically inert which is why it displaced "white lead", $2PbCO_3.Pb(OH)_2$: in industrial atmospheres this formed PbS (black) during the production of or weathering of the paint and was also a toxic hazard. Unfortunately the naturally occurring forms of TiO_2 are invariably coloured, sometimes intensely, by impurities, and expensive processing is required to produce pigments of acceptable quality. The two main processes in use are the *sulfate process* and the *chloride process* (Fig. A, p. 960), which account for approximately 56% and 44% respectively of total world production. The principal reactions of the chloride process are:

$$2TiO_2 + 3C + 4Cl_2 \xrightarrow{950°C} 2TiCl_4 + CO_2 + 2CO$$

and

$$TiCl_4 + O_2 \xrightarrow{1000-1400°} TiO_2 + 2Cl_2$$

It is most economical when high-grade ores are used, becoming less economical with poorer feed materials containing iron, because of the production of chloride wastes from which the chlorine cannot be recovered. By contrast the sulfate process cannot make use of rutile which does not dissolve in sulfuric acid, but is able to operate on lower grade ores. However, the capital cost of plant for the sulfate process is higher, and disposal of waste has proved environmentally more difficult, so that most new plant is designed for the chloride process.

The physical properties of the base pigments produced from both processes are further improved by slurrying in water and selectively precipitating on the finely divided particles a surface coating of SiO_2, Al_2O_3, or TiO_2 itself.

Table B Refractive indices of some pigments and other materials

Substance	Refractive index	Substance	Refractive index	Substance	Refractive index
NaCl	1.54	$BaSO_4$	1.64–1.65	Diamond	2.42
$CaCO_3$	1.53–1.68	ZnO	2.0	TiO_2(anatase)	2.49–2.55
SiO_2	1.54–1.56	ZnS	2.36–2.38	TiO_2(rutile)	2.61–2.90

Panel continues

---

[5] R. S. DARBY and J. LEIGHTON, in *The Modern Inorganic Chemicals Industry*, pp. 354–74, Special Publication No. 31, (1977), The Chemical Society, London. *Metals and Minerals Ann. Rev.*, 75–6 (1992).

[†] The smaller the particle size, the lower the wavelength at which maximum scattering occurs. Thus, ultrafine (20–50 nm) TiO_2 is used as a UV filter in skin care and cosmetic products. (Sec V. P. S. JUDIN, *Chem. Br.* **29**, 503–5 (1993).)

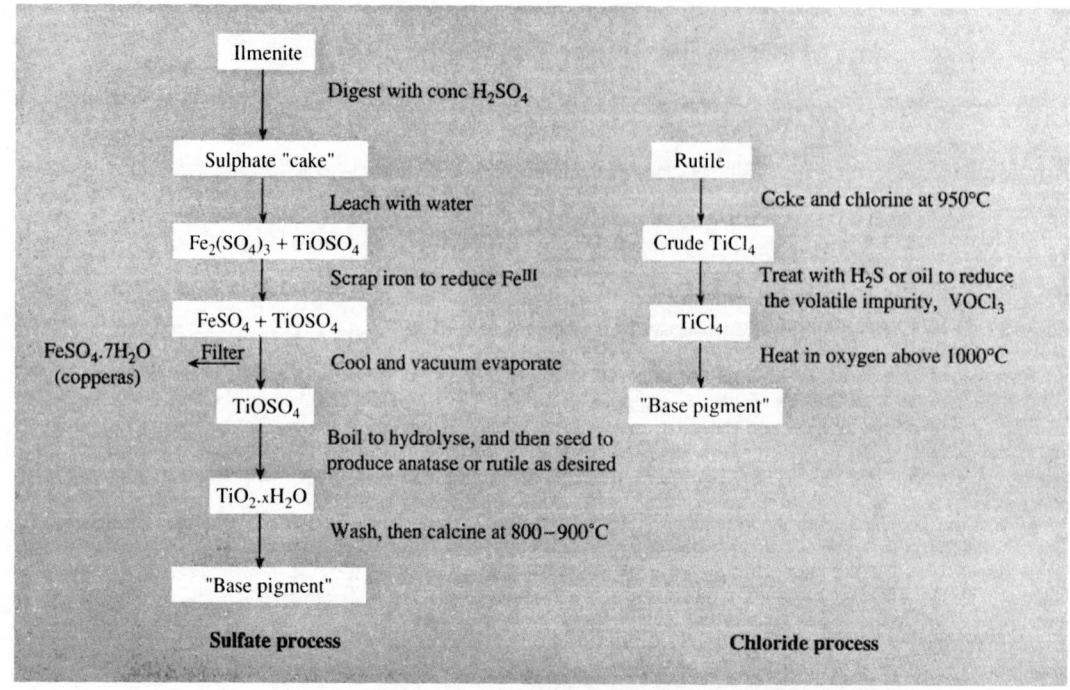

Figure A Flow diagrams for the manufacture of TiO_2 pigments.

Table 21.2 Oxidation states and stereochemistries of titanium, zirconium and hafnium

Oxidation state	Coordination number	Stereochemistry	Ti	Zr/Hf
−1 (d^5)	6	Octahedral	$[Ti(bipy)_3]^-$	$[Zr(bipy)_3]^-$
0 (d^4)	6	Octahedral	$[Ti(bipy)_3]$	$[Zr(bipy)_3]$
2 (d^2)	6	Octahedral	$TiCl_2$	Layer structures and clusters
	12	—	$[Ti(\eta^5\text{-}C_5H_5)_2(CO)_2]$	$[M(\eta^5\text{-}C_5H_5)_2(CO)_2]$
3 (d^1)	3	Planar	$[Ti\{N(SiMe_3)_2\}_3]$	
	5	Trigonal bipyramidal	$[TiBr_3(NMe_3)_2]$	
	6	Octahedral	$[Ti(urea)_6]^{3+}$	ZrX_3 (Cl, Br, I), HfI_3
4 (d^0)	4	Tetrahedral	$TiCl_4$	$ZrCl_4(g)$ (solid is octahedral)
	5	Trigonal bipyramidal	$[TiOCl_2(NMe_3)_2]$	—
		Square pyramidal	$[TiOCl_4]^{2-}$	--
	6	Octahedral	$[TiF_6]^{2-}$	$[ZrF_6]^{2-}$, $ZrCl_4(s)$
	7	Pentagonal bipyramidal	$[TiCl(S_2CNMe_2)_3]$	$[NH_4]^+_3[ZrF_7]^{3-}$
		Capped trigonal prismatic	$[TiF_5(O_2)]^{3-}$	$[Zr_2F_{13}]^{5-}$
	8	Dodecahedral	$[Ti(\eta^2\text{-}NO_3)_4]$	$[Zr(C_2O_4)_4]^{4-}$
		Square antiprismatic	—	$[Zr(acac)_4]$
	11	—	$[Ti(\eta^5\text{-}C_5H_5)(S_2CNMe_2)_3]$	$[Zr(\eta^5\text{-}C_5H_5)(S_2CNMe_2)_3]$
	12	—	—	$[M(\eta^3\text{-}BH_4)_4]$

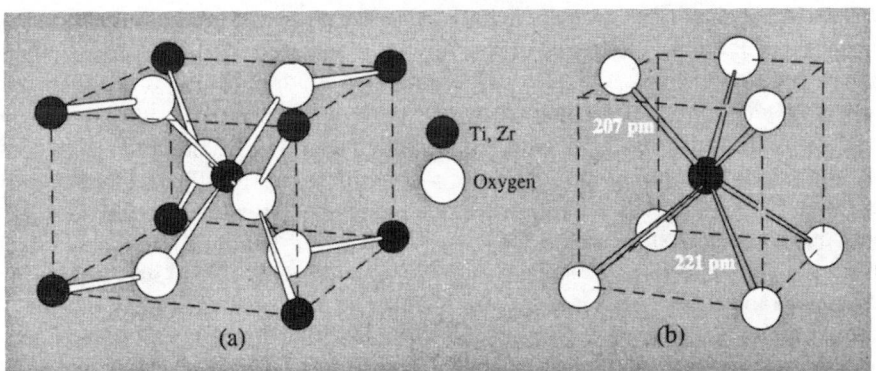

Figure 21.2   (a) The tetragonal unit cell of rutile, TiO_2. (b) The coordination of Zr^{IV} in baddeleyite ZrO_2; the 3
O atoms in the upper plane are each coordinated by 3 Zr atoms in a plane, whereas the 4 lower O
atoms are each tetrahedrally coordinated by 4 Zr atoms.

catalyse the polymerization of alkenes (olefins) turned organo-titanium chemistry into a topic of major commercial importance and has produced an extensive chemistry. The organometallic chemistry of Zr and Hf, though less developed than that of Ti, has grown rapidly in recent years.

21.3 Compounds of Titanium, Zirconium and Hafnium

The binary hydrides (p. 64), borides (p. 145), carbides (p. 299) and nitrides (p. 417) are hard, refractory, nonstoichiometric materials with metallic conductivities. They have already been discussed in relation to comparable compounds of other metals in earlier chapters.

21.3.1 Oxides and sulfides

The main oxides are the dioxides. In fact, TiO_2 is by far the most important compound formed by the elements of this group, its importance arising predominantly from its use as a white pigment (see Panel, p. 959). It exists at room temperature in three forms — rutile, anatase and brookite, each of which occurs naturally. Each contains 6-coordinate titanium but rutile is the most common form, both in nature and as produced commercially, and the others transform into it on heating. The rutile

structure is based on a slightly distorted hcp of oxygen atoms with half the octahedral interstices being occupied by titanium atoms. The octahedral coordination of the titanium atoms and trigonal planar coordination of the oxygen can be seen in Fig. 21.2. This is a structure commonly adopted by ionic dioxides and difluorides where the relative sizes of the ions are such as to favour 6-coordination (i.e. when the radius ratio of cation:anion lies in the range 0.73 to 0.41).[6] Anatase and brookite are both based on cubic rather than hexagonal close packing of oxygen atoms, but again the titanium atoms occupy half the octahedral interstices. TiO_2 melts at $1892 \pm 30°C$ when heated in an atmosphere of O_2; when heated in air the compound tends to lose oxygen and then melts at $1843 \pm 15°C$ ($TiO_{1.985}$).

Though it is unreactive, rutile can be reduced with difficulty to give numerous nonstoichiometric oxide phases, the more important of which are the Magnéli-type phases Ti_nO_{2n-1} ($4 \leq n \leq 9$), the lower oxides Ti_3O_5 and Ti_2O_3, and the broad, nonstoichiometric phase TiO_x ($0.70 \leq x \leq 1.30$). The Magnéli phases Ti_nO_{2n-1} are built up of slabs of rutile-type structure with a width of $nTiO_6$ octahedra and with adjacent slabs mutually related by a crystallographic shear which conserves oxygen atoms by an increased sharing

---
[6] A. F. Wells, *Structural Inorganic Chemistry*, 5th edn., Chap. 7, pp. 312–19, Oxford University Press, Oxford, 1984.

between adjacent octahedra. Ti_4O_7 is metallic at room temperature but the other members of the series tend to be semiconductors.

Of the lower oxides Ti_3O_5 is a blue-black material prepared by the reduction TiO_2 with H_2 at 900°C; it shows a transition from semiconductor to metal at 175°C. Ti_2O_3 is a dark-violet material with the corundum structure (p. 243); it is prepared by reacting TiO_2 and Ti metal at 1600°C and is generally inert, being resistant to most reagents except oxidizing acids. It has a narrow composition range ($x = 1.49–1.51$ in TiO_x) and undergoes a semiconductor-to-metal transition above $\sim$200°C.

TiO, a bronze coloured, readily oxidized material, is again prepared by the reaction of TiO_2 and Ti metal. It has a defect rock-salt structure which tolerates a high proportion of vacancies (Schottky defects) in both Ti and O sites and so is highly nonstoichiometric[7] with a composition range at 1700°C of $TiO_{0.75}$ to $TiO_{1.25}$. This range diminishes somewhat at lower temperatures and, at equilibrium below about 900°C, various ordered phases separate with smaller ranges of composition-variation, e.g. $TiO_{0.9}–TiO_{1.1}$ and $TiO_{1.25}$ (i.e. Ti_4O_5). In this latter compound the tetragonal unit cell can be thought of as being related to the NaCl-type structure: there are 10 Ti sites and 10 oxygen sites but 2 of the Ti sites are vacant in a regular or ordered way to generate the structure of Ti_4O_5. A high-temperature ($>$3000°C) form of TiO has been prepared with the unusual feature of Ti^{2+} in a trigonal prismatic array of oxygen atoms.[7a]

Finally, oxygen is soluble in metallic titanium up to a composition of $TiO_{0.5}$ with the oxygen atoms occupying octahedral sites in the hcp metal lattice: distinct phases that have been crystallographically characterized are Ti_6O, Ti_3O and Ti_2O. It seems likely that in all these reduced oxide phases there is extensive metal–metal bonding.

In the case of zirconium and hafnium there is little evidence of stable phases other than MO_2, and at room temperature ZrO_2 (baddeleyite) and the isomorphous HfO_2 have a structure in which the metal is 7-coordinate (Fig. 21.2(b)). ZrO_2 has at least two more high-temperature modifications (tetragonal above 1100°C and cubic, fluorite-type, above 2300°C) but it is notable that, presumably because of the greater size of Zr compared to Ti, neither of them has the 6-coordinate rutile structure. ZrO_2 is unreactive, has a low coefficient of thermal expansion, and a very high melting point (2710 $\pm$ 25°C) and is therefore a useful refractory material, being used in the manufacture of crucibles and furnace cores. However, the phase change at 1100° severely restricts the use of pure ZrO_2 as a refractory because repeated thermal cycling through this temperature causes cracking and disintegration — the problem is avoided by using solid solutions of CaO or MgO in the ZrO_2 since these retain the cubic fluorite structure throughout the temperature range. ZrO_2 has also recently been produced in fibrous form suitable for weaving into fabrics, as already mentioned for Al_2O_3 (p. 244), and its chemical inertness and refractivity — coupled with an apparent lack of toxicity — can be expected to lead to increasing applications as an insulator and for the filtration of corrosive liquids. Production of ZrO_2 concentrates in 1991 was about 870 000 t, Australia being the most important source.

The sulfides have been less thoroughly examined than the oxides but it is clear that a number of stable phases can be produced and nonstoichiometry is again prevalent (p. 679). The most important are the disulfides, which are semiconductors with metallic lustre. TiS_2 and ZrS_2 have the CdI_2 structure (p. 1211) in which the cations occupy the octahedral sites between alternate layers of hcp anions.

21.3.2 Mixed (or complex) oxides

Although the dioxides, MO_2, are notable for their inertness, particularly if they have been heated, fusion or firing at high temperatures (sometimes up to 2500°C) with the stoichiometric

[7] D. J. M. BEVAN, Chap. 49, pp. 453–540 in *Comprehensive Inorganic Chemistry*, Vol. 3, Pergamon Press, Oxford, 1973.

[7a] S. MÖHR and H. MÜLLER-BUSCHBAUM, *Z. anorg. allg. Chem.* **620**, 1175–8 (1994).

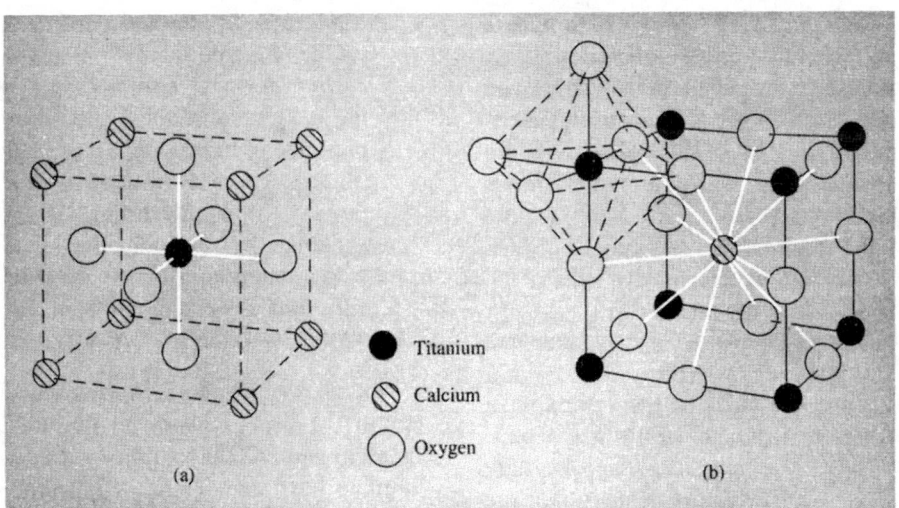

● Titanium

◍ Calcium

○ Oxygen

(a)   (b)

Figure 21.3   Two representations of the structure of perovskite, $CaTiO_3$, showing (a) the octahedral coordination of Ti, and (b) the twelve-fold coordination of Ca by oxygen. Note the relation of (b) to the cubic structure of ReO_3 (p. 1047).

amounts of appropriate oxides produces a number of "titanates", "zirconates", and "hafnates". The titanates are of two main types: the orthotitanates $M_2^{II}TiO_4$ and the metatitanates $M^{II}TiO_3$. The names are misleading since the compounds almost never contain the discrete ions $[TiO_4]^{4-}$ and $[TiO_3]^{2-}$ analogous to phosphates or sulfites. Rather, the structures comprise three-dimensional networks of ions which are of particular interest and importance because two of the metatitanates are the archetypes of common mixed metal oxide structures.

When M^{II} is approximately the same size as Ti^{IV} (i.e. M = Mg, Mn, Fe, Co, Ni) the structure is that of *ilmenite*, $FeTiO_3$, which consists of hcp oxygens with one-third of the octahedral interstices occupied by M^{II} and another third by Ti^{IV} This is essentially the same structure as corundum (Al_2O_3, p. 243) except that in that case there is only one type of cation which occupies two-thirds of the octahedral sites.

If, however, M^{II} is significantly larger than Ti^{IV} (e.g. M = Ca, Sr, Ba), then the preferred structure is that of *perovskite*,[8] $CaTiO_3$. This

can be envisaged as a ccp array of calcium and oxygen atoms, with the former regularly disposed, and the titanium atoms then occupying octahedral sites formed by oxygen atoms only and so being as remote as possible from the calciums (Fig. 21.3). The Ba^{II} ion is so large and expands the perovskite lattice to such an extent that the titanium is too small to fill the octahedral interstice which accommodates it. This leads to ferroelectric and piezoelectric behaviour as discussed in Chapter 3 (p. 57). In consequence, $BaTiO_3$ has found important applications in the production of compact capacitors (because of its high permittivity) and as a ceramic transducer in devices such as microphones and gramophone pick-ups. For such purposes it compares favourably with Rochelle salt (sodium potassium tartrate, $NaKC_4H_4O_6$) in terms of thermal stability, and with quartz in terms of the strength of the effect.

$M_2^{II}TiO_4$ (M = Mg, Zn, Mn, Fe, Co) have the *spinel* structure (MgAl_2O_4, p. 248) which is the third important structure type adopted by many mixed metal oxides; in this the cations occupy both octahedral and tetrahedral sites in a ccp array of oxide ions. Ba_2TiO_4, although having the same stoichiometry, is unique amongst titanates in that

[8] A. RELLER and T. WILLIAMS, *Chem. Br.*, **25**, 1227–30 (1989).

it contains discrete $[TiO_4]^{4-}$ ions which have a somewhat distorted tetrahedral structure.

High-temperature reduction of Na_2TiO_3 with hydrogen produces nonstoichiometric materials, Na_xTiO_2 ($x = 0.20$–0.25), called titanium "bronzes" by analogy with the better-known tungsten bronzes (p. 1016). They have a blue-black, metallic appearance with high electrical conductivity and are chemically inert (even hydrofluoric acid does not attack them).

"Zirconates" and "hafnates" can be prepared by firing appropriate mixtures of oxides, carbonates or nitrates. None of them are known to contain discrete $[MO_4]^{4-}$ or $[MO_3]^{2-}$ ions. Compounds $M^{II}ZrO_3$ usually have the perovskite structure whereas $M_2^{II}ZrO_4$ frequently adopt the spinel structure.

21.3.3 Halides

The most important of these are the tetrahalides, all 12 of which are known. The titanium compounds (Table 21.3) show an interesting gradation in colour, the charge-transfer band moving steadily to lower energies (i.e. absorbing increasingly in the visible region of the spectrum) as the anion becomes more easily oxidized (F^- to I^-) by the small, highly polarizing titanium cation. The larger Zr^{IV} and Hf^{IV}, however, do not have the same polarizing effect and their tetrahalides are all white solids; the fluorides are involatile but the other tetrahalides sublime readily at temperatures in the range 320–430°C.

Table 21.3 Some physical properties of titanium tetrahalides

Compound	Colour	MP/°C	BP/°C
TiF_4	White	284	—
$TiCl_4$	Colourless	−24	136.5
$TiBr_4$	Orange	38	233.5
TiI_4	Dark brown	155	377

Though numerous preparative methods are possible besides the direct action of the halogen on the metal, convenient general procedures are as follows:

tetrafluorides by the action of anhydrous HF on the tetrachloride;

tetrachlorides and tetrabromides by passing the halogen over the heated dioxide in the presence of a reducing agent such as carbon (this reaction is central to the chloride process for manufacturing TiO_2, p. 959);

tetraiodides by the iodination of the dioxide with aluminium triiodide at a temperature of 130–400° depending on the metal ($3MO_2 + 4AlI_3 \longrightarrow 3MI_4 + 2Al_2O_3$).

Not all the structures have been determined but in the vapour phase all the tetrahalides of titanium and probably all those of zirconium and hafnium have monomeric, tetrahedral structures. In the solid, TiF_4 is a polymer consisting of corner-sharing $\{TiF_6\}$ octahedra,[8a] but the other tetrahalides of titanium retain the tetrahedral configuration around the metal even in the solids. The larger zirconium exhibits higher coordination numbers. Thus solid MF_4 contain 8-coordinate (square antiprismatic) metal atoms while the tetrachlorides and bromides are polymers consisting of zigzag chains of edge-sharing $\{MX_6\}^{2-}$ octahedra.

All the tetrahalides, but especially the chlorides and bromides, behave as Lewis acids dissolving in polar solvents to give rise to series of addition compounds; they also form complex anions with halides. They are all hygroscopic and hydrolysis follows the same pattern as complex formation, with the chlorides and bromides being more vulnerable than the fluorides and iodides. $TiCl_4$ fumes in and is completely hydrolysed by moist air ($TiCl_4 + 2H_2O \longrightarrow TiO_2 + 4HCl$); a variety of intermediate hydrolysis products, such as the oxochlorides $MOCl_2$, can be formed with aqueous HCl of varying concentration. Even in conc HCl, $ZrCl_4$ gives $ZrOCl_2.8H_2O$. This contains the tetrameric cation $[Zr_4(OH)_8(H_2O)_{16}]^{8+}$ in which the 4 zirconium atoms are connected in a ring by 4 pairs of OH^- bridges and each zirconium atom is dodecahedrally coordinated to 8 oxygen atoms. The fluorides are less susceptible

---

[8a] H. BIALOWONS, M. MÜLLER and B. G. MÜLLER, Z. anorg. allg. Chem. **621**, 1227–31 (1995).

to hydrolysis and, though aqueous HF produces the oxofluorides, MOF_2, the hydrates $TiF_4.2H_2O$, $MF_4.H_2O$, and $MF_4.3H_2O$ (M = Zr, Hf) can be produced. Rather curiously the trihydrates of ZrF_4 and HfF_4 actually have different structures, though both contain 8-coordinated metal atoms. The zirconium compound is essentially dimeric $[(H_2O)_3F_3Zr(\mu\text{-}F)_2ZrF_3(H_2O)_3]$ with dodecahedral Zr, whereas the hafnium compound consists of infinite chains of octahedral $[>HfF_2(H_2O)_2(\mu\text{-}F)_2]$ with the third water molecule held in the lattice.

Besides being important as an intermediate in one of the processes for making TiO_2, $TiCl_4$ is also used to produce Ziegler–Natta catalysts (p. 972) for the polymerization of ethylene (ethene) and is the starting point for the production of most of the commercially important organic titanium compounds (in most cases these are actually titanium alkoxides rather than true organometallic compounds). The iodides MI_4 are all utilized in the van Arkel–de Boer process for producing pure metals (p. 956).

All the trihalides except HfF_3 have been prepared,[†] the most general method being the high-temperature reduction of the tetrahalide with the metal, though a variety of other methods have been used especially for the titanium compounds. Since the tetrahalides are quite stable to reduction, lower halides are not easily prepared in a pure state, incomplete reactions and the presence of excess metal being common. Apart from TiF_3, which, as expected for a d^1 ion, has a magnetic moment of 1.85 BM at room temperature, and only shows signs of magnetic interactions below about 60 K,[9] all compounds have low magnetic moments, indicative of appreciable M–M bonding. They are coloured, halogen-bridged polymers in which one third of the octahedral interstices of an hcp lattice of halide ions is occupied by metal atoms. In the cases of α-$TiCl_3$ and α-$TiBr_3$ this takes the form of the "BiI_3" structure which is comprised of layers of edge-sharing

octahedra; the remainder adopt the "β-$TiCl_3$" structure, comprised of chains of face-sharing octahedra.[10] In most, if not all, of the latter cases M–M bonds occur between pairs of metal atoms as a result of distortions leading, in the case of ZrI_3 for instance,[11] to alternate Zr–Zr distances of 317.2 and 350.7 pm. TiF_3 also differs in being stable in air unless heated whereas the others show reducing properties; indeed, ZrX_3 and HfX_3 reduce water and so have no aqueous chemistry, but aqueous solutions of TiX_3 are stable if kept under an inert atmosphere. Hexahydrates $TiX_3.6H_2O$ are well known and the chloride is notable in that, like its chromium(III) analogue, it exhibits hydrate isomerism, existing as violet $[Ti(H_2O)_6]^{3+}Cl_3^-$ and green $[TiCl_2(H_2O)_4]^+$- $Cl^-.2H_2O$.

TiX_2 (X = Cl, Br, I) have been prepared by reduction of TiX_4 with Ti metal and are black solids with the CdI_2 structure (p. 1211) but their low magnetic moments again indicate extensive M–M bonding. They are very strongly reducing and decompose water. Ti_7X_{16} (X = Cl, Br) have also been prepared. They are black crystalline solids sensitive to hydrolysis and oxidation and can be regarded as being composed of octahedrally coordinated Ti^{IV} and Ti^{II} in the ratio of 1:6 (i.e. $TiCl_4.6TiCl_2$) with the bivalent metal ions arranged in triangular groups involving Ti–Ti bonds. Incorporation of KCl in the chloride reaction mix yields[12] the structurally related KTi_4Cl_{11} but the structural diversity of reduced Ti halides does not yet match that of Zr.

Products of the high temperature (typically 750–850°C) reduction of ZrX_4 (X = Cl, Br, I) with Zr metal in various proportions, have provided intriguing structural problems. Black phases initially thought to be ZrX_2 and made up of Zr_6X_{12} clusters, isostructural with the well-known $[M_6X_{12}]^{n+}$ clusters of Nb and Ta, (p. 992), were subsequently shown to contain

[†] ZrF_3 may also be doubted (see p. 150 of D. SMITH, *Inorganic Substances*, Cambridge Univ. Press, Cambridge, 1990).

[9] R. HOPPE and ST. BECKER, *Z. anorg. allg. Chem.* **568**, 126–35 (1989).

[10] See pp. 167 and 196 of U. MÜLLER, *Inorganic Structural Chemistry*, 2nd edn., Wiley, New York, (1992).

[11] A. LACHGAR, D.S. DUDIS and J.D. CORBETT, *Inorg. Chem.* **29**, 2242–6 (1990).

[12] J. ZHANG, R.Y. QI and J.D. CORBETT, *Inorg. Chem.* **30**, 4794–8 (1991).

impurity atoms situated inside the Zr_6 octahedra which they actually stabilize. The materials are correctly formulated as $Zr_6X_{12}Z$ and, if alkali metal halides are incorporated in the reaction mix a whole series of phases based on the $[Zr_6X_{12}Z]$ cluster unit is obtained, of which the chlorides and iodides have so far been most thoroughly studied. Z is most commonly H, Be, B, C or N (dark orange to red products), but may also be Cr, Mn, Fe or Co (green, blue or purple products). In all cases the same basic $Zr_6X_{12}Z$ cluster unit is involved, though several structure types result from the differing ways in which these are connected.[13] In most cases it appears that stability is attained when 14 electrons are available for cluster bonding (i.e. total number of valence electrons from Zr_6 and Z, adjusted for overall charge, less 12 required by $X^-{}_{12}$) where Z is a main-group element, but 18 electrons where Z is a transition element. It has been suggested that the presence of Z is *essential* for the stabilisation of these clusters, but $Zr_6Cl_{12}(PMe_2Ph)_6$ appears to consist entirely of empty Zr_6Cl_{12} clusters with a phosphine attached externally to each Zr atom.[14]

By contrast, ZrCl and ZrBr, also prepared by the high temperature reduction of ZrX_4 with the metal, appear to be genuine binary halides. They are comprised of hcp double layers of metal atoms surrounded by layers of halide ions, leading to metallic conduction in the plane of the layers, and they are thermally more stable than the less reduced phases. ZrI has not been obtained, possibly because of the large size of the iodide ion, and, less surprisingly, attempts to prepare reduced fluorides have been unsuccessful.

21.3.4 Compounds with oxoanions

Because of the high ratio of ionic charge to radius, normal salts of Ti^{IV} cannot be prepared from aqueous solutions, which only yield basic, hydrolysed species. Even with Zr^{IV} and Hf^{IV}, normal salts such as $Zr(NO_3)_4.5H_2O$ and $Zr(SO_4)_2.4H_2O$ can only be isolated if the solution is sufficiently acidic, whilst basic salts and anionic complexes are readily obtained. Several oxometal(IV) compounds (i.e. "titanyl", "zirconyl") have been isolated but do not contain discrete MO^{2+} ions, being polymeric in the solid state. Thus, $TiOSO_4.H_2O$ contains chains of $-Ti-O-Ti-O-$ with each Ti being approximately octahedrally coordinated to 2 bridging oxygen atoms, 1 water molecule and an oxygen atom from each of 3 sulfates; $ZrO(NO_3)_2$ is also an oxygen-bridged chain, though hydroxy bridging, as in $ZrOCl_2.8H_2O$ mentioned above, is more common. By contrast, ion-exchange studies on aqueous solutions of Ti^{IV} in $2M$ $HClO_4$ are consistent with the presence of monomeric doubly-charged cationic species rather than polymers, though it is not clear whether the predominent species is $[TiO]^{2+}$ or $[Ti(OH)_2]^{2+}$.

The anhydrous nitrates can be prepared by the action of N_2O_5 on MCl_4. $Ti(NO_3)_4$ is a white sublimable and highly reactive compound (mp 58°C) in which the bidentate nitrate ions are disposed tetrahedrally around the titanium which thereby attains a coordination number of 8 (Fig. 21.4). Infrared evidence suggests that $Zr(NO_3)_4$ is isostructural but hafnium nitrate

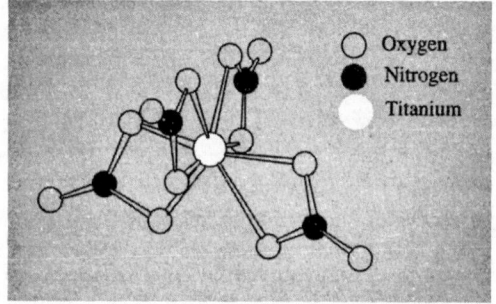

Figure 21.4 The molecular structure of $Ti(NO_3)_4$. Eight O atoms form a dodecahedron around the Ti and the 4 N atoms form a flattened tetrahedron.

[13] R. P. ZIEBARTH and J. D. CORBETT, *Acc. Chem. Res.* **22**, 256–62 (1989).

[14] F. A. COTTON, P. A. KIBALA and W. J. ROTH, *J. Am. Chem. Soc.* **110** 298–300 (1988).

sublimes under vacuum at 100°C as the adduct $Hf(NO_3)_4.N_2O_5$.

Zirconium phosphates (α-form: $Zr(HPO_4)_2$-H_2O, β-form: $Zr(HPO_4)_2.2H_2O$) have layered structures with cation-exchange properties due to the replaceable, acidic hydrogens. Intercalation of organic molecules causes swelling of the structures and increases their versatility as ion-exchangers.

In oxidation states lower than +4, only Ti^{III} forms a sulfate and this gives rise to the alums, $MTi(SO_4)_2.12H_2O$ (M = Rb, Cs), containing the octahedral hexaaquotitanium(III) ion.

21.3.5 Complexes [4, 15]

Oxidation state IV (d⁰)

A very large number of these complexes, particularly of titanium, have been prepared and, as is to be expected for the d^0 configuration, they are invariably diamagnetic. Hydrolysis, resulting in polymeric species with –OH– or –O– bridges, is common especially with titanium and is still a preparative problem with zirconium and hafnium, though acidic solutions if sufficiently dilute ($<10^{-4}$ M) probably contain the Zr^{4+}(aq) ion[16]. A coordination number of 6 is the most usual for Ti^{IV} but 7- and even 8-coordination is possible. However, these high coordination numbers are much more characteristic of Zr^{IV} and Hf^{IV}, whose complexes are more labile (consistent with greater electrostatic character in the bonding). Furthermore, because changes in geometry entail smaller changes in energy for higher coordination numbers, these include a greater variety of stereochemistries.

The neutral and anionic adducts of the halides constitute a large proportion of the complexes of Ti^{IV}, and the alkoxides (also prepared from $TiCl_4$) are of commercial importance (p. 968).

[15] N. Serpone, M. A. Jamieson and E. Pelizzeti, *Coord. Chem. Revs.* **90**, 243–315 (1988); R. Fay *ibid.* **80**, 131–56 (1987).

[16] D. H. Devia and A. G. Sykes, *Inorg. Chem.* **20**, 910–13 (1981).

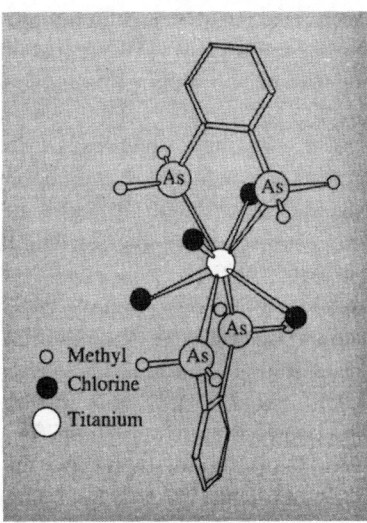

Figure 21.5 Molecular structure of $[TiCl_4(diars)_2]$. The dodecahedral coordination is produced by two interpenetrating tetrahedra (slightly distorted) of chlorine and arsenic atoms.

TiF_4 forms 6-coordinate adducts mainly with *O*- and *N*-donor ligands, and complexes of the type TiF_4L have all the appearances of fluorine-bridged polymers. $TiCl_4$ and $TiBr_4$ are especially prolific and are clearly "softer" acceptors than the fluoride. They form mainly yellow to red adducts of the types $[MX_4L_2]$ and $[MX_4(L-L)]$ with ligands such as ethers, ketones, $OPCl_3$, amines, imines, nitriles, thiols and thioethers. Zirconium and hafnium analogues occur but are often less well characterized because of insolubility and also difficulty in preparing samples suitable for X-ray analysis. Phosphorus- and *As*-donor ligands also complex readily with the chlorides of all three metals, particularly as chelates, and are of interest in that they produce coordination numbers which, for titanium, are unusually high. Thus *o*-phenylenebis(dimethyldiarsine), diars, and its phosphorus analogue form not only the 6-coordinate $[MX_4(L-L)]$ but also the 8-coordinate $[MX_4(L-L)_2]$. $[TiCl_4(diars)_2]$ (Fig. 21.5) was in fact one of the first examples of an 8-coordinate complex of a first-row transition element. The terdentate arsine, $MeC(CH_2AsMe_2)_3$, forms a 1:1

adduct with $TiCl_4$ which is monomeric and so presumably 7-coordinate. $[TiCl_4L]$ adducts are usually 6-coordinate dimers with double chloride bridges.

Octahedral, anionic complexes, $[MX_6]^{2-}$, show a marked increase in susceptibility to hydrolysis and consequent difficulty in preparation, in passing from the stable fluorides to the heavier halides, with the result that the hexaiodo complexes cannot be isolated. The fluorozirconates and fluorohafnates display considerable variety, complexes of the types $[MF_7]^{3-}$, $[M_2F_{14}]^{6-}$, and $[MF_8]^{4-}$ having been prepared, often by fusion of the appropriate fluorides. In Na_3ZrF_7 the anion has the 7-coordinate pentagonal bipyramidal structure; in $Li_6[BeF_4][ZrF_8]$ the zirconium anion is 8-coordinate, dodecahedral (distorted); in $Cu_6[ZrF_8].12H_2O$ it is 8-coordinate, square antiprismatic, and in $Cu_3[Zr_2F_{14}].18H_2O$ dimerization by the edge-sharing of two square antiprisms maintains 8-coordination. Stoichiometry does not, however, define coordination type, and this is very well illustrated by the ostensibly $[MF_6]^{2-}$ complexes which may contain 6-, 7-, or 8-coordinate Zr^{IV} or Hf^{IV} depending on the counter anion. In Rb_2MF_6, M is indeed octahedrally coordinated, but in $(NH_4)_2MF_6$ and K_2MF_6 polymerization occurs to give respectively 7- and 8-coordinate species.

Alkoxides of all 3 metals are well characterized but it is those of titanium which are of particular importance. The solvolysis of $TiCl_4$ with an alcohol yields a dialkoxide:

$$TiCl_4 + 2ROH \longrightarrow TiCl_2(OR)_2 + 2HCl$$

If dry ammonia is added to remove the HCl, then the tetraalkoxides can be produced:

$$TiCl_4 + 4ROH + 4NH_3 \longrightarrow Ti(OR)_4 + 4NH_4Cl$$

These alkoxides are liquids or sublimable solids and, unless the steric effects of the alkyl chain prevent it, apparently attain octahedral coordination of the titanium by polymerization (Fig. 21.6). The lower alkoxides are especially sensitive to moisture, hydrolysing to the dioxide. Application of these "organic titanates" (as they are frequently described) can therefore give a

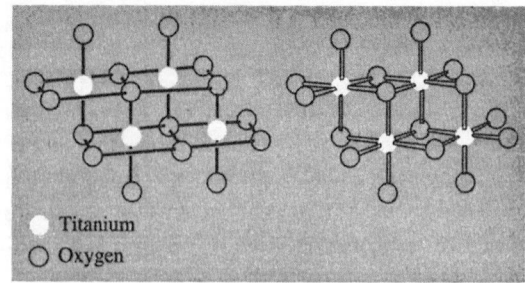

Figure 21.6 Two representations of the tetrameric structure of $[Ti(OEt)_4]_4$.

thin, transparent, and adherent coating of TiO_2 to a variety of materials merely by exposure to the atmosphere. In this way they are used to waterproof fabrics and also in heat-resistant paints. They are also used on glass and enamels which, after firing, retain a coating of TiO_2 which confers a resistance to scratching and often enhances the appearance. However, the most important commercial application is in the production of "thixotropic" paints which do not "drip" or "run". For this the $Ti(OR)_4$ is chelated with ligands such as β-diketonates to give products of the type $[Ti(OR)_2(L-L)_2]$ which are water soluble and more resistant to hydrolysis. In concentrations of 1% or less, they form gels with the cellulose ether colloids used to thicken latex paints and so produce the desired characteristics. Titanium tartrate complexes, probably dimeric species such as $[Ti_2(tartrate)_2(OR)_4]$, are also useful catalysts in asymmetric epoxidations of allylic alcohols.[17]

One of the most sensitive methods for estimating titanium (or, conversely, for estimating H_2O_2) is to measure the intensity of the orange colour produced when H_2O_2 is added to acidic solutions of titanium(IV). The colour is due[18] to the peroxo complex, $[Ti(O_2)(OH)(H_2O)_x]^+$, though alkaline solutions are needed before crystalline solids such as $M_3^I[Ti(O_2)F_5]$ or $M_2^I[Ti(O_2)(SO_4)_2]$

[17] R. A. JOHNSON and K. B. SHARPLESS, Chap. 3.2, pp. 389–436 in *Comprehensive Organic Synthesis*, Vol. 7, Pergamon Press, Oxford, 1991.

[18] E. M. NOUR and S. MORSY, *Inorg. Chim. Acta* **117**, 45–8 (1986).

can be isolated. The peroxo ligand is apparently bidentate, the 2 oxygen atoms being equidistant from the metal (see also p. 615).

Not surprisingly, in view of their greater size, zirconium and hafnium show a greater preference than titanium for O-donor ligands as well as for high coordination numbers, and this is shown by the greater variety of β-diketonates, carboxylates and sulfato complexes which they form. Bis-β-diketonates such as [$MCl_2(acac)_2$] of all 3 metals are made by the reaction of MCl_4 and the β-diketone in inert solvents such as benzene. They are octahedral with *cis*-chlorides. In addition, Zr and Hf form the monomeric, 7-coordinate [$MCl(acac)_3$] complexes which have a distorted pentagonal bipyramidal stereochemistry. Also, providing alkali is present to remove the labile proton, Zr and Hf will yield the tetrakis complexes in aqueous solution:

$$MOCl_2 \xrightarrow[+Na_2CO_3]{4acacH} [M(acac)_4]$$

These too are monomeric, and the 8-coordinate structure has a square-antiprismatic arrangement of oxygen atoms around M.

Monocarboxylates of the types [$Zr(carbox)_4$], [$ZrO(carbox)_3(H_2O)_x$] and [$ZrO(OH)(carbox)(H_2O)_x$] are well known, as are the corresponding dicarboxylates. It is interesting that the tetrakis(oxalates), $Na_4[M(C_2O_4)_4].3H_2O$, adopt the dodecahedral stereochemistry in contrast to the square-antiprismatic stereochemistry of [$M(acac)_4$], possibly because the smaller "bite" of the oxalate ion compared to that of acac favours the dodecahedral form (p. 916). It may also be noted that, although optical and geometrical isomerism is conceivable for these stereochemistries, intramolecular rearrangement of the ligands is too rapid for sets of isomers of the above compounds (or, indeed, of any compound of Zr^{IV} or Hf^{IV}) to have been isolated.

Intramolecular rearrangement evidently also occurs in the borohydride, [$Zr(BH_4)_4$] (p. 168). X-ray analysis of a single crystal at $-160°C$ (at which temperature thermal vibrations are sufficiently reduced to allow the positions of the hydrogen atoms to be determined) showed

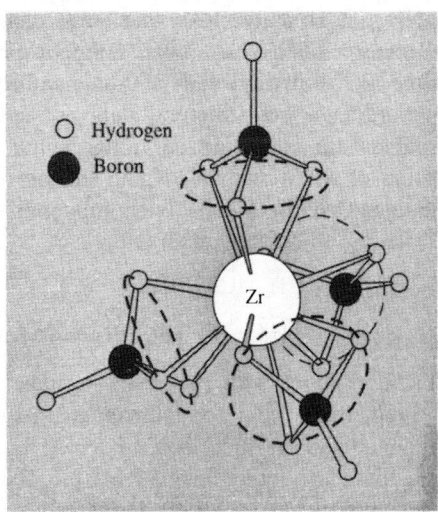

Figure 21.7 Molecular structure [$Zr(BH_4)_4$] showing 4 trihapto BH_4 groups.

it to have T_d symmetry (Fig. 21.7), with triple-hydrogen bridges, implying two types of hydrogen. Yet the proton nmr distinguishes only one type of proton, so that rapid intramolecular rearrangement is indicated. The structure of the hafnium compound has not been determined but its properties are so similar that its structure may be assumed to be the same. Both compounds are rather unstable, have virtually the same mp ($\sim29°C$) and are the most volatile compounds yet known for zirconium and hafnium. The type of bonding involved is a matter of some uncertainty. The volatility is indicative of covalency, but how many electrons the borohydride groups should be regarded as donating to the metal is open to doubt.

Oxidation state III (d^1)

The coordination chemistry of this oxidation state is virtually confined to that of titanium. Reduction of zirconium and hafnium from the quadrivalent to the tervalent state is not easy and cannot be attempted in water which is itself reduced by Zr^{III} and Hf^{III}. A few adducts of the trihalides of these two elements with N- or P- donor ligands have been prepared. $ZrBr_3$ treated with liquid ammonia yields a hexaammine stable to room temperature but NH_3 is readily lost and the chloride only retains $2.5NH_3$ at room temperature.[19] Pyridine, 2,2'-bipyridyl and 1,10-phenanthroline also coordinate, but structural data are sparse. Phosphines are characterized rather better and reduction of MCl_4 with Na/Hg in the presence of the ligand yields air-sensitive compounds with edge-sharing, bi-octahedral structures:[20]

$$[(PR_3)_2Cl_2M(\mu\text{-}Cl)_2MCl_2(PR_3)_2]$$

$$(M = Zr, Hf; PR_3 = PMe_2Ph)$$

Analogous iodides with $PR_3 = PMe_3$ have also been prepared,[21] and the diamagnetism of all these compounds is indicative of M–M bonds, though these are rather long (~310 pm for the chlorides and ~340 pm for the iodides).

Titanium(III) is also prone to aerial oxidation. Most of the complexes of titanium(III) are octahedral and are produced by reacting $TiCl_3$ with an excess of the ligand, giving rise to stoichiometries such as $[TiL_6]X_3$, $[TiL_4X_2]X$, $[TiL_3X_3]$ and $M_3^I[TiX_6]$ (L = neutral unidentate ligand, X = singly charged anion) (Table 21.4) together with corresponding complexes involving multidentate ligands.

The first of these types is most familiarly represented by the hexaaquo ion which is present in acidic aqueous solutions and, in the solid state, in the alum $CsTi(SO_4)_2.12H_2O$. In fact few other neutral ligands besides water form a $[TiL_6]^{3+}$ complex. Urea is one of these few and $[Ti(OCN_2H_4)_6]I_3$, in which the urea ligands coordinate to the titanium via their oxygen atoms, is one of the compounds of titanium(III) most resistant to oxidation.

Hydrate isomerism of $TiCl_3.6H_2O$, yielding $[TiCl_2(H_2O)_4]^+Cl^-$ as one of the isomers, has already been referred to (p. 965) and analogous complexes are formed by a variety of alcohols. Neutral complexes, $[TiL_3X_3]$ have been characterized for a variety of ligands such

as tetrahydrofuran (C_4H_8O), dioxan ($C_4H_8O_2$), acetonitrile, pyridine and picoline, while anionic complexes $[TiX_6]^{3-}$ (X = F, Cl, Br, NCS) have been prepared by electrolytic reduction of melts or by other nonaqueous methods. An interesting binuclear complex, $(NMe_4)[Ti(H_2O)_4F_2][TiF_6].H_2O$ is obtained by reacting $TiCl_3$ with NMe_4F in dimethylformamide. It contains *trans*-$[Ti^{III}(H_2O)_4F_2]^+$ cations and $[Ti^{IV}F_6]^{2-}$ anions.[22]

Interpretation of the electronic spectrum of Ti^{III} in aqueous solution was an early landmark in the development of Crystal Field Theory, the observed broad band being assigned to the $^2E_g \leftarrow 2T_{2g}$ transition (promotion of an electron from a t_{2g} to an e_g orbital). However, the absorption band actually observed for this and for other octahedral complexes of Ti^{III} is never of the symmetrical shape expected for a single transition, but is rather an asymmetrical peak with a (usually) distinct shoulder on the low-energy side[4]. The whole absorption "envelope" is apparently made up of two superimposed bands whose positions are indicated in Table 21.4 and which are generally assumed to be a consequence of the Jahn–Teller effect (p. 1021) acting on the excited term. The value of $10Dq$ is usually identified with the energy of the stronger of the two bands rather than an average, and the results in Table 21.4 indicate that this varies with the ligand in the order:

$$Br^- < Cl^- < urea < NCS^- < F^- < H_2O$$

which agrees with the spectrochemical series established for other metals.

The t_{2g}^1 ground configuration in a perfectly octahedral crystal field is expected to produce a magnetic moment of approx. 1.86 BM at room temperature, decreasing to zero at 0 K. Although observed magnetic moments of Ti^{III} compounds do indeed decrease with temperature, the effects of distortions (which split the ground $^2T_{2g}$ term) and partial covalency of the metal–ligand bond (which delocalizes the single electron from the

[19] E. L. BOYLE, E. S. DODSWORTH, D. NICHOLLS and T. A. RYAN, *Inorg. Chim. Acta* **100**, 281–4 (1985).

[20] F. A. COTTON, P. A. KIBALA and W. A. WOJTCZAK, *Inorg. Chim. Acta* **177**, 1–3 (1990).

[21] F. A. COTTON, M. SHANG and W. A. WOJTCZAK, *Inorg. Chem.* **30**, 3670–5 (1991).

[22] L. KIRIAZIS and R. MATTES, *Z. anorg. allg. Chem.* **593**, 90–8 (1991).

Table 21.4 Spectroscopic and magnetic properties of some complexes of titanium(III)

Complex	Colour	$^2E_g \leftarrow \,^2T_{2g}/(cm^{-1})$	μ (room temperature)/ BM
$[Cs(H_2O)_6][Ti(H_2O)_6][SO_4]_2$	Red-purple	19 900, 18 000	1.79
$[Ti(urea)_6]I_3$	Blue	17 550, 16 000	1.77
$[TiCl_3(NCMe)_3]$	Blue	17 100, 14 700	1.68
$[TiCl_3(NC_5H_5)_3]$	Green	16 600, Asym[a]	1.63
$[TiCl_3(thf)_3]$	Blue-green	14 700, 13 500	1.70
$[TiCl_3(dioxan)_3]$	Blue-green	15 150, 13 400	1.69
$[NH_4]_3[TiF_6]$	Purple	19 000, 15 100	1.78
$[C_5H_5NH]_3[TiCl_6]$	Orange	12 750, 10 800	1.78
$[C_5H_5NH]_3[TiBr_6]$	Orange	11 400, 9 650	1.81
$[NBu^n_4]_3[Ti(NCS)_6]$	Dark violet	18 400, Asym[a]	1.81

[a]The band "envelope" is asymmetrical with insufficient resolution to identify the position of the weaker component.

metal) lead to lower values at room temperature (see Table 21.4) and less temperature dependence than would have been expected.[23]

Amongst the few complexes of Ti^{III} which have been shown to be non-octahedral are $[TiBr_3(NMe_3)_2]$ and $[Ti\{N(SiMe_3)_2\}_3]$. The former has a 5-coordinate, trigonal bipyramidal structure while the latter is one of a series of complexes of tervalent metals which have a 3-coordinate, planar structure. It appears that the silylamide ligands are simply too bulky for the Ti^{III} ion to accommodate more than three of them, and this consideration overrides any preference which the metal might have for a higher coordination number.

Lower oxidation states

Apart from TiO and the lower halides already mentioned, the chemistry of these metals in oxidation states lower than 3 is not well established. Addition compounds of the type $[TiCl_2L_2]$ can be formed with difficulty with ligands such as dimethylformamide and acetonitrile, but their magnetic properties suggest that they also are polymeric with appreciable metal–metal bonding. However, the electronic spectra of Ti^{II} in $TiCl_2/AlCl_3$ melts and also of Ti^{II} incorporated in NaCl crystals (prepared by

the reaction of $CdCl_2$ and titanium in molten NaCl and subsequent sublimation of Cd metal) have been shown to be as expected for a d^2 ion in an octahedral field.

The versatility of cyanide and bipyridyl ligands has been used to stabilize low oxidation states. By using potassium in liquid ammonia, $K_3Ti^{III}(CN)_6$ is reduced to $K_2Ti^{II}(CN)_4$ and $TiBr_3 + KCN$ to $K_4Ti^0(CN)_4$. With $ZrBr_3$ and M^ICN ($M^I = $ K, Rb) in liquid ammonia, ammonolysis occurs and zerovalent Zr is produced:

$$4ZrBr_3 + 5M^ICN + 6NH_3 \rightarrow M^I_5Zr(CN)_5$$
$$+ 3ZrBr_3(NH_2) + 3NH_4Br$$

Reduction of MCl_4 (M = Ti, Zr) in tetrahydrofuran by lithium in the presence of bipyridyl yields a series of darkly coloured, very air-sensitive compounds of the types $[M(bipy)_3]$, $Li[M(bipy)_3]$ and $Li_2[M(bipy)_3]$ with varying amounts of solvent of crystallization, implying oxidation states of 0, −1 and −2. However, delocalization of charge in the π^* orbitals of the ligands facilitates reduction of the ligands and assigning oxidation states to the metals under these circumstances is a purely formal exercise. A more "realistic" claim to zero oxidation state in Zr and Hf compounds is provided by $[M(\eta\text{-PhMe})_2(PMe_3)]$. Metal vapour was produced from an "electron-gun furnace" and condensed with an excess of toluene and trimethylphosphine at −196°C. On warming up, a dark-green solution was produced from which the pure solids were isolated.

23 For a fuller account, see pp. 58–61 of R. L. CARLIN, *Magnetochemistry*, Springer-Verlag, Berlin (1986).

Ziegler–Natta Catalysts[27]

The original ICI process for producing polythene involved the use of high temperatures and pressures but K. Ziegler discovered that, in the presence of a mixture of TiCl$_4$ and AlEt$_3$ in a hydrocarbon solvent, the polymerization will take place at room temperature and atomospheric pressure. G. Natta then showed that by suitable modification of the catalyst stereoregular polymers of almost any alkene (olefin), CH$_2$=CHR, can be produced. In general, these catalysts can be formed from an alkyl of Li, Be or Al together with a halide of one of the metals of Groups 4 to 6 in an oxidation state less than its maximum. As a result of their work, Ziegler and Natta were jointly awarded the 1963 Nobel Prize for Chemistry. Because of its commercially sensitive nature, much of the voluminous literature on this subject is in the form of patents, but a great deal of work has also been directed at ascertaining the mechanism of the catalyst. The initial reaction of TiCl$_4$ and AlEt$_3$ produces insoluble TiCl$_3$ (alternatively, preformed TiCl$_3$ can be used). The most plausible sequence of events on the surface of this catalyst is then as illustrated in Fig. A:

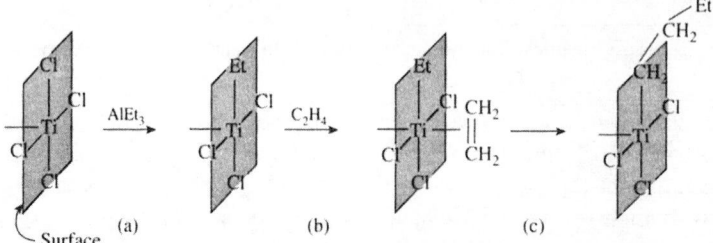

Figure A Possible mechanism of Ziegler–Natta catalyst.

(a) one of the chlorine atoms coordinated to a titanium atom is replaced by an ethyl group from AlEt$_3$,
(b) then, because the titanium atom on the surface of the solid has a vacant coordination site, a molecule of ethylene (ethene) can attach itself;
(c) migration of the ethyl group to the ethylene by a well-known process known as "*cis*-insertion" occurs.

The result of this *cis*-insertion is that a vacant site is left behind, and this can be occupied by another ethylene molecule and steps (a) and (b) repeated indefinitely.

The efficacy of the catalyst seems to lie in the fact that in the case of propylene (CH$_2$=CH–CH$_3$), for instance, the steric hindrance inherent in the surface coordination sites ensures that the polymer which is produced is stereoregular. Such a stereoregular polymer is stronger and has a higher mp than the non-regular (so-called "atactic") polymer. Furthermore, while the titanium provides bonds sufficiently strong to be able to hold the olefin and the alkyl in the correct orientations for reaction, they are not so strong as to prevent the migration which is essential to the reaction. For an alternative suggestion for the mechanism of catalysis, see p. 261.

21.3.6 Organometallic compounds[24,25]

Until the 1950s this was an unexplored area of chemistry, but then two events occurred:

ferrocene was discovered (pp. 937, 1109) and K. Ziegler[26] catalysed the polymerization of ethylene using an organo-titanium derivative. The first event initiated a systematic study of cyclopentadienyl compounds, and so led to the preparation of the most stable of the organometallic compounds of this group, while the second event provided a strong commercial incentive for the investigation of this field (see Panel).

[24] M. BOTTRILL, P. D. GAVENS J. W. KELLAND and J. MC-MEEKING, Chap. 22, pp. 271–547, and D. J. CARDIN, M. F. LAPPERT, C. L. RASTON and P. I. RILEY, Chap. 23, pp. 549–646, in *Comprehensive Organometallic Chemistry*, Vol. 3, Pergamon Press, Oxford, 1982.

[25] D. J. CARDIN, M. F. LAPPERT and C. L. RASTON, *Chemistry of Organo-Zirconium and -Hafnium Compounds*, Ellis Horwood, Chichester, 1986, 451 pp. D. COZAK and M. MELNIK. *Coord. Chem. Rev.* **74**, 53–99 (1986).

[26] K. ZIEGLER, E. HOLZKAMP, H. BREILAND and H. MARTIN, *Angew. Chem.* **67**, 541–7 (1955).

[27] See pp. 475–547 of ref. 24.

In sharp contrast to the Group 14 elements Ge, Sn and Pb, Group 4 metals form relatively few alkyl and aryl compounds and those which are known are very unstable to both air and water. Thermal stabilization is provided by ligands which lack β-hydrogens (p. 926) or are bulky. Thus MEt_4 are unknown; MMe_4 can be prepared by the reactions of LiMe and MCl_4 in ether at low temperatures, but the yellow titanium and the red zirconium compounds decompose to the metals at temperatures above -20 and $-15°C$ respectively; $M(CH_2SiMe_3)_4$ of all three metals are stable at room temperature. Another homoleptic alkyl is of interest because of its unusual structure. X-ray analysis has shown the anion of $[Li(tmed)]_2[ZrMe_6]$ to be the first ML_6 complex to have a trigonal bipyramidal structure and nmr studies indicate that this is retained in solution.[28]

Perhaps because of inadequate or non-existent back-bonding (p. 923), the only neutral, binary carbonyl so far reported is $Ti(CO)_6$ which has been produced by condensation of titanium metal vapour with CO in a matrix of inert gases at $10-15$ K, and identified spectroscopically. By contrast, if MCl_4 (M = Ti, Zr) in dimethoxyethane is reduced with potassium naphthalenide in the presence of a crown ether (to complex the K^+) under an atmosphere of CO, $[M(CO)_6]^{2-}$ salts are produced.[29] These not only involve the metals in the exceptionally low formal oxidation state of -2 but are thermally stable up to 200 and $130°C$ respectively. However, the majority of their carbonyl compounds are stabilized by π-bonded ligands, usually cyclopentadienyl,[30] as in $[M(\eta^5-C_5H_5)_2(CO)_2]$ (Fig. 21.8).

Indeed, it is the cyclopentadienyls which provide the major part of the organometallic chemistry of this group and they are known for metal oxidation states of IV, III and II though III

28 P. M. Morse and G. S. Girolami, *J. Am. Chem. Soc.* **111**, 4114–6 (1989).

29 K. M. Chi, S. R. Frerichs, S. B. Philson and J. E. Ellis, *Angew. Chem. Int. Edn. Engl.* **26**, 1190–1 (1987) and *J. Am. Chem. Soc.* **110**, 303–4 (1988).

30 D. J. Sikora, D. W. Macomber and M. D. Rausch, *Adv. Organometallic Chem.* **25**, 318–80 (1986).

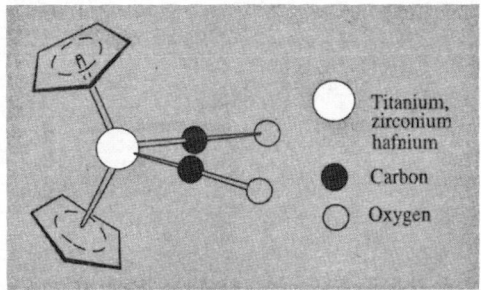

Figure 21.8 Molecular structure of $[M(\eta^5-C_5H_5)_2(CO)_2]$. For M = Ti the C_5H_5 rings are "eclipsed" as shown here, but for M = Hf they are "staggered". Essentially the same structure is found in other $[M(\eta^5-C_5H_5)_2L_2]$ molecules, but the conformation of the two C_5H_5 rings varies in an apparently unsystematic manner.

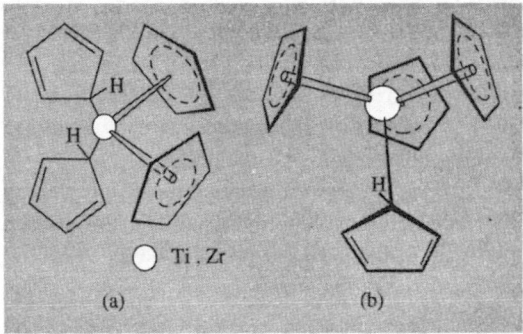

Figure 21.9 (a) Molecular structure of (a) $Ti(C_5H_5)_4$. (b) $Zr(C_5H_5)_4$.

and II are rather sparsely represented for Zr and Hf. The compounds $M(C_5H_5)_4$ are prepared from MCl_4 and NaC_5H_5 and the structure of the green-black titanium compound is shown in Fig. 21.9a. It is therefore formulated as $[Ti(\eta^1-C_5H_5)_2(\eta^5-C_5H_5)_2]$ (p. 940). Rather surprisingly, the ^1H nmr distinguishes only one type of proton at room temperature and it is evident that fluxional processes render all 20 protons indistinguishable. The yellow hafnium analogue is isostructural but the yellow-orange zirconium compound contains 1 monohapto- and 3 pentahapto-rings, $[Zr(\eta^1-C_5H_5)(\eta^5-C_5H_5)_3]$ Fig. 21.9b. This formulation is unexpected since it entails a formally 20-electron

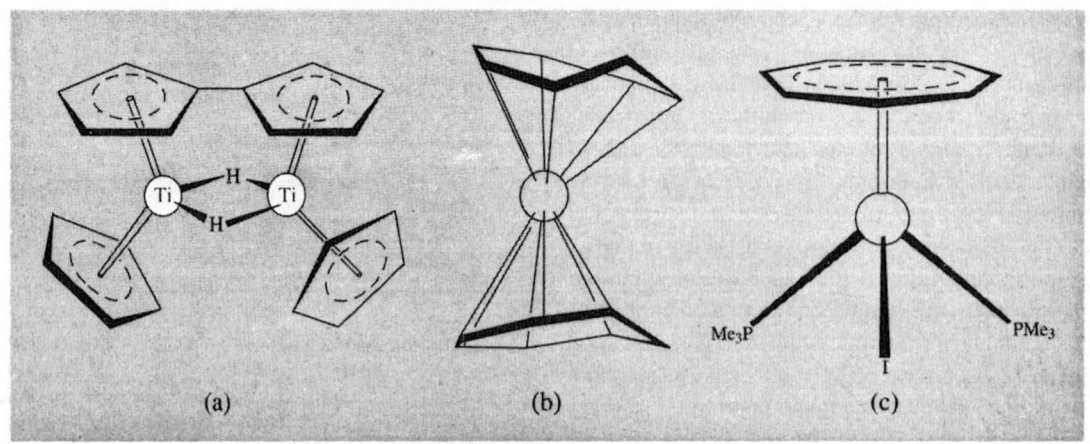

Figure 21.10 (a) "Dimeric" Ti(C$_5$H$_5$)$_2$, actually (μ-(η^5,η^5-fulvalene(-di-(μ-hydrido)-bis(η^5-cyclopentadienyl-titanium), (b) Zr(η^6-C$_7$H$_8$)$_2$ and (c) Zr(η^7-C$_7$H$_7$)(PMe$_3$)$_2$I.

configuration; the two compounds also provided the first authenticated example of a structural difference in the organometallic chemistries of Zr and Hf.

Best known of all are the bis(cyclopentadienyls) of the type [M(η^5-C$_5$H$_5$)$_2$X$_2$], the halides being prepared again by the action of NaC$_5$H$_5$ on MCl$_4$. [Ti(η^5-C$_5$H$_5$)$_2$Cl$_2$] is stable to air, has an extensive aqueous chemistry and is the starting point for most biscyclopentadienyl titanium chemistry. Replacement of X by SCN, N$_3$, $-$NR$_2$, $-$OR or $-$SR is also possible and in all cases the structures are distorted tetrahedral with both rings pentahapto (Fig. 21.8). Interesting derivatives of the type [(C$_5$H$_5$)$_2$Ti(CH$_2$)$_4$] have also been produced. Amongst the many other reactions of the dihalides, ring replacement to give compounds such as [Ti(C$_5$H$_5$)X$_3$] and reductions to [Ti(C$_5$H$_5$)$_2$X] and [Ti(C$_5$H$_5$)$_2$] may be noted. The last of these is of interest as a potential analogue of ferrocene. Several preparative routes have been suggested, and the usual product is a dark-green, pyrophoric, diamagnetic dimer, though a monomeric isomer may be produced in some cases as an intermediate. The structure of the dimer has been shown by X-ray crystallography[30a] to be that in Fig. 21.10a, confirming earlier results based on ^{13}C nmr. Attempts to prepare a zirconium analogue have yielded a variety of products, some dinuclear others polymeric but, as with titanium, no true mononuclear metallocene. A number of cyclopentadienyl and related compounds of titanium and zirconium have been found to absorb molecular nitrogen, which in some cases can be recovered in a reduced form (i.e. as ammonia or hydrazine) upon hydrolysis, and the first example of dinitrogen complexation by a non-cyclopentadienyl Ti system has recently been reported.[31] While this has obvious interest as a potential route to nitrogen fixation, a compound which can be regenerated and so act catalytically has so far proved elusive.

Although the chemistry of zirconium in its lower oxidation states is still relatively unexplored, it is developing. Examples which offer the possibility of further exploitation include the blue, paramagnetic zirconium(III) compound[32] [L$_2$Zr(μ-Cl)$_2$ZrL$_2$] {L = C$_5$H$_3$(SiMe$_3$)$_2$-1,3}, and the "sandwich" and "half-sandwich" compounds derived from cycloheptatriene: red

[30a] S. I. BEYDOUN, H. ANTROPIUSOVA and K. MACG, *J. Organometallic Chem.* **427**, 49–55 (1992).

[31] N. BEYDOUN, R. DUCHATEAU and S. GAMBAROTTA, *J. Chem. Soc., Chem. Commun.*, 244–6 (1992).

[32] P. B. HITCHCOCK, M. F. LAPPERT, G. A. LAWLESS, H. OLIVIER and E. J. RYAN, *J. Chem. Soc., Chem. Commun.*, 474–6 (1992).

$[Zr^0(\eta^6\text{-}C_7H_8)_2]^{(33)}$ and blue, $[Zr^{II}(\eta^7\text{-}C_7H_7)\text{-}(PMe_3)_2I]^{(34)}$ (Fig. 21.10b and c).

Considerable attention is also being given to the anti-tumor activity of titanium compounds.

Amongst these are bis(cyclopentadienyl) and bis(β-diketonate) derivatives, some of which are undergoing clinical trials,[35] in the hope that they will provide more extensive application than cisplatin (pp. 1163–4).

---

[33] M. L. H. GREEN and N. M. WALKER, *J. Chem. Soc., Chem. Commun.*, 850–2 (1989).

[34] *ibid.*, pp. 908–9.

---

[35] B. K. KEPPLER, C. FRIESEN, H. G. MORITZ, H. VONGERICH-TEN and E. VOGEL, *Struct. and Bonding* **78**, 97–127 (1991).

22
Vanadium, Niobium and Tantalum

22.1 Introduction

The discoveries of all three of these elements were made at the beginning of the nineteenth century and were marked by initial uncertainty and confusion due, in the case of the heavier pair of elements, to the overriding similarity of their chemistries. (See p. 1282 for element 105, dubnium.)

A. M. del Rio in 1801 claimed to have discovered the previously unknown element 23 in a sample of Mexican lead ore and, because of the red colour of the salts produced by acidification, he called it erythronium. Unfortunately he withdrew his claim when, 4 years later, it was (incorrectly) suggested by the Frenchman, H. V. Collett-Desotils, that the mineral was actually basic lead chromate. In 1830 the element was "rediscovered" by N. G. Sefström in some Swedish iron ore. Because of the richness and variety of colours found in its compounds he called it vanadium after Vanadis, the Scandinavian goddess of beauty. One year later F. Wöhler established the identity of vanadium and erythronium. The metal itself was isolated in a reasonably pure form in 1867 by H. E. Roscoe who reduced the chloride with hydrogen, and he was also responsible for much of the early work on the element.

In the same year that del Rio found his erythronium, C. Hatchett examined a mineral which had been sent to England from Massachusetts and had lain in the British Museum since 1753. From it he isolated the oxide of a new element which he named columbium, and the mineral columbite, in honour of its country of origin. Meanwhile in Sweden A. G. Ekeberg was studying some Finnish minerals and in 1802 claimed to have identified a new element which he named tantalum because of the difficulty he had had in dissolving the mineral in acids.[†] It was subsequently thought that the two elements were one and the same, and this view persisted until at least 1844 when H. Rose examined a columbite sample and showed that two distinct elements were involved.

[†] The classical allusion refers to Tantalus, the mythical king of Phrygia, son of Zeus and a nymph, who was condemned for revealing the secrets of the gods to man: one of his punishments was being made to stand in Tartarus up to his chin in water, which constantly receded as he stooped to drink. As Ekeberg wrote (1802): "This metal I call *tantalum* ... partly in allusion to its incapacity, when immersed in acid, to absorb any and be saturated."

One was Ekeberg's tantalum and the other he called niobium (Niobe was the daughter of Tantalus). Despite the chronological precedence of the name columbium, IUPAC adopted niobium in 1950, though columbium is still sometimes used in US industry. Impure niobium metal was first isolated by C. W. Blomstrand in 1866 by the reduction of the chloride with hydrogen, but the first pure samples of metallic niobium and tantalum were not prepared until 1907 when W. von Bolton reduced the fluorometallates with sodium.

22.2 The Elements

22.2.1 Terrestrial abundance and distribution

The abundances of these elements decrease by approximately an order of magnitude from V to Nb and again from Nb to Ta. Vanadium has been estimated to comprise about 136 ppm (i.e. 0.0136%) of the earth's crustal rocks, which makes it the nineteenth element in order of abundance (between Zr, 162 ppm, and Cl, 126 ppm); it is the fifth most abundant transition metal after Fe, Ti, Mn and Zr. It is widely, though sparsely, distributed; thus although more than 60 different minerals of vanadium have been characterized, there are few concentrated deposits and most of it is obtained as a coproduct along with other materials. Its major commercial source is the titanoferrous magnetites of South Africa, the former USSR and China. One of its important minerals is the polysulfide, patronite, VS_4, but, being a class-a metal, it is more generally associated with oxygen. For example, vanadinite approximates to lead chloride vanadate, $PbCl_2.3Pb_3(VO_4)_2$, and carnotite to potassium uranyl vanadate, $K(UO_2)(VO_4).1.5H_2O$. Vanadium is also found in some crude oils, in particular those from Venezuala and Canada, and can be recovered from the oil residues and from flue dusts after burning.

The crustal abundances of niobium and tantalum are 20 ppm and 1.7 ppm, comparable to N (19 ppm), Ga (19 ppm), and Li (18 ppm),

on the one hand, and to As (1.8 ppm) and Ge (1.5 ppm), on the other. Of course, in view of their chemical similarities. Nb and Ta usually occur together, and their most widespread mineral, $(Fe,Mn)M_2O_6$ (M = Nb, Ta), is known as columbite or tantalite, depending on which metal preponderates. Until the 1950s, this was the major source of both metals, with significant amounts obtained also as a byproduct of the extraction of tin in SE Asia and Nigeria. The discovery of a huge, high grade (2.5% Nb_2O_5) deposit of pyrochlore, $NaCaNb_2O_6F$, in Brazil totally changed the pattern. Nb is now obtained chiefly from Brazil; Ta from Australia, Canada and SE Asia but its production is heavily dependent on demand for Sn.

22.2.2 Preparation and uses of the metals

Because it is usually produced along with other metals, the availability of vanadium and the economics of its production[1] are intimately connected with the particular coproduct involved.

The usual extraction procedure is to roast the crushed ore, or vanadium residue, with NaCl or Na_2CO_3 at 850°C. This produces sodium vanadate, $NaVO_3$, which is leached out with water. Acidification with sulfuric acid to pH 2–3 precipitates "red cake", a polyvanadate which, on fusing at 700°C, gives a black, technical grade vanadium pentoxide. Reduction is then necessary to obtain the metal, but, since about 80% of vanadium produced is used as an additive to steel, it is usual to effect the reduction in an electric furnace in the presence of iron or iron ore to produce ferrovanadium, which can then be used without further refinement. Carbon was formerly used as the reductant, but it is difficult to avoid the formation of an intractable carbide, and so it has been superseded by aluminium or, more commonly, ferrosilicon (p. 330) in which case lime is also added to remove the silica as a slag of calcium silicate. If pure vanadium metal is required it can

---

[1] C. K. GUPTA and N. KRISHNAMURTHY, *Extractive Metallurgy of Vanadium*, Elsevier, Amsterdam, 1992, 689 pp.

be obtained by reduction of VCl_5 with H_2 or Mg, by reduction of V_2O_5 with Ca, or by electrolysis of partially refined vanadium in fused alkali metal chloride or bromide.

The benefit of vanadium as an additive in steel is that it forms V_4C_3 with any carbon present, and this disperses to produce a fine-grained steel which has increased resistance to wear and is stronger at high temperatures. Such steels are widely used in the manufacture of springs and high-speed tools. In 1995, world consumption of vanadium metal, alloys and concentrates exceeded 33 000 tonnes of contained vanadium.

Production of niobium and tantalum is on a smaller scale and the processes involved are varied and complicated. Alkali fusion, or digestion of the ore with acids can be used to solubilize the metals, which can then be separated from each other. The process originally developed by M. C. Marignac in 1866 and in use for a century utilized the fact that in dil HF tantalum tends to form the sparingly soluble K_2TaF_7, whereas niobium forms the soluble $K_3NbOF_5.2H_2O$. Nowadays it is more usual to employ a solvent extraction technique. For instance, tantalum can be extracted from dilute aqueous HF solutions by methyl isobutyl ketone, and increasing the acidity of the aqueous phase allows niobium to be extracted into a fresh batch of the organic phase. The metals can then be obtained, after conversion to the pentoxides, by reduction with Na or C, or by the electrolysis of fused fluorides. In 1995, world production of contained metal was in the region of 18 000 tonnes for Nb and 1000 tonnes for Ta.

Niobium finds use in the production of numerous stainless steels for use at high temperatures, and Nb/Zr wires are used in superconducting magnets. The extreme corrosion-resistance of tantalum at normal temperatures (due to the presence of an exceptionally tenacious film of oxide) leads to its application in the construction of chemical plant, especially where it can be used as a liner inside cheaper metals. Its complete inertness to body fluids makes it the ideal material for surgical use in bone repair and internal suturing.

It is widely used by the electronics industry in the manufacture of capacitors, where the oxide film is an efficient insulator, and as a filament or filament support. Indeed, it was for a while widely used to replace carbon as the filament in incandescent light bulbs but, by about 1911, was itself superseded by tungsten.

22.2.3 Atomic and physical properties of the elements

Some of the important properties of Group 5 elements are summarized in Table 22.1. Having odd atomic numbers, they have few naturally occurring isotopes; Nb only 1 and V and Ta 2 each, though the second ones are present only in very low abundance (^{50}V 0.250%, ^{180}Ta 0.012%). As a consequence (p. 17) their atomic weights have been determined with considerable precision. On the other hand, because of difficulties in removing all impurities, reported values of their bulk properties have often required revision.

All three elements are shiny, silvery metals with typically metallic bcc structures. When very pure they are comparatively soft and ductile but impurities usually have a hardening and embrittling effect. When compared to the elements of Group 4 the expected trends are apparent. These elements are slightly less electropositive and are smaller than their predecessors, and the heavier pair Nb and Ta are virtually identical in size as a consequence of the lanthanide contraction. The extra d electron again appears to contribute to stronger metal–metal bonding in the bulk metals, leading in each case to a higher mp, bp and enthalpy of atomization. Indeed, these quantities reach their maximum values in this and the following group. In the first transition series, vanadium is the last element before some of the $(n-1)$d electrons begin to enter the inert electron-core of the atom and are therefore not available for bonding. As a result, not only is its mp the highest in the series but it is the last element whose compounds in the group oxidation state (i.e. involving all $(n-1)$d and ns electrons) are not strongly oxidizing. In the second and

Table 22.1   Some properties of Group 5 elements

Property	V	Nb	Ta
Atomic number	23	41	73
Number of naturally occurring isotopes	2	1	2
Atomic weight	50.9415(1)	92.90638(2)	180.9479(1)
Electronic configuration	[Ar]$3d^34s^2$	[Kr]$4d^35s^2$	[Xe]$4f^{14}5d^36s^2$
Electronegativity	1.6	1.6	1.5
Metal radius (12-coordinate)/pm	134	146	146
Ionic radius (6-coordinate)/pm V	54	64	64
IV	58	68	68
III	64	72	72
II	79	—	—
MP/°C	1915	2468	2980
BP/°C	3350	4758	5534
ΔH_{fus}/kJ mol^{-1}	17.5	26.8	24.7
ΔH_{vap}/kJ mol^{-1}	459.7	680.2	758.2
ΔH_f (monoatomic gas)/kJ mol^{-1}	510 ($\pm$29)	724	782 ($\pm$6)
Density (20°C)/g cm^{-3}	6.11	8.57	16.65
Electrical resistivity (20°C)/μohm cm	~25	~12.5	(12.4)

third series the entry of $(n-1)$d electrons into the electron core is delayed somewhat and it is molybdenum and tungsten in Group 6 whose mps are the highest.

22.2.4 Chemical reactivity and trends

The elements of Group 5 are in many ways similar to their predecessors in Group 4. They react with most non-metals, giving products which are frequently interstitial and nonstoichiometric, but they require high temperatures to do so. Their general resistance to corrosion is largely due to the formation of surface films of oxides which are particularly effective in the case of tantalum. Unless heated, tantalum is appreciably attacked only by oleum, hydrofluoric acid or, more particularly, a hydrofluoric/nitric acid mixture. Fused alkalis will also attack it. In addition to these reagents, vanadium and niobium are attacked by other hot concentrated mineral acids but are resistant to fused alkali.

The most obvious factor in comparing the chemistry of the three elements is again the very close similarity of the second and third members although, in this group, slight differences can be discerned as will be discussed shortly. The

stability of the lower oxidation states decreases as the group is descended. As a result, although each element shows formal oxidation states from +5 down to −3, the most stable one in the case of vanadium under normal conditions is the +4, and even the +3 and +2 oxidation states (which are admittedly strongly reducing) have well-characterized cationic aqueous chemistries; by contrast most of the chemistries of niobium and tantalum are confined to the group oxidation state +5. Of the halogens, only the strongly oxidizing fluorine produces a pentahalide of vanadium, and the other vanadium(V) compounds are based on the oxohalides and the pentoxide. The pentoxide also gives rise to the complicated but characteristic aqueous chemistry of the polymerized vanadates (isopolyvanadates) which anticipates the even more extensive chemistry of the polymolybdates and polytungstates; this is only incompletely mirrored by niobium and tantalum.

The +4 oxidation state, which for Nb and Ta is best represented by their halides, is most notable for the uniquely stable VO^{2+} (vanadyl) ion which retains its identity throughout a wide variety of reactions and forms many complexes. Indeed it is probably the most stable diatomic ion known. The M^{IV} ions have only slightly smaller radii

Table 22.2   Oxidation states and stereochemistries of compounds of vanadium, niobium and tantalum

Oxidation state	Coordination number	Stereochemistry	V	Nb/Ta
-3 (d^8)	5	—	$[V(CO)_5]^{3-}$	$[M(CO)_5]^{3-}$
-1 (d^6)	6	Octahedral	$[V(CO)_6]^-$	$[M(CO)_6]^-$
0 (d^5)	6	Octahedral	$[V(CO)_6]$	—
1 (d^4)	6	Octahedral	$[V(bipy)_3]^+$	—
	7	Capped octahedral	—	$[TaH(CO)_2(diphos)_2]$
2 (d^3)	4	Square planar	—	NbO
	6	Octahedral	$[V(CN)_6]^{4-}$	TaO(?)
		Trigonal prismatic	VS	NbS
3 (d^2)	3	Planar	$[V\{N(SiMe_3)_2\}_3]$	—
	4	Tetrahedral	$[VCl_4]^-$	
	5	Trigonal bipyramidal	$[VCl_3(NMe_3)_2]$	
	6	Octahedral	$[V(C_2O_4)_3]^{3-}$	$[Nb_2Cl_9]^{3-}$
		Trigonal prismatic	—	LiNbO_2
	7	Complex	—	$[Ta(CO)Cl_3(PMe_2Ph)_3].EtOH$
	8	Dodecahedral	—	$[Nb(CN)_8]^{5-}$
4 (d^1)	4	Tetrahedral	VCl_4	$[Nb(NEt_2)_4]$ (not Ta)
	5	Trigonal bipyramidal	$[VOCl_2(NMe_3)_2]$	
		Square pyramidal	$[VO(acac)_2]$	
	6	Octahedral	$[VCl_4(bipy)]$	$[MCl_6]^{2-}$
	7	Pentagonal bipyramidal	—	$[NbF_7]^{3-}$
	8	Dodecahedral	$[VCl_4(diars)_2]$	$[NbCl_4(diars)_2]$ (not Ta)
		Square antiprismatic	$[V(S_2CMe)_4]^{(a)}$	$[Nb(\beta\text{-diketonate})_4]$
5 (d^0)	4	Tetrahedral	$VOCl_3$	$ScNbO_4$
	5	Trigonal bipyramidal	$VCl_5(g)$	$MF_5(g)$
		Square pyramidal	$[VOF_4]^-$	$[M(NMe_2)_5]$
	6	Octahedral	$[VF_6]^-$	$[MF_6]^-$
		Trigonal prismatic	—	$[M(S_2C_6H_4)_3]^-$
	7	Pentagonal bipyramidal	$[VO(S_2CNEt_2)_3]$	$[TaS(S_2CNEt_2)_3]$
		Capped trigonal prismatic	—	$[MF_7]^{2-}$
	8	Dodecahedral	$[V(O_2)_4]^{3-}$	$[M(O_2)_4]^{3-}$
				$[Ta(S_2CNMe_2)_4]^+$
		Square antiprismatic	—	$[MF_8]^{3-}$

[(a)]Tetrakis(dithioacetato)vanadium(IV) was originally classified as dodecahedral. Re-examination has shown that its unit cell in fact contains two independent metal sites. One is indeed dodecahedral but the other is square antiprismatic; C. W. HAIGH, *Polyhedron* **14**, 2871–8 (1995).

than those of Group 4, and, again, coordination numbers as high as 8 are found. In the +5 state, however, only Nb and Ta are sufficiently large to achieve this coordination number with ligands other than bidentate ones with very small "bites", such as the peroxo group. Table 22.2 illustrates the various oxidation states and stereochemistries of compounds of V, Nb and Ta.

Niobium and tantalum provide no counterpart to the cationic chemistry of vanadium in the +3 and +2 oxidation states. Instead, they form a series of "cluster" compounds based

on octahedral M_6X_{12} units. The occurrence of such compounds is largely a consequence of the strength of metal–metal bonding in this part of the periodic table (as reflected in high enthalpies of atomization), and similar cluster compounds are found also for molybdenum and tungsten.

Compounds containing M–C σ-bonds are frequently unstable and do not give rise to an extensive chemistry (p. 999). Vanadium forms a neutral (paramagnetic) hexacarbonyl which, though not very stable, contrasts with that of titanium in that it can at least be prepared in quantity. All three elements give a number of η^5-cyclopentadienyl derivatives.

22.3 Compounds of Vanadium, Niobium and Tantalum[2,3]

The binary hydrides (p. 67), borides (p. 148), carbides (p. 299), and nitrides (p. 418) of these metals have already been discussed and will not be described further except to note that, as with the analogous compounds of Group 4, they are hard, refractory and nonstoichiometric materials with high conductivities. The intriguing cryo-compound $[V(N_2)_6]$ has been isolated by cocondensing V atoms and N_2 molecules at 20–25 K; it has an infrared absorption at $2100 \, cm^{-1}$ and its d–d and charge-transfer spectra are strikingly similar to those of the isoelectronic 17-electron species $[V(CO)_6]$.

22.3.1 Oxides

Table 22.3 gives the principal oxides formed by the elements of this group. Besides the 4 oxides of vanadium shown, a number of other phases of intermediate composition have been identified and the lower oxides in particular have wide ranges of homogeneity. V_2O_5 is orange yellow when pure (due to charge transfer) and is the final product when the metal is heated in an excess of oxygen, but contamination with lower oxides is then common and a better method is to heat

Table 22.3   Oxides of Group 5 metals

Oxidation state:	+5	+4	+3	+2
V	V_2O_5	VO_2	V_2O_3	VO
Nb	Nb_2O_5	NbO_2	—	NbO
Ta	Ta_2O_5	TaO_2	—	(TaO)

[2] D. L. KEPERT, *The Early Transition Metals*, Chap. 3, V, Nb, Ta, pp. 142–254, Academic Press, London, 1972.

[3] R. J. H. CLARK, Chap. 34, pp. 491–551, and D. BROWN, Chap. 35, pp. 553–622, in *Comprehensive Inorganic Chemistry*, Vol. 3, Pergamon Press, Oxford, 1973.

ammonium "metavanadate":

$$2NH_4VO_3 \longrightarrow V_2O_5 + 2NH_3 + H_2O$$

On the basis of simple radius ratio arguments, vanadium(V) is expected to be rather large for tetrahedral coordination to oxygen, but rather small for octahedral coordination. It is perhaps not surprising therefore that, though the structure of V_2O_5 is somewhat complicated, it consists essentially of distorted trigonal bipyramids of VO_5 sharing edges to form zigzag double chains. Another, metastable, form has been prepared which differs from the normal one in the relative dispositions of adjacent parallel chains.[4] V_2O_5 is homogeneous over only a small range of compositions but loses oxygen reversibly on heating, which is probably why it is such a versatile catalyst. For instance, it catalyses the oxidation of numerous organic compounds by air or hydrogen peroxide, and the reduction of olefins (alkenes) and of aromatic hydrocarbons by hydrogen, but most importantly it catalyses the oxidation of SO_2 to SO_3 in the contact process for the manufacture of sulfuric acid (p. 708). For this purpose it replaced metallic platinum which, besides being far more expensive, was also prone to "poisoning" by impurities such as arsenic. V_2O_5 is amphoteric. It is slightly soluble in water, giving a pale yellow, acidic solution. It dissolves in acids producing salts of the pale-yellow dioxovanadium(V) ion, $[VO_2]^+$, and in alkalis producing colourless solutions which, at high pH, contain the orthovanadate ion, VO_4^{3-}. At intermediate pHs a series of hydrolysis-polymerization reactions occur yielding the isopolyvanadates to be discussed in the next section. It is also a mild oxidizing agent and in aqueous solution is reduced by, for instance, hydrohalic acids to vanadium(IV). In the solid, mild reduction with CO, SO_2, or fusion with oxalic acid gives the deep-blue VO_2.

At room temperature VO_2 has a rutile-like structure (p. 961) distorted by the presence of pairs of vanadium atoms bonded together. Above 70°C, however, an undistorted rutile

[4] J. M. COCCIANTELLI, P. GRAVEREAU, M. POUCHARD and P. HAGENMULLER, *J. Solid State Chem.*, **93**, 497–502 (1991).

structure is adopted as the atoms in each pair separate, breaking the localized V–V bonds and releasing the bonding electrons, so causing a sharp increase in electrical conductivity and magnetic susceptibility. It is again amphoteric, dissolving in non-oxidizing acids to give salts of the blue oxovanadium(IV) (vanadyl) ion $[VO]^{2+}$, and in alkali to give the yellow to brown vanadate(IV) (hypovanadate) ion $[V_4O_9]^{2-}$, or at high pH $[VO_4]^{4-}$. Like the vanadium(V) system, a number of polyanions are produced at intermediate pH. Between V_2O_5 and VO_2 is a succession of phases V_nO_{2n+1} of which V_3O_7, V_4O_9 and V_6O_{13} have been characterized.

Further reduction with H_2, C or CO produces a series of discrete chemical-shear phases (Magnéli phases) of general formula V_nO_{2n-1} based on a rutile structure with periodic defects (p. 961), before the black, refractory sesquioxide V_2O_3 is reached. Examples are V_4O_7, V_5O_9, V_6O_{11}, V_7O_{13} and V_8O_{15}. The oxides VO, V_2O_3 and V_3O_5 also conform to the general formula V_nO_{2n-1}, but this is a purely formal relation and their structures are not related by chemical-shear to those of the Magnéli phases.

V_2O_3 has a corundum structure (p. 243) and is notable for the transition occurring as it is cooled below about 170 K when its electrical conductivity changes from metallic to insulating in character. Chemically it is entirely basic, dissolving in aqueous acids to give blue or green vanadium(III) solutions which are strongly reducing. On still further reducing the oxide system, the corundum structure is retained down to compositions as low as $VO_{1.35}$, after which the grey metallic monoxide VO, with a defect rock-salt structure, is formed. This too is markedly nonstoichiometric with a composition range from $VO_{0.8}$ to $VO_{1.3}$. In all, therefore, at least 13 distinct oxide phases of vanadium have been identified between $VO_{\sim 1}$ and V_2O_5.

Niobium and tantalum also form various oxide phases but they are not so extensive or well characterized as those of vanadium. Their pentoxides are relatively much more stable and difficult to reduce. As they are attacked by conc HF and will dissolve in fused alkali, they may perhaps be described as amphoteric, but inertness is the more obvious characteristic. Their structures are extremely complicated and Nb_2O_5 in particular displays extensive polymorphism. It is interesting to note that the polymorphs of Nb_2O_5 and Ta_2O_5 are by no means all analogous.

High temperature reduction of Nb_2O_5 with hydrogen gives the bluish-black dioxide NbO_2 which has a distorted rutile structure. As in VO_2 the distortion is caused by pairs of metal atoms evidently bonded together, but the distortion is in a different direction. Between Nb_2O_5 and NbO_2 there is a homologous series of structurally related phases of general formula $Nb_{3n+1}O_{8n-2}$ with $n = 5$, 6, 7, 8 (i.e. Nb_8O_{19}, $Nb_{19}O_{46}$, $Nb_{11}O_{27}$ and $Nb_{25}O_{62}$). In addition, oxides of formula $Nb_{12}O_{29}$ and $Nb_{47}O_{116}$ have been reported: the numerical relationship to Nb_2O_5 is clear since $Nb_{12}O_{29}$ is $(12Nb_2O_5 - 2O)$ and $2Nb_{47}O_{116}$ (or $Nb_{94}O_{232}$) is $(47Nb_2O_5 - 3O)$. Further reduction produces the grey monoxide NbO which has a cubic structure and metallic conductivity but differs markedly from its vanadium analogue in that its composition range is only $NbO_{0.982}$ to $NbO_{1.008}$. The structure is a unique variant of the rock-salt NaCl structure (p. 242) in which there are vacancies (Nb) at the eight corners of the unit cell and an O vacancy at its centre (Fig. 22.1). The structure could therefore be described as a vacancy-defect NaCl structure $Nb_{0.75}\square_{0.25}O_{0.75}\square_{0.25}$, but as all the vacancies are ordered it is better to consider it as a new structure type in which both Nb and O form 4 coplanar bonds. The central feature is a 3D framework of Nb_6 octahedral clusters (Nb–Nb 298 pm, cf. Nb–Nb 285 pm in Nb metal) and this accounts for the metallic conductivity of the compound. The structure is reminiscent of the structure-motif of the lower halides of Nb and Ta (p. 992) and the retention of the Nb_6 clusters rather than the adoption of the ionic NaCl-type structure can similarly be related to the high heats of sublimation of Nb and neighbouring metals. (For a fuller discussion of the bonding, see ref. 5.)

---

[5] J. K. Burdett and T. Hughbanks, *J. Am. Chem. Soc.* **106**, 3101–13 (1984).

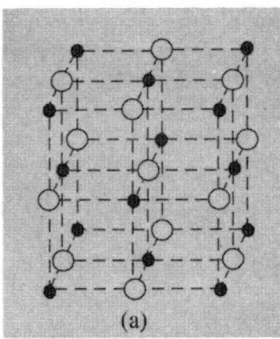 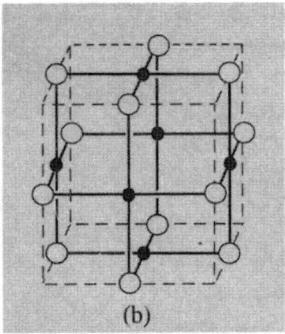 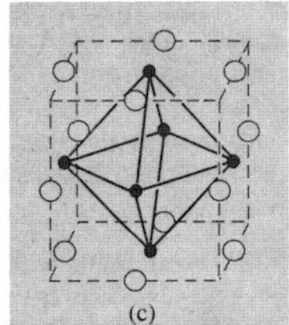

(a)   (b)   (c)

Figure 22.1   (a) NaCl (MgO) showing all sites occupied by M($\bullet$) and O($\bigcirc$). (b) NbO showing planar coordination of Nb (and O) and vacancies at the cube corners (Nb) and centre (O). (c) NbO as in (b), but emphasizing the octahedral Nb_6 cluster (joined by corner sharing to neighbouring unit cells).

The heavier metal tantalum is distinctly less inclined than niobium to form oxides in lower oxidation states. The rutile phase TaO_2 is known but has not been studied, and a cubic rock-salt-type phase TaO with a narrow homogeneity range has also been reported but not yet fully characterized. Ta_2O_5 has two well-established polymorphs which have a reversible transition temperature at 1355°C but the detailed structure of these phases is too complex to be discussed here.

22.3.2 Polymetallates [6-8b]

The amphoteric nature of V_2O_5 has already been noted. In fact, if the colourless solution produced by dissolving V_2O_5 in strong aqueous alkali such as NaOH is gradually acidified, it first deepens in colour, becoming orange to red as the neutral point is passed; it then darkens further and, around pH 2, a brown precipitate of hydrated V_2O_5 separates and redissolves at still lower pHs to give a pale-yellow solution. As a result of spectrophotometric studies there is general agreement that the predominant species in the initial colourless solution is the tetrahedral VO_4^{3-} ion and, in the final pale-yellow solution, the angular VO_2^+ ion. In the intervening orange to red solutions a complicated series of hydrolysis-polymerization reactions occur, which have direct counterparts in the chemistries of Mo and W and to a lesser extent Nb, Ta and Cr. The polymerized species involved are collectively known as isopolymetallates or isopolyanions. The determination of the equilibria involved in their formation, as well as their stoichiometries and structures, has been a confused and disputed area, some aspects of which are by no means settled even now. That this is so is perfectly understandable because:

(i) Some of the equilibria are reached only slowly (possibly months in some cases) and it is likely that much of the reported work has been done under non-equilibrium conditions.

(ii) Often in early work, solid species were crystallized from solution and their stoichiometries, quite unjustifiably as it turns out, were used to infer the stoichiometries of species in solution.

(iii) When a series of experimental measurements has been made it is usual to see what combination of plausible ionic species will best account for the

[6] M. T. POPE, Iso- and Hetero-polyanions, Chap. 38 in *Comprehensive Coordination Chemistry*, Vol. 3, pp. 1028–58, Pergamon Press, Oxford, 1987.

[7] M. T. POPE, *Heteropoly and Isopoly Oxometalates*, Springer Verlag, Berlin, 1983, 180 pp.

[8] M. T. POPE and A. MULLER, *Angew. Chem. Int. Edn. Engl.* **30**, 34–48 (1991).

[8a] G. M. MAKSIMOV, *Russ. Chem. Rev. (Engl. Transl.)* **64**, 445–61 (1995).

[8b] M. I. KHAN and J. ZUBIETA, *Prog. Inorg. Chem.* **43**, 1–149 (1995).

observed data. However, the greater the complexity of the system, the greater the number of apparently acceptable models there will be, and the greater the accuracy required if the measurements are to distinguish reliably and unambiguously between them.

Of the many experimental techniques which have been used in this field, the more important are: pH measurements, cryoscopy, ion-exchange and ultraviolet/visible spectroscopy for studying the stoichiometry of the equilibria, and infrared/Raman and nmr spectroscopy for studying the structures of the ions in solution, where oxygen-17 and metal atom nmr spectroscopy are playing an increasingly important role. Probably the best summary of our current understanding of the vanadate system is given by Fig. 22.2. This shows how the existence of the various vanadate species depends on the pH and on the total concentration of vanadium.[7] Their occurrence can be accounted for by protonation and condensation equilibria such as the following:

In alkaline solution:

$$[VO_4]^{3-} + H^+ \rightleftharpoons [HVO_4]^{2-}$$

$$2[HVO_4]^{2-} \rightleftharpoons [V_2O_7]^{4-} + H_2O$$

$$[HVO_4]^{2-} + H^+ \rightleftharpoons [H_2VO_4]^-$$

$$3[H_2VO_4]^- \rightleftharpoons [V_3O_9]^{3-} + 3H_2O$$

$$4[H_2VO_4]^- \rightleftharpoons [V_4O_{12}]^{4-} + 4H_2O$$

In acid solution:

$$10[V_3O_9]^{3-} + 15H^+ \rightleftharpoons 3[HV_{10}O_{28}]^{5-} + 6H_2O$$

$$[H_2VO_4]^- + H^+ \rightleftharpoons H_3VO_4$$

$$[HV_{10}O_{28}]^{5-} + H^+ \rightleftharpoons [H_2V_{10}O_{28}]^{4-}$$

$$H_3VO_4 + H^+ \rightleftharpoons VO_2^+ + 2H_2O$$

$$[H_2V_{10}O_{28}]^{4-} + 14H^+ \rightleftharpoons 10VO_2^+ + 8H_2O$$

In these equilibria the site of protonation in the species $[HVO_4]^{2-}$, $[H_2VO_4]^-$ etc., is an oxygen atom (not vanadium); a more precise representation would therefore be $[VO_3(OH)]^{2-}$, $[VO_2(OH)_2]^-$ etc. However, the customary formulation is retained for convenience (cf. HNO_3, HSO_4^-, H_2SO_4, etc.).

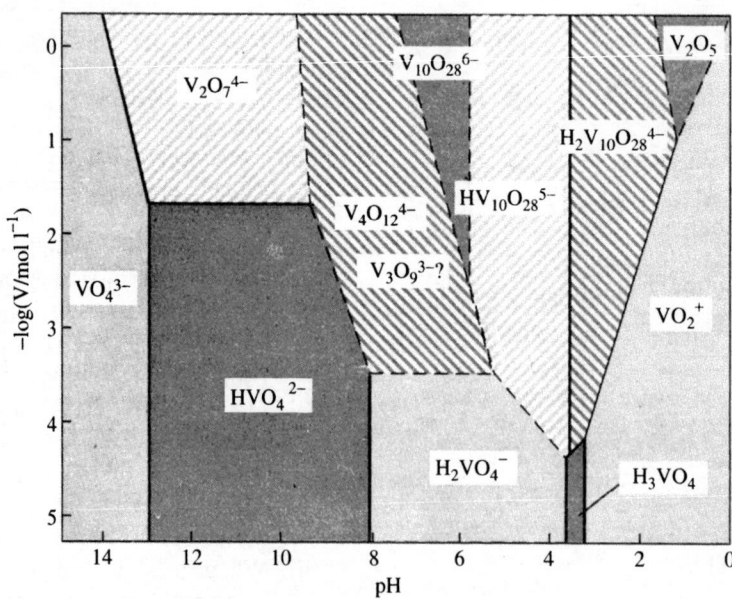

Figure 22.2   Occurrence of various vanadate and polyvanadate species as a function of pH and total concentration of vanadium.

It is evident from Fig. 22.2 that only in very dilute solutions are monomeric vanadium ions found and any increase in concentrations, particularly if the solution is acidic, leads to polymerization. ^{51}V nmr work indicates that, starting from the alkaline side, the various ionic species are all based on 4-coordinate vanadium(V) in the form of linked VO_4 tetrahedra until the decavanadates appear. These evidently involve a higher coordination number, but whether or not it is the same in solution as in the solids which can be separated is uncertain. However, it is interesting to note that similarities between the vanadate and chromate systems cease with the appearance of the decavanadates which have no counterpart in chromate chemistry. The smaller chromium(VI) is apparently limited to tetrahedral coordination with oxygen, whereas vanadium(V) is not.

More information is of course available on the structures of the various crystalline vanadates which can be separated from solution. Traditionally, the colourless salts obtained from alkaline solution were called ortho-, pyro-, or meta-vanadates by analogy with the phosphates of corresponding stoichiometry. "Ortho"-vanadates, $M_3^I VO_4(aq)$, apparently contain discrete, tetrahedral, VO_4^{3-} ions; "pyro"-vanadates, $M_4^I V_2O_7$ (aq), contain dinuclear $[V_2O_7]^{4-}$ ions consisting of 2 VO_4 tetrahedra sharing a corner; the structures of "meta"-vanadates depend on the state of hydration (Fig. 22.3) but in no cases do they involve discrete VO_3^- ions. Anhydrous metavanadates such as NH_4VO_3 contain infinite chains of corner-linked VO_4 tetrahedra, while hydrated metavanadates, such as $KVO_3.H_2O$, contain infinite chains of approximately trigonal bipyramidal VO_5 units, not unlike those in V_2O_5. From the bright orange, acidic solutions, orange, crystalline decavanadates such as $Na_6V_{10}O_{28}.18H_2O$ are obtained: the anion $[V_{10}O_{28}]^{6-}$ is made up of 10 VO_6 octahedra, two representations of which are shown in Fig. 22.3. ^{51}V and ^{17}O nmr evidence shows that this is present in solution, and it can be isolated with a variety of counter cations — indeed it occurs naturally in at least three minerals. Other compounds such as $(PyH)_4[V_{10}O_{28}H_2]$

can also be crystallized[9] in which outer oxygen atoms of the polyanion are protonated†, while refluxing the tetra-n-butyl ammonium salt of the decavanadate in acetonitrile has been shown[10] to yield the dark-red inclusion compound $[(n\text{-}C_4H_9N)]_4[MeCN \subset (V_{12}O_{32})^{4-}]$ in which the MeCN molecule sits inside the now basket-shaped polyanion.

Because of potential applications in catalysis and in providing convenient models for biological systems (for example, the chemical similarities of VO^{n+} and Fe^{n+} may be harnessed to study iron storage and transport proteins), a more diverse chemistry has so far been developed for reduced polyvanadates exhibiting a whole range of V^V to V^{IV} ratios. At the reduced extreme of this range, prolonged heating (4 days at 200°C) of NH_4VO_3 and $EtC(CH_2OH)_3$ produces black crystals of the V^{IV} compound[11] $(NH_4)_4[V_{10}O_{16}\{EtC(CH_2O)_3\}_4].4H_2O$, in the anion of which, twelve of the oxygen atoms in the $V_{10}O_{28}$ cluster are provided by bridging alkoxy groups. The same research workers have also used this hydrothermal technique to prepare another decavanadate(IV) material which contains chiral, interpenetrating double helices of vanadium phosphate units.[12] Still higher nuclearity is found in the dark brown $M_{12}^I[V_{18}O_{42}].nH_2O$ crystallized from alkaline solutions of VO_2. The anion consists this time of VO_5 square pyramids, the bases of which by corner- and edge-sharing form an almost spherical cavity of diameter ~450 pm (Fig. 22.3f). It has the extraordinary ability to encapsulate *negatively* charged ions, as in

---

† Although protonation usually occurs on outer oxygen atoms (Fig. 22.3e), an exception is provided by $[NH_3(C_6H_{13})][V_{10}O_{28}H_2]$ in which the protons have been located on triply linked, inner oxygen atoms. See P. ROMAN, A. ARANZABE, A. LUQUE, J. M. G.-ZORILLA and M. M.-RIPOLL, *J. Chem. Soc., Dalton Trans.*, 2225–31 (1995).

[9] J. M. ARRIETA, *Polyhedron* **11**, 3045–68 (1992).

[10] V. W. DAY, W. G. KLEMPERER and O. M. YAGHI, *J. Am. Chem. Soc.* **111**, 5959–61 (1989).

[11] M. I. KHAN, Q. CHEN and J. ZUBIETA, *J. Chem. Soc., Chem. Commun.*, 305–6 (1992).

[12] V. SOGHOMONIAN, Q. CHEN, R. C. HAUSHALTER, J. ZUBIETA and C. J. CONNOR, *Science* **259**, 1596–9 (1993).

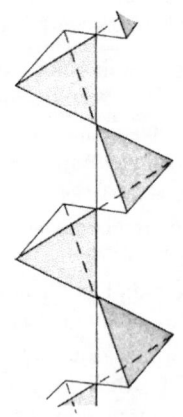
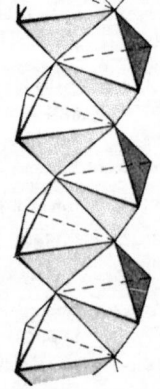
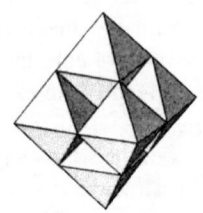

(a) Anhydrous metavanadates,   (b) Hydrated metavanadates,   (c) The $[M_6O_{19}]^{8-}$ (M = Nb.
  (e.g. NH_4VO_3) consisting of   (e.g. $KVO_3 \cdot H_2O$) consisting   Ta) ions made up of 6 MO_6
  infinte chains of corner-shared   of infinite chains of edge-shared   octahedra (one is obscured).
  VO_4 tetrahedra. VO_5 trigonal bipyramids.

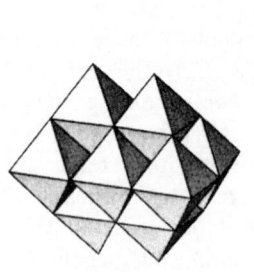
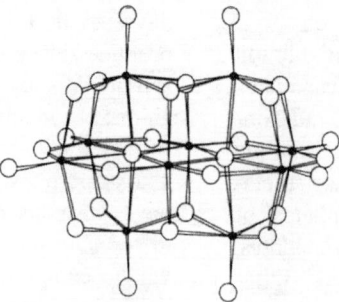
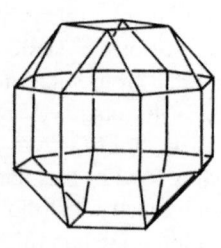

(d) The decavanadate, $[V_{10}O_{28}]^{6-}$. ion   (e) An alternative representation of   (f) Polyhedral cavity of $[V_{18}O_{42}]^{12-}$. Each
  made up of 10 VO_6 octahedra (2 are $[V_{10}O_{28}]^{6-}$ emphasizing the   square represents the base of a VO_5 unit
  obscured).   V–O bonds.   whose apex points outwards; and the
                                                                             triangles are "gaps" between pyramids.

Figure 22.3   The structures of some isopoly-anions in the solid state using, where relevant, the conventional representation in which each polyhedron contains a metal atom and each vertex of a polyhedron represents an oxygen atom.

the compounds,[13] $M_9[H_4V_{18}O_{42}X].nH_2O$ (M = Cs, $n = 12$, X = Br, I; M = K, $n = 16$, X = Cl). Amongst the mixed, V^V, V^{IV} polyvanadates nuclearities up to 34 have been attained,[14] as in $K_{10}[V_{34}O_{82}].20H_2O$. In these materials the coordination of the metal can be octahedral (V^V, V^{IV}), square pyramidal (V^V, V^{IV}), trigonal bipyramidal (V^V) and tetrahedral (V^V), and the

magnetic moment per V^{IV} atom decreases as the proportion of V^{IV} atoms increases (indicating increasing M–M interaction). To rationalize this rich variety of structures it has been suggested[15] that they may be conceptually derived from that of V_2O_5.

Heteropolyanions, in which an atom of a different element is incorporated, usually at the centre of a cage-like structure, are most abundant in Group 6 (p. 1013) but increasing numbers are to

[13] A. Müller, M. Penk, R. Rohlfing, E. Krickemeyer and J. Döring, *Angew. Chem. Int. Edn. Engl.* **29**, 926–7 (1990).

[14] A. Müller, R. Rohlfing, J. Döring and M. Penk. *Angew. Chem. Int. Edn. Engl.* **30**, 588–60 (1991).

[15] W. Klemperer. T. A. Marquart and O. M. Yaghi. *Angew. Chem. Int. Edn. Engl.* **31**. 49–51 (1992).

be found in this group also. For vanadium(V) the $[XV_{14}O_{42}]^{9-}$ ions (X = P, As) are composed of an X atom tetrahedrally coordinated to four oxygen atoms at the centre of a "Keggin" anion (p. 1014) which is capped by two VO groups.[16] Reduced species, because of their lower overall anionic charge, allow the formation of clusters of higher nuclearity and several of these have been reported.[8]

Fusion of Nb_2O_5 and Ta_2O_5 with an excess of alkali hydroxides or carbonates, followed by dissolution in water, produces solutions of isopolyanions but not in the variety produced with vanadium. It appears that, down to pH 11, $[M_6O_{19}]^{8-}$ ions are present; in the case of niobium protonation occurs at lower pH to give $[HNb_6O_{19}]^{7-}$. The presence of discrete MO_4^{3-} ions in strongly alkaline solutions is uncertain. Below pH $\sim$ 7 for Nb and pH $\sim$ 10 for Ta, precipitation of the hydrous oxides occurs. Salts such as $K_8M_6O_{19}.16H_2O$ can be crystallized from the alkaline solutions and contain $[M_6O_{19}]^{8-}$ ions which are made up of octahedral groupings of 6 MO_6 octahedra (Fig. 22.3). A decaniobate, exactly analogous to the decavanadate, has also been isolated and it is possible that such species exist also in solution at low pH.

Most niobates and tantalates, however, are insoluble and may be regarded as mixed oxides in which the Nb or Ta is octahedrally coordinated and with no discrete anion present. Thus KMO_3, known inaccurately (since they have no discrete MO_3^- anions) as metaniobates and metatantalates, have the perovskite (p. 963) structure. Several of these perovskites have been characterized and some have ferroelectric and piezoelectric properties (p. 57). Because of these properties, $LiNbO_3$ and $LiTaO_3$ have been found to be attractive alternatives to quartz as "frequency filters" in communications devices.

A number of nonstoichiometric "bronzes" are also known[17] which, like the titanium bronzes

already mentioned (p. 964) and the better known tungsten bronzes (p. 1016), are characterized by very high electrical conductivities and characteristic colours. For instance, Sr_xNbO_3 ($x = 0.7-0.95$) varies in colour from deep blue to red as the Sr content increases. Fusion of mixtures of appropriate oxides of niobium and alkali metals produces black powders (shiny, golden *single crystals*) of $NaNb_{10}O_{18}$ (metallic conductance)[18] and KNb_8O_{14} (semiconductor),[19] both of which are made up of Nb^VO_6 octahedra and Nb_6O_{12} clusters analogous to the M_6X_{12} halide cluster (p. 992). Li_xNbO_2 ($x \sim 0.5$) has been shown[20] to be a superconductor below 5 K, and is notable as the first superconductor involving an early transition metal oxide which has a layered rather than a 3D structure. It is, indeed, the search for better superconductors and battery electrode materials which is responsible for the upsurge in interest in early transition metal oxides, and further expansion of this area of chemistry is to be expected.

22.3.3 Sulfides, selenides and tellurides

All three metals form a wide variety of binary chalcogenides which frequently differ both in stoichiometry and in structure from the oxides. Many have complex structures which are not easily described, and detailed discussion is therefore inappropriate. The various sulfide phases are listed in Table 22.4: phases approximating to the stoichiometry MS have the NiAs-type structure (p. 556) whereas MS_2 have layer lattices related to MoS_2 (p. 1018), CdI_2, or $CdCl_2$ (p. 1212). Sometimes complex layer-sequences occur in which the 6-coordinate metal atom is alternatively octahedral and trigonal prismatic. Most of the phases exhibit

16 G.-Q. HUANG, S.-W. ZHANG, Y.-G. WEI and M.-C. SHAO, *Polyhedron* **12**. 1483–5 (1993).

17 P. HAGENMULLER, Chap. 50 in *Comprehensive Inorganic Chemistry*. Vol. 4. pp. 541–605, Pergamon Press, Oxford. 1973.

18 J. KÖHLER and A. SIMON, *Z. anorg. allg. Chem.* **572**, 7–17 (1989).

19 J. KÖHLER, R. TISCHTAN and A. SIMON, *J. Chem. Soc., Dalton Trans.*, 829–32 (1991).

20 M. GESELBRACHT. T. J. RICHARDSON and A. M. STACY, *Nature* **345**. 324–6 (1990).

Table 22.4 Sulfides of vanadium, niobium and tantalum

V_3S	$Nb_{21}S_8$	Ta_6S	V_2S_3	—	—
—	—	Ta_2S	V_5S_8	$Nb_{1+x}S_2$	$Ta_{1+x}S_2$
V_5S_4	—	—	—	NbS_2	TaS_2
VS	NbS_{1-x}	TaS	—	NbS_3	TaS_3
V_7S_8	—	—	VS_4	—	—
V_3S_4	Nb_3S_4	—			

Table 22.5 Selenides and tellurides of vanadium, niobium and tantalum

V_2Se	—	—	—	—	—
V_5Se_4	Nb_5Se_4	—	V_5Te_4	Nb_5Te_4	—
VSe	$NbSe$	—	VTe_{1+x}	—	$TaTe$
V_7Se_8	—	—	—	—	—
V_3Se_4	Nb_3Se_4	—	V_3Te_4	Nb_3Te_4	—
(V_2Se_3)	Nb_2Se_3	Ta_2Se_3	V_2Te_3	—	—
V_5Se_8	—	—	V_5Te_8	—	—
—	$Nb_{1+x}Se_2$	$Ta_{1+x}Se_2$	$V_{1+x}Te_2$	$Nb_{1+x}Te_2$	$Ta_{1-x}Te_2$
VSe_2	$NbSe_2$	$TaSe_2$	VTe_2	$NbTe_2$	$TaTe_2$
—	—	$TaSe_3$	—	—	—
—	$NbSe_4$	—	—	$NbTe_4$	$TaTe_4$

metallic conductivity and magnetic properties range from diamagnetic (e.g. VS_4), through paramagnetic (VS, V_2S_3), to antiferromagnetic (V_7S_8). Selenides and tellurides show a similar profusion of stoichiometries and structural types (Table 22.5).

In addition to these binary chalcogenides, many of which exist over wide ranges of composition because of the structural relation between the NiAs and CdI_2 structure types (p. 556), several ternary phases have been studied. Some, like $BaVS_3$ and $BaTaS_3$ have three-dimensional structures in which the Ba and V(Ta) are coordinated by 12 and 6 S atoms respectively. Other compounds such as the easily hydrolysed $(NH_4)_3VS_4$, which has been known for over a century, and $M_3^IVS_4$ (M = Na, K, Tl) prepared by heating stoichiometric amounts of the elements under vacuum[21] contain the discrete, tetrahedral $[VS_4]^{3-}$ anion. The cluster chemistry of the thiometallates of this group, however, is not comparable to that of the oxometallates. It is very limited and whereas, for instance, $(Et_4N)_4[M_6S_{17}].3CH_3CN$ (M = Nb,

Ta) contains a discrete $[M_6S_{17}]^{4-}$ anion,[22] the stoichiometrically analogous $M_4^INb_6O_{17}0.3H_2O$ has an extended structure.

22.3.4 Halides and oxohalides

The known halides of vanadium, niobium and tantalum, are listed in Table 22.6. These are illustrative of the trends within this group which have already been alluded to. Vanadium(V) is only represented at present by the fluoride, and even vanadium(IV) does not form the iodide, though all the halides of vanadium(III) and vanadium(II) are known. Niobium and tantalum, on the other hand, form all the halides in the high oxidation state, and are in fact unique (apart only from protactinium) in forming pentaiodides. However in the +4 state, tantalum fails to form a fluoride and neither metal produces a trifluoride. In still lower oxidation states, niobium and tantalum give a number of (frequently nonstoichiometric) cluster compounds which can be considered to involve fragments of the metal lattice.

[21] A. T. HARRISON and O. W. HAWORTH, *J. Chem. Soc., Dalton Trans.*, 1405–9 (1986).

[22] J. SOLA, Y. DO, J. M. BERG and R. H. HOLM, *Inorg. Chem.* **24**, 1706–13 (1985).

Table 22.6   Halides of vanadium, niobium and tantalum[a] (mp, bp/°C)

Oxidation state	Fluorides	Chlorides	Bromides	Iodides
+5	VF$_5$ colourless mp 19.5°, bp 48.3°	—	—	—
	NbF$_5$ white mp 79°, bp 234°	NbCl$_5$ yellow mp 203°, bp 247°	NbBr$_5$ orange mp 254°, bp 360°	NbI$_5$ brass coloured
	TaF$_5$ white mp 97°, bp 229°	TaCl$_5$ white mp 210°, bp 233°	TaBr$_5$ pale yellow mp 280°, bp 345°	TaI$_5$ black mp 496°, bp 543°
+4	VF$_4$ lime green (subl > 150°)	VCl$_4$ red-brown mp − 26°, bp 148°	VBr$_4$ magenta (d − 23°)	—
	NbF$_4$ black (d > 350°)	NbCl$_4$ violet-black	NbBr$_4$ dark brown	NbI$_4$ dark grey mp 503°
	—	TaCl$_4$ black	TaBr$_4$ dark blue	TaI$_4$
+3	VF$_3$ yellow-green mp 800°	VCl$_3$ red-violet	VBr$_3$ grey-brown	VI$_3$ brown-black
	NbF$_3$(?) blue	NbCl$_3$ black	NbBr$_3$ dark brown	NbI$_3$
	TaF$_3$(?) blue	TaCl$_3$ black	TaBr$_3$	—
+2	VF$_2$ blue	VCl$_2$ pale green (subl 910°)	VBr$_2$ orange-brown (subl 800°)	VI$_2$ red-violet

[a]Niobium and Ta also form a number of polynuclear halides in which the metal has non-integral oxidation states (see text).

VF$_5$ and all pentahalides of Nb and Ta can be prepared conveniently by direct action of the appropriate halogen on the heated metal. They are all relatively volatile, hydrolysable solids (indicative of the covalency to be anticipated in such a high oxidation state) in which the metals attain octahedral coordination by means of halide bridges (Fig. 22.4). VF$_5$ is an infinite chain polymer, whereas NbF$_5$ and TaF$_5$ are tetramers, and the chlorides and bromides are dimers. The colours vary from white fluorides, yellow chlorides, and orange bromides, to brown iodides. The decreasing energy of the charge-transfer bands responsible for these colours is a reflection of the increasing polarizability of the anions from F$^-$ to I$^-$, and for each anion usually the least readily reduced Ta produces the palest colour. All the pentahalides can be sublimed in an atmosphere of the appropriate halogen and they are then monomeric, probably trigonal bipyramidal. Potentially they are all Lewis acids but their ability to form adducts (LMX$_5$) diminishes and the iodides rarely do so.

The tetrahalides can be prepared by direct action of the elements. However, whereas VF$_4$ tends to disproportionate into VF$_5$ + VF$_3$ and must be sublimed from them, VCl$_4$ and VBr$_4$ tend to dissociate into VX$_3$ + $\frac{1}{2}$X$_2$ and so require the presence of an excess of halogen. Even so, VBr$_4$ has only been isolated by quenching the mixed vapours at −78°C. VF$_4$ is a bright-green hygroscopic solid, probably consisting of fluorine-bridged VF$_6$ octahedra. VCl$_4$ is a red-brown oil, rapidly hydrolysed by water to give solutions of oxovanadium(IV) chloride, and magnetic and spectroscopic evidence indicate that

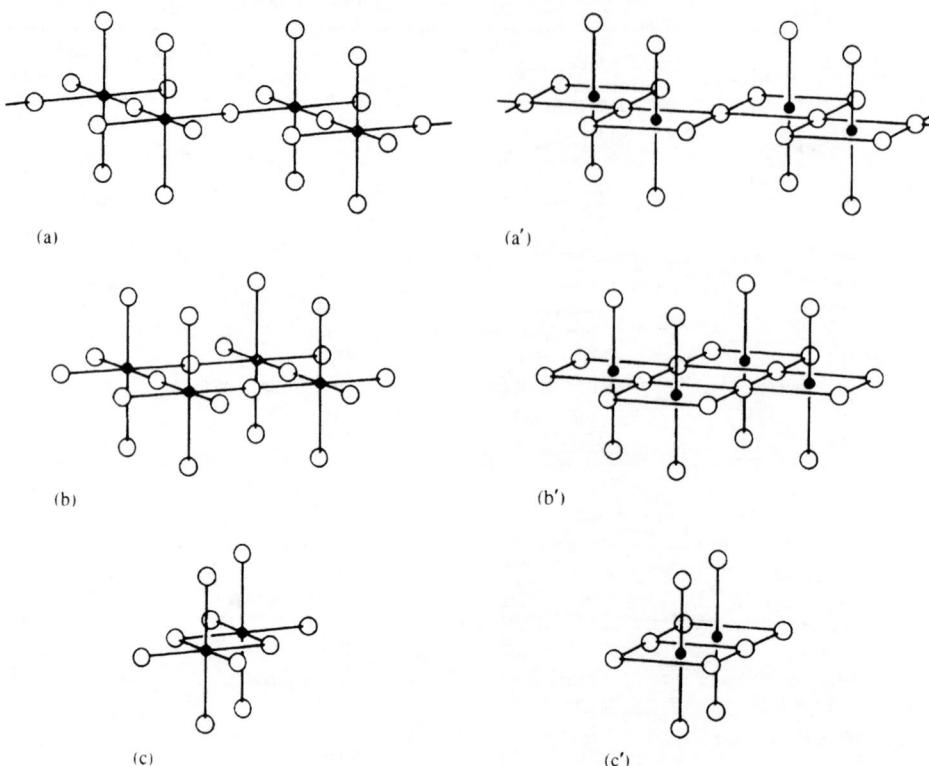

Figure 22.4   Alternative representations of: (a) infinite chains of vanadium atoms in VF_5, (b) tetrameric structures
of NbF_5 and TaF_5. and (c) dimeric structure of MX_5 (M = Nb, Ta; X = Cl, Br).

it consists of unassociated tetrahedral molecules.
As far as its properties are known, the magenta-
coloured VBr_4 is similar.

The Nb and Ta tetrahalides (except TaF_4
which is unknown, and NbI_4 which is
prepared by thermal decomposition of NbI_5)
are generally prepared by reduction of the
corresponding pentahalide and are all readily
hydrolysed. NbF_4 is a black involatile solid and
its low magnetic moment suggests extensive
metal–metal interaction, presumably via the
intervening F^- ions since it consists of infinite
sheets of NbF_6 octahedra (Fig. 22.5a). The
chlorides, bromides and iodides are brown to
black solids with a chain structure (Fig. 22.5b) in
which pairs of metal atoms are displaced towards
each other, so facilitating the interaction which
leads to their diamagnetism.

The vanadium trihalides are all crystalline,
polymeric solids in which the vanadium is 6-
coordinate. VF_3 is prepared by the action of HF
on heated VCl_3 and this, along with VBr_3 and
VI_3, can be prepared by direct action of the
elements under appropriate conditions. They are
coloured and have magnetic moments slightly
lower than the spin-only value of 2.83 BM
corresponding to 2 unpaired electrons. Apart
from the trifluoride, which is not very readily
oxidized nor very soluble in water, they are
easily oxidized by air and are very hygroscopic,
forming aqueous solutions of $[V(H_2O)_6]^{3+}$. As
with the other lower halides of Nb and Ta, the
trihalides are obtained by reduction or thermal
decomposition of their pentahalides. Despite
claims for the existence of NbF_3 and TaF_3
it is probable that these blue materials are

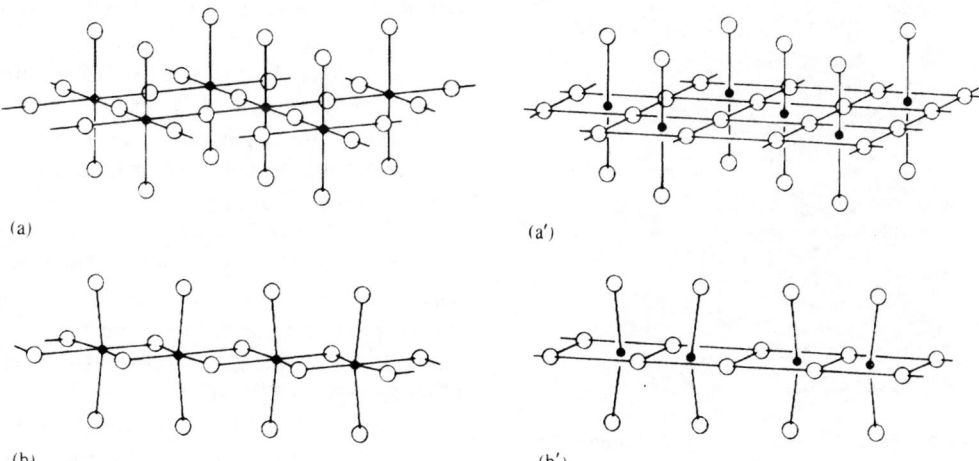

(a)   (a')

(b)   (b')

Figure 22.5   Alternative representations of: (a) the sheet structure of NbF$_4$ and (b) the chain structure of MX$_4$ (M = Nb, Ta; X = Cl, Br, I) showing the displacement of the metal atoms which leads to diamagnetism.

actually oxide fluorides but, because O^{2-} and F$^-$ are isoelectronic and very similar in size, they are difficult to distinguish by X-ray methods. The remaining 5 known trihalides of this pair of metals are dark coloured, rather unreactive materials. The Nb–Cl system has been the most thoroughly studied but the others appear to be entirely analogous. They are nonstoichiometric and the composition "MX$_3$" is best considered as a single unexceptional point within a broad homogeneous phase based on hcp halide ions. At one extreme is M$_3$X$_8$ (i.e. MX$_{2.67}$) in which one-quarter of the octahedral sites are empty and the others occupied by triangular groups of metal atoms. Of the 15 valence electrons provided by the 3 metal atoms, 8 are lost by ionization and transfer to the 8 Cl atoms and, of the remaining 7 available for metal–metal bonding, 6 are considered to be in bonding orbitals and 1 in a nonbonding orbital. This accounts for the magnetic moment of 1.86 BM for each trinuclear cluster in Nb$_3$Cl$_8$. Metal deficiency then produces stoichiometries to somewhat beyond MX$_3$ (i.e. M$_{2.67-x}$X$_8$) after which the MX$_4$ phase separates, containing pairs of interacting metal atoms, as already mentioned (i.e. M$_2$X$_8$).

In the still lower oxidation state, +2, the halides of vanadium on the one hand, and niobium and tantalum, on the other, diverge still further. The dihalides of V are prepared by reduction of the corresponding trihalides and have simple structures based on the close-packing of halide ions: the rutile structure (p. 961) for VF$_2$, and the CdI$_2$ structure (p. 1212) for the others. They are strongly reducing and hygroscopic, dissolving in water to give lavender-coloured solutions of [V(H$_2$O)$_6$]$^{2+}$. By contrast, high-temperature reductions of NbX$_5$ or TaX$_5$ with the metals (or Na or Al) yield a series of phases based on [M$_6$X$_{12}$]$^{n+}$ units consisting of octahedral clusters of metal atoms with the halogen atoms situated above each edge of the octahedra (Fig. 22.6). These may be surrounded by:

(a) Four similar units, with each of which a halogen atom is shared, producing a sheet structure with the composition [M$_6$X$_{12}$]X$_{4/2}$ = M$_6$X$_{14}$ (i.e. MX$_{2.3}$). These compounds are diamagnetic as a result of the metal–metal bonding.

(b) Six similar units, with each of which a halogen atom is shared, producing a

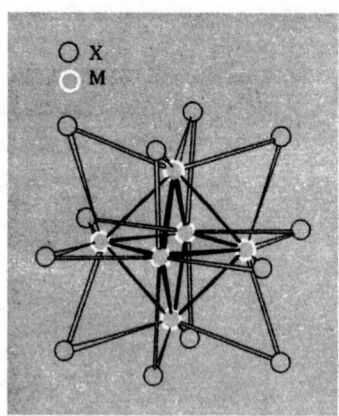

Figure 22.6 $[M_6X_{12}]^{n+}$ cluster with X bridges over each edge of the octahedron of metal ions.

three-dimensional array with the composition $[M_6X_{12}]X_{6/2} = M_6X_{15}$ (i.e. $MX_{2.5}$). These have magnetic moments corresponding to 1 unpaired electron per hexamer and so indicate the same metal–metal bonding within the cluster as in (a).

By incorporation of alkali metal halides in the reaction mix, materials of composition M_4^I-$[M_6X_{18}]$ can be produced in which each M_6X_{12} unit has a further six X atoms attached to its apices, so forming discrete clusters.

Many of these cluster compounds are water-soluble and yield solutions in which the clusters are retained throughout chemical reactions. These reactions include attachment of a variety of ligands at the apical (or "terminal") sites as well as reversible oxidations of the clusters. Thus, it has been possible[23] to isolate $Rb_4[Nb_6Br_{12}(N_3)_6].2H_2O$ from aqueous methanolic solutions, and from aqueous alcoholic solutions of $[M_6X_{12}]X_2.8H_2O$ (M = Nb, Ta; X = Cl, Br)[23a] the insoluble, diamagnetic compounds $[M_6X_{12}(ROH)_6]X_2$. In these compounds all the terminal coordination sites are occupied by azide groups and aliphatic alcohols respectively. In addition $[M_6X_{12}]^{2+}$ (diamagnetic) can also be

oxidized to $[M_6X_{12}]^{3+}$ (1 unpaired electron) and then to $[M_6X_{12}]^{4+}$ (diamagnetic), and compounds such as M_6X_{14}, M_6X_{15} and M_6X_{16}, usually with 7 or 8 molecules of H_2O, can be crystallized. Although terminal ligands are generally more labile than the bridging halogen atoms, isomers of the green $[Ta_6Cl_{12}(\mu\text{-}Cl)_2(PR_3)_4]$ in which the terminal chlorines are either *cis* or *trans* have been isolated by column chromatography. The isomerism was then retained[24] when the individual isomers were oxidized by $NOBF_4$ or $AgBF_4$ to the orange to brown BF_4^- salts of $[Ta_6Cl_{12}(\mu\text{-}Cl)_2(PR_3)_4]^{n+}$ (n = 1, 2).

The $[M_6X_8]$ cluster unit in which halogen atoms are situated above each *face* of the M_6 octahedron is far less common here than in Group 6 (p. 1022) but does occur in the unusual compound, Nb_6I_{11}. This consists of a 3D array of six $[Nb_6I_8]$ units joined by shared iodines: $[Nb_6I_8]I_{6/2} = Nb_6I_{11}$. It absorbs hydrogen and, in 1967, provided the first example of a metal atom cluster with an encapsulated H atom at its centre.[25] Both Nb_6I_{11} and HNb_6I_{11} exhibit a "spin-crossover": 1 to 3 unpaired electrons at 274 K for the former, and diamagnetic to 2 unpaired electrons at 324 K for the latter.[26]

The cluster compounds of this group may be regarded as intermediate between the $[M_6X_8]^{n+}$ type of Group 6 (p. 1022) which generally possess sufficient electrons (24) to allow M–M single bonds on each edge of the octahedron, and the comparatively electron-poor clusters of Groups 3 and 4 (p. 950 and 965) which generally require the presence of an interstitial atom to stabilize them.[27]

The known oxohalides are listed in Table 22.7. They are generally prepared from the oxides but are not particularly well known and, as can be seen, are limited almost entirely to the oxidation states of +4 and +5. Those in the

[23] H.-J. MEYER, *Z. anorg. allg. Chem.* **621**, 921–4 (1995).

[23a] A. KASHTA, N. BRNICEVIC and R. E. McCARLEY, *Polyhedron* **10**, 2031–6 (1991).

[24] H. IMOTO, S. HAYAKAWA, N. MORITA and T. SAITO, *Inorg. Chem.* **29**, 2007–14 (1990).

[25] A. SIMON, F. STOLLMAIER, D. GREGSON and H. FUESS, *J. Chem. Soc., Dalton Trans.*, 431–4 (1987).

[26] H. IMOTO and A. SIMON, *Inorg. Chem.* **21**, 308–19 (1982).

[27] A. SIMON, *Angew. Chem. Int. Edn. Engl.* **27**, 159–83 (1988).

Table 22.7   Oxohalides of vanadium, niobium and tantalum[28]

Oxidation state	Fluorides		Chlorides		Bromides		Iodides	
+5	VOF_3 yellow mp 300° bp 480°	VO_2F brown	$VOCl_3$ yellow mp −77° bp 127°	VO_2Cl orange	$VOBr_3$ deep red (d 180°)		—	
		NbO_2F white	$NbOCl_3$ white	NbO_2Cl white	$NbOBr_3$ yellow-brown	NbO_2Br brown	$NbOI_3$ black	NbO_2I red
	$TaOF_3$	TaO_2F	$TaOCl_3$ white	TaO_2Cl white	$TaOBr_3$ pale yellow	TaO_2Br orange-gold	$TaOI_3$	TaO_2I
+4	VOF_2 yellow		$VOCl_2$ green		$VOBr_2$ yellow-brown (d 180°)			
			$NbOCl_2$ black		$NbOBr_2$		$NbOI_2$ black	
			$TaOCl_2$		$TaOBr_2$ black		$TaOI_2$ black	
+3	—		$VOCl$ yellow-brown bp 127°		$VOBr$ violet (d 480°)			

former oxidation state are relatively stable but those in the latter are notably hygroscopic and hydrolyse vigorously to the hydrous pentoxides. The Nb(V) and Ta(V) compounds are rather volatile, though less so than the pentahalides. $NbOCl_3$ is the best known, mainly because of its propensity for occurring as an unwanted impurity in the preparation of VCl_5 if O_2 is not rigorously excluded or, more specially, if V_2O_5 is used.

22.3.5 Compounds with oxoanions

The group oxidation state of +5 is too high to allow the formation of simple ionic salts even for Nb and Ta, and in lower oxidation states the higher sublimation energies of these heavier metals, coupled with their ease of oxidation, again militates against the formation of simple salts of the oxoacids. As a consequence the only simple oxoanion salts are the sulfates of vanadium in the oxidation states +3 and +2. These can be crystallized from aqueous solutions as hydrates and are both strongly

reducing. They give rise to blue-violet alums, $MV(SO_4)_2.12H_2O$, the ammonium alum being air-stable when dry, and to the reddish-violet Tutton's salts, $M_2V(SO_4)_2.6H_2O$, the ammonium analogue of which is again relatively more stable to oxidation.

In the higher oxidation states partially hydrolysed species dominate the aqueous chemistry, the most important being the oxovanadium(IV), or vanadyl, ion VO^{2+}. This gives the sulfate $VOSO_4.5H_2O$, containing monodentate sulfate and octahedrally coordinated vanadium, and the polymeric $VOSO_4$. Oxovanadium(V) species are not well characterized, outside the oxohalides VOX_3, but in strongly acid solutions VO_2^+ is formed and reportedly gives the nitrate $VO_2(NO_3)$. The VO_2^+ ion is also found in anionic complexes such as $[VO_2(oxalate)_2]^{3-}$ and in all cases the oxygens are mutually *cis* as they are in the isoelectronic MoO_2^{2+} (p. 1024). Niobium and tantalum produce a variety of complicated and ill-defined, but probably polymeric, species which include the nitrates, $MO(NO_3)_3$, sulfates such as $Nb_2O(SO_4)$, and double sulfates such as $(NH_4)_6Nb_2O(SO_4)_7$, all of which are extremely readily hydrolysed.

[28] H. Schäfer, R. Gerken and L. Zylka, *Z. anorg. allg. Chem.* **534**, 209–15 (1986).

22.3.6 Complexes[(29,30)]

Oxidation state V (d⁰)

Vanadium (V) has a great affinity for O-donors: the extensive chemistry of the polyoxometallates has already been discussed and complexes not involving oxygen, such as the white diamagnetic hexafluorovanadates, MVF_6, are extremely susceptible to hydrolysis. If H_2O_2 is added to aqueous solutions of $[VO_4]^{3-}$ a series of substituted products is obtained depending on pH. Using Raman and ^{51}V nmr spectroscopy to compare the solutions with compounds of known compositions and structures, suggests[(31)] that the red-brown acidic solutions contain $[VO(O_2)(H_2O)_4]^+$ and that in progressively more alkaline solutions, $[VO(O_2)_2(H_2O)]^-$, $[VO_2(O_2)_2(H_2O)]^{3-}$, $[VO(O_2)_3]^{3-}$ and $[V(O_2)_4]^{3-}$ are among the species produced until, from strongly alkaline solutions, blue-violet crystals of $M^I_3[V(O_2)_4]$.- $nH_2O(M^I = Li, Na, K, NH_4)$ are deposited. Like the corresponding Cr ion (p. 637), $[V(O_2)_4]^{3-}$ is 8-coordinate and dodecahedral, but such a high coordination number is not common for vanadium. Niobium and tantalum produce similar peroxo-compounds, e.g. pale yellow $K_3[Nb(O_2)_4]$ and white $K_3[Ta(O_2)_4]$.

However, most complexes of Nb^V and Ta^V are derived from the pentahalides. NbF_5 and TaF_5 dissolve in aqueous solutions of HF to give $[MOF_5]^{2-}$ and, if the concentration of HF is increased, $[MF_6]^-$. This is normally the highest coordination number attained in solution though some $[NbF_7]^{2-}$ may form, and $[TaF_7]^{2-}$ definitely does form, in very high concentrations of HF. However, by suitably regulating the concentration of metal, fluoride ion and HF, octahedral $[MF_6]^-$, capped trigonal prismatic $[MF_7]^{2-}$, and even square-antiprismatic $[MF_8]^{3-}$ salts can all be isolated. By contrast with the fluorides, aqueous solutions of MCl_5 and MBr_5 (M = Nb, Ta) yield only oxochloro- and oxobromo-complexes, though the application of non-aqueous procedures allows their use as starting materials.

Niobium(V) is generally considered to be a class-a metal, but the SCN^- ligand yields a series of both N-bonded thiocyanato and S-bonded isothiocyanato complexes, e.g. $[Nb(NCS)_n(SCN)_{6-n}]^-$ ($n = 0, 2, 4, 5, 6$). Furthermore, dithiocarbamates, dodecahedral $[M(S_2CNR_2)_4]^+$, and dithiolates,[(32)] $[M(SCH_2CH_2S)_3]^-$ with stereochemistry midway between octahedral and trigonal-prismatic, are known for both Nb and Ta. The pentahalides of these two metals act as Lewis acids and form complexes of the type MX_5L with O, S, N, P. and As donor ligands.

Oxidation state IV (d¹)

The tetrahalides are Lewis acids and produce a number of adducts with a variety of donor atoms, the most common coordination number being 6. $[VF_4L]$ (L = NH_3, py) are insoluble in common organic solvents, have magnetic moments of about 1.8 BM, and are thought to be fluorine-bridged polymers. $[VCl_42L]$ (L = py, MeCN, aldehydes, etc.) and VCl_4- (L-L) (L-L = bipy, phen, diars) are brown paramagnetic, readily hydrolysed compounds assumed to be 6-coordinate monomers. Similar compounds of Nb and Ta are also paramagnetic and the metal–metal bonding which led to the diamagnetism of the parent tetrahalides is presumed to have been broken to give adducts which again are 6-coordinate monomers. Hexahalo-complexes $[MX_6]^{2-}$ (M = V, X = F, Cl; M = Nb, Ta, X = Cl, Br) are known, the vanadium compounds being especially sensitive to moisture though stable to air.

[29] L. V. Boas and L. C. Pessoa, Vanadium, Chap. 33, pp. 453–583, and L. G. Hubert-Pfalzgraf, M. Postel and J. G. Riess, Niobium and Tantalum, Chap. 34, pp. 585–697 in *Comprehensive Coordination Chemistry*, Vol. 3, Pergamon Press, Oxford, 1987.

[30] R. W. Berg, *Coord. Chem. Revs.* 113, 1–130 (1992).

[31] N. J. Campbell, A. C. Dengel and W. P. Griffith, *Polyhedron* 8, 1379–86 (1989). See also A. Butler, M. J. Clague and G. E. Meister, *Chem. Revs.* 94, 625–38 (1994).

[32] K. Tatsumi, Y. Sekiguchi, A. Nakamura, R. E. Cramer and J. J. Rupp, *Angew. Chem. Int. Edn. Engl.* 25, 86–7 (1986).

Higher coordination numbers are also found. Vanadium and Nb produce the dodecahedral $[MCl_4(diars)_2]$ just like the Group 4 metals. This is probably the most common stereochemistry for this coordination number but others are possible; differences in energy are slight and this facilitates non-rigidity. For example the yellow-coloured solid $K_4[Nb(CN)_8].2H_2O$ contains dodecahedral niobium(IV) (like its molybdenum isomorph), whereas esr and infrared data suggest that, in solution, the anion has the square-antiprismatic configuration. Likewise, the deep-red niobium(III) complex $K_5[Nb(CN)_8]$ adopts a dodecahedral (D_{2d}) configuration for the anion in the crystal whereas the single ^{13}C nmr signal in aqueous solution implies either a square-pyramidal (D_{4d}) or fluxional (D_{2d}) structure.

The major contrast with the Group 4 metals is the stability of VO^{2+} complexes which are the most important and the most widely studied of the vanadium(IV) complexes, and are the usual products of the hydrolysis of other vanadium(IV) complexes. VO^{2+} behaves as a class-a cation, forming stable compounds with F (especially), Cl, O, and N donor ligands. These "vanadyl" complexes are generally blue to green and can be cationic, neutral or anionic. They are very frequently 5-coordinate in which case the stereochemistry is almost invariably square pyramidal. $[VO(acac)_2]$ (Fig. 22.7) is the archetypal example of this geometry in coordination compounds. In this and in similar compounds the $V=O$ bond length is $\sim157-168$ pm which is about 50 pm shorter than the 4 equatorial V–O bonds. This, as well as spectroscopic evidence, is consistent with the

formulation of the bond as double. A sixth ligand may be weakly bonded *trans* to the $V=O$ to produce a distorted octahedral structure; the concomitant reduction in the stretching frequency of the $V=O$ bond generally within the range, $985 \pm 50\,cm^{-1}$ has been interpreted in terms of electron donation from this sixth ligand, thereby making the vanadium atom less able to accept charge from the oxygen and so reducing the bond order. Tetradentate Schiff bases, produced for instance by the condensation of salicylaldehyde with primary diamines, in most cases give entirely analogous compounds, but some are yellow and may be polymeric with the vanadium attaining 6-coordination by "stacking" so that the sixth position of each vanadium is occupied by the oxygen from the $V=O$ beneath. The black $[V(salen)_4(\mu-O)_3](BF_4)_2$ [H_2salen $= N,N'$-ethylenebis(salicylideneimine), p. 907] has recently been shown to be tetrameric with a linear V–O–V–O–V–O–V chain.[33]

In spite of the evident proclivity of VO^{2+} to form square pyramidal or distorted octahedral complexes, it must not be assumed that 5-coordination inevitably results in the former shape. $[VOCl_2(NMe_3)_2]$ is in fact trigonal bipyramidal (Fig. 22.8), no doubt because of a dominant steric effect of the bulky trimethylamine ligands rather than any electronic effect. Most oxovanadium(IV) complexes are magnetically simple, having virtually "spin-only" moments of 1.73 BM corresponding to 1 unpaired electron, but their electronic spectra are less easily understood. This is primarily due to the presence of a strong π contribution to the bond between the vanadium and the oxygen which makes it difficult to assign an unequivocal sequence to the molecular orbitals involved.[34]

Some square pyramidal derivatives of thio-vanadyl, $(V=S)^{2+}$, have also been prepared from the corresponding vanadyl complexes: deep magenta [VS(salen)] and [VS(acen)] [H_2acen $= N,N'$-ethylenebis(acetylacetonylideneimine)] by

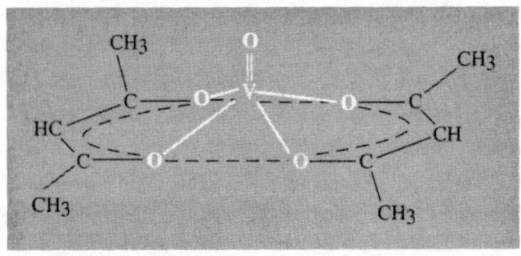

Figure 22.7 The square-pyramidal structure of $[VO(acac)_2]$.

[33] A. HILLS, D. L. HUGHES, G. J. LEIGH and J. R. SANDERS *J. Chem. Soc., Chem. Commun.*, 827–9 (1991).

[34] A. B. P. LEVER, *Inorganic Electronic Spectra*, 2nd edn., pp. 384–91, Elsevier Amsterdam, 1984.

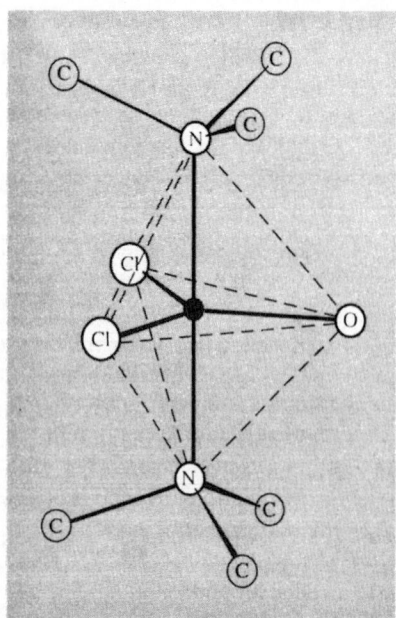

Figure 22.8 The trigonal bipyramidal structure of [$VOCl_2(NMe_3)_2$].

the action of B_2S_3 in CH_2Cl_2; brown [$VS(SCH_2$-$CH_2S)_2$]$^{2-}$ by the action of $(Me_3Si)_2S$ in MeCN.[35] The exclusion of air and moisture throughout these preparations is essential in order to avoid reversion to vandyl complexes.

Oxidation state III (d^2)

Until comparatively recently only vanadium had a significant M^{III} coordination chemistry and even so the majority of its compounds are easily oxidized and must be prepared with air rigorously excluded. The usual methods are to use VCl_3 as the starting material, or to reduce solutions of vanadium(V) or (IV) electrolytically. However, the reduction of pentahalides of Nb and Ta by Na amalgam or Mg, has facilitated the expansion of Nb^{III} and Ta^{III} chemistry particularly with S- and P-donor ligands.

---
[35] G. Christou, D. Heinrich, J. K. Money, J. R. Rambo, J. C. Huffman and K. Folting *Polyhedron*, **8**, 1723–7 (1989).

The chemistry of vanadium(III) closely parallels that of titanium(III) and it likewise favours octahedral coordination. The interpretation of the electronic spectra of its complexes, as the prime examples of d^2 ions in an octahedral field, provided the stimulus for early preparative work in this area. In general, the spectra are characterized by two bands in the visible region with a further much more intense absorption in the ultraviolet. The two former bands are believed to arise from d–d transitions and others from charge-transfer. Since the d^2 configuration in a cubic field is expected to give rise to three spin-allowed transitions it is assumed that the most energetic of these is obscured by the charge-transfer band. Table 22.8 gives data for some octahedral vanadium(III) complexes (see also ref. 34, pp. 400–6). It turns out, on examination of data such as these, that a coherent interpretation of the spectra is only possible if the bands are assigned (Fig. 22.9) as:

$$\nu_1 = {}^3T_{2g}(F) \leftarrow {}^3T_{1g}(F)$$
$$\nu_2 = {}^3T_{1g}(P) \leftarrow {}^3T_{1g}(F)$$

and the third, obscured one, therefore as:

$$\nu_3 = {}^3A_{2g}(F) \leftarrow {}^3T_{1g}(F)$$

B is the Racah "interelectronic repulsion parameter". It is included in Fig. 22.9 in order to retain generality and obviate the necessity of drawing separate diagrams for each d^2 metal ion. The expansion of d-electron charge on complexation reduces its value as compared to the value for the free-ion (860 cm^{-1}). In general the electronic spectra of these 6-coordinate complexes are accounted for moderately well on the assumption of basically octahedral crystal fields, but the inclusion of trigonal distortions gives more satisfactory results. The magnetic moments of d^2 ions in perfectly octahedral fields are expected to involve "orbital contribution" which varies with temperature. In practice the moments at room temperature rarely exceed the spin-only value and their variation with temperature is less than anticipated for a T ground term. This also is in accord with the presence of some distortion which splits the

Table 22.8   Typical octahedral complexes of vanadium(III)

Complex	Colour	ν_1/cm^{-1}	ν_2/cm^{-1}	$10Dq/cm^{-1}$	B/cm^{-1}	μ/BM (room temperature)
$[NH_4][V(H_2O_6)][SO_4]_2.6H_2O$	Blue-violet	17 800	25 700	19 200	620	2.80
$[VCl_3(MeCN)_3]$	Green	14 400	21 400	15 500	540	2.79
$[VCl_3(thf)_3]$	Orange	13 300	19 900	14 000	553	2.80
$K_3[VF_6]$	Green	14 800	23 250	16 100	649	2.79
$[pyH]_3[VCl_6]$	Purple-pink	16 650	18 350	12 650	513	2.71

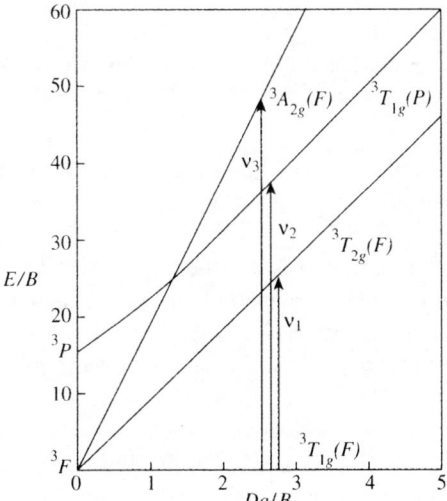

Figure 22.9   Energy Level diagram for a d^2 ion in an octahedral crystal field.

$^3T_{2g}$ ground term and so reduces the temperature dependence of the magnetic moment.

Cationic complexes of the type $[VL_6]^{3+}$ of which $[V(H_2O_6)]^{3+}$ is the best-known example are actually rather rare, the action of NH_3 on VX_3 for instance, causing ammonolysis of the V–X bond to produce $VX_2(NH_2).nNH_3$. Anionic $[VX_6]^{3-}$, $[VX_5L]^{2-}$, $[VX_4L_2]^-$ and neutral $[VCl_3L_3]$ are more common. Dithiolates $[V_2(SCH_2CH_2S)_4]^{2-}$ with four sulfur atoms bridging the two vanadium atoms are also known (Fig. 22.10a), their diamagnetism and short V–V distances (260 pm) indicating M–M bonding.

In spite of the preponderance of 6-coordinate complexes, other coordination numbers are known: the ions $[VCl_4]^-$ and $[VBr_4]^-$ are tetrahedral and are notable in that 4-coordination

with ligands other than O-donors is common only later in the transition series. Their spectra exhibit two bands in the regions of $9000\,cm^{-1}$ and $15\,000\,cm^{-1}$ which are assigned to $^3T_1(F) \leftarrow ^3A_2$ and $^3T_1(P) \leftarrow ^3A_2$ transitions respectively, corresponding quite reasonably to values of Δ_t of about 5000 to $5500\,cm^{-1}$. Their magnetic moments too are about 2.7 BM and independent of temperature, as expected.

Neutral complexes of the type $[VX_3(NMe_3)_2]$ (X = Cl, Br) are trigonal bipyramidal with the trimethylamines occupying the axial positions. By contrast $[V\{N(SiMe_3)_2\}_3]$ has a 3-coordinate, planar structure, presumably because the bis (trimethylsilyl)amido ligands are too big for the V^{III} to accommodate more. The 7-coordinate $K_4[V(CN)_7].2H_2O$ has a pentagonal bipyramidal structure and is a rare example of a 7-coordinated transition metal complex which persists in solution and in which the ligand is not F^-.

A few trinuclear oxo-centred carboxylates $[V_3O(RCOO)_6L_3]^+$ of a type more common for later transition metals (see Fig. 23.9, p. 1030) have been obtained,[36] as well as $[Nb_3O_2(MeCOO)_6(thf)_3]^+$ whose structure differs essentially only in that there are **two** bridging O atoms above and below the Nb_3 plane.[37]

With S- and P- donor ligands such as SMe_2 and PMe_3, $M_2Cl_6L_4$ (M = Nb, Ta) consisting of a pair of edge-sharing octahedra are formed. For Nb, but interestingly not for

[36] F. A. COTTON, M. W. EXTINE, L. R. FALVELLO, D. B. LEWIS, G. E. LEWIS, C. A. MURILLO, W. SCHWOTZER, M. TOMAS and J. M. TROUP, *Inorg. Chem.* **25**, 3505–12 (1986).

[37] F. A. COTTON, M. P. DIEBOLD, R. LLUSAR and W. J. ROTH, *J. Chem. Soc., Chem. Commun.*, 1276–8 (1986).

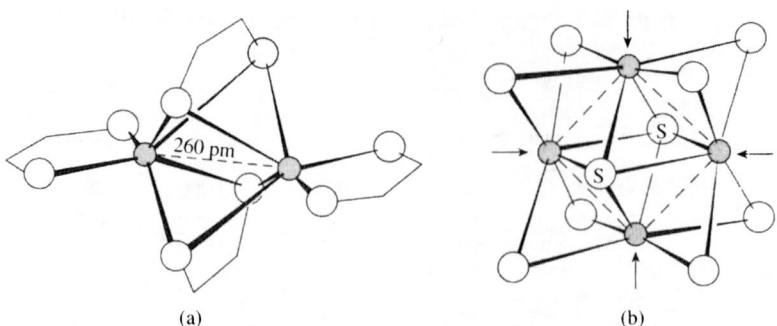

(a)   (b)

Figure 22.10   (a) dithiolates $[V_2(SCH_2CH_2S)_4]^{2-}$. (b) $[Nb_4S_2(SPh)_{12}]^{4-}$ and $[Nb_4S_2(SPh)_8(PMe_2R)_4]$ in which the four arrowed coordination sites are occupied by SPh^- and PMe_2R respectively. Unlabelled S atoms in (b) all have an attached Ph which is not shown. Nb–Nb(av) ~282 pm.

Ta, tetranuclear, orange coloured derivatives $Li_4[Nb_4S_2(SPh)_{12}]^{(38)}$ and $[Nb_4S_2(SPh)_8-(PMe_2R)_4]$ (R = Me, Ph)[39] have been shown to have a common and rather stable central unit of four Nb atoms in a square plane with two μ_4-S atoms above and below it (Fig. 22.10b). The diamagnetism and average Nb–Nb separations of approx 282 pm are consistent with single bonds between adjacent Nb atoms.

Oxidation state II (d³)

The coordination chemistry of this oxidation state is not well-developed. Vanadium(II) complexes are usually prepared by electrolytic or zinc reduction of acidic solutions of vanadium in one of its higher oxidation states. The resulting blue-purple solutions are strongly reducing, and reduction of the water is, in general, only prevented by the presence of acid. Several salts and double sulfates which contain the $[V(H_2O)_6]^{2+}$ ion are known and there are adducts of VCl_2 of the type $[VCl_2L_4]$, where L is one of a number of O- or N-donor ligands. The spectroscopic and magnetic properties of these compounds are typical of a d³ ion and their interpretation follows closely that for the chromium(III) ion (p. 1028). Also

typical of a d³ ion is the fact that vanadium(II) is kinetically inert and undergoes substitution reactions only slowly.

Other complexes of the type $[VCl_2L_2]$ are distinguished by their colour (green) and magnetic moment (~3.2 BM), well below the spin-only value for 3 unpaired electrons, and some at least are halogen-bridged oligomers. Carboxylate derivatives such as the trinuclear $[V_3(RCOO)_6(Me_2NCHCHNMe_2)_2]$ have recently been prepared[40] as has the binuclear $[V_2(RNCHNR)_4]$ (R = p-MeC$_6$H$_4$).[41] The former contains an almost linear chain of V atoms held together by carboxylate bridges and, in the latter, the pair of V atoms bridged by the four ligands, are so close (197.8 pm) that a V≡V bond is indicated (for single- and double-bonded V–V species, separations of approx. 260 and 220 pm, respectively, are common).

Organometallic compounds apart, oxidation states below +2 are best represented by complexes with tris-bidentate nitrogen-donor ligands such as 2,2′-bipyridyl. Reduction by $LiAlH_4$ in thf yields tris(bipyridyl) complexes in which the formal oxidation state of vanadium is +2 to −1. Magnetic moments are compatible with low-spin configurations of the metal but,

[38] J. L. SEELA, J. C. HUFFMAN and G. CHRISTOU, *J. Chem. Soc., Chem. Commun.*, 1258–60 (1987).
[39] E. B. KIBALA, F. A. COTTON and P. A. KIBALA, *Polyhedron* **9**, 1689–94 (1990).

[40] J. J. H. EDEMA, S. GAMBAROTTO, S. HAO and C. BENSIMON, *Inorg. Chem.* **30**, 2584–6 (1991).
[41] F. A. COTTON, L. M. DANIELS and C. A. MURILLO, *Angew. Chem. Int. Edn. Engl.* **31**, 737–8 (1992).

as with the analogous compounds of titanium, it may well be that they would be better regarded as complexes with reduced, i.e. anionic, ligands.

22.3.7 The biochemistry of vanadium[41a]

Certain vertebrates have an astonishing ability to accumulate vanadium in their blood. For example, the ascidian seaworm *Phallusia mammilata* has a blood concentration of V up to 1900 ppm, which represents more than a millionfold concentration with respect to the sea-water in which it lives. The related organism *Ascidia nigra* has an even more spectacular accumulation with concentrations up to 1.45% V (i.e. 14 500 ppm) in its blood cells, which also contain considerable concentrations of sulfuric acid (pH $\sim$ 0). One possibility that has been mooted is that the ascidia accumulates vanadate and polyvanadate ions in mistake for phosphate and polyphosphates (p. 528).

Indeed, the observation that vanadate is a potent inhibitor of phosphate-recognizing enzyme systems was a great stimulus to work in this area, but it now seems likely that its action is more complicated than simple mimicry of phosphates.[42] This is germane to obtaining an understanding of the antitumor activity of $[V(\eta^5\text{-}C_5H_5)_2Cl_2]$.

A number of nitrogen-fixing bacteria contain vanadium and it has been shown that in one of these, *Azotobacter*, there are three distinct nitrogenase systems based in turn on Mo, V and Fe, each of which has an underlying functional and structural similarity.[43] This discovery has prompted a search for models and the brown V^{-1} compound $[\text{Na(thf)}]^+[V(N_2)_2(\text{dppe})_2]$ (dppe = $Ph_2PCH_2CH_2PPh_2$) has recently been prepared by reduction of VCl_3 by sodium naphthalenide

in the presence of dppe.[44] Acidification achieves partial nitrogen fixation since one of the four N atoms is converted to NH_3.

22.3.8 Organometallic compounds[45]

The organometallic chemistry of this group developed rather slowly but there has been a surge of interest, especially in Nb and Ta, in the last decade or so. The chemistry of σ alkyls or aryls is less well developed than for many other elements but $[V^{III}\{CH(SiMe_3)_2\}_3]$, $[V^{IV}(CH_2SiMe_3)_4]$, and $[V^VO(CH_2SiMe_3)_3]$ have been isolated. In these compounds the possibility of decomposition by alkene elimination or other routes is circumvented by the absence of β hydrogen atoms (p. 926) and the bulkiness of the trimethylsilylmethyl groups. Complexes such as $[MMe_5(\text{dmpe})]$ (M = Nb, Ta; dmpe = $Me_2PCH_2CH_2PMe_2$) decompose spontaneously above room temperature and, although free $TaMe_5$ has been isolated, it can explode spontaneously at room temperature even in the absence of air. Despite this instability, the Ta–Me bond itself is rather strong: thermochemical studies have shown that the mean bond dissociation energy $D(\text{Ta–Me})$ in $TaMe_5$ is $261 \pm 6\,kJ\,mol^{-1}$, which is substantially greater than, for example, the mean dissociation energy $D(\text{W–CO})$ of $178 \pm 3\,kJ\,mol^{-1}$ in the kinetically much more stable $W(CO)_6$. Expanding the coordination sphere of the metal by the addition of other ligands such as $C_5H_5^-$, halides and phosphines often increases the thermal stability.

Reduction of MCl_5 or MCl_3 under an atmosphere of CO yields salts of the $[M(CO_6]^-$ ions (M = V, Nb, Ta)[46] which have the noble gas electron configuration. Using Na as reductant

[41a] H. Sigel and A. Sigel (eds.), *Metal Ions in Biological Systems*, Vol. 31, Marcel Dekker, New York, 1995, 779 pp.

[42] A. Butler and C. J. Carrano, *Coord. Chem. Revs.* **109**, 61–105 (1991).

[43] R. R. Eady, *Adv. Inorg. Chem.* **36**, 77–102 (1991).

[44] D. Rehder, C. Woitha, W. Priebsch and M. Gailus *J. Chem. Soc., Chem. Commun.*, 364–5 (1992).

[45] M. G. Connelly, Vanadium, Chap. 24, pp. 648–704, and J. A. Labinger, Niobium and Tantalum, Chap. 25, pp. 706–82 in *Comprehensive Organametallic Chemistry*, Vol. 3, Pergamon Press, Oxford, 1982.

[46] S. C. Srivastava and A. K. Shrimal, *Polyhedron* **7**, 1639–65 (1988).

with pyridine or diglyme as solvent requires high temperatures and pressures, but the application of high-energy ultrasound or the use of Mg/Zn as reductant allows less forcing conditions. In the case of the V salt, but not those of Nb and Ta, acidification and extraction with petroleum ether yields volatile, blue-green, pyrophoric crystals of $V(CO)_6$. Unlike other formally odd-electron transition metal carbonyls, this does not attain the noble gas configuration by dimerization and the formation of a M–M bond. It is in fact monomeric and isomorphous with Group 6 octahedral hexacarbonyls (p. 1037); it undergoes substitution reactions typical of metal carbonyls, but is unique amongst simple carbonyls in being paramagnetic with a moment at room temperature of 1.81 BM. Further reduction of $[Na(diglyme)_2][M(CO)_6]$ with Na metal in liquid NH_3 yields the super-reduced 18-electron species $[M(CO)_5]^{3-}$ which contain M in their lowest known formal oxidation state (-3).[47] Although sensitivity is somewhat dependent on the counter-cation involved, several of the salts of these ions are hazardously shock and temperature sensitive. Direct synthesis of $V(CO)_6$, $V_2(CO)_{12}$ and $M(CO)_n$ (M = V, n = 1–5; M = Ta, n = 1–6) by condensation of vanadium vapour with CO in a matrix of noble gases is possible. The same technique has also been used to prepare the hexakis(dinitrogen) compound, $[V(N_2)_6]$ (p. 981) which is isoelectronic and probably isostructural with the hexacarbonyl.

With the cyclopentadienyl ligand, vanadium forms the simple "sandwich" compound, "vanadocene". $[V(\eta^5-C_5H_5)_2]$ which is dark violet, paramagnetic (3 unpaired electrons) and extremely air-sensitive. Oxidative addition reactions are possible and provide compounds such as $[V(\eta^5-C_5H_5)_2Cl_n]$ (n = 1, 2, 3) and $[V(\eta^5-C_5H_5)_2R_2]$, while its reaction with dithioacetic acid produces the dark-brown tetramer $[V_4(\eta^5-C_5H_5)_4(\mu_3-S_4)$, Fig. 22.11.[48] With four V^{III} atoms, eight electrons are available for six V–V bonds and the implied bond order of 2/3

[47] J. E. ELLIS, *Adv. Organametallic Chem.* **31**, 1–52 (1990).
[48] S. A. DURAJ, M. T. ANDRAS and B. RIHTER, *Polyhedron* **8**, 2763–7 (1989).

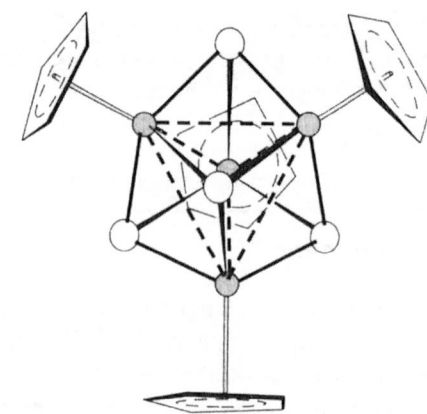

Figure 22.11 $[V_4(\eta^5-C_5H_5)_4(\mu_3-S)_4]$ the centre of which is a tetrahedron of V atoms face-capped by S atoms.

is consistent with the observed average V–V separation of 287.6 pm and magnetic moment of 2.65 BM at room temperature.

Niobium and tantalum do not form simple, thermally stable sandwich compounds. Niobocene is actually a dimer and a hydride (Fig. 22.12a). They do however form $[M(\eta^5-C_5H_5)_4]$ (p. 940) in which two rings are η^5- and two η^1-bonded, and there are many bis(cyclopentadienyl) compounds of the types $[M(\eta^5-C_5H_5)_2X_2]$ and $[M(\eta^5-C_5H_5)_2R_2]$ in which, if the C_5H_5 is taken as a single ligand, the coordination geometry is pseudo-tetrahedral. $[M(\eta^5-C_5H_5)_2X_3]$ and $[M(\eta^5-C_5H_5)_2R_3]$ are also known.

An important compound is the mixed methyl-methylene derivative of bis(cyclopentadienyl)tantalum(V) prepared by the following sequence of high-yield reactions:

$$[Ta(\eta^5-C_5H_5)_2Me_3] \xrightarrow{\ Ph_3C^+BF_4^-\ } [Ta(\eta^5-C_5H_5)_2Me_2]^+$$

$$\xrightarrow{\ +Me_3P\,=\,CH_2\ } [Ta(\eta^5-C_5H_5)_2(CH_3)(=CH_2)]$$

The structure of the pale buff-coloured product is shown in Fig. 22.12b and this allows a direct comparison between the three Ta–C distances: Ta=CH₂ 203 pm, Ta–CH₃ 225 pm, and Ta–C(C_5H_5) 216 pm. It will also be noted that the two cyclopentadienyl rings are eclipsed and that the CH₂ group orients perpendicular to the C–Ta–C plane.

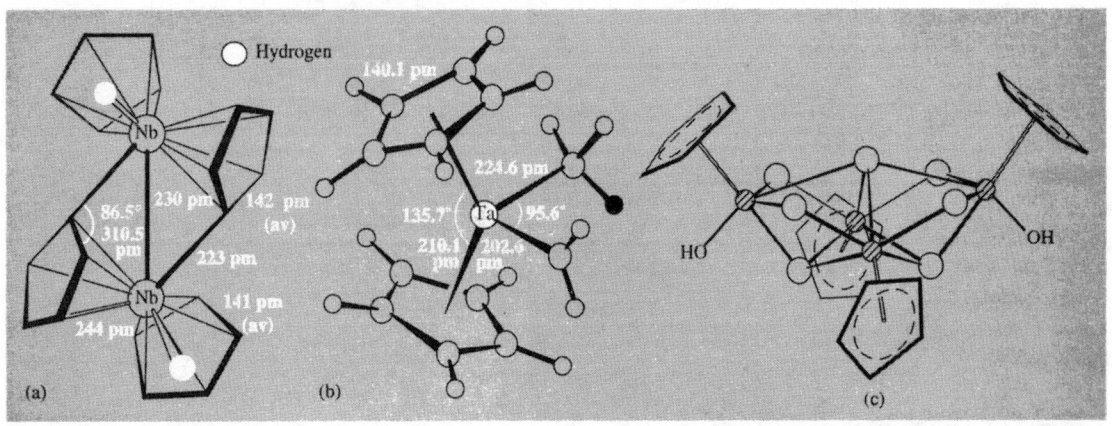

Figure 22.12   (a) The structure of dimeric $[Nb(\eta^5\text{-}C_5H_5)H\text{-}\mu\text{-}(\eta^5,\eta^1\text{-}C_5H_4)]_2$. The observed diamagnetism of this compound is consistent with the Nb–Nb bond shown. Each of the two bridging rings is η^5-bonded to one Nb and η^1-bonded to the other. (b) The structure of $[Ta(\eta^5\text{-}C_5H_5)_2(CH_3)(=CH_2)]$. (c) The structure of $[Ta_4(\eta^5\text{-}C_5Me_5)_4(\mu_2\text{-}O)_4(\mu_3\text{-}O)_2(\mu_4\text{-}O)(OH)_2]$.

Cationic cyclopentadienyl complexes are not common in this group, but recent examples whose structures have been determined include $[Nb^V(\eta^5\text{-}C_5H_5)_2Cl_2]BF_4$ [49] and $[Nb(\eta^5\text{-}C_5H_5)_2L_2](BF_4)_2$ (L = CNMe and NCMe),[50] which have pseudo-tetrahedral symmetry. Mono(cyclopentadienyl), or "half-sandwich" poly-oxo complexes are of interest as hydrocarbon-soluble models for oxide catalysts. The action of water on $[Ta(\eta^5\text{-}C_5Me_5)(PMe_3)_2]$ yields the colourless $[Ta_4(\eta^5\text{-}C_5Me_5)_4O_7(OH)_2]$ which has a tetranuclear "butterfly" core (Fig. 22.12c).[51]

The chemistry of these metals with ring systems other than cyclopentadienyl has been little developed but, since larger rings afford more bonding electrons it would seem that the relatively electron-poor, early transition elements (see p. 941) should provide a field of study ripe for expansion. Reduction of $NbCl_4$ by Na/Hg in thf in the presence of cycloheptatriene and PMe_3 provides a convenient route and several C_7-ring compounds have been prepared[52] including the blue-green, 17-electron complex $[Nb^{II}(\eta^7\text{-}C_7H_7)(PMe_3)_2I]$ which is isomorphous with the previously described Zr analogue (Fig. 21.10c).

[49] K. H. THIELE, W. KUBAK, J. SIELER, H. BORRMANN and A. SIMON, *Z. anorg. allgem. Chem.* **587**, 80–90 (1990).

[50] M. A. A. DE C. T. CARRONDO, J. MORAIS, C. C. ROMAO and M. J. ROMAO, *Polyhedron* **12**, 765–70 (1993).

[51] V. C. GIBSON, T. P. KEE and W. CLEGG, *J. Chem. Soc., Chem. Commun.*, 29–30 (1990).

[52] M. L. H. GREEN, P. MOUNTFORD, P. SCOTT and V. S. B. MTETWA, *Polyhedron* **10**, 389–92 (1991), and *J. Chem. Soc., Chem. Commun.*, 314–5 (1992).

23

Chromium, Molybdenum and Tungsten

23.1 Introduction

The discoveries of these elements span a period of about 20 y at the end of the eighteenth century. In 1778 the famous Swedish chemist C. W. Scheele produced from the mineral molybdenite (MoS_2) the oxide of a new element, thereby distinguishing the mineral from graphite with which it had hitherto been thought to be identical. Molybdenum metal was isolated 3 or 4 y later by P. J. Hjelm by heating the oxide with charcoal. The name is derived from the Greek word for lead (μόλυβδος, *molybdos*), owing to the ancient confusion between any soft black minerals which could be used for writing (this is further illustrated by the use of the names "plumbago" and "black lead" for graphite).

In 1781 Scheele, and also T. Bergman, isolated another new oxide, this time from the mineral now known as scheelite ($CaWO_4$) but then called "tungsten" (Swedish *tung sten*, heavy stone). Two years later the Spanish brothers J. J.

and F. d'Elhuyar showed that the same oxide was a constituent of the mineral wolframite and reduced it to the metal by heating with charcoal. The name "wolfram", from which the symbol of the element is derived, is still widely used in the German literature and is recommended by IUPAC, but the allowed alternative "tungsten" is used in the English-speaking world.

Finally, in 1797, the Frenchman L. N. Vauquelin discovered the oxide of a new element in a Siberian mineral, now known as crocoite ($PbCrO_4$), and in the following year isolated the metal itself by charcoal reduction. This was subsequently named chromium (Greek χρωμα, *chroma*, colour) because of the variety of colours found in its compounds. Since their discoveries the metals and their compounds have become vitally important in many industries and, as one of the biologically active transition elements, molybdenum has been the subject of a great deal of attention in recent years, especially in the field of nitrogen fixation (p. 1035).

23.2 The Elements

23.2.1 Terrestrial abundance and distribution

Chromium, 122 ppm of the earth's crustal rocks, is comparable in abundance with vanadium (136 ppm) and chlorine (126 ppm), but molybdenum and tungsten (both ~1.2 ppm) are much rarer (cf. Ho 1.4 ppm, Tb 1.2 ppm), and the concentration in their ores is low. The only ore of chromium of any commercial importance is chromite, $FeCr_2O_4$, which is produced principally in southern Africa (where 96% of the known reserves are located), the former Soviet Union and the Philippines. Other less plentiful sources are crocoite, $PbCrO_4$, and chrome ochre, Cr_2O_3, while the gemstones emerald and ruby owe their colours to traces of chromium (pp. 107, 242).

The most important ore of molybdenum is the sulphide molybdenite, MoS_2, of which the largest known deposit is in Colorado, USA, but it is also found in Canada and Chile. Less important ores are wulfenite, $PbMoO_4$, and powellite, $Ca(Mo,W)O_4$.

Tungsten occurs in the form of the tungstates scheelite, $CaWO_4$, and wolframite, $(Fe,Mn)WO_4$, which are found in China (thought to have perhaps 75% of the world's reserves), the former Soviet Union, Korea, Austria and Portugal.

23.2.2 Preparation and uses of the metals

Chromium is produced in two forms:[1]

(a) Ferrochrome by the reduction of chromite with coke in an electric arc furnace. A low-carbon ferrochrome can be produced by using ferrosilicon (p. 330) instead of coke as the reductant. This iron/chromium alloy is used directly as an additive to produce chromium-steels which are "stainless" and hard.

(b) Chromium metal by the reduction of Cr_2O_3. This is obtained by aerial oxidation of chromite in molten alkali to give sodium chromate, Na_2CrO_4, which is leached out with water, precipitated and then reduced to the Cr(III) oxide by carbon. The oxide can be reduced by aluminium (aluminothermic process) or silicon:

$$Cr_2O_3 + 2Al \longrightarrow 2Cr + Al_2O_3$$

$$2Cr_2O_3 + 3Si \longrightarrow 4Cr + 3SiO_2$$

The main use of the chromium metal so produced is in the production of non-ferrous alloys, the use of pure chromium being limited because of its low ductility at ordinary temperatures. Alternatively, the Cr_2O_3 can be dissolved in sulphuric acid to give the electrolyte used to produce the ubiquitous chromium-plating which is at once both protective and decorative.

The sodium chromate produced in the isolation of chromium is itself the basis for the manufacture of all industrially important chromium chemicals. World production of chromite ores approached 12 million tonnes in 1995.

Molybdenum is obtained as a primary product but mainly as a byproduct in the production of copper. In either case MoS_2 is separated by flotation and then roasted to MoO_3. In the manufacture of stainless steel and high-speed tools, which account for about 85% of molybdenum consumption, the MoO_3 may be used directly or after conversion to ferromolybdenum by the aluminothermic process. Otherwise, further purification is possible by dissolution in aqueous ammonia and crystallization of ammonium molybdate (sometimes as the dimolybdate, $[NH_4]_2[Mo_2O_7]$, sometimes as the paramolybdate, $[NH_4]_6[Mo_7O_{24}].4H_2O$, depending on conditions), which is the starting material for the manufacture of molybdenum chemicals. Pure molybdenum, which finds important applications as a catalyst in a variety of petrochemical processes and as an electrode material, can be

[1] *Kirk–Othmer, Encyclopedia of Chemical Technology*, 4th edn., Vol. 6, pp. 228–63, Interscience, New York, 1993.

obtained by hydrogen reduction of ammonium molybdate. In 1995 world production of molybdenum ores was equivalent to 130 000 tonnes of contained Mo.

The isolation of tungsten is effected by the formation of "tungstic acid" (hydrous WO_3), but the chemical route chosen depends on the ore being used. After pulverization and concentration of the ore:

(a) Wolframite is converted to soluble alkali tungstate either by fusing with NaOH and leaching the cooled product with water, or by protracted boiling with aqueous alkali. Acidification with hydrochloric acid then precipitates the tungstic acid.

(b) Scheelite is converted to insoluble tungstic acid by direct treatment with hydrochloric acid and separated from the soluble salts of other metals.

Tungstic acid is then roasted to WO_3 which is reduced to the metal by heating with hydrogen at 850°C. Half of the tungsten produced is used as the carbide, WC, which is extremely hard and wear-resistant and so ideal as a tool-tip. Other major uses are in the production of numerous heat-resistant alloys, but the most important use of the *pure* metal is still as a filament in electric light bulbs, in which role it has never been bettered since it was first used in 1908. In 1995, world production of tungsten ores contained 31 000 tonnes of tungsten.

Both molybdenum and tungsten are obtained initially in the form of powders and, since fusion is impracticable because of their high mps, they are converted to the massive state by compression and sintering under H_2 at high temperatures.

23.2.3 Properties of the elements

As can be seen from Table 23.1, which summarizes some of the important properties of Group 6, each of these elements has several naturally occurring isotopes which imposes limits on the precision with which their atomic weights have been determined, especially for Mo and W.

The elements all have typically metallic bcc structures and in the massive state are lustrous, silvery, and (when pure) fairly soft. However, the most obvious characteristic at least of

Table 23.1 Some properties of Group 6 elements

Property		Cr	Mo	W
Atomic number		24	42	74
Number of naturally occurring isotopes		4	7	5
Atomic weight		51.9961(6)	95.94(1)	183.84(1)
Electronic configuration		[Ar]3d^{5}4s^1	[Kr]4d^{5}5s^1	[Xe]4f^{14}5d^{4}6s^2
Electronegativity		1.6	1.8	1.7
Metal radius (12-coordinate)/pm		128	139	139
Ionic radius (6-coordinate)/pm	VI	44	59	60
	V	49	61	62
	IV	55	65	66
	III	61.5	69	—
	II[a]	73 (ls), 80 (hs)	—	—
MP/°C		1900	1620	3422
BP/°C		2690	4650	(5500)
ΔH_{fus}/kJ mol^{-1}		21(±2)	28(±3)	(35)
ΔH_{vap}/kJ mol^{-1}		342(±6)	590(±21)	824(±21)
ΔH_f (monatomic gas)/kJ mol^{-1}		397(±3)	664(±13)	849(±13)
Density (20°C)/g cm^{-3}		7.14	10.28	19.3
Electrical resistivity (20°C)/μohm cm		13	~5	~5

[a]Radius depends on whether Cr(II) is low-spin (ls) or high-spin (hs).

molybdenum and tungsten, is their refractive nature, and tungsten has the highest mp of all metals — indeed, of all elements except carbon. For this reason, metallic Mo and W are fabricated by the techniques of powder metallurgy and, in consequence, many of their bulk physical properties depend critically on the nature of their mechanical history.

As in the preceding transition-metal groups, the refractory behaviour and the relative stabilities of the different oxidation states can be explained by the role of the $(n-1)$d electrons. Compared to vanadium, chromium has a lower mp, bp and enthalpy of atomization which implies that the 3d electrons are now just beginning to enter the inert electron core of the atom, and so are less readily delocalized by the formation of metal bonds. This is reflected too in the fact that the most stable oxidation state has dropped to +3, while chromium(VI) is strongly oxidizing:

$$\tfrac{1}{2}Cr_2O_7{}^{2-} + 7H^+ + 3e^- \rightleftharpoons Cr^{3+} + 3\tfrac{1}{2}H_2O;$$

$$E° = 1.33 \text{ V}$$

For the heavier congenors, tungsten in the group oxidation state is much more stable to reduction, and it is apparently the last element in the third transition series in which all the 5d electrons participate in metal bonding.

23.2.4 Chemical reactivity and trends

At ambient temperatures all three elements resist atmospheric attack, which is why chromium is so widely used to protect other more reactive metals. They become more susceptible to attack at high temperatures, when they react with many non-metals giving frequently interstitial and non-stoichiometric products. Chromium reacts more readily with acids then does either molybdenum or tungsten though its reactivity depends on its purity and it can easily be rendered passive. Thus, it dissolves readily in dil HCl but, if very pure, will often resist dil H_2SO_4; again, HNO_3, whether dilute or concentrated, and aqua regia will render it passive for reasons which are by no means clear. In the presence of oxidizing agents such as KNO_3 or $KClO_3$, alkali melts rapidly attack the metals producing $MO_4{}^{2-}$.

Once again the two heavier elements are closely similar to each other and show marked differences from the lightest element. This is reflected particularly in the relative stabilities of the oxidation states, all of which are known from +6 down to −2.

The stability of the group oxidation state +6 was referred to above and it may be further noted that, while chromium(VI) tends to form poly oxoanions, the diversity of these is but a pale shadow of that of the polymolybdates and polytungstates (p. 1009). Oxidation states +5 and +4 are represented by chromium largely as unstable intermediates, and +3 is much its most stable oxidation state, the symmetrical t_{2g}^3 configuration leading to a coordination chemistry, the fecundity of which is exceeded only by that of cobalt(III). Chromium(II) is strongly reducing (Cr^{3+}/Cr^{2+}, $E° − 0.41$ V) but it still has an extensive cationic chemistry. By contrast, the chemistry of molybdenum and tungsten in oxidation states +5 to +2 is dominated by clusters and multiple-bonded species which, particularly in the case of molybdenum, has produced an effusion of publications in recent years. This is due not only to the intrinsically interesting chemistry involved but also because of molybdenum's role in biological processes and, catalytically, in the hydrodesulfurization (HDS) process for removing S-compounds from petroleum feedstocks. In the still lower oxidation states, found in compounds with π-acceptor ligands, the metals are quite similar.

Table 23.2 lists the oxidation states of the elements along with representative examples of their compounds. Coordination numbers as high as 12 can be attained, but those over 7 in the case of Cr and 9 in the cases of Mo and W involve the presence of the peroxo ligand or π-bonded aromatic rings systems such as η^5-$C_5H_5{}^-$ or η^6-C_6H_6.

Table 23.2 Oxidation states and stereochemistries of compounds of chromium, molybdenum and tungsten

Oxidation state	Coordination number	Stereochemistry	Cr	Mo/W
-4	4	Tetrahedral	$[Cr(CO)_4]^{4-}$	$[M(CO)_4]^{4-}$
-2 (d^8)	5	Trigonal bipyramidal(?)	$[Cr(CO)_5]^{2-}$	$[M(CO)_5]^{2-}$
-1 (d^7)	6	Octahedral	$[Cr_2(CO)_{10}]^{2-}$	$[M_2(CO)_{10}]^{2-}$
0 (d^6)	6	Octahedral	$[Cr(bipy)_3]$	$[M(CO)_6]$
	9	—	$[Cr(\eta^6\text{-}C_6H_6)(CO)_3]$	—
	12	—	$[Cr(\eta^6\text{-}C_6H_6)_2]$	—
1 (d^5)	6	Octahedral	$[Cr(CNR)_6]^+$	$[MoCl(N_2)(diphos)_2]$
	8	—	—	$[Mo(\eta^5\text{-}C_5H_5)(CO)_3]$
	11	—	—	$[Mo(\eta^5\text{-}C_5H_5)(\eta^6\text{-}C_6H_6)]$
	12	—	—	$[Mo(\eta^6\text{-}C_6H_6)_2]^+$
2 (d^4)	4	Tetrahedral	$[CrI_2(OPPh_3)_2]$	—
	4	Square Planar	$[Cr(acac)_2]$	—
	5	Trigonal bipyramidal	$[CrBr\{N(C_2H_4NMe_2)_3\}]^+$	—
		Square pyramidal	—	$[Mo_2Cl_8]^{4-}$, $[W_2Me_8]^{4-}$
	6	Octahedral	$[Cr(en)_3]^{2+}$	$[M(diars)_2I_2]$
	7	Capped trigonal prismatic	$[Cr(CO)_2(diars)_2X]^+$	$[Mo(CNR)_7]^{2+\dagger}$
		Pentagonal bipyramidal	—	$[MoH(\eta^2\text{-}O_2CCF_3)\{P(OMe)_3\}_4]$
	8	—	$[Cr(\eta^5\text{-}C_5H_5)Cl(NO)_2]$	—
	9	—	—	$[W(\eta^5\text{-}C_5H_5)(CO)_3Cl]$, M_6Cl_{12} clusters
	10	—	$[Cr(\eta^5\text{-}C_5H_5)_2]$	—
3 (d^3)	3	Planar	$[Cr(NPr_2)_3]$	—
	4	Tetrahedral	$[CrCl_4]^-$	$[(RO)_3Mo\equiv Mo(OR)_3]$, $[(R_2N)_3W\equiv W(NR_2)_3]$
	5	Trigonal bipyramidal	$[CrCl_3(NMe_3)_2]$	—
	6	Octahedral	$[Cr(NH_3)_6]^{3+}$	$[M_2Cl_9]^{3-}$
	7	?	—	$[WBr_2(CO)_3(diars)]^+$
	8	Dodecahedral(?)	—	$[Mo(CN)_7(H_2O)]^{4-}$
	8 or 12	—	—	$[Mo(\eta^1\text{-}C_5H_5)(\eta^x\text{-}C_5H_5)_2(NO)]$, $x=3$ or 5
4 (d^2)	4	Tetrahedral	$[Cr(OBu^t)_4]$	$[Mo(NMe_2)_4]$
	6	Octahedral	$[CrF_6]^{2-}$	$[MCl_6]^{2-}$
		Trigonal prismatic	—	MS_2
	8	Dodecahedral	$[CrH_4(dmpe)_2]^{(a)}$	$[M(CN)_8]^{4-}$
		Square antiprismatic(?)	—	$Mo(S_2CNMe_2)_4]$, $[M(picolinate)_4]$
	12	—	—	$[M(\eta^5\text{-}C_5H_5)_2X_2]$
5 (d^1)	4	Tetrahedral	$[CrO_4]^{3-}$	—
	5	Square pyramidal	$[CrOCl_4]^-$	—
		Trigonal bipyramidal	$CrF_5(g)$	$MoCl_5(g)$
	6	Octahedral	$[CrOCl_5]^{2-}$	$[MF_6]^-$
	8	Dodecahedral	$[Cr(O_2)_4]^{3-}$	$[M(CN)_8]^{3-}$
	13	—	—	$[W(\eta^5\text{-}C_5H_5)_2H_3]$
6 (d^0)	4	Tetrahedral	$[CrO_4]^{2-}$	$[MO_4]^{2-}$
	5	?	—	$[MOX_4]$
		Square pyramidal	—	$[W(\equiv CCMe_3)(=CHCMe_3)(CH_2CMe_3)\{(PMe_2CH_2\text{-})_2\}]$
	6	Octahedral	CrF_6	$\{MO_6\}$ in polymetallates
		Trigonal prismatic	—	$[M(S_2C_2H_2)_3]$
	7	Pentagonal bipyramidal	—	$[WOCl_4(diars)]$
	8	?	—	$[MF_8]^{2-}$
	9	Tricapped trigonal prismatic (C_{2v})	—	$[WH_6(PPhPr^i_2)_3]$

$\dagger$ The structure of these complexes is not regular and has been described as "4:3 (C_s) piano stool", which is obtained by slight distortion of a capped trigonal prism (C_{2v}).

(a) dmpe, 1,2-bis(dimethylphosphino)ethane, $Me_2PCH_2CH_2PMe_2$.

Table 23.3   Oxides of Group 6

Oxidation state:	+6	Intermediate	+4	+3
Cr	CrO_3	Cr_3O_8, Cr_2O_5, Cr_5O_{12}, etc.	CrO_2	Cr_2O_3
Mo	MoO_3	Mo_9O_{26}, Mo_8O_{23}, Mo_5O_{14}, $Mo_{17}O_{47}$, Mo_4O_{11}	MoO_2	—
W	WO_3	$W_{49}O_{119}$, $W_{50}O_{148}$, $W_{20}O_{58}$, $W_{18}O_{49}$	WO_2	—

23.3 Compounds of Chromium, Molybdenum and Tungsten[(2,3,3a)]

The binary borides (p. 145), carbides (p. 299), and nitrides (p. 418) have already been discussed. Suffice it to note here that the chromium atom is too small to allow the ready insertion of carbon into its lattice, and its carbide is consequently more reactive than those of its predecessors. As for the hydrides, only CrII is known which is consistent with the general trend in this part of the periodic table that hydrides become less stable across the d block and down each group.

23.3.1 Oxides [(2,4)]

The principal oxides formed by the elements of this group are given in Table 23.3 above.

CrO_3, as is to be expected with such a small cation, is a strongly acidic and rather covalent oxide with a mp of only 197°C. Its deep-red crystals are made up of chains of corner-shared CrO_4 tetrahedra. It is commonly called "chromic acid" and is generally prepared by the addition of conc H_2SO_4 to a saturated aqueous solution of a dichromate. Its strong oxidizing properties are widely used in organic chemistry. CrO_3 melts with some decomposition and, if heated above

220–250°, it loses oxygen to give a succession of lower oxides until the green Cr_2O_3 is formed.

Like the analogous oxides of Ti, V and Fe, Cr_2O_3 has the corundum structure (p. 243), and it finds wide applications as a green pigment. It is a semiconductor and is antiferromagnetic below 35°C. Cr_2O_3 is the most stable oxide of chromium and is the final product of combustion of the metal, though it is more conveniently obtained by heating ammonium dichromate:

$$(NH_4)_2Cr_2O_7 \longrightarrow Cr_2O_3 + N_2 + 4H_2O^{\dagger}$$

When produced by such dry methods it is frequently unreactive but, if precipitated as the hydrous oxide (or "hydroxide") from aqueous chromium(III) solutions it is amphoteric. It dissolves readily in aqueous acids to give an extensive cationic chemistry based on the $[Cr(H_2O)_6]^{3+}$ ion, and in alkalis to produce complicated, extensively hydrolysed chromate(III) species ("chromites").

The third major oxide of chromium is the brown-black, CrO_2, which is an intermediate product in the decomposition of CrO_3 to Cr_2O_3 and has a rutile structure (p. 961). It has metallic conductivity and its ferromagnetic properties lead to its commercial importance in the manufacture of magnetic recording tapes which are claimed to give better resolution and high-frequency response than those made from iron oxide. Other more or less stable phases with compositions between CrO_2 and CrO_3 have been identified but are of little importance.

The trioxides of molybdenum and tungsten differ from CrO_3 in that, though they are acidic and dissolve in aqueous alkali to give salts of

[2] E. R. Braithwaite and J. Haber (eds.), *Molybdenum: An Outline of its Chemistry and Uses*, Elsevier, Amsterdam 1994, 662 pp.

[3] C. L. Rollinson, Chap. 36 in *Comprehensive Inorganic Chemistry*, Vol. 3, pp. 623–769, Pergamon Press, Oxford, 1973.

[3a] *Encyclopedia of Inorganic Chemistry*, Wiley, Chichester, 1994: for Cr see Vol. 2, pp. 666–78; for Mo see Vol. 5, pp. 2304–30; for W see Vol. 6, pp. 4240–68.

[4] M. T. Pope, Molybdenum oxygen chemistry, *Prog. Inorg. Chem.* **39**, 181–257 (1991); pp. 181–94 deals with oxides.

† In 1986 the initial drying of the dichromate in a rotary vacuum drier, resulted in a serious explosion in Ohio. The cause was not obvious but the presence of an organic contaminant must be a possibility.

the $MO_4{}^{2-}$ ions, they are insoluble in water and have no appreciable oxidizing properties, being the final products of the combustion of the metals. MoO_3 and WO_3 have mps of 795 and 1473°C respectively (i.e. much higher than for CrO_3) and their crystal structures are different. The white MoO_3 has an unusual layer structure composed of distorted MoO_6 octahedra while the yellow WO_3 (like ReO_3 see p. 1047) consists of a three-dimensional array of corner-linked WO_6 octahedra. In fact, WO_3 is known in at least seven polymorphic forms and is unique in being the only oxide of any element that can undergo numerous facile crystallographic transitions near room temperature. Thus the monoclinic ReO_3-type phase (which is slightly distorted from cubic by W–W interactions) transforms to a ferroelectric monoclinic phase when cooled to −43°C, and transforms to another monoclinic variety above +20°C; there are further transitions to an orthorhombic phase at 325° and to a succession of tetragonal phases at 725°, 900° and 1225°.

If either MoO_3 or WO_3 is heated *in vacuo* or is heated with the powdered metal, reduction occurs until eventually MO_2 with a distorted rutile structure (p. 961) is formed. In between these extremes, however, lie a variety of intensely coloured (usually violet or blue) phases whose structural complexity has excited great interest over many years.[5] Following the pioneer work of the Swedish chemist A. Magnéli in the late 1940s these materials, which were originally thought to consist of a comparatively small number of rather grossly nonstoichiometric phases, are now known to be composed of a much larger number of distinct and accurately stoichiometric phases with formulae such as Mo_4O_{11}, $Mo_{17}O_{47}$, Mo_8O_{23}, $W_{18}O_{49}$ and $W_{20}O_{58}$. As oxygen is progressively eliminated, a whole series of M_nO_{3n-1} stoichiometries is feasible between the MO_3 structure containing *corner*-shared MoO_6 octahedra and the rutile structure consisting of

edge-shared MO_6 octahedra. These are produced as slabs of corner-shared octahedra move so as to share edges with the octahedra of identical adjacent slabs. This is the phenomenon of crystallographic shear and occurs in an ordered fashion throughout the solid.[6] The situation is further complicated by the formation of structures involving (a) 7-coordinate, and (b) 4-coordinate, alongside the more prevalent 6-coordinate, metal atoms. The reasons for the formation of these intermediate phases is by no means fully understood but, although their "nonstoichiometric" M:O ratios imply mixed valence compounds, their largely metallic conductivities suggest that the electrons released as oxygen is removed are in fact delocalized within a conduction band permeating the whole lattice.

Reduction of a solution of a molybdate(VI), or of a suspension of MoO_3, in water or acid by a variety of reagents including Sn^{II}, SO_2, N_2H_4, Cu/acid or Sn/acid, leads to the production of intense blue, sometimes transient, and probably colloidal products, referred to rather imprecisely as *molybdenum blues*. They appear to be oxide/hydroxide species of mixed valence, forming a series between the extremes of $Mo^{VI}O_3$ and $Mo^VO(OH)_3$, but a precise explanation of their colour is lacking. Their formation can be used as a sensitive test for the presence of reducing agents. The behaviour of tungsten is entirely analogous to that of molybdenum and, as will be seen presently, the reduction of heteropolyanions of these metals produces similar coloured products which may be distinguished from the above "blues" as "heteropoly blues" (though this is not always done).

The dioxides of molybdenum (violet) and tungsten (brown) are the final oxide phases produced by reduction of the trioxides with hydrogen; they have rutile structures sufficiently distorted to allow the formation of M–M bonds and concomitant metallic conductivity and diamagnetism. Strong heating causes disproportionation:

$$3MO_2 \longrightarrow M + 2MO_3$$

5 D. J. M. BEVAN, Chap. 49 in *Comprehensive Inorganic Chemistry*, Vol. 4, pp. 491–7, Pergamon Press, Oxford, 1973.

6 See p. 148 of ref. 2.

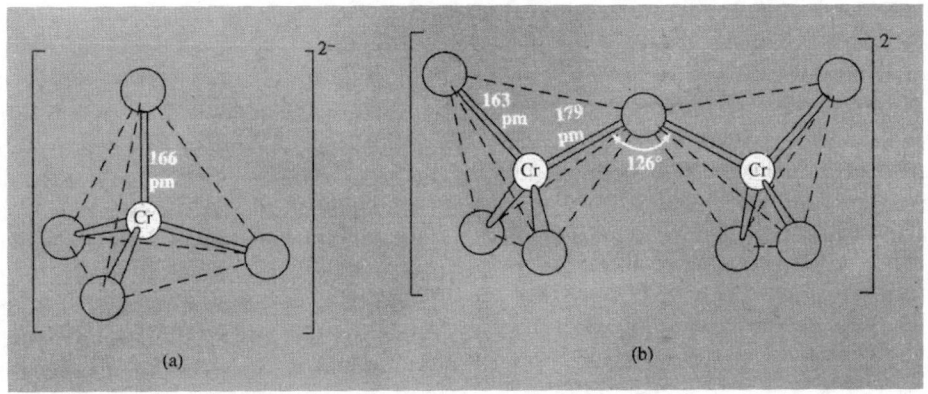

Figure 23.1   (a) CrO_4^{2-} ion, and (b) $Cr_2O_7^{2-}$ ion.

No other oxide phases below MO_2 have been established but a yellow "hydroxide", precipitated by alkali from aqueous solutions of chromium(II), spontaneously evolves H_2 and forms a chromium(III) species of uncertain composition. The sulfides, selenides and tellurides of this triad are considered on p. 1017.

23.3.2 Isopolymetallates [4,7,8,9,9a]

Acidification of aqueous solutions of the yellow, tetrahedral chromate ion, CrO_4^{2-}, initiates a series of labile equilibria involving the formation of the orange-red dichromate ion, $Cr_2O_7^{2-}$:

$$HCrO_4^- \rightleftharpoons CrO_4^{2-} + H^+$$

$$H_2CrO_4 \rightleftharpoons HCrO_4^- + H^+$$

$$Cr_2O_7^{2-} + H_2O \rightleftharpoons 2HCrO_4^-$$

$$HCr_2O_7^- \rightleftharpoons Cr_2O_7^{2-} + H^+$$

$$H_2CrO_4 \rightleftharpoons HCr_2O_7^- + H^+$$

However, estimates of equilibrium constants (see for instance, *Comprehensive Coordination Chemistry*, Vol. 3, p. 699) have been questioned and it appears that the concentration of $HCrO_4^-$ is much lower than was previously supposed, the ion being undetectable by Raman and uv-visible spectroscopic techniques.[9b] Because of the lability of these equilibria the addition of the cations Ag^I, Ba^{II} or Pb^{II} to aqueous dichromate solutions causes their immediate precipitation as insoluble chromates rather than their more soluble dichromates. Polymerization beyond the dichromate ion is apparently limited to the formation of tri- and tetra-chromates ($Cr_3O_{10}^{2-}$ and $Cr_4O_{13}^{2-}$), which can be crystallized as alkali-metal salts from very strongly acid solutions. These anions, as well as the dichromate ion, are formed by the corner sharing of CrO_4 tetrahedra, giving $Cr-O-Cr$ angles very roughly in the region of 120° (Fig. 23.1). The simplicity of this anionic polymerization of chromium, as compared to that shown by the elements of the preceding groups and the heavier elements of the present triad, is probably due to the small size of Cr^{VI}. This evidently limits it to tetrahedral rather than octahedral coordination with oxygen, whilst simultaneously favouring $Cr-O$ double bonds and so inhibiting the sharing of attached oxygens.

Sodium dichromate, $Na_2Cr_2O_7.2H_2O$, produced from the chromate is commercially much

[7] M. T. POPE, *Heteropoly and Isopoly Oxometalates*, Springer Verlag, Berlin, 1983, 180 pp. Also Chap. 38 in *Comprehensive Coordination Chemistry*, Vol. 3, pp. 1028–58, Pergamon Press, Oxford, 1987.

[8] Polyoxometalate Symposium Report (Engl.), *Comptes Rendus Acad. Sci. IIc*, **1**, 297–403 (1998).

[9] M. T. POPE and A. MÜLLER, *Angew. Chem. Int. Edn. Engl.* **30**, 34–48 (1991).

[9a] M. I. KHAN and J. ZUBIETA, *Prog. Inorg. Chem.* **43**, 1–149 (1995).

[9b] V. G. POULOPOULOU, E. VRACHNOU, S. KOINIS and D. KATAKIS, *Polyhedron* **16**, 521–4 (1997).

the most important compound of chromium. It yields a wide variety of pigments used in the manufacture of paints, inks, rubber and ceramics, and from it are formed a host of other chromates used as corrosion inhibitors and fungicides, etc. It is also the oxidant in many organic chemical processes; likewise, acidified dichromate solutions are used as strong oxidants in volumetric analysis:

$$Cr_2O_7{}^{2-} + 14H^+ + 6e^- \longrightarrow 2Cr^{3+} + 7H_2O;$$
$$E^\circ = 1.33 \text{ V}$$

For this purpose the potassium salt $K_2Cr_2O_7$ is preferred since it lacks the hygroscopic character of the sodium salt and may therefore be used as a primary standard.

The polymerization of acidified solutions of molybdenum(VI) or tungsten(VI) yields the most complicated of all the polyanion systems and, in spite of the fact that the tungsten system has been the most intensively studied, it is still probably the least well understood. This arises from the problem inevitably associated with studies of such equilibria, and which were noted (p. 983) in the discussion of the Group 5 isopolyanions. It must also be admitted that, whilst the observed structures of individual polyanions are reasonable, it is often difficult to explain why, under given circumstances, a particular degree of aggregation or a particular structure is preferred over other possibilities.

When the trioxides of molybdenum and tungsten are dissolved in aqueous alkali, the resulting solutions contain tetrahedral $MO_4{}^{2-}$ ions and simple, or "normal", molybdates and tungstates such as Na_2MO_4 can be crystallized from them. If these solutions are made strongly acid, precipitates of yellow "molybdic acid", $MoO_3.2H_2O$, or white "tungstic acid", $WO_3.2H_2O$ are obtained which convert to the monohydrates if warmed. At pHs between these two extremes, however, polymerization occurs and salts can be crystallized,[10] the anions of which are almost invariably made up of MO_6 octahedra. A plethora of

physical techniques[7] has been used to characterize these species and unravel the complexity of their structures. Examination of the alkali metal (or ammonium) and alkaline earth salts, particularly by X-ray analysis, forms the basis of classical studies of the isopoly-molybdates and -tungstates in the solid state. Modern nmr techniques (especially pulsed Fourier transform) have increasingly been used to study the solutions themselves. Even so it is only with great difficulty that the structure of an ion, determined in the solid, can be confirmed in solution.

Important differences distinguish the molybdenum and tungsten systems. In aqueous solution, equilibration of the molybdenum species is complete within a matter of minutes whereas for tungsten this may take several weeks; it also transpires that whereas the basic unit of most isopolymolybdates is an MO_6 octahedron with a pair of *cis*-terminal oxygens, that of the isopolytungstates is more commonly an MO_6 octahedron with only one terminal oxygen. The two must therefore be considered separately.

Undoubtedly the first major polyanion formed when the pH of an aqueous molybdate solution is reduced below about 6 is the heptamolybdate $[Mo_7O_{24}]^{6-}$, traditionally known as the paramolybdate:

$$7[MoO_4]^{2-} + 8H^+ \rightleftharpoons [Mo_7O_{24}]^{6-} + 4H_2O$$

This may be crystallized from aqueous solution and, by the addition of diethylenetriamine, $(H_3dien)_2[Mo_7O_{24}].4H_2O$ has been obtained[11] as two distinct polymorphs. Both contain discrete $[Mo_7O_{24}]^{6-}$ ions but differ in the way these are packed in the crystals.

Anions with 8, and probably 16–18, Mo atoms also appear to be formed, before increasing acidity suffices to precipitate the hydrous oxide. It is clear from the above equation that the condensation of MoO_4 polyhedra to produce these large polyanions requires large quantities of strong acid as the supernumary oxygen atoms are removed in the form of water molecules. Careful

[10] *Inorganic Syntheses*, **27**, Chap. 3 pp. 71–135 (1990), gives several detailed preparations.

[11] P. Roman, A. Luque, A. Aranzabe and J. M. Gutierrez-Zorrilla, *Polyhedron* **11**, 2027–38 (1992).

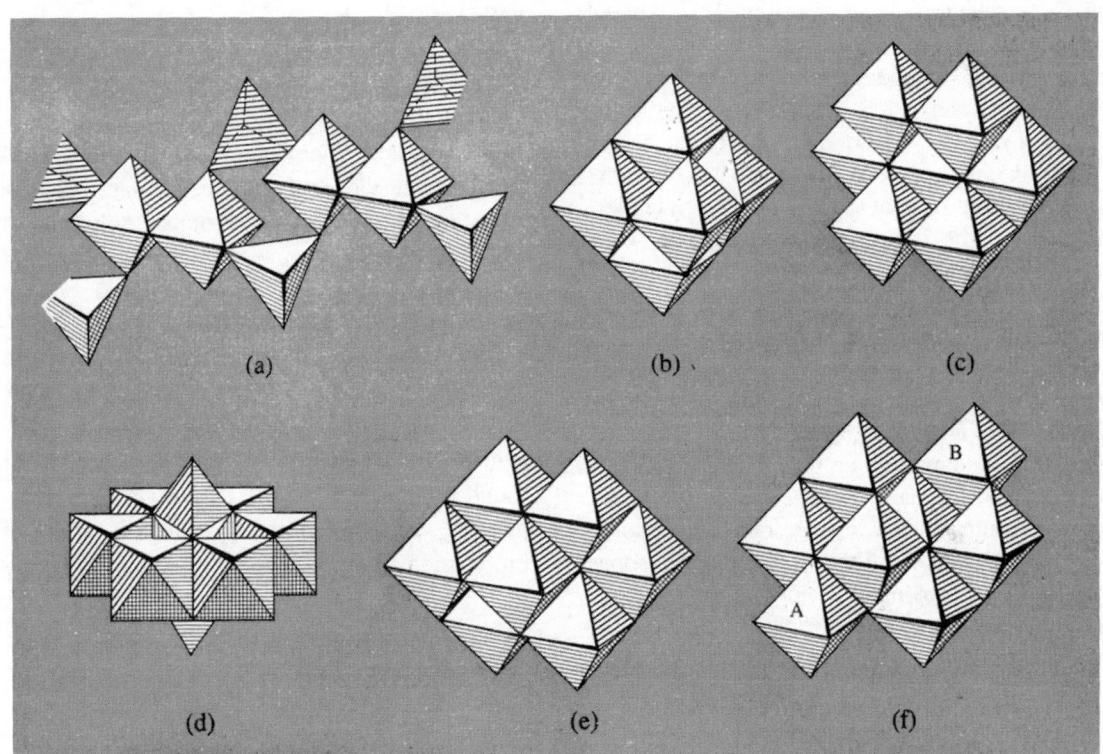

Figure 23.2 Idealized structures of isopolymolybdate ions. (a) Polymeric $[Mo_2O_7{}^{2-}]_n$ chain as found in the $NH_4{}^+$ salt. The $[NBu_4^n]^+$ salt contains discrete $[Mo_2O_7]^{2-}$ ions, comparable to $[Cr_2O_7]^{2-}$ (p. 1009) but with an M–O–M angle of 154° compared to 126°. (b) $[Mo_6O_{19}]^{2-}$ (the sixth octahedron is obscured). (c) Paramolybdate, $[Mo_7O_{24}]^{6-}$; this is the Anderson structure and can be viewed as an $M_{10}O_{28}$ structure (Fig. 22.3, p. 986) with a line of three octahedra removed. (d) α-$[Mo_8O_{26}]^{4-}$; a ring of six octahedra capped by two tetrahedra. (e) β-$[Mo_8O_{26}]^{4-}$ (one octahedron is obscured). (f) γ-$[Mo_8O_{26}]^{4-}$. One of the three terminal coordination positions in each octahedron A and B is unoccupied. Filling them with suitable ligands stabilizes this otherwise labile ion.

adjustment of acidity, concentration and temperature, often coupled with slow crystallization, can produce solids containing many other ions which are apparently not present in solution. Mixtures abound, but amongst the distinct species which have been characterized are: the dimolybdate, $[Mo_2O_7]^{2-}$; the hexamolybdate, $[Mo_6O_{19}]^{2-}$; and the octamolybdate, $[Mo_8O_{26}]^{4-}$, for which there are α- and β-isomers. The latter is the one usually obtained from aqueous solutions, but large counter ions or non-aqueous solvents have been used to prepare the former. A third (γ), coordinatively unsaturated form containing two 5-coordinate Mo atoms has been

suggested as an intermediate in the $\alpha \rightleftharpoons \beta$ equilibrium, and has been isolated[12] as the salt $[Me_3N(CH_2)_6NMe_3]_2[Mo_8O_{26}].2H_2O$. Stabilization of the γ-configuration is also possible by completing the octahedral coordination spheres of the 5-coordinate Mo atoms with suitable ligands such as pyridine or pyrazole.[13] Figure 23.2 depicts the structures of these ions and it can be seen that the basic units are

[12] M. L. NIVEN, J. J. CRUYWAGEN and J. B. B. HEYNS, *J. Chem. Soc., Dalton Trans.*, 2007–11 (1991).

[13] P. GILI, P. MARTIN-ZARZA, G. MARTIN-REYES, J. M. ARRIETA and G. MADARIAGA, *Polyhedron* **11**, 115–21 (1992).

MoO$_6$ octahedra which are joined by shared corners or shared edges, but not by shared faces. MoO$_4$ tetrahedra are also involved in $[Mo_2O_7^{2-}]_n$ and in a few other ions. The structure of $[Mo_{36}O_{112}(H_2O)_{16}]^{8-}$, one of the larger isopolyanions (but see Panel on p. 1015) consists predominantly of MoO$_6$ octahedra but includes, uniquely in the isopolymolybdates, MoO$_7$ pentagonal bipyramids.

The most important species produced by the progressive acidification of normal tungstate solutions are the paratungstates which, indeed, were the only ones reported prior to the mid-1940s. They are generally less soluble than the normal tungstates and can be crystallized over a period of several days. Further acidification produces metatungstates which are rather more soluble but will crystallize either on standing for some months or on prolonged heating of the solution. It seems that comparatively rapid condensation produces relatively soluble species which, if left,

will very slowly condense further into less-soluble species. Early evidence suggested that the first paratungstate, A, to be formed in solution is a hexamer but evidence later accumulated that a heptamer is produced, just as with molybdates. For instance, potentiometric data obtained from dilute (0.1 and 0.001 molar) solutions of Na$_2$WO$_4$.2H$_2$O in the range pH 7.8–5 and treated by a "best-fit program", indicated the presence of W$_6$, W$_7$ and W$_{12}$ species but with the W$_6$ always a minor component.[14] More recently, ^{183}W, ^{17}O and ^{1}H nmr spectra of 2 molar aqueous solutions of WO$_3$ and LiOH over the range pH 8–1.5 confirmed the presence of W$_7$ and W$_{12}$ species but found no evidence of W$_6$; they revealed a complicated series of equilibria in which a variety of protonations played a crucial role, and involving

---

[14] J. J. CRUYWAGEN and I. F. J. van der MERWE, *J. Chem. Soc., Dalton Trans.*, 1701–5 (1987).

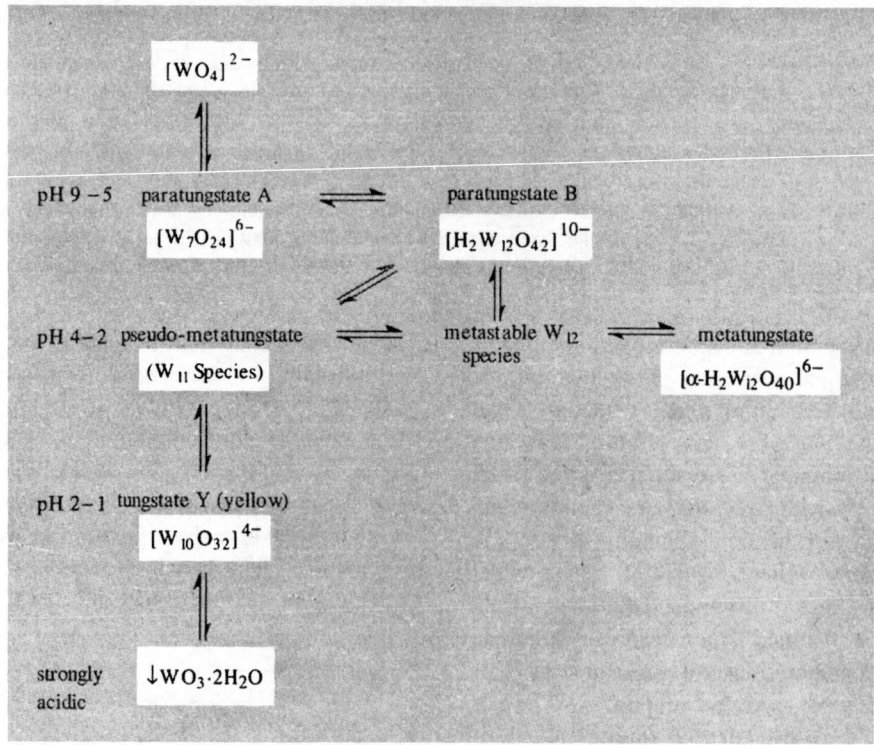

Reaction scheme for the condensation of tungstate ions in aqueous solution.

a W_{11} species of uncertain composition.[15] The much simplified reaction scheme at the foot of the previous page outlines the situation but it must be noted that concentration, temperature, rate of acidification and counter cation will all affect the details of a particular system.

Amongst the crystalline products obtained from aqueous solution are, $(NH_4)_{10}[H_2W_{12}O_{42}]$·$.10H_2O$, $Na_6[H_2W_{12}O_{40}].29H_2O$, $K_4[W_{10}O_{32}]$·$.4H_2O$ and $Na_6[W_7O_{24}].14H_2O$. The compound $Na_5[H_3W_6O_{22}].18H_2O$ has recently been precipitated by acetone from a non-equilibrated aqueous solution[15a] and the structure of the anion may be considered to be derived from that of $[W_7O_{24}]^{6-}$ (which is like that of its Mo analogue, Fig. 23.2c) by removal of an outer octahedron from the middle row of three. Another hexatungstate, $[W_6O_{19}]^{2-}$ isostructural with its Mo analogue, can be obtained from methanolic solutions. $Li_{14}(WO_4)_3(W_4O_{16}).4H_2O$ has also been crystallized from aqueous solution and shown to contain the discrete ion, $[W_4O_{16}]^{8-}$ though there is no direct evidence that this is present in solution. The structures† of these anions are described in Fig. 23.3.

Many attempts have been made to rationalize the structures and mechanisms of formation of polymetallates. Lipscomb observed that no individual MO_6 octahedral unit ever has more than two unshared, i.e. terminal oxygens (exceptions appear to be stable only in the solid state) and this has been explained on the basis of π-bonding between the metal and terminal oxygen atoms: more than two of these

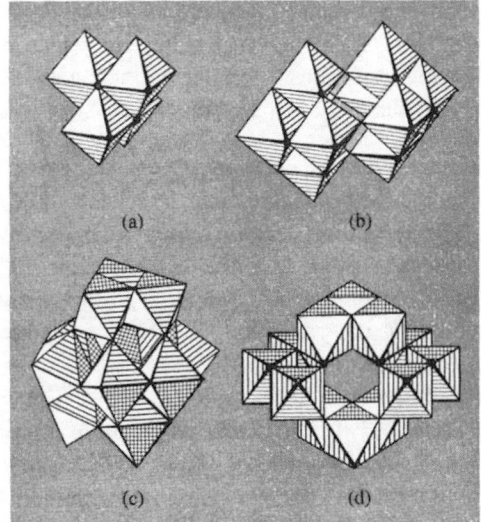

Figure 23.3 Idealized structures of isopolytungstate ions. (a) $[W_4O_{16}]^{8-}$ (b) $[W_{10}O_{32}]^{4-}$, composed of two identical W_5O_{16} groups. (c) The metatungstate ion, $[H_2W_{12}O_{40}]^{6-}$ (d) The paratungstate B ion, $[H_2W_{12}O_{42}]^{10-}$. As in the metatungstate, the protons appear to reside in the cavity of the ion but, unlike those of the metatungstate, exchange rapidly with protons from solvent water.

would so weaken and lengthen the *trans*-bonds holding the metal to the polyanion that it would become detached. Electrostatic repulsions between neighbouring metal ions will reinforce the distorting effect of M–O π-bonding, causing the metal ions to move off-centre in the MO_6 octahedra which are connected to each other. The effect increases as the mode of attachment changes from corner-sharing to edge-sharing. Thus, while the avoidance of unfavourably high, overall anionic charge favours edge-sharing as opposed to corner-sharing (thereby reducing the number of O^{2-} ions), the off-centre distortions become increasingly difficult to accommodate as the size of the polyanion increases. Ultimately edge-sharing is no longer possible, and this stage is reached by W^{VI} before it occurs with the smaller Mo^{VI}. Inspection of Figs. 23.2 and 23.3 shows the greater incidence of corner-sharing in the higher polytungstates than in

---

[15] J. J. HASTINGS and O. W. HOWARTH, *J. Chem. Soc., Dalton Trans.*, 209–15 (1992).

[15a] H. HARTL, R. PALM and J. FUCHS, *Angew. Chem. Int. Edn. Engl.* **32**, 1492–4 (1993).

$†$ It is instructive to recall a particular problem facing early workers in establishing these structures by X-ray diffraction. Large scattering by the heavy tungsten atoms made it extremely difficult to locate the positions of the lighter oxygen atoms and this sometimes led to ambiguity in the assignment of precise structures (relative scattering $O/W = (8/74)^2 = 1/86$, cf. $H/C = (1/6)^2 = 1/36$). This is no longer a problem because of the greater precision of modern techniques of X-ray data acquisition and processing, but good-quality crystals are still necessary and these may be very difficult to produce.

the polymolybdates. Also, except in $[M_7O_{24}]^{6-}$, linear sets of 3 MO_6 octahedra on which the distortions are most difficult to accommodate are not found, triangular M⌄⌄⌄⌄⌄⌄M sets being

preferred. Why so few structures are common to both molybdenum and tungsten is less readily explained and, in spite of numerous suggestions, there is little general agreement about the mechanism of formation of polyanions except that it occurs by the addition of MO_4 tetrahedra.

Several mixed metal species, Mo/W, Mo/V, W/V and W/Nb, in which some atoms of the parent metal are replaced, have been identified (see pp. 54–7 of ref. 7) but no new principles are as yet discernible.

23.3.3 Heteropolymetallates [7,8,9]

In 1826 J. J. Berzelius found that acidification of solutions containing both molybdate and phosphate produced a yellow crystalline precipitate. This was the first example of a heteropolyanion and it actually contains the phosphomolybdate ion, $[PMo_{12}O_{40}]^{3-}$, which can be used in the quantitative estimation of phosphate. Since its discovery a host of other heteropolyanions have been prepared, mostly with molybdenum and tungsten but with more than 50 different heteroatoms, which include many non-metals and most transition metals — often in more than one oxidation state. Unless the heteroatom contributes to the colour, the heteropoly-molybdates and -tungstates are generally of varying shades of yellow. The free acids and the salts of small cations are extremely soluble in water but the salts of large cations such as Cs^I, Ba^{II} and Pb^{II} are usually insoluble. The solid salts are noticeably more stable thermally than are the salts of isopolyanions. Heteropoly compounds have been applied extensively as catalysts in the petrochemicals industry, as precipitants for numerous dyes with which they form "lakes" and, in the case of the Mo compounds, as flame retardants.

In these ions the heteroatoms are situated inside "cavities" or "baskets" formed by MO_6 octahedra of the parent M atoms and are bonded to oxygen atoms of the adjacent MO_6 octahedra. The stereochemistry of the heteroatom is determined by the shape of the cavity which in turn depends on the ratio of the number of heteroatoms to parent atoms. Three major and a number of minor classes are found.

1:12, tetrahedral. These are found for both Mo and W but the latter are far more numerous and stable than the former. They occur with small heteroatoms such as P^V, As^V, Si^{IV} and Ge^{IV} which yield tetrahedral oxoanions, and they are the most readily obtained and best known of the heteropolyanions. Keggin[16] first determined the structure of the phosphotungstate, which was known to be isomorphous with the metatungstate, and his name is given to this structure type (Fig. 23.3c). The hetero-atom, or in the case of metatungstate a pair of protons, is situated in the tetrahedral inner cavity of the parent ion (Panel opposite). For the tungstates, Fe^{III}, Co^{II} and Zn^{II} derivatives are known, the second of which is of interest: it is readily formed, since tetrahedrally coordinated Co^{II} is not unusual, but oxidation yields $[Co^{III}W_{12}O_{40}]^{5-}$ in which the very unusual, high-spin, tetrahedral Co^{III} is trapped. Nor is tetrahedral coordination common for Cu^{II} but it is found in a recently reported[17] polyanion of this class containing both Cu^{II} and 2H as heteroatoms (giving an overall stoichiometry of $\{Cu_{0.4}(H_2)_{0.6}\}$ for the hetero "atom"). The structure of these compounds is now known as the α-Keggin structure since an isomeric β-Keggin structure has been identified for the heteropolyanions, "XMo_{12}" (X = Si, Ge, P, As) and "XW_{12}" (X = Si, Ge). Also β-$[H_2W_{12}O_{40}]^{6-}$ has been implicated in the isopolytungstate equilibria.[15] "Lacunary" ions, or their derivatives, are obtained by the nominal loss of one or more MO_6 octahedra (actually the stoichiometric loss of that number of MO

[16] J. F. KEGGIN, *Proc. R. Soc. A*, **144**, 75–100 (1934)
[17] H.-J. LUNK, S. GIESE, J. FUCHS and R. STÖSSER, *Z. anorg. allg. Chem.* **619**, 961–8 (1993).

Large Polymetallates

With the objective of producing model systems to mimic the metal oxide surfaces of catalysts, a great deal of effort has been devoted to the preparation of large polymetallate structures.

The α-Keggin structure of $[PW_{12}O_{40}]^{3-}$ and the metatungstate, $[H_2W_{12}O_{40}]^{6-}$ can be seen (Fig 23.3) to be composed of four identical "tritungstate" or W_3 groups. Each of these is made up of three edge-sharing WO_6 octahedra, and the four groups are linked to each other by corner-sharing so as to enclose the heteroatom. This is more clearly seen in A where one of the W_3 groups has been omitted and the oxygens which are nearest neighbours to the heteroatom are marked by dots. The β-Keggin structure, B, is derived from the α-form by rotation of one W_3 group (in this case the top one) through 60°. In principle, similar rotation of the other three W_3 groups would yield γ, δ and ε isomers.

The Dawson structure, C, can be visualized as being formed by removing the three basal octahedra from each of two α-Keggin ions which are then fused together. By omitting the four octahedra at the front, the oxygens associated with the 2 heteroatoms can be seen more clearly (D).

Still larger heteropolyanions are possible by using As^{III} as the heteroatom. The lone-pair of electrons of this atom makes it too large to fit inside the Keggin ion, and the lacunary $[AsW_9O_{33}]^{9-}$ is formed instead. By judicious use of this as a "building block," $[As_4W_{40}O_{140}]^{28-}$ has been prepared. Similar use of $[P_2W_{12}O_{48}]^{12-}$, produced by degrading the Dawson structure by raising the pH, has yielded[18] $[P_4W_{48}O_{184}]^{40-}$.

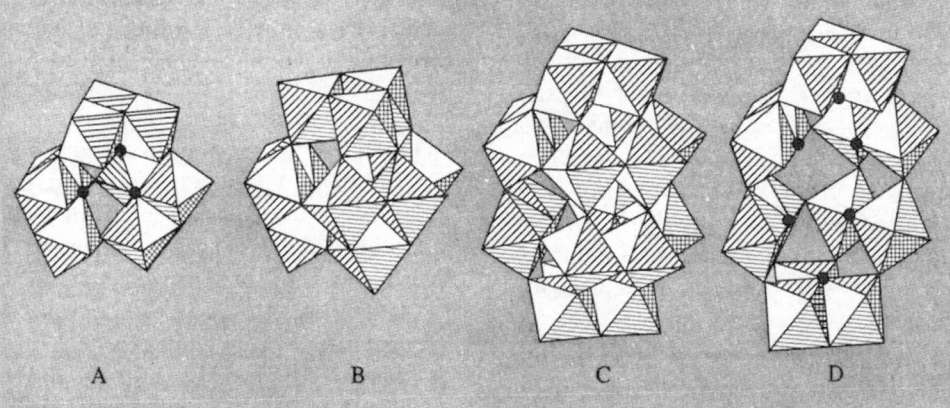

The largest polymetallates so far reported, however, are the mixed valence (Mo^{VI}, Mo^V) nitrosyls obtained by the more straightforward, if less systematic, method of heating acidified aqueous solutions of MoO_4^- and NH_2OH with VO_3^-. Depending on concentration and whether the solutions are refluxed or heated without stirring, a variety of products has been obtained[19] including the mixed metal $[Mo_{57}V_6O_{183}(NO)_6(H_2O)_{18}]^{6-}$ and the spectacular $[Mo_{154}O_{420}(NO)_{14}(H_2O)_{70}]^{n-}$ ($n = 25 \pm 5$). Both are dark blue and are composed of edge- and corner-sharing MoO_6 octahedra and $\{Mo(NO)O_6\}$ pentagonal bipyramids, along with $V^{IV}O_6$ octahedra in the case of the former. The latter has the overall shape of a car (automobile) tyre and, in spite of its large molar mass, its large surface area, bristling with H_2O and OH ligands, renders it readily soluble in water from which it can be recrystallized without decomposition in the absence of air.

units). The hetero atom is then held in an open "basket" rather than being totally enclosed. The

most numerous of such ions[9] are the Keggin derivatives, $[XM_{11}O_{39}]^{n-}$ (M = Mo, W; X = P,

[18] Y. JEANNIN, G. HERVE and A. PROUST, *Inorg. Chim. Acta* **198–200**, 319–36 (1992).
[19] S.-W. ZHANG, G.-Q. HUANG, M.-C. SHAO and Y.-Q. TANG, *J. Chem. Soc., Chem. Commun.*, 37–8

(1993). A. MÜLLER, E. KRICKEMEYER, J. MEYER, H. BÖGGE, F. PETERS, W. PLASS, E. DIEMANN, S. DILLINGER, F. NONNENBRUCH, M. RANDERATH and C. MENKE, *Angew. Chem. Int. Edn. Engl.* **34**, 2122–4 (1995).

As, Si, etc.) which are able to act as ligands to a variety of transition metal cations as well as to organometallic groups such as SnR, AsR and Ti (η^5-C_5H_5).

2:18, tetrahedral. If acidic solutions of the 1:12 anions $[X^VM_{12}O_{40}]^{3-}$ (X = P, As; M = Mo, W) are allowed to stand, the 2:18 $[X_2M_{18}O_{62}]^{6-}$ ions are gradually produced and can be isolated as their ammonium or potassium salts. The ion is best considered to be formed from two lacunary, 1:9 ions fused together and is generally known as the Dawson structure.

1:6, octahedral. These are formed with larger heteroatoms such as Te^{VI}, I^{VII}, Co^{III} and Al^{III} and are usually obtained from slightly acidic (pH 4–5) aqueous solutions. They adopt the Anderson structure in which the hetero-atom coordinates to 6 edge-sharing MO_6 octahedra in the form of a hexagon around the central XO_6 octahedron. It is noticeable that tungsten forms this type of ion less frequently than does molybdenum, which again probably reflects a greater readiness of molybdenum to form large structures based solely on edge-sharing, rather than corner-sharing, of octahedra. This is further reinforced by the less common, 1:9 octahedral type which is based solely on edge-sharing octahedra and of which tungsten apparently forms none. The best characterized examples are $[Mn^{IV}Mo_9O_{32}]^{6-}$ and $[Ni^{IV}Mo_9O_{32}]^{6-}$, prepared by the oxidation of X^{II} molybdate solutions with peroxodisulfate, the kinetics of which have been investigated.[20]

Mild and reversible reduction of 1:12 and 2:18 heteropoly-molybdates and -tungstates produces characteristic and very intense blue colours ("heteropoly blues") which find application in the quantitative determinations of Si, Ge, P and As, and commercially as dyes and pigments. The reductions are most commonly of 2 electron equivalents but may be of 1 and up to 6 electron equivalents. Many of the reduced anions can be isolated as solid salts in which the unreduced structure remains essentially unchanged and

the heteroatom is not normally involved; i.e. even $Fe^{III}W_{12}$ is reduced to $Fe^{III}W^VW_{11}^{VI}$ not to $Fe^{II}W_{12}$, although $Co^{III}W_{12}$ *is* reduced to $Co^{II}W_{12}$. 1- or 2-electron reductions evidently occur on individual M atoms, producing a proportion of M^V ions. Transfer of electrons from M^V to M^{VI} ions is then responsible for the intense "charge-transfer" absorption. In the highly reduced species, limited delocalization is probable.

23.3.4 Tungsten and molybdenum bronzes

These materials owe their name to their metallic lustre and are used in the production of "bronze" paints. They provide a further example of the formation of intense and characteristic colours by the reduction of oxo-species of Mo and W. The tungsten bronzes were the first to be discovered when, in 1823, F. Wöhler reduced a mixture of Na_2WO_4 and WO_3 with H_2 at red heat. The product was the precursor of a whole series of nonstoichiometric materials of general formula $M_x^IWO_3$ ($x < 1$) in which M^I is an alkali metal cation and W has an oxidation state between +5 and +6. Corresponding materials can also be obtained in which M is an alkaline earth or lanthanide metal. The alkali-metal molybdenum bronzes[21] are analogous to, but less well-known than, those of tungsten, being less stable and requiring high pressure for their formation; they were not produced until the 1960s. The lower stability of the molybdenum bronzes may be a consequence of the greater tendency of Mo^V to disproportionate as compared to W^V.

Tungsten bronzes can be prepared by a variety of reductive techniques but probably the most general method consists of heating the normal tungstate with tungsten metal. They are extremely inert chemically, being resistant both to alkalis and to acids, even when hot and concentrated. Their colours depend in the proportion of M and W present. In the case of sodium

---

[20] S. J. DUNNE, R. C. BURNS and G. A. LAWRANCE, *Aust. J. Chem.* **45**, 1943–52 (1992).

[21] M. GREENBLATT, *Chem. Revs.* **88**, 31–53 (1988).

tungsten bronze the colour varies from golden yellow, when $x \sim 0.9$, through shades of orange and red to bluish-black when $x \sim 0.3$. Within this range of x-values the structure consists of corner-shared WO_6 octahedra[†] as in WO_3 (p. 1008), with Na^I ions in the interstices — in other words an M-deficient perovskite lattice (p. 963). The observed electrical conductivities are metallic in magnitude and decrease linearly with increase in temperature, suggesting the existence of a conduction band of delocalized electrons. Measurements of the Hall effect (used to measure free electron concentrations) indicate that the concentration of free electrons equals the concentration of sodium atoms, implying that the conduction electrons arise from the complete ionization of sodium atoms. Several mechanisms have been suggested for the formation of this conduction band but it seems most likely that the t_{2g} orbitals of the tungsten overlap, not directly (since adjacent W atoms are generally more than 500 pm apart) but via oxygen $p\pi$ orbitals, so forming a partly filled π^* band permeating the whole WO_3 framework. If the value of x is reduced below about 0.3 the resulting electrical properties are semiconducting rather than metallic. This change coincides with structural distortions which probably disrupt the mechanism by which the conduction band is formed and instead cause localization of electrons in t_{2g} orbitals of specific tungsten atoms.

23.3.5 Sulfides [(2)], selenides and tellurides

The sulfides of this triad, though showing some similarities in stoichiometry to the principal

---

[†] This corner-sharing in tungsten bronzes is to be compared with a mixture of corner and edge-sharing in molybdenum bronzes which presumably occurs, as in the case of the polymetallates, because the increased electrostatic repulsion entailed in edge-sharing is less disruptive when the smaller Mo is involved. The prevalence of edge-sharing is still more marked in the vanadium and titanium bronzes (pp. 987, 964) where the smaller charges on the metal ions produce correspondingly smaller repulsions.

oxides (p. 1007), tend to be more stable in the lower oxidation states of the metals. Thus Cr forms no trisulfide and it is the di- rather than the tri-sulfides of Mo and W which are the more stable. However, tungsten (unlike Cr and Mo) does not form M_2S_3. Many of the compounds are nonstoichiometric, most are metallic (or at least semiconducting), and they exhibit a wide variety of magnetic behaviour encompassing diamagnetic, paramagnetic, antiferro-, ferri- and ferro-magnetic.

Cr_2S_3 is formed by heating powdered Cr with sulfur, or by the action of $H_2S(g)$ on Cr_2O_3, $CrCl_3$ or Cr. It decomposes to CrS on being heated, via a number of intermediate phases which approximate in composition to Cr_3S_4, Cr_5S_6 and Cr_7S_8. The structural relationship between these various phases can most readily be understood by reference to the $NiAs-CdI_2$ structure motif. Removal of all the M atoms from alternate layers of the NiAs structure (p. 555) yields the CdI_2 layer lattice (p. 1212). Between these two extremes, removal of a proportion of M atoms results in the above phases as follows: if one quarter of the Cr atoms are removed from *alternate* layers Cr_7S_8 results; if one third, Cr_5S_6 results; if two thirds, Cr_4S_6 (ie Cr_2S_3) results and if half, Cr_3S_4 results. Of these various phases Cr_2S_3 and CrS are semiconductors, whereas Cr_7S_8, Cr_5S_6 and Cr_3S_4 are metallic, and all exhibit magnetic ordering. The corresponding selenides CrSe, Cr_7Se_8, Cr_3Se_4, Cr_2Se_3, Cr_5Se_8 and Cr_7Se_{12} are broadly similar, as are the tellurides CrTe, Cr_7Te_8, Cr_5Te_6, Cr_3Te_4, Cr_2Te_3, Cr_5Te_8 and $CrTe_{\sim 2}$.

Of the many molybdenum sulfides which have been reported, only MoS, MoS_2 and Mo_2S_3 are well established. A hydrated form of the trisulfide of somewhat variable composition is precipitated from aqueous molybdate solutions by H_2S in classical analytical separations of molybdenum, but it is best prepared by thermal decomposition of the thiomolybdate, $(NH_4)_2MoS_4$. MoS is formed by heating the calculated amounts of Mo and S in an evacuated tube. The black MoS_2, however, is the most stable sulfide and, besides being the principal ore of Mo, is much the most important Mo compound commercially. In 1923 its structure was shown by R. G. Dickinson and L. Pauling (in the latter's first research paper) to consist of layers of MoS_2 in which the molybdenum atoms are each coordinated to 6 sulfides, but forming a trigonal prism rather than the more usual octahedron. This layer structure promotes easy cleavage and graphite-like lubricating properties, which have led to its widespread use as a lubricant both dry and in suspensions in oils and greases. It also has applications as a catalyst in many hydrogenation reactions and, even when the original catalyst takes the form of an oxide, it is likely that impurities (which often "poison" other catalysts) quickly produce a sulfide catalytic system. High-purity MoS_2 is normally prepared by heating the elements at 1000°C for several days. The reaction of anhydrous $MoCl_5$ and Na_2S offers a promising alternative.[22]

$$2MoCl_5 + 5Na_2S \longrightarrow 2MoS_2 + 10NaCl + S$$

It is so exothermic as to burst into flame on mixing, and is complete within seconds.

WS_3 and WS_2 are similar to their molybdenum analogues and all 4 compounds are diamagnetic semiconductors.

Selenides and tellurides are, again, broadly similar to the sulfides in structure and properties.

The oxygen atoms of MO_4^{2-} can be replaced successively by sulfur, and all four thiometallates, MO_3S^{2-}, $MO_2S_2^{2-}$, MOS_3^{2-} and MS_4^{2-} have been prepared; the thiomolybdates a century ago. They are useful reagents for the preparation of metal-sulfur clusters, and act as ligands, usually chelating but also as bridging groups.[23]

MSe_4^{2-} have also been known for a considerable time but are less familiar. They may be prepared conveniently by treating K_2Se_3 with $M(CO)_6$ in dmf.[24]

Remarkable physical properties are found in a series of ternary molybdenum chalcogenides, $M_xMo_6X_8$, known as Chevrel phases.[25] The first of these was $PbMo_6S_8$ but over 40 metals have been incorporated in the series, and both Se and Te analogues occur. These phases are black crystalline materials, prepared from the elements at temperatures of 1000–1100°C, and the $[Mo_6X_8]$ cluster, composed of an octahedron of Mo atoms face-capped by X atoms, is the basic structural unit (cf Mo, W dihalides, p. 1022). The clusters are linked because the otherwise free apical coordination site of each Mo is occupied by an X atom of an adjacent cluster, while the M_x atoms are intercalated in the channels between the clusters. That these bridges are strong, is evident from the observed intercluster Mo–Mo distances of only 310–360 pm compared to approx. 270 pm for Mo atoms within a cluster — which are not bridged. With $x = 0$, the metastable Mo_6X_8 (obtained by "deintercalation" of $M_xMo_6X_8$ with HCl, rather than by direct synthesis) has only 20 electrons per cluster (6 × 6 metal valence electrons less 2 × 8 used in bonding to X_8). This is 4 short of the 24 required for Mo–Mo single bonds along each of the edges of the cluster, and may be the cause of the observed trigonal distortion. Intercalation of M_x atoms provides up to 4 electrons which make good this deficit thereby strengthening and shortening the Mo–Mo bonds and reducing the distortion.[†] $PbMo_6S_8$ has 22 electrons per cluster. The electron "holes" facilitate conduction, and below 14 K it is a superconductor. This, and several other Chevrel phases retain their superconductivity in the presence of exceptionally strong magnetic fields, and attempts to produce technically acceptable superconductors by extruding filaments in a copper matrix have been

[22] P. R. BONNEAU, R. F. JARVIS and R. B. KANER, *Nature* **349**, 510–2 (1991).

[23] M. A. GREANEY and E. I. STIEFEL, *J. Chem. Soc.. Chem Commun.*, 1679–80 (1992).

[24] S. C. O'NEAL and J. W. COLIS, *J. Am. Chem. Soc.* **110**, 1971–3 (1988).

[25] R. CHEVREL, M. HIRRIEN and M. SERGENT, *Polyhedron* **5**, 87–94 (1986).

[†] An alternative interpretation, supported by evidence from relevant molecular compounds is that the distortions are the result of intercluster M–X interactions (see p. 1031)

promising. Apparently, no tungsten analogues are yet known.

23.3.6 Halides and oxohalides [2,3]

The known halides of chromium, molybdenum and tungsten are listed in Table 23.4. The observed trends are as expected. The group

oxidation state of +6 is attained by chromium only with the strongly oxidizing fluorine, and even tungsten is unable to form a hexaiodide. Precisely the same is true in the +5 oxidation state, and in the +4 oxidation state the iodides have a doubtful or unstable existence. In the lower oxidation states all the chromium halides are known, but molybdenum has not yet been induced to form a difluoride nor tungsten a di- or

Table 23.4　Halides of Group 6 (mp/°C)

Oxidation state	Fluorides	Chlorides	Bromides	Iodides
+6	CrF_6 yellow (d > −100°)			
	MoF_6 colourless (17.4°) bp 34°	$(MoCl_6)$ black		
	WF_6 colourless (1.9°) bp 17.1°	WCl_6 dark blue (275°) bp 346°	WBr_6 dark blue (309°)	
+5	CrF_5 red (34°) bp 117°			
	MoF_5 yellow (67°) bp 213°	$MoCl_5$ black (194°) bp 268°		
	WF_5 yellow	WCl_5 dark green (242°) bp 286°	WBr_5 black	
+4	CrF_4 violet-amethyst[a]	$CrCl_4$ (d > 600°, gas phase)	$CrBr_4$?	CrI_4
	MoF_4 pale green	$MoCl_4$ black	$MoBr_4$ black	MoI_4?
	WF_4 red-brown	WCl_4 black	WBr_4 black	WI_4?
+3	CrF_3 green (1404°)	$CrCl_3$ red-violet (1150°)	$CrBr_3$ very dark green (1130°)	CrI_3 very dark green
	MoF_3 brown (>600°)	$MoCl_3$ very dark red (1027°)	$MoBr_3$ green (977°)	MoI_3 black (927°)
		WCl_3 red	WBr_3 black (d > 80°)	WI_3
+2	CrF_2 green (894°)	$CrCl_2$ white (820°)	$CrBr_2$ white (842°)	CrI_2 red-brown (868°)
		$MoCl_2$ yellow (d > 530°)	$MoBr_2$ yellow-red (d > 900°)	MoI_2
		WCl_2 yellow	WBr_2 yellow	WI_2 brown

[a]It is probable that previously reported green samples were largely CrF_3; O. KRAMER and B. G. MÜLLER, *Z. anorg. allg. Chem.* **621**, 1969–72 (1995).

tri-fluoride. Similarly, in the oxohalides (which are largely confined to the +6 and +5 oxidation states, see p. 1023) tungsten alone forms an oxoiodide, while only chromium (as yet) forms an oxofluoride in the lower of these oxidation states.

All the known hexahalides can be prepared by the direct action of the halogen on the metal and all are readily hydrolysed. The yellow CrF_6, however, requires a temperature of 400°C and a pressure of 200–300 atms for its formation, and reduction of the pressure causes it to dissociate into CrF_5 and F_2 even at temperatures as low as −100°C. The monomeric and octahedral hexafluorides MoF_6 and WF_6 are colourless liquids and the former is strongly oxidizing. Only tungsten is known with certainty to produce other hexahalides and these are the dark-blue solids WCl_6 and WBr_6, the latter in particular being susceptible to reduction.

Of the pentahalides, chromium again forms only the fluoride which is a strongly oxidizing, bright red, volatile solid prepared from the elements using less severe conditions than for CrF_6. MoF_5 and WF_5 can be prepared by reduction of the hexahalides with the metal but the latter disproportionates into WF_6 and WF_4 if heated above about 80°C. They are yellow volatile solids, isostructural with the tetrameric $(NbF_5)_4$ and $(TaF_5)_4$ (Fig. 22.4b, p. 990). Similarity with Group 5 is again evident in the pentachlorides of Mo and W, $MoCl_5$ being the most extensively studied of the pentahalides. These, respectively, black and dark-green solids are obtained by direct reaction of the elements under carefully controlled conditions and have the same dimeric structure as their Nb and Ta analogues (Fig. 22.4c, p. 990). WBr_5 can be prepared similarly but is not yet well characterized.

The tetrahalides are scarcely more numerous or familiar than the hexa- and penta-halides, the 3 tetraiodides together with $CrBr_4$ and $CrCl_4$ being either of uncertain existence or occurring only at high temperatures in the gaseous phase. The most stable representatives are the fluorides: CrF_4 is an unreactive solid; MoF_4 is an involatile green solid; and WF_4 begins

to decompose only when heated above 800°. $MoCl_4$ exists in two crystalline modifications: α-$MoCl_4$ is probably made up of linear chains of edge-shared octahedra, whereas β-$MoCl_4$ has a unique structure composed of hexameric cyclic molecules $(MoCl_4)_6$ generated by edge-shared $\{MoCl_6\}$ octahedra with Mo–Cl_t 220 pm, Mo–Cl_μ 243 and 251 pm and Mo$\cdots$Mo 367 pm. General preparative methods include controlled reaction of the elements, reduction of higher halides, and halogenation of lower halides. The tetrahalides of Mo and W are readily oxidized and hydrolysed and produce some adducts of the form MX_4L_2.

The trihalides show major differences between the 3 metals. All 4 of the chromium trihalides are known, this being much the most stable oxidation state for chromium; they can be prepared by reacting the halogen and the metal, though CrF_3 is better obtained from HF and $CrCl_3$ at 500°C. The fluoride is green, the chloride red-violet, and the bromide and iodide dark green to black. In all cases layer structures lead to octahedral coordination of the metal. $CrCl_3$ consists of a ccp lattice of chloride ions with Cr^{III} ions occupying two-thirds of the octahedral sites of alternate layers. The other alternate layers of octahedral sites are empty and, without the cohesive effect of the cations, easy cleavage in these planes is possible and this accounts for the flaky appearance. Stable, hydrated forms of CrX_3 can also be readily obtained from aqueous solutions, and $CrCl_3$.-$6H_2O$ provides a well-known example of hydrate isomerism, mentioned on p. 920. In view of this clear ability of Cr^{III} to aquate it may seem surprising that anhydrous $CrCl_3$ is quite insoluble in pure water (though it dissolves rapidly on the addition of even a trace of a reducing agent). It appears that the reducing agent produces at least some Cr^{II} ions. Solubilization then follows as a result of electron transfer from $[Cr(aq)]^{2+}$ in solution via a chloride bridge to Cr^{III} in the solid, which leaves $[Cr(aq)]^{3+}$ in solution and Cr^{II} in the solid. The latter is kinetically far more labile than Cr^{III} and can readily leave the solid and aquate, so starting the cycle again and rapidly dissolving the solid.

The Mo trihalides are obtained by reducing a higher halide with the metal (except for the triiodide which, being the highest stable iodide, is best prepared directly). They are insoluble in water and generally inert. $MoCl_3$ is structurally similar to $CrCl_3$ but is distorted so that pairs of Mo atoms lie only 276 pm apart which, in view of the low and temperature-dependent magnetic moment, is evidently close enough to permit appreciable Mo–Mo interaction. Electrolytic reduction of a solution of MoO_3 in aqueous HCl changes the colour to green, then brown, and finally red, when complexes of the octahedral $[MoCl_6]^{3-}$, $[MoCl_5(H_2O)]^{2-}$ and $[Mo_2Cl_9]^{3-}$ can be isolated using suitable cations. The diversity of the coordination chemistry of molybdenum(III) is, however, in no way comparable to that of chromium(III).

By contrast, the tungsten trihalides (the trifluoride is not known) are "cluster" compounds similar to those of Nb and Ta. The trichloride and tribromide are prepared by halogenation of the dihalides. The structure of the former is based on the $[M_6X_{12}]^{n+}$ cluster (Fig. 22.6) with a further 6 Cl atoms situated above the apical W atoms. WBr_3, on the other hand, has a structure based on the $[M_6X_8]^{n+}$ cluster (see Fig. 23.5), but as it is formed by only a 2-electron oxidation of $[W_6Br_8]^{4+}$ it does not contain tungsten(III) and is best formulated as $[W_6Br_8]^{6+}(Br_4{}^{2-})(Br^-)_2$, where $(Br_4{}^{2-})$ represents a bridging polybromide group. Electrolytic reduction of WO_3 in aqueous HCl fails to produce the mononuclear complexes obtained with molybdenum, but forms the green $[W_2Cl_9]^{3-}$ ion. This and its Cr and Mo analogues provide an interesting reflection of the increasing strength of M–M bonding in the order $Cr^{III} < Mo^{III} < W^{III}$. The structure consists of 2 MCl_6 octahedra sharing a common face (Fig. 23.4) which allows the possibility of direct M–M bonding. In the Cr ion the Cr atoms are 312 pm apart, being actually displaced in their CrO_6 octahedra away from each other. The magnetic moment of $[Cr_2Cl_9]^{3-}$ is normal for a metal ion with 3 unpaired electrons and indicates the absence of Cr–Cr bonding. In $[Mo_2Cl_9]^{3-}$ the Mo atoms are 267 pm apart and the magnetic

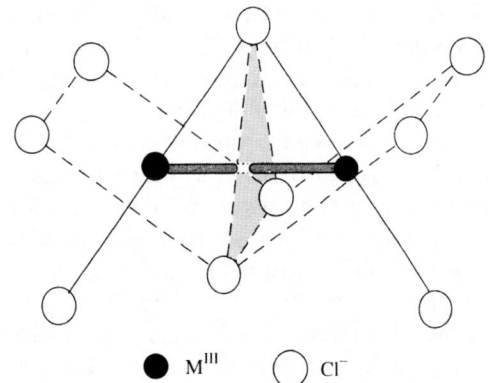

● M^{III} ○ Cl^-

Figure 23.4 Structure of $[M_2Cl_9]^{3-}$ showing the M–M bond through the shared face of two inclined MCl_6 octahedra. See also Fig. 7.9, p. 240, for an alternative representation of the confacial bioctahedral structure.

moment is low and temperature dependent, indicating appreciable Mo–Mo bonding. Finally, $[W_2Cl_9]^{3-}$ is diamagnetic: the metal atoms are displaced towards each other, being only 242 pm apart (compared to 274 pm in the metal itself), consistent with a W–W triple bond (p. 1030).

Anhydrous chromium dihalides are conveniently prepared by reduction of the trihalides with H_2 at 300–500°C, or by the action of HX (or I_2 for the diiodide) on the metal at temperatures of the order of 1000°C. They are all deliquescent and the hydrates can be obtained by reduction of the trihalides using pure chromium metal and aqueous HX. All have distorted octahedral structures as anticipated for a metal ion with the d^4 configuration which is particularly susceptible to Jahn–Teller distortion[†]. This is typified by CrF_2, which adopts a distorted rutile structure in which

---

[†] A theorem proposed by H. A. Jahn and E. Teller (1937) states that a molecule in a degenerate electronic state will be unstable and will undergo a geometrical distortion that lowers its symmetry and splits the degenerate state. *Jahn–Teller* distortions are particularly important and well-documented for octahedrally coordinated metal ions whose e_g (i.e. axial) orbitals are unequally occupied: $t_{2g}^3 e_g^1$ (high-spin Cr^{II} and Mn^{III}), $t_{2g}^6 e_g^1$ (low-spin Co^{II} and Ni^{III}) and $t_{2g}^6 e_g^3$ (Cu^{II}). They are generally manifested by an elongation of the bonds on one axis, and may be ascribed to the d_{z^2} orbital containing 1

4 fluoride ions are 200 pm from the chromium atom while the remaining 2 are 243 pm away. The strongly reducing properties of chromium(II) halides contrast, at first sight surprisingly, with the redox stability of the molybdenum(II) halides. Even the tungsten(II) halides, which admittedly are also strong reducing agents (being oxidized to their trihalides), may by their very existence be thought to depart from the expected trend.

Of the various preparative methods available for the dihalides of Mo and W, thermal decomposition or reduction of higher halides is the most general. The reason for their enhanced stability lies in the prevalence of metal–atom clusters, stabilized by M–M bonding. All 6 of these dihalides (Mo and W do not form difluorides) are isomorphous,[26] with a structure based on the $[M_6X_8]^{4+}$ unit briefly mentioned above for WBr$_3$ (see also Chevrel phases p. 1018). It can be seen (Fig. 23.5) that in this cluster each metal atom has a free coordination position. In the dihalides themselves, these positions are occupied by $6X^-$ ions, 4 of them bridging to other $[M_6X_8]^{4+}$ units, giving the composition $[M_6X_8]X_2X_{4/2} = MX_2$. Although precise details of the bonding scheme are not settled it is clear that in each cluster the 6 metals contribute $6 \times 6 = 36$ valence electrons of which 4 are transferred to the counter anions, so producing the net charge, and 8 are used in bonding to the 8 chlorines of the cluster. Twenty-four electrons remain which can provide M–M bonds along each of the 12 edges of the octahedron of metal atoms accounting for the observed diamagnetism. Unlike the M$_6$ clusters of the "electron-poor" elements of groups 3, 4 and 5 (pp. 950, 965 and 992) the incorporation of interstitial atoms offers no additional stability and is not observed.

The six outer halide ions are readily replaced, leaving the $[M_6X_8]^{4+}$ core intact throughout a

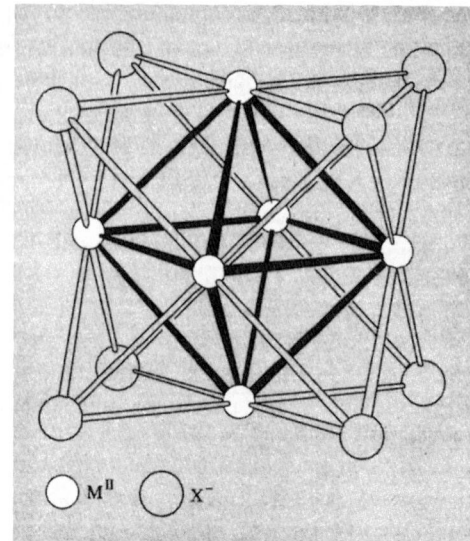

Figure 23.5 $[M_6X_8]^{4+}$ clusters with X bridges over each face of the octahedron of metal ions.

variety of substitution reactions. The eight core halogens are far less labile, but prolonged heating (16 h at 500C) of $[Mo_6Cl_8Br_4]^{2-}$ for instance, has been shown[27] by ^{19}F nmr spectroscopy to yield a mixture containing all 22 possible isomers of the $[Mo_6Br_nCl_{8-n}]^{4+}$ cluster. Oxidation of WBr$_2$ with Br$_2$ yields brownish-black crystals of the molecular cluster compound W$_6$Br$_{14}$ in which a non-bridging Br completes the coordination sphere of each metal atom in the {W$_6$Br$_8$} core.[27a]

The oxohalides of all three elements (Table 23.5) are very susceptible to hydrolysis and their oxidizing properties decrease in the order Cr > Mo > W. They are yellow to red liquids or volatile solids; probably the best known is the deep-red liquid, chromyl chloride, CrO$_2$Cl$_2$. It is most commonly encountered as the distillate in qualitative tests for chromium or chloride and can be obtained by heating a dichromate and chloride in conc H$_2$SO$_4$; it is an extremely aggressive oxidizing agent. The Mo and W oxohalides

electron more than the $d_{x^2-y^2}$, so preventing ligands on the z-axis approaching as close as those on the x and y

[26] An amorphous form of MoCl$_2$ is also known, whose spectroscopic properties suggest the presence of tetranuclear units; see W. W. BEERS and R. E. McCARLEY, *Inorg. Chem.* **24**, 472–5 (1985).

[27] P. BRÜCKNER, G. PETERS and W. PREETZ, *Z. anorg. allg. Chem.* **619**, 551–8 (1993).

[27a] J. SASSMANSHAUSEN and H.-G. VON SCHNERING, *Z. anorg. allg. Chem.* **620**, 1312–20 (1994).

Table 23.5　Oxohalides of Group 6 (mp/°C)

Oxidation state	Fluorides		Chlorides		Bromides	Iodides
+6	CrOF$_4$ red (55°)	CrO$_2$F$_2$ violet (32°)		CrO$_2$Cl$_2$ red (−96.5°) bp 117°	CrO$_2$Br$_2$ red (d < rt)	
	MoOF$_4$ white (97°) bp 186°	MoO$_2$F$_2$ white (subl 270°)	MoOCl$_4$ green (101°) bp 159°	MoO$_2$Cl$_2$ pale yellow (175°) bp 250°	MoO$_2$Br$_2$ purple- brown	
	WOF$_4$ white (101°) bp 186°	WO$_2$F$_2$ white	WOCl$_4$ red (209°) bp 224°	WO$_2$Cl$_2$ pale yellow (265°)	WOBr$_4$ dark brown (277°) or black (321°) WO$_2$Br$_2$ red	WO$_2$I$_2$ green
+5	CrOF$_3$		CrOCl$_3$ dark red			
	MoOF$_3$ green, also dark blue		MoOCl$_3$ black (d > 200°)	MoO$_2$Cl	MoOBr$_3$ black (subl 270° vac)	
			WOCl$_3$ olive green		WOBr$_3$ dark brown	WO$_2$I
+3			CrOCl green		CrOBr	

Cr^{IV}OCl$_2$ has been observed in the gaseous phase by means of mass spectrometry.[29]

are prepared by a variety of oxygenation and halogenation reactions which frequently produce mixtures, and many specific preparations have therefore been devised.[28] They are possibly best known as impurities in preparations of the halides from which air or moisture have been inadequately excluded, and their formation is indicative of the readiness with which metal–oxygen bonds are formed by these elements in high oxidation states.

23.3.7 Complexes of chromium, molybdenum and tungsten [3,30,31]

Oxidation state VI (d^0)

No halogeno complexes of the type [MX$_{6+x}$]$^{x-}$ are known and, although homoleptic imido complexes, Li$_2$[M(NBu$'$)$_4$] (M = Cr, Mo, W), containing tetrahedrally coordinated M^{VI} have been prepared,[32] the coordination chemistry of this oxidation state is centred mainly on oxo and peroxo complexes. The former class includes chromyl alkoxides[33] and adducts of tungsten oxohalides such as [WOX$_5$]$^-$ and [WO$_2$X$_4$]$^{2-}$ (X = F, Cl), but most are octahedral chelates of

[28] Ref. 2, pp. 275–81.

[29] V. PLIES. *Z. anorg. allg. Chem.* **602**, 97–104 (1991).

[30] L. F. LARKWORTHY, K. B. NOLAN and P. O'BRIEN, Chromium, Chap. 35, pp. 699–969, A. G. SYKES, G. J. HUNT, R. L. RICHARDS, C. D. GARNER, J. M. CHARNOCK and E. I. STIEFEL, Molybdenum, Chap. 36, pp. 1229–444, and Z. DORI, Tungsten, Chap. 37, pp. 973–1022, in *Comprehensive Coordination Chemistry*, Vol. 3, Pergamon Press, Oxford, 1987. For Chromium see also D. A. HOUSE, *Adv. Inorg. Chem.* **44**, 341–73 (1997).

[31] R. COLTON, *Coord. Chem. Revs.* **90**, 1–109 (1988).

[32] A. A. DANOPOULOS and G. WILKINSON, *Polyhedron* **9**, 1009–10 (1990).

[33] S. L. CHADHA, V. SHARMA and A. SHARMA, *J. Chem. Soc., Dalton Trans.*, 1253–5 (1987).

the types $[MoO_2X_2(L-L)]^{(34)}$ and $[MoO_2(L-L^-)_2]$ (M = Mo, W). In the MoO_2^{2+} group of these compounds the oxygen atoms are mutually *cis*, thereby maximizing the $O(p_\pi) \rightarrow M(d_\pi)$ bonding, and the group is reminiscent of the uranyl UO_2^{2+} ion (p. 1273), though its chemistry is by no means as extensive and the latter is a linear ion. The best-known example of this type of compound is $[MoO_2(oxinate)_2]$ used for the gravimetric determination of molybdenum; oxine is 8-hydroxyquinoline, i.e.

The peroxo-complexes provide further examples of the ability of oxygen to coordinate to the metals in their high oxidation states. The production of blue solutions when acidified dichromates are treated with H_2O_2 is a qualitative test for chromium.[†] The colour arises from the unstable CrO_5 which can, however, be stabilized by extraction into ether, and blue solid adducts such as $[CrO_5(py)]$ can be isolated. This is more correctly formulated as $[CrO(O_2)_2py]$ and has an approximately pentagonal pyramidal structure (Fig. 23.6a). Bidentate ligands, such as phenanthroline and bipyridyl produce pentagonal bipyramidal complexes in which the second N-donor atom is loosely bonded *trans* to the $=O$ (Fig. 23.6b). This 7-coordinate structure is favoured in numerous peroxo-complexes of Mo and W, and the dark-red peroxo anion $[Mo(O_2)_4]^{2-}$ is 8-coordinate, with Mo–O 197 pm and O–O 155 pm.

Oxidation state V (d^1)

This is an unstable state for chromium and, apart from the fluoride and oxohalides already

[34] K. DREISCH, C. ANDERSSON and C. STÅLHANDSKE, *Polyhedron* **11**, 2143–50 (1992).

[†] The acidity is important. In alkaline solution $[Cr^V(O_2)_4]^{3-}$ is produced, but from neutral solutions explosive violet salts, probably containing $[Cr^{VI}O(O_2)_2OH]^-$, are produced.

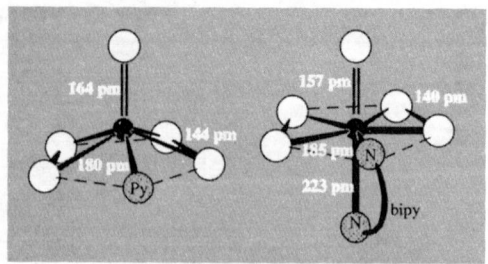

Figure 23.6   Molecular structures of (a) $[CrO(O_2)_2-py]$ and (b) $[CrO(O_2)_2(bipy)]$.

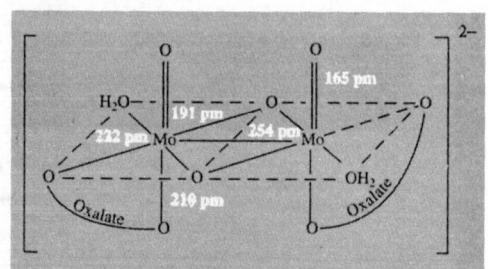

Figure 23.7   The dimeric, oxygen bridged, $[Mo_2O_4-(C_2O_4)_2(H_2O)_2]^{2-}$ showing the close approach of the 2 Mo atoms and unusually large range of Mo–O distances from 165 to 222 pm.

mentioned, it is represented primarily by the blue to black chromates of the alkali and alkaline earth metals and the red-brown tetraperoxochromate(V). The former contain the tetrahedral $[CrO_4]^{3-}$ ion and hydrolyse with disproportionation to Cr(III) and Cr(VI). The latter can be isolated as rather more stable salts from alkaline solutions of dichromate treated with H_2O_2. These red salts contain the paramagnetic 8-coordinate, dodecahedral, $[Cr(O_2)_4]^{3-}$ ion, which is isomorphous with the corresponding complex ions of the Group 5 metals (p. 994). The η^2-O_2 groups are unsymmetrically coordinated, with Cr–O 185 and 195 pm and the O–O distance 141 pm.

The heavier elements have a much more extensive +5 chemistry including, in the case of molybdenum, a number of compounds of considerable biological interest which will be discussed separately (p. 1035). A variety of reactions involving fusion and nonaqueous solvents has been used to produce octahedral hexahalogeno complexes. These are very susceptible to hydrolysis, and the affinity of Mo^V for oxygen is further demonstrated by the propensity of $MoCl_5$ to produce green oxomolybdenum(V) compounds by oxygen-abstraction from appropriate oxygen-containing materials. This leads to a number of well-characterized complexes of the type $[MoOCl_3L]$ and $[MoOCl_3L_2]$. Oxomolybdenum(V) compounds are also obtained from aqueous solution and include monomeric species such as $[MoOX_5]^{2-}$ (X = Cl, Br, NCS) and dimeric, oxygen-bridged complexes such as $[Mo_2O_4(C_2O_4)_2(H_2O)_2]^{2-}$ (Fig. 23.7) which may be considered to be derived from the orange-yellow aquo ion $[Mo_2O_4(H_2O)_6]^{2+}$. Whereas the monomeric compounds are paramagnetic with magnetic moments corresponding to 1 unpaired electron, the binuclear compounds are diamagnetic, or only slightly paramagnetic, suggesting appreciable metal–metal interaction occurring either directly or via the bridging oxygens.

Also of interest are the octacyano complexes, $[M(CN)_8]^{3-}$ (M = Mo, W), which are commonly prepared by oxidation of the M^{IV} analogues (using MnO_4^- or Ce^{IV}) and whose structures apparently vary, according to the environment and counter cation, between the energetically similar square-antiprismatic and dodecahedral forms.[35]

Oxidation state IV (d²)

As for the previous oxidation state, the chemistries of Mo^{IV} and W^{IV} are much more extensive than that of Cr^{IV} which is largely confined to peroxo- and fluoro- complexes. $[Cr(O_2)_2(NH_3)_3]$, which has a dark red-brown metallic lustre, may be obtained either by treating $[Cr(O_2)_4]^{3-}$ with warm aqueous ammonia or by the action of H_2O_2 on ammoniacal solutions of $(NH_4)_2CrO_4$. It has a pentagonal bipyramidal structure in which the peroxo- groups occupy

four of the planar positions, and the NH_3 molecules are replaceable by other ligands. The very hydrolysable salts of $[CrF_6]^{2-}$ are obtained by direct fluorination of anhydrous $CrCl_3$ and an alkali metal chloride.

More or less hydrolysable hexahalogeno salts of $[MX_6]^{2-}$ (M = Mo, X = F, Cl, Br; M = W, X = Cl, Br) are also known and the yellow octacyano compounds have provided structural interest ever since the classical work of J. L. Hoard in 1939 established $K_4[Mo(CN)_8].2H_2O$ as the first example of an 8-coordinate complex. This and its W analogue have dodecahedral (D_{2d}) structures and their diamagnetism arises from the splitting of their d-orbitals which stabilizes one (probably the d_{xy}) to such an extent that the two d electrons pair in it. The energy barrier between dodecahedral and square antiprismatic (D_{4d}) structures is, however, small and the latter is obtained if the K^+ counter cations are replaced by Cd^{2+}. ^{95}Mo and ^{14}N nmr studies show[35a] that the ion is dodecahedral in aqueous solution and that the equivalence of the eight CN groups (indicating the more symmetrical D_{4d} form), implied by earlier ^{13}C work, arises from rapid tumbling of the ion rather than fluxional rearrangement. Photolysis of the otherwise stable $[M(CN)_8]^{4-}$ solutions causes loss of four CN^- ions to give octahedral oxo compounds such as $K_4[MO_2(CN)_4].6H_2O$ (M = Mo, W).

Other mononuclear complexes include the tetrahedral $[Mo(NMe_2)_4]$ and the octahedral $Li_2[Mo(NMe_2)_6].2thf$[36] but recent interest in the chemistry of the M^{IV} ion has centred on the trinuclear oxo and thio complexes of Mo and W, particularly the former. They are of three main types. The first may be conceptually based on the $[M_3O_{13}]$ unit found in the aquo ions $[M_3O_4(H_2O_9)]^{4+}$ (M = Mo,[37] W). It contains a

[35] J. G. LEIPOLDT, S. S. BASSON and A. ROODT, *Adv. Inorg. Chem.* **40**, 241–322 (1994).

[35a] R. T. C. BROWNLEE, B. P. SHEHAN and A. G. WEDD, *Inorg. Chem.* **26**, 2022–4 (1987).

[36] M. H. CHISHOLM, C. E. HAMMOND and J. C. HUFFMAN, *Polyhedron* **7**, 399–400 (1988).

[37] Preparations of the various aquo ions of Mo in oxidation states II to V are given in D. T. RICHENS and A. G. SYKES, *Inorg. Synth.* **23**, 130–40 (1985).

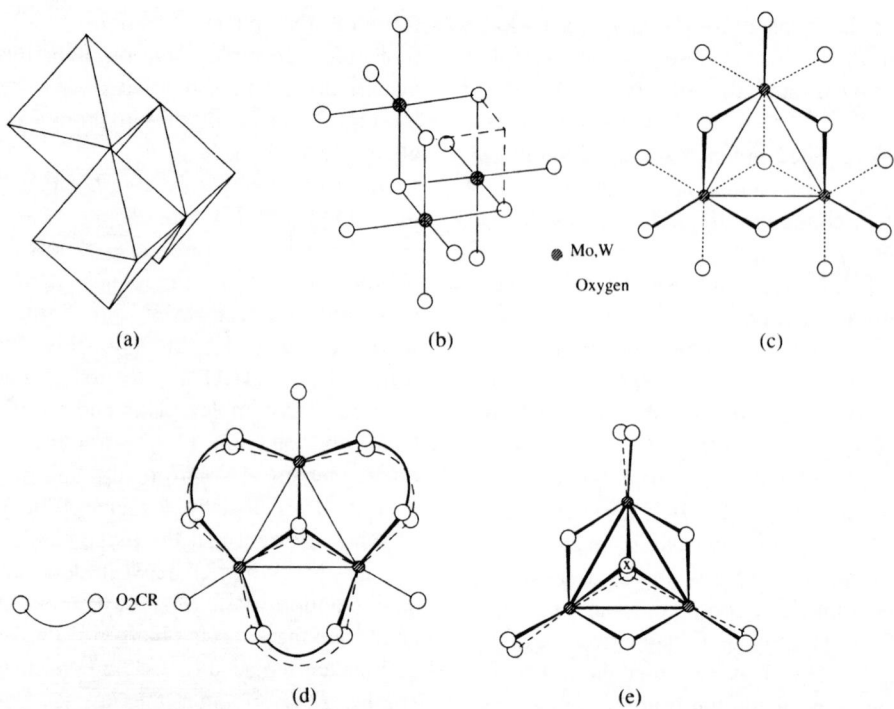

Figure 23.8 Trinuclear, M–M bonded species of Mo^{IV} and W^{IV}. (a) (b) and (c) are alternative representations of the M$_3$O$_{13}$ unit: (a) emphasizes its relationship to the edge-sharing octahedra of the M$_3$ group in polymetallate ions; (b) shows the (μ_3-O) (μ_2-O)$_3$ bridges and M–M bonds of its M$_3$O$_4$ "incomplete cubane" core; and (c) emphasizes its triangular centre by viewing from the unoccupied corner of the cuboid. (d) and (e) offer the same perspective as (c) but of [M$_3$O$_2$(O$_2$CR)$_6$(H$_2$O)$_3$]$^{2+}$ and [M$_3$(μ_3-X)(μ_3-OR)(OR)$_9$] structures respectively.

triangle of M–M bonded metals capped by a single oxygen on one side and on the other side three oxygens bridge each pair of metal atoms. It may be viewed either as ·a reduced form of the M$_3$ group found in polymetallate ions, or as an "incomplete cubane-type" of complex[38] (Fig. 23.8). Some, or all, of the nine water molecules of the aquo ion are replaceable by a variety of ligands including oxalate, edta and NCS$^-$, and thio derivatives[38a] containing M$_3$O$_3$S, M$_3$O$_2$S$_2$, M$_3$OS$_3$ and M$_3$S$_4$ cores have been prepared. In the mixed O/S species, S appears always to occupy the μ_3-position. M–M bond lengths are about 250 pm for M$_3$O$_4$ species increasing to 270–280 pm for M$_3$S$_4$ species, there

being very little difference between Mo and W compounds. Preparative routes vary but usually involve reduction from M^{VI} or M^V, often by the use of NaBH$_4$. Se and Te analogues of the Mo compounds are also known and an Se analogue for W has recently been reported.[39]

The second type of trinuclear compounds containing [M$_3$O$_2$(O$_2$CR)$_6$(H$_2$O)$_3$]$^{2+}$ and obtained by the reaction of M(CO)$_6$ (M = Mo, W) with carboxylic acids, features a similar triangle of M–M bonded metal atoms but this time capped on *both* sides by μ_3-O atoms (Fig. 23.8d). Complexes in which either one or both of these capping atoms are replaced by μ_3-CR, alkylidene,

[38] T. SHIBAHARA, *Adv. Inorg. Chem.* **37**, 143–73 (1991).
[38a] T. SAITO, *Adv. Inorg. Chem.* **44**, 45–92 (1997).

[39] V. P. FEDIN, M. N. SOKOLOV, A. V. VIROVETS, N. V. POD-BEREZSKAY and V. Y. FEDEROV, *Polyhedron* **11**, 2973–4 (1992).

groups are also obtainable and all these bicapped species are notable for their kinetic inertness. The third trinuclear type is that of the alkoxides $[M_3(\mu_3\text{-}X)(\mu_3\text{-}OR)(OR)_9]$ (M = Mo, W; X = O, NH)[40] which again are bicapped but with only single bridges spanning the M–M bonds (Fig. 23.8e).

Oxidation state III (d^3)

This is by far the most stable and best-known oxidation state for chromium and is characterized by thousands of compounds, most of them prepared from aqueous solutions. By contrast, unless stabilized by M–M bonding, molybdenum(III) compounds are sparse and hardly any are known for tungsten(III). Thus Mo, but not W, has an aquo ion $[Mo(H_2O)_6]^{3+}$, which gives rise to complexes $[MoX_6]^{3-}$ (X = F, Cl, Br, NCS). Direct action of acetylacetone on the hexachloromolybdate(III) ion produces the sublimable (Mo(acac)$_3$] which, however, unlike its chromium analogue, is oxidized by air to Mo^V products. A black Mo^{III} cyanide, $K_4Mo(CN)_7.2H_2O$, has been precipitated from aqueous solution by the addition of ethanol. Its magnetic moment ($\sim$1.75 BM) is consistent with 7-coordinate Mo^{III} in which the loss of degeneracy of the t_{2g} orbitals has caused pairing of 2 of the three d electrons.

Chromium(III) forms stable salts with all the common anions and it complexes with virtually any species capable of donating an electron-pair. These complexes may be anionic, cationic, or neutral and, with hardly any exceptions, are hexacoordinate and octahedral, e.g.:

$[CrX_6]^{3-}$ (X = halide, CN, SCN, N_3)

$[Cr(L\text{-}L)_3]^{3-}$ (L-L = oxalate)

$[CrX_6]^{3+}$ (X = H_2O, NH_3)

$[Cr(L\text{-}L)_3]^{3+}$ (L-L = en, bipy, phen)

$[Cr(L\text{-}L)_3]$ (L-L = β-diketonates, amino-acid anions)

40 M. H. CHISHOLM, D. L. CLARK, M. J. HAMPDEN-SMITH and D. H. HOFFMAN, *Angew. Chem. Int. Edn. Engl.* **28**, 432–44 (1989).

There is also a multitude of complexes with 2 or more different ligands, such as the pentaammines $[Cr(NH_3)_5X]^{n+}$ which have been extensively used in kinetic studies. These various complexes are notable for their kinetic inertness, which is compatible with the half-filled t_{2g} level arising from an octahedral d^3 configuration and is the reason why many thermodynamically unstable complexes can be isolated. Ligand substitution and rearrangement reactions are slow (half-times are of the order of hours), with the result that the preparation of different, solid, isomeric forms of a compound was the classical means of establishing stereochemistry and the reason why early coordination chemists devoted so much attention to Cr^{III} complexes. For precisely the same reason, however, the preparation of these complexes is not always straightforward. Salts such as the hydrated sulfate and halides, which might seem obvious starting materials, themselves contain coordinated water or anions and these are not always easily displaced. Simple addition of the appropriate ligand to an aqueous solution of a Cr^{III} salt is therefore not a usual preparative method, though in the presence of charcoal it is feasible in the case, for instance, of $[Cr(en)_3]^{3+}$. Some alternative routes, which avoid these pre-formed inert complexes, are:

(i) *Anhydrous methods*: ammine and amine complexes can be prepared by the reaction of CrX$_3$ with NH$_3$ or amine, and salts of $[CrX_6]^{3-}$ anions are best obtained by fusion of CrX$_3$ with the alkali metal salt.

(ii) *Oxidation of Cr(II)*: ammine and amine complexes can also be prepared by the aerial oxidation of mixtures of aqueous $[Cr(H_2O)_6]^{2+}$ (which is kinetically labile) and the appropriate ligands.

(iii) *Reduction of Cr(VI)*: CrO$_3$ and dichromates are commonly used to prepare such complexes as $K_3[Cr(C_2O_4)_3]$ and $NH_4[Cr(NH_3)_2(NCS)_4].H_2O$ (Reinecke's salt).

The violet hexaaquo ion, $[Cr(H_2O)_6]^{3+}$, occurs in the chrome alums, $Cr_2(SO_4)_3M_2^ISO_4.24H_2O$

Table 23.6　Spectroscopic data for typical octahedral complexes of chromium(III)

Complex	Colour	ν_1/cm^{-1}	ν_2/cm^{-1}	ν_3/cm^{-1}	$10Dq/cm^{-1}$	B/cm^{-1}	$\mu_n/BM^{(a)}$
$K[Cr(H_2O)_6][SO_4]_2.6H_2O$	Violet	17 400	24 500	37 800	17 400	725	3.84
$K_3[Cr(C_2O_4)_3].3H_2O$	Reddish-violet	17 500	23 900		17 500	620	3.84
$K_3[Cr(NCS)_6].4H_2O$	Purple	17 800	23 800		17 800	570	3.77
$[Cr(NH_3)_6]Br_3$	Yellow	21 550	28 500		21 550	650	3.77
$[Cr(en)_3]I_3.H_2O$	Yellow	21 600	28 500		21 600	650	3.84
$K_3[Cr(CN)_6]$	Yellow	26 700	32 200		26 700	530	3.87

[a] Room temperature value of μ_e.

(e.g. $[K(H_2O)_6][Cr(H_2O)_6][SO_4]_2)$, but in hydrated salts and aqueous solutions, green species, produced by the replacement of some of the water molecules by other ligands, are more usual. So, the common form of the hydrated chloride is the dark-green *trans*-$[CrCl_2(H_2O)_4]Cl.2H_2O$, and other isomers are known (see p. 920).

Chromium(III) is the archetypal d^3 ion and the electronic spectra and magnetic properties of its complexes have therefore been exhaustively studied[41] (see Panel). Data for a representative sample of complexes are given in Table 23.6.

One of the most obvious characteristics of Cr^{III} is its tendency to hydrolyse and form polynuclear complexes containing OH^- bridges. This is thought to occur by the loss of a proton from coordinated water, followed by coordination of the OH^- so formed to a second cation:

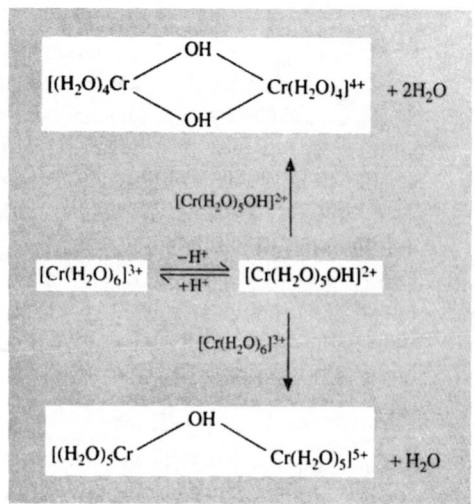

The ease with which the proton is removed can be judged by the fact that the hexaaquo ion ($pK_a \sim 4$) is almost as strong an acid as formic acid. Further deprotonation and polymerization can occur and, as the pH is raised, the final product is hydrated chromium(III) oxide or "chromic hydroxide". Formation of this is the reason why amine complexes are not prepared by simple addition of the amine base to an aqueous solution of Cr^{III}. By methods which commonly start with Cr^{II}, binuclear compounds such as $[(en)_2Cr(\mu_2\text{-}OH)_2Cr(en)_2]$ and $[(NH_3)_5Cr(\mu\text{-}OH)Cr(NH_3)_5]X_5$ are obtained. These have temperature-dependent magnetic moments, somewhat lower than those usual for octahedral Cr^{III} and indicative of weak antiferromagnetic interaction via the bent $Cr-O(H)-Cr$ bridges. Stronger antiferromagnetic interaction (magnetic moment per metal atom at room temperature ~ 1.3 BM falling to zero below 100 K) is found in the oxo-bridged derivative of the latter compound:

$$[(NH_3)_5Cr(\mu\text{-}OH)Cr(NH_3)_5]^{5+} \underset{H^+}{\overset{OH^-}{\rightleftharpoons}}$$
$$\text{red}$$
$$[(NH_3)_5Cr-O-Cr(NH_3)_5]^{4+}$$
$$\text{blue}$$

The linear $Cr-O-Cr$ bridge evidently permits pairing of the d electrons of the 2 metal atoms via $d_\pi-p_\pi$ bonds, much more readily than the bent $Cr-OH-Cr$ bridge. Blue $[LCr(\mu_2\text{-}O)(\mu_2\text{-}O_2CMe)_2CrL]$ (L = 1,4,7-trimethyl-1,4,7-triazacyclononane), produced similarly by

[41] A. B. P. LEVER *Inorganic Electronic Spectroscopy*, (2nd edn.), pp. 417–28, Elsevier, Amsterdam, 1984.

Electronic Spectra and Magnetic Properties of Chromium(III)

In an octahedral field the free-ion ground ^4F term of a d^3 ion is split into an A and two T terms which, along with the excited $^4T(P)$ term (Fig. A), give rise to the possibility of three spin-allowed d–d transitions of which the one of lowest energy is a direct measure of the crystal field splitting, Δ or 10 Dq:

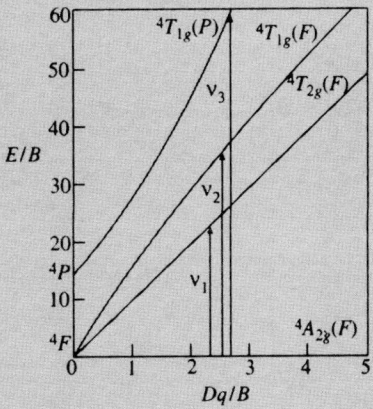

$$v_1 = {}^4T_{2g}(F) \leftarrow {}^4A_{2g}(F) = 10Dq$$
$$v_2 = {}^4T_{1g}(F) \leftarrow {}^4A_{2g}(F)$$
$$v_3 = {}^4T_{1g}(P) \leftarrow {}^4A_{2g}(F)$$

Figure A   Energy Level diagram for a d^3 ion in an octahedral crystal field.

Assignment of the observed bands to these transitions, provides an estimate of B, the Racah "interelectron repulsion parameter." Its value (Table 23.6) is invariably below that of the free-ion (1030 cm^{-1}) because the expansion of d-electron charge on complexation reduces the interelectronic repulsions.

The magnetic moment arising from the ground ^4A term is expected to be close to the spin-only value of 3.87 BM and independent of temperature. In practice, providing the compounds are mononuclear, these expectations are realized remarkably well apart from the fact that, as was noted for octahedral complexes of vanadium(III), the third high-energy band in the spectrum is usually wholly or partially obscured by more intense charge-transfer absorption.

In addition to the terms so far mentioned there are a number of spin doublets and, in the Cr^{3+} ions of ruby (α-Al$_2$O$_3$, corundum, in which a small proportion of Al^{3+} ions have been replaced by Cr^{3+}), two of these (^2E_g and $^2T_{1g}$) lie just below the $^4T_{2g}$. Ions excited to the $^4T_{2g}$ may decay back to the ground level with *spontaneous emission* of radiation but some will decay instead to the doublets, the small energy difference being converted to lattice vibrations. The rate of decay by spontaneous emission from the doublets to the ground level is however slow, being spin-forbidden, but can be induced by interaction with photons of the same energy as those to be emitted (i.e. *stimulated emission*). This situation is exploited in the ruby laser,[42] in which a rod of ruby is irradiated by intense light of appropriate frequency to continually excite and re-excite the Cr^{3+} ions to the $^4T_{2g}$ term. This *optical pumping* has the effect of steadily building up the population of the doublets. At suitable intervals the photons from the small proportion of ions which do spontaneously decay from the doublets are reflected by mirrors back through the rod where they interact with the excited ions, triggering their decay. This produces a burst of extremely intense radiation which is monochromatic, coherent and virtually non-divergent.

deprotonation of a pink, OH-bridged species but, crucially, with a 120° Cr–O–Cr bridge, shows only weak antiferromagnetic interaction.[43]

Examples of O atoms providing π pathways for antiferromagnetic interaction are also to be found among trinuclear compounds of Cr^{III}.

[42] J. A. DUFFY, *Bonding, Energy Levels and Bands*, pp. 72–7, Longman, Harlow, 1990.

[43] L. L. MARTIN, K. WIEGHARDT, G. BLONDIN, J.-J. GIRERD, B. NUBER and J. WEISS, *J. Chem. Soc., Chem. Commun.*, 1767–9 (1990).

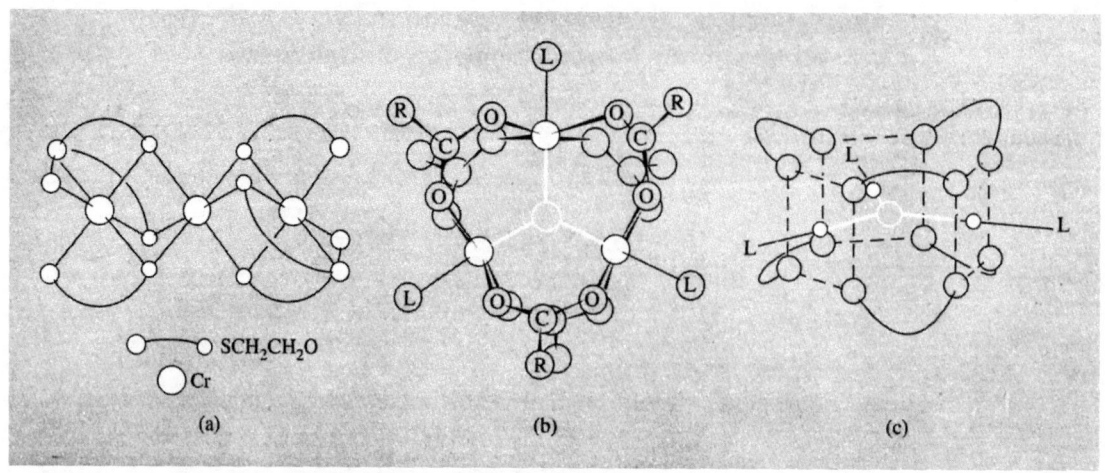

Figure 23.9 Trinuclear compounds of Cr^{III}: (a) $[Cr_3(SCH_2CH_2O)_6]^{3-}$. (b) and (c) are alternative representations of $[Cr_3(\mu_3\text{-}O)(O_2CR)_6]^+$.

$(PPh_4)_2Na[Cr_3(SCH_2CH_2O)_6]$, for instance, consists of three face-sharing octahedra in which the Cr^{III} atoms are linearly aligned and the O-, S-donor ligands are arranged so that all bridging atoms are oxygens[44] (Fig. 23.9a). A whole series of "basic" carboxylates of the general type $[Cr_3O(RCOO)_6L_3]^+$ show weak interactions and have the structure (Fig. 23.9b,c) common to carboxylates of other M^{III} atoms and containing a central μ_3-O.[45]

Hydrolysed, polynuclear Cr^{III} complexes are of considerable commercial importance in the dying and tanning industries. In the former the role is that of a mordant to the dye. In leather production it is necessary to treat animal hides to prevent putrefaction and to render them supple when dry. Traditionally, tannin was used, hence the name of the process, but this was superseded towards the end of the nineteenth century by solutions of chromium(III) sulfate. After soaking in sulfuric acid the hides are impregnated with the Cr^{III} solution. This is subsequently made alkaline, when the polynuclear complexes form and bridge

neighbouring chains of proteins, presumably by coordinating to the carboxyl groups of the proteins.

The bulk of the chemistry of Mo^{III} and W^{III} is associated with $M\equiv M$ bonded species[46] which have been extensively studied for over a decade. M_2X_6 compounds are commonly found with $X = NR_2$, OR, CH_2SiMe_3, SAr and more recently $SeAr$,[47] and are generally both oxygen- and moisture-sensitive. The usual preparative route is by reacting metal halides with $LiNR_2$ followed by ligand substitution of the $M_2(NR_2)_6$ so obtained, and the products are of the type $X_3M\equiv MX_3$ in which the two MX_3 halves are staggered with respect to each other. The $\sigma^2\pi^4$ triple bond is readily understood from the MO diagram of Fig. 23.12 (p. 1033), given that the two d^3 metal ions contribute six electrons for $M-M$ bonding. Neutral ligands can sometimes be added, to yield $LX_3M\equiv MX_3L$, and a series of tetranuclear products has been obtained by dimerization of $M_2(OR)_6$

[44] J. R. NICHOLSON, G. CHRISTOU, R.-J. WANG, J. C. HUFFMAN, H.-R. CHANG and D. N. HENDRICKSON, *Polyhedron* **19**, 2255–63 (1991).

[45] R. D. CANNON and R. P. WHITE, *Prog. Inorg. Chem.* **36**, 195–298 (1988).

[46] F. A. COTTON and R. A. WALTON, *Multiple Bands between Atoms*, 2nd edn., Oxford Univ. Press, Oxford, 1993, 787 pp.

[47] M. H. CHISHOLM, J. C. HUFFMAN, I. P. PARKIN and W. E. STREIB, *Polyhedron* **9**, 2941–52 (1990).

The precise shape of the M_4 core can be varied by partial substitution of OR with halide, and ranges from square to "butterfly" but apparently never tetrahedral[48]

Another type of triply bonded species is represented by the purple and unusually air-stable, $Cs_2[Mo_2(HPO_4)_4(H_2O)_2]$, prepared by the reaction of $K_4MoCl_8.2H_2O$ and CsCl in aqueous H_3PO_4. Here the cation has the dinuclear structure more commonly found in the divalent carboxylates (see below) and the $M\equiv M$ bond is supported by phosphate bridges.

Although having formal oxidation states of $2\frac{2}{3}$ per metal, it is opportune to mention here important molecular analogues of the Chevrel phases.[49] $M_6S_8(PEt_3)_6$, (M = Mo, W) have the same octahedral $[M_6S_8]$ core found in Chevrel phases (with the addition of terminal phosphines on each metal) but without the trigonal elongation found in the latter (p. 1018). That both are 20-electron clusters is compelling evidence that the distortion arises from intercluster interactions, which are absent in the molecular compounds, rather than because the number of cluster electrons is insufficient to form M–M bonds along all twelve edges of the octahedron.

Oxidation state II (d⁴)

For chromium, this oxidation state is characterized by the aqueous chemistry of the strongly reducing Cr^{II} cation, and a noticeable tendency to form dinuclear compounds with multiple metal–metal bonds. This tendency is even more

marked in the case of molybdenum but, perhaps surprisingly, is much less so in the case of tungsten,[†] though single M–M bonds are present in the $[M_6X_8]^{4+}$ clusters of the dihalides of both Mo and W (p. 1022).

With the exception of the nitrate, which has not been prepared because of internal oxidation–reduction, the simple hydrated, sky-blue, salts of chromium(II) are best obtained by the reaction of the appropriate dilute acid with pure chromium metal, air being rigorously excluded. A variety of complexes is formed, especially with N-donor chelating ligands which commonly produce stoichiometries such as $[Cr(L-L)_3]^{2+}$ and $[Cr(L-L)_2X_2]$. They (and other complexes of Cr^{II}) are generally extremely sensitive to atmospheric oxidation if moist, but are considerably more stable when dry, probably the most air-stable of all being the pale-blue hydrazinium sulfate, $(N_2H_5^{\oplus})_2Cr^{II}(SO_4)_2$. In the solid state this consists of linear chains of Cr^{II} ions, bridged by SO_4^{2-} ions:

The majority of Cr^{II} complexes are octahedral and can be either high-spin ($t_{2g}^3 e_g^1$) or low-spin (t_{2g}^4). The former are characterized by magnetic moments close to 4.90 BM and visible/ultraviolet spectra consisting typically of a broad band in the region of $16\,000$ cm^{-1} with another band around $10\,000$ cm^{-1}. Since a d⁴ ion in a perfectly octahedral field can give rise to only one d–d transition it is clear that some lowering of symmetry has occurred. Indeed, this is expected as a consequence of the Jahn–Teller effect, even when the metal is surrounded by 6 equivalent donor atoms. The splitting of the free-ion ^5D

[48] M. H. CHISHOLM, C. E. HAMMOND, J. C. HUFFMAN and J. D. MARTIN, *Polyhedron* **9**, 1829–41 (1990).

[49] T. SAITO, N. YAMAMOTO, T. NAGASE, T. TSUBOI, K. KOBAYASHI, T. YAMAGATA, H. IMOTO and K. UNOURA, *Inorg. Chem.* **29**, 764–70 (1990).

[†] A major reason for their comparative paucity is that the dinuclear acetate, which in the case of Mo is the most common starting material in the preparation of quadruply bonded dimeric complexes, is unknown for W.

term is shown in Fig. 23.10 and the two observed bands are assigned to superimposed $^5B_{2g} \leftarrow ^5B_{1g}$ and $^5E_g \leftarrow ^5B_{1g}$ transitions and to the $^5A_{1g} \leftarrow ^5B_{1g}$ transition respectively. The low-spin, intensely coloured compounds such as $K_4[Cr(CN)_6].3H_2O$ and $[Cr(L-L)_3]X_2.nH_2O$ (L-L = bipy, phen; X = Cl, Br, I) have magnetic moments in the range 2.74–3.40 BM and electronic spectra showing clear evidence of extensive π bonding, as is to be expected with such ligands.

Although distorted octahedral geometry is certainly the most usual, Cr^{II} has a varied stereochemistry, as indicated in Table 23.2 (p. 1006).

One of the best known of Cr^{II} compounds, and one which has often been used as the starting material in preparations of other Cr^{II} compounds, is the acetate, itself obtained by addition of sodium acetate to an aqueous solution of a Cr^{II} salt. The red colour of the hydrated acetate is in sharp distinction to the blue of the simple salts — a contrast reflected in its dinuclear, bridged structure (Fig. 23.11a). This structure is also found in the yellow $[Mo_2(\mu,\eta^2\text{-}O_2CMe)_4]$ which is obtained by the action of acetic acid on $[Mo(CO)_6]$. Other carboxylates of Cr and Mo are similar and the dinuclear structure is found also in the yellow alkali metal salts of $[Cr_2(CO_3)_4]^{4-}$ and the pink $K_4[Mo_2(SO_4)_4].2H_2O$ where the oxoanions CO_3^{2-} and SO_4^{2-} are the bridging groups. Although an exact structure determination is lacking it is likely that the violet dihydrate,

obtained by partial dehydration of the blue "double sulphate" $Cs_2SO_4.CrSO_4.6H_2O$, is of the same type in which case the formulation $Cs_4[Cr_2(\mu,\eta^2\text{-}SO_4)_4(H_2O)_2].2H_2O$ would be appropriate. $[NBu_4]_2[Cr(NCS)_4]$ exists in two forms in which the usual correlation between structure and colour of Cr^{II} salts is reversed.[49a] The red form contains the mononuclear, planar $[Cr(NCS)_4]^{2-}$ ion whereas the blue form contains the dinuclear $[(NCS)_3Cr(\mu\text{-}NCS)_2Cr(NCS)_3]^{4-}$ ion featuring bridging thiocyanates (p. 324).

The reaction of conc HCl and molybdenum acetate at 0°C produces the diamagnetic red anion $[Mo_2Cl_8]^{4-}$ (Fig. 23.11b) in which the 2 $MoCl_4$ are in the "eclipsed" orientation relative to each other and are held together solely by the Mo–Mo bond. At somewhat higher temperatures ($\sim$50°C) the above reactants also produce the $[Mo_2Cl_8H]^{3-}$ ion which has the $[M_2^{III}Cl_9]^{3-}$ structure (Fig. 23.4) but with one of the bridging Cl atoms replaced by a H atom.

An abundance of dinuclear compounds with a wide range of bridging groups involving not only the O–C–O unit of the carboxylates but also N–C–O, N–C–N, N–N–N and C–C–O, or like $[Mo_2Cl_8]^{4-}$ with no bridging groups at all, are now known for Cr^{II} and Mo^{II}, particularly the latter. W^{II} also forms a comparatively small number and analogues of the isoelectronic Re^{III} and Tc^{III} are well-known (p. 1058–9). The Cr^{II} compounds apart, all these compounds whether bridged or not are diamagnetic, have very short M–M distances and clearly involve M–M bonds the precise nature of which has excited considerable attention[46]. The best simple description of the d^4 systems is that shown in Fig. 23.12. The $d_{x^2-y^2}$ orbital is assumed to have been used in σ bonding to the ligands and the four d electrons on each metal atom are then used to form a M–M quadruple bond ($\sigma + 2\pi + \delta$) as originally proposed by B. N. Figgis and R. L. Martin for the bonding in dinuclear chromium(II) acetate (*J. Chem. Soc.* 3837–46 (1956). The characteristic

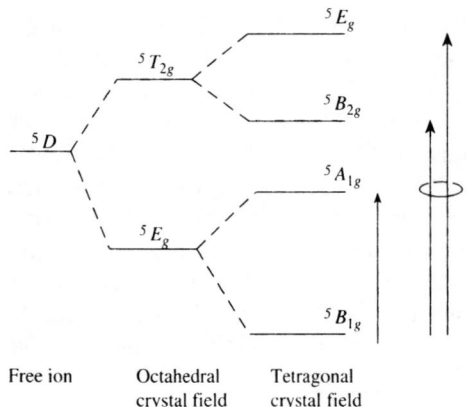

Free ion	Octahedral crystal field	Tetragonal crystal field

Figure 23.10   Crystal field splitting of the ^5D term of a d^4 ion.

49a L. F. LARKWORTHY,   G. A. LEONARD,   D. C. POVEY, S. S. TANDON, B. J. TUCKER and G. W. SMITH, *J. Chem. Soc., Dalton Trans.*, 1425–8 (1994).

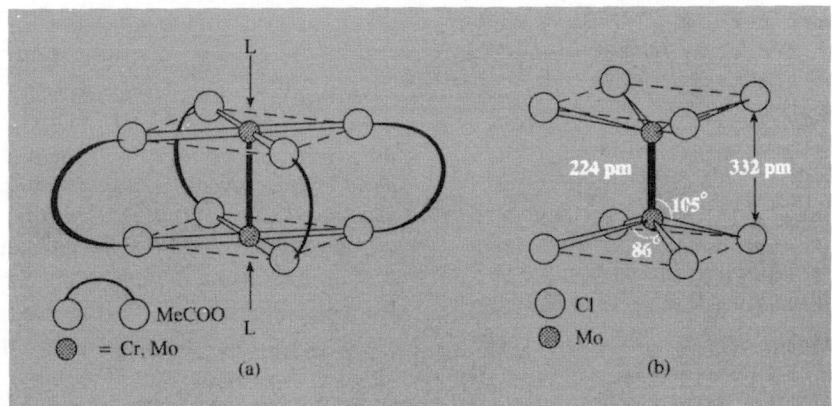

Figure 23.11   (a) $[M_2(\mu,\eta^2\text{-}O_2CMe)_4]$, M = Cr, Mo. In the case of Cr, but not Mo, the hydrate and other adducts can be formed by attachment of H_2O (or in general, L) molecules as arrowed. (b) $[Mo_2Cl_8]^{4-}$.

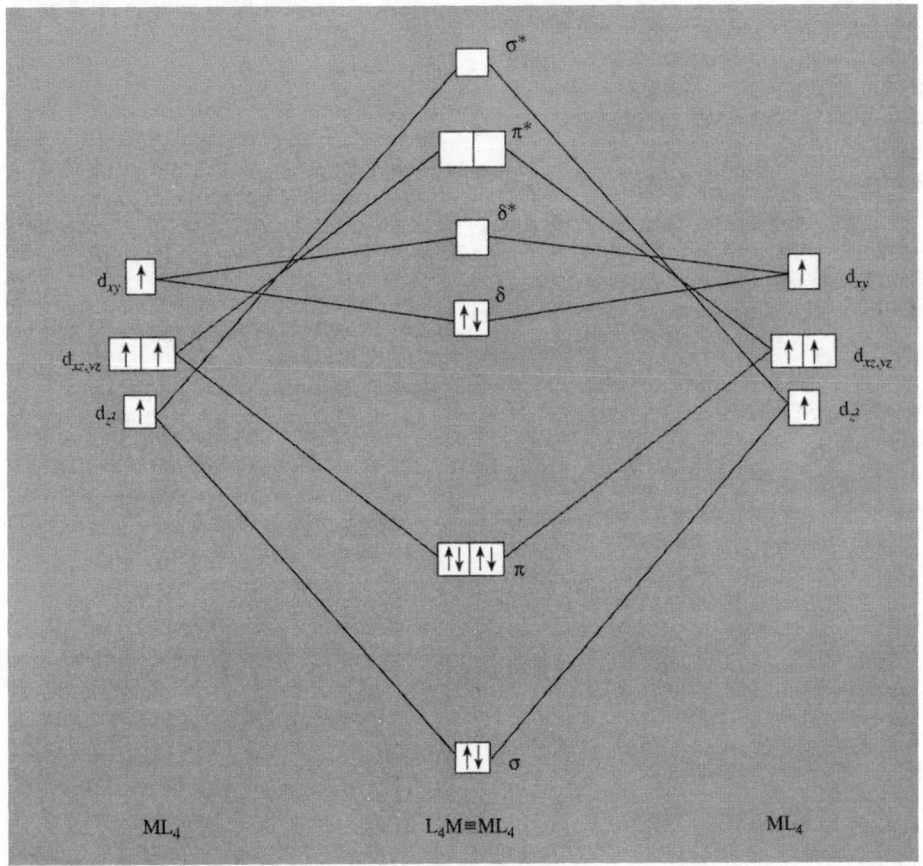

Figure 23.12   Simplified MO diagram showing the formation of an M–M quadruple bond in M_2L_8 systems of d^4 metal ions giving a ground configuration of $\sigma^2\pi^4\delta^2$ (the $d_{x^2-y^2}$, along with p_x, p_y and s orbitals of the metal ions are assumed to be used in the formation of M–L σ bonds).

red colour arises from the visible absorption at $19\,000\,cm^{-1}$ which is readily ascribed to the $\sigma^2\pi^4\delta\delta^* \leftarrow \sigma^2\pi^4\delta^2$ transition. The same assignment is also made for the absorption at $14\,300\,cm^{-1}$ which is responsible for the blue colour of $[Re_2Cl_8]^{2-}$ (p. 1058). The eclipsed orientation noted in $[Mo_2Cl_8]^{4-}$ provides strong confirmation of this bonding scheme since, without the δ bond, this configuration would be sterically unfavourable. A variety of experimental techniques, which includes polarized single-crystal spectroscopy, photoelectron spectroscopy, and X-ray emission spectroscopy, has been used to further substantiate this view of the bonding. Accurately determined M–M distances provide the most readily available indication of bond strength. The shortest, and therefore presumably the strongest, bonds are found in those compounds with no axial ligands (i.e. like Fig. 23.11b or a, without the Ls). Dimolybdenum(II) compounds, which bind axial ligands only reluctantly, have M–M distances in the approximate range 204–220 pm (where corresponding W^{II} compounds are known, the W–W distances are about 10 pm longer), whereas the M–M distances in dichromium(II) compounds fall into two distinct ranges: 183–200 and 220–250 pm. The longer Cr–Cr distances refer to the Cr^{II} carboxylates and, in spite of the smaller size of the metal atom, are longer than for the Mo^{II} carboxylates.[†] The Cr(II) carboxylates readily form axial adducts and measurements of magnetic susceptibility show that the acetate is inherently slightly paramagnetic, which has been confirmed recently

by variable temperature nmr.[50] This implies partial occupation of a low-lying spin triplet ($S = 1$, two unpaired electrons) and clearly indicates weaker M–M interaction than in the Mo^{II} and other Cr^{II} dinuclear compounds with shorter M–M distances. Whether this is a consequence, however, of the involvement of a different *type* of interaction in the Cr^{II} carboxylates — antiferromagnetic coupling between high-spin Cr^{2+} ions rather than just weak quadruple bonding — has not yet been unequivocally decided.

Interesting spin transitions are also observed: Although the reddish-purple $[CrI_2(dmpe)_2]$, (dmpe = 1,2-bis(dimethylphosphino)ethane) is low-spin, the purple-brown $[CrI_2(depe)_2]$, (depe = 1,2-bis(diethylphosphino)ethane) is high-spin ($\mu_{295} = 4.87\,BM$) at room temperature but quite suddenly becomes low-spin ($\mu_{90} = 2.82\,BM$) at *ca* 170 K[51]. A spin transition, the first one for a second row transition metal, is also displayed by *cis*-$[Mo(OPr^i)_2(bipy)_2]$, the reduction in μ_e being more gradual, from 1.96 BM at 305 K to 1.04 BM at 91 K. It is suggested[52] that the π-donor properties of the alkoxide ligands split the t_{2g} orbitals into "two below one" and that thermal equilibrium then results between the diamagnetic configuration in which the four d-electrons are paired in the lower two orbitals, and the paramagnetic configuration in which one electron is promoted to the upper orbital.

In contradistinction to this, weak ferromagnetism has been observed in a number of chloro and bromo complexes of the type $M_2[CrX_4]$ (M = a variety of protonated amines and alkali metal cations, X = Cl, Br), which are analogous to previously known copper(II) complexes (p. 1192). They have magnetic moments at room temperature in the region of 6 BM (compared

---

[†] To effect acceptable comparisons between compounds of different metals F. A. Cotton introduced the concept of the "formal shortness ratio" (FSR) which may be defined conveniently as (M–M distance in compound) : (M–M distance in metal). The compounds, $[Cr_2(2\text{-MeO-5-}MeC_6H_3)_4]$ and $Li_6[Cr_2(C_6H_4O)_4]Br_2.6Et_2O$ have virtually the same M–M distance of 183 pm, the shortest known and yielding the smallest FSR of 183/256 = 0.715. For $[Mo_2(\mu,\eta^2\text{-}O_2CMe)_4]$, FSR = 211/278 = 0.759 but, by contrast, for $[Cr_2(\mu,\eta^2\text{-}O_2CMe)_4].2H_2O$ FSR = 236/256 = 0.922. For comparison, the strongest homonuclear bonds for which bond energies are accurately known are N≡N and C≡C and their FSRs are 110/140 = 0.786 and 120.6/154 = 0.783 respectively.

[50] F. A. Cotton, H. Chen, L. M. Daniels and X. Feng, *J. Am. Chem. Soc.* **114**, 8980–3 (1992).

[51] D. M. Halepoto, D. G. L. Holt, L. F. Larkworthy, G. J. Leigh, D. C. Povey and G. W. Smith *J. Chem. Soc., Chem. Commun.*, 1322–3 (1989), *Polyhedron* **8**, 1821–2 (1989).

[52] M. H. Chisholm, E. M. Kober, D. J. Ironmonger and P. Thorton, *Polyhedron* **4**, 1869–74 (1985).

to 4.9 BM expected for magnetically dilute Cr^{II}) and these increase markedly as the temperature is lowered, the ferromagnetic interactions evidently being transmitted via Cr–Cl–Cr bridges. The electronic spectra consist of the usual absorptions expected for tetragonally distorted octahedral complexes of Cr^{II} but with two sharp and intense bands characteristically superimposed at higher energies (around 15 500 and 18 500 cm^{-1}). These are ascribed to spin-forbidden transitions intensified by the magnetic exchange.

Complexes in which the metal exhibits still lower oxidation states (such as I, 0, −I, −II) occur amongst the organometallic compounds (pp. 1006 and 1037).

23.3.8 Biological activity and nitrogen fixation

It appears that chromium(III) is an essential trace element[52a] in mammalian metabolism and, together with insulin, is responsible for the clearance of glucose from the blood-stream. Tungsten too has been found to have a role in some enzymes converting CO_2 into formic acid but, from the point of view of biological activity, the focus of interest in this group is unquestionably on molybdenum.

In animal metabolism, oxomolybdoenzymes catalyse a number of oxidation processes. These oxidases contain Mo^{VI} coordinated to terminal O and S atoms, and their action appears to involve loss of an O or S atom along with reduction to Mo^V or Mo^{IV}. It is, however, the role of molybdenum in nitrogen fixation which has received most attention.

It is estimated that each year approximately 150 million tonnes of nitrogen are fixed biologically compared to 120 million tonnes fixed industrially by the Haber process (p. 421). In both cases N_2 is converted to NH_3, requiring the rupture of the N≡N triple bond which has the highest dissociation energy (945.41 kJ mol^{-1})

of any homonuclear diatomic molecule. This is an inescapable toll exacted by N_2 no matter how the fixation is achieved. In the Haber process it is paid by using high temperatures and pressures. Nature pays it by consuming 1 kg of glucose for every 14 g of N_2 fixed, but does so *under ambient conditions*. It is this last fact which provides the economic spur to achieve an understanding of the mechanism of the natural process.

Nitrogen fixation takes place in a wide variety of bacteria, the best known of which is *rhizobium* which is found in nodules on the roots of leguminous plants such as peas, beans, soya and clover. The essential constituents of this and all other nitrogen-fixing bacteria are:

(i) adenosine triphosphate (ATP) which is a highly active energy transfer agent (p. 528), operating by means of its hydrolysis which requires the presence of Mg^{2+};

(ii) ferredoxin, $Fe_4S_4(SR)_4$ (p. 1102), which is an efficient electron-transfer agent that can be replaced in artificial systems by reducing agents such as dithionite, $[S_2O_4]^{2-}$;

(iii) a metallo-enzyme.

These metallo-enzymes are "nitrogenases" which have been isolated in an active form from several different bacteria and in a pure form from a number of these. The presence of Mo is not essential in all cases[53] (a vanadium nitrogenase is known — see p. 999) but is evidently a necessary component of most nitrogenases even though its precise function is unclear. These molybdenum nitrogenases consist of two distinct proteins. One, containing Fe but no Mo and therefore known as "Fe protein", is yellow and extremely air-sensitive. Its molecular weight is about 60 000 and its structure involves an Fe_4S_4, ferredoxin-like cluster. The other protein contains both Mo and Fe and is known as "MoFe protein." It is brown, air-sensitive, has a molecular weight in the approximate range 220 000 to 240 000, and

[52a] S. A. KATZ and H. SALEM, *The Biological and Environmental Chemistry of Chromium*, VCH, Weinheim, 1994, 214pp.

[53] R. R. EADY, *Adv. Inorg. Chem.* **36**, 77–102 (1991).

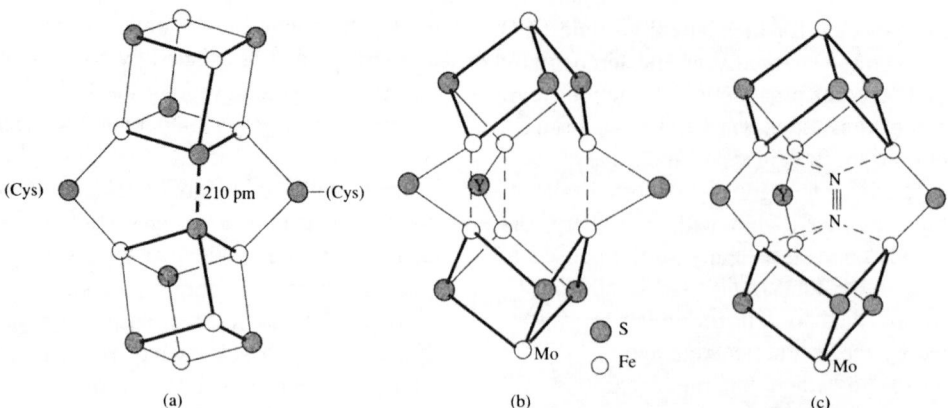

Figure 23.13 Metal centres in the FeMo protein of nitrogenase. (a) P-cluster pair. Each of the four outer Fe atoms is further coordinated to the S of a cysteine group. (b) FeMo cofactor. (Y is probably S, O or N.) Fe–Fe bridge distances are in the range 240–260 pm, suggesting weak Fe–Fe interactions. The Mo achieves 6-coordination by further bonds to N (of histidine) and two O atoms (of a chelating homocitrate), while the Fe at the opposite end of the cofactor is tetrahedrally coordinated by attachment of a cysteine. (c) Possible intermediate in the interaction of N_2 with FeMo cofactor.

contains the actual site of the N_2 reduction.[†] Most of the isolated forms of MoFe protein contain 2 atoms of Mo and about 30 atoms each of Fe and S. These atoms are arranged in 6 metal centres: 4 so-called P-clusters each made up of Fe_4S_4 units, and 2 Fe–Mo *cofactors* (FeMoco) in which the Mo is thought to be present as Mo^{IV}. Unfortunately, investigation of the structures of these proteins is hampered by the extreme sensitivity of nitrogenase to oxygen and the inherent difficulty of obtaining pure crystalline derivatives from biological materials. (Bacteria evidently protect nitrogenase from oxygen by a process of respiration, $O_2 \rightarrow CO_2$, but if too much oxygen is present the system cannot cope and nitrogen fixation ceases.) The recent determination of the structure of the nitrogenase from *Azotobacter vinelandii*[(54)] is therefore a remarkable achievement of X-ray crystallography, building upon results previously obtained from esr, Mössbauer spectroscopy and X-ray absorption spectroscopy (analysis of the

"extended X-ray absorption fine structure" or EXAFS).[(55)]

It turns out that each of the two FeMo cofactors consists of an Fe_4S_3 and an Fe_3MoS_3 incomplete cubane cluster. These are linked by two S bridges and a third bridging atom (Y), not identified with certainty, but possibly a well-ordered O or N or, alternatively, a less well-ordered S. Three atoms in each cluster are close enough to form interacting pairs across the bridge (Fig 23.13a). The P-clusters form two pairs, each pair consisting of two Fe_4S_4 cubane clusters linked by two cysteine thiol bridges and a disulfide bond (Fig. 23.13b). Cleavage and re-formation of this disulfide bridge *could* provide the mechanism for a $2e^-$ redox process. Mössbauer studies suggest that, in their most reduced form, the iron atoms of the P-clusters are in the 2+ oxidation state, unprecedented in biological Fe_4S_4 systems. The reduction of N_2 apparently involves the following steps:

(i) reduction by ferredoxin of the Fe protein's Fe_4S_4 cluster, which is situated in an exposed position at the surface of the protein;

[†] Isolated nitrogenases will also reduce other species such as CN^- and N_3^- containing a triple bond, as well as reducing acetylenes to olefins.

[54] D. C. REES, M. K. CHAN and J. KIM, *Adv. Inorg. Chem.* **40**, 89–119 (1993).

[55] C. D. GARNER, *Adv. Inorg. Chem.* **36**, 303–39 (1991).

(ii) one-electron transfer from the Fe protein to a P-cluster pair of the FeMo protein, by a process involving the hydrolysis of ATP;

(iii) two-electron transfer, within the FeMo protein, from a P-cluster pair (whose environment is essentially hydrophobic) to an FeMo cofactor (whose environent is essentially hydrophilic);

(iv) electron and proton transfer to N_2 which is almost certainly attached to the FeMo cofactor.

The overall reaction can be represented as:

$$N_2 + 8H^+ + 8e^- + 16Mg\text{-}ATP \longrightarrow 2NH_3 + H_2$$
$$+ 16(Mg\text{-}ADP + P_i), P_i = \text{inorganic phosphate.}$$

Aspects of the process still requiring clarification include details of the electron flow between redox centres; the pathways for entry and exit of N_2, NH_3 and H_2 (presumably structural rearrangements are needed); the role of Mg–ATP; and the nature of the interaction between N_2 and the FeMo cofactor which is central to the whole process. Persuasive arguments had been advanced for an intermediate involving 2 Mo atoms bridged by N_2[56], yet in the determined structure the Mo atoms are too far apart to form a binuclear intermediate of this kind. On the other hand it has been plausibly suggested[55] that a reduced form of the FeMo cofactor might be sufficiently open at its centre to allow the insertion of N_2 so forming a bridged intermediate in which Fe–N interactions replace weak Fe–Fe bonds (Fig. 23.13c). The concomitant weakening of the $N{\equiv}N$ bond would facilitate subsequent reduction of the N_2 bridge.

Further developments in this field may be confidently expected.

23.3.9 Organometallic compounds [57,58]

In this group a not-insignificant number of M–C σ-bonded compounds are known but are very unstable (MMe_6 is known only for W and this

explodes in air and can detonate in a vacuum) unless stabilized either by ligands lacking β-hydrogen atoms (p. 925) or by dimerizing and forming M–M bonds. Thus trimethylsilymethyl ($-CH_2SiMe_3$) yields $[Cr(tms)_4]$ and the dimers $[(tms)_3M{\equiv}M(tms)_3]$, (M = Mo, W). As with the preceding group, however, the bulk of organometallic chemistry is concerned with the metals in low oxidation states stabilized by π bonding ligands such as CO, cyclopentadienyl and, in this group, η^6-arenes. Cyanides have been discussed on pp. 1025–32.

Stable, colourless, crystalline hexacarbonyls, $M(CO)_6$, are prepared by reductive carbonylation of compounds (often halides) in higher oxidation states and are octahedral and diamagnetic as anticipated from the 18-electron rule (p. 1134). Replacement of the carbonyl groups by either π-donor or σ-donor ligands is possible, giving a host of materials of the form $[M(CO)_{6-x}L_x]$ or $[M(CO)_{6-2x}(L\text{-}L)_x]$ (e.g. L = NO, NH_3, CN, PF_3; L-L = bipy, butadiene). $[M(CO)_5X]^-$ ions (X = halogen, CN or SCN) are formed in this way. The low-temperature reaction ($-78°$) of the halogens with $[Mo(CO)_6]$ or $[W(CO)_6]$ (but not with $[Cr(CO)_6]$) produces the M^{II} carbonyl halides, $[M(CO)_4X_2]$ from which many adducts, $[M(CO)_3L_2X_2]$, are obtained. Although not all of these have been fully characterized, those that have are 7-coordinated and mostly capped octahedral. Reduction of the hexacarbonyls with a borohydride in liquid ammonia forms dimeric $[M_2(CO)_{10}]^{2-}$ which are isostructural with the isoelectronic $[Mn_2(CO)_{10}]$ (p. 1062). Hydrolysis of these dimers produces the yellow hydrides $[(CO)_5M\text{-}H\text{-}M(CO)_5]$ which maintain the 18 valence electron configuration by means of a 3-centre, 2-electron M–H–M bond. Neutron diffraction studies show these bridges to be non-linear as expected, the actual degree of bending probably being influenced by crystal-packing forces arising from different counter-cations. A

---

[56] A. E. Shilov, *Pure Appl. Chem.* **64**, 1409–20 (1992).

[57] S. W. Kirtley, R. Davis and L. A. P. Kane-Maguire, Chap. 26, pp. 783–1077, Chap. 27, pp. 1079–253 and Chap. 28, pp. 1255–384 in *Comprehensive Organometallic Chemistry*, Vol. 3, Pergamon Press, Oxford, 1982.

[58] pp. 277–402 of ref. 2.

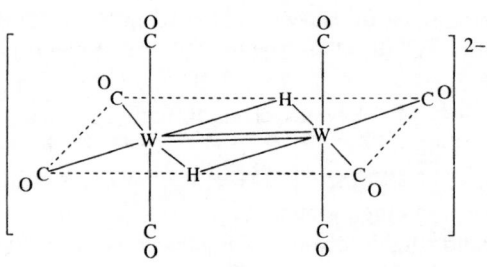

Figure 23.14 Structure of $[H_2W_2(CO)_8]^{2-}$.

related compound, $[NEt_4]_2^+[H_2W_2(CO)_8]^{2-}$ is of interest because it has 2 hydrogen bridges and a W–W distance indicative of a W–W double bond (301.6 pm compared to about 320 pm for a W–W single bond) (Fig. 23.14). The compound also illustrates the improved refinement now possible with modern X-ray methods (p. 1013) and it was, in fact, the first case of the successful location of hydrogens bridging third-row transition metals. Reduction of the hexacarbonyls using Na metal in liquid NH₃ yields the super-reduced, 18-electron species $[M(CO)_4]^{4-}$.

$M(CO)_6$ and other Mo and W compounds catalyse alkene metathesis† by the formation of

active alkylidene (p. 930) intermediates. This has stimulated the study of Mo and W alkylidenes (also alkylidynes which are similarly active in alkyne metathesis)[58]

Metallocenes, $[M^{II}(\eta^5\text{-}C_5H_5)_2]$, analogous to ferrocene would have only 16 valence electrons and could therefore be considered "electron deficient". Chromocene can be formed by the action of sodium cyclopentadienide on $[Cr(CO)_6]$. It is isomorphous with ferrocene but paramagnetic and much more reactive. Monomeric molybdocene and tungstocene polymerize above 10 K to red-brown polymeric solids, $[M^{II}(C_5H_5)_2]_n$. They are obtained by photolytic decomposition of yellow, $[M^{II}(\eta^5\text{-}C_5H_5)_2H_2]$ which are "bent" molecules (Fig 23.15a), themselves prepared by the action of NaBH₄ on MCl₅ and NaC₅H₅ in thf. With Mo and W hexacarbonyls, conditions similar to those used to prepare chromocene produce only $[(\eta^5\text{-}C_5H_5)M^I(CO)_3]_2$, (Fig. 23.15b) in which dimerization achieves the 18-valence-electron configuration by means of an M–M bond. The chromium analogue of these dimers has one of the longest M–M bonds found in dinuclear transition metal compounds (328.1 pm). Its reactivity allows ready insertion of a variety of groups which includes S and Se yielding

---

† This general reaction involves the cleavage of two C=C bonds and the formation of two new ones:

$$
\begin{array}{ccc}
CH_2{=}CHR & & CH_2 \quad CHR \\
+ & \rightleftharpoons & \parallel \quad + \quad \parallel \\
CH_2{=}CHR & & CH_2 \quad CHR
\end{array}
$$

---

and can be used to convert propylene into ethylene for subsequent polymerization or oligomerization.

[58] See for instance: J. KRESS and J. A. OSBORN, *Angew. Chem. Int. Edn. Engl.* **31**, 1585–7 (1992); A. MAYR and C. M. BASTOS, *Prog. Inorg. Chem.* **40**, 1–98 (1992).

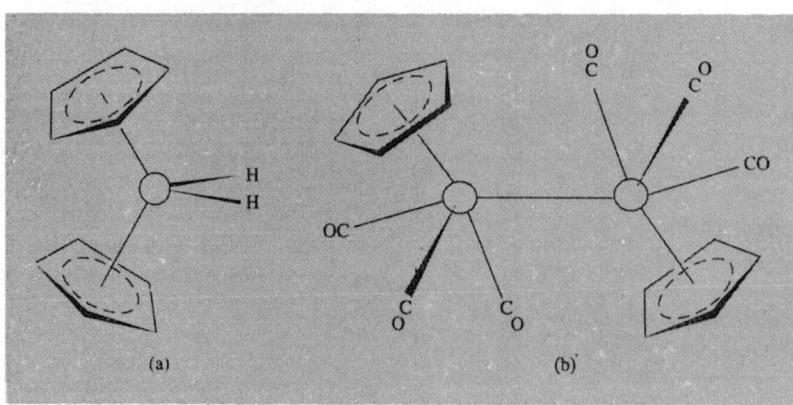

Figure 23.15 (a) The "bent" molecules $[M^{II}(\eta^5\text{-}C_5H_5)_2H_2]$ (b) $[M^I(\eta^5\text{-}C_5H_5)(CO)_3]_2$ (M = Mo, W).

products such as $[Cr_2(\eta^5\text{-}C_5H_5)_2(CO)_4E_2]$, while cleavage of the bond with Ph_2E_2 gives $[Cr(\eta^5\text{-}C_5H_5)(CO)_3(EPh)]$ (E = S, Se)[59]. Of the many other cyclopentadienyl derivatives the Mo and W halides $[M(\eta^5\text{-}C_5H_5)_2X_2]$ and dimeric $[M_2(\eta^5\text{-}C_5H_5)_2X_4]$, which are useful precursors in other syntheses[60] may be mentioned.

Of greater stability than the monomeric metallocenes in this group are the dibenzene sandwich compounds which are isoelectronic with ferrocene and of which the dark brown $[Cr(\eta^6\text{-}C_6H_6)_2]$ was the first to be prepared (p. 940) and remains the best known. The green $[Mo(\eta^6\text{-}C_6H_6)_2]$ and yellow-green $[W(\eta^6\text{-}C_6H_6)_2]$ are also well characterized and all contain the metal in the formal oxidation state of zero. As the 12 C atoms in $[M(\eta^6\text{-}C_6H_6)_2]$ are equidistant from the central metal atom, the coordination number of M is 12, though, of course, only 6 bonding molecular orbitals are primarily involved in linking the two ligand molecules to M. The compounds are more susceptible to oxidation than is the isoelectronic ferrocene and all are converted to paramagnetic salts of $[M^I(\eta^6\text{-}C_6H_6)_2]^+$: the ease with which this process takes place increases in the order Cr < Mo < W. Since CO groups are evidently better π-acceptors than C_6H_6, replacement of one of the benzene ligands in $[M(C_6H_6)_2]$ by three carbonyls giving, for instance, $[Cr(\eta^6\text{-}C_6H_6)(CO)_3]$, appreciably improves the resistance to oxidation because the electron density on the metal is lowered. $[W(\eta^6\text{-}C_6H_6)_2]$ is reversibly protonated by dilute acids to give $[W(\eta^6\text{-}C_6H_6)_2H]^+$.

As in the previous group, a potentially productive route into C_7-ring chemistry is provided by the reduction of a metal halide with Na/Hg in thf in the presence of cycloheptatriene. With $MoCl_5$, $[Mo(\eta^7\text{-}C_7H_7)(\eta^7\text{-}C_7H_9)]$ is produced and a variety of derivatives have already been obtained.[61]

[59] L. Y. GOH, Y. Y. LIM, M. S. TAY, T. C. W. MAK and Z. Y. ZHOU, *J. Chem. Soc., Dalton Trans.*, 1239–42 (1992).
[60] M. L. H. GREEN and P. MOUNTFORD, *Chem. Soc. Revs.* **21**, 29–38 (1992).

[61] M. L. H. GREEN, D. K. P. NG and R. C. TOVEY, *J. Chem. Soc., Chem. Commun.*, 918–9 (1992).

24

Manganese, Technetium and Rhenium

24.1 Introduction

In terms of history, abundance and availability, it is difficult to imagine a greater contrast than exists in this group between manganese and its congeners, technetium and rhenium. Millions of tonnes of manganese are used annually, and its most common mineral, pyrolusite, has been used in glassmaking since the time of the Pharaohs. On the other hand, technetium and rhenium are exceedingly rare and were only discovered comparatively recently, the former being the first new element to have been produced artificially and the latter being the last naturally occurring element to be discovered.

Metallic manganese was first isolated in 1774 when C. W. Scheele recognized that pyrolusite contained a new element, and his fellow Swede, J. G. Gahn, heated the MnO_2 with a mixture of charcoal and oil. The purity of this sample of the metal was low, and high-purity (99.9%) manganese was only produced in the 1930s when electrolysis of Mn^{II} solutions was used.

In Mendeleev's table, this group was completed by the then undiscovered eka-manganese ($Z = 43$) and dvi-manganese ($Z = 75$). Confirmation of the existence of these missing elements was not obtained until H. G. J. Moseley had introduced the method of X-ray spectroscopic analysis. Then in 1925 W. Noddack, I. Tacke (later Frau Noddack) and O. Berg discovered element 75 in a sample of gadolinite (a basic silicate of beryllium, iron and lanthanides) and named it rhenium after the river Rhine. The element was also discovered, independently by F. H. Loring and J. F. G. Druce, in manganese compounds, but is now most usually recovered from the flue dusts produced in the roasting of CuMo ores.

The Noddacks also claimed to have detected element 43 and named it masurium after Masuren in Prussia. This claim proved to be incorrect, however, and the element was actually detected in 1937 in Italy by C. Perrier and E. Segré in a sample of molybdenum which had been bombarded with deuterons in the cyclotron of E. O. Lawrence in California. It was present in the form of the β^- emitters ^{95m}Tc and ^{97m}Tc

with half-lives of 61 and 90 days respectively. The name technetium (from Greek τεχνικός, artificial) is clearly appropriate even though minute traces of the more stable ^{99}Tc (half-life = 2.11×10^5 y) do occur naturally as a result of spontaneous fission of uranium.

24.2 The Elements

24.2.1 Terrestrial abundance and distribution

The natural abundance of technetium is, as just indicated, negligibly small. The concentration of rhenium in the earth's crust is extremely low (of the order of $7 \times 10^{-8}\%$, i.e. 0.0007 ppm) and it is also very diffuse. Being chemically akin to molybdenum it is in molybdenites that its highest concentrations (0.2%) are found. By contrast, manganese (0.106%, i.e. 1060 ppm of the earth's crustal rocks) is the twelfth most abundant element and the third most abundant transition element (exceeded only by iron and titanium). It is found in over 300 different and widely distributed minerals of which about twelve are commercially important. As a class-a metal it occurs in primary deposits as the silicate. Of more commercial importance are the secondary deposits of oxides and carbonates such as pyrolusite (MnO_2), which is the most common, hausmannite (Mn_3O_4), and rhodochrosite ($MnCO_3$). These have been formed by weathering of the primary silicate deposits and are found in the former USSR, Gabon, South Africa, Brazil, Australia, India and China.

A further consequence of this weathering is that colloidal particles of the oxides of manganese, iron and other metals are continuously being washed into the sea where they agglomerate and are eventually compacted into the "manganese nodules" (so called because Mn is the chief constituent), first noted during the voyage of HMS *Challenger* (1872–6). Following a search in the Pacific organized by the University of California during the International Geophysical Year (1957), the magnitude and potential value of manganese nodules became apparent. More than 10^{12} tonnes are estimated to cover vast areas of the ocean beds and a further 10^7 tonnes are deposited annually. The composition varies but the dried nodules generally contain between 15 and 30% of Mn. This is less than the 35% normally regarded as the lower limit required for present-day commercial exploitation but, since the Mn is accompanied not only by Fe but more importantly by smaller amounts of Ni, Cu and Co, the combined recovery of Ni, Cu and Co, with Mn effectively as a byproduct could well be economical if performed on a sufficient scale. The technical, legal, and political problems involved are enormous, but perhaps even more importantly, overcapacity in conventional means of production has so far inhibited the exploitation of these reserves.

24.2.2 Preparation and uses of the metals

Over ninety per cent of all the manganese ores produced are used in steel manufacture, mostly in the form of ferromanganese.[1] This contains about 80% Mn and is made by reducing appropriate amounts of MnO_2 and Fe_2O_3 with coke in a blast furnace or, if cheap electricity is available, in an electric-arc furnace. Dolomite or limestone is also added to remove silica as a slag. Where the Mn content is lower (because of the particular ores used) the product is known as silicomanganese (65–70% Mn, 15–20% Si) or spiegeleisen (5–20% Mn). Where pure manganese metal is required it is prepared by the electrolysis of aqueous managanese(II) sulfate. Ore with an Mn content of over 8 million tonnes was produced in 1995, the most important sources being the former Soviet Union, the Republic of South Africa, Gabon and Australia.

All steels contain some Mn, and its addition in 1856 by R. Mushet ensured the success of the Bessemer process. It serves two main purposes. As a "scavenger" it combines with sulfur to form

---

[1] *Kirk–Othmer Encyclopedia of Chemical Technology*, 4th edn., Vol. 15, pp. 963–91, Interscience, New York, 1995.

Technetium in Diagnostic Nuclear Medicine[2]

[99m]Tc is one of the most widely used isotopes in nuclear medicine. It is injected into the patient in the form of a saline solution of a compound, chosen because it will be absorbed by the organ under investigation, which can then be "imaged" by an X-ray camera or scanner. Its properties are ideal for this purpose: it decays into ^{99}Tc by internal transition and γ-emission of sufficient energy to allow the use of physiologically insignificant quantities (nmol or even pmol — a permissible dose of 1 mCi corresponds to 1.92 pmol of ^{99m}Tc) and a half-life (6.01 h) short enough to preclude radiological damage due to prolonged exposure. It is obtained from [99]Mo ($t_{\frac{1}{2}}$ = 65.94 h), which in turn is obtained from the fission products of natural or reactor uranium, or else by neutron irradiation of [98]Mo.

Although details vary considerably, the [99]Mo is typically incorporated in a "generator" in the form of MoO_4^{2-} absorbed on a substrate such as alumina where it decays according to the scheme:

$$^{99}MoO_4^{2-} \xrightarrow{\beta} {}^{99m}TcO_4^{-} \xrightarrow{\gamma} {}^{99}TcO_4^{-}$$

These generators can be made available virtually anywhere and, when required, TcO_4^{-} is eluted from the substrate and reduced (Sn^{II} is a common, but not the sole, reductant) in the presence of an appropriate ligand, ready for immediate use. A wide range of N-, P- and S-donor ligands has been used to prepare complexes of Tc, mainly in oxidation states III, IV and V, which are absorbed preferentially by different organs. Though the circumstances of clinical usage mean that the precise formulation of the compound actually administered is frequently uncertain,[†] the imaging of brain, heart, lung, bone and tumours etc. is possible. It is the search for compounds of increased specificity which has stimulated most of the recent work on the coordination chemistry of Tc.

[†]Interconversion between different oxidation states occurs easily for Tc (see Section 24.2.4.), and its control often requires careful adjustment of pH and the relative excess of reductant used.

MnS which passes into the slag and prevents the formation of FeS which would induce brittleness, and it also combines with oxygen to form MnO, so preventing the formation of bubbles and pinholes in the cold steel. Secondly, the presence of Mn as an alloying metal increases the hardness of the steel. The hard, non-magnetic Hadfield steel containing about 13% Mn and 1.25% C, is the best known, and is used when resistance to severe mechanical shock and wear is required, e.g. for excavators, dredgers, rail crossings, etc.

Important, but less extensive, uses are found in the production of non-ferrous alloys. It is a scavenger in several Al and Cu alloys, while "manganin" is a well-known alloy (84% Cu, 12% Mn, 4% Ni) which is used in electrical instruments because the temperature coefficient of its resistivity is almost zero. A variety of other major uses have been found for Mn in the form of

its compounds and these will be dealt with later under the appropriate headings.

Technetium is obtained from nuclear power stations where it makes up about 6% of uranium fission products and is recovered from these after storage for several years to allow the highly radioactive, short-lived fission products to decay. The original process used the precipitation of $[AsPh_4]^+[ClO_4]^-$ to carry with it $[AsPh_4]^+[TcO_4]^-$ and so separate the Tc from other fission products, but solvent extraction and ion-exchange techniques are now used. The metal itself can be obtained by the high-temperature reduction of either NH_4TcO_4 or Tc_2S_7 with hydrogen. [99]Tc is the isotope available in kg quantities and the one used for virtually all chemical studies. Because of its long half-life it is not a major radiation hazard and, with standard manipulative techniques, can be safely handled in mg quantities. However, the main interest in Tc is its role in nuclear medicine, and here it is the metastable γ-emitting isotope ^{99m}Tc which is used (see Panel).

---

[2] S. JURISSON, D. BERNING, W. JIA and D. MA, *Chem. Revs.*, **93**, 1137–56 (1993). K. SCHWOCHALL, *Angew. Chem. Int. Edn. Engl.* **33**, 2258–67 (1994).

In the roasting of molybdenum sulfide ores, any rhenium which might be present is oxidized to volatile Re_2O_7 which collects in the flue dusts and is the usual source of the metal via conversion to $(NH_4)ReO_4$ and reduction by H_2 at elevated temperatures. Being highly refractory and corrosion-resistant, rhenium metal would no doubt find widespread use were it not for its scarcity and consequent high cost. As it is, uses are essentially small scale. These include bimetallic Pt/Re catalysts for the production of lead-free, high octane petroleum products, high temperature superalloys for jet engine components, mass spectrometer filaments, furnace heating elements and thermocouples. World production is about 35 tonnes annually.

24.2.3 Properties of the elements

Some of the important properties of Group 7 elements are summarized in Table 24.1. Technetium is an artificial element, so its atomic weight depends on which isotope has been produced. The atomic weights of Mn and Re, however, are known with considerable accuracy. In the case of

the former this is because it has only 1 naturally occurring isotope and, in the case of the latter, because it has only 2 and the relative proportions of these in terrestrial samples are essentially constant (^{185}Re 37.40%, ^{187}Re 62.60%).

In the solid state all three elements have typically metallic structures. Technetium and Re are isostructural with hcp lattices, but there are 4 allotropes of Mn of which the α-form is the one stable at room temperature. This has a bcc structure in which, for reasons which are not clear, there are 4 distinct types of Mn atom. It is hard and brittle, and noticeably less refractory than its predecessors in the first transition series.

In continuance of the trends already noticed, the most stable oxidation state of manganese is +2, and in the group oxidation state of +7 it is even more strongly oxidizing than Cr(VI). Evidently the 3d electrons are more tightly held by the Mn atomic nucleus and this reduced delocalization produces weaker metallic bonding than in Cr. The same trends are also starting in the second and third series with Tc and Re, but are less marked, and Re in particular is very refractory, having a mp which is second only to that of tungsten amongst transition elements.

Table 24.1   Some properties of Group 7 elements

Property		Mn	Tc	Re
Atomic number		25	43	75
Number of naturally occurring isotopes		1	—	2
Atomic weight		54.938049(9)	98.9063[a]	186.207(1)
Electronic configuration		$[Ar]3d^54s^2$	$[Kr]4d^65s^1$	$[Xe]4f^{14}5d^56s^2$
Electronegativity		1.5	1.9	1.9
Metal radius (12-coordinate)/pm		127	136	137
Ionic radius/pm	VII	46	56	53
(4-coordinate if marked*;	VI	25.5*	—	55
otherwise 6-coordinate)	V	33*	60	58
	IV	53	64.5	63
	III	58 (ls), 64.5 (hs)	—	—
	II	67	—	—
MP/°C		1244	2200	3180
BP/°C		2060	4567	(5650)
ΔH_{fus}/kJ mol^{-1}		(13.4)	23.8	34($\pm$4)
ΔH_{vap}/kJ mol^{-1}		221($\pm$8)	585	704
ΔH_f (monatomic gas)/kJ mol^{-1}		281($\pm$6)	—	779($\pm$8)
Density (25°C)/g cm^{-3}		7.43	11.5	21.0
Electrical resistivity (20°C)/μohm cm		185.0	—	19.3

[a] This refers to ^{99}Tc ($t_{\frac{1}{2}}$ 2.11 $\times$ 10^5 y). For ^{97}Tc ($t_{\frac{1}{2}}$ 2.6 $\times$ 10^6 y) and ^{98}Tc ($t_{\frac{1}{2}}$ 4.2 $\times$ 10^6 y) the values are 96.9064 and 97.9072 respectively.

24.2.4 Chemical reactivity and trends

Manganese is more electropositive than any of its neighbours in the periodic table and the metal is more reactive, especially when somewhat impure. In the massive state it is superficially oxidized on exposure to air but will burn if finely divided. It liberates hydrogen from water and dissolves readily in dilute aqueous acids to form manganese(II) salts. With non-metals it is not very reactive at ambient temperatures but frequently reacts vigorously when heated. Thus it burns in oxygen, nitrogen, chlorine and fluorine giving Mn_3O_4, Mn_3N_2, $MnCl_2$ and $MnF_2 + MnF_3$ respectively, and it combines directly with B, C, Si, P, As and S.

Technetium and rhenium metals are less reactive than manganese and, as is to be expected for the two heavier elements, they are closely similar to each other. In the massive form they resist oxidation and are only tarnished slowly in moist air. However, they are normally produced as sponges or powders in which case they are more reactive. Heated in oxygen they burn to give volatile heptaoxides (M_2O_7), and with fluorine they give $TcF_5 + TcF_6$ and $ReF_6 + ReF_7$ respectively. MS_2 can also be produced by direct action. Although insoluble in hydrofluoric and hydrochloric acids, the metals dissolve readily in oxidizing acids such as HNO_3 and conc H_2SO_4 and also in bromine water, when "pertechnetic" and "perrhenic" acids (HMO_4) are formed.

Because of the differing focus of interest in these elements their chemistries have not developed in parallel and the data on which strict comparisons might be based are not always available. Nevertheless many of the similarities and contrasts expected in the chemistry of transition elements are evident in this triad. The relative stabilities of different oxidation states in aqueous, acidic solutions are summarized in Table 24.2 and Fig. 24.1.

The most obvious features of Fig. 24.1 are the relative positions of the $+2$ oxidation states. For manganese this state, represented by the high-spin Mn^{II} cation, is much the most stable. This may be taken as an indication of the stability of the symmetrical d^5 electron configuration.

Table 24.2 $E°$ for some manganese, technetium and rhenium couples in acid solution at $25°C$

Couple	$E°/V$
$Mn^{2+}(aq) + 2e^- \rightleftharpoons Mn(s)$	-1.185
$Mn^{3+}(aq) + 3e^- \rightleftharpoons Mn(s)$	-0.283
$MnO_2 + 4H^+ + 4e^- \rightleftharpoons Mn(s) + 2H_2O$	0.024
$MnO_4^{2-} + 8H^+ + 4e^- \rightleftharpoons Mn^{2+}(aq) + 4H_2O$	1.742
$MnO_4^- + 8H^+ + 5e^- \rightleftharpoons Mn^{2+}(aq) + 4H_2O$	1.507
$Tc^{2+}(aq) + 2e^- \rightleftharpoons Tc(s)$	0.400
$TcO_2 + 4H^+ + 4e^- \rightleftharpoons Tc(s) + 2H_2O$	0.272
$TcO_3 + 2H^+ + 2e^- \rightleftharpoons TcO_2 + H_2O$	0.757
$TcO_4^- + 8H^+ + 5e^- \rightleftharpoons Tc^{2+}(aq) + 4H_2O$	0.500
$Re^{3+}(aq) + 3e^- \rightleftharpoons Re(s)$	0.300
$ReO_2 + 4H^+ + 4e^- \rightleftharpoons Re(s) + 2H_2O$	0.251
$ReO_3 + 6H^+ + 3e^- \rightleftharpoons Re^{3+}(aq) + 3H_2O$	0.318
$ReO_4^{2-} + 8H^+ + 3e^- \rightleftharpoons Re^{3+}(aq) + 4H_2O$	0.795
$ReO_4^- + 8H^+ + 4e^- \rightleftharpoons Re^{3+}(aq) + 4H_2O$	0.422

However, like the mp, bp and enthalpy of atomization, it also reflects the weaker cohesive forces in the metallic lattice since for Tc and Re, which have much stronger metallic bonding, the $+2$ state is of little importance and the occurrence of cluster compounds with M–M bonds is a dominant feature of rhenium(III) chemistry. The almost uniform slope of the plot for Tc presages the facile interconversion between oxidation states, observed for this element.

Another marked contrast is evident in the $+7$ oxidation state where the manganate(VII) (permanganate) ion is an extremely strong oxidizing agent but $(TcO_4)^-$ and $(ReO_4)^-$ show only mild oxidizing properties. Indeed, the greater stability of Tc and Re compared to Mn in any oxidation state higher than $+2$ is apparent, as will be seen more fully in the following account of individual compounds.

Table 24.3 lists representative examples of the compounds of these elements in their various oxidation states. The wide range of the oxidation states is particularly noteworthy. It arises from the fact that, in moving across the transition series, the number of d electrons has increased and, in this mid-region, the d orbitals have not yet sunk energetically into the inert electron core. The number of d electrons available for bonding is consequently maximized, and not

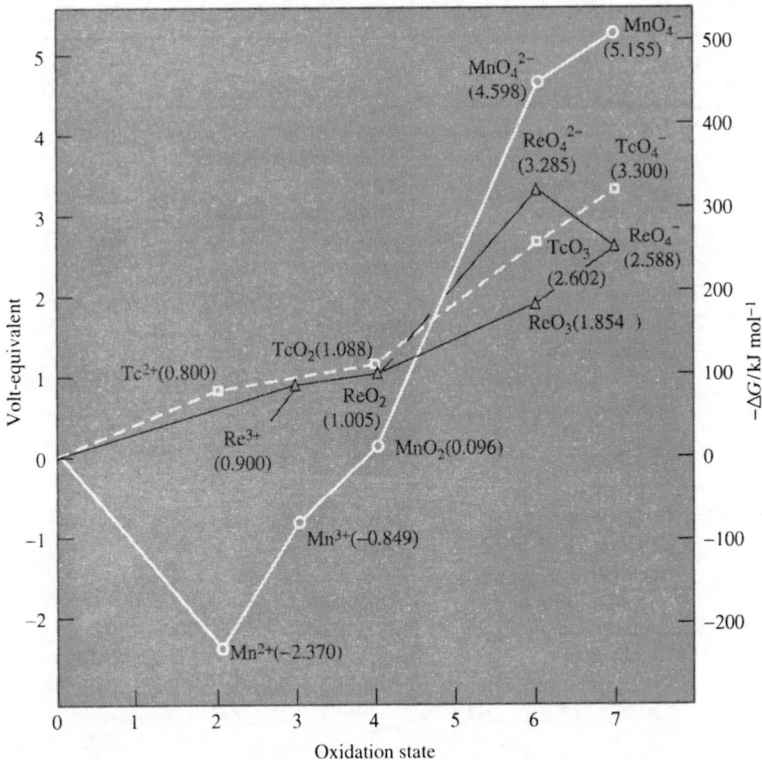

Figure 24.1   Plot of volt-equivalent versus oxidation state for Mn, Tc and Re.

only are high oxidation states possible, but back donation of electrons from metal to ligand is also facilitated with resulting stabilization of low oxidation states.

A further point of interest is the noticeably greater tendency of rhenium, as compared to either manganese or technetium, to form compounds with high coordination numbers.

24.3 Compounds of Manganese, Technetium and Rhenium[3]

Binary borides (p. 145), carbides (p. 297), and nitrides (p. 417) have already been mentioned.

[3] R. D. W. KEMMITT, Chap. 37, pp. 771–876; R. D. PEACOCK Chap. 38, pp. 877–903 and Chap. 39, pp. 905–78, in *Comprehensive Inorganic Chemistry*, Vol. 3, Pergamon Press, Oxford, 1973. (See also nine reviews devoted to the chemistry of Tc and Re in *Topics in Current Chemistry* **176**, 1996, 291 pp.)

Manganese, like chromium (and also the succeeding elements in the first transition series), is too small to accommodate interstitial carbon without significant distortion of the metal lattice. As a consequence it forms a number of often readily hydrolysed carbides with rather complicated structures.

Hydrido complexes are well-known but simple binary hydrides are not, which is in keeping with the position of these metals in the "hydrogen gap" portion of the periodic table (p. 67).

24.3.1 Oxides and chalcogenides

All three metals form heptoxides (Table 24.4) but, whereas Tc_2O_7 and Re_2O_7 are the final products formed when the metals are burned in an excess of oxygen, Mn_2O_7 requires prior oxidation of the manganese to the +7 state. It separates as a reddish-brown explosive oil from the green

Table 24.3 Oxidation states and stereochemistries of manganese, technetium and rhenium

Oxidation state	Coordination number	Stereochemistry	Mn	Tc/Re
-3 (d^{10})	4	Tetrahedral	$[Mn(NO)_3(CO)]$	$[M(CO)_4]^{3-}$
-2 (d^9)	4	Square planar	$[Mn(phthalocyanine)]^{2-}$	—
-1 (d^8)	5	Trigonal bipyramidal	$[Mn(CO)_5]^-$	$[M(CO)_5]^-$
	4	Square planar	$[Mn(phthalocyanine)]^-$	—
0 (d^7)	6	Octahedral	$[Mn_2(CO)_{10}]$	$[M_2(CO)_{10}]$
1 (d^6)	6	Octahedral	$[Mn(CN)_6]^{5-}$	$[M(CN)_6]^{5-}$
2 (d^5)	2	Linear	$[Mn\{C(SiMe_3)_3\}_2]^{(a)}$	
	4	Tetrahedral	$[MnBr_4]^{2-}$	
		Square planar	$[Mn(phthalocyanine)]$	
	5	Trigonal bipyramidal	$[MnBr\{N(C_2H_4NMe_2)_3\}]^+$	$[ReCl(dppe)_2]^+$
		Square pyramidal	$[Mn(CS_4)_2Cl]^{3-(b)}$	
	6	Octahedral	$[Mn(H_2O)_6]^{2+}$	$[M(diars)_2Cl_2]$
	7	Capped trigonal prismatic	$[Mn(edta)(H_2O)]^{2-}$	
	8	Dodecahedral	$[Mn(NO_3)_4]^{2-}$	
		Distorted square prismatic	$[MnL]^{2+(c)}$	
3(d^4)	5	Trigonal bipyramidal	$[Mn(PMe_3)_2I_3]$	
		Square pyramidal	$[MnCl_5]^{2-}$	$[Re_2Cl_8]^{2-}$
	6	Octahedral	$K_3[Mn(CN)_6]$	$[M(diars)_2Cl_2]^+$
	7	Pentagonal bipyramidal	$[Mn(NO_3)_3(bipy)]$	$[M(CN)_7]^{4-}$
	11	See Fig. 24.11a	—	$[Re(\eta^5-C_5H_5)_2H]$
4 (d^3)	5	—	—	$[(Me_3SiCH_2)_4Re(N_2)-Re(CH_2SiMe_3)_4]$
	6	Octahedral	$[MnF_6]^{2-}$	$[MI_6]^{2-}$
5 (d^2)	4	Tetrahedral	$[MnO_4]^{3-}$	—
	5	Trigonal bipyramidal (?)	—	ReF_5
		Square pyramidal	—	$[MOCl_4]^-$
	6	Octahedral	—	$[Tc(NCS)_6]^-$, $[ReNCl_2(PEt_2Ph)_3]$
	8	Dodecahedral	—	$[M(diars)_2Cl_4]^+$
6 (d^1)	4	Tetrahedral	$[MnO_4]^{2-}$	$[ReO_4]^{2-}$
	5	Square pyramidal		$ReOCl_4$
	6	Trigonal prismatic		$[Re(S_2C_2Ph_2)_3]$ (see p. 1055)
		Octahedral		ReF_6
	8	Dodecahedral		$[ReMe_8]^{2-}$
		Square antiprismatic		$[ReF_8]^{2-}$
7 (d^0)	4	Tetrahedral	$[MnO_4]^-$	$[MO_4]^-$
	5	Trigonal bipyramidal		$[ReO_2Me_3]$
	6	Octahedral		$[ReO_3Cl_3]^{2-}$
	7	Pentagonal bipyramidal		ReF_7
	9	Tricapped trigonal prismatic		$[ReH_9]^{2-}$

$^{(a)}$N. H. BUTTRUS, C. EABORN, P. B. HITCHCOCK, J. D. SMITH and A. C. SULLIVAN *J. Chem. Soc., Chem. Commun.* 1380–1 (1985).

$^{(b)}$S.-B. YU and R. H. HOLM, *Polyhedron* **12**, 263–6 (1993).

$^{(c)}$L = 1,4,7,10-tetrakis(pyrazol-1-ylmethyl)-1,4,7,10-tetraazacyclododecane. See M. DI VAIRA, F. MANI and P. STOPPIONI, *J. Chem. Soc., Dalton Trans.*, 1127–30 (1992).

Table 24.4   Oxides of Group 7

Ox. state	+7	+6	+5	+4	+3	+2
Mn	Mn_2O_7			MnO_2	Mn_2O_3 Mn_3O_4	MnO
Tc	Tc_2O_7	$TcO_3(?)$		TcO_2		
Re	Re_2O_7	ReO_3	Re_2O_5	ReO_2		

solutions produced by the action of conc H_2SO_4 on a manganate(VII) salt. On standing, it slowly loses oxygen to form MnO_2 but detonates around 95°C and will explosively oxidize most organic materials. The molecule is composed of 2 corner-sharing MnO_4 tetrahedra with a bent Mn–O–Mn bridge. The liquid solidifies at 5.9°C to give red crystals in which the dimeric units persist with an Mn–O–Mn angle[4] of 120.7°. The other 2 heptoxides are yellow solids whose volatility provides a useful means of purifying the elements and, as has been pointed out, is a crucial factor in the commercial production of rhenium (Tc_2O_7: mp 119.5°, bp 310.6°; Re_2O_7: mp 300.3°, bp 360.3°). In the vapour phase both consist of corner-sharing MO_4 tetrahedra but, whereas this structure is retained in the solid phase by Tc_2O_7 (linear Tc–O–Tc), solid Re_2O_7 has an unusual structure consisting of polymeric double layers of corner-sharing ReO_4 tetrahedra alternating with ReO_6 octahedra. The same basic unit, though this time discrete, is found in the dihydrate which is therefore best formulated as $[O_3Re–O–ReO_3(H_2O)_2]$ and is obtained by careful evaporation of an aqueous solution of the heptoxide. The structure breaks down, however, if the solution is kept for a period of months. Crystals of perrhenic acid monohydrate, $HReO_4.H_2O$, are deposited and consist of fairly regular ReO_4^- tetrahedra and H_3O^+ ions linked by hydrogen bridges.[5]

Only rhenium forms a stable trioxide. It is a red solid with a metallic lustre and is obtained by the reduction of Re_2O_7 with CO. ReO_3 has a structure in which each Re is

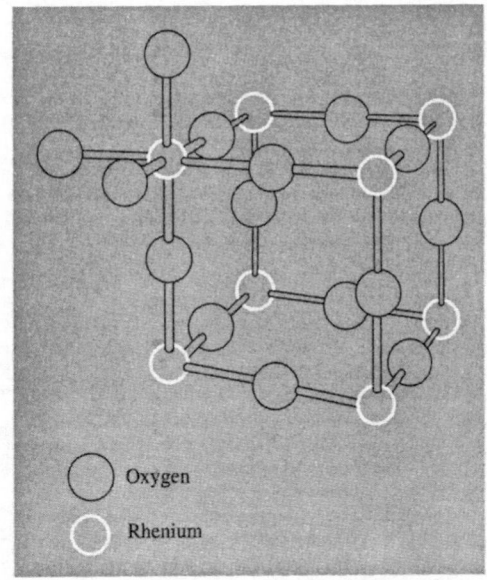

Oxygen

Rhenium

Figure 24.2   The structure of ReO_3. Note the similarity to perovskite (p. 963) which can be understood as follows: if the Re atom, which is shown here with its full complement of 6 surrounding O atoms, is imagined to be the small cation at the centre of Fig. 21.3(a), then the perovskite structure is obtained by placing the large cations (Ca^{II}) into the centre of the cube drawn above and in the 7 other equivalent positions around the Re.

octahedrally surrounded by oxygens (Fig. 24.2). It has an extremely low electrical resistivity which decreases with decrease in temperature like a true metal: ρ_{300K} 10 μohm cm, ρ_{100K} 0.6 μohm cm. It is clear that the single valency electron on each Re atom is delocalized in a conduction band of the crystal. ReO_3 is unreactive towards water and aqueous acids and alkalis, but when boiled with conc alkali it disproportionates into ReO_4^- and ReO_2. A blue pentoxide Re_2O_5 has been reported but is also prone to disproportionation into +7 and +4 species.

The +4 oxidation state is the only one in which all three elements form stable oxides, but only in the case of technetium is this the most stable oxide. TcO_2 is the final product when any Tc/O

[4] R. DRONSKOWSKI, B. KREBS, A. SIMON, G. MILLER and B. HETTICH, *Z. anorg. allg. Chem.* **558**, 7–20 (1988).

[5] G. WLTSCHEK, I. SVOBODA and H. FUESS, *Z. anorg. allg. Chem.* **619**, 1679–81 (1993).

Applications of Manganese Dioxide[6]

Although the primary use of manganese is in the production of steel it also finds widespread and important uses in non-metallurgical industries. These frequently use the manganese as MnO_2 but even where this is not the case the dioxide is invariably the starting material.

The largest non-metallurgical use of MnO_2 is in the manufacture of dry-cell batteries (p. 1204) which accounts for about half a million tonnes of ore annually. The most common dry batteries are of the carbon-zinc Leclanché type in which carbon is the positive pole. MnO_2 is incorporated as a depolarizer to prevent the undesirable liberation of hydrogen gas on to the carbon, probably by the reaction

$$MnO_2 + H^+ + e^- \longrightarrow MnO(OH)$$

Only the highest quality MnO_2 ore can be used directly for this purpose, and "synthetic dioxide", usually produced electrolytically by anodic oxidation of manganese(II) sulfate, is increasingly employed.

The brick industry is another major user of MnO_2 since it can provide a range of red to brown or grey tints. In the manufacture of glass its use as a decolourizer (hence "glassmaker's soap") is its most ancient application. Glass always contains iron at least in trace amounts, and this imparts a greenish colour; the addition of MnO_2 to the molten glass produces red-brown Mn^{III} which equalizes the absorption across the visible spectrum so giving a "colourless", i.e. grey glass. In recent times selenium compounds have replaced MnO_2 for this application, but in larger proportions the latter is still used to make pink to purple glass.

The oxidizing properties of MnO_2 are utilized in the oxidation of aniline for the preparation of hydroquinone which is important as a photographic developer and also in the production of dyes and paints.

In the electronics industry the advantages of higher electrical resistivity and lower cost of ceramic ferrites ($M^{II}Fe_2O_4$) (p. 1081) over metallic magnets have been recognized since the 1950s and the "soft" ferrites (M^{II} = Mn, Zn) are the most common of these. They are used on the sweep transformer and deflection yoke of a television set and, of course, MnO_2, either natural or synthetic, is required in their production.

system is heated to high temperatures, but ReO_2 disproportionates at 900°C into Re_2O_7 and the metal. Hydrated TcO_2 and ReO_2 may be conveniently prepared by reduction of aqueous solutions of MO_4^- with zinc and hydrochloric acid and are easily dehydrated. TcO_2 is dark brown and ReO_2 is blue-black: both solids have distorted rutile structures like MoO_2 (p. 1008).

It is MnO_2, however, which is by far the most important oxide in this group, though it is not the most stable oxide of manganese, decomposing to Mn_2O_3 above about 530°C and being a useful oxidizing agent. Hot concentrated sulfuric and hydrochloric acids reduce it to manganese(II):

$$2MnO_2 + 2H_2SO_4 \longrightarrow 2MnSO_4 + O_2 + 2H_2O$$

$$MnO_2 + 4HCl \longrightarrow MnCl_2 + Cl_2 + 2H_2O$$

the latter reaction being formerly the basis of the manufacture of chlorine. It is, however, extremely insoluble and, as a consequence, often unreactive. As pyrolusite it is the most plentiful ore of

manganese and it finds many industrial uses (see Panel).

The structural history of MnO_2 is complex and confused due largely to the prevalence of nonstoichiometry and the fact that in its hydrated forms it behaves as a cation-exchanger. Many of the various polymorphs which have been reported are probably therefore simply impure forms. The only stoichiometric form is the so-called β-MnO_2, which is that of pyrolusite and possesses the rutile structure (p. 961), but even here a range of composition from $MnO_{1.93}$ to $MnO_{2.0}$ is possible. β-MnO_2 can be prepared by careful decomposition of manganese(II) nitrate but, when precipitated from aqueous solutions, for instance by reduction of alkaline MnO_4^-, the hydrated MnO_2 has a more open structure which exhibits cation-exchange properties and cannot be fully dehydrated without some loss of oxygen.

Apart from the black $Re_2O_3.2H_2O$ (which is readily oxidized to the dioxide and is prepared by boiling $ReCl_3$ in air-free water) oxides of oxidation states below +4 are known only for manganese. Mn_3O_4 is formed when any

---

[6] *Ulmann's Encyclopedia of Industrial Chemistry*, Vol. A16, pp. 123-43, VCH, Weinheim, 1990.

oxide of manganese is heated to about $1000°C$ in air and is the black mineral, hausmannite. It has the spinel structure (p. 247) and as such is appropriately formulated as $Mn^{II}Mn^{III}_2O_4$, with Mn^{II} and Mn^{III} occupying tetrahedral and octahedral sites respectively within a ccp lattice of oxide ions; there is, however, a tetragonal distortion due to a Jahn–Teller effect (p. 1021) on Mn^{III}. A related structure, but with fewer cation sites occupied, is found in the black γ-Mn_2O_3 which can be prepared by aerial oxidation and subsequent dehydration of the hydroxide precipitated from aqueous Mn^{II} solutions. If MnO_2 is heated less strongly (say $<800°C$) than is required to produce Mn_3O_4, then the more stable α-form of Mn_2O_3 results which has a structure involving 6-coordinate Mn but with 2 Mn–O bonds longer than the other 4. This is no doubt a further manifestation of the Jahn–Teller effect expected for the high-spin d^4 Mn^{III} ion and is presumably the reason why Mn_2O_3, alone among the oxides of transition metal M^{III} ions, does not have the corundum (p. 242) structure.

Reduction with hydrogen of any oxide of manganese produces the lowest oxide, the grey to green MnO. This is an entirely basic oxide, dissolving in acids and giving rise to the aqueous Mn^{II} cationic chemistry. It has a rock-salt structure and is subject to nonstoichiometric variation ($MnO_{1.00}$ to $MnO_{1.045}$), but its main interest is that it is a classic example of an antiferromagnetic compound. If the temperature is reduced below about 118 K (its Néel point), a rapid fall in magnetic moment takes place as the electron spins on adjacent Mn atoms pair-up. This is believed to take place by the process of "superexchange" by which the interaction is transferred through intervening, non-magnetic, oxide ions. (MnO_2 is also antiferromagnetic below 92 K whereas the alignment in Mn_3O_4 results in ferrimagnetism below 43 K.)

The sulfides are fewer and less familiar than the oxides but, as is to be expected, favour lower oxidation states of the metals. Thus manganese forms MnS_2 which has the pyrite structure (p. 680) with discrete Mn^{II} and S_2^{-II} ions and is converted on heating to MnS and sulfur. This green MnS is the most stable manganese sulfide and, like MnO, has a rock-salt structure and is strongly antiferromagnetic ($T_N - 121°C$). Less-stable red forms are also known and the pale-pink precipitate produced when H_2S is bubbled through aqueous Mn^{II} solutions is a hydrated form which passes very slowly into the green variety. The corresponding selenides are very similar: $Mn^{II}Se_2$ (pyrite-type), and MnSe (NaCl-type), antiferromagnetic with $T_N - 100°C$.

Technetium and rhenium favour higher oxidation states in their binary chalcogenides. Both form black diamagnetic heptasulfides, M_2S_7, which are isomorphous and which decompose to $M^{IV}S_2$ and sulfur on being heated. These disulfides, unlike the pyrite-type $Mn^{II}S_2$, contain monatomic S^{-II} units. The diselenides are similar. TcS_2, $TcSe_2$ and ReS_2 feature trigonal prismatic coordination of M^{IV} by S (or Se) in a layer-lattice structure which is isomorphous with a rhombohedral polymorph of MoS_2. $ReSe_2$ also has a layer structure but the Re^{IV} atoms are octahedrally coordinated.

Lower formal oxidation states are stabilized, however, by M–M bonding in ternary chalcogenides such as $M_4^IM_6Q_{12}$, $M_4^IM_6Q_{13}$ ($M^I =$ alkali metal; M = Re, Tc; Q = S, Se) and the recently reported[7] $M_{10}^IM_6S_{14}$. Their structures are all based on the face-capped, octahedral M_6X_8 cluster unit found in Chevrel phases (p. 1018) and in the dihalides of Mo and W (p. 1022).

24.3.2 Oxoanions

The lower oxides of manganese are basic and react with aqueous acids to give salts of Mn^{II} and Mn^{III} cations. The higher oxides, on the other hand, are acidic and react with alkalis to yield oxoanion salts, but the polymerization which was such a feature of the chemistry of the preceding group is absent here.

---

[7] W. BRONGER, M. KANERT, M. LOVENICH and D. SCHMITZ, *Z. anorg. allg. Chem.* **619**, 2015–20 (1993).

Fusion of MnO_2 with an alkali metal hydroxide and an oxidizing agent such as KNO_3 produces very dark-green manganate(VI) salts (manganates) which are stable in strongly alkaline solution but which disproportionate readily in neutral or acid solution (see Fig. 24.1):

$$3MnO_4^{2-} + 4H^+ \longrightarrow 2MnO_4^- + MnO_2 + 2H_2O$$

The deep-purple manganate(VII) salts (permanganates) may be prepared in aqueous solution by oxidation of manganese(II) salts with very strong oxidizing agents such as PbO_2 or $NaBiO_3$. They are manufactured commercially by alkaline oxidative fusion of MnO_2 followed by the electrolytic oxidation of manganate(VI):

$$2MnO_2 + 4KOH + O_2 \longrightarrow 2K_2MnO_4 + 2H_2O$$

$$2K_2MnO_4 + 2H_2O \longrightarrow 2KMnO_4 + 2KOH + H_2$$

The most important manganate(VII) is $KMnO_4$ of which several tens of thousands of tonnes are produced annually. It is a well-known oxidizing agent, used analytically:

in acid solution:

$$MnO_4^- + 8H^+ + 5e^- \rightleftharpoons Mn^{2+} + 4H_2O;$$
$$E^\circ = +1.51 \text{ V}$$

in alkaline solution:

$$MnO_4^- + 2H_2O + 3e^- \rightleftharpoons MnO_2 + 4OH^-;$$
$$E^\circ = +1.23 \text{ V}$$

It is also important as an oxidizing agent in the industrial production of saccharin and benzoic acid, and medically as a disinfectant. It is increasingly being used also for purifying water, since it has the dual advantage over chlorine that it does not affect the taste, and the MnO_2 produced acts as a coagulant for colloidal impurities.

Reduction of $KMnO_4$ with aqueous Na_2SO_3 produces the bright-blue tetraoxomanganate(V) (hypomanganate), MnO_4^{3-}, which has also been postulated as a reaction intermediate in some organic oxidations; it is not stable, being prone to disproportionation.

All $[MnO_4]^{n-}$ ions are tetrahedral with Mn–O 162.9 pm in MnO_4^- and 165.9 pm in MnO_4^{2-}. K_2MnO_4 is isomorphous with K_2SO_4 and K_2CrO_4. By contrast, the only tetrahedral oxoanions of Tc and Re are the tetraoxotechnetate(VII) (pertechnetate) and tetraoxorhenate(VII) (perrhenate) ions. $HTcO_4$ and $HReO_4$ are strong acids like $HMnO_4$ and are formed when the heptoxides are dissolved in water. From such solutions dark-red crystals with the composition $HTcO_4$ in the case of technetium and, in the case of rhenium, yellowish crystals of $Re_2O_7.2H_2O$ or $HReO_4.H_2O$ (p. 1047) can be obtained.

$[TcO_4]^-$ and $[ReO_4]^-$ provide the starting point for virtually all the Tc and Re chemistry. They are produced whenever compounds of Tc and Re are treated with oxidizing agents such as nitric acid or hydrogen peroxide and, although reduced in aqueous solution by, for instance, Sn^{II}, Fe^{II}, Ti^{III} and I^-, they are much weaker oxidizing agents than $[MnO_4]^-$. In further contrast to $[MnO_4]^-$ they are also stable in alkaline solution and are colourless whereas $[MnO_4]^-$ is an intense purple. In fact, the absorption spectra of the 3 $[MO_4]^{-1}$ ions are very similar, arising in each case from charge transfer transitions between O^{2-} and M^{VII}, but the energies of these transitions reflect the relative oxidizing properties of M^{VII}. Thus the intense colour of $[MnO_4]^-$ arises because the absorption occurs in the visible region, whereas for $[ReO_4]^-$ it has shifted to the more energetic ultraviolet, and the ion is therefore colourless. $[TcO_4]^-$ is also normally colourless but the absorption starts on the very edge of the visible region and it may be that the red colour of crystalline $HTcO_4$, and other transient red colours which have been reported in some of its reactions, are due to slight distortions of the ion from tetrahedral symmetry causing the absorption to move sufficiently for it to "tail" into the blue end of the visible, thereby imparting a red coloration. $[MO_4]^-$ ions might be expected to act as Lewis bases (cf ClO_4^- p. 868) and, indeed, several mono- and bis- $[ReO_4]^-$ complexes with Co^{II}, Ni^{II} and Cu^{II} have been

Table 24.5   Halides of Group 7

Oxidation state	Fluorides	Chlorides	Bromides	Iodides
+7	ReF_7 yellow mp 48.3°, bp 73.7°			
+6	TcF_6 yellow mp 37.4°, bp 55.3° ReF_6 yellow mp 18.5°, bp 33.7°	$TcCl_6$ green mp 25° $ReCl_6$ red-green mp 29° (dichroic)		
+5	TcF_5 yellow mp 50°, bp (d) ReF_5 yellow-green mp 48°, bp(extrap) 221°	— $ReCl_5$ brown-black mp 220°	$ReBr_5$ dark brown (d 110°)	
+4	MnF_4 blue (d above rt) — ReF_4 blue (subl >300°)	— $TcCl_4$ red (subl >300°) $ReCl_4$ purple-black (d 300°)	— (?$TcBr_4$) (red-brown) $ReBr_4$ dark red	ReI_4 black (d above rt)
+3	MnF_3 red-purple —	— $[ReCl_3]_3$ dark red (subl 500°) (d)	— $[ReBr_3]_3$ red-brown	— $[ReI_3]_3$ lustrous black (d on warming)
+2	MnF_2 pale pink mp 920°	$MnCl_2$ pink mp 652°, bp ~1200°	$MnBr_2$ rose mp 695°	MnI_2 pink mp 613°

characterized, and both unidentate and bridging modes identified.[8]

Fusion of rhenates(VII) with a basic oxide yields so-called ortho- and meso-perrhenates (M_5ReO_6 and M_3ReO_5, M = Na, $\frac{1}{2}$Ca, etc.) while addition of rhenium metal to the fusion (and exclusion of oxygen) produces rhenate(VI) (e.g. Ca_3ReO_6). There is evidence suggesting the existence of $[ReO_6]^{5-}$ and $[ReO_6]^{6-}$ but it may be better to regard all these compounds as mixed oxides. In any case, it is clear that the coordination sphere of the metal has

expanded compared to that of the smaller Mn in the tetrahedral $[MnO_4]^{n-}$ ions. Comparable technetium compounds have also been prepared.

24.3.3 Halides and oxohalides

The known halides and oxohalides of this group are listed in Tables 24.5 and 24.6 respectively.

The highest halide of each metal is of course a fluoride: ReF_7 (the only thermally stable heptahalide of a transition metal), TcF_6, and MnF_4. This again indicates the diminished ability of manganese to attain high oxidation states when compared not only to Tc and Re but also to

[8] M. C. CHAKRAVORTY, *Coord. Chem. Revs.* **106**, 205–25 (1990).

Table 24.6 Oxohalides of Group 7

Oxidation state	Fluorides			Chlorides	Bromides
+7	—	—	MnO$_3$F dark green mp −78°, bp(extrap) 60°	MnO$_3$Cl vol green liq	—
	—	—	TcO$_3$F yellow mp 18.3°, bp ~100°	TcO$_3$Cl colourless	—
	ReOF$_5$ cream mp 43.8°, bp 73.0°	ReO$_2$F$_2$ yellow mp 90°, bp 185°	ReO$_3$F yellow mp 147°, bp 164°	ReO$_3$Cl colourless mp 4.5°, bp 130°	ReO$_3$Br colourless mp 39.5°
+6	—			MnO$_2$Cl$_2$ vol brown liq	—
	TcOF$_4$ blue mp 134° bp(extrap) 165°			TcOCl$_4$ blue	—
	ReOF$_4$ blue mp 108°, bp 171°			ReOCl$_4$ brown mp 30°, bp(extrap) 228°	ReOBr$_4$ blue
+5	—			MnOCl$_3$ vol liq	—
	—			TcOCl$_3$	TcOBr$_3$ black
	ReOF$_3$ black			—	—

chromium, which forms CrF$_5$ and CrF$_6$. The most interesting of the lower halides are the rhenium trihalides which exist as trimeric clusters which persist throughout much of the chemistry of Re^{III}.

Apart from ReF$_5$, which is produced when ReF$_6$ is reduced by tungsten wire at 600°C, all the known penta-, hexa- and hepta- halides of Re and Tc can be prepared directly from the elements by suitably adjusting the temperature and pressure, although various specific methods have been suggested. They are volatile solids varying in colour from pale yellow (ReF$_7$) to dark brown (ReBr$_5$), and are readily hydrolysed by water with accompanying disproportionation into the comparatively more stable [MO$_4$]$^-$ and MO$_2$, e.g.:

$$3ReCl_5 + 8H_2O \longrightarrow HReO_4 + 2ReO_2 + 15HCl$$

Because of the tendency to produce mixtures of the halides, and the facile formation of oxohalides if air and moisture are not rigorously excluded (or even, in some cases, also by attacking glass), not all of these halides have been characterized as well as might be desired. There is spectroscopic evidence that ReF$_7$ has a pentagonal bipyramidal structure, and ReX$_6$ are probably octahedral. ReCl$_5$ is actually a dimer, Cl$_4$Re(μ-Cl)$_2$ReCl$_4$, in which the rhenium is octahedrally coordinated.

The tetrahalides are made by a variety of methods. MnF$_4$, being the highest halide formed by Mn, can be prepared directly from the elements, as can TcCl$_4$, which is the only thermally stable chloride of Tc. TcCl$_4$ is a red sublimable solid consisting of infinite chains of edge-sharing TcCl$_6$ octahedra. By contrast the black $ReCl_4$, which is prepared by heating $ReCl_3$ and $ReCl_5$ in a sealed tube at 300°C, is made up of pairs of $ReCl_6$ octahedra which share faces (as in $[W_2Cl_9]^{3-}$, p. 1021), these dimeric units then being linked in chains by corner-sharing. The closeness of the Re atoms in each pair (273 pm) is indicative of a metal–metal bond though not so pronounced as the more extensive metal–metal bonding found in Re^{III} chemistry.

MnF_3 is a red-purple, reactive, but thermally stable solid; it is prepared by fluorinating any of the Mn^{II} halides and its crystal lattice consists of MnF_6 octahedra which are distorted, presumably because of the Jahn–Teller effect expected for d^4 ions. The Re^{III} halides are obtained by thermal decomposition of $ReCl_5$, $ReBr_5$ and ReI_4. The dark-red chloride is composed of triangular clusters of chloride-bridged Re atoms with 1 of the 2 out-of-plane Cl on each Re bridging to adjacent trimeric clusters (Fig. 24.3). After allowing for the Re–Cl bonds, each Re^{III} has a d^4 configuration and the observed diamagnetism can be accounted for by assuming that these four d electrons on each Re are used in forming

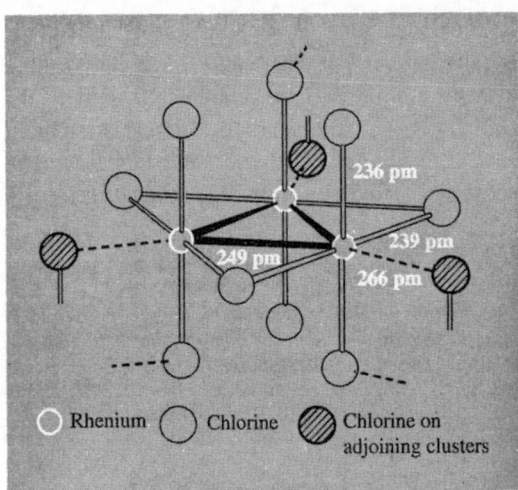

<Cl>O Rhenium   O Chlorine   ⦸ Chlorine on adjoining clusters</Cl>

Figure 24.3   Idealized structure of Re_3Cl_9; in crystalline $ReCl_3$ the trimeric units are linked into planar hexagonal networks. The coordination sites occupied by Cl from adjoining clusters can readily be occupied by a variety of other ligands instead.

double bonds ($\sigma + \pi$) to its 2 Re neighbours. The Re–Re distance of 249 pm is consistent with this (cf. 275 pm in Re metal). Re_3Cl_9 can be sublimed under vacuum but the green colour of the vapour probably indicates breakdown of the cluster in the vapour phase. The compound dissolves in water to give a red solution which slowly hydrolyses to hydrated Re_2O_3, and in conc hydrochloric acid it gives a red solution which is stable to oxidation and from which can be precipitated hydrates of Re_3Cl_9 and a number of complex chlorides in which the trimeric clusters persist.[9]

Re_3Br_9 is similar to Re_3Cl_9 but the iodide, which is a black solid and is similarly trinuclear, differs in that it is thermally less stable and only 2 Re atoms in each cluster are linked to adjacent clusters, thereby forming infinite chains of trimeric units rather than planar networks.

Except for the possible existence of ReI_2, the only simple dihalides of this group that are known (so far) are those of manganese. They are pale-pink salts obtained by simply dissolving the metal or carbonate in aqueous HX. MnF_2 is insoluble in water and forms no hydrate, but the others form a variety of very water-soluble hydrates of which the tetrahydrates are the most common.

The oxohalides of manganese are green liquids (except MnO_2Cl_2 which is brown); they are notable for their explosive instability. MnO_3F can be prepared by treating $KMnO_4$ with fluorosulfuric acid, HSO_3F, whereas reaction of Mn_2O_7 with chlorosulfuric acid yields $MnO_3Cl + MnO_2Cl_2 + MnOCl_3$.

The oxohalides of technetium and rhenium are more numerous than those of manganese and are not so unstable, although all of them readily hydrolyse (with dis-proportionation to $[MO_4]^-$ and MO_2 in the case of oxidation states +5 and +6). In this respect they may be regarded as being intermediate between the halides and the oxides which, in the higher oxidation states, are the more stable. Treatment of the oxides with the halogens, or the halides with oxygen are common preparative methods. The structures are not all

[9] M. IRMLER and G. MEYER, *Z. anorg. allg. Chem.* **581**, 104–10 (1990); B. JUNG, G. MEYER and E. HERDTWECK, *ibid.* **604**, 27–33 (1991).

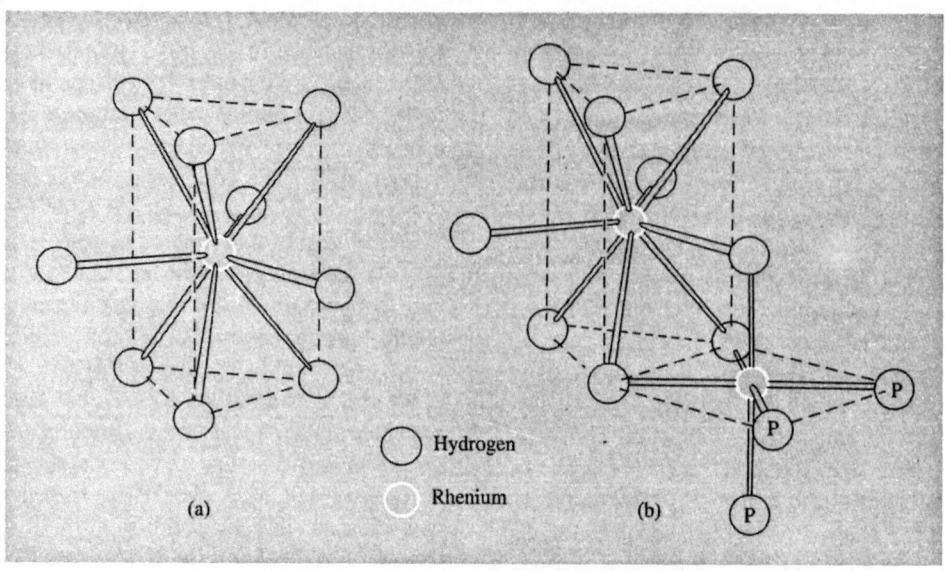

Figure 24.4 (a) The tricapped trigonal prismatic structure of the $[ReH_9]^{2-}$ anion. (b) $[Re_2(\mu\text{-}H)_3H_6MeC(CH_2\text{-}PPh_2)_3]$. For clarity, only the P atoms of the triphos ligand are shown.

known with certainty, but $ReOCl_4$ may be noted as an example of a square-pyramidal structure.

24.3.4 Complexes of manganese, technetium and rhenium[3,10,11]

Oxidation state VII (d⁰)

The coordination chemistry of this oxidation state is confined mainly to a few readily hydrolysed oxohalide complexes of Re such as $KReO_2F_4$. Exceptions to this limitation are provided by the isomorphous hydrides K_2MH_9 of Tc and Re which formally involve M^{VII} and H^-. The rhenium analogue was the first to be prepared as the colourless, diamagnetic product of the reduction of $KReO_4$ by potassium in aqueous diaminoethane (ethylenediamine). The

elucidation of its structure (Fig. 24.4a) illustrates vividly the problems associated with identifying a novel compound when its isolation in a pure form is difficult and when conventional chemical analysis is unable to establish the stoichiometry with accuracy.[†] Several other hydrido complexes are known, of which the reddish-orange, dinuclear $(Et_4N)[Re_2H_9(triphos)]$ may be mentioned. This is obtained by treatment of $(Et_4N)_2[ReH_9]$ with $MeC(CH_2PPh_2)_3$ in

[†] Only by using a wide range of physical techniques were these difficulties surmounted. The product was first thought to be $K[Re(H_2O)_4]$ containing Re^{-1} with a square-planar geometry, by analogy with the isoelectronic Pt^{II}. The nmr spectrum, however, indicated the presence of an Re–H bond so the compound was reformulated as $KReH_4.2H_2O$. Fresh analytical evidence then suggested that earlier products had been impure and a further reformulation, this time as K_2ReH_8, was proposed. The observed diamagnetism could then only be accounted for by assuming metal–metal bonding between the implied d^1 rhenium(VI) atoms, but X-ray analysis showing the Re atoms to be 550 pm apart, precluded this possibility. The problem was finally resolved when a neutron diffraction study established the formula as K_2ReH_9 and the structure is tricapped trigonal prismatic. The nmr spectrum actually shows only one proton signal in spite of the existence of distinct capping and prismatic protons, and this is thought to be due to rapid exchange between the sites.

[10] B. CHISWELL, E. D. MCKENZIE and L. F. LINDOY, Manganese, Chap. 41, pp. 1–122; K. A. CONNER and R. A. WALTON, Rhenium, Chap. 43, pp. 125–213 in *Comprehensive Coordination Chemistry*, Vol. 4, Pergamon Press, Oxford, 1987.
[11] J. BALDAS, *Adv. Inorg. Chem.* **41**, 2–123 (1994) and F. TISATO, F. REFOSCO and G. BANDOLI, *Coord. Chem. Revs.* **135/136**, 325–97 (1994) are devoted to technetium.

MeCN. The structure of the anion (Fig 24.4b) can be envisaged as a tridentate $[ReH_9]^{2-}$ ligand coordinated to $Re(triphos)^+$, and, since the metal atoms are only 259.4 pm apart, is said to involve an $Re\equiv Re$ triple bond[12] (in which case the $[ReH_9]^{2-}$ should be regarded as tetradentate and its Re atom as 10-coordinated).

Oxidation state VI (d¹)

Again, fluoro and oxo complexes of rhenium predominate. The reaction of KF and ReF_6 in an inert PTFE vessel yields pink $K_2[ReF_8]$, the anion of which has a square-prismatic structure; hydrolysis converts it to $K[ReOF_5]$.

An interesting compound which is usually included in discussions of Re^{VI} chemistry is the green crystalline dithiolate, $[Re(S_2C_2Ph_2)_3]$. This was the first authenticated example of a trigonal prismatic complex (Fig. 19.6, p. 915) but besides its structural interest it has, along with other complexes of such ligands, posed problems regarding the oxidation state of the metal. The ligand may be thought to coordinate in either of two extreme ways (or some intermediate state between them):

The difference between the two extremes is essentially that, in the former, the Re retains its valence electrons in its d orbitals whereas in the latter it loses 6 of them to delocalized ligand orbitals. In either case paramagnetism is anticipated since rhenium has an odd number of valence electrons. The magnetic moment of 1.79 BM corresponding to 1 unpaired electron, and esr evidence showing that this electron is situated predominantly on the ligands, indicates that an intermediate oxidation state is involved

but does not specify which one. Because of this uncertainty, dithiolate ligands, and others like them, have been expressively termed "non-innocent" ligands by C. K. Jørgensen.[13]

Oxidation state V (d²)

This oxidation state is sparse in the case of Mn but is important in the pharmaceutical applications of Tc, and an extensive chemistry has been developed. Some fluoro complexes of Tc and Re such as the salts of $[MF_6]^-$ are known, but oxo compounds predominate and, in $[MOCl_5]^{2-}$ and $[MOX_4]^-$ (X = Cl, Br, I) for instance, other halides are also able to coordinate. $[MOX_4]^-$ is square pyramidal with apical $M=O$ and the MO^{3+} moiety is reminiscent of VO^{2+}, being found in other compounds (particularly those containing phosphines) and labilizing whatever ligand is *trans* to it. The ir stretching frequency of the $M=O$ bond is conveniently used for its detection, lying in the range $890–1020\,cm^{-1}$ for $Tc=O$ and generally about $20\,cm^{-1}$ lower for $Re=O$. The $M\equiv N$ group also stabilizes the oxidation state, probably because the π bonds are able to reduce the charge on the M^V; it is found in compounds such as $[MNX_2(PR_3)_3]$ and $[MNX_2(PR_3)_2]$ (X = Cl, Br, I) produced when $[MO_4]^-$ is reduced by hydrazine in the presence of appropriate ligands, of which phosphines are especially useful.[14] The ir stretching frequency is again of diagnostic value being found in the approximate range of $1050–1100\,cm^{-1}$ for $Tc\equiv N$ and $20\,cm^{-1}$ or so lower for $Re\equiv N$. Eight-coordinate and probably dodecahedral $[ReCl_4(diars)_2]ClO_4$ has been prepared and the Tc analogue is notable as the first example of 8-coordinate technetium.

12 S. C. ABRAHAMS,   A. P. GINSBERG,   T. F. KOETZLE, P. MARSH and C. R. SPRINKLE, *Inorg. Chem.* **25**, 2500–10 (1986).

13 C. K. JÖRGENSEN, *Oxidation Numbers and Oxidation States*, Springer–Verlag, Berlin, 1969, 291 pp.

14 For other $Tc\equiv N$ compounds see for instance: G. A. WILLIAMS and J. BALDAS, *Aust. J. Chem.* **42**, 875–84 (1989); C. M. ARCHER, J. R. DILWORTH, J. D. KELLY and M. McPARTLIN, *Polyhedron* **8**, 1879–81 (1989).

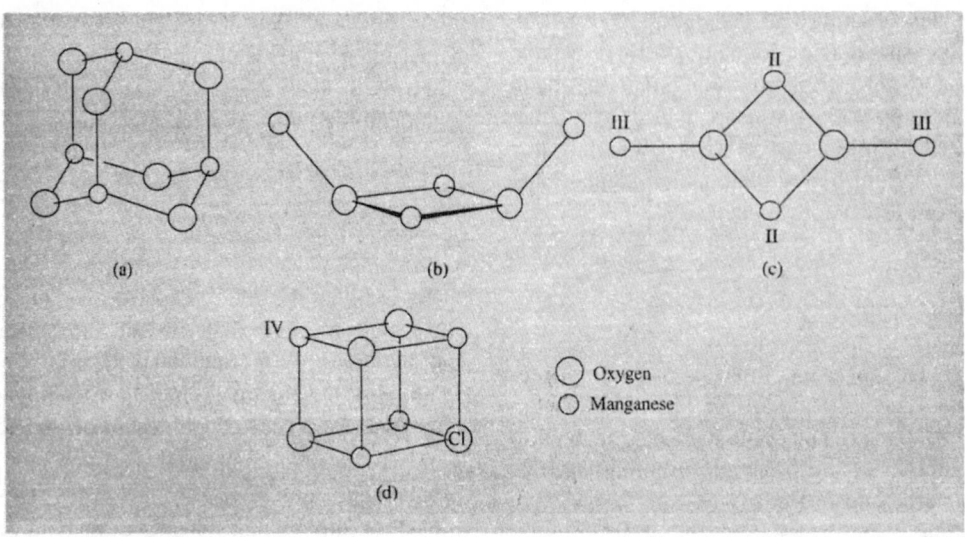

Figure 24.5   Cores of some Mn_4 complexes. (a) Adamantane $\{Mn_4^{IV}O_6\}$ in $[Mn_4O_6(tacn)_4]^{4+}$. (b) Butterfly $\{Mn_4^{III}O_2\}$ in $[Mn_4O_2(MeCOO)_7(bipy)_2]^+$. (c) Planar $\{Mn_2^{II}Mn_2^{III}O_2\}$ in $[Mn_4O_2(MeCOO)_6(bipy)_2]$. (d) Cubane $\{Mn_3^{III}Mn^{IV}O_3Cl\}$ in $[Mn_4O_3Cl_4(MeCOO)_3py_3]$.

Oxidation state IV (d³)

This is apparently the highest oxidation state in which manganese is able to form complexes. Monomeric complexes are sparse, though $K_2[MnX_6]$, where $X = F$, Cl, IO_3 and CN are known, but di- and poly-meric compounds are more numerous and have received attention as models for the water-oxidizing enzyme, *Photosystem II*,[15] important in plant photosynthesis. An $Mn(\mu\text{-}O)_2Mn$ core is thought to be involved and the redox behaviour of compounds such as $[(L\text{-}L)_2Mn(\mu\text{-}O)_2Mn(L\text{-}L)_2]^{n+}$ ($L\text{-}L = $ 1,10-phenanthroline, 2,2'-bipyridyl; $n = $ 2, 3, 4, implying $Mn^{III}\text{–}Mn^{III}$, $Mn^{III}\text{–}Mn^{IV}$ and $Mn^{IV}\text{–}Mn^{IV}$ pairings) has been studied.[16] Schiff bases and carboxylate ligands have also been used and complexes with OH bridges and also triply bridged complexes have been

produced. Fully oxidized $Mn^{IV}\text{–}Mn^{IV}$ species are often observed only electrochemically and not completely characterized. An exception is the Mn^{IV} tetramer, $[Mn_4O_6(tacn)_4]^{4+}$ prepared by aerial oxidation of Mn^{2+} in the presence of 1,4,7-triazacyclononane. The core of this has the adamantane structure, each Mn being facially coordinated to one tacn and three μ_2-oxygens (Fig. 24.5a).

Relatively few compounds of Tc^{IV} have radiopharmaceutical use, and its chemistry in this oxidation state has therefore been comparatively neglected. For both the heavier elements the preference for oxo compounds is diminishing while the tendency to form M–M multiple bonds has not yet acquired the importance to be found in more reduced states. The most important compounds are the salts of $[MX_6]^{2-}$ [M = Tc, Re; X = F, Cl, Br, I]. The fluoro complexes are obtained by the reaction of HF on one of the other halogeno complexes and these in turn are obtained by reducing $[MO_4]^-$ (commonly by using I^-) in aqueous HX. The corresponding Tc and Re complexes are closely similar, but an interesting difference between Tc^{IV} and Re^{IV} is found in their behaviour with CN^-. The reaction

[15] V. K. YACHANDRA, K. SAUER and M. P. KLEIN, *Chem. Revs.* **96**, 2927–50 (1996); R. MANCHANDA, G. W. BRUDVIG, and R. H. CRABTREE, *Coord. Chem. Revs.* **144**, 1–38 (1995).

[16] G. W. BRUDVIG and R. H. CRABTREE, *Prog. Inorg. Chem.* **37**, 99–142 (1989); J. B. VINCENT and G. CHRISTOU, *Adv. Inorg. Chem.* **33**, 197–258 (1989); K. WIEGHARDT, *Angew. Chem. Int. Edn. Engl.* **28**, 1153–72 (1989).

of KCN and K_2ReI_6 in methanol yields a mixture of $K_4[Re^{III}(CN)_7].2H_2O$ and $K_3[Re^VO_2(CN)_4]$ whereas the analogous reaction of KCN and K_2TcI_6 produces a reddish-brown, paramagnetic precipitate, thought to be $K_2[Tc(CN)_6]$.

Oxidation state III (d⁴)

Nearly all manganese(III) complexes are octahedral and high-spin with magnetic moments close to the spin-only value of 4.90 BM expected for 4 unpaired electrons. The d^4 configuration is also expected to be subject to Jahn–Teller distortions (p. 1021). For reasons which are not obvious, the $[Mn(H_2O_6)]^{3+}$ ion in the alum $CsMn(SO_4)_2.12H_2O$ does not display the appreciable distortion from octahedral symmetry (elongation of two *trans* bonds) found, for instance, in solid MnF_3, the octahedral Mn^{III} sites of Mn_3O_4, $[Mn(acac)_3]$ and in tris(tropolonato)manganese(III). Manganese(III) is strongly oxidizing in aqueous solution with a marked tendency to disproportionate into Mn^{IV} (i.e. MnO_2) and Mn^{II} (see Fig. 24.1). It is, however, stabilized by *O*-donor ligands, as evidenced by the way in which the virtually white $Mn(OH)_2$ rapidly darkens in air as it oxidizes to hydrous Mn_2O_3 or $MnO(OH)$, and by the preparation of $[Mn(acac)_3]$ via the aerial oxidation of aqueous Mn^{II} in the presence of acetylacetonate. $K_3[Mn(C_2O_4)_3].3H_2O$ is also known, while the complexing oxoanions, phosphate and sulfate, have a stabilizing effect on aqueous solutions. The main preparative routes to Mn^{III} are by reduction of $KMnO_4$ or oxidation of Mn^{II}. The latter may be effected electrolytically but a common method is by way of the red-brown acetate. This is similar to the "basic" acetate of chromium(III) and so involves the $[Mn_3O(MeCOO)_6]^+$ unit (see Fig. 23.9, p. 1030). The hydrate is prepared by oxidation of manganese(II) acetate with $KMnO_4$ in glacial acetic acid, and the anhydrous salt by the action of acetic hydride on hydrated manganese(II) nitrate.

The field of oxo-bridged polynuclear complexes of manganese, much of it involving mixed

oxidation states and facile redox behaviour, is expanding rapidly[16]. Oxidation of an ethanolic solution of Mn^{II} acetate by $(Bu_4^nN)MnO_4$ in the presence of acetic acid and pyridine can yield either the Mn^{III} compound, $[Mn_3O(MeCOO)_6py_3]^+$ or the $Mn^{II}Mn_2^{III}$ compound, $[Mn_3O(MeCOO)_6py_3]$. Addition of bipyridyl to solutions of these in MeCN gives the tetranuclear, $[Mn_4O_2(MeCOO)_7(bipy)_2]^+$ and $[Mn_4O_2(MeCOO)_6(bipy)_2]$ respectively. The structures of the cores of these and other Mn_4 complexes[17] are given in Fig. 24.5.

Still higher nuclearities, up to 12 in $[Mn_{12}O_{12}(RCOO)_{16}(H_2O)_4]$ (R = Me, Ph), have been reported.[18] The cores of these two compounds, which are of interest as potential building blocks in the preparation of molecular ferromagnets, consist of a central $\{Mn_4^{IV}(\mu\text{-O})_4\}$ cubane linked by O-bridges to eight Mn atoms.

The most important low-spin octahedral complex of Mn^{III} is the dark-red cyano complex, $[Mn(CN)_6]^{3-}$, which is produced when air is bubbled through an aqueous solution of Mn^{II} and CN^-. $[MnX_5]^{2-}$ (X = F, Cl) are also known; the chloro ion, at least when combined with the cation $[bipyH_2]^{2+}$, is notable as an example of a square pyramidal manganese complex.

Technetium(III) complexes are accessible especially if stabilized by back-bonding ligands, and are most commonly 6-coordinate. $[TcCl_2(diars)_2]ClO_4$, prepared by the reaction of *o*-phenylenebisdimethylarsine and HCl with $HTcO_4$ in aqueous alcohol, is probably the best known. The rhenium(III) analogue is isomorphous but requires the help of a reducing agent such as H_3PO_2 to effect the reduction from $[ReO_4]^-$. Other examples are $[Tc(NCS)_6]^{3-}$ and $[Tc(thiourea)_6]^{3+}$. However, 7-coordinate compounds such as $[M(CN)_7]^{4-}$ are also known and, more recently, it has been reported[19] that the

[17] V. McKee, *Adv. Inorg. Chem.* **40**, 323–410 (1994).

[18] P. D. W. Boyd, Q. Li, J. B. Vincent, K. Folting, H.-R. Chang, W. E. Streib, J. C. Huffman, G. Christou and D. N. Hendrickson, *J. Am. Chem. Soc.* **110**, 8537–9 (1988).

[19] C. M. Archer, J. R. Dilworth, P. Jobanputra, R. M. Thompson, M. McPartlin, P. C. Povey, G. W. Smith and J. D. Kelly, *Polyhedron* **9**, 1497–1502 (1990).

reaction of [MOCl$_4$]$^-$ with excess arylhydrazine and PPh$_3$ in ethanol gives 5-coordinate, diamagnetic, [MCl(N$_2$Ar)$_2$(PPh$_3$)$_2$].

In general Re^{III} is readily oxidized to Re^{IV} or Re^{VII} unless it is stabilized by metal–metal bonding[20] as in the case of the trihalides already discussed. Rhenium(III) complexes with Cl$^-$ and Br$^-$ have been characterized and are of two types, [Re$_3$X$_{12}$]$^{3-}$ and [Re$_2$X$_8$]$^{2-}$, both of which involve multiple Re–Re bonds. If Re$_3$Cl$_9$ or Re$_3$Br$_9$ are dissolved in conc HCl or conc HBr respectively, stable, red, diamagnetic salts may be precipitated by adding a suitable monovalent cation. Their stoichiometry is M^{I}ReX$_4$ and they were formerly thought to be unique examples of low-spin, tetrahedral complexes. X-ray analysis, however, showed that the anions are trimeric with the same structure as the halides (Fig. 24.3) and likewise incorporating Re=Re double bonds. Their chemistry reflects their structure since 3 halide ions per trimeric unit can be replaced by ligands such as MeCN, Me$_2$SO, Ph$_3$PO and PEt$_2$Ph yielding neutral complexes [Re$_3$X$_9$L$_3$].

The blue diamagnetic complexes [Re$_2$X$_8$]$^{2-}$ are produced when [ReO$_4$]$^-$ in aqueous HCl or HBr is reduced by H$_3$PO$_2$ and they can then be precipitated by the addition of a suitable cation. A more efficient method, which also yields a product soluble in polar organic solvents, is the reaction of (NBu$_4$)ReO$_4$ with refluxing benzoyl chloride followed by the addition of a solution of (NBu$_4$)Cl in ethanol saturated with HCl. Salts of [Re$_2$X$_8$]$^{2-}$ are the starting points for almost all dirhenium(III) compounds and the ion provided one of the first examples of a quadruple bond in a stable compound (see pp. 1032, 1034). The structure of [Re$_2$Cl$_8$]$^{2-}$ is shown in Fig. 24.6 and, as in [Mo$_2$Cl$_8$]$^{4-}$ (Fig. 23.11, p. 1033), the chlorine atoms are eclipsed. In both ions the metal has a d^4 configuration which is to be expected if a δ-bond is present. [Re$_2$Cl$_8$]$^{2-}$ can be reduced polarographically to unstable [Re$_2$Cl$_8$]$^{3-}$ and [Re$_2$Cl$_8$]$^{4-}$, and also undergoes a variety of substitution reactions (Fig. 24.6b,c,d).

One Cl on each Re may be replaced by phosphines, while MeSCH$_2$CH$_2$SMe (dth) takes up 4 coordination positions on 1 Re to give [Re$_2$Cl$_5$(dth)$_2$]. In this case the average oxidation state of the rhenium has been reduced to +2.5. The reduction in bond order from 4 to 3.5, which the addition of a δ* electron implies, causes some lengthening of the Re–Re distance and the configuration is staggered. Carboxylates are able to bridge the metal atoms forming complexes of the type [Re$_2$Cl$_2$(O$_2$CR)$_4$] which are clearly analogous to the dimeric carboxylates found in the previous group.

In the octachloro technetium system, by contrast, the paramagnetic [Tc$_2$Cl$_8$]$^{3-}$ is the most readily obtained species. The Tc has a formal oxidation state of +2.5 with a d(Tc–Tc) 210.5 pm and the configuration is eclipsed. The pale green [NBu$_4^n$]$_2^+$[Tc$_2^{III}$Cl$_8$]$^{2-}$ can be isolated from the products of reduction of [TcCl$_6$]$^{2-}$ with Zn/HCl(aq). The compound is strictly isomorphous with [NBu$_4^n$]$_2$[Re$_2$Cl$_8$] and has (Tc–Tc) 214.7 pm. The reason for the increase in Tc–Tc distance on removal of the δ* electron, and the consequent increase in the presumed bond order from 3.5 to 4, is not clear, but has been ascribed to a *decrease* in the strength of σ and π bonding caused by orbital contraction occurring as the charge on the metal core (and hence the bond order) increases.[21]

Oxidation state II (d^5)

The chemistry of technetium(II) and rhenium(II) is meagre and mainly confined to arsine and phosphine complexes. The best known of these are [MCl$_2$(diars)$_2$], obtained by reduction with hypophosphite and Sn^{II} respectively from the corresponding Tc^{III} and Re^{III} complexes, and in which the low oxidation state is presumably stabilized by π donation to the ligands. This oxidation state, however, is really best typified by manganese for which it is the most thoroughly studied and, in aqueous solution, by far the most

[20] F. A. COTTON and R. A. WALTON, *Multiple Bonds between Atoms*, 2nd edn., Oxford University Press, Oxford, 1993, 787 pp.

[21] p. 123 of ref. 20.

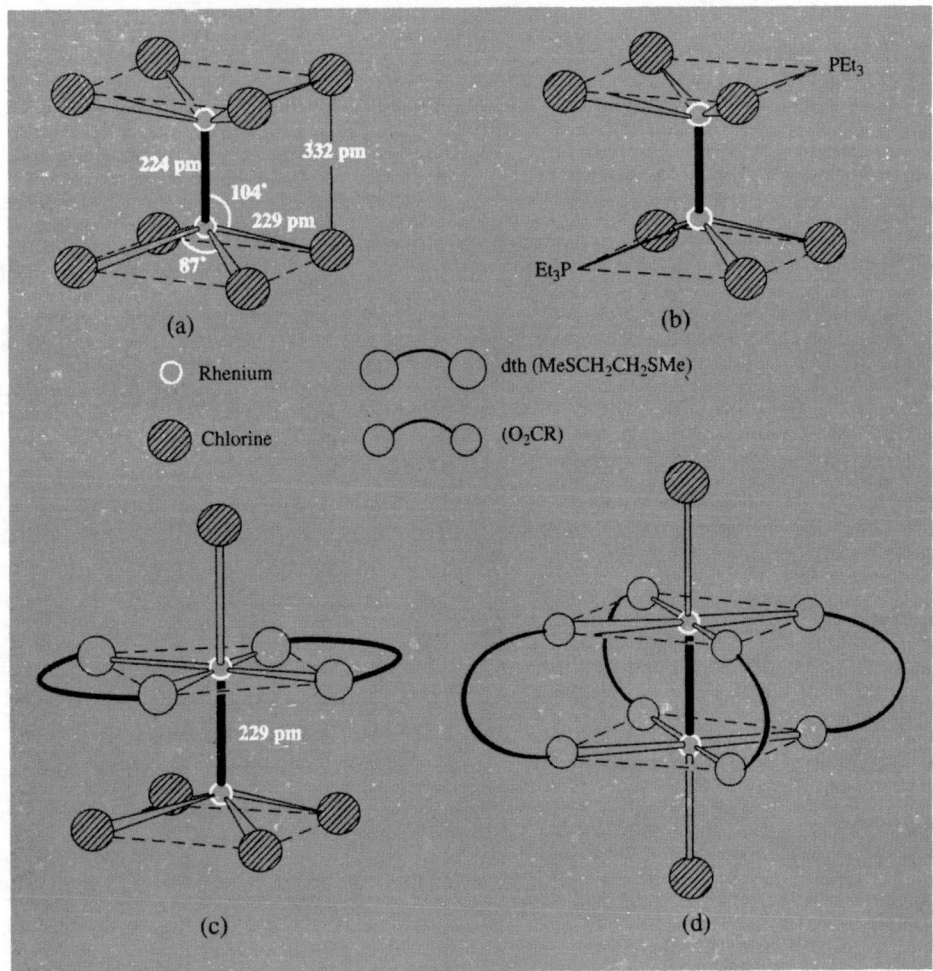

Figure 24.6 Some complexes of Re with multiple Re–Re bonds: (a) $[Re_2Cl_8]^{2-}$. (b) $[Re_2Cl_6(PEt_3)_2]$. (c) $[Re_2Cl_5(dth)_2]$. (d) $[Re_2(O_2CR)_4Cl_2]$.

stable; accordingly it provides the most extensive cationic chemistry in this group.

Salts of manganese(II) are formed with all the common anions and most are water-soluble hydrates. The most important of these commercially and hence the most widely produced is the sulfate, which forms several hydrates of which $MnSO_4.5H_2O$ is the one commonly formed. It is manufactured either by treating pyrolusite with sulfuric acid and a reducing agent, or as a byproduct in the production of hydroquinone (MnO_2 is used in the conversion of aniline to quinone):

$$PhNH_2 + 2MnO_2 + 2\tfrac{1}{2}H_2SO_4 \longrightarrow OC_6H_4O$$

$$+ 2MnSO_4 + \tfrac{1}{2}(NH_4)_2SO_4 + 2H_2O$$

It is the starting material for the preparation of nearly all manganese chemicals and is used in fertilizers in areas of the world where there is a deficiency of Mn in the soil, since Mn is an essential trace element in plant growth. The anhydrous salt has a surprising thermal stability; it remains unchanged even at red heat, whereas the sulfates of Fe^{II}, Co^{II} and Ni^{II} all decompose under these conditions.

Aqueous solutions of salts with non-coordinating anions contain the pale-pink, $[Mn(H_2O)_6]^{2+}$, ion which is one of a variety of high-spin octahedral complexes $(t_{2g}^3 e_g^2)$ which have been prepared more especially with chelating ligands such as en, edta, and oxalate. As is expected, most of these have magnetic moments close to the spin-only value of 5.92 BM, and are very pale in colour. This is a consequence of the fact that all electronic d–d transitions from a high-spin d^5 configuration must, of necessity, involve the pairing of some electrons and are therefore spin-forbidden. This is embodied in the interpretation[22] of the rather complex absorption spectrum of $[Mn(H_2O)_6]^{2+}$.

The resistance of Mn^{II} to both oxidation and reduction is generally attributed to the effect of the symmetrical d^5 configuration, and there is no doubt that the steady increase in resistance of M^{II} ions to oxidation found with increasing atomic number across the first transition series suffers a discontinuity at Mn^{II}, which is more resistant to oxidation than either Cr^{II} to the left or Fe^{II} to the right. However, the high-spin configuration of the Mn^{II} ion provides no CFSE (p. 1131) and the stability constants of its high-spin complexes are consequently lower than those of corresponding complexes of neighbouring M^{II} ions and are kinetically labile. In addition, a zero CFSE confers no advantage on any particular stereochemistry which must be one of the reasons for the occurrence of a wider range of stereochemistries for Mn^{II} than is normally found for M^{II} ions.

Green-yellow salts of the tetrahedral $[MX_4]^{2-}$ (X = Cl, Br, I) ions can be obtained from ethanolic solutions and are well characterized. Furthermore, a whole series of adducts $[MnX_2L_2]$ (X = Cl, Br, I) are known where L is an N-, P- or As-donor ligand, and both octahedral and tetrahedral stereochemistries are found. Of interest because of the possible role of manganese porphyrins in photosynthesis is $[Mn^{II}(phthalocyanine)]$ which is square planar. The reaction of aqueous edta with $MnCO_3$ yields

a number of complex species, amongst them the 7-coordinate $[Mn(edta)(H_2O)]^{2-}$ which has a capped trigonal prismatic structure. The highest coordination number, 8, is found in the anion $[Mn(\eta^2\text{-}NO_3)_4]^{2-}$ which, like other such ions, is approximately dodecahedral (p. 916).

A varied chemistry, centred on the phosphines $[MnX_2(PR_3)]$, is also developing. These are moisture sensitive and, frequently, air-sensitive, polymeric solids which can be obtained not only by the reaction of the phosphine with MnX_2 (X = Cl, Br, I), but also by the reaction of the phosphorane, R_3PX_2, with powdered metal.[23] In the case of $[MnI_2(PPhMe_2)]$ two isomers have been characterised. Both consist of chains of $[Mn(\mu\text{-}I)_2]$ units but whereas, in the one prepared from MnX_2 two phosphines are coordinated to alternate metals (4,6,4,6 coordination), in the one prepared from Mn metal, a single phosphine is coordinated to each metal (uniform 5,5,5,5 coordination).[23] $[MnX_2(PR_3)]$ have also been found to react reversibly with a variety of small molecules such as CO, NO, C_2H_4 and SO_2 (see for instance ref. 24). O_2 will also react reversibly in some cases but its controlled addition to the pale-pink $[MnI_2(PMe_3)]$ (obtained from PMe_3I_2 and Mn powder in dry ethyl ether as a 4,6,4,6 coordination polymer) yields successively[25] the dark-red dimer, $[Mn^{III}(PMe_3)I_2(\mu\text{-}I)Mn^{II}(PMe_3)_2I_2]$ (involving approximately tetrahedral Mn^{III} and trigonal bipyramidal Mn^{II}) and finally the dark-green, trigonal bipyramidal $[Mn^{III}(PMe_3)_2I_3]$.

Spin-pairing in manganese(II) requires a good deal of energy and is achieved only by ligands such as CN^- and CNR which are high in the spectrochemical series. The low-spin complexes. $[Mn(CN)_6]^{4-}$ and $[Mn(CNR)_6]^{2+}$ are presumed

22 A. B. P. Lever, *Inorganic Electronic Spectroscopy*, 2nd edn., pp. 448–52, Elsevier, Amsterdam, 1984.

23 S. M. Godfrey, D. G. Kelly, A. G. Mackie, P. P. Mac-Rory, C. A. McAuliffe, R. G. Pritchard and S. M. Watson, *J. Chem. Soc., Chem. Commun.* 1447–9 (1991).

24 D. S. Barratt, G. A. Gott and C. A. McAuliffe, *J. Chem. Soc., Dalton Trans.*, 2065–70 (1988).

25 C. A. McAuliffe, S. M. Godfrey, A. G. Mackie, and R. G. Pritchard. *J. Chem. Soc., Chem. Commun.* 483–5 (1992).

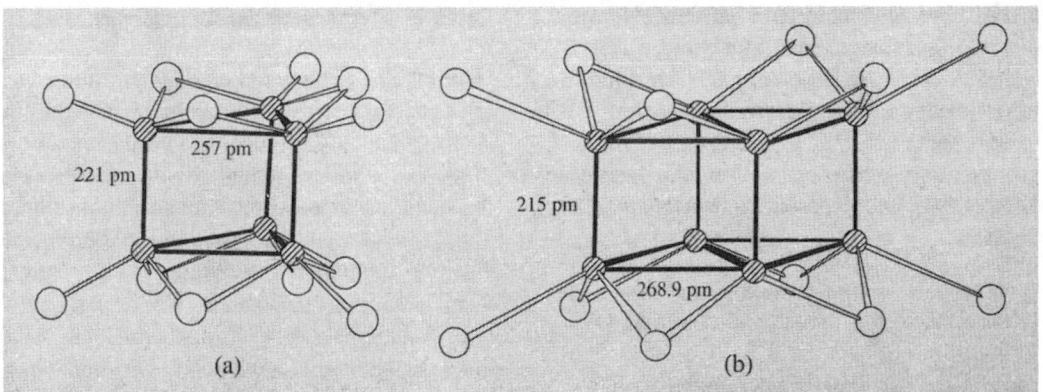

Figure 24.7 (a) Trigonal prismatic $[Tc_6Cl_{12}]^{2-}$ (b) $[Tc_8Br_{12}]^{n+}$. The bond lengths shown are for $n = 1$, i.e. $[Tc_8Br_{12}]Br.2H_2O$. The very short bonds holding together the triangular faces in (a) and the rhombohedral faces in (b) are consistent with $Tc{\equiv}Tc$ triple bonds.

to involve appreciable π bonding and this covalency brings with it a susceptibility to oxidation. Just as Mn^{II} hydroxide undergoes aerial oxidation to Mn^{III} so, in the presence of excess CN^-, aqueous solutions of the blue-violet $[Mn(CN)_6]^{4-}$ are oxidized by air to the dark red $[Mn(CN)_6]^{3-}$.

Lower oxidation states

Cyano complexes of the metals of this group in high oxidation states have already been referred to. The tolerance of CN^- to a range of metal oxidation states, arising, on the one hand, from its negative charge and, on the other, from its ability to act as a π-acceptor, is further demonstrated by the formation (albeit requiring reduction with potassium amalgam) of the M^I complexes, $K_5[M(CN)_6]$ (M = Mn, Tc, Re). However, claims for the formation of cyano complexes with oxidation state zero are less reliable.

Reduction of $[MO_4]^-$ in hydrohalic acid by H_2 under pressure is an alternative method for preparing $[Re_2X_8]^{2-}$. In the case of technetium, however, further reduction occurs, yielding $[Tc_2X_8]^{3-}$ along with higher nuclearity clusters in which the oxidation state of the metal is below 2.[26] Chloride species include $[Tc_6Cl_{14}]^{3-}$ and $[Tc_6Cl_{12}]^{2-}$

with the trigonal prismatic structure shown in Fig. 24.7a. Bromide species[27] additionally include hexanuclear octahedral species and the octanuclear prismatic, $[Tc_8X_{12}]^{n+}$ $(n = 0, 1)$ (Fig. 24.7b). Other examples of complexes in which Mn, Tc and Re are in lower oxidation states are considered in section 24.3.6 on organometallic compounds.

24.3.5 The biochemistry of manganese [16,18]

Traces of manganese are found in many plants and bacteria, and a healthy human adult contains about 10–20 mg of Mn.

In many manganoproteins the manganese is in the II oxidation state and can often be replaced by magnesium(II) without loss of function. In other cases, where redox activity is involved, some naturally occurring forms containing either manganese or iron are known. The most important natural role of manganese, however, is in the oxidation of water in green plant photosynthesis (p. 125) where its presence in photosystemII (PSII) is essential. Here, absorbed radiation provides the energy for the oxidation

---

[27] V. I. Spitzin, S. V. Kryutchkov, M. S. Grigoriev and A. F. Kuzina, *Z. anorg. allg. Chem.* **563**, 136–52 (1988).

of water, dioxygen being evolved and electrons transferred to photosystemI (PSI) where NADP is reduced. The oxidation proceeds by four 1-photon, 1-electron steps and it appears that it is the redox properties of a group of Mn atoms which provide stable stages for this stepwise oxidation. Manganese probably has two further functions:

(a) to act as a template holding two molecules of water close enough to facilitate O–O bond formation;
(b) to make the bound water more acidic, so facilitating loss of H^+

It is no doubt significant that the equilibrium constant for the reaction

$$H_2O-Mn^{III} + H_2O \rightleftharpoons HO-Mn^{III} + H_3O^+$$

is larger for Mn^{III} than for any other trivalent, first row transition metal ion.

Although definitive crystallographic data are lacking it seems clear that the "water oxidizing centre" (WOC) or "oxygen evolving complex" (OEC) of PSII contains four Mn atoms and it is believed that these are arranged in one of the cluster forms shown in Fig. 24.5. Physical techniques which have been used to study these proteins include esr, uv-visible spectroscopy, magnetic measurements and EXAFS. Two Mn–Mn distances, 270 and 330 pm are indicated, with O-, N- and possible Cl-donor atoms, giving a core of fairly low symmetry. A plausible sequence of oxidation state changes for the four Mn atoms consistent with, but by no means defined by, the available data would be:

$$(II)(III)_3 \longrightarrow (III)_4 \longrightarrow (III)_3(IV)$$
$$\longrightarrow (III)_2(IV)_2 \longrightarrow (III)(IV)_3$$

Efforts have been made to reproduce these characteristics in model systems, and molecules with the core structures already described have been prepared. Though none as yet has shown any photoredox activity the 270 pm distance has been shown to be consistent with $(\mu\text{-oxo})_2$ bridges and 330 pm with μ-oxo or μ-oxo-μ-carboxylate bridges. Several mechanistic proposals have been made incorporating these features.

24.3.6 Organometallic compounds

Carbonyls, cyclopentadienyls and their derivatives occupy a central position in the chemistry of this as of preceding groups, the bonding involved and even their stoichiometries having in some cases posed difficult problems. Increasingly, however, interest has focused on the chemistry of compounds involving M–C σ bonds, of which rhenium provides as rich a variety as any transition metal. It is also notable that, whereas the organometallic chemistry of manganese is largely limited to oxidation states 0, I and II, that of rhenium extends to VII.[28,29]

Only one well-characterized binary carbonyl is formed by each of the elements of this group. That of manganese is best prepared by reducing MnI_2 (e.g. with $LiAlH_4$) in the presence of CO under pressure. Those of technetium and rhenium are made by heating their heptoxides with CO under pressure. They are sublimable, isomorphous, crystalline solids: golden-yellow for $[Mn_2(CO)_{10}]$, mp 154°, and colourless for $[Tc_2(CO)_{10}]$, mp 160° and $[Re_2(CO)_{10}]$, mp 177°. Their stabilities in air show a regular gradation: manganese carbonyl is quite stable below 110°C, technetium carbonyl decomposes slowly and rhenium carbonyl may ignite spontaneously. The empirical stoichiometry $M(CO)_5$ would imply a paramagnetic molecule with 17 valence electrons, but the observed diamagnetism (for Mn and Re) suggests at least a dimeric structure. In fact, X-ray analysis reveals the structure shown in Fig. 24.8(a) in which two $M(CO)_5$ groups in staggered configuration are held together by an M–M bond, unsupported by bridging ligands (cf. S_2F_{10}, p. 684).

Very many derivatives of the carbonyls of Mn,[30] Tc and Re have been prepared since the parent carbonyls were first synthesized in 1949, 1961 and 1941 respectively:[3] among the more important are the carbonylate anions,

[28] C. P. Casey, *Science* **259**, 1552–8 (1993).
[29] W. A. Herrmann, *Angew. Chem. Int. Edn. Engl.* **27**, 1297–313 (1988).
[30] C. E. Holloway and M. Melnik, *J. Organometallic Chem.* **396**, 129–246 (1990).

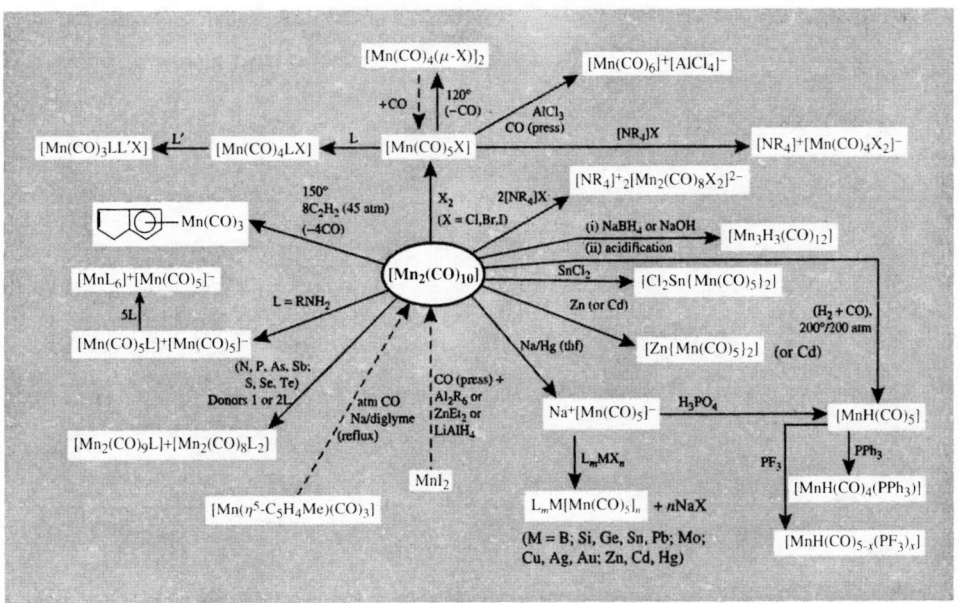

SCHEME A   Some reactions of [Mn$_2$(CO)$_{10}$] and its derivatives.[31]

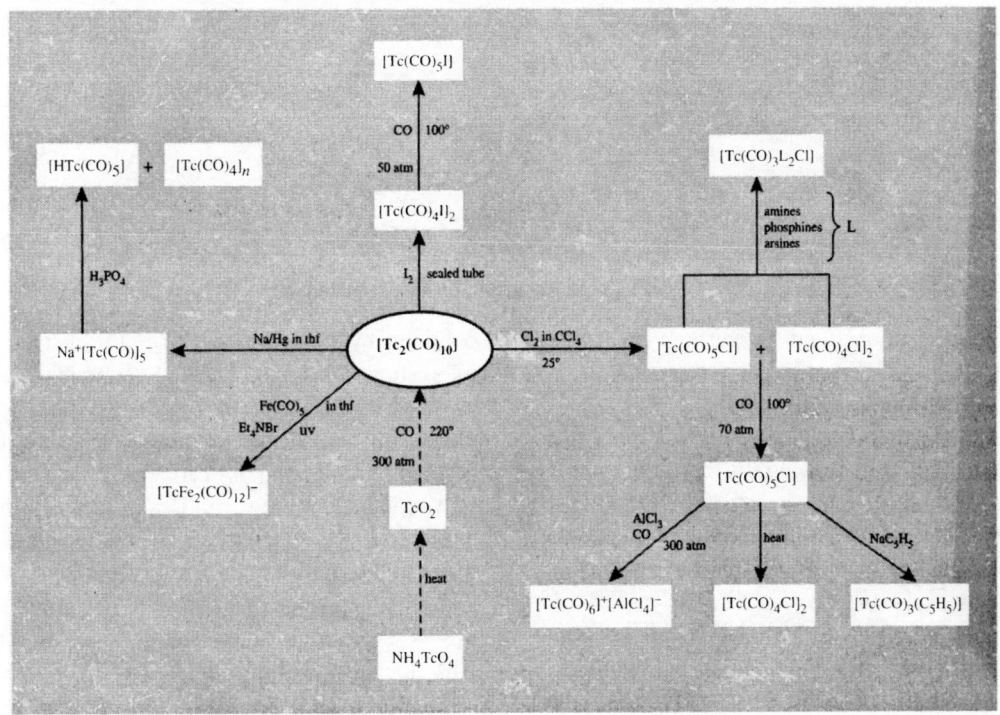

SCHEME B   Some reactions of [Tc$_2$(CO)$_{10}$] and its derivatives.[32]

[31] R. D. W. KEMMIT, pp. 839–51 in *Comprehensive Inorganic Chemistry*, Vol. 3, Pergamon Press, Oxford 1973.
[32] R. D. PEACOCK, *ibid*, p. 899 for Scheme B, p. 953 for Scheme C and p. 954 for Scheme D.

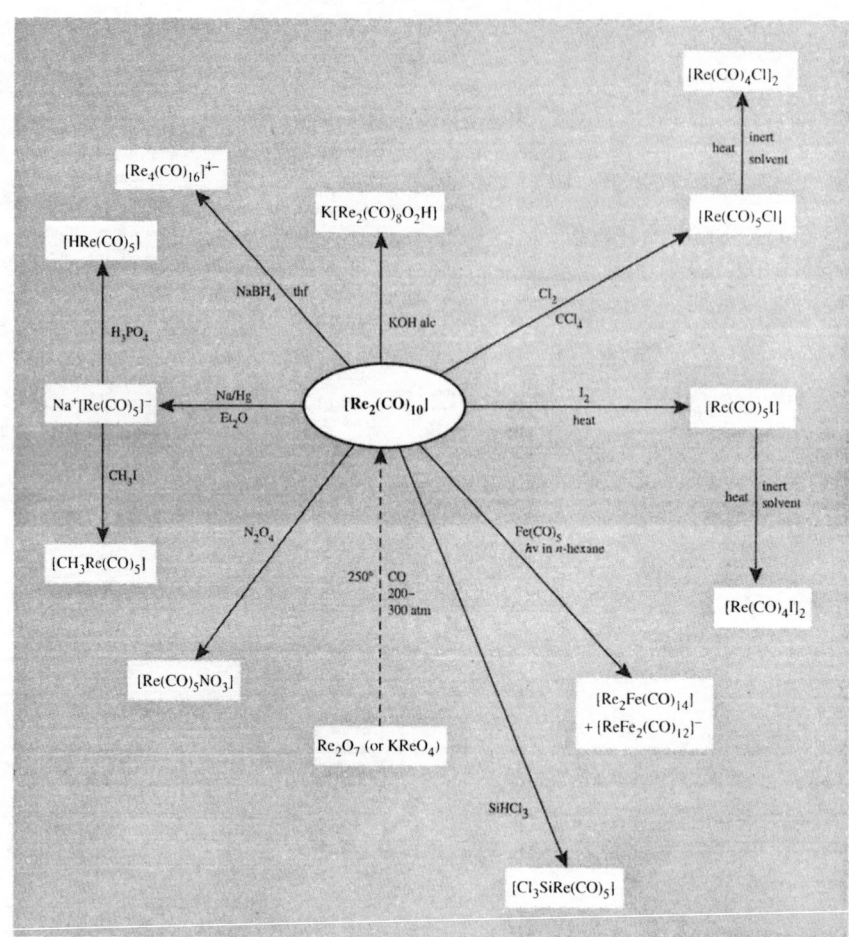

SCHEME C Some reactions of rhenium carbonyl.[32]

the carbonyl cations, and the carbonyl hydrides. Typical reactions are summarized in schemes A, B, C and D (this last on p. 1067).

Sodium amalgam reductions of $M_2(CO)_{10}$ give $Na^+[M(CO)_5]^-$ and, indeed, further reduction[33] leads to the "super reduced" species $[M(CO)_4]^{3-}$ in which the metals exhibit their lowest known formal oxidation state of -3. On the other hand, treatment of $[M(CO)_5Cl]$ with $AlCl_3$ and CO under pressure produces $[M(CO)_6]^+AlCl_4^-$ from which other salts of the cation can be obtained.

Acidification of $[M(CO)_5]^-$ produces the octahedral and monomeric, $[MH(CO)_5]$, and a number of polymeric carbonyls have been

obtained by reduction of $[M_2(CO)_{10}]$, including interesting hydrogen-bridged complexes such as $[H_3Mn_3(CO)_{12}]$ (the first transition metal cluster in which the H atoms were located), $[H_4Re_4(CO)_{12}]$ and $[H_6Re_4(CO)_{12}]^{2-}$ (Fig. 24.8). The tendency to form high nuclearity carbonyl clusters is, however, much less evident for Mn than for Re. The largest so far obtained for Mn is the heptanuclear, $[Mn_7(\mu_3\text{-}OH)_8(CO)_8]$[34] but this is exceptional, there being very few others with nuclearities higher than four.[30]

By contrast, the stronger M–M bonds characteristic of Re, help to provide a wider

[33] J. E. ELLIS, *Adv. Organometallic Chem.* **31**, 1–52 (1990).

[34] M. D. CLERK and M. J. ZAWOROTKO, *J. Chem. Soc., Chem. Commun.* 1607–8 (1991).

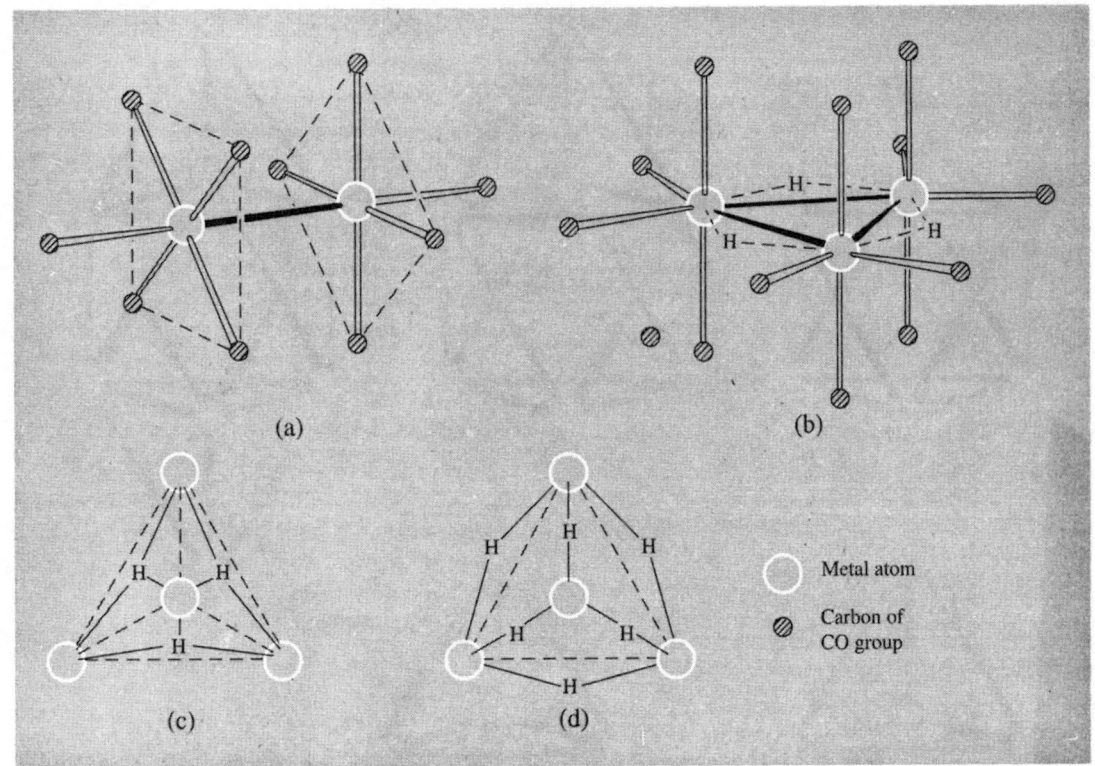

(a)

(b)

(c)

(d)

○ Metal atom

◍ Carbon of
   CO group

Figure 24.8 Some carbonyls and carbonyl hydrides of Group 7 metals. (a) [$M_2(CO)_{10}$], M = Mn, Tc. Re (Mn–Mn
293 pm, Tc–Tc 304 pm, Re–Re 302 pm). (b) [$H_3Mn_3(CO)_{12}$]. Mn–Mn 311 pm. (c) [$H_4Re_4(CO)_{12}$],
Re–Re 289.6–294.5 pm. (In this structure the 4 Re atoms lie at the corners of a tetrahedron, the faces
of which are bridged by 4 H atoms; the molecule is viewed from above one Re which obscures the
fourth H. For clarity the CO groups are not shown but 3 are attached to each Re so as to "eclipse"
the edges of the tetrahedron.) (d) [$H_6Re_4(CO)_{12}$]$^{2-}$, Re–Re 314.2–317.2 pm. (As in (c) the 4 Re
atoms lie at the corners of a tetrahedron and the CO groups have been omitted for clarity. The 3 CO
groups attached to each Re are now "staggered" with respect to the edges of the tetrahedron, whilst
the H atoms (6) are presumed to bridge these edges.)

variety[35] of which the carbon-centred clusters
[$H_2Re_6C(CO)_{18}$]$^{2-}$, [$Re_7C(CO)_{21}$]$^{3-}$ and [Re_8C-
$(CO)_{24}$]$^{2-}$ (Fig. 24.9), obtained by the pyrolytic
reduction of $Re_2(CO)_{10}$ with varying proportions
of Na in thf, may be mentioned. The H atoms in
the first of these clusters, though not positively
located, were thought to be face-capping (i.e. μ_3).
On the other hand [$Re_7HC(CO)_{21}$]$^{2-}$, which is
obtained by treating a salt of [$Re_7C(CO)_{21}$]$^{3-}$ in
acetone or thf with a strong acid such as HBF_4 or
H_2SO_4, exists in two isomeric forms and potential

energy computations suggest that both contain a
μ-H atom and differ in the cluster edge which
this bridges[36] (Fig. 24.9d and e).

When $MnCl_2$ in thf is treated with C_5H_5Na,
amber-coloured   crystals   of   manganocene,
[$Mn(C_5H_5)_2$], mp 172°, are produced. It is very
sensitive to both air and water and is a most
unusual compound. At room temperature it is
polymeric with $Mn(\eta^5\text{-}C_5H_5)$ units linked by
bridging C_5H_5 groups in a zig-zag arrangement.

35 T. J. HENLY, *Coord. Chem. Revs.* **93**, 269–95 (1989).

36 T. BERINGHELLI, G. D'ALFONSO, G. CIANI, A. SIRONI and
H. MOLINARI, *J. Chem. Soc., Dalton Trans.*, 1281–7 (1988).

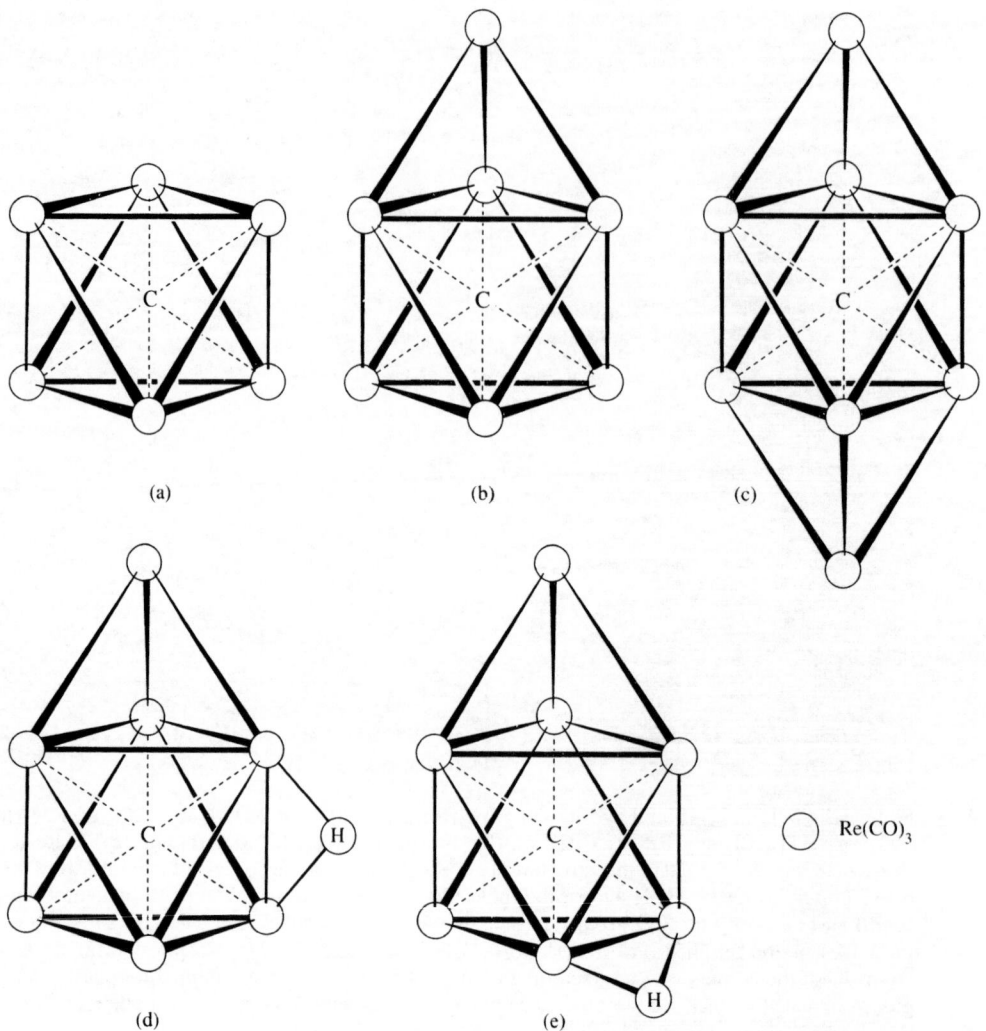

Figure 24.9 Cluster carbonyls of rhenium containing an encapsulated carbon atom. (a) Octahedral $[H_2Re_6C(CO)_{18}]^{2-}$. (b) Monocapped octahedral $[Re_7C(CO)_{21}]^{3-}$. (c) *trans*-bicapped octahedral $[Re_8C(CO)_{24}]^{2-}$. (d) and (e) isomers of $[Re_7HC(CO)_{21}]^{2-}$ differing in the position of their μ-H atom.

At about 159°C it turns pink and adopts the "sandwich" structure, expected for $[M(C_5H_5)_2]$ compounds, and this is retained in the gaseous phase and in hydrocarbon solutions. Using substituted cyclopentadienyls a variety of analagous sandwich compounds have been prepared[37] and their magnetic properties indicate that the

high-spin (5 unpaired electrons) and low-spin (1 unpaired electron) configurations are sufficiently close together to produce an equilibrium between the two in many cases (Fig. 24.10). The spin state depends on the nature and number of substituents in the C_5 ring and also on solvent and temperature. Electron donating substituents, such as methyl, enhance the covalent character of the Mn–C bonding and favour the low-spin configuration. Thus $[Mn(\eta^5\text{-}C_5Me_5)_2]$

[37] N. HEBENDANZ, F. H. KÖHLER, G. MÜLLER and J. REIDE, *J. Am. Chem. Soc.* **108**, 3281–9 (1986).

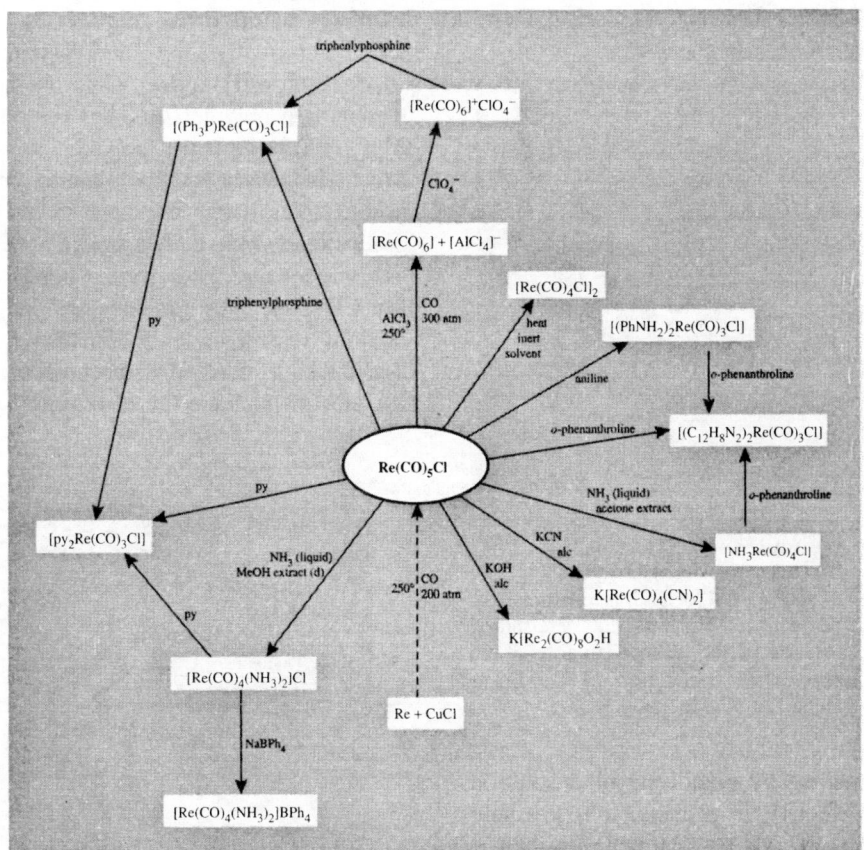

SCHEME D Some reactions of rhenium carbonyl chloride.

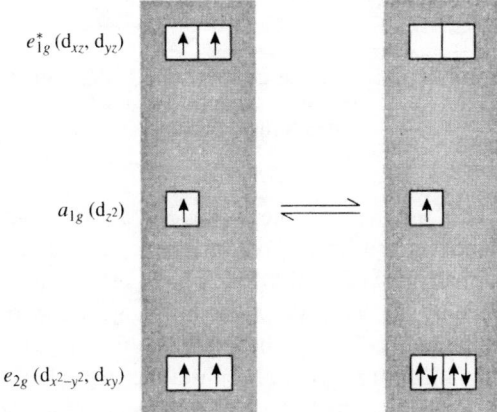

Figure 24.10 Spin equilibrium in $[Mn(\eta^5\text{-}C_5H_4\text{-}Me)_2]$: the orbitals shown here are the mainly metal-based orbitals in the centre of the MO diagram for metallocenes (see Fig. B, p. 939).

is exclusively low-spin, $[Mn(\eta^5\text{-}C_5H_4Me)_2]$ and other monoalkyl substituted ring systems exhibit spin-equilibria, while manganocene itself with a magnetic moment of 5.86 BM in hydrocarbon solvents at room temperature, is almost (but not entirely) high-spin.

Apart from the formation of $[Re(\eta^5\text{-}C_5H_5)_2]$ on N_2 matrices at 20 K, Tc and Re analogues of manganocene have not been prepared. Instead, when $TcCl_4$ or $ReCl_5$ are treated with NaC_5H_5 in thf, the diamagnetic, yellow crystalline hydrides, $[M(\eta^5\text{-}C_5H_5)_2H]$ are obtained (Fig. 24.11a). The protons on the cyclopentadienyl rings give rise to only one nmr signal, presumably because of rapid rotation of the rings about the metal-ring axis making the protons indistinguishable. As with Mn, however, methyl substitution has a stabilizing effect and purple $[Re(\eta^5\text{-}C_5Me_5)_2]$

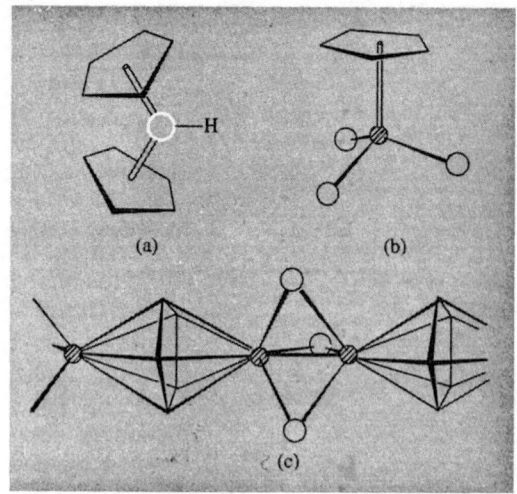

Figure 24.11 (a) $[M(\eta^5\text{-}C_5H_5)_2H]$ (M = Tc, Re) (b) $[Re(\eta^5\text{-}C_5Me_4Et)O_3]$ (The structure of $[Re(\eta^5\text{-}C_5Me_5)O_3]$ is presumed to be identical but was not determined because of the lack of suitable single crystals[29]. (c) Section of the linear chain $[Tc_2(C_5Me_5)O_3]_n$.

is readily obtained by photolysis of a solution of $[Re(\eta^5\text{-}C_5Me_5)_2H]$ in pentane. It is low-spin at low temperatures but has a minor contribution from the high-spin configuration at room temperature [38]

Pentamethylcyclopentadienyl compounds also provide a convenient route into high-valent organorhenium chemistry.[29] Oxidation of $[Re^I(\eta^5\text{-}C_5Me_5)(CO)_3]$ by H_2O_2 in a two-phase water–benzene system gives high yields of lemon yellow $[Re(\eta^5\text{-}C_5Me_5)O_3]$ (Fig. 24.11b) which, being stable in air even up to 140°C, demonstrates the remarkable stabilizing effect of oxygen on Re in high oxidation states. The same procedure[39] in the case of technetium raises its oxidation state only to 3.5, forming yellow $[Tc_2(C_5Me_5)O_3]_n$ (Fig. 24.11c) in which linear chains of Tc atoms are bridged alternately by $(\mu\text{-}C_5Me_5)$ and $(\mu\text{-}O)_3$

[38] J. A. BANDY, F. G. N. CLOKE, G. COOPER, J. P. DAY, R. B. GIRLING, R. G. GRAHAM, J. C. GREEN, R. GRINTER and R. N. PERUTZ, *J. Am. Chem. Soc.* **110**, 5039–50 (1988).

[39] B. KANELLAKOPULOS, B. NUBER, K. RAPTIS and M. L. ZIE-GLER, *Angew. Chem. Int. Edn. Engl.* **28**, 1055 (1989).

with Tc–Tc distances respectively of 407.7(4) and the unusually short 186.7(4) pm.

Manganese(II) forms alkyls with a distinct tendency to polymerize. Thus the bright orange $Mn(CH_2SiMe_3)_2$ is a polymer in which each Mn attains tetrahedral coordination, being doubly bridged to each adjacent metal by two CH_2SiMe_3 groups (each Mn–C–Mn bridge is best regarded as a three-centre, two-electron bond). Red-brown $Mn(CH_2CMe_3)_2$ is similarly bridged but, for no obvious reason, is only tetrameric, a terminal ligand being attached to each of the two outer Mn atoms which are therefore only 3-coordinate.

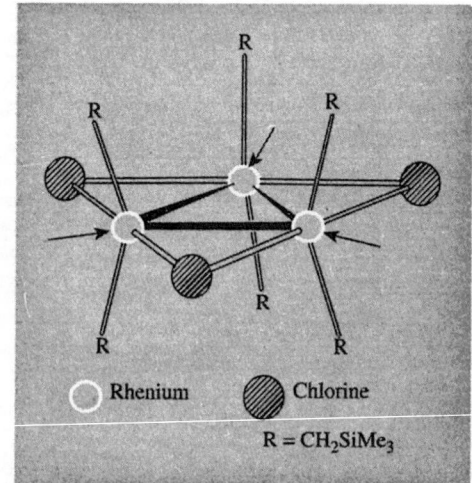

Figure 24.12 Rhenium clusters: $[Re_3Cl_3R_6]$: arrows indicate vacant coordination sites where further ligands can be attached.

The simplest of the σ-bonded Re–C compounds is the green, paramagnetic, crystalline, thermally unstable $ReMe_6$, which, after WMe_6, was only the second hexamethyl transition metal compound to be synthesized (1976). It reacts with LiMe to give the unstable, pyrophoric, $Li_2[ReMe_8]$, which has a square-antiprismatic structure, and incorporation of oxygen into the coordination sphere greatly increases the stability, witness $Re^{VI}OMe_4$, which is thermally stable up to 200°C, and $Re^{VII}O_3Me$, which is stable in air. The interaction of $[ReCl_4(thf)_2]$

with (o-tolyl)MgBr in thf yields the dark red, paramagnetic tetraaryl, $[Re(2\text{-}MeC_6H_4)_4]$[40] This highly air-sensitive compound, if treated with PMe_2R (R = Me, Ph), is converted into the thermally stable and rather inert benzyne, $[Re(\eta^2\text{-}C_6H_3Me)(PMe_2R)_2(2\text{-}MeC_6H_4)_2]$[41].

A whole series of alkyl cluster compounds $Re_3Cl_3R_6$ has been prepared by reacting Re_3Cl_9 with a large excess of RMgCl in

thf. The blue diamagnetic trimethylsilylmethyl complex (Fig. 24.12) is best known. A red isomer has been obtained in which the Cl bridges have exchanged positions with three of the terminal alkyls, and it is also possible to replace the Cl bridges by CH_3 to produce, $[Re_3(\mu\text{-}CH_3)_3(CH_2SiMe_3)_6]$. Adducts, $[Re_3Cl_3(CH_2SiMe_3)_6L_3]$ (L = CO, H_2O) can be obtained, but phosphines tend to cause cleavage of the Re_3 ring instead of forming adducts.

[40] P. Savage, G. Wilkinson, M. Motevalli and M. B. Hursthouse, *J. Chem. Soc., Dalton Trans.*, 669–73 (1988).

[41] J. Arnold, G. Wilkinson, B. Hussain and M. B. Hursthouse *J. Chem. Soc., Chem. Commun.* 704–5 (1988).

25

Iron, Ruthenium and Osmium

25.1 Introduction

The nine elements, Fe, Ru, Os; Co, Rh, Ir; Ni, Pd and Pt, together formed Group VIII of Mendeleev's periodic table. They will be treated here, like the other transition elements, in "vertical" triads, but because of the marked "horizontal" similarities it is not uncommon for Fe, Co and Ni to be distinguished from the other six elements (known collectively as the "platinum" metals) and the two sets of elements considered separately.

The triad Fe, Ru and Os is dominated, as indeed is the whole block of transition elements, by the immense importance of iron. This element has been known since prehistoric times and no other metal has played a more important role in man's material progress. Iron beads dating from around 4000 BC were no doubt of meteoric origin, and later samples, produced by reducing iron ore with charcoal, were not cast because adequate temperatures were not attainable without the use of some form of bellows. Instead, the spongy material produced by low-temperature reduction would have had to be shaped by prolonged hammering. It seems that iron was first smelted by the Hittites in Asia

Minor sometime in the third millennium BC, but the value of the process was so great that its secret was carefully guarded and it was only with the eventual fall of the Hittite empire around 1200 BC that the knowledge was dispersed and the "Iron Age" began.[1] In more recent times the introduction of coke as the reductant had far-reaching effects, and was one of the major factors in the initiation of the Industrial Revolution. The name "iron" is Anglo-Saxon in origin (iren, cf. German Eisen). The symbol Fe and words such as "ferrous" derive from the Latin ferrum, iron.

Biologically, iron plays crucial roles in the transport and storage of oxygen and also in electron transport, and it is safe to say that, with only a few possible exceptions in the bacterial world, there would be no life without iron. Again, within the last forty years or so, the already rich organometallic chemistry of iron has been enormously expanded, and work in the whole field given an added impetus by the discovery and characterization of ferrocene.[2]

---

[1] V. G. CHILDE, *What Happened in History*, pp. 182–5, Penguin Books, London, 1942.

[2] J. S. THAYER, *Adv. Organometallic Chem.* **13**, 1–49 (1975).

Ruthenium and osmium, though interesting and useful, are in no way comparable with iron and are relative newcomers. They were discovered independently in the residues left after crude platinum had been dissolved in aqua regia; ruthenium in 1844 from ores from the Urals by K. Klaus[2a] who named it after *Ruthenia*, the Latin name for Russia; and osmium in 1803 by S. Tennant who named it from the Greek word for odour (ὀσμή, *osme*) because of the characteristic and pungent smell of the volatile oxide, OsO_4. (CAUTION: OsO_4 is very toxic.)

25.2 The Elements Iron, Ruthenium and Osmium

25.2.1 Terrestrial abundance and distribution

Ruthenium and osmium are generally found in the metallic state along with the other "platinum" metals and the "coinage" metals. The major source of the platinum metals are the nickel–copper sulfide ores found in South Africa and Sudbury (Canada), and in the river sands of the Urals in Russia. They are rare elements, ruthenium particularly so, their estimated abundances in the earth's crustal rocks being but 0.0001 (Ru) and 0.005 (Os) ppm. However, as in Group 7, there is a marked contrast between the abundances of the two heavier elements and that of the first.

The nuclei of iron are especially stable, giving it a comparatively high cosmic abundance (Chap. 1, p. 11), and it is thought to be the main constituent of the earth's core (which has a radius of approximately 3500 km, i.e. 2150 miles) as well as being the major component of "siderite" meteorites. About 0.5% of the lunar soil is now known to be metallic iron and, since on average this soil is 10 m deep, there must be $\sim 10^{12}$ tonnes of iron on the moon's surface. In the earth's crustal rocks (6.2%, i.e. 62 000 ppm) it is the fourth most abundant element (after oxygen, silicon and aluminium) and the second most abundant metal. It is also widely distributed,

as oxides and carbonates, of which the chief ones are: haematite (Fe_2O_3), magnetite (Fe_3O_4), limonite ($\sim 2Fe_2O_3.3H_2O$) and siderite ($FeCO_3$). Iron pyrite (FeS_2) is also common but is not used as a source of iron because of the difficulty in eliminating the sulfur. The distribution of iron has been considerably influenced by weathering. Leaching from sulfide and silicate deposits occurs readily as $FeSO_4$ and $Fe(HCO_3)_2$ respectively. In solution, these are quickly oxidized, and even mildly alkaline conditions cause the precipitation of iron(III) oxide. Because of their availability, production of iron ores can be confined to those of the highest grade in gigantic operations.

25.2.2 Preparation and uses of the elements

Pure iron, when needed, is produced on a relatively small scale by the reduction of the pure oxide or hydroxide with hydrogen, or by the carbonyl process in which iron is heated with carbon monoxide under pressure and the $Fe(CO)_5$ so formed decomposed at 250°C to give the powdered metal. However, it is not in the pure state but in the form of an enormous variety of steels that iron finds its most widespread uses, the world's annual production being over 700 million tonnes.

The first stage in the conversion of iron ore to steel is the *blast furnace* (see Panel), which accounts for the largest tonnage of any metal produced by man. In it the iron ore is reduced by coke,[†] while limestone removes any sand or clay as a slag. The molten iron is run off to be cast into moulds of the required shape or into ingots ("pigs") for further processing — hence the names "cast-iron" or "pig-iron". This is an

---

[†] The actual reducing agent is, in the main, CO. Direct reduction of the ore using H_2, CO or CO + H_2 gas (produced from natural gas or fossil fuels) now accounts for about 4% of the world's total production of iron. With a much lower operating temperature than that of the blast furnace, reduction is confined to the ore, producing a "sponge" iron and leaving the gangue relatively unchanged. This offers a potential economy in fuel providing that the quantity and composition of the gangue do not adversely affect the subsequent conversion to steel — which is most commonly by the electric arc furnace.

[2a] V. N. PITCHKOV, *Platinum Metals Rev.* **40**, 181–8 (1996).

Iron[3,4] and Steel[5]

About 1773, in order to overcome a shortage of timber for the production of charcoal, Abraham Darby developed a process for producing carbon (coke) from coal and used this instead of charcoal in his blast furnace at Coalbrookdale in Shropshire. The impact was dramatic. It so cheapened and increased the scale of ironmaking that in the succeeding decades Shropshire iron was used to produce for the first time: iron cylinders for steam-engines, iron rails, iron boats and ships, iron aqueducts, and iron-framed buildings. The iron bridge erected nearby over the River Severn in 1779, gave its name to the small town which grew around it and still stands, a monument to the process which "opened up" the iron industry to the Industrial Revolution.

The blast furnace (Fig. A, opposite) remains the basis of ironmaking though the scale, if not the principle, has changed considerably since the eighteenth century: the largest modern blast furnaces have hearths 14 m in diameter and produce up to 10 000 tonnes of iron daily.

The furnace is charged with a mixture of the ore (usually haematite), coke and limestone, then a blast of hot air, or air with fuel oil, is blown in at the bottom. The coke burns and such intense heat is generated that temperatures approaching 2000°C are reached near the base of the furnace and perhaps 200°C at the top. The net result is that the ore is reduced to iron, and silicaceous gangue forms a slag (mainly $CaSiO_3$) with the limestone:

$$2Fe_2O_3 + 3C \longrightarrow 4Fe + 3CO_2$$

$$SiO_2 + CaCO_3 \longrightarrow CaSiO_3 + CO_2$$

The molten iron, and the molten slag which floats on the iron, collect at the bottom of the furnace and are tapped off separately. As the charge moves down, the furnace is recharged at the top, making the process continuous. Of course the actual reactions taking place are far more numerous than this and only the more important ones are summarized in Fig. A. The details are exceedingly complex and still not fully understood. At least part of the reason for this complexity is the rapidity with which the blast passes through the furnace ($\sim$10 s) which does not allow the gas-solid reactions to reach equilibrium. The main reduction occurs near the top, as the hot rising gases meet the descending charge. Here too the limestone is converted to CaO. Reduction to the metal is completed at somewhat higher temperatures, after which fusion occurs and the iron takes up Si and P in addition to C. The deleterious uptake of S is considerably reduced if manganese is present, because of the formation of MnS which passes into the slag. For this the slag must be adequately fluid and to this end the ratio of base (CaO):acid (SiO_2, Al_2O_3) is maintained by the addition, if necessary, of gravel (SiO_2). The slag is subsequently used as a building material (breeze blocks, wall insulation) and in the manufacture of some types of cement.

Traditionally, pig-iron was converted to wrought-iron by the "puddling" process in which the molten iron was manually mixed with haematite and excess carbon and other impurities burnt out. Some wrought-iron was then converted to steel by essentially small-scale and expensive methods, such as the Cementation process (prolonged heating of wrought-iron bars with charcoal) and the crucible process (fusion of wrought-iron with the correct amount of charcoal). In the mid-nineteenth century, production was enormously increased by the introduction of the *Bessemer process* in which the carbon content of molten pig-iron in a "converter" was lowered by blasting compressed air through it. The converter was lined with silica or limestone in order to form a molten slag with the basic or acidic impurities present in the pig-iron. Air and appropriate linings were also employed in the *Open-hearth process* which allowed better control of the steel's composition, but both processes have now been supplanted by the *Basic oxygen* and *Electric arc* processes.

Basic oxygen process (BOP). This process, of which there are several modifications, originated in Austria in 1952, and because of its greater speed has since become by far the most common means of producing steel. A jet of pure oxygen is blown through a retractable steel "lance" into, or over the surface of, the molten pig-iron which is contained in a basic-lined furnace. Impurities form a slag which is usually removed by tilting the converter.

Electric arc process. Patented by Siemens in 1878, this uses an electric current through the metal (direct-arc), or an arc just above the metal (indirect-arc), as a means of heating. It is widely used in the manufacture of alloy- and other high-quality steels.

World production of iron ore in 1995 was 1020 million tonnes (Mt) (China 25%, Brazil 18%, former USSR 14%, Australia 12.9%, India and USA 6% each). In the same year world production of raw steel was 748 Mt (Western Europe 22.7%, N. America 16.2%, Japan 13.6%, China 12.4%, former USSR 10.6% and S. America 4.7%).

---

[3] *Kirk–Othmer Encyclopedia of Chemical Technology*, 4th edn., Vol. 14, pp. 829–72, Interscience, New York, 1995.

[4] *Ullmann's Encyclopedia of Industrial Chemistry*, 5th edn., Vol. A21, pp. 461–590, VCH, Weinheim, 1989.

[5] Ref. 4, Vol. A25, pp. 63–307, 1994.

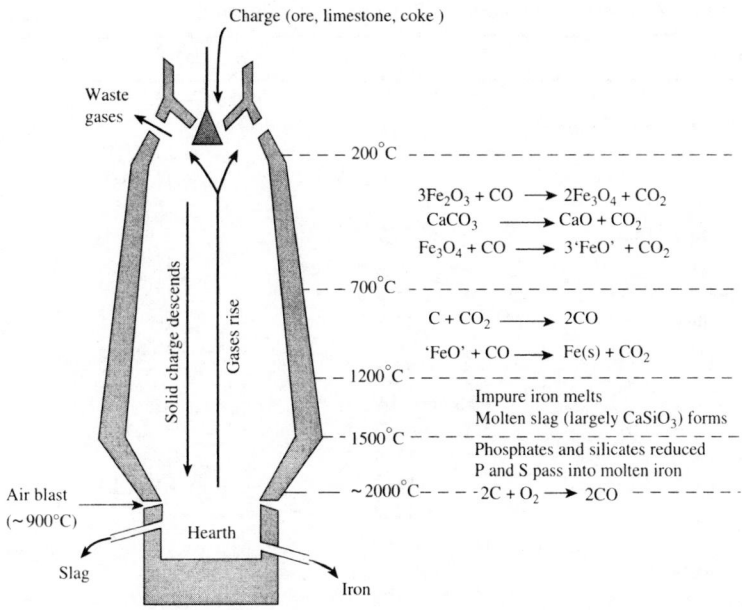

Figure A   Blast furnace (diagrammatic).

impure form of iron, containing about 4% of carbon along with variable amounts of Si, Mn, P and S. It is hard but notoriously brittle. To eradicate this disadvantage the non-metallic impurities must be removed. This can be done by oxidizing them with haematite in the now obsolete "puddling process", producing the much purer "wrought-iron", which is tough and malleable and ideal for mechanical working. Nowadays, however, the bulk of pig-iron is converted into steel containing 0.5–1.5% C but very little S or P. The oxidation in this case is most commonly effected in one of a number of related processes by pure oxygen (basic oxygen process, or BOP), but open-hearth and electric arc furnaces are also used, while the Bessemer Converter (see Panel) was of great historical importance. This "mild steel" is cheaper than wrought-iron and stronger and more workable than cast-iron; it also has the advantage over both that it can be hardened by heating to redness and then cooling rapidly (quenching) in water or mineral oil, and "tempered" by re-heating to 200–300°C and cooling more slowly. The hardness, resilience and ductility can be controlled by varying the temperature and the

rate of cooling as well as the precise composition of the steel (see below). Alloy steels, with their enormous variety of physical properties, are prepared by the addition of the appropriate alloying metal or metals.

All the platinum group metals are isolated from "platinum concentrates" which are commonly obtained either from "anode slimes" in the electrolytic refining of nickel and copper, or as "converter matte" from the smelting of sulfide ores.[6] The details of the procedure used differ from location to location and depend on the composition of the concentrate. Classical methods of separation, relying on selective precipitation, are still widely employed but solvent extraction and ion exchange techniques are increasingly being introduced to effect the primary separations (p. 1147).

Ru and Os are usually removed by distillation of their tetroxides immediately after the initial dissolution with hydrochloric acid and chlorine. Collection of the tetroxides in alcoholic NaOH and aqueous HCl respectively yields $OsO_2(NH_3)_4$-Cl_2 and $(NH_4)_3RuCl_6$ from which the metals are

---

[6] Ref. 4, Vol. A21, pp. 86–105, 1992.

Table 25.1   Some properties of the elements iron, ruthenium and osmium

Property		Fe	Ru	Os
Atomic number		26	44	76
Number of naturally occurring isotopes		4	7	7
Atomic weight		55.845(2)	101.07(2)	190.23(3)
Electronic configuration		$[Ar]3d^64s^2$	$[Kr]4d^75s^1$	$[Xe]4f^{14}5d^66s^2$
Electronegativity		1.8	2.2	2.2
Metal radius (12-coordinate)/pm		126	134	135
Effective ionic radius/pm	VIII	—	$36^{(a)}$	$39^{(a)}$
(4-coordinate if marked[a],	VII	—	$38^{(a)}$	52.5
otherwise 6-coordinate)	VI	$25^{(a)}$	—	54.5
	V	—	56.5	57.5
	IV	58.5	62	63
	III	55 (ls), 64.5 (hs)	68	—
	II	61 (ls), 78 (hs)	—	—
MP/°C		1535	2282($\pm$20)	3045($\pm$30)
BP/°C		2750	extrap 4050($\pm$100)	extrap 5025($\pm$100)
ΔH_{fus}/kJ mol^{-1}		13.8	~25.5	31.7
ΔH_{vap}/kJ mol^{-1}		340($\pm$13)	—	738
ΔH_f (monatomic gas)/kJ mol^{-1}		398($\pm$17)	640	791($\pm$13)
Density (20°C)/g cm^{-3}		7.874	12.37	22.59
Electrical resistivity (20°C)/μohm cm		9.71	6.71	8.12

[a]Refers to coordination number 4. ls = low spin, hs = high spin.

obtained by ignition in H_2. The metals are in the form of powder or sponge and are usually consolidated by powder-metallurgical techniques. Major uses of ruthenium are as a coating for titanium anodes in the electrolytic production of Cl_2 and, more recently, as a catalyst in the production of ammonia (p. 421). Osmium is used in dentistry as a hardening agent in gold alloys. However, Ru and Os, along with Ir, are regarded as the minor platinum metals, being obtained largely as byproducts in the production of Pt, Pd and Rh, and their annual world production is only of the order of tonnes. (Weights of Ru and Os, as of most precious metals, are generally quoted in troy ounces: 1 troy ounce = 1.097 avoirdupois ounce = 31.103 g.)

25.2.3 Properties of the elements

Table 25.1 summarizes some of the important properties of Fe, Ru and Os. The two heavier elements in particular have several naturally occurring isotopes, and difficulties in obtaining calibrated measurements of their relative abundances limit the precision with which their atomic weights can be determined. Osmium is the densest of all elements, surpassing iridium by the tiniest of margins.[7]

All three elements are lustrous and silvery in colour. Iron when pure is fairly soft and readily worked, but ruthenium and osmium are less tractable in this respect. The structures of the solids are typically metallic, being hcp for the two heavier elements and bcc for iron at room temperature (α-iron). However, the behaviour of iron is complicated by the existence of a fcc form (γ-iron) at higher temperatures (above 910°), reverting to bcc again (δ-iron) at about 1390°, some 145° below its mp. Technologically, the carbon content is crucial, as can be seen from the Fe/C phase diagram (Fig. 25.1), which also throws light on the hardening and tempering

---

[7] Densities are calculated from crystallographic data and depend on a knowledge of the wavelength of the X-rays, Avogadro's constant and the atomic weight of the element. Using the best available data the densities of Os and Ir are calculated to be 22.587 ± 0.009 and 22.562 ± 0.009 g cm^{-3} respectively at 20°C. J. W. ARBLASTER, *Platinum Metals Rev.* **33**, 14–16 (1989). *ibid.*, **39**, 164 (1995).

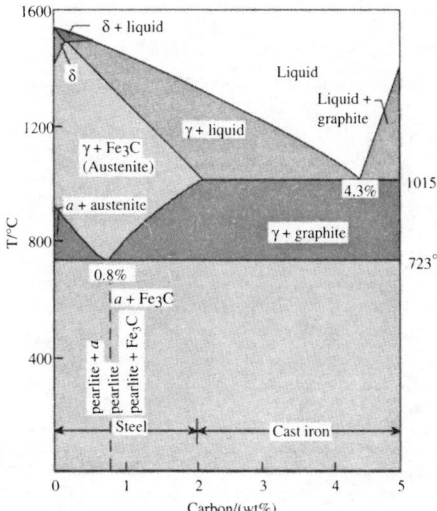

Figure 25.1 The iron-carbon phase diagram for low concentrations of carbon.

processes already referred to. The lowering of the mp from 1535° to 1015°C when the C content reaches 4.3%, facilitates the fusion of iron in the blast furnace, and the lower solubility of Fe_3C ("cementite") in α-iron as compared to δ- and γ-iron leads to the possibility of producing metastable forms by varying the rate of cooling of hot steels. At elevated temperatures a solid solution of Fe_3C in γ-iron, known as "austenite", prevails. If 0.8% C is present, slow cooling below 723°C causes Fe_3C to separate forming alternate layers with the α-iron. Because of its appearance when polished, this is known as "pearlite" and is rather soft and malleable. If, however, the cooling is rapid (quenching) the separation is suppressed and the extremely hard and brittle "martensite" is produced. Reheating to an intermediate temperature tempers the steel by modifying the proportions of hard and malleable forms. If the C content of the steel is below 0.8% then slow cooling gives a mixture of pearlite and α-iron and, if higher than 0.8% a mixture of pearlite and Fe_3C. Varying the proportion of carbon in the steel thereby further extends the range of physical properties which can be attained by appropriate heat treatment.

The magnetic properties of iron are also dependent on purity and heat treatment. Up to 768°C

(the Curie point) pure iron is ferromagnetic as a result of extensive magnetic interactions between unpaired electrons on adjacent atoms, which cause the electron spins to be aligned in the same direction, so producing exceedingly high magnetic susceptibilities and the characteristic ferromagnetic properties of "saturation" and "hysteresis". The existence of unpaired electrons on the individual atoms, as opposed to being delocalized in bands permeating the lattice, can be rationalized at least partly by supposing that in the bcc lattice the metal d_{z^2} and $d_{x^2-y^2}$ orbitals, which are not directed towards nearest neighbours, are therefore nonbonding and so can retain 2 unpaired electrons on the atom. On the other hand, electrons in the remaining three d orbitals participate in the formation of a conduction band of predominantly paired electrons. At temperatures above the Curie temperature, thermal energy overcomes the interaction between the electrons localized on individual atoms; their mutual alignment is broken, and normal paramagnetic behaviour ensues. This is sometimes referred to as β-iron (768–910°) though the crystal structure remains bcc as in ferromagnetic α-iron. For the construction of permanent magnets, cobalt steels are particularly useful, whereas for the "soft" irons used in electric motors and transformer cores (where the magnetization undergoes rapid reversal) silicon steels are preferred.

The mps and bps and enthalpies of atomization indicate that the $(n\text{-}1)d$ electrons are contributing to metal bonding less than in earlier groups although, possibly due to an enhanced tendency for metals with a d^5 configuration to resist delocalization of their d electrons, Mn and to a lesser extent Tc occupy "anomalous" positions so that for Fe and Ru the values of these quantities are actually higher than for the elements immediately preceding them. In the third transition series Re appears to be "well-behaved" and the changes from W $\rightarrow$ Re $\rightarrow$ Os are consequently smooth.

25.2.4 Chemical reactivity and trends

As expected, contrasts between the first element and the two heavier congeners are noticeable,

Rusting of Iron[8]

The economic importance of rusting can scarcely be overestimated. Although precision is impossible, it is likely that the cost of corrosion is over 1% of the world's economy.

Rusting of iron consists of the formation of hydrated oxide. $Fe(OH)_3$ or $FeO(OH)$, and is evidently an electrochemical process which requires the presence of water, oxygen and an electrolyte — in the absence of any one of these rusting does not occur to any significant extent. In air, a relative humidity of over 50% provides the necessary amount of water. The mechanism is complex[9] and will depend in detail on the prevailing conditions, but may be summarized as:

$$\text{the cathodic reduction: } 3O_2 + 6H_2O + 12e^- \longrightarrow 12(OH)^-$$

$$\text{and the anodic oxidations: } 4Fe \longrightarrow 4Fe^{2+} + 8e^-$$

$$\text{and } 4Fe^{2+} \longrightarrow 4Fe^{3+} + 4e^-$$

$$\text{i.e. overall: } 4Fe + 3O_2 + 6H_2O \longrightarrow \underbrace{4Fe^{3+} + 12(OH)^-}$$

$$4Fe(OH)_3 \text{ or } 4FeO(OH) + 4H_2O$$

The presence of the electrolyte is required to provide a pathway for the current and, in urban areas, this is commonly iron(II) sulfate formed as a result of attack by atmospheric SO_2 but, in seaside areas, airborne particles of salt are important. Because of its electrochemical nature, rusting may continue for long periods at a more or less constant rate, in contrast to the formation of an anhydrous oxide coating which under dry conditions slows down rapidly as the coating thickens.

The anodic oxidation of the iron is usually localized in surface pits and crevices which allow the formation of adherent rust over the remaining surface area. Eventually the lateral extension of the anodic area undermines the rust to produce loose flakes. Moreover, once an adherent film of rust has formed, simply painting over gives but poor protection. This is due to the presence of electrolytes such as iron(II) sulfate in the film so that painting merely seals in the ingredients for anodic oxidation. It then only requires the exposure of some other portion of the surface, where cathodic reduction can take place, for rusting beneath the paint to occur.

The protection of iron and steel against rusting takes many forms, including: simple covering with paint; coating with another metal such as zinc (galvanizing) or tin; treating with "inhibitors" such as chromate(VI) or (in the presence of air) phosphate or hydroxide, all of which produce a coherent protective film of Fe_2O_3. Another method uses sacrificial anodes, most usually Mg or Zn which, being higher than Fe in the electrochemical series, are attacked preferentially. In fact, the Zn coating on galvanized iron is actually a sacrificial anode.

both in the reactivity of the elements and in their chemistry. Iron is much the most reactive metal of the triad, being pyrophoric if finely divided and dissolving readily in dilute acids to give Fe^{II} salts; however, it is rendered passive by oxidizing acids such as concentrated nitric and chromic, due to the formation of an impervious oxide film which protects it from further reaction but which is immediately removed by acids such as hydrochloric. Ruthenium and osmium, on the other hand, are virtually unaffected by non-oxidizing acids, or even aqua regia. Iron also reacts fairly easily with most non-metals whereas ruthenium and osmium do so only with difficulty at high temperatures, except in the case of

oxidizing agents such as F_2 and Cl_2. Indeed, it is with oxidizing agents generally that Ru and Os metals are most reactive. Thus Os is converted to OsO_4 by conc nitric acid and both metals can be dissolved in molten alkali in the presence of air or, better still, in oxidizing flux such as Na_2O_2 or $KClO_3$ to give the ruthenates and osmates $[RuO_4]^{2-}$ and $[OsO_2(OH)_4]^{2-}$ respectively. If the aqueous extracts from these fusions are treated with Cl_2 and heated, the tetroxides distil off, providing convenient preparative starting materials as well as the means of recovering the elements.

Ruthenium and Os are stable to atmospheric attack though if Os is very finely divided it gives off the characteristic smell of OsO_4. By contrast, iron is subject to corrosion in the form of rusting which, because of its great economic importance, has received much attention (see Panel above).

[8] U. R. EVANS, *An Introduction to Metallic Corrosion*, Arnold, London, 3rd edn, 1981, 320 pp.

[9] T. E. GRAEDEL and R. P. FRANKENTHAL, *J. Electrochem. Soc.* **137**, 2385–94 (1990).

Table 25.2 Standard reduction potentials for iron, ruthenium and osmium in acidic aqueous solution[a]

Half reaction	$E°/V$	Volt-equivalent
$Fe^{2+} + 2e^- \rightleftharpoons Fe$	−0.447	−0.894
$Fe^{3+} + 3e^- \rightleftharpoons Fe$	−0.037	−0.111
$(FeO_4)^{2-} + 8H^+ + 3e^- \rightleftharpoons Fe^{3+} + 4H_2O$	2.20	6.49
$Ru^{2+} + 2e^- \rightleftharpoons Ru$	0.455	0.910
$Ru^{3+} + e^- \rightleftharpoons Ru^{2+}$	0.249	1.159
$RuO_2 + 4H^+ + 2e^- \rightleftharpoons Ru^{2+} + 2H_2O$	1.120	3.150
$(RuO_4)^{2-} + 8H^+ + 4e^- \rightleftharpoons Ru^{2+} + 4H_2O$	1.563	7.162
$(RuO_4)^- + 8H^+ + 5e^- \rightleftharpoons Ru^{2+} + 4H_2O$	1.368	7.750
$RuO_4 + 4H^+ + 4e^- \rightleftharpoons RuO_2 + 2H_2O$	1.387	8.698
$OsO_2 + 4H^+ + 4e^- \rightleftharpoons Os + 2H_2O$	0.687	2.748
$(OsO_4)^{2-} + 8H^+ + 6e^- \rightleftharpoons Os + 4H_2O$	0.994	5.964
$OsO_4 + 8H^+ + 8e^- \rightleftharpoons Os + 4H_2O$	0.85	6.80

[a]See also Table A (p. 1093) and Table 25.8 (p. 1101).

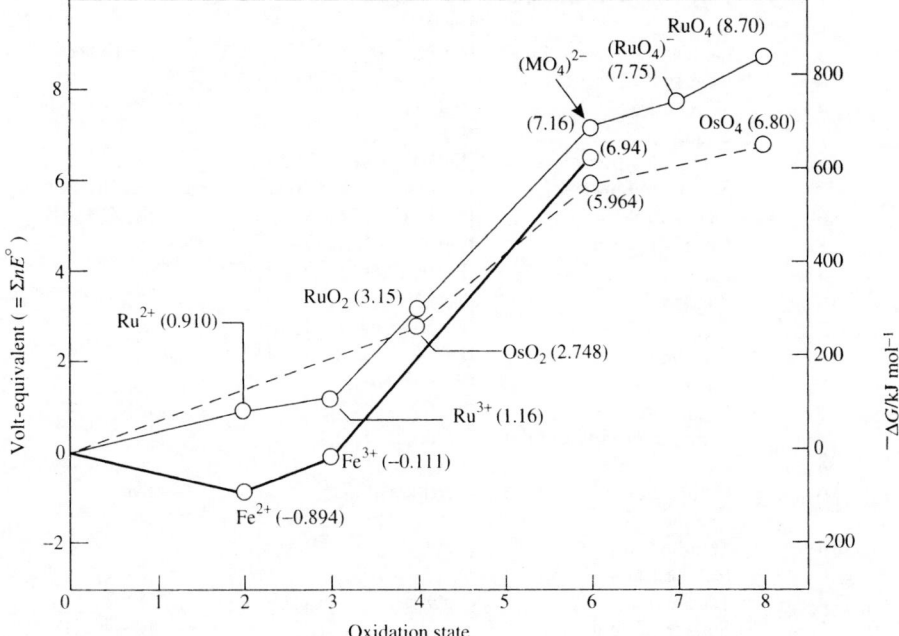

Figure 25.2 Plot of volt-equivalent against oxidation state for Fe, Ru and Os in acidic aqueous solution.

In moving across the transition series, iron is the first element which fails to attain its group oxidation state (+8). The highest oxidation state known (so far) is +6 in $[FeO_4]^{2-}$ and even this is extremely easily reduced. On the other hand, ruthenium and osmium do attain the group oxidation state of +8, though they are the last elements to do so in the second and third transition series, and this is consequently the highest oxidation state for any element (see also

Xe^{VIII}, p. 894). Ruthenium(VIII) is significantly less stable than Os^{VIII} and it is clear that the second- and third-row elements, though similar, are by no means as alike as for earlier element-pairs in the transition series. The same gradation within the triad is well illustrated by the reactions of the metals with oxygen. All react on heating, but their products are, respectively, Fe_2O_3 and Fe_3O_4, $Ru^{IV}O_2$ and $Os^{VIII}O_4$ In general terms it can be said that the most common oxidation states

for the three elements are +2 and +3 for Fe, +3 for Ru, and +4 for Os. And, while Fe (and to a lesser extent Ru) has an extensive aqueous cationic chemistry in its lower oxidation states, Os has none. Table 25.2 and Fig. 25.2 summarize the relative stabilities of the various oxidation states in acidic aqueous solution.

A selection of representative examples of compounds of the three elements is given in Table 25.3. As in the preceding group there is

Table 25.3   Oxidation states and stereochemistries of some compounds of iron, ruthenium and osmium

Oxidation state	Coordination number	Stereochemistry	Fe	Ru, Os
-2 (d^{10})	4	Tetrahedral	$[Fe(CO)_4]^{2-}$	$[M(CO)_4]^{2-}$
-1 (d^9)	5	Trigonal bipyramidal	$[Fe_2(CO)_8]^{2-}$	
0 (d^8)	5	Trigonal bipyramidal	$[Fe(CO)_5]$	$[M(CO)_5](?)$
	6	Octahedral (D_3)	$[Fe(bipy)_3]$	
	7	Face-capped octahedral	$[Fe_2(CO)_9]$	
1 (d^7)	2	Linear	$[FeO_2]^{3-}$	
	6	Octahedral	$[Fe(NO)(H_2O)_5]^{2+}$	$[Os(NH_3)_6]^+$
	9	(See Fig. 25.15(a))	$[\{Fe(\eta^5\text{-}C_5H_5)(CO)(\mu\text{-}CO)\}_2]$	
2 (d^6)	4	Tetrahedral	$[FeCl_4]^{2-}$	$[RuH\{N(SiMe_3)_2\}(PPh_3)_2]$
		Square planar	$BaFeSi_4O_{10}$	
	5	Trigonal bipyramidal	$[FeBr\{N(C_2H_4NMe_2)_3\}]^+$	
		Square pyramidal	$[Fe(OAsMe_3)_4(ClO_4)]^+$	$[RuCl_2(PPh_3)_3]$
	6	Octahedral	$[Fe(H_2O)_6]^{2+}$	$[M(CN)_6]^{4-}$
	7	(p. 174)	$[Fe(\eta^4\text{-}B_4H_8)(CO)_3]$	
	8	(See Fig. 25.15c)	$[Fe(\eta^1\text{-}C_5H_5)(\eta^5\text{-}C_5H_5)(CO)_2]$	
	10	Sandwich	$[Fe(\eta^5\text{-}C_5H_5)_2]$	$[M(\eta^5\text{-}C_5H_5)_2]$
3 (d^5)	3	Planar	$[Fe\{N(SiMe_3)_2\}_3]$	
	4	Tetrahedral	$[FeCl_4]^-$	
	5	Square pyramidal	$[Fe(acac)_2Cl]$	
	6	Octahedral	$[Fe(CN)_6]^{3-}$	$[MCl_6]^{3-}$
	7	Pentagonal bipyramidal	$[Fe(edta)(H_2O)]^-$	
	8	Dodecahedral	$[Fe(NO_3)_4]^-$	
4 (d^4)	6	Octahedral	$[Fe(diars)_2Cl_2]^{2+}$	$[MCl_6]^{2-}$
	4	Tetrahedral		$OsCy_4$
5 (d^3)	4	Tetrahedral	$[FeO_4]^{3-}$	
	6	Octahedral		$[MF_6]^-$
6 (d^2)	4	Tetrahedral	$[FeO_4]^{2-}$	$[RuO_4]^{2-}$
	5	Square pyramidal		$[OsNCl_4]^-$
		Trigonal bipyramidal		$[RuO_5]^{4-(a)}$
	6	Octahedral		$[OsO_2(OH)_4]^{2-}$
7 (d^1)	4	Tetrahedral		$[MO_4]^-$
	6	Octahedral		$[OsOF_5]$
	7	Pentagonal bipyramidal		OsF_7
8 (d^0)	4	Tetrahedral		MO_4
	6	Octahedral		$[OsO_4F_2]^{2-}$

(a)Both tetrahedral and trigonal bipyramidal Ru^{VI} occur in the single compound, $CsK_5[RuO_5][RuO_4]$; D. FISCHER and R. HOPPE, *Z. anorg. allg. Chem.* **617**, 37–44 (1992).

Table 25.4   Electronic spin-states of iron

Spin quantum number (S)	Ion	Electronic configuration	Typical compounds
0 (diamagnetic)	Low-spin Fe^{II}	t_{2g}^6	$K_4[Fe(CN)_6].3H_2O$
			HbO_2 (oxygenated haemoglobin)
$\frac{1}{2}$ (1 unpaired e^-)	Low-spin Fe^{III}	t_{2g}^5	$K_3[Fe(CN)_6]$, HbCN
	Low-spin Fe^I	$t_{2g}^6 e_g^1$	$[Fe(diars)(CO)_2I]$
1 (2 unpaired e^-)	Low-spin Fe^{IV}	t_{2g}^4	$[Fe(diars)_2Cl_2](ClO_4)_2$
	Tetrahedral Fe^{VI}	e^2	$Ba[FeO_4]$
$\frac{3}{2}$ (3 unpaired e^-)	Distorted square pyramidal Fe^{III}	$d_{x^2-y^2}^2\ d_{yz}^1\ d_{xz}^1\ d_{z^2}^1$	$[Fe(S_2CNR_2)_2Cl]$
2 (4 unpaired e^-)	High-spin Fe^{II}	$t_{2g}^4 e_g^2$	$[Fe(H_2O)_6]^{2+}$, deoxyhaemoglobin
$\frac{5}{2}$ (5 unpaired e^-)	High-spin Fe^{III}	$t_{2g}^3 e_g^2$	$[Fe(acac)_3]$, iron-transport proteins

a remarkably wide range of oxidation states, particularly for Ru and Os, and, although it is now evident that as the size of the atoms decreases across each period the tendency to form compounds with high coordination numbers is diminishing, Os has a greater tendency than Ru to adopt a coordination number of 6 in the higher oxidation states. Thus OsO_4 expands its coordination sphere far more readily than RuO_4 to form complexes such as $[OsO_4(OH)_2]^{2-}$, and Os has no 4-coordinate analogue of $[RuO_4]^{2-}$.

Iron is notable for the range of electronic spin states to which it gives rise. The values of S which are found include every integral and half-integral value from 0 to $\frac{5}{2}$ i.e. every value possible for a d-block element (Table 25.4).

25.3 Compounds of Iron[10], Ruthenium[11] and Osmium

The borides (p. 145), carbides (pp. 297, 1074), and nitrides (p. 417) have been discussed previously. Binary hydrides are not formed but prolonged heating of powdered Mg and Fe under a high pressure of H_2 yields $MgFeH_6$ containing the octahedral hydrido anion, $[FeH_6]^{4-}$ which satisfies the 18-electron rule.

25.3.1 Oxides and other chalcogenides

The principal oxides of the elements[12] of this group are given in Table 25.5.

Table 25.5   The oxides of iron, ruthenium and osmium

Oxidation state	+8	+4	+3	+2
Fe			Fe_2O_3 Fe_3O_4	'FeO'
Ru	RuO_4	RuO_2		
Os	OsO_4	OsO_2		

Three oxides of iron may be distinguished, but are all subject to nonstoichiometry. The lowest is FeO which is obtained by heating iron in a low partial pressure of O_2 or as a fine, black pyrophoric powder by heating iron(II) oxalate *in vacuo*. Below about 575°C it is unstable towards disproportionation into Fe and Fe_3O_4 but can be obtained as a metastable phase if cooled rapidly. It has a rock-salt structure but is always deficient in iron, with a homogeneity range of $Fe_{0.84}O$ to $Fe_{0.95}O$. Treatment of any aqueous solution of Fe^{II} with alkali produces a flocculent precipitate. If air is rigorously excluded this is the virtually white $Fe(OH)_2$ which is almost entirely basic in character, dissolving readily in non-oxidizing acids to give Fe^{II} salts but

[10] *Chemistry of Iron* (J. SILVER, ed.), Blackie, London, 1993, 306 pp.

[11] E. A. SEDDON and K. R. SEDDON, *The Chemistry of Ruthenium*, Elsevier, Amsterdam, 1984, 1374 pp.

[12] U. SCHWERTMANN and R. M. CORNELL, *Iron Oxides in the Laboratory*, VCH, Weinheim, 1991, 137 pp.

showing only slight reactivity towards alkali. It gradually decomposes, however, to Fe_3O_4 with evolution of hydrogen and in the presence of oxygen darkens rapidly and eventually forms the reddish-brown hydrated iron(III) oxide. Fe_3O_4 is a mixed Fe^{II}/Fe^{III} oxide which can be obtained by partial oxidation of FeO or, more conveniently, by heating Fe_2O_3 above about 1400°C. It has the inverse spinel structure. Spinels are of the form $M^{II}M_2^{III}O_4$ and in the normal spinel (p. 247) the oxide ions form a ccp lattice with M^{II} ions occupying tetrahedral sites and M^{III} ions octahedral sites. In the inverse structure half the M^{III} ions occupy tetrahedral sites, with the M^{II} and the other half of the M^{III} occupying octahedral sites.[†] Fe_3O_4 occurs naturally as the mineral magnetite or lodestone. It is a black, strongly ferromagnetic substance (or, more strictly, "ferrimagnetic" — see p. 1081), insoluble in water and acids. Its electrical properties are not simple, but its rather high conductivity may be ascribed to electron transfer between Fe^{II} and Fe^{III}.

Fe_2O_3 is known in a variety of modifications of which the more important are the α- and γ-forms. When aqueous solutions of iron(III) are treated with alkali, a gelatinous reddish-brown precipitate of hydrated oxide is produced (this is amorphous to X-rays and is not simple $Fe(OH)_3$, but probably FeO(OH)); when heated to 200°C, this gives the red-brown α-Fe_2O_3. Like V_2O_3 and Cr_2O_3 this has the corundum structure (p. 243) in which the oxide ions are hcp and the metal ions occupy octahedral sites. It occurs naturally as the mineral haematite and, besides its overriding importance as a source of the metal (p. 1072), it is used (a) as a pigment, (b) in the preparation of rare earth/iron garnets and

other ferrites (p. 1081), and (c) as a polishing agent — jewellers' rouge. The second variety γ-Fe_2O_3 is metastable and is obtained by careful oxidation of Fe_3O_4, like which it is cubic and ferrimagnetic. If heated *in vacuo* it reverts to Fe_3O_4 but heating in air converts it to α-Fe_2O_3. It is the most widely used magnetic material in the production of magnetic recording tapes.

The interconvertibility of FeO, Fe_3O_4 and γ-Fe_2O_3 arises because of their structural similarity. Unlike α-Fe_2O_3, which is based on a hcp lattice of oxygen atoms, these three compounds are all based on ccp lattices of oxygen atoms. In FeO, Fe^{II} ions occupy the octahedral sites and nonstoichiometry arises by oxidation, when some Fe^{II} ions are replaced by two-thirds their number of Fe^{III} ions. Continued oxidation produces Fe_3O_4 in which the Fe^{II} ions are in octahedral sites, but the Fe^{III} ions are distributed between both octahedral and tetrahedral sites. Eventually, oxidation leads to γ-Fe_2O_3 in which all the cations are Fe^{III} which are randomly distributed between octahedral and tetrahedral sites. The oxygen lattice remains intact throughout but contracts somewhat as the number of iron atoms which it accommodates diminishes.

Ruthenium and osmium have no oxides comparable to those of iron and, indeed, the lowest oxidation state in which they form oxides is +4. RuO_2 is a blue to black solid, obtained by direct action of the elements at 1000°C, and has the rutile (p. 961) structure. The intense colour has been suggested as arising from the presence of small amounts of Ru in another oxidation state, possibly +3. OsO_2 is a yellowish-brown solid, usually prepared by heating the metal at 650°C in NO. It, too, has the rutile structure.

The most interesting oxides of Ru and Os, however, are the volatile, yellow tetroxides, RuO_4 (mp 25°C, bp 130°C[(13)]) and OsO_4 (mp 40°C, bp 130°C). They are tetrahedral molecules and the latter is perhaps the best-known compound of osmium. It is produced by aerial oxidation of the heated metal or by oxidizing other compounds of osmium with

---

[†] Although Fe_3O_4 is an inverse spinel it will be recalled that Mn_3O_4 (pp. 1048–9) is normal. This contrast can be explained on the basis of crystal field stabilization. Manganese(II) and Fe^{III} are both d^5 ions and, when high-spin, have zero CFSE whether octahedral or tetrahedral. On the other hand, Mn^{III} is a d^4 and Fe^{II} a d^6 ion, both of which have greater CFSEs in the octahedral rather than the tetrahedral case. The preference of Mn^{III} for the octahedral sites therefore favours the spinel structure, whereas the preference of Fe^{II} for these octahedral sites favours the inverse structure.

[13] Y. KODA, *J. Chem. Soc., Chem. Commun.*, 1347–8 (1986).

nitric acid. It dissolves in aqueous alkali to give $[Os^{VIII}O_4(OH)_2]^{2-}$ and oxidizes conc (but not dil) hydrochloric acid to Cl_2, being itself reduced to H_2OsCl_6. It is used in organic chemistry to oxidize C=C bonds to *cis*-diols and is also employed as a biological stain. Unfortunately, it is extremely toxic and its volatility renders it particularly dangerous. RuO_4 is, appreciably less stable and will oxidize dil as well as conc HCl, while in aqueous alkali it is reduced to $[Ru^{VI}O_4]^{2-}$. If heated above 100°C it decomposes explosively to RuO_2 and is liable to do the same at room temperature if brought into contact with oxidizable organic solvents such as ethanol. Its preparation obviously requires stronger oxidizing agents than that of OsO_4; nitric acid alone will not suffice and instead the action of $KMnO_4$, KIO_4 or Cl_2 on acidified solutions of a convenient Ru compound is used.

The sulfides are fewer in number than the oxides and favour lower metal oxidation states. Iron forms 3 sulfides (p. 680). FeS is a grey, nonstoichiometric material, obtained by direct action of the elements or by treating aqueous Fe^{II} with alkali metal sulfide. It has a NiAs structure (p. 679) in which each metal atom is octahedrally surrounded by anions but is also quite close to 2 other metal atoms. It oxidizes readily in air and dissolves in aqueous acids with evolution of H_2S. FeS_2 can be prepared by heating Fe_2O_3 in H_2S but is most commonly encountered as the yellow mineral pyrites. This does not contain Fe^{IV} but is composed of Fe^{II} and S_2^{2-} ions in a distorted rock-salt arrangement, its diamagnetism indicating low-spin $Fe^{II}(d^6)$. It is very unreactive unless heated, when it gives $Fe_2O_3 + SO_2$ in air, or FeS + S in a vacuum. Fe_2S_3 is the unstable black precipitate resulting when aqueous Fe^{III} is treated with S^{2-}, and is rapidly oxidized in moist air to Fe_2O_3 and S.

Ruthenium and osmium form only disulfides. These have the pyrite structure and are diamagnetic semiconductors; this implies that they contain M^{II}. $RuSe_2$, $RuTe_2$, $OsSe_2$ and $OsTe_2$ are very similar. All 6 dichalcogenides are obtained directly from the elements.

25.3.2 Mixed metal oxides and oxoanions [14]

The "ferrites" and "garnets" of iron are mixed metal oxides of considerable technological importance. They are obtained by heating Fe_2O_3 with the carbonate of the appropriate metal. The ferrites have the general form $M^{II}Fe_2^{III}O_4$. Some adopt the *normal* spinel structure and others the *inverse* spinel structure (p. 248) as just described for Fe_3O_4 (which can itself be regarded as the ferrite $Fe^{II}Fe_2^{III}O_4$). In inverse spinels the unpaired electrons of all the cations in octahedral sites (M^{II} and half the M^{III}) are magnetically coupled parallel to give a ferromagnetic sublattice, while the unpaired electrons of all the cations in tetrahedral sites (the remaining M^{III}) are similarly but independently coupled parallel to give a second ferromagnetic sublattice. The spins of one sublattice, however, are antiparallel to those of the other. If the cations in the octahedral sites have the same total number of unpaired electrons as those in the tetrahedral sites, then the effects of 2 ferromagnetic sublattices are mutually compensating and "antiferromagnetism" results; but where the sublattices are not balanced then a type of ferromagnetism known as ferrimagnetism results, the explanation of which was first given by L. Néel in 1948 (Nobel Prize for Physics, 1970). Important applications of inverse spinel ferrites are as cores in high-frequency transformers (where they have the advantage over metals of being free from eddy-current losses), and in computer memory systems.

So-called "hexagonal ferrites" such as $BaFe_{12}O_{19}$ are ferrimagnetic and are used to construct permanent magnets. A third type of ferrimagnetic mixed oxides are the garnets, $M_3^{III}Fe_5O_{12}$, of which the best known is yttrium iron garnet (YIG) used as a microwave filter in radar.

Mixed oxides of Fe^{IV} such as $M_4^{I}FeO_4$ and $M_2^{II}FeO_4$ can be prepared by heating Fe_2O_3 with the appropriate oxide or hydroxide in

---

[14] A. F. WELLS, *Structural Inorganic Chemistry*, 5th edn., Complex oxides, pp. 575–625, Oxford University Press, Oxford, 1984.

oxygen. These do not contain discrete $[FeO_4]^{4-}$ anions and, as was seen above, mixed oxides of Fe^{III} are generally based on close-packed oxide lattices with no iron-containing anions. However, oxoanions of iron are known and are usually based on the FeO_4 tetrahedron.[†] Thus for iron(III), Na_5FeO_4, $K_6[Fe_2O_6]$ (2 edge-sharing tetrahedra), and $Na_{14}[Fe_6O_{16}]$ (rings of 6 corner-sharing tetrahedra), have been prepared and more recently, for iron(V), $K_3[FeO_4]$.[15] But the best-known oxoanion of iron is the ferrate(VI) prepared by oxidizing a suspension of hydrous Fe_2O_3 in conc alkali with chlorine, or by the anodic oxidation of iron in conc alkali. The tetrahedral $[FeO_4]^{2-}$ ion is red-purple and is an extremely strong oxidizing agent. It oxidizes NH_3 to N_2 even at room temperature and, although it can be kept for a period of hours in alkaline solution, in acid or neutral solutions it rapidly oxidizes the water, so liberating oxygen:

$$2[FeO_4]^{2-} + 5H_2O \longrightarrow 2Fe^{3+} + 10(OH)^- + \tfrac{3}{2}O_2$$

The distinction between the first member of the group and the two heavier members, which was seen to be so sharp in the early groups of transition metals, is much less obvious here. The only unsubstituted, discrete oxoanions of the heavier pair of metals are the tetrahedral $[Ru^{VII}O_4]^-$ and $[Ru^{VI}O_4]^{2-}$. This behaviour is akin to that of iron or, even more, to that of manganese, whereas in the osmium analogues the metal always increases its coordination number by the attachment of extra OH^- ions. If RuO_4 is dissolved in cold dilute KOH, or aqueous K_2RuO_4 is oxidized by chlorine, virtually black crystals of $K[Ru^{VII}O_4]$ ("perruthenate") are deposited. These are unstable unless dried and are reduced by water, especially if alkaline, to the orange

$[Ru^{VI}O_4]^{2-}$ ("ruthenate") by a mechanism which is thought to involve octahedral intermediates of the type $[RuO_4(OH)_2]^{3-}$ and $[RuO_4(OH)_2]^{2-}$. $K_2[RuO_4]$ is obtained by fusing Ru metal with KOH and KNO_3.

By contrast, dissolution of OsO_4 in cold aqueous KOH produces deep-red crystals of $K_2[Os^{VIII}O_4(OH)_2]$ ("perosmate"), which is easily reduced to the purple "osmate", $K_2[Os^{VI}O_2(OH)_4]$. The anions in both cases are octahedral with, respectively, *trans* OH and *trans* O groups.

By heating the metal with appropriate oxides or carbonates of alkali or alkaline earth metals, a number of mixed oxides of Ru and Os have been made. They include $Na_5Os^{VII}O_6$, $Li_6Os^{VI}O_6$ and the "ruthenites", $M^{II}Ru^{IV}O_3$, in all of which the metal is situated in octahedral sites of an oxide lattice. Ru^V (octahedral) has now also been established by ^{99}Ru Mössbauer spectroscopy as a common stable oxidation state in mixed oxides such as $Na_3Ru^VO_4$, $Na_4Ru_2^VO_7$, and the ordered perovskite-type phases $M_2^{II}Ln^{III}Ru^VO_6$.

25.3.3 Halides and oxohalides

The known halides of this group are listed in Table 25.6. As in the preceding group the highest halide is a heptafluoride, but OsF_7 (unlike ReF_7) is thermally unstable. It was for many years thought that OsF_8 existed but the yellow crystalline material to which the formula had been ascribed turned out to be OsF_6, the least unstable of the platinum metal hexafluorides. (In view of the propensity of higher fluorides to attack the vessels containing them, to disproportionate and to hydrolyse, it is not surprising that early reports on them sometimes proved to be erroneous.) The highest chloride is $OsCl_5$ and, rather unexpectedly perhaps, neither ruthenium nor iron form a chloride in an oxidation state higher than +3. Iron in fact does not form even a fluoride in an oxidation state higher than this and its halides are confined to the +3 and +2 states.

OsF_7 has been obtained as a yellow solid by direct action of the elements at 600°C

[†] An exception is $K_3[FeO_2]$ which contains the linear $[O-Fe^I-O]^{3-}$ anion (see p. 1166). It is surprisingly prepared as garnet-red crystals when a mixture of $K_6[CdO_4]$ and CdO is subjected to prolonged heating at 450°C in a closed iron cylinder and reacts with the cylinder walls! F. BERNARD and R. HOPPE, *Z. anorg. allg. Chem.* **619**, 969–75 (1993).

[15] R. HOPPE and K. MADER *Z. anorg. allg. Chem.* **586**, 115–24 (1990).

Table 25.6   Halides of iron, ruthenium and osmium (mp/°C)

Oxidation state	Fluorides	Chlorides	Bromides	Iodides
+7	OsF_7 yellow			
+6	RuF_6 dark brown (54°) OsF_6 yellow (33°)			
+5	RuF_5 dark green (86.5°) OsF_5 blue (70°)	$OsCl_5$ black (d > 160°)		
+4	RuF_4 yellow OsF_4 yellow (230°)	$OsCl_4$ red (also black form)	$OsBr_4$ black (d 350°)	
+3	FeF_3 pale green (>1000°) RuF_3 dark brown (d > 650°)	$FeCl_3$ brown-black (306°) $RuCl_3$ black (α) dark brown (β) $OsCl_3$ dark grey (d 450°)	$FeBr_3$ red-brown (d > 200°) $RuBr_3$ dark brown (d > 400°)	FeI_3 black RuI_3 black OsI_3 black
+2	FeF_2 white (>1000°)	$FeCl_2$ pale yellow (674°) $RuCl_2$ brown	$FeBr_2$ yellow-green (d 684°) $RuBr_2$ black	FeI_2 grey RuI_2 blue OsI_2 black
+1				OsI metallic grey

and a pressure of 400 atm, but under less drastic conditions OsF_6 is produced, as is RuF_6. This latter pair are low-melting, yellow and brown solids, respectively, hydrolysing violently with water and with a strong tendency to disproportionate into F_2 and lower halides. The pentafluorides are both polymeric, easily hydrolysed solids obtained by specific oxidations or reduction of other fluorides, and their structures involve $[MF_5]_4$ units in which 4 corner-sharing MF_6 octahedra form a ring (Fig. 25.3).

The tetrafluorides are yellow solids, probably polymeric, and are obtained by reducing RuF_5 with I_2, and OsF_6 with $W(CO)_6$. The tetrachloride and tetrabromide of osmium require pressure as well as heat in their preparations from the

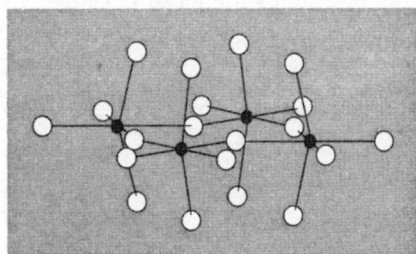

Figure 25.3   Tetrameric pentafluorides of Ru and Os, $[M_4F_{20}]$. Their structures are similar to, but more distorted than, those of the pentafluorides of Nb and Ta (see Fig. 22.4).

elements and are black solids, the bromide consisting of $OsBr_6$ octahedra connected by shared edges.

In the $+3$ and $+2$ oxidation states those halides of osmium which have been reported are poorly characterized, grey or black solids. The compound obtained by thermal decomposition of $OsBr_4$ and previously thought to be $OsBr_3$ has since been shown[16] to be Os_2OBr_6, the chloride analogue of which is also known. For ruthenium, $RuCl_3$ is well known and, as the anhydrous compound, exists in two forms: heating Ru metal at $330°C$ in CO and Cl_2 produces the dark-brown β-form which if heated above $450°C$ in Cl_2 is converted to the black α-form which is isomorphous with $CrCl_3$ (p. 1020). Evaporation of a solution of RuO_4 in hydrochloric acid in a stream of HCl gas produces red $RuCl_3.3H_2O$; aqueous solutions contain both $[Ru(H_2O)_6]^{3+}$ and chloro-substituted species and are easily hydrolysed and oxidized to Ru^{IV}. Where impurities due to such reactions are suspected, conversion back to Ru^{III} chloride can be effected by repeated evaporations to dryness with conc HCl. This gives a uniform though rather poorly characterized product that is widely used as the starting material in ruthenium chemistry.

All the anhydrous $+3$ and $+2$ halides of iron are readily obtained, except for iron(III) iodide, where the oxidizing properties of Fe^{III} and the reducing properties of I^- lead to thermodynamic instability. It has, however, been prepared[17] in mg quantities by the following reaction, with air and moisture rigorously excluded,

$$Fe(CO)_5 + I_2 \xrightarrow{\text{hexane}} \underset{\substack{\text{light red}\\\text{soln.}}}{Fe(CO)_4I_2} + CO \xrightarrow[-20°C]{\frac{1}{2}I_2 + h\nu}$$

$$\downarrow FeI_3 + 4CO$$
$$\text{black}$$

The other anhydrous FeX_3 can be prepared by heating the elements (though in the case of $FeBr_3$ the temperature must not rise above $200°C$ otherwise $FeBr_2$ is formed). The fluoride, chloride and bromide are respectively white, dark

brown and reddish-brown. The crystalline solids contain Fe^{III} ions octahedrally surrounded by halide ions and decompose to $FeX_2 + \frac{1}{2}X_2$ if heated strongly under vacuum. $FeCl_3$ sublimes above $300°C$ and vapour pressure measurements show the vapour to contain dimeric Fe_2Cl_6, like Al_2Cl_6 consisting of 2 edge-sharing tetrahedra. The trifluoride is sparingly soluble, and the chloride and bromide very soluble in water and they crystallize as white $FeF_3.4H_2O$ (converting above $50°C$ to the pink trihydrate),[18] yellow-brown $FeCl_3.6H_2O$ and dark-green $FeBr_3.6H_2O$. The chloride is probably the most widely used etching material, being particularly important for etching copper in the production of electrical printed circuits. It is also used in water treatment as a coagulant (by producing a "ferric hydroxide" floc which removes organic matter and suspended solids) in cases where the SO_4^{2-} of the more widely used iron(III) sulfate is undesirable.

Of the anhydrous dihalides of iron the iodide is easily prepared from the elements but the others are best obtained by passing HX over heated iron. The white (or pale-green) difluoride has the rutile structure the pale-yellow dichloride the $CdCl_2$ structure (based on ccp anions, p. 1212) and the yellow-green dibromide and grey diiodide the CdI_2 structure (based on hcp anions, p. 1212), in all of which the metal occupies octahedral sites. All these iron dihalides dissolve in water and form crystalline hydrates which may alternatively be obtained by dissolving metallic iron in the aqueous acid.

Apart from the pale green $RuOF_4$ and the oxochlorides already referred to, oxohalides are largely confined to the oxofluorides of osmium,[19] OsO_3F_2, OsO_2F_3, $OsOF_5$, $OsOF_4$ and the recently confirmed[20] OsO_2F_4, previously thought to be $OsOF_6$. The compounds of Os^{VIII} are orange and red solids and those of the lower oxidation states are yellow to green. Typical preparations involve

[16] H. SCHÄFER, *Z. anorg. allg. Chem.* **535**, 219–20 (1986).

[17] K. B. YOON and J. K. KOCHI, *Inorg. Chem.* **29**, 869–74 (1990).

[18] D. G. KARRAKER and P. K. SMITH, *Inorg. Chem.* **31**, 1119–20 (1992).

[19] J. H. HOLLOWAY and D. LAYCOCK, *Adv. Inorg. Chem. Radiochem.* **28**, 73–99 (1984).

[20] K. O. CHRISTE and R. BOUGON, *J. Chem. Soc., Chem. Commun.*, 1056 (1992).

the action of various fluorinating agents on OsO_4 but they are subject to disproportionation and not easily prepared in pure form.

25.3.4 Complexes [10,11,21,22,23]

Oxidation state VIII (d⁰)

Iron forms barely any complexes in oxidation states above +3, and in the +8, +7 and +6 states those of ruthenium are less numerous than those of osmium. Ru^{VIII} complexes are confined to a few unstable (sometimes explosive) amine adducts of RuO_4. The "perosmates" (p. 1082) are, of course, adducts of OsO_4, but the most stable Os^{VIII} complexes are the "osmiamates", $[OsO_3N]^-$ (p. 419). Pale-yellow crystals of $K[OsO_3N]$ are obtained when solutions of OsO_4 in aqueous KOH (i.e. the perosmate) are treated with ammonia: the compound has been known since 1847 and A. Werner formulated it correctly in 1901. The anion is isoelectronic with OsO_4 and has a distorted tetrahedral structure (C_{3v}), while its infrared spectrum shows $\nu_{Os-N} = 1023\,cm^{-1}$, consistent with an $Os\equiv N$ triple bond. Hydrochloric and hydrobromic acids reduce $K[OsO_3N]$ to red, $K_2[Os^{VI}NX_5]$.

Oxidation state VII (d¹)

Fluorides and oxo compounds of Ru^{VII} and Os^{VII} have already been mentioned, and salts such as $(R_4N)[RuO_4]$, (R = n-propyl, n-butyl) are useful reagents to oxidize a variety of organic materials without attacking double or allylic bonds.[24]

[21] P. N. HAWKER and M. V. TWIGG, Iron(II) and Lower States, Chap. 44.1, pp. 1179–288; S. M. NELSON, Iron(III) and Higher States, Chap. 44.2, pp. 217–76; M. SCHRÖDER and T. A. STEPHENSON, Ruthenium, Chap. 45, pp. 277–518; W. P. GRIFFITH, Osmium, Chap. 46, pp. 519–633 in *Comprehensive Coordination Chemistry*, Vol. 4, Pergamon Press, Oxford, 1987.

[22] C.-M. CHE and V. W.-W. YAM, High valent compounds of Ruthenium and Osmium, *Adv. Inorg. Chem.* **39**, 233–325 (1992).

[23] P. A. LAY and W. D. HARMAN, Recent advances in osmium chemistry, *Adv. Inorg. Chem.* **37**, 219–380 (1991).

[24] W. P. GRIFFITH, *Platinum Metals Rev.* **33**, 181–5 (1989).

Oxidation state VI (d²)

The most important members of this class are the osmium nitrido, and the "osmyl" complexes. The reddish-purple $K_2[OsNCl_5]$ mentioned above is the result of reducing the osmiamate. The anion has a distorted octahedral structure with a formal triple bond $Os\equiv N$ (161 pm) and a pronounced "*trans*-influence" (pp. 1163–4), i.e. the Os–Cl distance *trans* to Os–N is much longer than the Os–Cl distances *cis* to Os–N (261 and 236 pm respectively). The anion $[OsNCl_5]^{2-}$ also shows a "*trans*-effect" in that the Cl opposite the N is more labile than the others, leading, for instance, to the formation of $[Os^{VI}NCl_4]^-$, which has a square-pyramidal structure with the N occupying the apical position.

The osmyl complexes, of which the osmate ion $[Os^{VI}O_2(OH)_4]^{2-}$ may be regarded as the precursor, are a series of diamagnetic complexes containing the linear O=Os=O group together with 4 other, more remote, donor atoms which occupy the equatorial plane. That the Os–O bonds are double (i.e. 1σ and 1π) is evident from the bond lengths of 175 pm — very close to those of 172 pm in OsO_4. The diamagnetism can then be explained using the MO approach outlined in Chapter 19, but modified to allow for the tetragonal compression along the axis of the osmyl group (taken to define the z-axis). On this model, the effect of 6 σ interactions produces the molecular orbitals shown in Fig. 19.14 (p. 922). The tetragonal compression then splits the essentially metallic t_{2g} and e_g^* sets, as shown to the left of Fig. 25.4b. Two 3-centre π bonds are then formed, one by overlap of the metal d_{xz} orbital with the p_x orbitals of the 2 oxygen atoms (Fig. 25.4a), the second similarly by d_{yz} and p_y overlap. Each 3-centre interaction produces 1 bonding, 1 virtually nonbonding, and 1 antibonding MO, as shown. The metal d_{xy} orbital remains unchanged and, in effect, the two d electrons of the Os are obliged to pair-up in it since other empty orbitals are inaccessible to them.

The $\{Os^{VI}O_2\}^{2+}$ group has a formal similarity to the more familiar uranyl ion $[UO_2]^{2+}$ and is present in a variety of octahedral complexes

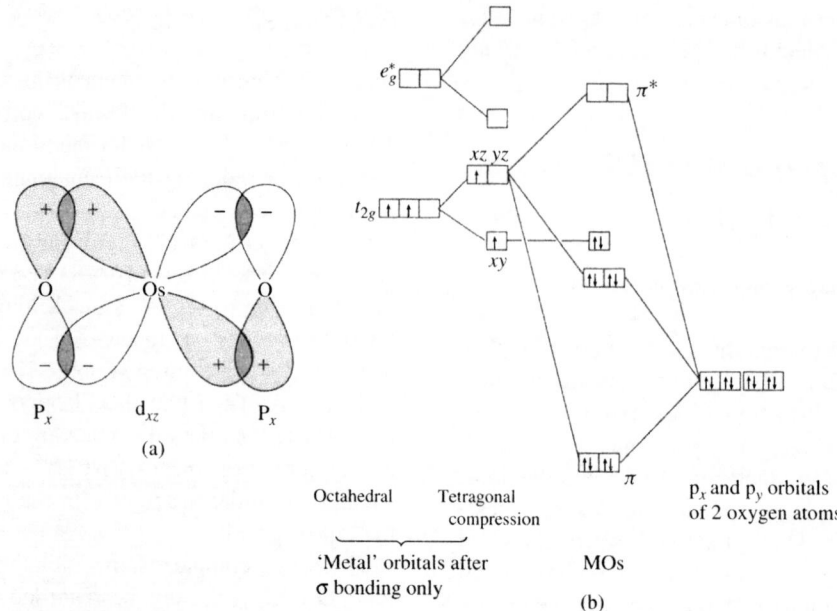

Figure 25.4 Proposed π bonding in osmyl complexes: (a) 3-centre π bond formed by overlap of ligand p_x and metal d_{zx} orbitals (a similar bond is produced by p_y and d_{yz} overlap), and (b) MO diagram (see text).

in which the 4 equatorial sites are occupied by ligands such as OH^-, halides, CN^-, $(C_2O_4)^{2-}$, NO_2^-, NH_3 and phthalocyanine. These are obtained from OsO_4 or potassium osmate.

A few analogous but less stable trans-dioxoruthenium(VI) compounds such as the bright yellow $[RuO_2(O_2CCH_3)_2py_2]$ (Ru–O = 172.6 pm) are also known.[25]

Oxidation state V (d³)

This is not a very stable state for this group of metals in solution, $[MF_6]^-$ and $[OsCl_6]^-$ being amongst the few established examples. It is, however, well-characterized and stable in numerous solid-state oxide systems (p. 1082).

Oxidation state IV (d⁴)

Under normal circumstances this is the most stable oxidation state for osmium and the

[25] S. PERRIER, T. C. LAU and J. K. KOCHI, *Inorg. Chem.* **29**, 4190–5 (1990).

$[OsX_6]^{2-}$ complexes (X = F, Cl, Br, I) are particularly well known. $[RuX_6]^{2-}$ (X = F, Cl, Br) are also familiar but can more readily be reduced to Ru^{III}. All these $[MX_6]^{2-}$ ions are octahedral and low-spin, with 2 unpaired electrons. Their magnetic properties are interesting and highlight the limitations of using "spin-only" values of magnetic moments in assessing the number of unpaired electrons (see Panel).

The action of hydrochloric acid on RuO_4 in the presence of KCl produces a deep-red crystalline material, of stoichiometry $K_2[RuCl_5(OH)]$, but its diamagnetism precludes this simple formulation. The compound is in fact $K_4[Cl_5Ru–O–RuCl_5]$ and is of interest as providing an early application of simple MO theory to a linear M–O–M system (not unlike the later treatment of the osmyl group). If the Ru–O–Ru axis is taken as the z-axis and each Ru^{IV} is regarded as being octahedrally coordinated, then the low-spin configuration of each Ru^{IV} ion is $d_{xy}^2 d_{xz}^1 d_{yz}^1$. The diamagnetism is accounted for on the basis of two 3-centre π bonds, one arising from overlap

Magnetic Properties of Low-spin, Octahedral d⁴ Ions

That halide ligands should cause spin-pairing may in itself seem surprising, but this is not all. The regular, octahedral complexes of Os^{IV} have magnetic moments at room temperature in the region of 1.48 BM and these decrease rapidly as the temperature is reduced. Even the moments of similar complexes of Ru^{IV} (which at around 2.9 BM are close to the "spin-only moment" expected solely from the angular momentum of 2 unpaired electrons) fall sharply with temperature. In the first place, low-spin configurations are much more common for the second- and third-row than for first-row transition elements and this is due to (a) the higher nuclear charges of the heavier elements which exert stronger attractions on the ligands so that a given set of ligands produces a greater splitting of the metal d orbitals, and (b) the larger sizes of 4d and 5d orbitals compared to 3d orbitals, with the result that interelectronic repulsions, which tend to oppose spin-pairing, are lower in the former cases. These factors explain why the halide complexes of Os^{IV} and Ru^{IV} are low-spin but what of the temperature dependence and their magnetic behaviour? This arises from the effect of "spin–orbit coupling" which can be summarized in a plot of μ_e versus $kT/|\lambda|$ (Fig. A). λ is the spin–orbit coupling constant for a particular ion and is indicative of the strength of the coupling between the angular momentum vectors associated with S and L, and also of the magnitude of the splitting of the ground term of the ion (^3T, in the case of low-spin d^4). When $|\lambda|$ is of comparable magnitude to kT, $\mu_e \sim 3.6$ BM, which is the spin-only moment (2.83 BM) plus a contribution from the orbital angular momentum. Thus, Cr^{II} ($\lambda = -115$ cm^{-1}) and Mn^{III} ($\lambda = -178$ cm^{-1}) at room temperature ($kT \sim 200$ cm^{-1}), lie on the flat portion of the curve and so have magnetic moments of about 3.6 BM which only begin to fall at appreciably lower temperatures. On the other hand, Ru^{IV} ($\lambda = -700$ cm^{-1}) and Os^{IV} ($\lambda \sim -2000$ cm^{-1}) have moments which at room temperature are already on the steep portion of the curve and so are extremely dependent on temperature. In each case, as the temperature approaches 0 K so also $\mu_e \rightarrow 0$, corresponding to a coupling of L and S vectors in opposition and their associated magnetic moments therefore cancelling each other.

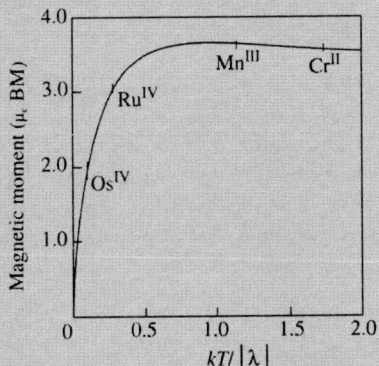

Figure A   The variation with temperature and spin-orbit coupling constant, of the magnetic moments of octahedral, low-spin, d⁴ ions. (The values of μ_e at 300 K are marked for individual ions).

All d^n configurations with T ground terms give rise to magnetic moments which are lower for second- and third-row than for first-row transition elements and are temperature dependent, but in no case so dramatically as for low-spin d^4.

of the oxygen p_x orbital and the two d_{xz} orbitals of the Ru ions, and the other similarly from p_y and d_{yz} overlap (Fig. 25.5). The bromo analogue apparently does not exist.[26]

---

[26] D. Appleby, R. I. Crisp, P. B. Hitchcock, C. L. Hussey, T. A. Ryan, J. R. Sanders, K. R. Seddon, J. E. Turp and J. A. Zora, *J. Chem. Soc., Chem. Commun.*, 483–5 (1986).

Ruthenium(IV) produces few other complexes of interest but osmium(IV) yields several sulfito complexes (e.g. $[Os(SO_3)_6]^{8-}$ and substituted derivatives) as well as a number of complexes, such as $[Os(bipy)Cl_4]$ and $[Os(diars)_2X_2]^{2+}$ (X = Cl, Br, I), with mixed halide and Group 15 donor atoms. The iron analogues of the latter complexes (with X = Cl, Br), are obtained by oxidation of

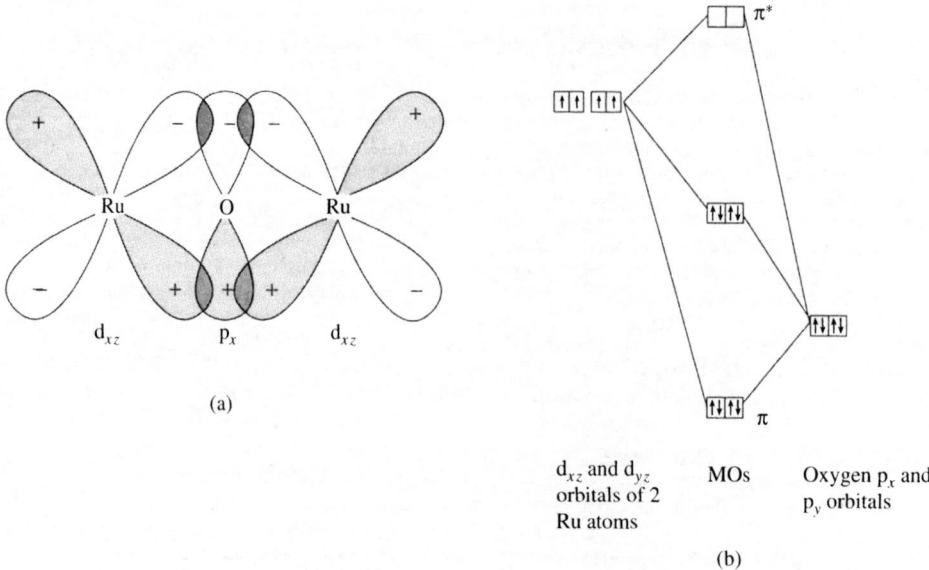

Figure 25.5 π bonding in $[Ru_2OCl_{10}]^{4-}$: (a) 3-centre π bond formed by overlap of an oxygen p_x and ruthenium d_{xz} orbitals (another similar bond is produced by p_y and d_{yz} overlap), and (b) MO diagram.

$[Fe(diars)_2X_2]^+$ with conc HNO_3 and provide rare examples of complexes containing iron in an oxidation state higher than +3. The halide ions are *trans* to each other and a reduction in the magnetic moment at 293 K from a value of ~3.6 BM (which might have been expected, since $\lambda = -260 \text{ cm}^{-1}$ for Fe^{IV} — see Panel) to 2.98 BM is explained by a large tetragonal distortion.

Oxidation state III (d^5)

Ruthenium(III) and osmium(III) complexes are all octahedral and low-spin with 1 unpaired electron. Iron(III) complexes, on the other hand, may be high or low spin, and even though an octahedral stereochemistry is the most common, a number of other geometries are also found. In other respects, however there is a gradation down the triad, with Ru^{III} occupying an intermediate position between Fe^{III} and Os^{III}. For iron the oxidation state +3 is one of its two most common and for it there is an extensive, simple, cationic chemistry (though the aquo ion, $[Fe(H_2O)_6]^{3+}$, is too readily hydrolysed to be really common). For ruthenium it is the best-known oxidation state and $[Ru(H_2O)_6]^{3+}$, which can be obtained by oxidation of the divalent ion (p. 1095), has been characterized[27] in the toluene sulfonate, $[Ru(H_2O)_6](tos)_3$ and the caesium alum (see below). For osmium, however, Os^{III} is a distinctly less-common oxidation state, being readily oxidized to Os^{IV} or even, in the presence of π-acceptor ligands such as CN^-, reduced to Os^{II}. There is no evidence of a simple aquo ion of osmium in this or indeed in any other oxidation state.

Except with anions such as iodide (but see p. 1084) which have reducing tendencies, iron(III) forms salts with all the common anions, and these may be crystallized in pale-pink or pale-violet hydrated forms. These presumably contain the $[Fe(H_2O)_6]^{3+}$ cation, and the iron alums certainly do. These alums have the composition $Fe_2(SO_4)_3M_2^ISO_4.24H_2O$ and can be formulated $[M^I(H_2O)_6][Fe^{III}(H_2O)_6][SO_4]_2$.

[27] F. JOENSEN and C. E. SCHAFFER, *Acta. Chem. Scand. Ser. A.* **38**, 819–20 (1984).

Like the analogous chrome alums they find use as mordants in dying processes. The sulfate is the cheapest salt of Fe^{III} and forms no less than 6 different hydrates (12, 10, 9, 7, 6 and 3 mols of H_2O of which $9H_2O$ is the most common); it is widely used as a coagulent in the treatment not only of potable water but also of sewage and industrial effluents.

In the crystallization of these hydrated salts from aqueous solutions it is essential that a low pH (high level of acidity) is maintained, otherwise hydrolysis occurs and yellow impurities contaminate the products. Similarly, if the salts are redissolved in water, the solutions turn yellow/brown. The hydrolytic processes are complicated, and, in the presence of anions with appreciable coordinating tendencies, are further confused by displacement of water from the coordination sphere of the iron. However, in aqueous solutions of salts such as the perchlorate the following equilibria are important:

$$[Fe(H_2O)_6]^{3+} \rightleftharpoons [Fe(H_2O)_5(OH)]^{2+} + H^+;$$
$$K = 10^{-3.05} \text{ mol dm}^{-3}$$

$$[Fe(H_2O)_5(OH)]^{2+} \rightleftharpoons [Fe(H_2O)_4(OH)_2]^+ + H^+;$$
$$K = 10^{-3.26} \text{ mol dm}^{-3}$$

and also $2[Fe(H_2O)_6]^{3+} \rightleftharpoons [Fe(H_2O)_4(OH)]_2^{4+}$
$$+ 2H^+ + 2H_2O; \quad K = 10^{-2.91} \text{ mol dm}^{-3}$$

(The dimer in the third equation is actually $[(H_2O)_4Fe\diagdown^{OH}_{OH}\diagup Fe(H_2O)_4]^{4+}$ and weakly coupled electron spins on the 2 metal ions reduce the magnetic moment per iron below the spin-only value for 5 unpaired electrons.)

It is evident therefore that Fe^{III} salts dissolved in water produce highly acidic solutions and the simple, pale-violet, hexaaquo ion only predominates if further acid is added to give pH ~ 0. At somewhat higher values of pH the solution becomes yellow due to the appearance of the above hydrolysed species and if the pH is raised above 2–3, further condensation occurs, colloidal gels begin to form, and eventually a reddish-brown precipitate of hydrous iron(III) oxide is formed (see p. 1080).

The colours of these solutions are of interest. Iron(III) like manganese(II), has a d^5 configuration and its absorption spectrum might therefore be expected to consist similarly of weak spin-forbidden bands. However, a crucial difference between the ions is that Fe^{III} carries an additional positive charge, and its correspondingly greater ability to polarize coordinated ligands produces intense, charge-transfer absorptions at much lower energies than those of Mn^{II} compounds. As a result, only the hexaaquo ion has the pale colouring associated with spin-forbidden bands in the visible region of the spectrum, while the various hydrolysed species have charge transfer bands, the edges of which tail from the ultraviolet into the visible region producing the yellow colour and obscuring weak d–d bands.[28] Even the hexaquo ion's spectrum is dominated in the near ultraviolet by charge transfer, and a full analysis of the d–d spectrum of this and of other Fe^{III} complexes is consequently not possible.

Iron(III) forms a variety of cationic, neutral and anionic complexes, but an interesting feature of its coordination chemistry is a marked preference (not shown by Cr^{III} with which in many other respects it is similar) for *O*-donor as opposed to *N*-donor ligands. Ammines of Fe^{III} are unstable and dissociate in water; chelating ligands such as bipy and phen which induce spin-pairing produce more stable complexes, but even these are less stable than their Fe^{II} analogues. Thus, whereas deep-red aqueous solutions of $[Fe(phen)_3]^{2+}$ are indefinitely stable, the deep-blue solutions of $[Fe(phen)_3]^{3+}$ slowly turn khaki-coloured as polymeric hydroxo species form. By contrast, the intense colours produced when phenols or enols are treated with Fe^{III}, and which are used as characteristic tests for these organic materials, are due to the formation of Fe–O complexes. Again, the addition of phosphoric acid to yellow, aqueous solutions of $FeCl_3$, for instance, decolourizes them because

28 A. B. P. LEVER, *Inorganic Electronic Spectroscopy*, 2nd edn., pp. 329–34 and 452–3, Elsevier, Amsterdam, 1984.

of the formation of phosphato complexes such as $[Fe(PO_4)_3]^{6-}$ and $[Fe(HPO_4)_3]^{3-}$. The deep-red $[Fe(acac)_3]$ and the green $[Fe(C_2O_4)_3]^{3-}$ are other examples of complexes with oxygen-bonded ligands although the latter, whilst very stable towards dissociation, is photosensitive due to oxidation of the oxalate ion by Fe^{III} and so decomposes to $Fe(C_2O_4)$ and CO_2.

Complexes with mixed *O*-and *N*-donor ligands such as edta and Schiff bases are well known and $[Fe(edta)(H_2O)]^-$ and $[Fe(salen)Cl]$ are examples of 7-coordinate (pentagonal bipyramidal) and 5-coordinate (square-pyramidal) stereochemistries respectively.

As in the case of Cr^{III}, oxo-bridged species with magnetic moments reduced below the spin-only value (5.9 BM in the case of high-spin Fe^{III}) are known. $[Fe(salen)]_2O$, for instance, has a moment of 1.9 BM at 298 K which falls to 0.6 BM at 80 K and the interaction between the electron spins on the 2 metal ions is transmitted across an Fe–O–Fe bridge, bent at an angle of 140°. Trinuclear, basic carboxylates, $[Fe_3O(O_2CR)_6L_3]^+$, are, however, entirely analogous to their Cr^{III} counterparts (p. 1030).[29]

Halide complexes decrease markedly in stability from F^- to I^-. Fluoro complexes are quite stable and in aqueous solutions the predominant species is $[FeF_5(H_2O)]^{2-}$ while isolation of the solid and fusion with KHF_2 yields $[FeF_6]^{3-}$. Chloro complexes are appreciably less stable, and tetrahedral rather than octahedral coordination is favoured.† $[FeCl_4]^-$ can be isolated in yellow salts with large cations such as $[RN_4]^+$ from ethanolic solutions or conc HCl. $[FeBr_4]^-$ and $[FeI_4]^-$ are also known but are readily reduced to Fe^{II} either by internal

oxidation–reduction or by the action of excess ligand.[30]

The blood-red colour produced by mixing aqueous solutions of Fe^{III} and SCN^- (and which provides a well-known test for Fe^{III}) is largely due to $[Fe(SCN)(H_2O)_5]^{2+}$ but, in addition to this, the simple salt $Fe(SCN)_3$ and salts of complexes such as $[Fe(SCN)_4]^-$ and $[Fe(SCN)_6]^{3-}$ can also be isolated.

The high-spin d^5 configuration of Fe^{III}, like that of Mn^{II}, confers no advantage by virtue of CFSE (p. 1131) on any particular stereochemistry. Some examples of its consequent ability to adopt stereochemistries other than octahedral have just been mentioned and further examples are given in Table 25.3 (p. 1078). These cover the range of coordination numbers from 3 to 8.

Further similarity with Mn^{II} may be seen in the fact that the vast majority of the compounds of Fe^{III} are high-spin. Only ligands such as bipy and phen (already mentioned) and CN^-, which are high in the spectrochemical series, can induce spin-pairing. The low-spin $[Fe(CN)_6]^{3-}$, which is best known as its red, crystalline potassium salt, is usually prepared by oxidation of $[Fe(CN)_6]^{4-}$ with, for instance, Cl_2. It should be noted that in $[Fe(CN)_6]^{3-}$ the CN^- ligands are sufficiently labile to render it poisonous, in apparent contrast to $[Fe(CN)_6]^{4-}$, which is kinetically more inert. Dilute acids produce $[Fe(CN)_5(H_2O)]^{2-}$, and other pentacyano complexes are known.

Fe^{III} complexes in general have magnetic moments at room temperature which are close to 5.92 BM if they are high-spin and somewhat in excess of 2 BM (due to orbital contribution) if they are low-spin. A number of complexes, however, were prepared in 1931 by L. Cambi and found to have moments intermediate between these extremes. They are the iron(III)-*N,N*-dialkyldithiocarbamates, $[Fe(S_2CNR_2)_3]$, in which the ligands are:

[29] R. D. CANNON and R. P. WHITE, *Prog. Inorg. Chem.* **36**, 195–298 (1988).

† In the compound, previously assumed to be (pyH)$_3$-[Fe$_2$Cl$_9$] with the anion composed of a pair of face-sharing octahedra, the iron is in fact coordinated tetrahedrally and the correct formulation is, [(pyH)$_3$Cl][FeCl$_4$]$_2$, see R. SHAVIV, C. B. LOWE, J. A. ZORA, C. B. AAKERÖY, P. B. HITCHCOCK, K. R. SEDDON and R. L. CARLIN, *Inorg. Chim. Acta* **198–200**, 613–21 (1992).

[30] S. POHL, U. BIERBACH and W. SAAK, *Angew. Chem. Int. Edn. Engl.* **28**, 776–7 (1989).

so that the Fe^{III} is surrounded octahedrally by 6 sulfur atoms. They provide well documented examples of high-spin/low-spin crossover (i.e. spin equilibria) (see Panel p. 1096).

Ruthenium(III) forms extensive series of halide complexes, the aquo-chloro series being probably the best characterized of all its complexes. The $Ru^{III}/Cl^-/H_2O$ system has received extensive study, especially by ion-exchange techniques. The ions $[RuCl_n(H_2O)_{6-n}]^{(n-3)-}$ from $n = 6$ to $n = 0$ have all been identified in solution and a number also isolated as solids. $K_3[RuF_6]$ can be obtained from molten $RuCl_3/KHF_2$. Several bromo complexes have been reported amongst them the dimeric anion $[Ru_2Br_9]^{3-}$ which, like its choloro analogue, is composed of a pair of face-sharing octahedra. There are, however, no iodo complexes and, whilst $[Os(CN)_6]^{3-}$ as well as the Fe^{III} analogue are known and some substituted cyano complexes of Ru^{III} have been prepared, the parent $[Ru(CN)_6]^{3-}$ has only recently been isolated as the brilliant yellow $(Bu^n{}_4N)^+$ salt by aerial oxidation of dmf solution of $[Ru(CN)_6]^{2+}$.[31] Ru^{III} is much more amenable to coordination with N-donor ligands than is Fe^{III}, and forms ammines with from 3 to 6 NH_3 ligands (the extra ligands making up octahedral coordination are commonly H_2O or halides) as well as complexes with bipy and phen. Treatment of "$RuCl_3$" with aqueous ammonia in air slowly yields an extremely intense red solution (ruthenium red) from which a diamagnetic solid can be isolated, apparently of the form:

$$[(NH_3)_5Ru^{III}-O-Ru^{IV}(NH_3)_4-O-Ru^{III}(NH_3)_5]^{6+}$$

Its diamagnetism can be explained on the basis of π overlap, producing polycentre molecular orbitals essentially the same as used for $[Ru_2OCl_{10}]^{4-}$ (see Fig. 25.5). It is stable in either acid or alkali and its acid solution can be used as an extremely sensitive test for oxidizing agents since even such a mild reagent as iron(III) chloride oxidizes the red, 6+ cation to a yellow, paramagnetic, 7+ cation of the same constitution (a change which is detectable in solutions containing less than 1 ppm Ru).

Trinuclear basic acetates $[Ru_3O(O_2CMe)_6L_3]^+$ have also been prepared apparently with the same constitution as the analogous Fe^{III} and Cr^{III} compounds (p. 1030).

For osmium, halogeno complexes are less diverse but the reaction of acetic acid/acetic anhydride with $[OsCl_6]^{2-}$ yields brown $Os_2(O_2CMe)_4-Cl_2$ which, if treated as a suspension in anhydrous ethanol with gaseous HX (X = Cl, Br), yields $[Os_2X_8]^{2-}$. These diamagnetic ions are notable for the presence of the $Os \equiv Os$ triple bond unsupported by bridging ligands. The triply bridged $[Os_2Br_9]^{3-}$ is also known.[32]

Oxidation state II (d⁶)

This is the second of the common oxidation states for iron and is familiar for ruthenium, particularly with Group 15-donor ligands (Ru^{II} probably forms more nitrosyl complexes than any other metal). Osmium(II) also produces a considerable number of complexes but is usually more strongly reducing than Ru^{II}.

Iron(II) forms salts with nearly all the common anions.† These are usually prepared in aqueous solution either from the metal or by reduction of the corresponding Fe^{III} salt. In the absence of other coordinating groups these solutions contain the pale-green $[Fe(H_2O)_6]^{2+}$ ion which is also present in solids such as $Fe(ClO_4)_2.6H_2O$, $FeSO_4.7H_2O$ and the well-known "Mohr's salt", $(NH_4)_2SO_4FeSO_4.6H_2O$ introduced into volumetric analysis by K. F. Mohr in the 1850s.‡

---

[31] S. ELLER and R. D. FISCHER, *Inorg. Chem.*, **29**, 1289–90 (1990).

[32] G. A. HEATH and D. G. HUMPHREY, *J. Chem. Soc., Chem. Commun.*, 672–3 (1990).

† An exception is NO_2^- which instantly oxidizes Fe^{II} to Fe^{III} and liberates NO. $Fe(BrO_3)_2$ and $Fe(IO_3)_2$ also are unstable.

‡ K. F. Mohr (1806–79) was Professor of Pharmacy at the University of Bonn. Among his many inventions were the specific gravity balance, the burette, the pinch clamp, the cork borer, and the use of the so-called Liebig condenser for refluxing. In addition to his introduction of iron(II) ammonium sulfate as a standard reducing agent he devised Mohr's method for titrating halide solutions with silver ions

The hydrolysis (which in the case of Fe^{III} produces acidic solutions) is virtually absent, and in aqueous solution the addition of CO_3^{2-} does not result in the evolution of CO_2 but simply in the precipitation of white $FeCO_3$. The moist precipitate oxidizes rapidly on exposure to air but in the presence of excess CO_2 the slightly soluble $Fe(HCO_3)_2$ is formed. It is the presence of this in natural underground water systems, leading to the production of $FeCO_3$ on exposure to air, followed by oxidation to iron(III) oxide, which leads to the characteristic brown deposits found in many streams.

The possibility of oxidation to Fe^{III} is a crucial theme in the chemistry of Fe^{II} and most of its salts are unstable with respect to aerial oxidation, though double sulfates are much less so (e.g. Mohr's salt above). However, the susceptibility of Fe^{II} to oxidation is dependent on the nature of the ligands attached to it and, in aqueous solution, on the pH. Thus the solid hydroxide and alkaline solutions are very readily oxidized whereas acid solutions are much more stable (see Panel opposite).

Iron(II) forms complexes with a variety of ligands. As is to be expected, in view of its smaller cationic charge, these are usually less stable than those of Fe^{III} but the antipathy to *N*-donor ligands is less marked. Thus $[Fe(NH_3)_6]^{2+}$ is known whereas the Fe^{III} analogue is not; also there are fewer Fe^{II} complexes with *O*-donor ligands such as acac and oxalate, and they are less stable than those of Fe^{III}. High-spin octahedral complexes of Fe^{II} have a free-ion ^5D ground term, split by the crystal field into a ground $^5T_{2g}$ and an excited ^5E_g term. A magnetic moment of around 5.5 BM (i.e. 4.90 BM + orbital contribution) is expected for pure octahedral symmetry but, in practice, distortions produce values in the range 5.2–5.4 BM. Similarly, in the electronic spectrum, the expected single band due to the $^5E_g(t_{2g}^3e_g^3) \leftarrow {}^5T_{2g}(t_{2g}^4e_g^2)$ transition is broadened

---

in the presence of chromate as indicator, and was instrumental in establishing titrimeric methods generally for quantitative analysis.

or split. Besides stereochemical distortions, spin–orbit coupling and a Jahn–Teller effect in the excited configuration (footnote p. 1021) help to broaden the band, the main part of which is usually found between 10 000 and 11 000 cm^{-1}. The d–d spectra of low-spin Fe^{II} (which is isoelectronic with Co^{III}) are not so well documented, being generally obscured by charge-transfer absorption (p. 1128).

Most Fe^{II} complexes are octahedral but several other stereochemistries are known (Table 25.3). $[FeX_4]^{2-}$ (X = Cl, Br, I, NCS) are tetrahedral. A single absorption around 4000 cm^{-1} due to the $^5T_2 \leftarrow {}^5E$ transition is as expected, but magnetic moments of these and other apparently tetrahedral complexes are reported to lie in the range 5.0–5.4 BM, and the higher values are difficult to explain.

Low-spin, octahedral complexes are formed by ligands such as bipy, phen and CN^-, and their stability is presumably enhanced by the symmetrical t_{2g}^6 configuration. $[Fe(bipy)_3]^{2+}$ and $[Fe(phen)_3]^{2+}$ are stable, intensely red complexes, the latter being employed as the redox indicator, "ferroin", due to the sharp colour change which occurs when strong oxidizing agents are added to it:

$$[Fe(phen)_3]^{2-} \rightleftharpoons [Fe(phen)_3]^{3+} + e^-$$
$$\text{red} \qquad\qquad\qquad \text{blue}$$

Mono- and bis-phenanthroline complexes can be prepared but these are both high-spin and, because of the increase in CFSE (p. 1131) accompanying spin pairing ($\frac{2}{5}\Delta_0 \rightarrow \frac{12}{5}\Delta_0$), addition of phenanthroline to aqueous Fe^{II} leads almost entirely to the formation of the tris complex rather than mono or bis, even though the Fe^{II} is initially in great excess. Pale-yellow $K_4[Fe(CN)_6].3H_2O$ can be crystallized from aqueous solutions of iron(II) sulfate and an excess of KCN: this is clearly more convenient than the traditional method of fusing nitrogeneous animal residues (hides, horn, etc.) with iron and K_2CO_3. The hexacyanoferrate(II) anion (ferrocyanide) is kinetically inert and is said to be non-toxic, but HCN is liberated by the addition of dilute acids.

The Fe^{III}/Fe^{II} Couples

A selection of the standard reduction potentials for some iron couples is given in Table A, from which the importance of the participating ligand can be judged (see also Table 25.8 for biologically important iron proteins). Thus Fe^{III}, being more highly charged than Fe^{II} is stabilized (relatively) by negatively charged ligands such as the anions of edta and derivatives of 8-hydroxyquinoline, whereas Fe^{II} is favoured by neutral ligands which permit some charge delocalization in π-orbitals (e.g. bipy and phen).

Table A　　$E°$ at 25°C for some Fe^{III}/Fe^{II} couples in acid solution

Fe^{III}	Fe^{II}	$E°/V$
$[Fe(phen)_3]^{3+} + e^- \rightleftharpoons$	$[Fe(phen)_3]^{2+}$	1.12
$[Fe(bipy)_3]^{3+} + e^- \rightleftharpoons$	$[Fe(bipy)_3]^{2+}$	0.96
$[Fe(H_2O)_6]^{3+} + e^- \rightleftharpoons$	$[Fe(H_2O)_6]^{2+}$	0.77
$[Fe(CN)_6]^{3-} + e^- \rightleftharpoons$	$[Fe(CN)_6]^{4-}$	0.36
$[Fe(C_2O_4)_3]^{3-} + e^- \rightleftharpoons$	$[Fe(C_2O_4)_2]^{2-} + (C_2O_4)^{2-}$	0.02
$[Fe(edta)]^- + e^- \rightleftharpoons$	$[Fe(edta)]^{2-}$	−0.12
$[Fe(quin)_3] + e^- \rightleftharpoons$	$[Fe(quin)_2] + quin^{-}$ [a]	−0.30

[a] $quin^- = $ 5-methyl-8-hydroxyquinolinate.

The value of $E°$ for the couple involving the simple aquated ions, shows that $Fe^{II}(aq)$ is thermodynamically stable with respect to hydrogen; which is to say that $Fe^{III}(aq)$ is spontaneously reduced by hydrogen gas (see p. 435). However, under normal circumstances, it is not hydrogen but atmospheric oxygen which is important and, for the process $\frac{1}{2}O_2 + 2H^+ + 2e^- \rightleftharpoons H_2O$, $E° = 1.229\,V$, i.e. oxygen gas is sufficiently strong an oxidizing agent to render $[Fe(H_2O)_6]^{2+}$ (and, indeed, all other Fe^{II} species in Table A) unstable wrt atmospheric oxidation. In practice the oxidation in acidic solutions is slow and, if the pH is increased, the potential for the Fe^{III}/Fe^{II} couple remains fairly constant until the solution becomes alkaline and hydrous Fe_2O_3 (considered here for convenience to be $Fe(OH)_3$) is precipitated. But here the change is dramatic, as explained below.

The actual potential E of the couple is given by the Nernst equation,

$$E = E° - \frac{RT}{nF}\ln\frac{[Fe^{II}]}{[Fe^{III}]}$$

where $E = E°$ when all activities are unity. However, once precipitation occurs, the activities of the iron species are far from unity; they are determined by the solubility products of the 2 hydroxides. These are:

$$[Fe^{II}][OH^-]^2 \sim 10^{-14}(mol\ dm^{-3})^3 \quad and \quad [Fe^{III}][OH^-]^3 \sim 10^{-36}(mol\ dm^{-3})^4$$

Therefore when $[OH^-] = 1\ mol\ dm^{-3}$, $\dfrac{[Fe^{II}]}{[Fe^{III}]} \sim 10^{22}$

Hence $E \sim 0.771 - 0.05916\log_{10}(10^{22}) = 0.771 - 1.301 = -0.530\ V$

Thus by making the solution alkaline the sign of E has been reversed and the susceptibility of Fe^{II} (aq) to oxidation (i.e. its reducing power) enormously increased. This is why white, precipitated $Fe(OH)_2$ and $FeCO_3$ are rapidly darkened by aerial oxidation and why Fe^{II} in alkaline solution will reduce nitrates to ammonia and copper(II) salts to metallic copper.

Addition of $K_4[Fe^{II}(CN)_6]$ to aqueous Fe^{III} produces the intensely blue precipitate, Prussian blue.[32a] The X-ray powder pattern and Mössbauer spectrum of this are the same as those of Turnbull's blue which is produced by the converse addition of $K_3[Fe^{III}(CN)_6]$ to aqueous Fe^{II}. By varying the conditions and proportions of the reactants, a whole range of these blue materials can be produced of varying composition with some, which are actually colloidal, described as soluble Prussian blue. They have found application as pigments in the manufacture of inks and paints since their discovery in 1704 and, in 1840, their formation on sensitized paper was utilized in the production of blueprints. It appears that all these materials have the same basic structure. This consists of a cubic lattice of low-spin Fe^{II} and high-spin Fe^{III} ions with cyanide ions lying linearly along the cube edges, and water molecules situated inside the cubes. The intense colour is due to charge-transfer from Fe^{II} to Fe^{III}. Unfortunately, detailed characterizations are bedevilled by difficulties in obtaining satisfactory single crystals and reproducible compositions. Good quality single crystals formulated as $Fe_4[Fe(CN)_6]_3.xH_2O$ ($x = 14-16$) can be produced by the slow diffusion of H_2O vapour into a solution of Fe^{III} and $[Fe(CN)_6]^{4-}$ in conc HCl. This has the same basic lattice but with some of the Fe^{II} and CN^- sites occupied by water. Less delicate methods lead to the absorption of alkali metal ions (particularly K^+) and to formulations such as $M^I Fe^{II} Fe^{III}(CN)_6.xH_2O$. The same structure motif is found in $Fe^{III} Fe^{III}(CN)_6$ and in the virtually white, readily oxidizable $K_2 Fe^{II} Fe^{II}(CN)_6$, the former having no counter cations while the K^+ ions of the latter fill all the lattice cubes. Having all their iron atoms in a uniform oxidation state, however, these two compounds lack the intense colour of the Prussian blues.

It is possible to replace 1 CN^- in the hexacyanoferrate(II) ion with H_2O, CO, NO_2^-, and, most importantly, with NO^+. The "nitroprusside" ion $[Fe(CN)_5NO]^{2-}$ can be produced by the

action of 30% nitric acid on either $[Fe(CN)_6]^{4-}$ or $[Fe(CN)_6]^{3-}$. That it formally contains Fe^{II} and NO^+ (rather than Fe^{III} and NO) is evident from its diamagnetism, although Mössbauer studies indicate that there is appreciable π delocalization of charge from the t_{2g} orbitals of the Fe^{II} to the nitrosyl and cyanide groups. The red colour of $[Fe(CN)_5(NOS)]^{4-}$, formed by the addition of sulfide ion, is used in a common qualitative test for sulfur. Another qualitative test involving an iron nitrosyl is the "brown ring" test for NO_3^-, using iron(II) sulfate and conc H_2SO_4 in which NO is produced. The brown colour, which appears to be due to charge-transfer, evidently arises from a cationic iron nitrosyl complex which has a magnetic moment $\sim$3.9 BM; it is therefore formulated as $[Fe(NO)(H_2O)_5]^{2+}$ in which the iron can be considered formally to be in the +1 oxidation state.

Roussin's "red" and "black" salts, formulated respectively as $K_2[Fe_2(NO)_4S_2]$ and $K[Fe_4(NO)_7S_3]$, are obtained by the action of NO on Fe^{II} in the presence of S^{2-} and are structurally interesting. In both cases the iron atoms are pseudo-tetrahedrally coordinated (Fig. 25.6) and, though the assignment of formal oxidation states has only doubtful significance, their diamagnetism and the presence of rather short Fe–Fe distances are indicative of some direct metal–metal interaction. The $[NEt_4]^+$ black salt in acetonitrile solution has been reversibly reduced electrochemically[33] to $[Fe_4(NO)_7S_3]^{n-}$ ($n = 1-4$), the $n = 2$ and 3 compounds being isolated and shown to retain essentially the same structure, though somewhat expanded, as expected with the extra charge.

These, and related, iron nitrosyl compounds have excited considerable interest because of their biological activity.[34] Nitroprusside induces muscle relaxation and is therefore used to control high blood pressure. Roussin's black salt has antibacterial activity under conditions relevant to

[32a] K. R. DUNBAR and R. A. HEINTZ, *Prog. Inorg. Chem.* **45**, 283–391 (1997).

[33] S. D'ADDARIO, F. DEMARTIN, L. GROSSI, M. C. IAPALUCCI, F. LASCHI, G. LONGONI and F. ZANELLO, *Inorg. Chem.* **32**, 1153–60 (1993).

[34] A. R. BUTLER, C. GLIDEWELL and S. M. GLIDEWELL, *Polyhedron*, **11**, 591–6 (1992).

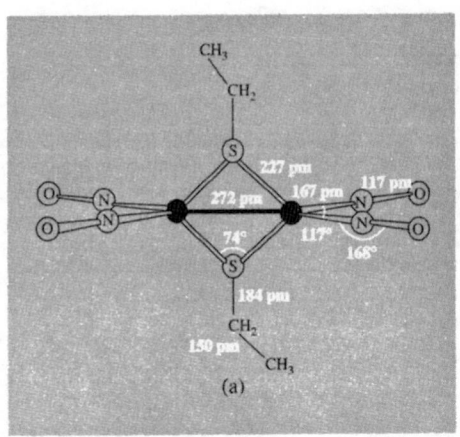 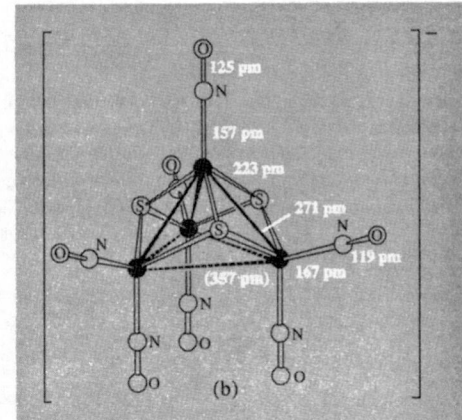

Figure 25.6   The structure of Roussin's salts: (a) the ethyl ester $[Fe(NO)_2SEt]_2$ of the red salt showing pseudo-tetrahedral coordination of each iron (Fe–Fe = 272 pm), and (b) the anion of the black salt $Cs[Fe_4(NO)_7S_3].H_2O$ showing a pyramid of 4 Fe atoms with an S atom above each of its three non-horizontal faces (Fe_{apex}–Fe_{base} = 271 pm, $Fe_{base}\cdots Fe_{base}$ 357 pm). (The anion may alternatively be viewed as an Fe_3S_3 ring with the "chair" conformation.) Note that even the short Fe–Fe distances are appreciably greater than the Fe–Fe "single-bond" distance of ~250 pm.

food-processing, while some of the red esters promote the activity of certain environmental carcinogens.

In addition to high-spin octahedral complexes with magnetic moments in excess of 5 BM, and diamagnetic, low-spin octahedral complexes, Fe^{II} affords further examples of high-spin/low-spin transitions within a given compound (see Panel, p. 1096). It has already been noted that a change from high-spin to low-spin accompanies the change,

$$[Fe(phen)_2(H_2O)_2]^{2+} \longrightarrow [Fe(phen)_3]^{2+}$$

so it is no great surprise that spin transitions have been found in $[Fe(phen)_2X_2]$ (X = NCS, NCSe) complexes and their bipy analogues. These evidently lie just to the high-field side of the crossover since at temperatures below −125°C the compounds are almost diamagnetic (what paramagnetism there is is probably due to impurity), while at some temperature between −125°C and −75°C depending on the compound, the moment quite suddenly rises to over 5 BM. Confirmation of the transition in these and other Fe^{II} complexes has been provided by electronic and Mössbauer spectroscopy.

Apart from compounds such as $[RuCl_2(PPh_3)_3]$, which is square pyramidal because the sixth coordinating position is stereochemically blocked, Ru^{II} compounds (and also Os^{II} compounds) are octahedral and diamagnetic. $[Ru(H_2O)_6]^{2+}$ can be prepared in aqueous solution by electrolytic reduction of $[RuCl_5(H_2O)]^{2-}$ using Pt/H_2 and, though readily oxidized to Ru^{III} (p. 1088), has been isolated and characterized[27] in the pink $[Ru(H_2O)_6](tos)_2$ and the sulfates $M_2[Ru(H_2O)_6](SO_4)_2$ (M = Rb, NH_4). The cyano complexes $[Ru(CN)_6]^{4-}$ and $[Ru(CN)_5NO]^{2-}$, analogous to their iron counterparts, are also known but the most notable compounds of Ru^{II} are undoubtedly its complexes with Group 15 donor ligands, such as the ammines and nitrosyls.

$[Ru(NH_3)_6]^{2+}$ and corresponding tris chelates with en, bipy and phen, etc., are obtained from "$RuCl_3$" with Zn powder as a reducing agent. The hexaammine is a strongly reducing substance and $[Ru(bipy)_3]^{2+}$, although thermally very stable, is capable of photochemical excitation involving the promotion of an electron from a molecular orbital of essentially metal character to one of an essentially ligand character, after which its oxidation is possible. A number of similar

Spin Equilibria[35–38]

Because the d-orbitals of a metal in an octahedral complex split into t_{2g} and e_g^* sets (p. 922), each of the d^4–d^7 configurations can exist in either high-spin or low-spin configurations, depending on whether the energy (P) required to force spin-pairing is greater or smaller than the orbital splitting (Δ_0 or $10Dq$). This is illustrated in the energy level diagrams (Figs. A and B) for d^5 and d^6 ions where in each case at a critical value of Δ_0 (the crossover point), the ground terms of the high- and low-spin configurations ($^6A_{1g}$ and $^2T_{2g}$ respectively for d^5, $^5T_{2g}$ and $^1A_{1g}$ for d^6) are equal. Close to the crossover point both terms are thermally accessible and a Boltzmann distribution of molecules between the two states can be envisaged.

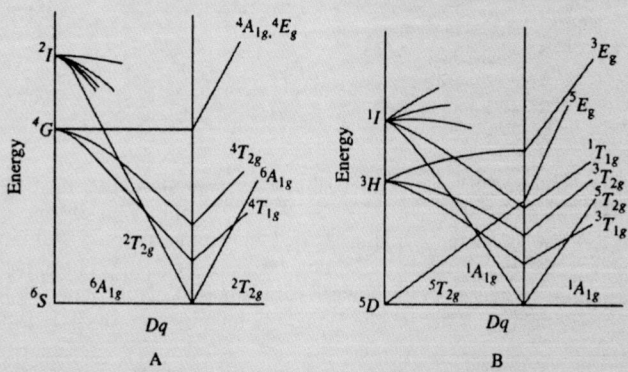

Energy level diagrams for, A d^5 ions and B d^6 ions.

This simple explanation accounts quite well for a variety of dithiocarbamato complexes of iron(III) whose magnetic moments rise gradually from about 2.3 BM (corresponding to low-spin d^5) at very low temperatures to > 4 BM (corresponding to roughly equal populations in the two states) above room temperature.

However, the emptying of the e_g^* orbitals in changing from high- to low-spin allows a shortening of metal-ligand distances with a corresponding increase in Δ_0. Such a situation does not correspond to the crossover point since the two isomers occupy different positions on the Δ_0 axis. In solutions, conversion of one isomer to the other is usually facile and equilibrium readily established. In solids, on the other hand, molecules are coupled by lattice vibrations and the conversion is often accompanied by a change of phase. The iron(II) compound [Fe(phen)$_2$(NCS)$_2$] is a good example of this, the change in magnetic moment being far too abrupt to be accounted for by a simple Boltzmann distribution between thermally accessible spin states.

Spin equilibria have been investigated by bulk magnetic measurements, X-ray crystallography, vibrational, electronic, Mössbauer, esr and nmr spectroscopy and also at high pressures. Besides their obvious intrinsic interest, they have biological relevance because of the change in spin when haemoglobin is oxygenated (p. 1099). Geologically, the high-spin iron(II) in minerals such as olivine (p. 347) becomes low-spin under high pressure in the earth's mantle. Since some spin-transitions can be induced optically, there are also possible light storage applications.

complexes with substituted bipyridyl ligands luminesce in visible light,[39] and considerable effort is being devoted to preparing suitable derivatives which could be used to catalyze the photolytic decomposition of water, with a view to the conversion of solar energy into hydrogen fuel.

$$2[\text{Ru(L-L)}_3]^{2+} + 2\text{H}^+ \longrightarrow$$
$$2[\text{Ru(L-L)}_3]^{3+} + \text{H}_2$$

then $2[\text{Ru(L-L)}_3]^{3+} + 2\text{OH}^- \longrightarrow$
$$2[\text{Ru(L-L)}_3]^{2+} + \text{H}_2\text{O} + \tfrac{1}{2}\text{O}_2$$

i.e. $\text{H}_2\text{O} \rightleftharpoons \text{H}^+ + \text{OH}^- \longrightarrow \text{H}_2 + \tfrac{1}{2}\text{O}_2$

[35] L. L. MARTIN, R. L. MARTIN and A. M. SARGESON, *Polyhedron* **13**, 1969–80 (1994).

[36] E. KÖNIG, *Structure and Bonding* **76**, 51–152 (1991).

[37] H. TOFLUND, *Coord. Chem. Revs.* **94**, 67–108 (1989).

[38] J. K. BEATTY, *Adv. Inorg. Chem.* **32**, 1–53 (1988).

[39] E. KRAUSZ and J. FERGUSON, *Prog. Inorg. Chem.* **37**, 293–390 (1989).

The pentaammine derivative, $[Ru(NH_3)_5N_2]^{2+}$, when prepared in 1965 by the reduction of aqueous $RuCl_3$ with N_2H_4, was the first dinitrogen complex to be produced (p. 414). It contains the linear Ru–N–N group ($\nu_{(N-N)}$ = 2140 cm^{-1}). The dinuclear derivative $[(NH_3)_5Ru-N-N-Ru(NH_3)_5]^{4+}$ with a linear Ru–N–N–Ru bridge ($\nu_{(N-N)}$ = 2100 cm^{-1} compared to 2331 cm^{-1} for N_2 itself) is also known (see pp. 414 and 1035 for a fuller discussion of the significance of N_2 complexes).

The nitrosyl complex $[Ru(NH_3)_5NO]^{3+}$, which is obtained by the action of HNO_2 on $[Ru(NH_3)_6]^{2+}$, is isoelectronic with $[Ru(NH_3)_5N_2]^{2+}$ and is typical of a whole series of Ru^{II} nitrosyls.[11,21] They are prepared using reagents such as HNO_3 and $NO_2{}^-$ and are invariably mononitrosyls, the 1 NO apparently sufficing to satisfy the π-donor potential of Ru^{II}. The RuNO group is characterized by a short Ru–N distance in the range 171–176 pm, and a stretching mode $\nu_{(N-O)}$ in the range 1930–1845 cm^{-1}, consistent with the formulation $Ru^{II}{=}\overset{+}{N}{=}O$. The other ligands making up the octahedral coordination include halides, O-donor anions, and neutral, mainly Group 15 donor ligands.

The stability of ruthenium nitrosyl complexes poses a practical problem in the processing of wastes from nuclear power stations. ^{106}Ru is a major fission product of uranium and plutonium and is a β^- and γ emitter with a half-life of 1 year (374d). The processing of nuclear wastes depends largely on the solvent extraction of nitric acid media, using tri-n-butyl phosphate (TBP) as the solvent (p. 1261). In the main, the uranium and plutonium enter the organic phase while fission products such as Cs, Sr and lanthanides remain in the aqueous phase. Unfortunately, by this procedure Ru is less effectively removed from the U and Pu than any other contaminant. The reason for this problem is the coordination of TBP to stable ruthenium nitrosyl complexes which are formed under these conditions. This confers on the ruthenium an appreciable solubility in the organic phase, thereby necessitating several extraction cycles for its removal.

Osmium(II) forms no hexaaquo complex and $[Os(NH_3)_6]^{2+}$, which may possibly be present in potassium/liquid NH_3 solutions, is also unstable. $[Os(NH_3)_5N_2]^{2+}$ and other dinitrogen complexes are known but only ligands with good π-acceptor properties, such as CN^-, bipy, phen, phosphines and arsines, really stabilize Os^{II}, and these form complexes similar to their Ru^{II} analogues.

Mixed Valence Compounds of Ruthenium [40]

Ruthenium provides more examples of dinuclear compounds in which the metal is present in a mixture of oxidation states (or in a non-integral oxidation state) than any other element.

Heating $RuCl_3.3H_2O$ in acetic acid/acetic anhydride under reflux yields brown $[Ru_2(O_2CCH_3)_4]-Cl$ (cf Os p. 1091) in which the metals are linked by four acetate bridges in the manner of Cr^{II} and Mo^{II} carboxylates (p. 1033). In this and analogous carboxylates, Ru = Ru 224–230 pm with magnetic moments indicative of three unpaired electrons; this can be explained by the assumption that the π^* and δ^* orbitals (see Fig. 23.14) are close enough in energy to afford the $\pi^{*2}\delta^*$ configuration.[41] Treatment of $[Ru(NH_3)_6]^{2+}$ in conc. HCl produces the intensely coloured ruthenium blue, $[(NH_3)_5Ru(\mu\text{-}Cl)_3Ru(NH_3)_5]^{2+}$ (Ru–Ru 275.3 pm). In all these cases the metal atoms are indistinguishable and are assigned an oxidation state of 2.5.

The "Creutz–Taube" anion, $[(NH_3)_5Ru-\{N(CH{=}CH)_2N\}Ru(NH_3)_5]^{5+}$ displays more obvious redox properties, yielding both 4+ and 6+ species, and much interest has focused on the extent to which the pyrazine bridge facilitates electron transfer. A variety of spectroscopic studies supports the view that low-energy electron tunnelling across the bridge delocalizes the charge, making the 5+ ion symmetrical. Other complexes, such as the anion $[(CN)_5Ru^{II}(\mu\text{-}CN)Ru^{III}(CN)_5]^-$, are asymmetric

[40] R. J. CRUTCHLEY, Adv. Inorg. Chem. **41**, 273–325 (1994).
[41] F. A. COTTON and R. A. WALTON, pp. 399–430 Multiple Bonds between Metal Atoms, Clarendon Press, Oxford (1993).

Table 25.7 Naturally occurring iron proteins

Name	Donor atoms. Stereochemisty of Fe	Function	Source	Approximate Mol wt	No. of Fe atoms
		Haem proteins			
Haemoglobin	$5 \times N$ Square pyramidal	O_2 transport	Animals	64 500	4
Myoglobin	$5 \times N$ Square pyramidal	O_2 storage	Animals	17 800	1
Cytochromes	$5 \times N + S$ Octahedral	Electron transfer	Bacteria, plants, animals	12 400	4
		NHIP (non-haem iron proteins)			
Transferrin		Scavenging Fe	Animals	80 000	2
Ferritin		Storage of Fe	Animals	460 000	20% Fe
Ferredoxins	$4 \times S$ Distorted tetrahedral	Electron transfer	Bacteria, plants, animals	6000–12 000	2–8
Rubridoxins	$4 \times S$ Distorted tetrahedral	Electron transfer	Bacteria	6000	1
"MoFe protein"		Nitrogen fixation		220 000–240 000	24–36
"Fe protein"	$4 \times S$ Distorted tetrahedral	(see p. 1035)	In nitrogenase	60 000	4

and are thought to have potential use in laser technology.[42]

Lower oxidation states

With rare exceptions, such as $[Fe(bipy)_3]^0$, oxidation states lower than $+2$ are represented only by carbonyls, phosphines, and their derivatives. These will be considered together with other organometallic compounds in Section 25.3.6.

25.3.5 The biochemistry of iron[43-45]

Iron is the most important transition element involved in living systems, being vital to both plants and animals. The stunted growth of the former is well known on soils which are either themselves deficient in iron, or in which high alkalinity renders the iron too insoluble to be accessible to the plants. Very efficient biological mechanisms exist to control the uptake and transport of iron and to ensure its presence in required concentrations. The adult human body contains about 4 g of iron (i.e. $\sim 0.005\%$ of body weight), of which about 3 g are in the form of haemoglobin, and this level is maintained by absorbing a mere 1 mg of iron per day — a remarkably economical utilization.

Proteins involving iron have two major functions:

(a) oxygen transport and storage;
(b) electron transfer.

Ancillary to the proteins performing these functions are others which transport and store the iron itself. All these proteins are conveniently categorized according to whether or not they contain haem, and the more important classes found in nature are listed in Table 25.7.

[42] W. M. LAIDLAW, R. G. DENNING, T. VERBIEST, E. CHAUCHARD and A. PERSOONS, *Nature* **363**, 58–60 (1993).

[43] J. G. LEIGH, G. R. MOORE and M. T. WILSON, Biological Iron, Chap. 6, pp. 181–243; A. K. POWELL, Models for Iron Biomolecules, Chap. 7, pp. 244–74, in ref. 10.

[44] R. CRICHTON, *Inorganic Biochemistry of Iron Metabolism*, Ellis Horwood, Hemel Hempstead, 1991, 212 pp.

[45] W. KAIM and B. SCHWEDERSKI, *Bioinorganic Chemistry: Inorganic Elements in the Chemistry of Life*, Wiley, Chichester, 1994, 401 pp.

Haemoglobin and myoglobin

Haemoglobin (see p. 126) is the oxygen-carrying protein in red blood-cells (erythrocytes) and is responsible for their colour. Its biological function is to carry O_2 in arterial blood from the lungs to the muscles, where the oxygen is transferred to the immobile myoglobin, which stores it so that it is available as and when required for the generation of energy by the metabolic oxidation of glucose. At this point the haemoglobin picks up CO_2, which is a product of the oxidation of glucose, and transports it in venous blood back to the lungs.[†]

In haemoglobin which has no O_2 attached (and is therefore known as deoxyhaemoglobin or reduced haemoglobin), the iron is present as high-spin Fe^{II} and the reversible attachment of O_2 (giving oxyhaemoglobin) changes this to diamagnetic, low-spin Fe^{II} without affecting the metal's oxidation state. This is remarkable, the more so because, if the globin is removed by treatment with HCl/acetone, the isolated haem in water entirely loses its O_2-carrying ability, being instead oxidized by air to haematin in which the iron is high-spin Fe^{III}:

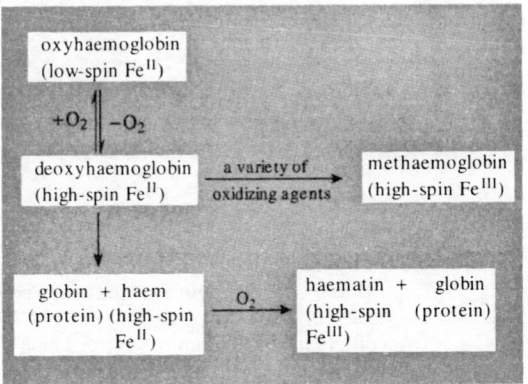

The key to the explanation lies in (a) the observation that in general the ionic radius of Fe^{II} (and also, for that matter, of Fe^{III}) decreases by roughly 20% when the configuration changes

from high- to low-spin (see Table 25.1), and (b) the structure of haemoglobin.

As a result of intensive study, enough is known about the structure of haemoglobin to allow the broad principles of its operation to be explained. It is made up of 4 subunits, each of which consists of a protein (globin), in the form of a folded helix or spiral, attached to 1 iron-containing group (haem). The proteins are of two types, one denoted as α consists of 141 amino acids, the other denoted as β consists of 146 amino acids. The polar groups of each protein are on the outside of the structure leaving a hydrophobic interior. The haem group, which is held in a protein "pocket" is therefore in a hydrophobic environment. Within the haem group the iron is coordinated to 4 nitrogen atoms of the planar group known as protoporphyrin IX (PIX). In the case of deoxyhaemoglobin the Fe^{II}, being high-spin, is too large to fit easily inside the hole provided by the porphyrin ring and is situated 55 pm above the ring which, in turn, is slightly bent into a domed shape, the better to accommodate the Fe^{II}. The fifth coordination site, away from the ring, is occupied by an imidazole nitrogen of a *proximal* histidine of the globin (Fig. 25.7). The vacant sixth site, below the ring, is essentially vacant, "reserved" for the O_2 but with another (*distal*) histidine restricting access. This is the so-called "tense" (deoxyT) form in which the 4 subunits of deoxyhaemoglobin are held together in an approximately tetrahedral arrangement by electrostatic $-NH_3^+ \cdots \overline{O}OC-$ "salt bridges."

In order that O_2 may bond to the haem, the *distal* histidine must swing away but, once the O_2 is attached, it swings back to form a hydrogen bond with the O_2. The Fe^{II} becomes low-spin and the oxyT form, which is still domed, "relaxes" to the planar oxyR form as the now smaller Fe^{II} slips into the ring which becomes planar again. When this occurs to one of the 4 subunits of deoxyhaemoglobin the movement of the Fe, and of the histidines attached to it, is communicated through the protein chains to the other subunits. This produces a rotation and linear movement of one $\alpha\beta$ pair w.r.t. the other which, crucially,

---

[†] Human arterial blood can absorb over 50 times more oxygen than can water, and venous blood can absorb 20 times more CO_2 than water can.

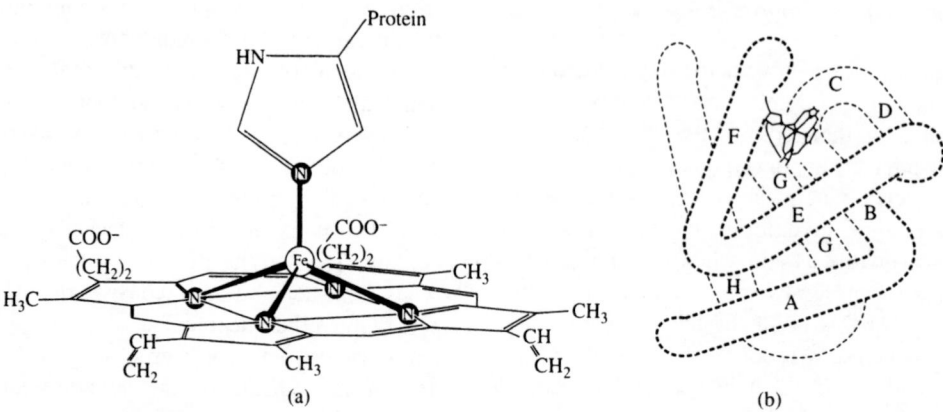

Figure 25.7   Haemoglobin: (a) The haem group, composed of the planar PIX molecule and iron, and shown here attached to the globin via an imidazole-nitrogen which completes the square pyramidal coordination of the Fe^{II}, and (b) myoglobin showing, diagrammatically, the haem group in a "pocket" formed by the folded protein. The globin chain is actually in the form of 8 helical sections, labelled A to H, and the haem is situated between the E and F sections. The 4 subunits of haemoglobin are similar.

converts the other 3 subunits to the deoxyR form, greatly increasing their affinity for O_2. The effect of attaching one O_2 to haemoglobin is therefore to greatly increase its affinity for more.

Conversely, as O_2 is removed from oxy-haemoglobin the reverse conformational changes occur and successively decrease its affinity for oxygen. This is the phenomenon of *cooperativity*, and its physiological importance lies in the fact that it allows the efficient transfer of oxygen from oxyhaemoglobin to myoglobin. This is because myoglobin contains only 1 haem group and can be regarded crudely as a single haemoglobin sub-unit. It therefore cannot display a cooperative effect and at lower partial pressures of oxygen it has a greater affinity than haemoglobin for oxygen. This can be seen in Fig. 25.8 which shows that, while haemoglobin is virtually sat-urated with O_2 in the lungs, when it experiences the lower partial pressures of oxygen in the mus-cle tissue its affinity for O_2 has fallen off so much more rapidly than that of myoglobin that oxy-gen transfer ensues. Indeed, the actual situation is even more effective than this, because the affinity of haemoglobin for oxygen decreases when the pH is lowered (this is called the Bohr effect and arises in a complicated manner from the effect

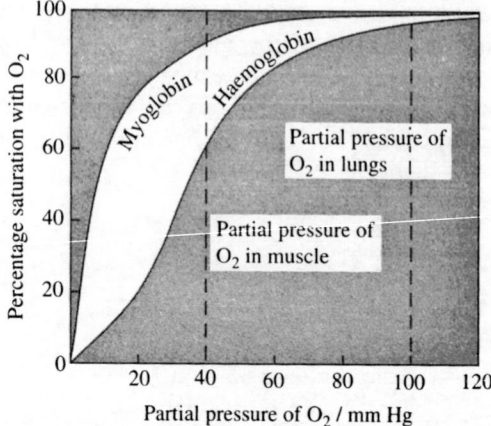

Figure 25.8   Oxygen dissociation curves for haemo-globin and myoglobin, showing how haemoglobin is able to absorb O_2 efficiently in the lungs yet transfer it to myoglobin in muscle tissue.

of pH on the salt bridges holding the subunits together). Since the CO_2 released in the muscle lowers the pH, it thereby facilitates the transfer of oxygen from the oxyhaemoglobin, and the greater the muscular activity the more the release of CO_2 helps to meet the increased demand for oxygen. Excess CO_2 is then removed from the tissue, predominantly in the form of soluble HCO_3^- ions whose formation is facilitated by the protein chains of deoxyhaemoglobin which act as a buffer by picking up the accompanying protons.

$$CO_2 + H_2O \rightleftharpoons HCO_3^- + H^+$$

The mode of bonding of the O_2 to Fe is important. In oxyhaemoglobin the hydrogen bonding to the *distal* histidine tilts the O_2 and produces an Fe–O–O angle of about 120°. This geometry (which hinders the formation of the Fe–O–Fe or Fe–O_2–Fe bridge believed to be an intermediate in Fe^{II} to Fe^{III} oxidations) along with the hydrophobic environment which inhibits electron transfer, together prevent the oxidation of Fe^{II} which would destroy the haemoglobin.

The poisoning effect of molecules such as CO and PF_3 (p. 495) arises simply from their ability to bond reversibly to haem in the same manner as O_2, but much more strongly, so that oxygen transport is prevented. The cyanide ion CN^- can also displace O_2 from oxyhaemoglobin but its very much greater toxicity at small concentrations stems not from this but from its interference with the action of cytochrome a.

Cytochromes [46]

The haem unit was evidently a most effective evolutionary development since it is found not only in the oxygen-transporting substances but also in electron transporters such as the cytochromes which are scattered widely throughout nature. There are three main types of cytochromes, a, b and c, members of each type being distinguished by subscripts, and their role is as intermediates in the metabolic oxidation of glucose by molecular oxygen. The iron of the haem group is attached to an associated protein by an imidazole N just as in haemoglobin and myoglobin. In most a and b cytochromes the sixth coordination site of the iron is also occupied by an imidazole N but, in type c and some type b cytochromes, it is occupied by a tightly bound

S from a methionine residue rendering these cytochromes inert not only to oxygen but also to the poisons which affect oxygen carriers. Electron transfer is effected in a series of steps, in each of which the oxidation state of the iron which is normally in a low-spin configuration oscillates between +2 and +3. Since the cytochromes are involved in the order b,c,a, the reduction potential of each step is successively increased (Table 25.8), so forming a "redox gradient". This allows energy from the glucose oxidation to be released gradually and to be stored in the form of adenosine triphosphate (ATP) (see also p. 528).

The link with the final electron acceptor, O_2, is the enzyme cytochrome c oxidase which spans the inner membrane of the mitochondrion. It consists of cytochromes a and a_3 along with two, or possibly three, Cu atoms. The details of its action are not fully established but the overall reaction catalysed by the enzyme is:

$$4Cytc^{2+} + O_2 + 8H_{inside}^+ \longrightarrow 4Cytc^{3+}$$
$$+ 2H_2O + 4H_{outside}^+$$

indicating the transport not only of electrons but also of protons across the mitochondrial membrane. As the end member of the redox gradient it differs from the other members in bonding O_2 directly and so being extremely susceptible to poisoning by CN^-.

Another important group of cytochromes, found in plants, bacteria and animals is cytochrome P-450, so-called because of the absorption at 450 nm characteristic of their complexes with CO. Their function is to activate

Table 25.8 Reduction potentials of some iron proteins

Iron protein	Oxidation states of Fe	$E°/V$
Cytochrome a_3	Fe^{III}/Fe^{II}	0.4
Cytochrome b	Fe^{III}/Fe^{II}	0.02
Cytochrome c	Fe^{III}/Fe^{II}	0.26
Rubredoxin	Fe^{III}/Fe^{II}	−0.06
2-Fe plant ferredoxins	Fe^{III}/fractional	−0.40
4-Fe bacterial ferredoxins	Fractional/ fractional	−0.37
8-Fe bacterial ferredoxins	Fractional/ fractional	−0.42

---

[46] See p. 206–8 of ref. 45.

O_2 sufficiently to facilitate its cleavage and so catalyse the reaction,

$$R-H + O_2 + 2H^+ + 2e^- \longrightarrow R-OH + H_2O$$

thus making R–H water soluble and aiding its elimination. They have molecular weights in the region of 50 000 and O_2 bonds to the haem in a manner similar to that in haemoglobin but with cysteine instead of histidine in the *proximal* position. The *S* donor atom of the cysteine is helpful in stabilizing an $Fe^{IV}{=}O$ group the oxygen of which is then inserted into the R–H bond.

Iron-sulfur proteins [47,48]

In spite of the obvious importance and diversity of haem proteins, comparable functions, especially that of electron transfer, are performed by non-haem iron proteins (NHIP).[†] These too are widely distributed (well over 100 are now known), different types being involved in nitrogen fixation (p. 1035) and photosynthesis as well as in the metabolic oxidation of sugars prior to the involvement of the cytochromes mentioned above. The NHIP responsible for electron transfer are the iron–sulfur proteins which are of relatively low molecular weight (6000–12 000) and contain 1, 2, 4 or 8 Fe atoms which, in all the structures which have been definitely established, are each coordinated to 4 S atoms in an approximately tetrahedral manner. As a consequence of the small ligand fields associated in the tetrahedral coordination, these all contain iron in the high-spin configuration. Nearly all NHIP are notable for reduction potentials in the unusually low range -0.05 to $-0.49\,V$ (Table 25.8), indicating their ability to act as reducing agents at the low-potential end of biochemical processes.

The simplest NHIP is rubredoxin, in which the single iron atom is coordinated (Fig. 25.9a) to 4 S atoms belonging to cysteine residues in the protein chain. It differs from the other Fe–S proteins in having no labile sulfur (i.e. inorganic sulfur which can be liberated as H_2S by treatment with mineral acid; sulfur atoms of this type are not part of the protein, but form bridges between Fe atoms.)

NHIP with more than one Fe are conveniently classified as [2Fe–2S], [3Fe–4S] and [4Fe–4S] types. The first of these, the so-called plant ferredoxins act as 1-electron transfer agents and contain 2 Fe atoms joined by S bridges with terminal cysteine groups (Fig. 25.9b). The 2 Fe atoms in the oxidized form are high-spin Fe(III) but very low magnetic moments are observed because of strong spin–spin interaction via the bridging atoms. The iron centres are not equivalent however, and esr evidence suggests that in the reduced form they exist as Fe(III) and Fe(II) rather than both having a fractional oxidation state of $+2.5$.

The existence of [3Fe–4S] ferredoxins has been established by Mössbauer spectroscopy only comparatively recently. The cluster consists essentially of the cubane [4Fe–4S] with one corner removed, the irons being high-spin Fe(III) in the oxidized form and Fe(II) + 2Fe(III) in the reduced. The most common and most stable of the ferredoxins, however, are the [4F–4S] type (Fig. 25.9c). In these clusters the 4 × Fe and 4 × S atoms form 2 interpenetrating tetrahedra which together make up a distorted cube in which each Fe atom is additionally coordinated to a cysteine sulfur to give it an approximately tetrahedral coordination sphere. The cluster, like the 2-Fe dimer, acts as a 1-electron transfer agent so that an 8-Fe protein, in which there are two [4Fe–4S] units with centres about 1200 pm apart can effect a 2-electron transfer. Why 4 Fe atoms are required to transfer 1 electron is not obvious. Synthetic analogues, prepared by reacting $FeCl_3$, NaHS and an appropriate thiol (or still better $FeCl_3$, elemental sulfur and the Li salt of a thiol), have properties similar to those of the natural proteins and have been used

[47] R. CAMMACK (ed.) *Adv. Inorg. Chem.* **38**, 1992, 487 pp. Whole volume devoted to Fe–S proteins.

[48] I. BERTINI, S. CUIRLI and C. LUCHINAT, *Structure and Bonding*, **83**, 1–53 (1995).

[†] The oxygen-carrying function is performed in some invertebrates by haemerythrin which, in spite of its name, does not contain haem. It is a diiron–oxygen protein. See K. K. ANDERSON and A. GRÄLUND, *Adv. Inorg. Chem.* **43**, 359–408 (1995).

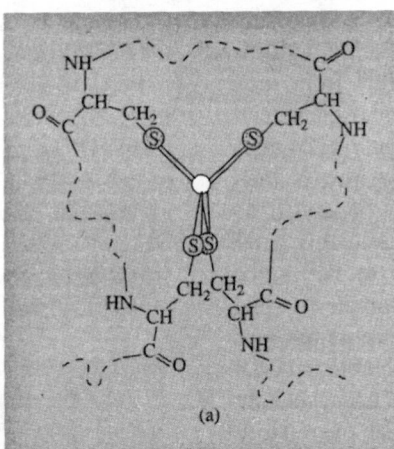

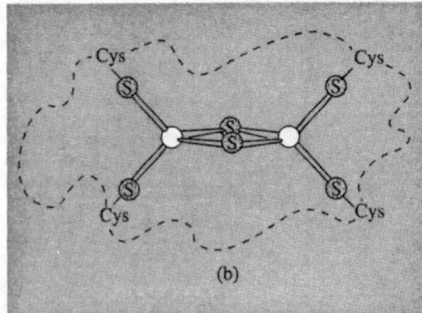

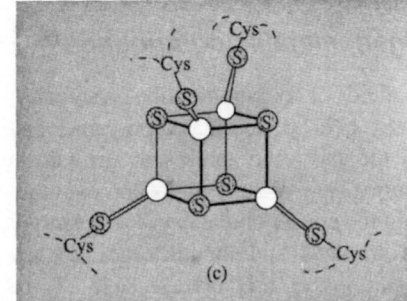

Figure 25.9   Some non-haem iron proteins: (a) rubredoxin in which the single Fe is coordinated, almost tetra-hedrally, to 4 cysteine-sulfurs, (b) plant ferredoxin, $[Fe_2S_2(S\text{-}Cys)_4]$, (c) $[Fe_4S_4(S\text{-}Cys)_4]$ cube of bacterial ferredoxins. (This is in fact distorted, the Fe_4 and S_4 making up the two interpenetrating tetrahedra, of which the latter is larger than the former).

extensively in attempts to solve this problem.[43] The esr, electronic, and Mössbauer spectra, as well as the magnetic properties of the synthetic $[Fe_4S_4(SR)_4]^{3-}$ anions, are similar to those of the reduced ferredoxins, whose redox reaction is therefore mirrored by:

$$[Fe_4S_4(SR)_4]^{3-} \rightleftharpoons [Fe_4S_4(SR)_4]^{2-}$$

$$\text{reduced ferredoxin} \underset{+e}{\overset{-e}{\rightleftharpoons}} \text{oxidized ferredoxin}$$

This indicates a change in the formal oxidation state of the iron from $+2.25$ to $+2.5$, and mixed Fe^{III}/Fe^{II} species have been postulated. However, it appears likely that these clusters are best regarded as electronically delocalized systems in which all the Fe atoms are equivalent.

4-Fe proteins are also known in which the diamagnetic, oxidized $[Fe_4S_4(SR)_4]^{2-}$ can be further oxidized at high potentials of about $+0.35\,V$ (hence "high potential iron sulfur proteins", HIPIP) to paramagnetic ($S = 1/2$), $[Fe_4S_4(SR)_4]^-$ species. Structural details and, indeed, biological function are still unclear.

Other non-haem proteins, distinct from the above iron-sulfur proteins are involved in the roles of iron transport and storage. Iron is absorbed as Fe^{II} in the human duodenum and passes into the blood as the Fe^{III} protein, transferrin.[49] The Fe^{III} is in a distorted octahedral environment consisting of $1 \times N$, $3 \times O$ and a chelating carbonate ion which

---

[49] E. N. BAKER, *Adv. Inorg. Chem.* **41**, 389–463 (1994)

apparently "locks" the iron into the binding site. This has a stability constant sufficiently high for the uncombined protein to strip Fe^{III} from such stable complexes as those with phosphate and citrate ions, and so it very efficiently scavenges iron from the blood plasma. The iron is then transported to the bone marrow where it is released from the transferrin (presumably after the temporary reduction of Fe^{III} to Fe^{II} since the latter's is a much less-stable complex), to be stored as ferritin, prior to its incorporation into haemoglobin. Ferritin is a water-soluble material consisting of a layer of protein encapsulating iron(III) hydroxyphosphate to give an overall iron content of about 20%.

25.3.6 Organometallic compounds [50]

Within the field of organometallic chemistry, iron has long held a dominant position, and the last decade has seen explosive growth in the organic chemistry of ruthenium and osmium, particularly in the cluster chemistry[51] of osmium carbonyls. Carbonyls and metallocenes occupy dominant positions in this diverse field. Thus, although alkyls and aryls are known, they are only obtained with bulky groups which cannot undergo β-elimination (p. 925) or if the M–C σ bonds are stabilized by π-bonding ligands such as CO and P-donors.

Carbonyls (see p. 926)

Having the d^6s^2 configuration, the elements of this triad are able to conform with the 18-electron rule by forming mononuclear carbonyls of the type $M(CO)_5$. These are volatile liquids which can be prepared by the direct action of CO on the powdered metal (Fe[†] and Ru) or by the action of

CO on the tetroxide (Os), in each case at elevated temperatures and pressures.

$Fe(CO)_5$ is a highly toxic substance discovered in 1891, the only previously known metal carbonyl being $Ni(CO)_4$. Like its thermally unstable Ru and Os analogues, its structure is trigonal bipyramidal (Fig. 25.10a) but its ^{13}C nmr spectrum indicates that all 5 carbon atoms are equivalent and this is explained by the molecules' fluxional behaviour (p. 914).

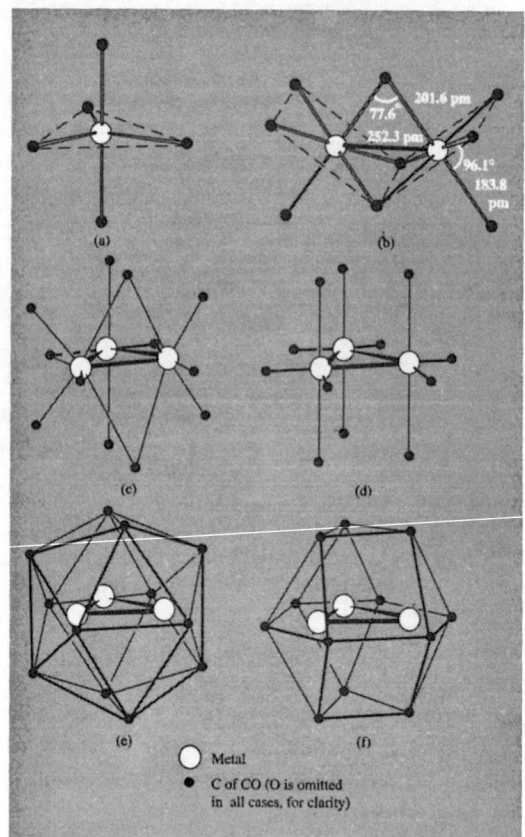

Figure 25.10 Some carbonyls of Fe, Ru and Os: (a) $M(CO)_5$; M = Fe, Ru, Os. (b) $Fe_2(CO)_9$; Fe–Fe = 252.3 pm. (c) $Fe_3(CO)_{12}$; 1 Fe–Fe = 256 pm, 2 Fe–Fe = 268 pm. (d) $M_3(CO)_{12}$; M = Ru, Os, Ru–Ru = 285 pm, Os–Os = 288 pm. (e) and (f) are alternative representations of (c) and (d) emphasizing respectively the icosahedral and anti-cubeoctahedral arrangements of the CO ligands.

[50] P. L. PAUSON, Chap. 4 in *Chemistry of Iron*, pp. 73–170, Blackie, London, 1993.

[51] A. J. AMOROSO, L. H. GADE, B. F. G. JOHNSON, J. LEWIS, P. R. RAITHBY and W. T. WONG, *Angew. Chem. Int. Edn. Engl.* **30**, 107–9 (1991); B. H. S. THIMMAPPA, *Coord. Chem. Revs.* **143**, 1–35 (1995).

[†] The presence of $Fe(CO)_5$ in commercial cylinders of carbon monoxide at levels of 50 ppm has been reported (*Chem, in Brit.* **28**, 517 (1992)).

Exposure of $Fe(CO)_5$ in organic solvents to ultraviolet light produces volatile orange crystals of the enneacarbonyl, $Fe_2(CO)_9$. Its structure consists of two face-sharing octahedra (Fig. 25.10b). An electron count shows that the dimer has a total of 34 valence electrons, i.e. 17 per iron atom. The observed diamagnetism is therefore explained by the presence of an Fe–Fe bond which is consistent with an interatomic separation virtually the same as in the metal itself. It is of interest that Ru and Os counterparts of $Fe_2(CO)_9$ are not only thermally less stable (the former especially so) but apparently are also structurally different, having an M–M bond supported by only 1 CO bridge. The carbonyls, which are produced along with the pentacarbonyls of Ru and Os and were initially thought to be enneacarbonyls, are in fact trimers, $M_3(CO)_{12}$, which also differ structurally from $Fe_3(CO)_{12}$ (Fig. 25.10c to f). This dark-green solid, which is best obtained by oxidation of $[FeH(CO)_4]^-$ (see below), has a triangular structure in which two of the iron atoms are bridged by a pair of carbonyl groups, and can be regarded as being derived from $Fe_2(CO)_9$ by replacing a bridging CO with $Fe(CO)_4$. The Ru and Os compounds (orange and yellow respectively), on the other hand, have a more symmetrical structure in which all the metal atoms are equivalent and are held together solely by M–M bonds. It has been suggested (Johnson's Ligand Polyhedral Model[52]) that the structure of the iron compound is determined not by the major bonding forces but by the interactions between the 12 CO ligands which in fact form an icosahedral array. This accommodates an Fe_3 triangle with Fe–Fe distances similar to those in the metal, but not the larger Ru_3 and Os_3 triangles which force the ligands to adopt the less dense anticubeoctahedral form. As with the mononuclear carbonyl, the ^{13}C nmr spectrum of the iron compound indicates C atom equivalence but this can be accounted for by oscillation of the Fe_3 triangle without disruption of the icosahedral

array of CO ligands.[52] In solution, a non-bridged isomer is formed, different from the Ru_3 and Os_3 carbonyls and again probably retaining the icosahedral arrangement of ligands.

The chemistry of these carbonyls, especially those of Os, is extensive and displays an astonishing structural diversity which has been exploited particularly by the Cambridge group of J. Lewis.[53] $Os_3(CO)_{12}$ is the starting material for the preparation of other Os_3 species and for clusters of higher nuclearity.[54] It is itself prepared by the reaction of OsO_4 and CO under high pressure and is more stable than its Ru counterpart, which has a weaker M–M bond enthalpy ($76 \, kJ \, mol^{-1}$ compared to $94 \, kJ \, mol^{-1}$ in $Os_8(CO)_{12}$) and fragments rather easily. Thermolysis of $Os_3(CO)_{12}$ at 200°C yields mainly $Os_6(CO)_{18}$ along with smaller quantities of $Os_5(CO)_{16}$, $Os_7(CO)_{21}$ (Fig. 25.11) and $Os_8(CO)_{23}$. By careful adjustment of conditions, thermal and photochemical methods can give good yields of selected products but more rational methods have also been developed. Nucleophilic attack, by amine oxides for instance, removes CO (as CO_2) allowing a vacant site to be filled by a donor solvent such as MeCN. The products may themselves be pyrolysed or the solvent molecules replaced by metal nucleophiles such as $H_2Os(CO)_4$:

$$Os_3(CO)_{12} + R_3NO \xrightarrow{MeCN} Os_3(CO)_{11}(MeCN)$$

$$\xrightarrow[\quad]{H_2Os(CO)_4} H_2Os_4(CO)_{13}$$

Carbonyl hydrides and carbonylate anions

The treatment of iron carbonyls with aqueous or alcoholic alkali can, by varying the conditions, be used to produce a series of interconvertible carbonylate anions: $[HFe(CO)_4]^-$, $[Fe(CO)_4]^{2-}$, $[Fe_2(CO)_8]^{2-}$, $[HFe_3(CO)_{11}]^-$ and $[Fe_4(CO)_{13}]^{2-}$. Of these the first has a distorted trigonal bipyramidal structure with axial H, the second

52 B. F. G. JOHNSON and Y. V. ROBERTS, *Polyhedron* **12**, 977–90 (1993).

53 J. LEWIS, *Chem. in Brit.* **24(5)**, 795–800 (1988).
54 A. J. DEEMING, *Adv. Organomet. Chem.* **26**, 1–96 (1986).

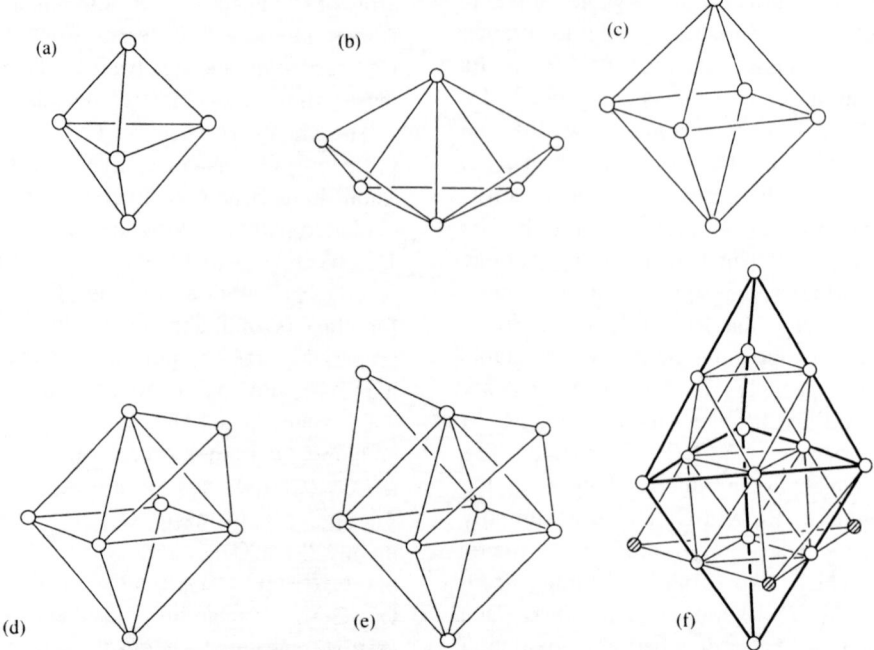

Figure 25.11   Metal frameworks of some high-nuclearity binary carbonyl and carbonylate clusters of osmium:
(a) $Os_5(CO)_{16}$ (trigonal bipyramid); (b) $Os_6(CO)_{18}$ (bicapped tetrahedron, or capped trigonal
bipyramid); (c) $[Os_6(CO)_{18}]^{2-}$ (octahedron); (d) $Os_7(CO)_{21}$ (capped octahedron); (e) $[Os_8(CO)_{22}]^{2-}$
(bicapped octahedron); (f) $[Os_{17}(CO)_{36}]^{2-}$ (3 shaded atoms cap an Os_{14} trigonal bipyramid).

is isoelectronic and isostructural with $Ni(CO)_4$,
the third is isoelectronic with $Co_2(CO)_8$ and
isostructural with the isomer containing no
CO bridges, while the trimeric and tetrameric
anions have the cluster structures shown in
Fig. 25.12. The related ruthenium complexes
$[HRu_3(CO)_{11}]^-$ and $[H_3Ru_4(CO)_{12}]^-$, are of
interest as possible catalysts for the "water-gas
shift reaction".[†]

[†] Water-gas is produced by the high-temperature reaction of
water and C:

$$C + H_2O \longrightarrow CO + H_2$$

and is therefore a mixture of H_2O. CO and H_2. By suitably
adjusting the relative proportions of CO and H_2, "synthesis gas" is obtained which can be used for the synthesis of
methanol and hydrocarbons (the Fischer–Tropsch process).
It is this catalytically controlled adjustment:

$$H_2O + CO \rightleftharpoons H_2 + CO_2$$

which is the water-gas shift reaction (WGSR) (see p. 421).

Reduction of the pH of solutions of carbonylate
anions yields a variety of protonated species
and, from acid solutions, carbonyl hydrides such
as the unstable, gaseous $H_2Fe(CO)_4$ and the
polymeric liquids $H_2Fe_2(CO)_8$ and $H_2Fe_3(CO)_{11}$
are liberated. The use of ligand-replacement
reactions to yield hydrides of higher nuclearity
has already been noted.

Thermolysis of binary carbonyls or of their
partially substituted derivatives, either under
vacuum or in solutions, has been used to
produce carbonyls and carbonylate anions with
an unparalleled range of structures (Fig. 25.11).
The Ru chemistry, though less well developed,
mostly parallels that of Os.[55] These compounds
are interesting not only for their catalytic
potential but also for the preparative and
theoretical problems they pose. Almost all these

---

[55] See for instance L. MA, G. WILLIAMS and J. R. SHAPLEY,
Coord. Chem. Revs. **128**, 261–84 (1993).

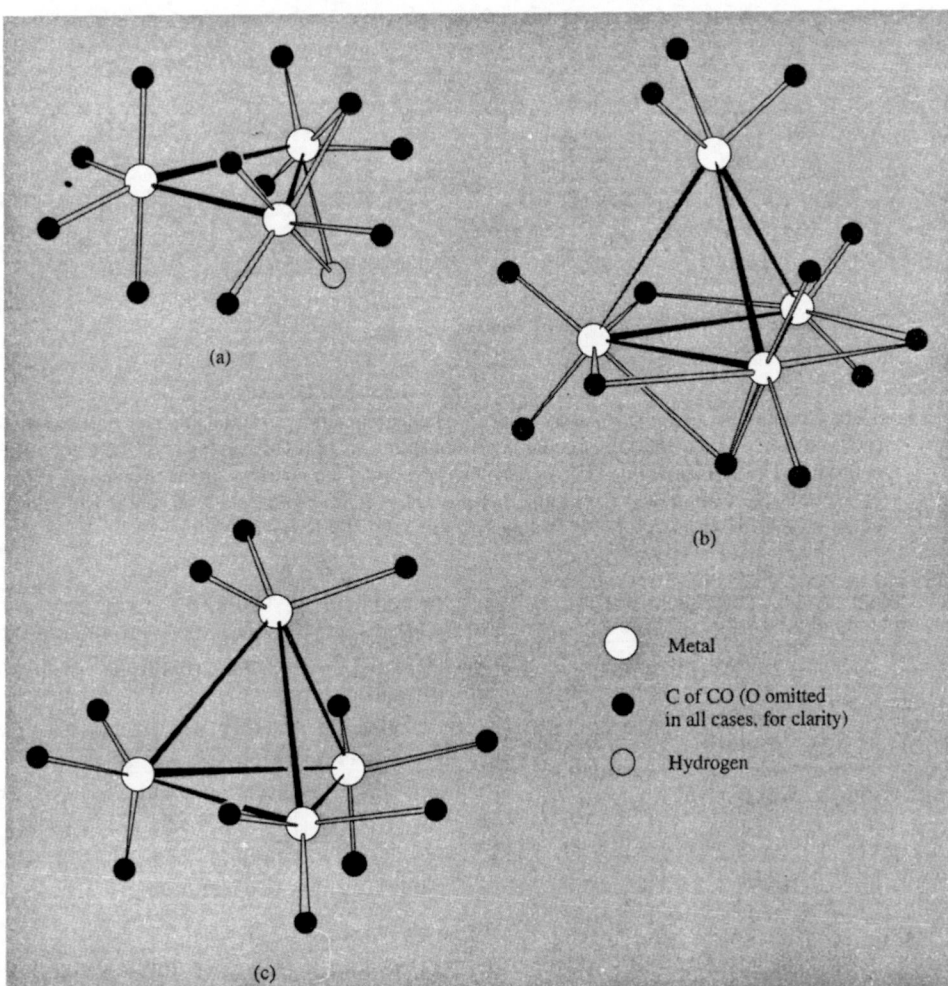

Figure 25.12 Some small carbonylate anion clusters of Fe, Ru and Os: (a) $[HM_3(CO)_{11}]^-$; M = Fe, Ru. (b) $[Fe_4(CO)_{13}]^{2-}$. (c) $[H_3Ru_4(CO)_{12}]^-$. [The H atoms are not shown in (c) because this ion exists in two isomeric forms: (i) the 3 H atoms bridge the edges of a single face of the tetrahedron, and (ii) the 3 H atoms bridge three edges of the tetrahedron which do not form a face.]

polyhedral clusters are networks of triangular faces, are diamagnetic and have structures which can be rationalized by electron-counting arguments. However, in applying these rules it has to be noted that where an $M(CO)_3$ group "caps" a triangular face it has no effect on the skeletal electron count of the central polyhedron. Nor do such rules predict structures *precisely*. The $[H_2M_6(CO)_{18}$, $[HM_6(CO)_{18}]^-$ and $[M_6(CO)_{18}]^{2-}$ clusters, for instance, while being stoichiometrically the same for M = Ru and M =

Os, and having the same essentially octahedral skeletons, nevertheless differ appreciably in the disposition of the attached carbonyl groups. The incorporation of interstitial (encapsulated) atoms such as C, H, S, N, P and, more recently, B[56] is a widespread and frequently stabilizing feature of these clusters. Carbido clusters are the most common the C contributing 4 electrons

---

[56] C. E. HOUSECROFT, D. A. MATTHEWS, A. RHEINGOLD and X. SONG, *J. Chem. Soc., Chem. Commun.*, 842–3 (1992).

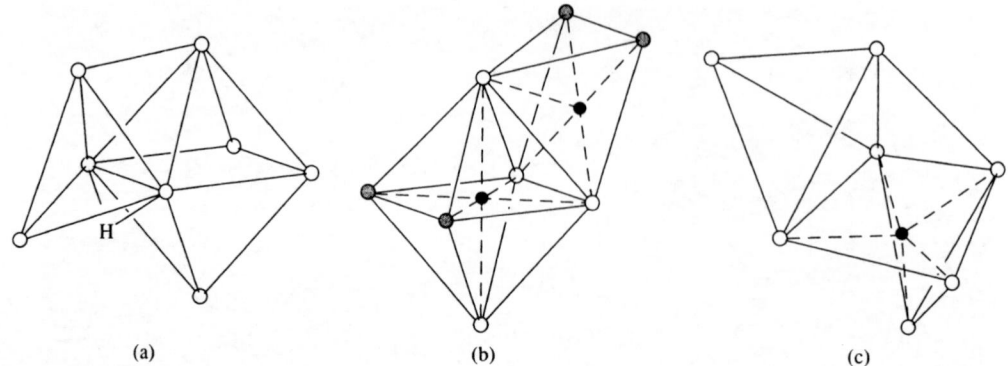

(a)   (b)   (c)

Figure 25.13   Metal frameworks of some Ru and Os carbonyl clusters with interstitial atoms. (a) $[Ru_8(H)_2(CO)_{21}]^{2-}$ (octahedron and face-sharing trigonal bipyramid); the second H is probably at the centre of the octahedron. (b) $[Ru_8(C)_2(CO)_{17}(PPh_2)_2]$ (octahedron and face-sharing square pyramid); PPh$_2$ ligands bridge the pairs of shaded Ru atoms. (c) $[Os_7(H)_2C(CO)_{19}]$ (tetrahedron and 3 irregularly spaced metal atoms); H atoms probably bridge two edges of the tetrahedron.

Table 25.9   Some metal carbonyl clusters with interstitial atoms

$[Fe_5C(CO)_{15}]$	black	square pyramidal*
$[Fe_6C(CO)_{16}]^{2-}$	black	octahedral
$[Ru_6C(CO)_{17}]$	deep red	octahedral
$[Ru_6H(CO)_{18}]^-$	red	octahedral
$[Ru_6(H)_2B(CO)_{18}]^-$	orange	trig.prism (H bridges)[55]
$[Ru_8C_2(CO)_{17}(PPh_2)_2]$	black	Fig. 25.13b
$[Ru_8(H)_2(CO)_{21}]^{2-}$	black	Fig. 25.13a
$[Ru_{10}C_2(CO)_{24}]^{2-}$	purple	bis oct.
$[Os_6P(CO)_{18}Cl]$	yellow	trig. prism (Cl bridge)
$[Os_7C(H)_2(CO)_{19}]$	green	Fig. 25.13c
$[Os_8C(CO)_{21}]$	purple	bicapped oct.
$[Os_9H(CO)_{24}]$	brown	tricapped oct.
$[Os_{10}C(CO)_{24}]^{2-}$	pink-red	tetracapped oct.

*corresponding Ru and Os compounds are red and orange respectively.

to the formal electron count and originating possibly from the solvent or, more often, from cleavage of a CO ligand. This is especially true for Ru where the formation of carbido clusters is a general consequence of thermolysis. Some illustrative examples of these compounds are listed in Table 25.9.

The encapsulated atom usually occupies the centre of the polyhedron of metals (or its base in the case of square pyramids). Its position can be located with precision by X-ray crystallography except for H, when it is possible only under the most favourable conditions, or by neutron diffraction.

A general property of these carbonyl clusters is their tendency to behave as electron "sinks", and their redox chemistry is extensive.[57] $[Os_{10}C(CO)_{24}]^{n-}$ has been characterized in no less than five oxidation states ($n = 0-4$); though admittedly this is exceptional.

Carbonyl halides and other substituted carbonyls

Numerous carbonyl halides, of which the best known are octahedral compounds of the type $[M(CO)_4X_2]$ are obtained by the action of halogen on Fe(CO)$_5$, or CO on MX$_3$ (M = Ru, Os). Stepwise substitution of the remaining CO groups is possible by X$^-$ or other ligands such as N, P and As donors.

Direct substitution of the carbonyls themselves is of course possible. Besides Group 15 donor ligands, unsaturated hydrocarbons give especially interesting products. The iron carbonyl acetylenes provided early examples of the use of carbonyls in organic synthesis. From them a wide variety

[57] S. R. DRAKE, *Polyhedron* **9**, 455–74 (1990).

of cyclic compounds can be obtained as a result of condensation of coordinated acetylenes with themselves and/or CO. The complexes involving the acetylenes alone are usually unstable intermediates which are only separable when bulky substituents are incorporated on the acetylene. More usually, complexes of the condensed cyclic products are isolated. These ring systems include quinones, hydroquinones, cyclobutadienes and cyclopentadienones, the specific product depending on the particular iron carbonyl used and the precise conditions of the reaction.

Ferrocene and other cyclopentadienyls

Bis(cyclopentadienyl)iron, $[Fe(\eta^5-C_5H_5)_2]$, or, to give it the more familiar name coined by M. C. Whiting, "ferrocene", is the compound whose discovery in the early 1950s utterly transformed the study of organometallic chemistry.[2] Yet the two groups of organic chemists who independently made the discovery, did so accidentally. P. L. Pauson and T. J. Kealy (*Nature* **168**, 1039 (1951)) were attempting to synthesize fulvalene, [diagram], by reacting the Grignard reagent cyclopentadienyl magnesium bromide with $FeCl_3$, but instead obtained orange crystals (mp 173°C) containing Fe^{II} and analysing for $C_{10}H_{10}Fe$. In a paper submitted simultaneously (*J. Chem. Soc.* 632 (1952)), S. A. Miller, T. A. Tebboth and J. F. Tremaine reported passing cyclopentadiene and N_2 over a reduced iron catalyst as part of a programme to prepare amines and they too obtained $C_{10}H_{10}Fe$.[†]

The initial structural formulation was [diagram] Fe [diagram], but the correct formulation, an unprecedented "sandwich" compound, was soon to follow. For this and for subsequent independent work in this field, G. Wilkinson and

E. O. Fischer shared the 1973 Nobel Prize for Chemistry.

The structure of ferrocene and an MO description of its bonding have already been given (p. 937). The rings are virtually eclipsed as they are in the analogous ruthenocene (light-yellow, mp 199°C) and osmocene (white, mp 229°C).

This is also the case in the decamethylmetallocenes of Ru and Os but not in the iron analogue which has a staggered conformation, presumably due to steric crowding around the smaller metal.

$[M(\eta^5-C_5H_5)_2]$ satisfy the 18-electron rule (p. 1134) and are stable to air and water but are readily oxidized. From ferrocene the blue-green, paramagnetic ferricinium ion, $[Fe^{III}(\eta^5-C_5H_5)_2]^+$, is produced whereas the Ru and Os monocations are unstable, oxidizing further to $[M^{IV}(\eta-C_5H_5)_2]^{2+}$ or dimerizing to $[(\eta^5-C_5H_5)_2M^{III}-M^{III}(\eta^5-C_5H_5)_2]^{2+}$. The decamethylferricinium salt, $[Fe(\eta^5-C_5Me_5)_2][tcne]$, (tcne = tetracyanoethylene) is a dark green crystalline material consisting of linear chains of alternating anions and cations.[58] It has the astonishing property of being a 1D molecular ferromagnet (with a saturation magnetisation greater than that of metallic iron itself on a molar basis), although the mechanism by which this originates is not yet settled.

The most notable chemistry of the bisclyopentadienyls results from the aromaticity of the cyclopentadienyl rings. This is now far too extensively documented to be described in full but an outline of some of its manifestations is in Fig. 25.14. Ferrocene resists catalytic hydrogenation and does not undergo the typical reactions of conjugated dienes, such as the Diels–Alder reaction. Nor are direct nitration and halogenation possible because of oxidation to the ferricinium ion. However, Friedel–Crafts acylation as well as alkylation and metallation reactions, are readily effected. Indeed, electrophilic substitution of ferrocene occurs with such facility compared to, say, benzene (3×10^6 faster) that some explanation is called for. It has been suggested that,

---

[†] In retrospect it seems likely that ferrocene was actually first prepared as volatile yellow crystals in the 1930s by chemists at Union Carbide who passed dicyclopentadiene through a heated iron tube, but the significance was not then realized.

[58] J. S. MILLER and A. J. EPSTEIN, *Chem. Brit.* **30**(6), 477–80 (1994).

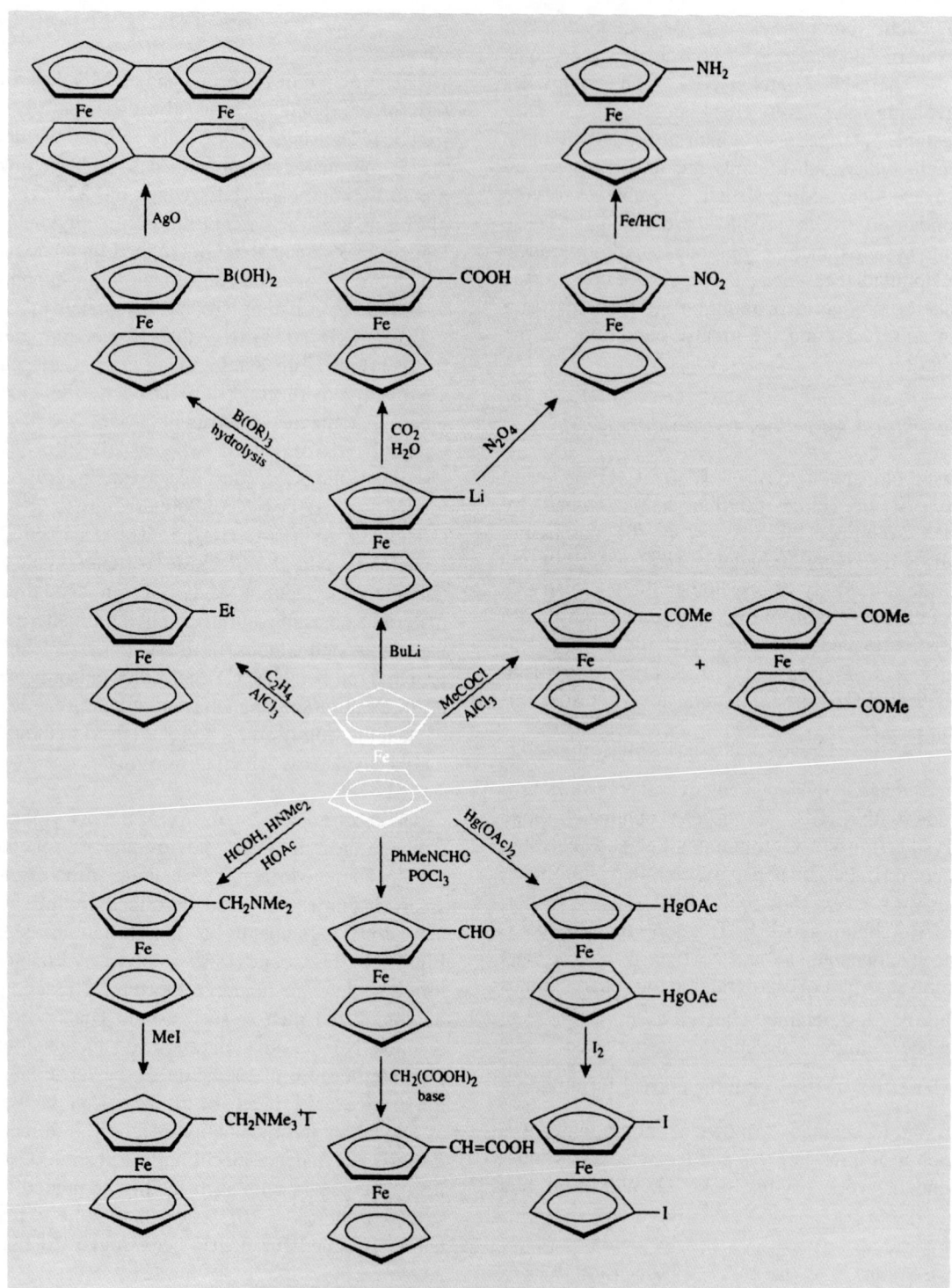

Figure 25.14   Some reactions of ferrocene.

in general, electrophilic substituents (E^+) interact first with the metal atom and then transfer to the C_5H_5 ring with proton elimination. Similar reactions are possible for ruthenocene and osmocene but usually occur less readily, and it appears that reactivity decreases with increasing size of the metal (see adjacent Scheme).

Many interesting cyclopentadienyl iron carbonyls have been prepared, the best known being the purple dimer, $[Fe(\eta^5\text{-}C_5H_5)(CO)_2]_2$ (Fig. 25.15a), prepared by reacting $Fe(CO)_5$ and dicyclopentadienyl at 135°C in an autoclave. Diamagnetism and an Fe–Fe distance of only 249 pm indicate the presence of an Fe–Fe bond. Prolonged reaction of the same reactants produces the very dark green, tetrameric cluster compound, $[Fe(\eta^5\text{-}C_5H_5)(CO)]_4$ (Fig. 25.15b), which involves CO groups which are triply bridging and so give rise to an exceedingly low (1620 cm^{-1}) ν_{CO} absorption. $[Fe(\eta^1\text{-}C_5H_5)(\eta^5\text{-}C_5H_5)(CO)_2]$ (Fig. 25.15c) is also of note as

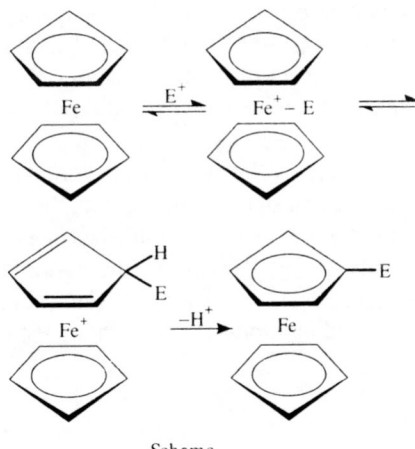

Scheme

an early example of a fluxional organometallic compound. The ^1H nmr spectrum consists of only two sharp lines, one for each ring. A single line is expected for the pentahapto ring since all its protons are equivalent, but it is clear that some averaging process must be occurring for the

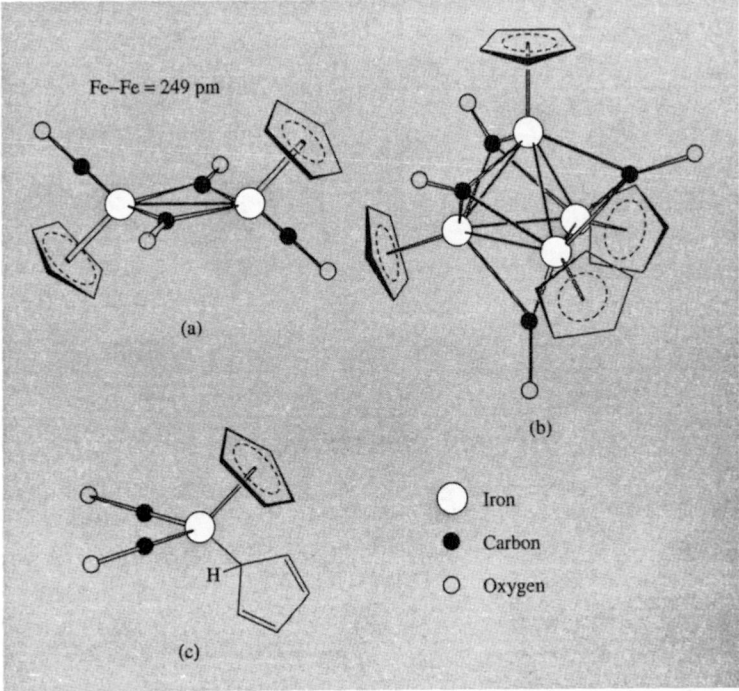

Fe–Fe = 249 pm

(a)

(b)

(c)

○ Iron

● Carbon

○ Oxygen

Figure 25.15　Some cyclopentadienyl iron carbonyls: (a) $[(\eta^5\text{-}C_5H_5)Fe(CO)_2]_2$, (b) $[(\eta^5\text{-}C_5H_5)Fe(CO)]_4$ and (c) $[(\eta^1\text{-}C_5H_5)(\eta^5\text{-}C_5H_5)Fe(CO)_2]$.

non-equivalent protons of the monohapto ring to produce just one line. It is concluded that the point of attachment of the monohapto ring to the metal must change repeatedly and rapidly ("ring whizzing") thus averaging the protons.

Although the cyclopentadienyls dominate the "aromatic" chemistry of this group, bis(arene) compounds are also well established. They are able to satisfy the 18-electron rule as the dications, $[M(arene)_2]^{2+}$ or by the two rings adopting different bonding modes; one η^6 the other η^4.

Other aspects of the organometallic chemistry of this triad have been referred to in Chapter 19 but for fuller details more extensive reviews should be consulted.[50,59]

---

[59] G. WILKINSON, F. G. A. STONE and E. W. ABEL (eds.), *Comprehensive Organometallic Chemistry*, Vol. 4, Pergamon Press, Oxford, 1982, Iron, pp. 243–649, Ruthenium, pp. 650–965, Osmium, pp. 967–1064. E. W. ABEL, F. G. A. STONE and G. WILKINSON, (eds.), *Comprehensive Organometallic Chemistry II*, Vol. 7, Iron, Ruthenium and Osmium, 1995.

26

Cobalt, Rhodium and Iridium

26.1 Introduction

Although hardly any metallic cobalt was used until the twentieth century, its ores have been used for thousands of years to impart a blue colour to glass and pottery. It is present in Egyptian pottery dated at around 2600 BC and Iranian glass beads of 2250 BC.[†] The source of the blue colour was recognized in 1735 by the Swedish chemist G. Brandt, who isolated a very impure metal, or "regulus", which he named "cobalt rex". In 1780 T. O. Bergman showed this to be a new element. Its name has some resemblance to the Greek word for "mine" but is almost certainly derived from the German word *Kobold* for "goblin" or "evil spirit". The miners of northern European countries thought that the spitefulness of such spirits was responsible for ores which, on smelting, not only failed unexpectedly to yield the anticipated metal but also produced highly toxic fumes (As_4O_6).

In 1803 both rhodium and iridium were discovered[(1)], like their preceding neighbours in the periodic table, ruthenium and osmium, in the black residue left after crude platinum had been dissolved in aqua regia. W. H. Wollaston discovered rhodium, naming it after the Greek word ῥόδον for "rose" because of the rose-colour commonly found in aqueous solutions of its salts. S. Tennant discovered iridium along with osmium, and named it after the Greek goddess Iris (ἶρις, ἰριδ-), whose sign was the rainbow, because of the variety of colours of its compounds.

26.2 The Elements

26.2.1 Terrestrial abundance and distribution

Rhodium and iridium are exceedingly rare elements, comprising only 0.0001 and 0.001 ppm of the earth's crust respectively, and even

[†] "Smalt", produced by fusing potash, silica and cobalt oxide, can be used for colouring glass or for glazing pottery. The secret of making this brilliant blue pigment was apparently lost, to be rediscovered in the fifteenth century. Leonardo da Vinci was one of the first to use powdered smalt as a "new" pigment when painting his famous "The Madonna of the Rocks".

[1] L. B. HUNT, *Platinum Metals Rev.* **31**, 32–41 (1987).

cobalt (29 ppm, i.e. 0.0029%), though widely distributed, stands only thirtieth in order of abundance and is less common than all other elements of the first transition series except scandium (25 ppm).

More than 200 ores are known to contain cobalt but only a few are of commercial value. The more important are arsenides and sulfides such as smaltite, $CoAs_2$, cobaltite (or cobalt glance), $CoAsS$, and linnaeite, Co_3S_4. These are invariably associated with nickel, and often also with copper and lead, and it is usually obtained as a byproduct or coproduct in the recovery of these metals. The world's major sources of cobalt are the African continent and Canada with smaller reserves in Australia and the former USSR. All the platinum metals are generally associated with each other and rhodium and iridium therefore occur wherever the other platinum metals are found. However, the relative proportions of the individual metals are by no means constant and the more important sources of rhodium are the nickel–copper–sulfide ores found in South Africa and in Sudbury, Canada, which contain about 0.1% Rh. Iridium is usually obtained from native osmiridium (Ir $\sim$ 50%) or iridiosmium (Ir $\sim$ 70%) found chiefly in Alaska as well as South Africa.

26.2.2 Preparation and uses of the elements [2]

The production of cobalt[2,3] is usually subsidiary to that of copper or nickel and the methods employed differ widely, depending on which of these it is associated with. In general the ore is subjected to appropriate roasting treatment so as to remove gangue material as a slag and produce a "speiss" of mixed metal and oxides. In the case of arsenical ores, As_2O_6 is condensed and provides a valuable byproduct. In the case of copper ores, the primary process

leaves a spent electrolyte from which iron is precipitated as the hydroxide by lime and the cobalt then separated by further electrolysis. Nickel ores yield acidic sulfate or chloride solutions and the methods used to separate the nickel and cobalt include: (a) precipitation of cobalt as the sulfide; (b) oxidation of cobalt and precipitation of $Co(OH)_3$; (c) making the solution alkaline with NH_3 and removal of nickel either as the sparingly soluble $(NH_4)_2Ni(SO_4)_2.6H_2O$ or by selective reduction to the metal by H_2 under pressure; (d) anion exchange, utilizing the preferential formation of $[CoCl_4]^{2-}$.

World production of cobalt in 1995 was about 20 000 tonnes, considerably below capacity. The major producing countries are Zaire, Zambia, Canada, Finland and the former Soviet Union.

The largest use of cobalt is in the production of chemicals for the ceramic and paint industries. In ceramics the main use now is not to provide a blue colour, but rather white by counterbalancing the yellow tint arising from iron impurities. Blue pigments are, however, used in paints and inks, and cobalt compounds are used to hasten the oxidation and hence the drying of oil-based paints. Cobalt compounds are also employed as catalysts in a range of organic reactions of which the "OXO" (or hydroformylation) reaction and hydrogenation and dehydrogenation reactions are the most important (pp. 1134–6).

Other uses include the manufacture of magnetic alloys. Of these the best known is "Alnico", a steel containing, as its name implies, aluminium and nickel, as well as cobalt. It is used for permanent magnets which are up to 25 times more powerful than ordinary steel magnets.

As already noted (p. 1073), the platinum metals are all isolated from concentrates obtained as "anode slimes" or "converter matte." In the classical process, after ruthenium and osmium have been removed, excess oxidants are removed by boiling, iridium is precipitated as $(NH_4)_2IrCl_6$ and rhodium as $[Rh(NH_3)_5Cl]Cl_2$. In alternative solvent extraction processes (p. 1147) $[IrCl_6]^{2-}$ is extracted in organic amines leaving rhodium in the aqueous phase to be precipitated, again, as $[Rh(NH_3)_5Cl]Cl_2$. In all cases ignition in H_2

[2] J. HILL, Chap. 2 in D. THOMPSON (ed.), *Insights into Speciality Inorganic Chemicals*, pp. 5–34, R.S.C., Cambridge, 1995.

[3] *Kirk–Othmer Encyclopedia of Chemical Technology*, 4th edn., Vol. 6, pp. 760–77, Interscience New York, 1993.

yields the metals as powders or sponges which can be consolidated by the techniques of powder metallurgy.

In 1996, consumption in the western world was 14.2 tonnes of rhodium and 3.8 tonnes of iridium. Unquestionably the main uses of rhodium (over 90%) are now catalytic, e.g. for the control of exhaust emissions in the car (automobile) industry and, in the form of phosphine complexes, in hydrogenation and hydroformylation reactions where it is frequently more efficient than the more commonly used cobalt catalysts. Iridium is used in the coating of anodes in chloralkali plant and as a catalyst in the production of acetic acid. It also finds small-scale applications in specialist hard alloys.

26.2.3 Properties of the elements

Some of the important properties of these three elements are summarized in Table 26.1.

The metals are lustrous and silvery with, in the case of cobalt, a bluish tinge. Rhodium and iridium are both hard, cobalt less so but still appreciably harder than iron. Rhodium and Ir have fcc structures, the first elements in the transition series to do so; this is in keeping with the view, based on band-theory calculations, that the fcc structure is more stable than either bcc or hcp when the outer d orbitals are nearly full. Cobalt, too, has an allotrope (the β-form) with this structure but this is only stable above 417°C; below this temperature the hcp α-form is the more stable. However, the transformation between these allotropes is generally slow and the β-form, which can be stabilized by the addition of a few per cent of iron, is often present at room temperature. This, of course, has an effect on physical properties and is no doubt responsible for variations in reported values for some properties even in the case of very pure cobalt. By contrast the atomic weights of cobalt and rhodium at least are known with considerable precision, since these elements each have but one naturally occurring isotope. In the case of cobalt this is ^{59}Co, but bombardment by thermal neutrons converts this to the radioactive ^{60}Co. The latter has a half-life of 5.271 y and decays by means of β^- and γ emission to non-radioactive ^{60}Ni. It is used in many fields of research as a concentrated source of γ-radiation, and also medically in the treatment of malignant growths. Iridium has two stable isotopes: ^{191}Ir 37.3% and ^{193}Ir 62.7%.

Table 26.1　Some properties of the elements cobalt, rhodium and iridium

Property		Co	Rh	Ir
Atomic number		27	45	77
Number of naturally occurring isotopes		1	1	2
Atomic weight		58.933200(9)	102.90550(2)	192.217(3)
Electronic configuration		[Ar]3d^{7}4s^2	[Kr]4d^{8}5s^1	[Xe]4f^{14}5d^{7}6s^2
Electronegativity		1.8	2.2	2.2
Metal radius (12-coordinate)/pm		125	134	135.5
Effective ionic radius (6-coordinate)/pm	V	—	55	57
	IV	53	60	62.5
	III	54.5 (ls), 61 (hs)	66.5	68
	II	65 (ls), 74.5 (hs)	—	—
MP/°C		1495	1960	2443
BP/°C		3100	3760	4550(±100)
ΔH_{fus}/kJ mol^{-1}		16.3	21.6	26.4
ΔH_{vap}/kJ mol^{-1}		382	494	612(±13)
ΔH_f (monatomic gas)/kJ mol^{-1}		425(±17)	556(±11)	669(±8)
Density (20°C)/g cm^{-3}		8.90	12.39	22.56
Electrical resistivity (20°C)/μohm cm		6.24	4.33	4.71

The mps, bps and enthalpies of atomization are lower than for the preceding elements in the periodic tables, presumably because the $(n-1)$d electrons are being drawn increasingly into the inert electron cores of the atoms. In the first series Co, like its neighbours Fe and Ni, is ferromagnetic (in both allotropic forms); while it does not attain the high saturation magnetization of iron, its Curie point ($>1100°C$) is much higher than that for Fe ($768°C$).

26.2.4 Chemical reactivity and trends

Cobalt is appreciably less reactive than iron, and so contrasts less markedly with the two heavier members of its triad. It is stable to atmospheric oxygen unless heated, when it is oxidized first to Co_3O_4; above $900°C$ the product is CoO which is also produced by the action of steam on the red-hot metal. It dissolves rather slowly in dil mineral acids giving salts of Co^{II}, and reacts on heating with the halogens and other non-metals such as B, C, P, As and S, but is unreactive to H_2 and N_2.

Rhodium and iridium will also react with oxygen and halogens at red-heat, but only slowly, and these metals are especially notable for their extreme inertness to acids, even aqua regia. Dissolution of rhodium metal is best effected by fusion with $NaHSO_4$, a process used in its commercial separation. In the case of iridium, oxidizing molten alkalis such as Na_2O_2 or $KOH + KNO_3$ will produce IrO_2 which can then be dissolved in aqua regia. Alternatively, a rather extreme measure which is efficacious with both metals, is to heat them with conc $HCl + NaClO_3$ in a sealed tube at $125-150°C$.

Table 26.2 is a list of examples of compounds of these elements in various oxidation states. The most striking feature of this, as compared to the corresponding lists for preceding triads, is that for the first time the range of oxidation states has diminished. This is a manifestation of the increasing stability of the $(n-1)$d electrons, whose attraction to the atomic nucleus is now sufficient to prevent the elements attaining the highest oxidation states and so to render irrelevant the concept of a "group" oxidation

state. No oxidation states are found above $+6$ for Rh and Ir, or above $+5$ for Co. Indeed, examples of cobalt in $+4$ and $+5$ and of rhodium or iridium in $+5$ and $+6$ oxidation states are rare and sometimes poorly characterized.

The most common oxidation states of cobalt are $+2$ and $+3$. $[Co(H_2O)_6]^{2+}$ and $[Co(H_2O)_6]^{3+}$ are both known but the latter is a strong oxidizing agent and in aqueous solution, unless it is acidic, it decomposes rapidly as the Co^{III} oxidizes the water with evolution of oxygen. Consequently, in contrast to Co^{II}, Co^{III} provides few simple salts, and those which do occur are unstable. However, Co^{III} is unsurpassed in the number of coordination complexes which it forms, especially with N-donor ligands. Virtually all of these complexes are low-spin, the t_{2g}^6 configuration producing a particularly high CFSE (p. 1131).

The effect of the CFSE is expected to be even more marked in the case of the heavier elements because for them the crystal field splittings are much greater. As a result the $+3$ state is the most important one for both Rh and Ir and $[M(H_2O)_6]^{3+}$ are the only simple aquo ions formed by these elements. With π-acceptor ligands the $+1$ oxidation state is also well known for Rh and Ir. It is noticeable, however, that the similarity of these two heavier elements is less than is the case earlier in the transition series and, although rhodium resembles iridium more than cobalt, nevertheless there are significant differences. One example is provided by the $+4$ oxidation state which occurs to an appreciable extent in iridium but not in rhodium. (The ease with which $Ir^{IV} \rightleftharpoons Ir^{III}$ sometimes occurs can be a source of annoyance to preparative chemists.)

Table 26.2 also reveals a diminished tendency on the part of these elements to form compounds of high coordination number when compared with the iron group and, apart from $[Co(NO_3)_4]^{2-}$, a coordination number of 6 is rarely exceeded. There is also a marked reluctance to form oxoanions (p. 1118). This is presumably because their formation requires the donation of π electrons from the oxygen atoms to the metal and the metals become progressively

Table 26.2 Oxidation states and stereochemistries of some compounds of cobalt, rhodium and iridium

Oxidation state	Coordination number	Stereochemistry	Co	Rh/Ir
−3	3		$[Co(CO)_3]^{3-}$	$[M(CO)_3]^{3-}$
−1 (d^{10})	4	Tetrahedral	$[Co(CO)_4]^-$	$[Rh(CO)_4]^-$, $[Ir(CO)_3(PPh_3)]^-$
0 (d^9)	4	Tetrahedral	$[Co(PMe_3)_4]$	
	6	Octahedral	$[Co_2(CO)_8]$	$[M_4(CO)_{12}]$
1 (d^8)	2	Linear	$[CoO_2]^{3-}$	
	3	Planar (?)		$[RhCl(PCy_3)_2]$
		T-shaped		$[Rh(PPh_3)_3]^+$
	4	Square planar		$[RhCl(PPh_3)_3]$ $[Ir(CO)Cl(PPh_3)_2]$
	5	Trigonal bipyramidal	$[Co(NCMe)_5]^+$	$[RhH(PF_3)_4]$, $[Ir(CO)H(PPh_3)_3]$
		Square pyramidal	$[Co(NCPh)_5]^+$	
	6	Octahedral	$[Co(bipy)_3]^+$	
2 (d^7)	2	Linear	$[Co\{N(SiMe_3)_2\}_2]$	
	3	Planar	$[Co\{N(SiMe_3)_2\}_2(PPh_3)]$	
	4	Tetrahedral	$[CoCl_4]^{2-}$	
		Square planar	$[Co(phthalocyanine)]$	$[RhCl_2\{P(o\text{-}MeC_6H_4)_3\}_2]$
	5	Trigonal bipyramidal	$[CoBr\{N(C_2H_4NMe_2)_3\}]^+$	$[Rh_2(O_2CMe)_4]$
		Square pyramidal	$[Co(CN)_5]^{3-}$	$[Rh_2(O_2CMe)_4(H_2O)_2]$
	6	Octahedral	$[Co(H_2O_6)]^{2+}$	
	8	Dodecahedral	$[Co(NO_3)_4]^{2-}$	
3 (d^6)	4	Tetrahedral	$[CoW_{12}O_{40}]^{5-}$	
	5	Trigonal bipyramidal		$[IrH_3(PR_3)_2]$
		Square pyramidal	$[Co(corrole)(PPh_3)]^{(a)}$	$[RhI_2Me(PPh_3)_2]$
	6	Octahedral	$[Co(NH_3)_6]^{3+}$	$[MCl_6]^{3-}$
4 (d^5)	4	Tetrahedral	$[Co(1\text{-norbornyl})_4]^{(b)}$	
	6	Octahedral	$[CoF_6]^{2-}$	$[MCl_6]^{2-}$
5 (d^4)	6	Octahedral		$[MF_6]^-$
	7	Pentagonal bipyramidal		$[IrH_5(PR_3)_2]$
6 (d^3)	6	Octahedral		$[MF_6]$

(a) Corrole is a tetrapyrrolic macrocycle
(b) 1-Norbornyl is a bicyclo[2.2.1]hept-l-yl

less able to act as π acceptors as their d orbitals are filled.

Hydrido complexes of all three elements, and covering a range of formal oxidation states, are important because of their roles in homogeneous catalysis either as the catalysts themselves or as intermediates in the catalytic cycles.

26.3 Compounds of Cobalt, Rhodium and Iridium

Binary borides (p. 147) and carbides (p. 297) have been discussed already.

26.3.1 Oxides and sulfides

As a result of the diminution in the range of oxidation states which has already been mentioned, the number of oxides formed by these elements is less than in the preceding groups, being confined to two each for cobalt (CoO, Co_3O_4) and rhodium (Rh_2O_3, RhO_2) and to just one for iridium (IrO_2) (though an impure sesquioxide Ir_2O_3 has been reported — see below). No trioxides are known.

The only oxide formed by any of these metals in the divalent state is CoO; this is prepared as an olive-green powder by strongly heating the metal in air or steam, or alternatively by heating the hydroxide, carbonate or nitrate in the absence of air. It has the rock-salt structure and is anti-ferromagnetic below 289 K. By reacting it with silica and alumina, pigments are produced which are used in the ceramics industry. CoO is stable in air at ambient temperatures and above 900°C but if heated at, say, 600–700°C, it is converted into the black Co_3O_4. This is $Co^{II}Co_2^{III}O_4$ and has the normal spinel structure with Co^{II} ions in tetrahedral and Co^{III} in octahedral sites within the ccp lattice of oxide ions. This is to be expected (p. 1080) because of the dominating advantage of placing the d^6 ions in octahedral sites, where adoption of the low-spin configuration gives it a decisively favourable CFSE. The ability of Co_3O_4 to absorb oxygen, and possibly also the retention of water in preparations from the hydroxide, have led to claims for the existence of Co_2O_3, but it is doubtful if these claims are valid. Oxidation of $Co(OH)_2$, or addition of aqueous alkali to a cobalt(III) complex, produces a dark-brown material which on drying at 150°C in fact gives cobalt(III) oxide hydroxide, CoO(OH).

Heating rhodium metal or the trichloride in oxygen at 600°C, or simply heating the trinitrate, produces dark-grey Rh_2O_3 which has the corundum structure (p. 242); it is the only stable oxide formed by this metal. The yellow precipitate formed by the addition of alkali to aqueous solutions of rhodium(III) is actually $Rh_2O_3.5H_2O$ rather than a genuine hydroxide. Electrolytic oxidation of Rh^{III} solutions and addition of alkali gives a yellow precipitate of $RhO_2.2H_2O$, but attempts to dehydrate this produce Rh_2O_3. Black anhydrous RhO_2 is best obtained by heating Rh_2O_3 in oxygen under pressure; it has the rutile structure, but it is not well characterized.

For iridium the position is reversed. This time it is the black dioxide, IrO_2, with the rutile structure (p. 961), which is the only definitely established oxide. It is obtained by heating the metal in oxygen or by dehydrating the precipitate produced when alkali is added to an aqueous solution of $[IrCl_6]^{2-}$. Contamination either by unreacted metal or by alkali is, however, difficult to avoid. The other oxide, Ir_2O_3, is said to be obtained by igniting K_2IrCl_6 with $NaCO_3$ or, as its hydrate, by adding KOH to aqueous $K_3[IrCl_6]$ under CO_2. However, even if it is a true compound, it is always impure and is readily oxidized to IrO_2.

Oxoanions are rare in this group; exceptions include the unstable $[Co^VO_4]^{3-}$ and $[Co^{II}O_3]^{4-}$. Heating mixtures of the appropriate oxides in oxygen, or under pressure, produces materials with the stoichiometry, $M_3^I CoO_4$, which, together with their oxidizing properties, suggests the presence of Co^V. When CoO is heated with 2.2 moles of Na_2O at 550° in a sealed tube under argon, bright-red crystals of $Na_4Co^{II}O_3$ are formed. The compound hydrolyses immediately on contact with atmospheric moisture and is notable in containing discrete planar $[CoO_3]^{4-}$ ions reminiscent of the carbonate ion (Co–O 186 ± 6 pm) and is similar to the red oxoferrate(II), $Na_4[FeO_3]$. The lustrous red tetracobaltate(II) $Na_{10}[Co_4^{II}O_9]$, with an anion analogous to the *catena*-tetracarbonate $[C_4O_9]^{2-}$, is also known. For iridium, prolonged heating of IrO_2 and Li_2O produces Li_2IrO_3 which, when heated with 2.2 moles of Na_2O at 800°C for 71 days, gives transparent red crystals of Na_4IrO_4 in which the Ir(IV) is surrounded by four O^{2-} in a square (Ir–O = 190.2 pm.)[4]

A larger number of sulfides have been reported but not all of them have been fully characterized. Cobalt gives rise to CoS_2 with the pyrites structure (p. 680), Co_3S_4 with the spinel structure (p. 247), and $Co_{1-x}S$ which has the NiAs structure (p. 555) and is cobalt-deficient. All are metallic, as is Co_9S_8 and the corresponding selenides and tellurides. The sulfides of rhodium and iridium are notable mainly for their inertness especially towards acids, and most of them are semiconductors. They are the disulfides MS_2, obtained from the elements; the "sesquisulfides" M_2S_3, obtained by passing H_2S through aqueous solutions of M^{III}; and Rh_2S_5 and IrS_3, obtained by heating $MCl_3 + S$ at 600°C. Numerous nonstoichiometric selenides and tellurides are also known.

⁴ K. MADERAND and R. HOPPE, *Z. anorg. allg. Chem.* **619**, 1647–54 (1993).

Table 26.3   Halides of cobalt, rhodium and iridium (mp/°C)

Oxidation state	Fluorides	Chlorides	Bromides	Iodides
+6	RhF_6 black (70°) IrF_6 yellow (44°) bp 53°			
+5	$[RhF_5]_4$ dark red $[IrF_5]_4$ yellow (104°)			
+4	CoF_4 RhF_4 purple-red IrF_4 dark brown	$IrCl_4$?	$IrBr_4$?	IrI_4?
+3	CoF_3 light brown RhF_3 red IrF_3 black	$RhCl_3$ red $IrCl_3$ red	$RhBr_3$ red-brown $IrBr_3$ red-brown	RhI_3 black IrI_3 dark brown
+2	CoF_2 pink (1200°)	$CoCl_2$ blue (724°)	$CoBr_2$ green (678°)	CoI_2 a blue-black (515°)

Because of possible catalytic and biological relevance of metal–sulfur clusters, several such compounds of cobalt have been prepared. The action of H_2S or M_2S (M = alkali metal) on a non-aqueous solution of a convenient cobalt compound (often containing, or in the presence of, a phosphine) is a typical route. Diamagnetic $[Co_6S_8(PR_3)_6]$ (R = Et, Ph) comprise an octahedral array of metal atoms (Co–Co in the range 281.7 to 289.4 pm), all faces capped by μ_3-S atoms,[5] and show facile redox behaviour

$$[Co_6S_8(PR_3)_6] \rightleftharpoons [Co_6S_8(PR_3)_6]^+$$

An indication of the range of such clusters which might possibly be synthesized is given by the observation[6] that mass spectroscopic analysis of the products of laser-ablation of CoS show no less than 83 gaseous ions ranging from $[CoS_2]^-$ to $[Co_{38}S_{24}]^-$.

26.3.2 Halides

The known halides of this triad are listed in Table 26.3. It can be seen that, apart from CoF_3, CoF_4 and the doubtful iridium tetrahalides, they fall into three categories:

(a) higher fluorides of Ir and Rh;
(b) a full complement of trihalides of Ir and Rh;
(c) dihalides of cobalt

The octahedral hexafluorides are obtained directly from the elements and both are volatile, extremely reactive and corrosive solids, RhF_6 being the least stable of the platinum metal hexafluorides and reacting with glass even when carefully dried. They are thermally unstable and must be frozen out from the hot gaseous reaction mixtures, otherwise they dissociate.

5 M. HONG, Z. HUANG, X. LEI, G. WEI, B. KANG and H. LIU, *Polyhedron*, **10**, 927–34 (1991).

6 J. EL NAKAT, K. J. FISHER, I. G. DANCE and G. D. WILLET, *Inorg. Chem.* **32** 1931–40 (1993).

The pentafluorides of Rh and Ir may be prepared by the deliberate thermal dissociation of the hexafluorides. They also are highly reactive and are respectively dark-red and yellow solids, with the same tetrameric structure as $[RuF_5]_4$ and $[OsF_5]_4$ (p. 1083).

RhF_4 is a purple-red solid, usually prepared by the reaction of the strong fluorinating agent BrF_3 on $RhBr_3$. The corresponding compound IrF_4 has had an intriguing and instructive history.[7] It was first claimed in 1929 and again in 1956 but this material was shown in 1965 to be, in reality, the previously unknown IrF_5. IrF_4 can now be made (1974) by reducing IrF_5 with the stoichiometric amount of iridium-black:

$$4IrF_5 + Ir \xrightarrow{400°} 5IrF_4$$

The dark-brown product disproportionates above 400° into IrF_3 and the volatile IrF_5. The structure features $\{IrF_6\}$ octahedra which share 4 F atoms, each with one other $\{IrF_6\}$ group, leaving a pair of *cis* vertices unshared: this is essentially a rutile type structure (p. 961) from which alternate metal atoms have been removed from each edge-sharing chain. It was the first 3D structure to have been found for a tetrafluoride.[7] Claims have been made for the isolation of all the other iridium tetrahalides, but there is some doubt as to whether these can be substantiated. This is an unexpected situation since +4 is one of iridium's common oxidation states and, indeed, the derived anions $[IrX_6]^{2-}$ (X = F, Cl, Br) are well known.

The most familiar and most stable of the halides of Rh and Ir, however, are the trihalides. Those of Rh range in colour from the red RhF_3 to black RhI_3 and, apart from the latter, which is obtained by the action of aqueous KI on the tribromide, they may be obtained in the anhydrous state directly from the elements. RhF_3 has a structure similar to that of ReO_3 (p. 1047), while $RhCl_3$ is isomorphous with $AlCl_3$ (p. 234). The anhydrous trihalides are generally unreactive and insoluble in water but, excepting the tri-iodide which is only known in this form,

water-soluble hydrates can be produced by wet methods. $RhF_3.6H_2O$ and $RhF_3.9H_2O$ can be isolated from aqueous solutions of Rh^{III} acidified with HF. Their aqueous solutions are yellow, possibly due to the presence of $[Rh(H_2O)_6]^{3+}$. The dark-red deliquescent $RhCl_3.3H_2O$ is the most common compound of rhodium and the usual starting point for the preparation of other rhodium compounds, and is itself best prepared from the metal sponge. This is heated with KCl in a stream of Cl_2 and the product extracted with water. The solution contains $K_2[Rh(H_2O)Cl_5]$ and treatment with KOH precipitates the hydrous Rh_2O_3 which can be dissolved in hydrochloric acid and the solution evaporated to dryness. $RhBr_3.2H_2O$ also is formed from the metal by treating it with hydrochloric acid and bromine.

The iridium trihalides are rather similar to those of rhodium. Anhydrous IrF_3 is obtained by reducing IrF_6 with the metal, $IrCl_3$ and $IrBr_3$ by heating the elements, and IrI_3 by heating its hydrate *in vacuo*. Water-soluble hydrates of the tri-chloride, -bromide, and -iodide are produced by dissolving hydrous Ir_2O_3 in the appropriate acid and, like its rhodium analogue, $IrCl_3.3H_2O$ provides a convenient starting point in iridium chemistry.

Lower halides of Rh and Ir have been reported and, whilst their existence cannot be denied with certainty, further substantiation is needed. Unquestionably, the divalent state is the preserve of cobalt. Apart from the strongly oxidizing CoF_3 (a light-brown powder isomorphous with $FeCl_3$ and the product of the action of F_2 on $CoCl_2$ at 250°C) and CoF_4 (identified[8] in the gaseous phase by mass spectometry, as the singly charged cation, when CoF_3 and TbF_4 are heated to 600–680 K), the only known halides of cobalt are the dihalides. In all of these the cobalt is octahedrally coordinated. The anhydrous compounds are prepared by dry methods: CoF_2 (pink) by heating $CoCl_2$ in HF; $CoCl_2$ (blue) and $CoBr_2$ (green) by the action of the halogens on the heated metal; CoI_2 (blue-black) by the action

[7] N. BARTLETT and A. TRESSAUD, *Comptes Rendus* **278C**, 1501–4 (1974).

[8] M. V. KOBOROV, L. N. SAVINOVA and L. N. SIDEROV, *J. Chem. Thermodynam.* **25**, 1161–8 (1993).

of HI on the heated metal. The fluoride is only slightly soluble in water but the others dissolve readily to give solutions from which pink or red hexahydrates can be crystallized. These solutions can alternatively and more conveniently be made by dissolving the metal, oxide or carbonate in the appropriate hydrohalic acid. The chloride is widely used as an indicator in the desiccant, silica gel, since its blue anhydrous form turns pink as it hydrates (see p. 1131).

The disinclination of these metals to form oxoanions has already been remarked and the same is evidently true of oxohalides: none have been authenticated.

26.3.3 Complexes

The chemistry of oxidation states above IV is sparse. Apart from RhF_6 and IrF_6, such chemistry as there is, is mainly confined to salts of $[RhF_6]^-$ and $[IrF_6]^-$. These are prepared respectively by the action of F_2 on $RhCl_3$ and KF under pressure,[9] and by fluorinating a lower halide of iridium with BrF_3 in the presence of a halide of the counter cation. Hydrido complexes of iridium in the formal oxidation state V are obtained by the action of $LiAlH_4$ or $LiBH_4$ on Ir^{III} compounds in the presence of phosphine or cyclopentadienyl ligands. $[IrH_5(PR_3)_2]$, in which the five hydrogens lie equatorially in a pentagonal bipyramid, and the "half sandwich", $[(\eta^5\text{-}C_5Me_5)IrH_4]$, are examples.

Oxidation state IV (d⁵)

Cobalt provides only a few examples of this oxidation state, namely some fluoro compounds and mixed metal oxides, whose purity is questionable and, most notably, the thermally stable, brown, tetraalkyl, $[Co(1\text{-norbornyl})_4]$. Prepared by the reaction of $CoCl_2$ and Li(1-norbornyl), it is the only one of a series of such compounds obtained for the first row transition metals Ti to Co which has been structurally characterized.[10] It is tetrahedral and, with a d^5 configuration, its room-temperature magnetic moment of 1.89 BM indicates that it is low-spin; the first example to be authenticated for a tetrahedral complex of a first row transition metal. Rhodium(IV) complexes are confined to salts of the oxidizing and readily hydrolysed $[RhX_6]^{2-}$ (X = F, Cl), the green solid $Cs_2[RhCl_6]$ being one of the few to be confirmed.[11] Only iridium(IV) shows appreciable stability.

The salts of $[IrX_6]^{2-}$ (X = F, Cl, Br) are comparatively stable and their colour deepens from red, through reddish-black to bluish-black with increasing atomic weight of the halogen. $[IrF_6]^{2-}$ is obtained by reduction of $[IrF_6]^-$, $[IrCl_6]^{2-}$ by oxidation of $[IrCl_6]^{3-}$ with chlorine, and $[IrBr_6]^{2-}$ by Br^- substitution of $[IrCl_6]^{2-}$ in aqueous solution. The hexachloroiridates in particular have been the subject of many magnetic investigations. They have magnetic moments at room temperature somewhat below the spin-only value for the t_{2g}^5 configuration (1.73 BM), and this falls with temperature. This has been interpreted as the result of antiferromagnetic interaction operating by a superexchange mechanism between adjacent Ir^{IV} ions via intervening chlorine atoms. More importantly, in 1953 in a short but classic paper,[12] J. Owen and K. W. H. Stevens reported the observation of hyperfine structure in the esr signal obtained from solid solutions of $(NH_4)_2[IrCl_6]$ in the isomorphous, but diamagnetic, $(NH_4)_2[PtCl_6]$. This arises from the influence of the chlorine nuclei and, from the magnitude of the splitting, it was inferred that the single unpaired electron, which is ostensibly one of the metal d^5 electrons, in fact spends only 80% of its time on the metal, the rest of the time being divided equally between the 6 chlorine ligands. This was the first unambiguous evidence that metal d electrons are able to move in molecular

[9] A. K. BRISDON, J. H. HOLLOWAY, E. G. HOPE and W. LEVASON, *Polyhedron* **11**, 7–11 (1992).

[10] E. K. BYRNE, D. S. RICHESON and K. H. THEOPOLD, *J. Chem. Soc., Chem. Commun.*, 1491–2 (1986).

[11] I. J. ELLISON and R. D. GILLARD, *Polyhedron* **15**, 339–48 (1996).

[12] J. OWEN and K. W. H. STEVENS, *Nature* **171**, 836 (1953).

Table 26.4 $E°$ for some Co^{III}/Co^{II} couples in acid solution

Couple	$E°/V$
$[Co(H_2O)_6]^{3+} + e^- \rightleftharpoons [Co(H_2O)_6]^{2+}$	1.83
$[Co(C_2O_4)_3]^{3-} + e^- \rightleftharpoons [Co(C_2O_4)_3]^{4-}$	0.57
$[Co(edta)]^- + e^- \rightleftharpoons [Co(edta)]^{2-}$	0.37
$[Co(bipy)_3]^{3+} + e^- \rightleftharpoons [Co(bipy)_3]^{2+}$	0.31
$[Co(en)_3]^{3+} + e^- \rightleftharpoons [Co(en)_3]^{2+}$	0.18
$[Co(NH_3)_6]^{3+} + e^- \rightleftharpoons [Co(NH_3)_6]^{2+}$	0.108
$[Co(CN)_6]^{3-} + H_2O + e^- \rightleftharpoons [Co(CN)_5(H_2O)]^{3-} + CN^-$	−0.8
$\frac{1}{2}O_2 + 2H^+ + 2e^- \rightleftharpoons H_2O$	1.229

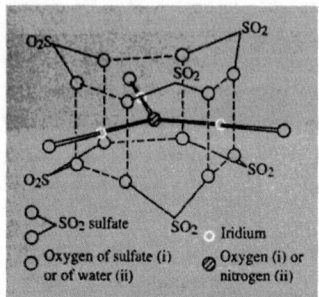

Figure 26.1 Trinuclear structure of (i) $[Ir_3O(SO_4)_9]^{10-}$ and (ii) $[Ir_3N(SO_4)_6(H_2O)_3]^{4-}$.

orbitals over the whole complex, and implies the presence of π as well as σ bonding.

In aqueous solution, the halide ions of $[IrX_6]^{2-}$ may be replaced by solvent and a number of aquo substituted derivatives have been reported. Other Ir^{IV} complexes with O-donor ligands are $[IrCl_4(C_2O_4)]^{2-}$, obtained by oxidizing Ir^{III} oxalato complexes with chlorine, and Na_2IrO_3, obtained by fusing Ir and Na_2CO_3.

Two interesting trinuclear complexes must also be mentioned. They are $K_{10}[Ir_3O(SO_4)_9].3H_2O$, obtained by boiling Na_2IrCl_6 and K_2SO_4 in conc sulfuric acid, and $K_4[Ir_3N(SO_4)_6(H_2O)_3]$, obtained by boiling Na_3IrCl_6 and $(NH_4)_2SO_4$ in conc sulfuric acid. They have the structure shown in Fig. 26.1, analogous to that of the basic carboxylates, $[M_3^{III}O(O_2CR)_6L_3]^+$ (see Fig. 23.9). The oxo species formally contains 1 Ir^{IV} and 2 Ir^{III} ions and the nitride species 2 Ir^{IV} ions and 1 Ir^{III} ion, but in each case the charges are probably delocalized over the whole complex.

Oxidation state III (d^6)

For all three elements this is the most prolific oxidation state, providing a wide variety of kinetically inert complexes. As has already been pointed out, these are virtually all low-spin and octahedral, a major stabilizing influence being the high CFSE associated with the t_{2g}^6 configuration ($\frac{12}{5}\Delta_o$, the maximum possible for any d^x configuration). Even $[Co(H_2O)_6]^{3+}$ is low-spin but it is such a powerful oxidizing agent that it is unstable in aqueous solutions and only a few simple salt hydrates, such as the blue $Co_2(SO_4)_3.18H_2O$ and $MCo(SO_4)_2.12H_2O$ (M = K, Rb, Cs, NH_4), which contain the hexaaquo ion, and $CoF_3.3\frac{1}{2}H_2O$ can be isolated. This paucity of simple salts of cobalt(III) contrasts sharply with the great abundance of its complexes, expecially with N-donor ligands[13], and it is evident that the high CFSE is not the only factor affecting the stability of this oxidation state.

Table 26.4 illustrates the remarkable sensitivity of the reduction potential of the Co^{III}/Co^{II} couple to different ligands whose presence renders Co^{II} unstable to aerial oxidation. The extreme effect of CN^- can be thought of as being due, on the one hand, to the ability of its empty π^* orbitals to accept "back-donated" charge from the metal's filled t_{2g} orbitals and, on the other, to its effectiveness as a σ donor (enhanced partly by its negative charge). The magnitudes of the

[13] P. HENDRY and A. LUDI, *Adv. Inorg. Chem.* **35**, 117–98 (1990).

changes in $E°$ are even greater than those noted for the Fe^{III}/Fe^{II} couple (p. 1093), though if the two systems are compared it must be remembered that the oxidation state which can be stabilized by adoption of the low-spin t_{2g}^6 configuration is $+3$ for cobalt but only $+2$ for iron. Nevertheless, the effect of increasing pH is closely similar, the M^{III} "hydroxide" of both metals being far less soluble than the M^{II} "hydroxide". In the case of cobalt this reduces $E°$ from 1.83 to 0.17 V:

$$Co^{III}O(OH) + H_2O + e^- \rightleftharpoons Co^{II}(OH)_2 + OH^-;$$
$$E° = 0.17 \text{ V}$$

thereby facilitating oxidation to the $+3$ state.

Complexes of cobalt(III), like those of chromium(III) (p. 1027), are kinetically inert and so, again, indirect methods of preparation are to be preferred. Most commonly the ligand is added to an aqueous solution of an appropriate salt of cobalt(II), and the cobalt(II) complex thereby formed is oxidized by some convenient oxidant, frequently (if an *N*-donor ligand is involved) in the presence of a catalyst such as active charcoal. Molecular oxygen is often used as the oxidant simply by drawing a stream of air through the solution for a few hours, but the same result can, in many cases, be obtained more quickly by using aqueous solutions of H_2O_2.

The cobaltammines, whose number is legion, were amongst the first coordination compounds to be systematically studied[†] and are undoubtedly the most extensively investigated class of cobalt(III) complex. Oxidation of aqueous mixtures of CoX_2, NH_4X and NH_3 (X = Cl, Br, NO_3, etc.) can, by varying the conditions and particularly the relative proportions of the reactants, be used to prepare complexes of types such as $[Co(NH_3)_6]^{3+}$, $[Co(NH_3)_5X]^{2+}$ and $[Co(NH_3)_4X_2]^+$. The range of these compounds

is further extended by the replacement of X by other anionic or neutral ligands. The inertness of the compounds makes such substitution reactions slow (taking hours or days to attain equilibrium) and, being therefore amenable to examination by conventional analytical techniques, they have provided a continuing focus for kinetic studies. The forward (aquation) and backward (anation) reactions of the pentaammines:

$$[Co(NH_3)_5X]^{2+} + H_2O \rightleftharpoons$$
$$[Co(NH_3)_5(H_2O)]^{3+} + X^-$$

must be the most thoroughly studied substitution reactions, certainly of octahedral compounds. Furthermore, the isolation of *cis* and *trans* isomers of the tetraammines (p. 914) was an important part of Werner's classical proof of the octahedral structure of 6-coordinate complexes. The kinetic inertness of cobalt(III) was also exploited by H. Taube to demonstrate the inner-sphere mechanism of electron transfer (see Panel on p. 1124).

Compounds analogous to the cobaltammines may be similarly obtained using chelating amines such as ethythenediamine or bipyridyl, and these too have played an important role in stereochemical studies. Thus *cis*-$[Co(en)_2(NH_3)Cl]^{2+}$ was resolved into $d(+)$ and $l(-)$ optical isomers by Werner in 1911 thereby demonstrating, to all but the most determined doubters, its octahedral stereochemistry.[‡] More recently, the absolute configuration of one of the optical isomers of $[Co(en)_3]^{3+}$ was determined (see Panel on p. 1125).

Another *N*-donor ligand, which forms extremely stable complexes, is the NO_2^- ion: its best-known complex is the orange "sodium cobaltinitrite", $Na_3[Co(NO_2)_6]$, aqueous solutions of which were used for the quantitative precipitation of K^+ as $K_3[Co(NO_2)_6]$ in classical analysis. Treatment of this with fluorine yields

---

[†] The observation by B. M. Tassaert in 1798 that solutions of cobalt(II) chloride in aqueous ammonia gradually turn brown in air, and then wine-red on being boiled, is generally accepted as the first preparation of a cobalt(III) complex. It was realized later that more than one complex was involved and that, by varying the relative concentrations of ammonia and chloride ion, the complexes $CoCl_3.xNH_3$ ($x = 6$, 5 and 4) could be separated.

[‡] So deep-seated at that time was the conviction that optical activity could arise only from carbon atoms that it was argued that the ethylenediamine must be responsible, even though it is itself optically inactive. The opposition was only finally assuaged by Werner's subsequent resolution of an entirely inorganic material (p. 915).

Electron Transfer (Redox) Reactions

Two mechanisms exist for the transfer of charge from one species to another:

1. *Outer-sphere.* Here, electron transfer from one reactant to the other is effected without changing the coordination sphere of either. This is likely to be the case if both reactants are coordinatively saturated and can safely be assumed to be so if the rate of the redox process is faster than the rates observed for substitution (ligand transfer) reactions of the species in question. A good example is the reaction,

$$[Fe^{II}(CN)_6]^{4-} + [Ir^{IV}Cl_6]^{2-} \rightleftharpoons [Fe^{III}(CN)_6]^{3-} + [Ir^{III}Cl_6]^{3-}$$

The observed rate law for this type of reaction is usually first order in each reactant. Extensive theoretical treatments have been performed, most notably by R. A. Marcus and N. S. Hush, details of which can be found in more specialized sources[14]

2. *Inner-sphere.* Here, the two reactants first form a bridged complex (*precursor*); intramolecular electron transfer then yields the *successor* which in turn dissociates to give the products. The first demonstration of this was provided by H. Taube. He examined the oxidation of $[Cr(H_2O)_6]^{2+}$ by $[CoCl(NH_3)_5]^{2+}$ and postulated that it occurs as follows:

$$[Cr^{II}(H_2O)_6]^{2+} + [Co^{III}Cl(NH_3)_5]^{2+} \rightleftharpoons [(H_2O)_5Cr^{II}-Cl-Co^{III}(NH_3)_5]^{4+}$$

precursor

↕ electron transfer

$$[Cr^{III}(H_2O)_5Cl]^{2+} + [Co^{II}(NH_3)_5H_2O]^{2+} \xleftarrow{H_2O} [(H_2O)_5Cr^{III}-Cl-Co^{II}(NH_3)_5]^{4+}$$

successor

↓ H_2O, H^+

$$[Co^{II}(H_2O)_6]^{2+} + 5NH_4^+$$

The superb elegance of this demonstration lies in the choice of reactants which permits no alternative mechanism. Cr^{II} (d^4) and Co^{II} (d^7) species are known to be substitutionally labile whereas Cr^{III} (d^3) and Co^{III} (low-spin d^6) are substitutionally inert. Only if electron transfer is preceded by the formation of a bridged intermediate can the inert cobalt reactant be persuaded to release a Cl^- ligand and so allow the quantitative formation of the (then inert) chromium product. Corroboration that electron transfer does not occur by an outer-sphere mechanism followed by loss of Cl^- from the chromium is provided by the fact that, if $^{36}Cl^-$ is added to the solution, none of it finds its way into the chromium product.

Demonstration of ligand transfer is crucial to the proof that *this particular reaction* proceeds via an inner-sphere mechanism, and ligand transfer is indeed a usual feature of inner-sphere redox reactions, but it is not an *essential* feature of *all* such reactions.

The observed rate law for inner-sphere, as for outer-sphere, reactions is commonly first order in each reactant but this does not indicate which step is rate-determining. Again, details should be obtained from more extensive accounts.[14]

For their work in this field, Taube and Marcus were awarded Nobel Prizes for Chemistry in 1983 and 1992 respectively.

$K_3[CoF_6]$, whose anion is notable not only as the only hexahalogeno complex of cobalt(III) but also for being high-spin and hence paramagnetic with a magnetic moment at room temperature of nearly 5.8 BM.

[14] R. G. WILKINS, *Kinetics and Mechanism of Reactions of Transition Metal Complexes*, 2nd edn., VCH, Weinhein, 1991, 465 pp. T. J. MEYER and H. TAUBE, Chap. 9 in *Comprehensive Coordination Chemistry*, Vol. 1, pp. 331–84, Pergamon Press, Oxford, 1987.

$[Co(CN)_6]^{3-}$ has already been mentioned and is extremely stable, being inert to alkalis and, like $[Fe(CN)_6]^{4-}$, which likewise involves the t_{2g}^6 configuration, it is reportedly nontoxic.

Complexes of cobalt(III) with *O*-donor ligands are generally less stable than those with *N*-donors although the dark-green $[Co(acac)_3]$ and $M_3^I[Co(C_2O_4)_3]$ complexes, formed from the chelating ligands acetylacetonate and oxalate, are stable. Other carboxylato complexes such as those of

Determination of Absolute Configuration

Because they rotate the plane of polarized light in opposite directions (p. 919) it is a relatively simple matter to distinguish an optical isomer from its mirror image. But to establish their absolute configurations is a problem which for long defeated the ingenuity of chemists. Normal X-ray diffraction techniques do not distinguish between them, but J. M. Bijvoet developed the absorption edge, or anomalous, diffraction technique which does. In this method the wavelength of the X-rays is chosen so as to correspond to an electronic transition of the central metal atom, and under these circumstances phase changes are introduced into the diffracted radiation which are different for the two isomers. An understanding of the phenomenon not only allows the isomers to be distinguished but also their configurations to be identified. Once the absolute configuration of one complex has been determined in this way. it can then be used as a standard to determine the absolute configuration of other, similar. complexes by the relatively simpler method of comparing their *optical rotary dispersion* (ORD) and *circular dichroism* (CD) curves.[15]

Normal measurements of optical activity are concerned with the ability of the optically active substance to rotate the plane of polarization of plane polarized light, its specific optical rotatory power (α_m) being given by

$$\alpha_m = \frac{\alpha V}{m\,l} \text{ rad m}^2 \text{kg}^{-1}$$

where α is the observed angle of rotation, V is the volume. m is the mass, and l is the path length.

The reason why this phenomenon occurs is that plane polarized light can be considered to be made up of left- and of right-circularly polarized components, and the nature of an optically active substance is such that, in passing through it, one component passes through greater electron density than does the other. As a result, that component is slowed down relative to the other and the two components emerge somewhat out-of-phase, i.e. the plane of polarization of the light has been rotated. If the wavelength of the polarized light is varied, and α_m then plotted against wavelength, the result is known as an *optical rotary dispersion* curve. For those wavelengths at which the substance is transparent, α_m is virtually constant, which is to say the ORD curve is flat. But what happens when the wavelength of the light is such that it is absorbed by the substance in question?

In absorbing light the molecules of a substance undergo electronic excitations which involve displacement of electron charge. Because of their differing routes through the molecules, the two circularly polarized components of the light produce these excitations to different extents and are consequently absorbed to different extents. The difference in extinction coefficients, $\epsilon_{left} - \epsilon_{right}$, can be measured and is known as the *circular dichroism.* If the CD is plotted against wavelength it is therefore zero at wavelengths where there is no absorption but passes through a maximum, or a minimum, where absorption occurs. Accompanying these changes in CD it is found that the ORD curve is like a first derivative, passing through zero at the absorption maximum (Fig. A). Such a change in sign of α_m highlights the importance of quoting the wavelength of the light used when classifying optical isomers as $(+)$ or $(-)$, since the classification could be reversed by simply using light of a different wavelength.[†]

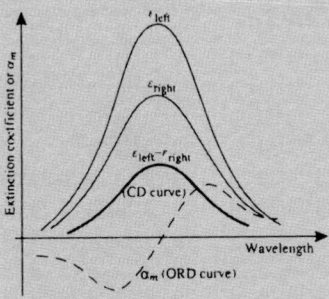

Figure A   Diagrammatic representation of the Cotton effect (actually "positive" Cotton effect. The "negative" effect occurs when the CD curve shows a minimum and the ORD curve is the reverse of the above).

Panel continues

[†]The situation is perhaps not quite so bad as is implied here. since *single* measurements of α_m are usually made at the sodium D line, 589.6 nm. Nevertheless. it is clearly better to state the wavelength than to assume that this will be understood.

---

[15] R. D. GILLARD. *Prog. Inorg. Chem.* **7**. 215-76 (1966).

The behaviours of CD and ORD curves in the vicinity of an absorption band are collectively known as the *Cotton effect* after the French physicist A. Cotton who discovered them in 1895. Their importance in the present context is that molecules with the same absolute configuration will exhibit the same Cotton effect for the same d-d absorption and, if the configuration of one compound is known, that of *closely similar* ones can be established by comparison.

The optical isomer of $[Co(en)_3]^{3+}$ referred to in the main text is the $(+)_{NaD}$ isomer, which has a left-handed *(laevo)* screw axis as shown in Fig. Ba, and according to the convention recommended by IUPAC is given the symbol Λ. This is in contrast to its mirror image (Fig. Bb) which has a right-handed *(dextro)* screw axis and is given the symbol Δ.

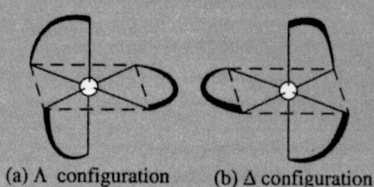

(a) Λ configuration   (b) Δ configuration

Figure B   The absolute configuration of the optical isomers of a metal tris-chelates complex such as $[Co(en)_3]^{3+}$. (a) Λ configuration and (b) Δ configuration.

the acetate are, however, less stable but are involved in the catalysis of a number of oxidation reactions by Co^{II} carboxylates.

A noticeable difference between the chemistries of complexes of chromium(III) and cobalt(III) is the smaller susceptibility of the latter to hydrolysis, though limited hydrolysis, leading to polynuclear cobaltammines with bridging OH^- groups, is well known. Other commonly occurring bridging groups are NH_2^-, NH^{2-} and NO_2^-, and singly, doubly and triply bridged species are known such as

the bright-blue $[(NH_3)_5Co-NH_2-Co(NH_3)_5]^{5+}$,

$$\text{garnet-red} \quad [(NH_3)_4]Co\underset{OH}{\overset{OH}{\diagdown\diagup}}Co(NH_3)_4]^{4+},$$

$$\text{and red} \quad [(NH_3)_3Co\underset{OH}{\overset{NH_2}{\diagdown\diagup}}Co(NH_3)_3]^{3+}$$

But probably the most interesting of the polynuclear complexes are those containing $-O-O-$ bridges (see also p. 616).

In the preparation of cobalt(III) hexaammine salts by the aerial oxidation of cobalt(II) in aqueous ammonia it is possible, in the absence

of a catalyst, to isolate a brown intermediate, $[(NH_3)_5Co-O_2-Co(NH_3)_5]^{4+}$. This is moderately stable in conc aqueous ammonia and in the solid, but decomposes readily in acid solutions to Co^{II} and O_2, while oxidizing agents such as $(S_2O_8)^{2-}$ convert it to the green, paramagnetic $[(NH_3)_5Co-O_2-Co(NH_3)_5]^{5+}(\mu_{300} \sim 1.7 BM)$. The formulation of the brown compound poses no problems. The 2 cobalt atoms are in the +3 oxidation state and are joined by a peroxo group, O_2^{2-}, all of which accords with the observed diamagnetism; moreover, the stereochemistry of the central $Co-O-O-Co$ group (Fig. 26.2a) is akin to that of H_2O_2 (p. 634). The green compound is less straightforward. Werner thought that it too involved a peroxo group but in this instance bridging Co^{III} and Co^{IV} atoms.

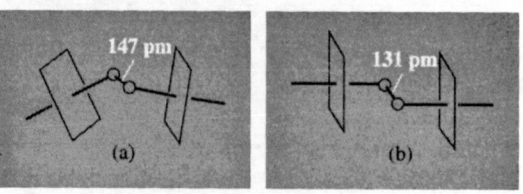

Figure 26.2 O_2 bridges in dinuclear cobalt complexes: (a) peroxo (O_2^{2-}) bridge, and (b) superoxo (O_2^-) bridge.

Table 26.5   Spectra of octahedral low-spin complexes of cobalt(III)

Complex	Colour	v_1/cm^{-1}	v_2/cm^{-1}	$10Dq/cm^{-1}$	B/cm^{-1}
$[Co(H_2O)_6]^{3+}$	Blue	16 600	24 800	18 200	670
$[Co(NH_3)_6]^{3+}$	Golden-brown	21 000	29 500	22 900	620
$[Co(C_2O_4)_3]^{3-}$	Dark green	16 600	23 800	18 000	540
$[Co(en)_3]^{3+}$	Yellow	21 400	29 500	23 200	590
$[Co(CN)_6]^{3-}$	Yellow	32 400	39 000	33 500	460

This could account for the paramagnetism, but esr evidence shows that the 2 cobalt atoms are actually equivalent, and X-ray evidence shows the central Co–O–O–Co group to be planar with an O–O distance of 131 pm, which is very close to the 128 pm of the superoxide, O_2^-, ion. A more satisfactory formulation therefore is that of 2 Co^{III} atoms joined by a superoxide bridge. Molecular orbital theory predicts that the unpaired electron is situated in a π orbital extending over all 4 atoms. If this is the case, then the π orbital is evidently concentrated very largely on the bridging oxygen atoms.

If $[(NH_3)_5Co-O_2-Co(NH_3)_5]^{4+}$ is treated with aqueous KOH another brown complex, $[(NH_3)_4Co(\mu-NH_2)(\mu-O_2)Co(NH_3)_4]^{3+}$ is obtained and, again, a 1-electron oxidation yields a green superoxo species, $[(NH_3)_4Co(\mu-NH_2)-(\mu-O_2)Co(NH_3)_4]^{4+}$ The sulfate of this latter is actually one component of Vortmann's sulfate — the other is the red $[(NH_3)_4Co(\mu-NH_2)-(\mu-OH)Co(NH_3)_4](SO_4)_2$. They are obtained by aerial oxidation of ammoniacal solutions of cobalt(II) nitrate followed by neutralization with H_2SO_4.

Apart from the above green superoxo-bridged complexes and the blue fluoro complexes, $[CoF_6]^{3-}$ and $[CoF_3(H_2O)_3]$, octahedral complexes of cobalt(III) (being low-spin) are diamagnetic. Their magnetic properties are therefore of little interest but, somewhat unusually for low-spin compounds, their electronic spectra have received a good deal of attention[16] (see Panel on p. 1128). Data for a representative sample of complexes are given in Table 26.5

Complexes of rhodium(III) are usually derived, directly or indirectly, from $RhCl_3.3H_2O$ and those of iridium(III) from $(NH_4)_3[IrCl_6]$. All the compounds of Rh^{III} and Ir^{III} are diamagnetic and low-spin, the vast majority of them being octahedral with the t_{2g}^6 configuration. Their electronic spectra can be interpreted in the same way as the spectra of Co^{III} complexes, though the second d–d band, especially in the case of Ir^{III}, is frequently obscured by charge-transfer absorption. The d–d absorptions at the blue end of the visible region are responsible for the yellow to red colours which characterize Rh^{III} complexes.

Similarity with cobalt is also apparent in the affinity of Rh^{III} and Ir^{III} for ammonia and amines. The kinetic inertness of the ammines of Rh^{III} has led to the use of several of them in studies of the *trans* effect (p. 1163) in octahedral complexes, while the ammines of Ir^{III} are so stable as to withstand boiling in aqueous alkali. Stable complexes such as $[M(C_2O_4)_3]^{3-}$, $[M(acac)_3]$ and $[M(CN)_6]^{3-}$ are formed by all three metals. Force constants obtained from the infrared spectra of the hexacyano complexes indicate that the M–C bond strength increases in the order Co < Rh < Ir. Like cobalt, rhodium too forms bridged superoxides such as the blue, paramagnetic, $[Cl(py)_4Rh-O_2-Rh(py)_4Cl]^{5+}$ produced by aerial oxidation of aqueous ethanolic solutions of $RhCl_3$ and pyridine.[17] In fact it seems likely that many of the species produced by oxidation of aqueous solutions of Rh^{III} and presumed to contain the metal in higher oxidation states, are actually superoxides of Rh^{III}.[18]

[16] A. B. P. Lever, *Inorganic Electronic Spectroscopy*, 2nd edn., pp. 473–7, Elsevier, Amsterdam, 1984.

[17] N. S. A. Edwards, I. J. Ellison, R. D. Gillard and B. Mile, *Polyhedron* **12**, 371–4 (1993).

[18] I. J. Ellison and R. D. Gillard, *J. Chem. Soc., Chem. Commun.*, 851–3 (1992).

Electronic Spectra of Octahedral Low-spin Complexes of Co(III)

It is possible to observe spin-allowed, d–d bands in the visible region of the spectra of low-spin cobalt(III) complexes because of the small value of $10Dq$, (Δ), which is required to induce spin-pairing in the cobalt(III) ion. This means that the low-spin configuration occurs in complexes with ligands which do not cause the low-energy charge transfer bands which so often dominate the spectra of low-spin complexes.

In practice two bands are generally observed and are assigned to the transitions: $\nu_1 = {}^1T_{1g} \leftarrow {}^1A_{1g}$ and $\nu_2 = {}^1T_{2g} \leftarrow {}^1A_{1g}$ (see Fig. A)

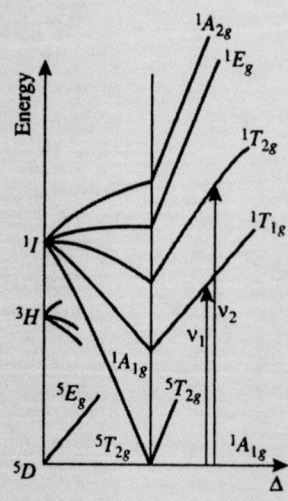

Figure A   Simplified Energy Level diagram for d^6 ions showing possible spin-allowed transitions in complexes of low-spin cobalt(III).

These transitions correspond to the electronic promotion $t_{2g}^6 \rightarrow t_{2g}^5 e_g^1$ with the promoted electron maintaining its spin unaltered. The orbital multiplicity of the $t_{2g}^5 e_g^1$ configuration is 6 and so corresponds to two orbital triplet terms ${}^1T_{1g}$ and ${}^1T_{2g}$. If, on the other hand, the promoted electron changes its spin, the orbital multiplicity is again 6 but the two T terms are now spin triplets, ${}^3T_{1g}$ and ${}^3T_{2g}$. A weak band attributable to the spin-forbidden ${}^3T_{1g} \leftarrow {}^1A_{1g}$ transition is indeed observed in some cases in the region of $11\,000–14\,000\,\text{cm}^{-1}$.

Data for some typical complexes are given in Table 26.5. The assignments are made, producing values of the inter-electronic repulsion parameter B as well as of the crystal-field splitting, $10Dq$.

The colours of *cis* and *trans* isomers of complexes $[CoL_4X_2]$ or $[Co(L-L)_2X_2]$ frequently differ and, although simple observation of colour will not alone suffice to establish a *cis* or *trans* geometry, an examination of the electronic spectra does have diagnostic value. Calculations of the effect of low-symmetry components in the crystal field show that the *trans* isomer will split the excited terms appreciably more than the *cis*, and the effect is most marked for ${}^1T_{1g}$, the lowest of the excited terms. In practice, if L-L and X are sufficiently far apart in the spectrochemical series (e.g. L-L = en and X = F which has been thoroughly examined), the ν_1 band splits completely, giving rise to three separate bands for the *trans* complex whereas the *cis* merely shows slight asymmetry in the lower energy band. Furthermore, because (like tetrahedral complexes) a *cis* isomer lacks a centre of symmetry, its spectrum is more intense than that of the centrosymmetric *trans* isomer.

It is relevant to note at this point that, because the metal ions are isoelectronic, the spectra of low-spin Fe^{II} complexes might be expected to be similar to those of low-spin Co^{III}. However, Fe^{II} requires a much stronger crystal field to effect spin-pairing and the ligands which provide such a field also give rise to low-energy charge-transfer bands which almost always obscure the d–d bands. Nevertheless, the spectrum of the pale-yellow $[Fe(CN)_6]^{4-}$ shows a shoulder at $31\,000\,\text{cm}^{-1}$ on the side of a charge transfer absorption and this is attributed to the ${}^1T_{1g} \leftarrow {}^1A_{1g}$ transition.

Despite the above similarities, many differences between the members of this triad are also to be noted. Reduction of a trivalent compound, which yields a divalent compound in the case of cobalt, rarely does so for the heavier elements where the metal, univalent compounds, or M^{III} hydrido complexes are the more usual products. Rhodium forms the quite stable, yellow $[Rh(H_2O)_6]^{3+}$ ion when hydrous Rh_2O_3 is dissolved in mineral acid, and it occurs in the solid state in salts such as the perchlorate, sulfate and alums. $[Ir(H_2O)_6]^{3+}$ is less readily obtained but has been shown to occur in solutions of Ir^{III} in conc $HClO_4$.

There is also clear evidence of a change from predominantly class-a to class-b metal charactristics (p. 909) in passing down this group. Whereas cobalt(III) forms few complexes with the heavier donor atoms of Groups 15 and 16, rhodium(III), and more especially iridium (III), coordinate readily with P-, As- and S-donor ligands. Compounds with Se- and even Te- are also known.[19] Thus infrared, X-ray and ^{14}N nmr studies show that, in complexes such as $[Co(NH_3)_4(NCS)_2]^+$, the NCS^- acts as an N-donor ligand, whereas in $[M(SCN)_6]^{3-}$ (M = Rh, Ir) it is an S-donor. Likewise in the hexahalogeno complex anions, $[MX_6]^{3-}$, cobalt forms only that with fluoride, whereas rhodium forms them with all the halides except iodide, and iridium forms them with all except fluoride.

Besides the thiocyanates, just mentioned, other S-donor complexes which are of interest are the dialkyl sulfides, $[MCl_3(SR_2)_3]$, produced by the action of SR_2 on ethanolic $RhCl_3$ or on $[IrCl_6]^{3-}$. Phosphorus and arsenic compounds are obtained in similar fashion, and the best known are the yellow to orange complexes, $[ML_3X_3]$, (M = Rh, Ir; X = Cl, Br, I; L = trialkyl or triaryl phosphine or arsine). These compounds may exist as either *mer* or *fac* isomers, and these are normally distinguished by their proton nmr spectra (a distinction previously made by the measurement of dipole moments). An especially interesting feature of their chemistry is the ease with which they afford hydride and carbonyl derivatives. For instance, the colourless, air-stable $[RhH(NH_3)_5]SO_4$ is produced by the action of Zn powder on ammoniacal $RhCl_3$ in the presence of $(NH_4)_2SO_4$:

$$[RhCl(NH_3)_5]Cl_2 \xrightarrow[SO_4{}^{2-}]{Zn} [RhH(NH_3)_5]SO_4$$

Ternary hydrides of Rh and Ir containing the octahedral $[MH_6]^{3-}$ anions have been prepared[20] by the reaction of LiH and the metal under a high pressure of H_2. It is however unusual for hydrides of metals in such a high *formal* oxidation state as +3 to be stable in the absence of π-acceptor ligands and, indeed, in the presence of π-acceptor ligands such as tertiary phosphines and arsines, the stability of rhodium(III) hydrides is enhanced. Thus H_3PO_2 reduces $[RhCl_3L_3]$ to either $[RhHCl_2L_3]$ or $[RhH_2ClL_3]$, depending on L; and the action of H_2 on $[Rh^I(PPh_3)_3X]$ (X = Cl, Br, I) yields $[RhH_2(PPh_3)_3X]$ which is, formally at least, an oxidation by molecular hydrogen. However, it is iridium(III) that forms more hydrido-phosphine and hydrido-arsine complexes than any other platinum metal. Using $NaBH_4$, $LiAlH_4$, EtOH or even $SnCl_2 + H^+$ to provide the hydride ligand, complexes of the type $[MH_nL_3X_{3-n}]$ can be formed for very many of the permutations which are possible from L = trialkyl or triaryl phosphine or arsine; X = Cl, Br or I. Many polynuclear hydride complexes are also known.[21]

Oxidation state II (d⁷)

There is a very marked contrast in this oxidation state between cobalt on the one hand, and the two heavier members of the group on the other. For cobalt it is one of the two most stable oxidation states, whereas for the others it is of only minor importance.

[19] A. Z. AL-RUBAIE, Y. N. AL-OBAIDI and L. Z. YOUSIF, *Polyhedron* **9**, 1141–6 (1990).

[20] W. BRONGER, M. GEHLEN and G. AUFFERMANN, *Z. anorg. allg. Chem.* **620**, 1983–5 (1994).

[21] T. M. G. CARNEIRO, D. MATT and P. BRAUNSTEIN, *Coord. Chem. Revs.* **96**, 49–88 (1989).

Many early reports of Rh^{II} and Ir^{II} complexes have not been verified and in some cases may have involved M^{III} hydrides. Monomeric compounds require stabilization by ligands such as phosphines or $C_6Cl_5^-$. Thus, the action of LiC_6Cl_5 on $[L_2M-Cl-ML_2]$, where $L_2 = 2[P(OPh)_3]$, cyclooctene or cycloocta-1,5-diene, affords *trans* square planar products of the type $[M^I(\eta^1\text{-}C_6Cl_5)_2(L_2)]^-$, oxidation of which yield monomeric paramagnetic compounds such as $[M^{II}(\eta^1\text{-}C_6Cl_5)_2(L_2)]$ and, in the case of iridium, square planar $[Ir^{II}(\eta^1\text{-}C_6Cl_5)_4]^{2-}$ isolated as its $(NBu_4)^+$ salt.[22] Rhodium(II) is somewhat more common than iridium(II). Paramagnetic, *trans* square planar phosphines $[RhCl_2L_2]$ and the alkyl $(RhR_2(tht)_2]$, $(R = 2,4,6\text{-}Pr_3^iC_6H_2$; tht = tetrahydrothiophene) have been characterized.[23] Also, depending on temperature and relative concentrations, the reaction of $Rh(NO)Cl_2(PPh_3)_2$ and $Na(S_2CNR_2)$ in benzene yields either $Rh(S_2CNR_2)_2$ or $Rh(S_2CNR_2)(PPh_3)$, characterized by spectroscopic methods as square planar and square pyramidal respectively.[24]

Rhodium(II), however, is most familiar in a series of green dimeric diamagnetic compounds.[25] If hydrous Rh_2O_3, or better still $RhCl_3.3H_2O$ and sodium carboxylate, is refluxed with the appropriate acid and alcohol, green or blue solvated $[Rh(O_2CR)_2]_2$ is formed. Compounds of this type are generally air-stable and have the same bridged structure as the carboxylates of Cr^{II}, Mo^{II} and Cu^{II}; in the case of the acetate this involves a Rh–Rh distance of 239 pm which is consistent with a Rh–Rh bond. If rhodium acetate is treated with a strong acid such as HBF_4, whose anion has little tendency to coordinate, green solutions apparently containing the diamagnetic Rh_2^{4+} ion are obtained but

no solid salt of this has been isolated. Why no comparable Ir^{II} carboxylates, and very few other dimeric species stabilized by metal–metal bonding, have yet been prepared is not clear.

By contrast, Co^{II} carboxylates such as the red acetate, $Co(O_2CMe)_2.4H_2O$, are monomeric and in some cases the carboxylate ligands are unidentate. The acetate is employed in the production of catalysts used in certain organic oxidations, and also as a drying agent in oil-based paints and varnishes. Cobalt(II) gives rise to simple salts with all the common anions and they are readily obtained as hydrates from aqueous solutions. The parent hydroxide, $Co(OH)_2$, can be precipitated from the aqueous solutions by the addition of alkali and is somewhat amphoteric, not only dissolving in acid but also redissolving in excess of conc alkali, in which case it gives a deep-blue solution containing $[Co(OH)_4]^{2-}$ ions. It is obtainable in both blue and pink varieties: the former is precipitated by slow addition of alkali at $0°C$, but it is unstable and, in the absence of air, becomes pink on warming (cf. p. 1131).

Complexes of cobalt(II) are less numerous than those of cobalt(III) but, lacking any configuration comparable in stability with the t_{2g}^6 of Co^{III}, they show a greater diversity of types and are more labile. The redox properties have already been referred to and the possibility of oxidation must always be considered when preparing Co^{II} complexes. However, providing solutions are not alkaline and the ligands not too high in the spectrochemical series, a large number of complexes can be isolated without special precautions. The most common type is high-spin octahedral, though spin-pairing can be achieved by ligands such as CN^- (p. 1133) which also favour the higher oxidation state. Appropriate choice of ligands can however lead to high-spin–low-spin equilibria as in $[Co(terpy)_2]X_2.nH_2O$ and some 5- and 6-coordinated complexes of Schiff bases and pyridines.[26]

Many of the hydrated salts and their aqueous solutions contain the octahedral, pink

[22] M. P. GARCIA, M. V. JIMENEZ, L. A. ORO and F. J. LAHOZ, *Organometallics* **12**, 4660–3 (1993).

[23] R. S. HAY-MOTHERWELL, S. U. KOSCHMIEDER, G. WILKINSON, B. HUSSAIN-BATES and M. B. HURSTHOUSE, *J. Chem. Soc., Dalton Trans.*, 2821–30 (1991).

[24] K. K. PANDEY, D. T. NEHETE and R. B. SHARMA, *Polyhedron* **9**, 2013–18 (1990).

[25] F. A. COTTON and R. A. WALTON, *Multiple Bonds Between Metal Atoms*, Clarendon Press, Oxford, 1993, 787 pp.

[26] P. THUERY and J. ZARAMBOWITCH, *Inorg. Chem.* **25**, 2001–8 (1986).

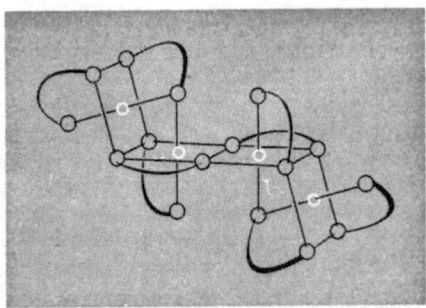

Figure 26.3 The tetrameric structure of [Co(acac)₂]₄.

$[Co(H_2O)_6]^{2+}$ ion, and bidentate N-donor ligands such as en, bipy and phen form octahedral cationic complexes $[Co(L\text{-}L)_3]^{3+}$, which are much more stable to oxidation than is the hexaammine $[Co(NH_3)_6]^{2+}$. Acac yields the orange $[Co(acac)_2(H_2O)_2]$ which has the *trans* octahedral structure and can be dehydrated to $[Co(acac)_2]$ which attains octahedral coordination by forming the tetrameric species shown in Fig. 26.3. This is comparable with the trimeric $[Ni(acac)_2]_3$ (p. 1157), like which it shows evidence of weak ferromagnetic interactions at very low temperatures. $[Co(edta)(H_2O)]^{2+}$ is ostensibly analogous to the 7-coordinate Mn^{II} and Fe^{II} complexes with the same stoichiometry, but in fact the cobalt is only 6-coordinate, 1 of the oxygen atoms of the edta being too far away from the cobalt (272 compared to 223 pm for the other edta donor atoms) to be considered as coordinated.

Tetrahedral complexes are also common, being formed more readily with cobalt(II) than with the cation of any other truly transitional element (i.e. excluding Zn^{II}). This is consistent with the CFSEs of the two stereochemistries (Table 26.6). Quantitative comparisons between the values given for CFSE(oct) and CFSE(tet) are not possible because of course the crystal field splittings, Δ_o and Δ_t differ. Nor is the CFSE by any means the most important factor in determining the stability of a complex. Nevertheless, where other factors are comparable, it can have a decisive effect and it is apparent that no configuration is more favourable than d^7 to the adoption of a tetrahedral as opposed to

Table 26.6 CFSE values[†] for high-spin complexes of d^0 to d^{10} ions

No. of d electrons	0	1	2	3	4	5	6	7	8	9	10
CFSE(oct)/(Δ_o)	0	$\frac{2}{5}$	$\frac{4}{5}$	$\frac{6}{5}$	$\frac{3}{5}$	0	$\frac{2}{5}$	$\frac{4}{5}$	$\frac{6}{5}$	$\frac{3}{5}$	0
CFSE(tet)/(Δ_t)	0	$\frac{3}{5}$	$\frac{6}{5}$	$\frac{4}{5}$	$\frac{2}{5}$	0	$\frac{3}{5}$	$\frac{6}{5}$	$\frac{4}{5}$	$\frac{2}{5}$	0

[†]The Crystal Field Stabilization Energy (CFSE) is the additional stability which accrues to an ion in a complex, as compared to the free ion, because its d-orbitals are split. In an octahedral complex a t_{2g} electron increases the stability by $2/5\Delta_o$ and an e_g electron decreases it by $3/5\Delta_o$. In a tetrahedral complex the orbital splitting is reversed and an e electron therefore increases the stability by $3/5\Delta_t$ whereas a t_2 electron decreases it by $2/5\Delta_t$.

an octahedral stereochemistry. Thus, in aqueous solutions containing $[Co((H_2O)_6]^{2+}$ there are also present in equilibrium, small amounts of tetrahedral $[Co(H_2O)_4]^{2+}$, and in acetic acid the tetrahedral $[Co(O_2CMe)_4]^{2-}$ occurs. The anionic complexes $[CoX_4]^{2-}$ are formed with the unidentate ligands, X = Cl, Br, I, SCN and OH, and a whole series of complexes, $[CoL_2X_2]$ (L = ligand with group 15 donor atom; X = halide, NCS), has been prepared in which both stereochemistries are found. $[CoCl_2py_2]$ exists in two isomeric forms: a blue metastable variety which is monomeric and tetrahedral, and a violet, stable form which is polymeric and achieves octahedral coordination by means of chloride bridges. Ligand polarizability is an important factor determining which stereochemistry is adopted, the more polarizable ligands favouring the tetrahedral form since fewer of them are required to neutralize the metal's cationic charge. Thus, if L = py, replacement of Cl^- by I^- makes the stable form tetrahedral and if L = phosphine or arsine the tetrahedral form is favoured irrespective of X.

The most obvious distinction between the octahedral and tetrahedral compounds is that *in general* the former are pink to violet in colour whereas the latter are blue, as exemplified by the well-known equilibrium:

$$[Co(H_2O)_6]^{2+} + 4Cl^- \rightleftharpoons [CoCl_4]^{2-} + 6H_2O$$
$$\text{pink} \qquad\qquad\qquad \text{blue}$$

This is not an infallible distinction (as the blue but octahedral $CoCl_2$ demonstrates) but is a useful

Electronic Spectra and Magnetic Properties of High-spin Octahedral and Tetrahedral Complexes of Cobalt(II)

Cobalt(II) is the only common d^7 ion and because of its stereochemical diversity its spectra have been widely studied. In a cubic field, three spin-allowed transitions are anticipated because of the splitting of the free-ion, ground ^4F term, and the accompanying ^4P term. In the octahedral case the splitting is the same as for the octahedral d^2 ion and the spectra can therefore be interpreted in a semi-quantitative manner using the same energy level diagram as was used for V^{3+} (Fig. 22.9, p. 997). In the present case the spectra usually consist of a band in the near infrared, which may be assigned as $\nu_1 = {}^4T_{2g}(F) \leftarrow {}^4T_{1g}(F)$, and another in the visible, often with a shoulder on the low energy side. Since the transition $^4A_{2g}(F) \leftarrow {}^4T_{1g}(F)$ is essentially a 2-electron transition from $t_{2g}^5 e_g^2$ to $t_{2g}^3 e_g^4$ it is expected to be weak, and the usual assignment is

$$\nu_2(\text{shoulder}) = {}^4A_{2g}(F) \leftarrow {}^4T_{1g}(F)$$

$$\nu_3 = {}^4T_{1g}(P) \leftarrow {}^4T_{1g}(F)$$

Indeed, in some cases it is probable that ν_2 is not observed at all, but that the fine structure arises from term splitting due to spin-orbit coupling or to distortions from regular octahedral symmetry.

In tetrahedral fields the splitting of the free ion ground term is the reverse of that in octahedral fields so that, for d^7 ions in tetrahedral fields $^2A_{2g}(F)$ lies lowest but three spin-allowed bands are still anticipated.In fact, the observed spectra usually consist of a broad, intense band in the visible region (responsible for the colour and often about 10 times as intense as in octahedral compounds) with a weaker one in the infrared. The only satisfactory interpretation is to assign these, respectively, as, $\nu_3 = {}^4T_1(P) \leftarrow {}^4A_2(F)$ and $\nu_2 = {}^4T_1(F) \leftarrow {}^4A_2(F)$ in which case $\nu_1 = {}^4T_2(F) \leftarrow {}^4A_2(F)$ should be in the region 3000–5000 cm^{-1}. Examination of this part of the infrared has sometimes indicated the presence of a band, though overlying vibrational bands make interpretation difficult.

Table 26.7 gives data for a number of octahedral and tetrahedral complexes, the values of $10Dq$ and B having been derived by analysis of the spectra.[27] It is clear from these data that the "anomolous" blue colour of octahedral CoCl$_2$ arises because 6 Cl$^-$ ions generate such a weak crystal field that the main band in its spectrum is at an unusually low energy, extending into the red region (hence giving a blue colour) rather than the green-blue region (which would give a red colour) more commonly observed for octahedral Co^{II} compounds.

Magnetic properties provide a complementary means of distinguishing stereochemistry. The T ground term of the octahedral ion is expected to give rise to a temperature-dependent orbital contribution to the magnetic moment whereas the A ground term of the tetrahedral ion is not. As a matter of fact, in a tetrahedral field the excited $^4T_2(F)$ term is "mixed into" the ground $^4A_2$ term because of spin-orbit coupling and tetrahedral complexes of Co^{II} are expected to have magnetic moments given by $\mu_e = \mu_{\text{spin-only}}(1 - 4\lambda/10Dq)$, where $\lambda = -170$ cm^{-1} and $\mu_{\text{spin-only}} = 3.87$ BM.

Thus the magnetic moments of tetrahedral complexes lie in the range 4.4–4.8 BM, whereas those of octahedral complexes are around 4.8–5.2 BM at room temperature, falling off appreciably as the temperature is reduced.

empirical guide whose reliability is improved by a more careful analysis of the electronic spectra[27] (see Panel). Data for some octahedral and tetrahedral complexes are given in Table 26.7.

Square planar complexes are also well authenticated if not particularly numerous and include [Co(phthalocyanine)] and [Co(CN)$_4$]$^-$ as well as [Co(salen)] and complexes with other Schiff bases. These are invariably low-spin with magnetic moments at room temperature in the range 2.1–2.9 BM, indicating 1 unpaired electron. They are primarily of interest because

of their oxygen-carrying properties, discussed already in Chapter 14 where numerous reviews on the subject are cited. The uptake of dioxygen, which bonds in the bent configuration,

$$\text{Co} - \text{O} \diagup \!\!\! \diagdown \;\; \overset{\text{O}}{}$$

is accompanied by the attachment of a solvent molecule *trans* to the O$_2$ and the retention of the single unpaired electron. There is fairly general agreement, based on esr evidence, that electron transfer from metal to O$_2$ occurs just as in the bridged complexes referred to on

---

[27] pp. 480-504 of ref. 16.

Table 26.7 Electronic spectra of complexes of cobalt(II)

(a) Octahedral

Complex	ν_1/cm^{-1}	ν_2/cm^{-1} (weak)	ν_3/cm^{-1} (main)	$10Dq/cm^{-1}$	B/cm^{-1}
$[Co(bipy)_3]^{2+}$	11 300		22 000	12 670	791
$[Co(NH_3)_6]^{2+}$	9000		21 100	10 200	885
$[Co(H_2O)_6]^{2+}$	8100	16 000	19 400	9200	825
$CoCl_2$	6600	13 300	17 250	6900	780

(b) Tetrahedral

Complex	ν_2/cm^{-1}	ν_3/cm^{-1} (main)	$10Dq/cm^{-1}$	B/cm^{-1}
$[Co(NCS)_4]^{2-}$	7780	16 250	4550	691
$[Co(N_3)_4]^{2-}$	6750	14 900	3920	658
$[CoCl_4]^{2-}$	5460	14 700	3120	710
$[CoI_4]^{2-}$	4600	13 250	2650	665

p. 1126, producing a situation close to the extreme represented by low-spin Co^{III} attached to a superoxide ion, O_2^-. (The opposite extreme, represented by $Co^{II}-O_2$, implies that the unpaired electron resides on the metal with the dioxygen being rendered diamagnetic by the loss of the degeneracy of its π^* orbitals with consequent spin pairing.) However, the precise extent of the electron transfer is probably determined by the nature of the ligand *trans* to the O_2.

The difficulty of assigning a formal oxidation state is more acutely seen in the case of 5-coordinate NO adducts of the type $[Co(NO)(salen)]$. These are effectively diamagnetic and so have no unpaired electrons. They may therefore be formulated either as $Co^{III}-NO^-$ or Co^I-NO^+. The infrared absorptions ascribed to the N–O stretch lie in the range 1624–1724 cm^{-1}, which is at the lower end of the range said to be characteristic of NO^+. But, as in all such cases which are really concerned with the differing polarities of covalent bonds, such formalism should not be taken literally.

Other 5-coordinate Co^{II} compounds which have been characterized include $[CoBr\{N(C_2H_4NMe_2)_3\}]^+$, which is high-spin with 3 unpaired electrons and is trigonal bipyramidal (imposed by the "tripod" ligand), and

$[Co(CN)_5]^{3-}$, which is low-spin with 1 unpaired electron and is square pyramidal. The latter complex is isolated from solutions of $Co(CN)_2$ and KCN as the yellow $[NEt_2Pr_2^i]^+$ salt, an extremely oxygen-sensitive and hygroscopic material. A further difficulty which hindered its isolation is its tendency to dimerize to the more familiar deep-violet, $[(CN)_5Co-Co(CN)_5]^{6-}$. The absence of a simple hexacyano complex is significant as it seems to be generally the case that ligands such as CN^-, which are expected to induce spin-pairing, favour a coordination number for Co^{II} of 4 or 5 rather than 6; the planar $[Co(diars)_2](ClO_4)$ is a further illustration of this. Presumably the Jahn–Teller distortion, which is anticipated for the low-spin $t_{2g}^6 e_g^1$ configuration is largely responsible.

Oxidation state I (d^8)

Oxidation states lower than +2 normally require the stabilizing effect of π-acceptor ligands and some of these are appropriately considered along with organometallic compounds in Section 26.3.5. Exceptions are the square pyramidal anion of the black, $Mg_2[CoH_5]$ (obtained by prolonged heating of the powdered metals under high pressure of H_2) and the linear anion of the garnet red $CsK_2[CoO_2]^{(27a)}$ (see p. 1166). However, although +1 is not a common oxidation state for cobalt, it is one of the two most common states for both rhodium and iridium and as such merits separate consideration.

Simple ligand-field arguments, which will be elaborated when M^{II} ions of the Ni, Pd, Pt triad are discussed on p. 1157, indicate that the d^8 configuration favours a 4-coordinate, square-planar stereochemistry. In the present group, however, the configuration is associated with a lower oxidation state and the requirements of the 18-electron rule,† which favour 5-coordination, are also to be considered. The upshot is that most Co^I complexes are 5-coordinate, like $[Co(CNR)_5]^+$, and square-planar Co^I is apparently unknown. On the other hand, complexes of Rh^I and Ir^I are predominantly square planar, although 5-coordination does also occur.

These complexes are usually prepared by the reduction of compounds such as $RhCl_3$.$3H_2O$ and K_2IrCl_6 in the presence of the desired ligand. It is often unnecessary to use a specific reductant, the ligand itself or alcoholic solvent being adequate, and not infrequently leading to the presence of CO or H in the product. A considerable proportion of the complexes of Rh^I and Ir^I are phosphines and of these, two in particular demand attention. They are Wilkinson's catalyst, $[RhCl(PPh_3)_3]$, and Vaska's compound, $trans$-$[IrCl(CO)(PPh_3)_2]$, both essentially square planar.

Wilkinson's catalyst, $[RhCl(PPh_3)_3]$. This red-violet compound$^{(28)}$, which is readily obtained by refluxing ethanolic $RhCl_3.3H_2O$ with an excess of PPh_3, was discovered$^{(29)}$ in 1965. It undergoes a variety of reactions, most of which involve either replacement of a phosphine ligand (e.g. with CO, CS, C_2H_4, O_2 giving *trans* products) or oxidative addition (e.g. with H_2, MeI) to form Rh^{III}, but its importance arises from its effectiveness as a catalyst$^{(30)}$ for highly selective hydrogenations of complicated organic molecules which are of great importance in the pharmaceutical industry. Its use allowed, for the first time, rapid *homogeneous* hydrogenation at ambient temperatures and pressures:

The precise mechanism is complicated and has been the subject of much speculation and controversy, but Fig. 26.4 shows a simplified but reasonable scheme. The essential steps in this are the oxidative addition of H_2 (if the hydrogen atoms are regarded as "hydridic", i.e. as H^-, the metal's oxidation state increases from +1 to +3); the formation of an alkene complex; alkene insertion and, finally, the reductive elimination of the alkane (i.e. the metal's oxidation state reverting to +1). The rhodium catalyst is able to fulfil its role because the metal is capable of changing its coordination number (loss of phosphine from the dihydro complex being encouraged by the large size of the ligand) and it possesses oxidation states (+1 and +3) which differ by 2 and are of comparable stability.

The discovery of the catalytic properties of $[RhCl(PPh_3)_3]$ naturally brought about a widespread search for other rhodium phosphines with catalytic activity. One of those which was found, also in Wilkinson's laboratory, was *trans*-$[Rh(CO)H(PPh_3)_3]$ which can conveniently be

---

† The filling-up of the bonding MOs of the molecule may be regarded, more simply, as the filling of the outer 9 orbitals of the metal ion with its own d electrons plus a pair of σ electrons from each ligand. A 4-coordinate d^8 ion is thus a "16-electron" species and is "coordinatively unsaturated". Saturation in this sense requires the addition of 10 electrons, i.e. 5 ligands, to the metal ion. By contrast rhodium(III) is a d^6 ion and so can expand its coordination sphere to accommodate 6 ligands with important consequences in catalysis which will be seen below.

^{27a} F. BERNHARD and R. HOPPE, *Z. anorg. allg. Chem.* **620**, 187–91 (1994).

^{28} The paramagnetic impurity which invariably accompanies Wilkinson's catalyst has proved difficult to identify. It is probably the air-stable, green, *trans*- $[RhCl(CO)(PPh_3)_2]$. see K. R. DUNBAR and S. C. HAEFNER, *Inorg. Chem.* **31**, 3676–9 (1992).

^{29} J. F. YOUNG, J. A. OSBORN, F. H. JARDINE, and G. WILKINSON, *J. Chem. Soc., Chem. Commun.*, 131–2 (1965).

^{30} R. S. DICKSON, *Homogeneous Catalysis with Compounds of Rhodium and Iridium*, D. Reidel, Dordrecht, 1985, 278 pp.

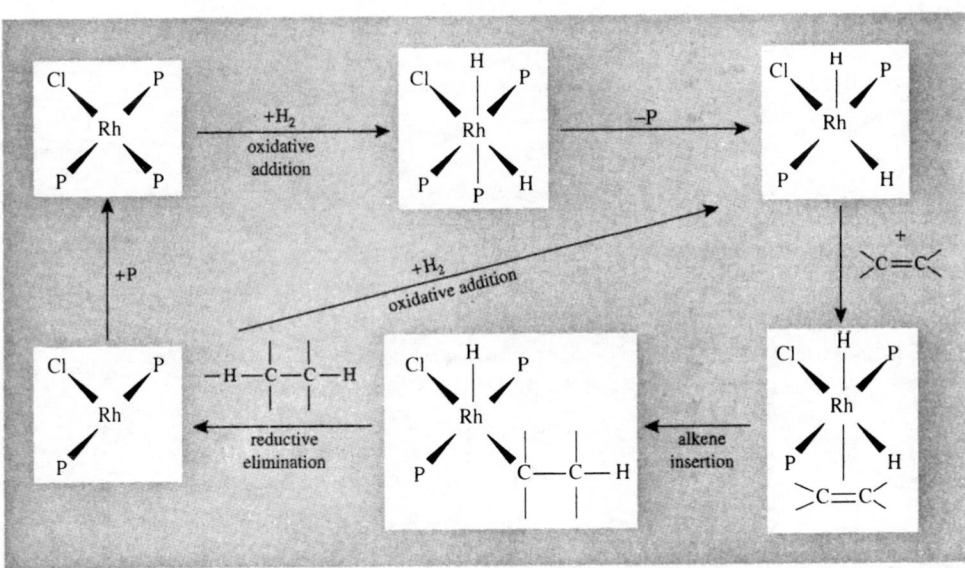

Figure 26.4 The catalytic cycle for the hydrogenation of an alkene, catalysed by [RhCl(PPh₃)₃] in benzene; possible coordination of solvent molecules has been ignored and the ligand PPh₃ has been represented as P throughout, for clarity.

dealt with here. It was found that, for steric reasons, it selectively catalyses the hydrogenation of alk-1-enes (i.e. terminal olefins) rather than alk-2-enes and it has been used in the *hydroformylation* of alkenes, (i.e. the addition of H and the formyl group, CHO) also known as the OXO process because it introduces oxygen into the hydrocarbon. This is a process of enormous industrial importance, being used to convert alk-1-enes into aldehydes which can then be converted to alcohols for the production of polyvinylchloride (PVC) and polyalkenes and, in the case of the long-chain alcohols, in the production of detergents:

$$RCH{=}CH_2 + H_2 + CO \xrightarrow{\text{catalyst}} RCH_2CH_2CHO$$

A simplified reaction scheme is shown in Fig. 26.5 Again, the ability of rhodium to change its coordination number and oxidation state is crucial, and this catalyst has the great advantage over the conventional cobalt carbonyl catalyst that it operates efficiently at much lower temperatures and pressures and produces straight-chain as opposed to branched-chain products.

The reason for its selectivity lies in the insertion step of the cycle. In the presence of the two bulky PPh₃ groups, the attachment to the metal of –CH₂CH₂R (anti-Markovnikov addition, leading to a straight chain product) is easier than the attachment of –CH(CH₃)R (Markovnikov addition, leading to a branched-chain product).

Vaska's compound, trans-[IrCl(CO)(PPh₃)₂]. This yellow compound can be prepared by the reaction of triphenylphosphine and IrCl₃ in a solvent such as 2-methoxyethanol which acts both as reducing agent and supplier of CO. It was discovered in 1961 by L. Vaska and J. W. di Luzio[31] and recognized as an ideal material for the study of oxidative addition reactions, since its products are generally stable and readily characterized. It is certainly the most thoroughly investigated compound of Ir[I]. It forms octahedral Ir[III] complexes in oxidative addition reactions with H₂, Cl₂, HX, MeI and RCO₂H, and ¹H nmr shows that in all cases the phosphine ligands are *trans* to each other. The 4 remaining ligands (Cl,

³¹ L. Vaska and J. W. Di Luzio, *J. Am. Chem. Soc.* **83**, 2784–5 (1961).

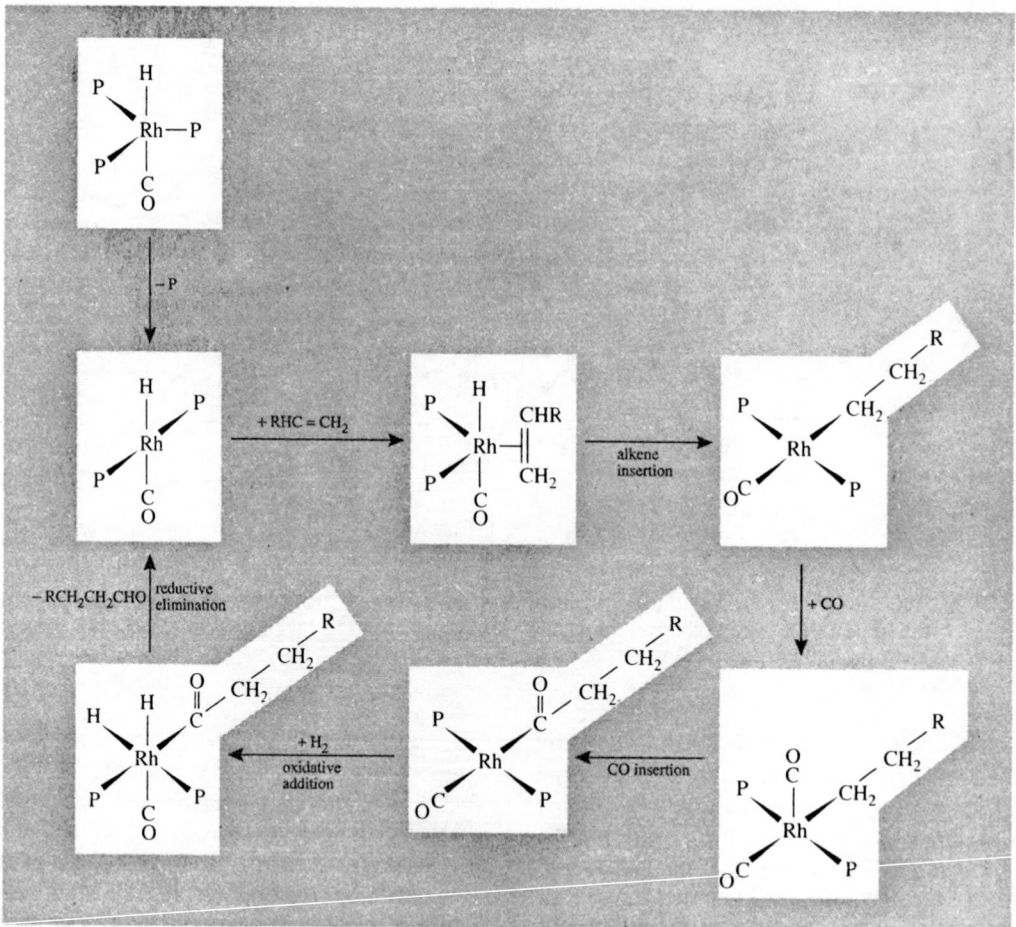

Figure 26.5 The catalytic cycle for the hydroformylation of an alkene catalysed by *trans*-[RhH(CO)(PPh₃)₃]. The tertiary phosphine ligand has been represented as P throughout.

CO and two components of the reactant) therefore lie in a plane and 3 isomers are possible:

There is apparently no simple way of predicting which of these will be formed and each case must be examined individually. The situation is further complicated by the fact that, when the Cl of Vaska's compound is replaced by H, Me or Ph, addition of H_2 gives products in which the phosphines are now *cis*. Various

theoretical models have been suggested to account for this.[32]

Addition reactions with ligands such as CO and SO_2 (the addition of which as an uncharged ligand is unusual) differ in that no oxidation occurs and 5-coordinate 18-electron Ir^I products are formed.

The facile absorption of O_2 by a solution of Vaska's compound is accompanied by a change in colour from yellow to orange which may be reversed by flushing with N_2. This

---

[32] M. J. BURK,   M. P. McGRATH,   R. WHEELER   and R. H. CRABTREE, *J. Am. Chem. Soc.* **110**, 5034–9 (1988).

is one of the most widely studied synthetic oxygen-carrying systems and has been discussed earlier (p. 615). The O–O distance of 130 pm in the oxygenated product (see Fig. 14.5b, p. 617) is rather close to the 128 pm of the superoxide ion, O_2^-, but this would imply Ir^{II} which is paramagnetic whereas the compound is actually diamagnetic. The oxygenation is instead normally treated as an oxidative addition with the O_2 acting as a bidentate peroxide ion, O_2^{2-}, to give a 6-coordinate Ir^{III} product. However, in view of the small "bite" of this ligand the alternative formulation in which the O_2 acts as a neutral unidentate ligand giving a 5-coordinate Ir^I product has also been proposed.

Oxygen-carrying properties are evidently critically dependent on the precise charge distribution and steric factors within the molecule. Replacement of the Cl in Vaska's compound with I causes loss of oxygen-carrying ability, the oxygenation being irreversible. This can be rationalized by noting that the lower electronegativity of the iodine would allow a greater electron density on the metal, thus facilitating $M \rightarrow O_2$ π donation: this increases the strength of the $M-O_2$ bond and, by placing charge in antibonding orbitals of the O_2, causes an increase in the O–O distance from 130 to 151 pm.

Lower oxidation states

Numerous complexes of Co, Rh and Ir are known in which the formal oxidation state of the metal is zero, −1, or even lower. Many of these compounds contain CO, CN^- or RNC as ligands and so are more conveniently discussed under organometallic compounds (Section 26.3.5). However, other ligands such as tertiary phosphines also stabilize the lower oxidation states, as exemplified by the brown, tetrahedral, paramagnetic complex $[Co^0(PMe_3)_4]$: this is made by reducing an ethereal solution of $CoCl_2$ with Mg or Na amalgam in the presence of PMe_3. Further treatment of the product with Mg/thf in the presence of N_2 gives $[Mg(thf)_4][Co^{-II}(N_2)(PMe_3)_4]$. Similar

reactions with $P(OMe)_3$ and $P(OEt)_3$ give both paramagnetic monomers $[Co^0\{P(OR)_3\}_4]$, and diamagnetic dimers $[Co_2^0\{P(OR)_3\}_8]$, whereas the more bulky $P(OPr^i)_3$ yields only the orange-red monomeric product. With an excess of sodium amalgam as reducing agent the product with this latter ligand is the white-crystalline $Na[Co^{-I}\{P(OPr^i)_3\}_5]$. In view of the ready solubility of this compound in pentane and the d^{10} configuration of Co^{-I} it may be that only 4 of the phosphite ligands are directly coordinated to the metal centre: one possible formulation would be

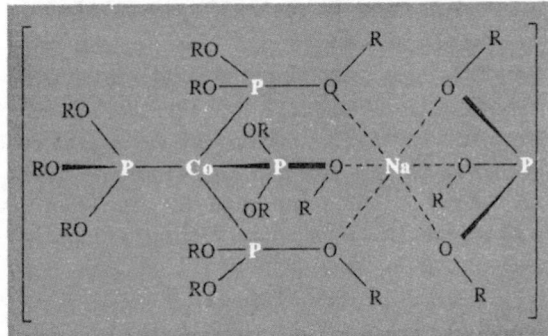

With the terdentate *P*-donor ligand, MeC-$(CH_2PPh_2)_3$, (tppme) excess sodium amalgam and an atmosphere of N_2 yields the deep-brown $[(tppme)Co-N-N-Co(tppme)]$ which, unusually for a dimer, is paramagnetic.[33] The N–N distance in the linear bridge is 118 pm compared with 109.8 pm in N_2 (p. 412).

Another technique for obtaining low oxidation states is by electrolytic reduction using cyclic voltametry. Some spectacular series can be achieved of which, perhaps, the most notable is based on $[Ir^{III}(bipy)_3]^{3+}$: this, when dissolved in MeCN, can be oxidized to $[Ir^{IV}(bipy)_3]^{4+}$ and reduced in successive 1-electron steps to give every oxidation state down to $[Ir^{-III}(bipy)_3]^{3-}$, a total of 8 interconnected redox complexes. However, by no means all have been isolated as solid products from solution. Many other

---

[33] F. CECCONI, C. A. GHILARDI, S. MIDOLLINI, S. MONETI, A. ORLANDINI and M. BACCI, *J. Chem. Soc., Chem. Commun.*, 731–3 (1985).

such redox series are known for these and other elements.

26.3.4 The biochemistry of cobalt[34]

The wasting disease in sheep and cattle known variously as "pine" (Britain), "bush sickness" (New Zealand), "coast disease" (Australia), and "salt sick" (Florida) has been recognized since the late eighteenth century. When it was realized to be an anaemic condition it was thought to be due to iron deficiency and was therefore treated, with mixed success, by administering iron salts. Then, in the 1930s, it was found by workers in Australia and New Zealand that the efficacious principle in the iron treatment was actually an impurity (cobalt) but its role was not understood. This became more evident when vitamin B_{12} was extracted from raw liver and shown to be responsible for the latter's well-known effectiveness in treating pernicious anaemia. It is now known that vitamin B_{12} is a coenzyme[†] in a number of biochemical processes, the most important of which is the formation of erythrocytes (red blood-cells). It obviously functions extremely effectively, the human body for instance containing a mere 2–5 mg, concentrated in the liver.

The structure of the diamagnetic, cherry-red vitamin B_{12} is shown in Fig. 26.6 and it can be seen that the coordination sphere of the cobalt has many similarities with that of iron in haem (see Fig. 25.7). In both cases the metal is coordinated to 4 nitrogen atoms of an unsaturated macrocycle (in this case part of a "corrin" ring which is less symmetrical and not so unsaturated as the porphyrin in haem) with an imidazole nitrogen in the fifth position. A major

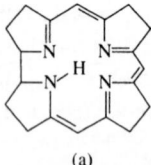

(a)

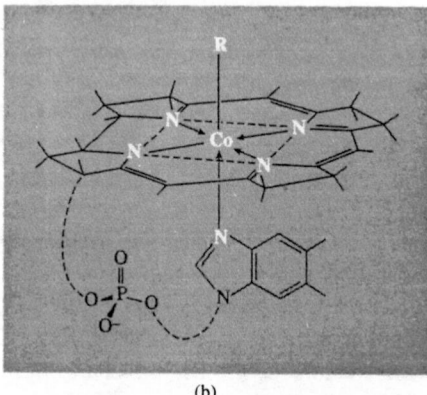

(b)

Figure 26.6 Vitamin B_{12}: (a) a *corrin* ring showing a square-planar set of N atoms and a replaceable H, and (b) simplified structure of B_{12}. In view of the H displaced from the corrin ring, the Co–C bond, and the charge on the ribose phosphate, the cobalt is formally in the +3 oxidation state. This and related molecules are conveniently represented as:

$$\text{R} \atop [\text{Co}^{\text{III}}]$$

difference is apparent, however, in the sixth coordination position which, in haemoglobin, is either vacant or occupied by O_2. Here it is filled by a σ-bonded carbon,[35] making vitamin B_{12} the first, and so far the only, fully established naturally occurring organometallic compound. The usual methods of isolation lead to a product known as *cyanocobalamin*, which is the same as vitamin B_{12} itself but with CN^- instead of deoxyadenosine in the sixth coordination position. This is a labile site, and other derivatives such as *aquocobalamin* can be prepared.

Incorporation of cobalt into the corrin ring system modifies the reduction potentials of

---

[34] W. KAIM and B. SCHWERDERSKI, pp. 39–55 of *Bioinorganic Chemistry:Inorganic Elements in the Chemistry of Life*, Wiley, Chichester, 1994; L. R. MILGROM, *Chem. in Brit.* **31**, 923–7 (1994).

[†] Enzymes are proteins which act as very specific catalysts in biological systems. Their activity may depend on the presence of substances, often metal complexes, of much lower molecular weight. These activators are known as "coenzymes".

[35] D. C. HODGKIN, *Proc. Roy. Soc.* A **288**, 294–305 (1965).

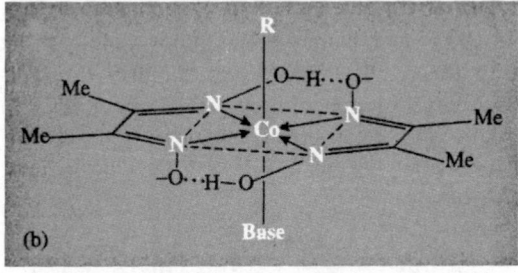

Figure 26.7 Model vitamin B_{12} compounds: (a) a Schiff base derivative, and (b) a cobaloxime, in this case derived from dimethylglyoxime.

cobalt giving it three accessible and consecutive oxidation states:

$$OH$$
$$|$$
$$[Co^{III}] \quad \underset{-e^-}{\overset{+e^-}{\rightleftarrows}} \quad [Co^{II}]$$

Hydroxocobalamin
purple

Vitamin B_{12r}
brown

$$-e^- \parallel +e^-$$

$$[Co^I]$$

Vitamin B_{12s}
blue-green

The reductions are effected in nature by ferredoxin (p. 1102). This behaviour can be reproduced surprisingly well by simpler, model compounds. Some of the best known of these are obtained by the addition of axial groups to the square-planar complexes of Co^{II} with Schiff bases, or substituted glyoximes (giving cobaloximes) as illustrated in Fig. 26.7. The reduced Co^I species of these, along with vitamin

B_{12s}, are amongst the most powerful nucleophiles known (hence, "supernucleophiles"), liberating H_2 from water.

Virtually all the biological processes, in which vitamin B_{12} is active, involve substituent exchange of the type:

$$
\begin{array}{ccc}
\underset{|}{\overset{H}{|}} \quad \underset{|}{\overset{R}{|}} & & \underset{|}{\overset{R}{|}} \quad \underset{|}{\overset{H}{|}} \\
-C-C- & \rightleftharpoons & -C-C- \\
| \quad | & & | \quad | \\
\end{array}
$$

which, significantly, does not involve solvent protons. The precise mechanism of these reactions is not settled but all involve cleavage of the Co–C bond and it is evident from the study of model systems that the lack of complete planarity of the corrin ring is an important factor in controlling this.[36]

26.3.5 Organometallic compounds [37]

Many of the organometallic compounds of the elements of this group show valuable catalytic activity and, as discussed above, much of the chemistry of vitamin B_{12} is the chemistry of the Co–Cσ bond. Simple homoleptic alkyls and aryls of cobalt, $[CoR_x]$, have not in fact been prepared, but this is evidently not due to thermodynamic instability of the Co–C bond. Compounds containing such bonds can be prepared in abundance, not only with $(\sigma + \pi)$-bonding ligands such as phosphines and CO but also with non-π-bonding ligands such as Schiff bases and glyoximes. These latter presumably owe their existence not to electronic but rather to steric factors, the additional ligands blocking what might otherwise be energetically favourable decomposition paths.

[36] M. RAVIKANTH and T. K. CHANRESHEKAR, *Structure and Bonding*, **82**, 105–88 (1995).

[37] R. S. DICKSON, *Organometallic Chemistry of Rhodium and Iridium*, Academic Press, New York, 1983, 432 pp.; C. WHITE, *Organometallic Compounds of Cobalt, Rhodium and Iridium*, Chapman & Hall, London 1985, 296 pp.

Carbonyls (see p. 926)

Because they possess an odd number of valence electrons the elements of this group can only satisfy the 18-electron rule in their carbonyls if M–M bonds are present. In accord with this, mononuclear carbonyls are not formed. Instead $[M_2(CO)_8]$, $[M_4(CO)_{12}]$ and $[M_6(CO)_{16}]$ are the principal binary carbonyls of these elements. But reduction of $[Co_2(CO)_8]$ with, for instance, sodium amalgam in benzene yields the monomeric and tetrahedral, 18-electron ion, $[Co(CO)_4]^-$, acidification of which gives the pale yellow hydride, $[HCo(CO)_4]$. Reductions employing Na metal in liquid NH_3 yield the "super-reduced" $[M(CO)_3]^{3-}$ (M = Co, Rh, Ir) containing these elements in their lowest formal oxidation state.[38]

The importance of cobalt carbonyls lies in their involvement in hydroformylation reactions discussed above. The original, and still widely used, process depends on the use of cobalt salts rather than the newer rhodium catalysts (pp. 1134–5). The mechanism of the cobalt cycle is more difficult to ascertain but it seems clear that the active agent is the hydride, $[HCo(CO)_4]$. It is, moreover, plausible that the cycle is basically the same as that outlined in Fig. 26.5 but starting with loss of CO from $[HCo(CO)_4]$ rather than loss of phosphine from $[Rh(CO)H(PPh_3)_3]$, so producing a comparable coordinatively unsaturated intermediate to which the alkene can attach itself. The disadvantages of the system, as already mentioned, are its lack of specificity, leading to branched-chain products, and the necessity of high temperatures (>150°C) and pressure (~200 atm). In addition the volatility of $[HCo(CO)_4]$ poses recovery problems.

The dinuclear octacarbonyls are obtained by heating the metal (or in the case of iridium, $IrCl_3$ + copper metal) under a high pressure of CO (200–300 atm). $Co_2(CO)_8$ is by far the best known, the other two being poorly characterized; it is an air-sensitive, orange-red solid melting at 51°C. The structure, which involves two bridging carbonyl groups as shown in Fig. 26.8a, can perhaps be most easily rationalized on the basis of a "bent" Co–Co bond arising from overlap of angled metal orbitals (d^2sp^3 hybrids). However, in solution this structure is in equilibrium with a second form (Fig. 26.8b) which has no bridging carbonyls and is held together solely by a Co–Co bond.

The most stable carbonyls of rhodium and iridium are respectively red and yellow solids of the form $[M_4(CO)_{12}]$ which are obtained by heating MCl_3 with copper metal under about 200 atm of CO. The black cobalt analogue is more simply obtained by heating $[Co_2(CO)_8]$ in an inert atmosphere

$$2[Co_2(CO)_8] \xrightarrow{50°C} [Co_4(CO)_{12}] + 4CO$$

The structures are shown in Fig. 26.8c and d and differ in that, whereas the Ir compound consists of a tetrahedron of metal atoms held together solely by M–M bonds, the Rh and Co compounds each incorporate 3 bridging carbonyls. A similar difference was noted in the case of the trinuclear carbonyls of Fe, Ru and Os (p. 1104) and can be explained in a similar way.[39] The M_4 tetrahedra of Co and Rh are small enough to be accommodated in an icosahedral array of CO ligands whereas the larger Ir_4 tetrahedron forces the adoption of the less dense cube octahedral array of ligands.

Of the $[M_6(CO)_{16}]$ carbonyls the very dark-brown Rh compound prepared simultaneously with and separated from $[Rh_4(CO)_{12}]$ is the best known. In the solid its structure consists of an octahedral array of $Rh(CO)_2$ units with the remaining 4 CO's bridging 4 faces of the octahedron (Fig. 26.8e). A black isomorphous, and presumably isostructural, Co analogue and an isostructural red Ir analogue are known. A second, black Ir isomer occurs which differs only in that it has 4 edge-bridging rather than face-bridging CO groups. Again rationalization is possible on the basis of the ligand polyhedral

[38] J. E. ELLIS, *Adv. Organometallic Chem.*, **31**, 1–52 (1990).

[39] B. F. G. JOHNSON and Y. V. ROBERTS, *Polyhedron*, **12**, 977–90 (1993).

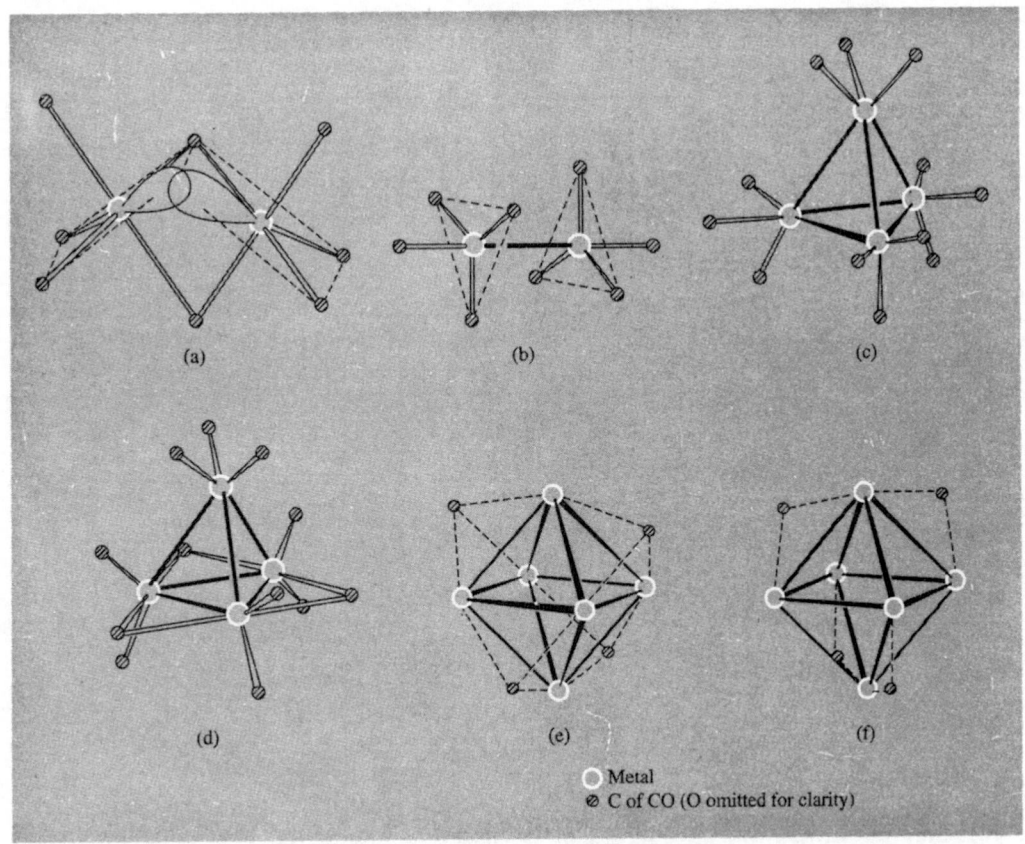

Figure 26.8   Molecular structures of some binary carbonyls of Co, Rh, and Ir. (a) $Co_2(CO)_8$ in solid state, showing the formation of a "bent" Co–Co bond. (b) $Co_2(CO)_8$ in solution. (c) $Ir_4(CO)_{12}$. (d) $M_4(CO)_{12}$, M = Co, Rh. (e) $M_6(CO)_{16}$ M = Co, Rh and Ir (for its red isomer). (f) black isomer of $Ir_6(CO)_{16}$.

model. In *both* structures the ligands occupy the 16 vertices of a tetracapped truncated tetrahedron. In one case the 4 caps are the face-bridging ligands, in the other the edge-bridging ligands. The two structures are related by a simple rotation of the M_6 octahedron about a C_4 axis.[39]

Carbonyl hydrides and carbonylate anions are obtained by reducing neutral carbonyls, as mentioned above, and in addition to mononuclear metal anions, anionic species of very high nuclearity have been obtained, often by thermolysis. These are especially numerous for Rh and in certain Rh_{13}, Rh_{14} and Rh_{15} anions have structures conveniently visualized either as polyhedra encapsulating further metal atoms, or alternatively as arrays of metal atoms forming portions of hexagonal close packed or body centred cubic lattices stabilized by CO ligands. $[Rh_{13}H_3(CO)_{24}]^{2-}$ (Fig 26.9a) is typical.

The anionic cluster $[Ir_6(CO)_{15}]^{2-}$ is octahedral and an increasing number of Ir clusters have been reported recently though their preparations are more difficult and yields usually smaller than for rhodium. $[Ir_{14}(CO)_{27}]^-$ has the highest nuclearity so far and is obtained as black crystals by oxidizing $[Ir_6(CO)_{15}]^{2-}$ with ferricinium ion[40] (Fig 26.9b).

The incorporation of interstitial or encapsulated heteroatoms is a common and stabilizing feature. Carbon is the most common and, as is the case in

40 R. D. PERGOLA, L. GARLASCHELLI, M. MANASSERO, N. MASCIOCCHI and P. ZANELLO, *Angew. Chem. Int. Edn. Engl.* **32**, 1347–9 (1993).

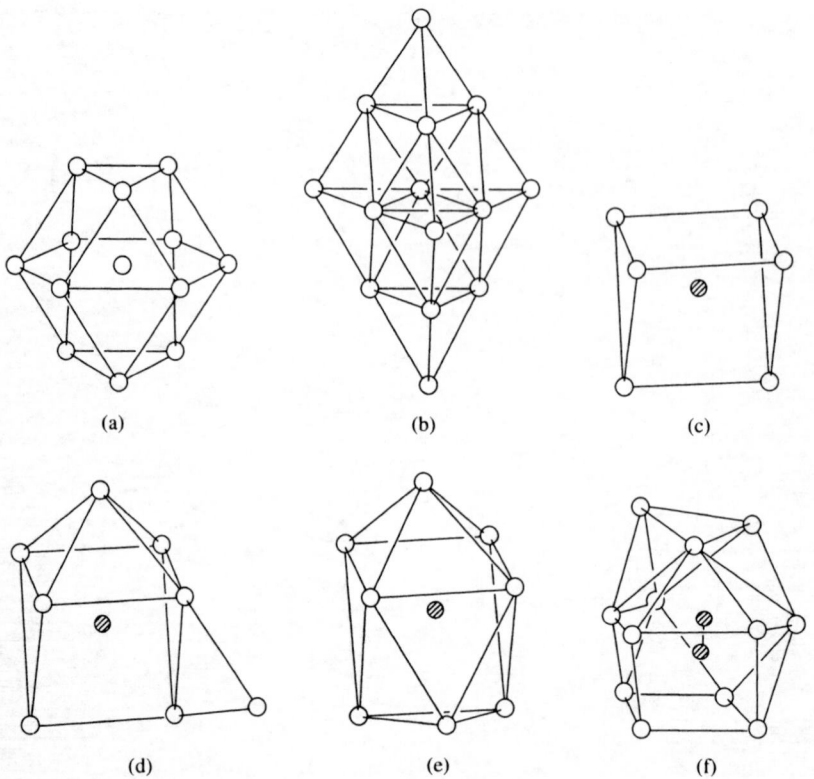

Figure 26.9 Schematic representations of the metal cores of some clusters of group 9 metals.
(a) $[Rh_{13}H_3(CO)_{24}]^{2-}$; the H atoms migrate within the cluster. (b) $[Ir_{14}(CO)_{27}]^-$. (c) $[Rh_6C(CO)_{15}]^{2-}$.
(d) $[Rh_8C(CO)_{19}]$; a trigonal prism of 6 Rh atoms has one face capped by a seventh Rh atom
and one edge bridged by the eighth Rh atom. (e) $[Co_8C(CO)_{18}]^{2-}$; the 8 Co atoms define a
distorted bicapped trigonal prism which, alternatively, can be viewed as a distorted square antiprism.
(f) $[Rh_{12}(C_2)(CO)_{25}]$.

group 8 (p. 1107), may originate from the solvent
or from cleavage of a CO ligand. The carbido C
contributes 4 electrons to the cluster bonding and
in the 90-electron species $[Rh_6C(CO)_{15}]^{2-}$ features trigonal prismatic coordination of Rh_6 about
the central C (Fig. 26.9c). More complex geometries are found for $[Rh_8C(CO)_{19}]$ (Fig. 26.9d)
and $[Co_8C(CO)_{18}]^{2-}$ (Fig. 26.9e): these two isoelectronic clusters are not isostructural though a
slight distortion would (hypothetically) transform
one into the other. The central carbido C in the
square antiprismatic $[Co_8C(CO)_{18}]^{2-}$ is formally
8-coordinate, the Co-C distances being in the
range 195–220 pm with a mean value of 207 pm.
Even more complicated structures are found
for the large Rh clusters containing 2 carbido

C atoms: $[Rh_{12}(C_2)(CO)_{25}]$ (Fig. 26.9f has no
symmetry elements but it is clear that the Rh_{12}
cluster surrounds an ethanide unit C_2 in which the
C–C distance is only 147 pm); the cluster also has
14 pendant terminal CO groups, 10 μ-CO groups
and one μ_3-CO. In contrast, $[Rh_{15}(C)_2(CO)_{28}]^-$
has individual 6-coordinate (octahedral) carbido
C atoms symmetrically placed on each side of a
central Rh which itself has 12 Rh nearest neighbours in addition to the 2 C atoms. Again, the
approach to metal structures is notable and is one
of the main interests in constructing large clusters
and studying their chemical and catalytic activity.

H, P, As, S have also been encapsulated in ions
such as $[Rh_{13}(H)_3(CO)_{24}]^{2-}$, $[Rh_9P(CO)_{21}]^{2-}$
$[Rh_{10}As(CO)_{22}]^{3-}$ and $[Rh_{17}(S)_2(CO)_{32}]^{3-}$.

More recently N has been encapsulated[41] in $[Rh_{14}(N)_2(CO)_{25}]^{2-}$ and $[Rh_{23}(N)_4(CO)_{38}]^{3-}$. The latter is the largest Rh cluster so far characterized. It consists of an irregular polyhedron of 21 Rh atoms encapsulating a pair of particularly close (257.1 pm) Rh atoms as well as 4 N atoms each of which is located in a semi octahedral site.

Other derivatives of the carbonyls are of course numerous; Ir forms many carbonyl halides of the types $[Ir^I(CO)_3X]$, $[Ir^I(CO)_2X_2]^-$, $[Ir^{III}(CO)_2X_4]^-$ and $[Ir^{III}(CO)X_5]^{2-}$, but the stability of carbonyl halides falls off in the sequence Ir > Rh > Co and those of Co are only of the type $[Co(CO)_4X]$ and are very unstable.

The bulk of derivatives are obtained by the displacement of CO by other ligands. These include phosphines and other group 15 donors, NO, mercaptans and unsaturated organic molecules such as alkenes, alkynes and cyclopentadienyls.

Cyclopentadienyls

Cobaltocene, $[Co^{II}(\eta^5\text{-}C_5H_5)_2]$, is a dark-purple air-sensitive material, prepared by the reactions of sodium cyclopentadiene and anhydrous $CoCl_2$ in thf. Having 1 more electron than ferrocene, it is paramagnetic with a magnetic moment of 1.76 BM and, while it is thermally stable up to 250°C, its most obvious characteristic is its ready loss of this electron to form the yellow-green cobalticenium ion, $[Co^{III}(\eta^5\text{-}C_5H_5)_2]^+$. This resists further oxidation, being stable even in conc HNO_3 but, like the isoelectronic ferrocene, is susceptible to nucleophilic attack on its rings.

Rhodocene, $[Rh(\eta^5\text{-}C_5H_5)_2]$, is also known but is unstable to oxidation and has a tendency to form dimeric species. Claims for the existence of iridocene probably refer to Ir^{III} complexes. However, the yellow rhodicenium and iridicenium cations are certainly known and are entirely analogous to the cobalticenium cation in their resistance to oxidation and susceptibility to nucleophilic attack.

Numerous "half-sandwich" compounds of the type $[M(\eta^5\text{-}C_5R_5)L_2]$, M = Rh, Ir; R = H, Me; L = CO, phosphine etc.) are known and are useful reagents. $[Ir(\eta^5\text{-}C_5Me_5)(CO)_2]$ for instance is an excellent nucleophile and is also used in the photochemical activation of C–H in alkanes. It is particularly effective in the latter role when supercritical CO_2 is the solvent.[42]

[41] S. MARTINENGO, G. CIANI and A. SIRONI, *J. Chem. Soc., Chem. Commun.*, 1405–6 (1992).

[42] M. JOBLING, S. M. HOWDLE, M. A. HEALY and M. POLIAKOFF, *J. Chem. Soc., Chem. Commun.*, 1287–90 (1990).

27

Nickel, Palladium and Platinum

27.1 Introduction

An alloy of nickel was known in China over 2000 years ago, and Saxon miners were familiar with the reddish-coloured ore, NiAs, which superficially resembles Cu_2O. These miners attributed their inability to extract copper from this source to the work of the devil and named the ore "Kupfernickel" (Old Nick's copper). In 1751 A. F. Cronstedt isolated an impure metal from some Swedish ores and, identifying it with the metallic component of Kupfernickel, named the new metal "nickel". In 1804 J. B. Richter produced a much purer sample and so was able to determine its physical properties more accurately.

Impure, native platinum seems to have been used unwittingly by ancient Egyptian craftsmen in place of silver, and was certainly used to make small items of jewellery by the Indians of Ecuador before the Spanish conquest. The introduction of the metal to Europe is a complex and intriguing story.[1] In 1736 A. de Ulloa, a Spanish astronomer and naval officer, observed an unworkable metal, *platina* (Spanish, little

silver), in the gold mines of what is now Colombia. Returning home in 1745 his ship was attacked by privateers and finally captured by the British navy. He was brought to London and his papers confiscated, but was fortunately befriended by members of the Royal Society and was indeed elected to that body in 1746 when his papers were returned. Meanwhile, in 1741, C. Wood brought to England the first samples of the metal and, following the eventual publication of de Ulloa's report in 1748, investigation of its properties began in England and Sweden. It became known as "white gold" (a term now used to describe an Au/Pd alloy) and the "eighth metal" (the seven metals Au, Ag, Hg, Cu, Fe, Sn and Pb having been known since ancient times). Great difficulty was experienced in working it because of its high mp and brittle nature (due to impurities of Fe and Cu). Powder metallurgical techniques of fabrication were developed† in great secrecy in Spain by the

---

† Precedence must in fact be given to the South American Indians to whom platinum was available only in the form of fine, hand-separated grains which must have been fabricated by ingenious, if crude, powder metallurgy.

[1] L. B. HUNT, *Platinum Metals Rev.* **24**, 31–9 (1980).

Frenchman P. F. Chabeneau, and subsequently in London by W. H. Wollaston,[2] who in the years 1800–21 produced well over 1 tonne of malleable platinum. These techniques were developed because the chemical methods used to isolate the metal produced an easily powdered spongy precipitate. Not until the availability, half a century later, of furnaces capable of sustaining sufficiently high temperatures was easily workable, fused platinum commercially available.

In 1803, in the course of his study of platinum, Wollaston isolated and identified palladium from the mother liquor remaining after platinum had been precipitated as $(NH_4)_2PtCl_6$ from its solution in aqua regia. He named it after the newly discovered asteroid, Pallas, itself named after the Greek goddess of wisdom ($\pi\alpha\lambda\lambda\acute{\alpha}\delta\iota o\nu$, palladion, of Pallas).

27.2 The Elements

27.2.1 Terrestrial abundance and distribution

Nickel is the seventh most abundant transition metal and the twenty-second most abundant element in the earth's crust (99 ppm). Its commercially important ores are of two types:

(1) *Laterites*, which are oxide/silicate ores such as garnierite, $(Ni,Mg)_6Si_4O_{10}(OH)_8$, and nickeliferous limonite, $(Fe,Ni)O(OH).nH_2O$, which have been concentrated by weathering in tropical rainbelt areas such as New Caledonia, Cuba and Queensland.

(2) *Sulfides* such as pentlandite, $(Ni,Fe)_9S_8$, associated with copper, cobalt and precious metals so that the ores typically contain about $1\frac{1}{2}\%$ Ni. These are found in more temperate regions such as Canada, the former Soviet Union and South Africa.

Arsenide ores such as niccolite (Kupfernickel (NiAs), smaltite ((Ni,Co,Fe)As$_2$) and nickel glance (NiAsS) are no longer of importance.

The most important single deposit of nickel is at Sudbury Basin, Canada. It was discovered in 1883 during the building of the Canadian Pacific Railway and consists of sulfide outcrops situated around the rim of a huge basin 17 miles wide and 37 miles long (possibly a meteoritic crater). Fifteen elements are currently extracted from this region (Ni, Cu, Co, Fe, S, Te, Se, Au, Ag and the six platinum metals).

Although estimates of their abundances vary considerably, Pd and Pt (approximately 0.015 and 0.01 ppm respectively) are much rarer than Ni. They are generally associated with the other platinum metals and occur either native in placer (i.e. alluvial) deposits or as sulfides or arsenides in Ni, Cu and Fe sulfide ores. Until the 1820s all platinum metals came from South America, but in 1819 the first of a series of rich placer deposits which were to make Russia the chief source of the metals for the next century, was discovered in the Urals. More recently however, the copper-nickel ores in South Africa and Russia (where the Noril'sk-Talnakh deposits are well inside the Arctic Circle) have become the major sources, supplemented by supplies from Sudbury.

27.2.2 Preparation and uses of the elements [3,3a,4]

Production methods for all three elements are complicated and dependent on the particular ore involved; they will therefore only be sketched in outline. In the case of nickel the oxide ores are not generally amenable to concentration by normal physical separations and so the whole ore has to be treated. By contrast the sulfide ores

---

[2] J. C. CHASTON, *Platinum Metals Rev.* **24**, 70–9 (1980).

[3] J. HILL in D. THOMPSON (ed.), *Insights into Speciality Inorganic Chemicals*, pp. 5–34, R.S.C., Cambridge, 1995.

[3a] *Kirk–Othmer Encyclopedia of Chemical Technology*, 4th edn., Interscience, New York: Ni, **17**, 1–47 (1996); Pt metals, **19**, 347–407 (1996).

[4] F. R. HARTLEY (ed.) *Chemistry of the Platinum Group Metals*, Elsevier, Amsterdam, 1991, 642 pp.

can be concentrated by flotation and magnetic separations, and for this reason they provide the major part of the world's nickel, though the use of laterite ores is appreciable.

A quarter of the world's nickel comes from Sudbury and there silica is added to the nickel/copper concentrates which are then subjected to a series of roasting and smelting operations. This reduces the sulfide and iron contents by converting the iron sulfide first to the oxide and then to the silicate which is removed as a slag. The resulting "matte" of nickel and copper sulfides is allowed to cool over a period of days, when Ni_3S_2, Cu_2S and Ni/Cu metal[†] form distinct phases which can be mechanically separated. (In the older, Orford, process the matte was heated with $NaHSO_4$ and coke, producing molten Na_2S which dissolved the copper sulfide and formed an upper layer, leaving the nickel sulfide below; on solidification the silvery upper layer was cut from the black lower layer — hence the process was commonly called the "tops and bottoms" process.) The matte may be cast directly as anode with pure nickel sheet as cathode and electrolysed using an aqueous $NiSO_4$, $NiCl_2$ electrolyte. Alternatively, the matte may be leached with hydrochloric acid, nickel chloride crystallized and converted to the oxide by high temperature oxidation with air, and finally the oxide reduced to the metal by H_2 at 600°C.

The carbonyl process developed in 1899 by L. Mond is still used, though it is mainly of historic interest. In this the heated oxide is first reduced by the hydrogen in water gas (H_2 + CO). At atmospheric pressure and a temperature around 50°C, the impure nickel is then reacted with the residual CO to give the volatile $Ni(CO)_4$. This is passed over nucleating pellets of pure nickel at a temperature of 230°C when it decomposes, depositing nickel of 99.95% purity and leaving CO to be recycled.

$$Ni + 4CO \underset{230°C}{\overset{50°C}{\rightleftharpoons}} Ni(CO)_4$$

[†] This metallic phase is worked for precious metals which are preferentially dissolved in it.

Somewhat higher pressures and temperatures (e.g. 20 atm and 150°C) are used to form the carbonyl in modern Canadian plant, but the essential principle of the Mond process is retained.

Total world production of nickel is in the region of 1.0 million tonnes pa of which (1995) 25% comes from the former Soviet Union, 18% from Canada, 12% from New Caledonia and 10% from Australia. The bulk of this is used in the production of alloys both ferrous and non-ferrous. In 1889 J. Riley of Glasgow published a report on the effect of adding nickel to steel. This was noticed by the US Navy who initiated the use of nickel steels in armour plating. Stainless steels contain up to 8% Ni and the use of "Alnico" steel for permanent magnets has already been mentioned (p. 1114).

The non-ferrous alloys include the misleadingly named nickel silver (or German silver) which contains 10–30% Ni, 55–65% Cu and the rest Zn; when electroplated with silver (electroplated nickel silver) it is familiar as EPNS tableware. *Monel* (68% Ni, 32% Cu, traces of Mn and Fe) is used in apparatus for handling corrosive materials such as F_2; cupro-nickels (up to 80% Cu) are used for "silver" coinage; *Nichrome* (60% Ni, 40% Cr), which has a very small temperature coefficient of electrical resistance, and *Invar*, which has a very small coefficient of expansion are other well-known Ni alloys. Electroplated nickel is an ideal undercoat for electroplated chromium, and smaller amounts of nickel are used as catalysts in the hydrogenation of unsaturated vegetable oils and in storage batteries such as the Ni/Fe batteries.

Ninety-eight per cent of the world's supply of platinum metals comes from three countries — the former Soviet Union (49%), the Republic of South Africa (43%), and Canada (6%). Because of the different proportions of Pt and Pd in their deposits, the Republic of South Africa is the major source of Pt and the former USSR of Pd. Only in the RSA (where the Bushveld complex contains over 70% of the world's reserves of the platinum metals at concentrations of 8–9 grams per tonne) are the platinum metals the primary products. Elsewhere, with concentrations of a mere fraction of a gramme per tonne, millions of tonnes of ore must be mined, milled and smelted each year. Precious metal concentrates are obtained either from the metallic phase of the sulfide matte (see above) or as anode slimes in the electrolytic refinement of the baser metals. From these, all six platinum metals as well as Ag and Au are obtained by a composite process. Traditional methods were based on selective precipitation and developed to suit the composition of the concentrate. Although these methods are still in use the efficiency of the separations is not high and costly recycling is required. Solvent extraction and ion exchange techniques offer superior efficiency and are increasingly replacing the classical processes. Fig. 27.1 outlines a typical solvent extraction process (see also p. 1073 and p. 1114).

Current annual world production of all platinum metals is around 380 tonnes of which perhaps 150 tonnes is platinum and 210 tonnes is palladium. 35–40% of Pt and about half as

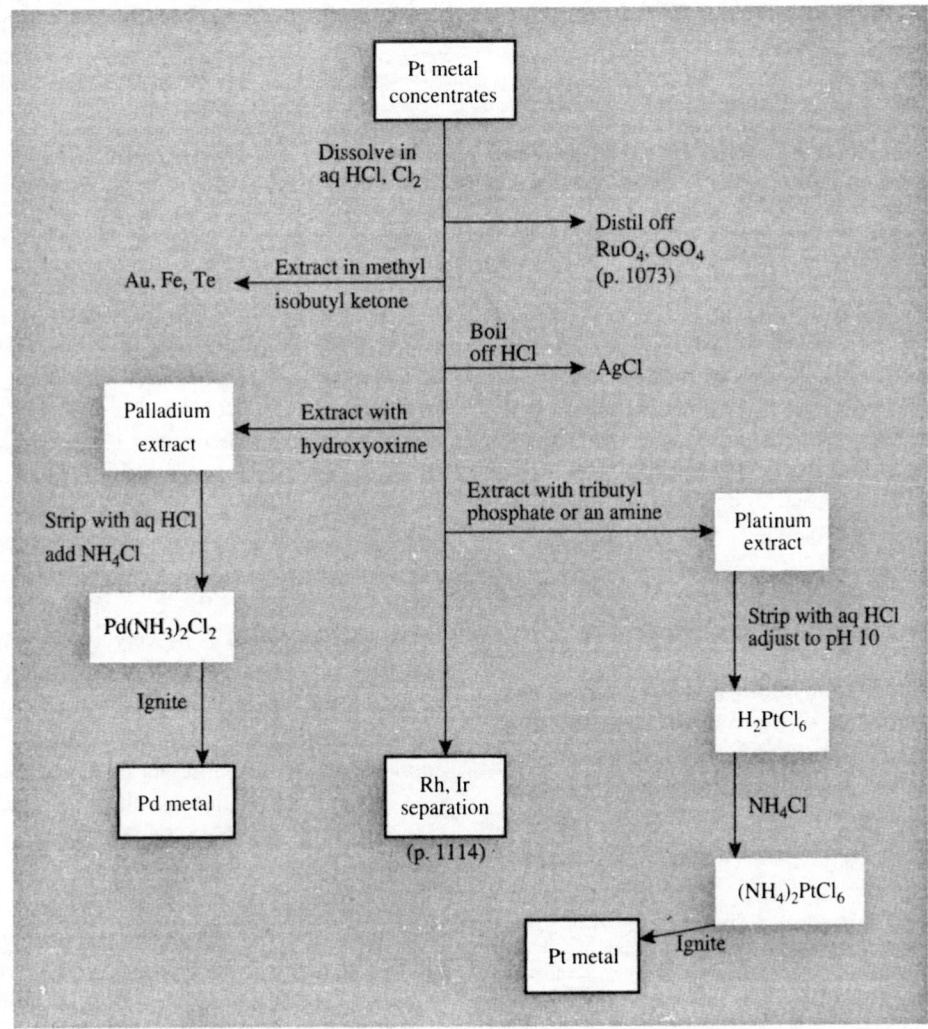

Figure 27.1 Flow diagram for refining palladium and platinum by solvent extraction.

Table 27.1 Some properties of the elements nickel, palladium and platinum

Property		Ni	Pd	Pt
Atomic number		28	46	78
Number of naturally occurring isotopes		5	6	6[a]
Atomic weight		58.6934(2)	106.42(1)	195.078(2)
Electronic configuration		$[Ar]3d^8 4s^2$	$[Kr]4d^{10}$	$[Xe]4f^{14}5d^9 6s^1$
Electronegativity		1.8	2.2	2.2
Metal radius (12-coordinate)/pm		124	137	138.5
Effective ionic radius (6-coordinate)/pm	V	—	—	57
	IV	48	61.5	62.5
	III	56 (ls), 60 (hs)	76	—
	II	69	86	80
MP/°C		1455	1552	1769
BP/°C		2920	2940	4170
ΔH_{fus}/kJ mol^{-1}		17.2($\pm$0.3)	17.6($\pm$2.1)	19.7($\pm$2.1)
ΔH_{vap}/kJ mol^{-1}		375($\pm$17)	362($\pm$11)	469($\pm$25)
ΔH_f (monatomic gas)/kJ mol^{-1}		429($\pm$13)	377($\pm$3)	545($\pm$21)
Density (20°C)/g cm^{-3}		8.908	11.99	21.45
Electrical resistivity (20°C)/μohm cm		6.84	9.93	9.85

[a] All have zero nuclear spin except ^{195}Pt (33.8% abundance) which has a nuclear spin quantum number $\frac{1}{2}$: this isotope finds much use in nmr spectroscopy both via direct observation of the ^{195}Pt resonance and even more by the observation of ^{195}Pt "satellites". Thus, a given nucleus coupled to ^{195}Pt will be split into a doublet symmetrically placed about the central unsplit resonance arising from those species containing any of the other 5 isotopes of Pt. The relative intensity of the three resonances will be ($\frac{1}{2} \times 33.8$):66.2:($\frac{1}{2} \times 33.8$), i.e. 1:4:1.

much Pd is used in the catalytic control of car-exhaust emissions. A similar amount of Pt is used for jewellery and 18% in the petroleum and glass industries. The largest single use for Pd is in the manufacture of electronic components (46%), but 25% is used in dentistry and 10% for hydrogenation and dehydrogenation catalysis.[†]

27.2.3 Properties of the elements

Table 27.1 lists some of the important atomic and physical properties of these three elements. The prevalence of naturally occurring isotopes in this triad limits the precision of their quoted atomic weights, though the value for Ni was improved by more than two orders of magnitude in 1989

[†] It should not be overlooked that platinum has played a crucial role in the development of many branches of science even though the amounts of metal involved may have been small. Reliable Pt crucibles were vital in classical analysis on which the foundations of chemistry were laid. It was also widely used in the development of the electric telegraph, incandescent lamps, and thermionic valves.

and that for Pt fifteen fold in 1995. Difficulties in attaining high purities have also frequently led to disparate values for some physical properties, while mechanical history has considerable effect on such properties as hardness. The metals are silvery-white and lustrous, and are both malleable and ductile so that they are readily worked. They are also readily obtained in finely divided forms which are catalytically very active. *Platinum black*, for instance, is a velvety-black powder obtained by adding ethanol to a solution of $PtCl_2$ in aqueous KOH and warming. Another property of platinum which has led to numerous laboratory applications is its coefficient of expansion which is virtually the same as that of soda glass into which it can therefore be fused to give a permanent seal.

Like Rh and Ir, all three members of this triad have the fcc structure predicted by band theory calculations for elements with nearly filled d shells. Also in this region of the periodic table, densities and mps are decreasing with increase in Z across the table: thus, although by comparison with the generality of members of the d block these elements are in each case to be considered as dense refractory metals, they are somewhat less so than their immediate predecessors, and palladium has the lowest density and melting point of any platinum metal.

Nickel is ferromagnetic, but less markedly so that either iron or cobalt and its Curie point (375°C) is also lower.

27.2.4 Chemical reactivity and trends

In the massive state none of these elements is particularly reactive and they are indeed very resistant to atmospheric corrosion at normal temperatures. However, nickel tarnishes when heated in air and is actually pyrophoric if very finely divided (finely divided Ni catalysts should therefore be handled with care). Palladium will also form a film of oxide if heated in air.

Nickel reacts on heating with B, Si, P, S and the halogens, though more slowly with F_2 than most metals do. It is oxidized at red heat by steam, and will dissolve in dilute mineral acids: slowly in most but quite rapidly in dil HNO_3. Conc HNO_3, on the other hand, renders it passive and dry hydrogen halides have little effect. It has a notable resistance to attack by aqueous caustic alkalis and therefore finds used in apparatus for producing NaOH.

Palladium is oxidized by O_2, F_2 and Cl_2 at red heat and dissolves slowly in oxidizing acids. Platinum is generally more resistant to attack than Pd and is, for instance, barely affected by mineral acids except aqua regia. However, both metals dissolve in fused alkali metal oxides and peroxides. It is also wise to avoid heating compounds containing B, Si, Pb, P, As, Sb or Bi in platinum crucibles under reducing conditions (e.g. the blue flame of a bunsen burner) since these elements form low-melting eutectics with Pt which cause the metal to collapse. All three elements absorb molecular hydrogen to an extent which depends on their physical state, but palladium does so to an extent which is unequalled by any other metal (section 27.3.1).

A list of typical compounds of these elements is given in Table 27.2 and it is noticeable that the reduction in the range of oxidation states compared to that in previous groups is continuing and differences between the two heavier elements are becoming increasingly evident. The maximum oxidation state is +6 but this is attained only by the heaviest element, platinum, in PtF_6; nickel and palladium only reach +4. At the other extreme, palladium and platinum provide no oxidation state below zero. The changes down the triad implied by these facts are also evidenced by those oxidation states which are the most stable for each element. For nickel, +2 is undoubtedly the most common and provides that element's most extensive aqueous chemistry. For palladium, +2 is again the most common, and $[Pd(H_2O)_4]^{2+}$ like $[Pt(H_2O)_4]^{2+}$ occurs in aqueous solutions from which potential ligands are excluded. For platinum, however, both +2 and +4 are prolific and form a vital part of early as well as more recent coordination chemistry.

Table 27.2 also reveals the reluctance of these elements to form compounds with high coordination numbers, a coordination number of 6 being rarely exceeded. In the divalent state nickel exhibits a wide and interesting variety of coordination numbers and stereochemistries which often exist simultaneously in equilibrium with each other, whereas palladium and platinum have a strong preference for the square planar geometry. The kinetic inertness of Pt^{II} complexes has led to their extensive use in studies of geometrical isomerism and reaction mechanisms. As will be seen presently, these differences between the lightest and heaviest members of the triad can be largely rationalized by reference to their CFSEs.

Also in the divalent state, Pd and Pt show the class-b characteristic of preferring CN^- and ligands with nitrogen or heavy donor atoms rather than oxygen or fluorine. Platinum(IV) by contrast is more nearly class-a in character and is frequently reduced to Pt^{II} by *P*- and *As*-donor ligands. The organometallic chemistry of these metals is rich and varied and that involving unsaturated hydrocarbons is the most familiar of its type.

Table 27.2   Oxidation states and stereochemistries of compounds of nickel, palladium and platinum

Oxidation state	Coordination number	Stereochemistry	Ni	Pd/Pt
−1	4	?	$[Ni_2(CO)_6]^{2-}$	
0 (d^{10})	3	Planar	$[Ni\{P(OC_6H_4\text{-}2\text{-}Me)_3\}_3]$	$[M(PPh_3)_3]$
	4	Tetrahedral	$[Ni(CO)_4]$	$[M(PF_3)_4]$
1 (d^9)	4	Tetrahedral	$[NiBr(PPh_3)_3]$	
	3	Trigonal planar	$[Ni(NPh_2)_3]^-$	
2 (d^8)	4	Tetrahedral	$[NiCl_4]^{2-}$	
		Square planar	$[Ni(CN)_4]^{2-}$	$[MCl_4]^{2-}$
	5	Trigonal bipyramidal	$[Ni(PPhMe_2)_3(CN)_2]$	$[M(qas)I]^{+(a)}$
		Square pyramidal	$[Ni(CN)_5]^{3-}$	$[Pd(tpas)Cl]^{+(b)}$
	6	Octahedral	$[Ni(H_2O)_6]^{2+}$	$[Pd(diars)_2I_2]$
		Trigonal prismatic	NiAs	
	7	Pentagonal bipyramidal	$[Ni(dapbH)_2(H_2O)_2]^{2+(c)}$	
3 (d^7)	4	Square planar	—	$[Pt(C_6Cl_5)_4]^-$
	5	Trigonal bipyramidal	$[NiBr_3(PEt_3)_2]$	
	6	Octahedral	$[NiF_6]^{3-}$	$[PdF_6]^{3-}$
4 (d^6)	6	Octahedral	$[NiF_6]^{2-}$	$[MCl_6]^{2-}$
	8	"Piano-stool"	—	$[Pt(\eta^5\text{-}C_5H_5)Me_3]$
5 (d^5)	6	Octahedral	—	$[PtF_6]^-$
6 (d^4)	6	Octahedral	—	PtF_6

[a] qas, tris-(2-diphenylarsinophenyl)arsine, $As(C_6H_4\text{-}2\text{-}AsPh_2)_3$.
[b] tpas, 1,2-phenylenebis{(2-dimethylarsinophenyl)-methylarsine}.
[c] dapbH, 2,6-diacetylpyridinebis(benzoic acid hydrazone).

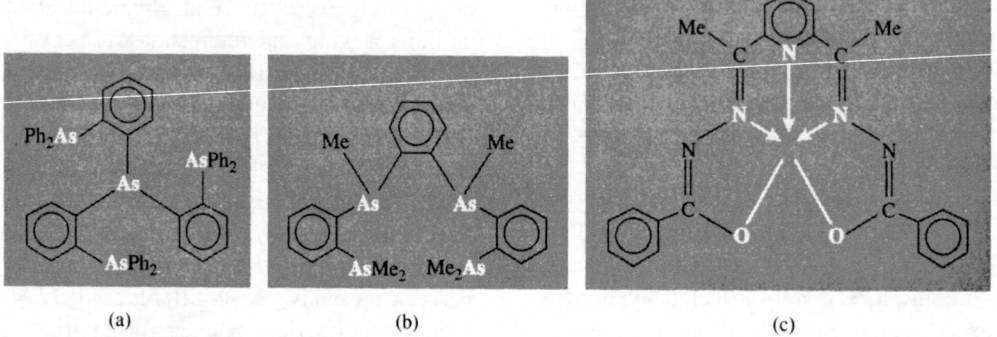

(a)   (b)   (c)

27.3 Compounds of Nickel, Palladium and Platinum

Such binary borides (p. 145), carbides (p. 297) and nitrides (p. 417) as are formed have been referred to already. The ability of the metals to absorb molecular hydrogen has also been alluded to above. While the existence of definite hydrides of nickel and platinum is in doubt the existence of definite palladium hydride phases is not.

27.3.1 The Pd/H₂ system

The absorption of molecular hydrogen by metallic palladium has been the subject of theoretical and practical interest ever since 1866 when T. Graham reported that, on being cooled from red heat, Pd can absorb (or "occlude" as

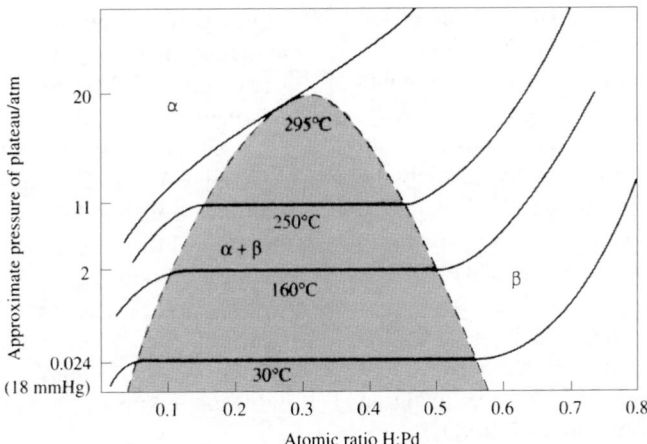

Figure 27.2 Pressure-concentration isotherms for the Pd/H$_2$ system: the biphasic region (in which the α- and β-phases coexist) is shaded. (From A. G. Knapton, *Plat. Met. Revs.* **21**, 44 (1977). See also F. A. Lewis, *ibid.* **38**, 112–18 (1994))

he called it) up to 935 times its own volume of H$_2$.[†] The gas is given off again on heating and this provides a convenient means of weighing H$_2$ — a fact utilized by E. W. Morley in his classic work on the composition of water (1895).

As hydrogen is absorbed, the metallic conductivity falls until the material becomes a semiconductor at a composition of about PdH$_{0.5}$. Palladium is unique in that it does not lose its ductility until large amounts of H$_2$ have been absorbed. The hydrogen is first chemisorbed at the surface of the metal but at increased pressures it enters the metal lattice and the so-called α- and β-phase hydrides are formed (Fig. 27.2). The basic lattice structure is not altered but, whereas the α-phase causes only a slight expansion, the β-phase causes an expansion of up to 10% by volume. The precise nature of the metal–hydrogen interaction is still unclear[‡] but the hydrogen has a high mobility within the lattice and diffuses rapidly through the metal. This process is highly specific to H$_2$ and D$_2$, palladium being virtually impervious to all other gases, even He, a fact which is utilized in the separation of hydrogen from mixed gases. Industrial installations with outputs of up to 9 million ft^3/day (255 million litres/day) are operated and it is of great importance in these that formation of the β-phase hydride is avoided, since the gross distortions and hardening which accompany it may result in splitting of the diffusion membrane. This can be done by maintaining the temperature above 300°C (Fig. 27.2), or alternatively by alloying the Pd with about 20% Ag which has the additional advantage of actually increasing the permeability of the Pd to hydrogen (p. 39).

27.3.2 Oxides and chalcogenides

The elements of this group form only one reasonably well-characterized oxide each, namely NiO, PdO and PtO$_2$, although claims for the existence of many others have been made. Formation of NiO by heating the metal in oxygen

---

[†] This approximates to a composition of Pd$_4$H$_3$ and represents a concentration of hydrogen approaching that in liquid hydrogen!

[‡] In March 1989 S. Pons and M. Fleischmann reported the production of excess heat from heavy water electrolysis using Pd cathode and Pt anode, and postulated nuclear fusion ("cold fusion") as the reason. In spite of widespread scepticism, work in many laboratories was quickly initiated and focused on: (a) measuring the excess heat effect, and (b) identifying any nuclear particles produced. Emissions of ^{4}He, ^{3}H and ^{1}n have been variously reported and it appears that production of

excess heat is associated with very heavy deuterium loading of Pd in the β-phase. Reproducibility is, however, poor and it seems probable that more than one effect is involved. The current consensus is against a "cold-fusion" explanation of the effects.

is difficult to achieve and incomplete conversion may well account for some of the claims for other nickel oxides, while grey to black colours probably arise from slight nonstoichiometry. It is best prepared as a green powder with the rock-salt structure (p. 242) by heating the hydroxide, carbonate or nitrate. $Ni(OH)_2$ is a green precipitate obtained by adding alkali to aqueous solutions of Ni^{II} salts and, like NiO, is entirely basic, dissolving easily in acids.

Black PdO can be produced by heating the metal in oxygen but it dissociates above about 900°C. It is insoluble in acids. However, addition of alkali to aqueous solutions of $Pd(NO_3)_2$ produces a gelatinous dark-yellow precipitate of the hydrous oxide which is soluble in acids but cannot be fully dehydrated without loss of oxygen. No other palladium oxide has been characterized although the addition of alkali to aqueous solutions of Pd^{IV} produces a strongly oxidizing, dark-red precipitate which slowly loses oxygen and, at 200°C, forms PdO.

Addition of alkali to aqueous solutions of $[Pt(H_2O)_4](ClO_4)_2$ under an atmosphere of argon gives a white amphoteric hydroxide of Pt^{II} at pH 4 which redissolves at pH 10.[5] The precipitate slowly turns black at room temperature (more rapidly when dried at 100°C) and has been formulated as $PtO_x.H_2O$, but it is too unstable to be properly characterized. The stable oxide of platinum is found, instead, in the higher oxidation state. Addition of alkali to aqueous solutions of $PtCl_4$ yields a yellow amphoteric precipitate of the hydrated dioxide which redissolves on being boiled with an excess of strong alkali to give solutions of $[Pt(OH)_6]^{2-}$; it also dissolves in acids. Dehydration by heating produces almost black PtO_2 but this decomposes to the elements above 650°C and cannot be completely dehydrated without some loss of oxygen.

Nickel sulfides are very similar to those of cobalt, consisting of NiS_2 (pyrites structure, p. 680), Ni_3S_4 (spinel structure, p. 247), and the black, nickel-deficient $Ni_{1-x}S$ (NiAs structure, p. 555), which is precipitated from aqueous

solutions of Ni^{II} by passing H_2S. There are also numerous metallic phases having compositions between NiS and Ni_3S_2.

Palladium and platinum both form a mono- and a di-sulfide. Brown PdS and black PtS_2 are obtained when H_2S is passed through aqueous solutions of Pd^{II} and Pt^{IV} respectively. Grey PdS_2 and green PtS are best obtained by respectively heating PdS with excess S and by heating $PtCl_2$, Na_2CO_3 and S. The crystal chemistry and electrical (and magnetic) properties of these phases and the many selenides and tellurides of Ni, Pd and Pt are complex.

27.3.3 Halides

The known halides of this group are listed in Table 27.3. This list differs from that of the halides of Co, Rh and Ir (Table 26.3) most obviously in that the +2 rather than the +3 oxidation state is now well represented for the heavier elements as well as for the lightest. The only hexa- and penta-halides are the dark-red PtF_6 and $(PtF_5)_4$ which are both obtained by controlled heating of Pt and F_2. The former is a volatile solid and, after RhF_6, is the least-stable platinum-metal hexafluoride. It is one of the strongest oxidizing agents known, oxidizing both O_2 (to $O_2^+[PtF_6]^-$) and Xe (to $XePtF_6$) (p. 892). The pentafluoride is also very reactive and has the same tetrameric structure as the pentafluorides of Ru, Os, Rh and Ir (Fig. 25.3). It readily disproportionates into the hexa- and tetra-fluorides.

Platinum alone forms all 4 tetrahalides and these vary in colour from the light-brown PtF_4 to the very dark-brown PtI_4. PtF_4 is obtained by the action of BrF_3 on $PtCl_2$ at 200°C and is violently hydrolysed by water. The others are obtained directly from the elements, the chloride being recrystallizable from water but the bromide and iodide being more soluble in alcohol and in ether. The only other tetrahalide is the red PdF_4 which is similar to its platinum analogue.

The most stable product of the action of fluorine on metallic palladium is actually $Pd^{II}[Pd^{IV}F_6]$, and true trihalides of Pd do not occur. Similarly, the diamagnetic "trichloride" and "tribromide" of Pt

[5] L. J. ELDING, *Inorg. Chim. Acta* **20**, 65–9 (1976).

Table 27.3   Halides of nickel, palladium and platinum (mp/°C)

Oxidation State	Fluorides	Chlorides	Bromides	Iodides
+6	$PtF_6^{(a)}$ dark red (61.3°)			
+5	$[PtF_5]_4$ deep red (80°)			
+4	PdF_4 brick-red			
	PtF_4 yellow-brown (600°)	$PtCl_4$ red-brown (d 370°)	$PtBr_4$ brown-black (d 180°)	PtI_4 brown-black (d 130°)
"+3"	$Pd[PdF_6]$ —	$PtCl_3$ green-black (d 400°) —	$PtBr_3$ green-black (d 200°) —	PtI_3 black (d 310°) —
+2	NiF_2 yellow (1450°)	$NiCl_2$ yellow (1001°)	$NiBr_2$ yellow (965°)	NiI_2 black (780°)
	PdF_2 pale violet	α-$PdCl_2^{(b)}$ dark red (d 600°)	$PdBr_2$ red-black	PdI_2 black
	—	α-$PtCl_2^{(b)}$ olive-green (d 581°)	$PtBr_2$ brown (d 250°)	PtI_2 black (d 360°)

$^{(a)}$ PtF_6 boils at 69.1°. $^{(b)}$ β-$PdCl_2$ and β-$PtCl_2$ (reddish-black) contain M_6Cl_{12} clusters (Fig. 27.3b).

contain Pt^{II} and Pt^{IV} and the triiodide probably does also. Trihalides of nickel are confined to impure specimens of NiF_3.

All the dihalides, except PtF_2, are known, fluorine perhaps being too strongly oxidizing to be readily compatible with the metal in the lower of its two major oxidation states. Except for NiF_2, the yellow to dark-brown dihalides of nickel can be obtained directly from the elements; they dissolve in water from which hexahydrates containing the $[Ni(H_2O)_6]^{2+}$ ion can be crystallized. These solutions may also be prepared more conveniently by dissolving $Ni(OH)_2$ in the appropriate hydrohalic acid. NiF_2 is best formed by the reaction of F_2 on $NiCl_2$ at 350°C and is only slightly soluble in water, from which the trihydrate crystallizes.

Violet, easily hydrolysed, PdF_2 is produced when $Pd^{II}[Pd^{IV}F_6]$ is refluxed with SeF_4 and is notable as one of the very few paramagnetic compounds of Pd^{II}. The paramagnetism arises from the $t_{2g}^6 e_g^2$ configuration of Pd^{II} which is consequent on its octahedral coordination in the rutile-type structure (p. 961). The dichlorides of both Pd and Pt are obtained from the elements and exist in two isomeric forms: which form is produced depends on the exact experimental conditions used. The more usual α-form of $PdCl_2$ is a red material with

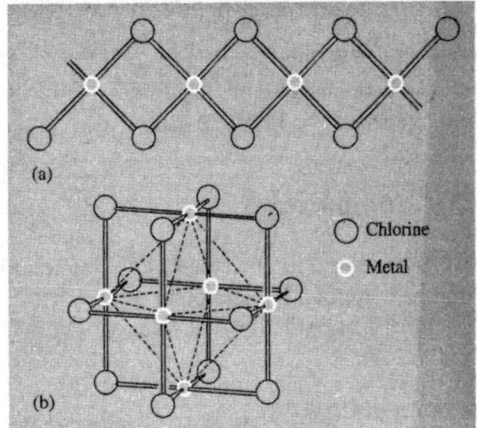

Figure 27.3   (a) The chain structure of α-$PdCl_2$, and (b) the M_6Cl_{12} structural unit of β-$PdCl_2$ and β-$PtCl_2$. (Note its broad similarity with the $[M_6X_{12}]^{n+}$ unit of the lower halides of Nb and Ta shown in Fig. 22.6 and to the unit cell of the three-dimensional structure of NbO.)

a chain structure (Fig. 27.3a) in which each Pd has a square planar geometry. It is hygroscopic and its aqueous solution provides a useful starting point for studying the coordination chemistry of Pd^{II}. β-$PdCl_2$ is also known and its structure is based on Pd_6Cl_{12} units in which, nevertheless, the preferred square-planar coordination of the Pd^{II} is still retained (Fig. 27.3b). Platinum dichlorides are less well-known. The high temperature modification, α-PtCl$_2$ is insoluble in water but dissolves in hydrochloric acid forming [PtCl$_4$]$^{2-}$ ions. It has been reported as both olive-green and black, the latter consisting of edge- and corner-sharing PtCl$_4$ units[6] (distinct from α-PdCl$_2$). The dark-red β-PtCl$_2$ is isomorphous with β-PdCl$_2$ and the Pt$_6$Cl$_{12}$ unit is retained on dissolution in benzene. Red PdBr$_2$ and black PdI$_2$, obtained respectively by the action of Br$_2$ on Pd and the addition of I$^-$ to aqueous solutions of PdCl$_2$, are both insoluble in water but form [PdX$_4$]$^{2-}$ ions on addition of HX (X = Br, I). PtBr$_2$ and α-PtI$_2$ are obtained by thermal decomposition of the tetrahalides, the latter being accompanied by Pt$_3$I$_8$ a mixed-valence (II, IV) iodide made up of octahedral PtI$_6$ and square planar PtI$_4$ units.[7] β-PtI$_2$ is prepared by hydrothermal synthesis from PtI$_4$, KI and I$_2$ at 420°C and is made up of planar PtI$_4$ and planar Pt$_2$I$_6$ units.[7]

Oxohalides in this group are apparently confined to the strongly oxidizing PtOF$_3$. The compound reported to be PtOF$_4$ is actually O$_2$$^+$[PtF$_6$].

27.3.4 Complexes [8]

Apart from the few Pt^{VI} and Pt^V fluoro and oxofluoro compounds mentioned above, there is no chemistry in oxidation states above IV.

Oxidation state IV (d^6)

All complexes in this oxidation state which have been characterized are octahedral and diamagnetic with the low-spin t_{2g}^6 configuration.

[6] B. KREBS, C. BRENDEL and H. SCHÄFER, *Z. anorg. allg. Chem.* **561**, 119–31 (1988).

[7] G. THIELE, W. WEIGL and H. WOCHNER, *Z. anorg. allg. Chem.* **539**, 141–53 (1986).

[8] L. SACCONI, F. MANI and A. BENCINI, Ni, Chap. 50, pp. 1–347; M. J. RUSSELL and C. F. J. BARNARD, Pd, Chap. 51, pp. 1099–130; A. T. HUTTON, Pd(II)–S-donor Complexes, Chap. 51.8, pp. 1131–55; A. T. HUTTON and C. P. MORLEY, Pd(II)–P-donor Complexes, Chap 51.9, pp. 1157–70; D. M. ROUNDHILL, Pt, Chap. 52, pp. 351–531 in *Comprehensive Coordination Chemistry.* Vol. 5, Pergamon Press, Oxford, 1987.

Fluorination of NiCl$_2$ + KCl produces red K$_2$NiF$_6$ which is strongly oxidizing and will liberate O$_2$ from water. Dark red complexes of the type [Ni^{IV}(L)](ClO$_4$)$_2$ (H$_2$L is a sexidentate oxime) have been obtained by the action of conc HNO$_3$ on [Ni^{II}(H$_2$L)](ClO$_4$)$_2$ and are stable indefinitely under vacuum but are reduced in moist air.

Palladium(IV) complexes are rather sparse and much less stable than those of Pt^{IV}. The best known are the hexahalogeno complexes [PdX$_6$]$^{2-}$ (X = F, Cl, Br) of which [PdCl$_6$]$^{2-}$, formed when the metal is dissolved in aqua regia, is the most familiar. In all of these the Pd^{IV} is readily reducible to Pd^{II}. In water, [PdF$_6$]$^{2-}$ hydrolyses immediately to PdO$_2$.xH$_2$O while the chloro and bromo complexes give [PdX$_4$]$^{2-}$ plus X$_2$. An organometallic chemistry of Pd^{IV} is developing (p. 1167).

By contrast Pt^{IV} complexes rival those of Pt^{II} in number, and are both thermodynamically stable and kinetically inert. Those with halides, pseudo-halides, and N-donor ligands are especially numerous. Of the multitude of conceivable compounds ranging from [PtX$_6$]$^{2-}$ through [PtX$_4$L$_2$] to [PtL$_6$]$^{4+}$, (X = F, Cl, Br, I, CN, SCN, SeCN; L = NH$_3$, amines) a large number have been prepared and characterized though, curiously, they do not include the [Pt(CN)$_6$]$^{2-}$ ion. K$_2$PtCl$_6$ is commercially the most common compound of platinum and the brownish-red, "chloroplatinic acid", H$_2$[PtCl$_6$](aq), is the usual starting material in Pt^{IV} chemistry. It is prepared by dissolving platinum metal sponge in aqua regia, followed by one or more evaporations with hydrochloric acid. A route to Pt^{II} chemistry also is provided by precipitation of the sparingly soluble K$_2$PtCl$_6$ followed by its reduction with hydrazine to K$_2$PtCl$_4$. The chloroammines were extensively used by Werner and other early coordination chemists in their studies on the nature of the coordinate bond in general and on the octahedral geometry of Pt^{IV} in particular.

O-donor ligands such as OH$^-$ and acac also coordinate to Pt^{IV}, but S- and Se-, and more especially P- and As-donor ligands, tend to reduce it to Pt^{II}.

Oxidation state III (d⁷)

Perhaps surprisingly, mononuclear M^{III} compounds are rather better represented by nickel than by either palladium or platinum. K_3NiF_6 has been prepared by fluorinating $KCl + NiCl_2$ at high temperatures and pressures. It is a violet crystalline material which is reduced by water with evolution of oxygen. The observed elongation of the $[NiF_6]^{3-}$ octahedron has been ascribed to the Jahn–Teller effect (p. 1021) to be expected for a $t_{2g}^6 e_g^1$ configuration although the reported magnetic moment of 2.5 BM at room temperature seems rather high for this configuration. Other examples include $[Ni(bipy)_3]^{3+}$, the black trigonal pyramidal $[NiBr_3(PEt_3)_2]$ and a number of compounds with N-donor macrocyclic ligands. Among the very few monomeric trivalent compounds of Pd and Pt, the blue $(NBu_4)[Pt(C_6Cl_5)_4]$ (obtained by oxidizing the Pt^{II} salt) and the red $[Pd(1,4,7-$trithiacyclononane)_2](ClO_4)_4.H_3O.3H_2O$ (obtained[9] by cyclovoltammetric oxidation in 70% aqueous $HClO_4$) should be mentioned.

The most abundant examples of this oxidation state, however, are the dinuclear Pt compounds[10] of the type, $[Pt_2(L-L)_4L_2]^{n-}$ with single Pt–Pt bonds and the same tetrabridged structure of Mo^{II} and Cr^{II} (p. 1032). The first of these was $K_2[Pt_2(SO_4)_4(H_2O)_2]$, prepared from $[Pt(NO_2)_2(NH_3)_2]$ and sulfuric acid, but those with phosphate or P-donor, pyrophosphito, $(P_2O_5H_2)^{2-}$, bridges are more numerous. Pt–Pt distances range from 278.2(1) pm, found with pyrophosphito bridges, down to 245.1(1) pm in $Cs_3[Pt_2(\mu-O_2CMe)_2(\mu-O_2CCH_2)_2]$. This yellow complex is obtained by a complex procedure[11] from K_2PtCl_4 and MeCOOAg and, besides a pair of O,O-donor acetate bridges, contains a pair of

unique C,O-donor, $-O.CO.CH_2-$, bridges. Stable tetraacetato bridged dimers are not found.

A number of compounds which have in the past been claimed to contain the trivalent metals have later turned out to contain them in more than one oxidation state. One such is H. Wolffram's red salt, $Pt(EtNH_2)_4Cl_3.2H_2O$, which has a structure (Fig. 27.4a) consisting of alternate octahedral Pt^{IV} and square-planar Pt^{II} linked by Cl bridges, i.e. $[Pt^{II}(EtNH_2)_4]^{2+}[trans-(\mu-Cl)_2-Pt^{IV}(EtNH_2)_4]^{2+}Cl^-_4.4H_2O$. Other examples are

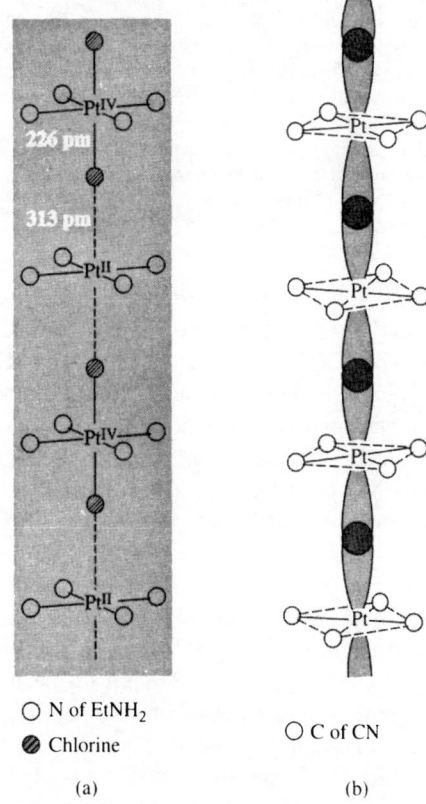

○ N of EtNH₂

◉ Chlorine

○ C of CN

(a)   (b)

Figure 27.4   Linear chain polymers of Pt. (a) The coordination of platinum in Wolffram's red salt, $Pt(EtNH_2)_4Cl_3.2H_2O$, showing alternating Pt^{II} and Pt^{IV} linked by Cl bridges. Four remaining Cl^- ions and 4 H_2O are situated within the lattice. (b) Stacking of square planar units in $[Pt(CN)_4]^{n-}$ showing the possible overlap of d_{z^2} orbitals. (Note the successive $45°$ rotations, or "staircase staggering", of these units.)

[9] A. J. Blake, A. J. Holder, T. I. White and M. Schroder, *J. Chem. Soc., Chem. Commun.*, 987–8 (1987).

[10] F. A. Cotton and R. A. Walton, *Multiple Bonds between Atoms*, 2nd Edn., Oxford University Press, Oxford, pp. 508–32 (1993); K. Umakoshi and Y. Sasaki, *Adv. Inorg. Chem.* **40**, 187–239 (1994).

[11] T. Yamaguchi, Y. Sasaki and T. Ito, *J. Am. Chem. Soc.* **112**, 4038–40 (1990).

Development of Ideas on the Stereochemistry of Nickel(II)

The way in which our present understanding of the stereochemical intricacies of Ni^{II} has evolved illustrates rather well the interplay of theory and experiment. On the basis of valence-bond theory, three types of complex of d^8 ions were anticipated. These were:

(i) *octahedral*, involving $sp^3d_{z^2}d_{x^2-y^2}$ hybridization and paramagnetism from 2 unpaired electrons;

(ii) *tetrahedral*, involving sp^3 hybridization and, again, paramagnetism from 2 unpaired electrons;

(iii) *square planar*, involving $d_{x^2-y^2}sp_xp_y$ hybridization which implies the confinement of all 8 electrons in four d orbitals, so producing diamagnetism.

Since X-ray determinations of structure were too time-consuming to be widely used in the 1930s and 1940s and, in addition, square-pianar geometry was a comparative rarity, any paramagnetic compound, which on the basis of stoichiometry appeared to be 4-coordinate, was presumed to be tetrahedral.

However, with the application in the 1950s of crystal field theory to transition-metal chemistry it was realized that CFSEs were unfavourable to the formation of tetrahedral d^8 complexes, and previous assignments were re-examined. A typical case was $[Ni(acac)_2]$, which had often been cited as an example of a tetrahedral nickel complex, but which was shown[12] in 1956 to be trimeric and octahedral. The over-zealous were then inclined to regard tetrahedral d^8 as non-existent until first L. M. Venanzi[13] and then N. S. Gill and R. S. Nyholm[14] demonstrated the existence of discrete tetrahedral species which in some cases were also rather easily prepared.

More comprehensive examination of spectroscopic and magnetic properties of d^8 ions followed which provided an explanation for the different types of Lifschitz salts (p. 1160) and led to studies of systems exhibiting anomalous properties. Rational explanations of these properties were eventually forthcoming.

provided by the one-dimensional conductors of platinum,[14a] of which the cyano complexes are the best known. Thus $K_2[Pt(CN)_4].3H_2O$ is a very stable colourless solid, but by appropriate partial oxidation it is possible to obtain bronze-coloured, "cation deficient", $K_{1.75}Pt(CN)_4.1.5H_2O$, and other partially oxidized compounds such as $K_2Pt(CN)_4Cl_{0.3}.3H_2O$. In these, square-planar $[Pt(CN)_4]^{n-}$ ions are stacked (Fig. 27.4b) to give a linear chain of Pt atoms in which the Pt–Pt distances of 280–300 pm (compared to 348 pm in the original $K_2[Pt(CN)_4].3H_2O$ and 278 pm in the metal itself) allow strong overlap of the d_{z^2} orbitals. This accounts for the metallic conductance of these materials along the crystal axis. Indeed, there is considerable current interest in such "one-dimensional" electrical conductors.

Oxalato complexes [e.g. $K_{1.6}Pt(C_2O_4)_2.1.2-H_2O$] originally prepared as long ago as 1888

by the German chemist H. G. Soderbaum, are also one-dimensional conductors with analogous structures.

Oxidation state II (d^8)

This is undoubtedly the most prolific oxidation state for this group of elements. The stereochemistry of Ni^{II} has been a topic of continuing interest (see Panel), and kinetic and mechanistic studies on complexes of Pd^{II} and Pt^{II} have likewise been of major importance. It will be convenient to treat Ni^{II} complexes first and then those of Pd^{II} and Pt^{II} (p. 1161).

Complexes of Ni^{II}. The absence of any other oxidation state of comparable stability for nickel implies that compounds of Ni^{II} are largely immune to normal redox reactions. Ni^{II} forms salts with virtually every anion and has an extensive aqueous chemistry based on the green[†] $[Ni(H_2O)_6]^{2+}$ ion which is always present in the absence of strongly complexing ligands.

[12] G. J. BULLEN, *Nature* **177**, 537–8 (1956).

[13] L. M. VENANZI, *J. Chem. Soc.* 719–24 (1958).

[14] N. S. GILL and R. S. NYHOLM, *J. Chem. Soc.* 3997–4007 (1959).

[14a] R. J. H. CLARK, *Chem. Soc. Rev.* **19**, 107–31 (1990).

[†] It was work on the absorption of light by solutions of nickel(II) which led A. Beer in 1852 to formulate the law which bears his name.

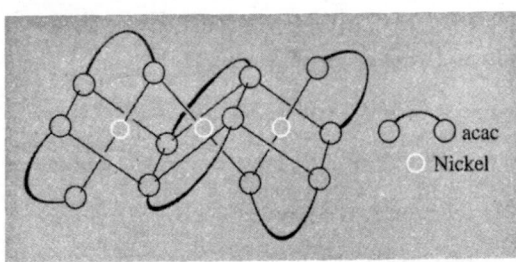

Figure 27.5   Trimeric structure of $[Ni(acac)_2]_3$.

The coordination number of Ni^{II} rarely exceeds 6 and its principal stereochemistries are octahedral and square planar (4-coordinate) with rather fewer examples of trigonal bipyramidal (5), square pyramidal (5), and tetrahedral (4). Octahedral complexes of Ni^{II} are obtained (often from aqueous solution by replacement of coordinated water) especially with neutral *N*-donor ligands such as NH_3, en, bipy and phen, but also with NCS^-, NO_2^- and the *O*-donor dimethylsulfoxide, dmso (Me_2SO).

The green trimer, $[Ni(acac)_2]_3$ (Fig 27.5), prepared by dehydrating the monomeric octahedral *trans*-dihydrate, $[Ni(acac)_2(H_2O)_2]$ and mentioned in the Panel opposite, has interesting magnetic properties. Down to about 80 K it behaves as a normal paramagnet but below that the magnetic moment per nickel atom rises from about 3.2 BM (as expected for 2 unpaired electrons, i.e. $S = 1$) to 4.1 BM at 4.3 K. This corresponds to the ferromagnetic coupling of all 6 unpaired electrons in the trimer (i.e. $S' = 3$). Replacement of the $-CH_3$ groups of acetylacetone by the bulkier $-C(CH_3)_3$ apparently prevents the formation of

the trimer and leads instead to the red square-planar monomer (Fig. 27.6a).

Of the four-coordinate complexes of Ni^{II}, those with the square planar stereochemistry are the most numerous. They include the yellow $[Ni(CN)_4]^{2-}$, the red bis(*N*-methyl-salicylaldiminato)nickel(II) and the well-known bis(dimethylglyoximato)nickel(II) (Fig. 27.6b and c) obtained as a flocculent red precipitate in gravimetric determinations of nickel. Actually, in the solid state, this last compound consists of planar molecules stacked above each other so that Ni–Ni interactions occur (Ni–Ni 325 pm), and the nickel atoms should therefore be described as octahedrally coordinated. However, in non-coordinating solvents it dissociates into the square-planar monomer, while in bis-(ethylmethylglyoximato)nickel(II) a much longer Ni–Ni separation (475 pm) indicates that even in the solid it must be regarded as square planar.

Although less numerous than the square-planar complexes, tetrahedral complexes of nickel(II) also occur. The simplest of these are the blue $[NiX_4]^{2-}$ (X = Cl, Br, I) ions, precipitated[14] from ethanolic solutions by large cations such as $[NR_4]^+$, $[PR_4]^+$ and $[AsR_4]^+$. Other examples include a number of those of the type $[NiL_2X_2]$ (L = PR_3, AsR_3, OPR_3, $OAsR_3$) amongst which were the first authenticated examples of tetrahedral nickel (II).[13]

A partial explanation, at least, can be provided for the relative abundances and ease of formation of the above stereochemical varieties of Ni^{II} complexes. It can be seen from Table 26.6 that the CFSEs of the d^8 configuration, unlike those of the d^7 configuration (e.g. Co^{II}), favour an

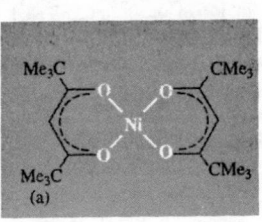
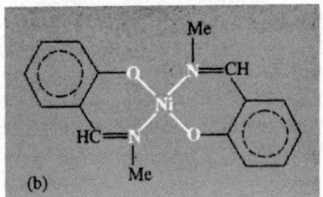
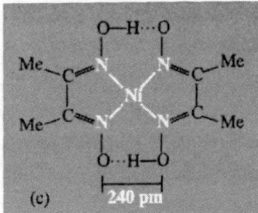

Figure 27.6   Some typical planar complexes of nickel (II): (a) $[Ni(Me_6\text{-}acac)_2]$, (b) $[Ni(Me\text{-}sal)_2]$ and (c) $[Ni(dmgH)_2]$. (Note the short O–O distance which is due to strong hydrogen bonding.)

Electronic Spectra and Magnetic Properties of Complexes of Nickel(II)[15]

Nickel(II) is the only common d^8 ion and its spectroscopic and magnetic properties have accordingly been extensively studied.

In a cubic field three spin-allowed transitions are expected because of the splitting of the free-ion, ground ^3F term and the presence of the ^3P term. In an octahedral field the splitting is the same as for the octahedral d^3 ion and the same energy level diagram (p. 1029) can be used to interpret the spectra as was used for octahedral Cr^{III}. Spectra of octahedral Ni^{II} usually do consist of three bands which are accordingly assigned as:

$$\nu_1 = {}^3T_{2g}(F) \leftarrow {}^3A_{2g}(F) = 10Dq; \quad \nu_2 = {}^3T_{1g}(F) \leftarrow {}^3A_{2g}(F); \quad \nu_3 = {}^3T_{1g}(P) \leftarrow {}^3A_{2g}(F)$$

with ν_1 giving the value of Δ, or $10Dq$, directly. Quite often there is also evidence of weak spin-forbidden (i.e. spin triplet → singlet) absorptions and, in $[Ni(H_2O)_6]^{2+}$ and $[Ni(dmso)_6]^{2+}$, for instance, the ν_2 absorption has a strong shoulder on it. This is ascribed to a transition to the spin singlet ^1E_g which occurs when the ^1E_g and $^3T_{1g}(F)$ terms are in close proximity.

For d^8 ions in tetrahedral fields the splitting of the free-ion ground term is the inverse of its splitting in an octahedral field, so that $^3T_{1g}(F)$ lies lowest. In this case three relatively intense bands are to be expected, arising from the transitions:

$$\nu_1 = {}^3T_2(F) \leftarrow {}^3T_1(F); \quad \nu_2 = {}^3A_2(F) \leftarrow {}^3T_1(F); \quad \nu_3 = {}^3T_1(P) \leftarrow {}^3T_1(F)$$

Table A gives data for a number of octahedral and tetrahedral complexes.

Table A   Electronic spectra of some complexes of nickel(II)

Complex	ν_1/cm^{-1}	ν_2/cm^{-1}	ν_3/cm^{-1}	$10Dq/cm^{-1}$
Octahedral				
$[Ni(dmso)_6]^{2+}$	7 730	12 970	24 040	7 730
$[Ni(H_2O)_6]^{2+}$	8 500	13 800	25 300	8 500
$[Ni(NH_3)_6]^{2+}$	10 750	17 500	28 200	10 750
$[Ni(en)_3]^{2+}$	11 200	18 350	29 000	11 200
$[Ni(bipy)_3]^{2+}$	12 650	19 200	(a)	12 650
Tetrahedral				
$[NiI_4]^{2-}$		7 040	14 030	3 820
$[NiBr_4]^{2-}$		7 000	13 230, 14 140	3 790
$[NiCl_4]^{2-}$		7 549	14 250, 15 240	4 090
$[NiBr_2(OPPh_3)_2]$		7 250	15 580	3 950

[a] Obscured by intense charge-transfer absorptions.

The T ground term of the tetrahedral ion is expected to lead to a temperature-dependent orbital contribution to the magnetic moment, whereas the A ground term of the octahedral ion is not, though "mixing" of the excited $^3T_{2g}(F)$ term into the $^3A_{2g}(F)$ ground term is expected to raise its moment to:

$$\mu_e = \mu_{spin-only}(1 - 4\lambda/10Dq)$$

where $\lambda = -315$ cm^{-1} and $\mu_{spin-only} = 2.83$ BM. (This is the exact reverse of the situations found for Co^{II}; p. 1132.) The upshot is that the magnetic moments of tetrahedral compounds are found to lie in the range 3.2–4.1 BM (and are dependent on temperature, and are reduced towards $\mu_{spin-only}$ by electron delocalization on to the ligands and by distortions from ideal tetrahedral symmetry) whereas those of octahedral compounds lie in the range 2.9–3.3 BM.

The spectra of square-planar d^8 complexes are usually characterized by a fairly strong band in the yellow to blue region (i.e. about 17 000–22 000 cm^{-1} or 600–450 nm) which is responsible for the reddish colour, and another band near the ultraviolet. The likelihood of π-bonding and attendant charge transfer makes a simple crystal-field treatment inappropriate, and unambiguous assignments are difficult.

---

[15] A. B. P. LEVER, *Inorganic Electronic Spectroscopy*, (2nd Edn.), pp. 507–611, Elsevier, Amsterdam, 1984.

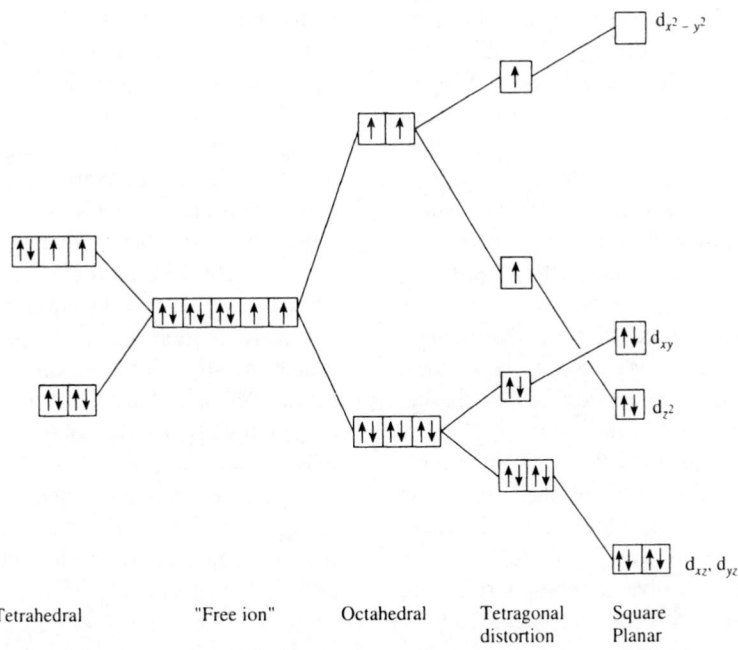

| Tetrahedral | "Free ion" | Octahedral | Tetragonal distortion | Square Planar |

Figure 27.7   The splitting of d orbitals in fields of different symmetries, and the resulting electronic configurations of the Ni^{II} d^8 ion.

octahedral as opposed to a tetrahedral stereochemistry. It is also evident from Fig 27.7 that the square-planar geometry offers the possibility, not available in either the octahedral or tetrahedral cases, of accommodating all 8 d electrons in 4 lower orbitals, thus leaving the uppermost ($d_{x^2-y^2}$) orbital empty. Providing therefore that the ligand field is of sufficiently low symmetry (or is sufficiently strong) to split the d orbitals enough to offset the energy required to pair-up 2 electrons, then the 4-coordinate, square-planar extreme can be energetically preferable not only to the tetrahedral but also to the 6-coordinate octahedral extreme. Thus, with the CN^- ligand which produces an exceptionally strong field, the square-planar $[Ni(CN)_4]^{2-}$ is formed rather than the tetrahedral isomer or the octahedral $[Ni(CN)_6]^{4-}$. Also, many compounds of the type $[NiL_2X_2]$, in which low-symmetry crystal fields are clearly possible, are planar. However, this selfsame formulation was mentioned above as including examples of tetrahedral complexes: evidently the factors which determine the geometry of a particular complex are finely balanced.

This balance, which apparently involves both steric and electronic factors, is well illustrated by the series of complexes $[Ni(PR_3)_2X_2]$ (X = Cl, Br, I). The diamagnetic, planar forms are favoured by R = alkyl, X = I, and the paramagnetic tetrahedral forms by R = aryl, X = Cl. When mixed alkylarylphosphines are involved, conformational isomerism may occur. For example, $[NiBr_2(PEtPh_2)_2]$ has been isolated in both a green, paramagnetic ($\mu_{300} = 3.20$ BM), tetrahedral form and a brown, diamagnetic, planar form.

These various stereochemistries are characterized by differing spectroscopic and magnetic properties (see Panel opposite). However, the crude traditional guidelines of colour and magnetism, namely that square planar compounds are red to yellow and diamagnetic whereas tetrahedral ones are green to blue and paramagnetic (due to the $t_{2g}^6 e_g^2$ and $e^4 t_2^4$ configurations respectively), cannot be regarded as rigorously diagnostic. The octahedral $[Ni(NO_2)_6]^{4-}$ and square planar $[NiI_2(quinoline)_2]$ for instance, are respectively paramagnetic and diamagnetic (expected) but are also brown-red and green (unexpected). Furthermore, the compounds, $[Bu_2^tP(\mu\text{-}O,\mu\text{-}NR)Ni(\mu\text{-}O,\mu\text{-}NR)PBu_2^t]$ ($R = Pr^i$, cyclohexyl) exist as both tetrahedral and square planar isomers of which not only the former but, uniquely, the latter also are paramagnetic.[16] Presumably the separation of $d_{x^2-y^2}$ and d_{xy} orbitals (Fig 27.7) is sufficiently small to allow both to be singly occupied.

Many compounds, of which $[NiBr_2(PEtPh_2)_2]$ mentioned above is one, exist in solution as mixtures of isomers giving rise to intermediate values of μ_e (0–3.2 BM). Such behaviour, previously regarded as "anomalous" is due to one of three possible types of equilibria:

1. *Planar–tetrahedral equilibria.* Compounds such as $[NiBr_2(PEtPh_2)_2]$ mentioned above as well as a number of *sec*-alkylsalicylaldiminato derivatives (i.e. Me in Fig. 27.6b replaced by a *sec*-alkyl group) dissolve in non-coordinating solvents such as chloroform or toluene to give solutions whose spectra and magnetic properties are temperature-dependent and indicate the presence of an equilibrium mixture of diamagnetic planar and paramagnetic tetrahedral molecules.

2. *Planar–octahedral equilibria.* Dissolution of planar Ni^{II} compounds in coordinating solvents such as water or pyridine frequently leads to the formation of octahedral complexes by the coordination of 2 solvent molecules. This can, on occasions, lead to solutions in which the Ni^{II} has an intermediate value of μ_e indicating the presence of comparable amounts of planar and octahedral molecules varying with temperature and concentration; more commonly the conversion is complete and octahedral solvates can be crystallized out. Well-known examples of this behaviour are provided by the complexes $[Ni(L\text{-}L)_2X_2]$ (L-L = substituted ethylenediamine, X = variety of anions) generally known by the name of their discoverer I. Lifschitz. Some of these Lifschitz salts are yellow, diamagnetic and planar, $[Ni(L\text{-}L)_2]X_2$, others are blue, paramagnetic, and octahedral, $[Ni(L\text{-}L)_2X_2]$ or

$[Ni(L\text{-}L)_2(solvent)_2]X_2$. Which type is produced depends on the nature of L-L, X, and the solvent.

3. *Monomer–oligomer equilibria.* [Ni(Mesal)$_2$], mentioned above as a typical planar complex, is a much studied compound. In pyridine it is converted to the octahedral bispyridine adduct ($\mu_{300} = 3.1$ BM), while in chloroform or benzene the value of μ_e is intermediate but increases with concentration. This is ascribed to an equilibrium between the diamagnetic monomer and a paramagnetic dimer, which must involve a coordination number of the nickel of at least 5; a similar explanation is acceptable also for the paramagnetism of the solid when heated above 180°C. The trimerization of Ni(acac)$_2$ to attain octahedral coordination has already been referred to but it may also be noted that it is reported to be monomeric and planar in dilute chloroform solutions.

Apart from the probably 5-coordinate Ni^{II} in the above oligomers, a number of well-characterized 5-coordinate complexes are known. These are either trigonal bipyramidal or square pyramidal, though the two forms are energetically similar and the stereochemistry is often imposed by the ligands. Thus the trigonal bipyramidal complexes, which are the more common, often involve tripod ligands (p. 907), while the quadridentate chain ligand,

$$Me_2As(CH_2)_3As(Ph)\text{-}CH_2\text{-}As(Ph)(CH_2)_3AsMe_2$$

(tetars) produces square pyramidal complexes of the type $[Ni(tetars)X]^+$. These 5-coordinate complexes can be of either high-spin or low-spin type. The former is found in $[NiBr\{N(C_2H_4NMe_2)_3\}]^+$ but with *P*- or *As*-donor ligands low-spin configurations are found.

The Ni^{II}/CN^- system illustrates nicely the ease of conversion of the two stereochemistries. Although, as already pointed out, there is no evidence of a hexacyano complex, a square pyramidal pentacyano complex is known:

$$Ni \xrightarrow{\ CN^-\ } \underset{\text{green ppt}}{[Ni(CN)_2aq]} \xrightarrow[\text{redissolves}]{\ CN^-\ } \underset{\text{yellow}}{[Ni(CN)_4]^{2-}}$$
$$\xrightarrow[\text{excess}]{\ CN^-\ } \underset{\text{red}}{[Ni(CN)_5]^{3-}}$$

[16] T. FRÖMMEL, W. PETERS, H. WUNDERLICH and W. KUCHERN, *Angew. Chem. Int. Edn. Engl.* **31**, 612–13 (1992); *ibid.* **32**, 907–9 (1993).

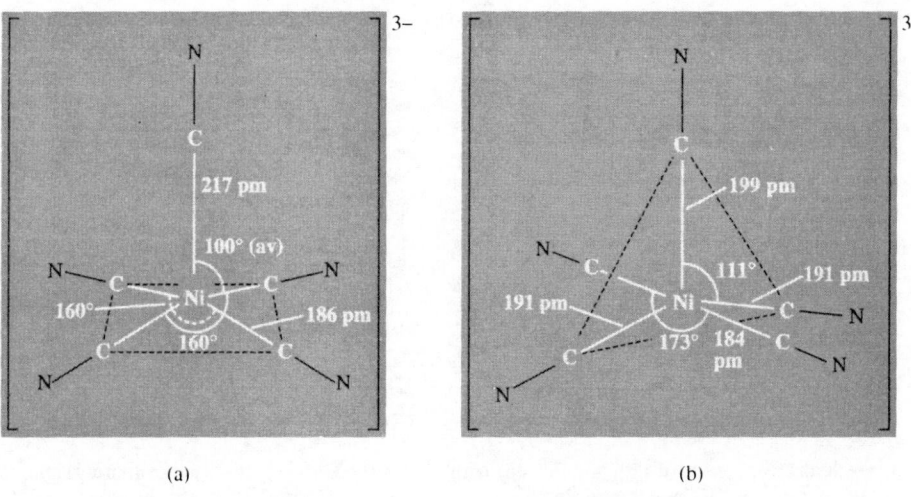

(a)   (b)

Figure 27.8   The structure of the distorted (a) square-pyramidal and (b) trigonal bipyramidal $[Ni(CN)_5]^{3-}$ ions in $[Cr(en)_3][Ni(CN)_5].1\frac{1}{2}H_2O$.

The fascinating crystalline compound $[Cr(en)_3]$-$[Ni(CN)_5].1\frac{1}{2}H_2O$ contains both square pyramidal and trigonal bipyramidal anions though each is distorted from true C_{4v} or D_{3h} symmetry as shown in Fig. 27.8.

Another interesting cyano derivative of nickel(II)[16a] which may conveniently be mentioned here is the *clathrate* compound, $[Ni(CN)_2$-$(NH_3)].xC_6H_6$ ($x \leq 1$). If CN^- is added to the blue-violet solution obtained by mixing aqueous solutions of Ni^{II} and NH_3, and this is then shaken with benzene, a pale-violet precipitate is obtained. This precipitate is soluble in conc NH_3. The benzene and ammonia can be removed by heating it above 150°C but not by washing or by application of reduced pressure. The benzene molecule is, in fact, trapped inside a cage formed by the lattice in which the nickel ions are coordinated to 4 cyanides situated in a square plane, and half are additionally coordinated to 2 ammonias (Fig. 27.9). The observed magnetic moment per Ni atom of 2.2 BM is entirely consistent with this since this average moment arises solely from the octahedrally coordinated Ni atoms, the square-planar Ni being diamagnetic.

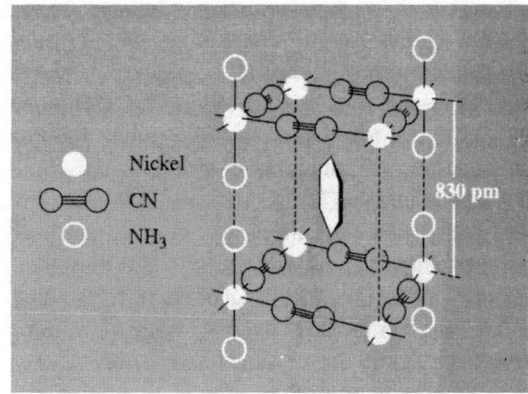

Figure 27.9   A "cage" in the structure of $[Ni(CN)_2$-$(NH_3)].x(C_6H_6)$, showing a trapped benzene molecule.

Complexes of Pd^{II} and Pt^{II}. The effect of complexation on the splitting of d orbitals is much greater in the case of second- and third-than for first-row transition elements, and the associated effects already noted for Ni^{II} are even more marked for Pd^{II} and Pt^{II}; as a result, their complexes are, with rare exceptions, diamagnetic and the vast majority are planar also. Not many complexes are formed with O-donor ligands but, of the few that are, $[M(H_2O)_4]^{2+}$ ions, and the polymeric anhydrous acetates $[Pd(O_2CMe)_2]_3$ and $[Pt(O_2CMe)_2]_4$ (Fig. 27.10), are the most

[16a] K. R. DUNBAR and R. A. HEINTZ *Prog. Inorg. Chem.* **45**, 283–391 (1997).

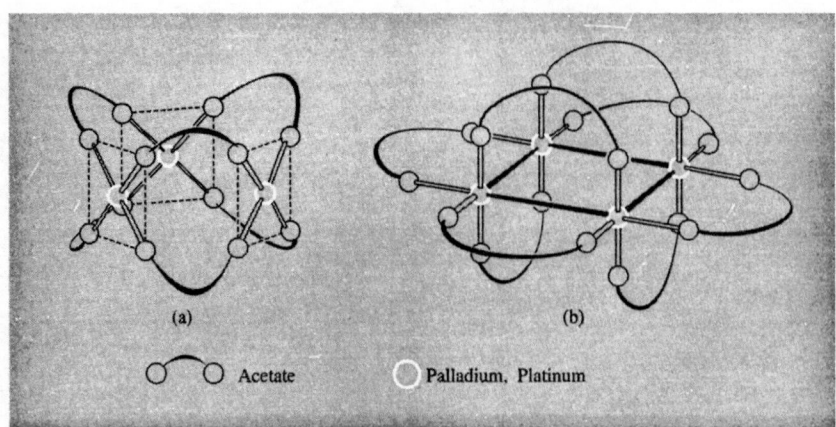

Figure 27.10   Anhydrous acetates of Pd^{II} and Pt^{II}: (a) trimeric $[Pd(O_2CMe)_2]_3$ involving square-planar coordinated Pd but no metal–metal bonding (average Pd–Pd = 315 pm), and (b) tetrameric $[Pt(O_2CMe)_2]_4$ involving octahedrally coordinated Pt and metal–metal bonds (average Pt–Pt = 249.5 pm). The four bridging ligands in the Pt_4 plane are much more labile than the others.

important.[17,18] Approximately square planar $[M(NO_3)_4]^{2-}$ anions containing the unusual unidentate nitrato ion are also known.[19] Fluoro complexes are even less prevalent, the preference of these cations being for the other halides, cyanide, N- and heavy atom-donor ligands.

The complexes $[MX_4]^{2-}$ (M = Pd, Pt; X = Cl, Br, I, SCN, CN) are all easily obtained and may be crystallized as salts of $[NH_4]^+$ and the alkali metals. By using $[NR_4]^+$ cations it is possible to isolate binuclear halogen-bridged anions $[M_2X_6]^{2-}$ (X = Br, I) which retain the square-planar coordination of M. Aqueous solutions of yellowish-brown $[PdCl_4]^{2-}$ and red $[PtCl_4]^{2-}$ are common starting materials for the preparation of other Pd^{II} and Pt^{II} complexes by successive substitution of the chloride ligands. In both $[M(SCN)_4]^{2-}$ complexes the ligands bond through their π-acceptor (S) ends, though in the presence of stronger π-acceptor ligands such as PR_3 and AsR_3 they tend to bond through their N ends.[†] Not surprisingly, therefore, several

instances of linkage isomerism (p. 920) have been established in compounds of the type *trans*-$[M(PR_3)_2(SCN)_2]$.

Complexes with ammonia and amines, especially those of the types $[ML_4]^{2+}$ and $[ML_2X_2]$, are numerous for Pd^{II} and even more so for Pt^{II}. Many of them were amongst the first complexes of these metals to be prepared and interest in them has continued since. For example, the colourless $[Pt(NH_3)_4]Cl_2.H_2O$ can be obtained by adding NH_3 to an aqueous solution of $PtCl_2$ and, in 1828, was the first of the platinum ammines to be discovered (by G. Magnus). Other salts of the $[Pt(NH_3)_4]^{2+}$ ion are easily derived, the best known being Magnus's green salt $[Pt(NH_3)_4][PtCl_4]$. That a green salt should result from the union of a colourless cation and a red anion was unexpected and is a consequence of the crystal structure, which consists of the square-planar anions and cations stacked

[17] D. P. BANCROFT, F. A. COTTON, L. R. FALVELLO and W. SCHWOTZER, *Polyhedron* **7**, 615–21 (1988).

[18] T. YAMAGUCHI, T. UENO and T. ITO, *Inorg. Chem.* **32**, 4996–7 (1993).

[19] L. I. ELDING, B. NORÉN and Å. OSKARSSON, *Inorg. Chim. Acta* **114**, 71–4 (1986).

[†] Steric, as well as electronic, effects are probably involved. When the ligand is N-bonded, $M{\leftarrow}N{\equiv}C{-}S$ is linear and so sterically undemanding. However, when the ligand is S-bonded, $M{-}S{-}C$ is nonlinear, the bonding and nonbonding electron pairs around the sulfur being more or less tetrahedrally disposed. On purely steric grounds, therefore, the latter type of bonding is expected to be less favoured than the former when bulky ligands such as PR_3 and AsR_3 are present.

alternately to produce a linear chain of Pt atoms only 325 pm apart. Interaction between these metal atoms shifts the d–d absorption of the $[PtCl_4]^{2-}$ ion from the green region (whence the normal red colour) towards the red, so producing the green colour.

Magnus's salt is an electrolyte and non-ionized polymerization isomers (p. 921) of the stoichiometry $PtCl_2(NH_3)_2$ are also known which can be prepared as monomeric *cis* and *trans* isomers:

$$[PtCl_4]^{2-} \xrightarrow{NH_3} cis\text{-}[PtCl_2(NH_3)_2]$$

$$[Pt(NH_3)_4]^{2+} \xrightarrow{HCl} trans\text{-}[PtCl_2(NH_3)_2]$$

Their existence led Werner to infer a square-planar geometry for Pt^{II}.

Many substitution reactions are possible with these ammines and were studied extensively in the 1920s by the Russian, I. I. Chernyaev (also transliterated from the Cyrillic as Tscherniaev, etc.). He noticed that when there are alternative positions at which an incoming ligand might effect a substitution; the position chosen depends not so much on the substituting or substituted ligand as on the nature of the ligand *trans* to that position. This became known as the "trans-effect" and has had a considerable influence on the synthetic coordination chemistry of Pt^{II} (see Panel).

A resurgence of interest in these seemingly simple complexes of platinum started in 1969 when B. Rosenberg and co-workers discovered the anti-tumour activity of *cis*-$[PtCl_2(NH_3)_2]$

The Trans Effect[20]

Because their rates of substitution are convenient for study, most work has been done with platinum complexes, and for these it is found that ligands can be arranged in a fairly consistent order indicating their relative abilities to labilize ligands *trans* to themselves:

$$F^-, \ OH^-, \ H_2O, \ NH_3, \ py < Cl^- < Br^- < I^-, \ -SCN^-, \ NO_2^-, \ C_6H_5^- <$$

$$S{=}C(NH_2)_2, \ CH_3^- < H^-, \ PR_3, \ AsR_3 < CN^-, \ CO, \ C_2H_4$$

The reason why the particular substitution reactions of $[PtC_4]^{2-}$ and $[Pt(NH_3)_4]^{2+}$, mentioned above, produce respectively *cis* and *trans* isomers is now evident. It is because, in both cases, in the second of the stepwise substitutions there is a choice of positions for the substitution and in each case it is a ligand *trans* to a Cl^- which is replaced in preference to a ligand *trans* to an NH_3:

Similar considerations have been invaluable in devising synthetic routes to numerous other isomeric complexes of Pt^{II} but, as can be seen in Fig. A, other considerations such as the relative stabilities of the different Pt–ligand bonds are also involved.

Panel continues

---

[20] A. K. Babkov, *Polyhedron* **7**, 1203–6 (1988).

Explanations for the *trans*-effect abound and it seems that either π or σ effects, or both, are involved. The ligands exerting the strongest *trans*-effects are just those (e.g. C_2H_4, CO, PR_3, etc.) whose bonding to a metal is thought to have most π-acceptor character and which therefore remove most π-electron density from the metal. This reduces the electron density most at the coordination site directly opposite, i.e. *trans*, and it is there that nucleophilic attack is most likely. This interpretation is not directly concerned with labilizing a particular ligand but rather with encouraging the attachment of a further ligand. It has consequently been applied most successfully to explaining kinetic phenomena such as reaction rates and the proportions of different isomers formed in a reaction (which depend on the rates of reaction), due to the stabilization of 5-coordinate reaction intermediates.

Figure A Preparation of the three isomers of [PtCl(NH$_3$)(NH$_2$Me)(NO$_2$)]. Where indicated these
steps can be explained by the greater *trans*-effect of the NO$_2^-$ ligand. Elsewhere the weakness
of the Pt–Cl as compared to the Pt–N bond must be invoked.

On the other hand, a ligand which is a strong σ-donor is expected to produce an axial polarization of the metal, its lone-pair inducing a positive charge on the near side of the metal and a concomitant negative charge on the far side. This will weaken the attachment to the metal of the *trans* ligand. This interpretation has been most successfully used to explain thermodynamic, "ground state" properties such as the bond lengths and vibrational frequencies of the *trans* ligands and their nmr coupling constants with the metal.

In order to distinguish between kinetic and thermodynamic phenomena it is convenient to refer to the former as the "*trans*-effect" and the latter as the "*trans*-influence" or "static *trans*-effect", though this nomenclature is by no means universally accepted. However, it appears that to account satisfactorily for the kinetic "*trans*-effect", both π (kinetic) and σ (thermodynamic) effects must be invoked to greater or lesser extents. Thus, for ligands which are low in the *trans* series (e.g. halides), the order can be explained on the basis of a σ effect whereas for ligands which are high in the series the order is best interpreted on the basis of a π effect. Even so, the relatively high position of H$^-$, which can have no π-acceptor properties, seems to be a result of a σ mechanism or some other interaction.

("cisplatin"). Binding of cisplatin to DNA appeared to be the central feature of the action and, since the *trans*-isomer is inactive, it was evident that chelation (or at least coordination to donor atoms in close proximity) is an essential part of the activity. Extensive studies, involving in particular proton nmr, suggested that Pt loses the Cl$^-$ ligands and binds to N-7

atoms of a pair of guanine bases on adjacent strands of DNA.[21] Recent X-ray work[22] on a 12-base-pair fragment of double stranded DNA

[21] J. L. van der VEER and J. REEDIJK, *Chem. in Brit.* **20** 775–80 (1988).

[22] P. M. TAKAHARA, A. C. ROSENZWEIG, C. A. FREDERICK and S. J. LIPPARD, *Nature* **377**, 649–52 (1995).

confirms that the binding of Pt distorts the local DNA structure therefore inhibiting the cell division inherent in the proliferation of cancer cells.

In order to avoid serious side effects of cisplatin (kidney- and neuro-toxicity) alternative Pt compounds have been developed. The most important of these is "carboplatin" in which the *cis*-chlorides are replaced by the *O*-chelate, cyclobutanedicarboxylate but all of them have ligands with NH groups which facilitate the hydrogen bonding thought to stabilize the distortions of the DNA structure.

Treatment of aqueous solutions of *cis*-$[PtCl_2(NH_3)_2]$ with a variety of pyrimidines yields blue, oligomeric (Pt_4) compounds of the type known since the early 20th century as "platinum blues." They are mostly, mixed valence, paramagnetic compounds and although some have been characterized[23] others are less well-defined and include green and violet materials.

Stable complexes of Pd^{II} and Pt^{II} are formed with a variety of *S*-donor ligands which includes the inorganic sulfite (SO_3^-) and thiosulfate $(S_2O_3^{2-}$ apparently coordinating through 1 S and 1 O) but those with organo-sulfur ligands such as 1,2-dithiolenes are of more interest. The anions $[M(mnt)_2]^{2-}$ (mnt = $S_2C_2(CN)_2$, M = Ni, Pd, Pt) have a facile redox chemistry yielding products with unusual electrical properties. Most salts of the square planar $[M(mnt)_2]^-$ crystallize in stacks, in which the anions associate in pairs, and are semiconductors but the nonstoichiometric $(H_3O)_{0.33}Li_{0.8}[Pt(mnt)_2]1.67H_2O$ is a linear conductor and $Cs_{0.82}[Pd(mnt)_2]0.5H_2O$ shows metallic conductance when subject to high pressure.[24]

The essentially class-b character of Pd^{II} and Pt^{II} is further indicated by the ready formation of complexes with phosphines and arsines. $[M(PR_3)_2X_2]$ and the arsine analogues are particularly well known. Zero dipole moments indicate that the palladium complexes are invariably *trans*, whereas those of platinum may be either *cis* or *trans* the latter being much the more soluble and having lower mps. When these bisphosphines and bisarsines are boiled in alcohol, or alternatively when they are fused with MX_2, the dimeric complexes $[MLX_2]_2$ are frequently obtained. Again, zero dipole moments (in some cases confirmed by X-ray analysis) indicate that these are all of the symmetrical *trans* form (a).

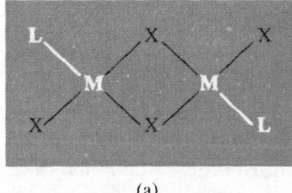

(a)

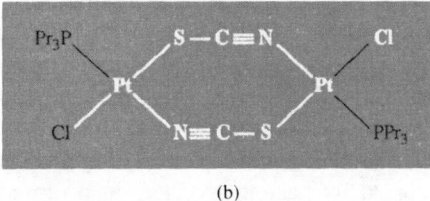

(b)

By involving SCN^- a novel 8-membered ring system has been produced (b).

Nuclear magnetic resonance has proved to be a particularly useful tool in studying phosphines of platinum. The nuclear spins of ^{31}P and ^{195}Pt (both equal to $\frac{1}{2}$) couple, and the strength of this coupling (as measured by the "coupling constant" J) is affected much more by ligands *trans* to the phosphine than by those which are *cis*. This has helped in determinations of structure and also in studies of the "*trans* influence". Platinum(II) also forms a number of quite stable monohydrido (H^-) phosphines which have proved similarly interesting, the $^1H-^{195}Pt$ coupling constants being likewise sensitive to the *trans* ligand.

It has already been pointed out that the overwhelming majority of complexes of Pd^{II} and Pt^{II} are square planar. However, 5-coordinate intermediates are almost certainly involved in many of the substitution reactions of these 4-coordinate complexes, and 5-coordinate trigonal

23 see for instance, T. V. O'HALLORAN, P. K. MASCHARAK, I. D. WILLIAMS, M. M. ROBERTS and S. J. LIPPARD, *Inorg. Chem.* **26** 1261–70 (1987).

24 M. B. HURSTHOUSE, R. L. SHORT, P. I. CLEMENSON and A. E. UNDERHILL, *J. Chem. Soc., Dalton Trans.*, 1101–4 (1989).

bipyramidal complexes with "tripod" ligands (p. 907) are well established. These ligands include the tetraarsine, $As(C_6H_4\text{-}2\text{-}AsPh_2)_3$ (qas, p. 1150), its phosphine analogue and also $N(CH_2CH_2NMe_2)_3$ i.e. (Me_6tren). The somewhat less-rigid tetraarsine,

$$1,2\text{-}C_6H_4\{As(Me)\text{-}C_6H_4\text{-}AsMe_2\}_2$$

(tpas), however forms a red, square-pyramidal complex $[Pd(tpas)Cl]ClO_4$ with palladium.

Oxidation state I (d⁹)

Although nickel(I) is thought to be involved in some nickel-containing enzymes, this oxidation state is best represented by yellow to red, tetrahedral phosphines such as $[Ni(PPh_3)_3X]$ (X = Cl, Br, I) which are paramagnetic, as expected for a d^9 configuration, and relatively stable. $[Ni(PMe_3)_4][BPh_4]$ has also been structurally characterized. A more recent[25] example is $K_3[NiO_2]$. This dark red, air- and water-sensitive compound, like the Fe^I (p. 1082 footnote) and Co^I (p. 1134) analogues, is prepared by heating K_6CdO_4 in a closed Ni cylinder at 500°C for 49 days when it reacts with the cylinder walls:

$$K_6CdO_4 + 2Ni \longrightarrow 2K_3[NiO_2] + Cd$$

These anions are remarkable not only for the low coordination number but also for the low oxidation state of the metals in combination with oxygen which is more commonly to be found stabilizing *high* oxidation states.

Oxidation state 0 (d¹⁰)

Besides $[Ni(CO)_4]$ and organometallic compounds discussed in the next section, nickel is found in the formally zero oxidation state with ligands such as CN^- and phosphines. Reduction of $K_2[Ni^{II}(CN)_4]$ with potassium in liquid ammonia precipitates yellow $K_4[Ni^0(CN)_4]$, which is sensitive to aerial oxidation. Being

isoelectronic with $[Ni(CO)_4]$ it is presumed to be tetrahedral. Similarity with the carbonyl is still more marked in the case of the gaseous and tetrahedral $[Ni(PF_3)_4]$, which also can be prepared directly from the metal and ligand:

$$Ni + 4PF_3 \xrightarrow[350\ atm]{1000°C} [Ni(PF_3)_4]$$

The pale yellow $[Ni(PEt_3)_4]$ is also tetrahedral but with some distortion.[26] In sharp contrast to nickel, palladium forms no simple carbonyl, $Pt(CO)_4$ is prepared only by matrix isolation at very low temperatures and reports of $K_4[M(CN)_4]$ (M = Pd, Pt) may well refer to hydrido complexes; in any event they are very unstable. The chemistry of these two metals in the zero oxidation state is in fact essentially that of their phosphine and arsine complexes and was initiated by L. Malatesta and his school in the 1950s. Compounds of the type $[M(PR_3)_4]$, of which $[Pt(PPh_3)_4]$ has been most thoroughly studied, are in general yellow, air-stable solids or liquids obtained by reducing M^{II} complexes in H_2O or $H_2O/EtOH$ solutions with hydrazine or sodium borohydride. They are tetrahedral molecules whose most important property is their readiness to dissociate in solution to form 3-coordinate, planar $[M(PR_3)_3]$ and, in traces, probably also $[M(PR_3)_2]$ species. The latter are intermediates in an extensive range of addition reactions (many of which may properly be regarded as *oxidative* additions) giving such products as $[Pt^{II}(PPh_3)_2L_2]$, (L = O, CN, N_3) and $[Pt^{II}(PPh_3)_2LL']$, (L,L' = H,Cl; R,I) as well as $[Pt^0(C_2H_4)(PPh_3)_2]$ and $[Pt^0(CO)_2(PPh_3)_2]$.

The mechanism by which this low oxidation state is stabilized for this triad has been the subject of some debate. That it is not straightforward is clear from the fact that, in contrast to nickel, palladium and platinum require the presence of phosphines for the formation of stable carbonyls. For most transition metals the π-acceptor properties of the ligand are thought to be of considerable importance and there is

[25] A. MÖLLER, M. A. HITCHMAN, E. KRAUSZ and R. HOPPE, *Inorg. Chem.* **34**, 2684–91 (1995).

[26] M. HURSTHOUSE, K. J. IZOD, M. MOTEVALLI and P. THORNTON, *Polyhedron* **13**, 151–3 (1994).

no reason to doubt that this is true for Ni^0. For Pd^0 and Pt^0, however, it appears that σ-bonding ability is also important, and the smaller importance of π backbonding which this implies is in accord with the higher ionization energies of Pd and Pt [804 and 865 kJ mol^{-1} respectively] compared with that for Ni [737 kJ mol^{-1}].

27.3.5 The biochemistry of nickel[27]

Until the discovery in 1975 of nickel in jack bean urease (which, 50 years previously, had been the first enzyme to be isolated in crystalline form and was thought to be metal-free) no biological role for nickel was known. Ureases occur in a wide variety of bacteria and plants, catalyzing the hydrolysis of urea,

$$OC(NH_2)_2 + H_2O \longrightarrow H_2NCOO^- + NH_4^+$$

Results from an array of methods, including X-ray absorption, EXAFS, esr and magnetic circular dichroism, suggest that in all ureases the active sites are a pair of Ni^{II} atoms. In at least one urease,[27a] these are 350 pm apart and are bridged by a carboxylate group. One nickel is attached to 2 N atoms with a fourth site probably used for binding to urea. The second nickel has a trigonal bipyramidal coordination sphere.

Three other Ni-containing enzymes found in bacteria have now been identified:
Hydrogenases, most of which also contain Fe and catalyse the reaction, $2H_2 + O_2 \longrightarrow 2H_2O$. The Ni has a coordination sphere of 5 or 6 mixed S-, N-, O-donors and is believed to undergo redox cycling between III, II and I oxidation states.
CO Dehydrogenase, also incorporating Fe and catalysing the oxidation of CO to CO_2. The attachment of CO to a nickel centre coordinated to perhaps four S-donors is postulated.

Methyl-coenzyme M reductase participates in the conversion of CO_2 to CH_4 and contains 6-coordinate nickel(II) in a highly hydrogenated and highly flexible porphyrin system. This flexibility is believed to allow sufficient distortion of the octahedral ligand field to produce low-spin Ni^{II} (Fig. 27.7) which facilitates the formation of a Ni^I–CH_3 intermediate.

27.3.6 Organometallic compounds[4,28]

All three of these metals have played major roles in the development of organometallic chemistry. The first compound containing an unsaturated hydrocarbon attached to a metal (and, indeed, the first organometallic compound if one excludes the cyanides) was $[Pt(C_2H_4)Cl_2]_2$, discovered by the Danish chemist W. C. Zeise as long ago as 1827 and followed 4 years later by the salt which bears his name, $K[Pt(C_2H_4)Cl_3].H_2O$. $[Ni(CO)_4]$ was the first metal carbonyl to be prepared when L. Mond and his co-workers discovered it in 1888. The platinum methyls, prepared in 1907 by W. J. Pope, were amongst the first-known transition metal alkyls, and the discovery by W. Reppe in 1940 that Ni^{II} complexes catalyse the cyclic oligomerization of acetylenes produced a surge of interest which was reinforced by the discovery in 1960 of the π-allylic complexes of which those of Pd^{II} are by far the most numerous.

σ-Bonded compounds

These are of two main types: compounds of M^{IV}, which for platinum have been known since the beginning of this century and commonly involve the stable {PtMe$_3$} group; and compounds of the divalent metals, which were first studied by J. Chatt and co-workers in the late 1950's and are commonly of the type $[MR_2L_2]$ (L = phosphine). In the Pt^{IV} compounds the metal is always octahedrally coordinated and this is frequently achieved in interesting ways. Thus the trimethyl halides, conveniently obtained

[27] A. F. KOLODZIEJ, *Prog. Inorg. Chem.* **41**, 493–597 (1994); J. R. LANCASTER (ed.), *The Bioinorganic Chemistry of Nickel*, VCH, Weinheim, 1988, 337 pp.; H. SIGEL (ed.), *Metal Ions in Biological Systems*, Vol. 23, *Nickel and its Role in Biology*, Dekker, New York, 1988, 488 pp.

[27a] S. J. LIPPARD, *Science*, **268**, 996–7 (1995); E. JABRI, M. B. CARR, R. P. HAUSINGER and P. A. KARPLUS, *ibid.* pp. 998–1004.

[28] G. WILKE, *Angew. Chem. Int. Edn. Engl.* **27**, 185–206 (1988).

by treating $PtCl_4$ with MeMgX in benzene, are tetramers, $[PtMe_3X]_4$, in which the 4 Pt atoms form a cube involving triply-bridging halogen atoms[†] (Fig. 27.11a). The dimeric $[PtMe_3(acac)]_2$ is also unusual in that the acac is both *O*- and *C*-bonded (Fig. 27.11b), while in $[PtMe_3(acac)(bipy)]$ 7-coordination is avoided because the acac coordinates merely as a unidentate *C*-donor. Pd^{IV} compounds such as $[PdI(bipy)Me_3]$ are also octahedral but are limited in number and much less stable than those of Pt^{IV}, being susceptible to reductive elimination.[29]

[†] The chequered history of compounds of this type makes salutory reading. H. Gilman and M. Lichtenwalter (1938, 1953) reported the synthesis of $PtMe_4$ in 46% yield by reacting Me_3PtI with NaMe in hexane. R. E. Rundle and J. H. Sturdivant determined the X-ray crystal structure of this product in 1947 and described it as a tetramer $[(PtMe_4)_4]$: this required the concept of a multicentred, 2-electron bond, and was one of the first attempts to interpret the bonding in a presumed electron-deficient cluster compound. In fact, tetramethylplatinum cannot be prepared in this way and is unknown; Gilman's compound was actually a hydrolysis product $[\{PtMe_3(OH)\}_4]$ and the mistaken identity of the crystal went undetected by the X-ray work because, at that time, the scattering curves for the 9-electron groups CH_3 and OH were indistinguishable in the presence of Pt. Interestingly, the compound $PtMe_3(OH)$ had, in reality, already been synthesized by W. J. Pope and S. J. Peachey as long ago as 1909, and its tetrameric structure was confirmed by subsequent X-ray work.[30] In a parallel study,[31] the transparent tan-coloured tetramer $[(PtMe_3I)_4]$ has now been shown to be the same compound as was previously erroneously reported in 1938 as hexamethyldiplatinum, $[Me_3Pt-PtMe_3]$. This was equally erroneously described in 1949 on the basis of an incomplete X-ray structural study as a methyl-bridged oligomer $[(PtMe_3)_{12}]$ or an infinite chain of methyl-bridged 6-coordinate $\{PtMe_3\}$-groups. A qualitative test for iodine would have revealed the error 30 years earlier.

Although $PtMe_4$ remains unknown it has more recently been shown that reaction of $[PtMe_2(PPh_3)_2]$ with LiMe yields the square-planar Pt^{II} complex $Li_2[PtMe_4]$, whereas reaction of $[PtMe_3I]_4$ with LiMe affords the octahedral Pt^{IV} complex $Li_2[PtMe_6]$.[32] The thermally stable, colourless, 8-coordinate complex $[PtMe_3(\eta^5\text{-}C_5H_5)]$ is also known.[33]

[29] A. J. CANTY, *Acc. Chem. Res.* **25**, 83–90 (1992); *Platinum Metals Rev.* **37**, 2–7 (1993).

[30] D. O. COWAN, N. G. KRIEGHOFF and G. DONNAY, *Acta Cryst.* **B24**, 287–8 (1968), and references therein.

[31] G. DONNAY, L. B. COLEMAN, N. G. KRIEGHOFF and D. O. COWAN, *Acta Cryst.* **B24**, 157–9 (1968), and references therein.

[32] G. W. RICE and R. S. TOBIAS, *J. Am. Chem. Soc.* **99**, 2141–9 (1977).

[33] O. HACKELBERG and A. WOJCICKI, *Inorg. Chim. Acta* **44**, L63–L64 (1980).

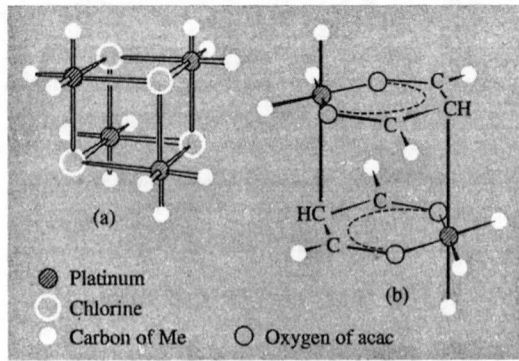

Platinum
Chlorine
Carbon of Me   Oxygen of acac

Figure 27.11 Schematic representation of the structures of compounds containing octahedrally coordinated Pt^{IV}:
(a) the tetramer, $[PtMe_3Cl]_4$, and
(b) the dimer, $[PtMe_3(acac)]_2$.

The stabilities of the $[ML_2R_2]$ phosphines increase from Ni^{II} to Pt^{II} and for Ni^{II} they are only isolable when R is an *o*-substituted aryl. Those of Pt^{II}, on the other hand, are amongst the most stable σ-bonded organo-transition metal compounds while those of Pd^{II} occupy an intermediate position.

Carbonyls (see p. 926)

On the basis of the 18-electron rule, the d^8s^2 configuration is expected to lead to carbonyls of formula $[M(CO)_4]$ and this is found for nickel. $[Ni(CO)_4]$, the first metal carbonyl to be discovered, is an extremely toxic, colourless liquid (mp $-19.3°$, bp $42.2°$) which is tetrahedral in the vapour and in the solid (Ni–C 184 pm, C–O 115 pm). Its importance in the Mond process for manufacturing nickel metal has already been mentioned as has the absence of stable analogues of Pd and Pt. It may be germane to add that the introduction of halides (which are σ-bonded) reverses the situation: $[NiX(CO)_3]^-$ (X = Cl, Br, I) are very unstable, the yellow $[Pd^{II}(CO)Cl_2]_n$ is somewhat less so, whereas the colourless $[Pt^{II}(CO)_2Cl_2]$ and $[PtX_3(CO)]^-$ are quite stable.

$[Ni(CO)_4]$ is readily oxidized by air and can be reduced by alkali metals in liquid ammonia or thf to yield a series of polynuclear carbonylate anion

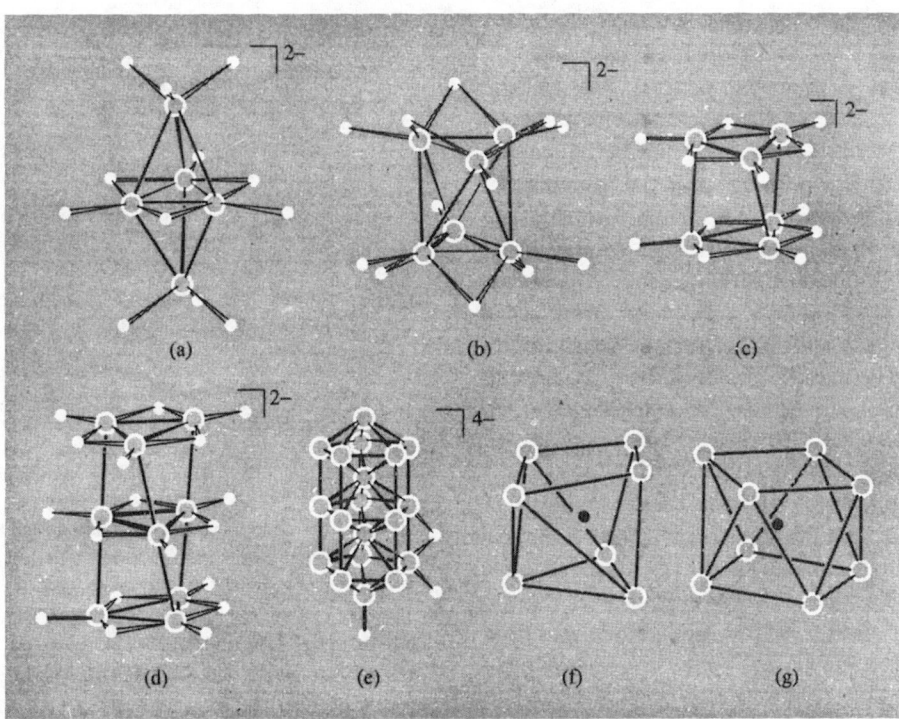

Figure 27.12   Some carbonylate anion clusters of nickel and platinum: (a) $[Ni_5(CO)_{12}]^{2-}$, (b) $[Ni_6(CO)_{12}]^{2-}$, (c) $[Pt_6(CO)_{12}]^{2-}$, (d) $[Pt_9(CO)_{18}]^{2-}$, (e) the Pt_{19} core of $[Pt_{19}(CO)_{22}]^{4-}$ showing one of the 10 bridging COs and 2 of the 12 terminal COs (which are attached to each of the 6 metal atoms at each end of the ion), (f) the Ni_7C core of $[Ni_7(CO)_{12}C]^{2-}$, (g) the Ni_8C core of $[Ni_8(CO)_{16}C]^{2-}$. Clusters (c) and (d) are structural motifs found in Ni clusters of nuclearities up to 34 and 38[35].

clusters but consisting mainly of $[Ni_5(CO_{12})]^{2-}$ and $[Ni_6(CO)_{12}]^{2-}$. The latter, being more stable and less toxic than the monomer, is a common starting material for the preparation of other clusters,[34] many of which are stabilized by encapsulated atoms of which carbon is especially efficacious. These clusters, which in general are intensely coloured and air-sensitive, have structures[35] based on the stacking of Ni_3 triangles and Ni_4 squares and, in carbon-centred clusters of higher nuclearities, based on Ni_7C and Ni_8C moieties (Fig. 27.12). Other clusters, derived from reactions of $[Ni_6(CO)_{12}]^{2-}$ and main group

reactants, have icosahedral frameworks[36] such as $Ni_{10}Se_2$, Ni_9Te_3 and $Ni_{10}Sb$. Some of these are centred with Ni, some centred with the main group element and others uncentred.

Reductions of $[PtCl_6]^{2-}$ in an atmosphere of CO provide a series of clusters, $[Pt_3(CO)_6]_n{}^{2-}$ ($n = 1-6, 10$) consisting of stacks of Pt_3 triangles in slightly twisted columns; $Pt-Pt = 266$ pm in triangles, $303-309$ pm between triangular planes (Fig. 27.12). A feature of these and other Pt clusters is that they mostly have electron counts lower than predicted by the usual electron counting rules. In the series just mentioned for instance, $n = 1$ and $n = 2$ have electron counts of 44 and 86 whereas 48 and 90 would

[34] J. K. BEATTIE, A. F. MASTERS and J. T. MEYER, *Polyhedron*, **14**, 829–68 (1995).

[35] A. F. MASTERS and J. T. MEYER, *Polyhedron* **14**, 339–65 (1995).

[36] A. J. KAHAIAN, J. B. THODEN and L. F. DAHL *J. Chem. Soc., Chem. Commun.*, 353–5 (1992).

be expected for a triangle and trigonal prism respectively. This is ascribed to the relatively large 6s–6p energy gap in this part of the periodic table and the consequently reduced involvement of p-orbitals in skeletal bonding. Heating salts of the $n = 3$ anion in acetonitrile under reflux produces $[Pt_{19}(CO)_{22}]^{4-}$ containing two encapsulated metal atoms (Fig. 27.12e). $[Pt_{26}(CO)_{32}]^{3-}$ and $[Pt_{38}(CO)_{44}H_x]^{2-}$, in which the metal atoms adopt a virtually cubic close packed arrangement, have also been characterized. In contrast to the Pt_6 cluster above, the brown-black $[Pt_6(CO)_6(\mu\text{-dppm})]^{2+}$ is the first octahedral platinum carbonyl cluster to be characterized. All its CO groups are terminal.[36a]

Palladium forms clusters of these types far less readily than nickel and platinum, unless they are stabilized by σ-donor ligands such as phosphines. This may be due to the lower energy of Pd–Pd bonds as reflected in the sublimation energies, 427, 354 and 565 kJ mol^{-1} for Ni, Pd and Pt.

Cyclopentadienyls

Nickelocene, $[Ni^{II}(\eta^5\text{-}C_5H_5)_2]$, is a bright green, reactive solid, conveniently prepared by adding a solution of $NiCl_2$ in dimethylsulfoxide to a solution of KC_5H_5 in 1,2-dimethoxyethane. It has the sandwich structure of ferrocene, and is similarly susceptible to ring-addition reactions, but its 2 extra electrons ($\mu_e = 2.86$ BM) must be accommodated in an antibonding orbital (p. 938). The orange-yellow, $[Ni(\eta^5\text{-}C_5H_5)_2]^+$, cation is therefore easily obtained by oxidation and the "triple-decker sandwich" cation, $[Ni_2(\eta^5\text{-}C_5H_5)_3]^+$ (Fig. 27.13), is produced by reacting nickelocene with a Lewis acid such as BF_3. This latter cation is a 34 valence electron species [i.e. $(2 \times 8) + (3 \times 6)$ for $2Ni^{II}$ and $3C_5H_5^-$] and there are theoretical grounds for supposing that this, and the 30-electron configuration, will offer the same sort of stability for binuclear sandwich compounds that the 18-electron configuration offers for mononuclear

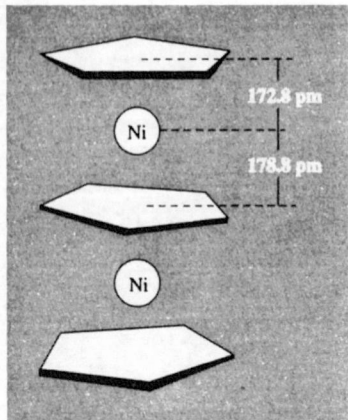

Figure 27.13 The "triple-decker sandwich" cation, $[Ni_2(\eta^5\text{-}C_5H_5)_3]^+$. Note that the C_5H_5 rings are neither "staggered" nor "eclipsed", and the nickel atoms are closer to the outer than to the central ring.

compounds. The cyclopentadienyls of palladium and platinum are less stable than those of nickel, and while the heavier pair of metals form some monocyclopentadienyl complexes, neither forms a metallocene.

Alkene and alkyne complexes [37]

These are important not only for their part in stimulating the development of bonding theory (for a fuller discussion, see p. 931) but also for their catalytic role in some important industrial processes.

Apart from some Pd^0 and Pt^0 biphosphine complexes, the alkene and alkyne complexes involve the metals in the formally divalent state. Those of Ni^{II} are few in number compared to those of Pd^{II}, but it is Pt^{II} which provides the most numerous and stable compounds of this type. These are of the forms $[PtCl_3Alk]^-$, $[PtCl_2Alk]_2$ and $[PtCl_2Alk_2]$. They are generally prepared by treating an M^{II} salt with the hydrocarbon when a less strongly bonded anion is displaced. Thus, Zeise's salt (p. 930) may be obtained by prolonged shaking of a solution of K_2PtCl_4 in

[36a] L. HAO, G. J. SPIVAK, J. XIAO, J. J. VITTAL and R. J. PUDDEPHATT *J. Am. Chem. Soc.* **117**, 7011–12 (1995).

[37] V. G. ALBANO, G. NATILE and A. PANUNZI, *Coord. Chem. Revs.* **133**, 67–114 (1994).

dil HCl with C_2H_4, though the reaction can be speeded-up by the addition of a small amount of $SnCl_2$. Treatment of an ethanolic solution of the product with conc HCl then affords the orange dimer, $[\{PtCl_2(C_2H_4)\}_2]$. If this is then dissolved in acetone at $-70°C$ and further treated with C_2H_4, yellow, unstable crystals of the *trans*-bis(ethene) are formed:

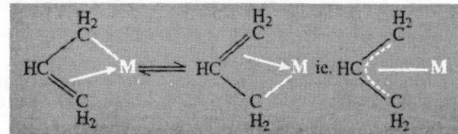

cis-Substituted dichloro complexes are obtained if chelating dialkenes such as *cis-cis*-cycloocta-1,5-diene (cod) are used (p. 932).

A common property of coordinated alkenes is their susceptibility to attack by nucleophiles such as OH^-, OMe^-, $MeCO_2^-$, and Cl^-, and it has long been known that Zeise's salt is slowly attacked by non-acidic water to give MeCHO and Pt metal, while corresponding Pd complexes are even more reactive.[38] This forms the basis of the Wacker process (developed by J. Smidt and his colleagues at Wacker Chemie, 1959–60) for converting ethene (ethylene) into ethanal (acetaldehyde) — see Panel overleaf.

Alkyne complexes are essentially similar to the alkenes (p. 932) and those of Pt^{II}, particularly when the alkyne incorporates the *t*-butyl group, are the most stable. Ni^{II} alkyne complexes are less numerous and generally less stable but are of greater practical importance because of their role as intermediates in the cyclic oligomerization of alkynes, discovered by W. Reppe (see Panel).

[38] A. HEUMANN, K.-J. JENS and M. REGLIER, *Prog. Inorg. Chem.* **42**, 483–576 (1994).

π-Allylic complexes

The preparation and bonding of complexes of the η^3-allyl group, $CH_2=CH-CH_2-$, have already been discussed (p. 933). This group, and substituted derivatives of it, may act as σ-bonded ligands, but it is as 3-electron π-donor ligands that they are most important. Crudely:

The π-allyl complexes of Pd^{II}, e.g. $[Pd(\eta^3\text{-}C_3H_5)X]_2$ (X = Cl, Br, I), are very stable and more numerous than for any other metal, and neither Ni nor Pt form as many of these complexes. Indeed, the contrast between Pd and Pt is such that in reactions with alkenes, where a particular compound of Pt is likely to form an alkene complex, the corresponding compound of Pd is more likely to form a π-allyl complex. The role of the Pd and Ni complexes as intermediates in the oligomerization of conjugated dienes (of which 1,3-butadiene, C_4H_6, is the most familiar) have been extensively studied, particularly by G. Wilke and his group. For instance in the presence of $[Ni(\eta^3\text{-}C_3H_5)_2]$ (or $[Ni(acac)_2]_3 + Al_2Et_6$), butadiene trimerizes, probably via the catalytic cycle:

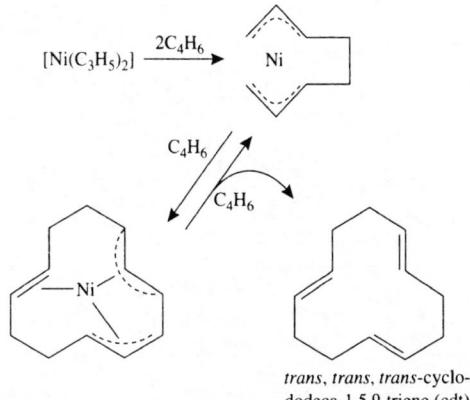

trans, trans, trans-cyclo-dodeca-1,5,9-triene (cdt)

Other isomers of cdt are also obtained and, if a coordination site on the nickel is blocked by the addition of a ligand such as a tertiary phosphine, dimerization of the butadiene, rather than trimerization, occurs.

Catalytic Applications of Alkene and Alkyne Complexes

The Wacker process

Ethanal is produced by the aerial oxidation of ethene in the presence of $PdCl_2/CuCl_2$ in aqueous solution. The main reaction is the oxidative hydrolysis of ethene:

$$C_2H_4 + PdCl_2 + H_2O \longrightarrow MeCHO + Pd\downarrow + 2HCl$$

The mechanism of this reaction is not straightforward but the crucial step appears to be nucleophilic attack by water or OH^- on the coordinated ethene to give σ-bonded —CH_2CH_2OH which then rearranges and is eventually eliminated as MeCHO with loss of a proton.

The commercial viability of the reaction depends on the formation of a catalytic cycle by reoxidizing the palladium metal *in situ*. This is achieved by the introduction of $CuCl_2$:

$$Pd + CuCl_2 \longrightarrow PdCl_2 + 2CuCl$$

Because the solution is slightly acidic, the $CuCl_2$ itself can be regenerated by passing in oxygen:

$$2CuCl + 2HCl + \tfrac{1}{2}O_2 \longrightarrow 2CuCl_2 + H_2O$$

The overall reaction is thus:

$$C_2H_4 + \tfrac{1}{2}O_2 \longrightarrow MeCHO$$

The Reppe Synthesis

Polymerization of alkynes by Ni^{II} complexes produces a variety of products which depend on conditions and especially on the particular nickel complex used. If, for instance, *O*-donor ligands such as acetylacetone or salicaldehyde are employed in a solvent such as tetrahydrofuran or dioxan, 4 coordination sites are available and cyclotetramerization occurs to give mainly cyclo-octatetraene (cot). If a less-labile ligand such as PPh_3 is incorporated, the coordination sites required for tetramerization are not available and cyclic trimerization to benzene predominates (Fig. A). These syntheses are amenable to extensive variation and adaptation. Substituted ring systems can be obtained from the appropriately substituted alkynes while linear polymers can also be produced.

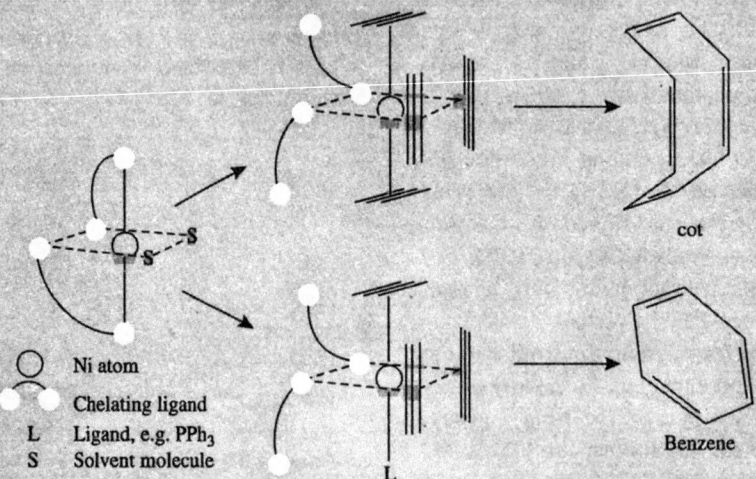

○	Ni atom
⊶	Chelating ligand
L	Ligand, e.g. PPh_3
S	Solvent molecule

Figure A   Cyclic oligomerizations of acetylene: tetramerization producing cyclooctatetraene (cot) and trimerization producing benzene.

28
Copper, Silver and Gold

28.1 Introduction[1]

Collectively known as the "coinage metals" because of their former usage, these elements were almost certainly the first three metals known to man. All of them occur in the elemental, or "native", form and must have been used as primitive money long before the introduction of gold coins in Egypt around 3400 BC.

Cold-hammering was used in the late Stone Age to produce plates of gold for ornamental purposes, and this metal has always been synonymous with beauty, wealth and power. Considerable quantities were accumulated by ancient peoples. The coffin of Tutankhamun (a minor Pharaoh who was only 18 when he died) contained no less than 112 kg of gold, and the legendary Aztec and Inca hoards in Mexico and Peru were a major reason for the Spanish conquests of Central and South America in the early sixteenth century. Today, the greatest hoard of gold is the 30 000 tonnes of bullion (i.e. bars) lying in the vaults of the US Federal Reserve Bank in New York and belonging to eighty different nations.

Estimates of the earliest use of copper vary, but 5000 BC is not unreasonable. By about 3500 BC it was being obtained in the Middle East by charcoal reduction of its ores, and by 3000 BC the advantages of adding tin in order to produce the harder bronze was appreciated in India, Mesopotamia and Greece. This established the "Bronze Age", and copper has continued to be one of man's most important metals.

The monetary use of silver may well be as old as that of gold but the abundance of the native metal was probably far less, so that comparable supplies were not available until a method of winning the metal from its ores had been discovered. It appears, however, that by perhaps 3000 BC a form of cupellation† was in operation in Asia Minor and its use gradually

---

† Cupellation processes vary but consist essentially of heating a mixture of precious and base (usually lead) metals in a stream of air in a shallow hearth, when the base metal is oxidized and removed either by blowing away or by absorption into the furnace lining. In the early production of silver, the sulfide ores must have been used to give first a silver/lead alloy from which the lead was then removed.

---

[1] R. F. TYLECOTE, *History of Metallurgy*, The Metals Society, London, 1976, 182 pp.

spread, so that silver coinage was of crucial economic importance to all subsequent classical Mediterranean civilizations.

The name *copper* and the symbol Cu are derived from *aes cyprium* (later Cuprum), since it was from Cyprus that the Romans first obtained their copper metal. The words *silver* and *gold* are Anglo-Saxon in origin but the chemical symbols for these elements (Ag and Au) are derived from the Latin *argentum* (itself derived from the Greek άργός, *argos*, shiny or white) and *aurum*, gold.

28.2 The Elements

28.2.1 Terrestrial abundance and distribution

The relative abundances of these three metals in the earth's crust (Cu 68 ppm, Ag 0.08 ppm, Au 0.004 pm) are comparable to those of the preceding triad — Ni, Pd and Pt. Copper is found mainly as the sulfide, oxide or carbonate, its major ores being copper pyrite (chalcopyrite), $CuFeS_2$, which is estimated to account for about 50% of all Cu deposits; copper glance (chalcocite), Cu_2S; cuprite, Cu_2O and malachite, $Cu_2CO_3(OH)_2$. Large deposits are found in various parts of North and South America, and in Africa and the former Soviet Union. The native copper found near Lake Superior is extremely pure but the vast majority of current supplies of copper are obtained from low-grade ores containing only about 1% Cu.

Silver is widely distributed in sulfide ores of which silver glance (argentite), Ag_2S, is the most important. Native silver is sometimes associated with these ores as a result of their chemical reduction, while the action of salt water is probably responsible for their conversion into "horn silver", AgCl, which is found in Chile and New South Wales. The Spanish Americas provided most of the world's silver for the three centuries after about 1520, to be succeeded in the nineteenth century by Russia. Appreciable quantities are now obtained as a byproduct in the production of other metals such as copper,

and the main producers are Mexico, the former Soviet Union, Peru, the USA and Australia.

Gold, too, is widely, if sparsely, distributed both native[†] and in tellurides, and is almost invariably associated with quartz or pyrite, both in veins and in alluvial or placer deposits laid down after the weathering of gold-bearing rocks. It is also present in sea water to the extent of around 1×10^{-3} ppm, depending on location, but no economical means of recovery has yet been devised. Prior to about 1830 a large proportion of the world's stock of gold was derived from ancient and South American civilizations (recycling is not a new idea), and the annual output of new gold was no more than 12 tonnes pa. This supply gradually increased with the discovery of gold in Siberia followed by "gold rushes" in 1849 (California: as a result of which the American West was settled), 1851 (New South Wales and Victoria: within 7 y the population of Australia doubled to 1 million), 1884 (Transvaal), 1896 (Klondike, North-west Canada) and, finally, 1900 (Nome area of Alaska) as a result of which by 1890 world production had risen to 150 tonnes pa. It is now 15 times that amount, ~2300 tonnes pa.

28.2.2 Preparation and uses of the elements[2,3]

A few of the oxide ores of copper can be reduced directly to the metal by heating with coke, but the bulk of production is from sulfide ores containing iron, and they require more complicated treatment. These ores are comparatively lean (often ~0.5% Cu) and their exploitation requires economies of scale. They are therefore obtained in huge, open-pit operations employing shovels

---

[†] The "Welcome Stranger" nugget found in Victoria, Australia, in 1869 weighed over 71 kg and yielded nearly 65 kg of refined gold but was, unfortunately, exceptional.

[2] *Kirk–Othmer Encyclopedia of Chemical Technology*, 4th edn., Interscience, New York; for Cu see Vol. 7, 1993, pp. 505–20; for Ag, Vol. 22, 1997, pp. 163–95; for Au, Vol. 12, 1994, pp. 738–67.

[3] J. MARSDEN and I. HOUSE, *The Chemistry of Gold Extraction*, Ellis Horwood, Chichester, 1992, 597 pp.

of up to $25 \, m^3$ (900 ft^3) and trucks of up to 250 tonnes capacity, followed by crushing and concentration (up to 15–20% Cu) by froth-flotation. (The environmentally acceptable disposal of the many millions of tonnes of finely ground waste poses serious problems.) Silica is added to the concentrate which is then heated in a reverberatory furnace (blast furnaces are unsuitable for finely powdered ores) to about 1400°C when it melts. FeS is more readily converted to the oxide than is Cu$_2$S and so, with the silica, forms an upper layer of iron silicate slag leaving a lower layer of copper matte which is largely Cu$_2$S and FeS. The liquid matte is then placed in a converter (similar to the Bessemer converter, p. 1072) with more silica and a blast of air forced through it. This transforms the remaining FeS first to FeO and then to slag, while the Cu$_2$S is partially converted to Cu$_2$O and then to metallic copper:

$$2FeS + 3O_2 \longrightarrow 2FeO + 2SO_2$$

$$2Cu_2S + 3O_2 \longrightarrow 2Cu_2O + 2SO_2$$

$$2Cu_2O + Cu_2S \longrightarrow 6Cu + SO_2$$

The major part of this "blister" copper is further purified electrolytically by casting into anodes which are suspended in acidified CuSO$_4$ solution along with cathodes of purified copper sheet. As electrolysis proceeds the pure copper is deposited on the cathodes while impurities collect below the anodes as "anode slime" which is a valuable source of Ag, Au and other precious metals.

About one-third of the copper used is secondary copper (i.e. scrap) but the annual production of new metal is nearly 8 million tonnes, the chief sources (1993) being Chile (22%), the USA (20%), the former Soviet Union (9%), Canada and China (7.5% each) and Zambia (5%). The major use is as an electrical conductor but it is also widely employed in coinage alloys as well as the traditional bronze (Cu plus 7–10% Sn), brass (Cu–Zn), and special alloys such as *Monel* (Ni–Cu).

Most silver is nowadays produced as a byproduct in the manufacture of non-ferrous metals such as copper, lead and zinc, when the silver follows the base metal through the concentration and smelting processes. In the case of copper production, for instance, the anode slimes mentioned above are treated with hot, aerated dilute H$_2$SO$_4$, which dissolves some of the base metal content, then heated with a flux of lime or silica to slag-off most of the remaining base metals, and, finally, electrolysed in nitrate solution to give silver of better than 99.9% purity. As with copper, much of the metal used is salvage but over 10 000 tonnes of new metal were produced in 1993, mainly from Mexico (19%) the former Soviet Union, the USA and Peru (~13% each) and Australia (9%). Photography accounts for the use of about one-third of this and it is also used in silverware and jewellery, electrically, for silvering mirrors, and in the high-capacity Ag–Zn, Ag–Cd batteries. A minor though important use from 1826 until recent times was as dental amalgam (Hg/γ–Ag$_3$Sn).

Traditionally, gold was recovered from river sands by methods such as "panning" which depend on the high density of gold (19.3 g cm^{-3}) compared with sand (~2.5 g cm^{-3})[†] but as such sources are largely worked out, modern production depends on the mining of the gold-containing rock (typically, 5–15 ppm of Au). This is crushed to a fine powder (the consistency of talcum powder) to liberate the metallic grains and these are extracted either by the cyanide process or, after gravity concentration, by amalgamation with mercury (after which the Hg is distilled off). In the former the gold and any silver present is leached from the crushed rock with an aerated, dilute solution of cyanide:

$$4Au + 8NaCN + O_2 + 2H_2O \longrightarrow 4Na[Au(CN)_2]$$
$$+ 4NaOH$$

It is then precipitated by adding Zn dust. Electrolytic refining may then be used to provide gold of 99.99% purity.[‡]

[†] In ancient times, gold-bearing river sands were washed over a sheep's fleece which trapped the gold. It seems likely that this was the origin of the Golden Fleece of Greek mythology.

[‡] Gold is commonly alloyed with other metals in order to make it harder and cheaper. (An appropriate mixture of Au

Table 28.1   Some properties of the elements copper, silver and gold

Property		Cu	Ag	Au
Atomic number		29	47	79
Number of naturally occurring isotopes		2	2	1
Atomic weight		63.546(3)	107.8682(2)	196.96655(2)
Electronic configuration		[Ar]$3d^{10}4s^1$	[Kr]$4d^{10}5s^1$	[Xe]$4f^{14}5d^{10}6s^1$
Electronegativity		1.9	1.9	2.4
Metal radius (12-coordinate)/pm		128	144	144
Effective ionic radius (6-coordinate)/pm	V	—	—	57
	III	54	75	85
	II	73	94	—
	I	77	115	137
Ionization energy/kJ mol^{-1}	1st	745.3	730.8	889.9
	2nd	1957.3	2072.6	1973.3
	3rd	3577.6	3359.4	(2895)
MP/°C		1083	961	1064
BP/°C		2570	2155	2808
ΔH_{fus}/kJ mol^{-1}		13.0	11.1	12.8
ΔH_{vap}/kJ mol^{-1}		307($\pm$6)	258($\pm$6)	343($\pm$11)
$\Delta H_{(monatomic\ gas)}$/kJ mol^{-1}		337($\pm$6)	284($\pm$4)	379($\pm$8)
Density (20°C)/g cm^{-3}		8.95	10.49	19.32
Electrical resistivity (20°C)/μohm cm		1.673	1.59	2.35

Total annual production of new gold is now about 2300 tonnes of which (1993) 27% comes from South Africa, 15% from the USA and 11% each from Australia and the former Soviet Union. The bulk of the gold from "Western" countries passes through the London Bullion Market which was established in 1666. Prices, which are quoted in troy oz,[†] are affected by speculative buying and can be subject to astonishing fluctuations.

The two main uses for gold are in settling international debts and in the manufacture of jewellery, but other important uses are in dentistry, the electronics industry (corrosion-free contacts), and the aerospace industry (brazing alloys and heat reflection), while in office buildings it has

been found that a mere 20 nm film on the inside face of windows cuts down heat losses in winter and reflects unwanted infrared radiation in summer.

28.2.3 Atomic and physical properties of the elements

Some important properties are listed in Table 28.1. As gold has only one naturally occurring isotope, its atomic weight is known with considerable accuracy; Cu and Ag each have 2 stable isotopes, and a slight variability of their abundance in the case of Cu prevents its atomic weight being quoted with greater precision. This is the first triad since Ti, Zr and Hf in which the ground-state electronic configuration of the free atoms is the same for the outer electrons of all three elements. Gold is the most electronegative of all metals: the value of 2.4 equals that for Se and approaches the value of 2.5 for S and I. Estimates of electron affinity vary considerably but typical values (kJ mol^{-1}) are Cu 119.2, Ag 125.6 and Au 222.8. These may be compared with values for

and Cu will maintain the golden hue.) The proportion of gold is expressed in *carats*, a *carat* being a twenty-fourth part by weight of the metal so that pure gold is 24 *carats*. In the case of precious stones the *carat* expresses mass not purity and is then defined as 200 mg. The term is derived from the name of the small and very uniform seeds of the carob tree which in antiquity were used to weigh precious metals and stones (p. 272).

[†] 1 troy (or fine) oz = 31.1035 g as distinct from 1 oz avoirdupois = 28.3495 g.

H 72.8, O 141.0 and I 295.2 kJ mol^{-1}. Consistent with this the compound CsAu has many salt-like rather than alloy-like properties and, when fused, behaves much like other molten salts. Similarly when Au is dissolved in solutions of Cs, Rb or K in liquid ammonia, the spectroscopic and other properties are best interpreted in terms of the solvated Au$^-$ ion (d^{10}s^2) analogous to a halide ion (s^{2}p^6).

The elements are obtainable in a state of very high purity but some of their physical properties are nonetheless variable because of their dependence on mechanical history. Their colours (Cu reddish, Ag white and Au yellow) and sheen are so characteristic that the names of the metals are used to describe them.† Gold can also be obtained in red, blue and violet colloidal forms by the addition of various reducing agents to very dilute aqueous solutions of gold(III) chloride. A remarkably stable example is the "Purple of Cassius", obtained by using SnCl$_2$ as reductant, which not only provides a sensitive test for Au^{III} but is also used to colour glass and ceramics. Colloidal silver and copper are also obtainable but are less stable.

The solid metals all have the fcc structure, like their predecessors in the periodic table, Ni, Pd and Pt, and they continue the trend of diminishing mp and bp. They are soft, and extremely malleable and ductile, gold more so than any other metal. One gram of gold can be beaten out into a sheet of ~1.0 m^2 only 230 atoms thick (i.e. 1 cm^3 to 18 m^2); likewise 1 g Au can be drawn into 165 m of wire of diameter 20 μm. The electrical and thermal conductances of the

---

† The colours arise from the presence of filled d bands near the electron energy surface of the s–p conduction band of the metals (Fermi surface). X-ray data indicate that the top of the d-band is ~220 kJ mol^{-1} (2.3 eV/atom) below the Fermi surface for Cu so electrons can be excited from the d band to the s–p band by absorption of energy in the green and blue regions of the visible spectrum but not in the orange or red regions. For silver the excitation energy is rather larger (~385 kJ mol^{-1}) corresponding to absorption in the ultraviolet region of the spectrum. Gold is intermediate but much closer to Cu, the absorption in the near ultraviolet and blue region of the spectrum giving rise to the characteristic golden yellow colour of the metal.

three metals are also exceptional, pre-eminence in this case belonging to silver. All these properties can be directly related to the d^{10}s^1 electronic configuration.

28.2.4 Chemical reactivity and trends

Because of the traditional designation of Cu, Ag and Au as a subdivision of the group containing the alkali metals (justified by their respective d^{10}s^1 and p^{6}s^1 electron configurations) some similarities in properties might be expected. Such similarities as do occur, however, are confined almost entirely to the stoichiometries (as distinct from the chemical properties) of the compounds of the +1 oxidation state. The reasons are not hard to find. A filled d shell is far less effective than a filled p shell in shielding an outer s electron from the attraction of the nucleus. As a result the first ionization energies of the coinage metals are much higher, and their ionic radii smaller than those of the corresponding alkali metals (Table 28.1 and p. 75). They consequently have higher mps, are harder, denser, less reactive, less soluble in liquid ammonia, and their compounds more covalent. Again, whereas the alkali metals stand at the top of the electrochemical series (with $E°$ between −3.045 and −2.714 V), the coinage metals are near the bottom: Cu$^+$/Cu +0.521, Ag$^+$/Ag + 0.799, Au$^+$/Au + 1.691 V. On the other hand, a filled d shell is more easily disrupted than a filled p shell. The second and third ionization energies of the coinage metals are therefore *lower* than those of the alkali metals so that they are able to adopt oxidation states higher than +1. They also more readily form coordination complexes. In short, Cu, Ag and Au are transition metals whereas the alkali metals are not. Indeed, the somewhat salt-like character of CsAu and the formation of the solvated Au$^-$ ion in liquid ammonia, mentioned above, can be regarded as halogen-like behaviour arising because the d^{10}s^1 configuration is 1 electron short of the closed configuration d^{10}s^2 (cf hydrogen, p. 43).

Copper, silver and gold are notable in forming an extensive series of alloys with many other metals and many of these have played an important part in the development of technology through the ages (p. 1173). In many cases the alloys can be thought of as nonstoichiometric intermetallic compounds of definite structural types and, despite the apparently bizarre formulae that emerge from the succession of phases, they can readily be classified by a set of rules first outlined by W. Hume-Rothery in 1926. The determining feature is the ratio of the number of electrons to the number of atoms ("electron concentration"), and because of this the phases are sometimes referred to as "electron compounds".

The fcc lattice of the coinage metals has 1 valency electron per atom ($d^{10}s^1$). Admixture with metals further to the right of the periodic table (e.g. Zn) increases the electron concentration in the primary alloy (α-phase) which can be described as an fcc solid solution

of M in Cu, Ag or Au. This continues until, as the electron concentration approaches 1.5 (i.e. 21/14), the fcc structure becomes less stable than a bcc arrangement which therefore crystallizes as the β-phase (e.g. β-brass, CuZn; see Fig. 28.1). Further increase in electron concentration results in formation of the more complex γ-brass phase of nominal formula Cu_5Zn_8 and electron concentration of $\{(5 \times 1) + (8 \times 2)\}/13 = 21/13 = 1.615$. The phase is still cubic but has 52 atoms in the unit cell (i.e. $4Cu_5Zn_8$). This γ-phase can itself take up more Zn until a third critical concentration is reached near 1.75 (i.e. 7/4 or 21/12) when the hcp ε-phase of $CuZn_3$ is formed. Hume-Rothery showed that this succession of phases is quite general (and also holds for Groups 8, 9 and 10 to the left of the coinage metals if they are taken to contribute no electrons to the lattice).

The reactivity of Cu, Ag and Au decreases down the group, and in its inertness gold

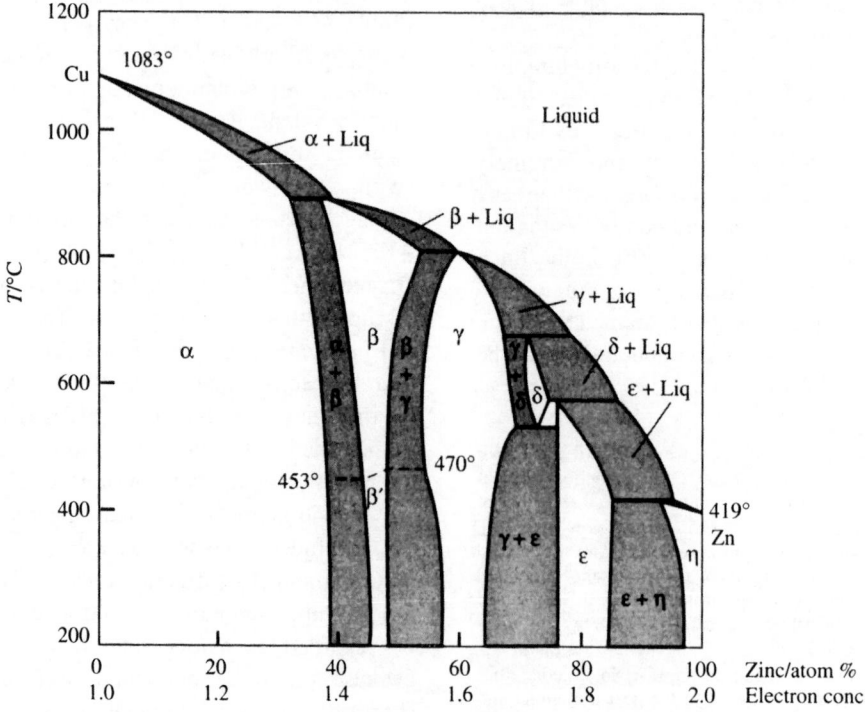

Figure 28.1 Phase diagram of the system Cu/Zn.

Table 28.2 Oxidation states and stereochemistries of copper, silver and gold

Oxidation state	Coordination number	Stereochemistry	Cu	Ag/Au
−1 ($d^{10}s^2$)	?	?		$[Au(NH_3)_n]^-$ (liq NH_3)
0 ($d^{10}s^1$)	3	Planar	$[Cu(CO)_3]$ (10 K)	$[Ag(CO)_3]$ (10 K)
	4	—	$[(CO)_3CuCu(CO)_3]$ (30 K)	$[(CO)_3AgAg(CO)_3]$ (30 K)
< +1	8	See Fig. 28.10(a)		$[(Ph_3P)Au\{Au(PPh_3)\}_7]^{2+}$
	10	See Fig. 28.10(c)		$[Au_{11}I_3\{P(C_6H_4\text{-}4\text{-}F)_3\}_7]$
	12	Icosahedral		$[Au_{13}Cl_{12}(PMe_2Ph)_{10}]^{3+}$
1 (d^{10})	2	Linear	$[CuCl_2]^-$, Cu_2O	$[M(CN)_2]^-$
	3	Trigonal planar	$[Cu(CN)_3]^{2-}$	$[AgI(PEt_2Ar)_2]$, $[AuCl(PPh_3)_2]$
	4	Tetrahedral	$[Cu(py)_4]^+$	$[M(diars)_2]^+$, $[Au(PMePh_2)_4]^+$
		Square planar		$[Au\{\eta^2\text{-}Os_3(CO)_{10}H\}_2]^-$
	6	Octahedral		AgX (X = F, Cl, Br)
2 (d^9)	4	Tetrahedral	$Cs_2[CuCl_4]^{(a)}$	
		Square planar	$[EtNH_3]_2[CuCl_4]^{(a)}$	$[Ag(py)_4]^{2+}$ $[Au\{S_2C_2(CN)_2\}_2]^{2-}$
	5	Trigonal bipyramidal	$[Cu(bipy)_2I]^+$	
		Square pyramidal	$[\{Cu(dmgH)_2\}_2]^{(b)}$	
	6	Octahedral	$K_2Pb[Cu(NO_2)_6]$	
	7	Pentagonal bipyramidal	$[Cu(H_2O)_2(dps)]^{2+(c)}$	
	8	Dodecahedral (dist.)	$[Cu(O_2CMe)_4]^{2+}$	
3 (d^8)	4	Square planar	$[CuBr_2(S_2CNBu^i_2)]$	$[AgF_4]^-$, $[AuBr_4]^-$
	5	Square pyramidal	$[CuCl(PhCO_2)_2(py)_2]^{(d)}$	$[Au(C_6H_4CH_2NMe_2\text{-}2)\text{-}$ $(phen)(PPh_3)]^{2+}$
	6	Octahedral	$[CuF_6]^{3-}$	$[AgF_6]^{3-}$, $[AuI_2(diars)_2]^+$
4 (d^7)	6	?	$[CuF_6]^{2-}$	
5 (d^6)	6	Octahedral (?)		$[AuF_6]^-$

(a)See text, p. 1193. (b)$dmgH_2$ = dimethylglyoxime: see also Fig. 28.6
(c)dps = 2,6-diacetylpyridine bissemicarbazone (d)G. SPEIER and V. FÜLÖP *J. Chem. Soc., Chem. Commun.*, 905–6 (1990).

resembles the platinum metals. All three metals are stable in pure dry air at room temperature but copper forms Cu_2O at red heat.† Copper is also attacked by sulfur and halogens, and the sensitivity of silver to sulfur and its compounds is responsible for the familiar tarnishing of the metal (black AgS) when exposed to air containing such substances. Under similar circumstances copper forms a green coating of a basic sulfate. In sharp contrast, gold is the only metal which will not react directly with sulfur. In general the reactions of the metals are assisted by the presence of oxidizing agents. Thus, in the absence of air, non-oxidizing acids have little effect, but

Cu and Ag dissolve in hot conc H_2SO_4 and in both dil and conc HNO_3, while Au dissolves in conc HCl if a strong oxidizing agent is present. Thus *aqua regia*, a 3:1 mixture of conc HCl and conc HNO_3, was so named by alchemists because it dissolves gold, the king of metals. More recently, solutions of Cl_2 and Me_3NHCl in MeCN have been shown[4] to be even better solvents of gold. In addition, the metals dissolve readily in aqueous cyanide solutions in the presence of air or, better still, H_2O_2.

Table 28.2 is a list of typical compounds of the elements, which reveals a further reduction in the range of oxidation states consequent on the stabilization of d orbitals at the end of the transition

---

† It was because of their resistance to attack by air, even when heated, that gold and silver were referred to as *noble* metals by the alchemists.

---

4 Y. NAKAO, *J. Chem. Soc., Chem. Commun.*, 426–7 (1992).

series. Apart from a single Cu^{IV} fluoro-complex and possibly one or two Cu^{IV} oxo-species, neither Cu nor Ag is known to exceed the oxidation state +3 and even Au does so only in a few Au^{V} fluoro-compounds (see below): these may owe their existence at least in part to the stabilizing effect of the t_{2g}^6 configuration. It is also significant that, in a number of instances, the +1 oxidation state no longer requires the presence of presumed π-acceptor ligands even though the M^I metals are to be regarded mainly as class b in character. Stable, zero-valent compounds are not found, but a number of cluster compounds with the metal in a fractional (<1) oxidation state, especially of gold, are of interest. The only aquo ions of this group are those of Cu^I (unstable), Cu^{II}, Ag^I and Ag^{II} (unstable). The best-known oxidation states, particularly in aqueous solution, are +2 for Cu, +1 for Ag, and +3 for Au. This accords with their ionization energies (Table 28.1) though, of course, few of the compounds are completely ionic. Silver has the lowest first ionization energy, while the sum of first and second is lowest for Cu and the sum of first, second, and third is lowest for Au. This is an erratic sequence and illustrates the most notable feature of the triad from a chemical point of view, namely that the elements are not well related either as three elements showing a monotonic gradation in properties or as a triad comprising a single lighter element together with a pair of closely similar heavier elements. "Horizontal" similarities with their neighbours in the periodic table are in fact more noticeable than "vertical" ones.

The reasons are by no means certain but no doubt involve several factors, of which size is probably a major one. Thus the Cu^{II} ion is smaller than Cu^I and, having twice the charge, interacts much more strongly with solvent water (heats of hydration are -2100 and $-580\,kJ\,mol^{-1}$ respectively). The difference is evidently sufficient to outweigh the second ionization energy of copper and to render Cu^{II} more stable in aqueous solution (and in ionic solids) than Cu^I, in spite of the stable d^{10} configuration of the latter. In the case of silver, however, the ionic radii are both much larger and

so the difference in hydration energies will be much smaller; in addition the second ionization energy is even greater than for copper. The +1 ion with its d^{10} configuration is therefore the more stable. For gold, the stability of the 6s orbital and instability of the 5d as compared to silver, and leading respectively to the possibility of Au^- and enhanced stability of Au^{III}, have been convincingly ascribed to relativistic effects operating on s and p electrons.[5] The high CFSE associated with square planar d^8 ions (see p. 1131) is a further factor favouring the +3 oxidation state.

Coordination numbers in this triad are again rarely higher than 6, but the univalent metals provide examples of the coordination number 2 which tends to be uncommon in transition metals proper (i.e. excluding Zn, Cd and Hg).

Organometallic chemistry (see p. 1199) is not particularly extensive even though gold alkyls were amongst the first organo-transition metal compounds to be prepared. Those of Au^{III} are the most stable in this group, while Cu^I and Ag^I (but not Au^I) form complexes, of lower stability, with unsaturated hydrocarbons.

28.3 Compounds of Copper, Silver and Gold

Binary carbides, M_2C_2 (i.e. acetylides), are obtained by passing C_2H_2 through ammoniacal solutions of Cu^+ and Ag^+. Both are explosive when dry but regenerate acetylene if treated with a dilute acid. Copper and silver also form explosive azides while the even more dangerous "fulminating" silver and gold, which probably contain M_3N, are produced by the action of aqueous ammonia on the metal oxides. None of the metals reacts significantly with H_2 but the reddish-brown precipitate, obtained when aqueous $CuSO_4$ is reduced by hypophosphorous acid (H_3PO_2), is largely CuH.

[5] P. Pyykkö and J.-P. Desclaux, *Acc. Chem. Res.* **12**, 276-81 (1979).

28.3.1 Oxides and sulfides [6]

Two oxides of copper, Cu_2O (yellow or red) and CuO (black), are known, both with narrow ranges of homogeneity and both form when the metal is heated in air or O_2, Cu_2O being favoured by high temperatures. Cu_2O (mp 1230°) is conveniently prepared by the reduction in alkaline solution of a Cu^{II} salt using hydrazine or a sugar.[†] CuO is best obtained by igniting the nitrate or basic carbonate of Cu^{II}. Addition of alkali to aqueous solutions of Cu^{II} gives a pale-blue precipitate of $Cu(OH)_2$. This will redissolve in acids and also in conc alkali (amphoteric) to give deep-blue solutions probably containing species of the type $[Cu(OH)_4]^{2-}$.

The lower affinities of silver and gold for oxygen lead to oxides of lower thermal stabilities than those of copper. Ag_2O is a dark-brown precipitate produced by adding alkali to a soluble Ag^I salt; AgOH is probably present in solution but not in the solid. It is readily reduced to the metal, and decomposes to the elements if heated above 160°C. The action of the vigorous oxidizing agent, $S_2O_8^{2-}$, on Ag_2O or other Ag^I compounds, produces a black oxide of stoichiometry AgO. That this is not a compound of Ag^{II} is, however, evidenced by its diamagnetism and by diffraction studies which show it to contain two types of silver ion, one with 2 colinear oxygen neighbours (Ag^I–O 218 pm) and the other with square-planar coordination (Ag^{III}–O 205 pm). It is therefore formulated as $Ag^I Ag^{III} O_2$. Anodic oxidation of silver salts yields two further black oxides, Ag_2O_3 (Ag^{III}–O = 202 pm) and, at lower potentials, Ag_3O_4. In both of these the silver atoms are in a square planar oxygen environment. It is tempting to formulate Ag_3O_4 as $Ag^{II} Ag_2^{III} O_4$ but the average Ag–O distances of 203 pm and 207 pm respectively are the wrong way round for this and instead imply non-integral oxidation states with the lower charge on the pair of silver atoms.[7] Hydrothermal treatment of AgO in a silver tube at 80°C and 4 kbar leads to an oxide which was originally (1963) incorrectly designated as $Ag_2O(II)$. The compound has a metallic conductivity and the stoichiometry is, in fact, Ag_3O; it can be described as an anti-BiI_3 structure (p. 559) in which oxide ions fill two-thirds of the octahedral sites in a hcp arrangement of Ag atoms (Ag-O 229 pm; Ag-Ag 276, 286, and 299 pm.

The action of alkali on aqueous Au^{III} solutions produces a precipitate, probably of $Au_2O_3.xH_2O$, which on dehydration yields brown Au_2O_3. This is the only confirmed oxide of gold. It decomposes if heated above about 160°C and, when hydrous, is weakly acidic, dissolving in conc alkali and probably forming salts of the $[Au(OH)_4]^-$ ion.

The sulfides are all black, or nearly so, and those with the metal in the +1 oxidation state are the more stable (p. 1174). Cu_2S (mp 1130°) is formed when copper is heated strongly in sulfur vapour or H_2S, and CuS is formed as a colloidal precipitate when H_2S is passed through aqueous solutions of Cu^{2+}. CuS, however, is not a simple copper(II) compounds since it contains the S_2 unit and is better formulated as $Cu_2^I Cu^{II} (S_2)S$. Ag_2S is very readily formed from the elements or by the action of H_2S on the metal or on aqueous Ag^I. The action of H_2S on aqueous Au^I precipitates Au_2S whereas passing H_2S through cold solutions of $AuCl_3$ in dry ether yield Au_2S_3, which is rapidly reduced to Au^I or the metal on addition of water. The relationships between the crystal structures of the oxides and sulfides of Cu, Ag and Au and the binding energies of the metals' d and p valence orbitals have been reviewed.[7a]

The selenides and tellurides of the coinage metals are all metallic and some, such as $CuSe_2$, $CuTe_2$, $AgTe_{\sim3}$ and Au_3Te_5 are superconductors at low temperature (as also are CuS and CuS_2).

6 T. P. DIRKSE, *Copper, Silver, Gold and Zinc, Cadmium, Mercury Oxides and Hydroxides*, Pergamon, Oxford, 1986, 380 pp.

† This is the basis of the very sensitive Fehling's test for sugars and other reducing agents. A solution of a copper(II) salt dissolved in alkaline tartrate solution is added to the substance in question. If this is a reducing agent then a characteristic red precipitate is produced.

7 B. STANDKE and M. JANSEN, *Angew. Chem. Int. Edn. Engl.* **25**, 77–8 (1986).

7a J. A. TOSSELL and D. J. VAUGHAN, *Inorg. Chem.* **20**, 3333–40 (1981).

Other phases are CuSe, CuTe; Cu_3Se_2, Cu_3Te_2; AgSe, AgTe; Ag_2Se_3, $AgSe_2$; Ag_5Te_3; Au_2Te_3 and $AuTe_2$. Most of these are nonstoichiometric.

28.3.2 High temperature superconductors [8-10]

Without doubt the main focus of interest in the field of copper oxide chemistry has, for the past decade, been on the production of high temperature superconductors of which $YBa_2Cu_3O_7$ is the most familiar (see Panel). Like all "cuprate superconductors", it is an oxygen deficient perovskite (if it were an "ideal" perovskite its six metal atoms would require the composition $YBa_2Cu_3O_9$. This massive oxygen deficiency results in a layered structure instead of the conventional 3-dimensional array — see p. 963). As shown in Fig. 28.2, the coordination of oxygen around copper is of two types, square planar for Cu(1) and square pyramidal for Cu(2). Due to the disparate effects of the large Ba^{2+} and the smaller more highly charged Y^{3+}, the Cu(2) are not situated at the centre of the square pyramid but only 30 pm above its base. They therefore lie in "puckered" or "dimpled" CuO_2 planes connected by the apical oxygens to chains of square planar Cu(1).

Esr results indicate that both Cu(1) and Cu(2) sites have a mixture of Cu^{2+} and Cu^{3+} ions. It is generally believed that superconduction occurs via positive holes in the conduction band of the CuO_2 planes and that the concentration of these holes is controlled, through the apical oxygens, by the non-conducting chains of Cu(1) which act as reservoirs of positive and negative charge. X-ray photoelectron spectroscopy shows that the conduction band has both copper (3d) and oxygen (2p) character, presumably as a result of π

[8] C. N. R. RAO (Ed.), *Chemistry of High Temperature Superconductors*, World Scientific, Singapore, 1991, 520 pp.

[9] J. T. S. IRVINE, Superconducting Materials, Chap. 11, pp. 275–301 in D. THOMPSON (ed.), *Insights into Speciality Inorganic Chemicals*, R.S.C., Cambridge, 1995.

[10] A series of articles on Superconductivity, *Chem. in Brit.* **30**, 722–48 (1994).

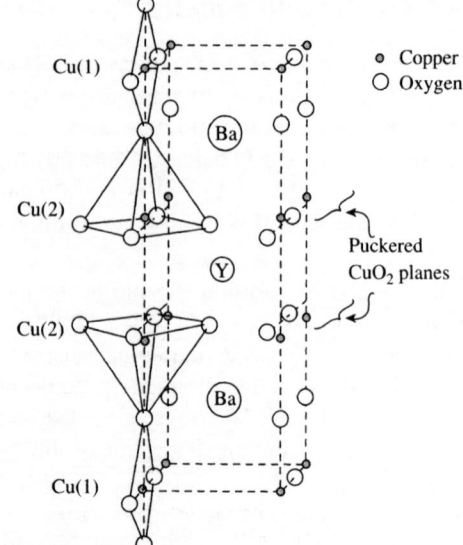

Figure 28.2 Structure of $YBa_2Cu_3O_7$.

interactions which would be at a maximum in the linear O–Cu–O bonds of perfect CuO_2 planes. The extent of puckering of these planes, as well as the nature and composition of the charge reservoirs, are evidently crucial factors affecting the value of T_c. To obtain a proper understanding of these factors Y and Ba have been replaced by a range of other elements producing compounds with up to seven different elements as in $Tl_{0.5}Pb_{0.5}Sr_2Ca_{1-x}Y_xCu_2O_7$. $La_{2-x}M_xCuO_4$ (M = Sr, Ba) and $HgBa_2Ca_2Cu_3O_{8+\delta}$ are other examples where the oxidation state of Cu > (II) and superconductivity occurs via positive holes, whereas in $Nd_{2-x}Ce_xCuO_4$, a so-called "electron superconductor", the oxidation state of Cu < (II) and excess electrons are the charge carriers. In each case, however, the path for conduction is provided by a CuO_2 plane.

The properties of these brittle ceramics depend critically on the preparative conditions. Intimate mixtures of the oxides, carbonates or nitrates of the relevant metals in the required proportions are heated at temperatures of 900–1000°C. For $YBa_2Cu_3O_{7-x}$, all compositions in the range $0 \leq x \leq 0.5$ superconduct and the highest T_c is found where $x \sim 0$. For others, the oxygen content must be stringently controlled. In all cases, the most

Superconductivity

H. Kammerling Onnes (Nobel Prize for Physics, 1913) discovered superconductivity in Leiden in 1911 when he cooled mercury to the temperature of liquid helium. Many other materials, mostly metals and alloys, were subsequently found to display superconductivity at very low temperatures.
Two properties characterize a superconductor:

1. It is perfectly conducting, i.e. it has zero resistance.
2. It is perfectly diamagnetic, i.e. it completely excludes applied magnetic fields. This is the Meissner effect and is the reason why a superconductor can levitate a magnet.

Superconductivity exists within the boundaries of three limiting parameters which must not be exceeded: the critical temperature (T_c), the critical magnetic field (H_c) and the critical current density (J_c).
Until 1986 the highest recorded value of T_c was ~23 K for Nb_3Ge but in that year Bednorz and Müller, in pioneering work for which they received the 1987 Nobel Prize for Physics, reported[11] $T_c = 30$ K in an entirely new Ba–La–Cu–O ceramic system quickly identified as $La_{2-x}Ba_xCuO_4$. This prompted an examination of other Cu–O systems and the technologically important breakthrough in 1987 by the Houston and Alabama teams of C. W. Chu and M. K. Wu, of superconductivity at temperatures attainable in liquid nitrogen.[12] $T_c = 95$ K in a material subsequently shown to be $YBa_2Cu_3O_7$, "YBCO". This, and other materials in which Y is replaced by a lanthanide, are referred to as "1,2,3" materials because of their stoichiometry. This produced a quite unprecedented explosion of activity amongst chemists, physicists and material scientists around the world. Though the highest T_c has been pushed up to 135 K (or 164 K under 350 kbar pressure) in $HgBa_2Ca_2Cu_3O_8$, YBCO is still the archetypal high temperature superconductor.
In spite of its long history, it was not until 1957 that Bardeen, Cooper and Schrieffer[13] provided a satisfactory explanation of superconductivity. This "BSC theory" suggests that pairs of electrons (Cooper pairs) move together through the lattice, the first electron polarizing the lattice in such a way that the second one can more easily follow it. The stronger the interaction of the two electrons the higher T_c, but it turns out as a consequence of this model that T_c should have an upper limit ~35 K. The advent of high-temperature superconductors therefore necessitated a new, or at least modified, explanation for the pairing mechanism. Various suggestions have been made but none has yet gained universal acceptance.

homogeneous products with the best grain alignment and the highest current density J_c, require the most careful control of sintering temperature, annealing and quenching rates. The major problems preventing large-scale practical applications therefore lie in the field of material processing. At present thin films of "YBCO" (see Panel), obtained for instance by its deposition on metal coated with ZrO_2 to provide flexible tapes, appear to offer the most promising way forward.

28.3.3 Halides

Table 28.3 is a list of the known halides: only gold forms a pentahalide and trihalides and, with

[11] J. G. BEDNORZ and K. A. MÜLLER, *Z. Phys. B* **64**, 189–93 (1986).
[12] M. K. WU, J. R. ASHBURN, C. J. TORNG, P. H. HOR, R. L. MENG, L. GAO, Z. J. HUANG, Y. Q. WANG and C. W. CHU, *Phys. Rev. Lett.* **58**, 908–10 (1987).
[13] J. BARDEEN, L. N. COOPER and J. R. SCHRIEFFER, *Phys. Rev.* **106**, 162–4 (1957).

the exception of AgF_2, only copper (as yet) forms dihalides.

AuF_5 is an unstable, polymeric, diamagnetic, dark-red powder, produced by heating $[O_2][AuF_6]$ under reduced pressure and condensing the product on to a "cold finger":

$$Au + O_2 + 3F_2 \xrightarrow[8\ atm]{370°} O_2AuF_6 \xrightarrow[(hot/cold)]{180°/20°}$$
$$AuF_5 + O_2 + \tfrac{1}{2}F_2$$

The compound tends to dissociate into AuF_3 and, when treated with XeF_2 in anhydrous HF solution below room temperature, yields yellow-orange crystals of the complex $[Xe_2F_3][AuF_6]$:

$$AuF_5 + 2XeF_2 \xrightarrow{HF/0°} [Xe_2F_3][AuF_6] \xrightarrow{>60°}$$
$$AuF_3 + XeF_2 + XeF_4$$

Again, in the +3 oxidation state, only gold is known to form binary halides, though AuI_3 has not been isolated. The chloride and the

Table 28.3   Halides of copper, silver and gold (mp/°C)

Oxidation state	Fluorides	Chlorides	Bromides	Iodides
+5	AuF_5 red (d > 60°)			
+3	AuF_3 orange-yellow (subl 300°)	$AuCl_3$ red (d > 160°)	$AuBr_3$ red-brown	
+2	CuF_2 white (785°) AgF_2 brown (690°)	$CuCl_2$ yellow-brown (630°)	$CuBr_2$ black (498°)	
+1	— AgF yellow (435°) —	$CuCl$ white (422°) $AgCl$ white (455°) $AuCl$ yellow (d > 420°)	$CuBr$ white (504°) $AgBr$ pale yellow (430°) $AuBr$ yellow	CuI white (606°) AgI yellow (556°) AuI yellow
$+\frac{1}{2}(0,+1)$	Ag_2F yellow-green (d > 100°)			

bromide are red-brown solids prepared directly from the elements and have a planar dimeric structure in both the solid and vapour phases. Dimensions for the chloride are as shown in Structure (1). On being heated, both compounds lose halogen to form first the monohalide and finally metallic gold. Au_2Cl_6 is one of the best-known compounds of gold and provides a convenient starting point for much coordination chemistry, dissolving in hydrochloric acid to give the stable $[AuCl_4]^-$ ion. Treatment of Au_2Cl_6 with F_2 or BrF_3 also affords a route to AuF_3, a powerful fluorinating agent. This orange solid consists of square-planar AuF_4 units which share *cis*-fluorine atoms with 2 adjacent AuF_4 units so as to form a helical chain (Structure (2)).

No halides are known for gold in the +2 oxidation state and silver only forms the difluoride; this is obtained by direct heating of silver in a stream of fluorine. AgF_2 is thermally stable but is a vigorous fluorinating agent used especially to fluorinate hydrocarbons. For copper, on the other hand, 3 dihalides are stable and the anhydrous difluoride, dichloride and dibromide can all be obtained by heating the elements. The white ionic CuF_2 has a distorted rutile structure

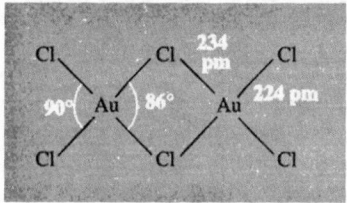

(1) Au_2Cl_6

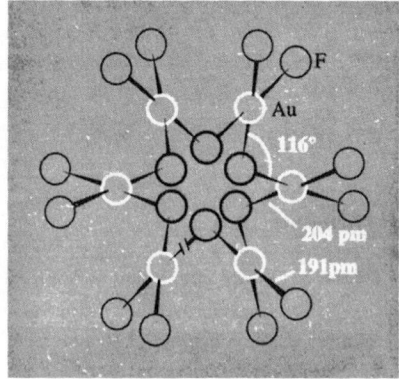

(2) Unique helical chain structure of AuF_3

(p. 961) with four shorter equatorial distances (Cu–F 193 pm) and two longer axial distances (Cu–F 227 pm). A similar distortion is found in the d^4 compound CrF_2 (p. 1021). When prepared from aqueous solution by dissolving copper(II) carbonate or oxide in 40% hydrofluoric acid, blue crystals of the dihydrate are obtained; these are composed of puckered sheets of planar *trans*-$[CuF_2(H_2O)_2]$ groups linked by strong H bonds to give distorted octahedral coordination about Cu with 2 Cu–O 194 pm, 2 Cu–F 190 pm, and 2 further Cu–F at 246.5 pm; the O–H$\cdots$F distance is 271.5 pm. With anhydrous $CuCl_2$ and $CuBr_2$ their increasing covalency is reflected in their polymeric chain structure, consisting of planar CuX_4 units with opposite edges shared, and by the deepening colours of brown and black respectively. The chloride and bromide are both very soluble in water, and various hydrates and complexes can be recrystallized. The solutions are more conveniently obtained by dissolution of the metal or $Cu(OH)_2$ in the relevant hydrohalic acid.

Iodide ions reduce Cu^{II} to Cu^{I}, and attempts to prepare copper(II) iodide therefore result in the formation of CuI. (In a quite analogous way attempts to prepare copper(II) cyanide yield CuCN instead.) In fact it is the electronegative fluorine which fails to form a salt with copper(I), the other 3 halides being white insoluble compounds precipitated from aqueous solutions by the reduction of the Cu^{II} halide. By contrast, silver(I) provides (for the only time in this triad) 4 well-characterized halides. All except AgI have the rock-salt structure (p. 242).[†] Increasing covalency from chloride to iodide is reflected in the deepening colour white → yellow, as the

energy of the charge transfer $(X^-Ag^+ \rightarrow XAg)$ is lowered, and also in increasing insolubility. In the latter respect, however, AgF is quite anomalous in that it is one of the few silver(I) salts which form hydrates ($2H_2O$ and $4H_2O$). That it is soluble in water is understandable in view of its ionic character and the high solvation energy of the small fluoride ion, but the *extent* of its solubility (1800 g per litre of water at 25°C) is astonishing. All 4 AgX can be prepared directly from the elements but it is more convenient to prepare AgF by dissolving AgO in hydrofluoric acid and evaporating the solution until the solid crystallizes; the others can be made by adding X^- to a solution of $AgNO_3$ or other soluble Ag^I compound, when AgX is precipitated. The most important property of these halides, particularly AgBr, is their sensitivity to light (AgF only to ultraviolet) which is the basis for their use in photography, discussed below.

All four monohalides of gold have been prepared but the fluoride only by mass spectrometric methods.[14] AuCl and AuBr are formed by heating the trihalides to no more than 150°C and AuI by heating the metal and iodine. At higher temperatures they dissociate into the elements. AuI is a chain polymer which features linear 2-coordinate Au with Au–I 262 pm and the angle Au–I–Au 72°.

28.3.4 Photography

Photography is a good example of a technology which evolved well in advance of a proper understanding of the principles involved (see

---

[†] At room temperature the stable form of silver iodide is γ-AgI which has the cubic zinc blende structure (p. 1210). β-AgI, which has the hexagonal ZnO (or wurtzite) structure (p. 1210), is the stable form between 136° and 146°. This structure is closely related to that of hexagonal ice (p. 624) and AgI has been found to be particularly effective in nucleating ice crystals in super cooled clouds, thereby inducing the precipitation of rain. β-AgI has another remarkable property: at 146° it undergoes a phase change to cubic α-AgI in which the iodide sublattice is rigid but the silver sublattice "melts". This has a dramatic effect on the (ionic) electrical conductivity of the solid which leaps from 3.4×10^{-4} to 1.31 ohm^{-1} cm^2, a factor of nearly 4000. The iodide sublattice in α-AgI is bcc and this provides 42 possible sites for each $2Ag^+$, distributed as follows:

---

6 sites having $2I^-$ neighbours at 252 pm
12 sites having $3I^-$ neighbours at 267 pm
24 sites having $4I^-$ neighbours at 286 pm

The silver ions are almost randomly distributed on these sites, thus accounting for their high mobility. Many other fast ion conductors have subsequently been developed on this principle, e.g.

$$Ag_2HgI_4 \text{ yellow hexag} \xrightarrow{50.7°} \text{orange-red cubic.}$$

[14] D. SCHRÖDER, J. HRUŠÁK, I. C. TORNIEPORTH-OETTING, T. M. KLAPÖTKE and H. SCHWARTZ. *Angew. Chem. Int. Edn. Engl.* **33**, 212–4 (1994).

History of Photography

In 1727 J. H. Schulze, a German physician, found that a paste of chalk and $AgNO_3$ was blackened by sunlight and, using stencils, he produced black images. At the end of the eighteenth century Thomas Wedgwood (son of the potter Josiah) and Humphry Davy used a lens to form an image on paper and leather treated with $AgNO_3$, and produced pictures which unfortunately faded rather quickly.

The first permanent images were obtained by the French landowner J. N. Niépce using bitumen-coated pewter (bitumen hardens when exposed to light for *several hours* and the unexposed portions can then be dissolved away in oil of turpentine). He then helped the portrait painter, L. J. M. Daguerre, to perfect the "daguerreotype" process which utilized plates of copper coated with silver sensitized with iodine vapour. The announcement of this process in 1839 was greeted with enormous enthusiasm but it suffered from the critical drawback that each picture was unique and could not be duplicated.

Reproducibility was provided by the "calotype" process, patented in 1841 by the English landowner W. H. Fox Talbot, which used semi-transparent paper treated with AgI and a "developer", gallic acid. This produced a "negative" from which any number of "positive" prints could subsequently be obtained. Furthermore it embodied the important discovery of the "latent image" which could be fully developed later. Even with Talbot's very coarse papers, exposure times were reduced to a few minutes and portraits became feasible, even if uncomfortable for the subject.

Though Talbot's pictures were undoubtedly much inferior in quality to Daguerre's, the innovations of his process were the ones which facilitated further improvements and paved the way for photography as we now know it. Sir John Herschel, who first coined the terms "photography", "negative" and "positive", suggested the use of "hyposulphite" (sodium thiosulfate) for "fixing" the image, and later the use of glass instead of paper — hence, photographic "plates". F. S. Archer's "wet collodion" process (1851) reduced the exposure time to about 10 s and R. L. Maddox's "dry gelatin" plates reduced it to only 0.5 s. In 1889 G. Eastman used a roll film of celluloid and founded the American Eastman Kodak Company.

Meanwhile the Scottish physicist, Clerk Maxwell (1861), recognizing that the sensitivities of the silver halides are not uniform across the spectrum, proposed a three-colour process in which separate negatives were exposed through red, green and blue filters, and thereby provided the basis for the later development of colour photography. Actually, the sensitivity is greatest at the blue end of the spectrum; a fact which seriously affected all early photographs. This problem was overcome when the German, H. W. Vogel, discovered that sensitivity could be extended by incorporating certain dyes into the photographic emulsion. "Spectral sensitization" at the present time is able to extend the sensitivity not only across the whole visible region but far into the infrared as well.

Panel). Most of the basic processes were established almost a century and a half ago, but a coherent theoretical explanation was not available until the publication in 1938 of the classic paper by R. W. Gurney and N. F. Mott. (*Proc. Roy. Soc.* **A164**, 151–67 (1938)). Since then the subject has stimulated a vast amount of fundamental research in wide areas of solid-state chemistry and physics.

A photograph is the permanent record of an image formed on a light-sensitive surface, and the essential steps in producing it are:

(a) production of light-sensitive surface;
(b) exposure to produce a "latent image";
(c) development of the image to produce a "negative";
(d) making the image permanent, i.e. "fixing" it;
(e) making "positive" prints from the negative.

(a) In modern processes the light-sensitive surface is an "emulsion" of silver halide in gelatine, coated on to a suitable transparent film, or support. The halide is carefully precipitated so as to produce small uniform crystals, ($< 1\ \mu m$ diameter, containing $\sim 10^{12}$ Ag atoms), or "grains" as they are normally called. The particular halide used depends on the sensitivity required, but AgBr is most commonly used on films; AgI is used where especially fast film is required and AgCl and certain organic dyes are also incorporated in the emulsion.

(b) When, on exposure of the emulsion to light, a photon of energy $h\nu$ impinges on a grain of AgX, a halide ion is excited and loses its electron to the conduction band, through which it passes rapidly to the surface of the grain where it is able to liberate an atom of silver:

$$X^- + h\nu \longrightarrow X + e^-; \quad Ag^+ + e^- \longrightarrow Ag$$

These steps are, in principle, reversible but in practice are not because the Ag is evidently liberated on a crystal dislocation, or defect, or at an impurity site such as may be provided by Ag_2S, all of which allow the electron to reduce its energy and so become "trapped". The function of the dye sensitizers is to extend the sensitivity of the emulsion across the whole visible spectrum, by absorbing light of characteristic frequency and providing a mechanism for transferring the energy to X^- in order to excite its electron. As more photons are incident on the grain, so more electrons migrate and discharge Ag atoms at the same point. A collection of just a few silver atoms on a grain (in especially sensitive cases a mere 4–6 atoms but, more usually, perhaps 10 times that number) constitutes a "speck", too small to be visible, but the concentration of grains possessing such specks varies across the film according to the varying intensity of the incident light thereby producing an invisible "latent image". The parallel formation of X atoms leads to the formation of X_2 which is absorbed by the gelatine.

(c) The "development" or intensification of the latent image is brought about by the action of a mild reducing agent whose function is to selectively reduce those grains which possess a speck of silver, while leaving unaffected all unexposed grains. To this end, such factors as temperature and concentration must be carefully controlled and the reduction stopped before any unexposed grains are affected. Hydroquinone, $1,6\text{-}C_6H_4(OH)_2$ is a common "developer" and the reduction is a good example of a catalysed solid-state reaction. Its mechanism is imperfectly understood but the complete reduction to metal of a grain (say 10^{12} atoms of Ag), starting from a single speck (say 10 or 100 atoms of Ag), represents a remarkable intensification of the latent image of about 10^{11} or 10^{10} times, allowing vastly reduced exposure times; this is the real reason for the superiority of silver halides over all other photosensitive materials, though an intensive search for alternative systems still continues.

(d) After development, the image on the negative is "fixed" by dissolving away all remaining silver salts to prevent their further reduction. This requires an appropriate complexing agent and sodium thiosulphate is the usual one since the reaction

$$AgX(s) + 2Na_2S_2O_3 \longrightarrow Na_3[Ag(S_2O_3)_2] + NaX$$

goes essentially to completion and both products are water-soluble.

(e) A positive print is the reverse of the negative and is obtained by passing light through the negative and repeating the above steps using a printing paper instead of a transparent film.

28.3.5 Complexes[15,16]

Oxidation states above +3 are attained only with difficulty and are confined mainly to AuF_5, mentioned above, together with salts of the octahedral anion $[AuF_6]^-$, and to $Cs_2[Cu^{IV}F_6]$, prepared by fluorinating $CsCuCl_3$ at high temperature and pressure.

Oxidation state III (d^8)

Copper(III) is generally regarded as uncommon, being very easily reduced, but because of its possible involvement in biological electron transfer reactions (p. 1199) a number of Cu^{III} peptides have been prepared. The pale-green, paramagnetic (2 unpaired electrons), K_3CuF_6, is obtained by the reaction of F_2 on $3KCl + CuCl$ and is readily reduced. This is the only high-spin Cu^{III} complex, the rest being low-spin, diamagnetic, and usually square planar, as is to be expected for a cation which, like Ni^{II}, has a d^8 configuration and is more highly charged. Examples are violet $[CuBr_2(S_2CNBu^i_2)]$, obtained by reacting $[Cu(S_2CNBu^i_2)]$ with Br_2

[15] B. J. HATHAWAY, Copper, Chap. 53, pp. 533–774; R. J. LANCASHIRE, Silver, Chap. 54, pp. 775–859; R. J. PUDDEPHATT, Gold, Chap. 55, pp. 861–923 in *Comprehensive Coordination Chemistry*, Vol. 5, Pergamon Press, Oxford, 1987.
[16] For gold in oxidation states other than III, see H. SCHMIDBAUR and K. C. DASH, *Adv. Inorg. Chem.* **25**, 239–66 (1982).

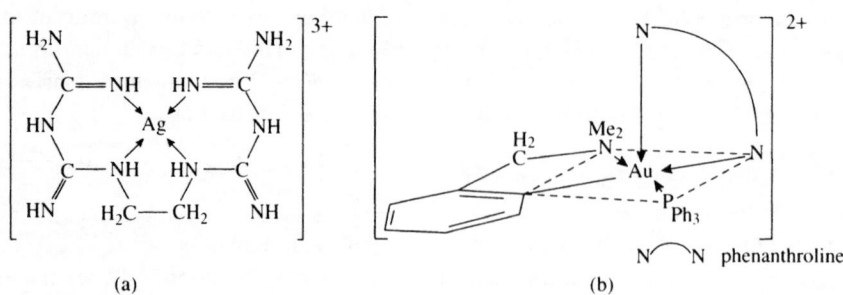

Figure 28.3 (a) Silver(III) ethylenedibiguanide complex ion; the counter anion can be HSO_4^-, ClO_4^-, NO_3^- or OH^-. (b) Gold(III) (dimethylamino)phenyl complex ion; the counter anion can be BF_4^- or ClO_4^-.

in CS_2, and bluish $MCuO_2$ (M = alkali metal), obtained by heating CuO and MO_2 in oxygen. The oxidation of Cu^{II} by alkaline ClO^- in the presence of periodate or tellurate ions yields salts in which chelated ligands apparently produce square-planar coordinated copper:

(X = I, Te) in complex ions such as, $[Cu(IO_5OH)_2]^{5-}$ and $[Cu\{TeO_4(OH)_2\}_2]^{5-}$

Silver(III) is quite similar to copper(III) and analogous, though more stable, periodate and tellurate complexes can be produced by the oxidation of Ag^I with alkaline $S_2O_8^{2-}$. The diamagnetic, red ethylenedibiguanide complex (Fig. 28.3a) is also obtained by peroxodisulfate oxidation and is again quite stable to reduction. However, yellow, diamagnetic, square-planar fluoro-complexes such as $K[AgF_4]$, obtained by fluorinating $AgNO_3 + KCl$ at 300°C, are much less stable; they attack glass and fume in moist air.

For gold, by contrast, +3 is the element's best-known oxidation state and Au^{III} is often compared with the isoelectronic Pt^{II} (p. 1161). The usual route to gold(III) chemistry is by dissolving the metal in aqua regia, or the compound Au_2Cl_6 in conc HCl, after which evaporation yields yellow chloroauric acid, $HAuCl_4.4H_2O$, from which numerous salts of the square-planar ion $[AuCl_4]^-$ can be obtained.

Other square-planar ions of the type $[AuX_4]^-$ can then be derived in which X = F, Br, I, CN, SCN and NO_3, the last of these being of interest as one of the few authenticated examples of the unidentate nitrate ion (cf. p. 1162). $[Au(SCN)_4]^-$ contains S-bonded SCN^- but, as with Pt^{II} (p. 1162), this ligand also gives rise to linkage isomers, this time in the K^+ and $(NEt_4)^+$ salts of $[Au(CN)_2(SCN)_2]^-$ and $[Au(CN)_2(NCS)_2]^-$. Numerous cationic complexes have been prepared with amines, both unidentate (e.g. py, quinoline, as well as NH_3) and chelating (e.g. en, bipy, phen). $[Au(C_6H_4-CH_2NMe_2-2)(phen)(PPh_3)]^{2+}$ (Fig. 28.3b) is an example with the additional interest that its distorted square pyramidal structure[17] provides a rare example of Au^{III} with a coordination number in excess of 4. Octahedral $[AuI_2(diars)_2]^+$ too has a "high" coordination number, though phosphine and arsine complexes are generally readily reduced to Au^I species. Reductions of Au^{III} to Au^I in aqueous solution by nucleophiles such as I^-, SCN^- and other S-donor ligands have been studied. Most take place by rapid ligand substitution followed by the rate determining electron transfer, though some reductions by I^- take place without substitution. With SCN^- the rates of substitution and electron transfer are finely balanced.[18]

[17] J. VICENTE, M. T. CHICOTE, M. D. BERMUDEZ, P. G. JONES, C. FITTSCHEN and G. M. SHELDRICK, *J. Chem. Soc., Dalton Trans.*, 2361–6 (1986).

[18] S. ELMROTH, L. H. SKIBSTED and L. I. ELDING, *Inorg. Chem.* **28**, 2703–10 (1989).

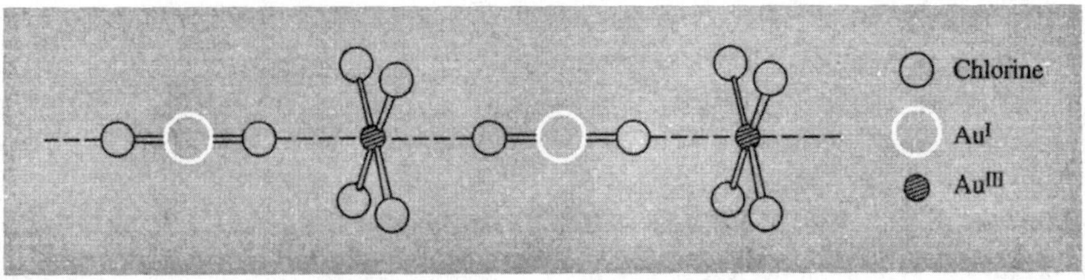

Figure 28.4   The anions of the chlorocomplex of stoichiometry, CsAuCl₃, showing linearly coordinated Au^I and (4 + 2) tetragonally distorted, octahedral Au^{III}, i.e. $Cs_2[Au^ICl_2][Au^{III}Cl_4]$.

In forming the fluoro complex $[AuF_4]^-$ mentioned above, and indeed in forming the simple fluoride AuF_3, Au^{III} differs from the isoelectronic Pt^{II} since the corresponding $[PtF_4]^{2-}$ and PtF_2 are unknown.

Oxidation state II (d⁹)

The importance of this oxidation state diminishes with increase in atomic number in the group, and most of the compounds ostensibly of Au^{II} are actually mixed valency Au^I/Au^{III} compounds. Examples include the sulfate $Au^IAu^{III}(SO_4)_2$ and the chlorocomplex, $Cs_2[Au^ICl_2][Au^{III}Cl_4]$, the anions of the latter being arranged so as to give linearly coordinated Au^I and tetragonally distorted, octahedral Au^{III} (Fig. 28.4). The analogous mixed-metal complex, $Cs_2AgAuCl_6$, has the same structure with Ag^I instead of Au^I. One of the few authenticated examples of Au^{II} is the maleonitriledithiolato complex

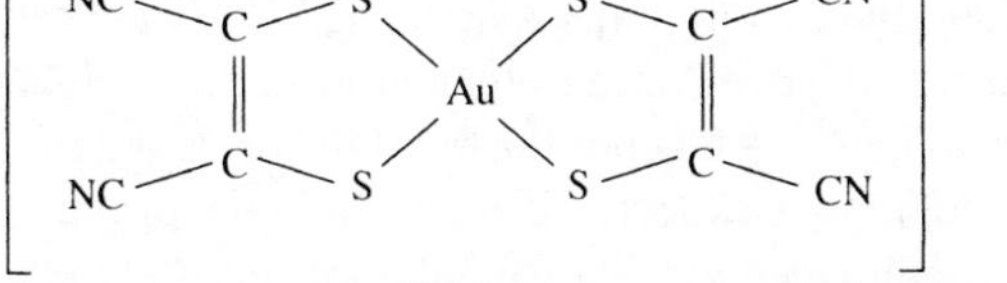

$$\left[\begin{array}{c} NC-C\overset{\|}{\underset{}{C}}-S \\ NC-C\underset{S}{\overset{\|}{}} \end{array} \;Au\; \begin{array}{c} S-C-CN \\ S-C\underset{}{\overset{\|}{}}-CN \end{array} \right]^{2-}$$

which has a magnetic moment at room temperature of 1.85 BM. Even here, however, esr evidence indicates appreciable delocalization of the unpaired electron on to the ligands and, in solution, the complex is readily oxidized to Au^{III}.

Compounds of Ag^{II} are more familiar and are, in general, square planar and paramagnetic ($\mu_e \sim$

1.7–2.2 BM); this is as expected for an ion which is isoelectronic with Cu^{II} (see below), particularly in view of the greater crystal field splitting associated with 4d (as opposed to 3d) electrons. The $Ag^{II}(aq)$ ion has a transitory existence when Ag^I salts are oxidized by ozone in a strongly acid solution, but it is an appreciably stronger oxidizing agent than MnO_4^- [$E°(Ag^{2+}/Ag^+) = +1.980$ V in 4M $HClO_4$; $E°(MnO_4^-/Mn^{2+}) = 1.507$ V] and oxidizes water even when strongly acidic.[†] Of the acidic solutions the most stable is that in phosphoric acid, no doubt because of complex formation, and even NO_3^- and ClO_4^- ions appear to coordinate in solution since the colours of these solutions depend on their concentrations. A variety of complexes, particularly with heterocyclic amines, has been obtained by oxidation of Ag^I salts with $[S_2O_8]^{2-}$ in aqueous solution in the presence of the ligand. They include $[Ag(py)_4]^{2+}$ and $[Ag(bipy)_2]^{2+}$ and are comparatively stable providing the counter-anion is a non-reducing ion such as NO_3^-, ClO_4^- or $S_2O_8^{2-}$. Other complexes include some with N-, O-donor ligands such as pyridine carboxylates, and also the violet $Ba[AgF_4]$.

However, in this oxidation state it is copper which provides by far the most familiar and extensive chemistry. Simple salts are formed with most anions, except CN^- and I^-, which instead form covalent Cu^I compounds which are insoluble in water. The salts are predominantly water-soluble, the blue colour of their solutions

---

[†] Solutions of this type have potential use in the destruction of a variety of waste organic materials by electrochemical oxidation — see D. F. STEELE, *Chem. in Brit.* **27**, 915–8 (1991).

arising from the $[Cu(H_2O)_6]^{2+}$ ion, and they frequently crystallize as hydrates. The aqueous solutions are prone to slight hydrolysis and, unless stabilized by a small amount of acid, are liable to deposit basic salts. Basic carbonates occur in nature (p. 1174), basic sulfates and chlorides are produced by atmospheric corrosion of copper, and basic acetates (verdigris) find use as pigments.

The best-known simple salt is the sulfate pentahydrate ("blue vitriol"), $CuSO_4.5H_2O$, which is widely used in electroplating processes, as a fungicide (in Bordeaux mixture) to protect crops such as potatoes, and as an algicide in water purification. It is also the starting material in the production of most other copper compounds. It is significant, as will be seen presently, that in the crystalline salt 4 of the water molecules form a square plane around the Cu^{II} and 2, more remote, oxygen atoms from SO_4^{2-} ions complete an elongated octahedron. The fifth water is hydrogen-bonded between one of the coordinated waters and sulfate ions (p. 626). On being warmed, the pentahydrate looses water to give first the trihydrate, then the monohydrate; above about 200°C the virtually white anhydrous sulfate is obtained and this then forms CuO by loss of SO_3 above about 700°C. Amongst the few salts of Cu^{II} which crystallize with 6 molecules of water and contain the $[Cu(H_2O)_6]^{2+}$ ion are the perchlorate, the nitrate (but the trihydrate is more easily produced) and Tutton salts.[†]

Attempts to prepare the anhydrous nitrate by dehydration always fail because of decomposition to a basic nitrate or to the oxide, and it was previously thought that $Cu(NO_3)_2$ could not exist. In fact it can be obtained by dissolving copper metal in a solution of N_2O_4 in ethyl acetate to produce $Cu(NO_3)_2.N_2O_4$, and then driving off the N_2O_4 by heating this at 85–100°C. The observation by C. C. Addison

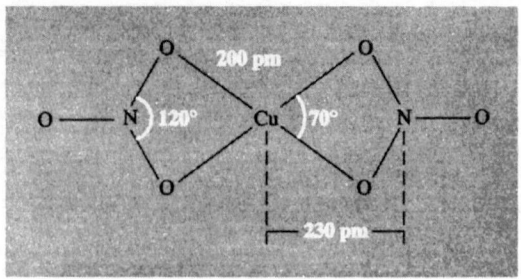

Figure 28.5 The $Cu(NO_3)_2$ molecule in the vapour phase (dimensions are approximate).

and B. J. Hathaway in 1958[19] that the blue $Cu(NO_3)_2$ could be sublimed (at 150–200°C under vacuum) and must therefore involve covalently bonded NO_3^-, was completely counter to current views on the bonding of nitrates and initiated a spate of work on the coordination chemistry of the ion (p. 469). Solid $Cu(NO_3)_2$ actually exists in two forms, both of which involve chains of copper atoms bridged by NO_3 groups, but its vapour is monomeric (Fig. 28.5).

The most common coordination numbers of copper(II) are 4, 5 and 6, but regular geometries are rare and the distinction between square-planar and tetragonally distorted octahedral coordination is generally not easily made. The reason for this is ascribed to the Jahn–Teller effect (p. 1021) arising from the unequal occupation of the e_g pair of orbitals (d_{z^2} and $d_{x^2-y^2}$) when a d^9 ion is subjected to an octahedral crystal field. Occasionally, as in solid $KAlCuF_6$ for instance, this results in a compression of the octahedron, i.e. "2 + 4" coordination (2 short and 4 long bonds).[20] The usual result, however, is an elongation of the octahedron, i.e. "4 + 2" coordination (4 short and 2 long bonds), as is expected if the metal's d_{z^2} orbital is filled and its $d_{x^2-y^2}$ half-filled. In its most extreme form this is equivalent to the complete loss of the axial ligands leaving a square-planar complex.

[†] Tutton salts are the double sulfates $M_2^I Cu(SO_4)_2.6H_2O$ which all contain $[Cu(H_2O)_6]^{2+}$ and belong to the more general class of double sulfates of M^I and M^{II} cations which are known as schönites after the naturally occurring K^I/Mg^{II} compound.

[19] C. C. ADDISON and B. J. HATHAWAY, *J. Chem. Soc.* 1958, 3099–106.
[20] M. ATANASOV, M. A. HITCHMAN, R. HOPPE, K. S. MURRAY, B. MOUBARAKI, D. REINEN and H. STRATEMEIER, *Inorg. Chem.* **32**, 3397–401 (1993).

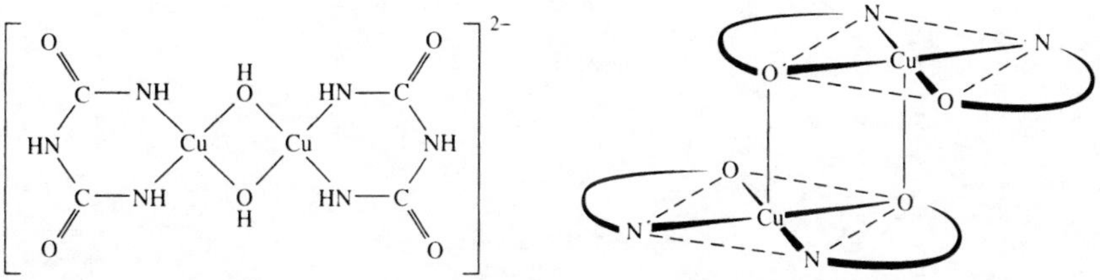

Figure 28.6   (a) Binuclear complex formed in biuret test (b) Schematic representation of square-pyramidal coordination of Cu^{II} in dimeric Schiff base complexes.

The effect of configurational mixing of higher-lying s orbitals into the ligand field d-orbital basis set is also likely to favour elongation rather than contraction.[21]

Elongation has the further consequence that the fifth and sixth stepwise stability constants (p. 908) are invariably much smaller than the first 4 for Cu^{II} complexes. This is clearly illustrated by the preparation of the ammines. Tetraammines are easily isolated by adding ammonia to aqueous solutions of Cu^{II} until the initial precipitate of $Cu(OH)_2$ redissolves, and then adding ethanol to the deep blue solution,[†] when $Cu(NH_3)_4SO_4.xH_2O$ slowly precipitates. Recrystallization of tetraammines from 0.880 ammonia yields violet-blue pentaammines, but the fifth NH_3 is easily lost; hexaammines can only be obtained from liquid ammonia and must be stored in an atmosphere of ammonia. Pyridine and other monoamines are similar in behaviour to ammonia. Likewise, chelating N-donor ligands such as en, bipy and phen show a reluctance to form tris complexes (though these can be obtained if a high concentration of ligand is used) and a number of 5-coordinate complexes such as $[Cu(bipy)_2I]^+$ with a trigonal bipyramidal structure are known. The structure of $[Cu(bipy)_3]^{2+}$ in its perchlorate has been described[22] as square pyramidal (4 short bonds, av. 202.6 pm, and 1 long, 222.3 pm) but, since the sixth N atom only 246.9 pm from

the Cu, distorted octahedral is perhaps a better description. The macrocyclic N-donor, phthalo-cyanine, forms a square-planar complex and substituted derivatives are used to produce a range of blue to green pigments which are thermally stable to over $500°C$, and are widely used in inks, paints and plastics.

In alkaline solution biuret, $HN(CONH_2)_2$ reacts with copper(II) sulfate to give a characteristic violet colour due to the formation of the complexes $[Cu_2(\mu\text{-}OH)_2(NHCONHCONH)_4]^{2-}$ (Fig. 28.6a) and $[Cu(NHCONHCONH)_2]^{2-}$. This is the basis of the "biuret test" in which an excess of NaOH solution is added to the unknown material together with a little $CuSO_4$ soln: a violet colour indicates the presence of a protein or other compound containing a peptide linkage.

Copper(II) also forms stable complexes with O-donor ligands. In addition to the hexaaquo ion, the square planar β-diketonates such as $[Cu(acac)_2]$ (which can be precipitated from aqueous solution and recrystallized from non-aqueous solvents) are well known, and tartrate complexes are used in Fehling's test (p. 1181).

Mixed O,N-donor ligands such as Schiff bases are of interest in that they provide examples not only of square-planar coordination but also, in the solid state, examples of square-pyramidal coordination by dimerization (Fig. 28.6(b)). A similar situation occurs in the bis-dimethylglyoximato complex, which dimerizes by sharing oxygen atoms, though the 4 coplanar donor atoms are all nitrogen atoms. Copper(II) carboxylates[15] are easily obtained by crystallization from aqueous solution or, in the case of the higher carboxylates, by precipitation with the appropriate acid from ethanolic solutions

[21] M. GERLOCH, *Inorg. Chem.* **20**, 638–40 (1981).

[†] This solution will dissolve cellulose which can be re-precipitated by acidification, a fact used in one of the processes for producing rayon.

[22] Z.-M. LIU, Z.-H. JIANG, D.-H. LIAO, G.-L. WANG, X.-K. YAO and H.-G. WANG, *Polyhedron* **10**, 101–2 (1991).

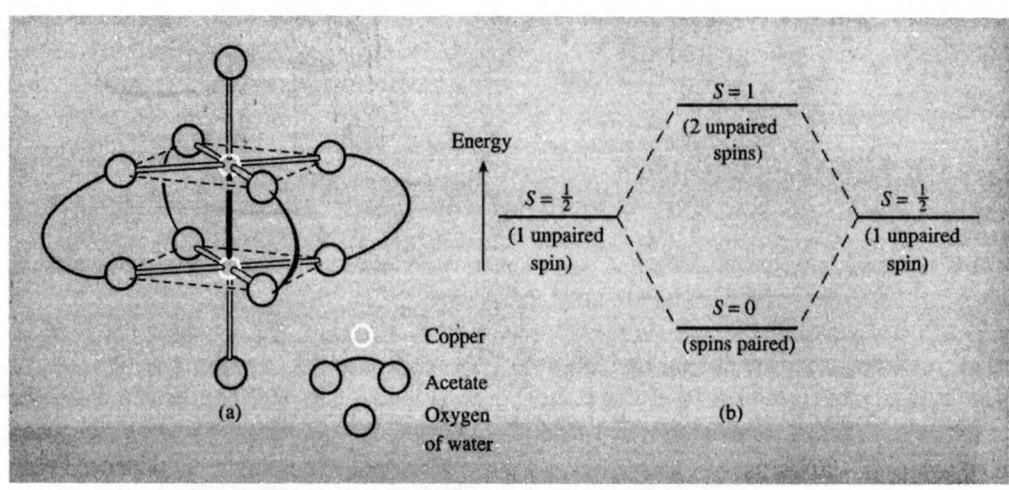

Figure 28.7   (a) Dinuclear structure of copper(II) acetate, and (b) spin singlet $(2S + 1 = 1)$ and spin triplet $(2S + 1 = 3)$ energy levels in dinuclear Cu^{II} carboxylates.

of the acetate. In the early 1950s it was found that the magnetic moment of green copper(II) acetate monohydrate is lower than the spin-only value (1.4 BM at room temperature as opposed to 1.73 BM) and that, contrary to the Curie law, its susceptibility reaches a maximum around 270 K but falls rapidly at lower temperatures. Furthermore, the compound has a dimeric structure in which 2 copper atoms are held together by 4 acetate bridges (Fig. 28.7a). Clearly the single unpaired electrons on the copper atoms interact, or "couple", antiferromagnetically to produce a low-lying singlet (diamagnetic) and an excited but thermally accessible triplet (paramagnetic) level (Fig. 28.7b). The separation is therefore only a few kJ mol⁻¹ (at room temperature, RT the thermal energy available to populate the higher level $\sim$2.5 kJ mol⁻¹) and as the temperature is reduced the population of the ground level increases and diamagnetism is eventually approached.

Similar behaviour is found in many other carboxylates of Cu^{II} as well as their adducts in which axial water is replaced by other O- or N-donor ligands. In spite of a continuous flow of work on these compounds there is still no general agreement as to the actual mechanism of the interaction nor on possible correlations of its magnitude with relevant

properties of the carboxylate and axial ligands.[23] The simplest interpretation is to assume that the singlet and triplet levels arise from a single interaction between the unpaired spins of the copper atoms and, with B. N. Figgis and R. L. Martin,[24] that this takes the form of "face-to-face" or δ overlap of the copper $d_{x^2-y^2}$ orbitals. However, σ overlap of d_{z^2} orbitals, or even a "superexchange" interaction transmitted via the π orbitals of the bridging carboxylates, are also feasible. It seems generally true that the magnetic interaction is greater for alkylcarboxylates than arylcarboxylates and for N-donor rather than O-donor axial ligands. More extensive correlations are unfortunately difficult to deduce from published results because of the existence of polymeric or other isomeric forms beside the dinuclear, and because of the possible presence of mononuclear impurities.

Mononuclear carboxylates such as $Ca[Cu(O_2-CMe)_4]$ and $[Cu(bet)_4](NO_3)_2$, (bet $= N^+Me_3$-CH_2COO^-) are also known.[25] In these

[23] M. KATO and Y. MUTO, *Coord. Chem. Revs.* **92**, 45–83 (1988).

[24] B. N. FIGGIS and R. L. MARTIN, *J. Chem. Soc.* 1956, 3837–46 (cf. quadruple bond in Cr(II) acetate (pp. 1032–4)).

[25] X.-M. CHEN and T. C. W. MAK, *Polyhedron* **10**, 273–6 (1991).

compounds each carboxylate ligand has one O close to the Cu (192–197 pm) and one much further away (277–307 pm) producing a distorted dodecahedral structure.

Other copper(II) complexes of stereochemical interests are the halogenocuprate(II) anions which can be crystallized from mixed solutions of the appropriate halides. The structures of the solids are markedly dependent on the counter cation. The compounds $MCuCl_3$ (M = Li, K, NH_4) contain red, planar $[Cu_2Cl_6]^{2-}$ ions, and $CsCuCl_3$ has a polymeric structure in which chains of $CuCl_6$ octahedra (4 + 2 coordination) share opposite faces.[26] With larger counter cations such as $[PPh_4]^+$, discrete $[Cu_2Cl_6]^{2-}$ ions are found which are distinctly non-planar, the coordination about each Cu being intermediate between square planar and tetrahedral.[27] The $[CuCl_5]^-$ salts present an even greater variety which includes 5-coordinate trigonal bipyramidal and square-pyramidal coordination, as well as $[dienH_3][CuCl_4]Cl$ which contains a square-planar anion and exhibits a curious mixture of ferro- and antiferro-magnetic properties. But it is the salts of $[CuX_4]^{2-}$ which have received most attention[28]: e.g. depending on the cation, $[CuCl_4]^{2-}$ displays structures ranging from square planar to almost tetrahedral (p. 913). The former is usually green and the latter orange in colour. $(NH_4)_2[CuCl_4]$ is an oft-quoted example of planar geometry, but 2 long Cu–Cl distances of 279 pm (compared to 4 Cu–Cl distances of 230 pm) make 4 + 2 coordination a more reasonable description. In the $[EtNH_3]^+$ salt the longer Cu–Cl distances increase still further to 298 pm, but the clearest example of square-planar $[CuCl_4]^{2-}$ is the methadone salt in which the fifth and sixth Cl atoms are more than 600 pm from the Cu^{II}. At the other extreme, $Cs[CuX_4]$ (X = Cl, Br) and $[NMe_4]_2[CuCl_4]$ approach a tetrahedral geometry and it appears that this geometry is retained in aqueous solution since the electronic spectra in the two phases are the same. For $[CuCl_4]^{2-}$ the Cu–Cl distance is close to 223 pm and the somewhat flattened (Jahn–Teller distorted) tetrahedron has four Cl–Cu–Cl angles in the range 100–103° and the other two enlarged to 124° and 130°. The angular distortions in $[CuBr_4]^{2-}$ are almost identical: 4 at 100–102° and the others at 126° and 130°.

Electronic spectra and magnetic properties of copper(II) [15,29]

Because the d^9 configuration can be thought of as an inversion of d^1, relatively simple spectra might be expected, and it is indeed true that the great majority of Cu^{II} compounds are blue or green because of a single broad absorption band in the region $11\,000$–$16\,000\,cm^{-1}$. However, as already noted, the d^9 ion is characterized by large distortions from octahedral symmetry and the band is unsymmetrical, being the result of a number of transitions which are by no means easy to assign unambiguously. The free-ion ^2D ground term is expected to split in a crystal field in the same way as the ^5D term of the d^4 ion (p. 1032) and a similar interpretation of the spectra is likewise expected. Unfortunately this is now more difficult because of the greater overlapping of bands which occurs in the case of Cu^{II}.

The T ground term of the tetrahedrally coordinated ion implies an orbital contribution to the magnetic moment, and therefore a value in excess of $\mu_{spin-only}$ (1.73 BM). But the E ground term of the octahedrally coordinated ion is also expected to yield a moment $[\mu_e = \mu_{spin-only}(1-2\lambda/10Dq)]$ in excess of 1.73 BM, because of "mixing" of the excited T term into the ground term, and the high value of λ ($-850\,cm^{-1}$) makes the effect significant. In practice, moments of magnetically dilute compounds are in the range 1.9–2.2 BM, with compounds whose geometry approaches octahedral having moments

[26] W. J. A. MAASKANT, *Struct. & Bond.* **83**, 55–87 (1995).

[27] L. P. BATTAGLIA, A. B. CORRADI, U. GEISER, R. D. WILLETT, A. MOTORI, F. SANDROLINI, L. ANTOLINI, T. MANFREDINI, L. MENABUE and G. C. PELLACANI, *J. Chem. Soc., Dalton Trans.*, 265–71 (1988) and refs. therein.

[28] see for instance, C. L. BOUTCHARD, M. A. HITCHMAN, B. W. SKELTON and A. H. WHITE, *Aust. J. Chem.* **48**, 771–81 (1995).

[29] A. B. P. LEVER, *Inorganic Electronic Spectroscopy* 2nd edn., pp. 554–72, Elsevier, Amsterdam (1984).

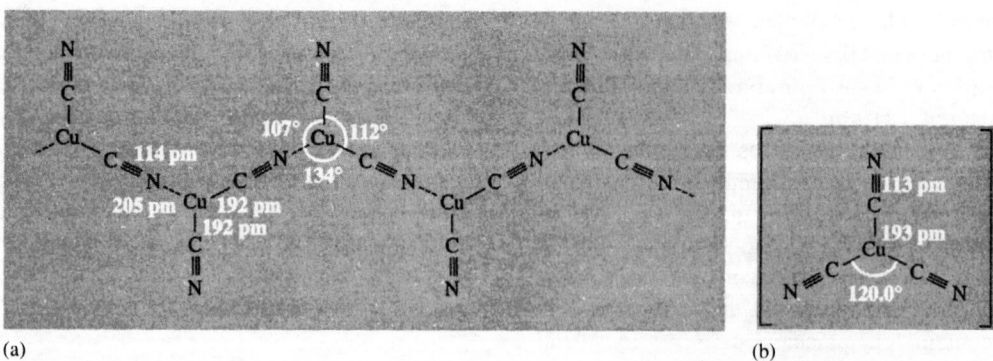

(a)   (b)

Figure 28.8   (a) Chain of Cu^I atoms linked by CN bridges to form the helical anion [Cu(CN)$_2$]$_\infty$ in KCu(CN)$_2$, and (b) one of the two types of [Cu(CN)$_3$]$^{2-}$ ions in Na$_2$[Cu(CN)$_3$].3H$_2$O — the other set have Cu–C 195 pm and C–N 116 pm.

at the lower end, and those with geometries approaching tetrahedral having moments at the higher end, but their measurements cannot be used diagnostically with safety unless supported by other evidence.

Oxidation state I (d^{10})

All M^I cations of this triad are diamagnetic and, unless coordinated to easily polarized ligands, colourless too. In aqueous solution the Cu^I ion is very unstable with respect to disproportionation (2Cu$^I \rightleftharpoons$ Cu^{II} + Cu(s)) largely because of the high heat of hydration of the divalent ion as already mentioned. At 25°C, K (= [Cu^{II}][Cu^I]$^{-2}$) is large, (5.38 ± 0.37) × 10^5 l mol^{-1}, and standard reduction potentials have been calculated[30] to be:

$$E°(Cu^+/Cu) = +0.5072 \text{ V}$$

and $$E°(Cu^{2+}/Cu^+) = +0.1682 \text{ V}$$

Nevertheless, Cu^I can be stabilized either in compounds of very low solubility or by complexing with ligands having π-acceptor character. Its solutions in MeCN are stable and electrochemical oxidation of the metal in this solvent provides a convenient preparative route. The usual stereochemistry is tetrahedral as in

complexes such as [Cu(CN)$_4$]$^{3-}$, [Cu(py)$_4$]$^+$, and [Cu(L-L)$_2$]$^+$ (e.g. L–L = bipy, phen), but lower coordination numbers are possible such as 2, in linear [CuCl$_2$]$^-$ formed when CuCl is dissolved in hydrochloric acid and 3, as in K[Cu(CN)$_2$], which in the solid contains trigonal, almost planar, Cu(CN)$_3$ units linked in a polymeric chain (Fig. 28.8). The discrete planar anion [Cu(CN)$_3$]$^{2-}$ is found in Na$_2$[Cu(CN)$_3$].3H$_2$O. In 2[Cu(C$_{25}$H$_{28}$N$_2$S$_2$)Cl]$^+$[Cu$_2$Cl$_4$]$^{2-}$ the bulky cation, consisting of an N$_2$S$_2$ type macrocycle and a chloride ion coordinated to Cu^{II}, stabilizes the Cu^I anion in an unusual, non-planar form[31] (Fig. 28.9a).

Polymers and oligomers form an expanding class of Cu^I complexes which, Cu^I being a d^{10} ion, are unlikely to involve M–M bonding. A wide range of structures, which frequently give rise to characteristic charge-transfer spectra,[32] is found. Stoichiometries of CuXL$_n$ (n = 0.5, 1, 1.5 and 2) are common and many different structures have been identified including "cubane", open "step" (or "chair") and "ladder" (Fig. 28.9b, c, d) depending on the nature of L and the particular halide involved as well as the stoichiometry.[33]

[30] L. Cravatta, D. Ferri and R. Palombari, *J. Inorg. Nucl. Chem.* **42**, 593–8 (1980).

[31] L. Escriche, N. Lucena, J. Casabo, F. Teixidor, R. Kivekäs and R. Sillapää, *Polyhedron* **14**, 649–54 (1995).

[32] M. Melnik, L. Macaskova and C. E. Holloway, *Coord. Chem. Revs.* **126**, 71–92 (1993).

[33] B. Skelton, A. F. Waters and A. H. White, *Aust. J. Chem.* **44**, 1207–15 (1991).

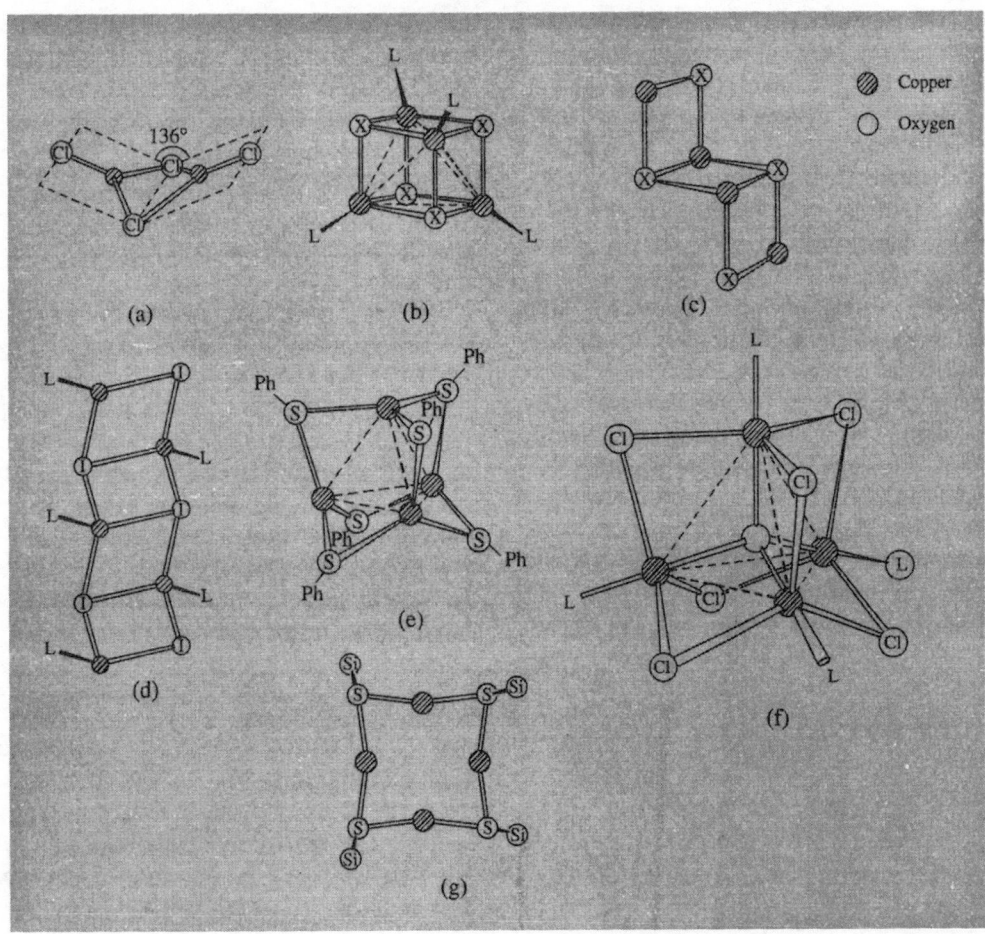

Figure 28.9 Some polymers and oligomers of Cu^I: (a) non-planar $[Cu_2Cl_4]^{2-}$. (b) "cubane" complexes $[CuXL]_4$; X = halide, L = phosphine or arsine. (c) "step" complexes $[CuXL]_4$; X = halide, L = phosphine or arsine. (d) extended "ladder" of $[CuI(NC_5H_4\text{-}2\text{-Me})]_x$. (e) $[Cu_4(SPh)_6]^{2-}$. (f) $[Cu_4OCl_6L_4]$, L = OPPh$_3$. (g) central portion of $[(Bu^tO)_3SiSCu]_4$.

Iodocuprates(I) provide a series of polymeric anions made up of planar $\{CuI_3\}$ or tetrahedral $\{CuI_4\}$ units, culminating in $(pyH)_{24}[Cu_{36}I_{56}]I_4$. The large anion in this consists of 36 $\{CuI_4\}$ tetrahedra joined by 2 or 3 edges, and may be visualized as a section of a c.c.p. lattice of iodides with Cu^I atoms occupying some of the tetrahedral interstices.[34]

S-donor ligands also contribute to this stereochemical diversity, Cu$_4$ tetrahedra being found in

$[Cu_4(SPh)_6]^{2-}$ and in $[Cu_4OCl_6(OPPh_3)_4]$, while $[(Bu^tO)_3SiSCu]_4$ provided[35] the first example of a square planar Cu$_4$S$_4$ ring (Fig. 28.9e, f, g).

The +1 state is by far the best-known oxidation state of silver and salts with most anions are formed. These reveal the reluctance of Ag^I to coordinate to oxygen for, with the exceptions of the nitrate, perchlorate and fluoride, most are insoluble in water. The last two of these salts are also among the very few Ag^I salts which form

[34] H. HARTL and J. FUCHS, *Angew. Chem. Int. Edn. Engl.* **25**, 569–70 (1986).

[35] B. BECKER, W. WOJNOWSKI, K. PETERS, E.-M, PETERS and H. G. VON SCHNERING, *Polyhedron* **9**, 1659–66 (1990).

hydrates and, paradoxically, their solubilities are actually noted for their astonishingly high values (respectively 5570 and $1800 \, g \, l^{-1}$ at 25°C). The hydrated ion is present in aqueous solution and a coordination number of 4 has been established.[36] Unlike Cu^I, however, Ag^I forms 4-coordinate tetrahedral complexes less readily than 2-coordinate linear ones. A wide variety of the latter are formed with *N*-, *P*- and *S*-donor ligands, some of them of great practical importance. The familiar dissolution of AgCl in aqueous ammonia is due to the formation of $[Ag(NH_3)_2]^+$; the formation of $[Ag(S_2O_3)_2]^{3-}$ in photographic "fixing" has already been mentioned (p. 1187), and the cyanide extraction process depends upon the formation of $[M(CN)_2]^-$ (M = Ag, Au) (contrast polymeric $[Cu(CN)_2]^-$, Fig. 28.8). AgCN itself is a linear polymer, $\{Ag–C \equiv N \rightarrow Ag–C \equiv N \rightarrow\}$ but AgSCN is non-linear mainly because the sp^3 hybridization of the sulfur forces a zigzag structure; there is also slight non-linearity at the Ag^I atom.

Because of their inability to form linear complexes, chelating ligands tend instead to produce polymeric species, but compounds with coordination numbers higher than 2 can be produced, e.g. the almost tetrahedral diphosphine and diarsine complexes $[Ag(L-L)_2]^+$ and the almost planar 5-coordinate $[Ag(quinquepyridine)][PF_6]$.[37] Four-coordination is also found in tetrameric phosphine and arsine halides $[AgXL]_4$ which occur in "cubane" and "step" (or "chair") forms like their copper analogues (Fig. 28.9). Indeed, $[AgI(PPh_3)]_4$ exists in both forms. As with Cu^I, sulfur and *S*-donor ligands yield many complexes

of high nuclearity. $[Ag_4(SCH_2C_6H_4CH_2S)_3]^{2-}$ contains the same tetrahedral $\{M_4S_6\}$ centre[38] found in $[Cu_4(SPh)_6]^{2-}$ (Fig. 28.9e), while in the dark-red $Na_2[Ag_6S_4]$ the metal atoms are disposed octahedrally.[39] The cyclohexanethiolato complex $[Ag(SC_6H_{11})]_{12}$ and $(PPh_3)_4[AgSBu^t]_{14}$[40] consist respectively of 24- and 28-membered puckered rings of alternate Ag and S atoms.

Like Ag^I, Au^I also readily forms linear 2-coordinate complexes such as $[AuX_2]^-$ (X = Cl, Br, I)[41] and also the technologically important $[Au(CN)_2]^-$. But it is much more susceptible to oxidation and to disproportionation into Au^{III} and Au^0 which renders all its binary compounds, except AuCN, unstable to water. It is also more clearly a class b or "soft" metal with a preference for the heavier donor atoms P, As and S. Stable, linear complexes are obtained when tertiary phosphines reduce Au^{III} in ethanol,

$$[AuCl_4]^- \xrightarrow{\text{PR}_3/\text{EtOH}} [AuCl(PR_3)].$$

The Cl ligand can be replaced by other halides and pseudo-halides by metathetical reactions. Trigonal planar coordination is found in phosphine complexes of the stoichiometry $[AuL_2X]$ but 4-coordination, though possible, is less prevalent. Diarsine gives the almost tetrahedral complex $[Au(diars)_2]^+$ but, for reasons which are not clear, the colourless complexes $[AuL_4]^+[BPh_4]^-$ with monodentate phosphines fail to achieve a regular tetrahedral geometry.

Complexes with dithiocarbamates involve linear S–Au–S coordination but are dimeric and the Au–Au distance of 276 pm compared with 288 pm in the metal and 250 pm in gaseous Au_2 is indicative of metal–metal bonding.[†]

[36] J. TEXTER, J. S. HASTRELTER and J. L. HALL, *J. Phys. Chem.* **87**, 4690–3 (1983). See also *Acta Chem. Scand.* A38, 437–51 (1984).

[37] E. C. CONSTABLE, M. G. B. DREW, G. FORSYTH and M. D. WARD, *J. Chem. Soc., Chem. Commun.*, 1450–1 (1988).

[38] G. HENKEL, P. BETZ and B. KREBS, *Angew. Chem. Int. Edn. Engl.* **26**, 145–6 (1987).

[39] J. HUSTER, B. BONSMANN and W. BRONGER, *Z. anorg. allg. Chem.* **619**, 70–2 (1993).

[40] I. DANCE, L. FITZPATRICK, M. SCUDDER and D. CRAIG, *J. Chem. Soc., Chem. Commun.*, 17–8 (1984).

[41] P. BRAUNSTEIN, A. MÜLLER and H. BÖGGE, *Inorg. Chem.* **25**, 2104–6 (1986).

[†] The stability of the 6s orbital in gold already referred to (p. 1180), allows it to participate in M–M interactions. This

In the thermal production of gold coatings on ceramics and glass, paints are used which comprise Au^{III} chloro-complexes and sulfur-containing resins dissolved in an organic solvent. It seems likely that polymeric species are responsible for rendering the gold soluble.

Gold cluster compounds [42-44]

Polymeric complexes of the types formed by copper and silver are not found for gold but instead a range of variously coloured cluster compounds, with gold in an average oxidation state < 1 and involving M–M bonds, can be obtained by the general process of reducing a gold phosphine halide, usually with sodium borohydride. Yellow $[Au_6\{P(C_6H_4-4-Me)_3\}_6]^{2+}$ consists of an octahedron of 6 gold atoms with a phosphine attached to each. Red $[Au_8(PPh_3)_8]^{2+}$ can be regarded as a chair-like, centred hexagon of gold atoms with an eighth gold situated above the chair, each gold atom having a phosphine attached to it (Fig. 28.10a). Clusters are known in which further gold atoms are added to the chair in a more or less spherical manner (e.g. $[Au_{11}\{P(C_6H_4-4-F)_3\}_7I_3]$ Fig. 28.10c in which the central gold has no attached ligand) and giving ultimately a centred icosahedron as found in the dark-red $[Au_{13}Cl_2(PMe_2Ph)_{10}]^{3+}$ (Fig. 28.10d). Another series of clusters can be distinguished with flatter, ring or torus shapes as in the red-brown $[Au_8(PPh_3)_7]^{2+}$ and

green $[Au_9\{P(C_6H_4-4-Me)_3\}_8]^{3+}$ (Fig. 28.10b). This latter series is characterized by lower electron counts than the former, reflecting a lower involvement of p-orbitals in M–M bonding and therefore less tangential skeletal bonding (cf. p. 1170 for Pt). This accords with the observation that only clusters with an icosahedral structure (stabilized by both tangential *and* radial skeletal bonding) are stereochemically rigid on the nmr time scale at room temperature [42].

Heteronuclear clusters [44] incorporating a range of other transition metals can be produced by the general method of reacting $AuPR_3$ with a carbonyl anion of the appropriate metal. "Clusters of clusters" of Au–Ag have been synthesized with metal frameworks based on vertex sharing icosahedra, the basic unit being an Au-centred $\{Au_7Ag_6\}$ icosahedron [43]. The largest of these is $[Au_{22}Ag_{24}(PPh_3)_{12}Cl_{10}]$ consisting of four $\{Au_7Ag_6\}$ icosahedra arranged tetrahedrally with six shared vertices. The spectacular, red-brown $[Au_{55}(PPh_3)_{12}Cl_6]$ is prepared by reducing $Au(PPh_3)Cl$ with B_2H_6 and is probably best viewed as a cubo-octahedral fragment of close-packed Au atoms. From it, water soluble $[Au_{55}(Ph_2PC_6H_4SO_3Na.2H_2O)_{12}Cl_6]$ can be obtained by ligand exchange. [45]

28.3.6 Biochemistry of copper [46,47]

Metallic copper and silver both have antibacterial properties[†] and Au^I thiol complexes have found increasing use in the treatment of rheumatoid arthritis, but only copper of this group has a biological role in sustaining life. It is widely distributed in the plant and animal worlds, and its redox chemistry is involved in a variety of

---

facilitates M–M bonding in compounds of Au^I, which would otherwise not be expected for d^{10} ions, and considerably enhances the strength of this bonding when the oxidation state of Au < 1.

[42] D. M. P. MINGOS pp. 189–97 in A. J. WELCH and S. K. CHAPMAN (eds.), *The Chemistry of the Copper and Zinc Triads*, R. S. C., Cambridge, 1993.

[43] B. K. TEO, H. ZHANG and X. SHI *ibid*. pp. 211–34.

[44] D. M. P. MINGOS and M. J. WATSON, *Adv. Inorg. Chem.* **39**, 327–99 (1992).

[45] G. SCHMID, N. KLEIN, L. KORSTE, U. KREIBIG and D. SCHÖNAUER, *Polyhedron* **7**, 605–8 (1988).

[46] K. D. KARLIN and Z. TYEKLAR (eds.), *Bioinorganic Chemistry of Copper*, Chapman & Hall, New York, 1993, 506 pp.

[47] pp. 187–214 of W. KAIM and B. SCHWEDERSKI, *Bioinorganic Chemistry: Inorganic Elements in the Chemistry of Life*, Wiley, Chichester, 1994.

[†] This was unknowingly utilized in ancient Persia where, by law, drinking water had to be stored in bright copper vessels.

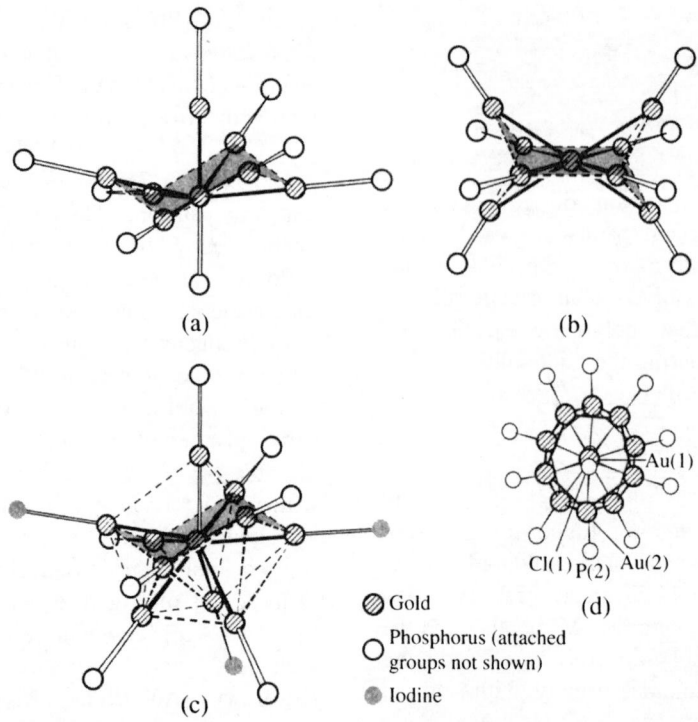

Gold

Phosphorus (attached groups not shown)

Iodine

Figure 28.10   Some gold cluster compounds. Note that a chair-like centred hexagon of gold atoms persists throughout these structures and is shaded in (a), (b), and (c): (a) $[Au_8(PPh_3)_8]^{2+}$, (b) $Au_9\{P(C_6H_4\text{-}4\text{-}Me)_3\}_8]^{3+}$, (c) $Au_{11}I_3\{P(C_6H_4\text{-}4\text{-}F)_3\}_7]$, and (d) $[Au_{13}Cl_2(PMe_2Ph)_{10}]^{3+}$. In (d) the 12th icosahedral gold atom and the 13th (central) gold atom are obscured by Au(l).

oxidation processes. A human adult contains around 100 mg of copper, mostly attached to protein, an amount exceeded only by iron and zinc amongst transition metals, and requiring a daily intake of some 3–5 mg. Copper deficiency results in anaemia, and the congenital inability to excrete Cu, resulting in its accumulation, is Wilson's disease. The presence of copper, along with haem, in the electron transfer agent cytochrome c oxidase has already been mentioned (p. 1101).

Although complete structural details are rare, considerable progress has been made in understanding the mode of action of copper proteins, synthetic modelling being a major factor in this.[48] Biologically active copper centres can be divided into three main types:

---
[48] N. KITAJIMA, *Adv. Inorg. Chem.* **39**, 1–77 (1992).

Type 1: "blue" monomeric Cu with very distorted "3 + 1" coordination of 2N- and 2S-donors. This is apparently a compromise between the square planar 4N preferred by Cu^{II} and the tetrahedral 4S preferred by Cu^I, with a degree of flexibility facilitating a Cu^{II}/Cu^I couple. This type of centre is characterized by an intense blue colour because of a strong absorption at 600 nm arising from $S \rightarrow Cu^{II}$ charge transfer.

Type 2: "normal" monomeric Cu^{II} in an essentially square planar environment with additional, very weak, tetragonal interactions and exhibiting normal esr.

Type 3: a pair of Cu^I atoms about 360 pm apart and attached to protein through histidine residues; these effect O_2 transport by means of the reversible reaction $2Cu^I \underset{}{\overset{O_2}{\rightleftharpoons}} Cu^{II}(\mu\text{-}O_2)Cu^{II}$. Whether the O_2 is bonded as a $\eta^1 : \eta^1$ linear Cu–O–O–Cu bridge or $\eta^2 : \eta^2$ (i.e. O–O

Organometallic compounds

perpendicular to the Cu–Cu axis) is still uncertain. The copper are esr inactive: Cu^I because of its d^{10} configuration and Cu^{II} because strong antiferromagnetic interaction between the two atoms renders them diamagnetic.

A further class, *Type 4*, has been proposed. It is composed of three Cu^{II} atoms two of which are strongly coupled, being only ~340 pm apart. The third Cu atom completes an isosceles triangle, being 390–400 pm from each of the first two, and is "normal".

In a large number of molluscs the oxygen-carrying pigment is not haemoglobin but a haemocyanin. These proteins, with molecular weights of the order of 10^6, are composed of differing numbers of subunits each containing a pair of type 3 copper centres. A limited cooperativity (p 1100) is displayed but its mechanism is not yet clear. The "blue proteins"[49] laccase and ascorbic oxidase are found in a variety of plants where they are involved in the oxidation of phenols, amines and ascorbate by O_2. They contain a type 1 copper, responsible for their colour and name, along with a type 4 trimer which together form a very distorted 4Cu tetrahedron. One-electron transfers by means of Cu^{II}/Cu^I couples are involved but the mechanism by which O_2 is reduced is far from clear. Ceruloplasmin is also a blue protein which is found in all mammals: it participates in copper transport and storage as well as in oxidation processes. It is the deficiency of this protein which is responsible for Wilson's disease.

Another oxidase, but non-blue, is galactose oxidase found in fungi where it catalyses the oxidation of $-CH_2OH$ in galactose to $-CHO$, simultaneously reducing O_2 to H_2O_2. With a molecular weight of 68 000 and containing a single type 2 Cu, it was thought likely that a Cu^{III}/Cu^I couple effected the 2-electron reduction of O_2. However, spectroscopic evidence appears to refute this. The coordination of the Cu is square pyramidal with two histidine nitrogens, two tyrosine oxygens and an acetate oxygen. The currently favoured interpretation is that the more tightly bound of the two tyrosines undergoes a 1-electron redox change which, together with a Cu^{II}/Cu^I couple, affords the required 2-electron transfer.

Cytochrome c oxidase contains two, or possibly three, copper atoms referred to as Cu_A and Cu_B since they do not fit into the usual classification. The former (possibly a dimer) is situated outside the mitochondrial membrane, whereas the latter is associated with an iron atom within the membrane. Both have electron transfer functions but details are as yet unclear.

28.3.7 Organometallic compounds [50]

Neutral binary carbonyls are not formed by these metals at normal temperatures[†] but copper and gold each form an unstable carbonyl halide, [M(CO)Cl]. These colourless compounds can be obtained by passing CO over MCl or, in the case of copper only (since the gold compound is very sensitive to moisture), by bubbling CO through a solution of CuCl in conc HCl or in aqueous NH_3. The latter reactions can in fact be used for the quantitative estimation of the CO content of gases. A silver carbonyl $[Ag(CO)][B(OTeF_5)_4]$ has also been prepared by mixing $AgOTeF_5$ and $B(OTeF_5)_3$ under CO[51] but the weakness of the Ag–C bond is indicated by the fact that the CO stretching frequency (2204 cm^{-1}) is the highest of any metal carbonyl. Complexes of the type [MLX], which are often polymeric, can be obtained for Cu^I and Ag^I with many olefins (alkenes) and acetylenes (alkynes) either by anhydrous methods or in solution. They are generally rather labile, often decomposing when

---

[50] F. P. PRUCHNIK, *Organometallic Chemistry of the Transition Elements*, Plenum Press, New York, 1990, 757 pp.

[†] Some have been synthesized by the condensation of Cu or Ag vapour and CO at temperatures of 6–15 K: e.g. $M(CO)_3$, $M_2(CO)_6$, $M(CO)_2$ and $M(CO)$. Thus $[Ag(CO)_3]$ is green, planar and paramagnetic; above 25–30 K it apparently dimerizes, perhaps by formation of an Ag–Ag bond (see D. MCINTOSH and G. A. OZIN, *J. Am. Chem. Soc.* **98**, 3167–75 (1976), and references therein).

[51] P. K. HURLBURT, O. P. ANDERSON and S. H. STRAUSS, *J. Am. Chem. Soc.* **113**, 6277–8 (1991).

---

[49] A. G. SYKES, *Adv. Inorg. Chem.* **36**, 377–408 (1991).

isolated. The silver complexes have received most attention and the silver–olefin bonds are found to be thermodynamically weaker than, for instance, corresponding platinum–olefin bonds. Since the former bonds are also found to be somewhat unsymmetrical it seems likely that π bonding is weaker for the group 11 metals. Gold also forms olefin complexes, but not nearly so readily as silver and then only with high molecular weight olefins.

M–C σ bonds can be formed by each of the M^I metals. The simple alkyls and aryls of Ag^I are less stable than those of Cu^I, while those of Au^I have not been isolated. Copper alkyls and aryls[52] are prepared by the action of LiR or a Grignard reagent on a Cu^I halide:

$$CuX + LiR \longrightarrow CuR + LiX$$

$$CuX + RMgX \longrightarrow CuR + MgX_2$$

CuMe is a yellow polymeric solid which explodes if allowed to dry in air, and CuPh, which is white and also polymeric, though more stable, is still sensitive to both air and water. Much greater stability is achieved by the σ-cyclopentadienyl complex $[Cu(\eta^1\text{-}C_5H_5)(PEt_3)]$ prepared by the reaction of C_5H_6, CuO and PEt_3 in petroleum ether; a similar Au^I compound, $[Au(\eta^1\text{-}C_5H_4Me)(PPh_3)]$, is also known. Au^I alkyls can be obtained like those of copper but only with an appropriate ligand present, e.g.:

$$[Au(PEt_3)X] + LiR \longrightarrow [Au(PEt_3)R] + LiX$$

The colourless solids are composed of linear monomers. A few anionic Au^I alkyls are known of which $[N(PPh_3)_2]^+[Au(acac)_2]^-$ might be mentioned.[53] In this it is the central C of the ligand, $HC(COMe)_2$ which is attached to the metal.

The alkyl derivatives of Au^{III} were discovered by W. J. Pope and C. S. Gibson in 1907; they include some of the most familiar and stable organo compounds of the group, and are notable for not requiring the stabilizing presence of π-bonding ligands. They are of three types:

AuR_3 (stable, when they occur at all, only in ether below $-35°C$);

AuR_2X (much the most stable); X = anionic ligand especially Br;

$AuRX_2$ (unstable, only dibromides characterized).

Corresponding aryl derivatives are rare and unstable. Thus, while $AuMe_3$ decomposes above $-35°C$ but is stabilized in $[AuMe_3(PPh_3)]$, $AuPh_3$ is unknown.

The dialkylgold(III) halides are generally prepared from the tribromide and a Grignard reagent:

$$AuBr_3 + 2RMgBr \longrightarrow AuR_2Br + 2MgBr_2$$

Many other anions can then be introduced by metathetical reactions with the appropriate silver salt:

$$AuR_2Br + AgX \longrightarrow AuR_2X + AgBr$$

In all cases where the structure has been determined, the Au^{III} attains planar four-fold coordination and polymerizes as appropriate to achieve this. The halides for instance are dimeric but with the cyanide, which forms linear rather than bent bridges, tetramers are produced:

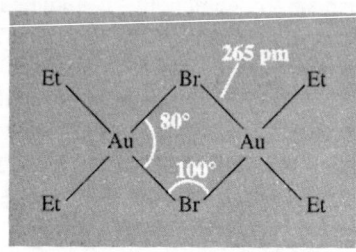

[52] P. P. Power, *Prog. Inorg. Chem.* **39**, 75–112 (1991).

[53] J. Vicente, M.-T. Chicote, I. Saura-Llamas and M.-C. Lagunas, *J. Chem. Soc., Chem. Commun.*, 915–6 (1992).

$$
\begin{array}{ccccc}
\text{R} & & & & \text{R} \\
| & & & & | \\
\text{R}-\text{Au}-\text{C}\!\equiv\!\text{N}-\text{Au}-\text{R} \\
| & & & & | \\
\text{N} & & & & \text{C} \\
\| & & & & \| \\
\text{C} & & & & \text{N} \\
| & & & & | \\
\text{R}-\text{Au}-\text{N}\!\equiv\!\text{C}-\text{Au}-\text{R} \\
| & & & & | \\
\text{R} & & & & \text{R}
\end{array}
$$

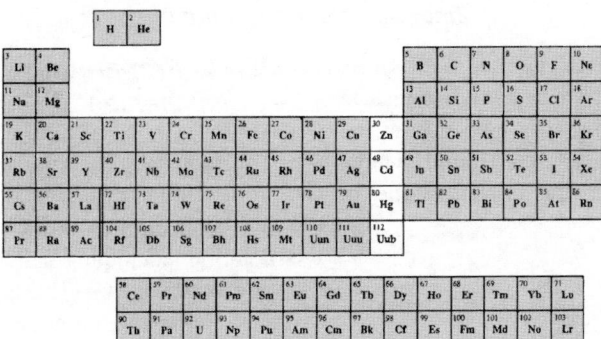

29

Zinc, Cadmium and Mercury

29.1 Introduction

The reduction of ZnO by charcoal requires a temperature of 1000°C or more and, because the metal is a vapour at that temperature and is liable to reoxidation, its collection requires some form of condenser and the exclusion of air. This was apparently first achieved in India in the thirteenth century. The art then passed to China where zinc coins were used in the Ming Dynasty (1368–1644). The preparation of alloyed zinc by smelting mixed ores does not require the isolation of zinc itself and is much more easily achieved. The small amounts of zinc present in samples of early Egyptian copper no doubt simply reflect the composition of local ores, but Palestinian brass dated 1400–1000 BC and containing about 23% Zn must have been produced by the deliberate mixing of copper and zinc ores. Brass was similarly produced by the Romans in Cyprus and later in the Cologne region of Germany.

Zinc was not intentionally made in medieval Europe, though small amounts were obtained by accidental condensation in the production of lead, silver and brass; it was imported from China by the East India Company after about 1605. The English zinc industry started in the Bristol area in the early eighteenth century and production quickly followed in Silesia and Belgium. The origin of the name is obscure but may plausibly be thought to be derived from *Zinke* (German for spike, or tooth) because of the appearance of the metal.

Mercury is more easily isolated from its ore, cinnabar, and was used in the Mediterranean world for extracting metals by amalgamation as early as 500 BC, possibly even earlier. Cinnabar, HgS, was widely used in the ancient world as a pigment (vermilion). For over a thousand years, up to AD 1500, alchemists regarded the metal as a key to the transmutation of base metals to gold and employed amalgams both for gilding and for producing imitation gold and silver. Because of its mobility, mercury is named after the messenger of the gods in Roman mythology, and the symbol, Hg, is derived from *hydrargyrum* (Latin, liquid silver).

Cadmium made its appearance much later. In 1817 F. Stromeyer of Göttingen noticed that a sample of "cadmia" (now known as "calamine"), used in a nearby smelting works, was yellow instead of white. The colour was not due to iron, which was shown to be absent, but arose instead from a new element which was named after the (zinc) ore in which it had been found (Greek καδμεία, cadmean earth, the ancient name of calamine).

29.2 The Elements

29.2.1 Terrestrial abundance and distribution

Zinc (76 ppm of the earth's crust) is about as abundant as rubidium (78 ppm) and slightly more abundant than copper (68 ppm). Cadmium (0.16 ppm) is similar to antimony (0.2 ppm); it is twice as abundant as mercury (0.08 ppm), which is itself as abundant as silver (0.08 ppm) and close to selenium (0.05 ppm). These elements are "chalcophiles" (p. 648) and so, in the reducing atmosphere prevailing when the earth's crust solidified, they separated out in the sulfide phase, and their most important ores are therefore sulfides. Subsequently, as rocks were weathered, zinc was leached out to be precipitated as carbonate, silicate or phosphate.

The major ores of zinc are ZnS (which is known as zinc blende in Europe and as sphalerite in the USA) and $ZnCO_3$ (calamine in Europe, smithsonite in the USA[†]). Large deposits are situated in Canada, the USA and Australia. Less important ores are hemimorphite, $Zn_4Si_2O_7(OH)_2.H_2O$ and franklinite, $(Zn,Fe)O.Fe_2O_3$. Cadmium is found as greenockite, CdS, but its only commercially important source is the 0.2–0.4% found in most zinc ores. Cinnabar, HgS, is the only important ore and source of mercury and is found along lines of previous volcanic activity. The most famous and extensive deposits are at Almaden in Spain; these contain up to 6–7% Hg and have been worked since Roman times. Other deposits, usually containing <1% Hg, are situated in the former Soviet Union, Algeria, Mexico, Yugoslavia and Italy.

29.2.2 Preparation and uses of the elements [1]

The isolation of zinc, over 90% of which is from sulfide ores, depends on conventional physical concentration of the ore by sedimentation or flotation techniques. This is followed by roasting to produce the oxides; the SO_2 which is generated is used to produce sulfuric acid. The ZnO is then either treated electrolytically or smelted with coke. In the former case the zinc is leached from the crude ZnO with dil H_2SO_4, at which point cadmium is precipitated by the addition of zinc dust. The $ZnSO_4$ solution is then electrolysed and the metal deposited — in a state of 99.95% purity — on to aluminium cathodes.

A variety of smelting processes have been employed to effect the reduction of ZnO by coke:

$$ZnO + C \longrightarrow Zn + CO$$

These formerly involved the use of banks of externally heated, horizontal retorts, operated on a batch basis. They were replaced by continuously operated vertical retorts, in some cases electrically heated. Unfortunately none of these processes has the thermal efficiency of a blast furnace process (p. 1072) in which the combustion of the fuel for heating takes place in the same chamber as the reduction of the oxide. The inescapable problem posed by zinc is that the reduction of ZnO by carbon is not spontaneous below the boiling point of Zn (a problem not encountered in the smelting of Fe, Cu or Pb, for instance), and the subsequent cooling to condense the vapour is liable, in the presence of the combustion products, to result in the reoxidation of the metal:

$$Zn + CO_2 \rightleftharpoons ZnO + CO$$

The problem can be overcome by spraying the zinc vapour with lead as it leaves the top of the furnace. This chills and dissolves the zinc

---

[†] After James Smithson, founder of the Smithsonian Institution, Washington. The name calamine is applied in the USA to a basic carbonate.

---

[1] *Kirk–Othmer Encyclopedia of Chemical Technology*, 4th edn., Interscience, New York. For Zn, see Vol. 25, 1998, pp. 789–853. For Cd, see Vol. 4, 1992, pp. 748–60. For Hg, see Vol. 16, 1995. pp. 212–28.

so rapidly that reoxidation is minimal. The zinc then separates as a liquid of nearly 99% purity and is further refined by vacuum distillation to give a purity of 99.99%. Any cadmium present is recovered in the course of this distillation. The use of a blast furnace has the further advantage that the composition of the charge is not critical, and mixed Zn/Pb ores can be used (ZnS and PbS are commonly found together) to achieve the simultaneous production of both metals, the lead being tapped from the bottom of the furnace.

World production of zinc (1995) is about 7 million tonnes pa: of this, about 1 million tonnes pa is produced by each of Canada and Australia and 800 000 tonnes pa by China. Cadmium is produced in much smaller quantities (~20 000 tonnes pa) and these are dependent on the supply of zinc.

Zinc finds a wide range of uses. The most important, accounting for 40% of output, is as an anti-corrosion coating. The application of the coating takes various forms: immersion in molten zinc (hot-dip galvanizing), electrolytic deposition, spraying with liquid metal, heating with powdered zinc ("Sherardizing"), and applying paint containing zinc powder. In addition to brasses (Cu plus 20–50% Zn), a rapidly increasing number of special alloys, predominantly of zinc, are used for diecasting and, indeed, the vast majority of *pressure* diecastings are now made in these alloys. Zinc sheeting is used in roof cladding and the manufacture of dry batteries (see Panel, p. 1204) is a further use, though this has declined considerably in recent years.

The major uses of cadmium are in batteries (67%) and coatings (7%). In the form of its compounds it is used in pigments (CdS −15%) and stabilizers, in PVC for instance, to prevent degradation by heat or ultraviolet radiation (10%).

The isolation of mercury is comparatively straightforward. The most primitive method consisted simply of heating cinnabar in a fire of brushwood. The latter acted as fuel and condenser, and metallic mercury collected in the ashes. Modern techniques are of course less crude than this but the basic principle is much the same. After being crushed and concentrated by flotation, the ore is roasted in a current of air and the vapour condensed:

$$HgS + O_2 \xrightarrow{600°C} Hg + SO_2$$

Alternatively, in the case of especially rich ores, roasting with scrap iron or quicklime is used:

$$HgS + Fe \longrightarrow Hg + FeS$$

$$4HgS + CaO \longrightarrow 4Hg + 3CaS + CaSO_4$$

Blowing air through the hot, crude, liquid metal oxidizes traces of metals such as Fe, Cu, Zn and Pb which form an easily removable scum. Further purification is by distillation under reduced pressure. About 4000 tonnes[†] of mercury are used annually but only half is from primary, mine production the other half being secondary production and sales from stockpiles. The main primary producer is now Spain, but several other countries, including the former Soviet Union, China and Algeria, have capacity for production.

The use of mercury for extracting precious metals by amalgamation has a long history and was extensively used by Spain in the sixteenth century when her fleet carried mercury from Almaden to Mexico and returned with silver. However, environmental concerns have resulted in falling demand and excess production capacity. It is still used in the extraction of gold and in the Castner–Kellner process for manufacturing chlorine and NaOH (p. 72), and a further major use is in the manufacture of batteries. It is also used in street lamps and AC rectifiers, while its small-scale use in thermometers, barometers and gauges of different kinds, are familiar in many laboratories.

29.2.3 Properties of the elements

A selection of some important properties of the elements is given in Table 29.1. Because the elements each have several naturally occurring isotopes their atomic weights cannot be quoted with great precision.

[†] Mercury is sold in iron *flasks* holding 76 lb of mercury and this is the unit in which output is normally measured.

Dry Batteries

A portable source of electricity, if not a necessity, is certainly a great convenience in modern life and is dependent on compact, sealed, dry batteries. The main types are listed below and they incorporate the metals Zn, Ni, Hg and Cd as well as MnO_2

(a) Carbon–zinc cell

The first dry battery was that patented in 1866 by the young French engineer, G. Leclanché. The positive pole consisted of carbon surrounded by MnO_2 (p. 1048) contained in a porous pot, and the negative pole was simply a rod of zinc. These were situated inside a glass jar containing the electrolyte, ammonium chloride solution thickened with sand or sawdust. This is still the basis of the most common type of modern dry cell in which a carbon rod is the positive pole, surrounded by a paste of MnO_2, carbon black, and NH_4Cl, inside a zinc can which is both container and negative pole. The reactions are:

negative pole: $\quad Zn \longrightarrow Zn^{2+} + 2e^-$
electrolyte: $\qquad Zn^{2+} + 2NH_4Cl + 2OH^- \longrightarrow [ZnCl_2(NH_3)_2] + 2H_2O$
positive pole: $\qquad 2MnO_2 + 2H_2O + 2e^- \longrightarrow 2MnO(OH) + 2OH^-$
net reaction: $\qquad Zn + 2NH_4Cl + 2MnO_2 \longrightarrow [ZnCl_2(NH_3)_2] + 2MnO(OH)$

(b) Mercury cell

The negative pole of pressed amalgamated zinc powder and the positive pole of mercury(II) oxide and graphite are separated by an absorbent impregnated with the electrolyte, conc KOH:

negative pole: $\quad Zn + 2OH^- \longrightarrow ZnO + H_2O + 2e^-$
positive pole: $\qquad HgO + H_2O + 2e^- \longrightarrow Hg + 2OH^-$
net reaction: $\qquad Zn + HgO \longrightarrow Hg + ZnO$

(c) Alkaline manganese cell

This is similar in principle to (a) but is constructed in a manner akin to (b). The negative pole of powdered zinc, formed into a paste with the electrolyte KOH, and the positive pole of compressed graphite and MnO_2 are separated by an absorbent impregnated with the electrolyte:

negative pole: $\quad Zn + 2OH^- \longrightarrow ZnO + H_2O + 2e^-$
positive pole: $\qquad 2MnO_2 + H_2O + 2e^- \longrightarrow Mn_2O_3 + 2OH^-$
net reaction: $\qquad Zn + 2MnO_2 \longrightarrow ZnO + Mn_2O_3$

(d) Nickel–cadmium cell

Unlike the cells above, which are all primary cells, this is a secondary (i.e. rechargeable) cell, and the two poles are composed in the uncharged condition of nickel and cadmium hydroxides respectively. These are each supported on microporous nickel, made by a sintering process, and separated by an absorbent impregnated with electrolyte. The charging reactions are:

negative pole: $\quad Cd(OH)_2 + 2e^- \longrightarrow Cd + 2OH^-$
positive pole: $\qquad Ni(OH)_2 + 2OH^- \longrightarrow NiO(OH) + 2H_2O + 2e^-$
net reaction: $\qquad Ni(OH)_2 + Cd(OH)_2 \longrightarrow NiO(OH) + Cd + 2H_2O$

During discharge these reactions are reversed. A crucial feature of the construction of this cell is that oxygen produced at the positive pole during charging by the side-reaction:

$$4OH^- \longrightarrow 2H_2O + O_2 + 4e^-$$

can migrate readily to the negative pole to be recombined in the reaction:

$$O_2 + 2H_2O + 2Cd \longrightarrow 2Cd(OH)_2$$

But for this rapid migration and recombination, the cell could not be sealed.

Table 29.1 Some properties of the elements zinc, cadmium and mercury

Property		Zn	Cd	Hg
Atomic number		30	48	80
Number of naturally occurring isotopes		5	8[a]	7
Atomic weight		65.39(2)	112.411(8)	200.59(2)
Electronic configuration		[Ar]$3d^{10}4s^2$	[Kr]$4d^{10}5s^2$	[Xe]$4f^{14}5d^{10}6s^2$
Electronegativity		1.6	1.7	1.9
Metal radius (12 coordinate)/pm		134	151	151
Effective ionic radius/pm	II	74	95	102
	I	—	—	119
Ionization energies/kJ mol^{-1}	1st	906.1	876.5	1007
	2nd	1733	1631	1809
	3rd	3831	3644	3300
$E°(M^{2+}/M)/V$		−0.7619	−0.4030	+0.8545
MP/°C		419.5	320.8	−38.9
BP/°C		907	765	357
ΔH_{fus}/kJ mol^{-1}		7.28(±0.01)	6.4(±0.2)	2.30(±0.02)
ΔH_{vap}/kJ mol^{-1}		114.2(±1.7)	100.0(±2.1)	59.1(±0.4)
$\Delta H_{(monatomic\ gas)}$/kJ mol^{-1}		129.3(±2.9)	111.9(±2.1)	61.3
Density (25°C)/g cm^{-3}		7.14	8.65	13.534(1)
Electrical resistivity (20°C)/μohm cm		5.8	7.5	95.8

[a]The half-life of $9.3 \pm 1.9 \times 10^{15}$ y for ^{113}Cd is the longest known for any β-emitter; note that this is 2 million times the age of the earth (4.6×10^9 y).

Their most noticeable features compared with other metals are their low melting and boiling points, mercury being unique as a metal which is a liquid at room temperature. Zinc and cadmium are silvery solids with a bluish lustre when freshly formed. Mercury is also unusual in being the only element, apart from the noble gases, whose vapour is almost entirely monatomic, while its appreciable vapour pressure (1.9×10^{-3} mmHg, i.e. 0.25 Pa, at 25°C), coupled with its toxicity, makes it necessary to handle it with care. The electrical resistivity of liquid mercury is exceptionally high for a metal, and this facilitates its use as an electrical standard (the international ohm is defined as the resistance of 14.4521 g of Hg in a column 106.300 cm long and 1 mm^2 cross-sectional area at 0°C and a pressure of 760 mmHg.

The structures of the solids, although based on the typically metallic hexagonal close-packing, are significantly distorted. In the case of Zn and Cd the distortion is such that, instead of having 12 equidistant neighbours, each atom has 6 nearest neighbours in the close-packed plane with the 3 neighbours in each of the adjacent planes

being about 10% more distant. In the case of (rhombohedral) Hg the distortion, again uniquely, is the reverse, with the coplanar atoms being the more widely separated (by some 16%). The consequence is that these elements are much less dense and have a lower tensile strength than their predecessors in Group 11. These facts have been ascribed to the stability of the d electrons which are now tightly bound to the nucleus: the metallic bonding therefore involves only the outer s electrons, and is correspondingly weakened.

29.2.4 Chemical reactivity and trends

Zinc and cadmium tarnish quickly in moist air and combine with oxygen, sulfur, phosphorus and the halogens on being heated. Mercury also reacts with these elements, except phosphorus and its reaction with oxygen was of considerable practical importance in the early work of J. Priestley and A. L. Lavoisier on oxygen (p. 601). The reaction only becomes appreciable at temperatures of about 350°C, but above about 400°C HgO decomposes back into the elements.

None of the three metals reacts with hydrogen, carbon or nitrogen.

Non-oxidizing acids dissolve both Zn and Cd with the evolution of hydrogen. With oxidizing acids the reactions are more complicated, nitric acid for instance producing a variety of oxides of nitrogen dependent on the concentration and temperature. Mercury is unreactive to non-oxidizing acids but dissolves in conc HNO_3 and in hot conc H_2SO_4 forming the Hg^{II} salts along with oxides of nitrogen and sulfur. Dilute HNO_3 slowly produces $Hg_2(NO_3)_2$. Zinc is the only element in the group which dissolves in aqueous alkali to form ions such as aquated $[Zn(OH)_4]^{2-}$ (zincates).

All three elements form alloys with a variety of other metals. Those of zinc include the brasses (p. 1178) and, as mentioned above, are of considerable commercial importance. Those of mercury are known as amalgams and some, such as sodium and zinc amalgams, are valuable reducing agents: in a number of cases, high heats of formation and stoichiometric compositions suggest chemical combination. Na_5Hg_8 and Na_3Hg for instance have been isolated and structurally characterized. They consist of "widespread" close-packed mercury (Hg–Hg > 500 pm) with respectively, all vacancies filled and all octahedral vacancies plus 5/6 tetrahedral vacancies filled with sodium atoms.[2] From caesium amalgams CsHg has been obtained and shown[3] to contain isolated square planar Hg_4 clusters (Hg–Hg ~ 300 pm whereas intercluster separation = 419 pm). Amalgams are most readily formed by heavy metals, whereas the lighter metals of the first transition series (with the exception of manganese and copper) are insoluble in mercury. Hence iron flasks can be used for its storage.

Chemically, it is clear that Zn and Cd are rather similar and that Hg is somewhat distinct. The lighter pair are more electropositive, as indicated both by their electronegativity coefficients and electrode potentials (Table 29.1), while Hg has a positive electrode potential and is comparatively inert. With the exception of the metallic radii, all the evidence indicates that the effects of the lanthanide contraction have died out by the time this group is reached. Compounds are characterized by the d^{10} configuration and, with the exception of derivatives of the Hg_2^{2+} ion, which formally involve Hg^I, they almost exclusively involve M^{II} (but see page 1213). The ease with which the s^2 electrons are removed compared with the more firmly held d electrons is shown by the ionization energies. The sum of the first and second is in each case smaller than for the preceding element in Group 11, whereas the third is appreciably higher. Even so the first two ionization energies are high for mercury (as they are for gold) — perhaps reflecting the poor nuclear shielding afforded by the filled 4f shell — and this, coupled with the small hydration energy associated with the large Hg^{II} cation, accounts for the positive value of its electrode potential.

In view of the stability of the filled d shell, these elements show few of the characteristic properties of transition metals (p. 905) despite their position in the d block of the periodic table. Thus zinc shows similarities with the main-group metal magnesium, many of their compounds being isomorphous, and it displays the class-a characteristic of complexing readily with *O*-donor ligands. On the other hand, zinc has a much greater tendency than magnesium to form covalent compounds, and it resembles the transition elements in forming stable complexes not only with *O*-donor ligands but with *N*- and *S*-donor ligands and with halides and CN^- (see p. 1216) as well. As mentioned above, cadmium is rather similar to zinc and may be regarded as on the class-a/b borderline. However, mercury is undoubtedly class b: it has a much greater tendency to covalency and a preference for *N*-, *P*- and *S*-donor ligands, with which Hg^{II} forms complexes whose stability is rarely exceeded by those of any other divalent cation. Compounds of the M^{II} ions of this group are characteristically diamagnetic and those of Zn^{II}, like those of Mg^{II}, are colourless. By contrast, many compounds of

[2] H. J. DEISEROTH and D. TOELSTEDE, *Z. anorg. allg. Chem.* **615**, 43–8 (1992).

[3] H. J. DEISEROTH, A. STRUNK and W. BAUHOFER, *Z. anorg. allg. Chem.* **575**, 31–8 (1989).

Table 29.2　Stereochemistries of compounds of Zn^{II}, Cd^{II} and Hg^{II}

Coordination number	Stereochemistry	Zn	Cd	Hg
2	Linear	$ZnEt_2$	$CdEt_2$	$[Hg(NH_3)_2]^{2+}$
3	Planar	$[ZnMe(NPh_3)]_2$		$[HgI_3]^-$
	T-shaped			$[Hg(SC_6H_2Bu^t_3)_2(py)]$
4	Tetrahedral	$[Zn(H_2O)_4]^{2+}$, $[Zn(NH_3)_4]^{2+}$	$[CdCl_4]^{2-}$	$[Hg(SCN)_4]^{2-}$
	Planar	$[Zn(glycinyl)_2]$		
5	Trigonal bipyramidal	$[Zn(terpy)Cl_2]$	$[CdCl_5]^{3-}$	$[Hg(terpy)Cl_2]$
	Square pyramidal	$[Zn(S_2CNEt_2)_2]_2$	$[Cd(S_2CNEt_2)_2]_2$	$[Hg\{N(C_2H_4NMe_2)_3\}I]^+$
6	Octahedral	$[Zn(en)_3]^{2+}$	$[Cd(NH_3)_6]^{2+}$	$[Hg(C_5H_5NO)_6]^{2+}$
7	Pentagonal bipyramidal	$[Zn(H_2dapp)(H_2O)_2]^{2+(a)}$	$[Cd(quin)_2(NO_3)_2H_2O]^{(b)}$	
8	Distorted dodecahedral	$[Zn(NO_3)_4]^{2-(c)}$		
	Distorted square antiprismatic			$[Hg(NO_2)_4]^{2-}$

[a] H_2dapp = 2,6-diacetylpyridinebis(2′-pyridylhydrazone).

[b] The 2 nitrate ions are not equivalent (both are bidentate but one is coordinated symmetrically, the other asymmetrically) and the structure of the complex is by no means regular (p. 1217).

[c] The distortion arises because the bidentate nitrate ions are coordinated asymmetrically to such an extent that the stereochemistry may alternatively be regarded as approaching tetrahedral (p. 1217).

Hg^{II}, and to a lesser extent those of Cd^{II}, are highly coloured due to the greater ease of charge transfer from ligands to the more polarizing cations. The increasing polarizing power and covalency of their compounds in the sequence, $Mg^{II} < Zn^{II} < Cd^{II} < Hg^{II}$, is a reflection of the decreasing nuclear shielding and consequent increasing power of distortion in the sequence: filled p shell < filled d shell < filled f shell.

A further manifestation of these trends is the increasing stability of σ-bonded alkyls and aryls in passing down the group (p. 1221). Those of Zn and Cd are rather reactive and unstable to both air and water, whereas those of Hg are stable to both. (The Hg–C bond is not in fact strong but the competing Hg–O bond is weaker.) However, the M^{II} ions do not form π complexes with CO, NO or olefins (alkenes), no doubt because of the stability of their d^{10} configurations and their consequent inability to provide electrons for "back bonding". Likewise their cyanides presumably owe their stability primarily to σ rather than π bonding. The filled d shell also prevents π acceptance and complexes with cyclopentadienide ions (which are good π donors) are σ- rather than π-bonded.

The range of stereochemistries found in compounds of the M^{II} ions is illustrated in Table 29.2. Since the d^{10} configuration affords no crystal field stabilization, the stereochemistry of a particular compound depends on the size and polarizing power of the M^{II} cation and the steric requirements of the ligands. Thus both Zn^{II} and Cd^{II} favour 4-coordinate tetrahedral complexes though Cd^{II}, being the larger, forms 6-coordinate octahedral complexes more readily than does Zn^{II}. However, the still larger Hg^{II} also commonly adopts a tetrahedral stereochemistry, and octahedral 6-coordination is less prevalent than for either of its congeners.[†] When it does occur it is usually highly distorted with 2 short and 4 long bonds, a distortion which in its extreme form produces the 2-coordinate, linear stereochemistry which is characteristic of

[†] An example of trigonal prismatic coordination has been reported for Hg in the green, zero-valent mixed-metal cluster $[Hg\{Pt(2,6-Me_2C_6H_3NC)\}_6]$; Y. YAMAMOTO, H. YAMAZAKI, and T. SAKURAI, *J. Am. Chem. Soc.* **104**, 2329–30 (1982). In $[Hg(mac)_2](HgBr_4)$, (mac = 1-thia-4,7-diazacyclononane) the coordination in the cation is intermediate between octahedral and trigonal prismatic; U. HEINZEL and R. MATTES, *Polyhedron* **11**, 597–600 (1992).

Hg^{II}. This is also found in organozinc and organocadmium compounds but only with Hg^{II} is it one of the predominant stereochemistries. Explanations of this fact have been given in terms of the promotional energies involved in various hybridization schemes, but it may be regarded pictorially as a consequence of the greater deformability of the d^{10} configuration of the large Hg^{II} ion. Thus, if 2 ligands are considered to approach the cation from opposite ends of the z-axis, the resulting deformation increases the electron density in the xy-plane and so discourages the close approach of other ligands. Coordination numbers greater than 6 are rare and generally involve bidentate, O-donor ligands with a small "bite", such as NO_3^- and NO_2^-.

29.3 Compounds of Zinc, Cadmium and Mercury[4-6]

Zinc hydride can be isolated from the reaction of LiH with $ZnBr_2$ or NaH with ZnI_2:

$$2MH + ZnX_2 \xrightarrow{\text{thf}} ZnH_2 + 2MX$$

The alkali metal halide remains in solution and ZnH_2 is precipitated as a white solid of moderate stability at or below room temperature.[7] CdH_2 and HgH_2 are much less stable and decompose rapidly even below $0°$. The complex metal hydrides $LiZnH_3$, Li_2ZnH_4 and Li_3ZnH_5 have each been prepared as off-white powders by the reaction of $LiAlH_4$ with the appropriate organometallic complex Li_nZnR_{n+2}.

The carbides of these metals (which are actually acetylides, MC_2, p. 297) and also the

nitrides are unstable materials, those of mercury explosively so.

29.3.1 Oxides and chalcogenides

The principal compounds in this category are the monochalcogenides, which are formed by all three metals. It is a notable indication of the stability of tetrahedral coordination for the elements of Group 12 that, of the 12 compounds of this type, only CdO, HgO and HgS adopt a structure other than wurtzite or zinc blende (both of which involve tetrahedral coordination of the cation — see below). CdO adopts the 6-coordinate rock-salt structure; HgO features zigzag chains of almost linear O–Hg–O units; and HgS exists in both a zinc-blende form and in a rock-salt form.

The normal oxide, formed by each of the elements of this group, is MO, and peroxides MO_2 are known for Zn and Cd. Reported lower oxides, M_2O, are apparently mixtures of the metal and MO.

ZnO is by far the most important manufactured compound of zinc[8] and, being an inevitable byproduct of primitive production of brass, has been known longer than the metal itself. It is manufactured by burning in air the zinc vapour obtained on smelting the ore or, for a purer and whiter product, the vapour obtained from previously refined zinc. It is normally a white, finely divided material with the wurtzite structure. On heating, the colour changes to yellow due to the evaporation of oxygen from the lattice to give a nonstoichiometric phase $Zn_{1+x}O$ ($x \leq 70\,ppm$); the supernumerary Zn atoms produce lattice defects which trap electrons which can subsequently be excited by absorption of visible light.[9] Indeed, by "doping" ZnO with an excess of 0.02–0.03% Zn metal, a whole range of colours — yellow, green, brown, red — can be obtained. The reddish hues of the naturally

[4] M. FARNSWORTH, *Cadmium Chemicals*, International Lead Zinc Research Org. Inc., New York, 1980, 158 pp.

[5] C. A. MCAULIFFE (ed.), *The Chemistry of Mercury*, Macmillan, London, 1977, 288 pp.

[6] B. J. AYLETT, Group IIB, Chap. 30, pp. 187–328, in *Comprehensive Inorganic Chemistry*, Vol. 3, Pergamon Press, Oxford, 1973.

[7] J. J. WATKINS and E. C. ASHBY, *Inorg. Chem.* **13**, 2350–4 (1974).

[8] See pp. 530–2 of W. BÜCHNER, R. SCHLIEBS, G. WINTER and K. H. BÜCHEL, *Industrial Inorganic Chemistry*, VCH, Weinheim 1989.

[9] N. N. GREENWOOD, *Ionic Crystals, Lattice Defects and Nonstoichiometry*, Chaps. 6 and 7, pp. 111–81, Butterworths, London, 1968.

occurring form, zincite, arise, however, from the presence of Mn or Fe.

The major industrial use of ZnO is in the production of rubber where it shortens the time of vulcanization. As a pigment in the production of paints it has the advantage over the traditional "white lead" (basic lead carbonate) that it is non-toxic and is not discoloured by sulfur compounds, but it has the disadvantage compared to TiO_2 of a lower refractive index and so a reduced "hiding power" (p. 959). It improves the chemical durability of glass and so is used in the production of special glasses, enamels and glazes. Another important use is in antacid cosmetic pastes and pharmaceuticals. In the chemical industry it is the usual starting material for other zinc chemicals of which the soaps (i.e. salts of fatty acids, such as Zn stearate, palmitate, etc.) are the most important, being used as paint driers, stabilizers in plastics, and as fungicides. An important small scale use is in the production of "zinc ferrites". These are spinels of the type $Zn_x^{II}M_{1-x}^{II}Fe_2^{III}O_4$ involving a second divalent cation (usually Mn^{II} or Ni^{II}). When $x = 0$ the structure is that of an inverse spinel (i.e. half the Fe^{III} ions occupy octahedral sites — see p. 1081). Where $x = 1$, the structure is that of a normal spinel (i.e. all the Fe^{III} ions occupy octahedral sites), since Zn^{II} displaces Fe^{III} from the tetrahedral sites. Reducing the proportion of Fe^{III} ions in tetrahedral sites lowers the Curie temperature. The magnetic properties of the ferrite can therefore be controlled by adjustment of the zinc content.

ZnO is amphoteric (p. 640), dissolving in acids to form salts and in alkalis to form zincates, such as $[Zn(OH)_3]^-$ and $[Zn(OH)_4]^{2-}$. The gelatinous, white precipitate obtained by adding alkali to aqueous solutions of Zn^{II} salts is $Zn(OH)_2$ which, like ZnO, is amphoteric.

CdO is produced from the elements and, depending on its thermal history, may be greenish-yellow, brown, red or nearly black. This is partly due to particle size but more importantly, as with ZnO, is a result of lattice defects — this time in an NaCl lattice. It is more basic than ZnO, dissolving readily in acids but hardly at all in alkalis. White $Cd(OH)_2$ is precipitated from aqueous solutions of Cd^{II} salts by the addition of alkali and treatment with very concentrated alkali yields hydroxocadmiates such as $Na_2[Cd(OH)_4]$. Cadmium oxide and hydroxide find important applications in decorative glasses and enamels and in Ni–Cd storage cells. CdO also catalyses a number of hydrogenation and dehydrogenation reactions.

Treatment of the hydroxides of Zn and Cd with aqueous H_2O_2 produces hydrated peroxides of rather variable composition. That of Zn has antiseptic properties and is widely used in cosmetics.

HgO exists in a red and a yellow variety. The former is obtained by pyrolysis of $Hg(NO_3)_2$ or by heating the metal in O_2 at about 350°C; the latter by cold methods such as precipitation from aqueous solutions of Hg^{II} by addition of alkali ($Hg(OH)_2$ is not known). The difference in colour is entirely due to particle size, both forms having the same structure which consists of zigzag chains of virtually linear O–Hg–O units with Hg–O 205 pm and angle Hg–O–Hg 107°. The shortest Hg$\cdots$O distance between chains is 282 pm.

Zinc blende, ZnS, is the most widespread ore of zinc and the main source of the metal, but ZnS is also known in a second naturally occurring though much rarer form, wurtzite, which is the more stable at high temperatures. The names of these minerals are now also used as the names of their crystal structures which are important structure types found in many other AB compounds. In both structures each Zn is tetrahedrally coordinated by 4 S and each S is tetrahedrally coordinated by 4 Zn; the structures differ significantly only in the type of close-packing involved, being cubic in zinc-blende and hexagonal in wurtzite (Fig. 29.1). Pure ZnS is white and, like ZnO, finds use as a pigment for which purpose it is often obtained (as "lithopone") along with $BaSO_4$ from aqueous solution of $ZnSO_4$ and BaS:

$$ZnSO_4 + BaS \longrightarrow ZnS\downarrow + BaSO_4\downarrow$$

Freshly precipitated ZnS dissolves readily in mineral acids with evolution of H_2S, but roasting renders it far less reactive and it is then an acceptable pigment in paints for children's toys since it is harmless if ingested. ZnS also has

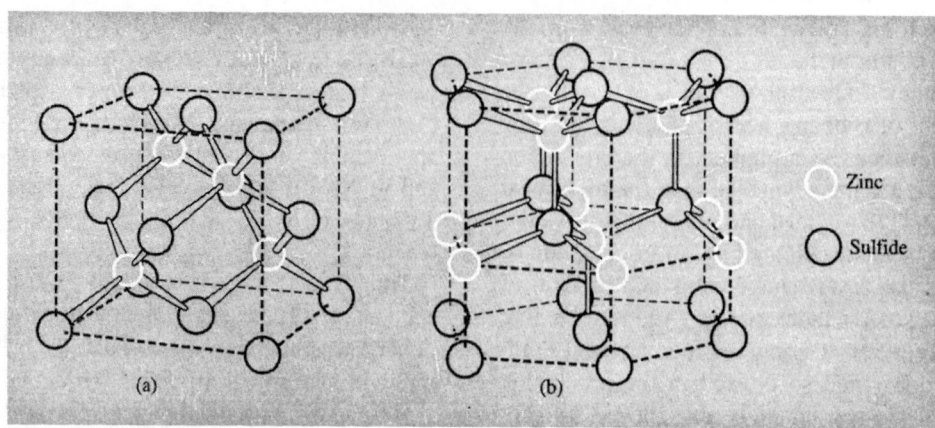

Figure 29.1 Crystal structures of ZnS. (a) Zinc blende, consisting of two, interpenetrating, ccp lattices of Zn and S atoms displaced with respect to each other so that the atoms of each achieve 4-coordination (Zn–S = 235 pm) by occupying tetrahedral sites of the other lattice. The face-centred cube, characteristic of the ccp lattice, can be seen — in this case composed of S atoms, but an extended diagram would reveal the same arrangement of Zn atoms. Note that if all the atoms of this structure were C, the structure would be that of diamond (p. 275). (b) Wurtzite. As with zinc blende, tetrahedral coordination of both Zn and S is achieved (Zn–S = 236 pm) but this time the interpenetrating lattices are hexagonal, rather than cubic, close-packed.

interesting optical properties. It turns grey on exposure to ultraviolet light, probably due to dissociation to the elements, but the process can be inhibited by trace additives such as cobalt salts. Cathode rays, X-rays and radioactivity also produce fluorescence or luminescence in a variety of colours which can be extended by the addition of traces of various metals or the replacement of Zn by Cd and S by Se. It is widely used in the manufacture of cathode-ray tubes and radar screens.

Yellow ZnSe and brown ZnTe are structurally akin to the sulfide and the former especially is used mainly in conjunction with ZnS as a phosphor.

Chalcogenides of Cd are similar to those of Zn and display the same duality in their structures. The sulfide and selenide are more stable in the hexagonal form whereas the telluride is more stable in the cubic form. CdS is the most important compound of cadmium and, by addition of CdSe, ZnS, HgS, etc., it yields thermally stable pigments of brilliant colours from pale yellow to deep red, while colloidal dispersions are used to colour transparent glasses.

CdS and CdSe are also useful phosphors. CdTe is a semiconductor used as a detector for X-rays and γ-rays,[10] and mercury cadmium telluride[11] has found widespread (particularly military) use as an ir detector for thermal imaging.

HgS is polymorphic. The red α-form is the mineral cinnabar, or vermilion, which has a distorted rock-salt structure and can be prepared from the elements. β-HgS is the rare, black, mineral metacinnabar which has the zinc-blende structure and is converted by heat to the stable α-form. In the laboratory the most familiar form is the highly insoluble[†] black precipitate obtained by the action of H_2S on aqueous solutions of Hg^{II}. HgS is an unreactive substance, being attacked only by conc HBr, HI or aqua regia. HgSe and

---

[10] M. HAGE-ALI and P. SIFFERT, pp. 219–334 of *Semiconductors and Semimetals*, Vol. 43, Academic Press, San Diego, 1995.

[11] *ibid.* Vol. 18, 1981, 388 pp. devoted to mercury cadmium telluride.

[†] The solubility product, $[Hg^{2+}][S^{2-}] = 10^{-52} \, mol^2 \, dm^{-6}$ but the actual solubility is greater than that calculated from this extremely low figure, since the mercury in solution is present not only as Hg^{2+} but also as complex species. In acid solution $[Hg(SH)_2]$ is probably formed and in alkaline

Table 29.3 Halides of zinc, cadmium and mecury (mp, bp, in parentheses)

Fluorides	Chlorides	Bromides	Iodides
ZnF_2 white (872°, 1500°)	$ZnCl_2$ white (275°, 756°)	$ZnBr_2$ white (394°, 702°)	ZnI_2 white (446°, d > 700°)
CdF_2 white (1049°, 1748°)	$CdCl_2$ white (568°, 980°)	$CdBr_2$ pale yellow (566°, 863°)	CdI_2 white (388°, 787°)
HgF_2 white (d > 645°)	$HgCl_2$ white (280°, 303°)	$HgBr_2$ white (238°, 318°)	HgI_2 α red, β yellow (257°, 351°)
Hg_2F_2 yellow (d > 570°)	Hg_2Cl_2 white (subl 383°)	Hg_2Br_2 White (subl 345°)	Hg_2I_2 yellow (subl 140°)

HgTe are easily obtained from the elements and have the zinc-blende structure.

29.3.2 Halides

The known halides are listed in Table 29.3. All 12 dihalides are known and in addition there are 4 halides of Hg_2^{2+} which are conveniently considered separately. It is immediately obvious that the difluorides are distinct from the other dihalides, their mps and bps being much higher, suggesting a predominantly ionic character, as also indicated by their typically ionic three-dimensional structures (ZnF_2, 6:3 rutile; CdF_2 and HgF_2, 8:4 fluorite). ZnF_2 and CdF_2, like the alkaline earth fluorides, have high lattice energies and are only sparingly soluble in water, while HgF_2 is hydrolysed to HgO and HF. The anhydrous difluorides can be prepared by the action of HF (in the case of Zn) or F_2 (Cd and Hg) on the metal.

The other halides of Zn^{II} and Cd^{II} are in general hygroscopic and very soluble in water ($\sim$400 g per 100 cm^3 for ZnX_2 and $\sim$100 g per 100 cm^3 for CdX_2). This is at least partly because of the formation of complex ions in solution, and the anhydous forms are best prepared by

the dry methods of treating the heated metals with HCl, Br_2 or I_2 as appropriate. Aqueous preparative methods yield hydrates of which several are known. Significant covalent character is revealed by their comparatively low mps, their solubilities in ethanol, acetone and other organic solvents, and by their layer-lattice (2D) crystal structures. In all cases these may be regarded as close-packed lattices of halides ions in which the Zn^{II} ions occupy tetrahedral, and the Cd^{II} ions octahedral, sites. The structures of $CdCl_2$ ($CdBr_2$ is similar) and CdI_2 are of importance (Fig. 29.2) since they are typical of MX_2 compounds in which marked polarization effects are expected (see chap. 3, pp. 37–61 of ref. 9). Electron diffraction studies show that ZnX_2 (X = Cl, Br, I) have linear X–Zn–X structures in the gas phase.[12]

Concentrated, aqueous solutions of $ZnCl_2$ dissolve starch, cellulose (and therefore cannot be filtered through paper!), and silk. Commercially $ZnCl_2$ is one of the important compounds of zinc. It has applications in textile processing and, because when fused it readily dissolves other oxides, it is used in a number of metallurgical fluxes as well as in the manufacture of magnesia cements in dental fillings. Cadmium halides are used in the preparation of electroplating baths and in the production of pigments.

Covalency is still more pronounced in HgX_2 (X = Cl, Br, I) than in the corresponding

---

solution, $[HgS_2]^{2-}$: the relevant equilibria are:

$$HgS(s) \rightleftharpoons Hg^{2+}(aq) + S^{2-}(aq); \quad pK_s \ 51.8$$

$$HgS(s) + 2H^+(aq) \rightleftharpoons Hg^{2+}(aq) + H_2S \ (1 \ atm); \quad pK' \ 30.8$$

$$HgS(s) + H_2S(g) \rightleftharpoons [Hg(SH)_2](aq); \quad pK \ 6.2$$

$$HgS(s) + S^{2-}(aq) \rightleftharpoons [HgS_2]^{2-}(aq); \quad pK \ 1.5$$

[12] M. HARGITTAI, J. TREMMEL and I. HARGITTAI, *Inorg. Chem.* **25**, 3163–6 (1986).

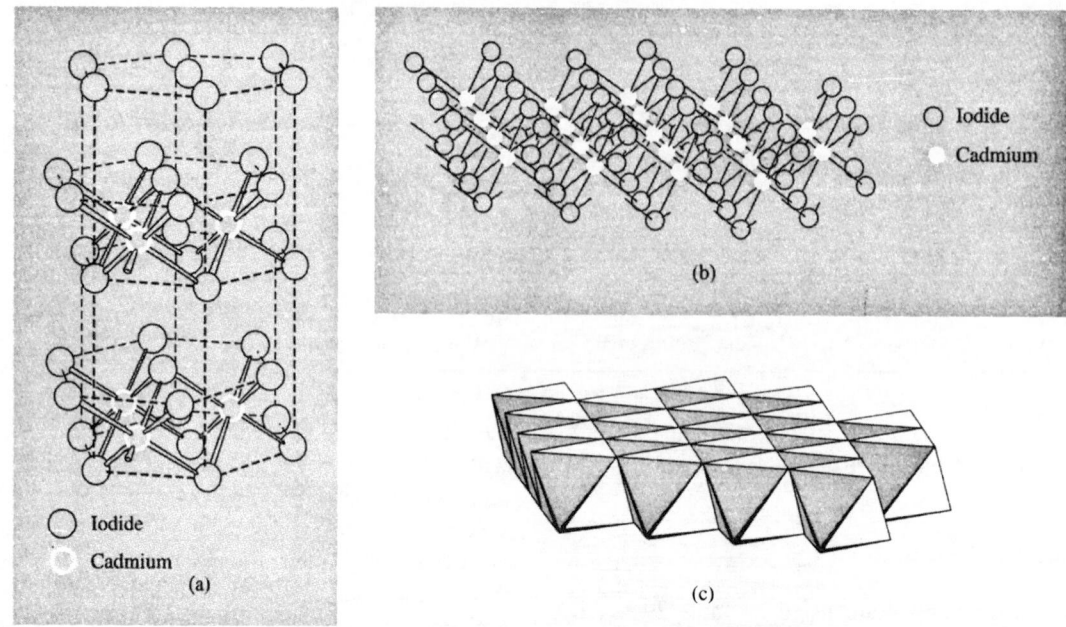

Figure 29.2 The layer structure of crystalline CdI_2: (a) Shows the hexagonal close-packing of I atoms with Cd atoms in alternate layers of octahedral sites sandwiched between layers of I atoms. In $CdCl_2$ the individual composite layers are identical with those in CdI_2, but they are arranged so that the Cl atoms are ccp. (b) Shows a portion of an individual composite layer of CdI_6 (or $CdCl_6$) octahedra. (c) Shows the same portion of a composite layer as in (b) and viewed from the same angle, but with CdI_2 (or $CdCl_2$) units represented by solid, edge-sharing octahedra.

halides of Zn and Cd. These compounds are readily prepared from the elements and are low-melting volatile solids, soluble in many organic solvents. Their solubilities in water, where they exist almost entirely as HgX_2 molecules, decrease with increasing molecular weight, HgI_2 being only slightly soluble, and they may be precipitated anhydrous from aqueous solutions by metathetical reactions. Their crystalline structures reveal an interesting gradation. $HgCl_2$ is composed of linear Cl–Hg–Cl molecules (Hg–Cl = 225 pm and the next shortest Hg$\cdots$Cl distance is 334 pm); $HgBr_2$ and HgI_2 have layer structures. However, in the bromide although the Hg^{II} may be regarded as 6-coordinated, two Hg–Br distances are much shorter than the other four (248 pm compared to 323 pm). In the red variety of the iodide the Hg^{II} is unambiguously tetrahedrally 4-coordinated (Hg–I = 278 pm). At temperatures above 126°C HgI_2 exists as a

less-dense, yellow form similar to $HgBr_2$. In the gaseous phase all 3 of these Hg^{II} halides exist as discrete linear HgX_2 molecules. Comparison of the Hg–X distances in these molecules (Hg–Cl = 228 pm, Hg–Br = 240 pm; Hg–I = 257 pm) with those given above, indicate an increasing departure from molecularity in passing from the solid chloride to the solid iodide.

$HgCl_2$ is the "corrosive sublimate" of antiquity, formerly obtained by sublimation from $HgSO_4$ and NaCl and used as an antiseptic. It is, however, a violent poison and was widely used as such in the Middle Ages.[5]

The halides are the most familiar compounds of mercury(I) and all contain the Hg_2^{2+} ion (see below). Hg_2F_2 is obtained by treating Hg_2CO_3 (itself precipitated by $NaHCO_3$ from aqueous $Hg_2(NO_3)_2$ which in turn is obtained by the action of dil HNO_3 on an excess of metallic mercury) with aqueous HF. It dissolves in water but is at once hydrolysed to the "black oxide" which is actually a mixture of Hg and HgO. On heating, it disproportionates to the metal and HgF_2. The other halides are virtually insoluble in water and so, being free from the possibility of hydrolysis, may be precipitated from aqueous solutions of $Hg_2(NO_3)_2$ by addition of X^-. Alternatively, they may be prepared by treatment of HgX_2 with the metal. Hg_2Cl_2 and Hg_2Br_2 are easily volatilized and their vapour densities correspond to "monomeric HgX". However, the diamagnetism of the vapour (Hg^I in HgX would be paramagnetic) and the ultraviolet absorption at the wavelength (253.7 nm) characteristic of Hg vapour, make it clear that decomposition to $Hg + HgX_2$ is the real reason for the halved vapour density. Hg_2I_2 decomposes similarly but even more readily, and the presence of finely divided metal is thought to be the cause of the greenish tints commonly found in samples of this otherwise yellow solid.

Calomel,[†] Hg_2Cl_2, has been widely used medicinally but possible contamination by the more soluble and poisonous $HgCl_2$ renders this a hazardous nostrum.

29.3.3 Mercury(I)

Raman spectra, indicative of $[M-M]^{2+}$ ions, are produced by the yellow glass obtained from the melt of Zn in $ZnCl_2$ and also by the colourless, very moisture sensitive crystals of $Cd_2Al_2Cl_8$ obtained from melts of Cd in $CdCl_2$ and $AlCl_3$. X-ray studies show that the latter contains "ethane-like" $[Cd_2Cl_6]^{4-}$ groups with Cd–Cd reported as 257.6 pm[13] and 256.1 pm[14] (cf 302 pm in the metal itself). The ^{113}Cd nmr

spectrum[15] of $[Cd\{HB(3,5-Me_2pz)_3\}]_2$ (pz = polycyclic pyrazolyl ligand) yields a $^{111}Cd-^{113}Cd$ coupling constant of 20 646 Hz, indicating a Cd–Cd bond; the first to be observed in a molecular complex of Cd. However, only for mercury is the formal oxidation state I of importance.

Mercury(I) compounds in general may be prepared, like the halides just discussed, by the reduction of the corresponding Hg^{II} salt, often by the metal itself, or by precipitation from aqueous solutions of the nitrate. The nitrate is known as the dihydrate, $Hg_2(NO_3)_2.2H_2O$, and is stable in water if this is acidified, otherwise basic salts such as $Hg(OH)(NO_3)$ and $Hg_2(OH)(NO_3)$ are precipitated. The perchlorate is the only other appreciably soluble salt, the rest being either insoluble or, like the sulfate, chlorate and salts of organic acids, only sparingly soluble. In all cases the dinuclear Hg_2^{2+} ion is present rather than mononuclear Hg^+. The evidence for this is overwhelming and includes the following:

(1) In crystalline mercury(I) compounds, instead of the sequence of alternate M^+ and X^- expected for MX compounds, Hg–Hg pairs are found in which the separation, though not constant, lies in the range 250–270 pm[5] which is shorter than the Hg–Hg separation of 300 pm found in the metal itself.

(2) The Raman spectrum of aqueous mercury(I) nitrate has, in addition to lines characteristic of the NO_3^- ion, a strong absorption at 171.7 cm^{-1} which is not found in the spectra of other metal nitrates and is not active in the infrared; it is therefore diagnostic of the Hg–Hg stretching vibration since homonuclear diatomic vibrations are Raman active not infrared active.[†] Similar data have subsequently been produced for a number of other compounds in the solid state and in solution.

[†] Calomel, derived from the Greek words καλό-ς (beautiful) and μέλας (black), seems an odd name for a white solid. It might arise from the colour of the material obtained when Hg_2Cl_2 is treated with ammonia; this is a product of variable composition (see below) which owes its colour to the presence of metallic mercury. Other more fanciful derivations are listed in the *Oxford English Dictionary* **2**, 41 (1970).

[13] R. FAGGIANI, R. J. GILLESPIE and J. E. VEKRIS, *J. Chem. Soc., Chem. Commun.*, 517–8 (1986).

[14] T. STAFFEL and G. MEYER, *Z. anorg. allg. Chem.* **548**, 45–54 (1987).

[15] D. L. REGER, S. S. MASON and A. L. RHEINGOLD, *J. Am. Chem. Soc.* **115**, 10406–7 (1993).

[†] Indeed, this is perhaps the earliest example of a new structural species to be established by Raman spectroscopy. (L. A. WOODWARD, *Phil. Mag.* **18**, 823–7 (1934).)

(3) Mercury(I) compounds are diamagnetic, whereas the monatomic Hg^+ ion would have a $d^{10}s^1$ configuration and so be paramagnetic.

(4) The measured emfs of concentration cells of mercury(I) salts are only explicable on the assumption that a 2-electron transfer is involved. This would not be the case if Hg^+ were involved: $[E = (2.303RT/nF)\log a_1/a_2$ where $n = 2$ for Hg_2^{2+} and $n = 1$ for $Hg^+]$.

(5) It is found that "equilibrium constants" are in fact only constant if the concentration $[Hg_2^{2+}]$ is employed rather than $[Hg^+]^2$, i.e. the equilibria must be of the type:

$$2Hg + 2Ag^+ \rightleftharpoons Hg_2^{2+} + 2Ag$$

(rather than

$$Hg + Ag^+ \rightleftharpoons Hg^+ + Ag)$$

or $Hg + Hg^{2+} \rightleftharpoons Hg_2^{2+}$

(rather than

$$Hg + Hg^{2+} \rightleftharpoons 2Hg^+)$$

In order to understand the formation and stability of mercury(I) compounds it is helpful to consider the relevant reduction potentials:

$$Hg_2^{2+} + 2e^- \rightleftharpoons 2Hg(l); \quad E^\circ + 0.7889\,V$$

and $\quad 2Hg^{2+} + 2e^- \rightleftharpoons Hg_2^{2+}; \quad E^\circ + 0.920\,V$

From this it follows that

$$Hg^{2+} + 2e^- \rightleftharpoons Hg(l); \quad E^\circ + 0.8545\,V$$

and $\quad Hg_2^{2+} \rightleftharpoons Hg(l) + Hg^{2+}; \quad E^\circ - 0.131\,V$

Now, $E^\circ = (RT/nF)\ln K$,

i.e. $\quad E^\circ = (0.0591/n)\log_{10} K$

Hence, $\log_{10} K = -(0.131/0.0591) = -2.217$,

i.e. $\quad K = [Hg^{2+}]/[Hg_2^{2+}] = 0.0061$

Thus, at equilibrium, aqueous solutions of mercury(I) salts will contain around 0.6% of mercury(II) and the rather finely balanced equilibrium is easily displaced. The presence of any reagent which reduces the activity (in effect the concentration) of Hg^{2+} more than that of Hg_2^{2+}, either by forming a less-soluble salt or a more-stable complex of Hg^{2+} will displace the equilibrium to the right and cause the disproportionation of the Hg_2^{2+}. There are many such reagents, including S^{2-}, OH^-, CN^-, NH_3 and acetylacetone. This is why the most stable Hg_2^{2+} salts are the insoluble ones and why there are few stable complexes. Those which are known all involve either *O*- or *N*-donor ligands,[†] the linear $O-Hg-Hg-O$ group being a common feature of the former.

Polycations of mercury

The $Hg-Hg$ bond in Hg_2^{2+} may be ascribed to overlap of the 6s orbitals with little involvement of 6p orbitals or of the filled d^{10} shell of each atom. If this is regarded as the coordination of Hg to an Hg^{2+} cation, the coordination of a second Hg ligand is also feasible. Accordingly, $Hg_3(AlCl_4)_2$ can be obtained from a molten mixture of $HgCl_2$, Hg and $AlCl_3$ and contains the discrete, virtually linear cation

$$[Hg \xrightarrow{255\,pm} Hg \longrightarrow Hg]^{2+}$$

in which the formal oxidation state of Hg is $+\frac{2}{3}$.

Still more interesting is the oxidation of Hg by AsF_5 in liquid SO_2:[16,17] in this process the AsF_5 serves both as an oxidant (being reduced to AsF_3) and also as a fluoride-ion acceptor to give AsF_6^-. In a matter of minutes the colour of the solution becomes bright yellow then deepens to red as the Hg simultaneously turns to a shiny golden-yellow solid; the solid then begins to dissolve to give an orange and, finally, a colourless solution. By controlling the quantity of oxidant, AsF_5, and removing the solution at the appropriate stages, it is possible to crystallize a series of extremely moisture-sensitive materials:

[†] For this reason, although Hg_2^{2+} must be regarded as a class-b cation (e.g. the aqueous solubilities of its halides decrease in the order F^- to I^-), it is evidently less so than Hg^{2+} which has a notable preference for *S* donors.

[16] I. D. BROWN, W. R. DATARS and R. J. GILLESPIE, pp. 1–41 in *Extended Linear Chain Compounds*, Plenum Press, New York, Vol. III (1982).

[17] R. J. GILLESPIE, P. GRANGER, K. R. MORGAN and G. J. SCHROBILGEN, *Inorg. Chem.* **23**, 887–91 (1984).

(a) deep red-black $Hg_4(AsF_6)_2$, the cation of which is the almost linear

$$[Hg \xrightarrow{255\,pm} Hg \xrightarrow{262\,pm} Hg \xrightarrow{259\,pm} Hg]^{2+}$$

with Hg in the formal average oxidation state $+\frac{1}{2}$;

(b) orange $Hg_3(AsF_6)_2$, containing the trimeric cation mentioned above; and

(c) colourless $Hg_2(AsF_6)_2$, containing the dimeric Hg^I cation.

By working at lower temperatures ($-20°C$) to reduce the reaction rate, or by using specially designed apparatus which limits the access of AsF_5 to the Hg, it has been possible to isolate large single crystals of the intermediate golden-yellow solid having dimensions up to $35 \times 35 \times 2\,mm^3$. X-ray analysis, supported by neutron diffraction, shows that it consists of a tetragonal lattice ($a = b \neq c$) of octahedral AsF_6^- anions with two non-intersecting and mutually perpendicular chains of Hg atoms running through it in the a and b directions. Chemical analysis suggests the composition $Hg_3(AsF_6)$ and a formal oxidation state of $Hg = +\frac{1}{3}$. However, the measured Hg–Hg separation of 264 pm along the chains is not commensurate with the parallel dimensions of the lattice unit cell, $a = b = 754$ pm (cf. 3×264 pm $= 792$ pm) and implies instead the nonstoichiometric composition $Hg_{2.82}(AsF_6)$ or more generally $Hg_{3-\delta}(AsF_6)$ since the composition apparently varies with temperature. Partially filled conduction bands formed by overlap of Hg orbitals produce a conductivity in the $a–b$ plane which approaches that of liquid mercury and the material becomes superconducting at 4 K.

Use of SbF_5 instead of AsF_5 produces a series of entirely analogous compounds including $Hg_{3-\delta}(SbF_6)$ but because the unit cell of the $(SbF_6)^-$ lattice is somewhat larger than that of $(AsF_6)^-$, it is formulated as $Hg_{2.90}(SbF_6)$. Oxidations of Hg by $Hg(MF_6)_2$ (M = Nb, Ta) in SO_2 also yield $Hg_{3-\delta}(MF_6)$ but, unlike the As and Sb compounds, these convert in a few hours into silver platelets of Hg_3MF_6 which consist of two

sheets of F atoms separated by hexagonal sheets (rather than linear chains) of Hg atoms.[18]

29.3.4 Zinc(II) and cadmium(II) [19]

The almost invariable oxidation state of these elements is +2 and, in addition to the oxides, chalcogenides and halides already discussed, salts of most anions are known. Oxo-salts are often isomorphous with those of Mg^{II} but with lower thermal stabilities. The carbonates, nitrates, and sulfates all decompose to the oxides on heating. Several, such as the nitrates, perchlorates and sulfates, are very soluble in water and form more than one hydrate. $[Zn(H_2O)_6]^{2+}$ is probably the predominant aquo species in solutions of Zn^{II} salts. Aqueous solutions are appreciably hydrolysed to species such as $[M(OH)(H_2O)_x]^+$ and $[M_2(OH)(H_2O)_x]^{3+}$ and a number of basic (i.e. hydroxo) salts such as $ZnCO_3.2Zn(OH)_2.H_2O$ and $CdCl_2.4Cd(OH)_2$ can be precipitated. Distillation of zinc acetate under reduced pressure yields a crystalline basic acetate, $[Zn_4O(OCOMe)_6]$. The molecular structure of this consists of an oxygen atom surrounded by a tetrahedron of Zn atoms bridged across each edge by acetates. It is isomorphous with the basic acetate of beryllium (p. 122) but, in contrast, the Zn^{II} compound hydrolyses rapidly in water, no doubt because of the ability of Zn^{II} to increase its coordination number above 4.

The coordination chemistry of Zn^{II} and Cd^{II}, although much less extensive than for preceding transition metals, is still appreciable. Neither element forms stable fluoro complexes but, with the other halides, they form the complex anions $[MX_3]^-$ and $[MX_4]^{2-}$, those of Cd^{II} being moderately stable in aqueous solution.[4] By using the large cation $[Co(NH_3)_6]^{3+}$ it is also possible to isolate the trigonal bipyramidal $[CdCl_5]^{2-}$

---

[18] I. D. BROWN, R. J. GILLESPIE, K. R. MORGAN, Z. TUN and P. K. UMMAT, *Inorg. Chem.* **23**, 4506–8 (1984).

[19] R. H. PRINCE, Zinc and Cadmium Chap. 56.1, pp. 925–1045, in *Comprehensive Coordination Chemistry*, Vol. 5, Pergamon Press, Oxford, 1987.

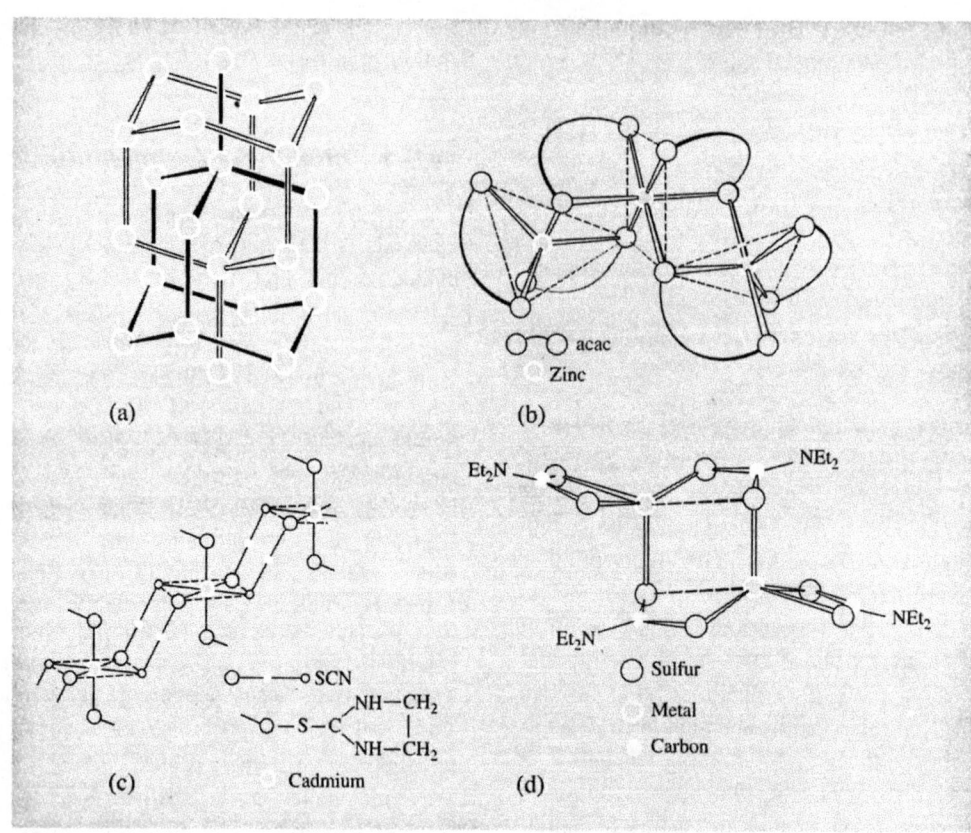

Figure 29.3 Some polymeric complexes: (a) Interpenetrating "adamantine" frameworks in M(CN)$_2$, M = Zn, Cd. (Only M shown; straight lines are CN forming linear MCNM "rods".) (b) [Zn(acac)$_2$]$_3$, (c) [Cd{S=C(NHCH$_2$)$_2$}$_2$(SCN)$_2$], and (d) [M(S$_2$CNEt$_2$)$_2$]$_2$, M = Zn, Cd, Hg. (Note that M is 5-coordinate but with one M–S distance appreciably greater than the other four.)

[MX$_3$]$^-$ and [MX$_4$]$^{2-}$ are formed in CH$_3$CN solutions also.[20] Tetrahedral complexes are the most common type and are formed with a variety of O-donor ligands (more readily with Zn^{II} than Cd^{II}), more stable ones with N-donor ligands such as NH$_3$ and amines. Some of the apparently 3-coordinate complexes have a higher coordination number because of aquation or association but, no doubt because the ligand is bulky, 2-coordinated Zn occurs in [Zn{N(CMe$_3$)(SiMe$_3$)}$_2$], the first homoleptic zinc amide to be structurally characterized.[21]

The ability of CN$^-$ to co-ordinate through either C or N has interesting stereochemical consequences. Crystalline M(CN)$_2$ consist of linear M–C–N–M "rods" and tetrahedrally co-ordinated M^{II}, arranged so as to form interpenetrating "adamantine" frameworks (Fig. 29.3a). Each "rod" projects through a cyclohexane-like "window" of the other framework with the M atoms at each end occupying cavities of the other framework.[22] When aqueous solutions of CdCl$_2$ + K[Cd(CN)$_4$] are left in contact with liquids such as CCl$_4$, CMeCl$_3$ ...... CMe$_4$, crystals of the clathrates Cd(CN)$_2$.G form at the interface

[20] D. P. GRADDON and C. S. KHOO, *Polyhedron* **7**, 2129–33 (1988).

[21] W. S. REES Jr., D. M. GREEN and W. HESSE, *Polyhedron*, **11**, 1697–9 (1992).

[22] B. F. HOSKINS and R. ROBSON, *J. Am. Chem. Soc.* **112**, 1546–54 (1990).

of the immiscible liquids.[23] In these, the guest molecules G, occupy the cavities of a single adamantine framework. $(NMe_4)[Cu^IZn(CN)_4]$ consists of a similar framework but this time half the cavities are occupied by NMe_4^+ cations. Another type of framework is found in $Cd(CN)_2.\frac{2}{3}H_2O.Bu^tOH$ which crystallizes from 50% aqueous Bu^tOH solutions of $Cd(CN)_2$. It contains CdCNCd "rods" but this time they are bent, $\frac{2}{3}$ of the Cd atoms are tetrahedrally co-ordinated by $4CN^-$, the other $\frac{1}{3}$ being octahedrally co-ordinated by $4CN^-$ and $2H_2O$. The result is a honeycomb framework with linear channels of hexagonal cross-section containing disordered Bu^tOH molecules.[24] Linear channels are also found in $Cd(CN)_2.G$ (G = dmf, dmso)[25] but the large cation in $(PPh_4)_3[(CN)_3CdCNCd(CN)_3]$ apparently prevents the formation of a 3D framework and instead stabilizes the discrete anion.[26]

Complexes of higher coordination number are often in equilibrium with the tetrahedral form and may be isolated by increasing the ligand concentration or by adding large counter ions, e.g. $[M(NH_3)_6]^{2+}$, $[M(en)_3]^{2+}$ or $[M(bipy)_3]^{2+}$. With acetylacetone, zinc achieves both 5- and 6-coordination by trimerizing to $[Zn(acac)_2]_3$ (Fig. 29.3b). Five-coordination is also found in adducts such as the distorted trigonal bipyramidal $[Zn(acac)_2(H_2O)]$ and $[Zn(glycinate)_2(H_2O)]$ while the hydrazinium sulfate $(N_2H_5)_2Zn(SO_4)_2$ contains 6-coordinated zinc. This is isomorphous with the Cr^{II} compound (p. 1031) and in the crystalline form consists of chains of Zn^{II} bridged by SO_4^{2-} ions, with each Zn^{II} additionally coordinated to two *trans*-$N_2H_5^+$ ions. The zinc porphyrin complex, $[Zn(porph)(thf)]$, (porph = *meso*-tetraphenyltetrabenzoporphyrin)

is approximately square pyramidal with thf at its apex. Being somewhat flexible the porphyrin is distorted into a saddle shape, 2 N being displaced above its mean plane and 2 N below it.[27]

Complexes with SCN^- throw light on the relative affinities of the two metals for N- and S-donors. In $[Zn(NCS)_4]^{2-}$ the ligand is N-bonded whereas in $[Cd(SCN)_4]^{2-}$ it is S-bonded. SCN^- can also act as a bridging group, as in $[Cd\{S=C(NHCH_2)_2\}_2(SCN)_2]$ when linear chains of octahedrally coordinated Cd^{II} are formed (Fig. 29.3c). A number of zinc–sulfur compounds are used as accelerators in the vulcanization of rubber. Among these are the dithiocarbamates, of which $[Zn(S_2CNEt_2)_2]_2$, and the isostructural Cd^{II} and Hg^{II} compounds achieve 5-coordination by dimerizing (Fig. 29.3d).

Coordination numbers higher than 6 are rare and in some cases are known to involve chelating NO_3^- ions which not only have a small "bite" but, may also be coordinated asymmetrically so that the coordination number is not well defined.

29.3.5 Mercury(II) [28]

The oxide (p. 1209), chalcogenides (p. 1210) and halides (p. 1211) have already been described. Of them, the only ionic compound is HgF_2 but other compounds in which there is appreciable charge separation are the hydrated salts of strong oxoacids, e.g. the nitrate, perchlorate, and sulfate. In aqueous solution such salts are extensively hydrolysed (HgO is only very weakly basic) and they require acidification to prevent the formation of polynuclear hydroxo-bridged species or the precipitation of basic salts such as $Hg(OH)(NO_3)$ which contains infinite zigzag chains:

23 T. Kitazawa, S. Nishikiori, A. Yamagishi, R. Kuroda and T. Iwamoto, *J. Chem. Soc., Chem. Commun.*, 413–5 (1992); T. Kitazawa, T. Kikoyama, M. Takeda and T. Iwamoto, *J. Chem. Soc., Dalton Trans.*, 3715–20 (1995).

24 B. F. Abrahams, B. F. Hoskins and R. Robson, *J. Chem. Soc., Chem. Commun.*, 60–1 (1990).

25 J. Kim, D. Whang, Y.-S. Koh and K. Kim, *J. Chem. Soc., Chem. Commun.*, 637–8 (1994).

26 T. Kitazawa and M. Takeda, *J. Chem. Soc., Chem. Commun.*, 309–10 (1993).

27 R.-J. Cheng, Y.-R. Chen, S. L. Wang and C. Y. Cheng, *Polyhedron*, **12**, 1353–60 (1993).

28 K. Brodersen and H.-U. Hummel, Mercury, Chap. 56.2, pp. 1047–1130, in *Comprehensive Coordination Chemistry*, Vol. 5, Pergamon Press, Oxford, 1987.

Their ionic character is symptomatic of the marked reluctance of Hg^{II} to form covalent bonds to oxygen. In the presence of excess NO_3^- ions the aqueous nitrate forms the complex anion $[Hg(NO_3)_4]^{2-}$ in which 8 oxygen atoms from the bidentate nitrate groups are equidistant from the mercury at 240 pm, which is almost precisely the sum of the ionic radii ($140 + 102$ pm). Also, the unusual regular octahedral coordination is found in complexes with O-donor ligands: $[Hg(C_5H_5NO)_6]^{2+}$ (Hg–O = 235 pm), $[Hg(H_2O)_6]^{2+}$ (Hg–O = 234 pm), and $[Hg(Me_2SO)_6]^{2+}$ (Hg–O = 234 pm). In contrast, the more covalently bonding β-diketonates do not form complexes.

The most usual type of coordination in compounds of Hg^{II} with other donor atoms is a distorted octahedron with 2 bonds much shorter than the other 4. In the extreme, this results in linear 2-coordination in which case the bonds are largely covalent. $Hg(CN)_2$ is actually composed of discrete linear molecules (C-bonded CN^-), whereas crystalline[†] $Hg(SCN)_2$ is built up of distorted octahedral units, all SCN groups being bridging:

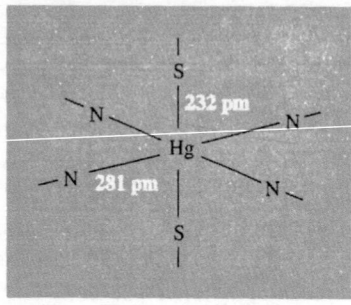

With both these pseudo halides, an excess produces complex anions $[HgX_3]^-$ and the tetrahedral $[HgX_4]^{2-}$.

Similar halogeno complexes are produced in solution, and several salts of $[HgX_3]^-$ have been isolated and characterized; they display a variety of stereochemistries. In $[HgCl_3]^-$ the environment of the Hg^{II} is either distorted octahedral (with small cations such as NH_4^+

or Na^+) or distorted trigonal bipyramidal (with larger cations such as $[NEt_4]^+$, $[SMe_3]^+$ or $[NH_2\{(CH_2)_2NH_3\}_2]^{3+(29)}$), whereas in salts of $[HgBr_3]^-$ and $[HgI_3]^-$ the coordination is more commonly distorted tetrahedral. In $[NBu_4^n][HgI_3]$ the anion is planar but, with one I–Hg–I angle 115°, its symmetry is C_{2v} rather than D_{3h}. In aqueous solution spectroscopic evidence suggests that $[HgCl_3]^-$ is planar with $2H_2O$ completing a trigonal bipyramidal coordination sphere; $[HgI_3]^-$ is pyramidal with H_2O completing a tetrahedral coordination sphere, while $[HgBr_3]^-$ shows features of both structures.[30]

In the presence of excess halide, $[HgX_4]^{2-}$ complex ions are produced and in comparison with those of Zn^{II} and Cd^{II} it can be seen that their stabilities increase with the sizes of the anion and the cation so that $[HgI_3]^{2-}$ is the most stable of all. Thus, the normally very insoluble HgI_2 will dissolve in aqueous solutions of I^- which can then be made strongly alkaline without precipitation occurring. Such solutions are known as Nessler's reagent, which is used as a sensitive test for ammonia since this produces a yellow or brown coloration due to the formation of $Hg_2NI.H_2O$, the iodo salt of Millon's base (see p. 1220). Adducts of the halides HgX_2, with N-, S-, and P-donor ligands are known, those with N-donors being especially numerous. Their stereochemistries are largely of the expected tetrahedral, or grossly distorted octahedral, types.

Hg^{II}–N compounds [5,28]

Mercury has a characteristic ability to form not only conventional ammine and amine complexes but also, by the displacement of hydrogen, direct covalent bonds to nitrogen, e.g.:

$$Hg^{2+} + 2NH_3 \rightleftharpoons [Hg{-}NH_2]^+ + NH_4^+$$

[†] Pellets of the dry powder, when ignited in air, form snake-like tubes of spongy ash of unknown composition — the so-called "Pharaoh's serpents".

[29] The compound $[NH_2\{(CH_2)_2NH_3\}_2]_2HgCl_8$ contains the trigonal bipyramidal anion $[HgCl_5]^{3-}$; see L. P. Battaglia, A. B. Corradi, L. Antolini, T. Manfredini, L. Menabue, G. C. Pellacani and G. Ponticelli, *J. Chem. Soc., Dalton Trans.*, 2529–33 (1986).

[30] T. R. Griffiths and R. A. Anderson, *J. Chem. Soc., Faraday*, **86**, 1425–35 (1990).

Thus in the presence of an excess of NH_4^+, which suppresses this forward reaction, and counteranions such as NO_3^- and ClO_4^-, which have little tendency to coordinate, complexes such as $[Hg(NH_3)_4]^{2+}$, $[Hg(L\text{-}L)_2]^{2+}$ and even $[Hg(L\text{-}L)_3]^{2+}$ (L-L = en, bipy, phen) can be prepared. But, in the absence of such precautions, amino, or imino-compounds are likely to be formed, often together. Because of this variety of simultaneous reactions and their dependence on the precise conditions, many reactions between Hg^{II} and amines, although first performed by alchemists in the Middle Ages, remained obscure until the application of X-ray crystallography and, still more recently, spectroscopic techniques such as nmr, infrared and Raman.

The action of aqueous ammonia on $HgCl_2$, for instance, may be described by the three reactions:

$$HgCl_2 + 2NH_3 \rightleftharpoons [Hg(NH_3)_2Cl_2] \qquad (1)$$

$$[Hg(NH_3)_2Cl_2] \rightleftharpoons [Hg(NH_2)Cl] + NH_4Cl \qquad (2)$$

$$2[Hg(NH_2)Cl] + H_2O \rightleftharpoons [Hg_2NCl(H_2O)]$$
$$+ NH_4Cl \qquad (3)$$

In general, all these products are obtained in proportions which depend on the concentrations of NH_3 and NH_4^+ and on the temperature, but more or less pure products can be prepared by suitably adjusting the conditions.

The diammine $[Hg(NH_3)_2Cl_2]$, descriptively known as "fusible white precipitate", can be isolated by maintaining a high concentration of NH_4^+, since reactions (2) and (3) are thereby inhibited, or better still by using non-polar solvents. It is made up of a cubic lattice of Cl^- ions with linear H_3N–Hg–NH_3 groups inserted so as to give the common, distorted octahedral coordination about Hg^{II} (Hg–N = 203 pm, Hg–Cl = 287 pm) (Fig. 29.4a).

By using a low concentration of NH_3 and with no NH_4^+ initially present, the amide $[Hg(NH_2)Cl]$, "infusible white precipitate" is

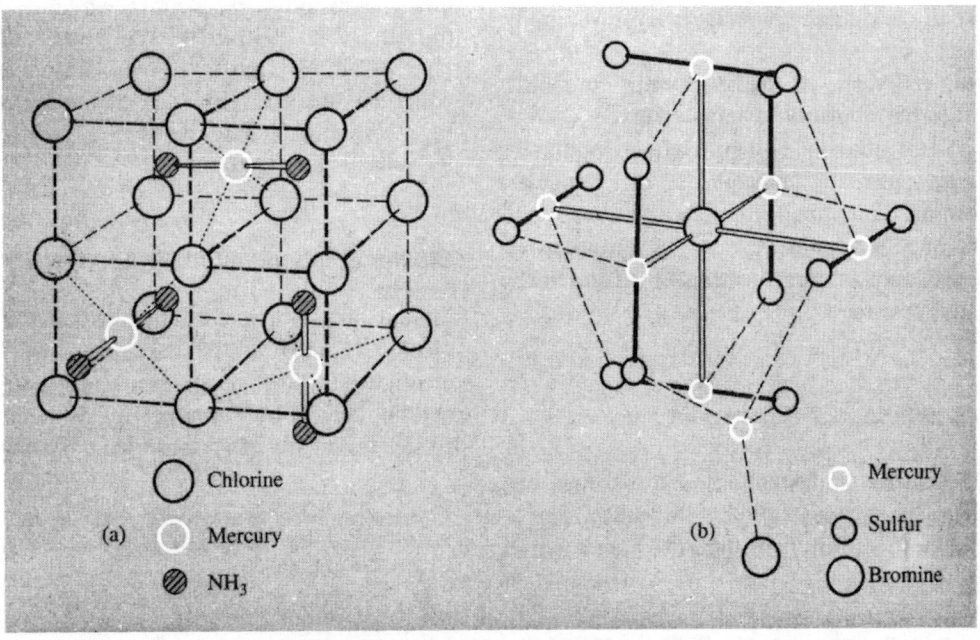

        ○ Chlorine   ○ Mercury

(a)   ○ Mercury   (b)   ○ Sulfur

       ◍ NH_3 ○ Bromine

Figure 29.4   (a) Crystal structure of $Hg(NH_3)_2Cl_2$ showing linear NH_3–Hg–NH_3 groups inside a lattice of chloride ions. (b) Central $Hg_7S_{12}Br_2$ core of $[Hg_7(SC_6H_{11})_{12}Br_2]$ showing, in an idealized manner, the octahedron of Hg atoms around a central Br. The tetrahedral coordination of the seventh Hg is completed with the second Br.

obtained. This consists of parallel chains of $\{Hg(NH_2)\}_\infty$ as above, separated by Cl^- ions.

$[Hg_2NCl(H_2O)]$ is the chloride of Millon's base, $[Hg_2N(OH).(H_2O)_2]$, and can be obtained either by heating the diammine, or amide with water or, better still, by the action of hydrochloric acid on Millon's base which is best prepared by the method, used in 1845 by its discoverer, of warming yellow HgO with aqueous NH_3. Replacement of the OH^- yields a series of salts, $[Hg_2NX(H_2O)]$, the structures of which (and that of the base itself) consist, with only minor variations, of a network of $\{Hg_2N\}^+$ units linked so that each N is tetrahedrally linked to 4 Hg and each Hg is linearly linked to 2 N (Hg–N = 204–209 pm depending on X).[31] The X^- ions and water molecules are accommodated interstitially and these materials behave as anion exchangers.

When Hg_2Cl_2 is treated with aqueous NH_3 disproportionation occurs ($Hg_2Cl_2 \longrightarrow HgCl_2 + Hg$); the $HgCl_2$ then reacts as outlined above to give a precipitate of variable composition. The liberated mercury, however, renders the precipitate black, as previously mentioned, and so forms the basis of a distinctive qualitative test for Hg_2^{2+}.

Hg^{II}–S compounds[32]

As indicated by the insolubility and inertness of HgS, Hg^{II} has a great affinity for sulfur. HgO reacts vigorously with mercaptans (which is why

RSH were given the name mercaptans[†]), displacing the H as with amines:

$$HgO + 2RSH \longrightarrow Hg(SR)_2 + H_2O$$

These mercaptides are low-melting solids, soluble in $CHCl_3$ and C_6H_6. Though their structures depend on R and some, such as $Hg(SR)_2$, (R = Bu^t, Ph) are polymers containing tetrahedral HgS_4 units, most contain linear (or nearly linear) S–Hg–S. Even in $[Hg(SC_6H_2Bu^t_3)_2(py)]$ where the Hg is 3-coordinate and T-shaped the S–Hg–S is still nearly linear (172°).[33] Most of the thioether (SR_2) complexes which have been prepared are adducts of the Hg^{II} halides and include both monomeric and polymeric (i.e. X-bridged) species as is the case with mixed thiolate–halide complexes. In $[Hg_7(SC_6H_{11})_{12}Br_2]$, which is obtained as colourless crystals when methanolic solutions of $HgBr_2$ and sodium cyclohexanethiolate are mixed, six Hg atoms are 4-coordinate but contain almost linear S–Hg–S (av. angle = 159.3°) and the seventh Hg is tetrahedrally coordinated. The six Hg atoms form a distorted octahedron around a central Br (Fig. 29.4b).[34] The dithiocarbamate $[Hg(S_2CNEt_2)_2]$ exists in two forms, one of which has the same structure as the corresponding Zn^{II} and Cd^{II} compounds (Fig. 29.3d), while the other is polymeric.

Cluster compounds involving mercury[35,36]

Mercury has a marked ability to bond to other metals. In addition to the amalgams already mentioned (p. 1206) it acts as a versatile structural building block by forming Hg–M bonds with cluster fragments of various types: e.g. reduction

[†] Mercaptans were discovered in 1834 by W. C. Zeise (pp. 930, 1167) who named them from the Latin *mercurium captans*, catching mercury.

[33] M. BOCHMANN, K. J. WEBB and A. K. POWELL, *Polyhedron* **11**, 513–6 (1992).

[34] T. ALSINA, W. CLEGG, K. A. FRASER and J. SOLA, *J. Chem. Soc., Chem. Commun.*, 1010–1 (1992).

[35] L. H. GADE, *Angew. Chem. Int. Edn. Engl.* **32**, 23–40 (1993).

[36] R. B. KING, *Polyhedron*, **7**, 1813–7 (1988).

[31] A. F. WELLS, *Structural Inorganic Chemistry*, 5th edn., Oxford University Press, Oxford, 1984: the structural chemistry of mercury is reviewed on pp. 1156–69.

[32] J. G. WRIGHT, M. J. NATAN, F. M. MACDONNELL, D. M. RALSTON and T. V. O'HALLORAN, *Prog. Inorg. Chem.* **38**, 323–412 (1990).

Table 29.4 Comparison of some typical organometallic compounds MR_2

R	Zn		Cd		Hg	
	MP/°C	BP/°C	MP/°C	BP/°C	MP/°C	BP/°C
Me	−29.2	46	−4.5	105.5	—	92.5
Et	−28	117	−21	64 (19 mmHg)	—	159
Ph	107	d 280	173	—	121.8 (subl)	204 (10 mmHg)

of [RhCl(PMe$_3$)$_3$] with Na amalgams gives Hg$_6$[Rh(PMe$_3$)$_3$]$_4$ which consists of an Hg$_6$ octahedron, four faces of which are capped by Rh(PMe$_3$)$_3$ groups. Again, Hg^{II} halides react with carbonylate anions yielding products such as [Os$_3$(CO)$_{11}$Hg]$_3$ comprising a most unusual "raft" structure in which three Os$_3$ triangles surround a central Hg$_3$ triangle in a planar array. From [Os$_{10}$C(CO)$_{24}$]$^{2-}$ it is possible to obtain [Os$_{20}$Hg(C)$_2$(CO)$_{48}$]$^{2-}$ the central portion of which is an HgOs$_2$ triangle. Whereas the "raft" cluster has no redox chemistry, the {Os$_{20}$Hg} cluster like the Os$_{10}$ cluster (p. 1108) from which it is formed, gives rise to five different redox states.

29.3.6 Organometallic compounds [37]

Although they were not the first organometallic compounds to be prepared (Zeise's salt was discovered in 1827) the discovery of zinc alkyls in 1849 by Sir Edward Frankland may be taken as the beginning of organometallic chemistry. Frankland's studies led to their employment as intermediates in organic synthesis, while the measurements of vapour densities led to his suggestion, crucial to the development of valency theory, that each element has a limited but definite combining capacity. After their discovery in 1900 Grignard reagents largely superseded the zinc alkyls in organic synthesis, but by then many of the reactions for which they are now used had already been worked out on the zinc compounds.

Alkyls of the types RZnX and ZnR$_2$ are both known and may be prepared by essentially the

original method of heating Zn with boiling RX in an inert atmosphere (CO$_2$ or N$_2$):

$$Zn + RX \longrightarrow RZnX$$

and then raising the temperature to distil the dialkyl:

$$2RZnX \longrightarrow ZnR_2 + ZnX_2$$

These reactions work best with X = I but the less-expensive RBr can be used in conjunction with a Zn–Cu alloy instead of pure Zn. Diaryls are best obtained from appropriate organoboranes or organomercury compounds:

$$3ZnMe_2 + 2BR_3 \longrightarrow 3ZnR_2 + 2BMe_3$$

or
$$Zn + HgR_2 \longrightarrow ZnR_2 + Hg$$

ZnR$_2$ are covalent, non-polar liquids or low-boiling solids (Table 29.4). They are invariably monomeric in solution with linear C–Zn–C coordination at the Zn atom. They are very susceptible to attack by air and those of low molecular weight are spontaneously flammable, producing a smoke of ZnO. Their reactions with water, alcohols and ammonia, etc., are generally similar to, but less vigorous than, those of Grignard reagents (p. 132) with the important difference that they are unaffected by CO$_2$; indeed, they are often prepared under an atmosphere of this gas.

Organocadmium compounds are normally prepared from the appropriate Grignard reagents:

$$CdX_2 + 2RMgX \longrightarrow CdR_2 + 2MgX_2$$

and then if desired:

$$CdR_2 + CdX_2 \longrightarrow 2RCdX$$

They are thermally less stable than their Zn counterparts but generally less reactive (not normally

---

[37] J. L. WARDELL, *Organometallic Compounds of Zinc, Cadmium and Mercury*, Chapman & Hall, London, 1985, 220 pp.

catching fire in air), and so their most important use (but see also ref. 38) is to prepare ketones from acid chlorides:

$$2R'COCl + CdR_2 \longrightarrow 2R'COR + CdCl_2$$

The use of Grignard reagents is impracticable here since they react further with the ketone.

An enormous number of organomercury compounds are known. They are predominantly of the same stoichiometries as those of Zn and Cd, viz. RHgX and HgR$_2$, and may be prepared by the action of sodium amalgam on RX:

$$2Hg + 2RX \longrightarrow HgR_2 + HgX_2$$

$$HgCl_2 + 2Na \longrightarrow Hg + 2NaCl$$

More usually they are made by the reaction of Grignard reagents on HgCl$_2$ in thf:

$$RMgX + HgCl_2 \longrightarrow RHgCl + MgXCl$$

$$RMgX + RHgCl \longrightarrow HgR_2 + MgXCl$$

or simply by the action of HgX$_2$ on a hydrocarbon:

$$HgX_2 + RH \longrightarrow RHgX + HX \text{ (mercuration).}$$

RHgX are crystalline solids, and HgR$_2$ are extremely toxic liquids or low-melting solids (Table 29.4). They are essentially covalent materials except when $X^- = F^-$, NO_3^- or SO_4^{2-}, in which cases the former are water-soluble and apparently ionic, $[RHg]^+X^-$. There are several reasons for the attention which these compounds have received. The search for pharmacologically valuable drugs has provided a continuing stimulus, and the existence of convenient preparative methods, coupled with their remarkable stability to air and water, has led to their extensive use in mechanistic studies. This stability sets them apart from the organic derivatives of Zn, Cd and Group 2 metals but arises from the extreme weakness of the Hg–O bond rather than an inherently strong Hg–C bond. In fact the latter ·is weak, being commonly only $\sim 60 \, kJ \, mol^{-1}$ and organomercury compounds are

thermally and photochemically unstable, in some cases requiring to be stored at low temperatures in the dark. Indeed, because of the weakness of the bond, Hg can be replaced by many metals which give stronger M–C bonds and the preparation of organo derivatives of other metals (e.g. of Zn and Cd as referred to above) is the most important application of these compounds.

It appears that all RHgX and HgR$_2$ compounds are made up of linear R–Hg–X or R–Hg–R units, which could arise from sp hybridization of the metal.[†] In some cases polymerization is necessary to achieve this linearity. Thus, for instance, *o*-phenylene-mercury, which could conceivably be formulated as

is in fact a cyclic trimer (Fig. 29.5a).[39] Organomercury compounds generally have little tendency to coordinate to further ligands. Exceptions include irregularly 3-coordinated [HgMe(bipy)]NO$_3$[40] and [HgR(Hdz)],[41] T-shaped [Hg(2-pyridylphenyl)Cl][42] (Fig. 29.5b, c, d) and the tetrahedral [HgMe(np$_3$)]$^+$ (np$_3$ is the "tripod" phosphine N{CH$_2$CH$_2$PPh$_2$}$_3$).[43]

Among the versatile and synthetically useful reactions are those typified by the absorption of alkenes (olefins) by methanolic solutions of salts, particularly, the acetate of Hg^{II}. The products are not π complexes, but σ-bonded addition

---

[†] Other possibilities which have been suggested include ds hybridization and minimization of interaction between metal d and non bonding ligand p orbitals — see pp. 351–2 of ref. 32.

[39] D. S. Brown, A. G. Massey and D. A. Wickens, *Acta. Cryst.* **B34**, 1695–7 (1978).

[40] A. J. Canty and B. M. Gatehouse, *J. Chem. Soc., Dalton Trans.*, 2018–20 (1976).

[41] A. T. Hutton and H. M. N. H. Irving, *J. Chem. Soc., Chem. Commun.*, 1113–4 (1979).

[42] E. C. Constable, T. A. Leese and D. A. Tocher, *J. Chem. Soc., Chem. Commun.*, 570–1 (1989).

[43] C. A. Ghilardi, P. Innocenti, S. Midollini, A. Orlandini and A. Vacca, *J. Chem. Soc., Chem. Commun.*, 1691–3 (1992).

[38] P. R. Jones and P. J. Desio, *Chem. Revs.* **78**, 491–516 (1978).

(a)

(b)

(c)

(d)

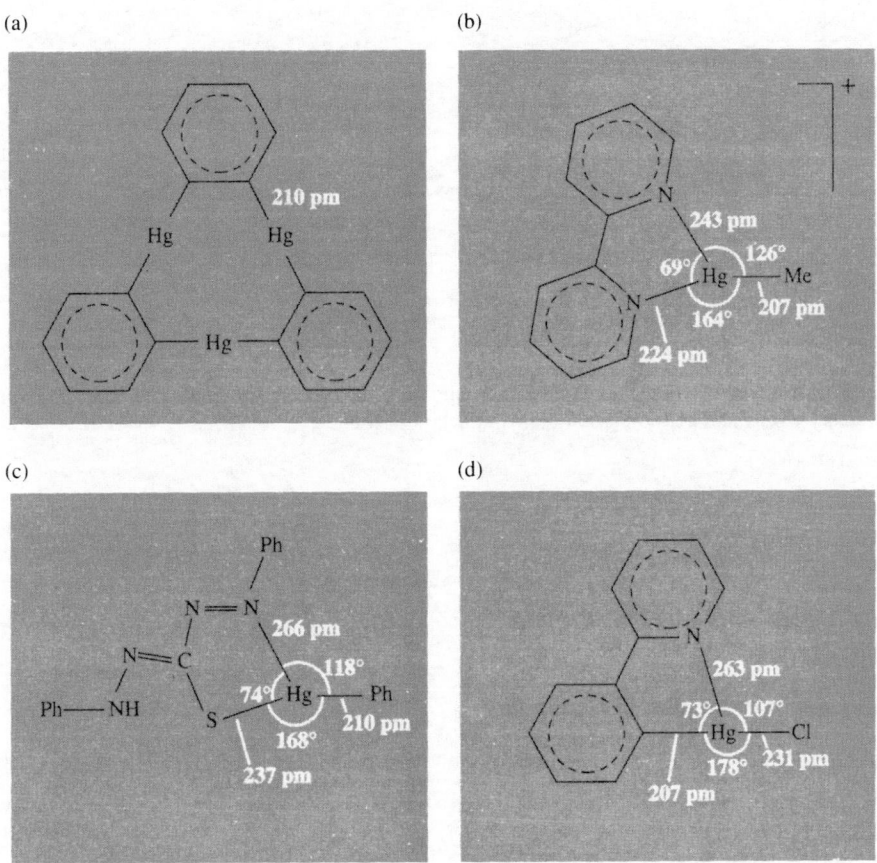

Figure 29.5   (a) *o*-Phenylenemercury trimer, (b) the planar cation in [HgMe(bipy)]NO₃, (c) phenylmercury(II)di-thizonate, and (d) the approximately T-shaped [Hg(2-pyridylphenyl)Cl].

compounds, e.g.:

$$R_2C{=}CR_2 + HgX_2 \rightleftharpoons X-CR_2-CR_2-Hg-X$$

$$\xrightarrow[\text{MeOH}]{(-HX)}$$

$$MeO-CR_2-CR_2-Hg-X$$

Regeneration of the alkene occurs on acidification, e.g. with HCl:

$$R_2C(OMe)C(HgX)R_2 + HCl \longrightarrow R_2C{=}CR_2$$

$$+ \,MeOH + HgXCl$$

Methanolic solutions of Hg^{II} also absorb CO and the products, of the type XHgC(=O)OMe are again σ-bonded.

A similar reluctance to form π bonds is seen in the cyclopentadienyls of mercury such as [Hg(η^1-C₅H₅)₂] and [Hg(η^1-C₅H₅)X]. As they are photosensitive and single crystals are very difficult to obtain, structural information has been derived mainly from infrared and nmr data. These show that the rings are monohapto and the compounds fluxional, i.e. the point of attachment of the Hg to the ring changes rapidly on the nmr time scale so that the 5 carbons are indistinguishable — the phenomenon of "ring whizzing". In the case of [Hg(η^1-C₅H₄PPh₃)I₂]₂ it has been possible to determine the structure by

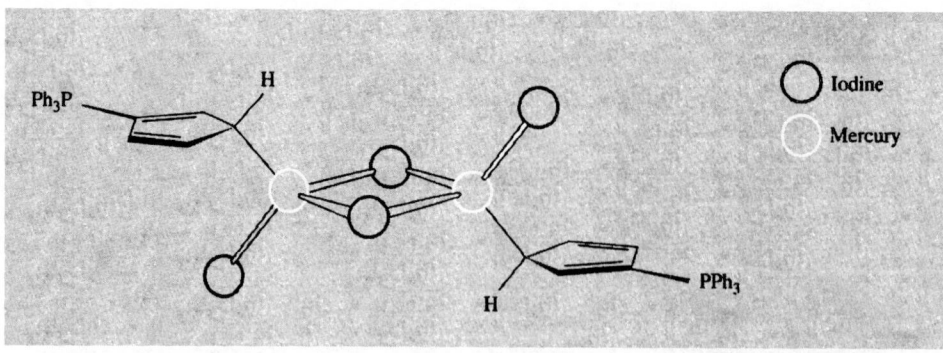

Figure 29.6 The structure of $[Hg(\eta^1\text{-}C_5H_4PPh_3)I_2]_2$ showing the essentially tetrahedral coordination of the mercury atoms and of the carbon atoms attached to them.

X-ray diffraction[44] which confirms the presence of an Hg–C σ bond (Fig. 29.6).

29.3.7 Biological and environmental importance [45,46,46a]

It is a remarkable contrast that, whereas Zn is biologically one of the most important metals and is apparently necessary to all forms of life,[47] Cd and Hg have no known beneficial biological role and are amongst the most toxic of elements.

The body of an adult human contains about 2 g of Zn but, as Zn enzymes are present in most body cells, its concentration is very low and realization of its importance was therefore delayed. The two Zn enzymes which have received most attention are carboxypeptidase A and carbonic anhydrase.

Carboxypeptidase A catalyses the hydrolysis of the terminal peptide bond in proteins during the process of digestion:

It has a molecular weight of about 34 000 and contains one Zn tetrahedrally coordinated to two histidine N atoms, a carboxyl O of a glutamate residue, and a water molecule. The precise mechanism of its action is not finally settled in spite of the intensive study of model systems,[48] but it is agreed that the first step is coordination of the terminal peptide to the Zn by its $\diagdown C{=}O$ group. This is thereby polarized, giving the C a positive charge and making it susceptible to nucleophilic attack. This attack is probably by the –OH of the attached water molecule, followed by proton-rearrangement and breaking of the C–N peptide bond,[49] though alternative possibilities,

[44] N. L. HOLY, N. C. BAENZIGER, R. M. FLYNN, and D. C. SWENSON, *J. Am. Chem. Soc.* **98**, 7823–4 (1976).

[45] W. KAIM and B. SCHWEDERSKI, *Bioinorganic Chemistry: Inorganic Elements in the Chemistry of Life*, Wiley, Chichester 1994; pp. 242–66 for Zn and pp. 335–43 for Cd, Hg.

[46] A. S. PRASAD, *Biochemistry of Zinc*, Plenum Press, New York, 1993, 303 pp.

[46a] A. SIGEL and H. SIGEL (eds.) *Metal Ions in Biological Systems*, Vol. 34, *Mercury and its Effects on the Environment and Biology*, Dekker, New York, 1997 604 pp.

[47] D. BRYCE-SMITH, *Chem. Brit.* **25**, 783–6 (1989) but see also *ibid.* p. 1207.

[48] E. KIMURA, *Prog. Inorg. Chem.* **41**, 443–91 (1994); E. KIMURA and T. KOIKE, *Adv. Inorg. Chem.* **44**, 229–61 (1997).

[49] D. W. CHRISTIANSON and W. N. LIPSCOMB, *Acc. Chem. Res.* **22**, 62–9 (1989).

such as attack by the carboxyl group of a second glutamate residue in the enzyme have also been considered. In any event it is evident that the conformation of the enzyme provides a hydrophobic pocket, close to the Zn, which accommodates the non-polar side-chain of the protein being hydrolysed, and that this protein is, throughout, held in the correct position by H bonding to appropriate groups in the enzyme.

Carbonic anhydrase was the first Zn metalloenzyme to be discovered (1940) and in its several forms is widely distributed in plants and animals. It catalyses the equilibrium reaction:

$$CO_2 + H_2O \rightleftharpoons HCO_3^- + H^+$$

In mammalian erythrocytes (red blood-cells) the forward (hydration) reaction occurs during the uptake of CO_2 by blood in tissue, while the backward (dehydration) reaction takes place when the CO_2 is subsequently released in the lungs. The enzyme increases the rates of these reactions by a factor of about one million.

The molecular weight of the enzyme is about 30 000 and the roughly spherical molecule contains just one zinc atom situated in a deep protein pocket, which also contains a number of water molecules arranged in an ice-like order. This Zn is coordinated tetrahedrally to 3 imidazole nitrogen atoms of histidine residues and to a water molecule. Once again the precise details of the enzyme's action are not settled, but it seems probable that the coordinated H_2O ionizes to give $Zn-OH^-$ and the nucleophilic OH^- then interacts with the C of CO_2 (which may be held in the correct position by H bonds to its two oxygen atoms) to yield HCO_3^-. This is equivalent to replacing the slow hydration of CO_2 with H_2O, by the fast reaction:

$$CO_2 + OH^- \longrightarrow HCO_3^-$$

The latter would normally require a high pH and the contribution of the enzyme is therefore presumed to be the provision of a suitable environment, within the protein pocket, which allows the dissociation of the coordinated H_2O to occur in a medium of pH 7 which would otherwise be much too low.

A more recently established function of zinc is in proteins responsible for recognizing base-sequences in DNA and so regulating the transfer of genetic information during the replication of DNA. These so-called "zinc-finger" proteins contain 9 or 10 Zn^{2+} ions each of which, by coordinating to 4 amino acids, stabilizes a protruding fold (finger) in the protein. The protein wraps around the double strand of DNA, each of the fingers binding to the DNA, their spacing matching the base sequence in the DNA and thus ensuring accurate recognition.[50]

Cadmium is extremely toxic and accumulates in humans mainly in the kidneys and liver; prolonged intake, even of very small amounts, leads to dysfunction of the kidneys. It acts by binding to the $-SH$ group of cysteine residues in proteins and so inhibits SH enzymes. It can also inhibit the action of zinc enzymes by displacing the zinc.

The toxic effects of mercury have long been known,[5] and the use of $HgCl_2$ as a poison has already been mentioned. The use of mercury salts in the production of felt[†] for hats and the dust generated in ill-ventilated workshops by the subsequent drying process, led to the nervous disorder known as "hatter's shakes" and possibly also to the expression "mad as a hatter".

The metal itself, having an appreciable vapour pressure, is also toxic, and produces headaches, tremors, inflammation of the bladder and loss of memory. The best documented case is that of Alfred Stock (p. 151) whose constant use of mercury in the vacuum lines employed in his studies of boron and silicon hydrides, caused him to suffer for many years. The cause was eventually recognized and it is largely due to Stock's publication in 1926 of details of his experiences that the need for care and adequate ventilation is now fully appreciated.

---

50 N. P. PAVLETICH and C. O. PABO, *Science* **261**, 1701–7 (1993).

† It was apparently helpful to add Hg^{II} to the dil HNO$_3$ used to roughen the surface of the animal hair employed in the making of felt which is a non-woven fabric of randomly oriented hairs.

Still more dangerous than metallic mercury or inorganic mercury compounds are organomercury compounds of which the methyl mercury ion HgMe$^+$ is probably the most ubiquitous.[51] This and other organomercurials are more readily absorbed in the gastrointestinal tract than Hg^{II} salts because of their greater ability to permeate biomembranes. They concentrate in the blood and have a more immediate and permanent effect on the brain and central nervous system, no doubt acting by binding to the −SH groups in proteins. Naturally occurring anaerobic bacteria in the sediments of sea or lake floors are able to methylate inorganic mercury (Co−Me groups in vitamin B$_{12}$ are able to transfer the Me to Hg^{II}) which is then concentrated in plankton and so enters the fish food chain.

The Minamata disaster in Japan, when 52 people died in 1952, occurred because fish, which formed the staple diet of the small fishing community, contained abnormally high concentrations of mercury in the form of MeHgSMe. This was found to originate from a local chemical works where Hg^{II} salts were used (inefficiently) to catalyse the production of

acetylene from acetaldehyde, and the effluent then discharged into the shallow sea. Evidence of a similar bacterial production of organomercury is available from Sweden where methylation of Hg^{II} in the effluent from paper mills has been shown to occur. The use of organomercurials as fungicidal seed dressings has also resulted in fatalities in many parts of the world when the seed was subsequently eaten.

It is now apparent that bacteria have developed resistance to heavy metals and the detoxifying process is initiated and controlled by *metalloregulatory* proteins which are able selectively to recognize metal ions. MerR is a small DNA-binding protein which displays a remarkable sensitivity to Hg^{2+}. The metal apparently binds to S atoms of cysteine and this has been a major incentive to recent work on Hg−S chemistry.[32]

Public concern about mercury poisoning has led to more stringent regulations for the use of mercury cells in the chlor-alkali industry (pp. 71−3, 798). The health record of this industry has, in fact, been excellent, but the added costs of conforming to still higher standards have led manufacturers to move from mercury cells to diaphragm cells, and this change has been made a legal requirement in Japan.

---

[51] S. Krishnamurthy, *J. Chem. Ed.* **69**, 347−50 (1992).

30

The Lanthanide Elements (Z = 58 – 71)

30.1 Introduction[1]

Not least of the confusions associated with this group of elements is that of terminology. The name "rare earth" was originally used to describe almost any naturally occurring but unfamiliar oxide and even until about 1920 generally included both ThO_2 and ZrO_2. About that time the name began to be applied to the elements themselves rather than their oxides, and also to be restricted to that group of elements which could only be separated from each other with great difficulty. On the basis of their separability it was convenient to divide these elements into the "cerium group" or "light earths" (La to about Eu) and the "yttrium group" or "heavy earths" (Gd to Lu plus Y which, though much lighter than the others, has a comparable ionic radius and is consequently found in the same ores, usually as the major component). It is now accepted that the "rare-earth elements" comprise the fourteen elements from $_{58}$Ce to $_{71}$Lu, but are commonly taken to include $_{57}$La and sometimes Sc and Y as well.

To avoid this confusion, and because many of the elements are actually far from rare, the terms "lanthanide", "lanthanon" and "lanthanoid" have been introduced. Even now, however, there is no general agreement about the position of La, i.e. whether the group is made up of the elements La to Lu or Ce to Lu. Throughout this chapter the term "lanthanide" and the general symbol, Ln, will be used to refer to the fourteen elements cerium to lutetium inclusive, the Group 3 elements, scandium, yttrium and lanthanum having already been dealt with in Chapter 20.

The lanthanides comprise the largest naturally-occurring group in the periodic table. Their properties are so similar that from 1794, when J. Gadolin isolated "yttria" which he thought was the oxide of a single new element, until 1907, when lutetium was discovered, nearly a hundred claims were made for the discovery of elements

---

[1] K. A. GSCHNEIDER Jr. and L. EYRING (eds.), *Handbook on the Physics and Chemistry of Rare Earths*, North-Holland, Amsterdam, Vol. 1, (1978) to Vol. 21, (1995). An authoritative source of information on all topics associated with lanthanide elements.

History of the Lanthanides[2–4]

In 1751 the Swedish mineralogist, A. F. Cronstedt, discovered a heavy mineral from which in 1803 M. H. Klaproth in Germany and, independently, J. J. Berzelius and W. Hisinger in Sweden, isolated what was thought to be a new oxide (or "earth") which was named *ceria* after the recently discovered asteroid, Ceres. Between 1839 and 1843 this earth, and the previously isolated *yttria* (p. 944), were shown by the Swedish surgeon C. G. Mosander to be mixtures from which, by 1907, the oxides of Sc, Y, La and the thirteen lanthanides other than Pm were to be isolated. The small village of Ytterby near Stockholm is celebrated in the names of no less than four of these elements (Table 30.1).

The classical methods used to separate the lanthanides from aqueous solutions depended on: (i) differences in basicity, the less-basic hydroxides of the heavy lanthanides precipitating before those of the lighter ones on gradual addition of alkali; (ii) differences in solubility of salts such as oxalates, double sulfates, and double nitrates; and (iii) conversion, if possible, to an oxidation state other than +3, e.g. Ce(IV), Eu(II). This latter process provided the cleanest method but was only occasionally applicable. Methods (i) and (ii) required much repetition to be effective, and fractional recrystallizations were sometimes repeated thousands of times. (In 1911 the American C. James performed 15 000 recrystallizations in order to obtain pure thulium bromate.)

The minerals on which the work was performed during the nineteenth century were indeed rare, and the materials isolated were of no interest outside the laboratory. By 1891, however, the Austrian chemist C. A. von Welsbach had perfected the thoria gas "mantle" to improve the low luminosity of the coal-gas flames then used for lighting. Woven cotton or artificial silk of the required shape was soaked in an aqueous solution of the nitrates of appropriate metals and the fibre then burned off and the nitrates converted to oxides. A mixture of 99% ThO_2 and 1% CeO_2 was used and has not since been bettered. CeO_2 catalyses the combustion of the gas and apparently, because of the poor thermal conductivity of the ThO_2, particles of CeO_2 become hotter and so brighter than would otherwise be possible. The commercial success of the gas mantle was immense and produced a worldwide search for thorium. Its major ore is monazite, which rarely contains more than 12% ThO_2 but about 45% Ln_2O_3. Not only did the search reveal that thorium, and hence the lanthanides, are more plentiful than had previously been thought, but the extraction of the thorium produced large amounts of lanthanides for which there was at first little use.

Applications were immediately sought and it was found that electrolysis of the fused chloride of the residue left after the removal of Th yielded the pyrophoric "mischmetall" (approximately 50% Ce, 25% La, 25% other light lanthanides) which, when alloyed with 30% Fe, is ideal as a lighter flint. Besides small amounts of lanthanides used in special glasses to control absorption at particular wavelengths, this was the pattern of usage until the 1940s. Before then there was little need for the pure metals and, because of the difficulty in obtaining them (high mps and very easily oxidized), such samples as were produced were usually impure. Attempts were also made to find element 61, which had not been found in the early studies, and in 1926 unconfirmed reports of its discovery from Illinois and Florence produced the temporary names *illinium* and *florentium*.

During the 1939–45 war, Mg-based alloys incorporating lanthanides were developed for aeronautical components and the addition of small amounts of mischmetall to cast-iron, by causing the separation of carbon in nodular rather than flake form, was found to improve the mechanical properties. But, more significantly from the chemical point of view, work on nuclear fission requiring the complete removal of the lanthanide elements from uranium and thorium ores, coupled with the fact that the lanthanides constitute a considerable proportion of the fission products, stimulated a great surge of interest. Solvent extraction and, more especially, ion-exchange techniques were developed, the work of F. H. Spedding and coworkers at Iowa State University being particularly notable.

As a result, in 1947, J. A. Marinsky, L. E. Glendenin, and C. D. Coryell at Oak Ridge, Tennessee, finally established the existence of element 61 in the fission products of ^{235}U and at the suggestion of Coryell's wife it was named *prometheum* (later *promethium*) after Prometheus who, according to Greek mythology, stole fire from heaven for the use of mankind. Since about 1955, individual lanthanides have been obtainable in increasing amounts in elemental as well as combined forms.

belonging to this group. In view of the absence at that time of a conclusive test to determine whether or not a mixture was involved, this is not surprising. Indeed, there was a general lack of understanding of the large number of elements

involved since the periodic table of the time could accommodate only one element, namely La. Not until 1913, as a result of H. G. J. Moseley's work on atomic numbers, was it realized that there were just fourteen elements between La and Hf, and in 1918 Niels Bohr interpreted this as an expansion of the fourth quantum group from 18 to 32 electrons. More information is in the Panel above and in Table 30.1.

[2] F. SZABADVARY, pp. 33–80, Vol. 11 (1988) of ref. 1.

[3] C. K. JØRGENSEN, pp. 197–215, Vol. 11 (1988) of ref. 1.

[4] C. H. EVANS, *Chem. in Brit.* **25**, 880–2 (1989).

Table 30.1 The discovery of the oxides of Group 3 and the lanthanide elements[2,4]

Element	Discoverer	Date	Origin of name
From ceria			
Cerium, Ce	C. G. Mosander	1839	The asteroid, Ceres
Lanthanum, La	C. G. Mosander	1839	Greek λανθάνειν, lanthanein, to escape notice
Praseodymium, Pr	C. A. von Welsbach	1885	Greek πρασιος + διδυμος praseos + didymos, leek green + twin
Neodymium, Nd	C. A. von Welsbach	1885	Greek νέος + διδυμος, neos + didymos, new twin
Samarium, Sm	L. de Boisbaudran	1879	The mineral, samarskite
Europium, Eu	E. A. Demarçay	1901	Europe
From yttria			
Yttrium, Y	C. G. Mosander	1843	Ytterby
Terbium, Tb[a]	C. G. Mosander	1843	Ytterby
Erbium, Er[a]	C. G. Mosander	1843	Ytterby
Ytterbium, Yb	J. C. G. de Marignac	1878	Ytterby
Scandium, Sc	L. F. Nilson	1879	Scandinavia
Holmium, Ho	P. T. Cleve	1879	Latin *Holmia*: Stockholm
Thulium, Tm	P. T. Cleve	1879	Latin *Thule*, "most northerly land"
Gadolinium, Gd	J. C. G. de Marignac	1880	Finnish chemist, J. Gadolin
Dysprosium, Dy	L. de Boisbaudran	1886	Greek δυσπροσιτος, dysprositos, hard to get
Lutetium, Lu[b]	G. Urbain		
	C. A. von Welsbach	1907	Latin *Lutetia*: Paris
	C. James		

[a]Terbium and erbium were originally named in the reverse order.
[b]Originally spelled lutecium, but changed to lutetium in 1949.

30.2 The Elements

30.2.1 Terrestrial abundance and distribution

Apart from the unstable ^{147}Pm (half-life 2.623 y) of which traces occur in uranium ores, the lanthanides are actually not rare. Cerium (66 ppm in the earth's crust) is the twenty-sixth most abundant of all elements, being half as abundant as Cl and 5 times as abundant as Pb. Even Tm (0.5 ppm), the rarest after Pm, is rather more abundant in the earth's crust than is iodine.

There are over 100 minerals known to contain lanthanides but the only two of commercial importance are monazite, a mixed La, Th, Ln phosphate, and bastnaesite, an La, Ln fluorocarbonate ($M^{III}CO_3F$). Monazite is widely but sparsely distributed in many rocks but, because of its high density and inertness, it is concentrated by weathering into sands on beaches and river beds, often in the presence of other similarly concentrated minerals such as ilmenite ($FeTiO_3$) and cassiterite (SnO_2). Deposits occur in southern India, South Africa, Brazil, Australia and Malaysia and, until the 1960s, these provided the bulk of the world's La, Ln and Th. Then, however, a vast deposit of bastnaesite, which had been discovered in 1949 in the Sierra Nevada Mountains in the USA, came into production. Bastnaesite is also now extracted in China in large quantities, and has become the most important single source of La and Ln.

The bulk of both monazite and bastnaesite is made up of Ce, La, Nd and Pr (in that order) but, whereas monazite typically contains around 5–10% ThO_2 and 3% yttrium earths, these and the heavy lanthanides are virtually absent in bastnaesite. Although thorium is only weakly radioactive it is contaminated with daughter elements such as ^{228}Ra which are more active and therefore require careful handling during the processing of monazite. This is a complication not encountered in the processing of bastnaesite.

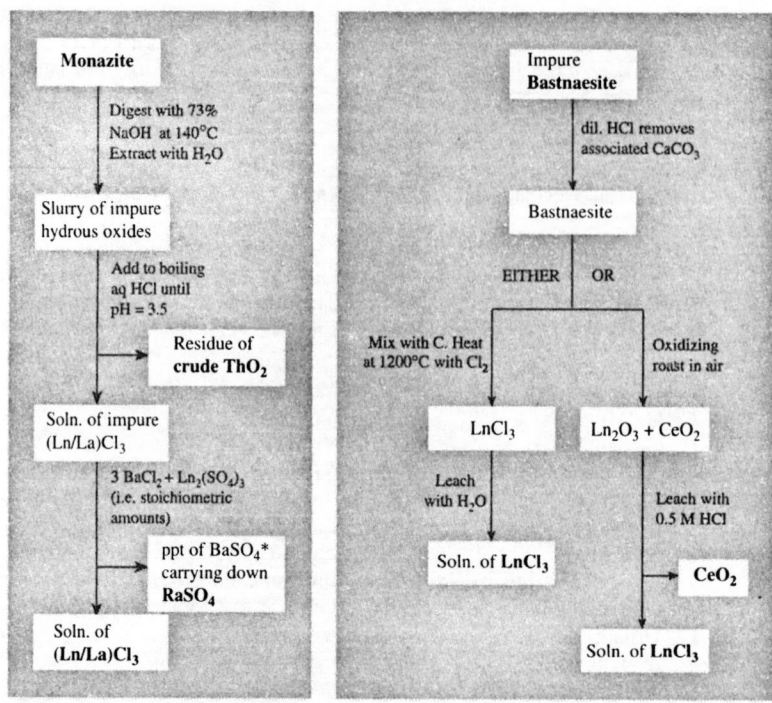

*These residues contain ^{228}Ra, a daughter element of Th and an active γ-emitter, and must therefore be handled with care

Figure 30.1 Flow diagram for the extraction of the lanthanide elements.

30.2.2 Preparation and uses of the elements [5–8]

Conventional mineral dressing yields concentrates of the minerals of better than 90% purity. These can then be broken down ("opened") by either acidic or alkaline attack, the latter being more usual nowadays. Details vary considerably since they depend on the ore being used and on the extent to which the metals are to be separated from each other, but the schemes

outlined in Fig. 30.1 are typical of those used for monazite and bastnaesite to obtain solutions of the mixed chlorides. At this point the classical methods (see Panel, p. 1228) were formerly employed to separate the individual elements where this was required and, indeed the separation of lanthanum by the fractional crystallization of La(NO$_3$)$_3$.2NH$_4$NO$_3$.4H$_2$O is still used. However the separations can now be effected on a large scale by solvent extraction[7,9] using aqueous solutions of the nitrates and a solvent such as tri-*n*-butylphosphate, (Bu^{n}O)$_3$PO (often with kerosene as an inert diluent), in which the solubility of Ln^{III} increases with its atomic weight. This type of process has the advantage of being continuous and is ideal where the product and feed are not to be changed.

Alternatively, for high-purity or smaller-scale production the more easily adapted ion-exchange

[5] *Kirk–Othmer Encyclopedia of Chemical Technology*, Vol. 14, pp. 1091–115 4th edn., Interscience, New York, 1995.

[6] B. JEZOWSKA-TRZEBIATOWSKA, S. KOPACZ and T. MIKULSKI, *The Rare Earth Elements, Occurrence and Technology*, Elsevier, Amsterdam, 1990, 540 pp.

[7] K. L. NASH and G. R. CHOPPIN (eds.), *Separations of Elements*, Plenum, New York, 1995, 286 pp.

[8] R. G. BAUTISTA and N. JACKSON (eds), *Rare Earths, Resources, Science Technology and Applications*, TMS, Warrendale USA, 1991, pp. 466.

[9] R. G. BAUTISTA, pp. 1–28, Vol. 21 (1995) of ref 1.

techniques are ideal, the best of these being "displacement chromatography". Two separate columns of cation exchange resin are generally employed for this purpose. The first column is loaded with the Ln^{III} mixture and the second, or development, column is loaded with a so-called "retaining ion" such as Cu^{II} (Zn^{II} and Fe^{III} have also been used), and the two columns are coupled together. An aqueous solution (the "eluant") of a complexing agent, of which the triammonium salt of $edta^{4-}$ is typical, is then passed through the columns, and Ln^{III} is displaced from the first column (barred species are bound to the resin):

$$\overline{Ln^{3+}} + (NH_4)_3(edta\cdot H) \rightleftharpoons \overline{3(NH_4^+)}$$
$$+ Ln(edta\cdot H)$$

The reaction at any point in the column becomes progressively displaced to the right as fresh complexing agent arrives and the reaction products are removed. The solution of $Ln(edta\cdot H)$ and $(NH_4)_3(edta\cdot H)$ then reaches the development column where Cu^{II} is displaced and Ln^{III} redeposited in a compact band at the top of the column:

$$\overline{3Cu^{2+}} + 2Ln(edta\cdot H) \longrightarrow \overline{2Ln^{3+}} + Cu_3(edta\cdot H)_2$$

This occurs because Cu^{II}, being smaller than Ln^{III}, is able to form in the solution phase, a complex with $(edta\cdot H)^{3-}$ of comparable stability, in spite of its lower charge. The Cu^{II} serves the additional purpose of keeping the complexing agent in a soluble form. If the resin were loaded instead with H^+, $edta\cdot H_4$ would be precipitated and would clog the resin. Even using Cu^{II} the composition of the eluant must be carefully controlled. The concentration of edta must not exceed 0.015 M, otherwise $Cu_2(edta).5H_2O$ precipitates, and it is to encourage the formation of the more soluble salt of $(edta\cdot H)^{3-}$ that an acidic rather than neutral ammonium salt of $edta^{4-}$ is used.

Once the Ln^{III} ions have been deposited on to the resin they are displaced yet again by the NH_4^+ in the eluant. Now, the affinity of Ln^{III} ions for the resin decreases with increasing atomic weight, but so slightly that elution of the development column

with NH_4^+ ions alone would not discriminate to an effective extent between the different lanthanides. However, the values of $\Delta G°$ (and therefore of log K) for the formation of $Ln(edta\cdot H)$ complexes, increase steadily along the series by a total of *ca.* 25% from Ce^{III} to Lu^{III}. Thus in the presence of the complexing agent, the tendency to leave the resin and go into solution is significantly greater for the heavy than for the light lanthanides. As a result, displacement of the Ln^{III} ions from the resin concentrates the heavier cations in the solution. The Ln^{III} ions therefore pass down the development column in a band, being repeatedly deposited and redissolved in what is effectively an automatic fractionation process, concentrating the heavier members in the solution phase. The result is that when all the copper has come off the column the lanthanides emerge in succession, heaviest first. They may then be precipitated from the eluant as insoluble oxalates and ignited to the oxides.

The production of mischmetall by the electrolysis of fused $(Ln,La)Cl_3$, and the difficulties in obtaining pure metals because of their high mps and ease of oxidation, have already been mentioned (Panel, p. 1228). Two methods are in fact available for producing the metals.

(i) *Electrolysis of fused salts.* A mixture of $LnCl_3$ with either NaCl or $CaCl_2$ is fused and electrolysed in a graphite or refractory-lined steel cell, which serves as the cathode, with a graphite rod as anode. This is used primarily for mischmetall, the lighter, lower-melting Ce, and for Sm, Eu and Yb for which method (ii) yields Ln^{II} ions.

(ii) *Metallothermic reduction.* This consists of the reduction of the anhydrous halides with calcium metal. Fluorides are preferred, since they are non-hygroscopic and the CaF_2 produced is stable, unlike the other Ca halides which are liable to boil at the temperatures reached in the process. $LnF_3 + Ca$ are heated in a tantalum crucible to a temperature 50° above the mp of Ln under an atmosphere of argon. After completion of the reaction, the charge is cooled and the slag and metal (of 97–99% purity) broken apart. The main impurity is Ca which is removed by melting under vacuum. With the exceptions of Sm, Eu and Yb this method has general applicability.

In 1995 total world production of "rare earth oxides" was 68 000 tonnes of which China and the USA produced 30 000 and 29 000 tonnes of bastnaesite respectively with smaller quantities of monazite from Australia (as a by-product of TiO_2 production) and India. The bulk of output is used without separation of individual lanthanides. Major uses are in the production of low alloy steels for plate and pipe where $< 1\%$ Ln/La added in the form of mischmetall or silicides greatly improves strength and workability, and in petroleum "cracking" catalysis where various mixed metal oxides are employed. The walls of domestic "self-cleaning" ovens are treated with CeO_2 which prevents the formation of tarry deposits, and CeO_2 of varying purity is used to polish glass. Other small-scale uses include that of mischmetall in Mg-based alloys to produce lighter flints, while Ln/Co alloys are used for the construction of permanent magnets, and individual Ln oxides are used as phosphors in television screens and similar fluorescent surfaces.

Current availability of individual lanthanides (plus Y and La) in a state of high purity and relatively low cost has stimulated research into potential new applications. These are mainly in the field of solid state chemistry and include solid oxide fuel cells, new phosphors and perhaps most significantly high temperature superconductors (p. 1182.)

30.2.3 Properties of the elements

The metals are silvery in appearance (except for Eu and Yb which are pale yellow, see p. 112 and below) and are rather soft, but become harder across the series. Most of them exist in more than one crystallographic form, of which hcp is the most common; all are based on typically metallic close-packed arrangements, but their conductivities are appreciably lower than those of other close-packed metals.

The more important physical properties of the elements are summarized in Table 30.2. The alternation between several and few stable

isotopes for even and odd atomic number respectively, is mirrored by an even–odd variation in the natural abundances of the elements (see p. 4) and in the uncertainty of their atomic weights (see p. 17).

The electronic configurations of the free atoms are determined only with difficulty because of the complexity of their atomic spectra, but it is generally agreed that they are nearly all $[Xe]4f^n5d^06s^2$. The exceptions are:

(1) Cerium, for which the sudden contraction and reduction in energy of the 4f orbitals immediately after La is not yet sufficient to avoid occupancy of the 5d orbital.
(2) Gd, which reflects the stability of the half-filled 4f shell;
(3) Lu, at which point the shell has been filled.

However, only in the case of cerium (see below) does this have any marked effect on the aqueous solution chemistry, which is otherwise dominated by the $+3$ oxidation state, for which the configuration varies regularly from $4f^1$ (Ce^{III}) to $4f^{14}$ (Lu^{III}). It is notable that a regular variation is found for any property for which this $4f^n$ configuration is maintained across the series, whereas the variation in those properties for which this configuration is not maintained can be highly irregular. This is illustrated dramatically in size variations (Fig. 30.2). On the one hand, the radii of Ln^{III} ions decrease regularly from La^{III} (included for completeness) to Lu^{III}. This "lanthanide contraction" occurs because, although each increase in nuclear charge is exactly balanced by a simultaneous increase in electronic charge, the directional characteristics of the 4f orbitals cause the $4f^n$ electrons to shield themselves and other electrons from the nuclear charge only imperfectly. Thus, each unit increase in nuclear charge produces a net increase in attraction for the whole extranuclear electron charge cloud and each ion shrinks slightly in comparison with its predecessor. On the other hand, although a similar overall reduction is seen in the metal radii, Eu and Yb are spectacularly irregular. The reason is that most of the metals are composed of a lattice of Ln^{III} ions with a $4f^n$ configuration and 3 electrons in the

Table 30.2 Some properties of the lanthanide elements

Property	Ce	Pr	Nd	Pm	Sm	Eu	Gd	Tb	Dy	Ho	Er	Tm	Yb	Lu
Atomic number	58	59	60	61	62	63	64	65	66	67	68	69	70	71
Number of naturally occurring isotopes	4	1	7	—	7	2	7	1	7	1	6	1	7	2
Outer electron configuration	$4f^15d^16s^2$	$4f^36s^2$	$4f^46s^2$	$4f^56s^2$	$4f^66s^2$	$4f^76s^2$	$4f^75d^16s^2$	$4f^96s^2$	$4f^{10}6s^2$	$4f^{11}6s^2$	$4f^{12}6s^2$	$4f^{13}6s^2$	$4f^{14}6s^2$	$4f^{14}5d^16s^2$
Atomic weight	140.116(1)	140.90765(2)	144.24(3)	—	150.36(3)	151.964(1)	157.25(3)	158.92534(2)	162.50(3)	164.93032(2)	167.26(3)	168.93421(2)	173.04(3)	174.967(1)
Metal radius (CN 6)/pm	181.8	182.4	181.4	183.4	180.4	208.4	180.4	177.3	178.1	176.2	176.1	175.9	193.3	173.8
Ionic radius (CN 6)/pm IV	87	85	—	—	—	—	—	76	—	—	—	—	—	—
III	102	99	98.3	97	95.8	94.7	93.8	92.3	91.2	90.1	89.0	88.0	86.8	86.1
II	—	—	129[a]	—	122[b]	117	—	—	107	—	—	103	102	—
$E^\circ(M^{4+}/M^{3+})$/V	1.72	3.2[c]	4.9[c]	—	—	—	—	3.1[c]	5.4[c]	—	—	—	—	—
$E^\circ(M^{3+}/M^{2+})$/V	—	—	−2.6	−2.29	−1.55	−0.35	—	—	−2.5	−2.33	—	−2.3	−1.05	—
$E^\circ(M^{3+}/M)$/V	−2.34	−2.35	−2.32	−2.29	−2.30	−1.99	−2.28	−2.31	−2.29	−2.33	−2.32	−2.32	−2.22	−2.30
MP/°C	798	931	1021	1042	1074	822	1313	1365	1412	1474	1529	1545	819	1663
BP/°C	3433	3520	3074	(3000)	1794	1429	3273	3230	2567	2700	2868	1950	1196	3402
ΔH_{fus}/kJ mol⁻¹	5.2(±1.2)	11.3(±2.1)	7.13	—	8.9(±0.4)	—	—	—	—	—	—	—	3.35	—
ΔH_{vap}/kJ mol⁻¹	398	331	289	—	165(±17)	176	301	293	280	280	280	247	159	414
ΔH_f (monatomic gas)/kJ mol⁻¹	419	356	328	301	207	178	398	389	291	301	317	232	152	—
Ionization energies/kJ mol⁻¹ 1st	541	522	530	536	542	547	595	569	567	574	581	589	603	513
2nd	1047	1018	1034	1052	1068	1085	1172	1112	1126	1139	1151	1163	1175	1341
3rd	1940	2090	2128	2140	2285	2425	1999	2122	2230	2221	2207	2305	2408	2054
ΔH(hydration Ln³⁺)/kJ mol⁻¹	3370	3413	3442	3478	3515	3547	3571	3605	3637	3667	3691	3717	3739	3760
Density(25°C)/g cm⁻³	6.770	6.773	7.007	—	7.520	5.234	7.900	8.229	8.550	8.795	9.066	9.321	6.965	9.840
Electrical resistivity (25°C)/μ ohm cm	73	68	64	(50)	88	90	134	114	57	87	87	79	29	79

[a] CN = 8.
[b] CN = 7.
[c] Estimated values since these M^{IV} are not stable in aqueous solution.

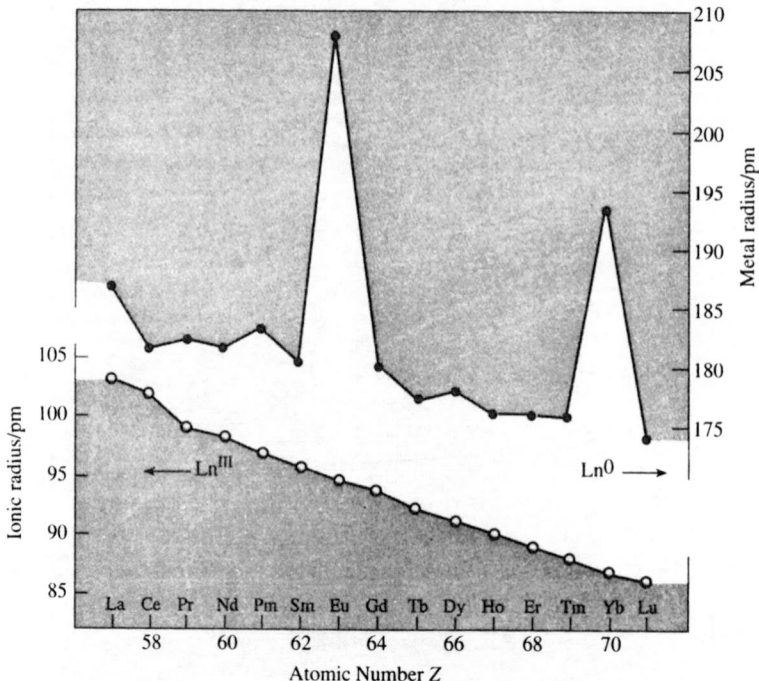

Figure 30.2   Variation of metal radius and 3+ ionic radius for La and the lanthanides. Other data for Ln^{II} and Ln^{IV} are in Table 30.2.

5d/6s conduction band. Metallic Eu and Yb, however, are composed predominantly of the larger Ln^{II} ions with $4f^{n+1}$ configurations and only 2 electrons in the conduction band. The smaller and opposite irregularity for metallic Ce is due to the presence of ions in an oxidation state somewhat above +3. Similar discontinuities are found in other properties of the metals, particularly at Eu and Yb.

A contraction resulting from the filling of the 4f electron shell is of course not exceptional. Similar contractions occur in each row of the periodic table and, in the d block for instance, the ionic radii decrease by 20.5 pm from Sc^{III} to Cu^{III}, and by 15 pm from Y^{III} to Ag^{III}. The importance of the lanthanide contraction arises from its consequences:

(1) The reduction in size from one Ln^{III} to the next makes their separation possible, but the smallness and regularity of the reduction makes the separation difficult.

(2) By the time Ho is reached the Ln^{III} radius has been sufficiently reduced to be almost identical with that of Y^{III} which is why this much lighter element is invariably associated with the heavier lanthanides.

(3) The total lanthanide contraction is of a similar magnitude to the expansion found in passing from the first to the second transition series, and which might therefore have been expected to occur also in passing from second to third. The interpolation of the lanthanides in fact almost exactly cancels this anticipated increase with the result, noted in preceding chapters, that in each group of transition elements the second and third members have very similar sizes and properties.

Redox processes, which of necessity entail a change in the occupancy of the 4f shell, vary in a very irregular manner across the series. Quantitative data from direct measurements are

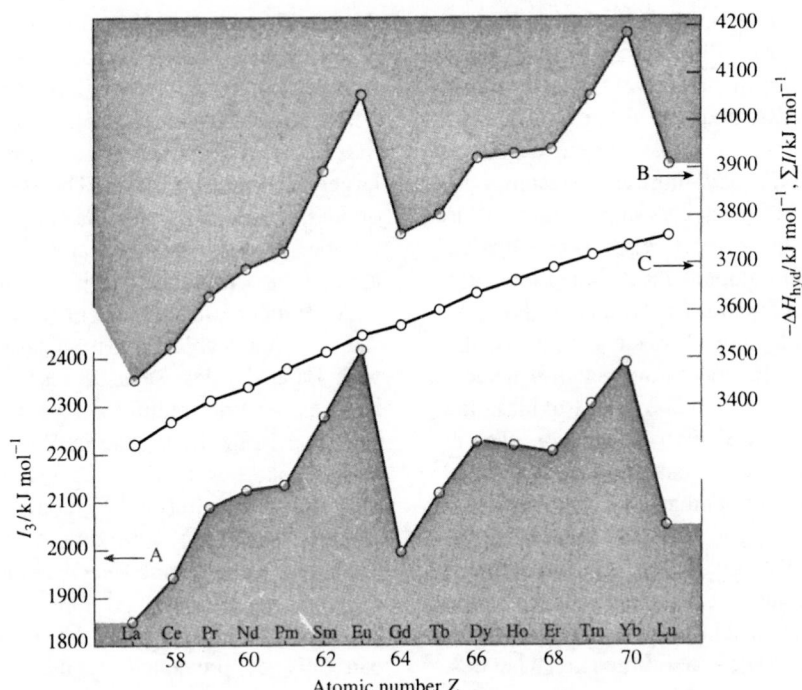

Figure 30.3   Variation with atomic number of some properties of La and the lanthanides: A, the third ionization energy (I_3); B, the sum of the first three ionization energies (ΣI); C, the enthalpy of hydration of the gaseous trivalent ions ($-\Delta H_{hyd}$). The irregular variations in I_3 and ΣI, which refer to redox processes, should be contrasted with the smooth variation in ΔH_{hyd}, for which the $4f^n$ configuration of Ln^{III} is unaltered.

far from complete for such processes, but the use of thermodynamic (Born–Haber) cycles[10] greatly improves the situation. Enthalpies of atomization (ΔH_f) and ionization energies are given in Table 30.2 and the variations of I_3 and ΣI are shown in Fig. 30.3. I_3 refers to the 1-electron change, $4f^{n+1}(Ln^{2+}) \rightarrow 4f^n(Ln^{3+})$ and the close similarity of the two curves indicates that this change is the dominant factor in determining the shape of the ΣI curve. The variation of I_3 across the series is in fact typical of the variation in energy of any process (e.g. $-\Delta H_f$ which refers essentially to $4f^{n+1}6s^2 \rightarrow 4f^n5d^16s^2$) which involves the reduction of Ln^{3+} to Ln^{2+}. It is characterized by an increase in energy, first as each of the 4f orbitals of the Ln^{II} ions are singly occupied and the stability of the 4f

shell steadily increases due to the corresponding increase in nuclear charge (La $\rightarrow$ Eu); then again as each 4f orbital is doubly occupied (Gd $\rightarrow$ Lu). The sudden falls at Gd and Lu reflect the ease with which it is possible to remove the single electrons in excess of the stable $4f^7$ and $4f^{14}$ configurations. Explanations have been given for the smaller irregularities at the quarter- and three-quarter-shell stages, but require a careful consideration of interelectronic repulsion, as well as exchange energy, terms.[11]

30.2.4 Chemical reactivity and trends

The lanthanides are very electropositive and reactive metals. With the exception of Yb

[10] D. A. JOHNSON, *J. Chem. Ed.* **57**, 475–7 (1980).

[11] D. A, JOHNSON, *Adv. Inorg. Chem. Radiochem.* **20**, 1–132 (1977).

their reactivity apparently depends on size so that Eu which has the largest metal radius is much the most reactive. They tarnish in air and, if ignited in air or O_2, burn readily to give Ln_2O_3 or, in the case of cerium, CeO_2 (praseodymium and terbium yield nonstoichiometric products approximating to Pr_6O_{11} and Tb_4O_7 respectively). When heated, they also burn in halogens producing LnX_3, and in hydrogen producing LnH_2 and LnH_3 (see below). They will, indeed, react, though usually less vigorously, with most non-metals if heated. Treatment with water yields hydrous oxides, and the metals dissolve rapidly in dilute acids, even in the cold, to give aqueous solutions of Ln^{III} salts.

The great bulk of lanthanide chemistry is of the +3 oxidation state where, because of the large sizes of the Ln^{III} ions, the bonding is predominantly ionic in character, and the cations display the typical class-a preference of O-donor ligands (p. 909). Three-dimensional lattices, characteristic of ionic character, are common and the coordination chemistry is quite different from, and less extensive than, that of the d-transition metals. Coordination numbers are generally high and stereochemistries, being determined largely by the requirements of the ligands and lacking the directional constraints of covalency, are frequently ill-defined, and the complexes distinctly labile. Thus, in spite of widespread opportunities for isomerism, there appears to be no confirmed example of a lanthanide complex existing in more than one molecular arrangement. Furthermore, only strongly complexing (i.e. usually chelating) ligands yield products which can be isolated from aqueous solution, and the comparative tenacity of the small H_2O molecule commonly leads to its inclusion, often with consequent uncertainty as to the coordination number involved. This is not to say that other types of complex cannot be obtained, but complexes with uncharged monodentate ligands, or ligands with donor atoms other than O, must usually be prepared in the absence of water.

Some typical compounds are listed in Table 30.3. Coordination numbers below 6 are found only with very bulky ligands and even

the coordination number of 6 itself is unusual, 7, 8 and 9 being more characteristic. Coordination numbers of 10 and over require chelating ligands with small "bites" (p. 917), such as NO_3^- or SO_4^{2-}, and are confined to compounds of the larger, lighter lanthanides. The stereochemistries quoted, especially for the high coordination numbers, are idealized and in most cases appreciable distortions are in fact found.

A number of trends connected with ionic radii are noticeable across the series. In keeping with Fajans' rules, salts become somewhat less ionic as the Ln^{III} radius decreases; reduced ionic character in the hydroxide implies a reduction in basic properties and, at the end of the series, $Yb(OH)_3$ and $Lu(OH)_3$, though undoubtedly mainly basic, can with difficulty be made to dissolve in hot conc NaOH. Paralleling this change, the $[Ln(H_2O)_x]^{3+}$ ions are subject to an increasing tendency to hydrolyse, and hydrolysis can only be prevented by use of increasingly acidic solutions.

However, solubility, depending as it does on the rather small difference between solvation energy and lattice energy (both large quantities which themselves increase as cation size decreases) and on entropy effects, cannot be simply related to cation radius. No consistent trends are apparent in aqueous, or for that matter nonaqueous, solutions but an empirical distinction can often be made between the lighter "cerium" lanthanides and the heavier "yttrium" lanthanides. Thus oxalates, double sulfates and double nitrates of the former are rather less soluble and basic nitrates more soluble than those of the latter. The differences are by no means sharp, but classical separation procedures depended on them.

Although lanthanide chemistry is dominated by the +3 oxidation state, and a number of binary compounds which ostensibly involve Ln^{II} are actually better formulated as involving Ln^{III} with an electron in a delocalized conduction band, genuine oxidation states of +2 and +4 can be obtained. Ce^{IV} and Eu^{II} are stable in water and, though they are respectively strongly oxidizing and strongly reducing, they have well-established

Table 30.3   Oxidation states and stereochemistries of compounds of the lanthanides[a]

Oxidation state	Coordination number	Stereochemistry	Examples
2	6	Octahedral	LnZ ($Ln = Sm, Eu, Yb$; $Z = S, Se, Te$)
	8	Cubic	LnF_2 ($Ln = Sm, Eu, Yb$)
3	3	Pyramidal	$[Ln\{N(SiMe_3)_2\}_3]$ ($Ln = Nd, Eu, Yb$)
	4	Tetrahedral	$[Lu(2,6\text{-dimethylphenyl})_4]^-$
		Distorted tetrahedral	$[Ln\{N(SiMe_3)_2\}_3(OPPh_3)]$ ($Ln = Eu, Lu$)
	6	Octahedral	$[LnX_6]^{3-}$ ($X = Cl, Br$); $LnCl_3$ ($Ln = Dy\text{–}Lu$)
	7	Capped trigonal prismatic	$[Dy(dpm)_3(H_2O)]$[b]
		Capped octahedral	$[Ho\{PhC(O)CH{=}C(O)Ph_3\}(H_2O)]$
	8	Dodecahedral	$[Ho(tropolonate)_4]^-$
		Square antiprismatic	$[Eu(acac)_3(phen)]$
		Bicapped trigonal prismatic	LnF_3 ($Ln = Sm\text{–}Lu$)
	9	Tricapped trigonal prismatic	$[Ln(H_2O)_9]^{3+}$, $[Eu(terpy)_3]^{3+}$
		Capped square antiprismatic	$[Pr(terpy)Cl_3(H_2O)_5]\cdot 3H_2O$
		Bicapped dodecahedral	$[Ln(NO_3)_5]^{2-}$ ($Ln = Ce, Eu$)
	12	Icosahedral	$[Ce(NO_3)_6]^{3-}$[c]
	15	See p. 1249	$[Sm(\eta^5\text{-}C_9H_7)_3]$
	16	See pp. 1248, 1249	$[Nd(\eta^5\text{-}C_5H_4Me)_3]_4$, $[Ln(\eta^8\text{-}C_8H_8)_2]^-$
4	6	Octahedral	$[CeCl_6]^{2-}$
	8	Cubic	LnO_2 ($Ln = Ce, Pr, Tb$)
		Square antiprismatic	$[Ce(acac)_4]$, LnF_4 ($Ln = Ce, Pr, Tb$)
	10	Complex	$[Ce(NO_3)_4(OPPh_3)_2]$[c]
	12	Icosahedral	$[Ce(NO_3)_6]^{2-}$[c]

[a]Except where otherwise stated, Ln is used rather loosely to mean most of the lanthanides; the Pm compound, for instance, is usually missing simply because of the scarcity and consequent expense of Pm.

[b]dpm = dipivaloylmethane, $Me_3CC(O)CH{=}C(O^-)CMe_3$.

[c]The structure can be visualized as octahedral if each NO_3^- is considered to occupy a single coordination site (p. 1245).

aqueous chemistries. Ln^{IV} ($Ln = Pr, Nd, Tb, Dy$) and Ln^{II} ($Ln = Nd, Sm, Eu, Dy, Tm, Yb$) also are known in the solid state but are unstable in water. The rather restricted aqueous redox chemistry which this implies is summarized in the oxidation state diagram (Fig. 30.4).

The prevalence of the +3 oxidation state is a result of the stabilizing effects exerted on different orbitals by increasing ionic charge. As successive electrons are removed from a neutral lanthanide atom, the stabilizing effect on the orbitals is in the order $4f > 5d > 6s$, this being the order in which the orbitals penetrate through the inert core of electrons towards the nucleus. By the time an ionic charge of +3 has been reached, the preferential stabilization of the $4f$ orbitals is such that in all cases the $6s$ and $5d$ orbitals have been emptied. Also, in most cases, the electrons remaining in the $4f$ orbitals are themselves so far

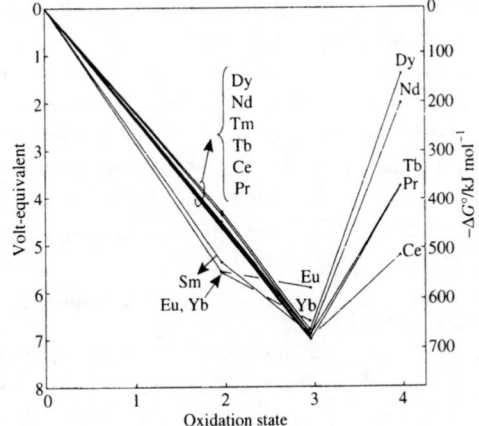

Figure 30.4   Volt-equivalent versus oxidation state for lanthanides with more than one oxidation state.

embedded in the inert core as to be immovable by chemical means. Exceptions are Ce and, to a lesser extent, Pr which are at the beginning of the series where, as already noted, the 4f orbitals are still at a comparatively high energy and can therefore lose a further electron. Tb^{IV} presumably owes its existence to the stability of the $4f^7$ configuration.

The stabilizing effects of half, and completely, filled shells can be similarly invoked to explain the occurrence of the divalent state in $Eu^{II}(4f^7)$ and $Yb^{II}(4f^{14})$ while these, and the other known divalent ions are of just those elements which occupy elevated positions on the I_3 plot (Fig. 30.3).

The absence of 5d electrons and the inertness of the lanthanides' 4f shell makes π backbonding energetically unfavourable and simple carbonyls, for instance, have only been obtained in argon matrices at 8–12 K. On the other hand, essentially ionic cyclopentadienides are well known and an increasing number of σ-bonded Ln–C compounds have been produced (see section 30.3.5).

30.3 Compounds of the Lanthanides[12-15]

The reaction between H_2 and the gently heated (300–350°C) metals produces black, reactive and highly conducting solids, LnH_2. These hydrides have the fcc fluorite structure (p. 118) and are evidently composed of Ln^{III}, $2H^-$, e^-, the electron being delocalized in a metallic conduction band. Further hydrogen can be accommodated in the interstices of the lattice and, with the exceptions of Eu and Yb, which are the two lanthanides

most favourably disposed to divalency, a limiting stoichiometry of LnH_3 can be achieved if high pressures are employed (p. 66). The composition of LnH_3 is Ln^{III}, $3H^-$ with conductivity correspondingly reduced as the additional H atom traps the previously delocalized electron (to form H^-).

Metallic conductivity, arising from the presence of Ln^{III} ions with the balance of electrons situated in a conduction band, is also found in some of the borides (p. 145) and carbides (p. 297).

30.3.1 Oxides and chalcogenides[16,17]

Ln_2O_3 are all well characterized. With three exceptions they are the final products of combustion of the metals or ignition of the hydroxides, carbonate, nitrate, etc. The exceptions are Ce, Pr and Tb, the most oxidized products of which are the dioxides, from which the sesquioxides can be obtained by controlled reduction with H_2. Ln_2O_3 adopt three structure types conventionally classified as:[18]

A-type, consisting of {LnO_7} units which approximate to capped octahedral geometry, and favoured by the lightest lanthanides.

B-type, also consisting of {LnO_7} units but now of three types, two are capped trigonal prisms and one is a capped octahedron; favoured by the middle lanthanides.

C-type, related to the fluorite structure but with one-quarter of the anions removed in such a way as to reduce the metal coordination number from 8 to 6 (but not octahedral); favoured by the middle and heavy lanthanides.

Ln_2O_3 are strongly basic and the lighter, more basic, ones resemble the oxides of Group 2

[12] S. COTTON, *Lanthanides and Actinides*, Macmillan, Basingstoke, 1991, 192 pp.

[13] G. MEYER and L. R. MORSS (eds.), *Synthesis of Lanthanide and Actinide Compounds*, Kluwer, Dordrecht, 1991, 367 pp.

[14] M. LESKALÄ and L. NIINISTÖ, pp. 203–334, Vol. 8 (1986) and pp. 91–320, Vol. 9 (1987) of ref. 1.

[15] T. MOELLER, The lanthanides, Chap. 44, pp. 1–101, in *Comprehensive Inorganic Chemistry*, Vol. 4, Pergamon Press, Oxford, 1973; Lanthanides and actinides, Vol. 7, *MTP International Review of Science, Inorganic Chemistry* (Series Two) (K. W. BAGNALL, ed.), Butterworths, London, 1975, 329 pp.

[16] R. G. HAIRE and L. EYRING, pp. 413–506, Vol. 18 (1994) of ref. 1.

[17] L. EYRING, pp. 187–224 of ref. 13 for oxides; M. GUITTARD and J. FLAHAUT, pp. 321–52 of ref. 13 for sulfides.

[18] A. F. WELLS, *Structural Inorganic Chemistry*, 5th edn., pp. 544–7, Oxford University Press, Oxford, 1984.

in this respect. All are insoluble in water but absorb it to form hydroxides. They dissolve readily in aqueous acids to yield solutions which, providing they are kept on the acid side of pH 5 to avoid hydrolysis, contain the $[Ln(H_2O)_x]^{3+}$ ions. Hydrous hydroxides can be precipitated from these solutions by addition of ammonia or aqueous alkali. Crystalline $Ln(OH)_3$ have a 9-coordinate, tricapped, trigonal prismatic structure, and may be obtained by prolonged treatment of Ln_2O_3 with conc NaOH at high temperature and pressure (hydrothermal ageing).

The pale-yellow CeO_2 is a rather inert material when prepared by ignition, but in the hydrous, freshly precipitated form it redissolves quite easily in acids. The analogous dark-coloured PrO_2 and TbO_2 can be obtained by ignition but require more extreme conditions (O_2 at 282 bar and 400°C for PrO_2, and atomic oxygen at 450°C for TbO_2). All three dioxides have the fluorite structure. Since this is the structure on which C-type Ln_2O_3 is based (by removing a quarter of the anions) it is not surprising that these three oxide systems involve a whole series of nonstoichiometric phases between the extremes represented by $LnO_{1.5}$ and LnO_2 (p. 643). The compositions and structures of these phases arise because the basic unit from which they are built is a so-called "coordination defect", $[M_2^{III}M_{1.5}^{IV}\square O_6]$.[19]

Claims for the existence of several lower oxides, LnO, have been made but most have been rejected, and it seems that only NdO, SmO (both lustrous golden yellow), EuO (dark red) and YbO (greyish-white) are genuine. They are obtained by reducing Ln_2O_3 with the metal at high temperatures and, except for EuO, at high pressures. They have the NaCl structure but whereas EuO and YbO are composed of Ln^{II} and are insulators or semiconductors, NdO and SmO like the dihydrides consist essentially of Ln^{III} ions with the extra electrons forming a conduction band. EuO was unexpectedly found to be ferromagnetic at low temperatures. The

absence of conduction electrons, and the presence of 4f orbitals which are probably too contracted to allow overlap between adjacent cations, makes it difficult to explain the mechanism of the ferromagnetic interaction. EuO and the monochalcogenides have potential applications in memory devices.[20]

Chalcogenides of similar stoichiometry to the oxides, but for a wider range of metals, are known, though their characterization is made more difficult by the prevalence of nonstoichiometry and the occurrence of phase changes in several instances. In general the chalcogenides are stable in dry air but are hydrolysed if moisture is present. If heated in air they oxidize (sulfides especially) to basic salts of the corresponding oxo-anion and they show varying susceptibility to attack by acids with evolution of H_2Z.

Monochalcogenides, LnZ (Z = S, Se, Te), have been prepared for all the lanthanides except Pm, mostly by direct combination.[17] They are almost black and, like the monoxides, have the NaCl structure. However, with the exceptions of SmZ, EuZ, YbZ, TmSe and TmTe, they have metallic conductivity and evidently consist of $Ln^{III} + Z^{2-}$ ions with 1 electron from each cation delocalized in a conduction band. EuZ and YbZ, by contrast, are semiconductors or insulators with genuinely divalent cations, but SmZ seem to be intermediate and may involve the equilibrium:

$$Sm^{II} + Z^{2-} \rightleftharpoons Sm^{III} + Z^{2-} + e^-$$

Trivalent chalcogenides, Ln_2Z_3, can be obtained by a variety of methods which include direct combination and, in the case of the sulfides, the action of H_2S on the chloride or oxide. As with Ln_2O_3, various crystalline modifications occur. When Ln_2Z_3 are heated with an excess of chalcogen in a sealed tube at 600°C, products with compositions up to or nearing LnZ_2 are obtained. They seem to be polychalcogenides, however, with the metal uniformly in the +3 state; Ln^{IV} chalcogenides are not known.

[19] B. F. HOSKINS and R. L. MARTIN, *Aust. J. Chem.* **48**, 709–39 (1995).

[20] Pages 23–41 of ref. 11.

30.3.2 Halides [12,13,21]

Halides of the lanthanides are listed in Table 30.4 and are of the types LnX_4, LnX_3 and LnX_2. Not surprisingly, LnX_4 occur only as the fluorides of Ce^{IV}, Pr^{IV} and Tb^{IV}. CeF_4 is comparatively stable and can be prepared either directly from the elements or by the action of F^- on aqueous solutions of Ce^{IV} when it crystallizes as the monohydrate. The other tetrafluorides are thermally unstable and, as they oxidize water, can only be prepared dry; TbF_4 from $TbF_3 + F_2$ at 320°C, and PrF_4 by the rather complex procedure of fluorinating a mixture of NaF and PrF_3 with F_2 ($\rightarrow Na_2PrF_6$) and then extracting NaF from the reaction mixture with liquid HF.

Promethium apart, all possible trihalides (52) are known. The trifluorides, being very insoluble, can be precipitated as $LnF_3 \cdot \frac{1}{2}H_2O$ by the action of HF on aqueous $Ln(NO_3)_3$. Aqueous solutions of the other trihalides are obtained by simply dissolving the oxides or carbonates in aqueous HX. Hydrated (6–8H_2O) salts can be crystallized, though with difficulty because of their high solubilities. Preparation of the anhydrous trihalides by thermal dehydration of these hydrates is possible for fluorides and chlorides of the lighter lanthanides, and an atmosphere of HX extends the applicability of the method to heavier lanthanides. Because of the possible formation of oxohalides in preparations involving halides and oxygen-containing materials, direct combination, which is a completely general method, is often preferred for the anhydrous halides.

The anhydrous trihalides are ionic, high melting, crystalline substances which, apart from the trifluorides are extremely deliquescent. As can be seen from Table 30.4, the coordination number of the Ln^{III} changes with the radii of the ions, from 9 for the trifluorides of the large lanthanides to 6 for the triiodides of the smaller lanthanides. Their chief importance has been as materials from which the pure metals can be prepared.

The dihalides are obtained from the corresponding trihalides, most generally by reduction with the lanthanide metal itself[22] or with an alkali metal[23,24] and also, in the case of the more stable of the diiodides (SmI_2, EuI_2, YbI_2), by thermal decomposition.[†] SmI_2 and YbI_2 can also be conveniently prepared in quantitative yield by reacting the metal with 1,2-diiodoethane in anhydrous tetrahydrofuran at room temperature:[25] $Ln + ICH_2CH_2I \rightarrow LnI_2 + CH_2{=}CH_2$. With the exception of EuX_2, all the dihalides are very easily oxidized and will liberate hydrogen from water. The occurrence of these dihalides parallels the occurrence of high values of the third ionization energy amongst the metals[10,11] (Fig. 30.3), with the reasonable qualification that, in this low oxidation state, iodides are more numerous than fluorides. The same types of structures are found as for the alkaline earth dihalides with the coordination number of the cation ranging from 9 to 6 and, like CaI_2, the diiodides of Dy, Tm and Yb form layer structures ($CdCl_2$, CdI_2; see Fig. 29.2) typical of compounds with large anions where marked polarization effects are expected.

The isomorphous diiodides of Ce, Pr and Gd stand apart from all the other, salt-like, dihalides. These three, like LaI_2, are notable for their metallic lustre and very high conductivities and are best formulated as $\{Ln^{III}, 2I^-, e^-\}$, the electron being in a delocalized conduction band. Besides the dihalides, other reduced species have been obtained such as Ln_5Cl_{11} (Ln = Sm, Gd, Ho). They have fluorite-related structures (p. 118) in which the anionic sublattice is partially rearranged to accommodate additional anions,

[21] H. A. EICK, pp. 365–412, Vol. 18 (1994) of ref. 1.

[22] J. D. CORBETT, pp. 159–73 of ref. 13.

[23] G. MEYER, *Chem. Rev.* **88**, 93–107 (1988); G. MEYER, and T. SCHLEID, pp. 175–85 of ref. 13.

[24] A. SIMON, H. MATTAUSCH, G. J. MILLER, W. BAUHOFFER and R. K. KREMER, pp. 191–285, Vol. 15 (1991) of ref. 1.

[†] Dilute solid solutions of Ln^{III} ions in CaF_2 may be reduced by Ca vapour to produce Ln^{II} ions trapped in the crystal lattice. By their use it has been possible to obtain the electronic spectra of Ln^{II} ions.

[25] P. GIRARD, J. L. NAMY and H. B. KAGAN, *J. Am. Chem. Soc.* **102**, 2693–8 (1980).

Table 30.4 Properties of lanthanide halides: colour, mp/°C and coordination[a]

	Ce	Pr	Nd	Sm	Eu	Gd	Tb	Dy	Ho	Er	Tm	Yb	Lu
LnF$_4$	white 400 dec 8 sa	—	—	—	—	—	white dec 8 sa	—	—	—	—	—	—
LnF$_3$	white 1430 9 ttp	green 1395 9 ttp	violet 1374 9 ttp	white 1306 9 ttp	white 1276 9 ttp	white 1231 8 btp	white 1172 8 btp	green 1154 8 btp	pink 1143 8 btp	pink 1140 8 btp	white 1158 8 btp	white 1157 8 btp	white 1182 8 btp
LnCl$_3$	white 817 9 ttp	green 786 9 ttp	mauve 758 9 ttp	yellow 682 9 ttp	yellow dec 9 ttp	white 602 9 ttp	white 582 8 btp	white 647 6 o	yellow 720 6 o	violet 776 6 o	yellow 824 6 o	white 865 6 o	white 925 6 o
LnBr$_3$	white 733 9 ttp	green 691 9 ttp	violet 682 8 btp	yellow 640 8 btp	grey dec 8 btp	white 770 6 o	white 828 6 o	white 879 6 o	yellow 919 6 o	violet 923 6 o	white 954 6 o	white dec 6 o	white 1025 6 o
LnI$_3$	yellow 766 8 btp	green 737 8btp	green 784 8 btp	orange 850 6 o	dec 6 o	yellow 925 6 o	957 6 o	green 978 6 o	yellow 994 6 o	violet 1015 6 o	yellow 1021 6 o	white dec 6 o	brown 1050 6 o
LnF$_2$	—	—	—	purple 1417 8 c	yellow 1416 8 c	—	—	—	—	—	—	grey (1407) 8 c	—
LnCl$_2$	—	—	green 841 9 ttp	brown 859 9 ttp	white 731 9 ttp	—	—	black 721 dec 8, 7	—	—	green 718 7 co	green 720 7 co	—
LnBr$_2$	—	—	green 725 9 ttp	brown 669 8, 7	white 683 8, 7	—	—	black 7 co	—	—	green 7 co	yellow 673 6 o	—
LnI$_2$	bronze 808	bronze 758	violet 562 8, 7	green 520 7 co	green 580 7 co	bronze 831	—	purple 721 dec 6 ol	—	—	black 756 6 ol	yellow 780 6 ol	—

[a] 9 ttp = 9-coordinate tricapped trigonal prismatic; 8 sa = 8-coordinate square antiprismatic; 8 btp = 8-coordinate bicapped trigonal prismatic; 8 c = 8-coordinate cubic (fluorite); 8, 7 = mixed 8- and 7-coordinate (SrBr$_2$ structure); 7 co = 7-coordinate capped octahedral; 6 o = 6-coordinate octahedral; 6 ol = 6-coordinate octahedral layered.

Table 30.5 Stoichiometries and structures of reduced halides ($X/M < 2$) of scandium, yttrium, lanthanum and the lanthanides

Average oxidation state	Examples	Structural features
1.714	Sc_7Cl_{12}	Discrete M_6X_{12} clusters
	M_7I_{12} (La, Pr, Tb)	Discrete M_6X_{12} clusters
1.600	Sc_5Cl_8	Single chains of edge-sharing metal octahedra with M_6X_{12}-type environment (edge-capped by X) along with parallel chains of edge-sharing MX_6 octahedra
1.500	M_2Cl_3 (Y, Gd, Tb, Er, Lu)	Single chains of edge-sharing metal octahedra with M_6X_8-type environment (face-capped by X)
	M_2Br_3 (Y, Gd)	
1.429	Sc_7Cl_{10}	Double chains of edge-sharing metal octahedra with M_6X_8-type environment with parallel chains of edge-sharing MCl_6 octahedra
1.000	MXH_n (X = Cl, Br)(Sc, Y, Gd, Lu and probably other Ln)	Double metal layers of edge-sharing metal octahedra, M_6X_8-type environment but with encapsulated H atoms

leading to irregular 7-and 8-coordination of the cations. In the case of Gd and Tb, further reduction gives rise to Ln_2Cl_3 phases which are constructed from Ln_6 octahedra sharing *trans*-edges and sheathed with chlorine atoms which bridge adjacent chains. Gd_2Cl_3 is a semiconductor and provided the first example of a lanthanide in an oxidation state $< +2$. Continued reduction finally produces "graphite-like" LnCl phases originally thought to be binary halides like ZrX (p. 966) but in fact, like ScCl (p. 950), requiring the presence of interstitial H atoms to stabilize the structure. They are therefore formulated as $LnXH_n$. Structural characteristics are summarised in Table 30.5.[22,26–28]

Other interstitial atoms stabilizing such clusters are B, C, N and O.[22] Examples of carbon stabilized clusters include: isolated metal octahedra in $Cs[Ln_6I_{12}C]$ (Ln = Er, Lu)[29] and $Gd[Gd_6Cl_{12}C]$; pairs of edge-sharing metal octahedra in $Gd_{10}Cl_{18}(C_2)_2$; and chains of edge-sharing metal octahedra in Gd_4I_5C.

[26] A. SIMON, *Angew. Chem. Int. Edn. Engl.* **27**, 159–83 (1988).

[27] R. P. ZIEBARTH and J. CORBETT, *Acc. Chem. Res.* **22**, 256–62 (1989).

[28] H. MATTAUSCH, R. EGER, J. D. CORBETT and A. SIMON, *Z. anorg. allg. Chem.* **616**, 157–61 (1992).

[29] H. M. ARTELT, T. SCHLEID and G. MEYER, *Z. anorg. allg. Chem.* **618**, 18–25 (1992).

30.3.3 Magnetic and spectroscopic properties [12]

The electronic configurations of the lanthanides are described by using the Russell–Saunders coupling scheme. Values of the quantum numbers S and L corresponding to the lowest energy are derived in the conventional manner.[12] These are then expressed for each ion in the form of a ground term with the symbolism that $S, P, D, F, G, H, I, \ldots$ correspond to $L = 0, 1, 2, 3, 4, 5, 6, \ldots$ in that order. The angular momentum vectors associated with S and L couple together (spin–orbit coupling) to produce a resultant angular momentum associated with an overall quantum number J. Because the 4f electrons of lanthanide ions are largely buried in the inner core, they are effectively shielded from their chemical environments. As a result, spin–orbit coupling is much larger than the crystal field (of the order of 2000 cm^{-1} compared to 100 cm^{-1}) and must be considered first. Note that this is precisely the reverse of the situation in the d-block elements where the d electrons are exposed directly to the influence of neighbouring groups and the crystal field is therefore much greater than the spin–orbit coupling.

J can take the values $J = L + S, L + S - 1, \ldots, L - S$ (or $S - L$ if $S > L$), each corresponding to a different energy, so that a "term" (defined

Table 30.6 Magnetic and spectroscopic properties of Ln^{III} ions in hydrated salts

Ln	Unpaired electrons	Ground state	Colour	μ_e/BM	
				$g\sqrt{J(J+1)}$	Observed
Ce	1 (4f^1)	$^2F_{5/2}$	Colourless	2.54	2.3–2.5
Pr	2 (4f^2)	$^3H_4$	Green	3.58	3.4–3.6
Nd	3 (4f^3)	$^4I_{9/2}$	Lilac	3.62	3.5–3.6
Pm	4 (4f^4)	$^5I_4$	Pink	2.68	—
Sm	5 (4f^5)	$^6H_{5/2}$	Yellow	0.85	1.4–1.7[a]
Eu	6 (4f^6)	$^7F_0$	Very pale pink	0	3.3–3.5[a]
Gd	7 (4f^7)	$^8S_{7/2}$	Colourless	7.94	7.9–8.0
Tb	6 (4f^8)	$^7F_6$	Very pale pink	9.72	9.5–9.8
Dy	5 (4f^9)	$^6H_{15/2}$	Yellow	10.65	10.4–10.6
Ho	4 (4f^{10})	$^5I_8$	Yellow	10.60	10.4–10.7
Er	3 (4f^{11})	$^4I_{15/2}$	Rose-pink	9.58	9.4–9.6
Tm	2 (4f^{12})	$^3H_6$	Pale green	7.56	7.1–7.5
Yb	1 (4f^{13})	$^2F_{7/2}$	Colourless	4.54	4.3–4.9
Lu	0 (4f^{14})	$^1S_0$	Colourless	0	0

[a] These are the values of μ_e at room temperature. The values fall as the temperature is reduced (see text).

by a pair of S and L values) is said to split into a number of component "states" (each defined by the same S and L values plus a value of J). The "ground state" of the ion is that with $J = L - S$ (or $S - L$) if the f shell is less than half-full, and that with $J = L + S$ if the f shell is more than half-full. It is indicated simply by adding this value of J as a subscript to the symbol for the "ground term".

The magnitude of the separation between the adjacent states of a term indicates the strength of the spin–orbit coupling, and in all but two cases (Sm^{III} and Eu^{III}) it is sufficient to render the first excited state of the Ln^{III} ions thermally inaccessible, and so the magnetic properties are determined solely by the ground state. It can be shown that the magnetic moment expected for such a situation is given by:

$$\mu_e = g\sqrt{J(J+1)} \text{ BM,}$$

where $g = \dfrac{3}{2} + \dfrac{S(S+1) - L(L+1)}{2J(J+1)}$

As can be seen in Table 30.6, this agrees very well with experimental values except for Sm^{III} and Eu^{III} and agreement is reasonable for these

also if allowance is made for the temperature-dependent population of excited states.

Electronic absorption spectra are produced when electromagnetic radiation promotes the ions from their ground state to excited states. For the lanthanides the most common of such transitions involve excited states which are either components of the ground term[†] or else belong to excited terms which arise from the same 4f^n configuration as the ground term. In either case the transitions therefore involve only a redistribution of electrons within the 4f orbitals (i.e. f→f transitions) and so are orbitally forbidden just like d→d transitions. In the case of the latter the rule is partially relaxed by a mechanism which depends on the effect of the crystal field in distorting the symmetry of the metal ion. However, it has already been pointed out that crystal field effects are very much smaller in the case of Ln^{III} ions and they

[†] The separation of these component states being, as pointed out above, of the order of a few thousand wavenumbers, such transitions produce absorptions in the infrared region of the spectrum. Ions which have no terms other than the ground term will therefore be colourless, having no transitions of sufficiently high energy to absorb in the visible region. This accounts for the colourless ions listed in Table 30.6.

cannot therefore produce the same relaxation of the selection rule. Consequently, the colours of Ln^{III} compounds are usually less intense. A further consequence of the relatively small effect of the crystal field is that the energies of the electronic states are only slightly affected by the nature of the ligands or by thermal vibrations, and so the absorption bands are very much sharper than those for d→d transitions. Because of this they provide a useful means of characterizing, and quantitatively estimating, Ln^{III} ions.

Nevertheless, crystal fields cannot be completely ignored. The intensities of a number of bands ("hypersensitive" bands) show a distinct dependence on the actual ligands which are coordinated. Also, in the same way that crystal fields lift some of the orbital degeneracy $(2L + 1)$ of the terms of d^n ions, so they lift some of the $2J + 1$ degeneracy of the sates of f^n ions, though in this case only by the order of $100 \, cm^{-1}$. This produces fine structure in some bands of Ln^{III} spectra.

Ce^{III} and Tb^{III} are exceptional in providing (in the ultraviolet) bands of appreciably higher intensity than usual. The reason is that the particular transitions involved are of the type $4f^n \rightarrow 4f^{n-1}5d^1$, and so are not orbitally forbidden. These 2 ions have 1 electron more than an empty f shell and 1 electron more than a half-full f shell, respectively, and the promotion of this extra electron is thereby easier than for other ions.

Sm, Dy but more especially Eu and Tb have excited states which are only slightly lower in energy than excited states of typical ligands. If electrons on the ligand are excited, the possibility therefore exists that, instead of falling back to the ground state of the ligand, they may pass first to the excited state of the Ln^{III} and *then* fall to the metal ground state, emitting radiation of characteristic frequency in doing so (fluorescence or, more generally, luminescence). This is the basis of the commercial use of oxide phosphors of these elements on TV screens where the excitation is provided by electrical discharge. Excitation by uv light produces luminescence spectra

which yield information about the donor atoms and co-ordination symmetry.[30,31]

It has been possible, as already noted (footnote, p. 1240) to study the spectra of Ln^{II} ions stabilized in CaF_2 crystals. It might be expected that these spectra would resemble those of the +3 ions of the next element in the series. However, because of the lower ionic charge of the Ln^{II} ions their 4f orbitals have not been stabilized relative to the 5d to the same extent as those of the Ln^{III} ions. Ln^{II} spectra therefore consist of rather broad, orbitally allowed, 4f→5d bands overlaid with weaker and much sharper f→f bands.

30.3.4 Complexes [12,14,32]

Oxidation state IV

The +4 oxidation state is found in LnO_2, LnF_4, the ternary oxides $M_2^I LnO_3$ and Li_8LnO_6 (Ln = Ce, Pr, Tb), and in the ternary fluorides $M_3^I LnF_7$ (Ln = Ce, Pr, Tb, Nd, Dy). $M^I TbIO_6.xH_2O$ has been obtained from aqueous alkaline solution[33] but Ce is the only lanthanide with a significant aqueous or co-ordination chemistry in this oxidation state. Fig. 30.4 shows that this situation is in no way surprising.

Aqueous "ceric" solutions are widely used as oxidants in quantitative analysis; they can be prepared by the oxidation of Ce^{III} ("cerous") solutions with strong oxidizing agents such as peroxodisulfate, $S_2O_8^{2-}$, or bismuthate, BiO_3^-. Complexation and hydrolysis combine to render $E(Ce^{4+}/Ce^{3+})$ markedly dependent on anion and acid concentration. In relatively strong perchloric acid the aquo ion is present but in other acids coordination of the anion is likely. Also, if the pH is increased, hydrolysis to

[30] N. SABBATINI, M. GUARDIGOLI and J.-M. LEHN, *Coord, Chem. Revs.* **123**, 201–28 (1993).

[31] J. V. BEITZ, pp. 159–96, Vol. 18 (1994) of ref. 1.

[32] F. A. HART, Scandium, Yttrium and the Lanthanides, Chap. 39, pp. 1059–127, in *Comprehensive Coordination Chemistry*, Vol. 3, Pergamon Press, Oxford, 1987.

[33] Y. YING and Y. RU-DONG, *Polyhedron* **11**, 963–6 (1992).

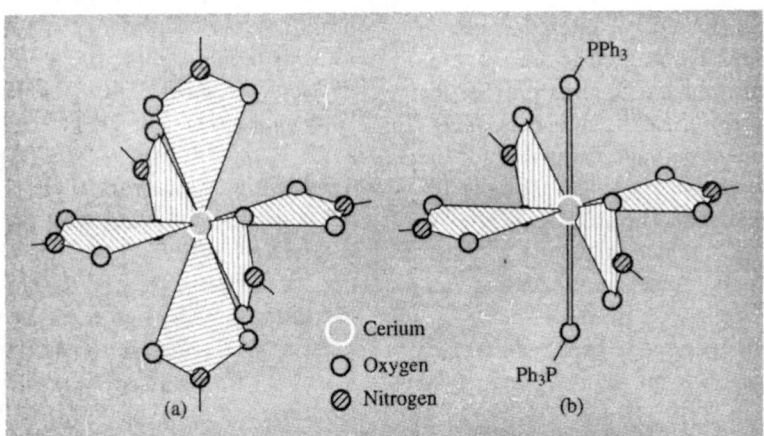

Figure 30.5 Nitrato complexes of Ce^{IV}. (a) [Ce(NO$_3$)$_6$]$^{2-}$: the Ce^{IV} is surrounded by 12 oxygen atoms from 6 bidentate nitrate ions in the form of an icosahedron (in each case the third oxygen is omitted for clarity). Note that this implies an octahedral disposition of the 6 nitrogen atoms. (b) [Ce(NO$_3$)$_4$(OPPh$_3$)$_2$].

Ce(OH)$^{3+}$ occurs followed by polymerization and finally, as the solution becomes alkaline, by precipitation of the yellow, gelatinous CeO$_2$.xH$_2$O.

Of the various salts which can be isolated from aqueous solution, probably the most important is the water-soluble double nitrate, (NH$_4$)$_2$[Ce(NO$_3$)$_6$], which is the compound generally used in Ce^{IV} oxidations. The anion involves 12-coordinated Ce (Fig. 30.5a). Two *trans*-nitrates of this complex can be replaced by Ph$_3$PO to give the orange 10-coordinate neutral complex [Ce(NO$_3$)$_4$(OPPh$_3$)$_2$] (Fig. 30.5b). The sulfates Ce(SO$_4$)$_2$.nH$_2$O ($n = 0$, 4, 8, 12) and (NH$_4$)$_2$Ce(SO$_4$)$_3$, and the iodate are also known. Also obtainable from aqueous solutions are complexes with other *O*-donor ligands such as β-diketonates, and fluoro complexes such as [CeF$_8$]$^{4-}$ and [CeF$_6$]$^{2-}$. This last ion is not in fact 6-coordinated but achieves an 8-coordinate, square-antiprismatic geometry with the aid of fluoride bridges. In the orange [CeCl$_6$]$^{2-}$ by contrast, the larger halide is able to stabilize a 6-coordinate, octahedral geometry. It is prepared by treatment of CeO$_2$ with HCl but, because Ce^{IV} in aqueous solution oxidizes HCl to Cl$_2$, the reaction must be performed in a nonaqueous solvent such as pyridine or dioxan.

Oxidation state III

The coordination chemistry of the large, electropositive Ln^{III} ions is complicated, especially in solution, by ill-defined stereochemistries and uncertain coordination numbers. This is well illustrated by the aquo ions themselves.[34] These are known for all the lanthanides, providing the solutions are moderately acidic to prevent hydrolysis, with hydration numbers probably about 8 or 9 but with reported values depending on the methods used to measure them. It is likely that the primary hydration number decreases as the cationic radius falls across the series. However, confusion arises because the polarization of the H$_2$O molecules attached directly to the cation facilitates hydrogen bonding to other H$_2$O molecules. As this tendency will be the greater, the smaller the cation, it is quite reasonable that the secondary hydration number increases across the series.

Hydrated salts with all the common anions can be crystallized from aqueous solutions and frequently, but by no means invariably, they contain the [Ln(H$_2$O)$_9$]$^{3+}$ ion. An enormous number of salts of organic acids such as oxalic, citric and

[34] E. N. RIZKALLA and G. R. CHOPPIN, pp. 529–58, Vol. 18 (1994) of ref. 1; T. KOWALL, F. FOGLIA, L. HELM and A. E. MERBACH, *J. Am. Chem. Soc.* **117**, 3790–9 (1995).

tartaric have been studied,[35] often for use in separation methods. These anions are, in fact, chelating *O* ligands which as a class provide the most extensive series of Ln^{III} complexes. NO_3^- is an inorganic counterpart and is notable for the high coordination numbers it yields, as in the 10-coordinate bicapped dodecahedral $[Ce(NO_3)_5]^{2-}$, and in $[Ce(NO_3)_6]^{3-}$ which like its Ce^{IV} analogue, has the 12-coordinate icosahedral geometry (Fig. 30.5a) (see also p. 469).

β-diketonates (L-L) provide further important examples of this class of ligand, and yield complexes of the type $[Ln(L-L)_3L']$ (L' = H$_2$O, py, etc.) and $[Ln(L-L)_4]^-$, which are respectively 7- and 8-coordinate. Dehydration, under vacuum, of the hydrated tris-diketonates produces $[Ln(L-L)_3]$ complexes which probably increase their coordination by dimerizing or polymerizing. They may be sublimed, the most volatile and thermally stable being those with bulky alkyl groups R in $[RC(O)CHC(O)R]^-$; they are soluble in non-polar solvents, and have received much attention as "nmr shift" reagents. Thus, in the case of organic molecules which are able to coordinate to Ln^{III} (i.e. if they contain groups such as –OH or –COO$^-$), the addition of one of these coordinatively unsaturated reagents produces a labile adduct; because this adduct is anisotropic the paramagnetic Ln^{III} ion shifts the resonance line of each proton by an amount which is critically dependent on the spatial relationship of the Ln^{III} and the proton. Greatly improved resolution is thereby obtained along with the possibility of distinguishing between alternative structures of the organic molecule.

Various crown ethers (p. 96) with differing cavity diameters provide a range of coordination numbers and stoichiometries, although crystallographic data are sparse. An interesting series, illustrating the dependence of coordination number on cationic radius and ligand cavity diameter, is provided by the complexes formed by the lanthanide nitrates and the 18-crown-6 ether (i.e. 1,4,7,10,13,16-

hexaoxacyclo-octadecane). For Ln = La–Gd the most thermally-stable product is that with a ratio of Ln:crown ether = 4:3, but the larger of these lanthanides (i.e. La, Ce, Pr and Nd) also form a 1:1 complex. This is $[Ln(NO_3)_3L]$ in which the Ln^{III} is 12-coordinate[36] (Fig. 30.6a). The 4:3 complex, on the other hand, is probably $[Ln(NO_3)_2L]_3[Ln(NO_3)_6]$ in which, compared to the 1:1 complex, the Ln^{III} in the complex cation has lost one NO_3^-, so reducing its coordination number to 10. The remaining, still smaller lanthanides (Tb–Lu) find the cavity of this ligand too large and form $[Ln(NO_3)_3(H_2O)_3]L$, in which the ligand is uncoordinated.

Unidentate *O* donors such as pyridine-*N*-oxide and triphenylphosphine oxide also form many complexes, as do alkoxides. This last group, like the alkoxides of Sc and Y (p. 951) is of special interest because of possible applications in the deposition of pure metal oxides by MOCVD techniques.[37] Attempts to prepare Ln(OR)$_3$ usually produce polynuclear clusters. Two examples will suffice: $[Nd_6(OPr^i)_{17}Cl]$, made up of 6 Nd atoms held together around a central Cl atom by means of bridging OCHMe$_2$ groups[38] (Fig. 30.6b). $[Yb_5O(OPr^i)_{13}]$ which consists of a square pyramid of Yb atoms containing a μ_5-O. Four μ_2-OPr^i groups cap the faces of the square pyramid. A single terminal alkoxide completes a distorted octahedral coordination sphere for each metal atom.[39]

Complexes with *O*-donor ligands are more numerous than those with *N* donors, probably because the former ligands are more often negatively charged — a clear advantage when forming essentially ionic bonds. However, by using polar organic solvents such as ethanol, acetone or acetonitrile in order to avoid competitive coordination by water, complexes with

[35] A. OUCHI, Y. SUZUKI, Y. OHKI and Y. KOIZUMI, *Coord. Chem. Revs.* **92**, 29–43 (1988).

[36] J.-C. G. BÜNZLI, B. KLEIN and D. WESSNER, *Inorg. Chim. Acta* **44**, L147–9 (1980).

[37] D. C. BRADLEY, *Chem. Revs.* **89**, 1317–22 (1989).

[38] R. A. ANDERSEN, D. H. TEMPLETON and A. ZALKIN, *Inorg. Chem.* **17**, 1962–5 (1978).

[39] D. C. BRADLEY, H. CHUDZYNSKA, D. M. FRIGO, M. E. HAMMON, M. B. HURSTHOUSE and M. A. MAZID, *Polyhedron* **9**, 719–26 (1990).

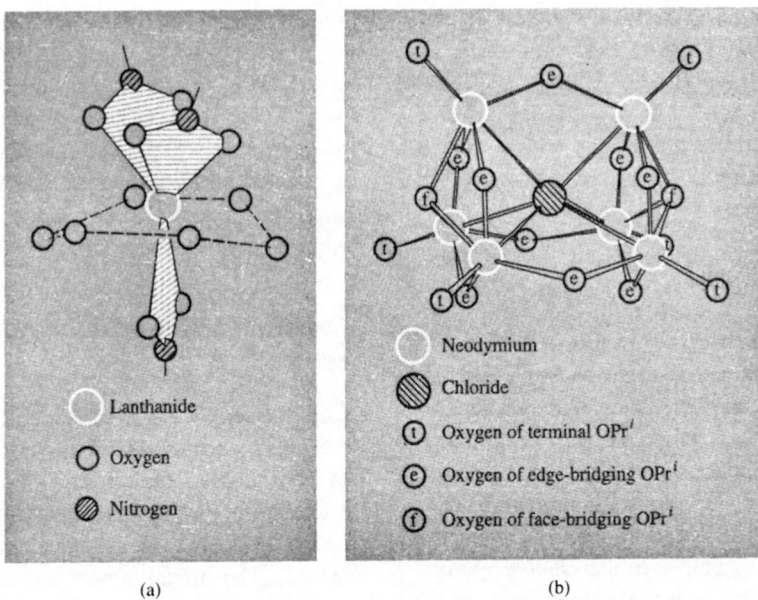

(a)　　　　　　　　　　　　　　　　　　　(b)

Figure 30.6　(a) $Ln(NO_3)_3$ (18-crown-6). For clarity only 2 of the oxygen atoms of each nitrate ion are shown, and only the 6 oxygen atoms of the crown ether. (Note the boat conformation of the crown ether which allows access to two NO_3^- on the open side and only one on the hindered side.) (b) $[Nd_6(OPr^i)_{17}Cl]$. Only the oxygens of the OPr^i groups are shown. Note that the 6 Nd atoms surrounding the Cl atom are situated at the corners of a trigonal prism, held together by 2 face-bridging and 9 edge-briding alkoxides.

chelating ligands such as en, dien, bipy,[39a] and terpy can be prepared. Coordination numbers of 8, 9 and 10 as in $[Ln(en)_4]^{3+}$, $[Ln(terpy)_3]^{3+}$ and $[Ln(dien)_4(NO_3)]^{2+}$ are typical. Nor do complexes such as the well-known $[Ln(edta)(H_2O)_3]^-$ show any destabilization because of the *N* donor atoms (edta has 4 oxygen and 2 nitrogen donor atoms). More pertinently, whereas the complexes of 18-crown-6-ethers mentioned above dissociate instantly in water, complexes of the *N*-donor analogues are sufficiently stable to remain unchanged.

As with other transition elements, the lanthanides can be induced to form complexes with exceptionally low coordination numbers by use of the very bulky ligand, $N(SiMe_3)_2^-$:

$$3LiN(SiMe_3)_2 + LnCl_3 \longrightarrow [Ln\{N(SiMe_3)_2\}_3]$$
$$+ 3LiCl$$

The volatile, but air-sensitive, and very easily hydrolysed products have a coordination number of 3, the lowest found for the lanthanides; they are apparently planar in solution (zero dipole moment) but pyramidal in the solid state. With Ph_3PO the 4-coordinate distorted tetrahedral adducts $[Ln\{N(SiMe_3)_2\}_3(OPPh_3)]$ are obtained. So difficult is it to expand the coordination sphere that attempts to prepare bis-(Ph_3PO) adducts produce instead the dimeric peroxo bridged complex, $[(Ph_3PO)\{(Me_3Si)_2N\}_2LnO_2$-$Ln\{N(SiMe_3)_2\}_2(OPPh_3)]$ (see p. 619).

Coordination by halide ions is rather weak, that of I^- especially so, but from non-aqueous solutions it is possible to isolate anionic complexes of the type $[LnX_6]^{3-}$. These are apparently, and unusually for Ln^{III}, 6-coordinate and octahedral. The heavier donor atoms S, Se, P[40] and As form only a few

[39a] E. C. CONSTABLE, *Adv. Inorg. Chem.* **34**, 1–64 (1989).

[40] M. D. FRYZUK, T. S. HADDAD and D. J. BERG, *Coord. Chem. Revs.* **99**, 137–212 (1990).

compounds. Chelating dithiocarbamate ligands provide the best known examples such as $[Ln(S_2CNMe_2)_3]$ and $[Ln(S_2CNMe_2)_4]^-$. Trigonal planar $[Sm(SAr)_3]$, $(Ar = C_6H_2Bu^t_3\text{-}2,4,6)$ is a rare example of an Ln complex with a unidentate S-donor ligand and also an unusually low coordination number.[40]

Oxidation state II[11]

The coordination chemistry in this oxidation state is essentially confined to the ions Sm^{II}, Eu^{II} and Yb^{II}. These are the only ones with an aqueous chemistry and their solutions may be prepared by electrolytic reduction of the Ln^{III} solutions or, in the case of Eu^{II}, by reduction with amalgamated Zn. These solutions are blood-red for Sm^{II}, colourless or pale greenish-yellow for Eu^{II} and yellow for Yb^{II}, and presumably contain the aquo ions. All are rapidly oxidized by air, and Sm^{II} and Yb^{II} are also oxidized by water itself although aqueous Eu^{II} is relatively stable, especially in the dark.

A number of salts have been isolated but, especially those of Sm^{II} and Yb^{II}, are susceptible to oxidation even by their own water of crystallization. Carbonates and sulfates, however, have been characterized and shown to be isomorphous with those of Sr^{II} and Ba^{II}.

Europium and Yb display further similarity with the alkaline earth metals in dissolving in liquid ammonia to give intense blue solutions, characteristic of solvated electrons and presumably also containing $[Ln(NH_3)_x]^{2+}$. The solutions are strongly reducing and decompose on standing with the precipitation of orange $Eu(NH_2)_2$ and brown $Yb(NH_2)_2$ (always contaminated with $Yb(NH_2)_3$) which are isostructural with the Ca and Sr amides.

30.3.5 Organometallic compounds[41]

The organometallic chemistry of lanthanides is far less extensive than that of transition elements

but, in spite of the lanthanides' inability to engage in π backbonding, it is one which has shown appreciable growth in the last quarter of a century. The compounds are of two main types: the predominantly ionic cyclopentadienides, and the σ-bonded alkyls and aryls. Organolanthanides of any type are usually thermally stable, but unstable with respect to water and air.

Cyclopentadienides and related compounds

The series $[Ln(C_5H_5)_3]$, $[Ln(C_5H_5)_2Cl]$ and the less numerous $[Ln(C_5H_5)Cl_2]$ are salts of the $C_5H_5^-$ anion and their most general preparation is by the reaction of anhydrous $LnCl_3$ and NaC_5H_5 in appropriate molar ratios in thf. The metal atoms in these compounds display an apparent tendency to increase their coordination numbers: solvates and other adducts are readily formed. In polar solvents, where they are no doubt solvated, they are monomeric but, in non-polar solvents the tris(C_5H_5) compounds are insoluble, while the bis(C_5H_5) compounds dimerize. In the solid state the tris-(C_5H_5) compounds show considerable structural diversity. Those of Er and Tm have η^5 rings arranged in a trigonal plane around the metal and those of Lu and Pr are isostructural with the Sc and La analogues respectively (p. 953). In the Sm compound each $C_5H_5^-$ ion is pentahapto towards 1 metal atom but some also act as bridges by presenting a ring vertex (η^1) or edge (η^2) towards an adjacent metal atom, so producing a chain structure.[†] In a less complicated way the blue $[Nd(C_5H_4Me)_3]$ is actually tetrameric, each Nd being attached to three rings in a pentahapto mode with one ring being further attached in a monohapto manner to an adjacent Nd. In spite of the steric bulk of the ligand, $[Sm(\eta^5\text{-}C_5Me_5)_3]$ has been obtained.[42] $[Ln(C_5H_5)_2Cl]$

[†] Ring bridges of these types are found in alkaline earth cyclopentadienides such as $[Ca(C_5H_5)_2]$ and are characteristic of the electrostatic nature of the bonding.

[41] C. J. SCHAVERIEN, *Adv. Organometallic Chem.* **36**, 283–362 (1994).

[42] W. J. EVANS, S. L. GONZALES and J. W. ZILLER, *J. Am. Chem. Soc.* **113**, 7423–4 (1991).

are actually dimers $[(\eta^5\text{-}C_5H_5)_2Ln(\mu\text{-}Cl)_2Ln(\eta^5\text{-}C_5H_5)_2]$. The Cl bridges can be replaced by, for instance, H, CN and OR and donor solvents will cleave the bridges. Most mono (C_5H_5) and (C_5Me_5) compounds are tris solvates such as $[Ln(\eta^5\text{-}C_5H_5)I_2(thf)_3]$.

Complexes with the two analogous ligands, indenide, $C_9H_7{}^-$,

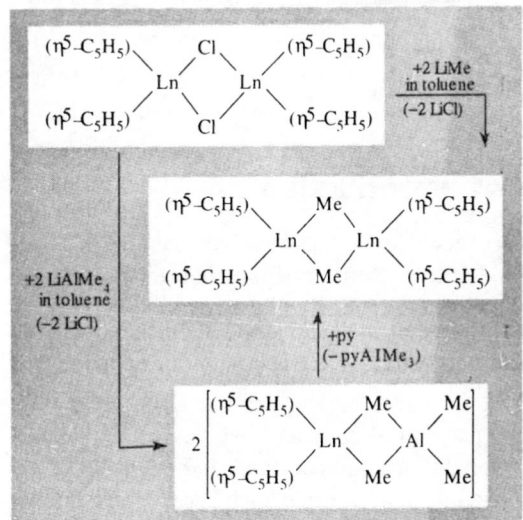

and cyclooctatetraenide, cot, $C_8H_8{}^{2-}$, ions can be prepared by similar means. In solid $[Sm(C_9H_7)_3]$ the 5-membered rings of the 3 ligands are bonded in a pentahapto manner and the compound shows little tendency to solvate, presumably because of the bulky nature of the $C_9H_7{}^-$ ions. The lighter (and therefore larger) Ln^{III} ions form $K[Ln(\eta^8\text{-}C_8H_8)_2]$. The Ce^{III} member of the series has a similar "sandwich" structure to the so-called "uranocene" (p. 1279). The other members of the series have the same infrared spectrum and so also are presumed to have this structure.

Cyclopentadienyl derivatives of divalent lanthanides are also known[43] $[Ln^{II}(\eta^5\text{-}C_5H_5)_2]$ (Ln = Sm, Eu, Yb) might be expected to be isostructural with ferrocene but are "bent" ie rather than the two rings being parallel they are tilted relative to each other.

Alkyls and aryls

These are prepared by metathesis in thf or ether solutions:

$$LnCl_3 + 3LiR \longrightarrow LnR_3 + 3LiCl$$
$$LnCl_3 + 4LiR \longrightarrow Li[LnR_4] + 3LiCl_3$$

43 W. J. EVANS, *Polyhedron*, **6**, 803–35 (1987).

The triphenyls are probably polymeric and the first fully-characterized compound was $[Li(thf)_4][Lu(C_6H_3Me_2)_4]$ in which the Lu is tetrahedrally coordinated to four σ-aryl groups. More stable products, of the form $[LnR_3(thf)_2]$, are obtained by the use of bulky alkyl groups such as $-CH_2CMe_3$ and $-CH_2SiMe_3$.

Methyl derivatives, octahedral $[LnMe_6]^{3-}$ species, are known for most of the lanthanides. The first homoleptic, neutral lanthanide alkyl[44] was obtained using the bulky alkyl $CH(SiMe_3)_2$:

$$Sm(OR)_3 + 3LiCH(SiMe_3)_2 \longrightarrow$$
$$[Sm\{CH(SiMe_3)_2\}_3] + 3LiOR$$

Compounds containing lanthanide–carbon σ-bonds have recently been reviewed.[45]

Novel, mixed alkyl cyclopentadienides have also been prepared for the heavy lanthanides:[46]

44 P. B. HITCHCOCK, M. F. LAPPERT, R. G. SMITH, R. A. BARTLETT and P. P. POWER, *J. Chem. Soc., Chem. Commun.*, 1007–9 (1988).

45 S. A. COTTON, *Coord. Chem. Revs.* **160**, 93–127 (1997).

46 J. HOLTON, M. F. LAPPERT, D. G. H. BALLARD, R. PEARCE, J. L. ATWOOD and W. E. HUNTER, *J. Chem. Soc., Dalton Trans.*, 45–61 (1979).

31

The Actinide and Transactinide Elements (Z = 90 –103 and 104 –112)

31.1 Introduction

The "actinides" ("actinons" or "actinoids") are the fourteen elements from thorium to lawrencium inclusive, which follow actinium in the periodic table. They are analogous to the lanthanides and result from the filling of the 5f orbitals, as the lanthanides result from the filling of the 4f. The position of actinium, like that of lanthanum, is somewhat equivocal and, although not itself an actinide, it is often included with them for comparative purposes.

Prior to 1940 only the naturally occurring actinides (thorium, protactinium and uranium) were known; the remainder have been produced artificially since then. The "transactinides" are still being synthesized and so far the nine elements with atomic numbers 104–112 have been reliably established. Indeed, the 20 manmade transuranium elements together with technetium and promethium now constitute one-fifth of all the known chemical elements.

In 1789 M. H. Klaproth examined pitchblende, thought at the time to be a mixed oxide ore of zinc, iron and tungsten, and showed that it contained a new element which he named *uranium* after the recently discovered planet, Uranus. Then in 1828 J. J. Berzelius obtained an oxide, from a Norwegian ore now known as "thorite"; he named this *thoria* after the Scandinavian god of war and, by reduction of its tetrachloride with potassium, isolated the metal *thorium*. The same method was subsequently used in 1841 by B. Peligot to effect the first preparation of metallic uranium.

The much rarer element, protactinium, was not found until 1913 when K. Fajans and O. Göhring identified ^{234}Pa as an unstable member of the ^{238}U decay series:

$$^{238}_{92}\text{U} \xrightarrow{-\alpha} \,^{234}_{90}\text{Th} \xrightarrow{-\beta^-} \,^{234}_{91}\text{Pa} \xrightarrow{-\beta^-} \,^{234}_{92}\text{U}$$

They named it brevium because of its short half-life (6.70 h). The more stable isotope ^{231}Pa

$(t_{\frac{1}{2}}$ 32 760 y) was identified 3 years later by O. Hahn and L. Meitner and independently by F. Soddy and J. A. Cranston as a product of ^{235}U decay:

$$^{235}_{92}U \xrightarrow{-\alpha} {}^{231}_{90}Th \xrightarrow{-\beta^-} {}^{231}_{91}Pa \xrightarrow{-\alpha} {}^{227}_{89}Ac$$

As the parent of actinium in this series it was named protoactinium, shortened in 1949 to *protactinium*. Because of its low natural abundance its chemistry was obscure until 1960 when A. G. Maddock and co-workers at the UK Atomic Energy Authority worked up about 130 g from 60 tons of sludge which had accumulated during the extraction of uranium from UO_2 ores. It is from this sample, distributed to numerous laboratories throughout the world, that the bulk of our knowledge of the element's chemistry was gleaned.

In the early years of this century the periodic table ended with element 92 but, with J. Chadwick's discovery of the neutron in 1932 and the realization that neutron-capture by a heavy atom is frequently followed by β^- emission yielding the next higher element, the synthesis of new elements became an exciting possibility. E. Fermi and others were quick to attempt the synthesis of element 93 by neutron bombardment of ^{238}U, but it gradually became evident that the main result of the process was not the production of element 93 but nuclear fission, which produces lighter elements. However, in 1940, E. M. McMillan and P. H. Abelson in Berkeley, California, were able to identify, along with the fission products, a short-lived isotope of element 93 ($t_{\frac{1}{2}}$ 2.355 days):[†]

$$^{238}_{92}U + {}^{1}_{0}n \longrightarrow {}^{239}_{92}U \xrightarrow{-\beta^-} {}^{239}_{93}Np$$

As it was the next element after uranium in the now extended periodic table it was named *neptunium* after Neptune, which is the next planet beyond Uranus.

The remaining actinide elements were prepared[1−4] by various "bombardment" techniques fairly regularly over the next 25 years (Table 31.1) though, for reasons of national security, publication of the results was sometimes delayed. The dominant figure in this field has been G. T. Seaborg, of the University of California, Berkeley, in early recognition of which, he and E. M. McMillan were awarded the 1951 Nobel Prize for Chemistry.

The isolation and characterization of these elements, particularly the heavier ones, has posed enormous problems. Individual elements are not produced cleanly in isolation, but must be separated from other actinides as well as from lanthanides produced simultaneously by fission. In addition, all the actinides are radioactive, their stability decreasing with increasing atomic number, and this has two serious consequences. Firstly, it is necessary to employ elaborate radiation shielding and so, in many cases, operations must be carried out by remote control. Secondly, the heavier elements are produced only in the minutest amounts. Thus mendelevium was first prepared in almost unbelievably small yields of the order of 1 to 3 atoms per experiment! Paradoxically, however, the intense radioactivity also facilitated the detection of these minute amounts: first by the development and utilization of radioactive decay systematics, which enabled the detailed properties of the expected radiation to be predicted, and secondly, by using the radioactive decay itself to detect and count the individual atoms synthesized. Accordingly, the separations were effected by ion-exchange techniques, and the elements

---

[†] $^{239}_{93}$Np itself also decays by β^- emission to produce element 94 but this was not appreciated until after that element (plutonium) had been prepared from $^{238}_{93}$Np.

[1] G. T. SEABORG (ed.), *Transuranium Elements; Products of Modern Alchemy*, Dowden, Hutchinson & Ross, Stroudsburg, 1978. This reproduces, in their original form, 122 key papers in the story of man-made elements.

[2] G. T. SEABORG and W. D. LOVELAND, *The Elements Beyond Uranium*, Wiley, New York, 1990, 359 pp.

[3] J. J. KATZ, L. R. MORSS and G. T. SEABORG (eds.) *The Chemistry of the Actinide Elements*, Chapman and Hall, London, 1986; Vol. 1, 1004 pp.; Vol 2, 912 pp.

[4] L. R. MORSS and J. FUGER (eds.), *Transuranium Elements: A Half Century*, Am. Chem. Soc., Washington, 1992, 700 pp.

Table 31.1   The discovery (synthesis) of the artificial actinides

Element	Discoverers	Date	Synthesis	Origin of name
93 Neptunium, Np	E. M. McMillan and P. Abelson	1940	Bombardment of $^{238}_{92}U$ with ^1_0n	The planet Neptune
94 Plutonium, Pu	G. T. Seaborg, E. M. McMillan, J. W. Kennedy and A. Wahl	1940	Bombardment of $^{238}_{92}U$ with ^2_1H	The planet Pluto (next planet beyond Neptune)
95 Americium, Am	G. T. Seaborg, R. A. James, L. O. Morgan and A. Ghiorso	1944	Bombardment of $^{239}_{94}Pu$ with ^1_0n	America (by analogy with Eu, named after Europe)
96 Curium, Cm	G. T. Seaborg, R. A. James and A. Ghiorso	1944	Bombardment of $^{239}_{94}Pu$ with ^4_2He	P. and M. Curie (by analogy with Gd, named after J. Gadolin)
97 Berkelium, Bk	S. G. Thompson, A. Ghiorso and G. T. Seaborg	1949	Bombardment of $^{241}_{95}Am$ with ^4_2He	Berkeley (by analogy with Tb, named after the village of Ytterby)
98 Californium, Cf	S. G. Thompson, K. Street, A. Ghiorso and G. T. Seaborg	1950	Bombardment of $^{242}_{96}Cm$ with ^4_2He	California (location of the laboratory)
99 Einsteinium, Es	Workers at Berkeley, Argonne and Los Alamos (USA)	1952	Found in debris of first thermonuclear explosion	Albert Einstein (relativistic relation between mass and energy)
100 Fermium, Fm	Workers at Berkeley, Argonne and Los Alamos (USA)	1952	Found in debris of first thermonuclear explosion	Enrico Fermi (construction of first self-sustaining nuclear reactor)
101 Mendelevium, Md	A. Ghiorso, B. H. Harvey, G. R. Choppin, S. G. Thompson and G. T. Seaborg	1955	Bombardment of $^{253}_{99}Es$ with ^4_2He	Dimitri Mendeleev (periodic table of the elements)
102 Nobelium, No[a]	Workers at Dubna, USSR[b]	1965	Bombardment of $^{243}_{95}Am$ with $^{15}_7N$ (or $^{238}_{92}U$ with $^{22}_{10}Ne$)	Alfred Nobel (benefactor of science)[a]
103 Lawrencium, Lr[c]	Workers at Berkeley and at Dubna[d]	1961– 1971[d]	Bombardment of mixed isotopes of $_{98}Cf$ with $^{10}_5B$, $^{11}_5B$; and of $^{243}_{95}Am$ with $^{18}_8O$, etc.	Ernest Lawrence (developer of the cyclotron)

[a] The first claim for element 102 was in 1957 by an international team working at the Nobel Institute for Physics in Stockholm. Their results could not be confirmed but their suggested name for the element was accepted.

[b] A full assessment of this work and that done at Berkeley and elsewhere has been carried out by the Transfermium Working Group, a neutral international group appointed jointly by IUPAC and IUPAP in 1987[5].

[c] Formerly Lw; the present symbol was recommended by IUPAC in 1965.

[d] The Transfermium Working Group concluded that "In the complicated situation presented by element 103, with several papers of varying degrees of completeness and conviction, none conclusive, and referring to several isotopes, it is impossible to say other than that full confidence was built up over a decade with credit attaching to work in both Berkeley and Dubna". The detailed analysis of the many relevant publications is given in ref. 5.

[5] R. C. BARBER, N. N. GREENWOOD, A. Z. HRYNKIEWICZ, Y. P. JEANNIN, M. LEFORT, M. SAKAI, I. ULEHLA, A. H. WAPSTRA and D. H. WILKINSON, Discovery of the Transfermium Elements, *Prog. Particle Nucl. Phys.* **29**, 453–530 (1992). Also published, with comments in *Pure Appl. Chem.* **63**, 879–86 (1991) and **65**, 1757–814, 1815–24 (1993).

identified by chemical tracer methods and by their characteristic nuclear decay properties. In view of the quantities involved, especially of californium and later elements, it is clear that this would not have been feasible without accurate predictions of the chemical properties also. It was Seaborg's realization in 1944 that these elements should be regarded as a second f series akin to the lanthanides that made this possible. (Thorium, protactinium and uranium had previously been regarded as transition elements belonging to groups 4, 5 and 6, respectively.)

Elements beyond 103 are expected to be 6d elements forming a fourth transition series, and attempts to synthesize them have continued during the past thirty years. All 10 (including, of course, actinium) are now known and are discussed in the section on transactinide elements on p. 1280. The work has required the dedicated commitment of extensive national facilities and has been carried out at the Lawrence-Berkeley Laboratories, the Joint Institute for Nuclear Research at Dubna, and the Heavy-Ion Research Centre (GSI) at Darmstadt, Germany.

Superheavy elements

Since the radioactive half-lives of the known transuranium elements and their resistance to spontaneous fission decrease with increase in atomic number, the outlook for the synthesis of further elements might appear increasingly bleak. However, theoretical calculations of nuclear stabilities, based on the concept of closed nucleon shells (p. 13) suggest the existence of an "island of stability" around $Z = 114$ and $N = 184$.[6] Attention has therefore been directed towards the synthesis of element 114 (a congenor of Pb in Group 14 and adjacent "superheavy" elements, by bombardment of heavy nuclides with a wide range of heavy ions, but so far without success.

Searches have been made for naturally occurring superheavies ($Z = 112$–15) in ores of Hg,

Tl, Pb and Bi, on the assumption that they would follow their homologues in their geochemical evolution and could be recognized by the radiation damage caused over geological time by their very energetic decay. Early claims to have detected such superheavies in natural ores have been convincingly discounted.[7] More recent uncorroborated claims to success have been made but, even if confirmed, the concentrations found in the samples examined, are exceedingly small[8] (less than 1 in 10^{13}).

31.2 The Actinide Elements[2.3.9–12]

31.2.1 Terrestrial abundance and distribution

Every known isotope of the actinide elements is radioactive and the half-lives are such that only ^{232}Th, ^{235}U, ^{238}U and possibly ^{244}Pu could have survived since the formation of the solar system. In addition, continuing processes produce equilibrium traces of some isotopes of which the most prominent is ^{234}U ($t_{\frac{1}{2}}$ 2.45×10^5 y,

[6] B. FRICKE, *Struct. Bonding, (Berlin)*, **21**, 89–144 (1975).

[7] F. BOSH, A. ELGORESY, W. KRÄTSCHMER, B. MARTIN, B. POVH, R. NOBILING, K. TRAXEL and D. SCHWALM, *Z. Physik* **A280**, 39–44 (1977); see also C. J. SPARKS, S. RAMAN, H. L. TAKEL, R. V. GENTRY and M. O. KRAUSE, *Phys. Rev. Letters* **38**, 205–8 (1977), for retraction of their earlier claim to have detected naturally occurring primordial superheavy elements.

[8] See, for instance, E. L. FIREMAN, B. H. KETELLE and R. W. STOUGHTON, *J. Inorg. Nucl. Chem.* **41**, 613–5 (1979).

[9] *Kirk–Othmer Encyclopedia of Chemical Technology*, 4th edn., Interscience, New York; for Actinides see Vol. 1, 1991, pp. 412–45; for Thorium see Vol. 24, 1997, pp. 68–88; for Uranium see Vol. 24, 1997, pp. 638–94; for Plutonium see Vol. 19, 1996, pp. 407–43.

[10] A. HARPER, Chap 17, pp. 435–56 in D. THOMPSON (ed.), *Insights into Speciality Inorganic Chemicals*, RSC, Cambridge, 1995.

[11] S. COTTON, *Lanthanides and Actinides*, Macmillan, Basingstoke, 1991, 192 pp.

[12] L. MANES (ed.) *Structure and Bonding*, Vol. 59/60, *Actinides – Chemistry and Physical Properties*, Springer, Berlin, 1985, 305 pp.

comprising 0.0054% of naturally occurring U isotopes). ^{231}Pa (and therefore ^{227}Ac) is formed as a product of the decay of ^{235}U, while ^{237}Np and ^{239}Pu are produced by the reactions of neutrons with, respectively, ^{235}U and ^{238}U. Traces of Pa, Np and Pu are consequently found, but only Th and U occur naturally to any useful extent. Indeed, these two elements are far from

rare: thorium comprises 8.1 ppm of the earth's crust, and is almost as abundant as boron, whilst uranium at 2.3 ppm is rather more abundant than tin. The radioactive decay schemes of the naturally occurring long-lived isotopes of ^{232}Th, ^{235}U and ^{238}U, together with the artificially generated series based on ^{241}Pu, are summarized in Fig 31.1.

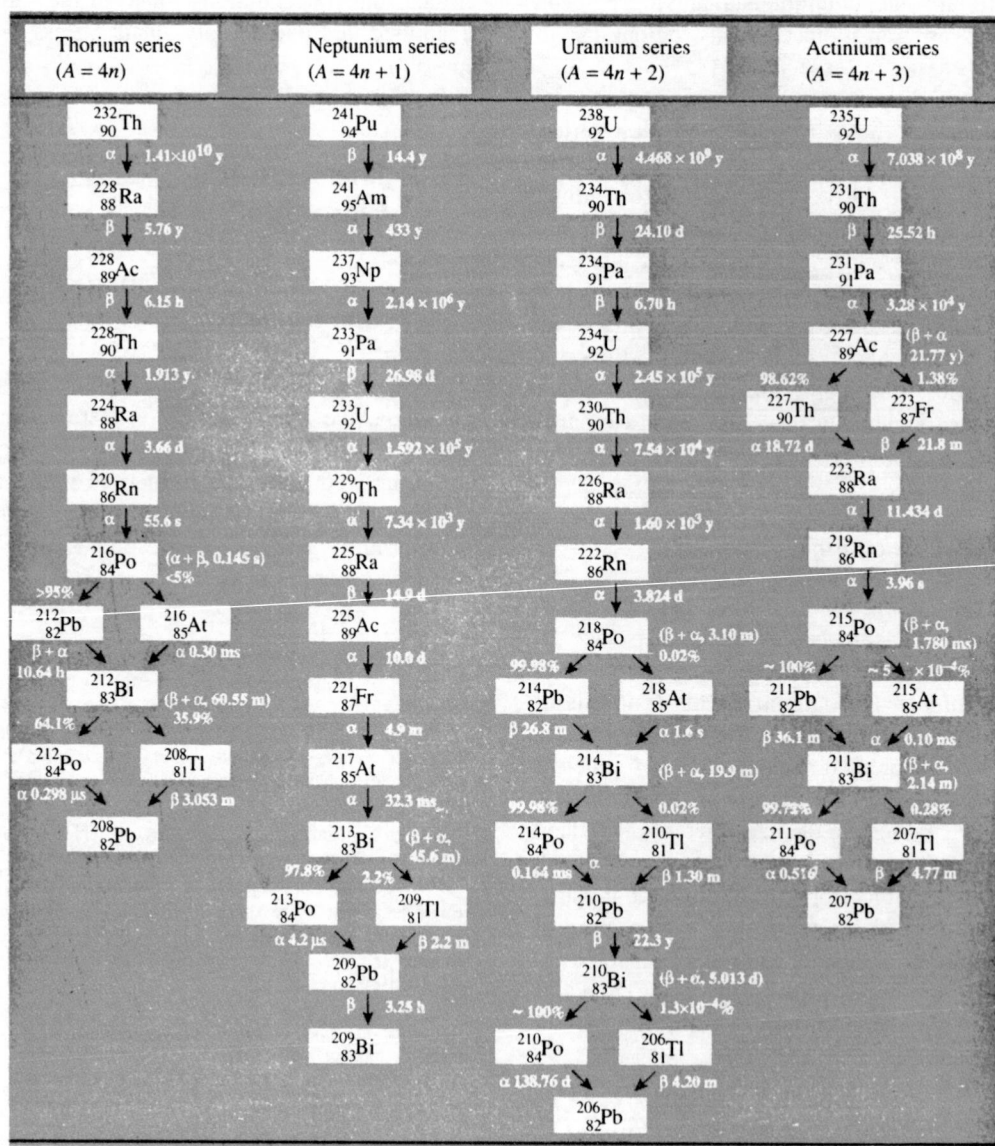

Figure 31.1 The radioactive decay series.

Thorium is widely but rather sparsely distributed and its only commercial sources are monazite sands (see p. 1229) and the mineral conglomerates of Ontario. The former are found in India, South Africa, Brazil, Australia and Malaysia, and in exceptional cases may contain up to 20% ThO_2 but more usually contain less than 10%. In the Canadian ores the thorium is present as uranothorite, a mixed Th,U silicate, which is accompanied by pitchblende. Even though present as only 0.4% ThO_2, the recovery of Th, as a co-product of the recovery of uranium, is viable.

Uranium, too, is widely distributed and, since it probably crystallized late in the formation of igneous rocks, tends to be scattered in the faults of older rocks. Some concentration by leaching and subsequent re-precipitation has produced a large number of oxide minerals of which the most important are pitchblende or uraninite, U_3O_8, and carnotite, $K_2(UO_2)_2(VO_4)_2.3H_2O$. However, even these are usually dispersed so that typical ores contain only about 0.1% U, and many of the more readily exploited deposits are nearing exhaustion. The principal sources are Canada, Africa and countries of the former USSR.

The transuranium elements must all be prepared artificially. In the case of plutonium about 1200 tonnes have so far been produced worldwide, about three-quarters of it in civilian reactors.

31.2.2 Preparation and uses of the actinide elements [2,9]

The separation of basic precipitates of hydrous ThO_2 from the lanthanides in monazite sands has been outlined in Fig. 30.1 (p. 1230). These precipitates may then be dissolved in nitric acid and the thorium extracted into tributyl phosphate, $(Bu^nO)_3PO$, diluted with kerosene. In the case of Canadian production, the uranium ores are leached with sulfuric acid and the anionic sulfato complex of U preferentially absorbed onto an anion exchange resin. The Th is separated from Fe, Al and other metals in the liquor by solvent extraction.

Metallic thorium can be obtained by reduction of ThO_2 with Ca or by reduction of $ThCl_4$ with Ca or Mg under an atmosphere of Ar (like Ti, finely divided Th is extremely reactive when hot).

The uses of Th are at present limited and only a few hundred tonnes are produced annually, about half of this still being devoted to the production of gas mantles (p. 1228). In view of its availability as a by-product of lanthanide and uranium production, output could be increased easily if it were to be used on a large scale as a nuclear fuel (see below).

Uranium production depends in detail on the nature of the ore involved but, after crushing and concentrating by conventional physical means, the ore is usually roasted and leached with sulfuric acid in the presence of an oxidizing agent such as MnO_2 or $NaClO_3$ to ensure conversion of all uranium to UO_2^{2+}. In a typical process the uranium is concentrated as a sulfato complex on an anion exchange resin from which it is eluted with strong HNO_3 and further purified by solvent extraction into tributyl phosphate (TBP) in either kerosene or hexane. The uranium is then stripped from the organic phase to give an aqueous sulfate solution from which so-called "yellow cake" is precipitated* by addition of ammonia. This is converted to UO_3 by heating at 300°C, and then to UO_2 by reducing in H_2 at 700°C. Conversion to the metal is generally effected by reduction of UF_4 with Mg at 700°C.

Apart from its long-standing though small-scale use for colouring glass and ceramics, uranium's only significant use is as a nuclear fuel. The extent of this use depends on environmental and political considerations. In 1994 world production after nearly a decade of decline was 31 000 tonnes, 30% of which came from Canada and 23% each from the former Soviet Union and African countries (Niger, Namibia, the Republic of South Africa and Gabon). This, however, represented only half the reactor requirements. The rest came from recycling and stockpiles

---

* Yellow cake is a complicated mixture of salts and oxides, the composition of which approximates to $(NH_4)_2U_2O_7$ but is dependent on the method by which it is produced (see p. 276 of ref. 2).

(which were expected to be exhausted within 4 or 5 years).

Nuclear reactors and atomic energy[13-15]

In the process of nuclear fission a large nucleus splits into two highly energetic smaller nuclei and a number of neutrons; if there are sufficient neutrons and they have the correct energy, they can induce fission of further nuclei, so creating a self-propagating chain reaction. The kinetic energy of the main fragments is rapidly converted to heat as they collide with neighbouring atoms, the amount being of the order of 10^6 times that produced by chemically burning the same mass of combustible material such as coal.

In practical terms, the only naturally occurring fissile nucleus is $^{235}_{92}U$ (0.72% abundant):

$$^{235}_{92}U + ^1_0n \longrightarrow 2 \text{ fragments} + x^1_0n \quad (x = 2-3)$$

The so-called "fast" neutrons which this fission produces have energies of about 2 MeV (190 × 10^6 kJ mol^{-1}) and are not very effective in producing fission of further $^{235}_{92}U$ nuclei. Better in this respect are "slow" or "thermal" neutrons whose energies are of the order of 0.025 eV (2.4 kJ mol^{-1}), i.e. equivalent to the thermal energy· available at ambient temperatures. In order to produce and sustain a chain reaction in uranium it is therefore necessary to counter the inefficiency of fast neutrons by either (a) increasing the proportion of $^{235}_{92}U$ (i.e. fuel enrichment) or (b) slowing down (i.e. moderating) the fast neutrons. In addition, there must be sufficient uranium to prevent excessive loss of neutrons from the surface (i.e. a "critical mass" must be exceeded). If the reaction is not to run out of control, an adjustable neutron absorber is also required to ensure that the rate

of production of neutrons is balanced by the rate of their absorption.

The first manmade self-sustaining nuclear fission chain reaction was achieved on 2 December 1942 in a disused squash court at the University of Chicago by a team which included E. Fermi. This was before nuclear-fuel enrichment had been developed: alternate sections of natural-abundance UO_2 and graphite moderator were piled on top of each other (hence, nuclear reactors were originally known as "atomic piles") and the reaction was controlled by strips of cadmium which could be inserted or withdrawn as necessary. In this crude structure, 6 tonnes of uranium metal, 50 tonnes of uranium oxide and nearly 400 tonnes of graphite were required to achieve criticality. The dramatic success of Fermi's team in achieving a self-sustaining nuclear reaction invited the speculation as to whether such a phenomenon could occur naturally.[16] In one of the most spectacular pieces of scientific detection work ever conducted, it has now unambiguously been established that such natural chain reactions have indeed occurred in the geological past when conditions were far more favourable than at present (see Panel).

If a chain reaction is to provide useful energy, the heat it generates must be extracted by means of a suitable coolant and converted, usually by steam turbines, into electrical energy. The high temperatures and the intense radioactivity generated within a reactor pose severe, and initially totally new, constraints on the design. The choices of fuel and its immediate container (cladding), of the moderator, coolant and controller involve problems in nuclear physics, chemistry, metallurgy and engineering. Nevertheless, the first commercial power station (as opposed to experimental reactors or those whose function was to produce plutonium for bomb manufacture) was commissioned in 1956 at Calder Hall in Cumberland, UK. Since then a variety of different types has been developed in several countries, as summarized in Fig. 31.2. At

[13] S. GLASSTONE and A. SESONSKE, *Nuclear Reactor Engineering*, 4th edn., Chapman and Hall, New York, 1994, 852 pp.

[14] R. L. MURRAY, *Nuclear Energy*, 4th edn., Pergamon, Oxford, 1993, 437 pp.

[15] *Kirk–Othmer Encyclopedia of Chemical Technology*, Vol. 17, 4th edn., 1996, pp. 369–465, Interscience, New York.

[16] P. K. KURODA, *Nature* **187**, 36–8 (1960).

Natural Nuclear Reactors — The Oklo Phenomenon[17]

Natural uranium consists almost entirely of the α emitters ^{235}U and ^{238}U. As ^{235}U decays more than six times faster than ^{238}U (Fig. 31.1) the proportion of ^{235}U is very slowly but inexorably decreasing with time. Prior to 1972, all analyses of naturally occurring uranium had shown this proportion to be notably constant at $0.7202 \pm 0.0006\%$.[†] In that year, however, workers at the French Atomic Energy laboratories in Pierrelatte performing routine mass spectrometric analyses recorded a value of 0.7171%. The difference was small but significant.

Contamination with commercially depleted U was immediately assumed, but it was gradually realized that the depletion was characteristic of the ore, which came from a mine at Oklo in Gabon, near the west coast ($1°$ $25'$S, $13°$ $10'$W). An intensive examination of the mine was quickly mounted and it was found that the depletion was not uniform but was greatest near those areas where the total U content was highest. The record depletion was an astonishingly low 0.296% ^{235}U from an area where the total U content of the ore rose to around 60%. Incredible as it may appear in view of the diverse and exacting requirements for the construction of a manmade nuclear reactor, the only satisfactory explanation is that the Oklo mine is the site of a spent, prehistoric, natural nuclear reactor. There are now known to have been 14 such reactors in the Franceville basin at Oklo, all of which have been mined, plus a further one some 30 km to the southeast at Bangombé, which it is hoped to preserve essentially undisturbed.

The Oklo ore bed consists of sedimentary rocks believed to have been laid down about 1.8×10^9 y ago. U^{IV} minerals in the igneous rocks, formed in the early history of the earth when the atmosphere was a reducing one, were converted to soluble U^{VI} salts by the atmosphere which had since become oxidizing. These were then re-precipitated as U^{IV} by bacterial reduction in the silt of a river delta and gradually buried under other sedimentary deposits. During this process the underlying granite rocks were tilted, the ores which contained about 0.5% U were fractured, and water percolating through the fissures created rich pockets of ore which in places consisted of almost pure UO_2. At that time the ^{235}U content of the uranium was about 3%, which is the value to which the fuel used in most modern water-moderated reactors is now artifically enriched.

Under these circumstances the critical mass could be attained and a nuclear chain reaction initiated, with water as the necessary moderator. The 15% water of hydration contained in the clays associated with the ore would be ideal for this purpose. As the reaction proceeded, the consequent rise in temperature would have driven off water, so producing "undermoderation" and slowing the reaction, thereby avoiding a "run away" reaction. As a result, a particular reactor may have operated in a steady manner or perhaps in a slowly pulsating manner, as water was alternately driven off (causing loss of criticality and cooling) and re-absorbed (recovering criticality and again heating).

Further control of the reactions must have been effected by neutron-absorbing "poisons", such as lithium and boron, which are nearly always present in clays. That these are present in the Oklo clays in comparatively low concentrations is one of the factors which allowed the reactions to take place. As the nuclear fuel in the original, rich pockets was being used up, the poisons in the surrounding ore would be simultaneously "burned out" by escaping neutrons. Thus ore of only slightly poorer quality, which was initially prevented only by the poisons from being critical, would gradually become so and the chain reaction would be propogated further through the ore bed. It is thought that these reactors operated for about $(0.2 - 1) \times 10^6$ y with output in the region of 10–100 kW, consuming altogether 4–6 tonnes of ^{235}U from a total deposit of the order of 400 000 tonnes of uranium. Subsequent preservation of the fossil reactors is a result of continued burial which protected the uranium from redissolution.

Confirmation of this explanation is unequivocally provided by the presence in the reactor zones of at least half of the more than 30 fission products of uranium. Although soluble salts, such as those of the alkali and alkaline earth metals, have been leached out, lanthanide and platinum metals remain along with traces of trapped krypton and xenon. Most decisively, the observed distribution of the various isotopes of these elements is that of fission products as opposed to the distribution normally found terrestrially. The reasons for the retention of these elements on this particular site is clearly germane to the problem of the long-term storage of nuclear wastes, and is therefore the subject of continuing study.

The circumstances which led to the Oklo phenomenon may well have occurred in other, as yet unidentified, places, but in view of the intervening natural depletion of ^{235}U, the possibility of a natural chain reaction being initiated at the present time or in the future may be discounted.

---

[17] *Le Phenomene d'Oklo*, Proceedings of a Symposium on the Oklo Phenomenon, International Atomic Energy Agency, Vienna, Proceedings Series, 1975. *Natural Fission Reactions*, IAEA, Vienna, Panel Proceedings Series STI/PUB/475, 1978, 754 pp. R. WEST, Natural nuclear reactors. *J. Chem. Ed.* **53**, 336–40 (1976).

[†] If, as is believed (p. 13), the earth was formed about 4.6×10^9 y ago it follows that the proportion of ^{235}U at that time must have been about 25%.

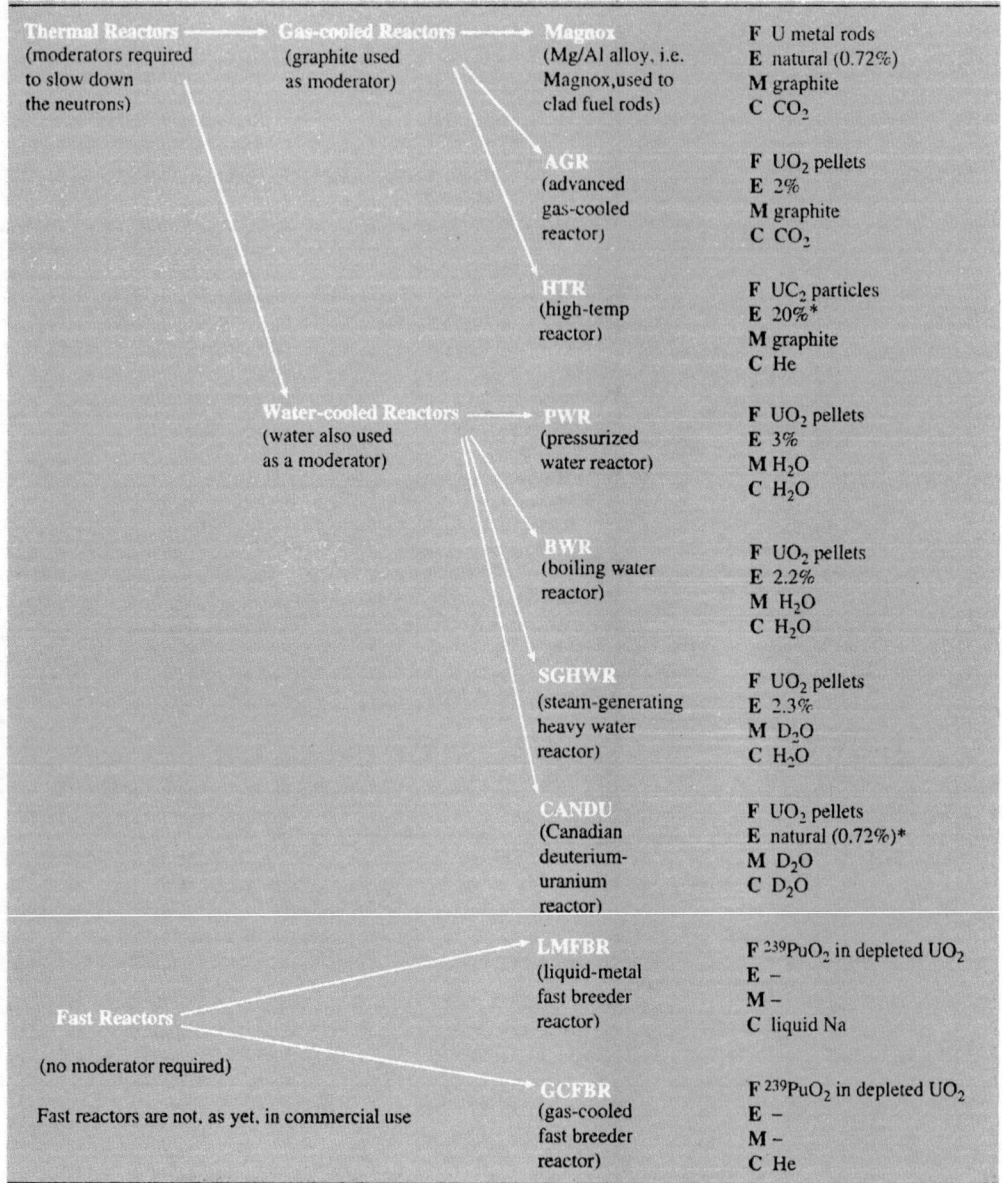

Thermal Reactors (moderators required to slow down the neutrons)	Gas-cooled Reactors (graphite used as moderator)	Magnox (Mg/Al alloy, i.e. Magnox, used to clad fuel rods)	F U metal rods E natural (0.72%) M graphite C CO_2
		AGR (advanced gas-cooled reactor)	F UO_2 pellets E 2% M graphite C CO_2
		HTR (high-temp reactor)	F UC_2 particles E 20%* M graphite C He
	Water-cooled Reactors (water also used as a moderator)	PWR (pressurized water reactor)	F UO_2 pellets E 3% M H_2O C H_2O
		BWR (boiling water reactor)	F UO_2 pellets E 2.2% M H_2O C H_2O
		SGHWR (steam-generating heavy water reactor)	F UO_2 pellets E 2.3% M D_2O C H_2O
		CANDU (Canadian deuterium-uranium reactor)	F UO_2 pellets E natural (0.72%)* M D_2O C D_2O
Fast Reactors (no moderator required) Fast reactors are not, as yet, in commercial use		LMFBR (liquid-metal fast breeder reactor)	F $^{239}PuO_2$ in depleted UO_2 E – M – C liquid Na
		GCFBR (gas-cooled fast breeder reactor)	F $^{239}PuO_2$ in depleted UO_2 E – M – C He

* HTR and CANDU could also possibly use ^{232}Th-^{233}U fuel

Figure 31.2 Various types of nuclear reactor currently in use or being developed (**F** fuel; **E** enrichment, expressed as %^{235}U present; **M** moderator; **C** coolant).

the present time (1996) some 30 countries are operating nuclear power stations to supply energy.

Fuels. Although the concentration of ^{235}U in natural uranium is sufficient to sustain a chain reaction, its effective dilution by the fuel cladding and other materials used to construct the reactor make fuel enrichment advantageous. Indeed, if ordinary (light) water is used as moderator or coolant, a concentration of 2–3% ^{235}U is necessary to compensate for the inevitable absorption of neutrons by the protons of the water. Enrichment also has the advantage of reducing the critical size of the reactor but this must be balanced against its enormous cost.

Early reactors used uranium in metallic form but this has been superseded by UO_2 which is chemically less reactive and has a higher melting point. UC_2 is also sometimes used but is reactive towards O_2.

In addition to $^{235}_{92}U$, which occurs naturally, two other fissile nuclei are available artificially. These are $^{239}_{94}Pu$ and $^{233}_{92}U$ which are obtained from $^{238}_{92}U$ and $^{232}_{90}Th$ respectively:

$$^{238}_{92}U + ^{1}_{0}n \longrightarrow ^{239}_{92}U \xrightarrow[23.5 \text{ min}]{-\beta^-} ^{239}_{93}Np \xrightarrow[2.36 \text{ days}]{-\beta^-}$$

$$^{239}_{94}Pu \xrightarrow[2.41 \times 10^4 \text{ y}]{-\alpha}$$

$$^{232}_{90}Th + ^{1}_{0}n \longrightarrow ^{233}_{90}Th \xrightarrow[22.3 \text{ min}]{-\beta^-} ^{233}_{91}Pa \xrightarrow[27.0 \text{ days}]{-\beta^-}$$

$$^{233}_{92}U \xrightarrow[1.59 \times 10^5 \text{ y}]{-\alpha}$$

^{239}Pu is therefore produced to some extent in all currently operating reactors because they contain ^{238}U, and this contributes to the reactor efficiency. More significantly, it offers the possibility of generating more fissile material than is consumed in producing it. Such "breeding" of ^{239}Pu is not possible in thermal reactors because the net yield of neutrons from the fission of ^{235}U is inadequate. But, if the moderator is dispensed with and the chain reaction sustained by using enriched fuel, then there are sufficient fast neutrons to "breed" new fissile material. Fast-breeder reactors are not yet in commercial use but prototypes are operating in France, the UK and Japan and use a core of PuO_2 in "depleted" UO_2 (i.e. $^{238}UO_2$) surrounded by a blanket of more depleted UO_2 in which the ^{239}Pu is generated. By making use of the ^{238}U as well as the ^{235}U, such reactors can extract 50–60 times more energy from natural uranium, so using more efficiently the reserves of easily accessible ores. Sadly there are possible dangers associated with a "plutonium economy" which

have led to well-publicized objections, and future developments will be determined by social and political as well as by economic considerations.

The net yield of thermal neutrons from the fission of ^{233}U is higher than from that of ^{235}U and, furthermore, ^{232}Th is a more effective neutron absorber than ^{238}U. As a result, the breeding of ^{233}U is feasible even in thermal reactors. Unfortunately the use of the $^{232}Th/^{233}U$ cycle has been inhibited by reprocessing problems caused by the very high energy γ-radiation of some of the daughter products.

Fuel enrichment. All practicable enrichment processes require the uranium to be in the form of a gas. UF_6, which readily sublimes (p. 1269), is universally used and, because fluorine occurs in nature only as a single isotope, the compound has the advantage that separation depends solely on the isotopes of uranium. The first, and until recently the only, large-scale enrichment process was by gaseous diffusion which was originally developed in the "Manhattan Project" to produce nearly pure ^{235}U for the first atomic bomb (exploded at Alamogordo, New Mexico, 5.30 a.m., 16 July 1945). UF_6 is forced to diffuse through a porous membrane and becomes very slightly enriched in the lighter isotope. This operation is repeated thousands of times by pumping, in a kind of cascade process in which at each stage the lighter fraction is passed forward and the heavier fraction backwards. Unfortunately gaseous diffusion plants are large, very demanding in terms of membrane technology, and extremely expensive in energy: alternatives have therefore actively been sought.[18] So far the only viable alternative is the gas centrifuge process currently operating in the UK, The Netherlands, Germany, Japan and Russia. In a cylindrical centrifuge $^{238}UF_6$ concentrates towards the walls and $^{235}UF_6$ towards the centre. In practice the radial concentration gradient is transformed into a axial gradient by injecting the UF_6 so as to set up an axial counter current so that both the enriched and depleted materials can be drawn off from

---

18 C. WHITEHEAD, *Chem. Brit.* **26**, 1161–4 (1990).

peripheral positions where the pressure is higher. The centrifuges rotate at about 1000 revolutions per second and are arranged in a cascade system.

A promising alternative is provided by "Laser isotope separation". Because the ionization energies of ^{235}U and ^{238}U differ slightly, it is possible to ionize the former selectively by irradiating U vapour with laser beams precisely tuned to the appropriate wavelength. The ions can then be collected at a negative electrode.

Cladding. The Magnox reactors get their name from the magnesium-aluminium alloy used to clad the fuel elements, and stainless steels are used in other gas-cooled reactors. In water reactors zirconium alloys are the favoured cladding materials.

Moderators. Neutrons are most effectively slowed by collisions with nuclei of about the same mass. Thus the best moderators are those light atoms which do not capture neutrons. These are ^2H, ^4He, ^9Be and ^{12}C. Of these He, being a gas, is insufficiently dense and Be is expensive and toxic, so the common moderators are highly purified graphite or the more expensive heavy water. In spite of its neutron-absorbing properties, which as mentioned above must be offset by using enriched fuel, ordinary water is also used because of its cheapness and excellent neutron-moderating ability.

Coolants. Because they must be mobile, coolants are either gases or liquids. CO_2 and He are appropriate gases and are used in conjunction with graphite moderators. The usual liquids are heavy and light water, with water also as moderator. In order to keep the water in the liquid phase it must be pressurized (PWR), otherwise it boils in the reactor core (BWR, etc.) in which case the coolant is actually steam. In the case of breeder reactors the higher temperatures of their more compact cores pose severe cooling problems and liquid Na (or Na/K alloy) is favoured, although highly compressed He is another possibility.

Control rods. These are usually made of boron steel or boron carbide (p. 149), but other good neutron absorbers which can be used are Cd and Hf.

Nuclear fuel reprocessing [3,10]

Many of the fission products formed in a nuclear reactor are themselves strong neutron absorbers (i.e. "poisons") and so will stop the chain reaction before all the ^{235}U (and ^{239}Pu which has also been formed) has been consumed. If this wastage is to be avoided the irradiated fuel elements must be removed periodically and the fission products separated from the remaining uranium and the plutonium. Such reprocessing is of course inherent in the operation of fast-breeder reactors, but whether or not it is used for thermal reactors depends on economic and political factors. Reprocessing is currently undertaken in the UK, France and Russia but is not considered to be economic in the USA.

Irradiated nuclear fuel is one of the most complicated high-temperature systems found in modern industry, and it has the further disadvantage of being intensely radioactive so that it must be handled exclusively by remote control. The composition of the irradiated nuclear fuel depends on the particular reactor in question, but in general it consists of uranium, plutonium, neptunium, americium and various isotopes of over 30 fission-product elements. The distribution of fission products is such as to produce high concentrations of elements with mass numbers in the regions 90–100 (second transition series) and 130–145 ($_{54}Xe$, $_{55}Cs$, $_{56}Ba$ and lanthanides). The more noble metals, such as $_{44}Ru$, $_{45}Rh$ and $_{46}Pd$, tend to form alloy pellets while class-a metals such as $_{38}Sr$, $_{56}Ba$, $_{40}Zr$, $_{41}Nb$ and the lanthanides are present in complex oxide phases.

The first step is to immerse the fuel elements in large "cooling ponds" of water for a hundred days or so, during which time the short-lived, intensely radioactive species such as $^{131}_{53}I$ ($t_{\frac{1}{2}} = 8.04$ days) lose most of their activity and the generation of heat subsides.

Then the fuel elements are dissolved in 7M HNO_3 to give a solution containing U^{VI} and Pu^{IV} which, in the widely used plutonium–uranium-reduction, or Purex process, are extracted into 20% tributyl phosphate (TBP) in kerosene leaving most of the fission products

(FP) in the aqueous phase. Subsequent separation of U and Pu depends on their differing redox properties (Fig. 31.3). The separations are far from perfect (see p. 1097), and recycling or secondary purification by ion-exchange techniques is required to achieve the necessary overall separations.

This reprocessing requires the handling of kilogram quantities of Pu and must be adapted to avoid a chain reaction (i.e. a criticality accident). The critical mass for an isolated sphere of Pu is about 10 kg, but in saturated aqueous solutions may be little more than 500 g. (Because of the large amounts of "inert" ^{238}U present, U does not pose this problem.)

The solution of waste products is concentrated and stored in double-walled, stainless steel tanks shielded by a metre or more of concrete.

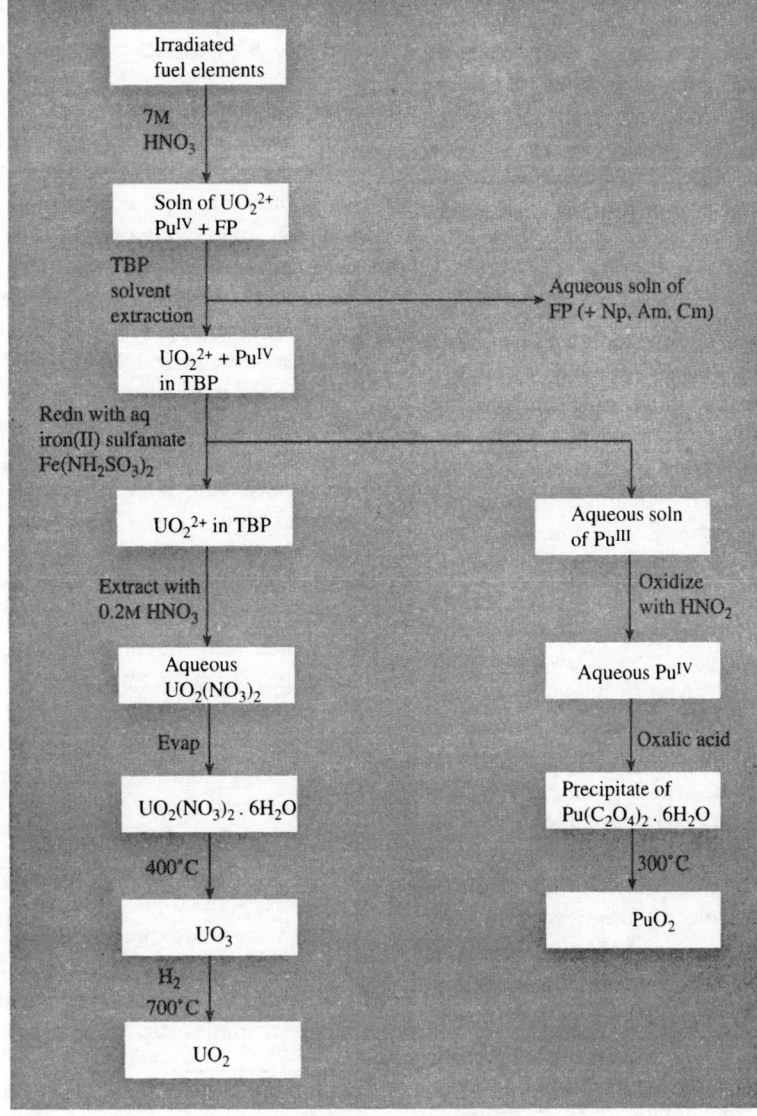

Figure 31.3 Flow diagram for the reprocessing of nuclear fuel [FP = fission products; TBP = $(Bu^nO)_3PO$].

Vitrification processes are being developed in several countries in which the dried waste is calcined and heated with ground glass "frit" to produce a borosilicate glass which can be stored or disposed of more permanently if there is agreement on suitable sites.

$^{237}_{93}$Np, $^{241}_{95}$Am and $^{243}_{95}$Am can be extracted from reactor wastes and are available in kg quantities. Prolonged neutron irradiation of $^{239}_{94}$Pu is used at the Oak Ridge laboratories in Tennessee to produce: $^{244}_{96}$Cm on a 100-g scale; $^{242}_{96}$Cm, $^{249}_{97}$Bk, $^{252}_{98}$Cf and $^{253}_{99}$Es all on a mg scale; and $^{257}_{100}$Fm on a μg scale. For trace amounts of these mixtures, dissolution in nitric acid, absorption of the +3 ions on to a cation exchange resin and elution with ammonium α-hydroxyisobutyrate provides an efficient separation of the elements from each other and from accompanying lanthanides, etc. The separation of macro amounts of these elements, however, is not feasible by this method because of radiolytic damage to the resin caused by their intense radioactivity. Much quicker solvent extraction processes similar to those used for reprocessing nuclear fuels are therefore used.

Because the sequence of neutron captures inevitably leads to $^{258}_{100}$Fm which has a fission half-life of only a few seconds, the remaining three actinides, $_{101}$Md, $_{102}$No and $_{103}$Lr, can only be prepared by bombardment of heavy nuclei with the light atoms $^{4}_{2}$He to $^{20}_{10}$Ne. This raises the mass number in multiple units and allows the $^{258}_{100}$Fm barrier to be avoided; even so, yields are minute and are measured in terms of the number of individual atoms produced.

Apart from $^{239}_{94}$Pu, which is a nuclear fuel and explosive, the transuranium elements have in the past been produced mainly for research purposes. A number of specialized applications, however, have led to more widespread uses. $^{238}_{94}$Pu (produced by neutron bombardment of $^{237}_{93}$Np to form $^{238}_{93}$Np which decays by β-emission to $^{238}_{94}$Pu) is a compact heat source (0.56 W g^{-1} as it decays by α-emission) which, in conjunction with PbTe thermoelectric elements, for instance, provides a stable and totally reliable source of electricity with no moving parts. It has been used in the form of PuO$_2$ in kg quantities in the American Apollo and Galileo spacecraft. Since its α-emission is harmless and is not accompanied by γ-radiation it is also used in heart pacemakers ($\sim$160 mg $^{238}_{94}$Pu) where it lasts about 5 times longer than conventional batteries before requiring replacements. $^{241}_{95}$Am is also widely used as an ionization source in smoke detectors and thickness gauges.

31.2.3 Properties of the actinide elements

The dominant feature of the actinides is their nuclear instability, as manifest in their radioactivity (mostly α-decay) and tendency to spontaneous fission; both of these modes of decay become more pronounced (shorter half-lives) with the heavier elements. The radioactivity of Th and U is probably responsible for much of the earth's internal heat, but is of a sufficiently low level to allow their compounds to be handled and transported without major problems. By contrast, the instability of the heavier elements not only imposes most severe handling problems[19] but drastically limits their availability. Thus, for instance, the crystal structures of Cf and Es were determined on only microgram quantities,[1] while the concept of "bulk" properties is not applicable at all to elements such as Md, No and Lr which have never been seen and have only been produced in unweighably small amounts. Even where adequate amounts are available, the constant build-up of decay products and the associated generation of heat may seriously affect the measured properties (see also p. 753). An indication of the difficulties of working with these elements can be gained from the fact that two phases described in 1974 as two forms of Cf metal were subsequently shown, in fact, to be hexagonal Cf$_2$O$_2$S and fcc CfS.[20]

Some of the more important known properties of the actinides are summarized in Table 31.2.

[19] R. A. BULMAN, *Coord. Chem. Revs.* **31**, 221–50 (1980).
[20] W. H. ZACHARIASEN, *J. Inorg. Nucl. Chem.* **37**, 1441–2 (1975).

Table 31.2 Some properties of the actinide elements

Property	Th	Pa	U	Np	Pu	Am	Cm	Bk	Cf	Es	Fm	Md	No	Lr
Atomic number	90	91	92	93	94	95	96	97	98	99	100	101	102	103
Number of naturally occurring isotopes	1	1	3	—	—	—	—	—	—	—	—	—	—	—
Most common isotope:														
Mass number	232	231	238	237	239	241	244	249	252	252	257	256	259	262
Half-life[a]	1.40×10^{10} y (α)	3.25×10^4 y (α)	4.47×10^9 y (α)	2.14×10^6 y (α)	2.41×10^4 y (α)	433 y (α)	18.1 y (α)	320 d (β^-)	2.64 y (α)	472 d (α)	100.5 d (α)	78 min (β^+/EC)	58 min (α, EC)	3.6 h (α)
Relative nuclidic mass	232.0380	231.0359	238.0289[b]	237.0482	239.0522	241.0568	244.0627	249.0750	252.0816	252.0830	257.0951	256.0941	259.1011	262.110
Electronic configuration, [Rn] plus	$6d^2 7s^2$	$5f^2 6d^1 7s^2$ or $5f^1 6d^2 7s^2$	$5f^3 6d^1 7s^2$	$5f^4 6d^1 7s^2$ or $5f^5 7s^2$	$5f^6 7s^2$	$5f^7 7s^2$	$5f^7 6d^1 7s^2$	$5f^9 7s^2$ or $5f^8 6d^1 7s^2$	$5f^{10} 7s^2$	$5f^{11} 7s^2$	$5f^{12} 7s^2$	$5f^{13} 7s^2$	$5f^{14} 7s^2$	$5f^{14} 6d^1 7s^2$
Metal radius (CN12)/pm	179	163	156	155	159	173	174	170	186 ± 2	186 ± 2	—	—	—	—
Ionic radius (CN6)/pm[c]														
VII	—	—	—	71	—	—	—	—	—	—	—	—	—	—
VI	—	—	73	72	71	—	—	—	—	—	—	—	—	—
V`	—	—	—	—	—	—	—	—	—	—	—	—	—	—
V	—	78	76	75	74	—	—	—	—	—	—	—	—	—
IV	94	90	89	87	86	85	85	83	82.1	—	—	—	—	—
III	—	104	102.5	101	100	97.5	97	96	95	—	—	—	—	—
II	—	—	—	110	—	126[d]	—	—	—	—	—	—	—	—
$E^\circ(MO_2^{2+}/MO_2^+)$/V	—	—	0.17	1.24	1.02	1.60	—	—	—	—	—	—	—	—
$E^\circ(MO_2^+/M^{4+})$/V	—	—	0.38	0.64	1.04	0.82	—	—	—	—	—	—	—	—
$E^\circ(M^{4+}/M^{3+})$/V	-3.8	-0.05	-0.52	0.15	1.01	2.62	3.1	1.67	3.2	4.5	5.2	—	—	—
$E^\circ(M^{4+}/M)$/V	-1.83	-1.4	-1.38	-1.30	-1.25	-0.90	—	—	—	—	—	—	—	—
$E^\circ(M^{3+}/M)$/V	—	-1.47	-1.66	-1.79	-2.00	-2.07	-2.06	-2.00	-1.91	-1.98	-2.07	-1.74	-1.26	-2.1
MP/°C	1750	1572	1135	644	640	1176	1345	1050	900	860	1527	827	827	1627
BP/°C	4788	(4722)	3818	(3902)	3228	(2607)	—	—	—	—	—	—	—	—
ΔH_{fus}/kJ mol^{-1}	16.11	16.7	12.6	(9.46)	2.80	14.4	—	—	—	—	—	—	—	—
ΔH_{vap}/kJ mol^{-1}	513.7	481	417	336	343.5	238.5	—	—	—	—	—	—	—	—
ΔH_{at} (monatomic gas)/kJ mol^{-1}	575	—	482	—	352	—	—	—	—	—	—	—	—	—
Density (25°C)/g cm^{-3}[e]	11.72	15.37	19.05	20.45	19.86	13.67	13.51	14.78	—	—	—	—	—	—
Electrical resistivity (22°C)/μohm cm	15.4	19.1	30.8	122	150	71	—	—	—	—	—	—	—	—

[a] The rate of decay by spontaneous fission increases with atomic number and is an important additional cause of instability in the later actinides (*trans*-Np).
[b] This value refers to the natural mixture of uranium isotopes, i.e. it is the atomic weight. Variations are possible because (i) some geological samples have anomalous isotopic compositions, and (ii) commercially available samples may have been depleted in ^{235}U. The value for ^{238}U itself is 238.0508.
[c] For Pa, CN = 10 and for U, Np and Pu the structures are rather irregular so that the coordination number is not a precise concept.
[d] For Am^{II}, radius refers to CN = 8.
[e] Polymorphism is common amongst the actinides and these data refer to the form most stable at room temperature.

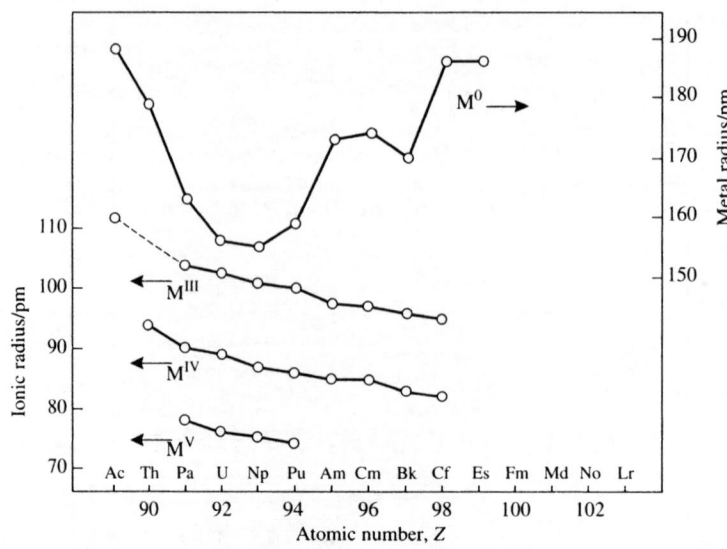

Figure 31.4 Metal and ionic radii of Ac and the actinides.

The metals are silvery in appearance but display a variety of structures. All except Cf have more than one crystalline form (Pu has six) but most of these are based on typically metallic close-packed arrangements. Structural variability is mirrored by irregularities in metal radii (Fig. 31.4) which are far greater than are found in lanthanides and probably arise from a variability in the number of electrons in the metallic bands of the actinide elements. From Ac to U, since the most stable oxidation state increases from +3 to +6, it seems likely that the sharp fall in metal radius is due to an increasing number of electrons being involved in metallic bonding. Neptunium and Pu are much the same as U but thereafter increasing metal radius is presumably a result of fewer electrons being involved in metallic bonding since it roughly parallels the reversion to a lanthanide-like preference for tervalency in the heavier actinides.

By contrast, the ionic radius in a given oxidation state falls steadily and, though the available data are less extensive, it is clear that an "actinide contraction" exists, especially for the +3 state, which is closely similar to the "lanthanide contraction" (see p. 1232).

31.2.4 Chemical reactivity and trends

The actinide metals are electropositive and reactive, apparently becoming increasingly so with atomic number. They tarnish rapidly in air, forming an oxide coating which is protective in the case of Th but less so for the other elements. Because of the self-heating associated with its radioactivity (100 g ^{239}Pu generates ~0.2 watts of heat) Pu is best stored in circulating dried air. All are pyrophoric when finely divided.

The metals react with most non-metals especially if heated, but resist alkali attack and are less reactive towards acids than might be expected. Concentrated HCl probably reacts most rapidly, but even here insoluble residues remain in the cases of Th (black), Pa (white) and U (black). Those of Th and U have the approximate compositions HThO(OH) and UH(OH)$_2$. Concentrated HNO$_3$ passivates Th, U and Pu, but the addition of F$^-$ ions avoids this and provides the best general method for dissolving these metals.

Reactions with water are complicated and are affected by the presence of oxygen. With boiling water or steam, oxide is formed on the surface of the metal and H$_2$ is liberated. Since the metals react readily with the latter, hydrides are produced which themselves react rapidly with

Table 31.3 Oxidation states of actinide elements

Oxidation states found only in solids are given in brackets; numbers in **bold** indicate the most stable oxidation states in aqueous solution. Colours refer to aqueous solutions[a]

Species present in H$_2$O	Th	Pa	U	Np	Pu	Am	Cm	Bk	Cf	Es	Fm	Md	No	Lr
M^{II}	—	—	—	—	—	(2)	—	—	(2)	(2)	2	2	**2**	—
M^{III}	3	(3)	3	3	3	**3**	**3**	**3**	**3**	**3**	**3**	**3**	3	**3**
			r	bl	v	pink	pale g	g	g					
M^{IV}	**4**	4	4	4	**4**	4	4	4	(4)	—	—	—	—	—
	c-less	c-less	g	y-g	br	pink	pale y	y						
MO$_2$$^+$	—	5	5	**5**	5	5	—	—	—	—	—	—	—	—
		c-less	unknown	g	purple[b]	y								
MO$_2$$^{2+}$	—	—	**6**	6	6	6	—	—	—	—	—	—	—	—
			y	p	o	br								
(MO$_5$$^{3-}$)[c]	—	—	—	7	7	—	—	—	—	—	—	—	—	—
				g	g									

[a]bl = blue; br = brown; c-less = colourless; gr = green; o = orange; r = red; v = violet; y = yellow.

[b]Because of disproportionation, PuO$_2$$^+$ is never observed on its own and its colour must therefore be deduced from the spectrum of a mixture involving Pu in several oxidation states.

[c]This is probably too simple, hydroxo species such as [MO$_4$(OH)$_2$]$^{3-}$ being more likely.

water and so facilitate further attack on the metals.

Knowledge of the detailed chemistry of the actinides is concentrated mainly on U and, to a lesser extent, Th and Pu.[21] Availability and safety are, of course, major problems for the remaining elements, but self-heating and radiolytic damage can be troublesome, the energy evolved in radioactive decay being far greater than that of chemical bonds. Thus in aqueous solutions of concentrations greater than 1 mg cm^{-3} (i.e. 1 g l^{-1}), isotopes with half-lives less than, say, 20 years, will produce sufficient H$_2$O$_2$ to produce appreciable oxidation or reduction where the redox behaviour of the element allows this. Fortunately, the nuclear instability which produces these problems also assists in overcoming them: by performing chemical reactions with appropriate, non-radioactive, carrier elements containing only trace amounts of the actinide in question, it is possible to detect the presence of the latter, and hence explore its chemistry because of the extreme sensitivity of radiation detectors. Such "tracer" techniques have

provided remarkably extensive information particularly about the aqueous solution chemistry of the actinides.

Table 31.3 lists the known oxidation states. For the first three elements (Th, Pa and U) the most stable oxidation state is that involving all the valence electrons, but after this the most stable becomes progressively lower until, in the second half of the series, the +3 state becomes dominant. Appropriate quantitative data for elements up to Am are summarized in Fig. 31.5. The highest oxidation state attainable by Th, and the only one occurring in solution, is +4. Data for Pa are difficult to obtain because of its propensity for hydrolysis which results in the formation of colloidal precipitates, except in concentrated acids or in the presence of complexing anions such as F$^-$ or C$_2$O$_4$$^{2-}$. However, it is clear that +5 is its most stable oxidation state since its reduction to +4 requires rather strong reducing agents such as Zn/H$^+$, Cr^{II} or Ti^{III} and the +4 state in solution is rapidly reoxidized to +5 by air. In the case of uranium the shape of the volt-equivalent versus oxidation state curve (pp. 435–8) reflects the ready disproportionation of UO$_2$$^+$ into the more stable U^{IV} and UO$_2$$^{2+}$; it should also be possible for atmospheric oxygen ($\frac{1}{2}$O$_2$ + 2H$^+$ +

---

[21] G. R. CHOPPIN and B. E. STOUT, *Chem. Brit.*, **27**, 1126–9 (1991).

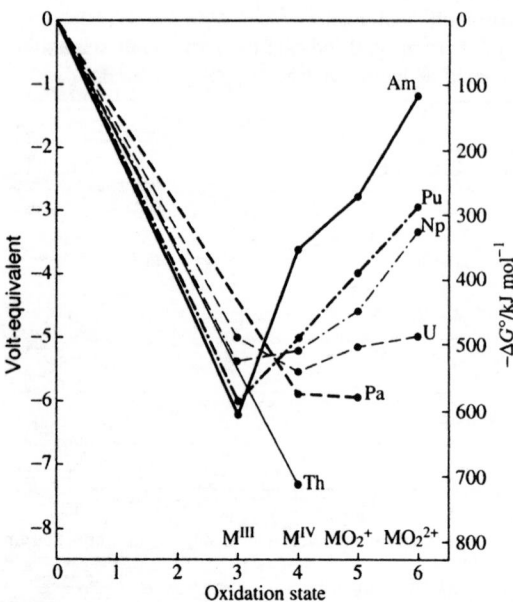

Figure 31.5   Volt-equivalent versus oxidation state for actinide ions.

$2e^- \rightleftharpoons H_2O$, $E° = 1.229$ V) to oxidize U^{IV} to UO_2^{2+} though in practice this occurs only slowly. For the heavier elements the increasingly steep-sided trough indicates the increasing stability of the +3 state.

The redox behaviour of Th, Pa and U is of the kind expected for d-transition elements which is why, prior to the 1940s, these elements were commonly placed respectively in groups 4, 5 and 6 of the periodic table. Behaviour obviously like that of the lanthanides is not evident until the second half of the series. However, even the early actinides resemble the lanthanides in showing close similarities with each other and gradual variations in properties, providing comparisons are restricted to those properties which do not entail a change in oxidation state. The smooth variation with atomic number found for stability constants, for instance, is like that of the lanthanides rather than the d-transition elements, as is the smooth variation in ionic radii noted in Fig. 31.4. This last factor is responsible for the close similarity in the structures of many actinide and lanthanide compounds especially noticeable in the +3 oxidation state for which

a given actinide ion is only about 4 pm larger than the corresponding Ln^{3+}.

It is evident from the above behaviour that the ionization energies of the early actinides, though not accurately known, must be lower than for the early lanthanides. This is quite reasonable since it is to be expected that, when the 5f orbitals of the actinides are beginning to be occupied, they will penetrate less into the inner core of electrons, and the 5f electrons will therefore be more effectively shielded from the nuclear charge than are the 4f electrons of the corresponding lanthanides (i.e. the relationship between 4f and 5f series may be compared to that between 3d and 4d). Because the outer electrons are less firmly held, they are all available for bonding in the actinide series as far as Np (4th member), but only for Ce (1st member) in the lanthanides, and the onset of the dominance of the +3 state is accordingly delayed in the actinides. That the 5f and 6d orbitals of the early actinides are energetically closer than the 4f and 5d orbitals of the early lanthanides is evidenced by the more extensive occupation of the 6d orbitals in the neutral atoms of the former (compare the outer electron configuration in Tables 31.2 and 30.2). These 5f orbitals also extend spatially further than the 4f and are able to make a covalent contribution to the bonding which is much greater than that in lanthanide compounds. This leads to a more extensive actinide coordination chemistry and to crystal-field effects, especially with ions in oxidation states above +3, much larger than those found for lanthanide complexes. It is also important to remember that relativistic effects on the atomic properties and chemistry of these heavy elements cannot be safely ignored in attempts to explain or predict their behaviour.

Table 31.4 is a list of typical compounds of the actinides and demonstrates the wider range of oxidation states compared to lanthanide compounds. High coordination numbers are still evident, and distortions from the idealized stereochemistries which are quoted are again general. However, no doubt at least partly because the early actinides have received most attention, the widest range of stereochemistries is

Table 31.4 Oxidation states and stereochemistries of compounds of the actinides
"An" is used as a general symbol for the actinide elements

Oxidation state	Coordination number	Stereochemistry	Examples
0	16	See Figs. 19.31 and 31.10	$[An(\eta^8-C_8H_8)_2]$ (An = Th $\rightarrow$ Pu), $[U(\eta^8-C_8H_4Ph_4)_2]$
3	6	Octahedral	$[AnCl_6]^{3-}$ (An = Np, Am, Bk)
	8	Bicapped trigonal prismatic	$AnCl_3$ (X = Br, An = Pu $\rightarrow$ Bk; X = I, An = Pa $\rightarrow$ Pu)
	9	Tricapped trigonal prismatic	$AnCl_3$ (An = U $\rightarrow$ Cm)
	15	See p. 1278	$[Th\{\eta^5-C_5H_3(SiMe_3)_2\}_3]$
4	4	Complex	$U(NPh_2)_4$
	5	Trigonal bipyramidal	$U_2(NEt_2)_8$
	6	Octahedral	$[AnX_6]^{2-}$ (An = U, Np, Pu; X = Cl, Br)
	7	Pentagonal bipyramidal	UBr_4
	8	Cubic	$[An(NCS)_8]^{4-}$ (An = Th $\rightarrow$ Pu)
		Dodecahedral	$[Th(C_2O_4)_4]^{4-}$, $[An(S_2CNEt_2)_4]$ (An = Th, U, Np, Pu)
		Square antiprismatic	$[An(acac)_4]$ (An = Th, U, Np, Pu)
	9	Tricapped trigonal prismatic	$(NH_4)_3[ThF_7]$
		Capped square antiprismatic	$[Th(tropolonate)_4(H_2O)]$
	10	Bicapped square antiprismatic	$K_4[Th(C_2O_4)_4].4H_2O$
		Complex	$[Th(NO_3)_4(OPPh_3)_2]^{(a)}$
	11	See Fig. 31.8a	$[Th(NO_3)_4(H_2O)_3].2H_2O$
	12	Icosahedral	$[Th(NO_3)_6]^{2-(a)}$
	14	Bicapped hexagonal antiprismatic	$[U(BH_4)_4]$
	20	See Fig. 31.9	$[An(\eta^5-C_5H_5)_4]$ (An = Th, U)
5	6	Octahedral	$Cs[AnF_6]$ (An = U, Np, Pu)
	7	Pentagonal bipyramidal	$PaCl_5$
	8	Cubic	$Na_3[AnF_8]$ (An = Pa, U, Np)
	9	Tricapped trigonal prismatic	$M_2[PaF_7]$ (M = NH_4, K, Rb, Cs)
6	6	Octahedral	AnF_6 (An = U, Np, Pu), UCl_6, $Cs_2[UO_2X_4]^{(b)}$ (X = Cl, Br)
	7	Pentagonal bipyramidal	$[UO_2(S_2CNEt_2)_2(ONMe_3)]^{(b)}$
	8	Hexagonal bipyramidal	$[UO_2(NO_3)_2(H_2O)_2]^{(b)}$
7	6	Octahedral	$Li_5[AnO_6]$ (An = Np, Pu)

$^{(a)}$These compounds are isostructural with the corresponding compounds of Ce (see Fig. 30.5, p. 1245) and can be visualized as octahedral if each NO_3^- is considered to occupy a single coordination site.
$^{(b)}$The polyhedra of these complexes are actually flattened because the two *trans* U–O bonds of the UO_2^{2+} group are shorter than the bonds to the remaining groups which form an equatorial plane.

now to be found in the +4 oxidation state rather than +3 as in the lanthanides.

31.3 Compounds of the Actinides[3,9,11,22-24]

Compounds with many non-metals are prepared, in principle simply, by heating the elements.

^{22} G. MEYER and L. R. MORSS (eds.) *Synthesis of Lanthanide and Actinide Compounds*, Kluwer, Dordrecht, 1991, 367 pp.
^{23} K. W. BAGNALL, Chap. 40, pp. 1129–228, in *Comprehensive Coordination Chemistry*, Vol. 3, Pergamon Press, Oxford, 1987.
^{24} I. SANTOS, A. P. de MATOS and A. G. MADDOCK, *Adv. Inorg. Chem.* **34**, 65–144 (1989).

Hydrides of the types AnH_2 (An = Th, Np, Pu, Am, Cm) and AnH_3 (Pa $\rightarrow$ Am), as well as Th_4H_{15} (i.e. $ThH_{3.75}$) have been so obtained but are not very stable thermally and are decidedly unstable with respect to air and moisture. Borides, carbides, silicides and nitrides (q.v.) are mostly less sensitive chemically and, being refractory materials, those of Th, U and Pu in particular have been studied extensively as possible nuclear fuels.[15,25] Their stoichiometries are very varied but the more important ones are the semi-metallic monocarbides, AnC, and mononitrides, AnN, all of which have the rock-salt structure: they are predominantly ionic

^{25} K. NAITO and N. KAGEGASHIRA, *Adv. Nucl. Sci. Tech.* **9**, 99–180 (1976).

Table 31.5 Oxides of the Actinide Elements[a]
The most stable oxide of each element is printed in **bold**.

Formal oxidation state of metal	Th	Pa	U	Np	Pu	Am	Cm	Bk	Cf	Es
+6	—	—	UO_3 o-y	—	—	—	—	—	—	—
	—	—	U_3O_8 dark g	—	—	—	—	—	—	—
+5	—	Pa_2O_5 white	U_2O_5 black	Np_2O_5 dark br	—	—	—	—	—	—
+4	ThO_2 white	PaO_2 black	UO_2 dark br	NpO_2 br-g	PuO_2 y-br	AmO_2 black	CmO_2 black	BkO_2 br	CfO_2 black	—
+3	—	—	—	—	Pu_2O_3 black	Am_2O_3 r-br	Cm_2O_3 white	Bk_2O_3 y-g	Cf_2O_3 pale g	Es_2O_3[b] white

[a] br = brown; g = green; o = orange; r = red; y = yellow.
[b] This is the only known oxide of Es. It is expected to be the most stable for this actinide but investigation of the Es/O system is hampered not only by low availability but also by the high α-activity ($t_{\frac{1}{2}} = 20.5$ days) which causes crystals to disintegrate. Es_2O_3 was characterized by electron diffraction using microgram samples measuring only about $0.03\,\mu m$ on edge.

but with supernumerary electrons in a delocalized conduction band.

31.3.1 Oxides and chalcogenides of the actinides [15.26]

Oxides of the actinides are refractory materials and, in fact, ThO_2 has the highest mp (3390°C) of any oxide. They have been extensively studied because of their importance as nuclear fuels.[25] However, they are exceedingly complicated because of the prevalence of polymorphism, nonstoichiometry and intermediate phases. The simple stoichiometries quoted in Table 31.5 should therefore be regarded as idealized compositions.

The only anhydrous trioxide is UO_3, a common form of which (γ-UO_3) is obtained by heating $UO_2(NO_3)\cdot6H_2O$ in air at 400°C; six other forms are also known.[27] Heating any of these, or indeed any other oxide of uranium, in air at 800–900°C yields U_3O_8 which contains pentagonal bipyramidal UO_7 units and can be used in gravimetric determinations of uranium. Reduction with H_2 or H_2S leads to a series of intermediate

nonstoichiometric phases (of which U_2O_5 may be mentioned) and ending with UO_2. Pentoxides are known also for Pa and Np. Pa_2O_5 is prepared by igniting Pa^V hydroxide in air, and the nonstoichiometric Np_2O_5 by treating Np^{IV} hydroxide with ozone and heating the resulting $NpO_3\cdot H_2O$ at 300°C under vacuum.

Dioxides are known for all the actinides as far as Cf. They have the fcc fluorite structure (p. 118) in which each metal atom has CN = 8; the most common preparative method is ignition of the appropriate oxalate or hydroxide in air. Exceptions are CmO_2 and CfO_2, which require O_2 rather than air, and PaO_2 and UO_2, which are obtained by reduction of higher oxides.

From Pu onwards, sesquioxides become increasingly stable with structures analogous to those of Ln_2O_3 (p. 1238); BkO_2 is out-of-sequence but this is presumably due to the stability of the f^7 configuration in Bk^{IV}. For each actinide the C-type M_2O_3 structure (metal CN = 6) is the most common but A and B types (metal CN = 7) are often also obtainable.

Reports of monoxides formed as surface layers on the metals have not been substantiated although their existence in the vapour phase is not disputed (see pp. 237–8 of ref. 22).

The oxides are basic in character but their reactivity is usually strongly influenced by their thermal history, being much more inert if they have

26 *J. Chem. Soc., Faraday Trans. II* **83**, 1065–285 (1987): a collection of papers on UO_2.
27 See for instance M. T. WELLER, P. G. DICKENS and D. J. PENNY, *Polyhedron* **7**, 243–4 (1988).

been ignited. Dioxides of Th, Np and Pu are best dissolved in conc HNO_3 with added F^-, but all oxides of U dissolve readily in conc HNO_3 or conc $HClO_4$ to yield salts of UO_2^{2+}.

Hydroxides are not well-characterized but gelantinous precipitates, which redissolve in acid, are produced by the addition of alkali to aqueous solutions of the actinides. Those of Th^{IV}, Pa^V, Np^V, Pu^{IV}, Am^{III} and Cm^{III} are stable to oxidation but lower oxidation states of these metals are rapidly oxidized. Aqueous solutions of hexavalent U, Np and Pu yield hydrous precipitates of $AnO_2(OH)_2$, which contain AnO_2^{2+} units linked by OH bridges, but they are often formulted as hydrated trioxides $AnO_3.xH_2O$.

Actinide chalcogenides can be obtained for instance by reaction of the elements, and thermal stability decreases S > Se > Te. Those of a given actinide differ from those of another in much the same way as do the oxides. Nonstoichiometry is again prevalent and, where the actinide appears to have an uncharacteristically low oxidation state, semimetallic behaviour is usually observed.

31.3.2 Mixed metal oxides

Alkali and alkaline earth metallates are obtained by heating the appropriate oxides, in the presence of oxygen where necessary. For instance, the reaction

$$\frac{5}{2} Li_2O + AnO_2 \xrightarrow[400-420°C]{O_2} Li_5AnO_6 \ [An = Np, Pu]$$

provides a means of stabilizing Np^{VII} and Pu^{VII} in the form of isolated $[AnO_6]^{5-}$ octahedra.

By suitable adjustment of the proportions of the reactants, An^{VI} species (An = U → Am) are obtained of which the "uranates" are the best known. These are of the types $M_2^I U_2O_7$, $M_2^I UO_4$, $M_4^I UO_5$ and $M_3^{II} UO_6$ in each of which the U atoms are coordinated by 6 O atoms disposed octahedrally but distorted by the presence of 2 short *trans* U–O bonds, characteristic of the uranyl UO_2^{2+} group. In view of the earlier inclusion of U in Group 6 it is interesting to note that, unlike Mo^{VI} and W^{VI}, U^{VI} apparently does

not show any tendency to form iso- or hetero-poly anions in aqueous solution.

$M^I An^V O_3$, $M_3^I An^V O_4$ and $M_7^I An^V O_6$ have been characterized for An = Pa → Am. Compounds of the first of these types have the perovskite structure (p. 963), those of the second a defect-rock-salt structure (p. 242), and those of the third have structures based on hexagonally close-packed O atoms. In all cases, therefore, the actinide atom is octahedrally coordinated. It is also notable that magnetic and spectroscopic evidence shows that, for uranium, these compounds contain the usually unstable U^V and not, as might have been supposed, a mixture of U^{IV} and U^{VI}.

$BaAn^{IV}O_3$ (An = Th → Am) all have the perovskite structure and are obtained from the actinide dioxide. In accord with normal redox behaviour, the Pa and U compounds are only obtainable if O_2 is rigorously excluded, and the Am compound if O_2 is present. Actinide dioxides also yield an extensive series of nonstoichiometric, mixed oxide phases in which a second oxide is incorporated into the fluorite lattice of the AnO_2. The UO_2/PuO_2 system, for example, is of great importance in the fuel of fast-breeder reactors.

31.3.3 Halides of the actinide elements [28]

The known actinide halides are listed in Table 31.6. They range from AnX_6 to AnX_2 and their distribution follows much the same trends as have been seen already in Tables 31.3 and 31.5. Thus the hexahalides are confined to the hexafluorides of U, Np and Pu (which are volatile solids obtained by fluorinating AnF_4) and the hexachloride of U, which is obtained by the reaction of $AlCl_3$ and UF_6. All are powerful oxidizing agents and are extremely sensitive to moisture:

$$AnX_6 + 2H_2O \longrightarrow AnO_2X_2 + 4HX$$

---

28 J. C. TAYLOR, *Coord. Chem. Rev.* **20**, 197–273 (1976).

Table 31.6 Properties of actinide halides[a]

	Th	Pa	U	Np	Pu	Am	Cm	Bk	Cf	Es
AnF_6			White 64° 6 o	Orange 54.7° 6 o	Brown 52° 6 o					
$AnCl_6$			Dark green 177° 6 o							
AnF_5		White na 7 pbp	Pale blue 348° 6 o	Pale blue na 7 pbp						
$AnCl_5$		Yellow 306° 7 pbp	Brown na 6 o							
$AnBr_5$		Dark red 6 o	Brown 6 o							
AnI_5		Black								
An_2F_9		Black (9)	Black (9)							
An_4F_{17}			Black		Red					
AnF_4	White 1068° 8 sa	Brown na 8 sa	Green 960° 8 sa	Green na 8 sa	Brown 1037° 8 sa	Tan na 8 sa	Brown na 8 sa	Yellow na 8 sa	Green na 8 sa	
$AnCl_4$	White 770° 8 d	Green-yellow na 8 d	Green 590° 8 d	Red-brown 517° 8 d						
$AnBr_4$	White 679° 8 d	Brown na 8 d	Brown 519° 7 pbp	Dark-red 464° 7 pbp						
AnI_4	Yellow 556° 8 sa	Black na	Black 506° 6 ol							
AnF_3			Black decomp. 9 ttp	Purple na 9 ttp	Violet 1425° 9 ttp	Pink 1395° 9 ttp	White 1406° 9 ttp	Yellow na 9 ttp	Green na 8 btp	‡ na 8btp
$AnCl_3$			Green 837° 9 ttp	Green 800° 9 ttp	Green 767° 9 ttp	Pink 715° 9 ttp	White 695° 9 ttp	Green 603° 9 ttp	Green 575° 9 ttp	White na 9 ttp
$AnBr_3$			Red 727° 9 ttp	Green na 9 ttp	Green 681° 8 btp	White na 8 btp	White 625° 8 bpt	Yellow-green na 8 btp	Pale-green na 6 o	Light-brown na 6 o
AnI_3	Black na 8	Brown na 8 btp	Black 766° 8 btp	Purple 760° 8 btp	Green (777°) 8 btp	Yellow 950° 8 btp	White na 6 o	Yellow na 6 o	Yellow na 6 o	‡ na 6 ol
$AnCl_2$						Black 9 ttp			Amber	‡
$AnBr_2$						Black 8,7			Amber 8,7	‡
AnI_2	Gold complex					Black 7 co			Violet	‡

[a]Key: Colour (‡ indicates preparation but no report of colour); mp/°C (na indicates value not reported); coordination 9 ttp = tricapped trigonal prismatic; 8 d = dodecahedral; 8 sa = square antiprismatic; 8 btp = bicapped trigonal prismatic; 8,7 = mixed 8- and 7-coordination (SrBr₂ structure); 7 cc = capped octahedral; 7 pbp = pentagonal bipyramidal; 6 o = octahedral; 6 och = octahedral chain, 6 ol = octahedral layered.

UF_6 is important in the separation of uranium isotopes by gaseous diffusion (p. 1259).

Pentahalides are, perhaps surprisingly, not found beyond Np (for which the pentafluoride alone is known) but all four are known for Pa. All the pentafluorides as well as $PaCl_5$ are polymeric and attain 7-coordination by means of double X-bridges between adjacent metal atoms (Fig. 31.6); by contrast UCl_5 and $PaBr_5$ consist of halogen-bridged dimeric An_2X_{10} units, e.g. $Cl_4U(\mu\text{-}Cl)_2UCl_4$. All are very sensitive to water, the hydrolysis of the U^V halides being complicated by simultaneous disproportionation. Fluorides of intermediate compositions An_2F_9 (An = Pa, U) and An_4F_{17} (An = U, Pu) have also been reported. U_2F_9 is the best known; its black colour probably results from charge transfer between U^{IV} and U^V.

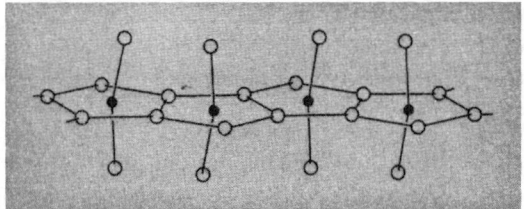

Figure 31.6   The polymeric structure of AnF_5 (An = Pa, U, Np) and $PaCl_5$, showing the distorted pentagonal bipyramidal coordination of the metal.

A much more extensive series is formed by the tetrahalides of which the tetrafluorides are known as far as Cf. The early tetrafluorides $ThF_4 \rightarrow PuF_4$ are produced by heating the dioxides in HF in the presence of H_2 for PaF_4 (in order to prevent oxidation) and in the presence of O_2 for NpF_4 and PuF_4 (in order to prevent reduction). The later tetrafluorides $AmF_4 \rightarrow CfF_4$ are obtained by heating the corresponding trifluoride with F_2. In all cases the metal is 8-coordinated, being surrounded by a slightly distorted square-antiprismatic array of F^- ions. The tetrachlorides (Th $\rightarrow$ Np) are prepared by heating the dioxides in CCl_4 or a similar chlorinated hydrocarbon, whereas the tetrabromides (Th $\rightarrow$ Np) and tetraiodides (Th $\rightarrow$ U) are obtained from the elements. Eight-coordination is again common (this time

dodecahedral) but a reduction to 7-coordination occurs with UBr_4 and $NpBr_4$, and to octahedral coordination for UI_4. AnF_4 are insoluble in water and, for Th, U and Pu at least, are precipitated as the hydrate $AnF_4.2\frac{1}{2}H_2O$ when F^- is added to any aqueous solution of An^{IV}. $AnCl_4$, $AnBr_4$ and AnI_4 are rather hygroscopic, and dissolve readily in water and other polar solvents. An extensive coordination chemistry is based on the actinide tetrahalides, and UCl_4 is one of the best-known compounds of uranium, providing the usual starting point for most studies of U^{IV} chemistry.

The trihalides are the most nearly complete series, all members having been obtained for the elements U $\rightarrow$ Es and the series could no doubt be extended. Preparative methods are varied and depend in particular on the actinide involved. For the heavier actinides (Am $\rightarrow$ Cf) heating the sesquioxide or dioxide in HX is generally applicable, but the lighter actinides require reducing conditions. For NpF_3 and PuF_3 the addition of H_2 to the reaction suffices, but UF_3 is best obtained by the reduction of UF_4 with metallic U or Al. Trichlorides and tribromides of these lighter actinides can be obtained by heating the actinide hydride with HX, and the triiodides by heating the metal with I_2 (U, Np) or HI (Pu). PaI_3 is said to be obtained by heating PaI_5 in a vacuum.

With the exception of their redox properties, the actinide trihalides form a homogeneous group showing strong similarities with the lanthanide trihalides. The ionic, high-melting trifluorides are insoluble in water, from which they can be precipitated as monohydrates; at Cf^{III} (ionic radius = 95 pm) they show the same structural change from CN 9 to CN 8 as the lanthanides do at Gd^{III} (ionic radius = 93.8 pm). The other trihalides are all hygroscopic, water-soluble solids, many of which crystallize as hexahydrates featuring 8-coordinate cations $[AnX_2(H_2O)_6]^+$. Reduction in coordination number as the cations get smaller, again parallels behaviour observed in the lanthanide trihalides but of course it occurs further along the series because of the larger size of the actinides.

Not surprisingly, in view of the stability of Th^{IV}, ThI_3 is quite different from the above trihalides. It is rapidly oxidized by air, reduces water with vigorous evolution of H_2, and is probably best regarded as $[Th^{IV}, 3I^-, e^-]$. The air-sensitive ThI_2, which is obtained by heating ThI_4 with stoichiometric amounts of the metal, is similarly best formulated as $[Th^{IV}, 2I^-, 2e^-]$. It has a complicated layer structure and its lustre and high electrical conductivity indicate a close similarity with the diiodides of Ce, Pr and Gd.

Halides of truly divalent americium, however, can be prepared:

$$Am + HgX_2 \xrightarrow{400-500°C} AmX_2 + Hg \ (X = Cl, Br, I)$$

Like those of Eu with which they are structurally similar, these dihalides presumably owe their existence to their f^7 configuration. $CfBr_2$ and CfI_2 are also known and it seems probable that actinide dihalides would be increasingly stable as far as No if the problems of availability, etc., were overcome.

Several oxohalides[3,22,23] are also known, mostly of the types $An^{VI}O_2X_2$, $An^{V}O_2X$, $An^{IV}OX_2$ and $An^{III}OX$, but they have been less thoroughly studied than the halides. They are commonly prepared by oxygenation of the halide with O_2 or Sb_2O_3, or in case of AnOX by hydrolysis (sometimes accidental) of AnX_3. As is to be expected, the higher oxidation states are formed more readily by the lighter actinides; thus AnO_2X_2, apart from the fluoro compounds, are confined to An = U. Conversely the lower oxidation states are favoured by the heavier actinides (from Am onwards).

31.3.4 Magnetic and spectroscopic properties[3,11]

As the actinides are a second f series it is natural to expect similarities with the lanthanides in their magnetic and spectroscopic properties. However, while previous treatments of the lanthanides (p. 1242) provide a useful starting point in discussing the actinides, important differences are to be noted. Spin–orbit coupling is again strong ($2000-4000\,cm^{-1}$) but, because of the greater exposure of the 5f electrons, crystal-field splittings are now of comparable magnitude and J is no longer such a good quantum number. Furthermore, as already mentioned (p. 1266), the energy levels of the 5f and 6d orbitals are sufficiently close for the lighter actinides at least, to render the 6d orbitals accessible. As a result, rigorous treatments of electronic properties must consider each actinide compound individually. They must allow for the mixing of "J levels" obtained from Russell–Saunders coupling and for the population of thermally accessible excited levels. Accordingly, the expression $\mu_e = g\sqrt{J(J+1)}$ is less applicable than for the lanthanides: the values of magnetic moment obtained at room temperature roughly parallel those obtained for compounds of corresponding lanthanides (see Table 30.6), but they are usually appreciably lower and are much more temperature-dependent.

The electronic spectra of actinide compounds arise from three types of electronic transition:

(i) *f→f transitions* (see p. 1243). These are orbitally forbidden, but the selection rule is partially relaxed by the action of the crystal field in distorting the symmetry of the metal ion. Because the field is stronger than for the lanthanides, the bands are more intense by about a factor of 10 and, though still narrow, are about twice as broad and are more complex than those of the lanthanides. They are observed in the visible and ultraviolet regions and produce the colours of aqueous solutions of simple actinide salts as given in Table 31.3.

(ii) *5f→6d transitions.* These are orbitally allowed and give rise to bands which are therefore much more intense than those of type (i) and are usually rather broader. They occur at lower energies than do the 4f → 5d transitions of the lanthanides but are still normally confined to the ultraviolet region and do not affect the colour of the ion.

(iii) *Metal→ligand charge transfer.* These again are fully allowed transitions and produce broad, intense absorptions usually found in the ultraviolet but sometimes trailing into the visible region. They produce the intense colours which characterize many actinide complexes, especially those involving the actinide in a high oxidation state with readily oxidizable ligands.

In view of the magnitude of crystal-field effects it is not surprising that the spectra of actinide ions are sensitive to the latter's environment and, in contrast to the lanthanides, may change drastically from one compound to another. Unfortunately, because of the complexity of the spectra and the low symmetry of many of the complexes, spectra are not easily used as a means of deducing stereochemistry except when used as "fingerprints" for comparison with spectra of previously characterized compounds. However, the dependence on ligand concentration of the positions and intensities, especially of the charge-transfer bands, can profitably be used to estimate stability constants.

31.3.5 Complexes of the actinide elements[3,11,23,29]

Because of the technical importance of solvent extraction, ion-exchange and precipitation processes for the actinides, a major part of their coordination chemistry has been concerned with aqueous solutions, particularly that involving uranium. It is, however, evident that the actinides as a whole have a much stronger tendency to form complexes than the lanthanides and, as a result of the wider range of available oxidation states, their coordination chemistry is more varied.

Oxidation state VII

This has been established only for Np and Pu, alkaline An^{VI} solutions of which can be electrolytically oxidized to give dark-green solutions probably containing species such as $[AnO_4(OH)_2]^{3-}$. Similar strongly oxidizing solutions (the more so if made acidic) are obtained when the mixed oxides Li_5AnO_6 are dissolved in water.

Oxidation state VI

Fluorocomplexes of U^{VI} are known of which $(NH_4)_4UF_{10}$ with a probable coordination number of ten is notable.[30] Otherwise, apart from UO_3 and the An^{VI} halides already discussed, this oxidation state is dominated by the dioxo, or "actinyl" AnO_2^{2+} ions which are found both in aqueous solutions and in solid compounds of U, Np, Pu and Am. These dioxo ions retain their identity throughout a wide variety of reactions and are present, for instance, in the oxohalides AnO_2X_2. The An–O bond strength and the resistance of the group to reduction decreases in the order U > Np > Pu > Am. Thus yellow uranyl salts are the most common salts of uranium and are the final products when other compounds of the element are exposed to air and moisture. The nitrate is the most familiar and has the remarkable property, utilized in the extraction of U, of being soluble in nonaqueous solvents such as tributyl phosphate. On the other hand, the formation of AmO_2^{2+} requires the use of such strong oxidizing agents as peroxodisulfate, $S_2O_8^{2-}$. Similarly, whereas the oxofluorides AnO_2F_2 are known for U, Np, Pu and Am, only U forms the corresponding oxochloride and oxobromide, Cl^- and Br^- reducing AmO_2^{2+} to Am^V species.

In aqueous solutions hydrolysis of the actinyl ions is important and such solutions are distinctly acidic. The reactions are complicated but, at least in the case of UO_2^{2+}, it appears that loss of H^+ from coordinated H_2O is followed by polymerization involving –OH– bridges and yielding species such as $[(UO_2)(OH)]^+$, $[(UO_2)_2(OH)_2]^{2+}$ and $[(UO_2)_3(OH)_5]^+$.

[29] N. B. MIKHEEV and A. N. KAMENSKAYA, *Coord. Chem. Revs.* **109**, 1–59 (1991).

[30] S. MILICEV and B. DRUZINA, *Polyhedron* **9**, 47–51 (1990).

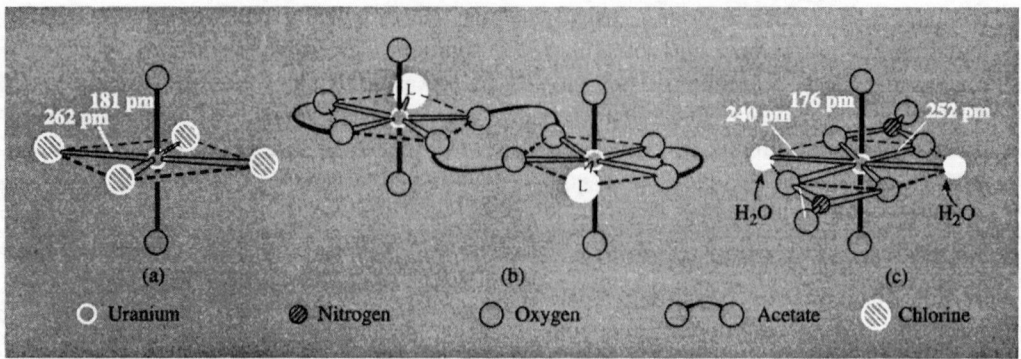

O Uranium   ⊘ Nitrogen   ◯ Oxygen   ◯◯ Acetate   ▨ Chlorine

Figure 31.7   (a) The octahedral anion in $Cs_2[UO_2Cl_4]$. (b) Pentagonal bipyramidal coordination of U in dinuclear $[UO_2(O_2CMe)_2L]_2$ (L = OPPh$_3$, OAsPh$_3$). (c) Hexagonal bipyramidal coordination of U in uranyl nitrate, $UO_2(NO_3)_2.6H_2O$.

Actinyl ions seem to behave rather like divalent, class-a, metal ions of smaller size (or metal ions of the same size but higher charge) and, accordingly, they readily form complexes with F$^-$ and O-donor ligands such as OH$^-$, SO$_4^{2-}$, NO$_3^-$ and carboxylates.[31] The O=An=O groups are in all cases linear, and coordination of a further 4, 5 or 6 ligands is possible in the equatorial plane. Octahedral, pentagonal bipyramidal, and hexagonal bipyramidal geometries result;[32] some examples are shown in Fig. 31.7. These ligands lying in the plane may be neutral molecules such as H$_2$O, OPR$_3$, OAsR$_3$, py or the anions mentioned above, many of which are bidentate.

The axial O–An bonds are clearly very strong. They cannot be protonated and are nearly always shorter than the equatorial bonds. In the case of UO$_2^{2+}$, for instance, it is likely that the U–O bond order is even greater than 2, since the U–O distance is only about 180 pm; in spite of the difference in the ionic radii of the metal ions (U^{VI} = 73 pm, Os^{VI} = 54.5 pm), this is close to that of the Os=O double bond found in the isostructural, osmyl group (175 pm, see p. 1085). It is usually assumed that combinations

of appropriate metal 6d and 5f orbitals overlap with the three p orbitals (or two p and one sp hybrid) of each oxygen to produce one σ and two π bonds, i.e. O⇌U⇋O. This interpretation implies that the change from bent to linear geometries in comparing MoO$_2^{2+}$ (p. 1024) and UO$_2^{2+}$ is due to the involvement of empty f orbitals in the latter case. More pertinently, the unstable ThO$_2$ which is isoelectronic with UO$_2^{2+}$, is bent (angle O–Th–O 122°) and the difference has been convincingly explained in a relativistic extended Hückel treatment, on the basis that d-orbitals favour bent and f-orbitals linear geometries; in UO$_2^{2+}$ the 6d orbitals are lower in energy than the 5f whereas in ThO$_2$ the order is reversed.[33]

Oxidation state V

In aqueous solution the AnO$_2^+$ ions (An = Pa → Am) may be formed, at least in the absence of strongly coordinating ligands. They are linear cations like AnO$_2^{2+}$ but are less persistent and, indeed, it is probable that PaO$_2^+$ should be formulated as [PaO(OH)$_2$]$^+$ and [PaO(OH)]$^{2+}$. Hydrolysis is extensive in aqueous solutions of Pa^V and colloidal hydroxo species are formed which readily lead to precipitation of

[31] J. LECIEJEWICZ, N. W. ALCOCK and T. J. KEMP, *Structure and Bonding* **82**, 43–84 (1995).
[32] See pp. 1424–31 of ref. 3.

[33] P. PYYKKÖ, L. S. LAAKKONEN and K. TATSUMI, *Inorg. Chem.* **28**, 1801–5 (1989).

$Pa_2O_5.nH_2O$. NpO_2^+ in aqueous $HClO_4$ is stable but UO_2^+, PuO_2^+ and AmO_2^+ are unstable to disproportionation:

$$2UO_2^+ \rightleftharpoons U^{IV} + UO_2^{2+} \quad \text{(very rapid}$$

$$\text{except in the range pH 2-4)}$$

$$2PuO_2^+ \rightleftharpoons Pu^{IV} + PuO_2^{2+}$$

and then $PuO_2^+ + Pu^{IV} \rightleftharpoons Pu^{III} + PuO_2^{2+}$.[†] Likewise:

$$3AmO_2^+ \rightleftharpoons Am^{III} + 2AmO_2^{2+}$$

Though the low charge on AnO_2^+ ions precludes the formation of very stable complexes, and disproportionation into An^{IV} and An^{VI} species is common, a number of complexes of NpO_2^+ have been prepared,[34] several containing the pentagonal bipyramidal $\{NpO_2(SO_4)_2L\}$ unit. In other cases, strongly coordinating ligands are able to replace the oxygen atoms of the AnO_2^+ ions and so inhibit disproportionation where this might otherwise occur. F^- is notable in this respect and complex ions, AnF_6^- (An = Pa, U, Np, Pu), PaF_7^{2-} and PaF_8^{3-} can be precipitated from aqueous HF solutions. However, in nonaqueous solvents, preparations such as the oxidation of M^IF and AnF_2 by F_2 are more common for U, Np and Pu and extend the range of complex ions to include AnF_7^{2-} (An = U, Np, Pu) and AnF_8^{3-} (An = U, Np). The stereochemistries of these anions are dependent on the particular counter cation as well as on An, and involve 6-, 7-, 8- and 9-coordination. The most remarkable of these complexes are the compounds Na_3AnF_8 (An = Pa, U, Np) in which the actinide ion is surrounded by 8 F^- at the corners of a nearly perfect cube in spite of the large inter-ligand repulsions which this entails.

[†] In the diagram of volt-equivalent versus oxidation state of Pu (Fig. 31.5) the oxidation states III to VI inclusive lie virtually on a straight line. It follows that if either Pu^{IV} or Pu^V is dissolved in water, disproportionations are thermodynamically feasible, and within a matter of hours mixtures of Pu in all four oxidation states are obtained.

34 M. S. GRIGOR'EV, I. A. CHARUSHNIKOV, N. N. KROT, A. I. YANOVSKII and Y. T. STRUCHNOV, *Russ. J. Inorg. Chem. (Engl. Trans.)* **39**, 1267–70 (1994).

Finally, the alkoxides $U(OR)_5$ must be mentioned.[35] Although easily hydrolysed, they are thermally stable and unusually resistant to disproportionation. They are usually dimeric, $[(RO)_4U(\mu\text{-}OR)_2U(OR)_4]$, and are best obtained by the reactions:

$$2[U(OEt)_4] \xrightarrow[(-2NaBr)]{Br_2 + 2NaOEt} [\{U(OEt)_5\}_2] \xrightarrow{10ROH}$$

$$[\{U(OR)_5\}_2]$$

Oxidation state IV

This is the only important oxidation state for Th, and is one of the two for which U is stable in aqueous solution; it is moderately stable for Pa and Np also. In water Pu^{IV}, like Pu^V, disproportionates into a mixture of oxidation states III, IV, V and VI, while Am^{IV} not only disproportionates into $Am^{III} + Am^VO_2^+$ but also (like the strongly oxidizing Cm^{IV}) undergoes rapid self-reduction due to its α-radioactivity. As a result, aqueous Am^{IV} and Cm^{IV} require stabilization with high concentrations of F^- ion. Berkelium(IV), though easily reduced, clearly has an enhanced stability, presumably due to its f^7 configuration, and the only other +4 ion is Cf^{IV}, found in the solids CfF_4 and CfO_2.

In aqueous solutions the hydrated cations are probably 8- or even 9-coordinated and, because they are the most highly charged ions in the actinide series, they have the greatest tendency to split-off protons and so function as quite strong acids (slightly stronger in most cases than H_2SO_3). This hydrolysis is followed by polymerization which has been most extensively studied in the case of Th. The aquated, dimeric ion, $[Th_2(OH)_2]^{6+}$, which probably involves two OH bridges, seems to predominate even in quite acidic solutions, but in solutions more alkaline than pH 3 polymerization increases considerably and eventually yields an amorphous precipitate of the hydroxide. Just before precipitation it is noticeable that the polymerization process slows down and equilibrium may take weeks to attain.

---

35 W. G. van der SLUYS and A. P. SATTELBERGER, *Chem. Revs.* **96**, 1027–40 (1990).

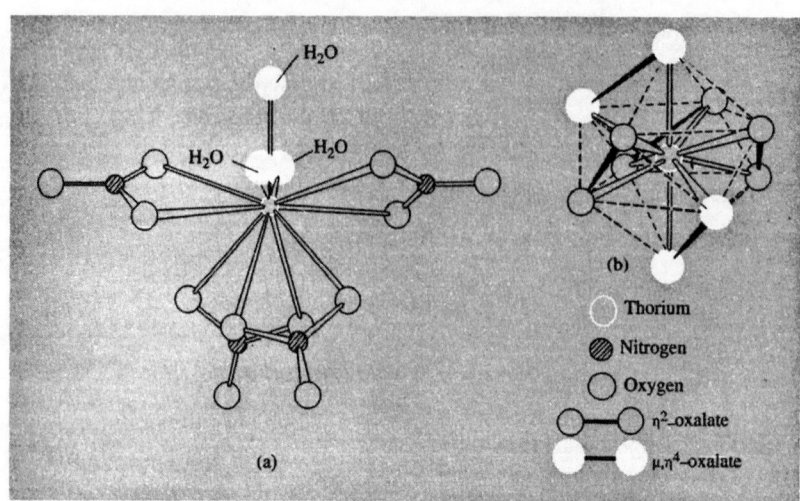

Figure 31.8   (a) Eleven-coordinate Th in Th(NO$_3$)$_4$.5H$_2$O: av. Th–O (of NO$_3$) = 257 pm; av. Th–O (of H$_2$O) = 246 pm. (b) The 10-coord. bicapped square antiprismatic anion in K$_4$[Th(C$_2$O$_4$)$_4$].4H$_2$O. Note that two pyramidal (267 pm) and three equatorial edges (276 pm) are spanned by oxalate groups, but none of the longer edges of the squares (311 pm). The oxalate groups on the pyramidal edges are actually quadridentate, being coordinated also to adjacent Th atoms.

The same effect is found also with Pu^{IV} where the persistence of polymers, even at acidities which would prevent their formation, can cause serious problems in the reprocessing of nuclear fuels.

The isolation of An^{IV} salts with oxoanions is limited by hydrolysis and redox compatibility. Thus, with the possible exception of Pu(CO$_3$)$_2$, carbonate ions furnish only basic carbonates or carbonato complexes such as [An(CO$_3$)$_5$]$^{6-}$ (An = Th, U, Pu). Stable tetranitrates are isolable only for Th and Pu, but Th(NO$_3$)$_4$.5H$_2$O is the most common salt of Th and is notable as the first confirmed example of 11-coordination (Fig. 31.8(a). Pu(NO$_3$)$_4$.5H$_2$O is isomorphous, and stabilization of Pu^{IV} by strong nitric acid solutions is crucial in the recovery of Pu by solvent extraction. *O*-donor ligands such as dmso, Ph$_3$PO and C$_5$H$_5$NO form adducts, of which [Th(NO$_3$)$_4$(OPPh$_3$)$_2$] is known to have a 10-coordinate structure like its Ce^{IV} analogue (Fig. 30.5b, p. 1245) and [Th(C$_5$H$_5$NO)$_6$(NO$_3$)$_2$]$^{2+}$ has a 10-coordinate distorted bicapped antiprismatic structure.[36]

Anionic complexes [An(NO$_3$)$_6$]$^{2-}$ (An = Th, U, Np, Pu) are also obtained, that of Th, and probably the others, having bidentate NO$_3^-$ ions forming a slightly distorted icosahedron similar to that of the Ce^{IV} analogue (see Fig. 30.5a). Th(ClO$_4$)$_4$.4H$_2$O is readily obtained from aqueous solutions but attempts to prepare the U^{IV} salt have produced a green explosive solid of uncertain composition. Hydrated sulfates are known for Th, U, Np and Pu. That of Np is of uncertain hydration but the others can be prepared with both 4H$_2$O and 8H$_2$O, PuSO$_4$.4H$_2$O having possible use as an analytical standard.

The actinides provide a wider range of complexes in their +4 oxidation state than in any other, and these display the usual characteristics of actinide complexes, namely high coordination numbers and varied geometry. Complexes with halides and with *O*-donor chelating ligands are particularly numerous. The main fluoro-complexes are of the types [AnF$_5$]$^-$, [AnF$_6$]$^{2-}$, [AnF$_7$]$^{3-}$, [AnF$_8$]$^{4-}$ and [An$_6$F$_{31}$]$^{7-}$ which are nearly all known for An = Th → Bk. Their stoichiometries have not all been determined but, in some cases at least, are known

^{36} D. M. L. GOODGAME, S. NEWNHAM, C. A. O'MAHONEY and D. J. WILLIAMS, *Polyhedron* **9**, 491–4 (1992).

to depend on the counter cation. For instance, $[UF_6]^{2-}$ has a distorted cubic structure in its K^+ salt and a distorted dodecahedral structure in its Rb^+ salt.

Several carboxylates, both simple salts and complex anions, have been prepared often as a means of precipitating the An^{IV} ion from solution or, as in the case of simple oxalates, in order to prepare the dioxides by thermal decomposition. In $K_4[Th(C_2O_4)_4].4H_2O$ the anion is known to have a 10-coordinate, bicapped square antiprismatic structure (Fig. 31.8b). β-diketonates are precipitated from aqueous solutions of An^{IV} and the ligand by addition of alkali, and nearly all are sublimable under vacuum. $[An(acac)_4]$, (An = Th, U, Np, Pu) are apparently dimorphic but both structures are based on an 8-coordinate, distorted square antiprism.

Complexes with S-donor ligands are generally less stable and more liable to hydrolysis than those with O-donors but can be obtained if the ligand is anionic and chelating. Diethyldithiocarbamates $[An(S_2CNEt_2)_4]$ (An = Th, U, Np, Pu) are the best known and possess an almost ideal dodecahedral structure.

Finally, the borohydrides $An(BH_4)_4$ must be mentioned.[37] Those of Th and U were originally prepared as part of the Manhattan Project and those of Pa, Np and Pu have been prepared more recently, all by the general reaction

$$AnF_4 + 2Al(BH_4)_3 \longrightarrow An(BH_4)_4 + 2AlF_2BH_4$$

The compounds are isolated by sublimation from the reaction mixture. Perhaps surprisingly the compounds fall into two quite distinct classes. Those of Np and Pu are unstable, volatile, monomeric liquids which at low temperatures crystallize with the 12-coordinate structure of $Zr(BH_4)_4$ (Fig. 21.7, p. 969). The borohydrides of Th, Pa and U, on the other hand, are thermally more stable and less reactive solids. They possess a curious helical polymeric structure in which each An is surrounded by 6 BH_4^- ions, 4 being bridging groups attached by 2 H atoms and

2 being *cis* terminal groups attached by 3 H atoms. The coordination number of the actinide is therefore 14 and the stereochemistry may be described as bicapped hexagonal antiprismatic.

Oxidation state III

This is the only oxidation state which, with the possible exception of Pa, is displayed by all actinides. From U onwards, its resistance to oxidation in aqueous solution increases progressively with increase in atomic number and it becomes the most stable oxidation state for Am and subsequent actinides (except No for which the f^{14} configuration confers greater stability on the +2 state).

Amber $Th^{3+}(aq)$ has recently been prepared from aqueous solutions of $ThCl_4$ and HN_3, and is stable for over 1 h before being oxidized by water.[37a] U^{III} can be obtained by reduction of $UO_2{}^{2+}$ or U^{IV}, either electrolytically or with Zn amalgam, but is thermodynamically unstable to oxidation not only by O_2 and aqueous acids but by pure water also.† It is nevertheless possible to crystallize double sulfates or double chlorides from aqueous solution and these can then be used to prepare other U^{III} complexes in nonaqueous solvents. Crystallographic data are not plentiful but it has been shown that in $(NH_4)U^{III}(SO_4)_2(H_2O)_4$ each $SO_4{}^{2-}$ is bidentate to one U and monodentate to a second. Three H_2O complete a coordination sphere of 9 oxygens for each uranium with a geometry intermediate between tricapped trigonal prismatic and monocapped square antiprismatic.[38] A number of cationic amide complexes are also known for which infrared evidence suggests[39]

---

† In pure water the activity of H^+ is only 10^{-7} mol dm^{-3}, and E for the $2H^+/H_2$ couple consequently falls to -0.414 V compared to $E^\circ = 0$. However, E° for U^{4+}/U^{3+} is even more negative (-0.607 V) and U^{III} will accordingly reduce water.

37a T. M. KLAPÖTKE and A. SCHULZ, *Polyhedron* **16**, 989–91 (1997).

38 J. I. BULLOCK,   M. F. C. LADD,   D. C. POVEY   and A. E. STOREY, *Inorg. Chim. Acta.* **43**, 101–8 (1980).

39 J. I. BULLOCK, A. E. STOREY and P. THOMPSON, *J. Chem. Soc., Dalton Trans.*, 1040–4 (1979).

---

37 R. H. BANKS and N. M. EDELSTEIN, *Lanthanide and Actinide Chemistry and Spectroscopy*, ACS Symposium, Series 131, Am. Chem. Soc., Washington, 1980, pp. 331–48.

the low symmetry coordination of 8 oxygen atoms to each uranium atom.

Instability also limits the number of complexes of Np^{III} and Pu^{III} but for Am^{III} the number so far prepared is apparently limited mainly by unavailability of the element. As has already been pointed out, the problem becomes still more acute as the series is traversed. While it is clear that lanthanide-like dominance by the tervalent state occurs with the actinides after Pu, the experimental evidence though compelling, is understandably sparse, being largely restricted to solvent extraction and ion-exchange behaviour.[40]

Oxidation state II

This state is found for the six elements Am and Cf → No, though in aqueous solution only for Fm, Md and No. However, for No, alone amongst all the f-series elements, it is the normal oxidation state in aqueous solution. The greater stabilization of the +2 state at the end of the actinides as compared to that at the end of the lanthanides which this implies, has been taken[40] to indicate a greater separation between the 5f and 6d than between the 4f and 5d orbitals at the ends of the two series. This is the reverse of the situation found at the beginnings of the series (p. 1266).

Reports of the observation of the +1 oxidation state in aqueous solutions of Md have not been substantiated despite attempts in several major laboratories, and it has been concluded that Md^I does not exist in either aqueous or ethanolic solutions.[41]

31.3.6 Organometallic compounds of the actinides [42]

The growth of organoactinide chemistry, like that of organolanthanide chemistry, is comparatively

recent. Attempts in the 1940s to prepare volatile carbonyls and alkyls of uranium for isotopic separations were unsuccessful though, as with the lanthanides, simple carbonyls of uranium have since been obtained in argon matrices quenched to 4 K. Subsequent work has mainly centred on cyclopentadienyls and, to a lesser extent, cyclooctatetraenyls; σ-bonded alkyl and aryl derivatives of the cyclopentadienyls have also been obtained. In general, these compounds are thermally stable, sublimable, but extremely air-sensitive solids which are sometimes water-sensitive also. Their bonding is evidently more covalent than that in organolanthanides, presumably because of the involvement of 5f orbitals, and relativistic effects.

The cyclopentadienyls are of the three main types: (a) $[An^{III}(C_5H_5)_3]$, (b) $[An^{IV}(\eta^5\text{-}C_5H_5)_4]$ and (c) derivatives of the type $[An^{IV}(\eta^5\text{-}C_5H_5)_3X]$ where X is a halogen atom, an alkyl or alkoxy group, or BH_4.

(a) $[An^{III}(C_5H_5)_3]$ (An = Th → Cf): the uranium compound is prepared directly from UCl_3 and $K(C_5H_5)$ but those of the heavier actinides are best made by the reaction:

$$2AnCl_3 + 3Be(C_5H_5)_2 \xrightarrow{65°C} 2An(C_5H_5)_3 + 3BeCl_2$$

Complete structural data are sparse but X-ray diffraction patterns suggest that both η^5 and η^1 bonding modes are involved (cf. $Sm(C_5H_5)_3$ p. 1248). In $[Th^{III}\{\eta^5\text{-}C_5H_3(SiMe_3)_2\}_3]$ the centres of three rings form a trigonal plane around the Th atom.[43] The spectroscopic properties of this blue paramagnetic compound imply a $6d^1$ rather than $5f^1$ configuration.[44]

(b) $[An^{IV}(C_5H_5)_4]$ (An = Th → Np): the Pa compound is prepared by treating $PaCl_4$ with $Be(C_5H_5)_2$ but the general method of preparation is:

$$AnCl_4 + 4K(C_5H_5) \xrightarrow[\text{in } C_6H_6]{\text{reflux}} [An(C_5H_5)_4] + 4KCl$$

[40] See, for instance, E. K. HULET, ref. 37, pp. 239–63.

[41] K. HULET, P. A. BAISEN, R. DOUGAN, J. H. LANDRUM, R. W. LOUGHEED and J. F. WILD, *J. Inorg. Nucl. Chem.* **43**, 2941–5 (1981).

[42] T. J. MARKS and R. D. ERNST, pp. 211–70 of Chap. 21 in *Comprehensive Organometallic Chemistry*, Vol. 3, Pergamon Press, Oxford, 1982. See also Vol. 4 of *COMC II*. 1995.

[43] P. C. BLAKE, M. F. LAPPERT, J. L. ATWOOD and H. ZHANG, *J. Chem. Soc., Chem. Commun.*, 1148–9 (1986).

[44] W. K. KOT, G. V. SHALIMOFF and N. M. EDELSTEIN, *J. Am. Chem. Soc.* **110**, 986–7 (1988).

$[M(C_5H_5)_4]$ $(M = Th, U)$ contain four identical η^5 rings arranged tetrahedrally around the metal atom (Fig. 31.9). The corresponding compounds of Pa and Np are probably the same since all four compounds have very similar nmr and ir spectra.

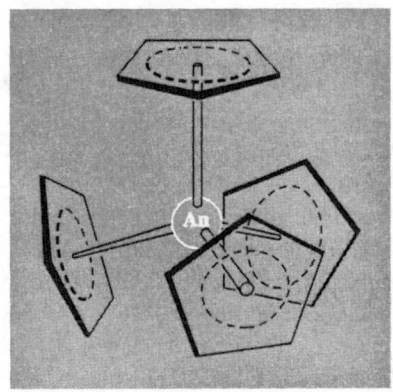

Figure 31.9   Structure of $[An(\eta^5\text{-}C_5H_5)_4]$ showing the tetrahedral arrangement of the four rings around the metal atom.

(c) Halide derivatives: the most plentiful are of the type $[An^{IV}(C_5H_5)_3X]$ $(An = Th, Pa, U, Np)$; they can be prepared by the general reaction:

$$AnX_4 + 3M^I(C_5H_5) \longrightarrow [An(C_5H_5)_3X] + 3M^IX$$

Indeed, the first report of an organoactinide was that of the pale brown $[U(C_5H_5)_3Cl]$ by L. T. Reynolds and G. Wilkinson in 1956. They showed that, unlike $Ln(C_6H_5)_3$, this compound does not yield ferrocene on reaction with $FeCl_2$, suggesting greater covalency in the bonding of $C_5H_5^-$ to U^{IV} than to Ln^{III}.

Replacement of Cl in $[U(C_5H_5)_3Cl]$ and $[Th(C_5H_5)_3Cl]$, by other halogens or by alkoxy, alkyl, aryl or BH_4 groups, provides the most extensive synthetic route in this field. An essentially tetrahedral disposition of three $(\eta^5\text{-}C_5H_5)$ rings and the fourth group around the metal appears to be general. The alkyl and aryl derivatives $[An(\eta^5\text{-}C_5H_5)_3R]$ $(An = Th, U)$, are of interest as they provide a means of investigating the An–C σ bond, and mechanistic studies of their thermal decomposition (thermolysis) have been prominent. The precise mechanism is not yet certain but it is clearly not β-elimination

(of an olefin, see p. 926) since the eliminated molecule is RH, the H of which originates from a cyclopentadienyl ring. The decomposition of the Th compounds are cleaner than those of U and a crystalline product can be isolated from the thermolysis at 170°C of a solution of $[Th(\eta^5\text{-}C_5H_5)_3Bu^n]$. This product is a dimer with the 2 Th atoms bridged by a pair of $(\eta^5,\eta^1\text{-}C_5H_5)$ rings, i.e. $[Th(\eta^5\text{-}C_5H_5)_2\text{-}\mu\text{-}(\eta^5,\eta^1\text{-}C_5H_5)]_2$. This remarkable bridge system is like that in niobocene (Fig. 22.12a, p. 1001) but each Th has two additional $(\eta^5\text{-}C_5H_5)$ rings instead of one $(\eta^5\text{-}C_5H_5)$ and an H atom.

It has not so far been possible to obtain either An^{III} or An^{IV} compounds with three C_5Me_5 rings around a single metal atom. However, $[M(\eta^5\text{-}C_5Me_4H)_3Cl]^{(45)}$ $(M = Th, U)$ and $[U(\eta^5\text{-}C_4Me_4P)_3Cl]^{(46)}$ have been prepared.

The complexes $[An(\eta^8\text{-}C_8H_8)_2]$ of cyclooctatetraene (cot) have been prepared for $An = Th \rightarrow Pu$ by the reactions:

$$AnCl_4 + 2K_2C_8H_8 \xrightarrow{\text{thf}} [An(C_8H_8)_2] + 4KCl$$

$$(An = Th \rightarrow Np)$$

and

$$[NEt_4]_2[PuCl_6] + 2K_2C_8H_8 \xrightarrow{\text{thf}} [Pu(C_8H_8)_2] + 4KCl + 2[NEt_4]Cl$$

followed by sublimation under vacuum. They are "sandwich" molecules with parallel and eclipsed rings (see Fig. 19.31, p. 942). This structure is strikingly similar to that of ferrocene (Fig. 19.27, p. 937), and extensive discussions on the nature of the metal-ring bonding suggests that this too is very similar.[3] In order to emphasise these resemblances with the d-series cyclopentadienyls, the names "uranocene", etc., have been coined. Although thermally stable, these compounds are extremely sensitive to air and, except for uranocene, are also decomposed by water.

[45] F. G. N. CLOKE, S. A. HAWKES, P. B. HITCHCOCK and P. SCOTT, *Organometallics* **13**, 2895–7 (1994).

[46] P. GRADOZ, C. BOISSON, D. BAUDRY, M. LANCE, M. NIERLICH, J. VIGNER and M. EPHRITIKHINE, *J. Chem. Soc., Chem. Commun.*, 1720–1 (1992).

However, uranocene can be made more air-stable by use of sufficiently bulky substituents, and 1,3,5,7-tetraphenylcyclo-octatetraene yields the completely air-stable [U(η^8-C$_8$H$_4$Ph$_4$)$_2$], in which the parallel ligands are virtually eclipsed but the phenyl substituents staggered and rotated on average 42° out of the C$_8$ ring plane (Fig. 31.10).

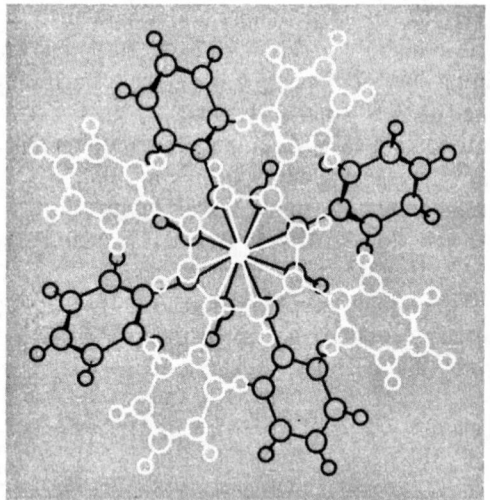

Figure 31.10   The structure of [U(η^8-C$_8$H$_4$Ph$_4$)$_2$].

31.4 The Transactinide Elements (Z = 104–112)

31.4.1 Introduction

The addition of nine further elements (Z = 104–112) to the Periodic Table during the past three decades has involved outstanding feats of intellectual and experimental virtuosity. Some of the discoveries have been widely accepted but others have been hotly contested and this has led to distressingly persistent disagreements concerning priority. For this reason IUPAC and IUPAP set up a neutral international group in 1987 to establish "the criteria that must be satisfied for the discovery of a new element to be recognised" and to apply these criteria to questions of priority in the discovery of the transfermium elements. Some of the conclusions of

this group have already been briefly mentioned (see Table 31.1). Their detailed Reports[5] were accepted by both IUPAC and IUPAP and the group's final recommendations, which form the basis of this Section, have been very widely though not universally accepted by the scientific community. Many subtle and difficult points are involved and the full reports repay careful reading. It is also worth noting that the word *discovery* is something of a misnomer in this context: *synthesis and characterization* of new elements would perhaps be a better discription.

The separate question of names and symbols for the new elements has, unfortunately, taken even longer to resolve, but definitive recommendations were ratified by IUPAC in August 1997 and have been generally accepted. It is clearly both unsatisfactory and confusing to have more than one name in current use for a given element and to have the same name being applied to two different elements. For this reason the present treatment refers to the individual elements by means of their atomic numbers. However, to help readers with the nomenclature used in the references cited, a list of the various names that are in use or that have been suggested from time to time is summarised in Table 31.7.

Two general types of nuclear reaction have been used to produce transfermium elements. The first type, hot fusion reactions, uses accelerated light particles with Z in the range 5–10 (typically $_5$B, $_6$C, $_7$N, $_8$O or $_{10}$Ne) to bombard targets with Z = 92–98 (typically $_{92}$U, $_{94}$Pu, $_{95}$Am, $_{96}$Cm or $_{98}$Cf). This method can be used effectively up to about element 106 but, increasingly, the compound nucleus is formed with such high excitation energy that many particles, including charged ones, evaporate off before the desired product nucleus is reached. To solve this problem the group at Dubna suggested an ingenious alternative route, cold fusion, which exploits the fact that nuclei such as $_{82}$Pb or $_{83}$Bi have high binding energies due to closed nuclear shells. If these nuclei are bombarded with moderately heavy ions which are preferably also near closed nuclear shells (e.g. $_{24}$Cr, $_{26}$Fe or $_{28}$Ni) at energies just above the Coulomb

Table 31.7 Names and symbols in current use (or proposed) for elements 104–112

Z	Systematic (1977)[a]	IUPAC (1997)	Other names suggested from time to time
104	Un-nil-quadium (Unq)	**Rutherfordium (Rf)**	Kurchatovium (Ku), Dubnium (Db)
105	Un-nil-pentium (Unp)	**Dubnium (Db)**	Nielsbohrium (Ns), Hahnium (Ha), Joliotium (Jl)
106	Un-nil-hexium (Unh)	**Seaborgium (Sg)**	Rutherfordium (Rf)
107	Un-nil-septium (Uns)	**Bohrium (Bh)**	Nielsbohrium (Ns)
108	Un-nil-octium (Uno)	**Hassium (Hs)**	Hahnium (Hn)
109	Un-nil-ennium (Une)	**Meitnerium (Mt)**	—
110	Un-un-nilium (Uun)	—	—
111	Un-un-unium (Uuu)	—	—
112	Un-un-bium (Uub)	—	—

[a]The hyphens in the systematic names have been inserted here to assist comprehension and pronunciation; they are not part of the names. The roots nil, un, bi, etc. were chosen to allow a unique set of three-letter symbols to be generated for any (atomic) number.

barrier, they produce compound product nuclei with much lower resultant excitation energies. As a result, the probability of (unwanted) fission is very much reduced and, under sufficiently fine-tuned conditions, neutron-only emission will dominate over all other light-particle emissions. This method has been outstandingly successful in producing elements with $Z > 106$.

31.4.2 Element 104

The first (inconclusive) work bearing on the synthesis of element 104 was published by the Dubna group in 1964. However, the crucial Dubna evidence (1969–70) for the production of element 104 by bombardment of $_{94}Pu$ with $_{10}Ne$ came after the development of a sophisticated method for rapid *in situ* chlorination of the product atoms followed by their gas-chromatographic separation on an atom-by-atom basis. This was a heroic enterprise which combined cyclotron nuclear physics and chemical separations. As we have seen, the actinide series of elements ends with $_{103}Lr$. The next element should be in Group 4 of the transition elements, i.e. a heavier congener of Ti, Zr and Hf.* As such it would be expected to have a chloride

---

* A happy consequence of nuclear systematics is that element 104 is in Group 4, element 105 is in Group 5, etc. This mnemonic holds to the end of the transition series at element 112 and presumably beyond; it can be compared with the similar relation between the group numbers of the post-transition main-group elements (13–18) and the group numbers of the preceding transition elements (3–8).

which is significantly more volatile than those of the actinide elements. After extensive preliminary work to develop and prove the method, the recoil products emitted from the target were chlorinated with a stream of gaseous $NbCl_5$ or $ZrCl_4$ within a fraction of a second from the instant of formation of the new atom, and then separated gas-chromatographically in a 4-metre-long quartz tube at either 250° or 300°C, before being detected by spontaneous fission. When part of the tube was replaced by a KCl capillary the activity in the detection zone ceased, because of the formation of an involatile complex, presumably $K_2[104]Cl_6$. As no nucleus with $Z > 104$ can be formed by bombarding $_{94}Pu$ with $_{10}Ne$, and no spontaneously fissioning atom with $Z < 104$ forms a volatile chloride, the new activity must be due to element 104. During the later stages of this work, and essentially contemporaneously with it, the Berkeley group established the reactions $^{249}Cf(^{12}C,4n)^{257}104$, $^{249}Cf(^{13}C,3n)^{259}104$ and $^{248}Cm(^{16}O,6n)^{258}104$ by elegant work which included the obsevation of generic parent–daughter α-decays to the known isotopes $^{253}102$ and $^{255}102$. It was concluded that credit for the discovery of element 104 should be shared between the groups at Dubna and Berkeley. Detailed references to the original papers, and an assessment of the many scientific points involved are in ref. 5. The name rutherfordium now recommended and adopted by IUPAC for element 104 was first suggested by the Berkeley group in 1969.

Nine isotopes of element 104 are now known with certainty in the mass range 255–264 and a tenth, ^{254}Rf, is possible. They have half-lives in the range 7 ms–65 s and can only be produced slowly one atom at a time. This clearly restricts chemical studies, though ingenious techniques have been developed to overcome some of the problems.[47] It has been found that element 104 is indeed a Group 4 homologue and tends to resemble Zr and Hf rather than Th in its aqueous solution chemistry and extractability. The predominant oxidation state is +4 and complexes such as $RfCl_6{}^{2-}$ have been confirmed. Distribution coefficients obtained for its extraction into thenoyltrifluoroacetone (TTA) lead to an ionic radius of 102 pm for 8-coordinated Rf, between those of Th and Pu. Gas-phase studies of element 104 by isothermal chromatography indicate that its bromides are more volatile than those of Hf, and that the chlorides of both Hf and Rf are more volatile than the bromides.[48,49]

31.4.3 Element 105

Attempts at the synthesis of element 105 were first reported from Dubna in 1968 but it was a further two years before cyclotron physics, combined with a thermal-gradient variant of gas-phase chromatography, plus parent–daughter α-particle generic relations finally succeeded in convincingly establishing its formation. The main reactions studied were ^{243}Am(^{22}Ne,4n)^{261}105 and ^{243}Am(^{22}Ne,5n)^{260}105. During the later stages of this work the Berkeley group published a convincing synthesis via ^{249}Cf(^{15}N,4n)^{260}105 which was also secured, amongst much other evidence, by an α-particle generic relation with ^{256}103. The independent work from the two laboratories was essentially contemporaneous and

credit for the discovery of element 105 was shared.[5] The name now internationally accepted for element 105 is dubnium.

The pioneering gas thermochromatographic studies of I. Zvara and his group in the mid-1970s suggested that element 105 was a homologue of Nb and Ta. No further work on its chemistry was reported until 1988 when the first studies of aqueous solutions of element 105 were published.[50] Using the 35 s isotope formed by the reaction ^{249}Bk(^{18}O,5n)^{267}105, some 800 manual experiments (taking about 50 s each) were performed. It was found that, after fuming with concentrated nitric acid, atoms of element 105, dubnium, sorbed on glass surfaces just like the Group 5 elements Nb and Ta but unlike Zr and Hf in the preceding Group. Extraction studies also confirmed the affinity to Group 5, though dubnium appeared closer to Nb than to Ta, perhaps due to the influence of relativistic effects. Later work using computer-controlled procedures reduced the timescale to less than 40 s per experiment;[49] halide complexation and extraction behaviour showed element 105 to be most like Pa, a pseudo Group 5 element.

31.4.4 Element 106

Work at Berkeley-Livermore in 1974 first convincingly demonstrated the synthesis of this element via the reaction ^{249}Cf(^{18}O,4n)^{263}106. Contemporaneous work at Dubna applied their novel cold fusion method (p. 1280) to reactions such as $_{82}$Pb + $_{24}$Cr: although this methodolgy was crucial to the synthesis of all later elements (107–112) it did not at that time demonstrate the formation of element 106 with adequate conviction. Very recently, element 106 was resynthesized by a new group at Berkeley using exactly the same reaction as employed in 1974.[51] The isotope ^{263}106 decays with a half-life of 0.8 ± 0.2 s to ^{259}104 and then by a second

[47] D. C. HOFFMAN, *Proc. Robert A. Welch Foundation Conference XXXIV. Fifty Years with Transuranium Elements,* October 1990, pp. 255–76. D. C. HOFFMAN, *Chem. & Eng. News,* May 2, 24–34 (1994).

[48] B. KADKHODAYAN, A. TÜRLER, K. E. GREGORICH, M. J. NURMIA, D. M. LEE and D. C. HOFFMAN, *Nucl. Instr. and Methods in Phys. Res.* **A317**, 254–61 (1992).

[49] D. C. HOFFMAN, *Radiochim. Acta* **61**, 123–8 (1993).

[50] K. E. GREGORICH (and 11 others), *Radiochim. Acta* **43**, 223–31 (1988).

[51] K. E. GREGORICH, M. R. LANE, M. F. MOHAR, D. M. LEE, C. D. CACHER, E. R. SILWESTER and D. C. HOFFMAN, *Phys. Rev. Lett.* **72**, 1423–6 (1994).

α-particle emission to ^{255}No, both of which were positively identified. The recommended name for element 106 is seaborgium, Sg.

Six isotopes of element 106 are now known (see Table 31.8) of which the most recent has a half-life in the range 10–30 s, encouraging the hope that some chemistry of this fugitive species might someday be revealed.[†] This heaviest isotope was synthsised by the reaction ^{248}Cm(^{22}Ne,4n)^{266}106 and the present uncertainty in the half-life is due to the very few atoms which have so far been observed. Indeed, one of the fascinating aspects of work in this area is the development of philosophical and mathematical techniques to define and deal with the statistics of a small number of random events or even of a single event.[52]

31.4.5 Elements 107, 108 and 109

These three elements were all first synthesized by the cold fusion method at GSI, Darmstadt,[5] using a very sophisticated set of techniques. For element 107 (1981) an accelerated beam of ionized ^{54}Cr atoms was made to impinge on a thin ^{209}Bi foil; the reaction recoils were separated in flight from the incoming beam and from the unwanted products of transfer reactions by a velocity filter consisting of a combination of magnetic and electric fields. This facility is known by the acronym SHIP, i.e. **s**eparated **h**eavy-**i**on reaction **p**roducts. The product atoms were then implanted in position-sensitive solid-state detectors which recorded α-particle decay energies or spontaneous fission events in position- and time-correlation with each other and with the time of implantation. Time-of-flight was also used to estimate the masses of these particles. Five atoms of ^{262}107 were detected and characterized in this way in the discovery experiments. Later work showed that

the half-life was 102 ± 26 ms and also established a second isotope, ^{261}107, with $t_{1/2}$ 11.8 ms having an (unsymmetrical) uncertainty at the 68% level of (+5.3, −2.8). The recommended name for element 107 is bohrium, Bh.

Element 108 was unequivocally established in 1984 using the SHIP facilities in Darmstadt to detect three atoms formed by the reaction ^{208}Pb(^{58}Fe,n)^{265}108. The half-life for α-decay was 1.8 ms with an uncertainty of (+2.2, −0.7) ms, and both the daughter and grand-daughter nuclides ^{261}106 and ^{257}104 were detected and characterized. Other isotopes of element 108 were in all probability obtained in Dubna at about the same time using reactions such as ^{209}Bi(^{55}Mn,n)^{263}108, ^{207}Pb(^{58}Fe,n)^{264}108 and ^{208}Pb(^{58}Fe,2n)^{264}108.[5] The recommended name for element 108 is hassium, Hs, after the latin name for Hesse, the region of Germany in which the GSI Laboratories are located.

Element 109 was also discovered by the Darmstadt GSI group in 1982 in an astonishingly virtuoso experiment which convincingly detected and unambiguously identified just *one atom* of ^{266}109 from the reaction ^{209}Bi(^{58}Fe,n). A further two atoms were synthesized at GSI six years later in 1988. The isotope is an α-emitter with a "half-life" of 3.4 ms (+1.6, −1.3 ms).[5] The recommended name for element 109 is meitnerium, Mt. It is salutory to contemplate the towering intellectual insights and prodigious technical achievements required to accomplish such experiments which can precisely identify a single atom amongst some 10^{18} accompanying events.

31.4.6 Elements 110, 111 and 112

These three elements were first made during a 15-month period of intense activity from late 1994 to early 1996 at GSI, Darmstadt. They therefore post-date the deliberations of the IUPAC/IUPAP international working group,[5] but the publications convincingly meet the stringent criteria for discovery elaborated by that group and have been widely accepted by the scientific community. So far, no names have been officially proposed or recommended for elements 110–112.

[†] The chemistry of 4 atoms of Sg in solution and of 3 atoms in the gas phase indicate that the element resembles its lighter homologues in Group 6, Mo and W; see M. SCHÄDEL and 17 others, *Nature* **388**, 55–7 (1997).

[52] K.-H. SCHMIDT,   C.-C. SAHM,   K. PIELENZ   and H.-G. CLERC, *Z. Phys. A* **316**, 19–26 (1984).

Initially, one atom of $^{269}110$ was detected on 9 November 1994 by the SHIP facilities at Darmstadt following the reaction $^{208}Pb(^{62}Ni,n)^{269}110$ and observation of the subsequent chain of four α-decays:[53,54]

$$^{269}110 \xrightarrow{393\,\mu s} {}^{265}108 \xrightarrow{583\,\mu s} {}^{261}106 \xrightarrow{72\,ms}$$
$$\xrightarrow{} {}^{257}104 \xrightarrow{779\,ms} {}^{253}No$$

A further three atoms of $^{269}110$ were observed during the next eight days leading to an average "half-life" of $170\,\mu s$ $(+160, -60\,\mu s)$. [Note that the decay times listed for the above single-atom observations are not identical with the best values of the statistical half-lives for the species mentioned.] Subsequent work also identified a second isotope $^{271}110$ with $t_{1/2}$ $623\,\mu s$.

Element 111 was synthesized and characterized by the same group during the period 8–17 December 1994 using the analogous cold-fusion reaction, $^{209}Bi(^{64}Ni,n)^{272}111$, followed by observation of up to five successive α-emissions which could be assigned to the chain:[54,55]

$$^{272}111 \xrightarrow{2.04\,ms} {}^{268}109 \xrightarrow{72\,ms} {}^{264}107 \xrightarrow{1.45\,s}$$
$$\xrightarrow{} {}^{260}105 \xrightarrow{0.57\,s} {}^{256}Lr \xrightarrow{66\,s} {}^{252}Md$$

Note also the production of new isotopes of elements 107 and 109 in this chain.

Element 112 emerged close to midnight on 9 February 1996 when the team at GSI unambiguously detected one atom of the new element after two weeks of bombarding a lead target with high-energy ionized atoms of zinc $^{208}Pb(^{70}Zn,n)^{277}112$.[56] The new element emitted an α-particle after $280\,\mu s$, followed by several

others which formed a coherent decay scheme down to Fm:

$$^{277}112 \xrightarrow{280\,\mu s} {}^{273}110 \xrightarrow{110\,\mu s} {}^{269}108 \xrightarrow{19.7\,s}$$
$$^{265}106 \longrightarrow {}^{263}104 \longrightarrow {}^{259}No \longrightarrow {}^{255}Fm$$

This work is particularly significant for a number of reasons. Not only does $^{277}112$ have the highest atomic number and the highest mass of any nuclide so far, but it is also expected to complete the 6d transition series of elements. Will the next elements 113, 114, etc. prove to be members of the boron and carbon groups or will relativistic effects supervene to stabilize other electronic configurations? Perhaps even more significantly, the new atomic species is approaching the "island of stability" which has been predicted on the basis of the expected nuclear closed sheels of 114 protons and 184 or 178 neutrons, and it does indeed show clear signs of this increasing stability (decreasing instability). Moreover, the decay chain generates two new isotopes of elements 110 and 108 which themselves are the heaviest (and most stable) isotopes of these elements so far. Further increases in stability might well make chemical experimentation feasible. Clearly, exciting prospects lie ahead.

At present, some 36 isotopes of the transactinide elements have been characterized and these are summarized in Table 31.8.

[53] S. HOFMANN (and 11 others), *Z. Phys. A* **350**, 277–80 (1995).

[54] M. FREEMANTLE, *Chem. & Eng. News*, 13 March, 35–40 (1995).

[55] S. HOFMANN (and 11 others), *Z. Phys. A* **350**, 281–2 (1995).

[56] S. HOFMANN (and 11 others), *Z. Phys. A* **354**, 229–30 (1996).

Table 31.8   Isotopes of the transactinide elements (1997)

Z (Discovered)	No. of isotopes	Mass range	$t_{1/2}$ range
104 (1969)	9(?10)	253–262	7 ms–65 s
105 (1970)	7	255–263	1.3 s–34 s
106 (1974)	6	259–266	3.6 ms–30 s
107 (1981)	3	261–264	12 ms–0.44 s
108 (1984)	3	264, 265, 269	80 μs–19.7 s
109 (1982)	2	266, 268	3.4 ms–70 ms
110 (1994)	3	269, 271, 273	0.1 ms–0.2 ms
111 (1994)	1	272	1.5 ms
112 (1996)	1	277	0.28 ms

Appendix 1
Atomic Orbitals

THE spacial distribution of electron density in an atom is described by means of atomic orbitals $\psi(r, \theta, \phi)$ such that for a given orbital ψ the function $\psi^2 dv$ gives the probability of finding the electron in an element of volume dv at a point having the polar coordinates r, θ, ϕ. Each orbital can be expressed as a product of two functions, i.e. $\psi_{n,l,m}(r, \theta, \phi) = R_{n,l}(r)A_{l,m}(\theta, \phi)$, where

(a) $R_{n,l}(r)$ is a radial function which depends only on the distance r from the nucleus (independent of direction) and is defined by the two quantum numbers n, l;

(b) $A_{l,m}(\theta, \phi)$ is an angular function which is independent of distance but depends on the direction as given by the angles θ, ϕ; it is defined by the two quantum numbers l, m.

Normalized radial functions for a hydrogen-like atom are given in Table A1.1 and plotted graphically in Fig. A1.1 for the first ten combinations of n and l. It will be seen that the radial functions for 1s, 2p, 3d, and 4f orbitals have no nodes and are everywhere of the same sign (e.g. positive). In general $R_{n,l}(r)$ becomes zero $(n - l - 1)$ times between r equals 0 and ∞. The probability of finding an electron at a distance r from the nucleus is given by $4\pi R_{n,l}^2(r)r^2 dr$, and this is also plotted in Fig. A1.1. However, the probability of finding an electron frequently depends also on the direction chosen. The probability of finding an electron in a given direction, independently of distance from the nucleus, is given by the square of the angular dependence function $A_{l,m}^2(\theta, \phi)$. The normalized functions $A_{l,m}(\theta, \phi)$ are listed in Table A1.2 and illustrated schematically by the models in Fig. A1.2. It will be seen that for s orbitals $(l = 0)$ the angular dependence function A is constant, independent of θ, and ϕ, i.e. the function is spherically symmetrical. For p orbitals $(l = 1)$ A comprises two spheres in contact, one being positive and one negative, i.e. there is one planar node. The d and f functions $(l = 2, 3)$ have more complex angular dependence with 2 and 3 nodes respectively.

Table A1.1 Normalized radial functions $R_{n,l}(r)$ for hydrogen-like atoms

$$R_{n,l}(r) = -\sqrt{\frac{4(n-l-1)!Z^3}{n^4[(n+l)!]^3 a_0^3}} \times \left(\frac{2Zr}{a_0 n}\right)^l L_{n+1}^{2l+1}\left(\frac{2Zr}{a_0 n}\right) \times e^{-Zr/a_0 n}$$

Orbital	n	l	$R_{n,l}$ =	Constant	×	Polynomial	×	Expon.
1s	1	0	$R_{1,0}$	$2(Z/a_0)^{3/2}$		1		e^{-Zr/a_0}
2s	2	0	$R_{2,0}$	$\dfrac{(Z/a_0)^{3/2}}{2\sqrt{2}}$		$\left(2 - \dfrac{Zr}{a_0}\right)$		$e^{-Zr/2a_0}$
2p	2	1	$R_{2,1}$	$\dfrac{(Z/a_0)^{3/2}}{2\sqrt{6}}$		$\dfrac{Zr}{a_0}$		$e^{-Zr/2a_0}$
3s	3	0	$R_{3,0}$	$\dfrac{2(Z/a_0)^{3/2}}{81\sqrt{3}}$		$\left(27 - 18\dfrac{Zr}{a_0} + 2\dfrac{Z^2 r^2}{a_0^2}\right)$		$e^{-Zr/3a_0}$
3p	3	1	$R_{3,1}$	$\dfrac{4(Z/a_0)^{3/2}}{81\sqrt{6}}$		$\left(6\dfrac{Zr}{a_0} - \dfrac{Z^2 r^2}{a_0^2}\right)$		$e^{-Zr/3a_0}$
3d	3	2	$R_{3,2}$	$\dfrac{4(Z/a_0)^{3/2}}{81\sqrt{30}}$		$\dfrac{Z^2 r^2}{a_0^2}$		$e^{-Zr/3a_0}$
4s	4	0	$R_{4,0}$	$\dfrac{(Z/a_0)^{3/2}}{768}$		$\left(192 - 144\dfrac{Zr}{a_0} + 24\dfrac{Z^2 r^2}{a_0^2} - \dfrac{Z^3 r^3}{a_0^3}\right)$		$e^{-Zr/4a_0}$
4p	4	1	$R_{4,1}$	$\dfrac{(Z/a_0)^{3/2}}{265\sqrt{15}}$		$\left(80\dfrac{Zr}{a_0} - 20\dfrac{Z^2 r^2}{a_0^2} + \dfrac{Z^3 r^3}{a_0^3}\right)$		$e^{-Zr/4a_0}$
4d	4	2	$R_{4,2}$	$\dfrac{(Z/a_0)^{3/2}}{768\sqrt{5}}$		$\left(12\dfrac{Z^2 r^2}{a_0^2} - \dfrac{Z^3 r^3}{a_0^3}\right)$		$e^{-Zr/4a_0}$
4f	4	3	$R_{4,3}$	$\dfrac{(Z/a_0)^{3/2}}{768\sqrt{35}}$		$\dfrac{Z^3 r^3}{a_0^3}$		$e^{-Zr/4a_0}$

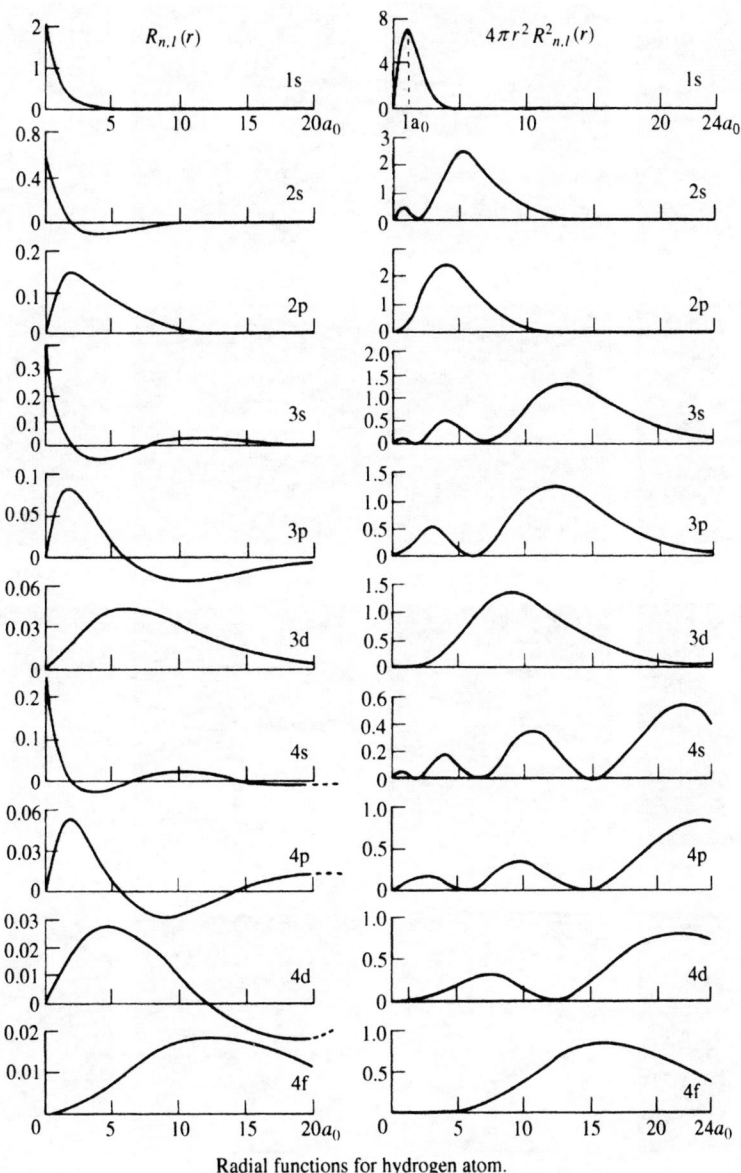

Radial functions for hydrogen atom.

Figure A1.1 Radial functions for a hydrogen atom. (Note that the horizontal scale is the same in each graph but the vertical scale varies by as much as a factor of 100. The Bohr radius $a_0 = 52.9\,\text{pm}$.)

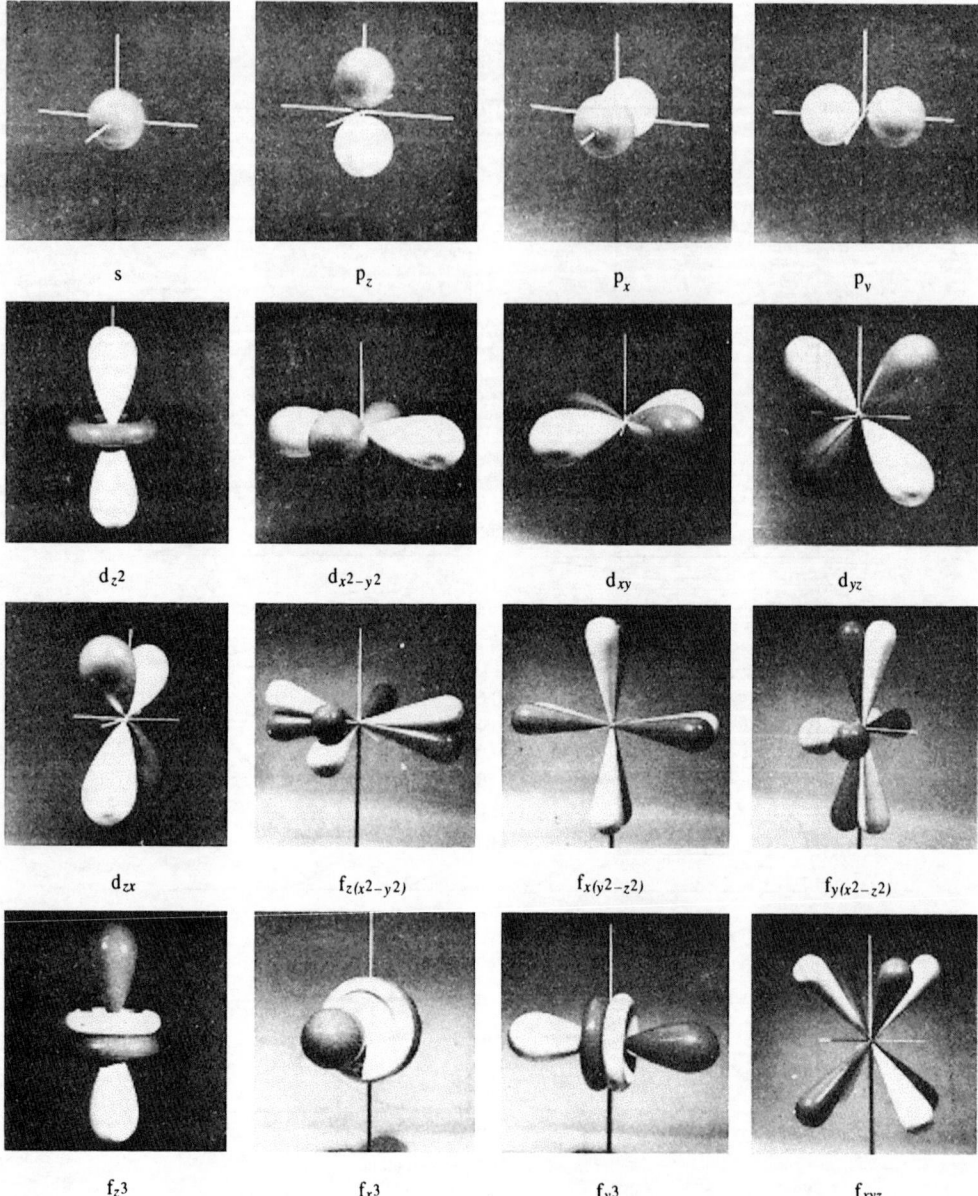

Figure A1.2   Models schematically illustrating the angular dependence functions $A_{l,m}(\theta, \phi)$. There is no unique way of representing the angular dependence functions of all seven f orbitals. An alternative to the set shown is one f_{z^3}, three f_{xz^2}, f_{yx^2}, f_{zy^2}, and three $f_{x(x^2-3y^2)}$, $f_{y(y^2-3z^2)}$, and $f_{z(z^2-3x^2)}$.

Table A1.2 Normalized angular dependence functions, $A_{l,m}(\theta, \phi) = \Theta_{l,m}(\theta)\Phi_m(\phi)$

Orbital	Angular dependence function	Orbital	Angular dependence function
s	$\dfrac{1}{2\sqrt{\pi}}$		
p_z	$\dfrac{\sqrt{3}}{2\sqrt{\pi}}\cos\theta$		
p_x	$\dfrac{\sqrt{3}}{2\pi}\sin\theta\cos\phi$	f_{z^3}	$\dfrac{\sqrt{7}}{4\sqrt{\pi}}(5\cos^3\theta - 3\cos\theta)$
p_y	$\dfrac{\sqrt{3}}{2\sqrt{\pi}}\sin\theta\sin\phi$	f_{z^2x}	$\dfrac{\sqrt{42}}{8\sqrt{\pi}}(5\cos^2\theta - 1)\sin\theta\cos\phi$
d_{z^2}	$\dfrac{\sqrt{5}}{4\sqrt{\pi}}(3\cos^2\theta - 1)$	f_{z^2y}	$\dfrac{\sqrt{42}}{8\sqrt{\pi}}(5\cos^2\theta - 1)\sin\theta\sin\phi$
$d_{x^2-y^2}$	$\dfrac{\sqrt{15}}{4\sqrt{\pi}}\sin^2\theta(2\cos^2\phi - 1)$	$f_{z(x^2-y^2)}$	$\dfrac{\sqrt{105}}{4\sqrt{\pi}}\cos\theta\sin^2\theta(2\cos^2\phi - 1)$
d_{zx}	$\dfrac{\sqrt{15}}{2\sqrt{\pi}}\cos\theta\sin\theta\cos\phi$	f_{zxy}	$\dfrac{\sqrt{105}}{2\sqrt{\pi}}\cos\theta\sin^2\theta\cos\phi\sin\phi$
d_{zy}	$\dfrac{\sqrt{15}}{2\sqrt{\pi}}\cos\theta\sin\theta\sin\phi$	f_{x^3}	$\dfrac{\sqrt{70}}{8\sqrt{\pi}}\sin^3\theta(4\cos^3\phi - 3\cos\phi)$
d_{xy}	$\dfrac{\sqrt{15}}{2\sqrt{\pi}}\sin^2\theta\sin\phi\cos\phi$	f_{y^3}	$\dfrac{\sqrt{70}}{8\sqrt{\pi}}\sin^3\theta(3\sin\phi - 4\sin^3\phi)$

Appendix 2
Symmetry Elements, Symmetry Operations and Point Groups

An object has *symmetry* when certain parts of it can be interchanged with others without altering either the identity or the apparent orientation of the object. For a discrete object such as a molecule 5 *elements of symmetry* can be envisaged:

> *axis* of symmetry, *C*;
> *plane* of symmetry, *σ*;
> *centre of inversion, i*;
> *improper axis* of symmetry, *S*; and
> *identity, E*.

These elements of symmetry are best recognized by performing various *symmetry operations*, which are geometrically defined ways of exchanging equivalent parts of a molecule. The 5·symmetry operations are:

C$_n$, *rotation* of the molecule about a symmetry *axis* through an angle of $360°/n$; *n* is called the *order* of the rotation (twofold, threefold, etc.);

σ   reflection of all atoms through a *plane* of the molecule;

i,   inversion of all atoms through a *point* of the molecule;

S$_n$, *Rotation* of the molecule through an angle $360°/n$ *followed by reflection* of all atoms through a plane perpendicular to the axis of rotation; the combined operation (which may equally follow the sequence *reflection then rotation*) is called *improper rotation*;

E,   the *identity* operation which leaves the molecule unchanged.

The rotation axis of highest order is called the *principal axis* of rotation; it is usually placed in the vertical direction and designated the *z*-axis of the molecule. Planes of reflection which are perpendicular to the principal axis are called *horizontal planes (h)*. Planes of reflection which contain the principal axis are called *vertical planes (v)*, or *dihedral planes (d)* if they bisect 2 twofold axes.

The complete set of symmetry operations that can be performed on a molecule is called the *symmetry group* or *point group* of the molecule and the *order* of the point group is the number of symmetry operations it contains. Table A2.1 lists the various point groups, together with their elements of symmetry and with examples of each.

Table A2.1   Point groups

Point group	Elements of symmetry	Examples
C_1	E	CHFClBr
C_s	E, σ	SO_2FBr, HOCl, BFClBr, $SOCl_2$, SF_5NF_2
C_i	E, i	CHClBr–CHClBr (staggered)
C_2	E, C_2	H_2O_2, *cis*-$[Co(en)_2X_2]$
C_3	E, C_3	PPh_3 (propeller)
C_{2v}	$E, C_2, 2\sigma_v$	H_2O (V-Shaped), H_2CO (Y-shaped), ClF_3 (T-shaped), SF_4 (see-saw), SiH_2Cl_2, *cis*-$[Pt(NH_3)_2Cl_2]$, C_6H_5Cl
C_{3v}	$E, C_3, 3\sigma_v$	GeH_3Cl, PCl_3, $O{=}PF_3$
C_{4v}	$E, C_4, 4\sigma_v$	SF_5Cl, IF_5, $XeOF_4$
C_{5v}	$E, C_5, 5\sigma_v$	$[Ni(\eta^5\text{-}C_5H_5)(NO)]$
C_{6v}	$E, C_6, 6\sigma_v$	$[Cr(\eta^6\text{-}C_6H_6)(\eta^6\text{-}C_6Me_6)]$
$C_{\infty v}$	$E, C_\infty, \infty\sigma_v$	NO, HCN, COS
C_{2h}	E, C_2, σ_h, i	*trans*-N_2F_4
C_{3h}	E, C_3, σ_h, i	$B(OH)_3$
C_{4h}	E, C_4, σ_h, i	$[Re_2(\mu,\eta^2\text{-}SO_4)_4]$
D_3	$E, C_3, 3C_2'$	trischelates $[M(chel)_3]$, C_2H_6 (*gauche*)
D_{2d}	$E, C_2, 2C_2', 2\sigma_d, S_4$	B_2Cl_4 (vapour, staggered), As_4S_4
D_{3d}	$E, C_3, 3C_2', 3\sigma_d, i, S_6$	$R_3W{\equiv}WR_3$ (staggered)
D_{4d}	$E, C_4, 4C_2', 4\sigma_d, S_8$	S_8 (crown), *closo*-$B_{10}H_{10}^{2-}$
D_{2h}	$E, C_2, 2C_2', 2\sigma_v, \sigma_h, i$	B_2Cl_4 (planar), B_2H_6, *trans*-$[Pt(NH_3)_2Cl_2]$, *trans*-$[Co(NH_3)_2Cl_2Br_2]^-$, 1,4-$C_6H_4Cl_2$
D_{3h}	$E, C_3, 3C_2', 3\sigma_v, \sigma_h, S_3$	BCl_3, PF_5, $B_3N_3H_6$, $[ReH_9]^{2-}$
D_{4h}	$E, C_4, 4C_2', 4\sigma_v, \sigma_h, i, S_4$	XeF_4, $PtCl_4^{2-}$, *trans*-$[Co(NH_3)_4Cl_2]^+$, $[Re_2Cl_8]^{2-}$, *closo*-1,6-$C_2B_4H_6$
D_{5h}	$E, C_5, 5C_2', 5\sigma_v, \sigma_h, S_5$	$[Fe(\eta^5\text{-}C_5H_5)_2]$ eclipsed, $B_7H_7^{2-}$, IF_7
D_{6h}	$E, C_6, 6C_2', 6\sigma_v, \sigma_h, i, S_6$	C_6H_6, $[Cr(\eta^6\text{-}C_6H_6)_2]$ (eclipsed)
$D_{\infty h}$	$E, C_\infty, \infty C_2', \infty\sigma_v, i$	Cl_2, CO_2
S_4	E, S_4	*cyclo*-$Cl_4B_4N_4R_4$
T	$E, 3C_2, 4C_3$	$Si(SiMe_3)_4$, $[Pt(PF_3)_4]$
T_d	$E, 4C_3, 6\sigma_d, 3S_4$	SiF_4, B_4Cl_4, $[Ni(CO)_4]$, $[Ir_4(CO)_{12}]$
T_h	$E, 4C_3, 3C_2, 3\sigma_h, i, 4S_6$	$[Co(NO_2)_6]^{3-}$ (*trans* NO_2 groups eclipsed), $[M(\eta^2\text{-}NO_3)_6]^{n-}$, $[W(NMe_2)_6]$
O_h	$E, 3C_4, 4C_3, 6C_2', 3\sigma_h, 6\sigma_d, i, 3S_4, 4S_6$	SF_6, $B_6H_6^{2-}$ (octahedron), C_8H_8 (cubane)
I_h	$E, 6C_5, 10C_3, 15C_2, 15\sigma_v, i, 12S_{10}, 10S_6$	$B_{12}H_{12}^{2-}$ (icosahedron)

It is instructive to add to these examples from the numerous instances of point group symmetry mentioned throughout the text. In this way a facility will gradually be acquired in discerning the various elements of symmetry present in a molecule.

A convenient scheme for identifying the point group symmetry of any given species is set out in the flow chart.[1] Starting at the top of the chart each vertical line asks a question: if the answer is "yes" then move to the right, if "no" then move to the left until the correct point group is arrived at. Other similar schemes have been devised.[2-5]

[1] J. DONOHUE, *Sov. Phys. Crystallogr.* **26**, 516 (1981); *Kristallografiya* **26**, 908–9 (1981).

[2] R. L. CARTER, *J. Chem. Educ.* **45**, 44 (1968).

[3] F. A. COTTON, *Chemical Applications of Group Theory*, 2nd edn., pp. 45–7, Wiley-Interscience, New York, 1971.

[4] J. D. DONALDSON and S. D. ROSS, *Symmetry and Stereochemistry*, pp. 35–49, Intertext Books, London, 1972.

[5] J. A. SALTHOUSE and M. J. WARE, *Point Group Character Tables and Related Data*, p. 29, Cambridge University Press, 1972.

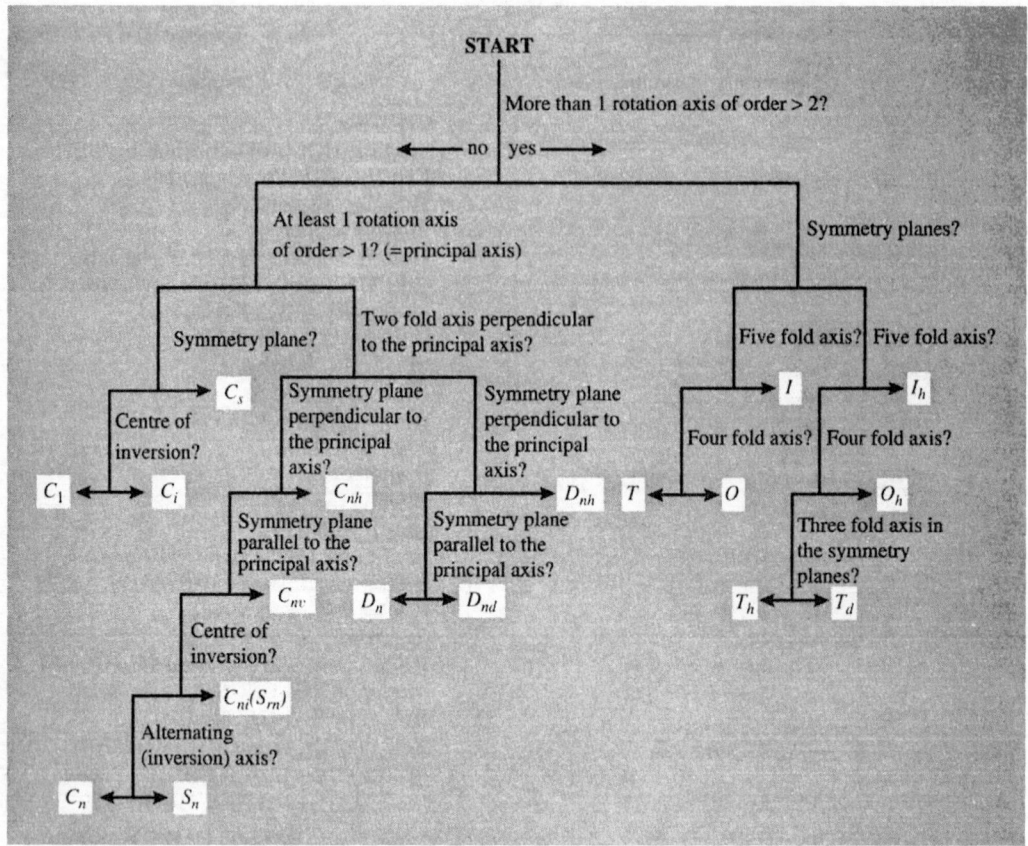

Figure A2.1 Point group symmetry flow chart.

Appendix 3
Some Non-SI Units[†]

Physical quantity	Name of unit	Symbol for unit	Definition of unit
Length	ångström	Å	10^{-10} m (100 pm)
Time	minute	min	60 s
	hour	h	3600 s
	day	d	86 400 s
Energy	erg	erg	10^{-7} J
	kilowatt hour	kWh	3.6×10^{6} J
	thermochemical calorie	cal_{th}	4.184 J
Force	dyne	dyn	10^{-5} N
Pressure	bar	bar	10^{5} Pa
	atmosphere	atm	101 325 Pa
	conventional millimetre of mercury	mmHg	13.5951×9.80665 Pa i.e. 133.322 Pa
	torr	Torr	(101 325/760) Pa
Magnetic flux	maxwell	Mx	10^{-8} Wb
Magnetic flux density (magnetic induction)	gauss	G, Gs	10^{-4} T
Dynamic viscosity	poise	P	10^{-1} Pa s
Concentration	–	M	mol dm^{-3}
Radioactivity	curie	Ci	3.7×10^{10} s^{-1}
Radioactive exposure	röntgen	R	2.58×10^{-4} C kg^{-1}
Absorbed dose	rad	rad	10^{-2} J kg^{-1}
Angle	degree	°	$1° = (\pi/180)$ radian

[†] The unit "degree Celsius" (°C) is identical with the kelvin (K). The Celsius temperature (t_C) is related to the thermodynamic temperature T by the definition: $t_C = T - 273.15$ K.

Some useful conversion factors:

1 m = 3.280 839 9 ft = 39.370 079 inches
1 inch = 25.4 mm (defined)
1 statute mile = 1.609 344 km
1 light year = $9.460\,55 \times 10^{12}$ km
1 acre = 4046.8564 m^2
1 gal (Imperial) = 1.200 949 gal (US) = 4.545 960 l
1 gal (US) = 0.832 674 7 gal (Imp.) = 3.785 411 8 l
1 lb (avoirdupois) = 0.453 592 37 kg
1 oz (avoirdupois) = 28.349 527 g
1 oz (troy, or apoth.) = 31.103 486 g
1 carat = 3.086 47 grains = 200 mg
1 tonne = 1000 kg = 2204.622 6 lb = 1.102 311 3 short tons
1 short ton = 907.184 74 kg = 2000 lb = 0.892 857 14 long tons
1 long ton = 1016.046 9 kg = 2240 lb = 1.120 short tons
1 atm = 101 325 Pa = 1.013 25 bar = 760 Torr = 14.695 95 lb/in^2
1 Pa = 10^{-5} bar $\sim 1.019\,716 \times 10^{-1}$ kg m^{-2} = $0.986\,923 \times 10^{-5}$ atm
1 mdyn Å^{-1} = 100 N m^{-1}
1 calorie (thermochem) = 4.184 J (defined)
1 eV = $1.602\,19 \times 10^{-19}$ J
1 eV/molecule = 96.484 56 kJ mol^{-1} = 23.060 36 kcal mol^{-1}

Appendix 4
Abundance of Elements in Crustal Rocks/ppm (i.e. g/tonne)[†]

No.	Elt.	ppm	Σ%	No.	Elt.	ppm	No.	Elt.	ppm	No.	Elt.	ppm
1	O	455 000	45.50	20	Cl	126	39	Th	8.1	58	Tl	0.7
2	Si	272 000	72.70	21	Cr	122	40	Sm	7.0	59	Tm	0.5
3	Al	83 000	81.00	22	Ni	99	41	Gd	6.1	60	I	0.46
4	Fe	62 000	87.20	23	Rb	78	42	Er	3.5	61	In	0.24
5	Ca	46 600	91.86	24	Zn	76	43	Yb	3.1	62	Sb	0.2
6	Mg	27 640	94.62	25	Cu	68	44	Hf	2.8	63	Cd	0.16
7	Na	22 700	96.89	26	Ce	66	45	Cs	2.6	64	⎰Ag	0.08
8	K	18 400	98.73	27	Nd	40	46	Br	2.5		⎱Hg	0.08
9	Ti	6320	99.36	28	La	35	47	U	2.3	66	Se	0.05
10	H	1520	99.51	29	Y	31	48	⎰Sn	2.1	67	Pd	0.015
11	P	1120	99.63	30	Co	29		⎱Eu	2.1	68	Pt	0.01
12	Mn	1060	99.73	31	Sc	25	50	Be	2	69	Bi	0.008
13	F	544	99.79	32	Nb	20	51	As	1.8	70	Os	0.005
14	Ba	390	99.83	33	⎰N	19	52	Ta	1.7	71	Au	0.004
15	Sr	384	99.86		⎱Ga	19	53	Ge	1.5	72	⎰Ir	0.001
16	S	340	99.90	35	Li	18	54	Ho	1.3		⎱Te	0.001
17	C	180	99.92	36	Pb	13		⎰Mo	1.2	74	Re	0.0007
18	Zr	162	99.93	37	Pr	9.1	55	⎨W	1.2	75	⎰Ru	0.0001
19	V	136	99.95	38	B	9		⎩Tb	1.2		⎱Rh	0.0001

[†]Taken from W. S. Fyfe, *Geochemistry,* Oxford University Press, 1974, with some modifications and additions to incorporate later data. The detailed numbers are subject to various assumptions in the models of the global distribution of the various rock types within the crust, but they are broadly acceptable as an indication of elemental abundances. See also Table 1 in C. K. JØRGENSEN, *Comments Astrophys.* **17**, 49–101 (1993).

Appendix 5
Effective Ionic Radii in pm for Various Oxidation States (in parentheses)[†]

s Block

Element	Radius	Element	Radius
Li (+1)	76	Be (+2)	45
Na (+1)	102	Mg (+2)	72.0
K (+1)	138	Ca (+2)	100
Rb (+1)	152	Sr (+2)	118
Cs (+1)	167	Ba (+2)	135
Fr (+1)	180	Ra (+2)^{VIII}	148

p Block

B	C	N	O	F	
(+3) 27	(+4) 16	(−3)^{IV} 146; (+3) 16; (+5) 13	(−2) 140	(−1) 133; (+7) 8	
Al (+3) 53.5	**Si** (+4) 40	**P** (+3) 44; (+5) 38	**S** (−2) 184; (+4) 37; (+6) 29	**Cl** (−1) 184; (+5)^{III} 12; (+7) 27	
Ga (+3) 62.0	**Ge** (+2) 73; (+4) 53.0	**As** (+3) 58; (+5) 46	**Se** (−2) 198; (+4) 50; (+6) 42	**Br** (−1) 196; (+3)$^{IV}_{sq}$ 59; (+5)^{III} 31; (+7) 39	
In (+3) 80.0	**Sn** (+2) 118; (+4) 69.0	**Sb** (+3) 76; (+5) 60	**Te** (−2) 221; (+4) 97; (+6) 56	**I** (−1) 220; (+5) 95; (+7) 53	**Xe** (+8) 48
Tl (+1) 150; (+3) 88.5	**Pb** (+2) 119; (+4) 77.5	**Bi** (+3) 103; (+5) 76	**Po** (+4) 94; (+6) 67	**At** (+7) 62	

d Block

First row

	Sc	Ti	V	Cr	Mn	Fe	Co	Ni	Cu (77)	Zn
(+1)									77	
(+2)		86	79	73 ls / 80 hs	67	61 ls / 78.0 hs	65 ls / 74.5 hs	69	73	74.0
(+3)	74.5	67.0	64.0	61.5	58 ls / 64.5 hs	55 ls / 64.5 hs	54.5 ls / 61 hs	56 ls / 60 hs	54 ls	
(+4)		60.5	58	55	53.0	58.5	53	48 ls		
(+5)			54	49	33^{IV}					
(+6)				44	25.5^{IV}	25^{IV}				
(+7)					46					

Second row

	Y	Zr	Nb	Mo	Tc	Ru	Rh	Pd (59^{II})	Ag (115)	Cd
(+2)								86	94	95
(+3)	90.0		72	69		68	66.5	76	75	
(+4)		72	68	65	64.5	62.0	60	61.5		
(+5)			64	61	60	56.5	55			
(+6)				59						
(+7)					56	38^{IV}				
(+8)						36^{IV}				

Third row

	La	Hf	Ta	W	Re	Os	Ir	Pt	Au (137)	Hg (119)
(+1)									137	119
(+2)								86	−	102
(+3)	103.2		72				68		85	−
(+4)		71	68	66	63	63.0	62.5	62.5	−	
(+5)			64	62	58	57.5	57	57	57	
(+6)				60	55	54.5				
(+7)					53	52.5				
(+8)						39^{IV}				

Ac	
+3	112

f Block

	Ce	Pr	Nd	Pm	Sm	Eu	Gd	Tb	Dy	Ho	Er	Tm	Yb	Lu
(+2)			129^{VIII}		122^{VII}				107			103	102	
(+3)	102	99	98.3	97	95.8	94.7	93.8	92.3	91.2	90.1	89.0	88.0	86.8	86.1
(+4)	87	85						76						

	Th	Pa	U	Np	Pu	Am	Cm	Bk	Cf	Es	Fm	Md	No	Lr
(+2)				110		126^{VIII}								
(+3)		104	102.5	101	100	97.5	97	96	95					
(+4)	94	90	89	87	86	85	85	83	82.1					
(+5)		78	78	75	74									
(+6)			73	72	71									
(+7)			71											

[†] For coord. no. 6 unless indicated by superscript numerals^{III},^{IV}, etc. (All data taken from R. D. Shannon, *Acta Cryst.* **A32**, 751–67 (1976).

Appendix 6
Nobel Prize for Chemistry

1901 **J. H. van't Hoff** (Berlin): discovery of the laws of chemical dynamics and osmotic pressure in solutions.

1902 **E. Fischer** (Berlin): sugar and purine syntheses.

1903 **S. Arrhenius** (Stockholm): electrolytic theory of dissociation.

1904 **W. Ramsay** (University College, London): discovery of the inert gaseous elements in air and their place in the periodic system.

1905 **A. von Baeyer** (Munich): advancement of organic chemistry and the chemical industry through work on organic dyes and hydroaromatic compounds.

1906 **H. Moissan** (Paris): isolation of the element fluorine and development of the electric furnace.

1907 **E. Buchner** (Berlin): biochemical researches and the discovery of cell-free fermentation.

1908 **E. Rutherford** (Manchester): investigations into the disintegration of the elements and the chemistry of radioactive substances.

1909 **W. Ostwald** (Gross-Bothen): work on catalysis and investigations into the fundamental principles governing chemical equilibria and rates of reaction.

1910 **O. Wallach** (Göttingen): pioneer work in the field of alicyclic compounds.

1911 **Marie Curie** (Paris): discovery of the elements radium and polonium, the isolation of radium, and the study of the nature and compounds of this remarkable element.

1912 **V. Grignard** (Nancy): discovery of the Grignard reagent.
P. Sabatier (Toulouse): method of hydrogenating organic compounds in the presence of finely disintegrated metals.

1913 **A. Werner** (Zürich): work on the linkage of atoms in molecules which has thrown new light on earlier investigations and opened up new fields of research especially in inorganic chemistry.

1914 **T. W. Richards** (Harvard): accurate determination of the atomic weight of a large number of chemical elements.

1915 **R. Willstätter** (Munich): plant pigments, especially chlorophyll.

1916 Not awarded

1917 Not awarded

1918 **F. Haber** (Berlin–Dahlem): the synthesis of ammonia from its elements.

1919 Not awarded

1920 **W. Nernst** (Berlin): work in thermochemistry.

1921 **F. Soddy** (Oxford): contributions to knowledge of the chemistry of radioactive substances and investigations into the origin and nature of isotopes.

1922 **F. W. Aston** (Cambridge): discovery, by means of the mass spectrograph, of isotopes in a large number of non-radioactive elements and for enunciation of the whole-number rule.

1923 **F. Pregl** (Graz): invention of the method of microanalysis of organic substances.

1924 Not awarded

1925 **R. Zsigmondy** (Göttingen): demonstration of the heterogeneous nature of colloid solutions by methods which have since become fundamental in modern colloid chemistry.

1926 **T. Svedberg** (Uppsala): work on disperse systems.

1927 **H. Wieland** (Munich): constitution of the bile acids and related substances.

1928 **A. Windaus** (Göttingen): constitution of the sterols and their connection with the vitamins.

1929 **A. Harden** (London) and **H. von Euler-Chelpin** (Stockholm): investigations on the fermentation of sugars and fermentative enzymes.

1930 **H. Fischer** (Munich): the constitution of haemin and chlorophyll and especially for the synthesis of haemin.

1931 **C. Bosch** and **F. Bergius** (Heidelberg): the invention and development of chemical high pressure methods.

1932 **I. Langmuir** (Schenectady, New York): discoveries and investigations in surface chemistry.

1933 Not awarded

1934 **H. C. Urey** (Columbia, New York): discovery of heavy hydrogen.

1935 **F. Joliot** and **Iréne Joliot-Curie** (Paris): synthesis of new radioactive elements.

1936 **P. Debye** (Berlin–Dahlem): contributions to knowledge of molecular structure through investigations on dipole moments and on the diffraction of X-rays and electrons in gases.

1937 **W. N. Haworth** (Birmingham): investigations on carbohydrates and vitamin C.
P. Karrer (Zürich): investigations of carotenoids, flavins, and vitamins A and B$_2$.

1938 **R. Kuhn** (Heidelberg): work on carotenoids and vitamins.

1939 **A. F. J. Butenandt** (Berlin): work on sex hormones.
L. Ruzicka (Zürich): work on polymethylenes and higher terpenes.

1940 Not awarded.

1941 Not awarded.

1942 Not awarded.

1943 **G. Hevesy** (Stockholm): use of isotopes as tracers in the study of chemical processes.

1944 **O. Hahn** (Berlin–Dahlem): discovery of the fission of heavy nuclei.

1945 **A. J. Virtanen** (Helsingfors): research and inventions in agricultural and nutrition chemistry, especially fodder preservation.

1946 **J. B. Sumner** (Cornell): discovery that enzymes can be crystallized.
J. H. Northrop and **W. M. Stanley** (Princeton): preparation of enzymes and virus proteins in a pure form.

1947 **R. Robinson** (Oxford): investigations on plant products of biological importance, especially the alkaloids.

1948 **A. W. K. Tiselius** (Uppsala): electrophoresis and adsorption analysis, especially for discoveries concerning the complex nature of the serum proteins.

1949 **W. F. Giauque** (Berkeley): contributions in the field of chemical thermodynamics, particularly concerning the behaviour of substances at extremely low temperatures.

1950 **O. Diels** (Kiel) and **K. Alder** (Cologne): discovery and development of the diene synthesis.

1951 **E. M. McMillan** and **G. T. Seaborg** (Berkeley): discoveries in the chemistry of the transuranium elements.

1952 **A. J. P. Martin** (London) and **R. L. M. Synge** (Bucksburn): invention of partition chromatography.

1953 **H. Staudinger** (Freiburg): discoveries in the field of macromolecular chemistry.

1954 **L. Pauling** (California Institute of Technology, Pasadena): research into the nature of the chemical bond and its application to the elucidation of the structure of complex substances.

1955 **V. du Vigneaud** (New York): biochemically important sulfur compounds, especially the first synthesis of a polypeptide hormone.

1956 **C. N. Hinshelwood** (Oxford) and **N. N. Semenov** (Moscow): the mechanism of chemical reactions.

1957 **A. Todd** (Cambridge): nucleotides and nucleotide co-enzymes.

1958 **F. Sanger** (Cambridge): the structure of proteins, especially that of insulin.

1959 **J. Heyrovský** (Prague): discovery and development of the polarographic method of analysis.

1960 **W. F. Libby** (Los Angeles): use of carbon-14 for age determination in archeology, geology, geophysics, and other branches of science.

1961 **M. Calvin** (Berkeley): research on the carbon dioxide assimilation in plants.

1962 **J. C. Kendrew** and **M. F. Perutz** (Cambridge): the structures of globular proteins.

1963 **K. Ziegler** (Mülheim/Ruhr) and **G. Natta** (Milan): the chemistry and technology of high polymers.

1964 **Dorothy Crowfoot Hodgkin** (Oxford): determinations by X-ray techniques of the structures of important biochemical substances.

1965 **R. B. Woodward** (Harvard): outstanding achievements in the art of organic synthesis.

1966 **R. S. Mulliken** (Chicago): fundamental work concerning chemical bonds and the electronic structure of molecules by the molecular orbital method.

1967 **M. Eigen** (Göttingen), **R. G. W. Norrish** (Cambridge) and **G. Porter** (London): studies of extremely fast chemical reactions, effected by disturbing the equilibrium by means of very short pulses of energy.

1968 **L. Onsager** (Yale): discovery of the reciprocity relations bearing his name, which are fundamental for the thermodynamics of irreversible processes.

1969 **D. H. R. Barton** (Imperial College, London) and **O. Hassel** (Oslo): development of the concept of conformation and its application in chemistry.

1970 **L. F. Leloir** (Buenos Aires): discovery of sugar nucleotides and their role in the biosynthesis of carbohydrates.

1971 **G. Herzberg** (Ottawa): contributions to the knowledge of electronic structure and geometry of molecules, particularly free radicals.

1972 **C. B. Anfinsen** (Bethesda): work on ribonuclease, especially concerning the connection between the amino-acid sequence and the biologically active conformation.
S. Moore and **W. H. Stein** (Rockefeller, New York): contributions to the understanding of the connection between chemical structure and catalytic activity of the active centre of the ribonuclease molecule.

1973 **E. O. Fischer** (Munich) and **G. Wilkinson** (Imperial College, London): pioneering work, performed independently, on the chemistry of the organometallic so-called sandwich compounds.

1974 **P. J. Flory** (Stanford): fundamental achievements both theoretical and experimental in the physical chemistry of macromolecules.

1975 **J. W. Cornforth** (Sussex): stereochemistry of enzyme-catalysed reactions.
V. Prelog (Zürich): the stereochemistry of organic molecules and reactions.

1976 **W. N. Lipscomb** (Harvard): studies on the structure of boranes illuminating problems of chemical bonding.

1977 **I. Prigogine** (Brussels): non-equilibrium thermodynamics, particularly the theory of dissipative structures.

1978 **P. Mitchell** (Bodmin, Cornwall): contributions to the understanding of biological energy transfer through the formulation of the chemiosmotic theory.

1979 **H. C. Brown** (Purdue) and **G. Wittig** (Heidelberg): for their development of boron and phosphorus compounds, respectively, into important reagents in organic synthesis.

1980 **P. Berg** (Stanford): the biochemistry of nucleic acids, with particular regard to recombinant-DNA.
W. Gilbert (Harvard) and **F. Sanger** (Cambridge): the determination of base sequences in nucleic acids.

1981 **K. Fukui** (Kyoto) and **R. Hoffmann** (Cornell): quantum mechanical studies of chemical reactivity.

1982 **A. Klug** (Cambridge): development of crystallographic electron microscopy and the structural elucidation of biologically important nucleic acid-protein complexes.

1983 **H. Taube** (Stanford): mechanisms of electron transfer reactions of metal complexes.

1984 **R. B. Merrifield** (Rockefeller, New York): development of methodology for the synthesis of peptides on a solid matrix.

1985 **H. A. Hauptman** (Buffalo, NY) and **J. Karle** (Washington, DC): outstanding achievements in the development of direct methods for the determination of crystal structures.

1986 **D. R. Herschbach** (Harvard), **Y. T. Lee** (Berkeley) and **J. C. Polanyi** (Toronto): contributions concerning the dynamics of chemical elementary processes.

1987 **D. J. Cram** (Los Angeles), **J.-M. Lehn** (Strasbourg) and **C. J. Pedersen** (Wilmington, Delaware): development and use of molecules with structure specific interactions of high selectivity.

1988 **J. Deisenhofer** (Dallas, Texas), **R. Huber** (Martinsried) and **H. Michel** (Frankfurt am Main): determination of the three-dimensional structure of a photosynthetic reaction centre.

1989 **S. Altman** (Yale) and **T. Cech** (Boulder, Colorado): discovery of the catalytic properties of RNA.

1990 **E. J. Corey** (Harvard): development of the theory and methodology of organic synthesis.

1991 **R. R. Ernst** (Eidgenössische Technische Hochschule, Zürich): contributions to the development of the methodology of high resolution nmr spectroscopy.

1992 **R. A. Marcus** (California Institute of Technology): contributions to the theory of electron transfer reactions in chemical systems.

1993 **K. B. Mullis** (La Jolla, California): invention of the polymerase chain reaction.
M. Smith (University of British Columbia): fundamental contributions to the establishment of oligonucleotide-based, site-directed mutagenesis and its development for protein studies.

1994 **G. A. Olah** (University of Southern California): contributions to carbocation chemistry.

1995 **P. Crutzen** (Max Planck Institute for Chemistry, Mainz), **M. Molina** (Massachusetts Institute of Technology) and **F. S. Rowland** (Irvine, California): work in atmospheric chemistry, particularly concerning the formation and decomposition of ozone.

1996 **R. F. Curl** (Rice University, Texas), **H. Kroto** (Sussex University) and **R. E. Smalley** (Rice University, Texas): discovery of a new form of carbon, the fullerenes.

1997 **P. D. Boyer** (Los Angeles) and **J. E. Walker** (Cambridge): pioneering work on enzymes that participate in the conversion of ATP.
J. C. Scou (Aarhus): discovery of the first molecular pump, an ion-transporting enzyme Na^+-K^+ ATPase.

Appendix 7
Nobel Prize for Physics

1901 **W. C. Röntgen** (Munich): discovery of the remarkable rays subsequently named after him.

1902 **H. A. Lorentz** (Leiden) and **P. Zeeman** (Amsterdam): influence of magnetism upon radiation phenomena.

1903 **H. A. Becquerel** (École Polytechnique, Paris): discovery of spontaneous radioactivity.
P. Curie and **Marie Curie** (Paris): researches on the radiation phenomena discovered by H. Becquerel.

1904 **Lord Rayleigh** (Royal Institution, London): investigations of the densities of the most important gases and for the discovery of argon in connection with these studies.

1905 **P. Lenard** (Kiel): work on cathode rays.

1906 **J. J. Thomson** (Cambridge): theoretical and experimental investigations on the conduction of electricity by gases.

1907 **A. A. Michelson** (Chicago): optical precision instruments and the spectroscopic and metrological investigations carried out with their aid.

1908 **G. Lippmann** (Paris): method of reproducing colours photographically based on the phenomenon of interference.

1909 **G. Marconi** (London) and **F. Braun** (Strasbourg): the development of wireless telegraphy.

1910 **J. D. van der Waals** (Amsterdam): the equation of state for gases and liquids.

1911 **W. Wien** (Würzburg): the laws governing the radiation of heat.

1912 **G. Dalén** (Stockholm): invention of automatic regulators for use in conjunction with gas accumulators for illuminating lighthouses and buoys.

1913 **H. Kamerlingh Onnes** (Leiden): properties of matter at low temperatures and production of liquid helium.

1914 **M. von Laue** (Frankfurt): discovery of the diffraction of X-rays by crystals.

1915 **W. H. Bragg** (University College, London) and **W. L. Bragg** (Manchester): analysis of crystal structure by means of X-rays.

1916 Not awarded.

1917 **C. G. Barkla** (Edinburgh): discovery of the characteristic Röntgen radiation of the elements.

1918 **M. Planck** (Berlin): services rendered to the advancement of physics by discovery of energy quanta.

1919 **J. Stark** (Greifswald): discovery of the Doppler effect on canal rays and of the splitting of spectral lines in electric fields.

1920 **C. E. Guillaume** (Sévres): service rendered to precise measurements in physics by discovery of anomalies in nickel steel alloys.

1921 **A. Einstein** (Berlin): services to theoretical physics, especially discovery of the law of the photoelectric effect.

1922 **N. Bohr** (Copenhagen): investigations of the structure of atoms, and of the radiation emanating from them.

1923 **R. A. Millikan** (California Institute of Technology, Pasadena): work on the elementary charge of electricity and on the photo-electric effect.

1924 **M. Siegbahn** (Uppsala): discoveries and researches in the field of X-ray spectroscopy.

1925 **J. Franck** (Göttingen) and **G. Hertz** (Halle): discovery of the laws governing the impact of an electron upon an atom.

1926 **J. Perrin** (Paris): the discontinuous structure of matter, and especially for the discovery of sedimentation equilibrium.

1927 **A. H. Compton** (Chicago): discovery of the effect named after him.
C. T. R. Wilson (Cambridge): method of making the paths of electrically charged particles visible by condensation of vapour.

1928 **O. W. Richardson** (King's College, London): thermionic phenomenon and especially discovery of the law named after him.

1929 **L. V. de Broglie** (Paris): discovery of the wave nature of electrons.

1930 **V. Raman** (Calcutta): work on the scattering of light and discovery of the effect named after him.

1931 Not awarded.

1932 **W. Heisenberg** (Leipzig): the creation of quantum mechanics, the application of which has, inter alia, led to the discovery of the allotropic forms of hydrogen.

1933 **E. Schrödinger** (Berlin) and **P. A. M. Dirac** (Cambridge): discovery of new productive forms of atomic theory.

1934 Not awarded.

1935 **J. Chadwick** (Liverpool): discovery of the neutron.

1936 **V. F. Hess** (Innsbruck): discovery of cosmic radiation.
C. D. Anderson (California Institute of Technology, Pasadena): discovery of the positron.

1937 **C. J. Davisson** (New York) and **G. P. Thomson** (London): experimental discovery of the diffraction of electrons by crystals.

1938 **E. Fermi** (Rome): demonstration of the existence of new radioactive elements produced by neutron irradiation and for the related discovery of nuclear reactions brought about by slow neutrons.

1939 **E. O. Lawrence** (Berkeley): invention and development of the cyclotron and for results obtained with it, especially with regard to artificial radioactive elements.

1940 Not awarded.

1941 Not awarded.

1942 Not awarded.

1943 **O. Stern** (Pittsburgh): development of the molecular ray method and discovery of the magnetic moment of the proton.

1944 **I. I. Rabi** (Columbia, New York): resonance method for recording the magnetic properties of atomic nuclei.

1945 **W. Pauli** (Zürich): discovery of the Exclusion Principle, also called the Pauli Principle.

1946 **P. W. Bridgman** (Harvard): invention of an apparatus to produce extremely high pressures and discoveries in the field of high-pressure physics.

1947 **E. V. Appleton** (London): physics of the upper atmosphere, especially the discovery of the so-called Appleton layer.

1948 **P. M. S. Blackett** (Manchester): development of the Wilson cloud chamber method and discoveries therewith in the field of nuclear physics and cosmic radiation.

1949 **H. Yukawa** (Kyoto): prediction of the existence of mesons on the basis of theoretical work on nuclear forces.

1950 **C. F. Powell** (Bristol): development of the photographic method of studying nuclear processes and discoveries regarding mesons made with this method.

1951 **J. D. Cockroft** (Harwell) and **E. T. S. Walton** (Dublin): pioneer work on the transmutation of atomic nuclei by artificially accelerated atomic particles.

1952 **F. Bloch** (Stanford) and **E. M. Purcell** (Harvard): development of new methods for nuclear magnetic precision measurements and discoveries in connection therewith.

1953 **F. Zernike** (Groningen): demonstration of the phase contrast method and invention of the phase contrast microscope.

1954 **M. Born** (Edinburgh): fundamental research in quantum mechanics, especially for the statistical interpretation of the wave function.
W. Bothe (Heidelberg): the coincidence method and discoveries made therewith.

1955 **W. E. Lamb** (Stanford): the fine structure of the hydrogen spectrum.
P. Kusch (Columbia, New York): precision determination of the magnetic moment of the electron.

1956 **W. Shockley** (Pasadena), **J. Bardeen** (Urbana) and **W. H. Brattain** (Murray Hill): investigations on semiconductors and discovery of the transistor effect.

1957 **T. Lee** (Columbia) and **C. Yang** (Princeton): penetrating investigation of the so-called parity laws, which has led to important discoveries regarding the elementary particles.

1958 **P. A. Cherenkov,** **I. M. Frank** and **I. E. Tamm** (Moscow): discovery and the interpretation of the Cherenkov effect.

1959 **E. Segrè** and **O. Chamberlain** (Berkeley): discovery of the antiproton.

1960 **D. A. Glaser** (Berkeley): invention of the bubble chamber.

1961 **R. Hofstadter** (Stanford): pioneering studies of electron scattering in atomic nuclei and discoveries concerning the structure of the nucleons.

R. L. Mössbauer (Munich): resonance absorption of gamma radiation and discovery of the effect which bears his name.

1962 **L. D. Landau** (Moscow): pioneering theories for condensed matter, especially liquid helium.

1963 **E. P. Wigner** (Princeton): the theory of the atomic nucleus and elementary particles, particularly through the discovery and application of fundamental symmetry principles.
Maria Goeppert-Mayer (La Jolla) and **J. H. D. Jensen** (Heidelberg): discoveries concerning nuclear shell structure.

1964 **C. H. Townes** (Massachusetts Institute of Technology), and **N. G. Basov** and **A. M. Prokhorov** (Moscow): fundamental work in the field of quantum electronics, which led to the construction of oscillators and amplifiers based on the maser-laser-principle.

1965 **S. Tomonaga** (Tokyo), **J. Schwinger** (Cambridge, Mass.,) and **R. P. Feynman** (California Institute of Technology, Pasadena): fundamental work in quantum electrodynamics, with deep-ploughing consequences for the physics of elementary particles.

1966 **A. Kastler** (Paris): discovery and development of optical methods for studying hertzian resonances in atoms.

1967 **H. A. Bethe** (Cornell): contributions to the theory of nuclear reactions, especially discoveries concerning the energy production in stars.

1968 **L. W. Alvarez** (Berkeley): decisive contributions to elementary particle physics, in particular the discovery of a large number of resonance states, made possible by the hydrogen bubble chamber technique and data analysis.

1969 **M. Gell-Mann** (California Institute of Technology, Pasadena): contributions and discoveries concerning the classification of elementary particles and their interactions.

1970 **H. Alfvén** (Stockholm): discoveries in magneto-hydrodynamics with fruitful applications in different parts of plasma physics.
L. Néel (Grenoble): discoveries concerning antiferromagnetism and ferrimagnetism which have led to important applications in solid state physics.

1971 **D. Gabor** (Imperial College, London): invention and development of the holographic method.

1972 **J. Bardeen** (Urbana), **L. N. Cooper** (Providence) and **J. R. Schrieffer** (Philadelphia): theory of superconductivity, usually called the BCS theory.

1973 **L. Esaki** (Yorktown Heights) and **I. Giaever** (Schenectady): experimental discoveries regarding tunnelling phenomena in semiconductors and superconductors respectively.
B. D. Josephson (Cambridge): theoretical predictions of the properties of a supercurrent through a tunnel barrier, in particular those phenomena which are generally known as the Josephson effects.

1974 **M. Ryle** and **A. Hewish** (Cambridge): pioneering research in radioastrophysics: Ryle for his observations and inventions, in particular of the aperture-synthesis technique, and Hewish for his decisive role in the discovery of pulsars.

1975 **A. Bohr** (Copenhagen), **B. Mottelson** (Copenhagen) and **J. Rainwater** (New York): discovery of the connection between collective motion and particle motion in atomic nuclei and the development of the theory of the structure of the atomic nucleus based on this connection.

1976 **B. Richter** (Stanford) and **S. C. C. Ting** (Massachusetts Institute of Technology): discovery of a heavy elementary particle of a new kind.

1977 **P. W. Anderson** (Murray Hill), **N. F. Mott** (Cambridge) and **J. H. van Vleck** (Harvard): fundamental theoretical investigations of the electronic structure of magnetic and disordered systems.

1978 **P. L. Kapitsa** (Moscow): basic inventions and discoveries in the area of low-temperature physics.
A. A. Penzias and **R. W. Wilson** (Holmdel): discovery of cosmic microwave background radiation.

1979 **S. L. Glashow** (Harvard), **A. Salam** (Imperial College, London) and **S. Weinberg** (Harvard): contributions to the theory of the unified weak and electromagnetic interaction between elementary particles, including, inter alia, the prediction of the weak neutral current.

1980 **J. W. Cronin** (Chicago) and **V. L. Fitch** (Princeton): discovery of violations of fundamental symmetry principles in the decay of neutral K-mesons.

1981 **K. M. Siegbahn** (Uppsala): development of high-resolution electron spectroscopy.
N. Bloembergen (Harvard) and **A. L. Schawlow** (Stanford): development of laser spectroscopy.

1982 **K. G. Wilson** (Cornell): theory for critical phenomena in connection with phase transitions.

1983 **S. Chandrasekar** (Chicago): theoretical studies of the physical processes of importance to the structure and evolution of the stars.
W. A. Fowler (California Institute of Technology, Pasadena): theoretical and experimental studies of the nuclear reactions of importance in the formation of the chemical elements in the universe.

1984 **C. Rubbia** and **S. Van der Meer** (CERN, Geneva): decisive contributions to the discovery of the field particles W and Z, communicators of weak interaction.

1985 **K. von Klitzing** (Stuttgart): discovery of the quantized Hall effect.

1986 **E. Ruska** (Berlin): fundamental work in electron optics and the design of the first electron microscope.
G. Binning and **H. Rohrer** (Zurich): design of the scanning tunneling microscope.

1987 **G. Bednorz** and **K. A. Müller** (Zürich): for their important breakthrough in the discovery of superconductivity in ceramic materials.

1988 **L. Lederman** (Batavia, Illinois), **M. Schwartz** (Mountain View, California) and **J. Steinberger** (Geneva): for the neutrino beam method and the demonstration of the doublet structure of the leptons through the discovery of the muon neutrino.

1989 **N. F. Ramsey** (Harvard): invention of the separated oscillatory fields method and its use in the hydrogen maser and other atomic clocks.

H. G. Dehmelt (University of Washington, Seattle) and **W. Paul** (Bonn): development of the ion trap technique.

1990 **J. I. Friedman** and **H. W. Kendall** (Massachusetts Institute of Technology) and **R. E. Taylor** (Stanford): pioneering investigations concerning deep elastic scattering of electrons on protons and bound neutrons, of essential importance for the development of the quark model in particle physics.

1991 **P.-G. de Gennes** (Collège de France, Paris): discovery that methods developed for studying order phenomena in simple systems can be generalized to more complex forms of matter, in particular to liquid crystals and polymers.

1992 **G. Charpak** (École Supérieure de Physique et Chemie, Paris, and CERN Geneva): invention and development of particle detectors, in particular the multiwire proportional chamber.

1993 **R. A. Hulse** and **J. H. Taylor** (Princeton): discovery of a new type of pulsar, that has opened up new possibilities for the study of gravitation.

1994 **B. N. Brockhouse** (McMaster University) and **C. G. Schull** (Massachusetts Institute of Technology): pioneering contributions to neutron scattering techniques for studies of condensed matter (namely neutron spectroscopy and neutron diffraction techniques, respectively).

1995 **M. L. Perl** (Stanford) and **F. Reines** (Irvine, California): pioneering experimental contributions to lepton physics (discovery of the tau particle and detection of the neutrino, respectively).

1996 **D. M. Lee** (Cornell), **D. D. Osheroff** (Stanford) and **R. C. Richardson** (Cornell): discovery of the superfluid phase of helium-3.

1997 **S. Chu** (Stanford), **C. Cohen-Tannoudji** (École Normal Supérieure, Paris) and **W. D. Phillips** (NIST, Gaithersburg): development of methods to cool and trap neutral atoms with laser light.

Index

1305

Recommended Consistent Values of Some Fundamental Physical Constants (1986)

(The numbers in parentheses are the standard deviation in the last digits of the quoted value.)

Quantity	Symbol	Value	Units	Uncertainty (ppm)
Permeability of vaccum	μ_0	$4\pi \times 10^{-7}$	$\mathrm{N\,A^{-2}}$	
		$= 12.566\,370\,614\ldots$	$10^{-7}\,\mathrm{N\,A^{-2}}$	(exact)
Speed of light in vaccum	c	$299\,792\,458$	$\mathrm{m\,s^{-1}}$	(exact)
Permittivity of vacuum	ε_0	$8.854\,187\,817\ldots$	$10^{-12}\,\mathrm{F\,m^{-1}}$	(exact)
Elementary charge	e	$1.602\,177\,33(49)$	$10^{-19}\,\mathrm{C}$	0.30
Planck constant	h	$6.626\,0755(40)$	$10^{-34}\,\mathrm{J\,s}$	0.60
	$\hbar = h/2\pi$	$1.054\,572\,66(63)$	$10^{-34}\,\mathrm{J\,s}$	0.60
Avogadro constant	N_A	$6.022\,136\,7(38)$	$10^{23}\,\mathrm{mol^{-1}}$	0.59
(Unified) atomic mass unit $1u = m_u = \frac{1}{12}\,m(^{12}C)$	u	$1.660\,540\,2(10)$	$10^{-27}\,\mathrm{kg}$	0.59
Electron mass	m_e	$9.109\,389\,7(54)$	$10^{-31}\,\mathrm{kg}$	0.59
		$0.510\,999\,06(15)$	MeV	0.30
Proton mass	m_p	$1.672\,623\,1(10)$	$10^{-27}\,\mathrm{kg}$	0.59
		$938.272\,31(28)$	MeV	0.30
Neutron mass	m_n	$1.674\,928\,6(10)$	$10^{-27}\,\mathrm{kg}$	0.59
		$939.565\,63(28)$	MeV	0.30
Proton-election mass ratio	m_p/m_e	$1836.152\,701(37)$		0.020
Faraday constant $N_A e$	F	$96\,485.309(29)$	$\mathrm{C\,mol^{-1}}$	0.30
Rydberg constant	R_∞	$10\,973\,731.534(13)$	$\mathrm{m^{-1}}$	0.0012
Bohr radius	a_o	$0.529\,177\,249(24)$	$10^{-10}\,\mathrm{m}$	0.045
Electron magnetic moment anomaly, μ_e/μ_{g-1}	a_e	$1.159\,652\,193(10)$	10^{-3}	0.0086
Electron g-factor, $2(1 + a_e)$	g_e	$2.002\,319\,304\,386(20)$		1×10^{-5}
Bohr magneton	μ_B	$9.274\,0154(31)$	$10^{-24}\,\mathrm{J\,T^{-1}}$	0.34
Nuclear magneton	μ_N	$5.050\,7866(17)$	$10^{-27}\,\mathrm{J\,T^{-1}}$	0.34
Electron magnetic moment	μ_e	$928.477\,01(31)$	$10^{-26}\,\mathrm{J\,T^{-1}}$	0.34
Proton magnetic moment	μ_p	$1.410\,607\,61(47)$	$10^{-26}\,\mathrm{J\,T^{-1}}$	0.34
in Bohr magnetons	μ_p/μ_B	$1.521\,032\,202(15)$	10^{-3}	0.010
Electron-proton magnetic moment ratio	μ_e/μ_p	$658.210\,688\,1(66)$		0.010
Proton gyromagnetic ratio	γ_p	$26\,752.2128(81)$	$10^4\,\mathrm{s^{-1}\,T^{-1}}$	0.30
Molar gas constant	R	$8.314\,510(70)$	$\mathrm{J\,mol^{-1}\,K^{-1}}$	8.4
Molar volume (ideal gas)	V_m	$22.414\,10(19)$	L/mol	8.4
Boltzmann constant R/N_A	k	$1.380\,658(12)$	$10^{-23}\,\mathrm{J\,K^{-1}}$	8.5
Constant of gravitation	G	$6.672\,59(85)$	$10^{-11}\,\mathrm{m^3\,kg^{-1}\,s^{-2}}$	128

Greek Alphabet

α	A	Alpha	η	H	Eta	ν	N	Nu	τ	T	Tau
β	B	Beta	θ	Θ	Theta	ξ	Ξ	Xi	υ	Y	Upsilon
γ	Γ	Gamma	ι	I	Iota	o	O	Omicron	ϕ	Φ	Phi
δ	Δ	Delta	κ	K	Kappa	π	Π	Pi	χ	X	Chi
ε	E	Epsilon	λ	Λ	Lambda	ρ	P	Rho	ψ	Ψ	Psi
ζ	Z	Zeta	μ	M	Mu	$\sigma\,\varsigma$	Σ	Sigma	ω	Ω	Omega